THE DANCING ANGEL

Also by Jack Casserly

THE FORD WHITE HOUSE

GOLDWATER

THE HEARSTS: FATHER AND SON

SCRIPPS: THE DIVIDED DYNASTY

ONCE UPON A TIME IN ITALY

THE DANCING ANGEL

a novel by

JACK CASSERLY

DONALD I. FINE, INC.

New York

 Published in the United States of America by Donald I. Fine, Inc. and in Canada by General Publishing Company Limited.

Library of Congress Catalogue Card Number: 94-68098

ISBN: 1-55611-429-X

Manufactured in the United States of America

10 9 8 7 6 5 4 3 2 1

Designed by Irving Perkins Associates

All of the characters and events in this novel are entirely fictional. The names of real people and places are used infrequently—none is in any manner meant to be part of the novel's storytelling content or characters—but are mentioned only to give the work an authentic time frame and atmosphere of Chicago. The author had neither the desire nor intention to reflect on any persons, living or dead, or any institutions. He is a lifelong practicing Catholic and wrote this novel in an attempt to show that the current divisions in the Church may better be resolved by face to face dialogue rather than by current recrimination and long-distance argument.

To my wife, Joy Ruth

CAST OF CHARACTERS

LEO DOLAN, father of the family and Chicago Police Department detective who is one year from retirement after thirty-nine years on the force.

NORA DOLAN, his wife of thirty-six years.

CARDINAL E. BRENDAN CARMODY, prelate of the Archdiocese of Chicago.

REVEREND TIMOTHY "CAPPY" CONLON, pastor of St. Malachy's Catholic Church.

MONSIGNOR THOMAS BRADY, private secretary of the cardinal.

SUPERINTENDENT JOSEPH ROSSI, chief of the Chicago Police Department and longtime friend of Leo Dolan.

MICHAEL DOLAN, thirty-four-year-old psychiatrist and eldest son.

JESSICA JANIS-LERNER, wife of Michael and owner-director of a Chicago advertising agency.

MARGARET DOLAN FELDMAN, twenty-nine-year-old daughter and nurse.

DR. DAVID FELDMAN, husband of Margaret and other member of his father's family medical practice.

DR. LEONARD FELDMAN, surgeon, father of David and active Orthodox Jew.

KATHLEEN DOLAN, twenty-seven, former nun, principal of a new, private, inner-city school.

DANIEL DOLAN, thirty-two, conservative Democratic alderman and lawyer.

ROBERT DOLAN, twenty-six, scheduled to be ordained to the priesthood.

EVANGELINE DOLAN, single, twenty-four, a Catholic-school teacher.

ROGER "RUSTY" CARMODY, twenty-nine-year-old nephew of the cardinal and rising Chicago lawyer involved with Evangeline.

MATT MORAN, detective partner of Leo Dolan.

ALDERMAN FRANCIS X. FAHEY, Chicago City Council leader and political fixer.

THOMAS "THUMBS" RAFFERTY, the alderman's gofer.

DR. EMERSON T. "BOOM BOOM" BRAITHWAITE, pastor of the Fourth Presbyterian Church and chairman of St. Malachy's parish council.

ELOISE BRAITHWAITE, his wife.

MAMMA X, Black Muslim leader and council member, also known as the Black Madonna, whose married name is Magnolia Gentry.

REGINALD THROWBRIDGE GENTRY, husband of Mamma X.

JOHN L. "SOCKS" SULLIVAN, deputy fire commissioner.

JOHN ELIXIR BABBINGTON, sometime actor, oftentime drunk, and member of St. Malachy's parish council.

FATHER PAT BROGAN, retired Jesuit professor at Loyola University and member of the same parish council.

RABBI IRVING "GOLDIE" GOLDMAN, retired, and council elder.

FATHER MARIO FORTUNATO, assistant pastor at St. Malachy's.

BRIDGET "BRIDIE" O'BRIEN, wealthy matron and council member.

K.C. WU, Chinese businessman and council member.

L.Y. WU, son of the council member.

JOAN SOLARI, former nun and friend of Kathleen Dolan.

CLAUDIA LALLY, reporter for the Chicago *Herald*.

F.X. WIGGINS, chairman and president of Midwest Oil & Gas.

BEAU BEAUCHAMPS, janitor at St. Malachy's.

MONSIGNOR RONALD BERTRAM, administrator of the archdiocese.

CARDINAL JUAN JOSÉ SALAZAR, archbishop of Rio de Janeiro.

KNOCKO KELLY, city building permits supervisor.

ANGELO BONI, owner of trattoria on Dearborn Street.

JIM GUNTH, seminary classmate of Robert Dolan.

JAMES QUINCY, the cardinal's chauffeur.

MRS. DOROTHY KOSLOWSKI, the cardinal's other secretary.

BILL CARMODY, an attorney and the cardinal's brother.

CHARLES CARMODY, his son, a teacher.

SERGEANT WILLIAM WELLER and OFFICER TOM KELLY, police officers in the Solari case.

PATROLMAN PHILIP ESPOSITO, on duty at St. Malachy's.

LIEUTENANT OSCAR VASILOV, LT. MIKE CRAWFORD, and SGT. HERMAN WITTENBERGER, police officers in Chicago's Loop.

RAY STREETER, a Cook County medical investigator.

ERNESTO FELICES, a drug dealer.

SERGEANT MARGARET HICKEY, secretary to the police superintendent.

MARIO MORETTI, the superintendent's driver.

CHARLES LOMBARDI, son of the demolition company owner.

ELIZABETH "BETTY" BLAKE, file clerk in the cardinal's office.

HOLLIS GRANBY, judge at the trial of Charles Carmody.

"FAST EDDIE" FLYNN, Chicago bookie.

SANDY LEVINE, managing editor of the Chicago *Herald*.

JUAN TORRES, Mexican gunman and robber.

DOCTOR JULIUS SCHMIDT, consulting engineer at St. Malachy's.

PATRICK and MARY DOLAN, of Clogher Head, County Kerry, Ireland, parents of Leo.

GAVIN FAMILY, friends of Patrick and Mary Dolan in Ireland.

SEAN O'HARA and JEREMIAH O'SULLIVAN, residents of Ireland's Blasket Islands.

Father Pat Brogan said: "I remember when Catholics described the differences in the Church as an angel dancing on the head of a pin: now the angel is dancing on the tip of a flaming candle."

—CHAPTER 14

In 1994 the archdiocese of Chicago celebrated its 150th anniversary.

CONTENTS

1. *The Storytellers* 1
2. *The Dilemma* 17
3. *The Cardinal* 41
4. *Boom Boom, Mamma X and Friends* 57
5. *The New Order* 74
6. *Authority vs. Conscience* 82
7. *S-O-S* 96
8. *The New Martyrs* 122
9. *The Power and the Glory* 148
10. *The Saints Go Marchin'* 164
11. *The Old Priesthood Is Dead* 183
12. *The Girl from Stony Brook* 200
13. *Fish in the Stream* 219
14. *The Dancing Angel* 229
15. *A Handshake* 235
16. *The Bells Toll* 249
17. *Love* 257
18. *Epilogue* 264

Chapter 1

THE STORYTELLERS

Leo Dolan dozed off and the Sunday newspapers fell to his feet. The Chicago *Herald* and the *News-Times* lay strewn on the living room floor. Leo's mouth was open, breathing heavily, and his old brown pipe had slid down his chest, hanging precariously on his thigh. Fortunately, the tobacco had flamed out.

Nora, his wife, had already placed her nine-pound baron of beef in the oven. Despite the blanket of gray clouds spread above her kitchen window, Nora knew it would be a glorious day. And why not? she mused in a soft Irish brogue. All six children and their families were coming to the Dolans' annual Easter dinner.

The reunion always seemed to end in uproarious argument. Even if it erupted into another 1916 Easter Rebellion, however, Nora would never become exasperated. She loved the gathering, saying it was the Dolans that counted—not

Leo, not herself, but the clan. The family was sacred like the Church—one, holy, catholic, and apostolic. *One* above all.

Leo and Nora lived alone in the house now. The large ten-room home on Troy Avenue off 103rd Street seemed vacant much of the time. The couple talked of selling and buying a smaller place in the South Side suburb of Oak Lawn, but nothing ever came of it. They wanted a large home for family reunions like this.

Nora could hear the creaky springs in Leo's old living room chair. He was squirming and talking to himself. Only the Good Lord knew what he was thinking. Probably about retirement from the police department in a year. He would then have forty years on the force. A policeman didn't last four decades anymore. They moved on or were eased out. Not Leo. He hung tough. And so long as Joe Rossi was police superintendent, Leo would have a place to hang his hat. Joe loved Leo like a brother. They had been Marines in Korea together and later partners as young patrolmen.

Joe had ridden to fame on two of the bushy-haired, six-foot Irishman's major busts—the kidnapping of a socialite and the murder of a prominent physician, his wife, and three children. Leo spoke sparingly and rarely of himself. He walked away from public attention, especially reporters and TV cameras. Rossi was eloquent. As Leo once said jokingly, "Joe is worthy of Virgil and the great Latin poets."

Nora heard Leo sigh. Ah, now she knew. He was dreaming of Ireland again. Leo's face had turned sad, heightening the whiteness of his hair. He had plodded back to that fateful Easter, fifty-five years before, in 1939. Paddy and Mary, his parents, were standing before the family cottage in the middle of Clogher Head. The hamlet was ten miles from the nearest town, Dingle, County Kerry, along a remote part of the southwest Irish coast.

The sixty-acre Dolan farm, stretching to the strand of

the Atlantic Ocean, was a rocky enclave of picturesque poverty. Most of the land was too poor for farming, but the Dolans and others ran cows, goats and pigs in the fields. Their garden plots dotted the hilly landscape.

The seven older Dolan children, like their neighbors, fled the impoverished soil to find work and a new life in America, England and Australia. Most of the Dolans had gone to Chicago. Each pulled the next across the ocean until only Leo was left. Their letters spoke of a grand reunion in Dingle one day, but the ink faded and the pages yellowed. The big, brawling giant on Lake Michigan had become their home.

Ireland and the Continent had closed their eyes on this westernmost outpost of Europe, lost in the mist, rain and wind of the far Atlantic. Yet these coastal peasants and poor fisherfolk of the nearby Blasket Islands remained faithful to the Gaelic language and passed down their history and culture as no other region in Ireland—all by word of mouth. Despite the barrenness of their rocky turf and godforsaken bleakness of their daily lives, they were among Ireland's greatest storytellers.

In his rambling reverie, Leo recalled that long-ago Sunday after Mass at St. Vincent's Church in the nearby village of Ballyferriter. A dozen men decided to take their wives on an Easter picnic to the Great Blasket Island. They shoved off that noon from the nearby village of Dunquin, and rowed their currachs, handmade canoes fashioned from lath and tarred canvas, across the three miles of Atlantic to the Blaskets.

Nine-year-old Leo helped his father row. A medal of St. Brendan the Navigator and a bottle of holy water were tied to the prow. The sky was beginning to turn gray and Paddy idly remarked:

"There's rain on the wind."

The Dolans and other families docked at the Great Blasket in less than an hour. Seals barked nearby while gannets, gadwall duck and chuffs fluttered out of their cliff homes.

The families climbed with picnic baskets to the summit of a panoramic hill, and spread blankets on the ground. Nora had prepared their Easter lunch—roast lamb, potatoes, bread, jam and tea. Cattle, shaggy goats, chickens and pigs grazed on the sandstone hills and valleys. Smoke plumed from peat fires in distant huts. The smell of cooked mackerel floated through the air. Of the small group of islands, only the Great Blasket was populated—home to about 150 souls.

Leo looked back at the mainland. "How magnificent Ireland is, Father!"

Paddy looked at the jagged cliffs above the coastline and said, "It holds more pity than promise."

The words struck Leo's face like a cold splash of sea. He never understood why his father and other men had so little good to say about Ireland. Paddy often said of his people:

"The Irish are happiest when they're sad. They rejoice in desperation and defeat. They're the only Christians for whom Easter is not the ultimate triumph. The Irish reserve that for Good Friday. The Resurrection is an afterthought."

Paddy said grace. Mary served her husband, then Leo, and finally herself. Paddy, as good a storyteller as anyone along the southwest coast, spoke of the Great Blasket and its people. He said these peasants were the purest and richest storehouse of Irish oral culture. By word of mouth alone, decade after decade, they carried forward the treasures of their folklore.

The old pipesmokers, male and female talking around the evening peat fires, were the voices of events—local birth and death, marriage and children, fishing, farm animals and weather. Their memories served as newspaper, radio, library, movie house and balladeer on the bleak wasteland marooned in the Atlantic. Generation after generation, unlettered but not unlearned, they became masters of proverb, poetry, song and prayer. Paddy viewed them as the caretakers of antiquity. He turned to Leo and said:

"Look back, Leo, wherever you may go. Remember who and what you are. Look closely at Ireland and its people. This is what you are. Plain, poor, with a history of sorrow. These are your people. They're rich only in the simplicity of their souls and lives. Their daily work and faith. God is our treasure. He's the richest thing we own, lad."

Bill and Peggy Gavin came by with their son, Tom. The two families strolled among the island huts. Sean O'Hara, a limping old fisherman, hailed them, and soon Jeremiah O'Sullivan, a scarecrow of a man, joined the group. O'Sullivan puffed an old pipe that would have been worthy of a prominent philosopher. Leo asked the pair about the local storytellers. O'Hara said:

"I sleep lightly. I listen for the Gaelic voices. Our grandfolk and the fairies talk to us from the past. Nothin's written. It's all in me head, lad. Time's our one luxury here. Everythin' has a price, from a candle to a touch of salt, but time comes and goes without asking for a beggar's coin."

"Tell me just a bit more," Leo pleaded. O'Sullivan replied:

"Here, the past is present and future. The twice-told tale is still gold. Bygone proverbs and the brittle lines of old poetry are fresh. Mem'ries are never put away. We're the pallbearers of Irish custom and tradition."

Bill Gavin thanked the men for sharing their thoughts, reminding the two families that it was almost time to shove off with the other currachs. They returned to the inlet.

The canoes were soon pushed from the strand. Paddy again stroked from aft but Mary took Leo's oar because the ocean current was strong. Mary had difficulty keeping the currach on course. It spun twice in the water within several minutes of leaving the inlet. No one spoke. They gauged progress by the lights at Dunquin.

Fifteen minutes into Blasket Sound, Leo saw that the undercurrent was dragging them away from Dunquin into the open Atlantic. The swells heaved and lashed the currachs. Suddenly, in the blackness that had sprung up around them, the Dolans' canoe was stood up by a wave and capsized, spinning madly in the sea. Leo was sucked under water, unable to control his twisting body. He held his breath. Something struck his head. Bill Gavin's oar had swiped his right temple. Gavin dropped the oar in his canoe and plunged his right hand into the water. He grabbed Leo's hair. The youngster screamed in pain as the ocean whipped him in the water, but Gavin held firm. Painstakingly, he pulled Leo into their currach and picked up his oar. They were already flowing past Clogher Head toward Ferriter's Cove, miles out of their way. The undercurrent slackened, fortunately, but the Gavins still rowed hard. They finally reached the cove.

All the canoes arrived safely except the Dolans'. A police motorboat, fishing boats and currachs plowed the coastline for nearly two days without a sign of the couple. The bodies of Paddy and Mary were finally found late in the second day by a fishing-boat crew along the strand north of Ferriter's Cove.

The wake was held in the Dolan home. Mike Ryan, Leo's cousin, hammered the wooden caskets. He also put out ten quarts of whiskey on the kitchen table. Friends and neighbors paid their respects and emptied the bottles long before departing.

After the funeral Mass at St. Vincent's, Paddy and Mary were buried at the old cemetery down the narrow country road leading from Ballyferriter to Clogher Head. The boxes were lowered with large ropes underneath each end. Leo was now alone.

Ryan wrote to the Dolans in America telling them the sad news. Nellie, the eldest of the family, agreed to take Leo. She was married with two children, but could easily feed one more mouth. Her husband was a fireman, and she ran a successful office-cleaning business.

The Dolan home and land were sold to pay for Leo's boat passage and train ticket. The remaining money would offer him some savings. A young woman from Tralee, headed for St. Louis, accompanied Leo as they sailed from Galway on May 10, 1939, and took the train from New York to Chicago.

Leo didn't want to leave home. The youngster promised he would return to be buried with his parents, facing the seas of St. Brendan and the Blasket Islands . . .

Nora abruptly awakened Leo. She reminded him the children would soon be arriving. He must pick up the scattered newspapers and put them away. She left a cup of coffee by the side of his chair. Leo cleared away the papers but was preoccupied.

The detective sergeant was proud of his children, but often felt lost among them. Most had passed him and Nora by with their mod clothes, computer jargon, combative ideas and changed lifestyles—especially their religious attitudes. The pope was about as infallible as the home-plate umpire at Comiskey Park.

Chicago and the world had changed dramatically since the couple were married in 1958, a year after Nora arrived in Chicago. It was shortly after her eighteenth birthday. They had met and married at St. Bridget's Back-o-the-Yards Church on the South Side. Father Brendan Carmody, a grade-school classmate of Leo who said their nuptial Mass, was now Cardinal E. Brendan Carmody, the primate of Chicago's Catholics.

Leo had come out of the U.S. Marine Corps and the war in Korea in 1953. He had made the Inchon landing in 1950 with the 1st Marine Division, 5th Regiment, as a corporal.

As most other whites, the Dolans had moved to the suburbs as the post-World War II black tide swept across the South Side. This was their twentieth Easter at Queen of Martyrs Catholic parish. The church, built in 1952, was a symbol of that white flight.

Catholicism had been transformed too. Since the Second Vatican Council of the 1960s, Catholics now debated what was once unthinkable—birth control, abortion, married and women priests. Underlying most of the differences was a confrontation between the individual conscience and Church authority.

Great altars had become bare tables; guitars had replaced church organs, and new communal confession was known as reconciliation. In a mass exodus from religious life, priests and nuns had left rectories and convents. Onetime priests now worked in social services for the city, and former nuns discarded their religious habits and taught in the public schools. The rock-bottom beliefs and traditions of two thousand years had become an argumentative inferno.

For Leo and Nora, born in Ireland and reared in ageless articles of faith, life had become a series of spiritual earthquakes. Yet they clung to the pillars of the past. Each still prayed the rosary in the Gaelic language during Mass and before going to bed at night. They would no more debate Church doctrine than tell a Polish joke about the pope. They had been married not only to each other but to a more deferential, obedient world.

Nora was seventeen when she cut her bonds to family and Ireland. She had finished the eighth grade in Dingle and, for the next three years, had worked cleaning fish catches on the town dock for sixty-five dollars a month. She left her parents, nine sisters and brothers, and sailed to Ellis Island, then traveled by train to join an older sister in Chicago. As her father said farewell to her on the dock at Galway, he remarked bitterly:

"Our biggest export is our own flesh and it's a bloody business. I'm ashamed of myself and Ireland. Remember, girl, that life's a miracle and 'tis given only once. The choices you make can never be made again. Never look back. Look forward and live the miracle."

Her father, tears in his eyes, walked away. That was her early life—hard and sometimes cruel. Yet Nora was always anchored to the Rock of Peter, the Roman Catholic Church. Now that rock was being battered by the waves of new times.

Still, with the family scraping together their nickels and dimes and the kids working, all six children were graduated from college. Three—Michael, Dan and Margaret—had won partial academic scholarships. Robert, a seminarian, had most of his education underwritten by the archdiocese. Kathleen and Evangeline had paid for most of their schooling by working.

The front doorbell rang now, and Kathleen, a twenty-seven-year-old nun, was the first to arrive. She hugged Leo at the door. Kathy, as she was called, introduced Joan Solari, a companion Sister of Mercy. Both had taught in St. Brendan's grade school at 67th and Racine Avenue before Cardinal Carmody had it demolished. The two young women, now at St. Leo's elementary, were naturally against the cardinal's plan to close more Catholic schools because of financial losses to the archdiocese. The two went to work helping Nora in the kitchen.

Margaret, who had become a nurse, arrived with her husband and six-year-old daughter. Marge had married a

Jewish physician, David Feldman, a soft-spoken, gentle man who practiced family medicine with his father near the University of Chicago. The couple had met on campus. Leonard, the father, planned to retire in a few years and turn the practice over to his son David.

It surely made for an interesting marriage and family relationship. The elder Feldman and his wife Sarah were practicing Orthodox Jews while their son David attended a Reform temple and Marge continued in her Catholic faith. The parents of both had learned to enjoy one another and often ate kosher at a Jewish deli on Sunday afternoon. Ecumenism of a special kind.

Twenty-four-year-old Evangeline, called "Evie," was the Dolans' youngest child. She taught fifth grade at Queen of Martyrs school. Evie was a shy, pretty young woman whose friends suggested she should have become a nun, but Evie made it clear that she wanted to have a family. Although Evie had her own apartment, mother and daughter were inseparable. Nora had named Evie after reading Henry Wadsworth Longfellow's epic poem *Evangeline*. The sad tale of unrequited love in Acadia reminded Nora of the young people of Ireland who sometimes waited decades to marry.

Michael, the eldest and kingpin of the brood, was the talker and self-appointed clan leader. He had attended Cornell Medical School on a scholarship and completed his training as a psychiatrist at New York Hospital. Thirty-four years old, he was married to Jessica Janis-Lerner. Lucy to friends and associates, she used her maiden name professionally. The tall, slim, elegantly dressed businesswoman directed her own advertising-public relations agency on Michigan Avenue. The only child of a Wall Street investor and his socialite wife, Lucy grew up on Manhattan's Upper East Side, was a Radcliffe graduate, a nonpracticing Jew and childless. Lucy and Michael's was a whirlwind four-week romance that developed while Michael was being interviewed for several New York medical posts in 1989. They were married on a Friday afternoon in New York's city hall and that evening Lucy's parents held a candlelight tent-wedding reception for some 350 guests at the couple's Manhasset, Long Island home. Caviar, lobster, Atlantic salmon, filet mignon and champagne flowed, as Nora put it, "like the Long Island Railroad." An orchestra played old-time big band music while a rock-and-roll group blasted between sets.

Michael planned to practice in Manhattan but returned to Chicago when he was unexpectedly offered a part-time teaching post at the University of Chicago. The psychiatrist later opened his own office in the Loop and in less than five years had become one of the best-known and most-respected practitioners in the city.

Michael came to the attention of Cardinal Carmody at a B'nai B'rith reception. His Eminence was a strong supporter of religious ecumenism. He also was impressed that Leo's son had such a wide circle of friends among the city's influential Jewish leaders. Carmody hired the "Irish lad" to counsel Catholic priests and nuns needing therapy, and Michael's name and practice became bywords among the city's psychiatric fraternity.

Robert, less than two months from ordination after completing his studies at the University of St. Peter in the Pines west of Chicago, arrived with a fellow seminarian, Jim Gunth. The two in sweaters and slacks reported that clearing skies and warm sun might push the temperature to sixty degrees, which in Chicago was an Easter miracle. Bob was a studious, self-effacing young man who spoke little and then usually about his studies.

Daniel came with his wife Emily and their two children. He had become a lawyer and the alderman on Dolan family turf, Chicago's Nineteenth Ward. Emily, the daughter of immigrants, grew up in a Polish neighborhood near 47th Street and Ashland Avenue, one of the city's more colorful melting pots. Her father still drove a bread truck. Strong-willed, she was a secretary in city hall when the two met, and they now had a boy and a girl. Dan and Emily seemed a very happy couple.

If Leo had a favorite son it was Dan, although the young attorney was in many ways different from his father. Dan was a thin, balding man four inches shorter than Leo, intellectually combative and a highly articulate and outspoken conservative, although he was a Democrat. He carried his conservative convictions on his sleeve but wasn't beyond trade-offs that typified Windy City politics. Only thirty-two, Dan often took on the mayor and city council in attacking the public-education establishment. "The important thing is that we not allow the twentieth century to remake the world in its own image," he had said rather challengingly.

Leo said grace before the meal that consisted of roast beef, mashed potatoes, thick brown gravy, peas, carrots and pickled beets, to be followed by apple pie a la mode and coffee. The children had already been served milk.

As usual, it was a boisterous gathering. Two tables seating fourteen Dolans and their two guests had been joined to bring the clan closer together. Leo watched and listened to his brood, and despite his pride at their success he was mystified by his children's break with the old ways—the custom and tradition of Church and country. They just didn't seem to comprehend, much less cherish the Church's and country's history. These were the lasting imports of life, he truly believed, not the so-called shock culture of American youth or the new notion of putting individual conscience over spiritual authority.

After dinner Dan, who loved to argue, started his usual brouhaha as soon as the family settled in the couches and armchairs. "Did anyone read the *Herald* this morning? The article quoting the Anglican minister in Ulster? Wasn't it Ian Paisley, head of the Protestant Ulster Defense Force? Anyway, he asked what did the Irish bring to the United States? Poverty, he said, that's what. All the leprechaun stories about the Irish breaking up the Anglo-Protestant leadership of America are so much blarney. The Irish were kings of the ghettos. You know who died with Custer at the Little Big Horn? Irishmen. Most of the Seventh Cavalry was Irish. That was the Irish ambition—a job. That's what the man said."

Dr. Feldman, who occasionally enjoyed needling his friends the Dolans, said with feigned innocence: "Is there any truth in what he said?" And his wife Marge, who liked intellectual combat as much as anyone in the family, said, "Yes, if you can believe Ian Paisley or the Archbishop of Canterbury." Everyone laughed. "Of course, we kicked the Protestants in the shins—in Chicago, Boston, New York and a lot of other places. The English Protestants were the enemy in Ireland, and the same here. They just changed accents and flags."

Kathy, the nun *and* the family activist, quickly was in her element. "The English have been on our backs and in our pockets since the Great Famine of 1845. That's why five million Irish came here."

Emily, Polish, urged Kathy on. "Go to it, kid." And Kathy did.

"The English hadn't let us learn any work skills so we became America's white slaves . . . its miners, cement-mixers, hod-carriers, iron and steel workers, janitors, bartenders."

Bob noted mildly that more than forty million Americans claimed Irish ancestry. No one accepted his signal for a truce.

Kathy fired up again. "Let's not forget the Irish working

girls. The pennies in our piggy banks built the Catholic institutional system across America—churches, schools, hospitals, orphanages. And don't forget those of us who became nuns. We created the best educational system in the country, no question."

The arrival of coffee mercifully called for a brief time out, but Dan was soon back on his stump, as he noted that the Irish didn't come to the United States as unskilled politicians. Daniel O'Connell's political movement in the early 1800s forced the Brits to allow Catholics to hold political office. "The Irish were ready for freewheeling American politics. They didn't just appear like the Holy Spirit. James Michael Curley of Boston and Jimmy Walker in New York climbed the Irish political ladder. "Bathhouse" John Coughlin, "Hinky Dink" Kenna, and later Pat Nash and Ed Kelly did here. So did Dick Daley. Remember what Daley said. ". . . We Irish, we're different from those Polacks. From them Krauts and Dagos. We understand power. We understand that if the other guy's got it, we don't!"

Feldman allowed himself a laugh.

Emily shot back, "You're not smarter than us Polacks!"

Everyone laughed with her.

Feldman then said matter-of-factly, "Jews went into business for themselves. I guess we felt it was the only way to go."

Michael, the realist, said the early Irish pols comforted the poor with money from gambling, saloons and prostitution payoffs. Dan quickly countered that the Chicago machine never ran on a platform of piety . . . "The Irish knew all about original sin. Most of them genuflected to the Ten Commandments only in the confessional. What Irishman ever supported temperance or the Sunday blue laws?"

The seminarian Bob quietly suggested that the best Irish talent went into the Church, that it became the largest, most powerful and wealthiest religious institution in the country.

He said the Catholic Church thought a lot like the Irish politicians. They didn't dwell on philosophy and theology so much as building an organization. And they were mighty good at it.

Dr. Feldman smiled. "Don't forget the Irish in sports—John L. Sullivan, Jack Dempsey, Gene Tunney, John McGraw—and Notre Dame!"

Nora said, "I didn't know you followed sports. Cheers for David!"

"I'm glad he didn't say Knute Rockne," Leo said. "Rockne was a Norwegian!"

Laughter swept the table, which then lapsed into a lull until Michael said, "Who and what are the Irish today? The suburbanites. The middle-class. Some of the richest and most powerful. We've moved to Wilmette, River Forest, Evanston and places so far south that we might as well be in Indiana. We've abandoned inner-city parishes like St. Bridget's and St. Mel's. The Church has gone south."

Dan nodded. "Catholic identity has gone down the tubes along with the rosary, novenas and the Irish jig. I don't even like to drink on St. Patrick's Day anymore. There are too many damn amateurs out there!"

"Amen!" Leo said, smiling.

"Chicagoans are a strange breed," Dr. Feldman said. "They'd rather be mayor than president or pope."

All laughed, and agreed.

Evie, who had said nothing at dinner, got up, bent over Nora and whispered, "Mom, I'm kind of tired. I'm going to lie down for a while."

"By all means, Evie," Nora said. "There's been enough big talk around here today to wear anybody out."

Michael, as he often did at these gatherings, then invoked the memory of James T. Farrell, the South Side Chicago novelist who wrote *Studs Lonigan*. The elder brother, who enjoyed playing family psychiatrist, claimed that the young Irish-American, Studs, had been damned by his own Catholic faith, and the same was happening to many of today's Catholics. Lonigan had rejected his religious background and chose to live by his own code, not hide behind the doctrines and direction of the Church. Lonigan's later life was ridden with the guilt preached by the priests and nuns of his boyhood. The psychiatrist went on, "The tragedy was that Studs never really defended himself. If only he could've convinced others that he was his own man, his own conscience, his life would be seen as a triumph. But Studs's voice failed, not his heart or his conscience. That was his sin—the cardinal sin. An Irishman must explain himself like the old Irish storytellers. We're the Studs Lonigans of today—Catholics made guilty because some of our ideas conflict with the Church. Are we like Studs? Will we go quietly into the night? Or will we challenge the hierarchy and not be *god*-damned by our silence?"

There was an uneasy quiet. Then, one by one, the family broke into small groups to exchange news of their work and friends. Nora carried dirty dishes to the kitchen sink and was alone when Marge slipped in. The nurse looked at her mother for a long time, then finally said, "Mother, Evie is pregnant."

Nora stood there in stunned silence. She placed both hands on her still-red hair, and finally stammered, "Jesus, Mary and Joseph!"

Chapter 2

THE DILEMMA

Evie met Marge in the cafeteria of St. Bernard's Hospital a few minutes after 4:00 P.M. She appeared calm, but her stomach was churning. Marge, who had just finished her nursing shift, got a cup of black coffee. Evie took hot tea. The sisters sat at a table in a far corner of the refectory where no one could hear them.

Marge smiled brightly, trying to ease the tension in Evie's face. "Dad always says the Dolans are born storytellers. You're a Dolan. Be a storyteller."

Evie laced her fingers and twisted them tightly. Her hands were trembling.

The nurse tried hard not to let her sister see that she could see her misery.

"Evie, I love you, sweetie, but I need to know more to help you. You've never told me much more that you're pregnant."

Evie looked away. "I'm so ashamed."

Marge took her sister's hand and said quietly, "Sweetie, I'll stand by you, every step of the way. Whatever . . . wherever."

Evie took a deep breath. "It was St. Patrick's evening. I'd invited Rusty Carmody to dinner at my apartment for the first time. I'd cooked corned beef and cabbage, just like mom makes it. She even came over to taste it before he got there and said it was perfect."

"You mean the cardinal's nephew? I didn't know you were seeing him."

"Yes."

The disclosure seemed to jolt Marge. "How long have you been dating him?"

"Five months."

"Why didn't you tell the family?"

"Rusty said we should wait to see how things worked out."

Marge's mind moved quickly. Charles "Rusty" Carmody was not only the cardinal's nephew, but his father was a well-known Chicago lawyer. Rusty's name was constantly in the newspapers as a rising young lawyer—a member of the chamber of commerce, the Lawyers Guild, Rotary, Kiwanis, Knights of Columbus, a seat on the cardinal's lay advisory board, the Boy Scouts. The irony of Rusty's leadership in the Boy Scouts stuck in the nurse's throat. Newspapers indicated the young civic leader planned to run for a seat on the city council.

Marge looked at her sister. "What happened? Tell me."

Marge took her sister's hand again as, slowly, Evie talked about the evening . . .

"I'd put on a tape of big band music. He brought a bottle of red wine. Dinner was the best I'd ever made, including fresh-baked apple strudel, his favorite. Even lighted candles and a vase of new tulips in the center of the table.

"After dinner, we sat on the living-room couch talking and listening to the music. He put his arm around me and rested his head on my shoulder. Then we kissed and after about five minutes . . . he picked me up and carried me into the bedroom.

"Rusty tried to do it once before at his place but I told him I wanted to wait for marriage. He backed off, but this time he put me on the bed and got on top of me and began kissing me. I could barely breathe and I told him no, I wanted to wait. He said there was nothing to worry about, he had a . . . condom. I pleaded with him, no, I want to get married. He began mumbling and finally said in September.

"It was the happiest moment of my life, Marge. A September wedding. I kissed him, I loved him—"

"The son of a bitch. Sweetie, are you *sure* you're pregnant?"

"Yes, I've seen a doctor . . . Marge, I'm very scared. Mom and dad are going to be so ashamed, it's so horrible."

"Have you told Rusty?"

"Yes."

"What did he say?"

"He seemed very surprised, but he was nice, at first. We had a cup of coffee in a restaurant near his office. He said we'd find the right answers. Later everything suddenly changed. He said we'd work something out. I asked him what that meant. He didn't answer so I said the right thing was to get married."

Evie began to cry, finally composed herself and went on.

"He blew up. I thought he'd gone crazy. He said he wasn't ready for marriage and hit the table with his fist. He was almost shouting. I asked him to calm down, other customers would hear. He said to hell with 'em. I couldn't believe he was saying these things. 'I'm going to have our child, yours and mine,' I told him. 'I come from a good Catholic family.' So did he. His uncle was the cardinal. We didn't have a choice . . ."

Marge saw battle flags in Rusty Carmody's behavior, and hunted for more facts:

"What else did he say?"

"He wouldn't calm down. He waved his arms around and said, 'I can't believe it,' he said, 'tough titty!' Can you imagine! I got angry and then said how could he use such stupid language. They didn't teach him that at Notre Dame. I won't forget what he said then . . . 'Well, the girls at Notre Dame know how to protect themselves.' "

"So he admitted not using the condom. The *bastard!*"

The nurse's mind was racing now. This could become not only an ugly confrontation between the two but a fierce fight involving the entire Dolan and Carmody clans. Marge knew she must move quickly. She got up from her chair. The answer was obvious—Michael. Their brother had trained for this sort of thing. Who better than Michael to think it through.

"I want you to see Michael before you decide anything," Marge said. "He deals with these problems in his psychiatric practice. I'll call and get you together with him."

Evie didn't hesitate. "Yes, Michael. He knows . . ."

Marge phoned her brother that evening and told him what Evie had said as well as her own opinion. The matter not only concerned Evie but could provoke a bitter public fight between the two families. Michael said little, but Marge knew that he was deeply upset by what he had heard.

Evie arrived at Michael's Loop office at 10 A.M. on Saturday following Easter. She parked in the lot beneath the Wacker Drive office building. Michael had not yet arrived. The security guard asked Evie to wait in a nearby lounge. Her brother walked in about ten minutes later with a cheery hello and an apology for his tardiness. He then led his sister to the elevator and they rode up to the eleventh floor.

"I haven't made one of the twelfth floor penthouse suites yet, sweetheart, but I'm working on it." He was trying for a light note.

Evie forced a smile.

"Just moved in about six months ago. How do you like the view?"

Evie could see the Chicago River and Lake Michigan. A steady drizzle was falling.

"It's very nice, Michael."

"Yes, my patients like it too. I'm glad they do. They're paying for it."

He took off his raincoat and began heating hot water for tea and instant coffee. He knew Evie preferred tea.

"Please take off your coat, sweetheart," Michael said. Evie nodded, embarrassed.

Michael poured the hot water over the instant coffee and the tea bag, handed her the cup of tea and sat back in his large leather swivel chair, stirring two cubes of sugar in his coffee. Finally he got to it.

"I've spoken with Rusty."

Evie stiffened. She hadn't asked her brother to do that. Michael didn't know what she thought and felt. That was the purpose of this meeting.

Michael continued: "Rusty thinks you should have an abortion."

Evie was too stunned to reply. "So do I."

Michael's abrupt matter-of-factness shocked her. Was this really happening? Rusty and *her own brother* advocating abortion? Was this modern Catholic psychiatry? Instant advice, and against the Church? Evie didn't really hear Michael for several moments until his words finally began to penetrate her disbelief.

"Evie, I want to talk to you as a Catholic—"

"As a Catholic! For the love of God, Michael, when did Catholics begin condoning abortion?"

Michael pulled back, realizing he had moved too quickly. She had always taken such pride in him . . . "Michael's done it, he's climbed the mountain for all of us. He's the family giant . . ." He loved her. She was always his buddy. He let her fix his tie before dates. She insisted on running errands for him. He would slip her money for the movie and popcorn. She would always be the girl with the lily in the little white dress. For him and the family, the fresh face of innocence.

"Let's take it one step at a time," he said.

He opened his briefcase, took out a legal-size pad filled with notes and began to read. "Rusty says he doesn't want to get married. He says he's too young and has to get his career started."

"He's over thirty, Michael."

Michael pressed on. "Rusty says it's going to take him several more years to get established. He's got to network, as he called it, get the right support. Chicago isn't the stockyards or the railroads anymore. It's international, with business ties to Europe, the Far East, Latin America. Rusty says he needs time to move, to put himself in the top circles—"

"Then why, Michael, didn't he go to bed with a Loop bar whore? He knew I was a *Catholic*. That I was a *virgin*. I'd made my virginity *very* clear to him. Let's use *your* language, Michael. It was Rusty's *intent* to convince me that we'd marry. He even set a date, next September, the night that we made love. For five months he whispered sweet nothings, held my hand and stroked my face, sent me telegrams, flowers and candy. He even said *September Song* was our song. No, Michael, he didn't pull out a contract and say this is a marriage license, let's sign it. I'd never have gone to bed with him without those two words: in September. That was a promise of marriage, Michael. I gave myself to him with every ounce of love in my body. When I learned that I was pregnant I told Rusty that I was ready to do the right thing. Or didn't they teach that when he went to Notre Dame?"

Michael looked steadily at his sister. "Evie, as a matter of fact, they didn't and they don't."

Evie looked at her brother through strained, increasingly confused eyes. She retreated into silence.

Michael tried to sound professional. "It happens that when couples face an unwanted pregnancy some find they have little or no relationship. They've never made any analysis of their particular feelings and goals. The truth is, they never knew or understood each other. Sex substituted for self-knowledge. Now this couple's in conflict. They're incompatible because it takes two to make a marriage. I'm not saying you're incompatible. Rusty is."

Michael paused to see if Evie wanted to speak. She didn't.

"Let's get one thing straight, Evie. There are two Catholic Churches—one in Rome and the other here in the U.S. They're acting and teaching as if we're living in two different worlds. Pope John Paul II and the Vatican condemn birth control and abortion. Here, some theologians, priests and prominent lay people say birth control and abortion are open questions, particularly contraception. The clergy waver on these issues as soon as individual conscience is mentioned. Not all, but many. Don't you see the confusion, the dilemmas that we have? The Church and clergy are talking out of both sides of their mouths. Millions of American Catholics and Church authority are on two completely different wavelengths."

Evie glared at her brother and said nothing. He pushed on.

"Rusty says the Church doesn't have a right to make statements on something so private as the sexual relationship between a man and a woman. The Vatican and many American theologians differ on the supremacy of the pope versus the individual conscience. Rusty says his conscience tells him abortion is acceptable under certain circumstances, particularly to save the life of the mother or when the man and woman are incompatible. He says the two of you aren't compatible."

The room had become very still. Michael stood, opened a window, returned to his chair and said across his large desk: "You know what dad once told me, sweetheart. He said the greatest confrontation we'll ever face is with our own consciences. He was right."

"Michael, I may be the family innocent, but I'm not stupid. I think you're saying it's okay for me to get an abortion."

Michael's reply was still elliptical. "You've heard dad say the Church has passed him by. He said that for a reason. Our theologians and some priests question Vatican teaching. They are our Church's leaders. If *they* can't make up their minds, we've got to take over responsibility for our lives—rely on our own individual consciences."

"Do you really believe that?"

"Yes, I do," Michael told her, his face very serious.

"Well, at least we're beginning to understand each other," she said.

Believing he may have made an opening, Michael went on. "Cardinal John Henry Newman, one of the Church's great minds, once said: 'Infallibility does not belong either to the hierarchy alone or to the believing people alone . . . but to the remarkable harmony of the Catholic bishops and faithful.' This harmony blew up twenty years ago. Eighty percent of a special commission created by Pope Paul VI, mostly bishops, told the pope that birth control was *not* intrinsically evil

—that the old rules should be relaxed. They did this after Paul said he wouldn't refuse absolution to a couple practicing contraception. Paul said he hoped the couple would realize they had chosen a lesser path in their moral life. Catholic theologians here and in Europe interpreted the papal statement as support for the rights of the individual conscience and for contraception. But then a year later Paul rejected the commission's report in his encyclical *Humanae Vitae*. He reemphasized traditional Church teaching, but theologians in the United States and Europe signed statements disagreeing with the encyclical. Karl Rahner, a Jesuit, publicly opposed the pope. Some ninety percent of this country's fifty-eight million Catholics have, in various polls, rejected Paul's views. The same surveys show that only fifteen percent of American priests will deny absolution to a Catholic who believes he or she has a good reason to practice contraception. No other encyclical in the history of the papacy has caused greater opposition. And none has caused more erosion of the Vatican's credibility among Catholics. Priests and bishops no longer preach about sex. It's almost like they're hiding a nuclear bomb in their closets. They know most Catholics here don't follow the encyclical. They're listening to Cardinal Newman and his belief that conscience could discount official but noninfallible teachings of the Church after prayer and reflection.

"And some American bishops and many priests privately disagree with the papal view. Paul's prohibition of birth control has been expressed even more strongly by Pope John Paul II. Yet if you go to confession to many European and American priests they'll tell you to listen to your conscience. Some even say the same about abortion, but they won't admit that in their Sunday sermons.

"You don't have to be St. Thomas Aquinas to know that Catholic teaching is in a quandary. Rather than face up to the real issues facing the Church, bishops and priests sermonize on Lazarus and the prodigal son. They're talking dead issues in a world that's passed them by. We rarely hear about what's important in our daily lives. The bishops and priests are caught in a Catch-22. They fear disagreeing with the pope or their bishop, and don't want to offend their congregations. So you and I—yes, I'm a psychiatrist but I'm also a Catholic—are listening to all of them—the pope, the Vatican Curia, the bishops, theologians, parish priests, lay leaders—and they're all singing a different hymn.

"I think a lot of priests are spiritually bankrupt. Every day, Evie, they come here to this office and pour out their miseries. Many are plain emotionally immature. They know damn little about life. Many are running on empty and lost in modern society while they pretend to have the answers to the world's needs."

He took a deep breath. "Okay, what does my sermon mean, Evie? What am I really trying to say in my long-winded roundabout way? I guess it comes down to this . . . You've got to do your own thinking, sweetheart. These guys have all they can do to save their own souls, much less yours. You've got to swim for yourself. They can't save you. They're too busy swimming to save themselves."

Evie was surprised by Michael's knowledge of the Church and clergy, but she also knew much of what he said was the voice of others. Then Michael played his last cards.

"Evie, the abortion rate among Catholic women is just as high as it is among other religious denominations. In some states it's even higher than for Protestants." He let that sink in, then said quietly, "Sweetheart, I suggest neither of us mention this meeting to mom and dad. I think mom could handle it, but I doubt Leo could. He just won't accept the new generation of Catholics. Some of us don't believe a human life is present during the first three months of pregnancy. We don't accept a lot of the thinking coming out of Imperial Rome. Dad's still listening to St. Patrick and the Irish storytellers."

Michael paused and spoke in barely audible tones. "Who'll take care of the child, Evie? If you're going to support it, that means you'll have to continue teaching. Where would you leave the baby during the day? With mom and dad? Is that what you want? There are serious consequences to carrying this fetus to term, among them that having the child may even close your door to marriage. Evie, there are new problems *and* new solutions. The old days of memorizing the catechism are over. They've even written a new catechism. Catholic theologians are in the forefront of this change—even a few bishops. Some priests are following them. So are many of the faithful. A new generation is speaking up. This isn't the Church of fish on Friday, confession on Saturday and Mass on Sunday. The Vatican is still trying to locate the twentieth century."

Evie heard him but felt more confused than ever. She tried not to show it.

"Thank you, Michael," was all she said.

"Dear Evie," he said, "I love you. I'm always here for you. You must remember that." And then he picked up the phone, invited his wife Lucy to lunch, walked around the desk and kissed his sister on the cheek.

As he walked her to the elevator he said, "Your big brother cares. Stay in touch."

Evie brooded for four days. Michael meant well, she knew, but it hadn't resolved anything for her. Abortion was still the ultimate act. There was no road back. No saints like Jude or Christopher reaching out a hand afterward. No dark corner of the soul to hide in. No words that could heal the terrible pain and sorrow of her parents. She could only see a black hole. For the first time in her life Evie felt the soft motionless ease with which thoughts of suicide infiltrate the brain. Some pills, sleep, no morning after.

She shook her head violently and reached for the phone on her kitchen wall. It was after eight on a Wednesday evening. Her sister should be home. Marge's husband David answered.

"Hi, David, this is Evie. Is Marge free?"

"Evening, Evie. Good to hear your voice. Yes, just a minute."

Marge took a long time to reach the phone and seemed out of breath when she did. "Hi, Evie. Sorry. I was upstairs sorting out some clothes in Dorothy's room. That kid makes a bigger mess than three girls at a pizza parlor."

"I'd like to see you, Marge."

"Okay, dear, when?"

"How about Saturday morning, say around nine?"

"Perfect, David will be making his rounds at the hospital. Why don't you come here? Dorothy has an aerobics class from nine to ten and a swimming lesson for forty-five minutes after that."

"Fine. See you about nine."

The sisters hung up.

Marge was carrying laundry from the basement when Evie rang her front doorbell. She had no household help by choice. From the age of fifteen she had always held a job. Although she was on a three-quarter academic scholarship throughout college, she helped Kathy and Evie through school. She worked part time as a salesgirl and later in the medical library at Loyola University, where she was graduated. Later she worked at Cook County Hospital, the assembly line of local hospital care. She had met David earlier at a University of Chicago dance and they began dating steadily when both worked at Cook County. They were married in a Catholic church and later at a Reform temple.

Marge wasn't crowned with the reddish blonde of most Dolans. Her hair was bushy brown. She was a handsome woman with a clean, open face. Her blue-gray eyes were striking, quick and knowing. As the eldest and most decisive of the girls she was looked up to by Kathy and Evie. Her mother Nora always called on her in a crisis. Marge was well aware that her meeting with Evie was such a time.

"Hi, kid!" Marge said, opening the front door. "I've put a pot of tea on for you. Come in and shake off the chill."

It was thirty-seven degrees this overcast Saturday. Winter still gripped the city. Leaden skies covered the entire suburb of Oak Lawn. Nevertheless, the White Sox were scheduled to play the Detroit Tigers at Comiskey Park. The optimism of Chicagoans about the weather pulled them through tough winters.

Marge poured tea and coffee as the two sat at the kitchen table. The kitchen had always been their meeting ground at home.

Evie, Marge noted, had lost weight. Her eyes seemed tired and her face pale.

"I won't keep you long," Evie said.

"Nonsense, sweetie. You're my sunshine today. I'd just be fussing over something unimportant if you weren't here."

Evie came quickly to the point. "I saw Michael." She paused, then blurted: "He advised me to get an abortion. Oh, he took a lot of words to say it, but it's what he meant."

Marge's eyes never flickered as Evie searched her face for some reaction. "You needn't make a decision today, Evie. Tell me what Michael said."

For the next several minutes, Evie did, and before she had finished Marge had become furious with Michael. She had no idea he'd gone so "modern." He meant well but it was clear that Evie was devastated.

"Evie, remember that a Dolan is *never* alone," she said. "We always have each other. Even when we disagree we're still a family. No one—not the bishops, not the theologians, not all those people remaking the Church—can break that bond." She moved to her difficult disclosure . . . "I told mom . . . I thought she should know . . ."

Evie closed her eyes, put her hand on her chest, and sat as though transfixed.

"Evie, she's your mother. She must know. You're going to need her. Oh, she was shocked at first, but after we talked awhile she recalled an old Irish saying. 'Any woman can lose her hat in a wind.' She smiled. We talked for a long time and at the end she said, 'Tell Evie that no matter how little or long a pitcher goes to water, it's broken in the end. My door and my heart are always open. I love her. She'll always be my child.' That's mom. She thinks David's father should tell dad. She said it should come from a man outside the family that Leo respects. It could be Chief Rossi but Joe would find it almost impossible. Leonard is a doctor and he can handle it."

"Will he do it?"

"Of course, dear. David and I will speak to him."

A huge burden seemed to have been lifted from Evie. And seeing it, Marge began something of a rebuttal to Michael. "Other than David, I've never told anyone the reason I went to St. Bernard's Hospital. After leaving Cook County I worked at a general-practice clinic with four doctors for almost a week. No one had ever said that two of the doctors performed abortions.

"I discovered a nurse flushing fetuses down a toilet. It's the same at other clinics. That same day I saw older, larger fetuses stashed into medical waste. These were carried away in a dump truck and buried in some landfill. Others were incinerated at the clinic.

"Later I was called in to help at an operation. The nurse who handled surgery was out sick. It was a hysterectomy. The woman, about twenty, was eight months pregnant. The doctor made the cut but had trouble lifting the fetus out. When he finally got the fetus unstuck, I thought I heard the baby whimper. I looked at him and he seemed furious that my eyes were on his. He dropped the child in a medical wastebasket. I walked out and never went back. The pro-choice people don't say much if anything about hysterectomy. The media don't tell the public that it's been legal under *Roe* v. *Wade* since 1975 for so-called social and health reasons. They're really matters of convenience."

"Do you believe abortion is murder?"

"Yes," Marge said, "because the fetus is a human being and it has rights like you and I do."

"But Michael says it's up to the individual conscience. And so do some Catholic theologians and clergy and lay leaders—"

"Has the Catholic Church said it?"

"No, but there are different opinions about it. Catholic politicians say they oppose abortion personally but support a woman's choice to have one."

"Her *legal* choice, Evie. They don't say it's moral to have an abortion."

Marge poured Evie more tea. After a pause to answer a phone call she returned and said, "Evie, my convictions didn't come from a flash of divine inspiration. I got them by thinking long and hard about this. By something that happened to me just before I left Cook County Hospital. I was standing outside the hospital one afternoon, I'd just left surgery and needed fresh air. High-school girls were parading in support of a nearby abortion clinic. They looked like good kids, and I'm sure they were. Then, I saw this sign. The big letters, painted in red, said THIS IS MY BODY. I choked and had a hard time breathing. I had to lean against a building. It took me a while to regain my composure.

"I understood what that teenager was trying to say. She could do with her body as she wanted. But those words suddenly reminded me of the sacred words of the priest in consecrating Christ's body at Mass . . . This is My Body. Was Allan Bloom, that professor at the University of Chicago, right? Have we closed the American mind and failed today's students? Both sides of the abortion debate aren't presented in too many schools. Something's wrong with the American soul. I believe that, Evie. But I realize it's a lot easier for me to talk . . . just like it is for Michael . . . than for you to make a decision. It's *your* life and I realize that. They say talk is cheap. I just hope I've at least given you something to think about. And, please, honey, whatever happens, I'm here for you. Just like I'm sure Michael is, even if I don't agree with him."

Young Dorothy burst in the front door from her swimming lesson and called out, "Mommy, I swam two whole lengths of the pool."

"Wonderful, dear. Now get ready for lunch."

Evie begged off lunch. As she fixed a fur-trimmed hat on her head she said, "Thanks, Marge. I'll think hard about what you said. And let me know about Dr. Feldman and dad. I love you, Marge . . ."

The sisters embraced, and Evie moved down the front steps in apparently better spirits than when she arrived. She started her car, waved at Marge, and drove off.

* * *

Dr. Leonard Feldman casually folded the luncheon napkin on his lap, seemingly relaxed, smiling at Leo and pointing to the luncheon menu at the Chicago Ridge Country Club. Feldman was a member in name only since he never played golf. His wife, Sarah, teed off twice a week through the spring, summer and even fall, weather permitting. The sun had sliced through the clouds after an early morning rain, and she was out on the course.

Leo had no idea why Feldman had invited him to lunch alone since the white-haired physician had never done so previously. For years they had always eaten with their wives. Leo asked himself what was so important on this April day that couldn't wait for their wives? And how could it involve him? Leo also wondered about Feldman's casual air. The physician usually was a rather formal, direct, plainspoken person.

Feldman was a thin five-feet-four with steady brown eyes and a face bronzed from being an avid outdoor gardener and a railbird at Chicago's racetracks one day a week. Spring and summer Wednesday mornings and Sundays he spent among his vegetables and flowers. On Wednesday afternoon he habitually went to one of the three tracks—Arlington Park International Race Course, Sportsman's Park or Hawthorne. Horses were his secret passion. He bet with a bookie during the week but never on the Sabbath or Sunday. He was a two-dollar bettor, two or three races on a given day, and with the same bookie for thirty years. To him, picking the nags was an intellectual challenge, like some people worked crossword puzzles, only he wanted action.

Leonard ordered first—a cup of chicken rice soup, a fruit plate and iced tea. He said to Leo with a grin, "Chicken soup . . . Jewish penicillin. Take it from the doctor."

Leo laughed but was convinced his host was preparing a

shot of something for him as well. He ordered beef barley soup with a bacon, lettuce and tomato sandwich and iced tea.

When the waiter left, Feldman said, "Did I ever tell you, Leo, that as a child I sang in the synagogue?"

"No, Leonard, I've always thought of us as shower Carusos."

"Well, starting in 1935," Leonard said, "I was five years old back in Warsaw. The rabbi and cantor heard me sing in school. We had a terrible cantor. You know all Jews are experts when it comes to chanting in the temple. We're the worst critics in the world. You'd think that half of us played the violin and the other half were symphony conductors. Anyway, *kvetch, kvetch,* that's all they ever did about our cantor. The poor man was in his eighties and was glad to turn the *Kol Nidre* over to me. They dressed me all in white because it was Yom Kippur, the Day of Atonement, the day of purity. So I chanted the *Kol Nidre.*"

"What is it?"

"It's sung at the evening service of Yom Kippur. I've memorized some of it in English.

Kol Nidre—chant of ages.
Chant of grief and chant of triumph,
Echoing, this night of mem'ries,
In the ears and heart of Israel.
Once again you draw together
All dispersed and all God's faithful
To return and humbly seek Him—
Suppliants for His grace and pardon . . .
For the dawn of peace and freedom.
When all hearts are purged of hatred.
Passions, lusts that rend asunder.
Then all men will stand together
To acknowledge God their father."

"I'm impressed. When did you come to the States?" Leo asked.

"In 1939, just after the Nazis marched into Warsaw, a friend of my father got us passports. As a matter of fact he was a Polish priest whose brother was a longtime politician. My father was the priest's doctor."

"Tell me about it." Leo was genuinely intrigued.

"My parents were Hasidic Jews. In Warsaw, the Gestapo, as you know, herded the Jews into a ghetto. My parents got out by train with me and my two sisters. The Nazis didn't know we were Jews, thanks to the fictitious names on the passports. We managed to get to London and finally to America at the end of 1939."

The waiter arrived with their soup and iced tea, and Feldman told Leo that his father had put great importance on the Sabbath. Men and women had to detach themselves from time and worldly pursuits. The Sabbath was God's. "They say it's only when we detach ourselves that we can fly to God."

Leo laughed. "Okay, but not cardinals."

Feldman had no way of knowing Leo was referring to his coming meeting with Cardinal Carmody. "You know, Leo, the more I pray, the more I see other aspects of living as less important . . ."

Feldman halted the thought and seemed lost in another corner of his mind as he stared out the dining room windows. Finally he apologized and said, "Excuse me, Leo, I was daydreaming. A human weakness. My father would never have approved. I was thinking about a horse."

"A horse?"

"Yes, a racehorse, Dr. Max. He's running out West. I follow horses, as I think you may know. To me, few things are more thrilling than seven or eight horses pounding around the final turn into the stretch. It is, as Damon Runyon used to say, worthy of a two-bob wager."

Leo smiled. He'd read Runyon, and anyway, the Irish loved horseracing.

They finished their soup and the waiter brought their entrees and more iced tea. When he left, Leonard took a deep breath and fired his broadside.

"Leo, I've been designated to tell you that your daughter Evie is expecting a child."

The detective choked the first bite of his BLT. His face flushed. Feldman nodded and jabbed his fork into a slice of banana, looked up, chewed slowly, took a sip of iced tea. Leo gripped his BLT and began to squeeze it, finally let the sandwich crumple to his plate. He took a long gulp of iced tea while studying Feldman's face. The doctor's expression showed nothing.

"You were *designated?*" Leo said. "By whom?"

"By your wife and children."

"My wife couldn't tell me?"

"Maybe not."

"My son Michael?"

"It didn't work out for whatever reason."

"Evie?"

"Apparently not, Leo."

"*Why,* Leonard?"

"I gather they had some problems handling it and thought it would be better if I helped out." Trying to soften it . . . "Men tend to take it hard when an unwed daughter gets pregnant. We often take it much harder than the mother. People think of a doctor at these times. They didn't want to see you hurt, Leo. Nora seemed to think I could help you."

"Who's the father?"

"Rusty Carmody, a young lawyer . . . and nephew of

the cardinal. I understand he isn't keen on marriage. Your son Michael has spoken with Evie and, I gather, left the door open to an abortion. Evie also has spoken with my son. David told her the decision was hers. Marge was against abortion."

Leo's head was swimming somewhere in the Irish Sea. Jesus, Mary and Joseph! He wanted to talk with Nora.

His friend went on as if he hadn't noticed Leo's torment. Dr. Feldman said he ordinarily didn't quote secondary opinions or sources but in this instance was forced to do so. If he could help Leo in any way, he would. He decided he should say nothing more.

Leo fumbled for words, said the word "abortion" had never been part of his vocabulary. Even the possibility that Evie would consider an abortion was . . . well, hard to imagine, for himself and his wife too. It was just against everything they believed. How could his daughter ever *consider* such an act? Abortion was murder.

"What's *your* opinion of all this, Leonard?"

"Are you asking me my opinion of abortion, or Evie's situation?"

"Both."

Feldman was very uncomfortable. He rarely if ever crossed the fine line between physician and rabbi or priest. He didn't mind discussing abortion but he decidedly didn't want to be offering moral advice to the Dolan family. To his friend Leo.

"Leo, I don't want to get into the moral or social aspects of this. That's something that you, your wife *and* Evie will have to sort out."

Leo was not happy with that. "Leonard, I've never understood how anyone could agree with *Roe* v. *Wade*. I'm amazed at what some Catholic theologians are saying about abortion, individualism and conscience. Hell, Leonard, I'm shocked that my own son Michael would suggest abortion. I respect you, Leonard, and I need to know more about your . . . your professional experience in this."

Feldman had heard Leo's dilemma many times in his nearly forty years as a doctor. Neither man spoke for a while. The silence grew more uncomfortable until the physician finally said, "Leo, on the morality of abortion, Catholics and Orthodox Jews are together. My beliefs are essentially yours with maybe a few exceptions. Orthodox biblical and Talmudic scholars believe that therapeutic abortions, abortions performed to save the life of the mother, are not only permissible but mandatory. The stage of pregnancy doesn't matter. In cases where there's a strong possibility that a child will be born deformed, where incest is involved, or there's the possibility of serious psychological or emotional problems for the mother, abortion is permitted.

"Rabbinical scholars agree with you that abortions for convenience, economics or other personal reasons are wrong and prohibited. This applies from the moment of conception. Although a fetus isn't considered a living soul until actual birth it does have *potential* life and its destruction is thought to be a grave moral wrong.

"What I've just said is not much different from what the pope and your bishops teach. If we were to go back into American history we'd find that abortion was condemned as wilful murder as early as the 1600s. A couple of hundred years later thirty states had banned abortion. Some said abortion was manslaughter. Those laws were overturned recently."

Feldman talked about a generation gap on the subject of abortion. His son, a Reform Jew, believed in the pro-choice option. David and Michael represented the modern world. "You and I are yesterday, Leo. We live at a time when a daughter may turn against her mother, and sons oppose their fathers. Maybe nothing in the Bible or Shakespeare rivals the current moral chasm."

Feldman paused. "I'm sorry, Leo. I'm lecturing. But today's generation doesn't understand history's fundamental fact—*life* is God's masterpiece."

"I agree," said Leo. His turmoil twisted his face. The physician agonized for Leo but remained cautious. Finally Leo asked what had been on his mind for several minutes . . . Would Feldman be willing to see Evie and talk about the moral implications of abortion?

Feldman was reluctant. He felt it was a family matter, that Leo, his wife and Evie should decide the outcome. Evie would probably want to make her own decision . . .

"That's why Nora and I need you, Leonard. My wife and I will accept the baby. Gladly."

Feldman felt the chicken soup backing up in his throat. He was becoming the point man, the soldier in the line of fire in somebody else's war, and he didn't like it. Yet what old religious Jew could say no to the grief on his friend Leo's face. Feldman's response was slow, as if he were seeking answers himself.

"You know, Leo, I keep thinking of my father in all this. He always talked in terms of God. He'd start off saying that being a Jew is a mystical thing. He talked about Jews who levitated on the history of family and kin. But Jews never quite fit into the easy categories used by old scholars or modern sociologists that define religions, nations, races. Jews aren't a race. But they're more than a religious faith and more than a nation. The only term for us is *people.* The devout Jew accepts that status but sees himself primarily as a servant of the Lord. That was my father. I'll do it, Leo, because I hear his voice."

Feldman laughed, then said, "But I have a request, Leo. Please ask Evie to write me a note asking for an appointment.

I'm too old to play with live hand grenades that backfire when the pin comes unstuck."

Leonard signed the check. Leo thanked him and the two men shook hands. As they walked to their cars in the club's parking lot, Feldman asked, "What are your plans now, Leo?"

"I'm going to see the cardinal."

Chapter 3

THE CARDINAL

The squat, matronly housekeeper who answered the door accepted Leo's hat and coat. She knew his name immediately because he had been summoned by the cardinal. Leo's letter asking for a meeting had been ignored. Her perfunctory good evening indicated His Eminence might be displeased with the guest. She knew that was the history of most command audiences.

The housekeeper turned, led the detective to a large parlor and closed the door as soon as his back heel allowed her to do so. The penetrating eyes of Cardinal George Mundelein looked down on Leo from the receiving room's portrait gallery. Mundelein was the most aristocratic of Chicago's long line of princes of the Church. Some attributed that to the fact that the prelate, a brilliant student, had studied in Rome. Yet the patrician had been a poor boy, born in New York in 1872 and raised on the Lower East Side. Mundelein was ordained for the Brooklyn diocese, was appointed the third leader of Chicago's Catholics in 1915 and remained the most powerful individual in the city until his death twenty-four years later.

Mundelein reminded Leo of his friend Cappy. Father Timothy "Cappy" Conlon was the longtime pastor of Old St. Malachy's Church at Ninth Street and South Wabash Avenue in the Loop. The pastor and prelate were brick-and-mortar men. Mundelein built most of the great edifices of the archdiocese—from seminaries and hospitals to a vast sweep of churches and schools. He was consecrated a cardinal in 1924. The honor represented the growing power of Chicago in America as well as in the global Catholic Church. Mundelein eventually died in 1939.

The cardinals who followed Mundelein assumed many of his traits and much of his influence. They had prided themselves more on building than books; they thought more about turf and less of theology; they knew the eternal value of their rosary beads but also the worth of a buck in the bank. Their views and voices made the walls of city hall tremble for decades. Bankers, lawyers and other pillars of the community quaked when they raised a hand. They were the power and glory of Chicago—until the aftershocks of the Second Vatican Council. Carmody was then faced with doctrinal, clerical, social and eventually financial chaos. And worse—he was viewed as a paper pusher.

The wait seemed eerie to Leo; the parlor was dark except for a single lamp near a distant desk. The sun, which had spun through openings in the dark red velvet drapes, had fallen as evening approached. Where was Fats? Leo asked himself. It had been more than forty years since he had called his grade-school chum that. His classmates had nicknamed Carmody "Fats" in the fifth grade when the redhead was eleven years old. Fats was about 160 pounds of peanut butter and jelly. He was far too slow for sports but had a quick mind and a booming voice that made him the class valedictorian. Only five years after he was ordained a priest, Carmody was named private secretary to Cardinal Albert Meyer and after a while became a monsignor. Carmody rode the royal wave and then became an associate bishop of the archdiocese. Many Chicago priests said the 280-pound insider raised himself to the bishopric by lifting his mind instead of his body.

Carmody, well known for his conservative views, was named by Pope John Paul II to succeed Cardinal Joseph Bernardin. Bernardin had possessed the gift of conciliation. Chicagoans didn't turn the other cheek unless they told someone to kiss it. However, Bernardin knew how to make peace among the tribe. The big question was whether Carmody could do the same.

The city's clergy, divided since the Second Vatican Council, played by new rules. The operative words in clerical circles—devotion, dedication and discretion—had new meaning. Being a devoted priest now meant avoiding public arguments about doctrinal change. A priest was dedicated when he didn't confront his pastor over one issue or another. A cleric was the soul of discretion when he kept his opinions to himself. The younger clergy wanted changes in the Church but didn't want to upset the ecclesiastical apple cart . . .

Leo asked himself about the pamphlet was on the nearby table? Didn't he recognize a face? Sure, it was Bill Carmody, the cardinal's younger brother. Leo picked up the pamphlet and began reading . . .

"Mr. William Carmody, distinguished Chicago attorney and brother of the cardinal, will address the Chicago Lawyers Guild on the relationship of the Second Vatican Council to the modern legal profession.

"Mr. Carmody, a longtime member of the Guild and other Chicago professional and civic organizations, will discuss the increased role of lawyers and the laity in Church affairs. Mr. Carmody, who has had private audiences with Popes Paul VI and John Paul II, has visited the Vatican on numerous occasions since the council to discuss the future of the U.S. laity with Church officials."

Leo returned the pamphlet to the table, squinted around the room as if trying to find an answer to a troubling question, then murmured to himself: "My God, Bill Carmody, *Rusty's father,* is one of the country's leading laymen."

Leo was glancing between the pamphlet and Fats's impressive portrait when the housekeeper reappeared and motioned to him to follow her. As he walked behind the woman, Leo was startled to see Cappy Conlon stepping gingerly down the deep dark rug of the central stairway. The stairway led to the cardinal's private reception room on the second floor. Cappy now pulled a flask from inside his suit coat and swigged a long whiskey, swishing it in his mouth. The swallow washed down with the rise and fall of his Adam's apple. His high cheeks glowed and the fire lit candles in his eyes. Cappy sighed his favorite aspiration: "Glory be to God!"

"Good evening, Cap," Leo said in the hushed tone of someone in church.

Startled, it took the St. Malachy's pastor several seconds to reply, "Glory be, Leo, it's good to see you. I hope you have better luck than I did. God bless."

Pure Cap, Leo thought. A blunt old-school priest. Sixty-eight years old. Some forty-five years at the venerable downtown church at Ninth Street and South Wabash. He wore an Irish cap with a peak like a jockey and so everyone called him Cappy. The pastor *looked* like a jockey too, about five feet on his tiptoes. A good gust of lakefront wind could lift him from the ground and drop the little fellow to his knees on the street, Leo thought. The drink never did that.

Everyone knew Cappy. No one forgot him. He said midnight Mass on Saturday for police and firemen as well as for the downtown acting and restaurant crowds. Some called it the Actors' Mass. Cappy walked the streets at all hours, pulling the homeless into the shelter of St. Malachy's basement. The little fellow gave the last rites to many a wounded cop or injured fireman. The wintry blasts, the whiskey in the cracks of his lips, the curses of the city and the cross of the Church—these were his world. He spit out nothing and would choke to death before coughing up a soul to hunger or damnation. A man of the chalice, the confessional and celibacy—they were his Holy Trinity. Cappy's mortal weaknesses were several devout morning, afternoon and nightly nips. The brand never mattered but he preferred Jameson's Irish whiskey. Bushmill's were a bunch of Black Irish Protestants.

What was Cappy doing here? Leo wondered. Why didn't the pastor have better luck? He must find out.

The housekeeper, who had seen the bottle, gave Cappy the glass eye, which he ignored as he picked up his coat and cap. He showed himself out onto the well-lit North State Parkway, where a squad car waited in front of the brownstone mansion to return the pastor to St. Malachy's. The cops took care of their own.

The woman opened the door to the cardinal's reception room and closed it quickly. Leo heard Carmody's soft welcome: "Good evening, Leo. Come over and sit down."

The Irishman saw the small lamp at the far end of the room and moved toward it, finally saw the cardinal's red robes in the light's reflection. Carmody's predecessors wore black suits except on church occasions; the cardinal wore his red often. Carmody didn't get up, he sat in a large gold-leaf chair. After Leo bent and kissed his ring the cardinal motioned him to sit on a nearby mahogany chair.

"Good to see you, Leo. It's been a while. I hope the family's well."

The detective swallowed. "Indeed, Your Eminence, five years, I believe, since we last met. The family's fine, thanks."

"Has it been that long?" sighed Carmody.

"Yes, the Police Association's Awards banquet back in 1989." Leo was too polite to mention Carmody had presented him with a service medal that evening.

The cardinal leaned back in his chair, entwined his fingers and noted the white stubble that speckled the detective's chin. Leo's suit looked like it came off a discount rack on the Far South Side, his shirt collar was yellowed with age and cheap starch, he still wore old-fashioned black high-top shoes with white socks. White socks! Leo's ears stood straight up, cocked, straining. His mop of white hair, jumbled like uncut grass, projected an awkward but acceptable dignity. He watched as the cardinal studied him. Carmody wore bright red slippers with gold-colored stitching. The needlework seemed to weave two crossed keys—the keys of the Kingdom. The cardinal's legs, stumpy and spread wide, revealed the bulge of his ankles. Leo noted Carmody's burgundy-colored silk hose. His cassock also was silk but the cardinal had shed his cape and wore a friendly wine-colored sweater. It took Leo several moments to recognize the knitting on the left chest of the wool. Stitched in papal gold and white, the dome of St. Peter's Basilica rose and fell on his chest as the cardinal breathed. Underneath Michelangelo's masterpiece, the detective saw Carmody's Latin motto—*Pater et Familia.* Beneath the motto the curvature of his personal signature spelled out CARDINAL CARMODY.

Leo swallowed hard and remembered seeing Presidents Johnson, Nixon, Ford, Reagan, Bush and now Clinton on television wearing a special presidential jacket. The emblematic eagle, quivers and olive branch of the presidency were emblazoned on the blue silk with these words encircling that stitching: PRESIDENT OF THE UNITED STATES OF AMERICA. Leo had recoiled from what seemed exceptional vanity.

Wisps of white hair leaped from the cardinal's head. Jagged lines of blue veins inched upward from the jowls of Fats's flush-red face. His thick, short neck weighed heavy with flesh. The character of the man sprang from his changing gray-green eyes. Swift, penetrating, cold, they were the image of Chicago on a chill cloudy day. The pupils swelled and evaporated like the city's weather, from pallid to light gray, from flat to a lush green. The green had now disappeared entirely. The eyes were enveloped in gray, casting a wintry pall over the flush of high blood pressure on Fats's face.

Carmody cleared his throat. The civilities had been exchanged. His dinner was getting cold. The housekeeper had left. He said, "Leo, I've asked you here this evening because of two important matters. You can help the archdiocese, old friend, and I'm sure everyone will be most appreciative of your assistance."

Carmody paused, allowing his expression of humility and need to take effect. Leo noted the cardinal was asking in the name of others, not himself. His back stiffened. The detective in him didn't like the distant approach, but he said nothing.

Carmody saw the hint of resistance on Leo's face. He wasn't an old office pro for nothing. His Eminence relented momentarily: "We shared a lot in the old days, Leo. Maybe our creased faces now seem more like maps of the city. The past has left us a great legacy. But a cardinal must forget friend or foe. He must be a man only in the service of the Church and God."

What the hell was Fats getting at? Leo didn't wait long for an answer.

"There is first the matter of Father Conlon at St. Malachy's. I believe you know Cappy."

Leo nodded, now more defensive than ever.

"Unfortunately, as you know, St. Malachy's is very old. The structure is defective and we're going to have to close it for the congregation's safety. I'm afraid Cap will have to retire."

"Jesus, Mary, and Joseph!" Leo's reaction echoed audibly around the room. He was overwhelmed. Fats was asking Cappy to dig his own grave by not only tearing down St. Malachy's but leaving two years before the mandatory retirement age of seventy. Leo turned away, silently talking to himself.

Both men had known Conlon for decades. Leo had met him when the two as youths worked summers in the onetime stockyard slaughterhouses. "Is Fats asking me to skin a lifetime friend like a pig?"

Upset and edging toward anger, Leo clenched his teeth. Instinctively Carmody knew Leo was thinking of earlier days when all were poor young Irishmen. Such reflection made the prelate uneasy. His immigrant parents had, as the greenhorn Irish used to say, little more than a pot to piss in. His father was a streetcar motorman who eventually rose to supervisor at the old 69th and South Ashland car barn. The Carmodys had five kids and lived from payday to payday, squeezing a buck like all their neighbors. They didn't have the means to push their eldest, Brendan, much further than a year or two at accounting school—certainly not to medical or law school. If the barriers were too great, what did the clever do? They leaped the hurdles and took the highest road—the priesthood, where the Church footed the educational bills. They became the nobility. Edward Brendan Carmody, who was uncomfortable with his common first name, was more like the city's Irish greenhorns than he liked to admit.

Leo was repelled by the notion of skinning Cappy. The detective hadn't had a drink in many years but he could feel Cappy's pint hidden inside his own dark suit. The bottle was pressing against his pounding heart. How he wanted to whip out the pint and lift it into the air. Mouth-to-mouth resuscitation. The whiskey would drain down his throat in hot bursts. He would press the last drops against the roof of his mouth with his tongue. The bottle was empty. So was Leo as he brooded. Cappy wasn't causing trouble like the intellectuals challenging the Church's doctrine. The liturgy, Church authority, married clergy, the ordination of women, and especially a definition of the Catholic conscience, were now fair game. But Cappy wasn't rocking the boat. He wasn't in a spiritual fix. No. The pastor boasted of Chicago with civic pride—the Art Institute, Adler Planetarium, Museum of Science and Industry, the John G. Shedd Aquarium, the Field Museum of Natural History, Orchestra Hall, the Opera House, Civic Center, Lincoln Park Zoo and Soldier Field. *His* Chicago wore a halo . . .

The cardinal was speaking again, softly. He said St. Malachy's parish council, composed mostly of lay people, including non-Catholics, unanimously refused his request to close the church and merge it with another parish. Cappy also declined to retire before his seventieth birthday. The cardinal then revealed his deep concern.

"St. Malachy's is losing more than six thousand dollars a month. The archdiocese, Leo, is picking up the losses."

Carmody was, however, holding back. The cardinal had already set in motion a plan whereby St. Malachy's would render the archdiocese millions of dollars. The enterprise wouldn't wash with many of the faithful so he kept it secret and planned to use the windfall to pay off large chunks of archdiocesan debt. He would also build more suburban churches where parishioners could support parishes.

Leo understood the need to reduce St. Malachy's large monthly losses but asked, "If the church is unsafe, can't you close it?"

"That's easier said than done, Leo. The parish council may call in their own structural engineers for another professional opinion and that could take months. They're also talking about raising money to fix the church. A rabbi on the council is suggesting an ecumenical movement of Protestants, Jews and Muslims to save the place. And there's some Black Muslim woman by the name of Magnolia Gentry who says she'll have a thousand Black Muslims marching outside the church against me." The cardinal hesitated then remembered. "She calls herself Mamma X. The parishioners call her the Black Madonna. Can you beat it?"

Magnolia. How did she get involved in this with all her troubles? Her husband was a Vietnam vet suffering from post traumatic stress disorder, commonly known as Vietnam Shock Syndrome. Carmody went on. "There's one more thing, Leo, and I'm sorry to mention it . . . your daughter Kathy has left the Sisters of Mercy and joined the rebellion at St. Malachy's. And she's accompanied by another nun, Joan Solari."

"Are you *sure,* Your Eminence?"

"Yes."

"Jesus mercy!" Leo sighed.

Carmody leaned forward and placed a soothing palm on the detective's left hand. He sat on the edge of his chair, waiting for Leo to say he would help him.

"What do you want me to do?" Leo asked.

Carmody outlined his plan. Public picketing around the church had to be stopped. He couldn't ask Police Superintendent Joseph Rossi to do that, although he knew Rossi, but the chief would listen to a trusted colleague like Leo. Block the pickets with some city ordinance that would keep the protest out of the media.

"Leo, I can't get into a public fight with Cappy *and* the Protestants, Jews and Muslims. To say nothing of Father Pat Brogan, the sociologist from Loyola University, and Alderman Francis X. Fahey. Brogan and Fahey are on the council."

Leo didn't want to ask Rossi, but Carmody persisted and reluctantly Leo agreed, but his mind's eye saw the scorn on his children's faces—the subservient sheep kisses the cardinal's ring again. And his police partner, Matt Moran, would add: "And kiss Carmody's fat arse."

Carmody, not ready to release Leo, forgot the detective was a member of Alcoholics Anonymous and offered him a drink, which Leo declined. The cardinal stood, walked to a cabinet, tumbled ice into a glass and poured Scotch—neat.

"It's been a long day," he said when he returned.

God. Leo looked upward, he could use a stiff one himself. He hadn't wanted a shot so much in more than twenty years—and a beer chaser. That would at least ease his conflict. He would have a second shot, then nurse the beer. The cardinal's voice cracked through.

"You can help us with a second problem, Leo."

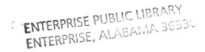

Carmody paused, waiting for Leo's positive reaction but it didn't come. His dinner was now completely cold; the prelate became impatient, took a strong swallow of Scotch and said, "It's Father Ralph Rebb. I'm sorry to say he's been picked up again for child molestation. I'm told it was an eleven-year-old altar boy. Leo, we just can't afford the scandal. I've already told Father Rebb that he must start rehabilitation. A place up in Massachusetts somewhere. We can't have this go to court, Leo. The publicity would undermine the archdiocese and all the work that we're doing. All the good work. Monsignor Tom Brady, my secretary, has spoken with the parents. We think they'll settle—"

"Settle?"

"Yes," the cardinal said, "a million-dollar out-of-court settlement."

"A *million?*"

Carmody raised his voice. "Yes, Leo, a million dollars. But the parents will never settle for that unless they think we might get the case thrown out of court. I'm thinking of the terrible publicity again, the scandal. *The harm to the archdiocese,* Leo. The money isn't an issue—"

"I thought the six thousand a month was an issue at St. Malachy's, Your Eminence."

Carmody glared, then turned away and sipped more of his Scotch.

"I'll speak with Superintendent Rossi," Leo said, "but I can't guarantee anything, especially in a case like this. Some people think we're corrupt, but not when it comes to sodomy and kids."

Leo's anger rose. Why didn't the cardinal do his own dirty work? If not himself, why not his secretary? No, the clergy must be clean. The laity should do it. After all, they're out there in the dirt. They're the unclean.

Carmody stood and extended his arm to shake hands. Leo didn't move. He sat and stared straight ahead. The cardinal withdrew his arm, tugging impatiently at the cuffs of his sweater.

"*I* have something to say, Your Eminence," Leo said. "Please give me a moment."

The cardinal was irritated, perhaps by the inflection in Leo's voice.

"I'll be brief. I believe your nephew, Rusty, should consider marrying our daughter, Evie. He made her pregnant. Are you aware of that?"

Carmody looked at him, still on his feet. "The subject has been mentioned to me, Leo, but I don't get involved in such matters. I'm running the archdiocese. Hundreds of institutions. Thousands of religious and other people. It's a huge administrative and financial responsibility—"

"Yes, I understand that six hundred thousand Catholic families of Cook County contribute more than one hundred fifty million dollars a year to the archdiocese."

Carmody ignored, or rejected, Leo's clear implication that the archdiocese was well-off. "Cardinal Bernardin has already sounded an alarm. He said the Church in Chicago would be broke in a few years unless its financial status changed for the better. *I* now have responsibility for that, and I'm not going to shirk or compromise it."

"Well, you asked me to get involved. To do your bidding. To keep your secrets about St. Malachy's and the sodomy of a priest. I'm not asking you to undercut a congregation or bury the case of a priest's sodomy. I'm trying to preserve the honor of a young woman, my daughter, who believes she was promised marriage by your nephew."

Carmody momentarily froze, then spoke metallically, as if he were reading from a Sunday church bulletin. "Rusty's father, Bill, has been to see me. My brother anticipated you would come here. Bill's one of the city's top attorneys and he told me he'll handle the matter. I must tell you that he said if you sued the case would never even get to court . . ."

"You mean someone would squash it like the Rebb sodomy case."

"I never said that, Leo."

"Yes, you did, Your Eminence. We're both from Chicago. We understand the language. As the spiritual leader of the archdiocese you refused to use your office, knowing that an abortion was possible. As my kids would put it, the cardinal copped out."

Carmody turned away, gritted his teeth, then took a long pull on his Scotch. Silence. The large standing clock ticked the only sound in the parlor. Finally Leo spoke:

"Nobody is *forcing* Rusty to marry my daughter. I'm asking that he consider it instead of having you and his father tell us how powerful they are. I can promise you one thing. *Carmody*"—he let the name linger nakedly in front of the cardinal—"may not marry my daughter, but the matter *will* go to court. We will publicly establish that he's the father. And Evie will ask him before the law, the Church, and the people of this city, including the chamber of commerce and his other clubs, to help support his child. That's a surer bet than Notre Dame on the football field."

Carmody said, "I understand your daughter is considering an abortion."

"Yes, and do you know who is asking her to do it, Your Eminence? Your nephew. Since Carmody has abandoned my daughter, I don't believe he should pressure her to have an abortion. Are you aware that he wants her to kill their child?"

The Cardinal's face flushed deep red, but he refused to answer. Leo pressed it.

"Do you know that? And didn't you say to Rusty's father, your brother, on the phone that you'd support whatever decision his son, your nephew, made? That's what all my children understand."

The prelate sat in embarrassed silence, hunched over like a man holding an indictment but refusing to read it.

Leo wouldn't be denied and burst out, "Answer the questions, Your Eminence. Is that what the Carmodys are about? Can a cardinal preach against murder and then be quiet when he sees it in his own family? Or does he send his secretary out to answer the questions? God Almighty, can't you face the facts?"

The cardinal's voice shook. "See here, Leo, I remind you to remember where you are and to whom you're talking—"

"Where am I? Who are you? Why don't you answer the question?"

There was a long silence. Finally Carmody said, "I'll speak with my brother. Perhaps Rusty can see your daughter and suggest a quiet adoption. There's no need for anyone to know about the child. She can have the baby out of state. That would be best for both of these young people. None of this must get out."

"That's a cop-out! Don't priests advocate *marriage* in such cases anymore?"

The deep anger and frustration in Leo's voice cut into the cardinal. It frightened him. Physically . . . he knew the detective carried a gun . . .

Leo knew he was unraveling. The hurt, the humiliation seemed to go through his entire body, and he said in an agonized voice, "Death . . . that's what you propose for me, for Cappy, for the child. Well, I'm not dead and I'm not a pallbearer. I'm an ex-Marine with balls. I'll die before my daughter is disgraced."

For some godforsaken reason the face of his father appeared to him. Paddy staring at the cardinal, said to Leo, He sells bad whiskey, son. Bad whiskey!

There was no greater sin in Ireland than to sell bad stuff. It was like breaking a sacred vow. Leo stared at the cardinal, who fidgeted more uncomfortably as Leo's eyes bore in on him. He was about to speak but could see that Leo was now staring off someplace, ignoring him. "Brendan Carmody sells bad whiskey . . . bad whiskey . . ."

The cardinal realized his visitor had come apart. "Can I help you, Leo?"

Leo didn't answer, his anguish submerged in a rising depression and contempt.

"What are you going to do?" the cardinal asked.

"I'm going to open up a saloon, Your Eminence."

The cardinal was momentarily confused. "What do you mean?"

"You wouldn't understand, Your Eminence. I was just thinking about Ireland, about my childhood, my father . . . and bad whiskey."

Carmody stood up, shaking his head. Dinner had waited too long. Leo did not kiss the cardinal's ring. He shook hands, and told himself, "We're strangers. In more than a half-century Brendan Carmody has never bothered to know me. And I've never known him."

The cardinal accompanied Leo to the door of the room. The two said good night and the detective ambled down the long staircase, picked up his coat and hat, walked out onto North State Parkway and lit his pipe.

Leo could not understand Carmody. Was *he* at fault? How in God's name could a prince of the Church not oppose abortion? Leo walked aimlessly along the street. Was this the new Catholic conscience?

Chapter 4

BOOM BOOM, MAMMA X AND FRIENDS

Superintendent Rossi broke a large chunk of *casareccio* from the thick loaf, stuffed slices of salami in the middle and chewed with a smile of satisfaction. Rossi especially liked Angelo's trattoria on Dearborn Street because it was a family-run place with homemade food, and Angelo reserved the back corner booth for him. The chief settled his most private business in that unpretentious square, never at his office in police headquarters at 1121 South State Street.

Rossi had ordered the same lunch for Leo Dolan—*pasta fagioli,* with white beans and ham bone. It was a Sicilian *zuppa,* much thicker than so-called soup, that Rossi's mother often made. A meal in itself. And fresh fruit for dessert.

Leo had arrived a few minutes late since Matt Moran, his

partner and driver, was slowed by heavy South Side traffic. Moran then drove on to get a corned-beef sandwich and coffee at a Madison Street deli.

"Sorry for the delay, Joe," Leo said. "You look hungry." The chief smiled and the two old friends shook hands.

"Good to see you, Leo. How are Nora and the family?" Leo said they were fine.

Since becoming superintendent Rossi had learned to get to the point quickly. "What's on your mind, Leo?" Two steaming bowls of *pasta fagioli* arrived, and Leo broke off a chunk of the Italian country bread.

"It's the cardinal, Joe."

Rossi, who had raised the steaming pasta and beans to his mouth, immediately put down his spoon. "The cardinal?" He shook his head and looked away. "What the hell does he want now? Forgive me, Leo, I mean no slight to you, but why doesn't he speak with me directly?"

"Deniability," Leo responded. "He never asked you."

"Well, give me the worst. Who do we cover for now?"

"You just about hit it on the head, Joe. First, he wants you to block any public marches around St. Malachy's. He says Cappy and his parish council plan to hit the bricks to stop him from tearing down the church. The publicity will make him and the archdiocese look bad. His message is Cappy and the church are gone."

Rossi still had not touched his *pasta fagioli.* "What else, Leo?"

"He wants you to get the city attorney to ditch the molestation charges against Father Ralph Rebb. Lose Rebb's confession or something. Anything. Carmody will ship him out somewhere."

Rossi exploded. "Rebb is a three-time loser. We warned him. What about the eleven-year-old altar boy? The last judge told Rebb he wouldn't get probation again. Where's Carmody coming from?"

"His Eminence says the case will create scandal among Catholics and cause a loss of respect for the priesthood. He says he'll ship Rebb out to a rehabilitation center. He left no doubt in my mind, Joe. He expects you to move for him on both counts."

"What do I say to the parents of that altar boy?"

"Carmody says they'll get a million bucks."

"And I take the dive?" Chief Rossi signaled Angelo, who hurried to the booth, and spoke to him in Italian. *"Mi dispiace tanto, Angelo, ma la zuppa è fredda. È la colpa mia. Per favore, puoi riscaldarla?"*

The owner promised to reheat it quickly, addressing Rossi as though he were an Italian don. He offered the chief a glass of red wine but Rossi declined.

Neither spoke. Finally Rossi pulled his chair closer to the table, leaned across to Leo and said very softly: "No."

The old friends looked one another in the eyes. Leo wasn't surprised. Rossi had always been a stand-up guy. The chief spoke in a low monotone. "No, because Cappy is one of us, and I'm not going to be a party to tearing down St. Malachy's. Not a cop, not a fireman, no one in the Loop would lift a finger against him or St. Malachy's. And 'no' on the Rebb case because the priest himself admits he stuck it to the kid four different times. We've got his confession on tape."

The chief, normally a composed individual, was angry. "Carmody and others like him have tried for years to ignore or cover up these cases. And I'm not talking just about the Catholics. It's the same for Protestants and Jews. The reason is always the same . . . their religion is more important than one priest, minister or rabbi. Or their victims. Hell, we've taken care of drunken priests, ministers and rabbis for decades. It's always for the good of the church or the temple or synagogue. Tell Carmody I said that, if he won't see the law through in these rape cases, and use the word *rape,* then the laity will do it. The days of our taking orders from the cardinal and his chancery officer are *over.* My wife and kids tell me the time of the laity has come. And from what I hear and read they may be on to something."

Angelo returned then with Rossi's steaming pasta and beans. The chief turned to the owner. *"Grazie, Angelo. Adesso, si: prendero quell' vino rosso."* He was thanking Angelo and saying he would now accept the glass of red wine. Angelo left and returned with two glasses, but Leo declined. Rossi leaned across the table again and lifted his glass.

"To Cappy and St. Malachy's!"

Leo lifted his cold water, the two clinked glasses and drank. Rossi asked about Nora, the rest of Leo's family. He could see that his old pal was uncomfortable with the question and asked, "Is anything wrong, Leo?"

The detective then blurted it out. "Evie's pregnant by Carmody's nephew. Rusty Carmody is a young lawyer on the way up. He won't marry her and suggests Evie get an abortion."

"Have you talked to the cardinal?"

"Yes."

"What did he say?"

"He *finally* said he'd speak to Rusty's father."

"And?"

"The cardinal's on the fence, Joe. Nothing will come of it."

"What's he going to do about his nephew wanting Evie to get an abortion?"

"I don't know, Joe. He mentioned an adoption but nothing definite."

"So when the clothes get dirty, it's you and me who wash

the laundry. The cardinals and bishops debate the theology of it but they don't get their hands dirty. They don't walk the streets like cops and the laity, Leo. They ride in chauffeur-driven cars. And if something breaks down or they get a flat, the grease is on our hands. They're always clean. The anointed. We're the unwashed."

The two finished their fruit, and Rossi eyed the large clock above the bar. "I'm sorry about Evie, Leo. Give Nora my best. The same from Gina. Let me know if I can do anything for you. By the way, the fireworks are about to start at St. Malachy's. The parish council meets this evening and they may vote to picket against the cardinal's plan to tear down the place."

Rossi shook Leo's hand, and Angelo presented no bill. The chief paid at the end of each month. As Angelo shook hands with both men he asked, *"Tutto è andato bene?"* All went well?

"Si, Angelo, abbiamo mangiato come due signori." Yes, Angelo, we ate like two gentlemen, Rossi told him.

The owner beamed and opened the door of the restaurant. *Ciao,* he said as the two men walked onto the sidewalk, shook hands again and parted. Rossi's driver waited nearby and the chief slid onto the front seat of his car. Moran waved to Leo from a half-block away, parked in a loading zone.

"Well?" Moran asked.

"Fats drew two deuces," Leo said.

Moran smiled. "What a great day for the church mice!"

When Leo arrived at the area he phoned the cardinal. Monsignor Thomas Brady, his private secretary, answered and said His Eminence was busy, but when Carmody heard who was on the phone he picked up the receiver and said in a formal tone, "Good afternoon. This is the cardinal."

Leo said, "The answer is no, on both counts."

An empty silence hung on the line. Leo waited. He could

hear Carmody take a deep breath. Then the receiver dropped into its cradle and the line went dead.

St. Malachy's parish council was assembling in the dank basement of the venerable house of worship. A boisterous mélange, the council was constituted by Cappy and themselves in a haphazard manner. St. Malachy's stood in the Loop and its parishioners, if they could be called that, came from all parts of Chicago and the suburbs. The church had become a rendezvous point for various groups and causes, Catholic and non-Catholic. The only apparent character reference for any council member was a willingness to serve. By various strokes of chance the group eventually embraced the world's four great faiths. Their doctrinal and moral differences were reflected far less than their most notable characteristic, a typically Chicago streak of independence. They were flamboyantly unpredictable yet fiercely loyal to their own.

Alderman Francis X. Fahey was the last to arrive at ten minutes past 7:00 P.M. Fahey was, by no account, a man fashioned after his namesake, Francis Xavier, the missionary saint. The alderman, who looked like a barrelhouse saloon bouncer, was a political good-timer, hale and well met. As all in the First Ward knew, however, the beefy Fahey shrewdly pushed all the right buttons at city hall. Indeed, it was often said he could get a blind man a driver's license.

Fahey was accompanied by Thomas "Thumbs" Rafferty, his bagman and gofer. Fahey always dealt in cash and Thumbs counted it. Thumbs often irritated some of the city's high-stakes players by counting every dollar before a deal was closed. The alderman and Rafferty assumed that everyone, in high or low stakes, was on the make. Their take, therefore, always came off the top. True, city hall and the city council were cleaner than in the old days but they still dealt many cards and took a percentage of the action across a wide array of questionable practices.

The eyes of everyone at the long, battered, coffee-stained table followed Fahey to his seat as the alderman waddled down to his favorite chair at the middle and sat down like an Old Testament Pharaoh, head high, eyes low, a hint of the imperiousness in his soft, flabby countenance. Fahey's political pedigree was long and proud by Chicago standards. He inherited the mantle of First Ward aldermen like "Bathhouse" John Coughlin and Mike "Hinky Dink" Kenna. The pair, with Big Jim Colosimo, the vice lord, brought downtown Chicago into the twentieth century. Politics and crime were blissfully wed. Scarface Al Capone, in his silk suits and large suite of offices, was a child of this marriage.

The motto of Chicago was *Urbs in Horto* or City in a Garden. City hall profiteers changed it to read *Ubi Est Mea?* or Where's Mine?

Dr. Emerson T. "Boom Boom" Braithwaite, pastor of the Fourth Presbyterian Church and current council chairman, called the meeting to order. Boom Boom, whose immaculate dickey was an extension of his precise personality, was a fastidious gentleman of the Old School. His nickname, so unlike his delicate character, was pinned on Braithwaite early in the game. It seemed young Emerson, as a boys' camp counselor, was appointed to sound reveille on his trumpet in the morning. Despite amplification over the camp's loudspeaker, half the camp never heard his wake-up calls. Emerson eventually triumphed through ingenuity, securing a small cannon. He moved the loudspeaker out onto the lawn and the rest was history.

The Reverend Braithwaite's diminutive, charming wife, Eloise, a true Southern honeysuckle, created the bond between her husband and Cappy Conlon.

"Poor Father Conlon," she would muse aloud at various civic and clerical gatherings. "He's not as big as a turnip seed. He's overworked and underfed. Somebody must care for him." That was twenty-five years earlier when she began sending Cappy her thick soups.

Boom Boom now called for attention with a studied cough and addressed the council in his customary meticulous fashion.

"I believe everyone is here and, therefore, we may begin. First of all, may I introduce a new member of the council, Kathleen Dolan. Kathy recently took leave of the Sisters of Mercy. I also wish to introduce another former Sister of Mercy, Joan Solari, who's also with us. Sisters, please stand."

The council members welcomed the pair with a healthy round of applause. Reverend Braithwaite continued:

"As all of you have been informed, Cappy is in St. Bernard's Hospital. He's been there for four days. Perhaps Father Pat Brogan can give us some news. Has he eaten anything yet, Pat?"

"No," the retired Jesuit professor from Loyola University answered. "He still refuses to eat or drink anything except water. Cap still won't call it a hunger strike or say it's a protest against the cardinal's plan to demolish St. Malachy's. But, pure and simple, that's what it is."

"Water?" boomed John L. "Socks" Sullivan, deputy fire commissioner. "What the hell is he using for a chaser?"

The room exploded in laughter.

"Is he on the wagon?" the incredulous voice of John Elixir Babbington rose from the end of the table. The longtime actor, now a local officer of Actors' Equity, was surprised. In mock humor, Babbington asked, "Is he delirious?"

Brogan replied with a wan smile. "He's mumbling something about taking the pledge."

More laughter.

The amusement deceived no one. The council was deeply grieved, and no one was more concerned than Socks Sullivan. Cappy had been his confessor as well as for scores of his fellow firemen for decades. They would confess to no one in the archdiocese, not even, or perhaps especially not, the cardinal.

Socks had pounded a beat as a cop before joining the fire department, and was fond of saying, "It wasn't the shoes that hurt. It was the socks!" Hence, the nickname.

Socks now warned the group, "If it gets out that Cappy isn't eating, people will put two and two together and get five."

The deputy often used his own unique logic. The wrong number meant trouble.

"Would you be more specific, deputy?" Boom Boom, as usual, requested precision.

"The rumor mill is no different than the gin mill." Socks spoke with his huge hands. "You start innocently with one and soon you're drowning in a half dozen. People will connect Cappy's state of mind with trouble at the church. Who knows what they'll come up with. We've got to keep the cork on this."

Rabbi Irving "Goldie" Goldman, some said the shrewdest but also most disarming of the group, agreed, though only to a point. Goldie, the former chief rabbi at three different synagogues in the city, was the council elder at seventy-nine years of age. He spoke little, but when he did everyone listened.

Goldie now surmised in his usual casual undertone, "We don't want to be accused of spreading the news that Cappy may be on a hunger strike against the cardinal. However, we must be prepared to move in advance of any adversary. We shouldn't be faced with a *fait accompli*. I mean, action by His

Eminence or one of his emissaries. We must keep St. Malachy's viable."

An air of conspiracy rose from the table and seemed to thicken as the dim ceiling lights began to tremble. Actually, the movement was caused by the Wabash Avenue traffic. For the first time, the full seriousness of the meeting fell across their faces.

Magnolia Gentry, known among council members as Mamma X and to parishioners as the Black Madonna, blew a soft low whistle. Mamma had become one of the best-known females among the city's Black Muslims thanks to her ability to fire up a crowd.

"Goldie," she said, "do you mean we're seriously fixin' to take on the Man? The big red cardinal?"

The rabbi reflected. "Sometimes, man is pursued by the inevitable."

Goldie and Mamma X had brought the holy water to a boil. The council might soon face a searing choice and their decision weighed heavily on each of them.

Mamma X sat back in her seat. It had been many years since she first met Cappy. As a young crusader she had led a strike of nurses at Cook County Hospital and met the pastor near St. Malachy's on a chilly December evening. She had said, "Reverend, I gotta pick the lock on your church. The nurses need a place to talk about our strike over at Cook County. It ain't right for us to have to meet on the street in the cold."

"You've got St. Malachy's basement," the pastor had replied.

The nurses at Cook County and other groups had met at St. Malachy's for years, and an unshakable bond developed between them and the little wishbone of a pastor. The big black woman and wisp of a white priest were an almost comical pair standing side by side, but they carried off their relationship with such elegance of manner that Socks once declared, "How these Christians and Muslims love one another!"

Father Mario Fortunato, Cappy's assistant, addressed Goldie now. "You seem to assume, rabbi, that we still have freedom to act. The cardinal sent the demolition contractor here last Monday. The contractor is getting the permits now and says the church will be down and the area cleared in a few weeks. *That* conversation put Cappy in the hospital. That's why he's on the hunger strike. He's sending a message to the cardinal."

Bridget "Bridie" O'Brien piped in, "Are we going to let the cardinal pull the strings on St. Malachy's from the chancery office? I'm sure His Eminence is already up to something. We've two questions before us—whether the contractor is going to receive those permits and whether we go public to save the church?"

Bridie, whose departed husband had left her an enormous windfall from his liquor-distribution business—some said in excess of fourteen million dollars—was no friend of the cardinal. He had variously ignored or rebuffed her efforts to become more involved with the Church and its leadership. Some said Carmody viewed Bridie's inheritance as "tainted money" because of her husband's freewheeling promotion of booze. It was suggested Bob O'Brien would, if he could, put a bourbon ad in every parish news bulletin in Chicago. Some also claimed that Bridie, whose father was a butcher in the stockyards and whose mother was a housemaid, could outswear any bartender on the South Side. The widow, now in her late sixties, had become a North Shore socialite and was spoiling for a fight with Fats Carmody. She said so in unmistakable terms.

"If the facts are properly presented, public opinion will be on our side. The cardinal will prevail if we play by his rules, silence and secret handshakes. So I think we've got to stick it to Fats by going public."

"Righto! Righto!" John Elixir Babbington, the former English actor and High Anglican, interrupted. He tapped his cane forcefully on the basement floor, which surprised the other council members because Babbington, usually a man of impeccable manners, rarely took the stage at these meetings. On occasion, however, he did, indulging a trait not uncommon among thespians.

Babbington's downfall had been quick and merciless. He had got pleasantly inebriated some years back, managed to assume his acting role on the Blackstone stage and turned the theater into a near public brawl. Shortly after the first act opened, Babbington began babbling, saying anything that came to his lips. The helpless cast tried to ad-lib. Babbington ridiculed them, saying the play was a farce anyway. The management tried to pull down the curtain but it got stuck at half-mast.

Babbington then began a monologue about theatrical treachery. The audience baited him with barbs of their own, which led to insults. By the time police arrived the evening performance had degenerated into a shouting match between the drunk onstage and tipplers in the audience.

As the cops carried him offstage, Babbington had closed his right fist and thrust up his middle finger at the packed house. That may have caused the greatest audience reaction of his long career. Police had to close down the place. Local politics taught Chicagoans to endure a lot, but they weren't prepared to accept the finger from a Limey.

Eventually it was Cappy who broke Babbington from the booze. He took the actor into his rectory for several months. It seemed surprising that a man like Cappy, who drank so much and apparently so happily, could turn another away from the bottle. The pastor explained it simply: "Prayer and self-pride. They're the best double-play combination on the South Side. The White Sox could use 'em."

K.C. Wu spoke little more than a Trappist monk, so no one knew how he and Cappy met. Wu seemed to be always smiling inscrutably to most of the council. The leader of the Chinese Businessman's Association was an enigma, but it was known that he had big chopsticks in Chinatown—a bank, three import-export stores, two real-estate offices, three restaurants, two jewelry shops, and rumors of additional holdings in San Francisco, Seattle and Hong Kong. No one appeared to know anything about Wu's family life although he once showed the rabbi a photo of a Chinese woman with seven children.

It was the pastor who bound the council together. Members traveled their separate ways and came together once each month, barring an emergency. This was the first such crisis in anyone's memory. Cappy never attempted to dominate the council. The pastor actually said little and wouldn't think of overruling a council decision. His presence was like a sanctuary lamp, keeping a steady vigil at the altar of St. Malachy's.

The current issue, though, was different. Council members viewed the conflict between Cappy and the cardinal as a critical, personal confrontation. They were convinced the little priest could die in his hunger strike. They understood Cappy was, like each of them, a frail human with a fault. The priest's long affair with the bottle had become an expression of that humanity. He was never drunk, nor was he ever perfectly sober. Cappy was God's imperfection in a religion that extolled and sanctified perfection. He was the blackened and bruised mouse in a Church that glorified saints and uplifted the cardinal red.

The Reverend Braithwaite turned to Kathy and asked, "Do you have any observations, Miss Dolan?"

The former nun was surprised at being recognized at her first meeting. When she hesitated Boom Boom urged her to speak. So after a pause, Kathy asked, "Is it possible to make St. Malachy's structurally sound? If so, how can we finance the undertaking?"

For some unexplainable reason the council hadn't discussed that possibility. The members buzzed with questions. Father Fortunato said, "The cardinal's secretary explained our problem. The roof girders are threatening the stability of the church's walls."

"Perhaps we can find an engineer to see if anything can be done," Kathy said.

Alderman Fahey piped up. "I make the motion that we hire an engineer and get a second opinion. You can send the tab to me!"

The council cheered the gesture. Fahey, nodding like a proud turkey, continued. "I also want to let the council know that, as of tonight, the wrecking contractor's requests for work permits are being delayed indefinitely. They will shortly be officially lost. I don't think they'll be found for at least thirty days."

Another round of cheers. Fahey beamed.

Bridie raised her hand and Boom Boom recognized her. "Perhaps we could get St. Malachy's declared an historic landmark? I'm a member of the Chicago Historical Society and the National Trust for Historic Preservation in Washington. If St. Malachy's is officially declared a historic landmark by the Chicago and national preservation societies we may be able to snap the cardinal's suspenders."

Kathy said, "We must still be certain that the structure can be made sound. The historic designations would hopefully follow."

"I take it then," said Boom Boom, "that the two proposals, finding an engineer and obtaining the historic designations, are ready for seconding and a vote."

Mamma X and Babbington seconded the motions and the council approved them with applause. Kathy, who now seemed to feel at home among the group, asked, "If the cardinal finds a way to obtain the permits for the church's destruction, no disrespect to you, Alderman Fahey, we may have to throw a picket line around St. Malachy's. Let's face it, the archdiocese is powerful."

Rabbi Goldman said, "Once the demolition teams arrive on the scene, the cardinal will have gone public. We've a right to respond. We must march before the wrecking ball starts bouncing off the walls of St. Malachy's."

Mamma X, who had been quieter than usual, spoke up. "If everybody agrees, we'll march," and Kathy immediately volunteered to be one of the pickets. It was clear that, without Cappy's presence, the council was a social and political powder keg.

Kathy was designated to find the engineer. She and Mamma X would prepare a contingent of marchers to picket the church, and Bridie would try to obtain the historic designations. The socialite cautioned it could take time to obtain the approvals, though she had some cards to call in. Presumably Birdie referred to her handsome political campaign contributions to all levels of government.

Beau Beauchamps, the church janitor, groaned in the darkness at the rear of the basement. Beau, a white-haired New Orleans-born half-Creole, had worked under Cappy for two decades. He was now seventy-six years old.

Boom Boom heard and asked, "Are you all right, Beau?"

Beau didn't respond. Boom Boom waited. The minister knew the janitor, even as a young man, couldn't be rushed. Beau had been a piano man, had come to town in 1922 with

Jelly Roll Morton. Morton, the composer of "Wolverine Blues" and "Chicago Breakdown," had turned South Side music upside down with his jazz improvisations. Beau played New Orleans music, sounds that grabbed 'em early and kept 'em late. Boom Boom remembered other greats who had hit South State Street in a musical shoot-out—Fatha Hines, Fats Waller, Tony Weatherford, Louis Armstrong, King Oliver. As Beau often put it, "Man, it was the mostest!"

Boom Boom called out now that Beau say a few words. No evening in the basement could be complete without him. Beau ate and lived there. He walked forward several paces to the edge of the light.

"Reverend Boom Boom, my soul's sick. Cappy's gotta start eatin'. Ah don't want that man walkin' away from us folks. Ah'm mighty upset. Thank ya, sir."

Boom Boom turned to Father Fortunato. "Perhaps you can tell us a bit more about Cappy."

"He just refuses to eat," Father Fortunato said. "He never says more than a word or two. We may have to force-feed him. He's already lost six pounds. That's a lot of Cappy. The doctors say visitors might cheer him up and change his mind, but he wants to be alone. He just props himself on a pillow in bed and recites the rosary. Over and over."

"What can we do?" Mamma X said.

"I don't know. He seems to be having a conversation with his conscience and God. I think Cappy wants to settle his accounts. Take me or give me back St. Malachy's."

Bridie came forward and laid twenty one-hundred dollar bills in front of Fortunato. Before walking away she said, "That's for Cappy's hospital bill."

Despite Bridie's generosity a sadness enveloped the room. Boom Boom summarized the evening's decisions and proposed that the council meet in a week. The minister would phone them if an earlier meeting were needed. All agreed.

The membership stood in a group. Kathy and Mamma X set up a meeting to organize their pickets. Other conversations developed, but one by one the members departed and Beau turned out the basement lights.

It had begun to drizzle when Thumbs, locating a number in his pocket address book, dialed the pay phone around the corner from the church. He handed the phone to the alderman when it began to ring at the other end.

"Hello, Knocko. This is Frank Fahey. Sorry to disturb you and the family at this late hour, but it's important. Knocko, you've got some applications there in city hall for work permits. They're to demolish Old St. Malachy's. It's important that we find those papers, all of them, as soon as possible . . . Good, Knocko. I knew we could count on your full cooperation. Now I want them deep-sixed. Every page, every line. The contractor will file again when he discovers the applications have been lost. Sit on his reapplication until I give you the word. Hell, lad, I know the archdiocese had to have hired the contractor. Kiss off the cardinal! We're taking care of Cappy on this one. The cardinal's out in the cold, boy!

"Fine, Knocko! You still got a punch, kid! My best to the Missus and all the Kellys. Tell the wife I'll be stopping by personally sometime before Christmas. A little holiday cheer, you might say. Good night, Knocko, and God bless."

Thumbs had been standing in the rain while the alderman delivered his message from inside the phone booth. Fahey, seeing the water drip down the middle-aged face of his errand boy, said, "C'mon, Thumbs. Let's lift one for Cappy."

Chapter 5

THE NEW ORDER

It was 6:00 P.M. Dr. Leonard Feldman had finished an hour earlier than usual with his last patient for the day. The streets of the city had darkened under the uncertain May sky. Feldman turned on a second set of lights in his office, said good night to his nurse, picked up his phone and dialed a long-distance number. A loud, energetic voice answered.

"Is that you, HiYo?" Feldman asked.

"Who the hell do you think it would be, Leonard?" The man behind the hoarse rasp knew Feldman's voice.

"I thought it might be one of your sons, HiYo. They've got strong voices and sound like you."

Dr. H.Y. Silverman laughed. "Never as strong as this old horse thief! Hey, Leonard, I met one of those Australian horse breeders the other day. Do you know what he dropped on me? He said he'd never met a Jewish cowboy before."

HiYo laughed loudly. Dr. H.Y. Silverman was called HiYo because his initials and family name reminded local folks of the Lone Ranger's call to his horse Silver. The physician's name was actually Harold Younger Silverman, the middle name connoting he was the younger of four sons.

Silverman, a tall, husky outdoorsman, owned the HiYo Silver Ranch in the back country of Chino Valley, Arizona. He was born there and had been a family doctor in central Arizona for nearly forty years. For two decades he had owned a stable of thoroughbred horses that raced at two tracks—Turf Paradise in Phoenix and Prescott Downs in nearby Prescott. Turf Paradise ran from early fall through much of the spring, and Prescott Downs followed throughout the summer. HiYo's horses raced all year and were never far from home.

Leonard Feldman had met Silverman at Turf Paradise a dozen years earlier. The Chicagoan and his wife took a week's vacation in February every year and went to Phoenix, she to play golf and he to play the ponies. Not surprisingly, the Chicago physician and the Arizona country doctor became friends. The Silvermans invited the Feldmans to their Chino Valley ranch and Prescott Downs in 1985, and Leonard and Sarah fell in love with the rolling hills, Silverman's racehorses and Prescott Downs only fifteen miles away. The country charm of Prescott Downs's aging stands, its unpretentious paddock and windblown stables called Leonard to the track every day.

Prescott was an historic city and track. The town was the old territorial capital of Arizona and held its first race there in 1866. America's first rodeo was performed on the grounds in 1888. The onetime mining town was one of the most colorful of the Old West.

The Feldmans purchased land to build a retirement home in Chino Valley near HiYo, the track and Antelope Hills golf course.

Leo now was explaining his phone call to HiYo. "I saw that Dr. Max is running today at Prescott Downs. You're running him at five and a half furlongs instead of seven. Why?"

"Leonard, Max is more than six years old now. He can run the seven furlongs, but we can't race him for at least a month after running that long. He's bone-dry and stretched. Why are you asking, are you playing him today?"

"I've already bet a sentimental two bucks, but I was surprised when you moved him down."

"Leonard, you and I are both getting old. So is Dr. Max."

The two men laughed.

"Okay," Leonard said, "I'll call you next week about that young filly, Little Star. I'm hoping for big things."

"All right," said HiYo, "but I'll be happy if she wins enough dough her first year to pay for her oats."

The receivers clicked amid laughter, and Feldman made a mental note. Dr. Max was running in the twelfth race. That would be about 7:00 P.M. Chicago time.

He opened his inner-office door and motioned Evie Dolan to come in. The teacher seemed so young, as if she were still a teenager. Feldman had to remind himself that Evie was twenty-four. The young woman stood now before him with little makeup, a plain brown skirt and blouse and an angelic face. She had reddish blonde hair and innocent blue eyes. She was a Dolan, all right. There was a freshness about her, a subdued but irrepressible vitality, and no apparent affectation.

Evie removed her poplin raincoat and sat in the center of three chairs spread in front of the physician's desk. She seemed calm but the doctor's practiced eyes saw traces of fear in her eyes.

Feldman was a no-nonsense professional who spoke plainly and directly with patients and their families. His mind was often so deep in a case that he sometimes even appeared brusque. Some patients needed several visits before becoming comfortable with him. But once they had overcome that initial hurdle none ever left his care. Feldman not only excelled in his profession but exuded unshakable personal integrity.

Evie was surprised when Feldman pulled a packet of chewing gum from a desk drawer and offered her a stick. She declined but he unwrapped one and stuck it in his mouth.

"My wife says I smell like an antiseptic ward when I come home for dinner, so now I breathe a little spearmint on her."

Evie smiled and squirmed in her seat, then said, "Thank you for seeing me, Dr. Feldman."

"No thanks needed. We're a family. I'm happy to be of whatever service I can to you, your mother and father, to *all* the Dolans. That's a fact. Now tell me what's on your mind."

"Of course, you know I'm pregnant—and single. The man involved doesn't want to marry me. I'm getting conflicting advice about whether to have the child. I just don't know what to do. I'm confused, and I know I'm not prepared to have a child out of wedlock." Evie paused and added, "Frankly, Dr. Feldman, I haven't been able to face my mother and father. I'm still ashamed, but I've no qualms about being here. Have you handled many abortion cases?"

"I don't perform abortions," the doctor said crisply, "but I've had patients who've had problems after abortions."

Evie told Feldman she needed a professional to help her understand the medical and moral aspects of abortion. He explained he wasn't a psychiatrist, priest or rabbi. He was a doctor, and offered ethical advice only when it was relevant to the medical case. Did she understand that?

Evie said she did but was having difficulty separating abortion from its moral consequences. She believed in God but couldn't understand why various religious beliefs differed so on abortion.

Feldman said, "Then I have a different role here this evening than I anticipated. I'm not primarily a doctor but someone counseling you as a friend of the family. Evie, I'm a little uncomfortable about talking about the morality of abortion with a Catholic. My dear, I am what I am, an elderly Orthodox Jewish doctor getting near his retirement. I'm not King Solomon, just a man who reads the Torah."

Feldman said he felt it necessary to explain a little about the Torah. Its Five Books of Moses represented the constitution of the Jewish people, he said, the terms of the Jews' Covenant with God. "I believe the words of the Torah are sacred. But do you as a Catholic?"

Evie said, "I need to hear your moral as well as medical viewpoint."

Feldman said a distinction had to be made between Catholics and Orthodox Jews. For Jews, holiness didn't mean embracing an ascetic saintliness. They stressed participation in human activity. Jews were obliged to contribute to the community. They emphasized sharing. "We must distinguish right from wrong, the clean from the unclean, the sacred from the profane. However, my dear, I don't discuss personal sanctity. I speak about community life."

The physician was telling her that he wasn't going to push any of his beliefs down her throat like a tonsil stick, and now Evie was steadily relaxing. Feldman told her that he was intellectually and morally convinced life existed from the moment of conception. He said that was because the sperm and egg created a unique genetic entity. Fourteen days after conception heart contractions could be traced, he said. Blood cells developed at about seventeen days. A day or so later the heart began to beat, and electrocardiographic examination showed a regular heart function in embryos as early as six weeks. He said that in fewer than seven weeks the sex of a fetus would be determined. Electronic recording established human brain activity at two months. By the twelfth week the brain structure was basically complete. The child, he said, would turn its head, kick its feet and open its mouth. Ultrasonography combined with other medical advances allowed doctors to diagnose the general health at eighteen to twenty weeks of gestation.

"There's no question for me. This is early human life. G.K. Chesterton put it succinctly when he said, 'I am.' The Supreme Court and many others say otherwise." Feldman added, "I believe if it's legitimate to legalize mothers' rights, it's also permissible—indeed, justice—to legalize those of the fetus."

He added an afterthought. "If the medical profession as well as the scientific and theological worlds can't agree on when life begins, how can a group of judges rule that life doesn't exist?" He returned to his chair and sat down.

Evie said he sounded a little like her brother Dan before the Chicago City Council.

Feldman smiled. "I'm afraid I'd never make a Chicago politician." He sat back in his chair and said other Western democracies had settled the abortion issue through the legislative process. In taking that decision out of the hands of the states in 1973 the Supreme Court justices, he felt, deprived the American people of the chance to acknowledge the interests involved. He said the pro-choice movement had stressed the separation of church and state, that abortion shouldn't be made a religious issue. Yet many of these pro-choice people supported the religious or moral rights advocated by Dr. Martin Luther King. And most backed the moral opponents of the war in Vietnam.

"Let me tell you a personal story," Feldman said. "After I finished my internship at Michael Reese Hospital here in Chicago I went out to California in the late 1950s to work for the state. A lot of my practice was among poor migrant farm workers from Mexico. I met Cesar Chavez, leader of the United Farm Workers, who was a devout Catholic. He asked for God's justice for the migrants. I remember the politicians and others who flocked to his side. Many weren't Catholic but they even went to Mass since Chavez's moral foundation was the Church. I never heard those activists call for the separation of church and state.

"The pro-choice people speak of the unwanted child, economic problems and other serious difficulties of an unwed mother. But there's a *shortage* of babies in the United States. American couples are going to Eastern Europe, the Far East and Latin America to adopt children. Wouldn't they accept an unwanted American child?

"They talk about the agony of a mother in surrendering her child to another family. Her guilt, shame, remorse. But what about the trauma from an abortion? Some women suffer nightmares, nervous collapse, and guilt.

"Evie, the Supreme Court has overturned Judeo-Christian principles according to which life has absolute value." His voice rasped and he appeared tired.

"Evie, I think we ought to call it a day. What do you think?"

"Oh, yes, of course. And I thank you."

Actually, Evie appeared torn by the many arguments, though she managed a pleasant smile and shook the physician's hand as if not wanting to let go.

"Evie, if you want to see me again, I'll be here. I'll deliver the baby if you want, and help you find an adoption agency if you ask."

On parting at the outer office door Feldman said, "I ask you only one favor. Have dinner with your parents. Will you do that?"

"I will," she said. She walked to her car in the parking garage, started the engine and turned on the lights. As she did so, Feldman's closing words returned:

"The Supreme Court has overturned Judeo-Christian principles according to which life has absolute value."

It was about 7:00 P.M. Feldman couldn't shake a distant image from his mind. He saw himself standing next to the rail at Prescott Downs, looking across the track at the eight open stalls where the horses were being saddled. Two large signs advertising chewing tobacco hung from the nearby judges' stand. An ambulance stood a few feet away. The green tote board listed eight horses. He could see the orange-and-white pole at the finish line.

He called his bookie "Fast Eddie" Flynn. "How did Dr. Max do in the twelfth at Prescott Downs?"

Eddie left the phone for a moment, returned and said, "Dr. Feldman, that old nag just won in a photo finish."

The physician's face lit up.

Well, well, there are still miracles. Was it a sign of hope for Evie?

Chapter 6

AUTHORITY VS. CONSCIENCE

Kathy Dolan smiled broadly as she walked with her parents to 11:00 A.M. Mass at Queen of Martyrs Church. It was, after all, the first time in years that she would spend a whole Sunday at home. The transition for Leo and Nora since Kathy left the convent had been difficult but they were happy to see her more often.

As usual the church was crowded and the three were fortunate to find themselves in the same pew. Monsignor Thomas Brady, the cardinal's private secretary, approached the altar to begin Mass.

Brady, a tall, robust man of 210 pounds, fifty-three years old, with silver-gray hair, was a distinguished-looking cleric with light blue eyes and soft skin. Like the cardinal, the monsignor was a Roman, having attended the Gregorian University for doctoral studies after ordination.

As Brady called on the congregation to offer each other the "peace-be-with you" greeting Kathy recalled that when she asked for a meeting with the cardinal before leaving the Sisters of Mercy it was the same Brady who turned her down.

The former nun still opposed the archdiocesan policy of closing inner-city Catholic schools because of financial problems. She believed Carmody could find the money to keep the schools open . . . special fund-raising efforts, cutting other archdiocesan expenses, particularly among the hierarchy, selling Holy Hills seminary near Niles, Illinois. The students could be transferred elsewhere. The cardinal had taken none of these options at St. Leo and St. Brendan elementary schools where she had served. He had refused to listen to Kathy who had been the second-ranked in her graduating class at Rosary College and was considered among the best and brightest of America's Catholic school system.

As Monsignor Brady now said the opening prayers of the Mass his silver hair seemed to glow in the late morning light that shimmered through a side window but his features were pallid. The secretary seemed older than his years, with twenty more pounds than needed and weak color in his eyes, though they moved alertly.

It was only yesterday that Kathy had met with Brady, and she recalled the long, distressful meeting in her office at Ogden Park School. She had founded the school with Joan Solari after the Sisters of Mercy had dispensed the two from their vows.

The monsignor had told her, "The cardinal asked me to see you. He was sorry that he couldn't meet you personally but he's quite busy, as you know."

No, she didn't know. That was Carmody's original excuse in not seeing her. However, she didn't challenge the secretary.

"He wanted me to discuss St. Malachy's with you," Brady said with an edge in his voice. He halted, apparently expecting Kathy to respond. She kept silent. The monsignor, an urbane man with officious manners, seemed unsettled by her aloofness. He measured her carefully, then Brady finally said, "His Eminence has heard rumors that you and others of St. Malachy's parish council plan to stage a protest march to stop the closing of the church. The cardinal feels that such picketing is inappropriate and could cause considerable problems for the Church. So he's asking that you call off the march."

"Why discuss the subject with me?" Kathy said curtly. "I think it's more appropriate that His Eminence take up the matter with Father Timothy Conlon, the pastor, and the full council."

Brady shot back, "But we understand that you and a Muslim woman are leaders of the march. His Eminence wants you to ask the parish council to stop it."

The tone of the monsignor's final sentence came across as harsh, demanding.

Kathy, unshaken, replied, "Monsignor, may I take a moment to refresh your memory and offer you some background about myself."

Brady nodded.

Kathy proceeded to explain she was shocked that the cardinal declined to see her to discuss closing the St. Leo and St. Brendan schools. The nuns had chosen her to explain their views and had used normal Church channels. Kathy and her colleague Joan had resigned as nuns because of the school closures and the cardinal's refusal to discuss them. They had opened the Ogden Park School to try to take the place of St. Brendan's grade school, which His Eminence had razed. And they did so at the expressed wish of the parents.

Kathy said she wanted the major differences between her, the cardinal and Brady out in the open. "Monsignor, I think we need to bring the Church into the twentieth century. I'm a new Christian. Out of the convent. I have my own conscience, not the mind of someone blindly following orders from the cardinal and the chancery office. I no longer just teach the difference between right and wrong. I think I can make a difference in real life. I'm trying to bring God and His goodness into the streets, where it seems you and the hierarchy refuse to go."

"Quite a speech, young lady. Did you make your decision to leave before His Eminence began closing the schools?"

She shot back, "My goal was and still is to keep Catholic schools alive as independent private schools. And to have former nuns run them with other laity. We're looking at a new lay apostolate among inner-city African-Americans and Hispanics . . ."

"Why did you leave the nuns?" the monsignor snapped at her in the meeting. The question startled Kathy. She had been explaining that for several moments. Didn't he *believe* her? Couldn't he understand what was tearing at her?

Brady was suggesting that something more basic than differences with the cardinal was stirring Kathy. He said he wasn't sure what that might be, but he was uncomfortable with his courtroom-style confrontation with the ex-nun. He suggested they go for a walk in Ogden Park. The sun and fresh air would do them both good, he said.

So they walked north to 67th Street and into the park, away from the loud traffic, strolled for several minutes before Kathy said:

"Church authority opposed and denigrated my individual conscience. That was the reason I left. It goes to the heart of all the problems among priests, nuns and the laity. It's at the root of every disagreement in the Church today. At least that's the way I see it."

Brady knew that Catholicism had always been a religion of authority, but he saw no purpose in explaining that now.

Today, she said, nearly thirty years after the close of the Second Vatican Council, most American Catholics approve of birth control and divorce. In certain circumstances even legalized abortion. Nearly three out of four Catholics went to Sunday Mass at the start of the Council. Now it is close to one out of three. And, she said, warming up, American Catholics are increasingly opposed to other Church positions . . . many favor a married clergy, the ordination of women, a greater role for the laity and more emphasis on individual conscience instead of the rigid pronouncements and rules of Rome. The hierarchy blames everyone but themselves for Catholicism's troubles. "The Catholic hierarchy copped out."

Brady interjected sharply: "*You* abandoned authority and became part of a church of ambiguity—Cafeteria Catholics who picked and chose what they'd believe." Brady said he was tired of priests and nuns challenging authority. "The bishops aren't boardroom directors looking at the bottom line. These are decent men who care about souls, Kathy."

Queen of Martyrs reverberated with the noise of the congregation sitting down. Leo nudged his daughter and she suddenly awoke from her recollections and seated herself with her mother and father. Brady was delivering the homily from the pulpit. Kathy missed his first few sentences but heard the monsignor say:

"Catholics once found certitude in the Church. Now theologians, other moralists and some of the laity turn away from the pope, the Vatican and the bishops. They seem to be trying to revise the Catholic moral tradition. There's a great gap today between their subjective conjecture and the Church's objective morality.

"Priests and nuns who place so-called conscience above the authority of the pope and bishops are dividing and demolishing much of the Church's foundation and strength.

They're creating a schism between Rome and the Church in the United States."

Kathy was angry at that. Brady and the cardinal were trying to destroy St. Malachy's. She was on her feet:

"The Church's great teachers have said we are *supposed* to follow our consciences, even in opposition to its leadership. Conscience is the final authority—*no question about that.*"

Brady was stunned by the outburst. He looked to see where the voice had come from and finally spotted Kathy. Everyone saw the young woman standing her ground. Two ushers hurried up the center aisle to where the Dolans were sitting and motioned to Kathy to leave her pew and the church. One usher tried to push past Nora to remove Kathy. Nora elbowed the man and wouldn't let him pass.

The monsignor, intelligent enough to be magnanimous, told the ushers to return to their places and said to Kathy:

"Is individual conscience *always* right? I didn't know that, my dear young lady. If that were accurate there would be no truth in moral matters. Judgments of conscience often contradict one another. There must be something more than conscience in the context of morality." He turned to Kathy, who refused to sit down although Leo tugged at her jacket. "The commandments, natural law and church teachings are objective truths. They can't be reduced to a private personal conscience. That would make us dependent on opinions that constantly changed."

"Well," said Kathy, "some Catholic theologians say morality is not set by the nature of an act. A man might rob because he needs the money to survive. It's the *intention* that counts."

The monsignor turned toward Kathy. "Listen to me carefully, Miss Dolan." An audible gasp swept up and down the aisles. The identification of Kathy Dolan by name intensified the confrontation. Brady then cited the debate between some U.S. theologians and the Vatican over birth control and abortion. The theologians argued that Catholics might disagree in good conscience with the Vatican's prohibition of both. He said these moralists were self-appointed and had no official teaching role in the Church.

An elderly man stood up and shouted across the pews at Kathy. "*He's* giving the sermon, not you. We haven't ordained women priests yet. Why don't you just *sit down?*"

A young woman's voice: "She speaks for many of us, not the old men at the Vatican and here."

The same two ushers hurried up the aisle and again asked Kathy to leave the church. Once more, Brady acted on her behalf.

Kathy then told him that his logic was contradictory, so far as she could see. On one hand bishops had the spiritual authority to bind their faithful. On the other, Catholics had a moral obligation to follow their consciences. There were a lot of gray areas in which the hierarchy and conscience conflicted. No wonder Catholics were confused. "Going to confession is a high-wire act!"

Brady said, "For someone to claim he or she has the right to act according to conscience without considering the law of God is absurd. Moral teaching comes from acknowledged authority, the pope and bishops, not contradictory voices competing for attention."

"That's right!" a voice shouted from the rear.

Another listener shot back, "Conscience may tell you differently even after you've heard the pope and bishops!"

Kathy challenged again. "There *are* alternatives to what the hierarchy are saying. You imply conscience and Church teaching always complement each other. That's just not true. There was strong movement during the Council to abolish many of the Vatican's pronouncements and cut its authority."

An elderly man got up and said, "This whole issue of

authority against conscience has done nothing but divide the Church. Theologians and bishops should meet face to face and settle their differences."

Applause.

Brady finally said: "Personal conscience is *not* and never will be the exclusive authority for deciding truth and morality."

He turned, left the pulpit to resume Mass, and Kathy sat down.

The service concluded without further incident. Four women and two men congratulated Kathy as she left the church. When the Dolans had walked two blocks and no one could hear them, Leo asked, "Kathy, *what* was that all about?"

"You mean, why did I stand up to Monsignor Brady?"

Leo nodded, and Kathy told her parents about the previous day's meeting at the secretary's request. Brady had arrived at the black and Hispanic Ogden Park School in the morning. She met him at the front door of the school, which once had been the main entrance to a supermarket. Brady was surprised that on a Saturday holiday scores of children were inside. Four African-American mothers were trying to keep order. The two shook hands and Kathy led the secretary to her office. She offered Brady an empty chair. He declined a cup of instant coffee.

Kathy saw that the secretary was studying the stark simplicity of her office—a wooden desk, five drawers of files, four chairs, a large jar filled with pens, pencils and erasers, and a phone. Kathy began easily.

"We're open six days a week from 9:00 A.M. to 6:00 P.M. We have 168 students from first through eighth grade. We use Ogden Park for recreation."

Brady nodded but said nothing.

"We don't tolerate any nonsense—no weapons, no dope,

no back talk. If kids don't behave or do their homework they're out. We have a demanding, all-black school board."

The monsignor looked around. The large room was divided by a series of temporary plastic and cardboard walls. Some youngsters were reading at desks despite the noise. Others were cutting and coloring books. Some were playing pin-the-tail-on-the-donkey.

"Is this an officially recognized school?"

Kathy told him that Alderman Frank Fahey had obtained the necessary permits and Ogden Park School was licensed by the city. They received funds from the city, state, and federal governments. *None* was offered by the archdiocese, although the school was an attempt to fill some of the void created by the cardinal's closing of St. Brendan's. Kathy waited for the secretary's reaction, but Brady avoided the challenge. He asked how Fahey got involved. Kathy said she knew the alderman since both served on St. Malachy's council. Fahey volunteered his help after she told him about the school's problems.

Brady tried to erase the coolness of the conversation by complimenting the former nun on her green dress. Kathy laughed.

"I bought the dress secondhand at the St. Vincent de Paul Thrift Store. It didn't come with a shamrock."

Brady then revealed his mission. The cardinal wanted Kathy to give him her word that she and others wouldn't picket at St. Malachy's to protest his plan to demolish the church. She immediately refused and Brady seemed to drop the subject. But he did ask a surprising question:

"Are you *sure,* Miss Dolan, that you made the right choice in leaving the Sisters of Mercy?" Kathy didn't hesitate. "The Church, including the cardinals, were abandoning the streets, the ghettos. They weren't builders anymore. They were just climbing behind high walls on a hill, like medieval men. Many nuns and priests weren't any better. They fled into teaching at the suburban public schools, government social service jobs, insurance companies, banks. I knew a priest who became an investment banker. A French-speaking nun became a European buyer for a New York cosmetics firm. The promises about a new Church came crashing down. They began a new life of sporty cars, chic clothes, golf clubs and a liquor cabinet. Our religious crusade ended before it began."

Brady changed the subject. "I'm not sure how many nuns have left the convents."

Kathy told him. "Over the last six years more than seventeen thousand. Many more since the mid-sixties. The older ones stayed because it was too late for them. The average age of a nun is now sixty-seven."

Then she coldly asked, "If the Church closes its schools and the churches, claiming the archdiocese is nearly broke, why not sell Cardinal Carmody's mansion, Chicago's ownership in Holy Hills College Seminary, which has only about seventy students, and some of the large rectories too? Sure, he's cut some from the top, but a lot more can go. Businesses are doing it. If we can't be a Church of the poor, let's at least be a Church of the *average* citizen."

Brady said, "Don't be too hard on the Church and hierarchy. True, some bishops mishandled the closing and merger of schools and churches. Many acted without consulting the pastors and people. They hurt a lot of Catholics. The hierarchy are learning it's no longer a Church of pray, pay and obey. The bishops aren't the autocrats of thirty or forty years ago. The healing will take time but they're still men of goodwill."

Kathy was startled. Brady's words clearly contradicted the cardinal's position. Carmody hadn't consulted the pastor and people of many parishes, including St. Malachy's. The monsignor was really telling her that he was just the messenger, not the message. Of course, he couldn't admit that.

The monsignor looked at her with a glint of admiration. "You didn't walk away, Kathy. You're still out here with your storefront school. You're to be commended."

"We're struggling for money here, Monsignor. The parents pay ten dollars a month for each child. Some can't come up with the tuition but we manage to cover the monthly rent with that revenue. But even with government funds the school has trouble meeting monthly electrical, heat and water bills. Also maintenance and salaries for me, Joan and six other teachers."

Kathy said the cost of sending a child to her school was about equal to that of a Catholic school. "We're an excellent investment."

"So you need funds to keep operating?"

"We need about fifty thousand dollars right now," Kathy admitted, somewhat embarrassed. "About forty thousand to pay off our debts and ten thousand to meet emergencies. We don't want to be forced to close."

"What if you get those funds? I can't make a commitment for His Eminence, but he might be able to help."

"But he doesn't have money for Catholic schools?"

"He might be able to find help somewhere."

Kathy was blunt. "What might the cardinal want in return?"

"This is just a hypothetical conversation, Kathy, but he probably would be pleased if there were no picketing at St. Malachy's."

So it all got down to the Church's and the cardinal's public image. Money had suddenly become secondary. Kathy told the secretary that she would have to think about the matter.

Brady said he needed an answer no later than Tuesday

morning since the picketing was set for Wednesday. He was well informed. Kathy said she would try to give an answer by then but wasn't sure she could.

The monsignor got up, the two shook hands. He slowly walked out among the screeching children. The sun shone brightly along Racine Avenue. Brady enjoyed the smell of barbecue sauce permeating the street. A black boy about seven years old asked, "Are you the pope, mister?"

Brady smiled benevolently. "No, son, just a messenger."

Kathy sat alone at her desk for more than a half-hour. Finally she picked up the phone and called her attorney brother, Dan. The alderman was a dedicated conservative, but she knew no one who could better advise her. When he answered she related the conversation with Monsignor Brady.

"Sit tight till you hear from me, sis."

Blood, Kathy told herself, was thicker than their philosophical differences.

Dan phoned Martin McHugh, who headed the mayor's education-grant office. "Hello, Marty, this is Dan. Sorry to bother you at home. How much dough do you have in the education-grant till? More than two hundred and seventy-five thousand? Good. Marty, I need a favor. Tell the mayor I'll give him the vote he needs for the Archer Avenue underpass if you'll send a fifty-thousand-dollar grant to the Ogden Park School on South Racine. The principal is Kathy Dolan. She's my sister. The mayor is there playing poker? Ask him, Marty."

Dan cupped the receiver to his ear and began reading the Saturday mail. Annie McGowan was furious with Mrs.

Alice McSweeney who was delivering Republican literature in the neighborhood. McGowan said no good Catholic would deliver Republican mail. Marty returned to the line:

"Okay, Dan, it's a deal. We'll hand deliver the check to Miss Dolan at the school next Tuesday."

Dan phoned Kathy. "Make sure you're in school next Tuesday. A man will come with a city check. Don't worry, it'll be good!"

Kathy laughed. "Does that mean I'm off the hook with the cardinal?"

"No," Dan said, "that's up to your conscience."

"God bless you, Dan." Her conscience versus the hierarchy again, she thought.

When Dan hung up he worried that Kathy would fail. She had the power of the archdiocese behind her as a nun. Now all she had were some blacks and Muslims. A lot of good they would do her . . . Still, he might be wrong. In 1993 lay black Catholics assumed the leadership of Hales Franciscan High School at 49th and Cottage Grove. The board of eighteen trustees effectively owned the school. Hales became the only officially recognized Catholic high school in the nation with such ownership. They had 380 students and were doing an excellent job—

His phone rang. Monsignor Brady, the cardinal's secretary, asked if Dan had heard that his sister Kathy and a Mamma X planned to lead picketers around St. Malachy's on Wednesday. The march was to protest the possibility that the church might be closed. The lawyer said he understood no final decision had been made. Brady ignored Dan's reply.

"His Eminence wants the protest stopped. Is that clear?"

"Eminently," Dan replied sarcastically. Brady hung up.

Cardinal Carmody, like any good city hall politician, was covering himself across the board.

* * *

Kathy was still at her desk. She was thinking back to the students who had been playing pin-the-tail-on-the-donkey when Brady arrived. The principal had a wicked smile on her face as she watched the kids sticking pins in Brendan Carmody's big fat Authority.

Chapter 7

S-O-S

The cardinal entered his large black Lincoln while James Quincy held the rear door. Quincy, a small, gray-haired fifty-nine-year-old, had been the chauffeur of Chicago's prelates for more than three decades. He was a quiet, discreet man with a wife and two sons, and his demeanor reflected his position. The chauffeur had the air-conditioning on even though it was only 8:20 A.M. His Eminence suffered from heat and humidity.

Quincy drove slowly because the night's heavy rain had left the streets slick. He could see the cardinal clearly in his rearview mirror. His Eminence was making notes on the day's schedule in red ink. The list had been delivered to his residence by his secretary, Mrs. Dorothy Koslowski, on Sunday evening. She handled Carmody's correspondence, visitors and the phones while Monsignor Brady was assigned the cardinal's private work. Mrs. Koslowski, a large, blonde, durable Polish woman, had worked in the chancery office for twenty years. Carmody chose Mrs. Koslowski because she was willing to work long hours, including several on Sunday, without overtime. There was one exception, Friday night, when she met her husband Stanley at his American Legion Post. Dorothy, who called herself a "hard-hat Polack," kicked up her heels. She and Stanley drank beer, danced the polka and, it was said, Dorothy could blow the head off a glass of beer from five feet away. She was also a sharp dart player. She ran everything and everyone in the cardinal's office to the minute—his schedule was inviolable, and he wanted it that way.

It was 8:40 A.M. when Quincy pulled in front of the chancery office on East Chicago Avenue. He had the door open before His Eminence could close his black briefcase. The elevator waited to take Carmody to the third floor. The cardinal would be behind his desk in less than two minutes, opening the *Herald* for the allotted quarter-hour of scanning the news.

Mrs. Koslowski offered His Eminence a loud "good morning" and poured the hot black coffee into his gold-white mug with the papal flag on it. The cardinal removed his Homburg and black raincoat with the red piping of his office while the secretary placed the hot mug to his right. The *Herald,* as usual, lay squarely at the center of his large mahogany desk.

His Eminence had lifted the mug to his lips and begun pulling down the brew when he suddenly spewed it across his desk with a loud whoosh, the hot liquid spilling down his chest and stomach.

"My God!" Mrs. Koslowski blurted, "is it too hot, Your Eminence?"

The cardinal didn't answer. His eyes were on the headline splashed across the top of the front page:

CHICAGO PRIEST ON HUNGER STRIKE

The big bold words leaped out at him, screaming, defying, damning. The headline above the lead story told the *Herald*'s million-plus readers:

PASTOR PROTESTS CARDINAL RAZING OLD CHURCH.

He read the lead and second paragraphs:

> The Rev. Timothy Conlon, 68-year-old pastor of St. Malachy's Roman Catholic Church, entered the seventh day of a hunger strike Tuesday in protest against Cardinal E. Brendan Carmody's reported plan to demolish the Loop landmark, according to church sources.
>
> Father Conlon entered St. Bernard's Hospital the day following a personal meeting with the archdiocesan leader, according to the same sources, and has not eaten solid food since. The priest is reported to be depressed at His Eminence's decision, and hopes the cardinal would yet change his mind. Father Conlon, better known as "Cappy." has indicated to friends that he will break his fast only when the church is "safe." The cardinal could not be reached for comment . . .

The secretary was bewildered by the cardinal's eruption. Ignoring Mrs. Koslowski's attempts at cleaning the coffee from his desk, Carmody ordered her to call Monsignor Brady to his office. Brady rushed in.

"Have you seen this tripe?"

Brady nodded.

"This is nonsense, of course." Carmody crunched the words. "I told Cappy no such thing. I merely said I was *thinking* about demolishing St. Malachy's because it was structurally unsound. I *also* told Cappy if he had any problems to come to see me, no one else. I want you to get to the bottom of this, Monsignor. I also want you to straighten out that reporter Donald Doherty. Tell him I'll call his managing editor if he keeps writing such speculation. Tell him his cardinal is speaking."

Carmody dismissed Brady with a wave of his hand.

Monsignor Roger Mahon was Cardinal Carmody's first appointment. Mrs. Koslowski knew the cardinal was running late and told Mahon it would be a quick meeting. His Eminence had transferred Mahon from St. Sabina's on the South Side to pastor at St. Francis of Rome in suburban Cicero. He had asked to see the cardinal.

After entering Carmody's office the pastor immediately accepted the transfer, and this pleased the cardinal . . . Mahon, called Pug because he was tough, could be a stone wall. Pug Mahon was close to the Gaelic for kiss my ass, and he had earned the recognition. Mahon now had a few chosen words for his successor:

"Your Eminence, please tell the new pastor not to be discouraged. Most of the blacks near St. Sabina's are Southern Baptists. Those who become Catholics are the hula-hoopers. Not one of them can stand still long enough for me to give them communion. It's their feet, Your Eminence. They'll dance on their own coffins!"

Mahon left with a smile on his face.

Carmody had some moments to think about the *Herald* story. He had been ambushed, he decided. Not by Cappy Conlon but . . . who? Who had the gall to take him on? Of course, Pat Brogan, that's who. Cappy's pal, that philosophizing, protesting Jesuit now retired from teaching at Loyola University. The rooster without a roost. Pat Brogan didn't conciliate—he asked questions. He didn't propose conclusions—he interrogated. And he did it in public auditoriums in front of thousands of good Catholics. Brogan's was an old line . . . no more power to Rome, no more pontificating by the Vatican curia, no more tongue-twisting pronouncements from Catholic bishops. All of which angered Carmody. A cardinal was supposed to protect the faith and the sanctity of his office, defend the archdiocese's Long Red Line. He hadn't become a prince of the Church to hand the keys of the kingdom to crazies in the priesthood and the streets. He'd become a cardinal because he was prepared to shed his blood in defense of the faith, and spill blood he would.

Mrs. Koslowski buzzed him. "Monsignor Brady needs a moment."

Brady burst into the room. "I spoke with Doherty, the *Herald* reporter who wrote the story on Cappy. He says he got the news from Cappy's housekeeper, Mrs. Kitty Flaherty, after last Saturday night's Actors' Mass. Cappy didn't celebrate it. Doherty met the housekeeper and asked why. Mrs. Flaherty said Cap was in St. Bernard's Hospital because he wasn't eating. Doherty egged her on. She said Cap was depressed because the cardinal was going to tear down St. Malachy's. The wrecking contractor had already examined the church—"

"Did you ask Doherty why he used the words hunger strike? And if he continues to write this wild speculation that I'm going to phone his managing editor?"

"I did, but Doherty was pretty snide about it. He said his managing editor was Jewish. Anyway, Doherty's going on vacation." Brady paused. He was obviously uncomfortable with the rest of his message and Carmody saw it.

"Just tell me."

"Doherty said Claudia Lally has been assigned to the story."

The cardinal almost leaped from his swivel chair. After a long sigh he slumped heavily back into it and spun the chair completely around without saying a word but thinking plenty.

How many years was it? he asked himself. About ten. He was still secretary and had been asked to issue a chancery office statement condemning a play at the Studebaker. It was written by some German who accused Pope Pius XII of complicity with the Nazis during World War II. Garbage. Then Claudia Lally wrote a review saying the play was bad history but good theater. She said the archdiocesan statement was silly. The two later got into a face-to-face argument at a reception in the Palmer House. It concerned not only Lally's review of the play but her opposition to a new archdiocesan rule that mandated six months of marriage counseling before anyone could get married in a Chicago Catholic church. Lally got married in Las Vegas. During the reception confrontation she told Carmody to go to hell. He turned his back on her and the two had not spoken since. And Lally was a friend of Cappy's as well, a regular at his midnight Actors' Mass. But why would she draw *this* assignment? She was a theater and movie critic. The cardinal fired the question at Brady.

"Doherty said she volunteered. Wanted a change during the summer months. The managing editor jumped at it. Lally's considered a very good reporter."

"Well, there's only one answer," Carmody said.

"St. Malachy's can stand!"

"No, Monsignor, that's why you're a secretary. I need the twelve million dollars from the sale of St. Malachy's land to meet the archdiocesan debt and help pay for some new churches."

Twelve million dollars! Now Brady understood the importance of demolishing St. Malachy's . . . except the cardinal hadn't mentioned the archdiocese's deficit. Never mind, he quickly got back on the cardinal's team. "Whew! I see, Your Eminence . . . but a word of caution?"

"About what?"

"The housekeeper told Doherty that Cappy would rather starve to death than see St. Malachy's torn down."

Carmody shot back: "Cappy's going to phone the *News-*

Times and deny the *Herald* story. As for the hunger strike, Cappy's word is surely more important than his housekeeper's." The cardinal buzzed Mrs. Koslowski and told her to phone St. Bernard's and get Father Conlon, a patient, on the phone. The secretary called him back in less than a minute. She said Father Conlon was unavailable but there was a priest on the line. Carmody jerked his receiver from its cradle and said sharply: "This is the cardinal. Who's this?"

"Good morning, Your Eminence. This is Father Pat Brogan. Cappy's being moved to another room at the moment. Leo Dolan's with him. Can we be of any help?"

"Why's he being moved?"

"To be closer to the nurses' desk. Apparently he's weaker and they want to look in on him more often."

Brogan relished stiffing the cardinal. He knew Carmody wasn't calling about Cappy's health. The prelate was about to issue some orders. Brogan also had a surprise for the cardinal: "A lady and gentleman have just arrived. Ms. Claudia Lally, I believe she's from the press. She has a photographer with her."

"I want them *out* of there. Do you hear me, Father Brogan, out!"

"Your Eminence, you'll have to speak with Sister Anne Le Compte. She's in charge of this floor."

"Tell that nun this is the wish of her cardinal. And ask Cappy to phone me as soon as possible. It's urgent. And while you're at it, advise Leo Dolan that his services aren't needed."

Carmody then ordered Brady to the hospital. "No more reporters, no visitors. Cappy's to see no one until I speak with him. That includes Brogan."

Brady left to do as ordered. Ten minutes later Mrs. Koslowski told His Eminence that Father Conlon was on the line but was able to speak only in a hoarse whisper.

Carmody's consoling voice eased over the line into the sickroom: "I hope you're feeling better, Cap. We mustn't let your strength weaken."

"It's all right . . ."

Carmody reached out, shepherd to his sheep. "We're all with you, Cap. All of your fellow priests."

Cappy's reply was inaudible. The cardinal, impatience tugging at his sleeve, said quietly, "Well, *Cap,* what's all this I hear about a hunger strike?"

The patient didn't respond; he seemed to be sleepy, perhaps under medication, or both. Finally, in a weary voice, Cappy said:

"Don't blame Kitty Flaherty, Your Eminence. The poor woman just said what came to mind. I told her I was offering it up, that I wouldn't eat solid food until God answered my prayers and saved St. Malachy's."

"Well now, Cap, I want you to take something to eat. We must have you up and about. Who else do we have to patrol downtown Chicago? You're the bishop of the Loop."

The cardinal's somewhat forced laugh was swallowed in silence. Cappy began to wheeze and cough. His only response was a wracking to loosen the grip of winter from his throat. The last coherent words Carmody heard from Cappy were ". . . in your hands, Your Eminence."

The phone receiver had turned cold in the cardinal's hand. He returned the mouthpiece to its cradle but the phone rang almost immediately. Brady had just arrived at St. Bernard's and was reporting in.

"There are four TV news crews here, six radio reporters, Lally, the *News-Times,* the Associated Press, United Press International, *Time, Newsweek,* even a reporter from the Catholic wire service. The hospital switchboard is jammed with news calls."

"Do they know who you are, Monsignor?"

"No, not yet."

"Good! Find Cappy. Tell him I said to see no one and say nothing. Then you get back here. I don't want them pointing any fingers about chancery office interference."

At that moment Mrs. Koslowski placed the first edition of the *News-Times* in the cardinal's workbasket and quickly departed. Another smash front-page headline: HUNGER PRIEST WEAKENING. Underneath was a large photo of Cappy standing outside St. Malachy's. The story, which began inside the tabloid, quoted church sources as saying Cappy was growing progressively weaker while the cardinal still had not denied that he planned to demolish St. Malachy's.

Carmody deep-sixed the newspaper into his wastebasket. The matter was getting out of hand. What did these people *want* from him? One church, a single priest, didn't constitute the archdiocese. His responsibility covered 2.3 million Catholics spread from Lake Michigan to Chicago's suburbs in ever-widening circles. That included more than 380 parishes with an official total of 767 diocesan priests, plus more from religious orders. He couldn't consult with each priest and congregation about every church and school. The good of the archdiocese came first, not slivers of individual opinion. The cardinalship was a killing job. Didn't they realize that? There had to be authority in the Church and it had to be obeyed if Catholicism was to survive and grow. This wasn't a matter of personal conscience, it was a decision of Church rule. Otherwise the archdiocese would be in chaos.

In July, the archdiocese would celebrate its 150th anniversary but Carmody had no heart for a large celebration. Nor did many religious or laity. The archdiocese and Church were in too much turmoil. The cardinal would have the Catholic World simply run a nice, neuteral, historical article.

Brady had come back and reported: "I met one of the

doctors. He said Cappy was suffering from severe mental depression . . ."

Carmody, undergoing his own depression, snapped, "Can't he find his pint?" Then, offended by his own remark, he excused himself, the signal for Brady to leave the room. He leaned over his desk and crumpled his face in his hands. He couldn't understand what was happening.

A week passed. Sister Anne Le Compte and Leo Dolan leaned over the slumped figure in the hospital bed. He was napping. Cappy slept only three hours a night, between two and five. Both marveled that such a frail creature could survive on so little sleep and no solid food for nearly two weeks.

The nurse had accepted Dolan's presence after Cappy had insisted on it. Whatever the detective was saying, he apparently gave the pastor strength. The nun had been told that Cappy respected Dolan because the policeman understood the sorrow in the hearts of his friends. Le Compte appreciated that. She shook Cappy slightly. He opened one eye and she immediately shoved the beef broth under his nose. His feet moved, then his hip, finally his shoulders and head.

"Father Conlon," the Canadian nun said, "you're getting my French up. I'll have no more of this. You either drink this soup or I'll send you out into the street in your nightshirt."

Cappy managed a faint smile.

Dolan urged him: "Cap, you've already lost more than ten pounds. You're down to less than ninety. The cardinal's mad as an Orangeman on St. Patrick's Day. Soup up, man, or he'll order all of us to say a half-dozen rosaries a day."

Leo's voice wasn't pushing his old pal. He figured no

man could force another in or out of the grave. Priests still had the liberty, in spite of Fats Carmody, to die.

The nun propped the priest's head high on his pillow but Cappy declined the broth. "I don't have a ticket."

"What're ye talking about?" Leo badgered him in his brogue. "Ye're not goin' anywhere. Drink, it's as good as Scotch!"

Cappy rubbed his white hair. "The trolley's leaving the barn and I've no place to go. Don't you see, Leo? There's no real mission ahead, only the end of the line for me."

Dolan pretended anger. "Ye mean ye're going to fall down because Fats hooked you with a left. He hasn't the shot of a flyweight. Are ye taking the count, man? Is that what ye're telling me? Ye're goin' down on the canvas without liftin' a hand?"

Boom Boom Braithwaite stood motionlessly at the door of the hospital room with his wife. Cappy nodded but didn't speak. Sister Le Compte was about to ask the two to leave but Dolan eased her away:

"He's a Presbyterian minister. Both are close friends."

The nun shrugged and left the room with the broth. The couple took seats at the side of the bed. Eloise Braithwaite berated Cappy in a falsetto ire:

"I'm *mad* at you, Cappy Conlon. I'm not going to speak with you unless you stop scaring all of us. Drink and eat your supper! Didn't your mother ever tell you that? Haven't I told you precisely that for years? You bachelors are *impossible.*"

Eloise thought she caught a glow in Cappy's eyes as her husband Boom Boom explained their visit.

"Has Leo told you about Dr. Julius Schmidt, the consulting architect and structural engineer?"

Cappy shook his head.

"I haven't had a chance," Dolan said.

"Well, tell him, my good man."

Dolan explained that his son Dan had found an engineering expert to see if, indeed, the roof and walls of St. Malachy's were unsound. Dr. Schmidt, who had an office on Wacker Drive, had designed and engineered many buildings in the downtown area. He was a German-born perfectionist with nearly fifty years experience and had examined St. Malachy's.

"Dr. Schmidt is outside in the hall. Will you see him, Cap?" Boom Boom asked.

The pastor raised himself on his pillow and was now wide-awake. He nodded. Eloise skipped into the corridor, and a large, silver-haired gentleman of about seventy-five years entered, shook hands with everyone and stood at the foot of Cappy's bed.

Schmidt said he and a colleague had examined the church structure on two separate occasions, a total of seven hours. He had been told the walls and roof were slowly collapsing. That was an accurate analysis as far as it went. However, steel plates could be placed along the large timbers or beams now used as roof girders. These plates would be bolted together. "Shoes," or reinforcements, could be set at the outside ends.

Cappy asked weakly, "What would that cost?"

Schmidt said that, including reinforcing the walls, the job could be done for about one hundred thousand dollars.

Cappy, the Braithwaites and Leo were dumbfounded. Schmidt had made it all so clear, so attainable. The architect-engineer said he would address a letter to Father Conlon as pastor stating his professional appraisal. Everyone agreed.

Schmidt concluded: "I'm an old man who cherishes old things. Believe me, St. Malachy's is not on its deathbed. It can live many more years." And with that, Schmidt walked briskly out of the room.

"Who's paying his fee?" Cappy asked.

Boom Boom told him: "We've taken up collections at my church, at a synagogue where Goldie once served and at Mamma X's mosque. We've raised four thousand dollars. Schmidt accepted that."

"Is any more lightning about to strike me today?" Cappy asked.

"Bridie O'Brien's trying to get St. Malachy's declared a national, state and Chicago landmark. That might stop the cardinal," Boom Boom said.

Cappy rolled his eyes in astonishment.

Braithwaite went on: "Mamma X and Kathy Dolan may throw pickets around St. Malachy's next Wednesday if the cardinal sends any work crews to tear down the church."

Cappy rolled his eyes again in disbelief. As for Leo, he was startled to learn his daughter was a leader in the ruckus.

"Of course, you have nothing to do with any of this," Boom Boom told Cappy. "The parish council's acting in your absence."

The pastor entwined his rosary more tightly in his chalky hands. Let his friends do their good deeds as they perceived them. In the end he would bend his knee to the cardinal as he had vowed and had been ordained a priest to do. Carmody was his superior, greedy perhaps, but a good man. He would not, however, halt the council. St. Malachy's was *their* church, too. He sank back in his pillow. He could only speak for himself. Sacrifice was the key to the Lord's kingdom. It was clear in his mind that if called on, he would swallow his medicine. Dropping his head, Cappy finally said, "Please tell Sister Le Compte that I'll drink my broth now."

Leo went out of the room and hurried to the kitchen and came back with the hot soup. End of meeting.

* * *

The swarm of reporters had left the hospital lobby days before since they were not allowed to interview Cappy. The cardinal decided to ride out the storm and was unavailable to the press. He concluded the media would eventually get tired of the story and it would only be a matter of time before he demolished St. Malachy's.

Claudia Lally thought otherwise. Every day she managed to dredge up a new source and score another *Herald* exclusive. She traced the cardinal's wrecking contractor, Lombardi & Sons, who admitted visiting the church but nothing more. Lally suggested to Anthony Lombardi, the gregarious father, that he had been gagged by Carmody, and the owner finally admitted the chancery office had put the lid on the cardinal's plans for the church.

Lally wrote a Sunday profile on Carmody, tracing his life back to boyhood. She listed her unreturned phone calls to the prelate, twenty-seven in all, her hours of empty pacing, sixteen, in front of his residence in hopes of an interview, her attempt to crash the cardinal's office only to have Dorothy Koslowski pounce on her a few feet from his door. The article included a laundry list of complaints from priests and nuns of the archdiocese. They claimed the cardinal failed to understand their desire to do greater Church service in the ghettos. Others, worried that hundreds of religious had left their ministry under Carmody, pleaded for a dialogue with the prelate to seek changes in his direction.

"These prayerful but desperate pleadings of the Cardinal's subordinates," she wrote, "indicate that His Eminence is sitting on a Church cauldron. Old St. Malachy's is only one example in endless kettles of hot water that boil on rectory and convent stoves across the archdiocese because, among other reasons, one man will not listen. It has long been said that the road to Paris is through Beijing. Can it be asked, as some religious now do, that the road to hell is through the Cardinal's Chancery Office?"

Lally concluded her tough five-thousand-word backgrounder: "The Cardinal appears to be a prisoner of his own words and deeds, a man whose vocation has turned from modesty and prayer to massive power in behind-the-scenes Chicago."

Chicagoans had rarely if ever seen such a brash assault on a prince of the Church. They had to return to the *Front Page* of Ben Hecht and Charles MacArthur and the escapades of the *Herald*'s Harry Romanoff to equal Lally's fiery ire.

Carmody exploded as he read the article in the sacristy of Holy Name Cathedral. He would admit that his long battle with the Association of Chicago Priests was a public rift, but they couldn't dictate the policies of the archdiocese and he wasn't in a position to grant most of what they demanded. He, above all, refused to accept that he was an unfair man.

He also insisted most of Chicago's priests were good and loyal to their spiritual leader. Didn't these other religious realize they must follow the pope's teachings on birth control and other moral issues? Not that Carmody would change a comma of the birth-control encyclical, mind you. Didn't they understand that a cardinal, above all, was a *good soldier?* Why should he meet face to face with priests who were leaving their ministry? For what? To give them his benediction? To say, go thou, good and faithful servant?

How could the priests' association attack him when some of them walked out of their rectories into secular money-grubbing jobs and soon were dancing on the nightclub floors and in the bars of Chicago? He was the faithful servant, not they. They would've burned down Fort Dearborn and there'd be no Chicago today.

It was time for His Eminence to begin the ten o'clock

Mass. He walked briskly to the altar but all he could see was the face of a middle-aged woman, her painted features wore a satisfied smile, the face of Claudia Lally . . .

Actually Lally was sitting before her computer in the *Herald* newsroom. She was looking at her notes on the screen and talking with Sandy Levine, her managing editor. Like the old pro she was, Lally told Levine her new information in brief bursts:

"I've got proof that Carmody intends to demolish St. Malachy's. Photocopies of the wrecking contractor's applications to the city. That's Lombardi & Sons. The cardinal plans to raze the church sometime during the last week in June. The salvage work, carrying out the altar, statues, stained-glass windows, pews, et cetera, would take place a week earlier. The address jumps out at you—Ninth Street and South Wabash. You want to know my source? Yes, it's confidential. Thumbs Rafferty, the gofer for Frank Fahey. Of course, I know Fahey's a fix man. So what? I've got Carmody's signature on Lombardi's records. It's in black and white!"

Levine's blast came over the line in best "Front-Page" fashion. "Go, girl! Go!"

The reporter's story revealed the cardinal's plan to raze St. Malachy's. She nailed Carmody good and sobbed all over the paper. She laced the story with mock reverence, referring to Carmody over and over as "His Eminence." The *Herald*'s entire editorial column was devoted to saving "one of Chicago's greatest landmarks." The commentary concluded:

"It is the American people who have always saved the United States. The people of Chicago have always rescued the Windy City from itself. And it is the people of faith, all faiths, who must now assure the salvation of historic old St. Malachy's church."

The *News-Times* followed with a devastating editorial cartoon that showed the cardinal poised over St. Malachy's with a sledgehammer in hand. The caption read: "Glory be to God!"

Fahey and Rafferty were having lunch at the Morrison Hotel when the alderman saw the cartoon, and Fahey gleefully interrupted his mushroom soup to tell Thumbs:

"The *Herald* and *News-Times* have stuck an enema up Carmody's ass. Be careful. Stay away from the papers for a while."

Rafferty gave Fahey thumbs up.

Meantime Bridie O'Brien was instructing her maid Gertrude, "I want the place especially clean this evening. Cocktails will begin at seven and we'll start dinner about eight."

O'Brien's Gold Coast apartment on Lake Michigan's North Lake Shore Drive had to be spotless; she was entertaining the Justin McGuires, the retired city judge and his wife; the Samuel Holmeses, the retired banker and spouse; and Dr. MacGregor Tuttle III and his new bride, both history professors—he at Northwestern and she at the University of Chicago. All were major players in the Chicago Historical Society.

Bridie then drove her new Cadillac to the Cafe Margarita on Rush Street, where she met Kitty Flaherty, Cappy's housekeeper. Both "adored"—that was Bridie's description—the Mexican restaurant's king-size knockout margaritas. While under the influence Bridie once admitted playing knees with Jorge, the tall waiter from Tijuana. Kitty and two blockbuster margaritas were waiting. The ladies said grace before hoisting the glass goblets, then Kitty pulled the *News-Times* from her lap and handed it to Bridie without comment. The black headline said:

S.O.S. SAVE OLD ST. MALACHY'S

The distress signal was explained by the photo below. Someone had spray-painted S-O-S across the front door of the church. Bridie laughed. "This should give His Eminence a good case of armpit sweats. It's beautiful!"

The two gulped from their goblets. The drink was already tickling Bridie's mind and thickening her tongue. "I love to see Carmody's fat fried."

The two ordered another blast, and Bridie was now joyfully inebriated: "The public is tired of a royal hierarchy in this town. We're tired of listening to Carmody speaking *ex cathedra*, as if he were the pope. I'm sick to death of his appeals for the poor when he lives like an Arabian oil king. To paraphrase somebody, the Church is too important to leave to the cardinals."

Kitty was worried because Bridie spoke more loudly with each long pull from her goblet, but the widow continued:

"Are we a one holy catholic and apostolic Church? Or are we a supermarket with everyone running in all directions, shopping for bargains? And who's running the store? The priests don't agree among themselves. Carmody tells the poor nuns . . . You're only women. Even the pope reminds 'em of that. No priesthood for *you!* And to the housewives, get rhythm or cross your legs! Listen to us old bachelors. We studied biology at the seminary."

Kitty, seeing the situation was getting out of hand, asked Jorge to bring their "*boracho* burritos" and quick.

The two chomped on the beef-bean-cheese-tomato-lettuce entree and as they finished the meal Bridie, blotto, predicted that Carmody would someday be forced to seek refuge in a Trappist monastery.

Finally O'Brien paid the tab and left Jorge a handsome tip. She promised to let Kitty know about her soiree when they next shared lunch. Somehow, she drove home without an accident and took a nap.

Three days later, at the invitation of Reverend Braithwaite, the parish council met to discuss the written report of Dr. Schmidt. Boom Boom had already showed it to Cappy at the hospital, and the pastor said the council's decision was his. After discussing the technicalities of steel-plating the roof girders and reinforcing St. Malachy's walls, Boom Boom said Schmidt had lowered his estimate of the work's cost to about ninety thousand dollars. He concluded:

"Dr. Schmidt said the church must eventually be demolished only if we don't fix it. He told me that when you have a toothache you go to the dentist—not a mortician."

Alderman Fahey, fumbling with his gold tie clasp portraying the saintly face of his namesake, St. Francis Xavier, spoke up. "This development raises important questions. Do we take this information to the cardinal for his reaction? Do we say we'll pay to restore the church? Or do we say nothing and fix the church?"

Bridie was irate. "His Eminence's intention is signed, sealed and almost delivered. Papal infallibility has been passed down to the Cardinal of Chicago, not only in matters of faith and morals but property values too. Carmody has sent word to suburban pastors that he'll soon have money to open new churches. So there's only one answer, Chicago's working motto: Fix it!"

Rabbi Goldman was either nodding asleep or agreeing with Bridie. He lifted a hand slightly and Boom Boom recognized him.

"Mrs. O'Brien is not without some persuasion," the rabbi said. "We know the archdiocese has asked the city for the permits to raze St. Malachy's. That's a sign of determined intention. We must also presume, and this is very significant, they know the material condition of the church as well as we do. Nevertheless, the cardinal has decided to proceed with the demolition. Why? It seems Mrs. O'Brien may have put her finger on the reason—finance. That, my dear friends, is reason unto itself."

Bridie pounced on the rabbi's words. "Thank you, Goldie. I assure you that I wouldn't have spoken about the cardinal's sale of St. Malachy's land unless it came from more than one source. We've got to fight on two fronts now—start our protest march and keep Claudia Lally informed about what His Eminence is up to behind the scenes."

The room was hushed. After a painfully long impasse Goldie ventured, "The media are fighting our battle for us. They appear to be committed. Is it wise to tell them their own business?"

The question hung in the air like a frozen icicle. The rabbi waited for the disturbing implications of his observations to be understood by all, then eased into his major concern:

"It'd be better for St. Malachy's if the hierarchy were convinced we weren't phoning the *Herald* and *News-Times* with leaks and distress signals. Remember, if we win, Cappy must still live with the cardinal."

Kathy said, "I'm not sure we're ever going to speak with one voice on tactics, and I'm not sure Cappy would want it that way. He never has in the past. We've got to coordinate as much as possible in order not to embarrass each other, but some of us must also act according to our consciences. I don't believe we've got the right to halt anyone's acting in good conscience."

Mamma X echoed Kathy's sentiments. The discussion on using the media continued without agreement. Boom Boom moved to the next item on the agenda and Bridie stood for her monologue. She had scheduled meetings in Chicago, Springfield and Washington on all three historic-landmark designations—local, state and national. She would meet with the mayor and governor shortly. She would then fly to Washington for meetings with Senators Paul Lyman and Barbara Ashley-Brown as well as every Illinois member of the House.

Mamma X shouted, "You're beautiful, baby. Bee-yoo-tee-full!"

Cheers burst across the room. Boom Boom recognized Mamma X, who said:

"*Salaam* an' all that, brothers and sisters. And *shalom* to you, Rabbi Goldman, since we're now together on the West Bank and Gaza Strip. Folks, we's ready to march. Twenty-four hours a day. We got the people, an' the schedule's all writ. Jes gimme the word an' we hit the bricks!"

A round of applause swept the table.

Boom Boom announced the council had a special speaker and introduced Leo Dolan, who had been sitting against the wall. Kathy, who hadn't yet noticed her father, stood and embraced him. Dolan, the quiet man, gave the longest speech of his life:

"I've managed a few hours a day with Cappy. He's taking orange juice now and tea and broth three times a day. Still no solid food, though. He's down to eighty-six pounds. He mumbles to himself a lot. I can't make out what he's saying. This is only a guess but I think he's asking God to butt in."

Babbington asked, "What about a Scotch?"

"He hasn't had a drop since he got to the hospital," Dolan said. "All he seems to care about is his rosary. He's turned outside in!"

The meeting ended as it had begun. No final decisions were made.

It was late when Beau Beauchamps turned out the basement lights and locked the church. The music man shuffled from the central door to the center aisle humming a New Orleans dirge and dancing slowly up the aisle toward the bare altar. Now he began to sing, "Gimme the horn, man, sweeter, sweeter, more sax, deep sax, brother . . . huumm, slow that stick, big man, make it cool, low down . . . lemme hear ya, piano fingers . . . bob-ah-doop, doop-a-doop . . . Bop-pop-pop . . . slow it, low it, blow yo' horn, big daddy . . ." Beau never appeared to touch the hardwood sacristy floor as he floated downstairs into the basement.

Cappy completed his last rosary and was about to extinguish his bedside lamp when the huge black figure slipped soundlessly into the room. He took off his Homburg before Cappy realized it was the cardinal standing at the foot of his bed.

Carmody nodded but didn't speak. He shed his raincoat and laid it across the back of an empty chair, then removed his red silk scarf. Cappy saw that the cardinal wore a wrinkled white shirt with no collar. A day's growth of white beard was etched across his puffed face. His Eminence moved to the right of the bed and blessed St. Malachy's pastor. Cappy couldn't see Carmody's face clearly because his bedside lamp was little more than a night light, but he heard the cardinal's voice:

"I've been thinking about you, Cap, praying for you . . ."

Carmody's voice trailed off and he looked away, and the pastor waited expectantly. Perhaps his prayers had been answered. God was merciful. God was good. Glory be to God!

The cardinal continued to look into the distance, which disturbed the pastor. Why didn't Carmody look him in the eye? A priest should never be distant, he should see other men's souls. His was supposed to be an immortal vision.

The cardinal noticed a pictorial history of Ireland on the small table to Cappy's right, picked it up and leafed through several pages. "Magnificent color! What a price you must've paid!"

A weak smile creased the pastor's face. "It was given me by Leo Dolan."

The cardinal had walked into that one. After their meeting about his daughter's pregnancy, Dolan seemed to be everywhere. Carmody changed the subject. "Didn't your mother come from Ireland, Cap?"

"Near the strand, the beach, at Inch."

"Ah, yes, County Kerry. Inch is about two hundred miles southwest of Dublin on the Atlantic. Purple mountains, emerald meadows, sapphire lakes. Ruddy faces polished by the wind. Thatch-roofed cottages. Sheep in the hills. Birds soaring above the cattle in the field. And plenty of salmon, too."

For the first time in years Cappy heard Carmody laugh.

"Talking like this," His Eminence said, "is like revisiting the old neighborhood, old friends. We haven't been able to leave the past behind us."

Cappy nodded. "It's our melancholy souls. The Irish love the romance of the past. We court it like some pursue the flesh. History is heaven. Everlasting light and eternal love. We embrace the long ago and far away as if it were our spiritual inheritance."

Carmody kept it going. "The Irish lyricize the past, the Americans invest in the future. One must seize time, bend it and use it. Otherwise one must simply live with it."

What was the cardinal saying? Cappy had accepted his limits. He had abandoned time. He had placed his whole life in the hands of God. Carmody, on the other hand, had seized time and used it to dominate the future. That was their difference. The cardinal's face seemed to be a mask without emotion, and Cappy recalled the only harsh words he had ever heard from Leo Dolan: "Carmody reminds me of Studs Lonigan's old man—mean."

The cardinal was a stark silhouette in the semidarkness, and seemed shrouded in a black mood. Cappy was seeing Fats Carmody tonight, an aged, angry man whose bile was thick in this throat.

"Faith," Carmody said. "That's what you and I've always been, Cap. Men of absolute faith. Absolute loyalty. Absolute trust. All this publicity's bad for Mother Church, Cap. The media think only about today's headlines, not tomorrow's truth—not our duty to the Good Lord, the Church, its future. What do you think about them, Cap?"

The trap had sprung and Cappy knew it. He also knew he was innocent.

"Your Eminence, I know nothing about the media. As you see, I have no TV, no radio here. I've read no newspapers or magazines since coming to St. Bernard's. For all practical purposes my only visitor is Leo Dolan. He's given me one order, relayed by Monsignor Brady in your name . . . don't speak with reporters. Your Eminence, I've spoken with no newsmen. To tell you the truth, I talk to myself most of the time."

The cardinal was set back by that. His mouth went dry, he tried to wet his lips, his jaw tightened. He had set a trap for himself . . . he should have known better. What was happening to him? Did he really believe he could stumble in here in the middle of the night and ask a priest to condemn his own spiritual life? Why was he threatening this old priest who had served him and the Church so well?

Fear. Men, even cardinals, didn't always exercise their power out of reason or intellect. Sometimes men use power out of emotion—from *fear*. But what and why did he fear? Was it that his domination, his control would be seen as slipping without total control of the archdiocese? Was it also a matter of expediency, quick money to cover Church debt and new suburban parishes? To rise above his priests and nuns and show them his leadership? What was it?

The prelate's right hand held the bedpost tightly. He would get a grip on himself. Fear was an imposter. A cardinal was by definition a leader. A man of decision. An administrator who lived by power.

Carmody saw that Cappy had begun to nap but was determined to complete his mission. He spoke bluntly:

"I want you to start eating solid food at breakfast this morning. That's an order, Cap."

Cappy didn't swallow the directive easily. God, it seemed, had closed His ears to his prayers. Carmody had become the will of God. The Good Lord wouldn't intervene. Mary, the mother of God, hadn't heard his rosaries. His mind cried out against the destruction of his church and his long priesthood, and he asked himself, Lord, why? Why?

The cardinal had put on his raincoat now and was leaving. Cappy called out: "And St. Malachy's?"

"That's my responsibility." He lessened the wallop. "St. Malachy's is in God's hands, Cappy. In the hands of Higher Authority."

The words knifed Cappy to his marrow.

His Eminence, Homburg in hand, stood over the pastor and said, "It's God's will, Cap." He blessed the priest, whose eyes had closed, then left.

In the morning, Cappy capitulated "I'll also take some scrambled eggs and toast. Maybe some orange juice, too."

Dolan broke into a broad smile. He rushed out to tell Sister Le Compte. On return Cappy explained his change:

"The cardinal was here. It's all right, Leo. I've given up. I surrendered to His Eminence about three this morning."

"He was here?" Dolan asked in surprise.

"Yes." Cappy squirmed. "He gave me his blessing and said St. Malachy's was in the hands of Higher Authority."

"And?"

"It's all over, Leo."

"Like hell it is. As soon as the wrecking crews arrive Mamma X and my daughter Kathy will throw pickets around the church. The media will be there. We're going to hand the cardinal a drum so he can join St. Malachy's victory parade up State Street."

"Leo," Cappy said in astonishment, "I've never heard you talk this way."

Dolan smiled.

"Leo," Cappy said, "I think I need a drink."

Chapter 8

THE NEW MARTYRS

Jim Gunth and Bob Dolan walked around the lake at the University of St. Peter in the Pines. A soft breeze cooled the June afternoon, the fragrance of evergreen filling the woods west of Chicago.

The two friends spoke about their old days at Wrigley Minor Seminary in Chicago, joked about the trials of translating Caesar's *Gallic Wars* from Latin and stumbling through trigonometry. The two had shared classes most of their seminary lives. "Slim Jim," as he was called, was almost like a brother to Bob Dolan.

They also recalled that first September day nearly four years ago when the bus slowly carried them through the wrought-iron gates of St. Peter's. Jim sat next to Bob during the ride. The blue-white vehicle wound around a long, narrow, twisting road before passing the imposing red-brick chapel and parking in front of Theology House, where they would live for four years before ordination to the priesthood. Bob had told Jim that he felt the presence of God there.

The two agreed they would never forget the red-brick facades of the buildings—especially the large chapel, library and Theology House. Most of the structures were colonial American, similar to Thomas Jefferson's University of Virginia. The imposing Memorial Library, with its old shaded lamps and 150,000 faded volumes—mostly on philosophy, theology and Church history—underlined St. Peter's educational attainment. It was one of only four institutions in the United States to grand canonical degrees in Sacred Theology.

Before the two arrived there had been sweeping changes in the seminary's life and curriculum that came in the 1960s and continued with some adjustments into their years. The changes reflected disagreements with old ways and teaching. Demands for a new era were launched by graduates throughout the Midwest who complained that St. Peter's studies had not prepared them for modern life. Graduates who abandoned their ministries agreed that they had faced unexpected temptations in the priesthood which their congregations had long faced daily.

To correct these concerns theology courses were revamped and the new study schedule included social and ethical issues. Professors from Loyola, DePaul and other local universities also taught at St. Peter's.

Some laymen still accused seminary graduates of living a rarified lifestyle, suffocated by the self-importance they attached to their religious education and priestly calling. Bob had heard it all, and like many of the young men being ordained he worried whether he was prepared for the real world. He had no idea what Jim thought.

Bob and Jim were scheduled to be ordained to the priesthood by Cardinal Carmody at Holy Name Cathedral in a few weeks. As they talked of that long-awaited day, Bob suddenly asked, "Jim, why did we come? Why?" He drew out the last word with a long question mark. Jim didn't answer, he never liked to be drawn out on personal questions. He was a man of issues, events of the moment. Bob finally responded to his own question: "I've never questioned my mother's explanation. It's a calling from God. I've always wanted to be a priest. Maybe my mother had something to do with it. Maybe it was Father Tom Gallagher who taught me to be an altar boy. I guess I just accepted it."

Gunth said he'd recently met a Saudi Arabian student on a Chicago bus who asked him who selected young men to be priests. Who interviewed them before they went to the seminary to find out what type of person each was? Gunth said he'd never really thought about being screened in an interview.

At Wrigley Minor for decades there was no screening process. Students entered with birth and baptismal certificates, a letter from their pastors and their marks from grammar school. Many priest-teachers at Wrigley never really knew their students. Early rectors and professors appeared to some students more interested in grades. In recent years rigorous screening had begun but it came too late to affect the many men already in the priesthood. Even if spiritual counselors at Holy Hills and St. Peter's eventually came to know seminarians well, they were bound by confessional silence if, for example, some students had sexual problems. When priests were ordained, some critics claimed, their superiors knew less about many of them than people being promoted in corporations or the military. Seminarians were God's chosen unless their conduct at the two seminaries was "unbecoming" or their scholastic grades were poor.

Gunth suddenly recalled: "Do you remember when Marty Scully quit in the middle of his first year in theology?

He came back to pick up his clothes and had that beautiful redhead with him. Her butt and breasts were busting out all over. Half the faculty couldn't take their eyes off her."

The two laughed. Jim put his arm around Bob's shoulders, hugging him. It was a good feeling, Bob told himself, to remember the past. He would never have a friend as fine as Jim Gunth, his closest link with the world over the past dozen years.

Geese flapped in the waters of a nearby lake. Someone was fishing from a small boat in the middle. The sun, lowering in the sky, still promised several hours of light. The dense forest covered the two with shade. Jim pressed his left hand into Bob's right and said quietly, "I love you, Bob."

Bob answered in innocence, "Hey, I love you too. You've been a real friend."

Such phrases were often shared among the seminarians; they were expressing God's love for one another. Jim squeezed Bob's hand. The turn of the road finally led to the Theology House. They still had an hour and a half before dinner. Jim wanted to take a spin, he said, in the new Chevy his parents had bought him and Bob agreed to go along. They drove off the seminary grounds and into a nearby forest. Jim stopped to "admire the sunset."

Jim suddenly ran one hand down Bob's neck and the other down his back. Bob, confused, felt Jim's hand on his chest, and then Jim pressed his penis against Bob's left thigh. Bob began to feel a rush of adrenalin, he had seen a similar scene at a risqué movie house in the Loop. Curiosity had got the better of him, but that was the only such theater he had ever gone to. Bob pulled away.

Jim had never behaved this way. He had fondled him just now the same way as males in that movie. And Bob suddenly realized that none of this seemed new to Jim Gunth. Had he been naive, misled—both?

Bob continued to ask himself questions. When Jim said he loved him as they walked in the pines, was his old friend suggesting they actually have sex?

He got his answer soon as Jim's hand reached up to Bob's shoulder and stroked it. And then in an instant Jim was on top of him and rolling him on his stomach and pulling at his clothes—and forcing himself inside . . . It was over in less than thirty seconds. A *rape* by his friend . . . friend? Oh, God . . .

Neither spoke until Jim finally said, "I don't want to talk about this now, neither do you. Let's just drive back."

Not a word was said during the return ride. Bob felt shaky, afraid he might go out of control. He couldn't think. And then he began to cry, quietly, covering his face with his hands.

When he got back to his room Bob tore off his clothes and stumbled into the shower, falling and just missing the glass door. He got up, turned on the hot water and soaped himself for what seemed hours, and it still wasn't enough.

He dressed, feeling like a zombie, and sat at his desk for a long time. He did not go to dinner or night-prayers. When it was time for Mass in the morning he walked mindlessly to chapel and didn't take his regular seat, remaining in the last pew. At Communion he was too upset to see if Jim had received the sacrament. Pale, shaking, Bob somehow got out of the chapel, avoiding going to Communion. His confessor, Father Richard Rivers, grabbed him by the arm in the hallway and asked if he was all right.

"I'm sick," Bob said abruptly, and continued walking.

He had been protected from life on the street during his four years at Wrigley, additional years at Holy Hills and finally during his final four years at St. Peter's. Now, about to be ordained a priest, he suddenly felt unprotected and terribly vulnerable.

He asked himself if it was possible that God was testing him just before his ordination? The ceremony had been scheduled, as was traditional, for mid-May. But two of those to be ordained had been killed in a car crash on Route 176 just ten days earlier and so ordination was postponed for a month's mourning.

That day now stood before him like a ticking clock.

He slumped into his weather-beaten 1987 Ford Escort. He was having more muffler trouble but drove on the highway. He got five dollars worth of unleaded and phoned his brother Michael at his home.

Michael's psychiatric antennae immediately recognized a crisis of some sort although Bob didn't tell him what had happened. He merely said he had to see Michael as soon as possible. All right, they would meet in Michael's office at 10:30 A.M., which would give Michael time to cancel several appointments. The office was best because Bob apparently was in no condition to have breakfast or meet in public.

The two met with a brief handshake.

"What's going on?" Michael said.

Bob spit it out. "I was raped by another seminarian . . . it was in the forest near St. Peter's . . . yesterday afternoon."

Michael tried to be professional. "Go on, Bob."

"You *know* what I mean. Do I have to draw you a picture?"

"Without your consent?"

"Yes."

"Anything else?"

"Isn't that *enough,* Michael?"

Michael knew in spite of his good intentions he was not handling this right. His protective concern in his brother's behalf had overcome his professional judgment. Let Bob talk instead of hammering him with questions. Right now his immediate role was to reassure Bob, ease his misery. Did Bob feel somehow guilty too? Probably. Guilt often went with the violation, especially at first. And too often others were inclined to blame the victim. Did he, she ask for it . . .

Michael quickly concluded that Bob was a true victim. The incident was not his brother's fault, he didn't initiate it. He knew he should send Bob to another psychiatrist, but looking at his brother, Michael decided he had to break the rules. Bob was emotionally devastated. It was his job to pull him out of this tailspin *fast* or Bob might be lost to the priesthood . . . to *himself.* He would go on with this emergency consultation because Bob, the family's silent son, might *never* seek or even agree to counseling. Michael kept his voice low, calm.

"Was this the first time this person or anyone else did this to you?"

"Yes."

"He was someone you knew fairly well?"

"Yes."

"Was it Jim Gunth?"

"I don't want to name him."

"All right. I said it. Bob, have you ever felt that you were gay?"

Bob hesitated, then: "No, but . . ."

"But what?"

"But maybe I misled him, my stupid naiveté. Or maybe . . ."

"Maybe you have suppressed your inclinations in the past?"

"I don't know, it raised some questions in my mind . . ."

"Aw, hell, Bob. You're a human being. That's all it told you. You aren't gay. More to the point, *you are not guilty.*"

"I still feel dirty."

Michael said again, "Bob, you're not gay. And this isn't a judgment. But I deal with homosexuals every day. Many tell me loving men is natural to them. That's not your inclination, not so long as I've known you, which is a pretty long time. Many gays still live a life of guilt and have severe psychiatric problems. You don't have those, that's not you."

A slow grin moved across Michael's face. "You know, little brother, you're still standing. Have a seat, this isn't the army."

Bob sat down next to Michael on a long black leather couch.

"Bob, do you just want to talk in general or do you want to talk about homosexuality?" He saw that his brother's tension seemed to be easing.

For the moment Michael would avoid the tough questions that he faced dealing with homosexual priests and the hierarchy's views of the problem: Why are so many clerics molesting young boys? Why do so many gay priests claim they are not responsible for their illegal actions? Why have bishops long protected clerical child molesters? What are the solutions to the financial damages facing the Church? Are the faithful expected to pay all these expenses? Why has it taken the Church so long to confront the issue of sex and priests? Shouldn't spiritual counselors discuss sex from the time a young man expresses a desire to enter a seminary or monastery through his career as a priest or brother? The same with nuns.

"I've decided not to be ordained," Bob said abruptly.

The declaration hit Michael like a blast of Lake Michigan wind. Suddenly he was a brother and a Dolan more than a psychiatrist. He reached for a handful of cashew nuts in a silver bowl on the nearby magazine table, chewed rapidly, crunching the nuts with a force that indicated his feelings. He thought of his father. Nora would survive but Bob's leaving would just about kill Leo. The old man was not the typical tough detective, streetwise as he was. Leo was a reverent man, a loyal son of the Catholic Church *and* a devoted father.

"Why don't you want to be ordained?"

"I feel *unworthy.* I've also lost some of the respect I had for the priesthood. My best friend's a hypocrite, still becoming a priest. He'll consecrate the Body and Blood of Christ in the morning and sodomize somebody that night. Twelve years in the seminary and my deacon internship have just blown up in my face."

Bob was on the verge of tears. Michael put his right hand on his brother's shoulder and said quietly, "Bob, your family loves you."

And Michael now began to try to get his brother to develop a broader context. Bob had, after all, spent three summer months at a clerical homosexual-treatment center in the Midwest helping the resident chaplain. Bob realized that two of the priests at the treatment center had made subtle, very subtle, sexual advances to him but he didn't take them seriously, didn't see them for what they were. He'd noticed, though, that some priests held hands and often stroked others who reciprocated the affection. He had originally been told that the men were there because of depression, nervous breakdowns. These priests were treated like visiting dignitaries. The lay staff, especially those who did menial work, were dealt with as inferiors. The priests never cleaned their rooms, washed dishes or did any other dirty work. Bob was struck by the unusual *cleanliness* of their hands, as though they washed their hands repeatedly. They attended a few classes, read, played cards, watched television and video movies and went for walks. Many of them drank, some were drunks.

"They acted like peacocks," he told Michael. "Even the ones who were being treated for homosexuality, and abuse, too, I suspect. They walked around with a superior air, like they were somehow better than the center's workers. I tell you, I began to understand why some people viewed priests warily. For the first time I began asking myself about my seminary life and training."

Just then the psychiatrist's secretary, Bonnie Biondi, knocked and peeked in the door. "Just letting you know I'm here, doctor. I've made coffee. Anybody want some?"

Michael got up from the couch. "I forgot about coffee. Would you like a cup, Bob?"

Bob accepted and Michael called for two blacks. He also told the secretary that he had already canceled his morning appointments. Then he asked his brother if he could tell him when he thought of leaving the priesthood. It sounded like Bob had been having some second thoughts before Jim Gunth's attack.

"I'm not sure exactly when, but it all seemed to coalesce the following morning. He'd committed a mortal sin, right? And I was directly involved. It brought the whole issue home. I asked myself how homosexual priests can say Mass, receive Communion, forgive sins and act as if they're living their vow of celibacy. I don't want any part of their priesthood."

Bob paused, then shook his head. "You know, the critics are right in saying the homosexuality of priests is the greatest Church scandal in four hundred years."

Michael wouldn't let go. He reminded his brother that Cardinal Carmody had made him a special medical counselor to the archdiocese. Priests with problems were now under his care . . . "I've learned things that may tell you something about yourself, whether *you* may be tempted by homosexuality and whether you have what it takes to be a priest.

"Many gay priests excuse homosexuality by intellectual and spiritual semantics. Most are emotionally immature. They've never really lived a regular life. I don't think you're one of these men, Bob.

"Some of these priests I've treated molest one boy after another—five, six, ten, twelve. They seek out children because youngsters are obviously easier to molest than adults. One priest who was sent to me molested *three* boys in a day. Many ignore that they're engaged in a criminal act. Others believe they'll never go to prison, their collar and the Church will protect them. We're dealing with men who feel they enjoy an untouchable status, above the law. They defend themselves by doing what they're best at—intellectualizing their actions, splitting moral hairs, making excuses for their behavior. Bob, I've never known you to make excuses for yourself. Just the opposite."

Michael sipped his coffee. "These guys talked about something they call proportionate reason to explain how they can do what they do and remain in the state of grace. They say that if the Catholic Church says it's wrong to perform a certain act and then you do it, there may have been some proportionate reason for your action and that's a mitigating moral factor. Some say the sexual attraction of young men is so great that they're powerless to stop it. They claim their private conscience allows them to stand back from the teachings of the Church and commit these acts. To put it bluntly, they screw a fellow priest or altar boy in the rectory at 6:00 A.M. and drink Christ's blood out of a sacred chalice less than an hour later. I don't believe *you're* such a man, Bob."

Michael paused to drink more coffee and allow his brother to think on what he had said, then pressed on:

"You have to wonder how they could take the vow of celibacy knowing, as some do, who and what they are. I don't make moral judgments. That's not my business. But I do feel these priests are psychologically damaging not only to themselves but to others. Some have drug and alcohol problems. Some suffer from severe depression, some have breakdowns. And some, guilty as sin of abuse, plainly deceive themselves and others. Priests are good at deception, and we're often dealing with very deceitful men. Such priests don't belong in the priesthood and I've told them so. Maybe I've overstepped my bounds there but psychiatrists are human too."

Michael was warmed up. "Much of the blame for the problems of priestly homosexuality and child molestation rests on the hierarchy, I believe. The bishops are almost as bad as the guilty ones named as sexual abusers. They've covered up by transferring pedophiles in molestation cases to new parishes. They've engaged in legal maneuvers to avoid paying financial damages to real victims. Their implicit threats to Catholic families suing the Church for medical bills and psychological damages are hardly Christian. And they don't understand that they've driven many of these families clear out of the Catholic faith.

"You know, Bob, we need a Curé d'Ars in the American priesthood. One St. Francis of Assisi. A single Mother Theresa? Hell, I'll settle for a good Anglican!"

Michael talked about the exodus of priests and nuns from the Church. In the mid-1960s there were about sixty thousand priests in the United States. By 1993 there were fewer than twenty-five thousand diocesan priests. "Eventually there may be more parishes than priests."

"What about priests marrying?" Bob asked. "Maybe that's the answer. I get the idea that a lot of priests want the right to marry."

Michael shook his head. "It won't happen in the life of this pope. He's made that clear."

Bob nodded. "I know. Isn't it true that at one time priests could marry?"

Michael picked it up. "Absolutely true. And I've read that thousands of priests now married are trying for the restoration of their positions . . ."

Bob still seemed very troubled and Michael understood that all this wasn't really going to be the answer to his brother's dilemma. A solution could come only in more human terms.

"I repeat, we love you, Bob. If the family knew about this incident, none of them would want you to walk away from your ordination."

Bob smiled, for the first time during his learned brother's long exposition.

"Well, Michael, you always seem to have a convincing close." The brothers smiled at one another as Bob stood and stuck out his right hand. "Thanks, big brother. A little windy, but I appreciate it."

"I know, I do go on. But what about it . . . are you going to be ordained?"

"I'm headed over to the chancery office now," Bob said seriously, "to ask for a meeting with the cardinal."

Mrs. Reginald Rebb handed her son the usual thermos bottle of cold root beer as their visit ended. The May afternoon sun warmed both of them. Father Ralph Rebb walked down the front steps of his mother's home in suburban Wilmette, then turned and waved to her. She stood against the front door and called out:

"Ralph, your father would be so proud of you."

"Thank you, Mother. God bless. See you next Thursday."

Rebb had Thursdays off and always had lunch with his

mother at her home. His father had died a decade earlier on the West Coast. Rebb had been ordained there but had gotten a transfer to Chicago when his mother came east to live with her sister, who passed away a year later. The sister left her home to Father Rebb's mother. Mother and son had always been close. Neither took a major decision without consulting the other. There was, however, one exception in his case—an admission he could *never* discuss with her.

Rebb opened the door of his silver Eldorado, a present from Gilbert Y. Truppete Jr., one of his longtime intimates. Gil was gone now. Died more than two years ago at fifty-one. AIDS. Fortunately, he and Gil had split. Gil Truppete, an insurance-company executive, had ended the relationship the day his doctor had told him he was HIV positive. He had bought Rebb the Cadillac that afternoon, in his own mind as a farewell. But Truppete had never told Rebb about his AIDS.

The two had seen less and less of one another during the last four years. Father Ralph Rebb had found youth—from nine to fourteen years old, first at San Guglielmo parish, until he was transferred. Then at St. Silverius parish, from which he was moved within six months. And then at Good Shepherd of God Church and another early transfer—all in less than four years. In two cases Rebb had been convicted of molesting boys but escaped prison. He was sent to semisecret Catholic treatment houses in New England and the Southwest for psychiatric help. In the third instance Rebb was caught by his pastor in the act of raping a nine-year-old boy in his car. The parents of the youth, who suffered severe psychological damage, threatened to bring suit against the archdiocese for more than four hundred thousand dollars in medical bills. The case was eventually settled out of court.

Rebb was now at St. Rosalie of Palermo on the South Side with its Boy Scouts and the youth choir, which recruited boys from public schools. No indication of his past was ever given to the congregation. Father Rebb was the maestro of the young hymnists. He had even taught them the *Ave Maria* and *Panis Angelicus* in Latin. The elders of the parish loved the two hymns, which reminded them of the past glories of the old Church. They loved Father Rebb's soft clear voice, his impeccable diction, his commitment to youth and his long, silvery hair. Only a handful at the parish, the Old Biddies as some called them, knew this was Rebb's fourth parish in a four-year span. But that was all they knew . . .

Rebb now started the Eldorado. His mother, a former nurse, was still waving to him. She had been much stronger willed than his father Reginald, an Englishman whom she had met at the end of World War II while serving with the Army Nursing Corps at a U.S. military hospital outside London. Reg, as his father was called, was a very proper sort. Elegant, he sometimes wore spats. Pinstripes, always. Silk ties. A restrained man who never raised his voice. Reg was the assistant director of a nursing home for wealthy elderly. He had been a male nurse in England. Rebb recalled a photograph of his father standing on the cliffs of Dover looking out on the English Channel; his grandfather had written these words on the back of the photo:

"To Reg, who never makes waves. Good luck, Father."

Rebb stopped the car in the parking lot of a liquor store three blocks from his mother's house, removed his suit coat, shirt and collar. He got out of the front seat, opened the trunk of the Cadillac and placed them in a carrying bag. He pulled a yellow sport shirt from a plastic holder, pulled it on and walked to the store, where he bought two miniature bourbons and a similar pair of gins that he slipped into the side pockets of a gray sports coat. After reentering his Eldorado he opened a gin, swigged it down and tossed the bottle in a nearby garbage can. Then he slipped the other three drinks into his glove compartment.

It was a twenty-five-minute drive to his old haunt, the Apollo X bar, a longtime gay hangout. He had not been there in more than two years. He didn't know precisely why but he had to go there today. For old times' sake, he told himself.

It was shortly after 3:00 P.M. and there were only two men in the Apollo X. D.D. was bartending. It took the owner a moment to recognize the figure in the darkness but he suddenly whooped:

"Foxy! Where the hell have you been?"

The two leaned across the bar and kissed.

D.D. had always called him the "Silver Fox." Rebb was already prematurely gray when he met D.D. in the bar in his prime at thirty-one. He called the next five years his education years. D.D., a night bartender then, was his first lover. Later D.D. bought the place.

The two of them were called the "She Wolf" and the "Silver Fox" in those days.

"Gin and tonic, right?" D.D. remembered.

"Right," Rebb echoed. He tossed three dollars on the bar.

"On the house," D.D. insisted, and returned the money to Rebb's right hand, which he squeezed, then picked up a shot of Scotch. "To the good old days!"

The two clinked glasses and downed the drinks.

"When was the first time you came in?" D.D. asked.

"More than twenty years ago."

"That long? But you look so well, Foxy. No pot. You can't weigh more than a hundred fifty-five. Good for a guy at five feet seven. Svelte but saucy."

A young man in his late thirties entered and sat down beside Rebb. "Weeell, helloo!"

Straights might call the elongated expression affectation. In the gay world it was more a friendship or perhaps a mating call.

Rebb stood to leave without acknowledging the newcomer. "You're looking well, too," Rebb said. "It's been great seeing you. I've got an appointment."

D.D. stood polishing the bar. "Anybody I know?"

Rebb shrugged. As he opened the door and walked out into the sunlight D.D. called after him, "Don't take so long to come back."

Rebb waved and closed the door. He thought of the intruder at the bar while walking back to the Caddy. A bejowled middle-ager with a big pouch. Nothing subtle or supple about him. No young eyes and tender skin. Ah, youth, so clean and fresh . . .

It was four o'clock. Perfect timing. Gene McDonner would be waiting for him. Well, he had seen the place again. Was he glad that he had broken with the old crowd? Of course. D.D. and that other guy had been around the block. They didn't smell the flowers anymore. The young innocent scent.

He drove forty-five minutes to the edge of Marquette Park and turned off the ignition. The street was deserted. He had ten to fifteen minutes. Rebb first removed his black shoes and silk stockings, then took off his black trousers and yellow shorts. He was deliberate, unhurried, meticulous. He took out a pair of green-and-white basketball trunks, white socks and tennis shoes from the same suitcase and dressed quickly. He opened the thermos and poured the two bourbons into the cold root beer. Young Gene turned the corner and walked toward the car, opened the right front door and climbed in the front seat.

"Afternoon, Father. Isn't it a great day!"

The priest acknowledged the warm sun and waited until

the fourteen-year-old had placed his schoolbooks in the back seat. Rebb patted Gene on the thigh.

"Good to see you, Gene. Here's your cold root beer."

Gene knew it was spiked. This was his third ride with the priest. But he liked getting high. Two of his best pals already drank beer every weekend.

"Ready to shoot a few buckets?" the priest asked.

"Yes, Father. I got my trunks on under my pants."

"You can just toss your pants in the back seat."

Gene, wearing sneakers, unzipped his khaki pants, removed them and draped the legs across the top of Rebb's closed suitcase. He took a long drink of root beer. It was strong.

"Choir tomorrow night, Father?"

"Yes," Rebb said, "we need the extra practice. The cardinal will be here in a month for confirmation."

Rebb had a ginger ale bottle stuffed between the seats. He lifted it up now, unscrewed the cap and took two slugs. It was eighty-five percent gin and ten percent tea. He held the open bottle in his hand and took one long final swallow, then screwed the cap back on and started the car.

The gin hit Rebb. It's the heat, he told himself. He was somewhat dizzy. He pulled over behind a deserted baseball field. Gene was still drinking his root beer, feeling the first hit of the bourbon.

"Well, pal, I got a little dizzy." Rebb placed his arm around the youngster's shoulder and pulled Gene toward him. He rubbed Gene's neck and back. A couple suddenly appeared and the young man looked squarely at the driver and youth. The couple stopped and Rebb panicked. He started the engine and pulled quickly away from the curb. The couple followed the Cadillac with a long questioning look.

Rebb was upset. He hadn't seen them. That was highly

unusual. He always kept his eyes peeled for snoops. Suddenly a siren sounded. The lights of a police car flashed behind him. The priest pulled to the curb.

The officer seemed relaxed as he asked for Rebb's driver's license. "Hey, buddy, didn't you see the stop sign at the last corner?"

"No, officer," Rebb replied. "Sorry, I guess I was thinking about choir practice."

There he was again, leaning on the Church. The crutch. No, the lifesaver. The shrinks had warned him time and again of that. He couldn't put all his weight on the Church's shoulder. He had to carry some of the burden himself. Invoking God and the Church was a cop-out.

"Excuse me," the officer said. "I didn't notice the Reverend in front of your name. Maybe the heat's got me today."

"Father Ralph Rebb," the priest said.

"Oh, a priest?"

"Yes, over at St. Rosalie of Palermo."

"I'm from St. Hal's, Father."

The officer, Tim Dalton, had not yet written a ticket and excused himself. He walked back to the squad car, where Dave Sturm, his senior by some ten years, waited. Rebb smiled. It had happened before. He wouldn't get a ticket from a Catholic cop. Instead Dalton snapped at Sturm.

"This one rocks me, Dave."

"What is it?" Sturm inquired.

"When I asked this guy for his driver's license he had to take his arm from around a kid. The kid can't be more than thirteen or fourteen and he's practically sitting in this guy's lap."

"And?"

"Then the guy talks about choir and tells me he's a Catholic priest. All the while I'm smelling booze. And, are you ready for this? He's only got basketball shorts on. It was like a thumb in my eye. Dave, you got to take a look."

Sturm got out of the car and came forward with his partner. He stood at the right front window while Dalton spoke on the left.

"Father, have you been drinking?"

Rebb did not respond.

Sturm took the root beer out of young Gene's hand and smelled the cup. "But you have, haven't you, son?"

"Well, I guess it's spiked a little."

"It's bourbon. Who gave it to you?"

"Father Rebb."

The two officers looked at one another. Dalton said, "Father, I have to ask you what that bottle is between the seats. Does it contain alcohol?"

Rebb remained silent. Dalton asked the priest and youth to step out of the Caddy. He reached in, unscrewed the bottle cap and smelled gin.

Sturm radioed for a special unit. He wanted no kickbacks and asked for blood and breath-analyzer tests. The tests were taken on the street about ten minutes later. The priest's alcohol content was nearly twice the legal limit. The McDonner youth also was analyzed as drinking.

Sturm walked to Rebb's side of the car and said quietly to the priest, "I'm not a particularly fastidious man, Father, but if your pecker is going to stand up you ought to wear more than basketball shorts." He halted for his words to take effect, then added: "Were you on your way to screwing the kid?"

"You'll hear about that remark from the chancery office," the priest snapped. Sturm about-faced and walked briskly back to the squad car and called on the radio.

"Do you have any rap on a Ralph Rebb? Says he's a Catholic priest."

Sturm waited for several minutes. Finally a new voice came on the line:

"Steve Rhymer here, Dave. Child molestation. A three-time loser. The last conviction was voided. He went to some behavioral clinic for priests. He's up for a third conviction now. An eleven-year-old altar boy."

"Thanks, Steve." Sturm closed off the call after conferring with his area lieutenant, then walked back to the priest. "You're under arrest, Father, for driving under the influence and contributing to the delinquency of a minor—giving him booze. You seem to know all about your rights on remaining silent so I don't think I have to read you every word."

Dalton drove Rebb and the youth to police headquarters at 11th and State streets. Standing orders from the top on clergymen. Their lieutenant had confirmed that on the radio. Sturm followed in the squad car.

Lieutenant Al Robb called ahead to headquarters and the phone report was sent up to Superintendent Rossi, who read it, groaned, phoned his wife and said he would be late for dinner.

Rossi saw Sturm and Dalton privately after they arrived with Rebb and the youngster. The police explained the lad had been briefly detained as a witness and was being sent home. The officers then told Rossi everything, including the sex angle. Rebb was brought up to the chief's private conference room after he had been booked for DUI downstairs. Rossi knew it wasn't smart to see Rebb but he had never met the priest and was curious. Once the priest arrived Rebb figured that from his Italian name Rossi was a Catholic.

Rebb never shut up. He spoke of his pastor, an elderly man, needing him. The choir would be waiting for practice. He always phoned his mother after visiting her. She would wonder and worry.

The priest was merely on his way to play basketball at

Marquette Park. A few games of "horse" with a fine young member of his choir. He needed more exercise. The hours of the priesthood were mostly cerebral, long and demanding. Sure, he had a few drinks. He certainly wasn't inebriated. He told Rossi, his eyebrows arched in a manner of certainty, there was a lot of tension in the work of a parish priest. Wandering into the night on sick calls. Listening to the grief of battered wives and unemployed husbands. The arguments of estranged couples seeking annulments of their marriages. Hearing confession was sometimes torture. Administering the last rites of the Church was a killer. A lot of good men were breaking down in the priesthood . . .

"I understand you're coming up on a third sodomy charge." Rossi smoked his fastball past Rebb, who sat speechless. The chief stared at the priest, the silence extending for nearly thirty seconds.

Rebb stood and asked: "May I wash my hands?"

Rossi motioned to the nearby bathroom. When the priest returned he carried a fistful of paper towels and dried his hands again and again.

Rossi asked: "How often do you get your hands manicured, Father?"

Rebb ignored the question, continuing to dry his hands, then said quietly that he had been away in treatment. Good psychiatrists. They had told him his cure would take time. "Are you going to throw away my priesthood? The long education, the sacrifices, the years of devotion and prayer. I'm not a sinner."

The superintendent asked, "No?"

Rebb casually remarked that Rossi probably hadn't read the Second Vatican Council statements on personal conscience. The chief turned over his hands negatively. The priest expounded that there were mitigating moral circumstances for men like him. He had been born a homosexual.

His father had been bisexual. He knew that his parents hadn't made love for the last fifteen years of their marriage. His mother had told him that. His parents passed on a latent homosexuality to him. There was nothing wrong with being gay and in any case he was powerless to deny his physical makeup, it was part of his existence.

Rossi then asked the priest why he had taken the vow of celibacy. Rebb said he only realized he was gay after entering the priesthood, through gay friends, several fellow priests. And they were still out there carrying on their ministry with dedication.

Rossi hid his deep skepticism. Most men he had known, even criminals, eventually took responsibility for their actions. Yet every gay priest that he had met, and there were dozens, intellectualized or rationalized his homosexuality, and behavior that was against his vows. Accountability, obligation, the vow of celibacy—they all became irrelevant to a changing conscience. Damn convenient, Rossi concluded.

Sergeant Hickey knocked on the door then and Rossi told her to enter. She reported that Officer Neal Rattigan had arrived and was waiting outside. The officer, a twenty-five-year-old redhead who stood six feet four inches tall, removed his hat and entered the conference room and Rossi introduced Father Rebb. The two men shook hands. The chief mentioned that Rattigan had graduated from Wrigley Minor and had completed his first year of theology at St. Peter's. He sometimes counseled Rossi on clerical matters.

Rossi briefly summarized Rebb's background. At a signal from the chief Rattigan began a low-key interrogation of the priest, which the officer prefaced by saying that American Catholic bishops, not always informed on the problem, had a long history of not removing priests from their ministry although some were *repeated* child molesters. This was in spite of the fact that such molestation had always been considered a serious felony. Rattigan said it wasn't true, as some claimed, that bishops or religious superiors were powerless to remove clerical child molesters from the priesthood. Canon law allowed them to do that. He asked why Rebb's faculties as a priest hadn't been suspended or revoked after his two convictions for child molestation. Rebb refused to respond, and kept silent.

"Was it because the priesthood is a club that shares a bond, protecting itself from the lay victims of its sexual crimes, even those whose lives are ruined and faith destroyed?"

The priest, obviously startled by the bluntness of the questions, remained silent.

Rattigan continued: "Hasn't it been true for decades that the Church, along with other nonprofit public-benefit groups, enjoyed a charitable status that gave it civil immunity? Bishops and priests could take many actions without fear of any civil damages. The crimes of some priests and nuns were thereby kept secret. True?"

Rebb lit a cigarette and Rossi told him to put it out.

Rattigan went on that if the public knew about priestly child molestation that took place twenty-five or more years ago, and the Church was then forced to pay millions of dollars in personal damages to victims, the modern Church probably wouldn't have tried to evade its responsibility in so many recent cases.

Rebb now angrily responded that he had been arrested on charges related to DUI and contributing to the delinquency of a minor.

"That's right," the officer said, "but society no longer allows the Church and priests, and the ministers of other faiths civil immunity."

Rebb again sulked.

Rattigan told him, for the record, that the legal profession now regarded religious institutions as having corporate liability because Church administrators had failed to carry out even minimal civil or ethical standards regarding priest pedophiles or other clerical crimes. Indeed, when confronted with a child molestation case, Church officials often asked parents not to contact police, lawyers or the courts. The victims were left twisting in the wind without medical or psychological aid. The evil, the crime committed was often ignored by the hierarchy. "That was among the last gasps of supreme autocracy in the American Church. Is that right, Father Rebb?"

The priest now began to respond, to rationalize in his standard fashion.

Rossi cut him off. "Do you always intellectualize sodomy on minors?"

Rebb then launched into a lecture on the education of a priest. Few men, he said, were more attuned to the teachings of Christ and the nature of sin than a priest. Few received this higher calling, this holy mission. People *needed* him, including doctors, lawyers, nurses, nuns *and* police. His healing words, his dispensation of the sacraments, his love. He was the voice of Christ—

"When you spoke to that youngster in the car, were you the voice of Christ?"

Rebb turned away, pouted and refused to respond.

"And *love?*" Rossi went on. "Does love include the molestation of children?" Rebb again clammed tight.

The chief halted the exchange and told Rebb that he would remain overnight in the tank. If he pleaded guilty to DUI at his arraignment in the morning his driver's license would probably be revoked for six months to a year. Rebb angrily said he was innocent of all charges, including contributing to the delinquency of a minor. He wanted to speak with one of the chancery office lawyers. Rossi told him the chancery was closed and wouldn't open until morning.

"Then I want to talk to the cardinal," Rebb said.

"Fine," Rossi said, "but you'll have to wait."

Rebb's bluff, threatening the chief with the power of the cardinal and Church, had failed and he knew it immediately. So did Rossi.

"Father, your collar, shirt, suitcoat and pants are downstairs. I suggest you go down, take off the shorts, and put your clerical clothes back on. And Father?"

"Yes?"

"Zip up your pants. And Father, no bullshit. That's not the voice of Christ."

Chapter 9

THE POWER AND THE GLORY

Leo arrived in his office at Area Two, Violent Crimes Unit, on East 111th Street shortly before 8:00 A.M. The phone rang and Sgt. William Weller, a calm, matter-of-fact man, spoke:

"We have a possible homicide out here near 113th and Kedzie. A young woman about twenty-four years old. White. No ID. Clean appearance. Well dressed. We found her in a locked black 1991 Ford Escort. Shot twice in the left side of the head with a .22. We got one slug. Ray Streeter, the investigator for the medical examiner, estimates she was killed about 1:30 A.M. A paper boy noticed her about six-thirty this morning as he was finishing his route. The kid phoned 911. When can you get here?"

Leo, seeing Matt Moran arrive, said he and his partner would be on the scene in twenty minutes. He asked Weller to keep the medical investigator there.

When they arrived Weller briefed the two before they

viewed the body. The woman had already been examined, photos taken, the car dusted for fingerprints and searched for evidence. The first police on the scene had found only two clues. Officers Tom Kelly and J.T. Walker discovered a syringe on the ground below the driver's side door. However, Investigator Streeter found no syringe marks on the victim's arms or body. There was no evidence to suggest she may have been on drugs. The officers also found four small white beads attached to a gold-plated chain on the car floor. The chain appeared to have been ripped at both ends. Weller recognized the beads. They had come from a rosary.

Weller had already sent Kelly, Walker and two other policemen to canvass homes in the area to see if anyone had heard shots during the night or if they had recently seen anyone suspicious in the neighborhood. Perhaps someone knew the woman. The police photographer provided Weller with six Polaroid shots of the victim's face, avoiding her head wounds as much as possible. The search had come up blank but the canvass continued.

Leo and Matt walked to the car where the victim was still seated.

Leo froze when he saw the face of the dead woman—it was Joan Solari.

"I know the victim," Leo said quietly. "Her name is Joan Solari. She's a former Sister of Mercy who works with my daughter Kathy at the Ogden Park grammar school at 67th and Racine."

Weller, aware that the veteran detective was truly shaken, said evenly, "The case is yours now. I'll drop a copy of my report in your office."

Leo nodded to Weller, unable to take his eyes off of Solari slumped in the front seat. She had brown hair, was about five feet five inches tall and weighed some one hundred fifteen pounds. He remembered how her closed brown eyes had once danced on her face. She reminded Leo of his own daughter Evie. Their physical similarity was slight but Joan, even in death, seemed to give off a fresh innocence.

Leo lit his pipe. It was not suicide, not only because of Joan's background but the former nun was shot twice from the left side at a distance of about a foot. Joan, it was established, was right-handed. The killing most likely was committed by someone in the driver's seat.

Since there was no purse or identification, Leo and Matt theorized the case might be robbery-murder, perhaps for drug money. They would have to await the medical exam and other reports for more information. Leo ordered that the car be taken away for further examination after the medical examiner's officer removed Joan's body to the morgue.

Leo saw Streeter and requested a detailed autopsy. He explained the victim was a friend of his family. Streeter promised to pass the word along to the examining physicians.

Leo kept the rosary beads and a police photo of the dead woman and then said to Moran: "Let's go get a drink."

Leo had never talked about having a drink in the years that the pair had worked together. Leo was still a member of AA and hadn't lifted a whiskey in three decades. Matt pretended not to have heard the remark and began driving back to the area.

"Let's try Dubliner's," Leo said. "It's not out of the way."

Matt eyed his partner uneasily. He wanted to stay on course to the area. However, watching Leo's blinking eyes, he headed for the saloon.

The two took seats at the far end of the long bar, and Matt noted Leo's hands were trembling slightly. Matt ordered a nonalcoholic beer for himself and a ginger ale for his partner. The two sat in silence for several minutes before Leo spoke:

"I saw our little girl Evie out there, Matt. That's what I saw. Her head bloody and her dreams wiped clean off her face." Leo picked up the ginger ale and took a long drink. "Don't you *see* it, Matt? Evie and Joan are the children of a crazy society. Lord, how I lay awake nights and think of going back to a civilized Ireland someday . . ." Leo's voice trailed off.

Matt tried to change the subject. "If whoever shot Joan Solari was on drugs we may get some prints. Let's go back to the area, Leo."

Leo ignored him, saying, "I remember when my first ten years on the force ended in 1965. There were, what, about eight thousand murders a year in the U.S.? Now they say there are twenty-five thousand. Today the statistics I see have it that there are over a million violent crimes, more than five times thirty years ago. Relatively few people were taking drugs then, the worst was getting drunk. A lot of kids still respected their parents, even went to church on Sunday, studied and lived fairly decent lives. Catholic kids today don't know the Stations of the Cross or the Act of Contrition. Twelve-year-old kids shoot drugs. Their older brothers and sisters have sex with strangers and expose themselves to AIDS. Pornography sells, alcoholism and suicides are now all too common among youngsters. They watch the most violent TV and movies ever made."

Matt knew that Leo's own world had gone badly wrong. His daughter Evie was unwed and pregnant, apparently considering an abortion. Marge was against abortion, so were Leo and Nora and brother Dan. Leo was upset with the cardinal because Carmody wouldn't talk to his nephew, who made Evie pregnant. Leo at least wanted Rusty Carmody to tell Evie to forget an abortion, he'd take financial responsibility for the baby. Now Kathy had left the Sisters of Mercy and was fighting the cardinal to save St. Malachy's from demolition and show Chicago that the laity could run an inner-city school abandoned by the Church. And Leo had joined Kathy and Cappy Conlon in their battle with His Eminence. And *now,* to top it off, Leo had hints from his daughter Kathy that his son Bob was threatening to forego ordination. Matt felt for Leo. The whole damn family had its britches on fire. One more hit and Leo might retire from the force and hightail it back to Ireland with Nora, just like he'd always planned after retirement.

As for himself, Matt figured he could handle the problems . . . he could tell the government, the cardinal and a lot of other people that he didn't give an Irish fart about their wishes and woes. He was probably the only Catholic in Chicago who would have the guts to tell the cardinal that he pissed icicles. But not Leo. Leo would play his harp and weep in his Old Country way that people would be better tomorrow than today. Except it wasn't better for Leo, it was getting worse and worse, at least as Matt saw it.

Matt knew Leo's troubles, one way or another, involved the Church, the sharp differences that had come out of the Second Vatican Council. There seemed to be a new Church squabble every few months. Now Leo was bemoaning the Apostolate of the Laity, except if forced to Leo would call them lay apostles. The Carmodys put themselves in this class. The Second Vatican Council endorsed the concept of a lay apostolate with some priests putting themselves in these roles without even taking off their collars.

Leo and Matt both felt the Church had too many self-appointed, self-righteous voices telling other people what to believe and do. But with the exodus of priests and more clerical losses to death and retirement, the laity became more significant each year. No question, whether they knew it or not, the Dolan children and grandchildren were creating a new Church.

Matt watched as Leo clenched and unclenched his right fist, stared at the booze against the bar mirror. Matt again tried to change the subject.

"Did you hear the latest about the Fightin' Irish of Notre Dame?" Leo didn't answer as Matt went on, "They're fightin' again."

Leo offered a weak smile.

"If the hiring trend goes on, the university will have a mostly non-Catholic faculty by the year 2000. The Holy Cross fathers, who own the university, believe the majority of the faculty should be Catholics. In a poll the faculty voted otherwise. The priests are concerned about the Catholic identity of the university and its religious mission."

Back in the area, there was little new in the case except a report that the Ford had been stolen that afternoon. Fingerprints of the owner and Joan were found on the car but no others. The syringe had been wiped clean. The inside was dry, so the syringe hadn't been used recently. Perhaps the murderer was unwilling to carry the syringe on his person as he—or she—walked from the scene. Leo now leaned heavily toward a drug-robbery-murder case.

Officer Kelly, who had continued interviewing neighbors, phoned Leo and reported that an elderly couple had seen a man about twenty-five years old pass them as they got out of their car in front of their 113th Street home about 1:35 A.M. He was of medium build, wore a light brown suit, a white shirt and tie and seemed to have sandy hair. Leo thanked Kelly and asked him for a written report as soon as possible. Weller was out on a robbery, so his report still wasn't ready, and the medical examiner's staff continued the autopsy.

The two detectives drove to Ogden Park School and confronted an upset Kathy. Joan hadn't arrived for class or phoned, highly unlike her, Kathy said. Leo asked her to step out of her office to the sidewalk. He didn't know how to explain except to say it plainly.

"Joan's gone, Kathy. She . . . died this morning."

He turned away then, not able to look at the pain and shock in his daughter's face.

It was Matt who told her that Joan had been found shot to death about six-thirty that morning in a stolen Ford near 113th Street and Kedzie. They had few clues except a syringe that had been discovered on the ground below the driver's seat and four white beads from a rosary that were found on the Escort's floor.

Kathy shook her head. Joan would *never* have taken drugs. She did own a rosary with white beads. Matt asked if Joan had any boyfriends. Kathy couldn't think of any, Joan was very shy.

"Do you think some guy could have taken her in, fooled her about himself and his feelings?"

Kathy thought for a moment. "Yes, I do think so. I think most men could fool her, she was a very trusting person who liked people, wanted to be accepted . . ."

Kathy took it on herself to notify Joan's mother Elena, who lived in Evergreen Park. Her father Frank had died when she was ten. Joan had no other family except some relatives in Sicily.

Kathy finally surrendered to tears, and Leo put his arm around his daughter's shoulders for several moments, then he and Matt left.

When the detectives returned to the area Leo found a phone message to call Streeter at the medical examiner's office. Streeter confirmed everything the two detectives had already surmised . . . Solari was still a virgin and had not been raped. No drugs were found in her system.

"I doubt that she committed suicide, for the same reasons that you do," Streeter said. "It looks like drugs were involved in some way; the syringe had traces of dried heroin."

Weller's report arrived with nothing new. The case was at a dead end.

The phone rang. It was Kathy, who told her father that she had forgotten to mention something. "It's very farfetched, Dad, but we do have a young man teaching here who has lunch with Joan and me once in a while. He's been with us for five months and teaches seventh grade. He just got his master's degree in sociology from DePaul. He took the job to have some time to decide whether he wanted to get his Ph.D. His name is Charles Carmody, Rusty's younger brother."

The mention of Rusty Carmody brought the old Marine to attention, and Leo casually asked: "What does he look like?"

"He's a very snappy dresser," Kathy said. "That's what everybody on the staff noticed about him. Always immaculate, well-cut suits. He's medium build with dishwater-blond hair."

"Well," Leo said, "I'm sure he's a fine young man with that DePaul background. Let me think about it. But, Kathy, don't mention to him that we talked. Okay?"

"All right, Dad."

Leo hung up, lit his pipe and checked the name on his computer. He scribbled down an address and said to Matt, "Get your suit coat, partner. Kathy's description of this guy is a dead ringer for the one we got from that elderly couple near the murder scene."

Leo was more upset than he let on. Of all the families in the world, he didn't want to accuse the Carmodys of something like this. Bad enough about Rusty and Evie. The Dolans and Carmodys were already at odds . . . he hated to think of a second confrontation.

As Leo and Matt drove to an apartment complex near 107th on South Pulaski Road they decided to place young Charles Carmody under surveillance rather than question him immediately.

After a half-hour wait they saw Carmody leave his apartment and drive a 1986 cream-colored Dodge Lancer to a large but seedy bar at 85th and Pulaski. They followed him into the saloon, a long, wide place with a female blonde bartender. A dozen customers sat at the bar and tables behind them. The woman appeared to know Carmody and poured him a white wine. Matt again ordered a nonalcoholic beer for himself and a ginger ale for Leo.

Kathy was right, Leo thought. The suit was made of fine Italian-cut silk, dark brown with a deep red handkerchief in the breast pocket. Carmody's tie was a lighter brown silk. He wore soft brown Italian loafers with tassels in the front. In less than five minutes another young man entered and Carmody left the bar to sit at a table with him. The newcomer, a Latino with a thin mustache, appeared barely twenty-one. As the two talked Matt overheard part of an exchange about a "milk" shipment. They agreed to meet in the bar at eleven that night to discuss delivery. The Latino then left and Carmody soon followed. The detectives decided not to follow the suspect and waited several minutes before leaving. The bartender, who Matt noted had been drinking screwdrivers, appeared to take little notice of the pair.

Matt agreed to pick Leo up about 10:30 P.M., when the detectives would go out dressed in old work clothes.

Kathy had arrived unexpectedly for dinner, and as she and Leo sat in the living room while Nora finished cooking dinner, Kathy said, "I want you to know something about Joan Solari, Dad.

"Joan was really special. We went to Rosary College and entered the Sisters of Mercy together. Joan had a four-point average at Rosary. She was not only brilliant but caring. Maybe it was in her Sicilian blood—she used to kid about that—but Joan was all about family. She was sorry she didn't have sisters and brothers. She used to say: '*La famiglia è tutto.*'

"She never talked about her scholastic honors. Individual honors meant nothing to her. She had no time for the authority versus conscience debate in the Church. She said the Church and society were family, that each of us was a child of God. She wasn't a so-called liberal Catholic like they call me. She left the convent because she wanted a husband and children. 'I'm Sicilian,' she said, and that said it all for her.

"I remember reading a newspaper clipping on her wall and I made a copy of it. The author was anonymous, but she felt his words were truly inspiring." Kathy pulled a photocopy from her purse. "I brought a copy to read to you.

" 'Be gentle with yourself. You are a child of the Universe no less than the trees and the stars. You have a right to be here . . . be at peace with God, whatever you conceive Him to be. And whatever your labors and aspirations, in the noisy confusion of life keep peace in your soul. With all its sham, drudgery and broken dreams, it is still a beautiful world.'

"She was the best, Dad."

Leo put his hand on her shoulder, trying to comfort her. She wasn't through, wanted the relief of talk.

"Dad, Joan was a fine woman. A fine *person.* I think women can be good priests. Maybe I'll be a priest someday. If we follow Vatican logic Joan of Arc would have been unworthy of the priesthood. Also St. Clare, Mother Cabrini, Ann Elizabeth Seton and Mother Teresa. Dad, I guess I'm trying to say Joan deserved better than the Church gave her. A lot of us do."

Leo knew when he was being proselytized. "Let me tell you something, girl. There's nothing to forbid these changes. They may come in time. Remember the Catholic Church thinks and acts in terms of centuries." And then Leo stunned Kathy with a question: "What about your mother and me? Parents set the consciences and values of their children. Have we failed? That's what bothers me. Where have your mother and I fallen short?"

Kathy shook her head. "All the kids are still Catholic, Dad."

Leo half-smiled ruefully. "Neither the Church nor many Catholics speak the same language today, Kathy." And then he brightened. "There's an old Irish toast that might be fitting. 'May you live to be a hundred years, with one extra year to repent.' "

Both grinned and Nora broke it up to call them to dinner—chicken, mashed potatoes and gravy, carrots, salad, apple pie and coffee.

Nora, seeing that Kathy looked worn, took the lead in dinner conversation. She had read an article in one of the newspapers about Helen Hayes. Asked about her younger actress colleagues before she died, Miss Hayes said: "I learned to be an actress. I never learned to be a star." Nora thought that was typical Irish sense.

Matt arrived about 10:15 P.M. He and Leo drove Kathy home, and after she walked away Leo recounted his daughter's description of Joan Solari.

"Matt, I think this young woman was in a car with an

apparently proper young man that she believed was totally trustworthy. Among other things, she was a trusting soul."

Moran agreed. It was evident to both that Charles Carmody, the cardinal's nephew, was now a prime suspect in Joan Solari's robbery and murder.

The detectives arrived at the bar in old work clothes at 11:00 P.M. Some two dozen customers were spread among the bar stools and tables. Neither Carmody nor the Latino had shown up. The two sat at opposite ends of the bar. About ten minutes later the Latino arrived wearing a straw hat, rancher's jacket and cowboy boots. Charles Carmody came in a few minutes later, dressed in a light blue suit and red tie. He joined the Latino at a table at the end of the bar and ordered white wine. The two sat near Matt, which was a break. Matt had good antennae.

Carmody appeared to be in a hurry while the Latino seemed indifferent to time and the surroundings. Neither, though, showed any concern. A new bartender had come on, a man about fifty years old.

From his close vantage point Matt caught snatches of conversation . . . The Latino was saying the milk had arrived. The cost of the shipment was a hundred and twenty dollars. Carmody said he was short. He had only a hundred and ten or so. The milk was already bottled, the Latino said, and the price couldn't change. Holding his wallet beneath the tabletop, Carmody counted his money. He had a hundred and sixteen dollars. The Latino said okay. Matt saw the money.

On those words, Matt nodded to Leo. The deal had been cut. Carmody handed the money to the Latino under the table. The young man pulled out a small open envelope and pushed it across the table. Then Carmody glanced at the contents, placed the envelope inside his jacket, stood and walked out the front door of the bar. Matt left immediately, Leo a few seconds later.

The partners followed Carmody to his car, although Leo also watched the bar door to see if the Latino was leaving. As Carmody opened the door Matt said:

"I'm a police officer. Put your hands up. Turn around, slowly."

Carmody slowly put up his hands and turned. His face was red, disbelieving. Matt flashed his badge, reached into Carmody's jacket and pulled out the envelope. Inside he found small plastic bags of white powder. The detective told Carmody he was under arrest for the possession of an illegal drug, and read him his rights on remaining silent. Matt then handcuffed Carmody, with Leo witnessing the arrest while watching the bar door. As soon as Carmody was cuffed Leo returned to the bar. Matt stood outside with the suspect.

Leo walked to the table where the Latino was still drinking his wine, flashed his badge and said: "I'm a narcotics officer, you're under arrest for the illegal sale of narcotics."

The Latino, clearly an old pro, offered no resistance.

Leo had called for a squad car on his portable radio, handcuffed the Latino and led him outside. The squad car, built with a wire grille and locked doors to hold prisoners in the back seat, arrived moments later. Leo told the two officers that he and Moran would follow them to the 111th Street area.

Matt booked the two men on drug charges. The Latino, who identified himself as Ernesto Felices, of Hermosillo, Mexico, phoned a lawyer. Leo and Moran were surprised when young Carmody declined. The detectives then led him to a detention room, where Matt surprised him:

"You got your masters in sociology from DePaul last January?"

Carmody didn't reply.

"Then you began teaching at Ogden Park School, right?"

Still no reply.

"How's your father and your brother Rusty?" Panic on Carmody's face, in his eyes.

"You going to call them? Eventually we'll notify your father if you don't."

"I don't want to see my father."

"Why not?"

"You know why not."

"Because you're on coke, heroin?"

No answer.

Matt told the prisoner to take off his jacket and roll up his shirtsleeves. Hesitatingly, Carmody complied. Needle marks ran up and down both arms.

"We're going to have to search your apartment," Matt said.

"It's not necessary," Carmody said, in the face of the inevitable. "I have some syringes there . . ."

"It is necessary," Matt told him. "We're looking for a certain type of syringe and a .22 calibre pistol."

The phone rang. A crime-lab technician reported to Matt: "The stuff you sent here is heroin."

Matt turned to Carmody. "Our lab says you bought heroin."

Carmody seemed paralyzed. Then Matt said almost in a whisper: "Did you shoot Joan Solari?"

Carmody broke then. Shortly after 4:00 A.M. he signed a confession to Joan Solari's robbery and killing. In the statement he said he was strung out, feverish, needed money for more heroin, out of his mind. She had a hundred and twenty-four dollars in her purse and refused to give it to him.

Carmody claimed he hadn't packed the .22 with any prior intent to kill her. It was protection for when he carried cash and bought drugs. Yes, the car was stolen. His Dodge was in the shop being worked on. He needed a vehicle to find drug money. He was burning up. His head, his throat, his veins were on fire . . .

"Don't you *understand?*" Carmody burst out. "I was *dying.*"

"How did you get her to meet you?" Matt asked, not impressed.

"I begged her," Carmody said. "I told her that I was desperate, had to speak to someone or else . . ."

Matt said bitterly: "Then you killed her, after she came out at that hour to help you."

No answer.

The Latino went free on ten thousand dollars bail. No sweat. Carmody refused to call his father. Leo phoned the lawyer at 4:30 A.M.:

"Mr. Carmody, this is Detective Leo Dolan at the East 111th Street area."

The lawyer erupted. "I'm not going to talk about my son Rusty unless we're in court. You've got a lot of goddamned nerve calling me at this hour—"

"I'm not calling about Rusty," Leo said evenly. "I'm phoning about your other son, Charles."

The mouthpiece lost his voice.

"As one of the arresting officers, I am notifying you that your son is being held here for the possession of an illegal drug and the murder of a young woman, Joan Solari, a teacher at the Ogden Park School."

Momentarily stunned into silence, Carmody returned to form. "You vengeful son of a bitch!" And slammed down the receiver.

* * *

The detectives then drove to an all-night coffee shop where Leo told Moran about his conversation with the elder Carmody. Matt said with even more than his normal bitterness: "The Carmodys believe they're the new power and glory. They figure they'll take over the American Church and tell the bishops what to do?"

Matt sipped his coffee. "Remember when we were kids we were told to keep our noses clean, work hard and have faith in God and the future. Hey, that's dead, Leo." He was getting warmed up on a subject not unfamiliar to his partner. "The Carmodys . . . they're the new Catholic aristocrats. The new leaders. But for all their money and position they're caught right between the old and the new, and down deep they don't really know what the hell to do.

"Rights over responsibility, notoriety is achievement. These are the *new* values. They're the Carmody faith. And, old pal, it's failing us, *and* them. Exhibits *A* and *B*—Rusty and Charles Carmody."

A church bell tolled. It was time for the 6:00 A.M. Mass and the two men walked toward the bells.

Chapter 10

THE SAINTS GO MARCHIN'

Bob Dolan entered the cardinal's outer office unannounced. His Eminence had arrived, and Mrs. Koslowski was carrying a cup of hot coffee into Carmody's office. When she returned, Dolan said he was scheduled to be ordained shortly and wished to see the cardinal on an urgent matter. The secretary told Dolan that he wasn't listed to see His Eminence and must make an appointment. Bob said the request was urgent, it involved his coming ordination, he was prepared to wait.

Mrs. Koslowski, a hard-nosed gatekeeper, suggested he see Monsignor Brady, the cardinal's private secretary, and Bob finally agreed.

Brady was reading the *Herald* when Bob entered his office. They shook hands and the secretary motioned to a large old chair. "I've seen you out at St. Peter's, Bob. Good to meet you personally. How can I help you?"

Bob said he wanted to see the cardinal on a personal

matter. It could take an hour of His Eminence's time. Brady then reverted to Carmody's standard reply: the prelate was very busy carrying out the work of the archdiocese.

Bob said: "I'm considering not being ordained in a few days and wanted to speak with the cardinal *himself.*"

"Why His Eminence?"

"I have some questions. Frankly, I believe only he can relieve my mind."

Brady was puzzled. What had happened? "Can you at least tell me the background so I can communicate some of your urgency to the cardinal? It'll remain private, of course."

Dolan trusted Brady but this was not how he wanted the matter handled. Still, it appeared he had little choice, so he finally told the monsignor that he had been raped by a fellow seminarian in a woods near St. Peter's. He refused to name Gunth. Shocked, Brady pressed Bob to disclose whether the rapist was in the present ordination class. Bob would not say. The monsignor had a difficult time controlling his anger at Dolan's reluctance.

Just then Brady's inter-office buzzer rang and Mrs. Koslowski said the cardinal wanted to see him. The secretary told Bob that he would phone him at St. Peter's. Dolan, very unhappy, left as Brady entered Carmody's office.

The prelate was flushed and almost sputtering. "The pickets are marching in front of St. Malachy's. I just got a call from the Lombardi Company that began work there this morning. Go over and see what you can find out. Now."

Brady, putting Dolan's problem aside, quickly did as told.

The cardinal sat brooding at his desk . . . the confrontation that he had so tried to avoid was now staring him in the face. He had talked to the mayor, the right people on the city council, Cappy Conlon and even had had Leo Dolan discuss the situation with police superintendent Rossi. Any *one* of them could have stopped the march. And all had turned away from him. Why? Did the Cardinal of Chicago no longer command enough respect to have his will obeyed by Catholic lay leaders? Was this part of the growing lay revolt? Surely they recognized that the protest was scandalous behavior? Or did it all just come down to their affection for Cappy, that pint-sized little pastor with a pint forever in his pocket? Had all those crazies on the parish council taken Cappy over and now effectively ran St. Malachy's?

Well, he would phone Chief Rossi himself. Joe Rossi owed him. At Rossi's request he had changed his schedule to attend the San Giuseppe dinner to benefit the Sons of Italy last March 19. Rossi had the power to act quickly. Perhaps he could shut down these protestors with just one more phone call.

Police Sergeant Margaret Hickey, still in the throes of a hangover, walked into the superintendent's office. The chief's secretary was trying to get Rossi off the phone where he had been for the past ten minutes. Rossi motioned that she sit down in one of the two old-fashioned hardwood chairs in front of his desk.

The chief and his longtime aide got along well. Both were low-keyed, quick-minded and neither pulled a punch. Maggie Hickey was a straight-shooting spinster cop who learned to say shit long before she had a bellyful. She had been raised in a Catholic orphanage, struggled to put herself through two years of accounting at DePaul night school, became a cop, walked a beat in the Loop for six years, later did juvenile work and took a secretarial class to help promote herself in the department.

"Hello, Maggie," Rossi said in a low whisper as he hung up the phone. "You look like hell."

Bulging from her blues, she shook her aching head. "I had a few at Willie Flynn's place last night with the vice boys.

Willie is still big on booze but cheap with the hors d'oeuvres. We had to send out for Chinese."

Rossi laughed. He loved to hear the tart descriptions of her barroom excursions. They brought back fond memories of earlier days when he too went out with the boys. That was finished now, and Maggie kept him in touch. She had drunk with many on the force, could spot a rotten cop the length of the bar but maintained a casual correctness that never allowed anyone to get too close. Rossi once characterized his secretary as "everybody's older sister."

"I'll bet it was those creamed drinks again," he told her now. "I've told you that they're for the Loop's bar whores, not you. Stay off the daiquiris and hoola-loops."

"Lord, help us!" Maggie fired back. "It's Moses on the Mount. And what're the other nine commandments?" Maggie smiled through the pain of her indulgence, then got to her mission. "Mamma X is on the phone. Says it's important. She's holding."

Rossi said he had been expecting her call and reached for the phone. "Hello, Mamma, I'm here and waiting."

"*Salaam* and all that, Chief. The Lombardi wreckers showed up about seven-thirty this mornin' at St. Malachy's. I got rousted outta bed an' jus got here five minutes ago with Kathy Dolan an' four other pickets. These demolition guys got a couple o' them big haulin' trucks an' are right now movin' out the altar, statues and Stations o' the Cross. Ah mean *movin'*. They're workin' fast."

Rossi could hear Mamma calling to someone in the distance. The bells of St. Malachy's tolled 9:00 A.M. The chief listened as Mamma argued with someone, then she returned to the line again.

"Mistah Lombardi, Junior, is here, an' he's got four black brothers workin' for him. He's wavin' a city permit and tellin' us that we gotta git outta their way. We been talkin' 'bout the Good Book an' to git if they know what's good for 'em." She paused to exchange words with someone. "So Lombardi called the cops, Chief. An' now we got two police here. An' *they're* tellin' *us* to git."

Rossi had been expecting this. He had been holding a picketing permit for St. Malachy's parish council in his desk drawer, waiting for the protest to begin. The permit was already stamped by the Corporation Commission but had the fingerprints of Alderman Frank Fahey all over it. The chief filled in the dates to cover the remainder of June and a week in July. He told Sergeant Hickey to call the commission's office manager, Joanne Bates, and give her the permit dates, then returned to the phone and advised Mamma to tell the officers that Sergeant Mario Moretti would soon arrive from police headquarters with instructions on the matter.

Mario Moretti, the chief's driver and point man, opened the rear door of the car as he saw Rossi emerge from headquarters. The chief told him "Old St. Malachy's" before the sergeant closed the door. As they drove north Rossi handed Moretti a permit, noting it was good for nearly two weeks. He explained to Moretti, a big-shouldered Italian with concrete in his fists, "Mario, hand the permit to the Muslim woman. Tell her to show it to the two police officers. By that time they should see me here in the back seat. Just suggest they ease off from the scene. You don't have to say more than that."

The two men had an unbreakable Sicilian bond. Both of their parents had come from Sicily and each understood *omertà*—the code of silence. In effect, it was an unspoken brotherhood. Sicilians absorbed silence as their ancestors consumed conquering legions. The Sicilians conquered them with tight lips and, according to some, closed minds.

Rossi straightened his black tie against his starched white collar. This was going to be a good day in spite of the wind. The skirts of working girls would take off, baring lace panties. Rossi watched now as an expensive Italian borsolino sailed north on Wabash and an elderly gentleman, apparently the owner, gloomily watched the hat climb above the traffic. Suddenly the man gave the hat the old Italian whammo, a slap of the hand across the muscle of his left arm. Moretti laughed out loud and gave the car the gas as the light turned green.

Rossi had made his name here in the Loop as head of downtown's robbery detail for nearly ten years. Then a captain, he put the brakes on shoplifting at a time when it was on the rise across the city and country. He trained crack squads and instituted new procedures that paid off in more arrests. He also kept the kleptomaniac wives of important figures out of the slammer. You did what you had to do, within reason.

The chief was still a street man. His diagnosis for a problem was often the right ear—influence. You remembered him, and he damn well didn't forget you. That was Chicago poker.

The cardinal, though, had alienated Rossi. Carmody was a distant figure, remote, a phone man who rarely if ever dealt face to face. He had Monsignor Brady make his calls for favors, and the chief detested that. He wanted to see if you squinted or shook his hand when you asked for help. He called Brady the cardinal's "finger man."

Nevertheless, the chief was obligated to put in many a fix for the cardinal . . . priests picked up for driving under the influence, nuns—the chief always called them "the poor things"—who stole gloves or sweaters for the good reason they were cold and had no money. Rossi ecumenically did the same for ministers and rabbis. The word on the street was to "check with downtown" before arresting a clergyman or nun.

A slight drizzle was beginning to fall as Rossi's car pulled up at the corner of Ninth and Wabash. Mamma X and Kathy

Dolan stood on the sidewalk with their pickets and held up two sets of signs:

S-O-S SAVE OLD ST. MALACHY'S and CHURCH UNITY, YES! THE CARDINAL, NO!

Statues of the Sacred Heart of Jesus and the Blessed Virgin Mary, both of Carrara marble, stood on the sidewalk in front of the church's vestibule. Two other statues, one of St. Joseph and the other of St. Patrick, were nearby.

Sergeant Moretti handed Mamma the permit, then approached the young officers who had already seen the chief in the rear seat and spoke with them while Mamma advanced on Rossi.

"Thanks, Chief. Can you wait till I speak with the wreckers?"

Rossi nodded. Moretti had finished his chat with the officers and returned to the driver's seat and signaled thumbs up to his boss. Charles Lombardi Jr., who had met the chief at a luncheon for onetime Italian prime minister Giulio Andreotti, told Rossi that he had seen the permit and didn't want a confrontation with the congregation or the police. He would withdraw his workmen after they returned the altar, statues and other property to the church. He spoke to Rossi in Italian:

"Ho capito tutto. Non vogliamo cominciare la terza guerra mondiale!" (I've understood everything. We don't want to start World War III!)

Mamma, with Kathy at her side, told the wrecking crew, "Ain't no other way, gentlemen, but law an' order. We don't want no trouble. We're gonna let the big folks settle this—the cardinal, your boss man, city hall. You git outta here. Ain't no foolin'. We got Allah on our side." The young police walked off, wondering what the hell Allah had to do with it.

Lombardi spoke with his men and they trucked the statues back inside St. Malachy's, then hauled the altar, vigil lights and other objects inside the church. Beau Beauchamps offered the men coffee but they declined. Rossi tapped Mario on the shoulder and the driver started the car. The chief waved to Mamma and Kathy, who returned his salute.

"His Eminence will probably be on the phone by noon," Rossi told Mario. "Can you handle it?"

Mario laughed. "No, but I think Sergeant Hickey can."

Rossi liked that and laughed as well.

As Catholics, Rossi and Moretti had been raised to consider a call from a cardinal, any cardinal, like a summons from the president of the United States. Maybe more important. You said yes three times over if you were a good Catholic. Until the Second Vatican Council, then Catholics learned to cough and say maybe.

Monsignor Brady watched the scene from a half-block away, where he had parked his car, and phoned the cardinal from a nearby street phone every half-hour.

The monsignor reported that Chief Rossi had arrived and that Lombardi & Company had departed. The Italians were a contradiction to Carmody. The cardinal could never quite understand or accept their strong reservations about the ruling clergy and kinship with little priests and a formless Church. He tended to overlook that the Church hierarchy had dominated Italy for centuries, using their power and influence to become the economic and political masters of the people. Once Garibaldi united the country back in the nineteenth century the average Italian was baptized, received first Holy Communion, was married and buried in the Church. Two of these four times they were carried into church. Otherwise they mostly ignored the institution. Carmody did appreciate Ireland's historical brand of Catholicity. The Irish often saw themselves as holier than the pope or Church. They applauded the regulations and most opinions of the clergy, and left the subtleties and distinctions for the philosophers and theologians. Every church, convent or cloister was a bit of heaven. Irishmen were soldiers of Christ—"to know, love, and serve the Lord"—backed by nearly one billion other Catholics. Now here he was being challenged by people who should have been his troops.

Shortly before noon, as Rossi prepared to leave his office for lunch, Maggie Hickey announced: "Carmody on Line Two. Excuse me, it'll probably be the *secretary* of the cardinal on Line Two."

The sergeant turned, clicked her low heels and saluted as she walked out the door.

Rossi poured himself a glass of ice water, drank half, picked up his phone and said mechanically, "Superintendent Rossi here."

Mrs. Koslowski said, "Hold for His Eminence, the cardinal, please."

The chief held. And held. He sipped water for about a minute before the voice blessed him:

"Good morning, Superintendent, this is Cardinal Carmody."

The chief merely said, "Good morning." He coughed and remained silent. The cardinal wasted no time:

"I'll come to the point, Superintendent. Some pickets are surrounding one of my downtown churches, Old St. Malachy's. A construction firm hired by the Church says these pickets are interfering with their work at the site. I would be most appreciative if you would take care of this matter."

Rossi had already decided what his response would be. Carmody's approach only changed the trappings of what he would say.

"Your Eminence, did you say construction or destruction? Our men at the scene understood this was a demolition job?"

Carmody hesitated. The split-second delay was well known to every policeman . . . the subject was trying to cop out of an unexpected question.

The cardinal, a master of indirection, answered: "Superintendent, it's essential work at the church and the contractor reports he has the necessary permits."

"Excuse me, Your Eminence," Rossi said, closing in on Carmody, "but weren't these permits originally granted by your chancery office?"

The cardinal was irritated. What difference did it make? He spoke for the Church and the contractor. He was the voice not only of St. Malachy's but every Catholic church for tens of miles around. The prelate, miffed, managed not to raise his voice.

"Ultimately, Superintendent, this is a project of the archdiocese. The Lombardi Company is acting in our name. It is essential that the work move forward in the name of the archdiocese."

Rossi smiled to himself. If only Cappy Conlon, Mamma X, Kathy Dolan and Frank Fahey could have heard that. In the name of the archdiocese? Lord, Fahey would belch with three double bourbons before lunch. He might even offer one to Thumbs!

The chief proceeded cautiously. "The reason that I raise any question at all, Your Eminence, is a legal one. I don't want to see your archdiocese office out on a limb." At that, Rossi noticed Sergeant Hickey was standing at his office door giving him one of her shame-on-you smiles. He ignored her. "You see, the pickets told our men that they're trying to stop someone from tearing down the church. They say the congregation opposes demolition and is threatening legal action. We don't want to get in the middle of a court fight. The only thing we know for sure, Your Eminence, is that the pickets have a city permit to march."

The cardinal came back quickly. "The only person who can speak for St. Malachy's in this instance is myself. As the sole representative of the legal entity involved, I assure you personally, Superintendent, that these people cannot speak or act for St. Malachy's. They have no legal rights with respect to the church and I am now asking that you use your good offices to allow us to continue our work without interference. The Lombardi Company wants to avoid a physical confrontation. It won't proceed with the pickets threatening them. And finally, Superintendent, I must carry out the Church's commitments."

Commitments! Carmody's punch line. Commitments, indeed. What commitments? Rossi decided to disengage swiftly, agreeably. He said in a slow, solemn tone:

"Your Eminence, let me consult our legal staff and community-relations people here. We want to facilitate the business"—he clenched his teeth—"of the Church but do it appropriately. Let me get back to you later in the day or tomorrow."

Carmody said, "I want it done today, Superintendent Rossi."

"We'll do our best," Rossi told him.

The cardinal hung up. There was no good luck or God bless, not even thanks or goodbye. Just the prelate's order, which rang in Rossi's ears.

The chief squeezed his water glass as he calmly told himself: "Fahey and Matt Moran are right. Fats Carmody pisses icicles."

Rossi dialed the city council chambers and asked for Frank Fahey, figuring the alderman could learn quickly if the land had been sold. Fahey wasn't there so the chief left an urgent message that Fahey call him back.

Rossi then phoned Rabbi Goldman. "Goldie, this is Joe Rossi. I just got off the phone with the cardinal. He wants the pickets removed—today. He said the work—he wouldn't say anything about demolition—must begin immediately because the Church has *commitments*."

Rabbi Goldman didn't hesitate, "He's probably sold the land. Let me speak with a few of the brethren. I presume you've already called Alderman Fahey."

Rossi confirmed his call to the council member. The two then agreed neither would, for the moment, tell Cappy of their suspicions about a land deal. They would proceed with extreme caution.

As the noon Angelus tolled from the bell tower of St. Malachy's, picket John Elixir Babbington's spirits were soaring. Why not? He was intoxicated. Mamma X had gone to get a sandwich and glass of milk in the rectory and left Kathy in charge. Kathy, less suspicious of the actor than her colleagues, noticed Babbington stumbling under his S-O-S sign. For some reason the actor had fallen off the wagon on his coffee break and was now emoting as a crowd gathered.

"Ladies and gentlemen, give us your hands and hearts. Let us defeat the legions of evil. I, John Elixir Babbington, implore you. Take wing! Fly with us in the name of St. Malachy!"

He then began singing "Fly Me to the Moon." Seeing the astonished face of an elderly woman, he regaled her with lines from his favorite Shakespearean play . . . *Love's Labour's Lost.*The fearful woman held out her black umbrella, ready to jab him as he pranced around her.

"I implore you, madame, in the name of St. Malachy, to take up a sign and follow us. Your voice must be our voice: *O, O, O, when the saints go marchin' in . . .*"

Babbington addressed the crowd: "Greatness must not die untouched and unknown by the masses. Was not even Shakespeare ignored by many of his contemporaries? People could see yet they were blind. Is that reflected in our own lives? Men and women are often idiots. That is what they have inherited—idiocy! Rise, good souls! Do battle in the name of St. Malachy! Sing, my fellow Christians, sing *O, O, O, when the saints go marchin' in—*"

A great bellow blasted from the corner to the middle of the sidewalk where Babbington was carrying on. "O, O, O, yourself, Elixir!" It was Mamma X and she was marching on Babbington. She took hold of him by the arm and led the fallen Falstaff toward the church entrance. "You're gonna sit in the last row with all the sinners. Now, you sit or you git! Which is it?"

Babbington dropped his sign on the pavement and trudged forlornly alongside Mamma X, shaking his head, talking to himself. He entered the church, sat in the last row on the left and promptly went to sleep facing the altar. None of the worshippers at the noon Mass seemed to notice the solitary figure transfixed in apparent worship.

The cardinal returned from his lunch at 2:00 P.M. Mrs. Koslowski was due back in the office at any moment, and Betty Blake, an office file clerk, was sitting in Koslowski's chair taking phone messages and chatting with Bob Dolan, who had returned and waited for His Eminence although Monsignor Brady had said he would phone him. Dolan had nonetheless decided he had to try to see the cardinal right away. Betty was under the impression that Dolan had an appointment.

The rising doubt about his worthiness for the priesthood ached through the young deacon's mind and body. In spite of the rigors of his long education, Bob Dolan was not a tough-willed man. He was, essentially, a follower. Yet Bob's frustration was pushing him. He was bursting. As the cardinal walked past, Bob rose from his seat and quickly followed Carmody into his office. Blake was too late to stop him. His Eminence looked up in surprise, saw the collar and thought Dolan was some young priest instead of a deacon. Carmody also saw the fear in the young man's face.

"Sit down, Father. Are you all right?"

"I'm only a deacon, Your Eminence, but am scheduled to be ordained by you a week from Saturday."

Mrs. Koslowski rushed into the cardinal's office and said, "Sorry for the interruption, Your Eminence, but I was at lunch . . ."

"That's all right," Carmody said. "We're just having a chat. I don't have anything on the schedule, as you know."

"Yes," his secretary said, "just waiting for the contract."

His Eminence frowned and Koslowski knew immediately that she had said too much. She was not supposed to indicate that the land beneath St. Malachy's had been sold. She quickly turned and left.

"Well now," Carmody said, "what's your name?"

"Robert Dolan."

The prelate paused and bit his lip, as if to say: My God, you Dolans are everywhere. Give me a break. "Is Leo your father?"

"Yes."

"I thought so," Carmody said with a trace of irony in his voice. "Did you know you need an appointment here?"

Bob admitted that he had seen Monsignor Brady and added, "I just couldn't wait, Your Eminence."

He avoided an immediate explanation of his mission . . . Cardinal Carmody had a reputation for avoiding priests in trouble. Several had resigned, claiming they might have remained priests if the prelate had been willing to meet with them. Yet in most instances, it was argued, the Church was better off when these men walked away. Carmody never argued the merits, but the clerical grapevine carried the message that he had little sympathy for rebellious priests and saw their departure as a blessing.

"What's the urgency?" the cardinal now asked.

And Bob finally gave the details of the rape by Jim Gunth without naming his classmate. "I feel I may no longer be worthy to serve as a priest. I could have fought the rape. I could have shouted and brought help. I didn't, and I believe I was wrong. I put friendship above what I thought was right."

He proceeded to spill out questions, one by one: Was he really still worthy of becoming a priest? Would the blot on his mind ever leave or would he, like some of the children sexually abused by priests, carry the horrible memory with him the rest of his life? Would his priesthood then be a nightmare?

"If I was wrong," he said, "I want to hear it from you directly. I don't want to have to look back twenty years from now and ask whether I made the right decision to leave or not."

Dolan seemed finally to have touched something deep inside Carmody as the prelate bit his lips repeatedly and looked away. As though to compose himself he buzzed his secretary and asked her on the intercom whether the written material he was expecting had arrived. Mrs. Koslowski said it hadn't, and the cardinal turned back to Dolan.

"You should stay, Robert."

The cardinal's words had a swift impact on Dolan. The cardinal, after all, was the voice of the Church, the conscience of God by virtue of his consecration by the pope. His Eminence had spoken. Bob Dolan felt his expiation was done.

"You may recall the episode at times for the rest of your life, Bob. But remember, it was only an incident, not a career. I propose a life's work for you, forty-five years or more of dedication to men, women and children who need a priest. As far as I can see you did nothing wrong. Who knows, perhaps what happened may make you a better priest. We all have terrifying incidents in our lives. If we quit, where would the Church and the world be? No, Robert, it's the future, not the past, that counts. Face whatever struggle is before you. You'll never become the Cardinal of Chicago unless you've gotten a bloody nose." Carmody actually smiled when he said it.

Dolan jumped to his feet, looked as if he might leap over the desk to shake hands with the cardinal. He did manage to grab Carmody's hand and almost break it with his new grip on life. Finally he sat down and said, "This is probably the greatest moment of my life . . ."

Bob's moment quickly became clouded when His Eminence said firmly, "You're going to have to tell me the name of the young man who attacked you. I'll tell you why. First, as far as I know, such an . . . episode has never occurred among St. Peter's seminarians. Second, I can't let this individual try to corrupt other priests and perhaps even rape young boys. Rape in any form is the murder of the human spirit. It's the killing of dreams like yours. If I can stop a rapist I may do more than in all my years of keeping the Archdiocese of Chicago financially solvent."

But Bob did not want to be a squealer. He asked himself what his father Leo would do in the circumstances. He couldn't hold off, though, not with the cardinal staring him down, and he named Jim Gunth.

Carmody quickly changed the subject.

"I'd like to return to something that you mentioned earlier. You said you put friendship above what you thought was right. I want to tell you something. I've given you more friendship here today than I've offered almost anyone as the Cardinal of Chicago. The man in this chair does not have friends. The job definition precludes real friendship. In many ways, so does the life of a priest. Your incident, Bob, should serve as a powerful lesson . . . I've never said this to anyone since assuming this office. Perhaps I'm getting old, tired or, as the Irish like to put it, a bit daft. But I will tell you something, in confidence. I've been tempted many times to put friendship above what I believe to be right. Churchmen don't always resist that. They promote friendships with powerful men—bankers, lawyers, politicians, even the president of the United States—and tell themselves that they're doing God's work. Clergymen wash the hands of the powerful while these leaders do the same for them. They use each other. Sometimes they corrupt one another. I've been guilty of that on occasions. One must go on and ask God's forgiveness."

For the first time since seeing Carmody years before, Bob Dolan began to perceive, as few did, the human dimension of the man. He started to understand what others had often described as the loneliness at the top. Although Carmody was still short of his sixty-fifth birthday he seemed as drained and weary as a man ten years older. Suddenly the cardinal stirred himself from his reflection.

"Did you ever hear the Irish proverb 'It's no use boiling cabbage twice'?"

Bob said his mother often quoted it when something frustrated her.

His Eminence said: "You may appreciate the irony of the language, but one American expression for money is cabbage. Money . . . cabbage . . . has been the curse of my tenure here because of the archdiocese's swiftly changing financial condition. The buck literally stops with me."

Dolan expected Carmody to launch into a defense of his efforts to tear down or do whatever else he had in mind for St. Malachy's. The cardinal, though, apparently had set his sights on a larger perspective.

"The Vatican, contrary to reports, is not well financially. Its overall deficit is approaching one hundred million dollars. Mostly from losses that have come from the Holy See's worldwide operations and charities. Yes, the Vatican itself operates at a small profit each year, some of that coming from its museums, coins, stamps and local donations. But the Holy See's major revenues come from investments and property. It also receives some sixty million a year from the annual worldwide Peter's Pence collection. Still, Peter's Pence is unreliable and can't be a foundation stone for keeping the Vatican financially stable. I give you this brief history because there's not a cardinal, not a bishop in the world who isn't worried about the Vatican's finances. I'm forced to think not only of Chicago but of Rome. I have to navigate an ocean of finance and money . . ." Carmody added in a low voice, "It isn't often that I get a chance to reach out and touch a soul, which is what I'm supposed to do. So go, Robert, be ordained and remember that I offered only one small piece of advice—the only attribute that a priest really needs is holiness. Try to be a holy priest."

Bob kissed the cardinal's ring and left, and Carmody buzzed for Brady. The monsignor, who had learned about Dolan's meeting, explained to His Eminence that he hadn't had time to brief him. The cardinal listed the necessary details and then asked Brady to drive immediately to St. Peter's to tell James Gunth what the cardinal knew. He was not to tell Gunth the source of the information. Brady was to advise the young man that the matter could be handled the easy way or the hard way. Which did he prefer?

* * *

As he lay in bed that night, Carmody asked himself a question not unlike the one Brady had, at his instruction, put to Gunth. St. Malachy's could yet be handled the easy way or the hard way. Which did he prefer?

Chapter 11

THE OLD PRIESTHOOD IS DEAD

The cardinal woke up early although the ordination ceremony did not begin until 10:00 A.M. Laymen and women had already arrived to prepare Holy Name Cathedral for the ceremony. The cathedral was a beautiful American Gothic structure, the scene of virtually every major Catholic religious event in Chicago over the past hundred and twenty years.

Carmody got up, put on his bathrobe and walked downstairs to the kitchen, where he made himself a cup of instant coffee . . . His mind wandered to the day's ordination and the cathedral itself. He smiled, recalling Holy Name's restoration in 1968–1969. He had lived in the rectory at the time and was working at the nearby chancery office. The cathedral's foundation had been severely weakened and was reconstructed with steel and concrete. This tidbit of archdiocesan history wasn't mentioned when he reported that St. Malachy's was unsound and must go.

In keeping with the liturgical changes called for by the Second Vatican Council, the ornately carved marble altar was removed during restoration and replaced by a free-standing altar at the center of the sanctuary. The tabernacle was shifted to a shrine on the sanctuary's left. The canopy was withdrawn and the bishop's throne moved to the back wall of the sanctuary. Stucco and multicolored decorations, including murals, were removed. The stained-glass windows, crafted in Milan, were, however, returned to their lofty perch. The cathedral was reborn at Christmas ceremonies in 1969. Carmody remembered every change. When he saw the wide-brimmed red hats of previous Chicago cardinals—those of Meyer, Stritch and Mundelein were particularly evident—he allowed himself to envision his own *galero* hanging there one day.

As the cardinal climbed the broad stairway to his room, Bridie O'Brien was eating breakfast in her suite at the Hay Adams Hotel near the White House. She had flown into Washington from Chicago the evening before and planned to spend the weekend touring the nation's capital, having never been to Washington.

Bridie would meet with Illinois senator Paul Lyman in his office at 9:00 A.M. on Monday and later with Senator Barbara Ashley-Brown at ten-thirty. By noon, she told herself, the name of Old St. Malachy's should be well on its way to placement in the National Register of Historic Places.

"Let Carmody swallow them onions. He can't touch us then," she had told her supporters.

* * *

As Bridie entered the northeast gate of the White House for her semiprivate tour with four other special guests, Cardinal Carmody prepared to begin the ordination ceremony. Jim Gunth had already left the seminary, telling his classmates he needed a rest and would vacation in Hawaii. He had, obviously, taken the easy way prescribed by His Eminence.

Eighteen young men were to be ordained to the priesthood for Chicago and other Midwest dioceses this Saturday morning as well as two from Africa. Seven were late vocations, men who only in later life decided to become priests. A generation before, ordination classes averaged some forty young men—double today's number.

The cathedral overflowed with more than a thousand worshippers, of which four hundred were official guests—family, friends, priests and nuns as well as former teachers and other dignitaries. Many of the unofficial congregation had come to receive the new priests' first blessings. The Dolan family and their friends were the largest official contingent—fifty-seven. Leo had bought himself a new navy blue suit, and Nora had purchased a beautiful new beige dress from a downtown boutique, complete with a corsage of white roses. Later the parents were to host a large reception for Bob at the Beverly Hills Country Club.

The organist played a prelude to the ceremony as the official procession of altar boys, priest-teachers, concelebrant priests, and candidates themselves and, finally, the cardinal began the procession up the center aisle. A half-dozen bishops knelt in pews inside the sanctuary. A choir of seminarians from St. Peter's chanted the "Festival Canticle" as the procession proceeded:

This is the feast of victory for our God, Alleluia . . .
Worthy is Christ, the Lamb who was claim,
whose blood set us free to be people of God,
This is the feast of victory for our God, Alleluia . . .

The Kyrie was sung in Latin, the Gloria in English, the Old Testament from Isaiah 61:1–3 was read in Spanish, and the Responsorial Psalm in English. The New Testament reading was taken from Hebrews 5:1–10:

> Every high priest is taken from among the people . . . They are able to deal patiently with erring sinners, for they themselves are beset by weakness and so must make sin offerings for themselves as well as for the people . . .

The gospel was from St. John 20:19–23. It recalled Jesus' appearance among the apostles who hid behind closed doors after His death and Resurrection. He bid them peace and showed the apostles His pierced hands and feet to prove His identity. The Savior then called on them to teach the word of God and, finally, told the men that the sins they pardoned would be pardoned, and those retained would be retained.

The rite of ordination began in the sanctuary, where Monsignor Anthony Magurski, rector of St. Peter in the Pines, announced the names of the candidates who presented themselves before the cardinal. When the names of all the young men had been called, the congregation applauded and Carmody then surprised everyone. He had asked Cardinal Juan José Salazar, Archbishop of Rio de Janeiro, Brazil, to deliver the homily. Salazar had been touring U.S. dioceses for the past six weeks in an attempt to learn more about modernizing and financing his religious institutions. In terms of Latin America's liberation theology, the Rio leader was viewed as a middle-of-the-roader.

Cardinal Salazar's bronzed face exuded a fresh spirit. Educated partly in the United States, the tall prelate spoke excellent English. Now Salazar climbed the stairs to the pulpit and addressed the new priests without notes:

"Welcome, my dear new priests, to the modern world. The old order of the priesthood is dead. Many of today's young priests are not the traditionalists of yesteryear's priesthood. The young wish change. The onetime order of unquestioned obedience has become an era of uncertainty.

"Most older priests resist modern civilization because it violates their longtime traditions and culture. These older men say the foundation stones of the priesthood—obedience, chastity and the spirit of poverty—are being crushed in the avalanche of a new age.

"Modern society claims its mores, not the Church's, speak for humanity today. Fraternalism and universal tolerance are the new gods of democratic reform. The venerable vows of religious men and women have become the relics of ancient tribes.

"In the minds of some priests, freedom and individual liberty now often replace restraint, the promise of obedience. They consider the individual conscience superior to human and divine authority. These men view the gospel and many functions of the Church as entrusted to all Catholics, not just the hierarchy.

"What then of the modern priesthood? Are lay people to do more in the Church and priests less? Are priests merely to administer the sacraments and become more the apostles of social change? These questions and issues are addressed to you and me. I believe we're asking the wrong questions. There is only one subject that is truly important in the life of a priest. It's not the Church versus modern civilization. Not individual freedom versus obedience. Not the clergy versus the laity. What we need more than anything else in the Church today are holy priests. Too many priests are spiritually bankrupt. There are three symptoms of this emptiness—priests have long been resigning; some priests' sexual and other behavior has caused public scandal, and the sermons of the majority are often sterile and meaningless in the modern world.

"Many diocesan priests are materialistic. They ignore the spirit of poverty and personal sacrifice. They spend much of their time in personal pursuits and less in helping their people. More priests than ever have an affinity for wealth. The incomes of U.S. diocesan priests average between fifteen and twenty thousand dollars a year, and that is not paltry since they pay no room and board. So-called luxuries—trips, vacations, fine dining, clothes, liquor and cars—are often paid for by friends. These clerics see themselves as elevated above the faithful, not as servants of their needs. The pursuit of material comfort has cost priests the closeness of the people.

"Modern priests face four major problems: first, lack of consistency in Church teaching; the need to change their lifestyle, including offering priests the option to marry; there must be a closer relationship among priests, nuns and bishops and laity; but foremost priests must face their own spiritual decline.

"Some may ask why I am addressing such controversial questions on this occasion? Because, my dear friends, the greatest of dreams must never hide reality. In our greatest moments of joy we must face life as it is.

"None of this is to condemn the many good priests who live and die by Christ's words. Indeed, it is to praise and honor them. These are the heroes of the Church—men of obedience, poverty, chastity, humility and love. Yet we must not ignore the fact that their example has been debased by some fellow priests who have turned away from Christ. The great sin of the priesthood today is to have publicly accepted and then betrayed the trust of Christ and His faithful.

"St. Thomas Aquinas said a thing is perfect only to the extent that it returns to its source. If we're to find holiness we must return to the ways of Him who above all is holy, Jesus Christ. If we believe St. Thomas, we will see the true meaning of life in this universe. Time and space will take on a divine dimension. Sanctity is possible only through belief in a divine plan. The art of living, of being holy, is to radiate that faith. Our Lord said, 'Unless a man be born again, he cannot see the kingdom of God.'

"To be good priests there is only one thing that we must know: The glory of God is the purpose and end of all creation. Each of you is a synthesis of that creation. You will be judged as priests by the degree of your union with God."

As Salazar ended his homily Carmody saw the face of Bob Dolan. Perhaps Dolan now understood better what he had tried to tell him. Carmody was bothered by some of the Brazilian's homily, especially the recognition of the laity's new power in the Church and future married priests. Still, Salazar had pinpointed the chief mission of the modern clergy—to be holy priests.

The ordination ceremony itself was swift and simple. The candidates vowed they intended without qualification to fulfill the duties of the priesthood. Each walked to the cardinal, knelt before him and joined hands with the prelate, promising obedience and respect. They then prostrated themselves before the altar as the congregation stood and joined in a prayer for them.

Later in the Mass each candidate knelt before the cardinal as the prelate laid his hands on their heads. The concelebrants and other priests in the sanctuary then placed their hands on the heads of the candidates, who concluded the most solemn moment of the ordination rite by kneeling again while the cardinal consecrated them as priests.

The Mass next moved to the Communion, and the choir concluded the ceremony singing "Rejoice, O Pilgrim Throng." The newly ordained priests soon appeared on the sidewalks outside the cathedral giving their first blessings to family and friends.

The cardinal watched closely as Bob Dolan blessed his parents and, one by one, gave his blessing to his sisters, brothers, their wives and children. Cappy Conlon, Joe Rossi and his wife, Matt Moran and his spouse. Frank Fahey and Thumbs Rafferty, Kitty Flaherty, Mamma X and Reggie and others knelt on the sidewalk to receive the new priest's blessing. The cardinal shook hands and offered congratulations to the newly ordained and their families, then entered the rear of his car with its closed drapes. His driver quickly closed the door. In the joyous, smiling throng, Cardinal E. Brendan Carmody left the scene as the lonely man that he was.

Bridie O'Brien was anything but forlorn in Washington. She visited the Smithsonian's Museum of Science and Industry, the Air and Space Museum, the Lincoln, Jefferson and Vietnam War memorials, Arlington Cemetery, the National Art Gallery in her weekend whirlwind tour of the city. She hired a private car both days and for the Monday morning drive to Senator Lyman's office on Capitol Hill. As they motored up Pennsylvania Avenue, Bridie was pleased at her political acumen. She had contributed thousands to the Lyman and Ashley-Brown campaigns by hosting fund-raising dinners and fall barbecues. She was no longer in love with the Democratic party but she knew her years of contributions to the party had not gone unnoticed. She was calling in her chips on this one and Lyman and Ashley-Brown knew it.

Lyman no sooner shook Bridie's hand and sat her on his office couch than he said in the language of Chicago politicians, "It's fixed, Bridie."

She gasped in surprise at the quick work. Chicagoans believed that Congress moved with all the speed of an Arlington Park long shot that hadn't run in three years.

"Yes, it is," Lyman said. "Barbara and I placed a joint call to the National Register nearly a month ago. There are some old Chicagoans over there. We sent them your originals plus photocopies of St. Malachy's documentary history, from the first building permits to the laying of the cornerstone and consecration of the church. I had no idea that St. Malachy's was a hundred and ten years old."

"Oh, *yes,*" Bridie said. "St. Malachy's was running before a White Sox ever stole a base."

Lyman laughed. "They phoned us back last Friday. Their exact words were: 'Everything is in order. St. Malachy's will be placed on the National Register of Historic Places.' "

Bridie had to restrain herself from throwing her arms around Lyman. "How long do we wait, Paul?"

"The registration will officially take place and be announced in a few months, say early December." Lyman straightened his glasses. "That's about as fast as it can be done."

Bridie swore a political oath. "I . . . all of us won't forget this, Paul." She gripped his hand to seal it.

"I always thought that the bells of St. Malachy's gave the Loop its best tone," Lyman said, smiling.

Bridie kissed the Illinois senator on the cheek and was off across the street to Senator Ashley-Brown's office, where the meeting was brief but very pleasant. The senator confirmed everything that Lyman had explained. The two women hugged and Ashley-Brown sent her best wishes to Mamma X. The two women made a date for dinner in Chicago as Bridie left the senator's office.

Back in her car Bridie told her driver to head for Duke Zeibert's, the famed hangout for much of Washington's sporting, journalistic and political crowd. It was only a little after 11:00 A.M. but Bridie told the driver to step on it, she was in a hurry.

The driver cut in front of the south lawn of the White House and swerved up 17th Street to Connecticut, hit the brakes at the corner of Connecticut and L. Bridie handed him traveler's checks for the two and a half days of service, plus a handsome cash tip.

"Good job, buddy. When I'm gonna get drunk I don't like to waste time."

Bridie took a stool at Duke's long bar and called out, "Bartender, give me a John Jameson's Irish whiskey in a snifter and a glass of water."

She glanced at her watch. It was 11:15 A.M. and only two other customers sat at the bar. The bartender returned with the Jameson's and a side glass of water.

"Do I know you, or should I?" he asked her.

Bridie could have kissed him. "My dear, you've always known me. The Irish invented whiskey so they wouldn't waste time trying to rule the world. I drink to running Chicago. By the way, have one with me. I'm drinking to the parish council of St. Malachy's church."

The bartender eyed Bridie. Better not, he told himself. He begged off on the drink but asked about Dick Daley.

"The old man is dead. His son is mayor now," Bridie said. "Didn't you know *that?*"

"I didn't know," the bartender said. "In this town you need a scorecard when you talk politics."

"Why were you asking about the old man?" Bridie asked.

The bartender, a man in his late forties, cased the bar before answering. "Because he wore his politics on his sleeve. In this town some guys change their politics as often as their shirts. The lawyers, the lobbyists, the headwaiters. At least Daley lived what he always was—a Chicago Democrat. And I got the idea he didn't give a damn who knew it."

Bridie lifted her glass. "*Some* people didn't realize that. God bless . . . what's your name, friend?"

"Nick."

"Okay, Nick, you're all right."

The bar had filled and a second bartender came on duty. Bridie had finished her second drink and ordered a third. She had time. It was only 12:15 P.M. and her plane didn't leave until four. She also ordered a cup of lobster bisque and a roast beef sandwich.

"I finally got to the Potomac for the first time in my life," she told Nick. "The Washington of George Washington, Abraham Lincoln, Jack Kennedy and Ronald Reagan. You know, Nick, this town has two of Chicago's main qualities."

"What're they?"

"A long history and the fix." So saying, she paid her bill in cash and left Nick a sawbuck tip. She walked to the door, turned and said goody-bye.

Nick nodded. "You take care of business. Chicago clout, honey!"

About the time Bridie's plane took off from National Airport, Charles Carmody was standing before Judge Hollis Granby in Criminal Court at 26th and South California Avenue. He was up for sentencing in the murder of Joan Solari. The fix was not in here. Charles had pled guilty at his arraignment, requesting an early sentencing hearing. He refused to speak with his father Bill or his brother Rusty. Bill Carmody, the powerful attorney, had twice attempted to talk with his son as well as to Judge Granby, who would rule on the case. Granby, aware of the pressure that Carmody might try to bring, declined the meeting.

The Carmody family anxiously eyed the judge as Granby prepared to read the sentence. He asked Charles if he had anything to say. The defendant replied in a quiet, modulated voice:

"I want to express my sorrow to Joan Solari's mother and friends. Joan was a fine young woman. She had a lot to offer her students. It was all my fault. That's why I refused my family's help. I was responsible. Thank you, Your Honor."

The courtroom, with over a hundred spectators, was hushed. Granby then declared:

"I hereby sentence you, Charles Carmody, to serve no less than twenty-five years for the murder of Joan Solari at Joliet State Penitentiary." The Carmody family gasped. The judge concluded: "And I hereby sentence you to five years at Joliet for the purchase and possession of an illegal drug. The case is closed."

Charles's mother burst into tears. The father clenched his teeth and glared at the judge. Rusty shifted nervously from foot to foot and did not look up.

Five of the Dolan family had come to hear the verdict—Leo and Nora as well as Marge, Kathy and Evie. All got up to leave the courtroom after the outburst. In leaving with his family Rusty's eyes met Evie's. Her first signs of pregnancy were evident. Rusty turned away and began to leave with his parents.

"Just a moment, Rusty," Evie called out, her voice clearly heard by Carmody and his parents. "I've been trying to speak with you, you're the father of my child. Why do you refuse to see me?"

Like the judge's verdict, the words pierced the feigned calm of those leaving the courtroom. The three Carmodys pressed on toward the elevator, not acknowledging Evie.

Leo's voice blistered the two Carmody men. "Why don't you answer my daughter's question?"

The father, Bill, turned and was about to answer when his wife tugged sharply at his sleeve and gripped his wrist, her face a mask.

Evie broke away from her family and went directly up to Rusty, grabbing hold of his left arm. *"I asked you a question, Rusty Carmody!"*

A dozen or so of the courtroom crowd halted, seemingly frozen in their tracks, to witness the extraordinary family drama.

"I *loved* you," Evie was saying, and her words ricocheted off the walls. ". . . loved you . . . love you . . ."

Rusty's face flushed. "Can't we talk about this another time—?"

"No, we can't. Why do you want an abortion?"

The crowd, mostly women, gasped.

Bill Carmody pulled away from his wife and moved toward Evie. "Get *away* from my son, you bitch . . ."

Nora and Marge had to restrain Leo. Marge pushed him back and confronted Bill Carmody, her face nearly touching his.

"Let's see who the bitch is, Mr. Carmody. Your son forcefully picked up my sister and carried her into her bedroom. He—"

"Shut up!" from Mrs. Carmody. "That's trash and you know it."

"Is it? My sister is pregnant, Mrs. Carmody. If you don't believe me ask your son. Ask him *now*. And ask him why he chose not even to wear a condom. Who's the bitch, madame?"

Mrs. Carmody stood in enraged silence as the word "madame" carried down the hall.

"Well," Marge continued, *"I'll* ask him. Rusty, true or not? Did you not force yourself on my sister while she told you that she was still a virgin? Didn't she beg you to wait for marriage?"

Rusty Carmody, his face now flushed red, did not answer. Marge demanded, "Rusty, didn't you tell my sister when she talked about marriage, and these were your exact words . . . 'In September'? Have you told your parents *that?* And, Mr. Carmody, when you spoke with your brother, the cardinal, did you tell him all this? You're goddamn right you didn't, you rotten hypocrite."

The elder Carmody tried to bluster his way out of this but his words were all but incoherent.

Marge kept at him. "Abortion. That's what you Carmodys want. And I say by his inaction, that includes the *cardinal.*"

"That's sacrilegious!" Mrs. Carmody yelled out.

Marge shook her head. "Rusty told my sister to get an abortion. Why? He said they were irreconcilable. He said his *conscience* told him that. When he penetrated her with his conscience-hardened penis they weren't so irreconcilable."

Mrs. Carmody shouted, "Shut *up.*"

Marge would not. "They only became irreconcilable when he talked about his wonderful career. He wasn't ready for marriage, he had to network, to move up in the right circles, and his *conscience* told him marriage was wrong for him now. Catholics like you Carmodys—with your money and position, you have the effrontery to call yourselves the

Church's new order. The New Conscience. What a laugh. My sister a bitch? You have some nerve. How *dare* you . . . ?"

Evie moved forward and touched Marge on the arm, then turned to Rusty.

"At least talk to me now, privately. You've avoided me for long enough. I am asking you . . ."

Finally Rusty said, "Where?"

Evie said there was a nearby conference room. They could use it.

"We'll all wait," Leo said.

Bill Carmody told his son, "I'm against this. She'll use anything you say against you."

Rusty hesitated, his mother shook her head no. Evie quickly told them, "I'm not going to *sue* anyone."

Rusty, hearing this, walked back to see if the conference room was empty, opened the door, looked inside and motioned to Evie, who followed him into the room and closed the door.

For a moment the two sat without speaking. Finally Rusty said, "All right, what do you want to say?"

Evie twisted a handkerchief in her hand. Her voice was low, nervous. "Just two questions, Rusty. First, I love you, at least I did. I think I could again if . . . is there any hope that we can be married?" Rusty's face was a blank. "Second, *why* do you want an abortion? This is your child too."

Rusty lit a small cigar. Evie had never seen him smoke before. As he lit it, his hands shook ever so slightly. He blew a cloud of smoke above his head. "Marriage is out of the question for me right now. You and I . . . we're heading in two different directions. That's all there is to it . . ."

"Don't you have any love . . . any respect for me at all? Am I hopelessly old-fashioned to ask that question?"

Rusty blew smoke out of the side of his mouth. "Evie, of course I care for you, but . . . well, you can't help me where

I'm going. That's a fact, and it's one of the reasons we're incompatible. You're not going where I'm going."

"Where are you going, Rusty? Are you saying you want a master of ceremonies for a wife?"

"That's sort of crude, but you're getting the idea. Look, I'm going to run for the city council, and eventually mayor. I already have name recognition through my father and the cardinal. To put it bluntly, the one thing I still need is a good dress."

"A good *what?*"

"A lady with smarts, ambition, maybe even money. You're a kid. I need someone more mature, more . . . modern."

"And that's it?"

"Yes, damn it. That's it. We're incompatible, like I said. My calling is to get into politics. We'd never make it together."

"What about our child? Is abortion still your answer?"

"If a couple isn't compatible I think abortion within the first three months of pregnancy is certainly a viable alternative." He had lapsed into his lawyerly manner. "Even some *Catholics* argue about when a fetus becomes a human. Well, I don't want the fetus *or* marriage now . . . Look, Evie, the pope is ill. He may only last another year or so. If he dies in the next few years all the old issues will be back on the front burner—birth control, married priests and women priests. Conscience versus Church authority. It'll be getting rid of meat on Friday all over again."

"It's not that simple, Rusty. I'm talking about us, people, not clerical rules."

A long pause, then Rusty said, "We've been here a long time."

Evie seemed emotionally drained.

"Well, are you going to have the child?"

"I don't know," she told him. Then she looked him in the eye. "As the Irish say, the day is not done."

"What the hell do you mean by *that?*"

"You said we were incompatible."

"So?"

"If we're incompatible, then I have every right to go my own way, listen to my own conscience. I believe the current phrase is 'do my own thing.' "

Angry and made uneasy by her burst of self-will, Rusty stood and said, "I don't want to see you again."

"And your child?"

Rusty threw his cigar on the floor and walked out the door.

After a moment Marge entered the room, and Evie, her eyes bright, told her sister:

"It's finished, Marge. Forever. To hell with Rusty Carmody. I'm free of him."

Chapter 12

THE GIRL FROM STONY BROOK

Nora was drinking a solitary morning cup of coffee at the breakfast table. "Hello, Mother." The voice came from behind her shoulder. Nora turned and saw Evie standing in the kitchen doorway. The family matriarch stood, held out her arms and Evie walked inside them. Mother and daughter held each other. It was their first meeting since the confrontation with the Carmodys and, indeed, Evie's first visit home in months.

Nora heated Evie a cup of tea. "It's good to see you, girl. Are you all right?"

"Yes, Mother. I'm fine. Really."

Nora didn't inquire about Evie's encounter with Rusty Carmody. The only family member to discuss the matter with Evie was Marge, and the nurse declined to disclose anything about their long talk. Mother and daughter spoke now about the family, especially Kathy's work at Ogden school, and the pickets at Old St. Malachy's.

Nora had to laugh. "Isn't Kathy *something*. A regular Eleanor Roosevelt! Well, Ireland's only fifty years behind the times. We finally got a woman up with the big boys. Mrs. Mary Robinson's been elected president and she's kicking over a few old milk pails."

Evie smiled. The house and kitchen were the same. The clean smell of fresh linens and well-scrubbed floors. The eternal coffeepot on the stove and the faded photo of Dingle, County Kerry, above the kitchen toaster. And, of course, the rosary hanging from the pocket of her mother's apron.

"Is dad okay? I've been worried about him," Evie said.

Nora said quietly, "He's missed you, Evie. He's worried about you. He talks less than he did. I guess we're all getting older."

"Are you?" Evie asked.

"I'm just fine, girl. I watch dad like a hawk 'cause he eats so little. He mentions retirement more often. I think he's plain tired."

"I saw Mario Moretti the other day," Evie said. "You know him, Chief Rossi's driver. One of his daughters was in my class last year. He said the chief, dad and Kathy were all at St. Malachy's when the pickets started marching. Dad stayed out of sight. He went to see Cappy Conlon in the rectory."

The two lifted their cups in silence. The radio was playing an old Rosemary Clooney song, "Tenderly." Nora asked quietly, "What happened, Evie, and where are you going, girl?"

"Do you want it all spread out, Mother?"

"Yes, I do."

Evie paused and took a deep breath. "I loved Rusty Carmody. Maybe a little part of me still does. Who knows? I do know that when I gave myself to him it was out of love . . ."

Nora quickly asked Evie if she had considered going back to teaching in the fall. Evie said she wanted to go back to her classroom at Queen of Martyrs but, pregnant and unwed, she wasn't sure the Catholic school would accept her. Nora hadn't thought about that, and wasn't sure what to say, not wanting to be a Pollyanna. She asked Evie if she wanted more tea but her daughter told her she had to go for a medical checkup and had another appointment afterward. The radio was playing "Music From Across the Way" now, one of Nora's favorites.

Evie looked at her mother. "I love you." Eyes moist, Evie was out the front door before Nora could kiss her.

Nora walked to her bedroom, knelt at the side of the bed, took out her rosary and prayed quietly as the day's full sun began to shine through the window.

Dr. Leonard Feldman pronounced Evie in excellent condition. He did not ask his patient if she planned to carry the child to term. He had already told Evie he wouldn't perform an abortion. He reported the news that his son David and Evie's sister Marge were expecting another child. The couple had learned only late yesterday afternoon, he said. Evie asked Feldman if he would convey her congratulations to his son, she would phone Marge herself.

As soon as Evie left, Feldman phoned his bookie Fast Eddie and bet two dollars to win on a new find, Dr. Music, running five and a half furlongs at Prescott Downs. He noted the two-year-old filly was owned by a physician, Dr. Martin Berman of Paso Robles, California. If Dr. Music played sweet today he would have another favorite to follow in the *Daily Racing Form*.

Outside a large black limousine waited for Evie as Michael's wife Lucy had promised. Lucy had phoned Evie two days earlier and invited her to lunch.

They drove now to the private posh Evergreen Club on Wacker Drive near Tribune Tower. The club was on the ninth floor of a bank building overlooking the Chicago River. Green vines and plants lined the walls of the club—Evie had never seen some of them—and spread a scent of pine throughout the room. A large green Chinese rug patterned in lotus covered the entire floor. The muted gold of the restaurant's indirect lighting gave the place a feeling of soft intimacy.

Jessica Janis-Lerner Dolan, known as Lucy to the family, stood and hugged Evie when the maitre d' led the schoolteacher to their table. Lucy, whose jet-black hair was beautifully combed, wore a dark blue satin Chinese dress with a long slit skirt and dark blue satin shoes. A strand of large matched pearls circled her neck. Evie noticed the third ring that always accompanied the advertising director's wedding and engagement rings. Lucy changed that ring each day along with her bracelet. Today both were lavender jade. So were her earrings.

Evie had once gone with Rusty to a downtown jeweler where he bought a three-thousand-dollar Swiss watch. As they were leaving the shop Evie spotted engagement rings and playfully asked Rusty to stop, then picked out a lavender jade, smaller than what Jessica now wore. She adored the ring and asked its price. The clerk casually mentioned ten thousand dollars. Evie took a deep breath and thanked him. Rusty, in retrospect, for obvious reasons had said nothing.

Lucy and Evie did not know one another well although they had met three or four times a year at family affairs. Neither had ever invited the other out.

Lucy and Michael traveled in very different circles from Evie. They were among the city's bright young people shooting to become stars of Chicago society. Lucy's Manhattan and Long Island family connections opened up many private doors along the Gold Coast and among Chicago's Jewish leaders. The professional status of the pair made them attractive guests among the city's more discreet movers and shakers as well as the upper-echelon business community. Lucy and Michael rode the social circuit at least three evenings a week and sometimes on weekends. As Lucy once put it to Nora, "We're riding a social merry-go-round." And she obviously liked it.

Lucy's advertising and public-relations agency had, in a few years, become one of the most prestigious in the Loop. Her accounts included a major department store, a leading bank, a national insurance agency and five different manufacturing firms. She had sixty-one clients, including TV personalities and five of the city's richest families. She had added two thousand square feet to her office space each year for the last four years. Her firm also undertook various charitable campaigns gratis. Lucy's dark beauty and Michael's Irish smile showed on local newspaper and society pages three or four times a month. They had it all—fame, wealth and acceptance into the atmosphere of the city's elite. So why, Evie asked herself for the umpteenth time, would her busy sister-in-law invite her to lunch?

"Lucy," Evie began, "this is a lovely club, I can't help but admire it . . ."

The conversation continued in this indirect noncommittal fashion along with several pauses. Lucy, who had a tendency to dominate other women with her quick mind, proceeded cautiously. The meeting was of special importance to her, although Evie had no idea of her intentions. The steward came and Lucy ordered a glass of Chardonnay while Evie, who rarely drank, asked for iced tea.

Lucy noticed that Evie couldn't take her eyes off her lavender jade ring. "You like it?"

"I didn't realize I was that obvious." Evie grinned. "It's beautiful."

"I got it last Christmas, a present to myself."

"Really?"

"Yes, and maybe there's more to that than meets the eye . . . Evie, are you happy?"

"I'm very happy in my job," Evie said emphatically. "I wouldn't want to do anything else."

The steward arrived with the wine and iced tea.

"That's great . . . some of us aren't so fortunate," Lucy said as the waiter hovered for their orders. Lucy told Evie her preferred choices, then ordered asparagus vinaigrette as an appetizer and filet mignon with buttered peas as her entree. Evie said she'd have the same.

Evie then asked Lucy why she felt less fortunate. "You're so successful. Your agency appears in the business pages all the time. You and Michael seem to own the society columns."

Lucy smiled. "Window dressing, Evie. Appearances. Doing things for effect. Like my going to Radcliffe. Don't get me wrong, it's a terrific college, but I went there because my *parents* wanted me to go there. Radcliffe was next door to Harvard. It's a joint degree. Both are in Cambridge. Prestige, social and academic. Actually, I wanted to go to Stony Brook on Long Island, where most of my friends went."

Lucy talked about the arguments with her parents. Her father said he hadn't worked his tail off in Wall Street for his daughter to go to a state school, and her mother pointed out that Stony Brook had no real *standing*. When Lucy moved into her Radcliffe dorm she found she was rooming with one Temple Cater-Willington of Charleston, South Carolina. Temple's family were Old South. The Willingtons had landed in Charleston in 1791 and established several businesses within their first decade, including a bank that eventually became one of the largest in the state. Like Lucy, Temple was an only child. She was to marry well because the young man would be taking over the family empires. A well-mannered Harvard man would do nicely. Lucy had to laugh as she told how Temple eloped with a Boston College Catholic. Eventually she went home, her husband was accepted and he took over the businesses. And Temple was now a Catholic lady with six children and expecting a seventh. Her one saving grace to the Willingtons and Caters was biological—Temple had produced five sons.

Lucy found herself confiding to Evie one of her own collegiate exploits. She had once made love to a Harvard crewman on the banks of the Charles River. And later he had adorned her bra with a stupid pen sketch of Gen. Ulysses S. Grant, a lousy likeness as she recalled. He wanted to borrow it to show and tell at a Hasty Pudding bash. "God, can you *believe* that . . . ?"

No, Evie couldn't, but she didn't say so. Instead she listened as Lucy said she had been subtly influenced to think of Radcliffe girls as being a cut above other college graduates. She knew intellectually that was hardly always true, but it got to her anyway. She had the Ivy League brand, no question.

Evie was tempted to suggest that wasn't so bad when the waiter interrupted with the appetizer plates.

"Sorry, Evie, I just sort of drifted off. But I do think if I'd gone to Stony Brook I'd probably care a lot less about my business and social notices in the newspapers. Radcliffe did a lot for me, I realize, but it also put a lot of pressure on me that I could do without."

The waiter arrived with the filet mignon and buttered peas and asked if they wished their drinks repeated. Both agreed. Lucy never took two drinks at lunch, but she knew why she had done so today. She needed a second Chardonnay and something stronger to get the real reason for her invitation to Evie. Finally she approached the subject.

"I want to have a family, Evie." Followed by a quick laugh and . . . "Of course, not five, six or seven like Temple! She's not only a good Catholic lady, she's got a sex drive that won't quit. At this rate she may have a dozen."

The two shared a laugh at that.

Abruptly the proper ambience of the room was interrupted by a hubbub at the maitre d's station. Three men and . . .

"That's Mamma X," Evie said, surprised.

"Who's Mamma X?" Lucy asked.

"She's a Black Muslim on the parish council at St. Malachy's church."

Mamma didn't want a table next to the palm tree at the side. She told the maitre d' that it reduced her view of the room. She wanted to absorb more of the atmosphere. She would like a table front and center. Her host, K.C. Wu, another member of the council, and his son, L.Y., agreed. Mr. Wu's other guest, Monsignor Thomas Brady, remained aloof from the exchange. Evie could tell Lucy who the Chinese men were because her sister Kathy had introduced them at a benefit dinner in St. Malachy's. She had seen Monsignor Brady at Queen of Martyrs Church.

The diners were looking, and trying not to be obvious, at Mamma X dressed in a large white silk turban and a flowing multicolored robe that stretched from her broad shoulders down to her open-sandal toes. Her short sleeves flowed above a purple silk undergarment whose large gold crescents flashed down to the wrists.

"What's that all about?" Lucy asked.

"I don't know," Evie told her, "but I'd bet the cardinal would like to know about it." She guessed maybe the meeting had to do with St. Malachy's.

The women went back to their meal, Evie feeling uneasy about responding to Lucy's desire for a family because her brother Michael was, after all, involved.

When they had finished their entree Lucy recommended fresh strawberries flown in from Sonora, Mexico. Lucy would have coffee after dessert and Evie more iced tea.

Evie couldn't help notice that Mamma X and Monsignor Brady were dominating the conversation with father and son Wu. It was a whispered but animated exchange but she couldn't hear a word of it.

Lucy then took a deep breath and got to the point of her invitation.

"Evie, if you're going to have your child and not raise it yourself . . . well, I would like to adopt it."

For the moment Evie was too stunned to reply.

"Of course, the name of the child would be Dolan. The entire matter would stay within the family. It could be done quietly and I honestly believe that most if not all of the family would approve. That is, of course, if *you* did . . ."

Evie stammered, "What does Michael say?"

"I haven't talked with Michael about this."

"Well . . . I . . ."

Lucy put her right hand in Evie's left. "We've tried for years. I went to see a gynecologist a few months ago and he told me, finally, that I'm incapable of having children. I know it's crazy, I've never told Michael. I just can't face his disappointment . . . not yet, anyway. I'm not a religious person, Evie. But I think I've been a caring and good wife. I think Michael would tell you that. Evie, if you would let me adopt your baby I would be forever grateful. I know how you feel about your religion so I'd bring the child up as a Catholic. It'd be the happiest moment of my life if you said yes . . ."

Neither woman spoke. Lucy waited for an answer. Evie

couldn't overlook the irony of the situation . . . Michael had suggested an abortion while his wife now pleaded for the child. Finally Evie said, "I did think about abortion and wanted to get that message back to the father of my baby. At the time I wanted Rusty Carmody on almost any terms. I loved him then, or at least thought I did. In these months he's completely turned away from me . . . he has other women now in his life . . . Considering abortion was mostly trying to win Rusty back. Love can do strange things to the mind. And, of course, I'm not unaware of the psychological damage that an abortion can have, never mind that it's still against my religion."

The waiter brought Lucy's coffee and when he left Evie went on. "I'll tell you now, Lucy, I'm not getting an abortion. I've had lots of advice, but it comes down to what *I* feel and believe. I can't do it. I won't do it."

Lucy was obviously pleased that Evie was not getting an abortion and said she thought Michael would be too. Evie didn't reveal her conversation with Michael about abortion for obvious reasons. There was a silence before Evie spoke again.

"I had a dream about ten days ago. The baby was a girl. I held her in my arms and rocked her . . . Lucy, I don't know what my feelings will be when the child is born. It seems so unreal that I'm even having a baby. I haven't been able to grasp the actual feeling of a child in my arms, although the dream gave me a vague notion of that. Maybe I won't be able to give up the baby. I may desperately want to keep her no matter what the consequences. But maybe I'd be wiser to consider adoption. If you did adopt the child I know you and Michael would raise her with love. But I'd want her to know . . . maybe on her twenty-first birthday . . . who her real mother and father were. Yes, she should know both of us. I want the truth out in the open. But right now, Lucy, I'm walking in a fog, I can't see where I'm going."

Lucy nodded, saying she understood.

"And Michael? When will you talk about this with Michael?" Evie asked.

"Only if and when you agree on an adoption."

"I'll let you know before the baby is born in December," Evie said. "I promise you that . . ."

The two chatted on for several more minutes before Lucy signed the check. On the way to the door they passed the Wu table. Mamma X and Monsignor Brady were still talking, and both women heard mention of St. Malachy's from Monsignor Brady:

"I've never seen an angel dance, either on a pin or a flame, much less a cardinal."

Claudia Lally sat at her desk at the *Herald,* trying to get her head straight over the call. She glanced around the city room, her professional home for more than two decades.

"It's politics, Claudia." That was the way Frank Fahey had framed the situation earlier over his roast beef. "And you know nothing is personal in politics." Fahey smiled with manufactured innocence. Why was the old charmer feeding her this remarkable story? Was it really politics, or something deeper and more personal?

Lally picked up her notebook and began rereading her notes. Rusty Carmody flew to Monaco about a week after his brother Charles had been sentenced to prison for the murder of Joan Solari. Rusty spent about an hour at the gaming tables, where he lost some one hundred and fifty dollars, left before midnight, then caught an early morning flight to Rome. He was traveling on a U.S. diplomatic passport. How?

Why? Where did Alderman Fahey get such confidential information? And why did Fahey want to fry Rusty Carmody?

Carmody, said Fahey, met Big Mike Cecci at the Excelsior Hotel on Rome's fashionable Via Veneto. After he checked in they immediately took a taxi to the Banco Italo-Americano on Via del Tritone with all of Carmody's luggage. Each man carried two suitcases. Rusty deposited more than $17 million in cash and negotiable securities with Dr. Federico Castagna, the bank's *direttore generale,* to the account of Comizio di Ricordo, the Meeting Place of Remembrance. There were many questions. The biggest was Cecci, *numero due* in Chicago's largest crime family. What was he up to? And what was Rusty Carmody doing in the company of the well-known mobster?

Fahey seemed to know the answers, but how did he know, and why was he spilling his guts to a reporter? Lally asked herself. And why *me?*

She stood and sauntered thirty feet to managing editor Sandy Levine's office. Levine had his hoofs up on the desk reading the paper's obituaries . . . his pet peeve was cliché-ridden obits.

"Sandy, I'm not scared but I am very confused," Lally began. She then went on to give him Fahey's story. When Claudia had finished, bearded and bespeckled Levine retreated into the high-backed deep leather of his swivel chair, then abruptly leaned forward.

"Go for it, Claudia. We'll back you. I'll call the lawyers. No, wait. Rusty's old man Bill Carmody may have a line in there. I'll tell the publisher—only him. Do it, kid."

Lally went back to her desk and dialed the number at the top of her notebook. She placed a new pad at the side of her old one. The city council was not in session, and she knew Fahey had returned to his apartment. The phone rang for more than a minute before Fahey's groggy voice sounded.

"Who the hell is this? I was taking a nap."

Lally identified herself. Fahey, suddenly alert, snapped, "Well, am I gonna read somethin' in the paper tomorrow?"

"No, I need to dig some more."

"Dig what? I thought we buried the guy over the rum cake."

Fahey laughed as though he had just drowned Rusty Carmody's ambitions. Actually, he had.

"I've got four questions, Mr. Fahey."

"Shoot."

"First, why me? Second, why Rusty Carmody? Third, who wants him out of the way? Fourth, how did you obtain the information on the passport and Italian bank?"

"First question: I trust you. You got a mouth, but you also protect your sources. You did that on St. Malachy's in spite of the pressure from the cardinal."

"Why Rusty Carmody?"

"I told you—politics."

"I need specifics, Mr. Fahey."

"Why?"

"Because I don't want to be a hit woman. I need facts, a reason."

The other end of the line fell silent. Lally could hear Fahey breathing. A clock chimed in the background. Fahey finally spoke.

"We're still on deep background, kid. I'm not the source. Nobody in politics is."

"Okay."

The alderman said Carmody planned to run against Dan Dolan in the Nineteenth Ward's Democratic primary. "We don't agree with Dolan a lot but we trust him. His word is his bond. We don't trust Carmody."

"Why not?"

"Are you kiddin'?"

"I need to hear it from you, Mr. Fahey."

"Look, kid, we owe Dolan."

Lally cut Fahey off. "Who's we?"

"City hall. The Democratic party."

"Why do you owe him?"

"Favors."

"What favors?"

"Look, I'm not gonna go into that. I'll just say that Dan Dolan may be a conservative but he plays by house rules. He backed a couple of bills we wanted badly. Let me put it simply. This is Chicago."

"Did he ask for this?"

"No, but we know he's hurtin'."

"Why?"

"Carmody poked his little sister."

Lally said, "I didn't think you fellows got so personal."

"Where've you been? Politics is people. And you know what didn't help young Carmody either? His uncle. His Eminence."

"Why?"

"Why? Of all people, you know why."

"I've got to hear it from you."

"The cardinal tried to stiff Cappy and St. Malachy's. It isn't going to work but he tried."

Lally smelled the climax to this drama. She fired the last question. "The passport and the Italian bank?"

"Did you know that Bill Carmody, the lawyer, worked for the U.S. State Department? That he takes on international cases for State? He hires local lawyers in, say, Italy but calls the shots. He got Rusty a State Department passport as an assistant and courier."

"And?"

"And, my ass. Bridie O'Brien could figure that one out even if she was drunk."

"I've got to hear it from you, Mr. Fahey."

"Rusty's passport made him untouchable. The mob found out. They approached him with big bucks. He became a courier for Mike Cecci and those other guys."

Stunned, Lally said, "Who found out about it? How much was Carmody paid?"

"The much maligned Chicago Police Department tailed Cecci to Rome a half-dozen times over the past year. Each time he met young Carmody at the Excelsior and they went to the Banco Italo-Americano and made a multimillion-dollar deposit. The mob deposited nearly a hundred million dollars. Carmody was paid a hundred and fifty thousand dollars a trip—a total of nine hundred thousand dollars or about one percent of the take. The Italian *carabinieri* grilled the bank director. They're building a case, right now."

"How'd you find out about the amount of money?"

"Joe Rossi. The chief knows a lot of people in the Italian police. All politics and police work are local—all over the world. Joe called in a marker."

"Whew!" Lally blew out a low whistle. "What's going to be done about it?"

"Rossi's told the Italian cops that it's up to them. The money is in Rome. He's also passed the word to the State Department."

"And?"

"This is not only the son of one of their most respected lawyers—and one of their own couriers—but the nephew of the Cardinal of Chicago. It's a hot church-politics potato. They call it a classified case and have backed off."

"Are they doing *anything?*"

"Oh, yeah, the department says it's investigating. Let me tell you, it's going to be one of the longest inquiries in history." Fahey laughed, then his voice changed character and tone. He became deadly serious. "Look, Mrs. Lally, the city council is not, as you well know, the College of Cardinals. However, we do have our better moments. We want to do two things—stop Cecci because that's dirty drug money he's exporting. If he's forced to find another route out of the country, Rossi has a chance of nailing him and the other mob leaders. And Joe wants them bad.

"Second, like I said—we owe Dan Dolan. In this town's politics, you pay your debts. If Carmody decides not to run for Dolan's seat we're square with Dan. And if he sends two dozen roses to Evie Dolan with a little note saying I'm sorry, that would be a bonus."

"I'm never going to be able to print this story," Lally said.

Fahey brightened. "Yes, you are. You've got the mob money-laundering story, quoting Chicago police sources—and no one will deny it. You can skip their names this time, but Cecci and Rusty may still be indicted. That would be a future scoop. Second, you've got Rusty dropping out of the Nineteenth Ward race. You may also have him leaving politics after a year telling a lot of people he's going to be mayor someday."

"I'd like to see Cecci and the mob in jail," Lally said.

"He who laughs last . . ." which Fahey did and hung up.

Lally checked a number in the phone book and dialed. The receptionist responded: "Carmody and Associates."

"Mr. Rusty Carmody, please."

"Who may I say is calling?"

"Claudia Lally of the *Herald*."

A strong male voice lowered now into intimacy. "Claudia . . . I feel as if I know you. Rusty Carmody here."

"Good afternoon, Mr. Carmody. I'm phoning on behalf of the *Herald*."

"I'm honored, Claudia. I've read many of your articles."

"Mr. Carmody, I'd like to make this brief—for both our sakes."

The lawyer waited.

"Mr. Carmody, when did you receive your diplomatic passport from the U.S. State Department?"

"Who said I had one?"

"Please, Mr. Carmody. It's not a secret. State and Customs have acknowledged it."

"Well, let's see . . . about a year ago. To do international legal work for my father and—"

"Mr. Carmody, when and where did you first meet Mike Cecci?"

Silence.

"Come on, Mr. Carmody, I have you meeting Cecci at the Excelsior Hotel in Rome and going with him to the Banco Italo-Americano where you deposited very large amounts of American dollars."

Carmody still said nothing.

"Money-laundering drug profits, Mr. Carmody?" Lally let him twist on the other end of the line. Then: "Did your father and perhaps your uncle know about these financial transactions?"

"Look, this is all outrageous. I don't know what you're implying but in any case I'm no longer doing any international work."

"Oh? Have you turned in your diplomatic passport?"

"It's in the mail."

"So you don't deny that you carried mob money to

Rome and accompanied Mike Cecci to deposit it in a Roman bank?"

"I'm not going to listen to any more of these slanderous—" Carmody's voice broke then. He was smart enough to know he had better cop a plea with her and hope to keep the lid on.

"My father . . . the cardinal . . . my mother . . . for God's sake . . ."

Lally took a deep breath. "How about Evie Dolan?"

Lally wanted a clear confession. She wanted this guy Carmody badly. She also wanted Cecci in the state prison.

Carmody's voice was barely audible. "I'm sorry about Evie. Things just didn't work out . . ."

Not good enough. "Let's get this over, Mr. Carmody. Are you still going to oppose Dan Dolan for alderman in the Democratic primary?"

"Who told you I was running?"

"Look, Cecci and the mob and their dirty money aren't going to elect you. *Are* you going to run?"

Carmody didn't respond. Lally could almost hear the gears grinding.

"I'm getting out of politics," Carmody said slowly. "I won't be running for any political office."

"Oh? You're withdrawing completely?"

"Yes . . ."

"One last thing," Lally said. "Send Evie Dolan a couple dozen roses and tell her to try to forgive you for being a real bastard."

On the following morning the *Herald* front-paged Lally's story on the mob's drug-money laundering operation in Italy. The reporter quoted "Chicago police sources." Rusty Carmody was not mentioned. He did make page one the next morning when Lally revealed he had dropped plans to run for alderman in the Nineteenth Ward. The young lawyer, a nephew of the cardinal, was quoted as saying he was withdrawing from politics to devote himself to his career in the law. And Evie Dolan received two dozen roses from Carmody with a card saying he was very sorry. He didn't add sorry for being a real bastard.

Chapter 13

FISH IN THE STREAM

Mr. K.C. Wu and his eldest son L.Y. entered the outer office of Cardinal Carmody at precisely five minutes before four o'clock of a July afternoon. It was now three weeks since the public protest against demolishing St. Malachy's had begun at the church and pickets were still carrying their banners.

The July heat and humidity lay heavily on the protestors, the chancery office and the city. The beaches along Lake Michigan were crowded with thousands fleeing the torrid temperatures. But the El sweltered with erratic air-conditioning on trains. In Chicago the dog days began in July, not August. It was also the time when the Cubs's fall to baseball oblivion usually started.

Mrs. Koslowski greeted the men and apologized for their ten-day wait to see the cardinal. His Eminence had been very busy. Nevertheless, he was pleased to receive them today. She told the guests that the cardinal was always on schedule and would receive them promptly at four o'clock.

Mr. Wu and his son had barely seated themselves in the red-cushioned chairs when the secretary buzzed the cardinal to remind him it was time for the Wu appointment. Mrs. Koslowski rose and motioned them to follow her and directed them into His Eminence's office. She closed the door behind them.

Carmody stepped around his desk and greeted father and son with warm handshakes. He seemed in a jovial mood. The visitors smiled but did not kiss his ring. The prelate had anticipated that and was already moving behind his desk.

"Gentlemen," the cardinal said, "I'm very pleased to see you. Please accept my apologies. I wanted to see you earlier, but my schedule . . . well, I understand you have a proposal for the archdiocese. Please tell me about it."

That was the phrase which Monsignor Brady used—a proposal for the archdiocese—when he explained the request to His Eminence. Brady said the Wu family had contacted him concerning a "property agreement" that they wished to discuss privately with the cardinal. Carmody was intrigued. Perhaps they wished to purchase some unused inner-city church or school near Chinatown. That would indeed be welcome. The blight of closed, boarded-up Catholic schools and churches across the city was a constant problem.

L.Y. Wu introduced his father, explaining the elder's humility about his English. He had come to America as a young man from Shanghai but hadn't gone to school in the United States. The son would translate his father's dialect. The elder Wu then nodded for L.Y. to begin and the Number One son addressed the cardinal in almost reverential tones:

"We are here, Your Holiness, in the name of my father's

wife and our respected mother, Mary C. Wu, a baptized Catholic."

Carmody made no attempt to correct their reference to him as the pope. It might embarrass his guests. Did he also experience a slight frisson of pleasure at the title being applied to him . . . ?

"We are also present in our own name, including six other sons, their wives and eighteen grandchildren. Mary C. Wu is now in the next life. She was converted to your faith at her birthplace, Shanghai. She took the name Mary from, as you know, the mother of Christ. Her Chinese name as a child was Hsu-djen, Precious Pearl. When she grew up the calligraphy was modified to mean Noble Woman."

Carmody found himself charmed, which was Wu's desired effect.

"The spirit of my mother has been appearing to my father over the past year. She comes in the form of a deer. It's a legendary white deer, the companion of a Taoist priest who befriended my father when he was lost in the mountains of China as a youth. The white deer symbolizes the elevation of the spirit. My father also now hears the voice of my mother in the poetry of Su Tungpo, who lived in the tenth century. Lin Yutang, our respected historical writer of this century, after whom I was named, has translated into English Su Tungpo's lament long after the passing of his wife."

L.Y. proceeded to pull a piece of paper from inside his breast pocket and read:

Ten years have we been parted,
the living and the dead.
Hearing no news,
Not thinking,
And yet forgetting nothing.
I cannot come to your grave a thousand miles away,

To converse with you and whisper my longing.
And even if we did meet
How would you greet
My weathered face, my hair a frosty white?
Last night I dreamed I had suddenly returned to our old home,
And saw you sitting there before the familiar dressing table,
With misty eyes before the candlelight.
May we year after year
In heartbreak meet
On the pine crest
In the moonlight.

The cardinal was fascinated, but what were these Chinese telling him? What did they *want*—yes, want. Carmody knew he must play the Chinese game—caution, indirection—and let the message evolve. After conferring with his father L.Y. continued:

"We are therefore here, Your Holiness, as a family in response to the spiritual call of Mary C. Wu. We wish to honor her in an appropriate manner."

"Appropriate manner?" These enigmatic Chinese certainly loved a mystery. He wondered what the eventual revelation would be.

K.C. spoke to his son. L.Y. nodded, turned to the cardinal and said matter-of-factly, "My father said to tell Your Holiness that we carry a modest proposal for your eminent consideration."

Carmody played the game, smiled, nodded, said nothing.

"We understand St. Malachy's church may soon expire. Rather than allow this honorable institution to be lost to the service of God, my father is willing to dismantle the church and remove it to another location. That would be in Chinatown near 22nd and Wentworth, where we are blessed with several parcels of land.

"We are prepared to extend to your chancery office the sum of one hundred thousand dollars for allowing us to purchase and remove the structure and its contents. In order to maintain the character of St. Malachy's we would wish the altar, tabernacles, sacred vessels, stations of the cross, confessionals and other accoutrements so the church would continue to function normally."

Carmody's eyes had widened with each sentence from L.Y. He hunched forward in anticipation. In contrast, K.C. Wu had closed his eyes, awaiting the decision. The two were surprised by the cardinal's question.

"May I ask what business Mr. K.C. is in?"

The son neither consulted with his father nor hesitated to reply, "Your Holiness, please forgive my directness but we are not in the church business. So we would not be starting a church of our own. St. Malachy's would remain what it is today, a Catholic place of worship. As for my father's business, we are a family corporation involved in import-export, banking, real estate, restaurants, grocery stores, laundry and other enterprises in Chinatown. You may inquire about our professional and personal character of anyone in Chinatown. I must reemphasize one fact. We are not Catholics. This is being done in memory of our mother, who, as I said, was a devout Catholic. For us this is a matter of ancestral respect."

Carmody now regretted his bluntness, although he needed some indication of the Wus' financial background. He tried to ease away from his question.

"Thanks to both of you. I merely wished to know how long your family had been established in the community."

"My parents' families came here from Shanghai some forty years ago," L.Y. told him.

To further ease any misapprehension, the cardinal laughed and said the only Chinese word he knew—*"Hao! Hao!"*

The Chinese knew, of course, that the word meant almost anything polite that one wished to attach to it. Both smiled. Carmody congratulated himself and nodded for L.Y. to continue. Young Wu then concluded the proposal:

"In addition to our payment of one hundred thousand dollars for the structure and its contents, including their removal, we are also prepared to sign an agreement promising that St. Malachy's will remain a Catholic institution. We will make up the six-to-seven-thousand-dollar monthly deficit to assure the church's continuing function. That should reassure you that St. Malachy's would not be a financial burden on your archdiocese."

The statement stuck in Carmody's craw, almost as much as Bridie O'Brien's mission to get the church made into some sort of national historic landmark that he couldn't sell or dispose of. He wasn't supposed to know about Bridie's trip to Washington but his Church contacts there had gotten wind of it and tipped him off. The Chinese were advising him they did not want the church dismantled or closed in the future. Still, he realized they didn't want to invest without a guarantee that the church would continue. L.Y. spelled it out.

"We recognize the feeling of the parish council that St. Malachy's is a neighborhood church and, as such, should remain where it is now located. However, that does not appear possible in view of its reported deficit and we don't believe in miracles. Therefore, moving the structure appears to be the only choice. My father is a modest man. He attempts only the possible, transferring the church and supporting it."

The cardinal, seeing their proposal as a way out of his dilemma, said, "I'm prepared to promise that the Church would function as it does today but, of course, I cannot speak for the next leader of the archdiocese."

K.C. Wu understood Carmody without his son's translation. He nodded. Young Wu said they would complete the job, brick by brick, within a month. They would sign a contract to that effect.

Carmody said in a friendly but firm voice: "Gentlemen, I'm humbled by the generosity of your offer and genuinely moved by the spirit in which it's undertaken. But I am obliged to point out some crucial legal considerations. I have signed an agreement which guarantees that the land will be completely cleared by August 31—"

L.Y. opened his brown briefcase and handed the cardinal a twelve-page document. "This contract covers all the legal obligations that you have mentioned except dates."

The prelate was startled; the Chinese apparently knew everything. How? Where was the leak? Had Midwest Oil & Gas betrayed him? Were they about to pull out of the land deal? L.Y. interrupted Carmody's thoughts.

"May we suggest that your attorneys study our proposal. In the meantime would you allow some of our workmen to ascend to the roof and study the various sections of St. Malachy's? Perhaps a phone call to the pastor would help?"

Would Cappy and the pickets block the workmen? Carmody wondered. The Chinese undoubtedly knew the marchers were outside St. Malachy's. But these men had come here informed and prepared. Yet they never asked about the pickets. Why? There could be only one reason . . . they already knew the answer.

Monsignor Brady, who had met with the Wus and Mamma X at the Evergreen Club, had secreted himself in his office all afternoon and had not been seen or heard from most of the day.

Carmody told Wu father and son that he would phone

Father Conlon and felt certain the pastor would approve of the workmen. K.C. Wu tugged at his son's arm, the two conversed briefly in Shanghai dialect and young Wu addressed the cardinal:

"Excuse us, please, Your Holiness. My father has a final thought. Perhaps we can offer you total assurance. If you would be so kind as to put us in contact with the new landowners we would formalize any needed legal assurances with them. This should relieve you of the slightest concern about any deadline liabilities. We will formally assume full responsibility with both of you, if that would reassure you."

The Wus already knew, of course, about the new landowner. Monsignor Brady had briefed them at their Evergreen Club lunch. The Wus were determined, however, to protect the secretary. They knew Brady respected the cardinal, but his conscience would not allow him to be a party to demolishing St. Malachy's.

Carmody now added up the financial and social ledger. First, he would receive one hundred thousand dollars where he had expected only archdiocesan expense. The chancery office would receive sufficient money each month to cover the parish deficit, signed and sealed. Next, he would finally shut up Cappy and those crazies on the parish council by giving them back their church and making Bridie's mission meaningless instead of an eventual embarrassment. True, St. Malachy's would be sitting somewhere out there in Chinatown but it would have reputable sponsors who wouldn't want it to drown somewhere in Lake Michigan. This was a seven-course Chinese dinner. His fortune cookie had become Chinese Precious Pudding. He could not refuse.

"You may contact Mr. J.R. Wiggins, chairman of the board and president of Midwest Oil & Gas. They bought the land and have an office in the Tribune Tower building. My secretary has their phone number. Midwest will be putting up its new headquarters at Ninth and Wabash. Of course, this is told you in confidence."

Mr. Wu and his son thanked the cardinal. They would phone him with developments in a few days. L.Y. handed Carmody the family business card and said the cardinal was free to contact them at any time. The Chinese obtained Wiggins's phone number from Mrs. Koslowski, thanked her and smiled at Carmody, who stood at his office door.

As father and son descended alone in the elevator shortly after 5:00 P.M., the son inquired, "Tell me, Father, what is the lesson that the family should learn from your meeting with the cardinal?"

The old man replied, "Wise is the dragon that would disguise itself in the form of a small fish."

"Would you explain that so I may tell my children someday in your own words?" L.Y. asked, knowing his father was waiting for the question.

K.C. began his answer as his son began to drive away in their fourteen-year-old Ford. "If there is dissension in the royal court, there must be a reason. Instead of seeking and remedying the cause, the unwise ruler tries to overcome the opposition with threats and perhaps even force. Since the beginnings of our history, unkind words and force have never suppressed the people.

"However, the rulers never seem to learn. Look at the tragic effects of Mao and his followers. Yet the people and China flow on like the Yangtze River. In all things one must never depend on threat or force. They are contrary to the nature of man and society. Even if change takes centuries, as it sometimes has in China, nature and reason will prevail. People will never be convinced by power—either by order or by the gun. The answer must be reason.

"In peasant terms, my son, ease the reins, feed the horse, wait patiently until the light of day and then proceed on the journey with a good map and prudent judgment. Speak well to all travelers along the road. Do not forget to water the horse at intervals. Do not tell those you meet that you are a king. Be their humble servant. Offer some of your food if they are hungry. Someday you may return on that road with the same horse. You may need those you befriend. Your horse also will not forget.

"You will then have become what our ancestors spoke of thousands of years ago, long before Mao, *the fish in the stream.* It is the fish that have fashioned and held together Chinese culture and history."

They drove south in the frenzied rush-hour traffic. The chaos swelled and spilled as cars turned in different directions. Rain splashed against the windshield as the Wus swam slowly in the river of traffic toward home, two humble fish in the stream.

Chapter 14

THE DANCING ANGEL

It was about nine-fifteen in the morning. Red Corrigan manned the assignment desk at WDDM-TV News. The phone rang and he picked up on Line Two.

"I got a hot one for you, Red."

Corrigan asked, "Who's this?"

"Phil Esposito," the patrolman barked.

"Oh," Corrigan recalled. Over in the First District. "You got a tip, Phil?"

"Yeah, and it's worth at least fifty bucks."

"We always pay, Phil, you know that. What's up?"

"Damndest thing. About two dozen Chinese are swinging from ropes all over St. Malachy's roof. The pickets let 'em pass. They dancing on ropes inside, too. They're everywhere."

"You drunk, Esposito?"

"Listen, you jerk, get your ass over here to Ninth and Wabash. You won't have to pay. I'll gladly kick the fifty bucks out of it. This is the last time I'll ever call you. From now on, it's WMAX."

Esposito hung up. Corrigan couldn't hesitate. This was a street-smart cop. This was also a dull news day. The newscasts needed something colorful. Besides, Claudia Lally and the *Herald* as well as the *News-Times* had taken TV and radio news to the cleaners on this story. That Lally never slept, and the *News-Times* must have bought the same alarm clock. Corrigan grabbed the intercom to Chuck Decker, who was in charge of Mobile Unit One, a TV studio on wheels. Corrigan briefly explained the story, told Decker to rush the crew over to St. Malachy's and start shooting.

Corrigan reached Skip Powers, a reporter, not the usual TV pretty boy with coiffed hair. In his late forties and two hundred pounds, he had come to television after fifteen years as a reporter on the *News-Times.* Powers thought cops were fleas.

Powers arrived before the mobile unit. It was a Chinese circus. The workmen had strung ropes from the church roof to nearby telephone poles, lampposts, fireplugs. They were acrobats swinging from one section of the roof to another, running measuring tapes in six different directions. Powers yelled to cameraman Zeke Klose to get it all. He spotted Cappy coming out the side door of the rectory; he recognized the pastor from his appearances at Loop crime and accident scenes and edged him against a wall.

"What's going on, Father?" Powers shoved his microphone into the pastor's face.

"You've heard of Chinese ropedancing?"

Powers had no time for Irish humor. "Please, Father, I'm in a hurry."

Cappy pointed to two Chinese hanging astride a wall of the church, assembling and reassembling figures with their arms and hands: "That's great *Tai Chi.*"

"What's that?"

"Some call it Chinese shadowboxing. They say it's good for the mind and body."

Powers wasn't charmed by this. The pastor talked in riddles like the Chinese. Suddenly he spotted Esposito on the street corner and went over to the patrolman. Esposito, still smarting from Corrigan's earlier put-down, gave him his don't-know-from-nuthin' look, until Powers ate crow and signed an extra fifty-dollar IOU. Then Esposito told him, interview-style, that the Chinese had explained to the pastor that "instead of seeing this old landmark demolished they're going to move it brick by brick and window by window to Chinatown. I happened to be standing nearby when their honcho said it."

"Where would they move it?"

"Near 22nd and Wentworth."

"Why won't the archdiocese save St. Malachy's?"

"Sonny, ask the cardinal."

Meanwhile the cardinal had sent Monsignor Brady to the work scene. Father Pat Brogan, the retired Jesuit professor at Loyola, had already arrived and was standing on the sidewalk watching the Chinese. It was a delicate moment for Carmody's secretary since the cardinal considered Brogan a wild-eyed liberation theology professor. The Jesuit also was a member of St. Malachy's parish council.

Brady took a chance, walked over to Brogan, put his right hand on the Jesuit's shoulder and stuck out his left. The irony of a leftie handshake wasn't lost on either, and both men burst into laughter.

It was now 10:45 A.M. and the scene had become an outdoor theater. Scores of bystanders crowded the sidewalk, gawking at the ropedancing Chinese.

Brogan kidded Brady, "My dear Monsignor, if the structure is so unsound, how can two dozen Chinese skip all across the roof?"

Brady was not about to be cornered. "It's a miracle, Pat! We're asking the Vatican to confirm it . . . By the way, I've thought a lot about Cappy these days. How is he?"

"He lives, bless him, in a world of mercy," Brogan said. "His watchword is forgiveness. He's always saying St. Malachy's is in the hands of God, the future's in the will of God. Can't argue with that." Brogan paused and sounded like the retired professor that he was. "Remember the saying of the old grammar school nuns? 'It's not just the act but the motive.' Sometimes motivation is more important than act."

Brady knew the meeting with Brogan would come to Brogan's lament about the priesthood's retreat from modern issues. A street corner suited Brogan fine. Why didn't the hierarchy and priests preach about birth control? Divorce? Individual conscience? Women and married priests? Church authority? The list was the proverbial mile long. Actually Brady agreed with some of what Brogan thought. The secretary was convinced, though, that many of the Jesuit's views often had unintended but serious consequences.

Brogan said something familiar to Brady. He'd used it himself in his own way. "I remember when Catholics described the differences in the Church as an angel dancing on the head of a pin. Now the angel is dancing on the tip of a flaming candle. In a generation or so Catholic congregations are going to become more like Protestants. No, Tom, I don't really believe American Catholics will abandon the pope and the Vatican or break with a less powerful U.S. hierarchy. They'll just agree to disagree. We'll have an open schism but one Church. In a less dramatic way that's what we have today."

"Pat," Brady said, "could it be that the cardinal is the

one who's living reality? Not trendy reality but plain reality. This isn't the first time the Church has been in trouble. We've had a lot of bad priests, corrupt cardinals and popes mired in their own pride and power. Rome wasn't built in a day, and the Church can't be *rebuilt* in a decade. Catholics aren't necessarily making revolutionary speeches against Vatican teaching. They're going their own way, in many cases the American way, and waiting for a new pope or time itself to change the Church. I believe that's where Carmody's coming from. He's battening down the hatches on a ship in a storm. Forgive the corny metaphor."

The Jesuit gave him a specific. "The best solution to abortion is birth control."

Brady shook his head and mockingly gave Brogan his blessing.

This time it was the Jesuit who put his hand on a shoulder.

"Tom, I don't know who'll be proved right. But I do know what I believe. Maybe in the end Carmody will have understood better than any of us. The Church and the cathedrals will stand majestic like they once did. The hierarchy and priesthood will restore their integrity. And all that we, the loyal opposition, will have created will be a patch of wildflowers. Not a monument or even a marker. Just a patch of wildflowers somewhere on a hillside in Arizona, or Utah, or Montana." He smiled. "End of speech."

The Chinese on the roof began descending to the ground on their ropes. A truck had pulled up to the curb and two women descended a ladder. They set up a table on the sidewalk and proceeded to take pots, pans, wooden bowls, plates and trays from a third woman still standing on the truck. It was like a military chow line. The Chinese lined up in short order, and the food was served on trays—hot and sour soup, mixed vegetables and chopped pork, chicken or beef. Hot tea and cookies were set on the side. Each worker had plastic packets of soy sauce, mustard, sweet sauce, a wooden spoon and chopsticks on his tray. The men paired off and sat against the wall of the structure as they ate lunch. They spoke in Chinese but in different dialects.

As the priest watched the Chinese settle down to lunch, Brogan said, "I'll tell you one thing, Tom. We liberals in the Church aren't making any big advances. I think I'm losing hope, Tom."

"The cardinal often says," Brady put in, "that the greatest horror of hell is no hope."

"How do you keep up your hope?" Brogan asked the secretary.

Brady answered: "I say the Beatitudes a lot . . . 'Blessed are the poor in spirit, for theirs is the kingdom of heaven. Blessed are the meek, for they shall possess the earth. Blessed are they who mourn, for they shall be comforted . . .' "

"Okay, okay, I surrender," Brogan said, smiling.

The Chinese were climbing their ropes now to resume work. Brady turned to Brogan. "Forgive the sermon, Pat, but I believe the greatest pain for good people, Catholic and non-Catholic, is to know God and not be able or willing to follow His message. That's why Cappy is great. He's understood the two secrets of Christianity—sacrifice and acceptance of God's will."

Brogan looked at him. "You're saying the cardinal and Cappy may represent the spiritual giants among us, different but good men with opposing views?"

"Maybe. And both have climbed to the mountaintop." He pointed to the Chinese on the church roof. "That's where Cappy and the cardinal are. Up there, Pat. Jousting for the soul of the Church."

Chapter 15

A HANDSHAKE

F.X. Wiggins, chairman of the board and president of Midwest Oil & Gas, didn't resemble the conventional image of a wildcatter. With soft white hair, rimless spectacles, starched white collar and narrow navy blue tie he looked more like a country preacher. Indeed, he grew up on a ranch outside Golden, Colorado, where, some forty years before, he was graduated magna cum laude in petroleum engineering from the Colorado School of Mines.

Golden, set in the foothills of the Rocky Mountains, had remained a sleepy town except for the presence of a brewing company. It enjoyed clean mountain air and spring water. Which were the reasons why F.X. and his wife Birdie returned to his family spread of a thousand acres every year for a two-week vacation. Birdie, originally Blanche, not surprisingly loved birds. Wiggins, who rejected any pretense of being an oil tycoon, liked long mountain hikes. He enjoyed studying Colorado's geological formations that climbed from the foothills to fourteen-thousand-foot peaks. Birdie, through her ever-present binoculars, searched for mountain bird sanctuaries. The two measured life by the feel of earth in their hands. Midwest Oil & Gas was Wiggins's big gusher. He earned more than $180 million in wildcat drilling across West Texas before purchasing the majority shares in Midwest some twenty years earlier.

K.C. Wu and his son L.Y. sat on the dark blue couch in Wiggins's office. A gray morning sky filtered through the windows. Wiggins sat a few feet away, facing them in a straight-back old-fashioned wooden chair. The oil executive needed the chair because he had a bad back from years of fieldwork. The Chinese stirred the fresh lemon in the tea that Wiggins had offered them on arrival.

L.Y., apologizing for his father's humble English, said he would translate the conversation for the elder Wu. He explained the family was about to purchase the structure of St. Malachy's church. The son repeated the proposal his father had made to Cardinal Carmody. They would move the church to Chinatown at their expense in loving memory of Mary C. Wu, the Roman Catholic wife and mother of the Wu family, who had passed away. The Wus would compensate the archdiocese for the structure and pay any future operating deficits. The purpose of their visit was to allay the cardinal's concerns that Midwest might hold the archdiocese legally liable if the church land were not cleared by August 31. The elder Wu was willing to sign a statement relieving the archdiocese of that obligation. He was also prepared to discuss any pertinent subject that Wiggins might wish to raise.

Wiggins rose, walked to his Tribune Tower office window and looked out on the Loop, then returned to his seat and disarmed the two:

"I'm a modest collector of Chinese art. It's not often that Chinese express interest in Western art, particularly religious."

K.C. Wu spoke quickly to his son in dialect and L.Y. translated. "My father humbly begs your indulgence on the subject of art. We appreciate Western art but ours depends on intimate symbolism. A symbolism is much more intricate. It involves capturing a sense of infinity not only in space and form but also in color. It is needed to fully relate man's creations to nature's surroundings. You are correct, Mr. Wiggins. We are attempting to combine Western and Chinese art and that is difficult. However, Mary C. Wu was a work of both arts. If I may go on a bit . . . some of the most remarkable examples of Chinese symbolism are the mausoleums within the enclosures of the great imperial tombs in Beijing. Mountain peaks, for example, guard the Ming tombs. These include many allusions to infinity and the Absolute in the form of historic events. We feel much wisdom is expressed in the delicate overtones of these works. So, too, is the art of the West, including religious works. We also are aware of Michelangelo, Raphael and more recent Italian masters who have created the art in your churches."

Wiggins nodded politely, waited for Wu to get to it.

"Mr. Wiggins, our removal of St. Malachy's church is a symbolic art with delicate overtones. It's an intimate family gesture. It is, so to speak, the moving of a mountain to guard a family ancestor, Mary C. Wu. It is the act born of respect and gratitude to both East and West. Chinese believe that in judging any work of art the view of one man will never contain the entire truth. The complexity, richness and symbolism of much Chinese art require the expertise of many individuals."

Wiggins smiled, understanding the unhurried delicacy of Chinese personal diplomacy. They were relieving him of the burden of a hasty response by talking around the business of the meeting. Wiggins, adjusting his spectacles, finally moved to assure the father and son:

"I'm in a position to respond to your proposal but I didn't want to interrupt your presentation. I don't often deal with Chinese businessmen, so excuse me if I react slowly to what you say. I want to be real sure about what you mean."

The oil man noted the puzzled expressions of the Chinese. Both indicated they didn't quite understand what he meant. They were doing business by American rules. It seemed to them as simple as that, but not to Wiggins.

"Many Americans believe your thinking is different than ours," Wiggins said. "So we're kind of cautious. You build houses with roofs that don't sit on walls. Compasses point south instead of north. You read your books from the back end. You write from the right in lines running perpendicular instead of horizontal. Your words of one syllable often take up as much room as longer words. Your coffin and grave clothes are prepared right after marriage. Differences like that can cause confusion and misunderstandings if we're not careful."

K.C. spoke quickly to his son and L.Y. translated his father's labyrinthine reasoning. "My father says you are correct. We consider ourselves normal American businessmen but often think and act according to our ancient traditions and customs. This can cause confusion. But our ends are much the same as Christians'. Taoism, for example—some call it a Chinese religion—is a search for the Absolute. Tao, however, is really indefinable. It speaks of Higher Virtue, distinguished from Common Virtue that is superficial and outward, not the inner soul. Tao discards the notions of benevolence and kindness on the scale of human measurement. Higher Virtue loses itself in the Absolute, to become good for the sake of goodness itself. If you think about it, Taoism is not so different from Western religions. We seek good, but because of our distinctions Americans think our business practices may be different."

The Chinese exchanged glances and the father motioned that his son come closer. K.C. whispered, the son nodded. L.Y. measured Wiggins carefully.

"May my father make an inquiry of you?"

Wiggins shifted in his chair but nodded. L.Y. asked, "Were you named after St. Francis Xavier?"

"Yes, my mother was a Catholic. However, I'm not."

"The question was not meant to be personal, Mr. Wiggins. My father, who spends most of his spare time reading, has a historian's sympathy for Francis Xavier. He says that in his view what Columbus dreamed, Francis realized. The Jesuit sailed from Europe to bring the Catholic faith to Japan and India. The saint's letters testify that his greatest wish was to bring Christ's gospel to China. Francis Xavier died four hundred years ago on the island of Sancien within sight of the China coast. My father has empathy for a man who undertakes such a long and difficult journey without fulfillment."

Wiggins understood the Wus didn't want to end their journey to his office without fulfillment. It took a lot of introduction to get to the first page.

"Gentlemen," he said, "I'm most sympathetic to your presentation. I believe you're sincere men and your project is a worthy one. In the light of your worthy project it's all the more difficult for me to report the circumstances of my company's position. We voted at a board meeting only two days ago to resell St. Malachy's. The company will keep its offices in this building. We've made a significant oil discovery through exploratory drilling along the shelf of the U.S. Atlantic coast and need all the funds that we can get to develop that lease. We're engaging a commercial real-estate company, and the entire property, including the building, will go on sale again within a few days."

Thunder appropriately, as if on cue, rumbled across the sky. Bursts of lightning flashed between the Loop's skyscrapers. Wiggins lowered his head, not wanting to look at father and son. He glanced at his left hand, once almost crushed in a rig accident.

"What are your considerations of the property's purchase?" K.C. finally asked.

Wiggins said his firm had no plans to demolish St. Malachy's but would do so if requested by a new owner. "The cost of the property is slightly more than what we paid for it, to cover the broker's fee and other closing costs. That would be nearly thirteen million dollars."

Father and son conferred, the exchange low-key but rapid-fire. Wiggins watched in fascination. The father's slightest inflection seemed to intensify L.Y.'s attention. K.C. turned to Wiggins. "Are we correct in assuming that you have not yet engaged a commercial real-estate company?"

Wiggins turned in his chair, picked up his phone and dialed an intraoffice number. "Walter, do we have a real-estate company yet on the church?"

Wiggins paused momentarily, then hung up. "No, but we expect to hire a firm this afternoon or tomorrow."

L.Y. said immediately, "My father now extends to you an offer to purchase the entire property for twelve million dollars. You would not need to pay a broker's fee and the two parties would share the usual closing costs. We are prepared to sign a contract to that effect—five million dollars down and the balance to be paid on August thirty-first. If that is acceptable we would ask you to draw up a contract."

L.Y. handed Wiggins his father's business card and said K.C. would sign the contract and make the first payment when Midwest completed the agreement. The speed of the Chinese stunned Wiggins. Pretty damn good, he said to himself, and nodded okay.

K.C. spoke for the first time: "It's old American custom. Handshake seals deal."

Wiggins roared with laughter. The two shook hands. K.C. said, "Deal final, yes?"

"Yes," Wiggins said. "For all practical purposes you own St. Malachy's—roof, altar and land. By the way, it's All Souls' Day."

Wiggins phoned two associates and told them St. Malachy's had been purchased, the company was to draw up a contract for the sale. The three shook hands again and Wiggins said, "Neither God nor the Absolute can change our handshake."

Everyone liked that.

Wiggins paused briefly. "Mr. Wu, if you'd allow me a personal note . . . I just wish it had been my pleasure to know your wife."

The two Chinese looked away and said nothing. What they were thinking, Wiggins could only guess as they shook hands again and the Chinese departed.

It was 1:00 P.M. when father and son Wu got in their car to drive home, and Claudia Lally was lifting a glass of red wine at a Jewish delicatessen near Wabash and Harrison streets.

"To the obstinate, indomitable Irish."

Cappy said, lifting a red wine, "I'll drink to that."

Lally said, "So you'll marry Arthur and me."

"If St. Malachy's is standing, I will," Cappy said. "But I'd like you to come to all the marriage-encounter sessions for the rest of this session. Three months or so."

"Done," Lally said, and they clinked glasses.

Cappy munched on a corned beef and rye, Lally on a lox, cream cheese, red onion and bagel sandwich. Izzy Weinstein blessed them with a smile and said from behind his counter: "Cappy's always munching. That's why I call him a munchkin."

Lally laughed politely and said to the pastor, "You're not afraid of Carmody?"

"You'll be registered as married in St. Malachy's church," Cappy said. "The only question is, why did it take you so long to become an honest woman?"

Lally smiled, said nothing.

"You're buying, I hope. I'm broke," Cappy said.

"I know that." Lally peered over the brown rims of her enormous sunglasses, which covered most of her face. "Consider it money I put in your poor box. Do you have more than two nickels in your pocket?"

Cappy stuck a hand in a pants pocket. "Not one."

Shouts from peddlers shoving their pushcarts toward Maxwell and Halsted streets pierced the deli. Two vendors shouted at one another in Yiddish. The smell of cooking cabbage steamed into the deli from a portable hot-lunch stand. In an apartment upstairs, someone played frenzied Hungarian gypsy music on a violin that wafted along the crowded street and carried into the sky. The sun had peeked through clouds about an hour before.

Cappy loved the old Maxwell Street, a great mélange of street counters and merchandise that ran west from Halsted. It reminded him of his early days at St. Malachy's. The neighborhood had been a melting pot of merchants—mostly Jews at first, and later Hispanics, blacks, Puerto Ricans, Koreans and a few Arkansas hillbillies. Seller and merchandise were suspect—from electric appliances and radios to auto fixtures, jewelry, shoes, socks, pants, bedspreads, a painting of an African Jesus, and a punch in the nose if you were looking for it. Some of the stuff was so hot the labels had peeled off.

Maxwell Street now made Cappy sad. The ethnic bazaar, long a Chicago landmark like St. Malachy's, had lost its battle to survive—except as a shell. Much of the old store area was gone, and the rest was being torn down to make way for additions to the Chicago campus of the University of Illinois.

Max Friedman entered the deli. The seventy-seven-year-old salesman was a Loop street fixture. Max had closed his clothing store on Maxwell Street seven years before, but his adrenalin seemed to flow only when he was selling—selling anything. So his rabbi told him to sell the books of the Talmud and Old Testament along Maxwell. Max was a practical man. He also stored bibles in his cart.

He put an Old Testament in Lally's hands now, saying, "I know Cappy prefers the New Testament. No sale there. But you could be a nice Jewish girl. Make me an offer."

The reporter laughed and riffled the pages, then handed the Old Testament back to Friedman.

"You missed the Book of Kings," Max said, and began to read from Kings, a strangely comforting recital amid the babble surrounding them:

> *And it came to pass . . . that Solomon began to build a house to the Lord.*
>
> *And the house which King Solomon built to the Lord was three seven cubits in length, and twenty cubits in breadth, and thirty cubits in height.*
>
> *And the house when it was in building, was built of stones hewed and made ready, that there was neither hammer nor axe nor any tool iron heard in the house while it was in building.*
>
> *So he built the house and finished it, and he covered the house with roofs of cedar.*
>
> *And the word of the Lord came to Solomon saying:*
>
> *This house, which thou buildest if thou wilt walk in my statutes and execute my judgments, and keep all my commandments, walking in them, I will fulfill my word to thee . . .*

Cappy looked up when Friedman had finished. "I think I know the question. Have I walked in the Lord's way, and will He fulfill the wishes of St. Malachy's?"

"You might put it that way," Lally said.

Friedman, who was acquainted with the church's troubles along with most other Chicagoans, told Cappy he had made the Kings' selection for him. He said good-bye to the two, walked outside, put the Old Testament on top of the other books in his cart and slowly pushed his cart along the street again.

Cappy then quoted, "Also from the Old Testament . . . *'The stone rejected by the builders has become the cornerstone . . .'* Or words to that effect. Memory fades, girl."

"Is St. Malachy's going to win, Cap?"

Unaware of the Wiggins-Wu agreement, the pastor said, "I've never lost faith, my dear." Cappy lifted his glass of white wine. "Christ spoke to his apostles of new wine that referred to the Beatific Vision. In our preoccupation with this world, we mustn't lose sight of our ultimate vision. If He doesn't answer me here He'll reply in His house."

Lally scolded Cappy. "You're talking in parables, Cap."

"Maybe. Let me mention a modern parable. Father Damien went to the island of Molokai off Hawaii to work among the lepers. He was a healthy man who labored there for many years. Then, one morning at Mass, Damien began his sermon with these words . . . 'We lepers . . .' Did he fail?" Cappy bit out each word.

Lally was silent, then finally asked, "Why do the Irish put so many things in terms of tragedy?"

"Not always, girl."

"Yes, you do."

"Not at all. My favorite quotation from Christ is 'I have loved you with an everlasting love . . .'"

Lally pressed, "Instead of Damien why not say 'Lord, that I may see'?"

"We do: 'Thy will be done . . .' or 'Thy sins are forgiven thee. Go and sin no more.' "

Claudia caught the tab and left a twenty-dollar bill on the table. "What'll I do with the marriage certificate from Las Vegas?" she asked.

"I'd frame it," the priest said, and smiled. "Right next to the one we're going to give you from St. Malachy's."

The two shook hands with Izzy, who said to Lally, "Come back. I got the lox. You got the looks."

Lally asked if she could drive Cappy anywhere but the pastor said he would walk. She kissed Cappy on the cheek and disappeared into a parking garage. Cappy hit the pavement north on Wabash.

Raucous laughter belched from the doorway of a crowded saloon. A white-haired man lay in the gutter and the priest tried to wake him. It was no use. Cappy walked to the police call box, pulled out the master key given him by Joe Rossi. A desk man answered:

"Hello, Wittenberger, this is Cappy. There's a poor old fellow in the gutter down here near Harrison and Wabash. Would you have him picked up before he rolls under the traffic?"

"What the hell are you doing there, Cap?" the sergeant asked.

"Herman, I'm buying myself one o' them fancy summer straw hats like the one your grandfather used to wear during Oktoberfest in the German beer halls."

Wittenberger said, "If the officers in the paddy wagon see you down there they're going to give you a free ride back here. I want to take a picture of you in cuffs and send it to the cardinal for the *Catholic World.*"

Both laughed and hung up.

First, Cappy would stop off to say a word or two to Jim Duffy at his law office on South Wabash near Madison. Duffy's wife had been ill. Next, over to LaSalle Street to see Rodney Williams, the investment banker, whose son had been hospitalized from a drug overdose. Over to the Blackstone Theater on East Balbo to see Digs Dorfman, the ticket-seller whose mother had gone to Lourdes in hopes of curing her arthritis. The stops seemed endless. Cappy walked more quickly and laughed to himself as he recalled a line attributed to Dick Daley in the sixties: "I love Chicago. You can't beat city living!" Cappy agreed.

The Loop was Cappy's city. State and Madison was its intersection. The compass never extended farther than two miles in any direction. As the pope blessed Rome and the world *"Urbi et Orbi,"* he had a special absolution for downtown Chicago. At least Cappy thought so. The Loop had, in fact, turned upside down. Parts had become tawdry despite its skyscrapers, meaner and, worse, dangerous.

In the distance now Cappy could see a crowd at Van Buren and Wabash where the elevated trains turned in their circle of the Loop. Police appeared to be pushing everyone south toward him and across to the west side of Wabash. The priest, sensing trouble, began to trot toward the commotion. He could hear the police shouting at people clogging the sidewalks and streets to move back.

Cappy edged through the bystanders and saw Lieutenant Oscar Vasilov.

"Oscar, what's up?"

The lieutenant said, "A young Hispanic. Mexican or Puerto Rican. He stuck up Manny's liquor store. He shot Manny. The kid's got a .45."

"Is Manny still alive in the store?"

"Yeah, we think so. But he could bleed to death. We already tried to rush the kid. He shot Bill Nichols and Brad

Wilhelm. They've been taken away by ambulance. We got another ambulance standing by. The kid's in the doorway next to the liquor store. We can't get a good shot at him."

Cappy's mind was racing. How long could Manny last without medical help? If the kid was Spanish, was he a Catholic? He might listen to a priest.

Cappy stood and began to walk across Wabash toward the doorway. Vasilov saw it was too late to stop him. The kid would soon see him, his Roman collar and black clothes. Cappy kept walking. The youth momentarily stuck his head out the doorway. The .45 was cocked in his right hand.

Cappy stopped some ten feet from the doorway. "I'm a priest. Do you speak English?"

The young man didn't reply so Cappy repeated the question. After some thirty interminable seconds the young Hispanic said, *"Un poco."*

SWAT team sharpshooters looked on from the roofs of nearby buildings. They were ordered not to fire until Cappy backed off and was safely away from the doorway.

Ten minutes passed. It was obvious to everyone that the pastor and thief were talking. After nearly twenty minutes of cajoling, the end came abruptly.

Cappy said, "You haven't killed anyone, son. Surrender. You'll have to go to jail but you can go home someday. Do you want to go home?"

The young Hispanic looked at Cappy like he was seeing an apparition . . . was this guy for real? . . . then abruptly threw his gun out toward Cappy, raised his hands and walked out onto the street. Police rushed him, pinned him to the ground and cuffed him, then put him into a squad car and sped away. Medics ran into the liquor store and found Manny shot in the right shoulder. They patched him, then took the liquor-store owner to the hospital.

Cappy lifted a flask from his hip pocket and took a long,

slow pull of Scotch, returned the flask to his hip pocket and said to Vasilov, "His name's Juan Torres, a Mexican, seventeen years old, from Cuernavaca, an illegal, eldest of nine kids, no job, no record in Mexico, his first stickup."

"Where did he get the gun?" Vasilov asked.

"From a friend," Cappy replied. "He said one thing over and over again. He wants to go home."

Vasilov's portable radio crackled. The report from the hospital said the two wounded officers would recover. So would Manny.

"Let's go home, Cappy," Vasilov said, taking the priest by the arm. "I'll give you a lift."

The two walked to the lieutenant's car. Cappy hesitated, then began walking away.

"Aren't you going home, Cap?"

The priest kept moving along, looking up at the Loop's tall buildings, and replied, "I am home."

Chapter 16

THE BELLS TOLL

The meeting of St. Malachy's parish council buzzed with excitement. Bridie O'Brien had just concluded her report—the church would be placed on Washington's National Register of Historic Places on December 5 and declared a historic landmark by both the city and state on December 8, Feast of the Immaculate Conception.

Bridie, her excitement enhanced by a pop or two, said, "It's three strikes on the archdiocese—national, city and state landmark designations!"

Cappy stood, asked the assembled to rise and recited an informal prayer of thanksgiving:

"Thank You, Lord. Forgive me for my wobbly, wishy-washy faith. It was human weakness. I give thanks not only to You but these devoted friends who have stayed strong at my side. We thank you with all our hearts."

The Reverend Braithwaite turned the meeting over to Rabbi Goldman. No one on the council knew about Goldie's announcement except the rabbi and Mr. Wu.

Goldie was about to make a stunning revelation when Beau Beauchamps called Alderman Fahey to the phone. "It's an emergency," Beau said. Kitty, the rectory housekeeper, had transferred the call to the phone extension in the rear of the basement near Beau's room. The rabbi sat down to wait for Fahey's return.

The alderman's reddish skin was ashen when he returned to face the council. He couldn't speak. He took a deep breath and finally got some control of himself . . .

"Members of the council . . . I've just been informed that Cardinal Carmody passed away . . . a heart attack . . . at his residence at about seven this evening, thirty minutes ago. That was a friend of mine on the phone, Dr. Robert Barrett, the cardinal's physician. He arrived a few moments after His Eminence closed the books. There's no doubt about it . . . the cardinal is dead."

As Fahey slumped into his seat, Cappy stood up and so did everyone else as the pastor said the Act of Contrition for the cardinal's soul:

"O, my God, I am heartily sorry for having offended Thee, and I detest all my sins because I dread the loss of heaven and the pains of hell; but most of all because they offend Thee my God Who art all good and deserving of all my love. I firmly resolve with the help of Thy grace to confess my sins, do penance, and amend my life." The council followed with "Amen."

Cappy paused, then solemnly recited three times, "My Jesus, mercy." Each time, the council repeated it. Cappy looked around the room and said, "The fact that we prayed the Act of Contrition and asked for mercy is no reflection on the cardinal. I'm used to the old ways, I don't put a halo on death, and it's hard to change. I believe His Eminence has joined his Maker."

He turned to Beau. "Beau, may we ring the bells in mourning for the next fifteen minutes."

Beau climbed the stairs to the sacristy and pushed the

red button on the left wall. The bells of St. Malachy's then tolled the cardinal's passing among the concrete canyons of the Loop. Passersby, surprised by the tolling at that hour, stopped and looked, wondering briefly, and continued on their way.

Rabbi Goldman stood and said, "Father Conlon and members of the council, I have the honor to advise you that this council now *owns* St. Malachy's, in addition to it being a landmark, thanks to Bridie."

The members seemed disbelieving. Everyone was silent, no one moved. Cappy seemed stunned. Even the unflappable Mamma X was halted in mid-movement. Rabbi Goldman went on in a calm, precise voice.

"This development has no relation whatever to the cardinal's sudden passing. It occurred before he died. An anonymous donor signed the contract and completed payment a few days ago. The church, the land, all the property has been deeded to us."

John Elixir Babbington leaped dramatically from his chair. Reverend Braithwaite and his wife Eloise did likewise. Boom Boom called out, "Glory be to God! Glory be to God!"

The minister and his wife knelt on the gray-painted concrete floor. Boom Boom's head was bowed but he lifted his hands.

Beau Beauchamps walked over and lifted Cappy from his seat, embracing the pastor. The aging black man and small priest hugged for a long time.

Mamma X embraced everyone. Kathy Dolan raised a clenched fist. "Hallelujah! We won!" Bridie O'Brien grabbed hold of Alderman Fahey by the hand and twirled him. Fahey, totally bewildered, had to sit down. The alderman ordered Thumbs Rafferty to send one hundred and fifty dollars' worth of red roses to the cardinal's residence, and Father Pat Brogan knelt in silent prayer. Evangeline Dolan, who had come with Kathy to the meeting, looked on and shared the pleasure.

Rabbi Goldman now raised his arms; the uproar subsided as he turned the meeting over to Cappy, who spoke in subdued tones:

"The Catholic Church doesn't have, to the best of my knowledge, any allowances for a church being owned by a congregation. There have been numerous lawsuits over this issue but the hierarchy has always prevailed. In this case, however, the Church took the initiative to sell its property. I doubt the chancery office can challenge the council's ownership. We've been engaged in a good cause, but that doesn't make our adversary, the cardinal, any less honorable. He lived by *his* principles. I'm happy about St. Malachy's but have regrets regarding His Eminence. Frankly, I feel some guilt about all this . . . I wonder if I somehow contributed to his passing. The man drove me half-crazy but I loved him as a man struggling like myself. Like you. Like the Church."

The room was silent until Goldie resumed quietly.

"I have a second announcement. Mr. K.C. Wu and his family have provided a grant of a million dollars to the Ogden Park School. Kathy Dolan, the principal, received the check this afternoon. She has decided to rename her school the Mary C. Wu school in honor of Mr. Wu's wife."

The council stood and clapped in honor of Mr. Wu. He also rose and clapped in return. Members of the council shook hands with Mr. Wu, whose stoic face was now wreathed in smiles.

They also congratulated Kathy. The former nun had accepted Mr. Wu's gift and agreed to rename her school only a few minutes before the council met. She still seemed dazed by the gift. Evie immediately agreed to Kathy's offer of a teaching post. Leo Dolan, who had been sitting along the wall with Evie and knew nothing of the grant, embraced his two daughters.

Kathy told her father: "I can now say, Dad, I haven't failed God or you and mom."

Kathy knew it was an experiment, but at least it would be funded. Lay Catholics would direct their own elementary school independent of the hierarchy. With St. Malachy's church, Hales High School and the Mary C. Wu school, the long pastoral domination of bishops and priests over the Catholic faithful was going to be tested for the first time. Would Catholics control the assets of other churches and schools, even universities, in the future? How many? When? By clerical default or their own initiative?

The greatest hidden fear of the Catholic hierarchy in America would come to the fore . . . the laity controlling the assets of the Church. Chicago, well, Catholics were launching what could become the greatest revolution in American Catholicism.

Kitty, the housekeeper, arrived with two large pots of hot coffee and two dozen plastic cups, plus cream, sugar and spoons. The council meeting had been adjourned moments before but the members stayed to talk about the startling developments.

No one, of course, was fooled by Mr. Wu's self-effacing silence. They knew he had purchased the church. But out of respect no one mentioned it to him or his son.

The council finally began to disperse about 10:00 P.M. and Beau turned out the lights after the last stragglers had left the basement. Bridie and Fahey decided to have a night-cap at the Drake Hotel, where Bridie drove the alderman.

Bridie ordered a margarita, Fahey a Jameson's neat with a glass of water. Bridie was coming off a heavy round of cocktails. She had attended a Democratic party benefit but had had to skip dinner. Fahey knew she was feeling no pain but waited to throw his verbal jabs. He loved to irritate the matron . . . maybe it was a sign that the old bachelor was drawn to Bridie. They were, after all, cut from the same cloth. The two proceeded to drink to Mr. Wu and spent at least ten minutes trying to fathom the "mysterious" Chinese. After a second round of drinks, Fahey couldn't resist needling her.

"Bridie, I understand you now wear them pearl-gray Turkish silk drawers embroidered in scarlet."

Bridie gave it right back. "Your ass! And even if I did, I wouldn't have the likes of you lookin' up there." "*Somebody* told me you wear those Geisha-district neon silk shorts, Frank. Aren't you a little old to be going about town like *that?* If you ever lose your pants you'll light up the Loop!"

Both knew they were going to get properly plastered after their fond exchange.

Meantime, Cappy was having a snort of his own. The pastor had just downed a second Scotch at his kitchen table when the phone rang. It was Msgr. Ronald Bertram, the archdiocesan administrator, the most officious member of the late cardinal's staff.

"Good evening, Father Conlon, we've some matters to discuss."

Cappy didn't reply.

"I'm now in charge of the archdiocese, and I have just read His Eminence's last will and testament. During the vacancy period, you will carry out my instructions."

Bertram stopped again, waiting for the pastor's acknowledgment, but got only more silence. The monsignor was irritated.

"Do you understand that, Father?"

"I do," Cappy finally said.

"Well, answer me then."

The pastor startled even himself with the bluntness of his reply. "I've been carrying out orders for over forty years in the priesthood, Monsignor. Those who've given me such orders have, as you know, come and gone."

The administrator, startled, tactfully retreated. "Cappy, I want you to know it has been my duty to read the cardinal's will. It in His Eminence states he wishes his wake and Resurrection Mass to be held at St. Malachy's. You are to make all the arrangements except the burial. The cardinal will be interred alongside his parents at Mount Olivet cemetery. Saturday seems the most likely day for the funeral. A concelebrated Mass of Resurrection, of course. You would say it with the cardinals and bishops in the sanctuary. Would 10:00 A.M. be agreeable?"

Cappy was caught downing a shot, and coughed before replying, "Ten is fine, Monsignor. I'll say the Mass and give the sermon. Father Fortunato will handle the other details."

Bertram did not want to turn the funeral details over to a minor cleric and couldn't hide his annoyance. "You're not going to turn this into a circus, are you, Conlon?"

Both knew he was referring to the pickets who previously marched outside the church.

"Excuse me, Monsignor, but I should tell you that our parish council now owns the church."

Bertram was stupefied at that and slammed his fist on his desk. "By damned, if you and your council own the church. This is the archdiocese of Chicago, not some bongo village in Africa. I'm in charge of the archdiocese. We'll straighten out St. Malachy's as soon as His Eminence is buried."

Cappy repeated, "The *council* now owns everything—the church, the land, the roof, the statues, the pews."

"What do you mean?"

"The archdiocese sold St. Malachy's, monsignor. The chancery office received, rumor has it, twelve million dollars for the place. The deed's now in the parish council's name. In effect, the church belongs to the congregation here at St. Malachy's."

Bertram began to comprehend the rebellious taunt, "Power to the laity." Cappy also recognized the meaning of the moment, yet was a little ashamed of tantalizing the administrator. He knew he should have written Bertram a formal letter about the change of ownership. He screwed the cap tightly on his bottle, bowed his head and prayed: "My Jesus, mercy."

Cappy then called it a night and climbed the stairs to his bedroom. He changed into pajamas and lay on the bed for several minutes, asking God to forgive his gamesmanship. At last the priest fell asleep, saying his rosary, a smile on his face.

Chapter 17

LOVE

Tuesday broke bright and clear over St. Malachy's. Cappy had received acceptances from six pallbearers, two clergy and four laity: Monsignors Brady and Bertram, Police Superintendent Rossi, Leo Dolan, Bill Carmody, the cardinal's brother, and K.C. Wu. Father Brogan smiled and said the choices had all the subtle craft of the Roman Curia and the old Daley machine. The U.S. cardinals were named honorary pallbearers.

All the American cardinals and twenty-six bishops would kneel in the sanctuary. The pallbearers, the cardinal's relatives and St. Malachy's council would occupy the first rows on each side of the aisle. They would be followed by the two U.S. senators and members of the House, the governor, the mayor and their family members, plus the cardinal's immediate staff and other top city and state officials. St. Peter's choir would occupy the church loft. The next announcement came as a shock: the rest of the church's nine hundred seats would be occupied on a first-come, first-served basis. There would be no reserved sections for priests and nuns. The church doors would open at 7:30 A.M., two and one-half hours before the Mass of Resurrection was to begin.

Overflow crowds spilled in and out of the church for most of the two-day wake. The religious, other mourners and the curious lit candles, touched the cardinal's bronze casket and some wept. Claudia Lally and her husband came to kneel and pray.

Saturday dawned cool and gray although August still clung to the city. It was 7:00 A.M. and Cappy was drinking coffee in the rectory kitchen, reading Claudia Lally's front-page commentary in the *Herald*. These paragraphs caught his eye:

> It is particularly fitting, several churchmen explained, that His Eminence chose Old St. Malachy's for his Mass of Resurrection. Chicago's cardinals have always wished that their red hats hang in death from the ceiling of Holy Name Cathedral. Carmody instead chose one of the oldest and most beloved churches in the city for this honor. Perhaps he was telling us all something, namely: he wished to be remembered and loved by the ordinary people of the city.

Cappy put the paper down and walked over to the church. The crowd outside St. Malachy's was already a half-mile long and the doors of the church would not open for a half-hour. The council and pallbearers had assembled in the basement. Everybody was somberly dressed except Mamma X, who wore a blazing red outfit with a red turban.

She told Cappy: "I know everybody's dressed like the undertaker but, Cap, you told me that red was the color of cardinals."

The pastor smiled and said "Mamma, don't worry about it. You're beautiful."

St. Peter's choir was preparing to chant the *Dies Irae,* the Day of Wrath, long gone from church liturgy, since the cardinal had requested it. Beau Beauchamps had been playing Chopin's funeral dirge on the organ for more than five minutes.

Shortly before 10:00 A.M. brother Bill Carmody and family walked past the casket one last time. Rusty Carmody was the last of the family to pass the coffin. Bill Mulberry, the mortician, closed the casket, then moved the gold-white Vatican flag with the keys of the kingdom and the American flag closer to the coffin. Mulberry lit six candles, three on each side of the casket. The candles, banned by Rome, were requested by His Eminence.

At precisely ten o'clock Mulberry asked the pallbearers, who had surrounded the casket, to move it from the front to the vestibule of the church. Cappy, as celebrant of the Mass, and his assistants, Father Fortunato and Monsignor Brady, waited for the coffin.

Draped in liturgical vestments, Cappy intoned, "The grace and peace of God our Father and the Lord Jesus Christ be with you."

The choir and pallbearers replied, "And also with you."

The sky had darkened. More than a hundred police and firemen stood at attention on the sidewalks and streets outside. Another five hundred worshippers stood to their rear and sides. Scores of priests and nuns knelt on the pavement. The Mass was being carried outside via loudspeaker.

WMAX-TV had drawn the straw to televise the Mass live from inside St. Malachy's. The Resurrection service was being fed to all of the city's television stations. Hundreds of thousands of Chicagoans watched as the ancient rites unfolded amid a panoply of religious splendor.

Cappy sprinkled the casket with holy water, saying, "I bless the body of Cardinal Edward Brendan Carmody with this holy water which recalls his baptism of which St. Paul writes: 'All of us who were baptized into Christ Jesus were baptized into His death. By baptism into His death we were buried together with Him, so that just as Christ was raised from the dead by the glory of the Father, we too might live a new life. For if we have been united with Him by likeness to His death, so shall we be united with Him by likeness to His resurrection.' "

The body moved up the center aisle in cadence with the chant of the choir, "I am the bread of life. He who comes to Me shall not hunger; he who believe in Me shall not thirst. No one can come to Me unless the Father draw him . . ."

Hundreds of Loop shoppers halted in front of store TV sets to witness the rites. Chicago mourned particularly because one of its own, not someone imposed from the outside by the Vatican, had passed on to glory.

Father Fortunato announced the first reading from the Book of Wisdom: "The souls of the just are in the hand of God, and no torment shall touch them. They seemed, in the view of the foolish, to be dead; and their passing away was thought an affliction and their going forth from us, utter destruction. But they are at peace. For if before men, indeed, they are punished, yet is their hope full of immortality . . ."

Monsignor Brady read the gospel according to John. He said Jesus had arrived at Bethany and found that Lazarus had already been in the tomb four days. Many people had come to console Martha and Mary over the loss of their brother. On his arrival, Jesus told Martha that Lazarus would rise again.

"I am the Resurrection and the life; whoever believes in Me, though he should die, will come to life; and whoever is alive and believes in Me will never die . . ."

Cappy climbed to the pulpit and began the eulogy. "Most eminent cardinals, excellencies, U.S. senators and representatives of the House, Governor and Mr. Mayor, distinguished city and state officials, the Carmody family, St.

Malachy's council and staff, friends . . . The one great question that Christ asks of each individual is, 'Do you love Me?' He responds on His part, 'I have loved you with an everlasting love.'

"I ask all of you today in the name of Christ: Do you love Me?

"Can you answer that question?

"Do you love me?

"Brendan Carmody answered it many years ago when he began his long scholastic journey to the priesthood.

"He replied at his ordination. He responded in a lifetime of work for the Church. For you, for me, for many.

"He provided us with churches, schools, hospitals and other institutions to nourish and lift up our lives.

"He left us houses in which to learn, hospitals in which to heal and even cemeteries in which we may be buried with decency and a friendly farewell. Brendan Carmody, for all the furor that sometimes accompanied his many difficult decisions" . . . he paused at that . . . "takes nothing with him.

"Each day this man performed his act of love. He took a piece of bread and a goblet of wine and transformed them into the Body and Blood of Christ at Mass. He participated in this ultimate sacrifice, the greatest act of love of all time, and watched in daily pain as Christ surrendered His life for us in blood and agony. He reminded us in the haunting words: 'Do this in memory of Me . . .'

"In all candor I am surprised that we are here at St. Malachy's today. As the Chicago media have told you in their own . . . expressive fashion *(restrained laughter),* the cardinal and I did not always see eye to eye. It was said that St. Malachy's was on the road to joining St. Peter *(more light laughter).* So we must ask ourselves this question to make today understandable and truthful. Why did His Eminence state in his will that he wished to have his Resurrection Mass in St. Malachy's and, so to speak, hang his hat here?

"I knew Brendan Carmody most of his life. Perhaps I can shed light on his motivation as we remember him today. He acted as he saw it for the good of the archdiocese, not for himself or public plaudits but for all of us. I think he chose St. Malachy's in death because he was unable to embrace it in life. In the cardinal's judgment his other responsibilities precluded that. He knowingly brought down public wrath on his own head. He made his own decisions, stuck by them and accepted the consequences. His reaction wasn't always with quiet jubilation *(mild laughter),* but always with a degree of good grace. He never publicly complained. And that's more than I can say for some of our more distinguished Chicagoans.

"I think the death of this cardinal comes at a critical time for the Catholic Church. The Church that many of us have known is changing—mightily, may I say. The young among us are swept up in that change. Tides of innovation and diversity are transforming the Church before our eyes. The new generation doesn't always see and appreciate much of the past.

"Where are we going? No one should profess to know the answer to that question. The cardinal is gone and need not reply. You and I are left to respond. Perhaps there's one reason for hope . . .

"*Love* is the basis for all religious belief, not just Catholic, but our Protestant, Jewish, Muslim, Buddhist and other brethren. Jesus Christ offered us infinite love. Love is a decision, a dedicated way of life. That's why He asks, 'Do you love Me?'

"Love, I believe, was the cardinal's ultimate motive.

"Yet, dear friends, no man or woman can live without forgiveness. Today, in the name of the people of Chicago, I ask God to have mercy on the cardinal and to pardon all our sins.

"Let us pray that, in begging His forgiveness, we will answer the question which Christ asks of each one of us: 'Do you love Me?' "

The Mass continued with the consecration of bread and wine. Most of the congregation went to Holy Communion. The choir sang *Panis Angelicus* as the angelic bread was distributed. Church bells pealed across Chicago and its suburbs. Cappy asked that Monsignor Brady, the cardinal's secretary, accompany the body to Mount Olivet cemetery, bless the gravesite and then commend the cardinal's body "to the earth from which it was made."

The church emptied. Leo Dolan met Matt Moran in the vestibule and the two detectives walked south on Wabash without exchanging a word. Leo lit his pipe, and Moran finally asked:

"Are you going back to Ireland, Leo?"

"Yes," Dolan said, "when I retire. The kids will visit us."

"When will you retire?"

"Next April."

"Why do you want to go, Leo? Chicago is your home now."

"No, it's not. There's too much pain in the Church here."

"Why do you say that, Leo?"

"Because, as Cappy said, Christ is asking Chicago 'Do you love Me?' Instead the priests, nuns and laity spend too much of their time arguing about what they believe. Other Catholics keep quiet about all this fighting. I think they . . . we . . . are confused and upset about all the conflicts in the Church. So we say nothing.

"Cappy, by God, was right, Matt. Only love can save the Church, and there's too little of it to go around."

EPILOGUE

On Christmas Eve, 1994, Evie Dolan gave birth to a six-pound, seven-ounce son named Michael J. Dolan Jr. Evie's brother Michael and his wife Lucy were completing the adoption papers and took the baby home with them when Evie left St. Bernard's Hospital.

Evie's decision was heartbreaking. She had long weeping bouts during the last three months of her pregnancy. She thought that if it weren't for the elder Dr. Feldman's kindness and professional experience in dealing with such cases she would probably have collapsed and might have lost the child.

The physician's months of care and advice moved Evie to focus on the future—whether she could give the child the time, care or opportunities that her brother and his wife offered. She wasn't able to make her final decision until a week before the baby was born. At Evie's request her brother Dan drew up an agreement in which the new parents promised to raise Michael Jr. a Catholic. Evie was guaranteed monthly visitation rights although Michael Jr. was not to be told she was his mother until he was twenty-one. At Evie's request the boy would also be told the name of his father at that time. By then he could deal with the reality of Rusty.

Evie began teaching at the Ogden Park Elementary School in mid-January, although her parents and family were worried about her health. They needn't have. She was stronger than they had ever imagined. Ogden Park became the Mary C. Wu School in September of 1995, with Kathy continuing as the principal.

Earlier, in May of 1995, Evie met a Donald Mackay, a bright young electrical engineer from Chicago's Beverly Hills. They dated for seven months, and time, as it usually did, healed the scar left by Rusty Carmody. Evie fell in love and married Mackay in November at St. Malachy's, the ceremony performed by Father Cappy Conlon. The reception, held in Leo and Nora's home, was an Irish blast.

On January 1, 1995, Cappy Conlon placed a gold-plated plaque in the sanctuary of St. Malachy's. It read: IN LOVING MEMORY OF MARY C. WU. The entire Wu family and two dozen Chinese friends as well as the parish council attended the afternoon ceremony. As the family departed, K.C. handed Cappy a check for ninety thousand dollars to underwrite engineering work that would make St. Malachy's structurally sound again.

In mid-January Claudia Lally of the *Herald* declined Lucy's offer to become executive director of her advertising-public relations firm. Claudia told her thanks but no thanks —the newsroom was in her blood. She did, though, recommend Henrietta R. Corbin of the *News-Times* for the post. Lucy hired Corbin, a veteran editor, but remained chairman of the board and worked part-time.

* * *

Marge Dolan Feldman and her husband David had a party at their home for Kathy and the teachers at the Mary C. Wu School. Many faculty members from Loyola, DePaul, Rosary, the University of Chicago and officials from the Chicago public school system attended. All said they were interested in the laity experiment. Marge had earlier given birth to Leonard Leo Feldman at St. Bernard's. Leonard Sr. said the excitement of a first grandson was better than picking the daily double at Arlington Park. Well, it was a close call . . .

The newspapers announced the engagement of Roger "Rusty" Carmody to one Rita Louise Hightower, the daughter of a wealthy Florida property-development executive. Rusty had not once contacted Evie after their child was born, although he had seen the birth announcement in the papers. Nor did he ever communicate with her about child support. A man who, if nothing else, stayed in character.

Ms. Hightower had been graduated from the University of Florida in liberal arts and had performed for the past two years with local and other amateur theater groups. The bride planned to continue her acting career while the bridegroom would join her father's firm as its legal counsel. They would be wed at the First Congregational Church near the Hightower family home in Naples, Florida, on July 4.

Nora Dolan never accepted or forgot Rusty's treatment of her daughter. She told Leo in her Irish ire: "I wish him not one day of Irish luck."

After ordination Father Bob Dolan was appointed a curate at St. Germaine's parish near Queen of Martyrs and became known among parishioners for his Sunday sermons.

Matt Moran and his wife, who often went to Bob's Mass to hear him preach, said the young priest was a born storyteller. His speaking abilities didn't surprise Leo and Nora. "All Dolans are storytellers," they said.

Bob's rape by Jim Gunth near St. Peter's remained a secret. After ordination the young priest appeared spiritually stronger than he had ever been. However, Bob never forgot the encounter and made the Stations of the Cross when he reminded himself of the incident.

The *News-Times* scooped the *Herald* with the news that Alderman Dan Dolan would run for mayor in the next Democratic primary.

Two weeks later both papers reported that Dr. Leonard Feldman, longtime family practitioner near the University of Chicago, had retired and was moving with his wife to Chino Valley, Arizona, where he had purchased a new home and two thoroughbred racehorses. The horses were named Dr. David and Nurse Marge. They were stabled at the HiYo Silver Ranch.

On Valentine's Day the society columns announced that Alderman Frank Fahey and Chicago socialite Bridget O'Brien had become engaged and would marry in May. In the same editions there were brief stories noting that John Elixir Barrington, onetime Chicago actor, was arrested and jailed for intoxication and creating a public disturbance outside the Blackstone Theater.

On March 5, the business pages carried a brief item reporting that James L. Gunth, a former seminarian at St. Peter's in the Pines, had joined the investment firm of Bookstedder & Redstone as a financial counselor.

On the following day, Father Ralph Rebb stood impeccably dressed in criminal court and pled for forty-five minutes against prison for his third conviction on the molestation of boys. Rebb maintained his priesthood would be so damaged by prison that he might no longer be in a position to save souls. He asked that he be allowed to spend six months to a year at a Catholic "rest home" for priests. Judge Thomas Donaghue said Rebb's three convictions did not call for, as he put it, a year at a country club. The judge then sentenced Rebb to from twelve to fifteen years at Joliet State Prison for molestation and three to five years for contributing to the delinquency of a minor, the sentences to run consecutively. Earlier, Rebb's driver's license was revoked for a year on the DUI charge. The priest broke down after the penitentiary verdicts and had to be carried from the courtroom. Nobody wept with him.

Several days later, in the same court, Ernesto Felices, of Hermosillo, Mexico, was sentenced to five years for selling heroin. Juan Torres, of Cuernavaca, Mexico, was given fifteen years for robbing Manny's downtown liquor store and wounding three persons during the holdup. The prisoner begged to be returned to Mexico but was told he could go there only after completing his sentence. A long and tough way to go home.

Charles Carmody had not reconciled with his parents although they visited him several times at Joliet prison. Father Bill, still missing the point, told Charles that he would have beaten both charges if he had placed the case in his hands. Charles, to his credit, said he was responsible for the murder of Joan Solari because of his drug addiction. In a bitter exchange Charles told his father that he had to pay the price for the Solari murder. What he wanted and needed was forgiveness, not his father's fix. The late cardinal's brother exploded and walked out of the visitor's reception room.

On March 15 Mamma X was appointed to two mayoral committees that concerned health and human services. Her husband, Reggie, had begun psychiatric treatment with Dr. Michael Dolan as a result of his Vietnam war experiences.

Monsignor Brady, former secretary of the late Cardinal Carmody, was appointed pastor of Queen of Martyrs parish on March 17.

In mid-April Rabbi Goldman and his wife were to be received by Pope John Paul II at the Vatican in honor of the rabbi's many contributions to ecumenism and the Catholic Church. The two would proceed to Israel, where they planned to consult with Talmudic scholars, spend a week on a kibbutz and travel throughout the country on a month's vacation.

In the last week of April, Chicago police arrested Big Mike Cecci and Fred Pottron, an attorney in Bill Carmody's legal firm, at O'Hare Airport. Although all four suitcases were covered by Pottron's U.S. diplomatic passport, Superintendent Rossi had forced the State Department to grant an exception in this case. The suitcases contained $13.5 million in cash and nearly $4 million in negotiable securities. Rossi also produced documentary evidence and a witness from the Banco Italo-Americano in Rome that showed that Cecci and an accomplice had previously laundered American drug money in Italy. Rusty Carmody was arrested in Naples, Florida, as that accomplice and also charged with laundering dirty drug income. Bill Carmody became their defense lawyer.

In a plea-bargain agreement, Rusty pled guilty to being an accomplice in the drug-money laundering operation but was given three years probation because he had never been arrested previously and had a civic record with the Boy Scouts and other groups. It appeared more than ironic to the Dolan family that Bill Carmody also mentioned to the prosecutor that Rusty's wife was expecting a baby.

Mike Cecci was found guilty and sentenced to three to five years in Joliet prison for drug-money laundering. Most police officers and legal observers considered the sentence much too light. The case also caused a sensation among Catholic laity involved with the Carmody family's leadership of the Catholic Church in Chicago.

On April 30, Leo Dolan retired from the police department and sold his home. A few weeks earlier, at the annual family Easter dinner, the Dolan children voted that Leo and Nora would spend their summers in Dingle, County Kerry, Ireland, but should return to Chicago each winter to be with the family. They would be housed with one of the married children's families. In a poignant meeting, the parents accepted.

In the first week of May the Dolans flew to Shannon Airport, where they rented a car and drove to Dingle. They rented a furnished home in the hamlet of Clogher Head, where Leo was born, for four months. Leo soon discovered that the old storytellers had abandoned the Blasket Islands in 1953 and had been resettled by the Irish government; the tale-spinners were scattered to the four winds of Ireland. Leo and Nora wondered who would now preserve the rich lore of Irish oral history? No one could tell them.

* * *

On May 20, according to the request in the cardinal's will, his red hat, his *galero,* was hung from the ceiling of St. Malachy's church. There was a brief ceremony attended by the parish council, the chancery office staff and relatives of His Eminence. Mr. and Mrs. William Carmody were, ironically, prominent attendees at the ceremony conducted, again, by Cappy Conlon.

Beau Beauchamps passed away two days after the cardinal's ceremony. Cappy arranged for a New Orleans jazz band, then performing in Chicago, to play at St. Mary's cemetery after the body was interred. The pastor broke down at the gravesite.

Cappy actually changed little. He still nipped Scotch and spent much of his time on the streets of the Loop ministering to the lost, rich and poor alike. The American clergy had still not produced a Curé d'Ars or St. Francis of Assisi, but Cappy was viewed by many as a good Chicago-style imitation.

The extent of the Church's financial problems in Chicago were finally disclosed after the death of Cardinal Carmody. The figures indicated the prelate had faced enormous economic pressures. The archdiocese reported that about 300 of its 382 parishes were financially sick. Church officials confirmed that the archdiocese was losing as much as $16 million a year. This was in spite of the fact that about sixty churches, schools and other Catholic institutions had been closed between 1990 and 1995.

Parishioners were contributing less than anticipated at both the regular Sunday and special collections. The annual rate of giving, which had historically always risen, had increased less than the rate of inflation. One unanticipated debt, said to be several million dollars a year, involved family settlements, legal fees and the cost of a new Church office associated with priestly molestation of children.

Chicago priests admitted there were other reasons why many Catholics contributed less to the archdiocese: the materialistic lifestyle of some of the hierarchy and priests; clerical infighting over Church doctrine and theology; dwindling attendance at Mass, and a general feeling among Catholics that too many clerics just didn't understand their spiritual mission, highlighted by the inability of priests to communicate in their Sunday sermons.

In spite of the annual debt, though, it was established that the net worth of the archdiocese was well over a billion dollars, mostly in land and real estate such as churches, schools and hospitals. But there was no plan to tap these large resources for the benefit of dead and dying inner-city churches and schools.

The Catholic Church across America continued in turmoil. The hierarchy and many dissenting theologians still had not met face to face in an attempt to moderate or heal their divisions. The guardian angel of the Church still danced on the flame of a candle.

THE
GREAT
WORLD
ATLAS

American Map Corporation

New York, N.Y.

THE
GREAT
WORLD
ATLAS

ATTRIBUTION

Publisher:

American Map Corporation, New York, N.Y.

Editorial:

Vera Benson, Director of Cartography,
American Map Corporation, in cooperation
with Kartographisches Institut Bertelsmann

Art and Design:

Vera Benson, American Map Corporation and
Kartographisches Institut Bertelsmann

Cartography:

Verlagsgruppe Bertelsmann GmbH,
Kartographisches Institut Bertelsmann, Gütersloh

Satellite Photos:

Photos: Deutsche Forschungs- und Versuchsanstalt für Luft- und Raumfahrt e.V., Oberpfaffenhofen, p. 9, 10; Map of Ptolemy, Staatsbibliothek, Preußischer Kulturbesitz, Berlin, Signatur Inc. 2640, p. 10; European Space Agency (ESA), Paris, and National Aeronautics and Space Administration (NASA), Washington, D.C.

Satellite Picture Processing: Dr. Rupert Haydn, Gesellschaft für Angewandte Fernerkundung mbH, Munich

Design: topic GmbH, Munich

The Nature of Our Planet:

Photos: Buxton/Survival Anglia (2); Everts/Zefa (1); Geoscience Features (1); Heather Angel (3); Hutchison Picture Library (3); NASA/Science Photo Library (1); Photri/Zefa (1); Regent/Hutchison Picture Library (1); Schneiders/Zefa (1); Schumacher/Zefa (1); Spectrum Colour Library (3); Steemans/Zefa (1); Swiss Tourist Office (2); van Grulsen (1); Willock/Survival Anglia (1).

Layout: Hubert Hepfinger, Freising

© Verlagsgruppe Bertelsmann International GmbH, Munich.

The Nature of Our Universe:

Arbeitsgemeinschaft Astrofotografie, Neustadt (4);
Joachim Herrmann, Recklinghausen (2);
Kartographisches Institut Bertelsmann, Gütersloh (6);
Barbara Michael, Hamburg (4);
Mount Wilson and Palomar Observatories (2);
NASA, Washington (1);
Günter Radtke, Uetze (1).

Text:

For Satellite Photos: Dr. Konrad Hiller,
Deutsche Forschungs- und Versuchsanstalt für Luft- und Raumfahrt e.V., Oberpfaffenhofen and Ulrich Münzer, University of Munich.

For Introduction: Helmut Schaub, Stuttgart.

For The Nature of Our Planet:
© Verlagsgruppe Bertelsmann International GmbH, Munich.

For The Nature of Our Universe: Joachim Herrmann, Recklinghausen.

Translations: Introduction Joseph Butler, Munich.
Satellite part Deirdre Hiller, Steinebach.
The Nature of Our Universe, Ann Hirst for German Language Services, New York.

Library of Congress Card Number 86-71065

Printed and bound in Germany by Mohndruck
Graphische Betriebe GmbH, Gütersloh.

ISBN 0-8416-2005-9

Fourth Edition

Printed in Germany

THE
GREAT
WORLD
ATLAS

INTRODUCTION

A world atlas is a condensed and systematic representation of human knowledge of the earth. The atlas, thus, fulfills two essential functions: first, it is a reference work of individual geographic facts; second, it sums up and comments upon our knowledge of various regions of the earth.

The means of cartographic representation are point, line and surface area, realized in color or pattern, and complemented by the written word, the explanatory element. Cartographers thus avail themselves of the same visual means of expression as graphic artists. Maps are scaled down, simplified, and annotated pictures of the earth and its regions. Cartographic representations number among the oldest cultural and artistic expressions of mankind. Maps are documents of man's contemplation of his environment and, as such, reveal his level of knowledge of his surroundings.

Like specialists in other areas, cartographers of today are faced with the difficult task of reducing a great diversity of complex information about the earth to a simplified, easy-to-understand form. The purpose of a world atlas is to present, clearly and concisely, those factors that shape the character of the whole earth or its regions – geofactors such as topography, climate, and vegetation; or the characteristics that result from the activities of mankind such as land use, economy, transportation, education, etc. In order to gain this comprehensive world picture, "The Great World Atlas" employs satellite photographs, topographic (physical) maps, thematic maps, as well as charts, illustrations, and text describing our world and universe.

"The Great World Atlas" is further distinguished by its clearly arranged sequence of maps, from north to south and from west to east, within the different continents, as well as by a unique system that uses fewer, chiefly true-to-area projections, and fewer scales. This facilitates the use of the atlas and the comparison of individual regions. Special attention has been paid to the United States by using the scale 1 : 3,750,000. This scale makes possible the complete reproduction of each individual state on one map. Continents are uniformly portrayed at a scale of 1 : 13,500,000. Numerous maps at a scale of 1 : 4,500,000 or 1 : 6,750,000 are devoted to countries and to important political, economic, and tourist regions. The worldwide phenomenon of the concentration of population in urban areas is taken into account by maps of major metropolitan centers (scale 1 : 225,000).

Satellite Photos: "The Great World Atlas" is unparalleled in its presentation of large regions of the earth through satellite photos. Satellite photos are "snapshots" of the surface of the earth. With the help of the topographic maps you can orient yourself in these landscapelike images. While topographic maps focus on the relief of the earth, satellite photos may emphasize the presence or absence of plant growth, or specific qualities of vegetation. The thematic maps, on the other hand, provide the facts behind the details in the images; e. g. climate maps may explain the reasons for the presence or absence of vegetation.

Satellite pictures and maps complement each other, neither one could replace the other. A separate chapter of this atlas looks into the technology of expensive high-tech satellite information gathering systems used to generate satellite imagery.

Topographic or physical maps: These constitute the major part of the atlas. The use of color and shading provide the impression of height and depth necessary to visualize various surface configurations of the earth. A great number of map symbols denote specific topographic forms such as deserts, swamps, glaciers and the like, but above all, the man-made topographic elements such as population centers, transportation routes or political borders. An additional characteristic of these topographic maps is the use of highly detailed nomenclature to identify the broad variety of geographic features.

Thematic maps: These maps either focus on single topics or form thematic groups, including precipitation or climate, soil, vegetation, population density, economy, nutrition, etc. Thematic data are built on simplified base maps containing major geographic features such as coast lines, waterways, political borders and important cities to assure spacial orientation and easy reference to the topographic maps. By comparing the topographic and thematic maps, the geographic forces, correlationships and interdependencies in the political, strategic, economic, and cultural spheres become evident.

Two sections new to this edition cover the topics of Earth Science and Astronomy. In The Nature of Our Planet we learn about the physical history and composition of our planet, and the processes of change it has undergone and continues to undergo. We can appreciate, for instance, that what transpires on a large scale over aeons – the destruction and creation of landforms – finds its counterpart, on a small scale, in the common, observable events of erosion by weathering, and deposition of eroded particles. Based on the latest scientific observations, The Nature of Our Universe offers insights into the structure and development of our solar system, our galaxy, and our ever-expanding universe.

"The Great World Atlas" makes a strong case for its claim as a special reference work with its extensive index of place names. It contains, in unabbreviated form, all the names that appear on the maps; in all, more than 100,000 entries.

All maps are up to date and reflect current scholarship and cartographic technology. Thus, "The Great World Atlas" meets the demands placed upon a modern map work with respect to both content and execution. For this achievement we extend our gratitude to all contributors, advisers, and institutions that have assisted us.

The Publisher

THE
GREAT
WORLD
ATLAS

CONTENTS OVERVIEW

EARTH FROM OUTER SPACE · SATELLITE PHOTOS
PAGES 9–48

THE WORLD
PAGES 49–53

NORTH AMERICA
PAGES 54–89

SOUTH AMERICA
PAGES 90–112

EUROPE
PAGES 113–130

ASIA
PAGES 131–155

AUSTRALIA · OCEANIA
PAGES 156–162

AFRICA
PAGES 163–176

THEMATIC MAPS OF THE WORLD
PAGES 177–195

THEMATIC MAPS OF NORTH AND SOUTH AMERICA
PAGES 197–198, 200–201

POLITICAL MAPS OF THE CONTINENTS
PAGES 196, 199, 202–208

THE NATURE OF OUR PLANET
PAGES 209–232

THE NATURE OF OUR UNIVERSE
PAGES 233–240

INDEX
PAGES 241–367

THE
GREAT
WORLD
ATLAS

TABLE OF CONTENTS

Page	Introduction to Atlas
1	Main Title
2	Attribution · Imprint
3	Introduction
4	Contents Overview
5-8	Table of Contents

PHOTO SECTION

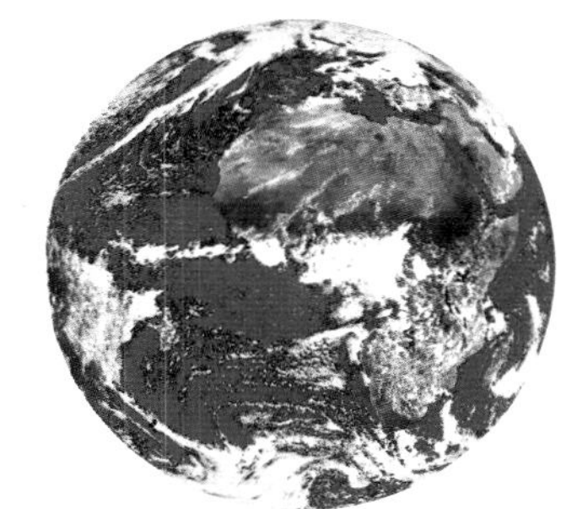

SATELLITE PHOTOS

Page	Photo
9	Earth from Outer Space
10-11	From Maps to Satellite Photos
12-13	Distant Reconnaissance of the Earth
14-15	New York
16-17	San Francisco
18-19	Denver
20-21	Mexico
22	Atacama Desert
23	Iceland
24-25	London
26-27	Mouth of the Rhone
28-29	Po Valley
30-31	Persian Gulf
32-33	Philippines
34	Beijing
35	Pilbara District
36-37	Red Sea
38-39	Namib Desert
40	Tibesti

Page	Introduction to Map Section
41-43	Key to Map Coverage
44-45	Description of Map Types and Scales
46	Map Projections
47	Abbreviations of Geographical Names and Terms
48	Explanation of Symbols

MAP SECTION

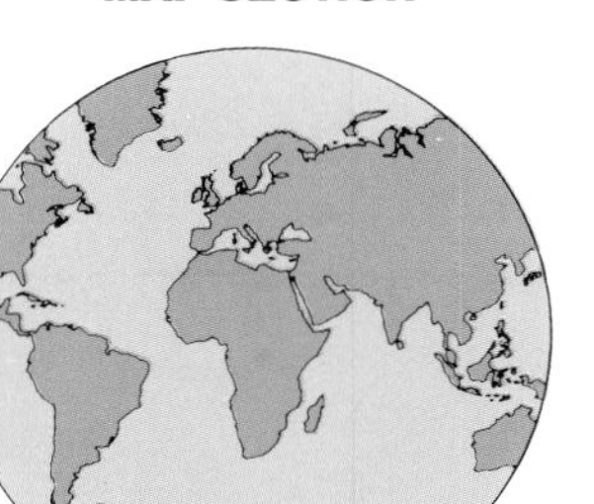

THE WORLD

Page	Map Title	Scale
49	World Map Section: Physical Maps	
50-51	World, physical	1 : 67,500,000
52	Arctic Region	1 : 27,000,000
53	Antarctic Region	1 : 27,000,000

THE
GREAT
WORLD
ATLAS

TABLE OF CONTENTS

MAP SECTION

NORTH AMERICA

Page	Map Title	Scale
54	North America, Vegetation	1 : 27,000,000
55	North America, physical	1 : 27,000,000
56-57	Northern North America	1 : 13,500,000
58-59	Alaska, Insets: Aleutian Islands	1 : 4,500,000
60	Canada, Pacific Provinces	1 : 4,500,000
61	Canada, Central Provinces West	1 : 4,500,000
62	Canada, Central Provinces East	1 : 4,500,000
63	Canada, Atlantic Provinces	1 : 4,500,000
64-65	Southern North America	1 : 13,500,000
	Inset: Panama Canal	1 : 900,000
66-67	U.S.A., Pacific States North	1 : 3,750,000
68-69	U.S.A., Central States Northwest	1 : 3,750,000
70-71	U.S.A., Central States Northeast	1 : 3,750,000
72-73	U.S.A., Atlantic States North	1 : 3,750,000
74-75	U.S.A., Pacific States South	1 : 3,750,000
76-77	U.S.A., Central States Southwest	1 : 3,750,000
78-79	U.S.A., Central States Southeast	1 : 3,750,000
	Inset: Hawaiian Islands	1 : 3,750,000
80-81	U.S.A., Atlantic States South, Inset: Florida	1 : 3,750,000
82	Montreal · Washington · New York	1 : 225,000
83	San Francisco · Chicago · Los Angeles	1 : 225,000
84	Boston · Detroit · Philadelphia	1 : 225,000
85	New Orleans · Atlanta · Houston	1 : 225,000
86-87	Mexico	1 : 6,750,000
88-89	Central America · West Indies	1 : 6,750,000

MAP SECTION

SOUTH AMERICA

Page	Map Title	Scale
90	South America, physical	1 : 27,000,000
91	Mexico City · Caracas · Bogotá	1 : 225,000
92-93	Northern South America	1 : 13,500,000
94-95	Venezuela · Colombia	1 : 4,500,000
96-97	Ecuador · Peru	1 : 4,500,000
98-99	Guyana · Suriname · Fr. Guiana · Northern Brazil	1 : 6,750,000
100-101	Eastern Brazil	1 : 4,500,000
102-103	Southern Brazil and Paraguay	1 : 4,500,000
104-105	Bolivia	1 : 4,500,000
106-107	Central Argentina, Central Chile and Uruguay	1 : 4,500,000
108-109	Southern Argentina and Southern Chile	1 : 4,500,000
110	Rio de Janeiro · São Paulo · Buenos Aires	1 : 225,000
111	Southern South America	1 : 13,500,000
112	Atlantic Ocean	1 : 60,000,000

MAP SECTION

EUROPE

Page	Map Title	Scale
113	Vienna · Rome · Madrid · Athens · Moscow	1 : 225,000
114-115	Europe, physical	1 : 13,500,000
116-117	Scandinavia, Insets: Iceland, Spitsbergen	1 : 4,500,000
118	Central Europe	1 : 4,500,000
119	British Isles	1 : 4,500,000
120-121	Western and Southwestern Europe	1 : 4,500,000
122-123	Southern and Southeastern Europe	1 : 4,500,000
124-125	Eastern Europe, Northern Part	1 : 4,500,000
126-127	Eastern Europe, Southern Part	1 : 4,500,000
128	Amsterdam · Brussels · Frankfurt · Zurich	1 : 225,000
129	Paris · London	1 : 225,000
130	Hamburg · Munich · Berlin	1 : 225,000

THE
GREAT
WORLD
ATLAS

TABLE OF CONTENTS

MAP SECTION

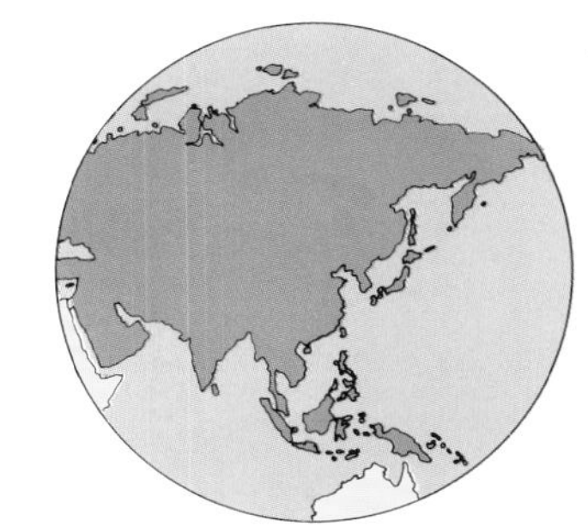

ASIA

Page	Map Title	Scale
131	Asia, physical	1 : 36,000,000
132-133	Northern Asia	1 : 13,500,000
134-135	Southwestern Asia	1 : 13,500,000
136-137	Near East	1 : 4,500,000
138-139	Northern India · Nepal	1 : 4,500,000
140	Southern India · Sri Lanka	1 : 4,500,000
141	Burma	1 : 4,500,000
142-143	Central and East Asia	1 : 13,500,000
144-145	Japan · Korea	1 : 4,500,000
146-147	Eastern China · Taiwan	1 : 4,500,000
148-149	Southeast Asia	1 : 13,500,000
	Insets: Fiji · Samoa · Hawaii · Solomon Islands	1 : 13,500,000
150-151	Thailand · Laos · Vietnam · Cambodia	1 : 4,500,000
152-153	Malaysia and Indonesia	1 : 6,750,000
154	Istanbul · Calcutta · Singapore · Jakarta	1 : 225,000
155	Hong Kong · Beijing · Tokyo	1 : 225,000

MAP SECTION

AUSTRALIA AND OCEANIA

Page	Map Title	Scale
156-157	Pacific Ocean	1 : 54,000,000
158-159	Australia · New Zealand	1 : 13,500,000
160	Southeastern Australia	1 : 6,750,000
	Inset: Tasmania	1 : 6,750,000
161	New Zealand	1 : 6,750,000
	Sydney · Melbourne	1 : 225,000
162	Australia and Oceania, physical	1 : 36,000,000

MAP SECTION

AFRICA

Page	Map Title	Scale
163	Africa, physical	1 : 36,000,000
164-165	Northern Africa, Inset: Somalia	1 : 13,500,000
166-167	Morocco · Algeria · Tunisia	1 : 4,500,000
168-169	West Africa	1 : 6,750,000
170	Algiers · Cairo · Lagos · Kinshasa · Johannesburg	1 : 225,000
171	East Africa	1 : 6,750,000
172	Southern Africa	1 : 13,500,000
173	Egypt	1 : 4,500,000
174-175	Republic of South Africa	1 : 4,500,000
176	Indian Ocean	1 : 60,000,000
	Inset: Maldive Islands	1 : 13,500,000

THE
GREAT
WORLD
ATLAS

TABLE OF CONTENTS

MAP SECTION

THEMATIC MAPS OF THE WORLD

Page	Map Title	Scale
177	World Map Section: Thematic Maps	
178-179	World, political	1 : 67,500,000
180	World, Geology · Earthquakes	1 : 135,000,000
181	World, Climate	1 : 90,000,000
182	World, Climate	1 : 162,000,000
183	World, Climate	1 : 162,000,000
184	World, Soils · Forest	1 : 135,000,000
185	World, Vegetation	1 : 90,000,000
186-187	World, Economy	1 : 67,500,000
188	World, Population	1 : 90,000,000
189	World, Education	1 : 90,000,000
190	World, Food	1 : 90,000,000
191	World, Traffic	1 : 90,000,000
192	World, Trade	1 : 90,000,000
193	World, Energy	1 : 90,000,000
194	World, Religions	1 : 90,000,000
195	World, Languages	1 : 90,000,000
196	North America, political	1 : 27,000,000
197	North America, Economy	1 : 27,000,000
198	North America, Economy	1 : 27,000,000
	Inset: U.S.A., Northeast	1 : 13,500,000
199	South America, political	1 : 27,000,000
200	South America, Economy	1 : 27,000,000
201	South America, Economy	1 : 27,000,000
202-203	Europe, political	1 : 13,500,000
204-205	Africa, political	1 : 27,000,000
206-207	Asia, political	1 : 27,000,000
208	Australia and Oceania, political	1 : 27,000,000

EARTH SCIENCE AND ASTRONOMY

OUR PLANET AND OUR UNIVERSE

Page	
209	The Nature of Our Planet
210–211	Structure and surface of the Earth
212	Plate tectonics
213	Structure of continents
214	Continental drift
215	Sedimentary rocks
216	Igneous rocks
217	Metamorphic rocks
218–219	Volcanoes
220	Geology and landscape
221	Caves and their formation
222–223	The weather
224	Weathering
225	Frost erosion
226–227	River action
228	Coral reefs and islands
229	The continental shelf
230	Ice caps
231	Mountain glaciers
232	Post-glaciation
233	The Nature of Our Universe
234	The Solar System
235	The Planetary System
236–237	The Sun
238–239	The Milky Way
240	Galaxies

241–367 INDEX

EARTH FROM OUTER SPACE

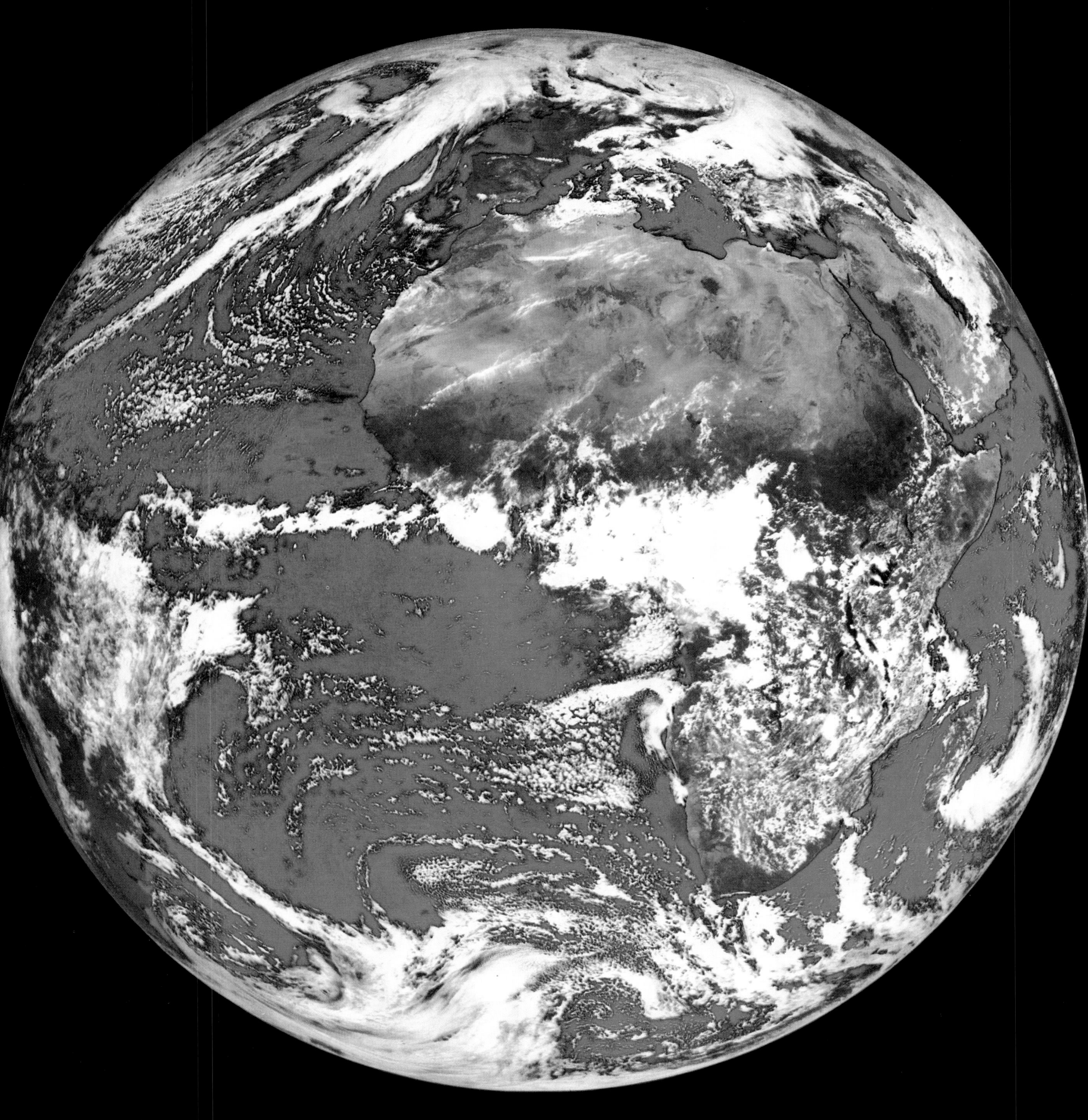

From Maps to Satellite Photos

Since early times man has tried to represent his environment pictorially. Today's familiar topographical maps are based on the concepts of the Greek natural scientist, Claudius Ptolemy. He first developed these during the second century in Alexandria, Egypt. Although his maps have not survived, his extant treatise, entitled "Geography," asserted great influence for centuries. It gives directions for presenting the spherical surface of the earth on a plane and for locating places on earth, using a grid with longitude and latitude lines. Ptolemy's directions reflect the knowledge of his time, yet maps reconstructed accordingly, around 1480, influenced official maps and geographical thinking for centuries thereafter. The world map below, printed in the 15th century, was drawn based upon Ptolemy's concept. It shows severe distortions in the proportions of some areas. The Black Sea, the Caspian Sea, and the Persian Gulf are each shown to be approximately the same size as the eastern Mediterranean. Geographers of that time had little reliable information and their ideas of the physical world were often influenced by imagination and legends. This accounts for non-existent mountain ranges and rivers in inner Africa and in the whole of eastern Asia. The distortion of features in the west-east direction caused Columbus to underestimate his western route to India by half of the real distance. Although he knew the correct circumference of the earth, his concept of geography was formed by such distorted maps. Fortunately, he reached land just as his supplies were running out. Thinking he was in India, he did not realize, at first, that he had discovered a new continent.

To satisfy the needs of the seafaring nations, coasts of newly discovered regions had priority over interior areas and were explored and surveyed first. The Englishman, Captain James Cook, made decisive contributions to coastal exploration, and geographical knowledge in general, during his three journeys between 1768 and 1779. He proved that no southern continent existed in the moderate climatic zone; discovered New Zealand and several other islands in the Pacific; and confirmed that Australia was a separate continent.

In the 18th and 19th centuries, the consequent seizure and division of newly discovered territories amongst the European powers stimulated detailed exploration, particularly of economically and strategically important areas. The publishing of larger-scaled maps and the introduction of thematic maps followed.

The development of a completely new dimension in cartography began with aerial photography. In 1858, the Parisian photographer, Nadar, working from a captive balloon, took the first aerial photo of the village of Bicètre, near Paris. Further developments followed fast, based upon developments in aviation. With the increasing distance and altitude capabilities of airplanes, larger and remoter areas could be surveyed (also see diagram p. 13). Concurrent advances in photography resulted in distortion- free lenses, precise shutters, and the use of a vacuum to keep film completely flat and in position. Progress in the development of materials resulted in a special fine-grained film, larger film formats, and the introduction of color film. The advanced state of this technology (at least militarily) was spotlighted in 1960 when the American U2-Pilot, Powers, was shot down over Russia. Films found in the wreck were published by the Soviet Union for propaganda purposes. These pictures, taken at a height of 15.5 mi., were able to distinguish a cyclist from a pedestrian!

In addition to maximum resolution, aerial photographs must meet other requirements. Minimum lens distortion is particularly important. This requires the lens to be calculated precisely and ground so that photographed landmarks do not appear displaced in the image. Distortions caused by imprecise lenses become immediately obvious during processing of the images by modern photogrammetric analyzing instruments. When viewing overlapping aerial photos through a stereoscope, a three-dimensional impression of the earth's surface is obtained. Such stereoscopic models may be used to derive exact locations and measurements of clearly defined points on the earth, and to determine topographic contour lines.

To obtain the overlapping aerial photos needed to produce a map, an airplane must fly on parallel courses, as many times as necessary, over the entire area. For control purposes, the position of the mid-point of each image is recorded on a small-scale diagram of the area. This pictorial information, together with data derived through the classic methods of photogrammetry, forms the basis for the production of topographical maps. First, the available image information is reduced according to the scale of the planned map and then it is transformed into drawings containing the familiar map symbols. Finally, color, shading, feature names, and explanatory technical notes are added.

Although generally unknown to the public, aerial photography is used in fields other than cartography. It aids in the planning of new highways and railway lines; redistribution of agricultural land; siting of landfill areas; expansion of suburbs; surveying of waste dumps; and damage to crops.

Nevertheless, aerial photographs cannot meet several requirements. It is impossible to photograph large areas, for example, the state of New York, in a short time and at a reasonable cost. Such a project would take days or weeks, during which time weather and lighting conditions would constantly change. The only solution to this problem is the use of satellites, flying high above the earth's surface. Satellite images of areas as large as 112 x 122 mi. can be taken in a few minutes, under constant lighting and weather conditions. The area photographed is large enough to carry out extensive, comparative investigations of vegetative or geological phenomena. In extreme cases, the whole of Europe, as on the weather satellite image opposite, or even an earth hemisphere, as on the Meteosat-Image (title page), can be covered by a single picture. With the aid of satellite photography, it is possible to record completely the earth's surface and to almost continually observe it. Current technology, methods, and applications of satellite photography are described on the following pages.

AFRICA
LIBIA INTERIOR
ETHIOPIA INTERIOR
MARE INDICVM

▷ *Europe*
Central Europe taken from the weather satellite NOAA – 7. Colors represent various surface temperatures. Blue represents low, yellow to red higher temperatures.

◁ *Map of Ptolemy*
During the Renaissance, maps drawn according to Claudius Ptolemy's concepts were widely used and influential. The one shown was published in 1482 in the "Cosmographia" by Linhart Holl in Ulm, Germany.

Distant Reconnaissance of the Earth

Techniques — Methods — Applications

In the last few years satellite images have become a common sight. Every evening television meteorologists use up-to-the-minute satellite maps to depict weather conditions across the continent. Reference books and magazines display satellite images of our cities or regional areas of interest. With few exceptions, these photos show strange, artificial red and gray tones dominating at our latitudes. The satellite imaging systems and the human eye obviously "see" things differently.

All substances whose temperatures register above absolute zero emit electromagnetic radiation. The higher the temperature, the shorter the emitted wavelength. Because the surface temperature of the sun averages 10,800°F, it radiates predominantly in the shorter wavelengths from ultraviolet to infrared. The human eye is adapted to a small portion of this radiation, which we sense as light.

Light coming directly from the sun appears colorless. Nevertheless when it strikes a body, some wavelengths are absorbed and others are reflected, resulting in color. The various characteristics of that body will determine the specific colors we see. A diagram of the range of electromagnetic radiation used in remote sensing from space is given opposite.

The earth's atmosphere strongly scatters and absorbs the blue part of the visible light. Therefore, remote sensing instruments do not register blue. They register the primary colors green and red, and a third component, shortwave infrared, which lies next to red in the spectrum, but is not visible to the eye.

Radiation from all three wavelengths is recorded separately in black and white. To reconstruct an image, the color blue is used to represent green light, green for red light, and red for infrared radiation. This results in the false color images previously mentioned. Fresh vegetation, for example, appears red because the chlorophyll in the leaves strongly reflects infrared wavelengths. Damaged vegetation loses this characteristic, causing the green band to predominate, thus, transitional colors from red to violet and blue are obtained.

In contrast, optoelectronic instruments operate without film. Light reflected from an object is recorded by a sensor and then transformed into electric signals. These are amplified and transmitted, in digital form, to a receiving station on the earth and are stored on magnetic tape. The conversion to a false color image can take place either directly on a computer screen or through point by point exposure of data on film.

In contrast to a conventional camera, which takes a photograph in a single exposure, an electronic sensor receives only one image point, that is, light from a small part of the earth's surface. Light from subsequent surface points is conducted point by point to the sensor by a rotating mirror (mirror scanner). Filters, placed in the path of light, or diverse sensors split the light into separate bands of the electromagnetic spectrum. The American Landsat and weather satellites use this type of scanning instrument.
The future of this field lies in the Charge Coupled Device scanners. In these CCDs, up to 4000 sensors are mounted in a single row. Each sensor measures about 16 thousandths of a millimeter and the complete chip about 5 cm. The chip is installed with the row of sensors perpendicular to the flight path of the satellite. The image is created by recording information point by point and row by row, with each scanning point corresponding to one of the sensors. An advantage of this system is that no moving mechanical parts are necessary. This greatly increases the reliability of such instruments, particularly important for long missions in outer space.
Scanner systems have several basic advantages over conventional film cameras. The signals are recorded in digital form and can be processed by a computer; also, wavelength which lie outside the sensitivity range of film can be registered. For example, rays in the thermal region, that is, warmth emitted from a body, can be recorded. The image of Central Europe, page 11, was recorded in this way. To make the temperature differences of the various surface types visible, the colors blue, green and red are used for the lowest to highest temperatures respectively. Water bodies and pine forests are relatively cold (dark blue), agricultural areas cool (green) to warm (yellow to orange), and urban areas are very warm (red). Clouds and snow in the alpine regions are extremely cold hence, pale blue.
The production and processing of modern satellite images would be impossible without high capacity computers. Each Landsat image contains 32 million pieces of information! The standard processing of this information results in the strangely colored images already discussed.
Nevertheless, sophisticated computer programs now make it possible to simulate the scattered blue not recorded by sensing instruments. A combination of the simulated blue and the original signals from the green and red bands results in an image with more or less natural colors, depending upon the quality of the processing. The examples on the opposite page clearly illustrate the difference between the false color image and its corresponding natural color image. The area pictured is San Francisco Bay and its surroundings. The most noticeable contrasts are that the green areas of vegetation appear red in the original image and the brown unforested mountains appear yellow.
All the previously described remote sensing techniques are based on "passive" methods – they record reflected (from light) or radiated (from warmth) electromagnetic waves from the observed object. In addition, various "active" procedures are used in remote sensing. Various wavelengths from the radar band (see the "Electromagnetic Spectrum" diagram below) are emitted from a transmitter, on board an airplane or satellite, via an antenna. The time the signal takes to travel from the transmitter to the object and back again is recorded and, following several intermediate steps, converted into an image. The advantage of this method is that the relatively longwave radar radiation travels through the atmosphere, practically without interference, so that one can "see" through clouds. This technique is very useful in areas such as the Amazon Basin, where year-round cloud cover makes conventional photography useless.
The equipment and methods of analysis described above could, in principle, be used at all altitudes. In fact, the equipment and the altitude selected are based upon the particular task requirements and environmental considerations such as image size, ground resolution, spectral range, probability of cloud coverage, etc. Dirigibles and helicopters fly at the lowest altitudes – from 3 to 5mi. Airplanes usually fly between 2 and 9 mi., and military spy planes up to 19 mi. high. Above the earth's atmosphere the space shuttle orbits at an altitude of 125 to 188 mi. and the earth observation satellites at 438 to 563 mi. They take about 90 minutes for one revolution around the earth. The meteorological and communication satellites appear fixed above a point over the equator, because at 22,400 mi. altitude, they orbit at exactly the same speed as the earth rotates at the equator. From this orbit, an overall view of half of the earth's sphere is possible.
Satellite images have multiple uses. Weather satellites, located above a fixed point on the earth's surface, transmit an image every half an hour, day and night, providing data on cloud type, altitude, and direction of movement, as well as air temperature. Satellite and aerial photographs have become indispensable to cartographers, particularly for recording inaccessible or quickly changing phenomena. Extensive areas can be economically, precisely and, if necessary, repeatedly recorded. Producing maps and monitoring icebergs are specific examples of this use.

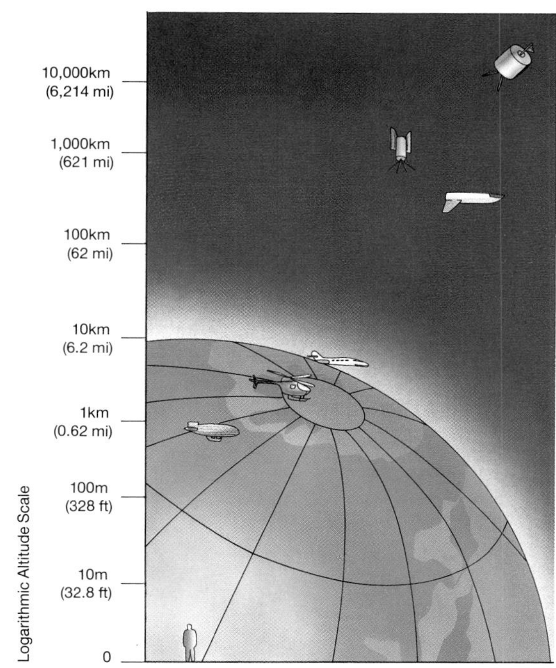
Logarithmic Altitude Scale
10,000km
(6,214 mi)
1,000km
(621 mi)
100km
(62 mi)
10km
(6.2 mi)
1km
(0.62 mi)
100m
(328 ft)
10m
(32.8 ft)
0

Multispectral analysis is used to distinguish between different materials. This is achieved by analyzing the different reflection characteristics of materials in the various wavelength ranges. It is mainly used in geology, forestry, and agriculture. In geology research is being carried out to determine the composition of rock and its tectonics through its spectral behavior. This can result in finding unknown ore deposits. The main applications in forestry and agriculture are the assessment of damage to forests and the estimation of expected harvest yields. In both cases periodically repeated surveys at different times of the year are necessary for accurate assessments. Important future applications will be in the field of environmental protection. Illegal discharges of oil from ships into the ocean or the release of toxic substance into rivers and lakes can be detected, and the responsible parties identified.
The images in this atlas were taken from the American satellites Landsat 1 to 4. The scales are 1:710,000 and 1:450,000. The orientation is north-northwest, picture size 112 x 112 mi. and 112 x 81 mi. respectively, and the ground resolution is 263 ft.

◁ San Francisco
Bay of San Francisco computer processed in two different ways: left false color image, right natural color version (see text).

△ Remote sensing platforms
The diagram displays the flight altitudes most commonly used for remote sensing platforms.

▷ Electromagnetic spectrum
Only part of the electromagnetic spectrum is used for remote sensing. It ranges from ultraviolet to the radar wavelengths, with visible light and short wave infrared being of particular importance.

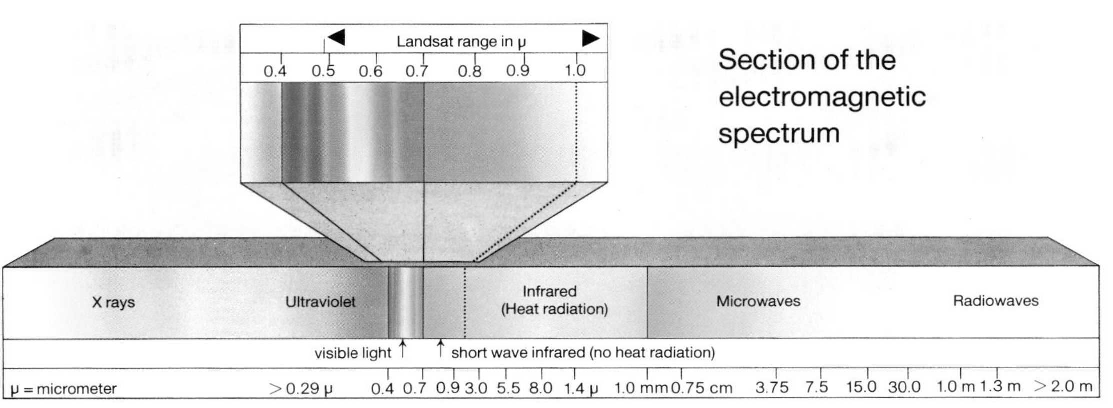
Landsat range in µ
0.4 0.5 0.6 0.7 0.8 0.9 1.0
Section of the electromagnetic spectrum
X rays
Ultraviolet
Infrared
(Heat radiation)
Microwaves
Radiowaves
visible light
short wave infrared (no heat radiation)
µ = micrometer
>0.29 µ
0.4 0.7 0.9 3.0 5.5 8.0 1.4 µ 1.0 mm 0.75 cm 3.75 7.5 15.0 30.0 1.0 m 1.3 m >2.0 m

22
2
6
11
12 A
12
16
9
7
21
15
5
14
8
19
13
4
18
17
3
20

Hub of Commerce and Culture

The New York City Metropolitan Area is the focal point of this satellite image. Its urban areas are characterized by gray; agricultural regions form a mosaic of browns and greens; while forests and meadows appear in gradations of green.
Long Island (1) is separated from the mainland by Long Island Sound (2). Above the ocean, the wind forms ribbons from vapor trails of high-flying jets (3). The Verrazano Narrows Bridge (4) appears as a thin line crossing the Narrows and marks the entrance to Upper New York Bay (5). The Hudson River (6) – the lower part of which is actually a fjord – is navigable by ocean-going vessels as far as Albany, the state capital, 150 miles upstream. In the photograph, the five boroughs of New York City are partially obscured by clouds. The island of Manhattan (7) is separated from Brooklyn (8) and Queens (9) by the East River, from the Bronx (11) – and the New York mainland – by the Harlem River (12), and from New Jersey (12 A) by the Hudson River. Manhattan is separated from Staten Island (13) by Upper New York Bay. The Staten Island ferry crosses the bay and provides a link for thousands of Staten Island residents who work in Manhattan. The densely populated areas west of the Hudson in New Jersey are Jersey City (14) and Hoboken (15).
The cultural and commercial center of the New York Metropolitan Area is the island of Manhattan (7). New York's famous Museum Mile – including the Metropolitan Museum, the Guggenheim Museum, and several others – runs along Fifth Avenue. This forms the eastern edge of Central Park (16) which is visible as a green rectangle. Complementing the fine arts are the performing arts, with a dazzling array of live theater staged in the Theater District, as well as other parts of the city. Broadway, Off Broadway, and Off-Off Broadway performances offer visitors and residents the widest range of entertainment possibilities found anywhere. The Wall Street area is the home of the New York Stock Exchange and contains the highest concentration of commercial and financial concerns in the world.
Because of the high contrast between the dark blue color of the sea and the gray of the building complexes, numerous details along the shore lines can be observed. A filigree of 3000 docks and piers – about 100 miles long – can be followed in New York City as well as in New Jersey. The shores toward the Atlantic are characterized by offshore barrier beaches including Sandy Hook (17) and Breezy Point (18). East of these, the wildlife refuge of Jamaica Bay (19) appears as brown lagoons. The mosaic of green and gray in New Jersey's Middlesex County (20) indicates its diverse composition of towns, suburbs, parks, and industrial areas. Further west and north, the forests of the Watchung Mountains (21) and Hudson Highlands (22) form swatches of deep green.

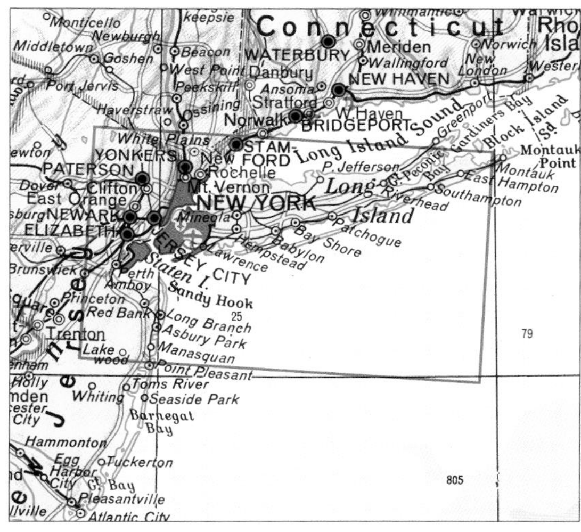
Connecticut
WATERBURY
Meriden
Wallingford
NEW HAVEN
Danbury
Norwalk
BRIDGEPORT
Long Island Sound
YONKERS
STAMFORD
PATERSON
Clifton
East Orange
NEWARK
ELIZABETH
NEW YORK
Long Island
Montauk Point
Sandy Hook
Red Bank
Long Branch
Asbury Park
Trenton
Toms River
Seaside Park
Tuckerton

15
17
7
8
6
10
9
2
14
13
11
20
1
19
12
3
16

16 San Francisco

The City on the Bay

Founded in 1779 by Spanish missionaries, San Francisco is known as the romantic city of the gold rush, sailing ships, and cable cars, but also as the center of a devastating earthquake. Overlooking the best natural harbor of the Pacific coast, the city is the center of a huge megalopolis. Surrounding the bay, residential areas, port facilities, military installations, and industrial complexes lie side by side to form the "Bay Area."

This satellite image shows the Pacific coast (1), the Bay Area (2) with the coastal ranges in the west (3) and the valleys of the Sacramento (4) and San Joaquin (5) rivers to the north-east.

Golden Gate (6), the strait which links the open waters of the Pacific Ocean with the bay, is easy to recognize. Measuring only 5 mi. long by 2 mi. wide, this gap experiences tidal changes of up to 7 ft. The severe currents caused by these tidal changes acted as a major deterrent to escape for the prisoners of the former jail on Alcatraz Island (7). The water of the bay is heavily polluted from industrial and agricultural waste and, therefore, appears gray. This image, taken at low tide, shows the contaminated water flowing out to the ocean, mixing with dark, clear water, and drifting south. The Golden Gate Bridge, supported by 745 ft high piers, spans the Golden Gate and is clearly visible as a white line (8). Within San Francisco city limits some landmarks are distinguishable: Golden Gate Park (9), the harbor docks (10), and just south of the city, the airport runways (11).

The bay of San Francisco is a geological syncline that forms part of the great San Andreas Fault system. Two continental plates are moving in opposite directions, one to the north-west (Pacific Plate), and the other south-east (North-American Plate). Over decades stress builds up along this 18 mi. deep fault until, at a critical point, pressure is released all at once. In 1906 an earthquake of this origin destroyed much of the city of San Francisco. Over a length of 125 mi. the western plate (Pacific Plate) moved 23 feet to the northwest. The San Andreas Fault (12) as well as other tectonic structures such as the Calaveras (13) and Hayward faults (14) show up as lines in the picture.

Bordering the bay and bounded by the Diablo (15) and Santa Cruz Mountains (16), flat alluvial land offers ideal conditions for settlement. Approximately 10 million people live in this area, shown here in gray tones. Because of their coarser pattern one is able to distinguish the city centers of Oakland (17) and San Jose (18) from their suburbs. On the southern end of the bay, rice fields, planted on recently drained marshes, are highlighted by a dense green color and enclosed by white borders (19). The deep brown patches in the same area are basins where sea water is evaporated to win salt (20).

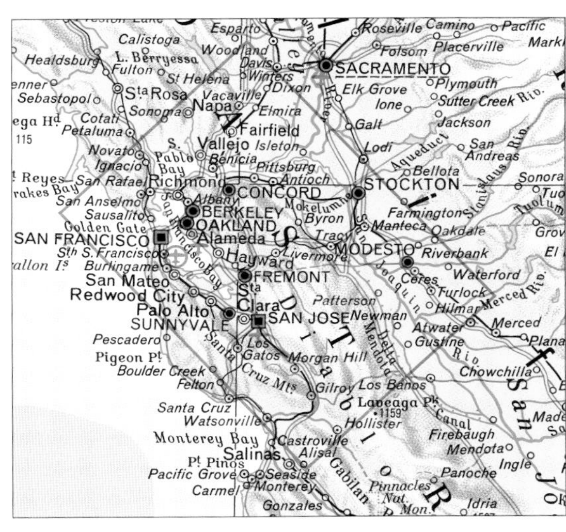

SACRAMENTO
Roseville
Folsom
Placerville
Davis
Woodland
Calistoga
L. Berryessa
Healdsburg
Sebastopol
Sta Rosa
Napa
Vacaville
Fairfield
Vallejo
Petaluma
Novato
San Rafael
Richmond
CONCORD
Antioch
Pittsburg
BERKELEY
OAKLAND
Alameda
SAN FRANCISCO
Golden Gate
Sausalito
Hayward
Livermore
Tracy
STOCKTON
Lodi
Manteca
MODESTO
Oakdale
Riverbank
Ceres
Turlock
FREMONT
San Mateo
Redwood City
Palo Alto
SUNNYVALE
Sta Clara
SAN JOSE
Los Gatos
Morgan Hill
Gilroy
Los Banos
Santa Cruz
Watsonville
Monterey Bay
Castroville
Salinas
Pacific Grove
Seaside
Monterey
Carmel
Gonzales
Hollister
Merced
Chowchilla
Firebaugh
Mendota

18 Denver

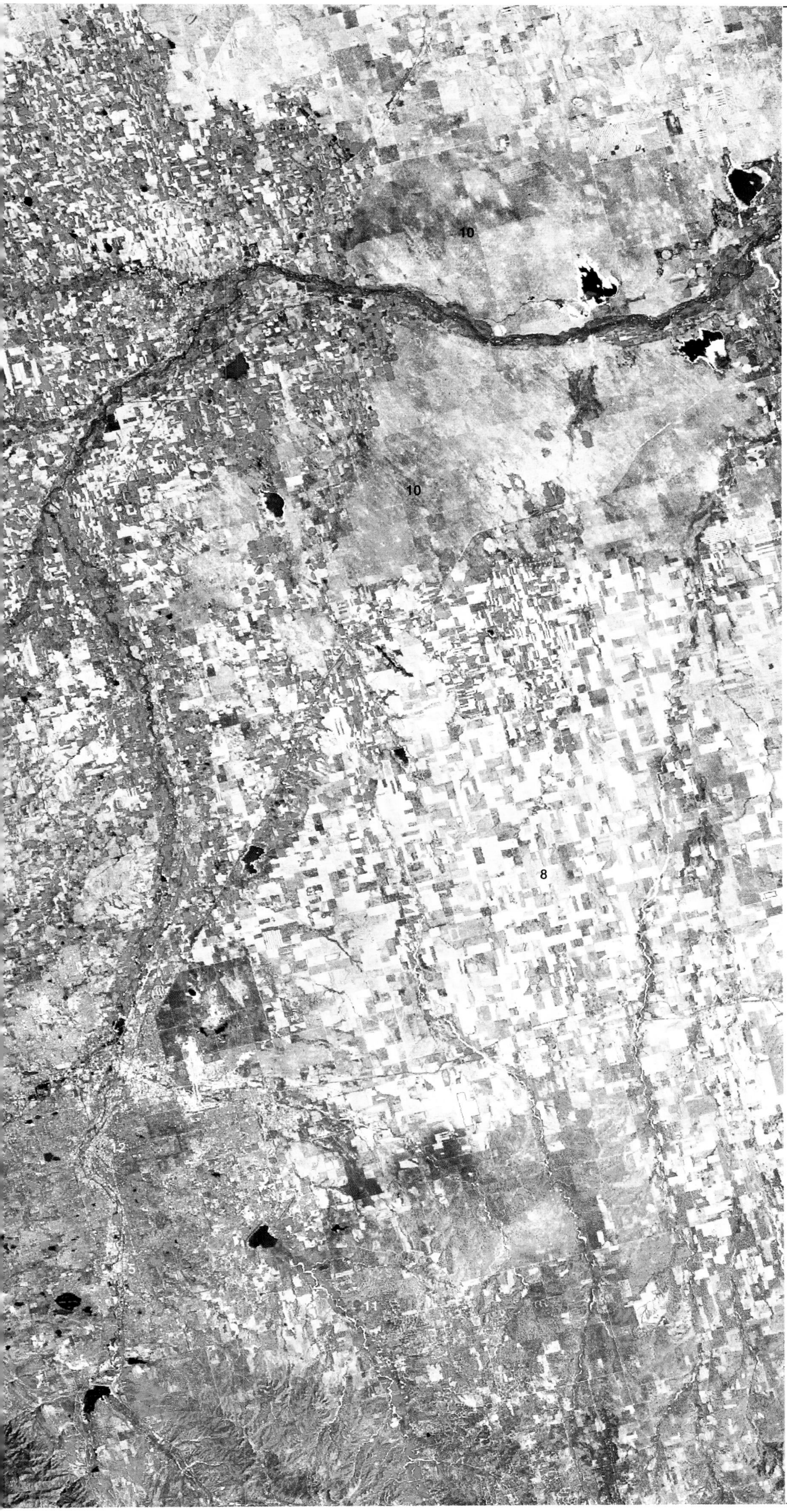

Mountains and Plains

The Front Ranges of the Rocky Mountains must have been an alarming sight for the early settlers traveling across the Great Plains. They rise up from the plains as a natural, seemingly insurmountable barrier, blocking the way west. Since there are no wide valleys, the few roads crossing the mountains have been constructed along deeply carved rivers and over high passes. Highway No. 40 (1), for example, follows Clear Creek (2) up to the 11,314 ft high Berthoud Pass (3) which is part of the continental divide. The continental divide runs from north to south and is roughly marked by the snowy peaks in the image. It separates water running west to the Colorado River (4), and eventually the Pacific Ocean, from that running east to the South Platte River (5) and the Gulf of Mexico. Aspen and coniferous trees, like Ponderosa pine, Douglas fir, and Rocky Mountain red cedar cover the mountains up to an altitude of 11,000 ft. Above this green zone brown meadows are found. High peaks such as Long's Peak rising to 14, 255 ft (6) and Hagues Peak (13,563 ft) (7), are covered with snow. Both are within the Rocky Mountain National Park.

In contrast to the dark green forests of the Rocky Mountains, one can see the multicolor checkered pattern of the Great Plains. This whole area is intensively farmed. The different types of land use can be recognized by the colors and sizes of the fields: yellow and brown represent winter wheat (8); green marks corn, beans and potatoes (9); and yellowish-brown indicates fallow land. Here the old field boundaries can barely be traced (10). The position of cultivated land along the South Platte River and its tributaries shows the area's dependence on the run-off water from the highlands. In fact, a substantial part of the irrigation water has to be diverted from the mountains east of the continental divide to the Great Plains by tunnel systems.

In 1858, a party of prospectors led by William Green Russell, discovered gold near Cherry Creek (11). This caused the Pikes Peak gold rush, during which about 50,000 people poured into the area. Cities such as Denver the capital of Colorado (12), Boulder (13), and Greeley (14) were founded during the late 19th century. Mining for gold was followed by mining for silver, but all these activities were short-lived, and by the end of the century the mountains were deserted, except for the operations of a few uranium and molybdenum mines.

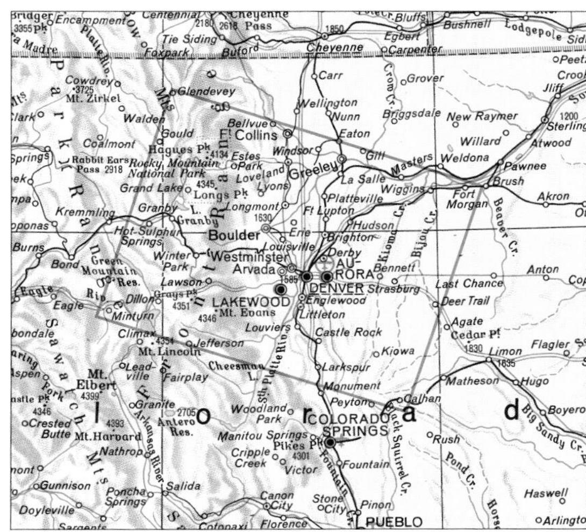
Cheyenne
Greeley
Boulder
Westminster
Arvada
DENVER
LAKEWOOD
Englewood
Littleton
Castle Rock
COLORADO SPRINGS
PUEBLO
Fort Morgan
Limon
Rocky Mountain National Park

16
15
14
1
1
14
13
10
9
12
10
11
7
5

Frontier in the Desert

This satellite photo shows part of the Sonora Desert at the northern end of the Gulf of California. The political boundary between Sonora, Mexico, in the south, and Yuma County, Arizona, in the north, is visible as a fine, pale diagonal line through the upper third of the picture (1). It consists of a fence, erected to prevent illegal immigration into the U.S.A.

In this desert and semi-desert landscape of white, beige, red and brown tones, little green is to be found as an indicator of vegetation. Irrigated crop cultivation (2) is only possible in the area on the lower edge of this image, where the Rio Concepcion flows into the Gulf. Also the upper course of the Rio Sonoita (3) creates, in places, green river oases. Other signs of vegetation appear only during a few months, in spring when torrential rain falls cause the desert to turn green and burst into blossom overnight. The giant saguaro cactuses (organ pipe cactuses) can also be found here. They grow up to 50 feet high and live for 150 to 200 years. Their white, wax-like flower is the state flower of Arizona. Organ Pipe Cactus National Monument (4), just north of the border, was established to protect these plants.

The coastal region is, in comparison, total desert. The people in the small towns of Porto Penasco (5) and La Salina (6) make their living from fishing. The form and location of the sandbanks in Bahia de Adair (7) and Bahia de San Jorge (8) show the existence of currents running parallel to the coast. These are influenced by the debouchment of the Colorado River which lies to the northwest, outside the boundary of the image. The fringes of the Gran Desierto, which stretches as far as the Colorado River, reach into this photo (9). Its sand fields, containing huge star dunes (10), can be clearly seen. White patches in the region of the dark brown shore marshlands (11), arise from the efflorescence of salt through evaporation of sea water. The most conspicuous formation is that of the Pinacate volcano field. The highest peak (12) reaches 4,560 ft. The volcanic activity in this area is relatively young. Some of the volcanoes, recognizable by their dark more or less circular forms, first erupted during the last 1000 years. The youngest lava fields are represented by very dark, almost black colors (13) which indicate a basaltic composition. In addition to the more common basaltic volcanism, explosive volcanism also occurs here. In the latter case lava, very rich in gas, explodes in the deep layers of the earth. On the surface it produces the familiar, usually circular conal structures (14). Black dots, indicating young volcanic activity, are also apparent in the Gila (15) and Coyote (16) Mountains.

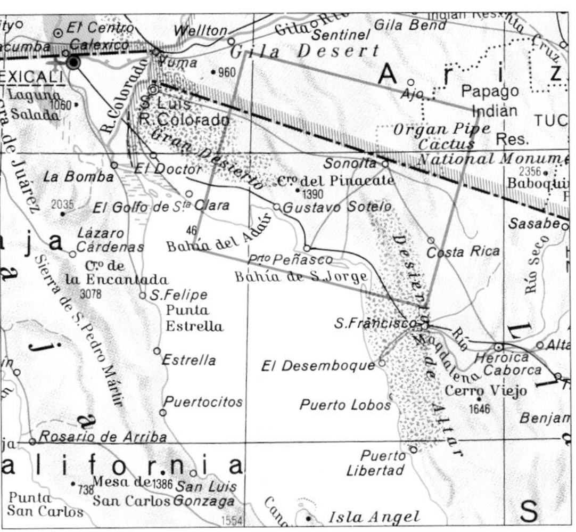

El Centro
Calexico
Wellton
Gila Bend
Sentinel
Gila Desert
Yuma
960
A r i z
Ajo
Papago
Indian
Res.
TUC
Laguna Salada
1060
R. Colorado
S. Luis R. Colorado
Gran Desierto
Organ Pipe Cactus National Monument
Sonoita
La Bomba
El Doctor
Cº del Pinacate
1390
2356
2035
El Golfo de Sta Clara
Gustavo Sotelo
Sasabe
Lázaro Cárdenas
46
Bahía del Adair
Costa Rica
Río Seco
Cº de la Encantada
3078
Prto Peñasco
Bahía de S. Jorge
Desierto de Altar
S. Felipe
Punta Estrella
S. Francisco
Río Magdalena
Sierra de S. Pedro Mártir
Estrella
El Desemboque
Heroica Caborca
Cerro Viejo
1646
Puertocitos
Puerto Lobos
Rosario de Arriba
Puerto Libertad
a l i f o r n i a
738
Mesa de San Carlos
1386
San Luis Gonzaga
Punta San Carlos
1554
Isla Angel
S

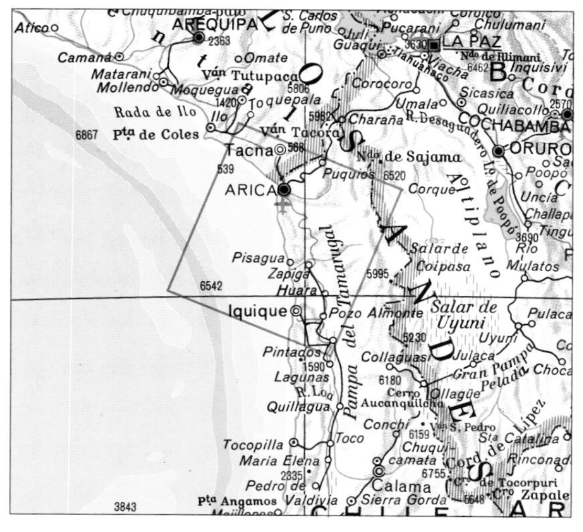
Atico
AREQUIPA
2363
S. Carlos de Puno
Juli
Pucarani
Chulumani
Guaqui
3630
LA PAZ
Ndo de Illimani
Inquisivi
Camaná
Omate
Tiahuanaco
Viacha
6462
Matarani
Mollendo
Moquegua
Ván Tutupaca
5806
Corocoro
Sicasica
1420
Toquepala
Umala
Quillacollo
2570
Rada de Ilo
Ilo
5982
Charaña
R. Desaguadero
COCHABAMBA
6867
Pta de Coles
Ván Tacora
Tacna
568
Ndo de Sajama
ORURO
539
Puquios
6520
Poopó
ARICA
Corque
Altiplano
Lº de Poopó
Uncía
Challapata
3690
Río Mulatos
Pisagua
Zapiga
Salar de Coipasa
5995
6542
Huara
Iquique
Pozo Almonte
Salar de Uyuni
Pulacayo
Pampa del Tamarugal
5230
Uyuni
Pintados
Collaguasi
Julaca
1590
Lagunas
6180
Gran Pampa Pelada
Chocaya
R. Loa
Cerro Aucanquilcha
Ollagüe
Quillagua
ANDES
Conchi
Ván S. Pedro
Cord. de Lípez
Tocopilla
Toco
6159
Chuquicamata
Sta Catalina
María Elena
Rinconada
2335
6755
Pedro de Valdivia
Calama
Crº de Tocorpuri
3843
Pta Angamos
Sierra Gorda
5648
Crº Zapaleri
CHILE

No Man's Land on the Pacific

Like a string of pearls, the surf separates the deep blue waters of the Pacific Ocean from the cliffs of Peru and Chile. This image depicts one of the driest areas on earth. In some parts of the Atacama Desert (1) it has never been known to rain. Annual rainfall of under 3 mm is measured in the town of Arica (2), on the coast. The main part of Bolivia's foreign trade is transacted in this Chilean port city. The piers (3) are just visible. The Atacama, also known as Pampa del Tamarugal, lies on a high plateau between two mountain ranges: the Cordillera de la Costa (4) to the west, recognizable by its hills and typical fault systems, and the Cordillera Occidental (5) to the east. The ground varies between pale yellow and rust brown. It consists mainly of rubble which has been washed down from the steep slopes of the volcanoes (6) in the Cordillera Occidental. Gravel slopes stand out as white threads in various places (7). Rivers, such as the Rio Azapa (8) and the Rio Camarones (9) have carved deeply into the land. Their tributaries (10) run parallel to each other which indicates that the land drops evenly but very steeply. Bright green, representing plant growth, is only apparent near the town of Tacna (11) and along a few river beds.

The Chilean province of Tarapacá is economically important because of its sodium nitrate (saltpeter) deposits. They appear as white salt pans (12) at the foot of the coastal cordillera.

Country of Fire and Ice

This natural color satellite image shows the southeastern part of Iceland. It is easy to recognize the glacial areas: the Vatnajökull or Water Glacier (1), the Myrdalsjökull (2), the Hofsjökull (3), and the Tungnafellsjökull (4). Black glacial outwash plains on the Atlantic coast and green, moss covered infertile land characterize this region.

With an area of approximately 3,205 sq.mi., the plateau glacier Vatnajökull forms Europe's largest ice sheet. The neovolcanic zone of the Mid-Atlantic Ridge stretches through Iceland as an active volcanic zone. It runs in a northeasterly direction in the south, and in a northerly direction in the north. This pattern is reflected by the location and orientation of river systems, lakes, craters, and volcanoes in the area. The chain of volcanic craters of the Eldgja fissure (5) and that of the Laki fissure (6) stretch over almost 25 mi.. In 1783 the Laki fissure (Lakagigar) erupted, emitting approximately 450,000 million cu.ft. of lava, one of the largest discharges ever recorded.

Two especially dangerous volcanic centers can be found within the boundaries of this image: Katla (7) lying underneath the Myrdalsjökull plateau glacier and Grimsvötn (8), under the Vatnajökull. Powerfull subglacial volcanic eruptions lead to the dreaded Jökullhlaup — an enormous outpour of melted ice, triggered by heat from lava and volcanic gases. Such an eruption occurred from Grimsvötn in 1934, when an estimated 247,000 million cu.ft. of melted ice thundered down at 13,200,000 gal. per second, flooding the Skeidararsandur (9). During the last eruption of the Katla in 1918 an even higher record discharge speed of 52,000,000 gal./s was reached.

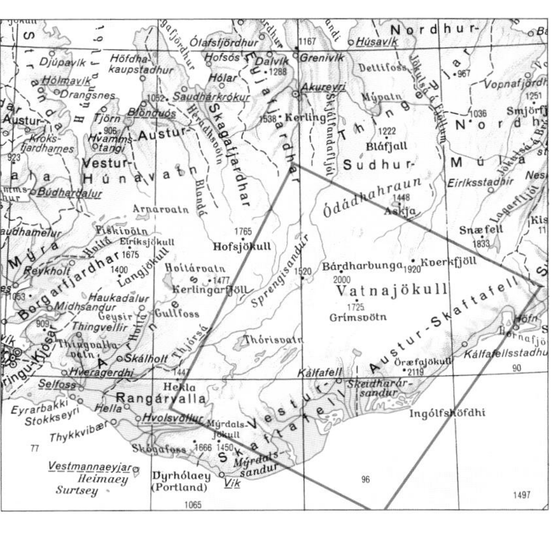

Nordhur-
Húsavík
Ólafsfjördhur
Hofsós
Dalvík
Grenivík
Höfdhakaupstadhur
Hólar
Akureyri
Djúpavík
Hólmavík
Drangsnes
Saudhárkrókur
Blönduós
Tjörn
Dettifoss
Mývatn
Vopnafjördh
Kerling
Austur-
Hvammstangi
Kroksfjardharnes
Vestur-
Húnavatn
Skagafjardhar
Eyjafjardhar
Thinge
Bláfjall
Sudhur-
Múla
Eirîksstadhir
Búdhardalur
Arnarvatn
Blandá
Ódádhahraun
Askja
Fiskivötn
Eiríksjökull
Hofsjökull
Snæfell
Borgarfjardhar
Langjökull
Hvítárvatn
Kerlingarfjöll
Sprengisandur
Bárdharbunga
Kverkfjöll
Reykholt
Vatnajökull
Haukadalur
Midhsandur
Geysir
Gullfoss
Grímsvötn
Thingvellir
Austur-Skaftafell
Höfn
Thingvallavatn
Skálholt
Thjórsá
Thórisvatn
Hveragerdhi
Kálfafell
Öræfajökull
Kálfafellsstadhur
Selfoss
Hekla
Rangárvalla
Skeidhárársandur
Eyrarbakki
Stokkseyri
Hella
Hvolsvöllur
Mýrdalsjökull
Vestur-Skaftafell
Ingólfshöfdhi
Thykkvibær
Skógafoss
Mýrdalssandur
Vestmannaeyjar
Heimaey
Surtsey
Dyrhólaey (Portland)
Vík

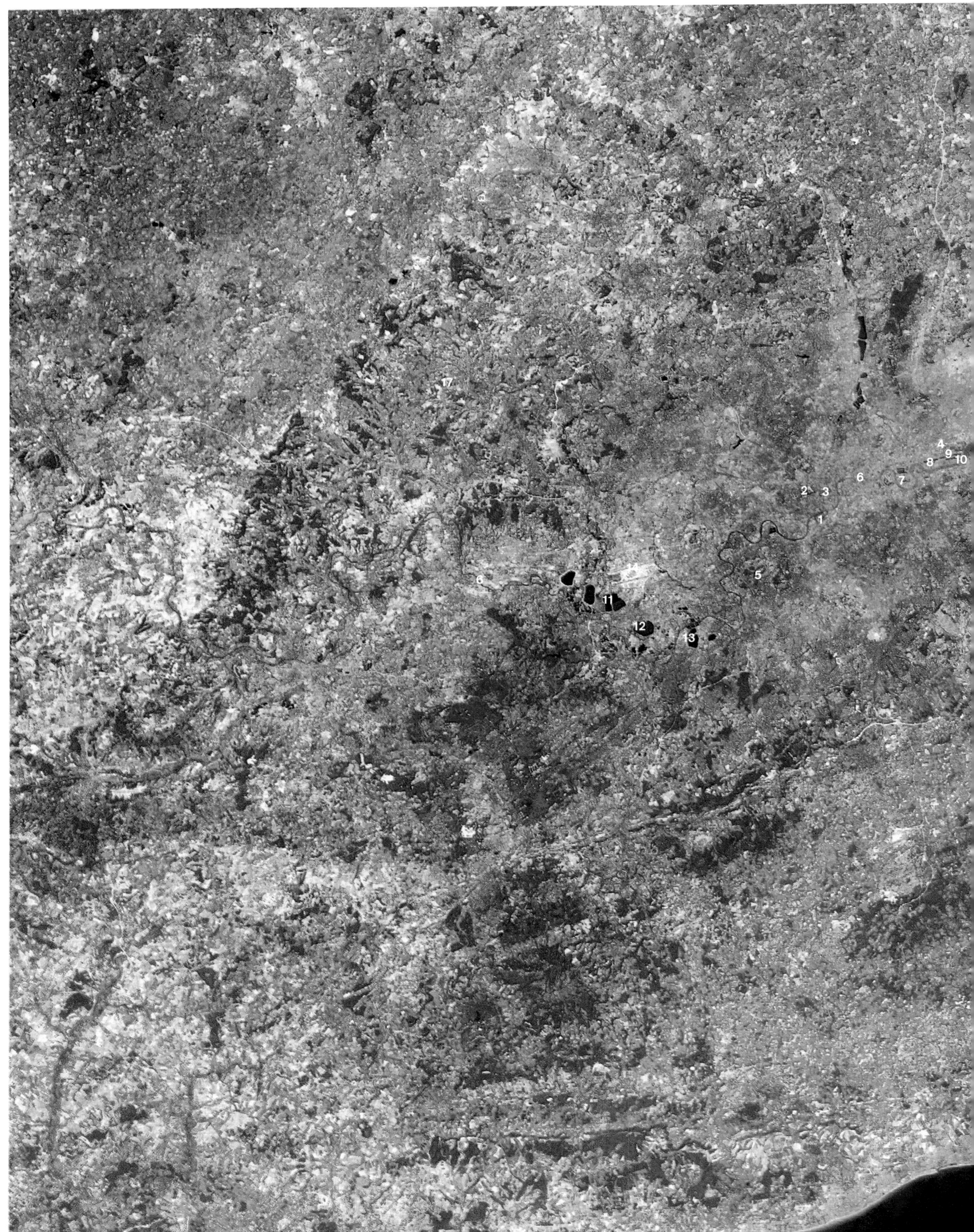
1
2
3
4
5
6
7
8
9
10
11
12
13
17

Old World Capital

Nestling in the hilly green countryside of southeast England, yet linked to the ocean by the Thames — the unique location of this metropolis is clearly reflected in our Landsat photograph.

Since 1884, London has been the hub of the world, both geographically and timewise. The old Royal Observatory in Greenwich (4) defines the geographical Prime Meridian. Times of the day throughout the world are determined by the Greenwich Mean Time (GMT), the time when the sun reaches its highest point at Greenwich.

Due to an image resolution of 80 m, and the presence of a thin veil of haze, the city center appears as a blue, more or less amorphous mass. Battersea Park (1), Hyde Park (2), and St. James Park (3) with Buckingham Palace, stand out as brown-green spots. Richmond Park and Wimbledon Common (5) together form a large forest area which is cut by a single road. The turns of the Thames, accentuated by light blue, and its harbor and docks are also easy to recognize: West India Docks (7), Victoria Dock (8), Royal Albert Dock (9) and King George Dock (10).

On the western perimeter of the city are several artificial and natural lakes. Among them are the reservoirs of King George VI (11), Queen Mary (12), and Queen Elizabeth (13). The dark blue color indicates that their water is relatively clear. In contrast, the light blue color of the Thames shows that it is heavily polluted and that it carries a high load of debris.

To the north of the King George VI Reservoir, London's international airport, Heathrow (14), can be seen in white and pale blue. Its runways and buildings cover an area of approx. 4.6 square miles.

Looking at the mouth of the Thames in the English Channel at Southend-on-Sea (15), different color shades are evident. Dark blue represents open, relatively clear water, and streaky light blue heavily polluted water. The even light blue marks the shallow water over the sand banks along the coast. When easterly winds cause a storm tide, the mouth of the Thames acts like a funnel through which water is pushed up the Thames. Hence, the center of London has been repeatedly flooded through the centuries.

In the surroundings of London one can distinguish several different types of land use: in the north, in Essex (16) and Buckingham (17) crops are grown; and in the south, in Sussex (18) and Kent (19), there are meadows and forests.

On the southern coast one can recognize the famous seaside resorts of Hastings (20) and Brighton (21). They show up as blue dots flanked by long white beaches reaching up and down the coast.

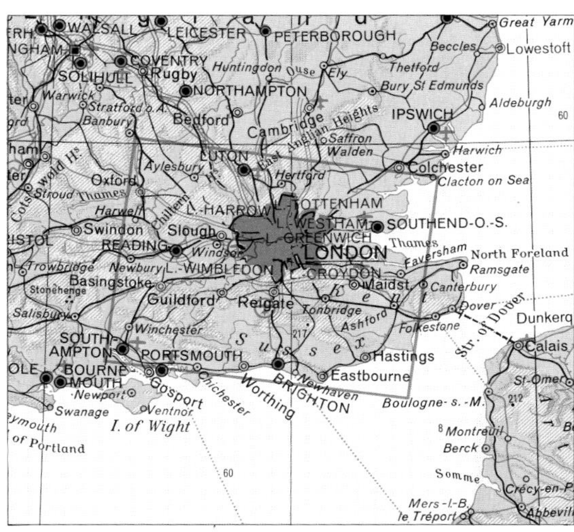

WALSALL
LEICESTER
PETERBOROUGH
Great Yarm
Lowestoft
COVENTRY
SOLIHULL
Rugby
NORTHAMPTON
Thetford
Bury St Edmunds
Aldeburgh
Bedford
Cambridge
IPSWICH
LUTON
Harwich
Colchester
Clacton on Sea
Oxford
TOTTENHAM
SOUTHEND-O.-S.
Swindon
Slough
READING
LONDON
North Foreland
Ramsgate
WIMBLEDON
CROYDON
Canterbury
Basingstoke
Guildford
Reigate
Maidst.
Dover
Dunkerq
Folkestone
Calais
PORTSMOUTH
Hastings
Eastbourne
BRIGHTON
Worthing
Newhaven
Boulogne-s.-M.
I. of Wight
Montreuil
Berck
Somme
Abbevill

4
11
17
17
12
15
14
13
2

26 Mouth of the Rhone

23
5
6
9
10
8
19
20
18
22
21
1
19

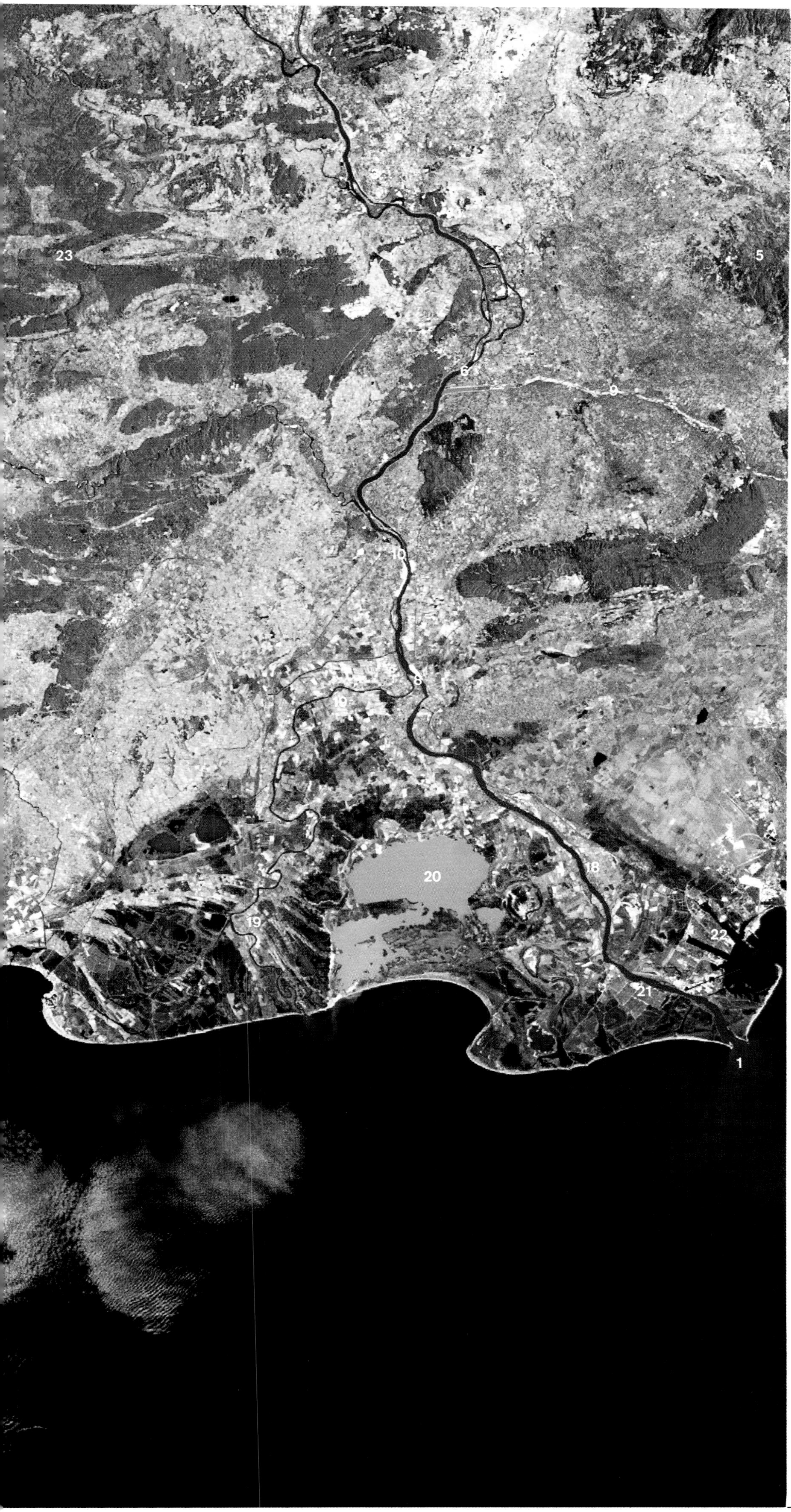

Mediterranean Landscapes

This image shows the French Riviera, from the mouth of the Rhone (1) to Béziers (2), the Rhone Valley (3) and its delta, as well as the Cévennes mountains (4). The foothills of the Maritime Alps are visible to the east (5).

The area of land which includes the coastal plains of Languedoc, as well as the Rhone Valley and Provence to the east, has been cultivated for centuries. Famous cities such as Avignon (6), Nîmes (7), and Arles (8) lie in the vast Rhone Valley. The river flows in a north-south direction and its winding path can easily be traced. Its waters are increased by the Durance (9), a main tributary coming from the Alps, which appears bright blue in its wide riverbed. This water is the lifeblood of the whole region. Through an extensive canal system, it irrigates this practically monocultural wine growing land. A recognizable example is the Bas-Rhone-Languedoc Canal which begins in Beaucaire (10) and ends in Montpellier (11). The rivers Hérault (12) and Orb (13), whose headwaters reach far into the Cévennes mountains, irrigate the southern Languedoc.

The coastline stands out through its almost continuous white fringe of sandy beaches. Étang de Thau (14), with the Port of Sète (15) and Étang de Mauguio (16) are the most important. In separated basins (17), recognizable by their slate gray color, water from the Mediterranean is evaporated to win salt.

Between the Grand Rhone (18), a branch of the Rhone delta which carries 85 percent of the water from the Rhone to the sea, and the Petit Rhone (19), and somewhat beyond it to the west, lies a unique area called the Camargue. Its landscape is characterized by numerous shallow lagoons. The largest of these is the Étang de Vaccàres (20). Because of their shallowness, the lagoons appear from pale to gray blue in the satellite photo. The large evaporation ponds of Salin-de-Giraud (21) can be recognized by their bordering dams. Further inland the yellow, brown and green shades represent a swamp and alluvial zone. Scrub land occurs in other parts of the Camargue due to the high salt content of the soil. These areas are used for the breeding of horses and fighting bulls.

To the east of the mouth of the Grand Rhone is the site of Fos-sur-Mer (22), an oil port that is still under construction.

The region to the west of the Rhone is conspicuous because of its unique green, wavy form (23). Rock folds have been exposed to the atmosphere through weathering. Plant growth, which differs in denseness according to the rock type, highlights the structure of the folding.

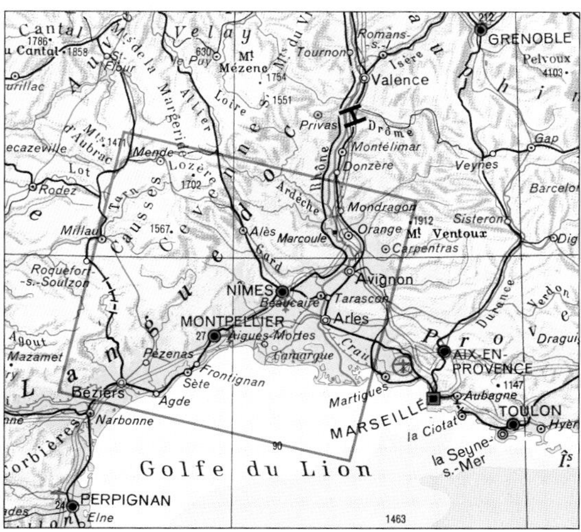

GRENOBLE
Valence
Privas
Montélimar
Donzère
Mende
Rodez
Millau
Alès
Marcoule
Orange
Mt Ventoux
Carpentras
Avignon
NÎMES
Beaucaire
Tarascon
Arles
MONTPELLIER
Aigues-Mortes
Camargue
Pézenas
Frontignan
Sète
Agde
Béziers
Narbonne
AIX-EN-PROVENCE
MARSEILLE
Aubagne
TOULON
la Ciotat
Golfe du Lion
PERPIGNAN
Elne
Gap
Sisteron

11
26
12
1
10
3
13
3
1
21
4
5
6
22
23
24
7
8
9

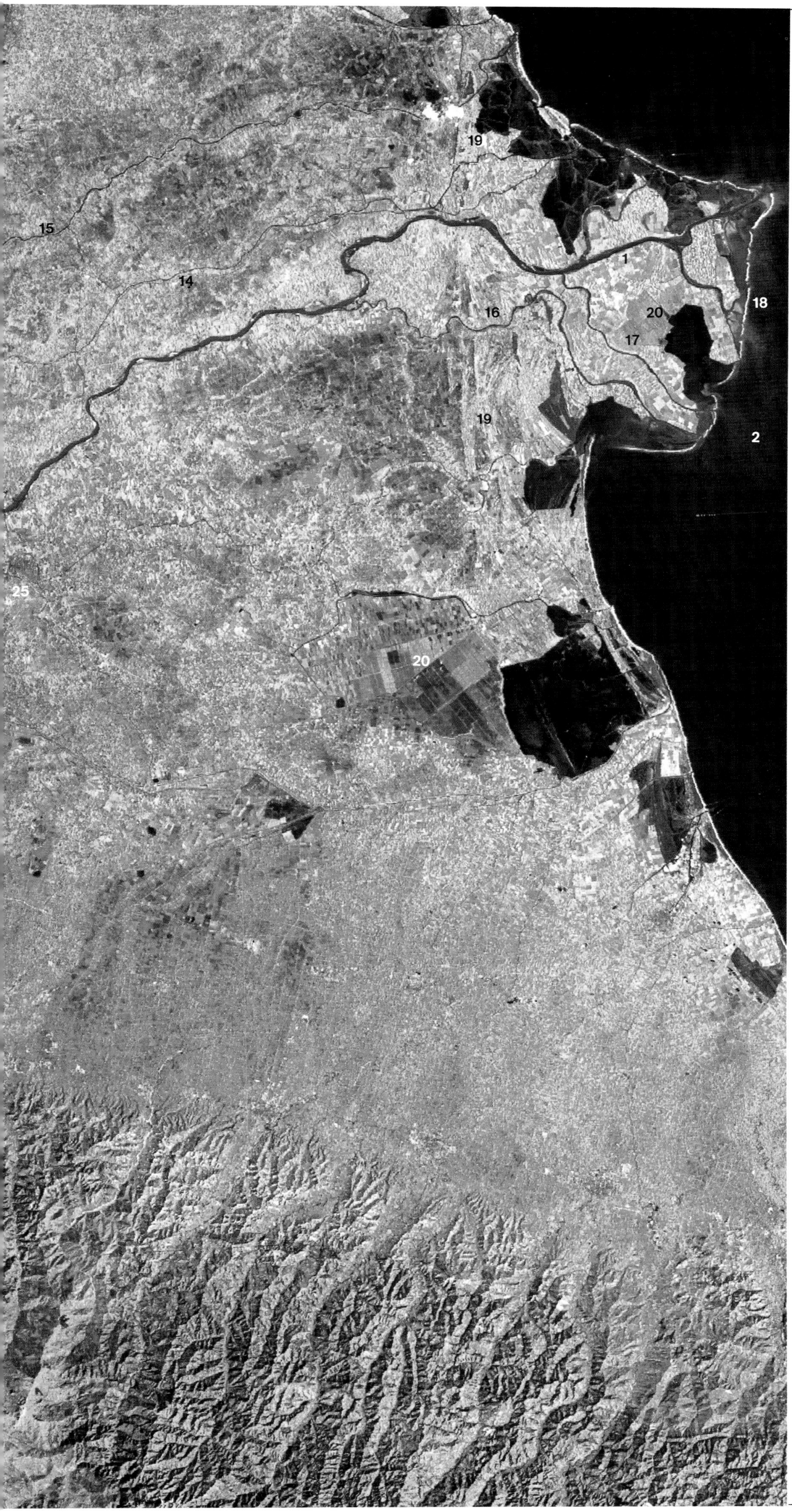

Farmland and Industrial Centers

The Po Valley, an alluvial plain, forms one of the largest natural complexes in Italy. It covers an area of approximately 19,300 sq.mi., one sixth of the total area of Italy. The valley is 310 mi. long and varies from 31 to 75 mi. in width. It stretches in a west–east direction, bordered in the north by the southern Alps, in the south by the Apennine Range, and in the east by the Adriatic Sea.

This satellite image covers the eastern part of the Po Valley with the Po delta (1) reaching into the Adriatic Sea (2). The river stands out against its surroundings like a black snake. The meandering nature of the river, and the numerous dark backwater curves (3) that were once part of the riverbed are sure signs of a slow-moving current, due to an extremely small gradient. The river descends only 1,312 ft over a length of 373 mi. The white sand banks in the river bed are quite conspicuous. Because these are continually changing, only small boats can navigate the river. The amount of water in the Po is determined by its tributaries from the Apennines, such as the Taro (4), Parma (5), Enza (6), Secchia (7), Panaro (8) and Setta (9); from the alpine rivers such as the Oglio (10); and from the river flowing out of Lake Garda (11), the Mincio (12). Artificial canals such as the Cavo Napoleonica (13) or the Canale Bianco (14) connect the tributaries of the Po and also form a link with the Adige River (15), to the north. They were built for irrigation purposes.

In the delta region, the Po divides into 14 branches of which the Po di Goro (16) and the Po di Gnocca (17) are the most significant. The delta consists of shallow lagoons which are separated from the Adriatic by a chain of white sand banks (18). Because of considerable debris, deposits, particularly from the Apennine rivers, the delta is growing out into the Adriatic Sea at a rate of about 230 to 260 ft annually. The coast lines from earlier centuries remain visible as prominent lines (19) on the mainland of today.

The intensive agricultural use of the land is apparent by the dense network of fields and meadows. Green tones in the west indicate orchards, vineyards and pastures; gray and red tones in the east are typical of crop growing areas. The land near the coast is predominantly used for the cultivation of rice. The noticeably large fields are surrounded by dams (20).

Industry is concentrated in a belt just north of the Apennines, including the cities of Parma (21), Reggio nell'Emilia (22), Modena (23), and Bologna (24). The road and railway track linking them is visible as a thin dark line. Ferrara (25) and Verona (26) are also of industrial importance.

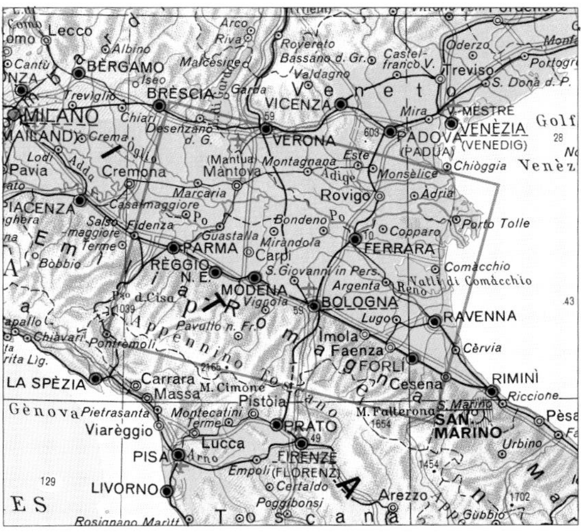

Lecco
BERGAMO
BRESCIA
VICENZA
MESTRE
VENEZIA (VENEDIG)
PADOVA (PADUA)
VERONA
Chioggia
Cremona
Mantova
Rovigo
Adria
Porto Tolle
PARMA
FERRARA
REGGIO
MODENA
BOLOGNA
Comacchio
RAVENNA
Imola
Faenza
FORLÌ
Cesena
Cèrvia
RIMINI
Riccione
SAN MARINO
LA SPEZIA
Carrara
Massa
Viarèggio
Lucca
PISA
PRATO
FIRENZE (FLORENZ)
LIVORNO
Arezzo

2
1
4
17
8
15
16
12
15
10
6
13
14

Swamps, Islands and Oil Fields

In ancient times, the Euphrates (1) and Tigris (2) rivers flowed independently into the Persian Gulf. Over the ages their estuaries have grown together forming the Shatt-al-Arab (3), whose river mouth is now approximately 106 miles from their confluence. With exception of the area on the lower left, the region shown in this image consists mainly of alluvial land, swamps and marshes.

In swamps, such as the Hawr-al-Hamar (4) or those in the region of the Jarrahi River (5), the black color shows clear, still water, and pale green represents polluted water. Young vegetation can be recognized by the bright green color, while darker green indicates older growth. The marshes (6) have gray tones and are covered by a multitude of dendritical rivers, which slowly meander over the flat land. The building of dams, artificial lakes, and irrigation plants in the upper Euphrates and Tigris rivers has heavily reduced the water volume and floating sediment in the Shatt-al-Arab. Hence, the first half of this river is a dark blue. The yellowish green, indicating sediment, first appears at the confluence of the Rud e-Karun River (7), which joins the Shatt-al-Arab near the city of Khorramshahr (8). Sediment from the other heavily loaded rivers such as the Khawr e-Bahmarshir (9) or Khawr-az-Zubayr (10) can be seen stretching far into the gulf. The huge amounts of mud which have been deposited can be understood if one considers that the city of Abadan (11) was an important port on the Persian Gulf during the tenth century. Today it lies 31 miles away from the coast.

Areas from three different countries appear in this image: Kuwait, Iraq, and the Iranian province of Khuzestan. A considerable part of the world's oil reserves are located in this region. The oil fields of Al-Rumaylah (12) in Iraq and As-Sabiriyah (13) in Kuwait are situated on the flat, loamy semi-desert of Ab-Dibdibah (14). Their platforms can be traced by following the black smoke trails which have been blown in a southeasterly direction. The drilling rigs and oil wells are linked by a network of streets (15) and pipelines (16). The latter run in straight lines and are mostly underground. Because of the closing of the ports of Al-Basrah (17) and Abadan on the Iraqi side, the loading of oil now takes place at the terminal of Khawr-al-Arnaiyah. This lies offshore and is not visible in the image. Before being shipped, the oil is stored in large tanks at Al-Faw (18). These tanks appear as orderly rows of pale dots.

The green area along both sides of the Shatt-al-Arab river marks the world's largest date producing area. Several hundred thousand tons of dates are harvested here annually.

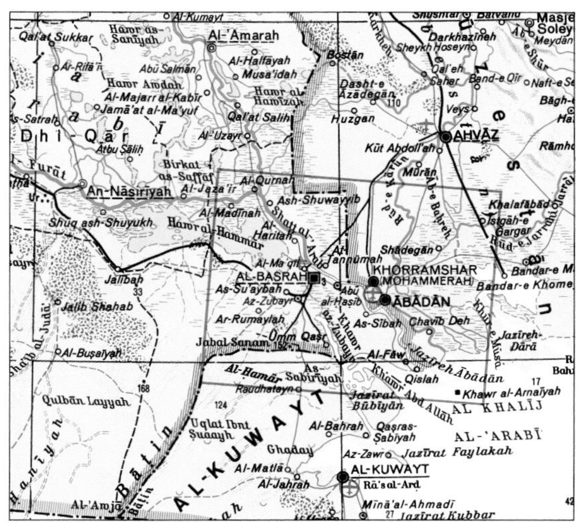

Al-'Amarah
AHVĀZ
An-Nāṣiriyah
AL-BAṢRAH
KHORRAMSHAHR
ĀBĀDĀN
AL-KUWAYT
AL-KUWAYT

8
5
9
2
6
9
7

Tropical Archipelago

Only a few of the 7107 islands, which comprise the Philippine archipelago are visible in this image. The eleven largest islands including Luzon (1) in the north, and Mindanao (not visible in photo) in the south, make up 96 percent of the total land area. Mindoro (2), the round island of Marinduque (3) and other, smaller islands seen as green spots, make up the remaining four percent.

The archipelago was first formed in the tertiary period, some 50 million years ago, when numerous volcanoes erupted through the ocean floor on the edge of the Pacific. Some of these can be recognized by their circular craters and radiating erosion grooves (4, 5).

Today there are twelve active volcanoes in the Philippines. These and frequent earthquakes show that the earth's crust in this region is not yet at rest. Consequently, the population is at times endangered by phenomena such as seismic sea waves, glowing clouds, ash rain, and lava flows.

As the Philippines are situated just north of the equator, they belong to the tropical climatic zone. Because of high temperatures throughout the year and substantial rainfall, the vegetation is lush. Hence, it is visible as deep dark green. Depending upon the altitude and respective rainfall, different types of forests are apparent: rain, monsoon and evergreen oak forest. However, due to the high monetary value of the timber, some areas have been completely deforested. This has led to erosion of the humus layer and the resulting barren mountainsides and deep ravines (6) can be seen on the island of Mindoro. The pale blue rivers (7) are also a part of this process. Their color indicates the presence of sediment that is transported from the eroded land into the sea.

The city of Calapan (8) is situated in the fertile lowlands to the east. Although these are partly covered by clouds, the settlements can be recognized by their purple-grey color. This is an intensively cultivated area where rice, pineapples, and coconut palms predominate.

Tourism is becoming an increasingly important economic factor here. The most popular attractions are the coral reefs just off the coast (9). The coral builds colonies of pipe-shaped lime secretions, which altogether form the coral reef. The animal requires clean, well-aerated saltwater at a temperature of 64 to 68°F, ample nourishment and a high intensity of light. As the reefs are aglow with a spectrum of colors, and provide shelter for many species of exotic fish, they are a favorite goal for scuba divers.

LUZÓN
Baguio
Dagupan
S. José
S. Carlos
Camiling
TARLAC
CABANATUAN
Iba
S. Fernando
S. Narciso
OLONGAPO
MANILA
Polillo Is
QUEZON CITY
Orani
Calagua Is
Cavite
Lamon Bay
Manila Bay
Paracale
Corregidor I.
S. Pablo
Lucena
Daet
Lubang Is
BATANGAS
Naga
Catanduanes I.
Iriga
Virac
Calapan
Marinduque I.
Tabaco
Mindoro
Bondoc Pen.
Burias I.
Legaspi
Pinamalayan
Sibuyan
Sorsogon
Donsol
Bulan
Mindoro Str.
Romblon
Odiongan
Sea
Masbate
Catarman
Busuanga I.
Tablas I.
Sibuyan I.
CALBAYOG
Culion I.
Mandaon
Samar
Semirara Is
Masbate
Catbalogan
Kalibo
Biliran I.
Panay
Roxas
Visayan Sea
Tacloban
El Nido
Cuyo Is
Bogo
Ormoc
Taytay
ILOILO
BACOLOD
Leyte
S. Carlos
S. José de Buenavista
Cebu
Baybay
Dinagat I.
Duma-ran I.
Guimaras I.
CEBU
Binalbagan
Siargao I.
Honda Bay
Negros
Carcar
Bohol
Puerto Princesa
Panaon I.
Surigao
Cagayan Is
Tanjay
Tagbilaran
Dumaguete
Camiguin
Cantilan

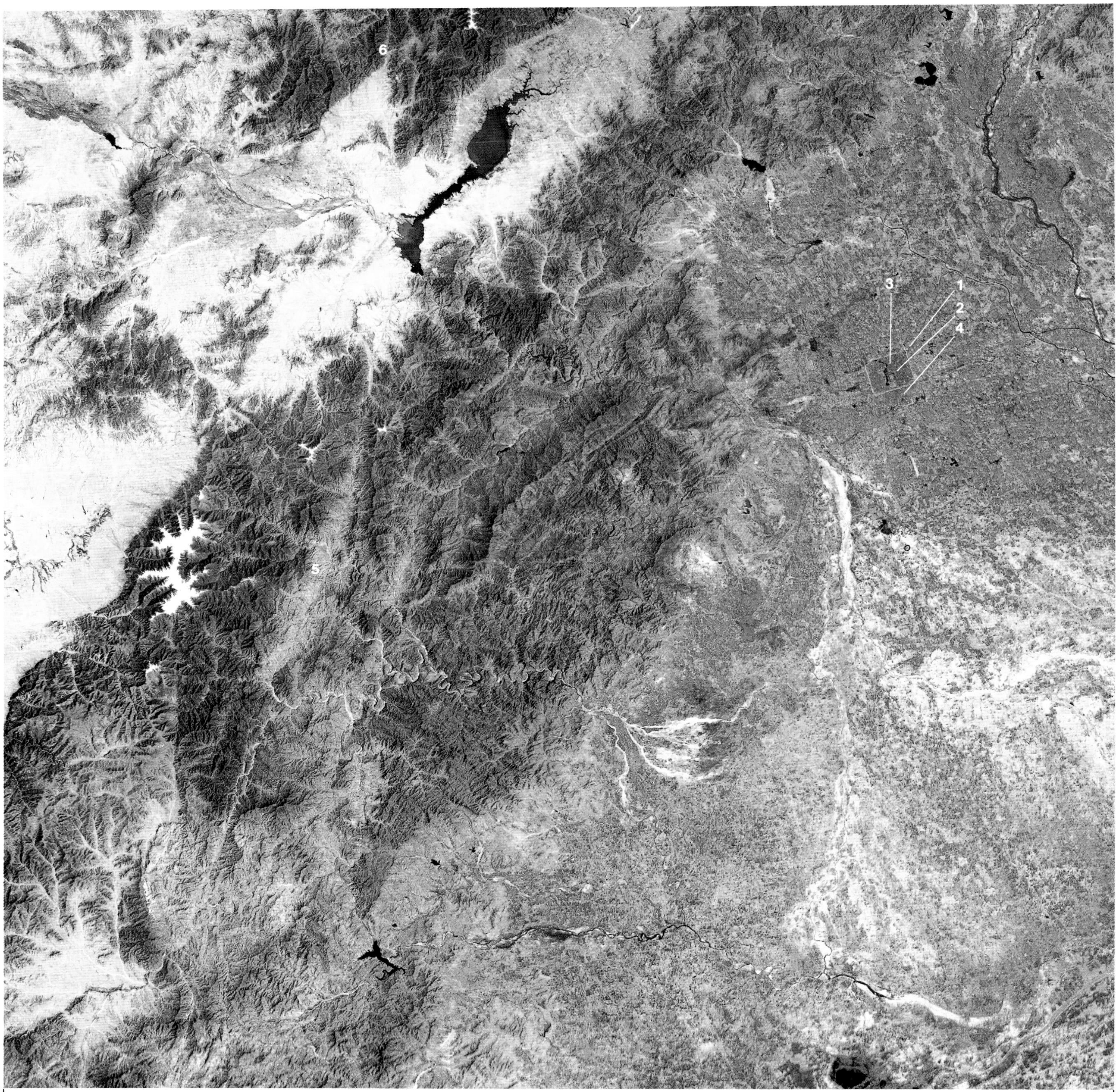

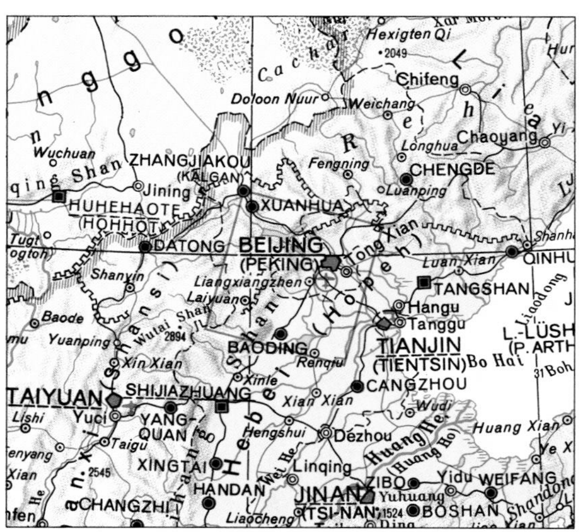
Hexigten Qi
Chifeng
Doloon Nuur
Weichang
Chaoyang
Wuchuan
ZHANGJIAKOU
(KALGAN)
Fengning
CHENGDE
Luanping
HUHEHAOTE
(HOHHOT)
Jining
XUANHUA
DATONG
BEIJING
(PEKING)
QINHU
Shanyin
Luan Xian
TANGSHAN
Hangu
Tanggu
Baode
Yuanping
TIANJIN
(TIENTSIN)
Bo Hai
Xin Xian
Xinle
Renqiu
TAIYUAN
SHIJIAZHUANG
CANGZHOU
Yuci
YANG-
QUAN
Hengshui
Dezhou
Huang Xian
XINGTAI
Linqing
HANDAN
Yidu
WEIFANG
CHANGZHI
JINAN
(TSI-NAN)
ZIBO
BOSHAN
Liaocheng

Civilization on Fertile Soil

One of the most noticeable features of this image is the center of the city of Beijing, which appears as a large gray spot. Its layout, based on a grid pattern, dates back to 1260. The white rectangle is the wall of the "Inner" or "Mongol" City (1). The dark, barely visible rectangle is the King's City with the "Forbidden City", the seat of the Chinese God-Emperors (2). The small black dots (3) are artificial lakes. The rectangle of the old "Chinese City" to the south is also just visible as its walls have been removed in recent times. The green patch inside the rectangle is the park of the Temple of Heaven (4).

Today, the city of Beijing has extended well outside its old walls. The multicolored mosaic appearance of the fields indicates intensive agricultural use. The high fertility of the "Great Plain" is due to its loess soil which has been deposited through flooding of the numerous rivers coming from the surrounding mountains.

The mountain range, lying on the diagonal of this image, is part of the larger Khingan Range. It consists of granite and basalt and is intersected by distinct faults (5). In one place (6), the left mountain block has been pushed southwards with respect to the right block. Although difficult to recognize at ground level, such large structures stand out well in satellite photographs.

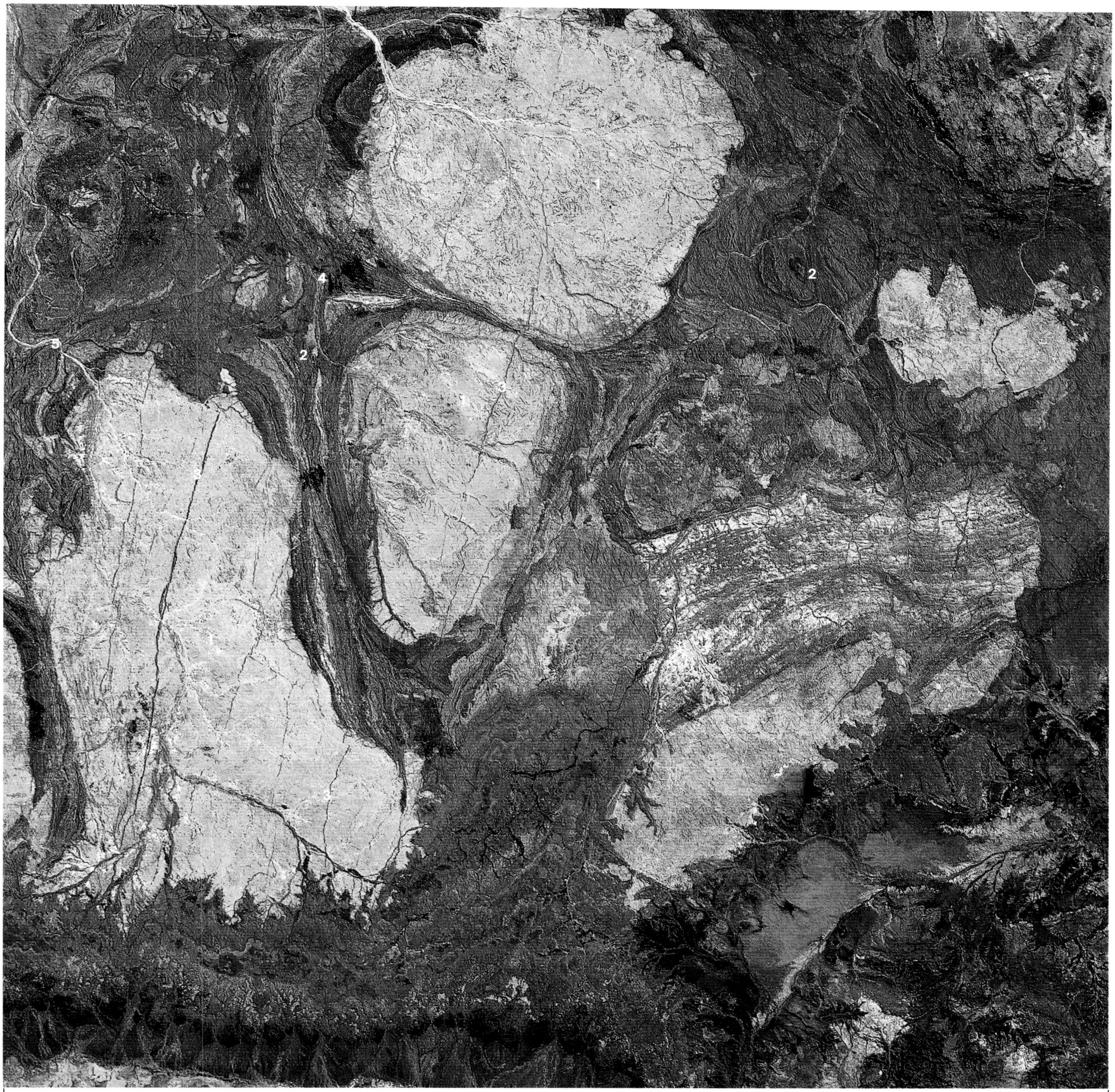

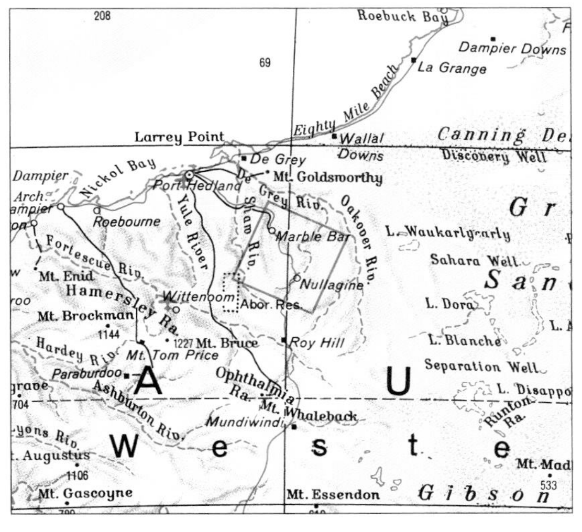

208
Roebuck Bay
Dampier Downs
69
La Grange
Eighty Mile Beach
Larrey Point
Wallal
Downs
Canning
Discovery Well
De Grey
Mt. Goldsworthy
Dampier
Nickol Bay
Port Hedland
Grey Riv.
Arch.
Roebourne
Yule River
Shaw Riv.
Oakover Riv.
Marble Bar
L. Waukarlycarly
Fortescue Riv.
Sahara Well
Mt. Enid
Hamersley Ra.
Nullagine
Wittenoom
Abor. Res.
L. Dora
Mt. Brockman
1144
1227 Mt. Bruce
Roy Hill
L. Blanche
Hardey Riv.
Mt. Tom Price
Separation Well
Paraburdoo
A
Ophthalmia Ra.
U
704
Ashburton Riv.
Mt. Whaleback
Runton Ra.
Mundiwindi
W e s t e
Mt. Augustus
1106
Mt. Gascoyne
Mt. Essendon
Gibson
533

Archaic Rock Formations

Lacking vegetation, this region reveals a part of the earth's early history. The rocks visible here were formed 2.5 to 3.5 billion years ago and belong to the oldest known formations on earth. At that time massive mountains reached heights of 12.5 miles. Over the ages the powers of erosion have reduced them to the truncated landscape of today.

Huge granite domes, called Plutons (1), were forced out of the deep layers of the earth's crust. Their bright yellow colors stand out well against the dark grayish-brown tones of the surrounding rocks (2). These belong to a so-called "mobile belt", a zone made up of gneisses, volcanic rock, and sedimentation, which were converted into metamorphic rock through heat and pressure. The original stratification can still be recognized from the bands of differing shades of color. The brown tones indicate the high iron content of the crusty surface layer.

Dark veins (3), up to 60 miles long, were created by basaltic lava which forced its way into the fissures formed during the cooling period of the granite.

The Pilbara District is a highly important economic region in Western Australia. The gold mining cities of Marble Bar (4) and Nullagine (5) were built in the 1920's. By 1972 a total of 11 tons of gold and 1041 tons of silver had been mined here.

3
3
4
3
3
10
9
8

Seam of two Continents

At its northern end, the Red Sea is divided into two branches: the Gulf of Akaba or Khalij al-Aqabah in Arabic, and the Gulf of Suez or Khalij as-Suways. This image shows the middle section of the latter. It is named after the Port of Suez or As-Suways which lies at the northern end.

The Gulf of Suez is part of a geological structure which has been intensively investigated for decades. A zone of weakness in the earth's crust stretches from Zimbabwe, over the long lakes of East Africa, the Rift valley in Kenya, and through the valley of Danikil in Ethiopia. Close to Djibouti this zone splits into three branches: in the east, the Gulf of Aden; in the north, the Red Sea with the Gulf of Suez; the third branch runs from the Gulf of Akaba through the Dead Sea as far the Jordan valley. Along this structure, the crust of the earth is broken apart by movements of the earth's mantle. This process, called plate tectonics, is basically a shifting apart of the two rock shelves. The drift rate has been measured by laser beam and amounts to 2 to 5 cm per year. Approximately one million years ago the two coasts seen in the photograph were joined together. Today, these two parts of Egypt belong to two different continents which continue to move away from each other.

Due to the lack of vegetation and variety of colors, the different types of rock can easily be determined from this image. Granite and gneiss are indicated by dark areas (1) with prominent fractures cutting through the rock. The light gray rock embedded in circular forms (2) is older, paler granite. The remaining red and gray toned rock (3) consists mainly of different types of old limestone. The way in which the limestone is deposited in layers can be seen on the edges of eroded areas (4) and in dry river beds (5). These rivers are characterized by several arms and branches, and form, in geological terms, a dendritical net. The highest mountains in the region are of granite which best withstands erosion. To name a few: the Jabal Kathrinah (8,652 ft) (6), named after the legend of the Moses mountain and on whose slopes the famous Katherine Monastery (Dayr Katrinah) lies; the Jabal Mosá (7,497 ft) (7); and the Jabal Gharib (5,145 ft) (8).

The region has recently gained industrial importance through the oil fields near Ra's Gharib (9) and Abu Darbah (10). These fields stretch out partly under the seabed. Recently, tourism has also become an important industry. The prominent attractions are the coral reefs (11) which appear light blue in the image.

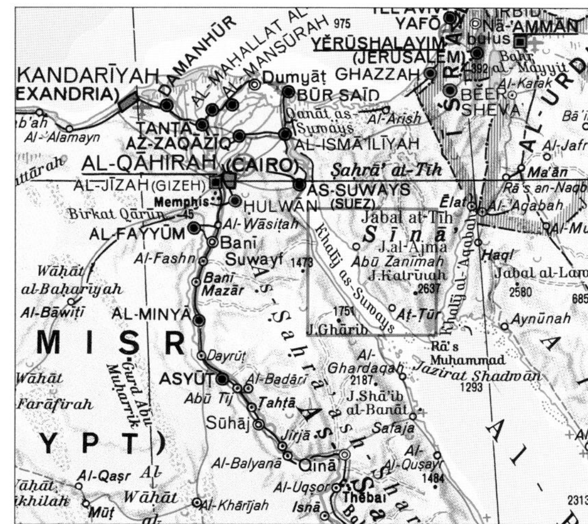

KANDARĪYAH
EXANDRIA)
DAMANHŪR
AL-MAHALLAT AL
AL-MANṢŪRAH
975
YAFO
Nā-
bulus
'AMMĀN
YĔRŪSHALAYIM
(JERUSALEM)
Dumyāṭ
GHAZZAH
BŪR SAʿĪD
BĔER-SHEVA
Al-Karak
Al-'Alamayn
TANṬA
AZ-ZAQĀZĪQ
Qanāt as-Suways
Al-'Arish
AL-ISMĀ'ĪLĪYAH
Al-Jafr
AL-QĀHIRAH (CAIRO)
Ṣaḥrā' al-Tīh
Ma'ān
AL-JĪZAH (GIZEH)
AS-SUWAYS (SUEZ)
Rā's an-Naqb
Memphis
HULWĀN
Ēlat
Al-'Aqabah
Birkat Qārūn
-45
Jabal at-Tīh
AL-FAYYŪM
Al-Wāsiṭah
Sīnā'
Banī Suwayf
1473
J.al-Ajma
Al-Fashn
Abū Zanīmah
Haql
Wāḥāt al-Baḥarīyah
Bani Mazār
J.Katrīnah
2637
Jabal al-Laro
2580
Al-Bāwiṭī
AL-MINYĀ
1751
Aṭ-Ṭūr
Aynūnah
J.Ghārib
Khalīj as-Suways
Khalīj al-'Aqabah
MISR
Rā's Muhammad
Dayrūṭ
Al-Ghardaqah
Jazirat Shadwān
Wāḥāt
ASYŪṬ
Al-Badārī
2187
1293
Ghurd Abū Muḥarrik
Farāfirah
Abū Tīj
Ṭahṭā
J.Shā'ib al-Banāt
Sūhāj
Safaja
YPT)
Jirjā
Al-Balyanā
Qinā
Al-Quṣayr
1484
Al-Qaṣr
Wāḥāt
Al-Uqṣor
Thebai
2313
Mūṭ
Al-Khārījah
Isnā

10
7
8
2
7
6
3
4

Diamond Deposits on the Shore

The region shown here is in southwestern Namibia, and includes part of the coastal strip comprising the Namib Desert. The climate of the region is extremely inhospitable.

The gray, yellow, and brown colors, and especially the complete lack of green tones, show that this area is total desert land. In spite of this however, the region is geologically and particularly economically interesting. The sand dunes, bordered by the sea and the mountains, contain the largest diamond deposits in the world. They stretch along the coast from Oranjerivier in the south, to Walvisbaai in the north, and are an average of 75 miles wide. The actual origin of the diamonds is still unknown. They probably originate from the Kimberlit rocks, which are located further inland. For a period of several million years, erosion debris from these rocks has moved to the coast. The hard diamonds withstood this movement while the rest of the material, being softer, was gradually ground up. The original deposit contained very few diamonds per cubic foot. The redeposition produced a diamond-rich secondary deposit which consists essentially of a lightly bound mixture of sand and pebbles.

To extract the diamonds, the wind-blown layer of the sand dunes is cleared away and then the diamond containing layers are washed. The yield of diamonds in 1978 was approximately 1.9 million carats (at approx. 0.2 g ea.). Ninety percent of this was of gemstone quality. Along with diamonds, lead, zinc, and copper (Sinclair coppermine) (1) are also mined in certain areas.

The fishing industry is of little importance, despite the fact that the cold Benguela current is rich in nutriments and hence rich in fish. Spencer Bay (2) and Hottentot Bay (3) are not suitable for the building of ports. The port town of Lüderitz (approx. 6,000 citizens) is the only one which has been able to develop in this region. It is situated on Lüderitz Bay (Angra Pequena) (4) which lies just below the lower part of this image. Roads and railway lines (5) end there.

The variety of forms and colors of the sand dunes are particularly fascinating. The longitudinal dunes (6) are clearly separated from each other and stretch out up to 30 miles. They mark the general wind direction north-north-east. The ripple dunes (7) are closer to each other and are aligned crosswise to the others. The star dunes (8) can be several hundred yards high. They extend far into the high country in the area of the Tirasduines (9). In the midst of this sea of sand, isolated mountains such as Hauchab (3,280 ft) (10) appear as islands.

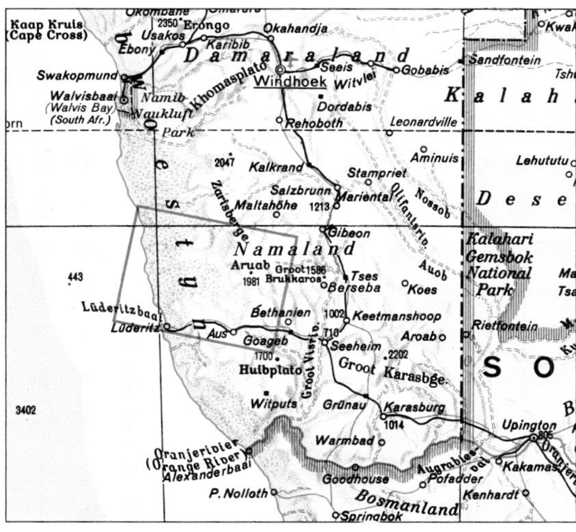
Kaap Kruis (Cape Cross)
Erongo
Usakos
Ebony
Karibib
Okahandja
Damaraland
Swakopmund
Walvisbaai (Walvis Bay) (South Afr.)
Namib-Naukluft Park
Khomasplato
Windhoek
Seeis
Witvlei
Gobabis
Sandfontein
Dordabis
Rehoboth
Leonardville
Kalah
Aminuis
Lehututu
Kalkrand
Stampriet
Salzbrunn
Mariental
Maltahöhe
Olifantsriv.
Nossob
Dese
Zaritsberge
Gibeon
Namaland
Aruab
Groot Brukkaros
Tses
Berseba
Koes
Auob
Kalahari Gemsbok National Park
Lüderitzbaai
Lüderitz
Aus
Bethanien
Keetmanshoop
Goageb
Seeheim
Aroab
Rietfontein
Huibplato
Groot Visriv.
Groot Karasbge.
Witputs
Grünau
Karasburg
Upington
Warmbad
Oranjerivier (Orange River)
Alexanderbaai
Goodhouse
Pofadder
Kakamas
Kenhardt
P. Nolloth
Bosmanland
Springbok

Volcanoes in the Sahara Desert

This image covers an area in the north of the Chad republic. The Tibesti Mountains, lying in the central Sahara, are "drowned" here in the adjoining gravel desert, the Serir de Tibesti (1). Different shades of yellow (2) represent parallel longitudinal sand dunes.

The Tibesti Mountains consist essentially of Precambrian rock, which was formed more than 600 million years ago. Over the ages the mountain tops of schist, phyllite and granite have been eroded, leaving the truncated forms of today. Most conspicuous are the faults (3) which run mainly in a north to northeasterly direction. They are accented by their light colored sand filling. The lengths and orientations of these faults have enabled researchers to draw conclusions about the powers which deformed the mountains. The angles at which the faults intersect each other (4) are also of particular significance to scientists.

In the Tertiary Age, about 50 million years ago, volcanoes erupted through the old rock. Their craters (5, 6, 7), in the lower part of the image, are easy to recognize by their circular shapes. The dark purple-gray of the volcanoes is typical of lava flows and volcanic ash. The age of the lava can be determined by the intensity of the color: the richer the color, the younger the lava. For example, relatively recent activity is indicated by the deep color of the Pic Toussidé volcano (8), the second highest mountain in the Sahara (10,712 ft). A small, strongly reflecting salt lake can be seen in the crater of Trou au Natron (9) nearby.

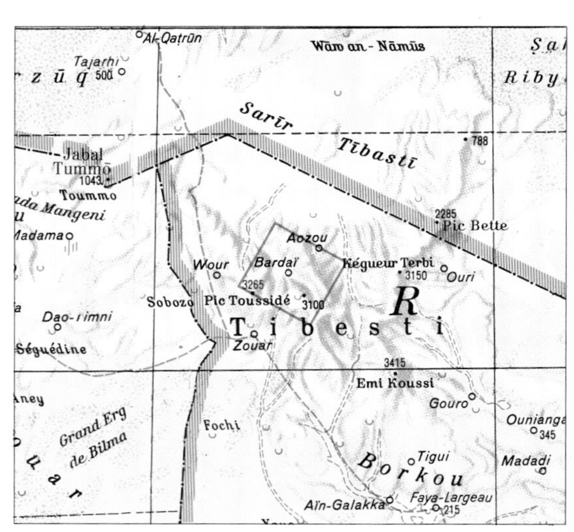

Al-Qaṭrūn
Wāw an-Nāmūs
Tajarhi
500
Riby
Sarīr Tībastī
788
Jabal Tummō
1043
Toummo
Mangeni
Madama
2285
Pic Bette
Aozou
Wour
Bardaï
Kégueur Terbi
3150
Ouri
3265
Sobozo
Pic Toussidé
3100
Dao-Timni
Tibesti
Séguédine
Zouar
3415
Emi Koussi
Aney
Gouro
Grand Erg de Bilma
Fochi
Ounianga
345
Tigui
Madadi
Borkou
Aïn-Galakka
Faya-Largeau
215

Key to Map Coverage

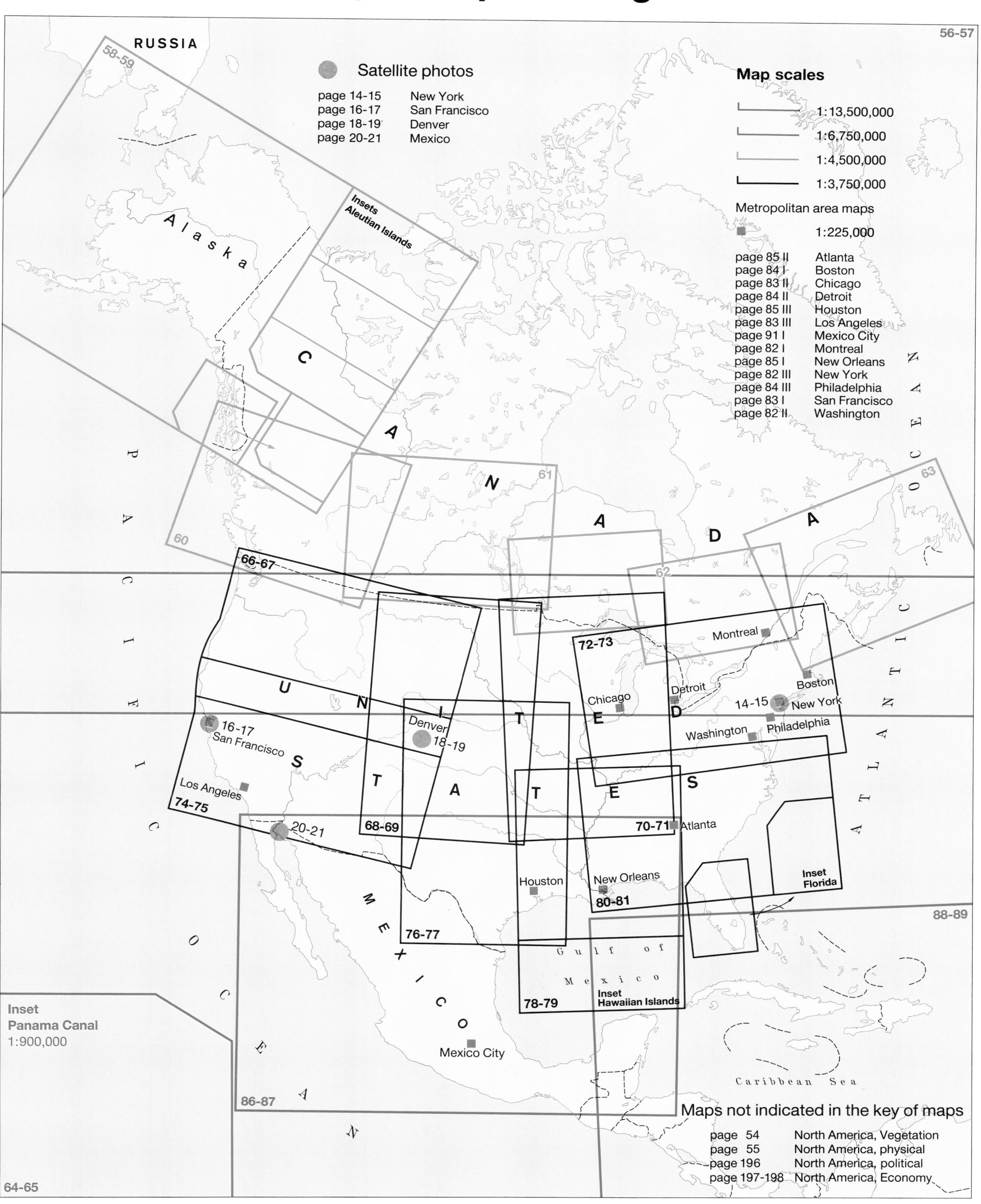
RUSSIA
Satellite photos
page 14-15 New York
page 16-17 San Francisco
page 18-19 Denver
page 20-21 Mexico
Map scales
1:13,500,000
1:6,750,000
1:4,500,000
1:3,750,000
Metropolitan area maps
1:225,000
page 85 II Atlanta
page 84 I Boston
page 83 II Chicago
page 84 II Detroit
page 85 III Houston
page 83 III Los Angeles
page 91 I Mexico City
page 82 I Montreal
page 85 I New Orleans
page 82 III New York
page 84 III Philadelphia
page 83 I San Francisco
page 82 II Washington
56-57
58-59
Alaska
Insets Aleutian Islands
CANADA
60
61
62
63
66-67
72-73
UNITED STATES
Montreal
Boston
Detroit
Chicago
14-15
New York
Philadelphia
Washington
16-17
San Francisco
Denver
18-19
Los Angeles
74-75
20-21
68-69
70-71
Atlanta
Houston
New Orleans
80-81
Inset Florida
76-77
MEXICO
Gulf of Mexico
78-79
Inset Hawaiian Islands
88-89
Mexico City
86-87
Caribbean Sea
Inset Panama Canal
1:900,000
64-65
PACIFIC OCEAN
ATLANTIC OCEAN
Maps not indicated in the key of maps
page 54 North America, Vegetation
page 55 North America, physical
page 196 North America, political
page 197-198 North America, Economy

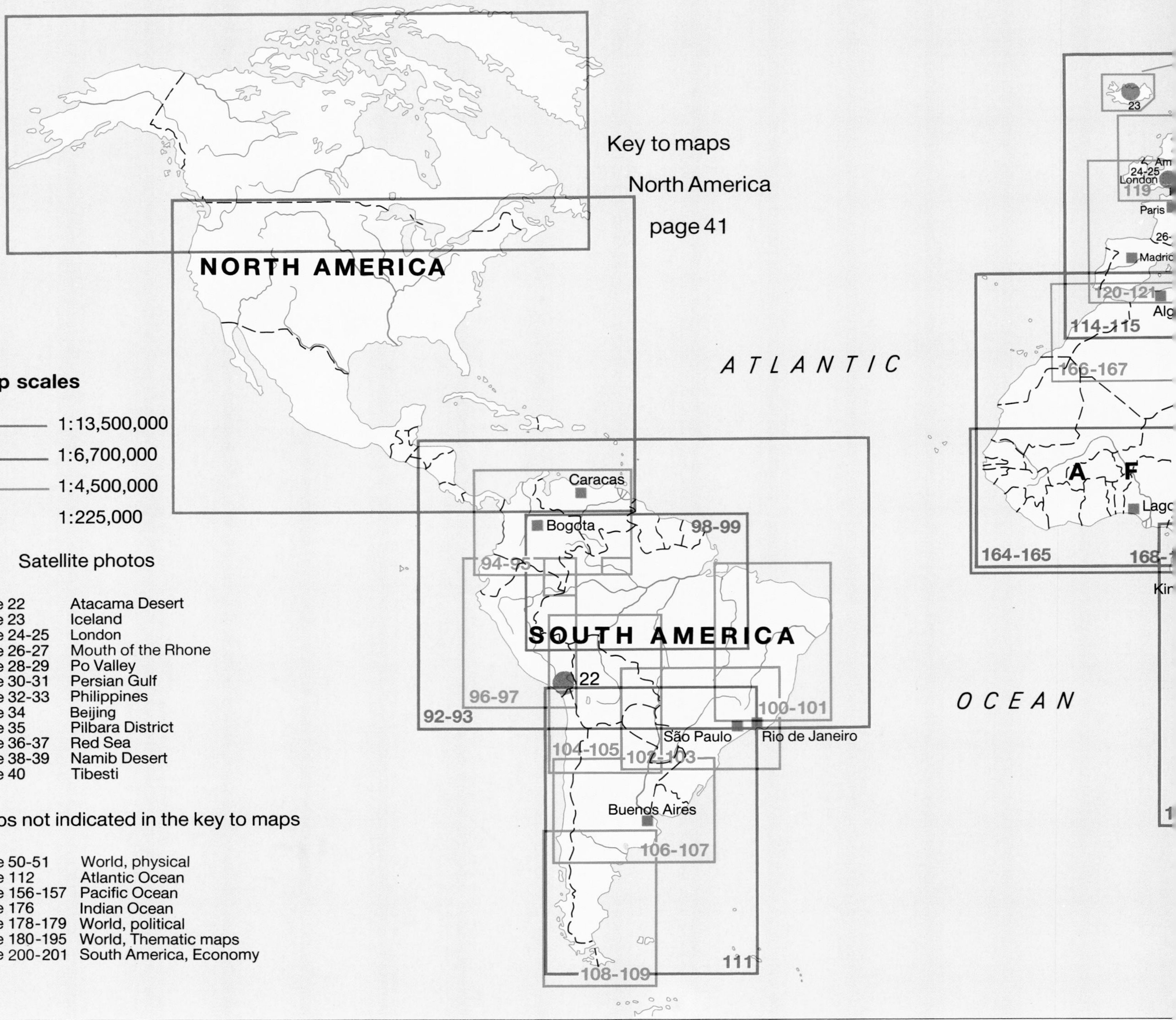

Key to maps
North America
page 41

NORTH AMERICA

SOUTH AMERICA

ATLANTIC

OCEAN

Caracas
Bogota
São Paulo
Rio de Janeiro
Buenos Aires

92-93
94-95
96-97
98-99
100-101
102-103
104-105
106-107
108-109
111
22

Map scales

- 1:13,500,000
- 1:6,700,000
- 1:4,500,000
- ■ 1:225,000
- ● Satellite photos

page 22	Atacama Desert
page 23	Iceland
page 24-25	London
page 26-27	Mouth of the Rhone
page 28-29	Po Valley
page 30-31	Persian Gulf
page 32-33	Philippines
page 34	Beijing
page 35	Pilbara District
page 36-37	Red Sea
page 38-39	Namib Desert
page 40	Tibesti

Maps not indicated in the key to maps

page 50-51	World, physical
page 112	Atlantic Ocean
page 156-157	Pacific Ocean
page 176	Indian Ocean
page 178-179	World, political
page 180-195	World, Thematic maps
page 200-201	South America, Economy

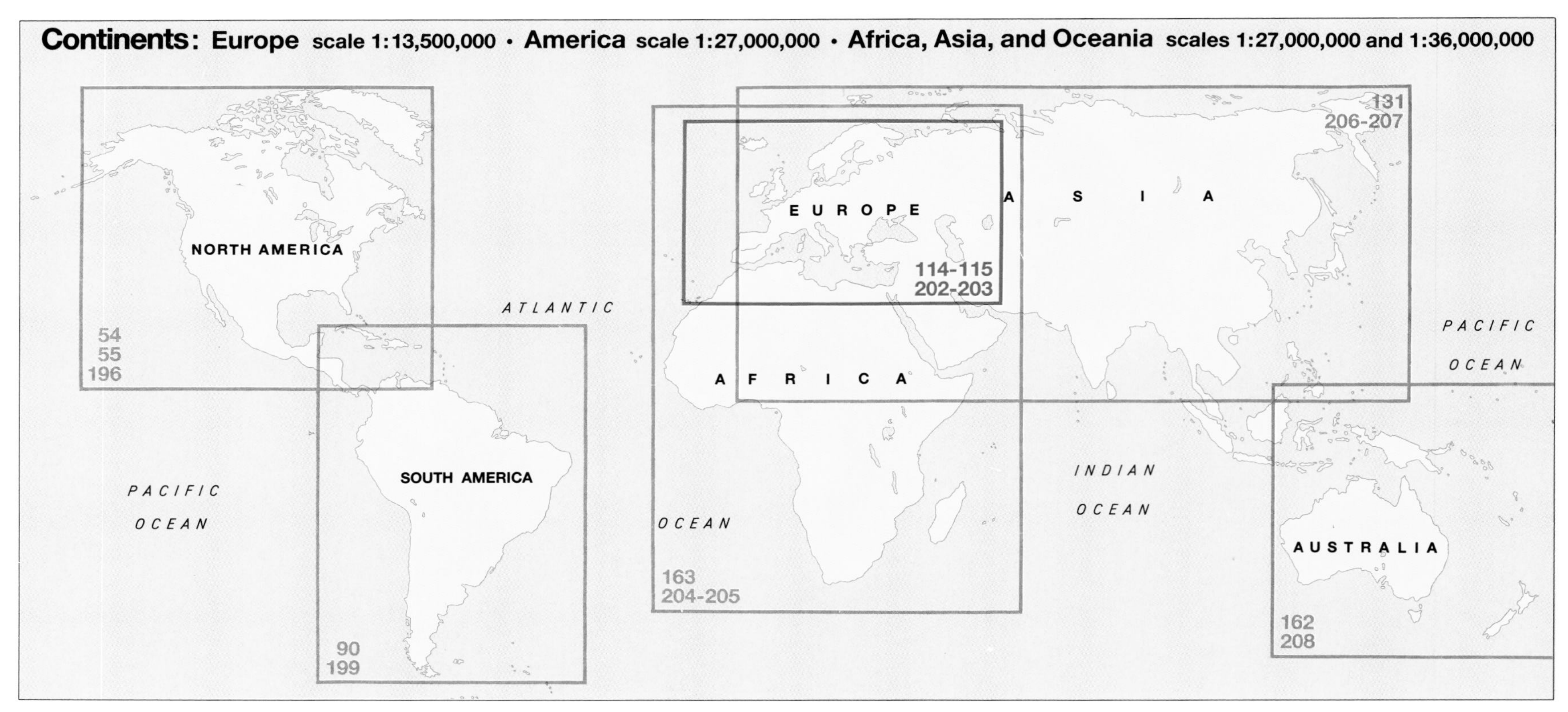
Continents: Europe scale 1:13,500,000 • America scale 1:27,000,000 • Africa, Asia, and Oceania scales 1:27,000,000 and 1:36,000,000
NORTH AMERICA
54
55
196
SOUTH AMERICA
90
199
ATLANTIC
PACIFIC
OCEAN
EUROPE
114-115
202-203
ASIA
131
206-207
AFRICA
OCEAN
163
204-205
INDIAN
OCEAN
PACIFIC
OCEAN
AUSTRALIA
162
208

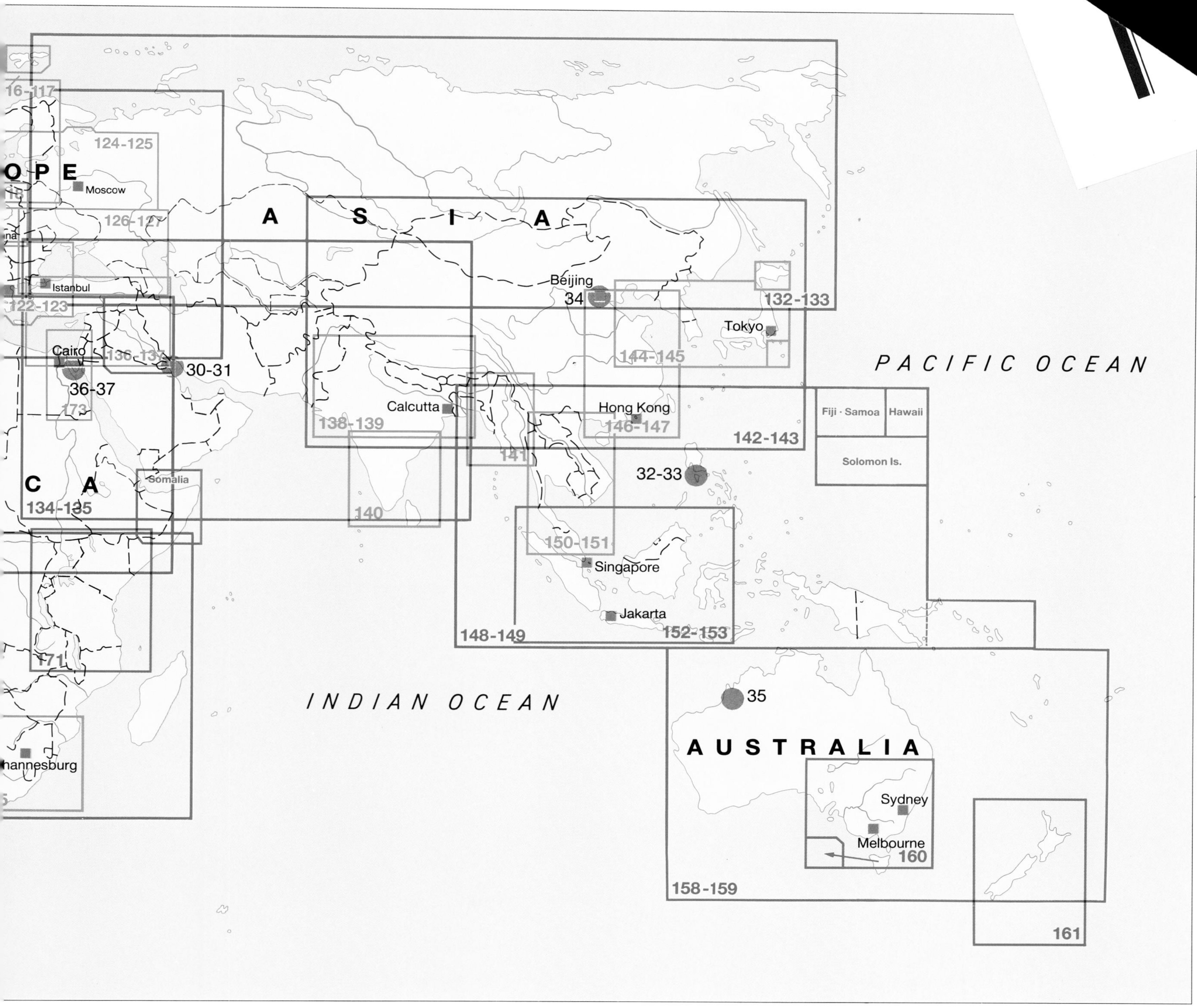

16-117
124-125
OPE
Moscow
126-127
A S I A
Istanbul
122-123
Beijing
34
132-133
Tokyo
Cairo
136-137
30-31
144-145
PACIFIC OCEAN
36-37
173
Calcutta
138-139
Hong Kong
146-147
142-143
Fiji · Samoa
Hawaii
141
Solomon Is.
32-33
C A
Somalia
134-135
140
150-151
Singapore
Jakarta
148-149
152-153
171
INDIAN OCEAN
35
AUSTRALIA
hannesburg
Sydney
Melbourne
160
158-159
161

Arctic Region · Antarctic Region **scale 1:27,000,000**

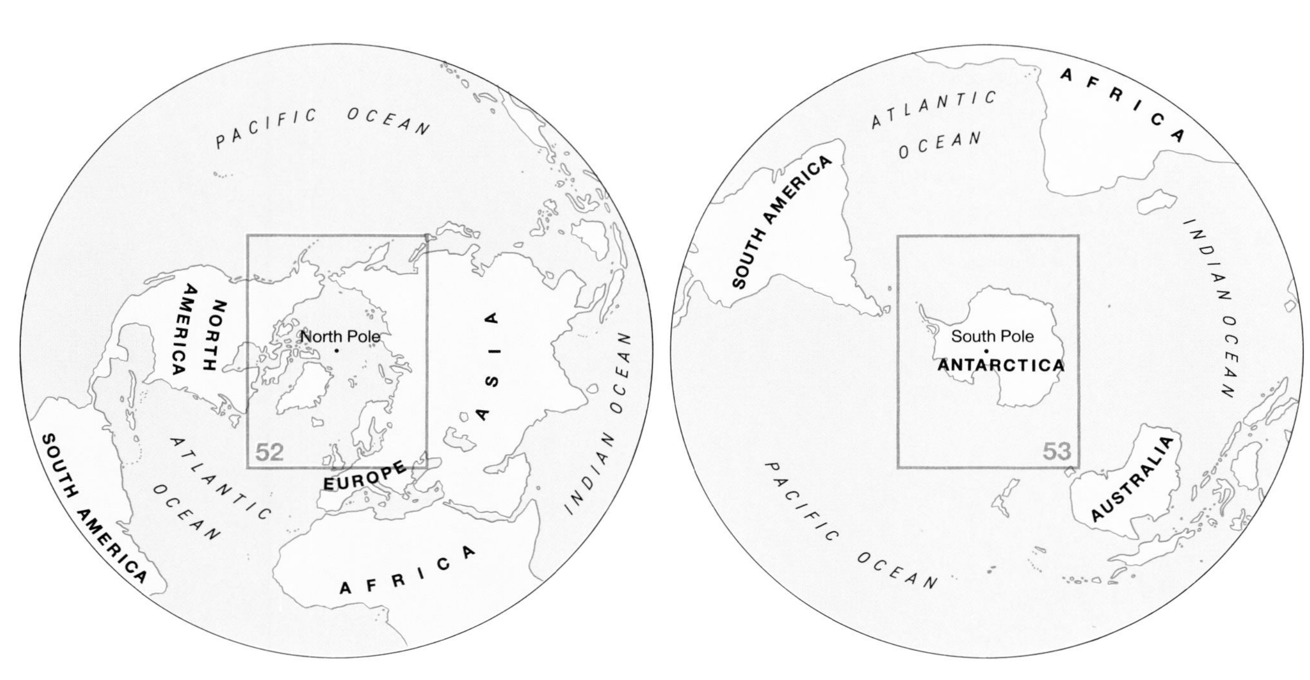
PACIFIC OCEAN
NORTH AMERICA
North Pole
ASIA
INDIAN OCEAN
52
SOUTH AMERICA
ATLANTIC OCEAN
EUROPE
AFRICA
ATLANTIC OCEAN
AFRICA
SOUTH AMERICA
South Pole
ANTARCTICA
INDIAN OCEAN
53
PACIFIC OCEAN
AUSTRALIA

Metropolitan area maps
1:225,000

page 170 I	Algiers
page 128 I	Amsterdam
page 113 IV	Athens
page 130 III	Berlin
page 91 III	Bogota
page 128 II	Brussels
page 110 III	Buenos Aires
page 170 II	Cairo
page 154 II	Calcutta
page 91 II	Caracas
page 128 III	Frankfurt
page 130 I	Hamburg
page 155 I	Hong Kong
page 154 I	Istanbul
page 154 IV	Jakarta
page 170 V	Johannesburg
page 170 IV	Kinshasa
page 170 III	Lagos
page 129 II	London
page 113 III	Madrid
page 161 II	Melbourne
page 113 V	Moscow
page 130 II	Munich
page 129 I	Paris
page 155 II	Beijing
page 110 I	Rio de Janeiro
page 113 II	Rome
page 110 II	São Paulo
page 154 III	Singapore
page 161 I	Sydney
page 155 III	Tokyo
page 113 I	Vienna
page 128 IV	Zürich

Description of Map Types and Scales

Hudson Bay
Labrador Pen.
Newfoundland
Newfoundland Basin
North American Basin
Bermuda Is.
Sargasso Sea
Bahama Is.
Gulf of Mexico
West Indies
Gr. Meteor Tablemount
Canary Basin
Cape Verde
Guiana
Chicago
Boston
Philadelphia
Washington
C.Hatteras
Jacksonville
Miami

Scale 1:67,500,000 ≙ One inch to 1,065 miles
Scale 1:60,000,000 ≙ One inch to 947 miles

HOUSTON
NEW ORLEANS
JACKSONVILLE
SAVANNAH
Charleston
Gulf of Mexico
BAHAMAS
LA HABANA
CUBA
JAMAICA
KINGSTON
HAITI
Caribbean
Campeche
Yucatán
BELIZE

Scale 1:36,000,000 ≙ One inch to 568 miles
Scale 1:27,000,000 ≙ One inch to 426 miles

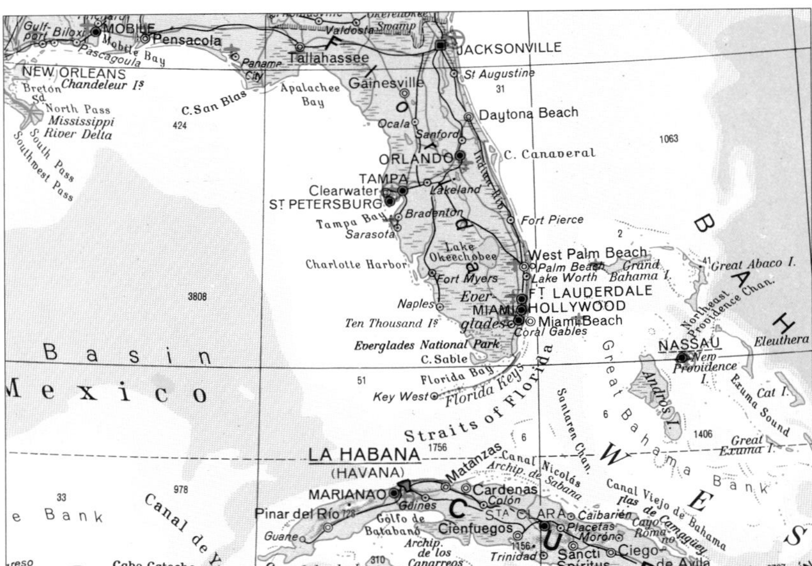

Pensacola
Tallahassee
JACKSONVILLE
NEW ORLEANS
St Augustine
Daytona Beach
ORLANDO
C. Canaveral
TAMPA
ST PETERSBURG
Fort Pierce
West Palm Beach
FT LAUDERDALE
HOLLYWOOD
Miami Beach
Key West
Straits of Florida
LA HABANA
(HAVANA)
MARIANAO
Cienfuegos
NASSAU

Scale 1:13,500,000 ≙ One inch to 213 miles

Lake Okeechobee
Punta Gorda
Charlotte Harbor
Naples
West Palm Beach
Boca Raton
Pompano Beach
FT LAUDERDALE
HOLLYWOOD
Miami Beach
MIAMI
Cape Florida
Big Cypress Swamp
Everglades National Park
Florida Bay
Key Largo
Key West
Dry Tortugas
Cape Romano
C. Sable

Scale 1:6,750,000 ≙ One inch to 107 miles
Scale 1:4,500,000 ≙ One inch to 71 miles
Scale 1:3,750,000 ≙ One inch to 59 miles

Topographic (Physical) Maps

Topographic maps combine natural (physical) features of the earth's surface with various man-made or "cultural" features.

The scale and coverage of a topographic map may depend on the need to depict features on a specific level of detail. For example, large-scale topographic maps may take into account the bridge, individual house, church, factory, a two-track railroad, footpath and copse of trees. Small-scale maps sketch a region in such comprehensive terms as coastlines, waterway networks, mountain ranges, towns and metropolises, railroad lines, or major roadways. On a relatively large-scale topographic map with a scale of 1:125,000, the District of Columbia occupies an area of 4 x 4 inches. At a much smaller scale of 1:60,000,000, the entire U.S. can be depicted in approximately the same space.

The term "physical" map commonly applied to topographic maps, although generally useful and descriptive, is not fully comprehensive. Topographic maps have two levels of presentation. The primary level depicts the "physis", i.e. the natural features of the earth, including coastlines, waterways, land elevation, sea depth, etc. The secondary level shows the effects of man: political borders, communities, transportation routes, and other elements of the civilized landscape. Language is an additional cultural feature which finds its expression in the geographic names and written comments on the map.

The map scale expresses the relationship between a certain distance in nature and the corresponding span on the map. The smaller the scale, the more cartographers are forced to simplify and to restrict themselves to the essentials. Cartography is an art of intelligent omission. The map user must be aware of this important fact when comparing maps of different scales, otherwise he or she runs the risk of obtaining a false picture of the world. Not a few misjudgements in history can be traced, in part, to distorted geographic conceptions.

In "The Great World Atlas", the continents, with the exception of the polar regions, are pictured at a scale of 1:13,500,000. This uniformity in scale, together with uniformity in map projections, enables easy comparisions between all continents.

For the United States 1:3,750,000 is the primary scale. Only for Alaska was it necessary to choose the scale of 1:4,500,000 in order to be able to depict the mainland on one double page.

For regions outside the United States, the scales of 1:4,500,000 and 1:6,750,000 were chosen based upon the criteria of population density, as well as political, economic and touristic significance. The key to map coverage, pp. 41-43, presents this regional division according to map pages and scales in an easy-to-understand manner.

The explanation of symbols on page 48 is the cartographic alphabet for understanding the contents of the maps; the index of names is the key to the geographic inventory of the atlas. The index of names and the number of entries are marks of quality of any atlas. The index of "The Great World Atlas" contains about 110,000 items.

Description of Map Types and Scales

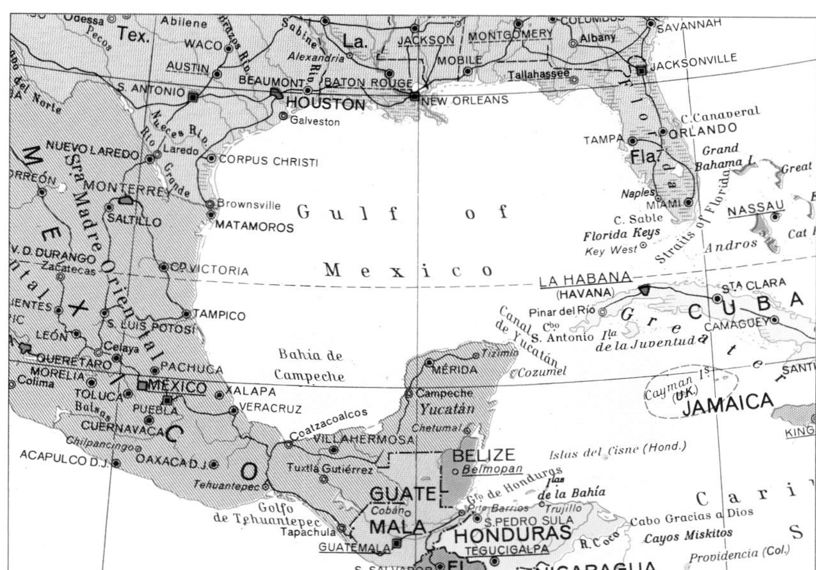
Tex.
Abilene
WACO
AUSTIN
La.
JACKSON
MONTGOMERY
Albany
SAVANNAH
JACKSONVILLE
MOBILE
Tallahassee
BEAUMONT
BATON ROUGE
S. ANTONIO
HOUSTON
NEW ORLEANS
Galveston
NUEVO LAREDO
Laredo
CORPUS CHRISTI
MONTERREY
SALTILLO
Brownsville
MATAMOROS
G u l f o f M e x i c o
TAMPA
ORLANDO
C. Canaveral
Grand Bahama I.
Fla.
Naples
MIAMI
NASSAU
C. Sable
Florida Keys
Key West
Andros
VICTORIA
LA HABANA (HAVANA)
STA CLARA
CUBA
TAMPICO
Pinar del Rio
C. S. Antonio
S. LUIS POTOSI
LEÓN
Bahía de Campeche
MÉRIDA
Cozumel
QUERÉTARO
MORELIA
PACHUCA
MÉXICO
XALAPA
VERACRUZ
Campeche
Yucatán
Cayman Is. (UK)
JAMAICA
TOLUCA
PUEBLA
CUERNAVACA
Coatzacoalcos
VILLAHERMOSA
ACAPULCO
OAXACA
BELIZE
Belmopan
Tuxtla Gutiérrez
Golfo de Tehuantepec
GUATE MALA
HONDURAS
S. PEDRO SULA
TEGUCIGALPA
Tapachula
GUATEMALA
S. SALVADOR
EL
NICARAGUA
Cabo Gracias a Dios
Cayos Miskitos
Providencia (Col.)

Scale 1:27,000,000 ≙ One inch to 426 miles
Scale 1:13,500,000 ≙ One inch to 213 miles

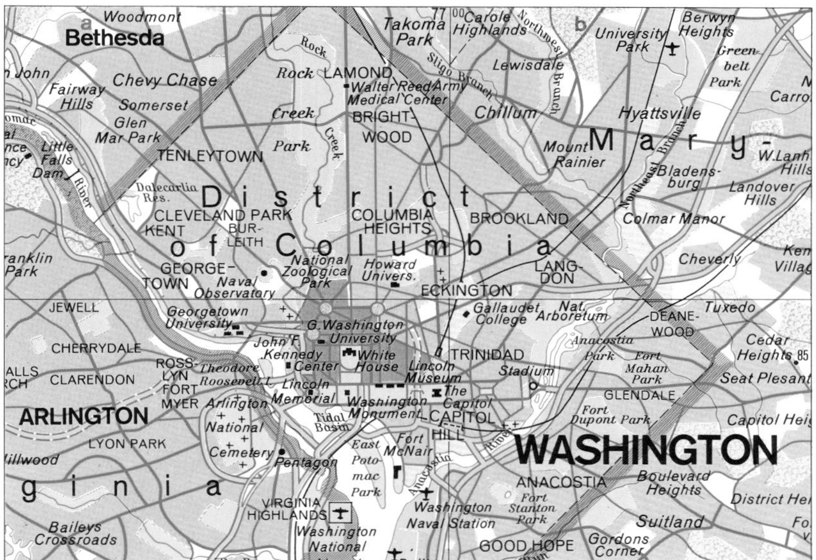
Woodmont
Bethesda
Chevy Chase
Somerset
Glen
Mar Park
Takoma Park
Carole Highlands
University Park
Berwyn Heights
Rock Creek
LAMOND
Walter Reed Army Medical Center
BRIGHTWOOD
Lewisdale
Chillum
Hyattsville
TENLEYTOWN
Park
Mount Rainier
Bladensburg
Landover Hills
CLEVELAND PARK
COLUMBIA HEIGHTS
BROOKLAND
Colmar Manor
D i s t r i c t o f C o l u m b i a
GEORGETOWN
National Zoological Park
Howard Univers.
Naval Observatory
LANGDON
Cheverly
ECKINGTON
JEWELL
Georgetown University
G. Washington University
Gallaudet College
Nat. Arboretum
DEANEWOOD
Tuxedo
CHERRYDALE
White House
Kennedy Center
TRINIDAD
Cedar Heights
Seat Plesant
CLARENDON
ROSSLYN
FORT MYER
Lincoln Memorial
Washington Monument
Capitol
GLENDALE
ARLINGTON
Arlington National Cemetery
Pentagon
LYON PARK
WASHINGTON
ANACOSTIA
Boulevard Heights
VIRGINIA HIGHLANDS
Washington Naval Station
Suitland
Baileys Crossroads
GOOD HOPE
Gordons Corner

Scale 1:225,000 ≙ One inch to 3.6 miles

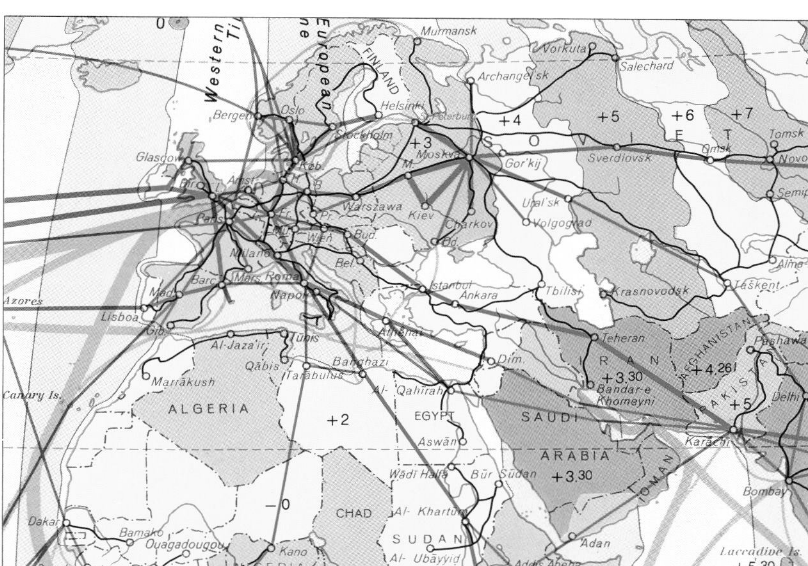
Murmansk
Vorkuta
Salechard
Archangel'sk
FINLAND
Helsinki
Oslo
Bergen
Glasgow
+3
+4
+5
+6
+7
Moskva
Sverdlovsk
Omsk
Tomsk
Gor'kij
Warszawa
Kiev
Ural'sk
Volgograd
Alma
Azores
Lisboa
Istanbul
Ankara
Tbilisi
Krasnovodsk
Taskent
Tunis
Teheran
IRAN
+3,30
+4,30
Bandar-e Khomeyni
Marrakush
ALGERIA
+2
EGYPT
SAUDI ARABIA
+3,30
Karachi
Bombay
Canary Is.
Aswan
Bur Sudan
CHAD
SUDAN
Adan
Dakar
Bamako
Ouagadougou
Kano
Addis Abeba
Laccadive Is.
+5,30

Scale 1:90,000,000 ≙ One inch to 1,420 miles
Scale 1:67,500,000 ≙ One inch to 1,065 miles

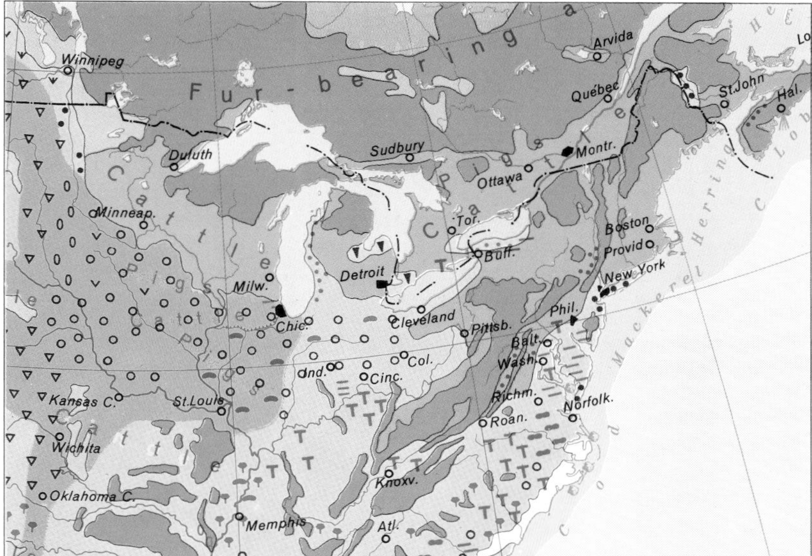
Winnipeg
F u r - b e a r i n g
Arvida
Quebec
St.John
Hal.
Duluth
Sudbury
Ottawa
Montr.
Minneap.
Tor.
Boston
Provid.
New York
Buff.
Detroit
Milw.
Chic.
Cleveland
Pittsb.
Phil.
Balt.
Wash.
Ind.
Col.
Cinc.
Kansas C.
St.Louis
Richm.
Norfolk.
Roan.
Wichita
Knoxv.
Oklahoma C.
Memphis
Atl.

Scale 1:27,000,000 ≙ One inch to 426 miles

Political Maps

The geographic location, the extension of the land area, and the interrelationships resulting from the relative locations of political powers, find their unique cartographic expression in political maps. By means of colored areas, the divisions of the earth into sovereign states and their dependent territories become apparent. In "The Great World Atlas" these political maps are placed, for easy orientation, in front of the maps of the individual continents. The assignment of a certain color to each state is maintained throughout. The political power of the individual states cannot be deduced from these maps. Deductions about the political and economic behavior of the various states can be made, however, by comparing maps of climate, density, and distribution of population, economy, and transportation.

Metropolitan Area Maps

The increasing concentration of population in urban centers is a global phenomenon. While the population of the world has approximately doubled in the last 100 years, the number of people living in cities has increased fivefold. In the year 2000 more than half of the population of the world is expected to be living in cities.
"The Great World Atlas" shows a selection of important metropolises from every corner of the world. All these maps make use of the same scale, 1:225,000, and the same legend, which makes possible immediate and global comparisons. The colored differentiation of built-up metropolitan areas, city centers and sprawling industrial parks, when viewed in conjunction with the scheme of the transportation network, allows conclusions to be drawn about the functional division of the cities and their surrounding area.

Thematic Maps

On thematic maps global phenomena and conditions are depicted. A distinction should be made between two groups of thematic maps: First, those maps whose topics are naturally occuring conditions such as geology, climate, and vegetation; second, those maps that deal with structures that have been created by man such as distribution of population, religion or the economy. These various aspects are transformed by cartographers into graphic representations. Not only the distribution of soil types, for example, or the occurence of petroleum are thus depicted, but bold or lightface arrows express the speed of ocean currents; shades of blue, the average temperature in January; the size of the symbol, the volume of production, and much more. Dynamic processes become apparent with regards to strength, direction, etc., as do differences in order of magnitude and, thus, in significance.

The study of geographic and thematic maps gives insight into the diverse relationships between mankind and his surroundings. Such study makes plain, furthermore, the connections and interdependencies among the different continents and regions and imparts understanding of the behavior of human groups, and of political and economic powers.

"The Great World Atlas" takes this into account with a series of thematic world maps, as well as economic maps of North and South America (pp. 197-198 and 200, 201), at the end of the topographical map section.

Projections

It is fundamentally impossible to depict without distortion the spherical surface of the earth on a flat surface. The curvature of the earth's surface can only be presented undistorted – that is, preserving areas, shapes, and angles – on a globe. In the three basic types of map projections, the parallels and meridians are projected onto a plane, or onto a cone or a cylinder which is subsequently cut and layed flat. In the first type, also known as an azimuthal projection, the earth's surface is projected onto a plane touching the globe at an arbitrary point. Distortion increases with distance from the point of contact. In the conical projection, the surface is projected onto an imaginary cone placed over the globe, usually so that it touches the parallel running through the center of the area to be depicted. In this case, distortion increases with distance from the line of contact. In the cylindrical projection, the cone is replaced by a cylinder surrounding the earth, normally touching the equator. Distortion here increases with distance from the equator. In the cylindrical projection, all parallels and meridians become straight lines. One example of this type is the Mercator projection, which preserves angle and is, accordingly, used for marine charts. On a Mercator map, the line connecting two points (the "loxodrome") is a straight line following the correct compass direction.

This atlas uses the following projections:

1 Polar projections for polar maps, scale 1:27,000,000
2 Azimuthal projections for all maps to scales 1:13,500,000 and 1:27,000,000, with the exception of the 1:27,000,000 maps of Asia and the polar regions
3 Conical projections (Albers) for all maps to scales 1:3,750,000, 1:4,500,000 and 1:6,750,000
4 Bonne equal-area projection for the map of Asia 1:27,000,000
5 Winkel triple projection has been used for all maps of the world

Polar projection

With this method, the earth's surface is projected onto a plane touching the globe at the pole, which is at the centre of the map. Meridians are shown as straight lines intersecting at the centre of the map. Parallels are concentric circles around the center of the map. This projection preserves areas.

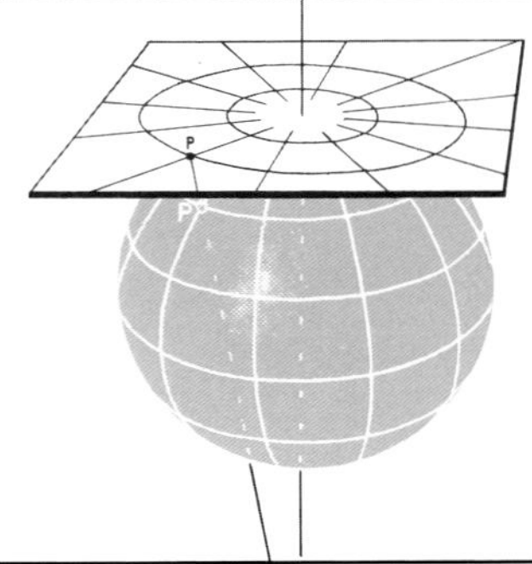

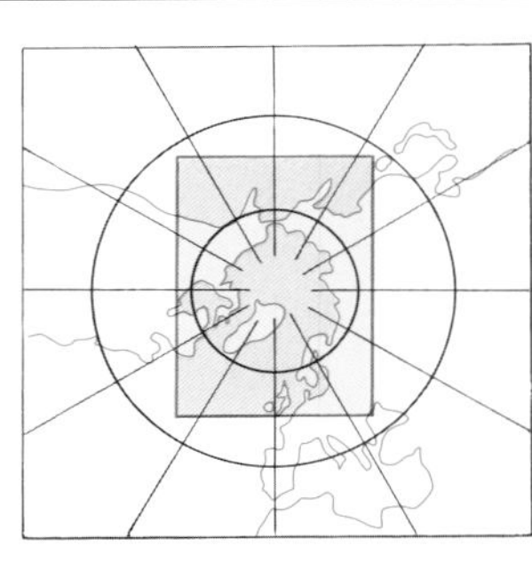

Equal-area azimuthal projection

With this method, the point of contact of the surface of projection is the equator (Africa 1:13 500 000) or an arbitrary latitude passing through the center of the area to be depicted.
These projections also approximately preserve angles, which is why they are called "azimuthal". Parallels and meridians are shown as curves generated from the combination of calculated and plotted coordinates.

The azimuthal projection is particularly suitable for depicting large regions. In the map of Asia, however, the distortions at the edges would be too great, therefore the Bonne Projection was preferred in this case.

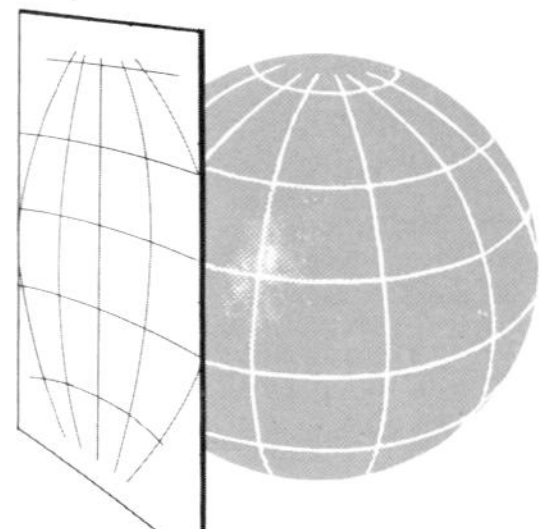

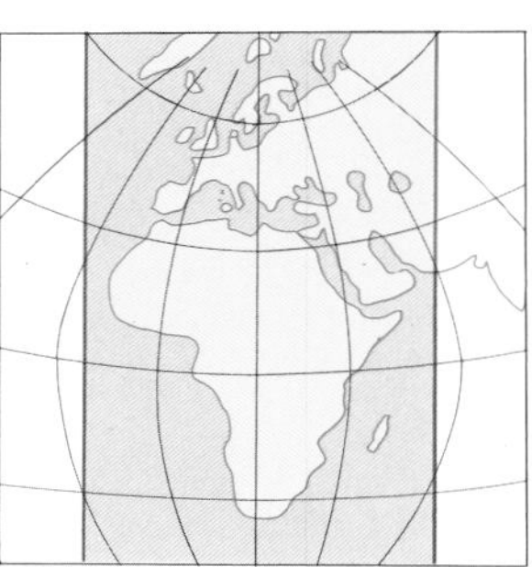

Conical projection (Albers)

In the conical projection, circles of longitude are depicted as straight lines. Parallels are concentric circles whose center is the point of intersection of the meridians, which lies outside the map's borders. Two of the parallels preserve distance, and the pair is selected for the individual maps to minimize overall distortion of distance and direction.
This relatively simple method is used for large scale maps, which show only a small section of the globe and involve correspondingly small distortion.

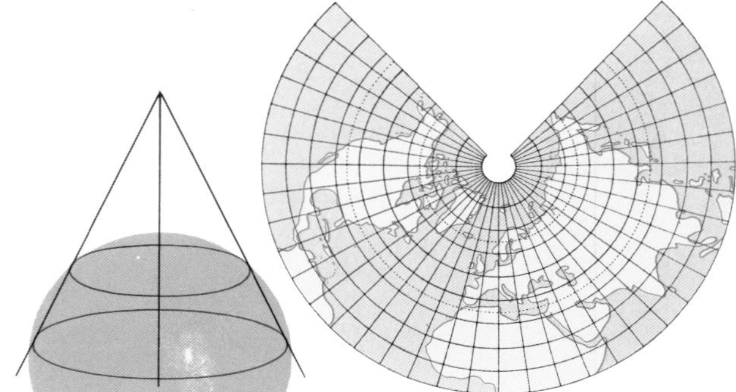

Bonne projection

This is also an equal-area method, based on a conical projection. The center meridian is shown as a straight line and divided to preserve lenght. One parallel is selected as a line of contact, and the other parallels are concentric circles, equally divided from the center meridian. The curves connecting corresponding segments generate the meridians.
This method is particularly suitable for depicting large areas of the earth.

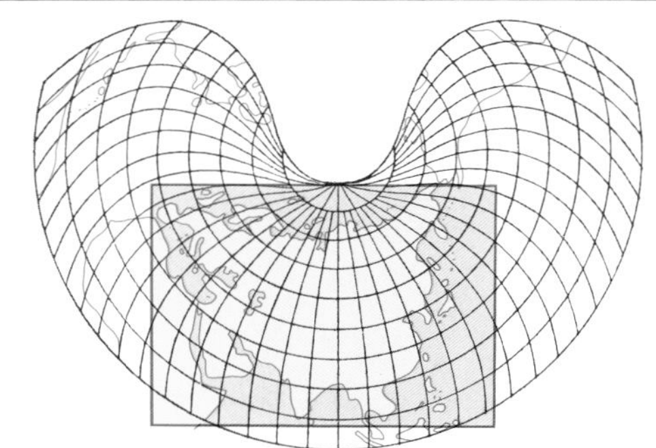

Winkel triple projection

This was used for world maps. The projection is based on Aitoff's method, which shows the poles as straight lines, with all meridians and parallels slightly curved.
While this projection does not preserve any attributes, it conveys an approximately equal-area impression of the earth's surface, particularly in the middle latitudes.

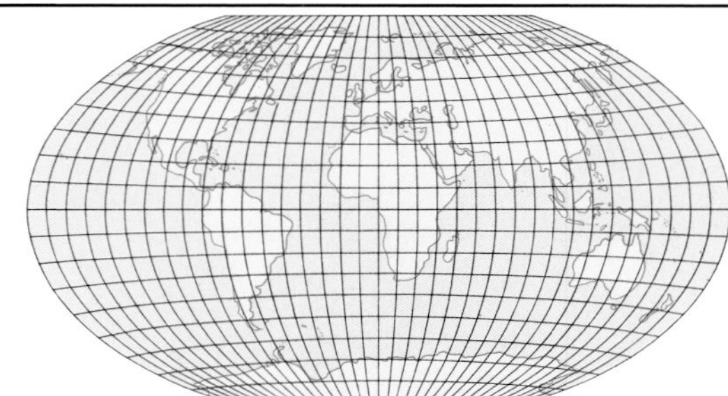

Abbreviations of Geographical Names and Terms

General

Bel.	Belyj, -aja	Mal.	Malyj, -aja, -oje	Sred.	Sredne,
	-oje,yje	Mc	Mac		-ij, -'aja,-eje
Bol.	Bol'šoj, -aja,	Nat.	National	St.	Sankt
	-oje, ije	nat.	national	S^{t}	Saint
Č.	Český, -á, -é	N$^{do(s)}$	Nevado(s)	Sta	Santa
Ea.	East	Niž.	Nižnij, -'aja,	Star.	Staryj, -aja
G$^{d(e)}$	Grand(e)		-eje, -ije		-oje, -yje
G^{des}	Grandes	N^{o}	Numero	S^{te}	Sainte
Gr.	Groß, -er, -e,	Nov.	Novo, -yj, -aja	Sth	South
	-es		-oje	S^{to}	Santo
G^{ral}	General	Nth	North	Sv.	Sveti, -a,
G^{t}	Great	N^{va}	Nueva		Sväty
Hag.	Hagia	N^{vo}	Nuevo	Upp.	Upper
Hág.	Hágios	P$^{it(e)}$	Petit(e)	V.	Veliki, -a, -o
H^{te}	Haute	Pr.	Prince	Vel.	Velikij, -aja,
Juž.	Južnyj, -aja,	Pres.	Presidente		-oje
	-oje	Prov.	Provincial	Vel.'	Vel'ká
Kr.	Krasno, -yj,	S....	San	Verch.	Verchne, -ij,
	-aja, oje, -yje	Sev.	Severnyj, -aja		-'aja, -eje, -ije
L^{le}	Little		-oje	W....	West;
				Zap.	Zapadnaja

Islands, Landscapes

ad.	adasi	Ì^{e}	Ìsole	o-va	ostrova
Arch.	Archipelago	I$^{la(s)}$	Isla(s)	P.	Pulau
arch.	archipelag	(-)I^{n}	(-)Inseln,	Pen.	Peninsula
Archip.	Archipiélago		(-inseln)	Poj.	Pojezierze
(-)I.	(-)Insel,	I^{s}	Islands	p-ov.	poluostrov
	(-insel)	Î^{s}	Îles	P.-p.	Pulau-pulau
I....	Isle	k.	kosa	Res.	Reservation,-e
....I.	Island	Kep.	Kepulauan	Rés.	Réservation
Î.	Île	L^{d}	Land	s.	sima
I^{a}	Ilha	(-)l$^{d(e)}$	(-)land(e)	V^{ey}	Valley
Ì^{a}	Ìsola	Mon.	Monument	y.ad.	yarimada, -si
I^{as}	Ilhas	o.	ostrov	zapov.	zapovednik

Hydrography

Arr.	Arroio, Arroyo	j.	joki	R^{ão}	Ribeirão
B.	Basin, Bay	Jez.	Jezioro	R^{ère}	Rivière
(-)B.	(-)Bucht,	j:vi	järvi	Res.	Reservoir
	(-bucht)	Kan.	Kanal; Kanaal	Rib^{a}	Ribeira
Bat.	Batang	(-)kan.	(-)kanal;	Riv.	River
Can.	Canal		-kanaal	-riv.	-rivier
Chan.	Channel	kör.	körfez, -i	...(-)S.	(-)See, (-see)
Cr.	Creek	L.	Lago, Lake	S^{ai}	Sungai
D.	Danau	Lim.	Limne	S^{d}	Sound
Est.	Estero	L$^{o(a)}$	Lago(a)	S^{ei}	Sungei
Est^{o}	Estrecho	L$^{una(s)}$	Laguna(s)	Sel.	Selat
Fj.; -fj.	Fjord; -fjord	n.	nehir, nehri	Str.	Strait
G.	Gulf	Ou.	Ouèd	Tel.	Teluk
g.	gawa	oz.	ozero	vdchr.	vodochra-
G^{fe}	Golfe	Pass.	Passage		nilišče
G^{fo}	Golfo	prol.	proliv	W^{di}	Wadī
g^{ü}	gölü	R.	rio	zal.	zaliv

Mountains

A....	Alpes; Alpi	g.	gora	M^{ts}	Monts
...A.	Alpen	G^{a}	Góra	n.	nos
Aig$^{lle(s)}$	Aiguille(s)	Geb.	Gebirge	N^{do}	Nevado
Akr.	Akrotérion	-geb.	-gebirge	Ór.	Óros
App.	Appennino	Gl.	Glacier	P.,	
Bg.; -bg.	Berg; -berg	G^{ng}	Gunung	P$^{c(o)}$	Pic(o)
Bge.; -bge.	Berge; -berge	H.	Hill	Peg.	Pegunungan
B^{t}	Bukit	h.	hory	per.	pereval
C.	Cape	H^{d}	Head	P$^{k(s)}$	Peak(s)
C^{bo}	Cabo	H^{s}	Hills	pl^{a}	planina
chr.	chrebet	J.	Jabal	Pl^{au}	Plateau
C$^{l(e)}$	Col(le)	K	Kap	pl^{e}	planine
C^{ma}	Cima	M.	Monte	pr.	prusmyk
C^{no}	Corno	m.	mys	P^{rto}	Puerto
Coll^{s}	Collines	M^{as}	Montanhas	Prz.	Przelecz
Cord.	Cordillera	M$^{gne(s)}$	Montagne(s)	P^{so}	Passo
C^{po}	Capo	Mt.	Mount	P$^{t(e)}$	Point(e)
C$^{ro(s)}$	Cerro(s)	M$^{t(i)}$	Mont(i)	P^{ta}	Punta
Cuch.	Cuchilla	Mt^{n}	Mountain	P^{zo}	Pizzo
dağl.	dağlar, -i	Mts.	Mounts	Ra$^{(s)}$	Range(s)
F^{êt}	Forêt	Mt^{s}	Mountains	R^{ca}	Rocca

Mountains

Ri.	Ridge	T^{ng}	Tanjung	-w.	-wald
S^{nia}	Serrania	V^{án}	Volcán	y.	yama
S$^{ra(s)}$	Sierra(s)	Vol.	Volcano		
S^{rra}	Serra	vozvyš.	vozvyšenn-		
			ost'		

Places

Arr.	Arroio, Arroyo	Hist.	Historical	P.	Port; Pulau
B.	Bad; Ban	-hm.	-heim	Pdg.	Padang
-bg.	-berg	Hqrs.	Headquarters	Ph.	Phum
-b^{u}g.	-burg	Hs.	House	P^{nte}	Puente
-bge.	-berge	-hsn.	-hausen	P^{rto}	Puerto
B^{io}	Balneario	Hts.	Heights	P^{so}	Passo
-br(n).	-brück(en)	J^{n}	Junktion	P^{t}	Point
Build.	Building	K.	Kuala	P^{ta}	Punta
C^{d}	Ciudad	-kchn.	-kirchen	P^{te}	Pointe
Ch^{au}	Château	Km	Kilómetro	P^{to}	Porto
C^{le}	Castle	K^{ng}	Kampung	R.	Rio
Co.	Country	Kp.	Kompong	Rec.	Recreation
Coll.	College	K^{r}	Kangkar	S^{i}	Sidi
Cor.	Coronel	-lbn.	-leben	-st.	-stadt
Cr.	Creek	M.	Monte; Mu'o'ng	Stat.	Station
-df.	-dorf	Mem.	Memorial	Tech.	Technical
E^{ción}	Estación	M^{gne}	Montagne	Univ.	University
-f^{d}	-field	Mt.	Mount	V^{a}	Vila
F^{rte}	Fuerte	M$^{t(s)}$	Mont(s)	V^{la}	Villa
F^{s}	Falls	Mt^{n}	Mountain	-wd.(e).	-wald(e)
F$^{t(e)}$	Fort(e)	Mt^{s}	Mountains		
F^{tin}	Fortin	Mus.	Museum		
-gn.	-ingen				

Administration

AK	Alaska	IL	Illinois	OR	Oregon
AL	Alabama	IN	Indiana	PA	Pennsylvania
A(O)	Autonome	Ind.	India	Port.	Portugal
	(Oblast)	Jap.	Japan	Reg.	Region
AR	Arkansas	KS	Kansas	Rep.	Republic
Austr.	Australia	KY	Kentucky	RI	Rhode Island
Aut.	Autonomous	LA	Louisiana	S. Afr.	South Africa
AZ	Arizona	MA	Massachusetts	SC	South
Braz.	Brazil	MD	Maryland		Carolina
CA	California	ME	Maine	SD	South Dakota
CO	Colorado	Mex.	Mexico	Terr.	Territor, -y,
Col.	Colombia	MI	Michigan		-ies
C.Rica	Costa Rica	MN	Minnesota	TN	Tennessee
CT	Connecticut	MO	Missouri	TX	Texas
DC	District of	MS	Mississippi	U.K.	United King-
	Columbia				dom
DE	Delaware	MT	Montana	U.S.A.	United States
Den.	Denmark	NC	North Carolina	UT	Utah
Dist.	District	ND	North Dakota	VA	Virginia
Ec.	Ecuador	NE	Nebraska	Vietn.	Vietnam
E.G.	Equatorial	Neth.	Netherlands	VT	Vermont
	Guinea	NH	New Hampshire	WA	Washington
Fed.	Federal;	Nic.	Nicaragua	WI	Wisconsin
	Federated	NJ	New Jersey	WV	West Virginia
FL	Florida	NM	New Mexico	WY	Wyoming
Fr.	France, French	Norw.	Norway		
GA	Georgia	NV	Nevada		
HI	Hawai	NY	New York		
Hond.	Honduras	N.Z.	New Zealand		
IA	Iowa	OH	Ohio		
ID	Idaho	OK	Oklahoma		

Explanation of Symbols

Symbols

River, stream
Drying river, stream
Intermittent river, stream
Canal
Canal under construction
Waterfall, rapids
Dam
Fresh-water or salt-water lake with permanent shore line
Fresh-water or salt-water lake with variable or undefined shore line
Intermittent lake
Well in dry area
Swamp, Bog
Salt marsh
Flood area
Mud flat
Reef, Coral reef
Glacier
Average pack ice limit in summer
Average pack ice limit in winter
Shelf ice
Sand desert, gravel desert, etc.
Inhabited spot, station
Ruins
Lighthouse

Railroad
Primary railroad } *on larger scale maps*
Secondary railroad
Suspended cable car
Railroad under construction
Train ferry
Tunnel
Major highway
Expressway } *on larger scale maps*
Expressway under construction
Caravan route, path, track
Ferry
Pass
Airport, Airfield
International boundary
Boundary of autonomous area
Boundary of subsidiary administrative unit
WASHINGTON — National capital
Harrisburg, *Nachičevan'* — Principal cities of subsidiary administrative units
Castle or fort
Nature reserve

Place		Locality
LOS ANGELES	over – 1,000,000 Inhabitants	L.-A.-HOLLYWOOD
BOSTON	500,000 – 1,000,000 Inhabitants	B.-DORCHESTER
ATLANTA	100,000 – 500,000 Inhabitants	A.-BOLTON
Malden	50,000 – 100,000 Inhabitants	*Edgeworth*
Jefferson	10,000 – 50,000 Inhabitants	
Cleveland	under – 10,000 Inhabitants	

Supplemental symbols of Metropolitan area maps

City center, Old town
Residential area
Industrial area, Waterfront
Park
Christian cemetery
Moslem cemetery
Forest (partly scrub)
Expressway
Main road, Secondary road
Railroad with station
Airport, Airfield
Important building, Point of interest
Municipal boundary
Town wall
Tower
Fort
Church
Temple
Mosque

Type Styles

CANADA	Independent country
Texas	Subordinate administrative unit
(U.S.A.) *(U.S.A.)*	Political affiliation
DENVER Columbia *Augusta*	Places
COAST RANGE Colorado Plateau	Mountain
Mt. Shasta	Mountain, cape, pass, glacier
MIDDLE WEST *Gila Desert* *Isle Royale*	Physical regions and islands
OCEAN Gulf of Mexico Mississippi River	Hydrography
Cayman Trench	Ocean basin, trench, ridge etc.
2789	Altitude and depth in meters
164	Depth of lakes below surface

Altitudes and depths

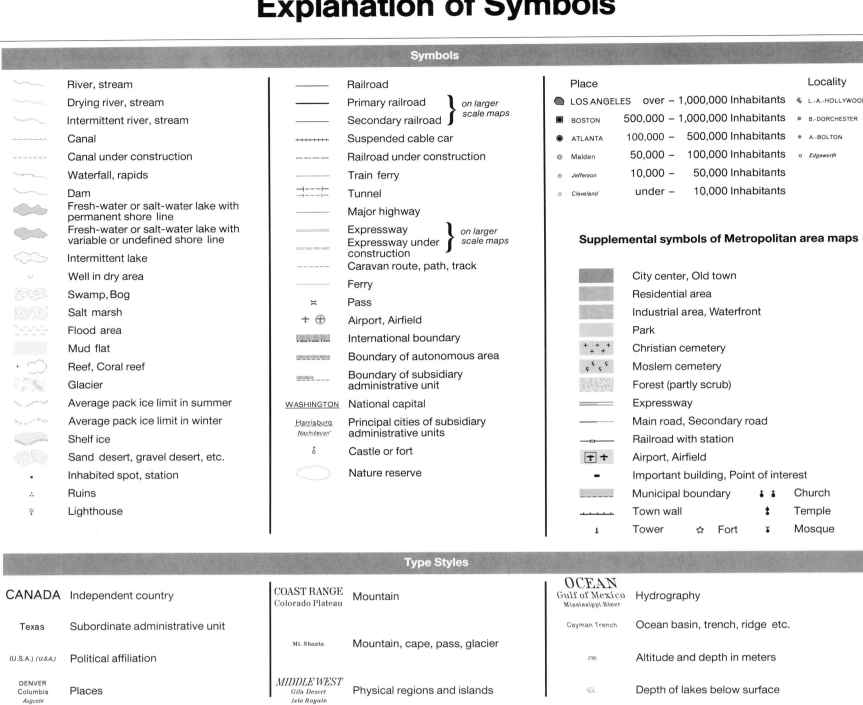

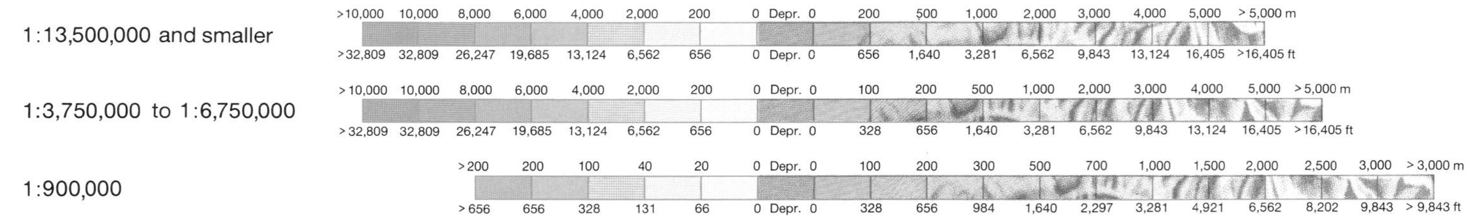
1:13,500,000 and smaller
>10,000 10,000 8,000 6,000 4,000 2,000 200 0 Depr. 0 200 500 1,000 2,000 3,000 4,000 5,000 >5,000 m
>32,809 32,809 26,247 19,685 13,124 6,562 656 0 Depr. 0 656 1,640 3,281 6,562 9,843 13,124 16,405 >16,405 ft
1:3,750,000 to 1:6,750,000
>10,000 10,000 8,000 6,000 4,000 2,000 200 0 Depr. 0 100 200 500 1,000 2,000 3,000 4,000 5,000 >5,000 m
>32,809 32,809 26,247 19,685 13,124 6,562 656 0 Depr. 0 328 656 1,640 3,281 6,562 9,843 13,124 16,405 >16,405 ft
1:900,000
>200 200 100 40 20 0 Depr. 0 100 200 300 500 700 1,000 1,500 2,000 2,500 3,000 >3,000 m
>656 656 328 131 66 0 Depr. 0 328 656 984 1,640 2,297 3,281 4,921 6,562 8,202 9,843 >9,843 ft

Conversion diagram

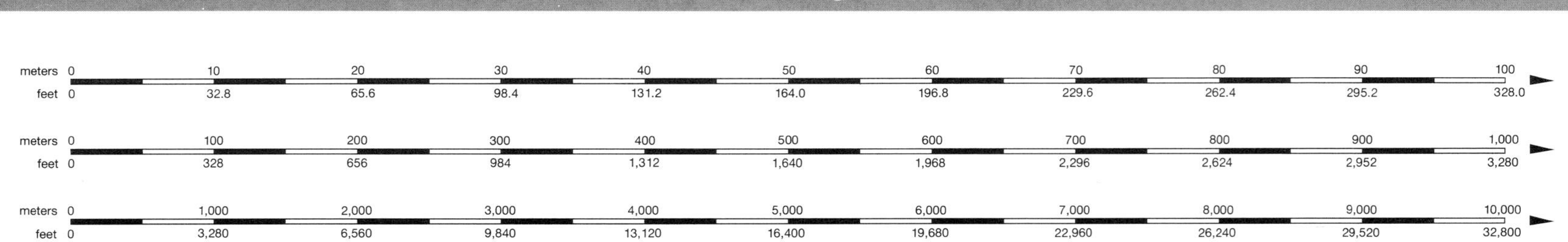
meters 0 10 20 30 40 50 60 70 80 90 100
feet 0 32.8 65.6 98.4 131.2 164.0 196.8 229.6 262.4 295.2 328.0
meters 0 100 200 300 400 500 600 700 800 900 1,000
feet 0 328 656 984 1,312 1,640 1,968 2,296 2,624 2,952 3,280
meters 0 1,000 2,000 3,000 4,000 5,000 6,000 7,000 8,000 9,000 10,000
feet 0 3,280 6,560 9,840 13,120 16,400 19,680 22,960 26,240 29,520 32,800

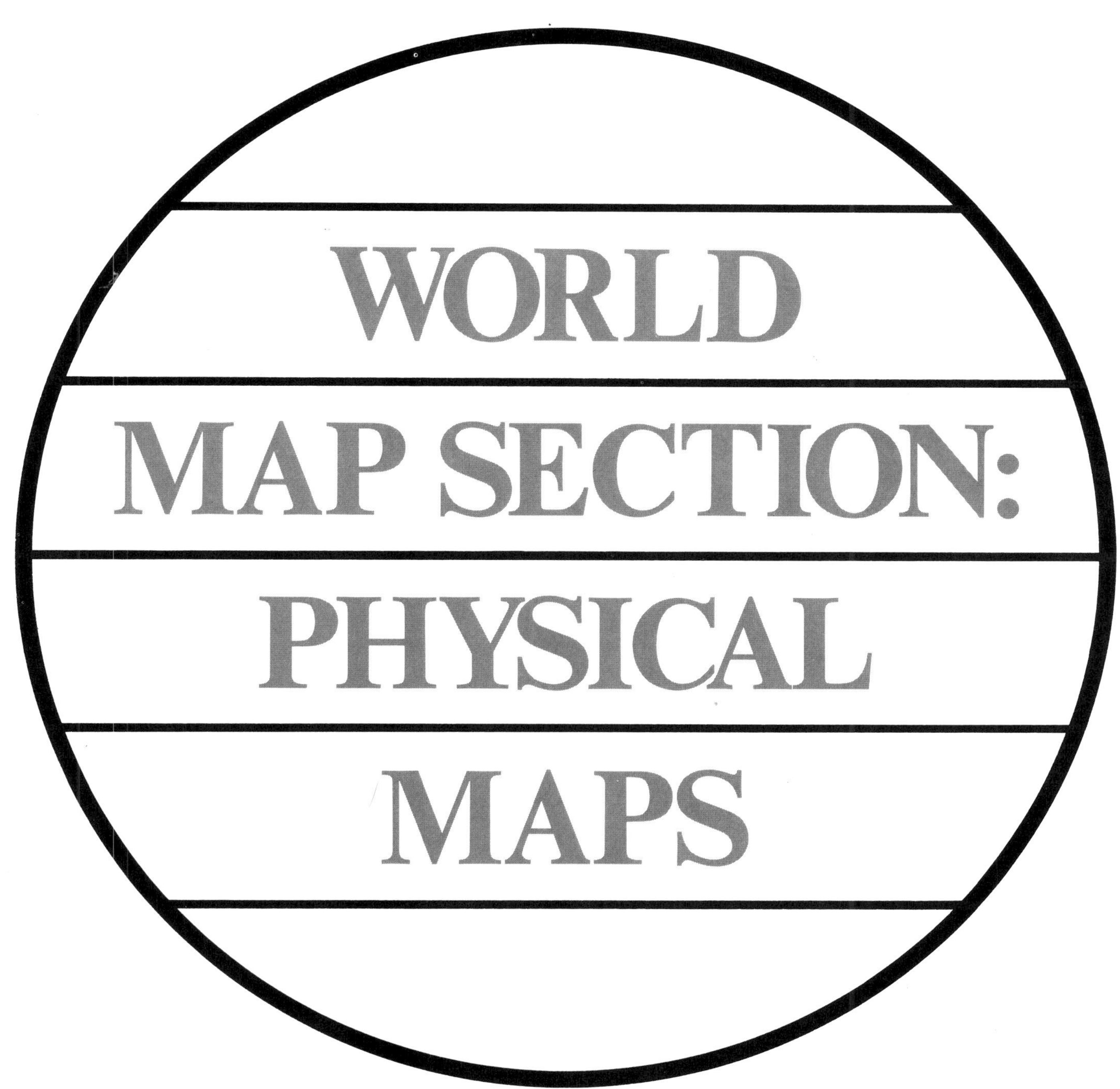
WORLD
MAP SECTION:
PHYSICAL
MAPS

A R C T I C
Amerasia Basin
Canada Basin
Beaufort Sea
Greenland
Baffin Bay
Hudson Bay
Labrador
Newfoundland
Davis Str.
Denmark Str.
Arctic Circle
Iceland
British Isles
Ireland
Alaska
Gulf of Alaska
Bering Sea
Aleutian Is.
Aleutian Trench
Victoria
Baffin
Labrador B.
NORTH AMERICA
North Pacific Basin
Mendocino Fracture Zone
Murray Fracture Zone
Tropic of Cancer
Hawaii
Hawaiian Is.
Gulf of Mexico
Mexico
Lower California
Gulf of California
Bermuda Is.
Bahama Is.
Sargasso Sea
West Indies
Cuba
Caribbean Sea
Guiana Basin
Cape Verde Basin
Is. Cabo Verde
Canary Basin
Iberian B.
West Europ. B.
North American Basin
Newfoundland Basin
Newfoundland Ridge
Azores Plateau
Madeira
Clarion Fracture Zone
Clipperton Fracture Zone
Central Pacific Basin
Guatemala Basin
P A C I F I C
O C E A N
ATLANTIC OCEAN
Cocos Rise
Equator
Is. Galápagos
Peru Basin
East Pacific Rise
Easter Plateau
Tropic of Capricorn
POLYNESIA
Is. Marquises
Tuamotu Basin
Society Is.
Tahiti
Cook Is.
Is. Tubuai
Pitcairn
Sala y Gómez
Easter I.
Is. Juan Fernandez
SOUTH AMERICA
Amazonas
Planalto do Brasil
Gran Chaco
Pampa
Patagonia
Brazil Basin
Argentine Basin
Rio Grande Rise
Falkland Is.
Tierra del Fuego
Scotia Ridge
West Scotia Basin
South Georgia
South Sandwich Is.
Drake Str.
South Shetlands
South Orkneys
Antarctic Pen.
Antarctic Circle
Weddell Sea
Bellingshausen Sea
South Pacific Basin
Southeast Pacific Basin
Mid Pacific Ridge
Byrd Land
Ross Ice Shelf
A N T A
Cities over 1,000,000 Population
Cities under 1,000,000 Population

Scale at the center meridian 1: 67,500,000 One inch to 1,065 miles
Conversion meters – feet see page 48

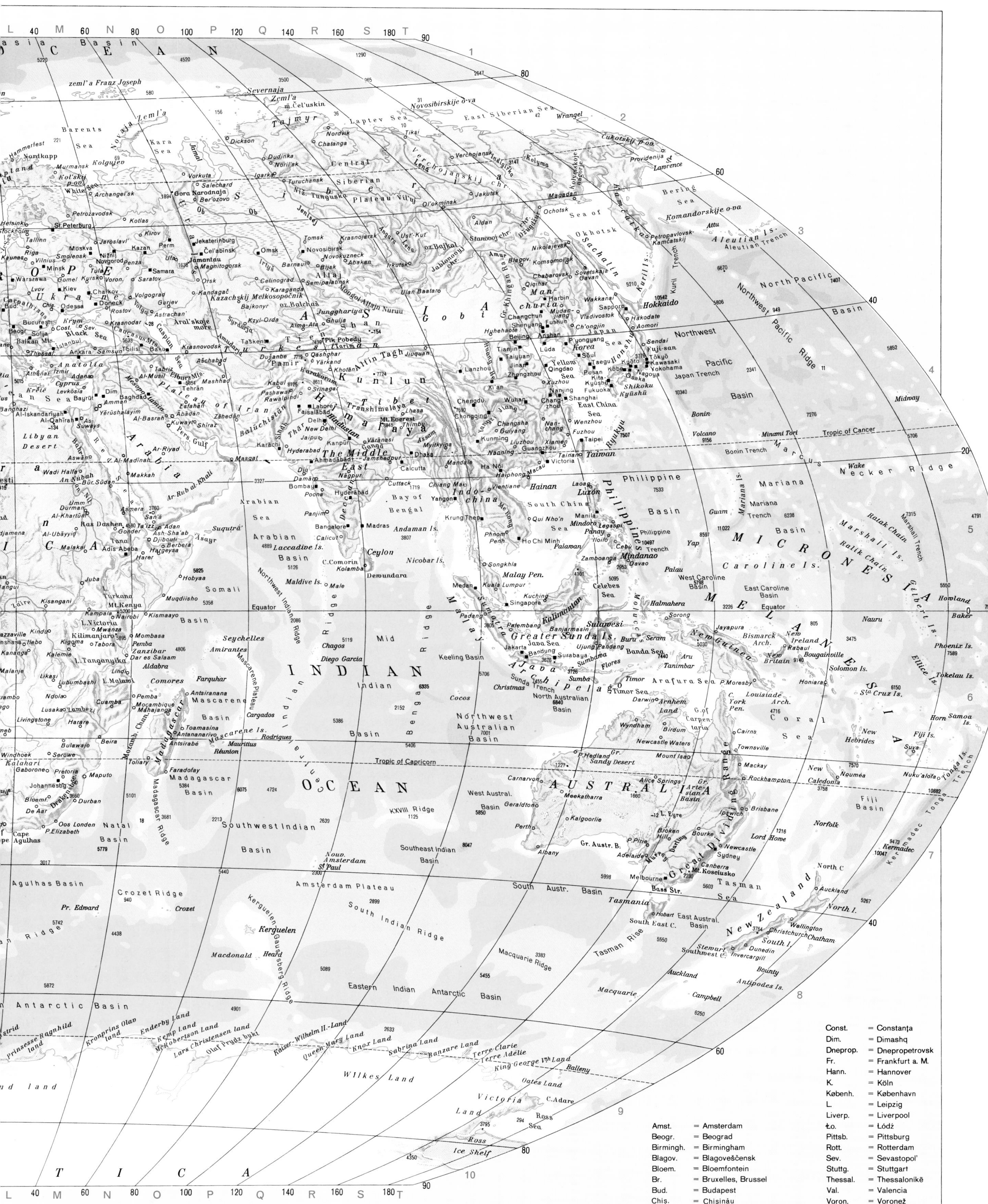
Amst. = Amsterdam
Beogr. = Beograd
Birmingh. = Birmingham
Blagov. = Blagoveščensk
Bloem. = Bloemfontein
Br. = Bruxelles, Brussel
Bud. = Budapest
Chiș. = Chișinău
Const. = Constanța
Dim. = Dimashq
Dneprop. = Dnepropetrovsk
Fr. = Frankfurt a. M.
Hann. = Hannover
K. = Köln
Københ. = København
L. = Leipzig
Liverp. = Liverpool
Ło. = Łódź
Pittsb. = Pittsburg
Rott. = Rotterdam
Sev. = Sevastopol'
Stuttg. = Stuttgart
Thessal. = Thessaloníkē
Val. = Valencia
Voron. = Voronež

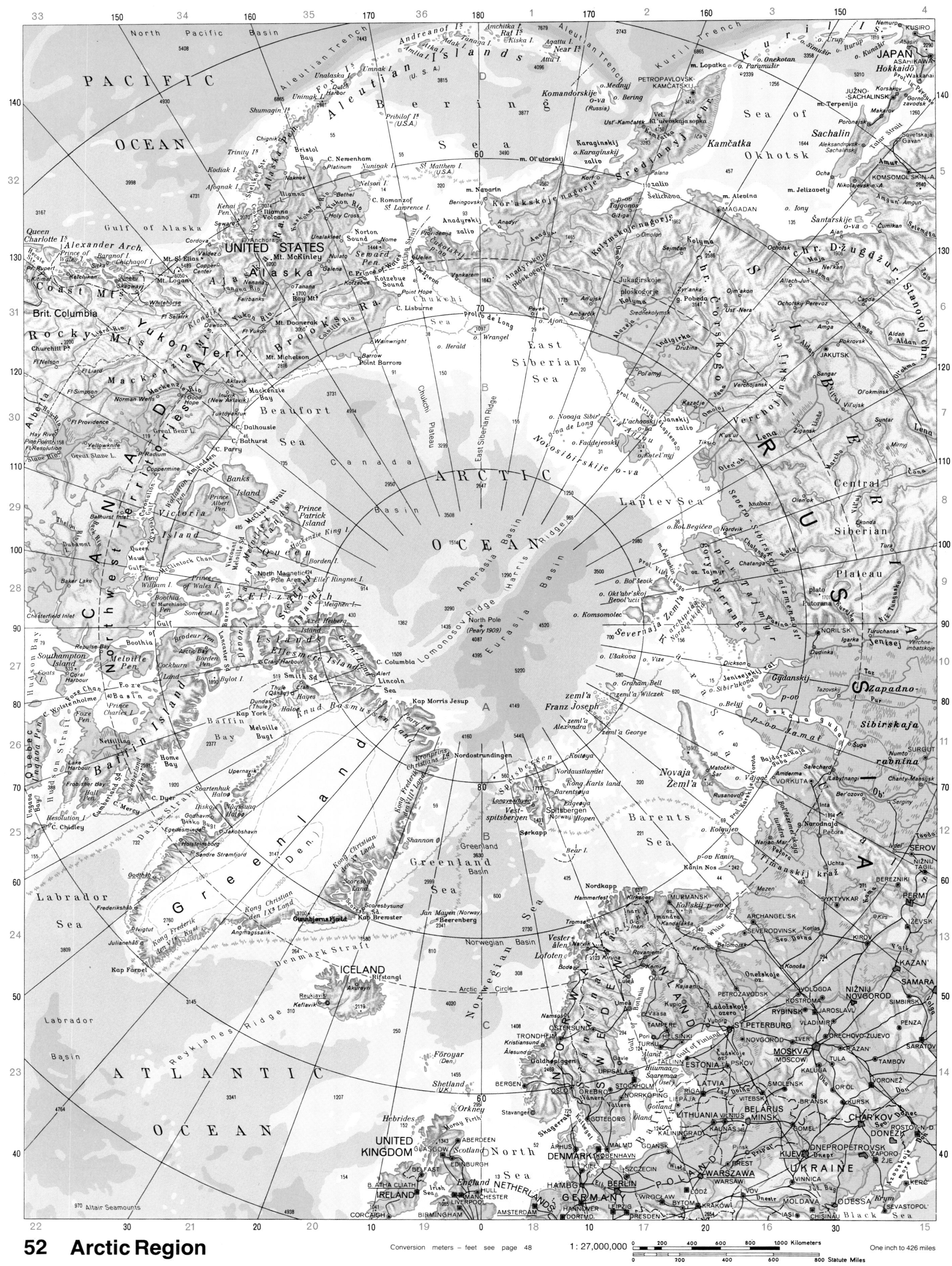
PACIFIC
OCEAN
North Pacific Basin
Aleutian Trench
Aleutian Islands
Bering Sea
Kuril Trench
Sea of Okhotsk
Gulf of Alaska
UNITED STATES
Alaska
Mt. McKinley
Brooks Ra.
Brit. Columbia
Rocky Mts.
Yukon Terr.
Mackenzie Mts.
Chukchi Sea
Beaufort Sea
Canada Basin
East Siberian Sea
ARCTIC
OCEAN
North Pole
(Peary 1909)
Lomonosov Ridge
Amerasia Basin
Eurasia Basin
Laptev Sea
Severnaja Zeml'a
Novosibirskije o-va
CANADA
Northwest Territories
Victoria Island
Banks Island
Queen Elizabeth Islands
Ellesmere Island
Baffin Island
Baffin Bay
Hudson Bay
Hudson Strait
Labrador Sea
Greenland
(Den.)
Greenland Sea
Greenland Basin
Denmark Strait
ICELAND
Norwegian Sea
Norwegian Basin
Arctic Circle
Barents Sea
Novaja Zeml'a
Kara Sea
zeml'a Franz Joseph
Spitsbergen
Jan Mayen (Norway)
Föroyar
(Den.)
Shetland
(U.K.)
Reykjanes Ridge
Labrador Basin
ATLANTIC
OCEAN
UNITED KINGDOM
IRELAND
North Sea
NORWAY
SWEDEN
FINLAND
ESTONIA
LATVIA
LITHUANIA
BELARUS
POLAND
GERMANY
DENMARK
NETHERLANDS
UKRAINE
RUSSIA
Central Siberian Plateau
Kamčatka
Sachalin
JAPAN
Hokkaidō
Black Sea
MOSKVA
ST. PETERBURG
Altair Seamounts

Conversion meters – feet see page 48

1 : 27,000,000 — Kilometers 0 200 400 600 800 1000 — Statute Miles 0 200 400 600 800

One inch to 426 miles

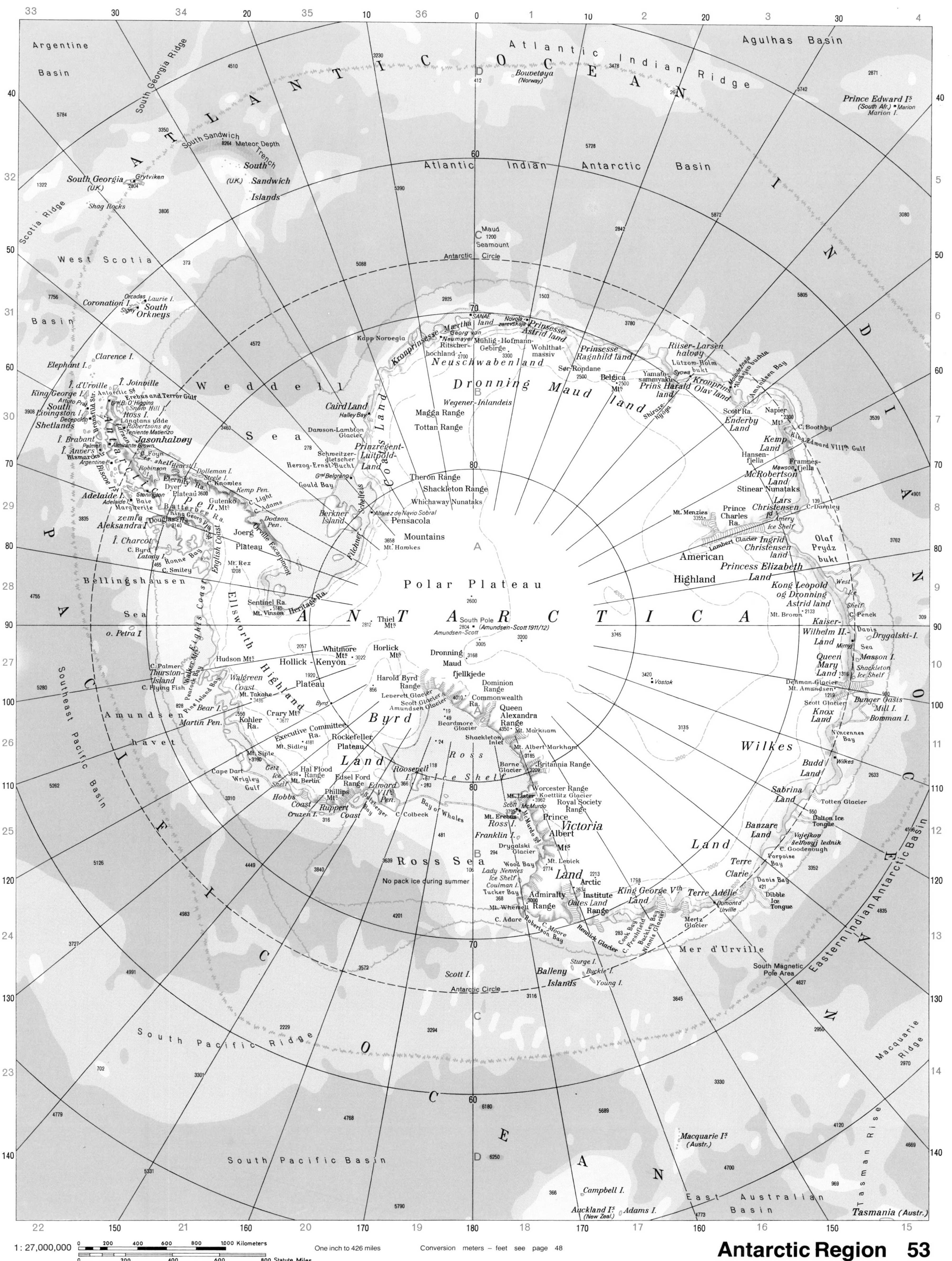

Argentine Basin
South Georgia Ridge
ATLANTIC OCEAN
Atlantic Indian Ridge
Agulhas Basin
Bouvetøya (Norway)
Prince Edward Is. (South Afr.)
Marion I.
South Sandwich Trench
Meteor Depth
South Sandwich Islands (U.K.)
South Georgia (U.K.)
Grytviken
Shag Rocks
Scotia Ridge
Atlantic Indian Antarctic Basin
Maud Seamount
Antarctic Circle
West Scotia Basin
Coronation I.
Orcadas
Laurie I.
Signy
South Orkneys
Elephant I.
Clarence I.
King George I.
South Shetlands
Livingston I.
Deception
Î. d'Urville
Î. Joinville
Erebus and Terror Gulf
Snow Hill I.
Ross I.
Jasonhaløoy
Î. Brabant
Î. Anvers
Palmer
Argentine I.
Biscoe Is.
Adelaide I.
Marguerite B.
Aleksandra I zemlja
Î. Charcot
Latady I.
Ronne Bay
Bellingshausen Sea
Weddell Sea
Kapp Norvegia
Kronprinsesse Märtha land
SANAE
Neuschwabenland
Ritscher-hochland
Mühlig-Hofmann-Gebirge
Wohlthat-massiv
Prinsesse Astrid land
Prinsesse Ragnhild land
Sør-Rondane
Belgica Mts.
Dronning Maud land
Wegener-Inlandeis
Riiser-Larsen halvøy
Lützow-Holm bukt
Syowa
Kronprins Olav land
Prins Harald land
Shirase-breen
Amundsen Bay
Scott Ra.
Napier Mts.
Enderby Land
Kemp Land
C. Boothby
King Edward VIIIth Gulf
Hansen-fjella
Framnes-fjella
Mawson
McRobertson Land
Stinear Nunataks
Lars Christensen
C. Darnley
Prince Charles Ra.
Mt. Menzies
Amery Ice Shelf
Lambert Glacier
Ingrid Christensen land
Olaf Prydz bukt
American Highland
Princess Elizabeth Land
Kong Leopold og Dronning Astrid land
West Ice Shelf
C. Penck
Mt. Brown
Caird Land
Halley Bay
Magga Range
Tottan Range
Dawson-Lambton Glacier
Prinzregent-Luitpold-Land
Coats Land
Schweitzer-gletscher
Herzog-Ernst-Bucht
Gould Bay
Gral Belgrano
Theron Range
Shackleton Range
Whichaway Nunataks
Berkner Island
Filchner-Schelfeis
Alférez de Navio Sobral
Pensacola Mountains
Mt. Hawkes
Antarctic Pen.
Dolleman I.
Steele I.
Hearst I.
Eternity Ra.
Dyer Plateau
Kemp Pen.
C. Knowles
C. Light
C. Adams
Gutenko Mts.
Dodson Pen.
Orville Escarpment
Joerg Plateau
English Coast
Mt. Rex
C. Smiley
Sentinel Ra.
Mt. Vinson
Heritage Ra.
Ellsworth Highland
Eights Coast
Polar Plateau
ANTARCTICA
Thiel Mts.
South Pole (Amundsen-Scott 1911/12)
Dronning Maud fjellkjede
Vostok
Sea
Davis
Drygalski-I.
Kaiser-Wilhelm II.-Land
Mirny
Queen Mary Land
Masson I.
Shackleton Ice Shelf
Denman Glacier
Mt. Amundsen
Bunger Oasis
Mill I.
Bowman I.
Scott Glacier
Knox Land
Vincennes Bay
Wilkes
Wilkes Land
Budd Land
Sabrina Land
Totten Glacier
Dalton Ice Tongue
Banzare Land
Vojejkov Selfovyj lednik
C. Goodenough
Porpoise Bay
Terre Clarie
Davis Bay
Dibble Ice Tongue
Terre Adélie
Dumont d'Urville
King George Vth Land
Mertz Glacier
Ninnis Glacier
Buckley Bay
C. Freshfield
Cook Bay
Rennick Glacier
Mer d'Urville
South Magnetic Pole Area
Eastern Indian Antarctic Basin
INDIAN OCEAN
o. Petra I
C. Palmer
Thurston Island
C. Flying Fish
Hudson Mts.
Walker Mts.
Peacock Bay
Walgreen Coast
Pine Island Bay
Mt. Takahe
Bear I.
Amundsen havet
Martin Pen.
Kohler Ra.
Crary Mts.
Whitmore Mts.
Hollick-Kenyon Plateau
Horlick Mts.
Harold Byrd Range
Leverett Glacier
Scott Glacier
Amundsen Glacier
Byrd
Byrd Land
Executive Committee Ra.
Mt. Sidley
Rockefeller Plateau
Mt. Siple
Getz Ice Shelf
Cape Dart
Wrigley Gulf
Hal Flood Range
Mt. Berlin
Edsel Ford Range
Hobbs Coast
Phillips Mts.
Ruppert Coast
Cruzen I.
Edward VII Pen.
Sulzberger Bay
C. Colbeck
Roosevelt I.
Ross Ice Shelf
Bay of Whales
Dominion Range
Commonwealth Ra.
Queen Alexandra Range
Beardmore Glacier
Mt. Markham
Shackleton Inlet
Mt. Albert Markham
Britannia Range
Barne Glacier
Worcester Range
Koettlitz Glacier
Royal Society Range
Mt. Lister
Scott
McMurdo
Mt. Erebus
Ross I.
McMurdo Sd.
Prince Albert Mts.
Victoria Land
Franklin I.
Drygalski Glacier
Mt. Lebick
Wood Bay
Lady Newnes Ice Shelf
Coulman I.
Tucker Bay
Mt. Whewell
Admiralty Range
Arctic Institute Range
Oates Land
C. Adare
C. Moore
Robertson Bay
Ross Sea
No pack ice during summer
Scott I.
Balleny Islands
Sturge I.
Buckle I.
Young I.
Southeast Pacific Basin
PACIFIC OCEAN
South Pacific Ridge
South Pacific Basin
Macquarie Is. (Austr.)
Macquarie Ridge
Campbell I.
Auckland Is. (New Zeal.)
Adams I.
East Australian Basin
Tasman Rise
Tasmania (Austr.)
1: 27,000,000
0 200 400 600 800 1000 Kilometers
0 200 400 600 800 Statute Miles
One inch to 426 miles
Conversion meters – feet see page 48

ARCTIC OCEAN
PACIFIC OCEAN
ATLANTIC
Hudson Bay
Gulf of Mexico
Caribbean Sea
Greenland Sea
Greenland
Labrador Sea
Baffin Bay
Davis Strait
Hudson Strait
Beaufort Sea
Chukchi Sea
Bering Sea
Gulf of Alaska
Queen Elizabeth Islands
Alaska
Alaska Range
Brooks Range
Rocky Mountains
Coast Range
Cascade Range
Sra Nevada
Great Plains
Appalachian Mts.
Sra Madre Occidental
Sra Madre Oriental
Lower California
Gulf of California
Yucatán
Greater Antilles
Bahamas
Great Bear L.
Great Slave L.
L. Athabasca
L. Winnipeg
L. Superior
L. Michigan
L. Huron
L. Erie
L. Ontario
Great Salt Lake
Anchorage
Fairbanks
Mt. McKinley
Whitehorse
Juneau
Vancouver
Seattle
Portland
San Francisco
Sacramento
Los Angeles
Las Vegas
Denver
Salt Lake City
Edmonton
Calgary
Winnipeg
Chicago
Detroit
Toronto
Montréal
Québec
Boston
New York
Philadelphia
Washington
Atlanta
Houston
New Orleans
Miami
México
Guadalajara
Monterrey
La Habana
Guatemala
Cultivated land (arable land, plantations, irrigated land)
Grassland and grassland farming
Forest of the temperate Zone
Tropical forest
Savannah
Steppe
Semi-desert, desert
Boreal forest
Tundra
Rock, snow and ice areas of mountain and polar regions

54 North America, Vegetation

Conversion meters – feet see page 48

1 : 27,000,000 — 0 200 400 600 800 1,000 Kilometers — 0 200 400 600 800 Statute Miles

One inch to 426 miles

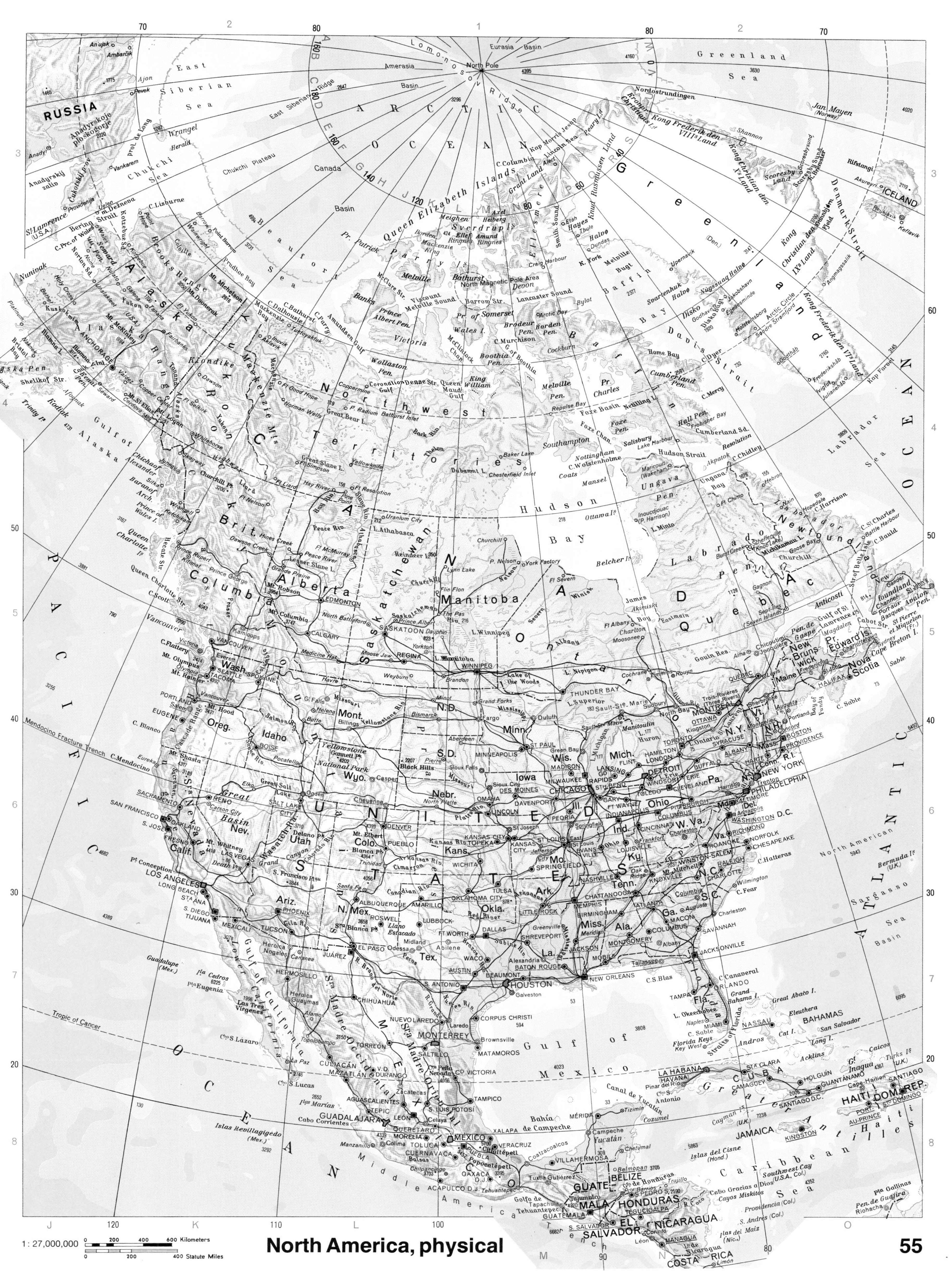
RUSSIA
North Pole
Eurasia Basin
Amerasia Basin
Lomonosov Ridge
East Siberian Sea
Chukchi Sea
Chukchi Plateau
Canada Basin
A R C T I C O C E A N
Greenland Sea
Jan Mayen (Norway)
ICELAND
Denmark Strait
Queen Elizabeth Islands
Beaufort Sea
Baffin Bay
Davis Strait
Labrador Sea
Greenland (Den.)
Alaska
Brooks Range
Alaska Range
Gulf of Alaska
ANCHORAGE
Mt. McKinley
Kodiak
Aleutian Is.
Northwest Territories
Great Bear L.
Great Slave L.
L. Athabasca
Yukon
Hudson Bay
Hudson Strait
James Bay
Labrador
Newfoundland
Quebec
Ontario
Manitoba
Saskatchewan
Alberta
Brit. Columbia
C A N A D A
Rocky Mts
VANCOUVER
Wash.
Oreg.
Calif.
Nev.
Idaho
Mont.
Wyo.
Utah
Colo.
Ariz.
N. Mex.
Tex.
Okla.
Kans.
Nebr.
S.D.
N.D.
Minn.
Iowa
Mo.
Ark.
La.
Miss.
Ala.
Ga.
Fla.
S.C.
N.C.
Tenn.
Ky.
Ill.
Ind.
Ohio
Mich.
Wis.
Pa.
N.Y.
Va.
W. Va.
U N I T E D S T A T E S
SEATTLE
PORTLAND
SAN FRANCISCO
LOS ANGELES
SAN DIEGO
SALT LAKE CITY
DENVER
PHOENIX
EL PASO
HOUSTON
DALLAS
NEW ORLEANS
CHICAGO
DETROIT
ST LOUIS
MINNEAPOLIS
TORONTO
MONTREAL
OTTAWA
QUEBEC
BOSTON
NEW YORK
PHILADELPHIA
WASHINGTON D.C.
BALTIMORE
ATLANTA
MIAMI
HALIFAX
Nova Scotia
New Bruns wick
Pr. Edward Is.
Anticosti
Great Salt L.
Great Basin
Mt. Whitney
Death Val.
L. Superior
L. Michigan
L. Huron
L. Erie
L. Ontario
Gulf of Mexico
Gulf of California
Sierra Madre Occidental
Sierra Madre Oriental
MEXICO
MONTERREY
GUADALAJARA
Yucatán
BAHAMAS
CUBA
LA HABANA
JAMAICA
HAITI
DOM. REP.
Caribbean Sea
Greater Antilles
BELIZE
GUATEMALA
HONDURAS
EL SALVADOR
NICARAGUA
COSTA RICA
Sargasso Sea
North American Basin
Bermuda Is. (U.K.)
Tropic of Cancer
Middle America Trench
Mendocino Fracture Trench
P A C I F I C O C E A N
A T L A N T I C O C E A N
1 : 27,000,000
0 200 400 600 Kilometers
0 200 400 Statute Miles

North America, physical

ARCTIC OCEAN
Chukchi Sea
Beaufort Sea
Canada Basin
Bering Strait
Bering Sea
Bristol Bay
Gulf of Alaska
PACIFIC OCEAN
North Pacific Basin
Mendocino Fracture Zone
Alaska (USA)
ALASKA RANGE
Brooks Range
Alaska Pen.
Aleutian Ra.
Yukon Territory
District of Mackenzie
Northwest Territories
District of Keewatin
Victoria Island
Banks Island
British Columbia
Alberta
Saskatchewan
Montana
Washington
Oregon
Idaho
Wyoming
California
Nevada
UNITED
ROCKY MOUNTAINS
COAST MTS.
RUSSIA
Amundsen Gulf
Great Bear L.
Great Slave L.
Lake Athabasca
Queen Charlotte Islands
Vancouver Island
ANCHORAGE
EDMONTON
CALGARY
SASKATOON
REGINA
VANCOUVER
Victoria
SEATTLE
TACOMA
SPOKANE
PORTLAND
EUGENE
BOISE
Mt. McKinley
Fairbanks
Whitehorse
Yellowknife

1 : 13,500,000 — 0 100 200 300 400 500 Kilometers; 0 100 200 300 400 Statute Miles

One inch to 213 miles

Conversion meters – feet see page 48

ICELAND
Reykjavík
Greenland
(Den.)
Denmark Strait
Reykjanes Ridge
Baffin Bay
Davis Strait
Labrador Sea
Labrador Basin
ATLANTIC OCEAN
Ellesmere Island
Devon Island
Jones Sound
Lancaster Sound
Bylot Island
Somerset Island
Baffin Island
Cumberland Sound
Cumberland Pen.
Frobisher Bay
Hall Pen.
Meta Incognita Pen.
Resolution I.
Foxe Basin
Foxe Channel
Foxe Pen.
Melville Pen.
Boothia Pen.
Gulf of Boothia
Prince Charles I.
Southampton Island
Coats I.
Mansel I.
Hudson Strait
Ungava Bay
Ungava Pen.
Hudson Bay
James Bay
Belcher Islands
Akimiski I.
LABRADOR
Coast of Labrador
Newfoundland
Anticosti I.
Gulf of St. Lawrence
Prince Edward Island
Cape Breton I.
Cabot Strait
Nova Scotia
New Brunswick
Bay of Fundy
Gulf of Maine
Sable I.
St. Pierre et Miquelon (France)
Quebec
Ontario
Manitoba
Keewatin
Lake Superior
Lake Huron
Lake Michigan
Lake Erie
Lake Ontario
Lake Nipigon
Lake of the Woods
Isle Royale
Georgian Bay
CANADA
UNITED STATES
Minnesota
Wisconsin
Michigan
New York
Pennsylvania
Vermont
New Hampshire
Maine
Massachusetts
Connecticut
Rhode Island
Ohio
QUEBEC
MONTREAL
OTTAWA
TORONTO
HAMILTON
DETROIT
CLEVELAND
CHICAGO
MILWAUKEE
MINNEAPOLIS
ST PAUL
THUNDER BAY
BOSTON
PROVIDENCE
HARTFORD
NEW HAVEN
BRIDGEPORT
NEW YORK
PHILADELPHIA
HALIFAX
St. John's
Dartmouth
Sydney
Charlottetown
Fredericton
Saint John
Churchill
Moosonee
Sudbury
North Bay
Sault Ste. Marie
Duluth
Kingston
Sherbrooke
Trois-Rivières
Chicoutimi
Sept-Îles
Goose Bay

Chukchi Sea
Bering Strait
Norton Sound
Bristol Bay
Gulf
North Slope
Brooks Range
De Long Mts
Baird Mts
Endicott Mts
Lookout Ridge
Lookwood Hills
Ray Mts
Kokrines Hills
Kaiyuh Mts
Kuskokwim Mts
Kilbuck Mts
Beaver Mts
Waring Mts
Schwatka Mts
Alaska Range
Chigmit Mts
Aleutian Range
Talkeetna Mts
Kenai Pen.
Seward Pen.
Yukon Delta
Kotzebue Sound
Kuskokwim Bay
Cook Inlet
Shelikof Str.
Alaska (U.S.)
RUSSIA
Arctic Circle
Barrow
Pt. Barrow
Wainwright
Icy Cape
Point Lay
C. Lisburne
Point Hope (Tigara)
Kivalina
Noatak
Kotzebue
Selawik
Kiana
Noorvik
Shishmaref
Wales
C. Prince of Wales
Teller
Nome
Solomon
Council
Golovnin
Elim
Koyuk
Unalakleet
Saint Michael
Stebbins
Kaltag
Nulato
Koyukuk
Galena
Ruby
Tanana
Rampart
Livengood
Fairbanks
College
Nenana
Healy
McKinley Park
Cantwell
Mt. McKinley
Mt. Foraker
Talkeetna
Wasilla
Palmer
ANCHORAGE
Girdwood
Whittier
Seward
Kenai
Soldotna
Homer
Seldovia
Iliamna L.
Iliamna Vol.
Dillingham
Naknek
King Salmon
Katmai Nat. Mon.
Mt. Katmai
Valley of 10 000 Smokes
Becharof L.
Kodiak I.
Afognak I.
Bethel
Aniak
McGrath
Nikolai
Holy Cross
Anvik
Russian Mission
Marshall (Fortuna Ledge)
Hooper Bay
Nunivak I.
Nelson I.
Saint Lawrence I. (U.S.A.)
King I.
Hagemeister I.
Bettles
Wiseman
Anaktuvuk Pass
Umiat
Prudhoe Bay
Colville Riv.
Noatak Riv.
Kobuk Riv.
Koyukuk Riv.
Yukon Riv.
Tanana Riv.
Kuskokwim Riv.
Nushagak Riv.
1:4,500,000
see inset for continuation

Aleutian Islands, East
Aleutian Islands, Central
Aleutian Islands, West
Continuation of main map
Bering Sea
PACIFIC OCEAN
Alaska Peninsula
Aleutian Range
Shumagin Is.
Kodiak I.
Chirikof I.
Unimak I.
Unalaska I.
Umnak I.
Islands of Four Mountains
Andreanof Is.
Near Is.
Aleutian Islands
Rat I.
Amchitka I.
Kiska I.
Attu
Agattu I.
Adak I.
Atka I.
Amlia I.
Seguam I.
Yukon Territory
Yukon Plateau
British Columbia
CANADA
Klondike
Dawson Ra.
Nisling Ra.
Ruby Ra.
Kluane Nat. Park
St. Elias Mts.
Wrangell Mts.
Mentasta Mts.
Nutzotin Mts.
Mackenzie Mts.
British Mts.
Davidson Mts.
Romanzof Mts.
Coast Mountains
Alexander Arch.
Chatham Str.
Frederick Sound
Clarence Str.
Prince of Wales I.
Revillagigedo I.
Dixon Entrance
Portland Canal
Coast Mts.
Gulf of Alaska
Beaufort Lagoon
Whitehorse
Juneau
Skagway
Haines
Sitka
Ketchikan
Prince Rupert
Petersburg
Wrangell
Dutch Harbor
Mt. Logan
Mt. St. Elias
Mt. Fairweather
Yakutat
Yakutat Bay
Icy Bay
Malaspina Glacier
Glacier Bay Nat. Mon.
Dyea
Atlin
Dease Lake
Telegraph Creek
Old Crow
Circle
Eagle
Fortymile
Tok Junction
Northway
Chisana
Alaska Highway
Yukon Riv.
Porcupine Riv.
Pelly Riv.
Stikine Riv.
Taku Riv.
see inset for continuation
conversion meters – feet see page 48

PACIFIC OCEAN
Queen Charlotte Sound
Hecate Strait
Vancouver Island
Queen Charlotte Islands
Prince of Wales I.
Dixon Entrance
Clarence Strait
ROCKY MOUNTAINS
COAST MOUNTAINS
Alberta
British Columbia
Washington
UNITED STATES
EDMONTON
CALGARY
VANCOUVER
Victoria
SEATTLE
SPOKANE
Prince George
Prince Rupert
Kamloops
Conversion meters – feet see page 48
1: 4,500,000
Kilometers
Statute Miles
One inch to 71 miles

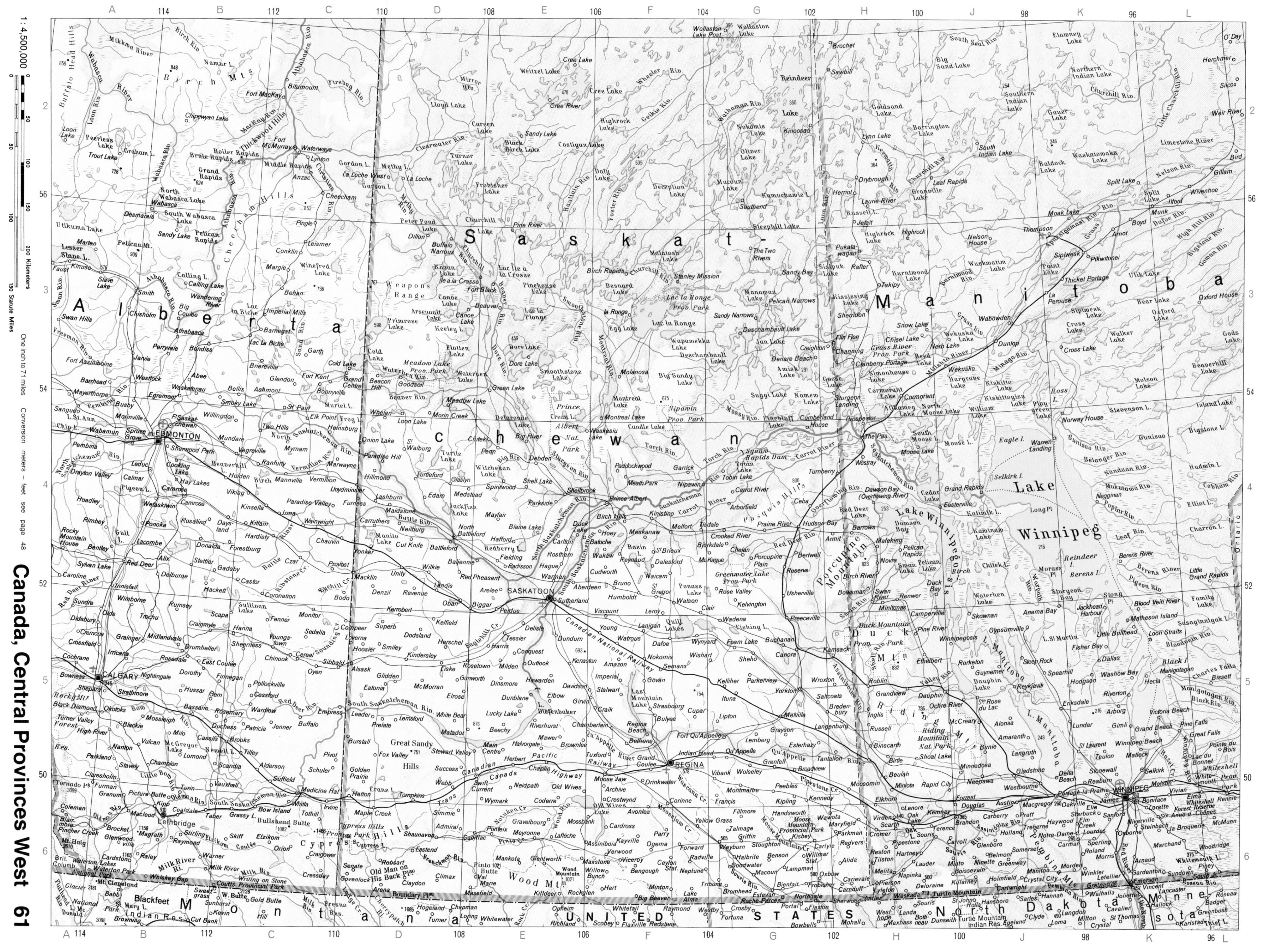
Alberta
Saskatchewan
Manitoba
Lake Winnipeg
Lake Winnipegosis
L. Manitoba
Reindeer Lake
UNITED STATES
North Dakota
Montana
Minnesota
Ontario
EDMONTON
CALGARY
SASKATOON
REGINA
WINNIPEG

1: 4,500,000 — 0 50 100 150 200 Kilometers — 0 50 100 150 Statute Miles

One inch to 71 miles Conversion meters - feet see page 48

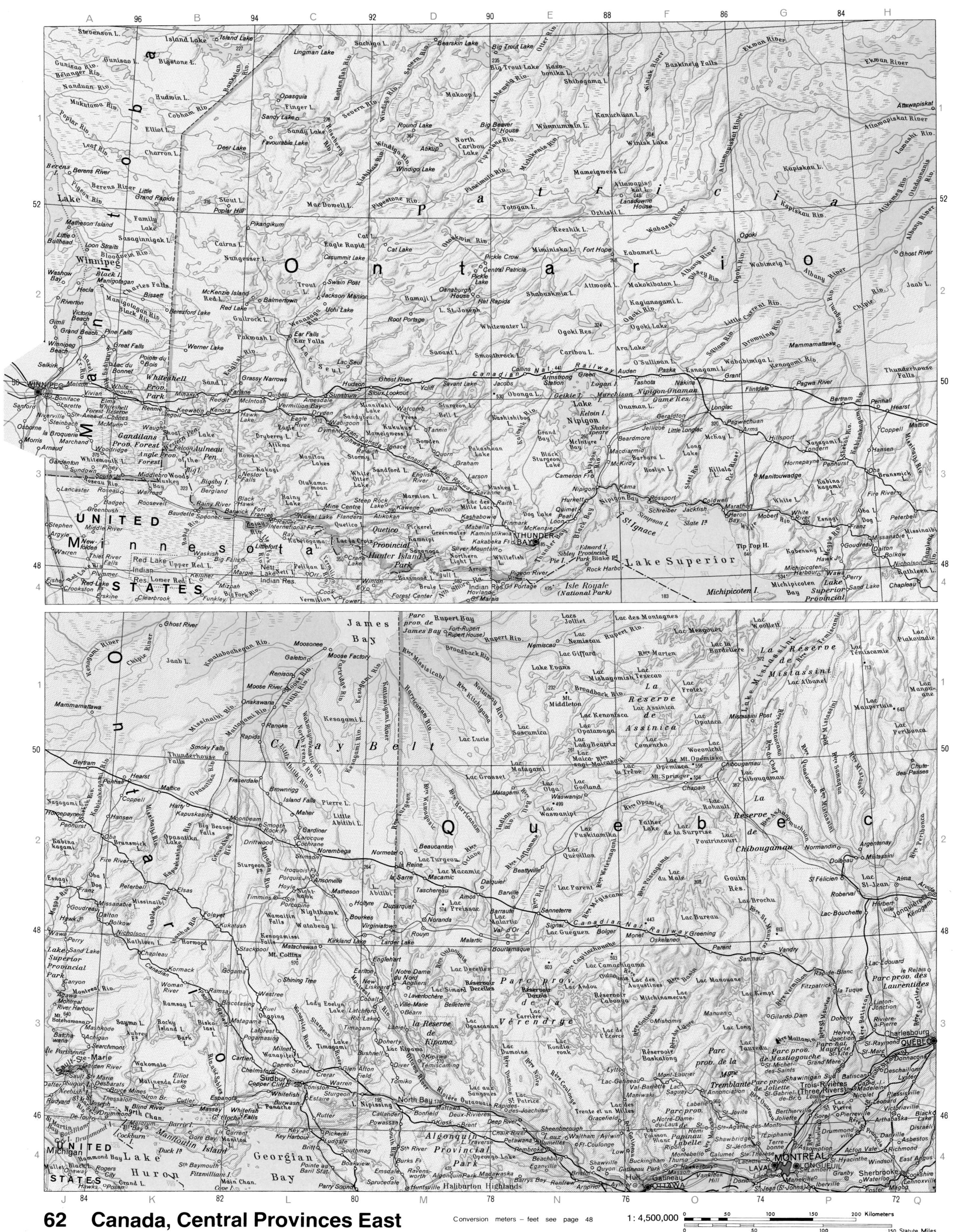

A 96 B 94 C 92 D 90 E 88 F 86 G 84 H
Manitoba
Patricia
Ontario
Lake Winnipeg
Winnipeg
Thunder Bay
Lake Superior
Isle Royale (National Park)
Lake Nipigon
UNITED STATES
Minnesota
James Bay
Clay Belt
Quebec
Ontario
Lake Huron
Georgian Bay
Manitoulin Island
Algonquin Provincial Park
Parc prov. de la Vérendrye
La Réserve de Mistassini
La Réserve de Chibougamau
Montreal
Québec
Ottawa
Sudbury
North Bay
Sault Ste-Marie
Canadian Nat. Railway
Canadian Pacific Railway
J 84 K 82 L 80 M 78 N 76 O 74 P 72 Q

 Canada, Central Provinces East

Conversion meters – feet see page 48

1: 4,500,000

0 50 100 150 200 Kilometers

0 50 100 150 Statute Miles

ATLANTIC OCEAN
Gulf of St Lawrence
Newfoundland
Quebec
New Brunswick
Prince Edward Island
Nova Scotia
Cape Breton I.
Cabot Strait
Anticosti I.
Gaspé Passage
Jacques Cartier Passage
Northumberland Strait
Bay of Fundy
Gulf of Maine
UNITED STATES
Maine
Îles de la Madeleine
St Pierre Bank
Misaine Bank
Banquereau Bank
Sable Island Bank
HALIFAX
Dartmouth
St John's
QUEBEC
1: 4,500,000
Kilometers
Statute Miles
One inch to 71 miles

Panama Canal
1: 900,000
Kilometer
Statute Miles
Caribbean Sea
PACIFIC OCEAN
Panama Canal
Colón
PANAMÁ
U N I T E D S T A T E S
M E X I C O
P A C I F I C O C E A N
Gulf of Mexico
Gulf of California
Tropic of Cancer
LOS ANGELES
SAN FRANCISCO
SEATTLE
PORTLAND
SALT LAKE CITY
DENVER
PHOENIX
EL PASO
HOUSTON
DALLAS
OKLAHOMA CITY
KANSAS CITY
MINNEAPOLIS
ST PAUL
MÉXICO
GUADALAJARA
MONTERREY
CHIHUAHUA
Guatemala Basin

1:13,500,000 Kilometers Statute Miles

One inch to 213 miles

Conversion meters – feet see page 48

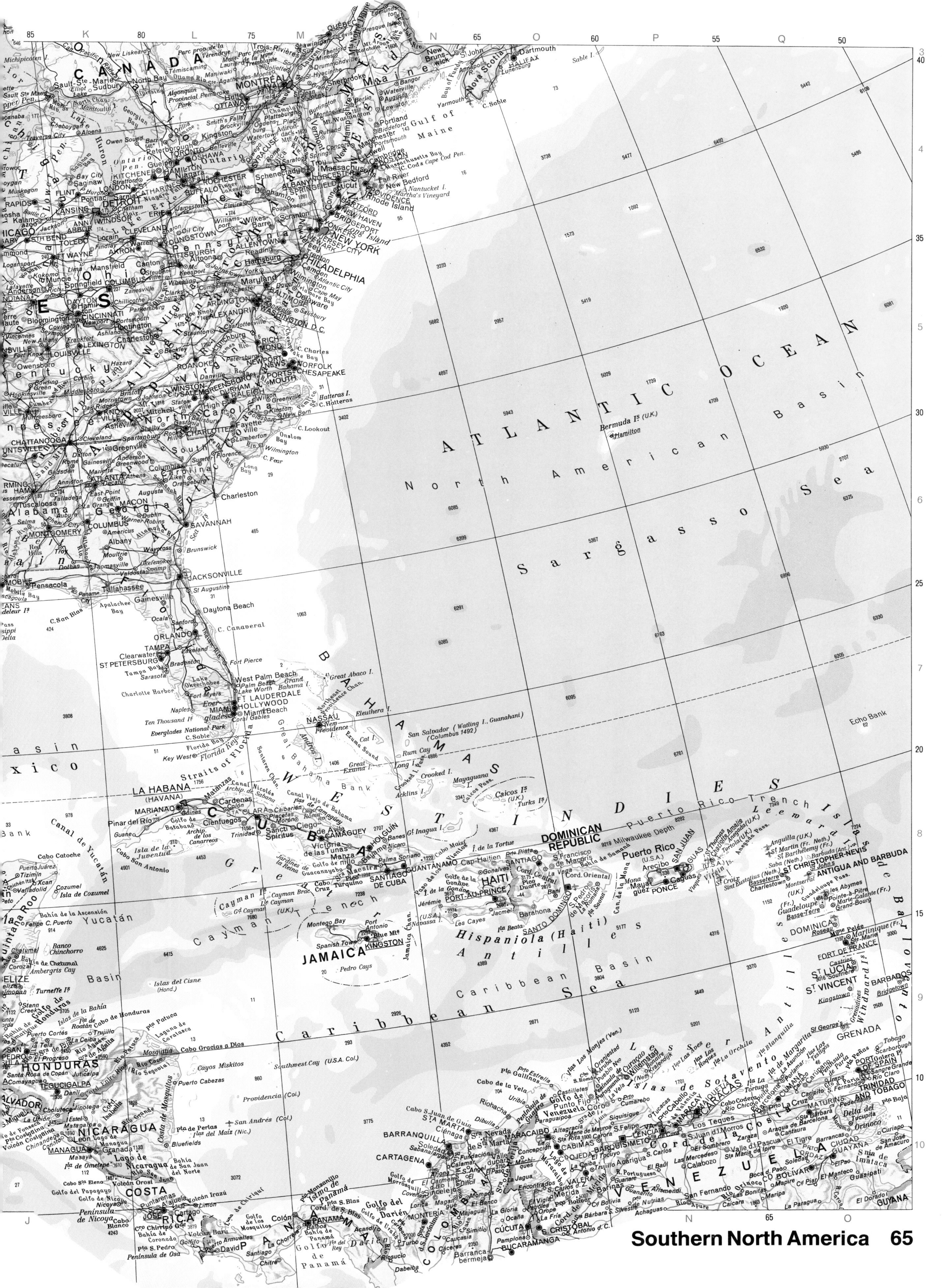
CANADA
ATLANTIC OCEAN
North American Basin
Sargasso Sea
Bermuda Is (U.K.)
Hamilton
Gulf of Maine
Nova Scotia
HALIFAX
Dartmouth
Sable I.
C. Sable
MONTREAL
OTTAWA
QUÉBEC
TORONTO
HAMILTON
BUFFALO
ROCHESTER
DETROIT
CLEVELAND
PITTSBURGH
COLUMBUS
CINCINNATI
LOUISVILLE
NEW YORK
PHILADELPHIA
BALTIMORE
WASHINGTON D.C.
RICHMOND
NORFOLK
CHESAPEAKE
BOSTON
PROVIDENCE
HARTFORD
Massachusetts
Rhode Island
Connecticut
Vermont
Maine
New Brunswick
Lake Ontario
Lake Erie
C. Hatteras
Hatteras I.
C. Lookout
C. Fear
Onslow Bay
Long Bay
CHARLOTTE
Charleston
ATLANTA
SAVANNAH
MACON
MONTGOMERY
JACKSONVILLE
Tallahassee
Pensacola
MOBILE
Daytona Beach
C. Canaveral
ORLANDO
TAMPA
ST PETERSBURG
Clearwater
West Palm Beach
FT LAUDERDALE
HOLLYWOOD
MIAMI
Fort Pierce
Everglades National Park
Key West
Florida Keys
Straits of Florida
BAHAMAS
NASSAU
Great Abaco I.
Grand Bahama I.
Eleuthera I.
Great Bahama Bank
San Salvador (Watling I., Guanahani) (Columbus 1492)
Rum Cay
Long I.
Crooked I.
Acklins I.
Mayaguana I.
Caicos Is (U.K.)
Turks Is
WEST INDIES
LA HABANA (HAVANA)
MARIANAO
Matanzas
Cardenas
Cienfuegos
CUBA
CAMAGÜEY
HOLGUÍN
SANTIAGO DE CUBA
GUANTÁNAMO
Isla de la Juventud
Cabo San Antonio
Canal de Yucatán
Cayman Is
Cayman Trench
JAMAICA
KINGSTON
Montego Bay
HAITI
PORT-AU-PRINCE
DOMINICAN REPUBLIC
SANTO DOMINGO
SANTIAGO
Hispaniola (Haiti)
Puerto Rico (U.S.A.)
SAN JUAN
PONCE
Puerto Rico Trench
Milwaukee Depth
Virgin Is.
Anguilla (U.K.)
ST CHRISTOPHER-NEVIS
ANTIGUA AND BARBUDA
Montserrat
Guadeloupe (Fr.)
DOMINICA
Martinique (Fr.)
FORT DE FRANCE
ST LUCIA
ST VINCENT
BARBADOS
GRENADA
TRINIDAD AND TOBAGO
PORT OF SPAIN
Antilles
Caribbean Basin
Caribbean Sea
Greater Antilles
Lesser Antilles
Leeward Islands
Windward Islands
Echo Bank
Yucatán
Yucatán Basin
Cozumel
HONDURAS
TEGUCIGALPA
NICARAGUA
MANAGUA
Lago de Nicaragua
COSTA RICA
SAN JOSÉ
PANAMÁ
PANAMA
Golfo de Panamá
Golfo del Darién
COLOMBIA
BARRANQUILLA
CARTAGENA
SANTA MARTA
CÚCUTA
BUCARAMANGA
VENEZUELA
MARACAIBO
Lago de Maracaibo
CARACAS
VALENCIA
MARACAY
BARQUISIMETO
Cordillera de la Costa
CIUDAD GUAYANA
CD BOLÍVAR
Isla de Margarita
GUYANA
Cabo Gracias a Dios
Golfo de Honduras
Islas de la Bahía
Golfo de Fonseca
Providencia (Col.)
San Andrés (Col.)
Gulf of Mexico
Atlantic Ocean

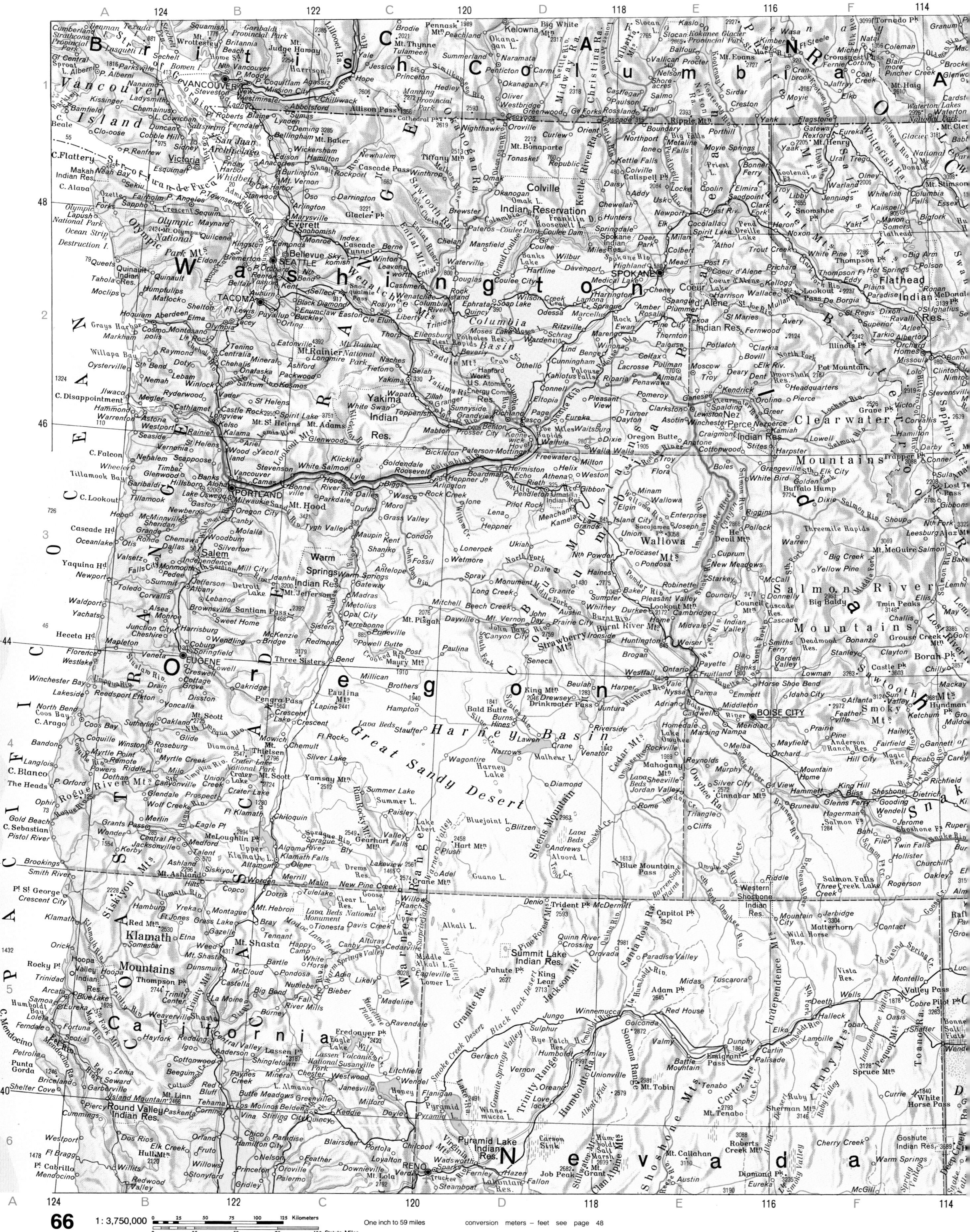
British Columbia
Washington
Oregon
California
Nevada
Idaho
PACIFIC OCEAN
CASCADE RANGE
COAST RANGES
Vancouver Island
VANCOUVER
Victoria
SEATTLE
TACOMA
Olympia
Everett
Bellingham
SPOKANE
Yakima
PORTLAND
Salem
EUGENE
BOISE CITY
RENO
Great Sandy Desert
Harney Basin
Blue Mountains
Salmon River Mountains
Klamath Mountains
Columbia Basin
Olympic Mts
Mt. Rainier
Mt. Hood
Mt. Shasta
Lassen Peak
Steens Mountain
Pyramid Lake
Crater Lake
Yakima Indian Res.
Warm Springs Indian Res.
Colville Indian Reservation
Nez Perce Indian Res.
Flathead Indian Res.
Columbia
Snake
Humboldt Riv.
A B C D E F
124 122 120 118 116 114
48 46 44 40
1 2 3 4 5 6

1 : 3,750,000 0 25 50 75 100 125 Kilometers 0 25 50 75 100 Statute Miles

One inch to 59 miles

conversion meters – feet see page 48

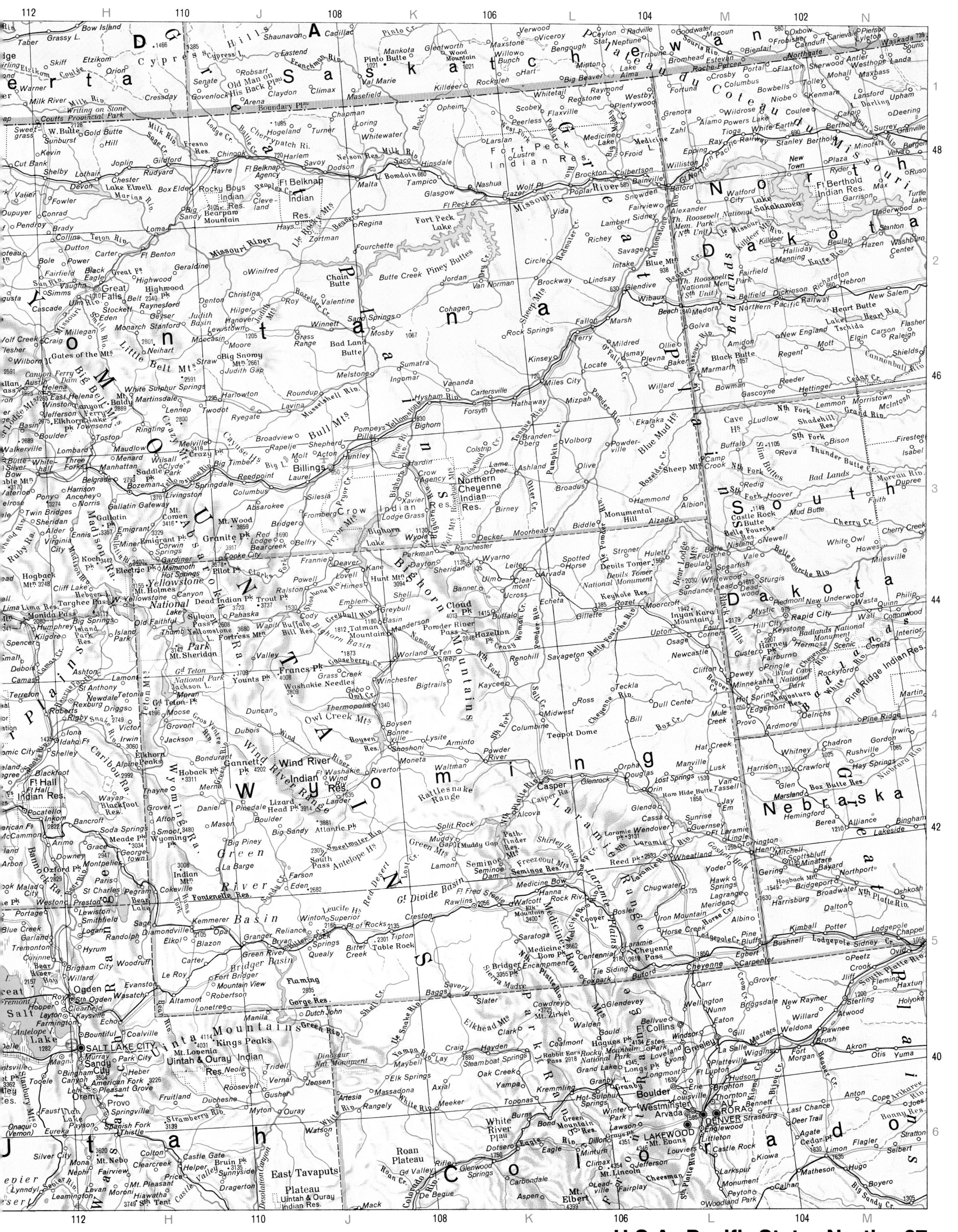

Saskatchewan
Alberta
Montana
Wyoming
North Dakota
South Dakota
Nebraska
Colorado
Utah
Rocky Mountains
Great Plains
Missouri Plateau du Coteau du Missouri
Yellowstone National Park
Grand Teton National Park
Bighorn Mountains
Wind River Range
Uinta Mountains
Laramie Range
Black Hills
Badlands
SALT LAKE CITY
DENVER
LAKEWOOD
AURORA
Great Falls
Billings
Casper
Cheyenne
Fort Peck Lake
Lake Sakakawea
Great Salt Lake
Fort Peck Indian Res.
Wind River Indian Res.
Crow Indian Res.
Northern Cheyenne Indian Res.
Pine Ridge Indian Res.
Uintah & Ouray Indian Res.
Rocky Mountain National Park
Bridger Basin
Great Divide Basin
Green River Basin
112
110
108
106
104
102
48
46
44
42
40

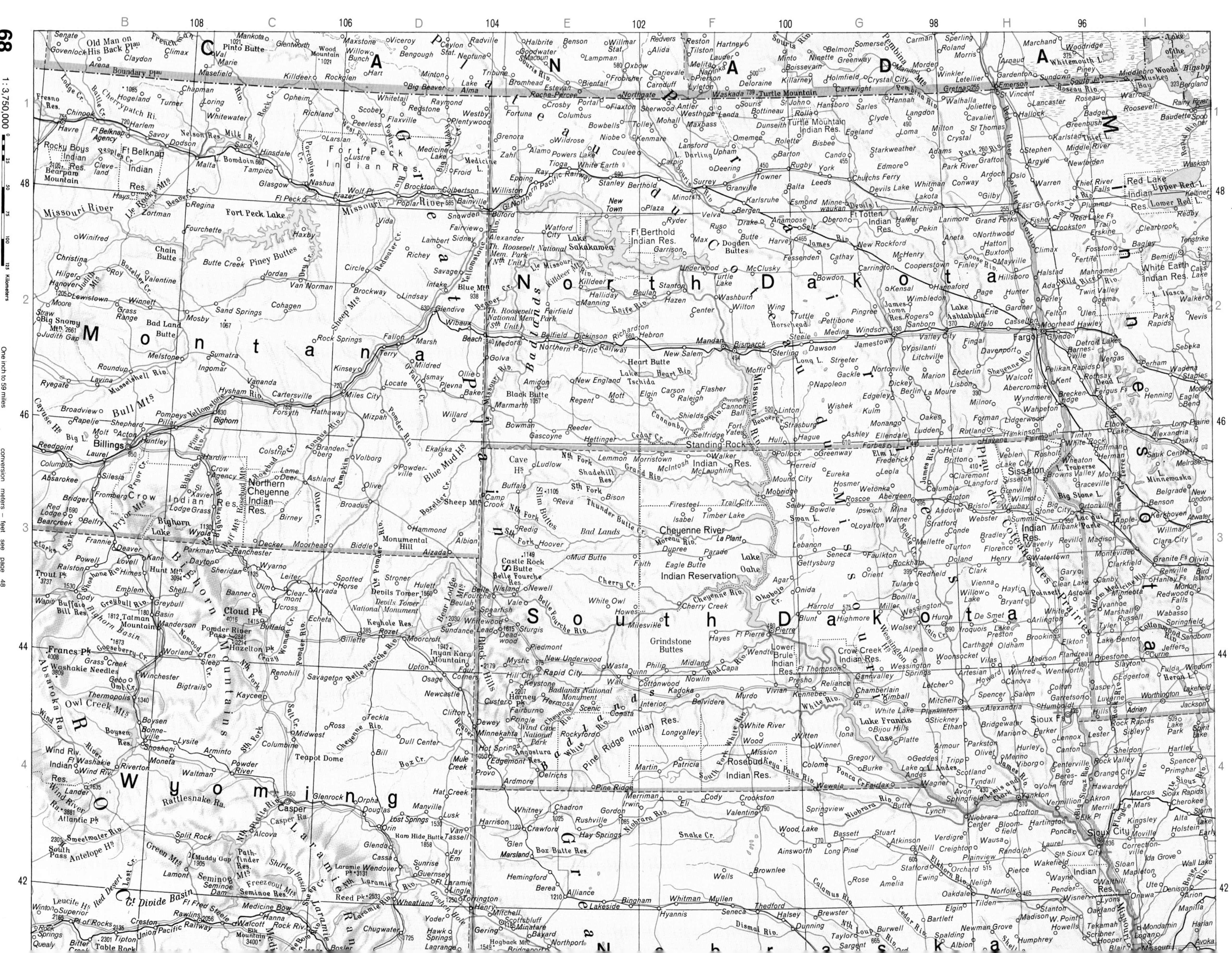
C A N A D A
M o n t a n a
N o r t h D a k o t a
S o u t h D a k o t a
W y o m i n g
M i n n e s o t a
Great Plains
Missouri Plateau
Coteau du Missouri
Coteau des Prairies
Badlands
Black Hills
Bighorn Mountains
Laramie Range
Fort Peck Lake
Lake Sakakawea
Lake Oahe
Fort Peck Indian Res.
Ft Berthold Indian Res.
Standing Rock Indian Res.
Cheyenne River Indian Reservation
Pine Ridge Indian Res.
Rosebud Indian Res.
Crow Indian Res.
Northern Cheyenne Indian Res.
Wind River Indian Res.
Billings
Bismarck
Fargo
Pierre
Rapid City
Sioux Falls
Sioux City
Casper
Boundary Plateau
Turtle Mountain

1 : 3,750,000 — 0 25 50 75 100 125 Kilometers — 0 25 50 75 100 Statute Miles — One inch to 59 miles — conversion meters - feet see page 48

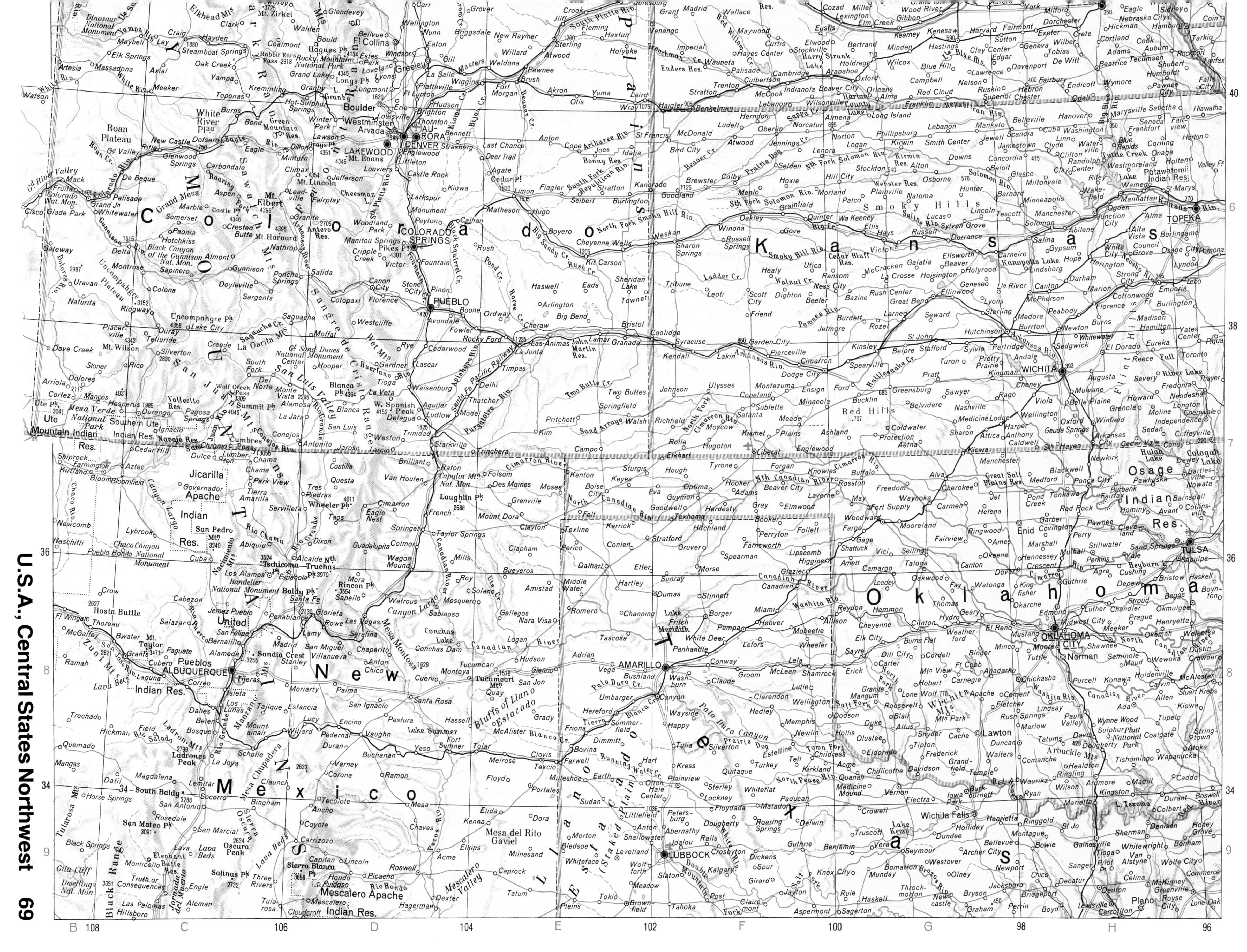
Colorado
Kansas
Oklahoma
Texas
New Mexico
TOPEKA
WICHITA
TULSA
OKLAHOMA CITY
DENVER
AURORA
LAKEWOOD
COLORADO SPRINGS
PUEBLO
AMARILLO
LUBBOCK
ALBUQUERQUE
Santa Fe
Smoky Hills
Red Hills
Plains
Sangre de Cristo Range
San Juan Mts.
Llano Estacado
Jicarilla Apache Indian Res.
Mescalero Apache Indian Res.
Osage Indian Res.

CANADA
Ontario
Lake Superior
Lake Michigan
Lake Huron
Michigan
Wisconsin
Minnesota
Iowa
North Dakota
South Dakota
MINNEAPOLIS
ST PAUL
MILWAUKEE
CHICAGO
MADISON
DULUTH
THUNDER BAY
GRAND RAPIDS
LANSING
FLINT
CEDAR RAPIDS
ROCKFORD

1: 3,750,000 — 0 25 50 75 100 125 Kilometers — 0 25 50 75 100 Statute Miles

One inch to 59 miles

conversion meters – feet see page 48

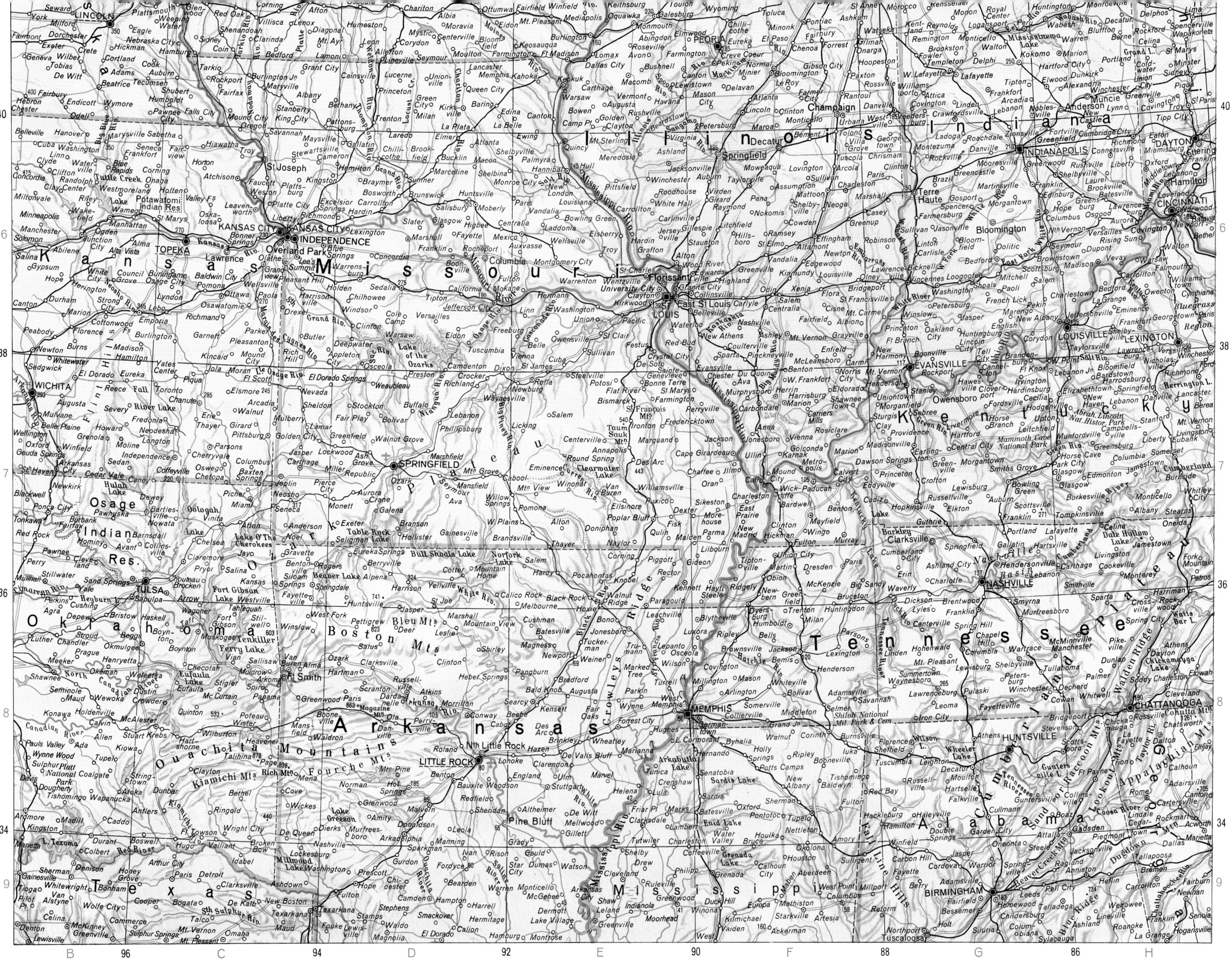

Illinois
Indiana
Kentucky
Tennessee
Missouri
Kansas
Arkansas
Oklahoma
Mississippi
Alabama
Texas
INDIANAPOLIS
CINCINNATI
DAYTON
LOUISVILLE
LEXINGTON
EVANSVILLE
NASHVILLE
CHATTANOOGA
HUNTSVILLE
BIRMINGHAM
MEMPHIS
LITTLE ROCK
ST. LOUIS
SPRINGFIELD
KANSAS CITY
INDEPENDENCE
TOPEKA
WICHITA
TULSA
LINCOLN
PEORIA
Springfield
Decatur
Champaign
Bloomington
Tuscaloosa
Ozark Plateau
Boston Mts
Ouachita Mountains
Osage Indian Res.
Lake of the Ozarks
Cumberland Plateau
Fall Line Hills

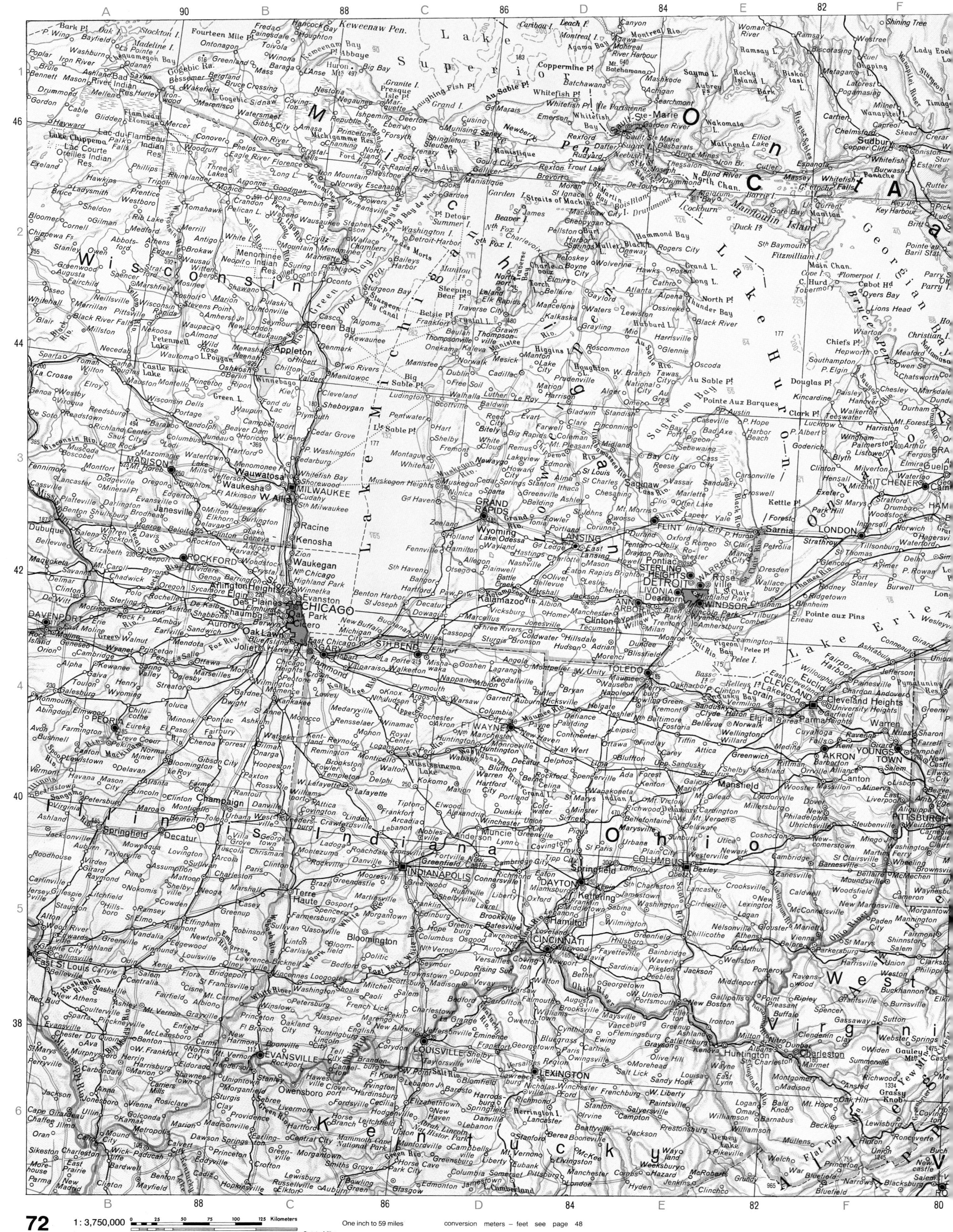

A
90
B
88
C
86
D
84
E
82
F
46
44
42
40
38
Lake Superior
Michigan
Wisconsin
Lake Michigan
Lake Huron
Georgian Bay
Lake Erie
Illinois
Indiana
Ohio
Kentucky
West Virginia
ONTARIO
CANADA
CHICAGO
MILWAUKEE
DETROIT
WINDSOR
TOLEDO
CLEVELAND
INDIANAPOLIS
CINCINNATI
LOUISVILLE
LEXINGTON
EVANSVILLE
COLUMBUS
DAYTON
GRAND RAPIDS
LANSING
FLINT
FT WAYNE
STH BEND
GARY
ROCKFORD
PEORIA
MADISON
DAVENPORT
AKRON
YOUNGSTOWN
PITTSBURGH
LONDON
KITCHENER
Green Bay
Appleton
Kalamazoo
Springfield
Champaign
Decatur
Terre Haute
Bloomington
Saginaw
Sault Ste Marie
Manitoulin Island
Keweenaw Pen.
Ohio River

1 : 3,750,000 0 25 50 75 100 125 Kilometers 0 25 50 75 100 Statute Miles

One inch to 59 miles

conversion meters – feet see page 48

Quebec
CANADA
Maine
New Hampshire
Vermont
Massachusetts
Connecticut
Rhode Island
New York
Pennsylvania
New Jersey
Delaware
Maryland
Virginia
ATLANTIC OCEAN
Lake Ontario
Lake Champlain
Adirondack Mountains
Catskill Mountains
Finger Lakes
Algonquin Provincial Park
Haliburton Highlands
Long Island
Long Island Sound
Cape Cod
Cape Cod Bay
Massachusetts Bay
Nantucket Island
Martha's Vineyard
Delaware Bay
Chesapeake Bay
Hudson Canyon
MONTRÉAL
QUÉBEC
OTTAWA
BOSTON
NEW YORK
PHILADELPHIA
BALTIMORE
WASHINGTON
RICHMOND
BUFFALO
ROCHESTER
SYRACUSE
ALBANY
PROVIDENCE
HARTFORD
NEW HAVEN
BRIDGEPORT
NEWARK
JERSEY CITY
PATERSON
YONKERS
ALLENTOWN
ARLINGTON
ALEXANDRIA
Wilmington
Trenton
Portland
Worcester
Springfield
Sherbrooke
Kingston
Harrisburg
Scranton
Binghamton
Utica
Schenectady
Burlington
Concord
Manchester
Lowell
Augusta
Bangor

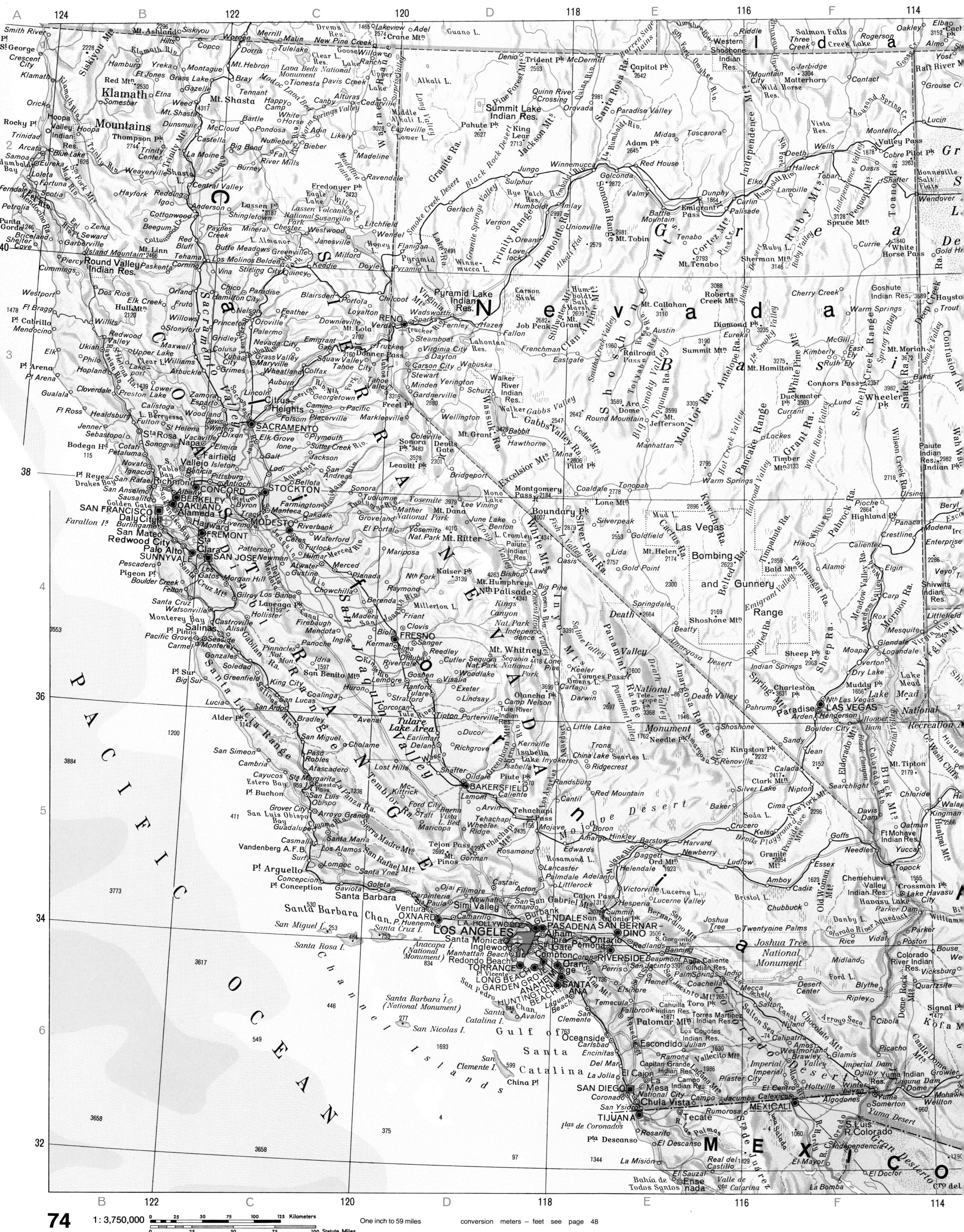

P A C I F I C   O C E A N
C h a n n e l   I s l a n d s
Gulf of Santa Catalina
N e v a d a
I d a h o
M E X I C O
SAN FRANCISCO
OAKLAND
BERKELEY
SAN JOSE
SACRAMENTO
STOCKTON
MODESTO
FRESNO
BAKERSFIELD
LOS ANGELES
PASADENA
LONG BEACH
SAN DIEGO
TIJUANA
MEXICALI
RENO
LAS VEGAS
Santa Barbara
Mojave Desert
Death Valley
Las Vegas Bombing and Gunnery Range
Mt. Whitney
Mt. Shasta
Lake Tahoe
Yosemite National Park
Santa Barbara Chan.
Salton Sea
Colorado Desert

1 : 3,750,000 0 25 50 75 100 125 Kilometers
0 25 50 75 100 Statute Miles
One inch to 59 miles
conversion meters – feet see page 48

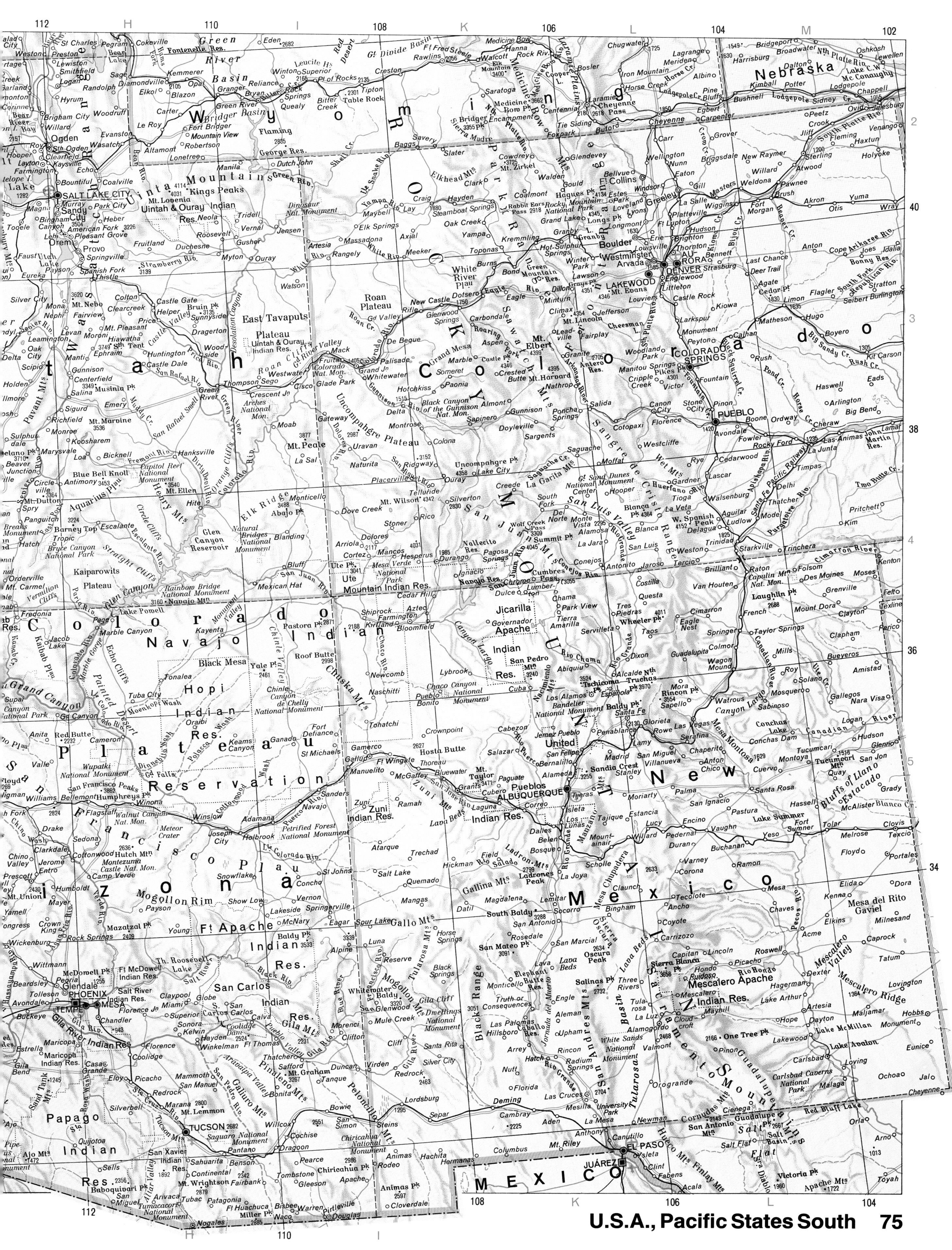
112
110
108
106
104
102
Wyoming
Nebraska
Colorado
Utah
New Mexico
Arizona
ROCKY MOUNTAINS
Colorado Plateau
Navajo Indian Reservation
Hopi Indian Res.
San Francisco Plau
Uintah & Ouray Indian Res.
Jicarilla Apache Indian Res.
Zuni Indian Res.
Ft Apache Indian Res.
San Carlos Indian Res.
Papago Indian Res.
Mescalero Apache Indian Res.
Ute Mountain Indian Res.
Green River Basin
Uinta Mountains
East Tavaputs Plateau
Roan Plateau
Uncompahgre Plateau
Kaiparowits Plateau
Mogollon Rim
Sacramento Mts
Guadalupe Mts
Llano Estacado
SALT LAKE CITY
Ogden
Provo
DENVER
AURORA
LAKEWOOD
Boulder
COLORADO SPRINGS
PUEBLO
Cheyenne
Laramie
Ft Collins
Greeley
ALBUQUERQUE
Santa Fe
Las Cruces
EL PASO
JUÁREZ
PHOENIX
TEMPE
MESA
Glendale
TUCSON
Flagstaff
Nogales
Douglas
Roswell
Carlsbad
Clovis
MEXICO

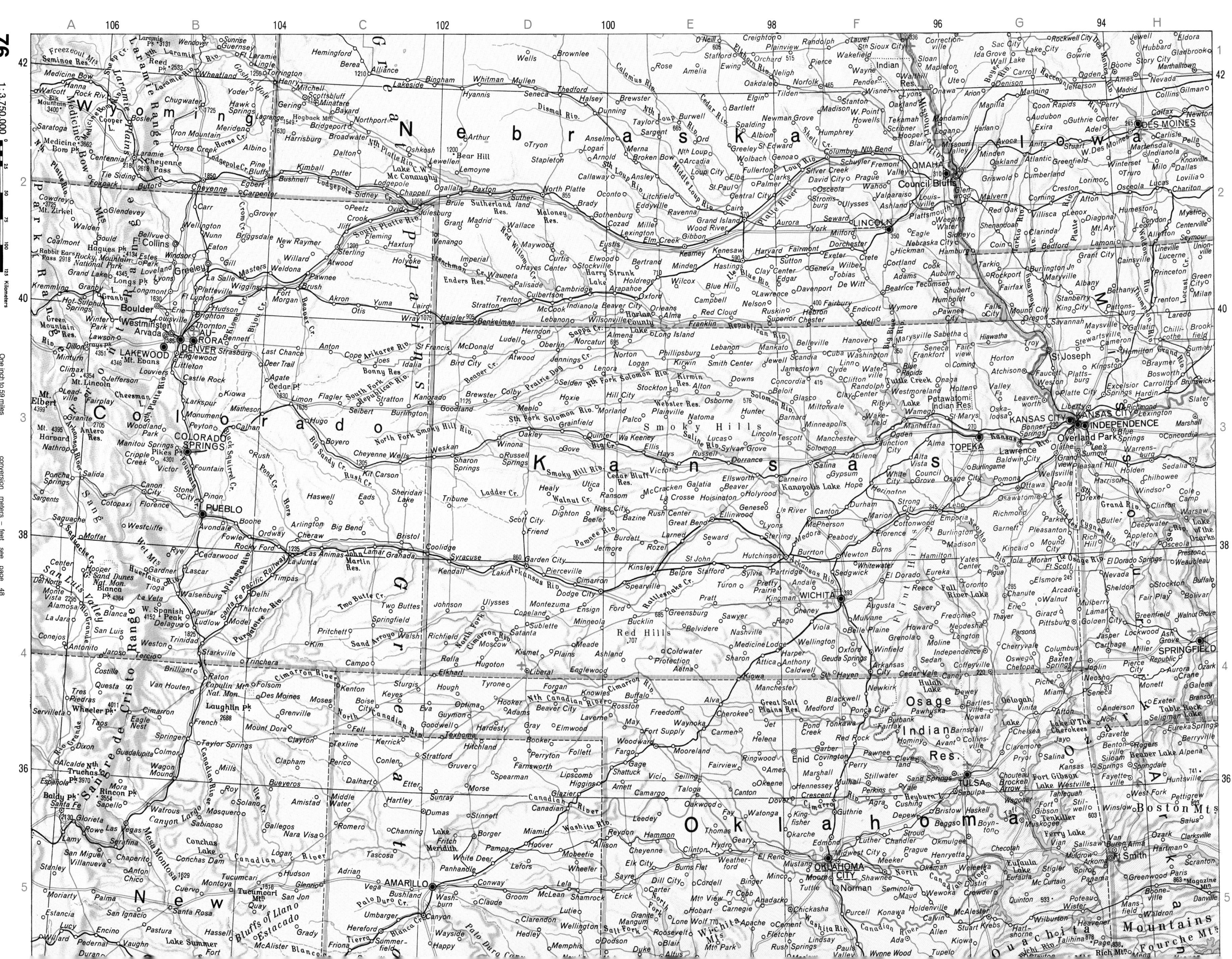

W y o m i n g
N e b r a s k a
I o w a
C o l o r a d o
K a n s a s
M i s s o u r i
O k l a h o m a
N e w
G r e a t P l a i n s
Laramie Range
Medicine Bow
Sangre de Cristo Range
Smoky Hills
Red Hills
Osage Indian Res.
Boston Mts
Ouachita Mountains
DES MOINES
OMAHA
Council Bluffs
LINCOLN
St Joseph
KANSAS CITY
INDEPENDENCE
Overland Park
TOPEKA
WICHITA
TULSA
OKLAHOMA CITY
AMARILLO
DENVER
AURORA
LAKEWOOD
Boulder
COLORADO SPRINGS
PUEBLO
SPRINGFIELD
Cheyenne

1 : 3,750,000 — 0 25 50 75 100 125 Kilometers — 0 25 50 75 100 Statute Miles

One inch to 59 miles

conversion meters - feet see page 48

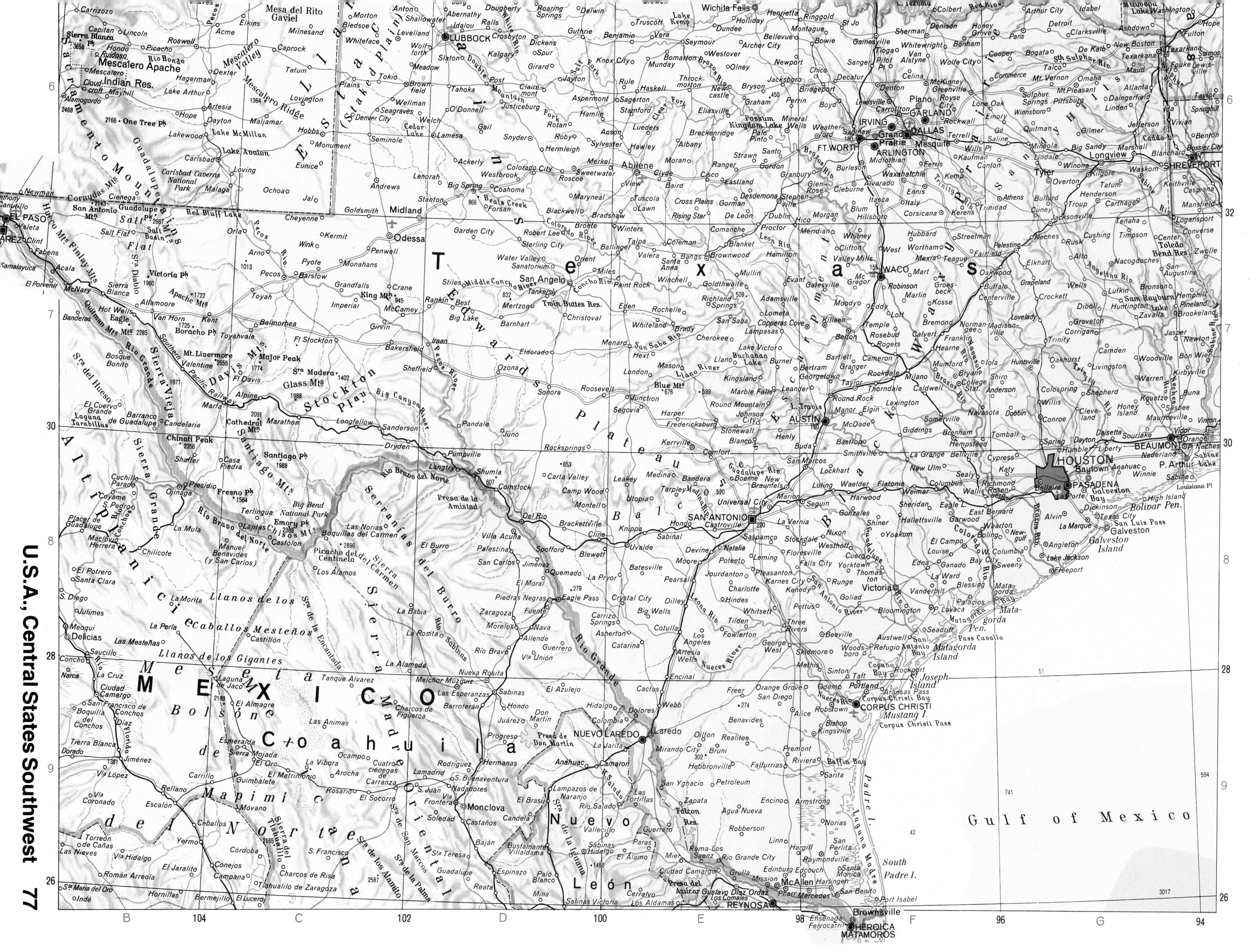
Texas
Gulf of Mexico
México
Coahuila
Nuevo León
Edwards Plateau
Llano Estacado
Balcones Escarpment
Sierra Madre Oriental
Bolsón de Mapimí
HOUSTON
DALLAS
SAN ANTONIO
AUSTIN
FT. WORTH
WACO
EL PASO
JUÁREZ
LUBBOCK
SHREVEPORT
BEAUMONT
CORPUS CHRISTI
NUEVO LAREDO
Laredo
Brownsville
HEROICA MATAMOROS
REYNOSA
McAllen
Abilene
Odessa
Midland
San Angelo
Río Grande
Pecos River
Brazos Riv.
Colorado Riv.
Padre I.
Galveston Island
Matagorda Island
Mustang I.

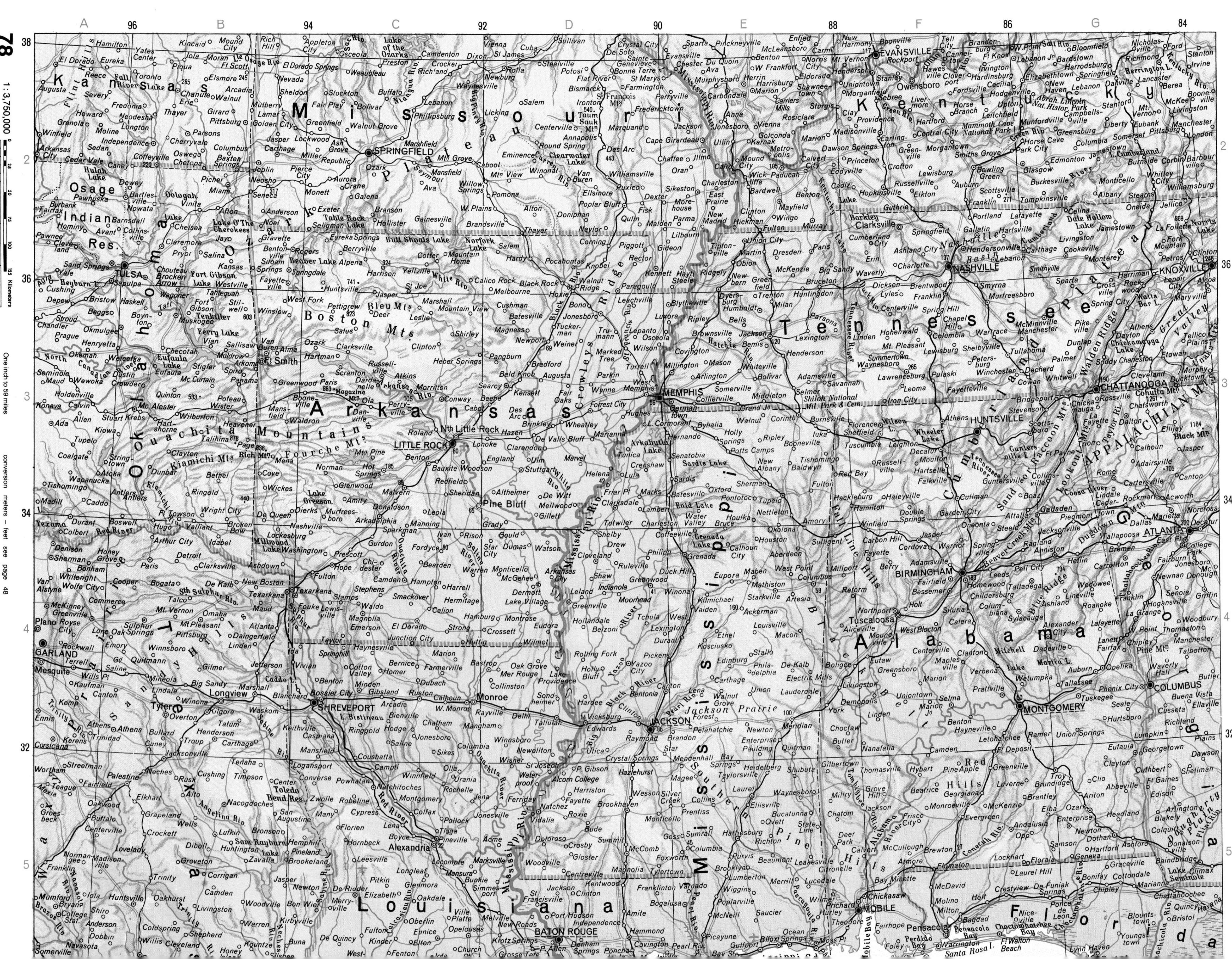

Kansas
Missouri
Kentucky
Tennessee
Oklahoma
Arkansas
Mississippi
Alabama
Georgia
Texas
Louisiana
Florida
Ozark Plateau
Boston Mts
Ouachita Mountains
Osage Indian Res.
APPALACHIAN MTS
Fall Line Hills
SPRINGFIELD
TULSA
LITTLE ROCK
MEMPHIS
NASHVILLE
KNOXVILLE
CHATTANOOGA
HUNTSVILLE
BIRMINGHAM
ATLANTA
MONTGOMERY
COLUMBUS
JACKSON
SHREVEPORT
BATON ROUGE
MOBILE
EVANSVILLE
GARLAND

1 : 3,750,000 — 0 25 50 75 100 125 Kilometers — 0 25 50 75 100 Statute Miles

One inch to 59 miles

conversion meters – feet see page 48

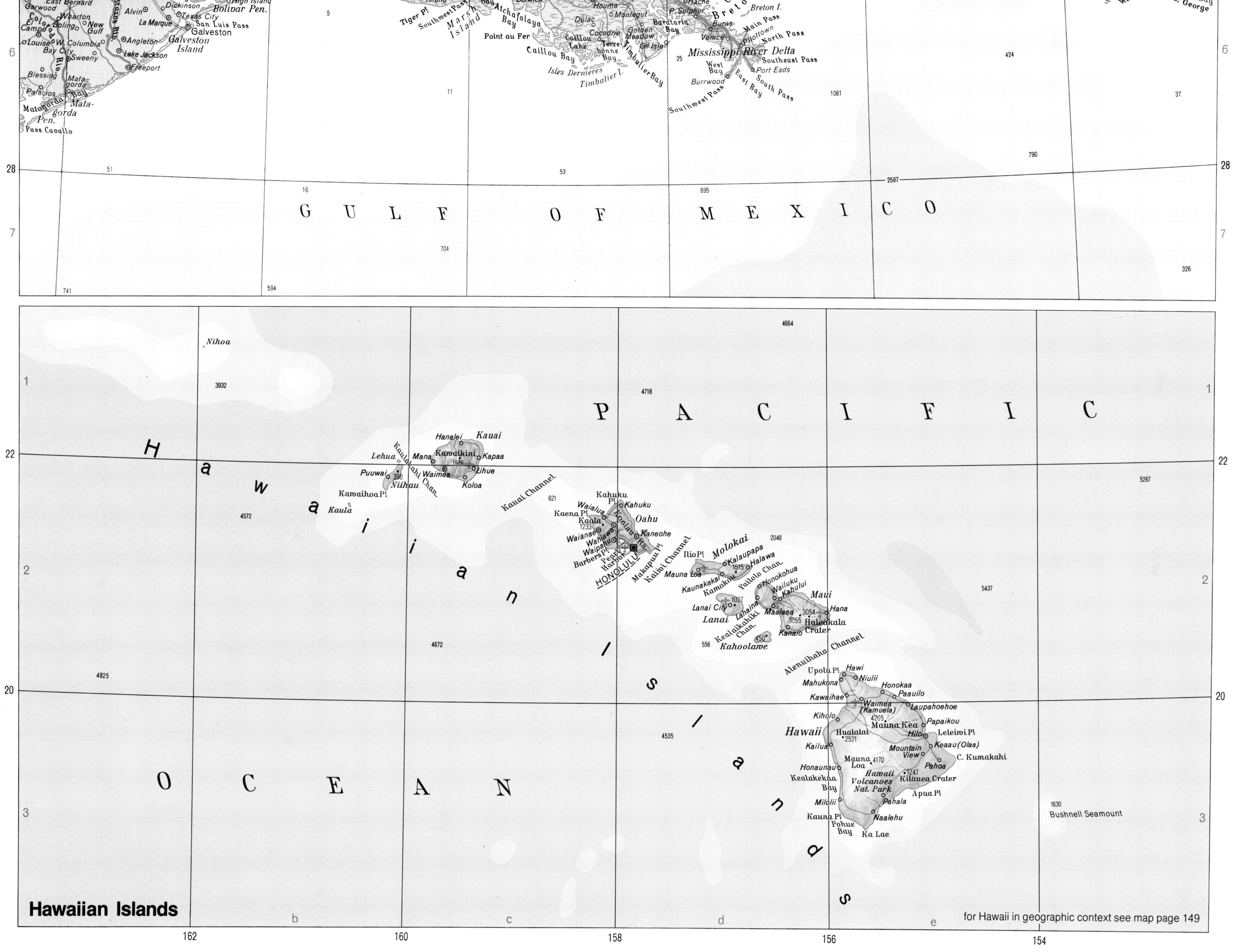
GULF OF MEXICO
Mississippi River Delta
Galveston Island
Bolivar Pen.
Isles Dernieres
Timbalier Bay
PACIFIC OCEAN
Hawaiian Islands
Nihoa
Niihau
Kauai
Kauai Channel
Oahu
HONOLULU
Kaiwi Channel
Molokai
Lanai
Maui
Haleakala Crater
Kahoolawe
Alenuihaha Channel
Hawaii
Mauna Kea
Mauna Loa
Hilo
Hawaii Volcanoes Nat. Park
Kilauea Crater
Bushnell Seamount
Hawaiian Islands
for Hawaii in geographic context see map page 149

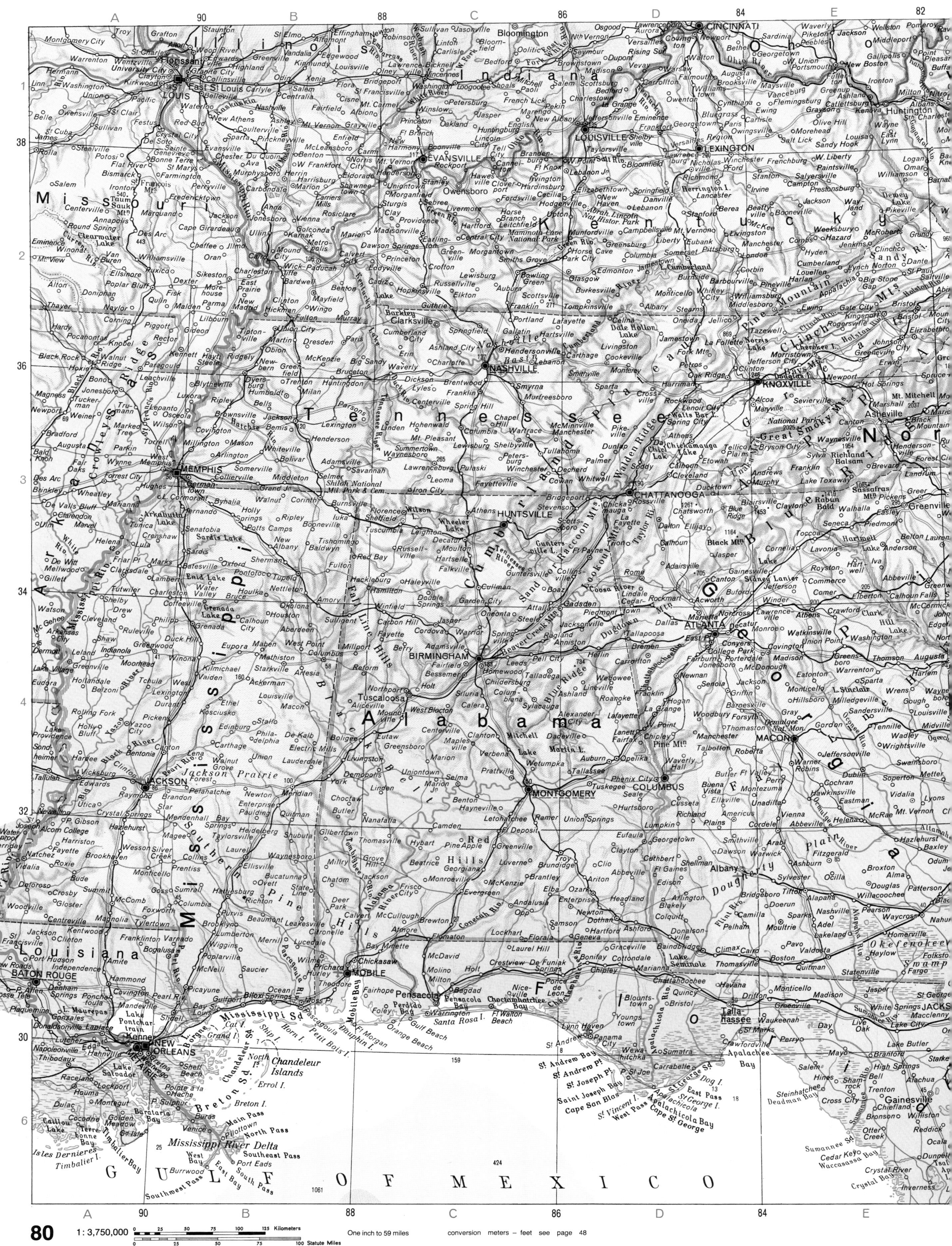

A
90
B
88
C
86
D
84
E
82
Illinois
Indiana
Ohio
Missouri
Kentucky
Tennessee
Arkansas
Mississippi
Alabama
Georgia
Louisiana
Florida
CINCINNATI
LOUISVILLE
LEXINGTON
EVANSVILLE
NASHVILLE
KNOXVILLE
MEMPHIS
CHATTANOOGA
HUNTSVILLE
BIRMINGHAM
ATLANTA
JACKSON
MONTGOMERY
COLUMBUS
MACON
MOBILE
BATON ROUGE
NEW ORLEANS
METAIRIE
Mississippi River Delta
Chandeleur Islands
GULF OF MEXICO
1 : 3,750,000
Kilometers
Statute Miles
One inch to 59 miles
conversion meters – feet see page 48

BALTIMORE
WASHINGTON
ARLINGTON
ALEXANDRIA
District of Columbia
Delaware
RICHMOND
HAMPTON
NEWPORT NEWS
NORFOLK
PORTSMOUTH
VIRGINIA BEACH
CHESAPEAKE
ROANOKE
Lynchburg
WINSTON-SALEM
GREENSBORO
High Point
DURHAM
RALEIGH
CHARLOTTE
Fayetteville
Columbia
North Charleston
Charleston
Cape Hatteras
Pamlico Sound
Albemarle Sd
Hatteras I.
C. Lookout
C. Fear
Onslow Bay
Long Bay
OCEAN
ATLANTIC
Continuation of main map
Florida
JACKSONVILLE
Gainesville
Daytona Beach
ORLANDO
TAMPA
ST PETERSBURG
Clearwater
Lake Okeechobee
West Palm Beach
FT LAUDERDALE
HOLLYWOOD
HIALEAH
MIAMI
Miami Beach
Everglades
Everglades National Park
Big Cypress Swamp
Key West
Key Largo
Florida Keys
Straits of Florida
Florida Bay
Dry Tortugas
Cape Canaveral
Okefenokee Swamp
GULF OF MEXICO
ATLANTIC OCEAN
Inset for continuation

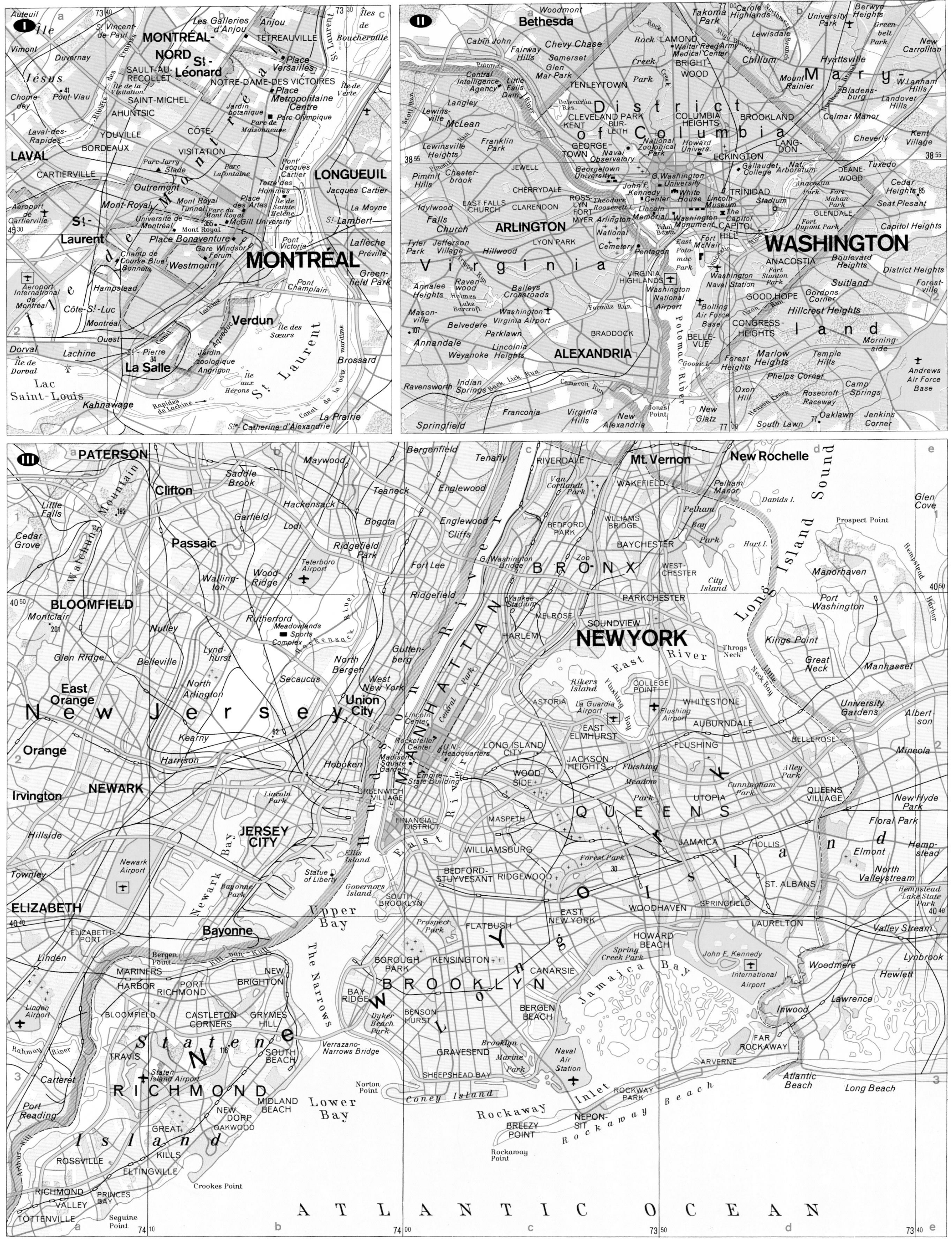
I
MONTRÉAL-NORD
St-Léonard
SAULT-AU-RECOLLET
NOTRE-DAME-DES VICTOIRES
Place Versailles
TÉTREAUVILLE
Anjou
Les Galleries d'Anjou
Île Jésus
Duvernay
Vimont
Chomedey
Pont-Viau
SAINT-MICHEL
AHUNTSIC
Laval-des-Rapides
YOUVILLE
BORDEAUX
LAVAL
CARTIERVILLE
VISITATION
Jardin botanique
Parc Olympique
Place Metropolitaine Centre
Parc de Maisonneuve
Outremont
Mont-Royal
Parc Jarry Stade
Parc Lafontaine
Terre des Hommes
Île de Sainte Hélène
LONGUEUIL
Jacques Cartier
La Moyne
St-Lambert
Aeroport de Cartierville
St-Laurent
McGill University
Université de Montréal
Place Bonaventure
Gare Windsor Forum
Westmount
MONTRÉAL
Pont Victoria
Laflèche
Préville
Greenfield Park
Aeroport International de Montréal
Hampstead
Côte-St-Luc
Montréal Ouest
Pont Champlain
Verdun
Île des Sœurs
St Laurent
Dorval
Île de Dorval
Lachine
St-Pierre
La Salle
Jardin zoologique Angrignon
Lac Saint-Louis
Kahnawage
Rapides de Lachine
Brossard
La Prairie
Ste-Catherine-d'Alexandrie
Canal de la Rive Sud
II
Bethesda
Woodmont
Chevy Chase
Cabin John
Fairway Hills
Somerset
Glen Mar Park
Central Intelligence Agency
Little Falls Dam
TENLEYTOWN
Takoma Park
Carole Highlands
LAMOND
Walter Reed Army Medical Center
BRIGHTWOOD
Rock Creek Park
Chillum
Hyattsville
University Park
Berwyn Heights
Greenbelt Park
New Carrollton
Lewisdale
Mount Rainier
Bladensburg
W. Lanham Hills
Landover Hills
District of Columbia
Maryland
CLEVELAND PARK
KENT
BURLEITH
COLUMBIA HEIGHTS
BROOKLAND
Colmar Manor
Langley
McLean
Lewinsville
Franklin Park
GEORGETOWN
National Zoological Park
Naval Observatory
Howard Univers.
ECKINGTON
LANGDON
Cheverly
Kent Village
Lewinsville Heights
Pimmit Hills
Chesterbrook
JEWELL
Georgetown University
G. Washington University
Gallaudet College
Nat. Arboretum
DEANEWOOD
Tuxedo
Cedar Heights
Seat Plesant
CHERRYDALE
ROSSLYN
FORT MYER
John F. Kennedy Center
White House
Lincoln Museum
The Capitol
TRINIDAD
Stadium
Idylwood
EAST FALLS CHURCH
CLARENDON
Theodore Roosevelt I.
Lincoln Memorial
Washington Monument
CAPITOL HILL
Falls Church
ARLINGTON
Arlington National Cemetery
Tidal Basin
Fort McNair
GLENDALE
Fort Dupont Park
Capitol Heights
Tyler Park
Jefferson Village
Hillwood
LYON PARK
Pentagon
WASHINGTON
ANACOSTIA
Boulevard Heights
District Heights
Virginia
VIRGINIA HIGHLANDS
Washington National Airport
Bolling Air Force Base
Washington Naval Station
Suitland
Forestville
Annalee Heights
Ravenwood
Baileys Crossroads
GOOD HOPE
Gordons Corner
Hillcrest Heights
Masonville
Lake Barcroft
Washington Virginia Airport
Belvedere
Parklawn
BRADDOCK
CONGRESS HEIGHTS
BELLEVUE
Annandale
Weyanoke
Lincolnia Heights
ALEXANDRIA
Potomac River
Forest Heights
Marlow Heights
Temple Hills
Morningside
Andrews Air Force Base
Phelps Corner
Ravensworth
Indian Springs
Oxon Hill
Rosecroft Raceway
Camp Springs
Franconia
Virginia Hills
New Alexandria
Jones Point
New Glatz
Oaklawn
Jenkins Corner
Springfield
South Lawn
III
PATERSON
Clifton
Saddle Brook
Maywood
Bergenfield
Tenafly
RIVERDALE
Mt. Vernon
New Rochelle
Teaneck
Englewood
Van Cortlandt Park
WAKEFIELD
Pelham Manor
Little Falls
Cedar Grove
Hackensack
Garfield
Lodi
Bogota
Englewood Cliffs
BEDFORD PARK
WILLIAMSBRIDGE
Pelham Bay Park
Davids I.
Long Island Sound
Glen Cove
Prospect Point
Passaic
Ridgefield Park
BAYCHESTER
Hart I.
Teterboro Airport
Fort Lee
G. Washington Bridge
BRONX
Zoo
WESTCHESTER
City Island
Manorhaven
Wallington
Wood-Ridge
Ridgefield
PARKCHESTER
Port Washington
BLOOMFIELD
Montclair
Yankee Stadium
MELROSE
SOUNDVIEW
Nutley
Rutherford
Meadowlands Sports Complex
HARLEM
NEW YORK
Kings Point
Glen Ridge
Lyndhurst
Guttenberg
North Bergen
East River
Throgs Neck
Great Neck
Manhasset
Belleville
North Arlington
Secaucus
West New York
Rikers Island
COLLEGE POINT
East Orange
Union City
ASTORIA
La Guardia Airport
WHITESTONE
Flushing Airport
University Gardens
New Jersey
Lincoln Center
AUBURNDALE
Albertson
Kearny
Rockefeller Center
U.N. Headquarters
LONG ISLAND CITY
EAST ELMHURST
FLUSHING
BELLEROSE
Orange
Harrison
Hoboken
Madison Square Garden
Empire State Building
JACKSON HEIGHTS
Flushing Meadow Park
Mineola
Irvington
NEWARK
Lincoln Park
GREENWICH VILLAGE
WOODSIDE
Alley Park
Cunningham Park
QUEENS VILLAGE
New Hyde Park
UTOPIA
QUEENS
Floral Park
Hillside
JERSEY CITY
FINANCIAL DISTRICT
MASPETH
MANHATTAN
Hudson
Central Park
JAMAICA
HOLLIS
Elmont
Hempstead
Newark Airport
Ellis Island
WILLIAMSBURG
Forest Park
North Valleystream
Townley
Statue of Liberty
Governors Island
BEDFORD-STUYVESANT
RIDGEWOOD
ST. ALBANS
Hempstead Lake State Park
ELIZABETH
Newark Bay
Bayonne Park
SOUTH BROOKLYN
Upper Bay
EAST NEW YORK
WOODHAVEN
SPRINGFIELD
Long Island
ELIZABETHPORT
Bayonne
Prospect Park
FLATBUSH
LAURELTON
Valley Stream
Linden
Bergen Point
Kill van Kull
HOWARD BEACH
Spring Creek Park
John F. Kennedy International Airport
Lynbrook
MARINERS HARBOR
PORT RICHMOND
NEW BRIGHTON
The Narrows
BOROUGH PARK
KENSINGTON
CANARSIE
Jamaica Bay
Woodmere
Hewlett
BROOKLYN
BAY RIDGE
Linden Airport
BLOOMFIELD
CASTLETON CORNERS
GRYMES HILL
BENSONHURST
BERGEN BEACH
Inwood
Lawrence
Dyker Beach Park
Rahway River
TRAVIS
Staten Island
SOUTH BEACH
Verrazano-Narrows Bridge
Brooklyn Marine Park
GRAVESEND
Naval Air Station
FAR ROCKAWAY
ARVERNE
Carteret
Staten Island Airport
RICHMOND
SHEEPSHEAD BAY
Atlantic Beach
Long Beach
Norton Point
MIDLAND BEACH
Lower Bay
Coney Island
Rockaway Inlet
ROCKAWAY PARK
Port Reading
NEW DORP
OAKWOOD
GREAT KILLS
Rockaway Beach
NEPONSIT
BREEZY POINT
Rockaway Point
ROSSVILLE
ELTINGVILLE
Arthur Kill
Crookes Point
RICHMOND VALLEY
PRINCES BAY
TOTTENVILLE
Sequine Point
ATLANTIC OCEAN

Conversion meters – feet see page 48

1:225,000 — 0 2.5 5 7.5 10 Kilometers — 0 2.5 5 7.5 Statute Miles

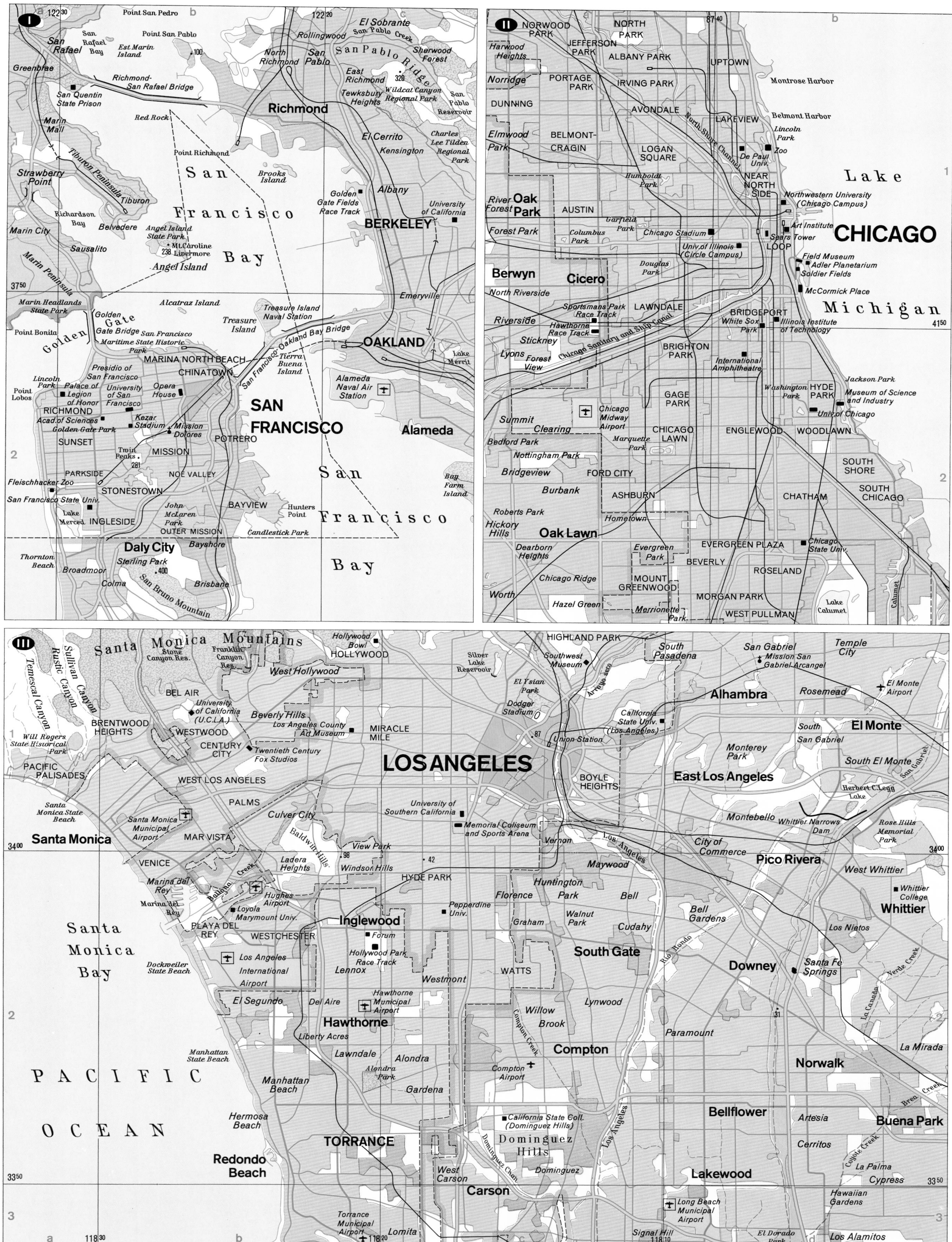

I
Point San Pedro
San Rafael
San Rafael Bay
Point San Pablo
Est Marin Island
Greenbrae
Richmond-San Rafael Bridge
San Quentin State Prison
Red Rock
Marin Mall
Tiburon Peninsula
Point Richmond
Strawberry Point
Tiburon
Richardson Bay
Marin City
Belvedere
Angel Island State Park
Mt.Caroline Livermore
Sausalito
Angel Island
Marin Peninsula
Marin Headlands State Park
Alcatraz Island
Golden Gate
Point Bonita
Golden Gate Bridge
San Francisco Maritime State Historic Park
Treasure Island
Treasure Island Naval Station
San Francisco-Oakland Bay Bridge
Yerba Buena Island
MARINA
NORTH BEACH
CHINATOWN
Presidio of San Francisco
Lincoln Park
Point Lobos
Palace of Legion of Honor
University of San Francisco
Opera House
RICHMOND
Acad.of Sciences
Golden Gate Park
Kezar Stadium
Mission Dolores
SUNSET
Twin Peaks
MISSION
POTRERO
SAN FRANCISCO
PARKSIDE
NOE VALLEY
Fleischhacker Zoo
STONESTOWN
San Francisco State Univ.
Lake Merced
INGLESIDE
John McLaren Park
BAYVIEW
Hunters Point
OUTER MISSION
Candlestick Park
Daly City
Bayshore
Thornton Beach
Sterling Park
Broadmoor
Colma
San Bruno Mountain
Brisbane
San Francisco Bay
El Sobrante
San Pablo Creek
Rollingwood
North Richmond
San Pablo
San Pablo Ridge
Sherwood Forest
East Richmond
Wildcat Canyon Regional Park
Tewksbury Heights
San Pablo Reservoir
Richmond
El Cerrito
Kensington
Charles Lee Tilden Regional Park
Brooks Island
Albany
Golden Gate Fields Race Track
University of California
BERKELEY
Emeryville
OAKLAND
Lake Merritt
Alameda Naval Air Station
Alameda
Bay Farm Island
II
NORWOOD PARK
NORTH PARK
JEFFERSON PARK
Harwood Heights
ALBANY PARK
UPTOWN
Montrose Harbor
Norridge
PORTAGE PARK
IRVING PARK
DUNNING
AVONDALE
North Shore Channel
LAKEVIEW
Belmont Harbor
Lincoln Park
Elmwood Park
BELMONT-CRAGIN
LOGAN SQUARE
De Paul Univ.
Zoo
Humboldt Park
NEAR NORTH SIDE
Lake Michigan
River Forest
Oak Park
AUSTIN
Northwestern University (Chicago Campus)
Garfield Park
Art Institute
Forest Park
Columbus Park
Chicago Stadium
Sears Tower
CHICAGO
Univ.of Illinois (Circle Campus)
LOOP
Field Museum
Adler Planetarium
Soldier Fields
Berwyn
Cicero
Douglas Park
McCormick Place
North Riverside
Sportsmans Park Race Track
LAWNDALE
BRIDGEPORT
White Sox Park
Illinois Institute of Technology
Riverside
Hawthorne Race Track
Stickney
Chicago Sanitary and Ship Canal
Lyons
Forest View
BRIGHTON PARK
International Amphitheatre
Jackson Park
Washington Park
HYDE PARK
Museum of Science and Industry
GAGE PARK
Univ.of Chicago
Chicago Midway Airport
Summit
Clearing
CHICAGO LAWN
ENGLEWOOD
WOODLAWN
Bedford Park
Marquette Park
Nottingham Park
SOUTH SHORE
Bridgeview
FORD CITY
Burbank
ASHBURN
CHATHAM
SOUTH CHICAGO
Roberts Park
Hometown
Hickory Hills
Oak Lawn
Evergreen Park
EVERGREEN PLAZA
Chicago State Univ.
Dearborn Heights
BEVERLY
ROSELAND
Chicago Ridge
MOUNT GREENWOOD
Worth
Hazel Green
MORGAN PARK
Merrionette Park
WEST PULLMAN
Lake Calumet
Calumet
III
Santa Monica Mountains
Stone Canyon Res.
Franklin Canyon Res.
Hollywood Bowl
HOLLYWOOD
HIGHLAND PARK
South Pasadena
San Gabriel
Temple City
Sullivan Canyon
Rustic Canyon
Temescal Canyon
West Hollywood
Silver Lake Reservoir
Southwest Museum
Mission San Gabriel Arcangel
BEL AIR
El Ysian Park
Arroyo Seco
Rosemead
El Monte Airport
University of California (U.C.L.A.)
Dodger Stadium
Alhambra
BRENTWOOD HEIGHTS
Beverly Hills
Los Angeles County Art Museum
MIRACLE MILE
California State Univ. (Los Angeles)
South San Gabriel
El Monte
Will Rogers State Historical Park
WESTWOOD
Union Station
CENTURY CITY
Twentieth Century Fox Studios
Monterey Park
PACIFIC PALISADES
LOS ANGELES
South El Monte
San Gabriel
WEST LOS ANGELES
BOYLE HEIGHTS
East Los Angeles
Herbert C.Legg Lake
PALMS
University of Southern California
Santa Monica State Beach
Culver City
Santa Monica Municipal Airport
Memorial Coliseum and Sports Arena
Montebello
Whittier Narrows Dam
Rose Hills Memorial Park
Santa Monica
MAR VISTA
Baldwin Hills
Vernon
City of Commerce
View Park
Los Angeles
Pico Rivera
VENICE
Ladera Heights
Windsor Hills
Maywood
West Whittier
HYDE PARK
Marina del Rey
Ballona Creek
Hughes Airport
Huntington Park
Whittier College
Florence
Bell
Pepperdine Univ.
Whittier
Loyola Marymount Univ.
Walnut Park
Bell Gardens
PLAYA DEL REY
Inglewood
Graham
Cudahy
Los Nietos
Santa Monica Bay
WESTCHESTER
Forum
Hollywood Park Race Track
South Gate
Los Angeles International Airport
Lennox
WATTS
Rio Hondo
Downey
Santa Fe Springs
Dockweiler State Beach
Westmont
Verde Creek
El Segundo
Del Aire
Hawthorne Municipal Airport
Lynwood
La Canada
Hawthorne
Willow Brook
Compton Creek
Liberty Acres
Paramount
Manhattan State Beach
Lawndale
Compton
La Mirada
Alondra
Alondra Park
Norwalk
PACIFIC OCEAN
Manhattan Beach
Compton Airport
Gardena
Brea Creek
Hermosa Beach
California State Coll. (Dominguez Hills)
Bellflower
Artesia
Buena Park
Dominguez Hills
TORRANCE
Coyote Creek
Redondo Beach
Dominguez Chan.
Cerritos
West Carson
Dominguez
Lakewood
La Palma
Cypress
Carson
Hawaiian Gardens
Torrance Municipal Airport
Lomita
Long Beach Municipal Airport
Signal Hill
El Dorado Park
Los Alamitos

1 : 225,000

0 2,5 5 7,5 10 Kilometers

0 2,5 5 7,5 Statute Miles

One inch to 3,6 miles

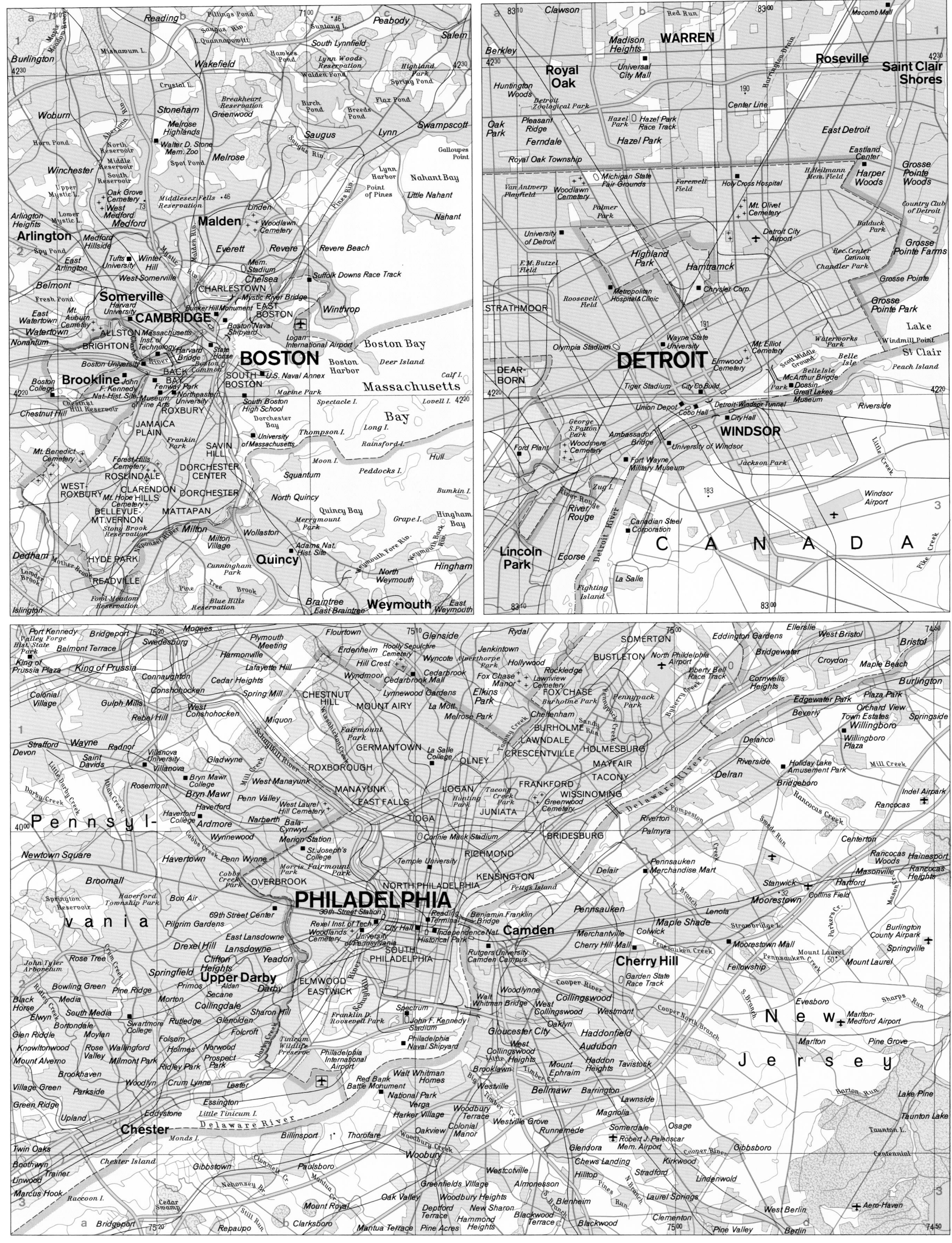

Conversion meters – feet see page 48

1 : 225,000

0 2.5 5 7.5 10 Kilometers

0 2.5 5 7.5 Statute Miles

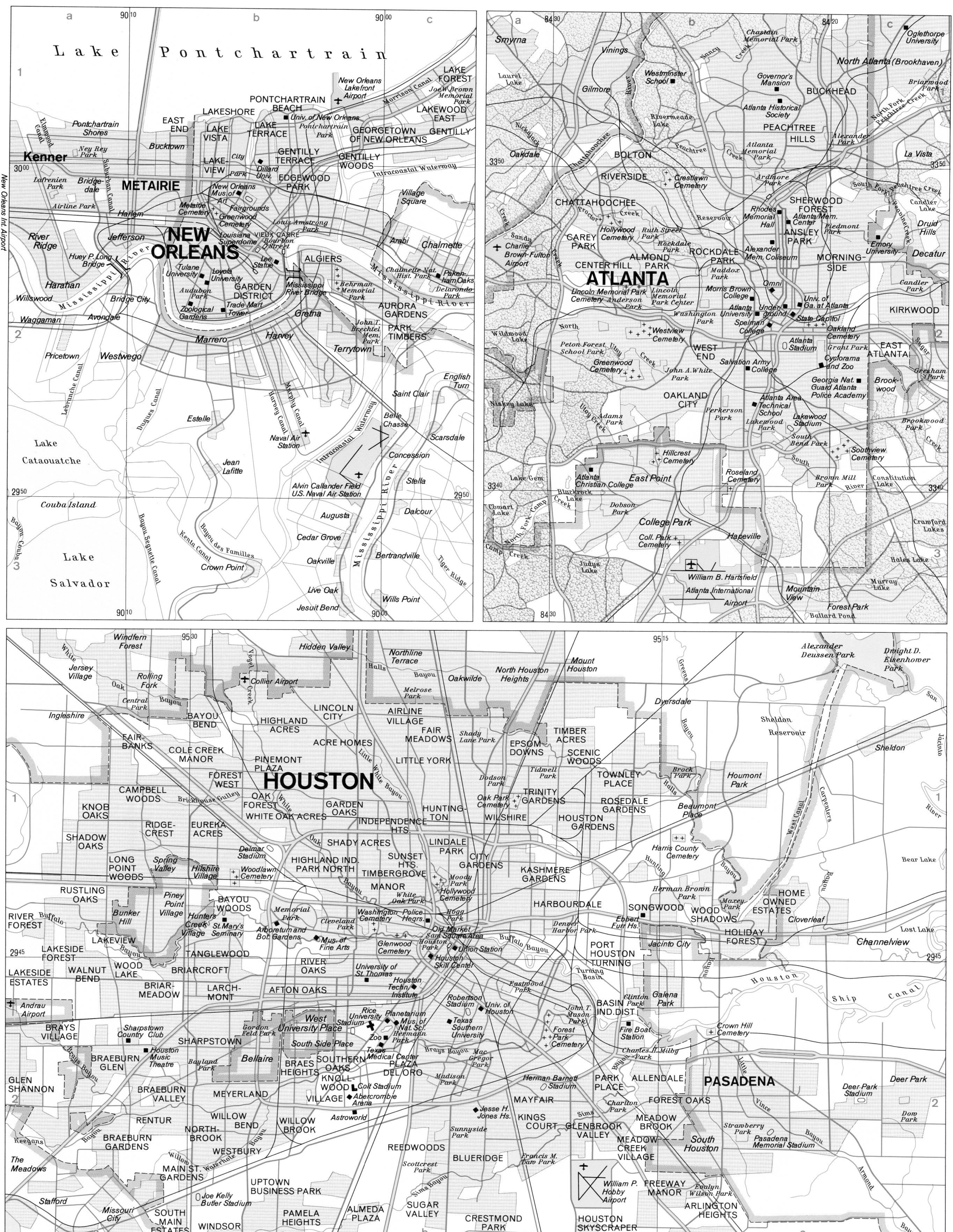

1 : 225,000 — 0, 2.5, 5, 7.5, 10 Kilometers — 0, 2.5, 5, 7.5 Statute Miles — One inch to 3.6 miles

California
Arizona
New Mexico
UNITED
Texas
SAN DIEGO
TIJUANA
MEXICALI
Chula Vista
Tecate
Calexico
Ensenada
Gila Desert
TUCSON
Nogales
Heroica Nogales
EL PASO
JUÁREZ
Las Cruces
Roswell
Odessa
LUBBOCK
Baja California
Gulf of California
Sonora
HERMOSILLO
Heroica Guaymas
CIUDAD OBREGÓN
Los Mochis
Isla Tiburón
Isla Angel de la Guarda
Bahía Sebastián Vizcaíno
Isla Cedros
Isla de Guadalupe
Baja California Sur
La Paz
San José del Cabo
Cabo San Lucas
Tropic of Cancer
SIERRA MADRE OCCIDENTAL
CHIHUAHUA
Chihuahua
Durango
VICTORIA DE DURANGO
TORREÓN
Gómez Palacio
Zacatecas
Sinaloa
CULIACÁN ROSALES
MAZATLÁN
Nayarit
TEPIC
AGUASCALIENTES
GUADALAJARA
Jalisco
Colima
Manzanillo
Puerto Vallarta
Islas Marías
Islas Revillagigedo (Mex.)
Isla Socorro
Isla Clarión
Roca Partida
Isla S.Benedicto
Rocas Alijos
PACIFIC OCEAN
Bolsón de Mapimí
Big Bend National Park
Llano Estacado

1 : 6,750,000 0 50 100 150 200 250 Kilometers 0 50 100 150 200 Statute Miles One inch to 107 miles Conversion meters – feet see page 48

GULF OF MEXICO
Mexico Basin
Campeche Bank
Bahía de Campeche
CARIBBEAN SEA
Yucatán Basin
Península de Yucatán
Golfo de Tehuantepec
Golfo de Honduras
Isla Desterrada
Isla Pérez
Cayo Arenas
Cayo Nuevo
Arrecifes Triángulos
Cayos Arcas
Isla Holbox
Cabo Catoche
Isla Contoy
Isla Mujeres
Cozumel
Banco Chinchorro
Islas de la Bahía
Arkansas
Louisiana
Mississippi
Alabama
Georgia
Florida
Texas
BELIZE
GUATEMALA
HONDURAS
EL SALVADOR
Tamaulipas
Veracruz
Tabasco
Chiapas
Oaxaca
Puebla
Hidalgo
Yucatán
Quintana Roo
Campeche
Guerrero
HOUSTON
DALLAS
FORT WORTH
ARLINGTON
WACO
AUSTIN
SAN ANTONIO
CORPUS CHRISTI
PASADENA
BEAUMONT
SHREVEPORT
JACKSON
BATON ROUGE
NEW ORLEANS
METAIRIE
MOBILE
MONTGOMERY
COLUMBUS
Tallahassee
MONTERREY
NUEVO LAREDO
Laredo
HEROICA MATAMOROS
Brownsville
REYNOSA
McAllen
CD VICTORIA
TAMPICO
Ciudad Madero
POZA RICA DE HIDALGO
JALAPA ENRÍQUEZ
HEROICA VERACRUZ
MEXICO
PUEBLA DE ZARAGOZA
CUERNAVACA
PACHUCA DE SOTO
QUERÉTARO
OAXACA DE JUÁREZ
ACAPULCO DE JUÁREZ
VILLAHERMOSA
MÉRIDA
Campeche
Chetumal
Belmopan
Tuxtla Gutiérrez
GUATEMALA
S.PEDRO SULA
TEGUCIGALPA
Coatzacoalcos
Minatitlán
Ciudad del Carmen
Progreso
Cancún
Tapachula
Mississippi River Delta
Matagorda Bay
Galveston Bay
Laguna Madre
Laguna de Términos
Sierra Madre del Sur
Istmo de Tehuantepec
Trench
Mexico 87

GULF OF MEXICO
UNITED STATES
Punta Gorda
Charlotte Harbor
Fort Myers
Sanibel I.
Naples
Immokalee
Lake Okeechobee
Pahokee
Belle Glade
West Palm Beach
Palm Beach
Lake Worth
Delray Beach
FT. LAUDERDALE
HOLLYWOOD
HIALEAH
MIAMI
Miami Beach
Coral Gables
Homestead
Cape Romano
Everglades
Ten Thousand Is.
Everglades National Park
Cape Sable
Key Largo
Florida Bay
Marathon
Florida Keys
Marquesas Keys
Dry Tortugas
Key West
Straits of Florida
Little Abaco I.
Cooper's Town
West End
Freeport
Grand Bahama I.
Marsh Harbour
Wilson City
Great Abaco I.
Mores I.
Cornwall
Northeast Providence Channel
Berry Is.
The Bluff
Hatchet Bay
Eleuthera I.
Nicholl's Town
NASSAU
New Providence I.
Andros Town
Andros I.
Great Bahama Bank
Bannerman Town
Hawksbill Cay
Fowl Cay
Gt. Guana Cay
Exuma Sound
Moss Town
Rolleville
Great Exuma I.
George Town
Canal Nicolás
Cay Sal
Anguilla Cays
Santaren Channel
LA HABANA (HAVANA)
MARIANAO
Matanzas
Cárdenas
La Isabela
Archipiélago de Sabana
Artemisa
Güira de Melena
Güines
Jovellanos
Colón
Sagua la Grande
STA. CLARA
Camajuaní
Caibarién
La Esperanza
Los Palacios
Pinar del Río
Ensenada de la Broa
Pen. de Zapata
Playa Larga
Jagüey Grande
Cayo Coco
Canal Viejo de Bahama
Archip. de Camagüey
Guane
Cortés
Golfo de Batabanó
Cienfuegos
Cruces
Placetas
Chambas
Cabo S. Antonio
Península de Guanahacabibes
Cabo Corrientes
Isla de la Juventud
Nueva Gerona
Santa Fé
Archipiélago de los Canarreos
Bahía de Cochinos
Trinidad
Sancti Spíritus
Cabaiguán
Morón
Ciego de Ávila
Cayo Romano
Cayo Guajaba
Cayo Sabinal
Nuevitas
Puerto Manatí
Puerto Padre
Gibara
Florida
Júcaro
Vertientes
CAMAGÜEY
Martí
Las Tunas
Victoria de las Tunas
HOLGUÍN
Jardines de la Reina
Sta. Cruz del Sur
Guayabal
Mayarí
Golfo de Guacanayabo
Manzanillo
Bayamo
Palma Soriano
Niquero
Granma
Sierra Maestra
Pico Turquino
Cabo Cruz
SANTIAGO DE CUBA
CUBA
GREATER
Little Cayman
Cayman Brac
Cayman Is. (U.K.)
Grand Cayman
Georgetown
Cayman Trench
JAMAICA
Montego Bay
Lucea
St. Ann's Bay
Port Maria
Annotto Bay
Port Antonio
North Negril Pt.
South Negril Pt.
Savanna-la-Mar
Cambridge
Mandeville
Spanish Town
Blue Mts.
KINGSTON
Morant Pt.
Portland Pt.
Pedro Cays
Campeche Bank
Isla Desterrada
Isla Pérez
Progreso
Celestún
MÉRIDA
Umán
Maxcanú
Izamal
Motul de Felipe Carillo Puerto
Dzilam de Bravo
Temax
Tizimín
Río Lagartos
Isla Holbox
Cabo Catoche
Isla Contoy
Isla Blanca
Isla Mujeres
Puerto Juárez
Ciudad Cancún
Playa del Carmen
Cozumel
Isla de Cozumel
Calotmul
Xcan
Valladolid
Chichén Itzá
Mayapán
Muna
Ticul
Uxmal
Oxkutzcab
Tekax
Peto
Calkiní
Tulum
Balankanché
Península de Yucatán
Campeche
Champotón
Hopelchén
Edzná
China
Tenabo
Laguna Chichancanab
Felipe Carillo Puerto
Vigía Chico
Bahía de la Ascensión
Bahía del Espíritu Santo
MEXICO
Quintana Roo
Meseta de Zohlaguna
Becan
Xpuhil
Laguna de Bacalar
Chetumal
Bahía de Chetumal
Cayo Centro
Banco Chinchorro
Cayo Lobos
Río Hondo
Corozal
Orange Walk Town
Cuello
Ambergris Cay
Calakmul
El Mirador
BELIZE
Belize
Belize Río
Belmopan
Turneffe Islands
Maya Mts.
Stann Creek
Dos Lagunas
Uaxactún
Paso Caballos
Tikal
Melchor de Mencos
Lago Petén Itzá
Flores
Río de la Pasión
Seibal
Poptun
Lubaantun
Punta Gorda
San Luis
Canal de Yucatán
Yucatán Basin
Golfo de Honduras
Bahía de Amatique
Isla de Roatán
Islas de la Bahía
Guanaja
Cabo de Honduras
Puerto Castilla
Trujillo
Cabo Camarón
Punta Patuca
Irona
Brus Laguna
Puerto Barrios
Puerto Cortés
Tela
La Ceiba
Lago de Izabal
Santo Tomás de C.
El Estor
S. PEDRO SULA
Sierra de Pija
Sierra de las Minas
Quiriguá
Río Motagua
La Lima
El Progreso
Yoro
Río Aguán
Río Sico
Wawina
Laguna de Caratasca
Cabo Falso
Puerto Lempira
Mosquitia
Cabo Gracias a Dios
Laguna Huani
Cayos Miskitos
Punta Gorda
Puerto Cabezas
GUATEMALA
Chisec
Guaján
Zacapa
Copán
Potrerillos
Santa Barbara
Sierra de Agalta
Wampú
Chiquimula
Jalapa
Santa Rosa de Copán
Nueva Ocotepeque
Gracias
Manto
Catacamas
Juticalpa
Auasbila
HONDURAS
Esquías
Comayagua
Río Patuca
Cord. Entre Ríos
San Ramón
Río Coco (Río Segovia)
Cerro Velucá
Río Huahua
Obrayeri
Ocuilí
Metapán
SANTA ANA
La Esperanza
Chalatenango
TEGUCIGALPA
La Paz
Jutiapa
Chalchuapa
Sonsonate
Acajutla
Nueva San Salvador
SAN SALVADOR
EL SALVADOR
Lago de Ilopango
Cojutepeque
S. Vicente
S. Francisco
S. Miguel
Zacatecoluca
Usulután
La Unión
Golfo de Fonseca
Yuscarán
Danlí
Cerro Mogotón
Choluteca
Ocotal
Cerro Kilambé
Cord. Isabella
Bonanza
Tunki
Carata
Prinzapolca
Laguna Huaunta
Salto de Pira
Estelí
Jinotega
Cord. de Darién
Matagalpa
Río Grande
Jockey
El Sauce
Costa de Mosquitos
Volcán Viejo
Chinandega
León
NICARAGUA
Lago de Managua
Boaco
Montañas de Huapí
Santo Domingo
Laguna de Perlas
Punta de Perlas
Las Perlas
Islas del Maíz (Nic.)
Bahía de Bluefields
MANAGUA
Masaya
Granada
Juigalpa
Rama
Bluefields
Jinotepe
Acoyapa
Cord. de Yolaina
Lago de Nicaragua
Isla de Ometepe
San Miguelito
S. Jorge
Rivas
San Juan del Sur
Punta del Mono
Bahía de S. Juan del Norte
S. Carlos
Río San Juan
Cabo Santa Elena
La Cruz
Golfo del Papagayo
Volcán Orosí
Liberia
Volcán Tonorio
Puerto Potrero
Santa Cruz
Nicoya
COSTA RICA
Altamira
S. Juan del Norte
Colorado
Tortuguero
Guápiles
Villa Quesada
Alajuela
Heredia
Puntarenas
Limón
Volcán Irazú
SAN JOSÉ
Cartago
Punta Guiones
Pen. de Nicoya
Golfo de Nicoya
Cabo Blanco
Punta Judas
Parrita
Cerro Chirripó Grande
Dominical
Cord. de Talamanca
Bahía de Coronado
Palmar
Puerto Cortés
Isla del Caño
Punta San Pedro
Península de Osa
Golfito
Golfo Dulce
Cabo Matapalo
Punta Mona
Archipiélago de Bocas del Toro
Pandora
Bocas del Toro
Laguna de Chiriquí
Pen. Valiente
Escudo de Veraguas
Golfo de los Mosquitos
Robalo
Volcán Barú
Chiriquí
Serranía de Tabasará
David
Puerto Armuelles
Punta Burica
Golfo de Chiriquí
Cerro Santiago
Tole
Veraguas
Santiago
S. Cristóbal
Penonomé
Coclé
Sona
Isla Coiba
Punta Naranjas
Golfo de Montijo
Divisa
Antón
Río Hato
Herrera
Chitré
Península de Azuero
Los Santos
Las Tablas
Pedasí
Punta Mala
Tonosí
Isla Raya
Morro de Puercos
Golfo de Parita
Panama Canal
Punta Manzanilla
Colón
Istmo de Panamá
Palenque
Punta San Blas
Archipiélago de San Blas
Donoso
San Miguelito
Balboa
La Chorrera
PANAMÁ
Chepo
Cord. de San Blas
Ailigandí
Bahía de Panamá
Chame
Archipiélago de las Perlas
Isla del Rey
Isla San José
Golfo de Panamá
Chimán
Sierra de Cañazas
Serranía del Darién
PANAMA
La Palma
Golfo de S. Miguel
Darién
Garachiné
El Real
Punta Caracoles
Punta Garachiné
Golfo del Darién
Permé
Acandí
Punta Caribana
Golfo de Urabá
Turbo
Tanela
Mulatos
Necoclí
Punta Rey
MONT
Córdob
Planeta R.
Punta de San Bernardo
Golfo de Morrosquillo
Coveñas
Lorica
CARTAGENA
BARRA
Islas del Cisne (Hond.)
Southwest Cay (U.S.A. Col.)
San Andrés y Providencia (Col.)
Providencia
San Andrés
Cayos de Albuquerque
CARI
Middle America Trench
PACIFIC OCEAN

1: 6,750,000

0 50 100 150 200 250 Kilometers

0 50 100 150 200 Statute Miles

One inch to 107 miles

Conversion meters – feet see page 48

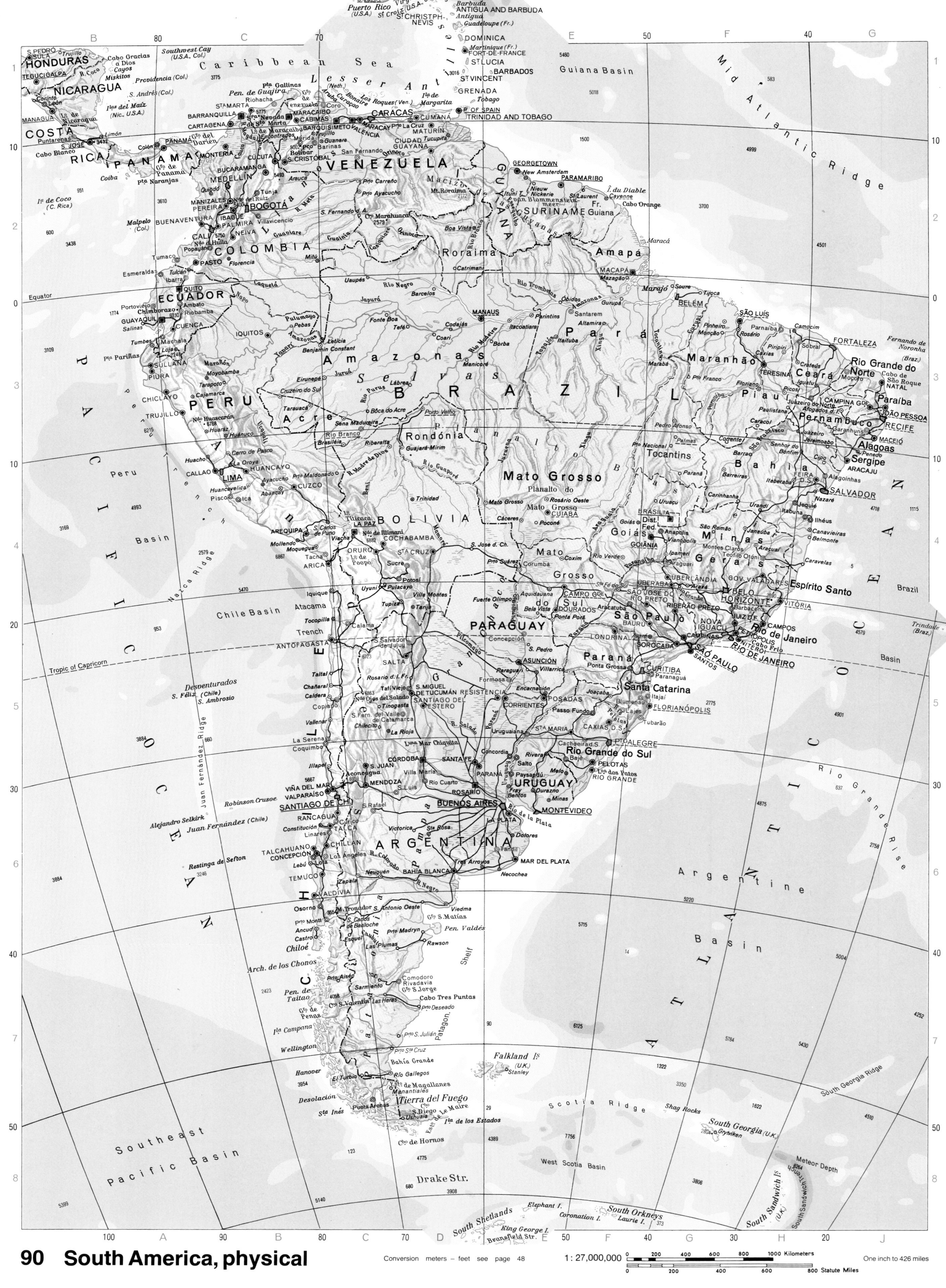

Conversion meters – feet see page 48

1 : 27,000,000

One inch to 426 miles

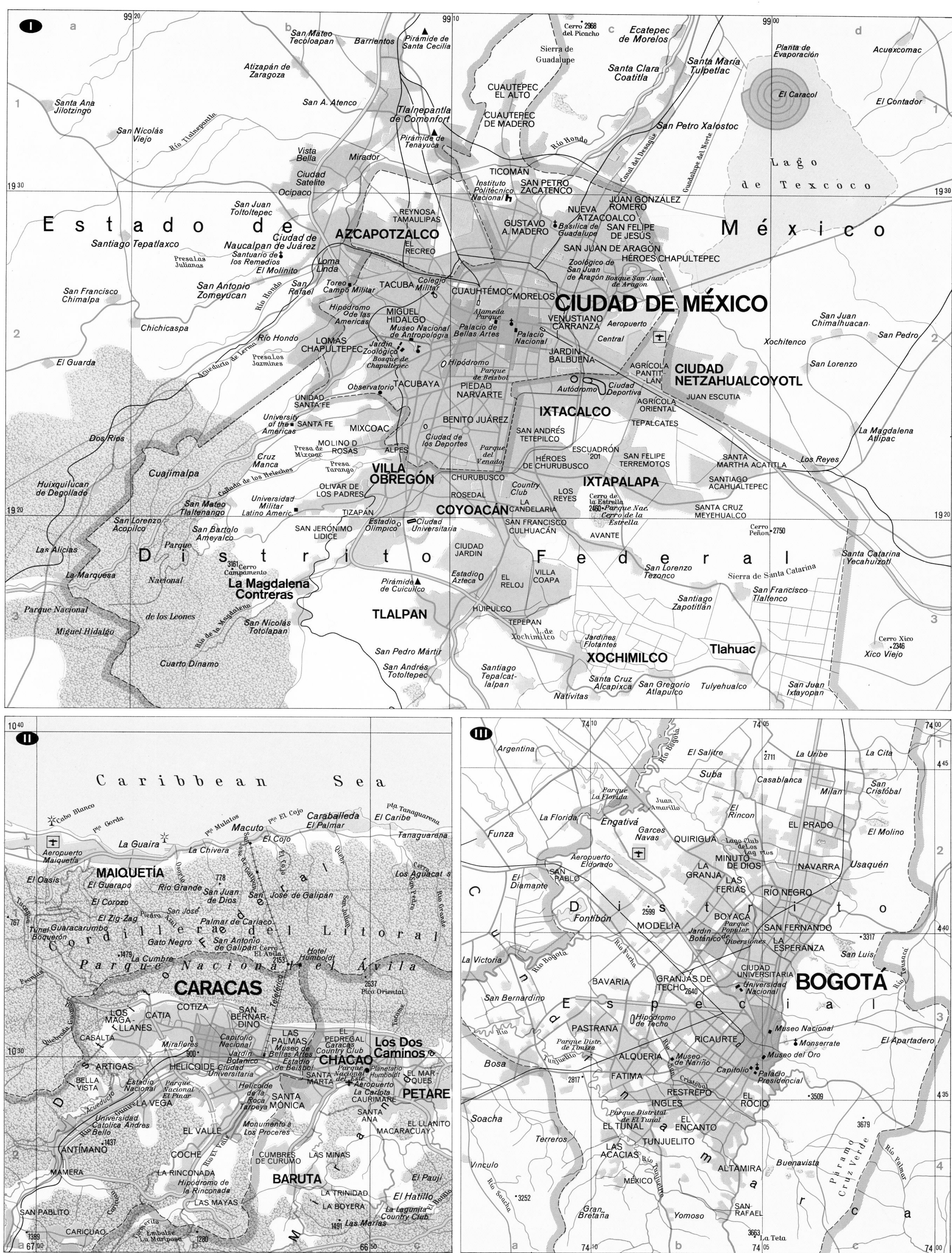

1 : 225,000 — 0 2.5 5 7.5 10 Kilometers; 0 2.5 5 7.5 Statute Miles — One inch to 3.6 miles — Conversion meters – feet see page 48

Caribbean Basin
Caribbean Sea
Lesser Antilles
HONDURAS
TEGUCIGALPA
NICARAGUA
MANAGUA
COSTA RICA
PANAMA
COLOMBIA
BOGOTÁ
VENEZUELA
CARACAS
ECUADOR
QUITO
GUAYAQUIL
PERU
LIMA
BOLIVIA
LA PAZ
Sucre
BRAZIL
CHILE
ARGENTINA
PACIFIC OCEAN
Peru Basin
Chile Basin
Peru Chile Trench
Atacama Trench
Nazca Ridge
Cocos Ridge
Archipiélago de Colón (Islas Galápagos) (Ecuador)
Equator
Amazon
Floresta Amazonica
Acre
Rondônia
Isla del Coco (Costa Rica)
Isla Malpelo (Col.)
MEDELLÍN
CALI
BARRANQUILLA
CARTAGENA
MARACAIBO
VALENCIA
MANAUS
IQUITOS
TRUJILLO
AREQUIPA
ARICA
ANTOFAGASTA
COCHABAMBA

1:13,500,000 — 0 100 200 300 400 500 Kilometers — 0 100 200 300 400 Statute Miles — One inch to 213 miles — conversion meters – feet see page 48

Guiana Basin
Cape Verde Basin
Mid Atlantic Ridge
ATLANTIC OCEAN
Pará Rise
Amazon Shelf
Equator
GEORGETOWN
PARAMARIBO
SURINAME
Fr. Guiana
Cayenne
Amapá
MACAPÁ
Pará
BELÉM
Santarém
Maranhão
SÃO LUÍS
TERESINA
Ceará
FORTALEZA (CEARÁ)
Rio Grande do Norte
NATAL
Paraíba
JOÃO PESSOA (PARAÍBA)
Pernambuco
RECIFE (PERNAMBUCO)
OLINDA
Alagoas
MACEIÓ
Sergipe
ARACAJU
Bahia
SALVADOR (BAHIA)
Fernando de Noronha
Atol das Rocas (Brazil)
Mato Grosso
CUIABÁ
Goiás
BRASÍLIA
GOIÂNIA
Minas Gerais
BELO HORIZONTE
Espírito Santo
VITÓRIA
Rio de Janeiro
RIO DE JANEIRO
São Paulo
SÃO PAULO
Mato Grosso do Sul
CAMPO GRANDE
Planalto do Mato Grosso
Planalto Brasileiro
Serra dos Carajás
Serra do Roncador
Tropic of Capricorn
Stocks Seamount
Groll Seamount
Brazil Basin
Iª da Trindade
Iªs Martim Vaz (Brazil)

CARIBBEAN SEA
PACIFIC OCEAN
Golfo de Venezuela
Lago de Maracaibo
Golfo del Darién
Golfo de Panamá
Golfo de Morrosquillo
Golfo de Cupica
Península de Guajira
Península de Azuero
Istmo de Panamá
Archipiélago de San Blas
Archipiélago de las Perlas
PANAMÁ
Colón
Darién
COLOMBIA
ECUADOR
PERU
Atlántico
Magdalena
Cesar
Bolívar
Sucre
Córdoba
Zulia
Norte de Santander
Táchira
Antioquia
Santander
Chocó
Boyacá
Casanare
Arauca
Caldas
Cundinamarca
Valle del Cauca
Cauca
Nariño
Meta
Guaviare
Caquetá
Putumayo
Napo
Amazonas
Vaupés
Esmeraldas
Imbabura
Pichincha
Cotopaxi
Manabí
Los Ríos
Pastaza
Sra Nevada de Sta Marta
Serranía de Perijá
Cordillera Occidental
Cordillera Central
Cordillera Oriental
Llanos
BARRANQUILLA
CARTAGENA
STA MARTA
MARACAIBO
CÚCUTA
BUCARAMANGA
MEDELLÍN
MANIZALES
PEREIRA
ARMENIA
IBAGUÉ
BOGOTÁ
CALI
BUENAVENTURA
NEIVA
Popayán
PASTO
QUITO
Villavicencio
MONTERÍA
Sincelejo
Valledupar
Ríohacha
Tunja
Quibdó
Florencia
Mocoa
Tumaco
Ibarra
Latacunga
Ambato
Tulcán
Río Magdalena
Río Cauca
Río Caquetá
Río Putumayo
Río Meta
Río Guaviare
Río Napo
Río Vaupés
Río Apaporis
A B C D E F
80 78 76 74 72
1: 4,500,000
0 50 100 150 200 Kilometers
0 50 100 150 Statute Miles
One inch to 71 miles
see inset for continuation

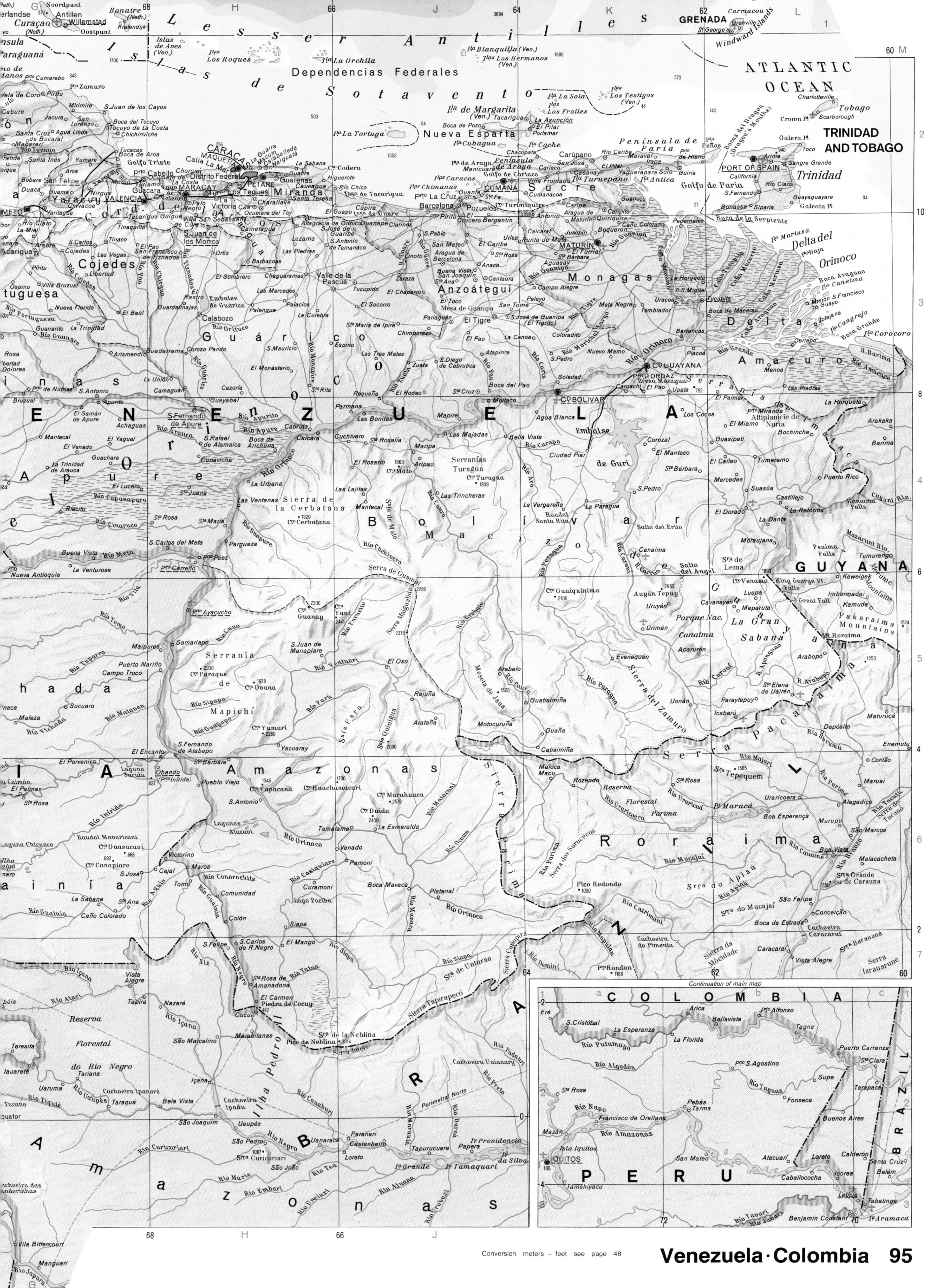
Lesser Antilles
Islas de Sotavento
Dependencias Federales
ATLANTIC OCEAN
GRENADA
TRINIDAD AND TOBAGO
Tobago
Trinidad
PORT OF SPAIN
Golfo de Paria
Península de Paria
Delta del Orinoco
Curaçao
Willemstad
Bonaire
Isla de Margarita
Nueva Esparta
Sucre
Miranda
CARACAS
Distrito Federal
MARACAY
VALENCIA
Yaracuy
Cojedes
Monagas
MATURÍN
Anzoátegui
CUMANÁ
Barcelona
Guárico
Calabozo
Delta Amacuro
Apure
S.Fernando de Apure
VENEZUELA
Orinoco
C.Bolívar
C.Guayana
Embalse de Guri
Bolívar
Sierra de Maigualida
Salto del Angel
Auyán Tepuy
Parque Nac. Canaima
La Gran Sabana
Mt.Roraima
Pakaraima Mountains
GUYANA
Sierra Pacaraima
Amazonas
Serranía Parima
Roraima
Boa Vista
Pto Ayacucho
Cº Duida
Pico de Neblina
Sierra Imeri
Río Negro
BRASIL
AMAZONAS
Continuation of main map
COLOMBIA
PERU
BRAZIL
IQUITOS
Leticia
Tabatinga
Río Putumayo
Río Amazonas
Río Napo
Río Yaguas

Conversion meters – feet see page 48

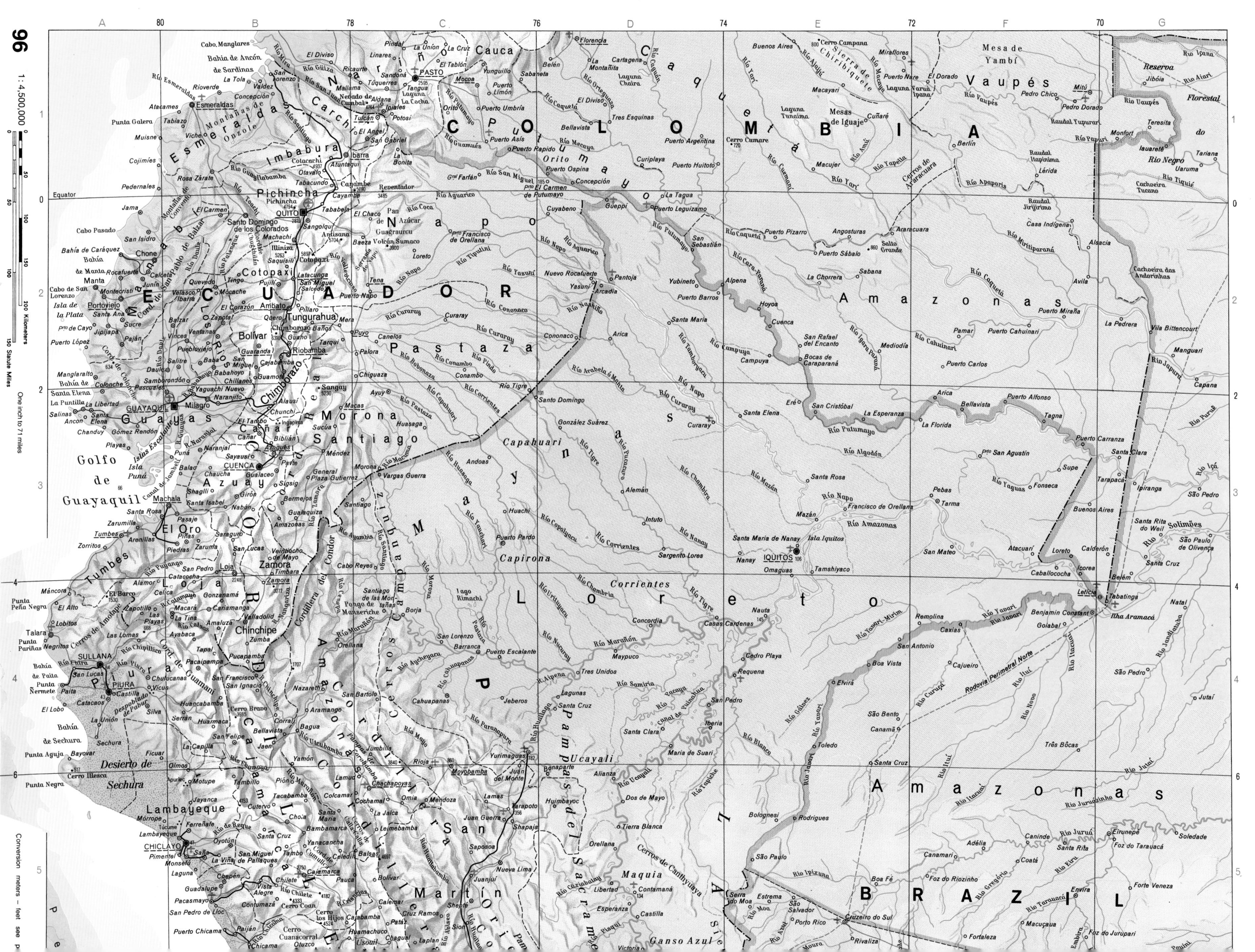
C O L O M B I A
E C U A D O R
B R A Z I L
Amazonas
Loreto
Vaupés
Caquetá
Putumayo
Napo
Pastaza
Morona Santiago
QUITO
GUAYAQUIL
CUENCA
PASTO
IQUITOS
PIURA
SULLANA
CHICLAYO
Golfo de Guayaquil
Desierto de Sechura
Equator
1: 4,500,000
200 Kilometers
150 Statute Miles
One inch to 71 miles
Conversion meters – feet see p

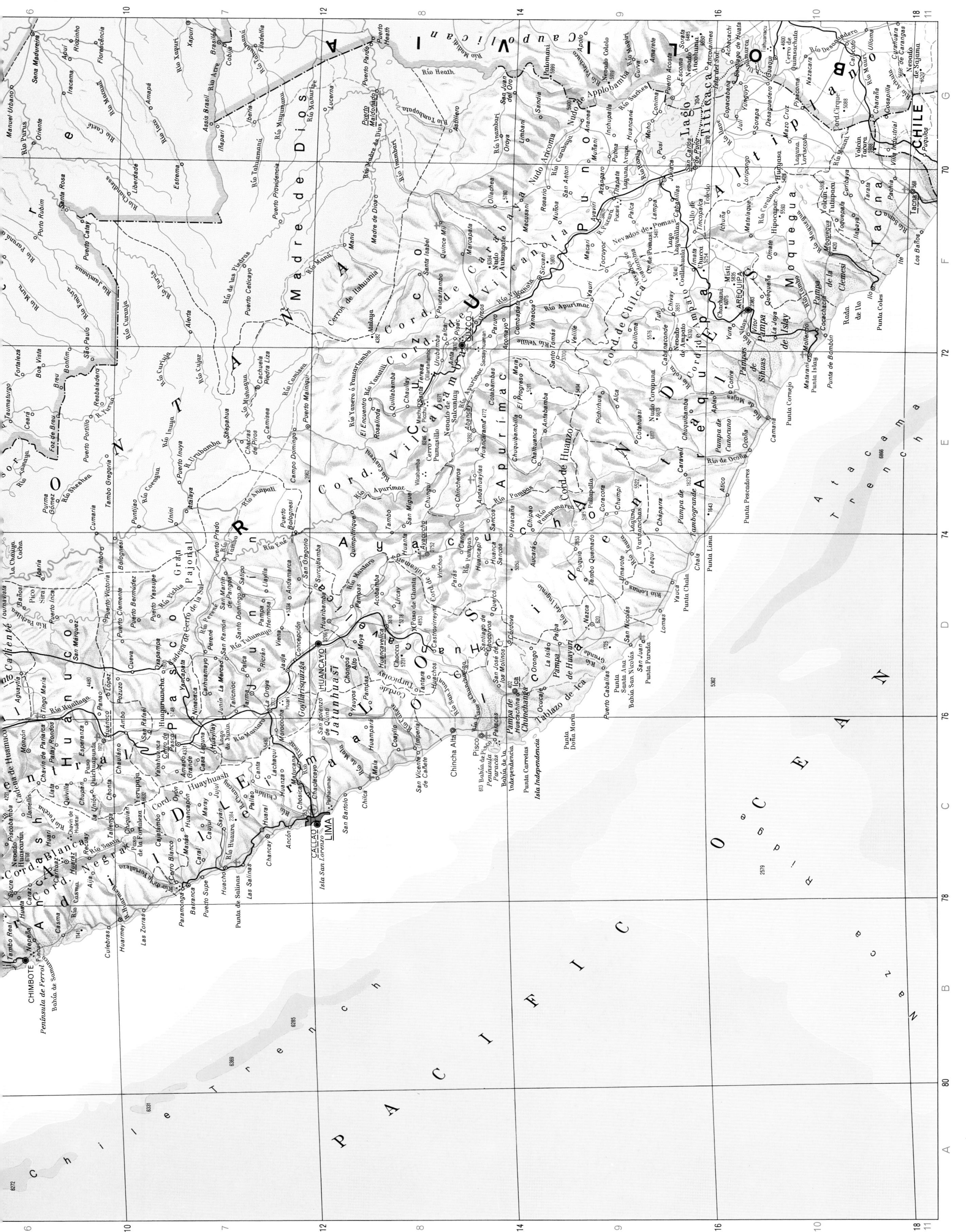
PACIFIC OCEAN
Chile-Peru Trench
LIMA
CALLAO
CHIMBOTE
HUANCAYO
CUZCO
AREQUIPA
Tacna
Pisco
Ica
Nazca
Lago Titicaca
CHILE
Madre de Dios
Altiplano
Isla San Lorenzo
Península de Ferrol

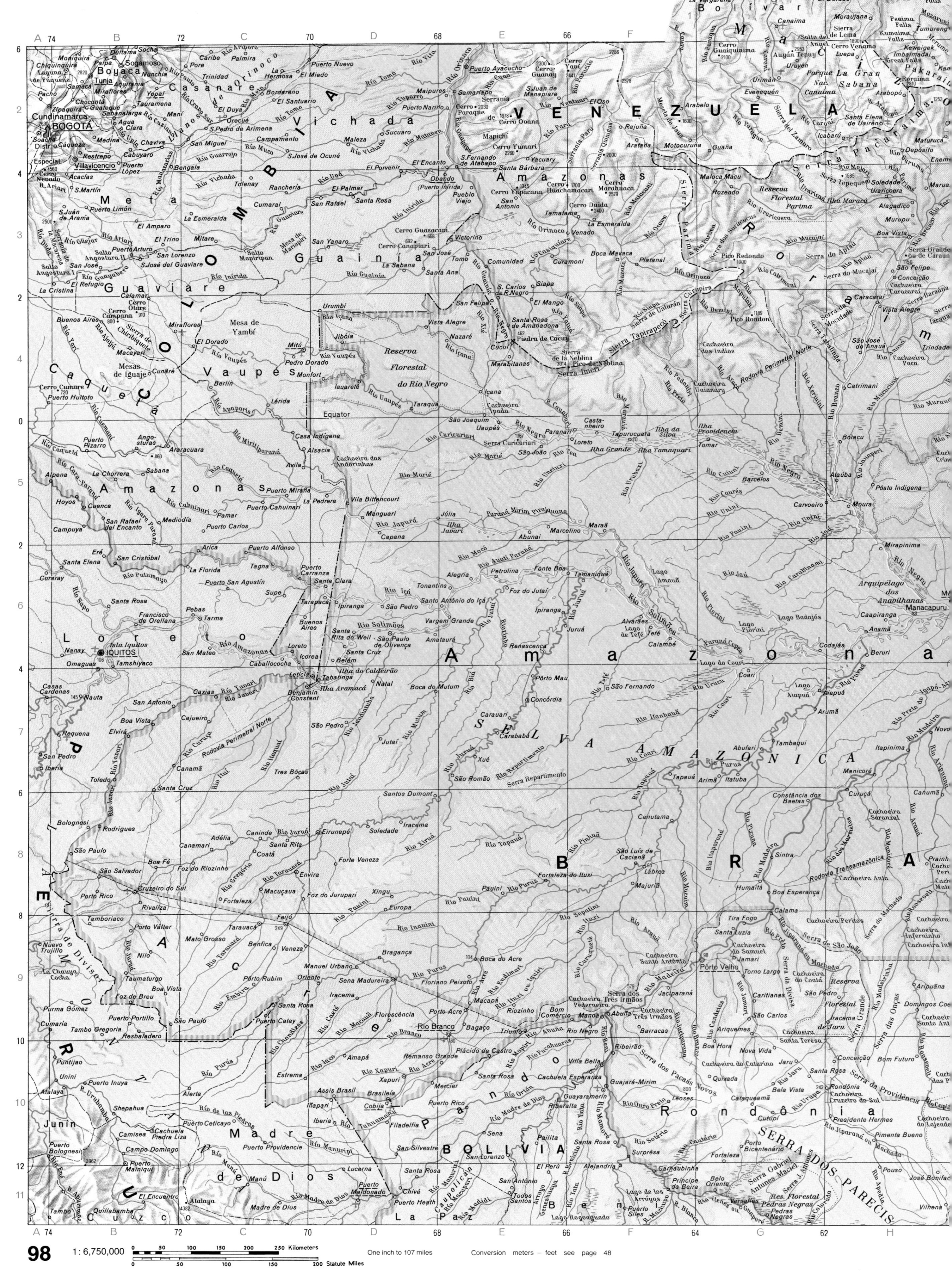

COLOMBIA
VENEZUELA
BRASIL
PERU
BOLIVIA
Amazonas
Vichada
Guainía
Guaviare
Vaupés
Caquetá
Meta
Casanare
Boyacá
Cundinamarca
BOGOTÁ
Bolívar
Loreto
IQUITOS
Roraima
Acre
Rondônia
Pando
Madre de Dios
Beni
La Paz
Cuzco
Junín
SELVA AMAZÔNICA
SERRA DOS PARECIS
Equator
Reserva Florestal do Rio Negro
Río Amazonas
Rio Solimões
Rio Negro
Rio Japurá
Rio Purus
Rio Juruá
Rio Madeira
Río Orinoco
Manaus
Pôrto Velho
Rio Branco
Boa Vista
Leticia

1: 6,750,000 — 0 50 100 150 200 250 Kilometers — 0 50 100 150 200 Statute Miles

One inch to 107 miles

Conversion meters – feet see page 48

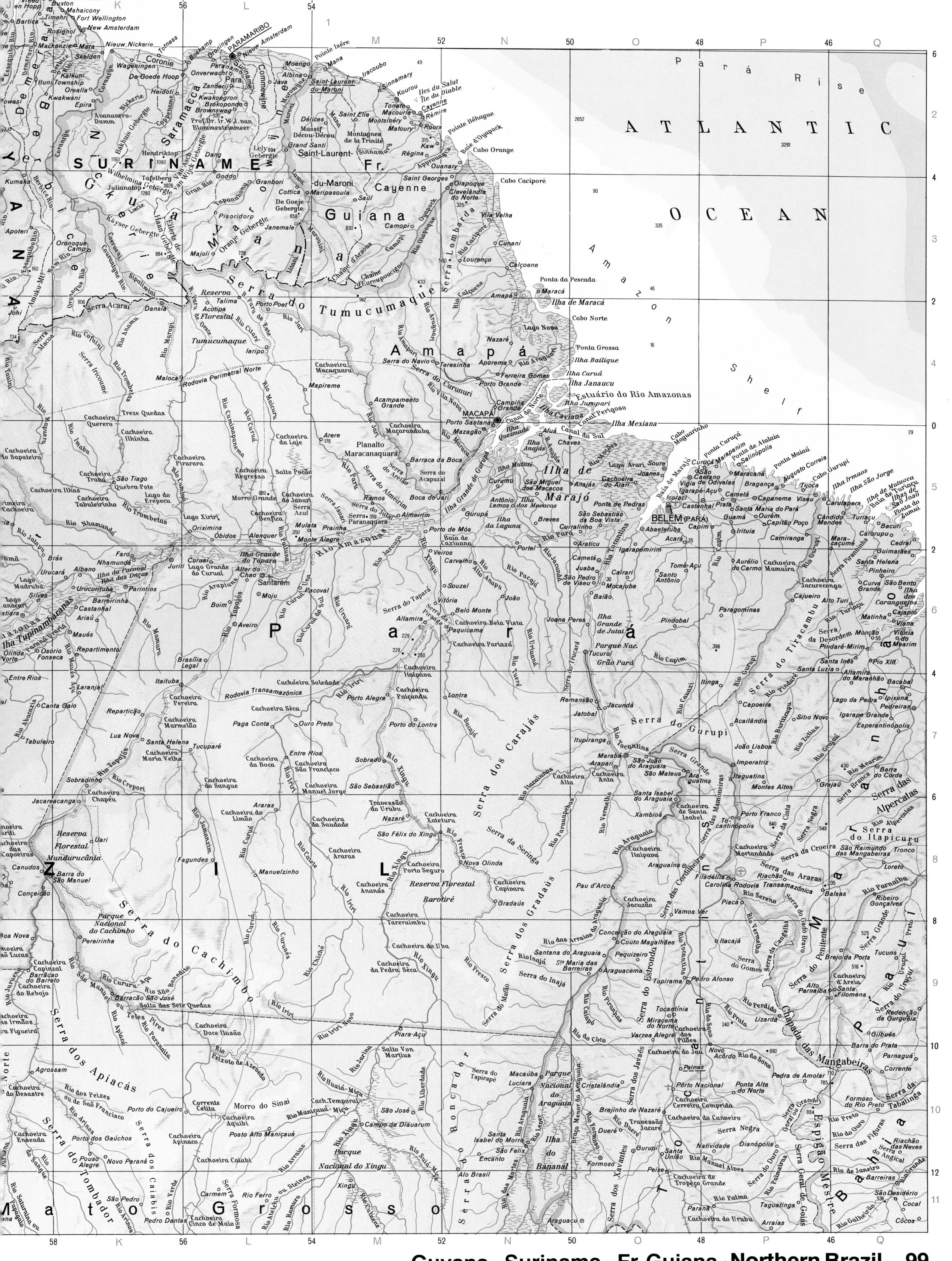

ATLANTIC OCEAN
Pará Rise
Amazon Shelf
SURINAME
Guiana
Fr.
Cayenne
GEORGETOWN
PARAMARIBO
MACAPÁ
BELÉM (PARÁ)
Amapá
Pará
Mato Grosso
Tocantins
Maranhão
Piauí
Bahia
Serra do Tumucumaque
Serra dos Carajás
Serra do Cachimbo
Serra dos Apiacás
Serra do Gurupi
Estuário do Rio Amazonas
Ilha de Marajó
Ilha Caviana
Ilha Mexiana
Rio Amazonas
Rio Xingu
Rio Tapajós
Rio Tocantins
Rio Araguaia
Santarém
Altamira
Marabá
Imperatriz
Itaituba
Óbidos
Oriximiná
Parintins
Macapá
Cabo Orange
Cabo Norte
Ilha do Bananal
Parque Nacional do Xingu
Parque Nacional do Araguaia
Rodovia Transamazônica
Rodovia Perimetral Norte

A T L A N T I C
FORTALEZA (CEARÁ)
RECIFE (PERNAMBUCO)
OLINDA
JOÃO PESSOA (PARAÍBA)
NATAL
MACEIÓ
CAMPINA GRANDE
CARUARU
TERESINA
SÃO LUÍS
Sobral
Parnaíba
Serra da Ibiapaba
Chapada do Araripe
Planalto da Borborema
Serra do Tiracambu
Serra das Alpercatas
Serra do Valentim
Serra do Itapicuru
Ceará
Rio Grande do Norte
Paraíba
Pernambuco
Alagoas
Maranhão
Piauí
B R A Z I L

1: 4,500,000 — 0 50 100 150 200 Kilometers — 0 50 100 150 Statute Miles — One inch to 71 miles — Conversion meters – feet see page 48

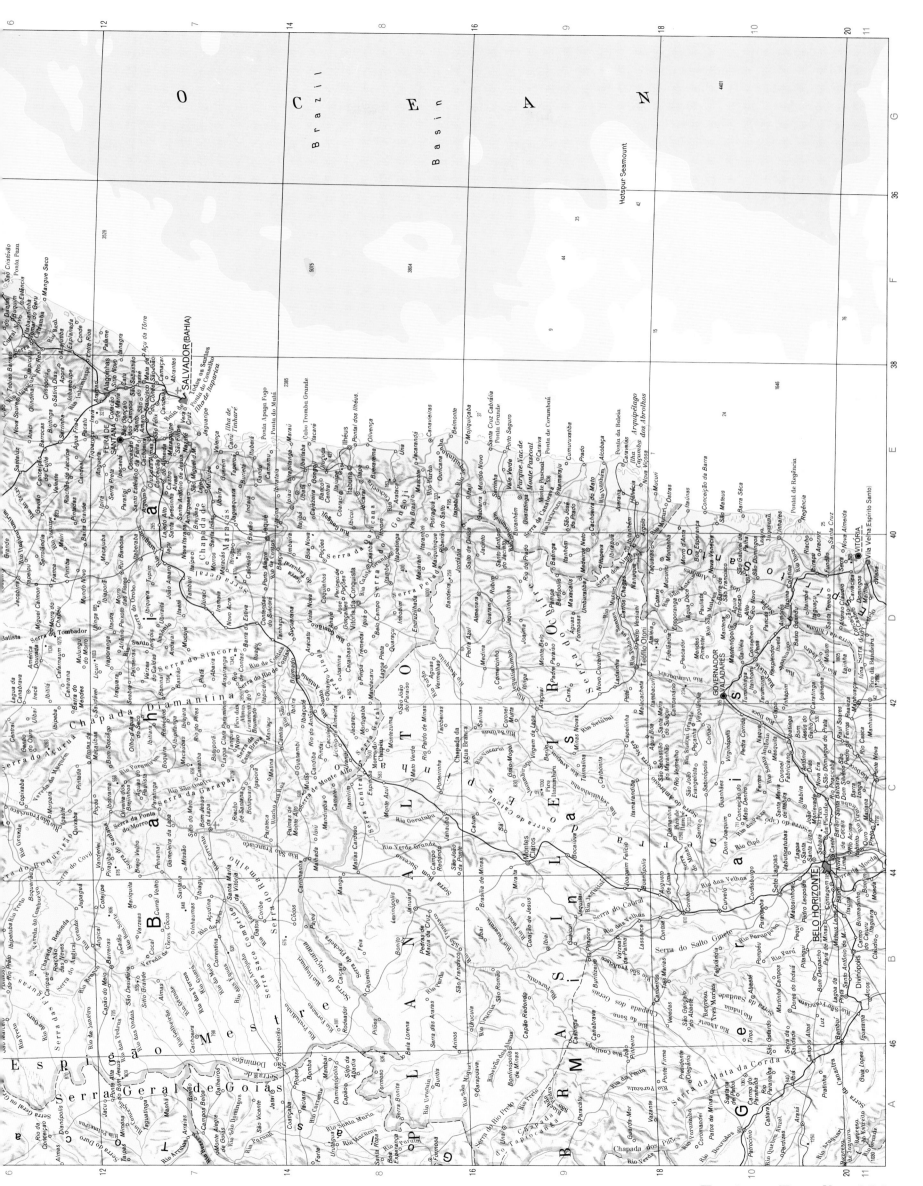

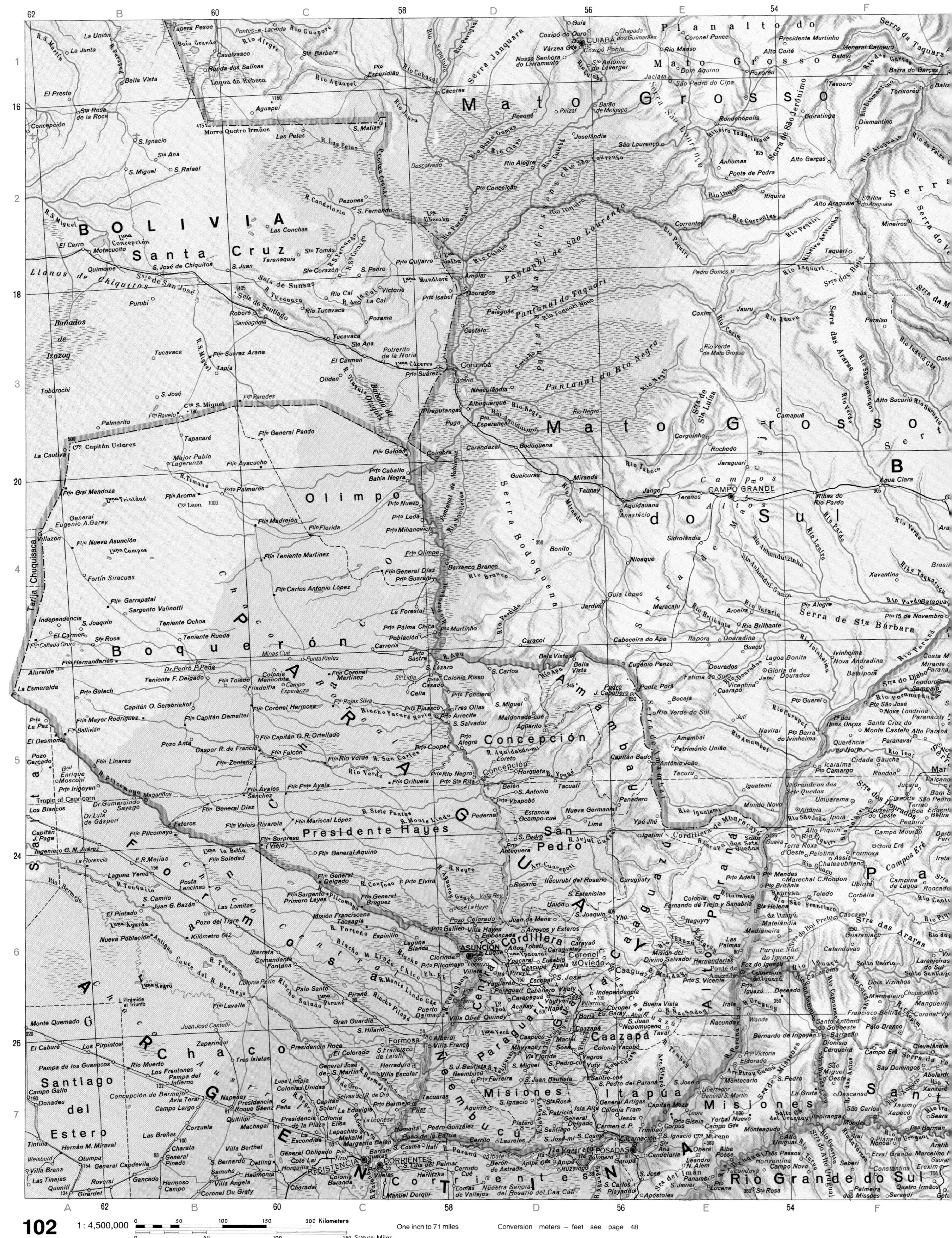
BOLIVIA
Santa Cruz
Mato Grosso
Mato Grosso do Sul
Planalto do Mato Grosso
CUIABÁ
CAMPO GRANDE
Corumbá
Pantanal de São Lourenço
Pantanal do Taquari
Pantanal do Rio Negro
Serra Bodoquena
Serra de Maracaju
Llanos de Chiquitos
Bañados de Izozog
Boquerón
Olimpo
Chaco
PARAGUAY
Presidente Hayes
Concepción
San Pedro
Amambay
Cordillera
Central
Paraguarí
Caaguazú
Caazapá
Ñeembucú
Misiones
Itapúa
Alto Paraná
Canendiyú
ASUNCIÓN
Tropic of Capricorn
Formosa
ARGENTINA
Chaco
Santiago del Estero
Corrientes
CORRIENTES
RESISTENCIA
POSADAS
Encarnación
Paraná
Santa Catarina
Rio Grande do Sul
Tarija
Chuquisaca
Salta
Rio Pilcomayo
Rio Paraguai
Rio Paraná
Rio Bermejo
Rio Iguaçu
Foz do Iguaçu

1: 4,500,000 — 0 50 100 150 200 Kilometers — 0 50 100 150 Statute Miles

One inch to 71 miles

Conversion meters – feet see page 48

BRASÍLIA
TAGUATINGA
Distr. Federal
GOIÂNIA
Anápolis
UBERLÂNDIA
UBERABA
Araguari
BELO HORIZONTE
Sete Lagoas
Montes Claros
GOVERNADOR VALADARES
Teófilo Otoni
JUIZ DE FORA
Barbacena
SÃO JOSÉ DO RIO PRETO
RIBEIRÃO PRETO
Araraquara
São Carlos
BAURU
Marília
PIRACICABA
CAMPINAS
JUNDIAÍ
SOROCABA
SÃO PAULO
GUARULHOS
OSASCO
SANTO ANDRÉ
SÃO BERNARDO D.C.
SÃO CAETANO D.S.
MAUÁ
SANTOS
SÃO VICENTE
SÃO JOSÉ DOS C.
TAUBATÉ
VOLTA REDONDA
PETRÓPOLIS
NOVA IGUAÇU
DUQUE DE CAXIAS
SÃO JOÃO D.M.
NITERÓI
SÃO GONÇALO
RIO DE JANEIRO
Teresópolis
Nova Friburgo
CAMPOS
LONDRINA
Ponta Grossa
CURITIBA
Paranaguá
Joinville
Blumenau
Itajaí
FLORIANÓPOLIS
Tubarão
Represa de Três Marias
Serra da Mantiqueira
Serra do Mar
Serra da Canastra
Serra do Espinhaço
Chapada dos Veadeiros
Rio Grande
Rio Paranaíba
Rio São Francisco
Rio Tietê
Rio Paraná
Rio Doce
Rio Paraíba do Sul
Baía de Guanabara
Baía de Sepetiba
Ilha Grande
Iª de São Sebastião
Ilha de Sta Catarina
Tropic of Capricorn
Cabo Frio
ATLANTIC
OCEAN

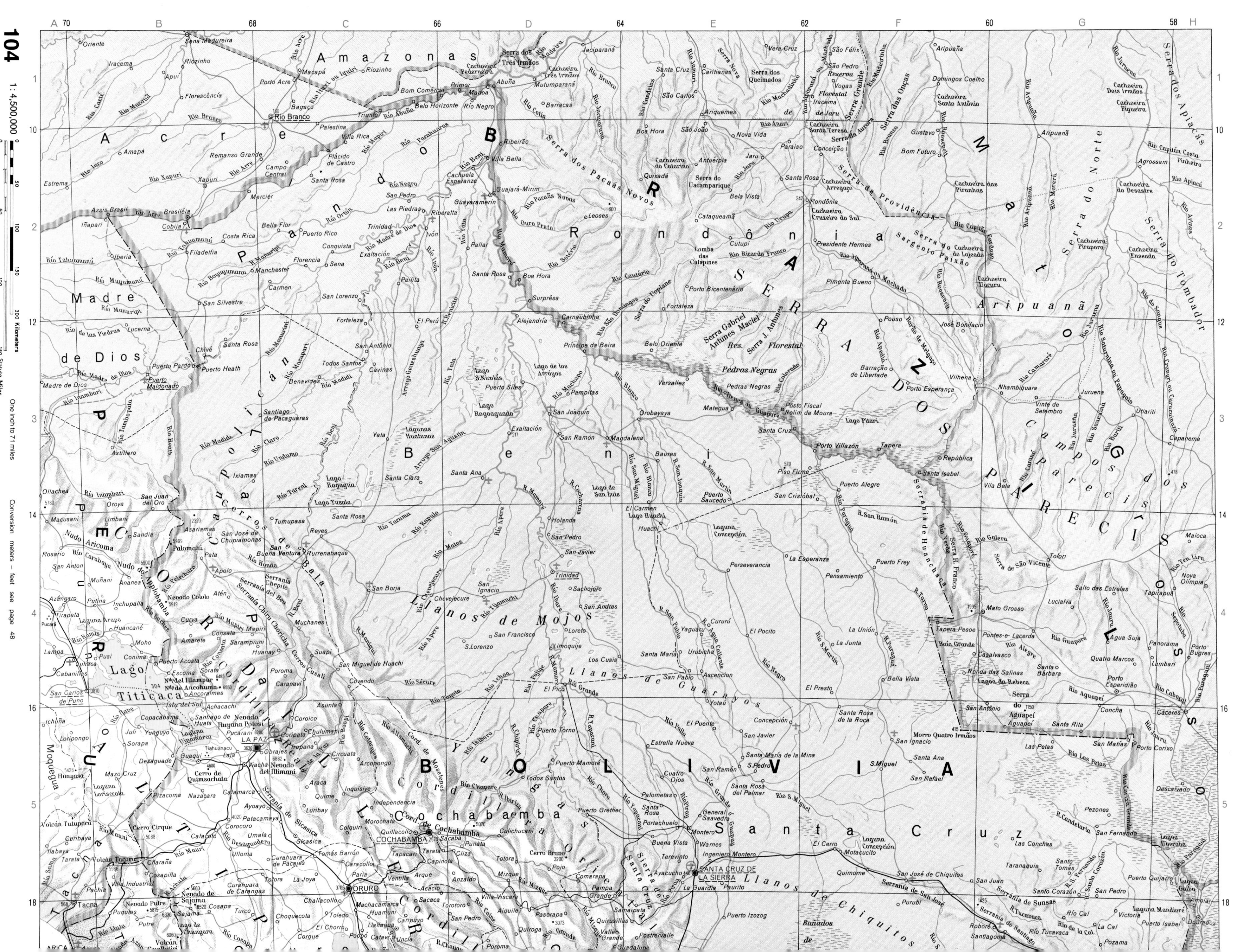

BOLIVIA
Amazonas
Acre
Pando
Beni
Rondônia
Mato Grosso
Santa Cruz
Madre de Dios
PERU
Campos dos Parecis
Serra dos Parecis
Aripuanã
Serra do Tombador
Serra dos Apiacás
Serra do Norte
Serra dos Pacaás Novos
Serra da Providência
Serranía de Huanchaca
Llanos de Mojos
Llanos de Chiquitos
Llanos de Guarayos
Cordillera Real
Cord. de Cochabamba
Lago Titicaca
LA PAZ
COCHABAMBA
SANTA CRUZ DE LA SIERRA
ORURO
Trinidad
Riberalta
Cobija
Rio Branco
Puerto Maldonado
Mato Grosso
Cáceres
Vila Bela
Guajará-Mirim
Moquegua
Tacna
Río Mamoré
Río Guaporé
Río Beni
Rio Abunã
Río Grande
Río Heath

1: 4,500,000 — 0 50 100 150 200 Kilometers; 0 50 100 150 Statute Miles

One inch to 71 miles

Conversion meters – feet see page 48

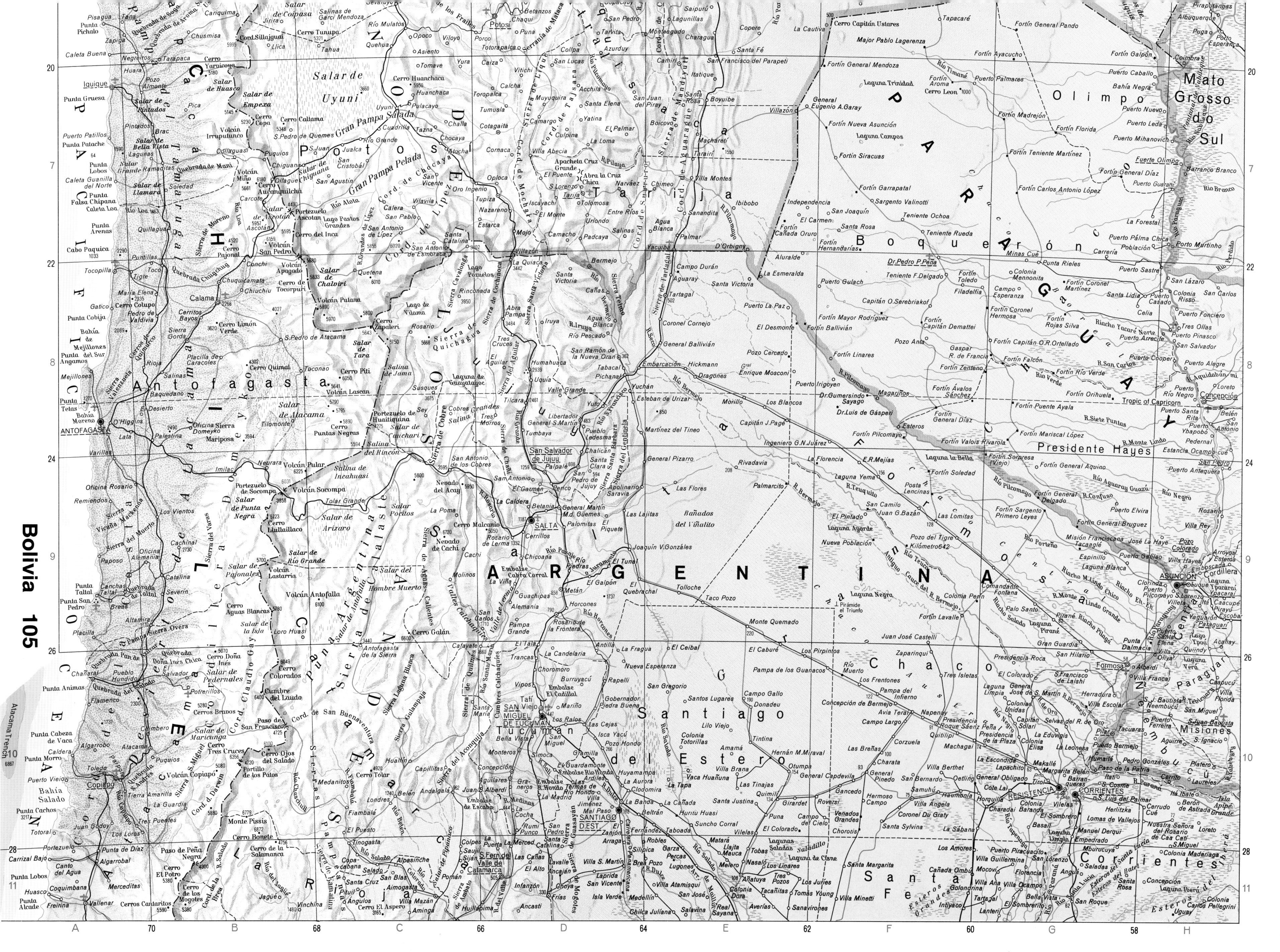
Mato Grosso do Sul
PARAGUAY
Olimpo
Boquerón
Presidente Hayes
ASUNCIÓN
Tropic of Capricorn
ARGENTINA
Formosa
Chaco
RESISTENCIA
CORRIENTES
Misiones
Corrientes
Santa Fe
Santiago del Estero
SANTIAGO DEL ESTERO
SAN MIGUEL DE TUCUMÁN
SALTA
San Salvador de Jujuy
La Rioja
Potosí
Tarija
Salar de Uyuni
CHILE
Antofagasta
ANTOFAGASTA
Calama
Iquique
Pampa del Tamarugal
Salar de Atacama
Copiapó
PACIFIC OCEAN
Atacama Trench

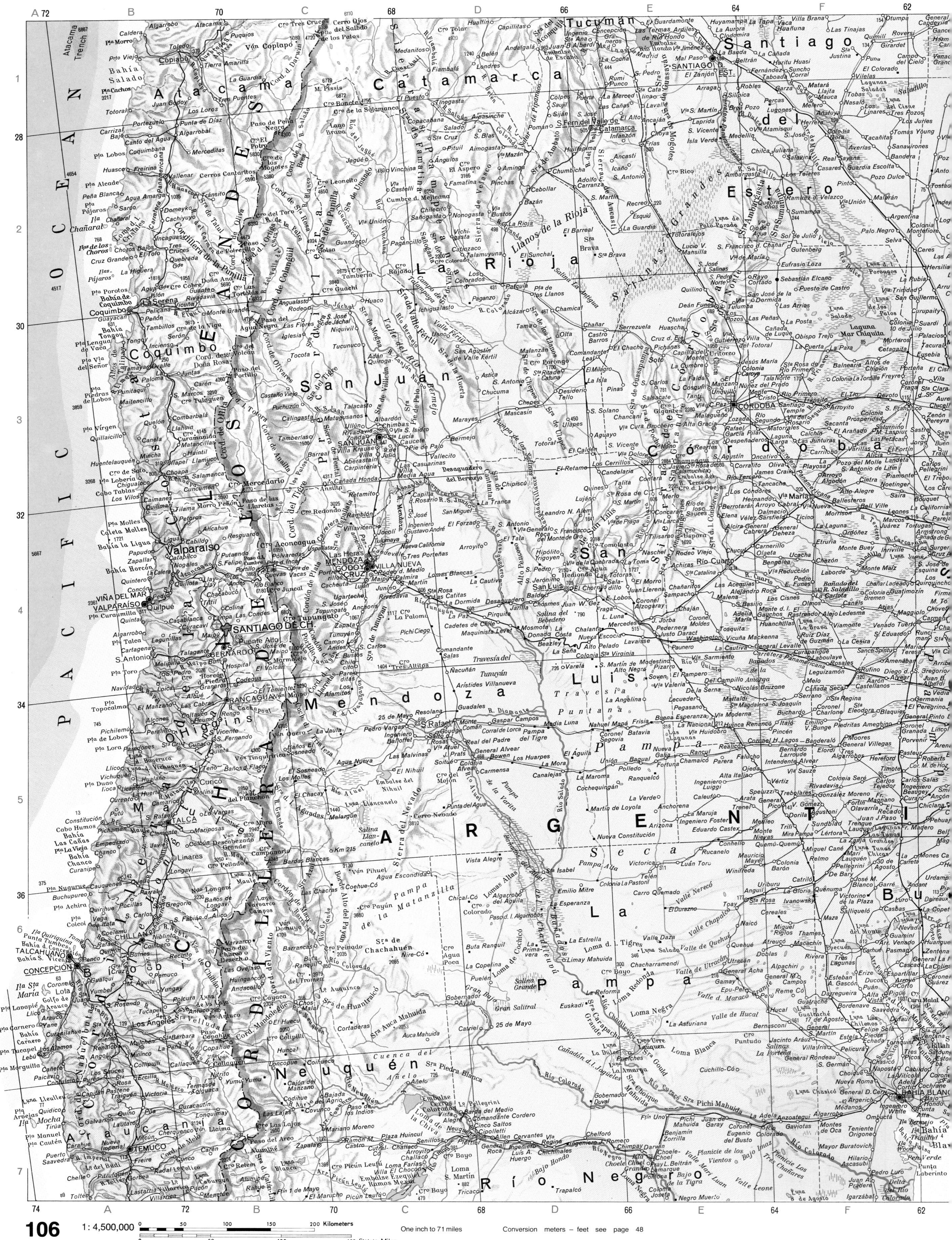
PACIFIC OCEAN
Atacama Trench
Atacama
Catamarca
Santiago del Estero
La Rioja
Coquimbo
San Juan
Córdoba
San Luis
Mendoza
ARGENTINA
La Pampa
Neuquén
Río Negro
Araucania
CORDILLERA DE LOS ANDES
Valparaíso
SANTIAGO DE CH.
MENDOZA
SAN JUAN
CÓRDOBA
TALCAHUANO
CONCEPCIÓN
TEMUCO
BAHÍA BLANCA
Tucumán
Laguna Mar Chiquita
Llanos de la Rioja
Salinas Grandes
Travesía Puntana
Pampa Seca
1:4,500,000
Kilometers
Statute Miles
One inch to 71 miles
Conversion meters - feet see page 48

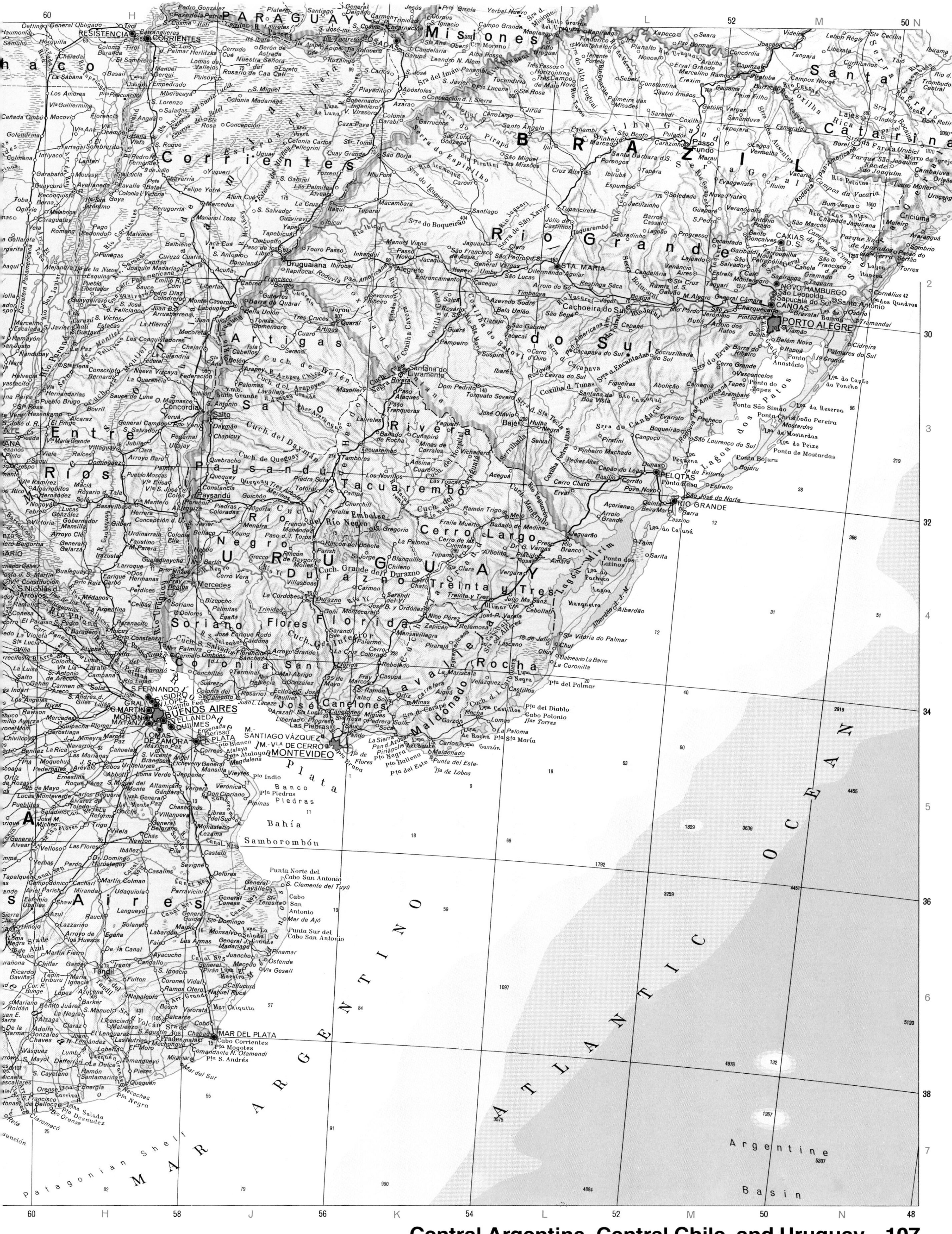
PARAGUAY
Misiones
BRAZIL
Santa Catarina
Corrientes
Rio Grande do Sul
Entre Ríos
Artigas
Salto
Rivera
Paysandú
Tacuarembó
Río Negro
URUGUAY
Cerro Largo
Durazno
Treinta y Tres
Soriano
Flores
Florida
Colonia
San José
Canelones
Lavalleja
Rocha
Maldonado
RESISTENCIA
CORRIENTES
POSADAS
PORTO ALEGRE
CAXIAS DO SUL
NOVO HAMBURGO
CANOAS
STA. MARIA
PELOTAS
RIO GRANDE
BUENOS AIRES
LA PLATA
MONTEVIDEO
MAR DEL PLATA
Lagoa dos Patos
Lagoa Mirim
Bahía Samborombón
Río de la Plata
MAR ARGENTINO
ATLANTIC OCEAN
Patagonian Shelf
Argentine Basin
Tandil
Quequén
Mercedes
Concordia
Uruguaiana
Alegrete
Bagé
Jaguarão
Chuy
Punta del Este
Cabo Polonio
Cabo San Antonio
Cabo Corrientes

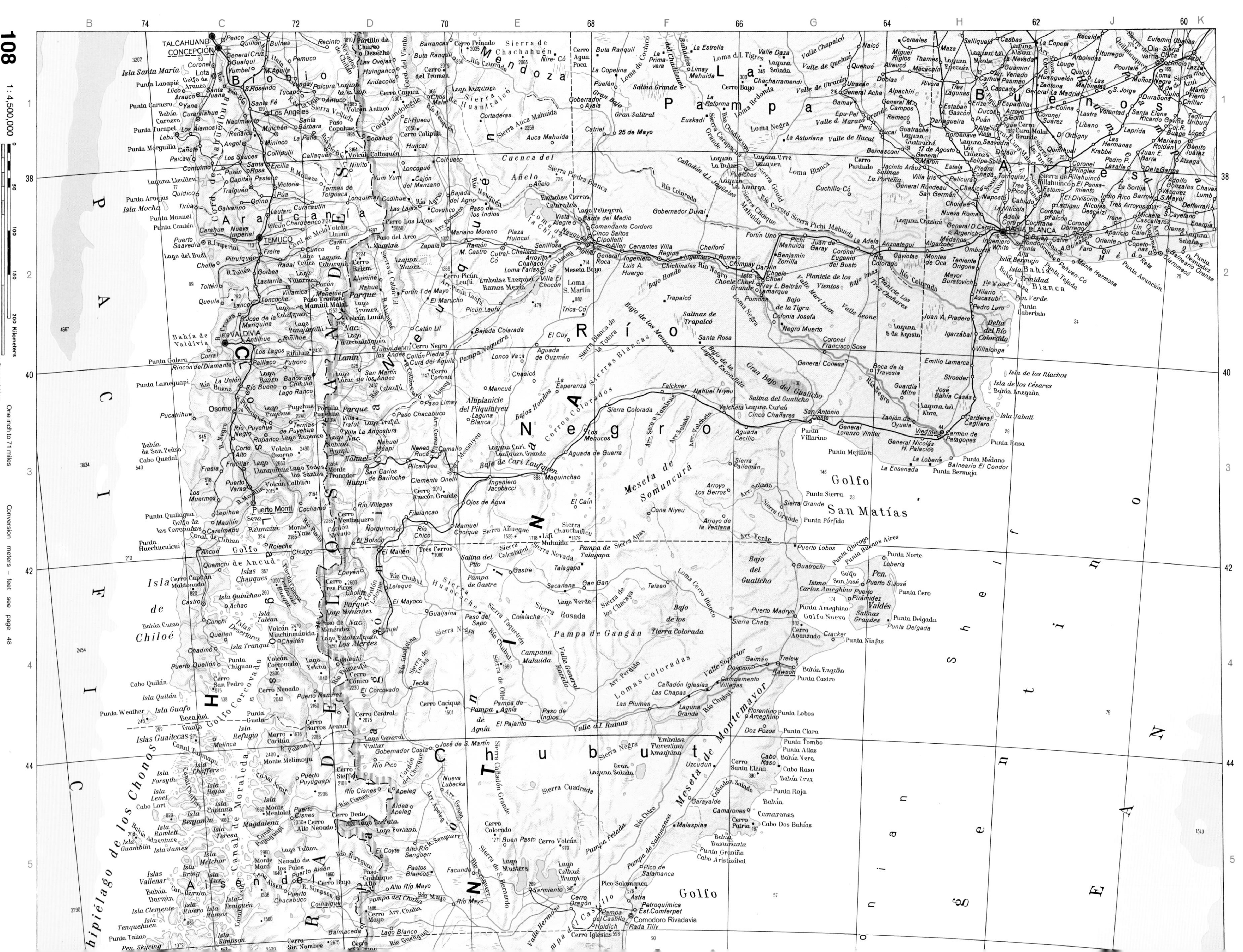
Mendoza
La Pampa
Buenos Aires
Río Negro
Neuquén
Chubut
Araucanía
Bío Bío
Golfo San Matías
Meseta de Somuncurá
Meseta de Montemayor
Pampa de Gangán
Isla de Chiloé
Archipiélago de los Chonos
Península Valdés
BAHIA BLANCA
TEMUCO
VALDIVIA
Puerto Montt
Comodoro Rivadavia
TALCAHUANO
CONCEPCIÓN

1: 4,500,000 — 0 50 100 150 200 Kilometers — 0 50 100 150 Statute Miles

One inch to 71 miles

Conversion meters – feet see page 48

Falkland Islands
(Islas Malvinas)
(U.K.)
West Falkland
East Falkland
Falkland Sound
Stanley
Burdwood Bank
Bahía Grande
Puerto Deseado
Puerto San Julián
Puerto Santa Cruz
Río Gallegos
Lago Argentino
Lago Viedma
Golfo de Peñas
Estrecho de Magallanes
Península Brunswick
Punta Arenas
Isla Grande de Tierra del Fuego
Ushuaia
Isla de los Estados
Cabo de Hornos

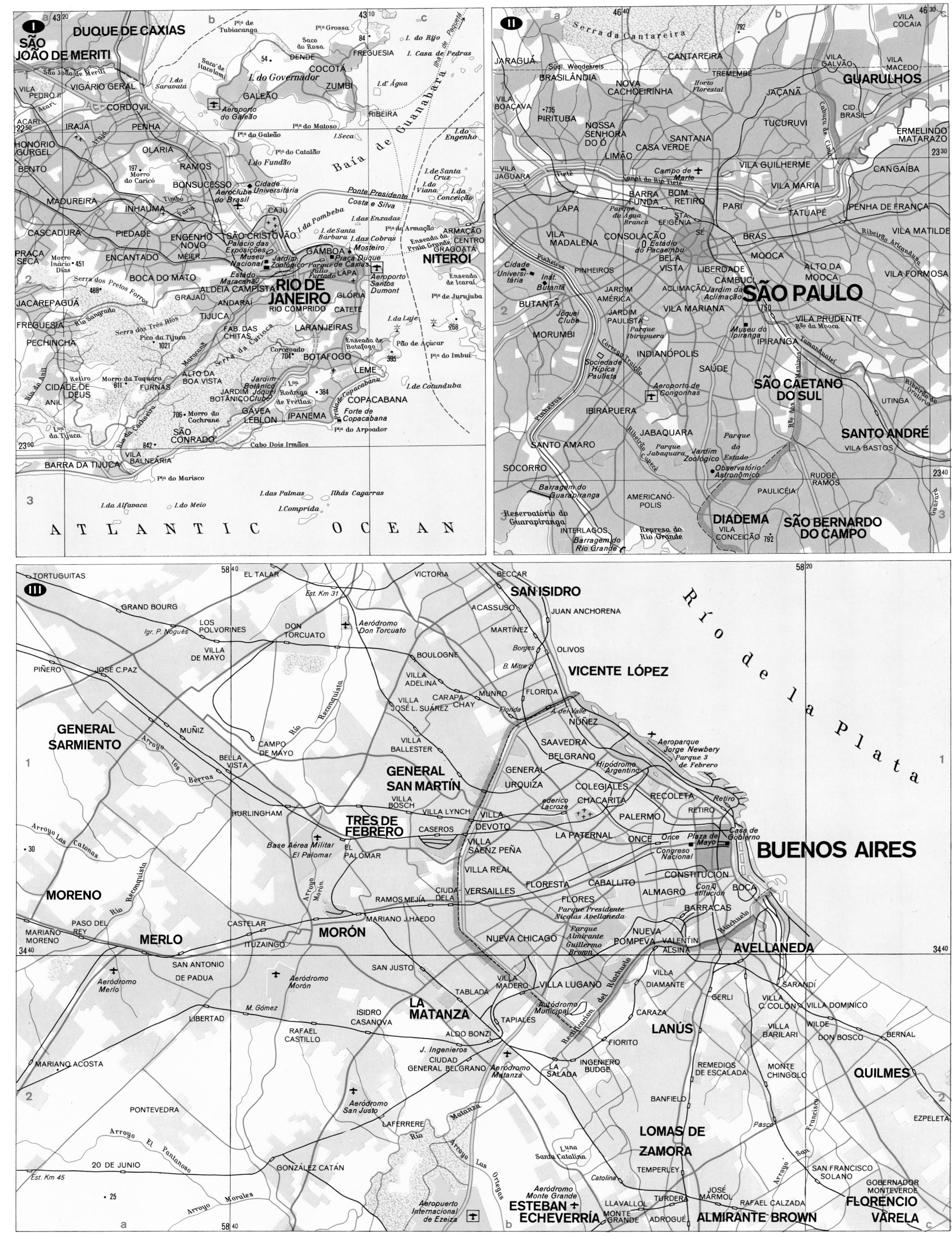
I
DUQUE DE CAXIAS
SÃO JOÃO DE MERITI
I. do Governador
Baía de Guanabara
RIO DE JANEIRO
NITERÓI
COPACABANA
IPANEMA
LEBLON
BARRA DA TIJUCA
ATLANTIC OCEAN
II
GUARULHOS
SANTANA
SÃO PAULO
SÃO CAETANO DO SUL
SANTO ANDRÉ
DIADEMA
SÃO BERNARDO DO CAMPO
III
SAN ISIDRO
VICENTE LÓPEZ
Río de la Plata
GENERAL SARMIENTO
GENERAL SAN MARTÍN
TRES DE FEBRERO
BUENOS AIRES
MORENO
MERLO
MORÓN
LA MATANZA
AVELLANEDA
LANÚS
QUILMES
LOMAS DE ZAMORA
ESTEBAN ECHEVERRÍA
ALMIRANTE BROWN
FLORENCIO VARELA

1 : 225,000
0 2.5 5 7.5 10 Kilometers
0 2.5 5 7.5 Statute Miles
One inch to 3.6 miles

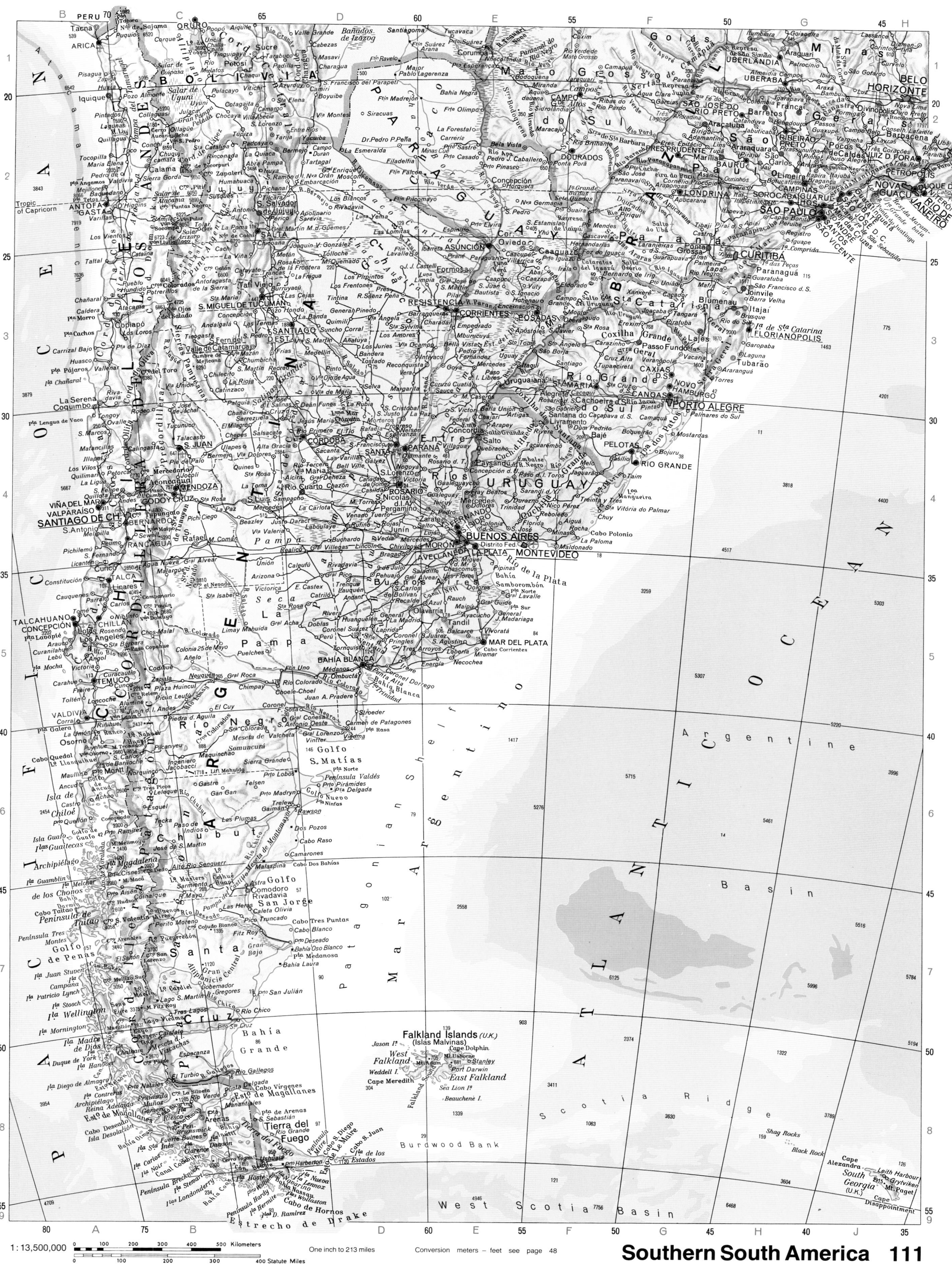

PACIFIC OCEAN
ATLANTIC OCEAN
BOLIVIA
PARAGUAY
BRAZIL
URUGUAY
ARGENTINA
CHILE
Tropic of Capricorn
ARICA
Tacna
ORURO
Sucre
Potosí
Iquique
ANTOFAGASTA
S. Salvador de Jujuy
SALTA
ASUNCIÓN
CURITIBA
SÃO PAULO
RIO DE JANEIRO
BELO HORIZONTE
S. MIGUEL DE TUCUMÁN
CORRIENTES
RESISTENCIA
POSADAS
FLORIANÓPOLIS
PORTO ALEGRE
PELOTAS
RIO GRANDE
CÓRDOBA
ROSARIO
SANTA FE
PARANÁ
MENDOZA
S. JUAN
VIÑA DEL MAR
VALPARAÍSO
SANTIAGO DE CH.
BUENOS AIRES
LA PLATA
MONTEVIDEO
Río de la Plata
MAR DEL PLATA
BAHÍA BLANCA
TALCAHUANO
CONCEPCIÓN
TEMUCO
VALDIVIA
Golfo S. Matías
Península Valdés
Golfo San Jorge
Comodoro Rivadavia
Isla de Chiloé
Archipiélago de los Chonos
Golfo de Penas
Bahía Grande
Río Gallegos
Estº de Magallanes
Tierra del Fuego
Cabo de Hornos
Estrecho de Drake
Falkland Islands (U.K.) (Islas Malvinas)
West Falkland
East Falkland
Stanley
Burdwood Bank
Scotia Ridge
West Scotia Basin
Argentine Basin
Patagonian Shelf
Mar Argentino
South Georgia (U.K.)
Shag Rocks
Black Rock

1:13,500,000 — Kilometers 0 100 200 300 400 500 — Statute Miles 0 100 200 300 400 — One inch to 213 miles — Conversion meters - feet see page 48

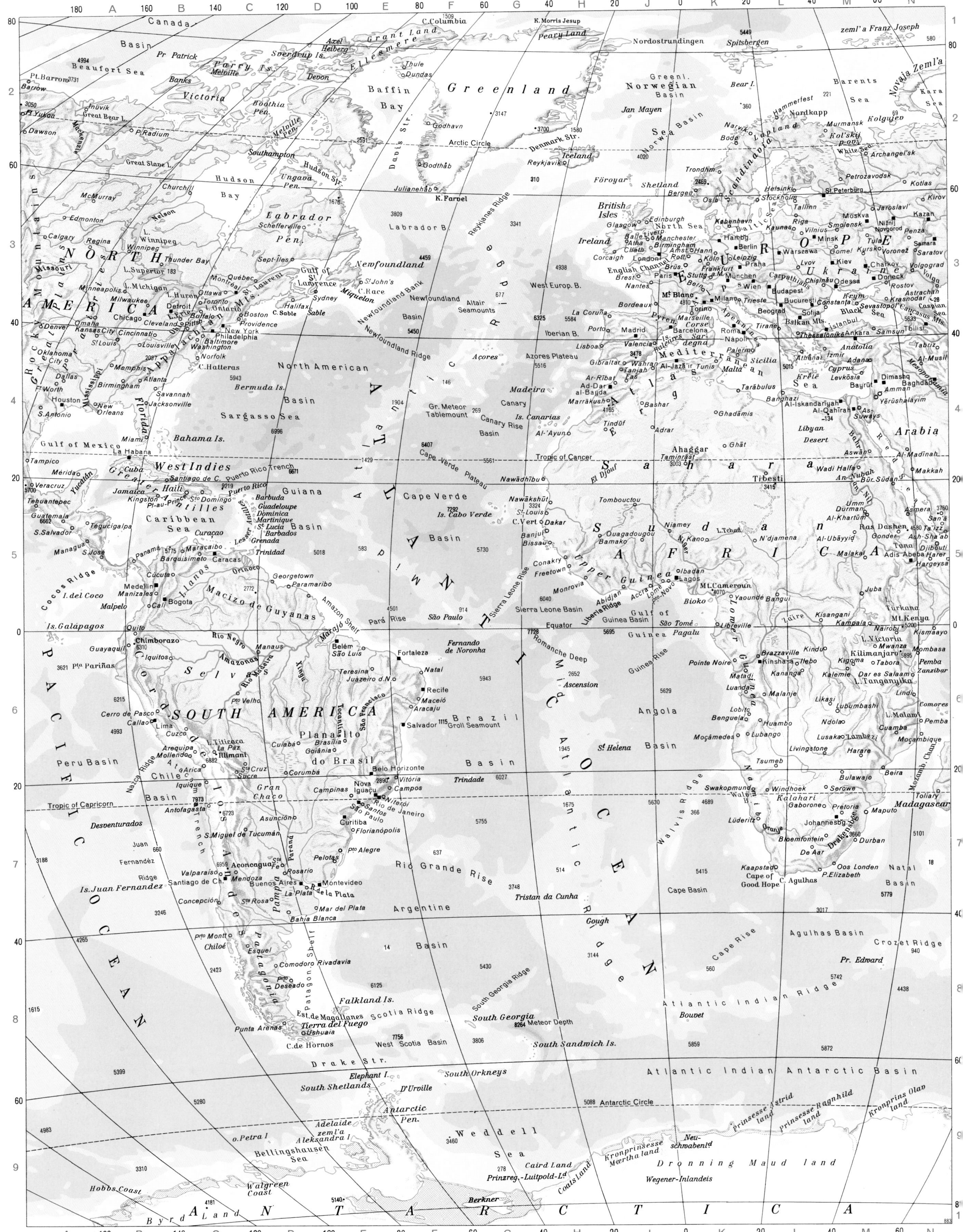
Greenland
Baffin Bay
Davis Str.
Denmark Str.
Iceland
Norwegian Basin
Norwegian Sea
Spitsbergen
Barents Sea
Kara Sea
Novaja Zeml'a
Hudson Bay
Hudson Str.
Labrador Pen.
Labrador B.
Newfoundland
Newfoundland Basin
Newfoundland Ridge
Reykjanes Ridge
British Isles
Ireland
North Sea
Baltic Sea
EUROPE
West Europ. B.
Iberian B.
Mediterranean Sea
Black Sea
Caspian Sea
NORTH AMERICA
Gulf of Mexico
Bahama Is.
West Indies
Caribbean Sea
Sargasso Sea
North American Basin
Bermuda Is.
Açores
Azores Plateau
Madeira
Canary Basin
Is. Canarias
Cape Verde Basin
Is. Cabo Verde
Tropic of Cancer
Puerto Rico Trench
Guiana Basin
ATLANTIC OCEAN
Mid Atlantic Ridge
AFRICA
Sahara
Gulf of Guinea
Guinea Basin
Sierra Leone Basin
Sierra Leone Rise
Equator
Romanche Deep
Ascension
Angola Basin
St Helena
Walvis Ridge
Cape Basin
Cape Rise
Agulhas Basin
Natal Basin
Madagascar
Arabia
SOUTH AMERICA
Amazon Shelf
Brazil Basin
Rio Grande Rise
Argentine Basin
Tristan da Cunha
Gough
Falkland Is.
Scotia Ridge
South Georgia
South Georgia Ridge
Meteor Depth
South Sandwich Is.
West Scotia Basin
Drake Str.
South Orkneys
South Shetlands
Atlantic Indian Ridge
Bouvet
Atlantic Indian Antarctic Basin
Antarctic Circle
Antarctic Pen.
Weddell Sea
Bellingshausen Sea
Dronning Maud land
ANTARCTICA
PACIFIC OCEAN
Peru Basin
Tropic of Capricorn
Scale at the center meridian 1 : 60,000,000
One inch to 947 miles

Conversion meters – feet see page 48

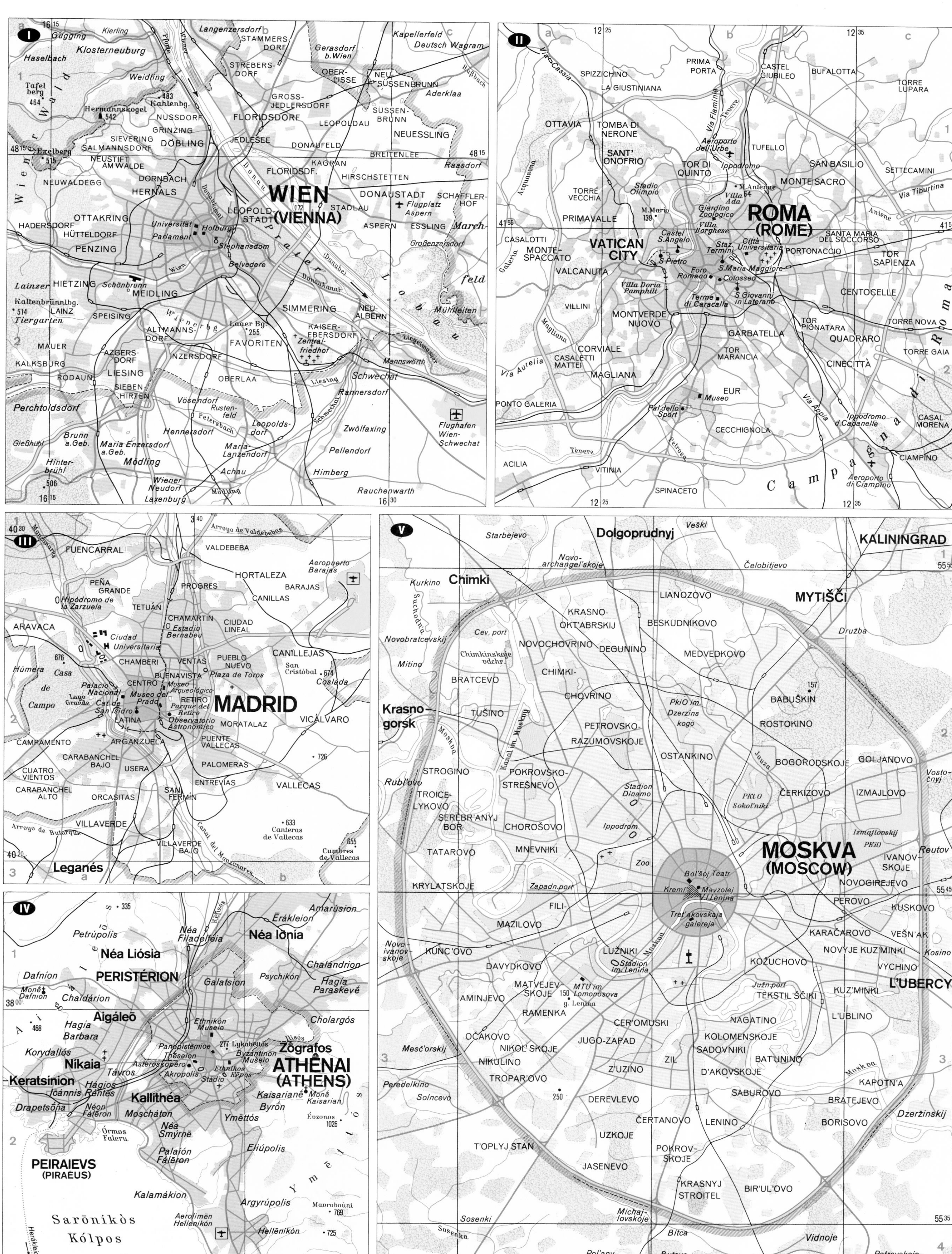

I
WIEN
(VIENNA)
Klosterneuburg
Gugging
Kierling
Haselbach
Langenzersdorf
STAMMERSDORF
Gerasdorf b.Wien
Kapellerfeld
Deutsch Wagram
STREBERSDORF
OBER-LISSE
NEU SÜSSENBRUNN
Aderklaa
Weidling
GROSS-JEDLERSDORF
SÜSSENBRUNN
Hermannskogel 542
483 Kahlenbg.
NUSSDORF
FLORIDSDORF
LEOPOLDAU
NEUESSLING
SIEVERING
GRINZING
SALMANNSDORF
DÖBLING
JEDLESEE
DONAUFELD
BREITENLEE
Exelberg 515
NEUSTIFT AM WALDE
KAGRAN
FLORIDSDF.
Raasdorf
HIRSCHSTETTEN
NEUWALDEGG
DORNBACH
HERNALS
DONAUSTADT
SCHAFFLERHOF
Flugplatz Aspern
LEOPOLDSTADT
STADLAU
OTTAKRING
HADERSDORF
HÜTTELDORF
PENZING
Universität
Parlament
Hofburg
Stephansdom
ASPERN
ESSLING
March
Großenzersdorf
Belvedere
Lainzer
HIETZING
Schönbrunn
MEIDLING
Kaltenbrünnlbg. 514
LAINZ
Tiergarten
SPEISING
SIMMERING
NEU-ALBERN
Mühlleiten
Laaer Bg. 255
KAISER-EBERSDORF
ALTMANNSDORF
FAVORITEN
Zentralfriedhof
MAUER
AZGERSDORF
INZERSDORF
KALKSBURG
Mannswörth
RODAUN
LIESING
OBERLAA
Schwechat
SIEBENHIRTEN
Rannersdorf
Perchtoldsdorf
Vösendorf
Rustenfeld
Brunn a.Geb.
Hennersdorf
Leopoldsdorf
Zwölfaxing
Flughafen Wien-Schwechat
Gießhübl
Maria Enzersdorf a.Geb.
Maria-Lanzendorf
Pellendorf
Hinterbrühl 506
Mödling
Achau
Himberg
Wiener Neudorf
Laxenburg
Rauchenwarth
Wienerwald
Donau
Prater
Lobau
II
ROMA
(ROME)
Via Cassia
SPIZZICHINO
LA GIUSTINIANA
PRIMA PORTA
CASTEL GIUBILEO
BUFALOTTA
TORRE LUPARA
OTTAVIA
TOMBA DI NERONE
Via Flaminia
Tevere
SANT' ONOFRIO
Aeroporto dell'Urbe
TUFELLO
TOR DI QUINTO
Ippodromo
SAN BASILIO
SETTECAMINI
TORRE VECCHIA
Stadio Olimpico
M.Antenne 64
Villa Ada
MONTE SACRO
Via Tiburtina
PRIMAVALLE
M.Mario 139
Giardino Zoologico
Villa Borghese
Aniene
CASALOTTI
VATICAN CITY
Castel S.Angelo
S.Pietro
Città Universitaria
Staz. Termini
SANTA MARIA DEL SOCCORSO
PORTONACCIO
MONTE-SPACCATO
TOR SAPIENZA
VALCANUTA
Foro Romano
S.Maria Maggiore
Colosseo
Villa Doria Pamphili
Terme di Caracalla
S.Giovanni in Laterano
CENTOCELLE
VILLINI
MONTVERDE NUOVO
TORRE NOVA
TOR PIGNATARA
GARBATELLA
QUADRARO
CORVIALE
TOR MARANCIA
TORRE GAIA
Via Aurelia
CASALETTI MATTEI
CINECITTÀ
MAGLIANA
EUR
Museo
PONTO GALERIA
Pal.dello Sport
Via Appia
Ippodromo d.Capanelle
CASAL MORENA
CECCHIGNOLA
ACILIA
VITINIA
SPINACETO
CIAMPINO
Aeroporto di Ciampino
Campagna di Roma
III
MADRID
Arroyo de Valdebebas
PUENCARRAL
VALDEBEBA
Aeropuerto Barajas
HORTALEZA
PEÑA GRANDE
PROGRES
BARAJAS
CANILLAS
Hipódromo de la Zarzuela
TETUÁN
CHAMARTIN
Estadio Bernabeu
CIUDAD LINEAL
ARAVACA
Ciudad Universitaria
VENTAS
PUEBLO NUEVO
CANILLEJAS
CHAMBERI
San Cristóbal 674
Húmera
Casa de Campo
BUENAVISTA
Plaza de Toros
Coslada
Palacio Nacional
CENTRO
Museo del Prado
Museo Arqueológico
Lago Grande
Cat. de San Isidro
RETIRO
Parque del Retiro
LATINA
Observatorio Astronómico
MORATALAZ
VICÁLVARO
CAMPAMENTO
ARGANZUELA
PUENTE VALLECAS
CARABANCHEL BAJO
USERA
PALOMERAS
CUATRO VIENTOS
ENTREVÍAS
VALLECAS
CARABANCHEL ALTO
ORCASITAS
SAN FERMÍN
Arroyo de Butarque
VILLAVERDE
Canal del Manzanares
633 Canteras de Vallecas
Cumbres de Vallecas 655
VILLAVERDE BAJO
Leganés
IV
ATHÊNAI
(ATHENS)
Amarúsion
Ērákleion
Petrúpolis
Néa Filadélfeia
Néa Iōnía
Néa Liósia
Chalándrion
Dafníon
PERISTÉRION
Galatsíon
Psychikón
Hagía Paraskevé
Chaïdárion
Aigáleō
Cholargós
Hagía Barbara
Ethnikón Muséion
Lykabēttós
Ilisós
Zōgrafos
Korydallós
Panepistēmíoe
Thēseion
Byzantinon Muséio
Nikaia
Távros
Akropolis
Stadio
Keratsínion
Hágios Ioánnis Rentes
Kaisarianē
Moné Kaisarian
Kallithéa
Drapetsõna
Néon Fáleron
Moscháton
Byrōn
Ymēttós
Evzonos 1026
Órmos Faleru
Néa Smyrnē
PEIRAIEVS
(PIRAEUS)
Palaión Fáleron
Eliúpolis
Kalamákion
Argyrúpolis
Sarōnikòs Kólpos
Aerolimēn Hellenikón
Hellēnikón
Ymēttós
V
MOSKVA
(MOSCOW)
Starbejevo
Dolgoprudnyj
Veški
KALININGRAD
Novoarchangel'skoje
Čelobitjevo
Kurkino
Chimki
LIANOZOVO
MYTIŠČI
Suchodnja
KRASNO-OKT'ABRSKIJ
BESKUDNIKOVO
Cev. port
Novobratcevskij
Družba
NOVOCHOVRINO
DEGUNINO
Chimkinskoje vdchr.
MEDVEDKOVO
Mitino
CHIMKI-CHOVRINO
BRATCEVO
BABUŠKIN
Krasnogorsk
TUŠINO
PkiO im. Dzerzinskogo
ROSTOKINO
Kanal im. Moskvy
PETROVSKO-RAZUMOVSKOJE
Moskva
Jauza
OSTANKINO
BOGORODSKOJE
GOLJANOVO
STROGINO
POKROVSKO-STREŠNEVO
Stadion Dinamo
Vostočnyj
Rubl'ovo
TROICE-LYKOVO
PKiO Sokol'niki
ČERKIZOVO
IZMAJLOVO
SEREBR'ANYJ BOR
CHOROŠOVO
Ippodrom
Izmajlovskij PKiO
TATAROVO
MNEVNIKI
Zoo
Reutov
IVANOVSKOJE
Bol'šoj Teatr
Kreml'
Mavzolej V.I.Lenina
NOVOGIREJEVO
KRYLATSKOJE
Zapadn.port
PEROVO
FILI-MAZILOVO
Tret'jakovskaja galereja
KUSKOVO
KARAČAROVO
VEŠN'AKI
Novo-ivanovskoje
KUNC'OVO
LUŽNIKI
Stadion im. Lenina
NOVYJE KUZ'MINKI
Kosino
KOŽUCHOVO
VYCHINO
DAVYDKOVO
L'UBERCY
MATVEJEVSKOJE
MTU im. Lomonosova
Južn.port
KUZ'MINKI
AMINJEVO
TEKSTIL'ŠČIKI
RAMENKA
L'UBLINO
CER'OMUŠKI
NAGATINO
OČAKOVO
JUGO-ZAPAD
KOLOMENSKOJE
NIKOL'SKOJE
SADOVNIKI
Mesč'orskij
BAT'UNINO
NIKULINO
ZIL
Z'UZINO
D'AKOVSKOJE
TROPAR'OVO
Peredelkino
KAPOTN'A
SABUROVO
Solncevo
DEREVLEVO
BRATEJEVO
Dzeržinskij
ČERTANOVO
LENINO
BORISOVO
UZKOJE
T'OPLYJ STAN
POKROVSKOJE
JASENEVO
KRASNYJ STROITEL
BIR'UL'OVO
Sosenki
Michajlovskoje
Bitca
Vidnoje
Pol'any
Butovo
Petrovskoje

1 : 225,000

0 2.5 5 7.5 10 Kilometers

0 2.5 5 7.5 Statute Miles

One inch to 3.6 miles

NORWEGIAN SEA
Lofoten Basin
Norwegian Basin
Arctic Circle
ICELAND
Reykjavík
Reykjanes Ridge
Iceland Basin
Mid-Atlantic Ridge
Rockall Plateau
ATLANTIC OCEAN
West European Basin
Iberian Basin
Azores Plateau
Canary Basin
Bay of Biscay
British Isles
UNITED KINGDOM
Scotland
England
Wales
IRELAND
North Sea
English Channel
Skagerrak
Kattegat
DENMARK
NETHERLANDS
BELGIUM
FRANCE
GERMANY
CZECH REP.
SWITZERLAND
AUSTRIA
SPAIN
PORTUGAL
ITALY
Adriatic Sea
Tyrrhenian Sea
Ligurian Sea
Corse
Sardegna
Sicilia
Baleares
MEDITERRANEAN
MOROCCO
ALGERIA
TUNISIA
High Atlas
Saharan Atlas
Tell Atlas
LONDON
PARIS
MADRID
BERLIN
ROMA
Madeira (Port.)
Is. Canarias (Spain)

1:13,500,000 — 0 100 200 300 400 500 Kilometers; 0 100 200 300 400 Statute Miles

One inch to 213 miles

Conversion meters – feet see page 48

Barents Sea
White Sea
Kol'skij p-ov
p-ov Kanin
o.Kolgujev
RUSSIA
KAZAKHSTAN
UZBEKISTAN
TURKMENISTAN
FINLAND
ESTONIA
LATVIA
LITHUANIA
BELARUS
UKRAINE
MOLDAVIA
ROMANIA
BULGARIA
GEORGIA
ARMENIA
AZERBAIJAN
TURKEY
SYRIA
IRAQ
IRAN
CYPRUS
LEBANON
Gulf of Finland
Ladožskoje oz.
Onežskoje oz.
Black Sea
Azovskoje more
Caspian Sea
Aral'skoje more
Kara-Bogaz-Gol
Aegean Sea
Caucasus Mts.
Elburz Mts.
Taurus Mts.
Pontic Mts.
Balkan Mts.
Rhodope Mts.
Krym
Ustjurt
Prikaspijskaja nizmennost'
Severnyje uvaly
Timanskij krjaž
Ural
Volga
Don
Dnepr
Ob
Persian Gulf
MOSKVA (MOSCOW)
ST.PETERBURG (ST.PETERSBURG)
ARCHANGEL'SK
MURMANSK
HELSINKI
TALLINN (REVAL)
RIGA
VILNIUS
MINSK
KIJEV
CHIŞINAU (KIŠINJOV)
BUCUREŞTI (BUCHAREST)
SOFIJA (SOFIA)
ISTANBUL
ANKARA
TBILISI
JEREVAN
BAKU
TEHRAN (TEHERAN)
BAGHDAD
DIMASHQ
BAYRŪT
LEVKOSIA (NICOSIA)
ATHENAI (ATHENS)

1 to Russia

BARENTS SEA
NORWEGIAN SEA
Iceland
ICELAND
Spitsbergen
Arctic Circle
Vatnajökull
Nordaustlandet
Vestspitsbergen
Lofoten
Vesterålen
Finnmarksvidda
Norrbotten
Västerbotten
BOTHNIA
MURMANSK
Oulu
Luleå
Umeå
Bodø
Kemi
Tromsø

 1: 4,500,000 0 50 100 150 200 Kilometers 0 50 100 150 Statute Miles One inch to 71 miles Conversion meters – feet see page 48

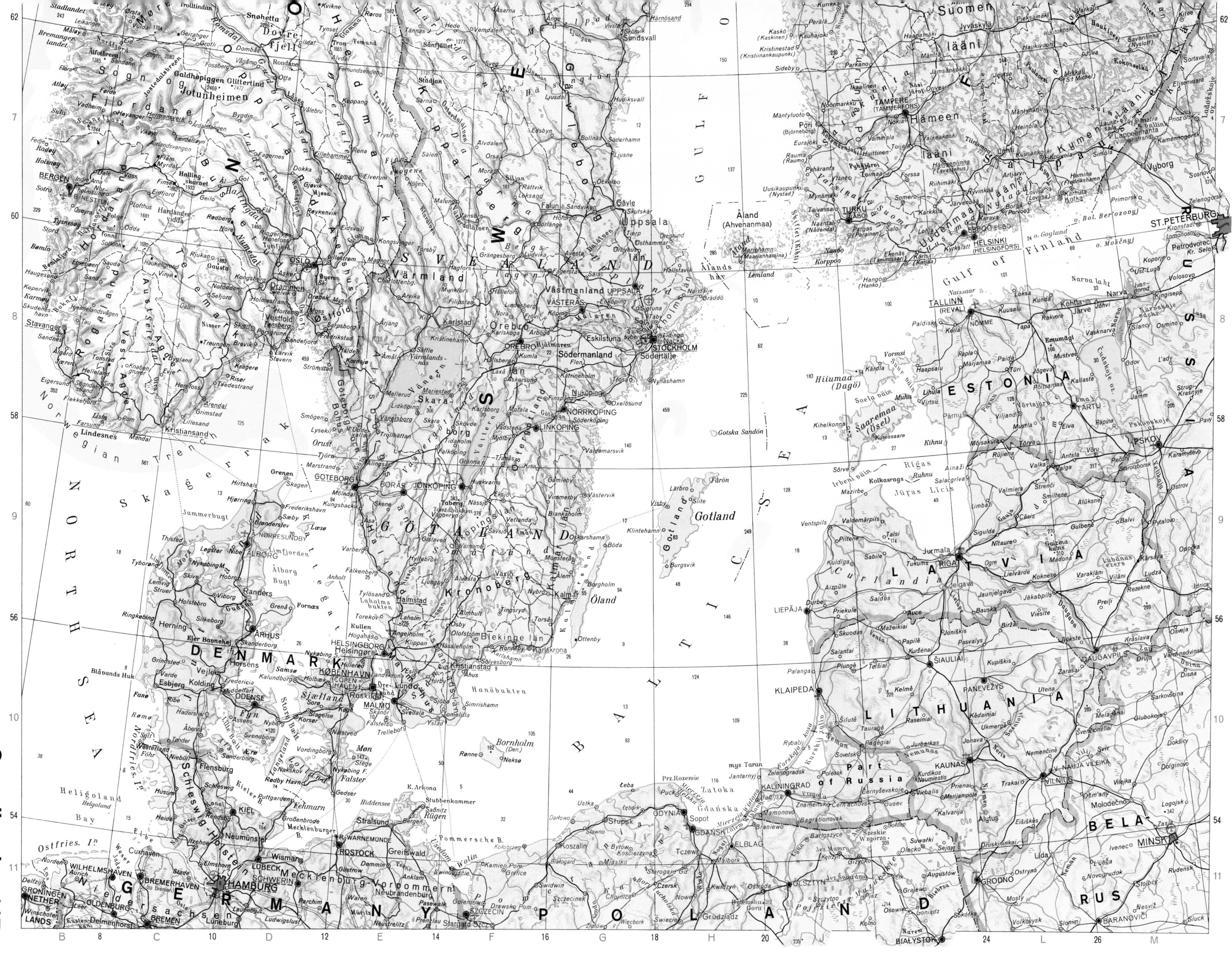

NORTH SEA
BALTIC SEA
GULF OF BOTHNIA
Gulf of Finland
Skagerrak
Kattegat
DENMARK
SWEDEN
ESTONIA
LATVIA
LITHUANIA
POLAND
GERMANY
RUSSIA
Part of Russia
BELARUS
Gotland
Öland
Bornholm
Åland (Ahvenanmaa)
Hiiumaa (Dagö)
Saaremaa (Ösel)
STOCKHOLM
OSLO
KØBENHAVN (COPENHAGEN)
HELSINKI (HELSINGFORS)
TALLINN (REVAL)
RIGA
VILNIUS
MINSK
ST.PETERBURG
GÖTEBORG
MALMÖ
BERGEN
Stavanger
Kristiansand
TURKU (ÅBO)
TAMPERE (TAMMERFORS)
KAUNAS
KLAIPEDA
LIEPĀJA
KALININGRAD
GDAŃSK
GDYNIA
SZCZECIN
ROSTOCK
LÜBECK
HAMBURG
KIEL
BREMEN
BREMERHAVEN
WILHELMSHAVEN
ÅRHUS
ÅLBORG
ODENSE
UPPSALA
NORRKÖPING
LINKÖPING
JÖNKÖPING
ÖREBRO
VÄSTERÅS
PSKOV
GRODNO
BIAŁYSTOK
DAUGAVPILS
ŠIAULIAI
PANEVĖŽYS
TARTU

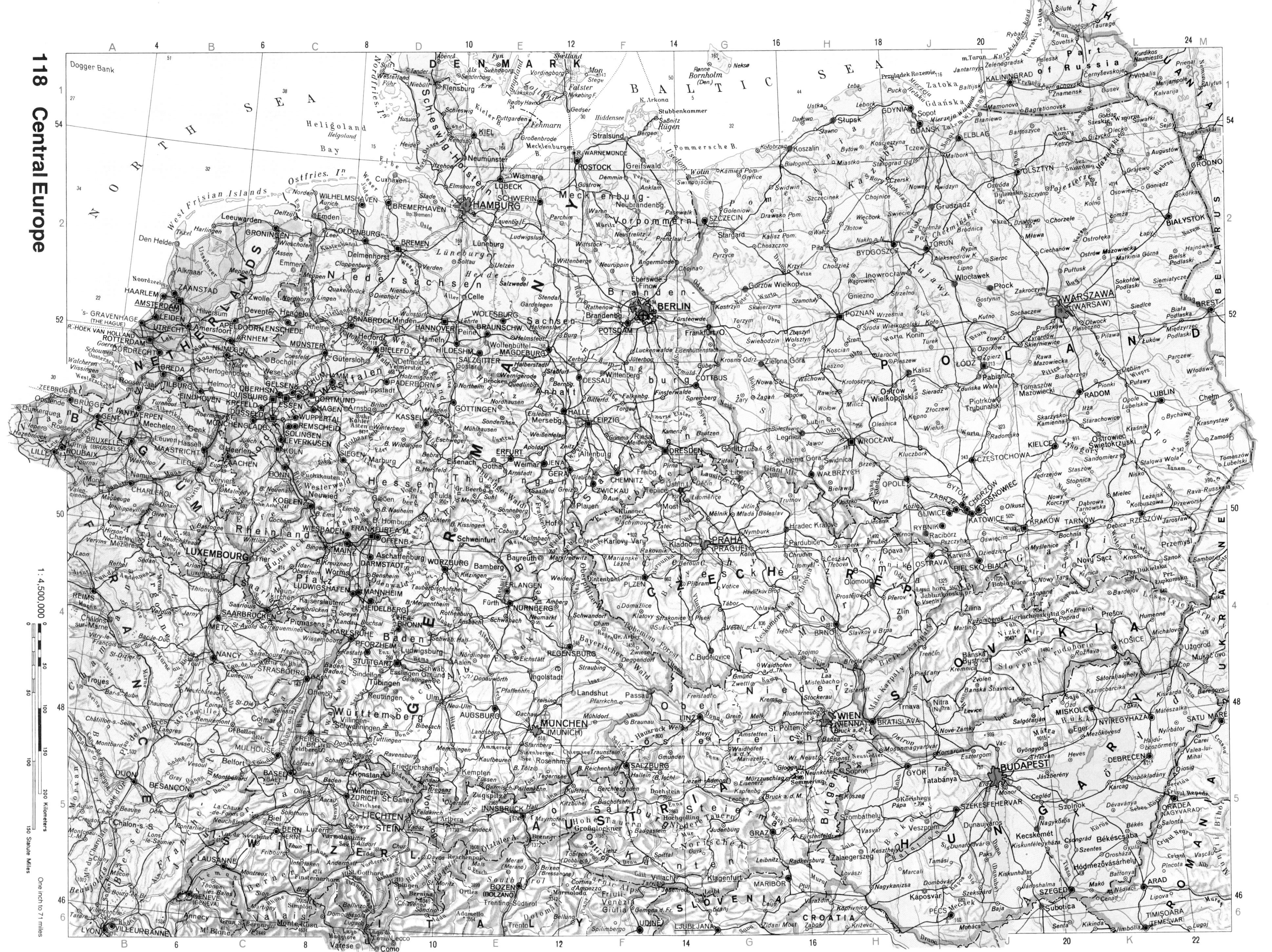

BERLIN
WARSZAWA (WARSAW)
PRAHA (PRAGUE)
WIEN (VIENNA)
BUDAPEST
MÜNCHEN (MUNICH)
HAMBURG
BRATISLAVA
LUXEMBOURG
AMSTERDAM
BRUXELLES (BRUSSEL)
LJUBLJANA
KALININGRAD
GDAŃSK
SZCZECIN
POZNAŃ
WROCŁAW
KRAKÓW
ŁÓDŹ
LUBLIN
DRESDEN
LEIPZIG
STUTTGART
NÜRNBERG
SALZBURG
GRAZ
BERN
ZÜRICH
STRASBOURG
KÖLN
BALTIC SEA
NORTH SEA
DENMARK
NETHERLANDS
BELGIUM
FRANCE
SWITZERLAND
LIECHTENSTEIN
AUSTRIA
SLOVENIA
CROATIA
HUNGARY
SLOVAKIA
CZECH REPUBLIC
POLAND
GERMANY
ITALY
ROMANIA
UKRAINE
BELARUS
LITHUANIA
Part of Russia
Dogger Bank
Heligoland Bay
West Frisian Islands
1 : 4,500,000
0 50 100 150 200 Kilometers
0 50 100 150 Statute Miles
One inch to 71 miles

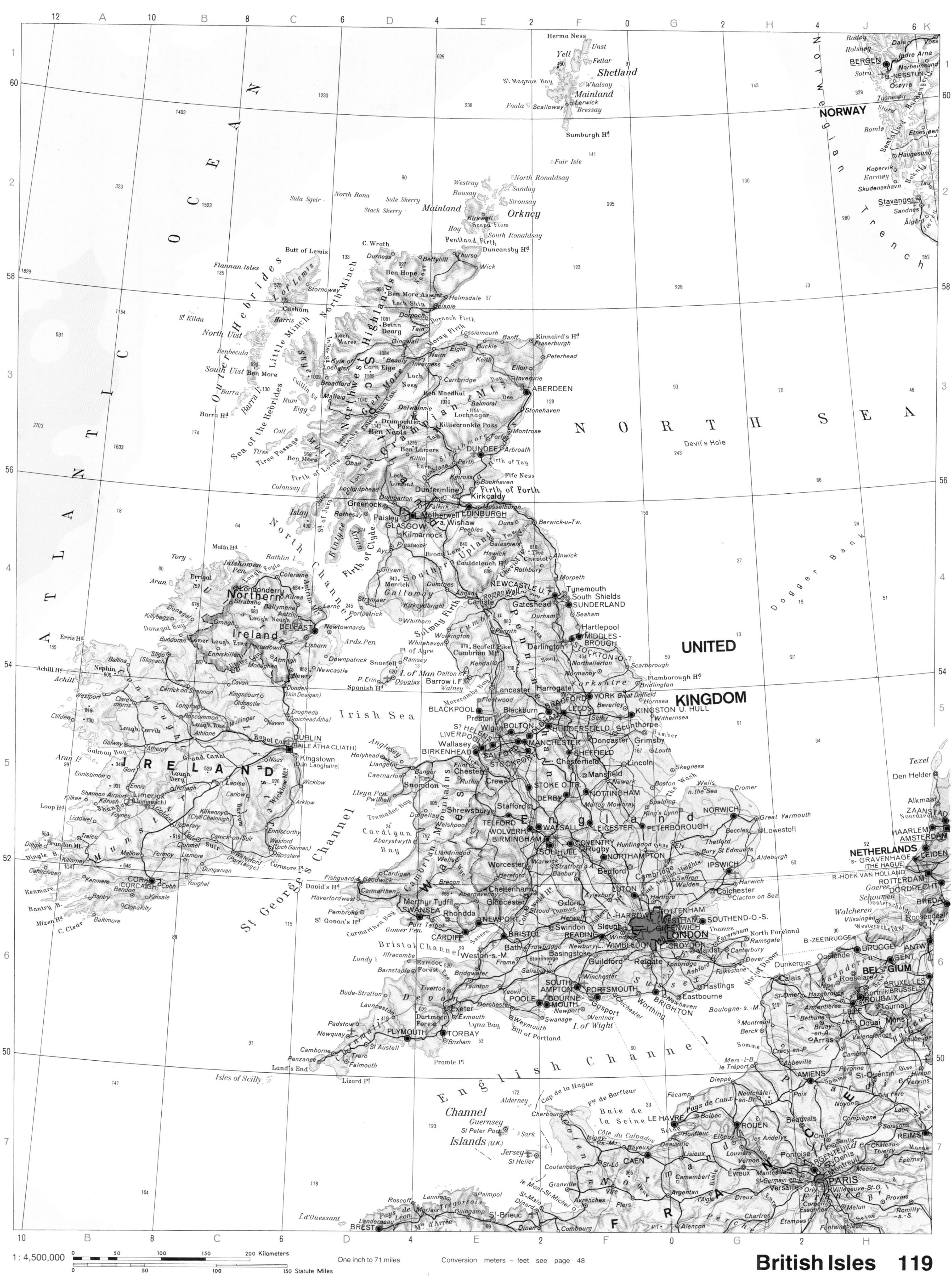
ATLANTIC OCEAN
NORTH SEA
NORWAY
Norwegian Trench
UNITED KINGDOM
IRELAND
Northern Ireland
NETHERLANDS
BELGIUM
FRANCE
Shetland
Mainland
Orkney
Outer Hebrides
Isle of Lewis
North Uist
South Uist
Inner Hebrides
Northwest Highlands
Grampian Mts.
Southern Uplands
Pennine Chain
Cambrian Mountains
North Channel
Irish Sea
St. George's Channel
Bristol Channel
English Channel
Channel Islands (U.K.)
Guernsey
Jersey
Isles of Scilly
I. of Man
I. of Wight
Dogger Bank
Devil's Hole
EDINBURGH
GLASGOW
ABERDEEN
DUNDEE
BELFAST
DUBLIN
CORK
NEWCASTLE
LIVERPOOL
MANCHESTER
LEEDS
SHEFFIELD
BIRMINGHAM
BRISTOL
CARDIFF
SWANSEA
PLYMOUTH
SOUTHAMPTON
PORTSMOUTH
LONDON
NORWICH
IPSWICH
BERGEN
AMSTERDAM
ROTTERDAM
BRUXELLES (BRUSSEL)
PARIS
ROUEN
LE HAVRE
AMIENS
LILLE
BREST

1: 4,500,000

0 50 100 150 200 Kilometers

0 50 100 150 Statute Miles

One inch to 71 miles

Conversion meters – feet see page 48

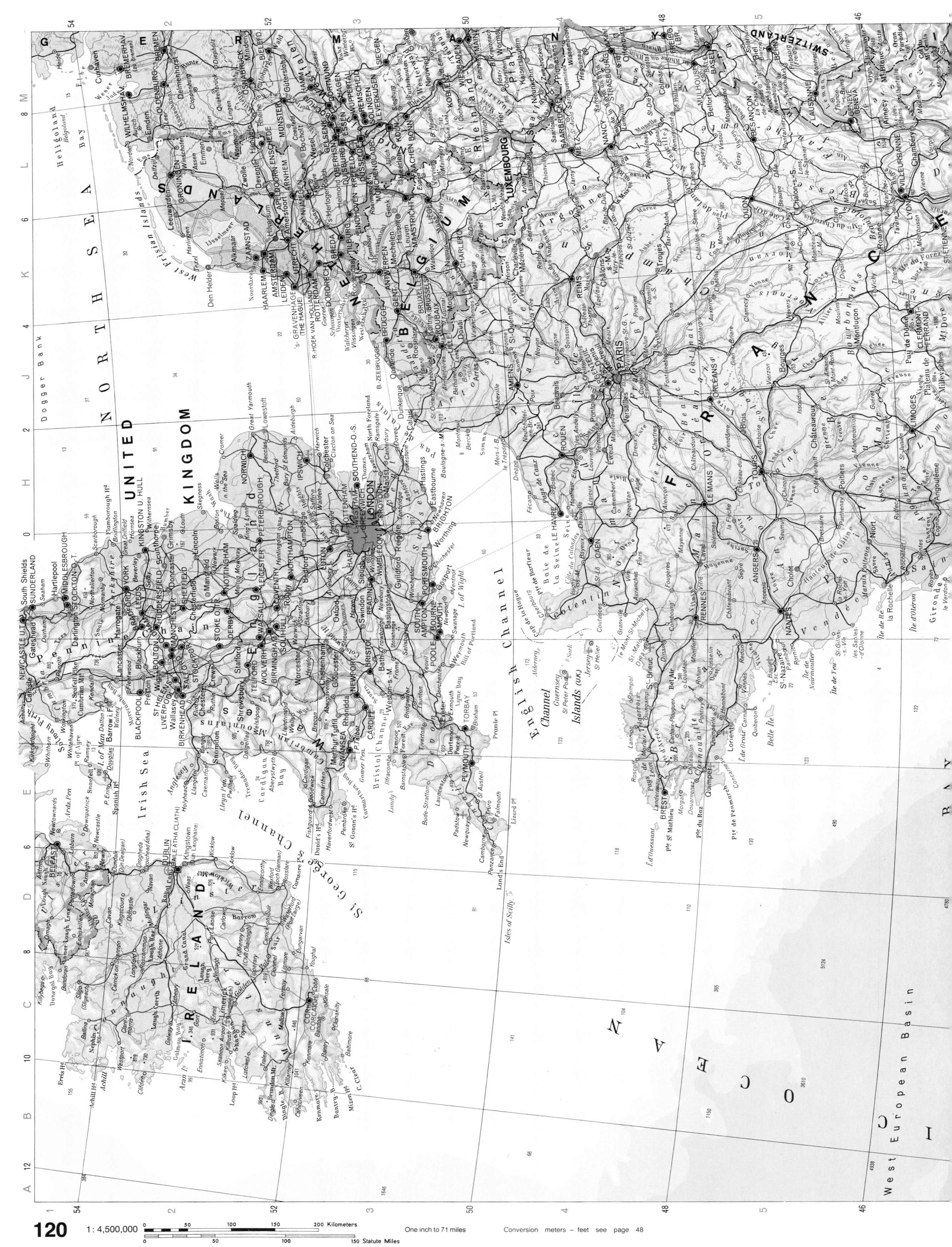
NORTH SEA
UNITED KINGDOM
English Channel
Irish Sea
St George's Channel
Bristol Channel
IRELAND
FRANCE
BELGIUM
LUXEMBOURG
PARIS
LONDON
BRUXELLES
AMSTERDAM
DUBLIN
West European Basin
Dogger Bank

1: 4,500,000

0 50 100 150 200 Kilometers

0 50 100 150 Statute Miles

One inch to 71 miles

Conversion meters – feet see page 48

ATLANTIC
MONACO
NICE
Cannes
Antibes
TOULON
MARSEILLE
AIX-EN-PROVENCE
Avignon
Arles
NÎMES
MONTPELLIER
Golfe du Lion
PERPIGNAN
TOULOUSE
ANDORRA
BARCELONA
BADALONA
HOSPITALET DE LLOBREGAT
TARRAGONA
LÉRIDA
ZARAGOZA
PAMPLONA
SAN SEBASTIÁN
BILBAO
VITORIA
SANTANDER
BARACALDO
BURGOS
VALLADOLID
LEÓN
OVIEDO
GIJÓN
LA CORUÑA
VIGO
Orense
SALAMANCA
MADRID
VALENCIA
ALICANTE
ELCHE
MURCIA
CARTAGENA
ALBACETE
ALMERÍA
GRANADA
MÁLAGA
CÓRDOBA
SEVILLA
JEREZ DE LA FRONTERA
CÁDIZ
HUELVA
BADAJOZ
LISBOA (LISBON)
Setúbal
PORTO
Coimbra
Mallorca
PALMA
Menorca
Ibiza
Formentera
Islas Baleares
MEDITERRANEAN SEA
Algerian Basin
(ALGIERS)
AL-JAZĀ'IR
WAHRĀN (ORAN)
TANJAH (TANGER)
TITWĀN (TETOUAN)
Ceuta (Spain)
Melilla (Spain)
Gibraltar (U.K.)
Strait of Gibraltar
MOROCCO
ALGERIA
PORTUGAL
SPAIN

GERMANY
SWITZERLAND
AUSTRIA
SLOVENIA
CROATIA
BOSNIA
HERCEGOVINA
ALGERIA
TUNISIA
SAN MARINO
MONACO
VATICAN CITY
MALTA
LIGURIAN SEA
TYRRHENIAN SEA
ADRIATIC SEA
IONIAN
MEDITERRANEAN
MÜNCHEN
WIEN
BRATISLAVA
SALZBURG
INNSBRUCK
GRAZ
LJUBLJANA
ZAGREB
TRIESTE
MILANO
TORINO
GENOVA
VENEZIA
BOLOGNA
FIRENZE
ROMA
NAPOLI
BARI
TARANTO
PALERMO
MESSINA
CATANIA
SIRACUSA
CAGLIARI
SASSARI
LYON
MARSEILLE
TOULON
NICE
GENÈVE
BERN
ZÜRICH
TUNIS
SPLIT
Sardegna
Corsica
Elba
Golfo di Gènova
Golfo di Venezia
Golfo di Taranto
Golfo di Squillace
Isole Eòlie o Lipari
Canale di Tunisi

1: 4,500,000 — 0 50 100 150 200 Kilometers — 0 50 100 150 Statute Miles — One inch to 71 miles

ROMANIA
MOLDAVA
UKRAINE
BULGARIA
MACEDONIA
ALBANIA
GREECE
TURKEY
BLACK SEA
AEGEAN SEA
Marmara Denizi
Transilvania
Kosovo
Makedonia
Chalkidikē
Sporades
Kyklades
Dōdekanēsos
Krētē
Levantine Basin
BUCUREŞTI (BUCHAREST)
BEOGRAD (BELGRADE)
SOFIJA (SOFIA)
SKOPJE
TIRANË (TIRANA)
ATHĒNAI (ATHENS)
THESSALONIKĒ (SALONIKA)
İSTANBUL
CHIŞINĂU
ODESSA
CONSTANŢA
VARNA
BURGAS
PLOVDIV
CLUJ-NAPOCA
TIMIŞOARA (TEMESVAR)
CRAIOVA
IAŞI
GALAŢI
BRĂILA
BURSA
İZMİR
ESKİŞEHİR
ANTALYA
ĒRAKLEION
20
22
24
26
28
30
32
J
K
L
M
N
O
P
2
3
4
5
6
7
8
36
38
40
42
44
46

Conversion meters – feet see page 48

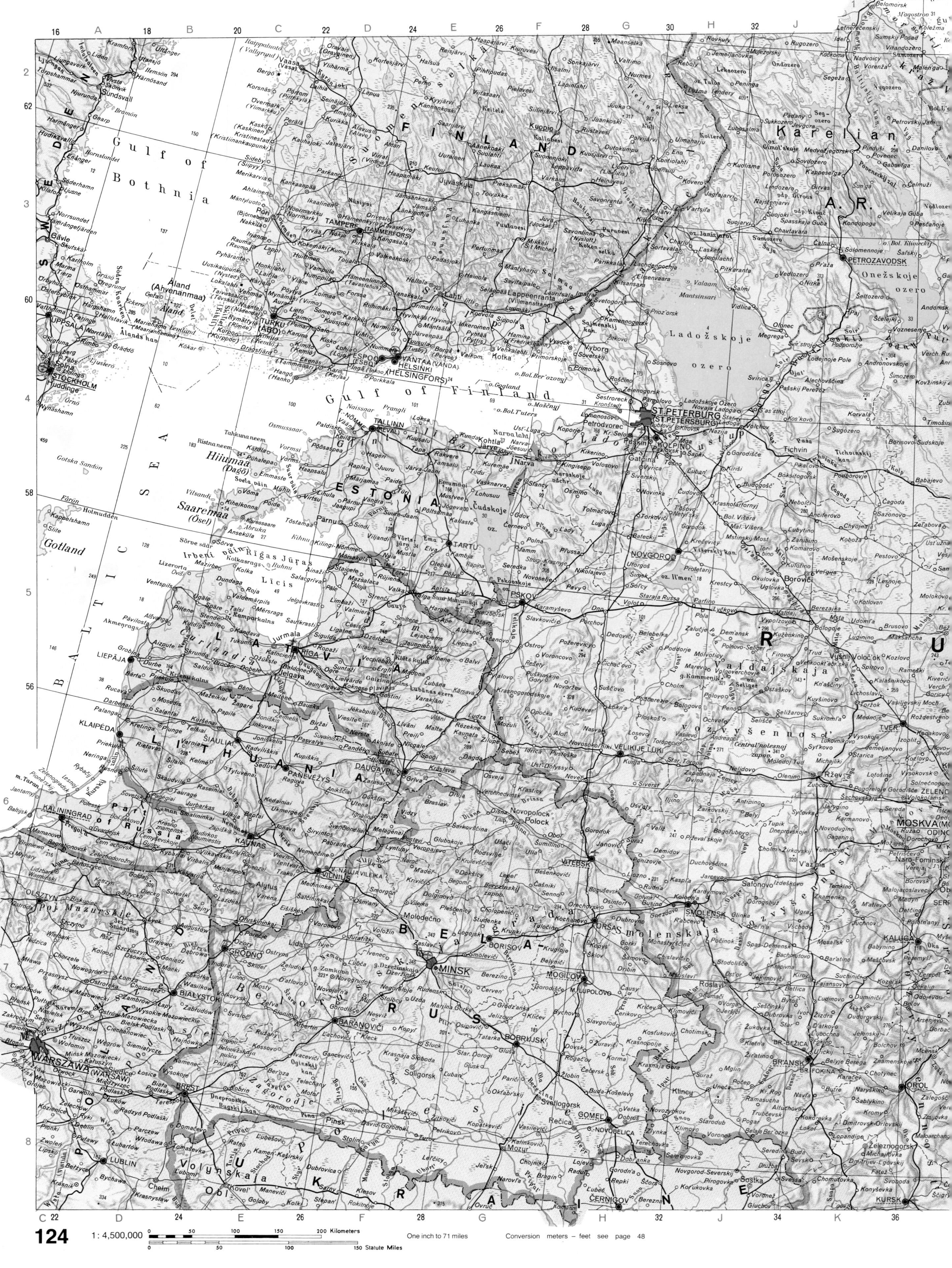
Gulf of Bothnia
Gulf of Finland
BALTIC SEA
FINLAND
ESTONIA
LATVIA
LITHUANIA
BELARUS
Kaliningrad Part of Russia
Karelian A.R.
Ladožskoje ozero
Onežskoje ozero
Gotland
Åland (Ahvenanmaa)
Hiiumaa (Dagö)
Saaremaa (Ösel)
Rīgas Jūras Līcis
Čudskoje oz.
STOCKHOLM
HELSINKI (HELSINGFORS)
TALLINN (REVAL)
RIGA
VILNIUS
MINSK
ST.PETERSBURG
MOSKVA
WARSZAWA (WARSAW)
KALININGRAD
KAUNAS
TURKU (ÅBO)
TAMPERE (TAMMERFORS)
PETROZAVODSK
NOVGOROD
PSKOV
TARTU
VITEBSK
SMOLENSK
GOMEL'
BREST
GRODNO
1: 4,500,000
Kilometers
Statute Miles
One inch to 71 miles
Conversion meters – feet see page 48

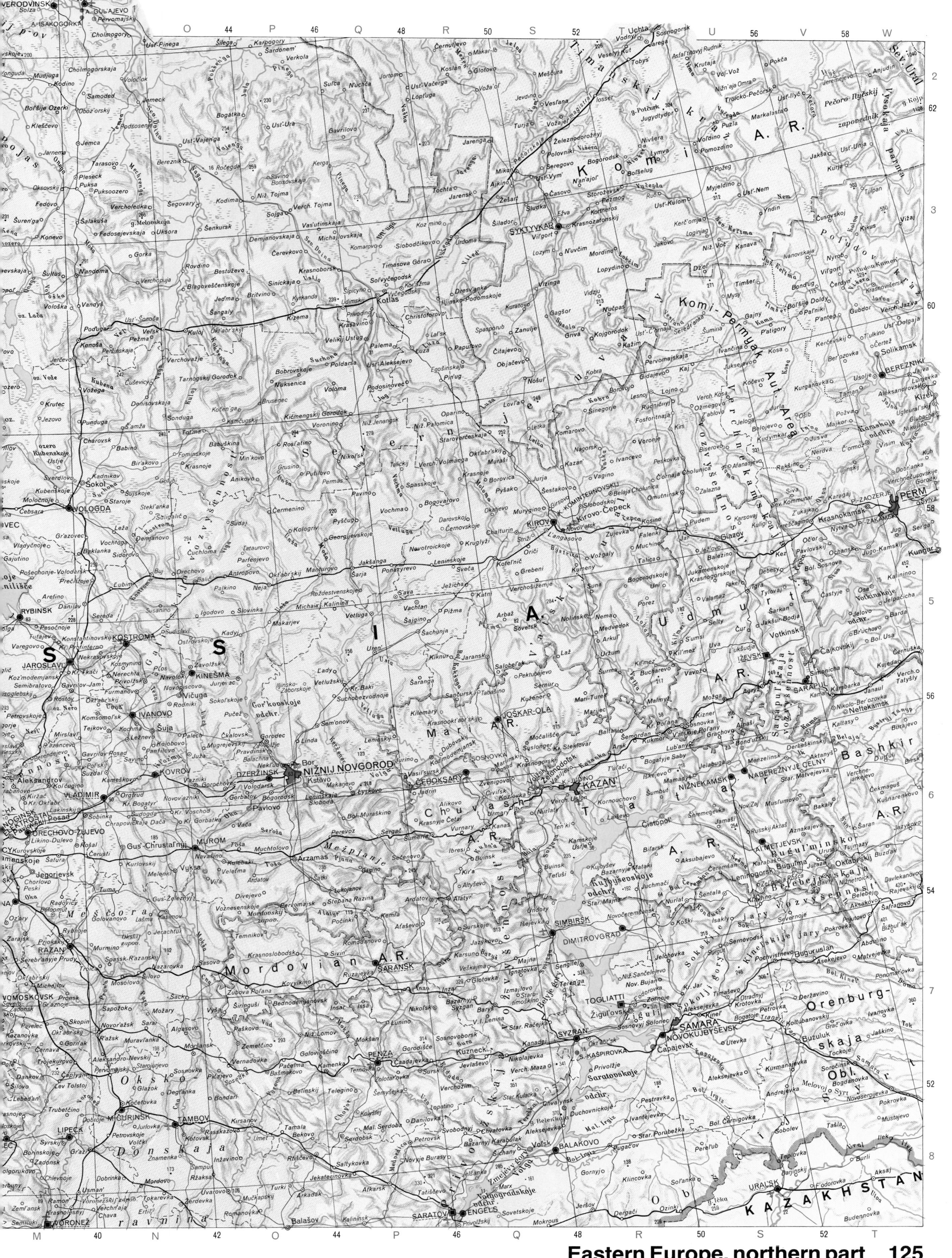

ARCHANGEL'SK
Komi A. R.
SYKTYVKAR
Kotlas
Komi-Permyak Aut. Area
Severnje Uvaly
Timanskij kr'až
BEREZNIKI
Solikamsk
PERM
KIROV
VOLOGDA
RYBINSK
JAROSLAVL'
KOSTROMA
KINEŠMA
IVANOVO
S S
I A
Udmurt A. R.
IŽEVSK
Mari A.R.
JOŠKAR-OLA
NIŽNIJ NOVGOROD
DZERŽINSK
KOVROV
VLADIMIR
MUROM
Arzamas
ČEBOKSARY
Chuvash A. R.
KAZAN'
Tatar A. R.
NABEREŽNYJE ČELNY
NIŽNEKAMSK
Bashkir A. R.
Mordovian A.R.
SARANSK
RJAZAN'
SIMBIRSK
DIMITROVGRAD
TOGLIATTI
SAMARA
NOVOKUJBYŠEVSK
SYZRAN'
PENZA
TAMBOV
MIČURINSK
LIPECK
VORONEŽ
SARATOV
ENGELS
BALAKOVO
Orenburgskaja Obl.
URAL'SK
KAZAKHSTAN

Volynskaja Obl.
POLAND
UKRAINE
MOLDAVA
ROMANIA
BULGARIA
GREECE
TURKEY
HUNG.
Crimea
BLACK SEA
AEGEAN SEA
AZOVSK
MOR
KIJEV
ČERNIGOV
LUCK
ROVNO
ŽITOMIR
LVOV
TERNOPOL
CHMEL'NICKIJ
VINNICA
BELAJA CERKOV
ČERKASSY
KREMENČUG
POLTAVA
SUMY
CHARKOV
KIROVOGRAD
DNEPRODZERŽINSK
DNEPROPETROVSK
NOVOMOSKOVSK
PAVLOGRAD
KRIVOJ ROG
ZAPOROŽJE
NIKOPOL
MELITOPOL
NIKOLAJEV
CHERSON
ODESSA
CHIŞINĂU
BELZY
BENDER
TIRASPOL
ČERNOVCY
SIMFEROPOL
SEVASTOPOL
Jalta
Feodosija
Kerč
CLUJ-NAPOCA
TÎRGU MUREŞ
IAŞI
BACĂU
SIBIU
BRAŞOV
PITEŞTI
PLOIEŞTI
BUZĂU
BRĂILA
GALAŢI
BUCUREŞTI (BUCHAREST)
CONSTANŢA
Tulcea
Delta Dunării
RUSE (RUSČUK)
PLEVEN
Varna
Burgas
STARA ZAGORA
PLOVDIV (FILIPOPOL)
EDIRNE
İSTANBUL
Marmara Denizi
BURSA
İZMİT
SAKARYA (ADAPAZARI)
ZONGULDAK
KASTAMONU
SAMSUN
ANKARA
ESKİŞEHİR
KÜTAHYA
BALIKESİR
MANİSA
İZMİR (SMYRNA)
KIRIKKALE
ÇORUM
Lesbos (Mytilēnē)
Lēmnos
Thásos
Samothrákē
Chíos

1: 4,500,000 0 50 100 150 200 Kilometers 0 50 100 150 Statute Miles
One inch to 71 miles Conversion meters - feet see page 48

KAZAKHSTAN
RUSSIA
GEORGIA
ARMENIA
AZERBAIJAN
CASPIAN SEA
Kalmyk A.R.
Chechen-Ingush A.R.
Dagestan A.R.
North Ossetian A.R.
Kabardino-Balkar A.R.
Karachayevo-Cherkess Aut. Reg.
Adygei Aut. Reg.
Abkhaz A.R.
Adjarian A.R.
South Ossetian Aut. Reg.
Nakhichevan A.R.
Nagorno-Karabagh Aut. Reg.
Ryn-peski
Prikaspijskaja nizmennost'
Nogajskaja step'
Stavropol'skaja vozvyšennost'
Kumo-Manyčskaja vpadina
Ergeni
Kurinskaja kosa
SARATOV
ENGEL'S
VORONEŽ
KAMYŠIN
VOLGOGRAD
VOLŽSKIJ
LUGANSK
ROSTOV-NA-DONU
NOVOČERKASSK
ŠACHTY
VOLGODONSK
KRASNODAR
STAVROPOL'
ARMAVIR
NEVINNOMYSSK
P'ATIGORSK
KISLOVODSK
NAL'ČIK
GROZNYJ
VLADIKAVKAZ
MACHAČKALA
ASTRACHAN'
GURJEV
AKTAU
SUMGAIT
BAKU
TBILISI
RUSTAVI
KUTAISI
BATUMI
SUCHUMI
SOČI
JEREVAN
KIROVAKAN
G'ANDŽA
TRAB'ZON
ERZURUM
Elista
Derbent
g. Elbrus
Ararat

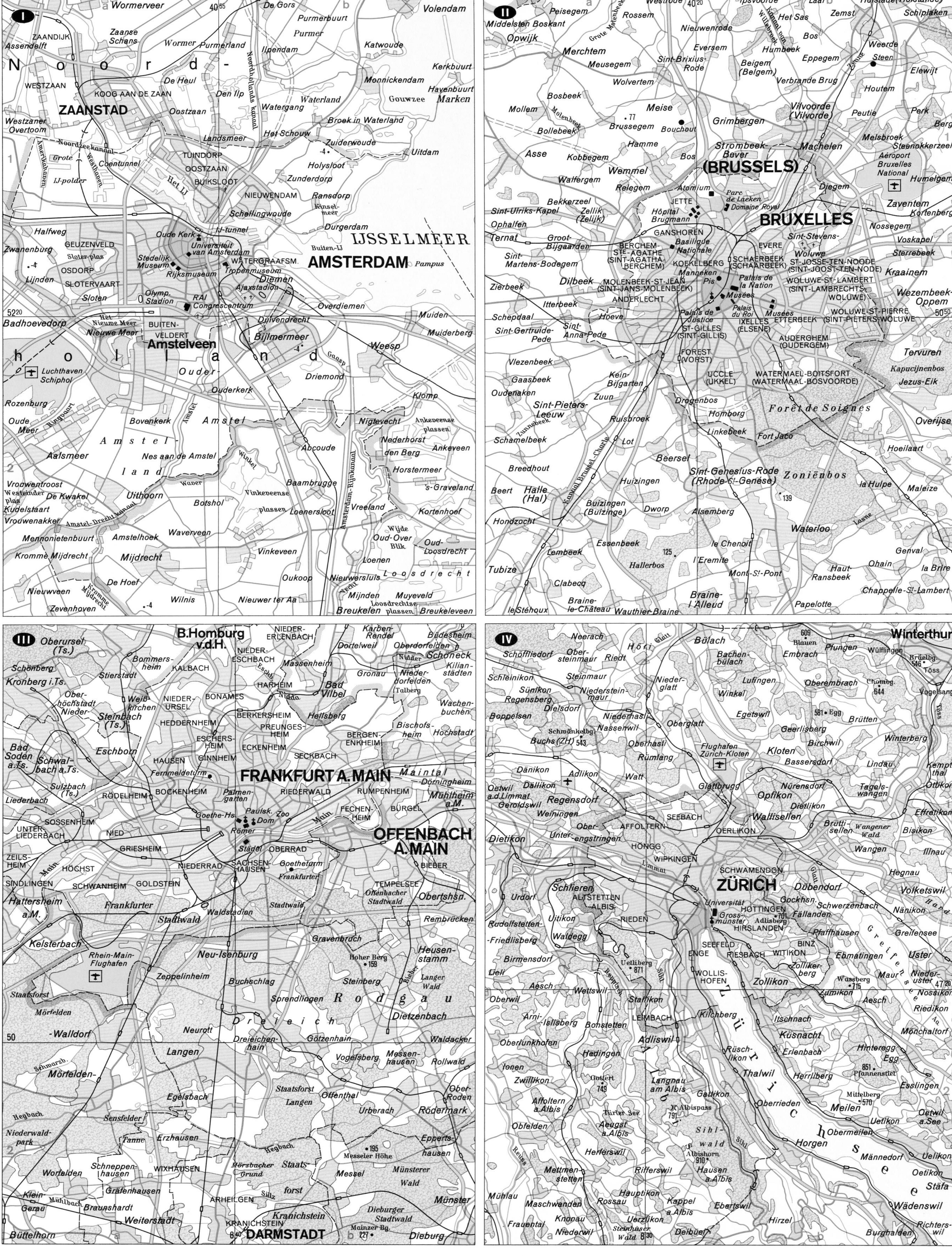

I
Wormerveer
Volendam
Zaanse Schans
ZAANDIJK
Assendelft
Purmerbuurt
Purmer
Wormer
Purmerland
Ilpendam
Katwoude
Noord-holland
WESTZAAN
KOOG AAN DE ZAAN
De Heul
Kerkbuurt
Monnickendam
Havenbuurt
Marken
Gouwzee
ZAANSTAD
Oostzaan
Den Ilp
Watergang
Waterland
Westzaner Overtoom
Broek in Waterland
Het Schouw
Zuiderwoude
Noordzeekanaal
Landsmeer
Uitdam
TUINDORP
OOSTZAAN
Coentunnel
Holysloot
BUIKSLOOT
Zunderdorp
IJ-polder
Het IJ
NIEUWENDAM
Ransdorp
Schellingwoude
Durgerdam
Halfweg
Oude Kerk
IJ-tunnel
IJSSELMEER
Zwanenburg
GEUZENVELD
Universiteit van Amsterdam
Buiten-IJ
Sloterplas
Stedelijk Museum
WATERGRAAFSM.
AMSTERDAM
Pampus
OSDORP
Rijksmuseum
Tropenmuseum
Lijnden
SLOTERVAART
Diemen
Ajaxstadion
Sloten
Olymp. Stadion
RAI Congrescentrum
Overdiemen
Badhoevedorp
Nieuwe Meer
BUITENVELDERT
Duivendrecht
Muiden
Muiderberg
Amstelveen
Bijlmermeer
Weesp
Luchthaven Schiphol
Ouder-Amstel
Ouderkerk
Driemond
Gaasp
Rozenburg
Klomp
Oude Meer
Bovenkerk
Amstel
Nigtevecht
Ankeveensche plassen
Amstelland
Abcoude
Nederhorst den Berg
Ankeveen
Aalsmeer
Nes aan de Amstel
Horstermeer
Vrouwentroost
Westeinder plas
De Kwakel
Uithoorn
Baambrugge
's-Graveland
Kudelstaart
Botshol
Vinkeveense plassen
Vreeland
Vrouwenakker
Amstel-Drecht kanaal
Loenersloot
Kortenhoef
Mennonietenbuurt
Amstelhoek
Waverveen
Wijde
Oud-Over
Blik
Oud-Loosdrecht
Kromme Mijdrecht
Mijdrecht
Vinkeveen
Loenen
De Hoef
Oukoop
Nieuwersluis
Loosdrecht
Nieuwveen
Wilnis
Nieuwer ter Aa
Mijnden
Muyeveld
Loosdrechtse plassen
Zevenhoven
Breukelen
Breukeleveen
II
Peisegem
Westrode
Ipsvoorde
Laar
Hofstade (Hofstande)
Middelsten Boskant
Rossem
Het Sas
Zemst
Schiplaken
Opwijk
Nieuwenrode
Bos
Merchtem
Eversem
Humbeek
Weerde
Steen
Meusegem
Sint-Brixius-Rode
Beigem (Belgem)
Eppegem
Elewijt
Wolvertem
Verbrande Brug
Houtem
Bosbeek
Meise
Vilvoorde (Vilvorde)
Peutie
Perk
Mollem
Brussegem
Bouchout
Grimbergen
Berg
Bollebeek
Hamme
Strombeek-Bever
Machelen
Melsbroek
Steenokkerzeel
Asse
Kobbegem
Bos
(BRUSSELS)
Aéroport Bruxelles National
Wemmel
Humelgem
Walfergem
Relegem
Atomium
Diegem
Bekkerzeel
Parc de Laeken
Domaine Royal
Zaventem
Sint-Ulriks-Kapel
Zellik (Zélik)
JETTE
Kortenberg
Ophalfen
Hôpital Brugmann
BRUXELLES
Nossegem
GANSHOREN
Ternat
Groot-Bijgaarden
Basilique Nationale
EVERE
Sint-Stevens-Woluwe
Voskapel
BERCHEM-STE-AGATHE (SINT-AGATHA-BERCHEM)
Sterrebeek
Sint-Martens-Bodegem
KOEKELBERG
SCHAERBEEK (SCHAARBEEK)
ST-JOSSE-TEN-NOODE (SINT-JOOST-TEN-NODE)
Manneken Pis
Dilbeek
MOLENBEEK-ST-JEAN (SINT-JANS-MOLENBEEK)
Palais de la Nation
WOLUWE-ST-LAMBERT (SINT-LAMBRECHTS-WOLUWE)
Kraainem
Zierbeek
Musées
Wezembeek-Oppem
ANDERLECHT
Itterbeek
Palais de Justice
Palais du Roi
Musées
ETTERBEEK
WOLUWE-ST-PIERRE (SINT-PIETERS-WOLUWE)
Schepdaal
Hoeve
ST-GILLES (SINT-GILLIS)
IXELLES (ELSENE)
Sint-Gertruide-Pede
Sint-Anna-Pede
AUDERGHEM (OUDERGEM)
FOREST (VORST)
Tervuren
Vlezenbeek
Kapucijnenbos
UCCLE (UKKEL)
WATERMAEL-BOITSFORT (WATERMAAL-BOSVOORDE)
Gaasbeek
Kein-Bijgaarten
Jezus-Eik
Oudenaken
Zuun
Drogenbos
Forêt de Soignes
Sint-Pieters-Leeuw
Homborg
Ruisbroek
Overijse
Linkebeek
Fort Jaco
Schamelbeek
Lot
Hoeilaart
Beersel
Breedhout
Sint-Genesius-Rode (Rhode-St-Genèse)
Zoniënbos
Halle (Hal)
Huizingen
la Hulpe
Maleize
Beert
Buizingen (Buizinge)
Dworp
Alsemberg
Hondzocht
Waterloo
Essenbeek
le Chenoit
Genval
Lembeek
Hallerbos
l'Eremite
Ohain
la Brire
Tubize
Mont-St-Pont
Haut-Ransbeek
Clabecq
Braine-le-Château
Braine-l'Alleud
Chappelle-St-Lambert
le Stéhoux
Wauthier-Braine
Papelotte
III
Oberursel (Ts.)
B.Homburg v.d.H.
NIEDER-ERLENBACH
Karben-Rendel
Bad Vilbel
Dortelweil
Bommersheim
NIEDER-ESCHBACH
Schöneck
Schönberg
KALBACH
Massenheim
Kronberg i.Ts.
Stierstadt
Gronau
Niederdorfelden
Kilianstädten
HARHEIM
Oberhöchstadt
Weißkirchen
BONAMES
NIEDER-URSEL
Nidda
Wachenbuchen
Steinbach (Ts.)
HEDDERNHEIM
BERKERSHEIM
Hellsberg
Bischofsheim
Hochstadt
PREUNGESHEIM
Bad Soden a.Ts.
Eschborn
ESCHERSHEIM
ECKENHEIM
BERGEN-ENKHEIM
Schwalbach a.Ts.
HAUSEN
GINNHEIM
SECKBACH
FRANKFURT A.MAIN
Maintal
Sulzbach (Ts.)
Fernmeldeturm
Dörnigheim
BOCKENHEIM
RIEDERWALD
RUMPENHEIM
Mühlheim a.M.
Liederbach
RÖDELHEIM
Palmengarten
FECHENHEIM
BÜRGEL
Goethe-Hs.
Paulsk.
Dom
Zoo
SOSSENHEIM
Main
UNTERLIEDERBACH
NIED
Römer
OFFENBACH A.MAIN
ZEILSHEIM
GRIESHEIM
Städel
OBERRAD
HÖCHST
NIEDERRAD
SACHSENHAUSEN
Goetheturm
BIEBER
SINDLINGEN
SCHWANHEIM
GOLDSTEIN
TEMPELSEE
Offenbacher Stadtwald
Obertshsn.
Hattersheim a.M.
Frankfurter Stadtwald
Waldstadion
Rembrücken
Kelsterbach
Gravenbruch
Rhein-Main-Flughafen
Neu-Isenburg
Heusenstamm
Hoher Berg
Zeppelinheim
Buchschlag
Steinberg
Langer Wald
Sprendlingen
Rodgau
Mörfelden
Dreieich
Dietzenbach
Walldorf
Neurott
Dreieichenhain
Götzenhain
Waldacker
Langen
Vogelsberg
Messenhausen
Rollwald
Mörfelden-
Staatsforst Langen
Ober-Roden
Egelsbach
Offenthal
Urberach
Rödermark
Sensfelder
Niederwald-park
Tanne
Erzhausen
Eppertshausen
Messeler Höhe
Worfelden
Schneppenhausen
WIXHAUSEN
Mörsbacher Grund
Staatsforst
Messel
Münsterer Wald
Gräfenhausen
Klein-Gerau
Braunshardt
ARHEILGEN
Kranichstein
Münster
Weiterstadt
KRANICHSTEIN
Dieburger Stadtwald
Büttelhorn
DARMSTADT
Mainzer Bg.
Dieburg
IV
Neerach
Höri
Bülach
Blauen
Pfungen
Winterthur
Schöfflisdorf
Obersteinmaur
Riedt
Bachenbülach
Embrach
Wülflingen
Schleinikon
Steinmaur
Niederglatt
Lufingen
Oberembrach
Töss
Sünikon
Niedersteinmaur
Regensberg
Dielsdorf
Winkel
Boppelsen
Niederhasli
Oberglatt
Egetswil
Egg
Brütten
Nassenwil
Buchs (ZH)
Oberhasli
Geerlisberg
Winterberg
Flughafen Zürich-Kloten
Birchwil
Rümlang
Kloten
Dänikon
Bassersdorf
Lindau
Adlikon
Watt
Kemptthal
Oetwil a.d.Limmat
Dällikon
Glattbrugg
Nürensdorf
Tagelswangen
Ottikon
Geroldswil
Regensdorf
Opfikon
Weiningen
Dietlikon
Effretikon
Ober-
AFFOLTERN
SEEBACH
Wallisellen
Brüttisellen
Dietikon
Unterengstringen
OERLIKON
Bisikon
HÖNGG
Wangen
WIPKINGEN
Illnau
Limmat
SCHWAMENDINGEN
Hegnau
Urdorf
Schlieren
ALTSTETTEN
ZÜRICH
Dübendorf
Volketswil
ALBIS-RIEDEN
Universität
Gockhsn.
Uitikon
Grossmünster
HOTTINGEN
Schwerzenbach
Nänikon
Rudolfstetten-Friedlisberg
Waldegg
HIRSLANDEN
Fällanden
Pfaffhausen
Greifensee
BINZ
Birmensdorf
SEEFELD
ENGE
RIESBACH
WITIKON
Ebmatingen
Uster
Uetliberg
Zollikerberg
Maur
WOLLISHOFEN
Zollikon
Aesch
Wettswil
Oberwil
Stallikon
Zumikon
Aesch
Nossikon
Riedikon
Arni-Islisberg
Bonstetten
LEIMBACH
Kilchberg
Itschnach
Mönchaltorf
Adliswil
Küsnacht
Oberlunkhofen
Hedingen
Erlenbach
Hinteregg
Rüschlikon
Thalwil
Egg
Zwillikon
Langnau am Albis
Herrliberg
Pfannenstiel
Gattikon
Esslingen
Affoltern a.Albis
Albispass
Oberrieden
Meilen
Obfelden
Aeugst a.Albis
Uetikon
Oetwil a.See
Sihlwald
Obermeilen
Horgen
Hedingen
Herferswil
Albishorn
Männedorf
Uelikon
Hausen a.Albis
Mettmenstetten
Rifferswil
Oetikon
Mühlau
Hauptikon
Stäfa
Maschwanden
Rossau
Kappel a.Albis
Ebertswil
Wädenswil
Knonau
Uerzlikon
Frauental
Hirzel
Niederwil
Steinhauser Wald
Deibüel
Burghalden
Richterswil
Zürichsee

Conversion meters – feet see page 48

1 : 225,000 — 0 2.5 5 7.5 Kilometers; 0 2.5 5 Statute Miles

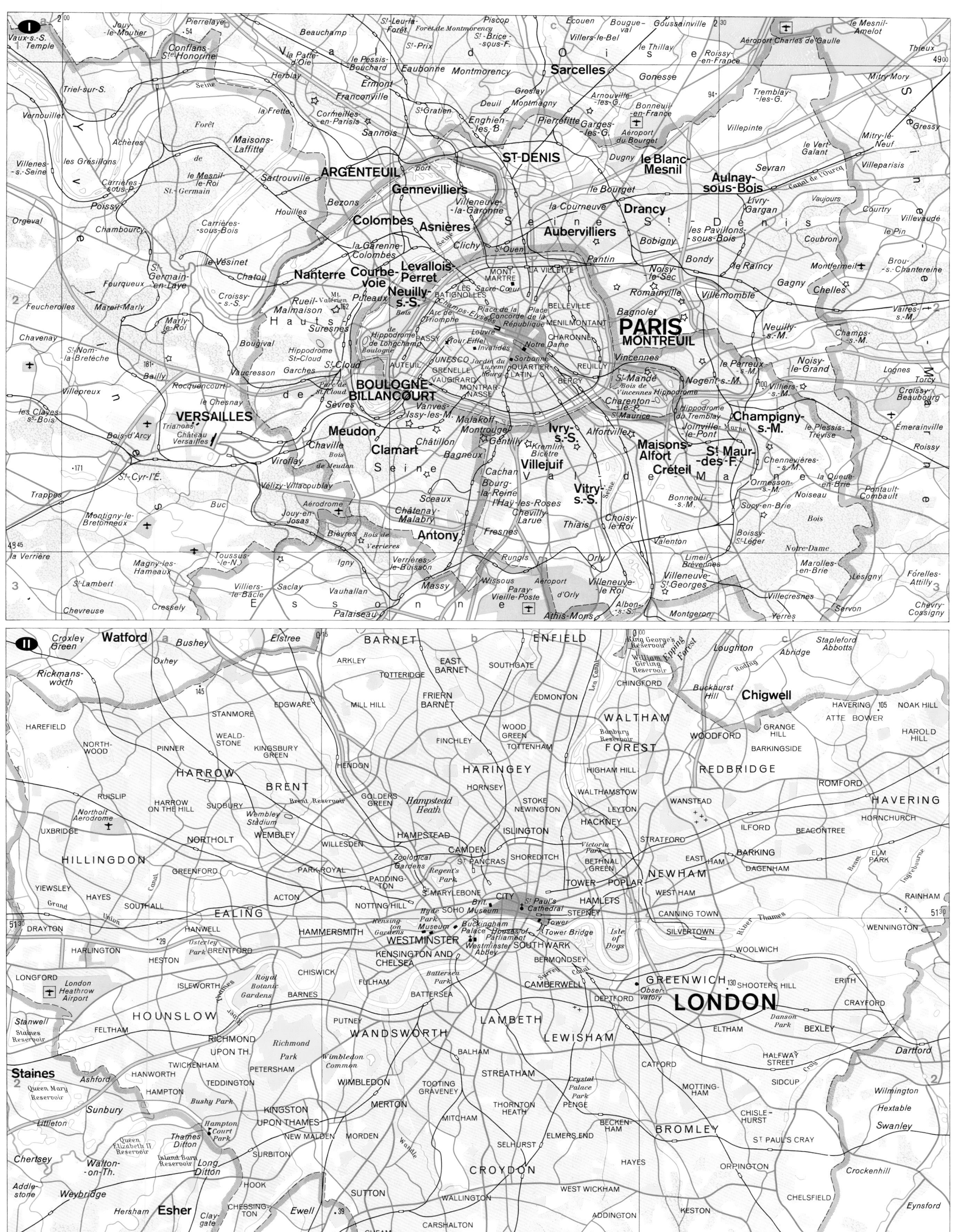

I
Vaux-s.-S.
Temple
Jouy-le-Moutier
Pierrelaye
Beauchamp
St-Leu-la-Forêt
Forêt de Montmorency
Piscop
St-Brice-sous-F.
Ecouen
Villiers-le-Bel
Bouqueval
Goussainville
le Mesnil-Amelot
Aéroport Charles de Gaulle
Conflans-Ste-Honorine
la Patte-d'Oie
le Plessis-Bouchard
St-Prix
Eaubonne
Montmorency
le Thillay
Roissy-en-France
Thieux
Herblay
Ermont
Sarcelles
Gonesse
Mitry-Mory
Triel-sur-S.
Franconville
Groslay
Montmagny
Arnouville-lès-G.
Tremblay-lès-G.
Vernouillet
la Frette
Cormeilles-en-Parisis
St-Gratien
Deuil
Enghien-les-B.
Pierrefitte
Garges-lès-G.
Bonneuil-en-France
Aéroport du Bourget
Villepinte
Gressy
Achères
Maisons-Laffitte
Sannois
ST-DENIS
Dugny
le Blanc-Mesnil
le Vert-Galant
Mitry-le-Neuf
Villenes-s.-Seine
les Grésillons
ARGENTEUIL
Sevran
Aulnay-sous-Bois
Villeparisis
Carrières-sous-P.
le Mesnil-le-Roi
St.-Germain
Sartrouville
Gennevilliers
Villeneuve-la-Garenne
le Bourget
Canal de l'Ourcq
Vaujours
Poissy
Houilles
Bezons
la Courneuve
Drancy
Livry-Gargan
Courtry
Villevaudé
Orgeval
Chambourcy
Carrières-sous-Bois
Colombes
Asnières
Aubervilliers
les Pavillons-sous-Bois
Coubron
le Pin
Clichy
St-Ouen
Bobigny
la Garenne-Colombes
le Vésinet
Chatou
Nanterre
Courbevoie
Levallois-Perret
MONTMARTRE
LA VILLETTE
Pantin
Noisy-le-Sec
Bondy
le Raincy
Montfermeil
Brou-s.-Chantereine
St-Germain-en-Laye
Fourqueux
Croissy-s.-S.
Rueil-Malmaison
Puteaux
Neuilly-s.-S.
BATIGNOLLES
Sacré Cœur
BELLEVILLE
Romainville
Villemomble
Gagny
Chelles
Feucherolles
Mareil-Marly
Marly-le-Roi
Hauts-de-Seine
Suresnes
Arc de Triomphe
Champs-Élysées
Place de la Concorde
Place de la République
MENILMONTANT
Bagnolet
PARIS
MONTREUIL
Neuilly-s.-M.
Vaires-s.-M.
Chavenay
Hippodrome de Longchamp
Bois de Boulogne
PASSY
Louvre
Tour Eiffel
Invalides
Notre Dame
CHARONNE
Champs-s.-M.
St-Nom-la-Bretèche
Bougival
Hippodrome St-Cloud
St-Cloud
AUTEUIL
UNESCO
Jardin du Luxembourg
Sorbonne
QUARTIER LATIN
Vincennes
le Perreux
Noisy-le-Grand
Lognes
Bailly
Vaucresson
Garches
GRENELLE
VAUGIRARD
REUILLY
Torcy
Villepreux
Rocquencourt
Parc de St-Cloud
BOULOGNE-BILLANCOURT
MONTPARNASSE
BERCY
St-Mandé
Bois de Vincennes
Hippodrome
Nogent-s.-M.
Villiers-s.-M.
Croissy-Beaubourg
les Clayes-s.-Bois
le Chesnay
Sèvres
Vanves
Issy-les-M.
Charenton-le-P.
St-Maurice
Hippodrome du Tremblay
Joinville-le-Pont
Champigny-s.-M.
VERSAILLES
Trianons
Château Versailles
Malakoff
Montrouge
Ivry-s.-S.
Alfortville
le Plessis-Trévise
Émerainville
Bois-d'Arcy
Meudon
Châtillon
Gentilly
Kremlin-Bicêtre
Maisons-Alfort
St-Maur-des-F.
Roissy
Chaville
Clamart
Bagneux
Villejuif
Créteil
Chennevières-s.-M.
Viroflay
Bois de Meudon
Cachan
Ormesson-s.-M.
la Queue-en-Brie
Trappes
St-Cyr-l'É.
Vélizy-Villacoublay
Bourg-la-Reine
Vitry-s.-S.
Pontault-Combault
Noiseau
Buc
Aérodrome
Sceaux
L'Haÿ-les-Roses
Bonneuil-s.-M.
Sucy-en-Brie
Montigny-le-Bretonneux
Jouy-en-Josas
Châtenay-Malabry
Chevilly-Larue
Thiais
Choisy-le-Roi
Bois
Bièvres
Bois de Verrières
Antony
Fresnes
Boissy-St-Léger
Valenton
Notre-Dame
la Verrière
Toussus-le-N.
Igny
Verrières-le-Buisson
Rungis
Orly
Limeil-Brévannes
Marolles-en-Brie
Lésigny
Férolles-Attilly
Magny-les-Hameaux
Saclay
Villiers-le-Bâcle
Vauhallan
Massy
Wissous
Paray-Vieille-Poste
Aéroport d'Orly
Villeneuve-le-Roi
Villeneuve-St-Georges
Villecresnes
St-Lambert
Chevreuse
Cressely
Palaiseau
Athis-Mons
Ablon-s.-S.
Montgeron
Yerres
Servon
Chevry-Cossigny
Essonne
Val-d'Oise
Val-de-Marne
Seine-St-Denis
Seine-et-Marne
Yvelines
II
Croxley Green
Watford
Bushey
Elstree
BARNET
ENFIELD
King George's Reservoir
William Girling Reservoir
Epping Forest
Loughton
Stapleford Abbotts
Abridge
Rickmansworth
Oxhey
ARKLEY
EAST BARNET
SOUTHGATE
TOTTERIDGE
CHINGFORD
Buckhurst Hill
Chigwell
HAREFIELD
STANMORE
EDGWARE
MILL HILL
FRIERN BARNET
EDMONTON
WALTHAM FOREST
HAVERING ATTE BOWER
NOAK HILL
NORTHWOOD
WEALDSTONE
PINNER
KINGSBURY GREEN
FINCHLEY
WOOD GREEN
TOTTENHAM
Banbury Reservoir
WOODFORD
GRANGE HILL
BARKINGSIDE
HAROLD HILL
HENDON
HARROW
BRENT
HARINGEY
HIGHAM HILL
REDBRIDGE
ROMFORD
HORNSEY
RUISLIP
HARROW ON THE HILL
SUDBURY
Brent Reservoir
GOLDERS GREEN
Hampstead Heath
STOKE NEWINGTON
WALTHAMSTOW
WANSTEAD
HAVERING
Northolt Aerodrome
Wembley Stadium
LEYTON
HORNCHURCH
UXBRIDGE
NORTHOLT
WEMBLEY
HAMPSTEAD
ISLINGTON
HACKNEY
ILFORD
BEACONTREE
WILLESDEN
CAMDEN
STRATFORD
HILLINGDON
Zoological Gardens
ST PANCRAS
SHOREDITCH
BETHNAL GREEN
EAST HAM
BARKING
GREENFORD
PARK ROYAL
Regent's Park
DAGENHAM
ELM PARK
YIEWSLEY
PADDINGTON
TOWER
POPLAR
NEWHAM
HAYES
ST MARYLEBONE
CITY
St Paul's Cathedral
HAMLETS
WEST HAM
RAINHAM
SOUTHALL
ACTON
NOTTING HILL
Brit. Museum
SOHO
STEPNEY
EALING
Hyde Park
Buckingham Palace
Houses of Parliament
Tower
Tower Bridge
CANNING TOWN
WENNINGTON
DRAYTON
HANWELL
HAMMERSMITH
WESTMINSTER
Westminster Abbey
Isle of Dogs
SILVERTOWN
HARLINGTON
Osterley Park
BRENTFORD
KENSINGTON AND CHELSEA
SOUTHWARK
BERMONDSEY
HESTON
WOOLWICH
River Thames
CHISWICK
Battersea Park
GREENWICH
Observatory
SHOOTERS HILL
ERITH
LONGFORD
London Heathrow Airport
ISLEWORTH
Royal Botanic Gardens
FULHAM
CAMBERWELL
BARNES
BATTERSEA
DEPTFORD
LONDON
CRAYFORD
HOUNSLOW
Stanwell
Staines Reservoir
FELTHAM
PUTNEY
LAMBETH
Danson Park
ELTHAM
BEXLEY
RICHMOND UPON TH.
Richmond Park
WANDSWORTH
LEWISHAM
Dartford
Wimbledon Common
BALHAM
HALFWAY STREET
Staines
Ashford
TWICKENHAM
PETERSHAM
CATFORD
HANWORTH
TEDDINGTON
WIMBLEDON
STREATHAM
SIDCUP
Queen Mary Reservoir
HAMPTON
TOOTING GRAVENEY
Crystal Palace Park
MOTTINGHAM
Wilmington
Bushy Park
Sunbury
KINGSTON UPON THAMES
MERTON
THORNTON HEATH
PENGE
Hextable
CHISLEHURST
Littleton
Hampton Court Park
MITCHAM
BECKENHAM
Swanley
BROMLEY
Queen Elizabeth II Reservoir
Thames Ditton
NEW MALDEN
MORDEN
SELHURST
ELMERS END
ST PAUL'S CRAY
Chertsey
Island Barn Reservoir
Long Ditton
SURBITON
HAYES
Walton-on-Th.
CROYDON
ORPINGTON
Crockenhill
Addlestone
Weybridge
HOOK
SUTTON
WALLINGTON
WEST WICKHAM
CHELSFIELD
Hersham
Esher
Claygate
CHESSINGTON
Ewell
ADDINGTON
KESTON
Eynsford
Byfleet
Oxshott
Epsom
CHEAM
CARSHALTON
PURLEY
SANDERSTEAD
FARNBOROUGH

1 : 225,000 — 0 2.5 5 7.5 10 Kilometers; 0 2.5 5 7.5 Statute Miles — One inch to 3.6 miles

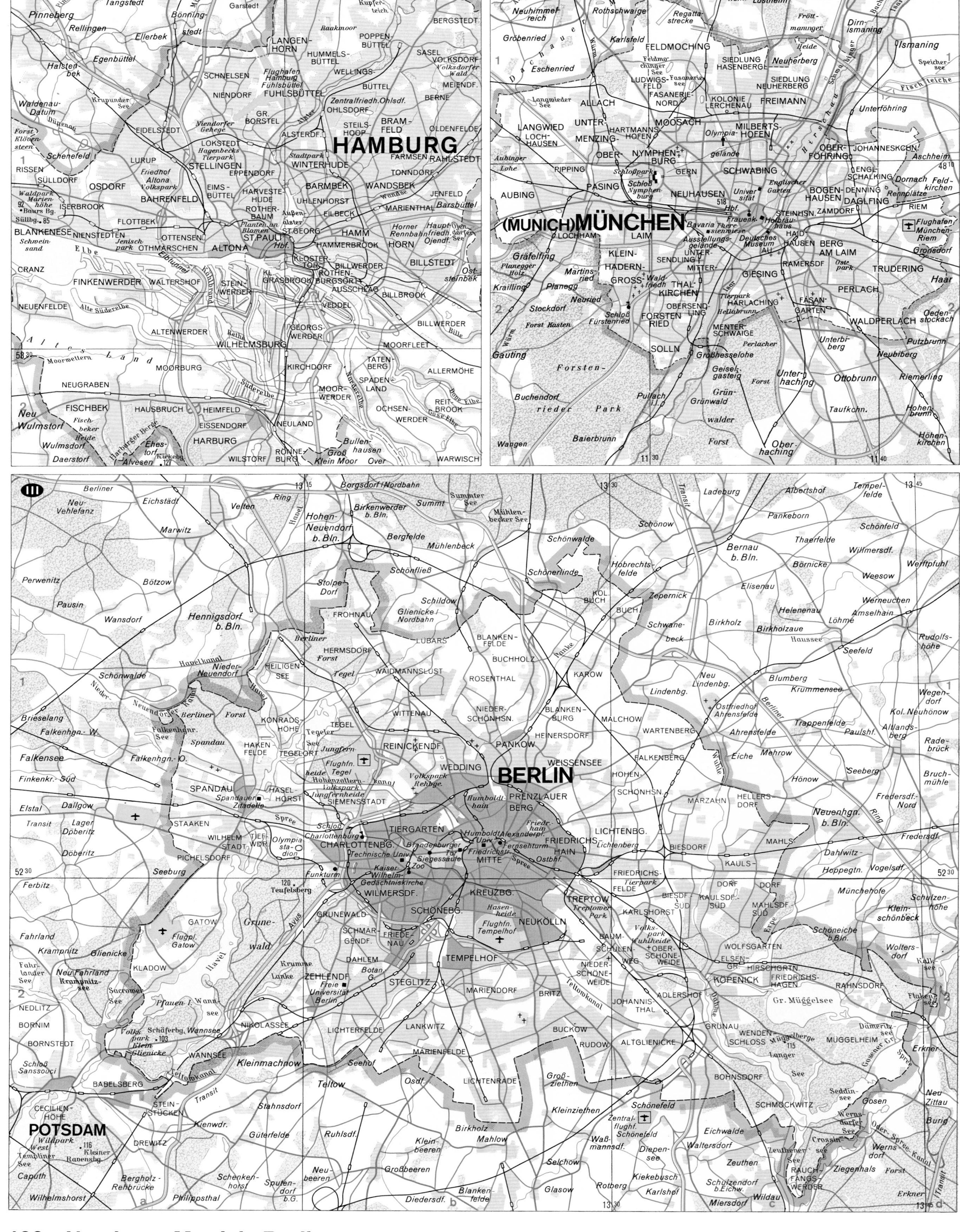
I
HAMBURG
Norderstedt
Pinneberg
Rellingen
Tangstedt
Ellerbek
Egenbüttel
Halstenbek
LANGENHORN
FUHLSBÜTTEL
OHLSDORF
BRAMFELD
WINTERHUDE
BARMBEK
WANDSBEK
EPPENDORF
STELLINGEN
LURUP
OSDORF
BAHRENFELD
RISSEN
BLANKENESE
ALTONA
ST.PAULI
ST.GEORG
HAMM
HORN
BILLSTEDT
FINKENWERDER
WALTERSHOF
WILHELMSBURG
ALTENWERDER
MOORBURG
NEUGRABEN
FISCHBEK
HAUSBRUCH
HEIMFELD
HARBURG
Neu Wulmstorf
BERGEDORF
II
(MUNICH)MÜNCHEN
Dachau
Oberschleißheim
Garching b.M.
Ismaning
FELDMOCHING
ALLACH
MOOSACH
UNTERMENZING
OBERMENZING
LANGWIED
AUBING
PASING
NYMPHENBURG
NEUHAUSEN
SCHWABING
BOGENHAUSEN
DAGLFING
LAIM
BERG AM LAIM
TRUDERING
PERLACH
GIESING
SENDLING
KLEINHADERN
GROSSHADERN
THALKIRCHEN
FORSTENRIED
SOLLN
Gräfelfing
Planegg
Gauting
Pullach
Grünwald
Unterhaching
Ottobrunn
Haar
III
BERLIN
Hennigsdorf b. Bln.
Hohen-Neuendorf b. Bln.
Bernau b. Bln.
SPANDAU
REINICKENDF.
PANKOW
WEDDING
WEISSENSEE
PRENZLAUER BERG
TIERGARTEN
CHARLOTTENBG.
MITTE
FRIEDRICHSHAIN
LICHTENBG.
KREUZBG.
WILMERSDF.
SCHÖNEBG.
NEUKÖLLN
TEMPELHOF
STEGLITZ
ZEHLENDF.
TREPTOW
KÖPENICK
Gr. Müggelsee
Falkensee
Kleinmachnow
Teltow
POTSDAM
Schönefeld
Grunewald
Wannsee

Conversion meters – feet see page 48

1: 225,000 0 2.5 5 7.5 10 Kilometers / 0 2.5 5 7.5 Statute Miles One inch to 3.6 miles

1 : 36,000,000
0 400 800 1200 km
0 400 800 Statute Miles One inch to 568 miles

Conversion meters – feet see page 48

BARENTS SEA
ARCTIC
Zeml'a Franz Joseph
Novaja Zemľa
Murmansk Rise
Novaya Zemlya Trough
Gulf of Bothnia
Gulf of Finland
SWEDEN
NORWAY
FINLAND
ESTONIA
TALLINN
HELSINKI
TURKU
TAMPERE
Oulu
MURMANSK
ARCHANGEL'SK
SEVERODVINSK
PETROZAVODSK
ST. PETERBURG
NOVGOROD
VOLOGDA
ČEREPOVEC
KOSTROMA
MOSKVA
KIROV
KAZAN'
SAMARA
TOGLIATTI
PENZA
SARANSK
SYZRAN'
UFA
PERM'
SYKTYVKAR
JEKATERINBURG
ČEL'ABINSK
MAGNITOGORSK
ORENBURG
URAL'SK
AKT'UBINSK
KUSTANAJ
KURGAN
TUMEN'
OMSK
PETROPAVLOVSK
KOKČETAV
CELINOGRAD
KARAGANDA
PAVLODAR
SEMIPALATINSK
UST'-KAMENOGORSK
BARNAUL
NOVOSIBIRSK
TOMSK
KEMEROVO
NOVOKUZNECK
KRASNOJARSK
ABAKAN
KANSK
NORIL'SK
SURGUT
NIŽNEVARTOVSK
VORKUTA
KZYL-ORDA
ČIMKENT
TAŠKENT
DŽAMBUL
BIŠKEK
ALMA-ATA
Arctic Circle
Jamal
Gydanskij p-ov
Obskaja guba
KAZAKHSTAN
UZBEKISTAN
TURKMENISTAN
RUSSIA
Aral'skoje more
oz. Balchaš
Betpak-Dala
Kyzylkum
Mujunkum
Baraba
Kulundinskaja step'
Západnyj Sajan
ALTAJ
MONGOLIA
CHINA
Evenki
Jamalo-Neneckij Aut. Area
Chanty-Mansijsk Aut. Area
Ural

1 : 13,500,000

0 100 200 300 400 500 Kilometers

0 100 200 300 400 Statute Miles

One inch to 213 miles

LAPTEV SEA
EAST SIBERIAN SEA
BERING SEA
SEA OF OKHOTSK
JAPAN SEA
Lomonosov Ridge
Novosibirskije o-va
o. Wrangel
Arctic Circle
Momskij chr.
Čerskogo
Verchojanskij chr.
chr. Suntar-Chajata
Jukagirskoje ploskogorje
Kolymskoje nagorje
Korjakskoje nagorje
Kamčatka
Sredinnyj chr.
Anadyrskij zaliv
Čukotskij p-ov
Chukot Aut. Area
Kolymskaja nizmennost'
Jano-Indigirskaja nizmennost'
Central'nojakutskaja ravnina
Aldanskoje nagorje
Stanovoj chr.
chr. Džagdy
Patomskoje nagorje
Jablonovyj chr.
Sachalin
Hokkaidō
Honshū
MANCHURIA
JAKUTSK
MAGADAN
PETROPAVLOVSK-KAMČATSKIJ
KOMSOMOLSK-NA-AMURE
CHABAROVSK
BLAGOVEŠČENSK
IRKUTSK
ULAN-UDE
ČITA
ULAANBAATAR (ULAN BATOR)
HARBIN
QIQIHAR (TSITSIHAR)
JILIN (KIRIN)
MUDANJIANG
USSURIJSK
VLADIVOSTOK
NACHODKA
JIAMUSI
HEGANG
JUŽNO-SACHALINSK
SAPPORO
ASAHIKAWA
HAKODATE
AOMORI
Lena
Amur
Kolyma
Aldan
Vil'uj
Indigirka
Jana
Olen'ok
Anadyr'
Occupied since 1945 by former U.S.S.R., claimed by Japan

Administrative units in the former Soviet Union:
1 Komi-Permyak Aut. Area
2 Udmurt A.S.S.R.
3 Mari A.S.S.R.
4 Chuvash A.S.S.R.
5 Mordovian A.S.S.R.
6 Tatar A.S.S.R.
7 Bashkir A.S.S.R.
8 Kirghiz S.S.R.
9 Gorno-Altai Aut. Reg.
10 Khakass Aut. Reg.
11 Ust-Ordynsky-Buryat Aut. Area
12 Aginsky-Buryat Aut. Area
13 Jewish Aut. Reg.

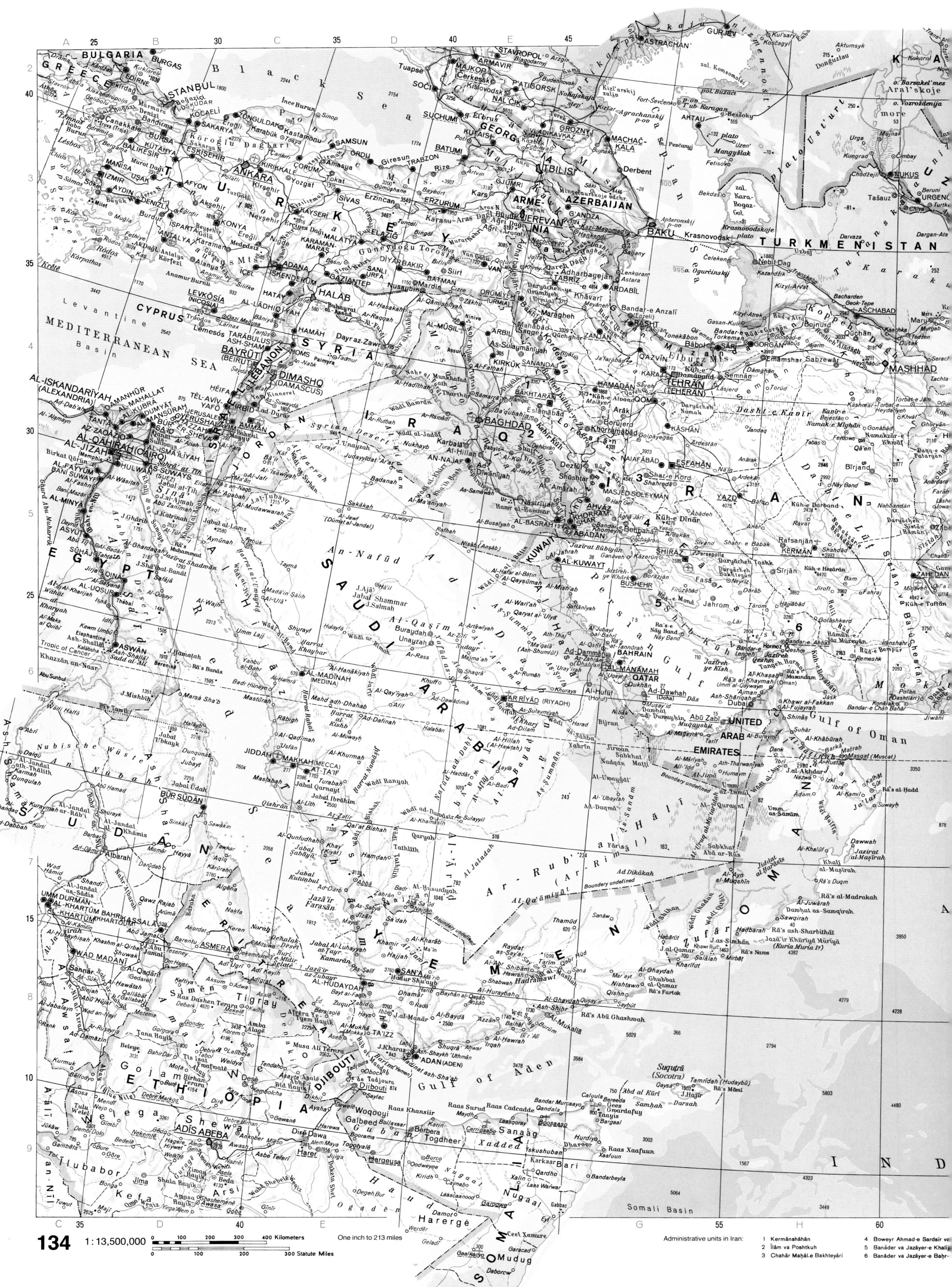

BULGARIA
GREECE
TURKEY
CYPRUS
MEDITERRANEAN SEA
Black Sea
Caspian Sea
GEORGIA
ARMENIA
AZERBAIJAN
TURKMENISTAN
SYRIA
LEBANON
ISRAEL
JORDAN
IRAQ
IRAN
KUWAIT
BAHRAIN
QATAR
UNITED ARAB EMIRATES
OMAN
SAUDI ARABIA
YEMEN
EGYPT
SUDAN
ERITREA
ETHIOPIA
DJIBOUTI
SOMALIA
Red Sea
Persian Gulf
Gulf of Oman
Gulf of Aden
Somali Basin
Administrative units in Iran:
1 Kermânshâhân
2 Îlâm va Poshtkuh
3 Chahâr Maḥâl.e Bakhteyârī
4 Boweyr Ahmad-e Sardsīr va
5 Banâder va Jazâyer-e Khalīj
6 Banâder va Jazâyer-e Baḥr-
1:13,500,000
One inch to 213 miles
400 Kilometers
300 Statute Miles

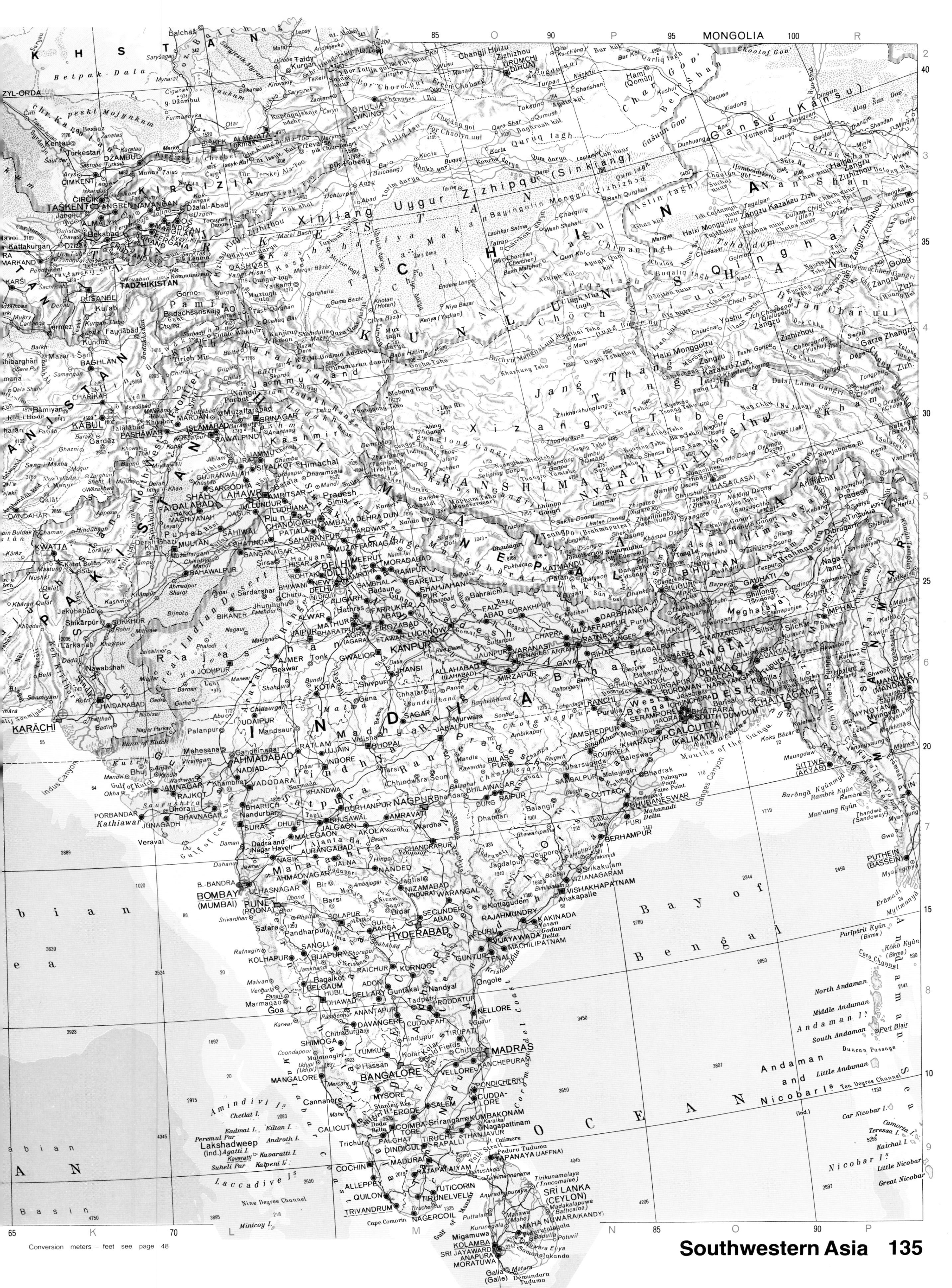
MONGOLIA
KIRGIZIA
TADZHIKISTAN
Uygur Zizhiqu (Sinkiang)
Xinjiang
Taklimakan
KUNLUN
Xizang (Tibet)
TRANSHIMALAYA
Nyanchhen-thangla
HIMALAYA
Qinghai
Gansu (Kansu)
ÜRÜMQI (DIHUA)
Turpan
Hami (Qomul)
Kašgar
Yarkand
Khotan (Hotan)
TAŠKENT
ALMA-ATA
BIŠKEK
DŽAMBUL
ČIMKENT
NAMANGAN
ANDIŽAN
OŠ
FERGANA
KOKAND
DUŠANBE
KABUL
CHARIKAR
Bamiyan
Gardez
Ghazni
Qandahar
KWATTA
PAKISTAN
AFGHANISTAN
PASHAWAR
ISLAMABAD
RAWALPINDI
SRINAGAR
Jammu and Kashmir
Karakoram
LAHAWR
FAISALABAD
MULTAN
BAHAWALPUR
SUKKHUR
HAIDARABAD
KARACHI
Punjab
Sind
Thar or Great Indian Desert
Rajasthan
AMRITSAR
LUDHIANA
CHANDIGARH
Simla
DEHRA DUN
MEERUT
DELHI (DILLI)
NEW DELHI (NI DILLI)
MORADABAD
BAREILLY
SHAHJAHANPUR
ALIGARH
AGRA
MATHURA
LUCKNOW
KANPUR
ALLAHABAD (ILAHABAD)
VARANASI (BENARES)
GORAKHPUR
PATNA
GAYA
Uttar Pradesh
Bihar
NEPAL
KATMANDU
Mt. Everest
Sagarmatha
BHUTAN
SIKKIM
Assam
Brahmaputra
GAUHATI
Shillong
Meghalaya
IMPHAL
Manipur
Mizoram
Tripura
BANGLADESH
DHAKA (DACCA)
CHATTAGAM
CALCUTTA (KALIKATA)
West Bengal
RANCHI
JAMSHEDPUR
Orissa
CUTTACK
BHUBANESWAR
PURI
SAMBALPUR
JAIPUR
AJMER
JODHPUR
BIKANER
UDAIPUR
KOTA
GWALIOR
JHANSI
INDIA
Madhya Pradesh
BHOPAL
INDORE
UJJAIN
JABALPUR
NAGPUR
RAIPUR
Gujarat
AHMADABAD
VADODARA
RAJKOT
JAMNAGAR
BHAVNAGAR
SURAT
Gulf of Kutch
Rann of Kutch
Gulf of Cambay
Kathiawar
Maharashtra
BOMBAY (MUMBAI)
PUNE (POONA)
NASIK
AURANGABAD
AHMADNAGAR
SOLAPUR
KOLHAPUR
Goa
Karnataka
BELGAUM
HUBLI
BANGALORE
MYSORE
MANGALORE
Andhra Pradesh
HYDERABAD
SECUNDERABAD
WARANGAL
VIJAYAWADA
GUNTUR
VISHAKHAPATNAM
RAJAHMUNDRY
KAKINADA
NELLORE
KURNOOL
Tamil Nadu
MADRAS
PONDICHERRY
SALEM
COIMBATORE
TIRUCHIRAPALLI
MADURAI
TUTICORIN
Kerala
CALICUT
COCHIN
ALLEPPEY
QUILON
TRIVANDRUM
Cape Comorin
Lakshadweep
Laccadive Is
Amindivi Is
Minicoy I.
Nine Degree Channel
Palk Strait
Gulf of Mannar
SRI LANKA (CEYLON)
JAPANAYA (JAFFNA)
Tirikunamalaya (Trincomalee)
Madakalapuwa (Batticaloa)
MAHA NUWARA (KANDY)
KOLAMBA
SRI JAYAWARDENEPURA
MORATUWA
Galla (Galle)
Bay of Bengal
Mouths of the Ganga
Ganges Canyon
Indus Canyon
OCEAN
Arabian Sea
Arabian Basin
Andaman Is
North Andaman
Middle Andaman
South Andaman
Port Blair
Little Andaman
Ten Degree Channel
Nicobar Is
Car Nicobar
Great Nicobar
Andaman and Nicobar Is
Andaman Sea
MYANMAR
SITTWE (AKYAB)
MANDALAY
PUTHEIN (BASSEIN)
Conversion meters – feet see page 48

BULGARIA
GREECE
BLACK SEA
TURKEY
CYPRUS
LEBANON
EGYPT
ISRAEL
JORDAN
SYRIA
AEGEAN SEA
MEDITERRANEAN SEA
Levantine Basin
Marmara Denizi
Antalya Körfezi
İSTANBUL
ANKARA
İZMIR
BURSA
KONYA
ADANA
ANTALYA
KAYSERİ
SAMSUN
ESKİŞEHİR
LEVKOSIA (LEFKOŞA) (NICOSIA)
BAYRŪT (BEIRUT)
DIMASHQ (DAMASCUS)
ḤALAB (ALEP)
ḤOMS (Emesa)
ḤAMĀH (Epiphania)
'AMMĀN
YERUSHALAYIM (JERUSALEM)
AL-QUDS
TEL-AVIV-YAFO (TEL AVIV-JAFFA)
AL-QAHIRAH (CAIRO)
AL-ISKANDARIYAH (ALEXANDRIA)
BŪR SA'ĪD (PORT SAID)
AS-SUWAYS (SUEZ)
AL-JIZAH
West Bank
Israeli occupied
Status to be determined
Krētē
Rhodes
Lésbos (Mytilēnē)
Chios
Sámos
Lēmnos
Kárpathos
Ródos
EDİRNE
Tekirdağ
Çanakkale
BALIKESİR
MANİSA
AYDIN
DENİZLİ
ISPARTA
AFYON
KÜTAHYA
SİVAS
KARAMANMARAŞ
HATAY (ANTAKYA)
İSKENDERUN
İÇEL (MERSİN)
TARSUS
AL-LĀDHIQĪYAH (LATAKIA)
TARĀBULUS ASH-SHAM (TRIPOLI)
ḤEFA (HAIFA)
GHAZZAH ('AZZA)
BE'ER-SHEVA (BEERSHEBA)
DUMYAT (DAMIETTA)
ṬANṬĀ
AL-MANṢŪRAH
AL-FAYYŪM
BANHĀ
Sinai
Ṣaḥrā' at-Tīh
Jabal at-Tīh
Jabal aṭ-Ṭubayq

1: 4,500,000 — 0 50 100 150 200 Kilometers — 0 50 100 150 Statute Miles

One inch to 71 miles

Conversion meters – feet see page 48

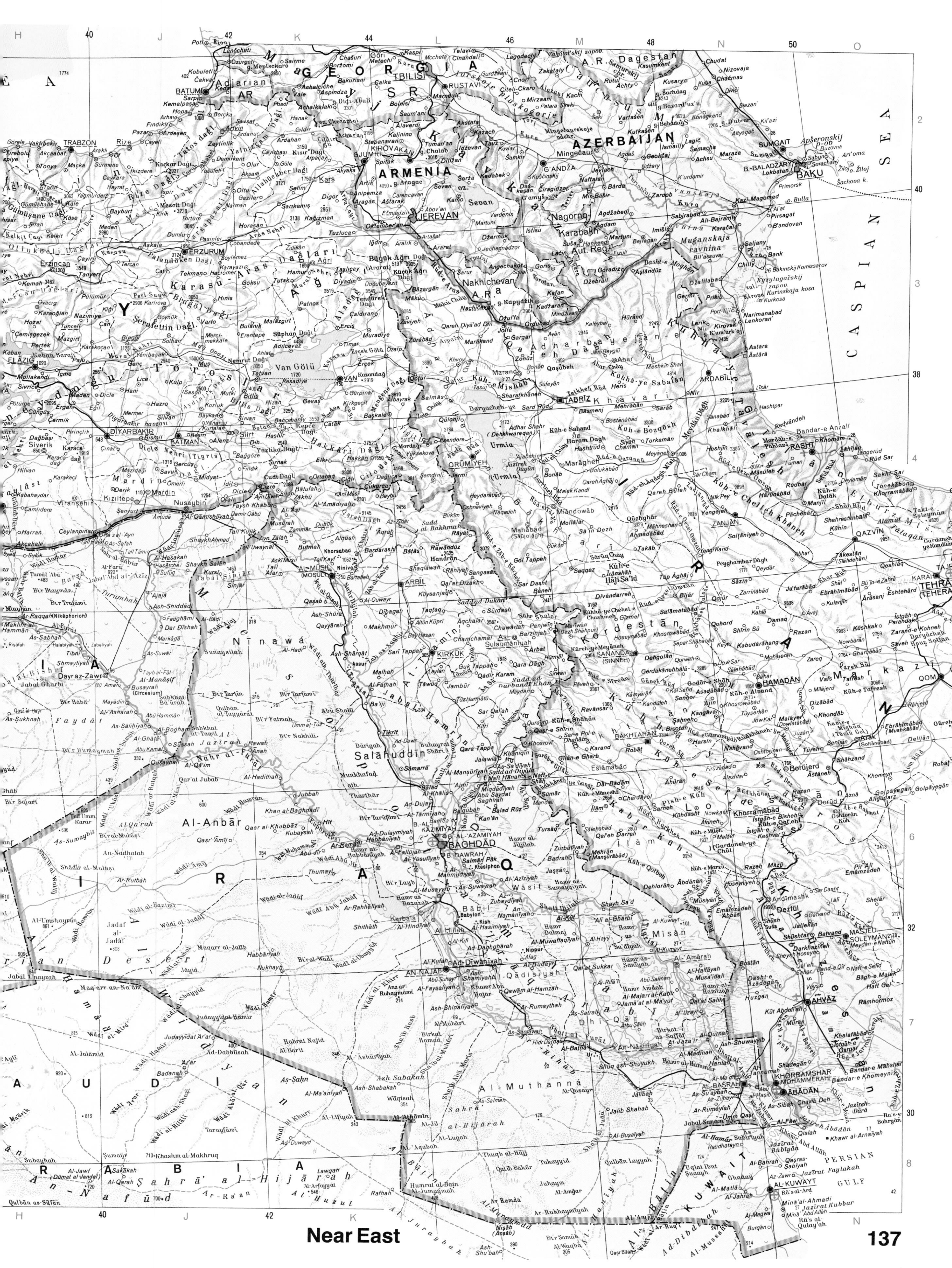

GEORGIA
S S R
TBILISI
RUSTAVI
BATUMI
Adjarian
AR
A.R. Dagestan
AZERBAIJAN
BAKU
SUMGAIT
ARMENIA
JEREVAN
Sevan
Nagorno-Karabakh
Aut. Reg.
Nakhichevan
A.R.
Kura
CASPIAN SEA
TRABZON
ERZURUM
Erzincan
ELÂZIĞ
DİYARBAKIR
BATMAN
Van Gölü
VAN
Siirt
Mardin
Nusaybin
TABRIZ
ARDABIL
RASHT
QAZVIN
ZANJAN
TEHRAN
QOM
HAMADAN
BAKHTARAN
ORŪMĪYEH
Urmia
Daryācheh-ye Urmia
SANANDAJ
Kordestān
Lorestān
Khorramābād
Borūjerd
Arāk
Dezfūl
Shūshtar
AHVĀZ
KHORRAMSHAHR
ĀBĀDĀN
I R A N
I R A Q
MOSUL
ARBĪL
KIRKŪK
As-Sulaymānīyah
BAGHDĀD
Sāmarrā'
Tikrīt
Salāhuddīn
Nīnawá
Al-Anbār
Ar-Ramādī
Al-Fallūjah
Karbalā'
Al-Hillah
An-Najaf
Ad-Dīwānīyah
Al-Qādisīyah
Wāsit
Al-Kūt
Misān
Al-'Amārah
Dhī Qār
An-Nāsirīyah
Al-Muthannā
As-Samāwah
Al-Basrah
AL-BASRAH
Dayr az-Zawr
Ar-Raqqah
Syrian Desert
Wādī al-Bātin
KUWAIT
AL-KUWAYT
PERSIAN GULF
S A U D I
A R A B I A
Sahrā' al Hijārah
An-Nafūd
Tigris
Euphrates
Nahr al-Furāt
Jabal Sinjār
Jabal Hamrīn
Kūhhā-ye Zāgros
Kūh-e Sahand
Kūh-e Sabalān
Elburz
Ağrı Dağı (Ararat)
Toros Dağları

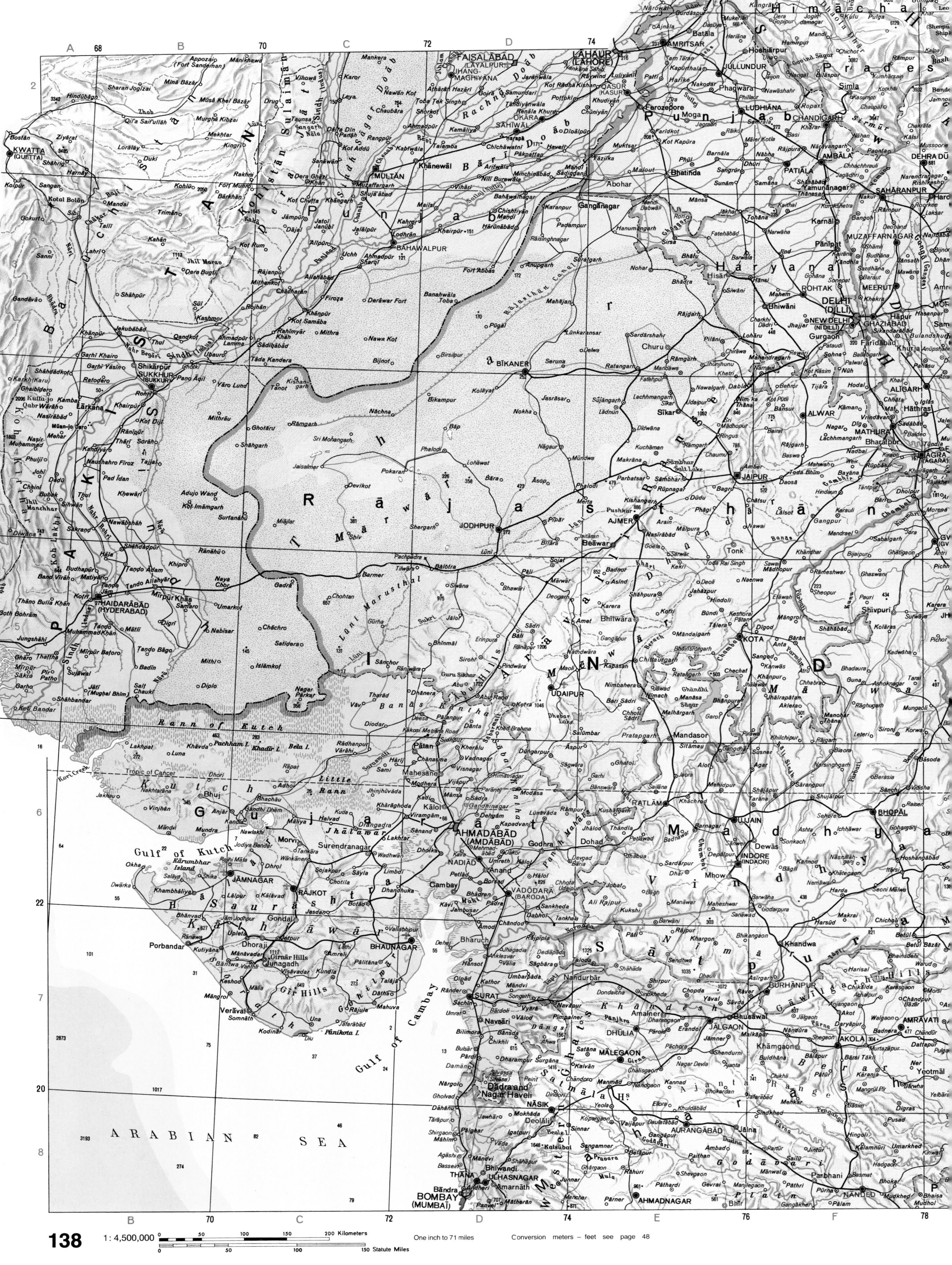

Himāchal Pradesh
Punjab
Haryana
Rājasthān
Mārwār
Thar
Gujarāt
Kutch
Saurāshtra
Kāthiāwār
Madhya Pradesh
Mālwa
Mewār
Satpura
Khāndesh
Ajanta Range
Berār
Baluchistān
Sind
Pakistan
Panjab
Rann of Kutch
Little Rann
Gulf of Kutch
Gulf of Cambay
ARABIAN SEA
Tropic of Cancer
Aravalli Hills
Gir Hills
Western Ghats
Lūni
Narmada
Tāpti
Chambal
Indus
Sutlej
FAISALĀBĀD (LAYALPUR)
LAHAUR (LAHORE)
AMRITSAR
JULLUNDUR
LUDHIANA
CHANDIGARH
AMBĀLA
PATIĀLA
SAHĀRANPUR
DEHRA DŪN
MUZAFFARNAGAR
MEERUT
DELHI (DILLI)
NEW DELHI (NI DILLI)
GHAZIABAD
ROHTAK
ALĪGARH
MATHURA
AGRA (AGARA)
Bharatpur
ALWAR
JAIPUR
AJMER
JODHPUR
BĪKANER
Jaisalmer
KOTA
UDAIPUR
BHOPĀL
UJJAIN
INDORE (INDAOR)
RATLĀM
AHMADĀBĀD (AMDĀBĀD)
VADODARA (BARODA)
SURAT
RĀJKOT
JĀMNAGAR
BHAUNAGAR
NĀSIK
BOMBAY (MUMBAĪ)
THĀNA
ULHASNAGAR
AURANGĀBĀD
AHMADNAGAR
JALGAON
DHŪLIA
MĀLEGAON
AKOLA
AMRAVATI
BURHĀNPUR
NĀNDED
MULTĀN
BAHĀWALPUR
KWATTA (QUETTA)
SUKKHUR (SUKKUR)
HAIDARĀBĀD (HYDERABAD)
Dādra and Nagar Haveli

138 1: 4,500,000 Kilometers / Statute Miles One inch to 71 miles Conversion meters – feet see page 48

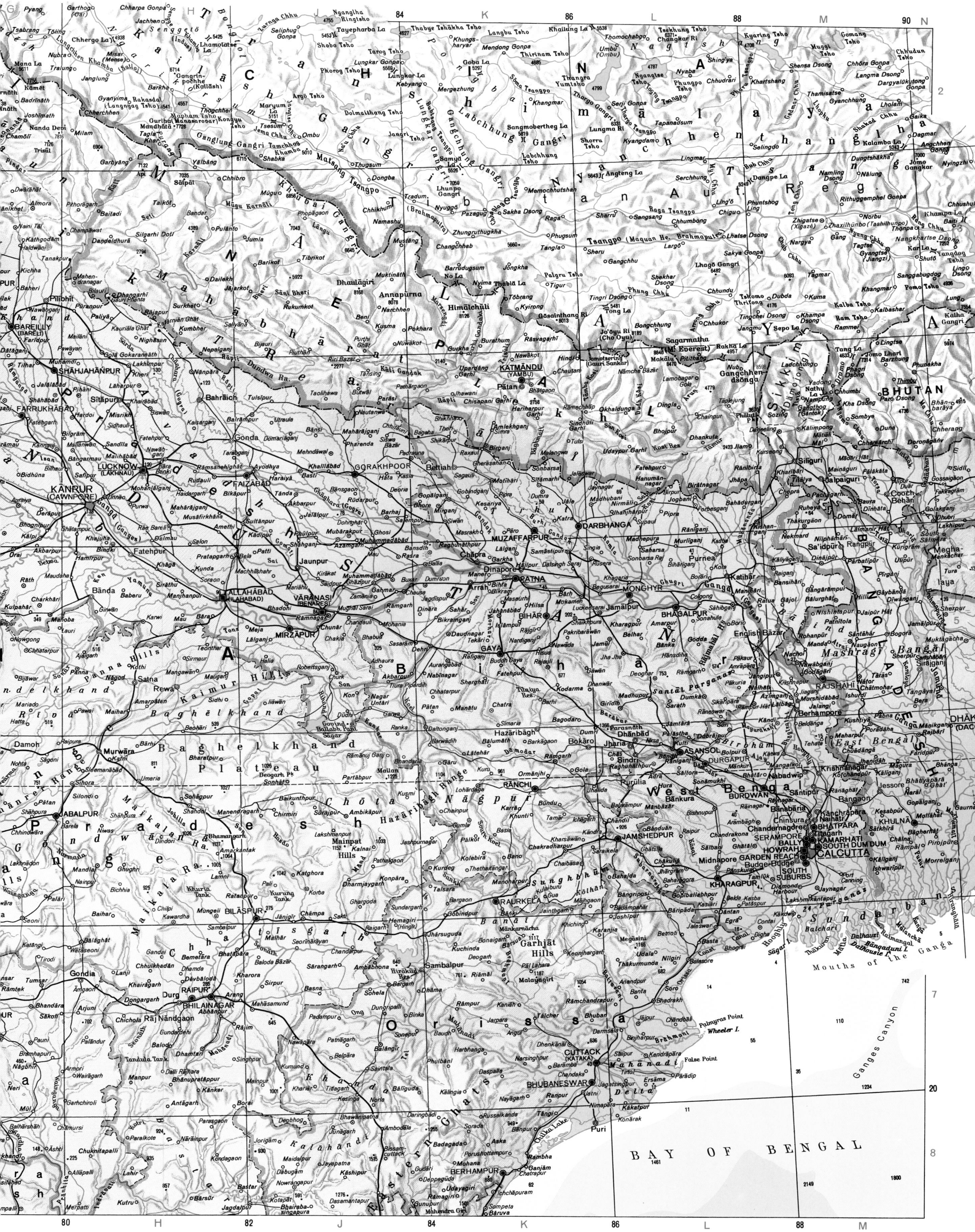

BHUTAN
KATMĀNDU (YAMBU)
Sagarmatha (Mt. Everest)
Annapūrna
Dhaulāgiri
Himālchūli
Gosāinthān
Jo'gu Ri (Cho Oyu)
Makālu
Jomo Lhari
Kāmet
Nanda Devi
Trisūl
Kailās
Mānasarovar
Rakas Tal
Tsangpo (Maquan He, Brahmaputra)
BAREILLY
SHĀHJAHĀNPUR
FARRUKHĀBĀD
LUCKNOW (LAKHNAU)
KĀNPUR (CAWNPORE)
ALLAHĀBĀD (ILAHABAD)
VĀRĀNASI (BENARES)
MIRZĀPUR
GORAKHPUR
FAIZĀBĀD
PATNA
GAYĀ
DARBHANGA
MUZAFFARPUR
MONGHYR
BHĀGALPUR
RĀNCHI
JAMSHEDPUR
ASANSOL
DURGĀPUR
BURDWĀN
CALCUTTA
HOWRAH
KHARAGPUR
RAURKELA
JABALPUR
BILĀSPUR
RAIPUR
BHILAINAGAR
CUTTACK (KATAKA)
BHUBANESWAR
BERHAMPUR
KHULNA
RAJSHĀHI
DHAKA
Puri
Darjeeling
Siliguri
Gangtok
Sikkim
West Bengal
Orissa
Bihār
Uttar Pradesh
Madhya Pradesh
Chhattīsgarh
Chota Nāgpur
Hazāribāgh Range
Baghelkhand Plateau
Kaimur Hills
Eastern Ghats
Mahānadi Delta
Chilka Lake
Sundarbans
Mouths of the Ganga
Ganges Canyon
BAY OF BENGAL
Palmyras Point
Wheeler I.
False Point

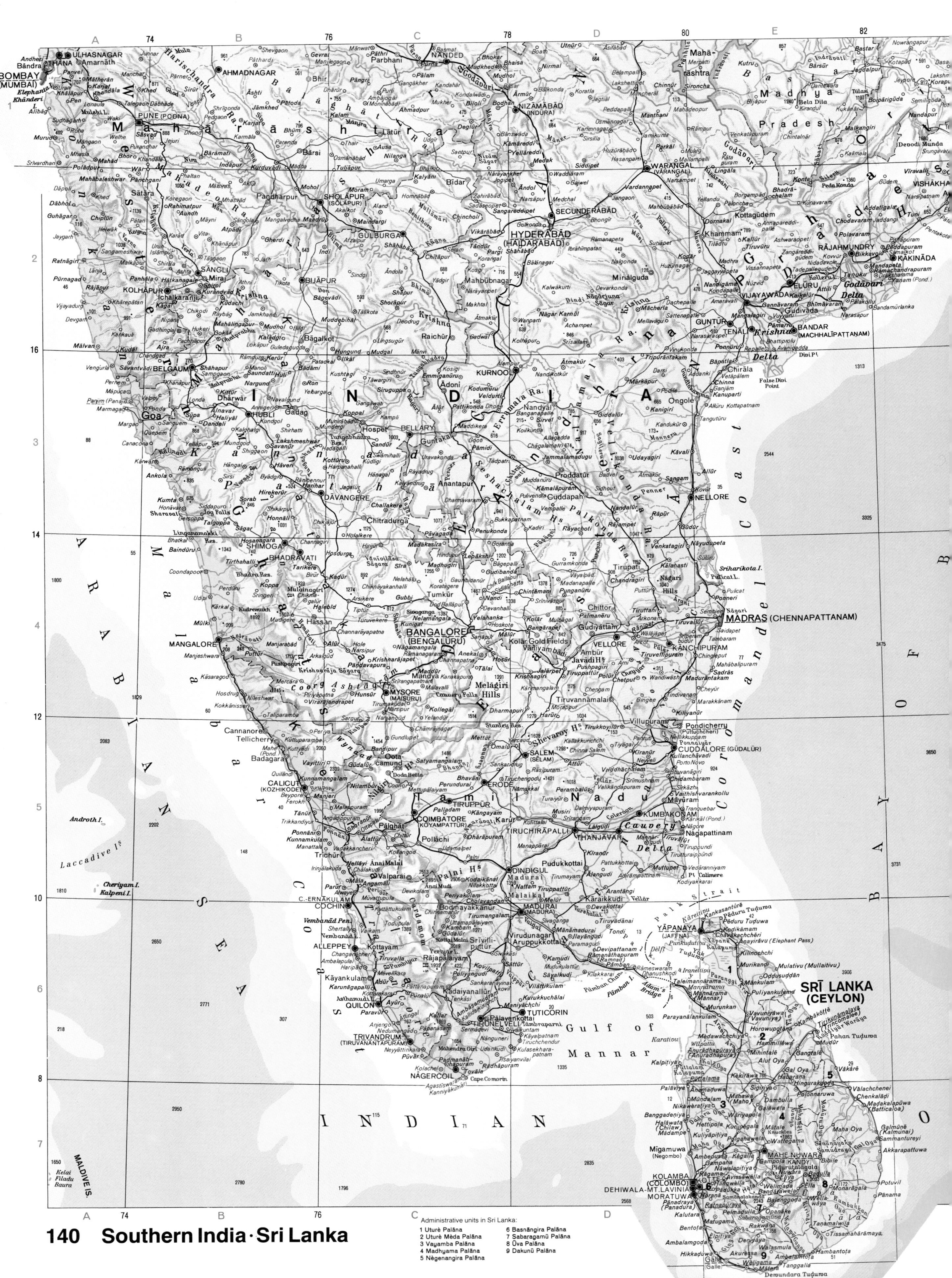

INDIA
SRĪ LANKA
(CEYLON)
ARABIAN SEA
INDIAN
BAY OF
Gulf of Mannar
Palk Strait
Laccadive Is
MALDIVE IS.
BOMBAY
(MUMBAI)
HYDERABAD
(HAIDARABAD)
MADRAS (CHENNAPATTANAM)
BANGALORE
(BENGALURU)
MYSORE
(MAISURU)
MANGALORE
COCHIN
TRIVANDRUM
(TIRUVANANTAPURAM)
MADURAI
TUTICORIN
KOLAMBA
(COLOMBO)
Cape Comorin
Administrative units in Sri Lanka:
1 Uturė Palāna
2 Uturė Mėda Palāna
3 Vayamba Palāna
4 Madhyama Palāna
5 Nėgenangira Palāna
6 Basnāngira Palāna
7 Sabaragamū Palāna
8 Ūva Palāna
9 Dakunū Palāna

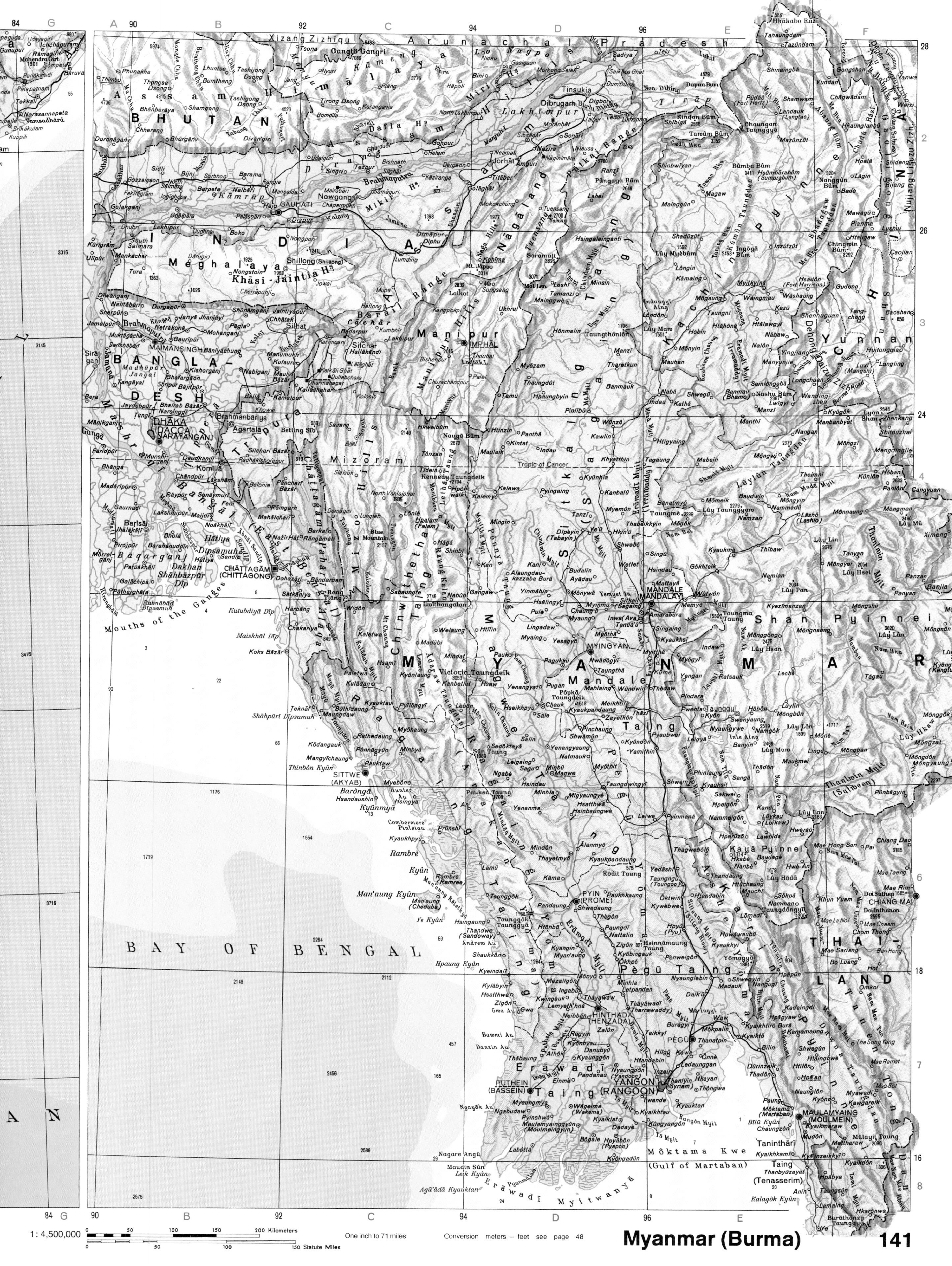
Xizang Zizhiqu
Arunachal Pradesh
BHUTAN
Assam
INDIA
Meghalaya
Khāsi - Jāintia Hs
Shillong
Manipur
IMPHĀL
Mizoram
Tripura
Nāgāland
Kohima
GAUHATI
Brahmaputra
BANGLA-DESH
DHAKA (DACCA)
NARAYANGANJ
CHĀTTAGĀM (CHITTAGONG)
Mouths of the Ganges
Tropic of Cancer
MYANMAR
MANDALE (MANDALAY)
MYINGYAN
SITTWE (AKYAB)
PYIN (PROME)
HINTHADA (HENZADA)
PEGU
YANGON (RANGOON)
PUTHEIN (BASSEIN)
MAULAMYAING (MOULMEIN)
Mandale Taing
Pègū Taing
Erāwadi Taing
Shan Pyinnei
Kayā Pyinnei
Yunnan
THAILAND
CHIANG MAI
BAY OF BENGAL
Mōktama Kwe (Gulf of Martaban)
Taing (Tenasserim)
Erāwadi Myitwanya
Myitkyinā
Bhamo
Lashio
Taunggyi
Magwe
Sagaing
Ava
Kalemyō
Ramree
Cheduba
Thanlwin Myit (Salween)
84
90
92
94
96
A
B
C
D
E
F
G

1: 4,500,000

0 50 100 150 200 Kilometers

0 50 100 150 Statute Miles

One inch to 71 miles

Conversion meters – feet see page 48

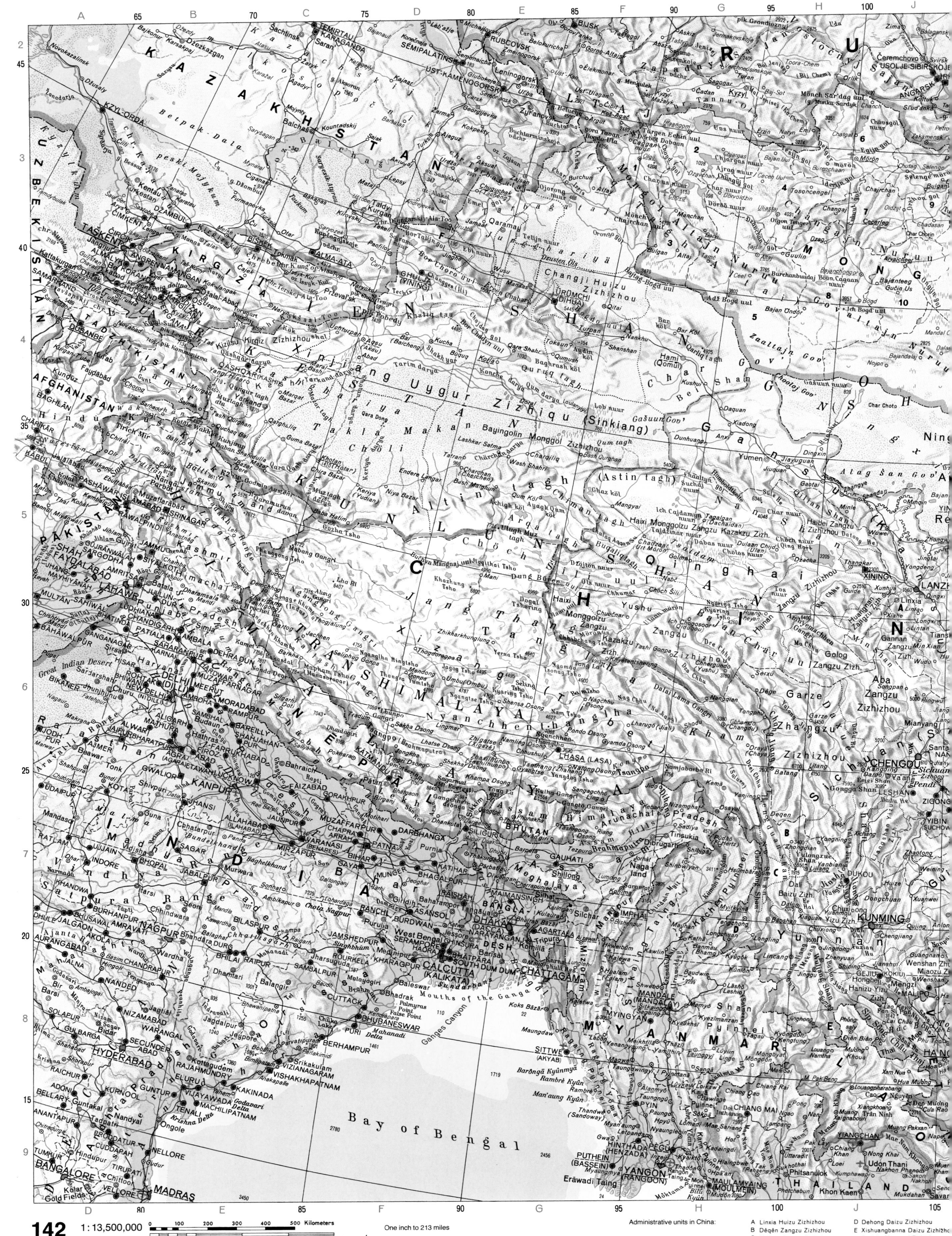
KAZAKHSTAN
KIRGIZIA
TADZHIKISTAN
AFGHANISTAN
PAKISTAN
INDIA
NEPAL
BHUTAN
BANGLADESH
MYANMAR
THAILAND
CHINA
MONGOLIA
RUSSIA
Xinjiang Uygur Zizhiqu (Sinkiang)
Xizang
Qinghai
Gansu
Sichuan
Yunnan
Takla Makan
Tarim darya
Tien Shan
Kunlun
Trans Himalaya
Himalaya
Nyanchhen thangha
Pamir
Hindu Kush
Karakoram
Altaj
Altin tagh
Bay of Bengal
Mouths of the Ganga
Ganges Canyon
Great Indian Desert
Rajasthan
Madhya Pradesh
Uttar Pradesh
Bihar
West Bengal
Assam
Arunachal Pradesh
Satpura Range
Vindhya Range
Andhra Pradesh
Betpak-Dala
Balchas
Alma-Ata
Taškent
Bišhek
Dušanbe
Kabul
Lahore
Delhi
New Delhi
Srinagar
Kathmandu
Lhasa
Dhaka (Dacca)
Calcutta (Kalikata)
Chattagam
Yangon (Rangoon)
Mandale (Mandalay)
Hyderabad
Madras
Bangalore
Chengdu
Kunming
Ürümchi (Dihua)
Kashgar
Xining
Lanzhou
Chiang Mai
Nagpur
Kanpur
Lucknow
Patna
Varanasi (Benares)
Allahabad
Jaipur
Sittwe (Akyab)
Pathein (Bassein)

 1:13,500,000

0 100 200 300 400 500 Kilometers
0 100 200 300 400 Statute Miles

One inch to 213 miles

Administrative units in China:
A Linxia Huizu Zizhizhou
B Dêqên Zangzu Zizhizhou
C Nujiang Lisuzu Zizhizhou
D Dehong Daizu Zizhizhou
E Xishuangbanna Daizu Zizhizhou
F Bortala Monggol Zizhizhou

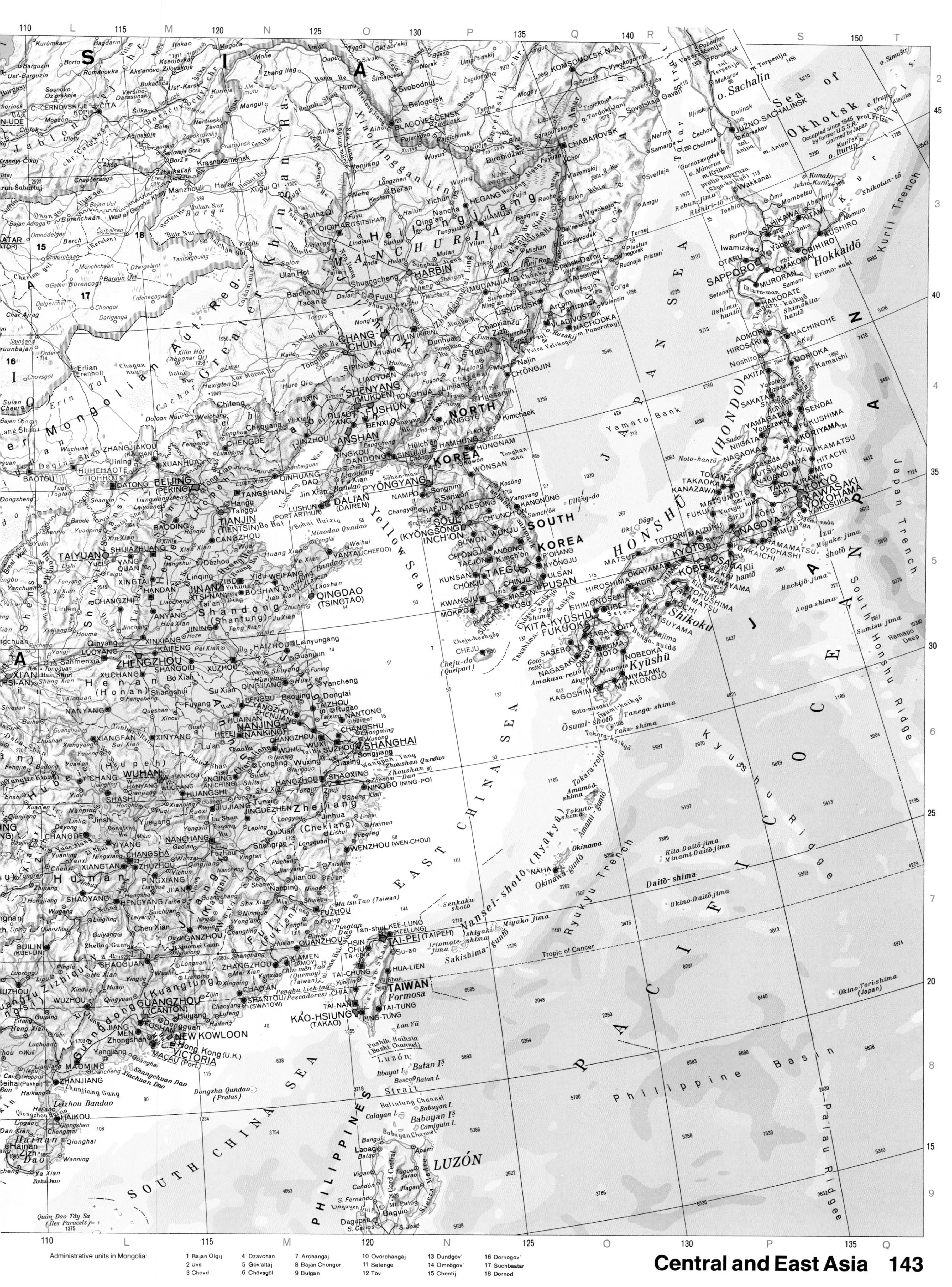

MANCHURIA
Heilongjiang
Greater Khingan Ra.
Inner Mongolian Aut. Reg.
HARBIN
CHANGCHUN
SHENYANG (MUKDEN)
FUSHUN
ANSHAN
DALIAN (DAIREN)
BEIJING (PEKING)
TIANJIN (TIENTSIN)
TAIYUAN
JINAN
QINGDAO (TSINGTAO)
ZHENGZHOU
NANJING (NANKING)
SHANGHAI
HANGZHOU
WUHAN
CHANGSHA
NANCHANG
FUZHOU
XIAMEN (AMOY)
GUANGZHOU (CANTON)
HONG KONG (U.K.)
VICTORIA
MACAU (Port.)
Hainan Dao
TAIWAN
Formosa
TAI-PEI (TAIPEH)
KAO-HSIUNG (TAKAO)
NORTH KOREA
SOUTH KOREA
P'YŎNGYANG
SŎUL
PUSAN
Yellow Sea
EAST CHINA SEA
SOUTH CHINA SEA
SEA OF JAPAN
Sea of Okhotsk
JAPAN
HONSHŪ (HONDO)
Hokkaidō
Shikoku
Kyūshū
TŌKYŌ
YOKOHAMA
KAWASAKI
NAGOYA
KYŌTO
ŌSAKA
KŌBE
HIROSHIMA
KITA-KYŪSHŪ
FUKUOKA
SAPPORO
o. Sachalin
JUŽNO-SACHALINSK
VLADIVOSTOK
CHABAROVSK
BLAGOVEŠČENSK
KOMSOMOLSK-N.-A.
PACIFIC OCEAN
Philippine Basin
Japan Trench
Kuril Trench
Ryukyu Trench
Nansei-shotō (Ryūkyū)
Okinawa
Tropic of Cancer
PHILIPPINES
LUZÓN
Bashi Channel
Luzon Strait

Administrative units in Mongolia:

1 Bajan Ölgij
2 Uvs
3 Chovd
4 Dzavchan
5 Gov'altaj
6 Chövsgöl
7 Archangaj
8 Bajan Chongor
9 Bulgan
10 Övörchangaj
11 Selenge
12 Töv
13 Dundgov'
14 Ömnögov'
15 Chentij
16 Dornogov'
17 Suchbaatar
18 Dornod

1: 4,500,000 — 0 50 100 150 200 Kilometers — 0 50 100 150 Statute Miles — One inch to 71 miles — Conversion meters – feet see page 48

HOKKAIDŌ
Japan Basin
JAPAN SEA
Yamato Bank
HONSHŪ (HONDO)
JAPAN
SHIKOKU
KYŪSHŪ
PACIFIC OCEAN
Japan Trench
Izu-shotō
Sea of Okhotsk
RUSSIA
Occupied since 1945 by former U.S.S.R. claimed by Japan
see inset for continuation
Continuation of main map
Hokkaido
TŌKYŌ
YOKOHAMA
KAWASAKI
NAGOYA
KYOTO
OSAKA
KOBE
HIROSHIMA
SENDAI
NIIGATA
AOMORI
HAKODATE
SAPPORO
ASAHIKAWA
KUSHIRO
MURORAN
OBIHIRO
KITAMI
VLADIVOSTOK
NACHODKA
Oki
Sado
Take-shima

1: 4,500,000 — 0, 50, 100, 150, 200 Kilometers; 0, 50, 100, 150 Statute Miles

One inch to 71 miles

Conversion meters – feet see page 48

PHILIPPINES
EAST CHINA
SOUTH CHINA SEA
TAIWAN
Formosa
TAIPEI
KAOHSIUNG
HUALIEN
TAICHUNG
TAINAN
FUZHOU (FOOCHOW)
XIAMEN (AMOY)
SHANTOU (SWATOW)
GUANGZHOU (CANTON)
Hong Kong
VICTORIA
MACAU
NANCHANG
CHANGSHA
HENGYANG
GUILIN
LIUZHOU
WUZHOU
ZHANJIANG
HAIKOU
WENZHOU
JINGDEZHEN
Tropic of Cancer

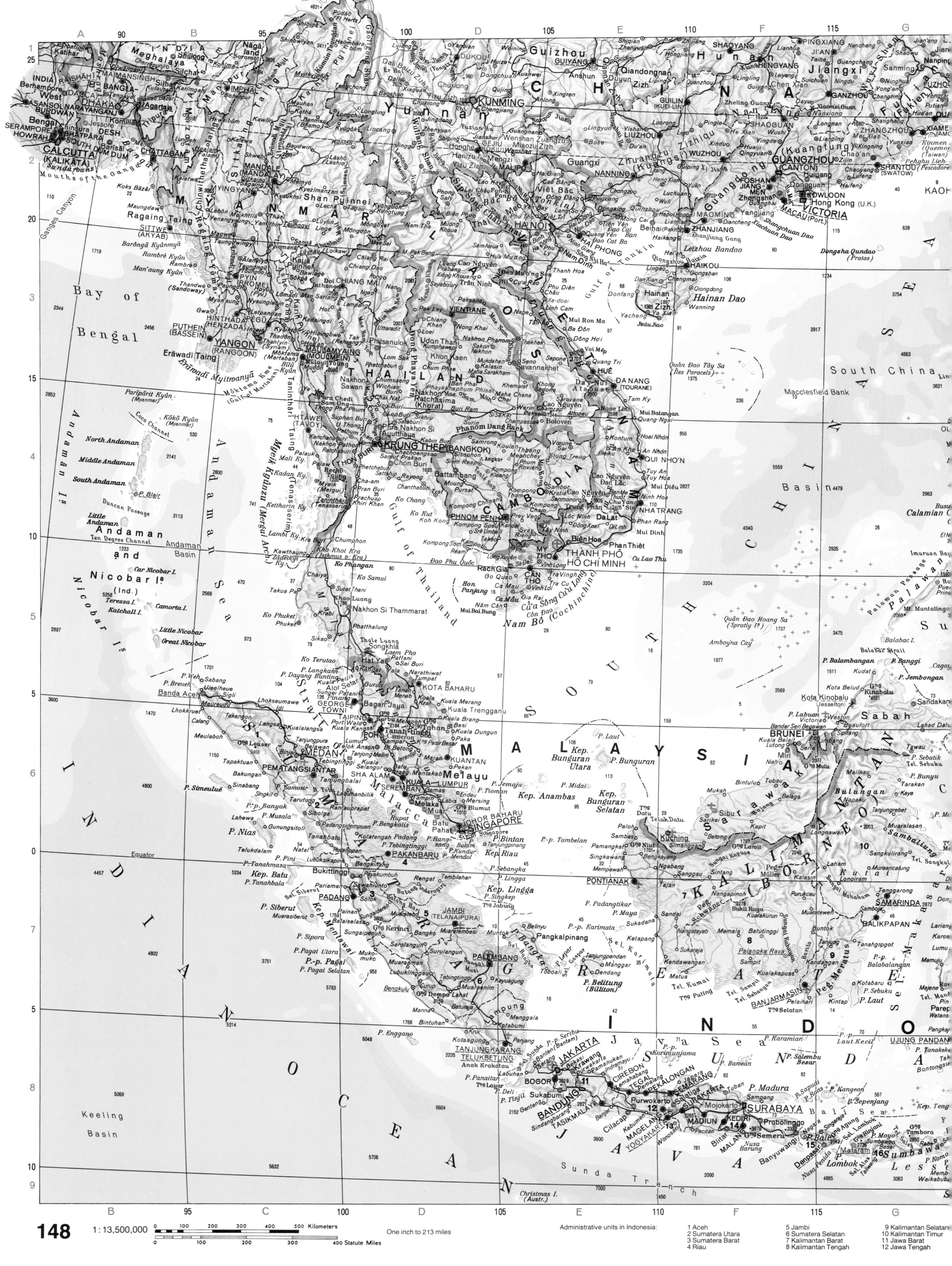

I N D I A
Meghalaya
Shillong
Nāga-land
Guizhou
GUIYANG
Hunan
Jiangxi
C H I N A
Yunnan
KUNMING
Guangxi
GUANGZHOU (CANTON)
Hong Kong (U.K.)
VICTORIA
MACAU (Port.)
BANGLADESH
DHAKA
CALCUTTA (KALIKATA)
HOWRAH
Mouths of the Ganges
CHITTAGONG
MANDALAY
M Y A N M A R
Shan
HANOI
HAI PHONG
Gulf of Tonkin
HAIKOU
Hainan Dao
L A O S
VIENTIANE
YANGON (RANGOON)
Bay of Bengal
T H A I L A N D
KRUNG THEP (BANGKOK)
C A M B O D I A
PHNOM PENH
V I E T N A M
HUE
DA NANG (TOURANE)
QUI NHO'N
NHA TRANG
THÀNH PHỐ HỒ CHÍ MINH
Gulf of Thailand
South China Sea
Macclesfield Bank
Basin
Andaman Sea
Andaman and Nicobar Is. (Ind.)
North Andaman
Middle Andaman
South Andaman
Little Andaman
Car Nicobar I.
Little Nicobar
Great Nicobar
Ten Degree Channel
S O U T H C H I N A S E A
Palawan
Sabah
Sarawak
BRUNEI
Kota Kinabalu
M A L A Y S I A
KUALA LUMPUR
Melayu
SINGAPORE
Strait of Malacca
Sumatera
MEDAN
PADANG
PAKANBARU
PALEMBANG
JAMBI
Equator
K A L I M A N T A N (B O R N E O)
PONTIANAK
BANJARMASIN
SAMARINDA
BALIKPAPAN
I N D O N E S I A
Java Sea
JAKARTA
BANDUNG
SEMARANG
SURAKARTA
SURABAYA
Jawa
Bali
Lombok
Sumbawa
Madura
I N D I A N O C E A N
Keeling Basin
Sunda Trench
Christmas I. (Austr.)

1 : 13,500,000 — 0 100 200 300 400 500 Kilometers — 0 100 200 300 400 Statute Miles

One inch to 213 miles

Administrative units in Indonesia:

1 Aceh	5 Jambi	9 Kalimantan Selatan
2 Sumatera Utara	6 Sumatera Selatan	10 Kalimantan Timur
3 Sumatera Barat	7 Kalimantan Barat	11 Jawa Barat
4 Riau	8 Kalimantan Tengah	12 Jawa Tengah

Fiji Islands
PACIFIC OCEAN
Vanua Levu
Viti Levu
Suva
TONGA
Tonga Trench
SAMOA
Savai'i
Upolu
Apia
Fiji – Samoa
Hawaiian Islands
Kauai
Oahu
HONOLULU
Pearl Harbor
Molokai
Maui
Lanai
Kahoolawe
Mauna Kea
Mauna Loa
Kilauea Crater
Hilo
Hawaii
Tropic of Cancer
Solomon Islands
Bismarck Sea
Bismarck Arch.
New Ireland
New Britain
Rabaul
Bougainville
Choiseul
Santa Isabel
New Georgia Group
Guadalcanal
Honiara
Malaita
San Cristóbal
Santa Cruz Is.
SOLOMON IS.
Louisiade Archipelago
d'Entrecasteaux Is.
Trobriand Is. (Kiriwina Is.)
Woodlark I.
PAPUA NEW GUINEA
Solomon Basin
Solomon Sea
New Britain Trench
Bougainville Trench
Continuation of main map
LUZÓN
Philippine Basin
PHILIPPINES
PACIFIC OCEAN
Philippine Trench
Ryukyu Trench
Okinawa
NAHA
Daito-jima
Samar
Leyte
Tacloban
Cebu
Bohol
Masbate
MINDANAO
DAVAO
Mt. Apo
Caroline Islands
BELAU
MICRONESIA
West Caroline Basin
East Caroline Basin
Halmahera
MANADO
Kep. Sangihe
Kep. Talaud
Molucca Sea
Ceram Sea
Seram
Ambon
Banda Sea
Banda Basin
South Banda Basin
Kep. Aru
Kep. Tanimbar
Kep. Kai
Arafura Sea
Timor Sea
Timor Trough
NEW GUINEA
Irian Jaya
Peg. Maoke
Peg. Sudirman
Peg. Jayawijaya
Jayapura (Hollandia)
Biak
Admiralty Is.
Manus
Bismarck Sea
Gulf of Papua
PORT MORESBY
Owen Stanley Ra.
Coral Sea
Torres Strait
AUSTRALIA
Equator
INDONESIA
ASIA
see inset for continuation

3 Yogyakarta
4 Jawa Timur
5 Bali
6 Nusa Tenggara Barat
17 Nusa Tenggara Timur
18 Sulawesi Utara
19 Sulawesi Tengah
20 Sulawesi Tenggara
21 Sulawesi Selatan
22 Maluku
23 Timor Timur

Conversion meters – feet see page 48

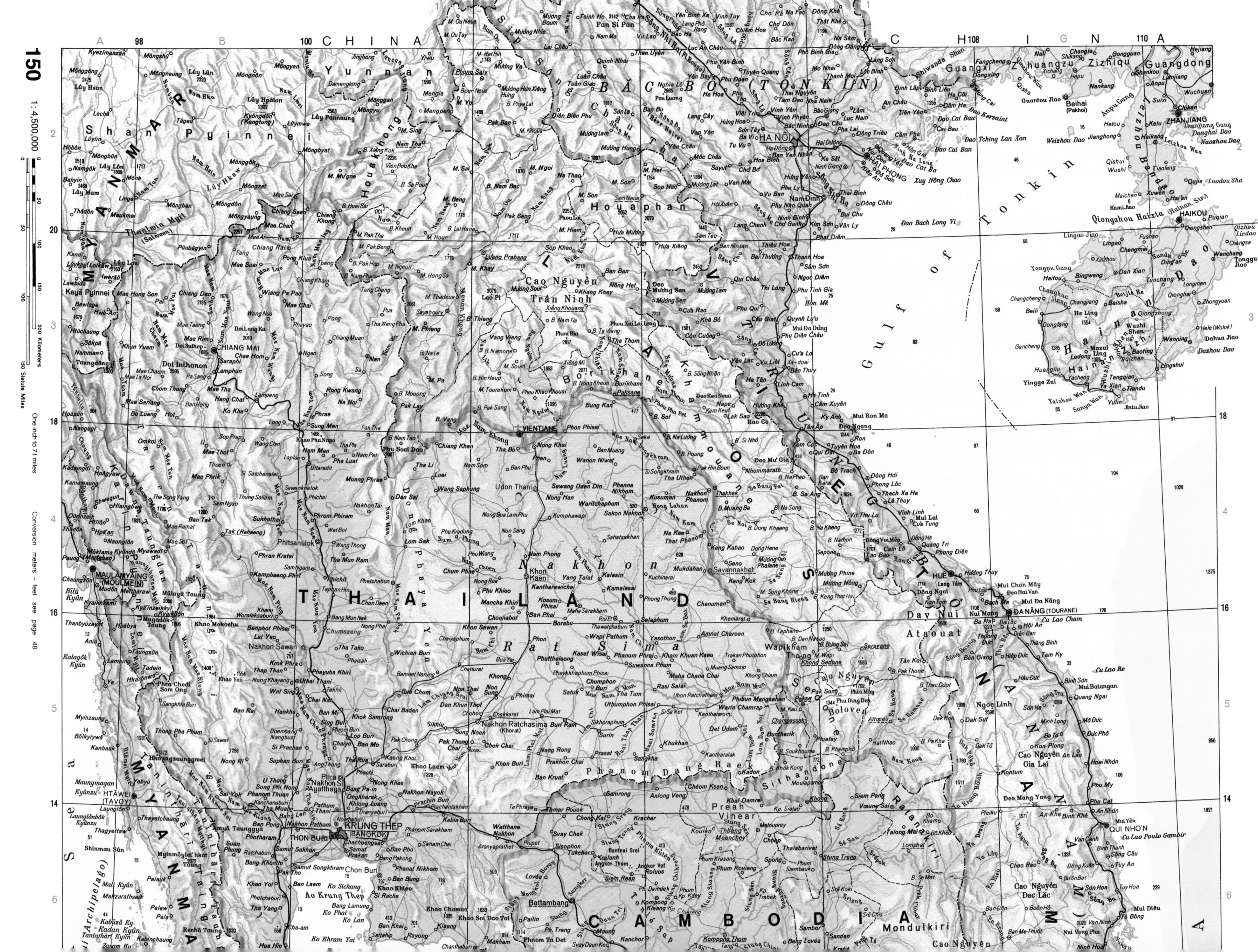
CHINA
THAILAND
CAMBODIA
MYANMA
Gulf of Tonkin
BĂC BỘ (TONKIN)
Yunnan
Guangdong
Guangxi Zhuangzu Zizhiqu
Hainan Dao
Leizhou Bandao
HÀ NỘI
HAI PHONG
HUẾ
ĐÀ NẴNG (TOURANE)
VIENTIANE
KRUNG THEP (BANGKOK)
THON BURI
CHIANG MAI
MAULAMYAING (MOULMEIN)
HAIKOU
ZHANJIANG
QUI NHƠN
HTAWEI (TAVOY)
Battambang
Nakhon Ratchasima (Khorat)
Savannakhet
Udon Thani
Phitsanulok
Nakhon Sawan
Menan Khong
Cao Nguyên Trân Ninh
Houaphan
Mondulkiri
Ao Krung Thep
Conversion meters – feet see page 48
One inch to 71 miles

1 : 4,500,000

0 50 100 150 200 Kilometers

0 50 100 150 Statute Miles

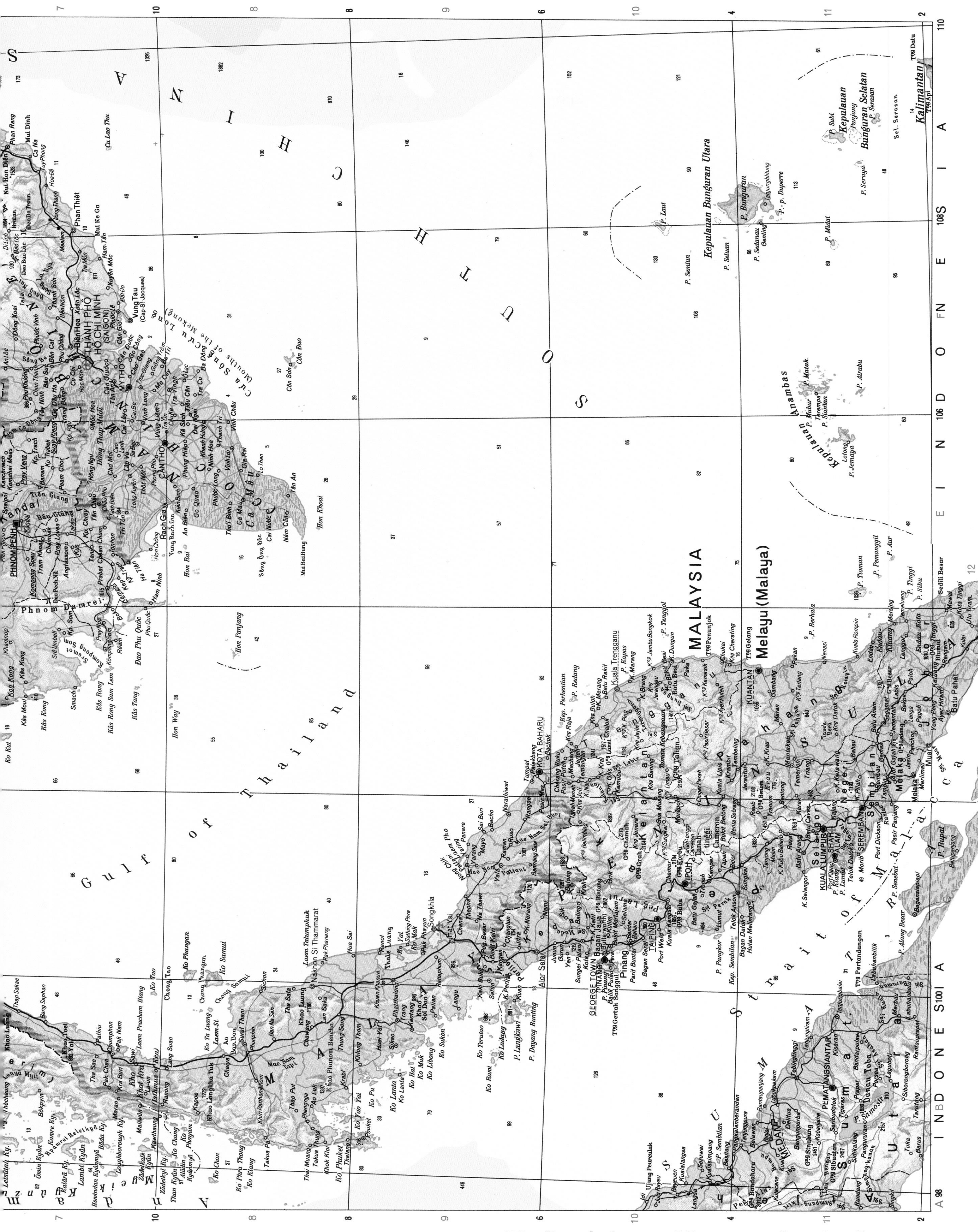

SOUTH CHINA
Gulf of Thailand
Strait of Malacca
MALAYSIA
Melayu (Malaya)
INDONESIA
Kepulauan Bunguran Utara
Kepulauan Anambas
Kepulauan Bunguran Selatan
Kalimantan
PHNOMPENH
THANH PHO HO CHI MINH (SAIGON)
KUALA LUMPUR
GEORGE TOWN
KOTA BAHARU
KUANTAN
MEDAN

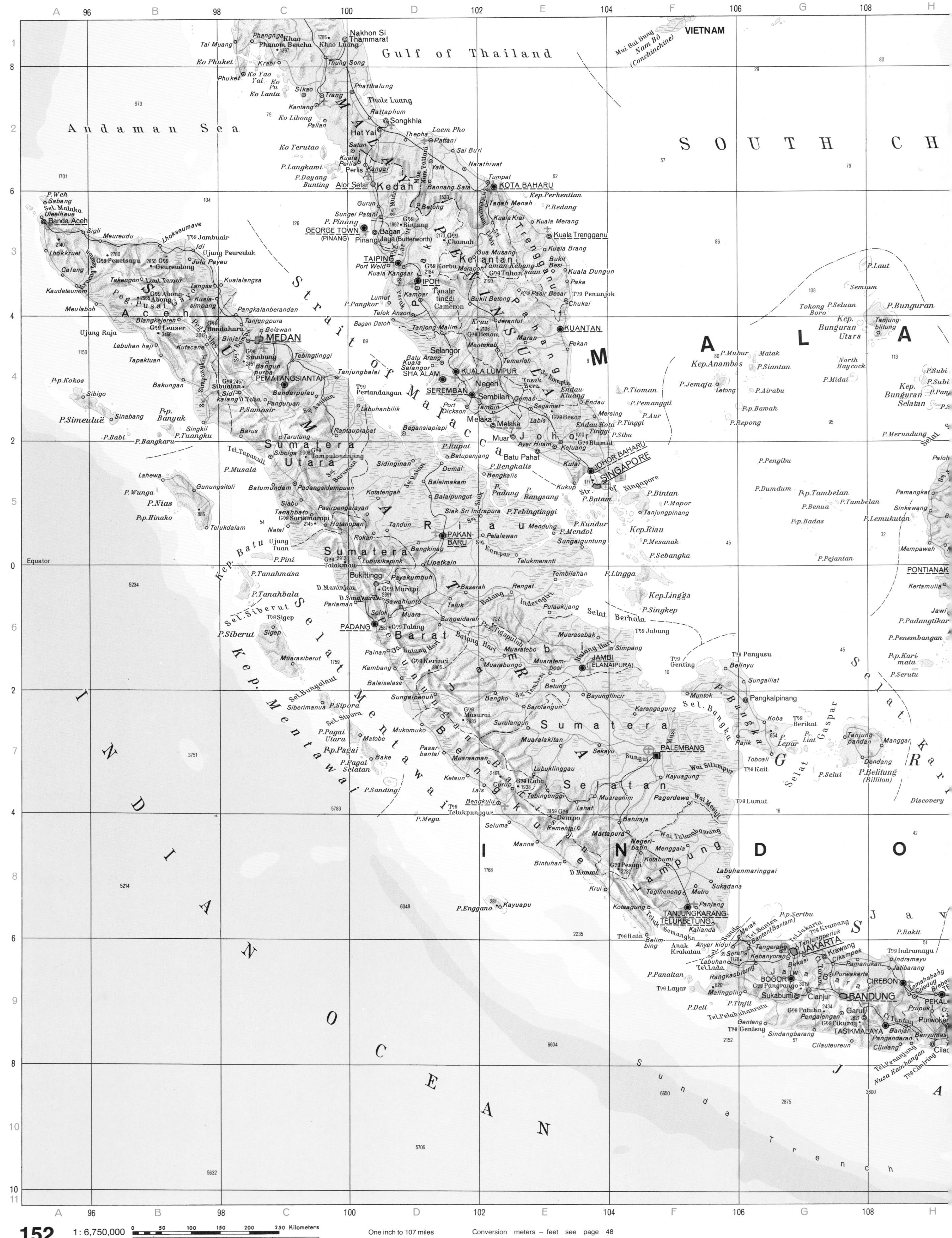

Gulf of Thailand
VIETNAM
Andaman Sea
SOUTH CH
Strait of Malacca
MALAYA
PENINSULA
M A L A
I N D O
INDIAN OCEAN
Sunda Trench
Nakhon Si Thammarat
Songkhla
Hat Yai
Pattani
Kedah
Alor Setar
GEORGE TOWN (PINANG)
TAIPING
IPOH
Kelantan
KOTA BAHARU
Kuala Trengganu
KUANTAN
KUALA LUMPUR
SEREMBAN
Melaka
Johor
JOHOR BAHARU
SINGAPORE
Kep.Anambas
P.Bunguran
Kep.Riau
Kep.Lingga
P.Singkep
Banda Aceh
Aceh
MEDAN
PEMATANGSIANTAR
Sumatera Utara
P.Simeulue
P.Nias
Riau
PAKAN-BARU
Sumatera Barat
PADANG
P.Siberut
Kep. Mentawai
JAMBI (TELANAIPURA)
Sumatera Selatan
PALEMBANG
P.Bangka
Pangkalpinang
P.Belitung (Billiton)
Bengkulu
Lampung
TANJUNGKARANG-TELUKBETUNG
P.Enggano
JAKARTA
BOGOR
BANDUNG
CIREBON
Jawa
PONTIANAK
Equator

1 : 6,750,000 — 0 50 100 150 200 250 Kilometers; 0 50 100 150 200 Statute Miles

One inch to 107 miles

Conversion meters – feet see page 48

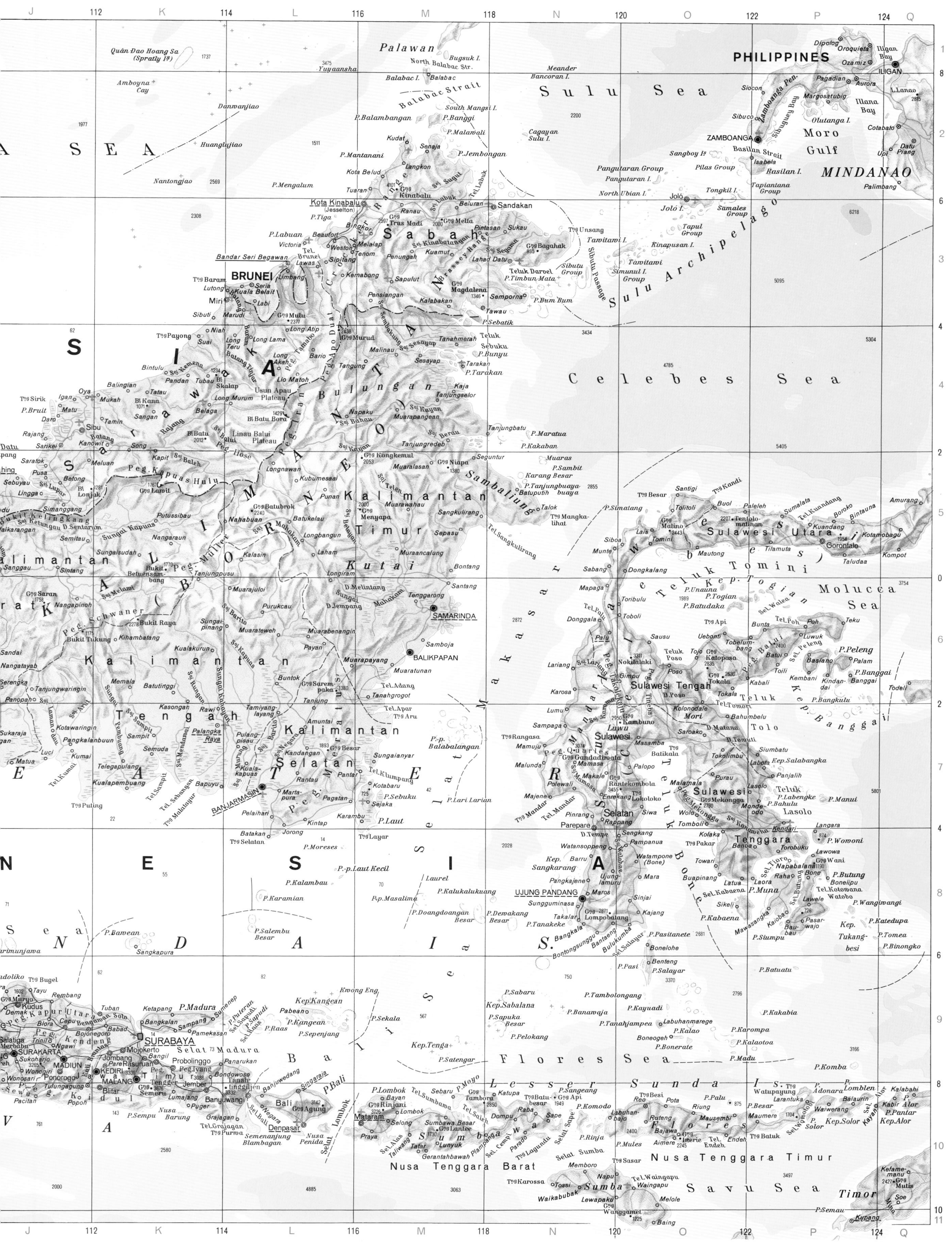

PHILIPPINES
Palawan
Sulu Sea
Balabac Strait
Basilan Strait
Moro Gulf
MINDANAO
ZAMBOANGA
ILIGAN
Sulu Archipelago
Celebes Sea
Kota Kinabalu (Jesselton)
Sandakan
Sabah
BRUNEI
Bandar Seri Begawan
Miri
Sarawak
Sibu
Kalimantan Timur
Kutai
SAMARINDA
BALIKPAPAN
Kalimantan Tengah
Kalimantan Selatan
BANJARMASIN
Kalimantan Barat
Sulawesi Utara
Gorontalo
Teluk Tomini
Molucca Sea
Sulawesi Tengah
Sulawesi Selatan
Sulawesi Tenggara
UJUNG PANDANG
Makasar Strait
Teluk Bone
Kendari
P.Butung
P.Muna
P.Peleng
Kep. Banggai
Flores Sea
Java Sea
SURABAYA
Selat Madura
P.Madura
SURAKARTA
MADIUN
KEDIRI
MALANG
Bali
Denpasar
P.Lombok
Mataram
Sumbawa Besar
Lesser Sunda Is.
Nusa Tenggara Barat
Nusa Tenggara Timur
Flores
Sumba
Savu Sea
Timor
Kupang
P.Alor
INDONESIA

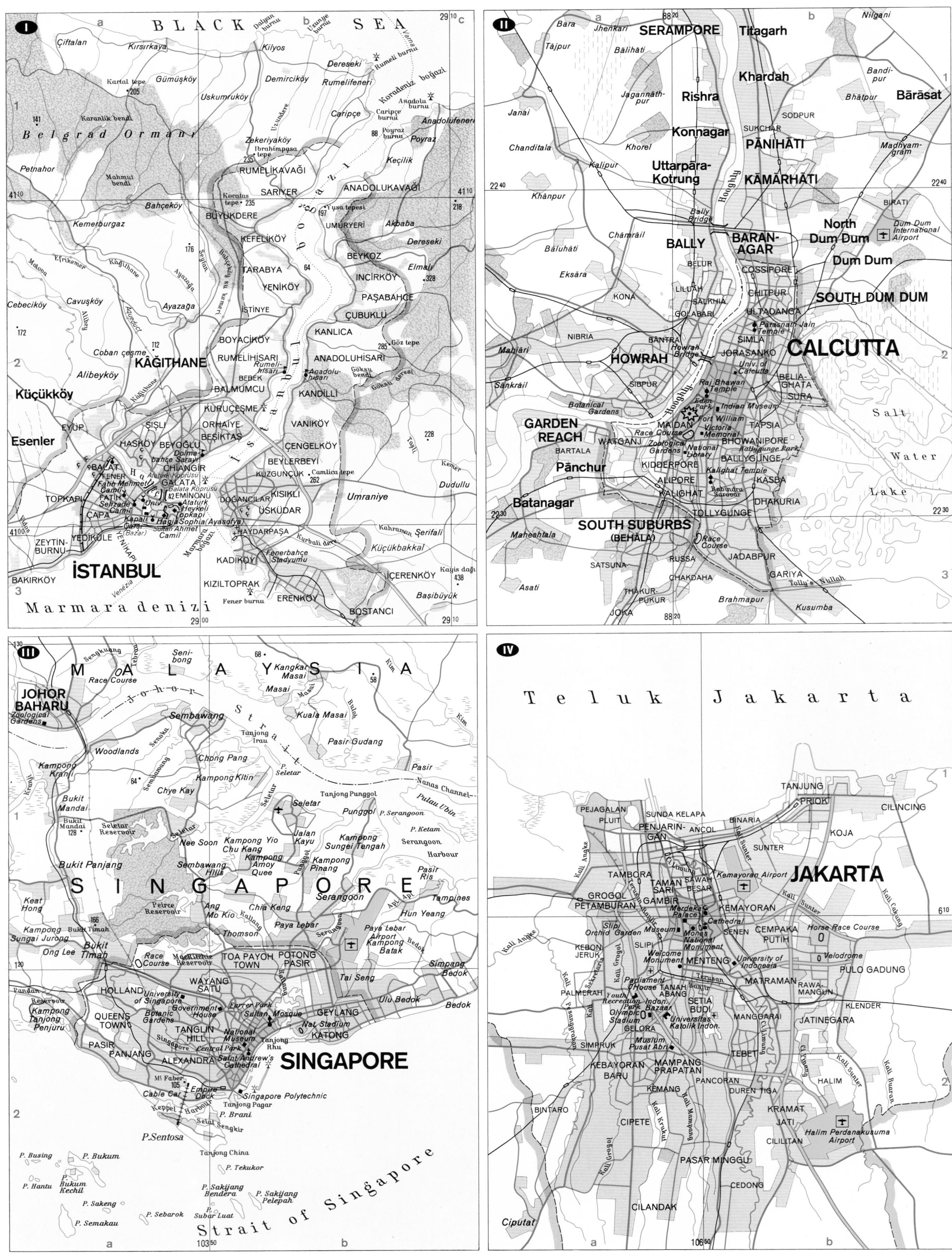
I
BLACK SEA
ISTANBUL
Marmara denizi
Kağıthane
Küçükköy
Esenler
Sarıyer
Büyükdere
Tarabya
Beykoz
Üsküdar
Kadıköy
II
CALCUTTA
HOWRAH
SERAMPORE
Titagarh
Khardah
Rishra
Konnagar
Uttarpara-Kotrung
BALLY
BARANAGAR
North Dum Dum
Dum Dum
SOUTH DUM DUM
Bārāsat
GARDEN REACH
Pānchur
Batanagar
SOUTH SUBURBS (BEHALA)
Salt Water Lake
III
MALAYSIA
JOHOR BAHARU
SINGAPORE
Johor Strait
Strait of Singapore
IV
Teluk Jakarta
JAKARTA
TANJUNG PRIOK
Kemayoran Airport
Halim Perdanakusuma Airport

Conversion meters – feet see page 48   1 : 225,000

0 2.5 5 7.5 10 Kilometers
0 2.5 5 7.5 Statute Miles

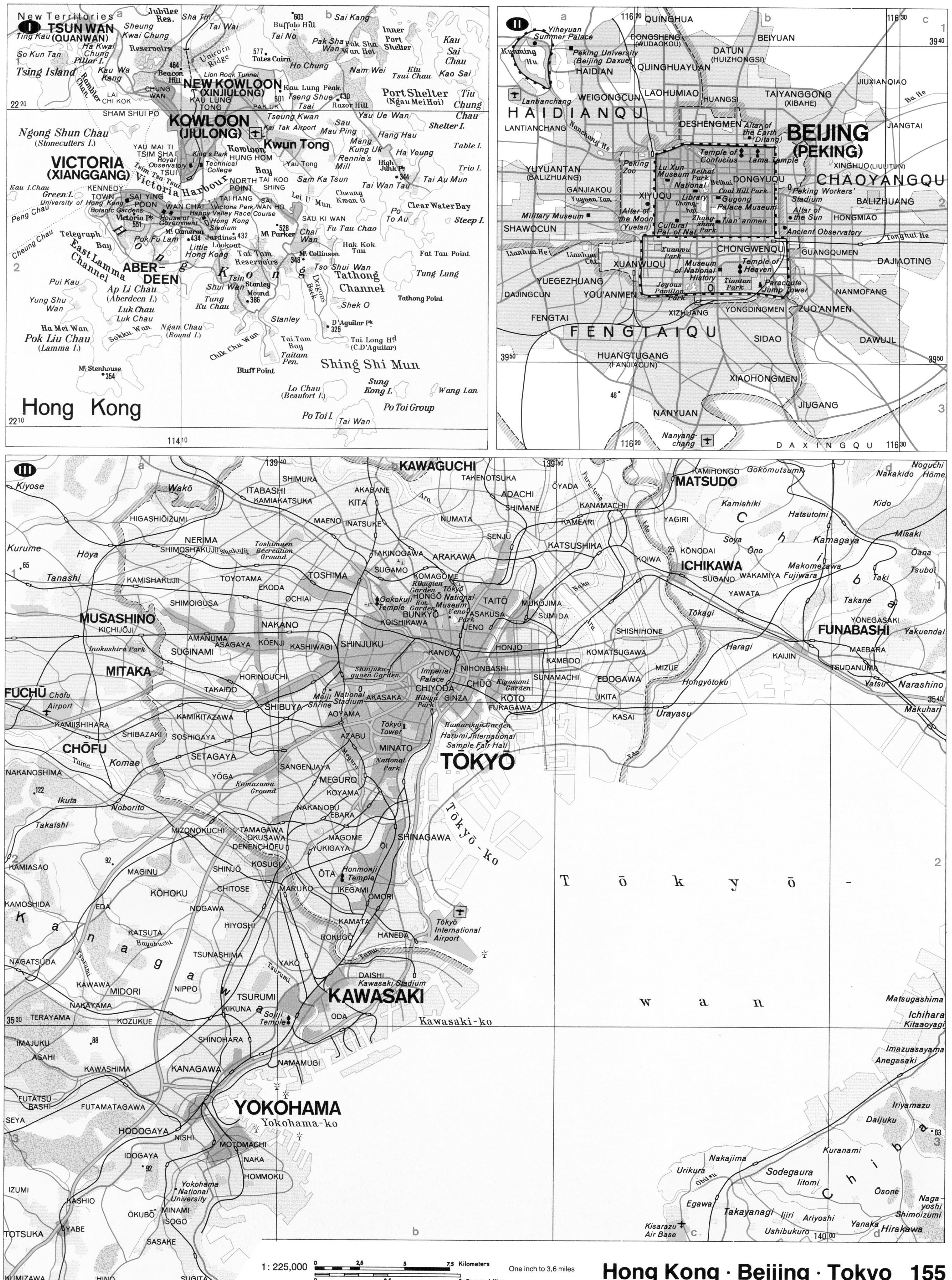

I
New Territories
TSUN WAN (QUANWAN)
Jubilee Res.
Sha Tin
Tai Wai
Sheung Kwai Chung
Ha Kwai Chung
Ting Kau
So Kun Tan
Pillar I.
Tsing Island
Kau Wa Kang
Reservoirs
Unicorn Ridge
Beacon Hill
Lion Rock Tunnel
NEW KOWLOON (XINJIULONG)
KAU LUNG TONG
CHUNG WAN
LAI CHI KOK
SHAM SHUI PO
Rambler Chan.
Buffalo Hill
Tai No
Sai Kang
Inner Port Shelter
Pak Sha Wan
Pak Sha Wan Hoi
Tates Cairn
Ho Chung
Nam Wei
Kiu Tsui Chau
Kau Sai Chau
Kao Sai
Kau Lung Peak
Tseng Shue Tsai
Razor Hill
Port Shelter (Ngau Mei Hoi)
Tiu Chung Chau
KOWLOON (JIULONG)
Tseung Kwan
Kai Tak Airport
Yau Ue Wan
Shelter I.
Ngong Shun Chau (Stonecutters I.)
Kwun Tong
Sau Mau Ping
Hang Hau
Mang Kung Uk
Ha Yeung
Table I.
YAU MA TI
TSIM SHA TSUI
Royal Observatory
King's Park
Technical College
Kowloon
HUNG HOM
Bay
Yau Tong
Rennie's Mill
High Junk Pk
Trio I.
VICTORIA (XIANGGANG)
Tsim Tsa Tsui
Victoria Harbour
NORTH POINT
TAI KOO SHING
Sam Ka Tsun
Tai Wan Tau
Tai Au Mun
Kau I. Chau
KENNEDY TOWN
Green I.
University of Hong Kong
Botanic Gardens
SAI YING POON
WAN CHAI
TAI HANG
Lei U Mun
Cheung Kwan O
Clear Water Bay
Peng Chau
Victoria Pk
House of Government
Happy Valley Race Course
Victoria Park
WAN HO
SAI WAN HO
SAU KI WAN
Po To Au
Steep I.
Mt Cameron
Hong Kong Stadium
Mt Parker
Chai Wan
Fu Tau Chao
Telegraph Bay
Pok Fu Lam
Jardines Lookout
Cheung Chau
East Lamma Channel
Little Hong Kong
Tai Tam Reservoirs
Mt Collinson
Hak Kok Tau
Fat Tau Point
ABERDEEN
Hong Kong
Tso Shui Wan
Tathong Channel
Tung Lung
Pui Kau
Ap Li Chau (Aberdeen I.)
Tsin
Stanley Mound
Dragons Back
Yung Shu Wan
Luk Chau
Shui Wan
Tung Ku Chau
Shek O
Tathong Point
Ha Mei Wan
Pok Liu Chau (Lamma I.)
Sok Kwu Wan
Ngan Chau (Round I.)
Chik Chu Wan
Stanley
D'Aguilar Pk
Tai Tam Bay
Tai Long Hd (C.D'Aguilar)
Taitam Pen.
Shing Shi Mun
Mt Stenhouse
Bluff Point
Sung Kong I.
Wang Lan
Lo Chau (Beaufort I.)
Po Toi Group
Po Toi I.
Tai Wan
Hong Kong
II
Yiheyuan Summer Palace
Kunming Hu
QUINGHUA
DONGSHENG (WUDAOKOU)
Peking University (Beijing Daxue)
DATUN (HUIZHONGSI)
BEIYUAN
QUINGHUAYUAN
HAIDIAN
Lantianchang
WEIGONGCUN
LAOHUMIAO
HUANGSI
TAIYANGGONG (XIBAHE)
JIUXIANQIAO
Ba He
HAIDIANQU
LANTIANCHANG
Nanchang He
DESHENGMEN
Altar of the Earth (Ditang)
BEIJING (PEKING)
JIANGTAI
Temple of Confucius
Lama Temple
Peking Zoo
Lu Xun Museum
Beihai Park
National Library
Beihai
DONGYUQU
XINGHUO (LIULITUN)
YUYUANTAN (BALIZHUANG)
CHAOYANGQU
GANJIAKOU
Yuyuan Tan
XIYUQU
Zhongnanhai
Coal Hill Park
Gugong Palace Museum
Peking Workers' Stadium
BALIZHUANG
Military Museum
Altar of the Moon (Yuetan)
Tian'anmen
Altar of the Sun
HONGMIAO
SHAWOCUN
Cultural Pal. of Nat.
Zhongshan Park
Ancient Observatory
Tonghui He
Lianhua He
CHONGWENQU
GUANGQUMEN
DAJIAOTING
XUANWUQU
Xuanwu Park
Museum of National History
Temple of Heaven
YUEGEZHUANG
Joyous Pavilion Park
Tiantan Park
Parachute Jump Tower
NANMOFANG
DAJINGCUN
YOU'ANMEN
YONGDINGMEN
ZUO'ANMEN
FENGTAI
XIZHUANG
FENGTAIQU
SIDAO
DAWUJL
HUANGTUGANG (FANJIACUN)
XIAOHONGMEN
NANYUAN
JIUGANG
Nanyangchang
DAXINGQU
III
KAWAGUCHI
Kiyose
SHIMURA
TAKENOTSUKA
KAMIHONGO
Gokōmutsumi
MATSUDO
Noguchi
Nakakido
Hōme
Wakō
ITABASHI
KAMIAKATSUKA
AKABANE
KITA
ADACHI
ŌYADA
SHIMANE
KANAMACHI
Kamishiki
Kido
HIGASHIŌIZUMI
MAENO
INATSUKE
NUMATA
KAMEARI
YAGIRI
Hatsutomi
Misaki
Kurume
NERIMA
SHIMOSHAKUJII
Shakujii
Toshimaen Recreation Ground
SENJU
KATSUSHIKA
KŌNODAI
Soya
Ōno
Kamagaya
Oana
Hōya
TAKINOGAWA
ARAKAWA
KOIWA
ICHIKAWA
Makomezawa
Fujiwara
Tsuboi
Tanashi
KAMISHAKUJII
TOYOTAMA
EKODA
TOSHIMA
SUGAMO
KOMAGOME
Rikugien Garden
SUGANO
WAKAMIYA
Taki
SHIMOIGUSA
OCHIAI
Gokokuji Temple
HONGŌ
Tōkyō National Museum
TAITŌ
MUKŌJIMA
YAWATA
Takane
MUSASHINO
KICHIJŌJI
BUNKYŌ
Bot. Garden
Ueno Park
ASAKUSA
SUMIDA
Tōkagi
YONEGASAKI
FUNABASHI
Yakuendai
AMANUMA
ASAGAYA
NAKANO
KOISHIKAWA
UENO
SHISHIHONE
Inokashira Park
SUGINAMI
KŌENJI
KASHIWAGI
SHINJUKU
KANDA
HONJO
KOMATSUGAWA
Haragi
MAEBARA
MITAKA
Shinjuku gyoen Garden
Imperial Palace
NIHONBASHI
KAMEIDO
MIZUE
KAIJIN
TSUDANUMA
HORINOUCHI
CHIYODA
CHŪŌ
Kiyosumi Garden
SUNAMACHI
EDOGAWA
Hongyōtoku
Yatsu
Narashino
FUCHŪ
Chōfu Airport
TAKAIDO
Meiji Shrine
National Stadium
AKASAKA
Hibiya Park
GINZA
KŌTO
UKITA
SHIBUYA
AOYAMA
FUKAGAWA
KASAI
Urayasu
Makuhari
KAMISHIHARA
KAMIKITAZAWA
Hamarikyu Garden
SHIBAZAKI
SOSHIGAYA
AZABU
Tōkyō Tower
Harumi International Sample Fair Hall
CHŌFU
SETAGAYA
MINATO
Komae
Tama
National Park
TŌKYŌ
NAKANOSHIMA
SANGENJAYA
Meguro
YŌGA
MEGURO
Komazawa Ground
KOYAMA
Ikuta
Noborito
NAKANOBU
EBARA
Tōkyō-ko
Takaishi
MIZONOKUCHI
TAMAGAWA
OKUSAWA
SHINAGAWA
DENENCHŌFU
MAGOME
YUKIGAYA
ŌI
KAMIASAO
MAGINU
SHINJŌ
KOSUGI
ŌTA
Honmonji Temple
KŌHOKU
CHITOSE
MARUKO
IKEGAMI
ŌMORI
Tōkyō-wan
KAMOSHIDA
EDA
NOGAWA
KAMATA
Tōkyō International Airport
Kanagawa
HIYOSHI
KATSUTA
Hayabuchi
ROKUGŌ
HANEDA
TSUNASHIMA
NAGATSUDA
Tsurumi
YAKŌ
DAISHI
Kawasaki Stadium
KAWAWA
NIPPO
KAWASAKI
MIDORI
TSURUMI
Matsugashima
NAKAYAMA
KIKUNA
Sojiji Temple
ODA
Ichihara
Kitaaoyagi
TERAYAMA
KOZUKUE
Kawasaki-ko
IMAJUKU
SHINOHARA
Imazuasayama
ASAHI
Anegasaki
KAWASHIMA
KANAGAWA
NAMAMUGI
FUTATSUBASHI
FUTAMATAGAWA
YOKOHAMA
Iriyamazu
Yokohama-ko
Daijuku
SEYA
HODOGAYA
NISHI
MOTOMACHI
Kuranami
IDOGAYA
NAKA
Nakajima
Urikura
Obitsu
Sodegaura
Iitomi
Chiba
Ōsone
IZUMI
HOMMOKU
Yokohama National University
KASHIO
MINAMI
Egawa
ŌKUBO
ISOGO
Takayanagi
Ijiri
Ariyoshi
Nagayoshi
Shimoizumi
TOTSUKA
YABE
Kisarazu Air Base
Ushibukuro
Yanaka
Hirakawa
SASAKE
KUMIZAWA
HINO
SUGITA
1 : 225,000
Kilometers
Statute Miles
One inch to 3,6 miles

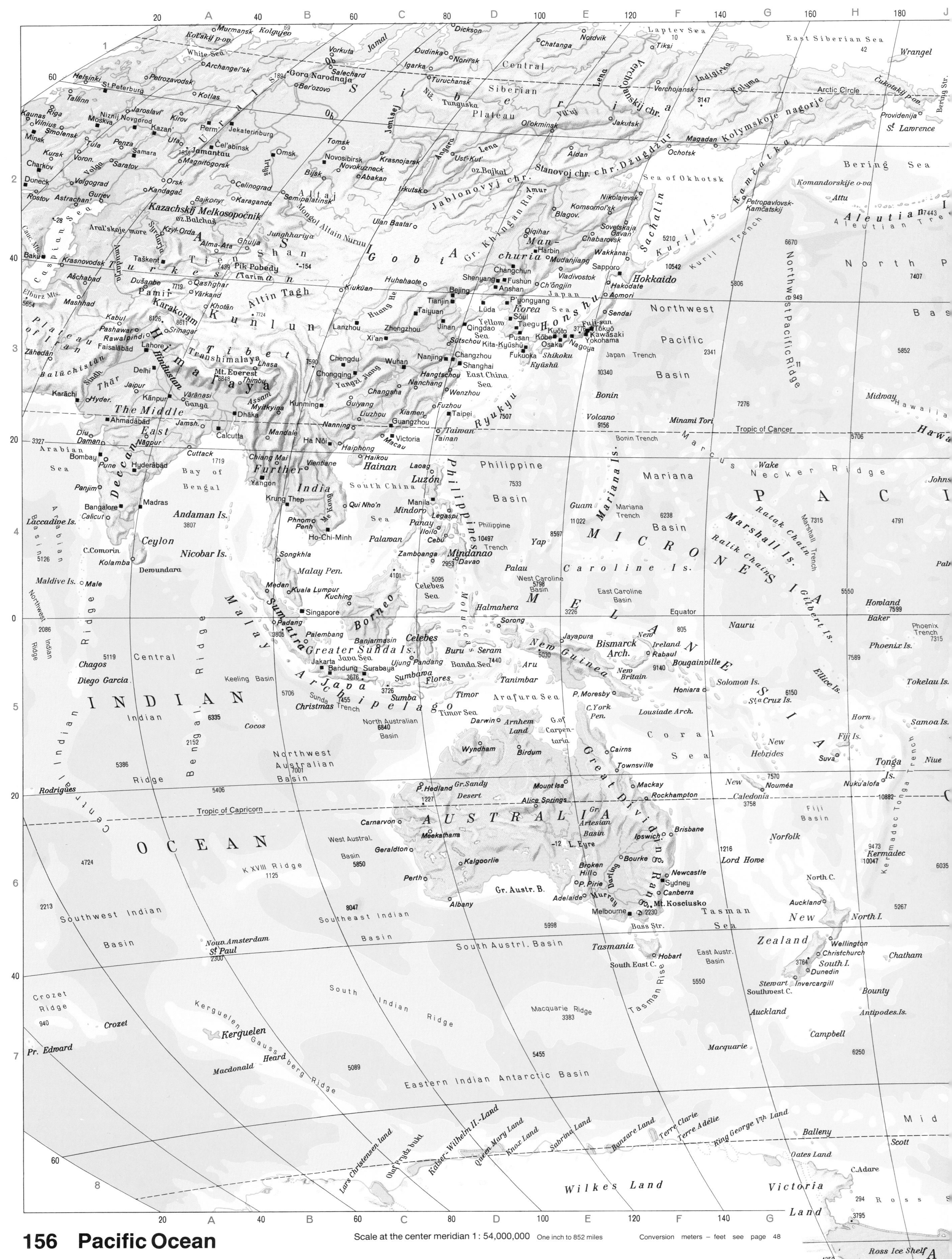
Laptev Sea
East Siberian Sea
Wrangel
Murmansk
Kolgujev
Kol'skij p-ov
White Sea
Archangel'sk
Vorkuta
Jamal
Dickson
Dudinka
Noril'sk
Chatanga
Nordvik
Tiksi
Central
Siberian
Plateau
Igarka
Turuchansk
Tunguska
Salechard
Gora Narodnaja
Ber'ozovo
Ob
Helsinki
St. Peterburg
Petrozavodsk
Kotlas
Tallinn
Riga
Vilnius
Minsk
Smolensk
Moskva
Nižnij Novgorod
Jaroslavl'
Kirov
Kazan'
Perm'
Jekaterinburg
Ural
Tula
Penza
Samara
Ufa
Čel'abinsk
Jamantau
Magnitogorsk
Kursk
Voron.
Saratov
Charkov
Doneck
Rostov
Volgograd
Astrachan'
Gurjev
Orsk
Kandagač
Omsk
Tomsk
Novosibirsk
Novokuzneck
Bijsk
Abakan
Krasnojarsk
Jenisej
Irtyš
Angara
Lena
Ust'-Kut'
oz. Bajkal
Irkutsk
Jablonovyj chr.
Stanovoj chr.
Džugdžur
Aldan
Ochotsk
Magadan
Kolymskoje nagorje
Verchojansk
Verchojanskij chr.
Jakutsk
Ol'okminsk
Vil'uj
Indigirka
Kolyma
Arctic Circle
Čukotskij p-ov
Bering Str.
Providenija
St. Lawrence
Bering Sea
Komandorskije o-va
Attu
Aleutian Is.
Aleutian Trench
Kamčatka
Petropavlovsk-Kamčatskij
Sea of Okhotsk
Sachalin
Kuril Is.
Kuril Trench
Nikolajevsk
Komsomol'sk
Blagov.
Amur
Sovetskaja Gavan'
Chabarovsk
Wakkanai
Sapporo
Hokkaido
Hakodate
Aomori
Sendai
Celinograd
Karaganda
Semipalatinsk
Altaj
Mongol Altain Nuruu
Ulan Baatar
Kazachskij Melkosopočnik
oz. Balchaš
Bajkonyr
Aral'skoje more
Syrdarja
Kzyl-Orda
Alma-Ata
Ghulja
Junghhariya
Caspian Sea
Baku
Krasnovodsk
Amudarja
Taškent
Tien Shan
Pik Pobedy
Tarim
Ašchabad
Dušanbe
Qashghar
Yarkand
Pamir
Elburz Mts.
Mashhad
Kabul
Pashawar
Rawalpindi
Srinagar
Faisalabad
Lahore
Karakoram
Khotān
Altin Tagh
Kunlun
Tibet
Plateau of Iran
Zāhedān
Balūchistān
Sindh
Thār
Delhi
Jaipur
Hindustan
Himalaya
Transhimalaya
Lhasa
Mt. Everest
Thimbu
Assam
Karāchi
Hyder.
Kānpur
Vārānasi
Ganga
Myitkyina
Dhāka
The Middle East
Ahmadābād
Jamsh.
Calcutta
Diu
Daman
Nāgpur
Mandalay
Arabian Sea
Bombay
Pune
Hyderābād
Cuttack
Bay of Bengal
Deccan
Panjim
Bangalore
Calicut
Madras
Andaman Is.
Laccadive Is.
Arabian Basin
C. Comorin
Kolamba
Ceylon
Dewundara
Nicobar Is.
Maldive Is.
Male
Gobi
Gr. Khingan Ra.
Manchuria
Qiqihar
Harbin
Mudanjiang
Changchun
Shenyang
Fushun
Anshan
Vladivostok
Ch'ŏngjin
Japan Sea
Hohehaote
Beijing
Tianjin
Taiyuan
Huang He
Lüda
P'yŏngyang
Korea
Sŏul
Taegu
Pusan
Honshu
Fuji-san
Tōkyō
Kawasaki
Yokohama
Nagoya
Kyōto
Kōbe
Ōsaka
Shikoku
Kyūshū
Fukuoka
Kita-Kyūshū
Yellow Sea
Qingdao
Jinan
Zhengzhou
Xi'an
Lanzhou
Chengdu
Chongqing
Wuhan
Nanjing
Changzhou
Shanghai
Hangtschou
East China Sea
Nanchang
Wenzhou
Changsha
Yangzi Jiang
Guiyang
Kunming
Liuzhou
Xiamen
Fuzhou
Taipei
Taiwan
Tainan
Guangzhou
Nanning
Victoria
Macau
Ha Nôi
Haiphong
Haikou
Hainan
Vientiane
Chiang Mai
Further India
Yangon
Krung Thep
South China Sea
Qui Nho'n
Me Kong
Phnom Penh
Ho-Chi-Minh
Songkhla
Malay Pen.
Medan
Kuala Lumpur
Singapore
Kuching
Borneo
Sumatra
Padang
Palembang
Malay Archipelago
Greater Sunda Is.
Jakarta
Bandung
Java Sea
Surabaya
Java
Banjarmasin
Celebes
Ujung Pandang
Sumbawa
Flores
Sumba
Sunda Trench
Christmas
Laoag
Luzon
Manila
Mindoro
Legaspi
Panay
Iloilo
Cebu
Palawan
Philippines
Philippine Trench
Zamboanga
Mindanao
Davao
Celebes Sea
Moluccas
Halmahera
Sorong
Buru
Seram
Banda Sea
Aru
Tanimbar
Timor
Timor Sea
Arafura Sea
Ryukyu
Philippine Basin
Bonin
Volcano
Bonin Trench
Minami Tori
Marcus Necker Ridge
Tropic of Cancer
Mariana Is.
Mariana Trench
Mariana Basin
Guam
Yap
Palau
West Caroline Basin
East Caroline Basin
Caroline Is.
Micronesia
Melanesia
Japan Trench
Northwest Pacific Basin
Northwest Pacific Ridge
North Pacific Basin
Midway
Hawaii
Wake
Pacific
Ratak Chain
Ralik Chain
Marshall Is.
Marshall Trench
Gilbert Is.
Equator
Nauru
Howland
Baker
Phoenix Trench
Phoenix Is.
Ellice Is.
Tokelau Is.
Samoa Is.
Horn
Fiji Is.
Suva
Tonga Is.
Niue
Nuku'alofa
Tonga Trench
Kermadec Trench
Kermadec
Fiji Basin
New Caledonia
Nouméa
New Hebrides
Solomon Is.
Sta Cruz Is.
Honiara
Bougainville
New Ireland
Rabaul
New Britain
Bismarck Arch.
New Guinea
Jayapura
P. Moresby
Louisiade Arch.
Coral Sea
C. York Pen.
G. of Carpentaria
Arnhem Land
Darwin
Wyndham
Birdum
Cairns
Townsville
Mackay
Rockhampton
Great Dividing Range
Mount Isa
Alice Springs
Gr. Sandy Desert
P. Hedland
Australia
Gr. Artesian Basin
L. Eyre
Brisbane
Ipswich
Bourke
Carnarvon
Meekatharra
Geraldton
Kalgoorlie
Perth
Albany
Gr. Austr. B.
Broken Hill
P. Pirie
Adelaide
Darling
Murray
Newcastle
Sydney
Canberra
Mt. Kosciusko
Melbourne
Bass Str.
Tasmania
Hobart
South East C.
Tasman Sea
Tasman Rise
Lord Howe
Norfolk
East Austr. Basin
New Zealand
North I.
North C.
Auckland
Wellington
Christchurch
South I.
Dunedin
Invercargill
Stewart
Southwest C.
Chatham
Bounty
Antipodes Is.
Auckland
Campbell
Macquarie
Indian Ocean
Central Indian Ridge
Northwest Indian Ridge
Chagos
Diego Garcia
Central Indian Basin
Keeling Basin
Cocos
Bengal Ridge
Ridge
North Australian Basin
Northwest Australian Basin
Rodrigues
Tropic of Capricorn
West Austral. Basin
K XVIII Ridge
Southwest Indian Basin
Southeast Indian Basin
Nouv. Amsterdam
St Paul
South Austr. Basin
Macquarie Ridge
South Indian Ridge
Crozet Ridge
Crozet
Pr. Edward
Kerguelen
Kerguelen Gaussberg Ridge
Heard
Macdonald
Eastern Indian Antarctic Basin
Mid
Balleny
Scott
Oates Land
C. Adare
Victoria Land
Ross Sea
Ross Ice Shelf
Lars Christensen land
Olaf Prydz bukt
Kaiser-Wilhelm II.-Land
Queen Mary Land
Knox Land
Sabrina Land
Banzare Land
Terre Clarie
Terre Adélie
King George Vth Land
Wilkes Land
20 A 40 B 60 C 80 D 100 E 120 F 140 G 160 H 180 J

Scale at the center meridian 1 : 54,000,000 One inch to 852 miles

Conversion meters – feet see page 48

Greenland
Baffin Bay
Baffin
Davis Str.
Godthavn
Godthåb
Julianehåb
K. Farvel
Denmark Str.
Iceland
Reykjavik
Reykjanes Ridge
Labrador B.
Norw. Basin
Bodø
Scandinavia
Trondheim
Oslo
Stockholm
Bergen
Shetland
Föroyar
British Isles
Glasgow
Edinburgh
København
North Sea
Manchester
Hamburg
Liverp.
Birmingh.
Amst.
Köln
Ireland
Baile Atha Cliath
Corcaigh
London
Rott.
Brüss.
English Channel
Brest
Paris
Nantes
West Europ. B.
La Coruña
Porto
Iberian B.
Lisboa
Açores
Açores Plateau
Madeira
Is. Canarias
Canary Rise
Canary Basin
Cape Verde Plateau
Cape Verde
Cape Verde Basin
Is. Cabo Verde
Beaufort Sea
Banks
Melville
Victoria
Boothia Pen.
Melville Pen.
Inuvik
Ft Yukon
Great Bear L.
P. Radium
Fairbanks
Dawson
Mackenzie
Anchorage
Whitehorse
Seward
Gulf of Alaska
Juneau
Great Slave L.
Southampton
Hudson Str.
Ungava Pen.
Hudson Bay
Churchill
Labrador
Schefferville
Labrador Pen.
Mc Murray
Nelson
Rocky Mountains
Queen Charlotte Is.
Prince Rupert
Edmonton
L. Winnipeg
Winnipeg
Sept-Iles
Gulf of St. Lawrence
Newfoundland
St John's
C. Race
Miquelon
Sydney
Halifax
Sable I.
C. Sable
Newfoundland Bank
Altair Seamounts
Vancouver
Calgary
Regina
Great Prairies
Thunder Bay
Québec
Montréal
Ottawa
St. Laurent
Seattle
Tacoma
Portland
Missouri
L. Superior
L. Michigan
L. Huron
Minneapolis
Milwaukee
Detroit
Toronto
L. Ontario
L. Erie
Buffalo
Boston
Providence
New York
Philadelphia
Baltimore
Washington
Norfolk
C. Hatteras
NORTH AMERICA
Appalachian Mts.
Great Salt Lake City
Great Basin
C. Mendocino
Mendocino Fracture Zone
Sacramento
San Francisco
Mt. Whitney
Colorado
Denver
Mt. Elbert
Omaha
Chicago
Cleveland
Pittsb.
Kansas City
St Louis
Cincinnati
Louisville
Ohio
Oklahoma City
Mississippi
Memphis
Atlanta
Albuquerque
Dallas
Ft Worth
Birmingh.
Los Angeles
S. Diego
El Paso
Cd Juárez
Savannah
Jacksonville
Rio Bravo
S. Antonio
Houston
New Orleans
Florida
North American Basin
Bermuda Is.
Sargasso Sea
Guadalupe
Lower California
Gulf of California
Rio Bravo del Norte
Monterrey
Torreón
Gulf of Mexico
Miami
Bahama Is.
Murray Fracture Zone
La Habana
Cuba
West Indies
Tampico
C.S. Lucas
S. Luis Potosí
Mérida
Guadalajara
Yucatán
Greater Antilles
Santiago de C.
Puerto Rico Trench
Puerto Rico
Haiti
Jamaica
Kingston
Pt-au-Prince
St Domingo
México
Veracruz
Tehuantepec
Is. de Revillagigedo
Middle America Trench
Guatemala
S. Salvador
Tegucigalpa
Managua
Caribbean Sea
Curaçao
Lesser Antilles
Barbuda
Guadeloupe
Dominica
Martinique
St Lucia
Barbados
Grenada
Guiana Basin
Trinidad
Clarion Fracture Zone
Central Pacific Basin
Clipperton Fracture Zone
Clipperton
Guatemala Basin
S. José
Panamá
Maracaibo
Barquisimeto
Caracas
Cúcuta
Llanos
Orinoco
Georgetown
Paramaribo
Cayenne
Cocos Rise
I. del Coco
Medellín
Manizales
Bogota
Macizo de Guyanas
Amazon Shelf
Malpelo
Equator
Quito
Chimborazo
Rio Negro
Marajó
Pará
Rise
São Paulo
Is. Galápagos
Guayaquil
Pta Pariñas
Iquitos
Manaus
Amazonas
Belém
São Luis
Teresina
Fortaleza
Fernando de Noronha
Natal
Crato
Selvas
Rio Madeira
Xingu
Pto Velho
Recife
Is. Marquises
Cerro de Pasco
Callao
Lima
SOUTH AMERICA
Tocantins
São Francisco
Maceió
Cuzco
Planalto do Brasil
Brazil Basin
Groll Seamount
Salvador
Puka Puka
Is. Tuamotu
Tahiti
Society Is.
Flint
Peru Basin
Arequipa
Mollendo
L. Titicaca
La Paz
Illimani
Cuiabá
Brasília
Goiânia
Arica
Sta Cruz
Corumbá
Belo Horizonte
Nazca Ridge
Chile Basin
Atacama Trench
Iquique
Sucre
Gran Chaco
Vitória
Tuamotu Basin
Tropic of Capricorn
Ducie
Pitcairn
Antofagasta
Nova Iguaçu
Trindade
Tubuai
Rapa
Sala y Gómez
Easter I.
Desventurados
S. Miguel de Tucumán
Asunción
Curitiba
Santos
Rio de Janeiro
São Paulo
Easter Plateau
East Pacific Ridge
Juan Fernández Ridge
Paraná
Florianópolis
Aconcagua
Valparaíso
Sta Fe
Rosario
Pto Alegre
Rio Grande Rise
Is. Juan Fernandez
Santiago de Ch.
Mendoza
Cord. de los Andes
Buenos Aires
Montevideo
R. de la Plata
La Plata
South Pacific Basin
Concepción
Sta Rosa
Pampa
Mar del Plata
Bahía Blanca
Tristan da Cunha
Argentine Basin
Pto Montt
Chiloé
Esquel
Gough
Patagonia
Comodoro Rivadavia
Pto Deseado
Patagon. Shelf
Falkland Is.
Southeast Pacific Basin
Punta Arenas
Est. de Magallanes
Tierra del Fuego
Scotia Ridge
Ushuaia
C. de Hornos
South Scotia Basin
South Georgia
Meteor Depth
South Sandwich Is.
Bouvet
Elephant I.
South Shetlands
South Orkneys
D'Urville
Atlantic Indian Antarctic Basin
Adelaide
Zeml'a Aleksandra I
o. Petra I
Antarctic Pen.
Bellingshausen Sea
Weddell Sea
Hobbs Coast
Walgreen Coast
Byrd Land
Berkner I.
Caird Land
Coats Land
Prinzreg.-Luitpold-Ld
Kronprinsesse Mærtha land
ANTARCTICA
ATLANTIC OCEAN
Mid Atlantic Ridge

I N D O N E S I A
Bali Sea
Flores Sea
Timor
Timor Trench
Arafura Sea
Timor Sea
Savu Sea
Sumbawa
Sumba
Flores
P. Lombok
Mataram
P. Roti
Cartier I.
Scott Reef
North Australian Trench
Rowley Shoals
I N D I A N O C E A N
Melville I.
Darwin
Cobourg Pen.
Arnhem Land
Aboriginal Reserve
Gulf of Carpentaria
Groote Eylandt
Wellesley Is
Cape York Pen.
Bonaparte Archipelago
Jos. Bonaparte Gulf
Kimberley
Dampier Land
Broome
Derby
Wyndham
Katherine
Daly Waters
Tennant Creek
Barkly Tableland
Tanami Desert
Northern Territory
Alice Springs
Macdonnell Ranges
Simpson Desert
Great Sandy Desert
Canning Desert
Gibson Desert
Great Victoria Desert
Nullarbor Plain
W E S T E R N A U S T R A L I A
S O U T H A U S T R A L I A
Q U E E N S L A N D
Great Artesian Basin
Port Hedland
Dampier
Onslow
North West Cape
Exmouth Gulf
Carnarvon
Shark Bay
Dirk Hartogs I.
Geraldton
Houtman Abrolhos
Kalgoorlie
Coolgardie
Norseman
Esperance
Archipelago of the Recherche
PERTH
FREMANTLE
Bunbury
Albany
Cape Leeuwin
Eucla
Hampton Tableland
Great Australian Bight
Eyre Pen.
Spencer Gulf
Yorke Pen.
ADELAIDE
Kangaroo I.
Lake Eyre
Flinders Ra.
Musgrave Ra.
Ayers Rock
Mt. Olga
Broken Hill
MELBOURNE
GEELONG
King I.
West Austral. Basin
South Australian Basin
Leeuwin Rise
Jeffrey Depth 5998

1 : 13,500,000 — 0 100 200 300 400 500 Kilometers — 0 100 200 300 400 Statute Miles

One inch to 213 miles

Conversion meters – feet see page 48

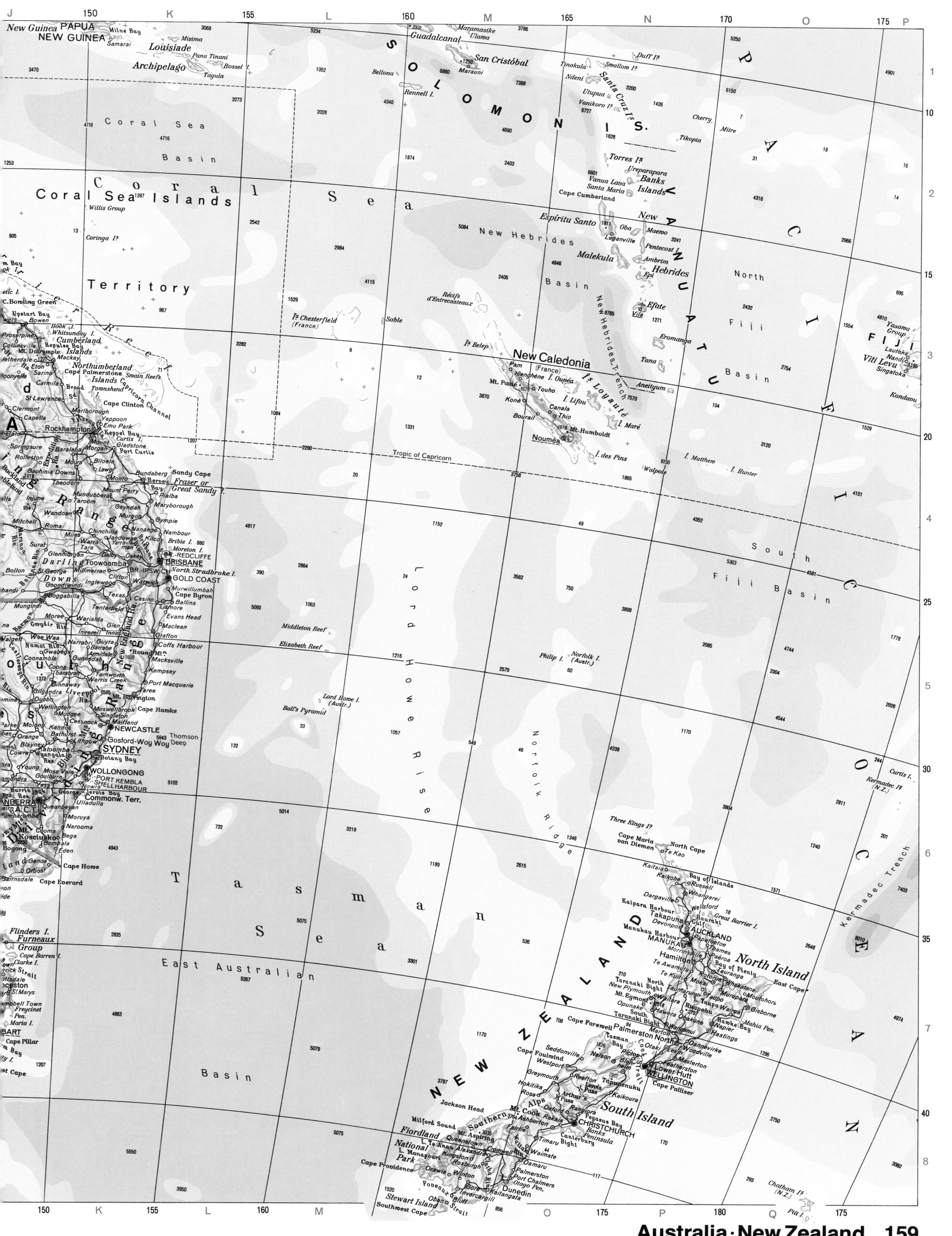

PAPUA NEW GUINEA
Louisiade Archipelago
SOLOMON IS.
Guadalcanal
San Cristóbal
Santa Cruz Is.
Coral Sea Basin
Coral Sea
Coral Sea Islands Territory
Willis Group
New Hebrides Basin
NEW HEBRIDES
Espíritu Santo
Malekula
Efate
Banks Islands
Torres Is.
PACIFIC OCEAN
North Fiji Basin
South Fiji Basin
FIJI
Viti Levu
New Caledonia (France)
Nouméa
Îs Loyauté
Tropic of Capricorn
Lord Howe Rise
Lord Howe I. (Austr.)
Norfolk I. (Austr.)
Norfolk Ridge
Tasman Sea
Tasman Basin
East Australian Basin
Kermadec Is. (N.Z.)
Kermadec Trench
Rockhampton
Brisbane
Gold Coast
Newcastle
Sydney
Wollongong
Canberra
Commonw. Terr.
Mt. Kosciusko
Flinders I.
Furneaux Group
Hobart
NEW ZEALAND
North Island
South Island
Auckland
Hamilton
Wellington
Christchurch
Dunedin
Stewart Island
Chatham Is. (N.Z.)

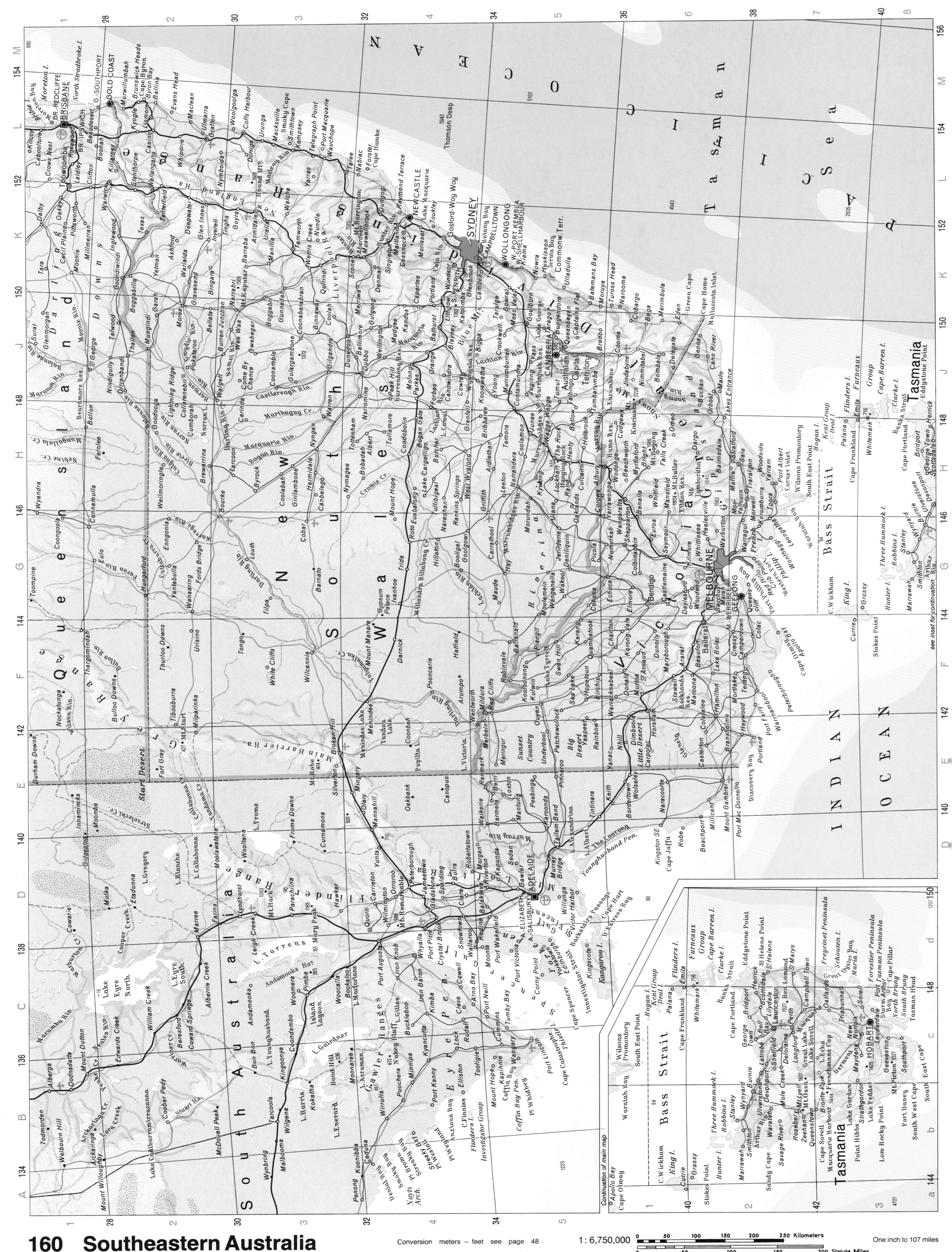
South Australia
New South Wales
Queensland
Victoria
Tasmania
Tasman Sea
Pacific Ocean
Indian Ocean
Bass Strait
Australian Capital Territory
SYDNEY
MELBOURNE
ADELAIDE
BRISBANE
CANBERRA
NEWCASTLE
WOLLONGONG
GEELONG
HOBART
GOLD COAST
Darling Downs
Great Dividing Range
Flinders Ranges
Gawler Ranges
Eyre Pen.
Yorke Pen.
Kangaroo I.
L. Torrens
Lake Eyre North
Sturt Desert
Riverina
Gippsland
Big Desert
Sunset Country
Continuation of main map
see inset for continuation

Conversion meters – feet see page 48

1: 6,750,000

0 50 100 150 200 250 Kilometers

0 50 100 150 200 Statute Miles

One inch to 107 miles

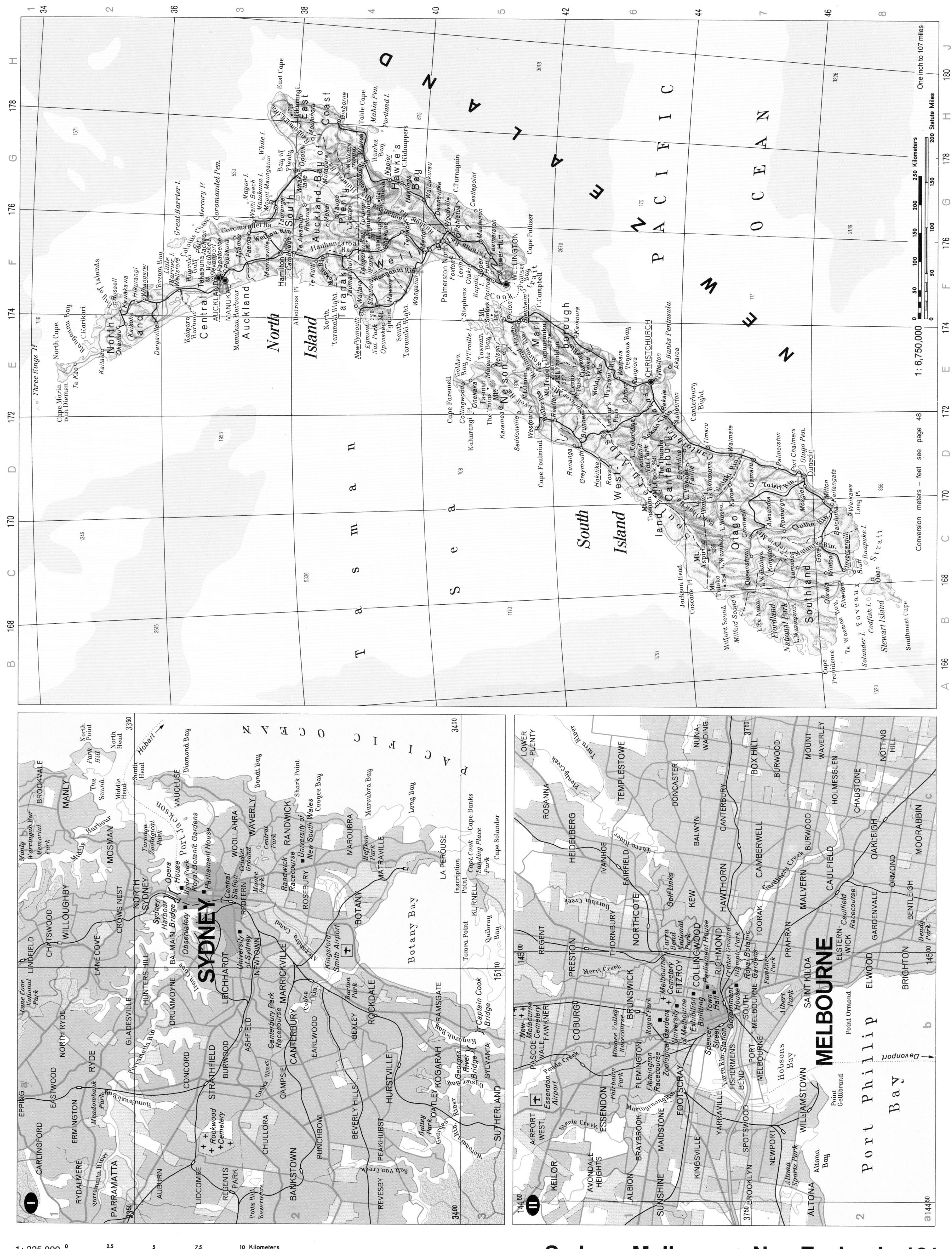

NEW ZEALAND
North Island
South Island
Tasman Sea
PACIFIC OCEAN
AUCKLAND
WELLINGTON
CHRISTCHURCH
Dunedin
Cook Strait
Foveaux Strait
Stewart Island
1 : 6,750,000
One inch to 107 miles
Conversion meters – feet see page 48
SYDNEY
Botany Bay
Port Jackson
MELBOURNE
Port Phillip Bay
Hobsons Bay
1 : 225,000
One inch to 3.6 miles
Kilometers
Statute Miles

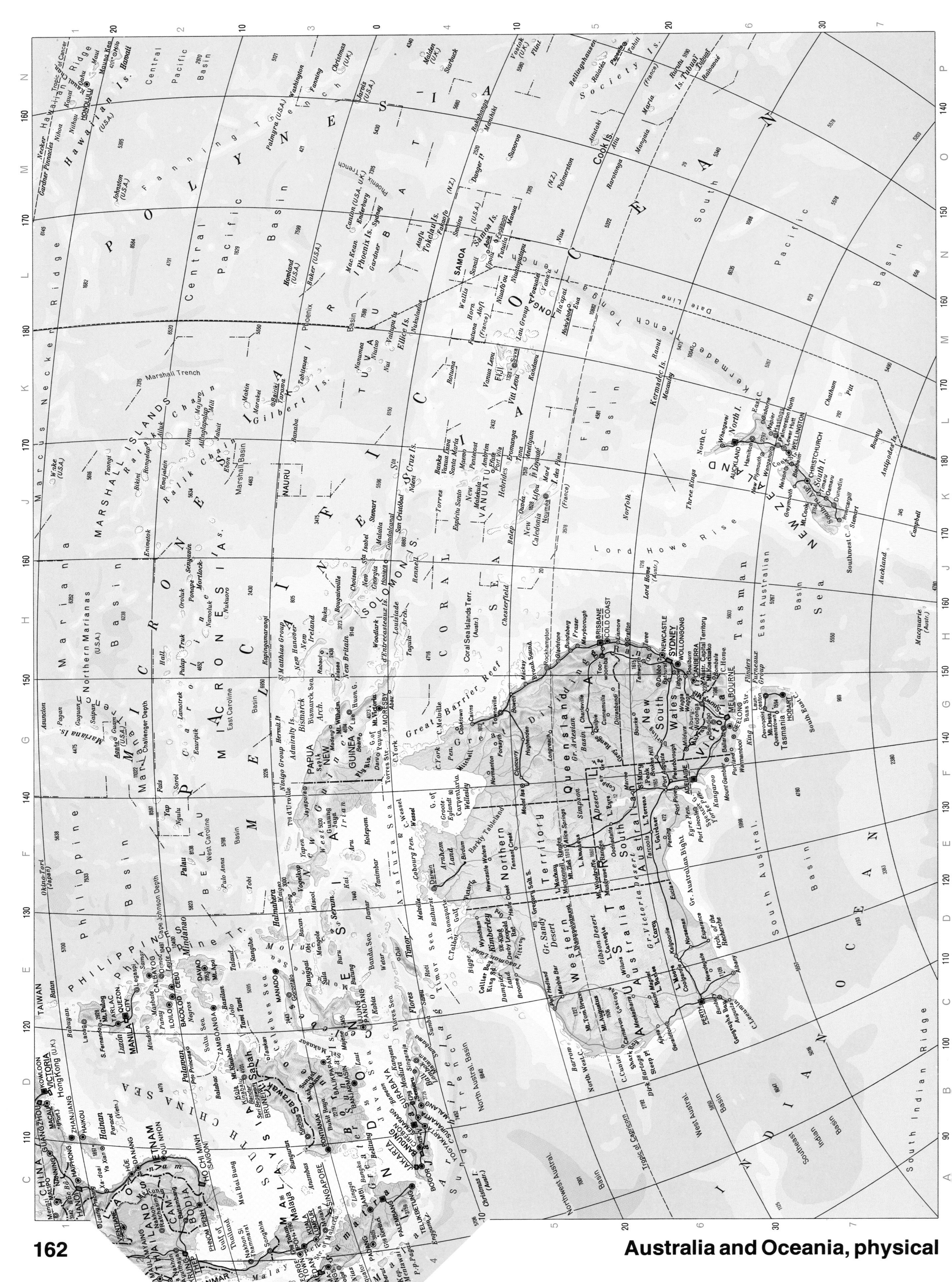

PACIFIC OCEAN
INDIAN OCEAN
POLYNESIA
MICRONESIA
MELANESIA
AUSTRALIA
NEW ZEALAND
CORAL SEA
Tasman Sea
Arafura Sea
Timor Sea
Java Sea
SOUTH CHINA SEA
PHILIPPINES
NEW GUINEA
PAPUA NEW GUINEA
SOLOMON IS.
VANUATU
FIJI
SAMOA
NAURU
MARSHALL ISLANDS
Hawaiian Is.
Hawaii
Cook Is.
Society Is.
Marshall Trench
Challenger Depth
Great Barrier Reef
Great Dividing Range
Queensland
New South Wales
Victoria
South Australia
Western Australia
Northern Territory
Tasmania
Gr. Sandy Desert
Gibson Desert
Gr. Victoria Desert
Simpson Desert
Lord Howe Rise
Kermadec Trench
South Australian Basin
Tropic of Capricorn
Tropic of Cancer
Equator
SYDNEY
MELBOURNE
BRISBANE
ADELAIDE
PERTH
CANBERRA
HOBART
DARWIN
WELLINGTON
AUCKLAND
CHRISTCHURCH
HONOLULU
MANILA
SINGAPORE
JAKARTA
HONG KONG

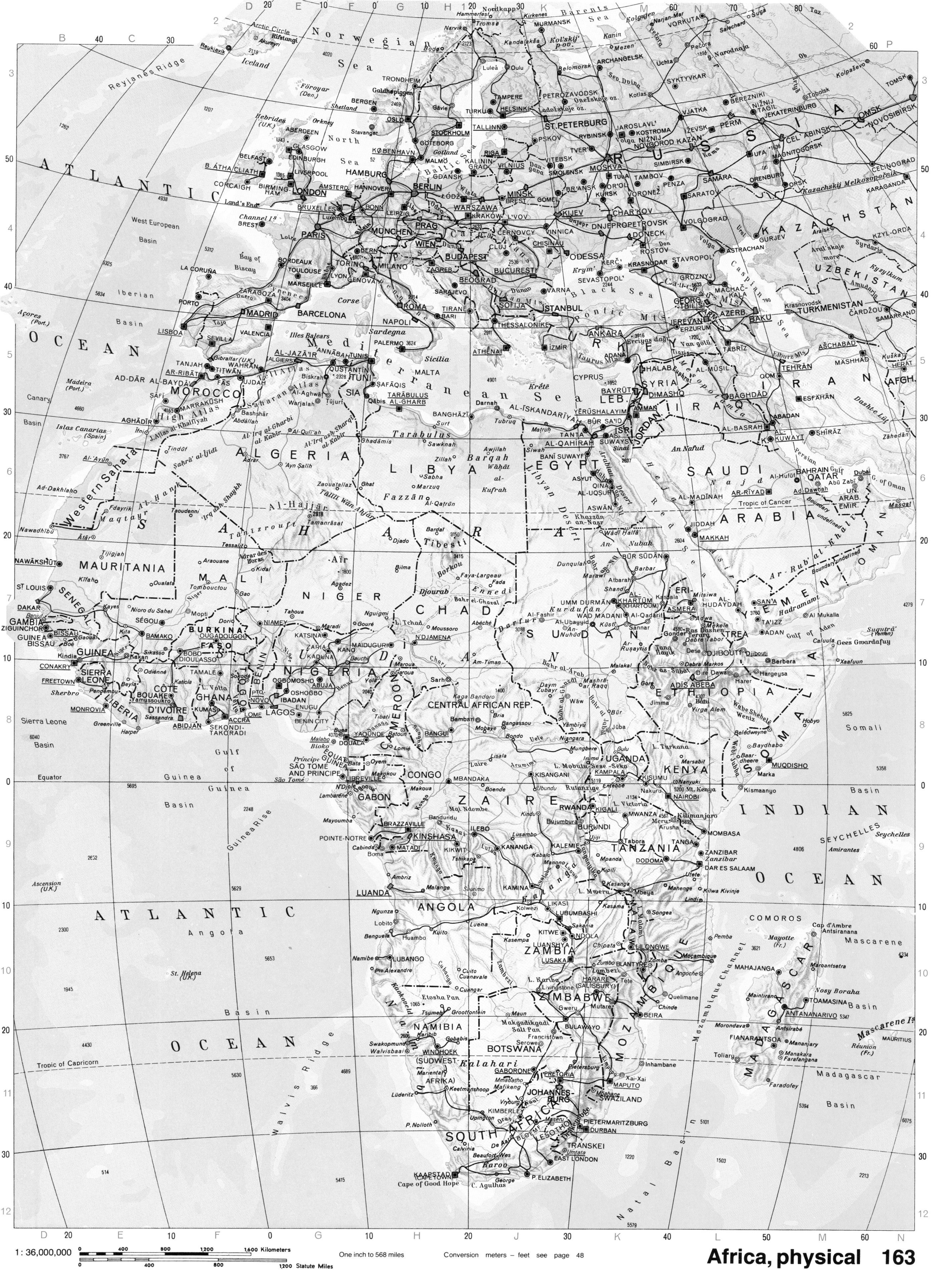
Norwegian Sea
Iceland
North Sea
Baltic Sea
ATLANTIC
OCEAN
West European Basin
Bay of Biscay
Iberian Basin
Mediterranean Sea
Black Sea
Caspian Sea
MOROCCO
ALGERIA
LIBYA
EGYPT
SAHARA
MAURITANIA
MALI
NIGER
CHAD
SUDAN
SENEGAL
GAMBIA
GUINEA
SIERRA LEONE
LIBERIA
CÔTE D'IVOIRE
GHANA
BURKINA FASO
NIGERIA
CAMEROON
CENTRAL AFRICAN REP.
ETHIOPIA
SOMALIA
KENYA
UGANDA
ZAIRE
CONGO
GABON
RWANDA
BURUNDI
TANZANIA
ANGOLA
ZAMBIA
MALAWI
MOZAMBIQUE
ZIMBABWE
NAMIBIA
BOTSWANA
SOUTH AFRICA
LESOTHO
SWAZILAND
MADAGASCAR
SAUDI ARABIA
YEMEN
OMAN
IRAN
IRAQ
SYRIA
JORDAN
TURKEY
RUSSIA
KAZACHSTAN
UZBEKISTAN
TURKMENISTAN
Gulf of Guinea
Guinea Basin
Angola Basin
Walvis Ridge
INDIAN OCEAN
Somali Basin
Mascarene Basin
Madagascar Basin
Natal Basin
Mozambique Channel
Tropic of Cancer
Tropic of Capricorn
Equator

1 : 36,000,000 — 0 400 800 1,200 1,600 Kilometers — 0 400 800 1,200 Statute Miles

One inch to 568 miles

Conversion meters – feet see page 48

ATLANTIC OCEAN
Azores Plateau
Canary Basin
PORTUGAL
SPAIN
Cabo de São Vicente
SEVILLA
GRANADA
Lorca
CARTAGENA
MÁLAGA
ALMERÍA
CÁDIZ
Gibraltar (UK)
Ceuta (Spain)
Melilla (Spain)
TANJAH (TANGER)
AL-JAZĀ'IR (ALGIERS)
QUSANTĪNAH (CONSTANTINE)
TŪNIS (TUNIS)
WAHRĀN (ORAN)
TILIMSĀN
AR-RIBĀṬ (RABAT)
AD-DĀR AL-BAYḌĀ' (CASABLANCA)
FĀS (FEZ)
MIKNĀS
MARRĀKUSH (MARRAKECH)
AṢFĪ (SAFI)
Agādīr
MOROCCO
Arquip. da Madeira (Port.)
Madeira
Funchal
Porto Santo
Ilhas Desertas
Ilhas Selvagens (Port.)
Islas Canarias (Spain)
La Palma
Tenerife
Gran Canaria
LAS PALMAS
Fuerteventura
Lanzarote
STA CRUZ DE TENERIFE
Western Sahara
Al-'Ayūn
Ad-Dakhlah
Tropic of Cancer
ALGERIA
Hammadat Tinghirt
Tādmāït
Aghlab
Tāniẓruft
Al-Hajjār
Tāsīlī Wān Ahjār
Tāsīlī Wān al-Hajjār
Adrār des Iforas
Erg in Sakkane
El Khenachich
El Mahia
Taoudenni
MAURITANIA
Adāfir
Al-Mrayyah
Nawākshūṭ
St-Louis
DAKAR
SENEGAL
GAMBIA
BANJUL
KAOLACK
THIÈS
Ziguinchor
GUINEA-BISSAU
BISSAU
Arquipélago dos Bijagós
GUINEA
CONAKRY
Fouta Djallon
SIERRA LEONE
FREETOWN
Sherbro I.
LIBERIA
MONROVIA
Grain Coast
CÔTE D'IVOIRE
ABIDJAN
BOUAKÉ
Côte d'Ivoire
MALI
BAMAKO
Tombouctou
Mopti
Gao
Ségou
BURKINA FASO
OUAGADOUGOU
BOBO-DIOULASSO
GHANA
KUMASI
ACCRA
SEKONDI-TAKORADI
Cape Coast
Gold Coast
TOGO
LOMÉ
BENIN
COTONOU
PORTO NOVO
Slave Coast
Bight of Benin
NIGER
NIAMEY
Aïr ou Azbine
Agadez
Ténéré du Tafassasset
Plateau du Djado
NIGERIA
LAGOS
IBADAN
ABUJA
KANO
KADUNA
ZARIA
MAIDUGURI
Jos Plateau
PORT HARCOURT
BENIN CITY
ONITSHA
ENUGU
CAMEROON
DOUALA
YAOUNDÉ
Mt Cameroun
Bioko
EQUATORIAL GUINEA
GABON
LIBREVILLE
SÃO TOMÉ AND PRINCIPE
Gfe de Bonny
Gulf of Guinea
Guinea Basin
Sierra Leone Basin
Liberia Ridge
Equator
LIBYA

1 : 13,500,000 — 0 100 200 300 400 500 Kilometers — 0 100 200 300 400 Statute Miles — One inch to 213 miles

Administrative unit in Nigeria: 1 Federal Capital Territory

conversion meters – feet see page 48

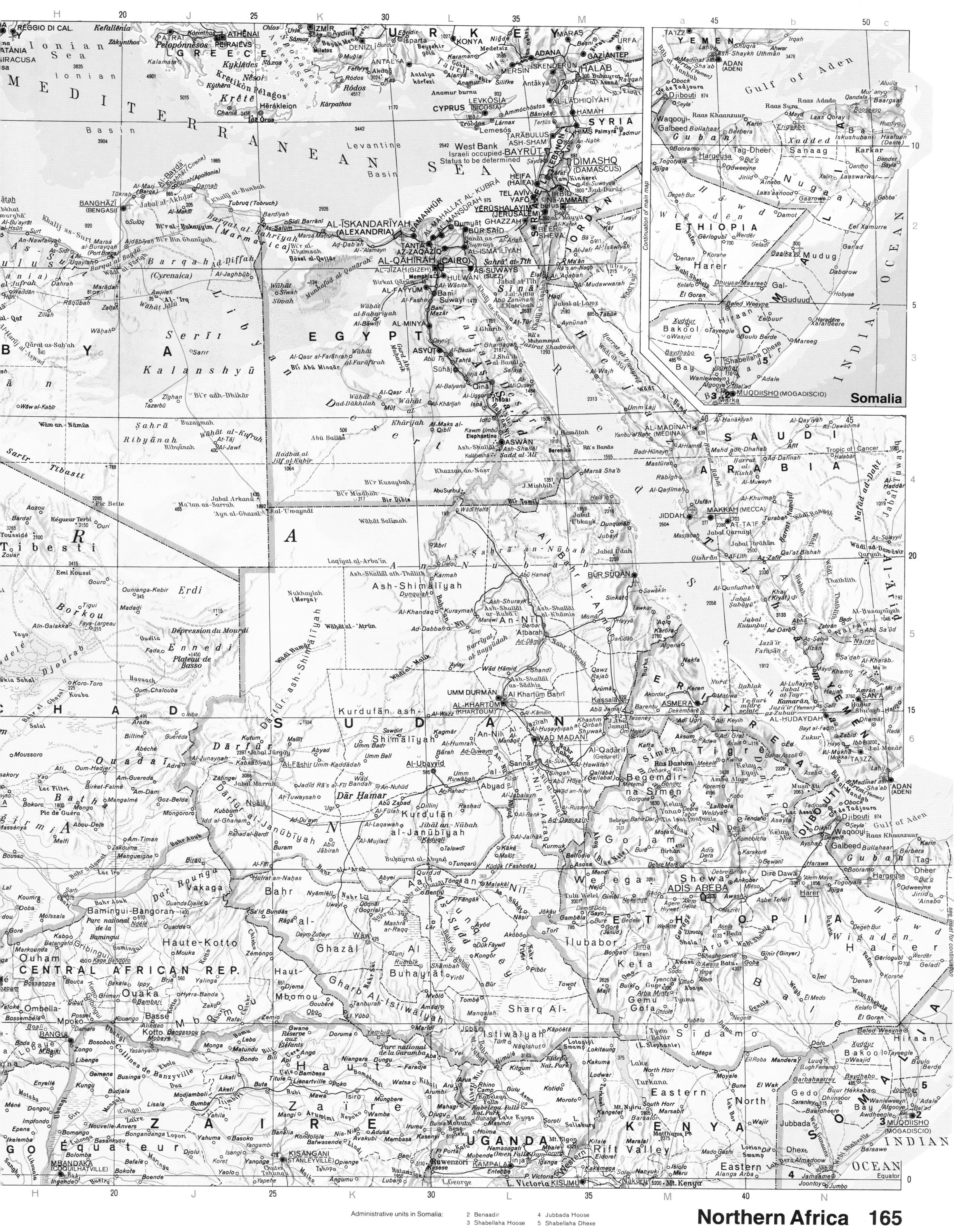
MEDITERRANEAN SEA
Ionian Sea
Levantine Basin
TURKEY
GREECE
CYPRUS
SYRIA
LEBANON
ISRAEL
JORDAN
West Bank
Israeli occupied-
Status to be determined
DIMASHQ (DAMASCUS)
BAYRŪT
YERŪSHALAYIM (JERUSALEM)
AL-ISKANDARĪYAH (ALEXANDRIA)
AL-QĀHIRAH (CAIRO)
BŪR SA'ĪD
AS-SUWAYS (SUEZ)
EGYPT
LIBYA
Libyan Desert
Serīr Kalanshyū
Arabian Desert
Sīnā'
Tibesti
Borkou
Ennedi
CHAD
SUDAN
Ash-Shimālīyah
An-Nīl
Kurdufān ash-Shimālīyah
Dārfūr
Dār Ḥamar
Janūb Kurdufān
Baḥr al-Ghazāl
Al-Istiwā'īyah
Sharq Al-Istiwā'īyah
UMM DURMĀN
AL-KHARṬŪM (KHARTOUM)
BŪR SŪDĀN
WAD MADANĪ
Kassalā
ERITREA
ASMERA
ETHIOPIA
ADIS ABEBA
Tigrē
Begemdir-na Simēn
Gojam
Welega
Shewa
Ilubabor
Kefa
Sīdamo
Harer
Bale
DJIBOUTI
Djibouti
SAUDI ARABIA
AL-MADĪNAH (MEDINA)
MAKKAH (MECCA)
JIDDAH
Tropic of Cancer
YEMEN
ADAN (ADEN)
Gulf of Aden
SOMALIA
MUQDIISHO (MOGADISCIO)
INDIAN OCEAN
Somalia
Continuation of main map
see inset for continuation
CENTRAL AFRICAN REP.
Haute-Kotto
Ouaka
Ouham
BANGUI
ZAIRE
Haut-Zaïre
Équateur
KISANGANI (STANLEYVILLE)
UGANDA
KAMPALA
L. Victoria
KENYA
Rift Valley
Eastern
North Eastern
L. Rudolf
Ruwenzori
Mt. Kenya
Equator

Administrative units in Somalia: 2 Benaadir 3 Shabellaha Hoose 4 Jubbada Hoose 5 Shabellaha Dhexe

ATLANTIC OCEAN
Azores Plateau
Canary Basin
PORTUGAL
SPAIN
MEDITERRANEAN
MOROCCO
ALGERIA
Western Sahara
MAURITANIA
MALI
CÓRDOBA
SEVILLA
GRANADA
MÁLAGA
CÁDIZ
ALMERÍA
CARTAGENA
Golfo de Cádiz
Gibraltar (U.K.)
Ceuta (Sebta) (Spain)
Melilla (Melilla) (Spain)
Strait of Gibraltar
Cabo de Trafalgar
Cabo de São Vicente
TANJAH (TANGER)
TITWĀN (TETOUAN)
AR-RIBĀṬ (RABAT)
AL-Q'NITRAH (KENITRA)
SLĀ (SALE)
AD-DĀR AL-BAYḌĀ' (CASABLANCA)
Al-Muhammadīyah (Fédala)
Al-Jadīdah (Mazagan)
ASFĪ (SAFI)
MARRĀKUSH (MARRAKECH)
Aṣ-Ṣawīrah (Mogador)
Agādīr
MIKNĀS (MEKNES)
FĀS (FEZ)
WAHRĀN (ORAN)
TILIMSĀN (TLEMCEN)
UJDAH (OUJDA)
Bashshār (Béchar)
Tindūf
Sabkhat Tindūf
Ar-Rīf
Al-Aṭlas al-Mutawassiṭ
Al-Jabal al-Aṭlas
Al-Aṭlas aṣ-Ṣaghīr
Jabal Bānī
Jabal Wārqzīz
Ḥammādat ad-Dara'
Ḥammādat Tūnasīn
Ḥammādat Tindūf
Ḥammādat al-Gīr
Tarfāyah (Tekna)
Al-'Irq
'Irq ar-Rāwī
Kaḥal Ṭābalbalah
'Irq Yābis
'Irq ash-Shāsh
Al-Ḥammādah
Wahilah
Iguidi
Al-Ḥank
Maṣhrāḥ
Aghlāb
Ṣaqīyat al-Ḥamrā'
Ar-Ruqaybah
Yaṭṭi
Sierra Nevada
Cordillera Penibética
Mulhacén

1 : 4,500,000 — 0 50 100 150 200 Kilometers — 0 50 100 150 Statute Miles

One inch to 71 miles

Conversion meters – feet see page 48

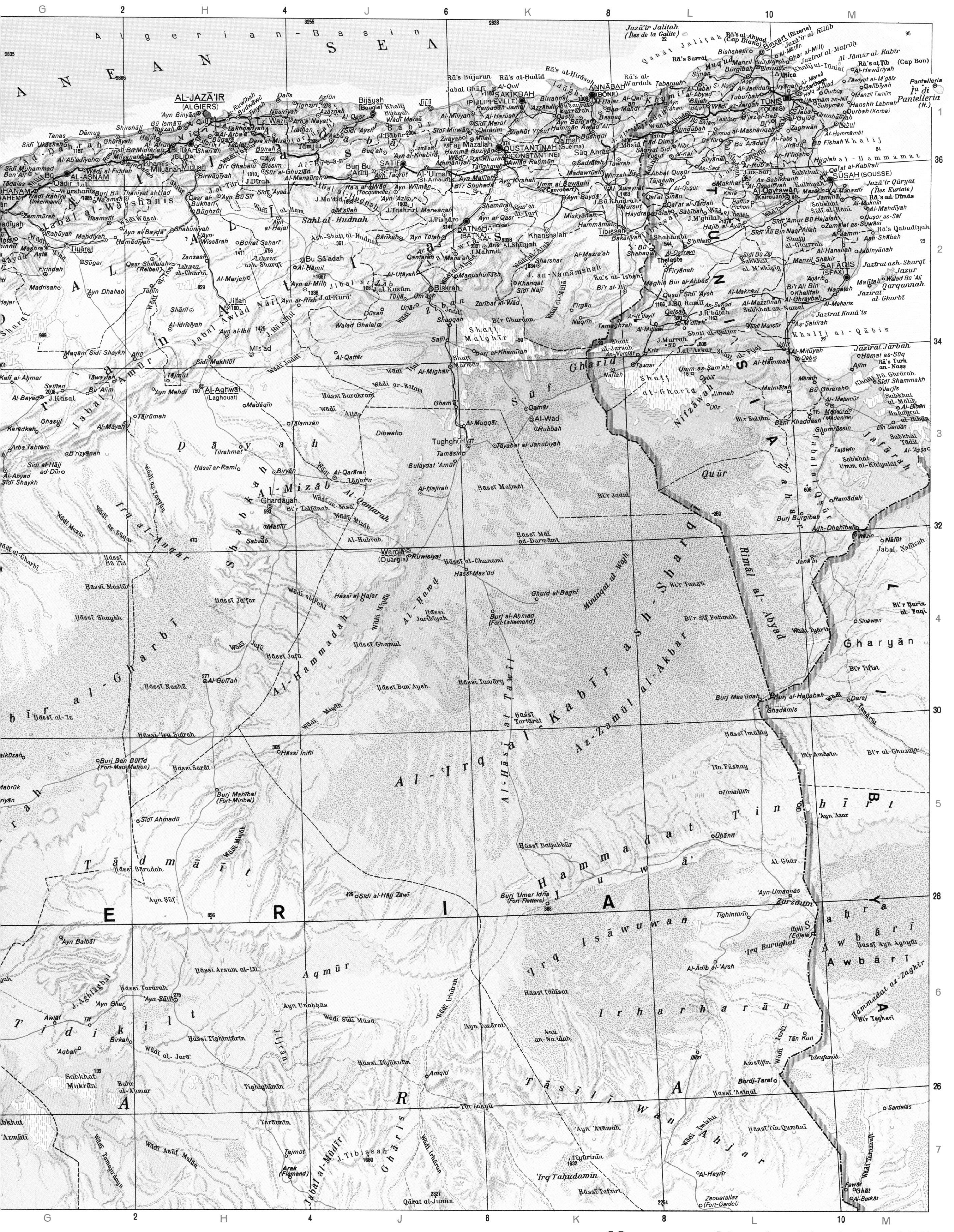

G
2
H
4
J
6
K
8
L
10
M
Algerian-Basin
SEA
AL-JAZĀ'IR
(ALGIERS)
AL-ASNAM
BLIDAH
Tizi Wazu
Bijāyah
(Bougie)
SAKIKDAH
(PHILIPPEVILLE)
ANNĀBAH
(BÔNE)
QUSTANTINAH
(CONSTANTINE)
SATIF
(SETIF)
BATNAH
(BATNA)
Biskrah
Tiyārat
Jilfah
Al-Aghwāt
(Laghouat)
Ghardāyah
Wargla
(Ouargla)
Tughghurt
Ghadāmis
Tūnis
(TUNIS)
Binzart (Bizerte)
SŪSAH (SOUSSE)
SAFĀQIS
(SFAX)
Al-Qayrawān
(Kairouan)
Qābis
Gafsa
Tibissah
Zarzaytin
Illizi
Bordj-Tarat
Burj 'Umar Idris
(Fort-Flatters)
Burj Ban Būl'īd
(Fort-Mac-Mahon)
Burj Mahībal
(Fort-Miribel)
Burj al-Ahmad
(Fort-Lallemand)
Al-Gul'ah
Arak
(Flamand)
Zaouatallaz
(Fort-Gardel)
Pantelleria
Jazā'ir Jalitah
(Îles de la Galite)
Jazīrat Jarbah
Sahl al-Hudnah
Al-Mizāb
Shatt Malghir
Shatt al-Gharid
Al-Hammadah
Al-Irq al Kabīr ash-Sharqī
Az-Zamūl al-Akbar
Al-Hāsī al-Tawīl
Rimāl al-Abyad
Hammadat Tinghīrt
Irq Isāwuwan
Irharharān
Tāsīlī Wan Ahjar
Tādmāīt
Tidikilt
Aqmūr
Awbārī
Hammādat az-Zaghir
Gharyān
Quūr
Nifzāwah
Sahrā Awbārī
ALGERIA
TUNISIA
LIBYA
28
30
32
34
36
26
1
2
3
4
5
6
7

MAURITANIA
At-Trārzah
Al-Brāknah
Al-Aṣābah
At-Taqānat
Al-Ḥawḍ al-Gharbī
Al-Ḥawḍ ash-Sharqī
Nawākshūt (Nouakchott)
Saint-Louis
SÉNÉGAL
DAKAR
THIÈS
Diourbel
KAOLACK
Sine-Saloum
Sénégal-Oriental
Casamance
Ziguinchor
Tambacounda
GAMBIA
Banjul
GUINEA BISSAU
BISSAU
Arquipélago dos Bijagós
GUINÉE
Fouta Djallon
CONAKRY
Kindia
Mamou
Labé
Kankan
Macenta
Guékédou
SIERRA LEONE
FREETOWN
Western Area
Northern
Southern
Eastern
Bo
Kenema
Makeni
LIBERIA
MONROVIA
Montserrado
Cape Mount
Bong
Nimba
Lofa
Grand Bassa
Sinoe
Grand Gedeh
Maryland
Harper
Buchanan
Greenville
MALI
BAMAKO
Kayes
Ségou
Mopti
Sikasso
Kita
Mandingue Plateau
Niger
CÔTE D'IVOIRE
ABIDJAN
BOUAKÉ
Korhogo
Man
Daloa
Odienné
San Pedro
Yamoussoukro
BOBO DIOULASSO
Hauts-Bassins
Volta Noire
Grain Coast
Côte d'Ivoire
Sierra Leone Basin
Liberia Ridge
ATLANTIC
Gulf
Guinea Basin
Equator

1 : 6,750,000 — 0 50 100 150 200 250 Kilometers — 0 50 100 150 200 Statute Miles

One inch to 107 miles

Conversion meters – feet see page 48

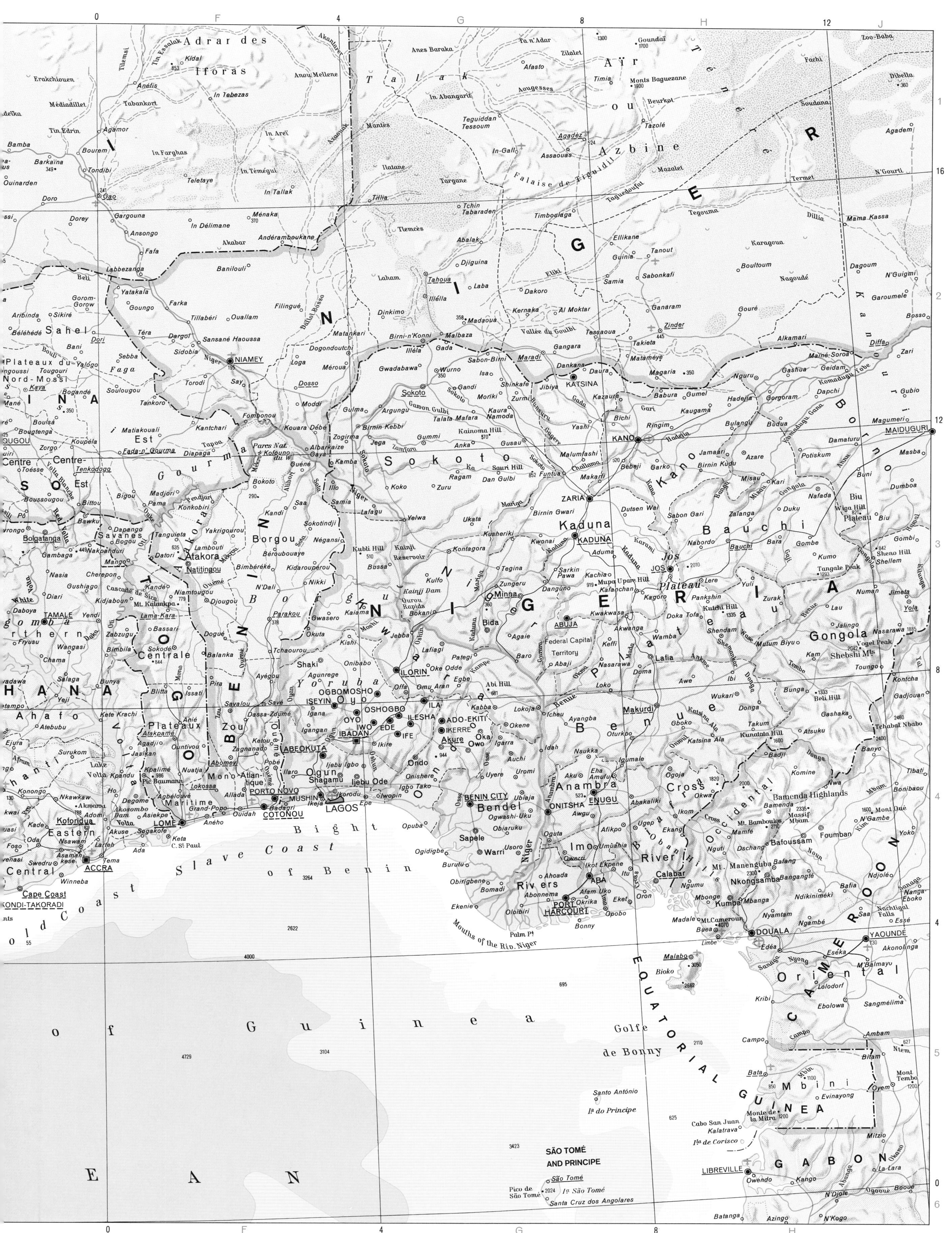

Adrar des Iforas
Aïr ou Azbine
Ténéré
Talak
Falaise de Tiguidit
NIGER
Sahel
Gourma
Sokoto
Kano
Bauchi
Borno
Plateau
Gongola
NIGERIA
Borgou
Atakora
Zou
Mono
Atlantique
Ouémé
BENIN
TOGO
Plateaux
Centrale
Maritime
GHANA
Ahafo
Ashanti
Volta
Eastern
Central
Yoruba
Oyo
Ogun
Ondo
Kwara
Bendel
Anambra
Imo
Rivers
Cross River
Benue
Niger
Kaduna
Bight of Benin
Slave Coast
Gold Coast
Gulf of Guinea
Golfe de Bonny
EQUATORIAL GUINEA
Mbini
CAMEROON
Oriental
Occidental
Bamenda Highlands
GABON
SÃO TOMÉ AND PRINCIPE
Ia do Principe
Santo António
Ia São Tomé
São Tomé
Pico de São Tomé
Santa Cruz dos Angolares
Ia de Corisco
Bioko
Malabo
LIBREVILLE
NIAMEY
KATSINA
KANO
ZARIA
KADUNA
Kaduna
JOS
Jos
MAIDUGURI
ABUJA
Federal Capital Territory
Minna
ILORIN
Ogbomosho
OYO
ISEYIN
OSHOGBO
ILESHA
ILA
IWO
EDE
IFE
IBADAN
ABEOKUTA
ADO-EKITI
IKERRE
Akure
Owo
Ondo
Ijebu Ode
Shagamu
MUSHIN
LAGOS
PORTO NOVO
COTONOU
Abomey
LOME
ACCRA
Koforidua
Cape Coast
SEKONDI-TAKORADI
Tamale
Bolgatanga
Natitingou
Parakou
Djougou
BENIN CITY
Sapele
Warri
ONITSHA
ENUGU
Makurdi
Lafia
Lokoja
Calabar
ABA
PORT HARCOURT
Bonny
Mouths of the Riv. Niger
DOUALA
YAOUNDÉ
Buea
Mt. Cameroun
Nkongsamba
Bafoussam
Bamenda
Sokoto
Gusau
Funtua
Bida
Zinder
Maradi
Tahoua
Agadez
Gao
Kidal
Dori
Fada-n'-Gourma
Kainji Reservoir
Yelwa
Jebba
Diffa
Nguru
Yola
Gombe
Bauchi
Vogel Peak
Shebshi Mts
Mt. Manenguba
Mbini
Bata
Ebolowa
Kribi

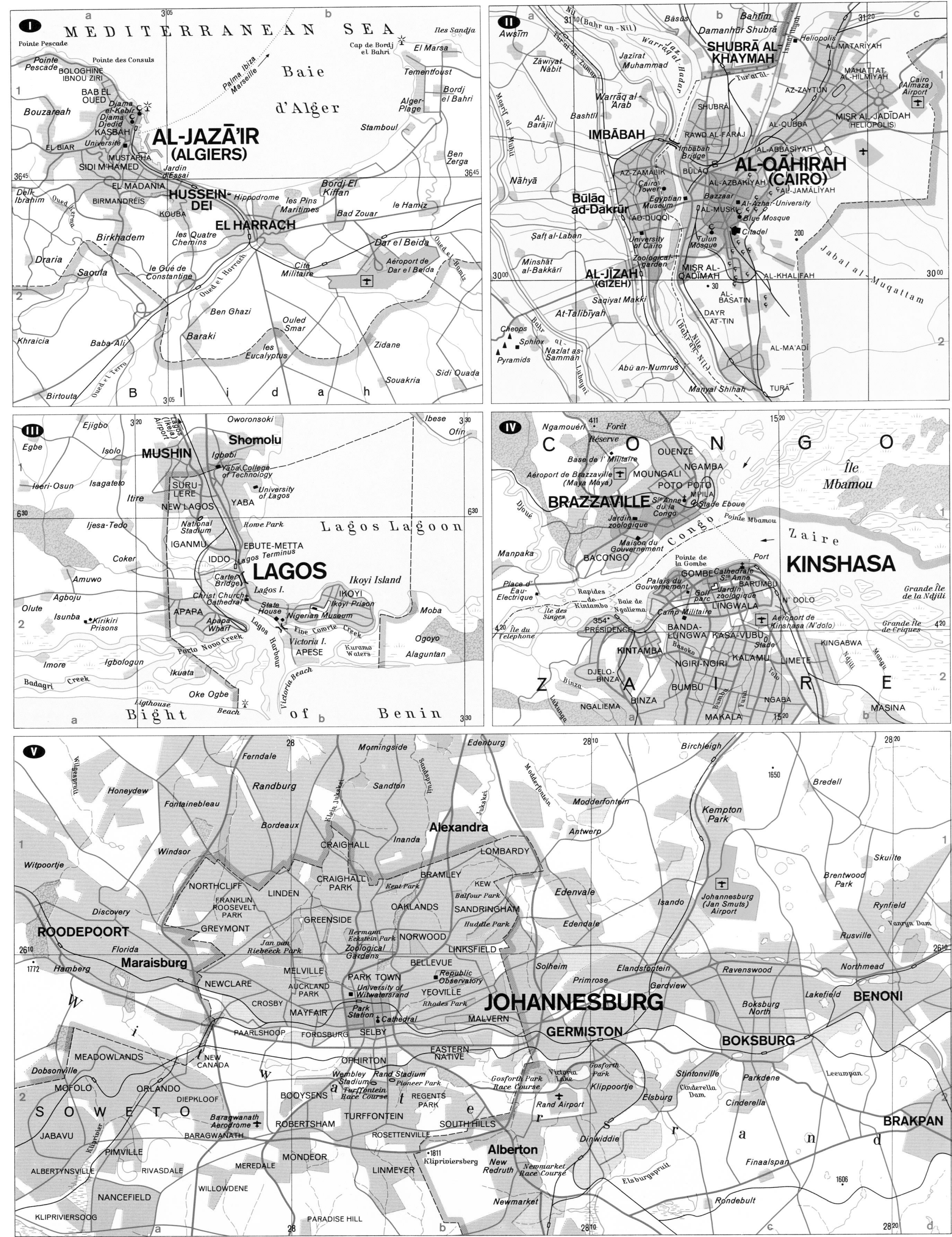

I
MEDITERRANEAN SEA
AL-JAZĀ'IR (ALGIERS)
II
AL-QĀHIRAH (CAIRO)
III
LAGOS
IV
BRAZZAVILLE
KINSHASA
V
JOHANNESBURG

1 : 225,000 — One inch to 3.6 miles — 0 2.5 5 7.5 Kilometers — 0 2.5 5 Statute Miles

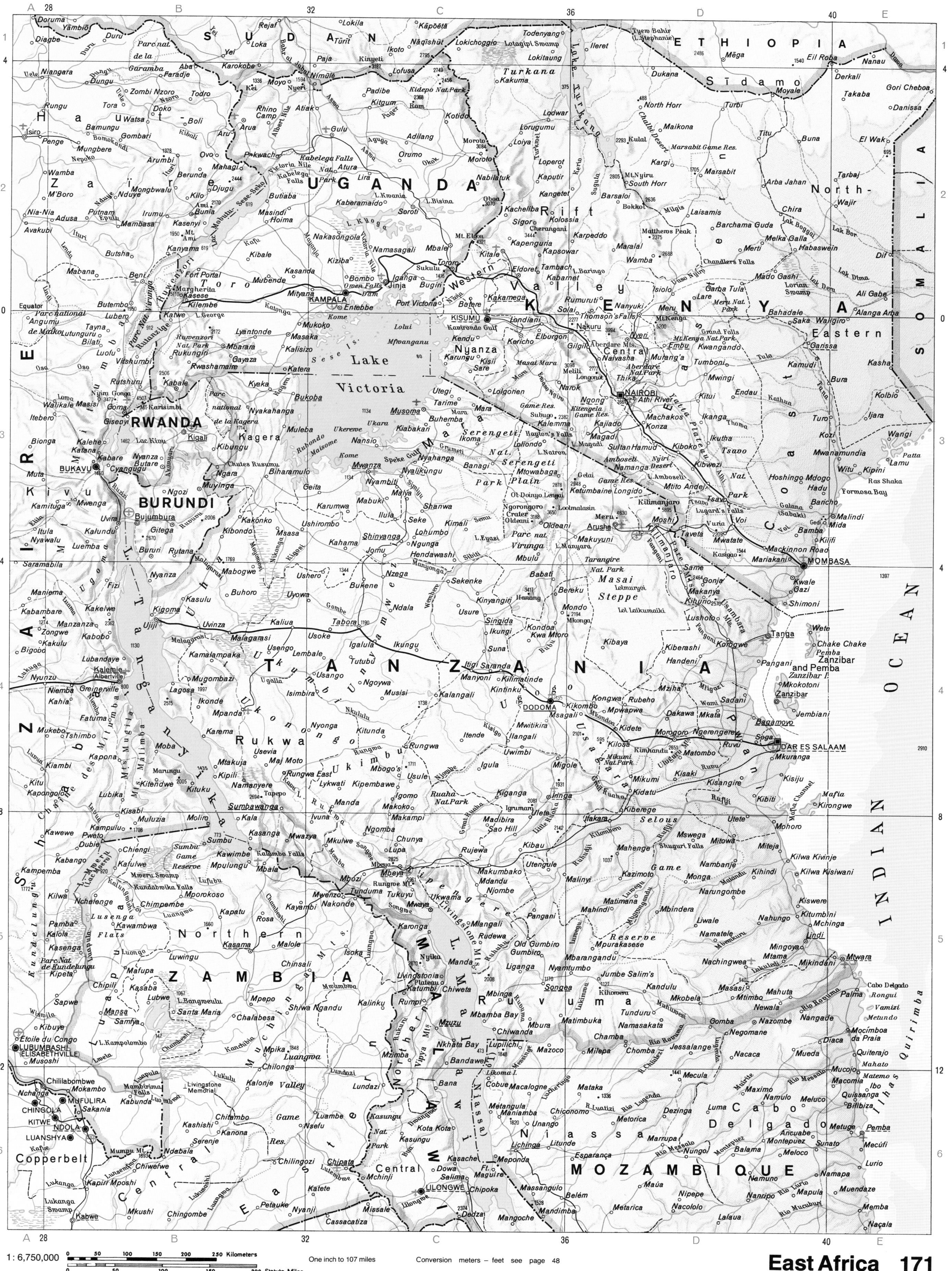
SUDAN
ETHIOPIA
Sīdamo
UGANDA
KENYA
Rift Valley
Turkana
Nyanza
Central
Eastern
North-Eastern
Coast
SOMALIA
Haute-Zaïre
ZAIRE
Kivu
RWANDA
BURUNDI
TANZANIA
Lake Victoria
L. Tanganyika
L. Rukwa
L. Turkana
Serengeti Plain
Masai Steppe
Selous Game Reserve
ZAMBIA
Northern
Central
Copperbelt
MALAWI
L. Malawi (Niassa)
MOZAMBIQUE
Niassa
Cabo Delgado
INDIAN OCEAN
Zanzibar and Pemba
KAMPALA
NAIROBI
DODOMA
DAR ES SALAAM
MOMBASA
KISUMU
Kigali
Bujumbura
LILONGWE
LUBUMBASHI
NDOLA
KITWE
CHINGOLA
Equator

1 : 6,750,000

0 50 100 150 200 250 Kilometers

0 50 100 150 200 Statute Miles

One inch to 107 miles

Conversion meters – feet see page 48

CENTRAL AFRICAN REP.
SUDAN
CAMEROON
EQUATORIAL GUINEA
GABON
CONGO
ZAIRE
UGANDA
RWANDA
BURUNDI
TANZANIA
ANGOLA
ZAMBIA
MALAWI
MOZAMBIQUE
ZIMBABWE
NAMIBIA
BOTSWANA
SOUTH AFRICA
LESOTHO
SWAZILAND
ATLANTIC OCEAN
Angola Basin
Cape Basin
Walvis Ridge
Tropic of Capricorn
Natal Ridge
DOUALA
YAOUNDÉ
LIBREVILLE
BANGUI
BRAZZAVILLE
KINSHASA (LEOPOLDVILLE)
POINTE NOIRE
MATADI
MBANDAKA (COQUILHATVILLE)
KISANGANI (STANLEYVILLE)
KAMPALA
KISUMU
BUKAVU
Bujumbura
DODOMA
LUANDA
KANANGA (LULUABOURG)
MBUJI-MAYI (BAKWANGA)
LUBUMBASHI (ELISABETHVILLE)
LIKASI (JADOTVILLE)
KITWE
NDOLA
MUFULIRA
LUSAKA
LILONGWE
BLANTYRE
HARARE (SALISBURY)
BEIRA
BULAWAYO
Windhoek
Walvis Bay
PRETORIA
JOHANNESBURG
KRUGERSDORP
GERMISTON
SPRINGS
VEREENIGING
MAPUTO
WELKOM
KIMBERLEY
BLOEMFONTEIN
PIETERMARITZBURG
DURBAN
EAST LONDON
PORT ELIZABETH
KAAPSTAD (CAPE TOWN)
Cape of Good Hope
Cape Agulhas
Kalahari Desert
Okavango Depression
Lake Victoria
Lake Mweru
Victoria Falls
Kaapland (Cape of Good Hope)
Oranje-Vrystaat (Orange Free State)
Transvaal
Natal
Conversion meters – feet see

Levantine
Basin
MEDITERRANEAN SEA
West Bank
Israeli occupied-
Status to be determined
BAYRŪT (BEIRUT)
LEBANON
DIMASHQ (DAMASCUS)
SYRIA
HEIFA (HAIFA)
IRBID
TEL AVIV-YAFO (TEL AVIV-JAFFA)
YERUSHALAYIM (JERUSALEM)
AL-QUDS
'AMMĀN
AZ-ZARQĀ'
GHAZZAH ('AZZA) (Aut. Region)
BEER SHEVA' (BEERSHEBA)
Negev
JORDAN
AL-ISKANDARĪYAH (ALEXANDRIA)
Dumyāt (Damietta)
BŪR SA'ĪD (PORT SAID)
DAMANHŪR
AL-MANSŪRA
AL-MAHALLAT AL-KUBRA
ṬANṬĀ
AZ-ZAQĀZĪQ
AL-ISMĀ'ĪLIYAH
Bilbays
Banha
IMBĀBAH
AL JĪZAH (GIZEH)
AL-QĀHIRAH (CAIRO)
Heliopolis
HULWĀN
AS-SUWAYS (SUEZ)
Memphis
Saqqārah
Birkat Qārūn
AL-FAYYŪM
Bani Suwayf
AL-MINYĀ
Mallawī
ASYŪṬ
Sawhāj
Akhmīm
Qinā
Naqādah
Qūṣ
Armant
Nekropolis
Al-Uqsur (Luxor)
Al-Karnak
Isnā
Idfū
Kawm Umbū
ASWĀN (Syene)
Elephantine
Sadd al-'Alī
Kalābsha
Abu Sunbul
Wādī Ḥalfā
Khazzān an-Naṣr
Tropic of Cancer
Sinā'
Jabal at-Tīh
Sahrā' at Tīh
Khalīj as-Suways
Khalīj al-'Aqabah
Elat
Al-'Aqabah
SAUDI ARABIA
Red Sea
Al-Quṣayr
Berenikē
Jazīrat Zabarjad
Al-Ghardaqah (Hurjadah)
Sharm ash-Shaykh
Al-Wāḥāt al-Khārijah
Al-Khārijah (El Kharga)
EGYPT
SUDAN
Ṣaḥrā' Ṣaḥ
Somali Basin
SOMALIA
MUQDISHO (MOGADISCIO)
Kismaanyo
Equator
Zanzibar and Pemba
SEYCHELLES
Aldabra Is.
COMOROS
Moroni
Mayotte (Fr.)
Mozambique Channel
MADAGASCAR
ANTANANARIVO
Toamasina
Fianarantsoa
Toliary
Madagascar Basin
INDIAN OCEAN

DAMARALAND
KALAHARI
BOTSWANA
NAMIBIA
Windhoek
Swakopmund
Walvis Bay
Rehoboth
Gibeon
Nama
Kalkplato
Warmbad
Keetmanshoop
Lüderitzbaai
Lüderitz
Kolmanskop
Mariental
Gobabis
Tropic of Capricorn
Game Reserve No.3
Herero
Twana
DESERT
Kalahari Gemsbok National Park
BETSJOEANALAND
SOUTH
Upington
Klein Namakwaland
Klein Bosmanland
Groot Bosmanland
NAMAKWALAND
Port Nolloth
Springbok
Kaalkaroo
Hantam
Hoë Karoo
Kaapland
(Cape of Good
Groot (Sentraal) Karoo
Klein Karoo
Klein Roggeveld
Middel Roggeveld
Nuweveldberge
Kaap Sint Martin
Kaap Colombine
Saldanha
Sint Helenabaai
KAAPSTAD
(CAPE TOWN)
Tafelberg
Cape of Good Hope
Kaap Hangklip
Cape Agulhas
Worcester
Swellendam
Oudtshoorn
George
Knysna
Beaufort-Wes
De Aar
Kimberley
ATLANTIC OCEAN
Cape Basin
Namib Woestyn
Oranjerivier (Orange River)
Tsau Tsau Flats
Molopo
Kuruman
Nossob
Auob
Swartrand
Hanamiplato
Noukloofberge
Hakos
Conception baai
Sandvisbaai
Hottentotsbaai
Elisabethbaai
Spencerbaai
Hollams Voëleil.
Sint Franziskusbaai
Oranjemund
Alexanderbaai
Hondeklipbaai
Groenriviermond
Bamboesbaai
Lambertsbaai
Langebaan
Dasseneiland
Robbeneiland
Calvinia
Vredenburg
Malmesbury
Paarl
Stellenbosch
Mosselbaai
Prieska
Brits

174 1 : 4,500,000 0 50 100 150 200 Kilometers 0 50 100 150 Statute Miles. One inch to 71 miles Conversion meters – feet see page 48

ZIMBABWE
MOZAMBIQUE
Inhambane
Gaza
SWAZILAND
LESOTHO
Transvaal
Natal
Oranje-Vrystaat
(Orange Free State)
INDIAN OCEAN
Kruger National Park
Drakensberg
Soutpansberge
Waterberge
Witwatersrand
Hoëveld
Maluti Mts
Natal Basin
Natal Ridge
PRETORIA
JOHANNESBURG
MAPUTO
DURBAN
PIETERMARITZBURG
OOS-LONDEN (EAST LONDON)
PORT ELIZABETH
BLOEMFONTEIN
Maseru
WELKOM
KRUGERSDORP
ROODEPORT
SOWETO
GERMISTON
BOKSBURG
BENONI
SPRINGS
VEREENIGING
Vanderbijlpark
Potchefstroom
Klerksdorp
Kroonstad
Ladysmith
Newcastle
Richard's Bay
Port Shepstone
Inhambane
Xai Xai
Baia do Maputo
Tongaland
Pondoland
Temboeland
Griekwaland-Oos
Transkei
Ciskei
Fingoland

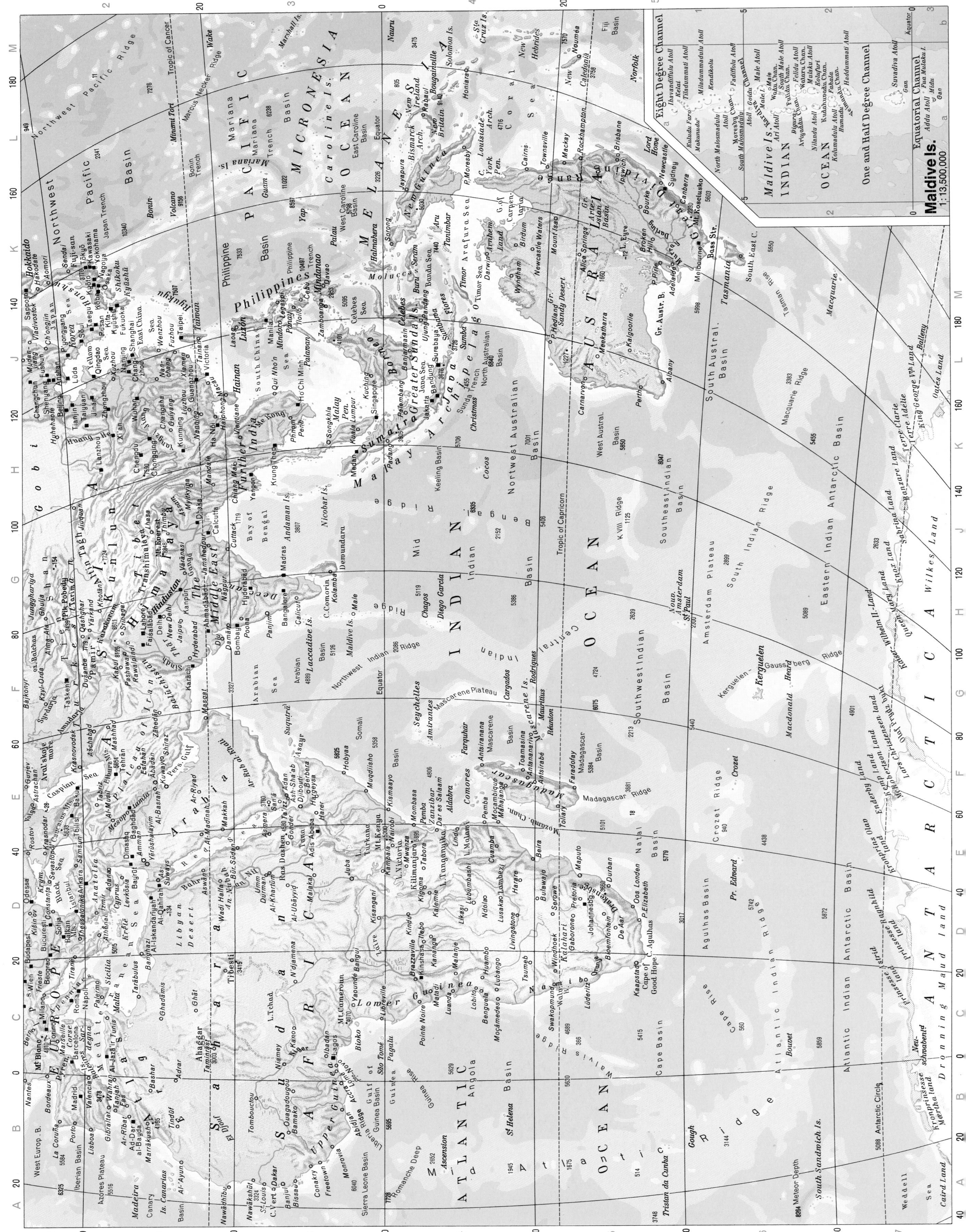

Conversion meters – feet see page 48

Scale at the center meridian 1 : 60,000,000 One inch to 947 miles

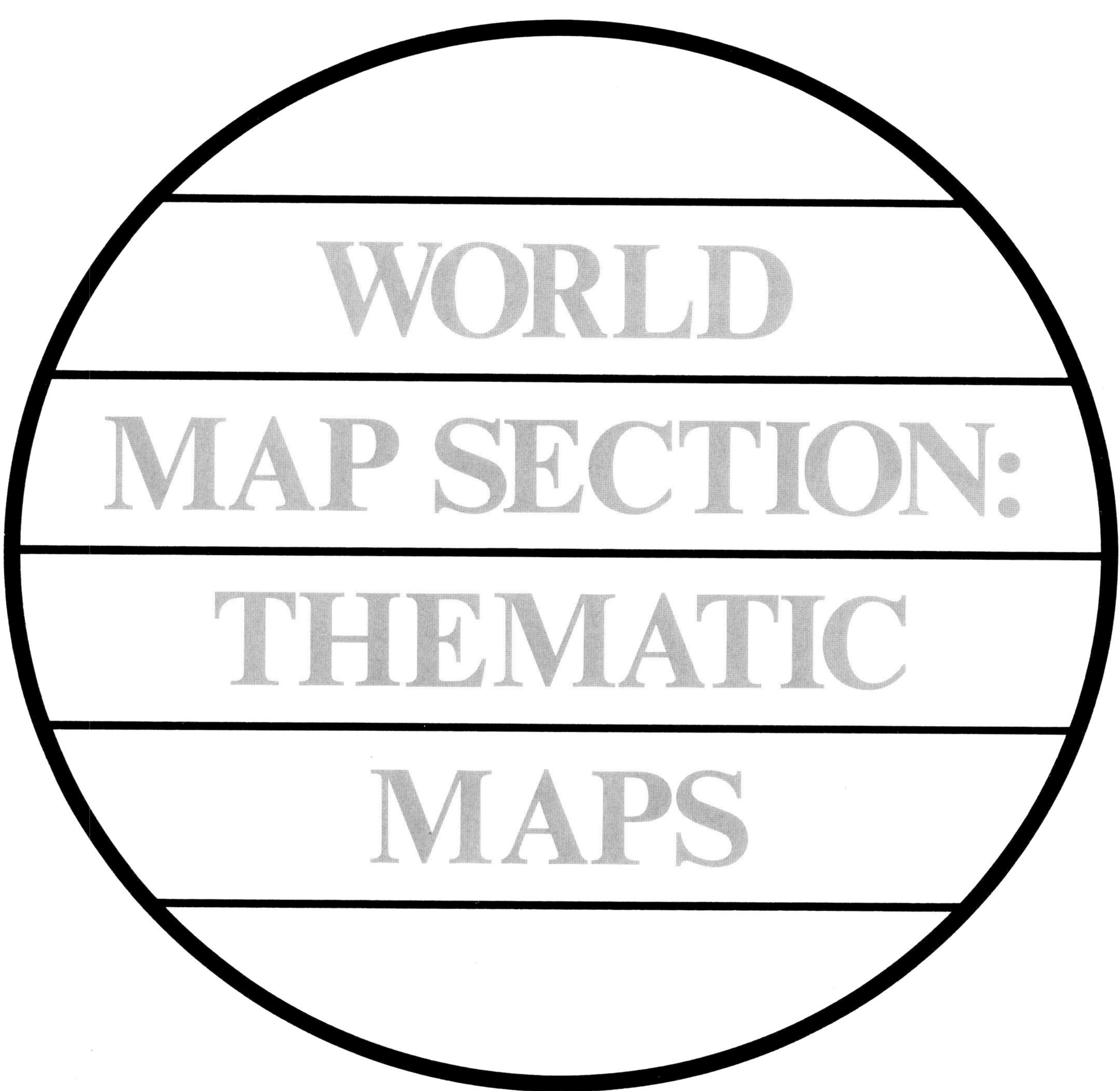
WORLD
MAP SECTION:
THEMATIC
MAPS

A. = Andorra
AFGHAN. = Afghanistan
ALB. = Albania
AR. = Armenia
AU. = Austria
AZ. = Azerbaijan
B. = Belgium
BA. = Bangladesh
BH. = Bhutan
BULG. = Bulgaria
CAM. = Cameroon
CAMB. = Cambodia
CR. = Croatia
DEN. = Denmark
DJ. = Djibouti
DOM.REP. = Dominican Republic
E. = Estonia
ER. = Eritrea
EQUAT.GUINEA = Equatorial Guinea
Fr.-G. = French Guiana
G. = Germany
1 Bosnia Hercegovina, Yugoslavia and Macedonia
2 Czech. Republic and Slovakia
ARCTIC
Greenland
(Den.)
Baffin Bay
Beaufort Sea
Bering Sea
Gulf of Alaska
Hudson Bay
Labrador
Newfoundland
CANADA
UNITED STATES
MEXICO
Gulf of Mexico
Sargasso Sea
Caribbean Sea
PACIFIC OCEAN
ATLANTIC OCEAN
Tropic of Cancer
Equator
Tropic of Capricorn
Arctic Circle
Antarctic Circle
Hawaiian Is.
Hawaii
KIRIBATI
CUBA
HAITI
DOM.REP.
JAMAICA
BAHAMAS
BELIZE
HONDURAS
GUATEMALA
EL SALVADOR
NICARAGUA
COSTA RICA
PANAMA
COLOMBIA
VENEZUELA
GUYANA
SURINAME
ECUADOR
PERU
BRAZIL
BOLIVIA
PARAGUAY
CHILE
ARGENTINA
URUGUAY
Falkland Is.
(U.K.)
South Georgia
South Sandwich Is.
Drake Str.
South Shetlands
South Orkneys
Weddell Sea
Bellingshausen Sea
Byrd Land
Ross Ice Shelf
ANTARCTICA
ICELAND
UNITED KINGDOM
IRELAND
PORTUGAL
MOROCCO
MAURITANIA
CAPE VERDE
SENEGAL
GAMBIA
GUINEA-BISSAU
GUINEA
SIERRA LEONE
LIBERIA
SÃO TOMÉ AND PRINCIPE
Ascension
St. Helena
Tristan da Cunha
Gough (U.K.)
Cities over 1,000,000 Population
Cities under 1,000,000 Population
Shipping trade routes

 Scale at the center meridian 1 : 67,500,000 One inch to 1,065 miles

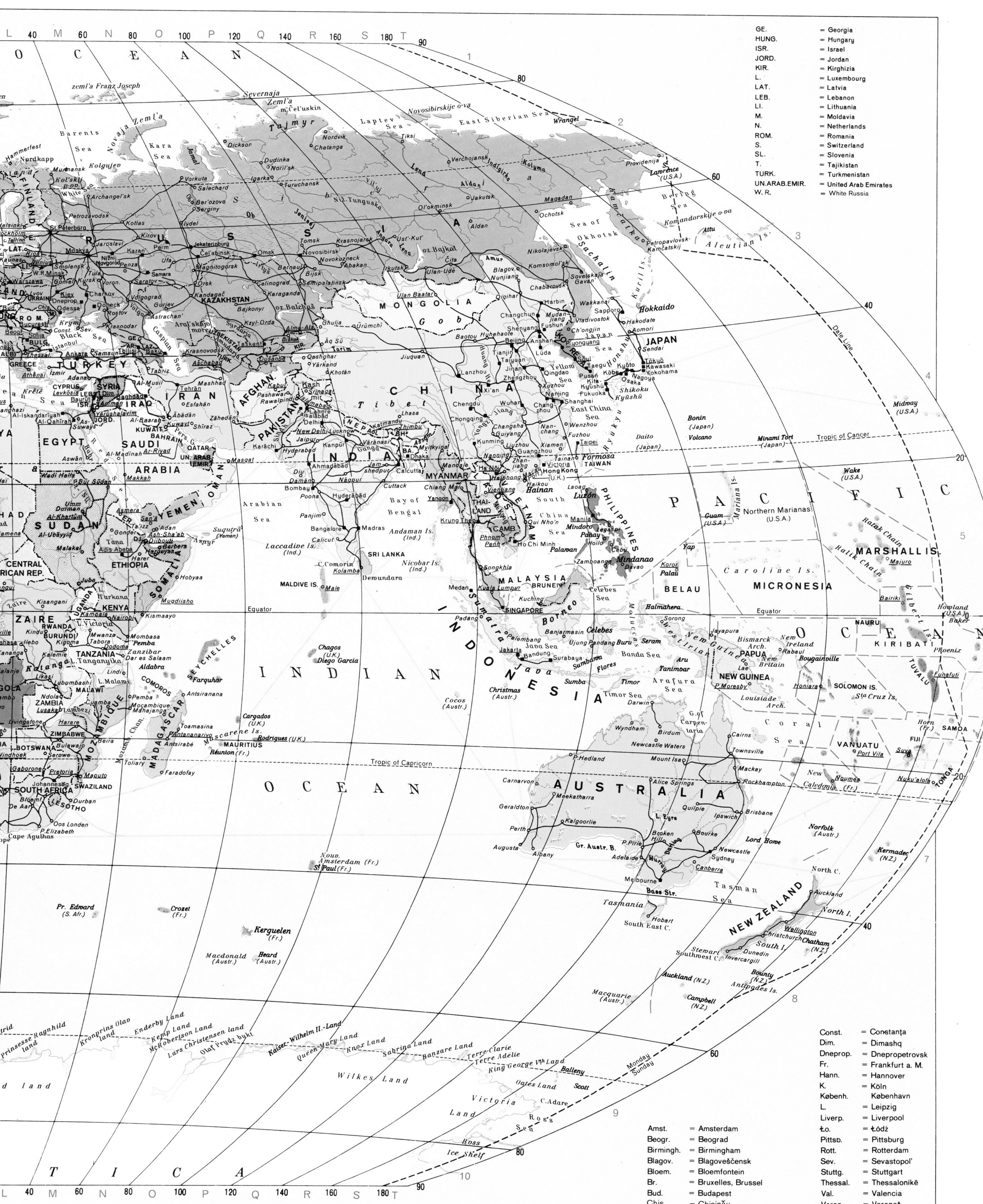

GE. = Georgia
HUNG. = Hungary
ISR. = Israel
JORD. = Jordan
KIR. = Kirghizia
L. = Luxembourg
LAT. = Latvia
LEB. = Lebanon
LI. = Lithuania
M. = Moldavia
N. = Netherlands
ROM. = Romania
S. = Switzerland
SL. = Slovenia
T. = Tajikistan
TURK. = Turkmenistan
UN.ARAB.EMIR. = United Arab Emirates
W. R. = White Russia
Amst. = Amsterdam
Beogr. = Beograd
Birmingh. = Birmingham
Blagov. = Blagoveščensk
Bloem. = Bloemfontein
Br. = Bruxelles, Brussel
Bud. = Budapest
Chiş. = Chişinău
Const. = Constanţa
Dim. = Dimashq
Dneprop. = Dnepropetrovsk
Fr. = Frankfurt a. M.
Hann. = Hannover
K. = Köln
Københ. = København
L. = Leipzig
Liverp. = Liverpool
Ło. = Łódź
Pittsb. = Pittsburg
Rott. = Rotterdam
Sev. = Sevastopol'
Stuttg. = Stuttgart
Thessal. = Thessalonikē
Val. = Valencia
Voron. = Voronež

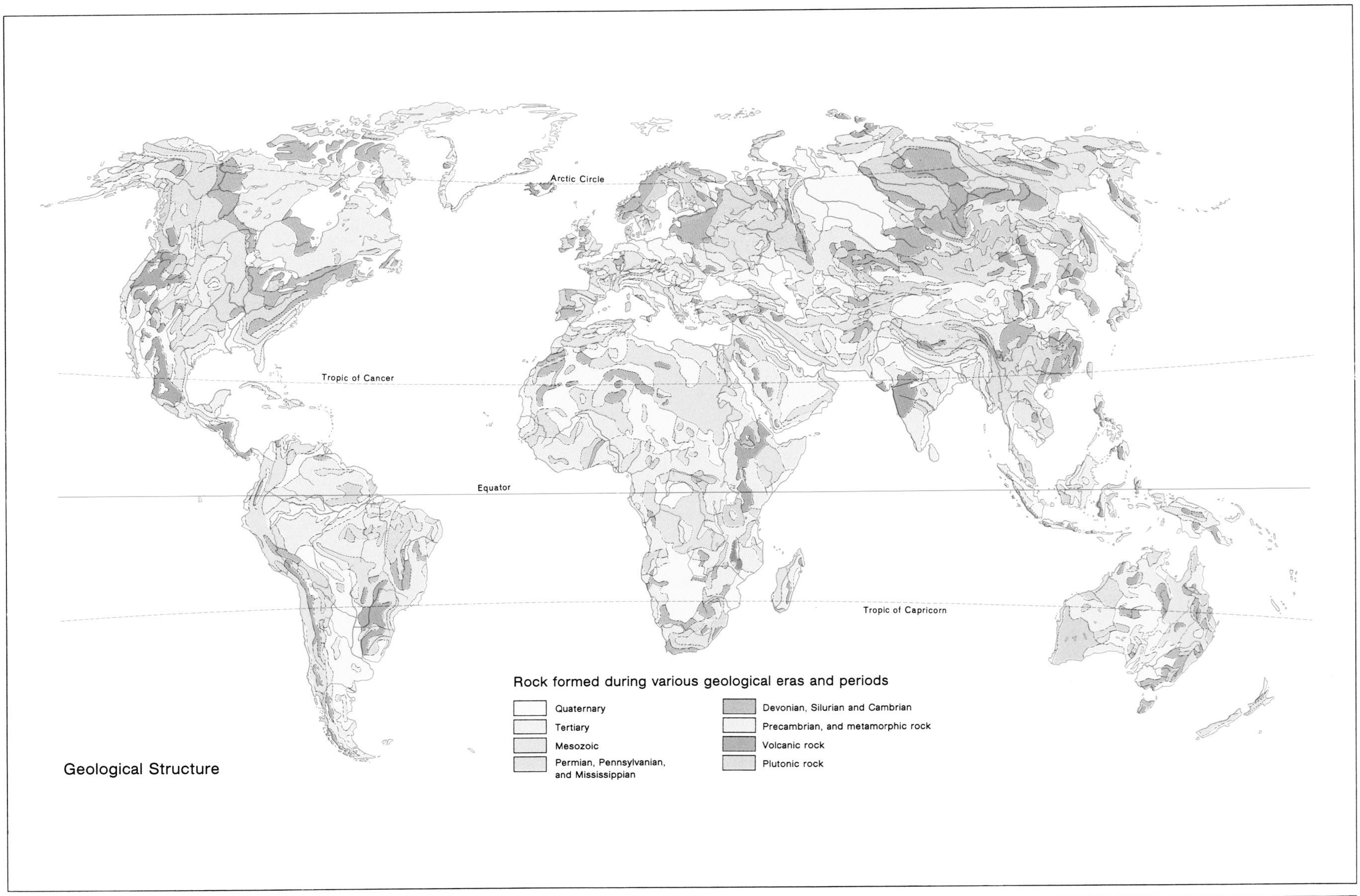

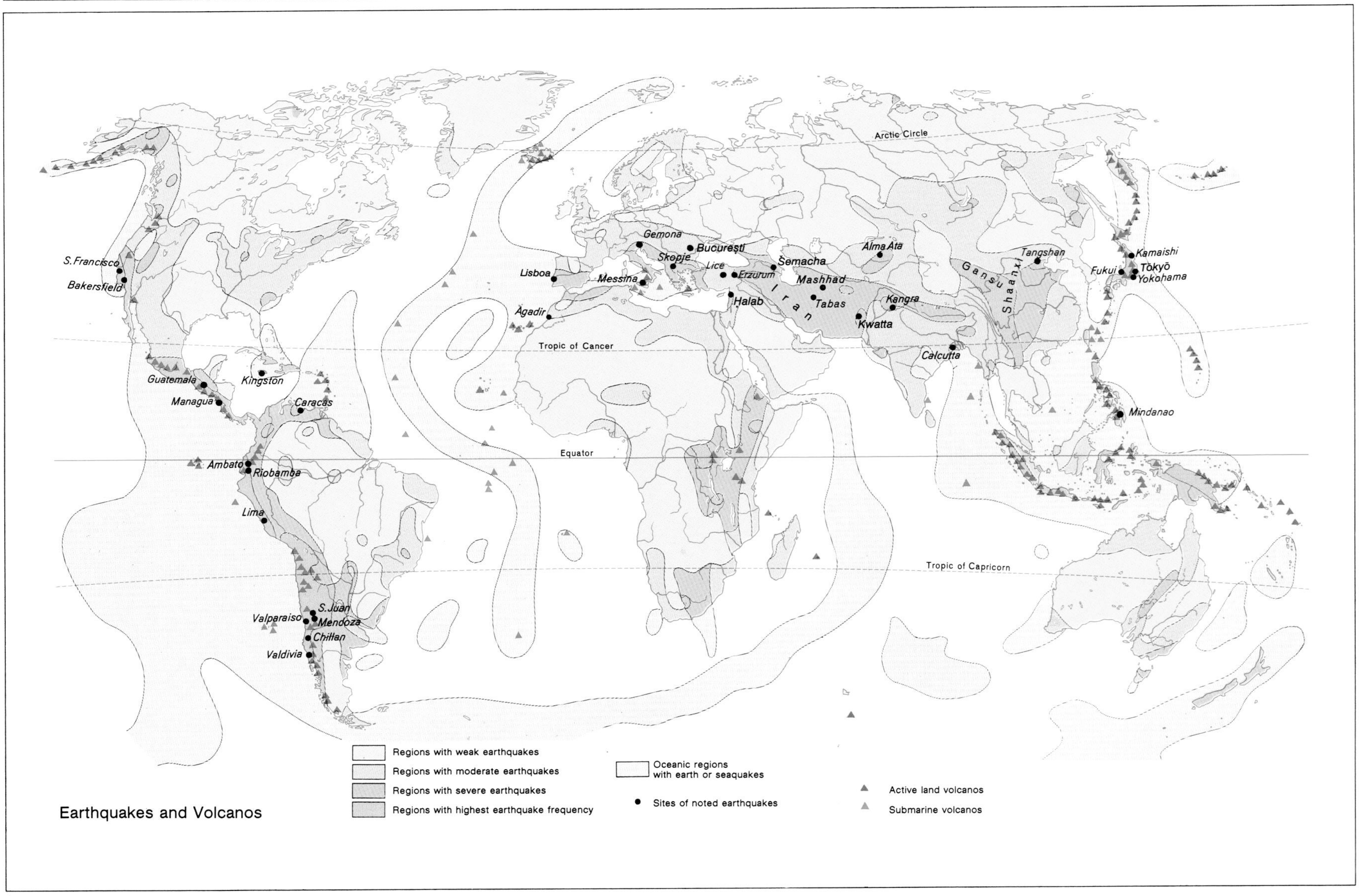

Geological Structure

Arctic Circle
Tropic of Cancer
Equator
Tropic of Capricorn

Rock formed during various geological eras and periods

- Quaternary
- Tertiary
- Mesozoic
- Permian, Pennsylvanian, and Mississippian
- Devonian, Silurian and Cambrian
- Precambrian, and metamorphic rock
- Volcanic rock
- Plutonic rock

Earthquakes and Volcanos

Arctic Circle
Tropic of Cancer
Equator
Tropic of Capricorn

S. Francisco
Bakersfield
Guatemala
Managua
Kingston
Caracas
Ambato
Riobamba
Lima
S. Juan
Valparaiso
Mendoza
Chillan
Valdivia
Lisboa
Agadir
Gemona
Bucureşti
Skopje
Messina
Lice
Erzurum
Halab
Šemacha
Mashhad
Tabas
Iran
Alma Ata
Kangra
Kwatta
Calcutta
Gansu
Shaanxi
Tangshan
Fukui
Kamaishi
Tōkyō
Yokohama
Mindanao

- Regions with weak earthquakes
- Regions with moderate earthquakes
- Regions with severe earthquakes
- Regions with highest earthquake frequency
- Oceanic regions with earth or seaquakes
- ● Sites of noted earthquakes
- ▲ Active land volcanos
- ▲ Submarine volcanos

Scale at the center meridian 1 : 135,000,000 One inch to 2,131 miles

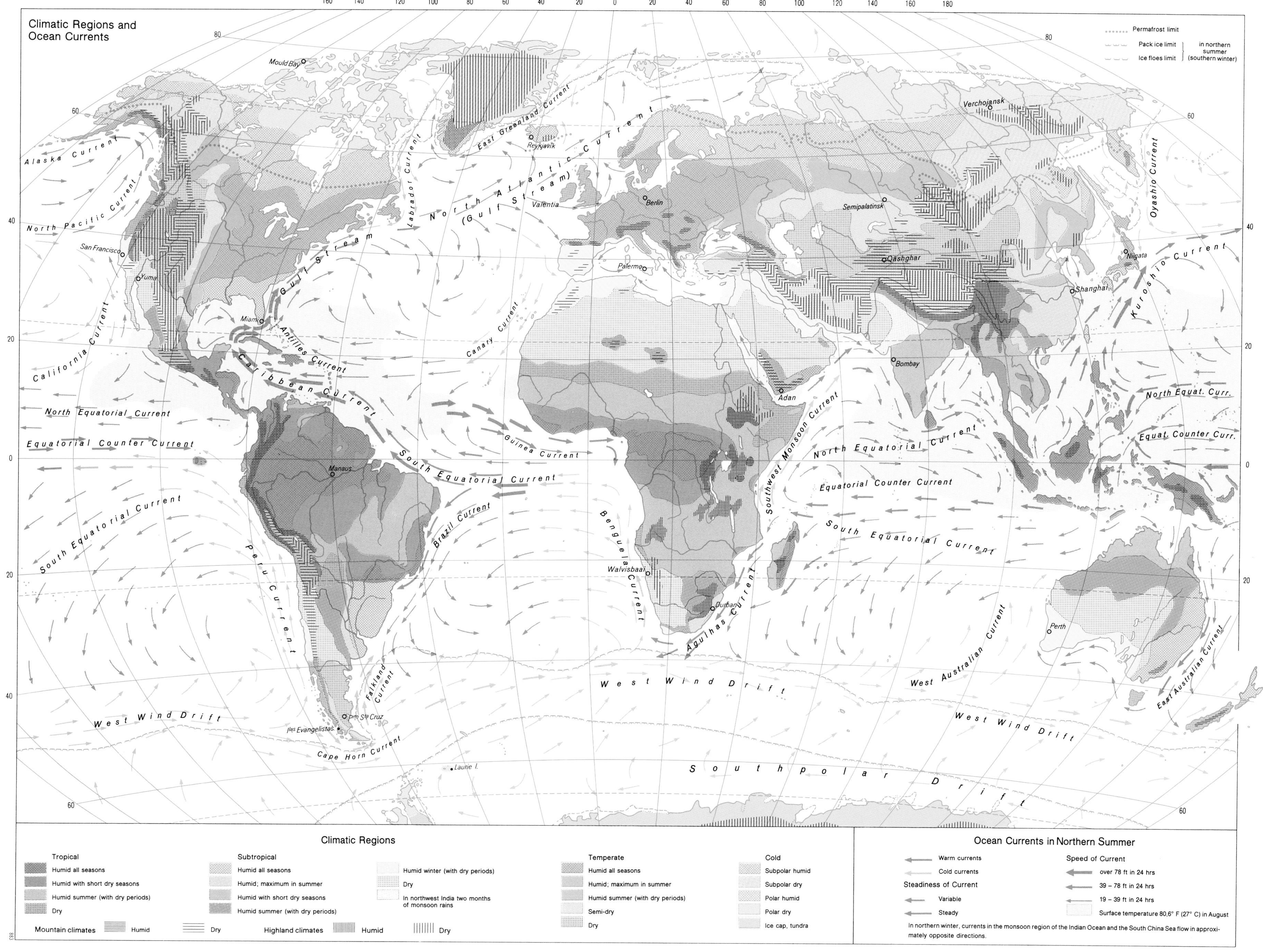

Climatic Regions and Ocean Currents
Permafrost limit
Pack ice limit
Ice floes limit
in northern summer (southern winter)
Alaska Current
North Pacific Current
California Current
North Equatorial Current
Equatorial Counter Current
South Equatorial Current
Peru Current
West Wind Drift
Cape Horn Current
Falkland Current
Labrador Current
Gulf Stream
Antilles Current
Caribbean Current
North Atlantic Current (Gulf Stream)
East Greenland Current
Canary Current
Guinea Current
South Equatorial Current
Brazil Current
Benguela Current
Agulhas Current
Southwest Monsoon Current
North Equatorial Current
Equatorial Counter Current
South Equatorial Current
West Australian Current
East Australian Current
West Wind Drift
Southpolar Drift
Oyashio Current
Kuroshio Current
North Equat. Curr.
Equat. Counter Curr.
Mould Bay
San Francisco
Yuma
Miami
Manaus
Pto Sta Cruz
Islas Evangelistas
Laurie I.
Reykjavik
Valentia
Berlin
Palermo
Walvisbaai
Durban
Adan
Bombay
Semipalatinsk
Qashghar
Verchojansk
Shanghai
Niigata
Perth
Climatic Regions
Tropical
Humid all seasons
Humid with short dry seasons
Humid summer (with dry periods)
Dry
Subtropical
Humid all seasons
Humid; maximum in summer
Humid with short dry seasons
Humid summer (with dry periods)
Humid winter (with dry periods)
Dry
In northwest India two months of monsoon rains
Temperate
Humid all seasons
Humid; maximum in summer
Humid summer (with dry periods)
Semi-dry
Dry
Cold
Subpolar humid
Subpolar dry
Polar humid
Polar dry
Ice cap, tundra
Mountain climates
Humid
Dry
Highland climates
Humid
Dry
Ocean Currents in Northern Summer
Warm currents
Cold currents
Steadiness of Current
Variable
Steady
Speed of Current
over 78 ft in 24 hrs
39 – 78 ft in 24 hrs
19 – 39 ft in 24 hrs
Surface temperature 80,6° F (27° C) in August
In northern winter, currents in the monsoon region of the Indian Ocean and the South China Sea flow in approximately opposite directions.

Scale at the center meridian 1 : 90,000,000 One inch to 1,420 miles

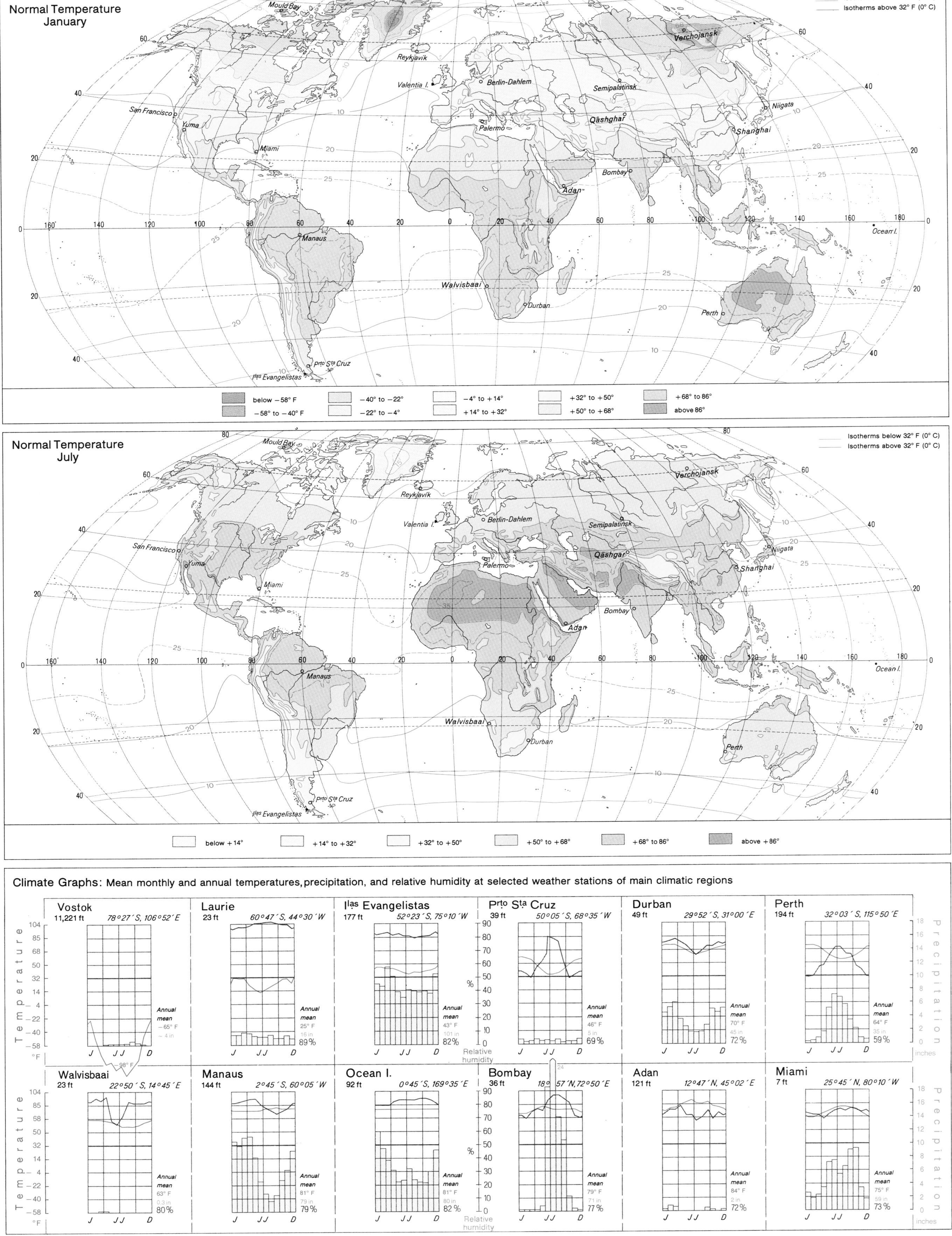

Normal Temperature
January
Isotherms below 32° F (0° C)
Isotherms above 32° F (0° C)
Mould Bay
Reykjavík
Valentia I.
Berlin-Dahlem
Verchojansk
Semipalatinsk
Niigata
Qāshghar
Shanghai
San Francisco
Yuma
Palermo
Miami
Bombay
Adan
Manaus
Ocean I.
Walvisbaai
Durban
Perth
Prto Sta Cruz
Ilas Evangelistas
below −58° F
−58° to −40° F
−40° to −22°
−22° to −4°
−4° to +14°
+14° to +32°
+32° to +50°
+50° to +68°
+68° to 86°
above 86°
Normal Temperature
July
Isotherms below 32° F (0° C)
Isotherms above 32° F (0° C)
below +14°
+14° to +32°
+32° to +50°
+50° to +68°
+68° to 86°
above +86°
Climate Graphs: Mean monthly and annual temperatures, precipitation, and relative humidity at selected weather stations of main climatic regions
Vostok 11,221 ft 78°27´S, 106°52´E
Laurie 23 ft 60°47´S, 44°30´W
Ilas Evangelistas 177 ft 52°23´S, 75°10´W
Prto Sta Cruz 39 ft 50°05´S, 68°35´W
Durban 49 ft 29°52´S, 31°00´E
Perth 194 ft 32°03´S, 115°50´E
Walvisbaai 23 ft 22°50´S, 14°45´E
Manaus 144 ft 2°45´S, 60°05´W
Ocean I. 92 ft 0°45´S, 169°35´E
Bombay 36 ft 18°57´N, 72°50´E
Adan 121 ft 12°47´N, 45°02´E
Miami 7 ft 25°45´N, 80°10´W
Temperature
°F
Precipitation
inches
%
Relative humidity
Annual mean
89%
82%
69%
72%
59%
80%
79%
82%
77%
72%
73%
883

Scale at the center meridian 1 : 162,000,000 One inch to 2,558 miles

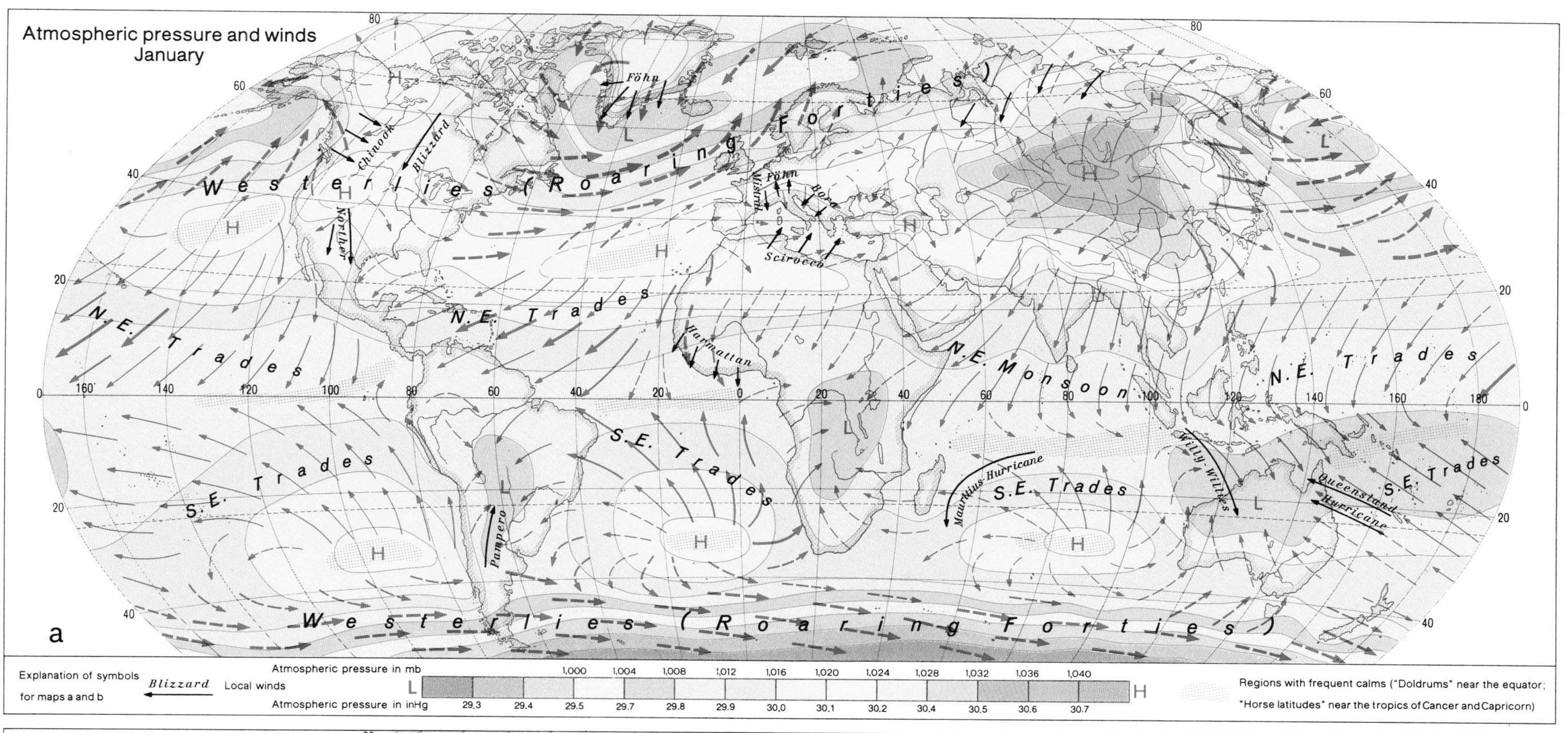
Atmospheric pressure and winds
January
Föhn
Chinook
Blizzard
Westerlies (Roaring Forties)
Norther
Mistral
Föhn
Bora
Scirocco
N.E. Trades
Harmattan
N.E. Monsoon
S.E. Trades
Pampero
Mauritius Hurricane
Willy Willies
Queensland Hurricane
a
Explanation of symbols for maps a and b
Blizzard Local winds
Atmospheric pressure in mb
1,000 1,004 1,008 1,012 1,016 1,020 1,024 1,028 1,032 1,036 1,040
Atmospheric pressure in inHg
29.3 29.4 29.5 29.7 29.8 29.9 30.0 30.1 30.2 30.4 30.5 30.6 30.7
Regions with frequent calms ("Doldrums" near the equator; "Horse latitudes" near the tropics of Cancer and Capricorn)

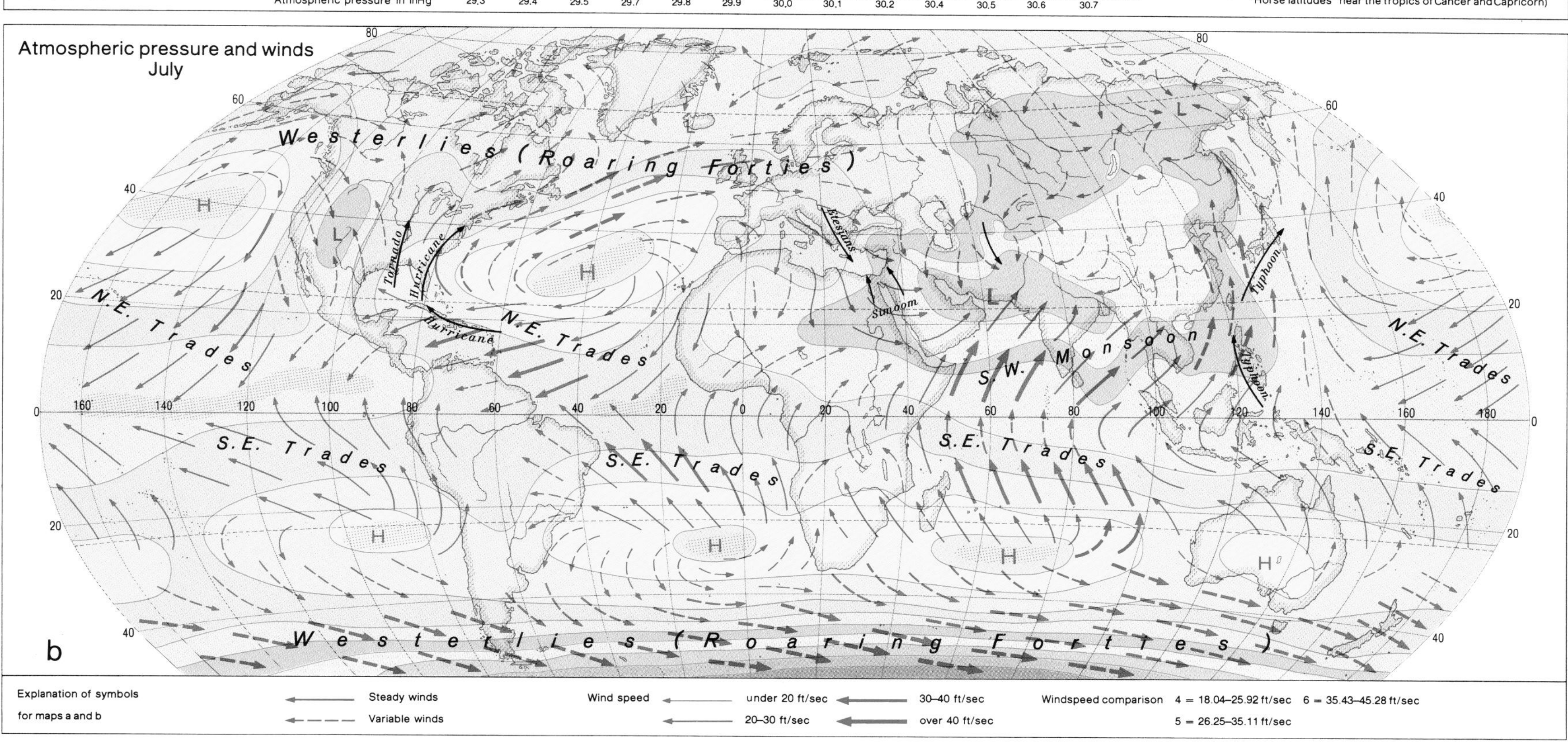
Atmospheric pressure and winds
July
Westerlies (Roaring Forties)
Tornado
Hurricane
Etesians
Simoom
N.E. Trades
S.W. Monsoon
Typhoon
S.E. Trades
b
Explanation of symbols for maps a and b
Steady winds
Variable winds
Wind speed
under 20 ft/sec
20–30 ft/sec
30–40 ft/sec
over 40 ft/sec
Windspeed comparison 4 = 18.04–25.92 ft/sec 6 = 35.43–45.28 ft/sec
5 = 26.25–35.11 ft/sec

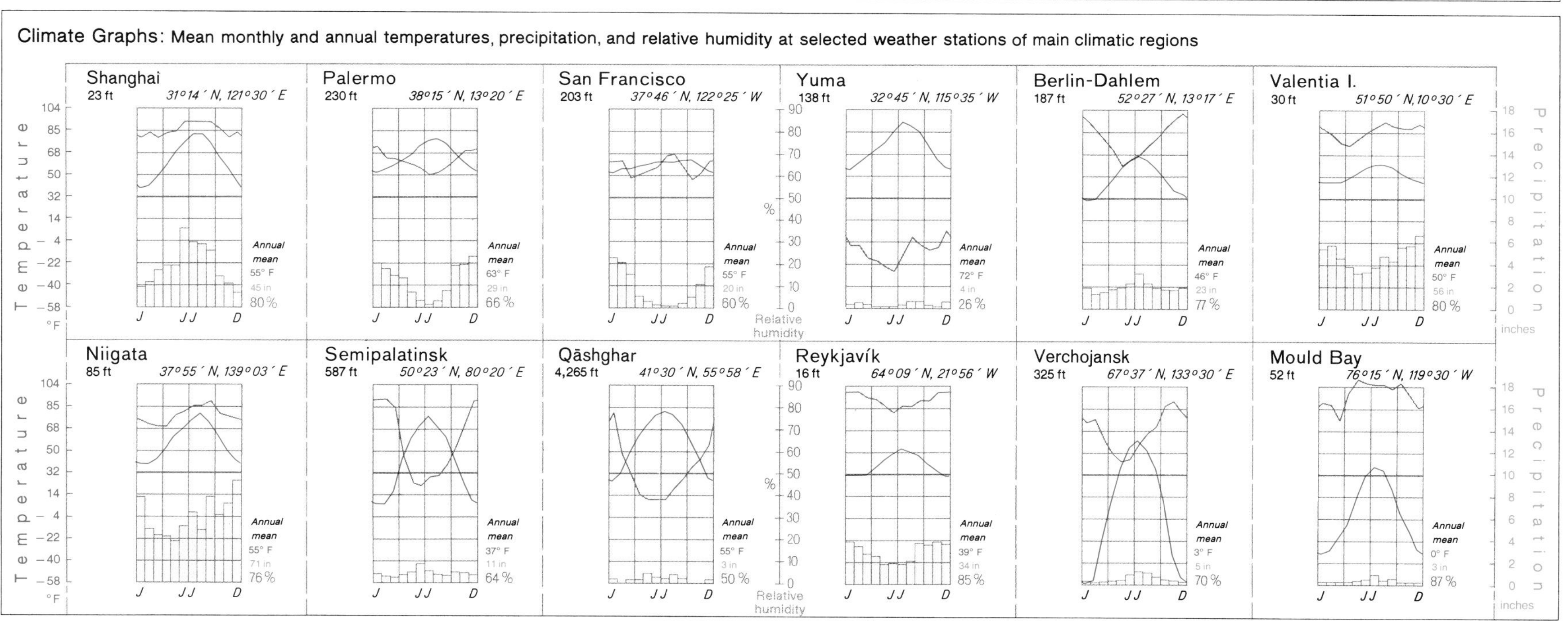
Climate Graphs: Mean monthly and annual temperatures, precipitation, and relative humidity at selected weather stations of main climatic regions
Temperature °F
Precipitation inches
Relative humidity %
Shanghai 23 ft 31°14′ N, 121°30′ E
Annual mean 55° F 45 in 80%
Palermo 230 ft 38°15′ N, 13°20′ E
Annual mean 63° F 29 in 66%
San Francisco 203 ft 37°46′ N, 122°25′ W
Annual mean 55° F 20 in 60%
Yuma 138 ft 32°45′ N, 115°35′ W
Annual mean 72° F 4 in 26%
Berlin-Dahlem 187 ft 52°27′ N, 13°17′ E
Annual mean 46° F 23 in 77%
Valentia I. 30 ft 51°50′ N, 10°30′ E
Annual mean 50° F 56 in 80%
Niigata 85 ft 37°55′ N, 139°03′ E
Annual mean 55° F 71 in 76%
Semipalatinsk 587 ft 50°23′ N, 80°20′ E
Annual mean 37° F 11 in 64%
Qāshghar 4,265 ft 41°30′ N, 55°58′ E
Annual mean 55° F 3 in 50%
Reykjavík 16 ft 64°09′ N, 21°56′ W
Annual mean 39° F 34 in 85%
Verchojansk 325 ft 67°37′ N, 133°30′ E
Annual mean 3° F 5 in 70%
Mould Bay 52 ft 76°15′ N, 119°30′ W
Annual mean 0° F 3 in 87%

Scale at the center meridian 1: 162,000,000 One inch to 2.558 miles

Soils

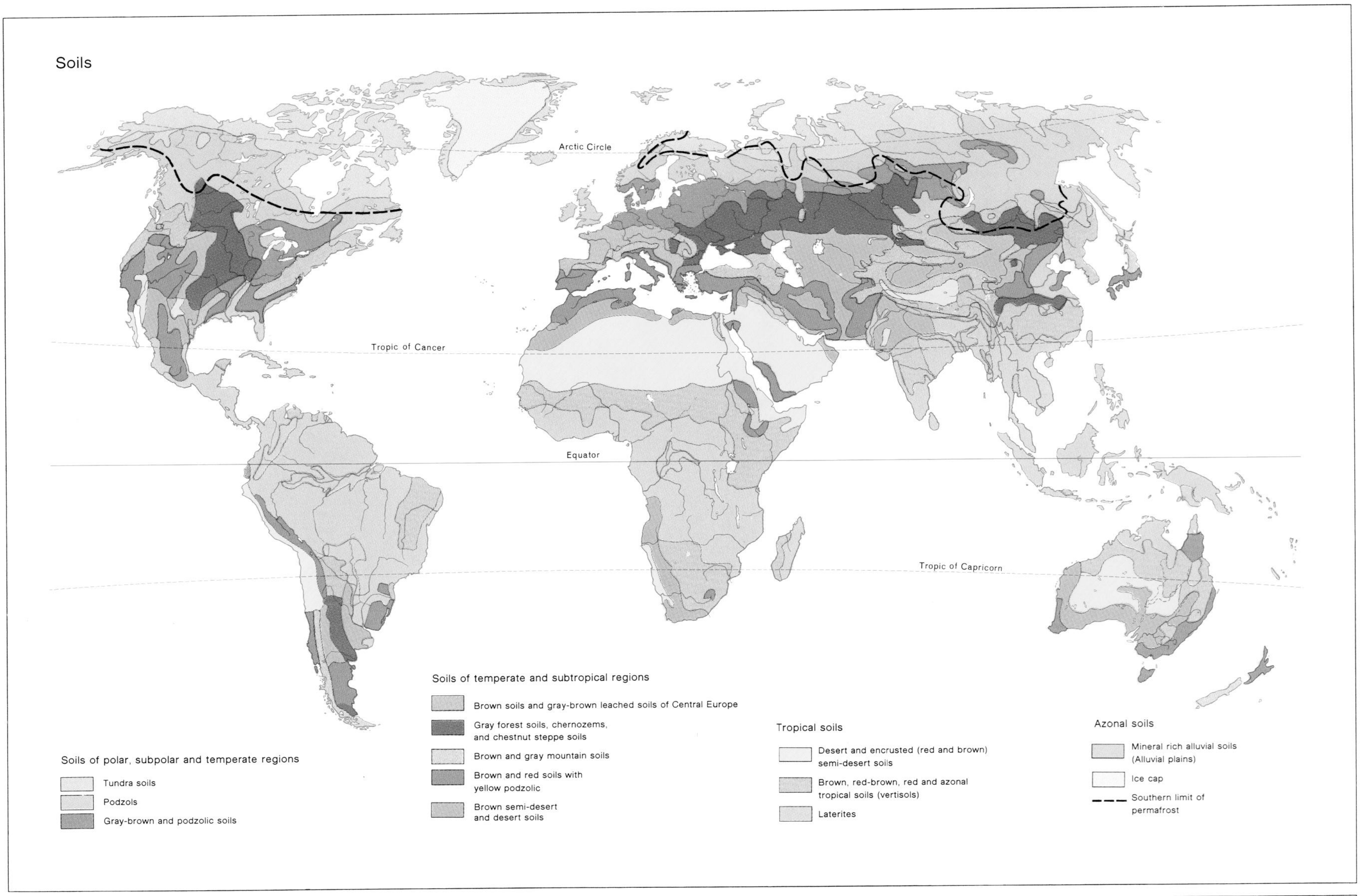

Arctic Circle

Tropic of Cancer

Equator

Tropic of Capricorn

Soils of polar, subpolar and temperate regions

- Tundra soils
- Podzols
- Gray-brown and podzolic soils

Soils of temperate and subtropical regions

- Brown soils and gray-brown leached soils of Central Europe
- Gray forest soils, chernozems, and chestnut steppe soils
- Brown and gray mountain soils
- Brown and red soils with yellow podzolic
- Brown semi-desert and desert soils

Tropical soils

- Desert and encrusted (red and brown) semi-desert soils
- Brown, red-brown, red and azonal tropical soils (vertisols)
- Laterites

Azonal soils

- Mineral rich alluvial soils (Alluvial plains)
- Ice cap
- Southern limit of permafrost

Forest

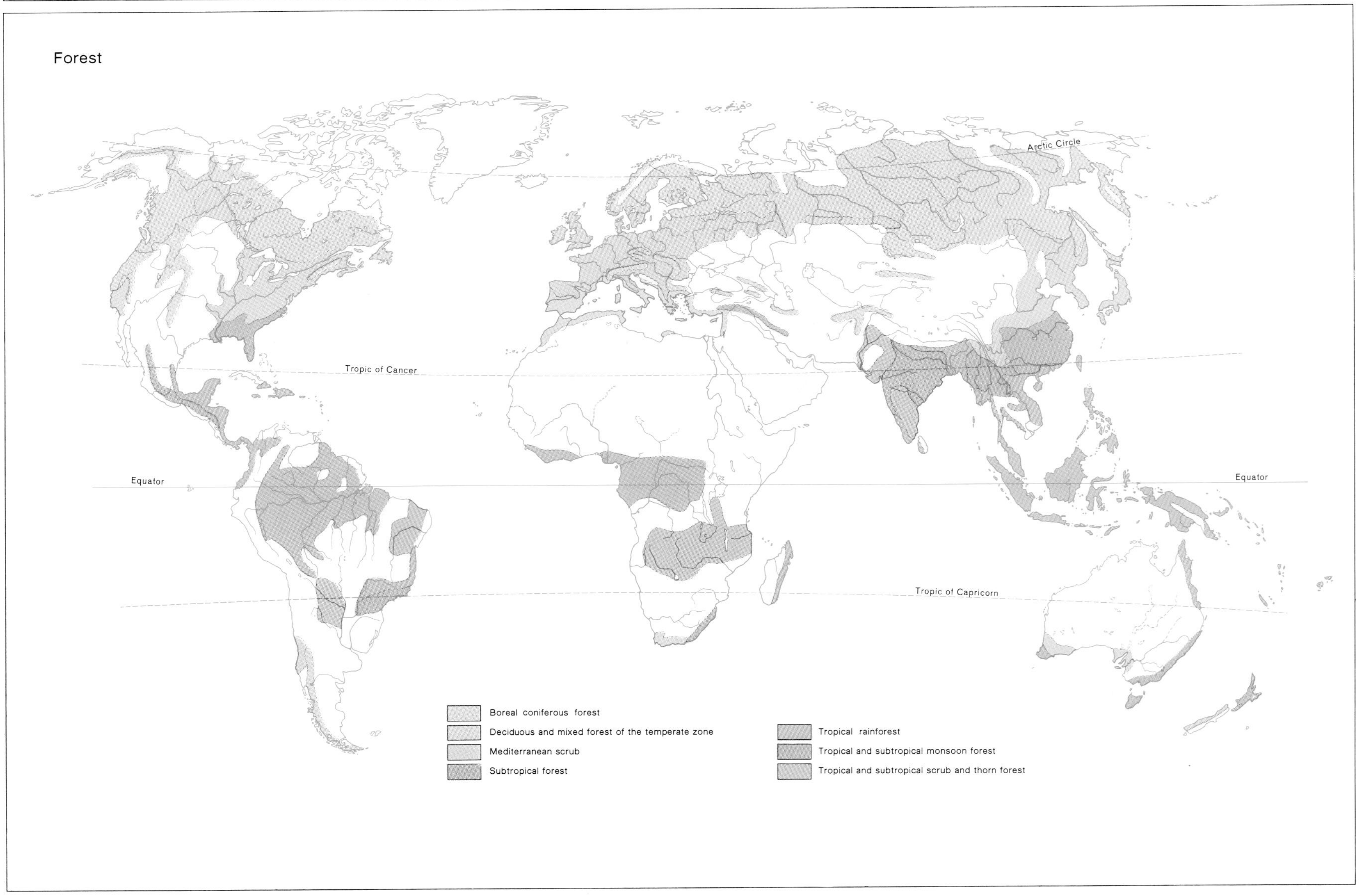

Arctic Circle

Tropic of Cancer

Equator

Equator

Tropic of Capricorn

- Boreal coniferous forest
- Deciduous and mixed forest of the temperate zone
- Mediterranean scrub
- Subtropical forest
- Tropical rainforest
- Tropical and subtropical monsoon forest
- Tropical and subtropical scrub and thorn forest

Scale at the center meridian 1 : 135,000,000 One inch to 2,131 miles

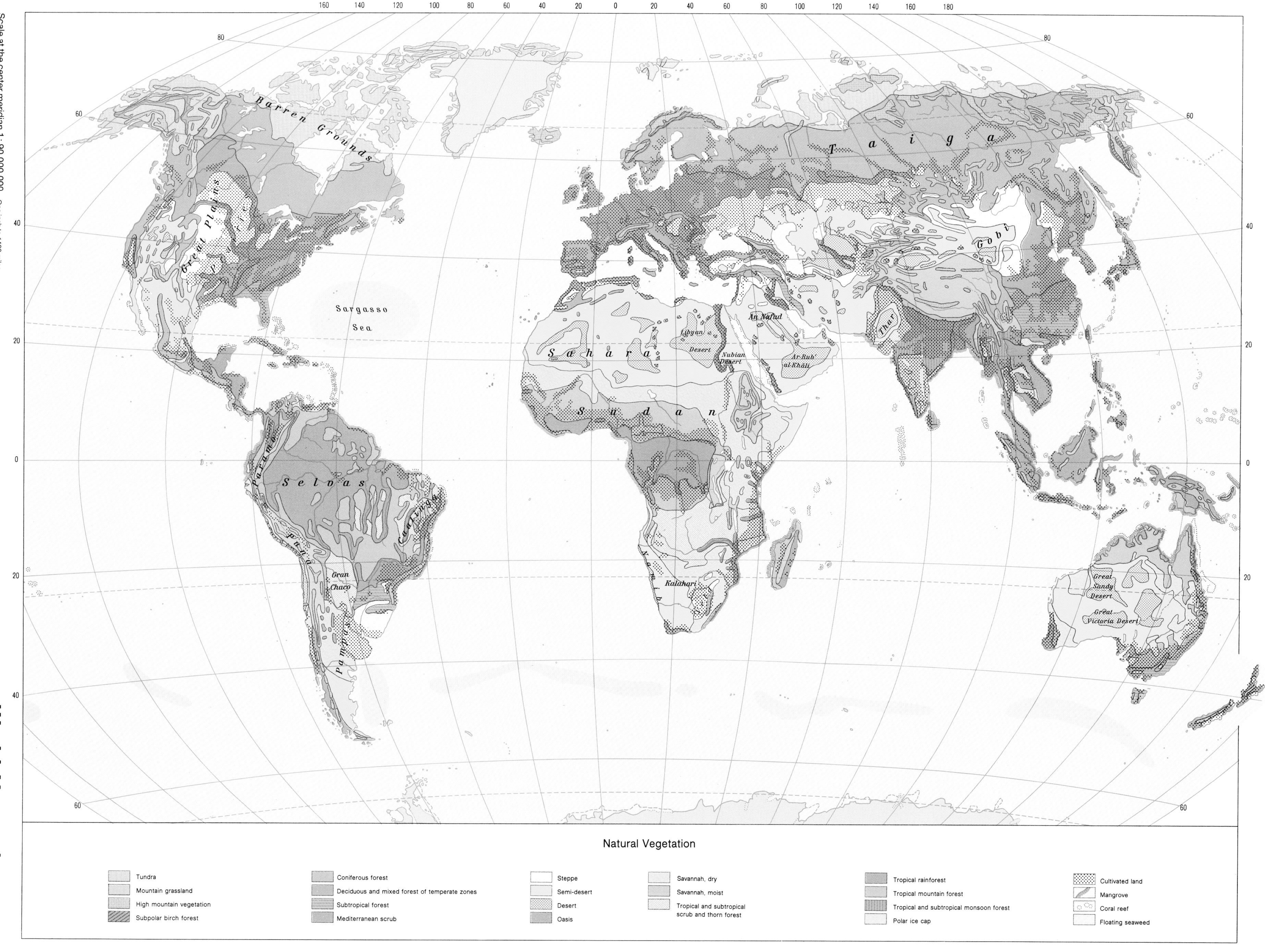

Barren Grounds
Great Plains
Sargasso Sea
Taiga
Gobi
Thar
Sahara
Libyan Desert
Nubian Desert
An Nafud
Ar-Rub' al-Khali
Sudan
Selvas
Paramo
Puna
Caatinga
Gran Chaco
Pampas
Namib
Kalahari
Great Sandy Desert
Great Victoria Desert
Natural Vegetation
Tundra
Mountain grassland
High mountain vegetation
Subpolar birch forest
Coniferous forest
Deciduous and mixed forest of temperate zones
Subtropical forest
Mediterranean scrub
Steppe
Semi-desert
Desert
Oasis
Savannah, dry
Savannah, moist
Tropical and subtropical scrub and thorn forest
Tropical rainforest
Tropical mountain forest
Tropical and subtropical monsoon forest
Polar ice cap
Cultivated land
Mangrove
Coral reef
Floating seaweed

Scale at the center meridian 1 : 90,000,000 One inch to 1,420 miles

Agricultural Resources
Grain
Wheat
Rice
Maize (corn)
Polar limit of grain cultivation
Limit of tropical and subtropical millet cultivation in Asia and Africa
Oil Plants
Oil palm distribution
Coconut tree distribution
Peanuts
Soy beans
Economy and Population Distribution
Industrial areas over 500 pop./sq. mile
Predominantly agrarian areas over 500 pop./sq. mile
Areas with 125–500 pop./sq. mile
Areas with 25–125 pop./sq. mile
Sparsely populated areas with 2–25 pop./sq. mile
Uninhabited or sparsely populated areas (steppes, savannahs, deserts and tundras)
Uninhabited or sparsely populated forest areas
Major fishing areas

 Scale at the center meridian 1 : 67,500,000 One inch to 1,065 miles

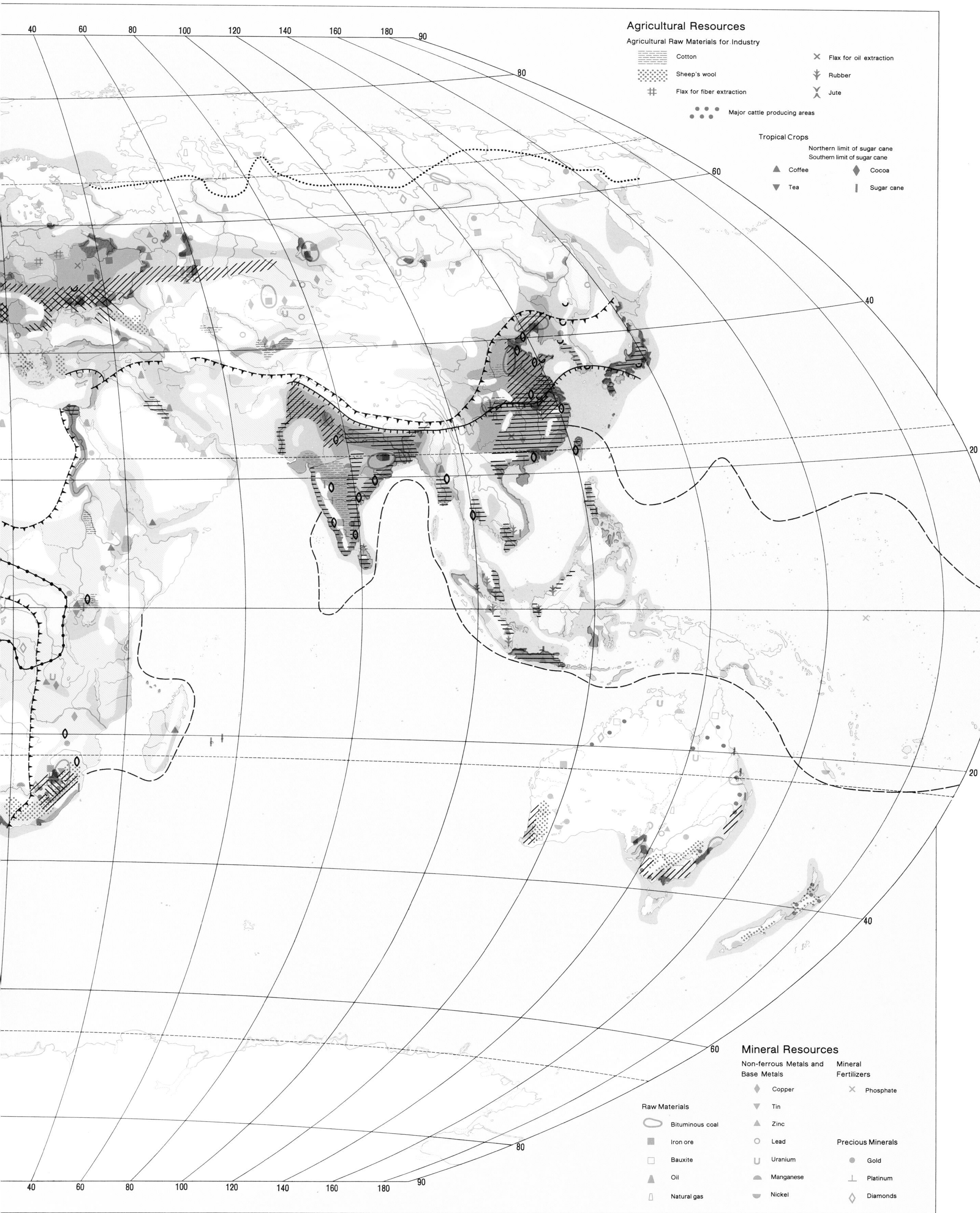
Agricultural Resources
Agricultural Raw Materials for Industry
Cotton
Sheep's wool
Flax for fiber extraction
Flax for oil extraction
Rubber
Jute
Major cattle producing areas
Tropical Crops
Northern limit of sugar cane
Southern limit of sugar cane
Coffee
Tea
Cocoa
Sugar cane
Mineral Resources
Non-ferrous Metals and Base Metals
Copper
Tin
Zinc
Lead
Uranium
Manganese
Nickel
Mineral Fertilizers
Phosphate
Raw Materials
Bituminous coal
Iron ore
Bauxite
Oil
Natural gas
Precious Minerals
Gold
Platinum
Diamonds
40
60
80
100
120
140
160
180
90
20

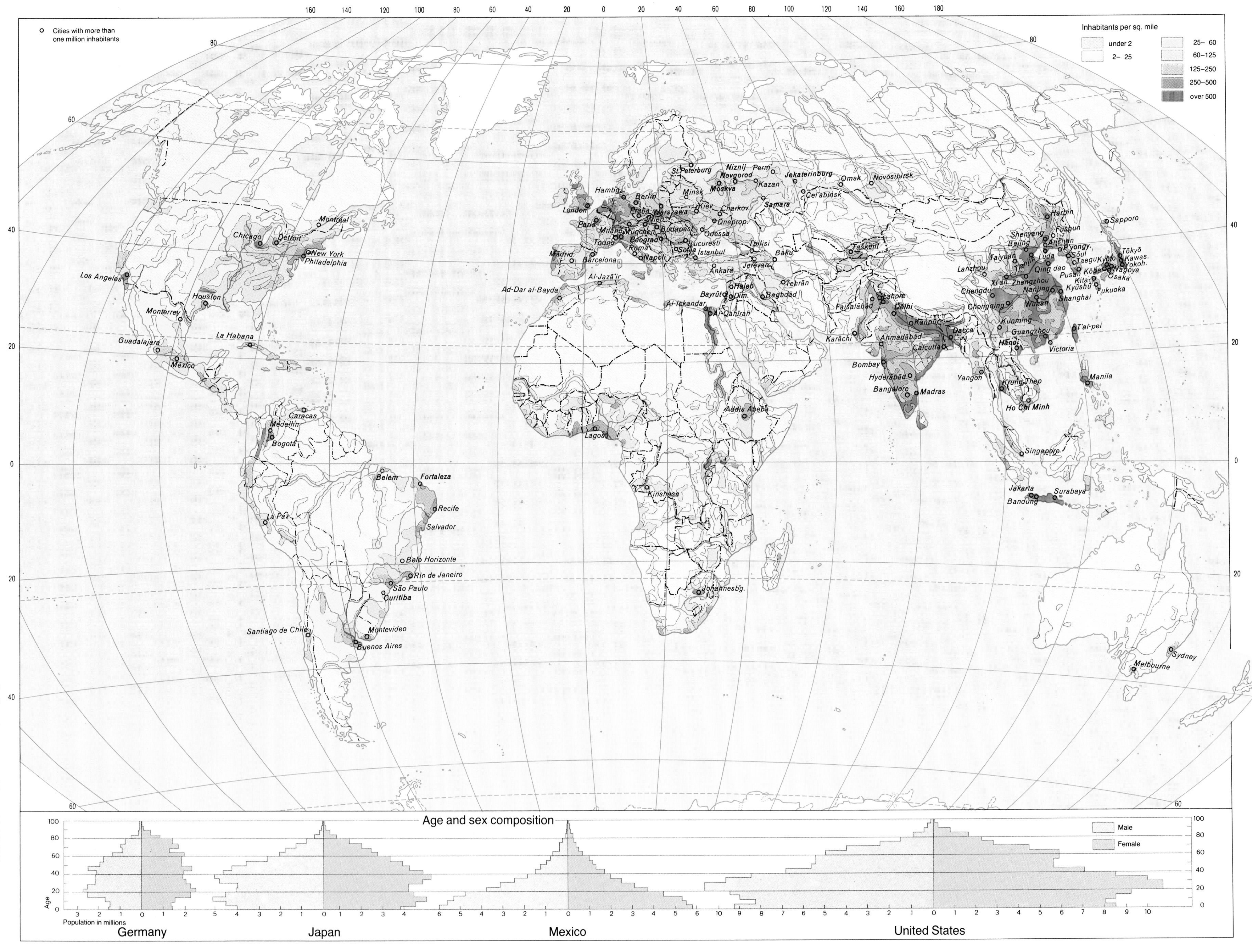
Cities with more than one million inhabitants
Inhabitants per sq. mile
under 2
2– 25
25– 60
60–125
125–250
250–500
over 500
Age and sex composition
Male
Female
Age
Population in millions
Germany
Japan
Mexico
United States

Scale at the center meridian 1 : 90,000,000 One inch to 1,420 miles

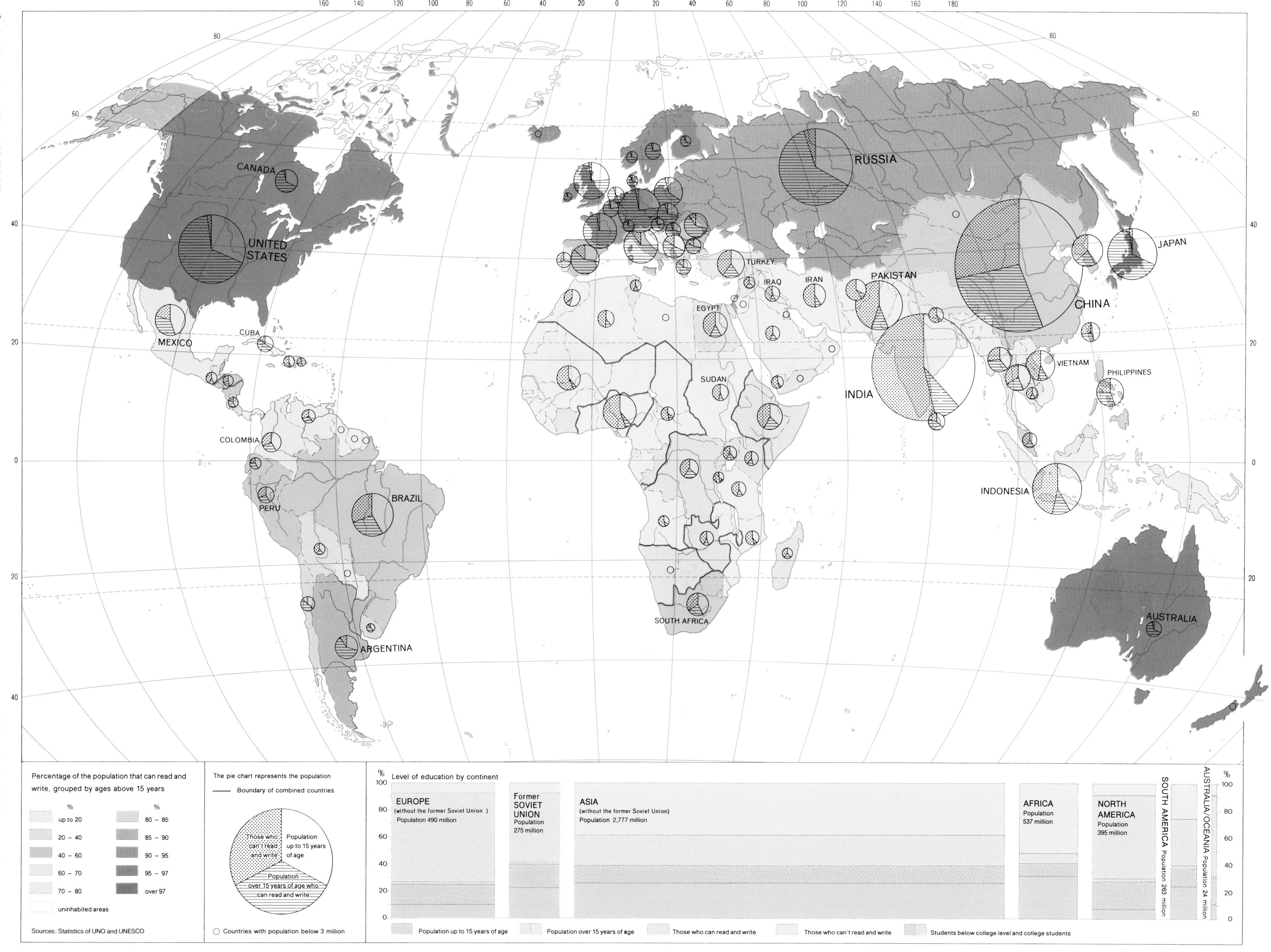

CANADA
UNITED STATES
MEXICO
CUBA
COLOMBIA
PERU
BRAZIL
ARGENTINA
RUSSIA
TURKEY
IRAQ
IRAN
EGYPT
SUDAN
SOUTH AFRICA
PAKISTAN
INDIA
CHINA
JAPAN
VIETNAM
PHILIPPINES
INDONESIA
AUSTRALIA
Percentage of the population that can read and write, grouped by ages above 15 years
%
up to 20
20 – 40
40 – 60
60 – 70
70 – 80
uninhabited areas
%
80 – 85
85 – 90
90 – 95
95 – 97
over 97
Sources: Statistics of UNO and UNESCO
The pie chart represents the population
Boundary of combined countries
Those who can't read and write
Population up to 15 years of age
Population over 15 years of age who can read and write
Countries with population below 3 million
Level of education by continent
EUROPE (without the former Soviet Union) Population 490 million
Former SOVIET UNION Population 275 million
ASIA (without the former Soviet Union) Population 2,777 million
AFRICA Population 537 million
NORTH AMERICA Population 395 million
SOUTH AMERICA Population 263 million
AUSTRALIA/OCEANIA Population 24 million
Population up to 15 years of age
Population over 15 years of age
Those who can read and write
Those who can't read and write
Students below college level and college students

Scale at the center meridian 1 : 90,000,000 One inch to 1420 miles

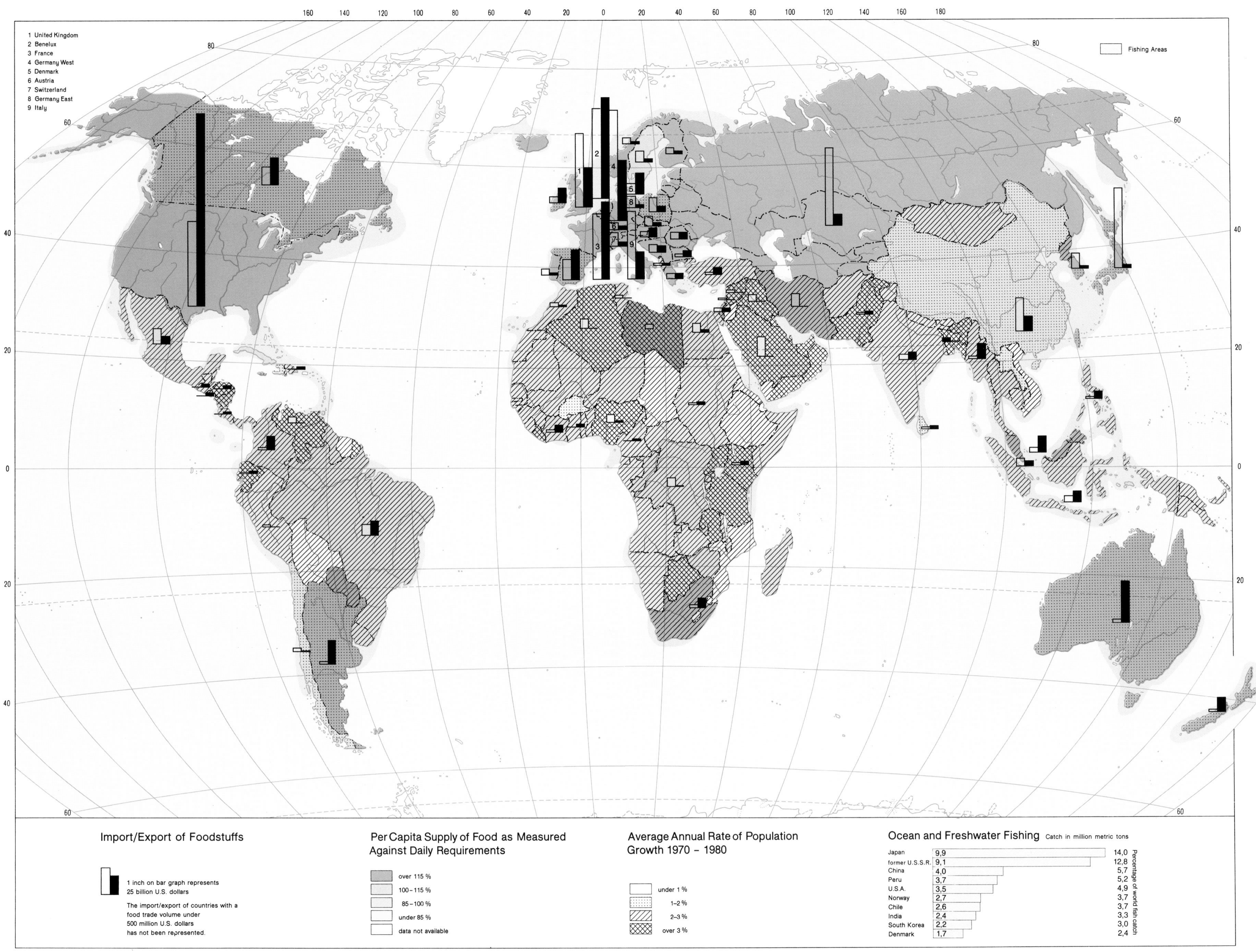
1 United Kingdom
2 Benelux
3 France
4 Germany West
5 Denmark
6 Austria
7 Switzerland
8 Germany East
9 Italy
Fishing Areas
Import/Export of Foodstuffs
1 inch on bar graph represents 25 billion U.S. dollars
The import/export of countries with a food trade volume under 500 million U.S. dollars has not been represented.
Per Capita Supply of Food as Measured Against Daily Requirements
over 115 %
100 - 115 %
85 - 100 %
under 85 %
data not available
Average Annual Rate of Population Growth 1970 - 1980
under 1 %
1-2 %
2-3 %
over 3 %
Ocean and Freshwater Fishing Catch in million metric tons
Percentage of world fish catch
Japan 9,9 14,0
former U.S.S.R. 9,1 12,8
China 4,0 5,7
Peru 3,7 5,2
U.S.A. 3,5 4,9
Norway 2,7 3,7
Chile 2,6 3,7
India 2,4 3,3
South Korea 2,2 3,0
Denmark 1,7 2,4

Scale at the center meridian 1 : 90,000,000 One inch to 1420 miles

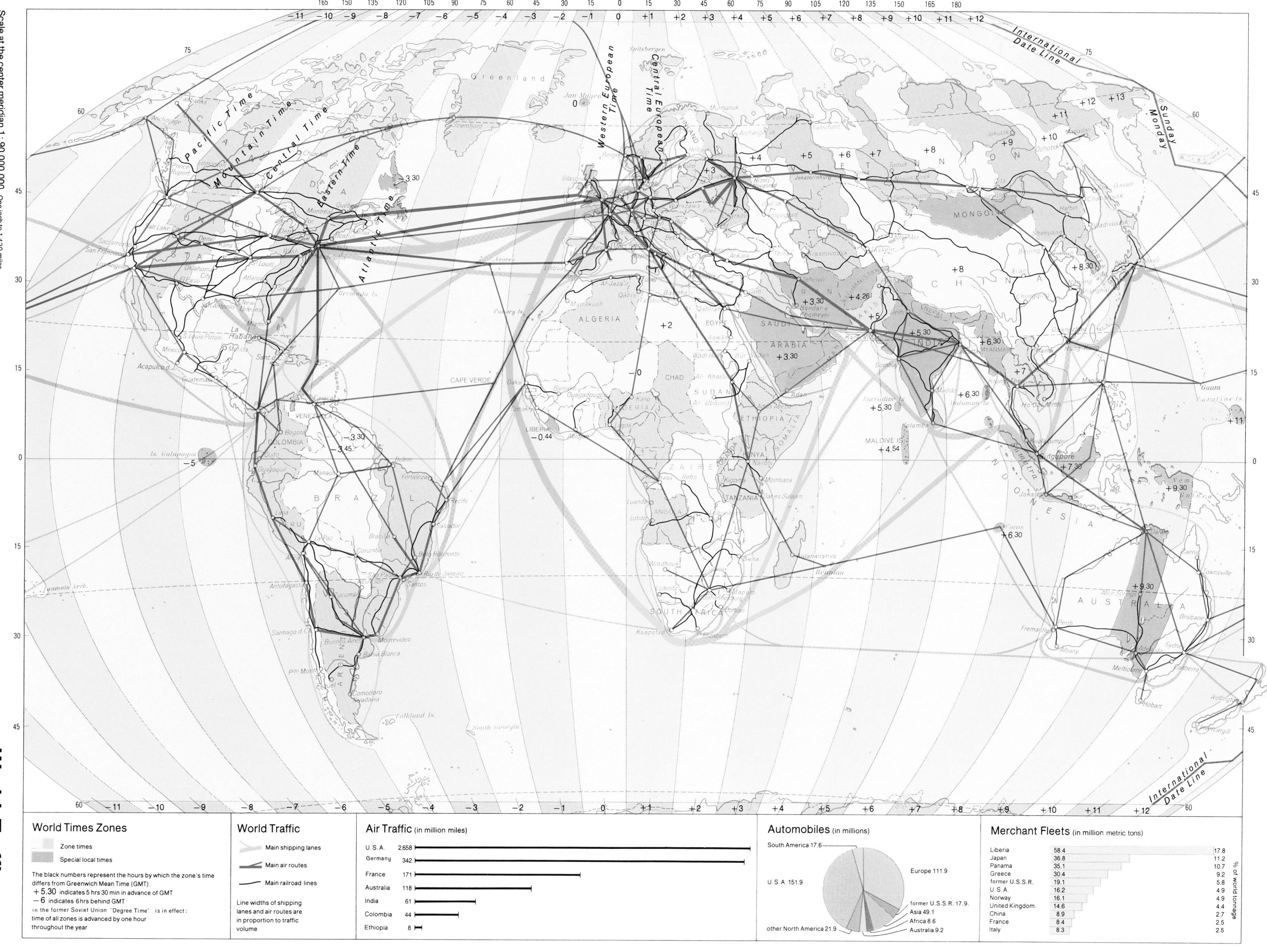

International Date Line
Sunday
Monday
Pacific Time
Mountain Time
Central Time
Eastern Time
Atlantic Time
Western European Time
Central European Time
Greenland
ALGERIA
EGYPT
CHAD
SUDAN
ETHIOPIA
SAUDI ARABIA
MONGOLIA
CHINA
INDIA
AUSTRALIA
INDONESIA
BRAZIL
COLOMBIA
VENEZUELA
ZAIRE
TANZANIA
SOUTH AFRICA
CAPE VERDE
LIBERIA
MALDIVE IS.
World Times Zones
Zone times
Special local times
The black numbers represent the hours by which the zone's time differs from Greenwich Mean Time (GMT):
+5.30 indicates 5 hrs 30 min in advance of GMT
−6 indicates 6hrs behind GMT
In the former Soviet Union "Degree Time" is in effect: time of all zones is advanced by one hour throughout the year
World Traffic
Main shipping lanes
Main air routes
Main railroad lines
Line widths of shipping lanes and air routes are in proportion to traffic volume
Air Traffic (in million miles)
U.S.A. 2,658
Germany 342
France 171
Australia 118
India 61
Colombia 44
Ethiopia 8
Automobiles (in millions)
South America 17.6
U.S.A. 151.9
other North America 21.9
Europe 111.9
former U.S.S.R. 17.9.
Asia 49.1
Africa 8.6
Australia 9.2
Merchant Fleets (in million metric tons)
% of world tonnage
Liberia 58.4 17.8
Japan 36.8 11.2
Panama 35.1 10.7
Greece 30.4 9.2
former U.S.S.R. 19.1 5.8
U.S.A. 16.2 4.9
Norway 16.1 4.9
United Kingdom 14.6 4.4
China 8.9 2.7
France 8.4 2.5
Italy 8.3 2.5

Scale at the center meridian 1: 90,000,000 One inch to 1,420 miles

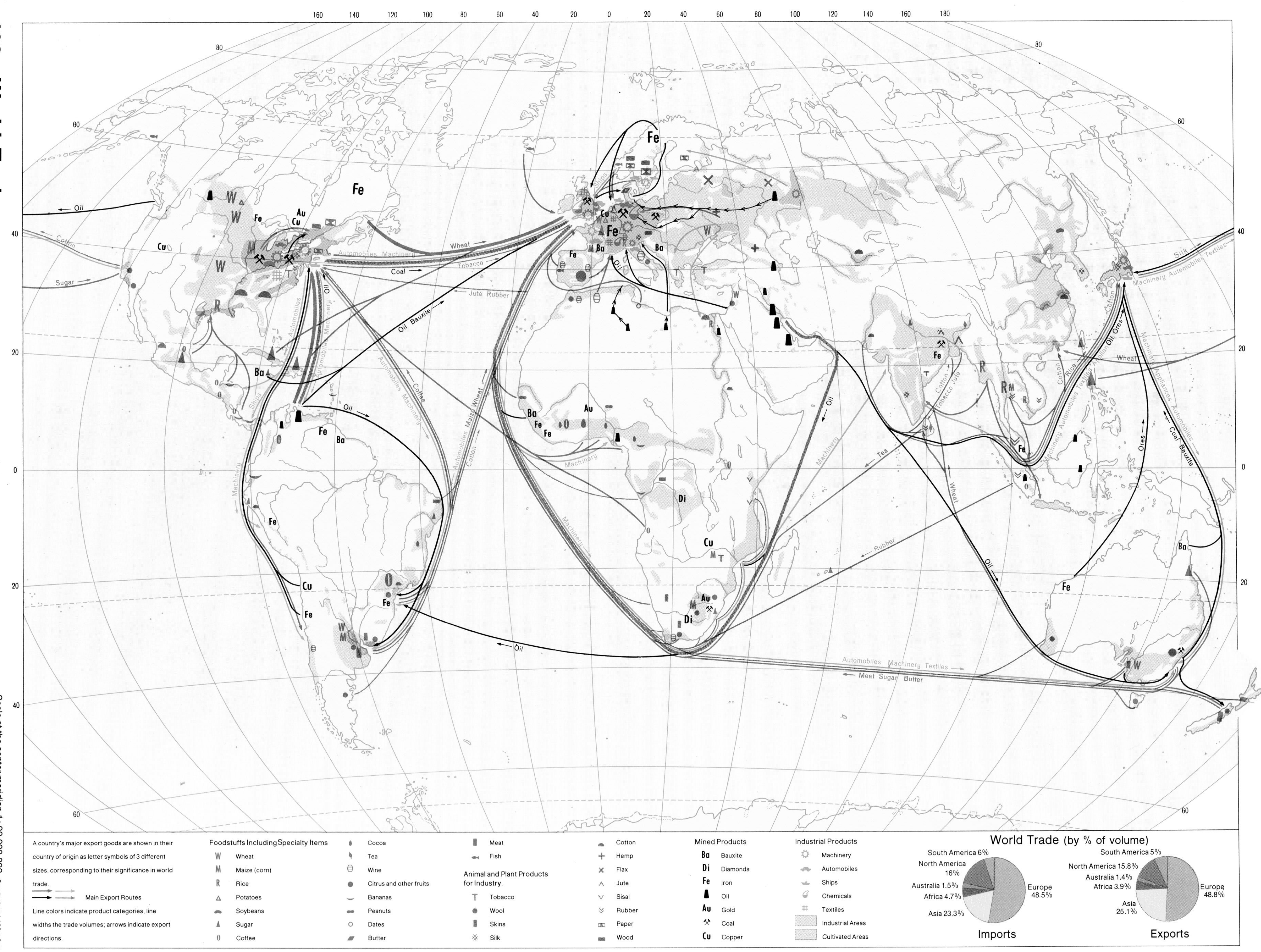

A country's major export goods are shown in their country of origin as letter symbols of 3 different sizes, corresponding to their significance in world trade.
Main Export Routes
Line colors indicate product categories, line widths the trade volumes; arrows indicate export directions.
Foodstuffs Including Specialty Items
W Wheat
M Maize (corn)
R Rice
Potatoes
Soybeans
Sugar
Coffee
Cocoa
Tea
Wine
Citrus and other fruits
Bananas
Peanuts
Dates
Butter
Meat
Fish
Animal and Plant Products for Industry
T Tobacco
Wool
Skins
Silk
Cotton
Hemp
Flax
Jute
Sisal
Rubber
Paper
Wood
Mined Products
Ba Bauxite
Di Diamonds
Fe Iron
Oil
Au Gold
Coal
Cu Copper
Industrial Products
Machinery
Automobiles
Ships
Chemicals
Textiles
Industrial Areas
Cultivated Areas
World Trade (by % of volume)
South America 6%
North America 16%
Australia 1.5%
Africa 4.7%
Asia 23.3%
Europe 48.5%
Imports
South America 5%
North America 15.8%
Australia 1.4%
Africa 3.9%
Asia 25.1%
Europe 48.8%
Exports

Scale at the center meridian 1 : 90,000,000 One inch to 1,420 miles

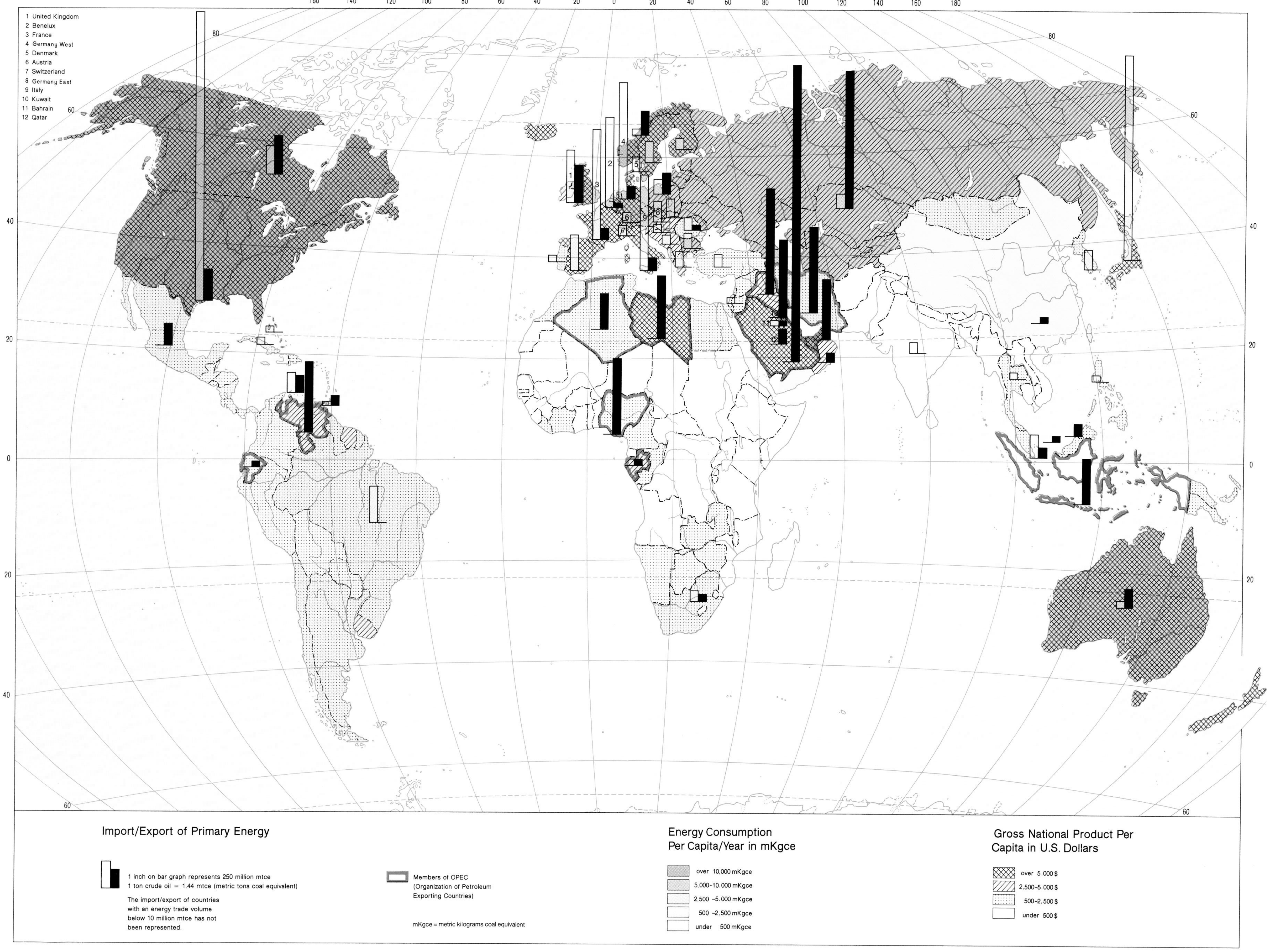
1 United Kingdom
2 Benelux
3 France
4 Germany West
5 Denmark
6 Austria
7 Switzerland
8 Germany East
9 Italy
10 Kuwait
11 Bahrain
12 Qatar
Import/Export of Primary Energy
1 inch on bar graph represents 250 million mtce
1 ton crude oil = 1.44 mtce (metric tons coal equivalent)
The import/export of countries with an energy trade volume below 10 million mtce has not been represented.
Members of OPEC (Organization of Petroleum Exporting Countries)
mKgce = metric kilograms coal equivalent
Energy Consumption Per Capita/Year in mKgce
over 10,000 mKgce
5,000–10,000 mKgce
2,500 –5,000 mKgce
500 –2,500 mKgce
under 500 mKgce
Gross National Product Per Capita in U.S. Dollars
over 5,000 $
2,500–5,000 $
500–2,500 $
under 500 $

Scale at the center meridian 1 : 90,000,000 One inch to 1420 miles

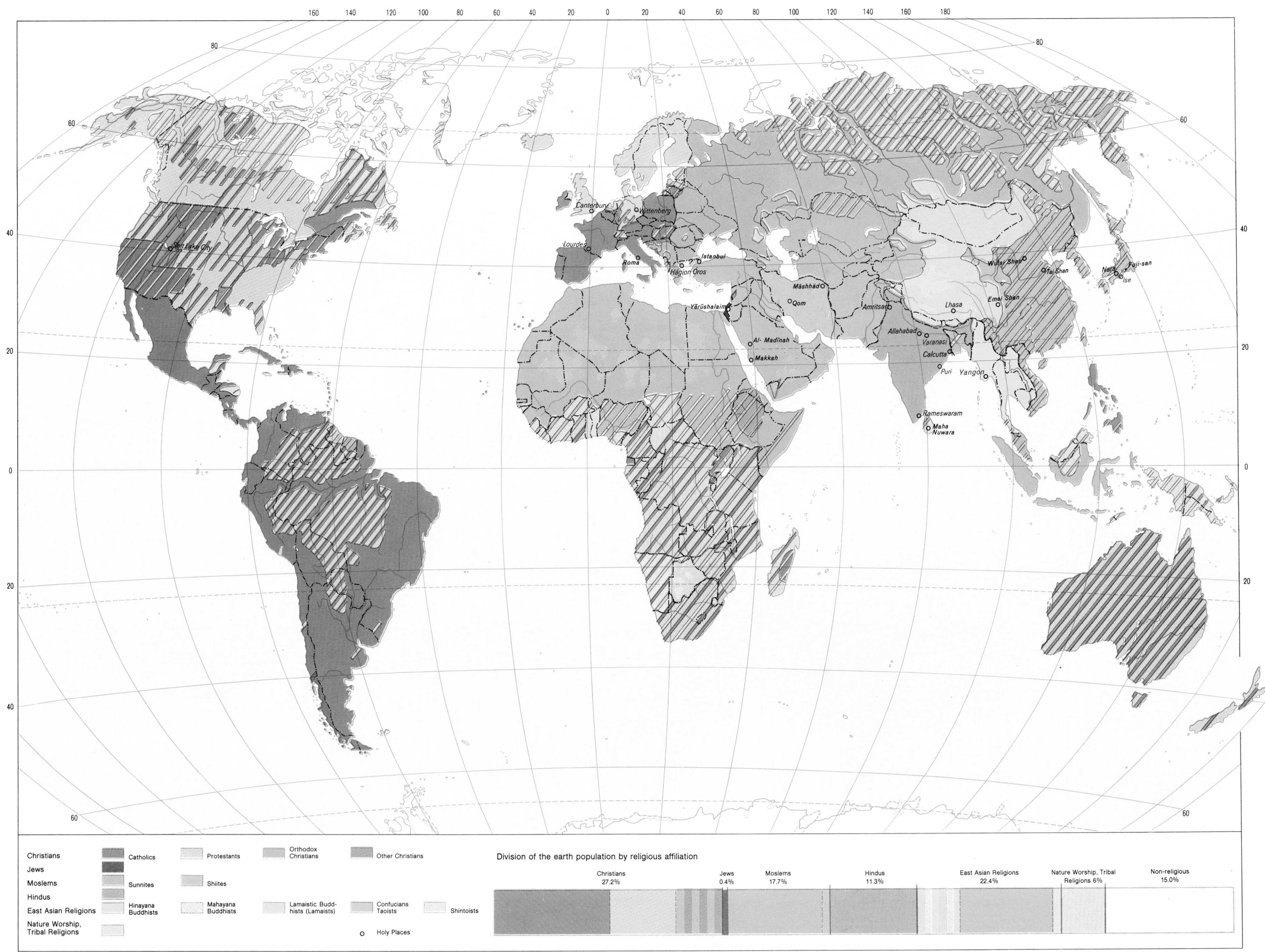
Salt Lake City
Canterbury
Wittenberg
Lourdes
Roma
Istanbul
Hagion Oros
Yĕrūshalaim
Al- Madīnah
Makkah
Mashhad
Qom
Amritsar
Allahabad
Varanasi
Calcutta
Puri
Yangon
Rameswaram
Maha Nuwara
Lhasa
Emei Shan
Wutai Shan
Tai Shan
Nara
Fuji-san
Ise
Christians
Catholics
Protestants
Orthodox Christians
Other Christians
Jews
Moslems
Sunnites
Shiites
Hindus
East Asian Religions
Hinayana Buddhists
Mahayana Buddhists
Lamaistic Buddhists (Lamaists)
Confucians Taoists
Shintoists
Nature Worship, Tribal Religions
Holy Places
Division of the earth population by religious affiliation
Christians 27.2%
Jews 0.4%
Moslems 17.7%
Hindus 11.3%
East Asian Religions 22.4%
Nature Worship, Tribal Religions 6%
Non-religious 15.0%

Scale at the center meridian 1 : 90,000,000 One inch to 1,420 miles

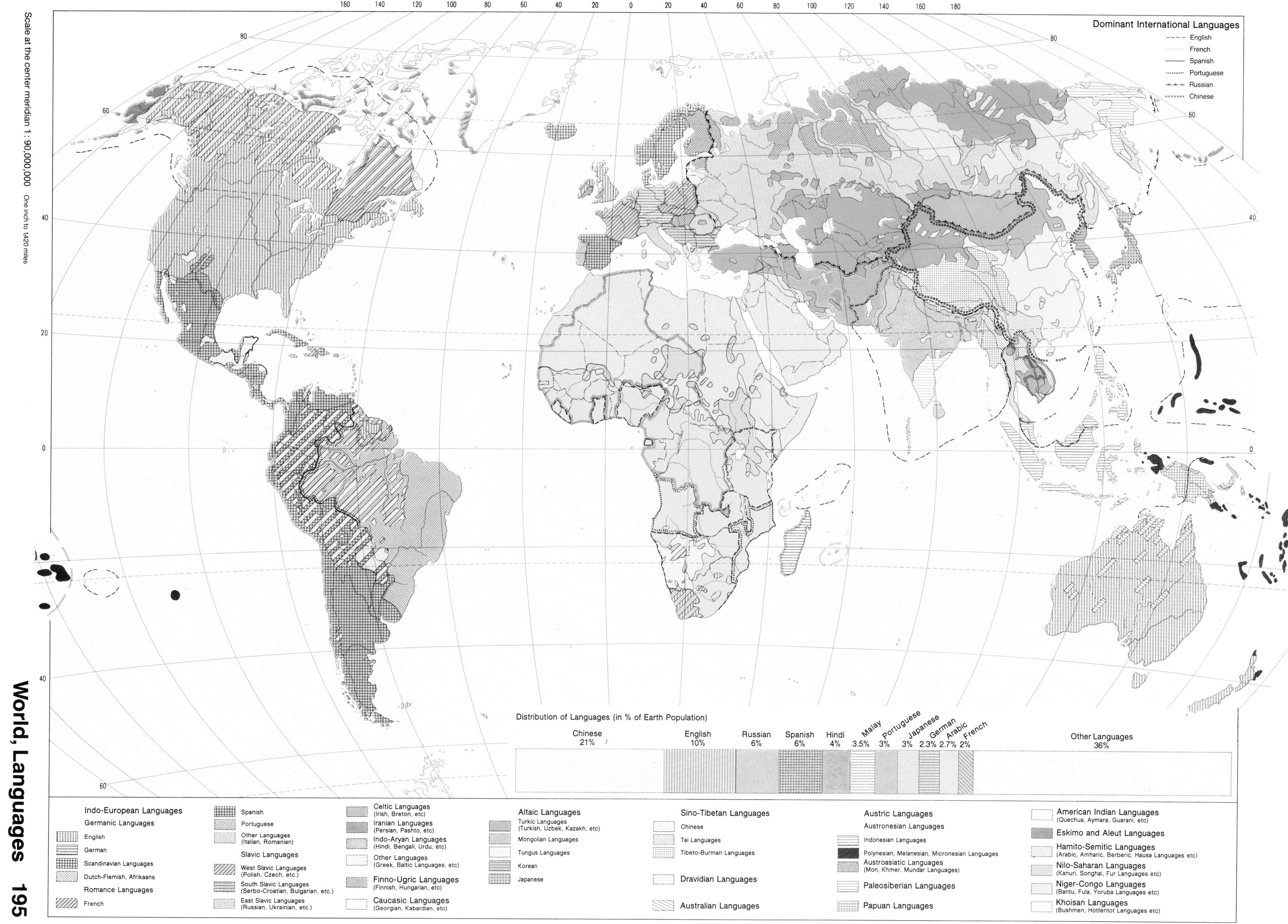
Dominant International Languages
English
French
Spanish
Portuguese
Russian
Chinese
Distribution of Languages (in % of Earth Population)
Chinese 21%
English 10%
Russian 6%
Spanish 6%
Hindi 4%
Malay 3.5%
Portuguese 3%
Japanese 3%
German 2.3%
Arabic 2.7%
French 2%
Other Languages 36%
Indo-European Languages
Germanic Languages
English
German
Scandinavian Languages
Dutch-Flemish, Afrikaans
Romance Languages
French
Spanish
Portuguese
Other Languages (Italian, Romanian)
Slavic Languages
West Slavic Languages (Polish, Czech, etc.)
South Slavic Languages (Serbo-Croatian, Bulgarian, etc.)
East Slavic Languages (Russian, Ukrainian, etc.)
Celtic Languages (Irish, Breton, etc)
Iranian Languages (Persian, Pashto, etc)
Indo-Aryan Languages (Hindi, Bengali, Urdu, etc)
Other Languages (Greek, Baltic Languages, etc)
Finno-Ugric Languages (Finnish, Hungarian, etc)
Caucasic Languages (Georgian, Kabardian, etc)
Altaic Languages
Turkic Languages (Turkish, Uzbek, Kazakh, etc)
Mongolian Languages
Tungus Languages
Korean
Japanese
Sino-Tibetan Languages
Chinese
Tai Languages
Tibeto-Burman Languages
Dravidian Languages
Australian Languages
Austric Languages
Austronesian Languages
Indonesian Languages
Polynesian, Melanesian, Micronesian Languages
Austroasiatic Languages (Mon, Khmer, Mundar Languages)
Paleosiberian Languages
Papuan Languages
American Indian Languages (Quechua, Aymara, Guarani, etc)
Eskimo and Aleut Languages
Hamito-Semitic Languages (Arabic, Amharic, Berberic, Hausa Languages etc)
Nilo-Saharan Languages (Kanuri, Songhai, Fur Languages etc)
Niger-Congo Languages (Bantu, Fula, Yoruba Languages etc)
Khoisan Languages (Bushmen, Hottentot Languages etc)
Scale at the center meridian 1 : 90,000,000 One inch to 1420 miles

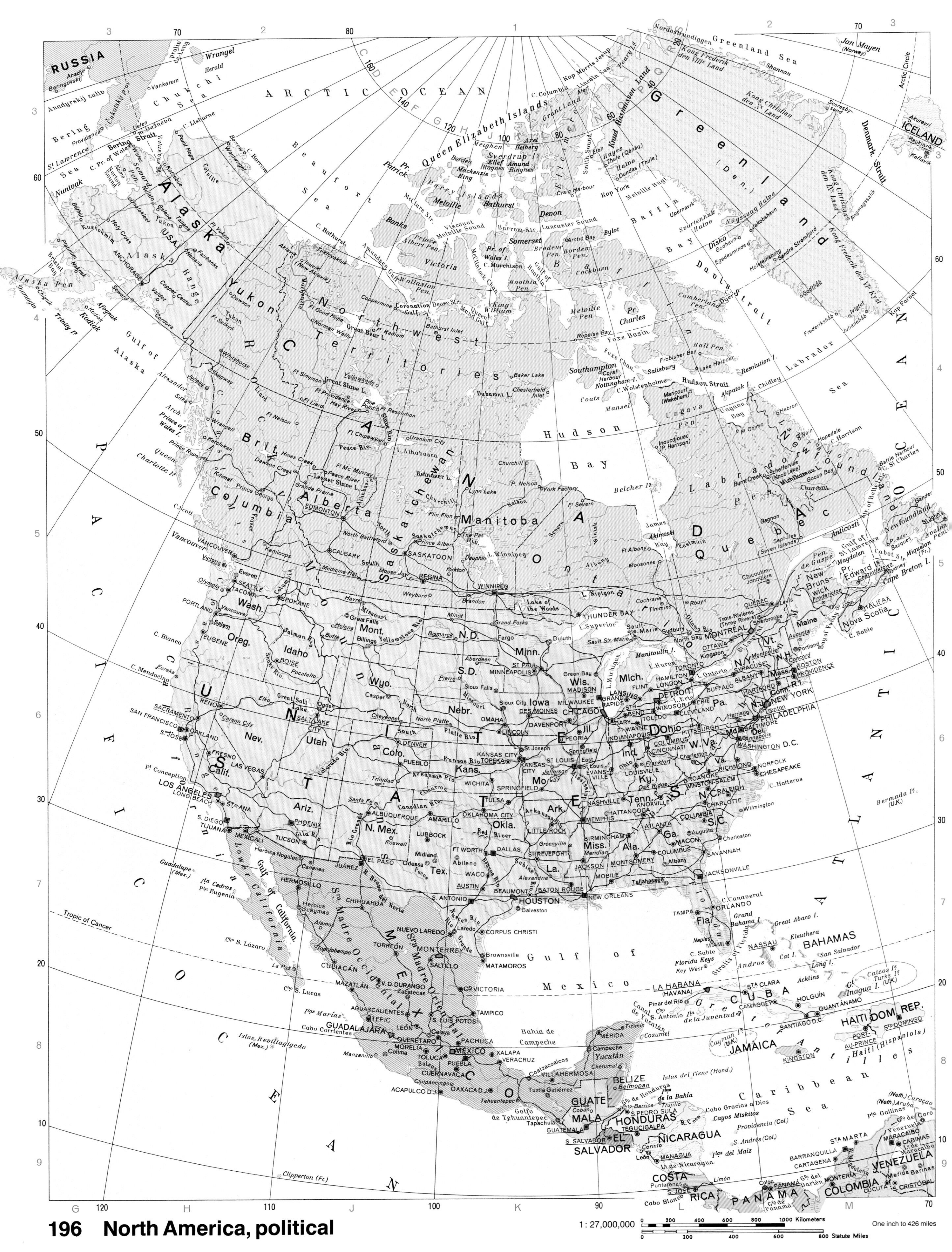
RUSSIA
ARCTIC OCEAN
Chukchi Sea
Bering Strait
Beaufort Sea
Queen Elizabeth Islands
Greenland Sea
Greenland (Den.)
Jan Mayen (Norway)
ICELAND
Denmark Strait
Arctic Circle
Baffin Bay
Davis Strait
Alaska
Gulf of Alaska
Yukon
Northwest Territories
CANADA
British Columbia
Alberta
Saskatchewan
Manitoba
Ontario
Quebec
Labrador
Newfoundland
Hudson Bay
Hudson Strait
Labrador Sea
New Brunswick
Nova Scotia
Wash.
Oreg.
Idaho
Mont.
Wyo.
N.D.
S.D.
Minn.
Wis.
Mich.
Iowa
Nebr.
Nev.
Utah
Colo.
Kans.
Calif.
Ariz.
N. Mex.
Okla.
Tex.
Mo.
Ark.
La.
Ill.
Ind.
Ohio
Ky.
Tenn.
Miss.
Ala.
Ga.
Fla.
S.C.
N.C.
Va.
W. Va.
Pa.
N.Y.
Maine
UNITED STATES
MEXICO
Gulf of Mexico
Gulf of California
Lower California
Tropic of Cancer
BAHAMAS
CUBA
JAMAICA
HAITI
DOM. REP.
BELIZE
GUATEMALA
HONDURAS
EL SALVADOR
NICARAGUA
COSTA RICA
PANAMA
COLOMBIA
VENEZUELA
Caribbean Sea
Greater Antilles
PACIFIC OCEAN
ATLANTIC OCEAN
1 : 27,000,000
One inch to 426 miles
0 200 400 600 800 1,000 Kilometers
0 200 400 600 800 Statute Miles

 North America, political

Land Use and Fishery
Arable land
Rich farmland
Tropical tillage
Irrigated farming
Steppe
Prairie, savannah
Good pastureland, pastureland farming
Tropical forest
Forest of the temperate and subtropical zone
Boreal forest
Tundra
Semi-desert and desert, rock and snow region, swamp (unproductive)
Wheat
Rye
Maize (corn)
Rice
Barley
Oats
Potatoes
Sugar beets
Sugar cane
Soybeans
Olives
Peanuts
Wine
Fruits
Vegetables
Citus fruits and pineapples
Bananas
Date palms
Cotton
Sisal
Coffee
Cocoa
Tobacco
Fishing areas
Fishing ports
Oysters
Pearls
Cities of over 1 million
Cities of under 1 million
Reindeer
Fur-bearing animals
Cattle
Sheep
Halibut
Salmon
Herring
Lobster
Sponges
Mackerel
Cod
Nome
Fairbanks
Anchorage
Valdez
Juneau
Sitka
Prince Rupert
Yellowknife
Lynn Lake
Flin Flon
Edmonton
Calgary
Regina
Winnipeg
Vancouver
Seattle
Tacoma
Spokane
Portland
Schefferville
Havre-St-Pierre
St.John's
Louisbourg
Arvida
Québec
St.John
Hal.
Montr.
Sudbury
Ottawa
Duluth
Tor.
Buff.
Boston
Provid.
New York
Phil.
Balt.
Wash.
Richm.
Norfolk
Roan.
Minneap.
Milw.
Chic.
Detroit
Cleveland
Pittsb.
Ind.
Cinc.
Col.
St.Louis
Kansas C.
Wichita
Oklahoma C.
Denver
Salt Lake City
San Francisco
Sacramento
Los Angeles
San Diego
Phoenix
Albuqu.
El Paso
Dallas
Memphis
Knoxv.
Atl.
Montg.
Jackson
New Orleans
Houston
S.Antonio
Miami
Heroica Guaymas
Chihuahua
Torreón
Mont.
Mazatlán
Aguascal.
Tampico
Guadalajara
Mexico
Veracruz
Mérida
Campeche
La Habana
Kingston
P.-au-Prince
Sto.Dom.
Guat.
S. Salv.
Teguc.
Managua
S.José
Panamá
Barranquilla
Cartagena
Maracaibo
Godhavn
Jakobshavn
Angmagssalik
Godthåb
Frederikshåb
Julianehåb
Akureyri
Reykj.
1 : 27,000,000
Kilometers
Statute Miles
One inch to 426 miles

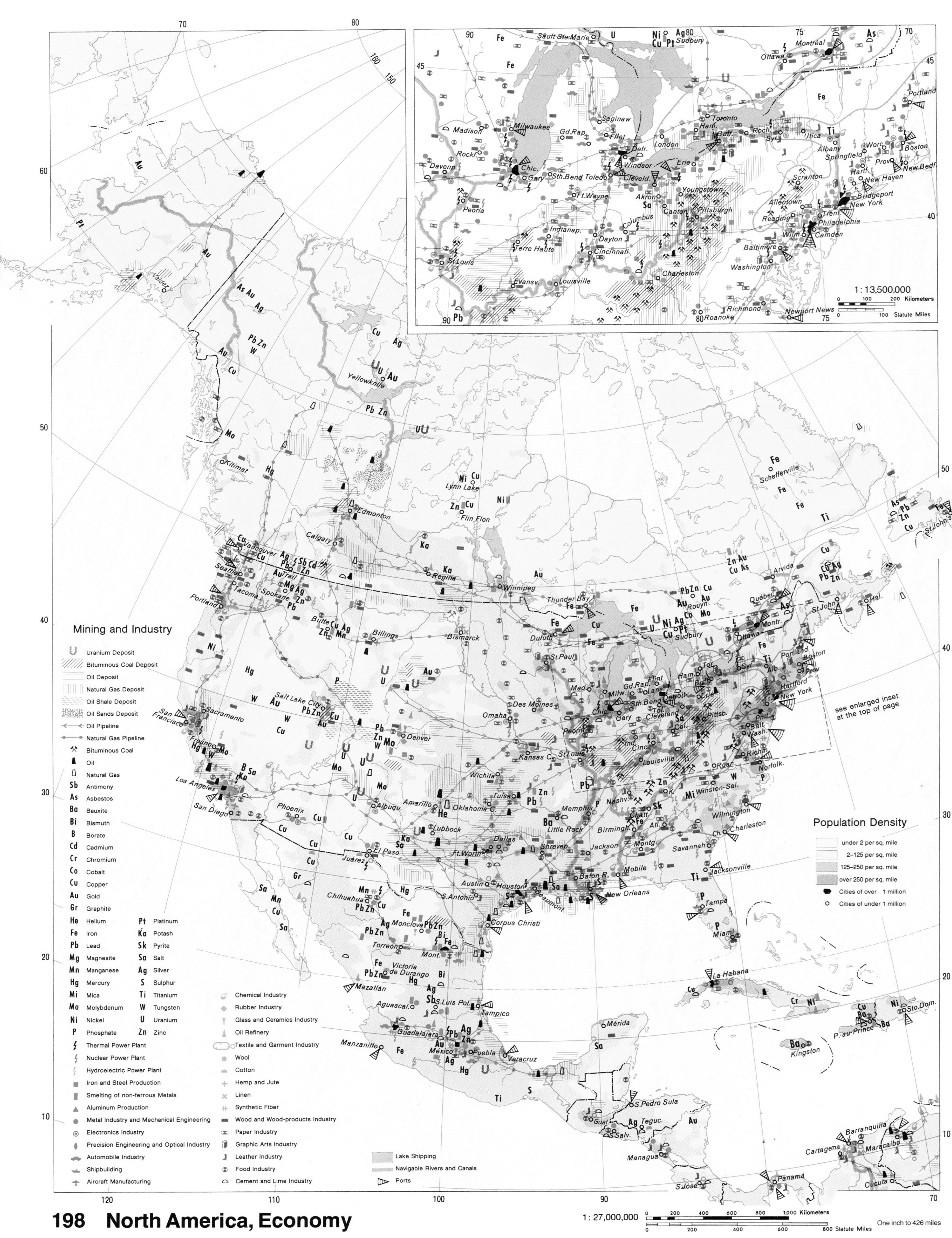
1: 13,500,000
0 100 200 Kilometers
0 100 Statute Miles
see enlarged inset at the top of page
Mining and Industry
Uranium Deposit
Bituminous Coal Deposit
Oil Deposit
Natural Gas Deposit
Oil Shale Deposit
Oil Sands Deposit
Oil Pipeline
Natural Gas Pipeline
Bituminous Coal
Oil
Natural Gas
Sb Antimony
As Asbestos
Ba Bauxite
Bi Bismuth
B Borate
Cd Cadmium
Cr Chromium
Co Cobalt
Cu Copper
Au Gold
Gr Graphite
He Helium
Fe Iron
Pb Lead
Mg Magnesite
Mn Manganese
Hg Mercury
Mi Mica
Mo Molybdenum
Ni Nickel
P Phosphate
Pt Platinum
Ka Potash
Sk Pyrite
Sa Salt
Ag Silver
S Sulphur
Ti Titanium
W Tungsten
U Uranium
Zn Zinc
Thermal Power Plant
Nuclear Power Plant
Hydroelectric Power Plant
Iron and Steel Production
Smelting of non-ferrous Metals
Aluminum Production
Metal Industry and Mechanical Engineering
Electronics Industry
Precision Engineering and Optical Industry
Automobile Industry
Shipbuilding
Aircraft Manufacturing
Chemical Industry
Rubber Industry
Glass and Ceramics Industry
Oil Refinery
Textile and Garment Industry
Wool
Cotton
Hemp and Jute
Linen
Synthetic Fiber
Wood and Wood-products Industry
Paper Industry
Graphic Arts Industry
Leather Industry
Food Industry
Cement and Lime Industry
Lake Shipping
Navigable Rivers and Canals
Ports
Population Density
under 2 per sq. mile
2–125 per sq. mile
125–250 per sq. mile
over 250 per sq. mile
Cities of over 1 million
Cities of under 1 million
1: 27,000,000
0 200 400 600 800 1000 Kilometers
0 200 400 600 800 Statute Miles
One inch to 426 miles

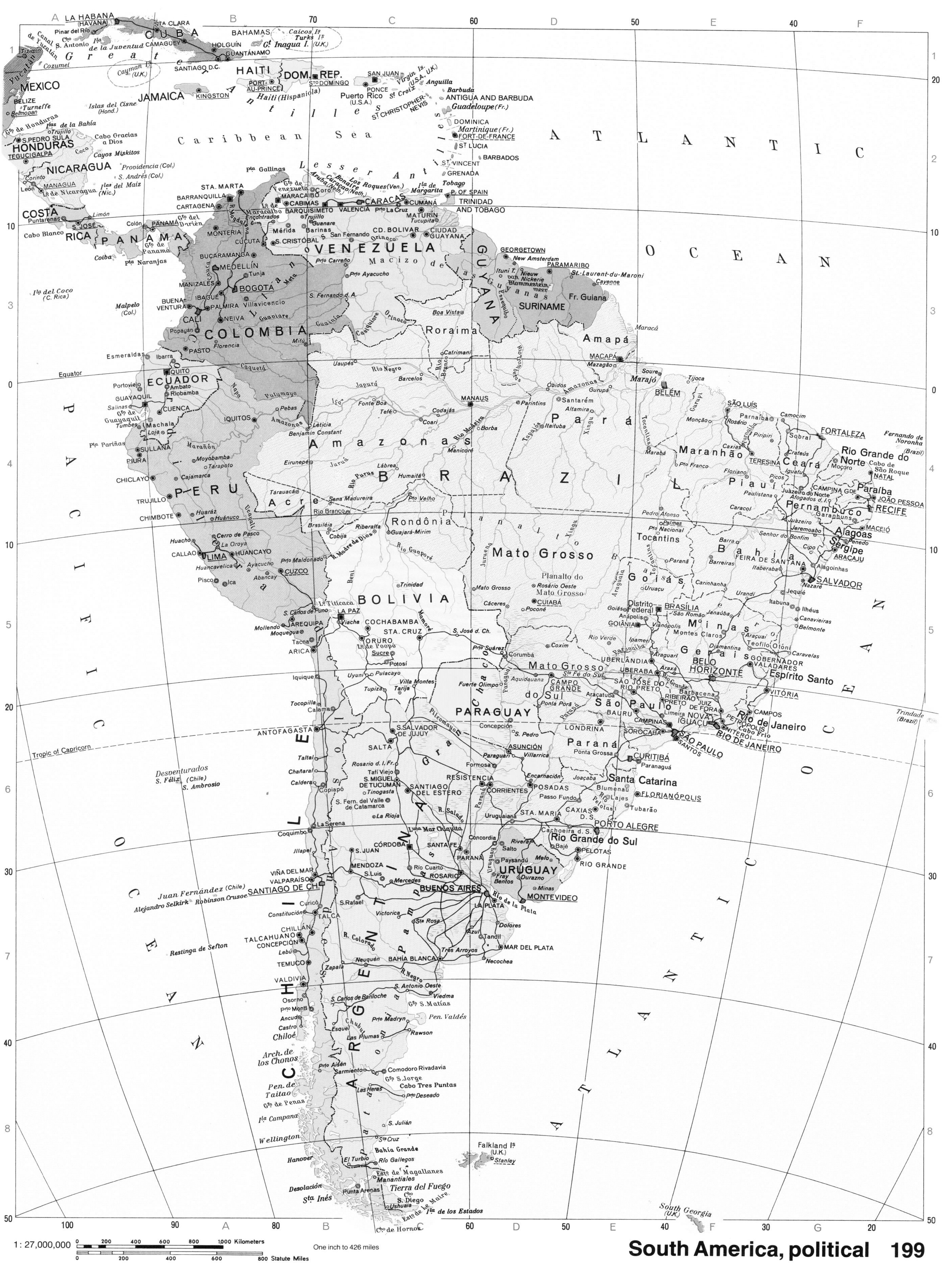

LA HABANA (HAVANA)
CUBA
STA CLARA
CAMAGÜEY
HOLGUÍN
GUANTÁNAMO
SANTIAGO D.C.
BAHAMAS
Caicos Is
Turks Is
Gt Inagua I. (U.K.)
Cayman Is (U.K.)
Great Antilles
MEXICO
BELIZE
Belmopan
HAITI
PORT-AU-PRINCE
DOM. REP.
STO DOMINGO
Haiti (Hispaniola)
JAMAICA
KINGSTON
SAN JUAN
PONCE
Puerto Rico (U.S.A.)
Virgin Is. (U.S.A. U.K.)
St Croix
Anguilla
Barbuda
ANTIGUA AND BARBUDA
ST. CHRISTOPHER-NEVIS
Guadeloupe (Fr.)
DOMINICA
Martinique (Fr.)
FORT-DE-FRANCE
ST LUCIA
BARBADOS
ST. VINCENT
GRENADA
Islas del Cisne (Hond.)
HONDURAS
TEGUCIGALPA
S.PEDRO SULA
Cabo Gracias a Dios
Cayos Miskitos
NICARAGUA
MANAGUA
Providencia (Col.)
S. Andrés (Col.)
Ilas del Maíz (Nic.)
COSTA RICA
S. JOSÉ
Limón
PANAMA
Colón
Caribbean Sea
Lesser Antilles
Los Roques (Ven.)
Bonaire
Curaçao (Neth.)
Aruba (Neth.)
Ila de Margarita
Tobago
P. OF SPAIN
TRINIDAD AND TOBAGO
ATLANTIC OCEAN
Pta Gallinas
Gfo de Venezuela
STA. MARTA
BARRANQUILLA
CARTAGENA
MARACAIBO
CABIMAS
CORO
CARACAS
CUMANÁ
BARQUISIMETO
VALENCIA
Pto La Cruz
MATURÍN
CD. BOLIVAR
CIUDAD GUAYANA
VENEZUELA
Macizo de las Guayanas
GEORGETOWN
New Amsterdam
GUYANA
PARAMARIBO
SURINAME
St-Laurent-du-Maroni
Cayenne
Fr. Guiana
MONTERÍA
CÚCUTA
S. CRISTÓBAL
Mérida
Barinas
San Fernando
Pto Carreño
Pto Ayacucho
BUCARAMANGA
MEDELLÍN
Tunja
MANIZALES
BOGOTÁ
IBAGUÉ
BUENAVENTURA
PALMIRA
Villavicencio
CALI
NEIVA
Popayán
COLOMBIA
PASTO
Florencia
Malpelo (Col.)
Ila del Coco (C. Rica)
Boa Vista
Roraima
Amapá
MACAPÁ
Esmeraldas
Ibarra
QUITO
ECUADOR
Equator
Ambato
Riobamba
GUAYAQUIL
CUENCA
Machala
Loja
Tumbes
IQUITOS
Marajó
BELÉM
SÃO LUÍS
Santarém
Óbidos
MANAUS
Amazonas
Pará
Maranhão
TERESINA
FORTALEZA
Ceará
Rio Grande do Norte
NATAL
Paraíba
JOÃO PESSOA
Pernambuco
RECIFE
MACEIÓ
Alagoas
Sergipe
ARACAJU
Bahia
SALVADOR
Piauí
Fernando de Noronha (Brazil)
SULLANA
PIURA
CHICLAYO
TRUJILLO
PERU
CHIMBOTE
Huaraz
Huánuco
Huacho
CALLAO
LIMA
HUANCAYO
Ayacucho
CUZCO
Pisco
Ica
Acre
Rio Branco
Rondônia
Mato Grosso
Tocantins
BRAZIL
Goiás
BRASÍLIA
GOIÂNIA
Minas Gerais
BELO HORIZONTE
Espírito Santo
VITÓRIA
Rio de Janeiro
RIO DE JANEIRO
SÃO PAULO
São Paulo
Paraná
CURITIBA
Santa Catarina
FLORIANÓPOLIS
PORTO ALEGRE
Rio Grande do Sul
PELOTAS
RIO GRANDE
Trindade (Brazil)
CUIABÁ
CAMPO GRANDE
Mato Grosso do Sul
BOLIVIA
LA PAZ
COCHABAMBA
STA. CRUZ
ORURO
Sucre
Potosí
Lago Titicaca
AREQUIPA
Tacna
ARICA
Iquique
Tocopilla
Calama
ANTOFAGASTA
PARAGUAY
ASUNCIÓN
Concepción
Tropic of Capricorn
S.SALVADOR DE JUJUY
SALTA
S. MIGUEL DE TUCUMÁN
SANTIAGO DEL ESTERO
RESISTENCIA
CORRIENTES
POSADAS
Copiapó
Caldera
La Serena
Coquimbo
CÓRDOBA
SANTA FE
PARANÁ
ROSARIO
S.JUAN
MENDOZA
VIÑA DEL MAR
VALPARAÍSO
SANTIAGO DE CH.
BUENOS AIRES
LA PLATA
URUGUAY
MONTEVIDEO
Río de la Plata
Juan Fernández (Chile)
Alejandro Selkirk
Robinson Crusoe
Desventurados
S. Félix (Chile)
S. Ambrosio
TALCA
CHILLÁN
TALCAHUANO
CONCEPCIÓN
TEMUCO
VALDIVIA
Osorno
Pto Montt
Chiloé
MAR DEL PLATA
BAHÍA BLANCA
Tandil
Neuquén
CHILE
ARGENTINA
Pampa
Patagonia
Pen. Valdés
Comodoro Rivadavia
Arch. de los Chonos
Pen. de Taitao
Wellington
Falkland Is (U.K.)
Stanley
Río Gallegos
Punta Arenas
Tierra del Fuego
Ushuaia
Ila de los Estados
Cbo de Hornos
South Georgia (U.K.)
PACIFIC OCEAN
ATLANTIC OCEAN
1: 27,000,000
Kilometers
Statute Miles
One inch to 426 miles

La Habana
Kingston
P.-au-Prince
Sto. Domingo
San Juan
Tegucig.
Managua
S.José
Panamá
Barranquilla
Cartagena
Maracaibo
Caracas
Barquisimeto
Barcelona
P.of Spain
Cúcuta
Medellín
Bucaramanga
Bogotá
Cali
Georgetown
Paramaribo
Quito
Guayaquil
Salinas
Belém
Manaus
Fortaleza
Natal
Recife
Maceió
Salvador
Chimbote
Callao
Lima
Arequipa
La Paz
Cochabamba
Arica
Iquique
Antofagasta
Brasília
Belo Horizonte
Vitória
São Paulo
Rio de Janeiro
Santos
Curitiba
Asunción
S.M.d.Tucumán
Resistencia
Porto Alegre
Rio Grande
S.Juan
Córdoba
Sta.Fé
Paraná
Mendoza
Rio Cuarto
Rosario
Valparaíso
Santiago de Ch.
Buenos Aires
Montev.
Maldonado
Mar d.Plata
Talcahuano
Conc.
Bahía Blanca
Necochea
Valdivia
Ancud
P.Madryn
Com.Rivadavia
Rio Gallegos
Pta Arenas
Ushuaia
Wild rubber
Brazil nuts
Cinchona bark
Yerba Buena
Sheep
Cattle
Whales
Land Use and Fishery
Arable land
Rich farmland
Tropical tillage
Irrigated farming
Steppe (Monte)
Alpine steppe (Puna, Paramo), Tundra
Poor pastureland (Llanos, Campos)
Good pastureland (Pampa)
Tropical rainforest
Forest of the temperate and subtropical zone
Savannah (Chaco, Caatinga)
Semi-desert and desert, swamp, rock an snow region (unproductive)
Wheat
Maize
Rice
Sweet potatoes, Maniok
Sugar cane
Wine
Fruits
Citrus fruits
Bananas
Cotton
Sisal
Coffee
Cocoa
Tobacco
Fishing areas
Fishing ports
Oysters
Pearls
Cities of over 1 million
Cities of under 1 million
1 : 27,000,000
0 200 400 600 800 1000 Kilometers
0 200 400 600 800 Statute Miles
One inch to 426 miles

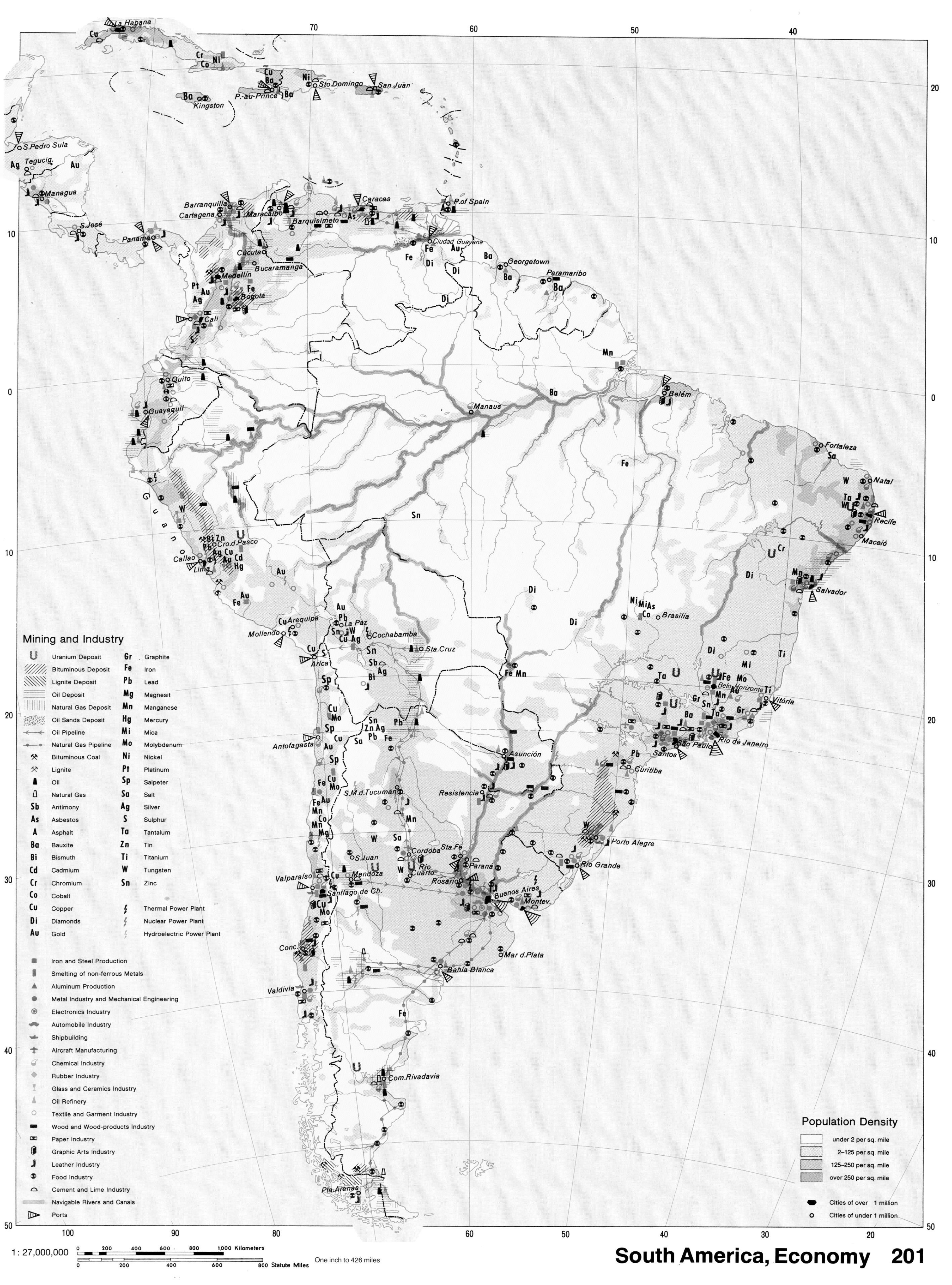
Mining and Industry
Uranium Deposit
Bituminous Deposit
Lignite Deposit
Oil Deposit
Natural Gas Deposit
Oil Sands Deposit
Oil Pipeline
Natural Gas Pipeline
Bituminous Coal
Lignite
Oil
Natural Gas
Sb Antimony
As Asbestos
A Asphalt
Ba Bauxite
Bi Bismuth
Cd Cadmium
Cr Chromium
Co Cobalt
Cu Copper
Di Diamonds
Au Gold
Gr Graphite
Fe Iron
Pb Lead
Mg Magnesit
Mn Manganese
Hg Mercury
Mi Mica
Mo Molybdenum
Ni Nickel
Pt Platinum
Sp Salpeter
Sa Salt
Ag Silver
S Sulphur
Ta Tantalum
Zn Tin
Ti Titanium
W Tungsten
Sn Zinc
Thermal Power Plant
Nuclear Power Plant
Hydroelectric Power Plant
Iron and Steel Production
Smelting of non-ferrous Metals
Aluminum Production
Metal Industry and Mechanical Engineering
Electronics Industry
Automobile Industry
Shipbuilding
Aircraft Manufacturing
Chemical Industry
Rubber Industry
Glass and Ceramics Industry
Oil Refinery
Textile and Garment Industry
Wood and Wood-products Industry
Paper Industry
Graphic Arts Industry
Leather Industry
Food Industry
Cement and Lime Industry
Navigable Rivers and Canals
Ports
Population Density
under 2 per sq. mile
2–125 per sq. mile
125–250 per sq. mile
over 250 per sq. mile
Cities of over 1 million
Cities of under 1 million
1: 27,000,000
0 200 400 600 800 1,000 Kilometers
0 200 400 600 800 Statute Miles
One inch to 426 miles
La Habana
Kingston
P.-au-Prince
Sto.Domingo
San Juan
S.Pedro Sula
Tegucig.
Managua
S.José
Panamá
Barranquilla
Cartagena
Maracaibo
Barquisimeto
Caracas
P.of Spain
Ciudad Guayana
Georgetown
Paramaribo
Cúcuta
Bucaramanga
Medellín
Bogotá
Cali
Quito
Guayaquil
Manaus
Belém
Fortaleza
Natal
Recife
Maceió
Salvador
Guano
Cro.d.Pasco
Callao
Lima
Arequipa
Mollendo
La Paz
Cochabamba
Sta.Cruz
Arica
Brasília
Belo Horizonte
Vitória
Rio de Janeiro
São Paulo
Santos
Curitiba
Antofagasta
Asunción
S.M.d.Tucumán
Resistencia
Porto Alegre
Rio Grande
Córdoba
Sta.Fe
Paraná
S.Juan
Mendoza
Rio Cuarto
Rosario
Valparaíso
Santiago de Ch.
Buenos Aires
Montev.
Mar d.Plata
Conc.
Bahía Blanca
Valdivia
Com.Rivadavia
Pta.Arenas

NORWEGIAN SEA
ICELAND
Reykjavík
Vatnajökull
Arctic Circle
Föroyar (Den.)
Shetland (U.K.)
Orkney
Hebrides
ATLANTIC OCEAN
UNITED KINGDOM
Scotland
ABERDEEN
DUNDEE
GLASGOW
EDINBURGH
Northern Ireland
BELFAST
NEWCASTLE
SUNDERLAND
Man
IRELAND
BAILE ÁTHA CLIATH (DUBLIN)
CORCAIGH
England
Wales
LIVERPOOL
MANCHESTER
LEEDS
SHEFFIELD
HULL
BIRMINGHAM
NORWICH
CARDIFF
BRISTOL
OXFORD
LONDON
PLYMOUTH
PORTSMOUTH
Dover
Wight
St George's Channel
Bristol Chan.
Land's End
Is of Scilly
English Channel
North Sea
NORWAY
SWEDEN
OSLO
BERGEN
TRONDHEIM
Skagerrak
Kattegat
DENMARK
KØBENHAVN (COPENHAGEN)
GÖTEBORG
MALMÖ
Bornholm (Den.)
Helgoland
HAMBURG
BREMEN
BERLIN
GERMANY
AMSTERDAM
'S-GRAVENHAGE (THE HAGUE)
ROTTERDAM
NETHERLANDS
BELGIUM
BRUXELLES (BRUSSELS)
ANTWERPEN
LUXEMBOURG
KÖLN
BONN
DÜSSELDORF
ESSEN
DORTMUND
FRANKFURT A. M.
LEIPZIG
DRESDEN
PRAHA (PRAGUE)
CZECH REP.
MÜNCHEN
STUTTGART
NÜRNBERG
WIEN
AUSTRIA
SWITZERLAND
ZÜRICH
BERN
GENÈVE (GENEVA)
LIECHT.
FRANCE
PARIS
LE HAVRE
ROUEN
BREST
RENNES
NANTES
LE MANS
ORLÉANS
TOURS
STRASBOURG
DIJON
LYON
BORDEAUX
TOULOUSE
MONTPELLIER
MARSEILLE
NICE
MONACO
Bay of Biscay
Pyrenees
ANDORRA
SPAIN
MADRID
BARCELONA
VALENCIA
SEVILLA
MÁLAGA
GRANADA
BILBAO
ZARAGOZA (SARAGOSSA)
VALLADOLID
SALAMANCA
LA CORUÑA
PORTUGAL
LISBOA (LISBON)
PORTO
Coimbra
Gibraltar (U.K.)
Str. of Gibraltar
Mallorca
Menorca
Ibiza
Is. Baleares
Corse
Sardegna
ITALY
MILANO (MILAN)
TORINO (TURIN)
GENOVA (GENOA)
VENEZIA (VENICE)
ROMA (ROME)
NÁPOLI (NAPLES)
FIRENZE (FLORENCE)
BOLOGNA
S. MARINO
VATICAN CITY
Sicilia
PALERMO
Ligurian Sea
Tyrrhenian Sea
Adriatic Sea
SLOVENIA
LJUBLJANA
CROATIA
ZAGREB
BOSNIA AND HERCEGOVINA
MALTA
Valletta
MEDITERRANEAN
MOROCCO
AR-RIBĀT (RABAT)
AD-DĀR AL-BAYDĀ (CASABLANCA)
MARRĀKUSH
High Atlas
ALGERIA
AL-JAZĀ'IR (ALGIERS)
Saharan Atlas
TUNISIA
TUNIS (TŪNIS)
Is. Canarias (Spain)
Madeira (Port.)

1 : 13,500,000

Kilometers 0 100 200 300 400 500

Statute Miles 0 100 200 300 400

One inch to 213 miles

Administrative units in the Soviet

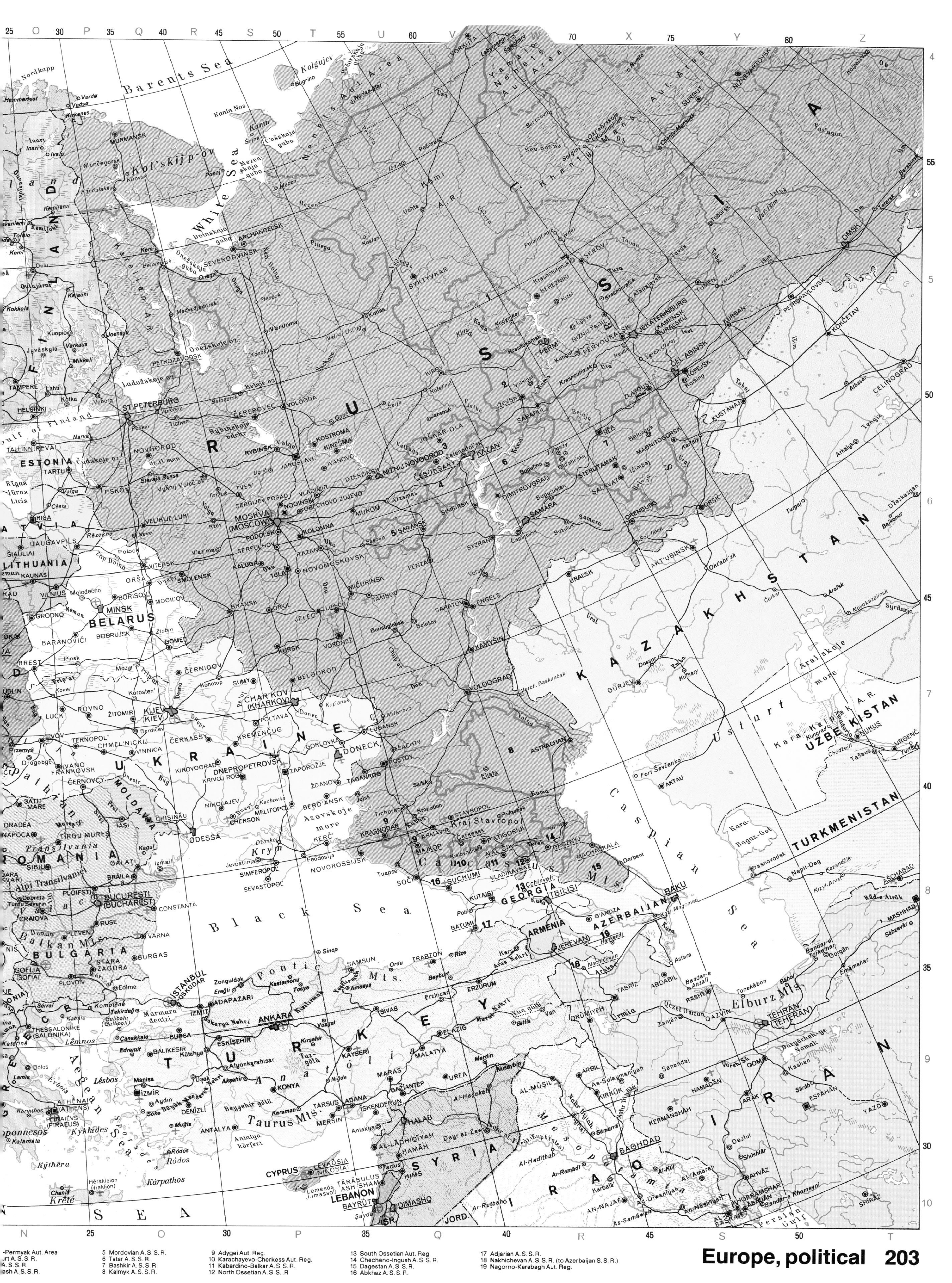

RUSSIA
KAZAKHSTAN
UKRAINE
BELARUS
TURKEY
IRAN
IRAQ
SYRIA
ROMANIA
BULGARIA
FINLAND
ESTONIA
LATVIA
LITHUANIA
MOLDAVA
GEORGIA
ARMENIA
AZERBAIJAN
UZBEKISTAN
TURKMENISTAN
LEBANON
CYPRUS
JORD.
ISR.
Barents Sea
White Sea
Black Sea
Caspian Sea
Azovskoje more
Aral'skoje more
Persian Gulf
Kol'skij p-ov
Caucasus Mts.
Pontic Mts.
Taurus Mts.
Elburz Mts.
Ustjurt
Mesopotamia
Anatolia
Krym
MOSKVA (MOSCOW)
ST.PETERBURG
KIJEV (KIEV)
MINSK
ANKARA
ISTANBUL
BUCURESTI (BUCHAREST)
TBILISI
BAKU
JEREVAN
TEHRAN (TEHERAN)
BAGHDAD
DIMASHQ
BAYRUT
LEVKOSIA (NICOSIA)
SOFIJA (SOFIA)
ATHENAI (ATHENS)
HELSINKI
TALLINN (REVAL)
RIGA
VILNIUS
-Permyak Aut. Area
-urt A. S. S. R.
A. S. S. R.
-ash A. S. S. R.
5 Mordovian A. S. S. R.
6 Tatar A. S. S. R.
7 Bashkir A. S. S. R.
8 Kalmyk A. S. S. R.
9 Adygei Aut. Reg.
10 Karachayevo-Cherkess Aut. Reg.
11 Kabardino-Balkar A. S. S. R.
12 North Ossetian A. S. S. R
13 South Ossetian Aut. Reg.
14 Checheno-Ingush A. S. S. R.
15 Dagestan A. S. S. R.
16 Abkhaz A. S. S. R.
17 Adjarian A. S. S. R.
18 Nakhichevan A. S. S. R. (to Azerbaijan S. S. R.)
19 Nagorno-Karabagh Aut. Reg.

1: 27,000,000

0 200 400 600 800 1000 Kilometers

0 200 400 600 800 Statute Miles

One inch to 426 miles

ATLANTIC
OCEAN
ARCTIC OCEAN
Norwegian Sea
Barents Sea
Greenland Sea
North Sea
Black Sea
Caspian Sea
MEDITERRANEAN SEA
Arctic Circle
Tropic of Cancer
Denmark Str.
CANADA
Greenland
Spitzbergen (Norway)
Jan Mayen (Norway)
ICELAND
UNITED KINGDOM
IRELAND
FRANCE
SPAIN
PORTUGAL
GERMANY
POLAND
HUNGARY
ROMANIA
BULGARIA
GREECE
ITALY
SWEDEN
FINLAND
ESTONIA
LATVIA
LITHUANIA
BELARUS
UKRAINE
RUSSIA
KAZAKHSTAN
UZBEKISTAN
TURKMENISTAN
AFGHANISTAN
TURKEY
SYRIA
LEBANON
ISRAEL
CYPRUS
IRAQ
IRAN
KUWAIT
QATAR
BAHRAIN
UNITED ARAB EMIRATES
SAUDI ARABIA
OMAN
EGYPT
LIBYA
TUNISIA
ALGERIA
MOROCCO
Western Sahara
MAURITANIA
CAPE VERDE
LONDON
PARIS
MADRID
LISBOA
ROMA
BERLIN
WARSZAWA
MOSKVA
ST.-PETERBURG
ISTANBUL
ANKARA
BAGHDAD
TEHRAN
AL-QAHIRAH (CAIRO)

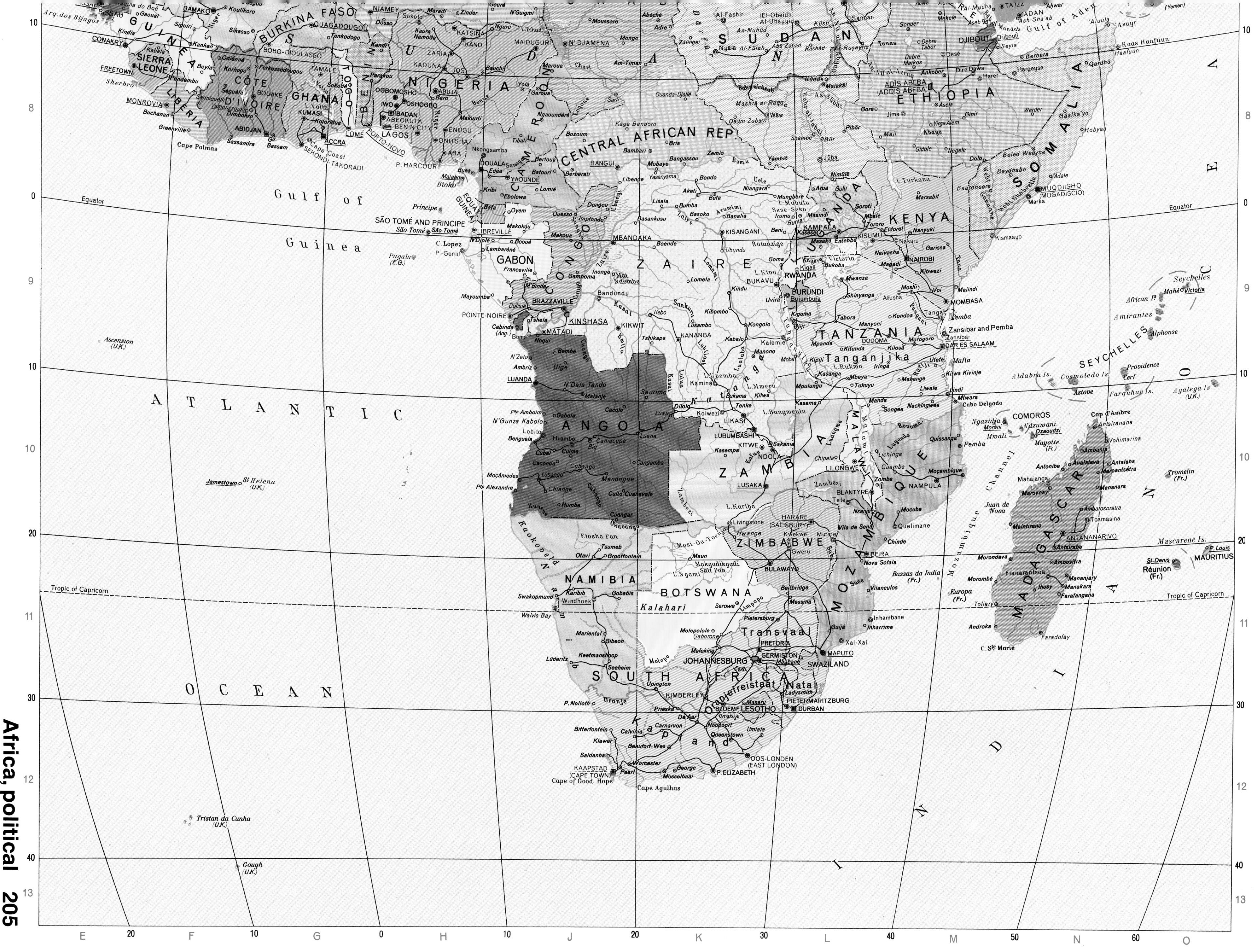
ATLANTIC
OCEAN
Gulf of
Guinea
Mozambique Channel
Equator
Tropic of Capricorn
SUDAN
ETHIOPIA
DJIBOUTI
SOMALIA
KENYA
UGANDA
RWANDA
BURUNDI
TANZANIA
ZAIRE
CONGO
GABON
EQUAT. GUINEA
CENTRAL AFRICAN REP.
NIGERIA
BURKINA FASO
GHANA
TOGO
BENIN
CÔTE D'IVOIRE
LIBERIA
SIERRA LEONE
GUINEA
ANGOLA
ZAMBIA
MALAWI
MOZAMBIQUE
ZIMBABWE
BOTSWANA
NAMIBIA
SOUTH AFRICA
LESOTHO
SWAZILAND
MADAGASCAR
COMOROS
SEYCHELLES
MAURITIUS
SÃO TOMÉ AND PRINCIPE
Réunion (Fr.)
St Helena (U.K.)
Ascension (U.K.)
Tristan da Cunha (U.K.)
Gough (U.K.)
Kalahari
Tanganjika
Transvaal
Oranjefreistaat
Natal
Kapland
ADIS ABEBA
NAIROBI
KAMPALA
KINSHASA
BRAZZAVILLE
LUANDA
LUSAKA
HARARE (SALISBURY)
MAPUTO
PRETORIA
JOHANNESBURG
KAAPSTAD (CAPE TOWN)
DURBAN
ANTANANARIVO
DAR ES SALAAM
MOMBASA
MUQDISHO (MOGADISCIO)
LAGOS
ACCRA
ABIDJAN
MONROVIA
FREETOWN
CONAKRY
BANGUI
LIBREVILLE
YAOUNDÉ
Windhoek
LILONGWE
BLANTYRE

1 : 27,000,000

0 200 400 600 800 1000 Kilometers

0 200 400 600 800 Statute Miles

One inch to 426 miles

Conversion meters – feet see page 48

UNITED STATES
Alaska
Bering Sea
Aleutian Is.
Sea of Okhotsk
Kamčatka
PETROPAVLOVSK-KAMČATSKIJ
MAGADAN
JAKUTSK
NORILSK
Tajmyr
Severnaja Zemlja
Novosibirskije o-va
East Siberian Sea
Laptev Sea
Wrangel
Chukchi Sea
SIBERIA
Lena
Bajkal
IRKUTSK
KRASNOJARSK
BRATSK
TOMSK
ULAN-UDE
KOMSOMOLSK
CHABAROVSK
VLADIVOSTOK
NACHODKA
Sachalin
JUŽNO-SACHALINSK
Hokkaidō
SAPPORO
Honshū
Shikoku
Kyūshū
TŌKYŌ (TOKIO)
YOKOHAMA
KAWASAKI
NAGOYA
KYOTO
OSAKA
KOBE
HIROSHIMA
KITA-KYUSHU
FUKUOKA
JAPAN
Sea of Japan
MONGOLIA
ULAAN BAATAR (ULAN BATOR)
Gobi
Manchuria
HARBIN
CHANGCHUN
SHENYANG (MUKDEN)
FUSHUN
ANSHAN
LÜDA
NORTH KOREA
P'YONG-YANG
SOUTH KOREA
SOUL
PUSAN
TAEGU
Yellow Sea
BEIJING (PEKING)
TIANJIN (TIENTSIN)
TAIYUAN
JINAN (TSI-NAN)
QINGDAO (TSINGTAO)
ZHENGZHOU
LUOYANG
XI'AN (HSI-AN)
LANZHOU
NANJING (NANKING)
SHANGHAI
CHANGZHOU
HANGZHOU
WUHAN
CHONGQING
CHENGDU
CHANGSHA
NANCHANG
FUZHOU
GUANGZHOU (CANTON)
Hong Kong (U.K.)
VICTORIA
KOWLOON
MACAU
KUNMING
CHINA
Xinjiang (Sinkiang)
Inner Mongolian Aut. Reg.
Tibetan Aut. Reg.
East China Sea
Ryukyu
Okinawa
TAIPEI
TAIWAN
Formosa
Tropic of Cancer
Bonin (Japan)
Volcano Is.
Northern Marianas (U.S.A.)
Guam (U.S.A.)
MICRONESIA
Caroline Is.
BELAU
PHILIPPINES
Luzon
MANILA
QUEZON CITY
Mindanao
DAVAO
CEBU
South China Sea
Hainan
HA NOI
HAI PHONG
VIETNAM
LAOS
VIENTIANE
THAILAND
KRUNG THEP (BANGKOK)
CAMBODIA
PHNOM PENH
HO CHI MINH (SAIGON)
MYANMAR
YANGON (RANGOON)
MANDALAY
BANGLADESH
DHAKA
CALCUTTA
BHUTAN
Himalaya
LHASA
Bay of Bengal
Andaman Sea
Andaman Is. (Ind.)
Nicobar Is. (Ind.)
Gulf of Thailand
MALAYSIA
KUALA LUMPUR
SINGAPORE
BRUNEI
Sabah
Sarawak
Borneo
Celebes Sea
Sulu Sea
Halmahera
New Guinea
PAPUA NEW GUINEA
INDONESIA
PACIFIC OCEAN
Equator

1 : 27,000,000 One inch to 426 miles
PACIFIC OCEAN
INDIAN OCEAN
AUSTRALIA
NEW ZEALAND
MICRONESIA
MELANESIA
INDONESIA
PHILIPPINES
PAPUA NEW GUINEA
SOLOMON IS.
VANUATU
FIJI
TONGA
SAMOA
NAURU
BELAU
Tasmania
Coral Sea
Tasman Sea
Arafura Sea
Timor Sea
Great Australian Bight
Tropic of Capricorn
Equator
Date Line
SYDNEY
MELBOURNE
BRISBANE
ADELAIDE
PERTH
HOBART
CANBERRA
Darwin
WELLINGTON
AUCKLAND
CHRISTCHURCH
PORT MORESBY

Australia and Oceania, political

THE NATURE OF OUR PLANET

Structure and surface of the Earth

The crust, the uppermost layer of the solid Earth, is a region of interaction between surface processes brought about by the heat of radioactive reactions deep in the Earth. Physically and chemically it is the most complex layer of the lithosphere. The Earth's crust contains a wide variety of rock types, ranging from sedimentary rocks dominated by single minerals, such as sandstone (which is mainly silica) and limestone (which is mainly calcite), to the mineral-chemical mixture igneous rocks such as basalt lavas and granite intrusions.

The crust is divided into ocean crust and continental crust. The average height of the two differs by about 2.8 mi. and the difference in their average total thickness is more exaggerated (continental crust is about 25 mi. thick, and oceanic crust about 4.4 mi.). The boundary between the crusts and the mantle is almost everywhere defined sharply by the Mohorovičić seismic discontinuity. There are further differences between the oceanic and continental crusts: They contrast strongly in structure, composition, average age, origin, and evolution. Vertical sections of both types of crust have been studied in zones of uplift caused by colliding tectonic plates. Combined with seismic evidence, these sections provide a unified view of crustal structure and composition.

Oceanic crust

Seismic studies of the ocean crust and upper mantle have identified four separate layers characterized by downward increases in wave propagation velocity, density, and thickness. The upper two layers were studied by the Deep Sea Drilling Project in 1968, whereas all that is known about the third and fourth layers has come only from ophiolites – uplifted ocean crust sections that are exposed on the Earth's surface. The top layer of the ocean crust, with an average thickness of nearly one third mile, comprises sedimentary muds (pelagic clays). They include the finest particles that were eroded from continents, and biochemically precipitated carbonate and siliceous deposits. The bottom three layers are made up of igneous materials formed during ocean-ridge processes. The chemical composition of these layers is that of basic igneous rocks, but their physical characteristics vary. The second layer, with an average thickness of one mile consists of basalt pillow lavas that were originally quenched by seawater when they erupted onto the sea floor. At the boundary between the second and third layers stratified lava is found that is interspersed with vertical dykes through which, originally, the pillow lava was ejected. These dykes lead to the third layer, a 2 mi. thick sequence of layered, coarse-grained, intrusive gabbros that must have cooled and crystallized slowly, with early formed crystals segregating into layers. The bottom layers includes layered peridotite which grades downwards into unlayered mantle peridotite.

Both layered perdotites and gabbros probably represent a fossilized magma chamber, which was originally created by the partial melting of the mantle beneath an ocean ridge. Molten material was probably ejected from the chamber roof, forming dykes that fed the pillow lava eruptions of the second layer. The Mohorovičić discontinuity lies between the two deepest layers.

Continental crust

In terms of seismic structure, the Earth's continental crust is much less regular than the ocean crust. A diffuse boundary called the Conrad discontinuity occurs between the upper and lower continental crusts at a depth of between 9 and 16 mi. The upper continental crust has a highly variable top layer which is a few miles thick and comprises relatively unmetamorphosed volcanic and sedimentary rocks. Most of the sedimentary rocks were laid down in shallow marine environments and subsequently uplifted. Beneath this superficial layer of the upper crust, most of the rock is similar in composition to granodiorite or diorite and is made up of intermediate, coarse-grained intrusive, igneous rocks. The total thickness of the upper continental crust reaches a maximum of about 16 mi. in zones of recent crustal thickening caused by igneous activity (as in the Andes mountain range in South America) and by tectonic overthrusting during collision (as in the Alps and Himalayas). This crust is of minimum thickness (about 9 mi.) in the ancient continental cratonic shield areas, where igneous rocks have been metamorphosed to form granite gneisses.

The lower continental crust extends down to the Mohorovičić discontinuity and comprises denser rocks that are only in their chemical composition similar to that of the upper crust. They include intermediate igneous rocks that have suffered intense metamorphism at high pressures, resulting in the growth of dense minerals; and basic igneous less metamorphosed rocks. This region is the least well-known, most inaccessible part of the Earth's crust.

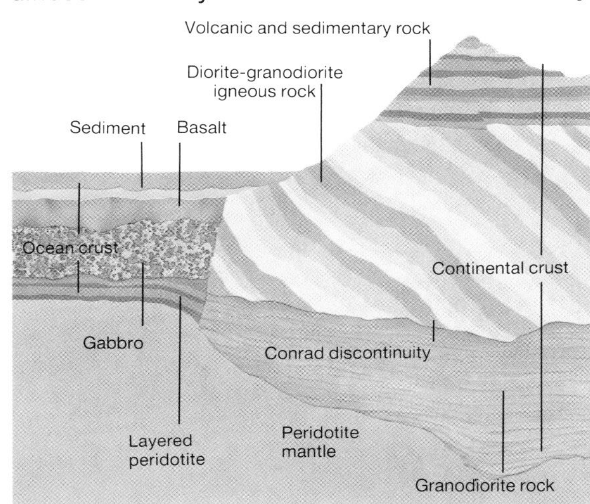
Volcanic and sedimentary rock
Diorite-granodiorite igneous rock
Sediment
Basalt
Ocean crust
Continental crust
Gabbro
Conrad discontinuity
Layered peridotite
Peridotite mantle
Granodiorite rock

The Earth's crust *is divided into oceanic and continental crust. Oceanic crust is about 2.5 mi. lower than continental crust and is about 20 per cent of its thickness. The structure of oceanic crust is uniform: a layer of sediment covers three layers of igneous rock of which the thickest is the layer of gabbro. These layers form from the partial melting of the underlying peridotite mantle. In contrast to the uniformity of oceanic crust, the structure of continental crust is varied and changes over short distances.*

The Earth's interior

Despite the information available about the surface of our planet, comparatively little is known about the state and composition of its inaccessible interior. The deepest boreholes (about 6 mi.) hardly scratch the Earth's outer skin and the deepest known samples of rock, nodules of unmolten material brought up in volcanic lavas, come from a depth of only about 60 mi., just 1.5 per cent of the distance to the center.

Our knowledge of the deeper interior relies on indirect evidence from physical measurements of the Earth's mass, volume and mean density, observations of seismic waves that have passed through the deep interior, observations of meteorites and

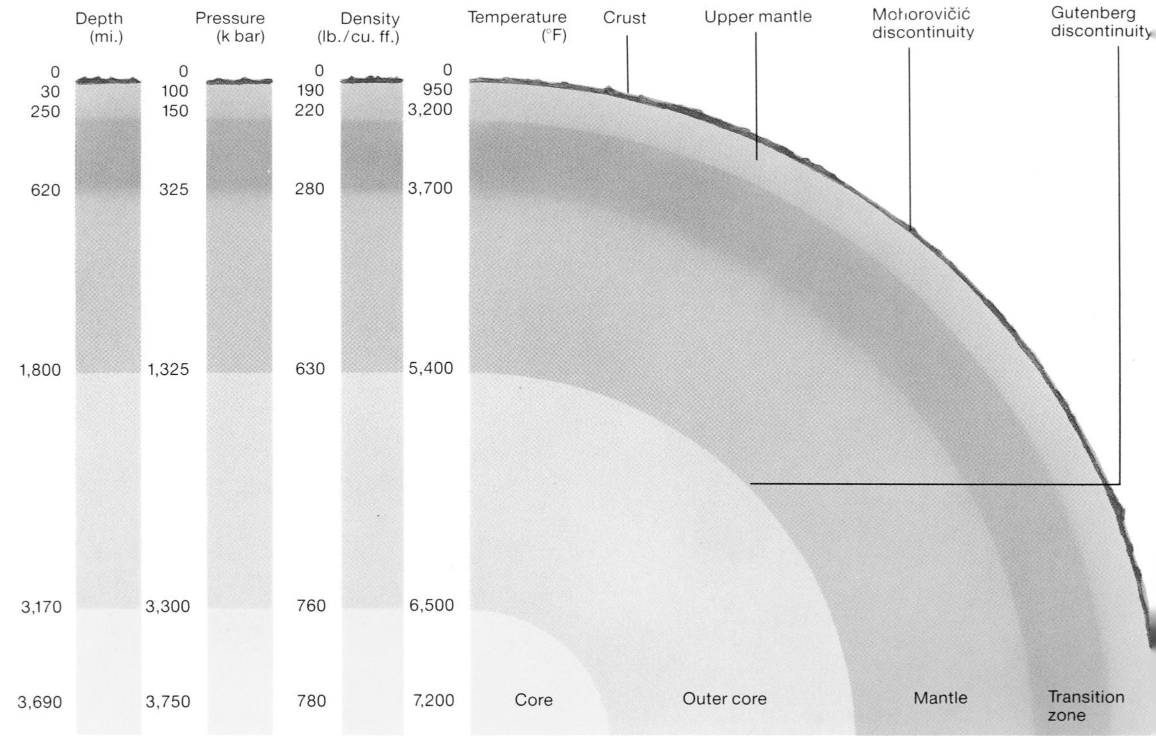
Depth (mi.)
Pressure (k bar)
Density (lb./cu. ff.)
Temperature (°F)
Crust
Upper mantle
Mohorovičić discontinuity
Gutenberg discontinuity
0
30
250
620
1,800
3,170
3,690
0
100
150
325
1,325
3,300
3,750
0
190
220
280
630
760
780
0
950
3,200
3,700
5,400
6,500
7,200
Core
Outer core
Mantle
Transition zone

The Earth *has four main structural components, namely the crust, the mantle and the outer and inner cores. The crust extends down to about 25 mi. and consists of rocks with a density of less than 190 lb./cu. ft. The mantle, divided by a transition zone, is made up of denser rocks than the crust. The temperature in this region rises rapidly, particularly between 62 and 124 mi. below the surface, where it reaches more than 1,800° F. At the core-mantle boundary (the Gutenberg discontinuity), 1,800 mi. below the surface, the pressure suddenly increases, as does the density (from 340 lb./cu. ft. to 620 lb./cu. ft.). The outer core is completely liquid, but the inner core is solid with an average density of 690 lb./cu. ft.*

other bodies in the Solar System, experimental studies of natural materials at the high pressures and temperatures of the Earth's interior, and studies of the Earth's magnetic field.

Seismic waves passing through the Earth's interior have revealed two major and three relatively minor discontinuities where changes in chemical and physical states occur. These data also help to determine the density and elastic properties of the materials through which the waves pass, since these properties govern wave velocities.

The seismic discontinuities are broadly concentric with the Earth's surface. Therefore, they mark the boundaries of spherical shells with successively greater density – the major subdivisions into crust, mantle, and core occur at the Mohorovičić and Gutenberg discontinuities.

The crust varies in thickness from about 4 mi. in oceanic areas to about 25 mi. under the continents and the mantle extends down to 1,800 mi. It contains a low-velocity layer which lies between 30 and 125 mi. below the surface, where seismic wave velocities are reduced by a few per cent, and it is most prominent and shallow beneath oceanic areas. The mantle also has a transition zone (from 250 to about 620 mi. under the surface), which is characterized by several sharp increases in wave velocity that are concurrent with an increase in density. The Earth's core is subdivided into outer and inner regions by a minor discontinuity at a depth of about 3,200 mi. The outer core does not transmit seismic shear waves and is the only totally fluid layer in the Earth.

The mantle

The combined evidence from volcanic nodules, exposed thrust slices of possible mantle rocks, physical data and meteorite studies, indicates that the upper mantle is made of silicate minerals. Among these minerals dark green olivine predominates, together with lesser amounts of black pyroxene, iron silicates and calcium aluminum silicates in a rock type known as peridotite.

Because temperature increases rapidly with depth in the outer 60 to 125 mi. of the Earth, there comes a point (at about 2,700° F) at which peridotite starts to melt. The presence of partial melt accounts for the low-velocity layer and basalt magmas that erupt, particularly from oceanic volcanoes. Because olivine has the highest melting temperature of the silicate minerals in peridotite it remains solid, while other, less abundant minerals contribute to the melt.

Temperature increases less rapidly with greater depth than does the melting point, so no further melting occurs at extreme depth although the hot, solid material is susceptible to plastic deformation and convects very slowly. This part of the mantle is the asthenosphere, or weak layer, which is distinct from the rigid uppermost mantle and crust, or lithosphere.

Increasing pressure is responsible for the transition zone where several rapid increases in density are probably caused by changes in the structure of the solids. In this zone the atomic structure of the compressed silicate minerals change to new forms in which the atoms are packed together more closely to occupy less volume. These new forms are thought to persist down to 1,800 mi.

Abundance of elements by volume

Oxygen 94.07 %
Silicon 0.88 %
Aluminium 0.44 %
Iron 0.34 %
Calcium 1.15 %
Potassium 1.17 %
Sodium 1.07 %
Magnesium 0.26 %

Abundance of elements by weigth

Oxygen 46.5 %
Silicon 28.9 %
Aluminium 8.3 %
Iron 4.8 %
Calcium 4.1 %
Potassium 2.4 %
Sodium 2.3 %
Magnesium 1.9 %

The chemical composition *of the Earth's crust is dominated by eight elements, which together make up more than 99 per cent by weight and by volume of the crust. Of these elements, oxygen is the most abundant, followed by silicon; most of the rock forming minerals of the crust are therefore silicates.*

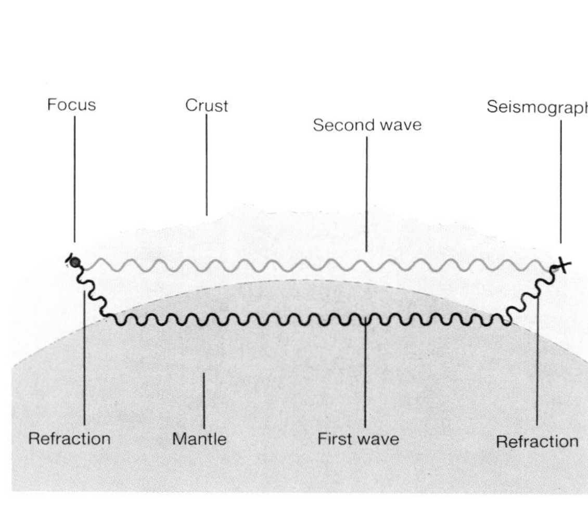
Focus
Crust
Second wave
Seismograph
Refraction
Mantle
First wave
Refraction

A seismic wave *moving through the crust arrives at a point on the surface later than a wave that has travelled farther but that has been refracted into the denser mantle and then refracted back to the surface. This phenomenon occurs because the denser the rock the faster the wave travels.*

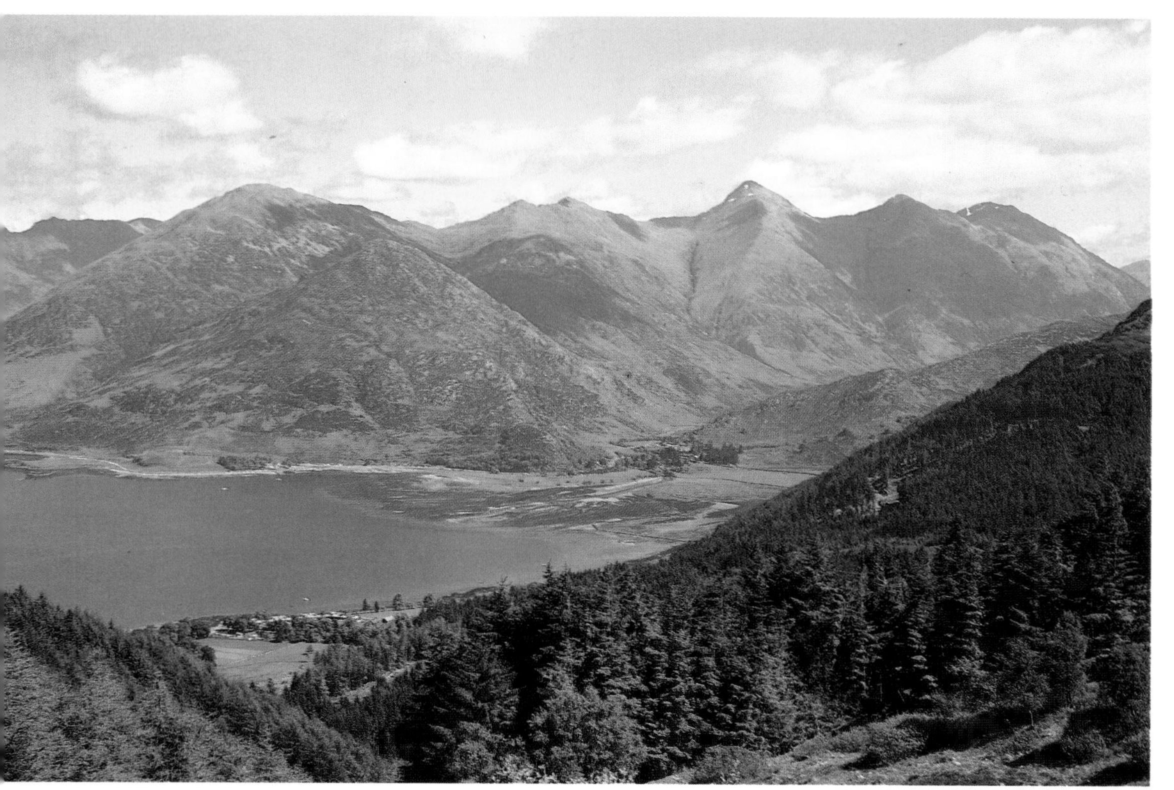

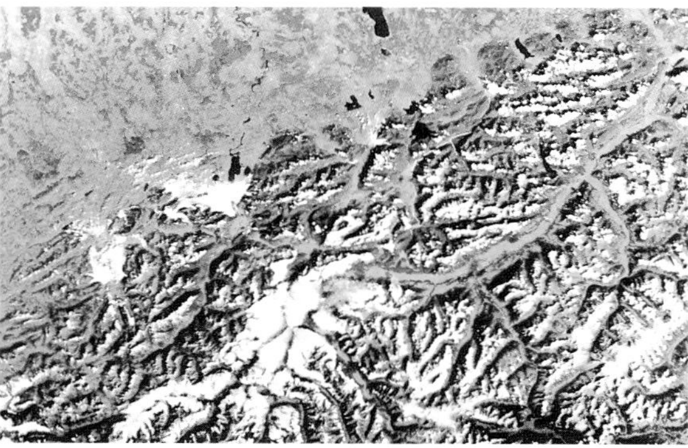

The Alps *are a typical example of a mountain chain formed by tectonic overthrusting. At some stage the strata of the Alpine region were subjected to compressive deformation from opposing plates which resulted in extensive faulting and elevation.*

Gneiss, *visible in the foreground and in the midle distance bordering the bay, is an igneous rock that is formed under intense metamorphism deep in the crust. It is exposed over time by uplift and erosion.*

Plate tectonics

On the human timescale most of the Earth seems passive and unchanging. But in some places – California, Italy, Turkey and Japan, for example – the Earth's crust is active and liable to move, producing earthquakes or volcanic eruptions. These and other dynamic areas lie on the major earthquake belts, most of which run along the middle of the ocean basins, although some are situated on the edges of oceans (around the Pacific Ocean, for instance) or pass across continental land masses (as along the Alpine-Himalayan belt).
It is this observation that there are several, relatively well-defined dynamic zones in the Earth's crust which forms the basis of plate tectonics. According to this theory, the crust consists of several large, rigid plates and the movements of the plates produce the Earth's major structural features, such as mountain ranges, mid-ocean ridges, ocean trenches and large faults. Stable areas with few or no earthquakes or active volcanoes lie in the middle of a plate, whereas active areas – where major structures are constantly being destroyed created – are situated along the plate boundaries.

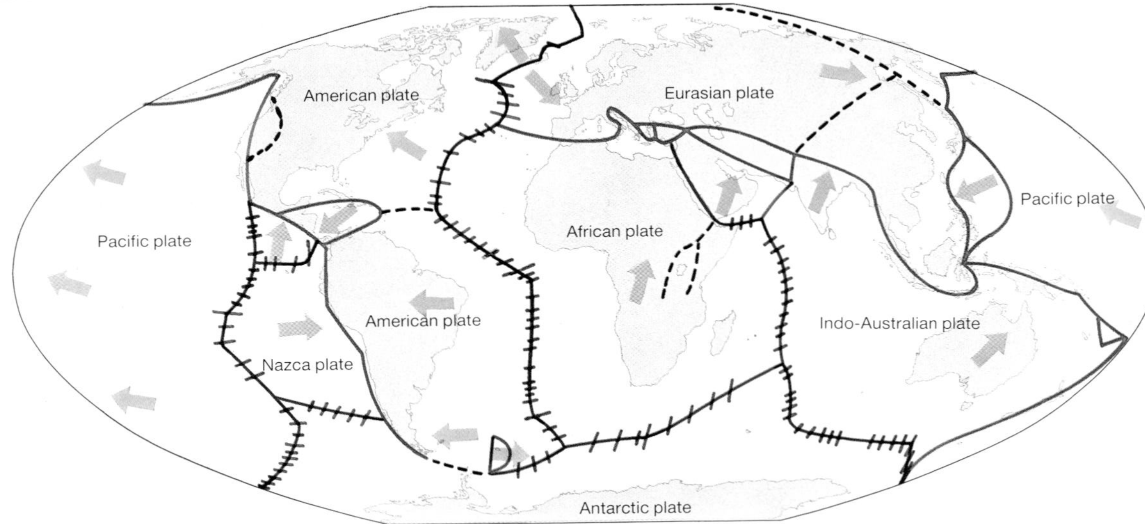
American plate
Eurasian plate
Pacific plate
Pacific plate
African plate
American plate
Nazca plate
Indo-Australian plate
Antarctic plate

The main plates *and their boundaries: Constructive boundaries are dark purple, destructive boundaries red, and transform faults green; broken black lines mark uncertain boundaries. Plate movements are shown with blue arrows.*

The extent and nature of crustal plates

The positions and sizes of the crustal plates can be determined by studying the paths of seismic waves (shock waves produced by earthquakes) that travel around and through the Earth. Such studies have also made it possible to estimate the thickness of the plates. Geologists have found that seismic waves tend to slow down and become less intense between about 60 and 250 mi. below the surface. From this observation they suggest that the solid lithosphere (which consists of the Earth's outermost layer, the crust, and the top part of the mantle, the layer below the crust) "floats" on a less rigid layer (the asthenosphere) which, because it is plastic, allows vertical and horizontal movements of the rigid lithospheric plates.
By collating the findings from various seismological studies, geologists have discovered that the lithosphere is divided into a relatively small number of plates. Most of them are very large – covering millions of square miles – but are less than about 60 mi. thick.

A spectacular demonstration *of the activity at a constructive plate boundary occurred in November 1963 when the volcanic island of Surtsey emerged from the sea, erupting lava and emitting large amounts of gas and dust. Situated off southern Iceland, Surtsey stands on the Mid-Atlantic Ridge, which marks the boundary between the slowly-separating Eurasian and American plates.*

Plate movements

The landforms, earthquake activity and vulcanism that characterize plate boundaries are caused by movements of the plates. There are three principal motions: the plates may move apart, collide or slide past each other.
Plate separation entails the formation of new lithosphere between the plates involved. This process occurs at constructive plate boundaries along the crests of mid-ocean ridges (and is therefore termed sea-floor spreading), where material from the mantle wells up to create the new crust.
Plate collision, on the other hand, necessitates the destruction of lithosphere at a plate boundary. Ocean trenches mark destructive plate boundaries, and at these sites the lithosphere of one plate is thrust beneath an overriding plate and resorbed into the mantle; this process is called subduction.

The Pyrenees *extend along the border between France and Spain. They were formed as a result of tectonic movements (which produced folding of the rock strata) during the Eocene and Oligocene periods (which together lasted from 54 to 26 million years ago).*

Ultimately, continued subduction of an ocean basin can lead to the complete disappearance of the basin and collision of the continents at its edges. In such collisions, mountain belts may be formed as the continents push against each other and force the intervening land upwards – as occurred when India collided with Asia some 50 million years ago creating the Himalayas.
After a continental collision, the momentum of the plates is initially absorbed by thickening and overthrusting of the continental crust. But there is a limit to which this process can occur and, because the continental crust is too bouyant to be subducted the momentum must be dissipated in other ways – by the sideways movements of small plates that form within the newly-created mountain belt or by a more general, probably world-wide, change in the boundaries and movements of the plates.
The other principal type of plate movement occurs when plates slide past each other (at what are called sites of transform faulting) which, unlike the first two types of movement, involves neither creation nor destruction of the intervening lithosphere often major faults, such as the San Andreas fault in California, mark these plate boundaries (which are called conservative plate boundaries).

Rates of plate movements

Most of our knowledge about the very slow rates of plate movements has come from studies of the Earth's magnetic field. In the past the magnetic field has repeatedly reversed direction (a phenomenon called polarity reversal). A record of the changing magnetic field has been preserved in the permanent "fossil" magnetism of the basalt rocks that form the ocean floor.
Around sites of sea-floor spreading, bands of rocks with normal polarity alternate with bands having a reversed polarity. By dating these different bands the rate of spreading can be deduced. Using this method it has been found that the rates of plate separation vary from about 9 mm a year in the northern Atlantic Ocean to 90 mm a year in the Pacific Ocean. From these determinations of separation rates geologists have calculated the relative motions of plates that are moving together or sliding past each other. They have thus determined the movements of almost all the plates on the surface of the Earth.

Structure of continents

The continents are large areas of crust that make up the solid surface of the Earth. They consist of comparatively low-density material called sial, and hence tend to float above other crustal material – the sima – in which they are embedded.
On a map of the globe each continent has a very different shape and appearance from the others, and each has its own climate zones and animal life. The geological structure of each one is, however, very much the same.

The simple continent

In its simplest form, a continent is older at the center than at the edges. The old center is known as a craton and is made up of rocks that were formed several billion years ago when the Earth's crust was thinner than it now is. The craton is not involved in any mountain building activity because it is already compact and tightly deformed by ancient mountain building, although the mountains that had been found on it have long since been worn away by the processes of erosion. Typical cratons include the Canadian Shield, covering northern and central Europa and the Siberian Shield in northern Asia. Several smaller cratons exist in South America, India, Africa, Antarctia and Australia.
The craton is the nucleus of the continent. It is flanked by belts of fold mountains, the oldest being nearer the craton and the youngest farther away. North America provides an excellent example, consisting of the Canadian Shield flanked in the east by the Appalachians and in the west by the Rockies. Close to the shield the Appalachians were formed about 400 million years ago, whereas farther east they were formed about 300 million years ago. The same is true of the mountains to the west, with the main part of the Rockies being about 200 million years old, whereas the coastal ranges are still geologically active today.
The reason for this structure is that when a continent lies at a subduction zone at the boundary between two crustal plates, its mass cannot be drawn down into the higher-density mantle. Instead it crumples up at the edge, the sedimentary areas around the coast being forced up into mountain chains which may be laced through with volcanic material from the plate tectonic activity. These movements may take place several times during a continent's history, with each subsequent mountain chain being attached to the one that was formed previously.

Supercontinents

In reality the situation is much more complicated. As the continents move about on the Earth's surface, two may collide with each other and become welded into a single mass. The result is a supercontinent, which has two or more cratons. The weld line between the two original continents is marked by a mountain range that was formed as their coastal ranges came together and crushed up any sediments that may have been between them. Europe and Asia together constitute such a supercontinent, the Urals having been formed when the two main masses came together about 30 million years ago.
On the other hand, a single continental mass may split, becoming two or more smaller continents. This has happened on a grand scale within the last 200 million years. Just before that thime all the continents of the Earth's crust had come together, forming one vast temporary supercontinent, known to geologists as Pangaea. Since then the single mass has fragmented into the distribution of continents we know today. Indeed the process is still continuing. The great Rift Valley of eastern Africa represents the first stage of a movement in which eastern Africa is breaking away from the main African landmass. The slumping structures found at the sides of a rift valley are also seen at the margins of the continents that are known to have split away and have not yet been subjected to any marginal mountain-building activity. The eastern coast of South America and the western coast of Africa show such features.
Not all continental masses are above sea level. The Indian Ocean contains many small continental fragments that have sheared off, just as India and Antarctica split away from Africa 200 million years ago. Such fragments include the Agulhas Plateau off South Africa, and the Seychelles and Kerguelen plateaux, each with islands representing their highest portions.

Areas of sedimentation

Another significant feature around the continents is their depositional basins. These are areas that have subsided and may even be below sea level. Because rivers tend to flow into such areas, the basins soon become thickly covered by sediments. The North Sea is an example of a sedimentary basin in northern Europe.

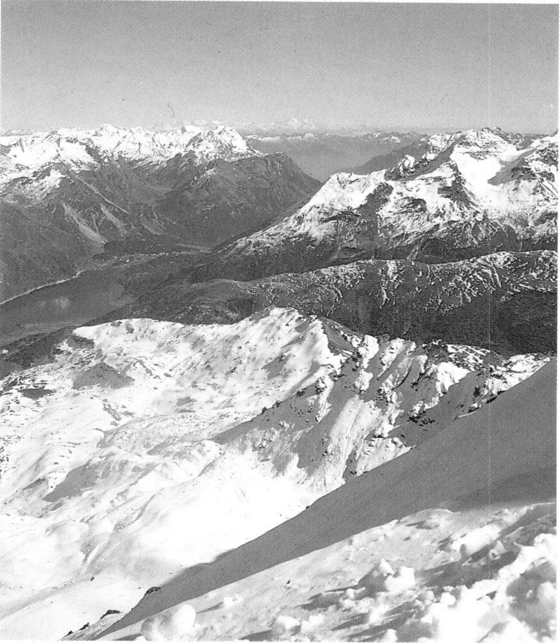

The Alps *are comparatively young mountains, in geological terms, in which the rock strata form complex patterns because of the folding and faulting that accompanied their formations.*

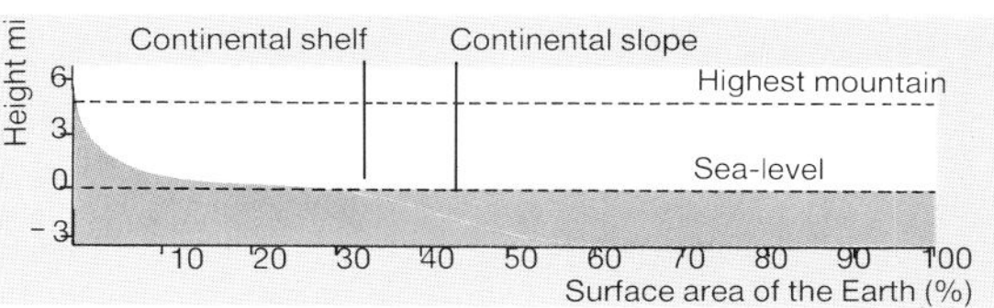

Continental shelf
Continental slope
Highest mountain
Sea-level
Height mi
6
3
0
-3
10
20
30
40
50
60
70
80
90
100
Surface area of the Earth (%)

The continents *– the land areas of the world – cover only about 30 per cent of the Earth's surface, and little of it rises to more than one half mile above sea-level.*

In some areas of the continental margin a large river may flow over the continental shelf and deposit its sediments in the ocean beyond. In such areas the edge of the continental shelf becomes extended beyond that of the rest of the area. The rivers Indus and Ganges produce shelf sediments in the Indian Ocean, and the Amazon and Zaire do the same on opposite sides of the Atlantic.
The actual land area of a continent may also be increased by these means, if the river builds up an extensive delta at its mouth. Considerable land areas have been built up in this way at the mouths of the rivers Mississippi and Niger.

At the edge of a continent *(below), where the continental crustal plate is riding over an oceanic plate, typical features include offshore island arcs (such as the Japanese islands) and relatively young mountain chains (such as the Andes). Farther inland a sedimentary basin (such as the North Sea), may form on tops of the older rocks of a craton. Rift valleys form in mid-continent.*

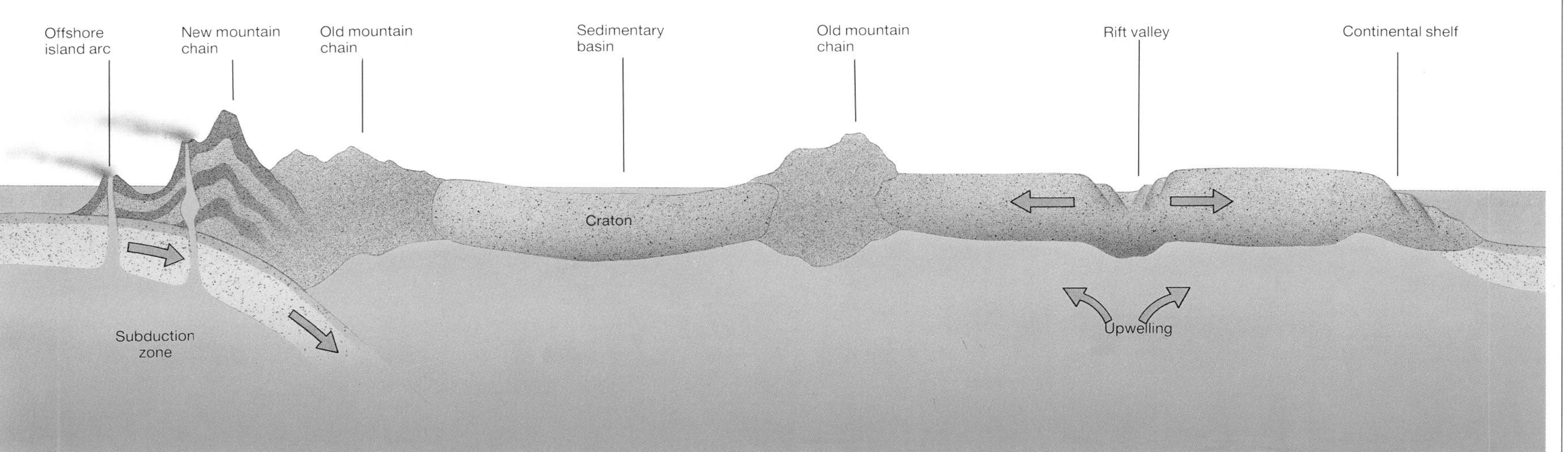

Offshore island arc
New mountain chain
Old mountain chain
Sedimentary basin
Old mountain chain
Rift valley
Continental shelf
Craton
Subduction zone
Upwelling

Continental drift

The continental masses that stand proud of their surrounding oceanic crust have never occupied fixed positions on the Earth's surface. They are constantly carried around on the tectonic plates rather like logs embedded in the ice-floes of a partly frozen river. The movement is going on at the present day, with North America moving away from Europe at a rate of about one inch per year. The movement of Africa against Europe is made evident by the intensity of earthquake activity and the presence of active volcanoes in the Mediterranean area.

The proof that this has been happening throughout geological time takes a number of forms.

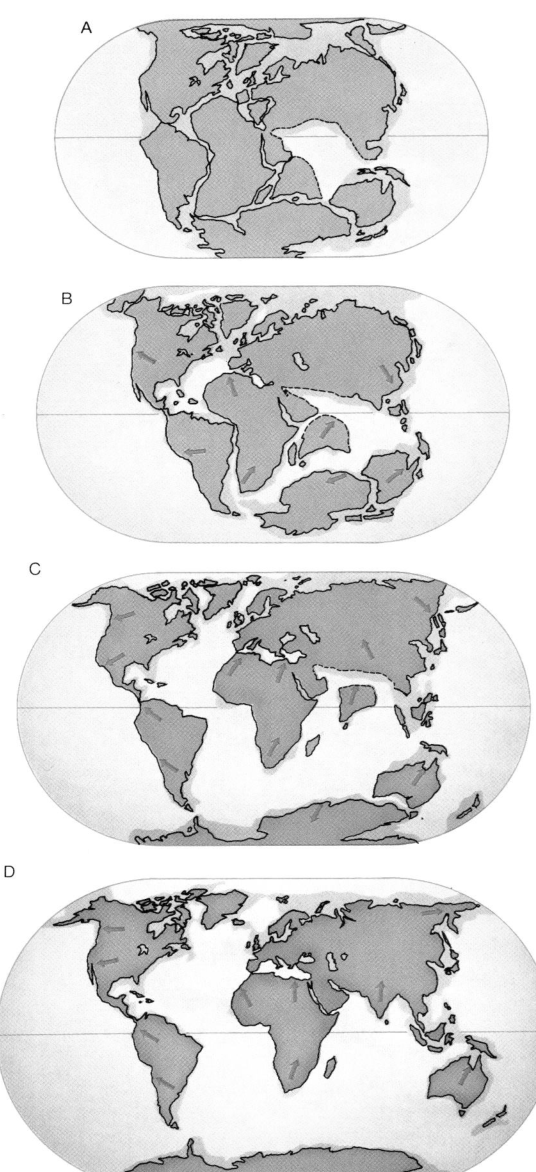
A
B
C
D

Nearly 200 million years ago, *the landmasses of the Earth were concentrated into one supercontinent, called Pangaea (A). Some geologists propose that, at that time, the Earth was only four-fifths its present size, and computer-plotted maps seem to support this view. Then, as Pangaea broke up and the continents began to move apart, the Earth as a whole gradually became larger. Map B is a reconstruction of the Earth of about 120 million years ago. By about 55 million years ago (C), the Atlantic Ocean had widened, India was on a collision course with Asia, and Australia was beginning to become detached from Antarctica. Map D shows the Earth as it is now, but even today the crustal plates are not static. Sea-floor spreading will continue to widen the Atlantic and Indian oceans, and Australia will continue on its north-easterly course. Seismic and volcanic activity, as along the eastern seaboard of the Pacific Ocean, result from subduction of the Pacific plate as it is being overridden by the westward-moving Americas. In northeastern Africa, there is evidence that Arabia is splitting off from the rest of the continent.*

Physical proof

The first line of evidence – in fact the first observation that suggested that the continents are in motion – is the apparent fit of one continental coastline with another. The eastern coast of South America and the western coast of Africa are so similar in shape that it seems quite obvious that the two once fitted together like the pieces of a jigsaw puzzle. The other continents can also be pieced together in a similar way, but usually the fit is not so obvious; for example, Africa, India, Antarctica and Australia would also mate together. It is the edges of the continental shelves, rather than the actual coastlines that provide the neat fit.

If the continents were placed together, certain physical features could be seen to be continuous from one to another across the joints. Mountains formed 400 million years ago and now found in south-eastern Canada and eastern Greenland would be continuous with those of the same age now found in Scotland and Norway, if North America and Europe were placed together. Mountain ranges in Brazil would be continuous with those in Nigeria if South America and Africa were brought together.

Evidence for ancient climates is also a good indicator of continental drift. Northern Europe went through a phase of desert conditions about 400 million years ago, followed by a phase of tropical forest 300 million years ago, and then another desert phase 200 million years ago. This is consistent with the movement of that area from the southern desert climate zone of the Earth, through the equatorial forest zone and into the northern desert zone.

About 280 million years ago an ice age gripped the Southern Hemisphere. The evidence for this includes ice-formed deposits and glacier marks from that period found in South America, southern Africa, Australia and, significantly, India – which is now in the Northern Hemisphere. If the continents were reassembled and the directions of ice movements analyzed, they would point to an ice cap with its center in Antarctica.

Biological proof

The evidence from fossils is just as spectacular. Fossils of the same land animals and plants have been found on all the southern continents in rocks dating from about 250 million years ago. These are creatures that could not have evolved independently on separate continents. *Mesosaurus* was a freshwater reptile, resembling a small crocodile, and its remains have been found both in South America and South Africa. *Lystrosaurus* was like a reptilian hippopotamus and its remains have been found in India, Africa and Antarctica. The fernlike plant *Glossopteris* is typical of the plants that lived at the same time as these creatures and its remains have been found in South America, Africa, India and Australia.

Similar biological evidence is found in the Northern Hemisphere where the dinosaurs of Europe, 150 million years ago, were similar to those of North America.

The mammals that developed in various parts of the world during the last 65 million years also reveal evidence of the movements of the continents. Up to about 10 million years ago the dominant mammals of South America were the pouched marsupials similar to those of Australia today. This suggests that their origin lies in a single southern continent. Later, most of the South American marsupials became extinct after a sudden influx of more advanced placental mammals from North America, suggesting that South and North America became attached to one another about 10 million years ago. India was a similar isolated continent, broken away from the southern landmass, until it collided with Asia about 50 million years ago. It would be interesting to see if the mammals of India before this date were marsupials or not, but no Indian mammal fossils have been found for the relevant period. In 1980 a fossil maruspial was found in Antarctica, helping to substantiate the theories.

Magnetic proof

The positions of the Earth's magnetic poles change over a long period of time. Clues to their location in any particular geological period lie in the way in which particles in the rocks that formed in that period have been magnetized. As rocks are formed the magnetic particles in them line up with the prevailing magnetic field of the Earth, and are then locked in position when the rock solidifies. This phenomenon is sometimes known as remanent magnetism and it has been actively studied since the 1960s. It has been found that the remanent magnetism for different periods in each of the continents point to a single north pole only if the continents are "moved" in relation to each other.

The mountains of the Himalayan *range were uplifted as a result of the impact between the Indian subcontinent and the Asian crustal plate about 50 million years ago.*

Sedimentary rocks

Sedimentary rocks are the most common types on the Earth's surface. In general, they were all formed in a similar way – by the deposition, compression and cementing together of numerous small particles of mineral, animal or plant origin. The details of these processes are best exemplified by clastic sedimentary rocks, which consist of mineral fragments derived from pre-existing rocks.

As soon as rocks are exposed on the Earth's surface they begin to be broken down by the forces of erosion. The rock fragments, and the minerals washed out of them, are carried by the wind, by streams or the sea, and finally come to rest as sediment. Eventually it becomes covered with more sediment, and the underlying layers are compressed and cemented together to form sedimentary rock – a process called lithification. After millions of years, this rock may be uplifted by Earth movements – thereby again exposed to the forces of erosion – and the entire process is repeated. This cycle of erosion, transportation, deposition, lithification and uplift is known as the sedimentary cycle.

Erosion, transportation and deposition

By studying the various features of a sedimentary rock, geologists can deduce a great deal about the conditions prevalent at the time of its formation. Sedimentary rocks typically occur as separate horizontal layers called beds, each formed as a result of fairly frequent changes in the sedimentation conditions. When sedimentation stops, the sediments settle; when it resumes, a new layer begins to form on top of the previous one. Unlayered sedimentary rocks – described as massive – therefore reflect long periods of unchanging conditions. Analysis of the grains that make up the rocks may reveal the composition of those from which the fragments originated. In some, the minerals are the same as those in the original rock, but more commonly they have been altered by reactions with water and chemicals in the atmosphere.

The sizes and shapes of the constituent particles reflect the distance they have travelled and the current conditions they encountered. For instance, the faster a current of water, the larger are the rock fragments that can be carried by it. Thus, large-grained sedimentary rocks were originally formed from large pebbles and boulders deposited by fast-flowing rivers or by the sea. Such rocks are called conglomerates if their fragments are rounded, or breccias if they are jagged and angular. Sandstones consist of their sediments that were laid down by weaker currents. Extremely small particles can be carried long distances by even very slow-moving water. The sediments that result are silts and muds, which occur in slow-flowing rivers or on the sea floor far away from a turbulent shoreline. When lithified, these very fine sediments form siltstones, mudstones or shales.

A mixture of different sized grains in the same rock may indicate that the current stopped abruptly, thereby suddenly depositing all of the various sized particles it was carrying. Such a sedimentary bed is termed poorly sorted. Well-sorted beds, in which all the particles are of approximately the same size, result from stable current conditions.

The shape of the particles in a sedimentary rock indicates the distance the eroded fragments travelled before being deposited and lithified. The farther the fragments travelled, the rounder they are because of the greater amount of abrasion from rubbing against other particles.

***Millions of years** of erosion have exposed the layers of sedimentary rocks in the Grand Canyon (in Arizona, USA), thereby providing a superb record of the area's geological history. The Grand Canyon is about 5,500 ft. deep at its deepest point, where the rocks are some 1.8 billion years old. Its walls consist chiefly of limestones, shales and sandstones.*

Rocks from sediment

It takes millions of years for a sediment to become rock. After deposition, the sediments are compressed beneath further layers that accumulate on top of them. The weight of the upper layers forces the underlying particles closer together, causing them to interlock and form a solid mass, but the mass is not yet rock at this stage, because the particles – although tightly packed together – are still separate. In the next phase – cementation – the particles are bonded together to form rock. Groundwater percolating through rock and sediment often has calcite dissolved in it, leached out of lime-rich rocks by the weak carbonic acid formed when carbon dioxide in the air reacts with water in rain. The dissolved calcite then precipitates in the minute spaces between grains, thereby cementing them together. The resulting compressed and cemented mass is the sedimentary rock.

Types of sedimentary rocks

In addition to clastic rocks, there are two other principal types of sedimentary rocks: chemical and organic (or biogenic). Chemical sedimentary rocks are formed when dissolved material precipitates out of water. For example, a bed of salt may be formed when part of the sea becomes cut off from the main body of water and eventually evaporates, leaving a deposit of salt, which may later be overlaid and compressed.

Organic sedimentary rocks are formed from the remains of animals or plants. One of the most common is limestone, which consists of the remains of small marine shellfish. When these creatures die, they sink to the sea bed, where their shells are broken up and then compressed and cemented together in the same way as clastic rocks.

Coal is probably the most familiar example of an organic sedimentary rock. It consists mainly of carbon, derived from masses of plant matter that accumulated in forested swamps aeons ago. Because of the lack of oxygen in the swamp water, the plants did not decompose; instead they became compressed and lithified into coal.

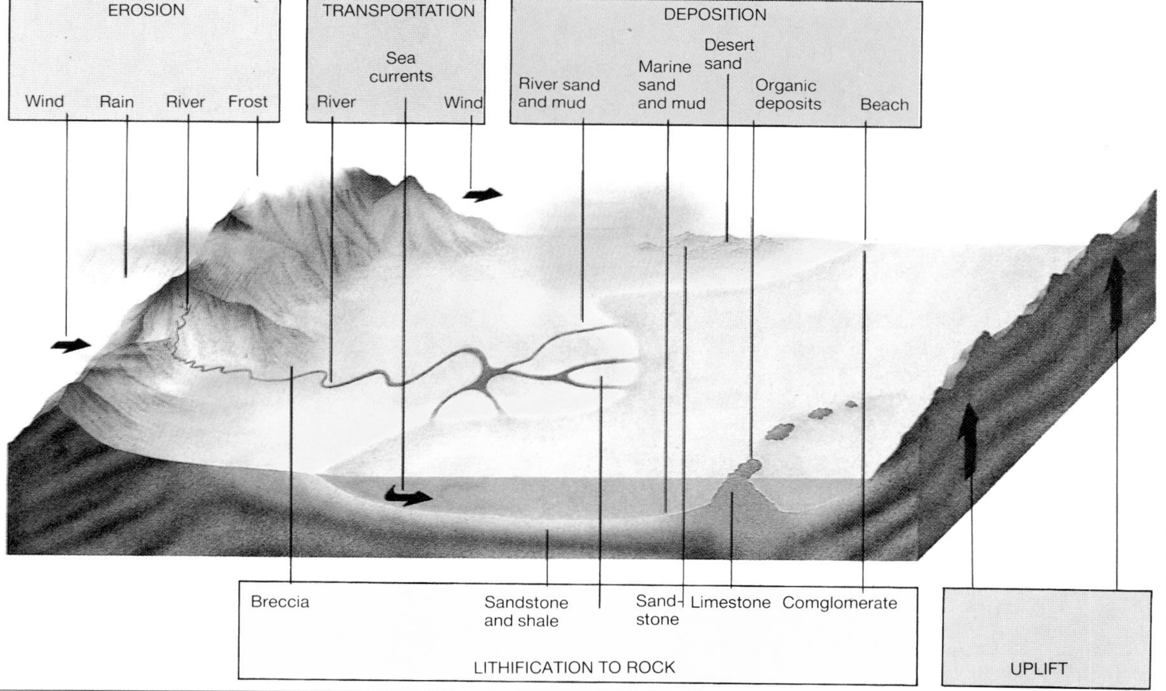
EROSION
Wind
Rain
River
Frost
TRANSPORTATION
Sea currents
River
Wind
DEPOSITION
River sand and mud
Marine sand and mud
Desert sand
Organic deposits
Beach
Breccia
Sandstone and shale
Sand-stone
Limestone
Comglomerate
LITHIFICATION TO ROCK
UPLIFT

***The sedimentary cycle** is the process that produces sedimentary rocks. Exposed rocks are broken down by the forces of weathering and erosion. The fragments are carried away by wind, rivers or sea currents and are then deposited as beds of sediment. Eventually these beds are buried and turned to rock (lithification). At a later time the beds of sedimentary rock are pushed upwards and exposed by mountain-building activity. The exposed rocks are then eroded and the cycle begins again.*

Igneous rocks

Igneous rocks orginate in masses of hot fluid that circulate deep within the Earth. This molten rock, called magma, may consist of part of the Earth's crust that has melted as a result of tectonic or mountain-building activity, or it may arise from the mantle (the layer immediately below the crust).

Rocks from magma

Igneous rocks are formed when molten magma cools and solidifies. Different types of igneous rocks may be produced out of the same mass of magma. As the magma cools, its components solidify in a set sequence. The first minerals to crystallize out of the melt are the high-temperature minerals – the olivines and pyroxenes, which are silicates of magnesium and iron. They tend to be the denser components and so they sink, leaving the remaining fluid deficient in magnesium and iron. The next group of minerals to solidify are the feldspars (silicate minerals of potassium, sodium, calcium and aluminum – the lighter metallic elements); the magma thus loses its metallic constituents first. Finally, any remaining silica crystallizes out as quartz. The entire solidification process, or differentation as it is called, therefore results in dense iron- and magnesium-rich rocks and less dense silica-rich rocks from the same original fluid. This is dramatically exemplified in the rare outcrops in which the different types of rock can be seen as layers in the same rock mass – as occurs in the approximately 980 ft. thick Palisade Sill in New Jersey in the United States, which has an olivine-rich layer at the bottom, and rocks with progressively less olivine above. Usually, however, an outcrop consists of only one type of igneous rock.

Geologists classify igneous rocks according to their composition. Those that have a low silica content (and are also usually rich in iron and magnesium) are called basic rocks; those with a high silica content are termed acid rocks. Basic rocks, such as gabbro, tend to be dark in colour because their constituent minerals are dark, whereas acid rocks (such as granite) are light in colour because they contain white and pink feldspars and glassy quartz.

Igneous rocks are also categorized according to their origin: intrusive rocks, formed from magma that solidified beneath the surface, and extrusive rocks, from magma that solidified above the surface.

***Magma** that cools quickly, as in a lava flow, forms a very fine-grained rock, such as basalt. Contraction of the cooling rock may cause it to crack and form a series of hexagonal columns that stand perpendicular to the lava surface. The classic example of this phenomenon is the Giant's Causeway on the north-eastern coast of Northern Ireland.*

Igneous textures

When hot magma cools slowly, the minerals in it have sufficient time to grow large crystals and hence, form coarse rock. The mineral crystals in rocks that have cooled quickly, on the other hand, are often too small to be seen with the naked eye. The coarseness of a rock depends on where it was formed. Very coarse-grained rocks, such as the gabbros and granites, solidified deep underground and therefore cooled slowly. Volcanic rocks, such as basalts and trachites, were formed from magma that cooled rapidly on the surface of the Earth and are therefore fine-grained. The finest-grained igneous rocks originated from volcanoes that erupted underwater or beneath glaciers, as a result of which the lava (magma ejected by a volcano) cooled extremely rapidly.

Occasionally, such igneous rocks are so fine-grained that no crystalline structure is visible, resulting in a natural glass called obsidian.

Sometimes an igneous rock has two textures. It may have large crystals (called phenocrysts) embedded in a matrix of very small ones. This type of two-textured rock forms when magma begins to differentiate slowly then, when some of the crystals have formed, solidifies much more rapidly – probably because it was forced into a cooler location. This texture is known as porphyritic, and the rock is called a porphyry.

The texture and composition of a rock can be studied by cutting a sample into thin transparent slices and examining them with a microscope. The rock's constituents can then be determined by viewing the sections using polarized light, a technique that causes each mineral crystal to appear as a different colour. This method reveals that the minerals which formed first have well-defined crystal shapes, whereas those that grew later tend to be distorted.

Igneous structures

It is not possible to observe igneous rocks while they form (except volcanic rocks, in which the crystallization and solidification can be particularly spectacular) because most igneous rocks form deep under the surface of the Earth in structures called intrusions. From these intrusions the magma can push its way through cracks, forcing aside or melting the surrounding rocks, and the resultant structures reflect this action.

The largest igneous intrusions are called batholiths and they form deep below the surface in active mountain chains. They may extend over hundreds of square miles. Underground cracks may fill with magma, forming sheets of igneous rock when the magma solidifies. The sheets are known as sills if they lie parallel to the strata of the surrounding rocks, or dykes if they cut across the strata. Igneous rocks may also form cylindrical structures – called stocks if they are broad and necks if they are narrow – which may once have led to volcanoes on the surface.

Igneous rocks (and metamorphic rocks) tend to be harder than any surrounding sedimentary formations. As a result, when a mass of rock containing both igneous and sedimentary types is eroded, the softer sedimentary rocks usually wear away first, leaving the igneous masses as hills and other landscape features that reflect their original shapes.

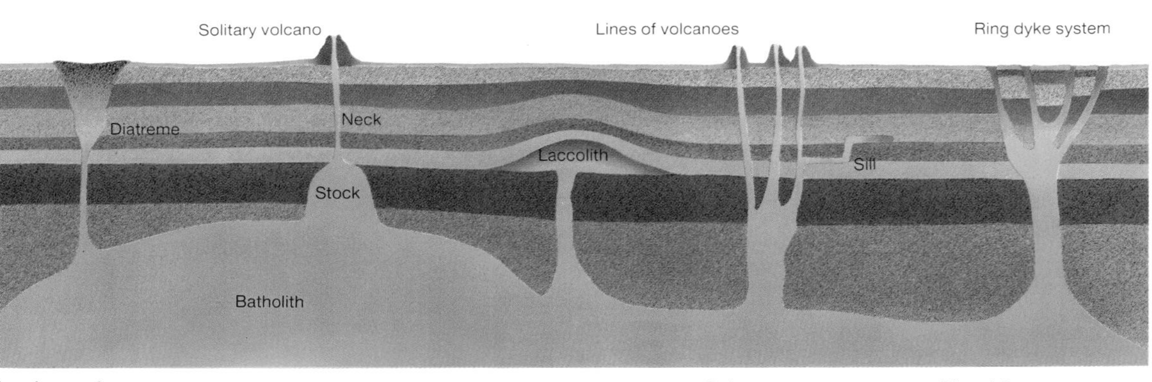

Solitary volcano
Lines of volcanoes
Ring dyke system
Diatreme
Neck
Laccolith
Sill
Stock
Batholith

Landscape forms

Diatreme
A diatreme is a funnel-shaped structure formed by the explosive expansion of magma as it rises through areas of lower pressure.

Neck
Erosion of the terrain down to a volcano's neck produces an isolated cylindrical hill, such as Devil's Tower in Wyoming, USA.

Laccolith
When a laccolith is exposed by erosion, it produces a rounded hill surrounded by circular scarps.

Dykes
A longitudinal dyke system results from erosion of a line of volcanoes.

Ring dykes
Ring dykes are concentric ridges of igneous rock that are formed when the land around a circular dyke system subsides.

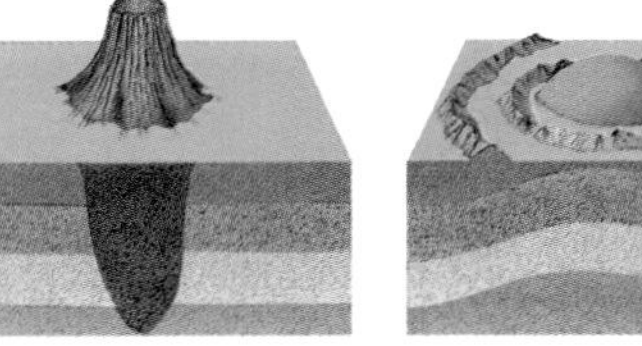

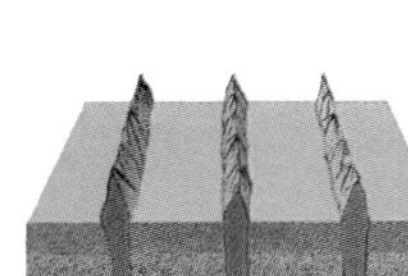

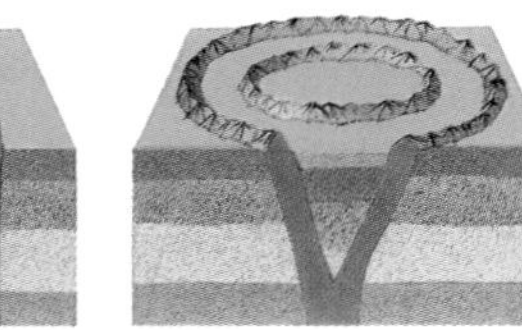

***Magma from a batholith** pushes its way through the overlying rocks and forms igneous intrusions (stocks, laccoliths and sills, for example) as it solidifies. Igneous rocks tend to be harder than the rocks surrounding them, and so, after the softer rocks have been eroded away, various igneous structures are exposed and form characteristic landscape features, some of which are illustrated on the left.*

Metamorphic rocks

When rocks are subjected to different conditions from those under which they originally formed, their minerals change. This alteration can happen when rocks are exposed at the Earth's surface and their minerals react with various chemicals in the atmosphere. Much more marked effects occur when rocks are buried deep in an emerging mountain range and subjected to very high temperatures and pressures. Under these conditions the rocks alter completely, becoming entirely different types of rocks with different mineral compositions. Such transformed rocks are called metamorphic rocks.

The characteristic feature of a metamorphic rock is that its mineral composition changes without the rock itself melting. If the rock does melt and then solidify again, the result is an igneous not a metamorphic rock.

Regional metamorphism

Regional (or dynamic) metamorphic rocks – one of the two main types – are those that have been altered by great pressure but low temperature – as occurs, for example, in the heart of a fold mountain belt while it is being compressed between moving crustal plates. The efforts of such a movement are usually extensive, hence regional metamorphic rocks tend to occupy large areas.

At depths in the order of tens of miles the weight of the overlying rocks produces sufficiently high pressures to alter the mineral structure of the rocks beneath. For example, the minerals in shale (the black, flaky sedimentary rock that is produced by the lithification of mud) recrystallize into the mineral mica as a result of great pressure. The flat, leaf-like mica crystals form in parallel bands (known as the rock's foliation). Earth movements associated with metamorphic processes may then deform the mica, forcing it to distort along the lines of foliation and producing, in turn, a schist, a typical regional metamorphic rock. The mineral bands in schist are very pronounced and are often distorted and jagged in appearance – evidence of the great stresses involved in their formation. A schist can usually be easily split along its foliation lines; this tendency to split along certain planes of weakness is called cleavage.

The cleavage of a regional metamorphic rock is exploited commercially in the quarrying and working of slate. Like schist, slate is formed by the metamorphism of shale, but under less extreme pressure. Compared with shale, the minerals in slate are small and are often invisible to the naked eye.

It is sometimes assumed – erroneously – that the cleavage of slate corresponds to the lines of the thin bedding in the shale from which it was originally formed. In fact the cleavage reflects the direction of the pressure to which the shale was subjected during its metamorphism rather than the original structure of the rock.

Thermal metamorphism

In the other main type of metamorphism – thermal (or contact) metamorphism – rocks are changed by the effects of great heat but low pressure. Thermal metamorphic rocks are formed when a hot igneous mass of magma forces its way through the Earth's crust, literally baking the rock surrounding it. In comparison with regional metamorphism, the volume of rock affected by thermal metamorphic processes is very small; the newly-formed thermal metamorphic rock may extend for only a few inches around the igneous intrusion (the affected area is called an aureole) or, occasionally, the new rock may be about one half mile wide around a very large batholith. There is usually a gradation of thermal metamorphic rocks around large intrusions; near such an intrusion there are high-temperature rocks, which gradually give way with increasing distance from the intrusion to low-temperature then unmetamorphosed rocks.

Probably the most familiar thermal metamorphic rock is marble, which is produced by the metamorphism of limestone, a sedimentary rock consisting almost entirely of calcite (calcium carbonate). When the calcite is subjected to great heat from a nearby igneous intrusion, it first gives off carbon dioxide then recombines with this gas, thereby re-forming new calcite crystals and transforming the limestone to marble. The newly-formed crystals have a regular form and grain size (as opposed to the random collection of fragments in the original limestone) which gives the marble strength and an even texture.

Usually, however, the elements in the minerals of the original rock recombine during metamorphism to form completely different minerals, as occurs in the formation of hornfels, which often contains cordierite (a silicate mineral found only in thermal metamorphic rocks).

__Vast slate quarries__ illustrate the great quantities of rock that can be altered by regional metamorphism. Slate, which is produced by the metamorphism of shale, is used to make roofing tiles and is one of the few metamorphic rocks of significant commercial importance.

Other types of metamorphism

Dislocation metamorphism is a relatively rare type that occurs when the rocks on each side of a major fault move against each other as the fault slips. In this situation the stresses can be so great that the minerals in the rocks at the fault break down and recrystallize, thereby giving rise to a hard, flinty metamorphic rock called mylonite.

Metasomatism is similar to – and often associated with – thermal metamorphism. As an igneous mass cools, it gives off hot liquids and gases, which may percolate through cracks and cavities in the surrounding rock. The hot fluids may then alter the surrounding rock by a combination of heat and deposition of minerals dissolved in the fluids. Many of the most productive deposits of metal ores are from veins that have been emplaced by metasomatic activity.

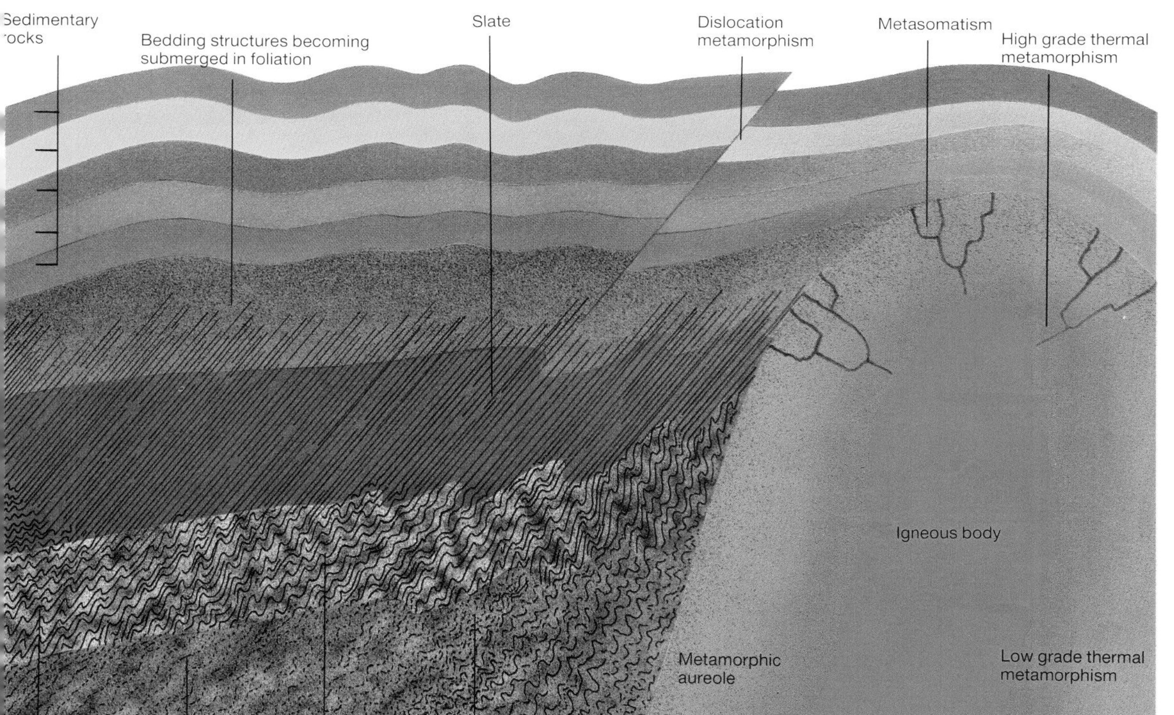

Sedimentary rocks
Bedding structures becoming submerged in foliation
Slate
Dislocation metamorphism
Metasomatism
High grade thermal metamorphism
Igneous body
Metamorphic aureole
Low grade thermal metamorphism
Contorted foliation
Coarse-grained foliation
Schist
Gneiss

__Regional metamorphism__ takes place deep underground where the pressure is great. The other main type – thermal metamorphism – occurs among the rocks "cooked" by the intrusion of a hot igneous body. Of the minor types, dislocation metamorphism occurs when a major fault slips, whereas metasomatism is caused by seepage of hot fluids (liquids and gases) from a igneous body into the surrounding rock.

Volcanoes

Volcanoes are holes or cracks in the Earth's crust through which molten rock erupts. They usually occur at structural weaknesses in the crust, often in regions of geological instability, such as the edges of crustal plates. Volcanoes are important to Man because they provide information about the Earth's interior, and because volcanically-formed soils are highly fertile and good for growing crops. Violent eruptions, however, can devastate huge areas, and accurate techniques for predicting eruptions are essential if major disasters are to be avoided.

Formation of volcanoes

Scientists do not fully understand the process by which volcanoes are formed. It seems that at points where the Earth's mantle (the layer immediately beneath the crust) is particularly hot (hot spots), or where part of the crust is being forced down into the mantle (e. g. where two crustal plates meet and one is forced down under the other), the heat causes the lower part of the crust or upper part of the mantle to melt. The molten rock – called magma – is under pressure as more magma forms and, being less dense than the surrounding rock, it rises, often along lines of weakness such as faults or joints in the crust. As the magma rises, it melts a channel for itself in the rock and accumulates, together with gases released from the melting rock, in a magma chamber a few miles below the Earth's surface.

Eventually the pressure from the magma and gas builds up to such an extent that an eruption occurs, blasting a vent through the surface rocks. Lava (magma after emission) piles up around the vent to form a volcanic mountain or, if the eruption is from a fissure, a lava plateau. The volcano then undergoes periodic eruptions of gases, lava and rock fragments. It is termed active, dormant or extinct, according to the frequency with which it erupts.

Vents associated with declining volcanic activity and the cooling of lava periodically emit steam or hot water, and are often valuable sources of energy or minerals: solfataras (which are rich in sulphur) and fumaroles give out steam and gas; geysers are hot springs that eject jets of hot water or steam at regular intervals as underground water is heated to the boiling point by the magma.

The characteristics of eruptions vary greatly from volcano to volcano, and those typical of any one volcano change over the years. Eruptions are classified according to their explosiveness, which depends on the composition (especially the gas content) and viscosity of the magma involved, which in turn depends largely on the depth at which the rock becomes molten. Relatively viscous magma causes explosive eruptions; sticky magma often forms a plug in the neck of the volcano, blocking further eruptions until enough magma and gas have accumulated for their pressure to blast away the plug and allow the emission of gas, lava and fragmented magma (tephra). This accumulation may take several decades, or even centuries. Some explosive eruptions are quite small, but others (those in which large amounts of gas are trapped in the magma) are so violent that they blast away a large part of a mountain or a whole island.

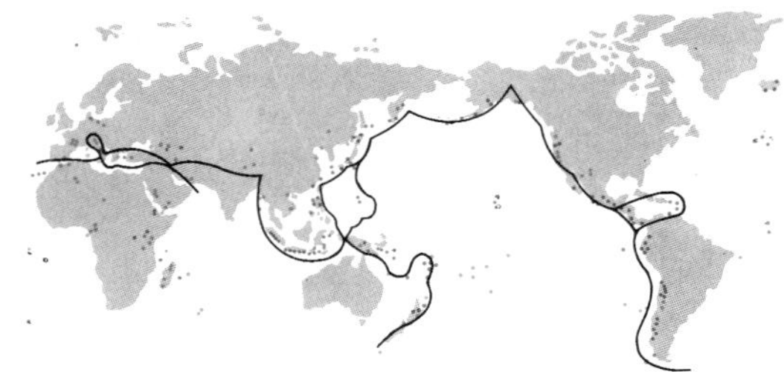

In the map of volcano distribution *active volcanoes are marked by red dots, extinct ones by blue dots. Most volcanoes are located at the edges of crustal plates (shown as black lines), where earthquakes and mountain building also take place. Some extinct volcanoes mark areas of former crustal instability, such as the Great Riff Valley in East Africa.*

Volcanoes formed mainly of rock fragments are generally steep-sided cones (with slopes of between 20° and 40° to the horizontal), because any fragments blasted into the air fall back near the vent. Those formed chiefly of viscous lava are usually highly convex domes (typically about 500 ft high and 1,300 ft. across), because the lava is too thick to flow far before solidifying. Exceptionally viscous lava may solidify in the vent. The solid mass may then be forced slowly upwards, forming a spine that rises several hundred feet above the summit This movement usually precedes a particularly violent eruption, caused by the sudden release of the accumulated pressure of the magma and gas In 1902, such an event accompanied the destructive eruption of Mont Pelée on the island of Martinique in the West Indies.

At the other extreme, relatively fluid magma is extruded quite freely and quietly, with small eruptions that occur at frequent intervals or even continuously. The lava flows for long distances before it solidifies, and therefore forms a low, broad dome, or shield volcano (usually with slopes of less than about 10°), such as Mauna Loa on Hawaii; the island rises about 32,800 ft. from a seafloor base 360 ft. in diameter.

Submarine volcanoes

Submarine volcanoes are particularly common near oceanic ridges, where magma is constantly extruded as the continental plates drift apart. Many also form over hot spots. As the crust moves, the volcano also moves away from the hot spot and becomes extinct; a new volcano forms directly over the original hot spot, and a chain of volcanoes gradually forms.

In oceanic ridges and hot spots the lava is formed from mantle material that is forced up by deep convection currents. This lava is dense but fluid, unlike the silica-rich lava produced by melting crustal material, found in continental areas and offshore island chains. Where it appears above the water surface – in Iceland and Hawaii, for example – it forms flat lava plateaux or shield volcanoes.

Marine volcanic activity may lead to the sudden creation of islands (e. g. Surtsey, off Iceland, in 1963). Volcanic islands are subject to severe erosion by the sea, and may also subside when they move away from a ridge or hot spot and cease to be active. There are more than 2,000 submerged – usually extinct – volcanoes (seamounts) in the world; those that have been eroded nearly to sea

A composite illustration *shows a section through a typical continental volcano (not to scale) and many features found in volcanic regions. Pahoehoe and aa are the two main types of lava; the former is relatively fluid, whereas the latter is more viscous and solidifies to form a rough surface. A tree mould is formed when a tree is covered with lava, which burns away the tree as the lava solidifies, leaving a mound of solid lava with a tree-shaped hole in the middle. Geysers periodically emit powerful jets of hot water. Fumaroles and solfataras give off steam and sulphurous gases. Other volcanic topographical features include crater lakes, hot springs, mud pools and mud pots.*

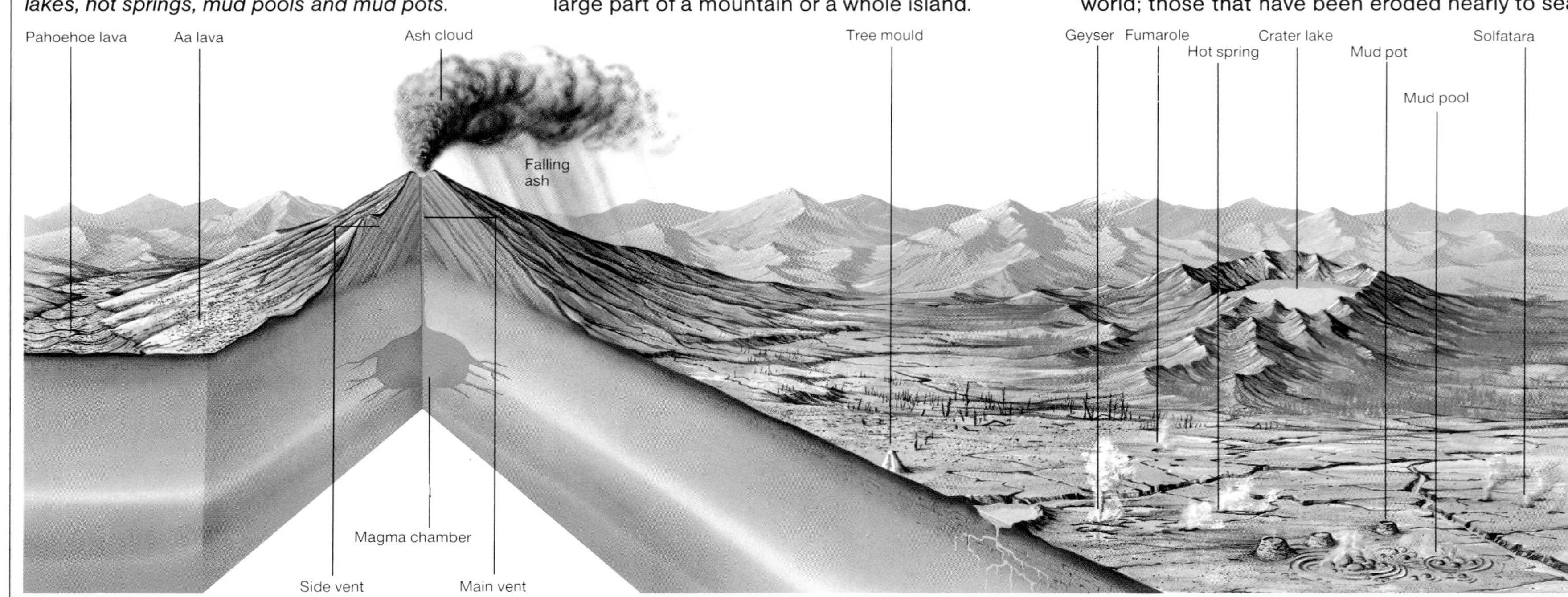
Pahoehoe lava
Aa lava
Ash cloud
Falling ash
Tree mould
Geyser
Fumarole
Hot spring
Crater lake
Mud pot
Mud pool
Solfatara
Magma chamber
Side vent
Main vent

***The section,** right, depicts Mount St. Helens before it erupted on May 18, 1980. On the far right is the volcano during the first eruption, when the north slope collapsed and hot volcanic gases, steam and dust* (a nuée ardente) *were blasted out sideways with explosive force. Simultaneously, a cloud of ash and dust was blown upwards.*

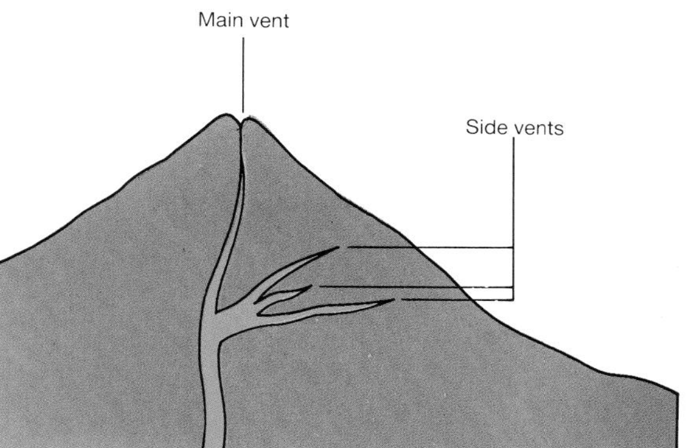

Main vent
Side vents

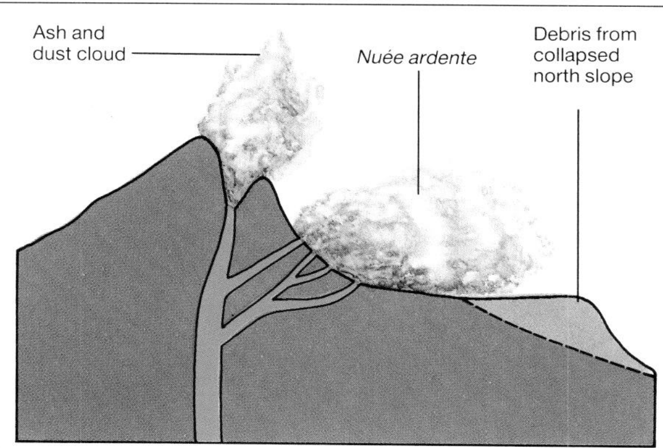

Ash and
dust cloud
Nuée ardente
Debris from
collapsed
north slope

level and then subsequently submerged, which are known as guyots, are also common.

Predicting volcanic eruptions

Prediction of eruptions is of great importance because of the extensive damage they can cause to surrounding areas, which are often fertile and densely populated. Volcanic activity used to be assessed in terms of temperature and pressure, measured by means of borings into the sides of the vent. Recently, however, geologists have come to rely instead on seismography, on measurements of changes in emissions of gas and its sulphur dioxide content, and on detecting activity inside the crater (monitored with mirrors). Most of all, they look for changes in the angle of the mountainside (measured with tiltmeters): any expansion in one part of the mountain indicates that an eruption there is likely. Further information is obtained from analyses of the mineral content of the local water, recordings of vertical ground swelling, and readings from geodimeters, which use lasers to measure minute swellings in the ground.

These techniques are, however, by no means perfect. They were in use on Mount St. Helens in the State of Washington, when it erupted in May 1980 but, despite the fact that scientists were aware that an eruption was imminent, they were not able to anticipate the time, force or exact direction of the blast.

***The most devastating** of Mount St. Helens' recent eruptions occurred in May 1980, but volcanic activity continued and there were several smaller eruptions during the later part of the year. The main explosion was estimated to have had the force of 500 Hiroshima atom bombs and was heard more than 185 mi. away.*

The Mount St. Helens eruption

Mount St. Helens is one of a chain of continental volcanoes in the Cascade Range in the northwestern United States. All the volcanoes in this mountain range are the result of the Pacific oceanic crustal plate being forced down into the mantle by the North American continental plate riding over it. The molten parts of the oceanic plate then rise through the crustal material, forming volcanoes. Normally an eruptive phase involves several of the Cascade Range volcanoes. During the nineteenth century, for example, Mount St. Helens erupted three times, simultaneously with nearby Mount Baker. Because of these coincident eruptions, some scientists believe that the two volcanoes may have a common origin where, at a depth of about 125 mi. below the surface, the Pacific crustal plate is being overridden by the North American plate.

After 123 years of dormancy, Mount St. Helens erupted in May 1980 – one of the most violent (and closely-monitored) eruptions in recent times. Volcanic activity was first noticed on March 20, when small tremors began and the mountain top started to bulge; about a week later fissures in the flank of the volcano emitted steam.

The first violent eruption occurred on May 18, when the slow accumulation of pressure within the volcano was released with explosive force. The north flank of the mountain collapsed and the contents of the vent were blasted out. The abrupt release of pressure caused the gas dissolved in the magma to come out of solution suddenly, forming bubbles throughout the hot mass – rather like the sudden formation of bubbles in champagne when the bottle is uncorked. A white-hot cloud of gas and pulverized magma (called *a nuée ardente*) then swept over the surrounding countryside, engulfing everything within a distance of about 5 mi. from the peak. (This phenomenon also occurred when Mont Pelée erupted in 1902; within a few minutes of the eruption the cloud had covered Saint-Pierre, then the capital of Martinique, killing its 30,000 inhabitants). At the same time, a vertical column of dust and ash was blown upwards. These two major effects were accompanied by a blast of air caused by the sudden expansion of the freed gases; the blast was so powerful that it flattened all trees near the volcano and knocked down some as far as 16 mi. away.

The *nuée ardente* and the vertical ash column produced cauliflower-shaped clouds 20 mi. wide that eventually reached a height of 15 mi. The ash in this cloud consisted mainly of silica, a reflection of the high silica content of the material emitted by continental volcanoes.

The ash falling back to earth and the debris of the collapsed flank (which amounted to about one cubic mile) combined with the water of nearby rivers and the meltwater of the mountain snows to form a mudflow (called *a lahar*). The mudflow plunged along the river valleys at speeds of up to about 50 m.p.h., destroying bridges and settlements as far as 12 mi. downstream; in some places, the mud deposited by this flow was as much as 425 ft. deep.

Although the May eruption is perhaps the best known, Mount St. Helens erupted several times during the later part of the year. Each eruption was preceded by the growth of a dome of volcanic material in the crater left by the initial explosion, and the general pattern of the subsequent eruptions resembled that of the first.

***Pahoehoe-lava** solidifies into characteristic ropy-textured folded sheets. In contrast, aa-lava – the other main type – is rough textured. The two types often have identical chemical compositions, and it is quite common for a lava flow that leaves a vent as pahoehoe to change to aa-lava as it progresses down a volcano's slopes.*

Geology and landscape

Most people consider the landscape to be unchanging whereas in fact our planet is a dynamic body and its surface is continually altering – slowly on the human timescale, but relatively rapidly when compared to the great age of the Earth (about 4,500 million years). There are two principal influences that shape the terrain: constructive processes such as uplift, which create new landscape features, and destructive forced such as erosion, which gradually wear away exposed landforms.

Hills and mountains are often regarded as the epitome of permanence, successfully resisting the destructive forces of nature, but in fact they tend to be relatively short-lived in geological terms. As a general rule, the higher a mountain is, the more recently it was formed; for example, the high mountains of the Himalayas, situated between the Indian subcontinent and the rest of Asia, are only about 50 million years old. Lower mountains tend to be older, and are often the eroded relics of much higher mountain chains. About 400 million years ago, when the present-day continents of North America and Europe were joined, the Caledonian mountain chain was the same size as the modern Himalayas. Today, however, the relics of the Caledonian orogeny (mountain-building period) exist as the comparatively low mountains of Greenland, the northern Appalachians in the United States, the Scottish Highlands, and the Norwegian coastal plateau.

Some mountains were formed as a result of the Earth's crustal plates moving together and forcing up the rock at the plate margins. In this process, sedimentary rocks that originally formed on the sea bed may be folded upwards to altitudes of more than 26,000 ft. Other mountains may be raised by faulting, which produces block mountains, such as the Ruwenzori Mountains on the border of Uganda and Zaire in Africa. A third type of mountain may be formed as a result of volcanic activity; these tend to occur in the regions of active fold mountain belts, such as the Cascade range of western North America, which contains Mount St Helens, Mount Rainier and Mount Hood. The other principal type of mountain is one that has been pushed up by the emplacement of an intrusion below the surface; the Black Hills in South Dakota were formed in this way.

***In deserts** and other arid regions the wind is the main erosive agent. It carries small particles that wear away any exposed landforms, thereby creating yet more material to bombard the rocks.*

As soon as land rises above sea level it is subjected to the destructive forces of denudation. The exposed rocks are attacked by the various weather processes and gradually broken down into fragments, which are then carried away and later deposited as sediments. Thus, any landscape represents only a temporary stage in the continuous battle between the forces of uplift (or of subsidence) and those of erosion.

The weather, in any of its forms, is the main agent of erosion. Rain washes away loose soil and penetrates cracks in the rocks. Carbon dioxide in the air reacts with the rainwater, forming a weak acid (carbonic acid) that may chemically attack the rocks. The rain seeps underground and the water may reappear later as springs. These springs are the sources of streams and rivers, which cut through the rocks and carry away debris from the mountains to the lowlands.

Under very cold conditions, rocks can be shattered by ice and frost. Glaciers may form in permanently cold areas, and these slowly-moving masses of ice scour out valleys, carrying with them huge quantities of eroded rock debris.

In dry areas the wind is the principal agent of erosion. It carries fine particles of sand, which bombard the exposed rock surfaces, thereby wearing them into yet more sand.

Even living things contribute to the formation of landscapes. Tree roots force their way into cracks in rocks and, in so doing, speed their splitting. In contrast, the roots of grasses and other small plants may help to hold loose soil fragments together, thereby helping to prevent erosion by the wind.

The nature of the rocks themselves determines how quickly they are affected by the various processes of erosion. The minerals in limestone and granite react with the carbonic acid in rain, and these rocks are therefore more susceptible to chemical breakdown than are other types of rocks containing minerals that are less easily affected by acidic rainwater. Sandstone tends to be harder than shale, and so where both are exposed in alternating beds, the shale erodes more quickly than the sandstone, giving the outcrop a corrugated or stepped appearance. Waterfalls and rapids occur where rivers pass over beds or intrusions of hard igneous rock which overlie softer rocks.

The erosional forces of the weather, glaciers, rivers, and also the waves and currents of the sea, are essentially destructive processes. But they also have a constructive effect by carrying the eroded debris to a new area and depositing it as sediment. Particles eroded by rivers may be deposited as beds of mud and sand in deltas and shallow seas; wind-borne particles in arid areas come to rest as desert sands; and the massive boulders and tiny clay particles produced and transported by glaciers give rise to spectacular landforms (terminal moraines, for example) after the glaciers have melted.

***The Himalayan range** contains some of the world's highest mountains, with more than 30 peaks rising to over 22,900 ft. above sea level – including Mount Everest (29,029 ft.). Situated along the northern border of India, the Himalayas were uplifted when a plate bearing the once-separate Indian landmass collided with Asia. This occurred comparatively recently in geological terms (about 50 million years ago) and so there has been relatively little time for the peaks to be eroded.*

Caves and their formation

As rainwater falls, it dissolves carbon dioxide from the air forming carbonic acid. This weak acid corrodes calcite (calcium carbonate), the main mineral component of limestone rocks. The acid dissolves the limestone and sculpts the rock, especially along joints and lines of weakness in the strata. Flowing rainwater makes its way through the dissolved gaps and holes and erodes caverns underground along the level of the water table. Where the water table reaches the surface, as on a slope, a spring forms and drainage is established. The place where the spring emerges is called the resurgence. At the level of the water table the pattern of linked caves is similar to that of a river, with converging branches and meanders formed by the flow of the water. Below the water table other caves are formed by solution effects, without current-formed features. These caves are full of water, joined to blind tunnels and hollows.

The cave system

When the water table drops, the current-formed cave system is left empty. Continuing solution effects undermine the rock and ceilings fall in, producing spacious caverns deep underground. Where a stream of water enters the caves, sink holes (also called potholes or swallow holes) form as the sides of the original gap are eroded and fall away.

Stalactites and stalagmites

When ground water, carrying dissolved calcite leached out of the rocks, seeps through to the ceiling of a cave it may hang there as a drip. Through loss of carbon dioxide the dissolved calcite is deposited on the ceiling as a minute mineral particle. This process happens also to the next and subsequent drips and over the years the accumulated particles produce a hanging icicle-like structure. It may take more than a thousand years to deposit one third inch of stalactite. The shapes of stalactites vary. Some are long and thin; others form curtain-like structures where the seeping water trickles down a sloping ceiling. A constant wind blowing through the cave may cause the stalactite to be crooked or eccentric.
Water from the stalactites drips to the floor. There the shock of the impact causes the calcite to separate from the water, which either flows away or evaporates. Constantly repeated, the result is the upward-growing equivalent of a stalactite – a stalagmite. Stalagmites also vary in shape; some resemble stacks of plates, whereas others have ledges and flutes that make them look like gigantic pine cones. Occasionally a stalactite and a stalagmite meet and grow into each other, producing a column. At times the calcite-rich water seeps through the wall into the cave, usually along a bedding plane, and gives rise to a cascade-like structure called a balcony, with stalactites and stalagmites that seem to flow over each other.
In the bed of an underground stream the calcite-rich water inevitably passes over ridges in the bed. A slight turbulence results and a particle of calcium carbonate is deposited on the ridge. This action is self-sustaining, because the more calcium carbonate there is deposited on an obstruction, the larger the obstruction becomes and the greater the turbulence. The result is a series of stalagmite ridges with horizontal crests, which act like dams that hold back the water in pools. These little dams are called gours, or rimstone pools.
The calcite that forms these features is a colorless mineral but impurities (mostly iron and manganese salts) stain the stalactites and stalagmites delicate shades of pink and yellow. The staining varies according to the composition of the rocks that the seeping water has passed through and it produces concentric patterns in the icicle-like stalactites, and bands of color on the curtain type.

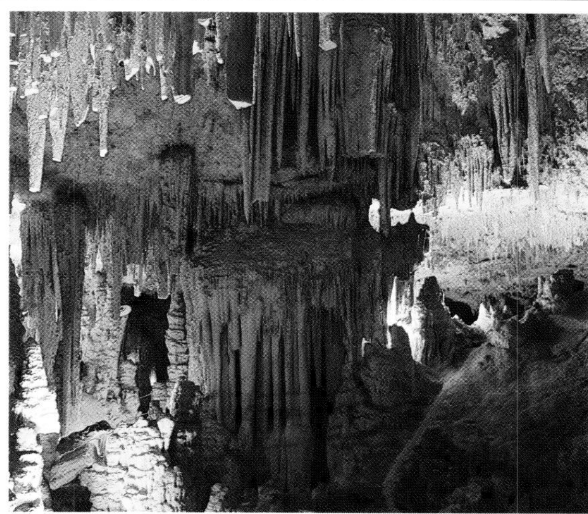

***Stalactites and stalagmites** develop in a variety of forms. The most common types are the thin straw stalactites and the broader icicle stalactites. Stalagmites, curtains, columns and gours (also called rimstone pools) are rarer. In the cave above are some fine examples of delicately-colored stalactites – and of a column. The red color of many of these is caused by iron impurities in the calcite; manganese impurities – the other main type – stain stalactites and stalagmites various shades of yellow.*

Caves and Man

Caves were the traditional homes of early Man; his artefacts have been found buried in floor debris, and his paintings have been found on walls. The most important of such sites are in the Spanish Pyrenees and the Dordogne valley in France, which have caves that were inhabited about 25,000 or 30,000 years ago.

Impervious rock
Joints
Bedding planes in easily-soluble limestone
Impervious rock

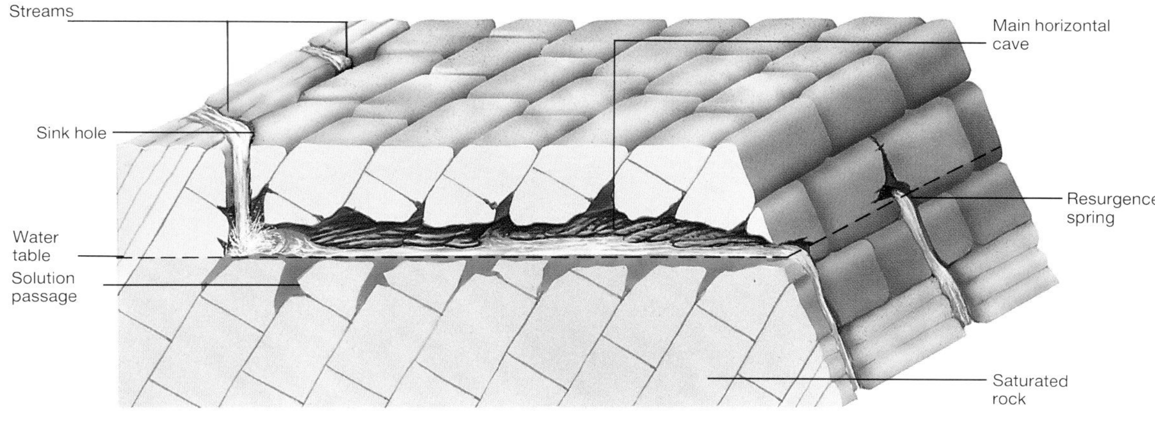
Streams
Main horizontal cave
Sink hole
Resurgence spring
Water table
Solution passage
Saturated rock

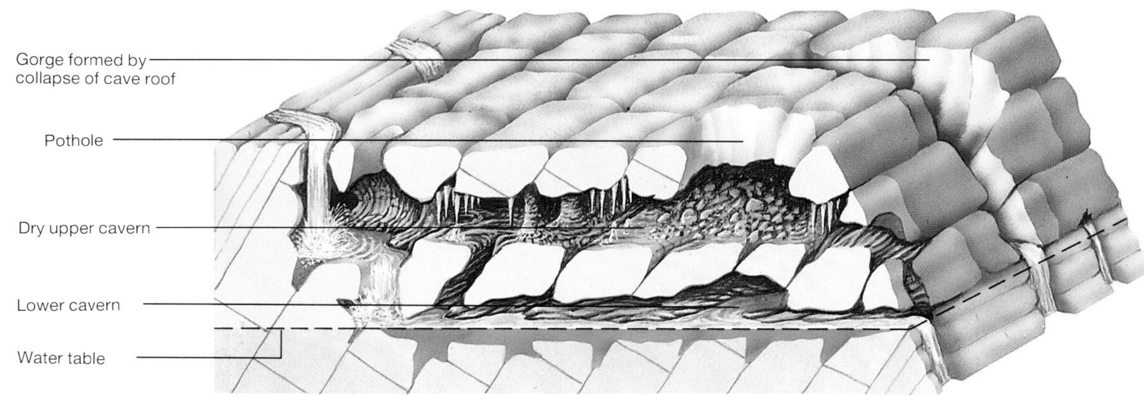
Gorge formed by collapse of cave roof
Pothole
Dry upper cavern
Lower cavern
Water table

***The horizontal network** of a cave system forms along joints and weakness in the rock. Carbonic acid (formed by carbon dioxide dissolving in rainwater) attacks the calcite in limestone rocks, eventually dissolving the rock. The rainwater then flows underground through dissolved sink holes and corrodes a horizontal cavern system at the level of the water table. Drainage is established when the water breaks through to the surface, forming a resurgence spring. Meanwhile, rainwater continues to flow into the cave system and eventually corrodes a second, lower cavern. Thus the upper caves become dry whereas the lower, more recent, caves are water-filled.*

The weather

The circulation of the atmosphere is essentially a gigantic heat exchange system, a consequence of the unequal heating of the Earth's surface by the Sun. The intensity of solar radiation is greatest around the equator and least near the poles. Thus the equator is the hottest region and, to balance the unequal heating, heat flows from the tropics to the poles.

Prevailing winds

Around the equator, radiation from the Earth's surface heats the lower layers of the atmosphere, causing them to expand and rise. This effect creates a permanent low-pressure zone (called the doldrums), with light to non-existent winds.

The light, warm air rises and eventually cools, spreading north and south to form convection currents. At around latitudes 30° North and 30° South the air in these current sinks, creating two belts of high pressure, called the horse latitudes. Like the doldrums, the horse latitudes are regions of light winds and calms. The dry, subsiding air and therefore stable atmospheric conditions of the horse latitudes tend to give rise to huge deserts on the Earth's surface – the Sahara, for example.

From the horse latitudes, air currents (winds) flow outwards across the Earth's surface. Those that flow towards the equator are the Trade Winds, and those moving towards the poles are the Westerlies. The Westerlies eventually meet cold air currents (the Polar Easterlies) flowing from the poles – areas of high atmospheric pressure caused by the sinking of cold, dense air. The regions between 30° and 65° North and South are transition zones with changeable weather, contrasting with the stable conditions in the tropics. The weather in these transition zones is influenced by the formation of large depressions, or cyclones, which result from the intermingling of polar and subtropical air.

Complicating factors

Although there is a continual heat exchange between the tropics and the poles, winds do not blow directly north-south. The Coriolis effect, caused by the rotation of the Earth on its axis, deflects winds to the right of their natural direction in the Northern Hemisphere, and to the left in the Southern Hemisphere. (The Coriolis effect also deflects ocean currents in a similar way.)

The paths of winds and the positions of the dominant low- and high-pressure systems also undergo seasonal changes. These result from the 23½° tilt of the Earth's axis, which causes the Sun to move northwards and southwards (as seen from the Earth) during the year. At the equinoxes (on about March 21 and September 23) the Sun is overhead at the equator, and solar radiation is equally balanced between the two hemispheres. But on about June 21, the summer solstice in the Northern Hemisphere, the Sun is overhead at the Tropic of Cancer (23½° North), and on December 21, the winter solstice in the Northern Hemisphere, the Sun is overhead at the Tropic of Capricorn (23½° South). The overall effect of these changes in heating is that the wind and pressure belts move north and south throughout the year. For example, Mediterranean regions come under the influence of the stable atmospheric conditions of the horse latitudes in summer, giving them hot, dry weather, but in winter the southward shift of wind belts brings cooler weather and cyclonic rain to Mediterranean lands. The astronomical dates pertaining to seasons do not coincide exactly with the actual seasons, however, because the Earth's surface is slow to warm up and cool down. As a result the summer months in the middle latitudes are June, July and August. Similarly, winter in the Northern Hemisphere occurs in December, January and February.

Winds are also affected by the fact that land heats up and cools faster than water. Rapid heating of coastal regions during the day creates an area relatively low air pressure on land, into which cooler air from the sea is drawn. At night, the land cools rapidly and cold air flows from the land towards the relatively warmer sea.

Differential heating of the land and seal also leads to the development of huge air masses over the continents and oceans. There are four main types of air masses. Polar maritime air is relatively warm and moist, because it is heated from below by the water. Polar continental air, by contrast, is cold and mainly dry in winter, but warm in summer when the land heats quickly. Tropical maritime air is warm and moist, whereas tropical continental air, such as that over the Sahara Desert, is warm and dry. The movements of these air masses and their interaction with adjacent masses along boundaries called fronts have important effects on the weather in transitional areas.

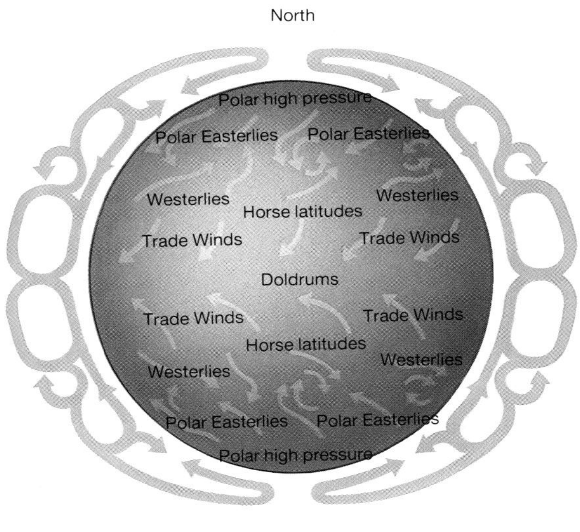
North
Polar high pressure
Polar Easterlies
Polar Easterlies
Westerlies
Horse latitudes
Westerlies
Trade Winds
Trade Winds
Doldrums
Trade Winds
Trade Winds
Horse latitudes
Westerlies
Westerlies
Polar Easterlies
Polar Easterlies
Polar high pressure
South

The atmosphere circulates *because of unequal heating of the Earth by the Sun. At the equator air is heated, rises and then flows towards the poles, creating a permanent low-pressure area (the doldrums) around the equator. At about 30° N and 30° S some of the air sinks, giving rise to the zones of high pressure called the horse latitudes. Continuing to move away from the equator, the air cools and sinks (creating high pressure) over the poles. It then flows back towards the equator. The overall effect of the atmosphere's circulation is to create a pattern of prevailing winds (grey arrows in the illustration) that blow from high- to low-pressure areas.*

Depressions

Depressions form along the polar front, the boundary between the polar and tropical air masses in the middle latitudes. They begin when undulations or waves develop in the front; warm air then flows into pronounced undulations, thereby forming depressions. The forward arc of the undulation is called the warm front, and the following arc is the cold front. Depressions are low-pressure air systems, and winds are therefore drawn towards their centers. But the deflection caused by the Coriolis effect makes winds circulate around rather than blow directly into the center of a depression. The wind circulation in depressions (cyclones) is in an anticlockwise direction in the Northern Hemisphere and clockwise in the Southern Hemisphere.

On weather maps depressions appear as a series of concentric isobars (lines joining places with equal atmospheric pressure – analogous to contour lines of height on land maps), with the lowest pressure at the center. When the isobars are close together the pressure gradient is steep, and the steeper the

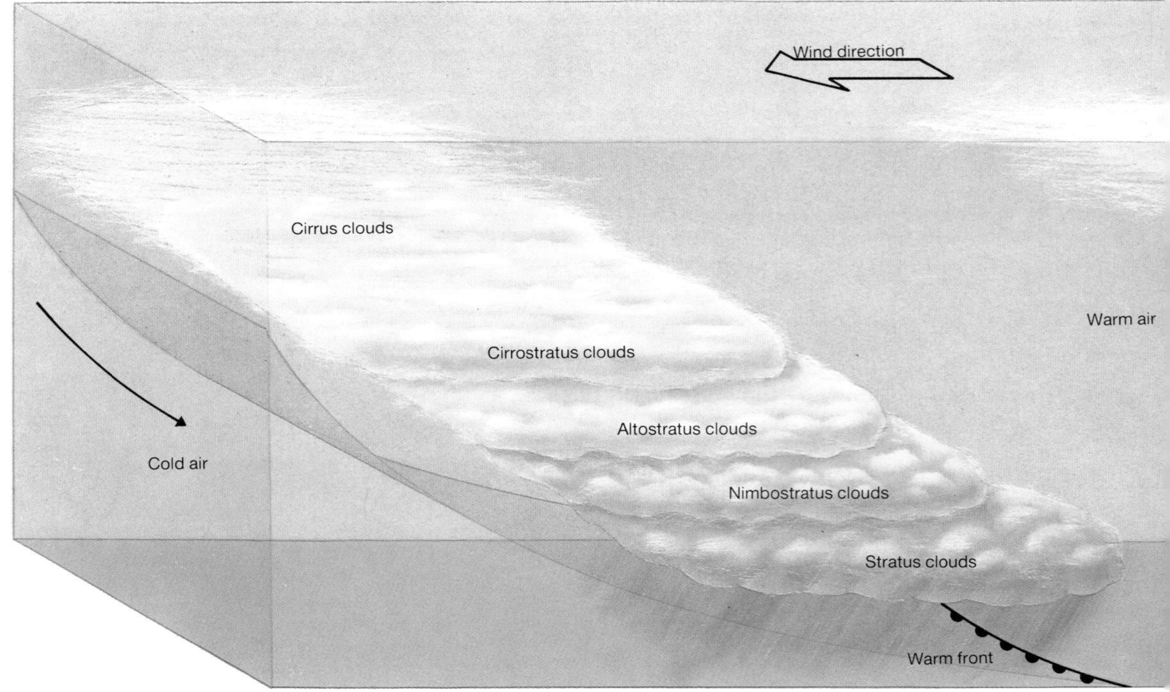
Wind direction
Cirrus clouds
Warm air
Cirrostratus clouds
Altostratus clouds
Cold air
Nimbostratus clouds
Stratus clouds
Warm front

A depression *consists of a wedge of warm air between masses of cold air. At the front edge of a depression is a warm front; a cold front marks the back edge. The approach of a depression is usually indicated by the appearance of high cirrus clouds, followed successively by cirrostratus, altrostratus, nimbostratus and stratus clouds, these last often bringing rain. When the warm front has passed, temperatures increase but thunderstorms often occur. The cold front is frequently marked by rain-bearing cumulonimbus clouds.*

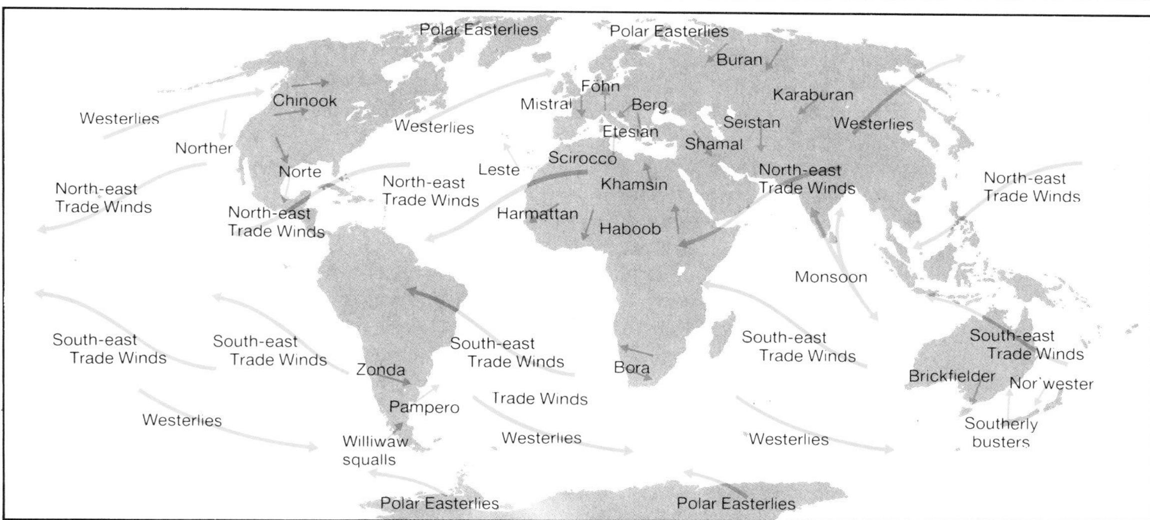
Polar Easterlies
Polar Easterlies
Buran
Westerlies
Chinook
Föhn
Mistral
Berg
Karaburan
Westerlies
Etesian
Seistan
Westerlies
Norther
Shamal
Sirocco
Norte
Leste
North-east Trade Winds
North-east Trade Winds
Khamsin
North-east Trade Winds
North-east Trade Winds
North-east Trade Winds
Harmattan
Haboob
Monsoon
South-east Trade Winds
South-east Trade Winds
South-east Trade Winds
South-east Trade Winds
South-east Trade Winds
Zonda
Bora
Brickfielder
Nor'wester
Pampero
Trade Winds
Westerlies
Williwaw squalls
Westerlies
Westerlies
Southerly busters
Polar Easterlies
Polar Easterlies

***The map** (above) shows the principal prevailing winds (large arrows) and various local winds (small arrows).*

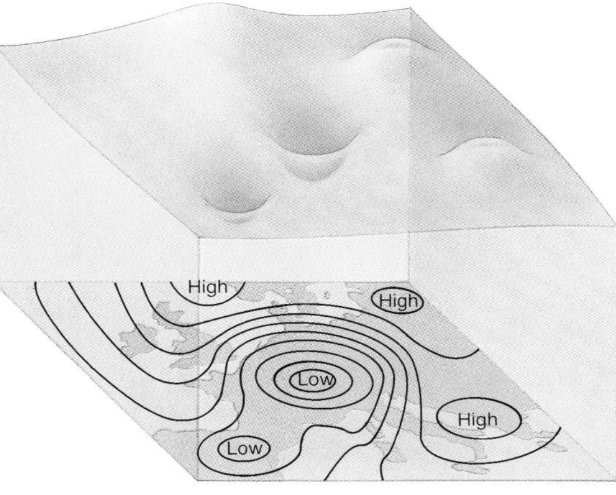
High
High
Low
High
Low

***Air pressure** is represented on weather maps by isobars – lines joining points of equal pressure. Depressions (or cyclones) are regions of low pressure, whereas anticyclones are high-pressure areas – as can be seen above where, on the graphical representation above the conventional isobar chart, depressions appear as troughs and anticyclones as mounds.*

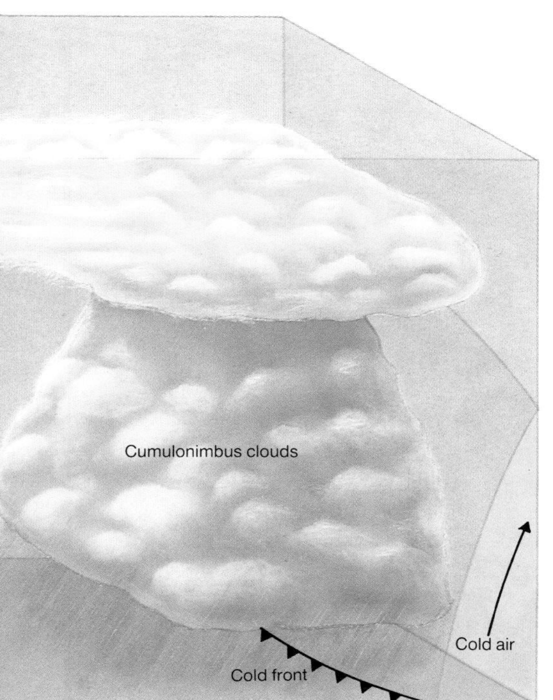
Cumulonimbus clouds
Cold air
Cold front

pressure gradient, the stronger are the winds, which tend to blow parallel to the isobars.

The formation of depressions is closely related to the paths of the jet streams in the upper atmosphere. On charts of the higher atmospheric layers, a poleward ripple in the westward-flowing jet stream usually indicates a depression below. The flow of the jet streams affects the development of depressions. When a jet stream broadens, it tends to suck air upwards, intensifying the low pressure below and causing wet, windy weather. When a jet stream narrows, it tends to push air down, thereby raising the pressure below. The jet streams are strongest in winter, when the temperature difference between polar and tropical regions is greatest; therefore the pressure gradient between these two regions is also steepest in winter. When a jet stream becomes strongly twisted, waves may break away. The jet stream soon connects up again, however, cutting off blocks of cold or warm air from the main flow. Such stationary blocks can bring spells of unseasonal weather, such as the so-called "Indian summer."

Within a depression warm air flows upwards over cold air along the warm front. Because the gradient is gradual, the clouds ahead of the warm front are usually stratiform in type. Along the cold front cold air undercuts the warm air, causing it to rise steeply; as a result, towering cumulonimbus clouds often form behind the cold front. Because the cold front moves faster than the warm front, the warm air is gradually pushed upwards, or occluded. Bands of cloud linger for some time above occluded fronts, but the depression soon weakens or is replaced by another.

Weather conditions in depressions

No two depressions bring exactly the same weather, but a knowledge of the general sequence of weather associated with these phenomena is an aid to forecasting. A depression is often heralded by the appearance of high cirrus clouds, usually drawn into long, hooked bands by the jet stream. As the warm front approaches, cloud cover increases as progressively lower clouds arrive: cirrostratus, altostratus, nimbostratus and stratus. The advance of the warm front is usually marked by increasingly heavy rain. After it has passed, air pressure stops falling and temperatures increase. After a few hours, however, thunderstorms often occur, associated with a narrow belt of squally weather along the cold front. After this belt has passed, the skies clear, pressure rises and humidity diminishes.

Anticyclones

Adding to the variety of weather conditions in the middle latitudes are anticyclones, or high-pressure air systems. Anticyclones appear on weather maps as a series of concentric isobars with the highest pressure at the center. Winds tend to blow outwards from the center of anticyclones (although not as strongly as winds blow into depressions) but are deflected by the Coriolis effect. As a result, the winds circulate around the center of an anticyclone in a clockwise direction in the Northern Hemisphere and in an anticlockwise direction in the Southern Hemisphere.

Anticyclones generally bring settled weather; warm weather with clear skies is typical in summer, whereas cold weather, frost and fogs are associated with anticyclones in winter.

Storms

The most common storms are thunderstorms, about 45,000 of which occur every day.

Thunderstorms, which are associated with cumulonimbus clouds formed in fast-rising air, are commonly accompanied by lightning, caused by the sudden release of accumulated static electricity in the clouds. The mechanisms by which static electricity forms in clouds is not known but, according to one popular theory, electrical charge is produced as a result of the freezing of supercooled droplets in clouds. The outer layers of these droplets freeze first and, in so doing, become positively charged (a phenomenon that has been observed in laboratory conditions); the warmer, still unfrozen cores acquire a negative charge. A fraction of a second later the cores freeze and expand, thus shattering the outer layers. Positively-charged fragments of the outer layers are then swept upwards to the top of the cloud while the still intact, negatively-charged cores remain in the cloud's lower levels. Eventually the total amount of charge in the cloud builds up sufficiently to overcome the electrical resistance of the air between the cloud and the ground, and the charge in the cloud is discharged as a huge electric spark – a flash of lightning. The violent expansion of the air molecules along the path of the lightning generates an intense sound wave, which is heard as thunder. Lightning is seen before thunder is heard because light travels faster than sound.

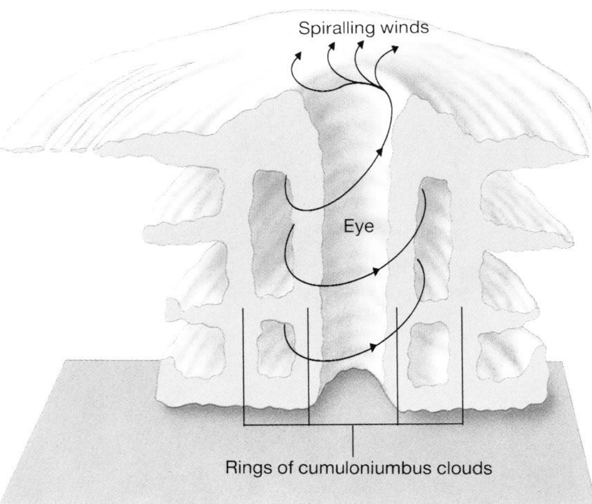
Spiralling winds
Eye
Rings of cumuloniumbus clouds

***A hurricane** is a large, intense low-pressure system consisting of concentric rings of mainly cumulonimbus clouds spiralling around a calm centre – the eye. Moist air circles and rises rapidly round the eye, generating winds that may reach speeds of 185 m. p. h. Within the eye, however, the sky is usually clear and the air almost stationary.*

Weathering

As soon as any rock is exposed at the surface of the earth it is subjected to various forces of erosion, which reduce the rock to fragments and carry the resulting debris to areas of deposition. The weather is the most significant agent of this erosion and can act in one of two ways. It can produce physical changes in which the rocks are broken down by the force of rain, wind or frost; or it can produce chemical changes in which the minerals of the rocks are altered and the new substances formed dissolve in water or crumble away from the main rock mass. The different processes involved do not act independently of each other; the resulting erosion is caused by a combination of physical and chemical effects, although in some areas one erosive force tends to predominate.

Effects of rain

The effects of rain erosion of the landscape are best seen in areas of loose topsoil. Rock or soil that is already loose is easily dislodged and washed away in heavy rainstorms. The most spectacular examples of this type of rain erosion occur in volcanic areas, where the soil consists of deep layers of volcanic ash deposited by recent eruptions. Streams of rainwater running down the slopes carry away fragments of the exposed volcanic topsoil, and the force of these moving fragments dislodges other fragments. As a result, the slopes become scarred with converging gullies and small gorges that form where the erosion is greatest. In some places, the lower slopes are worn away so rapidly that the higher ground is undercut, resulting in a landslip.

In regions that have a deep topsoil, small areas may be protected from rain erosion by the presence of large rocks on the surface. The soil around these rocks may be worn away, leaving the rocks supported on pedestals of undisturbed material.

Rain falling on grassy slopes may cause soil creep. The soil tends to be washed down the slope, but the interlocking roots of the grass prevent it from moving far, leading to the formation of a series of steps in the hillside where bands of turf have moved slowly downwards. (Soil creeps in bands because the force of gravity overcomes the roots' cohesion in the downwards direction whereas the root network remains strong in the sideways direction.)

The chemical effect of rain depends on the fact that carbon dioxide in the atmosphere dissolves in the rain, forming weak carbonic acid. The acid reacts with the calcite (a crystalline form of calcium carbonate, the substance responsible for "hardness" in water) in limestone and with certain other minerals, thereby dissolving them. This erosive effect may give rise to any of several geological features, such as grikes, which are widened cracks in the exposed rock, and swallow holes, where streams disappear underground – features that are particularly common in limestone areas, such as the county of Yorkshire in Britain.

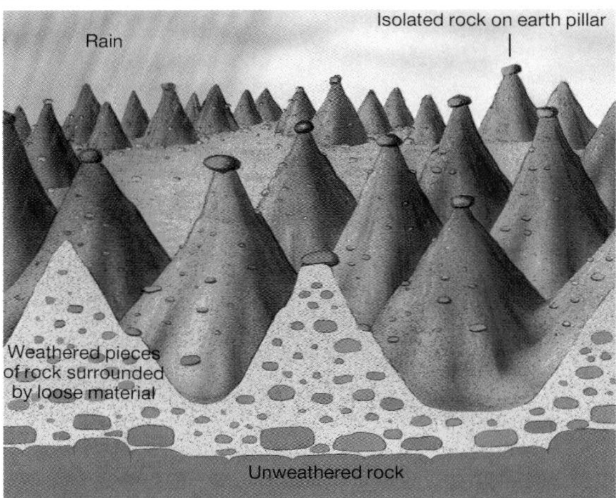

Rain
Isolated rock on earth pillar
Weathered pieces of rock surrounded by loose material
Unweathered rock

***Earth pillars** are unusual landscape features produced by rain erosion. In wet areas the rain is the principal agent of weathering. The chemical breakdown of the rock, helped by the action of vegetation, produces deep soil. Rain then washes the soil away, especially in areas where the vegetation has been removed. Where the soil has been protected by rocks resting on the surface, earth pillars may form as the surrounding soil is washed away.*

Effects of temperature

Temperature changes are an important part of the weathering process, particularly in arid areas where the air is so dry that its insulating effect is negligible; the lack of insulation results in a large daily range of temperature.

Repeated heating and cooling of the surface of a rock while the interior remains at a constant temperature weakens the rock's outer layers. When this effect is combined with the chemical action that takes place after the infrequent desert downpours, the outer layers of the rock peel off – a process called exfoliation. Exfoliation may occur on only a small scale, affecting individual rocks, or it may affect whole mountainsides, especially those in which the bedding planes of the rock are parallel to the surface. Exfoliation of entire mountains typically produces prominent, rounded hills called inselbergs, a well-known example of which is Ayers Rock in central Australia.

Effects of wind

As with heat, the weathering effects of the wind are also greatest in arid regions, because the soil particles are not stuck together or weighed down with water and are therefore light and easily dislodged. Coarser soil particles blown by the wind bounce along close to the ground, (a mode of travel called saltation), rarely rising more than 3 ft. above groundlevel. These moving particles can be highly abrasive and, where the top of an exposed rock is above the zone of attrition, can erode the rock into a pedestal shape. Stones and small boulders on the ground may be worn smooth on the side facing the prevailing wind, eventually becoming so eroded that they overbalance and present a new face to the wind. This process then repeats itself, resulting in the formation of dreikanters – stones with three or more sides that have been worn smooth.

The effect of the various abrasive processes is cumulative: particles that have been abraded from the surfaces of exposed rocks and stones further abrade the landscape features (thereby increasing the rate of erosion), eventually giving rise to a typical desert landscape.

Human influence and weathering

A natural landscape is a balance between the forces of uplift, which produce new topographical features, and erosion, which gradually wears away exposed surface features. Man's activities, especially farming, may alter this balance – sometimes with far-reaching effects. The removal of natural vegetation may weaken the topsoil, and when the soil particles are no longer held together by extensive root systems they can be washed away easily by the rain. This process may result in a "badlands" topography: initially, fields of deep, fertile soil are cut with gullies then, as erosion continues, the soil is gradually broken down into small particles that are eventually washed away by rain or blown away as dust.

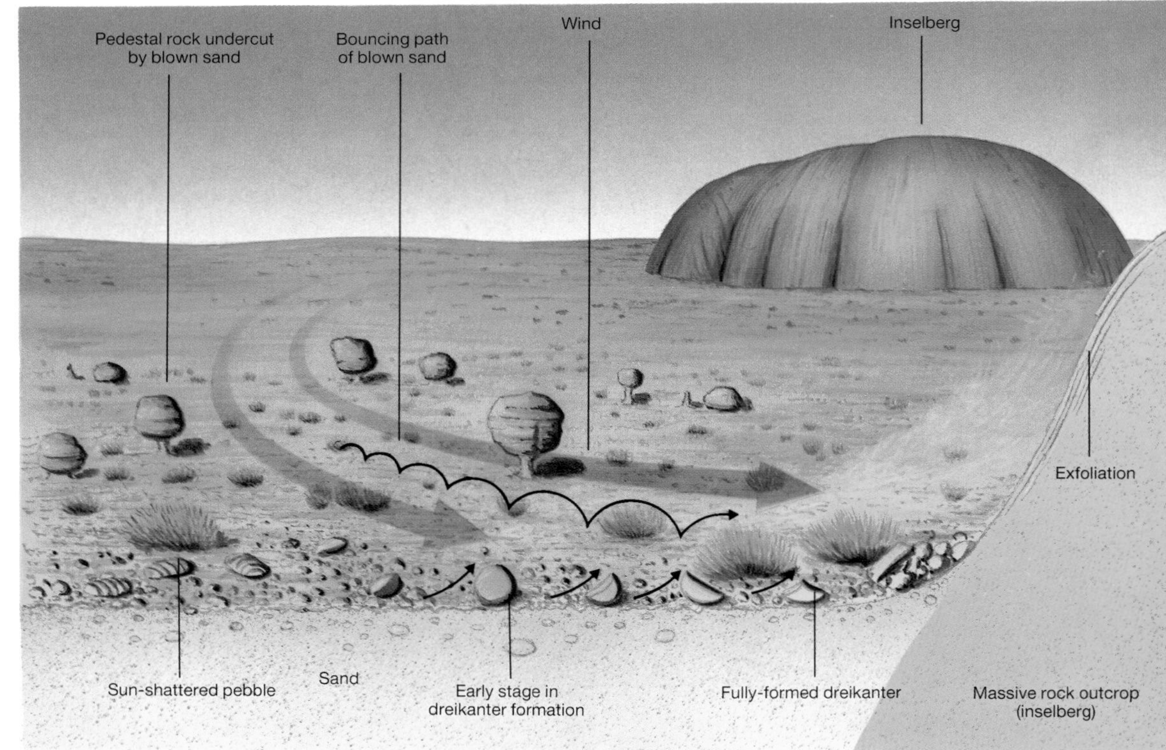

Pedestal rock undercut by blown sand
Bouncing path of blown sand
Wind
Inselberg
Exfoliation
Sun-shattered pebble
Sand
Early stage in dreikanter formation
Fully-formed dreikanter
Massive rock outcrop (inselberg)

***In arid regions** temperature changes and the wind are the strongest weathering forces. Chemical action may also affect the surface of exposed rock, although its effect is relatively minor. Temperature changes cause rapid expansion (during the day) and contraction (at night) of the rock surface, as a result of which fragments of rock break off. These fragments are then further eroded into small particles while they are being carried by the wind (a process called attrition). The various weathering processes in dry regions produce characteristic landscape features, such as pedestal rocks, rounded hills (inselbergs), dreikanters and, in hot areas, sun-shattered rocks.*

Frost erosion

Of all the forces of weathering that act on a landscape, water – particularly frozen water – produces the most dramatic topographical features. Water expands when it freezes, the expansion being accompanied by great outward pressure (it is this pressure that bursts pipes when the water in them freezes). This expansive force of frost can affect exposed terrain in two ways: rock may be broken into smaller fragments by freezing water expanding in its joints (a process called frost shattering), or the ground may be caused to expand and contract alternatively, known as frost heaving.

In order to be effective, the action of frost erosion must be strong enough to overcome the elasticity of the rock. The breakdown process starts when water seeps into pores or tiny cracks and joints in the rock. Then, when the water freezes, it forces the walls of the pores and joints further apart. On thawing, a slightly greater volume of water is able to enter the enlarged hole, and so a correspondingly stronger force is applied during the next freezing. Successive repetitions of this frost wedging process lead eventually to the shattering of a solid mass of rock into fragments.

Mountain landscapes

Frost erosion is particularly effective in mountainous areas, because temperatures are low and there is a wide daily variation in temperature. In some places, the eroded debris falls and collects in great quantities at the base of steep mountain slopes.

Mountains with needle-like peaks formed by frost action are known as "aiguilles" (meaning needles); they are often further worn away to a pyramidal "horn" by the erosive effect of frost and glaciers on the flanks. Material broken off the side of a mountain gathers towards the foot of the slopes, to form a scree (or talus) slope. Fragments of scree are always angular and the scree slopes are steep; the larger the fragments, the greater the erosion has been, and the steeper the slope. If the falling debris is guided by natural gullies and channels in the mountain, it comes to rest in a scree slope that resembles the rounded side of a cone as it fans out from its channel. Since they are forming continuously, scree slopes tend to have no soil or vegetation.

Mountain sculpting

Above the snowline any hollow in a mountainside is permanently occupied by snow. The steady accumulation and compression of the snow into ice in the bottom of the hollow eventually gives rise to a glacier. The erosive effect of the compressed snow in such a hollow acts in all directions at the same rate and, combined with the downward movement of the glacier, lowers the floor and cuts back the walls so that the hollow becomes a steep-sided, flat-bottomed feature called a cirque. Neighbouring cirques on the flanks of a mountain are divided by a ridge. As the cirque walls are cut back the ridge becomes steep and sharp-crested and forms an arête, several of which may radiate from all sides of a mountain – by now a pyramidal horn mountain.

Above a glacier the falling frost-shattered rocks do not form a scree. The blocks that land on the moving ice are carried away and eventually dumped as moraines, which are a significant feature of glacial action.

Layers of snow on the higher areas of mountains may occasionally tumble down steep eroded slopes in avalanches. They usually occur when the lower slopes of snow have melted or been blown away, leaving the top unsupported. The falling snow compacts to ice as soon as it hits anything and the great weights involved can tear away vast quantities of forest and rock from the lower slopes.

Frost effects on flat land

The more complex effects of frost erosion are seen in areas such as the tundra, where temperatures are below the freezing point for most of the year and nearly all the visible landscape features have been produced by frost action. The frost heaving that takes place does not break down the rocks, but moves and mixes the soil particles.

As the temperature drops from 32° F to –4° F, the already expanded ice begins to contract. When this occurs on the surface of the earth the result is a general shrinkage of soil in which the surface cracks up into polygonal sections. These sections may be about 33 ft. across and are bounded by deep cracks. During thaws, water enters the cracks and ice wedging takes place when the next freeze occurs. The expansion pressure of the surrounding ice causes the centre of the polygon to rise in the shape of a shallow dome.

A stone buried in the soil cools more quickly than the surrounding damp soil because it is a better conductor of heat. The first place in which ice forms during a freeze is therefore directly under any buried stone. The crystals of ice below the stone push it upwards slightly as they expand. Over a period of several years this process brings the stone to the surface. (This frost heaving effect is particularly noted by gardeners in cold weather.) In polygonally cracked ground, the stones are ultimately brought to the surface of the polygons. From there they move down the slopes of the domes and gather in the surrounding cracks.

The force of frost

Most of the effects of frost erosion derive from the peculiar behavior of water at temperatures near its freezing point, and from the unique properties of ice. Water contracts as it cools, reaching its maximum density at 39.2° F. On further cooling it expands and, as it freezes at 32° F, it reaches a volume greater than water. As the temperature falls even lower, ice expands further and can exert enormous pressure (a familiar example of the effect of this force is the bursting of frozen water pipes in winter). Then, well below the freezing point, at around –8° F, ice contracts again – to a volume less than water.

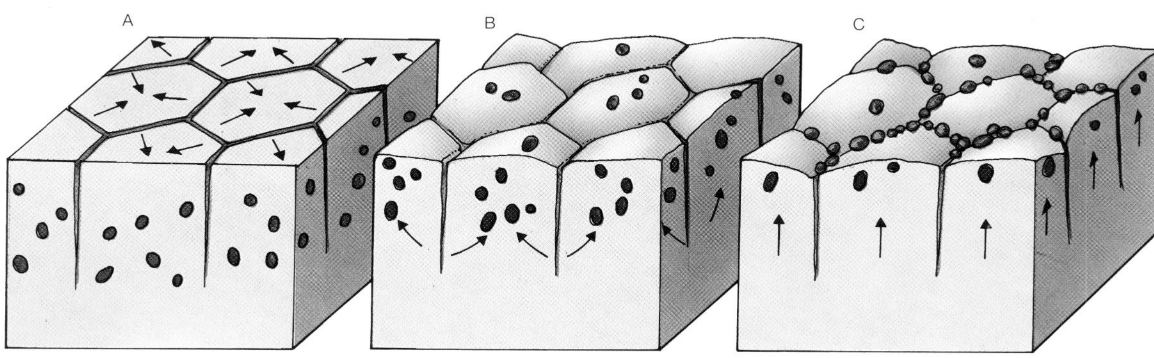

A
B
C

***Polygonal shrinking** in tundra occurs when the permafrost contracts and produces a series of interconnecting cracks in the soil surface. It is similar to the cracking that occurs in drying mud or cooling basalt, because when a homogeneous surface contracts, it does so towards a number of equally spaced centres on the surface. Cracks tend to appear at right angles to the forces (depicted by arrows) that act between each center (A). Expanding ice crystals under buried stones gradually push them to the surface (B), where they accumulate at the cracks (C).*

***The Matterhorn** (14,691 ft.) on the Swiss-Italian border shows the classic features of a frost-eroded mountain. Its peak is sharp; it has straight, steeply-sloping walls; and it has been carved into a pyramid shape by the development of cirques on its flanks.*

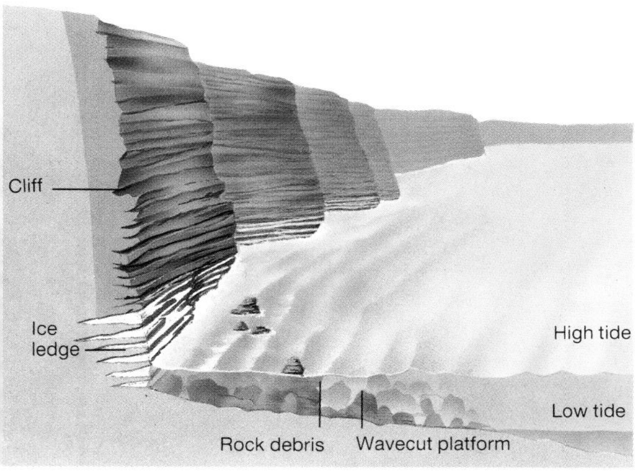

Cliff
Ice ledge
High tide
Low tide
Rock debris
Wavecut platform

***A strandflat** is a coastal feature that results from a combination of wave and frost action. A ledge of ice forms as a semi-permanent feature on a cliff just above the high tide level. Frost shattering takes place along this ledge, its effect accentuated by the lower temperatures of the salt water ice, and the cliff becomes undercut. In this way the cliff is worn back and the wavecut platform is extended.*

River action

Most streams are formed in mountains and hills from surface run-off, by the emergence of absorbed rainwater from the ground (as springs), or from melting glaciers. Over many years a stream becomes a river by eroding its bed. The course of a river can be divided into three sections: the upper course, where erosion is predominant mainly because the steep slopes increase the velocity of the water; the middle course, where most of the transportation of the eroded material occurs; and the lower course, where deposition is the major feature because the gentler slopes reduce the speed of the water so that it is not able to carry the debris any farther.

The processes of erosion

The force of flowing water, known as hydraulic action, removes loose material from the surface and forces apart cracks in rocks. Boulders and pebbles carried by the current scour and excavate the bed by corrasion. The rocks carried by the river are themselves worn down by abrasion as they collide with and rub against each other, so that abrasion of the boulders in the upper course provides the fine particles in the lower course. Fine particles are transported in suspension by the water. Rocks that are too large to be suspended are picked up from the bed of the river by the turbulence, only to be dropped again. This bouncing action is called saltation. Boulders are rolled along the river bed by traction.
Solution action is another form of weathering performed by a river. Weak acids in the water, such as carbonic acid, may dissolve the rocks over which the water passes. Most erosion occurs when the river is in spate, when its movement is most turbulent and its speed increases.

Gorges and canyons

In the upper part of its course a river erodes chiefly by vertical corrasion, cutting a steep V-shaped valley that winds between interlocking spurs of high land. The level of a river is changed when there is either an isostatic lift in the land or an eustatic fall in the sea level. In both cases the river is forced to regrade its course to a new base level and in so doing cuts a new valley in the original floodplain. This rejuvenated erosion results in the formation of river terraces.
Incised meanders occur with renewed downcutting so that bends in a river are etched into the bedrock. In some cases an asymmetrical valley is formed where lateral erosion on the outside of a bend produces river cliffs and a more gentle slip-off slope develops on the inside bend. If erosion is mainly vertical, then symmetrical valleys are formed. Localized undercutting by lateral erosion on both sides of the narrow neck of an incised meander can produce a natural bridge. When a passage is eventually excavated, the river bypasses the meander, leaving an abandoned meander loop beyond the bridge.
The Grand Canyon, one of the world's scenic wonders, was first cut in Miocene times (about 26 million years ago) as the Colorado Plateau was slowly uplifted by earth movements. The canyon has a maximum depth of about 5,500 ft. from the plateau top to the Colorado river. Differential erosion of the horizontal strata of sandstone, limestone and shales has formed a spectacular terraced valley up to 15 mi. wide.
River capture, which sometimes occurs in the upper course, results in an elbow-bend in the river and an H-shaped gorge. This happens when a stream erodes the land at its source until it breaks into the valley of another stream, and the adjacent stream is diverted into the new gorge.

Rapids and waterfalls

In the torrent stage of a stream, resistant bands of rock sometimes project transversely across the valley. If the hard band of rock dips gently downstream, then a series of rapids develop, as in the River Nile cataracts, where hard crystalline bands of rock cut across the rivers as it flows through the Nubian desert north of Khartoum. If the resistant layer is horizontal or dips upstream and covers a softer rock, then a waterfall may eventually result. In its outlet from Lake Erie, the Niagara River plunges 167 ft. over a hard dolomitic limestone ledge. The less resistant shales and sandstone beneath have been eroded by eddying in the plunge pool and by water and dripping back under the ledge, leaving the limestone unsupported. This process of headward erosion has resulted in the formation of a receding gorge about 7 mi. long, downstream from the falls.
Waterfalls are not only produced by erosion of softer layers of rock, but also by glacial action where, due to the gouging of the main valley by ice, the valleys of tributary streams are left hanging high above the main valley floor. These hanging valleys often produce magnificent falls which plunge down the side of the main glacial trough.
Potholes are also a feature of the upper course of a river. They are formed when eddies whirl around pebbles, causing them to spin and act as grinding tools on the rock below.

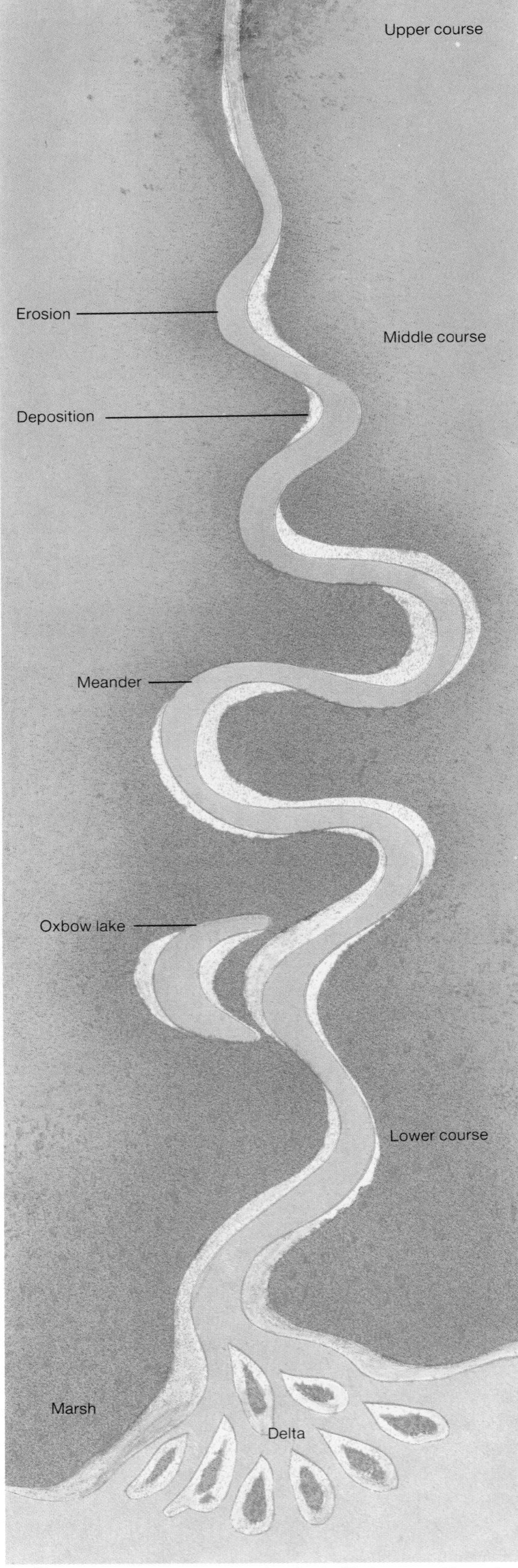
Upper course
Erosion
Middle course
Deposition
Meander
Oxbow lake
Lower course
Marsh
Delta

In its upper course, *particularly if the gradient is steep, a river channel is straight and narrow, and the river runs rapidly. But when the slope is reduced, the river slows down and moves around obstacles. In addition, the wave motion of the water moves the river from side to side. Eventually, the river erodes the outer bank of a slight bend and deposits material on the inner bank. The river channel is deepened towards the outer side of the bend and is widened at the same time by lateral erosion. As this process continues, the river widens the valley floor and the bends migrate downstream. When the river meets the sea or a lake, the reduction in velocity causes it to deposit sediment and a delta develops.*

The river terrace *of the Taramakau River on South Island in New Zealand probably resulted from a drop in the sea level, which caused the river to renew its downcutting. The step along the side of the valley marks the former level of the valley floor. The broad plains of gravel alluvium represent the floodplain as it is today.*

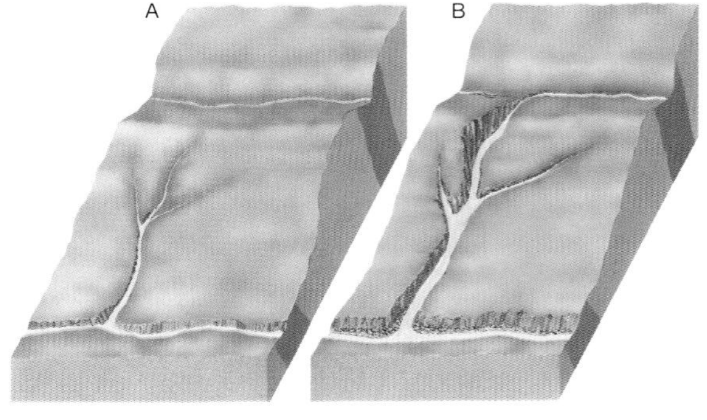
A
B

River capture *occurs when a major river and its tributaries (A) become so entrenched that they wear through a divide and intercept another river so that its course is diverted (B). When the gorge of the captured river beyond the bend at the point of diversion (elbow of capture) is completely drained, it becomes a wind gap.*

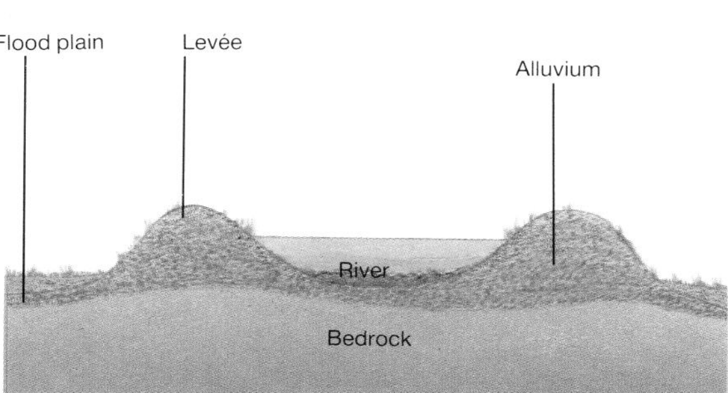
Flood plain
Levée
Alluvium
River
Bedrock

A levée, *a raised bank found on both sides of a meandering river, forms from the accumulation of sediment that the river deposits when it overflows its banks. The river bed is raised by deposited sediment until it is higher than the floodplain.*

River meanders

In the middle course of a river, most outcrops and formations are worn away and the bed is fairly flat. The current is just strong enough to carry debris from the upper course. But as a river flows onto flatter slopes it slows down and the coarsest debris is deposited. This debris may form sand and gravel bars around which the river is forced to flow. These deflections in its course develop into bends as the outer edges are eroded and as bars of sediment are deposited on the inner edges. In time, the curves become increasingly exaggerated and the river meanders.

The curves of a meandering river that flows across a wide flood plain slowly migrate downstream as erosion occurs on the outer bank of the bends and as sediments are deposited on the inner banks. The changing shape of the bends is due to the current, which usually follows a helical or corkscrew pattern as it goes downstream, flowing faster on the outer bank and sweeping more slowly towards the inner bank where it deposits a series of point bar sediments.

When a river is in spate, silt or alluvium may be spread over the floodplain. The river bed is raised higher than the surrounding land by deposition, while the river itself is contained by embankments, or levées, which are formed from the deposition of silt. Levées may break when the river is swollen and large areas of the floodplain may be inundated. At this time a river may alter its course, as did the Hwang Ho in China in 1852, when it shifted its mouth 300 mi. to the north of the Shantung Peninsula. On a smaller scale, individual meanders may be cut off if the river breaks through the narrow neck of land separating a meander loop. The river straightens its course at this point and the abandoned loop is left as an oxbow lake which gradually degenerates into a swamp as it is silted up by later floods.

A river is described as braided when it becomes wide and shallow and is split into several streams separated by mid-channels, bars of sand and shingle. Braiding often develops where a river emerges from a mountain region onto a bordering plain. The sudden flattening of the slope checks the velocity of the stream and sediment is deposited.

Deltas

Deposition is concentrated where a river is slowed on entering a lake or the sea. A delta forms at this point as long as no strong currents or tides prevent silt from settling. A typical cross-section through a delta shows a regular succession of beds in which fine particles of material – which are carried out farthest – create the bottom beds, whereas coarser material is deposited in a series of steep, angled wedges known as the foreset beds. As the delta progrades into the water, the coarsest sediment is carried through the river channel and laid down on the delta surface to form the top beds.

A good example of a lacustrine delta is found where the River Rhône enters Lake Geneva. The river is milky grey in colour because it is heavily charged with sediment acquired from its passage through the Bernese Oberland. The river plunges into the clear waters of the lake and slows down immediately, leaving the material it has transported to contribute to the outgrowth of the delta. Ultimately the lake may become completely silted up, although some lakes are initially divided by deltaic outgrowth. Derwentwater and Bassenthwaite in the English Lake District were originally one lake but are now separated by delta flats that were produced by the River Derwent.

Marine deltas are formed when the ocean currents at the river mouth are negligible, as in partially enclosed seas such as the Mediterranean and the Gulf of Mexico. The classic marine delta is exemplified by the arcuate type of the River Nile. Sediment is deposited in a broad arc surrounding the mouth of the river, which is made up of a series of distributary channels crossing the delta. Lagoons, marshes and coastal sand spits are also characteristic features of most deltas. The Mississippi delta has most of these features including levées, bayous (distributaries) and etangs (lagoons). The delta progrades seawards by way of several major channels which resemble outstretched fingers.

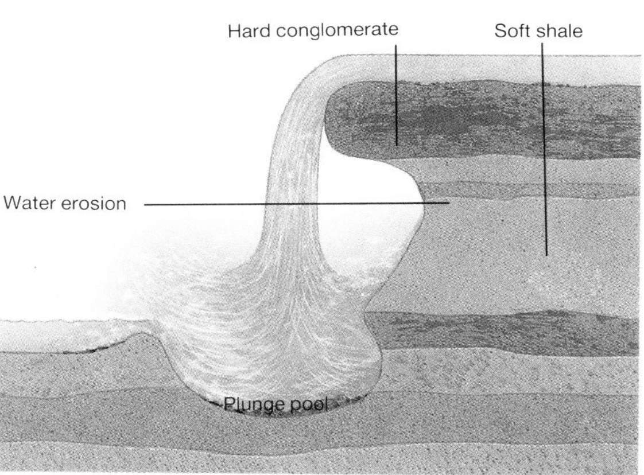
Hard conglomerate
Soft shale
Water erosion
Plunge pool

The Kaieteur Falls *in Guyana (above) are typical of receding waterfalls. Splashing water from the plunge pool erodes the soft shale as does water dripping back under the hard conglomerate and sandstone ledge which, unsupported, eventually falls away.*

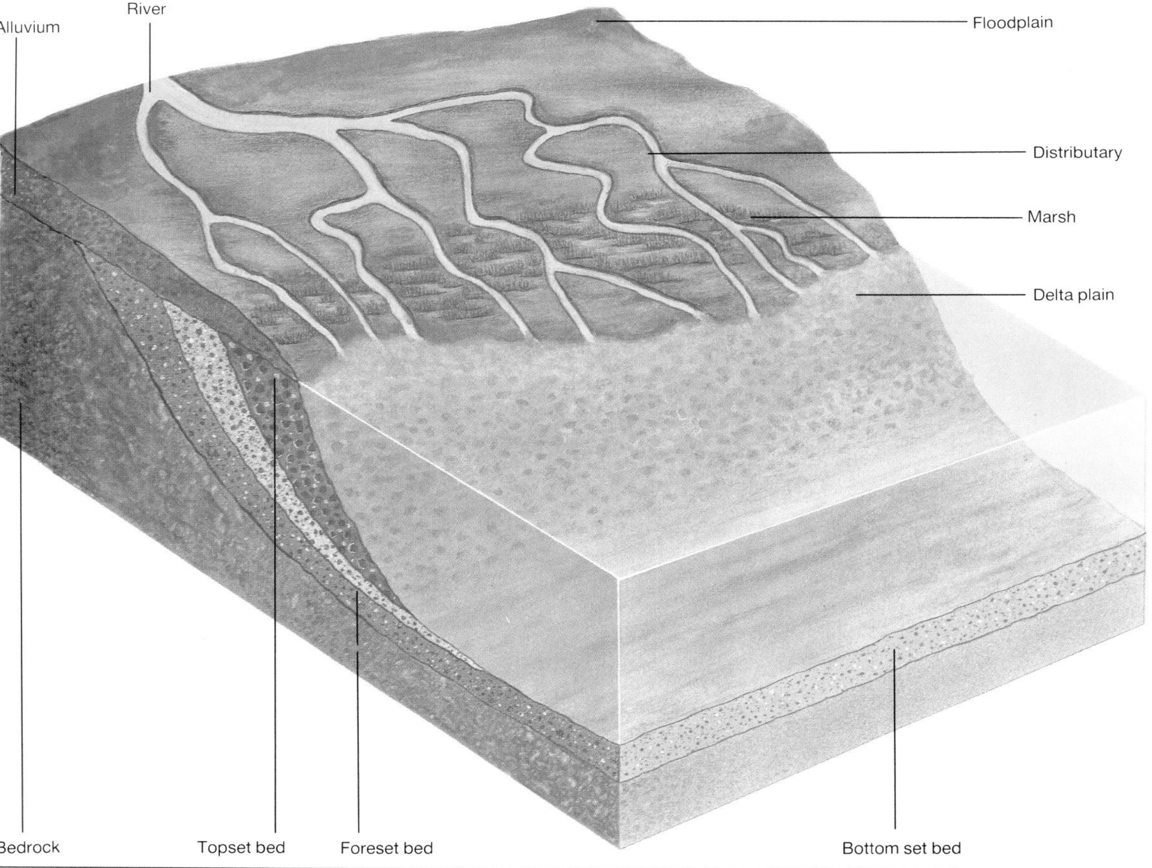
River
Alluvium
Floodplain
Distributary
Marsh
Delta plain
Bedrock
Topset bed
Foreset bed
Bottom set bed

A river delta *in cross-section can be seen to be composed of several layers of material. The bottom set beds are made up of the finest particles which are carried out farthest; the foreset beds comprise coarser material and the topset beds consist of the heaviest sediment that is deposited at an early stage as the river meets the sea. These layers form a sloping fan under water that gradually extends along the sea floor as more material accumulates.*

Coral reefs and islands

Not all rocks were formed hundreds of thousands of years ago. Enormous masses of limestone are being formed today in the warmer parts of the Indian and Pacific oceans, built up particle by particle through the activities of corals.

Corals are animals, relatives of the sea anemone that remain fixed to the same spot throughout life, feeding on organic material that drifts past in the water. They have a hard shell of calcite, formed by the extraction of calcium carbonate from sea water. A coral organism, called a polyp, can reproduce by budding and the result is a branching colony of thousands of individual creatures. Each colony is usually built up on the rocky skeletons of dead polyps, and in this way the coral mass can grow and spread to form a reef.

Corals flourish only in certain conditions. They live in sea water and grow best if the water is clear and silt-free, and at a temperature of between 73 and 77° F. Their tissues contain single-celled plants that help them to extract the calcite from water, and the plants must have sunlight to survive – in water less than 165 ft. deep. For these reasons, coral reefs are found in clear, shallow tropical seas.

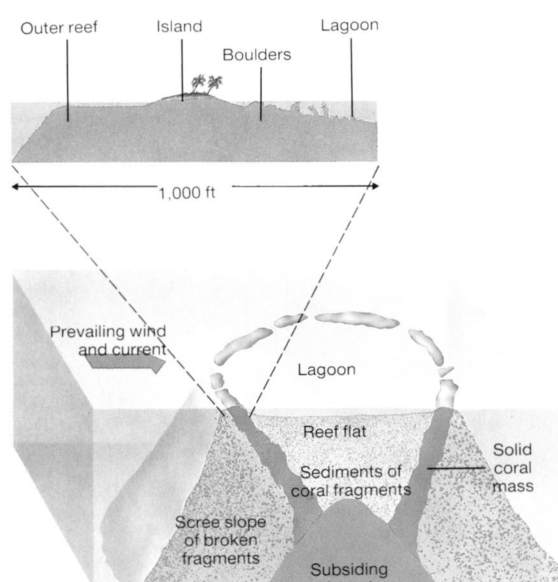

Outer reef
Island
Boulders
Lagoon
1,000 ft
Prevailing wind and current
Lagoon
Reef flat
Sediments of coral fragments
Solid coral mass
Scree slope of broken fragments
Subsiding island

An atoll *is a chain of coral islands, the remnants of a reef that once surrounded a volcanic island. Atolls are usually asymmetrical, growing more rapidly on the side to which the prevailing currents bring most nutrients.*

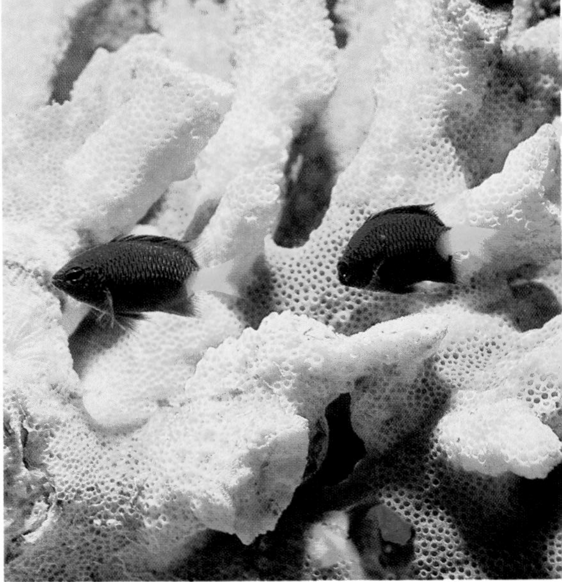

Colorful damsel fish *seek shelter among the finger-like growth of coral. The reefs support a wide variety of marine life, from the coral polyps themselves, through numerous species of molluscs and crustaceans, to the predatory fish that feed on them.*

Types of reefs

Most reefs tend to grow around islands. There are three main types of reefs. A fringing reef forms a shelf around an island, just below sea level. A barrier reef lies at a distance from the island, forming a rough ring around it and separated from it by a shallow lagoon. The third type of reef is the atoll, which is merely a ring of reef material without a central island. The three types can be considered as three stages in a single process.

Usually the island is volcanic, part of an island arc that rises from the sea floor where two crustal plates are converging. Once the island has appeared, corals begin to grow on its flanks, just below sea level. The outer limit of reef growth is defined by the depth (165 ft.) below which corals cannot grow. The result is a fringing reef.

As time passes the island may sink, possibly because, attached to its tectonic plate, it moves from a relatively shallow active area (such as an ocean ridge) towards deeper waters. Alternatively the "sinking" may be due to a rise in sea level caused by the melting of polar icecaps at the end of an ice age. As this occurs, the exposed part of the island – which is roughly conical in shape – becomes smaller. But the reef continues to build upwards from its original position. Sooner or later the island and reef become separated at the surface of the sea, producing a barrier reef. Eventually the island sinks completely, although the reef continues to grow and form the characteristic ring of an atoll.

If the atoll continues to sink and does so at such a rate that the growth of coral cannot keep ahead of it, then the coral dies and the whole reef is carried into depper water. This may account for the existence of guyots – flat-topped underwater hills whose summits may be 6,500 ft. below the surface of the sea.

The structure of a reef

A living reef forms a narrow plateau just below the surface of the water, producing an area of shallows that can be treacherous for swimmers and small craft. Where the reef crest is above the water it forms a small flat island, often crowned with coconut palms. The island is usually covered with white sand, made from the eroded fragments of coral skeletons. In the lagoon behind the reef there may be boulders of coral material that have been torn off the reef during storms and deposited in the calmer water. In the sheltered water of a lagoon, coral may grow into remarkable mushroom shapes and pinnacles and support a varied community of marine life.

The water in a lagoon is shallow, although not as shallow as over the reef itself. Its floor is covered by sediments of broken coral; this region is known as a flat reef. On the seaward side of the reef its edge may be composed of the skeletons of calcite-secreting algae, because these plants are better than corals at withstanding the rougher conditions. The outer edge forms a scree slope of fragments broken from the reef.

Fossil reefs

Geologically a reef is a mass of biogenic limestone whose porous nature makes it a good reservoir rock for oil and natural gas. In early times the reef organisms were very different from today's. Modern corals did not evolve until about 200 million years ago (in the Triassic period), yet the first reefs date from the Cambrian of 570 million years ago. Many of the early reefs were built by calcite-producing algae, or by shellfish that existed on the heaps of shells left by their ancestors.

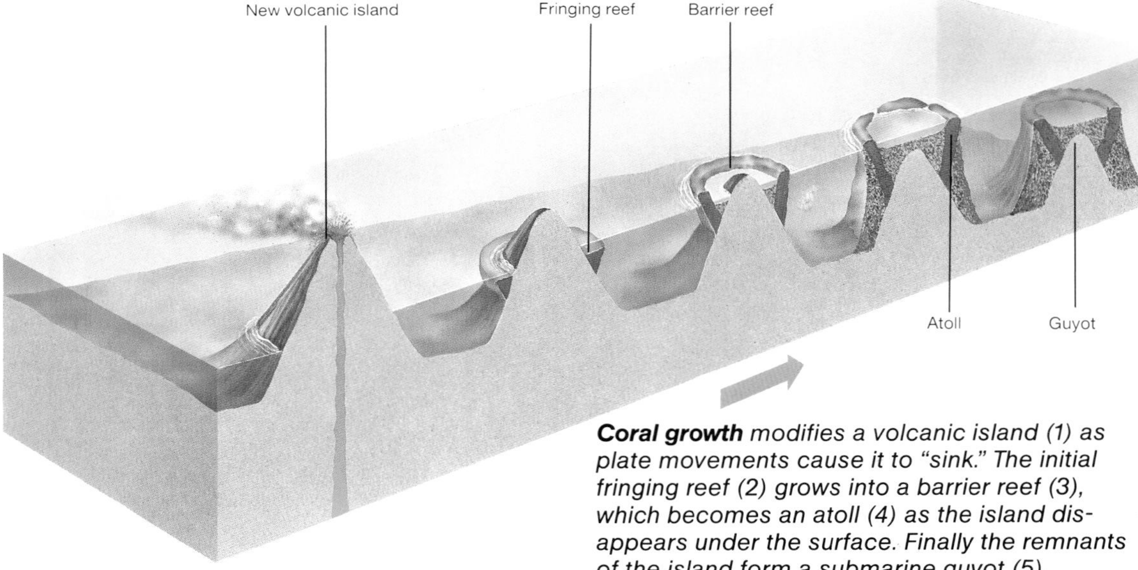

New volcanic island
Fringing reef
Barrier reef
Atoll
Guyot

Coral growth *modifies a volcanic island (1) as plate movements cause it to "sink." The initial fringing reef (2) grows into a barrier reef (3), which becomes an atoll (4) as the island disappears under the surface. Finally the remnants of the island form a submarine guyot (5).*

Turbulent shallow water *foams over the reef that fringes a small coral island in the Seychelles. Corals flourish in the warm waters of this part of the Indian Ocean.*

The continental shelf

A continental shelf is a submerged, gently-sloping ledge that surrounds the edge of a continent. On the landward side it is bordered by the coastal plain and on the seaward side by the shelf break, where the continental shelf gives way to the steeper continental slope. The coastal plain, continental shelf and continental slope together comprise what is caled the continental terrace. Farther out to sea beyond the continental slope is the continental rise and then the abyssal plain – the sea floor of the deep ocean.

Knowledge of the continental shelf has increased greatly since the 1950s, helped by geophysical techniques originally developed to prospect for offshore oil and gas reserves. Particularly valuable have been the various sonar mapping methods, which use ultrasonic sound to penetrate the sea water. The depth of the sea-bed can be measured using echo-sounders, and lateral sonar beams can be used to obtain pictorial views of the sea-bed that are similar to aerial photographs of the land.

Size and depth of the continental shelf

The continental shelf constitutes 7 to 8 per cent of the total area of the sea floor, forming the bottom of most of the world's shallow seas. The width of the shelf varies from place to place; off the coast of southern California, for example, the shelf is less than two thirds of a mile wide, whereas off South America, between Argentina and the Falkland Islands, it is more than 300 mi. wide. It is narrowest on active crustal-plate margins bordering young mountain ranges, such as those around the Pacific Ocean and Mediterranean Sea, and broadest on passive margins – around the Atlantic Ocean, for example.

The shelf slopes gradually (at an average of only 0.1° to the horizontal) down to the shelf break, the mean depth of which is 425 ft. below sea level. The continental slope, the other main part of the continental terrace, begins at the shelf break and extends to a depth of between one and two miles. The slope varies from about 12 to 60 mi. wide and is much steeper than the shelf, having an average inclination of 4°, although in some places it is as steep as 20°.

Influences on the continental shelf

The continental shelf is affected by two main factors: earth movements and sea-level changes. On passive crustal-plate margins the shelf subsides as the Earth's crust gradually cools after rifting and becomes thinner through stretching. These processes are often accompanied by infilling with sediments, the weight of which adds to the subsidence of the shelf. And in polar regions the weight of ice depresses the continents by a considerable amount, with the result that the shelf break may be more than 1,970 ft. below sea level.

Superimposed on the results of subsidence is the effect of worldwide changes in sea level which, during the Earth's history, have repeatedly led to drowning of the continental margins. During the last few million years, sea-level changes were caused mainly by the freezing of the seas in the ice ages. The last major change, the melting of ice at the end of the Pleistocene Ice Age several thousand years ago, released water into the oceans and submerged the shelf. Since then shorelines have remained comparatively unchanged.

Many of the earlier changes in sea level, however, were related to the Earth's activity. During quiescent phases, when the Earth's surface is being eroded and the resultant debris deposited in the seas, the sea level rises as water is displaced by the accumulating debris. During active mountain-building phases, on the other hand, the sea level falls. Changes in the rate at which the continents move apart also cause fluctuations in sea level. During times of rapid separation, the rocks near the center of spreading of the ocean floor (from where the continental movements originate) become hot and expand, thereby displacing sea water, which drowns the edges of the continents.

Topography of the continental shelf

The continental shelf has a varied relief. Drowned river valleys, cliffs and beaches – submerged by the recent (in geological terms) sea-level rise – are common, and in northern latitudes the characteristic features left by retreating ice sheets and glaciers (U-shaped valleys and moraines, for example) are apparent.

Furthermore the shelf is not unchanging even today. It is being altered by numerous influences that affect the sediments left behind by the sea-level rise at the end of the Pleistocene Ice Age. In strongly tidal areas, such as the Yellow Sea and the North Sea, currents sweep sand deposits into wave-like patterns that resemble the wind-blown dunes in deserts.

Earth movements *and sea-level changes can affect the continental shelf, as shown by the cliff (above) which was originally an off-shore coral reef but was raised by earth movements and became part of the land.*

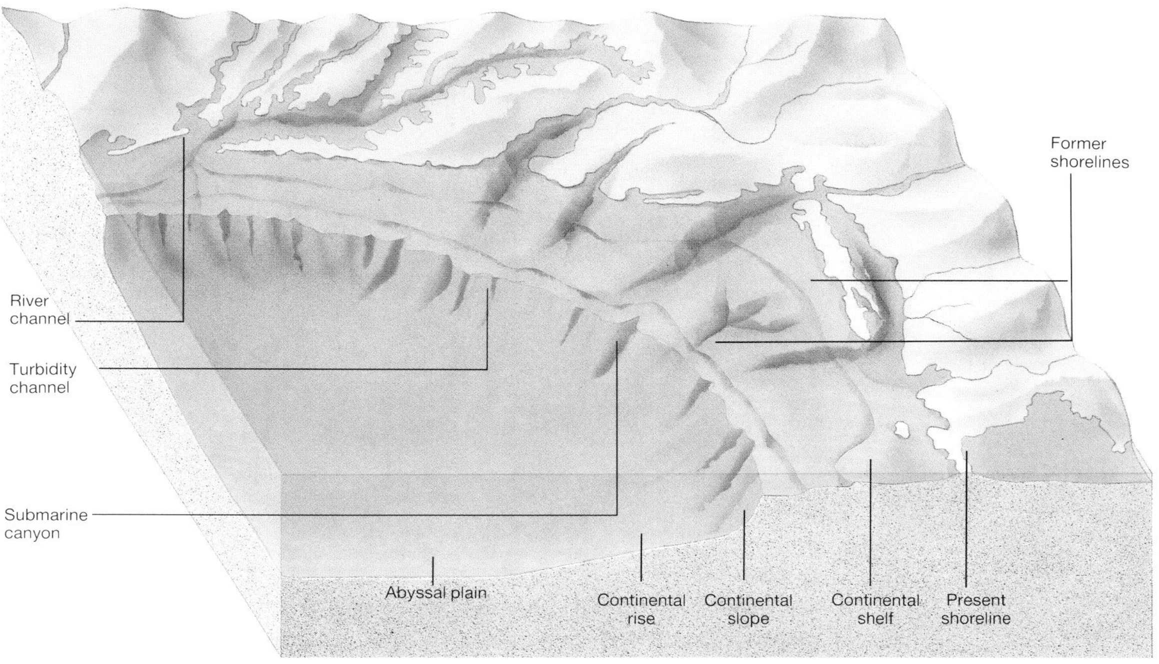

Former shorelines
River channel
Turbidity channel
Submarine canyon
Abyssal plain
Continental rise
Continental slope
Continental shelf
Present shoreline

The narrow margins *of the continents slope gradually before descending to the abyssal plain (the floor of the deep ocean). In the profile of the continental margin (below) the vertical scale has been exaggerated to enable the main zones to be clearly distinguishable.*

The continental margin *has a varied relief, with such features as submarine canyons and smaller turbidity and river channels. In some areas the former shorelines can also be seen.*

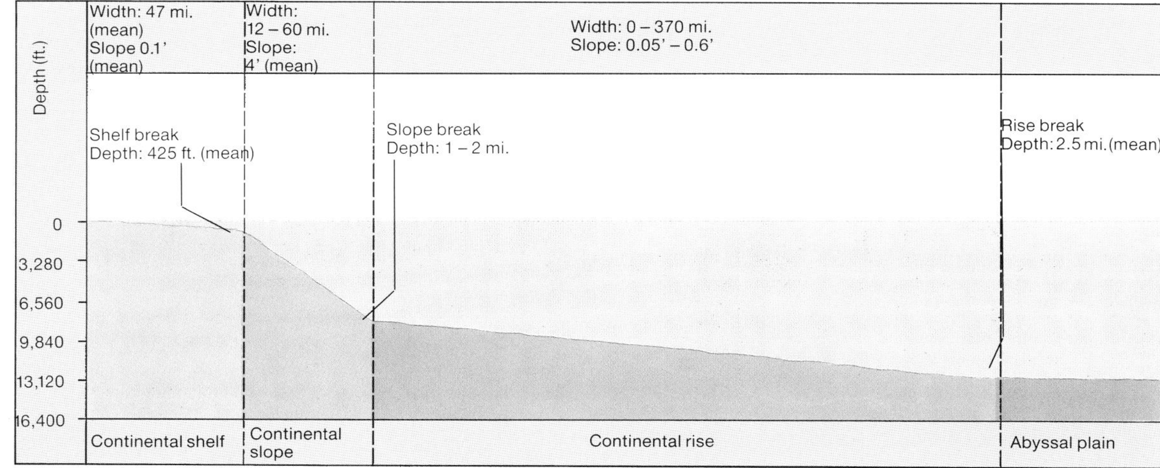

Width: 47 mi. (mean) Slope 0.1° (mean)
Width: 12 – 60 mi. Slope: 4° (mean)
Width: 0 – 370 mi. Slope: 0.05° – 0.6°
Depth (ft.)
Shelf break Depth: 425 ft. (mean)
Slope break Depth: 1 – 2 mi.
Rise break Depth: 2.5 mi. (mean)
0
3,280
6,560
9,840
13,120
16,400
Continental shelf
Continental slope
Continental rise
Abyssal plain

Ice caps

Within the last 1.6 million years the Earth has experienced an ice age during which almost one third of the land surface – about 11,600,000 sq. mi. – was covered by ice. Today the area of ice-covered land has dwindled to about 6,020,000 sq. mi., and continental ice sheets, such as those that were widespread during the last ice age, cover only Greenland and Antarctica. Smaller ice sheets, known as ice caps, occur in such northern landmasses as Iceland, Spitzbergen and the Canadian Islands. Valley glaciers that flow out over a plain and coalesce with others to form a broad sheet of ice are called piedmont glaciers; the classic examples of these are found along the southern coast of Alaska.

Ice movement

In very cold latitudes there is no summer thaw, and the snow that falls in winter is covered and compressed by snow in subsequent falls. The compressed snow eventually becomes glacier ice 2 to 2.5 mi. thick. The great pressure that builds up underneath the ice makes the ice crystals slide over each other and, because the pressure lowers the melting point of the ice, water is released which lubricates the mass. In addition, glacier ice under pressure can deform elastically like putty. As a result the ice sheet moves outwards, away from the build-up of pressure at the center. In Greenland the movement may be as great as 65 ft. per day, whereas in Antarctica it may only be 3 ft. per year. The bottom layers of the ice move and are deformed, but the top layers remain rigid and are carried along by them, cracking and splitting as they move.

The weight of a continental ice sheet depresses the land beneath it, so that a large percentage of the land surface of Greenland and Antarctica is below sea level. If these ice sheets were to melt, the level of the land below them would rise due to isostasy, as is happening in the areas of the Baltic Sea where the land is still recovering its isostatic balance after having lost the continental ice sheet that covered it during the last ice age. The restoration of balance does not just involve a simple raising of the land level; before this occurs the melting ice increases the volume of water in the oceans and raises the sea level at the same time.

When ice sheets pass over or through a mountain range and descend to a lower altitude, as they do in Iceland and the Canadian Islands, they squeeze through the passes and cols between the mountains in the form of lobes that may then become valley glaciers.

The various layers in an ice sheet can be detected by echo sounding, in which pulses of radio waves are sent down into the ice and the resulting echos analyzed. Reflections from different layers may come from thin layers of dirt, which are probably deposits of volcanic ash that may have periodically drifted into and fallen on the area.

Nunataks, *individual mountains that are completely surrounded by ice, occasionally protrude through the surface of an ice sheet. Lower mountains tend to be wholly engulfed and in such cases ice moving towards the sea can flow uphill.*

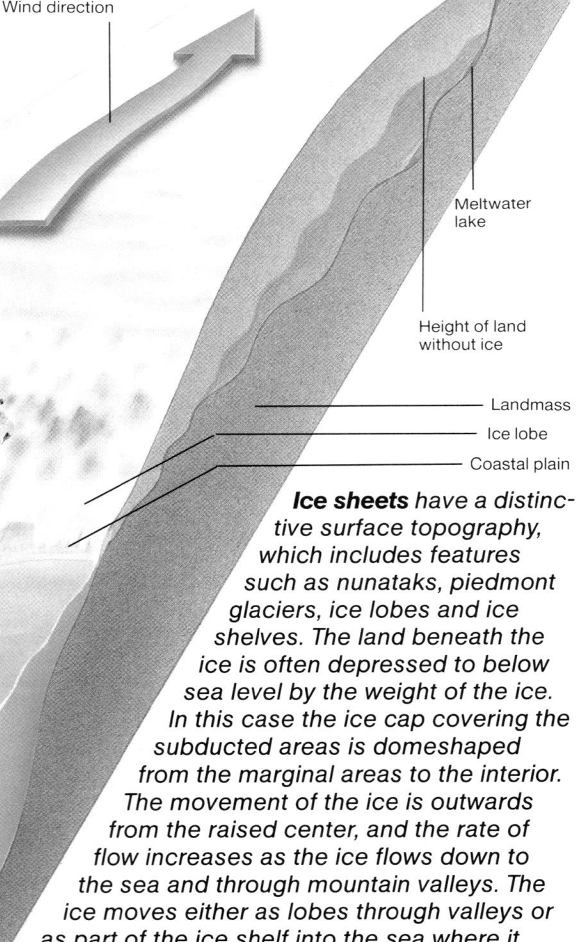
Icebergs
Ice shelf
Wind direction
Meltwater lake
Height of land without ice
Landmass
Ice lobe
Coastal plain
Nunatak
Piedmont glacier
Meltwater channels

Ice sheets *have a distinctive surface topography, which includes features such as nunataks, piedmont glaciers, ice lobes and ice shelves. The land beneath the ice is often depressed to below sea level by the weight of the ice. In this case the ice cap covering the subducted areas is domeshaped from the marginal areas to the interior. The movement of the ice is outwards from the raised center, and the rate of flow increases as the ice flows down to the sea and through mountain valleys. The ice moves either as lobes through valleys or as part of the ice shelf into the sea where it melts or calves into icebergs.*

Ice ages

The Earth has had a number of ice ages. The area covered by them can be mapped by the distribution of rocks, called tillites, which consist of the same type of material found in glacial deposition. At least three ice ages are known to have occurred in Precambrian times and one in the Upper Ordovician or Lower Silurian period – 430 million years ago – evidence of which has been found in South Africa. A particularly important one occurred in Carboniferous and Permian times – 280 million years ago – and the evidence for this has been found in South America, central and southern Africa, India and Australia. It therefore provides substance for the theory of continental drift and the break-up of Gondwanaland – the great southern continent that existed then.

The most recent ice age was during the Pleistocene era. It began 1,600,000 years ago and ended a mere 11,000 years ago. It consisted of about 18 different advances and retreats of the ice sheets, each one separated by a warm interglacial period during which the climate in the temperate latitudes was at times warmer than it is now. It is possible that the glacial advances are not over yet and that we are experiencing another interglacial period before the advance of the next ice sheet.

Causes of ice ages

Many theories have been proposed. It has been suggested that the distribution of continental masses may be responsible, for example by preventing the warm oceanic water from reaching the poles. Or the albedo of ice sheets reflects a high percentage of solar radiation and so reduces temperatures sufficiently to affect the world climate. Or there may be fluctuations in the proportion of carbon dioxide or dust particles in the atmosphere; a reduction in carbon dioxide or an increase in dust would allow more heat to be lost from the Earth and so result in lower temperatures. Others suggest that the reason must be found in space, such as in a fluctuation of the Sun's energy output or the presence of a cloud of dust between the Earth and the Sun.

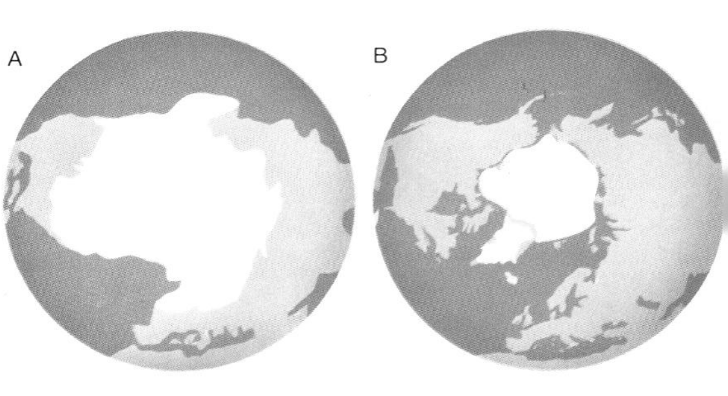
A
B

During the Pleistocene Ice Age, *about 18,000 years ago (A), two ice sheets covered land in the Northern Hemisphere; one had as its center Scandinavia, and covered the North Sea, most of Britain, the Netherlands, northern Germany and Russia; the other spread over the North American continent as far down as Illinois. These ice sheets froze enough water to reduce the sea level to about 250 ft. lower than it is at present. Today in the Northern Hemisphere (B), only Greenland is covered by an ice sheet, and ice caps lie over Iceland, parts of Scandinavia and the Canadian Islands.*

Mountain glaciers

The snowfields on mountain regions are constantly being replenished with fresh falls of snow, the weight of which compresses the underlying material into firn, or nevé. This material is composed of ice crystals separated from each other by small air spaces. With increasing depth and pressure, the firn gradually changes into much denser glacier ice which moves slowly out from the snowfields down existing valleys. The glacier becomes a river of moving ice, its surface marked by a series of deep cracks or crevasses. The cracks result from the fact that ice under pressure deforms and moves plastically, whereas the upper layers remain rigid and are therefore under tension and eventually shear. Transverse crevasses often occur where the slope of the glacier increases; these may be intersected by longitudinal crevasses, creating ice pinnacles, or seracs, between them. A large crevasse, known as a bergschrund, may also form near the head of a glacier in the firn zone where the ice pulls away from the mountain wall.

Glacial abrasion and plucking

Als a glacier moves it erodes the underlying rocks, mainly by abrasion and by plucking. Abrasion involves rock debris frozen into the sole of the glacier acting on the rocks underneath like coarse sandpaper. Plucking happens when the ice freezes onto rock projections, particularly in well-jointed rocks, and tears the blocks out as it moves.
Considerable evidence exists of glacial erosion having taken place during the Pleistocene Ice Age, when glaciers and ice sheets extended over much of northern Europe and North America. At that time, ice moved out of the high mountains and spread over the surrounding lowlands. It modified the shape of the land and left various distinctive landforms that can be seen today, long after the ice has receded.
In most glaciated valleys it is possible to find rock surfaces that have been grooved and scratched. These striations were caused by angular rock fragments frozen into the sole of a moving glacier. The marks give some indication of the direction of ice movement. Where a more resistant rock projects out of a valley floor it may have been moulded by the passage of ice so that it has a gentle slope on the upstream side (which is planed smooth by the glacier) and a steep ragged slope on the lee side (a result of ice plucking). Seen from a distance these rocks were thought to resemble the sheepskin wigs fashionable in early nineteenth-century Europe, and so were named roches moutonnées.

Corries

An aerial view of a glaciated highland reveals large amphitheater-like hollows arranged around the mountain peaks. These great hollows are called corries (cirques in France, and cwms in Wales) and are the point at which glaciers were first formed during an ice age, or where present-day glaciers start in areas such as the Alps or the Rockies. The Aletsch glacier, for example, begins on the south-eastern slopes of the Jungfrau in Switzerland and is fed by several tributary glaciers, each emerging from a corrie. Frost-shattering of the exposed walls of the corries results in their gradual enlargement; this process is accelerated by subglacial disintegration of the rock, which occurs when water reaches the rock floor through the bergschrund crevasse at the head of the glacier.
During an ice age most corries were probably filled to overflowing with glacier ice, and their walls and floors were subject to vigorous abrasion. When the ice melted, a corrie often became the site of a mountain lake, or tarn, with morainic material forming a dam at the outflow lip.
Corries are bordered by several precipitous knife-edged ridges known as arêtes. These develop when the walls of two adjoining corries meet after glacial erosion has taken place from both sides. When the arêtes themselves are worn back, the central mass may remain as an isolated peak where the heads of several corries meet. The Matterhorn in the Swiss Alps is a peak that was produced in this way.

Glacial valleys

When a glacier passes through a pre-existing river valley it actively erodes the valley to a characteristic U-shaped profile. The original interlocking spurs through which the former river wound are worn back and truncated. In this way the valley is straightened, widened and deepened, and its tributary valleys are left high above the main trough as hanging valleys. The streams in them often plunge down the valley side as spectacular waterfalls, as in the Lauterbrunnen valley between Interlaken and the Jungfrau in the Swiss Alps.
Where several tributary glaciers join the head of a major valley, the increased gouging by the extra ice flow results in the formation of a trough end, or steep step in the U-shaped trough. The floor of a glaciated valley is often eroded very unevenly and elongated depressions may become the sites of long, narrow, ribbon lakes. Some of the deeper ribbon lakes are dammed by morainic material at their outlets, as in lakes Como and Maggiore in northern Italy.
In mountainous regions glacial troughs may extend down to the coast where they form long steep-sided inlets, or fjords. The classic fjords of Norway, Scotland and British Columbia all result from intense glaciation, followed by a eustatic rise in sea level at the end of the Ice Age that flooded the lower ends of the U-shaped valleys.

***A melting glacier** in the Himalayas, near Sonamarg in Kashmir, lies in the U-shaped valley it has created. The typical rate of flow of a glacier is about 3 ft. a day and movement is due to slope and the plastic distortion of ice. Rock fragments that the glacier has plucked from the slopes of the valley can be seen littering the valley floor. They form the lateral moraine of the glacier and, at an earlier stage of glaciation, probably cut in and abraded the valley floor and sides as they were dragged along by the moving ice.*

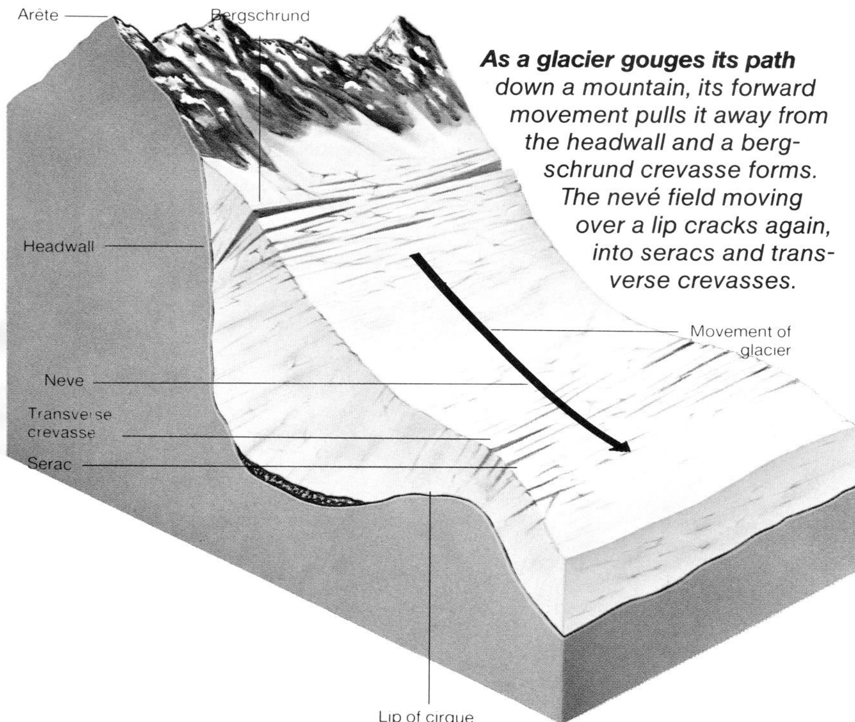
Arête
Bergschrund
Headwall
Movement of glacier
Neve
Transverse crevasse
Serac
Lip of cirque

***As a glacier gouges its path** down a mountain, its forward movement pulls it away from the headwall and a bergschrund crevasse forms. The nevé field moving over a lip cracks again, into seracs and transverse crevasses.*

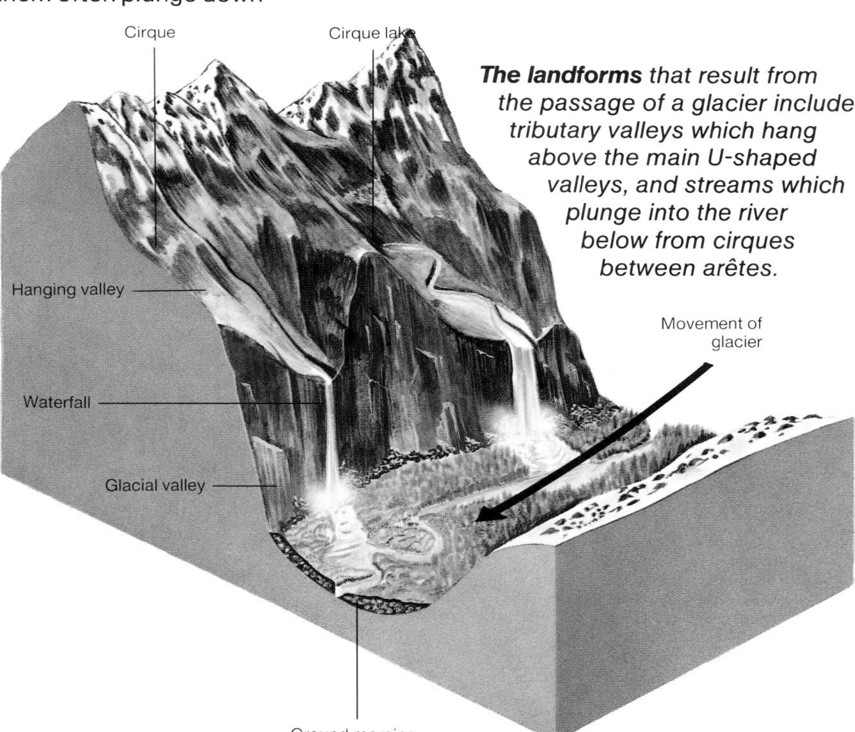
Cirque
Cirque lake
Hanging valley
Movement of glacier
Waterfall
Glacial valley
Ground moraine

***The landforms** that result from the passage of a glacier include tributary valleys which hang above the main U-shaped valleys, and streams which plunge into the river below from cirques between arêtes.*

Post-glaciation

When a glacier emerges from its U-shaped valley, it spreads out over the surrounding lowlands as an ice sheet. Much of the surface material eroded by the glacier and carried by it to the plains is deposited when the ice starts to melt. The pre-glacial lowland landscape is therefore often markedly modified by various deposits left behind by the ice.

Surface deposits

When the great northern continental ice sheets reached their most southerly extent, they deposited a ridge-like terminal moraine. Similar ridges, known as recessional moraines, have resulted from pauses during the retreat of the ice sheet. The North German Plain is traversed by a series of parallel crescent-shaped (arcuate) moraines which were formed as the Scandinavian ice sheet advanced across the Baltic. The main line of low morainic hills can be traced southwards through the Jutland peninsula, and then eastwards through northern Germany and Poland. The Baltic Heights represent the most clearly defined moraine, reaching more than 1,180 ft. in height near Gdańsk. Similarly, a series of moraines cross the plains to the south of the Great Lakes, marking the various halts in the recession of the North American ice sheet.
Behind each terminal moraine, groups of low, hummocky hills known as drumlins often occur. These hills were formed as the ice sheet retreated and most are elliptical mounds of sand and clay, sometimes up to 200 ft. high, and elongated in the direction of the ice movement. How they were formed is not known but it is thought that they were caused by the overriding of previous ground moraine. Drumlins are arranged in an echelon, or belt, and form a distinctive drumlin topography. A drumlin field may contain as many as 10,000 drumlins – one of the largest known is on the north-western plains of Canada. Around Strangford Lough in County Down, Ireland, drumlins form islands within the lough itself.
Winding across glaciated lowlands, there are often long, sinuous gravel ridges called eskers. They are thought to be deposits formed by subglacial streams at the mouths of the tunnels through which they flowed beneath the ice. Eskers are common in Finland and Sweden, where they run across the country between lakes and marshes.
When a delta is formed by meltwater seeping out from beneath the ice front, it develops into a mound of bedded sand and gravel known as a kame. In some areas kames are separated by water-filled depressions called kettle holes, formed originally as sediment piled up around patches of stranded ice which melted after the recession of the ice sheet.
The chief product of glacial deposition is boulder clay, which is the ground moraine of an ice sheet. It comprises an unstratified mixture of sand and clay particles of various sizes and origins. For example, deposits in south-eastern England contain both chalk boulders of local derivation and igneous rock from Scandinavia. Blocks of rock that are transported far from their parent outcrop are known as erratics. The largest blocks are commonly seen resting on the boulder clay surface or even perched on exposed rock platforms.
The unsorted ground moraine behind the ice front contrasts strongly with the stratified drift of the outwash plain beyond. Meltwater streams deposit sand and gravel on the outwash plains, to form the undulating topography so typical of the Luneburg Heath of Germany or the Geest of the Netherlands.

Erratics, *blocks of till or bedrock, have been known to be carried for more than 500 mi. by a glacier. They are prominent on glacial landscapes and their position often suggest the direction of the ice movement.*

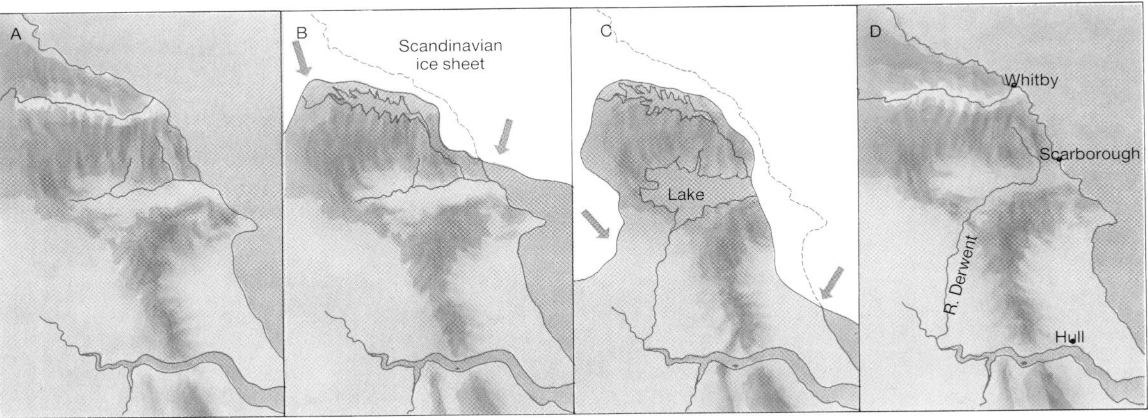
A
B
Scandinavian ice sheet
C
Lake
D
Whitby
Scarborough
R. Derwent
Hull

During the Ice Age, *encroaching ice sometimes diverted a river. In north-eastern England, originally (A) the land was drained by rivers flowing eastwards. The advancing Scandinavian ice cap dammed a river (B), creating a lake which overspilled southwards. Further ice movement created another lake (C), forcing the river further south. (D) The River Derwent still follows the diverted course.*

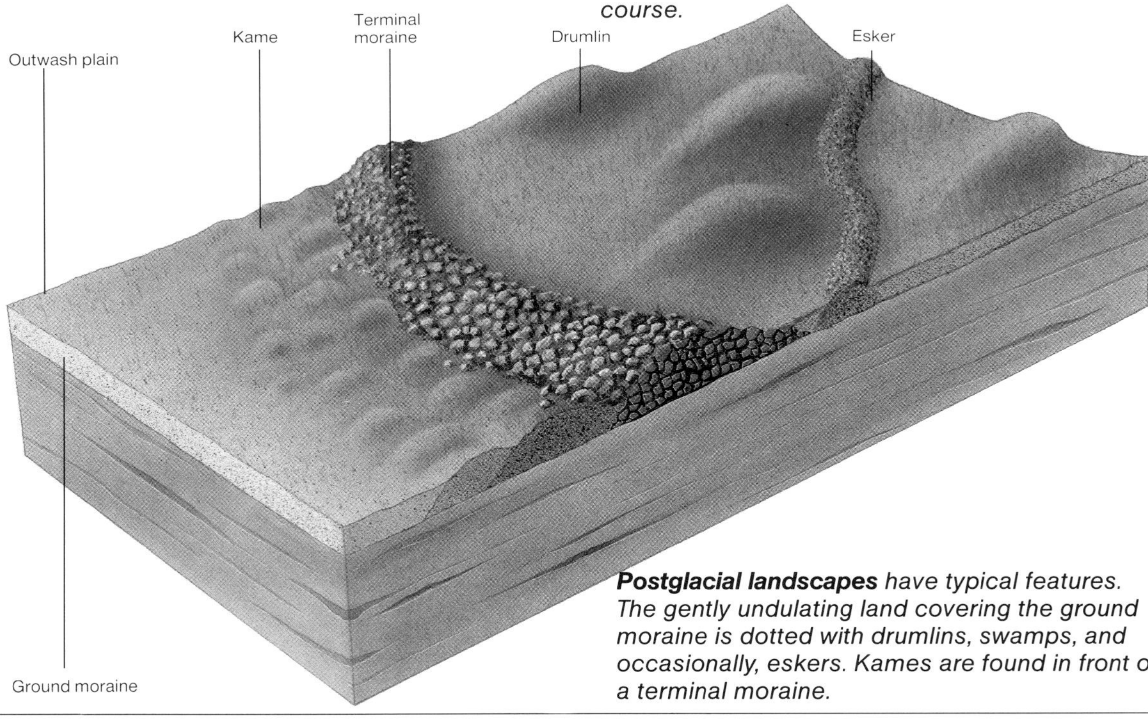
Outwash plain
Kame
Terminal moraine
Drumlin
Esker
Ground moraine

Postglacial landscapes *have typical features. The gently undulating land covering the ground moraine is dotted with drumlins, swamps, and occasionally, eskers. Kames are found in front of a terminal moraine.*

Proglacial lakes

At the end of the Ice Age, many rivers were dammed by ice and their waters formed proglacial lakes. During the retreat of the North American ice sheet, for example, a large lake – Lake Agassiz – was dammed up between the ice to the north and the continental watershed to the south. The remnants of this damming can be seen in Lake Winnipeg, which is now surrounded by lacustrine silts that were deposited on the floor of the ancient Lake Agassiz.
Beach strand lines are sometimes visible, which indicate the water levels at various stages in the draining of a lake. This probably occurred when the proglacial lake overflowed through spillways at successively lower levels, as the ice began to recede. In north-eastern England there is striking evidence of the diversion of drainage by ice. Preglacial rivers flowed eastwards into the North Sea, but were blocked by the Scandinavian ice front as it approached the base of the North York Moors. The Eskdale valley in the moors was turned into a lake which overflowed southwards via a spillway into Lake Pickering, about 16 mi. distant. This lake in turn drained through the Kirkham Abbey Gorge about 6 mi. away, and today the River Derwent still follows the southward route to the River Humber, having been diverted by ice from its pre-glacial eastwards course.

Periglacial features

Beyond the ice sheet margin lies the periglacial zone of permafrost, in which repeated freeze and thaw cycles result in the breaking of the soil surface and the differential sorting of loose fragments of rock, so that a pattern is produced. On flat surfaces, polygonal arrangements of stones occur, whereas on sloping surfaces, parallel lines are formed. Another periglacial landform is the pingo, or ice mound, created when a body of water freezes below ground and produces an ice core which raises the surface into a low hillock.

THE NATURE OF OUR UNIVERSE

The Solar System

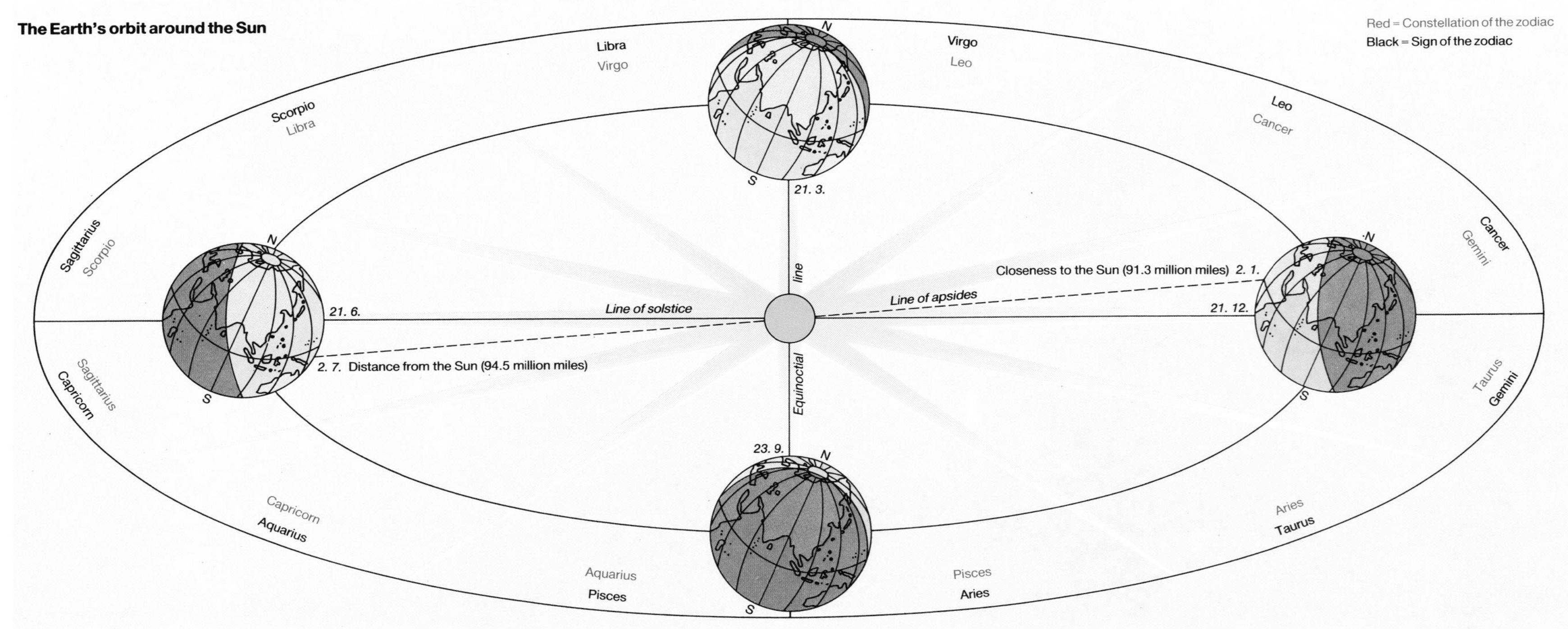
The Earth's orbit around the Sun
Red = Constellation of the zodiac
Black = Sign of the zodiac
Libra
Virgo
Virgo
Leo
Scorpio
Libra
Leo
Cancer
Sagittarius
Scorpio
Cancer
Gemini
Sagittarius
Capricorn
Taurus
Gemini
Capricorn
Aquarius
Aries
Taurus
Aquarius
Pisces
Pisces
Aries
21. 3.
21. 6.
21. 12.
23. 9.
2. 1.
2. 7. Distance from the Sun (94.5 million miles)
Closeness to the Sun (91.3 million miles)
Line of solstice
Line of apsides
Equinoctial line
N
S

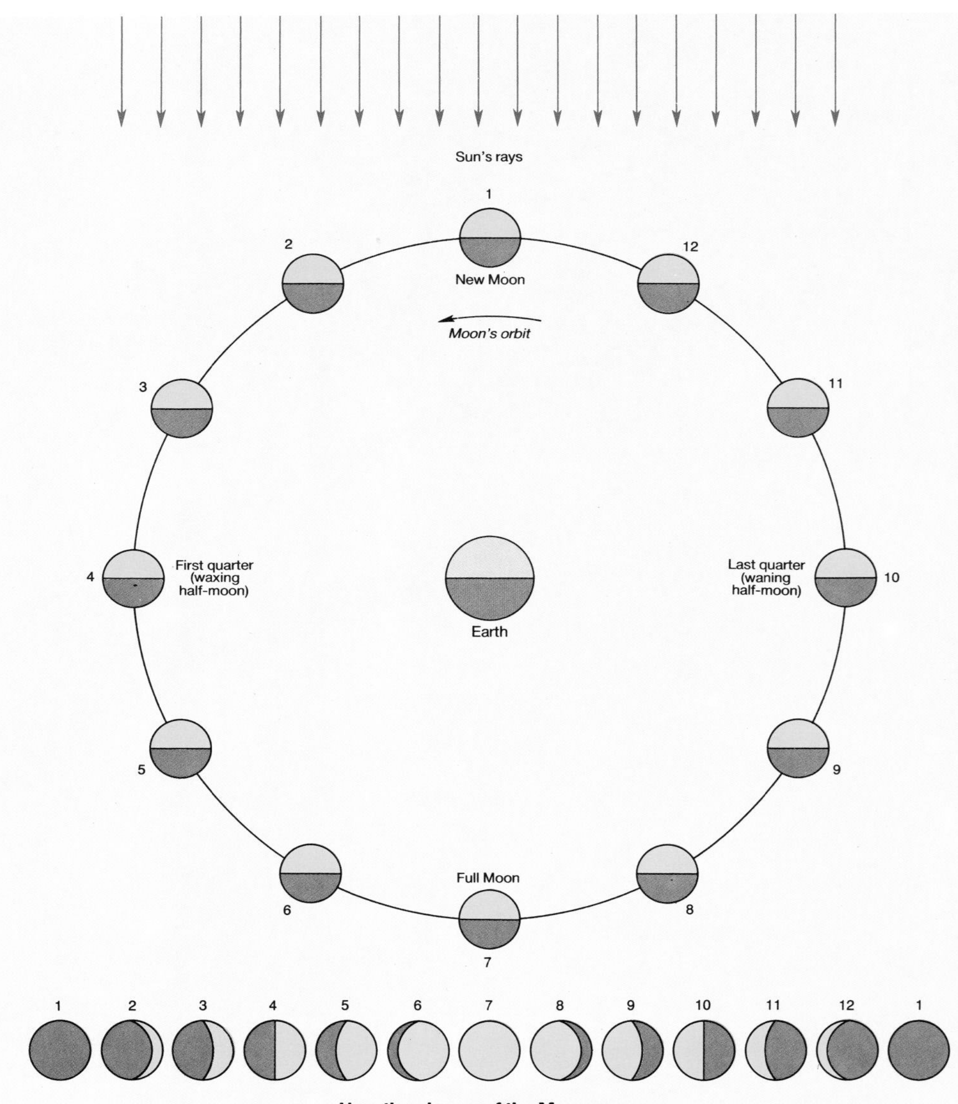
Sun's rays
New Moon
Moon's orbit
First quarter (waxing half-moon)
Last quarter (waning half-moon)
Earth
Full Moon
1
2
3
4
5
6
7
8
9
10
11
12

How the phases of the Moon occur

The origin of the seasons can be explained by the fact that on its orbit the Earth's axis is not vertical, but is tilted 23 ½ degrees from the vertical. Therefore, on June 21, our Earth's northern hemisphere is inclined slightly toward the Sun and is struck more directly by the rays of the Sun than the southern hemisphere. On December 21, the Earth's northern hemisphere is inclined slightly away from the Sun and is struck more obliquely by the Sun's rays than the southern hemisphere. It is then that winter begins in the northern hemisphere and summer in the southern hemisphere. Viewed from the perspective of the Earth rotating around the Sun, in the course of one year the Sun seems to pass before the backdrop of the twelve constellations of the zodiac.

For one revolution relative to the Sun, the Moon needs 29,531 days (the synodical month). During this time, the separate phases of the Moon also change. The waxing Moon can be observed more in the evening hours, the waning Moon after midnight and in the morning hours. At new Moon our satellite is invisible. The full Moon can be observed throughout the night. For one revolution relative to the stars, the Moon needs 27,322 days (the sidereal month). The average distance of the Moon from the Earth is 238,869 miles. This is only $1/389^{th}$ of the distance of the Sun from the Earth (92,960,000 miles). Therefore, in a scaled diagram of the Earth's orbit and of the Moon around our Sun, the orbit of the Moon is always bent concavely opposite the Sun.

***The movement of the Earth around the Sun** at an angle to the orbit of the Earth is shown above. The middle illustration shows the movement of the Moon around our Earth; the numbered row shows the phases of the Moon in its different positions. The bottom illustration shows the monthly orbit of the Moon.*

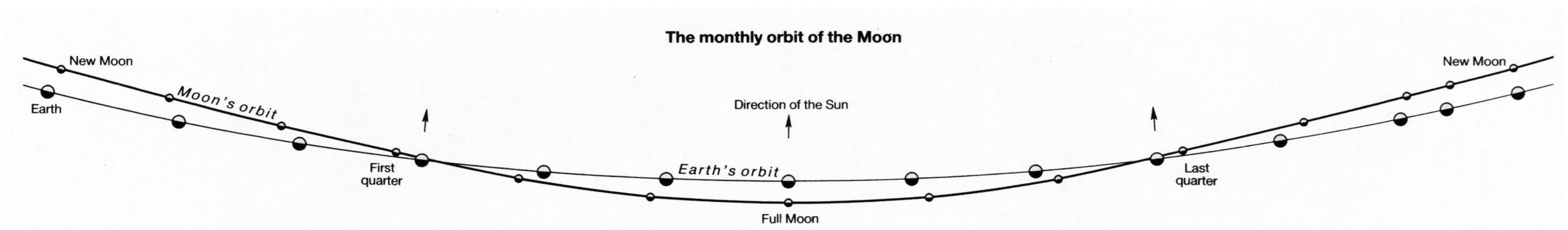
The monthly orbit of the Moon
New Moon
Earth
Moon's orbit
First quarter
Direction of the Sun
Earth's orbit
Full Moon
Last quarter
New Moon

The Planetary System

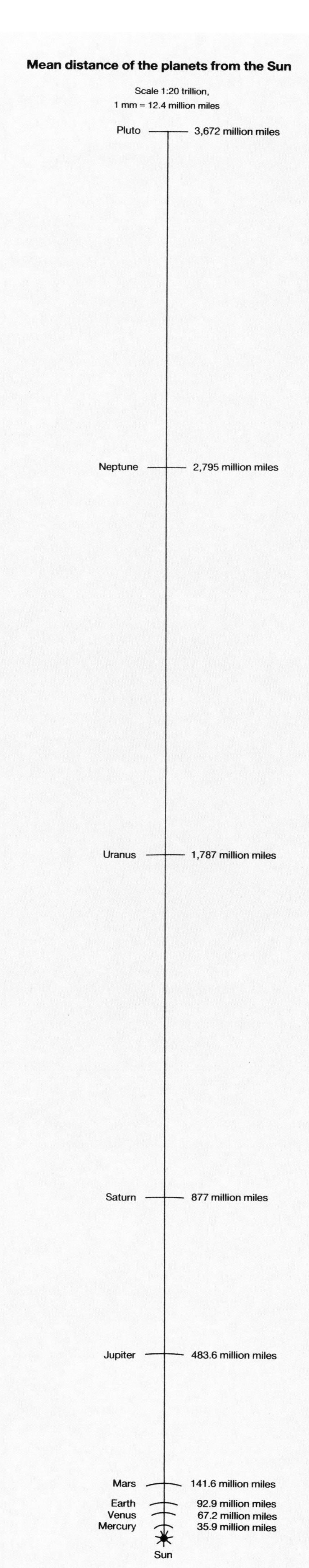
Mean distance of the planets from the Sun
Scale 1:20 trillion,
1 mm = 12.4 million miles
Pluto
3,672 million miles
Neptune
2,795 million miles
Uranus
1,787 million miles
Saturn
877 million miles
Jupiter
483.6 million miles
Mars
141.6 million miles
Earth
92.9 million miles
Venus
67.2 million miles
Mercury
35.9 million miles
Sun

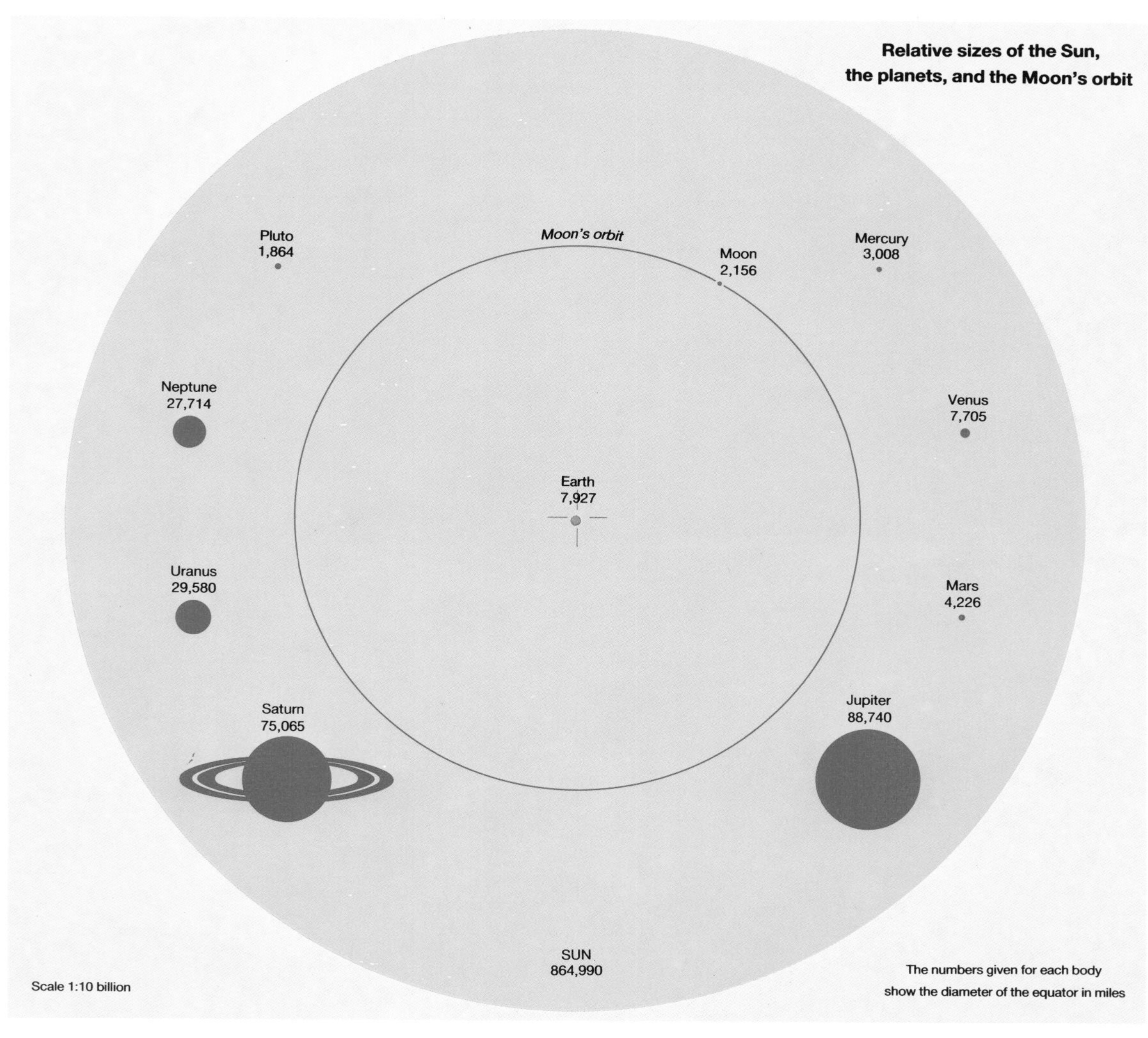
Relative sizes of the Sun, the planets, and the Moon's orbit
Pluto
1,864
Moon's orbit
Moon
2,156
Mercury
3,008
Neptune
27,714
Venus
7,705
Earth
7,927
Uranus
29,580
Mars
4,226
Saturn
75,065
Jupiter
88,740
SUN
864,990
Scale 1:10 billion
The numbers given for each body show the diameter of the equator in miles

The distances of the planets from our Sun vary so much that they can only be depicted accurately when drawn to scale. Using a scale of 1:20 trillion, the Sun, with a total diameter of 865,000,000 miles, shrinks to only 0.07 mm. The Earth then measures only 0.00068 mm and the largest planet, Jupiter, 0.007 mm. Nevertheless, one small part of Pluto's highly eccentric orbit still projects into Neptune's orbit. Pluto is the smallest of the nine large planets, measuring approximately 1,800 miles in diameter or 0.0002 mm on the aforementioned scale. The zone of the minor planets (asteroids and planetoids) lies between the planets Mars and Jupiter. Although almost 3,000 of these have been accurately identified, it is estimated that altogether they number 50,000, or more. Some of these minor planets rotate outside the main zone, deep within our planetary system, while others are in the outer regions.

Solar eclipses occur each time there is a new Moon, when the Moon is exactly incident with the line connecting the Sun to the Earth. Total darkness is observed within the umbra that the Moon casts on the Earth, while a partial solar eclipse is visible within the penumbra. A ring-shaped solar eclipse occurs when the Moon on its elliptical orbit is so far from the Earth that the point of the umbra no longer reaches the Earth's surface. As a result, the disc of the Moon appears to be slightly smaller than that of the Sun. An eclipse of the Moon takes place when the Moon enters into the shadow of the Earth. If the Moon passes completely through the Earth's umbra, then a total eclipse of the Moon occurs. A partial eclipse occurs when the Moon enters just slightly into the umbra. The Earth's penumbra has no significant effect.

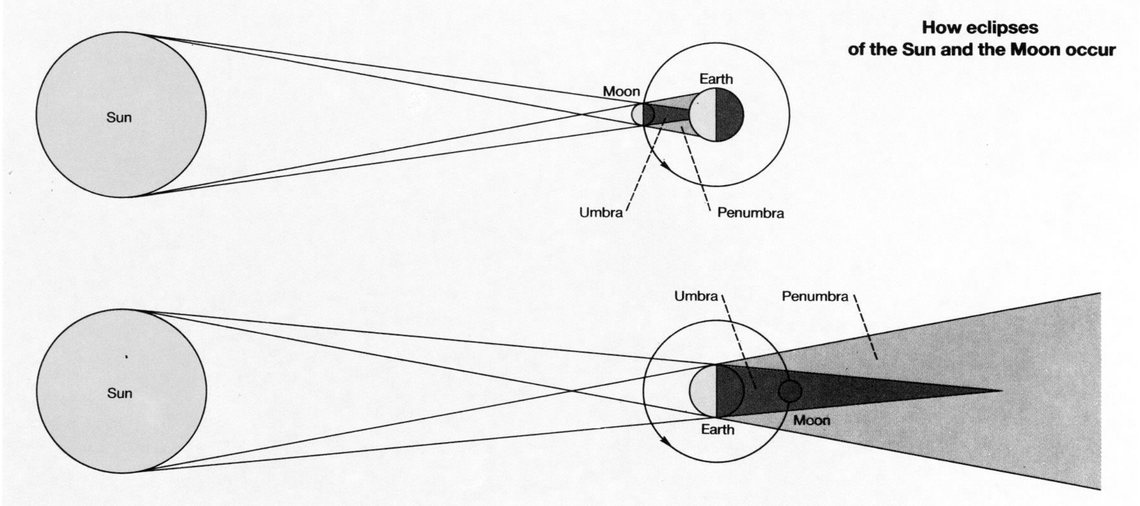
How eclipses of the Sun and the Moon occur
Sun
Moon
Earth
Umbra
Penumbra
Sun
Umbra
Penumbra
Earth
Moon

The Sun

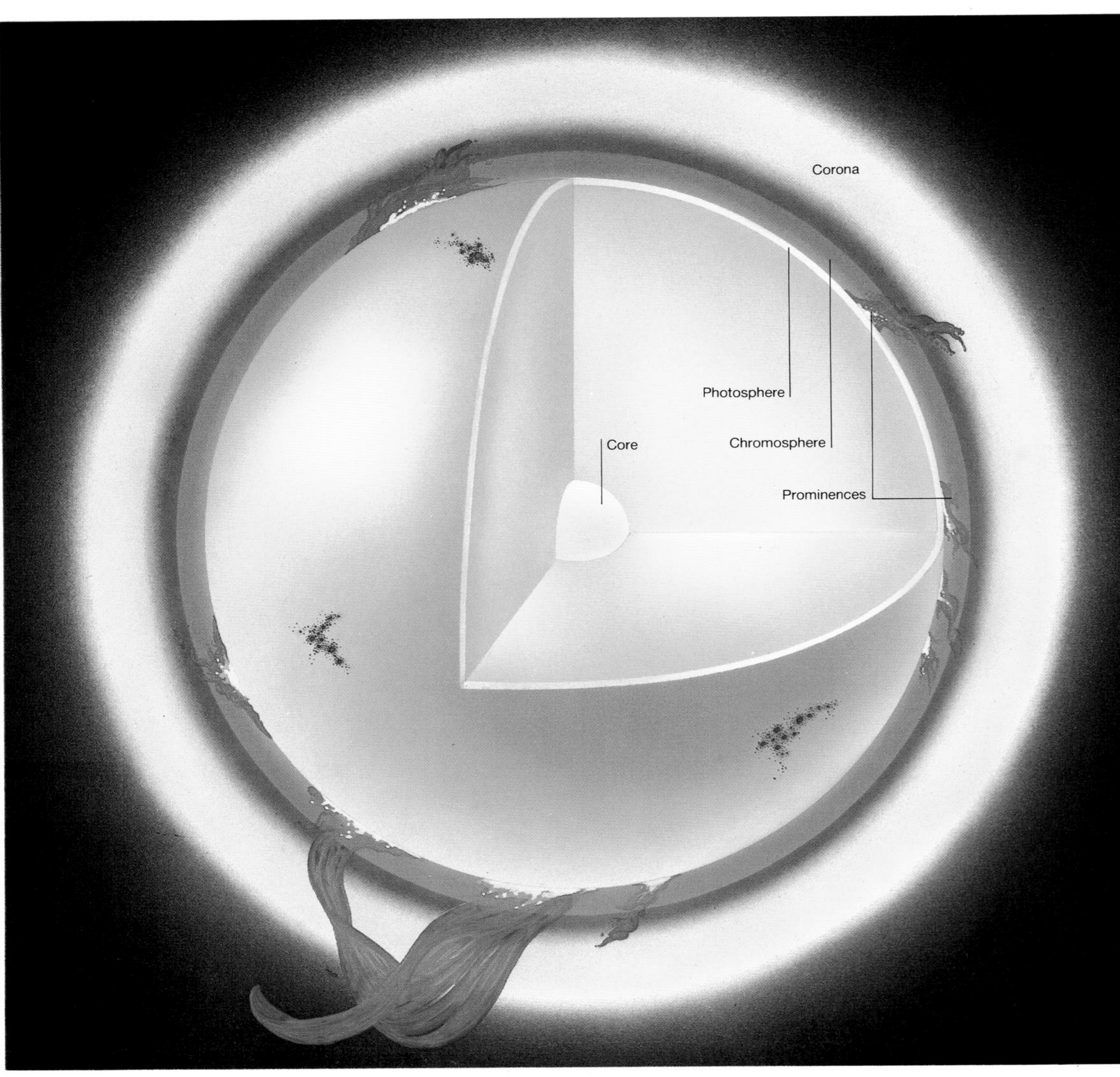
Corona
Photosphere
Core
Chromosphere
Prominences

The central star of our planet, the Sun, is an ordinary star, like other fixed stars we call suns. It is a globe of gases, made up of 75% hydrogen, 23% helium, and 2% heavy elements. We can directly observe and measure its surface, which has a temperature of about 9,900 °F. The interior of the Sun, however, can only be deduced mathematically, using the theory of stellar evolution. At high temperatures in the core of the Sun (up to a maximum of 27,000,000 °F), four hydrogen nuclei (protons) at a time fuse to form one helium nucleus consisting of two protons and two neutrons. During this nuclear merging (nuclear fusion), mass is transformed into energy. This process is the source of our Sun's energy, which can maintain its present state of equilibrium for a total of approximately 8 billion years. Now the Sun is just 5 billion years old. About 3 billion years from now the Sun will expand to a giant red star, and still later collapse to a compact white dwarf star.

The Sun requires 25 days at its equator to rotate on its axis. In medium and high latitudes, rotation time increases by a few days. Sunspots appear in the Sun's equatorial zone. The number of sunspots fluctuates, approximately on an eleven-year cycle. They generally occur more or less in large groups and last anywhere from a few days to several months. Their temperature is approximately 7,200 °F. Sunspots are caused by strong magnetic fields that penetrate and cool a region of the Sun's surface. Consequently, they appear to be darker than the rest of the surface. Near the sunspots' brighter spots, Sun flares, with a temperature of approximately 11,700 °F appear. As a result, a large number of sunspots does not alter the total intensity of our Sun.

The layer of the Sun visible with the naked eye or using a normal telescope is called the photosphere. The chromosphere that envelopes it can only be investigated using specialized instruments. Research reveals occasional powerful eruptions, especially in areas near active groups of sunspots. These are bright eruptions of light, accompanied by streams of particles, and they generally last only a few minutes or hours. Prominences are another form of ejection of matter, or movement above the Sun's surface. Caused by the structure of regional magnetic fields, these gas clouds often circulate in large swirls over the Sun's surface. Occasionally, too, eruptive prominences occur that flare up at great speed like flaming streamers into the Sun's upper atmosphere. During total solar eclipses a halo of light, the Sun's corona, can be discerned surrounding the disc of the Sun covered by the new Moon. This corona can be studied with specialized instruments. The temperature in the corona ranges from 1.8 to 5.4 million °F. It is from the corona that the Sun's X-rays radiate, a process that has been investigated in recent years using satellites. The Sun is also a powerful source of radio waves. Outbursts of radio waves often occur in conjunction with eruptions of the Sun.

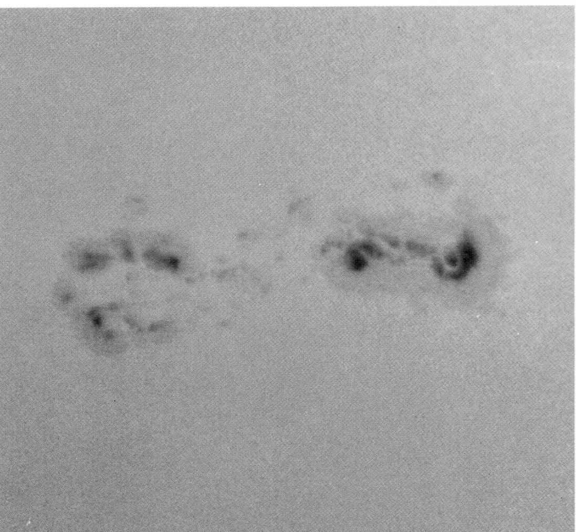

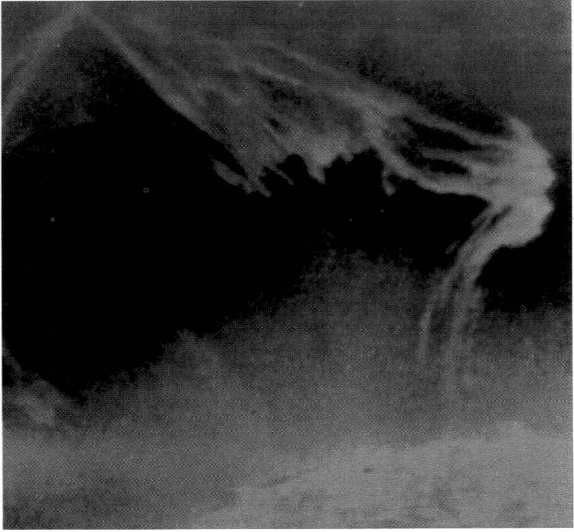

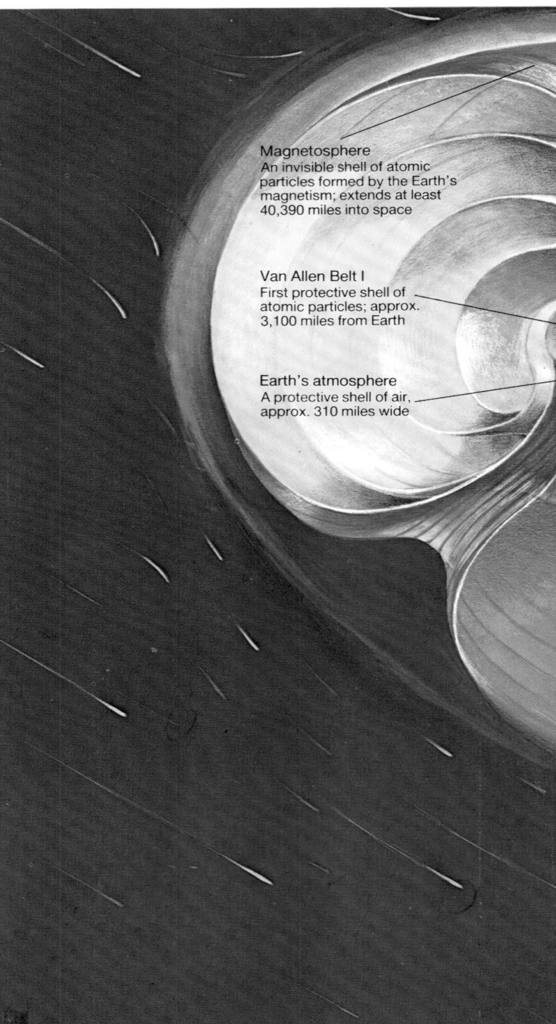
Magnetosphere
An invisible shell of atomic particles formed by the Earth's magnetism; extends at least 40,390 miles into space
Van Allen Belt I
First protective shell of atomic particles; approx. 3,100 miles from Earth
Earth's atmosphere
A protective shell of air, approx. 310 miles wide

The Sun interacts strongly with our Earth. The seasons are, of course, the most obvious manifestation of this connection. Sun activities such as sunspots, flares, and eruptions also give rise to certain events on Earth. For example, the Sun's X-ray radiation creates, in the Earth's atmosphere at a height of between 50 and 155 miles, several electrically charged layers – the ionosphere. The Sun is also able to reflect, and thereby transmit, short waves. Disturbances on our Sun cause disturbances in radio communications.

Our Earth is surrounded by a magnetic field extending far out into space. This magnetosphere is slightly indented on the side facing the Sun. On the side facing away from the Sun, a long tail of the Earth's magnetic field appears. The Van Allen Belts are found within the magnetosphere at heights of about 3,100 and 12,400 miles. Electrically charged particles that fly quickly back and forth between the magnetic north and south poles are trapped in them. Essentially, these particles were originally ejected from the Sun. The Sun radiates more than electromagnetic waves such as light or radio waves. It also emits the Sun's "wind," a fine stream of other electrically charged particles. These particles are generally so low in energy that they cannot penetrate the magnetosphere on the side facing the Sun. Instead, they are deflected sideways and gradually infiltrate the magnetosphere from the side facing away from the Sun. Higher energy particles ejected during eruptions of the Sun cause such enormous confusion in this system that the particles in the Van Allen Belts are "shaken out" and penetrate into the Earth's atmosphere, especially in the polar regions. There, they collide with the atoms of the atmosphere, causing them to glow. These polar lights (the northern and southern lights) appear most often at a height of between 56 and 80 miles. The lowest polar lights have been detected at 43 miles, the highest at about 620 miles.

Magnetic storms, disturbances of the Earth's magnetic field, occur simultaneously with these other phenomena. Additional connections between the Sun's activity and our Earth – especially concerning the influence of the Sun on our weather – are still hotly debated. To date it has not been possible to determine whether or not dry summers or cold winters can be predicted on the basis of the Sun's prevailing activity. It is clear that the Sun's activity is only one among numerous factors that determine the behavior of the weather.

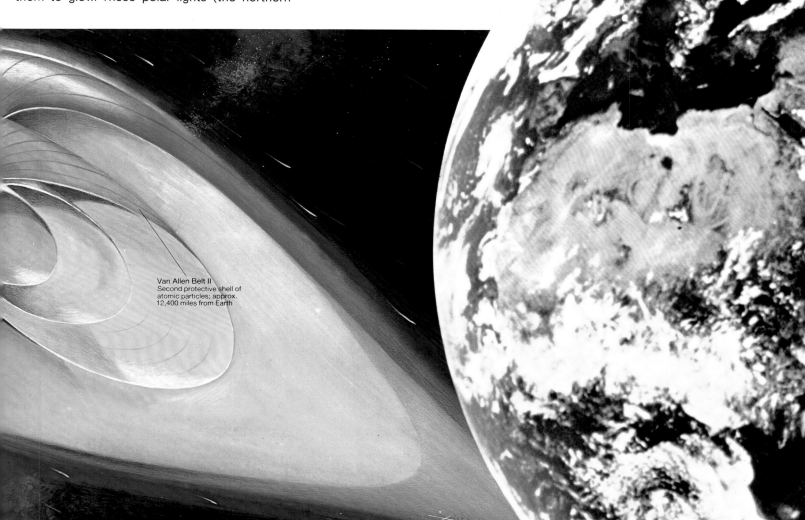

Van Allen Belt II
Second protective shell of atomic particles; approx. 12,400 miles from Earth

***The temperature of our Sun** increases markedly from the outside to the inside (see above left). Two photos on this page show a group of sunspots and a prominence (see below left). In the middle illustration, the Earth is shown surrounded by its magnetosphere, as well as the Van Allen Belts. Note the asymmetrical shape of the magnetosphere, with its geomagnetic tail on the side facing away from the Sun. On the right is a photo of the Earth, taken about halfway between the Earth and the Moon by Apollo II. In the middle is Africa, above right Arabia, and at the very top (under clouds) Europe. The yellow and reddish tones of the desert regions are particularly striking.*

The Milky Way

Stars are not randomly distributed, but often form groups or stellar clusters. The best-known are the two clusters in Taurus that can be seen with the naked eye: Hyades (the Rain Star) and Pleiades (the Seven Sisters). These are 130 to 410 light-years away from us and belong to the group of "open clusters." Open clusters generally consist of a few dozen to a few thousand stars clustered together so loosely that we can resolve them into individual stars through a telescope. They are relatively young collections of stars, up to a maximum of one billion years old. The globular clusters are considerably older. They contain 100,000 to 1 million stars and are arranged symmetrically, with stars strongly concentrated in the center. The brightest globular cluster, Omega Centauri, is found in the southern sky and is 17,000 light-years away. Globular clusters are approximately 12 billion years old.

The space between the stars is not completely empty. This is where the so-called interstellar matter (gas and dust) is found. As a rule, it contains only about 1 atom per cubic centimeter. In the bright and dark nebulae, visible through telescopes, the matter can, however, be concentrated to 100 to 10,000 atoms per cubic centimeter. Interstellar matter is the raw material for the creation of new stars. Phenomena like the Orion nebula of the Orion, the Rosette nebula of Monoceros, and the Omega nebula of Sagittarius are typical examples of such stellar birthplaces in the universe. So far, though, the causes of the compressions that lead to the creation of stars have not been completely explored. They may be gravitational waves of our Milky Way, or shock waves that emanate from supernova explosions and compress nearby interstellar dust. Our solar system may have originated in this way barely 5 billion years ago. Stars that can be seen today in the bright nebulae are especially young phenomena, between 10,000 and 1 million years old. A few infrared nebulae and infrared stars can even be regarded as stars in the process of creation. Such phenomena are often surrounded by thick cocoons of dust that may give rise to planetary systems. After a star compresses, the temperature inside increases causing atomic nuclear reactions, in particular the transformation of hydrogen into helium. An automatic balance is achieved: gravity, which might let the star collapse further, is counterbalanced by gas pressure operating from the inside out. If the generation of energy in the core of the star decreases as the hydrogen content decreases, gas pressure weakens simultaneously. The automatic balance is disturbed and gravity causes the core of the star to shrink. As a result the temperature rises. At present our Sun has a core temperature of 27 million °F. In about 3 billion years this will increase to between 90 and 180 million °F. At the same time, a new "ignition temperature" will be reached at which helium can transform into carbon. Then, even more energy will be produced in the core of the star. The gas pressure inside the star will cause it to expand into a red giant star. As the core temperature gradually rises, heavier and heavier elements, even iron, are formed. Then the star reaches the limits of its ability to maintain a stable balance and it collapses upon itself leaving a dense white dwarf star in its place. Stars with more than about 1.4 sun masses collapse into neutron stars. These measure approximately 12.5 miles in diameter and have a density of 10 trillion g/cm^3. Moreover, stars over 3 to 5 sun masses collapse into so-called black holes which can no longer be seen from the outside. The prevailing density inside these phenomena is up to 100,000 trillion g/cm^3.

The collapse of a star into a neutron star or a black hole is accompanied by a supernova explosion whereby the star's outer layers may be discarded. In this way, heavier elements formed earlier inside the star reach interstellar space. Stars that develop later from this substance will already contain a certain percentage of heavy elements.

All the stars visible to the naked eye (and most of those visible using a telescope) belong to our Milky Way or Galaxy. This is a flat spiral, 100,000 light-years in diameter. If we could view our Milky Way from the outside, it would look like a enormous Catherine wheel from above and like a flat disc from the side. The Sun and the planets lie about 30,000 light-years from the center of the Milky Way which, viewed from our perspective, is situated in the direction of Sagittarius. If we observe the sky from the Earth at the equatorial level of our Milky Way, we see a particularly large number of stars, and we can identify the band of the Milky Way with its myriad of stars. We can also see that the Milky Way (Galaxy) is clearly asymmetrical. It is brightest toward Sagittarius and weakest in the opposite direction (constellations Taurus and Auriga). With the aid of radio astronomy, it has been possible to detect a few spiral arms in the vicinity of the Sun; in particular the Perseus, Orion, and Sagittarius arms. Using techniques of radio astronomy, it has also been possible to explore the core of our Milky Way, which lies behind dark, light-absorbing clouds of interstellar

Two examples of stellar clusters: *the Pleiades or Seven Sisters in Taurus and the globular Omega Centauri cluster. The Rosette nebula of the constellation Monoceros and the Omega nebula of Sagittarius are examples of stellar birthplaces. We can clearly see bright young stars in them.*

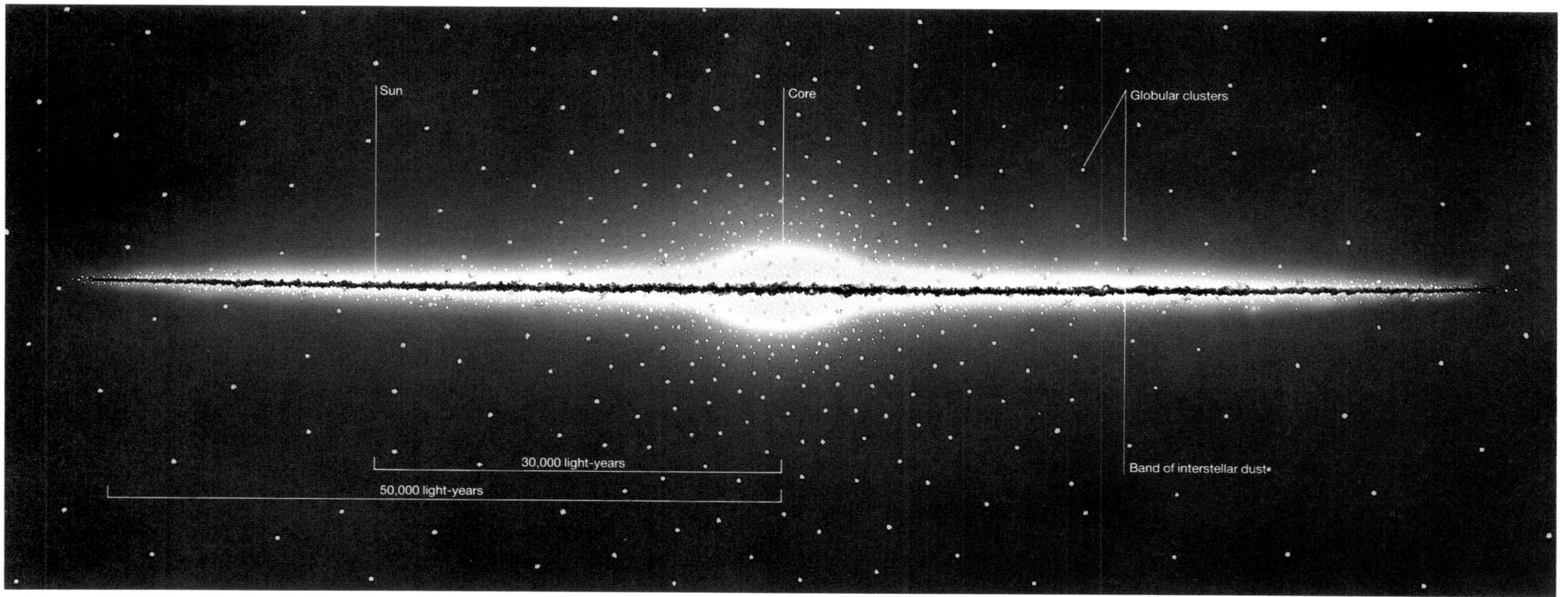
Sun
Core
Globular clusters
30,000 light-years
50,000 light-years
Band of interstellar dust

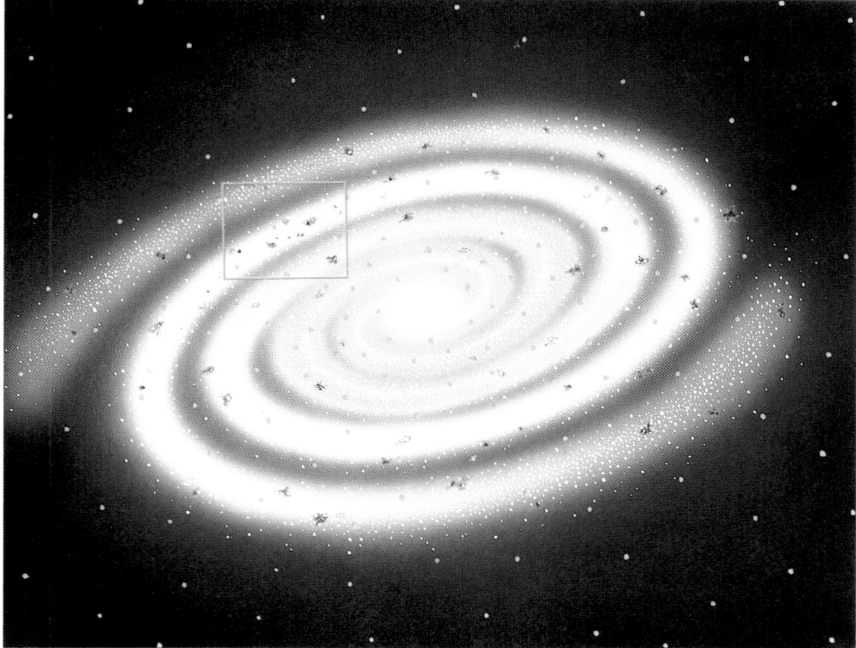

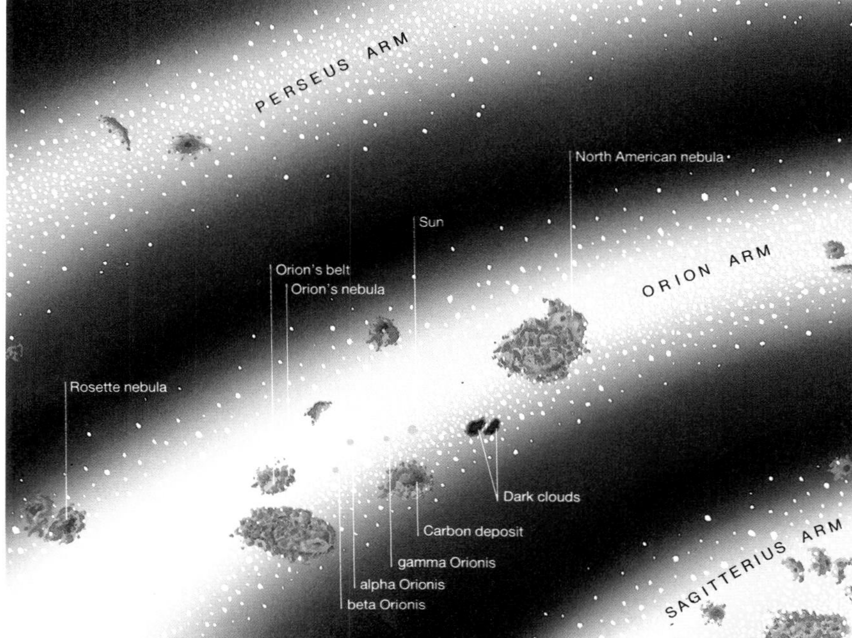
PERSEUS ARM
North American nebula
Sun
ORION ARM
Orion's belt
Orion's nebula
Rosette nebula
Dark clouds
Carbon deposit
gamma Orionis
alpha Orionis
beta Orionis
SAGITTERIUS ARM

matter. We know that a large mass is concentrated there in a relatively confined space. The exact structure of the Milky Way's core has, however, not yet been deciphered. Some researchers suspect it would reveal an enormous black hole.
Surrounding our own flat Milky Way is the galactic halo, where mainly globular stellar clusters are found. This halo extends far beyond the narrow confines of the Milky Way. If we include it, our galactic system might be 200,000 to 300,000 light-years in diameter. All stars rotate around the center of the galactic system. At an orbiting speed of about 155 miles per second, our Sun requires approximately 220 million years for this journey.

Two diagrams on this page show the ***structure of our Milky Way*** *system from above and from the side. Much of this information could only be obtained with the aid of radio astronomy and infrared astronomy. Our photo shows part of the Milky Way, with numerous stars, dark clouds, and bright nebulae. To the left is Sagittarius, to the right Cassiopeia.*

Galaxies

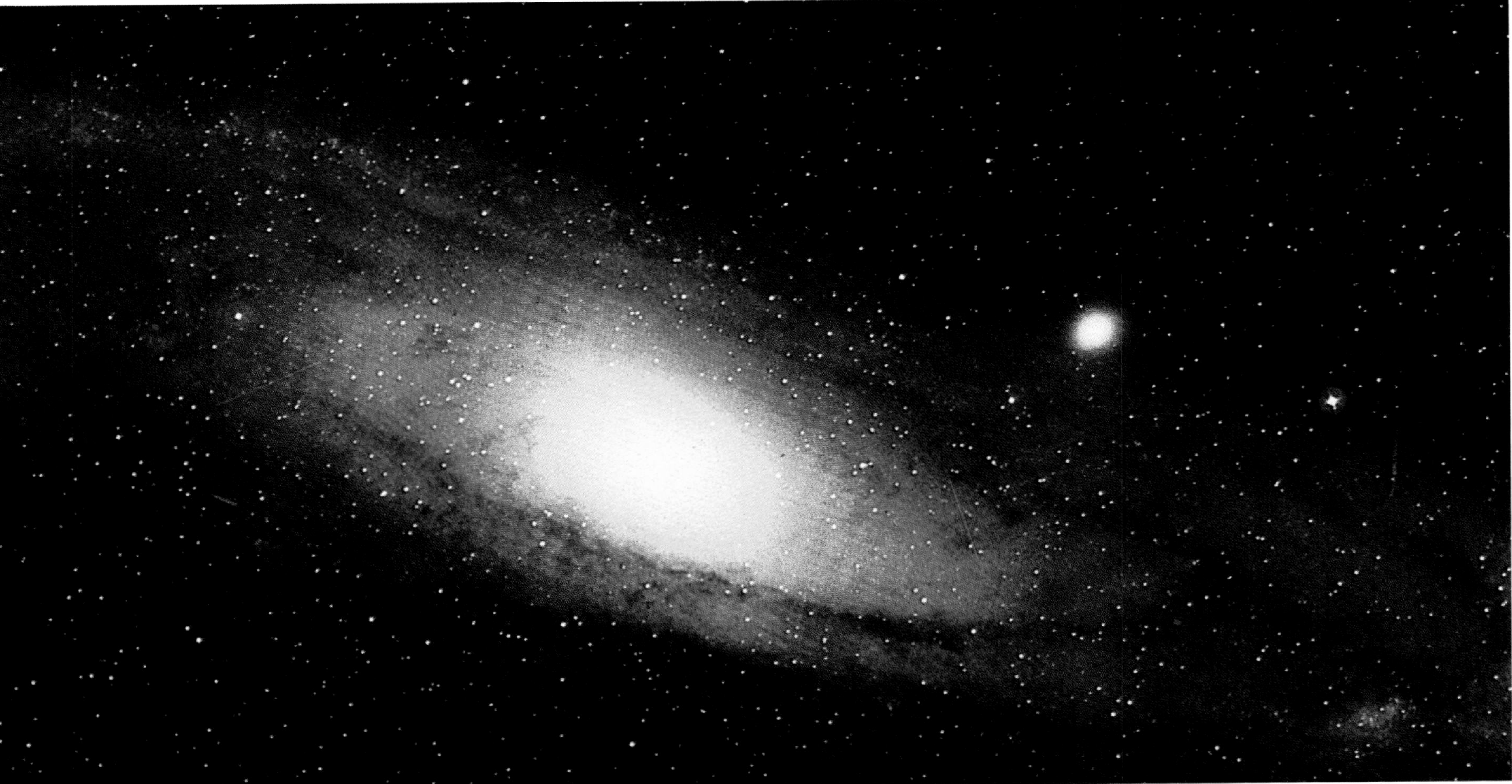

A large number of "nebulae" that can be observed in the sky using telescopes are not true nebulae (like the Orion and Rosette nebulae for example), but independent stellar systems – galaxies – lying outside our own Milky Way. The best-known galaxy is the Andromeda Spiral. On a clear night it is visible to the naked eye as a pale nebula patch in the constellation Andromeda. However, it has only been possible to resolve its individual stars with the aid of the largest telescopes and long-exposure photographs. The Andromeda Spiral is 2.3 million light-years away and similar in size to our own Milky Way: it is 150,000 light-years in diameter and consists of 200 billion sun masses. It contains practically the same phenomena as our system, e. g., open clusters, globular clusters, variable stars, bright nebulae, etc. The stars in the Andromeda Spiral rotate at speeds similar to stars in our galactic system. Andromeda is a spiral nebula. There are also elliptical and irregular nebulae. Our own Milky Way contains two irregular nebulae as satellites, the Large and Small Magellanic Clouds. These are visible virtually only from our Earth's southern hemisphere and are about 165,000 light-years away.

Galaxies often occur in clusters containing anywhere from several dozen to 10,000 galaxies. Our Milky Way belongs to the so-called local nebula group that includes 20 to 30 galaxies. There is also a large number of tiny dwarf galaxies, only a few of which are 1,000 light-years in diameter. Most of these are elliptical or irregular.

Another famous galaxy cluster – the Virgo cluster – lies in the direction of the constellation Virgo. There are several indications that many galaxy clusters recombine to form super clusters. Some galaxies emit very strong radio waves that indicate intense activity in the cores of the galaxies (radio galaxies). In addition, the quasars – dot-shaped phenomena that look like stars – and Seyfert galaxies are most likely extremely active galaxies. Quasars occur only at great distances from Earth. The most remote ordinary galaxies that can be captured on long-exposure photos are about 3 to 4 billion light-years away. The quasars are up to 15 billion light-years away.

As a result of extensive expansion of the universe, the galaxies are receding from us. The further away they are, the faster they recede. Nevertheless, we only seem to be in the center of this movement of flight. One would have the same impression from every other position in the universe. The universe has no center. Its curved, expanding space probably originated somewhat more that 15 billion years ago from a small, immensely dense mass of material in a process called the "big bang." This assumption has been supported by the discovery of so-called cosmic background radiation falling on us equally from all parts of the universe. Most of this radiation is found at a wavelength of approximately 4 mm, but some is also present in the centimeter range of radio wave radiation. It is believed to be residual radiation from the big bang. The quarks and the first elementary particles must have come into being just fractions of a second after the big bang. Shortly afterward, hydrogen atoms formed in addition to the atomic nuclei of deuterium and helium. There were no elements heavier than helium during this early phase of the universe. These elements formed inside the stars much later. We cannot construct a model of our universe as a finite, boundless, and curved space. At best, we can get some idea of the structure of the universe by picturing the surface of a sphere. Just as a sphere is curved two-dimensionally and turns back on itself, so is three-dimensional space – that is, the universe is curved and turns back on itself. There are no solid boundaries. The question of whether the expansion of the universe as observed today will continue for all time still remains to be answered. It is, to a large extent, dependent on the mass present in the universe. If this mass is large enough, then the expansion can later be transformed into a contraction. The universe would once more be a dense mass of material and then, perhaps, recreate itself with a big bang. To date however, the material found in the universe represents little more than one hundreth of the mass required to cause the expansion to eventually change to a contraction. It is possible though, that there is as yet unknown matter – in the form of black holes, for example. Some researchers suspect that neutrinos – particles that exist in huge numbers in the universe as a result of atomic nuclear reactions – are not completely massless, as was earlier thought, but rather possess a tiny mass. This may strongly contribute to the overall mass of the universe.

The Andromeda nebula *is a typical example of a close, spiral galaxy. It is 2.3 million light-years away, is 150,000 light-years in diameter, and contains approximately 200 billion sun masses. Our own Milky Way is quite similar in structure. Nearby, as satellites of the Andromeda nebula, we see two elliptical nebulae 2,300 and 7,800 light-years in diameter, respectively.*

Index

The index contains all the names that appear on the metropolitan area, country, regional, and world maps. It is ordered alphabetically. The umlauts ä, ö, and ü have been treated as the letters a, o, and u, and the ligatures æ and œ as ae and oe, while the German ß is alphabetized as ss.

The first number after the name entry indicates the page or double page where the name being looked up is to be found. The letters and numbers after the page reference designate the grid in which the name is located or those grids through which the name extends.

The names that have been abbreviated on the maps are listed unabbreviated in the index. Only with U.S. place names have the official abbreviations been inserted according to common U.S. practice, e.g. Washington, D.C. The alphabetic sequence includes the prefix, e.g. Fort, Saint.

In order to facilitate the search for names consisting of more than one element, these have consistently been given double entries in the index, e.g. Isle of Wight, and Wight, Isle of —; Le Havre, and Havre, Le-.

To a large extent official second forms, language variants, renamings, and other secondary designations are recorded in the index, followed by the names as they appear on the map, e.g. Persia = Iran, Venice = Venézia, Moscow = Moskva.

To differentiate identical names of features located in various countries, motor vehicle nationality letters for the respective countries have been added in brackets following these names. A complete listing of abbreviations is shown below.

A	Austria
AFG	Afghanistan
AL	Albania
AND	Andorra
AUS	Australia
B	Belgium
BD	Bangladesh
BDS	Barbados
BG	Bulgaria
BH	Belize
BOL	Bolivia
BR	Brazil
BRN	Bahrain
BRU	Brunei
BS	Bahamas
BUR	Burma
C	Cuba
CDN	Canada
CH	Switzerland
CI	Ivory Coast
CL	Sri Lanka
CO	Colombia
CR	Costa Rica
CS	Czech Rep. and Slovakia
CY	Cyprus
D	Germany
DK	Denmark
DOM	Dominican Republic
DY	Benin
DZ	Algeria
E	Spain
EAK	Kenya
EAT	Tanzania
EAU	Uganda
EC	Ecuador
ES	El Salvador
ET	Egypt
ETH	Ethiopia and Eritrea
F	France
FJI	Fiji
FL	Liechtenstein
GB	United Kingdom
GCA	Guatemala
GH	Ghana
GR	Greece
GUY	Guyana
H	Hungary
HK	Hong Kong
HV	Burkina Faso
I	Italy
IL	Israel
IND	India
IR	Iran
IRL	Ireland
IRQ	Iraq
IS	Iceland
J	Japan
JA	Jamaica
JOR	Jordan
K	Cambodia
KWT	Kuwait
L	Luxembourg
LAO	Laos
LAR	Libya
LB	Liberia
LS	Lesotho
M	Malta
MA	Morocco
MAL	Malaysia
MC	Monaco
MEX	Mexico
MS	Mauritius
MW	Malawi
N	Norway
NA	Netherlands Antilles
NIC	Nicaragua
NL	Netherlands
NZ	New Zealand
P	Portugal
PA	Panama
PAK	Pakistan
PE	Peru
PL	Poland
PNG	Papua New Guinea
PY	Paraguay
Q	Qatar
RA	Argentina
RB	Botswana
RC	Taiwan
RCA	Central African Republic
RCB	Congo
RCH	Chile
RFC	Cameroon
RH	Haiti
RI	Indonesia
RIM	Mauritania
RL	Lebanon
RM	Madagascar
RMM	Mali
RN	Niger
RO	Romania
ROK	South Korea
ROU	Uruguay
RP	Philippines
RSM	San Marino
RU	Burundi
RWA	Rwanda
S	Sweden
SD	Swaziland
SF	Finland
SGP	Singapore
SME	Suriname
SN	Senegal
SP	Somalia
SU	former Soviet Union
SUDAN	Sudan
SY	Seychelles
SYR	Syria
T	Thailand
TG	Togo
TJ	China
TN	Tunisia
TR	Turkey
TT	Trinidad and Tobago
USA	United States
V	Vatican City
VN	Vietnam
WAG	Gambia
WAL	Sierra Leone
WAN	Nigeria
WD	Dominica
WG	Grenada
WL	Saint Lucia
WS	Samoa
WV	Saint Vincent
Y	Yemen
YU	former Yugoslavia
YV	Venezuela
Z	Zambia
ZA	South Africa
ZRE	Zaire
ZW	Zimbabwe

A

Aachen 118 C 3
Aalen 118 E 4
Aalesund = Ålesund 116-117 AB 6
A'alī an-Nīl 164-165 KL 7
Aam, Daïa el — = Dayaṭ 'al-'Ām 166-167 B 6
Äänekoski 116-117 L 6
Aansluit 174-175 E 4
Aar, De — 172 D 8
Aarau 118 D 5
Aare 118 D 5
Aarón Castellanos 106-107 F 5
Aavasaksa 116-117 KL 4

Aba [WAN] 164-165 F 7
Aba [ZRE] 172 F 1
Abā' al-Qūr, Wādī — 136-137 J 7
Abā ar Rūs, Sabkhat — 134-135 GH 6
Abacaxis, Rio — 98-99 J 7
Abaco Island, Great — 64-65 L 6
Abad 142-143 E 3
Ābādān 134-135 F 4
Ābādān, Jazīreh — 136-137 N 7-8
Ābādeh 134-135 G 4
Abadia, El — = Al Ab'adīyah 166-167 G 1
Abadiânia 102-103 H 2
Ab'adīyah, Al- 166-167 G 1
Abadlah 164-165 D 2
Abaeté 102-103 K 3
Abaeté, Rio — 102-103 K 3
Abaetetuba 98-99 O 5
Abagnar Qi = Xilin Hot 142-143 M 3
Abaí 111 E 3
Abaiang 208 H 2
Abaira 100-101 D 7
Abaji 168-169 G 3
Abajo Peak 74-75 J 4
Abakaliki 168-169 H 4
Abakan 132-133 R 7
Abalak 168-169 G 2
Aban 132-133 S 6
Abancay 92-93 E 7
Abanga 168-169 H 5
Abangarit, In — 164-165 F 5
Abapó 104-105 E 6
Abār Ḥaymūr 173 CD 6
Abā Sa'ūd 134-135 EF 7
Abashiri 142-143 RS 3
Abashiriwan 144-145 d 1-2
Abasiri = Abashiri 142-143 RS 3
Abasolo 86-87 K 7
Abau 148-149 N 9
Abaung Bûm 141 F 2
Abay 164-165 M 6
Abaya 164-165 M 7
Abaza 132-133 R 7
Aba Zangzu Zizhizhou 142-143 J 5
Abbabis 174-175 B 2
Abbāsīyah, Al-Qāhirah-al- 170 II b 1
Abbat Quṣūr 166-167 L 1-2
Abbeville 120-121 HJ 3
Abbeville, AL 78-79 G 5
Abbeville, GA 80-81 E 4-5
Abbeville, LA 78-79 CD 5
Abbeville, SC 80-81 E 3
Abbey Peak 158-159 HJ 2
Abbotsford 66-67 BC 1
Abbotsford, WI 70-71 E 3
Abbott 106-107 H 5
Abbottabad = Ebuṭṭābād 134-135 L 4
'Abdah 166-167 B 3
'Abd al-'Azīz, Jabal — 136-137 HJ 4
'Abd al Kūrī 134-135 G 8
'Abd Allāh, Khawr — 136-137 N 8
Ābdānān 136-137 M 6
Ābdānān, Rūdkhāneh-ye — 136-137 M 6
'Abd an-Nabī, Bi'r — 136-137 B 8
Abdulino 132-133 J 7
'Abdullah = Minā' 'Abd Allāh 136-137 N 8
Abe, Kelay — 164-165 N 6
Āb-e Baḥreh 136-137 N 7
Abéché 164-165 J 6
Abécher = Abéché 164-165 J 6
Abed-Larache, El — = Al-'Ādib al-'Arsh 164-165 F 3
Abee 60 L 2
Ābe Estāda 134-135 K 4
Abeg, In- 164-165 D 4
Ab-e-Istādah = Ābe Estāda 134-135 K 4
Abejorral 94-95 D 5
Abelardo Luz 102-103 F 7
Abeløya 116-117 n 5
Abemama 208 H 2
Abengourou 164-165 D 7
Åbenrå 116-117 C 10
Abeokuta 164-165 E 7
Āb-e Raḥmat 136-137 N 6
Abercorn = Mbala 172 F 3
Abercrombie, ND 68-69 H 2
Abercrombie Arena 85 III b 2
Aberdare Mountains 172 G 1-2
Aberdare National Park 171 D 3
Aberdeen, ID 66-67 G 4
Aberdeen, MD 72-73 H 5
Aberdeen, MS 78-79 E 4
Aberdeen, NC 80-81 G 3
Aberdeen, SD 64-65 G 2
Aberdeen, WA 64-65 B 2
Aberdeen [AUS] 160 K 4
Aberdeen [CDN] 61 EF 4
Aberdeen [GB] 119 EF 3
Aberdeen [HK] 155 I a 2
Aberdeen [ZA] 172 D 8
Aberdeen Island = Ap Li Chau 155 I a 2
Aberdeen Lake 56-57 R 5
Aberfeldy [ZA] 174-175 H 5
Abergavenny 119 E 6
Aberjona River 84 I b 2
Abernathy, TX 76-77 D 6
Abert, Lake — 66-67 CD 4
Abertawe = Swansea 119 DE 6
Aberystwyth 119 D 5
Āb-e Shūr 136-137 N 7
Abez' 132-133 L 4
Āb-e Zimkān 136-137 LM 5
Abhā 134-135 E 7
Abhānpur 138-139 H 7
Ābhār 136-137 N 4
Abiaḍ, Râss el — = Rā's al-Abyaḍ 164-165 FG 1
Abibe, Serranía de — 94-95 C 3-4
'Abīd, Umm al- 164-165 H 3
'Abīd, Wād al- 166-167 CD 3-4
Ābīd al-'Arsh, Al- 164-165 F 3
Abidjan 164-165 CD 7
Abiekwasputs 174-175 D 4
Abi Hill 168-169 G 3
Abijan = Abidjan 164-165 CD 7
Abilene, KS 68-69 H 6
Abilene, TX 64-65 FG 5
Āb i Naft 136-137 L 6
Abingdon, IL 70-71 E 5
Abingdon, VA 80-81 EF 2
Abingdon = Isla Pinta 92-93 A 4
Abinsk 126-127 J 4
Abiod, Oued el — = Wādī al-Abyaḍ 166-167 JK 2
Abiod-Sidi-Cheikh, El- = Al-Abyaḍ 166-167 G 3
Abiquiu, NM 76-77 A 4
Abiseo, Río — 96-97 C 5
Ābi Sirwān 136-137 L 5
Abisko 116-117 H 3
Abitibi, Lake — 56-57 UV 8
Abitibi River 56-57 U 7-8
Abkhaz Autonomous Soviet Socialist Republic 126-127 K 5
Ābnāi Sandīp 141 B 4
Abnūb 173 B 4
Abo 144-145 H 1
Åbo = Turku 116-117 K 7
Abohar 138-139 E 2
Aboisso 164-165 D 7
Abolição 106-107 L 3
Abomé = Abomey 164-165 E 7
Abomey 164-165 E 7
Abong-Abong, Gunung — 152-153 B 3
Abong-Mbang 164-165 G 8
Abonnema 168-169 G 4
Aborigen, pik — 132-133 cd 5
Aboso 168-169 E 4
Abou-Deïa 164-165 H 6
Abou ed Douhour = Abū aẓ-Ẓuhūr 136-137 G 6
Abov'an 126-127 M 6
'Abr, Al — 134-135 F 7
Abra, Laguna del — 108-109 H 3
Abraham Bay 58-59 p 6
Abraham Lincoln National Historical Park 70-71 H 7
Abra la Cruz Chica 104-105 D 7
Abrantes [BR] 100-101 E 7
Abrantes [P] 120-121 CD 9
Abra Pampa 111 CD 2
Abrego 94-95 E 3
Abreojos, Punta — 64-65 CD 6
'Abrī 164-165 L 4
Abridge 129 II c 1
Abrigos, Bahía de los — = Bay of Harbours 108-109 K 9
Abrolhos, Arquipélago dos — 92-93 M 8
Abruka 124-125 D 4
Abruzzi 122-123 EF 4
Absaroka Range 64-65 D 2-E 3
Absarokee, MT 68-69 B 3
Abu 134-135 L 6
Abū 'Ajāj = Jalib Shahab 136-137 M 7
Abū al-Ḥaṣīb 136-137 MN 7
Abū al-Maṭāmīr 173 AB 2
Abū an-Numrus 170 II b 2
Abū 'Aweiqîla = Abū 'Uwayjīlah 173 CD 2
Abū aẓ-Ẓuhūr 136-137 G 5
Abū Bakr 166-167 F 2
Abū Ballāṣ 164-165 K 4
Abū Ḍahr, Jabal — 173 D 6
Abū Dārah, Rā's — 173 E 6
Abū Darbah 173 C 3
Abū Dhi'āb, Jabal — 173 D 5
Abū Durba = Abū Darbah 173 C 3
Abufari 98-99 G 7
Abū Ġashwah, Rā's — 134-135 G 8
Abū Gharādiq, Bi'r — 136-137 C 7
Abū Ḥādd, Wādī — 173 D 7
Abū Ḥaggāg = Rā's al-Ḥikmah 136-137 BC 7
Abū Ḥajār, Khawr — 136-137 L 7
Abū Ḥamad 164-165 L 5
Abū Ḥamāmīd, Jabal — 173 D 5
Abū Ḥammān 136-137 J 5
Abū Ḥarbah, Jabal — 173 C 4
Abū Ḥashū'ifah, Khalīj — 136-137 BC 7
Abu Hills 138-139 D 5
Abū Ḥjâr, Hôr — = Khawr Abū Ḥajār 136-137 L 7
Abū Hujar 164-165 LM 6
Abuja 164-165 F 7
Abū Jābirah 164-165 K 6
Abū Jahaf, Wādī — 136-137 K 6
Abū Jamal 164-165 M 5
Abū Jamal, Jabal — 164-165 M 6
Abū Jir 136-137 K 6
Abū Jir, Wādī — 136-137 K 6
Abū Jurdī, Jabal — 173 D 6
Abū Kabīr 173 B 2
Abū Kamāl 134-135 DE 4
Abū Khârga, Wâdi — = Wādī Abū Kharjah 173 BC 3
Abū Kharjah, Wādī — 173 BC 3
Abukuma-sammyaku 144-145 N 4
Abū Marīs, Sha'īb — 136-137 L 7
Abū Marw, Wādī — 173 C 6
Abū Minqār, Bi'r — 164-165 K 3
Abū Muḥarrik, Ghurd — 164-165 KL 3
Abu Mukharik Dunes = Gurd Abu Muḥarik 164-165 KL 3
Abunã 92-93 FG 6
Abunã, Rio — 92-93 F 7
Abunai 98-99 E 5
Abū Qīr 173 B 2
Abū Qīr, Khalīj — 173 B 2
Abū Qurqāṣ 173 B 4
Abū Rijmayn, Jabal — 136-137 H 5
Abu Road 138-139 D 5
Abū Sa'fah, Bi'r — 173 D 6
Abū Ṣaida = Abū Ṣaydat Ṣaghīrah 136-137 L 6
Abū Salmān 136-137 M 7
Abū Ṣaydat Ṣaghīrah 136-137 L 6
Abū Shalīl 136-137 K 5
Abū Shīl = Abū Shalīl 136-137 K 5
Abu Simbil = Abu Sunbul 164-165 L 4
Abū Sinbil = Abu Sunbul 164-165 L 4
Abū Şkhair = Abū Şuhayr 136-137 L 7
Abū Şuhayr 136-137 L 7
Abu Sunbul 164-165 L 4
Abū Tīj 164-165 L 3
Abū 'Uwayjīlah 173 CD 2
Abū Zabad 164-165 K 6
Abū Ẓabī 134-135 G 6
Abū Zanīmah 164-165 L 3
Abū Zawal, Bi'r — 173 C 4
Abū Zenîma = Abū Zanīmah 164-165 L 3
Abyad 164-165 K 6
Abyaḍ, Ar-Rā's al- 164-165 A 4
Abyaḍ, Rā's al- 164-165 FG 1
Abyaḍ, Rimāl al- 166-167 L 4
Abyaḍ, Wādī al- 166-167 JK 2
Abyad Sīdī Shaykh, Al- 166-167 G 3
Abyār, Al- 166-167 A 5
Abyei 164-165 K 7
Abymes, les — 64-65 O 8
Abyssinia = Ethiopia 164-165 MN 7

Acacías 94-95 E 6
Acacias, Bogotá-Las — 91 III b 4
Acacio 104-105 C 5-6
Academy of Sciences 83 I ab 2
Acadia National Park 72-73 M 2
Acadie 56-57 XY 8
Acahay 102-103 D 6
Açaí 102-103 G 5
Açailândia 98-99 P 7
Acajutiba 100-101 EF 6
Acajutla 64-65 HJ 9
Acala, TX 76-77 B 7
Acámbaro 64-65 FG 7
Acampamento Grande 98-99 M 4
Acandí 92-93 D 3
Acapetagua 86-87 O 10
Acaponeta 64-65 EF 7
Acapulco de Juárez 64-65 FG 8
Acapuzal, Serra do — 98-99 MN 5
Acará 92-93 K 5
Acará, Cachoeira — 98-99 J 7
Acaraí, Serra — 92-93 H 4
Acaraú 92-93 LM 5
Acaraú, Rio — 100-101 D 2
Acaray, Río — 102-103 E 6
Acaré 100-101 E 4
Acari [BR, place] 100-101 F 4
Acari [BR, river] 110 I a 1
Acari, Río — 98-99 J 7-8
Acari, Rio de Janeiro- 110 I a 1
Acarigua 92-93 F 3
Acassuso, San Isidro- 110 III b 1
Acay, Nevado de — 104-105 C 9
Acayucan 86-87 N 8-9
Acchila 104-105 D 7
Accomac, VA 80-81 J 2
Accra 164-165 DE 7
Acebal 106-107 G 4
Aceguá 106-107 K 3
Aceh = 1 ◁ 148-149 C 6
Acequias, Las — 106-107 EF 4
Acevedo 106-107 G 4
Achacachi 92-93 F 8
Achaguas 92-93 F 3
Achaïa 122-123 JK 6
Achalciche 126-127 L 6
Achalkalaki 126-127 L 6
Achalpur 138-139 F 7
Achampet 140 D 2
Achao 111 B 6
'Achâra, El — = Al-'Asharah 136-137 J 5
Acharnaí 122-123 K 6
Achau 113 I b 2
Achegour 164-165 G 5
Achelôos 122-123 J 6
Acheng 142-143 O 2
Achères 129 I b 2
Acherusia = Zonguldak 134-135 C 2
Achigan 70-71 HJ 2
Achigh Köl 142-143 F 4
Achill 119 A 5
Achill Head 119 A 4-5
Achira, Punta — 106-107 A 6
Achiras 106-107 E 4
Achōhampêta = Achampet 140 D 2
Achsu 126-127 O 6
Achter Roggeveld = Agter Roggeveld 174-175 D 6
Achtuba 126-127 N 3
Achtubinsk 126-127 MN 2
Achty 126-127 N 6
Achtyrka 126-127 G 1
Achur = Ātshūr 166-167 AB 6
Achur'an 126-127 L 6
Achuta, Rio — 104-105 B 5
Acı göl 136-137 CD 4
Acilia, Roma- 113 II a 2
Ačinsk 132-133 R 6
Acıpayam 136-137 C 4
Acireale 122-123 F 7
Ačisu 126-127 N 5
Ackerly, TX 76-77 D 6
Ackerman, MS 78-79 E 4
Ackley, IA 70-71 D 4
Acklins Island 64-65 LM 7
Aclimação, São Paulo- 110 II b 2
Acme, LA 78-79 D 5
Acme, NM 76-77 B 6
Acme, TX 76-77 E 5
Acobambo 96-97 D 8
Acomayo 92-93 E 7
Aconcagua 111 C 4
Aconcagua, Río — 106-107 B 4
Aconquija, Sierra del — 104-105 CD 10
Acopiara 92-93 M 6
Açores 50-51 H 4
Açoriana 106-107 L 4
Acornhoek 174-175 J 3
Acotipa 98-99 L 4
Acoyapa 88-89 D 9
Àcqui Terme 122-123 C 3
Acraman, Lake — 158-159 FG 6
Acre 92-93 EF 6
Acre = 'Akkô 136-137 F 6
Acre, Rio — 92-93 F 6
Acre Homes, Houston-, TX 85 III b 1
Acri 122-123 G 6
Actatlán de Osorio 86-87 LM 8
Acton 72-73 F 3
Acton, CA 74-75 D 5
Acton, MT 68-69 B 3
Acton, London- 129 II a 1
Acton Vale 72-73 K 2
Actopan 86-87 KL 6-7
Açu 100-101 F 3
Açu, Lagoa — 100-101 B 2
Açu, Rio — 100-101 F 3
Açú, Rio — = Rio Piranhas 92-93 M 6
Açúcar, Pão de — 110 I c 2
Açu da Tôrre 100-101 EF 7
Açude Aracatiaçu 100-101 DE 2-3
Açude Araras 100-101 D 3
Açude Coremas 100-101 F 4
Açude de Banabuiú 100-101 E 3
Açude de Orós 100-101 E 4
Açude Pentecoste 100-101 E 2
Açudina 100-101 B 7
Acueducto 91 II b 2
Acueducto de Lerma 91 I b 2
Acuexcomac 91 I d 1
Acuña 106-107 J 2
Acuña, Villa — 76-77 D 8
Açungui 102-103 H 6
Acuruá, Rio — 96-97 F 6
Açuruá, Serra do — 100-101 C 6
Acworth, GA 80-81 D 3

Ada, MN 68-69 H 2
Ada, OH 72-73 E 4
Ada, OK 64-65 G 5
Ada [GH] 164-165 E 7
Ada, Villa — 113 II b 1
'Adabīyah, Rā's — 173 C 3
Adachi, Tōkyō- 155 III b 1
Adado, Raas — 164-165 b 1
Adafir 164-165 BC 5
Adair, Bahía del — 86-87 CD 2
Adairsville, GA 78-79 G 3
Adak, AK 58-59 u 7
Adakale 136-137 K 2
Adak Island 52 D 36
Adak Strait 58-59 u 7
Adale 164-165 b 3
Adalia = Antalya 134-135 C 3
Ādam 134-135 H 6
Adam, Monte — = Mount Adam 111 DE 8
Adam, Mount — 111 DE 8
Adama = Nazrēt 164-165 M 7
Adamana, AZ 74-75 HJ 5
Adamantina 92-93 JK 9
Adamaoua 164-165 G 7
Adamaua = Adamaoua 164-165 G 7
Adamello 122-123 D 2
Adam Peak 66-67 E 5
Adams, MA 72-73 K 3
Adams, ND 68-69 GH 1
Adams, NE 68-69 H 5
Adams, NY 72-73 HJ 3
Adams, OK 76-77 D 4
Adams, Cape — 53 B 30-31
Adams, Mount — 64-65 B 2
Adam's Bridge 140 D 6
Adams Island 53 D 17
Adams Lake 60 H 4
Adams National Historical Site 84 I bc 3
Adams Park 85 II b 2
Adam's Peak = Samanaḷakanda 134-135 N 9
Adams River 60 H 4
Adamsville, AL 78-79 F 4
Adamsville, TN 78-79 E 3
Adamsville, TX 76-77 E 7
'Adan 134-135 F 8
Adana 136-137 F 4
Adang, Teluk — 152-153 M 6
Adán Quiroga 106-107 C 3
Adapazarı 134-135 C 2
Ādaraw Taungdan 141 C 5
Adare, Cape — 53 B 18
Adavale 158-159 HJ 5
Adda 122-123 C 3
Aḍ-Ḍab'ah 164-165 K 2
Ad-Dabbah 164-165 KL 5
Ad-Dabbūsah 136-137 J 7
Ad-Dafīnah 134-135 E 6
Ad-Daghgharah 136-137 L 6
Ad-Dahībah = Adh-Dhahībah 166-167 M 3
Ad-Dahnā' 134-135 E 5-F 6
Aḍ-Ḍahrah 166-167 G 1
Ad-Dakhlah 164-165 A 4
Ad-Damazīn 164-165 LM 6
Ad-Dāmir 164-165 L 5
Ad-Dammām 132-133 FG 5
Ad-Dāmūr 136-137 F 6
Addanki 140 DE 3
Ad-Daqmā' 134-135 FG 6
Addâr, Râss — = Rā's aṭ-Ṭīb 164-165 G 1
Ad-Dār al-Bayḍā' 164-165 BC 2
Ad-Darb 134-135 E 7
Addatīgala 140 EF 2
Aḍ-Ḍaw 136-137 G 5
Ad-Dawādimā 134-135 EF 6
Ad-Dawḥah 134-135 G 5
Ad-Dawr 136-137 KL 5
Ad-Dayr 173 C 5
Ad-Delaimiya = Ad-Dulaymīyah 136-137 K 6
Ad-Dibdibah 136-137 M 8
Aḍ-Ḍiffah 164-165 J 2
Ad-Dikākah 134-135 G 7
Ad-Dilam 134-135 F 6
Ad-Dilinjāt 173 B 2
Addington, London- 129 II b 2
Addis Alem = Alem Gena 164-165 M 7
Addison, NY 72-73 H 3
Addison = Webster Springs, WV 72-73 F 5
Ad-Dīwānīyah 134-135 EF 4
Addlestone 129 II a 2
Addo 174-175 F 7
Ad-Dôr = Ad-Dawr 136-137 KL 5
Addu Atoll 176 a 3
Ad-Du'ayn 164-165 K 6
Ad-Dujayl 136-137 KL 6
Ad-Dulaymīyah 136-137 K 6
Ad-Duwayd 134-135 E 5
Ad-Duwaym 164-165 L 6
Ad-Duwayr 173 B 4
Addy, WA 66-67 E 1
Adel, GA 80-81 E 5
Adel, IA 70-71 C 5
Adel, OR 66-67 D 4
Adela Corti 106-107 F 7
Adelaide [AUS] 158-159 GH 6-7
Adelaide [ZA] 174-175 G 7
Adelaide-Elizabeth 158-159 G 6
Adelaide Island 53 C 29-30
Adelaide Peninsula 56-57 R 4
Adelaide River 158-159 F 2
Adelanto, CA 74-75 E 5
Adélia 98-99 C 8
Adelia, La — 106-107 EF 7
Adelia María 106-107 E 4
Adélie, Terre — 53 C 14-15
Adélie Land = Terre Adélie 53 C 14-15
Ademuz 120-121 G 8
Aden, NM 76-77 A 6
Aden = 'Adan 134-135 EF 8
Aden, Gulf of — 134-135 F 8
Adendorp 174-175 F 7
Aderesso Rapides 168-169 E 3
Adghar = Adrār 164-165 DE 3
Adhaorā = Adhaura 138-139 J 5
Adhaura 138-139 J 5
Adh-Dhahībah 166-167 M 3
Adhibat, Sebkha el — = Sabkhat Tādit 166-167 M 3
Adhôi 138-139 C 6
Adi, Pulau — 148-149 K 7
Adib al-'Arsh, Al- 164-165 F 3
Adícora 94-95 FG 2
Adige 122-123 D 3
'Adi Grat 164-165 MN 6
Adi Kaye = Adi Keyih 164-165 MN 6
Adi Keyih 164-165 MN 6
Adilābād 138-139 G 8
Adilang 171 C 2
Adilcevaz 136-137 K 3
Adin, CA 66-67 C 5
Adirāmpattinam 140 D 5
Adiriyāt, Jabal al- 136-137 G 7
Adirondack Mountains 64-65 M 3
Adīs Abeba 164-165 M 7
Adīs Dera 164-165 M 6
'Adī Ugrī 164-165 M 6
Adıyaman 136-137 H 4
Adjai = Ajay 138-139 L 6
Adjaria = Adjarian Autonomous Soviet Socialist Republic 126-127 KL 6
Adjarian Autonomous Soviet Socialist Republic 126-127 KL 6
Adjim = Ajīm 166-167 M 3
Adjuntas, Presa de las — 86-87 LM 6
Adler, Soči- 126-127 J 5
Adler Planetarium 83 II b 1
Adlershof, Berlin- 130 III c 2
Adlikon 128 IV a 1
Adlisberg 128 IV b 1
Adliswil 128 IV ab 2
Admar, Irq — 164-165 F 4
Admiral 61 D 6
Admiralty Gulf 158-159 DE 2
Admiralty Inlet [CDN] 56-57 TU 3
Admiralty Inlet [USA] 66-67 B 1-2
Admiralty Island 56-57 K 6
Admiralty Islands 148-149 N 7
Admiralty Range 53 B 17
Admont 118 G 5
Ado-Ekiti 168-169 G 4
Adolfo E. Carranza 106-107 E 2
Adolfo Gonzales Chaves 106-107 GH 6-7
Adomi 168-169 EF 4
Adonara, Pulau — 148-149 H 8
Ādoni 134-135 M 7
Adour 120-121 G 7
Adra [E] 120-121 F 10
Adra [IND] 138-139 L 6
Adramúttion = Edremit 134-135 B 3
Adrār 164-165 DE 3
Adrar des Iforas 164-165 E 4-5
Adrar N Deren 166-167 BC 4
Adraskan, Dārya-ye — = Hārūt Rōd 134-135 J 4
Adré 164-165 J 6
Adri 164-165 G 3
Ádria 122-123 E 3
Adrian, MI 70-71 H 5
Adrian, MN 70-71 C 4
Adrian, OR 66-67 E 4
Adrian, TX 76-77 C 5
Adrianopel = Edirne 134-135 B 2
Adriatic Sea 114-115 LM 7
Adrogué, Almirante Brown- 110 III b 2
Adua 148-149 J 7
Adua = Adwa 164-165 M 6
Adujo Wanḍ 138-139 B 4
Aduma 168-169 GH 3
Adūr 140 C 6
Adusa 172 E 1
Aduwa = Adwa 164-165 M 6
Advance 174-175 D 6
Adventure, Bahía — 108-109 B 5
Adventure Bank 122-123 DE 7
Adventures Sound 108-109 K 9
Adwa 164-165 M 6
Adyča 132-133 a 4
Adygei Autonomous Region 126-127 JK 4
Adyk 126-127 M 4
Adžamka 126-127 F 2
Adž Bogd uul 142-143 GH 3

Aegean Sea 114-115 NO 8
Aegina, Gulf of — = Sarōnikòs Kólpos 122-123 K 7
Ærø 116-117 D 10
Aeroclube do Brasil 110 I b 2
Aerodrómo Don Torcuato 110 III b 1
Aeródromo Matanza 110 III b 2
Aeródromo Merlo 110 III a 2
Aeródromo Monte Grande 110 III b 2
Aeródromo Morón 110 III b 2
Aeródromo San Justo 110 III b 2
Aero-Haven 84 III d 3
Aerolimên Hellenikón 113 IV a 2
Aeroparque Jorge Newbery 110 III b 1
Aéroport Bruxelles National 128 II b 1
Aéroport Charles de Gaulle 129 I d 1
Aéroport de Brazzaville 170 IV a 1
Aéroport de Cartierville 82 I a 1
Aéroport de Dar el Beida 170 I b 2
Aéroport de Kinshasa 170 IV ab 1
Aéroport d'Orly 129 I c 3
Aéroport du Bourget 129 I c 2
Aeroporto de Congonhas 110 II b 2
Aeroporto di Ciampino 113 II bc 2
Aeroporto do Galeão 110 I b 1
Aeroporto Santos Dumont 110 I c 2
Aeropuerto Barajas 113 III b 2
Aeropuerto Central 91 I c 2
Aeropuerto Eldorado 91 III ab 2
Aeropuerto Internacional de Ezeiza 110 III b 2
Aeropuerto La Carlota 91 II bc
Aeropuerto Maiquetía 91 II b 1
Aesch [CH ↘ Zürich] 128 IV b 2
Aesch [CH ↙ Zürich] 128 IV a 1
Aetna, KS 76-77 E 4
Aeugst am Albis 128 IV ab 2

'Afag 136-137 L 6
Afal, Wādī al- = Wādī al-'Ifāl 173 D 3
Afallah 164-165 B 5
Afam Uko 168-169 G 4
Afanasjevo 124-125 T 4
Afántu 122-123 N 7
Afars et Issas = Djibouti 164-165 N 6
Afasto 168-169 G 1
Affery 168-169 DE 4
Affoltern, Zürich- 128 IV ab 1
Affreville = Khamīs-Milyānah 166-167 H 1
Affroun, El- = Al-'Afrūn 166-167 H 1
Afghānestān 134-135 J 4-L 3
Afgooye 164-165 ab 3
Afhjalar = Aqchalar 136-137 L 5
'Afif 134-135 E 6
Afikpo 164-165 F 7
Aflāj, Al — 134-135 F 6
Aflou = Aflū 166-167 H 2
Aflū 166-167 H 2
Afmadoow 164-165 N 8
Afogados da Ingázeira 92-93 M 6
Afognak, AK 58-59 L 7
Afognak Island 56-57 F 6
Afonso Bezerra 100-101 F 3
Afonso Cláudio 100-101 D 11
Afram 168-169 E 4
Afrânio 100-101 D 5
Afrânio Peixoto 100-101 D 7
Africa 50-51 J-L 5
African Islands 204-205 N 9
'Afrīn 136-137 G 4
Āfrīneh 136-137 M 6
'Afrūn, Al- 166-167 H 1
Afşin 136-137 G 3
'Afsō = 'Afsū 166-167 E 2
'Afsū 166-167 E 2
Afton, IA 70-71 C 5
Afton, OK 76-77 G 4
Afton, WY 66-67 H 4
Afton Oaks, Houston-, TX 85 III b 2
Aftout, Reg — = 'Irq Aflūt 166-167 DE 6
Aftut, Irq — 166-167 DE 6
Afuá 92-93 J 5
'Afūla 136-137 F 6
Afyonkarahisar 134-135 C 3
Afzalpur 140 C 2

Aga = Aginskoje 132-133 VW 7
Agadem 164-165 G 5
Agades = Agadèz 164-165 F 5
Agadèz 164-165 F 5
Agādīr 164-165 BC 2
Agādīr Tīssīnt 166-167 C 5
Agadji 168-169 F 4
Agadyr' 132-133 N 8
Agaie 164-165 F 7
Agalega Islands 204-205 N 10
Agalta, Sierra de — 64-65 J 8-9
Agamor 168-169 F 1
Agan 132-133 O 5
Agapa 132-133 Q 3
Agar 138-139 F 6
Agar, SD 68-69 F 3
Agarā = Agra 134-135 M 5
Agareb = 'Aqārib 166-167 M 2
Agartala 134-135 P 6
Agāshi 138-139 D 8
Agassiz 66-67 BC 1
Agastīswaram 140 C 6-7
Agata, ozero — 132-133 R 4
Agate, CO 68-69 E 6
Agathonêsion 122-123 M 7
Agats 148-149 L 8
Agatti Island 134-135 L 8
Agattu Island 52 D 1
Agattu Strait 58-59 p 6
Agawa 70-71 H 2
Agawa Bay 70-71 H 2
Agbélouvé 168-169 F 4
Agboju 170 III a 2
Agboville 164-165 D 7
Agdam 126-127 N 7
Agdaš 126-127 N 6
Agde 120-121 J 7
Agdz 166-167 C 4
Agdžabedi 126-127 N 6
Agen 120-121 H 6
Agere Hiywer 164-165 M 7
Āghā Jarī 134-135 FG 4
Aghiyuk Island 58-59 e 1
Aghlāghal, Jabal — 166-167 G 6
Aghwāt, Al- 164-165 E 2
Agiapuk River 58-59 DE 4
Agilmūs 166-167 D 3
Āğın 136-137 H 3
Agincourt = Penchia Hsü 146-147 HJ 9
Aginskoje 132-133 VW 7
Aginskoye = Aginskoje 132-133 VW 7
Aginsky-Buryat Autonomous Area = 12 ◁ 132-133 V 7
Aglagal, Djebel — = Jabal Aghlāghal 166-167 G 6
Ağlasun 136-137 D 4
Agnew 158-159 D 5
Agnía, Pampa de — 108-109 E 4
Agnibilekrou 168-169 E 4
Agnone 122-123 F 5
Agochi = Aoji 144-145 H 1
Agoj, gora — 126-127 J 4
8 de Agosto, Laguna — 108-109 H 2
Agosto, Laguna 8 de — 106-107 F 7
Agout 120-121 J 7
Āgra 134-135 M 5
Agra, OK 76-77 F 5
Agrachanskij poluostrov 126-127 NO 5
Agrado 94-95 D 6
Agrestina 100-101 G 5
Ağrı [TR] 136-137 K 3
Agrícola Oriental, Ixtacalco- 91 I c 2
Agrícola Pantitlán, Ixtacalco- 91 I c 2
Agrigento 122-123 E 7
Agrihan 206-207 S 8
Agrinion 122-123 J 6
Agrio, Río — 106-107 B 7
Agrópoli 122-123 F 5
Agrossam 98-99 JK 10
Agryz 132-133 J 6
Agter Roggeveld 174-175 D 6
Água, Ilha d' 110 I c 1
Agua Amarga 106-107 B 2
Agua Blanca [BOL] 104-105 E 7
Agua Blanca [RA] 104-105 D 8
Agua Blanca [YV] 94-95 K 4
Água Boa 102-103 L 2-3
Água Branca [BR, Alagoas] 100-101 F 5
Água Branca [BR, Piauí] 100-101 C 3
Água Branca, Chapada da — 102-103 L 1-2
Água Branca, Parque da — 110 II ab 2
Agua Brava, Laguna de — 86-87 GH 6

Agua Caliente 96-97 D 6
Agua Caliente, Río — 104-105 E 4
Agua Caliente Indian Reservation 74-75 E 6
Aguacatas, Los — 91 II c 1
Aguachica 94-95 E 3
Água Clara [BR] 92-93 J 9
Agua Clara [CO] 94-95 E 5
Aguada Cecilio 108-109 G 3
Aguada de Guerra 108-109 EF 3
Aguada de Guzmán 108-109 E 2-3
Aguada Grande 94-95 G 2
Agū'ādā Kyauktan 141 CD 8
Aguadas, Sierra de las — 106-107 BC 5
Agua de Dios 94-95 D 5
Aguadilla 88-89 N 5
Água Doce 100-101 D 10
Agua Dulce 86-87 NO 8
Agua Escondida 106-107 C 6
Água Fria 100-101 E 6
Agua Fria River 74-75 G 5-6
Agua Grande 106-107 B 2
Agua Hedionda, Cerro — 106-107 DE 4
Aguaí 102-103 J 5
Agua Linda 94-95 G 2
Aguán, Río — 64-65 J 8
Aguanaval, Río — 86-87 J 5
Agua Negra, Paso del — 106-107 BC 3
Aguanish 63 E 2
Agua Nueva 111 BC 4-5
Agua Nueva, TX 76-77 E 9
Aguanus, Rivière — 63 F 2
Aguapeí 102-103 C 2
Aguapeí, Rio — [BR, Mato Grosso] 102-103 C 1
Aguapeí, Rio — [BR, São Paulo] 102-103 G 4
Aguapey, Río — 106-107 J 1-2
Agua Poca, Cerro — 106-107 C 6
Agua Preta 100-101 G 5
Agua Prieta 64-65 DE 5
Aguaragüe, Cordillera de — 104-105 E 7
Aguaray 104-105 E 8
Aguaray Guazú, Río — 102-103 D 6
Aguarico, Río — 96-97 C 2
Aguasay 94-95 K 3
Águas Belas 100-101 F 5
Aguas Blancas, Cerro — 104-105 B 9
Aguascalientes [MEX, administrative unit] 64-65 F 7
Aguascalientes [MEX, place] 64-65 F 7
Aguas Calientes, Sierra de — 104-105 C 9
Águas da Prata 102-103 J 4
Águas do Paulista 100-101 C 7
Águas Formosas 92-93 L 8
Agua Suja 104-105 G 4
Água Vermelha 102-103 M 1
Água Vermelha, Represa de — 102-103 GH 3
Aguayita 96-97 D 6
Aguayo 106-107 E 3
Aguaytía 96-97 D 6
Aguaytía, Río — 96-97 D 6
Agudos 102-103 H 5
Águeda, Río — 120-121 D 8
Aguelmoûs = Agilmūs 166-167 D 3
Aguemour = Aqmūr 166-167 HJ 6
Agüerito 102-103 D 5
Aguga 171 C 2
Águia Branca 100-101 D 10
Aguiar 100-101 E 4
Aguila, AZ 74-75 G 6
Águila, Canal — = Eagle Passage 108-109 K 9
Águila, El — 106-107 D 5
Águila, Isla — = Speedwell Island 108-109 JK 9
Aguilar, CO 68-69 D 7
Aguilar, El — 104-105 D 8
Aguilar, Sierra de — 104-105 D 8
Aguilares 104-105 CD 10
Águilas 120-121 G 10
Aguirre 102-103 D 7
Aguirre, Bahía — 108-109 FG 10
Aguja, Cabo de la — 94-95 D 2
Aguja, Punta — 92-93 C 6
Agulhas, Cape — 172 D 8
Agulhas Basin 50-51 L 8
Agulhas Negras 92-93 K 9
Agung, Gunung — 148-149 G 8
Agunrege 168-169 F 3
Agusan 148-149 J 5
Agustín Codazzi 94-95 E 2-3
Agustoni 106-107 F 5
Agvali 126-127 N 5

Ahaggar = Al-Hajjār 164-165 EF 4
Ahaggar, Tassili Oua n' = Tāsīlī Wān al-Hajjār 164-165 E 5-F 4
Ahar 136-137 M 3
Ahar Chāy 136-137 M 3
Ahermoûmoû = Ahirmūmū 166-167 D 3
Aḥfīr 166-167 EF 2
Ahır dağı 136-137 G 4
Ahırlı 136-137 B 3
Ahirmūmū 166-167 D 3
Ahlat 136-137 K 3
Ahlat = Yusufeli 136-137 J 2
Ahlū, Al-Bi'r al- 166-167 B 6
Ahmadābād [IND] 134-135 L 6
Aḥmadābād [IR] 136-137 M 4
Aḥmadī, Al- = Mīnā' al-Aḥmadī 136-137 N 8
Ahmadnagar 134-135 LM 7
Ahmadpur [IND] 140 C 1
Aḥmadpūr [PAK] 138-139 CD 2
Ahmadpūr Lamma 138-139 BC 3
Aḥmadpūr Sharqī 134-135 L 5
Aḥmar, Bahr al- 166-167 GH 6
Aḥmar, Ḥāssī al- 166-167 E 3
Aḥmar, Jabal al- 173 B 3
Ahmednagar = Ahmadnagar 134-135 LM 7
Ahoada 168-169 G 4
Ahogayegua, Sierra de — 64-65 b 2-3
Ahom = Assam 138-139 N 4-5
Ahome 86-87 F 5
Ahoskie, NC 80-81 H 2
Ahousat 60 DE 5
Ahrensfelde, Ostfriedhof — 130 III c 1
Ahtopol 122-123 MN 4
Ahuntsic, Montréal- 82 I b 1
Āhūrān 136-137 M 6
Åhus 116-117 F 10
Ahuzhen 146-147 G 4
Ahvā = Ahwa 138-139 D 7
Ahvāz 134-135 F 4
Ahvenanmaa = Åland 116-117 HJ 7
Ahwa 138-139 D 7
Aḥwar 134-135 F 8
Ahwaz = Ahvāz 134-135 F 4

Aiaktalik Island 58-59 fg 1
Aiamitos, Los — 106-107 C 5
Aiapuá 98-99 GH 7
Aiapuá, Lago — 98-99 G 7
Aiari, Rio — 96-97 G 1
Āībak = Samangān 134-135 K 3
Aibetsu 144-145 c 2
Aichi 144-145 L 5
Aichilik River 58-59 Q 2
Aidin = Aydın 134-135 B 3
Aigáleō 113 IV a 2
Aigáleōs 113 IV a 1-2
Aigina [GR, island] 122-123 K 7
Aigina [GR, place] 122-123 K 7
Aigion 122-123 JK 6
Aigle, l' 120-121 H 4
Aiguá 111 F 4
Aigues-Mortes 120-121 JK 7
Aiguilete, Cerro — 108-109 C 8
Aigun = Aihun 142-143 O 1
Ai He 144-145 E 2
Ai Ho = Ai He 144-145 E 2
Aihsien = Yacheng 142-143 K 8
Aihui 142-143 O 1
Aija 92-93 D 6
Aijal 134-135 P 6
Aikawa 144-145 LM 3
Aiken, SC 64-65 K 5
Aileron 158-159 F 4
'Ailī, Sha'īb al- = Sha'īb al-'Aylī 136-137 H 7
Ailigandí 88-89 GH 10
Ailinglapalap 208 G 2
Aim 132-133 Z 6
Aimere 152-153 O 10
Aimogasta 106-107 D 2
Aimorés 92-93 L 8
Aimorés, Serra dos — 92-93 L 8
Ain 120-121 K 5
'Ain, Wādī al- = Wādī al-'Ayn 134-135 H 6
'Ainabo 164-165 b 2
'Aïn 'Aïcha = 'Ayn 'Ayshah 166-167 D 2
'Ain al-Barqah 166-167 M 7
'Ain al Muqshin, Al — = Al-'Ayn al-Muqshin 134-135 GH 7
Ainaza, Jebel — = Jabal 'Unayzah 134-135 GH 4
Aïn-Azel = 'Ayn 'Azl 166-167 J 2
Ainaži 124-125 DE 5
Aïn-Beïda = 'Ayn Baydā' 164-165 F 1
Aïn-ben-Khellil = 'Ayn Ban Khalīl 166-167 F 3
Aïn-ben-Tili = 'Ayn Bin Tīlī 164-165 C 3
Aïn-Berda = 'Ayn Bārd'ah 166-167 K 1
Aïn-Bessem = 'Ayn Bissim 166-167 H 1
Aïn-Boucif = 'Ayn Bū Sīf 166-167 H 2
Aïn Chaïr = 'Ayn ash-Sha'īr 166-167 E 3
Aïn-Defla = 'Ayn Daflah 166-167 GH 1
Aïn-Deheb = 'Ayn Dhahab 166-167 G 2
'Aïn Dîouâr = 'Ayn Dīwār 136-137 K 4
Aïne Belbela, Sebkra — = Sabkhat 'Ayn Balbālah 166-167 D 6
'Aïn ech Chaïr = 'Ayn ash-Sha'īr 166-167 E 3
'Aïn ed Defâlî = 'Ayn ad-Difālī 166-167 D 2
Aïn el Barka = 'Ayn al-Barqah 166-167 C 6
Aïn-el-Bel = 'Ayn al-Ibil 166-167 H 2
Aïn-el-Berd = 'Ayn al-Bard 166-167 F 2
Aïn El Guettara 164-165 D 4
Aïn-el-Hadjar = 'Ayn al-Ḥajar 166-167 G 2
Aïn-el-Hadjel = 'Ayn al-Ḥajal 166-167 H 2
Aïn-el-Khebira = 'Ayn al-Khabīrā 166-167 J 1
Aïn-el-Ksar = 'Ayn al-Qasr 166-167 K 2
Aïn-el-Melh = 'Ayn al-Milḥ 166-167 HJ 2
Aïn-el-Turk = 'Ayn al-Turk 166-167 F 1-2
Aïn-Galakka 164-165 H 5
'Aïn Garmashîn = 'Ayn Jarmashīn 173 B 5
Aïn-Kercha = 'Ayn Kirshah 166-167 K 1-2
Aïn Leuh = 'Ayn al-Lūḥ 166-167 D 3
'Aïn Loûḥ = 'Ayn al-Lūḥ 166-167 D 3
Aïn-Mahdi = 'Ayn Mahdī 166-167 H 3
Aïn-Melah = 'Ayn al-Milḥ 166-167 HJ 2
Aïn-M'lila = 'Ayn Malīlah 166-167 K 1-2
Aïn-Mokra = Birraḥḥāl 166-167 K 1
Aïn-Oulmène = 'Ayn Wilmān 166-167 J 2
Aïn-Oussera = 'Ayn Wissārah 166-167 H 2
'Aïn Remâda = Ramādah 166-167 M 3
Aïn-Rich = 'Ayn ar-Rīsh 166-167 HJ 2
Aïn-Roua = Buq'ah 166-167 J 1
Aïn-Salah = 'Ayn Ṣāliḥ 164-165 E 3
Aïn-Sefra = 'Ayn Ṣafrā 164-165 DE 2
Aïn Sfa = 'Ayn aṣ-Ṣafā' 166-167 EF 2
Aïn Souf = 'Ayn Ṣūf 166-167 H 5
Ainsworth, NE 68-69 FG 4
Aïn-Tagrout = 'Ayn Taqrūt 166-167 J 1
Aïn Tazzait = 'Ayn Tazārat 166-167 JK 6
Aïn-Tédelès = 'Ayn Tādalas 166-167 G 1-2
Aïn-Témouchent = 'Ayn Tamūshanat 164-165 D 1
Aïn-Touta = 'Ayn Tūtah 166-167 J 2
'Aïn Zorha = 'Ayn Zuraḥ 166-167 E 2
Aioi 144-145 K 5
Aion Island = ostrov Ajon 132-133 g 4
'Aïoûn, el — = Al-'Ayūn Dra'ah [MA, Agādīr] 166-167 A 5
'Aïoûn, el — = Al-'Ayūn Dra'ah [MA, Ujdah] 166-167 E 2
Aïoun du Draâ, el — = Al-'Ayūn Dra'ah 166-167 A 5
Aipe 94-95 D 6
Aipena 94-95 E 8
Aipena, Río — 96-97 CD 4
Aiquile 92-93 F 8
Aïr 164-165 F 5
Airabu, Pulau — 152-153 G 4
Airan Köl = Telijn nuur 142-143 F 2
Aire, Isla del — 120-121 K 9
Air Force Island 56-57 W 4
Airhitam, Teluk — 152-153 HJ 7
Airline Park 85 I a 2
Airline Village, Houston-, TX 85 III b 1
Airport West, Melbourne- 161 II b 1
Aisch 118 E 4
Aisega 148-149 g 6
Aisen, Sena — 108-109 C 5
Aisén del General Carlos Ibañez del Campo 108-109 B 5-C 6
Aishihik 56-57 J 5
Aishihik Lake 58-59 T 6
Aisne 120-121 J 4
Aïssa, Djebel — = Jabal 'Aysá 166-167 F 3
Aït 'Ammār 166-167 C 3
Aitana 120-121 G 9
Aitape 148-149 M 7
Aït 'Aysá, Wād — 166-167 E 3
Aitkin, MN 70-71 D 2
Aït Muḥammad 166-167 C 4
Aït Oûa Ballî = Aït Wa Ballī 166-167 B 5
Aït Ūrīr 166-167 C 4
Aitutaki 208 K 4
Aït Wa Ballī 166-167 B 5
Aiuaba 100-101 D 4
Aiud 122-123 K 2
Aiun, El — = Al-'Ayūn 164-165 B 3
Aiuruoca 102-103 K 4
Ai Vân, Đeo — = Đeo Hai Van 150-151 G 4
Aiwan Wan 146-147 H 7
Aix-en-Provence 120-121 KL 7
Aix-la-Chapelle = Aachen 118 C 3
Aix-les-Bains 120-121 KL 6
Aiyansh 60 C 2
Āīzāl = Aijal 134-135 P 6
Aizpute 124-125 C 5
Aizu-Wakamatsu 142-143 QR 4
Aizu-Wakamatsu = Aizu-Wakamatsu 142-143 QR 4

Ajā, Jabal — 134-135 E 5
'Ajab Shīr 136-137 L 4
Ajaccio 122-123 C 5
Ajaguz 132-133 P 8
Ajaigarh 138-139 H 5
Ajaijú, Río — 94-95 E 7
Ajaj, Wādī — 136-137 J 5
'Ajājā 136-137 J 4
Ajalpan 86-87 M 8
'Ajam, Al- 136-137 G 6
'Ajam, El — = Al-'Ajam 136-137 G 6
Ajan [SU, place Pribrežnyj chrebet] 132-133 a 6
Ajan [SU, place Sibirskoje ploskogorje] 132-133 U 6
Ajan [SU, river] 132-133 R 4
Ajana 158-159 BC 5
Ajanka 132-133 g 5
Ajanta 138-139 E 7
Ajanta Range 134-135 M 6
Ajax Mountain 66-67 G 3
Ajaxstadion 128 I b 1
Ajay 138-139 L 6
Ajaygarh = Ajaigarh 138-139 H 5
Ajdābiyah 164-165 J 2
Ajdar 126-127 J 2
Ajedabya = Ajdābiyah 164-165 J 2
Ājī Chāi = Rūd-e Āqdogh Mīsh 136-137 M 4
Ajigasawa 144-145 MN 2
Ajīm 166-167 M 3
Ājīn 136-137 M 5
Ajinṭhā = Ajanta 138-139 E 7
Ajjer, Tassili n' = Tāsīlī Wan Ahjār 164-165 F 3
Ajkino 124-125 R 2
'Ajlūn 136-137 FG 6
'Ajlūn, Jabal — 136-137 FG 6
'Ajmah, Jabal al- 164-165 L 3
'Ajmān 134-135 GH 5
Ajmer 138-139 E 4
'Ajmī 136-137 L 5-6
Ajnāla 138-139 E 2
Ajnis, Qārat — 136-137 BC 8
Ajo, AZ 74-75 G 6
Ajo Mountains 74-75 G 6
Ajon, ostrov — 132-133 g 4
Ajra 140 B 2
Ajrag nuur 142-143 GH 2
'Ajramīyah, Bi'r al- 173 BC 3
Ajtos 122-123 M 4
Aju, Kepulauan — 148-149 K 6
Ajuana, Rio — 94-95 J 8

Ak, Nam — 141 E 5
Akabah, Gulf of — = Khalīj al-'Aqabah 164-165 L 3
Akabane, Tōkyō- 155 III b 1
Akabar 168-169 F 2
Akabira 144-145 c 2
Akabli = 'Aqbalī 166-167 G 6
Akademii, zaliv — 132-133 a 7
Akaishi-sammyaku 144-145 LM 5
Akalkot 134-135 M 7
Akan ko 144-145 cd 2
Akantarer 164-165 E 5
Akanyaru 171 B 3
Akaroa 161 E 6
Akasaka, Tōkyō- 155 III b 1
Akasaki 144-145 J 5
'Akāsh, Wādī — = Wādī 'Ukāsh 136-137 J 5-6
Akashi 144-145 K 5
Akasi = Akashi 144-145 K 5
Äkäsjoki 116-117 KL 4
Akayu 144-145 N 3
Akba, Bou — = Bū 'Aqbah 166-167 C 5
Akbaba 154 I b 2
Akbarpur [IND, Bihār] 138-139 J 5
Akbarpur [IND, Uttar Pradesh ↙ Kānpur] 138-139 G 4-5
Akbarpur [IND, Uttar Pradesh ↖ Vārānasī] 138-139 J 4
Akbou = Akbū 166-167 J 1
Akbū 166-167 J 1
Akçaabat = Polathane 136-137 H 2
Akçadağ = Arğa 136-137 G 3
Akçakale 136-137 H 4
Akçakoca 136-137 D 2
Akçakoyunla 136-137 G 4
Akçan = Sakavi 136-137 J 3
Ak çay 136-137 C 4
Akchar = Āqshar 164-165 B 4
Akdağ [TR, Pontic Mts.] 136-137 J 2
Akdağ [TR, Taurus Mts.] 134-135 BC 3
Akdağlar 136-137 FG 3
Akdağmadeni 136-137 F 3
Ak deniz 136-137 B-E 5
Akera 126-127 N 7
Akershus 116-117 D 7-8
Aketi 172 D 1
Akhaïa = Achaïa 122-123 JK 6
Akhḍar, Jabal al- [LAR] 164-165 J 2
Akhḍar, Jabal al- [Oman] 134-135 H 6
Akhḍar, Wād al- 166-167 C 4
Akhiok, AK 58-59 f 1
Akhisar 136-137 BC 3
Akhmīm 173 BC 4
Aki 144-145 J 6
Akiachak, AK 58-59 FG 6
Akiak, AK 58-59 G 6
Akik = 'Aqiq 164-165 M 5
Akimiski Island 56-57 UV 7
Akimovka 126-127 G 3
Akita 142-143 QR 4
Akjoujt = Aqjawajat 164-165 B 5
Akka = 'Aqqah 166-167 B 5
Akka, Oued — = Wād 'Aqqah 166-167 B 5
Akka Iguirèn = 'Aqqat Igīrin 166-167 C 5
Akka Irhane = 'Aqqat Ighān 166-167 C 4
Akkajaure 116-117 G 4
Akka-mori 144-145 N 2
Akkani 58-59 B 4
Akkaraipattu = Akkarapattuwa 140 EF 7
Akkarapattuwa 140 EF 7
Akkaya 136-137 K 2
Akkerman = Belgorod-Dnestrovskij 126-127 DE 3
Akkeshi 144-145 d 2
Akkeshi wan 144-145 d 2
'Akkō 136-137 F 6
Akköy 136-137 B 4
Akku = Çaldere 136-137 G 2
Aklavik 56-57 J 4
Aklera 138-139 F 5
Aklūi 140 B 2
Akmal'-Abad = Gižduvan 132-133 L 9
Ak-Mečet' = Kzyl-Orda 132-133 M 9
Akmeṛags 124-125 C 5
Akmolinsk = Celinograd 132-133 MN 7
Akniste 124-125 EF 5
Aknūl 166-167 E 2
Akō 144-145 K 5
Akōbō 164-165 L 7
Akola 134-135 M 6
Akonolinga 164-165 G 8
Akor 168-169 D 2
Akordat 164-165 M 5
Akosombo Dam 168-169 F 4
Akot 138-139 F 7
Akoupé 168-169 E 4
Akpatok Island 56-57 X 5
Akpınar 136-137 J 4
Akranes 116-117 bc 2
Ákra Nkréko = Akrōtērion Gréko 136-137 F 5
Akrar 116-117 b 2
Akre = 'Āqrah 136-137 K 4
Akreyri = Akureyri 116-117 de 2
Akrítas, Akrōtērion — 122-123 JK 7
Akron, CO 68-69 E 5
Akron, IA 68-69 H 4
Akron, IN 70-71 GH 5
Akron, OH 64-65 K 3
Akropolis 113 IV a 2
Akrōtēri 122-123 L 8
Akrōtērion Akritas 122-123 JK 7
Akrōtērion Armevistēs 122-123 M 7
Akrōtērion Arnaûtēs 136-137 DE 5
Akrōtērion Gáta 136-137 E 5
Akrōtērion Grambûsa 122-123 K 8
Akrōtērion Gréko 136-137 F 5
Akrōtērion Hágios Andréa 136-137 F 5
Akrōtērion Hágios Iōánnēs 122-123 LM 8
Akrōtērion Kaférévs 122-123 L 6
Akrōtērion Kormakítēs 136-137 E 5
Akrōtērion Kriós 122-123 K 8
Akrōtērion Lidinon 122-123 L 8
Akrōtērion Maléas 122-123 K 7
Akrōtērion Prasonēsion 122-123 MN 8
Akrōtērion Síderos 122-123 M 8
Akrōtērion Spanta 122-123 KL 8
Akrōtērion Tainaron 122-123 K 7
Akrōtērion Zevgári 136-137 E 5
Akrōtēriu, Kólpos — 136-137 E 5
Akrotiri Bay = Kólpos Akrōtēriu 136-137 E 5
Akša 132-133 V 7
Aksaj [SU, place] 126-127 LM 3
Aksaj [SU, river] 126-127 N 5
Aksakovo 124-125 TU 6
Aksaray 136-137 EF 3
Akşehir 134-135 C 3
Akşehir gölü 136-137 D 3
Akseki 136-137 D 4
Aks'onovo-Zilovskoje 132-133 VW 7
Aksoran, gora — 132-133 O 8
Akstafa 126-127 M 6
Aksu [SU] 132-133 N 7
Aksu [TR] 136-137 G 4
Aksu = Aqsu 142-143 E 3
Aksuat 132-133 P 8
Aksubajevo 124-125 S 6
Aksu çay 136-137 D 4
Aksum 164-165 M 6
Aktanyš 124-125 TU 6
Aktogaj 132-133 O 8
Akt'ubinsk 132-133 K 7
Aktumsyk 132-133 K 9
Aktyubinsk = Akt'ubinsk 132-133 JK 7
Aku 168-169 G 4
Akulurak, AK 56-57 CD 5
Akune 142-143 OP 5
Akun Island 58-59 o 3
Akure 164-165 F 7
Akurèssa 140 E 7
Akureyri 116-117 de 2
Akuse 168-169 EF 4
Akutan, AK 58-59 o 3
Akutan Island 58-59 no 3
Akutan Pass 58-59 no 3
Akviran 136-137 E 4
Akwanga 168-169 GH 3
Akwawa 168-169 EF 4
Akyab = Sittwe 148-149 B 2
Akyazı 136-137 D 2

Ål 116-117 C 7
Al-Ab'adīyah 166-167 G 1
Alabama 64-65 J 5
Alabama River 64-65 J 5
Al-'Abīd al-'Arsh 164-165 F 3
Al 'Abr 134-135 F 7
Al-Abyad Sīdī Shaykh 166-167 G 3
Al-Abyār 166-167 A 5
Alaca 136-137 F 2
Alacadağ 136-137 DE 4
Alacahan 136-137 G 3
Alacahöyük 136-137 F 2
Alaçam 136-137 F 2
Alachadzy 126-127 JK 5
Alachua, FL 80-81 b 2
Aladağ [TR ↘ Karasu-Aras dağları] 136-137 K 3
Aladağ [TR ↑ Köroğlu dağları] 136-137 DE 2
Aladağ [TR ↗ Taurus Mts.] 136-137 F 4
Ālādāgh, Reshteh — 134-135 H 3
Aladdin Islands = Alādin Kyûnmyâ 150-151 AB 8
Al-Adib al-'Arsh 164-165 F 3
Alādin Kyûnmyâ 150-151 AB 8
Al Aflāj 134-135 F 6
Al-'Afrūn 166-167 H 1
Alagadiço 98-99 H 3
Al-Aghwāt 164-165 E 2
Alagir 126-127 LM 5
Alagnak River 58-59 J 7
Alagoa Grande 100-101 G 4
Alagoas 92-93 M 6-7
Alagoinha 100-101 F 5
Alagoinhas 92-93 M 7
Alagón 120-121 D 9
Alag Šan Gov' 142-143 J 4
Alaguntan 170 III b 2
Al-Aḥmadī = Mīnā' al-Aḥmadī 136-137 N 8
Alaid Island 58-59 pq 6
Al 'Ain al Muqshin = Al-'Ayn al-Muqshin 134-135 GH 7
Al-'Ajam 136-137 G 6
Alajuela 64-65 K 9-10
Alakanuk, AK 58-59 E 5
Alaknandā 138-139 G 2
Alakol', ozero — 132-133 P 8
Alaktak, AK 58-59 K 1
Al-'Alamayn 164-165 K 2
Alalaú, Rio — 92-93 G 5
Al-'Amādīyah 136-137 K 4
Al-'Amarah 134-135 F 4
'Alam ar-Rūm, Rā's — 136-137 B 7
'Alamayn, Al- 164-165 K 2
Alameda, CA 74-75 BC 4
Alameda, ID 66-67 G 4
Alameda, NM 76-77 A 5
Alameda, La — 76-77 CD 8
Alameda Naval Air Station 83 I c 2
Alameda Parque 91 I c 2
Al-Amgar 136-137 L 8
Al Amghar = Al-Amgar 136-137 L 8
Al-'Amirīyah 173 AB 2
Alamitos, Sierra de los — 86-87 JK 4
Alamo 86-87 M 7
Alamo, ND 68-69 E 1
Alamo, NV 74-75 F 4
Álamo, El — [MEX, Nuevo León] 76-77 E 9
Alamogordo, NM 64-65 E 5
Alamo Lake 74-75 G 5
Alamor 96-97 A 4
Alamo River 74-75 F 6
Alamos 64-65 E 6
Álamos, Los — [MEX] 86-87 J 3
Álamos, Los — [RCH] 106-107 A 6
Alamosa, CO 64-65 E 4
Álamos de Peña 76-77 A 7
Ālampur 140 CD 3
Al-Amsīd 164-165 B 3
Ālāmūt 136-137 O 4
Al-Anbār 136-137 J 6
Aland [IND] 140 C 2
Åland [SF, administrative unit] 116-117 HJ 7
Åland [SF, island] 116-117 HJ 7
Alaṅḍa = Aland 140 C 2
Al-Andarīn 136-137 G 5
Ålands hav 116-117 H 7-8
Åland Strait = Ålands hav 116-117 H 7-8
Alanga Arba 172 GH 1
Alanga Arba = Hagadera 172 GH 1
Alang Besar, Pulau — 150-151 C 11
Alangudi 140 D 5
Alanmyō 148-149 C 3
Alanya 134-135 C 3
Alaotra, Lac — 172 J 5
Alapaha, GA 80-81 E 5
Alapaha River 80-81 E 5
Alapajevsk 132-133 L 6
Alaplı = Yukarı Doğancılar 136-137 D 2
Ālappi = Alleppey 134-135 M 9
Alāq 164-165 B 5
Al-'Aqabah [IRQ] 136-137 KL 7
Al-'Aqabah [JOR] 134-135 CD 5
Al-'Aqabat aṣ-Ṣaghīrah 173 C 5
Alaquines 86-87 L 6
Al-'Arā'ish 164-165 C 1
Al 'Aramah 134-135 F 5-6
Al-'Arb'ā' [MA, Marrākush] 166-167 B 4
Al-Arba'ā' 166-167 H 1
Al-Arbā'wah 166-167 CD 2
Alarcón 120-121 FG 9
Al-Arfayyāt 136-137 K 8
Al-'Ārīḍ 134-135 F 6-7
Al-'Arīs 166-167 K 2
Al-'Arīsh 164-165 L 2
Al-'Arīshah 166-167 F 2
Al-'Arqūb 166-165 AB 4
Al Artāwīyah 134-135 EF 5
Alas, Pegunungan — 152-153 B 4
Alas, Selat — 148-149 G 8
Al-Aṣābah 168-169 BC 1
Alaşehir 136-137 C 3
Alašejev buchta 53 C 5
Al-'Asharah 136-137 J 5
Al-Ashmūnayn 173 B 4
Alashtar 136-137 MN 6
Al-'Āshūrīyah 136-137 K 7
Al-'Āṣī 136-137 G 5
Alaska 56-57 E-H 4
Alaska, Gulf of — 56-57 G-J 6
Alaska Highway 56-57 H 5
Alaska Peninsula 56-57 DE 6
Alaska Range 56-57 F-H 5
Al-Asnām 164-165 E 1
Al-'Aṣṣa 166-167 M 3
Alássio 122-123 C 3-4
Al'at 126-127 O 7
Al-'Athāmīn 136-137 K 7
Al-Aṭlas al-Kabīr 164-165 CD 2
Al-Aṭlas al-Mutawassiṭ 164-165 CD 2
Al-Aṭlas aṣ-Ṣaghīr 164-165 C 2-3
Al-Aṭlas aṣ-Ṣaḥrā' 164-165 D 2-F 1
Alatna, AK 58-59 L 3
Alatna River 58-59 L 3
Alatri 122-123 E 5
Ālattūr 140 C 5
Alatyr' [SU, place] 132-133 H 7
Alatyr' [SU, river] 124-125 P 6
Alaungdaukazzaba Burā 141 D 4
Alaungdaw Kathapa Pagoda = Alaungdaukazzaba Burā 141 D 4
Alausí 92-93 D 5
Alava, Cape — 66-67 A 1
Ālavāy = Alwaye 140 C 5
Alaverdi 126-127 M 6
Al-Awaynāt 166-167 KL 2
Al-'Awjā' 136-137 M 8
Alay, In — 164-165 D 5
Al-'Ayn al-Muqshin 134-135 GH 7
Al-'Ayun 164-165 B 3
Al-'Ayūn Dra'ah [MA, Ṭarfāyah] 166-167 A 5
Al-'Ayūn Dra'ah [MA, Ujdah] 166-167 E 2
Alayunt 136-137 D 3
Al-'Ayyāṭ 173 B 3
Al-'Azair = Al-'Uzayr 136-137 M 7
Alazani 126-127 N 6
Alazeja 132-133 d 3-e 4
Alazejskoje ploskogorje 132-133 c 4
Al-Azhar-University 170 II b 1
Al-'Azīzīyah [IRQ] 136-137 L 6
Al-'Azīzīyah [LAR] 164-165 G 2
Alba 122-123 C 3
Al-Bāb 136-137 G 4
Albacete 120-121 FG 9
Al-Badārī 164-165 L 3
Alba de Tormes 120-121 E 8
Al-Bādī [IRQ] 136-137 J 5
Al-Badī [Saudi Arabia] 134-135 F 6
Al-Baḥrah 136-137 MN 8
Al-Baḥr al-Aḥmar 164-165 L 4-M 5
Al-Baḥr al-Muḥīt 166-167 A 4-B 2
Alba Iulia 122-123 K 2
Al-Balqā 136-137 F 6-7
Al-Balyanā 164-165 L 3
Alban [CO] 94-95 D 5
Albanel, Lac — 62 P 1
Albania 122-123 J 5
Albano 98-99 K 6
Albany 158-159 C 6-7
Albany, CA 74-75 B 4
Albany, GA 64-65 K 5
Albany, KY 78-79 G 2
Albany, MN 70-71 C 3
Albany, MO 70-71 C 5
Albany, NY 64-65 LM 3
Albany, OR 64-65 B 3
Albany, TX 76-77 E 6
Albany Park, Chicago-, IL 83 II a 1
Albany River 56-57 U 7
Alba Posse 106-107 K 1
Al-Barāij 136-137 G 5
Al-Barājīl 170 II a 1
Albardão 106-107 L 4
Albardão do João Maria 106-107 L 4
Albardón 106-107 C 3
Al-Barīt 136-137 K 7
Albarkaize 168-169 F 2-3
Al-Barkāt 166-167 M 7
Albarracín 120-121 G 8
Al-Başalīyat Qiblī 173 C 5
Al-Başrah 134-135 F 4
Al-Baṭḥa 136-137 L 7
Al-Bāṭil 166-167 E 2
Al-Bāṭin [IRQ ↙ As-Salmān] 136-137 K 7-L 8
Al-Bāṭin [IRQ ↘ As-Salmān] 136-137 M 8
Al Bāṭinah 134-135 H 6
Albatross Bay 158-159 H 2
Albatross Point 161 EF 4
Al-Batrūn 136-137 F 5
Al-Bāwīṭī 164-165 K 3
Al-Bayāḍ [DZ] 164-165 E 2
Al-Bayāḍ [Saudi Arabia] 134-135 F 6
Al-Bayāḍīyah 173 C 5
Al-Bayḍā' [ADN] 134-135 EF 8
Al-Bayḍā' [LAR] 164-165 J 2
Albayrak = Sikefti 136-137 KL 3
Albemarle, NC 80-81 F 3
Albemarle = Isla Isabela 92-93 A 5
Albemarle Sound 80-81 HJ 2
Albenga 122-123 C 3
Alberche 120-121 E 8
Alberdi 102-103 CD 7
Alberga 160 B 1
Alberga River 158-159 FG 5
Alberni 66-67 A 1
Alberrie Creek 160 C 2
Albert [AUS] 160 H 4
Albert, Lake — 158-159 GH 7
Albert, Parc national — = Parc national Virunga 172 E 1-2
Alberta 56-57 NO 6
Alberta, VA 80-81 H 2
Alberti 106-107 G 5
Al'bertin 124-125 E 7
Albertinia 174-175 D 8
Albertkanaal 120-121 K 3
Albert Lea, MN 64-65 H 3
Albert Markham, Mount — 53 AB 17-15
Albert Nile 172 F 1
Alberton 170 V b 2
Alberton, MT 66-67 F 2
Albert Park 161 II b 2
Albertshof 130 III c 1
Albertson, NY 82 III de 2
Albert Town 88-89 JK 3
Albertville 120-121 L 6

Albertville = Kalemie 172 E 3
Albertynsville, Johannesburg- 170 V a 2
Albi 120-121 J 7
Albia, IA 70-71 D 5
Al-Bībān [DZ] 166-167 J 1
Al-Bībān [TN] 166-167 M 3
Al-Bid' 173 D 3
Albin, WY 68-69 D 5
Albina 92-93 J 3
Albino 122-123 CD 3
Albion, IL 70-71 F 6
Albion, IN 70-71 H 5
Albion, MI 70-71 H 4
Albion, MT 68-69 D 3
Albion, NE 68-69 GH 5
Albion, NY 72-73 GH 3
Albion, Melbourne- 161 II b 1
Al-Biqā' 136-137 FG 5-6
Al-Bi'r ad-Dīyāb 166-167 B 6
Al-Bi'r al-Ahlū 166-167 B 6
Al-Bi'r al-Jadīd 166-167 B 3
Albishorn 128 IV b 2
Albispass 128 IV b 2
Albisrieden, Zürich- 128 IV ab 1
Al-Biyāḍ = Al-Bayāḍ 134-135 F 6
Al-Bogham 136-137 J 5
Albon-sur-Seine 129 I c 3
Alborán 120-121 F 11
Ålborg 116-117 CD 9
Ålborg Bugt 116-117 D 9
Ålborg-Nørresundby 116-117 CD 9
Alborz, Reshteh Kūhhā-ye — 134-135 G 3
Al-Brāknah 168-169 B 1
Al-Bṣaiya = Al-Buṣaīyah 134-135 EF 4
Al-Bu'ayrāt al-Ḥsūn 164-165 H 2
Al-Budayr 136-137 L 7
Albuė 106-107 B 5
Albufera, La — 120-121 GH 9
Al-Buhayrāt 164-165 KL 7
Al-Buḥayrat al-Murrat al-Kubrā 173 C 2
Al-Bū'irḍah 166-167 C 5
Albuquerque 102-103 D 3
Albuquerque, NM 64-65 EF 4
Albuquerque, Cayos de — 88-89 F 8
Al-Buraymī 134-135 H 6
Alburquerque 120-121 D 9
Al-Burūj 166-167 C 3
Albury 158-159 J 7
Al-Buṣaīyah 134-135 EF 4
Al-Busaytā' 136-137 G 7-H 8
Alca 96-97 E 9
Alcácer do Sal 120-121 C 9
Alcade, Punta — 106-107 B 2
Alcalá de Guadaira 120-121 E 10
Alcalá de Henares 120-121 F 8
Alcalá la Real 120-121 F 10
Alcalde, NM 76-77 AB 4
Alcamo 122-123 E 7
Alcañiz 120-121 G 8
Alcântara [BR] 92-93 L 5
Alcántara [E] 120-121 D 9
Alcântaras 100-101 D 2
Alcantarilla 120-121 G 10
Alcantil 100-101 F 4
Alcaparra 76-77 AB 7
Alcaraz [E] 120-121 F 9
Alcaraz [RA] 106-107 H 3
Alcaraz, Sierra de — 120-121 F 9
Alcarria, La — 120-121 F 8
Alcatrazes, Ilha dos — 102-103 K 6
Alcatraz Island 83 I b 2
Alcázar 106-107 D 3
Alcázar de San Juan 120-121 F 9
Alcázarquivir = Al-Qṣar al-Kabīr 164-165 C 1
Alcazarseguer = Al-Qṣar aṣ-Ṣaghīr 166-167 D 2
Alcester Island 148-149 h 6
Al-Chebāyesh = Al-Jaza'ir 136-137 M 7
Alcira [E] 120-121 G 9
Alcira [RA] 111 D 4
Alcoa, TN 80-81 E 3
Alcobaça [BR] 92-93 M 8
Alcobaça [P] 120-121 C 9
Alcolea del Pinar 120-121 FG 8
Alcones 106-107 B 5
Alcoota 158-159 F 4
Alcorn College, MS 78-79 D 5
Alcorta 106-107 G 4
Alcova, WY 68-69 C 4
Alcoy 120-121 G 9
Aldabra Islands 172 J 3
Aldama [MEX, Chihuahua] 86-87 H 3
Aldama [MEX, Tamaulipas] 86-87 LM 6
Aldamas, Los — 76-77 E 9
Aldan, PA 84 III b 2
Aldan [SU, place] 132-133 XY 6
Aldan [SU, river] 132-133 Z 6
Aldana 94-95 C 7
Aldan Plateau = Aldanskoje nagorje 132-133 X-Z 6
Aldanskoje nagorje 132-133 X-Z 6
Aldea Apeleg 108-109 D 5
Aldeburgh 119 GH 5
Aldeia Campista, Rio de Janeiro- 110 I b 2
Alder, MT 66-67 GH 3
Alderney 119 E 7
Alder Peak 74-75 C 5
Alderson 61 C 5
Aldo Bonzi, La Matanza- 110 III b 2
Alduş = Temsiyas 136-137 H 3
Alechovščina 124-125 JK 3
Aledo, IL 70-71 E 5
Aleg = Alaq 164-165 B 5
Alegre 102-103 M 4
Alegrete 111 E 3-4
Alegria 98-99 E 6
Alejandra 106-107 H 2
Alejandra, Cabo — = Cape Alexandra 111 J 8
Alejandría 104-105 D 3
Alejandro Roca 106-107 EF 4
Alejandro Selkirk 199 A 7
Alejo Ledesma 106-107 F 4
Alejsk 132-133 P 7
Aleknagik, AK 58-59 HJ 7
Aleknagik, Lake — 58-59 H 7
Aleksandra, mys — 132-133 ab 7
Aleksandrija 126-127 F 2
Aleksandro-Nevskij 124-125 N 7
Aleksandrov 124-125 M 5
Aleksandrov Gaj 126-127 O 1
Aleksandrovka [SU, Rostovskaja Oblast'] 126-127 J 3
Aleksandrovsk [SU, Rossijskaja SFSR] 124-125 V 4
Aleksandrovsk = Belogorsk 132-133 YZ 7
Aleksandrovsk-Gruševskij = Šachty 126-127 K 3
Aleksandrovskoje [SU, Stavropol'skaja Oblast'] 126-127 L 4
Aleksandrovskoje [SU, Zapadno-Sibirskaja nizmennost'] 132-133 OP 5
Aleksandrovsk-Sachalinskij 132-133 bc 7
Aleksandrów Kujawski 118 J 2
Aleksejevka [SU, Kazachskaja SSR] 132-133 N 7
Aleksejevka [SU, Rossijskaja SFSR → Kujbyšev] 124-125 S 7
Aleksejevka [SU, Rossijskaja SFSR ↘ Kujbyšev] 124-125 S 7
Aleksejevka [SU, Rossijskaja SFSR Belgorodskaja Oblast'] 126-127 J 1
Aleksejevka [SU, Rossijskaja SFSR Saratovskaja Oblast'] 124-125 QR 7
Aleksejevka [SU, Ukrainskaja SSR] 126-127 GH 2
Aleksejevo-Lozovskoje 126-127 K 2
Aleksejevsk = Svobodnyj 132-133 YZ 7
Aleksin 124-125 L 6
Aleksinac 122-123 JK 4
Ålem 116-117 G 9
Alemán 96-97 D 3
Aleman, NM 76-77 A 6
Alemania 104-105 D 9
Alem Cué 106-107 J 2
Alem Gena 164-165 M 7
'Alem Maya 164-165 N 7
Além Paraíba 92-93 L 9
Alençon 120-121 H 4
Alenquer [BR] 92-93 HJ 5
Alentejo 120-121 C 10-D 9
Alenuihaha Channel 148-149 ef 3
Alenz 136-137 J 4
Aleppo = Halab 134-135 D 3
Alert 52 A 25
Alerta 92-93 E 7
Alert Bay 60 D 4
Āleru 140 D 2
Alès 120-121 K 6
Alessàndria 122-123 C 3
Ålesund 116-117 AB 6
Aleutian Islands 52 D 35-1
Aleutian Range 56-57 E 6-F 5
Aleutian Trench 156-157 HJ 2
Aleutka 142-143 T 2
Alevina, mys — 132-133 cd 6
Alevisik = Samandağ 136-137 F 4
Alexander, ND 68-69 E 2
Alexander, Kap — 56-57 WX 2
Alexander, Point — 158-159 G 2
Alexander Archipelago 56-57 J 6-K 7
Alexanderbaai 172 BC 7
Alexander City, AL 78-79 FG 4
Alexander Deussen Park 85 III c 1
Alexander Ist Island = zemľa Aleksandra I 53 C 29
Alexander Memorial Coliseum 85 II b 2
Alexander Park 85 II c 1
Alexanderplatz 130 III b 1
Alexandra [NZ] 158-159 N 9
Alexandra [ZA] 170 V b 1
Alexandra = Umzinto 174-175 J 6
Alexandra, Cape — 111 J 8
Alexandra, Singapore- 154 III ab 2
Alexandra, zemľa — 132-133 FG 1
Alexandra Canal 161 I b 2
Alexandra Fiord 56-57 VW 2
Alexandra land = zemľa Alexandra 132-133 FG 1
Alexandretta = İskenderun 134-135 D 3
Alexandrette = İskenderun 134-135 D 3
Alexandria, IN 70-71 H 5
Alexandria, LA 64-65 H 5
Alexandria, MN 70-71 C 3
Alexandria, SD 68-69 H 4
Alexandria, VA 64-65 L 4
Alexandria [AUS] 158-159 G 3
Alexandria [BR] 92-93 M 6
Alexandria [CDN] 60 F 3
Alexandria [RO] 122-123 L 4
Alexandria [ZA] 172 E 8
Alexandria = Al-Iskandarīyah 164-165 KL 2
Alexandria-Braddock, VA 82 II a 2
Alexandrina, Lake — 158-159 GH 7
Alexandrovsk = Poľarnyj 116-117 P 3
Alexandrúpolis 122-123 L 5
Alexis Creek 60 F 3
Al-Fahṣ 166-167 LM 1
Al-Fallūjah 136-137 JK 6
Alfambra 120-121 G 8
Al-Fant 173 B 3
Al-Faqīh Bin Ṣālaḥ 166-167 C 3
Al-Farā' 136-137 J 4
Alfarez de Navio Sobral 53 A 32-35
Al-Fāshir 164-165 K 6
Al-Fashn 164-165 KL 3
Alfatar 122-123 M 4
Al-Fatḥa = Al-Fatḥah 134-135 E 3
Alfavaca, Ilha da — 110 I b 3
Alfaville 166-167 G 3
Al-Fāw 136-137 N 7-8
Al-Fayṣalīyah 136-137 KL 7
Al-Fayyūm 164-165 KL 3
Alfeiós 122-123 J 7
Alfenas 102-103 JK 4
Alférez, Sierra de — 106-107 KL 4
Al-Fīfī 164-165 J 6
Alföld 118 J 5-L 4
Alfortville 129 I c 2
Ålfotbreen 116-117 A 7
Alfred, ME 72-73 L 3
Alfredo Chaves 102-103 M 4
Al-Fujairah = Al-Fujayrah 134-135 H 5
Al-Fujayrah 134-135 H 5
Al-Fūlah 164-165 K 6
Al-Funduq 166-167 D 2
Al-Furāt 134-135 DE 3
Alga 132-133 K 8
Algabas 126-127 Q 1
Al-Gadīdah = Al-Jadīdah [MA] 164-165 C 2
Al-Gadīdah = Al-Jadīdah [TN] 166-167 L 1
Al-Gamm = Al-Jamm 166-167 M 2
Al-Gāmūr al-Kabīr = Al-Jāmūr al-Kabīr 166-167 M 1
Al-Gārah 166-167 C 3
Ålgård 116-117 A 8
Algarrobal 106-107 B 2
Algarrobitos 106-107 GH 4
Algarrobo [RA] 106-107 F 7
Algarrobo [RCH, administrative unit] 106-107 AB 4
Algarrobo [RCH, place] 106-107 B 1
Algarrobo del Águila 106-107 D 6
Algarve 120-121 CD 10
Algasovo 124-125 N 7
Algeciras 120-121 E 10
Algena 164-165 M 5
Alger, MI 70-71 H 3
Alger, Baie d' 170 I b 1
Algeria 164-165 D-F 3
Algerian Basin 120-121 J 10-L 8
Alger-Plage 170 I b 1
Al-Ghāb 136-137 G 5
Al-Ghār 166-167 L 5
Alghar = Al-Ghār 166-167 L 5
Al-Gharaq as-Sulṭānī 173 AB 3
Al-Gharb 166-167 C 2
Al-Ghardaqah 164-165 L 3
Al-Gharīs 166-167 G 2
Al-Ghāṭā' 136-137 J 5
Al-Ghayḍah [ADN ← Sayḥūt] 134-135 FG 7-8
Al-Ghayḍah [ADN ↗ Sayḥūt] 134-135 G 7
Alghero 122-123 C 5
Al-Ghraybah 166-167 LM 2
Al-Ghūr 136-137 F 7
Algiers = Al-Jazā'ir 164-165 E 1
Algiers, New Orleans-, LA 85 I b 2
Algoabaai 172 E 8
Algoa Bay = Algoabaai 172 E 8
Algodón, Río — 96-97 E 3
Algodones 74-75 F 6
Algoma, OR 66-67 C 4
Algoma, WI 70-71 G 3
Algona, IA 70-71 CD 4
Algonquin Park 72-73 G 2
Algonquin Provincial Park 56-57 V 8
Algorte 106-107 J 4
Alguada Reef = Agū'ādā Kyauktan 141 CD 8
Al-Habrah 166-167 J 3
Al-Ḥad 166-167 D 2
Al-Haddār 134-135 EF 6
Al-Ḥadītah 134-135 F 4
Al-Ḥaḍr 136-137 K 5
Al-Ḥafar al-Bāṭin 134-135 F 5
Al-Ḥājab 166-167 D 3
Al-Ḥajar [DZ] 166-167 KL 1
Al-Ḥajar [Oman] 134-135 H 6
Al-Hajara = Ṣaḥrā' al-Hijārah 136-137 JK 8
Al-Ḥajīrah 166-167 J 3
Al-Ḥajjār 164-165 EF 4
Al-Ḥalfāyah 136-137 M 7
Al-Ḥalīl 136-137 F 7
Al-Ḥamād 136-137 H 6-J 7
Al-Ḥamār 136-137 M 8
Alhambra, CA 74-75 DE 5
Al-Ḥamdānīyah 136-137 G 5
Al-Ḥāmil 166-167 J 2
Al-Hamīs = Al-Khamīs 166-167 C 3
Al-Hammadah [DZ → Ghardāyah] 166-167 FG 4
Al-Hammadah [DZ ← Ghardāyah] 166-167 HJ 4
Al-Ḥammādat al-Ḥamrā' 164-165 G 2-3
Al-Ḥammah 166-167 L 3
Al-Ḥammām 136-137 C 7
Al-Ḥammāmāt 166-167 M 1
Al-Ḥammān 166-167 D 3
Al-Ḥamrā' [Saudi Arabia] 134-135 D 6
Al-Ḥamrā' [SYR] 136-137 G 5
Al-Ḥamūl 173 B 2
Al Ḥamza = Qawām al-Ḥamzah 136-137 L 7
Al Ḥanākīyah 134-135 E 6
Al-Handaq = Al-Khandaq 164-165 KL 5
Alhandra 100-101 G 4
Al-Ḥanīyah 136-137 LM 8
Al-Ḥank 164-165 C 3-4
Al-Hanshah 166-167 M 2
Al-Ḥaqūnīyah 164-165 B 3
Al-Ḥāritah 136-137 M 7
Al-Ḥarmal 136-137 G 5
Al Ḥarrah 134-135 D 4
Al-Ḥarūj al-Aswad 164-165 H 3
Al-Harūsh 166-167 K 1
Al 'Ḥasā' 134-135 F 5
Al-Ḥasakah 134-135 D 3
Al Hashemiya = Al-Hāshimīyah 136-137 L 6
Al-Hāshimīyah 136-137 L 6
Al-Ḥāsī aṭ-Ṭawīl 166-167 K 4-5
Al-Ḥaṭāṭibah 173 B 2
Al Ḥaurā = Al-Ḥawrah 134-135 F 8
Al-Hawārīyah 166-167 M 1
Al-Ḥawātah 164-165 LM 6
Al-Ḥawḍ [DZ] 166-167 J 4
Al-Ḥawḍ [RIM] 164-165 C 5
Al-Ḥawḍ al-Gharbī 168-169 C 1
Al-Ḥawḍ ash-Sharqī 168-169 D 1
Al-Ḥawrah 134-135 F 8
Al-Ḥawṭah = Al-Ḥillah 134-135 F 6
Al-Ḥawūz 166-167 B 4
Al-Ḥayrīr 166-167 L 7
Al-Ḥayy 134-135 F 4
Al-Ḥazīm 136-137 G 7
Al-Ḥazm 173 E 3
Al-Ḥazul = Al-Huzul 136-137 K 8
Al-Ḥijāz 134-135 D 5-6
Al-Ḥillah [IRQ] 134-135 E 4
Al-Ḥillah [Saudi Arabia] 134-135 F 6
Al-Hindīyah 136-137 KL 6
Al-Ḥomra = Al-Ḥumrah 164-165 L 6
Alhucemas = Al-Ḥusaymah 164-165 D 1
Alhucemas, Islas de — 166-167 E 2
Al-Ḥudaydah 134-135 E 8
Al-Hufūf 134-135 FG 5
Al-Ḥumaydah 173 D 3
Al-Ḥumrah 164-165 L 6
Al-Hums = Al-Khums 164-165 GH 2
Al-Huraybah 134-135 F 7
Al-Ḥuṣayḥiṣah 164-165 L 6
Al-Ḥusaymah 164-165 D 1
Al-Ḥusaynīyah 134-135 EF 7
Al-Huzul 136-137 K 8
Ali = Ngarikorsum 138-139 HJ 2
'Alī, Sadd al- 164-165 L 4
Aliákmon 122-123 JK 5
'Alī al-Garbī 136-137 M 6
Alianca 100-101 G 4
Alianza 96-97 D 5
Alībāg 140 A 1
Ali-Bajramly 126-127 O 7
Alibardak 136-137 J 3
Alibej, ozero — 126-127 E 4
Alibey 154 I a 2
Alibey adasi 136-137 B 3
Alibeyköy 154 I a 2
Alibori 168-169 F 3
Alibunar 122-123 J 3
Alicahue 106-107 B 4
Alicante 120-121 GH 9
Alice 174-175 G 7
Alice, TX 64-65 G 6
Alice, Punta — 122-123 G 6
Alice Arm 60 C 2
Alicedale 174-175 G 7
Alice Springs 158-159 FG 4
Aliceville, AL 78-79 EF 4
Alicia 106-107 F 3
Alicias, Las — 91 I a 3
Alicudi 122-123 F 6
Alida 68-69 F 1
Al-'Idd 134-135 G 6
Al-Idrīsīyah 166-167 H 2
Ali Gabe 171 E 2
Aliganj 138-139 G 4
Aligar = Alīgarh 134-135 M 5
Alīgarh 134-135 M 5
Alīgūdarz 136-137 NO 6
Alihe 142-143 N 1
Alijos, Rocas — 86-87 C 5
Alikovo 124-125 Q 6
Alima 172 BC 2
Alindao 164-165 J 7-8
Alingsås 116-117 E 9
Alipore, Calcutta- 154 II ab 2
'Alīpūr 138-139 C 3
Alīpur Duār 134-135 M 5
Aliquippa, PA 72-73 F 4
Ali Rājpur 138-139 E 6
Al-'Irq 164-165 J 3
Al-'Irq al-Kabīr al-Gharbī 164-165 D 3-E 2
Al-'Irq al-Kabīr ash-Sharqī 164-165 F 2-3
Alisal, CA 74-75 C 4
Al-'Isāwīyah 134-135 D 4
Al-Iskandarīyah 164-165 KL 2
Al-Ismā'īlīyah 164-165 L 2
Alisos, Río — 86-87 E 2
Alitak Bay 58-59 f 1
Alitus = Alytus 124-125 E 6
Aliwal-Noord 172 E 8
Aliwal Suid = Mosselbaai 172 D 8
Alix 60 L 3
Al-Jabal al-Abyaḍ 166-167 L 1
Al-Jabalayn 164-165 L 6
Al-Jabīlat 166-167 BC 4
Al-Jadīdah [MA] 164-165 G 2
Al-Jadīdah [TN] 166-167 L 1
Al-Jafr [JOR, place] 134-135 D 4
Al-Jafr [JOR, river] 136-137 G 7
Al-Jaghbūb 164-165 J 3
Al-Jahrah 134-135 F 5
Al-Jajah 173 B 5
Al-Jaladah 134-135 F 7
Al-Jalāmīd 136-137 HJ 7
Al-Jalhāk 164-165 L 6
Al-Jamm 166-167 M 2
Al-Jāmūr al-Kabīr 166-167 M 1
Al-Jarāwī 136-137 H 7
Al-Jauf = Al-Jawf 134-135 DE 5
Al-Jawf [LAR] 164-165 J 4
Al-Jawf [Saudi Arabia] 134-135 DE 5
Al-Jawf [Y] 134-135 EF 7
Al-Jaza'ir [DZ] 164-165 E 1
Al-Jaza'ir [IRQ] 136-137 M 7
Al-Jazā'ir-Bab el Oued 170 I a 1
Al-Jazā'ir-Birmandreïs 170 I a 2
Al-Jazā'ir-Bologhine Ibnou Ziri 170 I a 1
Al-Jazā'ir-El Biar 170 I a 1
Al-Jazā'ir-El Madania 170 I a 2
Al-Jazā'ir-Kasbah 170 I a 1
Al-Jazā'ir-Kouba 170 I ab 2
Al-Jazā'ir-Mustapha 170 I a 1
Al-Jazā'ir-Sidi M'Hamed 170 I a 1
Al-Jazīra = Arḍ al-Jazīrah 134-135 E 3-F 4
Al-Jazīrah [DZ] 166-167 F 2
Al-Jazīrah [IRQ] 136-137 J 5
Al-Jazīrah [Sudan] 164-165 L 6
Al-Jil 136-137 KL 7
Al-Jiladah = Al-Jaladah 134-135 F 6-7
Al-Jill = Al-Jil 136-137 KL 7
Al-Jiwā' 134-135 G 6
Al-Jīzah [ET] 164-165 KL 3
Al-Jīzah [JOR] 136-137 FG 7
Al-Jubail = Al-Jubayl al-Baḥrī 134-135 FG 5
Al-Jubayl al-Baḥrī 134-135 FG 5
Al Jumaima = Al-Jumaymah 136-137 KL 8
Al-Jumaymah 136-137 KL 8
Al-Junaynah 164-165 J 6
Al Juraiba = Al-Juraybah 136-137 KL 8
Al-Juraybah 136-137 KL 8
Al-Juwārah 134-135 H 7
Al-Kāf 164-165 F 1
Alkali Desert 66-67 EF 5
Alkali Flat 66-67 DE 5
Alkali Lake 66-67 D 5
Alkamari 168-169 H 2
Al-Kāmil 134-135 H 6
Al-Kamilīn 164-165 L 5
Al-Karak 134-135 D 4
Al-Karnak 173 C 5
Al-Kefil = Al-Kifl 136-137 L 6
Al-Khābūrah 134-135 H 6
Al-Khalj as-Sīntirā' 164-165 A 4
Al-Khalīj al-'Arabī 136-137 N 8
Al-Khālīṣ 136-137 L 6
Al-Khalūf 134-135 H 6
Al-Khamāsīn 134-135 EF 6
Al-Khamīs 166-167 C 3
Al-Khandaq 164-165 KL 5
Al-Kharāb 134-135 EF 7
Al-Khārījah 164-165 L 3
Al-Kharj 134-135 F 6
Al-Kharṭūm 164-165 L 5
Al-Kharṭūm Baḥrī 164-165 L 5
Al-Khaṣab 134-135 H 5
Al Khedir = Khiḍr Dardash 136-137 L 7
Al-Khums 164-165 GH 2
Al-Khurmah 134-135 E 6
Al-Khurub 166-167 K 1
Al-Kifl 136-137 L 6
Alkmaar 120-121 K 2
Al-Kūfah 136-137 L 6
Al-Kumayt 136-137 M 6
Al-Kunayt 136-137 M 6
Al-Kuntillā 173 D 3
Al-Kūt 134-135 F 4
Al-Kuwayt 134-135 F 5
Al Kwair = Al-Quwayr 136-137 K 4
Al-La'ā' = Al-Lu'ā'ah 136-137 L 7
Allach, München- 130 II a 1
Allach-Jun' 132-133 a 5
Allada 164-165 E 7
Al-Lādhiqīyah 134-135 CD 3
Āllagaḍa = Allagadda 140 D 3
Allagadda 140 D 3
Allagash, ME 72-73 M 1
Allagash River 72-73 M 1
Allāhābād [IND] 134-135 N 5
Allāhābād [PAK] 138-139 C 3
Al-Lajā' 136-137 G 6
Allakaket, AK 56-57 F 4
Allaküekber dağı 136-137 K 2
'Allāl at-Tāzī 166-167 C 2
Allal Tazi = 'Allāl at-Tāzī 166-167 C 2
Allamoore, TX 76-77 B 7
Allampūr = Ālampur 140 CD 3
Allanmyo = Ālanmyō 148-149 C 3
Allanridge 174-175 G 4
Allāpalli 138-139 H 8
Al-Laqawah 164-165 K 6
'Allāqī, Wadī al- 173 C 6
Allardville 63 D 4
Alldays 174-175 H 2
Allegan, MI 70-71 H 4
Alleghenies = Allegheny Mountains 64-65 K 4-L 3
Allegheny Mountains 64-65 K 4-L 3
Allegheny Plateau 72-73 F 5
Allegheny River 72-73 G 4
Allemanskraaldam 174-175 G 5
Allemorgens 174-175 D 7
Allen 106-107 D 7
Allen, OK 76-77 F 5
Allen, Mount — 58-59 QR 5
Allendale, SC 80-81 F 4
Allendale, Houston-, TX 85 III bc 2
Allende [MEX, Coahuila] 86-87 K 3
Allende [MEX, León] 86-87 KL 5
Allen Park, MI 72-73 E 3
Allen River 58-59 LM 3
Allentown, PA 64-65 L 3
Alleppey 134-135 M 9
Aller 118 D 2
Allermöhe, Hamburg- 130 I b 2
Allerton, IA 70-71 D 5
Alley Park 82 III d 2
Alliance, NE 64-65 F 3
Alliance, OH 72-73 F 4
Al-Lidām = Al-Khamāsīn 134-135 EF 6
Allier 120-121 J 6
Al-Līfīyah 136-137 K 7
Alliford Bay 60 B 3
Alligator Sound 80-81 HJ 3
Allison, IA 70-71 D 4
Allison, TX 76-77 DE 5
Allison Harbour 60 CD 4
Allison Pass 66-67 C 1
Alliston 72-73 G 2
Al-Līth 134-135 E 6
Allston, Boston-, MA 84 I b 2
Al-Lu'ā'ah 136-137 L 7
Al-Luhayyah 134-135 E 7
Allumettes, Île aux — 72-73 H 2
Allūr 140 E 3
Allūru Kottapatnam 140 E 3
Alma, AR 76-77 G 5
Alma, GA 80-81 E 5
Alma, KS 68-69 H 6
Alma, MI 70-71 H 4
Alma, NE 68-69 G 5
Alma, WI 70-71 E 3
Alma [CDN, New Brunswick] 63 D 5
Alma [CDN, Quebec] 56-57 W 8
Al'ma [SU] 126-127 F 4
Alma = Budwāwū 166-167 H 1
Alma, Lake — = Harlan County Reservoir 68-69 G 5-6
Al-Ma'anīyah 134-135 E 4
Al-Ma'arrah 136-137 G 4
Alma-Ata 132-133 O 9
Al-Mabrūk 166-167 G 5
Almada 120-121 C 9
Almadén 120-121 E 9
Al-Madīnah [IRQ] 136-137 M 7
Al-Madīnah [Saudi Arabia] 134-135 DE 6
Al-Mafraq 136-137 G 6
Al-Maghayrā' 134-135 G 6
Al-Māghrah 136-137 C 7
Almagre, El — 86-87 J 4
Almagro, Buenos Aires- 110 III b 1
Almaguer 94-95 C 7
Al-Maḥallat al-Kubrā 164-165 L 2
Al-Maḥamīd 166-167 D 5
Al-Mahārī = Al-Muhārī 136-137 L 7
Al-Maḥāriq 173 B 5
Al-Maḥaris 166-167 M 2
Al-Mahdīyah 164-165 G 1
Al-Maḥmūdīyah 136-137 L 6
Al-Ma'rījah 166-167 E 2-3
Al-Maisarī = Al-Maysarī 136-137 H 7
Al-Majarr al-Kabīr 136-137 M 7
Al-Makīlī 164-165 J 2
Al-Maknāsī 166-167 L 2
Al-Maks al-Baḥrī 173 AB 5
Al-Maks al-Qiblī 164-165 L 4
Al-Malaḥ 166-167 F 2
Almalyk 134-135 KL 2
Al-Manāmah 134-135 G 5
Al-Manāqil 164-165 L 6
Al-Manāṣif 136-137 J 5
Al-Manāstīr 166-167 M 2
Al Man'niyah = Al-Ma'anīyah 134-135 E 4
Almanor, Lake — 66-67 C 5
Almansa 120-121 G 9
Al-Manṣūr 166-167 F 6
Al-Manṣūrah [DZ] 166-167 HJ 1
Al-Manṣūrah [ET] 164-165 L 2
Al-Manṣūrīyah 136-137 L 5
Al-Manzilah 173 BC 2
Almanzora 120-121 F 10
Alma Peak 60 D 1
Al-Ma'qil 136-137 M 7
Al-Maqwa' 136-137 M 8
Al-Marāghah 173 B 4
Al-Marfa' = Al-Maghayrā' 134-135 G 6
Al-Mārīyah 134-135 G 6
Al-Marj 164-165 J 2
Al-Marjah 166-167 H 2
Al-Marsā 166-167 M 1
Almas [BR, Bahia] 100-101 B 7
Almas [BR, Goiás] 100-101 A 6
Almas, Pico das — 100-101 CD 7
Almas, Ribeirão das — 102-103 JK 2
Almas, Serra das — 100-101 D 4
Al-Maṭāmīr 166-167 M 3
Al-Maṭlā' 136-137 M 8
Al-Māṭlīn 166-167 M 1
Al-Māyah 166-167 G 3
Al-Maysarī 136-137 H 7
Almaza = Cairo Airport 170 II c 1
Almazán 120-121 F 8
Al-Mazār 136-137 F 7
Al-Mazr'a 136-137 F 7
Al-Mazra'ah 166-167 K 2
Al-Mazzūnah 166-167 L 2
Al-Mdaina = Al-Madīnah 136-137 M 7
Al-M'dīlah 166-167 L 2
Almeda, Houston-, TX 85 III b 2
Almeida 120-121 D 8
Almeidia Campos 92-93 K 8
Almeirim [BR] 92-93 J 5
Almeirim, Serra do — 98-99 M 5
Almena, KS 68-69 G 6
Almenara [BR] 92-93 LM 8
Almendralejo 120-121 D 9
Al-Meqdādiya = Al-Miqdādīyah 136-137 L 6
Almería 120-121 F 10
Almería, Golfo de — 120-121 F 10
Al'metjevsk 132-133 J 7
Älmhult 116-117 F 9
Al-Midhdharidhrah 164-165 A 5
Al-Mighāir 166-167 J 3
Al-Mijriyyah 164-165 B 5
Al-Mīlīyah 166-167 JK 1
Al-Minyā 164-165 KL 3
Almirantazgo, Seno — 108-109 DE 10
Almirante Brown [Antarctica] 53 C 30-31
Almirante Brown [RA] 110 III bc 2
Almirante Brown-Adrogué 110 III b 2
Almirante Brown-José Mármol 110 III b 2
Almirante Brown-Rafael Calzada 110 III b 2
Almirante Guillermo Brown, Parque — 110 III b 1
Almirante Montt, Golfo — 108-109 C 8
Al-Mish'āb 134-135 F 5
'Almis Marmūshah 166-167 D 3
Al-Mismīyah 136-137 G 6
Al-Miṣr 164-165 KL 3
Al-Mithūyah 166-167 LM 3
Al-Mitlawī 164-165 F 2
Al-Miṭūyah 166-167 LM 3
Al-Mizāb 166-167 J 3
Al-M'jārah 166-167 D 2
Almo, ID 66-67 G 4
Almodóvar del Campo 120-121 E 9
Al Moktar 168-169 G 2
Almond, WI 70-71 F 3
Almond Park, Atlanta-, GA 85 II b 2
Almonesson, NJ 84 III c 3
Almont, CO 68-69 C 6
Almonte [CDN] 72-73 H 2
Almora 138-139 G 3
Almorox 120-121 E 8
Almota, WA 66-67 E 2
Al-M'rāītī 164-165 C 4
Al-Mrayyah 164-165 C 5
Al-Mudawwarah 134-135 D 5
Al-Mughayrā' 136-137 G 8
Al-Mughrān 166-167 C 2
Al-Muḥammadīyah 166-167 C 3
Al-Muhārī 136-137 L 7
Al Mujlad 164-165 K 6
Al-Mukallā 134-135 FG 8
Al-Mukhā 134-135 E 8
Al-Muknīn 166-167 M 2
Almuñécar 120-121 F 10
Al-Muqayyar = Ur 134-135 F 4
Al-Muqqar 166-167 K 3
Al-Muraywad 136-137 L 8
Almus 136-137 G 2
Al-Musayyib 136-137 L 6
Al-Mūṣil 134-135 E 3
Al-Mussanāt 136-137 M 8
Al-Muthanna 136-137 L 7
Al-Muwaffaqīyah 136-137 L 6
Al-Muwayh 134-135 E 6
Al-Muwayliḥ 173 D 4
Alnaši 124-125 T 5
Alnavar 140 B 3
Alnīf 166-167 D 4
Alnwick 119 F 4
Alo Brasil 98-99 N 10-11
Alofi 148-149 b 1
Aloha, OR 66-67 B 3
Aloja 124-125 E 5
Al-'Ōja = Al-'Awjā 136-137 M 8
Alol' 124-125 G 5
Alondra, CA 83 III c 2
Alondra Park 83 III bc 2
Along, Baie d' = Vinh Ha Long 150-151 F 2
Alonsa 61 J 5
Alonso, Rio — 102-103 G 6
Alor, Kepulauan — 152-153 Q 10
Alor, Pulau — 148-149 HJ 8
Alor, Selat — 152-153 PQ 10
Álora 120-121 E 10
Alor Gajah 150-151 D 11
Alor Setar 148-149 CD 5
Alot 138-139 E 6
Alota, Río — 104-105 C 7
Alotau 148-149 NO 9
Aloûgoûm = Alūgūm 166-167 C 4
Al-Ousseukh = 'Ayn Dhahab 166-167 G 2
Aloysius, Mount — 158-159 E 5
Alpachiri 106-107 F 6
Alpasinche 106-107 D 2
Alpena 94-95 DE 8
Alpena, AR 78-79 C 2
Alpena, MI 64-65 K 2
Alpena, SD 68-69 G 3
Alpercatas, Rio — 92-93 KL 6
Alpercatas, Serra das — 100-101 B 3-4
Alpes, Villa Obregón- 91 I b 2
Alpes Cottiennes 120-121 G 6
Alpes Fueguinos 108-109 E 10
Alpes Graies 120-121 L 6
Alpes Maritimes 120-121 L 6
Alpet e Shqipërisë 122-123 HJ 4
Alpha 158-159 J 4
Alpha, IL 70-71 E 5
Alphonse 204-205 N 9
Alpine, AZ 74-75 J 6
Alpine, ID 66-67 H 4
Alpine, TX 64-65 F 5
Alpinópolis 102-103 J 4
Alpi Transilvanici 122-123 KL 3
Alps 122-123 A 3-E 2
Alpu 136-137 D 3
Al-Qa'āmiyāt 134-135 F 7

Al-Qa'ara = Al-Qa'rah 136-137 J 6
Al-Qabāb 166-167 D 3
Al-Qabāil 166-167 HJ 1
Al-Qaḍārif 164-165 M 6
Al-Qaḍīmah 134-135 DE 6
Al-Qādisiyah 136-137 L 7
Al-Qāhirah 164-165 KL 2
Al-Qāhirah-ad-Duqqi 170 II b 1
Al-Qāhirah-al-Abbāsīyah 170 II b 1
Al-Qāhirah-al-Azbakīyah 170 II b 1
Al-Qāhirah-al-Basatin 170 II b 2
Al-Qāhirah-al-Jamālīyah 170 II b 1
Al-Qāhirah-al-Khalifah 170 II b 1
Al-Qāhirah-al-Ma'adī 170 II b 2
Al Qāhirah-al-Matarīyah 170 II bc 1
Al-Qāhirah-al-Muski 170 II b 1
Al-Qāhirah-al-Qubba 170 II b 1
Al-Qāhirah-az-Zamālik 170 II b 1
Al-Qāhirah-az-Zaytun 170 II b 1
Al-Qāhirah-Būlāq 170 II b 1
Al-Qāhirah-Dayr at-Tin 170 II b 2
Al-Qāhirah-Maḥattat al-Hilmīyah 170 II bc 1
Al-Qāhirah-Miṣr al-Jadīdah 173 BC 2
Al-Qāhirah-Miṣr al-Qadīmah 170 II b 1
Al-Qāhirah-Rawd al-Faraj 170 II b 1
Al-Qāhirah-Shubrā 170 II b 1
Al-Qāhirah-Turā 170 II b 2
Al-Qā'im 136-137 J 5
Al-Qal'ah 164-165 F 1
Al-Qal'at al-Kabīrah 166-167 M 2
Al-Qal'at as-S'rāghnah 166-167 C 3-4
Al-Qāmishlīyah 134-135 E 3
Al-Qanṭarah [DZ, landscape] 166-167 J 3
Al-Qanṭarah [DZ, place] 166-167 J 2
Al-Qanṭarah [ET] 173 C 2
Al-Qa'rah [IRQ] 136-137 J 6
Al-Qārah [Saudi Arabia] 136-137 J 8
Al-Qarārah 166-167 J 3
Al-Qaryatayn 136-137 G 5
Al-Qaṣabah 136-137 B 7
Al-Qaṣābī 166-167 D 3
Al-Qaṣīm 134-135 E 5
Al-Qaṣr [DZ] 166-167 J 1
Al-Qaṣr [ET] 164-165 K 3
Al-Qaṣr al-Farāfirah 164-165 K 3
Al-Qaṣrayn 164-165 F 1-2
Al-Qaṭīf 134-135 F 5
Al-Qaṭrānah 136-137 FG 7
Al-Qaṭrūn 164-165 GH 4
Al-Qaṭṭār 166-167 J 2
Al-Qayīyah 134-135 E 6
Al-Qayrawān 164-165 FG 1
Al-Qayṣūmah 134-135 F 5
Al-Qiblī Qamūlā 173 C 5
Al-Q'nitrah 164-165 C 2
Al-Qōsh = Alqūsh 136-137 K 4
Al-Qṣar al-Kabīr 164-165 C 1
Al-Qṣar aṣ-Ṣaghīr 166-167 D 2
Al-Q'ṣībah 166-167 CD 3
Al-Qubayyāt 136-137 G 5
Al-Quds 136-137 F 7
Alqueria, Bogotá- 91 III b 3
Al-Qulī'ah 166-167 H 1
Al-Qull 166-167 K 1
Al-Qunfudhah 134-135 DE 7
Al-Qurayni 134-135 GH 6
Al-Qurayyah 173 DE 3
Al-Qurnah 136-137 M 7
Al-Quṣayr [ET] 164-165 L 3
Al-Quṣayr [IRQ] 136-137 L 7
Al-Quṣayr [SYR] 136-137 G 5
Alqūsh 136-137 K 4
Al-Qūṣīyah 173 B 4
Al-Quṣūr 166-167 L 2
Al-Quṭayfah 136-137 G 6
Al-Quwārib 164-165 A 5
Al-Quwaymāt 136-137 GH 6
Al-Quwayr 136-137 K 4
Al-Quwayrah 136-137 F 8
Alright, Île — 63 F 4
Alroy Downs 158-159 G 3
Als 116-117 C 10
Alsace 120-121 L 4-5
Alsacia 94-95 F 8
Alsask 61 D 5
Alsasua 120-121 FG 7
Alsea, OR 66-67 B 3
Alsek River 58-59 T 6-7
Alsemberg 128 II ab 2
Alsina, Laguna — 106-107 F 6
Alstahaug 116-117 DE 5
Alsterdorf, Hamburg- 130 I ab 1
Alšvanga 124-125 C 5
Alta 116-117 K 3
Alta, IA 70-71 C 4
Altaelv 116-117 K 3
Alta Gracia [RA] 111 CD 4
Altagracia [YV] 92-93 E 2
Altagracia de Orituco 94-95 HJ 3
Altair 102-103 H 4
Altair Seamounts 50-51 H 3
Alta Italia 106-107 E 5
Altaj [Mongolia, Altaj] 142-143 H 2
Altaj [Mongolia, Chovd] 142-143 G 2
Altaj [SU] 132-133 PQ 7
Altajn Nuruu = Mongol Altajn nuruu 142-143 F-H 2
Altamachi, Río — 104-105 C 5
Altamaha River 64-65 K 5
Altamira [BR] 92-93 J 5
Altamira [CO] 94-95 D 6
Altamira [CR] 88-89 DE 9
Altamira [RCH] 104-105 AB 9
Altamira, Bogotá 91 III b 4
Altamira, Cueva de — 120-121 EF 7
Altamira do Maranhão 100-101 B 3
Altamirano 106-107 H 5
Altamont, IL 70-71 F 6
Altamont, OR 66-67 BC 4
Altamont, WY 66-67 H 5
Altamura 122-123 G 5
Altamura, Isla — 86-87 F 5
Altanbulag 142-143 K 1-2
Altan Xiret = Ejin Horo Qi 146-147 BC 2
Altar 86-87 E 2
Altar, Desierto de — 86-87 D 2-3
Altar, Río — 86-87 E 2
Altar of the Earth 155 II b 2
Altar of the Moon 155 II ab 2
Altar of the Sun 155 II b 2
Altar Valley 74-75 H 7
Altata 86-87 FG 5
Alta Vista 106-107 F 6
Alta Vista, KS 68-69 H 6
Altavista, VA 80-81 G 2
Altay 142-143 F 2
Altay = Altaj 132-133 PQ 7
Altdorf 118 D 5
Altenburg 118 F 3
Altenwerder, Hamburg 130 I a 1
Alter do Chão [BR] 92-93 HJ 5
Alte Süderelbe 130 I a 1
Altevatn 116-117 H 3
Altglienicke, Berlin- 130 III c 2
Altheimer, AR 78-79 D 3
Altinho 100-101 F 5
Altinópolis 102-103 J 4
Altınözü = Fatikli 136-137 G 4
Altin Tagh 142-143 EF 4
Altıntaş 136-137 CD 3
Altiplanicie del Pilquiniyeu 108-109 E 3
Altiplanicie de Nuria 94-95 L 4
Altiplanicie Mexicana 64-65 E 5-F 7
Altiplano 92-93 F 8
Altiplano Barreras Blancas 108-109 E 8-F 7
Altmannsdorf, Wien- 113 I b 2
Altmühl 118 E 4
Alto, TX 76-77 G 7
Alto, El — [PE] 96-97 A 4
Alto, El — [RA] 104-105 D 11
Alto Alegre 106-107 F 4
Alto Anapu, Rio — 92-93 J 5
Alto Araguaia 102-103 F 2
Alto Baudó 94-95 C 5
Alto Coité 102-103 EF 1
Alto da Boa Vista, Rio de Janeiro- 110 I b 2
Alto da Mooca, São Paulo — 110 II b 2
Alto de Carrizal 94-95 C 4
Alto del Buey 94-95 C 4
Alto de Quimar 94-95 C 3
Alto de Toledo 96-97 F 9
Alto Garças 92-93 J 8
Alto Grande, Chapada do — 100-101 EF 5
Alto Longá 92-93 L 6
Alto Molócuè = Molócuè 172 G 5
Alton, IL 64-65 HJ 4
Alton, KS 68-69 G 6
Alton, MO 78-79 D 2
Altona, Friedhof — 130 I a 1
Altona, Melbourne- 161 II ab 2
Altona Bay 161 II b 2
Altona Sports Park 161 II b 2
Alto Nevado, Cerro — 108-109 C 5
Altônia 102-103 F 5
Altoona, PA 64-65 L 3
Alto Paraná [BR] 102-103 F 5
Alto Paraná [PY] 102-103 E 6
Alto Parnaíba 92-93 K 6
Alto Pelado 106-107 DE 4
Alto Pencoso 106-107 D 4
Alto Piquiri 111 F 2
Alto Rio Doce 102-103 L 4
Alto Río Mayo 108-109 D 5
Alto Rio Novo 100-101 D 10
Alto Río Senguerr 111 BC 6-7
Altos [BR] 100-101 C 3
Altos [PY] 102-103 D 6
Alto Santo 100-101 E 3
Altos de Chipión 106-107 F 3
Altos de María Enrique 64-65 bc 2
Altos de Talinay 106-107 B 3
Altos de Tarahumar 86-87 G 4-5
Alto Sucuriú 102-103 F 3
Alto Tamar 94-95 D 4
Alto Turi 100-101 B 2
Alto Uruguai 106-107 K 1
Alto Uruguai, Serra do — 106-107 L 1
Altstetten, Zürich- 128 IV a 1
Altuchovo 124-125 JK 7
Altunhisar = Ortaköy 136-137 F 4
Āltūn Kūprī 136-137 L 5
Alturas, CA 66-67 C 5
Alturitas 94-95 E 3
Altus, OK 64-65 G 5
Altyagać 126-127 O 6
Altyn Tagh = Altin tagh 142-143 EF 4
Altyševo 124-125 Q 6
Al-'Ubaylah 134-135 G 6
Al-Ubayyiḍ 164-165 KL 6
Alucra 136-137 H 2
Al-'Udaysāt 173 C 5
Alūgūm 166-167 C 4
Alūksne 124-125 F 5
Al-'Ulā' 134-135 D 5
Al-'Ulmah 166-167 J 1
Alumīné 111 B 5
Aluminé, Lago — 106-107 B 7
Aluminé, Río — 108-109 D 2
Al-'Umshaymin 136-137 H 6
Alung Gangri 142-143 E 5
Alupka 126-127 G 4
Al-'Uqaylah 164-165 H 2
Al-'Uqayr 134-135 FG 5
Al-Uqṣur 164-165 L 3
Alūr [IND, Andhra Pradesh] 140 C 3
Alūr [IND, Karnataka] 140 BC 4
Ālūra = Alūr 140 BC 4
Aluralde 102-103 A 5
Alūru = Ālūr 140 C 3
Al-'Urūq al-Mu'tariḍah 134-135 G 6-7
Al-Ussaltīyah 166-167 LM 2
Alušta 126-127 G 4
Al-Uṭāyah 166-167 J 2
Al-'Uthmānīyah 173 BC 4
Alut Oya 140 E 6
'Aluula 164-165 c 1
Al-'Uwayjā' 134-135 G 6
Al-'Uzayr 136-137 M 7
Alva, FL 80-81 c 3
Alva, OK 76-77 E 4
Alvalade 120-121 C 9-10
Alvand, Kūh-e — 134-135 FG 4
Alvar = Alwar 134-135 M 5
Alvarado 64-65 GH 8
Alvarado, TX 76-77 F 6
Alvarães 92-93 G 5
Álvares Machado 102-103 G 5
Álvarez do Toledo 106-107 H 5
Álvaro Obregón = Frontera 64-65 H 8
Alvaro Obregón, Presa — 86-87 F 4
Alvdal 116-117 D 6
Älvdalen 116-117 F 7
Alvear 106-107 J 2
Alverstone, Mount — 58-59 S 6
Alverthorpe Park 84 III c 1
Alvesen 130 I a 2
Alvesta 116-117 F 9
Alvin, TX 76-77 G 8
Alvin Callander Field United States Naval Air Station 85 I b 2
Alvord Lake 66-67 D 4
Älvsborgs län 116-117 E 8-9
Älvsbyn 116-117 J 5
Al-Wād 164-165 F 2
Al-Wadaḥ 173 D 6
Al-Wāḥāt al-Khārijah 164-165 KL 3-4
Al-Wajh 134-135 D 5
Al-Waqbā 136-137 L 8
Al-Waqf 173 C 4
Alwar 134-135 M 5
Al-Wari'ah 134-135 F 5
Al-Washm 134-135 EF 5-6
Al-Wāsiṭah 164-165 L 3
Alwaye 140 C 5
Al-Wazz 164-165 L 5
Al-Widyan 134-135 E 4
Al-Wūqbā = Al-Waqbā 136-137 L 8
Alys = Kızılırmak 134-135 D 3
Alytus 124-125 E 6
Al-Yūsufīyah 136-137 KL 6
Alzada, MT 68-69 D 3
Alzaga 106-107 H 7
Alzamaj 132-133 S 6
Amabele 174-175 G 7
Amacuro, Río — 94-95 L 3
Amada = 'Amādah 173 C 6
Amadabad = Ahmadābād 134-135 L 6
'Amādah 173 C 6
Amadeus, Lake — 158-159 F 4
Amādī 164-165 KL 7
'Amādīyah, Al- 136-137 K 4
Amadjuak Lake 56-57 W 4-5
Amado Grande 96-97 C 7
Amagā 94-95 D 4
Amagasaki 144-145 K 5
Amahai 148-149 J 7
Amaicha del Valle 110 III b 1
Amak Island 58-59 b 2
Amakusa nada 144-145 G 6
Amakusa-rettō 142-143 O 5
Amakusa syotō = Amakusa-rettō 142-143 O 5
Åmål 116-117 E 8
Amalfi [CO] 94-95 D 4
Amalfi [I] 122-123 F 5
Amaliás 122-123 J 7
Amalner 138-139 E 7
Amaluza 96-97 B 4
Amalyk 132-133 W 6
Amamā 104-105 E 10
Amambaí 102-103 E 5
Amambaí, Rio — 102-103 E 5
Amambaí, Serra de — 102-103 E 5
Amambay 102-103 DE 5
Amami-guntō 142-143 O 6
Amami-ō-shima 142-143 O 6
Amami-Ō sima = Amami-ō-shima 142-143 O 6
Amandola 122-123 E 4
Amangel'dy 132-133 M 7-8
Amaniú 100-101 CD 6
Amanos dağları = Nur dağları 136-137 G 4
Amantea 122-123 FG 6
Amanuma, Tōkyō- 155 III a 1
Amapá [BR, Acre] 98-99 D 10
Amapá [BR, Amapá administrative unit] 92-93 J 4
Amapá [BR, Amapá place] 92-93 J 4
Amapari, Rio — 98-99 M 4
Amar, Ḥāssī el — = Ḥāssī al-Aḥmar 166-167 E 3
Amara 164-165 M 6
Amarabūra 141 E 5
'Amarah, Al- 134-135 F 4
Amaraji 100-101 G 5
Amaramba, Lagoa — = Lagoa Chiuta 172 G 4
Amarante [BR] 92-93 L 6
Amarante do Maranhão 100-101 A 3
Amaranth 61 J 5
Amarapura = Amarabūra 141 E 5
Amarāvati [IND, Andhra Pradesh] 140 E 2
Amarāvati [IND, Tamil Nadu] 140 C 5
Amarāvatī = Amrāvati 134-135 M 6
Amarete 104-105 B 4
Amarga, Bañados de la — 106-107 EF 5
Amargo, CA 74-75 E 5
Amargosa 100-101 E 7
Amargosa Desert 74-75 E 4
Amargosa Range 74-75 E 4-5
Amargosa River 74-75 E 5
Amari, Laghi — = Al-Buḥayrat al-Murrat al-Kubrā 173 C 2
Amarillo, TX 64-65 F 4
'Amarina, Tel el- = Tall al-'Amārinah 173 B 4
'Amārinah, Tall al- 173 B 4
Amarkantak 138-139 HJ 6
Amarnāth 138-139 D 8
Amaro 106-107 L 4
Amaro Leite 92-93 JK 7
Amarpātan 138-139 H 5
Amarpatnam = Amarpātan 138-139 H 5
Amarpur 138-139 L 5
Amarpurā = Amrāpāra 138-139 L 5
Amarume 144-145 M 3
Amarūsion 122-123 KL 6-7
Amarvāṛā = Amarwāra 138-139 G 6
Amarwāra 138-139 G 6
Amasa, MI 70-71 F 2
Amāsin, Bi'r — 166-167 LM 5
Amasra 136-137 E 2
Amasya 134-135 D 2
Amatán 86-87 O 9
Amataurá 98-99 DE 6
Amatignak Island 58-59 t 7
Amatique, Bahía de — 64-65 J 8
Amatonga 174-175 K 2
Amauã, Lago — 92-93 G 5
Amazon 61 F 5
Amazon = Amazonas 92-93 F-H 5
Amazon, Mouth of the — = Estuário do Rio Amazonas 92-93 JK 4
Amazonas [BR] 92-93 F-H 5
Amazonas [CO] 94-95 EF 8
Amazonas [EC] 96-97 B 3
Amazonas [PE] 96-97 B 4-C 5
Amazonas [YV] 94-95 HJ 6
Amazonas, Estuário do Rio — 92-93 JK 4
Amazonas, Rio — [BR] 92-93 HJ 5
Amazonas, Río — [PE] 92-93 E 5
Amazon Shelf 50-51 G 5-6
Āmbā = Ambāh 138-139 G 4
Amba Alage 164-165 MN 6
Amba Alaji = Amba Alage 164-165 MN 6
Ambābhona 138-139 J 7
Ambad 138-139 E 8
Āmbādalā = Ambodala 138-139 J 8
Ambāh 138-139 G 4
Ambājogāi 134-135 M 7
Ambāla 134-135 M 4
Ambalamgoda 140 DE 7
Ambalamtota 140 E 7
Ambalapulai 140 C 6
Ambalavao 172 J 6
Ambalema 94-95 D 5
Ambam 164-165 G 8
Ambanja 172 J 4
Ambarčik 132-133 fg 4
Ambargasta 106-107 EF 2
Ambargasta, Sierra — 106-107 EF 2
Ambaro, Baie d' 172 J 4
'Ambarūsī, Ḥāssī — 166-167 F 6
Ambāsamudram 140 C 6
Ambassador Bridge 84 II b 3
Ambato 92-93 D 5
Ambato, Sierra de — 104-105 C 11
Ambatoboeny 172 J 5
Ambatolampy 172 J 5
Ambatondrazaka 172 J 5
Ambatosoratra 172 J 5
Ambelau, Pulau — 148-149 J 7
Ambepussa 140 DE 7
Amber 138-139 EF 4
Amber, WA 66-67 E 2
Amber Bay 58-59 e 1
Amberg 118 EF 4
Ambergris Cay 64-65 J 8
Ambidédi 168-169 C 2
Ambikāpur 134-135 N 6
'Ambikūl 173 B 7
Ambilobe 172 JK 4
Ambition, Mount — 58-59 W 8
Ambler River 58-59 J 3
Ambo 96-97 CD 7
Ambodāla 138-139 J 8
Ambodifototra 172 JK 5
Ambohibe 172 H 6
Ambohimahasoa 172 J 6
Amboim = Gabela 172 BC 4
Amboina = Pulau Ambon 148-149 J 7
Amboise 120-121 H 5
Amboland = Ovamboland 172 BC 5
Ambon 148-149 J 7
Ambon, Pulau — 148-149 J 7
Amboseli, Lake — 171 D 3
Amboseli Game Reserve 172 G 2
Ambositra 172 J 6
Ambovombe 172 J 7
Amboy, CA 74-75 F 5
Amboy, IL 70-71 F 5
Amboyna Cay 148-149 F 5
Ambrakikòs Kólpos 122-123 J 6
Ambre, Cap d' 172 JK 4
Ambre, Montagne d' 172 J 4
Ambridge, PA 72-73 FG 4
Ambrim 158-159 N 3
Ambriz 172 B 3
Ambrizete = N'Zeto 172 B 3
Ambrolauri 126-127 L 5
Ambrosini, Hassi — = Ḥāssī 'Ambarūsī 166-167 F 6
Ambrósio 100-101 B 4
Ambrósio, Serra do — 102-103 L 3
Āmbūr 140 D 4
Amchitka, AK 58-59 s 7
Amchitka Island 52 D 1
Amchitka Pass 58-59 t 7
Am-Dam 164-165 J 6
Amderma 132-133 L 4
Ameca 64-65 F 7
Ameca, Río — 86-87 H 7
Amedabad = Ahmadābād 134-135 L 6
Ameghino 106-107 F 5
Ameghino, Punta — 108-109 G 4
Amelia, NE 68-69 G 4
Amelia Court House, VA 80-81 GH 2
Amenābar 106-107 F 5
Aménas, In — = 'Ayn Umannās 164-165 F 3
Amenia, NY 72-73 K 4
Amer, Grand Lac — = Al-Buḥayrat al-Murrat al-Kubrā 173 C 2
Amerasia Basin 50-51 A-C 1
América Dourada 100-101 D 6
Americana 102-103 J 5
American Falls, ID 66-67 G 4
American Falls Reservoir 66-67 G 4
American Fork, UT 66-67 H 5
American Highland 53 B 8
Americanópolis, São Paulo — 110 II b 3
American River North Fork 74-75 C 3
Americas, Hipódromo de las — 91 I b 2
Americas, University of the — 91 I b 2
Americus, GA 64-65 K 5
Amerikahaven 128 I a 1
Amersfoort [NL] 120-121 K 2
Amersfoort [ZA] 174-175 HJ 4
Amery, WI 70-71 D 3
Amery Ice Shelf 53 BC 7-8
Amerzgān = Amirzgān 166-167 C 4
Ames, IA 64-65 H 3
Ames, OK 76-77 EF 4
Amesbury, MA 72-73 L 3
Amesdale 62 C 2-3
Ameṭ 138-139 DE 5
Amethi 138-139 H 4
Amfilochía 122-123 J 6
Ámfissa 122-123 K 6
Amga [SU, place] 132-133 Z 5
Amga [SU, river] 132-133 X 6
Amgaon 138-139 H 7
Amgar, Al- 136-137 L 8
Amghar, Al — = Al-Amgar 136-137 L 8
Amgu 132-133 a 8
Amguema 132-133 k 4
Am-Guereda 164-165 J 6
Amguid = Amqīd 166-167 J 6
Amgun' [SU, place] 132-133 a 7
Amgun' [SU, river] 132-133 a 7
Āmguri 141 D 2
Amhara = Amara 164-165 M 6
Amherst 56-57 XY 8
Amherst, MA 72-73 K 3
Amherst, VA 80-81 G 2
Amherst = Kyaikhkamī 141 E 7
Amherst, Île — 63 F 4
Amherst, Mount — 158-159 E 3
Amherstburg 72-73 E 3
Amherst Junction, WI 70-71 F 3
Ami, Mont — 171 B 2
Amiata, Monte — 122-123 D 4
Amidon, ND 68-69 E 2
Amiens 120-121 J 4
'Āmij, Wādī — 136-137 J 6
Amik gölü 136-137 G 4
Amīndīvi Islands 134-135 L 8
Aminga 106-107 D 2
Aminjevo, Moskva- 113 V b 3
Amino 144-145 K 5
Aminuis 172 C 6
Aminuis Reserve 174-175 C 2
Amirantes 204-205 N 9
'Amīrīyah, Al- 173 AB 2
Amirzgān 166-167 C 4
Amisk Lake 61 G 3
Amisós = Samsun 134-135 D 2
Amistad, NM 76-77 C 5
Amistad, Presa de la — 86-87 JK 3
Amite, LA 78-79 D 5
Amity, AR 78-79 C 3
Amīzmiz 166-167 B 4
Amlekhganj 138-139 K 4
Amlia Island 52 D 36
'Ammān 134-135 D 4
Ammarfjället 116-117 FG 4
Ammerman Mount 58-59 RS 2
Ammersee 118 E 5
Ammóchōstos 134-135 CD 3
Ammochōstu, Kólpos — 136-137 EF 5
Amnat Charoen 150-151 E 5
Amnok-kang 142-143 O 3
Amnyemachhen Gangri 142-143 HJ 5
Āmod 138-139 D 6-7
Amolar 102-103 D 3
Amontada 100-101 DE 2
Amores, Los — 111 DE 3
Amorgós 122-123 LM 7
Amory, MS 78-79 E 3-4
Amos 56-57 V 8
Amos, CA 74-75 F 6
Amotape, Cerros de — 96-97 A 4
'Amoûdâ = 'Āmudā 136-137 J 4
Amour, Djebel — = Jabal 'Amūr 166-167 G 3-H 2
Amoy = Xiamen 142-143 M 7
Ampanihy 172 H 6
Amparo 102-103 J 5
Amparo, El — 94-95 E 6
Amparo de Apure, El — 94-95 F 3
Ampasindava, Baie d' 172 J 4
Ampato, Cordillera de — 96-97 EF 9
Ampato, Nevado de — 92-93 E 8
Ampère = 'Ayn 'Azl 166-167 J 2
Amphípolis 122-123 K 5
Amphitrite Point 60 DE 5
Amposta 120-121 H 8
Ampurias 120-121 J 7
Amqīd 166-167 J 6
Amqui 63 C 3
Amrāpāra 138-139 L 5
Amrāvati 134-135 M 6
Amrawati = Amrāvati 134-135 M 6
Amreli 138-139 C 7
Amritsar 134-135 LM 4
Amroha 134-135 M 5
Amselhain 130 III c 1
Amsīd, Al- 164-165 B 3
Amstel 128 I a 2
Amstelhoek 128 I a 2
Amstelland 128 I a 2
Amsterdam, NY 72-73 JK 3
Amsterdam [NL] 120-121 K 2
Amsterdam [ZA] 174-175 J 4
Amsterdam, Universiteit van — 128 I ab 1
Amsterdam-Buiten Veldert 128 I a 2
Amsterdam-Geuzenveld 128 I a 1
Amsterdam Island = Nouvelle Amsterdam 204-205 NO 7
Amsterdam-Nieuwendam 128 I b 1
Amsterdam-Oostzaan 128 I ab 1
Amsterdam-Osdorp 128 I a 1
Amsterdam Plateau 50-51 NO 8
Amsterdam-Slotervaar 128 I a 1
Amsterdam-Tuindorp 128 I ab 1
Amstetten 118 G 4
Amt'ae-do 144-145 EF 5
Am-Timan 164-165 J 6
Amú, Río — 94-95 E 7
'Āmūdā 136-137 J 4
Amudarja 134-135 J 2
Amukta Island 58-59 l 4
Amukta Pass 58-59 kl 4
Amuku Mountains 98-99 J 3-4
Amund Ringnes Island 56-57 RS 2
Amundsen, Mount — 53 BC 11
Amundsen Bay 53 C 5
Amundsen Glacier 53 A 23-20
Amundsen Gulf 56-57 L-N 3
Amundsen havet 53 BC 25-26
Amundsen-Scott 53 A
Amuntai 152-153 L 7
Amur 132-133 Z 8
Amur = Heilong Jiang 142-143 P 2
Amurang 148-149 H 6
Amursk 132-133 a 7
Amurskij zaliv 144-145 H 1
Amuwo 170 III a 2
Amvrosijevka 126-127 HJ 3
Amyā Taunggyā 150-151 B 6
An 141 CD 6
Anabar 132-133 V 3
Anābib an-Nafṭ 134-135 DE 4
Ana Branch 158-159 H 6
Anabuki 144-145 K 5-6
Anacapa Island 74-75 D 6
Anaco 94-95 J 3
Anaconda, MT 64-65 D 2
Anaconda Range 66-67 G 2-3
Anacortes, WA 66-67 B 1
Anacostia, Washington-, DC 82 II b 2
Anacostia Park 82 II b 2
Anacostia River 82 II ab 2
Anadarko, OK 76-77 EF 5
Anadia [BR] 100-101 F 5
Anadolu burnu 154 I b 1
Anadolufeneri 154 I bc 1
Anadoluhisarı 154 I b 2
Anadoluhisarı, İstanbul- 154 I b 2
Anadolukavağı, İstanbul- 154 I b 1
Anadyr' [SU, place] 132-133 j 5
Anadyr' [SU, river] 132-133 hj 5
Anadyrskaja nizmennost' 132-133 j 4-5
Anadyrskij zaliv 132-133 j-l 5
Anadyrskoje ploskogorje 132-133 h 4
Anāfē 122-123 LM 7
Anagni 122-123 E 5
'Ānah 136-137 JK 5
Anaheim, CA 74-75 DE 6
Aṇahilvāḍ-Pātan = Pātan 138-139 D 6
Anahim Lake 60 E 3
Anahuac, TX 76-77 G 8
Anáhuac [MEX, Nuevo León] 86-87 K 4
Anáhuac [MEX, Zacatecas] 86-87 K 5
Anáhuac, Mesa de — 64-65 FG 7-8
Ānai Malai 140 C 5
Ānai Mudi 140 C 5
Anaiza, Jebel — = Jabal Unayzah 134-135 DE 4
Anajás 92-93 JK 5
Anajás, Ilha — 98-99 N 5
Anajás, Rio — 98-99 N 5
Anajatuba 100-101 B 2
Anajé 100-101 D 8
Anak 144-145 E 3
Anakāpalle 134-135 N 7
Anakāpaḷḷi = Anakāpalle 134-135 N 7
Anak Krakatau 148-149 DE 8
Anaktuk, AK 58-59 H 1
Anaktuvuk Pass, AK 58-59 KL 2
Anaktuvuk River 58-59 M 2
Analalava 172 J 4
Anamā 92-93 G 5
Anama Bay 61 J 5
Ānamaḍuwa 140 DE 7
Anamala = Ānai Malai 140 C 5
Anambas, Kepulauan — 148-149 E 6
Anambra [WAN, administrative unit] 164-165 F 7
Anambra [WAN, river] 168-169 G 4
Anamoose, ND 68-69 FG 2
Anamosa, IA 70-71 E 4
Anamu, Rio — 98-99 K 4
Anamur 134-135 C 3
Anamur burnu 134-135 C 3
Anan 144-145 K 6
Ananás, Cachoeira — 98-99 M 8
Ānand 138-139 D 6
Anandpur 138-139 L 7
Ananea 96-97 G 9
Ananjev 126-127 DE 3
Anantapur 134-135 M 8
Anantnāg 134-135 M 4
Anapa 126-127 H 4
Anapali, Rio — 96-97 E 7
Anápolis 92-93 K 8
Anapurna = Annapūrna 138-139 JK 3
Anār 134-135 GH 4
Anārak 134-135 G 4
Anārdara 134-135 J 4
Anari, Rio — 104-105 E 2
Anastácio 102-103 E 4
Anastácio, Ponta — 106-107 M 3
Anastasia Island 80-81 c 2
Anatolia 134-135 CD 3
Anatone, WA 66-67 E 2
Añatuya 111 D 3
Anauá, Rio — 98-99 HJ 4
Anavilhanas, Arquipélago dos — 98-99 H 6
Āṇayirāvu 140 E 6
Anaypazarı 136-137 E 4
Anbār, Al- 136-137 J 6
Anbianbu 146-147 AB 3
An Biên 150-151 E 8
Anbyŏn 144-145 F 3
Ancaján 106-107 E 2
Ancash 96-97 BC 6
Ancasti 104-105 D 11
Ancasti, Sierra de — 106-107 E 2
Ancenis 120-121 G 5
Anceny, MT 66-67 H 3
An Châu 150-151 F 2
An-chi = Anji 146-147 G 6
An-ch'i = Anxi 146-147 G 9
Anchieta 102-103 M 4
An-ching = Anqing 142-143 M 5
An-ch'iu = Anqiu 146-147 G 3
Ancho, NM 76-77 B 6
Ancho, Canal — 108-109 B 7-8
Anchorage, AK 56-57 FG 5
Anchorena 106-107 E 5
Anchoris 106-107 C 4
Anchor Point, AK 58-59 M 7
Anchuras 120-121 E 9
Anci 146-147 F 2
Ancient Observatory 155 II b 2
Anciferovo 124-125 JK 4
Anclote Keys 80-81 b 2
Ancober = Ankober 164-165 MN 7
Ancohuma, Nevado — 104-105 B 4
Ancol, Jakarta- 154 IV ab 1
Ancon [EC] 96-97 A 3
Ancón [PE] 96-97 C 7
Ancón [RA] 106-107 G 5
Ancona 122-123 E 4
Ancon de Sardinas, Bahía de — 96-97 B 1
Âncora, Ilha da — 102-103 M 5
Ancoraimes 104-105 B 4
Ancos 96-97 BC 6
Ancuabe 172 G 4
Ancud 111 B 6
Ancud, Golfo de — 111 B 6
Ancyra = Ankara 134-135 C 3
Anda 142-143 NO 2
Andacollo 106-107 B 6
Andahuaylas 96-97 E 8
Andale, KS 68-69 H 7
Andalgalá 111 C 3
Åndalsnes 116-117 BC 6
Andalucía [CO] 94-95 CD 5
Andalucía [E] 120-121 D-F 10
Andalusia, AL 78-79 F 5
Andalusia = Andalucía 120-121 D-F 10
Andalusia = Jan Kemp 174-175 F 4
Andaman and Nicobar Islands 134-135 OP 8
Andaman Basin 148-149 BC 4-5
Andamān Dvīp = Andaman Islands 134-135 P 8
Andamanensee 148-149 C 4-5
Andaman Islands 134-135 P 8
Andaman Sea 148-149 C 4-5
Andamarca [BOL] 104-105 C 6
Andamarca [PE] 96-97 D 7
Andamooka 158-159 G 6
Andamooka Ranges 160 C 3
Andant 111 D 5
Andara 172 D 5
Andaraí 100-101 D 7
Andaraí, Rio de Janeiro- 110 I b 2
Andarīn, Al- 136-137 G 5
Andelys, les — 120-121 H 4
Andenes 116-117 G 3
Andérambouka̱ne 168-169 F 2
Andermatt 118 D 5
Anderson, CA 66-67 BC 5
Anderson, IN 64-65 J 3
Anderson, MO 76-77 G 4

Anderson, SC 64-65 K 5
Anderson, TX 76-77 FG 7
Andersonkop 174-175 J 3
Anderson Park 85 II b 2
Anderson Ranch Reservoir 66-67 F 4
Anderson River 56-57 L 4
Andes 92-93 D 3
Andes, Cordillera de los — 92-93 E 3-F 9
Andes, Lake — 68-69 G 4
Andes, Los — 111 B 4
Andheri 138-139 D 8
Andhra 134-135 M 8-N 7
Andhra Pradesh 134-135 M 8-N 7
Andidanob, Jebel — = Jabal Asūtarībah 173 E 7
Andijskij chrebet 126-127 MN 5
Andijskoje Kojsu 126-127 MN 5
Andīmashk 136-137 N 6
Andırın 136-137 G 4
Andižan 134-135 L 2
Andizhan = Andižan 134-135 L 2
Andkhoy 134-135 JK 3
Andoas 92-93 D 5
Andoga 124-125 L 4
Āndol 140 D 2
Āndola 140 C 2
Āndōlā = Āndola 140 C 2
Andomskij Pogost 124-125 L 3
Andong 142-143 O 4
Andong = Dandong 142-143 N 3
Andongwei 146-147 G 4
Andorinha 100-101 DE 6
Andorinhas, Cachoeira das — 94-95 G 8
Andørja 116-117 GH 3
Andorra 120-121 H 7
Andorra la Vella 120-121 H 7
Andou, Lac — 72-73 H 1
Andover, OH 72-73 F 4
Andover, SD 68-69 GH 3
Andøy 116-117 FG 3
Andra = Āndhra 134-135 M 8-N 7
Andradina 92-93 J 9
Andrau Airport 85 III a 2
Andreafsky = Saint Marys, AK 58-59 F 5
Andreafsky, East Fork — 58-59 FG 5
Andreafsky River 58-59 F 5
Andreanof Islands 52 D 36
Andreapol' 124-125 J 5
Andreas, Cape — = Akrōthérion Hágios Andréas 136-137 F 5
Andréba = Ambatosoratra 172 J 5
Andrée land 116-117 j 5
Andréeneset 116-117 n 4
Andrejevka [SU, Kazachskaja SSR] 132-133 OP 8
Andrejevka [SU, Rossijskaja SFSR] 124-125 ST 7
Andrejevka [SU, Ukrainskaja SSR] 126-127 H 3
Andrelândia 102-103 KL 4
Andrés Bello, Universidad Catolica — 91 II b 2
Andréville 63 B 4
Andrew Au 141 CD 6
Andrews, NC 80-81 E 3
Andrews, OR 66-67 D 4
Andrews, SC 80-81 G 4
Andrews, TN 80-81 E 3
Andrews, TX 76-77 C 6
Andrews Air Force Base 82 II b 2
Ándria 122-123 FG 5
Andriba 172 J 5
Andringitra 172 J 6
Androka 172 H 7
Andronica Island 58-59 cd 2
Andronovskoje 124-125 K 3
Ándros 122-123 L 7
Androscoggin River 72-73 L 2
Andros Island 64-65 L 7
Andros Town 88-89 H 2
Androth Island 134-135 L 8
Andruševka 126-127 D 1
Andr'uškino 132-133 de 4
Andsfjord 116-117 G 3
Andújar 120-121 EF 9
Andulo 172 C 4
Anecón Grande, Cerro — 108-109 D 3
Anéfis 168-169 F 1
Anegada 64-65 O 8
Anegada, Bahía — 108-109 HJ 3
Anegada Passage 64-65 O 8
Anegasaki 155 III d 3
Anèho 164-165 E 7
Aneityum 158-159 N 4
Anekal 140 C 4
Añélo 111 C 5
Añelo, Cuenca del — 106-107 C 7
Anenous 174-175 B 5
Anes Baraka 168-169 G 1
Aneta, ND 68-69 GH 2
Aneto, Pico de — 120-121 H 7
Aney 164-165 G 5
Anezī = 'Anzī 166-167 B 5
Anfeng 146-147 H 5
Anfu 146-147 E 8
An-fu = Linli 142-143 L 6
Angādippuram 140 BC 5
Angamāli 140 C 5
Angamos, Isla — 108-109 B 7
Angamos, Punta — 111 B 2
Ang-ang-ch'i = Ang'angxi 142-143 N 2
Ang'angxi 142-143 N 2
Angara 132-133 S 6
Angarsk 132-133 T 7
Angarskij kr'až 132-133 S-U 6
Angatuba 102-103 H 5
Angchhen Gonpa 138-139 N 2-3
Ånge 116-117 F 6
Angechakot 126-127 M 7
Angel, El — 96-97 C 1
Angel, Salto del — 92-93 G 3
Ángel de la Guarda, Isla — 64-65 D 6
Ángeles, Los — [RA] 106-107 GH 5
Ángeles, Los — [RCH] 111 B 5
Ángel Etcheverry 106-107 HJ 5
Ängelholm 116-117 E 9
Angelina 102-103 H 7
Angelina, La — 106-107 E 5
Angelina River 76-77 G 7
Angel Island 83 I b 1
Angel Island State Park 83 I b 1
Angel Provincial Forest 62 B 3
Ångermanälven 116-117 G 5-6
Ångermanland 116-117 GH 6
Angermünde 118 FG 2
Angers 120-121 G 5
Ångesån 116-117 K 4
Angical 100-101 B 6-7
Angical, Serra do — 100-101 B 6
Angicos 100-101 F 3
Angka, Doi — = Doi Inthanon 148-149 C 3
Angke, Kali — 154 IV a 1
Angkor 148-149 D 4
Angkor Thom 150-151 D 6
Angkor Vat 150-151 DE 6
Anglesey 119 D 5
Angleton, TX 76-77 G 8
Anglialing Hu = Nganglha Ringtsho 138-139 J 2
Angliers 72-73 G 1
Angmagssalik = Angmagssaliq 56-57 de 4
Angmagssaliq 56-57 de 4
Ang Mo Kio 154 III ab 1
Ango 172 E 1
Angoche 172 GH 5
Angoche, Ilhas — 172 GH 5
Angol 111 B 5
Angola 172 CD 4
Angola, IN 70-71 H 5
Angola, NY 72-73 G 3
Angola Basin 50-51 JK 6
Angoon, AK 58-59 U 8
Angoon, AK 58-59 v 8
Angora = Ankara 134-135 C 3
Angostura = Ciudad Bolívar 92-93 G 3
Angostura I, Salto de — 92-93 E 4
Angostura II, Salto de — 92-93 E 4
Angostura Reservoir 68-69 E 4
Angosturas 92-93 E 5
Angoulême 120-121 H 6
Angoumois 120-121 GH 6
Angra do Heroismo 204-205 E 5
Angra dos Reis 102-103 K 5
Angrapa 118 KL 1
Angra Pequena = Lüderitzbaai 172 BC 7
Angren 134-135 KL 2
Angrenšachtstroj = Angren 134-135 KL 2
Angrignon, Jardin zoologique — 82 I b 2
Angtassom 150-151 E 7
Angteng La 138-139 L 3
Ang Thong 150-151 C 5
Anguá 106-107 H 2
Angualasto 106-107 C 3
Anguellou = 'Anqallaw 166-167 G 5
Anguera 100-101 E 7
Anguil 106-107 E 6
Anguila = Anguilla 64-65 O 8
Anguilla 64-65 O 8
Anguilla Cays 88-89 G 3
Anguille, Cape — 63 G 4
Angul 138-139 K 7
Ángulos 106-107 D 2
Angumu 172 E 2
Anguo 146-147 E 2
Angustora, Presa de la — 86-87 O 9-10
Anhandui-Guaçu, Rio — 102-103 EF 4
Anhanduízinho, Rio — 102-103 EF 4
Anholt 116-117 D 9
Anhsi = Anxi 142-143 H 3
An-hsiang = Anxiang 146-147 D 7
Anhua 146-147 C 7
An-Huei = Anhui 142-143 M 5
Anhuei = Anhui 142-143 M 5
Anhui 142-143 M 5
Anhumas 92-93 HJ 8
Ani 144-145 N 2-3
An-i = Anyi [TJ, Jiangxi] 146-147 E 7
An-i = Anyi [TJ, Shanxi] 146-147 C 4
Aniai = Ani 144-145 N 2-3
Aniak, AK 58-59 H 6
Aniakchak Volcano 58-59 de 1
Aniak River 58-59 H 6
Aníbal Pinto, Lago — 108-109 C 8-9
Anicuns 102-103 GH 2
Anié 168-169 F 4
Anie, Pic d' 120-121 G 7
Anikovo 124-125 O 4
Anikščiai 124-125 E 6
Anil 100-101 B 2
Anil, Rio de Janeiro- 110 I a 2
Anil, Rio do — 110 I a 2
Animas, NM 74-75 J 7
Animas, Las — 76-77 C 9
Animas, Punta — 104-105 A 10
Animas Peak 74-75 J 7
Anin 141 E 8
Anina 122-123 JK 3
Anipemza 126-127 LM 6
Anita, AZ 74-75 G 5
Anita, IA 70-71 C 5
Anitápolis 102-103 H 7
Aniuk River 58-59 J 2
Aniva, mys — 132-133 b 8
Aniva, zaliv — 132-133 b 8
Aniva Bay = zaliv Aniva 132-133 b 8
Anjangāńv = Anjangaon 138-139 F 7
Anjangaon 138-139 F 7
Añjankōḍ = Anjengo 140 C 6
Anjār 134-135 KL 6
An-jên = Anren 146-147 D 8
Anjengo 140 C 6
Anjer = Anyerkidul 152-153 F 9
Anji 146-147 G 6
Anjou [CDN] 82 I b 1
Anjou [F] 120-121 G 5
Anjou, Les Galleries d' 82 I b 1
Anjou, ostrova — 52 B 4-5
Anjouan = Ndzuwani 172 HJ 4
Anju 142-143 O 4
Anjudin 124-125 W 2
Anka 168-169 G 2
Ańkalēshvar = Anklesvar 138-139 D 7
Ankang 146-147 B 5
Ankara 134-135 C 3
Ankara suyu 136-137 DE 3
Ankaratra 172 J 5
Ankara-Yenidoğan 136-137 E 2
Ankara-Yenişehir 136-137 E 3
Ankazoabo 172 H 6
Ankeveen 128 I b 2
Ankeveense plassen 128 I b 2
An Khe 148-149 E 4
Anki = Anxi 146-147 G 9
Anking = Anqing 142-143 M 5
Ankiu = Anqiu 146-147 G 3
Anklam 118 F 2
Anklesvar 138-139 D 7
Ankober 164-165 MN 7
Ankola 140 B 3
Ankūr, Jabal — 173 DE 7
Ankwe 168-169 H 3
An Lao 150-151 G 5
An Lôc 150-151 F 7
Anlong 142-143 JK 6
Anlong Veng 150-151 E 5
Anlu 146-147 D 6
An-lu = Zhongxiang 146-147 D 6
Anlung = Anlong 142-143 JK 6
Anma-do 144-145 E 5
Ann, Cape — 72-73 L 3
Anna 126-127 K 1
Anna, IL 70-71 F 7
Annaba = Annābah 164-165 F 1
Annābah 164-165 F 1
An-Nabk [Saudi Arabia] 136-137 G 7
An-Nabk [SYR] 134-135 D 4
An-Nadhatah 136-137 J 6
An-Nadjaf = An-Najaf 134-135 E 4
An-Nāḍūr 166-167 E 2
An-Nafūd 134-135 E 5
An-Nahīlah = An-Nakhīlah 166-167 E 2
Annai 92-93 H 4
An-Najaf 134-135 E 4
An-Nakhīlah 166-167 E 2
Annalee Heights, VA 82 II a 2
Annam = Trung Bô 148-149 D 3-E 4
Annam, Porte d' = Đeo Ngang 150-151 F 3-4
An-Na'māh 164-165 C 5
An-Na'māniyah 136-137 L 6
Anna Maria Key 80-81 b 3
An-Namlāt 166-167 KL 2
Annan 119 E 4
Annandale, MN 70-71 C 3
Annandale, VA 82 II a 2
Annapareddipalle 140 E 2
Annapolis, MD 64-65 L 4
Annapolis, MO 70-71 E 7
Annapolis Royal 56-57 XY 9
Annapūrna 138-139 JK 3
Ann Arbor, MI 64-65 K 3
An-Nāṣirīyah 134-135 F 4
An-Naṣr 173 C 5
An-Nawfalīyah 164-165 H 2
Annecy 120-121 L 6
An Ne'māniya = An-Na'māniyah 136-137 L 6
Annenskij Most 124-125 L 3
Annette, AK 58-59 x 9
Annette Island 58-59 x 9
An-N'fidah 166-167 M 1
Anngueur, Erg el — = 'Irq al-'Anqar 166-167 G 3-H 4
An Nho'n 148-149 E 4
Annigeri 140 B 3
An-Nikhaib = Nukhayb 134-135 E 4
An-Nīl 164-165 L 5
An-Nīl al-Abyaḍ 164-165 L 6
An-Nīl al-Azraq [Sudan, administrative unit] 164-165 L 6
An-Nīl al-Azraq [Sudan, river] 164-165 L 6
An Niṣāb = Anṣāb 134-135 F 8
Anniston, AL 64-65 JK 5
Annobón = Pagalu 204-205 H 9
Annonciation, l' 72-73 J 1
Annotto Bay 88-89 H 5
Annu 168-169 H 3
An-Nubah 164-165 K-M 4-5
An-Nuhaylah 173 B 4
An-Nuhūd 164-165 K 6
Anoka, MN 70-71 D 3
Año Nuevo, Seno — 108-109 E 10
Anouâl = Anwāl [MA, An-Nāḍūr] 166-167 E 2
Anouâl = Anwāl [MA, Ar-Rashidīyah] 166-167 E 3
Anou Mellene 168-169 F 1
An-pien-pao = Anbianbu 146-147 AB 3
Anping 146-147 E 2
Anpu 146-147 C 11
Anpu Gang 146-147 B 11
Anqallaw 166-167 G 5
'Anqar, 'Irq al- 166-167 G 3-H 4
Anqing 142-143 M 5
Anqiu 146-147 G 3
Anren 146-147 D 8
Anṣāb 134-135 F 8
Anṣāb = Niṣāb 134-135 EF 5
Ansai 146-147 B 3
Anṣārīyah, Jabal al- 136-137 G 5
Ansbach 118 E 4
Anse-au-Loup, l' 63 H 2
Anse-aux-Griffons, l' 63 DE 3
Anse-aux-Meadows, l' 63 J 2
Ansekūla 124-125 D 4
Anselmo, NE 68-69 FG 5
Anserma 94-95 CD 5
Anse-Saint-Jean, l' 63 A 3
Anshan 146-147 G 2
Anshun 142-143 K 6
Ansiang = Anxiang 146-147 D 7
Ansilta, Cerro — 106-107 C 3-4
Ansilta, Cordillera de — 106-107 C 3
Ansina 106-107 K 3
Ansley, NE 68-69 G 5
Ansley Park, Atlanta-, GA 85 II b 2
Ansó 120-121 G 7
Anson, TX 76-77 DE 6
Anson Bay 158-159 EF 2
Ansongo 164-165 E 5
Ansonia, CT 72-73 K 4
Ansonville 62 L 2
Ansšong 144-145 F 4
Ansted, WV 72-73 F 5
Anta [IND] 138-139 F 5
Anta [PE] 92-93 E 7
An-ta = Anda 142-143 NO 2
Anta, Cachoeira — [BR, Amazonas] 98-99 H 8
Anta, Cachoeira — [BR, Pará] 98-99 O 7
Antabamba 92-93 E 7
Antāgarh 138-139 H 7
Antah = Anta 138-139 F 5
Antakya 134-135 D 3
Antalaha 172 K 4
Antālia = Antalya 134-135 C 3
Antalya 134-135 C 3
Antalya körfezi 134-135 C 3
Antananarivo 172 J 5
Antarctica 53 B 28-9
Antarctic Peninsula 53 BC 30-31
Antarctic Sound 53 C 31
Antarī = Antri 138-139 G 4
Antarktika 53 B 28-9
Antártica Chilena, Magallanes y — 108-109 B 7-E 10
Antas 100-101 E 6
Antas, Rio das — [BR, Rio Grande do Sul] 106-107 M 2
Antas, Rio das — [BR, Santa Catarina] 102-103 F 7
Antēgiri = Annigeri 140 B 3
Antelope, OR 66-67 C 3
Antelope Hills 66-67 J 4
Antelope Island 66-67 G 5
Antelope Range 74-75 E 3
Antenne, Monte — 113 II b 1
Antenor Navarro 100-101 E 4
Antequera 120-121 E 10
Antero Reservoir 68-69 CD 6
Anthony, KS 76-77 EF 4
Anthony, NM 76-77 A 7
Anthony Lagoon 158-159 FG 3
Anti Atlas = Al-Aṭlas aṣ-Ṣaghīr 164-165 C 2-3
Antibes 120-121 L 7
Anticosti Island 56-57 Y 8
Antigo, WI 70-71 F 3
Antigua 64-65 O 8
Antigua and Barbuda 64-65 OP 8
Antigua Guatemala 64-65 H 9
Antiguo Cauce del Río Bermejo 104-105 F 9
Antiguo Morelos 86-87 L 6
Antiguos, Los — 108-109 D 6
Antikýthēra 122-123 K 8
Anti Lebanon = Jabal Lubnān ash-Sharqī 136-137 G 5-6
Antilhue 108-109 C 2
Antilla 104-105 D 10
Antímano, Caracas- 91 II b 2
Antimēlos 122-123 KL 7
Antimony, UT 74-75 H 3
Antinopolis 173 B 4
Antioch, CA 74-75 C 3-4
Antioch, IL 70-71 F 4
Antioch = Antakya 134-135 D 3
Antiócheia = Antakya 136-137 FG 4
Antiokia = Antakya 136-137 FG 4
Antionio Pini 106-107 G 2
Antioquia [CO, administrative unit] 94-95 CD 4
Antioquia [CO, place] 92-93 D 3
Antíparos 122-123 L 7
Antipino 124-125 J 6
Antipodes Islands 156-157 HJ 7
Antisana 96-97 B 2
Antler, ND 68-69 F 1
Antlers, OK 76-77 G 5
Antofagasta [RCH, administrative unit] 104-105 BC 8
Antofagasta [RCH, place] 111 B 2
Antofagasta de la Sierra 111 C 3
Antofalla, Salar de — 104-105 C 9-10
Antofalla, Volcán — 104-105 BC 9
Antón 88-89 F 10
Anton, CO 68-69 E 6
Anton, TX 76-77 C 6
Anton Chico, NM 76-77 B 5
Antongila, Helodrona — 172 JK 5
Antonibe 172 J 4-5
Antonina 102-103 H 6
Antônio Carlos 102-103 L 4
Antonio de Biedma 108-109 FG 6
Antônio Dias 102-103 L 3
Antônio João 102-103 E 5
Antônio Lemos 98-99 N 5
Antônio Prado 106-107 M 2
Antonio Varas, Península — 108-109 C 8
Antonito, CO 68-69 CD 7
Anton Lizardo, Punta — 86-87 N 8
Antony 129 I c 2
Antri 138-139 G 4
Antrim 119 C 4
Antrim Mountains 119 CD 4
Antropologia, Museo Nacional de — 91 I b 2
Antropovo 124-125 O 4
Antsalova 172 H 5
Antseh = Anze 146-147 D 3
Antsirabé 172 J 5
Antsiranana 172 JK 4
Antsla 124-125 F 5
Antsohihy 172 J 4
An Tuc = An Khe 148-149 E 4
Antuco 106-107 B 6
Antuco, Volcán — 106-107 B 6
Antuérpia 104-105 E 2
Antung = Dandong 142-143 N 3
An-tung = Lianshui 146-147 G 5
An-tung-wei = Andongwei 146-147 G 4
Antuševo 124-125 L 4
Antwerp 170 V bc 1
Antwerp = Antwerpen 120-121 K 3
Antwerpen 120-121 J 3
'Anu an-Na'idah 166-167 K 6
Añueque, Sierra — 108-109 E 3
Anugula = Angul 138-139 K 7
Anūi 144-145 F 5
An'ujsk 132-133 f 4
An'ujskij chrebet 132-133 fg 4
Anunciación, Bahía de la — = Berkeley Sound 108-109 KL 8
Anūpgarh 138-139 D 3
Anupshahar = Anūpshar 138-139 FG 3
Anūpshahr 138-139 FG 3
Anuradhapura = Anurādhapūraya 134-135 MN 9
Anurādhapūraya 134-135 MN 9
Āńvalā = Aonla 138-139 G 3
Anvers = Antwerpen 120-121 J 3
Anvers, Île — 53 C 30
Anvik, AK 58-59 G 5
Anvik River 58-59 G 5
Anvil Peak 58-59 st 7
Anwāl [MA, An-Nāḍūr] 166-167 E 2
Anwāl [MA, Ar-Rashidīyah] 166-167 E 3
Anxi [TJ, Fujian] 146-147 G 9
Anxi [TJ, Gansu] 142-143 H 3
Anxiang 146-147 D 7
Anxious Bay 158-159 F 6
Anyang [ROK] 144-145 F 4
Anyang [TJ] 142-143 LM 4
Anyerkidul 152-153 F 9
Anyi [TJ, Jiangxi] 146-147 E 7
Anyi [TJ, Shanxi] 146-147 C 4
Anyox 60 C 2
Anyuan 146-147 E 9
Anzá [CO] 92-93 D 3
Anzac 61 C 2
Anzaldo 104-105 D 5
Anzarān, Bi'r — 164-165 B 4
'Anz ar-Ruḥaymāwī 136-137 K 7
Anze 146-147 D 3
Anžero-Sudženskij 132-133 PQ 6
Anzhero Sudzhensk = Anžero-Sudženskij 132-133 PQ 6
Anzhu = ostrova Anjou 132-133 a-d 2
'Anzī 166-167 B 5
Ánzio 122-123 E 5
Anzoategui 106-107 F 7
Anzoátequi 94-95 J 3
Aoba = Oba 158-159 N 3
Ao Ban Don 150-151 B 8
Aoga-shima 142-143 Q 5
Aoga sima = Aoga-shima 142-143 Q 5
Aoji 144-145 H 1
Aojiang 146-147 H 8
Ao Krung Thep 150-151 C 6
Ao Luk 150-151 B 8
Aomen = Macau 142-143 L 7
Aomori 142-143 QR 3
Aonae 144-145 a 2
Aonla 138-139 G 3
Aoraiyyā = Auraiya 138-139 G 4
Aorańgābād = Aurangābād [IND, Bihār] 138-139 K 5
Aorańgābād = Aurangābād [IND, Mahārāshtra] 138-139 E 8
Aoreora = Awrīūrā' 166-167 A 5
Aosta 122-123 B 3
Aougesses 168-169 G 1
Aouinet, El — = Al-Awaynāt 166-167 KL 2
Aouinet Legraa = 'Awīnat Laqra' 166-167 C 6
'Aouînêt Torkoz = 'Awīnat Turkuz 166-167 B 5
Aouk, Bahr — 164-165 HJ 7
Aouker = Āwkār 164-165 BC 5
Aoulef = Awlif 166-167 D 2
Aoulef-el-Arab = Awlāf 166-167 G 6
Aouriôra = Awrīūrā' 166-167 A 5
Aoussedjine = Awsūjīn 166-167 L 6
Aoya 144-145 JK 5
Aoyama, Tōkyō- 155 III b 2
Aozou 164-165 H 4
Apa, Río — 111 E 2
Apache, AZ 74-75 J 7
Apache, OK 76-77 E 5
Apache Mountains 76-77 B 7
Apacheta Cruz Grande 104-105 D 7
Apagado, Volcán — 104-105 BC 8
Apaga Fogo, Ponta — 100-101 E 7
Apalachee Bay 64-65 K 6
Apalachicola, FL 78-79 G 6
Apalachicola Bay 78-79 G 6
Apalachicola River 78-79 G 5
Apan 86-87 L 8
Apapa, Lagos- 170 III b 2
Apapa Wharf 170 III b 2
Apaporis, Río — 92-93 EF 5
Apar, Teluk — 152-153 M 7
Aparado, Salto do — 102-103 G 6
Aparados da Serra, Parque Nacional de — 106-107 MN 2
Aparecida 102-103 K 5
Aparecida do Taboado 102-103 G 4
Aparicio 106-107 G 7
Aparri 148-149 H 3
Apartadero, El — 91 III c 3
Aparurén 94-95 K 5
Apas, Sierra — 108-109 F 3-4
Apat 56-57 ab 4
Apatity 132-133 EF 4
Apatzingan de la Constitución 64-65 F 8
Ape 124-125 F 5
Apedia, Rio — 98-99 H 11
Apeldoorn 120-121 KL 2
Apeleg 108-109 D 5
Apeleg, Aldea — 108-109 D 5
Apeleg, Arroyo — 108-109 D 5
Apennines 122-123 C 3-G 5
Apere, Rio — 104-105 D 4
Apese, Lagos- 170 III b 2
Apeuzinho, Ilha — 100-101 B 1
Apex, NC 80-81 G 3
Aphajalapura = Afzalpur 140 C 2
Api [Nepal] 138-139 H 3
Api [ZRE] 172 E 1
Api, Gunung — 152-153 N 10
Api, Tanjung — 152-153 O 6
Apia 148-149 c 1
Apiacá, Rio — 98-99 K 9
Apiacás, Serra dos — 92-93 H 6-7
Apiaí 111 G 3
Apiaí, Rio — 102-103 H 5
Api Api 154 III b 1
Apiaú, Rio — 94-95 L 6
Apiaú, Serra do — 92-93 G 4
Api Passage = Selat Serasan 150-151 G 11
Apipé 106-107 J 1
Apipé Grande, Isla — 106-107 J 1
Apishapa River 68-69 D 7
Apiúna 102-103 H 7
Ap Iwan, Cerro — 108-109 D 6
Apizaco 86-87 LM 8
Aplao 96-97 E 10
Ap Li Chau 155 I a 2
Apo, Mount — 148-149 HJ 5
Apodi 100-101 F 3
Apodi, Chapada do- 92-93 M 6
Apo Duat, Pegunungan — 152-153 L 3-4
Apolda 118 E 3
Apolinario Saravia 111 D 2
Apollo Bay 160 F 7
Apollonia = Sūsah 164-165 J 2
Apolo 92-93 F 7
Apolyont gölü 136-137 C 2
Aponguao, Río — 98-99 H 3
Apopka, FL 80-81 c 2
Aporá 100-101 E 6
Aporé, Rio — 92-93 J 8
Aporema 98-99 N 4
Apostle Islands 64-65 HJ 2
Apóstoles 111 E 3
Apostolovo 126-127 FG 3
Apoteri 92-93 H 4
Appalachia, VA 80-81 E 2
Appalachian Mountains 64-65 K 5-N 2
Appennino Abruzese 122-123 E 4-F 5
Appennino Toscano 122-123 D 3-4
Appennino Umbro-Marchigiano 122-123 E 4
Appia, Via — 113 II b 2
Appleton, MN 70-71 BC 3
Appleton, WI 64-65 J 3
Appleton City, MO 70-71 CD 6
Applobamba, Nudo de — 104-105 B 4
Appomattox, VA 80-81 G 2
Appozai 134-135 K 4
Approuague 98-99 MN 2
Apšeronsk 126-127 JK 4
Apšeronskij poluostrov 126-127 OP 6
Apsheron Peninsula = Apšeronskij poluostrov 126-127 OP 6
Apsley Strait 158-159 EF 2
Apua Point 78-79 e 3
Apucarana 111 F 2
Apucarana, Serra de — 111 F 2
Apuí 104-105 B 1
Apuiarés 100-101 E 2
Apulia = Púglia 122-123 FG 5
Apure 94-95 GH 4
Apure, Río — 92-93 F 3
Apurímac 96-97 E 8
Apurímac, Río — 92-93 E 7
Apurito 94-95 G 4
Apurito, Río — 94-95 H 4
Apurlec 96-97 B 5
Apussigamasi River 61 K 3
Apyi = Api 138-139 H 2-3
'Aqabah, Al- [IRQ] 136-137 KL 7
'Aqabah, Al- [JOR] 134-135 CD 5
'Aqabah, Khalīj al- 134-135 C 5
'Aqabah, Wādī al- 173 CD 2-3
'Aqabat aṣ-Ṣaghīrah, Al- 173 C 5
Āqā Jarī = Āghā Jarī 134-135 FG 4
'Aqārib 166-167 M 2
'Aqbah, Bū — 166-167 C 5
'Aqbalī 166-167 G 6
Āqchalar 136-137 L 5
Āq Chāy 136-137 L 3
Āqdogh Mīsh, Rūd-e — 136-137 M 4
'Aqeila, el — = Al-'Uqaylah 164-165 H 2
'Aqīq 164-165 M 5
Aqjawajat 164-165 B 5
Aqmūr 166-167 HJ 6
'Aqqah 166-167 B 5
'Aqqah, Wād — 166-167 B 5
'Aqqa Īkirhene = 'Aqqat Igīrin 166-167 C 5
'Aqqa Īrhane = 'Aqqat Īghān 166-167 C 4
'Aqqat Īghān 166-167 C 4
'Aqqat Igīrin 166-167 C 5
'Aqrah 136-137 K 4
Aqshār 164-165 B 4
Āq Sū [IRQ] 136-137 L 5
Aqsu [TJ] 142-143 E 3
Aq Tagh Altai = Mongol Altajn Nuruu 142-143 F-H 2
Aquadas 94-95 D 5
Aquarius Plateau 74-75 H 3-4
Äquatorial-Guinea 164-165 FG 8
Aqueduc 82 I b 2
Aqueduct 154 I a 2
Aquidabã 100-101 F 6
Aquidabán-mí, Río — 102-103 D 5
Aquidauana 92-93 H 9
Aquidauana, Rio — 102-103 D 3
Aquila, L' 122-123 E 4
Aquiles Serdán 76-77 B 8
Aquio, Río — 94-95 GH 6
Aquiraz 100-101 E 2
Aquitania 94-95 E 5
Ara 155 III c 1
Ārā = Arrah 134-135 N 5
'Arab, Baḥr al- 164-165 K 6-7
'Arab, Khalīj al- 136-137 C 7
'Arab, Shaṭṭ al- 134-135 F 4
'Arab, Wādī al- 166-167 K 2
'Arabah, Wādī — 173 C 3
'Arabah, Wādī al- 136-137 F 7
Araban 136-137 G 4
Arabatskaja Strelka, kosa — 126-127 G 3-4
Arabela, Río — 96-97 D 2-3
Arabelo 94-95 J 5
'Arabestān = Khūzestān 134-135 F 4
Arabi, GA 80-81 E 5
Arabi, LA 85 I c 2
'Arabī, Al-Khalīj al- 136-137 N 8
Arabia 50-51 LM 4
Arabian Basin 50-51 N 5
Arabian Desert 164-165 L 3-4
Arabian Sea 134-135 JK 7
Arabistan = Khūzestān 134-135 F 4
Arabopó 94-95 L 5
Arabopó, Río — 94-95 L 5
Arabre 94-95 G 3
Araç 136-137 E 2
Araca 104-105 C 5
Araçá, Rio — 98-99 G 4
Aracaju 92-93 M 7
Aracataca 94-95 BE 2
Aracati 92-93 M 5
Aracatiaçu 100-101 D 2
Aracatiaçu, Açude — 100-101 DE 2-3
Aracatu 100-101 D 8
Araçatuba 92-93 JK 9
Araceli = Dumaran Island 148-149 GH 4
Aracena, Sierra de — 120-121 D 10
Arachthos 122-123 J 6
Araci 100-101 E 6
Aracoiaba 100-101 E 3
Aracruz 100-101 DE 10
Araçuaí 92-93 L 8
Araçuaí, Rio — 102-103 L 2
Arad 122-123 J 2
Arada 164-165 J 5-6
Arafura Sea 158-159 FG 2
Aragac 126-127 L 6
Aragac, gora — 126-127 M 6
Arago, Cape — 66-67 A 4
Aragón 120-121 G 7-8
Aragón, Río — 120-121 G 7
Aragonesa, La — 108-109 E 7
Aragua 94-95 H 2-3
Araguacema 92-93 K 6
Araguaçu 98-99 NO 11
Aragua de Barcelona 92-93 G 3
Aragua de Maturín 94-95 K 2-3
Araguaia, Parque Nacional do — 98-99 NO 10
Araguaia, Rio — 92-93 J 7
Araguaiana 102-103 FG 1
Araguaína 98-99 O 8
Araguao, Boca — 94-95 L 3
Araguao, Caño — 94-95 L 3
Araguari 92-93 K 8
Araguari, Rio — [BR, Amapá] 92-93 J 4
Araguari, Rio — [BR, Minas Gerais] 102-103 H 3
Araguatins 92-93 K 6
Arahoab = Aranos 174-175 C 3
Arai 144-145 M 4
'Araīch, el — = Al-'Arā'ish 164-165 C 1

Arain 138-139 E 4
Araioses 92-93 L 5
'Arā'ish, Al- 164-165 C 1
Araito = ostrov Altasova 132-133 de 7
'Araiyida, Bīr — = Bi'r 'Urayyiḍah 173 BC 3
Arak [DZ] 164-165 E 3
Arāk [IR] 134-135 F 4
Arakaka 94-95 L 4
Arakamčečen, ostrov — 132-133 I 5
Arakan = Ragaing Taing 148-149 B 2
Arakan Yoma = Ragaing Yôma 148-149 B 2-3
Arakawa 144-145 M 3
Arakawa, Tōkyō- 155 III b 1
Arakkalagūḍu = Arkalgūd 140 BC 4
Araklı 136-137 HJ 2
Araks 126-127 O 7
Araks = Rūd-e Aras 136-137 L 3
Aral, Lake — = Aral'skoje more 132-133 KL 8-9
Ara Lake 62 F 2
Aralda 126-127 P 4
Aralık = Başköy 136-137 L 3
Aral Sea = Aral'skoje more 132-133 KL 8-9
Aral'sk 132-133 L 8
Aral'skoje more 132-133 KL 8-9
Aralsor, ozero — 126-127 NO 2
Aralsul'fat 132-133 L 8
Aramac 158-159 HJ 4
Aramacá, Ilha — 94-95 c 3
'Aramah, Al — 134-135 F 5-6
Aramango 96-97 B 4
Aramari 100-101 E 7
Arāmbāgh 138-139 L 6
Arambaré 106-107 M 3
Aramberri 86-87 KL 5
Aran 119 B 4
Arañado, El — 106-107 F 3
Aranda de Duero 120-121 F 8
Arandas 86-87 J 7
Arandis 174-175 A 2
Arandjelovac 122-123 J 3
Arang 138-139 H 7
Āraṇi 140 D 4
Āraṇi = Arni 140 D 4
Aran Islands 119 AB 5
Aranjuez 120-121 F 8-9
Aranos 174-175 C 3
Aransas Pass, TX 76-77 F 9
Arantāngī 140 D 5
Arantes, Rio — 102-103 GH 3
Aranuka 208 H 2
Aranyaprathet 150-151 D 6
Aranzazu 94-95 D 5
Arao 144-145 H 6
Araouа, Chaîne d' 98-99 M 3
Araouane 164-165 D 5
Arapa, Laguna — 96-97 FG 9
Arapahoe, NE 68-69 G 5
Arapari 98-99 O 7
Arapey 111 E 4
Arapey Chico, Río — 106-107 J 3
Arapeyes, Cuchilla de los — 106-107 J 3
Arapey Grande, Río — 106-107 J 3
Arapiraca 100-101 F 5
Arapiranga 100-101 D 7
Arapiuns, Rio — 98-99 L 6
Arapkir 136-137 H 3
Arapongas 111 F 2
Arapoti 102-103 GH 6
Arapuá 102-103 F 4
Araquey 94-95 F 3
'Ar'ar 136-137 J 7
'Ar'ar, Wādī — 136-137 J 7
Araracuara 94-95 EF 8
Araracuara, Cerros de — 94-95 EF 7
Araranguá 111 G 3
Ararapira 102-103 HJ 6
Araraquara 92-93 K 9
Araraquara, Serra de — 102-103 HJ 4
Araras [BR, Pará] 92-93 J 6
Araras [BR, São Paulo] 92-93 K 9
Araras, Açude — 100-101 D 3
Araras, Cachoeira — 98-99 M 8
Araras, Monte das — 102-103 J 4
Araras, Serra das — [BR, Maranhão] 98-99 P 8
Araras, Serra das — [BR, Mato Grosso] 92-93 J 8
Araras, Serra das — [BR, Paraná] 111 F 2-3
Ararat [AUS] 158-159 H 7
Ararat [SU] 126-127 M 7
Ararat = Büyük Ağrı dağı 134-135 E 2-3
Arari 100-101 B 2
Arari, Cachoeira do — 92-93 K 5
Arari, Lago — 98-99 O 5
Araripe 100-101 D 4
Araripe, Chapada do — 92-93 LM 6
Araripina 100-101 D 4
Arariúna = Cachoeira do Arari 92-93 K 5
Araruama 102-103 L 5
Araruama, Lagoa de — 102-103 L 5
Araruna [BR, Paraíba] 100-101 G 4
Araruna [BR, Paraná] 102-103 G 5
Araruna, Serra da — 100-101 G 4
Aras, Rūd-e — 136-137 L 3
Arāsanj 136-137 O 5
Aras nehri 134-135 E 2
Arata 106-107 E 5
Arataca 100-101 E 8
Aratāna 94-95 J 5
Aratiba 106-107 L 1
Araticu 98-99 O 5
Arato = Shirataka 144-145 MN 3
Aratuba 100-101 E 3
Arauá, Rio — [BR ◁ Rio Madero] 98-99 H 8
Arauã, Rio — [BR ◁ Rio Purus] 98-99 F 9
Arauan = Araouane 164-165 D 5
Arauca [CO, administrative unit] 94-95 F 4
Arauca [CO, place] 92-93 E 3
Arauca, Río — 92-93 F 3
Araucanía 106-107 AB 7
Arauco 111 B 5
Arauco, Golfo de — 106-107 A 6
Arauquita 94-95 F 4
Aravaca, Madrid- 113 III a 2
Aravaipa Valley 74-75 H 6
Arāvaḷā Parvata = Arāvalli Range 134-135 L 6-M 5
Arāvalli Range 134-135 L 6-M 5
Arawa 148-149 j 6
Araxá 92-93 K 8
Araxes = Rūd-e Aras 136-137 L 3
Araya, Península de — 94-95 JK 2
Araya, Punta de — 94-95 J 2
Arazati 106-107 J 5
'Arb'ā', Al- [MA, Marrākush] 166-167 B 4
Arba'ā', Al- 166-167 H 1
Arb'ā' Amrān, el — = Tamdah 166-167 B 3
Arbaa-Naït-Iraten, L' = Arb'ā' Nāyat Īrāthan 166-167 J 1
Arba'īn, Lāqiyat al- 164-165 K 4
Arba Jahan 171 D 2
Arbaj Cheere = Arvajcheer 142-143 J 2
Arba Minch = Arba Minty 164-165 M 7
Arba Minty 164-165 M 7
Arb'ā Nāyat Trāthan 166-167 J 1
Arbat 136-137 L 5
Arba' Taḥtānī 166-167 G 3
Arbāwah, Al- 166-167 CD 2
Arbay Here = Arvajcheer 142-143 J 2
Arbaž 124-125 R 5
Arbīl 134-135 E 3
Arboga 116-117 F 8
Arboleda 94-95 C 7
Arboledas 106-107 G 6
Arboletes 94-95 C 3
Arbolito 106-107 K 4
Arbon, ID 66-67 G 4
Arboretum and Botanical Gardens 85 III b 1
Arborfield 61 G 4
Arborg 61 K 5
Arbroath 119 E 3
Arbuckle, CA 74-75 B 3
Arbuckle Mountains 76-77 F 5
Arbuzinka 126-127 E 3
Arcachon 120-121 G 6
Arcadia 96-97 D 2
Arcadia, FL 80-81 c 3
Arcadia, IN 70-71 G 5
Arcadia, KS 70-71 C 7
Arcadia, NE 68-69 G 5
Arcadia, TX 78-79 C 4
Arcadia, WI 70-71 E 3
Arcahaie, L' 88-89 K 5
Arcas, Cayos — 86-87 P 7
Arcata, CA 66-67 A 5
Arc de Triomphe 129 I c 2
Arc Dome 74-75 E 3
Arcelia 86-87 K 8
Archangaj 142-143 J 2
Archangel'sk 132-133 G 5
Archangel'sk-Gul'ajevo 124-125 N 1
Archangel'sk-Isakogorka 124-125 MN 1
Archangel'skoje [SU, Stavropol'skaja Oblast'] 126-127 M 4
Archangel'skoje [SU, Voronežskaja Oblast'] 126-127 K 1
Archenū, Gebel — = Jabal Arkanū 164-165 J 4
Archer Bay 158-159 H 2
Archer City, TX 76-77 E 6
Archer River 158-159 H 2
Arches National Monument 74-75 J 3
Arch Henda 168-169 DE 1
archipelag Nordenskiöld 132-133 RS 2
Archipelago of the Recherche 158-159 D 6
Archipel des Comores 172 HJ 4
Archipiélago de Bocas del Toro 88-89 EF 10
Archipiélago de Camagüey 64-65 L 7
Archipiélago de Colón 92-93 AB 5
Archipiélago de las Mulatas 94-95 B 3
Archipiélago de las Perlas 64-65 KL 10
Archipiélago de los Canarreos 64-65 K 7
Archipiélago de los Chonos 111 AB 6-7
Archipiélago de Sabana 64-65 KL 7
Archipiélago de San Blas 88-89 GH 10
Archipiélago Guayaneco 108-109 AB 6
Archipiélago Reina Adelaida 111 AB 8
Archive 61 F 5
Arciz 126-127 D 4
Arckaringa 158-159 FG 5
Arckaringa Creek 160 B 1-2
Arco 122-123 D 3
Arco, ID 66-67 G 4
Arco, El — 86-87 D 3
Arco, Paso del — 106-107 B 7
Arcola, IL 70-71 F 6
Arcopongo 104-105 C 5
Arcos 102-103 K 4
Arcot 140 D 4
Arcoverde 100-101 F 5
Arctic Bay 56-57 TU 3
Arctic Institute Range 53 B 16
Arctic Ocean 50-51 D-Q 1
Arctic Red River [CDN, place] 56-57 K 4
Arctic Red River [CDN, river] 56-57 K 4
Arctic Village, AK 58-59 OP 2
Arḍ, Rā's al- 136-137 N 8
Arda 122-123 L 5
Ardabīl 134-135 F 3
Ardahan 136-137 K 2
Ardakān 134-135 G 4
Ardakān = Ardekān 134-135 GH 4
Arḍ al-Jazīrah 134-135 E 3-F 4
Ardalstangen 116-117 BC 7
Ardanuç = Adakale 136-137 K 2
Ardar Gwagwa, Jabal — 173 D 6
Ardasa 136-137 H 2
'Arḍ aṣ-Ṣawwān 136-137 G 7
Ardatov [SU, Gor'kovskaja Oblast'] 124-125 O 6
Ardatov [SU, Mordovskaja ASSR] 124-125 PQ 6
Ardebil = Ardabīl 134-135 F 3
Ardèche 120-121 K 6
Ardekān 134-135 GH 4
Arden, NV 74-75 F 4
Ardennes 120-121 K 4-L 3
Ardennes, Canal des — 120-121 K 4
Ardeşen 136-137 J 2
'Arḍ eş Şuwwān = 'Arḍ aṣ-Ṣawwān 136-137 G 7
Ardestān 134-135 G 4
Ardila 120-121 D 9
Ardiles 106-107 E 1
Ardlethan 160 H 5
Ardmore, OK 64-65 G 5
Ardmore, PA 84 III b 1
Ardmore, SD 68-69 E 4
Ardmore Park 85 II b 2
Ardoch, ND 68-69 H 1
Ardon [SU] 126-127 M 5
'Ard Şafayn 136-137 H 5
Ards Peninsula 119 D 4
Ardud 122-123 K 2
Arduşin 136-137 J 3
Åre 116-117 E 6
Areado 102-103 J 4
Areal 102-103 L 5
Arecibo 64-65 N 8
Arecua 94-95 F 5
Arefino 124-125 M 4
Areia 100-101 G 4
Areia, Cachoeira d' 100-101 B 5
Areia, Rio da — 102-103 F 5-6
Areia Branca 92-93 M 5-6
Arelão, Serra do — 98-99 M 5
Arelee 61 E 4
Arena 68-69 B 1
Arena, Point — 74-75 AB 3
Arena de las Ventas, Punta — 86-87 F 5-6
Arenales, Cerro — 111 B 7
Arenas, Cayo — 86-87 P 6
Arenas, Punta — 104-105 A 7
Arenas, Punta de — 111 C 8
Arenaza 106-107 G 5
Arendal 116-117 C 8
Arenillas 96-97 A 3
Arequipa [PE, administrative unit] 96-97 EF 9
Arequipa [PE, place] 92-93 E 8
Arequito 106-107 G 4
Arere 92-93 J 5
Arerunguá, Arroyo — 106-107 J 3
Åreskutan 116-117 E 6
Arévalo 120-121 E 8
Arezzo 122-123 DE 4
Arfayyāt, Al- 136-137 K 8
Arfūd 166-167 D 4
Arğa 136-137 G 3
Argachtach 132-133 d 4
Arga-Muora-Sise, ostrov — 132-133 XY 3
Argāna = 'Arqānah 166-167 B 4
Arganzuela, Madrid- 113 III a 2
Argelès-sur-Mer 120-121 J 7
Argelia 94-95 C 6
Argent, Rivière l' 63 B 2
Argenta 122-123 D 3
Argentan 120-121 GH 4
Argentenay 62 PQ 2
Argenteuil 120-121 J 4
Argentia 56-57 Za 8
Argentina [CO] 91 III a 1
Argentina [RA, place] 106-107 FG 2
Argentina [RA, state] 111 C 7-D 2
Argentina, La — 106-107 H 4
Argentine Basin 50-51 GH 7-8
Argentine Islands 53 C 30
Argerich 106-107 F 7
Argeş 122-123 M 3
Arghandāb Rōd 134-135 K 4
Argoim 100-101 E 7
Argolikós Kólpos 122-123 K 7
Argolo 100-101 DE 9
Argonne 120-121 K 4
Argonne, WI 70-71 F 3
Árgos 122-123 K 7
Argos, IN 70-71 G 5
Argostólion 122-123 J 6
Argö Tsho 138-139 J 2
Arguello, Point — 74-75 C 5
Arguipélago dos Anavilhanas 98-99 H 6
Argun [SU, place] 126-127 MN 5
Argun' [SU, river ◁ Amur] 132-133 WX 7
Argun [SU, river ◁ Terek] 126-127 M 5
Argungu 164-165 EF 6
Argut 132-133 Q 8
Arguvan 136-137 H 3
Argyle, MN 68-69 H 1
Argyrúpolis 113 IV ab 2
Arhavi = Musazade 136-137 J 2
Århus 116-117 D 9
Ariake kai = Ariakeno-umi 144-145 H 6
Ariakeno-umi 144-145 H 6
Ariake-wan = Shibushi-wan 144-145 H 7
Ariamsvlei 174-175 C 5
Ariāna = Iryānah 166-167 M 1
Ariano Irpino 122-123 F 5
Ariari, Río — 94-95 E 6
Arias 106-107 F 4
Ari Atoll 176 a 2
Ariaú 98-99 K 6
Aribinda 164-165 D 6
Arica [CO] 92-93 E 5
Arica [PE] 96-97 D 2
Arica [RCH] 111 B 1
Aricanduva, Ribeirão — 110 II bc 2
Aricha, El- = Al-'Arīshah 166-167 F 2
Arichat 63 F 5
Aricoma, Nudo — 96-97 FG 9
'Ārid, Al- 134-135 E 6-7
Arid, Cape — 158-159 D 6
Ariège 120-121 H 7
Ariel 106-107 GH 6
Ariel, WA 66-67 B 3
Arifwāla 138-139 D 2
Arīha 136-137 F 7
Arikaree River 68-69 E 6
Arikawa 144-145 G 6
Arimā [BR] 92-93 G 6
Arima [TT] 94-95 L 2
Arimo, ID 66-67 GH 4
Arimu Mine 98-99 J 1
Arinos 92-93 K 8
Arinos, Rio — 92-93 H 7
Ario de Rosales 86-87 K 8
Arion, IA 70-71 C 5
Aripao 94-95 J 4
Ariporo, Río — 94-95 F 4
Aripuanã [BR, landscape] 98-99 J 10
Aripuanã [BR, place] 98-99 J 10
Aripuanã, Rio — 92-93 G 6
Ariquemes 92-93 G 6
Ariranha, Ribeiro — 102-103 F 2
Ariranha, Salto — 102-103 G 6
Aris [Namibia] 174-175 B 2
'Arīs, Al- 166-167 K 2
'Arīsh, Al- 164-165 L 2
'Arīsh, Wādī al- 173 C 2-3
'Arīshah, Al- 166-167 F 2
Arishīkkērē = Arsikere 140 C 4
Arismendi 92-93 F 3
Aristazabal Island 60 C 3
Arístides Villanueva 106-107 D 5
Aristizábal, Cabo — 108-109 FG 5
Arita 144-145 K 5
Ariton, AL 78-79 G 5
Arivaca, AZ 74-75 H 7
Ariyaddu Channel 176 a 2
Ariyoshi 155 III cd 3
Ariza 120-121 FG 8
Arizaro, Salar de — 111 C 2
Arizona [RA] 111 C 5
Arizona [USA] 64-65 D 5
Arizpe 86-87 E 2
Årjäng 116-117 E 8
Arjeplog 116-117 GH 4
Arjona [CO] 92-93 D 2
Arjuni 138-139 H 7
Arka 132-133 b 5
Arkabutla Lake 78-79 DE 3
Ārkāḍ = Arcot 140 D 4
Arkadak 124-125 O 8
Arkadelphia, AR 78-79 C 3
Arkadía 122-123 JK 7
Arkalgūd 140 BC 4
Arkalyk 132-133 M 7
Arkansas 64-65 H 4
Arkansas City, AR 78-79 D 4
Arkansas City, KS 76-77 F 4
Arkansas River 64-65 F 4
Arkanū, Jabal — 164-165 J 4
Arkell, Mount — 58-59 U 6
Arkenu, Jebel — = Jabal Arkanū 164-165 J 4
Arkhangelsk = Archangel'sk 132-133 G 5
Ārkkōṇam = Arkonam 140 D 4
Arkley, London- 129 II b 1
Arklow 119 CD 5
Arkoma, OK 76-77 G 5
Arkona, Kap — 118 F 1
Arkonam 140 D 4
Arktičeskogo Instituta, ostrova — 132-133 OP 2
Arkul' 124-125 S 5
Arlanzón 120-121 EF 7
Arlberg 118 E 5
Arlee, MT 66-67 F 2
Arles 120-121 K 7
Arlington 174-175 GH 5
Arlington, CO 68-69 E 6
Arlington, GA 78-79 G 5
Arlington, MA 84 I ab 2
Arlington, OR 66-67 CD 3
Arlington, SD 68-69 H 3
Arlington, TN 78-79 E 3
Arlington, TX 76-77 F 6
Arlington, VA 64-65 L 4
Arlington, WA 66-67 BC 1
Arlington-Cherrydale, VA 82 II a 2
Arlington-Clarendon, VA 82 II a 2
Arlington-East Falls Church, VA 82 II a 2
Arlington-Fort Myer, VA 82 II a 2
Arlington Heights, IL 70-71 FG 4
Arlington Heights, MA 84 I a 2
Arlington Heights, Houston-, TX 85 III c 2
Arlington-Jewell, VA 82 II a 2
Arlington-Lyon Park, VA 82 II a 2
Arlington National Cemetery 82 II a 2
Arlington-Rosslyn, VA 82 II a 2
Arlington-Virginia Highlands, VA 82 II a 2
Arlit 164-165 F 5
Arlon 120-121 K 4
Armação, Niterói- 110 I c 2
Armação, Punta da — 110 I c 2
Armadale 158-159 C 6
Armagh 119 C 4
Armagnac 120-121 GH 7
Arm'anskaja Sovetskaja Socialističeskaja Respublika = Armenian Soviet Socialist Republic 134-135 EF 2-3
Armant 173 C 5
Armas, Las — 106-107 HJ 6
Armavir 126-127 K 4
Armenia [CO] 92-93 D 4
Armenia [SU] 114-115 R 8-S 7
Armenian Soviet Socialist Republic 134-135 EF 2-3
Armentières 120-121 J 3
Armería, Río — 86-87 HJ 8
Armero 92-93 E 4
Armevistès, Akrōtērion — 122-123 M 7
Armidale 158-159 K 6
Arminto, WY 68-69 C 4
Armit 61 GH 4
Armōḍī = Armori 138-139 GH 7
Armond Bayou 85 III b 2
Armori 138-139 GH 7
Armour, SD 68-69 G 4
Arms 70-71 GH 1
Armstead, MT 66-67 G 3
Armstrong, IA 70-71 C 4
Armstrong, TX 76-77 EF 9
Armstrong [CDN] 60 H 4
Armstrong [RA] 106-107 G 4
Armstrong Station 62 E 2
Armuña, La — 120-121 DE 8
Ārmūr 140 D 1
Ārmūru = Ārmūr 140 D 1
Arnarfjördhur 116-117 ab 2
Arnarvatn 116-117 cd 2
Arnas dağı 136-137 K 4
Arnaud 62 A 3
Arnaûtēs, Akrōtērion — 136-137 DE 5
Arnauti, Cape — = Akrōthērion Chrysochûs 136-137 E 5
Arneirós 100-101 D 4
Årnes 116-117 cd 2
Arnett, OK 76-77 E 4
Arnhem 120-121 KL 2-3
Arnhem, Cape — 158-159 G 2
Arnhem Bay 158-159 G 2
Arnhem Land 158-159 FG 2
Arni 140 D 4
Arni-Islisberg 128 IV a 2
Arniston 174-175 D 8
Arno, TX 76-77 C 7
Arno [I] 122-123 D 4
Arno [Marshall Islands] 208 H 2
Arno Bay 160 C 4
Arnold, NE 68-69 FG 5
Arnold, PA 72-73 G 4
Arnot 61 K 3
Arnouville-lès-Gonesse 129 I c 2
Arnøy 116-117 J 2
Arnprior 72-73 H 2
Arnsberg 118 D 3
Arnstadt 118 E 3
Aro, Río — 94-95 K 4
Aroa 94-95 G 2
Aroab 172 C 7
Aroazes 100-101 D 3-4
Arocena 106-107 G 4
Arocha 76-77 C 9
Aroeira [BR, Mato Grosso do Sul] 102-103 E 4
Aroeira [BR, Piauí] 100-101 B 5
Aroeiras 100-101 G 4
Arômâ = Arūmâ 164-165 M 5
Aroma, Quebrada de — 104-105 B 6
Aroostook River 56-57 X 8
Aropuk Lake 58-59 EF 6
Arorae 208 H 3
Aros, Río — 86-87 F 3
Arourou 168-169 C 2
Arpa 126-127 M 7
Arpaçay 136-137 K 2
Arpa çayı 136-137 K 2
Arpoador, Ponta do — [BR, Rio de Janeiro] 110 I bc 2
Arpoador, Ponta do — [BR, São Paulo] 102-103 J 6
'Arqānah 166-167 B 4
Arqa tagh 142-143 FG 4
'Arqūb, Al- 164-165 AB 4
Arque 104-105 C 5
Arquipélago da Madeira 164-165 A 2
Arquipélago dos Abrolhos 92-93 M 8
Arquipélago dos Bijagós 164-165 A 6
Ar-Ra'an 136-137 J 8
Ar-Radīsīyat Baḥrī 173 C 5
Arrah [CI] 168-169 DE 4
Arrah [IND] 134-135 N 5
Ar-Rahāb = Ar-Rihāb 136-137 L 7
Ar-Rahad 164-165 L 6
Ar-Raḥḥālīyah 136-137 K 6
Arraias 92-93 K 7
Arraias, Rio — [BR, Goiás] 100-101 A 7
Arraias, Rio — [BR, Mato Grosso] 98-99 L 10-11
Arraias do Araguaia, Rio das — 98-99 N 9-O 8
Arraijān 64-65 b 3
Ar-Ramādī 134-135 E 4
Ar-Ramḍā' 136-137 L 8
Ar-Ramthā 136-137 FG 6
Arran 119 D 4
Arrandale 60 C 2
Ar-Rank 164-165 L 6
Ar-Raqqah 134-135 DE 3
Arras 120-121 J 3
Ar-Rā's al-Abyaḍ 164-165 A 4
Ar-Rāshidīyah 164-165 D 2
Ar-Rass 134-135 E 5
Ar-Rawḍah 173 B 4
Ar-Rawwāfah 173 E 4
Ar-R'dayif 164-165 F 2
Arrecife 164-165 B 3
Arrecifes 106-107 G 5
Arrecifes, Río — 106-107 G 5-H 4
Arrecifes Triangulos 86-87 OP 7
Arrée, Monts d' 120-121 EF 4
Ar-Refā'ī = Ar-Rifā'ī 136-137 M 7
Arregaço, Cachoeira — 104-105 F 2
Arrey, NM 76-77 A 6
Arriaga 64-65 H 8
Arrias, Las — 106-107 F 3
Ar-Ribaṭ 164-165 C 2
Arribeños 106-107 G 5
Ar-Rīf [MA, administrative unit] 166-167 DE 2
Ar-Rīf [MA, mountains] 164-165 CD 1-2
Ar-Rifā'ī 136-137 M 7
Ar-Rihāb 136-137 L 7
Ar-Rimāl = Ar-Rub' al-Khālī 134-135 F 7-G 6
Arriola, CO 74-75 J 4
Arris = Al-'Arīs 166-167 K 2
Ar-Rīṣānī 164-165 D 2
Ar-Rīsh 166-167 D 3
Ar-Riyāḍ 134-135 F 6
Ar-R'kīz 164-165 AB 5
Arroio da Palma 106-107 L 3
Arroio do Só 106-107 KL 2
Arroio dos Ratos 106-107 M 3
Arroio Grande 106-107 L 4
Arrojado, Rio — 100-101 B 7
Arrong Chhu 138-139 L 3
Arrouch, El- = Al-Harūsh 166-167 K 1
Arrowhead 60 J 4
Arrow Lake 70-71 EF 1
Arroyito [RA, Córdoba] 106-107 F 3
Arroyito [RA, Mendoza] 106-107 D 4
Arroyito Challacó 106-107 C 7
Arroyo Algodón 106-107 F 4
Arroyo Apeleg 108-109 D 5
Arroyo Arerunguá 106-107 J 3
Arroyo Barrancoso 106-107 G 4
Arroyo Barú 106-107 H 3
Arroyo Cabral 106-107 F 4
Arroyo Chalia 108-109 D 5
Arroyo Claromecó 106-107 G 7
Arroyo Clé 106-107 H 4
Arroyo Comallo 108-109 D 3
Arroyo Corto 106-107 F 6
Arroyo Covunco 106-107 BC 7
Arroyo Cuarepoti 102-103 D 6
Arroyo de Butarque 113 III a 2
Arroyo de las Flores 106-107 GH 5-6
Arroyo de la Ventana 108-109 F 3
Arroyo del Medio 106-107 G 4
Arroyo de los Huesos 106-107 H 6
Arroyo del Rey 106-107 H 2
Arroyo de Maillín 106-107 F 2
Arroyo de Valdebebas 113 III b 2
Arroyo El Pantanoso 110 III a 2
Arroyo El Toba 106-107 GH 2
Arroyo Feliciano 106-107 H 3
Arroyo Geneshuaya 104-105 C 3
Arroyo Genoa 108-109 D 5
Arroyo Golondrinas 106-107 G 2
Arroyo Grande, CA 74-75 CD 5
Arroyo Grande [RA] 106-107 HJ 6
Arroyo Grande [ROU] 106-107 J 4
Arroyo Las Catonas 110 III a 1
Arroyo Las Ortegas 110 III b 2
Arroyo los Berros 110 III a 1
Arroyo Los Berros 108-109 F 3
Arroyo Morales 110 III ab 2
Arroyo Moróno 110 III b 1
Arroyo Perdido 108-109 F 4
Arroyo Picún Leufú 106-107 BC 7
Arroyo Pigüé 106-107 F 6
Arroyo Pirapó 102-103 E 7
Arroyo Piray Guazú 102-103 E 7
Arroyos, Lago de los — 104-105 D 3
Arroyo Salado [RA ◁ Bajo de la Laguna Escondida] 108-109 F 3
Arroyo Salado [RA ◁ Golfo San Matías] 108-109 G 3
Arroyo San Agustín 104-105 CD 3
Arroyo San Francisco 110 III bc 2
Arroyo Sarandí 106-107 H 2-3
Arroyo Sauce Corto 106-107 G 6
Arroyo Seco [RA] 108-109 F 3
Arroyo Seco [USA ◁ Colorado River] 74-75 F 6
Arroyo Seco [USA ◁ Los Angeles] 83 III c 1
Arroyos y Esteros 102-103 D 6
Arroyo Urquiza 106-107 HJ 4
Arroyo Valcheta 108-109 F 3
Arroyo Vallimanca 106-107 G 5-6
Arroyo Venado 106-107 F 6
Arroyo Verde 108-109 G 3
Ar-Rub'ah 166-167 L 1
Ar-Rub' al-Khālī 134-135 F 7-G 6
Arrufó 106-107 G 3
Ar-Rukhaimiyah = Ar-Rukhaymīyah 136-137 L 8
Ar-Rukhaymīyah 136-137 L 8
Ar-Rumāh 134-135 F 5
Ar-Rumaylah 136-137 M 7
Ar-Rumaythah 136-137 L 7
Ar-Rummānī 166-167 C 3
Ar-Ruqaybah 166-167 AB 7
Ar-Ruqī 136-137 M 8
Ar-Ruṣayriş 164-165 LM 6
Ar-Rustāq 134-135 H 6
Ar-Ruṭbah [IRQ] 134-135 DE 4
Ar-Ruṭbah [SYR] 136-137 G 6
Ar-Ruwībah 166-167 H 1
Arša Nuur = Chagan nuur 142-143 L 3
Arsenault Lake 61 D 3
Arsenjev 132-133 Z 9
Arsenjevo 124-125 L 7
Arsikere 140 C 4
Arsila = Aṣīlah 166-167 C 2
Aršincevo 126-127 H 4
Arsk 124-125 RS 5
Arsum al-Līl, Ḥāssī — 166-167 H 6
Arsuz 136-137 F 4
Årta 122-123 J 6
Arta, Gulf of — = Ambrakikòs Kólpos 122-123 J 6
Artaki = Erdek 136-137 B 2
Artašat 126-127 M 7
Arṭāwīyah, Al — 134-135 EF 5
Artemisa 88-89 E 3
Artesia 174-175 FG 3
Artesia, CA 83 III d 2
Artesia, CO 66-67 J 5
Artesia, MS 78-79 E 4
Artesia, NM 64-65 EF 5
Artesian, SD 68-69 GH 3
Artesia Wells, TX 76-77 E 8
Arthabaska 72-73 KL 1
Arthur 72-73 F 3
Arthur, NE 68-69 F 5
Arthur City, TX 76-77 G 6
Arthur Kill 82 III a 3
Arthur River 160 b 2
Arthur's Pass 158-159 O 8
Artigas [ROU, administrative unit] 106-107 J 3
Artigas [ROU, place] 111 E 4
Artigas, Caracas- 91 II b 2
Artik 126-127 LM 6
Art Institute 83 II b 1
Artjärvi 116-117 LM 7
Artois 120-121 J 3
Art'om 132-133 Z 9
Art'omovka 126-127 G 2
Art'omovsk [SU, Rossijskaja SFSR] 132-133 R 7
Art'omovsk [SU, Ukrainskaja SSR] 126-127 HJ 2
Art'omovskij [SU ↗ Bodajbo] 132-133 VW 6
Art'omovskij [SU ↗ Sverdlovsk] 132-133 L 6
Artova 136-137 G 2
Artur de Paiva = Capelongo 172 C 4
Artur de Paiva = Cubango 172 C 4
Arturo Prat 53 C 30-31
Artvin 134-135 E 2
Aru 172 F 1
Aru, Kepulauan — 148-149 KL 8
Aru, Tanjung — 152-153 M 7
Arua 172 F 1
Aruab 172 C 7
Aruacá, Ponta do — 100-101 B 1
Aruanã 92-93 J 7
Aruaru 100-101 E 3
Aruba 64-65 N 9
Arumā [BR] 92-93 G 5
Arūmā [Sudan] 164-165 M 5
Arumbi 172 EF 1
Arumpo 160 F 4
Aruṇ 134-135 O 5
Arunachal Pradesh 134-135 P Q 5
Arundel [ZA] 174-175 F 6
Arunta Desert = Simpson Desert 158-159 G 4-5
Aruppukkottai 140 D 6
Arusha 172 G 2
Arusī 164-165 M 7
Arut, Sungai — 152-153 J 6-7
Aruvi Āru 140 E 6
Aruwimi 172 E 1
Arvada, CO 68-69 D 6
Arvada, WY 68-69 CD 3
Arvajcheer 142-143 J 2
Arvejas, Punta — 106-107 A 7
Arverne, New York-, NY 82 III d 3
Arvi 138-139 G 7
Arvida 63 A 3
Arvidsjaur 116-117 H 5
Arvika 116-117 E 8
Arvin, CA 74-75 D 5
Arvoredo, Ilha do — 102-103 HJ 7
Arys' 132-133 M 9
Arzamas 132-133 GH 6
Arzew = Arzū 166-167 F 2
Arzgir 126-127 M 4
Arzila = Aṣīlah 166-167 C 2
Arzū 166-167 F 2
Åsa [S] 116-117 E 9
Asab 174-175 B 3
Aṣābah, Al- 168-169 BC 1
Asadābād [AFG] 134-135 L 4
Asadābād [IR] 136-137 MN 5
Asador, Pampa del — 108-109 D 6-7
Asagaya, Tōkyō- 155 III a 1
Aşağıçıgıl 136-137 DE 3

Aşağıpınarbaşi 136-137 E 3
Asahan, Sungai — 152-153 C 4
Asahi 144-145 N 5
Asahi, Yokohama- 155 III a 3
Asahi dake [J, Hokkaidō] 142-143 R 3
Asahi dake [J, Yamagata] 144-145 M 3
Asahigava = Asahikawa 142-143 R 3
Asahi gawa 144-145 J 5
Asahikawa 142-143 R 3
Asakusa, Tōkyō- 155 III b 1
Asalē 164-165 MN 6
Asam 134-135 P 5
Asamankese 168-169 E 4
Asángaro = Azángaro 92-93 EF7
Asansol 134-135 O 6
Asante = Ashanti 164-165 D 7
Asariamas 104-105 B 4
Åsarna 116-117 F 6
Asati 154 II a 3
'Asayr 134-135 G 8
Asayta 164-165 N 6
Asbesberge 174-175 E 5
Asbest 132-133 L 6
Asbestos 72-73 L 2
Asbestos Mountains = Asbesberge 174-175 E 5
Asbe Teferī 164-165 N 7
Asbury Park, NJ 72-73 JK 4
Ascensión [BOL] 92-93 G 8
Ascension [GB] 204-205 F 9
Ascensión [MEX] 86-87 FG 2
Ascensión [RA] 106-107 G 5
Ascensión, Bahía de la — 64-65 J 8
Aščhabad 134-135 HJ 3
Aschaffenburg 118 D 4
Aschheim 130 II c 1
Aščiozek 126-127 N 2
Ascoli-Piceno 122-123 E 4
Ascotán 104-105 B 7
Ascotán, Portezuelo — 104-105 BC 7
Ascotán, Salar de — 104-105 B 7
Aseb 164-165 N 6
Asekejevo 124-125 T 7
Asela 164-165 M 7
Åsele 116-117 G 5
Aselle = Asela 164-165 M 7
Asenovgrad 122-123 L 4-5
Aserraderos 86-87 GH 6
Asfal'titovyj Rudnik 124-125 U 2
Asfī 164-165 C 2
Asfūn 173 C 5
Ashanti 164-165 D 7
Ashaqār, Rā's — 166-167 CD 2
Ashāqif, Tulūl al- 136-137 G 6
'Asharah, Al- 136-137 J 5
Ashburn, GA 80-81 E 5
Ashburn, Chicago-, IL 83 II a 2
Ashburton 158-159 O 8
Ashburton River 158-159 C 4
Ashcroft 60 G 4
Ashdōd 136-137 F 7
Ashdown, AR 76-77 G 6
Asheboro, NC 80-81 FG 3
Asherton, TX 76-77 DE 8
Asheville, NC 64-65 K 4
Asheweig River 62 DE 1
Ashe Yōma 148-149 C 3
Ashfield, Sydney- 161 I a 2
Ashford, AL 78-79 G 5
Ashford, WA 66-67 BC 2
Ashford [AUS] 160 K 2
Ashford [GB, Kent] 119 G 6
Ashford [GB, Surrey] 129 II a 2
Ash Fork, AZ 74-75 G 5
Ash Grove, MO 78-79 C 2
Ashibetsu 144-145 c 2
Ashikaga 144-145 M 4
Ashizuri-zaki 144-145 J 6
Ashkelon = Ashqělōn 136-137 F 7
Ashkhabad = Aščhabad 134-135 HJ 3
Ashkum, IL 70-71 FG 5
Ashland, AL 78-79 FG 4
Ashland, IL 70-71 E 6
Ashland, KS 76-77 DE 4
Ashland, KY 64-65 K 4
Ashland, ME 72-73 M 1
Ashland, MT 68-69 CD 3
Ashland, NE 68-69 H 5
Ashland, OH 72-73 EF 4
Ashland, OR 66-67 B 4
Ashland, VA 80-81 H 2
Ashland, WI 64-65 H 2
Ashland, Mount — 66-67 B 4
Ashland City 78-79 F 2
Ashley 70-71 F 6
Ashley, MI 70-71 H 4
Ashley, ND 68-69 G 2
Ashmont 61 C 3
Ashmūn 173 B 2
Ashmūnayn, Al- 173 B 4
Ashoknagar 138-139 F 5
Ashqělōn 136-137 F 7
Ash-Shābah 166-167 M 2
Ash-Shabakah [IRQ, landscape] 136-137 K 7
Ash-Shabakah [IRQ, place] 136-137 K 7
Ash-Shallāl [ET, place] 164-165 L 3
Ash-Shallāl [ET, river] 164-165 L 3
Ash-Shallāl al-Khāmis 164-165 L 5
Ash-Shallāl as-Sādhis 164-165 L 5
Ash-Shallāl ath-Thālith 164-165 KL 5
Ash-Shāmah = Al-Ḥarrah 136-137 GH 7
Ash-Shamāʼīyah 166-167 B 3
Ash-Shāmīyah 136-137 L 7
Ash-Shaqqāt 164-165 C 3
Ash-Sharāh 136-137 F 7
Ash-Shāriqah 134-135 GH 5
Ash-Sharmah 173 D 3-4
Ash-Sharqāṭ 136-137 K 5
Ash-Shaṭrah 136-137 LM 7
Ash-Shaṭṭ al-Gharbī 166-167 F 3
Ash-Shaṭṭ al-Hudnah 166-167 EF 1
Ash-Shaṭṭ ash-Sharqī 164-165 DE 2
Ash-Shawbak 136-137 F 7
Ash-Shāwīyah 166-167 C 3
Ash-Shaykh 'Uthmān 134-135 EF 8
Ash-She'aiba = Ash-Shu'aybah 136-137 M 7
Ash-Shenāfiya = Ash-Shināfiyah 136-137 L 7
Ash-Shiādmā' 166-167 B 4
Ash-Shibicha = Ash-Shabakah 136-137 K 7
Ash-Shiddādī 136-137 J 4
Ash-Shīḍīyah 136-137 FG 8
Ash-Shiḥr 134-135 F 8
Ash-Shimālīyah 164-165 KL 5
Ash-Shināfiyah 136-137 L 7
Ash-Shirqāṭ = Ash-Sharqāṭ 136-137 K 5
Ash-Shōra = Ash-Shūr'a 136-137 K 5
Ash-Shu'aybah 136-137 M 7
Ash-Shu'bah 136-137 L 8
Ash-Shumlūl = Ma'qalā' 134-135 F 5
Ashshur = Assur 134-135 E 3
Ash-Shūr'a 136-137 K 5
Ash-Shurayk 164-165 L 5
Ash-Shuwayyib 136-137 MN 7
Ashta [IND, Madhya Pradesh] 138-139 F 6
Ashta [IND, Mahārāshtra] 140 B 2
Ashtabula, OH 72-73 F 3-4
Ashtabula, Lake — = Baldhill Reservoir 68-69 GH 2
Ashtāgrām 140 C 4
Ashtha = Ashta 138-139 F 6
Āshti [IND, Andhra Pradesh] 138-139 G 8
Ashti [IND, Mahārāshtra] 138-139 G 7
Ashton 174-175 CD 7
Ashton, ID 66-67 H 3
Ashton, IL 70-71 F 5
Ashuanipi Lake 56-57 X 7
Ashuapmuchuan, Rivière — 62 P 2
'Āshūrīyah, Al- 136-137 K 7
Ashvarāvapēṭa = Ashwaraopet 140 E 2
Ashwaraopet 140 E 2
'Āṣī, Al- 136-137 K 4
'Āṣī, Nahr al- 136-137 G 5
Asia 50-51 N-P 3
Asia, Estrecho — 108-109 BC 8
Asia, Kepulauan — 148-149 K 6
Asiekpe 168-169 F 4
Asiento 104-105 C 6
Āsifābād 138-139 G 8
Asike 148-149 LM 8
Aṣīlah 166-167 C 2
Asinara 122-123 BC 5
Asinara, Golfo dell' 122-123 C 5
Asīnd 138-139 E 5
Asi nehri 136-137 G 4
Asino 132-133 PQ 6
Āsiphābād = Āsifābād 138-139 G 8
'Asīqāl, Ḥāssī — 166-167 L 6-7
'Asīr 134-135 E 7
Asīrgarh 138-139 F 7
Asiut = Asyūṭ 164-165 L 3
Aska [IND] 138-139 K 8
Aşkale 136-137 J 3
Askalon = Ashqělōn 136-137 F 7
Askanija-Nova 126-127 FG 3
'Askar, Jabal al- 166-167 L 2
Askāūn 166-167 C 4
Asker 116-117 D 8
Askersund 116-117 F 8
Askham 174-175 D 4
Askī Mūṣil 136-137 K 4
Askinuk Mountains 58-59 E 6
Askiz 132-133 R 7
Askja 116-117 e 2
Askol'd, ostrov — 144-145 J 1
Aşlāndūz 136-137 M 3
Asmaca 136-137 F 4
Asmara = Asmera 164-165 M 5
Asmera 164-165 M 5
Asnām, Al- 164-165 E 1
Asnī 166-167 BC 4
Åsop 138-139 D 4
Asosa 164-165 LM 6
Asotin, WA 66-67 E 2
Asouf Mellene, Ouëd — = Wādī Asūf Malān 166-167 H 7
Aso zan 144-145 H 6
Aspen, CO 68-69 C 6
Aspen Hill, MD 72-73 H 5
Aspermont, TX 76-77 D 6
Aspern, Flugplatz — 113 I c 2
Aspid, Mount — 58-59 n 4
Aspindza 126-127 L 6
Aspiring, Mount — 158-159 N 8
Aspromonte 122-123 FG 6
Āspur 138-139 DE 6
Aspy Bay 63 FG 4
'Aṣr, Jabal al- 173 B 6
Assa 126-127 M 5
'Aṣṣa, Al- 166-167 M 3
Assab = Aseb 164-165 N 6
As-Sabhah 136-137 H 5
As-Sabikhanh 166-167 LM 2
As-Ṣābirīyah 136-137 M 8
As-Sabt G'zūlah 166-167 B 3
Aş-Şabyā' 134-135 E 7
Assad, Buḥayrat al- 134-135 D 3
As-Sa'dīyah 136-137 L 5
Aş-Şafā 136-137 G 6
Aş-Şafaḥ 136-137 J 4
Aş-Şaff 173 B 3
'Assah 166-167 B 5
Aş-Şahīrah 166-167 M 2
Aş-Şaḥn 136-137 K 7
Aş-Şaḥrā' an-Nūbah 164-165 LM 4
Aş-Şa'īd 164-165 L 3-4
As-Sa'dīyah 166-167 EF 2
Assaitta = Asaita 164-165 N 6
Assal, Lac — 164-165 N 6
Assale = Asalē 164-165 MN 6
Aş-Şalīf 134-135 E 7
Aş-Şāliḥīyah [ET] 173 BC 2
Aş-Şāliḥīyah [SYR] 136-137 J 5
As-Salmān 136-137 L 7
As-Salṭ 136-137 F 6
As-Salūm 164-165 K 2
Assam = Asam 134-135 P 5
As-Samāwah 134-135 EF 4
Assam Hills 134-135 P 5
Assam Himālaya 134-135 OP 5
As-Sanad 166-167 L 2
As-Sanām 134-135 G 6
Assaouas 168-169 G 1
As-Sars 166-167 L 1
Assateague Island 72-73 J 5
Aş-Şawīrah 164-165 BC 2
Aş-Şawrah 173 D 4
Assegai = Mkondo 174-175 J 4
Assen 120-121 L 2
Assendelft 128 I a 1
Assens 116-117 CD 10
As-Sībah 136-137 N 7
As-Sibā'īyah 173 C 5
As-Sibū 'Gharb 173 C 6
As-Sidr 164-165 H 2
Assiguel, Hassi — = Ḥāssī 'Asīqāl 166-167 L 7
As-Sinbillāwayn 173 BC 2
Assiniboia 61 F 6
Assiniboine, Mount — 56-57 NO 7
Assiniboine River 56-57 Q 7
Assinica, Lac — 62 O 1
Assinica, la Réserve de — 62 O 1
Assis 92-93 J 9
Assis Brasil 98-99 D 10
Assis Chateaubriand 102-103 F 6
Assisi 122-123 E 4
Assiut = Asyūṭ 164-165 L 3
Assomption, L' 72-73 K 2
Assoûl = Assūl 166-167 D 4
Assuan = Aswān 164-165 L 4
As Sūbāṭ 164-165 L 7
As Sudd 164-165 L 7
Aş-Şukhnah 136-137 H 5
As-Sūki 164-165 L 6
Assūl 166-167 D 4
As-Sulaymīyah 134-135 F 6
As-Sulayyil 134-135 F 6
Aş-Şulb 134-135 F 5
Aş-Şummān [Saudi Arabia ↑ Ar-Riyāḍ] 134-135 F 5
Aş-Şummān [Saudi Arabia ↘ Ar-Riyāḍ] 134-135 F 6
Assumption, IL 70-71 F 6
Assumption Island 172 J 3
Assunção 100-101 D 3
Assur 134-135 E 3
As-Surt 164-165 H 2-3
As-Sūs 166-167 B 4
Aş-Şuwār 136-137 J 5
As-Suwaybit 136-137 H 6
As-Suwaydā' 134-135 D 4
Aş-Şuwayrah 136-137 L 6
As-Suways 164-165 L 2-3
As Swaib = Ash-Shuwayyib 136-137 MN 7
As Swaibit = As-Suwaybit 136-137 H 6
Aş Şwaira = Aş-Şuwayrah 136-137 L 6
Astakós 122-123 J 6
Āstāneh 136-137 N 6
Āstārā [IR] 136-137 N 3
Astara [SU] 126-127 O 7
Aštarak 126-127 M 6
Asteroskopéro 113 IV a 2
Asthamudi Lake 140 C 6
Astica 106-107 D 3
Astillero 96-97 G 8
Astin tagh = Altin tagh 142-143 EF 4
Astorga 120-121 DE 7
Astoria, OR 64-65 B 2
Astoria, SD 68-69 H 3
Astoria, New York-, NY 82 III c 2
Astove Island 172 J 4
Astra 111 C 7
Astrachan' 126-127 O 3
Astrachan Bazar = Džalilabad 126-127 O 7
Astrachanskij zapovednik 126-127 O 3
Astrakhan = Astrachan' 126-127 O 3
Astrida 172 E 2
Astrolabe Bay 148-149 N 7-8
Astroworld 85 III b 2
Asturiana, La — 106-107 E 6
Asturias 120-121 DE 7
Astypálaia 122-123 LM 7
Asūf Malān, Wādī — 166-167 H 7
Asunción [PY] 111 E 3
Asuncion [USA] 206-207 S 8
Asunción, La — 92-93 G 2
Asunción, Punta — 106-107 G 7
Asunta 104-105 C 5
Asūtarībah, Jabal — 173 E 7
Aswa 172 F 1
Aswān 164-165 L 4
'Aswān, Sad el — = Sadd al-'Ālī 164-165 L 3
Asyūṭ 164-165 L 3
Asyūṭī, Wādī al- 173 B 4
Ata 208 J 5
Atacama [RA] 111 BC 3
Atacama [RCH] 104-105 A 11-B 10
Atacama, Desierto de — 111 B 3-C 2
Atacama, Salar de — 111 C 2
Atacama Trench 156-157 O 5-6
Atacames 96-97 AB 1
Atacavi, Lagunas — 94-95 H 6
Ataco 94-95 D 6
Atacuari 96-97 F 3
Atafu 208 J 3
Atakor = Atākūr 164-165 F 4
Atakora [DY, administrative unit] 168-169 F 3
Atakora [DY, mountains] 164-165 E 6-7
Atakpamé 164-165 E 7
Atākūr 164-165 F 4
Atalaia 100-101 FG 5
Atalaia, Ponta de — 98-99 P 5
Atalanti Channel = Evboïkòs Kólpos 122-123 KL 6
Atalaya [PE, mountain] 96-97 F 8
Atalaya [PE, place] 92-93 E 7
Atalaya [RA] 106-107 J 5
Atalaya, Punta — 106-107 J 5
Ataleia 92-93 L 8
Atami 144-145 M 5
Atanik, AK 58-59 GH 1
Ataniya = Adana 134-135 D 3
Ataouat, Day Nui — 148-149 E 3
Atapirire 94-95 J 3
Atapupu 148-149 H 8
'Atāqah, Jabal — 173 C 2-3
Atār 164-165 B 4
Ataran River = Zami Myit 141 F 8
Ataraolā = Utraula 138-139 J 4
Atarque, NM 74-75 J 5
Atarū = Atru 138-139 F 5
Atascadero, CA 74-75 C 5
At'aševo 124-125 PQ 6
Atasta 86-87 O 8
Atasu 132-133 N 8
Atatürk Heykeli 154 I ab 2
Atatürk Köprüsü 154 I a 2
Ataúba 98-99 H 5
Ataúro, Ilha de — 148-149 J 8
'Aṭbarah 164-165 L 5
'Aṭbarah, Nahr — 164-165 LM 5
Atbasar 132-133 M 7
Atbu Şāliḥ 136-137 M 7
Atchafalaya Bay 78-79 D 6
Atchison, KS 70-71 C 6
Atchueelinguk River 58-59 G 5
Atebubu 168-169 E 4
Atelchu, Rio — 98-99 L 11
Atén 104-105 B 4
Ater 138-139 G 4
Atessa 122-123 F 4-5
Atfārītī 164-165 B 3
Aṭfīḥ 173 B 3
Athabasca [CDN, administrative unit] 56-57 O 7
Athabasca [CDN, place] 60 L 2
Athabasca, Lake — 56-57 OP 6
Athabasca River 56-57 O 6
'Athāmīn, Al- 136-137 K 7
Athanī = Athni 140 B 2
Aṭhārān Hazārī 138-139 D 2
Athena, OR 66-67 D 3
Athēnai 122-123 KL 7
Athenry 119 B 5
Athens, AL 78-79 F 3
Athens, GA 64-65 K 5
Athens, OH 72-73 E 5
Athens, PA 72-73 H 4
Athens, TN 78-79 G 3
Athens, TX 76-77 FG 6
Athens, WI 70-71 EF 3
Athens = Athēnai 122-123 KL 7
Atherton 158-159 HJ 3
Athi 172 G 2
Athil, Khurb al- 166-167 CD 5
Athi River 171 D 3
Athis-Mons 129 I c 3
Athlone 119 C 5
Athni 140 B 2
Athōk 141 D 7
Athol, ID 66-67 E 2
Áthos 122-123 L 5
Ath-Thaj 134-135 F 5
Ath-Thalātha' [MA, Marrākush] 166-167 BC 3-4
Ath-Thalātha' [MA, Miknās] 166-167 D 2
Ath-Tharwānīyah 134-135 GH 6
Ath-Thnīn Rīāt 166-167 B 3
Ati 164-165 H 6
Atiak 171 BC 2
Atibaia 102-103 J 5
Atibaia, Rio — 102-103 J 5
Atico 92-93 E 8
Aticonipi, Lac — 63 G 2
Atikameg 60 JK 2
Atikameg Lake 61 H 3
Atikameg River 62 H 1-2
Atkins, AR 78-79 C 3
Atikokan 70-71 E 1
Atikup 62 D 1
Atikwa Lake 62 C 3
Atitlán, Volcán — 64-65 H 9
Atizapán de Zaragoza 91 I b 1
Atka 132-133 d 5
Atka, AK 58-59 j 4
Atka Island 52 D 36
Atka Pass 58-59 j 4-5
Atkarsk 124-125 P 8
Atkinson, NE 68-69 G 4
Atlanta, GA 64-65 K 5
Atlanta, ID 66-67 F 4
Atlanta, IL 70-71 F 5
Atlanta, MI 70-71 HJ 3
Atlanta, MO 70-71 D 6
Atlanta, TX 76-77 G 6
Atlanta-Almond Park, GA 85 II b 2
Atlanta-Ansley Park, GA 85 II b 2
Atlanta Area Technical School 85 II b 2
Atlanta-Bolton, GA 85 II b 1
Atlanta-Buckhead, GA 85 II bc 1
Atlanta-Carey Park, GA 85 II b 2
Atlanta-Center Hill, GA 85 II b 2
Atlanta-Chattahoochee, GA 85 II b 2
Atlanta Christian College 85 II b 2
Atlanta-East Atlanta, GA 85 II c 2
Atlanta Historical Society 85 II b 1
Atlanta-Kirkwood, GA 85 II c 2
Atlanta Memorial Center 85 II b 2
Atlanta Memorial Park 85 II b 1
Atlanta-Morningside, GA 85 II bc 2
Atlanta-Oakland City, GA 85 II b 2
Atlanta-Peachtree Hills, GA 85 II b 1
Atlanta Police Academy 85 II bc 2
Atlanta-Riverside, GA 85 II b 2
Atlanta-Rockdale Park, GA 85 II b 2
Atlanta-Sherwood Forest, GA 85 II bc 2
Atlanta Stadium 85 II b 2
Atlanta University 85 II b 2
Atlanta-Westend, GA 85 II b 2
Atlantic, IA 70-71 C 5
Atlantic Beach, NY 82 III d 3
Atlantic City, NJ 64-65 M 4
Atlantic Coastal Plain 64-65 K 5-L 4
Atlantic Indian Antarctic Basin 50-51 J-M 9
Atlantic Indian Ridge 50-51 J-L 8
Atlántico 94-95 D 2
Atlantic Ocean 50-51 G 4-J 7
Atlantic Peak 68-69 B 4
Atlantique 168-169 F 4
Atlas, Punta — 108-109 G 5
Aṭlas al-Kabīr, Al- 164-165 CD 2
Aṭlas al-Mutawassiṭ, Al- 164-165 CD 2
Aṭlas aş-Şaghīr, Al- 164-165 C 2-3
Atlas aş-Şaḥrā', Al- 164-165 D 2-F 1
Atlasova, ostrov — 132-133 de 7
Atlin 56-57 K 6
Atlin Lake 56-57 K 6
Atlixco 64-65 G 8
Atløy 116-117 A 7
Ātmagūru = Ātmakūr 140 D 3
Ātmakūr [IND → Kurnool] 140 D 3
Ātmakūr [IND ↑ Kurnool] 140 C 2
Ātmakūru = Ātmakūr [IND ↑ Kurnool] 140 C 2
Ātmākūru = Ātmakūr [IND → Kurnool] 140 D 3
Atmore, AL 78-79 F 5
Atna Peak 60 CD 3
Atna Range 60 D 2
Atnarko 60 E 3
Atocha 104-105 C 7
Atoka, OK 76-77 FG 5
Atol das Rocas 92-93 N 5
Atoleiros 100-101 B 5
Atomic City, ID 66-67 G 4
Atomium 128 II ab 1
Atotonilco el Alto 86-87 JK 7
Atouat, Massif d' = Day Nui Ataouat 148-149 E 3
Atoyac, Río — 86-87 L 8
Atoyac de Álvarez 86-87 K 9
Atpādi 140 B 2
Atrai 138-139 M 5
Atrāk, Rūd-e 134-135 H 3
Atraolī = Atrauli 138-139 G 3-4
Aṭrash, Wādī al- 173 C 4
Atrato, Río — 92-93 D 3
Atrauli 138-139 G 3-4
Atreucó 106-107 EF 6
Atrōtérion Súnion 122-123 KL 7
Atru 138-139 F 5
'Aṭrūn, Wāḥāt al- 164-165 K 5
Atshūr 166-167 AB 6
Atsuku 168-169 H 4
Atsumi 144-145 M 3
Atsumi-hantō 144-145 L 5
Atsunai 144-145 cd 2
Atsuta 144-145 b 2
Atsutoko 144-145 d 2
Aṭ-Ṭafīlah 136-137 F 7
At-Taḥrīr 173 AB 2
Aṭ-Ṭā'if 134-135 E 6
At-Tāj 164-165 J 4
At-Talātā' = Ath-Thalātha' [MA, Marrākush] 166-167 BC 3-4
At-Talātā' = Ath-Thalātha' [MA, Miknās] 166-167 D 2
Attalea = Antalya 134-135 C 3
Attaléia = Antalya 134-135 C 3
At-Talībīyah 170 II ab 2
Attalla, AL 78-79 F 3-4
At-Ta'mīn 136-137 KL 5
At-Tannūmah 136-137 MN 7
At-Taqānat 168-169 C 1
Attar, Oued — = Wādī 'Aṭṭār 166-167 J 3
'Aṭṭār, Wādī — 166-167 J 3
Aṭ-Ṭārmīyah 136-137 KL 6
Attawapiskat 62 H 1
Attawapiskat Lake 62 F 1
Attawapiskat River 56-57 TU 7
Atte Bower, London- 129 II c 1
Attica, IN 70-71 G 5
Attica, KS 76-77 E 4
Attica, OH 72-73 E 4
Attili 140 E 2
Attingal 140 C 6
Attopeu 148-149 E 3-4
Attopo' = Attopeu 148-149 E 3-4
At-Trārzah 164-165 AB 5
Attu, AK 58-59 p 6
Attu Island 52 D 1
Āttūr 140 D 5
Aṭ-Ṭūr 164-165 L 3
At-Tuwāt 164-165 DE 3
Aṭ-Ṭuwaysah 164-165 K 6
Attwood Lake 62 E 2
Atuabo 168-169 EF 4
Atucha 106-107 H 4
Atuel, Bañados del — 106-107 D 5-6
Atuel, Río — 106-107 D 5
Atuila = Atwīl 166-167 B 6
Atuntaqui 96-97 BC 1
Atūwī, Wād — 164-165 B 4
Atwater, CA 74-75 C 4
Atwater, MN 70-71 C 3
Atwīl 166-167 B 6
Atwood, CO 68-69 E 5
Atwood, KS 68-69 F 6
Au, München- 130 II b 2
Auasberge 174-175 B 2
Auasbila 88-89 D 7
Auas Mountains = Auasberge 174-175 B 2
Auati Paraná, Rio — 92-93 F 5
Aubagne 120-121 K 7
Aube 120-121 K 4
Aubing, München- 130 II a 2
Aubinger Lohe 130 II a 1-2
Aubrac, Monts d' 120-121 J 6
Aubrey Falls 62 K 3
Auburn, AL 64-65 J 5
Auburn, CA 74-75 C 3
Auburn, IL 70-71 F 6
Auburn, IN 70-71 H 5
Auburn, KY 78-79 F 2
Auburn, ME 72-73 L 2
Auburn, NE 70-71 BC 5
Auburn, NY 72-73 H 3
Auburn, WA 66-67 B 2
Auburn, Sydney- 161 I a 2
Auburndale, FL 80-81 c 2-3
Auburndale, New York-, NY 82 III d 2
Auca Mahuida 106-107 C 6
Auca Mahuida, Sierra — 106-107 C 6
Aucanquilcha, Cerro — 111 C 2
Aucará 96-97 D 9
Auce 124-125 D 5
Auch 120-121 H 7
Auchi 168-169 G 4
Auckland 158-159 OP 7
Auckland Islands 53 D 17-18
Auckland Park, Johannesburg- 170 V ab 2
Aude 120-121 J 7
Auden 62 F 2
Auderghem 128 II b 2
Audubon, IA 70-71 C 5
Audubon, NJ 84 III c 2
Audubon Street 85 I b 2
Aue 118 F 3
Auenat, Gebel — = Jabal al-'Uwaynāt 164-165 K 4
Auf, Ras el- = Rā's Banās 164-165 M 4
Augathella 158-159 J 5
Augila = Awjilah 164-165 J 3
Augrabies Falls = Augrabiesval 172 CD 7
Augrabiesval 172 CD 7
Au Gres, MI 70-71 J 3
Augsburg 118 E 4
Augusta, AR 78-79 D 3
Augusta, GA 64-65 K 5
Augusta, IL 70-71 E 5
Augusta, KS 68-69 H 7
Augusta, KY 72-73 DE 5
Augusta, LA 85 I b 3
Augusta, ME 64-65 N 3
Augusta, MT 66-67 G 2
Augusta, WI 70-71 E 3
Augusta [AUS] 158-159 BC 6
Augusta [I] 122-123 F 7
Augustine Island 58-59 L 7
Augustines, Lac des — 72-73 J 1
Augusto Correia 98-99 P 5
Augusto Correira 100-101 A 1
Augusto de Lima 102-103 KL 3
Augusto Severo 100-101 F 3
Augustów 118 L 2
Augustów = Virbalis 124-125 D 6
Augustów = Virbalis 124-125 D 6
Augustus, Mount — 158-159 C 4
Augustus Downs 158-159 GH 3
Augustus Island 158-159 D 3
Auisigghin = Awsījīn 166-167 L 6
Auisigghin = Awsījīn 166-167 L 6
Auja, El- = Qěẓī'ōt 136-137 F 7
Auk = Bahr Aouk 164-165 HJ 7
Auki 148-149 k 6
Aulander, NC 80-81 H 2
Auld, Lake — 158-159 D 4
Aulnay-sous-Bois 129 I cd 2
Aulneau Peninsula 62 B 3
Aumale = Sūr al-Ghuzlān 166-167 HJ 1
Aundh 140 B 2
Aunis 120-121 G 5
Auob 172 C 7
Auquinco, Lago — 106-107 C 6
Aur 208 H 2
Aur, Pulau — 150-151 E 11
Auraiya 138-139 G 4
Aurangābād [IND, Bihār] 138-139 K 5
Aurangābād [IND, Mahārāṣhṭra] 134-135 LM 6-7
Aurelia 106-107 G 3
Aurelia, Via — 113 II a 2
Aurélio do Carmo 98-99 P 6
Aurès = Jabal al-Awrās 166-167 JK 2
Aurich 118 C 2
Aurignac 120-121 H 7
Aurilândia 102-103 G 2
Aurillac 120-121 J 6
Aurizona 100-101 B 1
Aurlandsvangen 116-117 B 7
Aurora, AK 58-59 EF 4
Aurora, CO 68-69 D 6
Aurora, IL 64-65 J 3
Aurora, IN 70-71 H 6
Aurora, MN 70-71 DE 2
Aurora, MO 78-79 C 2
Aurora, NC 80-81 H 3
Aurora, NE 68-69 GH 5
Aurora, OH 72-73 D 5
Aurora [BR] 100-101 E 4
Aurora [CDN] 72-73 G 2-3
Aurora [RP] 152-153 P 2
Aurora [ZA] 174-175 C 7
Aurora, La — 106-107 EF 1
Aurora, Serra da — 104-105 F 1-2
Aurora Gardens, New Orleans-, LA 85 I c 2
Aurora Lodge, AK 58-59 OP 4
Aurukun 158-159 H 2
Aus 172 C 7
Ausa 140 C 1
Au Sable Point [USA, Lake Huron] 72-73 E 2
Au Sable Point [USA, Lake Superior] 70-71 G 2
Au Sable River 70-71 HJ 3
Ausangate = Nudo Ausangate 92-93 E 7
Ausentes, Serra dos — 106-107 M 1-2
Ausiait 56-57 Za 4
Aussenalster 130 I ab 1
Ausstellungsgelände München 130 II b 2
Aust-Agder 116-117 BC 8
Austfonna 116-117 m 4
Austin 61 J 6
Austin, MN 64-65 H 3
Austin, MT 66-67 GH 2
Austin, NV 74-75 E 3
Austin, OR 66-67 D 3
Austin, TX 64-65 G 5
Austin, Chicago-, IL 83 II a 1
Austin, Lake — 158-159 C 5
Australia 158-159 C-J 4
Australian Capital Territory 158-159 J 7
Australien 158-159 C-J 4
Austria 118 E-G 5
Austur-Bardhastrandar 116-117 bc 2
Austur-Húnavatn 116-117 cd 2
Austur-Skaftafell 116-117 ef 2
Austvågøy 116-117 F 3
Austwell, TX 76-77 F 8
Auteuil 82 I a 1
Auteuil, Paris- 129 I c 2
Autlán de Navarro 64-65 EF 8
Autódromo de México 91 I c 2
Autódromo Municipal 110 III b 2
Autun 120-121 K 5
Auvergne [AUS] 158-159 EF 3
Auvergne [F] 120-121 J 6
Auxerre 120-121 J 5
Auxvasse, MO 70-71 DE 6
Auyama 94-95 E 2
Auyán Tepuy 94-95 K 5
Ava, IL 70-71 F 7
Ava, MO 78-79 C 2
Ava = Inwa 141 D 5
Avadh 134-135 N 5
Avaí 102-103 H 5
Āvaj 136-137 N 5
Avakubi 172 E 1
Avalik River 58-59 H 1
Avalon, CA 74-75 D 6
Avalon, Lake — 76-77 BC 6
Avalon Peninsula 56-57 a 8
Avān 136-137 M 3
Avanavero Dam 98-99 K 2
Avanhandava 102-103 GH 4
Avanigadda 140 E 2
Avanos 136-137 F 3
Avant, OK 76-77 F 4
Avante, Ixtapalapa- 91 I c 3
Avanzado, Cerro — 108-109 G 4
Avaré 92-93 K 9
Avarskoje Kojsu 126-127 N 5
Avatanak Island 58-59 o 3-4
Aveiro [BR] 92-93 HJ 5
Aveiro [P] 120-121 C 8
Avej = Āvaj 136-137 N 5
Avelino Lopes 100-101 BC 5
Avellaneda [RA, Buenos Aires] 111 DE 4-5
Avellaneda [RA, Santa Fe] 106-107 H 2
Avellaneda-Gerli 110 III b 2
Avellaneda-Sarandí 110 III bc 2
Avellaneda-Valentín Alsina 110 III b 1
Avellaneda-Villa Barilari 110 III b 2
Avellaneda-Villa Cristóbal Colón 110 III b 2
Avellaneda-Villa Dominico 110 III c 2
Avellaneda-Wilde 110 III c 2
Avellino 122-123 F 5
Avenal, CA 74-75 CD 4
Averías 106-107 F 2
Averøy 116-117 B 6
Aversa 122-123 EF 5
Avery, ID 66-67 F 2
Aves 88-89 P 7
Avesta 116-117 G 7
Aveyron 120-121 HJ 6
Avezzano 122-123 E 4
Avia Terai 104-105 F 10
Avignon 120-121 K 7
Ávila [CO] 94-95 F 8
Ávila [E] 120-121 E 8
Ávila, Parque Nacional el — 91 II bc 1
Avilés 120-121 DE 7

Avión, Faro de — 120-121 CD 7
Avis 120-121 D 9
Avispas, Las — 106-107 G 2
Avissåwêlla 140 E 7
Avlije-Ata = Džambul 132-133 MN 9
Avoca, IA 70-71 C 5
Avola [CDN] 60 H 4
Àvola [I] 122-123 F 7
Avon, IL 70-71 E 5
Avon, MT 66-67 G 2
Avon, SD 68-69 GH 4
Avondale, AZ 74-75 G 6
Avondale, CO 68-69 D 6
Avondale, LA 85 I a 2
Avondale, Chicago-, IL 83 II b 1
Avondale Heights, Melbourne- 161 II b 1
Avon Downs 158-159 G 4
Avondrust 174-175 DE 8
Avonlea 61 F 6
Avon Park, FL 80-81 c 3
Avontuur 172 D 8
Avranches 120-121 G 4

Awabes = Abbabis 174-175 B 2
Awadh = Avadh 134-135 N 5
Awâdî 164-165 B 4
Awaji-shima 144-145 K 5
'Awânah 164-165 C 5
Awanla = Aonla 138-139 G 3
Awasa [ETH, lake] 164-165 M 7
Awasa [ETH, place] 164-165 M 7
Awash [ETH, place] 164-165 MN 7
Awash [ETH, river] 164-165 M 7
Awa-shima 144-145 M 3
Awasibberge 174-175 A 3
Awasib Mountains = Awasibberge 174-175 A 3
Awaso 164-165 D 7
Awaya 144-145 K 5
Awaynât, Al- 166-167 KL 2
Awbârî 164-165 G 3
Awbârî, Şaḥrâ' — 164-165 G 3
Awdah, Hawr — 136-137 M 7
Awdheegle 164-165 N 8
Awe 168-169 H 3
Awe, Loch — 119 D 3
Aweil = Uwayl 164-165 K 7
Awgu 168-169 G 4
A'wînat Laqra' 166-167 C 6
'Awînat Turkuz 166-167 B 5
'Awjâ', Al- 136-137 M 8
Awjilah 164-165 J 3
Åwkâr 164-165 BC 5
Awlâd Abû 166-167 BC 3
Awlâd Mîmûn 166-167 F 2
Awlâd Nâîl, Jabal — 166-167 H 2
Awlâd Raḥmûn 166-167 K 1
Awlâd Sa'îd 166-167 BC 3
Awlâf 166-167 G 6
Awlaytîs, Wâd — 164-165 B 3
Awlif 166-167 D 2
Awrâs, Jabal al- 166-167 JK 2
Awrîûrâ' 166-167 A 5
Awsart 164-165 B 4
Awsîm 170 II a 1
Awsûjîn 166-167 L 6
Awţât Awlâd al-Ḥâjj 166-167 E 3
Awul 148-149 h 6
Awuna River 58-59 J 2

Axarfjördhur 116-117 e 1
Axel Heiberg Island 56-57 ST 1-2
Axial, CO 68-69 C 5
Axim 164-165 D 8
Axinim 98-99 J 6
Ax-les-Thermes 120-121 HJ 7
Axochiapán 86-87 L 8

Ayabaca 92-93 CD 5
Ayabe 144-145 K 5
Ayacucho [BOL] 104-105 E 5
Ayacucho [PE, administrative unit] 96-97 D 8-E 9
Ayacucho [PE, place] 92-93 E 7
Ayacucho [RA] 111 E 5
Ayâdau 141 D 4
Ayadaw = Ayâdau 141 D 4
Ayagh Qum köl 142-143 F 4
Ayambis, Río — 96-97 BC 3
Ayamonte 120-121 D 10
Ayancık 136-137 F 2
Ayangba 168-169 G 4
Ayapel 94-95 D 3
Ayapel, Ciénaga de — 94-95 D 3
Ayapel, Serranía de — 94-95 D 4
Ayarde, Laguna — 104-105 F 9
Ayas [TR] 136-137 E 2
'Ayashî, Jabal — 164-165 CD 2
Ayasofya = Hagia Sophia 154 I ab 2
Ayaviri 92-93 E 7
Ayazağa [TR, place] 154 I a 2
Ayazağa [TR, river] 154 I a 2
Aybastı = Esenli 136-137 G 2
Aycheyacu, Río — 96-97 C 4
Ayden, NC 80-81 H 3
Aydın 134-135 B 3
Aydın dağları 136-137 B 4-C 3
Aydın köl 142-143 F 3
Ayégou 168-169 F 3
Ayer Hitam 150-151 D 12
Ayer Puteh = Kampung Ayer Puteh 150-151 D 10
Ayers Rock 158-159 F 5
Ayiyak River 58-59 L 2
'Aylay 164-165 L 5
Aylesbury 119 F 6
'Aylî, Sha'îb al- 136-137 H 7
Aylmer [CDN, Ontario] 72-73 F 3
Aylmer [CDN, Quebec] 72-73 HJ 2
Aylwin 72-73 H 2
'Ayn, Wâdî al- 134-135 H 6
'Aynabo 164-165 O 7
'Ayn ad-Difâlî 166-167 D 2
'Ayn Aghyût, Ḥâssî — 166-167 M 6
'Ayn al-Bard 166-167 F 2
'Ayn al-Bayḍâ 166-167 GH 2
'Ayn al-Bayḍâ' 136-137 GH 7
'Ayn al-Bayḍâh 136-137 GH 5
'Ayn al-Ghazâl [ET] 173 B 5
'Ayn al-Ghazal [LAR] 164-165 J 4
'Ayn al-Hajal 166-167 H 2
'Ayn al-Ḥajar 166-167 G 2
'Ayn al-Ibil 166-167 H 2
'Ayn al-Khabîrâ 166-167 J 1
'Ayn al-Lûḥ 166-167 D 3
'Ayn al-Milḥ 166-167 HJ 2
'Ayn al-Muqshîn, Al- 134-135 GH 7
'Ayn al-Qasr 166-167 K 2
'Ayn ar-Rîsh 166-167 HJ 2
'Ayn ash-Sha'îr 166-167 E 3
'Ayn aş-Şafâ' 166-167 EF 2
'Ayn at-Turk 166-167 F 1-2
'Ayn 'Ayshah 166-167 D 2
'Ayn 'Ayssah 136-137 H 4
'Ayn 'Azar 166-167 M 5
'Ayn 'Azâwah 166-167 K 7
'Ayn 'Azl 166-167 J 2
'Ayn Azzân 164-165 G 4
'Ayn Balbâl 166-167 G 6
'Ayn Balbâlah, Sabkhat — 166-167 D 6
'Ayn Ban Khalîl 166-167 F 3
'Ayn Bârdah 166-167 K 1
Ayn Bin Tîlî, Wâd — 166-167 B 6-7
'Ayn Binyân 166-167 H 1
'Ayn Bissim 166-167 H 1
'Ayn Bû Sîf 166-167 H 2
'Ayn Daflah 166-167 GH 1
'Ayn Dhahab 166-167 G 2
'Ayn Dîwâr 136-137 K 4
'Ayn Drâham 166-167 L 1
'Ayn Ghar 166-167 G 6
Aynı 136-137 JK 4
'Ayn Jarmashîn 173 B 5
'Ayn Kirshah 166-167 K 1-2
'Ayn Mahdî 166-167 H 3
'Ayn Mâlilah 166-167 K 1-2
'Ayn Qazzân 164-165 EF 5
'Ayn Şafrâ 164-165 DE 2
'Ayn Şâliḥ 164-165 E 3
'Ayn Şûf 166-167 H 5
'Ayn Tâdalas 166-167 G 1-2
'Ayn Tâdîn 164-165 E 4
'Ayn Taqrût 166-167 J 1
'Ayn Tazârat 166-167 JK 6
'Ayn Tûtah 166-167 J 2
'Ayn-Umannâs 164-165 F 3
Aynunâh 132-133 D 5
'Ayn Unaḥḥâs 166-167 HJ 6
'Ayn Wilmân 166-167 J 2
'Ayn Wissârah 166-167 H 2
'Ayn Zâlah 136-137 K 4
'Ayn Zuraḥ 166-167 E 2
Ayoaya 104-105 B 5
Ayôd 164-165 L 7
Ayodhya 138-139 J 4
Ayr [AUS] 158-159 J 3
Ayr [GB] 119 D 4
Ayrancı 136-137 E 4
Ayre, Point of — 119 DE 4
Ayrig Nur = Ajrag nuur 142-143 GH 2
'Aysa, Jabal — 166-167 F 3
Aysha 164-165 N 6
Ayu Islands = Kepulauan Aju 148-149 K 6
'Ayun, Al- 164-165 B 3
Ayun, Ja — = Ya Ayun 150-151 G 6
Ayun, Ya — 150-151 G 6
'Ayûn al-'Atrûs 164-165 C 5
'Ayûn Dra'ah, Al- [MA, Ţarfâyah] 166-167 A 5
'Ayûn Dra'ah, Al- [MA, Ujdah] 166-167 E 2
Ayûr 140 C 6
Ayutla 86-87 L 9
Ayuy 96-97 C 3
Ayvacık [TR, Çanakkale] 136-137 B 3
Ayvalık 136-137 B 3
'Ayyâţ, Al- 173 B 3

Azabu, Tôkyô- 155 III b 2
Azafal 164-165 AB 4
'Azair, Al- = Al-'Uzayr 136-137 M 7
Azamganj = Azîmganj 138-139 LM 5
Azamgarh 138-139 J 4-5
'Azamîyah, Baghdâd-Al- 136-137 L 6
Azángaro 92-93 EF 7
Azaoua, In — 164-165 F 4
Azaoua, In — = 'Ayn 'Azâwah 166-167 K 7
Azaouad 164-165 D 5
Azaouak 164-165 E 5
Azapa 104-105 AB 6
Azapa, Quebrada — 104-105 B 6
Azara 106-107 K 2
Âžarbayejân-e Bâkhtarî 134-135 EF 3
Âžarbâyejân-e-Khâvarî 134-135 EF 3
Azare 164-165 FG 6
Âzar Shahr 136-137 LM 4
'Azâwah, 'Ayn — 166-167 K 7
Azawak, Wadi — = Azaouak 164-165 E 5
A'zâz 136-137 G 4
Azazga = 'Azâzgah 166-167 J 1
Azâzgah 166-167 J 1
Azbakîyah, Al-Qâhirah-al- 170 II b 1
Azbine 164-165 F 5
Azcapotzalco 91 I b 2
Azcapotzalco-El Recreo 91 I b 2
Azcapotzalco-Reynosa Tamaulipas 91 I b 2
Azdavay 136-137 E 2
Azéfal = Azafal 164-165 AB 4
Azeffoun = Azfûn 166-167 J 1
Azemmoûr = Azimûr 166-167 B 3
Azerbaijan Soviet Socialist Republic 126-127 NO 6
Azerbajdžanskaja Sovetskaja Socialističeskaja Respublika = Azerbaijan Soviet Socialist Republic 126-127 NO 6
Azerbaydzhan Soviet Socialist Republic 134-135 F 2
Azero, Río — 104-105 D 6
Azevedo Sodré 106-107 K 3
Azfûn 166-167 J 1
Azgersdorf, Wien- 113 I b 2
Azgir 126-127 N 3
Azhar-University, Al- 170 II b 1
Azîlâl 166-167 C 4
Azîmganj 138-139 LM 5
Azimgarh = Azamgarh 138-139 J 4-5
Azimûr 166-167 B 3
Azingo 168-169 H 6
'Azîzîyah, Al- [IRQ] 136-137 L 6
'Azîzîyah, Al- [LAR] 164-165 G 2
Aziziye 136-137 D 4
Azlam, Wâdî — 173 DE 4
'Azmâtî, Sabkhat — 164-165 DE 3
Aznâ 136-137 N 6
Aznakajevo 124-125 T 6
Azogues 92-93 D 5
Azores = Açores 204-205 E 5
Azores Plateau 50-51 HJ 4
Azoûrkî, Jbel — = Jabal Azûrkî 166-167 C 4
Azouzetta Lake 60 F 2
Azov 126-127 J 3
Azov, Sea of — = Azovskoje more 126-127 GH 3-4
Azovskoje more 126-127 GH 3-4
Azraq, El — = Azraq ash-Shîshân 136-137 G 7
Azraq ash-Shîshân 136-137 G 7
Azroû = Azrû 164-165 CD 2
Azrû 164-165 CD 2
Aztec, AZ 74-75 G 6
Aztec, NM 68-69 BC 7
Azua de Compostela 88-89 L 5
Azuaga 120-121 E 9
Azuay 96-97 B 3
Azúcar Guagraurcu, Pan de — 96-97 C 2
Azucena 106-107 H 6
Azuero, Península de — 64-65 K 10
Azul [MEX] 86-87 K 4
Azul [RA] 111 E 5
Azul, Cordillera — 92-93 D 6
Azul, Sierra — 106-107 BC 5-6
Azul, Sierra de — 106-107 GH 6
Azulejo, El — 76-77 D 9
Azuma-yama 144-145 MN 4
Azurduy 92-93 G 8-9
Azûrkî, Jabal — 166-167 C 4
Azz, Hassi el — = Ḥâssî al-'Iz 166-167 G 4
Azza = Ghazzah 134-135 C 4
Azzaba = 'Azzâbah 166-167 K 1
'Azzâbah 166-167 K 1
Az-Za'farânah 173 C 3
Az-Zahlîqah 166-167 C 3
Az-Zahrân 134-135 FG 5
Az-Zamûl al-Akbar 166-167 K 5-L 4
'Azzân 134-135 F 8
Az-Zaqâzîq 164-165 KL 2
Az-Zarqâ' 136-137 G 6
Az-Zatîr 134-135 E 6-7
Az-Zâwîyah 164-165 G 2
Az-Zawr 136-137 N 8
Azzel Matti, Sebkra — = Sabkhat 'Azmâtî 164-165 DE 3
Az-Zîbâr 136-137 KL 4
Az-Ziltî 134-135 EF 5
Az-Zubaydîyah 136-137 L 6
Az-Zubayr 136-137 M 7

B

Baa 148-149 H 9
Ba'abdâ 136-137 F 6
Baalbek = Ba'labakk 136-137 G 5-6
Baambrugge 128 I b 2
Ba'an = Batang 142-143 H 6
Baardheere 164-165 N 8
Baargaal 164-165 c 1
Bâb, Al- 136-137 G 4
Baba [EC] 96-97 B 2
Bâbâ, Kûh-e — 134-135 J 4
Baba-Ali 170 I a 2
Baba burnu [TR, Black Sea] 136-137 D 2
Baba burnu [TR, Ege denizi] 134-135 B 3
Babad 152-153 K 9
Babadag 122-123 N 3
Babadag, gora — 126-127 O 6
Babaeski 136-137 B 2
Baba Hatim 142-143 E 4
Babahoyo 92-93 CD 5
Babahoyo, Río — 96-97 B 2-3
Babajevo 132-133 F 6
Babajurt 126-127 N 5
Bâb al-Mandab 134-135 E 8
Bab al-Mandeb = Bâb al-Mandab 134-135 E 8
Babanango 174-175 J 5
Babar, Kepulauan — 148-149 JK 8
Babati 171 C 4
Babb, MT 66-67 G 1
Babbage River 58-59 S 2
Babbitt, NV 74-75 D 3
Babbitt, MN 70-71 E 2
Babel = Babylon 134-135 EF 4
Bab el Mandeb = Bâb al-Mandab 134-135 E 8
Bab el Oued, Al-Jazâ'ir- 170 I a 1
Babelthuap 148-149 KL 5
Baberu 138-139 H 5
Babi, Pulau — 152-153 B 4
Babia, La — 76-77 CD 8
Babia Góra 118 J 4
Babícora, Laguna de — 86-87 FG 3
Babil 136-137 L 6
Bâbil = Babylon 134-135 EF 4
Babinda 158-159 J 3
Babine Lake 56-57 L 6-7
Babine Portage 60 E 2
Babine Range 56-57 L 6-7
Babine River 60 D 2
Babino [SU, Vologodskaja Oblast'] 124-125 N 4
Bâbol 134-135 G 3
Baboquivari Peak 74-75 H 7
Babor, Djebel — = Jabal Bâbûr [DZ, mountain] 166-167 J 1
Babor, Djebel — = Jabal Bâbûr [DZ, mountains] 166-167 J 1
Baboua 164-165 G 7
Bâb Tâzah 166-167 D 2
Bâbul = Bâbol 134-135 G 3
Bâbûr, Jabal — [DZ, mountain] 166-167 J 1
Bâbûr, Jabal — [DZ, mountains] 166-167 J 1
Babura 168-169 H 2
Babuškin 132-133 U 7
Babuškin, Moskva- 124-125 LM 5-6
Babuškina 124-125 O 4
Babuškina, zaliv — 132-133 de 6
Babuyan Channel 148-149 H 3
Babuyan Island 148-149 H 3
Babuyan Islands 148-149 H 3
Babylon 134-135 EF 4
Babylon, NY 72-73 K 4
Babynino 124-125 K 6
Bacabal 100-101 B 3
Bacajá, Rio — 98-99 N 7
Bacalar, Laguna de — 86-87 Q 8
Bacamuchi, Río — 86-87 EF 2-3
Bacan, Pulau — 148-149 J 7
Bacău 122-123 M 2
Băc Bô 148-149 DE 2
Bacchus Marsh 160 G 6
Bac Giang 150-151 F 2
Bachaquero 94-95 F 3
Bacharden 134-135 H 3
Bachchâr 164-165 D 2
Bachenbülach 128 IV b 1
Bachíniva 86-87 G 3
Bach Long Vi, Dao — 150-151 F 2
Bach Ma 150-151 FG 4
Bachmač 126-127 F 1
Bachmutovo 124-125 JK 6
Bacho 150-151 C 9
Bachok 150-151 D 9
Bachtemir 126-127 N 3-4
Bachu = Maral Bashi 142-143 D 3-4
Bačka 122-123 H 3
Băc Kan 150-151 E 1
Bačka Palanka 122-123 H 3
Bačka Topola 122-123 HJ 3
Back Bay 80-81 J 2
Back Bay, Boston-, MA 84 I b 2
Back Lick Run 82 II a 2
Back River 56-57 R 4
Backriver 174-175 C 4
Backstairs Passage 158-159 G 7
Bac Lio' = Vinh Lo'i 148-149 E 5
Băc Ninh 150-151 EF 2
Bacolod 148-149 H 4
Bacongo, Brazzaville- 170 IV a 1
Bacuit = El Nido 148-149 G 4
Bacuri 100-101 B 1
Bad', Wâdî — 173 C 3
Badaâmpahâḍ = Bâdâmpahâr 138-139 L 6
Badagada 138-139 K 8
Badagara 140 B 5
Badagri 168-169 F 4
Badagri Creek 170 III a 2
Badajia 146-147 H 5
Badajos, Lago — 92-93 G 5
Badajoz 120-121 D 9
Badakhšân 134-135 L 3
Bâda Kyûn 150-151 B 7
Badalona 120-121 J 8
Baḍambâgaḍa = Barâmba 138-139 K 7
Bâdâmî 140 B 3
Badâmî = Bâdâmî 140 B 3
Bâdâmpahâr 138-139 L 6
Badanah 134-135 E 4
Badârî, Al- 164-165 L 3
Badarpur 141 C 3
Badas, Pulau-pulau — 152-153 G 5
Badavêlu = Badvel 140 D 3
Bad Axe, MI 72-73 E 3
Badâyûn = Budaun 134-135 M 5
Baddeck 63 F 4
Baddûzzah, Râ's al- 164-165 BC 2
Badè 141 F 2
Bad Ems 118 C 3
Baden [A] 118 H 4
Baden [CH] 118 D 5
Baden-Baden 118 D 4
Baden-Württemberg 118 D 4
Badgâṅ = Bargaon 138-139 K 6
Badgastein 118 F 5
Badger, MN 70-71 BC 1
Bad Hersfeld 118 D 3
Badhoevedorp 128 I a 2
Bad Homburg 118 D 3
Badî, Al- [IRQ] 136-137 J 5
Badî', Al- [Saudi Arabia] 134-135 F 6
Badikaha 168-169 D 3
Badîn 134-135 K 6
Badin, NC 80-81 F 3
Badiraguato 86-87 G 5
Bad Ischl 118 F 5
Badji 168-169 H 4
Bad Kissingen 118 E 3
Bad Kreuznach 118 CD 4
Bad Land Butte 68-69 BC 2
Badlands [USA, North Dakota] 64-65 F 2
Badlands [USA, South Dakota] 64-65 F 3
Badlands National Monument 68-69 E 4
Bad Mergentheim 118 DE 4
Bad Nauheim 118 D 3
Badnâvar = Badnâwar 138-139 E 6
Badnâwar 138-139 E 6
Badnera 138-139 F 7
Bad Neuenahr 118 C 3
Badnor 138-139 E 5
Baḍoḍêñ = Vaḍôdarâ 134-135 L 6
Ba Đôn 148-149 E 3
Badong [TJ] 142-143 KL 5
Ba Đông [VN] 150-151 F 8
Badou 146-147 F 3
Badoumbé 168-169 C 2
Badplaas 174-175 J 3
Badr 134-135 E 7
Badra = Bhâdra 138-139 A 3
Badrah 136-137 L 6
Bad Reichenhall 118 F 5
Badr Ḥûnayn 134-135 D 6
Badriane = Badriyân 166-167 G 5
Badrînâth [IND, mountain] 138-139 G 2
Badrînâth [IND, place] 138-139 G 2
Bad River 68-69 F 3
Bad River Indian Reservation 70-71 E 2
Badriyân 166-167 G 5
Bad Tölz 118 E 5
Badu Danan = Denan 164-165 N 7
Badulla 134-135 N 9
Badvel 140 D 3
Bad Wildungen 118 D 3
Bad Zouar 170 I b 2
Baependi 102-103 K 4-5
Baerâţ = Bairat 138-139 F 4
Baerâṭh = Bairat 138-139 F 4
Baeza [EC] 96-97 C 2
Bafang 164-165 G 7-8
Bafatá 164-165 B 6
Baffin Bay [CDN] 56-57 W-Y 3
Baffin Bay [USA] 76-77 F 9
Baffin Island 56-57 V 3-X 5
Baffin Island National Park 56-57 XY 4
Baffin Land = Baffin Island 56-57 V 3-X 5
Bafia 164-165 G 8
Bafing 164-165 B 6
Bafing Makana 168-169 C 2
Bafoulabé 164-165 BC 6
Bafoussam 164-165 G 7
Bâfq 134-135 GH 4
Bafra 136-137 FG 2
Bafra burnu 136-137 G 2
Bafwasende 172 E 1
Bagabag Island 148-149 N 7
Bagaço 98-99 E 9
Bagaha 138-139 K 4
Bagahak, Gunung — 152-153 N 3
Bagajevskij 126-127 K 3
Bâgalakôṭṭê = Bâgalkot 134-135 LM 7
Bâgalkot 134-135 LM 7
Bagalpur = Bhâgalpur 134-135 O 5-6
Bagamojo = Bagamoyo 172 G 3
Bagamoyo 172 G 3
Bagan Datoh 150-151 C 11
Bagan Jaya 148-149 D 5
Bagan Serai 150-151 C 10
Bagase Burnu = İncekum burnu 136-137 EF 4
Bagbe 168-169 CD 3
Bagdad, AZ 74-75 G 5
Bagdad, FL 78-79 F 5
Bagdâd = Baghdâd 134-135 EF 4
Bagdarin 132-133 VW 7
Bâgêpali = Bâgepalli 140 CD 4
Bâgepalli 140 CD 4
Bâgevâdi 140 BC 2
Baggs, WY 68-69 C 5
Bâgh 138-139 E 6
Baghdâd 134-135 EF 4
Baghdâd-Al-'Azamîyah 136-137 L 6
Baghdâd-Al-Kâzimîyah 136-137 L 6
Baghdâd-Dawrah 136-137 L 6
Baghdâd-Dôra = Baghdâd-Dawrah 136-137 L 6
Bâghdâdî, Râs — = Râ's Ḥunkurâb 173 D 5
Baghêlkhaṇḍ 134-135 N 6
Baghelkhand Plateau 138-139 HJ 6
Bâgh-e Malek 136-137 N 7
Bâgherhâṭ 138-139 M 6
Bagheria 122-123 E 6
Baghlân 134-135 K 3
Bâghmatî 138-139 K 4
Baghrash köl 142-143 F 3
Bagirmi 164-165 H 6
Bagley, MN 70-71 C 2
Bagley Icefield 58-59 QR 6
Bâgli 138-139 F 6
Bağlum 136-137 E 2
Bâgmatî = Bâghmatî 138-139 K 4
Bagnères-de-Bigorre 120-121 H 7
Bagnères-de-Luchon 120-121 H 7
Bagneux 129 I c 2
Bagnolet 129 I c 2
Bagodar 138-139 K 5
Bagoé 164-165 C 6
Bagotville 63 A 3
Bagrationovsk 118 K 1
Bagru 138-139 E 4
Bagua 96-97 B 4
Bagual 106-107 E 5
Baguezane, Monts — 164-165 F 5
Baguinéda 168-169 D 2
Baguio 148-149 H 3
Baguirmi = Bagirmi 164-165 H 6
Bagur, Cabo — 120-121 J 8
Bâh 138-139 G 4
Bâhâḍâgôḍâ = Baharâgora 138-139 L 6
Bahadale 171 D 2-3
Bahâdurganj 138-139 LM 4
Bahalda 138-139 L 6
Bahama, Canal Viejo de — 64-65 L 7
Bahama Island, Grand — 64-65 L 6
Bahamas 64-65 L 6-M 7
Bâhâr 136-137 N 5
Baharâgora 138-139 L 6
Baharâich = Bahrâich 134-135 N 5
Bahar Assoli 164-165 N 6
Bahar Dar = Bahir Dar 164-165 M 6
Bahar el Hammar = Bahr al-Aḥmar 166-167 GH 6
Baḥarîyah, Wâḥât al- 164-165 K 3
Baharu, Kota — 148-149 D 5
Bahau 150-151 D 11
Bahau, Sungai — 152-153 LM 4
Bahâwalnagar 138-139 D 2-3
Bahâwalpûr 134-135 L 5
Bahçe 136-137 G 4
Bahçeköy 154 I a 2
Bahçeköy su kemeri 154 I b 2
Ba He 155 II c 2
Baheri 138-139 G 3
Bahia 92-93 LM 7
Bahia = Salvador 92-93 M 7
Bahía, Isla de la — 64-65 J 8
Bahía, Islas de la — 64-65 J 8
Bahía Adventure 108-109 B 5
Bahía Aguirre 108-109 FG 10
Bahía Anegada 108-109 HJ 3
Bahía Asunción 86-87 C 4
Bahía Blanca [MEX] 86-87 C 3
Bahía Blanca [RA, bay] 111 D 5
Bahía Blanca [RA, place] 111 D 5
Bahía Bustamante 108-109 FG 5
Bahía Camarones 108-109 G 5
Bahía Carnero 106-107 A 6
Bahía Chanco 106-107 A 5
Bahía Cook 111 B 9
Bahía Cruz 108-109 G 5
Bahía Cucao 108-109 B 4
Bahía Darwin 111 AB 7
Bahía de Amatique 64-65 J 8
Bahía de Ancon de Sardinas 96-97 B 1
Bahía de Banderas 64-65 E 7
Bahía de Bluefields 88-89 E 8
Bahía de Buenaventura 92-93 D 4
Bahía de Campeche 64-65 GH 7
Bahía de Caráquez 92-93 CD 5
Bahía de Chetumal 64-65 J 8
Bahía de Cochinos 88-89 F 3-4
Bahía de Concepción 106-107 A 6
Bahía de Coquimbo 106-107 B 2
Bahía de Coronado 64-65 K 10
Bahía de la Anunciación = Berkeley Sound 108-109 KL 8
Bahía de la Ascensión 64-65 J 8
Bahía de la Concepción 86-87 E 4
Bahía del Adair 86-87 CD 2
Bahía de la Independencia 96-97 C 8-9
Bahía de La Paz 64-65 DE 7
Bahía del Espíritu Santo 86-87 R 8
Bahía del Labertino = Adventures Sound 108-109 K 9
Bahía de los Abrigos = Bay of Harbours 108-109 K 9
Bahía de Los Ángeles 86-87 CD 3
Bahía de los Nodales 108-109 G 7
Bahía de Magdalena 86-87 C 5-6
Bahía de Manta 92-93 C 5
Bahía de Mejillones del Sur 104-105 A 8
Bahía de Nipe 88-89 J 4
Bahía de Paita 96-97 A 4
Bahía de Palma 120-121 J 9
Bahía de Panamá 64-65 bc 3
Bahía de Pisco 92-93 D 7
Bahía de Portete 94-95 EF 1
Bahía de Samaná 64-65 N 8
Bahía de Samanco 96-97 B 6
Bahía de San Blas 86-87 H 7
Bahía de San Jorge 86-87 D 2
Bahía de San Juan del Norte 64-65 K 9
Bahía de San Pedro 108-109 BC 3
Bahía de San Quintín 86-87 BC 2
Bahía de San Rafael 86-87 D 3
Bahía de Santa Elena 96-97 A 2-3
Bahía de Santa María 86-87 F 5
Bahía de Sechura 92-93 C 6
Bahía de Todos Santos 86-87 B 2
Bahía de Valdivia 108-109 C 2
Bahía Dineley 108-109 AB 7
Bahía Dulce 86-87 L 9
Bahía Engaño 108-109 G 4
Bahía Falsa 106-107 FG 7
Bahía Grande 111 C 8
Bahía Honda 94-95 EF 1
Bahía Horcón 106-107 AB 4
Bahía Inútil 111 BC 8
Bahía la Ligua 106-107 AB 4
Bahía Las Cañas 106-107 A 5
Bahía Las Minas 64-65 b 2
Bahía Laura 111 CD 7
Bahía Limón 64-65 b 2
Bahía Lomas 108-109 E 9
Bahía Magdalena 64-65 D 7
Bahía Moreno 104-105 A 8
Bahía Nassau 111 C 9
Bahía Negra 111 E 2
Bahía Oso Blanco 111 CD 7
Bahía Otway 111 AB 8
Bahía Petacalco 86-87 JK 9
Bahía Posesión 108-109 E 9
Bahía Salado 106-107 B 1
Bahía Salvación 108-109 B 8
Bahía Samborombón 111 E 5
Bahía San Carlos 86-87 D 3-4
Bahía San Felipe 108-109 DE 9
Bahía San Francisco de Paula = Byron Sound 108-109 J 8
Bahía San Julián = Queen Charlotte Bay 108-109 J 8
Bahía San Nicolás 96-97 D 9
Bahía San Sebastián 108-109 EF 9
Bahía San Vicente 106-107 A 6
Bahía Sebastián Vizcaíno 64-65 CD 6
Bahía Solano 94-95 C 4
Bahía Solano [CO, place] 92-93 D 3
Bahía Stokes 108-109 C 10
Bahía Thetis 108-109 FG 10
Bahía Tongoy 106-107 B 3
Bahía Tortugas 86-87 C 4
Bahía Trinidad 64-65 b 2
Bahía Vera 108-109 G 5
Bahir Dar 164-165 M 6
Baḥrah, Al- 136-137 MN 8
Bahrâich 134-135 N 5
Bahrain 134-135 G 5
Bahr al-Aḥmar 166-167 GH 6
Baḥr al-Aḥmar, Al- 164-165 L 4-M 5
Baḥr al-'Arab 164-165 K 6-7
Baḥr al-Ghazâl [Sudan, administrative unit] 164-165 JK 7
Baḥr al-Ghazâl [Sudan, river] 164-165 KL 7
Baḥr al-Jabal 164-165 L 7
Baḥr al-Lubaynî 170 II ab 2
Baḥr al-Mayyit 134-135 D 4
Baḥr al-Muḥîṭ, Al- 166-167 A 4-B 2
Bahrampur = Berhampore 134-135 O 6
Baḥr an-Nîl 164-165 L 3-4
Bahr Aouk 164-165 HJ 7
Bahr ash-Shârî = Buhayrat Shârî 136-137 L 5
Bahr ath Tharthâr = Munkhafad ath-Tharthâr 134-135 E 4
Bahr Dar Giorgis = Bahir Dar 164-165 M 6
Baḥreh, Âb-e — 136-137 N 7
Bahrein = Bahrain 134-135 G 5
Baḥr el Jebel = Baḥr al-Jabal 164-165 L 7
Baḥr el-Miyet = Baḥr al-Mayyit 134-135 D 4
Baḥr el Mouḥîṭ = Al-Baḥr al-Muḥîṭ 166-167 A 4-B 2
Bahrenfeld, Hamburg- 130 I a 1
Bahrgân, Ra's-e — 136-137 N 7-8
Bahrôṭ = Behror 138-139 F 4
Bahr Salamat 164-165 H 6-7
Baḥr Siniqal 168-169 B 2
Baḥr Yûsef = Baḥr Yusuf 173 B 3
Baḥr Yusuf 173 B 3
Baḥt, Wad — 166-167 D 3
Bahtîm 170 II b 1
Ba Hu = Po Hu 146-147 F 6
Bahulu, Pulau — 152-153 P 7
Bahumbelu 148-149 H 7
Bai 142-143 E 3
Baia = Salvador 92-93 M 7
Baía da Ilha Grande 102-103 K 5
Baía de Caxiuana 92-93 J 5
Baía de Cumã 100-101 B 1-2
Baía de Guanabara 102-103 L 5
Baía de Guaratuba 102-103 HJ 6
Baía de Inhambane 174-175 L 2
Baía de Lourenço Marques = Baía do Maputo 172 F 7
Baía de Mangunça 100-101 B 1
Baía de Marajó 92-93 K 4-5
Baía de Paranaguá 102-103 HJ 6
Baía de Santos 102-103 JK 6
Baía de São Francisco 102-103 HJ 7
Baía de São José 100-101 BC 2
Baía de São Marcos 92-93 L 5
Baía de Sepetiba 102-103 KL 5
Baía de Setúbal 120-121 C 9
Baía de Sofala 172 FG 6
Baía de Tijucas 102-103 H 7
Baía de Todos os Santos 92-93 M 7
Baía de Trapandé 102-103 J 6
Baía de Turiaçu 92-93 KL 5
Baía do Caeté 100-101 A 1
Baía do Emborai 100-101 AB 1
Baía do Maputo 172 F 7
Baía dos Lençóis 100-101 B 1
Baía dos Tigres 172 B 5
Baía Grande 102-103 B 1
Baia Mare 122-123 KL 2
Baião 92-93 JK 5
Baia Sprie 122-123 KL 2
Baibiene 106-107 H 2
Baïbokoum 164-165 H 7
Baibû = Baybû 136-137 KL 4
Bai Bung, Mui — 148-149 D 5
Baicha 146-147 E 7
Baicheng 142-143 N 2
Baicheng = Bai 142-143 E 3
Baidaratskaya Bay = Bajdarackaja guba 132-133 M 4
Baidu 146-147 F 9
Baie, la — 63 A 3
Baie Bradore 63 H 2
Baie Comeau 56-57 X 8
Baie de Bombetoka 172 HJ 5
Baie de Gaspé 63 DE 3
Baie de la Seine 120-121 G 4

Baie de Ngaliema 170 IV a 1
Baie de Saint Augustin 172 H 6
Baie des Sept-Îles 63 CD 2-3
Baie-Johan-Beetz 63 E 2
Baie Marguerite 53 C 29-30
Baie Moisie 63 D 2
Baierbrunn 130 II a 2
Baie-Sainte-Catherine 63 AB 2-3
Baie-Sainte-Claire 63 DE 3
Baie-Saint-Paul 63 A 4
Baie-Trinité 63 C 3
Baie Verte 63 HJ 2-3
Baigezhuang 146-147 G 2
Baihar 138-139 H 6
Baihe [TJ, place] 142-143 KL 5
Bai He [TJ, river] 146-147 D 5
Bai Hu 146-147 F 6
Ba'iji 136-137 K 5
Baiju 146-147 H 5
Baikunthpur 138-139 J 6
Baile Átha Cliath = Dublin 119 CD 5
Băileşti 122-123 K 3
Bailey 174-175 G 6
Baileys Crossroads, VA 82 II a 2
Baileys Harbor, WI 70-71 G 3
Bailique, Ilha — 98-99 O 4
Bailly 129 I b 2
Bailundo 172 C 4
Baima Shan 146-147 D 9-10
Bainbridge, OH 72-73 E 5
Baindbridge, GA 78-79 G 5
Baindūru 140 B 4
Baing 148-149 H 9
Bain-Tumen = Čojbalsan 142-143 L 2
Bainville, MT 68-69 D 1
Baipeng 146-147 B 9
Baipu 146-147 H 5
Baiqibao = Baiqipu 144-145 D 2
Baiqipu 144-145 D 2
Bā'ir 134-135 D 4
Bā'ir, Wādī — 136-137 G 7
Bairat 138-139 F 4
Bairath = Bairat 138-139 F 4
Baird, TX 76-77 E 6
Baird Inlet 58-59 EF 6
Baird Mountains 56-57 DE 4
Bairiki 208 H 2
Bairnsdale 158-159 J 7
Baïse 120-121 H 7
Baisha [TJ, Guangdong ↙ Haikou] 150-151 G 3
Baisha [TJ, Guangdong ← Macau] 146-147 D 10
Baisha [TJ, Hunan] 146-147 D 8
Baishi Guan 146-147 CD 9
Baishui [TJ, Hunan] 146-147 C 8
Baishui [TJ, Shaanxi] 146-147 B 4
Baitadi 138-139 H 3
Baitarani 138-139 KL 7
Bai Thu'o'ng 150-151 E 3
Baiti 138-139 N 3
Baitou Shan 144-145 FG 2
Baitou Shan = Changbai Shan 142-143 O 3
Bait Range 60 D 2
Baituchangmen 144-145 CD 2
Baitul = Bĕtūl 138-139 F 7
Baiwen 146-147 C 2
Baixa Grande 100-101 DE 6
Baixão 100-101 DE 7
Baixiang 146-147 E 3
Baixo Guandu 100-101 D 10
Baiyang Dian 146-147 EF 2
Baiyanjing 146-147 A 2
Baiyu Shan 146-147 B 3
Baja 118 J 5
Baja California Norte 64-65 CD 6
Baja California Sur 64-65 D 6
Bajada, La — 108-109 E 7
Bajada Colarada 108-109 E 2
Bajada del Agrio 106-107 BC 7
Bājah 164-165 F 1
Baján [MEX] 76-77 D 9
Bajan [Mongolia] 142-143 K 2
Bajan Adraga 142-143 KL 2
Bajanaul 132-133 O 7
Bajan Char uuul 142-143 H 5
Bajan Chej = Baiyanjing 146-147 A 2
Bajanchongor 142-143 HJ 2
Bajan Choto 142-143 JK 4
Bajandaj 132-133 U 7
Bajandalaj 142-143 J 3
Bajangol [Mongolia] 142-143 K 2
Bajan Gol [TJ] 142-143 K 3
Bajan Obo 142-143 K 3
Bajan Olgi 142-143 FG 2
Bajan Öndör 142-143 H 3
Bajan Sum = Bajan 142-143 K 2
Bajanteeg 142-143 J 2
Bajan Tümen = Čojbalsan 142-143 L 2
Bajan Ulaa = Bajan Uul 142-143 H 2
Bajan Ülegei = Ölgij 142-143 FG 2
Bajan Uul [Mongolia, Dornod] 142-143 L 2
Bajan Uul [Mongolia, Dzavchan] 142-143 H 2
Bajawa 148-149 GH 8
Baj-Baj = Budge-Budge 138-139 LM 6
Bajdarackaja guba 132-133 M 4
Bajé 111 F 4
Bajeuen 150-151 AB 10
Bajī 138-139 B 3
Bajío, El — 64-65 F 7
Bajirge 136-137 L 4
Bājitpūr 141 B 3
Bajkal, ozero — 132-133 U 7
Bajkal'skij chrebet 132-133 U 6-7
Bajkal'skoje 132-133 UV 6
Bajkit 132-133 S 5
Bajkonyr 132-133 M 8
Bajmak 132-133 K 7
Bajo Baudó 92-93 D 3
Bajo Caracoles 108-109 D 6
Bajo de Cari Laufquen 108-109 E 3
Bajo de la Laguna Escondida 108-109 F 2-G 3
Bajo de la Tigra 106-107 E 7
Bajo del Gualicho 108-109 G 4
Bajo del Guanaco 108-109 E 6
Bajo de los Menucos 108-109 F 2-3
Bajo de los Tierra Colorada 108-109 F 4
Bajo del Río Seco 108-109 EF 7
Bajo Hondo [RA, Buenos Aires] 106-107 G 7
Bajo Hondo [RA, Río Negro] 106-107 D 7
Bajo Imaz 106-107 E 7
Bajo Picaso 108-109 EF 7
Bajos Hondos 108-109 E 3
Bajram-Ali 134-135 J 3
Bajšint = Chongor 142-143 L 2
Baj-Sot 132-133 S 7
Bajtag Bogd uul 142-143 G 2-3
Bakal 132-133 K 6-7
Bakala 164-165 HJ 7
Bakal'skaja kosa 126-127 F 4
Bakaly 124-125 TU 6
Bakanas 132-133 O 8-9
Bakarganj = Bāqarganj 141 B 4
Bakārīyah 166-167 KL 2
Bakčar 132-133 P 6
Bake 152-153 D 7
Bakel [SN] 164-165 B 6
Baker 50-51 T 6
Baker, CA 74-75 E 5
Baker, ID 66-67 G 3
Baker, MT 68-69 D 2
Baker, NV 74-75 FG 3
Baker, OR 64-65 C 3
Baker, Canal — 111 B 7
Baker, Mount — 66-67 C 1
Baker Foreland 56-57 ST 5
Baker Island 58-59 vw 9
Baker Lake [CDN, lake] 56-57 R 5
Baker Lake [CDN, place] 56-57 R 5
Bakersfield, CA 64-65 C 4
Bakersfield, TX 76-77 CD 7
Bakerville 174-175 G 3-4
Bakhmah, Sadd al- 136-137 L 4
Bākhtarī, Āžarbayejān-e — 134-135 EF 3
Bakhtegān, Daryācheh — 134-135 G 5
Bakhuis Gebergte 98-99 K 2
26 Bakinskij Komissarov 126-127 OP 7
Bakır çayı 136-137 B 3
Bakırdağı = Taşcı 136-137 F 3
Bakırköy, İstanbul- 136-137 C 2
Bakkafjördhur 116-117 fg 1
Bakkaflói 116-117 f 1
Bakkagerdhi 116-117 g 2
Baklanka 124-125 N 4
Bako 168-169 D 3
Bakony 118 HJ 5
Bakool 164-165 a 3
Bakres 126-127 M 4
Baksan [SU, place] 126-127 L 5
Baksan [SU, river] 126-127 L 5
Baksar = Buxar 138-139 JK 5
Baku 126-127 OP 6
Baku-Baladžary 126-127 O 6
Baku-Buzovna 126-127 P 6
Bakungan 148-149 C 6
Bakuriani 126-127 L 6
Baku-Sabunči 126-127 OP 6
Baku-Surachany 126-127 P 6
Bakwanga = Mbuji-Mayi 172 D 3
B'ala [BG] 122-123 L 4
Bala [CDN] 72-73 G 2
Bâlâ [TR] 136-137 E 3
Bala, Cerros de — 92-93 F 7-8
Balabac 152-153 M 3
Balabac Island 148-149 G 5
Balabac Strait 148-149 G 5
Balabaia 172 B 4
Ba'labakk 136-137 G 5-6
Balabalangan, Pulau-pulau — 148-149 G 7
Balabanovo 124-125 L 6
Balabino 126-127 G 3
Balachna 124-125 O 5
Bala-Cynwyd, PA 84 III b 1
Balad [IRQ] 136-137 L 5-6
Bal'ad [SP] 164-165 b 3
Balad'ok 132-133 Z 7
Balad Rūz 136-137 L 6
Baladžary, Baku- 126-127 O 6
Balagansk 132-133 T 7
Bālāghāt 134-135 N 6
Bālāghāt Range 140 BC 1
Bālāgī = Bhālki 140 C 1
Balaguer 120-121 H 8
Balaikarangan 152-153 J 5
Balā'im, Rā's al- 173 C 3
Balaipungut 152-153 D 5
Balaiselasa 148-149 CD 7
Balaklava [AUS] 158-159 G 6
Balaklava [SU] 126-127 F 4
Balakleja [SU, Čerkasskaja Oblast'] 126-127 H 2
Balakleja [SU, Char'kovskaja Oblast'] 126-127 H 2
Balakovo 132-133 HJ 7
Balama 171 D 6
Balambangan, Pulau — 148-149 G 5
Bālānagar 140 D 2
Balança, Serra da — 100-101 E 4
Balancán de Domínguez 86-87 P 9
Balanças, Serra das — 100-101 DE 3
Balanda 126-127 M 1
Balangan, Kepulauan — = Pulau-pulau Balabalangan 148-149 G 7
Ba Lang An, Mui — = Mui Batangan 148-149 EF 3
Balanggoda 140 E 7
Balāngīr 134-135 N 6
Balanka 168-169 F 3
Balankanche 86-87 QR 7
Balao 96-97 B 3
Bālāpur 138-139 F 7
Balarāmpur 138-139 L 6
Balashov = Balašov 126-127 L 1
Balašicha 124-125 LM 5-6
B'ala Slatina 122-123 K 4
Balasore 134-135 O 6
Balašov 126-127 L 1
Balat, İstanbul- 154 I a 2
Balaton 118 HJ 5
Balaurin 152-153 P 10
Balboa 64-65 b 3
Balboa Heights 64-65 b 3
Balcarce 111 E 5
Bal'cer = Krasnoarmejsk 126-127 M 1
Balchari 138-139 M 7
Balchaš 132-133 N 8
Balchaš, ozero — 132-133 NO 8
Balčik 122-123 MN 4
Balclutha 161 C 8
Balcones Escarpment 64-65 F 6-G 5
Bald Butte 66-67 D 4
Balde 106-107 D 4
Baldeo 138-139 FG 4
Bald Head 158-159 C 7
Baldhill Reservoir 68-69 GH 2
Bald Knob, AR 78-79 D 3
Bald Knob, WV 80-81 F 2
Bald Mountain 74-75 F 4
Baldock Lake 61 K 2
Baldone 124-125 DE 5
Balduck Park 84 II c 2
Baldwin, MI 70-71 H 4
Baldwin, WI 70-71 D 3
Baldwin City, KS 70-71 C 6
Baldwin Hills 83 III b 1-2
Baldwin Peninsula 58-59 F 3
Baldwinsville, NY 72-73 H 3
Baldwyn, MS 78-79 E 3
Baldy, Mount — 66-67 H 2
Baldy Peak [USA, Arizona] 64-65 DE 5
Baldy Peak [USA, New Mexico] 76-77 AB 5
Balé 164-165 N 7-8
Bâle = Basel 118 C 5
Baléa 168-169 C 2
Baleares, Islas — 120-121 H 9-K 8
Balearic Islands = Islas Baleares 120-121 H 9-K 8
Baleh, Sungei — 152-153 K 5
Baleia, Ponta da — 100-101 E 9
Baleimakam 152-153 D 7
Balej 132-133 W 7
Báleshvara = Balasore 134-135 O 6
Balezino 124-125 T 5
Balfour [CDN] 66-67 E 1
Balfour [ZA, Kaapland] 174-175 G 7
Balfour [ZA, Transvaal] 174-175 H 4
Balfour North = Balfour 174-175 H 4
Balfour Park 170 V b 1
Balḥāf 134-135 F 8
Balham, London- 129 II b 2
Balharshāh 138-139 G 8
Bāli [IND] 138-139 D 5
Bali [RI = 15 ◁] 148-149 F 8
Bālī = Bally 138-139 M 6
Bali, Pulau — 148-149 FG 8
Bali, Selat — 152-153 L 10
Bāliguda 138-139 J 7
Baligura = Bāliguda 138-139 J 7
Balīh, Nahr — 136-137 H 4
Bālihāti 154 II a 1
Balıkesir 134-135 B 3
Balikpapan 148-149 G 7
Balik Pulau 150-151 BC 10
Baling 150-151 C 10
Balingian 152-153 K 4
Balintang Channel 148-149 H 3
Bali Sea 148-149 FG 8
Baliyā = Ballia 138-139 K 5
Baliza 102-103 F 2
Balizhuang = Beijing-Yuyuantan 155 II a 2
Balizhuang, Beijing- 155 II bc 2
Baljabbūr, Ḥāssī — 166-167 K 5
Baljennie 61 DE 4
Balkan = Dedeköy 136-137 C 3-4
Balkan Mountains 122-123 K-M 4
Balkh 134-135 K 3
Balkh Āb 134-135 K 3
Balkhash, Lake — = ozero Balchaš 132-133 NO 8
Bālkonda 140 D 1
Ballā 141 B 3
Balla Balla = Mbalabala 172 EF 6
Ballabgarh 138-139 F 3
Balladonia 158-159 D 6
Ballarat 158-159 H 7
Ballard, Lake — 158-159 D 5
Ballard Pond 85 II b 3
Ballāri = Bellary 134-135 M 7
Ballé 164-165 C 5
Ballena, Punta — 106-107 K 5
Ballenas, Canal de — 86-87 D 3
Ballenero, Canal 108-109 D 10
Balleny Islands 53 C 17
Ballesteros 106-107 F 4
Ballia 138-139 K 5
Balliguda = Bāliguda 138-139 J 7
Ballimore 160 J 4
Ballina [AUS] 158-159 K 5
Ballina [IRL] 119 B 4
Ballinger, TX 76-77 DE 7
Ballivián = Fortín Ballivián 102-103 AB 5
Ballona Creek 83 III b 2
Ball's Pyramid 158-159 L 6
Ballstad 116-117 EF 3
Bally 138-139 M 6
Bally Bridge 154 II b 2
Ballygunge, Calcutta- 154 II b 2
Ballygunge Park 154 II b 2
Ballymena 119 C 4
Balmaceda 108-109 CD 5
Balmaceda, Cerro — 108-109 C 8
Balmaceda, Sierra — 108-109 DE 9
Balmain, Sydney- 161 I b 2
Balmertown 62 C 2
Balmoral [GB] 119 E 3
Balmoral [ZA] 174-175 H 3
Balmorhea, TX 76-77 C 7
Balmumcu, İstanbul- 154 I b 2
Balnearia 106-107 F 3
Balneario El Condor 108-109 H 3
Balneario La Barre 106-107 L 4
Balneario Orense 106-107 H 7
Balod 138-139 H 7
Baloda Bāzār 138-139 J 7
Bālōdbāzār = Baloda Bāzār 138-139 J 7
Balombo 172 B 4
Balonne River 158-159 J 5
Bālōtra 138-139 D 5
Balovale 172 D 4
Balqā, Al- 136-137 F 6-7
Balrāmpur 138-139 HJ 4
Balrāmpur = Balarāmpur 138-139 L 6
Balranald 158-159 H 6
Balsa 106-107 G 5
Balsāḍ = Bulsār 138-139 D 7
Balsar = Bulsār 138-139 D 7
Balsas [BR] 92-93 K 6
Balsas [MEX] 86-87 KL 8-9
Balsas [PE] 96-97 BC 5
Balsas, Río — 64-65 F 8
Balsas, Rio das — 100-101 B 4
Balsas ó Mezcala, Río — 86-87 KL 8-9
Balsfjord 116-117 HJ 3
Balta, ND 68-69 FG 1
Balta [RO] 122-123 MN 3
Balta [SU] 126-127 D 3
Baltasi 124-125 RS 5
Bālṭī = Bel'cy 126-127 CD 3
Baltic Port = Paldiski 124-125 DE 4
Baltic Sea 114-115 L 5-M 4
Baltijsk 118 J 1
Baltijskoje more 124-125 B 6-C 4
Baltijsko-Ladožskij ustup 124-125 E-J 4
Baltīm 173 B 2
Baltimore, MD 64-65 L 4
Baltimore [GB] 119 B 6
Baltimore [ZA] 174-175 H 2
Bāltistān 134-135 M 3-4
Bāltit 134-135 L 3
Balūchestān, Sīstān va — 134-135 H 4-J 5
Balūchistān 134-135 J 5-K 4
Bāluhāti 154 II a 2
Balui, Sungei — 152-153 KL 4
Bālumāth 138-139 K 6
Bālurghāt 138-139 M 5
Balvi 124-125 F 5
Balwyn, Melbourne- 161 II c 1
Balya 136-137 B 3
Balyanā, Al- 164-165 L 3
Balygyčan 132-133 d 5
Balykši 126-127 PQ 3
Balyul = Nēpāl 134-135 NO 5
Balzar 96-97 B 2
Bam 134-135 H 5
Bama 164-165 G 6
Bamaco = Bamako 164-165 C 6
Bamaji Lake 62 D 2
Bamako 164-165 C 6
Bamba [EAK] 171 D 3
Bamba [RMM] 164-165 D 5
Bamba [ZRE] 172 C 3
Bambamarca 96-97 B 5
Bambara-Maoundé 168-169 E 2
Bambari 164-165 J 7
Bamberg 118 E 4
Bamberg, SC 80-81 F 4
Bambesa 172 E 1
Bambinga 172 C 2
Bamboesbaai 174-175 BC 6
Bamboi 168-169 E 3
Bambouk 164-165 B 6
Bamboulos, Mount — 168-169 H 4
Bambuí 92-93 K 8-9
Bamenda 164-165 G 7
Bamenda Highlands 168-169 H 4
Bamfield 66-67 A 1
Bamingui 164-165 HJ 7
Bamingui, Parc national de la — 164-165 HJ 7
Bamingui-Bangoran 164-165 HJ 7
Bāmiyān 134-135 K 4
Bamnet Narung 150-151 C 5
Bampu, Sungai — 152-153 C 4
Bampūr, Rūd-e 134-135 HJ 5
Ba mTsho 142-143 G 5
Bamūdā = Garhākota 138-139 G 6
Bamum = Foumban 164-165 G 7
Bamungu 171 B 2
Bana [MW] 171 C 6
Ba Na [VN] 150-151 FG 5
Baña, Punta de la — 120-121 H 8
Banabuiú, Açude de — 100-101 E 3
Banabuiú, Rio — 100-101 E 3
Banāder va Jazāyer-e Baḥr-e 'Omān = 6 ◁ 134-135 H 5
Banāder va Jazāyer-e Khalīj-e Fārs = 5 ◁ 134-135 G 5
Banadia 92-93 E 3
Bañado del Río Saladillo 106-107 F 4
Bañado de Medina 106-107 KL 4
Bañado de Rocha 106-107 K 3
Bañados de Izozog 92-93 G 8
Bañados de la Amarga 106-107 EF 5
Bañados del Atuel 106-107 D 5-6
Bañados del Chadileuvú 106-107 D 6
Bañados del Viñalito 104-105 E 9
Bañados Otuquis 104-105 G 6
Banagi 171 C 3
Banahwāla Ṭoba 138-139 D 3
Banāi 138-139 K 7
Banāigaḍa = Bonaigarh 138-139 K 7
Banalia 172 DE 1
Banam 150-151 E 7
Banamana, Lago — 174-175 KL 2
Banamba 168-169 D 2
Banana 172 B 3
Banana Islands 168-169 B 3
Bananal 102-103 K 5
Bananal, Ilha do — 92-93 J 7
Bananeiras 92-93 M 6
Bāṇapura = Bānpur 138-139 K 8
Ban ar-Ramād, Wādī — 166-167 F 3
Banās 138-139 F 4
Banās Kāntha 138-139 CD 5
Banat 122-123 J 3
Banātmyō 141 E 4
Banatului, Munții — 122-123 JK 3
Banawaja, Pulau — 152-153 N 9
Ban 'Aysh, Ḥāssī — 166-167 J 4
Banaz 136-137 C 3
Banaz çayı 136-137 C 3
Ban Ban 150-151 D 3
Ban Bat = Buôn Bat 150-151 G 6
Ban Bu 150-151 E 2
Ban Bung 150-151 C 6
Ban Bu'ng Sai 150-151 F 5
Banbury 119 F 5
Banbury Reservoir 129 II b 1
Banc du Geyser 172 J 4
Banco, El — 92-93 E 3
Banco Central 100-101 E 8
Banco Chinchorro 64-65 J 8
Banco Piedras 106-107 J 5
Bancoran Island 152-153 N 2
Bancroft 72-73 H 2
Bancroft, ID 66-67 H 4
Banḍā [IND, Madhya Pradesh] 138-139 G 5-6
Bānda [IND, Uttar Pradesh] 138-139 H 5
Banda = Sainte-Marie 172 B 2
Banda, Kepulauan — 148-149 J 7
Banda, La — 111 D 3
Banda, Punta — 64-65 C 5
Banda Aceh 148-149 BC 5
Bandahara, Gunung — 152-153 BC 4
Banda-Lungwa, Kinshasa- 170 IV a 1-2
Bandama 164-165 CD 7
Bandama Blanc 168-169 D 3
Bandama Rouge 168-169 D 4
Bandamūrlangkā = Bandamūrlanka 140 EF 2
Bandamūrlanka 140 EF 2
Ban Dan Na Lao 150-151 EF 5
Bandar [IND] 134-135 N 7
Bandar [Nēpāl] 138-139 H 3
Bandāra = Bandar 134-135 N 7
Bandar 'Abbās 134-135 H 5
Bandārawela 140 E 7
Bandar Baharu 150-151 C 10
Bāndarban 141 C 4
Bandar Banhā = Banhā 173 B 2
Bandar-e Anzalī 134-135 FG 3
Bandar-e Būshehr 134-135 G 5
Bandar-e Chāh Bahār 134-135 HJ 5
Bandar-e Khomeynī 134-135 FG 4
Bandar-e Lengeh 134-135 GH 5
Bandar-e Māhshar 136-137 N 7
Bandar-e Shāh 134-135 G 3
Bandar Maharani = Muar 148-149 D 6
Bandar Penggaram = Batu Pahat 148-149 D 6
Bandarpulau 152-153 C 4
Bandarpūnch 138-139 G 2
Bandar Rompin = Kuala Rompin 150-151 D 11
Bandar Seri Begawan 148-149 FG 5-6
Banda Sea 148-149 JK 8
Bandawe 172 F 4
Bande Bābā 134-135 J 4
Bandeira 100-101 D 8
Bandeira, Pico da — 92-93 L 9
Bandeirante 92-93 JK 7
Bandeirantes 102-103 GH 5
Bandelierkop 174-175 H 2
Bandelier National Monument 76-77 A 5
Band-e Qir 136-137 N 7
Bandera 111 D 3
Bandera, TX 76-77 E 8
Banderaló 106-107 F 5
Banderas 76-77 B 7
Banderas, Bahía de — 64-65 E 7
Bānd-e Turkestān = Tirbande Turkestān 134-135 JK 3
Bandiagara 164-165 D 6
Bandipur [IND, Karnataka] 140 C 5
Bandipur [IND, West Bengal] 154 II b 1
Bandırma 134-135 B 2
Bandjarmasin = Banjarmasin 148-149 F 7
Bandjermassin = Banjarmasin 148-149 F 7
Bandon, OR 66-67 A 4
Bandon [IRL] 119 B 6
Ban Đôn [VN] 150-151 FG 6
Ban Don, Ao — 150-151 B 8
Ban Dong Khaang 150-151 E 4
B'andovan 126-127 O 7
Bāndra 134-135 L 7
Bānduān 138-139 L 6
Bandundu [ZRE, administrative unit] 172 C 2-3
Bandundu [ZRE, place] 172 C 2
Bandung 148-149 E 8
Band Vīrāh 138-139 AB 5
Bāneh 136-137 L 4-5
Banes 64-65 L 7
Bañeza, La — 120-121 DE 7
Banff [CDN] 56-57 NO 7
Banff [GB] 119 E 3
Banff National Park 56-57 NO 7
Banfield, Lomas de Zamora- 110 III b 2
Banfora 164-165 D 6
Bang, Kompong — 150-151 E 6
Banga 168-169 H 3
Bāngaduni Island 138-139 M 7
Bangāl Khārī = Bay of Bengal 134-135 N-P 7
Bangalore 134-135 M 8
Banganapalle 140 D 3
Baṅganāpalli = Banganapalle 140 D 3
Bangangté 168-169 H 4
Bangaon 138-139 M 6
Bangap, Lau — 150-151 AB 11
Bangārapet 140 D 4
Bāngarmaū 138-139 H 4
Bangarpet = Bangārapet 140 D 4
Bangassou 164-165 J 8
Bangassu = Bangassou 164-165 J 8
Bang Fai, Se — 150-151 E 4
Bangfou = Bengbu 142-143 M 5
Banggadeniya 140 D 7
Banggai 148-149 H 7
Banggai, Kepulauan — 148-149 H 7
Banggai, Pulau — 148-149 H 7
Banggala Au = Bay of Bengal 134-135 N-P 7
Banggi, Pulau — 148-149 G 5
Banghāzī 164-165 HJ 2
Bang Hieng, Se — 150-151 E 4
Bangil 152-153 K 9
Bangka, Pulau — 148-149 E 7
Bangka, Selat — 148-149 E 7
Bangkala 152-153 N 8
Bangkalan 152-153 K 9
Bangkaru, Pulau — 152-153 B 4-5
Bang Khonthi 150-151 B 6
Bangkinang 148-149 D 6
Bangko 148-149 D 7
Bangkok = Krung Thep 148-149 D 4
Bangkok, Bay of — = Ao Krung Thep 150-151 C 6
Bangkulu, Pulau — 152-153 P 6
Bangladesh 134-135 OP 6
Bang Lamung 150-151 C 6
Bang Len 150-151 BC 5-6
Bang Mun Nak 150-151 C 4
Bangolo 168-169 D 4
Bangor 119 DE 5
Bangor, ME 64-65 N 3
Bangor, MI 70-71 G 4
Bangor, PA 72-73 J 4
Bang Pahan = Phachi 150-151 C 5
Bang Pa-in 150-151 C 5
Bang Pakong 150-151 C 6
Bang Pakong, Mae Nam — 150-151 C 6
Bāngriposi 138-139 L 6
Bangs, TX 76-77 E 7
Bang Saphan 150-151 B 7
Bangu, Rio de Janeiro- 102-103 L 5
Bangui [RCA] 164-165 H 8
Bangui [RP] 148-149 GH 3
Bangunpurba 152-153 C 4
Bangweulu, Lake — 172 EF 4
Banhā 173 B 2
Ban Hin Heup 150-151 D 3
Ban Hong 150-151 B 3
Ban Huei Sai 150-151 C 2
Baní [DOM] 64-65 M 8
Bani [HV] 168-169 E 2
Bani [RMM] 164-165 C 6
Banī, Jabal — 166-167 C 2-3
Banī Abbās 164-165 D 2
Baniara 148-149 NO 8
Banī Khaddāsh 166-167 LM 3
Banī Lant 166-167 D 2
Banilouli 168-169 F 2
Banī Mallāl 164-165 C 2
Banī Mazār 164-165 L 3
Baning, Kampung — 150-151 D 10
Banī Sa 'd 136-137 L 6
Banī Šāf 166-167 F 2
Banī Shuqayr 173 B 4
Ban Island 58-59 L 7
Banī Suwayf 164-165 L 3
Banī Tajīt 166-167 E 3
Banī Wanīf 164-165 D 2
Bāniyāchung 141 B 3
Bāniyās [SYR, Al-Lādiqīyah] 134-135 D 3
Bāniyās [SYR, Dimashq] 136-137 FG 6
Banja Luka 122-123 G 3
Banjar 148-149 E 8
Banjarmasin 148-149 F 7
Banjermassin = Banjarmasin 148-149 F 7
Banjia 141 F 4
Banjo = Banyo 164-165 G 7
Banjul 164-165 A 6
Banjuwangi = Banyuwangi 148-149 F 8
Banjuwedang 152-153 L 9-10
Bank 126-127 O 7
Bānka [IND] 138-139 L 5
Banka = Pulau Bangka 148-149 E 7
Banka Banka 158-159 F 3
Bankaner = Wānkāner 138-139 C 6
Ban Karai 150-151 F 4
Bankass 168-169 E 2
Ban Ken = Ban Kheun 150-151 C 2
Ban Keng That Hai 150-151 EF 4
Ban Khai 150-151 C 6
Ban Khamphô 150-151 F 5
Ban Kha Panang 150-151 F 6
Ban Kheng = Ban Na Kheng 150-151 EF 4
Ban Kheun 150-151 C 2
Ban Khôk Kong 150-151 E 5
Bānki 138-139 K 6
Banko 168-169 D 2
Ban Kruat 150-151 D 5
Banks, ID 66-67 E 3
Banks, OR 66-67 B 3
Banks, Cape — 161 I b 3
Banksian River 62 B 1
Banks Island [AUS] 158-159 H 2
Banks Island [CDN, British Columbia] 56-57 KL 7
Banks Island [CDN, District of Franklin] 56-57 MN 3
Banks Islands 158-159 N 2
Banks Lake 66-67 D 2
Banks Peninsula 158-159 O 8
Banks Strait 158-159 J 8
Banks Strait = MacClure Strait 56-57 MN 2-3
Bankstown, Sydney- 161 I a 2
Bānkura 138-139 L 6
Ban Laem 150-151 BC 6
Ban Lat Hane 150-151 CD 2
Ban Mae = Mae Sariang 150-151 AB 3
Ban Mahdī 166-167 KL 1
Banmau 148-149 C 2
Banmauk 141 D 3
Ban Me Thuôt 148-149 E 4
Ban Mi 150-151 C 5
Ban Mo 150-151 C 5
Ban Mouong = Ban Muong 150-151 C 3
Ban Muang 150-151 D 4
Ban Muang = Pong 148-149 CD 3
Ban Mu'ang Ba 150-151 E 4
Ban Muong 150-151 C 3
Bannack, MT 66-67 G 3
Ban Na Kheng 150-151 EF 4
Ban Na Le 150-151 C 3
Ban Na Lu'ong 150-151 E 4
Ban Nam Bac 150-151 D 2
Ban Namone 150-151 D 3
Ban Nam Phao 150-151 C 3
Ban Nam Tao 150-151 C 4
Ban Nam Tia 150-151 D 3
Bannang Sata 150-151 C 9
Bannang Star = Bannang Sata 150-151 C 9
Ban Na Phao 150-151 E 4
Ban Na San 150-151 B 8
Ban Na Song 150-151 E 4
Ban Nathon 150-151 F 4
Banner, WY 68-69 C 3
Bannerman Town 88-89 HJ 2
Banning, CA 74-75 E 6
Banningville = Bandundu 172 C 2
Ban Nin Lan 150-151 E 3
Bannockburn [CDN] 72-73 GH 2
Bannockburn [ZW] 172 EF 6
Bannock Range 66-67 G 4
Ban Nong Kheun 150-151 D 3
Bannū 134-135 KL 4
Bano 138-139 K 6
Baños [EC] 96-97 B 2
Baños [PE] 96-97 D 6
Baños, Los — 96-97 F 11
Baños de Chihuio 108-109 CD 3
Baños del Flaco 106-107 B 5
Baños de Longaví 106-107 B 6
Baños El Sosneado 106-107 BC 5
Ban Pa Kha 150-151 F 5
Ban Pak Hop 150-151 C 3
Ban Pak Sang 150-151 D 3
Ban Pak Thone 150-151 F 5
Ban Phai 148-149 D 3
Ban Pho 150-151 C 6
Banphot Phisai 150-151 B 5
Ban Phu 150-151 D 4
Ban Phya Lat 150-151 D 2
Ban Pong 150-151 B 6
Ban Poung 150-151 E 4
Bānpur 138-139 K 8
Banquereau Bank 63 GH 5
Ban Rai 150-151 B 5
Ban Sa Ang 150-151 EF 4
Ban Sa Pout 150-151 C 2
Bāṅsavāḍā = Bānswāda 140 CD 1
Bānsbāria 138-139 LM 6
Bānsda 138-139 D 7
Bānsdīh 138-139 JK 5
Ban Se Mat 150-151 F 6
Bānsgāṅv = Bānsgaon 138-139 J 4
Bānsgaon 138-139 J 4
Bānsi [IND → Gonda] 138-139 J 4
Bānsi [IND ↓ Jhānsi] 138-139 G 5
Bansihāri 138-139 M 5
Ban Si Nhô 150-151 E 4
Banská Bystrica 118 J 4
Banská Štiavnica 118 J 4
Ban Sông Khôn 150-151 E 3
Ban Sot 150-151 E 3
Ban Soukhouma 150-151 E 5
Bānsur 138-139 F 4
Bāṅsvāṛā = Bānswāra 138-139 E 6
Bānswāda 140 CD 1
Bānswāra 138-139 E 6
Banta 138-139 L 7

Bantaeng 148-149 GH 8
Ban Tak 150-151 B 4
Bantam = Banten 148-149 E 8
Ban Taphane 150-151 E 5
Ban Ta Viang 150-151 D 3
Banteai Srei 150-151 D 6
Banten 148-149 E 8
Banten, Teluk — 152-153 G 8
Ban Thac Du'ot 150-151 F 5
Banthali = Vanthli 138-139 C 7
Ban Thieng 150-151 CD 3
Bāntra, Howrah- 154 II ab 2
Ban Tring = Buôn Hô 150-151 G 6
Bantry 119 B 6
Bantry Bay 119 AB 6
Bantul 152-153 J 9-10
Bāntva = Bāntwa 138-139 BC 7
Bāntwa 138-139 BC 7
Banūd 166-167 G 3
Ban Vang 150-151 C 3
Ban Waeng = Phong Thong 150-151 DE 4
Ban Xiêng Kok 150-151 C 2
Banyak, Pulau-pulau — 148-149 C 6
Banyak Islands = Pulau-pulau Banyak 148-149 C 6
Ban Yen Nhân 150-151 EF 2
Banyin 141 E 5
Banyo 164-165 G 7
Banyumas 152-153 H 9
Banyuwangi 148-149 F 8
Banzaburō-dake 144-145 M 5
Banzare Land 53 C 13
Ban Zīriq 166-167 F 4
Banzystad = Yasanyama 172 D 1
Banzyville = Yasanyama 172 D 1
Banzyville, Collines des — 172 D 1
Bao'an [TJ, Guangdong] 146-147 DE 10
Bao'an [TJ, Shaanxi] 146-147 BC 4
Baode 146-147 L 4
Baodi 146-147 F 2
Baoding 142-143 LM 4
Baofeng 146-147 D 5
Bao Ha 150-151 E 1
Baohe = Mengla 150-151 C 2
Baohu Jiao 146-147 C 11
Baoji 142-143 K 5
Baojidun = Badajia 146-147 H 5
Baojing 142-143 K 6
Baokang 146-147 C 6
Bao Lôc 150-151 FG 7
Bao Lôc, Đeo — 150-151 F 7
Baoqing 142-143 P 2
Baoshan [TJ, Shanghai] 146-147 H 6
Baoshan [TJ, Yunnan] 142-143 HJ 6
Baoting 150-151 G 3
Baotou 142-143 KL 3
Baoulé 164-165 C 6
Baoying 142-143 M 5
Bāp 138-139 D 4
Bapatla 140 E 3
Baptai 124-125 DE 6
Baptiste 72-73 GH 2
Bapuyu 152-153 KL 7
Bāqarganj 141 B 4
Bāqir, Jabal — 136-137 F 8
Baqqah 168-169 B 1
Ba'qūbah 134-135 EF 4
Baquedano 111 BC 2
Bar [SU] 126-127 C 2
Bar [YU] 122-123 H 4
Bāra [IND, Rājasthān] 138-139 D 4
Bāra [IND, Uttar Pradesh] 138-139 H 5
Bara [IND, West Bengal] 154 II a 1
Bara [WAN] 168-169 H 3
Baraawe 164-165 N 8
Bāra Banki 138-139 H 4
Barabinsk 132-133 OP 6
Barabinskaja step' 132-133 O 6-7
Barābir, 'Uqlat — 166-167 E 4
Baraboo, WI 70-71 F 4
Baracaldo 120-121 F 7
Barachois 63 DE 3
Baracoa 88-89 J 4
Baradero 106-107 H 4
Baraga, MI 70-71 F 2
Baragaḍa = Bargarh 138-139 J 7
Bārāganul 122-123 M 3
Baragwanath, Johannesburg- 170 V a 2
Baragwanath Aerodrome 170 V a 2
Bārah 164-165 L 6
Baṛahānuddīn 141 B 4
Barahī = Barhi 134-135 O 6
Barahona [DOM] 64-65 M 8
Barai 150-151 E 6
Barāij, Al- 136-137 G 5
Barail Range 141 C 3
Baraily = Bareilli 138-139 G 6
Barajas, Aeropuerto — 113 III b 2
Barajas, Madrid- 113 III b 2
Barājīl, Al- 170 II a 1
Barāk 141 C 3
Barak = Karkamış 136-137 G 4
Baraka = Barka 164-165 M 5
Barākar 138-139 L 5
Baraki [AFG] 134-135 K 4
Baraki [ET] 170 I b 2
Barakram, Ḥāssī — 166-167 J 3
Baralaba 158-159 JK 4
Baram, Batang — 152-153 L 3-4
Barama 141 B 2
Bārāmati 140 B 1
Bārāmba 138-139 K 7
Bārāmūlā 134-135 L 4
Bārān 138-139 F 5
Baranagar 154 II b 2
Barā Nikōbār = Great Nicobar 134-135 P 9
Barā Nikōbār = Little Nicobar 134-135 P 9
Baranoa 94-95 D 2
Baranof, AK 58-59 v 8
Baranof Island 56-57 JK 6
Baranoviči 124-125 EF 7
Barão de Cocais 102-103 L 3-4
Barão de Grajaú 92-93 L 6
Barão de Melgaço 104-105 F 3
Barão de Melgaço [BR, place] 102-103 E 2
Baraot = Baraut 138-139 F 3
Baraqua, Sierra de — 94-95 FG 2
Barārī = Borāri 138-139 L 5
Bārāsat 154 II b 1
Barāsiā = Berasia 138-139 F 6
Barataria Bay 78-79 DE 6
Bar'atino 124-125 K 6
Barauanã, Serra — 98-99 H 3-4
Baraut 138-139 F 3
Baraya 94-95 D 6
Barbacena 92-93 L 9
Barbacoas [CO, Guajira] 94-95 E 2
Barbacoas [CO, Nariño] 94-95 B 7
Barbacoas [YV] 94-95 H 3
Barbados 64-65 OP 9
Barbalha 100-101 E 4
Barbar 164-165 L 5
Barbara Lake 70-71 G 1
Barbastro 120-121 GH 7
Barberspan 174-175 F 4
Barbers Point 78-79 c 2
Barberton 172 F 7
Barberton, OH 72-73 F 4
Barborá = Berbera 164-165 O 6
Barbosa [CO, Antioquia] 94-95 D 4
Barbosa [CO, Boyacá] 92-93 E 3
Barbosa Ferraz 102-103 F 6
Barbourville, KY 72-73 DE 6
Barbūshī, Ḥāssī — 166-167 E 5
Barca = Al-Marj 164-165 J 2
Barca, La — 86-87 J 7
Barcaldine 158-159 HJ 4
Barce = Al-Marj 164-165 J 2
Barcellona Pozzo di Gotto 122-123 F 6
Barcelona [E] 120-121 J 8
Barcelona [YV] 92-93 G 2
Barcelonnette 120-121 L 6
Barcelos [BR] 92-93 G 5
Barchama Guda 171 D 2
Barchöl Choto = Bar köl 142-143 G 3
Barco 94-95 E 3
Barco, El — [PE] 96-97 A 4
Barcoo River 158-159 H 4-5
Barcroft, Lake — 82 II a 2
Barda [SU, Azerbajdžanskaja SSR] 126-127 N 6
Barda [SU, Rossijskaja SFSR] 124-125 U 5
Barda del Medio 106-107 CD 7
Bardaï 164-165 H 4
Bardarash 136-137 K 4
Bardas Blancas 106-107 BC 5
Bardawīl, Sabkhat al- 173 C 2
Barddhmān = Burdwān 134-135 O 6
Bardejov 118 K 4
Bardeliere, Lac la — 62 OP 1
Bárdharbunga 116-117 e 2
Bardīs 173 B 4
Bardīyah 164-165 K 2
Bardiz 136-137 K 2
Bārdoli 138-139 D 7
Bardstown, KY 70-71 H 7
Barduba 64-65 O 8
Bardwell, KY 78-79 E 2
Baré 168-169 E 2
Bareilly 134-135 MN 5
Barela 138-139 GH 6
Bareli 138-139 G 6
Barelī = Bareilly 134-135 MN 5
Barentsburg 116-117 jk 5
Barents Island = Barentsøya 116-117 l 5
Barentsøya 116-117 l 5
Barents Sea 132-133 D-J 2-3
Barentu 164-165 M 5
Barfleur, Pointe de — 120-121 G 4
Barga [TJ] 142-143 M 2
Bargaon 138-139 K 6
Bargarh 138-139 J 7
Barguzin 132-133 UV 7
Barguzinskij chrebet 132-133 U 7-V 6
Bārh 138-139 K 5
Barhāḍ = Berar 138-139 F 7
Barhaj 138-139 J 4
Barhampura = Berhampur 134-135 NO 7
Barhār = Berar 138-139 F 7
Bar Harbor, ME 72-73 M 2
Barhi [IND, Bihār] 134-135 O 6
Bārhi [IND, Madhya Pradesh] 138-139 H 6
Bari [I] 122-123 G 5
Bāri [IND] 138-139 F 4
Bari [SP] 164-165 bc 1
Baria = Devgad Bāria 138-139 DE 6
Baricho 171 DE 3
Barī Dihing = Burhi Dihing 141 D 2
Barī Doāb 138-139 D 2
Barika = Bārīkah 166-167 J 2
Bārīkah 166-167 J 2
Barīkot 138-139 J 3
Barillas 86-87 P 10
Bariloche, San Carlos de — 111 B 6
Barīm 134-135 E 8
Barima 94-95 L 4
Barima, Río — 94-95 L 3
Barinas [YV, administrative unit] 94-95 FG 3
Barinas [YV, place] 92-93 EF 3
Bārind 138-139 M 5
Baring, IA 70-71 D 5
Baring, Cape — 56-57 MN 3
Baringo, Lake — 171 D 2
Barinitas 94-95 F 3
Bario 152-153 L 4
Baripāda 138-139 L 6-7
Bariri 102-103 H 5
Bāris 173 B 5
Bari Sādri 138-139 E 5
Barisāl 134-135 OP 6
Barisan, Pegunungan — 152-153 D 6-E 8
Barīt, Al- 136-137 K 7
Barito 148-149 F 7
Bāriyā = Devgad Bāria 138-139 DE 6
Barka [ETH] 164-165 M 5
Barkā' [Oman] 134-135 H 6
Barka = Al-Marj 164-165 J 2
Barka, Aïn el — = 'Ayn al-Barqah 166-167 C 6
Barkāgāṅv = Barkāgaon 138-139 K 6
Barkāgaon 138-139 K 6
Barkaïna 168-169 E 1
Barkal 141 C 4
Barkan, Rās-e — = Ra's-e Bahrgān 136-137 N 7-8
Barkāt, Al- 166-167 M 7
Barke = Barkha 138-139 H 2
Barker 106-107 H 6
Barkerville 60 G 3
Barkha 138-139 H 2
Bārkhān 138-139 B 3
Barkīn 166-167 E 3
Barking, London- 129 II c 1
Barkingside, London- 129 II c 1
Bark Lake 62 K 3
Barkley, Lake — 78-79 EF 2
Barkley Sound 66-67 A 1
Barkly East = Barkly-Oos 174-175 G 6
Barkly-Oos 174-175 G 6
Barkly-Pas 174-175 G 6
Barkly Pass = Barkly-Pas 174-175 G 6
Barkly Tableland 158-159 FG 3
Barkly-Wes 174-175 F 5
Barkly West = Barkly-Wes 174-175 F 5
Bar köl [TJ, lake] 142-143 G 3
Bar Köl [TJ, place] 142-143 G 3
Bark Point 70-71 E 2
Barla dağı 136-137 D 3-4
Bar-le-Duc 120-121 K 4
Barlee, Lake — 158-159 C 5
Barletta 122-123 G 5
Barlovento, Islas de — 64-65 OP 8-9
Barmbek, Hamburg- 130 I b 1
Bāṛmēr 134-135 L 5
Barmera 158-159 H 6
Barmhān 138-139 G 6
Barnabus, WV 80-81 EF 2
Barnagar 138-139 E 6
Barnāla 138-139 E 2
Barnard, KS 68-69 GH 6
Barnato 160 G 3
Barnaul 132-133 P 7
Barnegat 61 C 3
Barnegat Bay 72-73 JK 5
Barne Glacier 53 A 17-18
Barnes, London- 129 II a 2
Barnesville, GA 80-81 DE 4
Barnesville, MN 68-69 H 2
Barnesville, OH 72-73 F 4-5
Barnet, London- 129 II b 1
Barney Top 74-75 GH 4
Barnhart, TX 76-77 D 7
Barnsdall, OK 76-77 FG 4
Barnstable, MA 72-73 L 4
Barnstaple 119 D 6
Barnwell, SC 80-81 F 4
Baro 164-165 F 7
Baroda 174-175 F 7
Baroda = Vadōdarā 134-135 L 6
Baroe 174-175 F 7
Barōngā Kyûnmya 148-149 B 3
Barotiré, Reserva Florestal — 98-99 MN 8
Barouda, Hassi — = Ḥāssī Bārudah 166-167 GH 5
Barpeta 134-135 P 5
Barqa = Al-Marj 164-165 J 2
Bārqa = Bārqah 166-167 C 2
Barqah [LAR] 164-165 J 2
Bārqah [MA] 166-167 C 2
Barqah, 'Ain al- 166-167 M 7
Barqah, Jabal al- 173 C 5
Barqat al-Baḥrīyah 164-165 JK 2
Barqat al-Bayḍā' 164-165 HJ 2-3
Barquisimeto 92-93 EF 2-3
Barra [BR, Bahia] 92-93 L 7
Barra [BR, Piauí] 100-101 D 2
Barra [BR, Rio Grande do Sul] 106-107 LM 4
Barra [GB] 119 C 3
Barra, Ponta da — 174-175 L 2
Barraba 158-159 K 6
Barra Bonita 102-103 H 5
Barraca da Boca 98-99 MN 5
Barracão [BR, Rio Grande do Sul] 106-107 M 1
Barracão [BR, Santa Catarina] 102-103 F 7
Barração de Libertade 104-105 F 3
Barracão do Barreto 92-93 H 6
Barracão São José 98-99 K 9
Barracas [BR] 98-99 F 9
Barracas, Buenos Aires- 110 III b 1
Barra da Estiva 100-101 D 7
Barra da Tijuca, Rio de Janeiro- 110 I ab 3
Barra de Icaparra 102-103 J 6
Barra de Santa Rosa 100-101 FG 4
Barra de São Francisco 100-101 D 10
Barra de São João 102-103 LM 5
Barra do Bugres 92-93 H 7-8
Barra do Corda 92-93 KL 6
Barra do Garças 92-93 J 8
Barra do Mendes 100-101 CD 6
Barra do Piraí 102-103 KL 5
Barra do Prata 100-101 B 6
Barra do Quaraí 106-107 J 3
Barra do Ribeiro 106-107 M 3
Barra do São Manuel 92-93 H 6
Barra Falsa, Ponta da — 174-175 L 2
Barra Funda, São Paulo- 110 II b 2
Barrage 164-165 C 6
Barrage de Gatun = Presa de Gatún 64-65 ab 2
Barragem do Guarapiranga 110 II a 3
Barragem do Rio Grande 110 II a 3
Barrage Sansanding 168-169 D 2
Barra Head 119 BC 3
Barra Islands 119 C 3
Barra Longa 102-103 L 4
Barra Mansa 102-103 KL 5
Barranca [PE] 92-93 D 5
Barranca [RCH] 96-97 BC 7
Barrancabermeja 92-93 E 3
Barrancas [RA, Neuquén] 106-107 BC 6
Barrancas [RA, Santa Fe] 106-107 G 4
Barrancas [YV, Barinas] 94-95 F 3
Barrancas [YV, Monagas] 92-93 G 3
Barrancas, Río — 106-107 BC 6
Barrancas Santa Rita 94-95 F 2
Barranco Branco 102-103 D 4
Barranco de Guadalupe 86-87 H 2
Barranco de Loba 94-95 DE 3
Barrancoso, Arroyo — 106-107 G 4
Barranqueras 111 DE 3
Barranquilla 92-93 DE 2
Barranquitas 94-95 E 3
Barras 100-101 C 3
Barra Seca 100-101 E 10
Barraute 62 N 2
Barra Velha 111 G 3
Barre, VT 72-73 K 2
Barre, Wilkes — , PA 64-65 L 3
Barreal 106-107 C 3
Barreal, El — 106-107 DE 2
Barreiras 92-93 KL 7
Barreirinha 92-93 H 5
Barreirinhas 92-93 L 5
Barreiro 120-121 C 9
Barreiros 92-93 MN 6
Barren Grounds 56-57 O 4-S 5
Barren Islands 58-59 LM 7
Barrenland = Barren Grounds 56-57 O 4-S 5
Barren Sage Plains 66-67 E 4
Barreras Blancas, Altiplano — 108-109 E 8-F 7
Barretos 92-93 K 9
Barrhead 60 K 2
Barrie 56-57 UV 9
Barrie Island 62 K 3
Barrientos 91 I b 1
Barrière 60 GH 4
Barrington, IL 70-71 F 4
Barrington, NJ 84 III c 2
Barrington, Mount — 158-159 K 6
Barrington Lake 61 HJ 2
Barrīyat al-Bayyūdah 164-165 L 5
Barro [BR] 100-101 E 4
Barro [Guinea Bissau] 168-169 B 2
Barrocas 100-101 E 6
Barro Colorado, Isla — 64-65 b 2
Barron, WI 70-71 DE 3
Barros, Lagoa dos — 106-107 M 2
Barros, Tierra de — 120-121 D 9
Barros Arana, Cerro — 108-109 CD 4
Barros Cassal 106-107 L 2
Barroterán 76-77 D 9
Barro Vermelho 100-101 E 5
Barrow, AK 56-57 E 3
Barrow [IRL] 119 C 5
Barrow [RA] 106-107 G 7
Barrow, Point — 56-57 EF 3
Barrow Creek 158-159 FG 4
Barrow in Furness 119 E 4
Barrow Island 158-159 BC 4
Barrows 61 H 4
Barrow Strait 56-57 RS 3
Barru 152-153 N 8
Barrudugsum 138-139 K 3
Barrydale 174-175 D 7
Barrys Bay 62 N 4
Barşā' 136-137 H 4
Barsakel mes, ostrov — 132-133 KL 8
Barsaloi 172 G 1
Barsalpur = Birsilpur 138-139 D 3
Baršatas 132-133 O 8
Bārshī = Bārsi 134-135 M 7
Bārsi 134-135 M 7
Bārsi Tākli 138-139 F 7
Barstow, CA 64-65 C 4-5
Barstow, TX 76-77 C 7
Bārsua 138-139 K 7
Bārsūr 138-139 H 8
Bar-sur-Aube 120-121 K 4
Bārta [SU, place] 124-125 C 5
Bartala, Garden Reach- 154 II a 2
Barṭallah 136-137 K 4
Bartau = Bārta 124-125 C 5
Barter Island 58-59 Q 1
Bartibog 63 CD 4
Bartica 92-93 H 3
Bartın [TR] 136-137 E 2
Bartın çayı = Koca ırmak 136-137 E 2
Bartle, CA 66-67 C 5
Bartlesville, OK 64-65 G 4
Bartlett, NE 68-69 G 5
Bartlett, TX 76-77 F 7
Bartlett's Harbour 63 H 2
Bartolome Mitre 110 III b 1
Bartolomeu Dias 172 G 6
Barton, ND 68-69 FG 1
Barton Park 161 I a 2
Barton Run 84 III d 2
Bartoszyce 118 K 1
Bartow, FL 80-81 bc 3
Barú, Volcán — 64-65 K 10
Bārudah, Ḥāssī — 166-167 GH 5
Barumbu, Kinshasa- 170 IV a 1
Barumun, Sungai — 152-153 CD 5
Barung, Nusa — 152-153 K 10
Barus 152-153 C 4
Baruta 91 II b 2
Baruta-Cumbres de Curumo 91 II b 2
Baruta-La Boyera 91 II b 2
Baruta-Las Minas 91 II b 2
Baruta-La Trinidad 91 II b 2
Baruta-Santa Marta 91 II b 2
Baruun Urt 142-143 L 2
Bāruva 138-139 K 8
Barvāḍīh = Barwādih 138-139 K 6
Baṛvāhā = Barwāha 138-139 F 6
Baṛvāla = Barwāla 138-139 E 3
Baṛvānī = Barwāni 138-139 E 6
Barvenkovo 126-127 H 2
Barville 62 N 2
Barwādih 138-139 K 6
Barwāha 138-139 F 6
Barwāla 138-139 E 3
Barwāni 138-139 E 6
Barwick 62 BC 3
Barwon River 158-159 J 5
Barwon River = Darling River 158-159 H 6
Bary, De — 106-107 F 6
Barykova, mys — 132-133 jk 5
Barylas 132-133 Z 4
Baryš [SU, place] 124-125 Q 7
Baryš [SU, river] 124-125 Q 6
Barzanja = Barzinjah 136-137 L 5
Barzas 132-133 Q 6
Barzhung 138-139 M 4
Barzinjah 136-137 L 5
Basail 104-105 G 10
Başalīyat Qiblī, Al- 173 C 5
Basankusu 172 CD 1
Bašanta 126-127 K 3
Bāsar 140 CD 1
Basatin, Al-Qāhirah-al- 170 II b 2
Basavilbaso 106-107 H 4
Başbaş 166-167 KL 1
Basco 142-143 N 7
Base Aérea Militar El Palomar 110 III b 1
Base de l'Militaire 170 IV a 1
Basel 118 C 5
Baserah 152-153 DE 6
Bashahar 138-139 G 2
Bashahr = Bashahar 138-139 G 2
Basharrī 136-137 G 5
Basheerivier 174-175 H 7
Bashi Haixia = Pashih Haihsia 142-143 N 7
Bāshim = Bāsim 134-135 M 5
Bashkir Autonomous Soviet Socialist Republic = 7 <| 132-133 K 6
Bash Kurghan = Bash Qurghan 142-143 G 4
Bash Malghun 142-143 F 4
Bash Qurghan 142-143 G 4
Bashshār 164-165 D 2
Bashtīl 170 II ab 1
Ba Shui 146-147 E 6
Basi 138-139 F 2
Basia 138-139 K 6
Basiano 148-149 H 7
Başıbüyük 154 I bc 3
Basilan Island 148-149 H 5
Basilan Strait 148-149 H 5
Basilica de Guadalupe 91 I c 2
Basilicata 122-123 FG 5
Basilio 111 F 4
Basilique Nationale 128 II ab 1
Basim 134-135 M 6
Basin, MT 66-67 G 2
Basin, WY 68-69 BC 3
Basin, Rivière — 62 O 3
Basingstoke 119 F 6
Basin Ind Dist, Houston-, TX 85 III b 2
Basin Lake 61 F 4
Basīṭ, Rā's al- 136-137 F 5
Basiyā = Basia 138-139 K 6
Başkale 136-137 KL 3
Baskatong, Réservoir — 72-73 J 1
Baskineig Falls 62 F 1
Baškirskaja Avtonomnaja Sovetskaja Socialističeskaja Respublika = Bashkir Autonomous Soviet Socialist Republic 132-133 K 7
Başköy 136-137 L 3
Baskunčak, ozero — 126-127 N 2
Basle = Basel 118 C 5
Bašmakovo 124-125 O 7
Basmat 138-139 F 8
Bāsmenj 136-137 M 4
Basna 138-139 J 7
Basnāngira Palāna <| 140 E 7
Bāsoda 138-139 FG 6
Basoko [ZRE, Haute Zaïre] 172 D 1
Basoko [ZRE, Kinshasa] 170 IV a 2
Basra = Al-Başrah 134-135 F 4
Başrah, Al- 134-135 F 4
Bassac = Champassak 148-149 DE 4
Bassain 138-139 D 8
Bassala 168-169 D 2
Bassano 61 B 5
Bassano del Grappa 122-123 D 3
Bassari 168-169 F 3
Bassas da India 172 GH 6
Bassein 138-139 D 8
Bassein = Puthein 148-149 B 3
Bassein = Puthein Myit 141 D 7
Basse Kotto 164-165 J 7-8
Bassersdorf 128 IV b 1
Basse Santa Su 168-169 B 2
Basse-Terre [Guadeloupe, island] 88-89 PQ 6
Basse-Terre [Guadeloupe, place] 64-65 O 8
Basseterre [Saint Christopher-Nevis] 64-65 O 8
Bassett, NE 68-69 G 4
Bassett, VA 80-81 F 2
Bass Islands 72-73 E 4
Basso, Plateau de — 164-165 J 5
Bass Strait 158-159 HJ 7
Basswood Lake 70-71 E 1
Basta 138-139 L 7
Bastar [IND, landscape] 138-139 H 8
Bastar [IND, place] 138-139 HJ 8
Bastī 138-139 J 4
Bastia 122-123 C 4
Bastianøyane 116-117 l 5
Bastião 100-101 D 7
Bastioes, Serra dos — 100-101 DE 4
Bastogne 120-121 KL 3-4
Bastos 102-103 G 4
Bastrop, LA 64-65 H 5
Bastrop, TX 76-77 F 7
Bastuträsk 116-117 HJ 5
Bāsūs 170 II b 1
Basutoland = Lesotho 172 E 7
Basutos 172 E 5
Basvā = Baswa 138-139 F 4
Baswa 138-139 F 4
Bas-Zaïre 172 BC 3
Bata [CO] 94-95 E 4
Bata [Equatorial Guinea] 164-165 F 8
Batabanó, Golfo de — 64-65 K 7
Batac 148-149 GH 3
Batagaj 132-133 Za 4
Batagaj-Alyta 132-133 YZ 4
Bataguaçu 102-103 F 4
Bataiporã 102-103 F 5
Batajsk 126-127 JK 3
Batakan 152-153 L 8
Bataklik 136-137 E 4
Batāla 134-135 M 4
Batalha [BR] 100-101 C 2-3
Batalha [P] 120-121 C 9
Batam, Pulau — 148-149 D 6
Batamaj 132-133 YZ 5
Batan 146-147 GH 4
Batanagar 154 II a 2
Batang [RI] 152-153 JK 4
Batang [TJ] 142-143 H 6
Batanga 168-169 H 6
Batangafo 164-165 H 7
Batangan, Mui — 148-149 EF 3
Batangas 148-149 H 4
Batang Baram 152-153 L 3-4
Batang Hari 148-149 D 7
Batang Inderagiri 148-149 D 7
Batang Kuantan = Batang Inderagiri 148-149 D 7
Batang Tinjar 152-153 L 4
Batan Island 142-143 N 7
Batan Islands 142-143 N 7
Batanta, Pulau — 148-149 JK 7
Batao = Batan 146-147 GH 4
Bāţās 136-137 L 4
Batatais 102-103 J 4
Batatchatu = Chulaq Aqqan Su 142-143 G 4
Batavia, NY 72-73 GH 3
Batavia, OH 72-73 DE 5
Batavia [RA] 106-107 E 5
Batavia = Jakarta 148-149 E 8
Batbakkara = Amangel'dy 132-133 M 7
Batchawana 62 J 3
Batchawana, Mount — 70-71 H 2
Bateckij 124-125 H 4
Bāţel = Al-Bāţil 166-167 E 2
Batel, Esteros del — 106-107 HJ 2
Batemans Bay 160 K 5
Batesburg, SC 80-81 F 4
Batesville, AR 78-79 D 3
Batesville, IN 70-71 H 6
Batesville, MS 78-79 E 3
Batesville, OH 72-73 D 5
Batesville, TX 76-77 E 8
Bath 119 E 6
Bath, ME 72-73 M 3
Bath, NY 72-73 H 3
Batha 164-165 H 6
Baṭḥa, Al- 136-137 L 7
B'athar Zajū, Jabal — 173 C 7
Bathéay 150-151 E 6-7
Bathurst [AUS] 158-159 JK 6
Bathurst [CDN] 56-57 XY 8
Bathurst [ZA] 174-175 G 7
Bathurst = Banjul 164-165 A 6
Bathurst, Cape — 56-57 KL 3
Bathurst Inlet [CDN, bay] 56-57 P 4
Bathurst Inlet [CDN, place] 56-57 P 4
Bathurst Island [AUS] 158-159 EF 2
Bathurst Island [CDN] 56-57 R 2
Batié 164-165 D 6-7
Batignolles, Paris-les — 129 I c 2
Batikala, Tanjung — 152-153 O 7
Bāţil, Al- 166-167 E 2
Bāţin, Al- [IRQ ↙ As-Salmān] 136-137 K 7-L 8
Bāţin, Al- [IRQ ↘ As-Salmān] 136-137 M 8
Baţin, Humrat al- 136-137 KL 8
Bāţin, Wādī al- 134-135 F 5
Bāţinah, Al- 134-135 H 6
Batinga 100-101 D 3
Batiscan 72-73 K 1
Batiscan, Rivière — 72-73 K 1
Batista, Serra do — [BR, Bahia] 100-101 D 6
Batista, Serra do — [BR, Piauí] 100-101 D 4
Batlow 160 HJ 5
Batman 134-135 E 3
Batna = Batnah 164-165 F 1
Batnah 164-165 F 1
Ba To' 150-151 G 5
Batoche 56-57 PQ 7
Baton Rouge, LA 64-65 H 5
Batouri 164-165 G 8
Batovi 102-103 F 1
Batovi, Coxilha do — 106-107 K 3
Batrā, Jabal al- 136-137 F 8
Ba Tri 150-151 F 7-8
Batrūn, Al- 136-137 F 5
Battambang 148-149 D 4
Battambang, Stung — = Stung Sangker 150-151 D 6
Batterbee Range 53 BC 30
Battersea, London- 129 II b 2
Battersea Park 129 II b 2
Batticaloa = Maḍakalapūwa 134-135 N 9
Battle Creek, MI 64-65 J 3
Battle Creek [USA <| Milk River] 68-69 B 1
Battle Creek [USA <| Owyhee River] 66-67 E 4
Battle Harbour 56-57 Za 7
Battle Mountain, NV 66-67 E 5
Battle River 56-57 OP 7
Battonya 118 K 5
Batu 164-165 M 7
Batu, Bukit — 152-153 K 4
Batu, Kepulauan — 148-149 C 7
Batu Anam 150-151 D 11
Batu Arang 148-149 D 6
Batuatu, Pulau — 152-153 P 8
Batubesar, Tanjung — 152-153 N 10
Batu Besi 150-151 D 10
Batu Bora, Bukit — 152-153 L 4
Batubrok, Gunung — 152-153 L 5
Batu Caves 150-151 C 11
Batudaka, Pulau — 152-153 O 6
Bāţūfah 136-137 K 4
Batu Gajah 150-151 C 10
Batui 152-153 P 6
Batui, Pegunungan — 152-153 OP 6
Batuk, Tanjung — 152-153 P 10
Batukelau 152-153 L 5
Batumi 126-127 K 6
Batumundam 152-153 C 5
Bat'unino, Moskva- 113 V c 3
Batu Pahat 148-149 D 6
Batupanjang 152-153 D 5
Batuputih 152-153 N 5
Baturaja 148-149 D 7
Batu Rakit 150-151 D 10
Baturi = Batouri 164-165 G 8
Baturino 132-133 Q 6
Baturité 92-93 M 5
Baturité, Serra do — 100-101 E 3
Batutinggi 148-149 F 7
Batvand 136-137 N 6-7
Bau [MAL] 152-153 J 5
Baú, Pico — 102-103 K 5
Baubau 148-149 H 8
Baucau 148-149 J 8
Bauchi [WAN, administrative unit] 168-169 H 3
Bauchi [WAN, place] 164-165 FG 6
Baudette, MN 70-71 C 1
Baudh 134-135 N 6
Baudó, Río — 94-95 C 5
Baudó, Serranía de — 94-95 C 4-5
Baudouinville = Moba 172 E 3
Baudwin 148-149 C 2
Bauhinia 158-159 J 4
Baúl, El — 92-93 F 3
Bauld, Cape — 56-57 Za 7
Baule = Baoulé 164-165 C 6
Baule-Escoublac, la — 120-121 F 5
Baumann, Pic — 168-169 F 4
Baumschulenweg, Berlin- 130 III bc 2
Baura [BD] 138-139 M 4
Baura [IND] 140 A 7
Bā'ūrah, Sabkhat — 136-137 J 5
Baures 92-93 G 7
Baurs Berg 130 I a 1
Bauru 92-93 K 9
Baús 102-103 F 3
Bauska 124-125 E 5
Bauske = Bauska 124-125 E 5
Bautino 126-127 OP 4
Bautzen 118 G 3
Bauxite, AR 78-79 C 3
Bauya 164-165 B 7
Bavaria 130 II b 2
Bavaria = Bayern 118 E 4
Bavaria, Bogotá- 91 III b 3
Bavarian Forest = Bayerischer Wald 118 F 4
Ba Vi 150-151 E 2
Bavispe 86-87 F 2
Bavispe, Río — 86-87 F 2-3
Bavispe, Río de — 74-75 J 7
Bavly 124-125 T 6
Bawah, Pulau-pulau — 152-153 G 4
Bawal, Pulau — 152-153 H 7
Bawean, Pulau — 148-149 F 8
Bāwīţī, Al- 164-165 K 3
Bawku 164-165 D 6
Bawlagè 148-149 C 3
Bawlei Myit 141 DE 7
Bawmi Au 141 D 7
Ba Xian 146-147 F 2
Baxten Springs 76-77 G 4
Baxter State Park 72-73 M 1-2
Bay 164-165 a 3

Bayāḍ, Al- [DZ] 164-165 E 2
Bayāḍ, Al- [Saudi Arabia] 134-135 F 6
Bayāḍīyah, Al- 173 C 5
Bay al-Kabīr, Wādī — 164-165 GH 2
Bayamo 64-65 L 7
Bayamón 88-89 N 5
Bayan 152-153 M 10
Bayāna 138-139 F 4
Bayan Tumen = Čojbalsan 142-143 L 2
Bayard, NE 68-69 E 5
Bayas 86-87 H 6
Bayat [TR, Afyonkarahisar] 136-137 D 3
Bayat [TR, Çorum] 136-137 F 2
Bayauca 106-107 G 5
Baybay 148-149 HJ 4
Bayboro, NC 80-81 H 3
Baybū 136-137 KL 4
Bayburt 134-135 E 2
Baychester, New York-, NY 82 III cd 1
Bay City, MI 64-65 K 3
Bay City, TX 76-77 FG 8
Bayḍā', Al- [ADN] 134-135 EF 8
Bayḍā', Al- [LAR] 164-165 J 2
Bayḍā', 'Ayn al- 136-137 GH 7
Bayḍā', Bi'r — 173 CD 4
Bayḍā', Jabal — 173 D 6
Baydāh, 'Ayn al- 136-137 GH 5
Baydhabo 164-165 a 3
Bayerischer Wald 118 F 4
Bayern 118 E 4
Bayeux [BR] 100-101 G 4
Bayeux [F] 120-121 G 4
Bay Farm Island 83 I c 2
Bayfield, WI 70-71 E 2
Bayḥān al-Qaṣab 134-135 F 8
Bay Ḥasan 136-137 L 5
Bayiji 146-147 F 4
Bayındır 136-137 B 3
Bayingolin Monggol Zizhizhou 142-143 FG 4
Bayland Park 85 III b 2
Bay Minette, AL 78-79 F 5
Bay Mountains 80-81 E 2
Bay of Bangkok = Ao Krung Thep 150-151 C 6
Bay of Fundy 56-57 X 8-9
Bay of Harbours 108-109 K 9
Bay of Islands [CDN] 63 G 3
Bay of Islands [NZ] 158-159 OP 7
Bay of Pelusium = Khalīj aṭ-Ṭīnah 173 C 2
Bay of Plenty 158-159 P 7
Bay of Whales 53 B 19-20
Bayonne 120-121 G 7
Bayonne, NJ 82 III b 3
Bayonne Park 82 III b 2
Bayou Bend, Houston-, TX 85 III ab 1
Bayou Couba 85 I a 3
Bayou des Familles 85 I b 3
Bayou Segnette Canal 85 I b 3
Bayou Woods, Houston-, TX 85 III b 1
Bayovar 96-97 A 4
Bay Port, MI 72-73 E 3
Bayraktar 136-137 JK 3
Bayramiç 136-137 B 3
Bayrāt, Ḥāssī al- 166-167 B 6
Bayreuth 118 E 4
Bay Ridge, New York-, NY 82 III b 3
Bayrūt 134-135 CD 4
Bays, Lake of — 72-73 G 2
Bay Saint Louis, LA 78-79 E 5
Bayshore, CA 83 I b 2
Bay Shore, NY 72-73 K 4
Bays Mountains 80-81 E 2
Bay Springs, MS 78-79 E 4-5
Bayt al-Faqīh 134-135 E 8
Bayt Laḥm 136-137 F 7
Baytown, TX 64-65 GH 6
Bayunglincir 152-153 EF 7
Bayview, San Francisco-, CA 83 I b 2
Bayyūḍ, Bi'r al- 136-137 H 5
Bayyūḍah, Barrīyat al- 164-165 L 5
Bayzaḥ, Wādī — 173 C 5
Baza 120-121 F 10
Bazai 146-147 E 9
Bazán 106-107 D 2
Bazar = Kapalı Çarşı 154 I a 2-3
Bazar Dere 142-143 D 4
Bazard'uzi, gora — 126-127 N 6
Bāzargān 136-137 L 3
Bazarnyje Mataki 124-125 RS 6
Bazarnyj Karabulak 124-125 Q 7
Bazarnyj Syzgan 124-125 Q 7
Bazaršulan 126-127 PQ 2
Bazartobe 126-127 PQ 2
Bazaruto, Ilha do — 172 G 6
Bazas 120-121 G 6
Bāzdar 134-135 JK 5
Bazhao Dao = Pachao Tao 146-147 G 10
Bazias 122-123 J 3
Bazine, KS 68-69 G 6
Baziya 174-175 H 6
Bazzar 170 II b 1
Be, Sông — 150-151 F 7
Beach, ND 68-69 DE 2
Beachburg 72-73 H 2
Beachport 158-159 G 7
Beacon, NY 72-73 K 4
Beacon Hill [CDN] 61 D 3
Beacon Hill [HK] 155 I ab 1
Beacontree, London- 129 II c 1
Beagle, Canal — 111 C 8
Beagle Bay 158-159 D 3
Bealanana 172 J 4
Beale, Cape — 60 E 5
Beale Lake 138-139 D 8
Beals Creek 76-77 D 6
Beam 129 II c 1
Beara 148-149 MN 8
Bear Creek 58-59 ST 6
Bearcreek, MT 66-67 J 3
Bearden, AR 78-79 C 4
Beardmore 70-71 G 1
Beardmore Glacier 53 A 20-18
Beardmore Reservoir 160 HJ 1
Beardsley, AZ 74-75 G 6
Beardstown, IL 70-71 EF 5
Bear Hill 68-69 F 5
Bear Island 53 B 26
Bear Islands = ostrova Medvežji 132-133 f 3
Bear Lake [CDN] 61 KL 3
Bear Lake [CDN, lake] 60 D 1
Bear Lake [CDN, place] 60 D 1
Bear Lake [USA, Houston] 85 III c 1
Bear Lake [USA, Idaho, Utah] 64-65 D 3
Bear Lodge Moutains 68-69 D 3
Beārma 138-139 G 6
Bear Mount 58-59 QR 2
Bēarn [CDN] 72-73 G 1
Béarn [F] 120-121 G 7
Bearpaw, AK 58-59 M 4
Bearpaw Mountain 66-67 J 1
Bear River [CDN] 63 D 5
Bear River [USA] 64-65 D 3
Bear River Bay 66-67 G 5
Bearskin Lake 62 D 1
Bēas [IND] 138-139 E 2
Beata, Cabo — 88-89 L 6
Beata, Isla — 64-65 M 8
Beatrice 172 F 5
Beatrice, AL 78-79 F 5
Beatrice, NE 64-65 G 3
Beatrice, Cape — 158-159 G 2
Beatty, NV 74-75 E 4
Beattyville 62 N 2
Beattyville, KY 72-73 E 6
Beaucaire 120-121 K 7
Beaucanton 62 M 2
Beauce 120-121 HJ 4
Beauceville 63 A 4
Beauchamp 129 I b 1
Beauchene Island 111 E 8
Beaudesert 160 L 1
Beaufort, NC 80-81 H 3
Beaufort, SC 80-81 F 4
Beaufort [AUS] 160 F 6
Beaufort Inlet 80-81 H 3
Beaufort Island = Lo Chau 155 I b 2
Beaufort Lagoon 58-59 Q 2-R 1
Beaufort Sea 56-57 G-L 3
Beaufort-Wes 172 D 8
Beaufort West = Beaufort-Wes 172 D 8
Beauharnois 72-73 JK 2
Beaujolais 120-121 K 5
Beauly 119 D 3
Beaumont, CA 74-75 E 6
Beaumont, MS 78-79 E 5
Beaumont, TX 64-65 GH 5
Beaumont Place, TX 85 III c 1
Beaune 120-121 K 5
Beauty 174-175 GH 2
Beauvais 120-121 HJ 4
Beauval 61 DE 3
Beaver, AK 58-59 O 3
Beaver, KS 68-69 G 6
Beaver, UT 74-75 G 3
Beaver Bay, MN 70-71 E 2
Beaver City, NE 68-69 FG 5
Beaver City, OK 76-77 D 4
Beaver Creek [CDN] 58-59 R 5
Beaver Creek [USA] 58-59 O 3-4
Beaver Creek [USA ◁ Cheyenne River] 68-69 D 4
Beaver Creek [USA ◁ Little Missouri River] 68-69 DE 2
Beaver Creek [USA ◁ Milk River] 66-67 J 1
Beaver Creek [USA ◁ Missouri River] 68-69 F 2
Beaver Creek [USA ◁ Republican River] 68-69 F 6
Beaver Creek [USA ◁ South Platte River] 68-69 E 5-6
Beaver Creek Mountain 78-79 F 4
Beaverdam, VA 80-81 GH 2
Beaver Dam, WI 70-71 F 4
Beaver Falls, PA 72-73 F 4
Beaverhead Range 66-67 G 3
Beaverhead River 66-67 G 3
Beaverhill Lake [CDN, Alberta] 61 BC 4
Beaverhill Lake [CDN, Manitoba] 61 L 3
Beaver Inlet 58-59 no 4
Beaver Island [Falkland Islands] 108-109 J 8
Beaver Island [USA] 70-71 H 3
Beaver Lake 76-77 GH 4
Beaverlodge 60 GH 2
Beaver Mountains 58-59 J 5
Beaver River 56-57 P 7
Beaverton 72-73 G 2
Beāwar 134-135 LM 5
Beazley 111 C 4
Beba, La — 106-107 G 5
Bebedero, Salina del — 106-107 D 4
Bebedó 94-95 C 5
Bebedouro 92-93 K 9
Bebeji 168-169 H 3
Bebek, İstanbul- 154 I b 2
Beberibe 100-101 EF 3
Bebra 118 D 3
Becan 86-87 Q 8
Beccar, San Isidro- 110 III b 1
Beccles 119 G 5
Bečej 122-123 HJ 3
Bečevinka 124-125 LM 4
Béchar = Bashshār 164-165 D 2
Becharof Lake 56-57 EF 6
Bechevin Bay 58-59 ab 2
Bechuanaland = Betsjoeanaland 172 D 7
Beckenham, London- 129 II b 2
Beckley, WV 64-65 K 4
Beclean 122-123 KL 2
Beda 164-165 M 7
Beddington, ME 72-73 MN 2
Bedeau = Ra's-al-Mā' 166-167 F 2
Bedele 164-165 M 7
Bedestadpan 174-175 D 4
Bedford, IA 70-71 C 5
Bedford, IN 70-71 G 6
Bedford, KY 70-71 H 6
Bedford, PA 72-73 G 4
Bedford, VA 80-81 G 2
Bedford [CDN, Nova Scotia] 63 DE 5
Bedford [CDN, Quebec] 72-73 K 2
Bedford [GB] 119 F 5
Bedford [ZA] 174-175 FG 7
Bedford Park, IL 83 II a 2
Bedford Park, New York-, NY 82 III c 1
Bedford-Stuyvesant, New York-, NY 82 III c 2
Bedi = Rojhi Māta 138-139 BC 6
Bedirli 136-137 G 3
Bēdja = Bājah 164-165 F 1
Bednesti 60 F 3
Bednodemjanovsk 124-125 OP 7
Bedok [SGP, place] 154 III b 2
Bedok [SGP, river] 154 III b 1
Bedourie 158-159 GH 4
Beebe, AR 78-79 CD 3
Beech Creek, OR 66-67 D 3
Beechey Point, AK 58-59 MN 1
Beechworth 160 H 6
Beechy 61 E 5
Beegum, CA 66-67 B 5
Beeler, KS 68-69 FG 6
Beerenberg 52 B 19
Bēer-Mĕnūḥa 136-137 F 7
Beersel 128 II a 2
Beersheba = Bĕer-Sheva' 134-135 C 4
Bĕer-Sheva' 134-135 C 4
Beers Mine, De — 174-175 F 5
Beert 128 II a 2
Beeshoek 174-175 E 5
Beestekraal 174-175 G 3
Beeville, TX 64-65 G 6
Befale 172 D 1
Befandriana-atsimo 172 H 6
Befandriana-avaratva 172 J 5
Bega [AUS] 158-159 JK 7
Bega, Canal — 122-123 J 3
Begadó 94-95 C 5
Begamganj 138-139 G 6
Begārī, Nahr — 138-139 B 3
Begemdir-na Simen 164-165 M 6
Beggs, OK 76-77 F 5
Begičeva, ostrov — = ostrov Bol'šoj Begičev 132-133 VW 3
Begna 116-117 C 7
Begoml' 124-125 FG 6
Begorītis, Límnē — 122-123 JK 5
Begumganj = Begamganj 138-139 G 6
Begusarai 138-139 L 5
Behagle, De — = Laï 164-165 H 7
Behāgue, Pointe — 92-93 J 3-4
Behāla = South Suburbs 154 II ab 3
Behan 61 C 3
Behara 172 J 6
Behbahān 134-135 G 4
Behm Canal 58-59 x 9
Behn, Mount — 158-159 E 3
Behrman Memorial Park 85 I b 2
Behror 138-139 F 4
Beht, Ouēd — = Wād Baḥt 166-167 D 3
Bei, Nam — 141 E 4
Bei'an 142-143 O 2
Beibei 142-143 K 6
Beibu Wan 142-143 K 7-8
Beichuan He 146-147 C 3
Beida, Bîr — = Bi'r Bayḍā' 173 CD 4
Beidā', El — = Al-Bayḍā' 164-165 J 2
Beida, Gebel — = Jabal Bayḍā' 173 D 6
Beidachi 146-147 A 2-3
Beifei He 146-147 F 5
Beigem 128 II b 1
Beihai [TJ, Beijing] 155 II b 2
Beihai [TJ, Guangxi Zhuangzu Zizhiqu] 142-143 K 7
Beihai Park 155 II b 2
Bei Jiang 146-147 D 10
Beijiang = Peichiang 146-147 H 10
Beijie He 150-151 G 3
Beijing 142-143 LM 3-4
Beijing-Balizhuang 155 II bc 2
Beijing-Beiyuan 155 II b 1
Beijing-Chaoyangqu 155 II bc 2
Beijing-Chongwenqu 155 II b 2
Beijing-Dajiaoting 155 II bc 2
Beijing-Dajingcun 155 II a 2
Beijing-Datun 155 II b 2
Beijing-Dawuji 155 II b 2
Beijing Daxue = Peking University 155 II ab 2
Beijing-Deshengmen 155 II b 2
Beijing-Dongsheng 155 II ab 1
Beijing-Dongyuqu 155 II b 2
Beijing-Fengtai 155 II a 2
Beijing-Fengtaiqu 155 II ab 2
Beijing-Ganjiakou 155 II a 2
Beijing-Guanqumen 155 II b 2
Beijing-Haidian 155 II a 2
Beijing-Haidianqu 155 II ab 2
Beijing-Hongmiao 155 II b 2
Beijing-Huangsi 155 II b 2
Beijing-Huangtugang 155 II ab 2
Beijing-Jiangtai 155 II bc 2
Beijing-Jiugang 155 II b 3
Beijing-Jiuxianqiao 155 II bc 2
Beijing-Lantianchang 155 II a 2
Beijing-Laohumiao 155 II b 2
Beijing-Nanmofang 155 II b 2
Beijing-Nanyuan 155 II b 3
Beijing-Quinghua 155 II b 1
Beijing-Quinghuayuan 155 II b 2
Beijing-Shawocun 155 II a 2
Beijing-Sidao 155 II b 2
Beijing-Taiyanggong 155 II b 2
Beijing-Weigongcun 155 II ab 2
Beijing-Xiaohongmen 155 II b 3
Beijing-Xinghuo 155 II b 2
Beijing-Xiyuqu 155 II a 2
Beijing-Xizhuang 155 II b 2
Beijing-Xuanwuqu 155 II ab 2
Beijing-Yongdingmen 155 II b 2
Beijing-You'anmen 155 II ab 2
Beijing-Yuegezhuang 155 II a 2
Beijing-Yuyuantan 155 II a 2
Beijingzi 144-145 DE 3
Beijing-Zuo'anmen 155 II b 2
Beiji Shan 146-147 H 8
Beili 150-151 G 3
Beiliu 146-147 C 10
Beiliu Jiang 146-147 C 10
Beinn Dearg 119 D 3
Beipa'a 148-149 N 8
Beipiao 144-145 C 2
Beira [Mozambique] 172 FG 5
Beira [P] 120-121 CD 8
Beira Mar 106-107 L 4
Beirāt, Ḥassī el — = Ḥāssī al-Bayrāt 166-167 B 6
Beiroût = Bayrūt 134-135 CD 4
Beiru He 146-147 D 4
Beirut = Bayrūt 134-135 CD 4
Beisan = Bēt Sheān 134-135 F 6
Beisbol, Estadio de — 91 II b 2
Beisbol, Parque de — 91 I c 2
Bei Shan 142-143 GH 3
Beishanchengzhen = Caoshi 144-145 E 1
Beitbridge 172 EF 6
Beit Laḥm = Bayt Laḥm 136-137 F 7
Beiyuan, Beijing- 155 II b 1
Beizaḥ, Wādī — = Wādī Bayzaḥ 173 C 5
Beizhen [TJ, Liaoning] 144-145 C 2
Beizhen [TJ, Shandong] 146-147 FG 3
Beja 120-121 D 9-10
Beja = Bājah 164-165 F 1
Bēja = Bājah 164-165 F 1
Bejaïa = Bijāyah 164-165 EF 1
Bejaïa, Golfe de — = Khalīj Bijāyah 166-167 J 1
Béjar 120-121 E 8
Bejestān 134-135 H 4
Beji = Bajī 138-139 B 3
Bejsug 126-127 J 4
Bekabad 134-135 KL 2
Bekasi 148-149 E 8
Bek-Budi = Karši 134-135 K 3
Bekdaš 134-135 G 2
Békés 118 K 5
Békéscsaba 118 K 5
Beketovka, Volgograd- 126-127 M 2
Bekily 172 J 6
Bekkaria = Bakārīyah 166-167 KL 2
Bekkerzeel 128 II a 1
Bekok 150-151 D 11
Bekovo 124-125 O 7
Bekwai 168-169 E 4
Bela [IND] 138-139 HJ 5
Belā [PAK] 134-135 K 5
Bela Crkva 122-123 J 3
Bela Cruz 100-101 D 2
Bela Dila 140 E 1
Belā Dvīp = Bela Island 138-139 C 6
Belaga 148-149 F 6
Belagām = Belgaum 134-135 LM 7
Belaia = Beleye 164-165 b 2-3
Bel Air 120-121 F 4
Bel Air, MD 72-73 H 5
Bel Air, Los Angeles-, CA 83 III b 1
Bela Island 138-139 C 6
Belaja [SU, place] 126-127 GH 1
Belaja [SU, river] 132-133 J 6
Belaja Ber'ozka 124-125 JK 7
Belaja Cerkov' 126-127 E 2
Belaja Cholunica 124-125 S 4
Belaja Glina 126-127 K 3
Belaja Kalitva 126-127 K 2
Belaja Zemľa, ostrova — 132-133 L-N 1
Bel'ajevka 126-127 E 3
Bela Lorena 102-103 JK 1
Belampalli 138-139 G 8
Belang 148-149 HJ 6
Bélanger River 62 A 1
Bela Palanka 122-123 K 4
Belāpur 138-139 E 8
Belau 148-149 KL 5
Bela União 106-107 K 3
Bela Vista [BR, Amazonas] 94-95 H 7
Bela Vista [BR, Mato Grosso do Sul] 92-93 H 9
Bela Vista [BR, Rondônia] 98-99 G 10
Bela Vista [Mozambique] 172 F 7
Bela Vista, Cachoeira — 92-93 J 5
Bela Vista, São Paulo- 110 II b 2
Bela Vista de Goiás 92-93 K 8
Bela Vista do Paraíso 102-103 G 5
Belawan 148-149 C 6
Belayan, Sungai — 152-153 L 5
Belcher Channel 56-57 RS 2
Belcher Islands 56-57 U 6
Belchite 120-121 G 8
Belcik = Yavi 136-137 G 3
Bel'cy 126-127 CD 3
Belda 138-139 L 6
Beldānga 138-139 M 6
Belden, CA 66-67 C 5
Belding, MI 70-71 H 4
Belebej 132-133 J 7
Belebelka 124-125 H 5
Beléco 168-169 D 2
Beled Weeyne 164-165 O 8
Béléhédé 168-169 E 2
Belém [BR, Amazonas] 94-95 c 2
Belém [BR, Pará] 92-93 K 5
Belém [BR, Paraíba] 100-101 F 4
Belém [Mozambique] 171 CD 6
Belém de São Francisco 100-101 E 5
Belém Novo 106-107 M 3
Belen, NM 64-65 E 5
Belén [CO] 94-95 D 7
Belén [PY] 102-103 D 5
Belén [RA] 104-105 C 10
Belén [ROU] 106-107 J 3
Belén, Cuchilla de — 106-107 J 3
Belén, Río — 104-105 C 10-11
Belep, Îles — 158-159 M 3
Beleye 164-165 M 6
Belfair, WA 66-67 B 2
Belfast, ME 72-73 M 2
Belfast [GB] 119 CD 4
Belfast [ZA] 174-175 HJ 3
Belfield, ND 68-69 E 2
Belfodio 164-165 LM 6
Belfort 120-121 L 5
Bel Freissat = Bin al-Fraysāt 166-167 E 3
Belfry, MT 68-69 B 3
Bēlgāṅv = Belgaum 134-135 LM 7
Belgaon = Belgaum 134-135 LM 7
Belgaum 134-135 LM 7
Belgem = Beigem 128 II b 1
Belgica Mountains 53 B 3-4
Belgium 120-121 JK 3
Belgorod 126-127 H 1
Belgorod-Dnestrovskij 126-127 DE 3
Belgrade, MN 70-71 C 3
Belgrade, MT 66-67 H 3
Belgrade = Beograd 122-123 J 3
Belgrad Ormanı 154 I a 1
Belgrano, Buenos Aires- 110 III b 1
Belgrano, Cerro — 108-109 D 6
bel Guebbour, Hassi — = Ḥāssī Baljabbūr 166-167 K 5
Bel Guerdane = Bi'r al-Qird'an 166-167 A 7
Belhā = Bela 138-139 HJ 5
Belhar 138-139 L 5
Belhaven, NC 80-81 H 3
Beli 168-169 EF 2
Beliaghata, Calcutta- 154 II b 2
Beli Hill 168-169 H 4
Belīkh, Nahr — = Nahr Balīh 136-137 H 4
Beliki 126-127 FG 2
Beli Lom 122-123 LM 4
Belimbing 152-153 F 8-9
Belinskij 124-125 O 7
Belinyu 148-149 E 7
Beli Timok 122-123 K 4
Belitung, Pulau — 148-149 E 7
Belize [BH, place] 64-65 J 8
Belize [BH, state] 64-65 J 8
Belize River 86-87 Q 9
Belkofski, AK 58-59 bc 2
Bel'kovskij, ostrov — 132-133 Za 2
Bell, CA 83 III c 2
Bell, FL 80-81 b 2
Bell, Rivière — 62 N 2
Bella, Laguna la — 102-103 B 6
Bella Bella 60 C 3
Bellaco 106-107 HJ 4
Bella Coola 56-57 L 7
Bella Flor 104-105 C 2
Bellaire, MI 70-71 H 3
Bellaire, OH 72-73 F 4-5
Bellaire, TX 76-77 G 8
Bellary 134-135 M 7
Bellas Artes, Palacio de — 91 I c 2
Bellata 160 J 2
Bella Unión 111 E 4
Bella Vista [BOL] 92-93 G 8
Bellavista [BR, Amazonas] 98-99 D 6
Bellavista [BR, Magdalena] 94-95 D 2
Bellavista [CO] 94-95 D 7
Bellavista [PE] 96-97 B 4
Bella Vista [PY] 102-103 D 5
Bella Vista [RA, Corrientes] 111 E 3
Bella Vista [RA, Tucumán] 104-105 D 10
Bella Vista [YV] 94-95 JK 4
Bella Vista, Caracas- 91 II b 2
Bella Vista, General Sarmiento- 110 III ab 1
Bella Vista, Salar de — 104-105 B 7
Bell Bay 160 c 2
Belle, MO 70-71 E 6
Bellefontaine, OH 72-73 E 4
Bellefonte, PA 72-73 GH 4
Belle Fourche, SD 68-69 DE 3
Belle Fourche Reservoir 68-69 E 3
Belle Fourche River 68-69 E 3
Belle Glade, FL 80-81 c 3
Belle Île 120-121 F 5
Belle Isle [CDN] 56-57 Za 7
Belle Isle [USA] 84 II c 2
Belle Isle, Strait of — 56-57 Z 7
Belle Isle Park 84 II c 2
Bellemont, AZ 74-75 GH 5
Belleoram 63 J 4
Belle Plaine, IA 70-71 D 5
Belle Plaine, KS 68-69 H 7
Belle Plaine, MN 70-71 D 3
Bellerose, New York-, NY 82 III d 2
Belles Artes, Museo de — 91 II b 1
Belleterre 72-73 G 1
Belleville, IL 70-71 F 6
Belleville, KS 68-69 H 6
Belleville, NJ 82 III ab 2
Belleville [CDN] 56-57 V 9
Belleville, Paris- 129 I c 2
Bellevue, IA 70-71 E 4
Bellevue, MI 70-71 H 4
Bellevue, OH 72-73 E 4
Bellevue, TX 76-77 E 6
Bellevue, WA 66-67 BC 2
Bellevue, Johannesburg- 170 V b 2
Bellevue, Washington-, DC 82 II a 2
Bellevue-Mount Vernon, Boston-, MA 84 I b 3
Belle Yella 168-169 C 4
Bellflower, CA 83 III d 2
Bell Gardens, CA 83 III d 2
Bellin [CDN] 56-57 WX 5
Bellingham, WA 66-67 BC 1
Bellingshausen Sea 53 BC 28
Bellinzona 118 D 5
Bell Irving River 60 C 1
Bellis 61 C 3
Bell Island 63 J 2
Bell Island = Wabana 56-57 a 8
Bell Island Hot Springs, AK 58-59 x 8-9
Bell Lake 62 D 3
Bellmawr, NJ 84 III c 2
Bello [CO] 92-93 DE 3
Bellocq 106-107 G 5
Bello Horizonte = Belo Horizonte 92-93 L 8
Bellona 148-149 j 7
Bellota, CA 74-75 C 3
Bellows Falls, VT 72-73 K 3
Belloy 60 H 2
Bell Peninsula 56-57 U 5
Bells, TN 78-79 E 3
Belluno 122-123 DE 2
Bellville, TX 76-77 F 8
Bell Ville [RA] 111 D 4
Bellville [ZA] 174-175 C 7
Bellvue, CO 68-69 D 5
Belmez 120-121 E 9
Belmond, IA 70-71 D 4
Belmont, MA 84 I ab 2
Belmont, NY 72-73 GH 3
Belmont [CDN] 68-69 G 1
Belmont [ZA] 174-175 F 5
Belmont Cragin, Chicago-, IL 83 II a 1
Belmonte [BR] 92-93 M 8
Belmont Harbor 83 II b 1
Belmont Terrace, PA 84 III a 1
Belmopan 64-65 J 8
Belo Campo 100-101 D 8
Belogorsk [SU, Rossijskaja SFSR] 132-133 YZ 7
Belogorsk [SU, Ukrainskaja SSR] 126-127 G 4
Belogradčik 122-123 K 4
Belo Horizonte [BR, Minas Gerais] 92-93 L 8
Belo Horizonte [BR, Rondônia] 104-105 CD 1
Beloit, KS 68-69 GH 6
Beloit, WI 64-65 J 3
Belo Jardim 100-101 F 5
Beloje ozero 132-133 F 5
Belojevo 124-125 TU 4
Belokuricha 132-133 PQ 7
Belo Monte 98-99 N 6
Belomorsk 132-133 EF 5
Belomorsko-Baltijskij kanal 124-125 K 1-2
Belonia 141 B 4
Beloomut 124-125 M 6
Belo Oriente 98-99 G 11
Belopolje 126-127 G 1
Belopúla 122-123 K 7
Beloreˇcensk 126-127 J 4
Beloreck 132-133 K 7
Belorussian Soviet Socialist Republic 124-125 E-H 6-7
Belorusskaja gr'ada 124-125 E 7-G 6
Belorusskaja Sovetskaja Socialističeskaja Respublika = Belorussian Soviet Socialist Republic 124-125 E-H 7
Belosarajskaja kosa 126-127 H 3
Belo-Tsiribihina 172 H 5
Bel'ov 124-125 L 7
Belo Vale 102-103 K 4
Beloveżskaja pušča, zapovednik — 124-125 E 7
Belovo 132-133 Q 7
Belovodsk 126-127 J 2
Belozersk 132-133 F 5-6
Belpaḍā = Belpāra 138-139 J 7
Belpāra 138-139 J 7
Belpre, KS 68-69 G 7
Belpre, OH 72-73 F 5
Belrhiada = Bin al-Ghiadah 166-167 E 3
Belsund 116-117 j 6
Belt, MT 66-67 H 2
Belted Range 74-75 E 4
Belton, SC 80-81 E 3
Belton, TX 76-77 F 7
Beltrán 106-107 EF 1
Belucha, gora — 132-133 Q 8
Beluchistan = Balūchistān 134-135 J 5-K 4
Beluga Lake 58-59 M 6
Beluja Guba 132-133 HJ 3
Belum 152-153 D 3
Belur, Howrah- 154 II b 2
Beluran 152-153 M 3
Belvedere, CA 83 I b 1
Belvedere, VA 82 II a 2
Belvedere [A] 113 I b 2
Belveren 136-137 G 4
Belvidere, IL 70-71 F 4
Belvidere, KS 68-69 G 7
Belvidere, SD 68-69 F 4
Belyj 124-125 J 6
Belyj, ostrov — 132-133 MN 3
Belyj Byček = Čagoda 132-133 EF 6
Belyje Berega 124-125 K 7
Belyje gory 124-125 QR 7
Belyj Gorodok 124-125 L 5
Belyj Jar 132-133 Q 6
Belyniči 124-125 G 6-7
Belzoni, MS 78-79 D 4
Bemaraha 172 HJ 5
Bembe 172 BC 3
Bembéreké = Bimbéreké 164-165 E 6
Bembou 168-169 C 2
Bement, IL 70-71 F 6
Bemetāra 138-139 H 7
Bemidji, MN 64-65 GH 2
Bemis, TN 78-79 E 3
Bena, MN 70-71 CD 2
Benaadir [SP, administrative unit = 2 ◁] 164-165 O 8
Benaadir [SP, landscape] 164-165 ab 3
Benāb = Bonāb 136-137 M 4
Bena-Dibele 172 D 2
Benalla 158-159 J 7
Benares = Vārānasi 134-135 N 5
Benas, Ras — = Rā's Banās 164-165 M 4
Benavente 120-121 DE 7
Benavides 104-105 C 3
Benavides, TX 76-77 E 9
Ben Baṭāī, Ḥassī — = Ḥāssī Bin Baṭāī 166-167 AB 5
Benbecula 119 BC 3
Bến Cat 150-151 F 7
Bend 60 G 3
Bend, OR 64-65 B 3
Bendaja 168-169 C 4
Bendel 164-165 F 7
Bendeleben Mountains 58-59 EF 4
Bender Abas = Bandar 'Abbās 134-135 H 5
Bender Bayla 164-165 c 2
Bendery 126-127 D 3
Bendigo 158-159 HJ 7
Bēne 124-125 D 5
Beneditinos 100-101 C 3
Benedito Leite 100-101 B 4
'Ben er Rechīd = Bin Rashīd 166-167 BC 3
Benevento 122-123 F 5
Benfica [BR, Acre] 98-99 C 9
Benfica [BR, Minas Gerais] 102-103 L 4
Benfica, Cachoeira — 98-99 L 5
Beng, Nam — 150-151 C 2
Benga 172 F 5
Bengal, Bay of — 134-135 N-P 7
Bengala 94-95 EF 5
Bengalian Ridge 50-51 O 5-6
Bengalore = Bangalore 134-135 M 8
Bengaḷūru = Bangalore 134-135 M 8
Ben Gardân = Bin Qardān 166-167 M 3
Bengasi = Banghāzī 164-165 HJ 2
Bengawan Solo 152-153 JK 9
Bengbu 142-143 M 5
Benge, WA 66-67 D 2
Ben Ghazi [DZ] 170 I b 2
Benghazi = Banghāzī 164-165 HJ 2
Beng He 146-147 G 4
Bến Giang 150-151 F 5
Bengkalis 152-153 E 5
Bengkalis, Pulau — 148-149 D 6
Bengkayang 148-149 EF 6
Bengkule 152-153 D 7-E 8
Bengkulu 148-149 D 7
Beng Lovéa 150-151 E 6
Bến Goi, Vung — = Vung Hon Khoi 150-151 G 6
Bengolea 106-107 F 4
Bengough 68-69 D 1
Benguela 172 B 4
'Ben Guerīr = Bin Gharīr 164-165 C 2
Benguérua, Ilha — 174-175 L 1
'Ben Ḥamed = Bin Aḥmad 166-167 C 3
Ben Hope 119 D 2
Beni [BOL] 104-105 C-E 3
Beni [Nepal] 138-139 J 3
Beni [ZRE] 172 E 1
Beni, Río — 92-93 F 7
Beni-Abbès = Banī Abbās 164-165 D 2
Benicia, CA 74-75 BC 3
Benicito, Río — 104-105 D 2-3
Beni Kreddache = Banī Khaddāsh 166-167 LM 3
'Beni Lent = Banī Lant 166-167 D 2
Benī Mazār = Banī Mazār 164-165 L 3
'Benī Mellāl = Banī Mallāl 164-165 C 2
Benin 164-165 E 6-7
Bénin = Benin 164-165 E 6-7
Benin, Bight of — 164-165 E 7-8
Benin City 164-165 F 7
Béni-Saf = Banī Ṣāf 166-167 F 2
Benī Shigeir = Banī Shuqayr 173 B 4
Bēni Souef = Banī Suwayf 164-165 L 3
Benī Suēf = Banī Suwayf 164-165 L 3
'Benī Tajjīt = Banī Tajīt 166-167 E 3
Benítez 106-107 GH 5

Benithora 140 C 2
Benito Juárez 111 DE 5
Benito Juárez, Ciudad de México- 91 I bc 2
Benjamim Constant 92-93 EF 5
Benjamin, TX 76-77 DE 6
Benjamin, Isla — 108-109 BC 5
Benjamin Franklin Bridge 84 III c 2
Benjamin Hill 86-87 E 2
Benjamin Zorrilla 106-107 E 7
Benkelman, NE 68-69 F 5
Benkulen = Bengkulu 148-149 D 7
Ben Lawers 119 DE 3
Ben Lomond [AUS] 160 cd 2
Ben Macdhui [GB] 119 DE 3
Ben Macdhui [LS] 174-175 GH 6
Ben-Mehidi = Ban Mahdī 166-167 KL 1
Ben More [GB, Mull] 119 C 3
Ben More [GB, Outer Hebrides] 119 C 3
Benmore, Lake — 161 D 7
Ben More Assynt 119 DE 2
Bennett 58-59 U 7
Bennett, CO 68-69 D 6
Bennett, WI 70-71 E 2
Bennett, ostrov — 132-133 cd 2
Bennett's Harbour 88-89 J 2
Bennettsville, SC 80-81 G 3
Ben Nevis 119 D 3
Bennington, VT 72-73 K 3
Bên Nôm 150-151 F 7
Ben Ohau Range 161 C 7-D 6
Benom = Gunung Benom 150-151 CD 11
Benom, Gunung — 150-151 CD 11
Benoni 174-175 H 4
Benoud = Banūd 166-167 G 3
Bénoué 164-165 G 7
Benqi = Benxi 142-143 N 3
Bensheim 118 D 4
'Ben Slîmân = Bin Sulīmān 166-167 C 3
Benson 68-69 E 1
Benson, AZ 74-75 H 7
Benson, MN 70-71 C 3
Bên Suc 150-151 F 7
Benta Sebrang 150-151 CD 10
Benteng 152-153 O 9
Bên Thuy 150-151 EF 3
'Ben Tieb = Bin Ṭiyab 166-167 E 2
Bentinck Island 158-159 GH 3
Bentinck Island = Pyinzabu Kyûn 150-151 A 7
Bentiū 164-165 KL 7
Bent Jebaïl = Bint Jubayl 136-137 F 6
Bentleigh, Melbourne- 161 II c 2
Bentley 60 K 3
Bento, Rio de Janeiro- 110 I a 2
Bento Gomes, Rio — 102-103 D 2
Bento Gonçalves 106-107 M 2
Benton, AL 78-79 F 4
Benton, AR 78-79 C 3
Benton, CA 74-75 D 4
Benton, IL 70-71 F 6-7
Benton, KY 78-79 E 2
Benton, LA 78-79 C 4
Benton, WI 70-71 E 4
Benton City, WA 66-67 D 2
Bentong 150-151 CD 11
Benton Harbor, MI 70-71 G 4
Bentonia, MS 78-79 D 4
Bentonville, AR 76-77 G 4
Bentoṭa 140 DE 7
Benty 168-169 B 3
Benua 152-153 OP 8
Benua, Pulau — 152-153 G 5
Benue 164-165 F 7
Benué = Benue 164-165 F 7
Benue Plateau 164-165 F 7
Benxi 142-143 N 3
ben Yaïch, Hassi — = Ḥāssī Ban 'Aysh 166-167 J 4
Ben Zerga 170 I b 1
Ben-Zireg = Ban Zīriq 166-167 F 4
Benzoû = Benzū 166-167 D 2
Benzū 166-167 D 2
Beograd 122-123 J 3
Beograd-Zemun 122-123 HJ 3
Beohāri 138-139 H 5
Béoumi 168-169 D 4
Beppu 144-145 H 6
Bēppūr = Beypore 140 BC 5
Beqā', El — = Al-Biqā' 136-137 FG 5-6
Bequia 88-89 Q 8
Beṛa 138-139 M 5
Beraber, Oglat — = 'Uqlat Barābir 166-167 E 4
Berach 138-139 E 5
Beraïje = Al-Barāij 136-137 G 5
Beram, Tanjung — 152-153 KL 3
Berar 138-139 F 7
Berasia 138-139 F 6
Berat 122-123 H 5
Berau, Sungai — 152-153 M 4
Berau, Teluk — 148-149 K 7
Berau Gulf = Teluk Berau 148-149 K 7
Berber = Barbar 164-165 L 5
Berbera 164-165 b 1
Berbérati 164-165 a 1
Berbice 98-99 J 2-K 3
Berbice River 98-99 JK 3
Berbouchi, Hassi — = Ḥāssī Barbūshī 166-167 E 5
Berch 142-143 L 2
Berchem-Sainte-Agathe 128 II a 1
Berchtesgaden 118 F 5
Berck 120-121 H 3
Bercy, Paris- 129 I c 2
Berd'ansk 126-127 H 3
Berd'anskaja kosa 126-127 H 3
Berd'anskij zaliv 126-127 H 3
Berdičev 126-127 D 2
Berdichev = Berdičev 126-127 D 2
Berdigest'ach 132-133 XY 5
Berdjansk = Berd'ansk 126-127 H 3
Berea, KY 70-71 H 7
Berea, NE 68-69 E 4
Berea, OH 72-73 F 4
Béréba 168-169 E 3
Bérèby 168-169 D 4
Bereg [SU, Vologodskaja Oblast'] 124-125 LM 4
bereg Charitona Lapteva 132-133 Q 3-R 2
Beregomet 126-127 B 2
Beregovo 126-127 A 2
bereg Prončiščeva 132-133 UV 2-3
Bereku 171 CD 4
Berenda, CA 74-75 CD 4
Berendejevo 124-125 M 5
Berenike 164-165 LM 4
Berens Island 61 K 4
Berens River [CDN, place] 56-57 R 7
Berens River [CDN, river] 56-57 R 7
Beresford 160 C 2
Beresford, SD 68-69 H 4
Beresford Lake 62 B 2
Beresina = Berezina 124-125 G 6-7
Beresniki = Berezniki 132-133 JK 6
Berestečko 126-127 B 1
Beretău 122-123 JK 2
Berezajka [SU, place] 124-125 JK 4-5
Berežany 126-127 B 2
Berezina 124-125 G 6-7
Berezino [SU, Kazachskaja SSR] 126-127 O 1
Berezino [SU, Rossijskaja SFSR] 124-125 G 7
Berezinskij zapovednik 124-125 G 6
Berezna 124-125 HJ 8
Bereznik 124-125 O 2
Berezniki [SU, Perm'skaja Oblast'] 132-133 JK 6
Berezno 126-127 C 1
Berezovka = Ber'ozovka [SU, Odesskaja SSR] 126-127 E 3
Berezovka = Ber'ozovka [SU, Perm'skaja Oblast'] 124-125 UV 4
Berg [B] 128 II b 1
Berga = Birkah 166-167 G 6
Bergama 134-135 B 3
Berg am Laim, München- 130 II b 2
Bèrgamo 122-123 CD 3
Bergantín 94-95 J 2-3
Bergen, ND 68-69 F 1-2
Bergen [DDR] 118 F 1
Bergen [N] 116-117 A 7
Bergen Beach, New York-, NY 82 III c 3
Bergenfield, NJ 82 III c 1
Bergen-Nesttun 116-117 AB 7
Bergen Point 82 III b 3
Bergerac 120-121 H 6
Bergfelde 130 III b 1
Bergholz-Rehbrücke 130 III a 2
Bergland, MI 70-71 F 2
Bergland [CDN] 70-71 C 1
Bergland [Namibia] 174-175 B 2
Bergslagen 116-117 F 7-8
Bergstedt, Hamburg- 130 I b 1
Berguennt = Birjant 166-167 EF 2-3
Bergville 174-175 H 5
Berhala, Pulau — 150-151 DE 11
Berhala, Selat — 152-153 EF 6
Berhampore 134-135 O 6
Berhampur 134-135 NO 7
Berhampur = Berhampore 134-135 O 6
Berikat, Tanjung — 152-153 G 7
Berilo 102-103 L 2
Bering, mys — 132-133 k 5
Bering, ostrov — 132-133 fg 7
Bering Glacier 56-57 H 5
Bering Lake 58-59 P 6
Beringovskij 132-133 j 5
Bering Sea 132-133 k 5-g 6
Bering Strait 56-57 B 5-C 4
Beris = Bāris 173 B 5
Berisso 106-107 J 5
Beristain 86-87 LM 7
Berja 120-121 F 10
Berjozovo = Ber'ozovo 132-133 LM 5
Berkan = Birkān 166-167 E 2
Berkeley, CA 64-65 B 4
Berkeley Sound 108-109 KL 8
Berkersheim, Frankfurt am Main- 128 III b 1
Berkīn = Barkīn 166-167 E 3
Berkley, MI 84 II ab 1
Berkner Island 53 B 31-32
Berkovica 122-123 K 4
Berland River 60 J 2
Berlengas, Rio — 100-101 C 4-5
Berlevåg 116-117 N 2
Berlin, MD 72-73 J 5
Berlin, ND 68-69 G 2
Berlin, NH 64-65 M 3
Berlin, NJ 84 III d 3
Berlin, WI 70-71 F 4
Berlín [CO] 94-95 F 7
Berlin [D] 118 FG 2
Berlin [ZA] 174-175 G 7
Berlin, Mount — 53 B 23
Berlin-Adlershof 130 III c 2
Berlin-Altglienicke 130 III c 2
Berlin-Baumschulenweg 130 III bc 2
Berlin-Biesdorf 130 III c 1
Berlin-Biesdorf-Süd 130 III c 2
Berlin-Blankenburg 130 III b 1
Berlin-Blankenfelde 130 III b 1
Berlin-Bohnsdorf 130 III c 2
Berlin-Britz 130 III b 2
Berlin-Buchholz 130 III b 1
Berlin-Buckow 130 III b 2
Berlin-Dahlem 130 III b 2
Berlin-Elsengrund 130 III c 2
Berliner Forst Spandau 130 III a 1
Berliner Forst Tegel 130 III ab 1
Berliner Ring 130 III c 1
Berlin-Falkenberg 130 III c 1
Berlin-Friedenau 130 III b 2
Berlin-Friedrichsfelde 130 III c 1-2
Berlin-Friedrichshain 130 III b 1
Berlin-Frohnau 130 III b 1
Berlin-Grunewald 130 III b 2
Berlin-Hakenfelde 130 III a 1
Berlin-Haselhorst 130 III a 1
Berlin-Heiligensee 130 III a 1
Berlin-Heinersdorf 130 III b 1
Berlin-Hellersdorf 130 III c 1
Berlin-Hirschgarten 130 III c 2
Berlin-Hohenschönhausen 130 III c 1
Berlin-Johannisthal 130 III c 2
Berlin-Karow 130 III b 1
Berlin-Kaulsdorf 130 III c 1-2
Berlin-Kaulsdorf-Süd 130 III c 2
Berlin-Kladow 130 III a 2
Berlin-Kolonie Buch 130 III b 1
Berlin-Konradshöhe 130 III a 1
Berlin-Kreuzberg 130 III b 2
Berlin-Lankwitz 130 III b 2
Berlin-Lübars 130 III b 1
Berlin-Mahlsdorf-Süd 130 III c 2
Berlin-Malchow 130 III bc 1
Berlin-Mariendorf 130 III b 2
Berlin-Marienfelde 130 III b 2
Berlin-Marzahn 130 III c 1
Berlin-Müggelheim 130 III c 2
Berlin-Niederschöneweide 130 III b 2
Berlin-Niederschönhausen 130 III b 1
Berlin-Nikolassee 130 III a 2
Berlin-Oberschöneweide 130 III c 2
Berlin-Prenzlauer Berg 130 III b 1
Berlin-Rahnsdorf 130 III c 2
Berlin-Rauchfangswerder 130 III c 2
Berlin-Rosenthal 130 III b 1
Berlin-Rudow 130 III b 2
Berlin-Schmargendorf 130 III b 2
Berlin-Siemensstadt 130 III b 1
Berlin-Staaken 130 III a 1
Berlin-Steinstücken 130 III a 2
Berlin-Tegelort 130 III ab 1
Berlin-Tiefwerder 130 III a 1
Berlin-Tiergarten 130 III b 1
Berlin-Treptow 130 III b 2
Berlin-Waidmannslust 130 III b 1
Berlin-Wannsee 130 III a 2
Berlin-Wartenberg 130 III c 1
Berlin-Wedding 130 III b 1
Berlin-Wendenschloss 130 III c 2
Berlin-Wilhelmstadt 130 III a 1
Berlin-Wilmersdorf 130 III b 2
Berlin-Wittenau 130 III b 1
Berlin-Wolfsgarten 130 III c 2
Bermejillo 86-87 J 5
Bermejo [BOL] 92-93 G 9
Bermejo [RA] 111 C 4
Bermejo, Desaguadera del — 106-107 D 3-4
Bermejo, Isla — 106-107 FG 7
Bermejo, Río — [RA ◁ Río Desaguadero] 106-107 C 3
Bermejo, Río — [RA ◁ Río Paraguay] 111 D 2
Bermejo, Río — = Río Colorado 106-107 D 2
Bermejos 96-97 B 3
Bermeo 120-121 F 7
Bermondsey, London- 129 II b 2
Bermuda Islands 64-65 NO 5
Bermudas = Bermuda Islands 64-65 NO 5
Bern 118 C 5
Berna 106-107 GH 2
Bernabeu, Estadio — 113 III ab 2
Bernal, Quilmes- 110 III c 2
Bernalillo, NM 76-77 A 5
Bernardino de Campos 102-103 H 5
Bernardo de Irigoyen 111 F 3
Bernardo Larroude 106-107 F 5
Bernasconi 106-107 EF 6
Bernburg 118 EF 3
Berne, IN 70-71 H 5
Berne, WA 66-67 C 2
Berne = Bern 118 C 5
Berne, Hamburg- 130 I b 1
Berner Alpen 118 C 5
Bernese Alps = Berner Alpen 118 C 5
Bernhardina 174-175 H 4
Bernice, LA 78-79 C 4
Bernier Bay 56-57 ST 3
Bernier Island 158-159 B 4
Bernina 118 D 5
Beṛoia 122-123 JK 5
Berón de Astrada 106-107 J 1
Beroroha 172 HJ 6
Béroubouaye 168-169 F 3
Beroun 118 FG 4
Berounka 118 F 4
Ber'oza 124-125 E 7
Ber'ozovka [SU, Odesskaja SSR] 126-127 E 3
Ber'ozovka [SU, Perm'skaja Oblast'] 124-125 UV 4
Ber'ozovo 132-133 LM 5
Ber'ozovskaja 126-127 LM 1
Berrahal = Birraḥḥāl 166-167 K 1
Berras, Arroyo los — 110 III a 1
Ber Rechid = Bin Rashīd 166-167 BC 3
Berrekrem, Hassi — = Ḥāssī Barakram 166-167 J 3
Berri 160 E 5
Berriane = Biryān 166-167 HJ 3
Berrotarán 106-107 EF 4
Berrouaghia = Birwāgīyah 166-167 H 1
Berry 120-121 HJ 5
Berry, AL 78-79 F 4
Berryessa, Lake — 74-75 B 3
Berry Islands 88-89 GH 2
Berryville, AR 78-79 C 2
Berryville, VA 72-73 GH 5
Bersā' = Barṣā' 136-137 H 4
Bersabee = Bēer Sheva' 134-135 C 4
Beršad' 126-127 D 2
Berseba 172 C 7
Bersimis 63 B 3
Berté, Lac — 63 BC 2
Berthierville 72-73 K 1
Berthold, ND 68-69 EF 1
Bertioga 102-103 J 5
Bertiskos 122-123 K 5
Bertolínia 92-93 L 6
Bertópolis 100-101 D 3
Bertoua 164-165 G 8
Bertram 62 G 3
Bertram, TX 76-77 EF 7
Bertrand, NE 68-69 G 5
Bertrand, Cerro — 108-109 C 8
Bertrandville, LA 85 I bc 3
Bertua = Bertoua 164-165 G 8
Bertwell 61 G 4
Beru 208 H 3
Berunda 171 B 2
Beruri 92-93 G 5
Berwick, LA 78-79 D 6
Berwick, PA 72-73 H 4
Berwick [CDN] 63 D 5
Berwick-upon-Tweed 119 EF 4
Berwyn, IL 70-71 FG 5
Berwyn Heights, MD 82 II b 1
Beryl, UT 74-75 G 4
Berytus = Bayrūt 134-135 CD 4
Berzekh el Jadîd = Rā's al-Jadīd 166-167 E 2
Berzekh el Kilâtes = Rā's Qilātis 166-167 E 2
Berzekh Rhîr = Rā's Ghīr 166-167 AB 4
Berzekh Sbartel = Rā's Ashaqār 166-167 CD 2
Berzekh Thlèta Madârî = Rā's Wūruq 164-165 D 1
Besalampy 172 H 5
Besançon 120-121 L 5
Besar, Gunung — [MAL] 150-151 D 11
Besar, Gunung — [RI] 152-153 LM 7
Besar, Pulau — 152-153 P 10
Besar, Tanjung — 152-153 O 5
Besbes = Başbaş 166-167 KL 1
Besboro Island 58-59 G 4
Besed' 124-125 H 7
Bešenkoviči 124-125 G 6
Besi, Tanjung — 152-153 O 10
Beşiktaş, İstanbul- 154 I b 2
Beşirê, El — = Buşayrah 136-137 J 5
Beşiri = Kobin 136-137 J 4
Besitang 150-151 B 10
Beskids = Beskidy 118 JK 4
Beskidy 118 JK 4
Beşkonak = Bozyaka 136-137 D 4
Beskudnikovo, Moskva- 113 V bc 2
Beslan 126-127 M 5
Besna Kobila 122-123 K 4
Besnard Lake 61 F 3
Besni 134-135 D 3
Beşparmak dağı 136-137 BC 4
Bessa Monteiro 172 B 3
Bessarabia = Bessarabija 126-127 C 2-D 3
Bessarabija 126-127 C 2-D 3
Bessarabka 126-127 D 3
Bessaz gora 132-133 M 9
Bessels, Kapp — 116-117 lm 5
Bessemer, AL 64-65 J 5
Bessemer, MI 70-71 EF 2
Bessemer City, NC 80-81 F 3
Besshi 144-145 J 6
Bessoky, gora — 134-135 G 2
Best, TX 76-77 D 7
Bestobe 132-133 N 7
Bestuževo [SU, Archangel'skaja Oblast'] 124-125 O 3
Bêṭ = Okha 134-135 K 6
Betaf 148-149 L 7
Betafo 172 J 5
Betânia [BR] 100-101 EF 5
Betania [RA] 104-105 D 9
Betanzos [BOL] 104-105 D 6
Betanzos [E] 120-121 CD 7
Bétaré-Oya 164-165 G 7
Bethal 172 F 7
Bethanië = Bethanien 172 C 7
Bethanien 172 C 7
Bethany, MO 70-71 CD 5
Bethel, AK 56-57 D 5
Bethel, ME 72-73 L 2
Bethel, MN 70-71 D 3
Bethel, NC 80-81 H 3
Bethel, OH 72-73 DE 5
Bethel, OK 76-77 G 5
Bethel, VT 72-73 K 3
Bethesda, MD 82 II a 1
Bethlehem 172 E 7
Bethlehem, PA 72-73 J 4
Bethnal Green, London- 129 II b 1
Beth Shaan = Bêt Shĕ'ān 134-135 F 6
Bethulie 172 E 8
Bethune [CDN] 61 F 5
Béthune [F] 120-121 J 3
Betijoque 94-95 F 3
Betim 102-103 K 3-4
Betioky 172 H 6
Betiyā = Bettiah 138-139 K 4
Betlehem = Bayt Laḥm 136-137 F 7
Betlica 124-125 JK 6-7
Betling Sīb 141 BC 4
Betnoti 138-139 L 7
Betong 150-151 C 10
Betoota 158-159 H 5
Betpak-Dala 132-133 MN 8
Betroka 172 J 6
Bêt Shĕ'ān 134-135 F 6
Betsiamites 63 B 3
Betsiamites, Rivière — 63 B 3
Betsiboka 172 J 5
Betsie Point 70-71 G 3
Betsjoeanaland 172 D 7
Bette, Pic — 164-165 HJ 4
Bettiah 138-139 K 4
Bettié 168-169 E 4
Bettles, AK 58-59 M 3
Bettles Field = Evansville, AK 58-59 LM 3
Bettyhill 119 DE 2
Betuensambang, Bukit — 152-153 K 5-6
Betūl 138-139 F 7
Betūl Bāzār 138-139 FG 7
Betung 152-153 E 6
Betvā = Betwa 134-135 M 6
Betwa 134-135 M 6
Beu, Serranía del — 104-105 BC 4
Beuharī = Beohāri 138-139 H 5
Beulah 61 H 5
Beulah, MI 70-71 G 3
Beulah, ND 68-69 EF 2
Beulah, OR 66-67 D 4
Beulah, WY 68-69 D 3
Beurkot 168-169 H 1
Beverley 119 F 5
Beverley, Lake — 58-59 H 7
Beverly, MA 72-73 L 3
Beverly, NJ 84 III d 1
Beverly, WA 66-67 D 2
Beverly, Chicago-, IL 83 II ab 2
Beverly Hills, CA 83 III b 1
Beverly Hills, Houston-, TX 85 III c 2
Beverly Hills, Sydney- 161 I a 2
Bexiga 106-107 L 2
Bexley, OH 72-73 E 4-5
Bexley, London- 129 II c 2
Bexley, Sydney- 161 I a 2
Beyābān, Kūh-e- 134-135 H 5
Beyce 136-137 C 3
Bey dağları 136-137 D 4
Beydili = Gerede 136-137 D 2
Bey el Kebir, Wadi — = Wādī Bey al-Kabīr 164-165 GH 2
Beykoz, İstanbul- 136-137 C 2
Beyla 164-165 C 7
Beylerbeyi, İstanbul- 154 I b 2
Beylikahır 136-137 D 3
Beyoğlu, İstanbul- 154 I a 2
Beypazarı 136-137 DE 2
Beypore [IND, place] 140 B 5
Beypore [IND, river] 140 BC 5
Beyrouth = Bayrūth 134-135 CD 4
Beyşehir 136-137 DE 4
Beyşehir gölü 134-135 C 3
Beyt = Okhā 134-135 K 6
Beytişebap = Elki 136-137 K 4
Bežeck 124-125 L 5
Bezerra, Rio — 100-101 A 7
Bezerros 100-101 G 5
Bežica, Br'ansk- 124-125 JK 7
Beziers 120-121 J 7
Bezons 129 I b 2
Bezwada = Vijayavādā 134-135 N 7
Bhabua 138-139 J 5
Bhachāu 138-139 C 6
Bhadaorā = Bhadaura 138-139 F 5
Bhadaura 138-139 F 5
Bhadohi 138-139 J 5
Bhādra [IND] 138-139 E 3
Bhādra [PAK] 138-139 A 3
Bhadrāchalam 140 E 2
Bhadrakh 134-135 O 6
Bhādran 138-139 D 6
Bhadra Reservoir 140 B 4
Bhadrāvati 140 B 4
Bhaeṅsdehi = Bhainsdehi 138-139 F 7
Bhāgalpur 134-135 O 5-6
Bhāgīrathi [IND, Uttar Pradesh] 138-139 G 2
Bhāgīrathi [IND, West Bengal] 138-139 M 5-6
Bhainsdehi 138-139 F 7
Bhainsrorgarh 138-139 E 5
Bhairabasingapura 138-139 J 8
Bhairab Bāzār 134-135 P 6
Bhaisa 138-139 FG 8
Bhālki 140 C 1
Bhamangarh 138-139 HJ 6
Bhamo = Banmau 148-149 C 2
Bhānbarāya 138-139 N 4
Bhandāra 134-135 MN 6
Bhandaria 138-139 JK 6
Bhānder 138-139 G 5
Bhānga 138-139 MN 6
Bhānpura 138-139 E 5
Bhānrer Range 138-139 GH 6
Bhānurpratāppur 138-139 H 7
Bhānvad 138-139 B 7
Bhaoṅgāṅv = Bhongaon 138-139 G 4
Bharatpur [IND, Madhya Pradesh] 138-139 H 6
Bharatpur [IND, Rājasthān] 134-135 M 5
Bhāreli 141 C 2
Bharthana 138-139 G 4
Bharuch 134-135 L 6
Bhaṭakal = Bhatkal 140 B 4
Bhātapāra 138-139 HJ 7
Bhātār 138-139 L 6
Bhāṭgāṅv = Bhātgaon 134-135 O 5
Bhatgaon 134-135 O 5
Bhatiapara Ghat = Bhāṭiyāpārā Ghāṭ 138-139 MN 6
Bhatinda 134-135 L 4
Bhāṭiyāpārā Ghāṭ 138-139 MN 6
Bhatkal 140 B 4
Bhāṭpāra 134-135 O 6
Bhātpur 154 II b 1
Bhattiprolu 140 E 2
Bhatu 138-139 E 3
Bhaunagar 134-135 L 6
Bhavāni [IND, place] 140 C 5
Bhavānī [IND, river] 140 C 5
Bhavānīpāṭnā = Bhawānipatna 134-135 N 7
Bhāvarī = Bhawāri 138-139 D 5
Bhawānipatna 134-135 N 7
Bhawāri 138-139 D 5
Bhelsā = Vidisha 134-135 M 6
Bheri 138-139 J 3
Bheri, Sāni — 138-139 J 3
Bhīkangāṅv = Bhikangaon 138-139 EF 7
Bhikangaon 138-139 EF 7
Bhiker = Bhōkar 138-139 F 8
Bhikhna 138-139 K 4
Bhilainagar 134-135 N 6
Bhilsa = Vidisha 134-135 M 6
Bhīlvāṛā = Bhīlwāra 138-139 E 5
Bhīlwāra 138-139 E 5
Bhīma 134-135 M 7
Bhīmāvaram 140 E 2
Bhind 138-139 G 4
Bhīnmāl 138-139 D 5
Bhīr 134-135 M 7
Bhivānī = Bhiwāni 134-135 M 5
Bhiwandi 138-139 D 8
Bhiwani 134-135 M 5
Bhognīpur 138-139 G 4
Bhograi 138-139 L 7
Bhojpur 138-139 L 4
Bhokar 138-139 F 8
Bhokardan 138-139 E 7
Bhokardhan = Bhokardan 138-139 E 7
Bhoker = Bhokar 138-139 F 8
Bholā 141 B 4
Bhongaon 138-139 G 4
Bhongir 140 D 2
Bhopāl 134-135 M 6
Bhor 134-135 L 7
Bhore 138-139 K 4
Bhowanipore, Calcutta- 154 II b 2
Bhuban 138-139 KL 7
Bhubana = Bhuban 138-139 KL 7
Bhubanēshvara = Bhubaneswar 134-135 O 6
Bhubeneswar 134-135 O 6
Bhuj 134-135 KL 6
Bhūm 140 B 1
Bhūrgāṅv 141 B 2
Bhurgaon = Bhurgāṅv 141 B 2
Bhusāvaḷ = Bhusāwal 134-135 M 6
Bhusāwal 134-135 M 6
Bhutan 134-135 OP 5
Bhuvanāgiri 140 DE 5
Bia [CI] 168-169 E 4
Bia, Phou — 150-151 D 3
Bia, Pu — = Phou Bia 150-151 D 3
Biá, Rio — 98-99 E 7
Bīābān, Kūh-e — = Kūh-e Beyābān 134-135 H 5
Biafra 164-165 F 7
Biak, Pulau — 148-149 L 7
Biała Podlaska 118 L 2-3
Białobrzegi 118 K 3
Białogard 118 GH 1-2
Białystok 118 L 2
Biankouma 168-169 CD 4
Biaora 138-139 F 6
Biar = Bihār 134-135 NO 6
Biar, Al-Jazā'ir-El — 170 I a 1
Biaro, Pulau — 148-149 J 6
Biarritz 120-121 G 7
Bias Bay = Daya Wan 146-147 E 10
Bias Fortes 102-103 KL 4
Biasso = Bissau 164-165 A 6
Bibā 173 B 3
Bibai 144-145 bc 2
Bibala 172 B 4
Bībān, Al- [DZ] 166-167 J 1
Bībān, Al- [TN] 166-167 M 3
Bībān, Bouḥeïret el — = Buḥayrat al-Bībān 166-167 M 3
Bībān, Buḥayrat al- 166-167 M 3
Bibans = Al-Bībān 166-167 J 1
Biberach 118 D 4
Bibiani 168-169 E 4
Bibile 140 E 7
Bibliān 96-97 B 3
Bic 63 B 3
Bicaner = Bīkaner 134-135 L 5
Bicas 102-103 L 4
Biche, Lac la — 61 BC 3
Bichhia 138-139 H 6
Bichi 168-169 H 2
Bickerdike 60 J 3
Bickerton Island 158-159 G 2
Bickleton, WA 66-67 CD 2
Bicknell, IN 70-71 G 6
Bicknell, UT 74-75 H 3
Bīḍ = Bhīr 134-135 M 7
Bid', Al- 173 D 3
Bida 164-165 F 7
Bīdar 134-135 M 7
Bidara = Bīdar 134-135 M 7
Biddeford, ME 64-65 MN 3
Biddle, MT 68-69 D 3
Bidele Depression = Djourab 164-165 H 5
Bidhūna 138-139 G 4
Bidor 150-151 C 10
Bi Doup 150-151 G 6
Bi Dup = Bi Doup 150-151 G 6
Bié = Kuito 172 C 4
Bieber 128 III b 1
Bieber, CA 66-67 C 5
Bieber, Offenbach- 128 III b 1
Biebrza 118 L 2
Biel 118 C 5
Bielawa 118 H 3
Bielefeld 118 D 2
Biele Karpaty 118 HJ 4
Biella 122-123 BC 3
Bielsko-Biała 118 J 4
Bielsk Podlaski 118 L 2
Bienfait 68-69 E 1
Biên Hoa 148-149 E 4
Bienne = Biel 118 C 5
Bienville, LA 78-79 C 4
Bienville, Lac — 56-57 W 6
Biesdorf, Berlin- 130 III c 1
Biesdorf-Süd, Berlin- 130 III c 2
Biesiesfontein 174-175 B 6
Biesiespoort 174-175 E 6
Biesjespoort = Biesiespoort 174-175 E 6
Bièvres 129 I b 2
Bifuka 144-145 c 1
Biğa 136-137 B 2
Bigadiç 136-137 C 3
Bigand 106-107 G 4
Big Arm, MT 66-67 FG 2
Big Baldy 66-67 F 3
Big Bar Creek 60 FG 4
Big Bay, MI 70-71 G 2
Big Bay de Noc 70-71 G 3
Big Beaver 68-69 D 1
Big Beaver Falls 62 K 2
Big Beaver House 62 DE 1
Big Bell 158-159 C 5
Big Belt Mountains 66-67 H 2
Big Bend, CA 66-67 C 5
Big Bend, CO 68-69 E 6
Big Bend National Park 64-65 F 6
Big Black River 78-79 D 4
Big Blue River 68-69 H 5-6
Big Canyon River 76-77 CD 7
Big Chino Wash 74-75 G 5
Big Coulee 61 B 3
Big Creek, ID 66-67 F 3
Big Creek [CDN] 60 F 4
Big Creek [USA] 68-69 FG 6
Big Cypress Indian Reservation 80-81 c 3
Big Cypress Swamp 80-81 c 3-4
Big Delta, AK 56-57 GH 5
Big Desert 160 E 5
Big Falls 66-67 E 1
Big Falls, MN 70-71 CD 1
Bigfork, MT 66-67 FG 1
Big Fork River 70-71 CD 2
Bigga 160 J 5
Biggar [CDN] 56-57 P 7
Biggs Island 158-159 DE 2
Biggs, OR 66-67 C 3
Bigha = Biğa 136-137 B 2
Big Hole River 66-67 G 3
Bighorn, MT 68-69 C 2
Bighorn Basin 68-69 B 3
Bighorn Lake 68-69 BC 3
Bighorn Mountains 64-65 E 2-3
Bighorn River 68-69 C 3
Bight of Benin 164-165 E 7-8
Big Island [CDN, Hudson Strait] 56-57 WX 5
Big Island [CDN, Lake of the Woods] 70-71 C 1
Big Koniuji Island 58-59 d 2
Big Lake 68-69 B 3
Big Lake, AK 58-59 N 3
Big Lake, TX 76-77 D 7
Big Lost River 66-67 G 4
Big Muddy Creek 68-69 D 1
Big Muddy River 70-71 F 6-7
Bignona 168-169 A 2
Bigobo 171 A 4
Bigot, Lac — 63 D 2
Bigou 168-169 F 3
Big Pine, CA 74-75 DE 4
Big Pine Key, FL 80-81 c 4
Big Piney, WY 66-67 HJ 4
Big Piney River 70-71 DE 7
Big Port Walter, AK 58-59 v 8
Biğrān 134-135 G 6
Big Rapids, MI 70-71 H 4
Big River [CDN, place] 61 E 4
Big River [CDN, river] 61 E 4
Big River [USA] 58-59 K 5
Big Sable Point 70-71 G 3
Big Salmon Range 56-57 K 5
Big Salmon River 58-59 U 6
Big Sand Lake 61 J 2
Big Sandy, MT 68-69 AB 1
Big Sandy, TN 78-79 EF 2
Big Sandy, TX 76-77 G 6
Big Sandy, WY 66-67 J 4
Big Sandy Creek 68-69 E 6
Big Sandy Lake [CDN] 61 F 3
Big Sandy Lake [USA] 70-71 D 2
Big Sandy River 74-75 G 5
Bigsby Island 70-71 C 1
Big Sioux River 68-69 H 4
Big Smoky Valley 74-75 E 3
Big Snowy Mountain 68-69 B 2
Big Spring, TX 64-65 F 5
Big Springs, ID 66-67 H 3
Big Squaw Lake = Chandalar, AK 58-59 NO 3
Big Stone City, SD 68-69 H 3
Big Stone Gap, VA 80-81 E 2
Bigstone Lake [CDN] 62 B 1
Big Stone Lake [USA] 68-69 H 3
Bigstone River 61 L 3

Big Sur, CA 74-75 BC 4
Big Timber, MT 66-67 J 3
Big Timber Creek 84 III c 2
Big Timber Creek South Branch 84 III c 3
Bigtrails, WY 68-69 C 4
Big Trout Lake [CDN, lake] 56-57 T 7
Big Trout Lake [CDN, place] 62 E 1
Biguaçu 102-103 H 7
Big Wells, TX 76-77 E 8
Big White Mountain 66-67 D 1
Big Wood River 66-67 F 4
Bihać 122-123 F 3
Bihār [IND, administrative unit] 134-135 NO 6
Bihār [IND, place] 134-135 O 6
Biharamulo 172 F 2
Bihāriganj 138-139 L 5
Bihor 122-123 K 2
Bihor, Munţii — 122-123 K 2
Bihoro 144-145 d 2
Bihta 138-139 K 5
Bihu 146-147 G 7
Bijagós, Arquipélago dos — 164-165 A 6
Bijaipur 138-139 F 4
Bijang 141 F 2
Bijaori = Bijauri 138-139 J 3
Bijāpur [IND, Karnataka] 134-135 LM 7
Bījāpur [IND, Madhya Pradesh] 140 E 1
Bijāpura = Bijāpur 134-135 LM 7
Bījār 134-135 F 3
Bijauri 138-139 J 3
Bijāvar = Bijāwar 138-139 G 5
Bijāwar 138-139 G 5
Bijāyah, Khalīj — 166-167 J 1
Bij-Chem = Bol'šoj Jenisej 132-133 S 7
Bijie 142-143 K 6
Bījistān = Bejestān 134-135 H 4
Bijlmermeer 128 I b 2
Bijnaor = Bijnor 138-139 G 3
Bijni 141 B 2
Bijnor 138-139 G 3
Bijnoṭ 134-135 L 5
Bijou Creek 68-69 D 5-6
Bijou Hills, SD 68-69 G 4
Bijrān 134-135 G 6
Bijsk 132-133 Q 7
Bikampur 138-139 D 4
Bīkaner 134-135 L 5
Bīkāpur 138-139 HJ 4
Bikin [SU, place] 132-133 Za 8
Bikin [SU, river] 132-133 a 8
Bikkavolu 140 EF 2
Bikkevels Mountains = Bokkeveldberge 174-175 C 6
Bikoro 172 C 2
Bikram 138-139 K 5
Bikramganj 138-139 K 5
Bilac 102-103 G 4
Bilagi = Bilgi 140 B 2
Bilāra 138-139 D 4
Bilāri 138-139 G 3
Bil'arsk 124-125 S 6
Bilāspur [IND, Himāchal Pradesh] 138-139 F 2
Bilāspur [IND, Madhya Pradesh] 134-135 N 6
Bilāspur [IND, Uttar Pradesh] 138-139 G 3
Bilati 171 B 3
Bilauktaung Range = Tanintharī Taungdan 150-151 B 5-6
Bilauri 138-139 H 3
Bilbao 120-121 F 7
Bilbays 173 B 2
Bildudalur 116-117 ab 2
Bileća 122-123 H 4
Bilecik 136-137 C 2
Bilgi 140 B 2
Bilgrām 138-139 H 4
Bilhaor = Bilhaur 138-139 GH 4
Bilhaur 138-139 GH 4
Bili [ZRE, place] 172 DE 1
Bili [ZRE, river] 172 DE 1
Bilibiza 171 E 6
Bilimora 138-139 D 7
Bilin [BUR] 141 E 7
Bilin Myit 141 E 7
Biliran Island 148-149 H 4
Bill, WY 68-69 D 4
Billbrook, Hamburg- 130 I b 1
Billefjord 116-117 k 5
Billings, MT 64-65 E 2
Billinsport, NJ 84 III b 2
Billiton = Pulau Belitung 148-149 E 7
Bill of Portland 119 EF 6
Billstedt, Hamburg- 130 I b 1
Billwerder Ausschlag, Hamburg- 130 I b 1
Bill Williams River 74-75 FG 5
Bilma 164-165 G 5
Bilma, Grand Erg de — 164-165 G 5
Biloela 158-159 K 4
Bilo gora 122-123 G 2-3
Biloli 140 C 1
Biloxi, MS 64-65 J 5
Bilqās 173 B 2
Bilqas Qism Auwal = Bilqās 173 B 2
Biltine 164-165 J 6
Bilugyn = Bilū Kyūn 148-149 C 3
Bilū Kyūn 148-149 C 3
Bimbéréké 164-165 E 6
Bimbila 168-169 F 3
Bimlipatam 134-135 M 7
Bīna [IND] 138-139 G 5
Bin Aḥmad 166-167 C 3
Binakā = Binka 138-139 J 7
Binalbagan 148-149 H 4
Bin al-Fraysāt 166-167 E 3
Bin al-Ghīadah 166-167 E 3
Binaria, Jakarta- 154 IV b 1
Bin Baṭāʾi = Ḥāssī Bin Baṭāʾi 166-167 AB 5
Bin Baṭāʾi, Ḥāssī — 166-167 AB 5
Binboğa 136-137 G 3
Bindki 138-139 H 4-5
Bindloe = Isla Marchena 92-93 AB 4
Binga, Mount — 172 F 5
Bin Ganīyah, Biʾr — 164-165 J 2
Bingara 160 K 2
Bingen 118 C 4
Binger, OK 76-77 E 5
Bingerville 168-169 DE 4
Bingham, ME 72-73 M 2
Bingham, NE 68-69 EF 4
Bingham, NM 76-77 A 6
Bingham Canyon, UT 66-67 GH 5
Binghamton, NY 64-65 LM 3
Bin Gharīr 164-165 C 2
Binghui = Tianchang 146-147 G 5
Bingkor 152-153 LM 3
Bingo Bay = Hiuchi-nada 144-145 J 5
Bingöl 134-135 E 3
Bingöl dağları 136-137 J 3
Bingwang 150-151 G 3
Binhai 146-147 GH 4-5
Binh Khê 150-151 G 6
Binh Liêu 150-151 F 2
Bin Ho'p = Ban Hin Heup 150-151 D 3
Binh So'n 150-151 G 5
Binh Thanh 150-151 G 6
Binī 141 D 2
Binjai 148-149 C 6
Binjharpur 138-139 L 7
Binjhārpura = Binjharpur 138-139 L 7
Bin Jiang 146-147 D 9-10
Binka 138-139 J 7
Binnaway 158-159 JK 6
Binongko, Pulau — 152-153 Q 8
Bin Qardān 166-167 M 3
Bin Rashīd 166-167 BC 3
Binscarth 61 H 5
Bin Sulīmān 166-167 C 3
Bintan, Pulau — 148-149 DE 6
Bintang, Gunung — 150-151 C 10
Bintaro, Jakarta- 154 IV a 2
Bintauna 152-153 P 5
Bin Ṭiyab 166-167 E 2
Bint Jubayl 136-137 F 6
Bintuhan 148-149 D 7
Bintulu 148-149 F 6
Bin Xian [TJ, Shaanxi] 146-147 AB 4
Bin Xian [TJ, Shandong] 146-147 FG 3
Binz, Zürich- 128 IV b 1
Binza 170 IV a 2
Binza, Kinshasa- 170 IV a 2
Binzart 164-165 FG 1
Binzart, Buḥayrat — 166-167 LM 1
Binzert = Binzart 164-165 FG 1
Biobío 106-107 AB 6
Bío Bío, Río — 111 B 5
Biograd 122-123 F 4
Bioko 164-165 F 8
Biola, CA 74-75 CD 4
Bionga 171 AB 3
Biorka, AK 58-59 no 4
Bioūgra = Bīūkrā 166-167 B 4
Bīpūr = Beypore 140 B 5
Biqāʿ, Al- 136-137 FG 5-6
Bīr = Bhīr 134-135 M 7
Bira 132-133 Z 8
Biʾr ʿAbd an-Nabī 136-137 B 8
Biʾr Abū Gharādiq 136-137 C 7
Biʾr Abū Minqār 164-165 K 3
Biʾr Abū Saʿfah 173 D 6
Biʾr Abū Zawal 173 C 4
Biʾr ad-Dīyāb, Al- 166-167 B 6
Biʾr adh-Dhahab 166-167 F 7
Biʾr adh-Dhikār 164-165 J 3
Birāk 164-165 G 3
Bir'akovo 124-125 N 4
Biʾr al-Abd 173 C 2
Biʾr al-ʿAjramīyah 173 BC 3
Biʾr al-Bayyūḍ 136-137 H 5
Biʾr al-Ghuzayl 166-167 M 5
Biʾr al-Ḥajāj 166-167 F 6
Biʾr al-Hamsah = Biʾr al-Khamsah 164-165 K 2
Biʾr al-Ḥaysī 173 D 3
Biʾr al-Ḥukayyim 164-165 J 2
Biʾr ʿAlī 134-135 F 8
Biʾr ʿAlī Bin Khalīfah 166-167 M 2
Biʾr al-ʿItir 166-167 KL 2
Biʾr al-Jadīd, Al- 166-167 B 3
Biʾr al-Jiḍāmī 173 C 4
Biʾr al-Khamsah 164-165 K 2
Biʾr al-Khamsha 164-165 K 2
Biʾr al-Mashāriqah 166-167 L 1
Biʾr al-Mulūṣī 136-137 J 6
Biʾr al-Mʾwīsāt 166-167 A 7
Biʾr al-Qaf 164-165 H 3
Biʾr al-Qirdʾan 166-167 A 7
Biʾr al Wādī 136-137 K 6
Biʾr Amāsīn 166-167 LM 5
Biʾr an-Naʿām 136-137 G 7
Biʾr Anzarān 164-165 B 4
Birao 164-165 J 6
Biʾr ʿAraiyiḍa = Biʾr ʿUrayyiḍah 173 BC 3
Birati, Dum Dum- 154 II b 2
Birāṭnagar 138-139 L 4
Biʾr Baydāʾ 173 CD 4
Bîr Beiḍa = Biʾr Baydāʾ 173 CD 4
Bîr Ben Gania = Biʾr Bin Ganīyah 164-165 J 2
Bīrbhūm 138-139 L 6
Biʾr Bin Ganīyah 164-165 J 2
Biʾr Btaymān 136-137 H 4
Birch Creek 58-59 P 3
Birch Creek, AK 58-59 P 3
Birches, AK 58-59 L 4
Birch Hills 61 F 4
Birchip 160 F 5
Birch Island [CDN, island] 61 J 4
Birch Island [CDN, place] 60 H 4
Birch Lake [CDN] 61 C 4
Birch Lake [USA] 70-71 E 2
Birchleigh 170 V c 1
Birch Mountains 56-57 O 6
Bir-Chouhada = Biʾr Shuhadāʾ 166-167 K 2
Birch Pond 84 I c 2
Birch Rapids 61 EF 3
Birch River [CDN, place] 61 H 4
Birch River [CDN, river] 61 B 2
Birchwil 128 IV b 1
Bird 61 L 2
Bird Cape 58-59 s 7
Bird City, KS 68-69 F 6
Bir Diab = Al-Biʾr ad-Dīyāb 166-167 B 6
Biʾr Dibis 164-165 K 4
Bird Island 58-59 cd 2
Bird Island, MN 70-71 C 3
Bird Island = Voëleiland 174-175 G 7
Bir Djedid = Biʾr Jadīd 166-167 K 3
Bir Djenèien = Janāʿin 166-167 LM 4
Birdsville 158-159 G 5
Birdum 158-159 F 3
Birecik 136-137 GH 4
Bir ed Dacar = Biʾr ad-Dhikār 164-165 J 3
Bir ed Deheb = Biʾr adh-Dhahab 166-167 F 7
Bir-el-Ater = Biʾr al-ʿItir 166-167 KL 2
Bir el Gar = Biʾr al-Qaf 164-165 H 3
Bir el Ghazeil = Biʾr al-Ghuzayl 166-167 M 5
Bir el Hadjaj = Biʾr al-Ḥajāj 166-167 F 6
Bîr el-Ḥeisî = Biʾr al-Ḥaysī 173 D 3
Bir el-Khamsa = Biʾr al-Khamsah 164-165 K 2
Birestik 136-137 GH 3
Biʾr Fatmah 136-137 K 5
Birganj 134-135 NO 5
Biʾr Ghabālū 166-167 H 1
Biʾr Ghallah 173 C 3
Biʾr Ghardan 166-167 K 2
Bir-Ghbalou = Biʾr Ghabālū 166-167 H 1
Bir Guerdane = Biʾr Ghardan 166-167 K 2
Biʾr Gulbān at-Ṭaiyārāt = Qulbān aṭ-Ṭayyārāt 136-137 JK 5
Biʾr Hābā 136-137 H 5
Bir Hacheim = Biʾr al-Ḥukayyim 164-165 J 2
Biʾr Hālidah 136-137 B 7
Birhan 164-165 M 6
Biʾr Ḥariz al-Faqī 166-167 M 4
Biʾr Ḥasmat ʿUmar 173 CD 7
Bîr Ḥismet ʿUmar = Biʾr Ḥasmat ʿUmar 173 CD 7
Biʾr Hooker 173 B 2
Bîr Ḥoumaïmâ = Biʾr Ḥumaymah 136-137 HJ 5
Biʾr Hûker = Biʾr Hooker 173 B 2
Biʾr Ḥumaymah 136-137 HJ 5
Birigui 92-93 J 9
Biril'ussy 132-133 QR 6
Birimşe 136-137 H 3
Biritinga 100-101 E 6
Biʾr Jadīd 166-167 K 3
Birjand 134-135 H 4
Birjant 166-167 EF 2-3
Bir Jdid Chavent = Al-Biʾr al-Jadīd 166-167 B 3
Birkah 166-167 G 6
Birkān 166-167 E 2
Birkat as-Saffāf 136-137 M 7
Birkat Hamad 136-137 KL 7
Birkat Qārūn 164-165 KL 3
Birkenhead 119 E 5
Birket-Fatmé 164-165 HJ 6
Birkhadem 170 I a 2
Bîr Khâlda = Biʾr Hālidah 136-137 B 7
Birkholz [DDR, Frankfurt] 130 III c 1
Birkholz [DDR, Potsdam] 130 III b 2
Birkholzaue 130 III c 1
Birkim 136-137 L 4
Biʾr Kusaybah 164-165 K 4
Bîrlad [RO, place] 122-123 M 2
Bîrlad [RO, river] 122-123 M 2-3
Bir Lehlû = Al-Biʾr al-Ahlū 166-167 B 6
Bir Lemouissate = Biʾr al-Mʾwīsāt 166-167 A 7
Birma 148-149 BC 2
Biʾr Majal 173 C 6
Birmandreïs, Al-Jazāʾir- 170 I a 2
Bir Mashash = Biʾr Mushāsh 136-137 G 7
Bir Mcherga = Biʾr al-Mashāriqah 166-167 L 1
Birmensdorf 128 IV a 1
Biʾr Miaws 173 D 6
Biʾr Mineiga = Biʾr Munayjah 173 D 6
Birmingham, AL 64-65 J 5
Birmingham [GB] 119 EF 5
Biʾr Misāḥah 164-165 K 4
Biʾr Mlayḥān 136-137 H 4
Biʾr Munayjah 173 D 6
Biʾr Murr 173 B 6
Biʾr Mushāsh 136-137 G 7
Biʾr Nābah 173 C 7
Biʾr Nāhid 136-137 C 7
Biʾr Nakhīlī 136-137 K 5
Biʾr Nakhlāy 173 B 6
Birney, MT 68-69 C 3
Birnie [CDN] 61 J 5
Birnie [Kiribati] 208 J 3
Birnin Gwari 168-169 G 3
Birnin Kebbi 164-165 EF 6
Birni-n'Konni 164-165 EF 6
Birnin Kudu 168-169 H 3
Bîr Nukheila = Nukhaylah 164-165 K 5
Birobidžan 132-133 Z 8
Birpur 138-139 L 4
Biʾr Qulayb 173 CD 5
Bîr Quleib = Biʾr Qulayb 173 CD 5
Birraḥhāl 166-167 K 1
Birrie River 160 H 2
Birrindudu 158-159 EF 3
Biʾr Sajarī 136-137 H 6
Biʾr Samāh 136-137 L 8
Biʾr Sararāt Sayyāl 173 D 6
Bîr Sejrî = Biʾr Sajarī 136-137 H 6
Biʾr Shināy 173 D 6
Biʾr Shuhadāʾ 166-167 K 2
Biʾr Sīf Fatimah 166-167 L 4
Birsilpur 138-139 D 3
Birsk 132-133 K 6
Birskij = Obluč'e 132-133 Z 8
Bîr Solṭān = Biʾr Sulṭān 166-167 L 3
Bir Soltane = Biʾr Soltān 166-167 L 3
Biʾr Sulṭān 166-167 L 3
Biʾr Tābah 173 D 3
Biʾr Takhlīs 173 AB 6
Biʾr Ṭamṭam 166-167 D 3
Bir Tangueur = Biʾr Tanqūr 166-167 L 4
Biʾr Tanqūr 166-167 L 4
Biʾr Ṭarfāwī 136-137 K 5
Biʾr Ṭarṭīn 136-137 J 5
Biʾr Tarūfāwī 136-137 K 6
Birtavarre 116-117 J 3
Biʾr Ṭawīl 164-165 L 4
Biʾr Tegherī 166-167 M 6
Biʾr Tifist 166-167 M 4
Birtle 61 H 5
Birtouta 170 I a 2
Biʾr Trafāwī 136-137 H 4
Bir Trefâouî = Biʾr Trafāwī 136-137 H 4
Bir'učij ostrov 126-127 G 3
Bir'ulovo, Moskva- 124-125 LM 6
Biʾr Umm Bishtīt 173 DE 6
Biʾr Umm Ḥibāl 173 C 6
Biʾr Umm Qarayn 164-165 B 3
Biʾr Umm Saʿīd 173 CD 3
Biruni 132-133 L 9
Birūr 140 B 4
Biʾr ʿUrayyiḍah 173 BC 3
Birūru = Birūr 140 B 4
Bir'usa 132-133 S 6
Birwāgīyah 166-167 H 1
Biryān 166-167 HJ 3
Biržai 124-125 E 5
Biʾr Zalfānah 166-167 HJ 3
Biʾr Zayb 136-137 K 6
Bir Zelfana = Biʾr Zalfānah 166-167 HJ 3
Bisa, Pulau — 148-149 J 7
Bisaliya, El — = Al-Basalīyat Qiblī 173 C 5
Bisaolī = Bisauli 138-139 G 3
Bisauli 138-139 G 3
Bisbee, AZ 74-75 HJ 7
Bisbee, ND 68-69 G 1
Biscay, Bay of — 114-115 GH 6
Biscayne Bay 80-81 c 4
Bisceglie 122-123 G 5
Bischofsheim 128 III b 1
Bischofshofen 118 F 5
Biscoe Islands 53 C 30
Biscotasing 62 KL 3
Biscra = Biskrah 164-165 F 2
Biscucuy 94-95 G 3
Biserovo 124-125 T 4
Biševo 122-123 F 4
Bīshah, Wādī — 134-135 E 6-7
Bishamkaṭaka = Bissamcuttack 138-139 J 8
Bīsheh, Istgah-e — 136-137 N 6
Bishenpur 134-135 P 6
Bishnāth 141 C 2
Bishnupur 138-139 L 6
Bishop, CA 74-75 D 4
Bishop, TX 76-77 F 9
Bishopville, SC 80-81 F 3
Bishrī, Jabal al- 136-137 H 5
Bishshāṭīr 166-167 L 1
Bisikon 128 IV b 1
Bisinaca 94-95 G 5
Biskayerhuken 116-117 hj 5
Biskotasi Lake 62 K 3
Biskrah 164-165 F 2
Bisling 148-149 J 5
Bismagar = Visnagar 138-139 D 6
Bismarck, MO 70-71 E 7
Bismarck, ND 64-65 F 2
Bismarck Archipelago 148-149 gh 5
Bismarckburg = Kasanga 172 F 3
Bismarck Range 148-149 M 7-N 8
Bismarck Sea 148-149 gh 5
Bismil 136-137 J 4
Bison, SD 68-69 E 3
Bisotūn 136-137 M 5
Bissagos Islands = Arquipélago dos Bijagós 164-165 A 6
Bissamcuttack 138-139 J 8
Bissau 164-165 A 6
Bissett 62 B 2
Bistcho Lake 56-57 N 6
Bistineau, Lake — 78-79 C 4
Bistōnis, Limnē — 122-123 L 5
Bistriţa [RO, place] 122-123 L 2
Bistriţa [RO, river] 122-123 M 2
Bisvān = Biswān 138-139 H 4
Biswān 138-139 H 4
Bitam 172 B 1
Bitca 113 V c 4
Bitely, MI 70-71 GH 4
Bitik 126-127 P 1
Bitlis 134-135 E 3
Bitlis dağları 136-137 JK 3
Bitola 122-123 J 5
Bitonto 122-123 G 5
Bitter Creek 66-67 J 5
Bitter Creek, WY 68-69 B 5
Bitterfeld 118 F 3
Bitterfontein 172 C 8
Bitterroot Range 64-65 C 2-D 3
Bitterroot River 66-67 F 2
Bittou 168-169 E 3
Bit'ug 126-127 K 1
Bitumount 61 C 2
Bitung 148-149 J 6
Bitupitá 100-101 D 2
Bituruna 102-103 G 7
Biu 164-165 G 6
Bīūkrā 166-167 B 4
Biu Plateau 168-169 HJ 3
Biviraka 148-149 M 8
Biwa-ko 142-143 Q 4
Biyāḍ, Al- = Al-Bayāḍ 134-135 F 6
Biyalā 173 B 2
Biyang 146-147 D 5
Biysk = Bijsk 132-133 Q 7
Bizana 174-175 HJ 6
Bižbul'ak 124-125 U 7
Bizcocho 106-107 J 4
Bizerta = Binzart 164-165 FG 1
Bizerte = Binzart 164-165 FG 1
Bjargtangar 116-117 a 2
Bjelovar 122-123 G 3
Bjelowo = Belovo 132-133 Q 7
Bjelucha = gora Beluchа 132-133 Q 8
Björkdale 61 F 4
Björkholmen 116-117 H 4
Björkö = Bol'šoj Ver'ozovyj ostrov 124-125 FG 3
Björkö = Primorsk 124-125 G 3
Björna 116-117 H 6
Björneborg = Pori 116-117 J 7
Bjuröklubb 116-117 JK 5
Bla 168-169 D 2
Blaauwberg = Blouberg 174-175 H 2
Blaauwkop = Bloukop 174-175 H 4
Blaauwpan 174-175 D 4
Black, AK 58-59 E 5
Blackall 158-159 HJ 4
Black Bay 70-71 F 1
Black Belt 64-65 J 5
Black Birch Lake 61 E 2
Blackburn 119 EF 5
Blackburn, Mount — 56-57 H 5
Black Butte 68-69 E 2
Black Canyon 74-75 F 5
Black Canyon of the Gunnison National Monument 68-69 C 6
Black Diamond 60 K 4
Black Diamond, WA 66-67 BC 2
Black Duck 56-57 ST 6
Black Eagle, MT 66-67 H 2
Blackfeet Indian Reservation 66-67 G 1
Blackfoot, ID 66-67 GH 4
Blackfoot, MT 66-67 G 1
Blackfoot Reservoir 66-67 H 4
Blackfoot River 66-67 G 2
Black Forest = Schwarzwald 118 D 4-5
Black Gobi = Char Gov' 142-143 GH 3
Black Hawk 62 C 3
Black Hills 64-65 F 3
Black Horse, PA 84 II a 2
Blackie 60 L 4
Black Island 62 A 2
Black Lake [CDN] 72-73 L 1-2
Black Lake [USA] 70-71 HJ 3
Black Lake [USA, Alaska] 58-59 d 1
Blackleaf, MT 66-67 G 1
Black Mbuluzi 174-175 J 4
Black Mesa 74-75 H 4
Black Mountain, NC 80-81 EF 3
Black Mountain [USA] 78-79 G 3
Black Mountains [USA] 64-65 D 4-5
Black Nossob = Swart Nossob 174-175 C 2
Black Pine Peak 66-67 G 4
Black Point 58-59 g 1
Blackpool [CDN] 60 G 4
Blackpool [GB] 119 E 5
Black Range 76-77 A 6
Black Rapids, AK 58-59 P 5
Black River, MI 72-73 E 2
Black River [CDN] 62 AB 2
Black River [USA < Henderson Bay] 72-73 J 3
Black River [USA < Mississippi River] 70-71 E 3
Black River [USA < Porcupine River] 58-59 Q 3
Black River [USA < Saint Clear River] 72-73 E 3
Black River [USA < Salt River] 74-75 HJ 6
Black River [USA < White River] 78-79 D 2-3
Black River = Sông Đa 148-149 D 2
Black River Falls, WI 70-71 E 3
Black Rock 111 H 8
Black Rock, AR 78-79 D 2
Black Rock, UT 74-75 G 3
Black Rock Desert 64-65 C 3
Blackrock Lake 85 II b 3
Blacksburg, VA 80-81 F 2
Black Sea 114-115 PQ 7
Blackshear, GA 80-81 EF 5
Black Springs, NM 74-75 J 6
Black Squirrel Creek 68-69 D 6
Blackstone, VA 80-81 GH 2
Black Sturgeon Lake 70-71 F 1
Black Umfolozi = Swart Umfolozi 174-175 J 4-5
Blackville 63 CD 4
Blackville, SC 80-81 F 4
Black Volta 164-165 D 7
Black Waxy Prairie 64-65 G 5
Blackwell, OK 76-77 F 4
Blackwell, TX 76-77 D 6
Blackwood, NJ 84 III c 3
Blackwood Terrace, NJ 84 III c 3
Bladensburg, MD 82 II b 1
Bladgrond 174-175 CD 5
Blåfjall 116-117 e 2
Blåfjorden 116-117 lm 5
Blagodarnoje 126-127 L 4
Blagodatnoje 126-127 G 3
Blagoevgrad 122-123 K 4-5
Blagoveščensk 132-133 YZ 7
Blagoveščenskij proliv 132-133 c 2-d 3
Blagoveščenskoje 124-125 O 3
Blagoveshchensk = Blagoveščensk 132-133 YZ 7
Blaine, WA 66-67 B 1
Blaine Lake 61 E 4
Blair, NE 68-69 H 5
Blair, OK 76-77 E 5
Blair, WI 70-71 E 3
Blair Athol 158-159 J 4
Blairbeth 174-175 G 3
Blairmore 66-67 F 1
Blairsden, CA 74-75 C 3
Blairsville, GA 80-81 DE 3
Blairsville, PA 72-73 G 4
Blakely, GA 78-79 G 5
Blake Point 70-71 F 1
Blambagan = Semenanjung Blambagan 152-153 L 10
Blanca, CO 68-69 D 7
Blanca Grande 106-107 G 6
Blanca Peak 64-65 E 4
Blanchard, LA 76-77 GH 6
Blanche, Lake — [AUS, South Australia] 158-159 GH 5
Blanche, Lake — [AUS, Western Australia] 158-159 D 4
Blanc-Mesnil, le — 129 I c 2
Blanco 174-175 E 7-8
Blanco, TX 76-77 E 7
Blanco Creek 76-77 C 5
Blancos, Los — [RA] 111 D 2
Blanc-Sablon 63 H 2
Blandá 116-117 d 2
Blanding, UT 74-75 J 4
Blaney 174-175 G 7
Blangkejeren 152-153 B 4
Blankaholm 116-117 FG 9
Blankenburg, Berlin- 130 III b 1
Blankenfelde, Berlin- 130 III b 1
Blanket, TX 76-77 E 7
Blanquillo 106-107 K 4
Blantyre 172 FG 5
Blao, Đeo- = Đeo Bao Lộc 150-151 F 7
Blaquier 106-107 F 5
Blauen [CH] 128 IV b 1
Blåvands Huk 116-117 BC 10
Blavet 120-121 F 4-5
Blaye 120-121 G 6
Blayney 158-159 J 6
Blaze, Point — 158-159 EF 2
Blazon, WY 66-67 H 5
Bleaker Island 108-109 K 9
Blednaja, gora — 132-133 M 2
Bledsoe, TX 76-77 C 6
Blejeşti 122-123 L 3
Blekinge län 116-117 F 9
Blenheim, NJ 84 III c 3
Blenheim [CDN] 72-73 F 3
Blenheim [NZ] 158-159 O 8
Blenque, Río — 96-97 B 2
Blessing, TX 76-77 F 8
Bleu Mountains 78-79 C 3
Blewett, TX 76-77 D 8
Blida = Blīdah 164-165 E 1
Blīdah [DZ, administrative unit] 170 I ab 2
Blīdah [DZ, place] 164-165 E 1
Blidet-Amor = Bulaydat ʿAmūr 166-167 J 3
Bikana 174-175 G 6
Blind River 62 K 3
Bliss, ID 66-67 F 4
Blissfield, MI 72-73 E 4
Blitar 148-149 F 8
Blitong = Pulau Belitung 148-149 E 7
Blitta 164-165 E 7
Blitzen, OR 66-67 D 4
Block Island 72-73 L 4
Block Island Sound 72-73 KL 4
Bloedrivier [ZA, place] 174-175 J 4
Bloedrivier [ZA, river] 174-175 J 4-5
Bloemfontein 172 E 7
Bloemhof 174-175 F 4
Bloemspruitrivier 174-175 G 4-5
Blois 120-121 H 5
Blomspruit = Bloemspruitrivier 174-175 G 4-5
Blönduós 116-117 cd 2
Blood Vein River [CDN, place] 61 K 5
Bloodvein River [CDN, river] 62 AB 2
Bloody Falls 56-57 NO 4
Bloomer, WI 70-71 E 3
Bloomfield, IA 70-71 D 5
Bloomfield, IN 70-71 G 6
Bloomfield, KY 70-71 H 7
Bloomfield, NE 68-69 H 4
Bloomfield, NJ 82 III a 2
Bloomfield, NM 74-75 JK 4
Bloomfield, New York-, NY 82 III ab 3
Blooming Prairie, MN 70-71 D 4
Bloomington, IL 64-65 HJ 3
Bloomington, IN 64-65 J 4
Bloomington, MN 70-71 D 3
Bloomington, TX 76-77 F 8
Bloomsburg, PA 72-73 H 4
Blora 152-153 J 9
Blosseville Kyst 56-57 ef 4
Blossom, mys — 132-133 jk 3
Blouberg [ZA, mountain] 174-175 H 2
Blouberg [ZA, place] 174-175 H 2
Bloukop 174-175 H 4
Blountstown, FL 78-79 G 5
Bloupan 174-175 C 6
Bloupan = Blaauwpan 174-175 D 4
Blouwberg = Blouberg 174-175 H 2
Bloxom, VA 80-81 J 2
Blūdān 136-137 G 6
Blue Bell Knoll 74-75 H 3
Blueberry 60 G 1
Blue Bonnets, Champ de Course — 82 I b 2
Bluecliff 174-175 F 7
Blue Creek, UT 66-67 G 5
Blue Earth, MN 70-71 CD 4
Bluefield, VA 80-81 F 2
Bluefield, WV 80-81 F 2
Bluefields 64-65 K 9
Bluefields, Bahía de — 88-89 E 8
Bluegrass Region 70-71 H 6
Blue Hill, NE 68-69 G 5
Blue Hills of Couteau 63 GH 4
Blue Hills Reservation 84 I b 3
Blue Island, IL 70-71 FG 5
Bluejoint Lake 66-67 D 4
Blue Knob 72-73 G 4
Blue Lake, CA 66-67 B 5
Blue Mosque 170 II b 1
Blue Mountain [BUR] 141 C 4
Blue Mountain [USA, Montana] 68-69 DE 2
Blue Mountain [USA, Pennsylvania] 72-73 HJ 4
Blue Mountain Pass 66-67 E 4
Blue Mountains [JA] 64-65 L 8
Blue Mountains [USA, Maine] 72-73 L 2
Blue Mountains [USA, Oregon] 64-65 C 2-3
Blue Mountains [USA, Texas] 76-77 E 7
Blue Mud Bay 158-159 G 2
Blue Mud Hills 68-69 D 3
Blue Nile = An-Nīl al-Azraq 164-165 L 6
Bluenose Lake 56-57 N 4
Blue Rapids, KS 68-69 H 6
Blue Ridge, GA 80-81 D 3
Blue Ridge [CDN] 60 K 2
Blue Ridge [USA, Alabama] 78-79 FG 4
Blue Ridge [USA, New York] 72-73 J 3
Blue Ridge [USA, North Carolina] 64-65 KL 4
Blueridge, Houston-, TX 85 III b 2
Blue River 74-75 J 6
Blue Springs, MO 70-71 CD 6
Bluewater, NM 74-75 JK 5
Bluff 158-159 N 9
Bluff, AK 58-59 F 4
Bluff, UT 74-75 J 4
Bluff, The — 88-89 H 2
Bluff Point 155 I b 2
Bluffs of Llano Estacado 76-77 C 5
Bluffton, IN 72-73 D 4
Bluffton, OH 72-73 E 4
Blufton, IN 70-71 H 5
Blum, TX 76-77 F 6
Blumenau [BR] 111 FG 3
Blumut, Gunung — 148-149 D 6
Blunt, SD 68-69 FG 3
Bly, OR 66-67 C 4
Blying Sound 58-59 N 7
Blyth [CDN] 72-73 F 3
Blythe, CA 74-75 F 6
Blytheville, AR 64-65 HJ 4
B. Mitre 110 III b 1
Bo [WAL] 164-165 B 7
Boa Água 100-101 E 3
Boaco 88-89 D 8
Boaçu 100-101 D 8
Boa Esperança [BR, Amazonas] 98-99 G 8
Boa Esperança [BR, Ceará] 100-101 D 3
Boa Esperança [BR, Espírito Santo] 100-101 DE 10
Boa Esperança [BR, Goiás] 100-101 A 8
Boa Esperança [BR, Minas Gerais] 102-103 K 4
Boa Esperança [BR, Piauí] 100-101 C 5
Boa Esperança [BR, Roraima] 94-95 L 6
Boa Esperança, Represa da — 100-101 B 4
Boa Esperança do Sul 102-103 H 4
Boa Fé 98-99 B 8
Boa Hora 98-99 G 10
Bo ʿai 146-147 D 4
Boajibu 168-169 C 3
Boakview 72-73 FG 2
Boali 164-165 H 8
Boame 174-175 K 4

Boa Morada 100-101 B 4
Boa Nova [BR, Bahia] 92-93 LM 7
Boa Nova [BR, Pará] 98-99 J 9
Boardman, OR 66-67 D 3
Boa Sorte, Rio — 100-101 B 7
Boath 138-139 G 8
Boa Viagem 100-101 E 3
Boa Vista [BR, Acre] 98-99 BC 9
Boa Vista [BR, Amazonas] 98-99 B 7
Boa Vista [BR, Roraima] 92-93 G 4
Boa Vista [Cape Verde] 204-205 E 7
Boa Vista, Morro da — 102-103 K 5
Boa Vista, Serra da — 100-101 EF 4
Boaz, AL 78-79 FG 3
Bobadah 160 H 4
Bobai 146-147 BC 10
Bobare 94-95 G 2
Bobbejaanskloofberge 174-175 EF 7
Bobbili 134-135 N 7
Bòbbio 122-123 C 3
Bobigny 129 I c 2
Bobo-Dioulasso 164-165 D 6
Bobo-Diulasso = Bobo-Dioulasso 164-165 D 6
Bobonaza, Río — 96-97 C 2
Bobonong 172 E 6
Bóbr 118 G 3
Bobrik 124-125 F 7
Bobriki = Novomoskovsk 124-125 M 6
Bobrinec 126-127 F 2
Bobrka 126-127 B 2
Bobrof Island 58-59 u 6-7
Bobrov 126-127 J 1
Bobrovica 126-127 E 1
Bobrovskoje 124-125 P 3
Bobrujsk 124-125 G 7
Bobures 94-95 F 3
Bocá, Buenos Aires- 110 III b 1
Boca, Cachoeira da — 98-99 L 7
Boca, La — 64-65 b 3
Boca Araguao 94-95 L 3
Boca da Estrada 94-95 L 6
Boca de Arichuna 94-95 H 4
Boca de Aroa 94-95 GH 2
Boca de Jesus María 86-87 M 5
Boca de la Serpiente 92-93 G 2-3
Boca de la Travesía 108-109 GH 3
Boca del Pao 92-93 FG 3
Boca del Río 86-87 MN 8
Boca del Tocuyo 94-95 GH 2
Boca de Macareo 94-95 L 3
Boca de Pozo 94-95 J 2
Boca do Acre 92-93 F 6
Boca do Jari 92-93 J 5
Boca do Mato, Rio de Janeiro- 110 I b 2
Boca do Mutum 98-99 DE 7
Boca do Tapauá = Tapauá 92-93 FG 6
Boca Grande 94-95 L 3
Boca Grande, FL 80-81 b 3
Bocaina 102-103 H 5
Bocaina, Serra da — 102-103 GH 7-8
Bocaiuva 92-93 L 8
Bocaiuva do Sul 102-103 H 6
Bocajá 102-103 E 5
Boca Mavaca 94-95 J 6
Bocanda 168-169 DE 4
Bocaranga 164-165 H 7
Boca Raton, FL 80-81 cd 3
Bocas 86-87 K 6
Boca Santa María 86-87 M 5
Bocas de Caraparaná 94-95 E 8
Bocas del Dragon 94-95 L 2
Bocas del Toro 88-89 E 10
Bocas del Toro, Archipiélago de — 88-89 EF 10
Bocche di Bonifàcio 122-123 C 5
Bochina 118 K 4
Bochinche 94-95 L 4
Bocholt 118 C 3
Bochum 118 C 3
Bockenheim, Frankfurt am Main- 128 III a 1
Boconito 94-95 FG 3
Bocono 94-95 F 3
Boconó, Río — 94-95 G 3
Boçoroca 100-101 D 5
Boda [RCA] 164-165 H 8
Böda [S] 116-117 G 9
Bodajbo 132-133 VW 6
Bodega Head 74-75 B 3
Bodelé 164-165 H 5
Boden 116-117 JK 5
Bodensee 118 D 5
Bodhan 140 CD 1
Bodināyakkanūr 140 C 6
Bodo [CDN] 61 C 4
Bodø [N] 116-117 EF 4
Bodocó 100-101 E 4
Bodogodo = Badagada 138-139 K 8
Bodoquena 92-93 H 8
Bodoquena, Serra — 92-93 H 9
Bodrum 136-137 B 4
Bô Đu'c 150-151 F 6-7
Bod Zizhiqu 141 BC 1
Boekittingi = Bukittingi 148-149 CD 7
Boende 172 D 2
Boerne, TX 76-77 E 8
Boesakrivier 174-175 E 6
Boesakspruit = Boesakrivier 174-175 E 6
Boezak River = Boesakrivier 174-175 E 6
Bofete 102-103 H 5
Boffa 164-165 B 6
Bōfu = Hōfu 144-145 H 5-6
Bogale 141 D 7
Bogalusa, LA 64-65 HJ 5
Bogandé 164-165 DE 6
Bogan Gate 160 H 4
Bogan River 158-159 J 6
Bogarnes 116-117 bc 2
Bogata, TX 76-77 G 6
Bogatka 124-125 OP 2
Bogatoje 124-125 S 7
Bogatyje Saby 124-125 S 6
Boğazkale 136-137 F 2-3
Boğazköprü 136-137 F 3
Boğazlıyan 136-137 F 3
Bogd 142-143 J 2
Bogdanovka 124-125 T 7
Bogdo uul 142-143 FG 3
Bogenfels 174-175 A 4
Bogenhausen, München- 130 II b 2
Boget 126-127 NO 2
Boggabilla 158-159 JK 5
Boggabri 160 JK 3
Boggai, Lak — 171 D 2
Bogham, Al- 136-137 J 5
Boghari = Qasr al-Bukharī 164-165 E 1
Bogia 148-149 MN 7
Boğlan 136-137 J 3
Bogo [RP] 148-149 H 4
Bogoduchov 126-127 G 1
Bogol'ubovo [SU, Smolenskaja Oblast'] 124-125 J 6
Bogong, Mount — 158-159 J 7
Bogor 148-149 E 8
Bogorā 138-139 M 5
Bogorodick 124-125 LM 7
Bogorodsk [SU, Gor'kovskaja Oblast'] 124-125 O 5
Bogorodsk [SU, Komi ASSR] 124-125 ST 2
Bogorodskoje [SU, Kirovskaja Oblast'] 124-125 S 5
Bogorodskoje, Moskva- 113 V cd 2
Bogoslof Island 58-59 m 4
Bogotá 92-93 E 4
Bogota, NJ 82 III b 1
Bogotá, Río — 91 III b 1
Bogotá-Alqueria 91 III b 3
Bogotá-Bavaria 91 III b 3
Bogotá-Boyaca 91 III b 2
Bogotá-Ciudad Universitaria 91 III bc 3
Bogotá-El Encanto 91 III b 4
Bogotá-El Prado 91 III c 2
Bogotá-El Rocio 91 III bc 3-4
Bogotá-El Tunal 91 III b 4
Bogotá-Fatima 91 III b 3
Bogotá-Granjas de Techo 91 III b 3
Bogotá-Ingles 91 III b 4
Bogotá-La Esperanza 91 III c 3
Bogotá-La Granja 91 III b 2
Bogotá-Las Acacias 91 III b 4
Bogotá-Las Ferias 91 III b 2
Bogotá-México 91 III b 4
Bogotá-Minuto de Dios 91 III b 2
Bogotá-Navarra 91 III c 2
Bogotá-Pastrana 91 III ab 3
Bogotá-Quirigua 91 III b 2
Bogotá-Restrepo 91 III b 3
Bogotá-Ricaurte 91 III b 3
Bogotá-San Fernando 91 III c 2
Bogotá-San Pablo 91 III a 2
Bogotá-San Rafael 91 III b 4
Bogotá-Tunjuelito 91 III b 4
Bogotol 132-133 Q 6
Bogou 168-169 F 3
Bogovarovo 124-125 Q 4
Bogra = Bogorā 138-139 M 5
Bogučany 132-133 S 6
Bogučar 126-127 K 2
Boguševsk 124-125 H 6
Boguslav 126-127 E 2
Bogyi Ywa = Bôlkyīywā 150-151 A 5
Bo Hai 142-143 M 4
Bohai Haixia 142-143 N 4
Bohai Wan 146-147 FG 2
Bohemian Forest 118 F 4
Bohemian Forest = Böhmerwald 118 FG 4
Bohemian-Moravian Height = Českomoravská vrchovina 118 GH 4
Bohnsdorf, Berlin- 130 III c 2
Bohol 148-149 H 5
Bo Hu = Po Hu 146-147 F 6
Boi, Ponta do — 102-103 K 6
Boiaçu 98-99 H 5
Boibeïs, Límnē — 122-123 K 6
Boicovo 104-105 E 7
Boigu Island 148-149 M 8
Boim 92-93 H 5
Boipārīguḍā 140 F 1
Boi Preto, Serra do — 102-103 F 6
Bois, Lac des — 56-57 M 4
Bois, Rio dos — 102-103 G 3
Bois Blanc Island 70-71 HJ 3
Bois-d'Arcy 129 I b 2
Boise City, ID 64-65 G 3
Boise City, OK 76-77 C 4
Boise River 66-67 E 4
Bois le Duc = 's-Hertogenbosch 120-121 KL 3
Bois Notre-Dame 129 I d 2
Boissevain 68-69 FG 1
Boissy-Saint-Léger 129 I d 2
Boituva 102-103 J 5
Bojador, Cabo — = Rā's Bujdūr 164-165 AB 3
Bojarka 132-133 S 3
Bojnūrd 134-135 H 3
Bojonegoro 152-153 JK 9
Boju = Baiju 146-147 H 5
Bojuru 111 F 4
Bojuru, Ponta — 106-107 M 3
Bokani 168-169 G 3
Bokāro 138-139 K 6
Boké 164-165 B 6
Bo Kham 150-151 F 6
Bô Kheo 150-151 F 6
Bokkeveldberge 174-175 C 6
Bokkol 171 D 2
Bokkraal 174-175 C 6
Boknfjord 116-117 A 8
Boko 141 B 3
Bokong 174-175 H 5
Bokor 150-151 DE 7
Bokoro 164-165 H 6
Bokote 172 D 1-2
Bokoto 168-169 F 3
Bokovskaja 126-127 K 2
Bôkpyin 150-151 B 7
Boksburg 174-175 H 4
Boksburg North 170 V c 2
Boksitogorsk 124-125 J 4
Bokungu 172 D 2
Bolaiti 172 DE 2
Bolama 164-165 A 6
Bolān, Kotal — 134-135 K 5
Bolangir = Balāngīr 134-135 N 6
Bolan Pass = Kotal Bolān 134-135 K 5
Bólbē, Límnē — 122-123 K 6
Bolbec 120-121 H 4
Bolchov 124-125 KL 7
Bole 164-165 D 7
Bole, MT 66-67 GH 2
Bolechov 126-127 AB 2
Boles, ID 66-67 E 3
Bolesławiec 118 GH 3
Bolgatanga 164-165 D 6
Bolger 62 N 2
Bolgrad 126-127 D 4
Boli [TJ] 142-143 P 2
Boli [ZRE] 171 B 2
Boliden 116-117 J 5
Boligee, AL 78-79 E 4
Boling, TX 76-77 FG 8
Bolissós 122-123 L 6
Bolivar, MO 70-71 D 7
Bolivar, TN 78-79 E 3
Bolívar [CO, Antioquia] 94-95 CD 5
Bolívar [CO, Armenia] 94-95 C 5
Bolívar [CO, Bolívar] 94-95 D 3
Bolívar [CO, Popayán] 94-95 C 7
Bolívar [EC] 96-97 B 1
Bolívar [PE] 92-93 D 6
Bolívar [YV] 94-95 JK 4
Bolívar, Pico — 92-93 E 3
Bolivar Peninsula 76-77 G 8
Bolivia 92-93 F-H 8
Bolkar dağları 136-137 F 4
Bolkow [CDN] 70-71 J 1
Bôlkyīywā 150-151 A 5
Bollebeek 128 II a 1
Bolling Air Force Base 82 II ab 2
Bollnäs 116-117 G 7
Bollon 158-159 J 5
Bolnisi 126-127 M 6
Bolobo 172 C 2
Bolochovo 124-125 LM 6
Bologhine Ibnou Ziri, Al-Jazā'ir- 170 I a 1
Bologna 122-123 D 3
Bolognesi [BR] 96-97 E 5
Bolognesi [PE] 96-97 D 7
Bologoje 132-133 EF 6
Bologovo 124-125 H 5
Bolomba 172 C 1
Bolor = Bāltistān 134-135 M 3-4
Bolo-retto = Penghu Lieh-tao 142-143 M 7
Bólos 122-123 K 6
Bolotnoje 132-133 P 6
Boloven, Cao Nguyên — 148-149 E 3-4
Bolpur 138-139 L 6
Bolsa, Cerro — 106-107 C 2
Bol'šaja — = Velikaja 132-133 h 5
Bol'šaja Černigovka 124-125 S 7
Bol'šaja Kinel' 124-125 T 7
Bol'šaja Kokšaga 124-125 Q 5
Bol'šaja L'ovgora 124-125 L 2
Bol'šaja Martynovka 126-127 KL 3
Bol'šaja Orlovka 126-127 K 3
Bol'šaja Sosnova 124-125 U 5
Bol'šaja Usa 124-125 U 5
Bol'šaja Višera 124-125 J 4
Bol'šaja Vys' 126-127 E 2
Bol'šekrepinskaja 126-127 JK 3
Bol'šelug 124-125 T 2
Bolsena, Lago di — 122-123 DE 4
Bol'ševik, ostrov — 132-133 T-V 2
Bol'šezemel'skaja tundra 132-133 JK 4
Bolshevik = ostrov Bol'ševik 132-133 T-V 2
Bol'šije Abuli, gora — 126-127 LM 6
Bol'šije Doldy 124-125 UV 3
Bol'šije Ozerki [SU, Archangel'skaja Oblast'] 124-125 MN 2
Bol'šije Uki 132-133 N 6
Bol'šinka 126-127 K 2
Bol'šoj An'uj 132-133 fg 4
Bol'šoj Čeremšan 124-125 S 6
Bol'šoje Muraškino 124-125 P 6
Bol'šoj Irgiz 124-125 R 8
Bol'šoj Jenisej 132-133 S 7
Bol'šoj Klimeckij, ostrov — 124-125 KL 3
Bol'šoj Oloj = Oloj 132-133 f 4
Bol'šoj Šantar, ostrov — 132-133 ab 7
Bol'šoj Teatr 113 V c 2
Bol'šoj T'uters, ostrov — 124-125 FG 4
Bol'šoj Uluj 132-133 R 6
Bol'šoj Uzen' 126-127 O 2
Bol'šoj Ver'ozovyj, ostrov — 124-125 FG 3
Bolsón, El — 108-109 D 3
Bolsón de Mapimí 64-65 F 6
Bolton 119 E 5
Bolton, NC 80-81 G 3
Bolton, Atlanta-, GA 85 II b 1
Bolu 136-137 D 2
Bo Luang 150-151 B 3
Bolukābād 136-137 M 4
Bolungarvík 116-117 ab 1
Boluo 146-147 E 10
Bolvadin 136-137 D 3
Bolzano 122-123 D 2
Boma 172 B 3
Boma, Gulf of — = Khalīj al-Bunbah 164-165 JK 2
Bomadi 168-169 G 4
Bomarton, TX 76-77 E 6
Bomba 100-101 A 8
Bómba, Khalig — = Khalīj al-Bunbah 164-165 J 2
Bomba, La — 86-87 C 2
Bombaim = Bombay 134-135 L 7
Bombala 158-159 JK 7
Bombarai 148-149 K 7
Bombay 134-135 L 7
Bombetoka, Baie de — 172 HJ 5
Bombo 171 C 2
Bom Comércio 92-93 F 6
Bom Conselho 100-101 F 5
Bom Despacho 92-93 KL 8
Bomdila 141 C 2
Bom Futuro 98-99 H 10
Bomi Hills 164-165 B 7
Bom Jesus [BR, Piauí] 92-93 L 6
Bom Jesus [BR, Rio Grande do Sul] 106-107 M 2
Bom Jesus da Gurguéia, Serra — 92-93 L 6-7
Bom Jesus da Lapa 92-93 L 7
Bom Jesus do Galho 102-103 LM 3
Bom Jesus do Norte 102-103 M 4
Bømlafjord 116-117 A 8
Bømlo 116-117 A 8
Bommersheim 128 III a 1
Bomokandi 172 E 1
Bomongo 172 C 1
Bom Princípio 100-101 D 2
Bom Retiro 102-103 H 7
Bom Retiro, São Paulo- 110 II b 2
Bom Sossêgo 100-101 C 7
Bom Sucesso 102-103 K 4
Bom Sucesso, Serra — 102-103 KL 1
Bom Sucessu 102-103 FG 5
Bomu 172 D 1
Bon, Cap — = Rā' aṭ-Ṭīh 164-165 G 1
Bona = Annābah 164-165 F 1
Bona, Mount — 58-59 QR 6
Bonāb [IR ↖ Tabrīz] 136-137 LM 3
Bonāb [IR ↙ Tabrīz] 136-137 M 4
Bon Accord 174-175 H 3
Bonai = Banāī 138-139 K 7
Bonaigarh 138-139 K 7
Bon Air, PA 84 III b 2
Bonaire 64-65 N 9
Bonames, Frankfurt am Main- 128 III ab 1
Bonampak 86-87 P 9
Bonanza 88-89 D 8
Bonanza, ID 66-67 F 3
Bonaparte 96-97 D 5
Bonaparte, Mount — 66-67 D 1
Bonaparte Archipelago 158-159 DE 2
Bonasila Dome 58-59 G 5
Bonasse 94-95 L 2
Bonaventura 63 D 3
Bonavista 56-57 a 8
Bonavista Bay 63 K 3
Bon Bon 160 BC 3
Bond, CO 68-69 C 6
Bondari 124-125 O 7
Bondelswarts Reserve 174-175 C 4-5
Bondeno 122-123 D 3
Bond Hill 160 B 3
Bondi Bay 161 I b 2
Bondiss 60 L 2
Bondo [ZRE] 172 D 1
Bondoc Peninsula 148-149 H 4
Bondoukou 164-165 D 7
Bondowoso 152-153 KL 9
Bond'ug 124-125 U 3
Bondurant, WY 66-67 HJ 4
Bond'užskij 124-125 T 6
Bondy 129 I c 2
Bone 152-153 P 8
Bône = Annābah 164-165 F 1
Bone = Watampone 148-149 GH 7
Bone, Teluk — 148-149 H 7
Bonelipu 152-153 P 8
Bonelohe 152-153 O 8
Boneogeh 152-153 O 9
Bonerate, Pulau — 152-153 O 9
Bonete, Cerro — 106-107 C 1
Bonfield 72-73 G 1
Bonfim [BR, Amazonas] 96-97 E 6
Bonfim [BR, Gerais] 102-103 K 4
Bonfinópolis de Minas 102-103 JK 2
Bong [LB, administrative unit] 168-169 C 4
Bong [LB, place] 168-169 C 4
Bonga 164-165 M 7
Bongandanga 172 D 1
Bongāṅv = Bangaon 138-139 M 6
Bongaon = Bangaon 138-139 M 6
Bongchhung 138-139 L 3
Bongo 172 AB 2
Bongolave 172 J 5
Bongor 164-165 H 6
Bongouanou 168-169 DE 4
Bongtol 138-139 HJ 2
Bonham, TX 76-77 F 6
Bonhu 100-101 E 3
Boni, Gulf of — = Teluk Bone 148-149 H 7
Bonibaou 168-169 J 4
Bonifacio 122-123 C 5
Bonifàcio, Bocche di — 122-123 C 5
Bonifay, FL 78-79 G 5
Bonilla, SD 68-69 G 3
Bonin 206-207 RS 7
Boninal 100-101 D 7
Bonin Trench 156-157 G 3
Bonita, AZ 74-75 HJ 6
Bonita, La — 96-97 C 1
Bonita, Point — 83 I a 2
Bonitas, Las — 92-93 FG 3
Bonito [BR, Mato Grosso do Sul] 102-103 D 4
Bonito [BR, Minas Gerais] 102-103 K 1
Bonito [BR, Pernambuco] 100-101 G 5
Bonn 118 C 3
Bonne Bay 63 H 2
Bonner, MT 66-67 G 2
Bonners Ferry, ID 66-67 E 1
Bonner Springs, KS 70-71 C 6
Bonne Terre, MO 70-71 E 7
Bonneuil-en-France 129 I c 2
Bonneuil-sur-Marne 129 I c 2
Bonneville, OR 66-67 C 3
Bonneville, WY 68-69 BC 4
Bonneville Salt Flats 66-67 G 5
Bonnie Rock 158-159 C 6
Bonnievale 174-175 CD 7
Bönningstedt 130 I a 1
Bonny 164-165 F 8
Bonny, Golfe de — 164-165 F 8
Bonny Reservoir 68-69 E 6
Bonnyville 56-57 O 7
Bono, AR 78-79 D 3
Bō-no misaki 144-145 GH 7
Bonoua 168-169 E 4
Bonpland 106-107 J 2
Bonstetten 128 IV a 2
Bonsucesso, Rio de Janeiro- 110 I b 2
Bont = Banta 138-139 L 7
Bontang 152-153 M 5
Bonthe 164-165 B 7
Bontongssunggu 148-149 G 8
Bontongsunggu 152-153 N 8-9
Bon Wier, TX 78-79 C 5
Bookabie 158-159 F 6
Bookaloo 158-159 G 6
Booker, TX 76-77 D 4
Book Plateau = Roan Plateau 68-69 B 6
Booligal 158-159 H 6
Boomrivier 174-175 D 5
Boonah 160 L 1-2
Böön Cagaan nuur 142-143 HJ 2
Boone, CO 68-69 D 6
Boone, IA 70-71 CD 4
Boone, NC 80-81 F 2
Booneville, AR 76-77 GH 5
Booneville, KY 72-73 E 6
Booneville, MS 78-79 E 3
Boons 174-175 G 3
Boonville, IN 70-71 G 6
Boonville, MO 70-71 D 6
Boonville, NY 72-73 J 3
Boopi, Río — 104-105 C 5
Booramo 164-165 a 2
Boosaaso 164-165 bc 1
Boothbay Harbor, ME 72-73 M 3
Boothby, Cape — 53 C 6-7
Boothia, Gulf of — 56-57 ST 3-4
Boothia Isthmus 56-57 S 4
Boothia Peninsula 56-57 RS 3
Boothwyn, PA 84 III a 3
Booué 172 B 1-2
Boowagendrift = Bo-Wadrif 174-175 CD 7
Booysens, Johannesburg- 170 V ab 2
Boping 146-147 F 3
Boping Ling 146-147 F 9
Boppelsen 128 IV a 1
Boqueirão [BR, Bahia ↘ Jataí] 100-101 AB 7
Boqueirão [BR, Bahia ↙ Xiquexique] 100-101 BC 6
Boqueirão [BR, Rio Grande do Sul] 111 F 4
Boqueirão, Serra do — [BR, Bahia] 92-93 L 7
Boqueirão, Serra do — [BR, Pernambuco] 100-101 F 5
Boqueirão, Serra do — [BR, Piauí] 100-101 C 4
Boqueirão, Serra do — [BR, Rio Grande do Sul] 106-107 K 2
Boqueirão dos Cochos 100-101 E 4
Boquerón [PY] 102-103 BC 4
Boqueron [YV] 94-95 K 3
Boquerón, Túnel — 91 II ab 1
Boquilla del Conchos 86-87 H 4
Boquillas del Carmen 86-87 J 3
Boquira 100-101 C 7
Bor [SU] 124-125 P 5
Bor [TR] 136-137 F 4
Bor [YU] 122-123 K 3
Bōr = Būr 164-165 L 7
Bor, Lak — 172 G 1
Borabu 150-151 D 4-5
Boracho Peak 76-77 B 7
Borah Peak 64-65 D 3
Borai 138-139 HJ 7
Borāri 138-139 L 5
Borås 116-117 E 9
Borāzjān 134-135 G 5
Borba [BR] 92-93 H 5
Borbón, Isla de — = Pebble Island 108-109 K 8
Borborema 102-103 H 4
Borborema, Planalto da — 92-93 M 6
Bor Chadyn uul 142-143 EF 3
Bor Choro uul 142-143 E 3
Borçka = Yeniyol 136-137 JK 2
Borcu = Borkou 164-165 H 5
Borda da Mata 102-103 JK 5
Bordareno 94-95 F 5
Borde Alto del Payún 106-107 C 6
Bordeaux [F] 120-121 G 6
Bordeaux [ZA] 170 V ab 1
Bordeaux, Montréal- 82 I ab 1
Bordenave 106-107 F 6
Borden Island 56-57 NO 2
Borden Peninsula 56-57 U 3
Border 174-175 F 4
Bordertown 160 E 6
Bordighera 122-123 BC 4
Bordj-bou-Arréridj = Burj Bū 'Arīrij 166-167 J 1
Bordj Boûrguîba = Burj Būrgībah 166-167 LM 3
Bordj-de-Chegga = Shaqqah 166-167 JK 2
Bordj-de-Stil = Saṭīl 166-167 J 2
Bordj el Bahri 170 I b 1
Bordj el Bahri, Cap de — 170 I b 1
Bordj-el-Hamraïa = Burj al-Khamīrah 166-167 K 2
Bordj el Kiffan 170 I b 2
Bordj-Flye-Sainte-Marie = Burj Falāy 166-167 E 6
Bordj-Maïa = Al-Māyah 166-167 G 3
Bordj-Messouda = Burj Mas'ūdah 166-167 L 4
Bordj-Taguine = Tāḥīn 166-167 H 2
Bordj-Tarat 166-167 L 6
Bordj-Welvert = 'Ayn al-Ḥajal 166-167 H 2
Bordo, El — = Patía 94-95 C 6
Bordzongijn Gov' 142-143 K 3
Bóreioi Sporádes 122-123 KL 6
Bóreiron Stenòn Kerkýras 122-123 HJ 6
Borel 102-103 G 8
Borgå 116-117 LM 7
Borgampād 140 E 2
Borgarfjardhar 116-117 c 2
Børgefjell 116-117 EF 5
Borger, TX 64-65 F 4
Borges 110 III b 1
Borghese, Villa — 113 II b 1-2
Borgholm 116-117 G 9
Borgne, Lake — 78-79 E 5-6
Borgomanero 122-123 BC 3
Borgou 168-169 F 3
Borgsdorf/Nordbahn 130 III b 1
Borgu 168-169 FG 3
Bōrhāz Jbel Ṭāroq = Bughāz Jabal Ṭāriq 164-165 CD 1
Bori 138-139 G 7
Borikhane 150-151 DE 3
Borinskoje 124-125 M 7
Borio 138-139 L 5
Borislav 126-127 A 2
Borisoglebsk 126-127 KL 1
Borisoglebskij 124-125 M 5
Borisov 124-125 G 6
Borisova, mys — 132-133 a 6
Borisovka 126-127 GH 1
Borisovo, Moskva- 113 V cd 3
Borisovo-Sudskoje 124-125 KL 4
Borispol' 126-127 E 1
Bōriyō = Borio 138-139 L 5
Borja [PE] 92-93 D 5
Borja [PY] 102-103 D 6
Borj es Sedra = 'Uqlat Ṣudrā' 166-167 E 3
Borkhaya Bay = guba Buor-Chaja 132-133 Z 3
B'ork'o = Primorsk 124-125 G 3
Borkou 164-165 H 5
Borku = Borkou 164-165 H 5
Borlänge 116-117 FG 7
Borlu 136-137 C 3
Bòrmida 122-123 C 3
Bornemouth 119 F 6
Borneo = Kalimantan 148-149 F 7-G 6
Bornholm 116-117 F 10
Börnicke [DDR, Frankfurt] 130 III c 1
Bornim, Potsdam- 130 III a 2
Borno [WAN] 164-165 G 6
Bornou = Borno 164-165 G 6
Bornstedt, Potsdam- 130 III a 2
Bornu = Borno 164-165 G 6
Borogoncy 132-133 Z 5
Borojó 94-95 F 2
Boroko 152-153 P 5
B'or'ol'och = Susuman 132-133 cd 5
Boromo 168-169 E 3
Boron, CA 74-75 E 5
Borough Park, New York-, NY 82 III bc 3
Boroûj, el — = Al-Burūj 166-167 C 3
Borovaja 126-127 HJ 2
Borovica 124-125 R 4
Boroviči 132-133 EF 6
Borovl'anka 132-133 P 7
Borovoj 124-125 S 4
Borovsk 124-125 L 6
Borovskoj 132-133 LM 7
Borrazópolis 102-103 G 5
Borroloola 158-159 G 3
Borša 122-123 L 2
Borsad 138-139 D 6
Boršč'ov 126-127 C 2
Borščovočnyj chrebet 132-133 W 7
Bortala Monggol Zizhizhou 142-143 E 2-3
Bor Talijn gol 142-143 E 3
Borto 132-133 V 7
Bortondale, PA 84 III a 2
Borūjerd 134-135 FG 4
Borusa Strait = proliv Vil'kickogo 132-133 S-U 2
Boryo = Fangliao 146-147 H 10
Bory Tucholskie 118 HJ 2
Borz'a 132-133 W 7
Borzna 126-127 F 1
Boržomi 126-127 L 6
Borzya = Borz'a 132-133 W 7
Bos [B ↖ Bruxelles] 128 II a 1
Bos [B ↗ Bruxelles] 128 II b 1
Bosa [CO] 94-95 D 5
Bosa [I] 122-123 C 5
Bosanska Gradiška 122-123 G 3
Bosanska Krupa 122-123 G 3
Bosanski Novi 122-123 FG 3
Bosanski Petrovac 122-123 G 3
Bosbeek [B, place] 128 II a 1
Bosbulten, De — 174-175 DE 5
Bosch 106-107 H 6
Bosch Bulten, De — = De Bosbulten 174-175 DE 5
Boschpoort 174-175 G 4
Boscobel, WI 70-71 E 4
Bosconia 94-95 E 2
Bose 142-143 K 7
Boshan 142-143 M 4
Bosho Boholu 174-175 E 3
Boshoek 174-175 G 3
Boshof 174-175 F 5
Boskamp 98-99 L 1-2
Bosler, WY 68-69 D 5
Bosluissoutpan 174-175 C 5
Bosmanland 172 C 7
Bosmanland, Groot — 174-175 CD 5
Bosmanland, Klein — 174-175 C 5
Bosmanskop 174-175 G 6
Bosmansriviermond 174-175 G 7
Bosna [BG] 122-123 M 4
Bosna [YU] 122-123 GH 3
Bosnia Hercegovina 122-123 GH 3-4
Bosobolo 172 C 1
Bōsō hantō 144-145 N 5
Bosporus = Karadeniz boğazı 134-135 BC 2
Bosque, NM 76-77 A 5
Bosque Bonito 76-77 B 7
Bosque de Chapultepec 91 I b 2
Bosque San Juan de Aragón 91 I c 2
Bossangoa 164-165 H 7
Bossembélé 164-165 H 7
Bossier City, LA 64-65 H 5
Bosso 164-165 G 6
Bostān [IR] 136-137 MN 7
Bostān [PAK] 138-139 A 2
Bostānābād 136-137 M 4
Bostancı, İstanbul- 154 I b 3
Boston, GA 80-81 E 5
Boston, MA 64-65 MN 3
Boston [GB] 119 FG 5
Boston-Allston, MA 84 I b 2
Boston-Back Bay, MA 84 I b 2
Boston Bay 84 I c 2
Boston-Bellevue-Mount Vernon, MA 84 I b 3
Boston-Brighton, MA 84 I b 2
Boston-Charlestown, MA 84 I b 2
Boston-Clarendon Hills, MA 84 I b 3
Boston College 84 I a 3
Boston Common 84 I b 2
Boston-Dorchester, MA 84 I b 3
Boston-Dorchester Center, MA 84 I b 3
Boston-East Boston, MA 84 I b 2
Boston Harbor 84 I c 2
Boston-Hyde Park, MA 84 I b 3
Boston-Jamaica Plain, MA 84 I b 3
Boston-Mattapan, MA 84 I b 3
Boston Mountains 64-65 H 4
Boston Naval Shipyard U.S.S. Constitution 84 I b 2
Boston-Readville, MA 84 I b 3
Boston-Roslindale, MA 84 I b 3
Boston-Roxbury, MA 84 I b 3
Boston-Savin Hill, MA 84 I b 3
Boston-South Boston, MA 84 I b 2
Boston Tea Party Ship 84 I b 2
Boston University 84 I b 2
Boston-West Roxbury, MA 84 I b 3
Bosveld 172 E 6
Boswell, OK 76-77 G 5-6
Bosworth, MO 70-71 D 6
Bōta = Boath 138-139 G 8
Botād 138-139 C 6
Botafogo, Enseada de — 110 I bc 2
Botafogo, Rio de Janeiro- 110 I b 2
Botan çayı 136-137 K 4
Botanical Gardens 154 II a 2
Botanic Garden of Tōkyō 155 III b 1
Botanic Gardens of Singapore 154 III a 2
Botanic Gardens of Victoria 155 I a 2
Botanischer Garten Berlin 130 III b 2
Botany, Sydney- 161 I b 2
Botany Bay 158-159 K 6
Botar = Botād 138-139 C 6
Botejevo 126-127 G 3
Botelhos 102-103 J 4
Botersleegte 174-175 D 6
Botev 122-123 L 4
Bothasberg 174-175 H 4
Bothaspas 174-175 H 4
Bothaville 174-175 G 4
Bothnia, Gulf of — 114-115 MN 3
Botkul', ozero — 126-127 N 2
Botletle 172 D 6
Botlich 126-127 N 5
Botoşani 122-123 M 2
Botou = Bozhen 146-147 F 2
Bô Trach 150-151 F 4

Botshol 128 I ab 2
Botswana 172 DE 6
Botte Donato 122-123 G 6
Bottineau, ND 68-69 F 1
Botucaraí, Serra — 106-107 L 2
Botucatu 92-93 K 9
Botulu 132-133 W 5
Botuporã 100-101 C 7
Botuquara 100-101 C 7
Botwood 63 J 3
Bou 168-169 D 3
Bouaflé 164-165 C 7
Bou Akba = Bū 'Aqbah 166-167 C 5
Bouaké 164-165 CD 7
Boualem = Bū 'Alim 166-167 G 3
Bou-Ali = Bū 'Alī 166-167 F 6
Boû 'Amaroû = Bu 'Amarū 136-137 HJ 5
Bouar 164-165 H 7
Boû 'Arâda = Bū 'Arādah 166-167 L 1
Boû 'Arfa = Bū 'Arfah 166-167 F 3
Boû 'Azzer = Bū Azīr 166-167 C 4
Boubker = Abū Bakr 166-167 F 2
Boubo 168-169 D 4
Bouca 164-165 H 7
Boucau 120-121 G 7
Bou-Chebka = Bū Shabaqah 166-167 L 2
Bouchegouf = Būshqūf 166-167 K 1
Boucheron = Al-Gārah 166-167 C 3
Boucherville, Îles de — 82 I bc 1
Boucle du Baoulé, Parc National de la — 168-169 C 2
Boûdenîb = Bū Danīb 166-167 E 4
Boudewijnstad = Moba 172 E 3
Bou Djébéha 164-165 D 5
Boudouaou = Budwāwū 166-167 H 1
Boû el Ja'd = Bū al-J'ad 166-167 CD 3
Boû el Louân = Bū al-'Awn 166-167 B 3
Bouerda, El — = Al-Bū'irdah 166-167 C 5
Boufarik = Būfarīk 166-167 H 1
Boû Fîcha = Bū Fīshah 166-167 M 1
Bougaa = Buq'ah 166-167 J 1
Bougainville 148-149 j 6
Bougainville, Cape — 108-109 KL 8
Bougainville, Isla — = Lively Island 108-109 KL 9
Bougaroun, Cap — = Rā's Būjarun 166-167 JK 1
Bou-Ghezoul = Būghzūl 166-167 H 2
Bougie = Bijāyah 164-165 EF 1
Bougie, Golfe de — = Khalīj Bijāyah 166-167 J 1
Bougival 129 I b 2
Bougouni 164-165 C 6
Bou Grara = Bū Ghrārah 166-167 M 3
Bou Grara, Golfe de — = Khalīj Bū Ghrārah 166-167 M 3
Bougtenga 168-169 E 2
Bougtob = Bū Kutub 164-165 E 2
Bouguerra = Būgarā 166-167 H 1
Bouguelval 129 I c 1
Boû Haïâra, Hâssî — = Ḥassī Bū Ḥayārah 166-167 D 4
Bouheïret el Bîbân = Buḥayrat al-Bībān 166-167 M 3
Bouïra = Būirah 166-167 H 1
Bouira-Sakary = Būīrat Ṣaḥarī 166-167 H 2
Bou-Ismaïl = Bū Ismāʿīl 166-167 H 1
Boû Izakârn = Bū Izakārn 166-167 B 5
Boujad = Bū al-J'ad 166-167 C 3
Bou-Kadir = Bū Qādir 166-167 G 1
Bou Kadra, Djebel — = Jabal Bū Khaḍrah 166-167 KL 2
Bou Kahil, Djebel — = Jabal Bū Kāhil 166-167 HJ 2
Boukân = Būkān 136-137 LM 4
Boukhanefis = Bū Khanāfis 166-167 F 2
Bou Khelala, Hassi — = Ḥāssī Bū al-Khallalah 166-167 F 4
Bou-Ktoub = Bū Kutub 164-165 E 2
Boulain, Lac — 63 F 2
Boulal 168-169 C 2
Boulaouane = Bū al-'Awn 166-167 B 3
Boulder 158-159 D 6
Boulder, CO 64-65 EF 3-4
Boulder, MT 66-67 GH 2
Boulder, WY 66-67 HJ 4
Boulder City, NV 64-65 CD 4
Boulder Creek, CA 74-75 B 4
Boulder Dam = Hoover Dam 64-65 D 4
Boulevard Heights, MD 82 II b 2
Boulhaut = Bin Sulīmān 166-167 C 3
Bouli 168-169 E 2
Boulia 158-159 G 4
Boulmân = Būlmān 166-167 D 3
Boulogne, San Isidro- 110 III b 1
Boulogne-sur-Mer 120-121 H 3
Boulsa 168-169 E 2
Boultoum 168-169 H 2
Boumâln = Būmāln Dādis 166-167 CD 4
Boumba 164-165 H 8
Bou-Medfaa = Bū Midfār'ah 166-167 H 1
Bouna 164-165 D 7
Bouna, Réserve de Faune de — 164-165 D 7
Boû Naṣr, Jbel — = Jabal Bū Naṣr 166-167 E 3
Boundary, AK 58-59 R 4
Boundary Mountains 72-73 L 2
Boundary Peak 64-65 C 4
Boundary Plateau 66-67 J 1
Boundary, WA 66-67 E 1
Boundiali 164-165 C 7
Boundji 172 C 2
Boundou 164-165 B 6
Boung, Sông — 150-151 F 5
Boun Neua 150-151 CD 2
Bounoum 168-169 B 2
Bountiful, UT 66-67 H 5
Bounty 156-157 HJ 7
Bouquet 106-107 G 4
Bouraghet, Erg — = 'Irq Buraghat 166-167 L 6
Bourail 158-159 MN 4
Bourbonnais 120-121 J 5
Bourbon Street 85 I b 2
Bourem 164-165 DE 5
Bourg-en-Bresse 120-121 K 5
Bourges 120-121 J 5
Bourg-la-Reine 129 I c 2
Bourgogne 120-121 K 5-6
Bourgogne, Canal de — 120-121 K 5
Boû Rhrâra = Bū Ghrārah 166-167 M 3
Bourke 158-159 J 6
Bourkes 62 LM 2
Bourlamaque 62 N 2-3
Bou-Saâda = Bū Sa'ādah 166-167 J 2
Boû Salem = Bū Sālām 166-167 L 1
Bouse, AZ 74-75 FG 6
Bouṣrâ ech Châm = Buṣrat ash-Shām 136-137 G 6
Bousso 164-165 H 6
Boussougou 168-169 E 3
Boutilimit = Bū Tilimīt 164-165 B 5
Bou-Tlelis = Būtīlīs 166-167 F 2
Bouvard, Cape — 158-159 BC 6
Bouvet 50-51 K 8
Bouvetøya 53 D 1
Bouzareah 170 I a 1
Bou Zid, Hassi — = Ḥāssī Bū Zīd 166-167 G 4
Boûznîqa = Bū Z'nīqah 166-167 C 3
Bovenkerk 128 I a 2
Bovey, MN 70-71 D 2
Boviaanskloof Mountains = Bobbejaans-kloofberge 174-175 EF 7
Bovill, ID 66-67 E 2
Bovina, TX 76-77 C 5
Bovril 106-107 H 3
Bo-Wadrif 174-175 CD 7
Bowbells, ND 68-69 E 1
Bowdle, SD 68-69 G 3
Bowdoin, Lake — 68-69 C 1
Bowdon, ND 68-69 G 2
Bowen, IL 70-71 E 5
Bowen [AUS] 158-159 J 3-4
Bowen [RA] 106-107 D 5
Bowen Island 66-67 B 1
Boweyr Ahmad-e Sardsīr va Kohkīlūyeh = 4 ◁ 134-135 G 4
Bowie, AZ 74-75 J 6
Bowie, TX 76-77 F 6
Bow Island 66-67 H 1
Bowker's Park 174-175 G 6
Bowling Green, KY 64-65 J 4
Bowling Green, MO 70-71 E 6
Bowling Green, OH 72-73 E 4
Bowling Green, PA 84 III a 2
Bowling Green, VA 72-73 H 5-6
Bowling Green, Cape — 158-159 J 3
Bowman, ND 68-69 E 2
Bowman Island 53 C 11
Bowmanville 72-73 G 3
Bowness 60 K 4
Bowral 160 JK 5
Bowron Lake Provincial Park 60 G 3
Bowron River 60 G 3
Bow Rover 56-57 O 7
Bowsman 61 H 4
Box Butte Reservoir 68-69 E 4
Box Creek 68-69 D 4
Box Elder, MT 68-69 A 1
Boxelder Creek [USA ◁ Little Missouri River] 68-69 D 3
Boxelder Creek [USA ◁ Musselshell River] 68-69 B 2
Box Hill, Melbourne- 161 II c 1-2
Bo Xian 142-143 LM 5
Boxing 146-147 G 3
Boyabat 136-137 F 2
Boyacá 94-95 E 5
Boyaca, Bogotá- 91 III b 2
Boyacıköy, İstanbul- 154 I b 2
Boyalık = Çiçekdağı 136-137 F 3
Boyang 146-147 F 7
Boyce, LA 78-79 C 5
Boyd 61 K 3
Boyd, TX 76-77 F 6
Boydton, VA 80-81 G 2
Boyera, Baruta-La — 91 II b 2
Boyero, CO 68-69 E 6
Boyer River 70-71 C 4
Boyeruca, Laguna de — 106-107 AB 5
Boykins, VA 80-81 H 2
Boyle Heights, Los Angeles-, CA 83 III c 1
Boyne City, MI 70-71 H 3
Boynton, OK 76-77 G 5
Boynton Beach, FL 80-81 cd 3
Boysen, WY 68-69 BC 4
Boysen Reservoir 68-69 B 4
Boyuibe 92-93 G 9
Boyuyumanu, Río — 104-105 B 2
Bozburun 136-137 C 4
Bozca ada [TR, island] 136-137 AB 3
Bozdağ [TR, mountains] 136-137 D 2-3
Boz Dağı 136-137 C 4
Boz dağlar 136-137 C 3
Bozdoğan 136-137 C 4
Bozeman, MT 64-65 D 2
Bozen = Bolzano 122-123 D 2
Bozhen 146-147 F 2
Bozkır 136-137 E 4
Bozkurt 136-137 F 1-2
Bozok yaylâsı 136-137 F 2-3
Bozoum 164-165 H 7
Bozova = Hüvek 136-137 H 4
Bozqūsh, Kūh-e — 136-137 M 4
Bozüyük 136-137 CD 3
Bra 122-123 B 3
Brabant, Île — 53 C 30
Brac [RCH] 104-105 B 7
Brač [YU] 122-123 G 4
Bracciano, Lago di — 122-123 DE 4
Bracebridge 72-73 G 2
Bräcke 116-117 F 6
Brackettville, TX 76-77 D 8
Brackwater = Brakwater 174-175 B 2
Braclav 126-127 D 2
Braço do Norte, Rio — 102-103 H 7-8
Braço Menor de Araguia 92-93 JK 7
Brad 122-123 K 2
Brădano 122-123 G 5
Braddock, Alexandria-, VA 82 II a 2
Bradenton, FL 64-65 K 6
Bradford, AR 78-79 D 3
Bradford, PA 72-73 G 4
Bradford [CDN] 72-73 G 2
Bradford [GB] 119 F 5
Bradley, CA 74-75 C 5
Bradley, SD 68-69 H 3
Bradore, Baie — 63 H 2
Bradore Hills 63 H 2
Bradshaw, TX 76-77 DE 6
Brady, MT 66-67 H 1-2
Brady, NE 68-69 F 5
Brady, TX 76-77 E 7
Brady Glacier 58-59 T 7
Braeburn Gardens, Houston-, TX 85 III a 2
Braeburn Glen, Houston-, TX 85 III a 2
Braeburn Valley, Houston-, TX 85 III a 2
Braes Heights, Houston-, TX 85 III b 2
Braga 120-121 C 8
Braga, Serra do — 100-101 E 4
Bragado 111 D 5
Bragança 120-121 D 8
Bragança [BR, Amazonas] 98-99 D 9
Bragança [BR, Pará] 92-93 K 5
Bragança Paulista 92-93 K 9
Bragin 124-125 GH 8
Braham, MN 70-71 D 3
Brahestad = Raahe 116-117 L 5
Brahmanbaria = Brahmaṇbāriyā 141 B 4
Brahmaṇbāriyā 141 B 4
Brāhmani 134-135 O 6
Brahmapur 154 II b 3
Brahmapurī = Bramhapuri 138-139 G 7
Brahmaputra 134-135 P 5
Brahmaputra = Matsang Tsangpo 138-139 J 2-3
Brahmaputra = Tamchhog Khamba 138-139 J 2
Brahmaputra = Tsangpo 138-139 L 3
Brah Yang = Bralan 150-151 G 7
Brăila 122-123 M 3
Brainerd, MN 64-65 H 2
Braintree, MA 84 I bc 3
Brak = Birāk 164-165 G 3
Brākṇah, Al- 168-169 B 1
Brakpan 174-175 H 4
Brakpoort 174-175 E 6
Brakrivier [ZA, Kaapland] 174-175 E 5
Brakrivier [ZA, Transvaal] 174-175 H 2
Brakwater 174-175 B 2
Bralan 150-151 G 7
Bralorne 60 F 4
Bramaputra = Brahmaputra 134-135 P 5
Bramaputra = Tsangpo 138-139 L 3
Bramfeld, Hamburg- 130 I b 1
Bramhapuri 138-139 G 7
Bramley, Johannesburg- 170 V b 1
Brampton 72-73 FG 3
Branch 63 JK 4
Branchville, SC 80-81 F 4
Brandberg 172 B 6
Brandenberg, MT 68-69 CD 3
Brandenburg, KY 70-71 G 6-7
Brandenburg [DDR, landscape] 118 FG 2
Brandenburg [DDR, place] 118 F 2
Brandenburger Tor 130 III b 1
Brandfort 174-175 G 5
Brandon, FL 80-81 b 3
Brandon, MS 78-79 DE 4
Brandon, VT 72-73 K 3
Brandon [CDN] 56-57 Q 8
Brandon Mount 119 AB 5
Brandsen 106-107 H 5
Brandsville, MO 78-79 CD 2
Brandvlei 174-175 D 6
Brandywine, MD 72-73 H 5
Branford, FL 80-81 b 1-2
Brang, Kuala — 148-149 D 5-6
Brani, Pulau — 154 III b 2
Braniewo 118 JK 1
Bransfield Strait 53 C 30-31
Br'ansk [SU] 124-125 JK 7
Br'ansk-Bežica 124-125 JK 7
Branson, MO 78-79 C 2
Brantas, Kali — 152-153 JK 9
Brantford 72-73 FG 3
Brantley, AL 78-79 FG 5
Branxholme 160 EF 6
Brás [BR] 98-99 JK 6
Brás, São Paulo- 110 II b 2
Brâsc = Birāk 164-165 G 3
Bras d'Or Lake 56-57 YZ 8
Brasil, El — 76-77 D 9
Brasilândia 102-103 FG 4
Brasilândia, São Paulo- 110 II a 1
Brasiléia 92-93 F 7
Brasília 92-93 K 8
Brasília de Minas 102-103 KL 2
Brasília Legal 92-93 H 5
Braslav 124-125 F 6
Brașov 122-123 L 3
Brassey Range 152-153 MN 3
Bråsvellbreen 116-117 lm 5
Bratcevo, Moskva- 113 V ab 2
Bratejevo, Moskva- 113 V cd 3
Bratislava 118 H 4
Bratsk 132-133 T 6
Bratskoje 126-127 E 3
Bratskoje vodochranilišče 132-133 T 6
Brattieboro, VT 72-73 K 3
Brațul Chilia 122-123 N 3
Brațul Sfîntu Gheorghe 122-123 N 3
Brațul Sulina 122-123 N 3
Braunau 118 F 4
Braunschweig 118 E 2
Braunshardt 128 III a 2
Brava 204-205 E 7
Brava = Baraawe 172 H 1
Brawley, CA 64-65 C 5
Bray, CA 66-67 C 5
Braybrook, Melbourne- 161 II b 1
Bray Island 56-57 V 4
Braymer, MO 70-71 D 6
Brays Bayou 85 III a 2
Brays Village, Houston-, TX 85 III a 2
Brazeau 60 J 3
Brazeau, Mount — 60 J 3
Brazeau River 60 K 3
Brazil 92-93 F-M 6
Brazil, IN 70-71 G 6
Brazil Basin 50-51 H 6
Brazilian Plateau = Planalto Brasileiro 92-93 KL 8
Brazlândia 102-103 H 1
Brazo de Gatún 64-65 b 2
Brazo del Chagres 64-65 b 2
Brazo de Loba 94-95 D 3
Brazo Noroeste 108-109 DE 10
Brazo Norte 108-109 B 7
Brazos River 64-65 G 5-6
Brazos River, Clear Fork — 76-77 E 6
Brazos River, Salt Fork — 76-77 D 6
Brazo Sur del Río Coig 108-109 D 8
Brazza = Brač 122-123 G 4
Brazzaville 172 BC 2
Brazzaville, Aéroport de — 170 IV a 1
Brazzaville-Bacongo 170 IV a 1
Brazzaville-Moungali 170 IV a 1
Brazzaville-Mpila 170 IV a 1
Brazzaville-Ngamba 170 IV a 1
Brazzaville-Ouenzé 170 IV a 1
Brazzaville-Poto Poto 170 IV a 1
Brčko 122-123 H 3
Brdy 118 FG 4
Brea, Cordillera de la — 106-107 C 2
Brea Creek 83 III d 2
Breakheart Reservation 84 I b 2
Bream Bay 161 F 2
Brea Pozo 106-107 EF 2
Breas 104-105 A 9
Breaux Bridge, LA 78-79 D 5
Brebes 152-153 H 9
Brechin [CDN] 72-73 G 2
Breckenridge, MN 68-69 H 2
Breckenridge, TX 76-77 E 6
Brecknock, Peninsula — 111 B 8-9
Břeclav 118 H 4
Brecon 119 E 5-6
Breda 120-121 K 3
Bredasdorp 172 D 8
Bredbo 160 J 5
Bredell 170 V c 1
Bredenbury 61 H 5
Bredy 132-133 KL 7
Breedhout 128 II a 2
Breeds Pond 84 I c 2
Breërivier 174-175 D 8
Breezy Point, New York-, NY 82 III c 3
Bregalnica 122-123 K 5
Bregenz 118 DE 5
Bregovo 122-123 K 3
Breidhafjördhur 116-117 ab 2
Breidhavik 116-117 a 2
Breidi Fjord = Breidhafjördhur 116-117 ab 2
Breipaal 174-175 G 6
Breitenlee, Wien- 113 I bc 1
Brejão [BR, Goiás] 100-101 A 7
Brejão [BR, Pernambuco] 100-101 F 5
Brejinho 100-101 D 5
Brejinho do Nazaré 92-93 K 7
Brejo 100-101 C 2
Brejo, Riacho do — 100-101 C 5
Brejo da Madre de Deus 100-101 F 5
Brejo da Porta 100-101 B 5
Brejo da Serra 100-101 C 6
Brejo de São Félix 100-101 C 3
Brejo do Cruz 100-101 F 4
Brejões 100-101 E 7
Brejo Santo 100-101 E 4
Brejo Velho 100-101 C 7
Brejtovo 124-125 LM 4
Brekstad 116-117 C 6
Bremangerlandet 116-117 A 7
Bremen 118 D 2
Bremen, GA 78-79 G 4
Bremen, Colonia — 106-107 F 4
Bremerhaven 118 D 2
Bremerton, WA 64-65 B 2
Bremond, TX 76-77 F 7
Brem River 60 E 4
Breñas, Las — 104-105 F 10
Brenham, TX 76-77 F 7
Brenne 120-121 H 5
Brenner 118 E 5
Brennero = Brenner 118 E 5
Brennevinsfjord 116-117 k 4
Brent 72-73 G 1
Brent, London- 129 II a 1
Brentford, London- 129 II a 2
Brentwood, TN 78-79 F 2-3
Brentwood Heights, Los Angeles-, CA 83 III ab 1
Brentwood Park 170 V c 1
Brèscia 122-123 D 3
Bressanone 122-123 DE 2
Bressay 119 F 1
Bresse 120-121 K 5
Bressuire 120-121 G 5
Brest [F] 120-121 E 4
Brest [SU] 124-125 D 7
Bretagne 120-121 F 4-G 5
Breton, Cape — 56-57 Z 8
Breton Island 78-79 E 6
Breton Sound 64-65 J 6
Breu 96-97 E 6
Breueh, Pulau — 148-149 B 5
Breukeleveen 128 I b 2
Brevard, NC 80-81 E 3
Breves 92-93 J 5
Brevik 116-117 C 8
Brevort, MI 70-71 H 2
Brewarrina 158-159 J 5
Brewer, ME 72-73 M 2
Brewersville 168-169 C 4
Brewster, KS 68-69 F 6
Brewster, NE 68-69 G 5
Brewster, WA 66-67 CD 1
Brewster, Kap — 52 BC 20-21
Brewton, AL 78-79 F 5
Breyten 174-175 H 4
Brezina = B'rizyānah 166-167 G 3
Bria 164-165 J 7
Briançon 120-121 L 6
Brian Head 74-75 G 4
Briarcroft, Houston-, TX 85 III b 2
Briare 120-121 J 5
Briarmeadow, Houston-, TX 85 III a 2
Briarwood Park 85 II c 1
Bribbaree 160 HJ 5
Bribie Island 158-159 K 5
Bričany 126-127 C 2
Briceland, CA 66-67 AB 5
Bricelyn, MN 70-71 CD 4
Brickaville = Vohibinany 172 JK 5
Brickhouse Gulley 85 III b 1
Briconnet, Lac — 63 F 2
Bridesburg, Philadelphia-, PA 84 III c 2
Bridge, ID 66-67 G 4
Bridgeboro, GA 80-81 DE 5
Bridgeboro, NJ 84 III d 1
Bridge City, LA 85 I ab 2
Bridgedale, LA 85 I a 2
Bridgeport, AL 78-79 FG 3
Bridgeport, CA 74-75 D 3
Bridgeport, CT 64-65 M 3
Bridgeport, IL 70-71 FG 6
Bridgeport, NE 68-69 E 5
Bridgeport, NJ 84 III a 3
Bridgeport, PA 84 III a 1
Bridgeport, TX 76-77 F 6
Bridgeport, Chicago-, IL 83 II b 1
Bridger, MT 68-69 B 3
Bridger Basin 66-67 HJ 5
Bridge River 60 F 4
Bridger Peak 68-69 C 5
Bridgeton, NC 80-81 H 3
Bridgeton, NJ 72-73 J 5
Bridgetown [AUS] 158-159 C 6
Bridgetown [BDS] 64-65 OP 9
Bridgetown [CDN] 63 D 5
Bridgeview, IL 83 II a 2
Bridgewater 63 D 5
Bridgewater, PA 84 III d 1
Bridgewater, SD 68-69 H 4
Bridgton, ME 72-73 L 2
Bridgwater 119 E 6
Bridlington 119 FG 4
Bridport [AUS] 160 c 2
Brie 120-121 J 4
Brieréville 61 C 3
Brig 118 CD 5
Briggsdale, CO 68-69 DE 5
Brigham City, UT 64-65 D 3
Bright 160 H 6
Brighton, IA 70-71 DE 5
Brighton, MI 70-71 HJ 4
Brighton, NY 72-73 H 3
Brighton [CDN] 72-73 GH 2
Brighton [GB] 119 FG 6
Brighton, Boston-, MA 84 I b 2
Brighton, Melbourne- 161 II bc 2
Brighton Indian Reservation 80-81 c 3
Brighton Park, Chicago-, IL 83 II a 2
Brightwood, Washington-, DC 82 II a 1
Brigthon, CO 68-69 D 5-6
Brigue = Brig 118 CD 5
Brigus 63 K 4
Brijnagar = Jhālawār 138-139 EF 5
Brijuni 122-123 E 3
Brikama 168-169 A 2
Brilhante, Rio — 102-103 E 4
Brilliant, NM 76-77 B 4
Brilon 118 D 3
Brimson, MN 70-71 DE 2
Brindaban = Vrindāvan 138-139 F 4
Brindakit 132-133 a 5-6
Brindisi 122-123 GH 5
Brinkley, AR 78-79 D 3
Brinkspan 174-175 E 6
Brion, Île — 63 F 4
Brisbane 158-159 K 5
Brisbane, CA 83 I b 2
Brisbane-Ipswich 158-159 K 5
Brisbane-Redcliffe 158-159 K 5
Brisbane River 158-159 K 5
Bristol, CO 68-69 E 6
Bristol, FL 78-79 G 5
Bristol, PA 84 III d 1
Bristol, RI 72-73 L 4
Bristol, SD 68-69 H 3
Bristol, TN 80-81 E 2
Bristol, VA 64-65 K 4
Bristol [CDN] 72-73 H 2
Bristol [GB] 119 EF 6
Bristol Bay 56-57 DE 6
Bristol Channel 119 DE 6
Bristol Lake 74-75 EF 5
Bristow, OK 76-77 F 5
Britannia Beach 66-67 B 1
Britannia Range 53 AB 15-16
British Columbia 56-57 L 6-N 7
British Isles 114-115 F 5-G 4
British Mountains 56-57 HJ 4
British Museum 129 II b 1
Brits 174-175 G 3
Britstown 172 D 8
Britt 72-73 F 2
Britt, IA 70-71 D 4
Brittany = Bretagne 120-121 F 4-G 5
Britton, SD 68-69 GH 3
Britvino 124-125 OP 3
Britz, Berlin- 130 III b 2
Brive, la — 128 II b 2
Brive-la-Gaillarde 120-121 H 6
Brixen = Bressanone 122-123 DE 2
Brixham 119 E 6
B'rizyānah 166-167 G 3
Brjansk = Br'ansk [SU] 124-125 JK 7
Brno 118 H 4
Broa, Ensenada de la — 88-89 EF 3
Broach = Bharuch 134-135 L 6
Broadback, Rivière — 62 MN 1
Broadford 119 CD 3
Broad Law 119 E 4
Broadmoor, CA 83 I b 2
Broad Pass, AK 58-59 N 5
Broad River 80-81 F 3
Broad Sound 158-159 JK 4
Broadus, MT 68-69 D 3
Broadview 61 GH 5
Broadview, MT 68-69 B 2
Broadwater, NE 68-69 E 5
Broceni 124-125 D 5
Brochet 56-57 Q 6
Brochet, Lac — 63 B 3
Brochu, Lac — 62 OP 2
Brocken 118 E 3
Brocket 60 L 5
Brock Island 56-57 N 2
Brocklyn Marine Park 82 III c 3
Brockman, Mount — 158-159 C 4
Brock Park 85 III c 1
Brockport, NY 72-73 GH 3
Brockton, MA 72-73 L 3
Brockton, MT 68-69 D 1
Brockville 56-57 V 9
Brockway, MT 68-69 D 2
Brockway, PA 72-73 G 4
Brodeur Peninsula 56-57 T 3
Brodhead, WI 70-71 F 4
Brodie 66-67 C 1
Brodnax, VA 80-81 GH 2
Brodnica 118 J 2
Brodósqui 102-103 J 4
Brody [SU, Ukrainskaja SSR] 126-127 B 1
Brogan, OR 66-67 E 3
Brokaw, WI 70-71 F 3
Broken Arrow, OK 76-77 G 4
Broken Bow, NE 68-69 G 5
Broken Bow, OK 76-77 G 5-6
Broken Hill 158-159 H 6
Broken Hill = Kabwe 172 E 4
Brokopondo 92-93 HJ 3
Bromhead 68-69 E 1
Brønderslev 116-117 CD 9
Bronevskaja 124-125 M 3
Brong-Ahafo 168-169 E 4
Bronkhorstspruit 174-175 H 3
Brønnøysund 116-117 DE 5
Bronson, FL 80-81 b 2
Bronson, MI 70-71 H 5
Bronson, TX 76-77 G 7
Bronte 122-123 F 7
Bronte, TX 76-77 D 7
Bronte Park 158-159 J 8
Bronx, New York-, NY 82 III c 1
Broodsnyersplaas 174-175 H 4
Brookeland, TX 76-77 GH 7
Brookfield, MO 70-71 D 6
Brookhaven, MS 78-79 D 5
Brookhaven, PA 84 III a 2
Brookhaven = North Atlanta, GA 85 II c 1
Brookings, OR 66-67 A 4
Brookings, SD 64-65 G 3
Brookland, Washington-, DC 82 II b 1
Brooklawn, NJ 84 III c 2
Brookline, MA 72-73 L 3
Brooklyn, IA 70-71 D 5
Brooklyn, MS 78-79 E 5
Brooklyn, Melbourne- 161 II ab 1-2
Brooklyn, New York-, NY 82 III bc 3
Brooklyn Park, MN 70-71 D 3
Brookneal, VA 80-81 G 2
Brooks 61 C 5
Brooks, Lake — 58-59 K 7
Brooks, Mount — 58-59 MN 5
Brooks Bay 60 CD 4
Brooks Island 83 I b 1
Brooks Mount 58-59 D 4
Brooks Range 56-57 E-H 4
Brookston, IN 70-71 G 5
Brookston, MN 70-71 D 2
Brooksville, FL 80-81 b 2
Brooksville, KY 72-73 DE 5
Brookton 158-159 C 6
Brookvale, Sydney- 161 I b 1
Brookville, IN 70-71 H 6
Brookville, OH 72-73 D 5
Brookville, PA 72-73 G 4
Brookwood, GA 85 II c 2
Brookwood Park 85 II c 2
Broomall, PA 84 III a 2
Broome 158-159 D 3
Broquerie, la — 61 KL 6
Brossard 82 I bc 2
Brotas 102-103 H 5
Brotas de Macaúbas 92-93 L 7
Brothers, OR 66-67 C 4
Brothers, The — = Jazā'ir al-Ikhwān 173 D 4
Brothers, The — = Samḥah, Darsah 134-135 G 8
Brou-sur-Chantereine 129 I d 2
Brovary 126-127 E 1
Brovio 168-169 C 4
Brovki 126-127 D 2
Brown, Mount — 53 BC 9
Brown, Point — 160 A 4
Brownfield, TX 76-77 CD 6
Browning, MT 66-67 G 1
Brownlee 61 E 5
Brownlee, NE 68-69 F 4
Brownlow Point 58-59 P 1
Brown Mill Park 85 II bc 2
Brownrigg 62 L 2
Brown's Bank 63 D 6
Brownstown, IN 70-71 GH 6
Browns Valley, MN 68-69 H 3
Brownsville, OR 66-67 B 3
Brownsville, PA 72-73 FG 4
Brownsville, TN 78-79 E 3
Brownsville, TX 64-65 G 6
Brownsweg 92-93 H 3-4
Brownville Junction, ME 72-73 M 2
Brownwood, TX 64-65 G 5
Broxton, GA 80-81 E 5
Bruay-en-Artois 120-121 J 3
Bruce, MS 78-79 E 3-4
Bruce, WI 70-71 E 3
Bruce, Mount — 158-159 C 4
Bruce Crossing, MI 70-71 F 2
Bruce Mines 70-71 J 2
Bruce Peninsula 72-73 F 2
Bruce Rock 158-159 C 6
Bruceton, TN 78-79 E 2
Bruchmühle 130 III d 1
Br'uchoveckaja 126-127 J 4
Br'uchovo 124-125 U 5
Bruchsal 118 D 4
Bruck an der Leitha 118 H 4
Bruck an der Mur 118 G 5
Brüelberg 128 IV b 1
Brug, De — 174-175 F 5
Bruges = Brugge 120-121 J 3
Brugge 120-121 J 3
Brugge-Zeebrugge 120-121 J 3
Brugmann, Hôpital — 128 II a 1
Bruin Peak 74-75 H 3
Bruit, Pulau — 152-153 J 4
Bruja, Cerro — 64-65 b 2
Brukkaros, Mount — = Groot Brukkaros 172 C 7
Brule, NE 68-69 F 5
Brule, WI 70-71 E 2
Brule Lake 70-71 E 2
Brule Rapids 60 L 1
Brumadinho 102-103 K 4
Brumado 92-93 L 7
Brundidge, AL 78-79 FG 5
Bruneau, ID 66-67 F 4
Bruneau River 66-67 F 4
Brunei 148-149 F 6
Brunei = Bandar Seri Begawan 148-149 FG 5-6
Brunei, Teluk — 152-153 L 3
Brunette Island 63 HJ 4
Bruni, TX 76-77 E 9
Brunner 161 DE 6
Bruno 61 F 4
Brunswick, GA 64-65 K 5
Brunswick, MD 72-73 H 5
Brunswick, ME 72-73 LM 3
Brunswick, MO 70-71 D 6
Brunswick = Braunschweig 118 E 2
Brunswick, Melbourne- 161 II b 1
Brunswick, Península — 111 B 8
Brunswick Bay 158-159 D 3
Brunswick Heads 160 LM 2
Brunswick Lake 70-71 J 1
Bruny Island 158-159 J 8
Brusenec 124-125 OP 3
Brush, CO 68-69 E 5
Brushy Mountains 80-81 F 2-3
Brus Laguna 88-89 DE 7

Brusovo 124-125 K 5
Brusque 111 G 3
Brussegem 128 II a 1
Brussel = Bruxelles 120-121 JK 3
Brussel-Charleroi, Kanaal — 128 II a 2
Brussels 174-175 F 4
Brussels = Bruxelles 120-121 JK 3
Brütten 128 IV b 1
Brüttisellen 128 IV b 1
Bruxelles 120-121 JK 3
Bruxelles National, Aéroport — 128 II b 1
Bruyns Hill 174-175 J 5
Bruzual 94-95 G 3-4
Bryan, OH 70-71 H 5
Bryan, TX 64-65 G 5
Bryan, WY 66-67 J 5
Bryansk = Br'ansk 124-125 JK 7
Bryant, SD 68-69 H 3
Bryce Canyon National Park 74-75 GH 4
Bryn Mawr, PA 84 III b 1
Bryn Mawr College 84 III b 1
Bryson, TX 76-77 E 6
Bryson City, NC 80-81 E 3
Bryson City, TN 80-81 E 3
Brzeg 118 H 3
Bşaiya, Al- = Al-Buşaiyah 134-135 EF 4
Bsharri = Basharrī 136-137 G 5
Btaymān, Bi'r — 136-137 H 4
Bua 171 C 6
Bua Chum 150-151 C 5
Buake = Bouaké 164-165 CD 7
Buala 148-149 jk 6
Bū al-'Awn 166-167 B 3
Bū 'Alī 166-167 F 6
Bū 'Alim 166-167 G 3
Bū al-J'ad 166-167 CD 3
Bū al-Khallalah, Ḥāssī — 166-167 G 2-3
Bū'Amarū 136-137 HJ 5
Buapinang 152-153 O 8
Bū 'Aqbah 166-167 C 5
Bū 'Arādah 166-167 L 1
Buaran, Kali — 154 IV b 2
Bū 'Arfah 166-167 F 3
Bua Yai 150-151 D 5
Bu'ayrāt al-Ḥsūn, Al- 164-165 H 2
Bū Azīr 166-167 C 4
Bubak 138-139 A 4
Bub Chhu 138-139 LM 3
Būbīyan, Jazīrat — 134-135 FG 5
Bubtsang Tsangpo 138-139 K 2
Bubu 171 C 4
Bubu, Gunung — 150-151 C 10
Buc 129 I b 2
Bučač 126-127 B 2
Bucak 136-137 D 4
Bucakkışla 136-137 E 4
Bucaramanga 92-93 E 3
Bucatunna, MS 78-79 E 5
Buccaneer Archipelago 158-159 D 3
Buchan [AUS] 160 J 6
Buchanan, MI 70-71 G 5
Buchanan, NM 76-77 B 5
Buchanan, VA 80-81 FG 2
Buchanan [CDN] 61 G 5
Buchanan [LB] 164-165 B 7
Buchanan Lake 76-77 E 7
Buchans 56-57 Z 8
Buchara 134-135 JK 3
Buchardo 111 D 4
Bucharest = Bucureşti 122-123 L 3
Bucharevo 124-125 S 5
Buchendorf 130 III a 2
Buchholz, Berlin- 130 III b 1
Buchon, Point — 74-75 C 5
Buchschlag 128 III ab 1
Buchs (Zürich) 128 IV a 1
buchta Marii Prončiščevoj 132-133 VW 2
Buchtarma 132-133 Q 8
Buchtarminskoje vodochranilišče 132-133 PQ 8
Buchupureo 106-107 A 6
Buchyn Mangnaj uul 124-143 EF 4-5
Buckeye, AZ 74-75 G 6
Buckhannon, WV 72-73 F 5
Buckhaven 119 E 3
Buckhead, Atlanta-, GA 85 II bc 1
Buckhorn Lake 72-73 G 2
Buckhurst Hill 129 II c 1
Buckie 119 E 3
Buckingham [CDN] 72-73 J 2
Buckingham Palace 129 II b 2
Buckland, AK 58-59 G 4
Buckland River 58-59 G 4
Buckland Tableland 158-159 J 4-5
Buckleboo 158-159 G 6
Buckle Island 53 C 16-17
Buckley, WA 66-67 BC 2
Buckley Bay 53 C 15-16
Buckley Ranges 60 D 2
Bucklin, KS 68-69 G 7
Bucklin, MO 70-71 D 6
Buckow, Berlin- 130 III b 2
Bucksport, ME 72-73 M 2
Bucktown, LA 85 I b 1
Bucovina 122-123 LM 2
Buco Zau 172 B 2
Buctouche 63 D 4
Bucureşti 122-123 LM 3
Bucureşti-Jilava 122-123 M 5
Bucyrus, OH 72-73 E 4
Buda, TX 76-77 F 7
Budai = Putai 146-147 GH 10
Buda-Košelevo 124-125 H 7
Budakskij liman 126-127 E 4
Budalin 141 D 4
Bū Danīb 166-167 E 4
Budapest 118 J 5
Budarino 126-127 P 1
Budaun 136-135 M 5
Budayr, Al- 136-137 L 7
Buddh Gaya 138-139 K 5
Budd Land 53 C 12
Bude, MS 78-79 D 5
Budennovka 124-125 T 8
Büdesheim 128 III b 1
Bude-Stratton 119 D 6
Budge-Budge 138-139 LM 6
Budhāna 138-139 F 3
Budhapūr 138-139 AB 5
Būdhardalur 116-117 c 2
Būdhīyah, Jabal — 173 C 3
Budi, Lago del — 106-107 A 7
Budjala 172 CD 1
Budogošč' 124-125 J 4
Bud'onnovskaja 126-127 KL 3
Budop = Bô Đu'c 150-151 F 6-7
Budua 168-169 H 2
Budva 122-123 H 4
Budwāwū 166-167 H 1
Buea 164-165 F 8
Buena Esperanza 106-107 E 5
Buena Park, CA 83 III d 2
Buenaventura [CO] 92-93 D 4
Buenaventura [MEX] 86-87 G 3
Buenaventura, Bahía de — 92-93 D 4
Buena Vista, GA 78-79 G 4
Buena Vista, VA 80-81 G 2
Buena Vista [BOL] 104-105 E 5
Buenavista [CO] 91 III c 4
Buena Vista [PE] 96-97 B 6
Buena Vista [PY] 102-103 E 6
Buena Vista [YV, Anzoátegui] 94-95 J 3
Buena Vista [YV, Apure] 94-95 G 4
Buena Vista, Cordillera de — 94-95 FG 2
Buenavista, Madrid- 113 III ab 2
Buenavista, San José de — 148-149 H 4
Buena Vista Lake Bed 74-75 D 5
Buenolândia 102-103 GH 1
Buenópolis 102-103 KL 2
Buenos Aires [CO, administrative unit] 94-95 E 7
Buenos Aires [CO, place] 94-95 bc 2
Buenos Aires [PA] 64-65 b 2
Buenos Aires [RA, administrative unit] 111 DE 5
Buenos Aires [RA, place] 111 E 4
Buenos Aires, Lago — 111 B 7
Buenos Aires, Punta — 108-109 G 4-H 3
Buenos Aires-Almagro 110 III b 1
Buenos Aires-Barracas 110 III b 1
Buenos Aires-Belgrano 110 III b 1
Buenos Aires-Bocá 110 III b 1
Buenos Aires-Caballito 110 III b 1
Buenos Aires-Chacarita 110 III b 1
Buenos Aires-Colegiales 110 III b 1
Buenos Aires-Constitución 110 III b 1
Buenos Aires-Flores 110 III b 1
Buenos Aires-Floresta 110 III b 1
Buenos Aires-General Urquiza 110 III b 1
Buenos Aires-La Paternal 110 III b 1
Buenos Aires-Nueva Chicago 110 III b 1
Buenos Aires-Nueva Pompeya 110 III b 1
Buenos Aires-Núñez 110 III b 1
Buenos Aires-Once 110 III b 1
Buenos Aires-Palermo 110 III b 1
Buenos Aires-Recoleta 110 III b 1
Buenos Aires-Retiro 110 III b 1
Buenos Aires-Saavedra 110 III b 1
Buenos Aires-Versailles 110 III b 1
Buenos Aires-Villa Devoto 110 III b 1
Buenos Aires-Villa Lugano 110 III b 2
Buenos Aires-Villa Real 110 III b 1
Buenos Aires-Villa Sáenz Peña 110 III b 1
Buen Pasto 108-109 E 5
Buen Retiro 64-65 b 3
Buen Tiempo, Cabo — 108-109 EF 8
Buerarema 100-101 E 8
Buey, Alto del — 94-95 C 4
Bueyeros, NM 76-77 C 4-5
Bufalotta, Roma- 113 II b 1
Būfarīk 166-167 H 1
Buffalo 61 C 5
Buffalo, MN 70-71 D 3
Buffalo, MO 70-71 D 7
Buffalo, ND 68-69 H 2
Buffalo, NY 64-65 L 3
Buffalo, OK 76-77 E 4
Buffalo, SD 68-69 E 3
Buffalo, TX 76-77 FG 7
Buffalo, WV 72-73 F 5
Buffalo, WY 68-69 C 3
Buffalo Bayou 85 III b 1
Buffalo Bill Reservoir 68-69 B 3
Buffalo Head Hills 61 A 2
Buffalo Hill 155 I b 1
Buffalo Hump 66-67 F 3
Buffalo Lake 56-57 NO 5
Buffalo Narrows 61 D 3
Buffalo River = Bloedrivier 174-175 J 4-5
Buffalorivier = Buffelsrivier 174-175 J 4
Buffelsrivier [ZA, Drakensberge] 174-175 J 4
Buffelsrivier [ZA, Groot Karoo] 174-175 D 7
Buffelsrivier [ZA, Namakwaland] 174-175 C 6
Bū Fīshah 166-167 M 1
Buford, GA 80-81 DE 3
Buford, ND 68-69 E 1-2
Buford, WY 68-69 D 5
Buford Reservoir = Lake Sidney Lanier 80-81 DE 3
Bug 118 L 2
Bug = Južnyj Bug 126-127 E 2
Bug, Južnyj — 126-127 E 3
Buga 92-93 D 4
Bugalagrande 94-95 CD 5
Bugant 142-143 K 2
Būgarā 166-167 H 1
Bugel, Tanjung — 152-153 J 9
Bughāz Jabal Tāriq 164-165 CD 1
Bū Ghrārah 166-167 M 3
Bū Ghrārah, Khalīj — 166-167 M 3
Būghzūl 166-167 H 2
Bugiri 171 C 2
Bugorkan 132-133 U 5
Bugrino 132-133 H 4
Bugsuk Island 152-153 M 1
Bugt 142-143 N 2
Bugul'ma 132-133 J 7
Bugul'minsko-Belebejevskaja vozvyšennost' 124-125 TU 6
Buguruslan 132-133 J 7
Buhăeşti 122-123 M 2
Bū Ḥayārah, Ḥāssī — 166-167 D 4
Buhayrat, Al- 164-165 KL 7
Buḥayrat al-Abyaḍ 164-165 KL 6
Buhayrat al-Assad 134-135 D 3
Buḥayrat al-Bībān 166-167 M 3
Buḥayrat al-Burullus 173 B 2
Buḥayrat al-Manzilah 173 BC 2
Buḥayrat at-Timsāḥ 173 C 2
Buḥayrat Binzart 166-167 LM 1
Buḥayrat Fazrārah 166-167 K 1
Buḥayrat Idkū 173 B 2
Buḥayrat Maryūṭ 173 AB 2
Buhayrat Shārī 136-137 L 5
Buḥeiret el Murrat el-Kubrâ = Al-Buḥayrat al-Murrat al-Kubrā 173 C 2
Buhemba 171 C 3
Buhl, ID 66-67 F 4
Buhl, MN 70-71 D 2
Buhoro 171 B 4
Bū Iblān, Jabal — 166-167 D 3
Bui Chu 150-151 F 2
Bui Dam 168-169 E 3
Buin [PNG] 148-149 j 6
Buin [RCH] 106-107 B 4
Bū'īn-e Zahrā' 136-137 O 5
Buinsk [SU, Čuvašskaja ASSR] 124-125 Q 6
Buinsk [SU, Tatarskaja ASSR] 124-125 R 6
Buíque 100-101 F 5
Būīrah 166-167 H 1
Būīrat Şaḥarī 166-167 H 2
Bū'irdah, Al- 166-167 C 5
Buir Nur 142-143 M 2
Bū Ismā'īl 166-167 H 1
Buiten-IJ 128 I b 1
Buiten Veldert, Amsterdam- 128 I a 2
Buitenzorg = Bogor 148-149 E 8
Bū Izākārn 166-167 B 5
Buizinge = Buizingen 128 II a 2
Buizingen 128 II a 2
Buj 132-133 G 6
Bujalance 120-121 EF 10
Būjarun, Rā's — 166-167 JK 1
Bū Jaydūr, Rā's — 164-165 AB 3
Buji 148-149 M 8
Bujnaksk 126-127 N 5
Bujumbura 172 EF 2
Bukačača 132-133 W 7
Bū Kāhil, Jabal — 166-167 HJ 2
Buka Island 148-149 hj 6
Bukama 172 E 3
Būkān 136-137 LM 4
Bukavu 172 E 2
Bukene 172 F 2
Bū Khaḍrah, Jabal — 166-167 KL 2
Bū Khanāfis 166-167 F 2
Bukit Batu 152-153 K 4
Bukit Batu Bora 152-153 L 4
Bukit Besi 148-149 D 6
Bukit Betong 148-149 D 6
Bukit Betuensambang 152-153 K 5-6
Bukit Kana 152-153 K 4
Bukit Kelingkang 152-153 J 5
Bukit Ketri 150-151 C 9
Bukit Lonjak 152-153 JK 5
Bukit Mandai 154 III a 1
Bukit Mandai [SGP, place] 154 III a 1
Bukit Mertajam 150-151 C 10
Bukit Panjang 154 III a 1
Bukit Raya 148-149 F 7
Bukit Skalap 152-153 KL 4
Bukit Timah 154 III a 1
Bukit Timah [SGP, place] 154 III a 1
Bukittinggi 148-149 CD 7
Bukit Tukung 152-153 JK 6
Bükk 118 K 4-5
Bukkapatnam 140 CD 3
Bukoba 172 F 2
Bukum, Pulau — 154 III a 2
Bukum Kechil, Pulau — 154 III a 2
Bū Kutub 164-165 E 2
Bula [RI] 148-149 K 7
Bula [SU] 124-125 R 6
Bulagan = Bulgan 142-143 J 2
Bulan 148-149 H 4
Bulancak 136-137 GH 2
Bulandshahar = Bulandshur 138-139 FG 3
Bulandshur 138-139 FG 3
Bulangu 168-169 H 2
Bulanık 136-137 K 3
Būlāq 173 B 5
Būlāq, Al-Qāhirah- 170 II b 1
Būlāq ad-Dakrūr 170 II ab 1
Bulawayo 172 E 6
Bulaydat 'Amūr 166-167 J 3
Buldan 136-137 C 3
Buldhāna 138-139 F 7
Bulghānā = Buldhāna 138-139 F 7
Buldir Island 58-59 r 6
Bulgan [Mongolia, administrative unit = 9 ◁] 142-143 J 2
Bulgan [Mongolia, place Bulgan] 142-143 J 2
Bulgan [Mongolia, place Chovd] 142-143 G 2
Bulgaria 122-123 K-M 4
Buli = Puli 146-147 H 10
Buli, Teluk — 148-149 J 6
Bulkī 164-165 M 7
Bulla, ostrov — 126-127 O 6
Bullahaar 164-165 a 1
Bullard, TX 76-77 G 6
Bullenhausen 130 I b 2
Buller, Mount — 160 H 6
Buller River 161 DE 5
Bullfinch 158-159 C 6
Bull Mountains 68-69 B 2
Bulloo Downs 158-159 H 5
Bulloo River 158-159 H 5
Bulls Bay 80-81 G 4
Bullshead Butte 61 C 6
Bull Shoals Lake 78-79 C 2
Būlmān 166-167 D 3
Bulnes 106-107 A 6
Buloh 154 III b 1
Buloh, Kampung — 150-151 D 10
Bulsār 138-139 D 7
Bultfontein 174-175 FG 5
Bulu 148-149 J 6
Buluan 148-149 H 5
Bulucan = Emirhan 136-137 GH 3
Bulukumba 148-149 GH 8
Bulungan 148-149 G 6
Buluntou Hai = Ojorong nuur 142-143 F 2
Bulwater 174-175 D 7
Bulwer 174-175 H 5
Bulyea 61 F 5
Bum, Mu'o'ng — = Mu'o'ng Boum 150-151 D 1
Būmālin Dādis 166-167 CD 4
Bumba [ZRE, Bandundu] 172 C 3
Bumba [ZRE, Équateur] 172 D 1
Bumba = Boumba 164-165 H 8
Būmba Būm 141 E 2
Bumbeni 174-175 K 4
Bumbu 170 IV a 2
Bumbu, Kinshasa- 170 IV a 2
Bum Bum, Pulau — 152-153 N 3
Bū Midfār'ah 166-167 H 1
Bumkin Island 84 I c 3
Bumthang 141 B 2
Bumthang Chhu 141 B 2
Buna, TX 78-79 C 5
Buna [EAK] 172 G 1
Buna [PNG] 148-149 N 8
Bū Naṣr, Jabal — 166-167 E 3
Bunbah, Khalīj al- 164-165 J 2
Bunbury 158-159 BC 6
Bundaberg 158-159 K 4
Bundelkhand 134-135 MN 6
Būndi 134-135 M 5
Bundooma 158-159 FG 4
Bundoran 119 B 4
Būndu 138-139 K 6
Bung, Sông — = Sông Boung 150-151 F 5
Bunga 168-169 H 4
Bungalaut, Selat — 152-153 C 6-7
Bunge, zemľa — 132-133 b 2-3
Bungendore 160 JK 5
Bunger Oasis 53 C 11
Bung Kan 150-151 D 3
Bungo-suidō 142-143 P 5
Bungotakada 144-145 H 6
Bu'ng Sai = Ban Bu'ng Sai 150-151 F 5
Bunguran, Pulau — 148-149 E 6
Bunguran Selatan, Kepulauan — 148-149 E 6
Bunguran Utara, Kepulauan — 148-149 E 6
Buni 168-169 HJ 3
Bunia 172 F 1
Bunker Hill, AK 58-59 E 4
Bunker Hill, TX 85 III a 2
Bunker Hill Monument 84 I b 2
Bunkeya 172 E 4
Bunkie, LA 78-79 CD 5
Bunkyō, Tōkyō- 155 III b 1
Bunnell, FL 80-81 c 2
Bun No'a = Boun Neua 150-151 CD 2
Bunsuru 168-169 G 2
Bunta 148-149 H 7
Buntharik 150-151 E 5
Buntok 148-149 FG 7
Bunya 168-169 EF 3
Bunyan 136-137 F 3
Bunyu, Pulau — 148-149 G 6
Buol 148-149 H 6
Buolkalach 132-133 W 3
Buôn Bat 150-151 G 6
Buôn Hô 150-151 G 6
Buôn Ma Thuôt = Ban Mê Thuôt 148-149 E 4
Buôn Plao Sieng 150-151 FG 6
Buor-Chaja, guba — 132-133 Z 3
Buor-Chaja, mys — 132-133 Z 3
Bū Qadir 166-167 G 1
Buq'ah 166-167 J 1
Buqaliq tagh 142-143 G 4
Buqian = Puqian 146-147 C 11
Buquim 100-101 F 6
Buquq 142-143 E 3
Būr 164-165 L 7
Bura 172 GH 2
Bur Acaba = Buur Hakkaba 164-165 N 8
Buraghat, 'Irq — 166-167 L 6
Bū Raghragh, Wād — 166-167 C 3
Burāgyī 141 E 7
Burajevo 124-125 U 6
Buram 164-165 K 6
Bū Ramlī, Jabal — 166-167 L 2
Buranhém 100-101 DE 9
Buranhém, Rio — 100-101 DE 9
Burao = Bur'o 164-165 O 7
Buras, LA 78-79 E 6
Burāthônzū Taunggyā 141 EF 8
Burathum 138-139 K 3
Bur'atskaja Avtonomnaja Sovetskaja Socialističeskaja Respublika = Buryat Autonomous Soviet Socialist Republic 132-133 T 7-V 6
Būr Atyan = Nawādhību 164-165 A 4
Buraydah 134-135 E 5
Buraymī, Al- 134-135 H 6
Burbank, CA 74-75 DE 5
Burbank, IL 83 II a 2
Burbank, OK 76-77 F 4
Burchanbuudaj 142-143 H 2
Burcher 160 H 4
Burchun 142-143 F 2
Burdeau = Mahdīyah 164-165 E 1
Burdekin River 158-159 J 4
Burdett, KS 68-69 G 6
Burdur 134-135 BC 3
Burdur gölü 136-137 CD 4
Burdwān 134-135 O 6
Burdwood Bank 111 DE 8
Burê [ETH, Gojam] 164-165 M 6
Bure [ETH, Ilubabor] 164-165 M 7
Bureā 116-117 J 5
Bureau, Lac — 62 O 2
Büreen = Büren 142-143 K 2
Bureinskij chrebet 132-133 Z 7-8
Bureja 132-133 Z 7
Büren [Mongolia] 142-143 K 2
Burenchaan [Mongolia, Chentij] 142-143 L 2
Burenchaan [Mongolia, Chövsgöl] 142-143 H 2
Bürencogt 142-143 L 2
Būr Fu'ād = Būr Sādāt 173 C 2
Burg 118 EF 2
Būr Gābo = Buur Gaabo 172 H 2
Burgampahāḍ = Borgampād 140 E 2
Bur Gao = Buur Gaabo 172 H 2
Burgas 122-123 M 4
Burgaski zaliv 122-123 MN 4
Burgaw, NC 80-81 GH 3
Bürgel, Offenbach- 128 III b 1
Burg el-'Arab = Burj al-'Arab 136-137 C 7
Burgenland 118 H 5
Burgeo 63 H 4
Burgeo Bank 63 GH 4
Burgersdorp 172 E 8
Burgersfort 174-175 J 3
Burgerville 174-175 F 6
Burgess, Mount — 58-59 S 3
Burgfjället 116-117 F 5
Burghalden 128 IV b 2
Burghersdorp = Burgersdrop 172 E 8
Bürgio 122-123 E 7
Burgos 120-121 F 7
Burgsvik 116-117 H 9
Būr Hakkaba 172 H 1
Burḥānā = Budhāna 138-139 F 3
Burhaniye 136-137 B 3
Burhānpur 134-135 M 6
Burhi Dihing 141 D 2
Burhi Gandak 138-139 K 4-5
Būrhi Gandaki 138-139 K 3-4
Burholme, Philadelphia-, PA 84 III c 1
Burholme Park 84 III c 1
Buri 102-103 H 5
Buria Gandak = Burhi Gandak 138-139 K 4-5
Burias Island 148-149 H 4
Burica, Punta — 64-65 K 10
Burietá 100-101 E 7
Burig 130 III d 2
Burin 63 J 4
Burin Peninsula 56-57 Z 8
Buri Ram 148-149 D 3-4
Buriti [BR, Maranhão] 92-93 L 5
Buriti [BR, Minas Gerais] 102-103 H 3
Buriti, Rio — 104-105 G 3
Buriti Alegre 102-103 H 3
Buriti Bravo 92-93 L 6
Buriticupu, Rio — 100-101 A 3
Buriti dos Lopes 92-93 L 5
Buritirama 100-101 C 6
Buritis 102-103 J 1
Buritizeiro 102-103 K 2
Burj al-Ahmad 166-167 K 4
Burj al-'Arab 136-137 C 7
Burj al-Haṭṭabah 164-165 F 2
Burj al-Khamīrah 166-167 K 2
Burj Ban Būl'īd 164-165 E 3
Burj Bu 'Arīrij 166-167 J 1
Burj Bū Na'amah 166-167 G 2
Burj Būrgībah 166-167 LM 3
Burj Falāy 166-167 E 6
Burjing = Burchun 142-143 F 2
Burj Luṭfī 164-165 F 3-4
Burj Mahībal 166-167 H 5
Burj Mas'ūdah 166-167 L 4
Burj 'Umar Idrīs 166-165 EF 3
Burkburnett, TX 76-77 E 5
Burke, SD 68-69 G 3
Burkesville, KY 78-79 G 2
Burketown 158-159 GH 3
Burkeville, VA 80-81 GH 2
Burkina Faso 164-165 D 6
Burks Falls 72-73 G 2
Burleith, Washington-, DC 82 II a 1
Burleson, TX 76-77 F 6
Burley, ID 66-67 G 4
Burli 124-125 T 8
Burlingame, CA 74-75 B 4
Burlingame, KS 70-71 BC 6
Burlington 72-73 G 3
Burlington, CO 68-69 E 6
Burlington, IA 64-65 H 3
Burlington, KS 70-71 BC 6
Burlington, MA 84 I a 1
Burlington, NC 80-81 G 2
Burlington, NJ 84 III d 1
Burlington, VT 64-65 M 3
Burlington, WA 66-67 BC 1
Burlington, WI 70-71 F 4
Burlington County Airpark 84 III de 2
Burlington Junction, MO 70-71 C 5
Burma 148-149 BC 2
Burma = Birma 148-149 BC 2
Burma Road 141 F 3
Burnaby Island 60 B 3
Burnet, TX 76-77 E 7
Burney, CA 66-67 C 5
Burney, Monte — 108-109 C 9
Burnie 158-159 HJ 8
Burns, CO 68-69 C 6
Burns, KS 68-69 H 6
Burns, OR 66-67 D 4
Burns Flat, OK 76-77 E 5
Burnside, KY 70-71 H 7
Burns Lake 56-57 LM 7
Burnsville, MS 78-79 E 3
Burnsville, WV 72-73 F 5
Burnt Creek 56-57 X 6-7
Burnt Ground 88-89 J 3
Burnt Lake 63 E 1
Burntop 174-175 J 4
Burnt Paw, AK 58-59 QR 3
Burnt River 66-67 DE 3
Burnt River Mountains 66-67 DE 3
Burntwood Lake 61 H 3
Burntwood River 61 J 3
Bur'o 164-165 b 2
Buron [SU] 126-127 M 5
Burqah, Khahrat — 136-137 GH 6
Burqān 136-137 M 8
Burra 158-159 G 6
Burra, Cape — = Ponta da Barra 174-175 L 3
Burra Falsa, Cape — = Ponta da Barra Falsa 174-175 L 2
Burrendong Reservoir 160 J 4
Burren Junction 160 J 3
Burrinjuck Reservoir 158-159 J 7
Burro, El- 76-77 D 8
Burro, Serranías del — 64-65 F 6
Burrton, KS 68-69 H 6
Burruyacú 111 CD 3
Burrwood, LA 78-79 E 6
Bursa 134-135 B 2-3
Būr Sādāt 173 C 2
Būr Safāga = Safājah 164-165 L 3
Būr Sa'īd 164-165 L 2
Burstall 61 D 5
Burštyn 126-127 B 2
Būr Sūdān 164-165 M 5
Burt, IA 70-71 C 4
Būr Tawfīg 173 C 3
Burt Lake 70-71 H 3
Buru, Pulau — 148-149 J 7
Burūj, Al- 166-167 C 3
Burullus, Buḥayrat al- 173 B 2
Burūm 134-135 F 8
Burundi 172 EF 2
Burun-Šibertuj, gora — 132-133 UV 8
Bururi 172 E 2
Burutu 168-169 G 4
Burwash 72-73 F 1
Burwash Landing 58-59 RS 6
Burwell, NE 68-69 G 5
Burwood, Sydney- 161 I a 2
Buryat Autonomous Soviet Socialist Republic 132-133 T 7-V 6
Burye = Burê 164-165 M 6
Buryn' 126-127 F 1
Burynšik 126-127 P 4
Bury Saint Edmunds 119 G 5
Busa, Cape — = Akrotérion Grambûsa 122-123 K 8
Bū Sa'ādah 166-167 J 2
Buşaiyah, Al- 134-135 EF 4
Bū Sālām 166-167 L 1
Buşayrah 136-137 J 5
Busayṭā', Al- 136-137 G 7-H 8
Busby 60 KL 3
Bus Cagaan Nuur = Böön Cagaan nuur 142-143 HJ 2
Būsh 173 B 3
Bū Shabaqah 166-167 L 2
Būshehr = Bandar-e Būshehr 134-135 G 5
Bushey 129 II a 1
Bushire = Bandar-e Būshehr 134-135 G 5
Bushland, TX 76-77 CD 5
Bushnell 72-73 FG 1
Bushnell, IL 70-71 E 5
Bushnell, NE 68-69 E 5
Bushnell Seamount 78-79 f 3
Būshqūf 166-167 K 1
Bushy Park 129 II a 2
Busing, Pulau — 154 III a 2
Businga 172 D 1
Busira 172 C 1-2
Buskerud 116-117 C 7-D 8
Buşrat ash-Shām 136-137 G 6
Bussa 168-169 G 3
Busselton 158-159 BC 6
Bustamante 76-77 D 9
Bustamante, Bahía — 108-109 FG 5
Bustleton, Philadelphia-, PA 84 III c 1
Busto Arsizio 122-123 C 3
Busuanga Island 148-149 G 4
Busuluk = Buzuluk 132-133 J 7
Buta 172 D 1
Butantã, São Paulo- 110 II a 2
Buta Ranquil [RA, La Pampa] 106-107 D 6
Buta Ranquil [RA, Mendoza] 106-107 BC 6
Butare 171 B 3
Butarque, Arroyo de — 113 III a 2
Butedale 60 C 3
Bute Inlet 60 E 4
Butembo 171 B 2
Butere 171 C 2
Butha Buthe 174-175 H 5
Butha Qi 142-143 N 2
Būthīdaung 141 C 5
Bū Th'rārah, Khalīj — 166-167 M 3
Butiaba 172 F 1
Bū Tilimīt 164-165 B 5
Butler, AL 78-79 E 4
Butler, GA 78-79 G 4
Butler, IN 70-71 H 5
Butler, MO 70-71 C 6
Butler, PA 72-73 G 4
Būtīlīs 166-167 F 2
Buṭmah 136-137 K 4
Butovo 113 V c 4
Bu Toy 150-151 F 6
Butre 124-125 K 7
Butsha 171 B 2
Butsikáki 122-123 J 6
Butte, MT 64-65 D 2
Butte, ND 68-69 F 2
Butte, NE 68-69 G 4
Butte Creek, MT 68-69 C 2
Büttelhorn 128 III a 2
Butte Meadows, CA 66-67 BC 5
Butterworth = Bagan Jaya 148-149 D 5
Butterworth = Gcuwa 172 E 8
Butt of Lewis 119 C 2
Butuan 148-149 HJ 5
Butung, Pulau — 148-149 H 7-8
Butung, Selat — 152-153 P 8
Buturlinovka 126-127 K 1
Buṭvāl = Butwāl 138-139 J 4
Butwāl 138-139 J 4
Buulo Berde 164-165 b 3
Buwārah, Jabal — 173 D 3
Buxar 138-139 JK 5
Buxton, ND 68-69 H 2
Buxton [GUY] 98-99 JK 1
Buxton [ZA] 174-175 F 4
Buyo 168-169 D 4
Buyr Nur = Buir Nur 142-143 M 2
Büyükada, İstanbul- 136-137 C 2
Büyük Ağrı dağı 134-135 E 2-3
Büyükdere, İstanbul- 154 I b 2
Büyük Doğanca 136-137 B 2
Büyük Köhne 136-137 F 3
Büyük Mahya 136-137 B 2
Büyük Menderes nehri 134-135 B 3
Buzači 134-135 G 1-2
Buzău [RO, place] 122-123 M 3
Buzău [RO, river] 122-123 M 3
Buzaymah 164-165 J 4
Buzd'ak 124-125 U 6
Buzi 146-147 G 5
Buzi = Potzu 146-147 H 10
Bū Zīd, Ḥāssī — 166-167 GH 4
Búzios, Cabo dos — 102-103 M 5
Búzios, Ilha dos — 102-103 K 5
Bū Z'nīqah 166-167 C 3
Bužory 126-127 D 3
Buzuluk 132-133 J 7
Buzzards Bay 72-73 L 4
Byādagī = Byādgi 140 B 3
Byādgi 140 B 3
Byam Martin Channel 56-57 PQ 2
Byam Martin Island 56-57 Q 2-3
Byar 138-139 G 2
Byārmā = Beārma 138-139 G 6
Byās = Beās 138-139 E 2
Byāurā = Biaora 138-139 F 6
Byāvar = Beāwar 134-135 LM 5
Byawar = Beāwar 134-135 LM 5
Byberry Creek 84 III cd 1
Býblos = Jubayl 136-137 F 5
Bychawa 118 L 3
Bychov 124-125 GH 7
Bydgoszcz 118 HJ 2
Byely Island = Belyj ostrov 132-133 MN 3
Byfleet 129 II a 2
Bygdin 116-117 C 7
Bygland 116-117 BC 8
Byhalia, MS 78-79 E 3
Byk 126-127 D 3
Bykovo [SU, Volgogradskaja Oblast'] 126-127 M 2
Bylot Island 56-57 V 3
Byōhyī = Beohāri 138-139 H 5
Byoritsu = Miaoli 146-147 H 9
Byrd 53 AB 25
Byrd, Cape — 53 C 29
Byrd Land 53 AB 23-22
Byrock 158-159 J 6
Byrōn 113 IV b 2
Byron, CA 74-75 C 4
Byron, IL 70-71 F 4
Byron, Cape — 158-159 K 5
Byrōn, Isla — 108-109 B 6
Byron Bay 160 LM 2
Byron Sound 108-109 J 8
Byrranga, gory — 132-133 Q 3-V 2
Byske 116-117 J 5
Byssa 132-133 Z 7
Bystrica 124-125 R 4
Bystryj Tanyp 124-125 U 6
Bytom 118 J 3

Bytoš' 124-125 JK 7
Bytów 118 H 1
Byzantinon Museio 113 IV ab 2

Bzémā = Buzaymah 164-165 J 4
Bzura 118 J 2
Bzyp 126-127 K 5

C

Ca, Sông — 150-151 E 3
Caacupé 111 E 3
Čaadajevka 124-125 P 7
Caaguazú [PY, administrative unit] 102-103 DE 6
Caaguazú [PY, place] 111 EF 3
Caaguazú, Cordillera de — 111 E 3
Caála 172 BC 4
Caamaño Sound 60 BC 3
Caapiranga 98-99 H 6
Caapucú 111 E 3
Caarapó 102-103 E 5
Caatiba 100-101 D 8
Caatinga 92-93 K 8
Caatinga, Rio — 102-103 JK 2
Caatinga, Serra da — 100-101 EF 3
Caatingas 92-93 L 7-M 6
Caazapá [PY, administrative unit] 102-103 DE 7
Caazapá [PY, place] 111 E 3
Cabaçal, Rio — 102-103 CD 1
Cabaiguán 88-89 G 3
Caballería, Cabo de — 120-121 K 8
Caballero 102-103 D 6
Cáballito, Buenos Aires- 110 III b 1
Caballococha 92-93 E 5
Caballo Reservoir 76-77 A 6
Caballos Mesteños, Llanos de los — 76-77 BC 8
Cabana 96-97 BC 6
Cabanaconde 96-97 EF 9
Cabanatuan 148-149 H 3
Cabanillas 96-97 F 9
Cabano 63 B 4
Cabecão 102-103 L 5
Cabeceira do Apa 102-103 E 4-5
Cabeceras 94-95 C 5
Cabedelo 92-93 N 6
Cabeza del Buey 120-121 E 9
Cabeza del Mar 108-109 D 9
Cabeza de Vaca, Punta — 104-105 A 10
Cabeza Negra 86-87 HJ 8
Cabezas 92-93 G 8
Cabezon, NM 76-77 A 5
Cabildo [RA] 106-107 FG 7
Cabildo [RCH] 106-107 B 4
Cabimas 92-93 E 2
Cabinda [Angola, administrative unit] 172 B 3
Cabinda [Angola, place] 172 B 3
Cabinet Mountains 66-67 E 1
Cabin John, MD 82 II a 1
Cable, WI 70-71 E 2
Cable Car of Singapore 154 III a 2
Cabo Alejandra = Cape Alexandra 111 J 8
Cabo Alto = Cape Bougainville 108-109 KL 8
Cabo Alto = Cape Dolphin 111 E 8
Cabo Aristizábal 108-109 FG 5
Cabo Bagur 120-121 J 8
Cabo Beata 88-89 L 6
Cabo Blanco [CR] 64-65 J 10
Cabo Blanco [RA] 111 CD 7
Cabo Blanco [YV] 91 II b 1
Cabo Bojador = Rā's Bujdūr 164-165 AB 3
Cabo Branco 92-93 N 6
Cabo Buen Tiempo 108-109 EF 8
Cabo Cabrón 88-89 M 5
Cabo Caçiporé 92-93 JK 4
Cabo Camarón 88-89 D 6
Cabo Carvoeiro 120-121 C 9
Cabo Castro 108-109 B 8
Cabo Catoche 64-65 J 7
Cabo Codera 92-93 F 2
Cabo Colnett 86-87 B 2
Cabo Corrientes [C] 88-89 DE 4
Cabo Corrientes [CO] 92-93 D 3
Cabo Corrientes [MEX] 64-65 E 7
Cabo Corrientes [RA] 111 E 5
Cabo Corrientes = Cape Carysfort 108-109 L 8
Cabo Creus 120-121 J 7
Cabo Cruz 64-65 L 8
Cabo Curioso 108-109 F 7
Cabo Dañoso 108-109 F 7
Cabo da Roca 120-121 C 9
Cabo Dartuch 120-121 J 9
Cabo de Caballería 120-121 K 8
Cabo Decepción = Cape Disappointment 111 J 8-9
Cabo de Espichel 120-121 C 9
Cabo de Finisterre 120-121 BC 7
Cabo de Gata 120-121 FG 10
Cabo de Honduras 64-65 JK 8
Cabo de Hornos 111 CD 9
Cabo de la Aguja 94-95 D 2
Cabo de la Nao 120-121 H 9
Cabo de la Vela 92-93 E 2
Cabo Delgado [Mozambique, administrative unit] 172 GH 4
Cabo Delgado [Mozambique, cape] 172 H 4
Cabo de Palos 120-121 G 10
Cabo de Peñas 120-121 E 7
Cabo de Salinas 120-121 J 9
Cabo de San Juan de Guía 92-93 DE 2
Cabo de San Lorenzo 92-93 C 5
Cabo de Santa Maria 120-121 CD 10
Cabo de Santa Maria = Cap Sainte-Marie 172 J 7
Cabo de Santa Pola 120-121 GH 9
Cabo de Santo Agostinho 100-101 G 5
Cabo de São Roque 92-93 MN 6
Cabo de São Tomé 92-93 LM 9
Cabo de São Vicente 120-121 C 10
Cabo Deseado 111 AB 8
Cabo de Sines 120-121 C 10
Cabo de Tortosa 120-121 H 8
Cabo de Trafalgar 120-121 D 10
Cabo Dois Irmãos 110 I b 2
Cabo Dos Bahías 111 CD 7
Cabo dos Búzios 102-103 M 5
Cabo Dyer 108-109 AB 7
Cabo Engaño 88-89 MN 5
Cabo Espíritu Santo 108-109 EF 9
Cabo Esteban 108-109 B 8
Cabo Falso [Honduras] 88-89 E 7
Cabo Falso [MEX] 64-65 D 7
Cabo Farallón = Cabo Santa Elena 64-65 J 9
Cabo Formentor 120-121 J 8
Cabo Frio [BR, cape] 92-93 L 9
Cabo Frio [BR, place] 92-93 L 9
Cabo Glouster 108-109 BC 10
Cabo Gracias a Dios 64-65 K 8
Cabo Guardián 108-109 FG 7
Cabo Gurupi 98-99 PQ 5
Cabo Hall 108-109 G 10
Cabo Haro 64-65 D 6
Cabo Humos 106-107 A 5
Cabo Jorge 108-109 B 8
Cabo Lort 108-109 B 5
Cabo Lucrecia 88-89 J 4
Cabo Maguari 92-93 K 4-5
Cabo Maisi 64-65 M 7
Cabo Manglares 92-93 CD 4
Cabo Marzo 92-93 D 3
Cabo Matapalo 64-65 K 10
Cabo Meredit = Cape Meredith 111 D 8
Cabo Mondego 120-121 C 8
Cabonga, Réservoir — 72-73 HJ 1
Cabo Norte 92-93 K 4
Cabo Nuevo = Rā's al-Jadīd 166-167 E 2
Cabool, MO 78-79 CD 2
Caboolture 160 L 1
Cabo Orange 92-93 J 4
Cabo Ortegal 120-121 CD 7
Cabo Pakenham 108-109 AB 7
Cabo Pantoja = Pantoja 92-93 DE 5
Cabo Paquica 104-105 A 7
Cabo Pasado 92-93 C 5
Cabo Peñas 108-109 F 9
Cabo Polonio 111 F 4
Cabo Primero 108-109 AB 7
Cabo Prior 120-121 C 7
Cabo Quedal 111 AB 6
Cabo Quilán 108-109 B 4
Cabora Bassa 172 F 5
Cabo Raper 108-109 AB 6
Cabo Raso [RA, cape] 108-109 G 5
Cabo Raso [RA, place] 111 CD 6
Cabo Raso = Cabo Norte 92-93 K 4
Cabo Reyes 96-97 BC 3
Cabo Rizzuto 122-123 G 6
Cabo Rojo [MEX] 64-65 G 7
Cabo Rojo [Puerto Rico] 88-89 N 6
Cabo Samaná 88-89 M 5
Cabo San Antonio [C] 64-65 K 7
Cabo San Antonio [RA] 106-107 J 6
Cabo San Bartolomé 108-109 G 10
Cabo San Diego 111 CD 8
Cabo San Francisco de Paula 108-109 F 7
Cabo San Juan [Equatorial Guinea] 164-165 F 8
Cabo San Juan [RA] 111 D 8
Cabo San Lázaro 64-65 D 7
Cabo San Lucas 64-65 E 7
Cabo San Quintín 64-65 C 5
Cabo San Román 92-93 EF 2
Cabo Santa Elena 64-65 J 9
Cabo Santa Marta Grande 102-103 H 8
Cabo Santiago 108-109 AB 8
Cabo San Vicente 108-109 FG 10
Cabo Silleiro 120-121 C 7
Cabot, AR 78-79 CD 3
Cabo Tablas 106-107 AB 3
Cabo Taitao 111 A 7
Cabo Tate 108-109 BC 9
Cabot Head 72-73 F 2
Cabo Toriñana 120-121 C 7
Cabo Tres Puntas 111 CD 7
Cabo Tromba Grande 100-101 E 8
Cabot Strait 56-57 YZ 8
Cabo Verde, Islas — 50-51 H 5
Cabo Vidio 120-121 DE 7
Cabo Vigia 108-109 F 7
Cabo Vírgenes 111 C 8
Cabra 120-121 E 10
Cabra, Monte — 64-65 b 3
Cabra Corral, Embalse — 104-105 D 9
Cabral, La — 106-107 G 3
Cabral, Serra do — 102-103 K 2
Cabras [BR] 102-103 J 5
Cabras, Las — 106-107 B 5
Cabred 106-107 J 3
Cabrera 88-89 M 5
Cabrera, Isla — 120-121 J 9
Cabriel 120-121 G 9
Cabrillo, Point — 74-75 AB 3
Cabrobó 100-101 E 5
Cabrón, Cabo — 88-89 M 5
Cabruta 94-95 H 4
Cabuçu de Cima 110 II b 1
Cabul = Kabul 134-135 K 4
Cabure 94-95 G 2
Caburé, El — 104-105 E 10
Caburgua, Laguna — 108-109 D 2
Cabusa Island = Kabūzā Kyūn 150-151 AB 6
Cabuyaro 94-95 E 5
Caca 126-127 M 2
Caçador 111 F 3
Cacahual, Isla — 94-95 BC 5
Čačak 122-123 J 4
Cacaoui, Lac — 63 C 2
Caçapava 102-103 K 5
Caçapava, Serra de — 106-107 L 3
Caçapava do Sul 111 F 4
Càccia, Capo — 122-123 BC 5
Cacequi 111 F 3
Cáceres [BR] 92-93 H 8
Cáceres [CO] 92-93 D 3
Cáceres [E] 120-121 D 9
Cáceres, Laguna — 104-105 GH 6
Cachan 129 I c 2
Cachapoal, Río — 106-107 B 5
Cāchār [IND] 141 C 3
Cachar [TJ] 142-143 M 3
Cachari 106-107 H 6
Cache, OK 76-77 E 5
Cache Creek 60 G 4
Cachegar = Qāshqār 142-143 CD 4
Cachemire = Kashmīr 134-135 LM 4
Cache Peak 66-67 G 4
Cacheu [Guinea Bissau, place] 164-165 A 6
Cacheu [Guinea Bissau, river] 168-169 B 2
Cacheuta 106-107 C 4
Cachi 111 C 3
Cachi, Nevado de — 111 C 2
Cachimbo, Parque Nacional do — 98-99 K 8-9
Cachimbo, Serra do — 92-93 HJ 6
Cachimo 172 D 3
Cachinal 104-105 B 9
Cáchira 94-95 E 4
Cachiyuyo 106-107 B 2
Cachoeira [BR ↙ Barreiras] 100-101 B 7
Cachoeira [BR ↓ Feira de Santana] 92-93 M 7
Cachoeira, Rio — 100-101 E 8
Cachoeira, Rio da — 110 I b 2
Cachoeira Acará 98-99 J 7
Cachoeira Alta [BR, Goias] 98-99 NO 7
Cachoeira Alta [BR, Paraná] 102-103 G 3
Cachoeira Ananás 98-99 M 8
Cachoeira Anta [BR, Amazonas] 98-99 H 8
Cachoeira Anta [BR, Pará] 98-99 O 7
Cachoeira Araras 98-99 M 8
Cachoeira Arregaço 104-105 F 2
Cachoeira Bela Vista 92-93 J 5
Cachoeira Benfica 98-99 L 5
Cachoeira Caiabi 98-99 L 10
Cachoeira Capinzal 98-99 JK 9
Cachoeira Capivara 92-93 J 6
Cachoeira Caracaraí 92-93 G 4
Cachoeira Cerreira Comprida 98-99 OP 10
Cachoeira Chapéu 98-99 K 7-8
Cachoeira Cinco de Maio 98-99 L 11
Cachoeira Comprida = Treze Quedas 92-93 H 4
Cachoeira Criminosa 98-99 HJ 5
Cachoeira Cruzeiro do Sul 98-99 H 10
Cachoeira da Boca 98-99 L 7
Cachoeira da Laje 98-99 L 5
Cachoeira da Pedra da Amolar 100-101 B 5
Cachoeira da Pedra Sêca 98-99 M 8
Cachoeira das Andorinhas 94-95 G 8
Cachoeira da Saudade 98-99 M 8
Cachoeira das Capoeiras 92-93 H 6
Cachoeira das Piranhas 98-99 HJ 10
Cachoeira de Paulo Afonso 92-93 M 6
Cachoeira de Rebojo 98-99 J 9
Cachoeira de Santa Isabel 98-99 OP 8
Cachoeira de São Lucas 98-99 J 9
Cachoeira de Tropêço Grande 98-99 OP 11
Cachoeira do Arari 92-93 K 5
Cachoeira do Catarino 98-99 G 10
Cachoeira Doce Ilusão 98-99 L 9
Cachoeira do Coatá 92-93 G 6
Cachoeira do Desastre 98-99 J 10
Cachoeira do Infernão 92-93 G 6
Cachoeira Dois Irmãos 98-99 J 9
Cachoeira do Jaú 98-99 OP 10
Cachoeira do Javari 98-99 LM 5
Cachoeira do Lajeado 98-99 H 10
Cachoeira do Limão 92-93 J 6
Cachoeira do Maribondo 102-103 H 4
Cachoeira do Mato 100-101 DE 9
Cachoeira do Pacu 92-93 J 9
Cachoeira do Periquito 92-93 G 6
Cachoeira do Pimenta 94-95 K 7
Cachoeira do Praião 92-93 K 8
Cachoeira do Samuel 98-99 G 9
Cachoeira do Sangue 98-99 L 7
Cachoeira do Sapateiro 92-93 H 5
Cachoeira dos Índios 92-93 G 4
Cachoeira dos Pilões 98-99 OP 9
Cachoeira do Sul 111 F 3-4
Cachoeira do Uba 98-99 MN 9
Cachoeira Dourada 102-103 H 3
Cachoeira do Urubu 98-99 OP 11
Cachoeira Figueira 98-99 J 9
Cachoeira Ilhas 98-99 JK 5
Cachoeira Ilhinha 98-99 K 5
Cachoeira Ipadu 92-93 F 4
Cachoeira Ipanoré 94-95 GH 7
Cachoeira Itaipava [BR, Rio Araguaia] 92-93 K 6
Cachoeira Itaipava [BR, Rio Xingu] 92-93 J 5
Cachoeira Jacureconga 100-101 A 2
Cachoeira Jaianary 94-95 J 7
Cachoeira Jararaca 102-103 G 6
Cachoeira Macaquara 98-99 M 4
Cachoeira Maçaranduba 92-93 J 4-5
Cachoeira Macuco 102-103 GH 4
Cachoeira Mamuira 98-99 P 6
Cachoeira Manuel Jorge 98-99 LM 7
Cachoeira Maria Velha 98-99 K 7
Cachoeira Marmelão 98-99 KL 7
Cachoeira Matamatá 98-99 HJ 8
Cachoeira Miriti 98-99 J 8
Cachoeira Mortandade 98-99 P 8
Cachoeira Paca 98-99 H 4
Cachoeira Paiçandu 92-93 J 5
Cachoeira Pariaxá 98-99 N 6
Cachoeira Patauá 98-99 FG 5
Cachoeira Paulista 102-103 K 5
Cachoeira Pederneira 92-93 FG 6
Cachoeira Pereira 98-99 KL 7
Cachoeira Peritos 98-99 GH 9
Cachoeira Pirapora 104-105 G 2
Cachoeira Pirarara 98-99 KL 5
Cachoeira Porto Seguro 98-99 MN 8
Cachoeira Querero 98-99 K 4-5
Cachoeira Regresso 92-93 HJ 5
Cachoeira Santa Teresa 98-99 G 9-10
Cachoeira Santo Antônio [BR, Rio Madeira] 92-93 FG 6
Cachoeira Santo Antônio [BR, Rio Roosevelt] 98-99 HJ 9
Cachoeira São Francisco 98-99 LM 7
Cachoeira Saranzal 98-99 H 8
Cachoeiras de Macacu 102-103 LM 5
Cachoeira Sêca 98-99 L 7
Cachoeira Soledade 98-99 LM 7
Cachoeira Tareraimbu 92-93 J 6
Cachoeira Temporal 92-93 J 7
Cachoeira Trava 92-93 H 5
Cachoeira Tucano 94-95 G 7
Cachoeira Uacuru 98-99 HJ 10
Cachoeira Uaianary 98-99 FG 4
Cachoeira Xateturu 98-99 MN 8
Cachoeiro de Itapemirim 92-93 LM 9
Cachoeiro do Canoeiro 98-99 OP 10
Cachoeiro Enseada 98-99 J 10
Cachoeiro Jacuzão 98-99 O 8
Cachoeiro Pereira 92-93 H 5
Cachos, Punta — 111 B 3
Cachuela Esperanza 104-105 D 2
Cachuela Piedra Liza 96-97 E 7
Cacimba de Dentro 100-101 G 4
Cacine 168-169 B 3
Caçiporé, Cabo — 92-93 JK 4
Caçiporé, Rio — 92-93 J 4
Cacique, Cerro — 108-109 D 4
Cacitúa, Morro — 108-109 C 4
Çaçmak 136-137 F 4
Cacolo 172 C 3-4
Caconda 172 BC 4
Cácota 94-95 E 4
Cactus, TX 76-77 E 9
Cactus Range 74-75 E 4
Caçu 102-103 G 3
Caculé 92-93 L 7
Caçumba, Ilha — 100-101 E 9
Cacuso 172 C 3
Čadan 132-133 R 7
Caddo, OK 76-77 F 5
Caddo Lake 76-77 GH 6
Cadena de Cerro de la Sal 96-97 D 7
Cadena de Huamuco 96-97 C 6
Cadereyta Jiménez 86-87 KL 5
Cadetes de Chile 106-107 D 4
Cadibarrawirracanna, Lake — 160 AB 2
Cadillac, MI 70-71 H 3
Cadillac [CDN] 66-67 JK 1
CaĐinh, Nam — = Nam Theun 150-151 E 3
Cádiz 120-121 D 10
Cadiz, CA 74-75 F 5
Cadiz, KY 78-79 EF 2
Cádiz, Golfo de — 120-121 D 10
Čadobec [SU, place] 132-133 S 6
Čadobec [SU, river] 132-133 S 6
Cadomin 60 J 3
Cadotte River 60 J 1
Cadret 106-107 G 5
Čadyr-Lunga 126-127 D 3
Caém 100-101 D 6
Caen 120-121 G 4
Caerdydd = Cardiff 119 E 6
Caerfyrddin = Carmarthen 119 D 6
Caernarfon 119 D 5
Caesarea 136-137 F 6
Caesarea = Kayseri 134-135 D 3
Caesarea Philippi = Bāniyās 136-137 FG 6
Caeté, Baía do — 100-101 A 1
Caeté, Rio — 98-99 D 9
Caetés 100-101 F 5
Caetité 92-93 L 7
Cafarnaum 100-101 D 6
Cafayate 111 C 3
Café, Serra do — 100-101 G 6
Cafelândia 102-103 H 4
Cafta = Kafta 164-165 M 6
Cagaan Cherem = Wanli Changcheng 142-143 K 4
Cagarras, Ilhas — 110 I b 3
Cagayan de Oro 148-149 HJ 5
Cagayan Islands 148-149 H 5
Cagayan Sulu Island 148-149 GH 5
Čagda 132-133 Z 6
Cageri 126-127 L 5
Caggan nuur 142-143 FG 2
Càgliari 122-123 C 6
Càgliari, Golfo di — 122-123 C 6
Čagoda [SU, place] 132-133 EF 6
Čagoda [SU, river] 124-125 K 4
Çağrankaya 136-137 J 2
Cag Sum = Dzag 142-143 H 2
Caguán, Río — 92-93 E 4
Caguas 64-65 N 8
Cahama 172 BC 5
Cahirciveen 119 AB 6
Cahors 120-121 H 6
Cahuapanas 92-93 D 6
Cahuapanas, Río — 96-97 C 4
Cahuilla Indian Reservation 74-75 E 6
Cahuinari, Río — 94-95 EF 8
Cahungula = Caungula 172 C 3
Caí 106-107 M 2
Caia [Mozambique] 172 G 5
Caiabi, Cachoeira — 98-99 L 10
Caiabis, Serra dos — 92-93 H 7
Caiambé 92-93 FG 5
Caiapó, Rio — 102-103 G 2
Caiapó, Serra do — 102-103 FG 2
Caiapônia 102-103 FG 2
Cai Ban, Đao — 148-149 E 2
Caibarién 64-65 L 7
Cai Bau 150-151 F 2
Cai Be 150-151 EF 7
Caiçara [BR, Bahia] 100-101 B 8
Caiçara [BR, Paraíba] 100-101 G 4
Caicara [YV] 92-93 F 3
Caicaral 94-95 K 3
Caicedonia 94-95 CD 5
Caicó 100-101 F 4
Caicos Islands 64-65 M 7
Caicos Passage 64-65 M 7
Cai Lây 150-151 EF 7
Cailloma 96-97 F 9
Caillou Bay 78-79 D 6
Caillou Lake 78-79 D 6
Caimán, Laguna — 94-95 G 6
Caimanero, Laguna del — 86-87 G 6
Caimanes 106-107 B 3-4
Caimito 64-65 b 3
Caimito, Río — 64-65 b 3
Caín, El — 108-109 E 3
Cain Creek 68-69 G 3
Caine, Río — 104-105 D 6
Cainsville, MO 70-71 D 5
Cai Nu'o'c 150-151 E 8
Cairari 92-93 K 5
Caird Land 53 B 33-34
Cairn Mount 58-59 K 6
Cairns 158-159 J 3
Cairns Lake 62 B 2
Cairo, GA 80-81 D 5
Cairo, IL 64-65 J 4
Cairo, NE 68-69 G 5
Cairo = Al-Qāhira 164-165 KL 2
Cairo Airport 170 II c 1
Cairo Tower 170 II b 1
Cairú 100-101 E 7
Cais, Rio — 100-101 D 3
Caiundo 172 C 5
Caiuvá, Lagoa do — 106-107 LM 4
Caiza 104-105 D 7
Caizi Hu 146-147 F 6
Cajabamba 92-93 D 6
Cajamar 102-103 J 5
Cajamarca [PE, administrative unit] 96-97 B 4-5
Cajamarca [PE, place] 92-93 D 6
Cajapió 92-93 KL 5
Cajarí 100-101 B 2
Cajatambo 92-93 D 7
Cajàzeira 100-101 E 8
Cajazeiras 100-101 E 4
Cajdamyn nuur, Ich — 142-143 GH 4
Čajek 134-135 L 2
Čajkovskij 124-125 U 5
Cajón del Manzano 106-107 B 7
Cajon Pass 74-75 E 5
Caju, Ilha do — 100-101 CD 2
Caju, Rio de Janeiro- 110 I b 2
Cajuás, Ponta dos — 92-93 M 5
Cajueiro [BR, Amazonas] 98-99 C 7
Cajueiro [BR, Maranhão] 100-101 A 2
Cajueiros, Lago dos — 100-101 CD 2
Cajuí 100-101 CD 6
Cajuru 102-103 J 4
Çakıralan 136-137 F 2
Cakung, Kali — 154 IV b 1-2
Čakva 126-127 K 6
Çal = Demirciköy 136-137 C 3
Cal, La — 104-105 G 6
Cal, Río de la — 104-105 G 6
Cala [ZA] 174-175 G 6
Calabar 164-165 F 7-8
Calabogie 72-73 H 2
Calabozo 92-93 F 3
Calabozo, Ensenada de — 94-95 F 2
Calàbria 122-123 FG 5
Calacoto 104-105 B 5
Calada, CA 74-75 F 5
Calafat 122-123 K 3-4
Calafate 111 B 8
Calafquen, Lago — 108-109 C 2
Calagua Islands 148-149 H 4
Calahari = Kalahari Desert 172 CD 6
Calahorra 120-121 G 7
Calais 120-121 H 3
Calais, Pas de — 120-121 HJ 3
Calakmul 86-87 Q 9
Calalaste, Sierra de — 111 C 2-3
Calama [BR] 92-93 G 6
Calama [RCH] 111 C 2
Calamar [CO ↘ Bogotá] 92-93 E 4
Calamar [CO ↘ Cartagena] 94-95 D 2
Calamarca 104-105 B 5
Calamian Group 148-149 G 4
Calamus River 68-69 G 4
Calandria, La — 106-107 H 3
Calang 148-149 C 6
Calansho Sand Sea = Serīr Kalanshyū 164-165 J 3
Calapan 148-149 H 4
Călăraşi 122-123 M 3
Calarcá 94-95 D 5
Cala Road = Calaweg 174-175 G 6
Calatayud 120-121 G 8
Calate = Qalāt 134-135 K 5
Călăţele 122-123 K 2
Calaweg 174-175 G 6
Calayan Island 148-149 H 3
Calbayog 148-149 HJ 4
Calbuco, Volcán — 108-109 C 3
Calca 92-93 E 7
Calcanhar, Ponta do — 92-93 M 6-N 5
Calcasieu Lake 78-79 C 6
Calcasieu River 78-79 C 5
Calcatapul, Sierra — 108-109 E 4
Calceta 96-97 AB 2
Calcha 104-105 D 7
Calchaquí 106-107 G 2
Calchaquíes, Cumbres — 104-105 D 10
Calchaquíes, Valles — 104-105 CD 9
Calchín 106-107 F 3
Calçoene 92-93 J 4
Calçoene, Rio — 98-99 N 3-4
Calcutta 134-135 O 6
Calcutta-Alipore 154 II ab 2
Calcutta-Ballygunge 154 II b 2
Calcutta-Beliaghata 154 II b 2
Calcutta-Bhowanipore 154 II b 2
Calcutta-Chitpur 154 II b 2
Calcutta-Cossipore 154 II b 2
Calcutta-Dhakuria 154 II b 2
Calcutta-Gariya 154 II b 3
Calcutta-Jadabpur 154 II b 3
Calcutta-Jorasanko 154 II b 2
Calcutta-Kalighat 154 II ab 2
Calcutta-Kasba 154 II b 2
Calcutta-Kidderpore 154 II ab 2
Calcutta-Maidan 154 II ab 2
Calcutta-Simla 154 II b 2
Calcutta-Sura 154 II b 2
Calcutta-Tapsia 154 II b 2
Calcutta-Ultadanga 154 II b 2
Calcutta-Watganj 154 II a 2
Caldas [BR] 102-103 J 4
Caldas [CO, administrative unit] 94-95 D 5
Caldas [CO, place] 94-95 D 4
Caldas da Rainha 120-121 C 9
Caldas Novas 102-103 H 2
Caldeirão 100-101 D 7
Caldeirão, Ilha do — 98-99 D 7
Caldeirão Grande 100-101 D 6
Caldén, El — 106-107 DE 3
Caldera 111 B 3
Caldera, La — 104-105 D 9
Çaldere 136-137 G 2
Calderón 94-95 bc 2
Çaldıran 136-137 K 3
Caldono 94-95 C 6
Caldwell, ID 66-67 E 4
Caldwell, KS 76-77 F 4
Caldwell, OH 72-73 F 5
Caldwell, TX 76-77 F 7
Calecute = Calicut 134-135 LM 8
Caledon 172 CD 8
Caledon Bay 158-159 G 2
Caledonia, MN 70-71 E 4
Caledonia [CDN, Nova Scotia] 63 D 5
Caledonia [CDN, Ontario] 72-73 G 3
Caledonian Canal 119 D 3
Caledonrivier 172 E 7-8
Calemar 96-97 C 5
Calera 104-105 C 7
Calera, AL 78-79 F 4
Calera, La — 106-107 B 4
Caleta Buena 104-105 A 6
Caleta Clarencia 108-109 DE 9
Caleta de Vique 64-65 b 3
Caleta Guanilla del Norte 104-105 A 7
Caleta Josefina 108-109 E 9
Caleta Loa 104-105 A 7
Caleta Molles 106-107 AB 4
Caleta Olivia 111 C 7
Caleufú 111 D 5
Caleufú, Río — 108-109 D 3
Calexico, CA 74-75 F 6
Calf Island 84 I c 2
Calfucurá 106-107 J 6
Çalgan 136-137 H 4
Calgary 56-57 O 7
Calhan, CO 68-69 D 6
Calhoun, GA 78-79 G 3
Calhoun, LA 78-79 C 4
Calhoun, TN 80-81 D 3
Calhoun City, MS 78-79 E 4
Calhoun Falls, SC 80-81 E 3
Cali 92-93 D 4
Calico Rock, AR 78-79 CD 2
Calicut 134-135 LM 8
Caliente, CA 74-75 D 5
Caliente, NV 64-65 CD 4
California, MO 70-71 D 6
Califórnia [BR] 102-103 G 6
California [TT] 94-95 L 2
California [USA, administrative unit] 64-65 B 3-C 5
California [USA, landscape] 196 G 5-H 7
California, Gulf of — 64-65 D 5-E 7
California, La — 106-107 FG 4
California, University of — [USA, Los Angeles] 83 III b 1
California, University of — [USA, San Francisco] 83 I c 1
California State College 83 III c 2
California State University 83 III c 1
Căliman, Munţii — 122-123 L 2
Calimere, Point — 134-135 MN 8
Călineşti 122-123 L 3
Calingasta 111 BC 4
Calion, AR 78-79 C 4
Calipatria, CA 74-75 F 6
Calispell Peak 66-67 E 1
Calistoga, CA 74-75 B 3
Calitzdorp 174-175 D 7
Calka 126-127 M 6
Calkiní 64-65 H 7
Callabonna, Lake — 158-159 G 5
Callabonna Creek 160 E 2
Calla-Calla, Cerros de — 96-97 BC 5
Callafo = Kelafo 164-165 N 7
Callahan, FL 80-81 c 1
Callahan, Mount — 74-75 E 3
Callander [CDN] 72-73 G 1
Callao 92-93 D 7
Callao, El — 94-95 L 4
Callaquén 106-107 B 6
Callaquén, Volcán — 106-107 B 6
Callaway, NE 68-69 FG 5
Calle Larga 94-95 E 3
Calling Lake [CDN, lake] 60 L 2
Calling Lake [CDN, place] 60 L 2
Callison Ranch 58-59 W 7
Calmar 60 L 3
Calmar, IA 70-71 DE 4
Calmon 102-103 G 7
Čalna 124-125 JK 3
Calógeras 102-103 GH 5
Caloosahatchee River 80-81 c 3
Calotmul 86-87 QR 7
Caltagirone 122-123 F 7
Caltama, Cerro — 104-105 BC 7
Caltanissetta 122-123 EF 7
Calulo 172 BC 3-4
Calumet, MI 70-71 F 2
Calumet [CDN] 72-73 J 2
Calumet [USA] 83 II b 2
Calumet, Lake — 83 II b 2
Calva, AZ 74-75 HJ 6
Calvados, Côte du — 120-121 G 4
Calvas, Río — 96-97 B 4
Calve 106-107 G 7
Calvert, AL 78-79 EF 5
Calvert, TX 76-77 F 7
Calvert City, KY 78-79 E 2
Calvert Island 60 C 4
Calvi 122-123 C 4
Calvin, OK 76-77 F 5
Calvinia 172 CD 8
Camabatela 172 C 3
Camaçari 100-101 E 7
Camachigama, Lac — 62 NO 3
Camacho [BOL] 104-105 D 7
Camacho [MEX] 86-87 JK 5
Camacupa 172 C 4
Camaguán 94-95 H 3
Camagüey 64-65 L 7
Camagüey, Archipiélago de — 64-65 L 7
Camajuaní 88-89 G 3
Çamalan 136-137 F 4
Camalaú 100-101 F 4
Camamu 100-101 E 7
Camaná 92-93 E 8
Camapuã 92-93 J 8
Camapuã, Sertão de — 92-93 J 8-9
Camaquã 111 F 4
Camaquã, Rio — 106-107 L 3
Camararé, Rio — 98-99 J 11
Çamardı 136-137 F 4
Camargo, OK 76-77 E 4-5
Camargo [BOL] 92-93 FG 9
Camargo [MEX] 64-65 E 6
Camargo, Ciudad — 76-77 E 9
Camargue 120-121 K 7
Camarico 106-107 B 5
Camarillo, CA 74-75 D 5
Camariñas 120-121 C 7
Camarón [MEX] 76-77 DE 9
Camarón [PA] 64-65 b 3
Camarón, Cabo — 88-89 D 6
Camarones 111 CD 6
Camarones, Bahía — 108-109 G 5
Camarones, Río — 104-105 AB 6
Camas, ID 66-67 G 3
Camas, WA 66-67 B 3
Camas Creek 66-67 GH 3
Camataquí = Villa Abecia 92-93 FG 9
Camateí 100-101 C 8
Ca Mâu 148-149 DE 5
Ca Mau = Quan Long 148-149 DE 5
Ca Mau, Mui — = Mui Bai Bung 148-149 D 5
Cambaia = Cambay 134-135 L 6
Cambajuva 106-107 N 2
Cambará 102-103 G 5
Cambay 134-135 L 6
Cambay, Gulf of — 134-135 L 6
Cambé 102-103 G 5
Camberwell, London- 129 II b 2
Camberwell, Melbourne- 161 II c 2
Cambing = Ilha de Ataúro 148-149 J 8
Cambodia 148-149 DE 4
Camboriú 102-103 H 7
Camborne 119 D 6
Cambrai 120-121 J 3
Cambray, NM 76-77 A 6
Cambria, CA 74-75 C 5
Cambrian Mountains 119 D 5-E 6
Cambridge, ID 66-67 E 3
Cambridge, IL 70-71 EF 5

Cambridge, MA 64-65 NM 3
Cambridge, MD 72-73 H 5
Cambridge, MN 70-71 D 3
Cambridge, NE 68-69 F 5
Cambridge, OH 72-73 EF 4
Cambridge [CDN] 72-73 FG 3
Cambridge [GB] 119 FG 5
Cambridge [JA] 88-89 H 5
Cambridge [NZ] 161 F 3
Cambridge Bay 56-57 PQ 4
Cambridge City, IN 70-71 H 6
Cambridge City, OH 72-73 D 5
Cambridge Gulf 158-159 E 2-3
Cambuci, São Paulo- 110 II b 2
Cambuí 102-103 J 5
Camden 160 K 5
Camden, AL 78-79 F 4-5
Camden, AR 64-65 H 5
Camden, ME 72-73 M 2
Camden, NJ 64-65 LM 4
Camden, SC 80-81 F 3
Camden, TX 76-77 G 7
Camden, Islas — 108-109 C 10
Camden, London- 129 II b 1
Camden Bay 58-59 P 1
Camdenton, MO 70-71 D 6-7
Cameia = Lumeje 172 D 4
Camelback Mount 58-59 HJ 5
Çameli 136-137 C 4
Camembert 120-121 H 4
Cameron, AZ 74-75 H 5
Cameron, LA 78-79 C 6
Cameron, MO 70-71 CD 6
Cameron, TX 76-77 F 7
Cameron, WI 70-71 E 3
Cameron, WV 72-73 F 5
Cameron, Mount — 155 I ab 2
Cameron, Tanah-tinggi — 148-149 D 6
Cameron Falls 70-71 F 1
Cameron Run 82 II a 2
Cameroon 164-165 G 8-7
Camerota 122-123 F 5-6
Cameroun, Mont — 164-165 F 8
Cameroun Occidental 164-165 FG 7
Cameroun Oriental 164-165 G 7
Cametá [BR ↙ Belém] 92-93 JK 5
Cametá [BR ↗ Belém] 98-99 P 5
Cametagua 94-95 H 3
Camfer 174-175 E 7
Camiguin Island [RP, Babuyan Channel] 148-149 H 3
Camiguin Island [RP, Mindanao Sea] 148-149 H 5
Camiling 148-149 GH 3
Camilla, GA 80-81 D 5
Camiña 104-105 B 6
Camino, CA 74-75 C 3
Caminreal 120-121 G 8
Camira = Camiri 92-93 G 9
Camiranga 92-93 K 5
Camiri 92-93 G 9
Camirim 100-101 D 6
Camisea 96-97 E 7
Camisea, Río — 96-97 E 7
Cam Lâm 150-151 G 7
Çamlıbel = Çiftlik 136-137 G 2
Çamlıbel dağları 136-137 G 3
Camlica tepe 154 I b 2
Camlıdere 136-137 E 2
Cam Lô 150-151 F 4
Camocim 92-93 L 5
Camooweal 158-159 G 3
Camopi [French Guiana, place] 98-99 M 3
Camopi [French Guiana, river] 98-99 M 3
Camorta Island 134-135 P 9
Camoruco 94-95 F 4
Camoxilo 172 C 4
Camp 19, AK 58-59 FG 4
Campagna 122-123 F 5
Campagne = Campània 122-123 F 5
Campamento 94-95 F 5
Campamento, Cerro — 91 I b 3
Campamento, Madrid- 113 III a 2
Campamento Villegas 108-109 FG 4
Campana [MEX] 76-77 C 9
Campana [RA] 106-107 H 5
Campana, Cerro — 94-95 E 7
Campana, Isla — 111 A 7
Campana Mahuida 108-109 E 4
Campanário [BR] 100-101 CD 10
Campanario, Cerro — 111 BC 5
Campanha 102-103 K 4
Campania 122-123 F 5
Campania Island 60 C 3
Campanquiz, Cerros de — 92-93 D 5-6
Campbell 174-175 E 5
Campbell, NE 68-69 G 5
Campbell, OH 72-73 F 4
Campbell, Cape — 161 F 5
Campbellford 72-73 H 2
Campbell Island 53 D 17
Campbell River 56-57 L 7
Campbellsport, WI 70-71 F 4
Campbellsville, KY 70-71 H 7
Campbellton 56-57 X 8
Campbell Town 158-159 J 8
Campbell Woods, Houston-, TX 85 III a 1
Camp-Berteaux = Mal'qat al-Widān 166-167 E 2
Camp Creek 85 II a 3
Camp Creek, North Fork — 85 II a 3
Camp Crook, SD 68-69 DE 3
Camp Douglas, WI 70-71 EF 4
Campeche 64-65 H 8
Campeche, Bahía de — 64-65 GH 7
Campeche, Gulf of — = Bahía de Campeche 64-65 GH 7
Campeche Bank 64-65 HJ 7
Camperdown [AUS] 160 F 7
Camperdown [ZA] 174-175 J 5
Camperville 61 H 5
Cẩm Pha 150-151 F 2
Campidano 122-123 C 6
Campillo, Del — 106-107 E 5
Campiña, La — [E, Andalucía] 120-121 E 10
Campina da Lagoa 102-103 F 6
Campiña del Henares, La — 120-121 F 8
Campina Grande [BR, Amapá] 92-93 MN 6
Campina Grande [BR, Paraíba] 98-99 N 4
Campinas 92-93 K 9
Campinas do Piauí 100-101 D 4
Campina Verde 102-103 H 3
Campli 122-123 E 4
Camp Militaire 170 IV a 1
Camp Nelson, CA 74-75 D 4
Campo, CA 74-75 E 6
Campo, CO 76-77 C 4
Campo [RFC, place] 164-165 F 8
Campo [RFC, river] 164-165 G 8
Campo, Casa de — 113 III a 2
Campo Alegre [BR] 102-103 H 7
Campoalegre [CO] 94-95 D 6
Campo Alegre [YV] 94-95 K 3
Campo Alegre de Goiás 102-103 J 2
Campobasso 122-123 F 5
Campo Belo 92-93 KL 9
Campo Central 104-105 C 2
Campo de Diauarum 92-93 J 7
Campo de la Cruz 94-95 D 2
Campo del Cielo 106-107 FG 1
Campo de Marte 110 II b 2
Campo de Mayo, General Sarmiento- 110 III b 1
Campo de Talampaya 106-107 CD 2-3
Campo do Brito 100-101 F 6
Campo Domingo 96-97 E 7
Campodónico 106-107 GH 6
Campo do Tenente 102-103 H 6-7
Campo Duran 111 D 2
Campo Erê 102-103 F 7
Campo Esperanza 102-103 C 5
Campo Florido 102-103 H 3
Campo Formoso 100-101 D 6
Campo Gallo 104-105 E 10
Campo Garay 106-107 G 2
Campo Grande [BR] 92-93 J 9
Campo Grande [RA] 111 EF 3
Campo Indian Reservation 74-75 E 6
Campo Largo [BR] 102-103 H 6
Campo Largo [RA] 102-103 B 7
Campo Los Andes 106-107 C 4
Campo Maior [BR] 92-93 L 5
Campo Maior [P] 120-121 D 9
Campo Mara 94-95 EF 2
Campo Mourão 102-103 F 6
Campo Novo 102-103 EF 7
Campo Redondo 102-103 L 1
Campo Rico, Isla — 106-107 G 4
Campos [BR, landscape] 92-93 L 7
Campos [BR, place] 92-93 L 9
Campos, Laguna — 102-103 B 4
Campos, Tierra de — 120-121 E 7-8
Campos Altos [BR, Mato Grosso] 92-93 HJ 9
Campos Altos [BR, Minas Gerais] 102-103 JK 3
Campos Belos 100-101 A 7
Campos da Vacaria 106-107 M 2
Campos de Cima da Serra 106-107 M 2
Campos de Lapa 102-103 GH 6
Campos do Jordão 102-103 K 5
Campos dos Parecis 92-93 H 7
Campos Erê 102-103 F 6
Campos Gerais [BR, Minas Gerais] 102-103 K 4
Campos Gerais [BR, Paraná] 102-103 GH 6
Campos Novos 102-103 G 7
Campos Novos Paulista 102-103 GH 5
Campos Sales 100-101 DE 4
Campo Troco 94-95 G 5
Camp Point, IL 70-71 E 5
Campsie, Sydney- 161 I a 2
Camp Springs, MD 82 II b 2
Campti, LA 78-79 C 5
Campton, KY 72-73 E 6
Campton Airport 83 III c 2
Campton Creek 83 III c 2
Campuya 96-97 E 2
Campuya, Río — 96-97 DE 2
Camp Verde, AZ 74-75 H 5
Camp Wood, TX 76-77 DE 8
Cam Ranh 150-151 G 7
Cam Ranh, Vinh — 150-151 G 7
Camrose 56-57 O 7
Camulenba 172 C 3
Cẩm Xuyên 150-151 EF 3
Çan [TR, Çanakkale] 136-137 B 2
Çan [TR, Elâzığ] 136-137 J 3
Ca Na 150-151 G 7
Cana-Brava 102-103 K 2
Canabrava, Serra da — [BR, Rio Jucurucu] 100-101 DE 9
Cana Brava, Serra da — [BR, Rio São Onofre] 100-101 C 7
Canacari, Lago — 98-99 J 6
Canada 56-57 M 5-W 7
Cañada, La — 106-107 F 1
Canada Basin 50-51 BC 1-2
Canada Bay 63 HJ 2
Cañada de Gómez 111 D 4
Cañada de los Helechos 91 I b 2
Cañada de Luque 106-107 F 3
Cañada de Villance 106-107 D 4
Cañada Honda 106-107 C 3
Cañada Ombú 106-107 GH 2
Cañada Oruro = Fortín Cañada Oruro 102-103 AB 4
Cañada Rica 106-107 GH 1
Cañada Rosquín 106-107 G 4
Cañada Seca 106-107 F 5
Canadian, TX 76-77 D 5
Canadian Channel = Jacques Cartier Passage 56-57 Y 7-8
Canadian National Railways 56-57 PQ 7
Canadian Pacific Railway 56-57 OP 7
Canadian River 64-65 F 4
Canadian Steel Corporation 84 II b 3
Cañadón de la Cancha 108-109 E 7
Cañadón de las Vacas 108-109 E 8
Cañadón de los Jagüeles 106-107 D 7
Cañadón El Pluma 108-109 D 6
Cañadón Grande, Sierra — 108-109 E 5
Cañadón Iglesias 108-109 F 4
Cañadón Salado 108-109 FG 5
Cañadón Seco 108-109 F 6
Canaima 94-95 K 4
Canaima, Parque Nacional — 94-95 KL 5
Çanakkale 134-135 B 2
Çanakkale boğazı 134-135 B 2-3
Canal, De la — 106-107 H 6
Canala 158-159 N 4
Canal Águila = Eagle Passage 108-109 K 9
Canal Ancho 108-109 B 7-8
Canal Baker 111 B 7
Canal Beagle 111 C 8
Canal Bega 122-123 J 3
Canal Chaffers 108-109 B 5
Canal Cheap 108-109 B 6
Canal Cockburn 111 B 8
Canal Concepción 111 AB 8
Canal Costa 108-109 C 5
Canal Darwin 108-109 B 5
Canal de Ballenas 86-87 D 3
Canal de Bourgogne 120-121 K 5
Canal de Chacao 108-109 C 3
Canal de Jambelí 96-97 AB 3
Canal de la Galite = Qanāt Jaliṭah 166-167 L 1
Canal de la Marne au Rhin 120-121 K 4
Canal de la Mona 64-65 N 8
Canal de la voie maritime 82 I b 2
Canal del Desagüe 91 I c 1
Canal del Manzanares 113 III b 2-3
Canal de Macaé à Campos 102-103 M 4-5
Canal de Moçambique 172 H 6-4
Canal de Moraleda 111 B 6-7
Canal de Panamá 64-65 b 2
Canal de Puinahua 96-97 D 4
Canal de São Sebastião 102-103 K 5-6
Canal des Ardennes 120-121 K 4
Canal des Pangalanes 172 J 5-6
Canal de Yucatán 64-65 J 7
Canal do Geba 168-169 AB 3
Canal do Norte 92-93 JK 4
Canal do Rio Tietê 110 II b 2
Canal do Sul 92-93 K 4-5
Canal du Midi 120-121 HJ 7
Canal du Rhône au Rhin 120-121 L 4-5
Canale di Tunisi 122-123 D 7
Canalejas 106-107 D 5
Canal Flats 60 JK 4
Canal Jacaf 108-109 C 5
Canal Lachine 82 I b 2
Canal Messier 108-109 B 7
Canal Nicolás 64-65 KL 7
Canal Número 1 106-107 HJ 6
Canal Número 11 111 E 5
Canal Número 12 106-107 H 6
Canal Número 15 106-107 J 5-6
Canal Número 16 106-107 H 5
Canal Número 2 106-107 J 6
Canal Número 5 106-107 J 6
Canal Número 9 106-107 HJ 6
Canal Octubre 108-109 B 7
Canal Perigoso 92-93 K 4
Canal Puyuguapi 108-109 C 5
Canals 106-107 F 4
Canal Smyth 108-109 B 8-C 9
Canal Tuamapu 108-109 B 4-C 5
Canal Viejo de Bahama 64-65 L 7
Canal Whiteside 108-109 D 9-10
Canamã 98-99 BC 7
Canamari 98-99 C 8
Canandaigua, NY 72-73 H 3
Cananea 64-65 DE 5
Cananeia 102-103 HJ 6
Cananeia, Ilha de — 102-103 J 6
Canaṇor = Cannanore 134-135 LM 8
Canapiare, Cerro — 94-95 G 6
Canápolis 102-103 H 3
Cañar [EC, administrative unit] 96-97 B 3
Cañar [EC, place] 92-93 D 5
Canarana 100-101 D 6
Canárias, Ilha das — 92-93 L 5
Canarias, Islas — 164-165 A 3
Canarreos, Archipiélago de los — 64-65 K 7
Canarsie, New York-, NY 82 III c 3
Canary Basin 50-51 HJ 4
Canary Islands = Islas Canarias 164-165 A 3
Canary Rise 50-51 HJ 4
Cañas 104-105 D 8
Cañas, Las — 104-105 D 11
Canastota, NY 72-73 HJ 3
Canastra, Serra da — [BR, Bahia] 100-101 E 6
Canastra, Serra da — [BR, Minas Gerais] 92-93 K 9
Canasvieiras 102-103 H 7
Canatiba 100-101 C 7
Canatlán 86-87 H 5
Canaveral, FL 80-81 c 2
Canaveral, Cape — 64-65 KL 6
Canavieiras 92-93 M 8
Cañazas, Sierra de — 88-89 G 10
Canbelego 160 H 3
Canberra 158-159 J 7
Canby, CA 66-67 C 5
Canby, MN 68-69 H 3
Canby, OR 66-67 B 3
Cancela, Ponta da — 100-101 G 4
Cancha, Cañadón de la — 108-109 E 7
Cancha Carrera 108-109 CD 8
Canché 100-101 E 5
Canchenjunga = Gangchhendsönga 134-135 O 5
Çandarlı körfezi 136-137 B 3
Candeal 100-101 E 6
Candeias [BR, Bahia] 100-101 E 7
Candeias [BR, Minas Gerais] 102-103 K 4
Candeias, Rio — 98-99 G 9-10
Candela [MEX] 76-77 D 9
Candelaria, TX 76-77 B 7
Candelária [BR] 106-107 L 2
Candelaria [RA, Misiones] 106-107 K 1
Candelaria [RA, San Luis] 106-107 E 4
Candelaria, Coyoacán-la — 91 I c 2
Candelaria, La — 104-105 D 10
Candelaria, Río — [BOL] 104-105 G 5
Candelaria, Río — [MEX] 86-87 P 8
Candi = Maha Nuwara 134-135 N 9
Candia = Hērákleion 122-123 L 8
Candiba 100-101 C 8
Cândido de Abreu 102-103 G 6
Cândido Mendes 92-93 KL 5
Cândido Mota 102-103 G 5
Çandili tepe 136-137 G 3
Çandır 136-137 E 2
Candle, AK 58-59 G 4
Candle Lake 61 F 4
Candler Lake 85 II c 2
Candler Park 85 II c 2
Candlestick Park 83 I b 2
Cando, ND 68-69 G 1
Candói 102-103 FG 6
Candón 148-149 GH 3
Candravasih 148-149 K 7
Cần Đư'o'c 150-151 F 7
Canehas 104-105 A 9
Caneima, Isla — 94-95 L 3
Canela [BR] 106-107 M 2
Canela [RCH] 106-107 B 3
Canelas, Serra — 100-101 AB 4
Canelones 106-107 JK 5
Canelos 92-93 D 5
Cañete [PE] 92-93 D 7
Cañete [RCH] 106-107 A 6
Cañete, Río — 96-97 CD 8
Caney, KS 76-77 FG 4
Cangaíba, São Paulo- 110 II b 2
Cangalha, Serra da — [BR, Goiás] 98-99 P 9
Cangalha, Serra da — [BR, Piauí] 100-101 D 3
Cangallo [PE] 92-93 DE 7
Cangallo [RA] 106-107 H 6
Cangamba 172 C 4
Cangas 120-121 C 7
Cangas de Narcea 120-121 D 7
Cân Gio' 150-151 F 7
Cân Giuôc 150-151 F 7
Cangombe 172 C 4
Cangrejo, Cerro — 108-109 C 7
Cangrejo, Isla — 94-95 L 3
Canguaretama 92-93 MN 6
Canguçu 106-107 L 3
Canguçu, Serra do — 106-107 L 3
Cangwu 146-147 C 10
Cangxien = Cangzhou 142-143 M 4
Cangyuan 141 F 4
Cangzhou 142-143 M 4
Canhotinho 100-101 FG 5
Cani, Îles — = Jazā'ir al-Kilāb 166-167 M 1
Caniçado 174-175 K 3
Canicattì 122-123 E 7
Canigou, Mont — 120-121 J 7
Canik 136-137 K 3
Canik dağları 136-137 G 2
Canillas, Madrid- 113 III b 2
Canillejas, Madrid- 113 III b 2
Canim Lake [CDN, lake] 60 G 4
Canim Lake [CDN, place] 60 G 4
Caninde [BR, Amazonas] 98-99 C 8
Canindé [BR, Ceará] 92-93 M 5
Canindé, Rio — 100-101 C 4
Canisteo, NY 72-73 H 3
Cañitas de Felipe Pescador 86-87 J 6
Çankırı 134-135 C 2
Canmore 60 K 4
Cannae 122-123 G 5
Cannanore 134-135 LM 8
Cannelton, IN 70-71 G 7
Cannes 120-121 L 7
Canning Desert 158-159 D 3
Canning River 58-59 O 2
Canning Town, London- 129 II c 1
Cannon Ball, ND 68-69 F 2
Cannonball River 68-69 F 2
Cannon Falls, MN 70-71 D 3
Cannon Recreation Center 84 II c 2
Cann River 160 J 6
Cano = Kano 164-165 F 6
Caño, Isla del — 88-89 DE 10
Canoa, La — 94-95 JK 3
Caño Araguao 94-95 L 3
Canoas 111 F 3
Canoas, Punta — 94-95 D 2
Canoas, Rio — 102-103 G 7
Canobie 158-159 H 3
Caño Branco 94-95 F 3
Caño Colorado [CO] 94-95 G 6
Caño Colorado [YV] 94-95 K 3
Canoe 60 H 4
Canoeiro, Cachoeiro do — 98-99 OP 10
Canoeiros 102-103 K 2-3
Canoe Lake [CDN, lake] 61 D 3
Canoe Lake [CDN, place] 61 D 3
Canoinhas 102-103 G 7
Caño Mácareo 94-95 L 3
Caño Manamo 92-93 G 3
Caño Mariusa 94-95 L 3
Canon City, CO 64-65 EF 4
Canopus 160 E 4
Caño Quebrado, Río — [PA, Colón] 64-65 a 2
Caño Quebrado, Río — [PA, Panamá] 64-65 b 2-3
Canora 56-57 Q 7
Caño Tucupita 94-95 L 3
Canouan 88-89 Q 8
Canova, SD 68-69 H 4
Canowindra 160 J 4
Canrobert = Umm al-Bawāghī 166-167 K 2
Cansanção 100-101 E 6
Canso 56-57 Y 8
Canso, Strait of — 56-57 YZ 8
Canso Bank 63 F 5
Cansu = Gansu 142-143 G 3-J 4
Canta 92-93 D 7
Cantabrian Mountains = Cordillera Cantábrica 120-121 D-F 7
Cantábrica, Cordillera — 120-121 D-F 7
Cantagallo 94-95 DE 4
Canta Galo 98-99 JK 7
Cantagalo, Ponta — 102-103 H 7
Cantal 120-121 J 6
Cantal, Plomb du — 120-121 J 6
Cantanhede [BR] 100-101 B 2
Cantantal, Sierra de — 106-107 D 3-4
Cantareira, São Paulo- 110 II b 1
Cantareira, Serra da — 110 II ab 1
Cantaritos, Cerros — 106-107 BC 2
Cantaura 92-93 G 3
Canteras de Vallecas 113 III b 2
Canterbury [CDN] 63 C 5
Canterbury [GB] 119 G 7
Canterbury [NZ] 161 D 6
Canterbury, Melbourne- 161 II c 1
Canterbury, Sydney- 161 I a 2
Canterbury Bight 158-159 O 8
Canterbury Park Racecourse 161 I a 2
Canterbury Plains 161 D 7-E 6
Cần Thơ 148-149 E 5
Canthyuaya, Cerros de — 96-97 D 5
Cantil, CA 74-75 DE 5
Cantilan 148-149 J 5
Cantin, Cap — = Rā's al-Baddūzah 164-165 BC 2
Cantin, Cape — = Rā's Ṭarfāyah 164-165 B 3
Canto del Agua 106-107 B 2
Canto do Buriti 92-93 L 6
Canton 208 J 3
Canton, CA 78-79 G 3
Canton, GA 80-81 D 3
Canton, IL 70-71 EF 5
Canton, KS 68-69 H 6
Canton, MA 72-73 L 3
Canton, MO 70-71 E 5
Canton, MS 78-79 DE 4
Canton, NC 80-81 E 3
Canton, NY 72-73 J 2
Canton, OH 64-65 K 3
Canton, OK 76-77 E 4
Canton, PA 72-73 H 4
Canton, SD 68-69 H 4
Canton, TX 76-77 FG 6
Canton = Guangzhou 142-143 LM 7
Cantón, El — 94-95 F 4
Cantù 122-123 C 3
Cantu, Rio — 102-103 F 6
Cantu, Serra do — 102-103 FG 6
Cantwell, AK 58-59 N 5
Canudos [BR, Bahia] 100-101 E 5
Canudos [BR, Pará] 98-99 J 8
Cañuelas 106-107 H 5
Canumã 92-93 H 5
Canumã, Rio — 98-99 J 7
Canumã, Rio — = Rio Sucunduri 92-93 H 6
Canuri = Kanouri 164-165 G 6
Canutama 92-93 G 6
Canutillo, TX 76-77 A 7
Čany, ozero — 132-133 O 7
Canyon, TX 76-77 D 5
Canyon, WY 66-67 H 3
Canyon [CDN, Ontario] 70-71 H 2
Canyon [CDN, Yukon Territory] 58-59 T 6
Canyon City, OR 66-67 D 3
Canyon de Chelly National Monument 74-75 J 4-5
Canyon Ferry Dam 66-67 GH 2
Canyon Ferry Reservoir 66-67 H 2
Canyon Largo [USA ← Jicarilla Apache Indian Reservation] 76-77 A 4
Canyon Largo [USA ↑ Mesa Montosa] 76-77 B 5
Canyonville, OR 66-67 B 4
Cao Bằng 148-149 F 2
Caocheira Inferninho 98-99 H 9
Caohe = Qichun 146-147 E 6
Caojian 141 F 3
Cao Lanh 150-151 E 7
Caombo 172 C 3
Cao Nguyên Boloven 148-149 E 3-4
Cao Nguyên Đac Lăc 148-149 E 4
Cao Nguyên Gia Lai 150-151 G 5
Cao Nguyên Lâm Viên 150-151 G 6-7
Cao Nguyên Trần Ninh 148-149 D 3
Cao Nguyên Trung Phần 148-149 E 4
Caopacho, Rivière — 63 C 2
Caoshi 144-145 E 1
Cao Xian 146-147 E 4
Capa, SD 68-69 F 3
Çapa, İstanbul- 154 I a 2
Cap-à-Foux 88-89 K 5
Capahuari 96-97 C 3
Capahuari, Río — 96-97 C 3
Čapajevka 124-125 S 7
Čapajevo 132-133 J 7
Čapajevsk 132-133 HJ 7
Çapakçur = Bingöl 134-135 E 3
Capana 98-99 D 5
Capanaparo, Río — 94-95 G 4
Capané 106-107 L 3
Capanelle, Ippodromo — 113 II bc 2
Capanema [BR, Mato Grosso] 92-93 H 7
Capanema [BR, Pará] 92-93 K 5
Capanema [BR, Paraná] 102-103 F 6
Capanema, Rio — 102-103 F 6-7
Capão 100-101 A 8
Capão Bonito 111 G 2
Capão do Leão 106-107 L 3
Capão do Meio 100-101 B 7
Capão do Poncho, Lagoa do — 106-107 MN 3
Caparão, Serra do — 92-93 L 8-9
Capatárida 94-95 F 2
Cap-aux-Meules 63 F 4
Cap Blanc = Ar-Rā's al-Abyaḍ 164-165 A 4
Cap Bon = Rā' aṭ-Ṭīh 164-165 G 1
Cap Bougaroun = Rā's Būjarun 166-167 JK 1
Cap Cantin = Rā's al-Baddūzah 164-165 BC 2
Cap-Chat 63 C 3
Cap Chon May = Mui Cho'n Mây 150-151 G 4
Cap Corse 122-123 C 4
Cap Dame Marie 88-89 J 5
Cap de Bordj el Bahri 170 I b 1
Cap de Fer = Rā's al-Ḥadīd 166-167 K 1
Cap de la Hague 120-121 G 4
Cap-de-la-Madeleine 56-57 W 8
Cap des Hirondelles = Mui Yên 150-151 G 6
Capdeville 106-107 C 4
Cap de Whittle 63 F 2
Cape Adams 53 B 30-31
Cape Adare 53 B 18
Cape Alava 66-67 A 1
Cape Alexandra 111 J 8
Cape Anguille 63 G 4
Cape Ann 72-73 L 3
Cape Arago 66-67 A 4
Cape Arid 158-159 D 6
Cape Arnhem 158-159 G 2
Cape Banks 161 I b 3
Cape Baring 56-57 MN 3
Cape Barren Island 158-159 JK 8
Cape Basin 50-51 K 7
Cape Bathurst 56-57 KL 3
Cape Bauld 56-57 Za 7
Cape Beale 60 E 5
Cape Beatrice 158-159 G 2
Cape Blanco 64-65 AB 3
Cape Boothby 53 C 6-7
Cape Bougainville 108-109 KL 8
Cape Bougainville 158-159 E 2
Cape Bouvard 158-159 BC 6
Cape Bowling Green 158-159 J 3
Cape Breton 56-57 Z 8
Cape Breton Highlands National Park 63 FG 4
Cape Breton Island 56-57 X-Z 8
Cape Byrd 53 C 29
Cape Byron 158-159 K 5
Cape Campbell 161 F 5
Cape Canaveral 64-65 KL 6
Cape Carysfort 108-109 L 8
Cape Catastrophe 158-159 F 7-G 6
Cape Chacon 58-59 wx 9
Cape Charles 64-65 LM 4
Cape Charles, VA 80-81 HJ 2
Cape Chichagof 58-59 HJ 7
Cape Chidley 56-57 Y 5
Cape Chiniak 58-59 LM 8
Cape Chiniak 58-59 gh 1
Cape Chunu 58-59 u 7
Cape Churchill 56-57 S 6
Cape Clarence 56-57 S 3
Cape Clear 119 B 6
Cape Cleare 58-59 NO 7
Cape Clinton 158-159 K 4
Cape Coast 164-165 D 7
Cape Cod 64-65 N 3
Cape Cod Bay 72-73 L 3-4
Cape Cod Peninsula 64-65 N 3
Cape Colbeck 53 B 20-21
Cape Columbia 52 A 25-26
Cape Comorin 134-135 M 9
Cape Constantine 56-57 DE 6
Cape Cook 60 CD 4
Cape Coral, FL 80-81 bc 3
Cape Corwin 58-59 E 7
Cape Crawford 56-57 TU 3
Cape Cross = Kaap Kruis 172 B 6
Cape Cumberland 158-159 N 2
Cape Cuvier 158-159 B 4
Cape D'Aguilar = Tai Long Head 155 I b 2
Cape Dalhousie 56-57 KL 3
Cape Darby 58-59 F 4
Cape Darnley 53 C 7-8
Cape Dart 53 B 24
Cape Denbigh 58-59 FG 4
Cape Disappointment [Falkland Islands] 111 J 8-9
Cape Disappointment [USA] 66-67 A 2
Cape Dolphin 111 E 8
Cape Dorchester 56-57 V 4
Cape Dorset 56-57 VW 5
Cape Douglas 58-59 L 7
Cape Dyer 56-57 YZ 4
Cape Elizabeth 72-73 LM 3
Cape Elizabeth = Cape Pillar 158-159 J 8
Cape Elvira 56-57 P 3
Cape Espenberg 58-59 F 3
Cape Etolin 58-59 D 6
Cape Everard 158-159 JK 7
Cape Fairweather 58-59 ST 7
Cape Falcon 66-67 A 3
Cape Farewell 158-159 O 8
Cape Farewell = Kap Farvel 56-57 c 6
Cape Farina = Ghar al-Milḥ 166-167 M 1
Cape Fear 64-65 L 5
Cape Fear River 64-65 L 4-5
Cape Finnis 160 B 4
Cape Flattery [AUS] 158-159 J 2
Cape Flattery [USA] 66-67 A 1
Cape Florida 80-81 cd 4
Cape Flying Fish 53 BC 26
Cape Ford 158-159 E 2
Cape Foulwind 158-159 NO 8
Cape Fourcroy 158-159 E 2
Cape Foyn 53 C 30
Cape Frankland 160 c 1
Cape Freels 63 K 3
Cape Freshfield 53 C 16
Cape Gargantua 70-71 H 2
Cape Girardeau, MO 64-65 HJ 4
Cape Goodenough 53 C 13
Cape Graham Moore 56-57 V-X 3
Cape Grenvill 158-159 H 2
Cape Grim 158-159 H 8
Cape Halkett 58-59 LM 1
Cape Hangklip = Kaap Hangklip 174-175 C 8
Cape Harrison 56-57 Z 7
Cape Hart 160 D 5-6
Cape Hatteras 64-65 LM 4
Cape Hawke 158-159 K 6
Cape Henlopen 72-73 J 5
Cape Henrietta Maria 56-57 U 6
Cape Henry 80-81 J 2
Cape Hermes = Kaap Hermes 174-175 H 6
Cape Hollmann 148-149 gh 5
Cape Hopes Advance 56-57 X 5
Cape Howe 158-159 K 7
Cape Hurd 72-73 EF 2
Cape Igvak 58-59 f 1
Cape Ikolik 58-59 f 1
Cape Infanta = Kaap Infanta 174-175 D 8
Cape Inscription 158-159 B 5
Cape Isachsen 56-57 OP 2
Cape Izigan 58-59 n 4
Cape Jaffa 160 D 6
Cape Johnson Depth 148-149 J 4
Cape Jones 56-57 UV 7
Cape Kamliun 58-59 e 1
Cape Karikari 161 EF 1
Cape Kellett 56-57 L 3
Cape Kidnappers 161 GH 4
Cape Knowles 53 B 30-31
Cape Krusenstern 58-59 EF 3
Cape Kumakahi 78-79 e 3
Cape Kutuzof 58-59 c 1
Capela [BR, Alagoas] 100-101 FG 5
Capela [BR, Sergipe] 100-101 F 6
Cape Lambton 56-57 M 3
Cape Leeuwin 158-159 B 6
Cape Le Grand 158-159 D 6
Cape Leontovich 58-59 b 2
Cape Leveque 158-159 D 3
Capelinha 102-103 L 2
Cape Light 53 B 30-31
Cape Lisburne 56-57 C 4
Capella 158-159 J 4
Cape Londonderry 158-159 E 2
Capelongo 172 C 4
Cape Lookout [USA, North Carolina] 64-65 L 5
Cape Lookout [USA, Oregon] 66-67 A 3
Cape Low 56-57 T 5
Cape Maria van Diemen 158-159 O 6
Cape May, NJ 64-65 M 4
Cape May Court House, NJ 72-73 JK 5
Cape May Point 72-73 J 5
Cape Melville 158-159 HJ 2
Cape Mendenhall 58-59 DE 7
Cape Mendocino 64-65 AB 3
Cape Mercy 56-57 Y 5
Cape Meredith 111 D 8
Cape Mohican 56-57 C 5
Cape Moore 53 BC 17
Cape Mount 168-169 C 4
Cape Murchison 56-57 S 3
Cape Muzon 58-59 w 9
Cape Naturaliste 158-159 B 6

Cape Negrais = Nagare Angû 141 CD 7
Cape Newenham 56-57 D 6
Cape Nome 58-59 E 4
Cape North 56-57 YZ 8
Cape Oksenof 58-59 a 2
Cape Ommaney 58-59 v 8
Cape Otway 158-159 H 7
Cape Palliser 158-159 P 8
Cape Palmas 164-165 C 8
Cape Palmer 53 B 27
Cape Palmerstone 158-159 JK 4
Cape Pankof 58-59 b 2
Cape Parry 56-57 M 3
Cape Pasley 158-159 D 6
Cape Peirce 58-59 FG 7
Cape Penck 53 C 9
Cape Pillar 158-159 J 8
Cape Pine 63 K 4
Cape Pingmar = Lingao Jiao 150-151 G 3
Cape Pole, AK 58-59 vw 9
Cape Portland 160 c 2
Cape Prince Alfred 56-57 KL 3
Cape Prince of Wales 56-57 C 4-5
Cape Providence [NZ] 158-159 MN 9
Cape Providence [USA] 58-59 ef 1
Cape Province = Kaapland 172 DE 8
Cape Race 56-57 a 8
Cape Raper 56-57 XY 4
Cape Ray 56-57 Z 8
Cape Recife = Kaap Recife 174-175 FG 8
Cape Rise 50-51 K 8
Cape Rodney 58-59 D 4
Cape Romain 80-81 G 4
Cape Romano 80-81 bc 4
Cape Romanzof 56-57 C 5
Capertee 160 JK 4
Cape Sabak 58-59 pq 6
Cape Sable [CDN] 56-57 XY 9
Cape Sable [USA] 64-65 K 6
Cape Sable Island 63 D 6
Cape Saint-Blaize = Kaap Sint Blaize 174-175 E 8
Cape Saint Charles 56-57 Za 7
Cape Saint Elias 58-59 P 7
Cape Saint Francis = Sealpunt 174-175 F 8
Cape Saint George 78-79 G 5
Cape Saint George [CDN] 63 G 3
Cape Saint James 56-57 K 7
Cape Saint John 63 J 3
Cape Saint Lawrence 63 F 4
Cape Saint Martin = Kaap Sint Martin 174-175 B 7
Cape Saint Mary's 63 J 4
Cape Saint Paul 168-169 F 4
Cape Salatan = Tanjung Selatan 148-149 F 7
Cape San Agustin 148-149 J 5
Cape San Blas 64-65 J 6
Cape Sasmik 58-59 u 7
Cape Scott 56-57 L 7
Cape Seal = Kaap Seal 174-175 E 8
Cape Sebastian 66-67 A 4
Cape Sifa = Dahua Jiao 150-151 H 3
Cape Simpson 58-59 KL 1
Cape Smiley 53 B 29
Cape Smith 56-57 UV 5
Cape Solander 161 I b 3
Cape Sorell 158-159 HJ 8
Cape Spencer [AUS] 158-159 G 7
Cape Spencer [USA] 58-59 T 7
Cape Stephens 161 EF 5
Cape Suckling 58-59 Q 7
Cape Swinburne 56-57 R 3
Cape Talbot 158-159 E 2
Cape Tanak 58-59 m 4
Cape Tatnam 56-57 ST 6
Cape Tavoy = Shinmau Sûn 150-151 AB 6
Cape Thompson 58-59 D 2
Cape Three Points 164-165 D 8
Cape Tormentine 63 DE 4
Cape Town = Kaapstad 172 C 8
Cape Turnagain 161 G 5
Cape Van Diemen 158-159 EF 2
Cape Verde 178-179 H 5
Cape Verde = Cap Vert 164-165 A 6
Cape Verde Basin 50-51 GH 4-5
Cape Verde Plateau 50-51 H 4-5
Cape Vincent, NY 72-73 HJ 2
Cape Ward Hunt 148-149 N 8
Cape Wessel 158-159 G 2
Cape Weymouth 158-159 HJ 2
Cape Wickham 160 b 1
Cape Wolstenholme 56-57 VW 5
Cape Wrath 119 D 2
Cape Yakak 58-59 u 7
Cape Yakataga, AK 58-59 QR 6
Cape York 158-159 H 2
Cape York Peninsula 158-159 H 2
Cap Falaise = Mui Đa Du'ng 150-151 EF 3
Cap Falcon = Rā's Falkun 166-167 F 2
Cap Figalo = Rā's Fiqālu 166-167 F 2
Cap Gaspé 56-57 Y 8
Cap Ghir = Rā's Ghīr 166-167 AB 4
Cap-Haïtien 64-65 M 8
Capibara 92-93 F 4
Capilla, La — 96-97 B 4
Capilla del Monte 106-107 E 3
Capilla del Rosario 106-107 CD 4
Capillitas 104-105 C 10
Capim 98-99 OP 5
Capim, Rio — 92-93 K 5
Capinota 104-105 CD 5
Capinzal 102-103 G 7
Capinzal, Cachoeira — 98-99 JK 9
Capira 94-95 B 3
Capirona 96-97 CD 3
Capistrano 100-101 E 3
Capitachouahe, Rivière — 62 N 2-3
Capital Territory, Australian — 158-159 J 7
Capitan, NM 76-77 B 6
Capitán Aracena, Isla — 108-109 D 10
Capitán Bado 102-103 E 5
Capitão Costa Pinheiro, Rio — 104-105 GH 2
Capitan Grande Indian Reservation 74-75 E 6
Capitán Joaquín Madariaga 106-107 H 2
Capitán Juan Pagé 104-105 E 8
Capitán Maldonado, Cerro — 108-109 BC 4
Capitán Meza 102-103 E 7
Capitán O. Serebriakof 102-103 B 5
Capitán Pastene 106-107 A 7
Capitán Solari 104-105 G 10
Capitán Ustares, Cerro — 102-103 B 3
Capitão Cardoso, Rio — 98-99 HJ 10
Capitão de Campos 100-101 CD 3
Capitão-Mór, Serra do — 100-101 F 4-5
Capitão Poço 98-99 P 5
Capitol, The — 82 II ab 2
Capitol Heights, MD 82 II b 2
Capitol Hill, Washington-, DC 82 II ab 2
Capitolio 91 III b 3
Capitolio Nacional 91 II b 1
Capitol Peak 66-67 E 5
Capitol Reef National Monument 74-75 H 3
Capivara 106-107 G 3
Capivara, Cachoeira — 92-93 J 6
Capivara, Represa de — 102-103 G 5
Capivari 102-103 J 5
Capiz = Roxas 148-149 H 4
Čaplino 126-127 GH 2
Cap Lopez 172 A 2
Čaplygin 124-125 M 7
Cap Masoala 172 K 5
Cap Nuevo = Rā's al-Jadīd 166-167 E 2
Capo Càccia 122-123 BC 5
Capo Carbonara 122-123 CD 6
Capo Comino 122-123 CD 5
Capo de Frasca 122-123 BC 6
Capo delle Colonne 122-123 G 6
CApodí, Chapada do — 92-93 M 6
Capo di Muro 122-123 C 5
Capoeira 98-99 P 7
Capoeiras 100-101 F 5
Capoeiras, Cachoeira das — 92-93 H 6
Capo Falcone 122-123 BC 5
Capo Pàssero 122-123 F 7
Capo San Marco 122-123 BC 6
Capo Santa Maria di Leuca 122-123 H 6
Capo San Vito 122-123 E 6
Capo Spartivento [I, Calàbria] 122-123 G 7
Capo Spartivento [I, Sardegna] 122-123 G 6
Cappari = Psérimos 122-123 M 7
Capràia 122-123 CD 4
Capreol 72-73 F 1
Caprera 122-123 C 5
Capri 122-123 EF 5
Capricorn Channel 158-159 K 4
Caprivistrook 172 D 5
Caprock, NM 76-77 C 6
Cap Rosa = Rā's al-Wardah 166-167 L 1
Cap Saint-André 172 H 5
Cap Sainte-Marie 172 J 7
Cap-Saint-Jacques = Vung Tau 150-151 F 7
Cap Saint-Sebastien 172 J 4
Cap Spartel = Rā's Ashaqār 166-167 CD 2
Cap Tafelney = Rā's Tafalnī 166-167 AB 4
Captain Cook Bridge 161 I a 3
Captain Cook Landing Place Park 161 I b 3
Captains Flat 160 JK 5
Captiva, FL 80-81 b 3
Cap Tourane = Mui Đa Năng 150-151 G 4
Cap Tres Forcas = Rā's Wūruq 164-165 D 1
Càpua 122-123 EF 5
Capulin Mountain National Monument 76-77 BC 4
Capunda 172 C 4
Cap Varella = Mui Diêu 148-149 EF 4
Cap Verga 168-169 B 3
Cap Vert 164-165 A 6
Caquetá 94-95 DE 7
Caquetá, Río — 92-93 E 5
Cáqueza 94-95 E 5
Čara [SU, place] 132-133 W 6
Čara [SU, river] 132-133 W 6
Carababá 98-99 E 7
Caraballeda 94-95 H 2
Carabanchel Alto, Madrid- 113 III a 2
Carabanchel Bajo, Madrid- 113 III a 2
Carabaya, Cordillera de — 92-93 EF 7
Carabaya, Río — 96-97 FG 9
Carabinami, Rio — 98-99 G 6
Caracal 122-123 KL 3
Caracalla, Terme di — 113 II b 2
Caracaraí 92-93 G 4
Caracaraí, Cachoeira — 92-93 G 4
Caracas 92-93 F 2
Caracas, Islas — 94-95 J 2
Caracas-Antímano 91 II b 2
Caracas-Artigas 91 II b 2
Caracas-Bella Vista 91 II b 2
Caracas-Caricuao 91 II b 2
Caracas-Casalta 91 II b 1
Caracas-Catia 91 II b 1
Caracas-Coche 91 II b 2
Caracas-Cotiza 91 II b 1
Caracas Country Club 91 II b 1
Caracas-El Pedregal 91 II b 1
Caracas-El Valle 91 II b 2
Caracas-Helicoide 91 II b 2
Caracas-La Rinconada 91 II b 2
Caracas-Las Mayas 91 II b 2
Caracas-Las Palmas 91 I b 1
Caracas-La Vega 91 II b 2
Caracas-Los Magallanes 91 II b 1
Caracas-Mamera 91 II b 2
Caracas-San Bernardino 91 II b 1
Caracas-San Pablito 91 II ab 2
Caracas-Santa Mónica 91 II b 2
Carache 94-95 F 3
Carachi = Karāchī 134-135 K 6
Caracol [BR, Mato Grosso do Sul] 102-103 D 4
Caracol [BR, Piauí] 92-93 L 6
Caracol, El — 91 I d 1
Caracol, Rio — 100-101 A 5-6
Caracol, Serra do — 100-101 C 5
Caracoles, Punta — 88-89 G 11
Caracolí 94-95 E 2
Caracollo 104-105 C 5
Caracórum = Karakoram 134-135 L 3-M 4
Caraguatá, Cuchilla del — 106-107 K 3-4
Caraguatatuba 102-103 K 5
Caraguatay [PY] 102-103 D 6
Caraguatay [RA] 106-107 GH 2
Carahue 111 B 5
Caraí 102-103 M 2
Caraíbas 100-101 D 8
Caraiva 100-101 E 9
Carajás, Serra dos — 92-93 J 5-6
Caral 96-97 C 7
Caramanta 94-95 CD 5
Caraná, Rio — 104-105 G 3
Caranavi 104-105 C 4
Carandaí 102-103 L 4
Carandazal 102-103 D 3
Carangas 104-105 B 6
Carangola 102-103 L 4
Caranguejos, Ilha dos — 100-101 B 2
Caransebeş 122-123 K 3
Carapa, Río — 102-103 E 6
Carapacha Grande, Sierra — 106-107 DE 6-7
Carapachay, Vicente López- 110 III b 1
Cara-Paraná, Río — 94-95 E 8
Carapé, Sierra de — 106-107 K 5
Carapebus, Lagoa — 102-103 M 5
Carapeguá 102-103 D 6
Carapicuíba 102-103 J 5
Carapo, Río — 94-95 K 4
Caraquet 63 D 4
Carata 88-89 E 8
Caratasca, Laguna de — 64-65 K 8
Caratinga 92-93 L 8
Caratunk, ME 72-73 LM 2
Carauari 92-93 F 5
Caraúbas [BR, Ceara] 92-93 M 6
Caraúbas [BR, Paraíba] 100-101 F 4
Carauna, Serra de — 98-99 H 3
Caravaca de la Cruz 120-121 FG 9
Caravela, Ilha — 168-169 A 3
Caravelas 92-93 M 8
Caravelí 92-93 E 8
Carayaó 102-103 D 6
Caraz 96-97 C 6
Caraza, Lanús- 110 III b 2
Carazinho 111 F 3
Carballo 120-121 C 7
Carberry 61 J 6
Carbonara, Capo — 122-123 CD 6
Carbon Creek 58-59 H 2
Carbondale, CO 68-69 C 6
Carbondale, IL 70-71 F 7
Carbondale, PA 72-73 J 4
Carbonear 56-57 a 8
Carbonera, Cuchilla de la — 106-107 KL 4-5
Carbon Hill, AL 78-79 F 4
Carbònia 122-123 C 6
Carbonita 102-103 L 2
Carcajou Mountains 56-57 L 4-5
Carcar 148-149 H 4-5
Carcaraña 106-107 G 4
Carcarañá, Río — 106-107 FG 4
Carcassonne 120-121 J 7
Carchi 96-97 BC 1
Carcoss Island 108-109 J 8
Carcote 104-105 B 7
Carcross 56-57 K 5
Çardak 136-137 C 4
Cardamom Hills 141 C 5-6
Cardamum Island = Kadmat Island 134-135 L 8
Cardenal Cagliero 108-109 H 3
Cárdenas [C] 64-65 K 7
Cárdenas [MEX] 64-65 G 7
Çardı 136-137 C 3
Cardiel, Lago — 111 B 7
Cardiff 119 E 6
Cardigan 119 D 5
Cardigan Bay 119 D 5
Cardington, OH 72-73 E 4
Cardona [E] 120-121 H 8
Cardona [ROU] 106-107 J 4
Cardos, Los — 106-107 G 4
Cardoso, Ilha do — 102-103 J 6
Cardross 61 F 6
Cardston 56-57 O 8
Čardžou 134-135 J 3
Careen Lake 61 DE 2
Carei 122-123 K 2
Careiro 92-93 H 5
Careiro, Ilha do — 98-99 J 6
Carelmapu 108-109 C 3
Carén [RCH, La Serena] 106-107 B 3
Carén [RCH, Temuco] 106-107 B 7
Čarencavan 126-127 M 6
Carevokokšajsk = Joškar-Ola 132-133 H 6
Carey, ID 66-67 G 4
Carey, OH 72-73 E 4
Carey, Lake — 158-159 D 5
Carey Park, Atlanta-, GA 85 II b 2
Careysburg 164-165 BC 7
Cargados 50-51 N 6
Carhaix-Plouguer 120-121 F 4
Carhuamayo 96-97 D 7
Carhuaz 96-97 C 6
Cariacica 100-101 D 11
Cariaco 92-93 G 2
Cariaco, Golfo de — 94-95 JK 2
Cariamanga 96-97 B 4
Caribana, Punta — 92-93 D 3
Caribbean Basin 64-65 MN 8
Caribbean Sea 64-65 K-N 8
Caribe 94-95 F 5
Caribe, El — [YV, Anzoátegui] 94-95 J 3
Caribe, El — [YV, Distrito Federal] 91 II c 1
Caribe, Río — 86-87 P 8
Cariboo Mountains 56-57 M 7
Cariboo River 60 G 3
Caribou, AK 58-59 P 4
Caribou, ME 72-73 MN 1
Caribou, Lac — = Rentiersee 56-57 Q 6
Caribou Hide 58-59 XY 8
Caribou Island 70-71 H 2
Caribou Lake 62 E 2
Caribou Mountains 56-57 NO 6
Caribou Range 66-67 H 4
Caribou River 58-59 c 2
Caricó, Morro do — 110 I b 2
Caricuao, Caracas- 91 II b 2
Caricuau 91 II b 2
Caridade 100-101 E 3
Carievale 68-69 F 1
Cari Laufquen, Bajo de — 108-109 E 3
Cari Laufquen Grande, Laguna — 108-109 E 3
Carinda 160 HJ 3
Carinhanha 92-93 L 7
Carinthia = Kärnten 118 FG 5
Carioca, Serra da — 110 I b 2
Caripare 100-101 B 6
Caripçe 154 I b 1
Caripçe burnu 154 I b 1
Caripe 94-95 K 2
Caripito 92-93 G 2
Caripuyo 104-105 C 6
Cariquima 104-105 B 6
Carira 100-101 F 6
Cariré 100-101 D 2
Caririaçu 100-101 E 4
Cariris Novos, Serra dos — 100-101 D 3-4
Carirubana 94-95 F 2
Caris, Río — 94-95 K 3
Caritianas 98-99 G 9
Cariús 100-101 E 4
Cariús, Riacho — 100-101 E 4
Carleton 63 C 3
Carleton, Mount — 63 C 4
Carleton Place 72-73 HJ 2
Carletonville 174-175 G 4
Carlin, NV 66-67 EF 5
Carlingford, Sydney- 161 I a 1
Carlinville, IL 70-71 EF 6
Carlisle 119 E 4
Carlisle, IA 70-71 D 5
Carlisle, IN 70-71 G 6
Carlisle, KY 72-73 DE 5
Carlisle, PA 72-73 H 4
Carlisle, SC 80-81 F 3
Carlisle Island 58-59 I 4
Carlo, AK 58-59 N 5
Carlópolis 102-103 H 5
Carlos, Isla — 111 B 8
Carlos Ameghino, Istmo — 108-109 G 4
Carlos Beguerie 106-107 H 5
Carlos Casares 106-107 G 5
Carlos Chagas 92-93 LM 8
Carlos M. Naón 106-107 G 5
Carlos Pellegrini 106-107 G 4
Carlos Salas 106-107 FG 5
Carlos Tejedor 106-107 F 5
Carlota, La — [RA] 111 D 4
Carlow 119 C 5
Carlsbad, CA 74-75 E 6
Carlsbad, NM 64-65 F 5
Carlsbad = Karlovy Vary 118 F 3
Carlsbad Caverns National Park 76-77 B 6
Carlsruhe = Karlsruhe 118 D 4
Carlton, MN 70-71 D 2
Carlton [CDN] 61 E 4
Carlton [ZA] 174-175 F 6
Carlyle 61 GH 6
Carlyle, IL 70-71 F 6
Carmacks 56-57 J 5
Carmagnola 122-123 BC 3
Carman 68-69 GH 1
Carmânia = Kermān 134-135 H 4
Carmanville 63 JK 3
Carmarthen 119 D 6
Carmarthen Bay 119 D 6
Carmaux 120-121 J 6
Carmel, CA 74-75 BC 4
Carmelo 106-107 HJ 4-5
Carmelo, El — 94-95 EF 2
Carmen, OK 76-77 E 4
Carmen [BOL] 104-105 C 2
Carmen [BR] 98-99 L 11
Carmen [RA, Jujuy] 104-105 D 9
Carmen [RA, Santa Fe] 106-107 G 4
Carmen [ROU] 106-107 JK 4
Carmen, Ciudad del — 64-65 H 8
Carmen, El — [BOL, Beni] 104-105 E 3-4
Carmen, El — [BOL, Santa Cruz] 104-105 G 6
Carmen, El — [CO, Amazonas] 94-95 H 7
Carmen, El — [CO, Chocó] 94-95 C 5
Carmen, El — [CO, Norte de Santander] 94-95 E 3
Carmen, El — [EC] 96-97 B 2
Carmen, El — [PY] 102-103 AB 4
Carmen, Isla — 64-65 DE 6
Carmen, Isla del — 86-87 OP 8
Carmen, Río del — [MEX] 86-87 G 2-3
Carmen, Río del — [RCH] 106-107 B 2
Carmen, Sierra del — 86-87 J 3
Carmen de Areco 106-107 H 5
Carmen de Bolívar, El — 92-93 DE 3
Carmen del Paraná 102-103 DE 7
Carmen de Patagones 111 D 6
Carmensa 106-107 D 5
Carmen Silva, Río Chico — 108-109 E 9
Carmen Silva, Sierra de — 108-109 E 9
Carmi 66-67 D 1
Carmi, IL 70-71 F 6
Carmila 158-159 J 4
Carmo 102-103 L 4
Carmo da Cachoeira 102-103 K 4
Carmo da Mata 102-103 K 4
Carmo do Cajuru 102-103 K 4
Carmo do Paranaíba 102-103 J 3
Carmo do Rio Claro 102-103 JK 4
Carmona [Angola] 172 BC 3
Carmona [E] 120-121 E 10
Carmópolis 100-101 F 6
Carnac 120-121 F 5
Carnaíba 100-101 EF 4
Carnamah 158-159 C 5
Carnarvon [AUS] 158-159 B 4
Carnarvon [ZA] 172 D 8
Carnarvon Range 158-159 CD 5
Carnatic 134-135 M 8-9
Carnaubais 100-101 F 3
Carnaubal 100-101 D 3
Carnaubas 100-101 E 3
Carnaubinha 98-99 FG 11
Carnduff 68-69 F 1
Carnegie, OK 76-77 E 5
Carnegie, PA 72-73 F 4
Carnegie, Lake — 158-159 D 5
Carn Eige 119 D 3
Carneiro, KS 68-69 GH 6
Carnerillo 106-107 EF 4
Carnero, Bahía — 106-107 A 6
Carnero, Punta — 106-107 A 6
Carnic Alps 122-123 E 2
Car Nicobar Island 134-135 P 9
Carnoió 100-101 FG 4
Carnot 164-165 H 8
Carnot = Al-Abādīyah 166-167 G 1
Carnot Bay 158-159 D 3
Carnsore Point 119 CD 5
Caro, AK 58-59 NO 3
Caro, MI 72-73 E 3
Carole Highlands, MD 82 II b 1
Carolina [BR] 92-93 K 6
Carolina [CO] 94-95 D 4
Carolina [Puerto Rico] 88-89 O 5
Carolina [ZA] 172 EF 7
Carolina, La — [E] 120-121 F 9
Carolina, La — [RA] 106-107 G 4
Carolina, North — 64-65 KL 4
Carolina, South — 64-65 K 5
Caroline 60 K 3
Caroline Islands 206-207 RS 9
Caroline Livermore, Mount — 83 I b 1
Carol Springs, FL 80-81 c 3
Caroní, Río — 92-93 G 3
Carora 92-93 EF 2
Carovi 106-107 K 2
Čarozero 124-125 M 3
Carp 72-73 HJ 2
Carp, NV 74-75 F 4
Carpathians 122-123 L 2-M 3
Carpentaria, Gulf of — 158-159 GH 2
Carpenter, WY 68-69 DE 5
Carpenters Bayou 85 III c 1
Carpentras 120-121 K 6
Carpi 122-123 D 3
Carpina 92-93 M 6
Carpintería 106-107 C 3
Carpinteria, CA 74-75 D 5
Carpio, ND 68-69 F 1
Carp Lake 60 F 2
Carpolac 158-159 H 7
Carr, CO 68-69 D 5
Carrabelle, FL 78-79 G 6
Carrao, Río — 94-95 K 4
Carrapateiras 100-101 D 3
Carrara 122-123 D 3
Carrasquero 94-95 EF 2
Carrathool 160 G 5
Carrbridge 119 E 3
Carrería 111 E 2
Carreta, La — 106-107 FG 6
Carretas, Punta — 96-97 C 9
Carretera Interamericana 88-89 E 10
Carretera Panamericana 106-107 B 2
Carriacou 94-95 L 1
Carrick on Shannon 119 BC 5
Carrick-on-Suir 119 C 5
Carrière, Lac — 72-73 H 1
Carrières-sous-Bois 129 I b 2
Carrières-sous-Poissy 129 I b 2
Carriers Mills, IL 70-71 F 7
Carrieton 160 D 4
Carrillo 76-77 BC 9
Carrilobo 106-107 F 3
Carrington, ND 68-69 G 2
Carrión 120-121 E 7
Carrizal 94-95 E 1
Carrizal, Alto de — 94-95 C 4
Carrizal, Laguna del — 106-107 H 7
Carrizal Bajo 111 B 3
Carrizo Springs, TX 76-77 DE 8
Carrizozo, NM 76-77 B 6
Carroll 61 HJ 6
Carroll, IA 70-71 C 4
Carrollton, GA 78-79 G 4
Carrollton, IL 70-71 E 6
Carrollton, KY 70-71 H 6
Carrollton, MO 70-71 D 6
Carrollton, TX 76-77 F 6
Carro Quemado 106-107 E 6
Carrot River [CDN, place] 61 G 4
Carrot River [CDN, river] 61 GH 4
Carruthers 61 D 4
Çarşamba 136-137 G 2
Çarşamba suyu 136-137 DE 4
Čaršanga 134-135 K 4
Carshalton, London- 129 II b 2
Čarsk 132-133 P 8
Carson, CA 83 III c 3
Carson, ND 68-69 F 2
Carson City, NV 64-65 C 4
Carson Sink 74-75 D 3
Carsonville, MI 72-73 E 3
Cartagena [CO, Bolívar] 92-93 D 2
Cartagena [CO, Caquetá] 94-95 D 7
Cartagena [E] 120-121 G 10
Cartagena [RCH] 106-107 B 4
Cartago, CA 74-75 DE 4
Cartago [CO] 92-93 D 4
Cartago [CR] 64-65 K 10
Carta Valley, TX 76-77 D 8
Carter, MT 66-67 H 2
Carter, OK 76-77 E 5
Carter, WY 66-67 H 5
Carter Bridge 170 III b 2
Carteret, NJ 82 III a 3
Cartersville, GA 78-79 G 3
Cartersville, MT 68-69 C 2
Carthage 164-165 G 1
Carthage, IL 70-71 E 5
Carthage, MO 64-65 H 4
Carthage, MS 78-79 E 4
Carthage, NC 80-81 G 3
Carthage, NY 72-73 J 2-3
Carthage, SD 68-69 H 3
Carthage, TN 78-79 G 2
Carthage, TX 76-77 G 6
Carthago 164-165 G 1
Cartier 62 L 3
Cartier Island 158-159 D 2
Cartierville, Aéroport de — 82 I a 1
Cartierville, Montréal- 82 I a 1
Cartum = Al Kharṭūm 164-165 L 5
Cartwright [CDN, Manitoba] 68-69 G 1
Cartwright [CDN, Newfoundland] 56-57 Z 7
Caru, Rio — 100-101 A 2
Caruachi 94-95 K 3
Caruaru 92-93 M 6
Carúpano 92-93 G 2
Carutapera 92-93 K 5
Carvalho 98-99 N 6
Carvoeiro 98-99 GH 5
Carvoeiro, Cabo — 120-121 C 9
Cary, NC 80-81 G 3
Čaryn 132-133 OP 9
Čaryš 132-133 P 7
Carysfort, Cape — 108-109 L 8
Casabe [CO, landscape] 94-95 D 4
Casabe [CO, place] 94-95 DE 4
Casablanca [CO] 91 III bc 2
Casablanca [RCH] 106-107 B 4
Casablanca = Ad-Dār al-Bayḍā' 164-165 BC 2
Casa Branca [BR] 102-103 J 4
Casacajal, Punta — 94-95 B 6
Casa de Campo 113 III a 2
Casa de Gobierno 110 III b 1
Casa de Janos 86-87 F 2
Casadepaga, AK 58-59 EF 4
Casa de Pedras, Ilha — 110 I c 1
Casa Grande, AZ 74-75 H 6
Casa Indígena 94-95 F 8
Casa Laguna 96-97 C 7
Casal di Principe 122-123 EF 5
Casale Monferrato 122-123 C 3
Casaletti Mattei, Roma- 113 II a 2
Casalins 106-107 H 6
Casalmaggiore 122-123 CD 3
Casal Morena, Roma- 113 II c 2
Casalotti, Roma- 113 II a 2
Casalta, Caracas- 91 II b 1
Casalvasco 102-103 BC 1
Casamance [SN, administrative unit] 168-169 B 2
Casamance [SN, river] 168-169 AB 2
Casanare 94-95 EF 5
Casanare, Río — 92-93 E 3
Casanay 94-95 K 2
Casa Nova 92-93 L 6
Casa Piedra, TX 76-77 BC 8
Casares [RA] 106-107 F 2
Casas Cardenas 96-97 DE 4
Casas Grandes, Río — 64-65 E 5-6
Casa Verde, São Paulo- 110 II b 1
Casbas 106-107 F 6
Cascada 106-107 FG 6
Cascadas, Las — 64-65 b 2
Cascade 66-67 DE 1
Cascade, IA 70-71 E 4
Cascade, ID 66-67 EF 3
Cascade, MT 66-67 GH 2
Cascade de Sica 168-169 F 3
Cascade Head 66-67 A 3
Cascade Pass 66-67 C 1
Cascade Point 161 BC 7
Cascade Range 64-65 B 2-3
Cascade Reservoir 66-67 EF 3
Cascade Tunnel 66-67 C 2
Cascadura, Rio de Janeiro- 110 I ab 2
Cascapédia, Rivière — 63 C 3
Cascata 100-101 A 5
Cascatinha 102-103 L 5
Cascavel [BR, Ceará] 100-101 E 3
Cascavel [BR, Paraná] 111 F 2
Casco, WI 70-71 G 3
Casco Bay 72-73 LM 3
Cascumpeque Bay 63 DE 4
Časel'ka 132-133 P 4-5
Caseros, General San Martín- 110 III b 1
Caserta 122-123 F 5
Casetas 120-121 G 8
Caseville, MI 72-73 E 3
Casey, IL 70-71 FG 6
Cashmere, WA 66-67 C 2
Casigua [YV, Falcón] 94-95 F 2
Casigua [YV, Zuila] 94-95 E 3
Casilda 111 D 4
Casimiro de Abreu 102-103 L 5
Casino 158-159 K 5
Casiquiare, Río — 92-93 F 4
Casireni, Río — 96-97 E 8
Casma 92-93 D 6
Casma, Río — 96-97 BC 6
Casmalia, CA 74-75 C 5
Čašniki 124-125 G 6
Časovo 124-125 S 2
Caspe 120-121 GH 8
Casper, WY 64-65 E 3
Casper Range 68-69 C 4
Caspiana, LA 78-79 C 4
Caspian Sea 134-135 F 1-G 3
Cass, WV 72-73 FG 5
Cassa, WY 68-69 D 4
Cassacatiza 171 C 6
Cassai = Kasai 172 C 2
Cassai, Rio — 172 CD 4
Cassamba 172 D 4
Cass City, MI 72-73 E 3
Cassel = Kassel 118 D 3
Casselton, ND 68-69 H 2
Cássia 102-103 J 4
Cassia, Via — 113 II a 1
Cassiar Mountains 56-57 KL 6
Cassilândia 102-103 FG 3
Cassils 61 B 5
Cassinga = Kassinga 172 C 5
Cassino [BR] 106-107 LM 4
Cassino [I] 122-123 EF 5
Cass Lake, MN 70-71 C 2
Cassopolis, MI 70-71 GH 5
Cass River 70-71 J 4
Cassville, WI 70-71 E 4
Castaic, CA 74-75 D 5
Castanhal [BR, Amazonas] 98-99 K 6
Castanhal [BR, Pará] 92-93 K 5
Castanheiro 92-93 F 5
Castaños 76-77 D 9
Castaño Viejo 106-107 C 3
Castejón 120-121 FG 7
Castelar, Morón- 110 III ab 1
Castelfranco Veneto 122-123 DE 3
Castel Giubileo, Roma- 113 II b 1
Castella, CA 66-67 B 5
Castellammare, Golfo di — 122-123 E 6
Castellammare del Golfo 122-123 E 6
Castellammare di Stàbia 122-123 EF 5
Castellana Grotte 122-123 G 5
Castelli 106-107 J 6
Castelli = Juan José Castelli 111 DE 3
Castellón de la Plana 120-121 GH 9
Castelnaudary 120-121 HJ 7
Castelo [BR, Espírito Santo] 102-103 M 4
Castelo [BR, Mato Grosso do Sul] 102-103 D 3
Castelo, Serra do — 100-101 D 11
Castelo Branco 120-121 D 9
Castelo do Piauí 100-101 D 3
Castelrosso = Mégistē 136-137 C 4
Castel Sant'Angelo 113 II b 2
Castelsarrasin 120-121 H 6
Castelvetrano 122-123 E 7
Casterton 158-159 H 7
Castilla [PE, Loreto] 96-97 D 5
Castilla [PE, Piura] 96-97 A 4
Castilla la Nueva 120-121 E 9-F 8
Castilla la Vieja 120-121 E 8-F 7
Castillejo 94-95 L 4
Castilletes 92-93 E 2
Castillo, Pampa del — 111 C 7
Castillo de San Marcos National Monument 80-81 c 1
Castillón 86-87 J 3
Castillos 106-107 L 5
Castillos, Laguna — 106-107 KL 5
Castle Dale, UT 74-75 H 3
Castle Dome Mountains 74-75 FG 6
Castlegar 66-67 DE 1
Castle Gate, UT 74-75 H 3

Castle Hayne, NC 80-81 H 3
Castlemaine 158-159 HJ 7
Castle Mount 58-59 LM 2
Castle Mountain 60 K 4
Castle Peak [USA, Colorado] 68-69 C 6
Castle Peak [USA, Idaho] 66-67 F 3
Castlepoint 161 G 5
Castlereagh Bay 158-159 FG 2
Castlereagh River 158-159 J 6
Castle Rock, CO 68-69 D 6
Castle Rock, WA 66-67 B 2
Castle Rock Butte 68-69 E 3
Castle Rock Lake 70-71 F 4
Castleton Corners, New York-, NY 82 III b 3
Castle Valley 74-75 H 3
Castolon, TX 76-77 C 8
Castor 61 C 4
Castres 120-121 J 7
Castries 64-65 O 9
Castro [BR] 111 F 2
Castro [RCH] 111 B 6
Castro, Cabo — 108-109 B 8
Castro, Punta — 108-109 G 4
Castro Alves 100-101 E 7
Castro Barros 106-107 E 3
Castro-Urdiales 120-121 F 7
Castrovillari 122-123 G 6
Castroville, CA 74-75 C 4
Castroville, TX 76-77 E 8
Castrovirreyna 92-93 DE 7
Častyje 124-125 U 5
Casuarinas, Las — 106-107 CD 3
Casuarinenkust 148-149 L 8
Casummit Lake 62 C 2
Casupá 106-107 K 5
Caswell, AK 58-59 MN 6
Çat = Yavı 136-137 J 3
Catacamas 88-89 D 7
Catacaos 96-97 A 4
Catacocha 96-97 B 3-4
Cataguases 102-103 L 4
Çatak 136-137 K 3-4
Catalão 102-103 J 3
Catalão, Punta do — 110 I b 2
Çatalca 136-137 C 2
Catalina 111 C 3
Catalina, Punta — 108-109 EF 9
Catalonia = Cataluña 120-121 H 8-J 9
Cataluña 120-121 H 8-J 7
Çatalzeytin 136-137 F 1-2
Catamarca 104-105 B 9-C 11
Catamarca = San Fernado del Valle de Catamarca 111 C 3
Catamayo, Río — 96-97 AB 4
Catandica 172 F 5
Catanduanes Island 148-149 HJ 4
Catanduva 92-93 K 9
Catanduvas 102-103 F 6
Catânia 122-123 F 7
Catán Lil 108-109 D 2
Catán-Lil, Sierra de — 106-107 B 7
Catanzaro 122-123 G 6
Catão 100-101 B 7
Cataouatche, Lake — 85 I a 2
Catapilco 106-107 B 4
Cataqueamã 98-99 G 10
Catar = Qaṭar 134-135 G 5
Cataratas del Iguazú 111 F 3
Catarina 100-101 DE 4
Catarina, TX 76-77 E 8
Catarina, Gebel — = Jabal Katrīnah 164-165 L 3
Catarina, Raso da — 100-101 E 5
Catarino, Cachoeira do — 98-99 G 10
Catarman 148-149 HJ 4
Cat Arm River 63 H 2
Catastrophe, Cape — 158-159 F 7-G 6
Catatumbo, Río — 94-95 EF 3
Catavi 104-105 C 6
Cat Ba, Dao — 150-151 F 2
Catbalogan 148-149 HJ 4
Catedral, Monte — 108-109 BC 6
Catedral de San Isidro 113 III a 2
Catemaco 86-87 N 8
Catena Costiera = Coast Mountains 56-57 K 6-M 7
Catende 100-101 G 5
Catete 172 B 3
Catete, Rio — 98-99 LM 8
Catete, Rio de Janeiro- 110 I b 2
Catford, London- 129 II c 2
Cathay, ND 68-69 G 2
Cathcart 174-175 G 7
Cathedrale Sainte Anne 170 IV a 1
Cathedral Mountain 76-77 C 7
Cathedral of Jakarta 154 IV b 2
Cathedral of Johannesburg 170 V b 2
Cathedral Peak [LS] 174-175 H 5
Cathedral Peak [USA] 64-65 B 2-3
Cathkin Peak 172 EF 7
Cathlemat, WA 66-67 B 2
Cathro, MI 70-71 J 3
Catia, Caracas- 91 II b 1
Catiaeum = Kütahya 134-135 BC 3
Catia La Mar 94-95 H 2
Catiara 102-103 J 3
Catinzaco 111 C 3
Catió 164-165 AB 6
Catisimiña 94-95 K 5
Cat Island [BS] 64-65 L 7
Cat Island [USA] 78-79 E 5
Catitas, Las — 106-107 CD 4
Cativá 64-65 b 2
Cat Lake [CDN, lake] 62 CD 2
Cat Lake [CDN, place] 62 D 2
Catlettsburg, KY 72-73 E 5
Catmandu = Katmāndū 134-135 NO 5
Catoche, Cabo — 64-65 J 7
Catolé Grande, Rio — 100-101 D 8
Catolina 110 III b 2
Catramba, Serra do — 100-101 F 6
Catriel 106-107 CD 6
Catriló 111 D 5
Catrimani 92-93 G 4
Catrimani, Rio — 92-93 G 4
Catskill, NY 72-73 JK 3
Catskill Mountains 72-73 J 3
Cattaraugus, NY 72-73 G 3
Catu 100-101 E 7
Catuane 174-175 K 4
Catulé do Rocha 100-101 F 4
Catumbela 172 B 4
Catunda 100-101 DE 3
Catuni 102-103 L 2
Catuni, Serra do — 102-103 L 2
Caturai 102-103 H 2
Câu, Sông — 150-151 E 2
Cauaburi, Rio — 98-99 E 4-F 5
Cauamé, Rio — 94-95 L 6
Cauaxi, Rio — 98-99 O 7
Cauca 94-95 C 6
Cauca, Río — 92-93 E 3
Caucagua 94-95 H 2
Caucaia 92-93 M 5
Caucasia 92-93 D 3
Caucasus Mountains 134-135 EF 2
Cauchari, Salar de — 104-105 C 8
Caughnawage 82 I ab 2
Câu Giat 150-151 E 3
Caujul 96-97 C 7
Câu Ke 150-151 EF 8
Cauldcleuch Head 119 E 4
Caulfield, Melbourne- 161 II c 2
Caulfield Racecourse 161 II c 1
Caungula 172 C 3
Caunpore = Kānpur 134-135 MN 5
Čaunskaja guba 132-133 gh 4
Caupolicán 92-93 F 7
Cauquenes 111 B 5
Caura, Río — 92-93 G 3
Caurés, Rio — 98-99 G 5
Caurimare, Petare- 91 II bc 2
Causapscal 63 C 3
Causapscal, Parc provincial de — 63 C 3
Causse du Kelifely 172 HJ 5
Causses 120-121 J 6
Čausy 124-125 H 7
Cautário, Rio — 98-99 FG 10
Cautén, Punta — 106-107 A 7
Cauterets 120-121 G 7
Cautiva, La — [BOL] 104-105 EF 6
Cautiva, La — [RA, Córdoba] 106-107 E 4
Cautiva, La — [RA, San Luis] 106-107 D 4
Cauvery 140 C 5
Cauvery Delta 140 D 5
Cauvery Falls 140 C 4
Caux, Pays de — 120-121 H 4
Cavalcante 92-93 K 7
Cavalheiros 102-103 HJ 2
Cavalier, ND 68-69 H 1
Cavally 164-165 C 7-8
Cavalonga, Sierra — 104-105 C 8
Cavan 119 C 4-5
Cavanayén 94-95 KL 5
Cave Hills 68-69 E 3
Caveiras, Rio — 102-103 G 7
Caverá, Coxilha — 106-107 K 3
Caviana, Ilha — 92-93 K 4
Cavinas 104-105 C 3
Cavite 148-149 H 4
Cavtat 122-123 GH 4
Çavuşçu gölü 136-137 DE 3
Cavuşköy 154 I a 2
Cawnpore = Kānpur 134-135 MN 5
Caxambu 102-103 K 4
Caxiabatay, Río — 96-97 D 5
Caxias [BR, Amazonas] 98-99 C 7
Caxias [BR, Maranhão] 92-93 L 5
Caxias do Sul 111 F 3
Caxito 172 B 3
Caxiuana, Baía de — 92-93 J 5
Çay 136-137 D 3
Çay = Okam 136-137 K 2
Cayaca, Cerro — 106-107 B 6
Cayambe [EC, mountain] 92-93 D 5
Cayambe [EC, place] 92-93 D 4
Cayar 168-169 A 2
Cayar, Lac — = Ar-R'kīz 164-165 AB 5
Cayastacito 106-107 G 3
Çaybaşı 136-137 J 2
Çaycuma 136-137 E 2
Çayeli = Çaybaşı 136-137 J 2
Cayenne [French Guiana, administrative unit] 98-99 M 3
Cayenne [French Guiana, place] 92-93 J 3-4
Cayes, Les — 64-65 M 8
Cayey 88-89 N 5
Çayıralan = Çayırşehri 136-137 F 3
Çayırhan 136-137 DE 2
Çayırlı 136-137 HJ 3
Cayırlıahmetçiler 136-137 D 2
Çayırşehri 136-137 F 3
Çaykara 136-137 J 2
Cayman Brac 64-65 L 8
Cayman Islands 64-65 KL 8
Cayman Trench 64-65 KL 8
Cayo Arenas 86-87 P 6
Cayo Centro 86-87 R 8
Cayo Coco 88-89 G 3
Cayo Guajaba 88-89 H 4
Cayo Lobos 86-87 R 8
Cayo Nuevo 86-87 O 7
Cayo Romano 64-65 L 7
Cayo Sabinal 88-89 H 4
Cayos Arcas 86-87 P 7
Cayos de Albuquerque 88-89 F 8
Cayos Miskito 64-65 K 9
Cay Sal 88-89 F 3
Cayucos, CA 74-75 C 5
Cayuga Lake 72-73 H 3
Cayungo = Nana Candundo 172 D 4
Cayuse Hills 68-69 B 2-3
Cazador, Cerro — 108-109 CD 8
Cazalla de la Sierra 120-121 E 10
Caza Pava 106-107 J 2
Cazombo 172 D 4
Cazorla [YV] 94-95 H 3
Cchaltubo 126-127 L 5
Cea 120-121 E 7
Ceahlău, Muntele — 122-123 LM 2
Ceará [BR, administrative unit] 92-93 LM 6
Ceará [BR, place] 96-97 E 6
Ceará = Fortaleza 92-93 M 5
Ceará-Mirim 100-101 G 3
Ceba 61 G 4
Ceballos 86-87 HJ 4
Çebeciköy 154 I a 2
Čeboksary 132-133 H 6
Čeboksary-Sosnovka 124-125 QR 5
Cebollar 106-107 D 2
Cebollati 106-107 L 4
Cebollati, Río — 106-107 K 4
Cebrikovo 126-127 E 3
Čebsara 124-125 M 4
Cebú [RP, island] 148-149 H 4
Cebú [RP, place] 148-149 H 4
Cecchignola, Roma- 113 II b 2
Çeçeli 136-137 F 4
Čečel'nik 126-127 D 2
Čečen', ostrov — 126-127 N 4
Čečeno-Ingušskaja Avtonomnaja Sovetskaja Socialističeskaja Respublika = Checheno-Ingush Autonomous Soviet Socialist Republic 126-127 MN 5
Cecen Uul 142-143 H 2
Cecerleg 142-143 J 2
Čečersk 124-125 H 7
Čechov [SU, Sachalin] 132-133 b 8
Cecilia, KY 70-71 GH 7
Cecilienhöhe, Potsdam- 130 III a 2
Cecil Lake 60 GH 1
Cecil Plains 160 K 1
Cécina 122-123 D 4
Čečujsk 132-133 U 6
Cedar Bluff Reservoir 68-69 G 6
Cedar Breaks National Monument 74-75 G 4
Cedarbrook, PA 84 III c 1
Cedarbrook Mall 84 III bc 1
Cedarburg, WI 70-71 FG 4
Cedar City, UT 64-65 D 4
Cedar Creek [USA, North Dakota] 68-69 EF 2
Cedar Creek [USA, Virginia] 72-73 G 5
Cedar Falls, IA 70-71 D 4
Cedar Grove, LA 85 I b 3
Cedar Grove, NJ 82 III a 1
Cedar Grove, WI 70-71 G 4
Cedar Heights, MD 82 II b 2
Cedar Heights, PA 84 III b 1
Cedar Hill, NM 68-69 C 7
Cedar Island [USA, North Carolina] 80-81 H 3
Cedar Island [USA, Virginia] 80-81 J 2
Cedar Key, FL 80-81 b 2
Cedar Lake [CDN] 56-57 Q 7
Cedar Lake [USA] 76-77 C 6
Cedar Mountains [USA, Nevada] 74-75 E 3
Cedar Mountains [USA, Oregon] 66-67 E 4
Cedar Point 68-69 E 6
Cedar Rapids, IA 64-65 H 3
Cedar River [USA ◁ Iowa River] 70-71 E 4-5
Cedar River [USA ◁ Loup River] 68-69 G 5
Cedar Springs, MI 70-71 H 4
Cedar Swamp 84 III ab 3
Cedartown, GA 78-79 G 3-4
Cedar Vale, KS 76-77 F 4
Cedarville 174-175 H 6
Cedarville, CA 66-67 C 5
Cedarwood, CO 68-69 D 7
Cedong, Jakarta- 154 IV b 2
Cedral [BR, Maranhão] 100-101 B 1
Cedral [BR, São Paulo] 102-103 H 4
Cedro 92-93 M 6
Cedro Playa 96-97 E 4
Cedros, Isla — 64-65 C 6
Ceduna 158-159 F 6
Ceel 142-143 H 2
Cefalù 122-123 F 6
Cega 120-121 E 8
Čegdomyn 132-133 Z 7
Čegitun 58-59 B 3
Cegléd 118 J 5
Ceiba, La — [Honduras] 64-65 J 8
Ceiba, La — [YV] 92-93 E 3
Ceiba Grande 86-87 O 9
Ceibal, El — 104-105 E 10
Ceibas 106-107 H 4
Ceja, La — 94-95 D 5
Cejal 94-95 H 6
Cejas, Las — 111 D 3
Čekalin 124-125 L 6
Čekanovskogo, kr'až — 132-133 XY 3
Çekerek = Hacıköy 136-137 F 2
Çekerekırmağı 136-137 F 3-G 2
Čekmaguš 124-125 U 6
Cela = Uaco Cungo 172 C 4
Čel'abinsk 132-133 L 6
Celaya 64-65 F 7
Čelbas 126-127 J 3
Celebes = Sulawesi 148-149 G 7-H 6
Celebes Sea 148-149 GH 6
Celebessee 148-149 GH 6
Çelebiler 136-137 E 2
Celedín 96-97 B 5
Čeleken 134-135 G 3
Celestún 86-87 P 7
Celia 102-103 C 5
Celikan 136-137 GH 4
Celina, OH 70-71 H 5
Celina, TN 78-79 G 2
Celina, TX 76-77 F 6
Celinograd 132-133 MN 7
Celje 122-123 F 2
Čelkar 132-133 KL 8
Celle 118 E 2
Čelmuži 124-125 KL 2
Čelobitjevo 113 V c 1
Çeltik 136-137 DE 3
Çeltikçi = Aziziye 136-137 D 4
Celuo = Chira Bazar 142-143 DE 4
Čel'uskin, mys — 132-133 T-V 2
Cement, OK 76-77 EF 5
Çemişgezek 136-137 H 3
Çemlidere = Mecrihan 136-137 H 4
Cempaka Putih, Jakarta- 154 IV b 2
Cempi, Selat — 152-153 N 10
Cenad 122-123 J 2
Cencia = Tyencha 164-165 M 7
Cenepa, Río — 96-97 B 4
Çengelköy, İstanbul- 154 I b 2
Centane 174-175 H 7
Centennial 84 III de 2
Centennial, WY 68-69 CD 5
Centeno 106-107 G 4
Center, CO 68-69 C 7
Center, ND 68-69 F 2
Center, NE 68-69 GH 4
Center, TX 76-77 GH 7
Centerfield, UT 74-75 H 3
Center Hill, Atlanta-, GA 85 II b 2
Center Line, MI 84 II b 2
Centerton, NJ 84 III d 2
Centerville, AL 78-79 F 4
Centerville, IA 70-71 D 5
Centerville, MO 70-71 E 7
Centerville, SD 68-69 H 4
Centerville, TN 78-79 F 3
Centerville, TX 76-77 FG 7
Centinela, Picacho del — 64-65 F 6
Centinela, Sierra del — 104-105 D 8-9
Centocelle, Roma- 113 II bc 2
Central, AK 58-59 P 4
Central, NM 74-75 JK 6
Central [BR] 100-101 C 6
Central [EAK] 172 G 2
Central [GH] 168-169 E 4
Central [MW] 171 C 6
Central [PY] 102-103 D 6
Central [Z] 172 E 4
Central, Plateau — = Cao Nguyên Trung Phân 148-149 E 4
Central African Republic 164-165 HJ 7
Central Auckland 161 EF 3
Central City, KY 70-71 G 7
Central City, NE 68-69 GH 5
Centrale 168-169 F 3
Central Falls, RI 72-73 L 4
Centralia, IL 64-65 J 4
Centralia, MO 70-71 DE 6
Centralia, WA 66-67 B 2
Central Indian Ridge 50-51 N 5-7
Central Intelligence Agency 82 II a 1
Central Karroo = Groot Karoo 172 D 8
Central Mount Stuart 158-159 F 4
Central'nojakutskaja ravnina 132-133 WX 5
Central'nolesnoj zapovednik 124-125 J 5
Central Pacific Basin 156-157 KL 4
Central Park [AUS] 161 I b 2
Central Park [USA, New York] 82 III c 2
Central Park [USA, Philadelphia] 85 III a 1
Central Park of Singapore 154 III ab 2
Central Patricia 62 DE 2
Central Point, OR 66-67 B 4
Central Province = Madhyama Palāna = 4 ◁ 140 E 7
Central Range 174-175 H 5
Central Siberian Plateau 132-133 R-X 4-5
Central Station [AUS] 161 I b 2
Central Valley, CA 66-67 BC 5
Centre 168-169 E 2-3
Centre-Est 168-169 E 2-3
Centre-Ouest 168-169 E 3
Centreville 63 BC 4
Centreville, MD 72-73 HJ 5
Centreville, MS 78-79 D 5
Centro, El — 94-95 E 4
Centro, Niterói- 110 I c 2
Century City, Los Angeles-, CA 83 III b 1
Cenxi 146-147 C 10
Čepca 124-125 S 4
Cepeda [RA] 106-107 G 4
Cephalonia = Kefallēnia 122-123 J 6
Cepu 152-153 J 9
Ceram = Seram 148-149 JK 7
Ceram Sea 148-149 J 7
Cerbatana, Serranía de la — 92-93 F 3
Cerbatano, Cerro — 94-95 H 4
Cerbère 120-121 J 7
Cercen = Chärchän 142-143 F 4
Čerdyn' 124-125 V 3
Cereal 61 C 5
Cereales 106-107 EF 6
Čeremchovo 132-133 T 7
Čeremisinovo 124-125 L 8
Čeremšan 124-125 S 6
Čerepanovo 132-133 P 7
Čerepet' 124-125 L 6
Čerepovec 132-133 F 6
Ceres, CA 74-75 C 4
Ceres [RA] 106-107 G 2
Ceres [ZA] 172 C 8
Céret 120-121 J 7
Cereté 94-95 CD 3
Čerevkovo 124-125 P 3
Cerf Island 172 K 3
Cerignola 122-123 F 5
Cerigo = Kýthēra 122-123 K 7
Cerigotto = Antikýthēra 122-123 K 8
Čerikov 124-125 H 7
Cerillos 86-87 P 8
Cerillos, Los — 106-107 E 3
Čerkassy 126-127 EF 2
Çerkeş 136-137 E 2
Čerkessk 126-127 L 4
Čerkizovo, Moskva- 113 V c 2
Čerlak 132-133 N 7
Čermenino 124-125 OP 4
Çermik 136-137 H 3
Čern' 124-125 L 7
Čern'achov 126-127 D 1
Čern'achovsk 118 K 1
Čern'anka 126-127 HJ 1
Černatica 122-123 L 4-5
Cernăuţi = Černovcy 126-127 B 2
Černava 124-125 M 7
Cernavodă 122-123 MN 3
Černevo 124-125 FG 4
Černigov 126-127 E 1
Černigovka 132-133 Z 9
Černobyl' 126-127 DE 1
Černogorsk 132-133 R 7
Černomorskoje 126-127 F 4
Černorečje = Dzeržinsk 132-133 GH 6
Černovcy 126-127 B 2
Černovskije Kopi, Čita- 132-133 V 7
Černuška 124-125 UV 5
Černutjevo 124-125 R 2
Černyševskij 132-133 V 5
Černyševskoje 118 KL 1
Černyškovskij 126-127 KL 2
Cero, Punta — 108-109 H 4
Čer'omuski, Moskva- 113 V bc 3
Cerralvo [MEX, island] 76-77 E 9
Cerralvo [MEX, place] 86-87 KL 4
Cerralvo, Isla — 64-65 E 7
Cerreira Comprida, Cachoeira — 98-99 OP 10
Cerrillos 104-105 D 9
Cerrito [BR] 106-107 L 3
Cerrito [CO] 94-95 E 4
Cerrito [PY] 102-103 D 7
Cerrito, El — 94-95 CD 6
Cerritos 64-65 FG 7
Cerritos, CA 83 III d 2
Cerritos Bayos 104-105 B 8
Cerro, El — 92-93 G 8
Cerro Agua Hedionda 106-107 DE 4
Cerro Agua Poca 106-107 C 6
Cerro Aguas Blancas 104-105 B 9
Cerro Aiguilete 108-109 C 8
Cerro Alto Nevado 108-109 C 5
Cerro Anecón Grande 108-109 D 3
Cerro Ansilta 106-107 C 3-4
Cerro Ap Iwan 108-109 D 6
Cerro Arenales 111 B 7
Cerro Aucanquilcha 111 C 2
Cerro Avanzado 108-109 G 4
Cerro Azul [BR] 102-103 H 6
Cerro Azul [MEX] 86-87 M 7
Cerro Balmaceda 108-109 C 8
Cerro Barros Arana 108-109 CD 4
Cerro Bayo [RA, La Pampa] 106-107 DE 6
Cerro Bayo [RA, Río Negro ↑ Loma San Martín] 106-107 C 7
Cerro Bayo [RA, Río Negro ← Loma San Martín] 106-107 C 7
Cerro Bayo [RCH] 108-109 CD 5
Cerro Belgrano 108-109 D 6
Cerro Bertrand 108-109 C 8
Cerro Blanco [PE] 96-97 C 7
Cerro Blanco [RA] 108-109 F 6
Cerro Blanco, Loma — 108-109 F 4
Cerro Bolsa 106-107 C 2
Cerro Bonete 106-107 C 1
Cerro Bravo [BOL] 104-105 D 5
Cerro Bravo [PE] 96-97 B 4
Cerro Bruja 64-65 b 2
Cerro Cacique 108-109 D 4
Cerro Caltama 104-105 BC 7
Cerro Campamento 91 I b 3
Cerro Campana 94-95 E 7
Cerro Campanario 111 BC 5
Cerro Canapiare 94-95 G 6
Cerro Cangrejo 108-109 C 7
Cerro Capitán Maldonado 108-109 BC 4
Cerro Capitán Ustares 102-103 B 3
Cerro Cayaca 106-107 B 6
Cerro Cazador 108-109 CD 8
Cerro Central 108-109 D 4
Cerro Cerbatano 94-95 H 4
Cerro Cerrón 94-95 F 2
Cerro Champaquí 106-107 E 3
Cerro Chato [BR] 106-107 L 3
Cerro Chato [ROU] 106-107 K 4
Cerro Chirripó Grande 64-65 K 10
Cerro Chorreras 86-87 GH 4
Cerro Cirque 104-105 B 5
Cerro Coan 96-97 B 5
Cerro Cobre 106-107 B 2
Cerro Coipasa 104-105 B 6
Cerro Cojudo Blanco 111 BC 7
Cerro Colipilli 106-107 B 6
Cerro Colorado [RA, Chubut] 108-109 E 5
Cerro Colorado [RA, La Pampa] 106-107 D 6
Cerro Colorado [RA, La Rioja] 106-107 D 2
Cerro Colorado [ROU] 106-107 K 4
Cerro Colupo 104-105 AB 8
Cerro Cónico 108-109 D 4
Cerro Copa 104-105 B 7
Cerro Corá 100-101 F 4
Cerro Corona 108-109 D 3
Cerro Crucero 86-87 H 7
Cerro Cuanacorral 96-97 B 5
Cerro Cumare 94-95 E 7
Cerro Cumbrera 108-109 C 7
Cerro Curamalal Grande 106-107 FG 6
Cerro Curamavida 106-107 B 3
Cerro Dedo 111 B 6
Cerro de La Encantada 64-65 C 5
Cerro de la Estrella 91 I c 2
Cerro de la Estrella, Parque Nacional — 91 I c 2-3
Cerro de la Sal, Cadena de — 96-97 D 7
Cerro de la Salamanca 106-107 C 2
Cerro de las Cuentas 106-107 K 4
Cerro de las Ovejas 106-107 E 4
Cerro de la Viga 106-107 B 3
Cerro del Inca 104-105 BC 7
Cerro del León 64-65 G 8
Cerro del Mojón 106-107 CD 5
Cerro de los Mogotes 106-107 C 2
Cerro del Picacho 91 I c 1
Cerro del Pinacate 86-87 D 2
Cerro del Toro 111 C 3
Cerro del Tromen 106-107 B 6
Cerro del Volcán 106-107 BC 3
Cerro de Pasco 92-93 D 7
Cerro de Pomasi 92-93 E 8
Cerro de Quimsachota 104-105 B 5
Cerro de San Antonio 94-95 D 2
Cerro de Soto 106-107 B 3
Cerro de Tocorpuri 92-93 F 9
Cerro Divisadero 108-109 C 8
Cerro Doce Grande 108-109 E 6
Cerro Doña Ana 106-107 B 2
Cerro Doña Ines 104-105 B 10
Cerro d'Ouro 106-107 KL 3
Cerro Dragón 108-109 E 5
Cerro Duida 94-95 J 6
Cerro El Aspero 106-107 D 2
Cerro El Avila 91 II b 1
Cerro El Ford 108-109 D 9
Cerro El Nevado 92-93 E 4
Cerro el Nevado [RA, mountain] 111 C 5
Cerro El Potro 106-107 C 2
Cerro El Viejo 94-95 E 4
Cerro Finger 108-109 C 9
Cerro Galán 111 C 3
Cerro Grande [BR] 106-107 M 3
Cerro Grande [MEX] 86-87 K 8-9
Cerro Guachi 106-107 C 2
Cerro Guaiquinima 92-93 G 3
Cerro Guanay 94-95 H 5
Cerro Guasacavi 94-95 G 6
Cerro Hatscher 108-109 C 7
Cerro Hermanos 108-109 C 6
Cerro Horcón de Piedra 106-107 B 4
Cerro Huachamacari 94-95 HJ 6
Cerro Huanchaca 104-105 C 7
Cerro Huchuento 64-65 E 7
Cerro Hudson 111 B 7
Cerro Hyades 108-109 C 6
Cerro Iglesias 108-109 EF 6
Cerro Illesca 96-97 A 4-5
Cerro Jeinemeni 108-109 C 6
Cerro Juncal 106-107 BC 4
Cerro Kilambé 88-89 CD 8
Cerro La Paloma 106-107 C 4
Cêrro Largo [BR] 106-107 K 2
Cerro Largo [ROU] 106-107 KL 4
Cerro las Casitas 64-65 E 7
Cerro La Silveta 111 B 8
Cerro Las Lajas 106-107 B 7
Cerro Las Tórtolas 106-107 BC 2
Cerro Leiva 94-95 D 6
Cerro Leon 102-103 B 4
Cerro Leoncito 106-107 C 2
Cerro Limón Verde 104-105 B 8
Cerro Lloron 86-87 H 7
Cerro los Gigantes 106-107 E 3
Cerro los Hijos 96-97 B 5
Cerro Malcanio 104-105 CD 9
Cerro Marahuaca 92-93 FG 4
Cerro Marmolejo 106-107 BC 4
Cerro Mato 94-95 J 4
Cerro Mayo 108-109 D 5
Cerro Mellizo Sur 111 B 7
Cerro Mercedario 111 BC 4
Cerro Mesa 108-109 D 7
Cerro Mogotón 88-89 C 8
Cerro Mora 106-107 B 5
Cerro Moreno 106-107 K 1
Cerro Moro, Pampa del — 108-109 F 6-7
Cerro Munchique 94-95 C 6
Cerro Murallón 111 B 7
Cerrón, Cerro — 94-95 F 2
Cerro Negro 108-109 D 2
Cerro Nevado 108-109 C 4
Cerro Osborne = Mount Usborne 111 E 8
Cerro Otare 92-93 E 4
Cerro Otatal 86-87 E 3
Cerro Ovana 94-95 H 5
Cerro Paine 111 B 8
Cerro Pajonal 104-105 B 7
Cerro Paraque 94-95 H 5
Cerro Pata de Gallo 96-97 B 6
Cerro Patria 108-109 G 5
Cerro Payún 111 BC 5
Cerro Peinado 106-107 C 6
Cerro Pellado 106-107 B 5
Cerro Peña Nevada 64-65 FG 7
Cerro Peñon 91 I c 3
Cerro Picún Leufú 106-107 C 7
Cerro Pináculo 108-109 CD 8
Cerro Piramide 108-109 C 7
Cerro Pirre 94-95 C 4
Cerro Piti 111 C 2
Cerro Porongo 106-107 D 3
Cerro Pumasillo 96-97 E 8
Cerro Puntas Negras 111 C 2
Cerro Puntodo 106-107 E 7
Cerro Quimal 104-105 B 8
Cerro Rajado 106-107 C 2
Cerro Redondo 106-107 C 4
Cerro Relem 111 B 5
Cerro Rico 106-107 E 2
Cerro Río Grande 91 II c 1
Cerro San Lorenzo 111 B 7
Cerro San Miguel 104-105 F 6
Cerro San Pedro 108-109 C 4
Cerro Santa Elena 108-109 G 5
Cerro Santiago 88-89 EF 10
Cerro San Valentín 111 B 7
Cerros Bravos 104-105 B 10
Cerros Cantaritos 106-107 BC 2
Cerros Colorados [RA] 111 C 6
Cerros Colorados [RCH] 111 C 3
Cerros Colorados, Embalse — 106-107 C 7
Cerros Cusali 104-105 C 4
Cerros de Amotape 96-97 A 4
Cerros de Araracuara 94-95 EF 7
Cerros de Bala 92-93 F 7-8
Cerros de Calla-Calla 96-97 BC 5
Cerros de Campanquiz 92-93 D 5-6
Cerros de Canthyuaya 96-97 D 5
Cerros de Itahuania 96-97 F 8
Cerros de Quimurcu 104-105 AB 8
Cerro Sin Nombre 108-109 C 5-6
Cerro Steffen 108-109 D 5
Cerro Tacarcuna 94-95 C 3
Cerro Tamaná 94-95 CD 5
Cerro Tambería 106-107 C 2
Cerro Teotepec 64-65 FG 8
Cerro Tolar 104-105 C 10
Cerro Tomolasta 106-107 DE 4
Cerro Tres Altitos 106-107 C 4
Cerro Tres Cruces 106-107 C 1
Cerro Tres Picos 111 B 6
Cerro Tulaguen 106-107 B 3
Cerro Tunupa 104-105 C 6
Cerro Tupungato 111 BC 4
Cerro Turagua 94-95 J 4
Cerro Turimiquire 94-95 JK 2
Cerro Uritorco 106-107 E 3
Cerro Uspara 106-107 E 4
Cerro Velucá 88-89 D 7
Cerro Venamo 94-95 L 5
Cerro Ventisquero 108-109 D 3
Cerro Vera 106-107 J 4
Cerro Viejo 86-87 DE 2
Cerro Volcán 108-109 E 5
Cerro Xico 91 I d 3
Cerro Yapacana 94-95 H 6
Cerro Yarvicoya 104-105 B 6-7
Cerro Yaví 92-93 F 3
Cerro Yogan 111 BC 8
Cerro Yumari 92-93 F 4
Cerro Zanelli 108-109 C 9
Cerro Zapaleri 111 C 2
Cerro Zempoaltepec 64-65 GH 8
Cerrudo Cué 106-107 J 1
Čerskij 132-133 f 4
Certaldo 122-123 D 4
Čertanovo, Moskva- 113 V bc 3
Čertež 124-125 V 4
Čertkovo 126-127 K 2
Čerusti 124-125 N 6
Cervantes 106-107 D 7
Cervati, Monte — 122-123 F 5
Červen' 124-125 G 7
Červen br'ag 122-123 KL 4
Cervera 120-121 H 8
Cervèteri 122-123 E 4
Cèrvia 122-123 E 3
Červonoarmejskoje [SU, Zaparožskaja Oblast'] 126-127 GH 3
Červonograd 126-127 B 1
Červonozavodskoje 126-127 FG 1
Cesar 94-95 E 3
César, Río — 94-95 E 2
Cesareia = Caesarea 136-137 F 6
Césares, Isla de los — 108-109 HJ 3
Cesena 122-123 DE 3
Cesira, La — 106-107 F 4
Cēsis 124-125 E 5
Česká Třebova 118 G 4
České Budějovice 118 G 4
České země 118 F-H 4
Českomoravská vrchovina 118 GH 4
Çeşme 136-137 B 3
Cessford 56-57 O 7
Cessnock 158-159 K 6
Cess River 164-165 C 7
Cetinje 122-123 H 4
Çetinkaya 136-137 GH 3
Cetraro 122-123 F 6
Ceuta 164-165 CD 1
Cevennes 120-121 JK 6
Cevernyj port 113 V b 2
Cevizlik 136-137 H 2
Ceyhan 136-137 FG 4
Ceyhan nehri 136-137 G 4
Ceylânpınar 136-137 HJ 4
Ceylon = Srī Langka 134-135 N 9
Ceylon Station 61 F 6
Chaaltyn gol 142-143 GH 4

Cha-am [T] 148-149 CD 4
Chaamba, Hassi — = Ḥāssī Sha'ambah 166-167 D 5
Chaapsalu = Haapsalu 124-125 D 4
Chaba 142-143 F 2
Chabar = Bandar-e Chah Bahār 134-135 HJ 5
Chabarovo 132-133 L 4
Chabarovsk 132-133 a 8
Chabás 106-107 G 4
Chab Chhu 138-139 M 3
Chablis 120-121 J 5
Chaca 104-105 AB 6
Chacabuco [RA] 106-107 G 5
Chacabuco [RCH] 106-107 B 4
Chacao 91 II bc 1-2
Chacao, Canal de — 108-109 C 3
Chacarita, Buenos Aires- 110 III b 1
Chacay, El — 106-107 BC 5
Chacays, Sierra de los — 108-109 F 4
Chachahuen, Sierra de — 106-107 C 6
Chachani 96-97 F 10
Chachapoyas 92-93 D 6
Chācharān 64-65 K 4
Chacharramendi 106-107 E 6
Ch'a-chên = Chazhen 146-147 B 5
Cha-ching = Zhajiang 146-147 D 8
Cha-ching = Zhajin 146-147 E 7
Chacho, El — 106-107 E 3
Chāchro 138-139 C 5
Chachyoṭ = Chichot 138-139 F 2
Chaclacayo 96-97 C 7-8
Chačmas 126-127 O 6
Chaco 111 D 3
Chaco, El — 96-97 C 2
Chaco Austral 111 DE 3
Chaco Boreal 111 DE 2
Chaco Canyon National Monument 74-75 JK 4-5
Chaco Central 111 D 2-E 3
Chacon, Cape — 58-59 wx 9
Chacopata 94-95 JK 2
Chaco River 74-75 J 4
Chacras, Las — 106-107 BC 6
Chacras de Piros 96-97 E 7
Chad 164-165 HJ 5
Chad, Lake — = Lac Tchad 164-165 G 6
Chadasan 142-143 J 2
Chadchal = Chatgal 142-143 HJ 1
Chadileuvú, Bañados del — 106-107 D 6
Chadileuvú, Río — 106-107 DE 6
Chadmó 108-109 BC 4
Chadron, NE 68-69 E 4
Chadstone, Melbourne- 161 II c 2
Chadum 172 D 5
Chadwick, IL 70-71 F 4
Chadzaar 142-143 G 4
Chae Hom 150-151 B 3
Chaem, Nam Mae — 150-151 B 3
Chaenpur = Chainpur 138-139 K 6
Chaeryŏng 144-145 EF 3
Chafarinas, Islas — 166-167 EF 2
Chaffee, MO 78-79 DE 2
Chaffers, Canal — 108-109 B 5
Chaffers, Isla — 108-109 BC 5
Chāgalamarri 140 D 3
Chagang-do 144-145 EF 2
Chagan nuur 142-143 L 3
Chagas 102-103 H 1
Chageri = Hageri 124-125 E 4
Chagny 120-121 K 5
Cha Gonpa = Chhōra Gonpa 138-139 M 2
Chagos 50-51 N 6
Chagres [PA, place] 64-65 b 2
Chagres [PA, river] 64-65 ab 2
Chagres, Brazo del — 64-65 b 2
Chagres, Río — 64-65 bc 2
Chagres Arm = Brazo del Chagres 64-65 b 2
Chagual 96-97 C 5
Chaguaramas 94-95 H 3
Chagulak Island 58-59 l 4
Chāgwādam 141 F 2
Chāhār Burjak = Chār Burjak 134-135 J 4
Chahār Maḥāl-e Bakhteyārī = 3 ◁ 134-135 G 4
Chahbā = Shahbā' 136-137 G 6
Chāh Bāhār = Bandar-e Chāh Bahār 134-135 HJ 5
Chahbounia = Shābūnīyah 166-167 H 2
Ch'aho 144-145 G 2
Chai Badan 150-151 C 5
Chaibāsa 138-139 K 6
Chaidamu Pendi = Tsaidam 142-143 GH 4
Chaïdárion 113 IV a 1
Chailar = Hailar 142-143 M 2
Ch'ail-bong 144-145 F 2
Chai Nat 148-149 D 3
Chain Butte 68-69 B 2
Chaîne des Mitumba 172 E 3-4
Chainpur [IND] 138-139 K 6
Chainpur [Nepal] 138-139 L 4
Chaiqiao 146-147 HJ 7
Chaira, Laguna — 94-95 D 7
Chaitén 108-109 C 4
Chai Wan 155 I b 2
Chaiya 148-149 C 5
Chaiyaphum 150-151 CD 5
Chaiyeru = Punchu 140 D 4
Chaiyo 150-151 C 5
Chaiyyār = Cheyyar 140 D 4
Chaján 106-107 E 4
Chajarí 111 E 4
Chajdag gol 142-143 EF 3
Chajian 146-147 G 5
Chajlar 142-143 M 2
Chajlar = Hailar 142-143 M 2
Chajlar gol = Hailar He 142-143 MN 2
Chajrchan 142-143 J 2
Chajr'uzovo 132-133 e 6
Chakachamna Lake 58-59 L 6
Chakaktolik, AK 58-59 F 6
Chaka Nor = Chöch nuur 142-143 H 4
Chākar 138-139 AB 3
Chakaria = Chakariya 141 C 5
Chakariya 141 C 5
Chakdaha, South Suburbs- 154 II ab 3
Chake Chake 171 DE 4
Chakhcharān 134-135 K 4
Chakia 138-139 J 5
Chakkarat 150-151 D 5
Chakkra Rat = Chakkarat 150-151 D 5
Chakradharpur 138-139 K 6
Chakraotā = Chakrāta 138-139 FG 2
Chakrāta 138-139 FG 2
Chaksu = Chātsu 138-139 EF 4
Chākuliā 138-139 L 6
Chakwaktolik, AK 58-59 EF 6
Chāl = Shāl 136-137 N 5
Chala 92-93 E 8
Chala, Punta — 96-97 D 9
Chalab, gora — 126-127 M 6
Chalabesa 171 B 5
Chālakudi 140 C 5
Chalanta 106-107 DE 4
Cha-lan-tun = Yalu 142-143 N 2
Chalatenango 88-89 B 7-8
Chalbi Desert 171 D 2
Chalchuapa 88-89 B 8
Chalchyn gol 142-143 M 2
Chalcidice = Chalkidikḗ 122-123 K 5
Chaleur Bay 56-57 XY 8
Chalhuanca 92-93 E 7
Chalia, Arroyo — 108-109 D 5
Chalia, Pampa del — 108-109 D 5
Chalía, Río — 108-109 DE 7
Chalicán 104-105 D 9
Chaling 146-147 D 8
Cha-ling Hu = Kyaring Tsho 142-143 H 5
Chālīsgā̃v = Chālisgaon 138-139 E 7
Chālisgaon 138-139 E 7
Chalkē 122-123 M 7
Chalkidikḗ 122-123 K 3
Chalkís 122-123 K 6
Chalk River 72-73 H 1-2
Chalkyitsik, AK 58-59 PQ 3
Challa 104-105 C 7
Challacó 106-107 C 7
Challacollo 104-105 C 6
Challacota 104-105 C 6
Challakere 140 C 3
Challapata 92-93 F 8
Challawa 168-169 G 3
Challis, ID 66-67 F 3
Chal'mer-Ju 132-133 L 4
Chalmer-Sede = Tazovskij 132-133 OP 4
Chalmette, LA 85 I c 2
Chalmette Natural Historical Park 85 I c 2
Chālna 138-139 M 6
Chalok 150-151 D 10
Châlons-sur-Marne 120-121 JK 4
Chalon-sur-Saône 120-121 K 5
Chalosse 120-121 G 7
Chalturin 132-133 H 6
Chalviri, Salar de — 104-105 C 8
Cham 118 F 4
Cham, Cu Lao — 150-151 G 5
Chama 168-169 E 3
Chama, NM 68-69 C 7
Chama, Rio — 76-77 A 4
Chamah, Gunung — 150-151 C 10
Chamaicó 106-107 E 5
Chamaites 174-175 B 4
Chaman 134-135 K 4
Chamao, Khao — 150-151 C 6
Chāmarājanagara = Chāmrājnagar 140 C 5
Chamartín, Madrid- 113 III ab 2
Chamaya, Río — 96-97 B 4-5
Chamba [EAT] 171 D 5
Chamba [IND] 134-135 M 4
Chambak 150-151 E 7
Chambal [IND ◁ Kālī Sindh] 134-135 M 5-6
Chambal [IND ◁ Yamunā] 134-135 M 5-6
Chambas 88-89 G 3
Chamberí, Madrid- 113 III a 2
Chamberlain 61 EF 5
Chamberlain, SD 68-69 G 4
Chamberlain Lake 72-73 M 1
Chamberlain River 158-159 E 3
Chamberlin, Mount — 58-59 P 2
Chambersburg, PA 72-73 GH 4
Chambers Island 70-71 G 3
Chambéry 120-121 K 6
Chambeshi 172 F 4
Chambī, Djebel — = Jabal Shaḥambī 166-167 L 2
Chambira, Río — 96-97 D 3
Chambourcy 129 I b 2
Chambres Pass = Cumbres Pass 68-69 C 7
Chambria, Río — 96-97 D 4
Chamchamāl 136-137 L 5
Chamdo = Chhamdo 142-143 H 5
Chame 88-89 G 10
Chamela 86-87 H 8
Chamical 106-107 DE 3
Chami Choto = Hami 142-143 G 3
Chamiss Bay 60 D 4
Chamo, Lake — = Tyamo 164-165 M 7
Chamōlī 138-139 G 2
Chāmpa [IND] 134-135 N 6
Champa [SU] 132-133 X 5
Champagne [CDN] 58-59 TU 6
Champagne [F] 120-121 J 5-K 4
Champagne Castle 174-175 H 5
Champagny Islands 158-159 D 3
Champaign, IL 64-65 J 3-4
Champaquí, Cerro — 106-107 E 3
Champara, Nevado de — 96-97 C 6
Champāran = Mōtihāri 134-135 NO 5
Champassak 148-149 DE 4
Champāvat = Champāwat 138-139 H 3
Champāwat 138-139 H 3
Champ de Course Blue Bonnets 82 I b 2
Champigny-sur-Marne 129 I d 2
Champion 61 B 5
Champlain, Lake — 64-65 LM 3
Champlain, Pont — 82 I b 2
Champotón 64-65 H 8
Champotón, Río — 86-87 P 8
Champs-Elysées 129 I c 2
Champs-sur-Marne 129 I d 2
Champur = Chainpur 138-139 L 4
Chāmrāil 154 II a 2
Chāmrājnagar 140 C 5
Chāmursi 138-139 GH 8
Chan, Ko — 150-151 AB 8
Chana 150-151 C 9
Chanāb 138-139 C 3
Chanāb = Chenāb 134-135 M 4
Chanak Kalessi = Çanakkale 134-135 B 2
Chañar 111 C 4
Chañaral [RCH ↖ Copiapó] 111 B 3
Chañaral [RCH ↙ Copiapó] 106-107 B 2
Chañaral, Isla — 111 B 3
Chañaritos 106-107 E 4
Chānasma 138-139 D 6
Chan Bogd 142-143 K 3
Chancaní 106-107 E 3
Chancay 92-93 D 7
Chancay, Río — 96-97 C 7
Chance Island = Ko Chan 150-151 AB 8
Chanch 142-143 J 1
Chan Chan 96-97 B 6
Chan-chiang = Zhanjiang 142-143 L 7
Chanchoengsao 148-149 D 4
Chanco 106-107 A 5
Chanco, Bahía — 106-107 A 5
Chānd 138-139 G 7
Chānda = Chandrapur 134-135 M 7
Chandaka 138-139 K 7
Chandalar, AK 58-59 NO 3
Chandalar, East Fork — 58-59 P 2
Chandalar, Middle Fork — 58-59 O 2-3
Chandalar, North Fork — 58-59 N 2-3
Chandalar Lake 58-59 NO 3
Chandalar River 56-57 G 4
Chandannagar = Mangalkōṭ 138-139 LM 6
Chandaolī = Chandauli 138-139 J 5
Chandaosī = Chandausi 138-139 G 3
Chandarpur 138-139 J 7
Chandauli 138-139 J 5
Chandausi 138-139 G 3
Chāndbāli 138-139 L 7
Chandeleur Islands 64-65 J 6
Chandeleur Sound 78-79 E 5-6
Chandernagore 138-139 LM 6
Chāndgad 140 AB 3
Chandīgarh 134-135 LM 4
Chāndil 138-139 L 6
Chanditala 154 II a 1
Chandler 56-57 Y 8
Chandler, AZ 74-75 H 6
Chandler, OK 76-77 F 5
Chandler Lake 58-59 LM 2
Chandler Park 84 II c 2
Chandler River 58-59 L 2
Chandlers Falls 171 D 2
Chandless, Rio — 98-99 C 9-10
Chāndod 138-139 D 6-7
Chāndor 138-139 DE 7
Chāndpūr [BD] 141 B 4
Chāndpur [IND] 138-139 G 3
Chāndpur = Chāndpur Bāzār 138-139 FG 7
Chāndpur Bāzār 138-139 FG 7
Chandrā 138-139 F 1
Chandragiri 140 D 4
Chandrakona 138-139 L 6
Chandranagar = Chandernagore 138-139 LM 6
Chandrapur 134-135 M 7
Chāndūr 138-139 FG 7
Chāndūr = Chāndor 138-139 DE 7
Chanduy 96-97 A 3
Chandyga 132-133 a 5
Chang, Ko — [T, Andaman Sea] 150-151 B 8
Chang, Ko — [T, Gulf of Thailand] 148-149 D 4
Changai = Shanghai 142-143 N 5
Changaj 142-143 H 2
Changajn Nuruu 142-143 HJ 2
Changalane 174-175 K 4
Changam = Chengam 140 D 4
Chang'an 146-147 B 4
Ch'ang-an = Xi'an 142-143 K 5
Changanācheri 140 C 6
Changane, Rio — 172 F 6
Chang'ankou = Laopukou 146-147 B 9
Chang'anzhen = Rong'an 146-147 B 9
Changara 172 F 5
Changbai 144-145 FG 2
Changbai Shan 142-143 O 3
Changcheng 150-151 G 3
Changchhab 138-139 K 3
Chang-chia-k'ou = Zhangjiakou 142-143 L 3
Ch'ang Chiang = Changhua Jiang 150-151 G 3
Ch'ang Chiang = Chang Jiang 146-147 F 7
Chang-chia-p'ang = Zhangjiapang 146-147 E 6
Changchih = Changzhi 142-143 L 4
Ch'ang-chih = Changzhi 142-143 L 4
Ch'ang-ch'ing = Changqing 146-147 F 3
Chang-ch'iu = Zhangqiu 146-147 F 3
Changchow = Zhangzhou 142-143 M 7
Changchun 142-143 NO 3
Changdang Hu 146-147 G 6
Changdao 146-147 H 3
Changde 142-143 L 6
Changdu = Chhamdo 142-143 H 5
Change Islands 63 JK 3
Changfeng 146-147 F 5
Changge 146-147 D 4
Chang-hai = Shanghai 142-143 N 5
Changhang 144-145 F 4-5
Chang Ho = Zhang He 146-147 E 3
Changhowŏn 144-145 F 4
Ch'ang-hsing = Changxing 146-147 G 6
Ch'ang-hsing Tao = Changxing Dao 144-145 C 3
Chang Hu 146-147 D 6
Changhua [RC] 146-147 H 9
Changhua [TJ] 146-147 G 6
Changhua Jiang 150-151 G 3
Chang-huang = Zhanghuang 146-147 B 10
Changhŭng 144-145 F 5
Changhŭng-ni 144-145 FG 2
Changhwa = Changhua 146-147 H 9
Ch'ang-i = Changyi 146-147 G 3
Changjiang [TJ, place] 150-151 G 3
Chang Jiang [TJ, river ◁ Dong Hai] 142-143 K 5-6
Chang Jiang [TJ, river ◁ Poyang Hu] 146-147 F 7
Changji Huizu Zizhizhou 142-143 FG 3
Changjin 144-145 F 2
Changjin-gang 144-145 F 2
Changjin-ho 144-145 F 2
Changjŏn 144-145 G 3
Changkar Ri 138-139 L 2
Changkiakow = Zhangjiakou 142-143 L 3
Changkou = Zhangqiu 146-147 F 3
Chang-kuang-ts'ai Ling = Zhangguangcai Ling 142-143 O 2-3
Changkung 146-147 H 10
Changle [TJ, Fujian] 146-147 G 9
Changle [TJ, Guangdong] 146-147 B 11
Changle [TJ, Shandong] 146-147 G 3
Changli 146-147 G 2
Ch'ang-lo = Changle [TJ, Guangdong] 146-147 B 11
Ch'ang-lo = Changle [TJ, Shandong] 146-147 G 3
Changlun 150-151 C 9
Changluo = Changle 146-147 G 9
Changngnanāshērī = Changanācheri 140 C 6
Changngāṭ = Manattala 140 BC 5
Changnim-ni 144-145 F 3
Changning 146-147 D 8
Ch'angnyŏng 144-145 G 5
Ch'ang-pai = Changbai 144-145 FG 2
Ch'ang-pai Shan = Changbai Shan 142-143 O 3
Changping 146-147 F 1
Changping = Zhangping 146-147 F 9
Changpu = Zhangpu 146-147 F 9
Chang-p'u = Zhangpu 146-147 F 9
Changqing 146-147 F 3
Changsa 150-151 H 3
Chang-san-ying = Zhangsanying 144-145 AB 2
Changsha 142-143 L 6
Changshan 146-147 G 7
Changshan Dao = Miao Dao 146-147 H 3
Changsheng 146-147 EF 8
Changshu 142-143 N 5
Changshui 146-147 C 4
Chang Shui = Zhang Shui 146-147 E 9
Ch'angsŏng = Chongsŏng 144-145 GH 1
Changtai 146-147 F 9
Chang Tang = Jang Thang 142-143 E-G 5
Ch'ang-tê = Anyang 142-143 LM 4
Ch'ang-tê = Changde 142-143 L 6
Changteh = Changde 142-143 L 6
Changting 142-143 M 6
Changtsing = Changqing 146-147 F 3
Ch'ang-tu = Chhamdo 142-143 H 5
Changtutsung = Chhamdo 142-143 H 5
Chang-tzŭ = Zhangzi 146-147 D 3
Ch'angwŏn 144-145 G 5
Changxi = Changsa 150-151 H 3
Changxing 146-147 G 6
Changxing Dao [TJ, Dong Hai] 146-147 HJ 6
Changxing Dao [TJ, Liaodong Wan] 144-145 C 3
Changyang 146-147 C 6
Changyeh = Zhangye 142-143 J 4
Changyi 146-147 G 3
Changyŏn 142-143 NO 4
Changyuan 146-147 E 4
Changzhi 142-143 L 4
Changzhou 142-143 M 5
Chan-hua = Zhanhua 146-147 FG 3
Chañi, Sierra de — 104-105 D 8-9
Chaniá 122-123 KL 8
Chaniṓn, Kólpos — 122-123 KL 8
Chanka, ozero — 132-133 Z 9
Chaṅkam = Chengam 140 D 4
Chankiang = Zhanjiang 142-143 L 7
Chankliut Island 58-59 de 1
Channāb = Chenāb 134-135 M 4
Channagiri 140 BC 3-4
Channapatna 140 C 4
Channapattana = Channapatna 140 C 4
Channarāyapatna 140 C 4
Chañar Ladeado 106-107 F 4
Channel Islands [GB] 119 E 7
Channel Islands [USA] 74-75 CD 6
Channel Islands National Monument = Anacapa Island, Santa Barbara Island 74-75 D 6
Channel-Port-aux-Basques 56-57 Z 8
Channelview, TX 85 III c 1
Channing 61 H 3
Channing, MI 70-71 FG 2
Channing, TX 76-77 CD 5
Chansi = Shanxi 142-143 L 4
Chanskoje, ozero — 126-127 J 3
Chantaburi = Chanthaburi 148-149 D 4
Chantada 120-121 CD 7
Chantajka 132-133 PQ 4
Chantajskoje, ozero — 132-133 QR 4
Chantanika River 58-59 O 4
Chan Tengri, pik — 134-135 MN 2
Chanthaburi 148-149 D 4
Chantong = Shandong 142-143 M 4
Chantrey Inlet 56-57 RS 4
Chanty-Mansijsk 132-133 M 5
Chanty-Mansijskij Nacional'nyj Okrug = Khanty-Mansi Autonomous Area 132-133 L-P 5
Chanuman 150-151 E 4
Chanute, KS 70-71 C 7
Chanzy = Sīdī 'Alī Ban Yūb 166-167 F 2
Chao 96-97 B 6
Chao'an 142-143 M 7
Chao-an = Zhao'an 146-147 F 10
Chao-an Wan = Zhao'an Wan 146-147 F 10
Chao-ch'êng = Jiaocheng 146-147 CD 3
Chaochow = Chao'an 142-143 M 7
Chaohsien = Zhao Xian 146-147 E 3
Chao-hsien = Zhao Xian 146-147 G 4
Chao Hu 142-143 M 5
Chao-i = Chaoyi 146-147 BC 4
Chao Phraya, Mae Nam — 148-149 CD 3-4
Chaoping = Zhaoping 146-147 C 9
Chaor He 142-143 N 2
Chaosā = Chausa 138-139 JK 5
Chaotarā = Chautara 138-139 KL 4
Chaotung = Zhaotong 142-143 J 6
Chao-t'ung = Zhaotong 142-143 J 6
Chao Xian 146-147 FG 6
Chaoyang [TJ, Guangdong] 142-143 M 7
Chaoyang [TJ, Liaoning] 142-143 MN 3
Ch'ao-yang-chên = Huinan 142-143 O 3
Chaoyangqu, Beijing- 155 II bc 2
Chaoyi 146-147 BC 4
Chao-yüan = Zhaoyuan 146-147 H 3
Cha Pa 150-151 DE 1
Chapada 106-107 M 2
Chapada da Água Branca 102-103 L 1-2
Chapada da Serra Verde 100-101 FG 3
Chapada das Mangabeiras 92-93 K 6-L 7
Chapada de Maracás 100-101 DE 7
Chapada Diamantina 92-93 L 7
Chapada do Alto Grande 100-101 EF 5
Chapada do Apodí 92-93 M 6
Chapada do Araripe 92-93 LM 6
Chapada do CApodí 92-93 M 6
Chapada dos Guimarães 102-103 E 1
Chapada dos Parecis 92-93 GH 7
Chapada dos Pilões 102-103 J 2-3
Chapada dos Veadeiros 92-93 K 7-8
Chapada do Tapiocanga 102-103 J 2
Chapada Grande 100-101 C 4
Chapada Redonda 100-101 B 6
Chapadinha 92-93 L 5
Chapadmalal 106-107 J 6-7
Chapado dos Gerais 92-93 K 8
Chapais 62 O 2
Chapala 86-87 J 7
Chapala, Lago de — 64-65 F 7
Chapalcó, Valle — 106-107 E 6
Chapare, Río — 104-105 D 5
Chāparmukh 141 C 2
Cháparra 96-97 E 9
Chaparral 94-95 D 6
Chaparro, El — 94-95 J 3
Chapas, Las — 108-109 F 4
Chapčeranga 132-133 V 8
Chapel Hill, NC 80-81 G 3
Chapel Hill, TN 78-79 F 3
Chaperito, NM 76-77 B 5
Chapéu, Cachoeira — 98-99 K 7-8
Chapéu, Morro do — 100-101 C 8
Chapicuy 106-107 J 3
Chapleau 62 H 4
Chapleau River 62 H 3
Chaplin 61 E 5
Chapman, MT 68-69 BC 1
Cha-p'o = Zhapo 146-147 C 11
Chappell, NE 68-69 E 5
Chappelle-Saint-Lambert 128 II b 2
Chāpra 134-135 N 5
Chã Preta 100-101 F 5
Chapultepec, Bosque de — 91 I b 2
Chapuy 106-107 G 4
Chaqui 92-93 F 8
Chā'r, Jebel — = Jabal Shā'r 136-137 GH 5
Charabali 126-127 N 3
Charadai 111 E 3
Charagua 92-93 G 8
Charagua, Cordillera de — 92-93 G 8-9
Char Ajrag 142-143 KL 2
Charalá 94-95 E 4
Charallave 94-95 H 2
Charaña 92-93 F 8
Charata 104-105 F 10
Charbin = Harbin 142-143 O 2
Chār Burjak 134-135 J 4
Charcas 64-65 F 7
Chärchän 142-143 F 4
Chärchän Darya 142-143 F 4
Char Chorin 142-143 J 2
Char Choto 142-143 J 3
Charcos de Figueroa 76-77 CD 9
Charcos de Risa 76-77 C 9
Charcot, Île — 53 C 29
Chardāvol 136-137 M 6
Chardon, OH 72-73 F 4
Charef = Shārif 166-167 H 2
Chāref, Ouèd — = Wād Shārif 166-167 E 3
Charente 120-121 G 6
Charenton-le-Pont 129 I c 2
Chargla = Hargla 124-125 F 5
Char Gov' 142-143 GH 3
Chari 164-165 H 6
Chārikār 134-135 K 3-4
Char Irčis 142-143 F 2
Chariton, IA 70-71 D 5
Charitona Lapteva, bereg — 132-133 Q 3-R 2
Chariton River 70-71 D 5-6
Charity 92-93 H 3
Charkhāri 138-139 G 5
Charkhi Dādri 138-139 EF 3
Charkhlik = Charqiliq 142-143 F 4
Char'kov 126-127 H 1-2
Charleroi 120-121 K 3
Charles, Cape — 64-65 LM 4
Charlesbourg 63 A 4
Charles City, IA 70-71 D 4
Charles de Gaulle, Aéroport — 129 I d 1
Charles Falls 62 B 2
Charles Fuhr 108-109 D 8
Charles H. Milby Park 85 III b 2
Charles Island 56-57 VW 5
Charles Lee Tilden Regional Park 83 I c 1
Charles River 84 I b 2
Charles River Basin 84 I b 2
Charleston, IL 70-71 FG 6
Charleston, MO 78-79 E 2
Charleston, MS 78-79 DE 3
Charleston, SC 64-65 KL 5
Charleston, TN 78-79 G 3
Charleston, WV 64-65 K 4
Charleston Peak 74-75 F 4
Charlestown, IN 70-71 H 6
Charlestown [Saint Christopher-Nevis] 64-65 O 8
Charlestown [ZA] 174-175 HJ 4
Charlestown, Boston-, MA 84 I b 2
Charlesville 172 D 3
Charleville [AUS] 158-159 J 5
Charleville-Mézières 120-121 K 4
Charlevoix, MI 70-71 H 3
Charlevoix, Lake — 70-71 H 3
Charley River 58-59 Q 4
Charlie Brown-Fulton Airport 85 II a 2
Charlie Lake 60 G 1
Charlotte, MI 70-71 H 4
Charlotte, NC 64-65 KL 4-5
Charlotte, TN 78-79 F 2
Charlotte, TX 76-77 E 8
Charlotte Amalie 64-65 O 8
Charlotte Harbor 64-65 K 6
Charlotte Lake 60 E 3
Charlottenberg 116-117 E 8
Charlottenburg, Schloss — 130 III b 1
Charlottesville, VA 64-65 L 4
Charlottetown 56-57 Y 8
Charlottetown = Roseau 64-65 O 8
Charlotteville 94-95 L 2
Charlton 160 F 6
Charlton Island 56-57 UV 7
Charlton Park 85 III b 2
Charlu 124-125 H 3
Char Narijn uul 142-143 K 3
Char nuur [Mongolia] 142-143 G 2
Char nuur [TJ] 142-143 H 4
Charny [CDN] 63 A 4
Charolais, Monts du — 120-121 K 5
Charon = Bū Qādir 166-167 G 1
Charonne, Paris- 129 I c 2
Charouïne = Shārwīn 166-167 F 5
Charovsk 132-133 G 6
Charqī, Jebel ech — = Jabal ar-Ruwāq 136-137 G 5-6
Charqiliq 142-143 F 4
Charquecada 106-107 M 2
Charron Lake 62 B 1
Charters Towers 158-159 J 3-4
Chartres 120-121 H 4
Char us nuur 142-143 G 2
Chās [IND] 138-139 L 6
Chās [RA] 106-107 H 5
Chasan 144-145 H 1
Chasavjurt 126-127 N 5
Chaschuil, Río — 104-105 B 10
Chascomús 111 E 5
Chase 60 H 4
Chase City, VA 80-81 G 2
Chasicó [RA, Buenos Aires] 106-107 F 7
Chasicó [RA, Río Negro] 108-109 E 3
Chasicó, Laguna — 106-107 F 7
Chasm 60 G 4
Chasŏng 144-145 F 2
Chassahowitzka Bay 80-81 b 2
Chastain Memorial Park 85 II b 1
Chašuri 126-127 L 5-6
Chatanga 132-133 TU 3
Chatan gol 142-143 K 3
Chatangskij zaliv 132-133 UV 3
Chatanika, AK 58-59 O 4
Châteaubriant 120-121 G 5
Château-du-Loir 120-121 H 5
Châteaudun 120-121 H 4
Châteaulin 120-121 EF 4
Châteauroux 120-121 H 5
Château-Thierry 120-121 J 4
Château Versailles 129 I b 2
Châtellerault 120-121 H 5
Châtenay-Malabry 129 I c 2
Chatfield, MN 70-71 D 4
Chatgal 142-143 HJ 1
Chatham, AK 58-59 U 8
Chatham, LA 78-79 C 4
Chatham, NY 72-73 K 3
Chatham, VA 80-81 G 2
Chatham [CDN, New Brunswick] 56-57 XY 8
Chatham [CDN, Ontario] 56-57 U 9
Chatham = Isla San Cristóbal 92-93 B 5
Chatham, Chicago-, IL 83 II b 2
Chatham, Isla — 111 B 8
Chatham Islands 158-159 Q 8
Chatham Sound 60 B 2
Chatham Strait 56-57 K 6
Cha Thing Phra = Sathing Phra 150-151 C 9
Châtillon [F] 129 I c 2
Châtillon [I] 122-123 B 3
Châtillon-sur-Seine 120-121 K 5
Chātmohar 138-139 M 5
Chatom, AL 78-79 E 5
Chatou 129 I b 2
Chatra 138-139 K 5
Chatrapur 138-139 K 8
Chātsu 138-139 EF 4
Chatswood, Sydney- 161 I b 1
Chatsworth 72-73 F 2
Chatsworth, GA 78-79 G 3
Chāṭṭagām 134-135 P 6
Chāṭṭagām Pahāṛī 'Alāqa 141 C 4-5
Chattahoochee, FL 78-79 G 5
Chattahoochee, Atlanta-, GA 85 II b 2
Chattahoochee River 64-65 JK 5
Chattanooga, TN 64-65 J 4
Chattarpur = Chhatarpur 134-135 M 6
Chatturat 150-151 CD 5
Chaubāra 138-139 C 2
Chaucha 96-97 B 3
Chauchaiñeu, Sierra — 108-109 E 3
Chaudière, Rivière — 63 A 4-5
Châu Đốc = Châu Phu 148-149 E 4
Chauekuktuli Lake 58-59 HJ 6
Chauk 141 D 5
Chaulán 96-97 C 7
Chaullay 96-97 E 8
Chaumont 120-121 K 4
Chaumu 138-139 E 4
Chaun-do 144-145 EF 5
Chaungan Taunggya 141 E 2
Chaungʼū 141 D 5
Chaungzōn 141 E 7
Chaupāl 138-139 F 2
Châu Phu 148-149 E 4
Chauques, Islas — 108-109 C 4
Chausa 138-139 JK 5
Chautara 138-139 KL 4
Chautauqua Lake 72-73 G 3
Chautavara 124-125 J 2
Chauvin 61 C 4
Chauwīs-Parganā = 24-Parganas 138-139 M 6-7
Chaux-de-Fonds, La — 118 C 5
Chauya Cocha, La — 96-97 D 6
Chāvākachchēri 140 E 6
Chaval 100-101 D 2
Chavarria 106-107 H 2
Chavast 134-135 K 2
Chavenay 129 I a 2
Chaves, NM 76-77 B 6

Chaves [BR] 92-93 K 5
Chaves [P] 120-121 D 8
Chaves, Isla — = Isla Santa Cruz 92-93 AB 5
Chavīb Deh 136-137 N 7
Chaville 129 I b 2
Chavín de Huántar 96-97 C 6
Chavín de Pariarca 96-97 C 6
Chaviva 92-93 E 4
Chawang 150-151 B 8
Chây, Sông — 150-151 E 1
Chaya = Drayā 142-143 H 5
Chayanta, Río — 104-105 CD 6
Chaynpur = Chainpur 138-139 L 4
Ch'a-yü = Dsayul 142-143 H 6
Chazhen 146-147 B 5
Chazón 111 D 4
Chbar, Prêk — 150-151 F 6
Cheam, London- 129 II b 2
Cheap, Canal — 108-109 B 6
Cheat Mountain 72-73 FG 5
Cheat River 72-73 G 5
Cheb 118 F 3
Chebāyesh, Al- = Al-Jaza'ir 136-137 M 7
Chèbba, Ech — = Ash-Shābah 166-167 M 2
Chebii, Uâu el — = Wādī Bay al-Kabīr 164-165 GH 2
Chebka, Région de la — = Shabkah 166-167 H 3-4
Cheboksary = Čeboksar 132-133 H 6
Cheboygan, MI 64-65 K 2
Chech, Erg — = Irq ash-Shāsh 164-165 D 3-4
Chechaouène = Shifshawn 164-165 CD 1
Chechat 138-139 E 5
Checheng = Zhecheng 146-147 E 4
Checheno-Ingush Autonomous Soviet Socialist Republic 126-127 MN 5
Chech'on 144-145 G 4
Checotah, OK 76-77 G 5
Chedabucto Bay 63 F 5
Chedādī, El- = Ash-Shiddādī 136-137 J 4
Cheduba = Man'aung 141 C 6
Cheduba Strait = Man'aung Reletkyā 141 CD 6
Cheecham 61 C 2
Cheecham Hills 61 B 3-C 2
Cheeching, AK 58-59 E 6
Cheektowaga, NY 72-73 GH 3
Cheepie 158-159 HJ 5
Cheesman Lake 68-69 D 6
Chef, Rivière du — 62 P 1-2
Chefoo = Yantai 142-143 N 4
Chefornak, AK 58-59 E 6
Chefu = Yantai 142-143 N 4
Chegar Prah = Chigar Perah 150-151 CD 10
Chegga = Ash-Shaqqāt 164-165 C 3
Chegga = Shaqqah 166-167 JK 2
Chegutu 172 EF 6
Chehalis, WA 66-67 B 2
Chehalis River 66-67 B 2
Chehel-e Chashmeh, Kūhhā-ye — 136-137 M 5
Cheikh, Hassi — = Ḥāssī Shaykh 166-167 G 4
Cheikh Aḥmed = Shaykh Ahmad 136-137 J 4
Cheikh Hilâl = Shaykh Hilāl 136-137 G 5
Cheikh Ṣalâḥ = Shaykh Salāh 136-137 J 4
Cheikh Zerâfâ = Zilāf 136-137 G 6
Chējarļā = Mellavāgu 140 D 2
Cheju 142-143 O 5
Cheju-do 142-143 NO 5
Cheju-haehyŏp 142-143 O 5
Chê-jung = Zherong 146-147 GH 8
Chekiang = Zhejiang 142-143 MN 6
Chekkâ, Râs — = Rā's ash-Shikk'ah 136-137 F 5
Chela, Serra da — 172 B 5
Chelan 61 G 4
Chelan, WA 66-67 CD 2
Chelan, Lake — 66-67 C 1
Chê-lang Chiao = Zhelang Jiao 146-147 E 10
Chelforó 106-107 D 7
Cheli = Jinghong 150-151 C 2
Chélia, Djebel — = Jabal Shīlyah 164-165 F 1
Chéliff, Ouèd — = Shilif 166-167 G 1
Cheline 174-175 L 2
Chê-ling Kuan = Zheling Guan 142-143 L 6
Chellala = Qaṣr Shillalah 166-167 H 2
Chellala-Dahrania = Shallālat Ḍahrānīyah 166-167 G 3
Chelle 106-107 A 7
Chelleh Khāneh, Kūh-e — 136-137 N 4
Chelles 129 I d 2
Chełm 118 L 3
Chełmińskre, Pojezierze — 118 J 2
Chelmsford [CDN] 62 L 3
Chełmża 118 J 2
Chelsea, MA 84 I b 2
Chelsea, MI 70-71 HJ 4
Chelsea, OK 76-77 G 4
Chelsea, VT 72-73 K 2-3
Chelsfield, London- 129 II c 2
Cheltenham 119 EF 6
Cheltenham, PA 72-73 J 4
Chelyabinsk = Čel'abinsk 132-133 L 6
Chema ia, ech — = Ash-Shamā'iyah 166-167 B 3
Chemainus 66-67 AB 1
Chemawa, OR 66-67 B 3
Chemba 172 F 5
Chemehuevi Valley Indian Reservation 74-75 F 5
Chemmora = Shamūrah 166-167 K 2
Chemnitz 118 F 3
Chemor 150-151 C 10
Chemulpo = Inch'ŏn 142-143 O 4
Chemult, OR 66-67 C 4
Chenāb 134-135 M 4
Chenab = Chanāb 138-139 C 3
Chenachane, Ouèd — = Wādī Shanāshīn 166-167 E 7
Chena Hot Springs, AK 58-59 OP 4
Chên-an = Zhen'an 146-147 B 5
Chena River 58-59 OP 4
Ch'ên-ch'i = Chenxi 142-143 L 6
Ch'ên-chia-chiang = Chenjiajiang 146-147 GH 4
Chên-chiang = Zhenjiang 142-143 M 5
Ch'ên-chou = Yuanling 142-143 L 6
Chencoyi 86-87 PQ 8
Chenega, AK 58-59 NO 6
Cheney, KS 68-69 H 7
Cheney, WA 66-67 E 2
Chên-fan = Minqin 142-143 J 4
Cheṅgalpeṭṭai = Chingleput 140 DE 4
Chengam 140 D 4
Chengbu 146-147 C 8
Chengcheng 146-147 BC 4
Chêng-chia-i = Zhengjiayi 146-147 C 7
Ch'êng-chiang = Chengjiang 142-143 J 7
Chengde 142-143 M 3
Chengdong Hu 146-147 F 5
Chengdu 142-143 J 5
Chenghai 146-147 F 10
Chengjiang 142-143 J 7
Chengkiang = Chengjiang 142-143 J 7
Chengkou 142-143 K 5
Chengmai 142-143 KL 8
Chêng-ning = Zhengning 146-147 B 4
Chêng-pu = Chengbu 146-147 C 8
Ch'êng-shan Chiao = Chengshan Jiao 146-147 J 3
Chengshan Jiao 146-147 J 3
Chengteh = Chengde 142-143 M 3
Chengting = Zhengding 146-147 E 2
Chengtu = Chengdu 142-143 J 5
Chengwu 146-147 E 4
Cheng-Xian = Sheng Xian 142-143 N 6
Chengxi Hu 146-147 EF 5
Chengyang 146-147 GH 7
Chengyang = Zhengyang 146-147 E 5
Chêng-yang-kuan = Zhengyangguan 146-147 F 5
Chengzitan 144-145 D 3
Chenhai = Zhenhai 146-147 H 6-7
Chên-hsi = Bar Köl 142-143 G 3
Chenik, AK 58-59 KL 7
Chenjiajiang 146-147 GH 4
Chenjiazhuang 146-147 G 3
Chenkalāḍi 140 E 7
Cheṅkam = Chengam 140 D 4
Chenkiang = Zhenjiang 142-143 M 5
Chennagiri = Channagiri 140 BC 3-4
Chennapaṭṭaṇam = Madras 134-135 N 8
Chennarāyapaṭṭaṇā = Channarāyapatna 140 C 4
Chennevières-sur-Marne 129 I d 2
Chêng-ho = Zhenghe 146-147 G 8
Chenoa, IL 70-71 F 5
Chenoit, le — 128 II b 2
Chenping = Zhenping 146-147 D 5
Chensi = Bar Köl 142-143 G 3
Chensi = Shanxi 142-143 L 4
Chentiin Nuruu 142-143 K 2
Chentij 142-143 L 2
Chên-t'ung = Zhentong 146-147 GH 5
Chenxi 142-143 L 6
Chen Xian 142-143 L 6
Chenyang = Shenyang 142-143 NO 3
Chenyuan = Zhenyuan [TJ, Guizhou] 146-147 B 8
Chenyuan = Zhenyuan [TJ, Yunnan] 142-143 J 7
Chên-yüan = Zhenyuan [TJ, Yunnan] 142-143 J 7
Chên-yüeh = Yiwu 150-151 C 2
Chéom Ksan 150-151 E 5
Cheops Pyramids 170 II a 2
Cheo Reo 150-151 G 6
Chepan 146-147 FG 8
Chepelmut, Lago — 108-109 F 10
Chepén 96-97 B 5
Chepes 111 C 4
Chepes, Sierra de — 106-107 D 3
Chepite, Serrania — 104-105 BC 4
Chepo 88-89 G 10
Chequamegon Bay 70-71 E 2
Cher 120-121 J 5
Chērammādēvi = Sermādevi 140 C 6
Cherangani 171 C 2
Cherang Ruku 150-151 D 10
Cheratting, Kampung — 150-151 D 10
Cheraw, CO 68-69 E 6
Cheraw, SC 80-81 FG 3
Cherbourg 120-121 G 4
Cherchar = Sharshar 166-167 K 2
Cherchell = Shirshāll 166-167 GH 1
Cherchen = Chärchän 142-143 F 4
Cheremkhovo = Čeremchovo 132-133 T 7
Cheren = Keren 164-165 M 5
Cherepon 168-169 EF 3
Chergui, Chott ech — = Ash-Shaṭṭ ash-Sharqī 164-165 DE 2
Chergui, Île — = Jazīrat ash-Sharqī 166-167 M 2
Cheribon = Cirebon 148-149 E 8
Cheriyam Island 140 AB 5
Cherkassi = Čerkassy 126-127 EF 2
Cherlen gol 142-143 KL 2
Cherlen gol = Herlen He 142-143 M 2
Chernabura Island 58-59 d 2
Chernigov = Černigov 126-127 E 1
Chernogorsk = Černogorsk 132-133 R 7
Chernovtsy = Černovcy 126-127 B 2
Cherokee, IA 70-71 C 4
Cherokee, OK 76-77 E 4
Cherokee, TX 76-77 E 7
Cherokee Lake 80-81 E 2
Cherque, Cordón del — 108-109 D 5
Cherquenco 106-107 AB 7
Cherrapunj = Cherrāpunji 134-135 P 5
Cherrapunji 134-135 P 5
Cherry 158-159 N 2
Cherry Creek 68-69 E 3
Cherry Creek, NV 74-75 F 3
Cherry Creek, SD 68-69 F 3
Cherrydale, Arlington-, VA 82 II a 2
Cherry Hill, NJ 84 III c 2
Cherry Hill Mall 84 III c 2
Cherrypatch Ridge 68-69 B 1
Cherryvale, KS 76-77 G 4
Cherryville 60 H 4
Cherskogo Mountains = chrebet Čorskogo 132-133 a 4-c 5
Cherso = Cres 122-123 F 3
Cherson [SU] 126-127 F 3
Chersonesskij, mys — 126-127 F 4
Chertsey 129 II a 2
Chesaning, MI 70-71 HJ 4
Chesapeake, VA 64-65 LM 4
Chesapeake Bay 64-65 L 4
Cheshire, OR 66-67 B 3
Cheshskaya Bay = Čošskaja guba 132-133 H 4
Chesley 72-73 F 2
Chesnay, le — 129 I b 2
Chessington, London- 129 II a 2
Chester, CA 66-67 C 5
Chester, IL 70-71 F 7
Chester, MT 66-67 H 1
Chester, NE 68-69 H 5
Chester, PA 72-73 J 5
Chester, SC 80-81 F 3
Chester [CDN] 63 D 5
Chester [GB] 119 E 5
Chesterbrook, VA 82 II a 2
Chesterfield 119 F 5
Chesterfield, Île — 172 H 5
Chesterfield, Îles — 158-159 L 3
Chesterfield Inlet [CDN, bay] 56-57 ST 5
Chesterfield Inlet [CDN, place] 56-57 ST 5
Chester Island 84 III a 3
Chestertown, MD 72-73 HJ 5
Chestnut Hill, MA 84 I ab 3
Chestnut Hill, Philadelphia-, PA 84 III b 1
Chestnut Hill Reservoir 84 I a 2
Chesuncook Lake 72-73 LM 1
Cheta [SU, place] 132-133 S 3
Cheta [SU, river] 132-133 S 3
Chetek, WI 70-71 E 3
Chéticamp 63 F 4
Chetlat Island 134-135 L 8
Chetopa, KS 76-77 G 4
Chetput 140 D 4
Chetumal 64-65 J 8
Chetumal, Bahía de — 64-65 J 8
Chetwynd 60 FG 2
Cheung Chau 155 I a 2
Cheung Kwan O 155 I b 2
Chevak, AK 58-59 E 6
Chevejecure 104-105 CD 4
Chevejecure, Río — 104-105 C 4
Cheverly, MD 82 II b 1
Chevilly-Larue 129 I c 2
Cheviot, The — 119 EF 4
Cheviot Hills 119 E 4
Chevreuse 129 I b 3
Chevry-Cossigny 129 I d 3
Chevy Chase, MD 82 II a 1
Chewelah, WA 66-67 DE 1
Chews Landing, NJ 84 III c 3
Chê-yang = Zherong 146-147 GH 8
Cheyenne, OK 76-77 E 5
Cheyenne, TX 76-77 C 7
Cheyenne, WY 64-65 F 3
Cheyenne Pass 68-69 D 5
Cheyenne River 64-65 F 3
Cheyenne River Indian Reservation 68-69 F 3
Cheyenne Wells, CO 68-69 E 6
Cheyūr 140 E 4
Cheyyar 140 D 4
Cheyyūr = Cheyūr 140 E 4
Chezacut 60 EF 3
Chhabaṛā = Chhabra 138-139 F 5
Chhabra 138-139 F 5
Chhachhrauli 138-139 F 2
Chhagtag Tsangpo 138-139 K 3
Chhamārchī 138-139 M 4
Chhamdo 142-143 H 5
Chhaprā = Chāpra 134-135 N 5
Chhārikār = Chārikār 134-135 K 3-4
Chharpa Gonpa 138-139 H 2
Chhāta 138-139 F 4
Chhātak 141 B 3
Chhatarpur [IND, Bihār] 138-139 K 5
Chhatarpur [IND, Madhya Pradesh] 134-135 M 6
Chhatrapura = Chatrapur 138-139 K 8
Chhattīsgarh 134-135 N 6
Chhep 150-151 E 6
Chherang 138-139 N 4
Chherchhen 138-139 H 2
Chhergo La 138-139 H 2
Chhergundo 142-143 H 5
Chhergundo Zhou = Yushu Zangzu Zizhizhou 142-143 GH 5
Chhibchang Tsho 142-143 G 5
Chhibrāmau 138-139 G 4
Chhibro 138-139 HJ 3
Chhikhum 138-139 J 3
Chhindvāṛā = Chhindwāra [IND ↙ Jabalpur] 138-139 G 6
Chhindvāṛā = Chhindwāra [IND ← Seoni] 134-135 M 6
Chhindwāra [IND ↙ Jabalpur] 138-139 G 6
Chhindwāra [IND ← Seoni] 134-135 M 6
Chhinī 138-139 A 4
Chhinnamanūr = Chinnamanūr 140 C 6
Chhinnasēlam = Chinna Salem 140 D 5
Chhitāuni 138-139 J 4
Chhlong 150-151 EF 6
Chhōra Gonpa 138-139 M 2
Chhōṭā Andamān = Little Andaman 134-135 P 8
Chhōṭā Nikōbār = Little Nicobar 134-135 P 9
Chhota Udaipur 138-139 DE 6
Chhōṭā Udaypur = Chhota Udaipur 138-139 DE 6
Chhotī Sādri 138-139 E 5
Chhudrari 138-139 L 2
Chhudun Tsho 138-139 MN 2
Chhuīkhadān 138-139 H 7
Chhukor 138-139 L 3
Chhumar 142-143 G 4-5
Chhumbi 138-139 M 4
Chhumbong 138-139 L 3
Chhundu 138-139 L 3
Chhushul 142-143 FG 6
Chi, Lam — 150-151 D 5
Chi, Nam — 150-151 DE 5
Chía 94-95 DE 5
Chiachi Island 58-59 d 2
Chiaḏma, ech — = Ash-Shiādmā' 166-167 B 4
Chia-ho = Jiahe 146-147 D 9
Chia-hsien = Jia Xian [TJ, Henan] 146-147 D 5
Chia-hsien = Jia Xian [TJ, Shanxi] 146-147 C 2
Chia-hsing = Jiaxing 142-143 N 5
Chia-i 142-143 MN 7
Chia Keng 154 III b 1
Chiali 146-147 GH 10
Chia-li = Lharugö 142-143 G 5
Chia-li-chuang = Chiali 146-147 GH 10
Chia-ling Chiang = Jialing Jiang 142-143 K 5
Chia-lu Ho = Jialu He 146-147 E 4
Chia-mu-szŭ = Jiamusi 142-143 P 2
Chi-an = Ji'an [TJ, Jiangxi] 142-143 LM 6
Chi-an = Ji'an [TJ, Jilin] 144-145 EF 2
Chiang-chou = Xinjiang 142-143 L 4
Chiang Dao 148-149 CD 3
Chiange 172 B 5
Chiang-hsi = Jiangxi 142-143 LM 6
Chiang-hung = Jianghong 146-147 B 11
Chiangir, İstanbul- 154 I ab 2
Chiang Kham 150-151 BC 3
Chiang Khan 148-149 D 3
Chiang Khong 150-151 C 2
Chiang-k'ou = Jiangkou [TJ, Guangxi Zhuangzu Zizhiqu] 146-147 C 10
Chiang-k'ou = Jiangkou [TJ, Guizhou] 146-147 B 8
Chiang Krai, Lam — 150-151 C 5
Chiang-ling = Jiangling 146-147 CD 6
Chiang-lo = Jiangle 146-147 F 8
Chiang Mai 148-149 C 3
Chiang-mên = Xinhui 146-147 D 10
Chiang Muan 150-151 C 3
Chiang-ning-chên = Jiangning 146-147 G 6
Chiang-p'u = Jiangpu 146-147 G 5
Chiang Rai 148-149 CD 3
Chiang Saen 150-151 BC 2
Chiang-shan = Jiangshan 146-147 G 7
Chiang-su = Jiangsu 142-143 MN 5
Chiang-yin = Jiangyin 146-147 H 6
Chiao-chou Wan = Jiaozhou Wan 146-147 H 3-4
Chiao-ho-k'ou = Jiaohekou 146-147 B 4
Chiao-ling = Jiaoling 146-147 EF 9
Chiapa, Río — = Río Grande 64-65 H 8
Chiapas 64-65 H 8
Chiari 122-123 CD 3
Chia-shan = Jiashan [TJ, Anhui] 146-147 G 5
Chia-shan = Jiashan [TJ, Zhejiang] 146-147 H 6
Chia-ting = Jiading 146-147 H 6
Chiau 174-175 K 3
Chi-aün Ho = Jiyun He 146-147 F 2
Chiàvari 122-123 C 3
Chiavenna 122-123 C 2
Chiayi 142-143 MN 7
Chia-yü = Jiayu 146-147 D 6-7
Chiba 144-145 N 5
Chibabava 172 F 6
Chibata, Serra da — 100-101 D 10-11
Chibemba 172 BC 5
Chibia 172 B 5
Chibinogorsk = Kirovsk 132-133 EF 4
Chibougamau 56-57 VW 7-8
Chibougamau, Lac — 62 OP 2
Chibougamau, la Réserve de — 62 OP 2
Chiburi-jima 144-145 J 5
Chibuto 172 F 6
Chica, Costa — 86-87 L 9
Chicacole = Shrīkākulam 134-135 N 7
Chicago, IL 64-65 J 3
Chicago, University of — 83 II b 2
Chicago-Albany Park, IL 83 II a 1
Chicago-Ashburn, IL 83 II a 2
Chicago-Austin, IL 83 II a 1
Chicago-Avondale, IL 83 II b 1
Chicago-Belmont Cragin, IL 83 II a 1
Chicago-Beverly, IL 83 II ab 2
Chicago-Bridgeport, IL 83 II b 1
Chicago-Brighton Park, IL 83 II a 2
Chicago Campus = Northwestern University 83 II b 1
Chicago-Chatham, IL 83 II b 2
Chicago-Chicago Lawn, IL 83 II a 2
Chicago-Dunning, IL 83 II b 1
Chicago-Englewood, IL 83 II b 2
Chicago-Evergreen Plaza, IL 83 II ab 2
Chicago-Ford City, IL 83 II a 2
Chicago-Gage Park, IL 83 II a 2
Chicago Heights, IL 70-71 G 5
Chicago-Hyde Park, IL 83 II b 2
Chicago-Irving Park, IL 83 II b 1
Chicago-Jefferson Park, IL 83 II a 1
Chicago-Lakeview, IL 83 II ab 1
Chicago Lawn, Chicago-, IL 83 II a 2
Chicago-Lawndale, IL 83 II a 1
Chicago-Logan Square, IL 83 II a 1
Chicago-Loop, IL 83 II b 1
Chicago Midway Airport 83 II a 2
Chicago-Morgan Park, IL 83 II ab 2
Chicago-Mount Greenwood, IL 83 II a 2
Chicago-Near North Side, IL 83 II b 1
Chicago-North Park, IL 83 II a 1
Chicago-Norwood Park, IL 83 II a 1
Chicago-Portage Park, IL 83 II b 1
Chicago Ridge, IL 83 II a 2
Chicago-Roseland, IL 83 II b 2
Chicago Sanitary and Ship Canal 83 II a 1-2
Chicago-South Chicago, IL 83 II b 2
Chicago-South Shore, IL 83 II b 2
Chicago Stadium 83 II a 1
Chicago State University 83 II b 2
Chicago-Uptown, IL 83 II ab 1
Chicago-West Pullman, IL 83 II b 2
Chicago-Woodlawn, IL 83 II b 2
Chical-Có 106-107 CD 6
Chicama 96-97 B 5
Chicama, Río — 96-97 B 5
Chicapa, Rio — 172 D 3
Chic-Chocs, Monts — 56-57 X 8
Ch'i-ch = Qiqihar 142-143 N 2
Chichagof, AK 58-59 T 8
Chichagof, Cape — 58-59 HJ 7
Chichagof Island 56-57 J 6
Chichancanab, Laguna — 86-87 Q 8
Chīchāoua = Shishāwah 166-167 B 4
Chīchāwatnī 138-139 D 2
Chiché, Rio — 98-99 LM 9
Chichén Itzá 64-65 J 7
Chichester 119 F 6
Chi-ch'i = Jixi 146-147 G 6
Chichicaspa 91 I b 2
Chichinales 106-107 D 7
Chichiriviche 94-95 GH 2
Chichocane 174-175 L 2
Chichola 138-139 H 7
Chicholi 138-139 F 6
Chichot 138-139 F 2
Ch'i-chou Tao = Qizhou Liedao 150-151 H 3
Chickaloon, AK 58-59 NO 6
Chickamauga, GA 78-79 G 3
Chickamauga Lake 78-79 G 3
Chickasaw, AL 78-79 EF 5
Chickasha, OK 64-65 G 4-5
Chicken, AK 58-59 QR 4
Chiclana 106-107 G 5
Chiclayo 92-93 CD 6
Chico, CA 64-65 B 4
Chico, TX 76-77 F 6
Chico, Río — [RA, Chubut] 111 C 6
Chico, Río — [RA, Santa Cruz ◁ Bahía Grande] 111 C 7
Chico, Río — [RA, Santa Cruz ◁ Río Gallegos] 111 C 7
Chico, Río — [YV] 92-93 F 2
Chicoa 172 F 5
Chicoana 111 CD 3
Chicoma Peak = Tschicoma Peak 76-77 AB 4
Chicomo 174-175 KL 3
Chiconomo 171 CD 6
Chicontepec de Tejeda 86-87 LM 7
Chicopee, MA 72-73 K 3
Chicotte 63 E 3
Chicoutimi 56-57 WX 8
Chicuaco, Laguna — 94-95 G 6
Chicualacuala 174-175 JK 2
Chidambaram 140 DE 5
Chidenguele 174-175 L 3
Chidester, AR 78-79 C 4
Chidley, Cape — 56-57 Y 5
Chi-do 144-145 EF 5
Chiefland, FL 80-81 b 2
Chiefs Point 72-73 F 2
Chieh-hsiu = Jiexiu 146-147 CD 3
Chiehmo = Chärchän 142-143 F 4
Chieh-shih = Jieshi 146-147 E 10
Chieh-shih Wan = Jieshi Wan 146-147 E 10
Chieh-shou = Jieshou 146-147 E 5
Chieh-yang = Jieyang 146-147 F 10
Chiêm Hoa 150-151 E 1
Chiemsee 118 F 5
Ch'i en-an = Qian'an 146-147 G 1
Chien-ch'ang = Jianchang [TJ → Benxi] 144-145 E 2
Chien-ch'ang = Jianchang [TJ ↙ Jinzhou] 144-145 B 2
Chien-ch'ang = Nancheng 146-147 F 8
Chien-ch'ang-ying = Jianchangying 146-147 G 1
Ch'ien-chi = Qianji 146-147 G 4-5
Ch'ien-chiang = Qianjiang [TJ, Guangxi Zhuangzu Zizhiqu] 146-147 B 10
Ch'ien-chiang = Qianjiang [TJ, Hubei] 142-143 L 5
Ch'ien-chiang = Qianjiang [TJ, Sichuan] 146-147 B 7
Chiengi 172 E 3
Chieng Kong = Chiang Khong 150-151 C 2
Chiengmai = Chiang Mai 148-149 C 3
Chien-ho = Jianhe [TJ, place] 146-147 B 8
Chien-Ho = Jian He [TJ, river] 144-145 D 2
Ch'ien-hsi = Qianxi 146-147 G 1
Ch'ien-hsien = Qian Xian 146-147 B 4
Chien-ko = Jiange 142-143 JK 5
Chien-li = Jianli 146-147 D 7
Chien-ning = Jianning 146-147 F 8
Chien-ning = Jian'ou 142-143 M 6
Chien-ou = Jian'ou 142-143 M 6
Chien-p'ing = Jianping 144-145 B 2
Chien-p'ing = Langxi 146-147 G 6
Ch'ien-shan = Qianshan 146-147 F 6
Chien-shui = Jianshui 142-143 J 7
Chien-tê = Jiande 146-147 G 7
Ch'ien-wei = Qianwei 144-145 C 2
Chien-yang = Jianyang [TJ, Fujian] 146-147 FG 8
Chien-yang = Jianyang [TJ, Sichuan] 142-143 JK 5
Ch'ien-yang = Qianyang 146-147 C 8
Ch'ien-yu Ho = Qianyou He 146-147 B 5
Chieti 122-123 F 4
Chifeng 142-143 M 3
Chifre, Serra do — 92-93 L 8
Chiftak, AK 58-59 EF 6
Chigar Perah 150-151 CD 10
Chiginagak, Mount — 58-59 e 1
Chigmit Mountains 58-59 L 6
Chignecto Bay 63 D 5
Chignik, AK 56-57 EF 6
Chignik Lake 58-59 de 1
Chigorodó 94-95 C 4
Chigu 138-139 L 3
Chigualoco 106-107 B 3
Chiguana 104-105 BC 7
Chiguana, Salar de — 104-105 C 7
Chiguao, Punta — 108-109 C 4
Chiguaza 96-97 C 2
Chigubo 174-175 K 2
Chigwell 129 II c 1
Chigyŏng 144-145 F 3
Ch'ih-ch'i = Chixi 146-147 D 10-11
Chih-chiang = Zhijiang [TJ, Hubei] 146-147 C 6
Chih-chiang = Zhijiang [TJ, Hunan] 142-143 KL 6
Chihe 146-147 FG 5
Ch'ih-fêng = Chifeng 142-143 M 3
Chih-fu = Yantai 142-143 N 4
Ch'ih-ho = Chihe 146-147 FG 5
Ch'ih-k'an = Chikan 146-147 C 11
Chihkiang = Zhijiang 142-143 KL 6
Chih-li Wan = Bo Hai 142-143 M 4
Chi-hsi = Jixi 142-143 P 2
Chi-hsien = Ji Xian [TJ, Hebei → Beijing] 146-147 F 1
Chi-hsien = Ji Xian [TJ, Hebei ↘ Shijiazhuang] 146-147 E 3
Chi-hsien = Ji Xian [TJ, Henan] 146-147 E 4
Chi-hsien = Ji Xian [TJ, Shanxi] 146-147 C 3
Ch'i-hsien = Qi Xian [TJ, Henan ↘ Kaifeng] 146-147 E 4
Ch'i-hsien = Qi Xian [TJ, Henan ↗ Xinxiang] 146-147 DE 4
Ch'i-hsien = Qi Xian [TJ, Shanxi] 146-147 D 3
Chihtan = Zhidan 146-147 B 3
Chihu 146-147 H 9-10
Chihuahua 64-65 E 6
Ch'i-i = Qiyi 146-147 D 5
Chiingij gol 142-143 GH 2
Chii-san = Chiri-san 144-145 F 5
Chikalda 138-139 F 7
Chikan 146-147 C 11
Chik Chu Wan 155 I b 2
Chike = Xunke 142-143 O 2
Chikhalī = Chikhli 138-139 F 7
Chikhli [IND, Gujarāt] 138-139 D 7
Chikhli [IND, Mahārāshtra] 138-139 F 7
Chikjājūr 140 BC 3
Chikkai = Chixi 146-147 D 10-11
Chikkamagaļūru = Chikmagalūr 140 B 4
Chikkanāyakanahaļļi = Chiknayakanhalli 140 C 4
Chikmagalūr 140 B 4
Chiknayakanhalli 140 C 4
Chikodi 140 B 2
Chikrang, Stung — 150-151 E 6
Chikreng = Kompong Chikreng 150-151 E 6
Chikugo 144-145 H 6
Chikuminuk Lake 58-59 HJ 6
Chikwawa 172 FG 5
Chilako River 60 F 3
Chilapa de Alvarez 64-65 G 8
Chilās 134-135 L 3
Chilaw = Halāwata 140 D 7
Chilca 92-93 D 7
Chilca, Cordillera de — 96-97 EF 9
Chilca Juliana 106-107 F 2
Chilcoot, CA 74-75 CD 3
Chilcotin River 60 F 3-4
Childersburg, AL 78-79 F 4
Childress, TX 76-77 DE 5
Chile 111 B 5-C 2
Chile Basin 156-157 O 5-6
Chile Chico 108-109 D 6
Chilecito [RA, La Rioja] 111 C 3
Chilecito [RA, Mendoza] 106-107 C 4
Chileno 106-107 K 4
Chilete 92-93 D 6
Chilete, Río — 96-97 B 5
Chilhowee, MO 70-71 D 6
Chilia, Braţul — 122-123 N 3
Chilibre 64-65 b 2
Ch'i-li-chên = Qilizhen 146-147 B 4
Chilicote 76-77 B 8
Ch'i-lien Shan = Qilian Shan 142-143 HJ 4
Chilikadrotna River 58-59 K 6
Chilikā Hrada = Chilka Lake 134-135 NO 7
Chililabombwe 172 E 4
Chi-lin = Jilin [TJ, administrative unit] 142-143 N 2-O 3
Chi-lin = Jilin [TJ, place] 142-143 O 3
Chilivani 122-123 C 5
Chilka Lake 134-135 NO 7
Chilk Ballāpur 140 CD 4
Chilko Lake 56-57 M 7
Chillán 111 B 5
Chillán, Nevados de — 106-107 B 6
Chillanes 96-97 B 2
Chillar 106-107 H 6
Chill Chainnigh = Kilkenny 119 C 5
Chillicothe, IL 70-71 F 5
Chillicothe, MO 64-65 H 3-4
Chillicothe, OH 64-65 K 4
Chillicothe, TX 76-77 E 5
Chilliwack 66-67 C 1
Chillón, Río — 96-97 C 7
Chillum, MD 82 II b 1
Chilly 126-127 O 7
Chilly, ID 66-67 FG 3
Chiloé, Isla de — 111 AB 6
Chilok 132-133 UV 7
Chilonga 171 B 5-6
Chilongozi 171 BC 6
Chiloquin, OR 66-67 C 4
Chilpancingo de los Bravos 64-65 G 8
Chilpi 138-139 H 6
Chiltern Hills 119 F 6
Chilton, WI 70-71 F 3
Chilung 142-143 N 6
Chilwa, Lake — 172 G 5
Chima 94-95 E 4
Chiman 88-89 G 10
Chimanas, Islas — 94-95 J 2
Chiman tagh 142-143 FG 4
Chimbas 106-107 C 3
Chimbero 104-105 AB 10
Chimborazo [EC, administrative unit] 96-97 B 2-3
Chimborazo [EC, mountain] 92-93 D 5
Chimborazo [YV] 94-95 J 3
Chimbote 92-93 D 6
Chimei Hsü 146-147 G 10
Ch'i-mên = Qimen 146-147 F 7
Chimeo 104-105 E 7
Chimichagua 94-95 DE 3
Chi-ming-ho = Jiminghe 146-147 E 6
Chimkent = Čimkent 132-133 M 9
Chimki 124-125 L 5-6
Chimki-Chovrino, Moskva- 113 V b 2
Chimkinskoje vodochranilišče 113 V b 2
Chimney Peak = One Tree Peak 76-77 B 6
Chi-mo = Jimo 146-147 H 3
Chimoio 172 F 5
Chimpay 111 C 5
Chimpembe 171 B 5

Chiná [MEX, Campeche] 86-87 P 8
China [MEX, Nuevo León] 86-87 L 5
China [TJ] 142-143 E-K 5
China, Tanjong — 154 III ab 2
Chinácota 94-95 E 4
China Lake, CA 74-75 E 5
Chinan 144-145 F 5
Chinan = Jinan 142-143 M 4
Ch'in-an = Qin'an 142-143 K 5
Chinandega 64-65 J 9
China Point 74-75 D 6
Chinati Peak 76-77 B 8
Chinatown, San Francisco-, CA 83 I b 2
Chinbo 144-145 G 4
Chincha Alta 92-93 D 7
Chin-ch'êng = Jincheng 142-143 L 4
Chincheros 96-97 E 8
Chin-ch'i = Jinxi [TJ, place] 146-147 F 8
Chin Ch'i = Jin Xi [TJ, river] 146-147 F 8
Chin Chiang = Jin Jiang 146-147 E 7
Chinchilla 158-159 K 5
Chinchilla de Monte-Aragón 120-121 G 9
Chinchiná 94-95 D 5
Chin-ching = Jinjing 146-147 D 7
Chinchipe 96-97 B 4
Chinchipe, Río — 96-97 B 4
Chincholi 140 C 2
Chinchorro, Banco — 64-65 J 8
Chinchow = Jinzhou 142-143 N 3
Chincoteague, VA 80-81 J 2
Chincoteague Bay 72-73 J 5
Chinde 172 G 5
Chin-do [ROK, island] 144-145 EF 5
Chindo [ROK, place] 144-145 F 5
Chindwin Myit 148-149 C 1-2
Ching-an = Jing'an 146-147 E 7
Ch'ing-chang Ho = Qingzhang Dongyuan 146-147 D 3
Ching-chi = Jingzhi 146-147 G 3
Ching-chiang = Jingjiang 146-147 H 5-6
Ch'ing Chiang = Qing Jiang 146-147 C 6
Ch'ing-chien = Qingjian 146-147 C 3
Ching-ch'uan = Yinchuan 142-143 JK 4
Ch'ing-fêng = Qingfeng 146-147 E 4
Chingford, London- 129 II bc 1
Ch'ing Hai = Chöch nuur 142-143 H 4
Ching-hai = Jinghai 146-147 F 2
Chinghai = Qinghai 142-143 GH 4
Ching-ho = Jinghe [TJ, place] 142-143 E 3
Ching Ho = Jing He [TJ, river] 146-147 B 4
Ch'ing-ho = Qinghe 146-147 E 3
Ch'ing-ho-chên = Qinghezhen 146-147 F 3
Ch'ing-ho-ch'êng = Qinghecheng 144-145 E 2
Ch'ing-ho-mêng = Qinghemen 144-145 C 2
Ching-hsien = Jing Xian [TJ, Anhui] 146-147 G 6
Ching-hsien = Jing Xian [TJ, Hunan] 146-147 B 8
Ching-hsing = Jingxing 146-147 DE 2
Ching-ku = Jinggu 142-143 J 7
Chingleput 140 DE 4
Ch'ing-lien = Qinglian 146-147 D 9
Ch'ing-liu = Qingliu 146-147 F 8
Ching-lo = Jingle 146-147 CD 2
Ching-mên = Jingmen 146-147 CD 6
Ching-ning = Jingning 142-143 K 4
Chingola 172 E 4
Chingombe 171 B 6
Chingovo, Rio — 174-175 K 2
Ching-pien = Jingbian 146-147 B 3
Ching-po Hu = Jingbo Hu 142-143 O 3
Ch'ing-p'u = Qingpu 146-147 H 6
Ching Shan = Jing Shan [TJ, mountains] 146-147 C 6
Ching-shan = Jingshan [TJ, place] 146-147 D 6
Ch'ing-shui-ho = Qingshuihe [TJ, place] 146-147 C 2
Ch'ing-shui Ho = Qingshui He [TJ, river] 146-147 B 2
Ching-t'ai = Jingtai 142-143 J 4
Ch'ing-tao = Qingdao 142-143 N 4
Ching-tê = Jingde 146-147 G 6
Ch'ing-t'ien = Qingtian 146-147 H 7
Ch'ing-tui-tzŭ = Qingduizi 144-145 D 3
Ching-tung = Jingdong 142-143 J 7
Ching-tzŭ-kuan = Jingziguan 146-147 C 5
Chingwin Bûm 141 F 3
Ching-yang = Jingyang 146-147 B 4
Ch'ing-yang = Qingyang [TJ, Anhui] 146-147 FG 6
Ch'ing-yang = Qingyang [TJ, Gansu] 142-143 K 4
Ching-yüan = Jingyuan 142-143 JK 4
Ch'ing-yüan = Qingyuan [TJ, Fujian] 146-147 G 8
Ch'ing-yüan = Qingyuan [TJ, Guangdong] 146-147 D 10
Ch'ing-yüan = Qingyuan [TJ, Liaoning] 144-145 E 1
Ch'ing-yün = Qingyun 146-147 F 3
Chinhae 144-145 G 5
Chinhae-man 144-145 G 5
Ch'in Ho = Qin He 146-147 D 4
Chinhoyi 172 EF 5
Chin-hsiang = Jinxiang [TJ, Shandong] 146-147 EF 4
Chin-hsiang = Jinxiang [TJ, Zhejiang] 146-147 H 8
Chin-hsien = Jinxian [TJ, Hebei] 146-147 E 2
Chin-hsien = Jinxian [TJ, Jiangxi] 146-147 F 7
Chin-hsien = Jin Xian [TJ, Liaoning ↗ Jinzhou] 144-145 C 2
Chin-hsien = Jin Xian [TJ, Liaoning ↑ Lüda] 142-143 N 4
Chinhsien = Jinzhou 142-143 N 3
Chinhsien = Qin Xian 146-147 D 3
Chin-hua = Jinhua 142-143 MN 6
Ch'in-huang-tao = Qinhuangdao 142-143 MN 3-4
Chiniak, Cape — 58-59 LM 8
Chiniak, Cape — 58-59 gh 1
Chi-ning = Jining [TJ, Inner Mongolia Aut. Reg.] 142-143 L 3
Chi-ning = Jining [TJ, Shandong] 142-143 M 4
Chinit, Stung — 150-151 E 6
Chinitna Bay 58-59 L 7
Chinju 142-143 O 4
Chinko 164-165 J 7
Chin-k'ou = Jinkou 146-147 E 6
Chinle, AZ 74-75 J 4
Chinle Valley 74-75 J 4
Ch'in Ling = Qin Ling 142-143 KL 5
Chin-mên = Kinmen Dao 142-143 M 7
Chinna Ganjām 140 E 3
Chinnamanūr 140 C 6
Chinnamp'o = Nampo 142-143 NO 4
Chinna Salem 140 D 5
Chin-niu = Jinniu 146-147 E 6-7
Chinnūr 140 D 1
Chinnūru = Chinnūr 140 D 1
Chinon 120-121 H 5
Chinook 61 C 5
Chinook, MT 68-69 B 1
Chinook Valley 60 HJ 1
Chino Valley, AZ 74-75 G 5
Chin-p'ing = Jinping 146-147 B 8
Chinquião = Zhenjiang 142-143 M 5
Chins, Île des — = Jazā'ir al-Kilāb 166-167 M 1
Chinsali 172 F 4
Chin-sha Chiang = Jinsha Jiang 142-143 J 6
Chin-shan = Jinshan 146-147 H 6
Ch'in Shui = Qingshui Jiang 146-147 B 8
Ch'in-shui = Qinshui 146-147 D 4
Chinsiang = Jinxiang 146-147 EF 4
Chinsura 134-135 O 6
Chintalnār 140 E 1
Chintāmaṇi 140 D 4
Chin-t'an = Jintan 146-147 G 6
Chinú 94-95 D 3
Chinwangtao = Qinhuangdao 142-143 MN 3-4
Chinwithetha Taing 148-149 B 2
Ch'in-yang = Qinyang 142-143 L 4
Chinyŏng 144-145 G 5
Chin-yüan = Jinyuan 146-147 D 3
Chinyuan = Qinyuan 146-147 D 3
Ch'in-yüan = Qinyuan 146-147 D 3
Chin-yün = Jinyun 146-147 H 7
Chiôco 172 F 5
Chióggia 122-123 E 3
Chíos [GR, island] 122-123 L 6
Chíos [GR, place] 122-123 M 6
Chipao 96-97 E 9
Chipata 172 F 4
Chipewyan Lake 61 B 2
Chipie River 62 GH 2
Chipili 171 B 5
Chipillico, Río — 96-97 A 4
Chipinge 172 F 6
Chipiriri, Río — 104-105 D 5
Chipiscú 106-107 D 4
Chip Lake 60 K 3
Chipley, FL 78-79 G 5
Chipley, GA 78-79 G 4
Chiplūn 140 A 2
Chipman 63 D 4
Chipoka 171 C 6
Chiporiro 172 F 5
Chippewa Falls, WI 70-71 E 3
Chippewa Flowage 70-71 E 3
Chippewa Reservoir = Chippewa Flowage 70-71 E 3
Chippewa River [USA, Michigan] 70-71 H 4
Chippewa River [USA, Wisconsin] 70-71 DE 3
Chipurupalle 140 F 1
Chiputneticook Lakes 72-73 MN 2
Chiquian 96-97 C 7
Chiquimula 64-65 HJ 9
Chiquinquirá 94-95 DE 5
Chiquita, Mar — [RA, Buenos Aires ← Junín] 106-107 G 5
Chiquita, Mar — [RA, Buenos Aires ↑ Mar del Plata] 106-107 J 6
Chiquitos, Llanos de — 92-93 G 8
Chira 171 D 2
Chira, Río — 96-97 A 4
Chira Bazar 142-143 DE 4
Chirāla 140 E 3
Chirāwa = Chirāwa 138-139 E 3
Chirāwa 138-139 E 3
Chiraz = Shīrāz 134-135 G 5
Chiredzi 172 F 6
Chirfa 164-165 G 4
Chirgua, Río — 94-95 H 3
Chiribiquete, Sierra de — 94-95 E 7
Chiricahua National Monument 74-75 J 6-7
Chiricahua Peak 74-75 J 7
Chiriguaná 94-95 E 3
Chirikof Island 56-57 EF 6
Chiriquí 88-89 E 10
Chiriquí, Golfo de — 64-65 K 10
Chiriquí, Laguna de — 64-65 K 9-10
Chiri-san 144-145 F 5
Chirmiri 138-139 J 6
Chiromo 172 G 5
Chirripó Grande, Cerro — 64-65 K 10
Chiru Choricha, Serrania — 104-105 BC 4
Chirundu 172 E 5
Chisamba 172 E 4-5
Chisana, AK 58-59 Q 5
Chisana River 58-59 R 5
Chisapani Gaṛhī 138-139 K 4
Chisec 86-87 P 10
Chisel Lake 56-57 QR 7
Ch'i-sha = Qisha 150-151 G 2
Chishan 146-147 H 10
Chi-shih Shan = Amnyemachhen Gangri 142-143 HJ 5
Chisholm 60 KL 2
Chishtian Mandi = Chishtiyān Maṇḍī 134-135 L 5
Chishtiyān Maṇḍī 134-135 L 5
Chi-shui = Jishui 146-147 E 8
Chisimaio = Kismaanyo 172 H 2
Chişinău = Kišin'ov 126-127 D 3
Chislaviči 124-125 HJ 6
Chislehurst, London- 129 II c
Chisos Mountains 76-77 C 8
Chistochina, AK 58-59 PQ 5
Chiswick, London- 129 II ab 2
Chita 94-95 E 4
Chita = Čita 132-133 V 7
Chitado 172 B 5
Chitagá 94-95 E 4
Chitagōḍē = Chikodi 140 B 2
Chita-hantō 144-145 L 5
Ch'i-t'ai = Qitai 142-143 FG 3
Chitambo 171 B 6
Chitanana River 58-59 L 4
Chitāpur 140 C 2
Chitek 61 DE 4
Chitek Lake 61 J 4
Chitembo 172 C 4
Chitina, AK 58-59 P 6
Chitina River 58-59 Q 6
Chitkal 138-139 G 2
Chitogarh = Chittaurgarh 134-135 L 6
Chitose 144-145 b 2
Chitose, Kawasaki- 155 III a 2
Chitpur, Calcutta- 154 II b 2
Chitradurga 134-135 M 8
Chitrāl 134-135 L 3
Chitrāvati 140 CD 3
Chitré 64-65 K 10
Chi-tsê = Jize 146-147 E 3
Chittagong = Chāṭṭagām 134-135 P 6
Chittagong Hill Tracts = Chāṭṭagām Pahāṛī 'Alāqa 141 C 4-5
Chittaldurga = Chitradurga 134-135 M 8
Chittaorgarh = Chittaurgarh 134-135 L 6
Chittaurgarh 134-135 L 6
Chittor 134-135 M 8
Chittūr 140 C 5
Chittūru = Chittor 134-135 M 8
Ch'i-tung = Qidong [TJ, Jiangsu] 146-147 H 6
Ch'i-tung = Qidong [TJ, Shandong] 146-147 F 3
Chiu-chiang = Jiujiang 146-147 D 10
Chiuchiu 104-105 B 8
Chiuchuan = Jiuquan 142-143 H 4
Chiu-ho-hsü = Jiuhe 146-147 E 10
Chiu-hsien = Qiu Xian 146-147 E 3
Chiulezi, Rio — 171 D 5-6
Chiu-ling Shan = Jiuling Shan 146-147 E 7
Chiu-lung Ch'i = Jiulong Xi 146-147 F 8
Chiu-lung Chiang = Jiulong Jiang 146-147 F 9
Chiu-lung Shan = Jiulong Shan 146-147 G 7
Chiuma, ostrov — = Hiiumaa 124-125 CD 4
Chiumbe, Rio — 172 D 3
Chiume 172 D 4
Ch'iung-chou Hai-hsia = Qiongzhou Haixia 142-143 KL 7
Chiungshan = Qiongshan 142-143 L 8
Ch'iung-tung = Qionghai 142-143 L 8
Chiu-shan Lieh-tao = Jiushan Liedao 146-147 J 7
Chiuta, Lagoa — 172 G 4
Chiuta, Lake — 172 G 4
Chiu-tao-liang = Jiudaoliang 146-147 BC 6
Chiva [SU] 132-133 L 9
Chiva, Loma de la — 106-107 C 7
Chivacoa 94-95 G 2
Chivasso 122-123 B 3
Chivay 92-93 E 8
Chivé 104-105 B 3
Chivera, La — 91 II b 1
Chivilcoy 111 DE 4
Chivu 172 F 5
Chiwanda 172 FG 4
Chiwefwe 171 B 6
Chiweta 172 F 4
Chixi 146-147 D 10-11
Chixoy, Río — 64-65 H 8
Chi-yang = Jiyang [TJ, Fujian] 146-147 FG 8
Chi-yang = Jiyang [TJ, Shandong] 146-147 F 3
Ch'i-yang = Qiyang 146-147 CD 8
Chiyoda, Tōkyō- 155 III b 1
Chi-yüan = Jiyuan 146-147 D 4
Chiza, Quebrada de — 104-105 AB 6
Chjargas 142-143 G 2
Chjargas nuur 142-143 GH 2
Chlevnoje 124-125 M 7
Chloride, AZ 74-75 F 5
Chmeiṭīyé = Shmayṭīyah 136-137 H 5
Chmelevoje 126-127 E 2
Chmel'nickij 126-127 C 2
Chmel'nickij, Perejaslav- 126-127 EF 1
Chmel'nik 126-127 CD 2
Choachí 94-95 E 5
Choapa 106-107 B 3
Choapa, Río — 106-107 B 3
Choapas, Las — 86-87 NO 9
Chobe 172 D 5
Chobe National Park 172 DE 5
Cho' Bo' 150-151 E 2
Chocaya 92-93 F 9
Chocaya, Cordillera de — 104-105 C 7
Chocca 92-93 D 7
Cho-chang Ho = Zhuozhang He 146-147 D 3
Chochiang = Charqiliq 142-143 F 4
Choch'iwŏn 144-145 F 4
Chöch nuur 142-143 H 4
Chochol'skij 126-127 J 1
Chöch Šili 142-143 G 4
Chöch Šili uul 142-143 FG 4
Chocó 94-95 C 4-5
Chocolate Mountains 74-75 F 6
Chocontá 92-93 E 3
Choctaw, AL 78-79 E 4
Choctawhatchee Bay 78-79 F 5
Choctawhatchee River 78-79 FG 5
Chodavaram [IND ↑ Rājahmundry] 140 EF 2
Chodavaram [IND ↖ Vishākhapatnam] 140 F 2
Ch'o-do [North Korea] 144-145 E 3-4
Ch'o-do [ROK] 144-145 F 5
Cho' Dôn 150-151 E 1
Chodorov 126-127 B 2
Chodžambas 134-135 JK 3
Chodžejli 132-133 K 9
Chodžent = Leninabad 134-135 KL 2-3
Chodzież 118 H 2
Choele-Choel 111 CD 5
Choele Choel Grande, Isla — 106-107 DE 7
Choen, Nam — 150-151 CD 4
Chōfu 155 III a 2
Chōfu Airport 155 III a 1-2
Chōfu-Kamiishihara 155 III a 2
Chōfu-Shibazaki 155 III a 2
Cho' Ganh 150-151 E 2
Cho' Gao 150-151 F 7
Cho' Giông Trôm = Giông Trôm 150-151 F 7-8
Choho 150-151 CD 5
Chohsien = Zhuo Xian 146-147 E 2
Chohtan 138-139 C 5
Choibalsan = Čojbalsan 142-143 L 2
Choiqué 106-107 F 7
Choique Mahuida, Sierra — 106-107 E 7
Choiseul 148-149 j 6
Choiseul, Seno — = Choiseul Sound 108-109 KL 8
Choiseul Sound 108-109 KL 8
Choisy-le-Roi 129 I c 2
Chojna 118 G 2
Chojnice 118 HJ 2
Chojniki 124-125 G 8
Chōkai-zan 144-145 MN 3
Chok Chai 150-151 D 5
Chōḷamaṇḍala = Coromandel Coast 134-135 N 7-8
Cholame, CA 74-75 CD 5
Cholargós 113 IV b 2
Cholavandan 140 C 5
Chold = Chuld 142-143 K 2-3
Cholet 120-121 G 5
Cholgo 108-109 C 3-4
Cholita 108-109 D 4
Chŏlla-namdo 144-145 F 5
Chŏlla-pukto 144-145 F 5
Cholm 124-125 H 5
Cholmogorskaja 124-125 N 2
Cholmogory 132-133 G 5
Cholmsk 132-133 b 8
Cholm-Žirkovskij 124-125 JK 6
Cholopeniči 124-125 G 6
Cholos nuur 142-143 H 4
Ch'ŏlsan 144-145 E 3
Cho-lu = Zhuolu 146-147 E 1
Cholula 86-87 L 8
Choluteca 64-65 J 9
Choma 172 E 5
Chomba 171 D 5
Chomberg 128 IV b 1
Chomedey 82 I a 1
Cho' Mo'i 150-151 E 7
Chomolungma = Sagarmatha 138-139 L 3
Chom Thong 150-151 B 3
Chomū = Chaumu 138-139 E 4
Chomutovka 124-125 K 8
Ch'ŏnan 144-145 F 4
Chon Buri 148-149 D 4
Chŏnch'ŏn 144-145 F 2
Chon Daen 150-151 C 4
Chone 92-93 CD 5
Chong'an 146-147 F 8
Ch'ŏng'chŏn-gang 144-145 EF 2-3
Chongde 146-147 H 6
Chongdjin = Ch'ŏngjin 142-143 OP 3
Chŏnggŏ-dong 144-145 E 3
Ch'ŏngha 144-145 G 4
Ch'ŏngjin 142-143 OP 3
Chongjin = Ch'ŏngjin 142-143 OP 3
Chŏngju 142-143 O 4
Chong Kal 150-151 D 6
Chongling Shui 146-147 D 8-9
Chongming 142-143 N 5
Chongming Dao 146-147 HJ 6
Chongoene 174-175 KL 3
Chongor 142-143 L 2
Chongor = Bajan Adraga 142-143 KL 2
Chongor Oboo Sum = Bajandalaj 142-143 J 3
Chongor Tagh = Qungur tagh 142-143 D 4
Chongos Alto 96-97 D 8
Chong Pang 154 III ab 1
Chong Phangan 150-151 BC 8
Chong Pha-ngan = Chong Phangan 150-151 BC 8
Ch'ŏngp'yŏngch'ŏn 144-145 FG 4
Chongqing 142-143 K 6
Chongren 146-147 EF 8
Chong Samui 150-151 BC 8
Ch'ŏngsan-do 144-145 F 5
Chongshan = Chongzuo 142-143 K 7
Chongshanpai = Jitan 146-147 E 9
Ch'ongsŏktu-ri 144-145 EF 3
Chongsŏng 144-145 GH 1
Chong Tao 150-151 BC 8
Chŏngŭp 144-145 F 5
Chongwenqu, Beijing- 155 II b 2
Chongwu 146-147 G 9
Ch'ŏngyang [ROK] 144-145 F 4
Chongyang [TJ] 146-147 E 7
Chongyang = Zhongyang 146-147 C 3
Chongyang Xi 146-147 FG 8
Chongyi 146-147 E 9
Chongzuo 142-143 K 7
Chŏnju 142-143 O 4
Chon May, Cap — = Mui Cho'n Mây 150-151 G 4
Cho'n Mây, Mui — 150-151 G 4
Chonnabot 150-151 D 4
Chonos, Archipiélago de los — 111 AB 6-7
Chonta 96-97 C 6-7
Chonta, Paso de — 96-97 D 8
Chon Thanh 150-151 F 7
Chonuu 132-133 b 4
Chooloj Gov' 142-143 H 3
Cho Oyu = Jo'öyu Ri 138-139 L 3
Chōpāl = Chaupāl 138-139 F 2
Chopda 138-139 E 7
Chopim, Rio — 102-103 F 6-7
Chopinzinho 102-103 F 6
Chop'or 124-125 P 7
Chopra 138-139 M 4
Choquecota 104-105 C 6
Chor 132-133 Za 8
Cho' Râ [VN] 150-151 E 1
Chorasan = Khorāsān 134-135 H 3-4
Chôra Sfakíon 122-123 L 8
Chordogoj 132-133 W 5
Chor He 142-143 N 2
Chorillo, El — 106-107 DE 4
Chorinsk 132-133 U 7
Chorlovo 124-125 M 6
Choró 100-101 E 3
Choro, Río — [BOL] 104-105 D 5
Choró, Rio — [BR] 100-101 E 3
Chorog 134-135 L 3
Chorol 126-127 F 2
Choromoro 104-105 D 10
Choroní 94-95 H 2
Choros, Islas de los — 106-107 B 2
Choros Bajos 106-107 B 2
Chorošovo, Moskva- 113 V b 2
Chorotis 104-105 F 10
Chorrera, La — [CO] 94-95 E 8
Chorrera, La — [PA] 64-65 b 3
Chorreras, Cerro — 86-87 GH 4
Chorro, El — 104-105 C 6
Chorsabad = Khorsabad 136-137 K 4
Chŏrwŏn 144-145 F 3
Chŏryŏng-do = Yŏng-do 144-145 G 5
Chorzele 118 K 2
Chorzów 118 J 3
Chŏsen-kaikyō 142-143 O 5
Chōshi 144-145 N 5
Chosica 96-97 C 7
Chos-Malal 111 BC 5
Chosmes 106-107 D 4
Chosŏn-man = Tonghan-man 142-143 O 4
Choszczno 118 GH 2
Chota 92-93 D 6
Chotan = Chohtan 138-139 C 5
Chota Nāgpur 134-135 NO 6
Choteau, MT 66-67 G 2
Chotila 138-139 C 6
Chotimsk 124-125 J 7
Chotin 126-127 C 2
Chott ech Chergui = Ash-Shaṭṭ ash-Sharqī 164-165 DE 2
Chott el Djerid = Shaṭṭ al-Jarīd 164-165 F 2
Chott el Fedjedj = Shaṭṭ al-Fijāj 166-167 L 2-3
Chott el Gharsa = Shaṭṭ al-Jarsah 166-167 KL 2
Chott el Guetter = Shaṭṭ al-Qaṭṭār 166-167 L 2
Chott el Hodna = Ash-Shaṭṭ al-Hudnah 164-165 EF 1
Chott el Qeṭṭâr = Shaṭṭ al-Qaṭṭār 166-167 L 2
Chott en Nouâl = Sabkhat an-Nawāl 166-167 LM 2
Chott Melrhir = Shaṭṭ Malghīr 164-165 F 2
Chott Mṭâ el Rhèrra = Shaṭṭ al-Ghurrah 166-167 M 2
Chott Rharbi = Ash-Shaṭṭ al-Gharbī 166-167 F 3
Chott Rharsa = Shaṭṭ al-Jarsah 166-167 KL 2
Chotynec 124-125 K 7
Chou-chih = Zhouzhi 146-147 AB 4
Chou-k'ou-tien = Fangshan 146-147 E 2
Chou-ning = Zhouning 146-147 G 8
Chou Shan = Zhoushan Dao 142-143 N 5-6
Chou-shan Ch'ün-tao = Zhoushan Qundao 142-143 N 5
Chou-tang-p'an = Zhoudangfan 146-147 E 6
Chouteau, OK 76-77 G 4
Chou-ts'un = Zhoucun 146-147 FG 3
Chovd [Mongolia, administrative unit = 3 ◁] 142-143 G 2
Chovd [Mongolia, place] 142-143 G 2
Chovd gol 142-143 G 2
Chovet 106-107 G 4
Chövsgöl [Mongolia, administrative unit = 6 ◁] 142-143 J 1
Chövsgöl [Mongolia, place] 142-143 KL 3
Chövsgöl nuur 142-143 J 1
Chowan River 80-81 H 2
Chowchilla, CA 74-75 C 4
Chowiet Island 58-59 e 1
Choya 106-107 E 2
Choybalsan = Čojbalsan 142-143 L 2
Chozapini, ozero — 126-127 L 6
Chrapovickaja Dača 124-125 N 6
chrebet Čorskogo 132-133 a 4-c 5
chrebet Džagdy 132-133 YZ 7
chrebet Džugdžur 132-133 Z-b 6
chrebet Džungarskij Alatau 132-133 O 9-P 8
chrebet Karatau 132-133 MN 9
chrebet Kokšaal-Tau 134-135 M 2
chrebet Kular 132-133 Z 4
chrebet Kungej-Alatau 132-133 O 9
chrebet Nuratau 132-133 M 9
chrebet Pekul'nej 132-133 hj 4
chrebet Sette-Daban 132-133 a 5
chrebet Sunnagyn 132-133 Y 6
chrebet Suntar-Chajata 132-133 ab 5
chrebet Tarbagataj 132-133 PQ 8
chrebet Terskej-Alatau 134-135 M 2
chrebet Ulan-Burgasy 132-133 UV 7
Chrenovoje 126-127 K 1
Chrisman, IL 70-71 G 6
Chrissiesmeer 174-175 J 4
Christchurch [NZ] 158-159 OP 8
Christ Church Cathedral 170 III b 2
Christian, AK 58-59 P 3
Christian = Az-Zahīliqah 166-167 C 3
Christiana 174-175 F 4
Christiania = Oslo 116-117 D 8
Christian Island 72-73 F 2
Christian River 58-59 P 3
Christiansburg, VA 80-81 FG 2
Christianshåb = Qasigiánguit 56-57 ab 4
Christian Sound 58-59 v 8-9
Christiansted 88-89 OP 6
Christie Bay 56-57 O 5
Christina, MT 68-69 B 2
Christina Range 66-67 D 1
Christina River 61 C 2
Christinovka 126-127 DE 2
Christmas 156-157 K 4
Christmas, Isla — 108-109 D 10
Christmas Creek 158-159 E 3
Christmas Island [AUS] 148-149 E 9
Christmas Island [CDN] 63 F 5
Christmas Mount 58-59 GH 4
Christoforovo 124-125 QR 3
Christoval, TX 76-77 D 7
Christóvão Pereira, Ponta — 106-107 M 3
Chromo, CO 68-69 C 7
Chromtau 132-133 K 7
Chrudim 118 GH 4
Chrysē 122-123 LM 8
Chrysler Corporation 84 II b 2
Chrysochûs, Kólpos — 136-137 E 5
Chu, Sông — 150-151 E 3
Chuādāngā 138-139 M 6
Chuali, Lagoa — 174-175 K 3
Chuambo 174-175 L 1
Chuanchang He 146-147 GH 5
Ch'üan-ch'i = Quanxishi 146-147 D 8
Ch'üan-chiao = Quanjiao 146-147 FG 5
Ch'üan-chou Chiang = Quanzhou Gang 146-147 G 9
Chuangchow = Jinjiang 146-147 H 5-6
Chuang-ho = Zhuanghe 144-145 D 3
Chuansha 146-147 HJ 6
Chubb Crater = New Quebec Crater 56-57 VW 5
Chubbuck, CA 74-75 F 5
Chubisgalt = Chövsgöl 142-143 KL 3
Chubsugul = Chövsgöl nuur 142-143 J 1
Chūbu 144-145 LM 4-5
Chubut 111 BC 6
Chubut, Río — 111 C 6
Chucca 96-97 F 9
Chucheng = Zhucheng 142-143 MN 4
Chu-chi = Zhuji 142-143 N 6
Chu-ch'i = Zhuxi 146-147 BC 5
Chu-chia Chien = Zhujia Jian 146-147 J 7
Chu-ch'iao = Zhuqiao 146-147 GH 3
Ch'ü-chieh = Qujie 146-147 C 11
Ch'ü-ching = Qujing 142-143 J 6
Ch'ü-chou = Qu Xian 142-143 M 6
Ch'ü-chou = Quzhou 146-147 E 3
Chu-chou = Zhuzhou 142-143 L 6
Chuchow = Zhuzhou 142-143 L 6
Chuchwa 174-175 D 3
Chučni 126-127 N 6
Chucul 106-107 E 4
Chucuma 106-107 D 3
Chucunaque, Río — 94-95 C 3
Chudat 126-127 O 6
Chŭdŭ Rāzī 141 F 2
Ch'üeh-shan = Queshan 142-143 L 5
Ch'ü-fou = Qufu 146-147 F 4
Chugach Islands 58-59 M 7
Chugach Mountains 56-57 GH 5
Chugchilán, Cordillera de — 96-97 B 2
Chugchug, Quebrada — 104-105 B 8
Chuginadak Island 58-59 l 4
Chugoku 144-145 HJ 5
Chūgoku-sammyaku 144-145 JK 5
Chuguchak 142-143 E 2
Chuguchak = Tarbagataj 142-143 EF 2
Chugwater, WY 68-69 D 5
Chuhsien = Chu Xian 146-147 FG 5
Chuhsien = Ju Xian 146-147 G 4
Ch'ü-hsien = Ju Xian 146-147 G 4
Chuhsien = Qu Xian 142-143 M 6
Ch'u-hsiung = Chuxiong 142-143 J 7
Chü-hua Tao = Juhua Dao 144-145 C 2
Chuí 106-107 L 4
Chuilnuk Mountains 58-59 HJ 6
Ch'uja-do 144-145 F 6
Ch'ü-jung = Jurong 146-147 G 6
Chukai 150-151 D 10
Chukchi Peninsula = Čukotskij poluostrov 132-133 kl 4
Chukchi Plateau 52 B 35
Chukchi Sea 52 BC 35-36
Chuki = Zhuji 142-143 N 6
Chuknitapalli 138-139 H 8
Chukot Autonomous Area 132-133 g-k 4
Chukotskiy, Cape — = mys Čukotskij 132-133 l 5
Ch'ü-k'ou-p'u = Jukoupu 146-147 C 8
Chu-kuang Shan = Zhuguang Shan 146-147 DE 8-9
Chukudu Kraal 172 D 6
Chūl, Gardaneh-ye — 136-137 MN 6
Chulaq Aqqan Su 142-143 G 4
Chula Vista, CA 64-65 C 5
Chulchuta 126-127 N 3
Chuld 142-143 K 2-3
Chulitna, AK 58-59 N 5
Chulitna River 58-59 MN 5
Ch'u-liu-ho = Juliuhe 144-145 D 1
Chullora, Sydney- 161 I a 2
Chulp'o 144-145 F 5
Chü-lu = Julu 146-147 E 3
Chulucanas 92-93 CD 6
Chulumani 92-93 F 8
Chu-lung Ho = Zhulong He 146-147 E 2
Chu-ma-tien = Zhumadian 146-147 DE 5
Chumbicha 111 C 3
Chum Phae 148-149 D 3
Chumphon 148-149 CD 4
Chumphon Buri 150-151 D 5
Chumpi 96-97 E 9
Chumsaeng 148-149 D 3
Chumunjin 144-145 G 4
Chuña 106-107 E 3
Chuna = Čun'a 132-133 ST 5
Chun'an 146-147 G 7
Chunār 138-139 J 5
Chunchanga, Pampa de — 96-97 CD 9
Chunchi 96-97 B 3
Ch'unch'ŏn 142-143 O 4
Chunchuri 96-97 D 6
Chungam-ni 144-145 G 5
Chungan = Chong'an 146-147 F 8
Chungara, Lago de — 104-105 B 6
Ch'ung Ch'i = Chongyang Xi 146-147 FG 8
Ch'ungch'ŏng-namdo 144-145 F 4
Ch'ungch'ŏng-pukto 144-145 FG 4
Chüngges 142-143 E 3
Chung-hsiang = Zhongxiang 146-147 D 6

Chung-hsin-hsü = Zhongxin 146-147 E 9
Chunghwa 144-145 EF 3
Ch'ung-i = Chongyi 146-147 E 9
Ch'ung-jên = Chongren 146-147 EF 8
Ch'ungju 144-145 FG 4
Chungking = Chongqing 142-143 K 6
Chungli 146-147 H 9
Ch'ung-ming = Chongming 142-143 N 5
Ch'ung-ming Tao = Chongming Dao 146-147 HJ 6
Chung-mou = Zhongmou 146-147 DE 4
Ch'ungmu 144-145 G 5
Chung-pu = Huangling 146-147 B 4
Chŭngsan 144-145 E 3
Chungshan = Zhongshan 142-143 L 7
Chungsiang = Zhongxiang 146-147 D 6
Chung-t'iao Shan = Zhongtiao Shan 146-147 CD 4
Chung-tien = Zhongdian 142-143 HJ 6
Chung-tu = Zhongdu 146-147 B 9
Chungui 96-97 E 8
Chüngüj gol 142-143 GH 2
Chung Wan, Kowloon- 155 I a 1
Chung-wei = Zhongwei 142-143 JK 4
Ch'ung-wu = Chongwu 146-147 G 9
Chungyang = Chongyang 146-147 E 7
Chungyang Shanmo 142-143 N 7
Chün-hsien = Jun Xian 146-147 C 5
Chunhua 146-147 B 4
Chunian = Chūniyān 138-139 DE 2
Chūniyān 138-139 DE 2
Chunu, Cape — 58-59 u 7
Chunya 172 F 3
Chunzach 126-127 N 5
Chūō, Tōkyō- 155 III b 1
Chupadera, Mesa — 76-77 A 5-6
Chupán 96-97 C 6
Ch'ü-qu = Quwo 146-147 C 4
Chuquibamba 92-93 E 8
Chuquibambilla 96-97 E 9
Chuquicamata 111 C 2
Chuquichuqui 104-105 D 6
Chuquisaca 104-105 D 6-E 7
Chuquisaca = Sucre 92-93 FG 8
Chur 118 D 5
Churāchāndpur 141 C 3
Churchill, ID 66-67 FG 4
Churchill [CDN] 56-57 RS 6
Churchill [ROU] 106-107 JK 4
Churchill, Cape — 56-57 S 6
Churchill Falls 56-57 XY 7
Churchill Lake 61 DE 2-3
Churchill Peak 56-57 LM 6
Churchill River [CDN ◁ Hamilton Inlet] 56-57 Y 7
Churchill River [CDN ◁ Hudson Bay] 56-57 RS 6
Church Point, LA 78-79 CD 5
Churchs Ferry, ND 68-69 G 1
Chureo, Paso de — 106-107 B 6
Churk 138-139 J 5
Churu 134-135 LM 5
Churubusco, Coyoacán- 91 I c 2
Churuguara 94-95 G 2
Chusei-hokudō = Ch'ungch'ŏng-pukto 144-145 FG 4
Chusei-nandō = Ch'ungch'ŏng-namdo 144-145 F 4
Ch'ü Shan = Daqu Shan 146-147 J 6
Chu-shan = Zhushan 142-143 KL 5
Chusistan = Khūzestān 134-135 F 4
Chuska Mountains 74-75 J 4-5
Chusmisa 104-105 B 6
Chust 126-127 A 2
Chutag 142-143 J 2
Chu-t'an = Zhutan 146-147 E 7
Chute-aux-Outardes 63 BC 3
Chute-des-Passes 63 A 3
Chutes François Joseph 172 C 3
Chutes Rusumu 171 B 3
Chutes Tshungu 172 DE 1
Chutes Wissmann 172 CD 3
Chutes Wolff 172 D 3
Chu-t'ing = Zhuting 146-147 D 8
Chutorskoj 126-127 L 3
Chutung 146-147 H 9
Ch'ü-tzŭ-chên = Quzi 146-147 A 3
Chuučnar 142-143 G 5
Chuŭronjang 144-145 GH 2
Chuvash Autonomous Soviet Socialist Republic = 4 ◁ 132-133 H 6
Chuwārtah 136-137 L 5
Chu Xian 146-147 FG 5
Chuxiong 142-143 J 7
Chuxiong Yizu Zizhizhou 142-143 J 6
Chuxiong Zizhizhou 142-143 J 6
Chuy 111 F 4
Ch'ü-yang = Quyang [TJ, Hebei] 146-147 E 2
Ch'ü-yang = Quyang [TJ, Jiangxi] 146-147 E 8
Chu Yang Sin 148-149 E 4
Chü-yeh = Juye 146-147 F 4
Chužir 132-133 U 7
Chvalynsk 124-125 QR 7
Chvatovka 124-125 Q 7
Chvojnaja 124-125 K 4
Chwansha = Chuansha 146-147 HJ 6
Chwārta = Chuwārtah 136-137 L 5
Chye Kay 154 III a 1
Ciampino, Aeroporto di — 113 II bc 2
Ciampino, Roma- 113 II c 2
Cianjur 152-153 G 9
Cianorte 102-103 F 5
Čiatura 126-127 L 5
Čibit 132-133 Q 7
Čibju = Uchta 124-125 T 2
Cibola, AZ 74-75 F 6
Cibuta 74-75 H 7
Çiçekdağı 136-137 F 3
Cicero, IL 70-71 G 5
Cícero Dantas 92-93 M 7
Čichačovo 124-125 GH 5
Čičikleja 126-127 E 3
Cidade Brasil, Guarulhos- 110 II b 1
Cidade de Deus, Rio de Janeiro- 110 I ab 2
Cidade Universitária [BR, Rio de Janeiro] 110 I b 2
Cidade Universitária [BR, São Paulo] 110 II a 2
Cide 136-137 E 2
Cidreira 106-107 MN 3
Ciechanów 118 K 2
Ciego de Ávila 64-65 L 7
Ciénaga 92-93 DE 2
Ciénaga de Ayapel 94-95 D 3
Ciénaga de Oro 94-95 D 3
Ciénaga de Zapatosa 94-95 E 3
Ciénaga Grande 94-95 D 3
Ciénaga Grande de Santa Marta 94-95 DE 2
Ciénage La Raya 94-95 D 3
Cienega, NM 76-77 B 6
Cienfuegos 64-65 K 7
Cieza 120-121 G 9
Çiftalan 154 I a 1
Çifteler 136-137 D 3
Çiftlik [TR, Gümüşane] 136-137 H 2
Çiftlik [TR, Sivas] 136-137 G 2
Cifuentes 120-121 F 8
Čiganak 132-133 N 8-9
Çiğli 136-137 K 4
Cihanbeyli = İnevi 136-137 E 3
Cihanbeyli yaylâsı 136-137 E 3
Cihuatlán 86-87 H 8
Čiili 132-133 M 9
Cijara, Embalse de — 120-121 E 9
Cijulang 152-153 H 9
Cikampek 152-153 G 9
Čikola 126-127 L 5
Cikuray, Gunung — 152-153 G 9
Cilacap 148-149 E 8
Cilandak, Jakarta- 154 IV a 2
Cilauteureun 152-153 G 9
Çıldır = Zurzuna 136-137 K 2
Çıldır gölü 136-137 K 2
Ciledug 152-153 H 9
Cili 146-147 C 7
Cililitan, Jakarta- 154 IV b 2
Cilincing, Jakarta- 154 IV b 1
Ci Liwung 154 IV a 1
Cilo dağı 136-137 KL 4
Cima, CA 74-75 F 5
Cima da Serra, Campos de — 106-107 M 2
Cimaltepec 64-65 G 8
Cimarron, KS 68-69 FG 7
Cimarron, NM 76-77 B 4
Cimarron River, North Fork — 76-77 D 4
Čimbaj 132-133 KL 9
Çimen dağı 136-137 H 3
Cimiring, Tanjung — 152-153 H 9-10
Čimkent 132-133 M 9
Ciml'ansk 126-127 KL 3
Ciml'anskoje vodochranilišče 126-127 L 2-3
Cimmarron River 64-65 F 4
Cimone, Monte — 122-123 D 3
Cîmpina 122-123 LM 3
Cîmpulung 122-123 L 3
Cîmpulung Moldovenesc 122-123 LM 2
Cinandali 126-127 M 6
Çınar = Akpınar 136-137 J 4
Cinaruco, Río — 94-95 G 4
Cinca 120-121 H 8
Cincinnati, OH 64-65 K 4
Cinco Chañares 108-109 G 3
Cinco de Maio, Cachoeira — 98-99 L 11
Cinco Saltos 106-107 CD 7
Cinderella 170 V c 2
Cinderella Dam 170 V c 2
Cinder River 58-59 de 1
Çine 136-137 BC 4
Cinecittà, Roma- 113 II bc 2
Cinema 60 FG 3
Cingaly 132-133 MN 5
Cinnabar Mountain 66-67 E 4
Cinta, Serra da — 92-93 K 6
Cintalapa de Figueroa 86-87 NO 9
Cinto, Mont — 122-123 C 4
Cintra 106-107 F 4
Cintra = Sintra [BR] 92-93 G 6
Ciotat, la — 120-121 K 7
Čiovo 122-123 G 4
Cipete, Jakarta- 154 IV a 2
Cipikan 132-133 V 7
Ci Pinang 154 IV b 2
Cipó 92-93 M 7
Cipó, Rio — 102-103 L 3
Cipó, Serra do — 102-103 L 3
Cipolletti 106-107 D 7
Ciputat 154 IV a 2
Čir 126-127 L 2
Čiragidzor 126-127 N 6
Circel Campus = University of Illinois 83 II ab 1
Circeo, Monte — 122-123 E 5
Čirčik 132-133 M 9
Circle, AK 56-57 H 4
Circle, MT 68-69 D 2
Circle Cliffs 74-75 H 4
Circle Hot Springs, AK 58-59 PQ 4
Circleville, OH 72-73 E 5
Circleville, UT 74-75 G 3
Circuata 104-105 C 5
Cirebon 148-149 E 8
Cirenaica = Barqah 164-165 J 2
Cirene = Shaḥḥāt 164-165 J 2
Cirí, Río — 64-65 a 3
Cirò Marina 122-123 G 6
Čirpan 122-123 L 4
Cirque, Cerro — 104-105 B 5
Cisa, Passo della — 122-123 CD 3
Cisco, TX 76-77 E 6
Cisco, UT 74-75 J 3
Cisne, IL 70-71 F 6
Cisne, El — 106-107 G 3
Cisne, Ilhas del — = Swan Islands 64-65 K 8
Cisne, Laguna del — 106-107 FG 2
Cisneros 92-93 DE 3
Cisnes, Laguna de los — 108-109 D 6
Cisnes, Los — 106-107 F 4
Cisnes, Río — 108-109 D 5
Čist'akovo = Thorez 126-127 J 2-3
Cisterna di Latina 122-123 E 5
Cisternino 122-123 G 5
Čistopol' 132-133 HJ 6
Čita 132-133 V 7
Cita, La — 91 III c 1
Čita-Černovskije Kopi 132-133 V 7
Citadelle, La — 88-89 K 5
Citadel of Cairo 170 II b 1
Čitajevo 124-125 R 3
Ci Tanduy 152-153 H 9
Citaré, Rio — 98-99 L 4
Ci Tarum 152-153 G 9
Citeli-Ckaro 126-127 MN 6
Cité Militaire 170 I b 2
Citlaltépetl 64-65 G 8
Citra, FL 80-81 bc 2
Citronelle, AL 78-79 E 5
Citrusdal 172 CD 8
Citrus Height, CA 74-75 C 3
Citrus Heights, CA 64-65 B 4
Cittanova 122-123 FG 6
Città Universitaria 113 II b 2
City County Building 84 II b 2
City Gardens, Houston-, TX 85 III b 1
City Hall [CDN] 84 II b 3
City Hall [USA] 84 III bc 2
City Island 82 III d 1
City of Commerce, CA 83 III d 1-2
City Park 85 I b 1-2
Ciucaş 122-123 LM 3
Ciuciulco, Pirámide de — 91 I b 3
Ciudad Altamirano 86-87 K 8
Ciudad Bolívar 92-93 G 3
Ciudad Bolivia 92-93 E 3
Ciudad Camargo 76-77 E 9
Ciudad Camargo = Camargo 64-65 E 6
Ciudad Cancún 86-87 R 7
Ciudad del Carmen 64-65 H 8
Ciudad Delicias = Delicias 64-65 E 6
Ciudad del Maíz 86-87 L 6
Ciudad de los Deportes 91 I bc 2
Ciudad de México-Benito Juárez 91 I bc 2
Ciudad de México-Cuauhtémoc 91 I c 2
Ciudad de México-Cuautepec de Madero 91 I c 1
Ciudad de México-Cuautepec el Alto 91 I c 1
Ciudad de México-Gustavo A. Madero 91 I c 2
Ciudad de México-Héroes Chapultepec 91 I c 2
Ciudad de México-Jardín Balbuena 91 I c 2
Ciudad de México-Juan González Romero 91 I c 2
Ciudad de México-Lomas Chapultepec 91 I b 2
Ciudad de México-Miguel Hidalgo 91 I b 2
Ciudad de México-Morelos 91 I c 2
Ciudad de México-Nueva Atzacoalco 91 I c 2
Ciudad de México-Piedad Narvarte 91 I c 2
Ciudad de México-San Felipe de Jesús 91 I c 2
Ciudad de México-San Juan de Aragón 91 I c 2
Ciudad de México-San Petro Zacatenco 91 I c 1
Ciudad de México-Tacuba 91 I b 2
Ciudad de México-Tacubaya 91 I b 2
Ciudad de México-Ticomán 91 I c 1
Ciudad de México-Venustiano Carranza 91 I c 2
Ciudad de Naucalpan de Juárez 91 I b 2
Ciudad Deportiva 91 I c 2
Ciudadela 120-121 J 8-9
Ciudadela, Tres de Febrero- 110 III b 1
Ciudad General Belgrano, La Matanza- 110 III b 2
Ciudad Guayana 92-93 G 3
Ciudad Guayana-Puerto Ordaz 92-93 G 3
Ciudad Guerrero 86-87 G 3
Ciudad Guzmán 64-65 F 8
Ciudad Hidalgo 86-87 K 8
Ciudad Jardín, Coyoacán- 91 I c 3
Ciudad Juárez = Juárez 64-65 E 5
Ciudad Lerdo 64-65 EF 6
Ciudad Linares = Linares 64-65 G 7
Ciudad Lineal, Madrid- 113 III b 2
Ciudad Madero 64-65 G 7
Ciudad Mante 64-65 G 7
Ciudad Mendoza 86-87 M 8
Ciudad Mier 86-87 L 4
Ciudad Netzahualcóyotl 86-87 L 8
Ciudad Netzahualcoyotl-Juan Escutia 91 I C 2
Ciudad Obregón 64-65 DE 6
Ciudad Ojeda 92-93 E 2-3
Ciudad Pemex 86-87 O 9-P 8
Ciudad Piar 92-93 G 3
Ciudad Real 120-121 EF 9
Ciudad Río Bravo 86-87 LM 5
Ciudad Río Grande 86-87 J 6
Ciudad-Rodrigo 120-121 DE 8
Ciudad Satélite 91 I b 1
Ciudad Serdán 86-87 LM 8
Ciudad Trujillo = Santo Domingo 64-65 MN 8
Ciudad Universitaria [E] 113 III a 2
Ciudad Universitaria [MEX] 91 I bc 3
Ciudad Universitaria [YV] 91 II b 2
Ciudad Universitaria, Bogotá- 91 III bc 3
Ciudad Valles 64-65 G 7
Ciudad Victoria 64-65 G 7
Civa burnu 136-137 G 2
Civil'sk 124-125 Q 6
Cìvita Castellana 122-123 E 4
Civitanova Marche 122-123 EF 4
Civitavècchia 122-123 D 4
Çivril 136-137 C 3
Cixi 146-147 H 6
Ci Xian 146-147 E 3
Čiža 132-133 G 4
Čiža II 126-127 OP 1
Cizre 134-135 E 3

Čkalov = Orenburg 132-133 JK 7
Čkalovsk 124-125 O 5

Clacton on Sea 119 G 6
Clain 120-121 H 5
Clair 61 FG 4
Claire, Lake — 56-57 O 6
Clairefontaine = Al-Awaynāt 166-167 KL 2
Clairemont, TX 76-77 D 6
Clairton, PA 72-73 FG 4
Clamart 129 I bc 2
Clamecy 120-121 J 5
Clan Alpine Mountains 74-75 DE 3
Clanton, AL 78-79 F 4
Clanwilliam 172 C 8
Clanwilliamdam 174-175 C 7
Clapham, NM 76-77 C 4
Clara [BR] 106-107 K 2
Clara [RA] 106-107 H 3
Clara City, MN 70-71 C 3
Clara Island = Kalāra Kyūn 150-151 AB 7
Clara River 158-159 H 3
Claraz 106-107 H 6
Clare, MI 70-71 H 4
Clare [AUS] 158-159 G 6
Claremont, NH 72-73 KL 3
Claremont, SD 68-69 GH 3
Claremore, OK 76-77 G 4
Claremorris 119 B 5
Clarence, Cape — 56-57 S 3
Clarence, Isla — 111 B 8
Clarence Island 53 C 31
Clarence River 161 E 6
Clarence Strait [AUS] 158-159 F 2
Clarence Strait [USA] 58-59 w 8-x 9
Clarendon, AR 78-79 D 3
Clarendon, TX 76-77 D 5
Clarendon, Arlington-, VA 82 II a 2
Clarendon Hills, Boston-, MA 84 I b 3
Clarenville 63 J 3
Claresholm 60 KL 4
Clarinda, IA 70-71 C 5
Clarines 94-95 J 3
Clarion, IA 70-71 CD 4
Clarion, PA 72-73 G 4
Clarión, Isla — 86-87 C 8
Clarión Fracture Zone 156-157 KL 4
Clark, CO 68-69 C 5
Clark, SD 68-69 H 3
Clark, Lake — 58-59 K 6
Clarkdale, AZ 74-75 G 5
Clarke 106-107 G 4
Clarkebury 174-175 H 6
Clarke City 56-57 X 7
Clarke Island 158-159 J 8
Clarke River 158-159 HJ 3
Clarkfield, MN 70-71 BC 3
Clark Fork, ID 66-67 E 1
Clark Fork River 64-65 CD 2
Clark Hill Lake 80-81 E 4
Clarkia, ID 66-67 EF 2
Clark Mountain 74-75 F 5
Clark Point 72-73 EF 2
Clarks, NE 68-69 GH 5
Clarksboro, NJ 84 III b 3
Clarksburg, WV 64-65 K 4
Clarksdale, MS 64-65 HJ 5
Clarks Fork 68-69 B 3
Clarks Fork Yellowstone River 68-69 B 3
Clark's Harbour 63 CD 6
Clarkson 174-175 F 8
Clarks Point, AK 58-59 HJ 7
Clarkston, WA 66-67 E 2
Clarksville, AR 78-79 C 3
Clarksville, IA 70-71 D 4
Clarksville, TN 64-65 J 4
Clarksville, TX 76-77 G 6
Clarksville, VA 80-81 G 2
Claromecó 106-107 GH 7
Claromecó, Arroyo — 106-107 G 7
Claude, TX 76-77 D 5
Cláudio 102-103 K 4
Claudio Gay, Cordillera — 104-105 B 9-10
Claunch, NM 76-77 AB 5
Clawson, MI 84 II b 1
Claxton, GA 80-81 EF 4
Clay, KY 70-71 G 7
Clay, WV 72-73 F 5
Clay Belt 56-57 T-V 7
Clay Center, KS 68-69 H 6
Clay Center, NE 68-69 GH 5
Claydon 68-69 B 1
Clayes-sous-Bois, les — 129 I a 2
Claygate 129 II a 2
Claymont, DE 72-73 J 5
Claypool, AZ 74-75 H 6
Clayton, AL 78-79 G 5
Clayton, GA 80-81 E 3
Clayton, ID 66-67 F 3
Clayton, IL 70-71 E 5
Clayton, MO 70-71 E 6
Clayton, NC 80-81 G 3
Clayton, NM 76-77 C 4
Clayton, NY 72-73 HJ 2
Clayton, OK 76-77 G 5
Clearbrook, MN 70-71 C 2
Clear Creek 58-59 O 4
Clearcreek, UT 74-75 H 3
Cleare, Cape — 58-59 NO 7
Clearfield, PA 72-73 G 4
Clearfield, UT 66-67 GH 5
Clear Fork Brazos River 76-77 E 6
Clear Hills 56-57 N 6
Clearing, IL 83 II a 2
Clear Lake 74-75 B 3
Clear Lake, IA 70-71 D 4
Clear Lake, MN 70-71 G 3
Clear Lake, SD 68-69 H 3
Clear Lake, WI 70-71 DE 3
Clear Lake Reservoir 66-67 C 5
Clearmont, WY 68-69 C 3
Clear Prairie 60 H 1
Clearwater 60 G 4
Clearwater, FL 64-65 C 6
Clear Water Bay 155 I b 2
Clearwater Lake [CDN] 56-57 VW 6
Clearwater Lake [USA] 78-79 D 2
Clearwater Mountains 66-67 F 2-3
Clearwater River [CDN ◁ Athabasca River] 61 D 2
Clearwater River [CDN ◁ North Saskatchewan River] 60 K 3-4
Clearwater River [USA] 66-67 E 2
Clearwater River, North Fork — 66-67 F 2
Clearwater River, South Fork — 66-67 F 3
Cleburne, TX 64-65 G 3
Cle Elum, WA 66-67 C 2
Clemente, Isla — 108-109 B 5
Clemente Onelli 108-109 D 3
Clementon, NJ 84 III cd 3
Clemesi, Pampa de la — 96-97 F 10
Clen Cove, NY 82 III e 1
Clendenin, WV 72-73 F 5
Clermont, FL 80-81 bc 2
Clermont [AUS] 158-159 J 4
Clermont [CDN] 63 A 4
Clermont-Ferrand 120-121 J 6
Cleve 160 C 4
Cleveland, MS 78-79 D 4
Cleveland, MT 68-69 B 1
Cleveland, OH 64-65 K 3
Cleveland, OK 76-77 F 4
Cleveland, TN 64-65 K 4
Cleveland, TX 76-77 G 7
Cleveland, WI 70-71 G 4
Cleveland, Mount — 64-65 D 2
Cleveland Heights, OH 72-73 F 4
Clevelândia 102-103 F 7
Clevelândia do Norte 98-99 N 3
Cleveland Park 85 III b 1
Cleveland Park, Washington-, DC 82 II a 1
Clewiston, FL 80-81 c 3
Clichy 129 I c 2
Clifden 119 A 5
Cliff, NM 74-75 J 6
Cliff Lake, MT 66-67 H 3
Cliffs, ID 66-67 E 4
Clifton 158-159 K 5
Clifton, AZ 74-75 J 6
Clifton, KS 68-69 H 6
Clifton, NJ 72-73 J 4
Clifton, TX 76-77 F 7
Clifton, WY 68-69 D 4
Clifton Forge, VA 80-81 G 2
Clifton Heights, PA 84 III b 2
Clifton Hills 158-159 G 5
Climax 68-69 B 1
Climax, CO 68-69 C 6
Climax, GA 78-79 G 5
Climax, MN 68-69 H 2
Clinchco, VA 80-81 E 2
Clinch Mountain 80-81 E 2
Clinch Mountains 80-81 E 2
Clinch River 80-81 E 2
Cline 86-87 KL 3
Cline, TX 76-77 D 8
Clint, TX 76-77 A 7
Clinton, AR 78-79 C 3
Clinton, IA 64-65 H 3
Clinton, IL 70-71 F 5
Clinton, IN 70-71 G 6
Clinton, KY 78-79 E 2
Clinton, LA 78-79 D 5
Clinton, MI 70-71 H 4
Clinton, MO 70-71 D 6
Clinton, MS 78-79 D 4
Clinton, MT 66-67 G 2
Clinton, NC 80-81 G 3
Clinton, OK 76-77 E 5
Clinton, SC 80-81 F 3
Clinton, TN 78-79 GH 2
Clinton, WI 70-71 F 4
Clinton [CDN, British Columbia] 60 G 4
Clinton [CDN, Ontario] 72-73 F 3
Clinton, Cape — 158-159 K 4
Clinton Creek 58-59 R 4
Clinton Park 85 III b 2
Clintonville, WI 70-71 F 3
Clio, AL 78-79 G 5
Clio, MI 70-71 J 4
Clipperton, Île — 64-65 E 9
Clipperton Fracture Zone 156-157 LM 4
Clisham 119 C 3
Cliza 104-105 D 5
Cloates, Point — 158-159 B 4
Clocolan 174-175 G 5
Clodomira 106-107 EF 1
Clonakilty 119 B 6
Cloncurry 158-159 H 4
Cloncurry River 158-159 H 3
Clonmel 119 BC 5
Clonmelt Creek 84 III b 2-3
Clo-oose 66-67 A 1
Cloppenburg 118 CD 2
Cloquet, MN 70-71 D 2
Cloquet River 70-71 DE 2
Clorinda 104-105 GH 9
Cloucester, VA 80-81 H 2
Cloudcroft, NM 76-77 B 6
Cloud Peak 64-65 E 3
Cloudy Mount 58-59 J 5
Clover, VA 80-81 G 2
Cloverdale, CA 74-75 B 3
Cloverdale, NM 74-75 J 7
Cloverleaf, TX 85 III c 1
Cloverport, KY 70-71 G 7
Clovis, CA 74-75 D 4
Clovis, NM 64-65 F 5
Clucellas 106-107 G 3
Cluj-Napoca 122-123 KL 2
Cluny 120-121 K 5
Clutha River 158-159 N 9
Clyde 56-57 X 3
Clyde, KS 68-69 H 6
Clyde, ND 68-69 G 1
Clyde, OH 72-73 E 4
Clyde, TX 76-77 E 6
Clyde, Firth of — 119 D 4
Clyde Park, MT 66-67 H 3
Clydesdale 174-175 GH 4
Clyo, GA 80-81 F 4

C. M. Naón 106-107 G 5

Cna [SU ◁ Mokša] 124-125 O 6
Cna [SU ◁ Prip'at'] 124-125 F 7
Cnori 126-127 MN 6
Cnossos = Knōssós 122-123 L 8

Coa 120-121 D 8
Coachella, CA 74-75 E 6
Coachella Canal 74-75 EF 6
Coahoma, TX 76-77 D 6
Coahuayutla de Guerrero 86-87 K 8
Coahuila 64-65 F 6
Coalbrook 174-175 GH 4
Coalcomán, Sierra de — 86-87 J 8
Coal Creek 66-67 F 1
Coal Creek, AK 58-59 PQ 4
Coaldale 66-67 G 1
Coaldale, NV 74-75 E 3
Coalgate, OK 76-77 F 5
Coal Harbour 60 CD 4
Coal Hill Park 155 II b 2
Coalinga, CA 74-75 C 4
Coallahuala 96-97 F 9
Coalmont, CO 68-69 C 5
Coalville, UT 66-67 H 5
Coamo 88-89 N 5-6
Coan, Cerro — 96-97 B 5
Coaraci 100-101 E 8
Coari 92-93 G 5
Coari, Lago do — 98-99 G 6-7
Coari, Rio — 92-93 G 5-6
Coast 172 GH 2
Coastal Cordillera = Cordillera de la Costa 111 B 4-5
Coast Mountains 56-57 K 6-M 7
Coast of Labrador 56-57 YZ 6-7
Coast Range 64-65 B 2-C 5
Coatá 98-99 C 8
Coatá, Cachoeira do — 92-93 G 6
Coatepec 64-65 G 8
Coatesville, PA 72-73 HJ 4
Coatiçaba 100-101 A 7-8
Coaticook 72-73 KL 2
Coats Island 56-57 U 5
Coats Land 53 B 33-34
Coatzacoalcos 64-65 H 8
Coayllo 96-97 C 8
Cobalt 72-73 G 1
Cobán 64-65 H 8
Coban çeşme 154 I a 2
Cobar 158-159 J 6
Cobargo 160 JK 6
Cobble Hill 66-67 AB 1
Cobbo = Kobo 164-165 MN 6
Cobbs Creek 84 III b 1-2
Cobbs Creek Park 84 III b 2
Cobe = Kōbe 142-143 PQ 5
Cobequid Mountains 63 DE 5
Cobh 119 B 6
Cobham River 62 B 1
Cobija 92-93 F 7
Cobija, Punta — 104-105 A 8
Coblence = Koblenz 118 C 3
Cobleskill, NY 72-73 J 3
Cobo 106-107 J 6
Coboconk 72-73 G 2
Cobo Hall 84 II b 3
Cobourg 72-73 GH 3
Cobourg Peninsula 158-159 F 2
Cobras, Ilha das — 110 I bc 2
Cobre, NV 66-67 F 5
Cobre, Cerro — 106-107 B 2
Cobre, Rio do — 102-103 FG 6
Cobre, Sierra del — 104-105 C 8-9
Cobres 104-105 C 8
Cobres, San Antonio de los — 111 C 2
Cobue 171 C 6
Coburg 118 E 3
Coburg, OR 66-67 B 3
Coburg, Melbourne- 161 II b 1
Coburg Island 56-57 V 2
Coca 120-121 E 8
Coca, Río — 96-97 C 2
Cocachacra 96-97 F 10
Cocal [BR, Bahia] 100-101 B 7
Cocal [BR, Piauí] 100-101 D 2
Cocalcomán de Matamoros 86-87 J 8
Cocalzinho, Serra do — 102-103 H 1
Cocanada = Kākināda 134-135 N 7
Cocha, La — 104-105 D 10
Cochabamba [BOL, administrative unit] 104-105 CD 5
Cochabamba [BOL, place] 92-93 F 8
Cochabamba, Cordillera de — 104-105 CD 5
Cochamal 96-97 C 5
Cochamó 108-109 CD 3
Cocharcas, Río — 104-105 D 3-4
Coche, Caracas- 91 II b 2
Coche, Isla — 94-95 K 2
Cochem 118 C 3
Cochequingán 106-107 DE 5
Cochi = Kōchi 142-143 P 5
Cochicó, Loma de — 106-107 D 6
Cochim = Cochin 134-135 M 9
Cochin 134-135 M 9
Cochinchina = Nam Bộ 148-149 DE 5
Cochin-Ernākulam 140 BC 5-6
Cochinoca, Sierra de — 104-105 D 8
Cochinos, Bahía de — 88-89 F 3-4
Cochise, AZ 74-75 J 6
Cochran, GA 80-81 E 4
Cochrane [CDN, Alberta] 60 K 4
Cochrane [CDN, Ontario] 56-57 U 8
Cochrane [RA] 106-107 FG 7
Cochrane, Lago — 108-109 C 6
Cochrane, Morro de — 110 I b 2
Cochrane River 56-57 Q 6
Cockburn, Canal — 111 B 8
Cockburn Island 62 K 4
Cockburn Land 56-57 UV 3
Cockeysville, MD 72-73 H 5
Coclé 88-89 F 10
Coco, Cayo — 88-89 G 3
Coco, El — 64-65 b 3
Coco, Isla del — 92-93 B 3
Coco, Punta — 94-95 C 6
Coco, Río — 64-65 K 9
Côco, Rio do — 98-99 O 9
Cocoa, FL 80-81 c 2
Coco Channel 148-149 B 4
Cocodrie, LA 78-79 D 6
Cocolalla, ID 66-67 E 1
Coconho, Ponta do — 100-101 G 3
Coconino Plateau 74-75 G 4-5
Cocos [AUS] 50-51 O 6
Côcos [BR, Bahia] 100-101 B 7
Côcos [BR, Minas Gerais] 100-101 B 8
Cocos = Isla del Coco 92-93 B 3
Cocos, Los — 94-95 KL 4
Côcos, Vereda de — 100-101 B 7
Coco Solo 64-65 b 2
Cocos Rise 156-157 N 4
Cocotá, Rio de Janeiro- 110 I b 1
Cocula 86-87 HJ 7
Cocuy, El — 92-93 E 3
Cocuy, Piedra de — 94-95 H 7
Cod, Cape — 64-65 N 3
Codajás 92-93 G 5
Codegua 106-107 B 4-5
Codera, Cabo — 92-93 F 2
Coderre 61 E 5
Codfish Island 161 B 8
Codihue 111 BC 5
Codó 92-93 L 5
Codorniz, Paso — 108-109 C 6
Codózinho 100-101 BC 3
Codózinho, Rio — 100-101 B 3
Codpa 104-105 B 6
Codroy 63 G 4
Cody, NE 68-69 F 4
Cody, WY 68-69 B 3
Coehue-Có 106-107 C 6
Coelemu 106-107 A 6
Coelho Neto 100-101 C 3
Coeli 172 C 4
Coello 94-95 D 5
Coen 158-159 H 2
Coengua, Río — 96-97 E 7
Coentunnel 128 I a 1
Coerney 174-175 F 7
Coeroeni 98-99 K 3
Coesfeld 118 C 3
Coeur d'Alene, ID 64-65 C 2
Coeur d'Alene Indian Reservation 66-67 E 2
Coeur d'Alene Lake 66-67 E 2
Coffee Bay 174-175 H 6
Coffee Creek 58-59 S 5
Coffeeville, MS 78-79 DE 4
Coffeyville, KS 64-65 G 4
Coffin Bay 158-159 FG 6
Coffin Bay Peninsula 158-159 FG 6
Coffs Harbour 158-159 K 6
Cofimvaba 174-175 G 7
Cofrentes 120-121 G 9
Cofu = Kōfu 142-143 Q 4

Cofuini, Río — 98-99 K 4
Cogealac 122-123 N 3
Cognac 120-121 G 6
Čogujev 126-127 H 2
Çoğun 136-137 F 3
Coguno 174-175 L 3
Cohagen, MT 68-69 C 2
Cohoes, NY 72-73 K 3
Cohuna 158-159 HJ 7
Cohutta Mountian 78-79 G 3
Coi, Sông = Sông Nhi Ha 148-149 D 2
Coiba, Isla — 64-65 K 10
Coicoi, Punta — 106-107 A 6
Coig, Río — 108-109 D 8
Coihaique 111 B 7
Coihaique Alto, Paso — 108-109 D 5
Coihueco [RA] 106-107 BC 7
Coihueco [RCH] 106-107 AB 6
Coimbatore 134-135 M 8
Coimbra [BR] 102-103 L 4
Coimbra [P] 120-121 C 8
Coín 120-121 E 10
Coin, IA 70-71 C 5
Coipasa, Cerro — 104-105 B 6
Coipasa, Lago de — 104-105 C 6
Coipasa, Salar de — 92-93 F 8
Coire = Chur 118 D 5
Coité, Rio — 100-101 E 6
Čojbalsan 142-143 L 2
Čojbalsangijn Ajmag = Dornod ◁ 142-143 LM 2
Cojedes [YV, administrative unit] 94-95 G 3
Cojedes [YV, place] 94-95 G 3
Cojedes, Río — 94-95 G 3
Cojimies 92-93 C 4
Cojo, El — [YV, place] 91 II b 1
Cojo, El — [YV, river] 91 II b 1
Cojoro 94-95 F 2
Cojudo Blanco, Cerro — 111 BC 7
Cojutepeque 88-89 B 8
Çokak 136-137 G 4
Cokato, MN 70-71 C 3
Coker 170 III a 2
Cokeville, WY 66-67 H 4
Čokurdach 132-133 cd 3
Colac 158-159 H 7
Colachel = Kolachel 140 C 6
Colangüil, Cordillera de — 106-107 C 2-3
Colap dere 136-137 H 4
Colapur = Kōlhāpur 134-135 L 7
Cólar = Kōlār Gold Fields 134-135 M 8
Colares 120-121 C 9
Colatina 100-101 D 10
Colbeck, Cape — 53 B 20-21
Colbert, OK 76-77 F 6
Colbert, WA 66-67 E 2
Colbert = 'Ayn Wilmān 166-167 J 2
Colbinabbin 160 G 6
Colbún 106-107 B 5
Colby, KS 68-69 F 6
Colca, Río — 92-93 E 8
Colcamar 96-97 BC 5
Colchester, VT 72-73 K 2
Colchester [GB] 119 G 6
Colchester [ZA] 174-175 FG 7
Cold Bay 58-59 b 2
Cold Bay, AK 58-59 b 2
Col des Nuages = Đeo Hai Van 150-151 G 4
Cold Lake [CDN, lake] 61 D 3
Cold Lake [CDN, place] 61 C 3
Cold Spring, MN 70-71 C 3
Coldspring, TX 76-77 G 7
Coldstream [ZA] 174-175 E 7-8
Col du Mont Cenis 120-121 L 6
Coldwater 72-73 G 2
Coldwater, KS 76-77 E 4
Coldwater, MI 70-71 H 5
Coldwater, OH 70-71 H 5
Coldwell 70-71 G 1
Colebrook, NH 72-73 L 2
Cole Camp, MO 70-71 D 6
Cole Creek Manor, Houston-, TX 85 III ab 1
Coleen Mount 58-59 Q 3
Coleen River 58-59 Q 2
Colegiales, Buenos Aires- 110 III b 1
Colégio = Porto Real do Colégio 92-93 M 6-7
Colegio Militar 91 I b 2
Colelache 108-109 E 4
Coleman 66-67 F 1
Coleman, MI 70-71 H 4
Coleman, TX 76-77 E 7
Coleman River 158-159 H 2-3
Çölemerik 136-137 K 4
Colenso 174-175 H 5
Coleraine [AUS] 160 EF 6
Coleraine [GB] 119 C 4
Coleridge, Lake — 161 D 6
Coleroon 140 D 5
Coles, Punta de — 92-93 E 8
Colesburg 172 DE 8
Colesville, CA 74-75 D 3
Colfax, CA 74-75 C 3
Colfax, IA 70-71 D 5
Colfax, LA 78-79 C 5
Colfax, WA 66-67 E 2
Colfax, WI 70-71 E 3
Colgong 138-139 L 5
Colhué Huapí, Lago — 111 C 7
Colico, Lago — 106-107 AB 7
Coligny 174-175 G 4
Colima 64-65 F 8
Colima, Nevado de — 64-65 EF 8
Colina [BR] 102-103 H 4
Colina [RCH] 106-107 B 4
Colina, La — 106-107 G 6
Colinas 92-93 L 6
Colinet 63 K 4
Colipilli, Cerro — 106-107 B 6
Coll 119 C 3
Collaguasi 111 C 2
Collarenebri 160 HJ 2
Colle di Tenda 122-123 B 3
College, AK 56-57 G 4-5
College Park, GA 80-81 DE 4
College Park Cemetery 85 II b 3
College Point, New York-, NY 82 III cd 2
College Station, TX 76-77 F 7
Colles 86-87 L 6
Colleymount 60 D 2
Collie 158-159 C 6
Collier Airport 85 III b 1
Collier Bay 158-159 D 3
Collierville, TN 78-79 E 3
Collines des Banzyville 172 D 1
Collingdale, PA 84 III b 2
Collingswood, NJ 84 III c 2
Collingwood [CDN] 72-73 FG 2
Collingwood [NZ] 161 DE 5
Collingwood, Melbourne- 161 II bc 1
Collins 62 E 2
Collins, IA 70-71 D 5
Collins, MS 78-79 E 5
Collins, MT 66-67 H 2
Collins, Mount — 62 L 3
Collins Field 84 III d 2
Collinson, Mount — 155 I b 2
Collinson Peninsula 56-57 Q 3-4
Collinston, LA 78-79 D 4
Collinsville 158-159 J 4
Collinsville, AL 78-79 FG 3
Collinsville, IL 70-71 F 6
Collinsville, OK 76-77 G 4
Collipulli 106-107 A 6
Collo = Al-Qull 166-167 K 1
Collón Curá 108-109 D 3
Collón Curá, Río — 108-109 D 3
Collpa 104-105 D 6
Colma, CA 83 I b 2
Colmar 120-121 L 4
Colmar Manor, MD 82 II b 1
Colmena 106-107 G 2
Colmor, NM 76-77 B 4
Colnett, Cabo — 86-87 B 2
Cologne = Köln 118 C 3
Cololo, Nevado — 92-93 F 7
Colomb-Béchar = Bashshār 164-165 D 2
Colombes 129 I bc 2
Colômbia [BR] 92-93 K 9
Colombia [CO] 92-93 D-F 4
Colombia [MEX] 76-77 DE 9
Colombine, Kaap — 174-175 B 7
Colombo 102-103 H 6
Colombo = Kolamba 134-135 M 9
Colome, SD 68-69 G 4
Colón [C] 64-65 K 7
Colón [PA, administrative unit] 64-65 ab 2
Colón [PA, place] 64-65 b 2
Colón [RA, Buenos Aires] 106-107 G 4
Colón [RA, Entre Ríos] 106-107 H 4
Colón [YV] 94-95 H 6
Colón, Archipiélago de — 92-93 AB 5
Colona 158-159 F 6
Colona, CO 68-69 C 6
Colonche 96-97 A 2-3
Colonche, Cordillera de — 96-97 A 2-3
Colonia 106-107 HJ 5
Colonia, La — 108-109 C 6
Colonia Alvear 106-107 D 5
Colonia Baranda 104-105 G 10
Colonia Barón 106-107 F 6
Colonia Benjamín Aceval = Benjamín Aceval 102-103 D 6
Colonia Bremen 106-107 F 4
Colonia Cabildo = Cabildo 106-107 FG 7
Colonia Carlos Pellegrini 106-107 J 2
Colonia Caroya 106-107 EF 3
Colonia 10 de Julio 106-107 FG 3
Colonia del Sacramento 111 E 4
Colonia 25 de Mayo 111 C 5
Colonia Diez de Julio 106-107 FG 3
Colonia Dora 106-107 F 2
Colonia Elía 106-107 H 4
Colonia Elisa 104-105 G 10
Colonia Fernando de Trejo y Sanabria 102-103 E 6
Colonia Fram 102-103 DE 7
Colonia Garabí 106-107 JK 2
Colonia Isabel Victoria 106-107 H 2
Colonia Josefa 106-107 E 7
Colonia La Pastoril 106-107 DE 6
Colonia Las Heras = Las Heras 111 C 7
Colonia La Tordilla 106-107 F 3
Colonial Beach, VA 72-73 H 5
Colonial Heights, VA 80-81 H 2
Colonia Libertad = Libertad 106-107 HJ 3
Colonial Manor, NJ 84 III c 2
Colonial Village, PA 84 III a 1
Colonia Madariaga 106-107 J 2
Colonia Mennonita 102-103 C 5
Colonia Montefiore 106-107 FG 2
Colonia Osório 100-101 AB 2
Colonia Perín 104-105 FG 9
Colonia Prosperidad 106-107 F 3
Colonia Risso 102-103 D 5
Colonia Santa Virginia 106-107 DE 4-5
Colonia Seré 106-107 F 5
Colonias Unidas 104-105 G 10
Colonia Totorillas 104-105 E 10
Colonia Yacubó 102-103 DE 7
Colonia Yeruá = Yeruá 106-107 H 3
Colonne, Capo delle — 122-123 G 6
Colonsay 119 C 3
Colorada, La — 86-87 EF 3
Coloradito 94-95 K 3
Colorado [CR] 88-89 E 9
Colorado [USA] 64-65 EF 4
Colorado, El — [RA, Chaco] 104-105 G 10
Colorado, El — [RA, Santiago del Estero] 106-107 F 1
Colorado, Río — [RA, La Rioja] 106-107 D 2
Colorado, Río — [RA, Neuquén Río Negro] 111 D 5
Colorado City, TX 76-77 D 6
Colorado Desert 74-75 EF 6
Colorado National Monument 74-75 J 3
Colorado Plateau 64-65 DE 4
Colorado River [USA ◁ Gulf of California] 64-65 E 4
Colorado River [USA ◁ Gulf of Mexico] 64-65 G 5
Colorado River Aqueduct 74-75 F 5
Colorado River Indian Reservation 74-75 F 6
Colorados, Cerros — [RA] 111 C 6
Colorados, Cerros — [RCH] 111 C 3
Colorados, Los — 106-107 HJ D 2
Colorado Springs, CO 64-65 F 4
Colo River 160 K 4
Colosseo 113 II b 2
Colotlán 86-87 J 6-7
Colpes 106-107 D 2
Colquechaca 104-105 CD 6
Colquiri 104-105 C 5
Colquitt, GA 78-79 G 5
Colstrip, MT 68-69 C 3
Coltauco 106-107 B 5
Colton, SD 68-69 H 4
Colton, UT 74-75 H 3
Colt Stadium 85 III b 2
Columbia, KY 70-71 H 7
Columbia, LA 78-79 CD 4
Columbia, MD 72-73 H 5
Columbia, MO 64-65 H 4
Columbia, MS 78-79 E 5
Columbia, NC 80-81 H 3
Columbia, PA 72-73 H 4
Columbia, SC 64-65 K 5
Columbia, SD 68-69 GH 3
Columbia, TN 78-79 F 3
Columbia, Cape — 52 A 25-26
Columbia, District of — 72-73 H 5
Columbia, Mount — 56-57 N 7
Columbia Basin 66-67 D 2
Columbia City, IN 70-71 H 5
Columbia Falls, MT 66-67 FG 1
Columbia Glacier 58-59 O 6
Columbia Heights, Washington-, DC 82 II a 1
Columbiana, AL 78-79 F 4
Columbia Plateau 64-65 C 2-3
Columbia River 64-65 BC 2
Columbia River, WA 66-67 C 2
Columbine, WY 68-69 C 4
Columbretes, Islas — 120-121 H 9
Columbus, GA 64-65 K 5
Columbus, IN 70-71 H 6
Columbus, KS 76-77 G 4
Columbus, MS 64-65 J 5
Columbus, MT 68-69 B 3
Columbus, ND 68-69 E 1
Columbus, NE 64-65 G 3
Columbus, NM 76-77 A 7
Columbus, OH 64-65 K 3-4
Columbus, TX 76-77 F 8
Columbus, WI 70-71 F 4
Columbus Junction, IA 70-71 E 5
Columbus Park 83 II a 1
Čolun-Chamur 126-127 M 4
Colupo, Cerro — 104-105 AB 8
Colusa, CA 74-75 BC 3
Colville, WA 66-67 E 1
Colville Bar, AK 58-59 K 2
Colville Channel 161 F 3
Colville Indian Reservation 66-67 D 1
Colville River 56-57 EF 4
Colwick, NJ 84 III c 2
Comácchio 122-123 E 3
Comácchio, Valli di — 122-123 E 3
Comalcalco 86-87 O 8
Comales, Los — 76-77 E 9
Comallo 108-109 DE 3
Comallo, Arroyo — 108-109 D 3
Comana 122-123 LM 3
Comanche, OK 76-77 F 5
Comanche, TX 76-77 E 7
Comandante Cordero 106-107 CD 7
Comandante Fontana 104-105 G 9
Comandante Leal 106-107 DE 3
Comandante Luis Piedra Buena [RA ← Río Gallegos] 108-109 DE 8
Comandante Luis Piedra Buena [RA ↑ Río Gallegos] 108-109 E 7
Comandante N. Otamendi 106-107 J 7
Comandante Salas 106-107 CD 4
Comarapa 104-105 D 5
Comau, Fiordo — 108-109 C 4
Comayagua 64-65 J 9
Combapata 96-97 F 9
Combarbalá 106-107 B 3
Comber 72-73 E 3
Combermere Bay = Combermere Pinleiau 141 C 6
Combermere Pinleiau 141 C 6
Combomune 174-175 K 2
Combourg 120-121 G 4
Combs, KY 72-73 E 6
Comeau, Baie — 56-57 X 8
Come By Chance 160 J 3
Comechingones, Sierra de — 106-107 E 4
Comencho, Lac — 62 O 1
Comer, GA 80-81 E 3
Comercinho 102-103 M 2
Cometala 174-175 L 1
Comfort, TX 76-77 E 7-8
Comilla = Komillā 134-135 P 6
Comino, Capo — 122-123 CD 5
Comiso 122-123 F 7
Comitán de Domínguez 64-65 H 8
Commadagga = Kommadagga 174-175 F 7
Commerce, GA 80-81 E 3
Commerce, TX 76-77 FG 6
Commewijne 98-99 L 2
Commissionerssoutpan 174-175 C 6
Committee Bay 56-57 T 4
Commonwealth Range 53 A
Commonwealth Territory 158-159 K 7
Como 122-123 C 3
Como, Lago di — 122-123 C 2-3
Comodoro Rivadavia 111 C 7
Comoé = Komoe 164-165 D 7
Comondú 86-87 DE 4
Comores, Archipel des — 172 HJ 4
Comorin, Cape — 134-135 M 9
Comoro Islands = Archipel des Comores 172 HJ 4
Comoros 172 HJ 4
Compeer 61 CD 5
Compiègne 120-121 J 4
Compostela 86-87 H 7
Comprida, Cachoeira — = Treze Quedas 92-93 H 4
Comprida, Ilha — [BR, Atlantic Ocean] 111 G 2-3
Comprida, Ilha — [BR, Rio de Janeiro] 110 I b 3
Comprida, Ilha — [BR, Rio Paraná] 102-103 G 4
Comprida, Lago — = Lagoa Nova 92-93 J 4
Compton, CA 74-75 DE 6
Comstock, TX 76-77 D 8
Comundú 86-87 DE 4
Comunidad 94-95 H 6
Čona 132-133 V 5
Conakry 164-165 B 7
Conambo 96-97 C 2
Conambo, Río — 96-97 C 2
Cona Niyeu 108-109 F 3
Conata, SD 68-69 E 4
Conca = Cuenca 92-93 D 5
Concarán 106-107 E 4
Concarneau 120-121 EF 5
Conceição [BR, Maranhão] 100-101 C 3
Conceição [BR, Mato Grosso] 92-93 H 6
Conceição [BR, Paraíba] 100-101 E 4
Conceição [BR, Rondônia] 98-99 H 10
Conceição [BR, Roraima] 98-99 H 3
Conceição, Ilha da — 110 I c 2
Conceição, Riacho — 100-101 D 4
Conceição, Rio — 100-101 A 7
Conceição da Barra 92-93 M 8
Conceição da Feira 100-101 E 7
Conceição das Alagoas 102-103 HJ 3
Conceição de Castelo 102-103 M 4
Conceição do Almeida 100-101 E 7
Conceição do Araguaia 92-93 JK 6
Conceição do Canindé 100-101 D 4
Conceição do Castelo 100-101 D 11
Conceição do Cuité 100-101 E 6
Conceição do Rio Verde 102-103 K 4
Concelho = Inhambane 172 G 6
Concepcion, CA 74-75 C 5
Concepción [BOL] 92-93 G 8
Concepción [CO, Putumayo] 92-93 DE 4
Concepcion [CO, Santander] 94-95 E 4
Concepción [EC] 96-97 B 1
Concepción [PE] 96-97 D 7
Concepción [PY, administrative unit] 102-103 D 5
Concepción [PY, place] 111 E 2
Concepción [RA, Corrientes] 106-107 J 2
Concepción [RA, Tucumán] 111 C 3
Concepción [RCH] 111 AB 5
Concepción, Bahía de — 106-107 A 6
Concepción, Bahía de la — 86-87 E 4
Concepción, Canal — 111 AB 8
Concepción, La — 92-93 E 2
Concepción, Laguna — [BOL → Santa Cruz de la Sierra] 104-105 F 5
Concepción, Laguna — [BOL ↑ Santa Cruz de la Sierra] 104-105 E 4
Concepción de Bermejo 104-105 F 10
Concepción de la Sierra 106-107 K 1
Concepción del Oro 64-65 F 7
Concepción del Uruguay 111 E 4
Conception, Point — 64-65 B 5
Conceptionbaai 174-175 A 2
Conception Bay 63 K 4
Conception Bay = Conceptionbaai 174-175 A 2
Concession, LA 85 I c 2
Concha 94-95 F 3
Conchas 102-103 J 5
Conchas, Las — 104-105 G 5
Conchas Dam, NM 76-77 B 5
Conchas Lake 76-77 B 5
Conchi [RCH, Antofagasta] 111 C 2
Conchi [RCH, Lagos] 108-109 C 4
Conchillas 106-107 HJ 5
Concho 76-77 B 9
Concho, AZ 74-75 J 5
Concho River 76-77 DE 7
Conchos, Río — 64-65 EF 6
Concón 106-107 B 4
Concord, CA 74-75 BC 4
Concord, NC 80-81 F 3
Concord, NH 64-65 M 3
Concord, Sydney- 161 I a 2
Concordia, KS 68-69 GH 6
Concordia, MO 70-71 D 6
Concórdia [BR, Amazonas] 98-99 E 7
Concórdia [BR, Santa Catarina] 102-103 FG 7
Concordia [CO] 94-95 CD 4
Concordia [PE] 96-97 D 4
Concordia [RA] 111 E 4
Concordia [ZA] 174-175 BC 5
Côn Cuông 150-151 E 3
Côn Đao 148-149 E 5
Conde 92-93 M 7
Conde, SD 68-69 GH 3
Conde de Araruama 102-103 M 5
Condes, Las — 106-107 B 4
Condé-Smedou = Zīghūt Yūsuf 166-167 K 1
Condobolin 158-159 J 6
Condon, OR 66-67 C 3
Condor, Cordillera del — 96-97 B 3-4
Cóndor, El — 108-109 E 9
Cóndores, Los — 106-107 EF 4
Cóndores, Sierra de los — 106-107 E 4
Condoroma, Nevados de — 96-97 F 9
Condoto 94-95 C 5
Cône, Ilôt — = Kås Moul 150-151 D 7
Conecuh River 78-79 F 5
Coneição do Mato Dentro 102-103 L 3
Conejera, Isla — 120-121 J 9
Conejos 76-77 C 9
Conejos, CO 68-69 C 7
Conejos River 68-69 C 7
Conesa 106-107 G 4
Coney Island 82 III c 3
Conflans-Sainte-Honorine 129 I b 1
Confucius, Temple of — 155 II b 2
Confusion Range 74-75 G 3
Confuso, Río — 102-103 C 6
Conghua 146-147 D 10
Congjiang 146-147 B 9
Congo 172 B 2-C 1
Congo = Zaïre 172 D 1
Congonhas, Aeroporto de — 110 II b 2
Congreso Nacional 110 III b 1
Congress, AZ 74-75 G 5
Congress Heights, Washington-, DC 82 II b 2
Conhello 106-107 E 5-6
Cônia = Konya 134-135 C 3
Conima 96-97 G 9
Coniston [CDN] 72-73 F 1
Conjeeveram = Kānchipuram 134-135 MN 8
Conklin 61 C 3
Conlara 106-107 E 4
Conlara, Río — 106-107 E 4
Conlen, TX 76-77 C 4
Connaught 119 B 4-5
Connaughton, PA 84 III ab 1
Conneaut, OH 72-73 F 3-4
Connecticut 64-65 M 3
Connecticut River 72-73 K 3-4
Connell, WA 66-67 D 2
Connellsville, PA 72-73 G 4
Conner, MT 66-67 FG 3
Conner, Mount — 158-159 F 5
Connersville, IN 70-71 H 6
Connersville, OH 72-73 D 5
Connie Mack Stadium 84 III c 2
Connors 63 B 4
Connors Pass 74-75 F 3
Cononaco 96-97 D 2
Cononaco, Río — 96-97 C 2
Conorochite, Río — 94-95 H 6
Conover, WI 70-71 F 2
Conquest 61 E 5
Conquista [BOL] 104-105 C 2
Conquista [BR] 102-103 J 3
Conquistadores, Los — 106-107 H 3
Conrad, MT 66-67 H 1
Conroe, TX 76-77 G 7
Consata 104-105 B 4
Consata, Río — 104-105 B 4
Conscripto Bernardi 106-107 H 3
Conselheiro Lafaiete 92-93 L 9
Conselheiro Pena 102-103 M 3
Conselho, Ponta do — 100-101 E 7
Conshohocken, PA 84 III ab 1
Consolação, São Paulo- 110 II ab 2
Côn So'n 150-151 F 8
Constable = Konstabel 174-175 CD 7
Constance = Konstanz 118 D 5
Constance, Lake — = Bodensee 118 D 5
Constancia [ROU] 106-107 HJ 4
Constância dos Baetas 92-93 G 6
Constanța 122-123 M 3
Constantina [BR] 106-107 L 1
Constantina = Qusantīnah 164-165 F 1
Constantine, Cape — 56-57 DE 6
Constantinople = İstanbul 134-135 BC 2
Constantinovka = Konstantinovka 126-127 H 2
Constanza 106-107 G 3
Constitución 111 B 5
Constitución, Buenos Aires- 110 III b 1
Constitution Lake 85 II c 2
Consuls, Pointe des — 170 I a 1
Contact, NV 66-67 F 5
Contador, El — 91 I d 1
Contagem 102-103 K 3
Contai 138-139 L 7
Contamana 92-93 DE 6
Contão 94-95 L 6
Contas, Rio de — 92-93 L 7
Contendas do Sincorá 100-101 D 7
Continental, AZ 74-75 H 7
Continental, OH 70-71 H 5
Con Tom = Kon Tom 150-151 F 4
Contoy, Isla — 86-87 R 7
Contratación 92-93 E 3
Contreras, Isla — 111 AB 8
Contria 102-103 K 3
Controller Bay 58-59 P 6
Contulmo 106-107 A 6
Contumazá 96-97 B 5
Contwoyto Lake 56-57 OP 4
Convención 94-95 E 3
Convento, Montañas de — 96-97 B 1-2
Converse, LA 78-79 C 5
Conway, AR 78-79 C 3
Conway, ND 68-69 H 1
Conway, NH 72-73 L 3
Conway, SC 80-81 G 4
Conway, TX 76-77 D 5
Conyers, GA 80-81 DE 4
Coober Pedy 158-159 F 5
Cooch Behār 138-139 M 4
Coogee Bay 161 I b 2
Cook 158-159 F 6
Cook, MN 70-71 D 2
Cook, NE 68-69 H 5
Cook, Bahía — 111 B 9
Cook, Cape — 60 CD 4
Cook, Mount — [NZ] 158-159 NO 8
Cook, Mount — [USA] 58-59 RS 6
Cook Bay 53 C 16
Cooke City, MT 66-67 J 3
Cookeville, TN 78-79 G 2
Cookhouse = Kookhuis 174-175 FG 7
Cooking Lake 60 L 3
Cook Inlet 56-57 F 5-6
Cook Islands 156-157 K 6
Cooks, MI 70-71 G 3
Cook's Harbour 63 HJ 2
Cookshire 62 Q 4
Cooks River 161 I a 2
Cook Strait 158-159 O 8
Cooktown 158-159 HJ 3
Coolabah 160 H 3
Coolah 160 J 3
Coolamon 160 H 5
Coolgardie 158-159 CD 6
Coolidge, AZ 74-75 H 6
Coolidge, KS 68-69 EF 6
Coolidge Dam 74-75 H 6
Coolin, ID 66-67 E 1
Cooma 158-159 J 7
Coonabarabran 158-159 JK 6
Coonamble 158-159 J 6
Coonana 158-159 D 6
Coonbah 160 EF 4
Coondambo 160 BC 3
Coondapoor 134-135 L 8
Coongoola 158-159 HJ 5
Coonoor 140 C 5
Coon Rapids, IA 70-71 C 5
Cooper 174-175 DE 8
Cooper, TX 76-77 G 6
Cooper Creek 158-159 G 5
Cooper Lake 68-69 CD 5
Cooper Landing, AK 58-59 N 6
Cooper North Branch 84 III cd 2
Cooper River 84 III c 2
Cooper's Town 88-89 GH 1
Cooperstown, ND 68-69 GH 2
Cooperstown, NY 72-73 J 3
Coorg 140 BC 4
Coorong, The — 158-159 G 7
Coosa River 78-79 G 3
Coos Bay 66-67 A 4
Coos Bay, OR 64-65 AB 3
Cootamundra 158-159 J 6
Čop 126-127 A 2
Copa, Cerro — 104-105 B 7
Copacabana 104-105 B 5
Copacabana [CO] 94-95 D 4
Copacabana [RA] 104-105 C 11
Copacabana, Forte de — 110 I bc 2
Copacabana, Rio de Janeiro- 110 I bc 2
Copahue 106-107 B 6
Copahue, Paso — 111 BC 5
Copalyacu, Río — 96-97 D 3
Copán 64-65 J 9
Copán, Santa Rosa de — 64-65 J 9
Copano Bay 76-77 F 8
Copco, CA 66-67 B 4-5
Cope, CO 68-69 E 6
Copeland, KS 68-69 F 7
Copelina, La — 106-107 D 6
Copenhagen = København 116-117 DE 10
Copere 104-105 E 6
Copeta, La — 106-107 G 6
Copetonas 106-107 G 7
Copiapó 111 BC 3
Copiapó, Río — 106-107 B 1
Copiapó, Volcán — 106-107 C 1
Copixaba 100-101 C 6
Čopoviči 126-127 D 1
Copparo 122-123 DE 3
Coppell 62 K 2
Coppename 98-99 K 2
Copperas Cove, TX 76-77 EF 7
Copperbelt 172 E 4
Copper Center, AK 56-57 G 5
Copper Cliff 62 L 3
Copper Harbor, MI 70-71 G 2
Coppermine 56-57 N 4
Coppermine Point 70-71 H 2
Coppermine River 56-57 NO 4
Copper River 56-57 GH 5
Copşa Mică 122-123 L 2
Coqueiros, Ponta do — 100-101 G 4
Coquilhatville = Mbandaka 172 C 1-2
Coquille, OR 66-67 AB 4
Coquille River 66-67 AB 4
Coquimbana 106-107 B 2
Coquimbo [RCH, administrative unit] 106-107 B 3
Coquimbo [RCH, place] 111 B 3
Coquimbo, Bahía de — 106-107 B 2
Coquinhos 100-101 D 8
Corabia 122-123 L 4
Coração de Jesus 102-103 K 2
Coração de Maria 100-101 E 7
Coracora 92-93 E 7-8
Corais, Ilhas dos — 102-103 HJ 6
Coralaque, Río — 96-97 F 10
Coral Gables, FL 64-65 KL 6
Coral Harbour 56-57 U 5
Coral Sea 158-159 K-M 3
Coral Sea Basin 158-159 K 2
Coral Sea Islands Territory 158-159 JK 3
Corantijn 92-93 H 4
Corato 122-123 G 5
Corazón, El — 96-97 B 2
Corbeil-Essonnes 120-121 HJ 4
Corbélia 102-103 F 6
Corbières 120-121 J 7
Corbin 66-67 F 1
Corbin, KY 64-65 K 4
Corcaigh = Cork 119 B 6
Corcoran, CA 74-75 D 4
Corcovado 110 I b 2
Corcovado, El — 108-109 D 4
Corcovado, Volcán — 111 B 6
Corcubión 120-121 C 7
Corda, Rio — 100-101 B 3-4
Cordeiro 102-103 L 4-5
Cordele, GA 80-81 DE 4
Cordell, OK 76-77 E 5
Cordilheiras, Serra das — 98-99 OP 8
Cordillera 102-103 D 6
Cordillera Azul 92-93 D 6
Cordillera Blanca 92-93 D 6
Cordillera Cantábrica 120-121 D-F 7
Cordillera Central [BOL] 92-93 F 8-G 9
Cordillera Central [CO] 92-93 D 4-E 3
Cordillera Central [DOM] 64-65 M 8
Cordillera Central [PE] 92-93 D 6
Cordillera Central [RP] 148-149 H 3
Cordillera Claudio Gay 104-105 B 9-10
Cordillera Darwin [RCH, Cordillera Patagónica] 108-109 C 7-8
Cordillera Darwin [RCH, Tierra del Fuego] 108-109 DE 10
Cordillera de Aguaragüe 104-105 E 7
Cordillera de Ampato 96-97 EF 9
Cordillera de Ansilta 106-107 C 3
Cordillera de Buena Vista 94-95 FG 2
Cordillera de Caaguazú 111 E 3
Cordillera de Carabaya 92-93 EF 7
Cordillera de Charagua 92-93 G 8-9
Cordillera de Chilca 96-97 EF 9
Cordillera de Chocaya 104-105 C 7
Cordillera de Chugchilán 96-97 B 2
Cordillera de Cochabamba 104-105 CD 5
Cordillera de Colangüil 106-107 C 2-3
Cordillera de Colonche 96-97 A 2-3
Cordillera de Cumullca 96-97 B 5
Cordillera de Darién 88-89 D 8
Cordillera de Darwin 104-105 B 10
Cordillera de Doña Rosa 106-107 B 3
Cordillera de Guamani 96-97 AB 4
Cordillera de Huanzo 96-97 E 9
Cordillera de Julcamarca 96-97 D 8
Cordillera de la Brea 106-107 C 2
Cordillera de la Costa [RCH] 111 B 2-3
Cordillera de la Costa [YV] 92-93 FG 3
Cordillera de la Ortiga 106-107 BC 2
Cordillera de la Punilla 106-107 B 2
Cordillera de las Llarretas 106-107 C 4-5
Cordillera de la Totora 106-107 BC 3
Cordillera del Condor 96-97 B 3-4
Cordillera de Lípez 92-93 F 9
Cordillera del Litoral 91 II bc 1
Cordillera de los Andes 92-93 E 3-F 9
Cordillera de los Frailes 104-105 CD 6
Cordillera del Tigre 106-107 C 3-4
Cordillera del Viento 106-107 B 6
Cordillera de Mbaracayú 102-103 E 5-6
Cordillera de Melo 106-107 AB 7
Cordillera de Mérida 92-93 EF 3
Cordillera de Mochara 104-105 D 7
Cordillera de Mosetenes 104-105 C 5
Cordillera de Nahuelbuta 106-107 A 6-7
Cordillera de Oliva 111 BC 3
Cordillera de Olivares 106-107 C 3
Cordillera de Ollita 111 B 4
Cordillera de San Blas 64-65 L 10

Cordillera de San Buenaventura 104-105 BC 10
Cordillera de San Pablo de Balzar 96-97 AB 2
Cordillera de Santa Rosa 106-107 C 2
Cordillera de Suaruro 104-105 DE 7
Cordillera de Tajsara 104-105 D 7
Cordillera de Talamanca 88-89 E 10
Cordillera de Turco 96-97 C 6
Cordillera de Turpicotay 96-97 D 8
Cordillera de Vilcanota 96-97 E 8-F 9
Cordillera de Yolaina 88-89 D 9
Cordillera Domeyko 111 C 2-3
Cordillera Entre Rios 64-65 J 9
Cordillera Huayhuash 96-97 C 7
Cordillera Iberica 120-121 F 7-G 8
Cordillera Isabella 64-65 J 9
Cordillera Mandolegüe 106-107 B 6
Cordillera Negra 92-93 D 6
Cordillera Occidental [CO] 92-93 D 3-4
Cordillera Occidental [PE] 92-93 D 6-E 8
Cordillera Oriental [BOL] 92-93 FG 8
Cordillera Oriental [CO] 92-93 D 4-E 3
Cordillera Oriental [DOM] 64-65 N 8
Cordillera Oriental [PE] 92-93 D 5-E 7
Cordillera Patagónica 111 B 8-5
Cordillera Penibética 120-121 E 9-G 8
Cordillera Real [BOL] 104-105 B 4-C 5
Cordillera Real [EC] 92-93 D 5
Cordillera Riesco 108-109 D 9
Cordillera Sarmiento 108-109 C 8-9
Cordillera Sillajguai 104-105 B 6
Cordillera Vilcabamba 92-93 E 7
Cordisburgo 102-103 KL 3
Córdoba [CO] 94-95 D 3
Córdoba [E] 120-121 E 10
Córdoba [MEX, Durango] 76-77 C 9
Córdoba [MEX, Veracruz] 64-65 G 8
Córdoba [RA] 111 D 4
Córdoba, Sierra de — [RA] 111 C 4-D 3
Cordobesa, La — 106-107 J 4
Cordón Alto [RA ↙ Puerto Santa Cruz] 108-109 D 8
Cordón Alto [RA ↑ Puerto Santa Cruz] 108-109 E 7
Cordón del Cherque 108-109 D 5
Cordón de Mary 106-107 BC 6
Cordón de Plata 106-107 C 4
Cordón de Portillo 106-107 C 4
Cordón El Pluma 108-109 D 6
Cordón Esmeralda 108-109 C 6
Cordón Leleque 108-109 D 4
Cordón Nevado 108-109 D 3
Córdova 92-93 DE 7
Cordova, AK 56-57 G 5
Cordova, AL 78-79 F 4
Córdova, Península — 108-109 C 9
Cordova Bay 58-59 w 9
Cordova Peak 58-59 P 6
Cordovil, Rio de Janeiro- 110 I b 1
Coreaú 100-101 D 2
Coreaú, Rio — 100-101 D 2
Coremas 100-101 F 4
Coremas, Açude — 100-101 F 4
Core Sound 80-81 H 3
Corfield 158-159 H 4
Corfu = Kérkyra 122-123 H 6
Corguinho 102-103 E 3
Coria 120-121 D 8-9
Coria del Río 120-121 D 10
Coribe 100-101 B 7
Coringa Islands 158-159 K 3
Corinne 61 F 5
Corinne, UT 66-67 G 5
Corinth, MS 78-79 E 3
Corinth = Kórinthos 122-123 K 7
Corinth, Gulf of — = Korinthiakòs Kólpos 122-123 JK 6
Corinto [BR] 92-93 KL 8
Corinto [CO] 94-95 C 6
Corinto [NIC] 64-65 J 9
Coripata 104-105 C 5
Corire 96-97 E 10
Corisco, Isla de — 164-165 F 8
Corixa Grande, Rio — 102-103 C 2
Corixão 102-103 D 3
Cork 119 B 6
Corleone 122-123 E 7
Corleto Perticara 122-123 FG 5
Çorlu 136-137 B 2
Çorlu suyu 136-137 B 2
Cormeilles-en-Parisis 129 I b 2
Cormoranes, Rocas — = Shag Rocks 111 H 8
Cormorant 61 HJ 3
Cormorant Lake 61 H 3
Čormoz 124-125 UV 4
Cornaca 104-105 D 7
Čornaja [SU, Rossijskaja SFSR] 132-133 Q 3
Čornaja Cholunica 124-125 ST 4
Čornaja Sloboda 124-125 LM 3
Corneille = Marwānah 166-167 J 2
Cornejo, Punta — 96-97 E 10
Cornelia 174-175 H 4
Cornelia, GA 80-81 E 3
Cornélio Procópio 111 FG 2
Cornelius 106-107 MN 2
Cornell, WI 70-71 E 3
Corner Brook 56-57 Z 8
Corner Inlet 160 H 7
Corning, AR 78-79 D 2
Corning, CA 74-75 B 3
Corning, IA 70-71 C 5
Corning, KS 70-71 BC 6
Corning, NY 72-73 H 3
Cornish, Seno — 108-109 B 6
Corn Islands = Islas del Maíz 64-65 K 9
Cornouaille 120-121 EF 4
Čornovskoje 124-125 QR 4
Cornudas Mountains 76-77 B 6-7
Cornwall [BS] 88-89 H 2
Cornwall [CDN] 56-57 VW 8
Cornwall [GB] 119 D 6
Cornwallis Island 56-57 RS 2-3
Cornwall Island 56-57 RS 2
Cornwells Heights, PA 84 III d 1
Čornyje zemli 126-127 N 3-4
Čornyj Jar 126-127 MN 2
Corny Point 160 C 5
Coro 92-93 EF 2
Coro, Golfete de — 94-95 F 2
Coroaci 102-103 L 3
Coroados 102-103 G 4
Coroatá 92-93 L 5
Corobamba, Pampas de — 96-97 B 4-C 5
Corocoro 92-93 F 8
Corocoro, Isla — 94-95 LM 3
Coroico 92-93 F 8
Coromandel 102-103 J 3
Coromandel Coast 134-135 N 7-8
Coromandel Peninsula 161 FG 3
Coromandel Range 161 F 3
Corona, CA 74-75 E 6
Corona, NM 76-77 B 5
Corona, Cerro — 108-109 D 3
Coronado, CA 74-75 E 6
Coronado, Bahía de — 64-65 K 10
Coronados, Golfo de los — 108-109 BC 3
Coronados, Islas de — 74-75 E 6
Coronation 61 C 4
Coronation Gulf 56-57 OP 4
Coronation Island [Orkney Is.] 53 CD 32
Coronation Island [USA] 58-59 v 9
Coronation Islands 158-159 D 2
Coronda 106-107 G 3
Coronda, Laguna — 106-107 G 3-4
Coronel 106-107 A 6
Coronel Alzogaray 106-107 E 4
Coronel Charlone 106-107 F 5
Coronel Cornejo 104-105 E 8
Coronel Dorrego 111 DE 5
Coronel Du Graty 104-105 F 10
Coronel Eugenio del Busto 106-107 E 7
Coronel Eugenio Garay 102-103 DE 6
Coronel Fabriciano 92-93 L 8
Coronel Falcón 106-107 G 7
Coronel Fraga 106-107 FG 3
Coronel Francisco Sosa 111 CD 5-6
Coronel Galvão = Rio Verde de Mato Grosso 92-93 HJ 8
Coronel Granada 106-107 FG 5
Coronel H. Lagos 106-107 EF 5
Coronel Martínez de Hoz 106-107 FG 5
Coronel Moldes 106-107 E 4
Coronel Mom 106-107 G 5
Coronel Murta 102-103 L 2
Coronel Oviedo 92-93 E 2-3
Coronel Ponce 102-103 E 1
Coronel Pringles 111 D 5
Coronel R. Bunge 106-107 GH 6
Coronel Segovia 106-107 DE 5
Coronel Suárez 111 D 5
Coronel Vidal 106-107 HJ 6
Coronel Vivida 102-103 F 6-7
Coronie 98-99 K 2
Coronilla, La — 106-107 L 4
Coropuna, Nudo — 92-93 E 8
Corowa 160 H 5-6
Corozal [BH] 64-65 J 8
Corozal [CO] 94-95 D 3
Corozal [YV] 94-95 K 4
Corozo, El — 91 II b 1
Corozo Pando 94-95 H 3
Corps Mort, Île de — 63 E 4
Corpus 106-107 K 1
Corpus Christi, TX 64-65 G 6
Corpus Christi Bay 76-77 F 9
Corpus Christi Pass 76-77 F 9
Corque 92-93 F 8
Corral [PE] 96-97 B 4
Corral [RCH] 111 B 5
Corral de Lorca 106-107 D 5
Corralito 106-107 EF 4
Correa 106-107 G 4
Correas, Los — 106-107 J 5
Correctionsville, IA 70-71 BC 4
Corregidor Island 148-149 GH 4
Córrego Bacuri-mirim 102-103 G 4
Córrego Traição 110 II ab 2
Corrente 92-93 KL 7
Corrente, Riacho — 100-101 B 4-5
Corrente, Rio — [BR, Bahia] 92-93 L 7
Corrente, Rio — [BR, Goiás ◁ Rio Paraná] 100-101 A 8
Corrente, Rio — [BR, Goiás ◁ Rio Paranaíba] 102-103 G 3
Corrente, Rio — [BR, Piauí] 100-101 D 3
Correntes [BR, Mato Grosso] 92-93 HJ 8
Correntes [BR, Pernambuco] 100-101 F 5
Correntes, Rio — 102-103 E 2
Correntina 92-93 KL 7
Correo, NM 76-77 A 5
Corrib, Lough — 119 B 5
Corrientes [PE] 96-97 D 4
Corrientes [RA, administrative unit] 106-107 HJ 2
Corrientes [RA, place] 106-107 H 1
Corrientes, Cabo — [C] 88-89 DE 4
Corrientes, Cabo — [CO] 92-93 D 3
Corrientes, Cabo — [MEX] 64-65 E 7
Corrientes, Cabo — [RA] 111 E 5
Corrientes, Cabo — = Cape Carysfort 108-109 L 8
Corrientes, Río — [EC] 96-97 C 3
Corrientes, Río — [RA] 106-107 H 2
Corrigan, TX 76-77 G 7
Corrigin 158-159 C 6
Corry, PA 72-73 G 4
Corse 122-123 C 4
Corse, Cap — 122-123 C 4
Corsica = Corse 122-123 C 4
Corsicana, TX 64-65 G 5
Čorskogo, chrebet — 132-133 a 4-c 5
Cortaderas 106-107 C 6
Cortazar 86-87 K 7
Corte 122-123 C 4
Cortês [BR] 100-101 G 5
Cortès [C] 88-89 E 3
Cortez, CO 74-75 J 4
Cortez Mountains 66-67 E 5
Cortina d'Ampezzo 122-123 E 2
Čortkov 126-127 BC 2
Cortland, NE 68-69 H 5
Cortland, NY 72-73 HJ 3
Corto Alto 108-109 C 3
Cortona 122-123 D 4
Corubal 168-169 B 3
Çoruh = Artvin 134-135 E 2
Çoruh dağları 136-137 J 2
Çoruh nehri 136-137 J 2
Çorum 134-135 CD 2
Corumbá 92-93 H 8
Corumbá, Rio — 92-93 K 8
Corumbá de Goiás 102-103 H 1
Corumbaíba 102-103 H 3
Corumbataí, Rio — 102-103 G 6
Corumbaú, Ponta de — 100-101 E 9
Corumiquara, Ponta — 100-101 E 2
Coruña, La — 120-121 C 7
Corundum 174-175 J 3
Corunna, MI 70-71 H 4
Corunna = La Coruña 120-121 C 7
Corupá 102-103 H 7
Coruripe 100-101 F 6
Corvallis, MT 66-67 FG 2
Corvallis, OR 64-65 B 3
Corviale, Roma- 113 II ab 2
Corwin, AK 58-59 E 2
Corwin, Cape — 58-59 E 7
Corwin Springs, MT 66-67 H 3
Corydon, IA 70-71 D 5
Corydon, IN 70-71 GH 6
Corzuela 104-105 F 10
Cos = Kōs 122-123 M 7
Cosala 86-87 G 5
Cosamaloapan 86-87 MN 8
Cosapa 104-105 B 6
Cosapa, Río — 104-105 B 6
Cosapilla 104-105 B 5
Cosenza 122-123 FG 6
Coshocton, OH 72-73 EF 4
Cosigüina, Punta — 64-65 J 9
Cosigüina, Volcán — 64-65 J 9
Coslada 113 III b 2
Cosmoledo Islands 172 J 3
Cosmópolis 102-103 J 5
Cosmopolis, WA 66-67 B 2
Cosmos, MN 70-71 C 3
Cosna River 58-59 M 4
Cosquín 106-107 E 3
Cossipore, Calcutta- 154 II b 2
Čošskaja guba 132-133 H 4
Costa 100-101 C 4
Costa, Canal — 108-109 C 5
Costa, Cordillera de la — [RCH] 111 B 2-3
Costa, Cordillera de la — [YV] 92-93 FG 3
Costa, La — 106-107 D 4
Costa Brava 120-121 J 8
Costa Chica 86-87 K 9
Costa del Sol 120-121 EF 10
Costa de Mosquitos 64-65 K 9
Costa Grande 64-65 F 8
Costa Machado 102-103 FG 5
Costa Rica [BOL] 104-105 B 2
Costa Rica [CR] 64-65 JK 9-10
Costa Rica [MEX, Sinaloa] 86-87 FG 5
Costa Rica [MEX, Sonora] 86-87 D 2
Costera del Golfo, Llanura — 86-87 L-N 5-8
Costera del Pacífico, Llanura — 86-87 E-H 2-7
Costermansville = Bukavu 172 E 2
Costigan Lake 61 EF 2
Costilla, NM 76-77 B 4
Cotabambas 96-97 E 8
Cotabato 148-149 H 5
Cotacachi 96-97 B 1
Cotacajes, Río — 104-105 C 5
Cotagaita [BOL] 92-93 F 9
Cotagaita [RA] 106-107 F 3
Cotahuasi 92-93 E 8
Cotati, CA 74-75 B 3
Cotaxé 100-101 D 10
Coteau des Prairies, Plateau du — 64-65 G 2-3
Coteau du Missouri, Plateau du — 64-65 FG 2
Côteau-Station 72-73 J 2
Cote Blanche Bay 78-79 D 6
Côte d'Azur 120-121 L 7
Côte du Calvados 120-121 G 4
Côte du Poivre = Malabar Coast 134-135 L 8-M 9
Cotegipe, Rio — 102-103 F 6
Cotejipe 100-101 B 7
Coté-Lai 104-105 G 10
Cotentin 120-121 G 4
Côte-Saint-Luc 82 I ab 2
Côte-Visitation, Montréal- 82 I b 1
Cotia 102-103 J 5
Cotia, Rio — 104-105 D 1
Cotiza, Caracas- 91 II b 1
Cotonou 164-165 E 7
Cotonu = Cotonou 164-165 E 7
Cotopaxi, CO 68-69 D 6
Cotopaxi [EC, administrative unit] 96-97 B 2
Cotopaxi [EC, mountain] 92-93 D 5
Cotswold Hills 119 EF 6
Cottage Grove, OR 66-67 B 4
Cottageville, SC 80-81 F 4
Cottbus 118 G 3
Cotter, AR 78-79 C 2
Cottian Alps = Alpes Cottiennes 120-121 L 6
Cottica 92-93 J 4
Cottondale, FL 78-79 G 5
Cotton Valley, LA 78-79 C 4
Cottonwood, AZ 74-75 GH 5
Cottonwood, CA 66-67 B 5
Cottonwood, ID 66-67 E 2
Cottonwood, SD 68-69 F 4
Cottonwood Creek 66-67 B 5
Cottonwood Falls, KS 68-69 H 6
Cottonwood River 70-71 C 3
Cottonwood Wash 74-75 HJ 5
Cotulla, TX 76-77 E 8
Cotunduba, Ilha de — 110 I c 2
Couba Island 85 I a 3
Coubron 129 I d 2
Coudersport, PA 72-73 GH 4
Coudres, Île aux — 63 A 4
Coulee, ND 68-69 EF 1
Coulee City, WA 66-67 D 2
Coulee Dam, WA 66-67 D 1-2
Coulman Island 53 B 18
Coulonge, Rivière — 72-73 H 1
Coulterville, IL 70-71 F 6
Council, AK 58-59 F 4
Council, ID 66-67 E 3
Council Bluffs, IA 64-65 GH 3
Council Grove, KS 68-69 H 6
Council Mountain 66-67 E 3
Country Club 91 I c 2
Country Club of Detroit 84 II c 2
Courantyne River 98-99 K 3
Courbevoie 129 I bc 2
Courland = Curlandia 124-125 CD 5
Courneuve, la — 129 I c 2
Courtenay [CDN] 56-57 LM 8
Courtrai = Kortrijk 120-121 J 3
Courtry 129 I d 2
Coushatta, LA 78-79 C 4
Coutances 120-121 G 4
Coutinho 100-101 D 3
Couto Magalhães 98-99 O 9
Coutts 66-67 H 1
Couves, Ilha das — 102-103 K 5
Covadonga, Isla — 108-109 BC 9
Cove, AR 76-77 G 5
Cove Island 62 KL 4
Coveñas 92-93 D 3
Covendo 104-105 C 4
Coventry 119 F 5
Covil, Serra do — 100-101 BC 6
Covilhã 120-121 D 8
Covington, GA 80-81 E 4
Covington, IN 70-71 G 5
Covington, KY 64-65 JK 4
Covington, LA 78-79 D 5
Covington, MI 70-71 F 2
Covington, OH 70-71 H 5
Covington, OK 76-77 F 4
Covington, TN 78-79 E 3
Covington, VA 80-81 FG 2
Covunco 106-107 BC 7
Covunco, Arroyo — 106-107 BC 7
Cowal, Lake — 158-159 J 6
Cowan, TN 78-79 FG 3
Cowan, Lake — 158-159 D 6
Cowansville 72-73 K 2
Coward Springs 158-159 G 5
Cowarie 158-159 G 5
Cowart Lake 85 II a 3
Cowden, IL 70-71 F 6
Cowdrey, CO 68-69 C 5
Cowell 160 C 4
Cowen, Mount — 66-67 H 3
Cowlitz River 66-67 B 2
Cowra 158-159 J 6
Coxilha 106-107 LM 2
Coxilha Caverá 106-107 K 3
Coxilha da Santana 111 E 3-F 4
Coxilha das Tunas 106-107 L 3
Coxilha do Batovi 106-107 K 3
Coxilha Geral 106-107 K 3
Coxilha Grande 111 F 3
Coxilha Pedras Altas 106-107 L 3
Coxilha Rica 102-103 G 7
Coxim 92-93 J 8
Coxim, Rio — 102-103 E 3
Coxipó do Ouro 102-103 D 1
Coxipó Ponte 102-103 DE 1
Cox River 158-159 FG 3
Cox's Bazar = Koks Bāzār 134-135 P 6
Cox's Cove 63 GH 3
Coyame 86-87 H 3
Coyle = Río Coig 108-109 D 8
Coyoacán 91 I bc 2
Coyoacán-Churubusco 91 I c 2
Coyoacán-Ciudad Jardín 91 I c 3
Coyoacán-la Candelaria 91 I c 2
Coyoacán-Rosedal 91 I c 2
Coyoacán-San Francisco Culhuacán 91 I c 3
Coyote, NM 76-77 B 6
Coyote Creek 83 III d 2
Coyotes Indian Reservation, Los — 74-75 E 6
Coyte, El — 108-109 D 5
Coyuca de Catalán 86-87 K 8
Cozad, NE 68-69 G 5
Cozumel 64-65 J 7
Cozumel, Isla de — 64-65 J 7
Cozzo Pellegrino 106-107 HJ 5
Crab Creek 66-67 D 2
Cracker 108-109 G 4
Cradock 172 E 8
Craig, CO 68-69 C 5
Craig, MT 66-67 GH 2
Craighall, Johannesburg- 170 V b 1
Craighall Park, Johannesburg- 170 V b 1
Craig Harbour 56-57 UV 2
Craigmont, ID 66-67 E 2
Craigmyle 61 B 5
Craigower 61 CD 6
Craik 61 F 5
Craiova 122-123 K 3
Crakow = Kraków 118 JK 3
Crampel = Ra's al-Mā' 164-165 D 2
Cranberry Portage 61 H 3
Cranbrock 56-57 NO 8
Cranbrook 60 JK 5
Crandon, WI 70-71 F 3
Crane, MO 78-79 C 2
Crane, OR 66-67 D 4
Crane, TX 76-77 C 7
Crane Lake 61 D 5
Crane Lake, MN 70-71 DE 1
Crane Mountain 66-67 CD 4
Cranston, RI 72-73 L 4
Cranz, Hamburg- 130 I a 1
Crary Mountains 53 B 25
Crasna [RO, place] 122-123 M 2
Crasna [RO, river] 122-123 K 2
Crater Lake 64-65 B 3
Crater Lake, OR 66-67 BC 4
Crater Lake National Park 66-67 BC 4
Craters of the Moon National Monument 66-67 G 4
Crateús 92-93 LM 6
Crato [BR] 92-93 M 6
Crau 120-121 K 7
Crauford, Cape — 56-57 TU 3
Cravari, Rio — 104-105 GH 3
Cravinhos 102-103 J 4
Cravo Norte 92-93 EF 3
Cravo Norte, Río — 94-95 F 4
Cravo Sur, Río — 94-95 EF 5
Crawford, GA 80-81 E 4
Crawford, NE 68-69 E 4
Crawford Lakes 85 II c 3
Crawfordsville, IN 70-71 G 5
Crawfordville, FL 80-81 DE 4
Cray 129 II c 2
Crayford, London- 129 II c 2
Crazy Mountains 66-67 H 2-3
Crazy Peak 66-67 HJ 3
Crazy Woman Creek 68-69 C 3
Crean Lake 61 E 3
Creciente, Isla — 86-87 DE 5
Creede, CO 68-69 C 7
Creedmoor, NC 80-81 G 2
Creel 86-87 G 4
Cree Lake [CDN, lake] 56-57 P 6
Cree Lake [CDN, place] 61 E 2
Cree River 61 E 2
Crefeld = Krefeld 118 BC 3
Creighton 61 GH 3
Creighton, NE 68-69 GH 4
Creil 120-121 J 4
Crema 122-123 C 3
Cremona [CDN] 61 A 5
Cremona [I] 122-123 CD 3
Crenshaw, MS 78-79 D 3
Crepori, Rio — 98-99 K 7
Crerar 72-73 F 1
Cres [YU, island] 122-123 F 3
Cres [YU, place] 122-123 F 3
Crescent, OK 76-77 F 4-5
Crescent, OR 66-67 C 4
Crescent, Lake — 66-67 B 1
Crescent City, CA 66-67 A 5
Crescent City, FL 80-81 c 2
Crescent Junction, UT 74-75 J 3
Crescent Lake, OR 66-67 C 4
Crescent Spur 60 GH 3
Crescentville, Philadelphia-, PA 84 III c 1
Cresciente, Isla — 86-87 DE 5
Cresco, IA 70-71 DE 4
Crespo 106-107 G 4
Cressday 68-69 A 1
Cressely 129 I b 3
Cressy 160 F 7
Crested Butte, CO 68-69 C 6
Crestlawn Cemetery 85 II b 2
Crestline, NV 74-75 F 4
Crestmond Park, Houston-, TX 85 III b 2
Creston 66-67 E 1
Creston, IA 70-71 C 5
Creston, WY 68-69 BC 5
Crestview, FL 78-79 F 5
Crestwynd 61 F 5
Creswell, OR 66-67 B 4
Crete, NE 68-69 H 5
Crete = Krētē 122-123 L 8
Créteil 129 I c 2
Crétéville = Jabal al-Gulūd 166-167 M 1
Creus, Cabo — 120-121 J 7
Creuse 120-121 H 5
Creusot, le — 120-121 K 5
Creve Coeur, IL 70-71 F 5
Crevice Creek, AK 58-59 LM 3
Crewe 119 E 5
Crewe, VA 80-81 G 2
Cribi = Kribi 164-165 F 8
Crib Point 160 G 7
Crichna = Krishna 134-135 M 7
Criciúma 106-107 N 2
Cricket Ground [AUS, Melbourne] 161 II bc 1
Cricket Ground [AUS, Sydney] 161 I b 2
Crikvenica 122-123 F 3
Crillon, Mount — 58-59 T 7
Crillon, mys — 132-133 b 8
Crimea = Krym 126-127 FG 4
Criminosa, Cachoeira — 98-99 HJ 5
Criolla, La — 106-107 G 3
Cripple, AK 58-59 JK 5
Cripple Creek, CO 68-69 D 6
Criques, Grande Île de — 170 IV b 1-2
Crişana 122-123 JK 2
Crisfield, MD 72-73 J 5-6
Crisnejas, Río — 96-97 BC 5
Crisópolis 100-101 E 6
Criss Creek 60 G 4
Cristais, Serra dos — 102-103 J 2
Cristalândia 98-99 O 10
Cristalândia do Piauí 100-101 B 5-6
Cristales, Loma de los — 106-107 B 2
Cristalina 102-103 J 2
Cristina 102-103 K 5
Cristina, La — 106-107 E 6
Cristino Castro 100-101 B 5
Cristobal 64-65 b 2
Cristóbal Colón, Pico — 94-95 E 2
Crişul Alb 122-123 J 2
Crişul Negru 122-123 JK 2
Crivitz, WI 70-71 FG 3
Crna Reka 122-123 J 5
Croatia 122-123 F-H 3
Crockenhill 129 II c 2
Crocker, MO 70-71 D 7
Crocker Range 152-153 L 3-M 2
Crockett, TX 76-77 G 7
Crocodile Islands 158-159 FG 2
Croeira, Serra da — 100-101 A 4
Crofton, KY 78-79 F 2
Crofton, NE 68-69 H 4
Croissy-Beaubourg 129 I d 2
Croissy-sur-Seine 129 I b 2
Croix, Lac à la — 63 A 2
Croix, Lac la — 70-71 DE 1
Croker Island 158-159 F 2
Cromer [CDN] 61 H 6
Cromer [GB] 119 G 5
Cromwell 158-159 NO 8-9
Cromwell, MN 70-71 D 2
Crook, CO 68-69 E 5
Crooked Creek 66-67 DE 4
Crooked Creek, AK 58-59 QR 4
Crooked Creek, AK 58-59 H 6
Crooked Island 64-65 M 7
Crooked Island Passage 64-65 LM 7
Crooked River [CDN] 61 G 4
Crooked River [USA] 66-67 C 3
Crookes Point 82 III b 3
Crookston, MN 68-69 H 2
Crookston, NE 68-69 F 4
Crooksville, OH 72-73 E 5
Crookwell 160 J 5
Crosby, MN 70-71 CD 2
Crosby, MS 78-79 D 5
Crosby, ND 68-69 E 1
Crosby, Johannesburg- 170 V a 2
Crosbyton, TX 76-77 D 6
Cross 168-169 H 4
Cross, Cape — = Kaap Kruis 172 B 6
Cross City, FL 80-81 b 2
Crosse, La —, WI 64-65 H 3
Crossett, AR 78-79 D 4
Crossfield 60 K 4
Crossinsee 130 III c 2
Cross Lake [CDN, lake] 61 K 3
Cross Lake [CDN, place] 61 K 3
Crossman Peak 74-75 FG 5
Cross Plains, TX 76-77 E 6
Cross River 164-165 F 7-8
Cross Sound 56-57 J 6
Crossville, TN 78-79 G 3
Croswell, MI 72-73 E 3
Crotone 122-123 G 6
Crow Agency, MT 68-69 C 3
Crow Creek 68-69 D 5
Crow Creek Indian Reservation 68-69 G 3
Crowder, OK 76-77 FG 5
Crowell, TX 76-77 E 6
Crowie Creek 160 H 4
Crow Indian Reservation 68-69 BC 3
Crowley, LA 64-65 H 5-6
Crowley, Lake — 74-75 D 4
Crowleys Ridge 78-79 D 2-3
Crown Hill Cemetery 85 III c 2
Crown King, AZ 74-75 G 5
Crown Point 94-95 L 2
Crown Point, IN 70-71 G 5
Crown Point, LA 85 I b 3
Crownpoint, NM 74-75 JK 5
Crown Prince Christian Land = Kronprins Christians Land 52 AB 20-21
Crows Nest 160 L 1
Crows Nest, Sydney- 161 I b 1
Crowsnest Pass 66-67 F 1
Croxley Green 129 II a 1
Croydon 158-159 H 3
Croydon, PA 84 III d 1
Croydon, London- 119 FG 7
Crozet 50-51 M 8
Crozet Ridge 50-51 M 8
Crucero, CA 74-75 EF 5
Crucero, Cerro — 86-87 H 7
Crucero, El — 94-95 J 2-3
Cruces 88-89 FG 3
Cruces, Las — 64-65 b 2
Cruces, Las —, NM 64-65 E 5
Cruces, Punta — 94-95 C 4
Crum Creek 84 III a 2
Crum Lynne 84 III b 2
Cruxati, Rio — 100-101 E 2
Cruz, Bahia — 108-109 G 5
Cruz, Cabo — 64-65 L 8
Cruz, La — [CO] 94-95 C 7
Cruz, La — [CR] 88-89 CD 9
Cruz, La — [MEX] 76-77 B 9
Cruz, La — [RA] 106-107 J 2
Cruz, La — [ROU] 106-107 JK 4
Cruz, Serra da — 100-101 A 5
Cruz Alta [BR] 111 F 3
Cruz Alta [RA] 106-107 G 4
Cruz das Almas 100-101 E 7
Cruz del Eje 111 CD 4
Cruz de Malta 100-101 DE 5
Cruz de Taratara, La — 94-95 G 2
Cruz do Espírito Santo 100-101 G 4
Cruzeiro 92-93 L 9
Cruzeiro do Oeste 102-103 F 5
Cruzeiro do Sul 92-93 E 6
Cruzeiro do Sul, Cachoeira — 98-99 H 10
Cruzen Island 53 B 22-23
Cruzes, Río — 108-109 C 2
Cruz Grande [MEX] 86-87 L 9
Cruz Grande [RCH] 106-107 B 2
Cruzília 102-103 K 4
Cruz Machado 102-103 G 6
Cruz Manca 91 I b 2
Cruz Ramos 96-97 C 5
Cruz Verde, Páramo — 91 III c 4
Crysdale, Mount — 60 F 2
Crystal, ND 68-69 H 1
Crystal Bay 80-81 b 2
Crystal Brook 160 CD 4
Crystal City 68-69 G 1
Crystal City, MO 70-71 E 6
Crystal City, TX 76-77 E 8
Crystal Falls, MI 70-71 F 2-3
Crystal Lake, IL 70-71 FG 4
Crystal Lake [CDN] 70-71 GH 3
Crystal Lake [USA] 84 I b 2
Crystal Palace Park 129 II b 2
Crystal River, FL 80-81 b 2
Crystal Springs, MS 78-79 D 4-5
Csongrád 118 K 5
Ctesiphon = Ktesiphon 136-137 L 6
Ču 132-133 N 9
Cúa 94-95 H 2
Cuadrada, Sierra — 108-109 E 5
Cuadrilla 104-105 C 7
Cuajimalpa 91 I b 2
Cuajiniculipa 86-87 L 9
Cu'a Lo 150-151 E 3
Cuamba 172 G 4
Cuanacorral, Cerro — 96-97 B 5
Cuando, Rio — 172 D 5
Cuando-Cubango 172 C 4-D 5
Cuangar 172 C 5
Cuango 172 C 3
Cuango, Rio — 172 C 3
Cuanza Norte 172 BC 3-4
Cuanza Sul 172 BC 3-4
Cuao, Río — 94-95 H 5
Cu'a Rao 148-149 DE 3
Cuarein, Río — 106-107 J 3
Cuarepoti, Arroyo — 102-103 D 6
Cuaró [ROU, Artigas] 106-107 J 3
Cuaró [ROU, Tucuarembó] 106-107 K 3
Cuarto Dinamo 91 I b 3
Cu'a Sông Cu'u Long 148-149 E 5
Cuatro Ciénegas de Carranza 86-87 J 4
Cuatro Ojos 104-105 E 5
Cuatro Vientos, Madrid- 113 III a 2
Cu'a Tung 150-151 F 4
Cuauhtémoc 64-65 C 6
Cuauhtémoc, Ciudad de México- 91 I c 2
Cuautepec de Madero, Ciudad de México- 91 I c 1
Cuautepec el Alto, Ciudad de México- 91 I c 1
Cuay Grande 106-107 J 2
Cuba 64-65 KL 7
Cuba, KS 68-69 H 6
Cuba, MO 70-71 E 6
Cuba, NM 76-77 A 4
Cubagua, Isla — 94-95 J 2
Cubal 172 B 4
Cubango 172 C 4
Cubango, Rio — 172 C 5
Cubará 94-95 E 4
Čubartau = Baršatas 132-133 O 8
Cubatão 102-103 J 5
Cubero, NM 76-77 A 5
Cubo 174-175 K 2
Cubuk 136-137 E 2
Çubuklu, İstanbul- 154 I b 2
Cucao, Bahía — 108-109 B 4
Cu Chi 150-151 F 7
Cuchi, Rio — 172 C 4-5
Cuchilla de Belen 106-107 J 3
Cuchilla de Haedo 111 E 4
Cuchilla de la Carbonera 106-107 KL 4-5
Cuchilla de la Tristeza 106-107 C 5
Cuchilla del Caraguatá 106-107 K 3-4
Cuchilla del Daymán 106-107 J 3
Cuchilla del Hospital 106-107 K 3
Cuchilla de los Arapeyes 106-107 J 3
Cuchilla de Montiel 106-107 H 3
Cuchilla de Queguay 106-107 J 3
Cuchilla Grande [RA] 106-107 H 2-3
Cuchilla Grande [ROU] 111 EF 4
Cuchilla Grande del Durazno 106-107 JK 4
Cuchilla Grande Inferior 106-107 JK 4

Cuchilla Mangrullo 106-107 KL 4
Cuchilla Negra 106-107 K 3
Cuchilla San Salvador 106-107 HJ 4
Cuchillo-Có 106-107 E 7
Cuchillo Parado 76-77 B 8
Cuchivero 94-95 J 4
Cuchivero, Río — 94-95 J 4
Čuchloma 124-125 O 4
Cucuí 92-93 F 4
Cucumbi 172 C 4
Cucunor = Chöch nuur 142-143 H 4
Cucurrupí 94-95 C 5
Cúcuta 92-93 E 3
Cudahy, CA 83 III c 2
Cudahy, WI 70-71 G 4
Cuddalore 134-135 MN 8
Cuddapah 134-135 M 8
Cudgewa 160 HJ 6
Cudi dağı 136-137 K 4
Cudinamarca 94-95 DE 5
Čudovo 132-133 E 6
Čudskoje ozero 132-133 O 6
Cudworth 61 EF 4
Cue 158-159 C 5
Cuello 86-87 Q 8
Cuemaní, Río — 94-95 E 7-8
Cuenca [CO] 94-95 E 8
Cuenca [E] 120-121 FG 8
Cuenca [EC] 92-93 D 5
Cuenca, Serranía de — 120-121 F 8-G 9
Cuenca del Añelo 106-107 C 7
Cuencamé de Ceniceros 86-87 J 5
Cuenlum = Kunlun Shan 142-143 D-H 4
Cuernavaca 64-65 FG 8
Cuero, TX 76-77 F 8
Cuervo, NM 76-77 B 5
Cuervo Grande, El — 76-77 B 7
Cuesta Pass 74-75 C 5
Cueva 96-97 D 7
Cueva, La — 94-95 E 2
Cueva de Altamira 120-121 EF 7
Cuevas, Las — 106-107 BC 4
Cuevas del Almanzora 120-121 G 10
Cuevitas 94-95 C 5
Cufra, Wāhāt el — = Wāḥāt al-Kufrah 164-165 J 4
Čuguš, gora — 126-127 JK 5
Cuiabá [BR, Amazonas] 92-93 H 6
Cuiabá [BR, Mato Grosso] 92-93 H 8
Cuiabá, Rio — 92-93 H 8
Cuicas 94-95 F 3
Cuieté, Rio — 102-103 M 3
Cuil, El — 94-95 B 6
Cuilapa 86-87 P 10
Cuillin Sound 119 C 3
Cuilo, Rio — 172 C 3
Cuíma 172 C 4
Cuipo 64-65 a 2
Cuité 100-101 F 4
Cuité, Serra do — 100-101 F 4
Cuito, Rio — 172 CD 5
Cuito Cuanavale 172 CD 5
Cuitzeo, Laguna de — 86-87 K 8
Cuiuni, Rio — 98-99 G 5
Cujar, Río — 96-97 E 7
Čukotskij, mys — 132-133 l 5
Čukotskij Nacional'nyj Okrug = Chukot Autonomous Area 132-133 g-k 4
Čukotskij poluostrov 132-133 kl 4
Çukurca 136-137 K 4
Çukurova 136-137 F 4
Cu Lao Cham 150-151 G 5
Cu Lao Hon = Cu Lao Thu 148-149 EF 4
Cu Lao Poulo Gambir 150-151 GH 6
Cu Lao Rê 150-151 G 5
Cu Lao Thu 148-149 EF 4
Cu Lao Xanh = Cu Lao Poulo Gambir 150-151 GH 6
Culbertson, MT 68-69 D 1
Culbertson, NE 68-69 F 5
Culcairn 158-159 J 7
Culebra [PA] 64-65 b 2
Culebra [Puerto Rico] 88-89 O 5
Culebra, La — 94-95 H 3
Culebras 96-97 B 6
Culgoa River 158-159 J 5
Culiacán 64-65 E 6-7
Culiacán Rosales = Culiacán 64-65 E 6-7
Culichucani 104-105 D 5
Culion Island 148-149 G 4
Čulkovo 132-133 Q 5
Cúllar de Baza 120-121 F 10
Cullera 120-121 GH 9
Cullinan 174-175 H 3
Cullman, AL 78-79 F 3
Čul'man 132-133 XY 6
Culpeper, VA 72-73 GH 5
Culpina 104-105 D 7
Culta 104-105 C 6
Cultural Palace of Nationalities 155 II b 2
Culuene, Rio — 92-93 J 7
Čuluut gol 142-143 J 2
Culver, Point — 158-159 DE 6
Culver City, CA 83 III b 1
Čulym [SU, place] 132-133 P 6
Čulym [SU, river] 132-133 Q 6
Cum = Qom 134-135 G 4
Cumã, Baía de — 100-101 B 1-2
Cumae 122-123 EF 5
Cumamoto = Kumamoto 142-143 P 5
Cumaná 92-93 G 2
Cumanacoa 94-95 K 2
Cumaral 94-95 F 6
Cumare, Cerro — 94-95 E 7
Cumari 102-103 HJ 3
Cumaria 96-97 DE 6
Cumaribo 94-95 G 5
Cumassia = Kumasi 164-165 D 7
Cumbal, Nevado de — 94-95 BC 7
Cumberland 66-67 A 1
Cumberland, IA 70-71 C 5
Cumberland, KY 80-81 E 2
Cumberland, MD 64-65 L 4
Cumberland, VA 80-81 GH 2
Cumberland, WI 70-71 DE 3
Cumberland, Cape — 158-159 N 2
Cumberland, Lake — 70-71 H 7
Cumberland City, TN 78-79 F 2
Cumberland House 61 GH 3-4
Cumberland Island 80-81 F 5
Cumberland Islands 158-159 JK 4
Cumberland Peninsula 56-57 XY 4
Cumberland Plateau 64-65 J 5-K 4
Cumberland Point 70-71 F 2
Cumberland River 64-65 J 4
Cumberland Sound [CDN] 56-57 X 4-Y 5
Cumberland Sound [USA] 80-81 c 1
Cumborah 160 H 2
Cumbre, La — [RA] 106-107 E 3
Cumbre, La — [YV] 91 II b 1
Cumbre, Paso de la — 111 BC 4
Cumbre del Laudo 104-105 B 10
Cumbre de Mejicana 111 C 3
Cumbrera, Cerro — 108-109 C 7
Cumbres Calchaquíes 104-105 D 10
Cumbres de Curumo, Baruta- 91 II b 2
Cumbres de Vallecas 113 III b 2
Cumbres Pass 68-69 C 7
Cumbria 119 F 4
Cumbrian Mountains 119 E 4
Cumbum = Kambam 140 C 6
Čumikan 132-133 Za 7
Cuminá, Rio — 92-93 H 5
Cuminapanema, Rio — 98-99 L 4-5
Cummings, CA 74-75 B 3
Cummins 158-159 G 6
Çumra 136-137 E 4
Cumullca, Cordillera de — 96-97 B 5
Cumuruxaiba 100-101 E 9
Čuna [SU ◁ Angara] 132-133 S 6
Čun'a [SU ◁ Podkamennaja Tunguska] 132-133 ST 5
Cunaco 106-107 B 5
Cunani 92-93 J 4
Cuñapirú 106-107 K 3
Cuñaré 94-95 E 7
Cunaviche 94-95 H 4
Cunco 111 B 5
Cuncumén 106-107 B 3
Cunene 172 C 5
Cunene, Rio — 172 B 5
Cúneo 122-123 B 3
Cuney, TX 76-77 G 6
Çüngüş 136-137 H 3
Cunha 102-103 K 5
Cunnamulla 158-159 HJ 5
Cunningham, WA 66-67 D 2
Cunningham Park [USA, Boston] 84 I b 3
Cunningham Park [USA, New York] 82 III d 2
Cunocuno, Pampa de — 96-97 E 10
Čuokkarašša 116-117 KL 2
Cupar 61 F 5
Cupecê, Ribeirão — 110 II b 2
Cupica 94-95 C 4
Cupica, Golfo de — 92-93 D 3
Cupira [BR] 100-101 G 5
Cúpira [YV] 94-95 J 2
Cuprum, ID 66-67 E 3
Cuptana, Isla — 108-109 C 5
Cupupira, Sierra — 94-95 J 6-7
Čur 124-125 T 5
Curaçá [BR, Amazonas] 92-93 G 6
Curaçá [BR, Bahia] 92-93 LM 6
Curaçá, Rio — 100-101 E 5
Curaçao 64-65 N 9
Curacautín 111 B 5
Curacaví 106-107 B 4
Curacó, Río — 106-107 E 7
Curahuara de Carangas 104-105 B 5
Curahuara de Pacajes 104-105 C 5
Cura Mala, Sierra de — 106-107 FG 6-7
Curamalal Grande, Cerro — 106-107 FG 6
Curamavida, Cerro — 106-107 B 3
Curamoni 94-95 H 6
Curanilahue 111 B 5
Curanipe 106-107 A 5
Curanja, Río — 96-97 F 7
Curapaligüe 106-107 F 5
Čurapča 132-133 Z 5
Curaray [EC] 96-97 C 2
Curaray [PE] 96-97 D 3
Curaray, Río — 92-93 D 5
Curarigua 94-95 FG 3
Curarú 106-107 FG 5
Curaumilla, Punta — 106-107 AB 4
Curdistán = Kordestān 134-135 F 3
Curepto 106-107 A 5
Curiapo 92-93 G 3
Curibaya 96-97 F 10
Curicó 111 B 4
Curicó, Laguna — 108-109 G 3
Curicuriari, Rio — 98-99 DE 5
Curicuriari, Serra — 98-99 E 5
Curimatá 100-101 B 6
Curimatá, Rio — 100-101 B 5-6
Curioso, Cabo — 108-109 F 7
Curiplaya 94-95 D 7
Curitiba 111 G 3
Curitibanos 102-103 G 7
Curiuja, Río — 96-97 E 7
Curiúva 102-103 G 6
Curlandia 124-125 CD 5
Curlew, WA 66-67 D 1
Curnamona 158-159 GH 6
Currais Novos 92-93 M 6
Curralinho 98-99 NO 5
Curral Novo 100-101 CD 5
Curral Novo, Serra — 100-101 EF 6
Curral Velho 100-101 B 7
Currant, NV 74-75 F 3
Current River 78-79 D 2
Currie 158-159 H 7-8
Currie, MN 70-71 C 3
Currie, NV 66-67 F 5
Currituck Sound 80-81 J 2
Curry, AK 58-59 MN 5
Curtea-de-Argeș 122-123 L 3
Curtin Springs 158-159 F 5
Curtis, NE 68-69 F 5
Curtis Island [AUS] 158-159 K 4
Curtis Island [NZ] 158-159 Q 6
Curuá, Ilha — 98-99 NO 4
Curuá, Rio — [BR ◁ Rio Amazonas] 98-99 L 4-5
Curuá, Rio — [BR ◁ Rio Iriri] 92-93 J 6
Curuá do Sul, Rio — 98-99 LM 6
Curuaés, Rio — 98-99 L 9
Curuai 92-93 H 5
Curuai, Lago Grande do — 98-99 L 6
Curuá Una, Rio — 98-99 L 6
Curuçá 92-93 K 5
Curuçá, Ponta — 98-99 P 5
Curuçá, Rio — 98-99 C 7
Curucuinazá, Rio — 104-105 GH 3
Curuguaty 102-103 E 6
Curumani 94-95 E 3
Curumu 98-99 N 5
Curunuri, Serra do — 98-99 MN 4
Curup 148-149 D 7
Curupá 100-101 AB 5
Curupai, Rio — 102-103 EF 5
Curupaity 106-107 G 3
C'urupinsk 126-127 F 3
Curupira 100-101 E 3
Curuquetê, Rio — 98-99 F 9
Cururú 92-93 G 8
Cururu-Açu, Rio — 98-99 K 9
Cururupu 92-93 L 5
Curuzú Chali, Isla — 106-107 H 3
Curuzú Cuatiá 111 E 3
Curva 104-105 B 4
Curva Grande 92-93 K 5
Curvelo 92-93 L 8
Curzola = Korčula 122-123 G 4
Cusali, Cerros — 104-105 C 4
Čuševicy 124-125 N 3
Cushing, OK 76-77 F 5
Cushing, TX 76-77 G 7
Cushman, AR 78-79 D 3
Cusiana, Río — 94-95 E 5
Cusino, MI 70-71 G 2
Cusis, Los — 104-105 D 4
Čusovoj 132-133 K 6
Čusovskoj 124-125 V 3
Cusseta, GA 78-79 G 4
Čust 134-135 L 2
Custer, SD 68-69 E 4
Custódia 100-101 F 5
Cutanga, Volcán — 94-95 C 7
Cutapines, Lomba das — 104-105 E 2
Cut Bank, MT 66-67 GH 1
Cutch = Kutch 134-135 K 6
Cutervo 92-93 D 6
Cuthbert, GA 78-79 G 5
Cut Knife 61 D 4
Cutler 62 K 3
Cutler, CA 74-75 D 4
Cutler River 58-59 HJ 3
Cutral-Có 106-107 C 7
Cuttaburra Creek 160 G 2
Cuttack 134-135 NO 6
Cutupí 98-99 G 10
Cutzamala, Río — 86-87 K 8
Cu'u Long, Cu'a Sông — 148-149 E 5
Čuvašskaja Avtonomnaja Sovetskaja Socialističeskaja Respublika = Chuvash Autonomous Soviet Socialist Republic 132-133 H 6
Cuvelai 172 C 5
Cuvier, Cape — 158-159 B 4
Cuvo, Rio — 172 B 4
Cuxhaven 118 D 2
Cuy, El — 111 C 5
Cuyabeno 96-97 D 2
Cuyahoga Falls, OH 72-73 F 4
Cuyama River 74-75 C 5
Cuyo Islands 148-149 H 4
Cuyuni River 92-93 G 3
Cuzco [PE, administrative unit] 96-97 EF 8
Cuzco [PE, place] 92-93 E 7

C. W. MacConaughy, Lake — 68-69 E 5

Cyangugu 171 B 3
Cybulev 126-127 DE 2
Cyclorama and Zoo 85 II bc 2
Cymru = Wales 119 E 5-6
Cynthiana, KY 72-73 DE 5
Cyphergat = Syfergat 174-175 G 6
Cyp-Navolok 116-117 PQ 3
Cypress, CA 83 III d 2
Cypress, LA 78-79 C 5
Cypress, TX 76-77 FG 8
Cypress Hills 56-57 OP 8
Cypress Hills Provincial Park 61 CD 6
Cypress Lake 66-67 J 1
Cyprus 134-135 C 4
Cyrenaica = Barqah 164-165 J 2
Cyrene = Shaḥḥat 164-165 J 2

Czar 61 C 4
Czechoslovakia 118 F-K 4
Czersk 118 J 2
Częstochowa 118 JK 3

D

Đa, Sông — 148-149 D 2
Da'an 146-147 C 10
Ḍab'ah 136-137 G 7
Ḍab'ah, Aḍ- 164-165 K 2
Ḍab'ah, Rā's, aḍ- 136-137 C 7
Dabaidi 146-147 E 8
Dabajuro 94-95 F 2
Dabakala 164-165 D 7
Daba Shan 142-143 KL 5
Dabas nuur 142-143 H 4
Dabat = Debark 164-165 MN 7
Dabbā = Jabal Jarbī 136-137 H 5
Dabbah, Ad- 164-165 KL 5
Dabbūsah, Ad- 136-137 J 7
Dabdū 166-167 E 3
Dabeiba 92-93 D 3
Dabhoi 138-139 D 6
Dābhol 140 A 2
Dabie Shan [TJ, mountain] 146-147 EF 6
Dabie Shan [TJ, mountains] 142-143 M 5
Dabla 138-139 E 4
Dabola 164-165 B 6
Daborow 164-165 b 2
Dabou 168-169 D 4
Daboya 168-169 E 3
Dąbrowa Tarnowska 118 K 3
Dabu 146-147 F 9
Dābugām 138-139 J 8
Dabul = Dābhol 140 A 2
Dabuxun Hu = Dabas nuur 142-143 H 4
Dacaidan = Tagalgan 142-143 H 4
Dacar = Dakar 164-165 A 6
Dacar, Bir ed — = Bi'r ad-Dhikār 164-165 J 3
Dacca = Ḍhāka [BD, administrative unit] 138-139 N 5-6
Dacca = Ḍhāka [BD, place] 134-135 OP 6
Dachaidan = Tagalgan 142-143 H 4
Dachangshan Dao 144-145 D 3
Dachangtu Shan 146-147 J 6
Dachau 118 E 4
Dachen Dao 146-147 HJ 7
Dacheng = Daicheng 146-147 F 2
Dachepalle 140 DE 2
Dachovskaja 126-127 JK 4
Dachstein 118 F 5
Đac Lăc, Cao Nguyên — 148-149 E 4
Dadache, Rio — 174-175 K 2
Dadaituan = Shentuan 146-147 G 4
Dadanawa 98-99 HJ 3
Daday 136-137 E 2
Dade City, FL 80-81 b 2
Dadeville, AL 78-79 FG 4
Dadian [TJ, Anhui] 146-147 F 5
Dadian [TJ, Shandong] 146-147 G 4
Dādis, Wād — 166-167 C 4
Dadra and Nagar Haveli 134-135 L 6
Dādrī = Charkhi Dādri 138-139 EF 3
Da Drin = Sông Tra 150-151 G 5
Dādū 134-135 K 5
Dadu He 142-143 J 5
Dadukou 146-147 F 6
Đa Dung 150-151 FG 7
Đa Du'ng, Mui — 150-151 EF 3
Daduru Oya 140 DE 7
Dadynskoje, ozero — 126-127 M 4
Daerstorf 130 I a 2
Daet 148-149 H 4
Dafan 146-147 E 7
Dafdaf, Jabal — 173 D 3
Dafeng 146-147 H 5
Dafeng Shan = Shinaibeidong 146-147 H 7
Dafinah, Ad- 134-135 E 6
Dafla Hills 141 C 2
Dafnion 113 IV a 1
Dafoe 61 F 5
Dafoe River 61 L 3
Dafou = Wangmudu 146-147 E 9
Dafter, MI 70-71 H 2
Dafu Shui 146-147 D 6
Dagabur = Degeh Bur 164-165 N 7
Daga Myit 141 D 7
Dagana 164-165 AB 5
Dagangtou 146-147 G 7
Dağbaşı 136-137 H 4
Dagda 124-125 F 5
Dagelet = Ullŭng-do 142-143 P 4
Dagenham, London- 129 II c 1
Dagestan Autonomous Soviet Socialist Republic 126-127 MN 5
Dagestanskije Ogni 126-127 O 5
Daggett, CA 74-75 E 5
Daghgharah, Ad- 136-137 L 6
Daglfing, München- 130 II bc 2
Dağlıca = Oramar 136-137 KL 4
Dagmar 138-139 MN 2
Dagö = Hiiumaa 124-125 CD 4
Dagomba 164-165 D 7
Dagomys, Soči- 126-127 J 5
Dagoum 168-169 J 2
Dagu 146-147 F 2
Dagua [CO] 94-95 C 6
Dagua [PNG] 148-149 M 7
Dagu He 146-147 H 3
D'Aguilar, Cape — = Tai Long Head 155 I b 2
D'Aguilar Peak 155 I b 2
Dagujia 144-145 E 1
Dagverdharnes 116-117 b 2
Dāhānu 134-135 L 6-7
Dahao Dao 146-147 DE 10
Dahar = Ẓahar 166-167 LM 3
Daheishan Dao 146-147 GH 3
Dahej = Dehej 138-139 D 7
Dahī, Nafūd ad- 134-135 EF 6
Dahībah, Ad- = Adh-Dhahībah 166-167 M 3
Dahlak desēt 164-165 N 5
Dahlem, Berlin- 130 III b 2
Dahnā', Ad- 134-135 E 5-F 6
Dāhōd = Dohad 138-139 E 6
Dahomey = Benin 164-165 E 6-7
Dahongcheng 146-147 CD 1
Dahong Shan 146-147 D 6
Dahra = Aḍ-Ḍahrah 166-167 G 1
Ḍahrah 164-165 H 3
Ḍahrah, Aḍ- 166-167 G 1
Ḍahr Walātah 164-165 C 5
Dahshūr = Minshāt Dahshūr 173 B 3
Dahua Jiao 150-151 H 3
Dahūk 136-137 K 4
Dahushan 144-145 D 2
Daïa, Monts de — = Jabal aḍ-Ḍāyah 166-167 F 2
Daïa, Région des — = Ḍāyah 166-167 HJ 3
Daïa el Aam = Dayat 'al-'Âm 166-167 B 6
Daïa el Maïda = Ḍaya al-Mā'idah 166-167 D 4
Daibang Wand = Dapeng Wan 146-147 E 10
Daïet el Khadra = Ḍayat al-Khaḍrah 166-167 BC 6
Daijuku 155 III d 3
Daik'ū 141 E 7
Dailekh 138-139 H 3
Đai Lôc 150-151 G 5
Daimiel 120-121 F 9
Đai Ngai 150-151 EF 8
Daingerfield, TX 76-77 G 6
Daiō zaki 144-145 L 5
Daipingqiao = Taipingshao 144-145 E 2
Dāira Dīn Panāh 138-139 C 2
Daireaux 106-107 G 6
Dairen = Lüda-Dalian 142-143 N 4
Dairūṭ = Dayrūṭ 164-165 L 3
Dai-sen 144-145 J 5
Dai-Sengen dake 144-145 ab 3
Daisetta, TX 76-77 G 7
Dai Shan 146-147 HJ 6
Dai Shan = Taishan Liedao 146-147 H 8
Daishi, Kawasaki- 155 III b 2
Dais hōji = Kaga 144-145 L 4
Daisy, WA 66-67 DE 1
Daito-jima 142-143 P 6
Daitō-shima 142-143 P 6
Daitō sima = Daitō-shima 142-143 P 6
Dai Xian 146-147 D 2
Dājal 138-139 C 3
Dajarra 158-159 G 4
Dajiangkou = Jiangkou 146-147 C 8
Dajiangtou = Dagangtou 146-147 G 7
Dajiaoting, Beijing- 155 II bc 2
Dajing [TJ, Guangdong] 146-147 C 10
Dajing [TJ, Zhejiang] 146-147 H 7
Dajingcun, Beijing- 155 II a 2
Daka 168-169 E 3
Dakar 164-165 A 6
Dakawa 171 D 4
Dakaye 168-169 E 3
Daketa 164-165 N 7
Dakhan = Deccan 134-135 M 6-8
Dakhan Shāhbāzpūr Dīp 141 B 4
Dākhilah, Wāḥāt ad- 164-165 K 3
Dakhin Shahbazpur Island = Dakhan Shāhbāzpūr Dīp 141 B 4
Dakhlah, Ad- 164-165 A 4
Dakhla Oasis = Wāḥāt ad-Dākhilah 164-165 K 3
Dak Hon 150-151 F 5
Dakka = Ḍhāka 134-135 OP 6
Dākor 138-139 D 6
Dakoro 168-169 G 2
Dakota, North — 64-65 FG 2
Dakota, South — 64-65 FG 3
D'akovskoje, Moskva- 113 V c 3
Dak Po'kô 150-151 F 5
Dakshin Andamān = South Andamān 134-135 P 8
Dakshinī Koil = South Koel 138-139 K 6
Dakshin Paṭhār = Deccan 134-135 M 6-8
Dakshin Shālmāra = South Sālmāra 138-139 N 5
Dak Sut 150-151 F 5
Dak Tô 150-151 F 5
Dakunū Palāna ◁ 140 E 7
Dākur = Dākor 138-139 D 6
Dala 116-117 bc 2
Dalaba 164-165 B 6
Dalafi 168-169 B 2
Dalai 142-143 N 2
Dalai Lama Gangri 142-143 GH 5
Dalai Nur 142-143 M 3
Dalaj Nuur = Hulun Nur 142-143 M 2
Dalāk, Kūh-e — 136-137 N 4
Dalälven 116-117 G 7
Dalaman nehri 136-137 C 4
Dalandzadgad 142-143 JK 3
Dalangwan 146-147 D 11
Dalarna 116-117 EF 7
Da Lat 148-149 E 4
Dalavakasır 136-137 J 4
Dālbandīn 134-135 J 5
Dalby [AUS] 158-159 K 5
Dalcour, LA 85 I c 3
Dale 116-117 AB 7
Dale, OR 66-67 D 3
Dale, PA 72-73 G 4
Dalecarlia Reservoir 82 II a 1
Dale Hollow Lake 78-79 G 2
Dalen 116-117 C 8
Dalesford 61 F 4
Dalgaranger, Mount — 158-159 C 5
Dalhart, TX 76-77 C 4
Dalhauzī 138-139 M 7
Dalhousie 63 C 3
Dalhousie = Dalhauzī 138-139 M 7
Dalhousie, Cape — 56-57 KL 3
Dalhousie Island 138-139 M 7
Dali [TJ, Shaanxi] 146-147 B 4
Dali [TJ, Yunnan] 142-143 HJ 6
Dalian, Lüda- 142-143 N 4
Dalias 120-121 F 10
Dali Baizu Zizhizhou 142-143 HJ 6
Dalies, NM 76-77 A 5
Dali He 146-147 B 3
Daling He 144-145 C 2
Dalis 166-167 HJ 1
Daljā' 173 B 4
Ḍalkūt = Kharīfūt 134-135 G 7
Dall, Mount — 58-59 LM 5
Dallas 61 K 5
Dallas, GA 78-79 G 4
Dallas, IA 70-71 D 5
Dallas, OR 66-67 B 3
Dallas, TX 64-65 G 5
Dallas City, IL 70-71 E 5
Dällikon 128 IV a 1
Dalli Rājhara 138-139 H 7
Dall Island 56-57 K 7
Dall Lake 58-59 F 6
Dall Mount 58-59 N 3
Dallol Bosso 164-165 E 5-6
Dall River 58-59 N 3
Dalmacija 122-123 F 3-H 4
Dalmacio Vélez Sarsfield 106-107 EF 4
Dalmaj, Hawr — 136-137 L 6
Dalmatia = Dalmacija 122-123 F 3-H 4
Dalmau 138-139 H 4
Dalmiyapuram 140 D 5
Dalnegorsk 132-133 a 9
Dalnerečensk 132-133 Za 8
Dal'nij = Lüda-Dalian 142-143 N 4
Daloa 164-165 C 7
Dalqū 164-165 L 4-5
Dalquier 62 MN 2
Dalrymple, Mount — 158-159 J 4
Dalsingh Saraj 138-139 K 5
Dalton 70-71 HJ 1
Dalton, GA 64-65 JK 5
Dalton, MA 72-73 K 3
Dalton, NE 68-69 E 5
Daltonganj 134-135 N 6
Dalton Ice Tongue 53 C 12-13
Dalton in Furness 119 E 4
Dalvík 116-117 d 2
Dalwhinnie 119 DE 3
Dalyan burnu 154 I b 1
Daly City, CA 74-75 B 4
Daly Lake 61 F 2
Daly River 158-159 F 2
Daly Waters 158-159 F 3
Damā, Wādī — 173 DE 4
Damakanya 168-169 B 3
Damān 134-135 L 6
Damanhūr 164-165 L 2
Damanhūr Shubrā 170 II b 1
Damão = Damān 134-135 L 6
Damaq 136-137 N 5
Damar, Pulau — 148-149 J 8
Damara 164-165 H 8
Damaraland 172 C 6
Damascus, VA 80-81 F 2
Damascus = Dimashq 134-135 D 4
Damaturu 164-165 G 6
Damāvand, Kūh-e — 134-135 G 3
Damazīn, Ad- 164-165 LM 6
Damba 172 BC 3
Dambuki 142-143 S 3-T 2
Dambulla 140 E 7
Dam Dam = South Dum Dum 134-135 OP 6
Damdek = Phum Damdek 150-151 DE 6
Dame Marie, Cap — 88-89 J 5
Damenglong 150-151 C 2
Dämeritzsee 130 III c 2
Dāmghān 134-135 GH 3
Đâm Ha 150-151 F 2
Damianópolis 100-101 A 8
Damiaoshan = Rongshui 146-147 B 9
Damietta = Dumyāṭ 164-165 L 2
Damietta Mouth = Maṣabb Dumyāṭ 173 BC 2
Daming 146-147 E 3
Dāmīr, Ad- 164-165 L 5
Damīr Qābū 136-137 JK 4
Dammām, Ad- 132-133 FG 5
Damnāt 166-167 C 4
Dāmodar 134-135 O 6
Damoh 138-139 G 6
Damongo 168-169 E 3
Damot 164-165 b 2
Damous = Dāmus 166-167 G 1
Dampier 158-159 C 4
Dampier, Selat — 148-149 K 7
Dampier Archipelago 158-159 C 4
Dampier Downs 158-159 D 3
Dampier Land 158-159 D 3
Damrei, Phnom — 150-151 DE 7
Dāmūr, Ad- 136-137 F 6
Dāmus 166-167 G 1
Dan, Kap — 56-57 d 4
Dana, Mount — 74-75 D 4
Danané 168-169 CD 4
Đa Năng 148-149 E 3
Đa Năng, Mui — 150-151 G 4
Dānāpur = Dinapore 138-139 K 5
Danau Jempang 152-153 LM 6
Danau Maninjau 152-153 CD 6
Danau Matana 152-153 O 7
Danau Melintang 152-153 LM 6
Danau Poso 152-153 O 6
Danau Ranau 152-153 E 8
Danau Sentarum 152-153 JK 5
Danau Singkarak 152-153 CD 6
Danau Tempe 148-149 GH 7
Danau Toba 148-149 C 6
Danau Towuti 148-149 H 7
Danau Wissel 148-149 L 7
Danbury, CT 72-73 K 4
Danbury, WI 70-71 D 2-3
Danby Lake 74-75 F 5
Dancharia 120-121 G 7
Dandarah 173 C 4
Daṇḍeldhurā 138-139 H 3
Dandeli 140 B 3
Dandelli = Dandeli 140 B 3
Dandoldhura = Daṇḍeldhurā 138-139 H 3
Dandong 142-143 N 3
Danfeng 146-147 C 5
Danforth, ME 72-73 MN 2
Danfu 148-149 h 5
Dang 98-99 L 2
Dangan Liedao 146-147 E 10-11
Dangaripalli = Dungripalli 138-139 J 7
Dange, Rio — 172 B 3
Danger 208 K 4
Dangpe La 138-139 M 3
Dang Raek, Phanom — 148-149 DE 4
Dangraek, Phnom — = Phanom Dong Raek 148-149 DE 4
Dāngs 138-139 D 7
Dangs, The — = Dāngs 138-139 D 7
Dangshan 146-147 F 4
Dangtu 146-147 G 6
Dan Gulbi 168-169 G 3
Danguno 164-165 F 6-7
Dangyang 146-147 CD 6
Danhao Dao 146-147 DE 10
Dan He 146-147 D 4
Da Nhim 150-151 G 7
Daniel, WY 66-67 H 4
Daniel's Harbour 63 GH 2
Dänikon 128 IV a 1
Danilov 132-133 G 6
Danilovka 124-125 P 7
Danilovo 124-125 KL 2
Daning 146-147 C 3
Danissa 171 E 2
Dan Jiang 146-147 C 5
Danjo-shotō 144-145 G 6
Ḍank 134-135 H 6
Dankana 168-169 GH 2
Dankhar Gömpa 138-139 G 1
Dan Khun Thot 150-151 CD 5
Dankov 124-125 M 7
Danlí 64-65 J 9
Dan Na Lao = Ban Dan Na Lao 150-151 EF 5
Dannemora, NY 72-73 JK 2
Dannevirke 158-159 P 8
Dannhauser 174-175 HJ 4-5
Dañoso, Cabo — 108-109 F 7
Dan River 80-81 FG 2
Dan Sai 150-151 C 4
Danshui 146-147 E 10
Danshui = Tanshui 142-143 N 6
Danshui He = Tanshui Chiang 146-147 H 9
Dansia 92-93 H 4
Danson Park 129 II c 2
Dansville, NY 72-73 H 3
Dānta 138-139 D 5
Danta, La — 94-95 L 4
Dāntan 138-139 L 7
Dānta Rāmgarh = Rāmgarh 138-139 E 4
Dante, VA 80-81 E 2
Dante = Haafuun 164-165 c 1
Dantewāra 140 E 1
Dantyaorā = Dantewāra 140 E 1
Danube = Duna 118 J 5
Danubyū 141 D 7
Danushkodi 134-135 MN 9
Danville 72-73 KL 2
Danville, AR 78-79 C 3
Danville, IL 64-65 J 3
Danville, IN 70-71 G 6
Danville, KY 70-71 H 7
Danville, ME 72-73 L 2-3
Danville, VA 64-65 L 4
Danwanjiao 152-153 KL 2
Dan Xian 142-143 K 8
Danyang 146-147 G 6
Danzin Au 141 D 7
Đao Bach Long Vi 150-151 F 2
Đao Cai Ban 148-149 E 2
Đao Cat Ba 150-151 F 2
Đao Kersaint 150-151 FG 2
Daolatābād = Daulatābād 138-139 E 8
Daoli 146-147 H 3
Dao Ly So'n = Cu Lao Rê 150-151 G 5
Đao Phu Quôc 148-149 D 4
Daosā 138-139 F 4
Dao Shui 146-147 E 6
Đao Tching Lan Xan 150-151 FG 2
Dao-Timni 164-165 G 4
Ḍaou, Eḍ — = Aḍ-Ḍaw 136-137 G 5
Daouadi 168-169 B 2

Daoura, Hamada de la — = Hammadat ad-Dawrah 166-167 DE 5
Daoura, Oued ed — = Wādī ad-Dawrah 166-167 DE 5
Đao Vinh Thu'c = Đao Kersaint 150-151 FG 2
Dao Xian 146-147 C 9
Dapango 168-169 F 3
Đap Câu 150-151 F 2
Dapchi 168-169 H 2
Dapeng 146-147 E 10
Dapeng Wan 146-147 E 10
Dapingzu = Huitongqiao 141 F 3
Dapna Bum 141 E 2
Dapodi = Dabaidi 146-147 E 8
Dāpoli 140 A 2
Dapsang = K2 134-135 M 3
Dapu = Dabu 146-147 F 9
Dāpung = Brāpung 138-139 N 3
Dapupan 148-149 GH 3
Daqi = Ta-ch'i [RC ✓ Taipei] 146-147 H 9
Daqi = Ta-ch'i [RC ✓ Taitung] 146-147 H 10
Daqiao 146-147 E 7
Daqing Shan 142-143 L 3
Daqmā', Ad- 134-135 FG 6
Daqq-e Patargān 134-135 J 4
Daquan 142-143 H 3
Daqu Shan 146-147 J 6
Dar'ā 136-137 G 6
Darā, Jazīreh — 136-137 N 7
Daraā, Rio — 94-95 J 7-8
Dara' al-Mizān 166-167 HJ 1
Dārāb 134-135 GH 5
Darabani 122-123 M 1
Darad = Dardistān 134-135 L 3
Darag = Legaspi 148-149 H 4
Daraj 164-165 G 2
Dār al-Bayḍā', Ad- 164-165 BC 2
Dār al-Qā'id al-Midbūh 166-167 DE 2
Darang = Dirang 141 C 2
Dār ash-Shāfa'i 166-167 C 3
Darašun = Veršino-Darasunskij 132-133 VW 7
Darau = Darāw 173 C 5
Darāw 173 C 5
Darb, Ad- 134-135 E 7
Dār Bādām 136-137 M 6
Darband, Kūh-e — 134-135 H 4
Darbandī Khan, Sadd ad- 136-137 L 5
Darbanga = Darbhanga 134-135 O 5
Darbėnai 124-125 C 5
Darbhanga 134-135 O 5
Darbi = Darvi 142-143 G 2
Darby, MT 66-67 FG 2
Darby, PA 84 III b 2
Darby, Cape — 58-59 F 4
Darby Creek 84 III b 2
Darby Mountains 58-59 E 4
Dar Caid Medboh = Dār al-Qā'id al-Midbūh 166-167 DE 2
Dar Chafaï = Dār ash-Shāfa'i 166-167 C 3
Darchan 142-143 K 2
Dardanelle, AR 78-79 C 3
Dardanelles = Çanakkale boğazı 134-135 B 2-3
Dār Dīshah 136-137 J 5
Dardo = Kangding 142-143 J 5-6
Dār Dryūs 166-167 E 2
Darebin Creek 161 II c 1
Dār ech Chāfaï = Dār ash-Shāfa'i 166-167 C 3
Dar el Beida 170 I b 2
Dar el Beida, Aéroport de — 170 I b 2
Dār el Beiḍā', ed — = Ad-Dār al-Bayḍā' 164-165 BC 2
Darende 136-137 G 3
Dar es Salaam 172 GH 3
Dārfūr 164-165 J 6
Dārfūr al-Janūbīyah 164-165 JK 6
Dārfūr ash-Shimālīyah 164-165 J 6-K 5
Dargagā, Jebel ed — = Jabal Ardar Gwagwa 173 D 6
Dargan-Ata 134-135 J 2
Dargaville 158-159 O 7
Dargo 160 H 6
Dargol 168-169 F 2
Dargyalükutong Gonpa 138-139 MN 2
Dār Ḥamar 164-165 K 6
Dar Hu = Dalaj Nur 142-143 M 3
Darien, GA 80-81 F 5
Darién [PA, landscape] 64-65 L 10
Darien [PA, place] 64-65 b 2
Darien = Lüda-Dalian 142-143 N 4
Darién, Cordillera de — 88-89 D 8
Darién, Golfo del — 92-93 D 3
Darién, Serranía del — 88-89 H 10
Dārigah 136-137 K 5
Dariganga 142-143 L 2
Daringbādi 138-139 JK 8
Darjeeling 134-135 O 5
Dārjiling = Darjeeling 134-135 O 5
Darjinskij 124-125 S 8
Darkhazīneh 136-137 N 7
Darling 174-175 C 7
Darling, Lake — 68-69 F 1
Darling Downs 158-159 JK 5
Darling Range 158-159 C 6
Darling River 158-159 H 6
Darlington 119 EF 4
Darlington, SC 80-81 FG 3
Darlington, WI 70-71 EF 4
Darlowo 118 H 1
Darmsāla 138-139 KL 7
Darmstadt 118 D 4
Darmstadt-Kranichstein 128 III b 2
Darnah 164-165 J 2
Darnall 174-175 J 5
Darnick 158-159 H 6
Darnley, Cape — 53 C 7-8
Daro 152-153 J 4
Daroca 120-121 G 8
Darovskoj 124-125 Q 4
Darregueira 106-107 F 6
Darrington, WA 66-67 C 1
Dar Rounga 164-165 J 6-7
Dar Runga = Dar Rounga 164-165 J 6-7
Darsah 134-135 G 8
Darshi = Darsi 140 D 3
Darsi 140 D 3
Dart, Cape — 53 B 24
Dartford 129 II c 2
Dartmoor Forest 119 E 6
Dartmouth [CDN] 56-57 Y 9
Dartuch, Cabo — 120-121 J 9
Daru 148-149 M 8
Darūdāb 164-165 M 5
Dārugiri 141 B 3
Dār Ūld Zīdūḥ 166-167 C 3
Daruvar 122-123 G 3
Darvaza 134-135 H 2
Darvel, Teluk — 152-153 N 3
Dārvhā = Dārwha 138-139 F 7
Darvi 142-143 G 2
Darwešān 134-135 JK 4
Dārwha 138-139 F 7
Darwin, CA 74-75 E 4
Darwin [AUS] 158-159 F 2
Darwin [RA] 106-107 E 7
Darwin, Bahía — 111 AB 7
Darwin, Canal — 108-109 B 5
Darwin, Cordillera — [RCH, Cordillera Patagónica] 108-109 C 7-8
Darwin, Cordillera — [RCH, Tierra del Fuego] 108-109 DE 10
Darwin, Cordillera de — 104-105 B 10
Darwin zapovednik 124-125 LM 4
Daryācheh Bakhtegān 134-135 G 5
Daryācheh Ḥowḍ Solṭān 136-137 O 5
Dāryācheh i Niriz = Daryācheh Bakhtegān 134-135 G 5
Daryācheh Namak 134-135 G 4
Daryācheh Reḍā'īyeh = Daryācheh-ye Orūmīyeh 134-135 F 3
Daryācheh Sīstān 134-135 HJ 4
Daryācheh Ṭashk 134-135 GH 5
Daryācheh Urmia = Daryācheh Orūmīyeh 134-135 F 3
Daryācheh-ye Orūmīyeh 134-135 E 3
Daryāpur 138-139 F 7
Dāryā-ye Adraskan = Hārūt Rōd 134-135 J 4
Dārya-ye-Hilmānd = Helmand Rōd 134-135 K 4
Dāryā-ye 'Omān = Khalīj 'Umān 134-135 HJ 6
Dās 134-135 G 5
Dasamantapur 138-139 J 8
Dašava 126-127 AB 2
Dašev 126-127 D 2
Dasha He 146-147 E 2
Dashamantpura = Dasamantapur 138-139 J 8
Dashen, Ras — 164-165 M 6
Dashiqiao 144-145 D 2
Dasht 134-135 J 5
Dasht-e Āzādegān 136-137 N 7
Dasht-e Kavīr 134-135 GH 4
Dasht-e Lūṭ 134-135 H 4
Dasht-e Marg 134-135 J 4
Dasht-e Margoh = Dasht-e Marg 134-135 J 4
Dasht-e Moghān 134-135 F 3
Dashtiāri = Polān 134-135 J 5
Daškesan 126-127 MN 6
Daspalla 138-139 K 7
Dassa-Zoumé 168-169 F 4
Dassel, MN 70-71 C 3
Dasseneiland 174-175 BC 7
Dasūā = Dasūya 138-139 E 2
Dasūya 138-139 E 2
Dātāganj 138-139 G 3
Datang 146-147 B 9
Dataran Tinggi Cameron = Tanah-tinggi Cameron 148-149 D 6
Datça = Reşadiye 136-137 B 4
Đât Đo 150-151 F 7
Date 144-145 b 2
Dātha 138-139 C 7
Datia 134-135 M 5
Datian 146-147 F 9
Datil, NM 76-77 A 5
Datiyā = Datia 134-135 M 5
D'atkovo 124-125 K 7
D'atlovo 124-125 E 7
Datok, Kampung — 150-151 D 11
Datong [TJ, Anhui] 146-147 F 6
Datong [TJ, Shanxi] 142-143 L 3
Datong He 142-143 J 4
Datori 168-169 F 3
Da Troun, Đeo — 150-151 G 7
Da Trun, Đeo — = Đeo Da Troun 150-151 G 7
Dattapur 138-139 FG 7
Datu, Tanjung — 148-149 E 6
Datu, Teluk — 148-149 EF 6
Datun, Beijing- 155 II b 2
Datu Piang 148-149 H 5
Dau'an = Al-Huraybah 134-135 F 7
Daudkaṇḍi 141 B 4
Daudmannsodden 116-117 hj 5
Daudnagar 138-139 K 5
Daugava 124-125 E 5
Daugava = Severnaja Dvina 132-133 G 5
Daugavpils 124-125 EF 6
Daulagiri = Dhaulāgiri 134-135 N 5
Daulatābād 138-139 E 8
Daule 96-97 AB 2
Daule, Río — 92-93 CD 5
Dauna Parma = Dawa 164-165 M 7-8
Daun Tri, Stung — 150-151 D 6
Dauphin 56-57 QR 7
Dauphiné 120-121 KL 6
Dauphin Island 78-79 EF 5
Dauphin Lake 61 J 5
Daura 168-169 GH 2
Daura, Wed ed — = Wādī ad-Dawrah 166-167 DE 5
Daurskij chrebet 132-133 V 7
Dausā = Daosā 138-139 F 4
Dautlatābād = Malāyer 134-135 F 4
Davalguiri = Dhaulāgiri 134-135 N 5
Davalinskogo = Ararat 126-127 M 7
Dāvangere 140 BC 3
Davao 148-149 J 5
Davao Gulf 148-149 J 5
Dāvariyā = Deoria 138-139 J 4
Davel 174-175 H 4
Davenport, AK 58-59 JK 5
Davenport, IA 64-65 H 3
Davenport, ND 68-69 H 2
Davenport, NE 68-69 H 5
Davenport, WA 66-67 D 2
Davenport Downs 158-159 H 4
Davenport Range 158-159 FG 4
Davey, Port — 158-159 HJ 8
David 64-65 K 10
David City, NE 68-69 H 5
David-Gorodok 124-125 F 7
Davidof Island 58-59 s 6-7
Davids Island 82 III d 1
Davidson 61 E 5
Davidson, OK 76-77 E 5
Davidson Mountains 56-57 H 4
Daviesville 174-175 HJ 2
Davignab 174-175 C 4
Davis, CA 74-75 BC 3
Davis, IL 70-71 F 4
Davis, OK 76-77 F 5
Davis, WV 72-73 G 5
Davis Bay 53 C 14
Davis Creek, CA 66-67 C 5
Davis Dam, AZ 74-75 F 5
Davis Island = Than Kyūn 150-151 A 8
Davis Mountains 76-77 BC 7
Davis Sea 53 C 10
Davis Strait 56-57 Z 4-5
Davlekanovo 132-133 JK 7
Davo 168-169 D 4
Davos 118 DE 5
Davydkovo, Moskva- 113 V b 3
Davydovka 126-127 J 1
Ḍaw, Aḍ- 136-137 G 5
Dawa 164-165 M 7-8
Dawadawa 168-169 E 3
Dawādimā, Ad- 134-135 EF 6
Dawan 146-147 B 10
Dawangjia Dao 144-145 D 3
Dawanle = Dewelē 164-165 N 6
Dawarah, Wād ad- 166-167 D 4
Dawāsir, Wādī ad- 134-135 EF 6
Dawenkou 146-147 F 3-4
Dawḥah, Ad- 134-135 G 5
Dawhat aḍ-Ḍuwayḥin 134-135 G 6
Dawḥat as-Sawqirah 134-135 H 7
Dawingnab = Davignab 174-175 C 4
Dawna Taungdan 141 EF 7
Dawr, Ad- 136-137 KL 5
Dawrah, Baghdād- 136-137 L 6
Dawrah, Hammadat ad- 166-167 DE 5
Dawrah, Wādī ad- 166-167 DE 5
Dawson 56-57 J 5
Dawson, GA 78-79 G 5
Dawson, ND 68-69 G 2
Dawson, Isla — 111 BC 8
Dawson Bay [CDN, bay] 61 H 4
Dawson Bay [CDN, place] 61 H 4
Dawson Creek 56-57 M 6
Dawson-Lambton Glacier 53 B 33-34
Dawson Range 56-57 J 5
Dawson Springs, KY 70-71 FG 7
Dawu 146-147 E 6
Dawu = Tawu 146-147 H 10
Dawuji, Beijing- 155 II b 2
Dawwah 134-135 H 6
Dawwāya = Jamā'at al-Ma'yuf 136-137 M 7
Dax 120-121 G 7
Da Xi 146-147 G 7-8
Da Xi = Longquan Xi 146-147 G 7-8
Da Xian 142-143 K 5
Daxindian 146-147 H 3
Daxing 146-147 F 2
Daxinggu 155 II b 3
Daxue Shan 142-143 J 5-6
Day, FL 80-81 b 1
Ḍāya al-Ma'īdah 166-167 D 4
Ḍāyah 166-167 HJ 3
Ḍāyah, Jabal aḍ- 166-167 F 2
Dayang Bunting, Pulau — 148-149 C 5
Dayang He 144-145 D 2
Dayat 'al-Ām 166-167 B 6
Ḍayat al-Khadrah 166-167 BC 6
Daya Wan 146-147 E 10
Daye 146-147 E 6
Daying Jiang 141 EF 3
Daylesford 160 G 6
Daymān 106-107 J 3
Daymān, Cuchilla del — 106-107 J 3
Daym Zubayr 164-165 K 7
Day Nui Ataouat 148-149 E 3
Dayong 142-143 L 6
Dayr, Ad- 173 C 5
Dayr as-Suryānī 173 AB 2
Dayr at-Tin, Al-Qāhirah- 170 II b 2
Dayr az-Zawr 134-135 DE 3
Dayr Ḥāfir 136-137 G 4
Dayr Katrīnah 173 C 3
Dayr Māghar 136-137 H 4
Dayr Mawās 173 B 4
Dayr Samū'īl 173 B 3
Dayrūṭ 164-165 L 3
Daysland 61 BC 4
Dayton, NM 76-77 B 6
Dayton, NV 74-75 D 3
Dayton, OH 64-65 K 4
Dayton, TN 78-79 G 3
Dayton, TX 76-77 G 7
Dayton, WA 66-67 E 2
Dayton, WY 68-69 C 3
Daytona Beach, FL 64-65 KL 6
Dayu 142-143 L 6
Dayu Ling 146-147 DE 9
Da Yunhe [TJ, Jiangsu] 142-143 M 5
Da Yunhe [TJ, Shandong] 146-147 EF 3
Dayu Shan 146-147 H 6
Dayville, OR 66-67 D 3
Dazhang Xi 146-147 G 9
Dazhou Dao 150-151 H 3
Dazkırı 136-137 CD 4
De Aar 172 D 8
Dead Indian Peak 66-67 HJ 3
Dead Lake 70-71 BC 2
Deadman Bay 80-81 b 2
Deadman Mount 58-59 NO 5
Dead Sea = Yām Hammelah 136-137 F 7
Deadwood, SD 68-69 E 3
Deadwood Reservoir 66-67 F 3
Dealesville 174-175 F 5
Deal Island 160 cd 1
De'an 146-147 EF 7
Deanewood, Washington-, DC 82 II b 2
Deān Funes 111 D 4
Dean River 56-57 L 7
Dearborn, MI 72-73 E 3
Dearborn Heights, IL 83 II a 2
Dearg, Beinn — 119 D 3
Deary, ID 66-67 E 2
Dease Arm 56-57 MN 4
Dease Inlet 58-59 K 1
Dease Lake 56-57 KL 6
Dease Strait 56-57 P 4
Death Valley 64-65 C 4
Death Valley, CA 74-75 E 4
Death Valley National Monument 74-75 E 4-5
Deauville 120-121 GH 4
Deaver, WY 68-69 B 3
Debal'cevo 126-127 J 2
Debar 122-123 J 5
Debark 164-165 M 6
De Bary 106-107 F 6
Debden 61 E 4
Debdoū = Dabdū 166-167 E 3
De Beers Mine 174-175 F 5
Debeeti 174-175 G 2
De Behagle = Laï 164-165 H 7
De Beque, CO 68-69 BC 6
Debert 63 E 5
Debesy 124-125 T 5
Dēbgada = Deogarh 138-139 K 7
Dębica 118 K 3-4
Dęblin 118 KL 3
Debo, Lac — 164-165 D 5
Deborah, Mount — 58-59 O 5
De Borgia, MT 66-67 F 2
De Bosbulten 174-175 DE 5
De Bosch Bulten = De Bosbulten 174-175 DE 5
Debra Birhan = Debre Birhan 164-165 MN 7
Debra Marcos = Debre Markos 164-165 M 6
Debre Birhan 164-165 MN 7
Debrecen 118 K 5
Debre Markos 164-165 M 6
Debre Tabor 164-165 M 6
De Brug 174-175 F 5
Decamere = Dekemḥarē 164-165 M 5
Decatur, AL 64-65 J 5
Decatur, GA 64-65 K 5
Decatur, IL 64-65 HJ 3-4
Decatur, IN 70-71 H 5
Decatur, MI 70-71 GH 4
Decatur, TX 76-77 F 6
Decazeville 120-121 J 6
Decelles, Lac — 62 M 3
Decelles, Réservoir — 72-73 GH 1
Decepción, Cabo — = Cape Disappointment 111 J 8-9
Deception 53 C 30
Deception Lake 61 F 2
Decherd, TN 78-79 FG 3
Děčín 118 G 3
Decker, MT 68-69 C 3
Declo, ID 66-67 G 4
Decorah, IA 70-71 E 4
Decoto, CA 74-75 BC 4
Décou-Décou, Massif — 98-99 LM 2
Deda 122-123 L 2
Dedayé 141 D 7
Dedeagach = Alexandrúpolis 122-123 L 5
Dedeköy 136-137 C 3-4
Dedham, MA 84 I a 3
Dediāpāda 138-139 D 7
Ḍēḍiyāpāḍā = Dediāpāda 138-139 D 7
Dedo, Cerro — 111 B 6
De Doorns 174-175 CD 7
Dédougou 164-165 D 6
Dedoviči 124-125 GH 5
Dedovsk 124-125 L 6
Dedza 172 F 4
Deeg = Dīg 138-139 F 4
Deelfontein 174-175 E 6
Deep Creek Range 74-75 G 2-3
Deep River [CDN] 72-73 GH 1
Deep River [USA] 80-81 G 3
Deepwater 160 K 2
Deepwater, MO 70-71 D 6
Deer, AR 78-79 C 3
Deerfield Beach, FL 80-81 cd 3
Deering, AK 58-59 F 3
Deering, ND 68-69 F 1
Deering, Mount — 158-159 E 5
Deer Island [USA, Boston Bay] 84 I c 2
Deer Island [USA, Pacific Ocean] 58-59 b 2
Deer Lake [CDN, Newfoundland] 63 H 3
Deer Lake [CDN, Ontario] 62 B 1
Deer Lodge, MT 66-67 G 2
Deer Lodge Mountains 66-67 G 2
Deer Lodge Pass 66-67 G 3
Deer Park, AL 78-79 E 5
Deer Park, TX 85 III c 2
Deer Park, WA 66-67 E 2
Deer Park Stadium 85 III c 2
Deer River, MN 70-71 CD 2
Deerton, MI 70-71 G 2
Deer Trail, CO 68-69 DE 6
Deerwood, MN 70-71 D 2
Deesa 138-139 D 5
Deeth, NV 66-67 F 5
Deffa, ed — = Aḍ-Ḍiffah 164-165 J 2
Defferrari 106-107 H 7
Defiance, OH 70-71 H 5
De Funiak Springs, FL 78-79 FG 5
Degaon = Dehgām 138-139 D 6
Dēge 142-143 H 5
Degeh Bur 164-165 N 7
Dēgelis 63 B 4
Dēgēn Zangzu Zizhizhou 142-143 H 6
Deggendorf 118 F 4
Deglūr 140 C 1
De Goede Hoop 98-99 K 2
De Goeje Gebergte 98-99 L 3
Degome 168-169 F 4
De Gors 128 I b 1
De Gouph = Die Koup 174-175 E 7
De Grey 158-159 CD 4
De Grey River 158-159 CD 4
Degt'anka 124-125 N 7
Degunino, Moskva- 113 V b 2
Dehbat = Adh-Dhahībah 166-167 M 3
Deheb, Bir ed — = Bi'r adh-Dhahab 166-167 F 4
Dehej 138-139 D 7
De Heul 128 I a 1
Dehgām 138-139 D 6
Dehgolān 136-137 M 5
Dehibat = Adh-Dhahībah 166-167 M 3
Dehiwala-Mount Lavinia 134-135 M 9
Dehkhwareqan = Āzar Shahr 136-137 LM 4
Dehlorān 134-135 F 4
Dehna = Ad Dahnā' 134-135 E 5-F 6
Dehna, Ed- = Ad-Dahnā' 134-135 E 5-F 6
De Hoef 128 I a 2
Dehōk = Dahūk 136-137 K 4
Dehong Daizu Zizhizhou 142-143 H 6
Dehra Dūn 134-135 M 4
Dehrā Gōpīpur = Dera Gopipur 138-139 F 2
Dehri 138-139 JK 5
Dehua 146-147 G 9
Deibüel 128 IV b 2
Deir, Ed — = Ad-Dayr 173 C 5
Deir es-Suryānī = Dayr as-Suryānī 173 AB 2
Deir ez Zōr = Dayr az-Zawr 134-135 DE 3
Deir Ḥāfir = Dayr Ḥāfir 136-137 G 4
Deir Katerīna = Dayr Katrīnah 173 C 3
Deir Māghar = Dayr Māghar 136-137 H 4
Deir Mawās = Dayr Mawās 173 B 4
Deir Samweil = Dayr Samū'īl 173 B 3
Dej 122-123 K 2
De Jong, Tanjung — 148-149 L 8
De Kalb, IL 70-71 F 5
De Kalb, MS 78-79 E 4
De Kalb, TX 76-77 G 6
De-Kastri 132-133 ab 7
Dekemḥarē 164-165 M 5
Dekese 172 D 2
Dekoūa, Tell — = Tall adh-Dhakwah 136-137 G 6
De Kwakel 128 I a 2
De la Canal 106-107 H 6
De la Garma 106-107 G 6-7
Delagoa Bay = Baía do Maputo 172 F 7
Delagua, CO 68-69 D 7
Delaimiya, Ad- = Ad-Dulaymīyah 136-137 K 6
Delair, NJ 84 III c 2
Del Aire, CA 83 III b 2
Delanco, NJ 84 III d 1
De Land, FL 80-81 c 2
Delano, CA 74-75 D 5
Delano, MN 70-71 CD 3
Delano Peak 64-65 D 4
Delareyville 174-175 F 4
Delarof Islands 58-59 t 7
Delaronde Lake 61 E 3-4
Delarondeo Park 85 I c 2
De la Serna 106-107 E 5
Delavan, IL 70-71 F 5
Delavan, WI 70-71 F 4
Delaware 64-65 LM 4
Delaware, OH 72-73 E 4
Delaware Bay 64-65 LM 4
Delaware Lake 72-73 E 4
Delaware Reservoir 72-73 E 4
Delaware River 72-73 J 5
Delburne 60 L 3
Delcambre, LA 78-79 CD 6
Del Campillo 106-107 E 5
Delčevo 122-123 K 4-5
Delegate 160 J 6
De Leon, TX 76-77 E 6
Delfi = Delphoí 122-123 K 6
Delfim Moreira 102-103 K 5
Delfino 100-101 D 6
Delfinópolis 102-103 J 4
Delft [CL] 140 D 6
Delfzijl 120-121 L 2
Delgerchet 142-143 L 2
Delger mörön 142-143 H 1-2
Delgo = Delqū 164-165 L 4-5
Delhi, CO 68-69 DE 7
Delhi, LA 78-79 D 4
Delhi, NY 72-73 J 3
Delhi [CDN] 72-73 F 3
Delhi [IND] 134-135 M 5
Delhi = Dili 148-149 J 8
Deli, Pulau — 148-149 DE 8
Delice 136-137 E 3
Deliceırmak 136-137 F 3
Délices 92-93 J 4
Delicias 64-65 E 6
Deli-Ibrahim 170 I a 2
Delījān 136-137 O 5-6
Delingde 132-133 VW 4
Delipuna Miao = Brāpung 138-139 N 3
Delisle 61 E 5
Delitua 150-151 B 11
Dell, MT 66-67 G 3
Della Rapids 60 DE 5
Delle, UT 66-67 G 5
Dellys = Dalis 166-167 HJ 1
Del Mar, CA 74-75 E 6
Delmar, IA 70-71 E 4-5
Delmar Stadium 85 III b 1
Delmas 174-175 H 4
Delmenhorst 118 CD 2
Delmiro Gouveia 100-101 F 5
Del Norte, CO 68-69 C 7
de Long, proliv — 132-133 j 3-4
De Long Mountains 56-57 D 4
Deloraine [AUS] 160 c 2
Deloraine [CDN] 68-69 F 1
Délos 122-123 L 7
Delphi, IN 70-71 G 5
Delphoí 122-123 K 6
Delphos, OH 70-71 H 5
Delportshoop 174-175 EF 5
Delran, NJ 84 III d 1
Delray Beach, FL 80-81 cd 3
Del Rio, TX 64-65 F 6
Delta, CO 68-69 B 6
Delta, UT 74-75 G 3
Delta Amacuro 94-95 L 3
Delta Beach 61 JK 5
Delta del Ebro 120-121 H 8
Delta del Orinoco 92-93 G 3
Delta del Río Colorado 108-109 H 2
Delta del Río Paraná 106-107 H 4-5
Delta Dunarii 122-123 N 3
Delta Junction, AK 58-59 OP 4
Delta Mendota Canal 74-75 C 4
Delta River 58-59 OP 5
Delvā = Delwa 138-139 DE 3
Del Valle 106-107 G 5
Delvinë 122-123 HJ 6
Delwa 138-139 DE 3
Delwin, TX 76-77 D 6
Demachi = Tonami 144-145 L 4
Demāgiri 141 C 4
Demak 152-153 J 9
Dem'ansk 124-125 J 5
Demarcation Point 58-59 RS 2
Demarchi 106-107 G 5
De Mares 94-95 DE 4
Demavend = Kūh-e Damāvand 134-135 G 3
Demba 172 D 3
Dembī Dolo 164-165 LM 7
Demchhog 142-143 D 5
Ḍemeir = Ḍumayr 136-137 G 6
Demeke 168-169 C 2
Demēr, Djebel — = Jabal al-Qṣūr 166-167 M 3
Demerara 98-99 J 1-2
Demerara = Georgetown 92-93 H 3
Demerara River 98-99 J 1-2
Demidov 124-125 H 6
Deming, WA 66-67 BC 1
Demini, Rio — 92-93 G 4-5
Demirci 136-137 C 3
Demirciköy [TR, Denizli] 136-137 C 3
Demirciköy [TR, İstanbul] 154 I b 1
Demirköprü barajı 136-137 C 3
Demirköy 136-137 BC 2
Demir Qābū = Damīr Qābū 136-137 JK 4
Demjanka 132-133 N 6
Demjanovo 124-125 N 4
Demjanovskaja 124-125 P 3
Demjanskoje 132-133 MN 6
Demmin 118 F 2
Demmitt 60 H 2
Demnate = Damnāt 166-167 C 4
Demopolis, AL 78-79 EF 4
De Morhiban, Lac — 63 E 2
Dempo, Gunung — 148-149 D 7
Demta 148-149 M 7
De Naauwte 174-175 DE 6
Denali, AK 58-59 O 5
Denan 164-165 N 7
Denare Beach 61 GH 3
Denau 134-135 K 3
Denbigh [CDN] 72-73 H 2
Denbigh, Cape — 58-59 FG 4
Dendang 148-149 E 7
Dende, Rio de Janeiro- 110 I b 1
Dendy Park 161 II c 2
Denenchōfu, Tōkyō- 155 III ab 2
Dengkou = Bajan Gol 142-143 K 3
Denglou Jiao = Kami Jiao 146-147 B 11
Deng Xian 146-147 D 5
Den Haag = 's-Gravenhage 120-121 JK 2
Denham 158-159 B 5
Denham Springs, LA 78-79 D 5
Den Helder 120-121 K 2
Denia 120-121 H 9
Denial Bay 160 A 4
Denikil 164-165 N 6
Deniliquin 158-159 HJ 7
Den Ilp 128 I ab 1
Denio, OR 66-67 D 5
Denison, IA 70-71 C 4-5
Denison, TX 64-65 G 5
Denison, Mount — 58-59 KL 7
Denisovskaja 124-125 NO 3
Deṇiyāya 140 E 7
Denizli 134-135 B 3
Denman 160 K 4
Denman Glacier 53 BC 10-11
Denman Island 66-67 A 1
Denmark, SC 80-81 F 4
Denmark, WI 70-71 G 3
Denmark [AUS] 158-159 C 6
Denmark [DK] 116-117 CD 10
Denmark Strait 56-57 f 4-e 5
Denndoudi 168-169 B 2
Denning, München- 130 II bc 2
Denpasar 148-149 FG 8
Dent, ID 66-67 E 2
Dent du Tigre = Dông Voi Mêp 148-149 F 4
Denton, MD 72-73 HJ 5
Denton, MT 68-69 B 2
Denton, NC 80-81 FG 3
Denton, TX 64-65 G 5
d'Entrecasteaux Islands 148-149 h 6
Denver, CO 64-65 EF 4
Denver City, TX 76-77 C 6
Denver Harbor Park 85 III b 1
Denzil 61 D 4
Đeo Ai Vân = Đeo Hai Van 150-151 G 4
Deoband 138-139 F 3
Đeo Bao Lôc 150-151 F 7
Deobhog 138-139 J 8
Đeo-Blao = Đeo Bao Lôc 150-151 F 7
Deodar = Diodar 138-139 C 5
Đeo Da Troun 150-151 G 7
Đeo Da Trun = Đeo Da Troun 150-151 G 7
Deodrug 140 C 2
Deogarh [IND, Orissa] 138-139 K 7
Deogarh [IND, Rājasthān] 138-139 D 5
Deogarh Peak 138-139 J 6
Deoghar 134-135 O 6
Đeo Hai Van 150-151 G 4
Đeo Keo Neua 150-151 E 3
Deolāli 138-139 D 8
Deoli [IND, Mahārāshtra] 138-139 G 7
Deoli [IND, Rājasthān] 138-139 E 5
Đeo Lô Qui Hô = Đeo Hai Yân 150-151 D 1
Đeo Mang Yang 150-151 G 5
Đeo Mu' Gia 150-151 E 4
Đeo Mu'o'ng Sen 148-149 DE 3
Đeo Ngang 150-151 F 3-4
Đeo Pech Nil 150-151 E 7
Deoprayag = Devaprayāg 138-139 G 2
Deori 138-139 G 6
Deoria 138-139 J 4
Depālpur 138-139 E 6
De Paul University 83 II b 1
Dependencias Federales 94-95 HJ 2
Depew, OK 76-77 F 5
Deping 146-147 F 3
Depósito 98-99 H 2
Deppegūda 138-139 JK 8
Dépression du Mourdi 164-165 J 5
Deptford, London- 129 II b 2
Deptford Terrace, NJ 84 III c 3
De Put = Die Put 174-175 E 6
Deqen 142-143 H 6
Deqen Zizhizhou = B ◁ 142-143 H 6
Deqing [TJ, Guangdong] 146-147 C 10
Deqing [TJ, Zhejiang] 146-147 GH 6
De Queen, AR 76-77 G 5
De Quincy, LA 78-79 C 5
Der'ā = Dar'ā 136-137 G 6
Dera, Lak — 172 H 1
Dērā Bassī = Basi 138-139 F 2
Ḍera Bugṭī 138-139 B 3
Ḍera Ghāzi Khān 134-135 L 4
Ḍera Gopipur 138-139 F 2
Ḍera Ismāīl Khān 134-135 L 4
Ḍera Jāt 138-139 C 2
Derajat = Ḍera Jāt 138-139 C 2-3
Derāpur 138-139 G 4
Derāwar Forṭ 138-139 C 3
Derazn'a 126-127 C 2
Derbent 126-127 O 5

Derbesiye 136-137 J 4
Derbeškinskij 124-125 T 6
Derby [AUS] 158-159 D 3
Derby [GB] 119 F 5
Derby [ZA] 174-175 G 3
Derdepoort 174-175 G 3
Dereköy [TR, Sivas] 136-137 G 2
Dereli 136-137 H 2
Deren, Adrar N — 166-167 BC 4
Dereseki [TR ↑ İstanbul] 154 I b 1
Dereseki [TR ↗ İstanbul] 154 I b 2
Derevlevo, Moskva- 113 V b 3
Derg' = Daraj 164-165 G 2
Derg, Lough — 119 BC 5
Dergači [SU, Rossijskaja SFSR] 124-125 R 8
Dergači [SU, Ukrainskaja SSR] 126-127 H 1
Ḍergāṅv = Dergaon 141 C 2
Dergaon 141 C 2
De Ridder, LA 78-79 C 5
Derik 136-137 J 4
Derinkuyu 136-137 F 3
Derj = Daraj 164-165 G 2
Derkali 171 E 2
Derm 174-175 C 2
Dermott, AR 78-79 D 4
Derna = Darnah 164-165 J 2
Derry, NH 72-73 L 3
Derūdēb = Darūdāb 164-165 M 5
De Rust 174-175 E 7
Derventa 122-123 G 3
Derwent [AUS] 160 c 3
Derwent [ZA] 174-175 H 3
Deržavino 124-125 T 7
Deržavinskij 132-133 M 7
Desaguadera del Bermejo 106-107 D 3-4
Desaguadero [PE] 96-97 G 10
Desaguadero [RA] 106-107 D 4
Desaguadero, Río — [BOL] 92-93 F 8
Desaguadero, Río — [RA] 106-107 D 4
Desagüe, Canal del — 91 I c 1
Des Arc, AR 78-79 D 3
Des Arc, MO 78-79 D 2
Desastre, Cachoeira do — 98-99 J 10
Desbarats 70-71 J 2
Descabezado Grande, Volcán — 106-107 B 5
Descalvado 102-103 D 2
Descanso 102-103 F 7
Descanso, El — 86-87 B 1
Descanso, Punta — 86-87 B 1
Deschaillons 72-73 KL 1
Deschambault Lake [CDN, lake] 61 FG 3
Deschambault Lake [CDN, place] 61 G 3
Deschutes River 66-67 C 3
Desdemona, TX 76-77 E 6
Desē 164-165 MN 6
Deseado 102-103 EF 6
Deseado = Puerto Deseado 111 CD 7
Deseado, Cabo — 111 AB 8
Deseado, Río — 111 BC 7
Desecho, Paso de — 106-107 B 6
Desemboque, El — 86-87 D 2
Desengaño, Punta — 108-109 F 7
Desenzano del Garda 122-123 D 3
Deseret Peak 66-67 G 5
Deseronto 72-73 H 2
Desertas, Ilhas — 164-165 A 2
Desert Center, CA 74-75 F 6
Desertores, Islas — 108-109 C 4
Deserto Salato = Dasht-e Kavīr 134-135 GH 4
Desful = Dezfūl 134-135 F 4
Deshengmen, Beijing- 155 II b 2
Deshler, OH 72-73 E 4
Deshu 134-135 J 4
Desiderio Tello 106-107 DE 3
Desierto, El — 104-105 B 8
Desierto de Altar 86-87 D 2-3
Desierto de Atacama 111 B 3-C 2
Desierto de Sechura 96-97 A 4-5
Desierto de Vizcaíno 86-87 CD 4
Desirade, La — 88-89 Q 6
Desmarais 60 KL 2
De Smet, SD 68-69 H 3
Des Moines, IA 64-65 GH 3
Des Moines, NM 76-77 C 4
Des Moines River 64-65 GH 3
Des Moines River, East Fork — 70-71 C 4
Des Moines River, West Fork — 70-71 C 4
Desmonte, El — 104-105 E 8
Desna 124-125 K 7
Desnudez, Punta — 106-107 H 7
Desolación, Isla — 111 AB 8
Desolation Canyon 74-75 J 3
Desordem, Serra da — 100-101 AB 2
De Soto, MO 70-71 E 6
De Soto, WI 70-71 E 4
Despatch 174-175 F 7
Despeñaderos 106-107 EF 3
Despeñaperros, Puerto de — 120-121 F 9
Des Plaines, IL 70-71 FG 4
Despoblado de Pabur 96-97 A 4
Dessau 118 F 3
Desterrada, Isla — 86-87 Q 6
Destêrro 100-101 F 4
D'Estrees Bay 160 CD 5-6
Destruction Bay 58-59 S 6
Destruction Island 66-67 A 2
Desventurados 199 AB 6
Desvio El Sombrero = El Sombrero 106-107 H 1
Detčino 124-125 KL 6
Dete 172 E 5
Detmold 118 D 3
De Tour, MI 70-71 HJ 2-3
Detrital Valley 74-75 F 4-5
Detroit, MI 64-65 K 3
Detroit, TX 76-77 G 6
Detroit, Country Club of — 84 II c 2
Detroit, University of — 84 II b 2
Detroit City Airport 84 II bc 2
Detroit Harbor, WI 70-71 G 3
Detroit Lake 66-67 B 3
Detroit Lakes, MN 70-71 BC 2
Detroit River 72-73 E 3-4
Detroit-Strathmoor, MI 84 II a 2
Detroit-Windsor Tunnel 84 II bc 3
Detroit Zoological Park 84 II ab 2
Dettifoss 116-117 e 2
Det Udom 150-151 E 5
Deuil 129 I c 2
Deutsches Museum 130 II b 2
Deux-Rivières 72-73 G 1
Deva 122-123 K 3
Devakottai 140 D 6
De Valls Bluff, AR 78-79 D 3
Devanahaḷḷi = Devanhalli 140 CD 4
Devanhalli 140 CD 4
Devaprayāg 138-139 G 2
Dēvarakoṇḍā = Devarkonda 140 D 2
Devarkonda 140 D 2
Dēvās = Dewās 138-139 F 6
Dévaványa 118 K 5
Dēvbaḍodā 138-139 H 7
Dēvband = Deoband 138-139 F 3
Deveci dağları 136-137 FG 2
Develi [TR, Kayseri] 136-137 F 3
Deventer 120-121 L 2
Devgad Bāria 138-139 DE 6
Devgarh 140 A 2
Devikolam 140 C 5
Devīkot 138-139 C 4
Devil Mount 58-59 E 3
Devils Elbow 58-59 JK 5
Devils Gate 74-75 D 3
Devil's Hole 114-115 HJ 4
Devils Lake 68-69 G 1
Devils Lake, ND 68-69 G 1
Devils Paw 58-59 UV 7
Devils Playground 74-75 EF 5
Devil's Point = Yak Tuḍuwa 140 DE 6
Devils Tower 68-69 D 3
Devils Tower National Monument 68-69 D 3
Devin 122-123 L 5
Devine, TX 76-77 E 8
Devipatam = Devipattanam 140 D 6
Devipattanam 140 D 6
Dēvlāli = Deolāli 138-139 D 8
Dēvlī = Deoli [IND, Mahārāshtra] 138-139 G 7
Dēvlī = Deoli [IND, Rājasthān] 138-139 E 5
Devodi Munda 140 F 1
Devoll 122-123 J 5
Devon, MT 66-67 H 1
Devon, PA 84 III a 1
Devon [GB] 119 DE 6
Devon Island 56-57 S-U 2
Devonport [AUS] 158-159 J 8
Devonport [NZ] 158-159 O 7
Devonshire = Devon 119 DE 6
Devoto 106-107 F 3
Devrek 136-137 DE 2
Devrekâni 136-137 EF 2
Devrez çayı 136-137 EF 2
de Vries, proliv — 142-143 S 2
Dēvrī-Khās = Deori 138-139 G 6
Dewakang Besar, Pulau — 152-153 N 8
Dewās 138-139 F 6
Dewdar = Diodar 138-139 C 5
Dewelē 164-165 N 6
Dewetsdorp 174-175 G 5
Dewey, OK 76-77 FG 4
Dewey, SD 68-69 DE 4
Dewey Lake 80-81 E 2
De Witt, AR 78-79 D 3
De Witt, IA 70-71 E 5
De Witt, NE 68-69 H 5
Dewli = Deoli 138-139 G 7
Dewundara Tuḍuwa 134-135 N 9
Dexian = Dezhou 142-143 M 4
Dexing 146-147 F 7
Dexter, ME 72-73 M 2
Dexter, MO 78-79 DE 2
Dexter, NM 76-77 B 6
Deyālā = Diyālā 134-135 EF 4
Dey Dey, Lake — 158-159 F 5
Deylamān 136-137 NO 4
Dez, Rūd-e — 136-137 N 6
Dezadeash Lake 58-59 T 6
Dezfūl 134-135 F 4
Dezhou 142-143 M 4
Dezh Shāhpur = Marīvān 136-137 M 5
Dezinga 171 D 6
Dežneva, mys — 132-133 lm 4

Dhahab 173 D 3
Dhahab, Bi'r adh- 166-167 F 7
Dhahar = Ẓahar 166-167 LM 3
Dhahībah, Adh- 166-167 M 3
Dhahran = Aẓ-Ẓahrān 134-135 FG 5
Ḍhaka 138-139 N 6
Ḍhākā = Ḍhaka [BD, administrative unit] 138-139 N 5-6
Ḍhākā = Ḍhaka [BD, place] 138-139 N 6
Dhakuria, Calcutta- 154 II b 2
Dhakwah, Tall adh- 136-137 G 6
Dhāma 138-139 JK 7
Dhamār 134-135 EF 8
Dhamda 138-139 H 7
Dhāmpur 138-139 G 3
Dhamtari 134-135 N 6
Dhānbād 138-139 L 6
Dhandhuka 138-139 CD 6
Dhānera 138-139 D 5
Dhangarhī 138-139 H 3
Dhankuta 134-135 O 5
Dhansiri 141 C 2
Dhanushkodi 134-135 MN 9
Dhanuṣhkōṭi = Dhanushkodi 134-135 MN 9
Dhanvār = Dhanwār 138-139 KL 5
Dhanwār 138-139 KL 5
Dhaola Dhār 138-139 F 1-2
Dhaolāgiri = Daulāgiri 134-135 N 5
Dhār 134-135 M 6
Dharampur 138-139 D 7
Dharamsālā 134-135 M 4
Dhārangāṅv = Dharangaon 138-139 E 7
Dharangaon 138-139 E 7
Dhārāpuram 140 C 5
Dhārāshiva = Osmānābād 140 C 1
Dhārāvāda = Dhārwār 134-135 LM 7
Dharlā 138-139 M 5
Dharmanagar 141 C 3
Dharmapuri 140 CD 4
Dharmavaram 140 C 3
Dharmjaygarh 138-139 J 6
Dharmsala = Dharamsālā 134-135 M 4
Dharmshala = Dharamsālā 134-135 M 4
Dharoor 164-165 c 1
Dhārūr 140 BC 1
Dhārvāḍ = Dhārwār 134-135 LM 7
Ḍhar Walātah 164-165 C 5
Dhārwār 134-135 LM 7
Dhasān 138-139 G 5
Dhāt al-Ḥājj = Ḥājj 173 DE 3
Dhāṭ yā Thar = Great Indian Desert 134-135 L 5
Dhauladhar = Dhaola Dhār 138-139 F 1-2
Dhaulāgiri 134-135 N 5
Dhauli 138-139 E 7
Dhāvan'gerē = Dāvangere 134-135 M 8
Dhawladhar = Dhaola Dhār 138-139 F 1-2
Dhebar Lake 138-139 D 5
Ḍhēnkānal = Dhenkānāl 138-139 K 7
Dhenkānāl 138-139 K 7
Dhiinsoor 164-165 N 8
Dhikār, Bi'r adh- 164-165 J 3
Dhi-Qār 136-137 LM 7
Dholpur 138-139 F 4
Dhōnā = Dhone 140 C 3
Dhond 134-135 L 7
Dhone 140 C 3
Dhorāji 134-135 L 6
Dhori 138-139 B 6
Dhrāṅgadhra = Drangadra 138-139 C 6
Dhrangadhra = Drangadra 138-139 C 6
Dhrbarī = Dhubri 134-135 OP 5
Dhrol 138-139 C 6
Dhubri 134-135 OP 5
Dhufar = Ẓufār 134-135 G 7
Dhulēṅ = Dhūlia 134-135 L 6
Dhūlia 134-135 L 6
Dhūliyā = Dhūlia 134-135 L 6
Dhūndār 138-139 E 5-F 4
Dhūri 138-139 EF 2
Dhuusa Mareeb 164-165 b 2

Dia 122-123 L 8
Diable, Île du — 92-93 J 3
Diablo, Punta del — 106-107 L 5
Diablo, Sierra — 76-77 B 7
Diablo Heights 64-65 b 3
Diablo Range 64-65 BC 4
Diabo, Serra do — 102-103 F 5
Diaca 171 DE 5
Diadema 102-103 J 5
Diadema-Paulicéia 110 II b 3
Diadema-Vila Conceição 110 II b 3
Diagbe 171 AB 1
Diagonal, IA 70-71 CD 5
Dialafara 168-169 C 2
Dialloubé 168-169 DE 2
Diamante [RA] 111 DE 4
Diamante, El — 91 III a 2
Diamante, Río — 106-107 D 5
Diamantina 92-93 L 8
Diamantina River 158-159 H 4
Diamantino [BR ↗ Alto Garças] 102-103 F 2
Diamantino [BR ↖ Cuiabá] 92-93 H 7
Diamantino, Rio — 102-103 F 2
Diamond, OR 66-67 D 4
Diamond Bay 161 I b 2
Diamond Harbour 138-139 LM 6
Diamond Island = Leik Kyûn 141 CD 8
Diamond Lake 66-67 B 4
Diamond Peak 74-75 EF 3
Diamondville, WY 66-67 H 5
Diamou 168-169 C 2
Dianbai 146-147 C 11
Diancheng 142-143 L 7
Dian Chi 142-143 J 7
Dianfou = Feidong 146-147 F 6
Dianópolis 92-93 K 7
Dianra 168-169 D 3
Diaocha Hu 146-147 D 6
Diapaga 164-165 E 6
Diari 168-169 E 3
Díaz [MEX] 76-77 B 9
Díaz [RA] 106-107 G 4
Dībaga = Dībagah 136-137 KL 5
Dībagah 136-137 KL 5
Dibai 138-139 G 3
Dibaya 172 D 3
Dibbāgh, Jabal — 173 D 4
Dibble Ice Tongue 53 C 14
Dibdibah, Ad- 136-137 M 8
Dibele, Bena- 172 D 2
Dibella 164-165 G 5
Dibeng 174-175 E 4
Dibis, Bi'r — 164-165 K 4
Diboll, TX 76-77 G 7
Dibrugarh 134-135 PQ 5
Dibsah 136-137 GH 5
Dibulla 92-93 E 2
Dibwah 166-167 J 3
Dickens, TX 76-77 D 6
Dickey, ND 68-69 G 2
Dickinson, ND 64-65 F 2
Dickinson, TX 76-77 G 8
Dick's Head = Raas Jumbo 172 H 2
Dickson 132-133 P 3
Dickson, AK 58-59 E 4
Dickson, TN 78-79 F 2-3
Dickson City, PA 72-73 HJ 4
Dickson Harbour = P'asinskij zaliv 132-133 PQ 3
Dicle = Piran 136-137 J 3
Dicle nehri 136-137 J 4
Didiéni 164-165 C 6
Didirhine, Djebel — = Jabal Tidighin 166-167 D 2
Didsbury 60 K 4
Dīḍvānā = Dīdwāna 138-139 E 4
Dīdwāna 138-139 E 4
Didymóteichon 122-123 LM 5
Diébougou 168-169 E 3
Dieburger Stadtwald 128 III b 2
Dieciocho de Julio 106-107 L 4
Dieciséis de Julio 106-107 G 6
Diecisiete de Agosto 106-107 F 6
Diedersdorf 130 III b 2
Diefenbaker, Lake — 61 E 5
Diego de Alvear 106-107 F 5
Diego de Amagro, Isla — 111 A 8
Diego Garcia 50-51 N 6
Diego Ramírez, Islas — 111 C 9
Diégo-Suarez = Antsiranana 172 JK 4
Die Koup 174-175 E 7
Diéma 168-169 C 2
Diemen 128 I b 1
Diemensland, Van — = Tasmania 158-159 HJ 8
Điên Ban 150-151 G 5
Điên Biên Phu 148-149 D 2
Điên Khanh 150-151 G 6
Diepensee 130 III c 2
Diepholz 118 D 2
Diepkloof, Johannesburg- 170 V a 2
Dieppe 120-121 H 4
Die Put 174-175 E 6
Dierks, AR 76-77 GH 5
Dietlikon 128 IV b 1
Dietrich, ID 66-67 F 4
Dietrich River 58-59 N 3
Diêu, Mui — 148-149 EF 4
Diez de Julio, Colonia — 106-107 FG 3
Dif 172 H 1
Diffa 164-165 G 6
Ḍiffah, Aḍ- 164-165 J 2
Difícil, El — 92-93 E 3
Dīg 138-139 F 4
Digboi 141 D 2
Digby 63 CD 5
Digha 138-139 L 7
Dighton, KS 68-69 F 6
Digne 120-121 L 6
Digod 138-139 F 5
Digoin 120-121 JK 5
Digor 136-137 K 2
Digos 148-149 J 5
Digras 138-139 F 7
Digrī 138-139 B 5
Digul 148-149 M 8
Digura 176 a 2
Dih 136-137 K 4
Dihang 134-135 PQ 5
Dihri = Dehri 138-139 JK 5
Dihua = Ürümchi 142-143 F 3
Di'īb, Wādī — 173 DE 6-7
Dijlah, Nahr — 134-135 E 3
Dijlah, Shaṭṭ — 134-135 F 4
Dijon 120-121 K 5
Dikabi 174-175 G 2
Dikākah, Ad- 134-135 G 7
Dikanäs 116-117 F 5
Dikeman, AK 58-59 J 5
Dikhil 164-165 N 6
Dikili 136-137 B 3
Dikoa = Dikwa 164-165 G 6
Díktē Óros 122-123 L 8
Dikwa 164-165 G 6
Dila 164-165 M 7
Dilam, Ad- 134-135 F 6
Dilbeek 128 II a 1
Dilermando Aguiar 106-107 KL 2
Di Linh 148-149 E 4
Dilinjāt, Ad- 173 B 2
Dilizan 126-127 M 6
Dillard University 85 I b 1
Dill City, OK 76-77 E 5
Dilley, TX 76-77 E 8
Dilli 148-149 J 8
Dillī = Delhi 134-135 M 5
Dillia 164-165 G 5-6
Dillingham, AK 56-57 DE 6
Dillinj 164-165 KL 6
Dillman = Shāhpūr 136-137 L 3
Dillon 61 D 3
Dillon, CO 68-69 C 6
Dillon, MT 66-67 G 3
Dillon, SC 80-81 G 3
Dillwyn, VA 80-81 G 2
Dilolo 172 D 4
Dima, Lak — 171 E 2
Dimāpur 141 C 3
Dīmās, Rā's ad- 166-167 M 2
Dimashq 134-135 D 4
Dimbokro 164-165 D 7
Dimboola 160 EF 6
Dime Landing, AK 58-59 FG 4
Dimitrijevskoje = Talas 134-135 L 2
Dimitrovgrad [BG] 122-123 LM 4
Dimitrovgrad [SU] 132-133 HJ 7
Dimmitt, TX 76-77 C 5
Dimōna 136-137 F 7
Dimpo 174-175 D 3
Dina 94-95 CD 6
Dinagat Island 148-149 J 4
Dinājpūr 138-139 M 5
Dinamo, Stadion — 113 V b 2
Dinan 120-121 F 4
Dinapore 138-139 K 5
Dinar 136-137 CD 3
Dīnār, Kūh-e — 134-135 G 4
Dinara 122-123 G 3-4
Dināra [IND] 138-139 K 5
Dinard 120-121 F 4
Dinaric Alps = Dinara 122-123 G 3-4
Dindi 140 D 2
Dindigul 134-135 M 8
Dindivanam = Tindivanam 140 DE 4
Dindori [IND, Madhya Pradesh] 138-139 H 6
Dindori [IND, Mahārāshtra] 138-139 D 7
Diṇḍukkal = Dindigul 134-135 M 8
Dineley, Bahía — 108-109 AB 7
Ding 142-143 M 4
Ding'an 150-151 H 3
Dingbian 146-147 A 3
Ding Den, Phu — 150-151 F 5
Dinghai 146-147 J 6-7
Dingjiang = Qingjiang 146-147 E 7
Dingla 138-139 L 4
Dingle 119 A 5
Dingle Bay 119 A 5
Dingnán 146-147 E 9
Dingqiang = Dingxiang 146-147 D 2
Dingri Zong = Tingri Dsong 138-139 L 3
Dingshan = Qingshuzhen 146-147 G 6
Dingshuzhen 146-147 G 6
Dingtao 146-147 E 4
Dinguiraye 164-165 BC 6
Dingwall 119 D 3
Dingxi 142-143 J 4
Ding Xian 146-147 E 2
Dingxiang 146-147 D 2
Dingxin 142-143 H 3
Dingxing 146-147 E 2
Dingyuan 146-147 F 5
Dingzi Gang 146-147 H 3
Dingzi Wan = Dingzi Gang 146-147 H 3
Dinh, Mui — 148-149 E 4
Dīnhāta 138-139 M 4
Đinh Lâp 150-151 F 2
Dinkimo 168-169 G 2
Dinnebito Wash 74-75 H 5
Dinosaur National Monument 66-67 J 5
Dinsmore 61 E 5
Dinuba, CA 74-75 D 4
Dinwiddie 170 V bc 2
Diodar 138-139 C 5
Diogo Island 146-147 H 11
Dioïla 164-165 C 6
Dioka 168-169 C 2
Diomida, ostrova — 56-57 C 4-5
Dionísio Cerqueira 102-103 F 7
Diosig 122-123 JK 2
Diougani 168-169 E 2
Diouloulou 164-165 A 6
Dioura 168-169 D 2
Diourbel 164-165 A 6
Dīpālpūr 138-139 D 2
Dīpēyin 141 D 4
Dipfaryas = Rizokárpason 136-137 EF 5
Diphu 141 C 3
Diplo 138-139 B 5
Dipolog 148-149 H 5
Dipurdú 94-95 C 5
Dīr 134-135 L 3
Dira, Djebel — = Jabal Dīrah 166-167 H 1
Diradawa = Dirē Dawa 164-165 N 7
Dīrah, Jabal — 166-167 H 1
Dirang 141 C 2
Dīrat at-Tulūl 136-137 G 6
Dirē 164-165 D 5
Dirē Dawa 164-165 N 7
Direkli 136-137 G 3
Dîret et Touloûl = Dīrat at-Tulūl 136-137 G 6
Dirfys 122-123 KL 6
Dirico 172 D 5
Dirk Hartogs Island 158-159 B 5
Dirkiesdorp 174-175 J 4
Dirkou 164-165 G 5
Dirnismaning 130 II bc 1
Dirranbandi 158-159 J 5
Dirty Devil River 74-75 H 3-4
Dīsā = Deesa 138-139 D 5
Disappointment, Cape — [Falkland Islands] 111 J 8-9
Disappointment, Cape — [USA] 66-67 A 2
Disappointment, Lake — 158-159 DE 4
Discovery [RI] 152-153 H 7
Discovery [ZA] 170 V a 1
Discovery Bay 158-159 GH 7
Discovery Well 158-159 D 4
Dishkakat, AK 58-59 J 5
Dishnā 173 C 4
Dishna River 58-59 J 5
Disko 56-57 a 4
Disko Bugt 56-57 a 4
Diskobukta 116-117 l 6
Dismal River 68-69 F 5
Dismal Swamp 80-81 H 2
Disna [SU, place] 124-125 G 6
Disna [SU, river] 124-125 FG 6
Disraëli 72-73 L 2
Disston, OR 66-67 B 4
District Heights, MD 82 II b 2
District of Columbia 72-73 H 5
District of Franklin 56-57 N-V 3
District of Keewatin 56-57 RS 4-5
District of Mackenzie 56-57 L-P 5
Distrito Especial 94-95 D 5
Distrito Federal [BR] 92-93 K 8
Distrito Federal [MEX] 86-87 L 8
Distrito Federal [RA] 111 E 4
Distrito Federal [YV] 94-95 H 2
Disūq 173 B 2
Ditang = Altar of the Earth 155 II b 2
Ditu, Mwene- 172 D 3
Diu 134-135 L 6
Dīvāndarreh 136-137 M 5
Divāṅgiri 134-135 P 5
Divejevo 124-125 O 6
Diver 72-73 G 1
Diversiones, Parque Popular de — 91 III bc 2-3
Diviči 126-127 O 6
Divide, MT 66-67 G 3
Dividive, El — 94-95 F 3
Divino 102-103 L 4
Divinópolis 92-93 KL 9
Divi Point 140 E 3
Divisa 88-89 F 10
Divisa, Monte da — 102-103 J 4
Divisa, Serra da — 98-99 G 9
Divisadero, Cerro — 108-109 C 8
Divisa Nova 102-103 J 4
Diviso, El — [CO, Nariño] 94-95 B 7
Diviso, El — [CO, Putumayo] 94-95 D 7
Divisões, Serra das — 92-93 JK 8
Divisor, Sierra de — 92-93 E 6
Divisorio, El — 106-107 G 7
Divnoje 126-127 L 4
Divo 168-169 D 4
Divriği 136-137 GH 3
Diwāna 138-139 A 4
Dīwānganj 134-135 OP 5
Dīwānīyah, Ad- 134-135 EF 4
Diweir, Ed — = Ad-Duwayr 173 B 4
Dixfield, ME 72-73 L 2
Dixie, ID 66-67 F 3
Dixie, WA 66-67 DE 2
Dixon, CA 74-75 C 3
Dixon, IL 70-71 F 5
Dixon, MO 70-71 DE 6
Dixon, MT 66-67 F 2
Dixon, NM 76-77 B 4
Dixon Entrance 56-57 K 7
Diyadin 136-137 K 3
Diyālā 134-135 EF 4
Diyālā, Nahr — 134-135 EF 4
Diyālā, Sadd ad- 136-137 L 5
Diyarbakır 134-135 DE 3
Diyarbakır havzası 136-137 J 3
Dīzābād 136-137 N 5
Dize 136-137 L 4
Dizful = Dezfūl 134-135 F 4

Dja 164-165 G 8
Djado 164-165 G 4
Djado, Plateau du — 164-165 G 4
Djafar, Hassi — = Ḥassī Ja'far 166-167 H 4
Djafou, Hassi — = Ḥāssī Jafū 164-165 E 2
Djafou, Ouêd — = Wādī Jafū 166-167 H 4
Djakarta = Jakarta 148-149 E 8
Djakovica 122-123 J 4
Djakovo 122-123 H 3
Djala 122-123 J 2
Djâlita, Djezîret — = Jazā'ir Jaliṭah 166-167 L 1
Djâlita, Qanât — = Qanāt Jaliṭah 166-167 L 1
Djamaa = Gham'ā 166-167 J 3
Djama Djedid 170 I a 1
Djama el-Kebir 170 I a 1
Djambala 172 BC 2
Djardjîr = Jarjīs 166-167 M 3
Djaret, Ouêd el — = Wādī al-Jarā' 166-167 H 6
Djebel Abiod = Al-Jabal al-Abyaḍ 166-167 L 1
Djebel Aglagal = Jabal Aghlāghal 166-167 G 6
Djebel Aïssa = Jabal 'Aysā 166-167 F 3
Djebel Amour = Jabal 'Amūr 166-167 G 3-H 2
Djebel Babor = Jabal Bābūr [DZ, mountain] 166-167 J 1
Djebel Babor = Jabal Bābūr [DZ, mountains] 166-167 J 1
Djebel Bou Kadra = Jabal Bū Khaḍrah 166-167 KL 2
Djebel Bou Kahil = Jabal Bū Kāhil 166-167 HJ 2
Djebel Chambi = Jabal Shaḥāmbī 166-167 L 2
Djebel Chélia = Jabal Shīlyah 164-165 F 1
Djebel Demer = Jabal al-Qṣūr 166-167 M 3
Djebel Didirhine = Jabal Tidighīn 166-167 D 2
Djebel Dira = Jabal Dīrah 166-167 H 1
Djebel Dough = Jabal ad-Dūgh 166-167 F 3
Djebel el Abiaḍ = Al-Jabal al-Abyaḍ 166-167 L 1
Djebel el Goufi = Jabal Ghūfī 166-167 KL 1
Djebel el Koraa = Jabal al-Kurā' 166-167 J 2
Djebel el Ksoum = Jabal al-Kusūm 166-167 J 2
Djebel es Serdj = Jabal as-Sarj 166-167 L 2
Djebel Idget = Jabal 'Ikdat 166-167 B 4
Djebel Idjerane = Jabal Ijrān 166-167 H 6
Djebel Ksel = Jabal Kasal 166-167 G 3
Djebel Maâdid = Jabal Ma'ḍīd 166-167 J 2
Djebel Morra = Jabal Murrah 166-167 L 2
Djebel Msid = Jabal Masīd 166-167 L 1
Djebel Mzi = Jabal Mazī 166-167 F 3
Djebel Nefoussa = Jabal Nafusah 164-165 G 2
Djebel Orbâṭa = Jabal R'bāṭah 166-167 L 2
Djebel Ouarsenis = Jabal al-Wārshanīs 166-167 GH 2
Djebel Sargho = Jabal Ṣaghrū' 164-165 C 2
Djebel Sarro = Jabal Ṣaghrū 164-165 C 2
Djebel Tachrirt = Jabal Tashrirt 166-167 J 2
Djebel Tenouchfi = Jabal Tanūshfī 166-167 F 2
Djebel Tessala = Jabal Tasalah 166-167 F 2
Djebel Tichao = Jabal Tīshāro 166-167 JK 2
Djebilet = Al-Jabīlat 166-167 BC 4
Djebilet, Hassi — = Ḥassī Jabīlāt 166-167 BC 6
Djebiniâna = Jabinyānah 166-167 M 2
Djedeïda, El- = Al-Jadīdah 166-167 L 1
Djedi, Ouêd — = Wādī Jaddī 166-167 JK 2
Djedid, Bir — = Bi'r Jadīd 166-167 K 3
Djeffâra = Jafārah 166-167 M 3
Djelfa = Jilfah 164-165 E 2
Djelo-Binza, Kinshasa- 170 IV a 2
Djem, El — = Al-Jamm 166-167 M 2
Djema 164-165 K 7
Djemel, Hassi — = Ḥāssī Ghamal 166-167 J 4
Djemila = Jamīlah 166-167 J 1
Djemmâl = Jammāl 166-167 M 2
Djemna = Jimnah 166-167 L 3
Djeneïen = Janā'in 166-167 LM 4
Djenien-bou-Rezg = Ghanāin Bū Rizq 166-167 F 3
Djenné 164-165 D 6
Djenoun, Garet el — = Qārat al-Junūn 166-167 J 7
Djerâdoû = Jirādū 166-167 M 1
Djerba = Ḥūmat as-Sūq 166-167 M 3
Djerba, Djezîret — = Jazīrat Jarbah 166-167 M 3
Djérém 164-165 G 7
Djeribia, Hassi — = Ḥāssī Jarībiyah 166-167 J 4
Djerîd = Gharīd 166-167 K 3
Djerîd, Chott el — = Shaṭṭ al-Jarīd 164-165 F 2
Djezîra el Rharbî = Jazīrat al-Gharbī 166-167 M 2
Djezîrat el Maṭroûḥ = Jazīrat al-Maṭrūḥ 166-167 M 1
Djezîra Zembra = Al-Jāmūr al-Kabīr 164-165 M 1
Djezîret Djâlita = Jazā'ir Jaliṭah 166-167 L 1
Djezîret Djerba = Jazīrat Jarbah 166-167 M 3
Djezîret Qerqena = Jazur Qarqannah 166-167 M 2
Djezîr Qoûrait = Jazā'ir Qūryāt 166-167 M 2
Djibhalanta = Uliastaj 142-143 H 2
Djibo 164-165 D 6
Djibouti [Djibouti, place] 164-165 N 6
Djibouti [Djibouti, state] 164-165 N 6
Djibuti = Djibouti 164-165 N 6
Djidda = Jiddah 134-135 D 6
Djidjelli = Jījlī 164-165 F 1
Djiguina 168-169 G 2
Djiledug = Ciledug 152-153 H 9
Djilolo = Halmahera 148-149 JK 6
Djirgalanta = Chovd 142-143 G 2
Djokjakarta = Yogyakarta 148-149 EF 8
Djolu 172 D 1
Djoua = Juwā' 166-167 KL 5
Djouah 172 B 1
Djoué 170 IV a 1
Djougou 164-165 E 7
Djourab 164-165 H 5

Djuba = Webi Ganaane 164-165 N 8
Djugu 172 EF 1
Djúpavik 116-117 c 2
Djúpivogur 116-117 fg 2
Djurdjura = Jurjurah 164-165 EF 1

Dmitrija Lapteva, proliv — 132-133 a-c 3
Dmitrijevka [SU, Černigov] 126-127 F 1
Dmitrijevka = Talas 134-135 L 2
Dmitrijev-L'govskij 124-125 KL 7
Dmitrov 132-133 F 6
Dmitrovsk-Orlovskij 124-125 KL 7

Dnepr 124-125 H 7
Dneprodzerzhinsk = Dneprodzeržinsk 126-127 FG 2
Dneprodzeržinsk 126-127 FG 2
Dneprodzeržinskoje vodochranilišče 126-127 F 2
Dnepropetrovsk 126-127 GH 2
Dneprorudnoje 126-127 G 3
Dneprovskij liman 126-127 EF 3
Dneprovsko-Bugskij kanal 124-125 E 7
Dneprovskoje 124-125 JK 6
Dnestr 126-127 D 2-3
Dnestrovskij liman 126-127 DE 3
Dnieper = Dnepr 124-125 H 7
Dniester = Dnestr 126-127 D 2-3
Dnjepr = Dnepr 124-125 H 7
Dnjestr = Dnestr 126-127 D 2-3
Dno 124-125 G 5

Doab 134-135 MN 5
Doaktown 63 CD 4
Doangdoangan Besar, Pulau — 152-153 M 8
Doba 164-165 H 7
Dobbiaco 122-123 E 2
Dobbin, TX 76-77 G 7
Dobbyn 158-159 GH 3
Dobele 124-125 D 5
Döberitz [DDR ← Berlin] 130 III a 1
Doblas 111 D 5
Dobo 148-149 K 8
Doboj 122-123 GH 3
Dobovka 126-127 M 2
Dobr'anka [SU, Rossijskaja SFSR] 124-125 V 4
Dobr'anka [SU, Ukrainskaja SSR] 124-125 H 7
Dobreta Turnu Severin 122-123 K 3
Dobrinka [SU] 124-125 N 7
Dobroje [SU, Rossijskaja SFSR] 124-125 MN 7
Dobroje [SU, Ukrainskaja SSR] 126-127 F 3
Dobropolje [SU] 126-127 H 2
Dobruja 122-123 M 4-N 3
Dobruš 124-125 H 7
Dobson Park 85 II b 3
Dobsonville 170 V a 2
Doč 126-127 F 1
Docampadó, Ensenada de — 94-95 C 5
Doce Grande, Cerro — 108-109 E 6
Doce Ilusão, Cachoeira — 98-99 L 9
Dockweiler State Beach 83 III b 2
Doctor, El — 86-87 C 2
Doctor Domingo Haróstegui 106-107 H 6
Doctor Gumersindo Sayago 102-103 B 5
Doctor Luis de Gásperi 102-103 B 5
Doctor Pedro P. Peña 111 D 2
Doda Betta 134-135 M 8
Dod Ballāpur 140 C 4
Dodecanese = Dōdekánēsos 122-123 M 7-8
Dōdekánēsos 122-123 M 7-8
Dodge Center, MN 70-71 D 3-4
Dodge City, KS 64-65 FG 4
Dodgeville, WI 70-71 EF 4
Dodoma 172 G 3
Do Doorns 174-175 CD 7
Dodsland 61 D 5
Dodson, MT 68-69 BC 1
Dodson, TX 76-77 DE 5
Dodson Park 85 III b 1
Dodson Peninsula 53 B 30-31
Dodurga 136-137 C 3
Doembang Nangbuat 150-151 BC 5
Doe River 60 G 1
Doerun, GA 80-81 E 5
Dofar = Zufār 134-135 G 7
Dogai Tshoring 142-143 F 5
Doğancılar, İstanbul- 154 I b 2
Doğanhisar 136-137 D 3
Doğanşehir 136-137 G 3
Dog Creek 60 FG 4
Dogden Buttes 68-69 F 2
Doger Stadium 83 III c 1
Dogger Bank 114-115 J 4-5
Dog Island 78-79 G 6
Dog Lake [CDN ↖ Missanabie] 70-71 HJ 1
Dog Lake [CDN ↖ Thunder Bay] 70-71 F 1
Dōgo 142-143 P 4
Dogondoutchi 164-165 E 6
Dogoni 168-169 D 2
Dōgo yama 144-145 J 5
Dogs, Isle of — 129 II b 2
Doğubayazıt 136-137 KL 3
Dogué 168-169 F 3
Doha = Ad-Dawhah 134-135 G 5
Dohad 138-139 E 6
Dohazārī 141 BC 4
Doheny 72-73 K 1
Doherty 72-73 G 1
Dohlka 138-139 D 6
Dohrīghāt 138-139 J 4
Doi Angka = Doi Inthanon 148-149 C 3
Doi Inthanon 148-149 C 3
Doi Lang Ka 150-151 B 3
Doi Pui = Doi Suthep 150-151 B 3
Dois Córregos 102-103 HJ 5
Dois Irmãos, Cabo — 110 I b 2
Dois Irmãos, Cachoeira — 98-99 J 9
Dois Irmãos, Serra — 92-93 L 6
Doi Suthep 150-151 B 3
Dois Vizinhos 102-103 F 6
Dokan, Sad ad- = Sadd ad-Dukān 136-137 L 4-5
Doka Tofa 168-169 H 3
Dokka 116-117 D 7
Doko 171 B 2
Dokós 122-123 K 7
Dokšicy 124-125 FG 6
Doland, SD 68-69 GH 3
Dolavon 108-109 FG 4
Dolbeau 56-57 W 8
Dôle 120-121 K 5
Dolgaja kosa 126-127 HJ 3
Dolgano-Nenets Autonomous Area 132-133 P-U 3
Dolgellau 119 DE 5
Dolgij, ostrov — 132-133 K 4
Dolgij ostrov [SU, Azovskoje more] 126-127 HJ 3
Dolgij'ostrov [SU, Black Sea] 126-127 E 3
Dolginovo 124-125 F 6
Dolgoi Island 58-59 c 2
Dolgoje [SU, Rossijskaja SFSR Orlovskaja Oblast'] 124-125 L 7
Dolgoprundnyj 113 V bc 1
Dolgorukovo 124-125 M 7
Dolhasca 122-123 M 2
Dolina 126-127 AB 2
Dolinsk 132-133 b 8
Dolinskaja 126-127 F 2
Dolinskoje 126-127 DE 3
Dolleman Island 53 B 30-31
Dolmabahçe Sarayi 154 I a 2
Dolmaithang Tsho 138-139 JK 2
Dolo 164-165 N 8
Dolomites = Dolomiti 122-123 DE 2
Dolomiti 122-123 DE 2
Doloon Choolojn Gobi = Zaaltajn Gov' 142-143 H 3
Doloon Nuur 142-143 LM 3
Dolores, CO 74-75 J 4
Dolores, TX 76-77 E 9
Dolores [CO] 94-95 D 6
Dolores [RA] 111 E 5
Dolores [ROU] 111 E 4
Dolores [YV] 94-95 G 3
Dolores Hidalgo 86-87 K 7
Dolores River 64-65 E 4
Doloroso, MS 78-79 D 5
Dolphin, Cape — 111 E 8
Dolphin and Union Strait 56-57 NO 4
Đô Lu'o'ng 150-151 E 3
Dolžanskaja 126-127 HJ 3
Dom [D] 128 III b 1
D'oma [SU] 124-125 U 7
Doma [WAN] 168-169 H 3
Domačevo 124-125 DE 8
Domaine Royale 128 II b 1
Domanevka 126-127 E 3
Dom Aquino 102-103 E 1
Domār 138-139 M 4
Domariāganj 138-139 J 4
Domazlice 118 F 4
Dombaj-Ul'gen, gora — 126-127 KL 5
Dombarovskij 132-133 K 7
Dombås 116-117 C 6
Dombe Grande 172 B 4
Dombóvár 118 HJ 5
Dome, AZ 74-75 F 6
Dôme, Puy de — 120-121 J 6
Dome Creek 60 G 3
Dōmēl = Muzaffarābād 134-135 LM 4
Domel Island = Letsûtau Kyûn 150-151 AB 7
Dome Rock Mountains 74-75 F 6
Domesnäs = Kolkasrags 124-125 D 5
Domeyko 106-107 B 2
Domeyko, Cordillera — 111 C 2-3
Domingos Coelho 98-99 HJ 9
Domingos Martins 100-101 D 11
Dominguez 106-107 H 3
Dominguez, CA 83 III c 2
Dominguez Channel 83 III c 2
Dominguez Hills 83 III c 2
Dominica 64-65 O 8
Dominical 88-89 DE 10
Dominican Republic 64-65 MN 7-8
Dominica Passage 88-89 Q 7
Dominion Range 53 A 18-19
Dom Joaquim 102-103 L 3
Dom Noi, Lam — 150-151 E 5
Domodóssola 122-123 C 2
Dom Pedrito 111 F 4
Dom Pedro 100-101 B 3
Dompu 152-153 N 10
Dom Silverio 102-103 L 4
Domsjö 116-117 H 6
Domuyo, Volcán — 111 BC 5
Dom Yai, Lam — 150-151 E 5
Don [GB] 119 E 3
Don [IND] 140 BC 2
Don [SU] 124-125 M 7
Doña Ana, Cerro — 106-107 B 2
Donadeu 104-105 E 10
Donado 106-107 D 4
Doña Ines, Cerro — 104-105 B 10
Doña Inés Chica, Quebrada — 104-105 B 10
Donald 158-159 H 7
Donalda 61 B 4
Donald Landing 60 E 2
Donaldson, AR 78-79 C 3
Donaldsonville, LA 78-79 D 5
Donalsonville, GA 78-79 G 5
Doña María, Punta — 92-93 D 7
Doña Rosa, Cordillera de — 106-107 B 3
Donau 118 G 4
Donaueschingen 118 D 5
Donaufeld, Wien- 113 I b 1
Donaustadt, Wien- 113 I bc 2
Donauwörth 118 E 4
Donbei 146-147 D 9
Don Benito 120-121 E 9
Don Bosco, Quilmes- 110 III c 2
Doncaster 119 F 5
Doncaster, Melbourne- 161 II c 1
Don Cipriano 106-107 J 5
Dondaicha 138-139 E 7
Dondo [Angola] 172 BC 3
Dondo [Mozambique] 172 FG 5
Dondra Head = Dewundara Tuduwa 134-135 N 9
Đơn Du'o'ng 150-151 G 7
Doneck 126-127 H 2-3
Doneckij kr'až 126-127 H-K 2
Donegal 119 B 4
Donegal Bay 119 B 4
Donets = Severnyj Donec 126-127 J 2
Donetsk = Doneck 126-127 H 2-3
Donez = Severnyj Donec 126-127 J 2
Donga 164-165 G 7
Dong'a = Dong'ezhen 146-147 F 3
Dong'an 146-147 C 8
Dongara 158-159 B 5
Dongargarh 138-139 H 7
Dongba 138-139 J 3
Dongbei 146-147 D 9
Dongbei = Xinfeng 146-147 EF 8
Dongbi = Dongbei 146-147 D 9
Dongbo = Dongbei 146-147 D 9
Đông Châu 150-151 F 2
Dongchuan 142-143 J 6
Đông Đăng 148-149 E 2
Dong'ezhen 146-147 F 3
Dongfang 142-143 K 8
Donggala 148-149 G 7
Donggou 144-145 DE 3
Dongguan 142-143 LM 7
Dongguang 146-147 F 3
Đông Ha 150-151 F 4
Donghai 146-147 G 4
Donghai Dao 146-147 C 11
Dong He 146-147 A 3
Dong Hene 150-151 E 4
Đông Hoi 148-149 E 3
Dong Hu = Chengdong Hu 146-147 F 5
Dong Jiang 146-147 DE 10
Dongjiang = Congjiang 146-147 B 9
Dongjiang = Tungchiang 146-147 H 10
Dong Jiang = Xu Jiang 146-147 F 8
Dongjin = Dongjing 146-147 BC 10
Dongjing 146-147 BC 10
Dongjing Wan = Beibu Wan 142-143 K 7-8
Dongjinping = Zuo'an 146-147 E 8
Dongkalang 148-149 GH 6
Đông Khê 150-151 F 1
Dong Khiang = Ban Dong Khaang 150-151 E 4
Dong Khoang = Ban Dong Khaang 150-151 E 4
Dong Khuang = Ban Dong Khaang 150-151 E 4
Dongkou 146-147 C 8
Dongliu 146-147 F 6
Dongming 146-147 E 4
Đông Nai 150-151 F 7
Đông Ngai 150-151 F 4
Dongola = Dunqulah 164-165 KL 5
Dongou 172 C 1
Dong Phaya Yen 148-149 D 3
Dongping 146-147 F 4
Dongping = Anhua 146-147 C 7
Dongping Hu 146-147 F 3-4
Dong Qi = Songxi 146-147 G 8
Dongshan 146-147 F 10
Dongshan Dao 146-147 F 10
Dongshannei Ao 146-147 F 10
Dongsha Qundao 142-143 LM 7
Dongsheng 142-143 KL 4
Dongsheng, Beijing- 155 II ab 1
Dongtai 142-143 N 5
Dông Thap Mu'o'i 150-151 EF 7
Dongting Hu 142-143 L 6
Dongtou Shan 146-147 H 8
Đông Trang 150-151 G 6
Đông Triều 150-151 F 2
Đông Voi Mêp 148-149 E 3
Dongxiang 146-147 F 7
Dongxi Lian Dao 146-147 GH 4
Dongxing 142-143 K 7
Đông Xoai 148-149 E 4
Đông Xuân 150-151 G 6
Dongyang 146-147 H 7
Dong Yunhe = Chuanchang He 146-147 GH 5
Dongyuqu, Beijing- 155 II b 2
Dongzhen = Xinyi 146-147 C 10
Dongzhi 146-147 F 6
Doniphan, MO 78-79 D 2
Donjek River 58-59 S 5
Donji Vakuf 122-123 G 3
Donkerpoort 174-175 F 6
Dôn Kyûn 150-151 AB 6
Don Martín 76-77 D 9
Dønna 116-117 DE 4
Donnacona 63 A 4
Donnely, ID 66-67 EF 3
Donner Pass 64-65 B 4
Donnybrook 174-175 H 5
Donoso 88-89 F 10
Don Peninsula 60 C 3
Donskoj 124-125 M 7
Donsol 148-149 H 4
Dônthami 141 E 7
Don Torcuato, Tigre- 110 III b 1
Donûsa 122-123 LM 7
Donuzlav, ozero — 126-127 F 4
Donyztau 132-133 K 8
Donzère 120-121 K 6
Doonerak, Mount — 56-57 FG 4
Doornbosch = Doringbos 174-175 C 6
Doornik = Tournai 120-121 J 3
Doornriver = Doringrivier 174-175 C 6
Doorns, De — 174-175 CD 7
Doorns, Do — 174-175 CD 7
Door Peninsula 70-71 G 3
Dōr, Ad- = Ad-Dawr 136-137 KL 5
Dora, NM 76-77 C 6
Dōra, Baghdād- = Baghdād-Dawrah 136-137 L 6
Dora, Lake — 158-159 D 4
Dora Bāltea 122-123 B 3
Dorada, La — 92-93 E 3
Dorado 76-77 B 9
Dorado, El —, AR 64-65 H 5
Dorado, El — [CO] 92-93 E 4
Dorado, El — [RA] 106-107 G 5
Dorado, El — [YV] 92-93 G 3
Doral 142-143 F 3
D'Orbigny [BOL] 104-105 E 7
D'Orbigny [RA] 106-107 G 6
Dorbjany = Darbėnai 124-125 C 5
Dörböt Dabaan 142-143 FG 2
Dorchester 119 E 6
Dorchester, NE 68-69 H 5
Dorchester, Boston-, MA 84 I b 3
Dorchester, Cape — 56-57 V 4
Dorchester Bay 84 I b 3
Dorchester Center, Boston-, MA 84 I b 3
Dordabis 172 C 6
Dordogne 120-121 GH 6
Dordrecht [NL] 120-121 JK 3
Dordrecht [ZA] 174-175 G 6
Dore 120-121 J 6
Dore, Mont — 120-121 J 6
Doré Lake [CDN, lake] 61 E 3
Doré Lake [CDN, place] 61 E 3
Dore River 61 E 3
Dores do Indaiá 102-103 K 3
Dorey 168-169 E 2
Dorgali 122-123 C 5
Dori 164-165 DE 6
Doria Pamphili, Villa — 113 II b 2
Dorila 106-107 F 5
Doringberge 174-175 E 5
Doringbos 174-175 C 6
Doringrivier 174-175 C 6
Dorion 72-73 J 2
Dormida, La — 106-107 D 4
Dornach [D, Oberbayern] 130 II c 2
Dornakal 140 E 2
Dornbach, Wien- 113 I b 2
Dörnigheim 128 III b 1
Dornoch 119 D 3
Dornoch Firth 119 E 3
Dornod ◁ 142-143 LM 2
Dornogov 142-143 K 3
Doro 168-169 E 1
Dorochovo 124-125 L 6
Dorofejevskaja 132-133 P 3
Dorogobuž 124-125 J 6
Dorohoi 122-123 M 2
Doroŋāgāṅv 138-139 MN 4
Doronagaon = Doroŋāgāṅv 138-139 MN 4
Döröö nuur 142-143 GH 2
Dorotea 116-117 G 5
Dorothy 61 B 5
Dorrance, KS 68-69 G 6
Dorreen 60 C 2
Dorre Island 158-159 B 5
Dorrigo 160 L 3
Dorris, CA 66-67 C 5
Dortelweil 128 III b 1
Dortmund 118 CD 3
Dortmund-Ems-Kanal 118 C 2-3
Dörtyol 136-137 G 4
Dorūd 136-137 N 6
Doruma 172 E 1
Dorval 82 I a 2
Dorval, Île de — 82 I a 2
Dörvöldžin 142-143 GH 2
Dorya, Ganale — = Genale 164-165 N 7
Dorylaeum = Eskişehir 134-135 C 2-3
Dos Bahías, Cabo — 111 CD 7
Dos Caminos, Los — 91 II c 2
Dos de Mayo 92-93 DE 6
Dos Hermanas [RA] 106-107 H 4
Dos Lagunas 86-87 PQ 9
Đô So'n 150-151 F 2
Dos Pozos 111 CD 6
Dos Rios, CA 74-75 B 3
Dos Rios [MEX] 91 I a 2
Dossin Great Lakes Museum 84 II c 2-3
Dosso 164-165 E 6
Doswell, VA 80-81 H 2
Dothan, AL 64-65 J 5
Dothan, OR 66-67 B 4
Dot Lake, AK 58-59 PQ 5
Dotsero, CO 68-69 C 6
Doty, WA 66-67 B 2
Doua = Cavally 164-165 C 7-8
Douāb, Rūd-e — = Qareh Sū 134-135 FG 3-4
Douai 120-121 J 3
Douala 164-165 FG 8
Douarnenez 120-121 E 4
Double Mountain Fork 76-77 D 6
Double Peak 58-59 LM 6
Double Springs, AL 78-79 F 3-4
Doubs 120-121 L 5
Doucen = Dūsan 166-167 J 2
Doudaogoumen = Yayuan 144-145 F 2
Douentza 164-165 D 6
Dough, Djebel — = Jabal ad-Dūgh 166-167 F 3
Dougherty, OK 76-77 F 5
Dougherty, TX 76-77 D 6
Dougherty Plain 80-81 DE 5
Douglas, AK 58-59 UV 7
Douglas, AZ 64-65 E 5
Douglas, GA 80-81 E 5
Douglas, WA 66-67 CD 2
Douglas, WY 68-69 D 4
Douglas [CDN] 61 J 6
Douglas [GB] 119 D 4
Douglas [ZA] 172 D 7
Douglas, Cape — 58-59 L 7
Douglas, Mount — 58-59 KL 7
Douglas Channel 60 C 3
Douglas Lake [CDN] 60 GH 4
Douglas Lake [USA] 80-81 E 2-3
Douglas Park 83 II a 1
Douglas Point 72-73 EF 2
Douglas Range 53 BC 29-30
Douglastown 63 D 3
Dougou 146-147 E 5
Doûh, Jbel ed — = Jabal ad-Dūgh 166-167 F 3
Douhudi = Gong'an 146-147 D 6-7
Doûmâ = Dūmā 136-137 G 6
Doumé 164-165 G 8
Douna [HV] 168-169 D 2
Douna [RMM] 168-169 E 2
Dounan = Tounan 146-147 H 10
Dourada, Cachoeira — 102-103 H 3
Dourada, Serra — 92-93 K 7
Douradina 102-103 E 4
Dourado 102-103 H 5
Dourados [BR ↑ Corumbá] 102-103 D 3
Dourados [BR ↖ Ponta Porã] 92-93 J 9
Dourados, Rio — [BR, Mato Grosso do Sul] 102-103 E 5
Dourados, Rio — [BR, Minas Gerais] 102-103 J 3
Dourados, Serra dos — 111 F 2
Douro 120-121 C 8
Dou Rūd = Dorūd 136-137 N 6
Dou Sar = Dow Sar 136-137 N 5
Doûz = Dūz 166-167 L 3
Dovbyš 126-127 C 1
Dove Creek, CO 74-75 J 4
Dove Elbe 130 I b 2
Dover, DE 64-65 L 4
Dover, GA 80-81 F 4
Dover, NC 80-81 H 3
Dover, NH 72-73 L 3
Dover, NJ 72-73 J 4
Dover, OH 72-73 F 4
Dover, OK 76-77 EF 4
Dover [GB] 119 G 7
Dover [ZA] 174-175 G 4
Dover, Strait of — 119 GH 6
Dover-Foxcroft, ME 72-73 M 2
Doveyrīch, Rūd-e — 136-137 M 6
Dovrefjell 116-117 C 6
Dovsk 124-125 H 7
Dow, Lake — 172 D 6
Dowa 172 F 4
Dowagiac, MI 70-71 GH 4
Dowlatābād = Malāyer 134-135 F 4
Downey, CA 83 III d 2
Downey, ID 66-67 GH 4
Downieville, CA 74-75 C 3
Downpatrick 119 D 4
Downs, KS 68-69 G 6
Downton, Mount — 60 E 3
Dow Park 85 III c 2
Dows, IA 70-71 D 4
Dow Sar 136-137 N 5
Doyle, CA 66-67 C 5
Doyleville, CO 68-69 C 6
Dōzen 142-143 P 4
Dozois, Réservoir — 72-73 H 1
Dozornoje 126-127 F 4

Dra, Hamada du — = Hammadat ad-Dara' 164-165 CD 3
Drâ, Oued ed — = Wad Dra'ah 164-165 BC 3
Draa, Oued — = Wād Dra'ah 166-167 C 5
Dra'ah, Wād — 164-165 BC 3
Dracena 102-103 G 4
Dra-el-Mizan = Dara' al-Mizān 166-167 HJ 1
Drăgăneşti-Vlaşca 122-123 L 3
Drăgăşani 122-123 L 3
Dragerton, UT 74-75 H 3
Draghoender 174-175 E 5
Dragon, Bocas del — 94-95 L 2
Dragonera, Isla — 120-121 HJ 9
Dragones 104-105 E 8
Dragons Back 155 I b 2
Dragon's Mouths = Bocas del Dragon 94-95 L 2
Dragoon, AZ 74-75 HJ 6
Draguignan 120-121 L 7
Drain, OR 66-67 B 4
Drake, AZ 74-75 G 5
Drake, ND 68-69 F 2
Drake, Estrecho de — 111 B-D 9
Drakensberge 172 E 8-F 7
Drakes Bay 74-75 B 4
Drākṣharama 140 F 2
Dráma 122-123 KL 5
Drammen 116-117 CD 8
Dran = Đo'n Du'o'ng 150-151 G 7
Dranda 126-127 K 5
Drang, Ya — 150-151 F 6
Drangajökull 116-117 bc 1
Drangsnes 116-117 c 2
Draper, NC 80-81 G 2
Draper, Mount — 58-59 S 7
Drapetsŏna 113 IV a 2
Dräpung = Bräpung 138-139 N 3
Draria 170 I a 2
Drau 118 F 5
Drava 118 H 6
Drawa 118 G 2
Drawsko Pomorskie 118 GH 2
Drayā 142-143 H 5
Drayton Plains, MI 72-73 E 3
Drayton Valley 60 K 3
Dre Chhu = Mōronus 142-143 G 5
Dreieichenhain 128 III ab 1-2
Dreikikir 148-149 M 7
Drepung = Bräpung 138-139 N 3
Dresden, TN 78-79 E 2
Dresden [CDN] 72-73 E 3
Dresden [DDR] 118 FG 3
Dresv'anka 124-125 R 3
Dreunberg 174-175 FG 6
Dreux 120-121 H 4
Drew, MS 78-79 D 4
Drewitz, Potsdam- 130 III a 2
Drewsey, OR 66-67 D 4
Drews Reservoir 66-67 C 4
Drexel, MO 70-71 C 6
Drexel Hill, PA 84 III b 2
Dribin 124-125 H 6
Driemond 128 I b 2
Drifton, FL 80-81 DE 5
Driftpile 60 JK 2
Driggs, ID 66-67 H 4
Drin 122-123 J 4
Drina 122-123 H 3
Dring, Isla — 108-109 B 5
Drini i Bardhë 122-123 J 4
Drini i Zi 122-123 J 5
Drinit, Gjiri i — 122-123 H 5
Drinkwater 61 F 5
Drinkwater Pass 66-67 D 4
Drissa 124-125 G 6
Drøback 116-117 D 8
Drogenbos 128 II ab 2
Drogheda 119 CD 5
Drogobyč 126-127 AB 2
Droichead Átha = Drogheda 119 CD 5
Drôme 120-121 K 6
Dromo 138-139 M 4
Dronne 120-121 H 6
Dronning Maud fjellkjede 53 A
Dronning Maud land 53 B 36-4
Droupolé, Monts de — 168-169 CD 4
Drowning River 62 G 2
Drug 138-139 C 2
Drug = Durg 138-139 H 7
Druid Hills, GA 85 II c 2
Druja 124-125 F 6
Drumbo 72-73 F 3
Drumheller 56-57 O 7
Drummond, MI 70-71 J 2
Drummond, MT 66-67 G 2
Drummond, WI 70-71 E 2
Drummond Island 70-71 HJ 3
Drummondlea 174-175 H 3
Drummondville 56-57 W 8
Drummoyne, Sydney- 161 I a 2
Drumochter Pass 119 D 3
Drury Lake 58-59 U 5
Druskininkai 124-125 DE 6-7
Druskininkaj = Druskininkai 124-125 DE 6-7
Druso, Gebel — = Jabal ad-Durūz 134-135 D 4
Družba [SU, Kazachskaja SSR] 132-133 P 8
Družba [SU, Moskva] 113 V cd 2
Družba [SU, Ukrainskaja SSR] 124-125 J 7
Družina 132-133 bc 4
Drvar 122-123 G 3
Dry Bay 58-59 S 7
Dryberry Lake 62 C 3
Drybrough 61 H 2
Dry Creek 68-69 C 2
Dryden 56-57 K 1
Dryden, TX 76-77 C 7-8
Drygalski Glacier 53 B 17-18
Drygalskiinsel 53 C 10
Dry Lake, NV 74-75 F 4
Drysdale River 158-159 E 2-3
Dry Tortugas 80-81 b 4

Dsayul 142-143 H 6
Dschang 164-165 G 7

Dua 172 D 1
Duaca 94-95 G 2
Duala = Douala 164-165 FG 8
Du'an 142-143 K 7
Duanshi 146-147 D 4
Duao, Punta — 106-107 A 5
Duarte, Pico — 64-65 M 8
Duartina 102-103 H 5
Duas Igrejas 120-121 DE 8
Duas Onças, Ilha das — 102-103 F 5
Du'ayn, Ad- 164-165 K 6
Ḍubā 173 D 4
Dubach, LA 78-79 C 4
Dubawnt Lake 56-57 Q 5
Dubawnt River 56-57 Q 5
Dubay 134-135 GH 5
Dubbo 158-159 J 6
Dubda 138-139 M 3
Dübendorf 128 IV b 1
Dubie 171 B 5
Dublin 119 CD 5
Dublin, GA 64-65 K 5
Dublin, MI 70-71 GH 3
Dublin, TX 76-77 E 6
Dubli River 58-59 JK 4
Dubna [SU, place Moskovskaja Oblast'] 124-125 L 5
Dubna [SU, place Tul'skaja Oblast'] 124-125 L 6
Dubna [SU, river] 124-125 M 5
Dubno 126-127 B 1
Dubois, ID 66-67 G 3
Du Bois, PA 72-73 G 4
Dubois, WY 66-67 J 4
Dubossary 126-127 D 3
Dubov'azovka 126-127 F 1
Dubovskij 124-125 Q 5
Dubovskoje 126-127 L 3
Dubovyj Ovrag 126-127 LM 2
Dubrājpur 138-139 L 6
D'ubrar, gora — 126-127 O 6
Dubréka 164-165 B 7
Dubrovica 124-125 EF 8
Dubrovka [SU, Br'anskaja Oblast'] 124-125 JK 7
Dubrovka [SU, Leningradskaja Oblast'] 124-125 H 4
Dubrovnik 122-123 GH 4
Dubrovno 124-125 H 6
Dubuque, IA 64-65 H 3
Dubysa 124-125 D 6
Duchang 146-147 F 7
Duchesne, UT 66-67 H 5
Duchess [AUS] 158-159 G 4
Duchess [CDN] 61 BC 5
Duchovnickoje 124-125 R 7
Duchovščina 124-125 J 6
Ducie [GH] 168-169 E 3
Ducie [Pitcairn] 156-157 L 6
Duck Bay 61 H 4
Duck Hill, MS 78-79 DE 4
Duck Islands 62 K 4
Duck Lake 61 EF 4
Duck Mountain 61 H 5
Duck Mountain Provincial Park 61 H 5
Duck River 78-79 F 2-3
Ducktown, TN 78-79 G 3
Duckwater Peak 74-75 F 3
Ducor, CA 74-75 D 5
Ducos 106-107 F 6
Đu'c Phô 150-151 G 5
Đu'c Trong 150-151 G 7
Duda, Rio — 94-95 D 6
Dudčany 126-127 F 3
Duddhi = Dūdhi 138-139 J 5
Dūdhi 138-139 J 5
Dudh Kōsī 138-139 L 4
Dudhnā = Dudna 138-139 E 8
Dudhnai 141 B 3
Dudignac 106-107 G 5
Dudinka 132-133 PQ 4
Dudna 138-139 E 8
Dudnaī = Dudhnai 141 B 3
Dudorovskij 124-125 K 7
Dūdu 138-139 E 4
Dudullu 154 I bc 2
Duékoué 168-169 D 4
Duende, Península — 108-109 B 6
Dueré, Rio — 98-99 O 10
Duero 120-121 F 8
Duevé 98-99 O 10
Dufaur 106-107 F 6
Dufayt, Wādī — 173 D 6
Duff Islands 148-149 I 6
Dūfiri 166-167 F 3
Dufresne Lake 63 D 2
Dufur, OR 66-67 C 3
Duga-Zapadnaja, mys — 132-133 bc 6
Dugdown Mountain 78-79 G 3-4
Dūgh, Jabal ad- 166-167 F 3
Dugi Otok 122-123 F 4
Dugna 124-125 L 6
Dugny 129 I c 2
Dugo Selo 122-123 G 3
Dugues Canal 85 I b 2
Duğur 136-137 K 2
Du He 146-147 C 5
Duida, Cerro — 94-95 J 6
Duifken Point 158-159 H 2
Duisburg 118 C 3
Duitama 94-95 E 5
Duivelskloof = Duiwelskloof 174-175 J 2
Duivendrecht 128 I b 2
Duiwelskloof 174-175 J 2
Dujail = Ad-Dujayl 136-137 KL 6
Dujayl, Ad- 136-137 KL 6
Dujiawobu = Ningcheng 144-145 B 2
Dukān, Sadd ad- 136-137 L 4-5
Dukana 171 D 2
Duk Ayod = Ayōd 164-165 L 7
Duke, OK 76-77 E 5
Duke Island 58-59 x 9
Dūk Fāywīl 164-165 L 7
Dukhān 134-135 G 5
Dukī 138-139 B 2
Dukielska, Przełęcz — 118 KL 4
Dukkālah 164-165 C 2
Dukla Pass = Dukelský průsmyk 118 KL 4
Dukou 142-143 J 6
Dūkštas 124-125 EF 6
Duku 168-169 H 3
Dulaanchaan 142-143 JK 1-2
Dulaan Chijd 142-143 H 4
Dulac, LA 78-79 D 6
Dulawan = Datu Piang 148-149 H 5
Dulaymīyah, Ad- 136-137 K 6
Dulce, NM 68-69 C 7

Dulce, La — 106-107 H 7
Dulce, Río — 111 D 3-4
Dulgalach 132-133 Z 4
Duliu Jiang 146-147 B 9
Dullabchara 141 C 3
Dull Center, WY 68-69 D 4
Dullstroom 174-175 J 3
Dulovo 122-123 M 4
Duluth, MN 64-65 H 2
Dūmā 136-137 G 6
Dumaguete 148-149 H 5
Dumai 152-153 D 5
Dumaran Island 148-149 GH 4
Ḍumariyāganj = Domariāganj 138-139 J 4
Dumas, AR 78-79 D 4
Dumas, TX 76-77 D 5
Dumas, Península — 108-109 E 10
Dūmat al-Jandal = Al-Jawf 134-135 DE 5
Dumayj, Sharm — 173 DE 4
Ḍumayr 136-137 G 6
Dumbarton 119 D 3-4
Dumboa 168-169 J 3
Dum Dum 154 II b 2
Dumdum, Pulau — 152-153 G 5
Dum Duma 141 D 2
Dumduma = Dum Duma 141 D 2
Dum Dum-Birati 154 II b 2
Dum Dum International Airport 154 II b 2
Dume = Doumé 164-165 G 8
Dumfries 119 E 4
Duminići 124-125 K 7
Dumkā 138-139 L 5
Dumlu = Hınș 136-137 J 2
Dumlupınar 136-137 CD 3
Dumoine, Lac — 72-73 H 1
Dumoine, Rivière — 72-73 H 1
Dumont d'Urville 53 C 14-15
Dumra 138-139 K 4
Dumrāňv = Dumraon 138-139 K 5
Dumraon 138-139 K 5
Ḍumrī 138-139 KL 6
Dumyāṭ 164-165 L 2
Dumyāṭ, Maṣabb — 173 BC 2
Duna [Bhutan] 138-139 M 4
Duna [H] 118 J 5
Dunaföldvár 118 J 5
Dunaj [SU] 144-145 J 1
Dunaj, ostrova — 132-133 XY 3
Dunajec 118 K 4
Dunajevcy 126-127 C 2
Dunareă 122-123 M 3
Dunarii, Delta — 122-123 N 3
Dunas 106-107 L 3
Dunaújváros 118 J 5
Dunav 122-123 J 3
Dunbar, AK 58-59 N 4
Dunbar, OK 76-77 G 5
Dunbar, WV 72-73 F 5
Dunblane [CDN] 61 E 5
Dunblane [GB] 119 DE 3
Duncan 66-67 AB 1
Duncan, AZ 74-75 J 6
Duncan, OK 64-65 G 5
Duncan, WY 66-67 J 4
Duncan Passage 134-135 P 8
Duncansby Head 119 E 2
Dundaga 124-125 D 5
Dund Ajmang = Töv ◁ 142-143 K 2
Dundalk, MD 72-73 H 5
Dundalk [CDN] 72-73 F 2
Dundalk [IRL] 119 CD 4-5
Dundas 56-57 X 2
Dundas, Lake — 158-159 D 6
Dundas Island 60 B 2
Dundas Peninsula 56-57 O 2-3
Dundas Strait 158-159 F 2
Dún Dealgan = Dundalk 119 CD 4-5
Dundee, MI 72-73 E 4
Dundee, TX 76-77 E 6
Dundee [GB] 119 E 3
Dundee [ZA] 172 F 7
Dundgov' ◁ 142-143 K 2
Dundurn 61 E 5
Dundwa Range 138-139 J 4
Dunedin 158-159 O 9
Dunedin, FL 80-81 b 2
Dunedoo 160 J 4
Dunfermline 119 DE 3
Dūngarpur 138-139 D 6
Dungarvan 119 C 5
Dung Büree uul 142-143 FG 4-5
Dungeness, Punta — 108-109 EF 9
Dungog 160 KL 4
Dungripalli 138-139 J 7
Dungtshākha 138-139 M 3
Dungu [ZRE, place] 172 E 1
Dungu [ZRE, river] 171 B 2
Dungun, Kuala — 148-149 D 6
Dungun, Sungei — 150-151 D 10
Dungunab = Dunqunāb 164-165 M 4
Dunhua 142-143 O 3
Dunhuang 142-143 GH 3
Dunière, Parc provincial de — 63 C 3
Dunkerque 120-121 HJ 3
Dunkirk, IN 70-71 H 5
Dunkirk, NY 72-73 G 3
Dunkirk = Dunkerque 120-121 HJ 3
Dunkwa 164-165 D 7
Dún Laoghaire = Kingstown 119 CD 5
Dunlap, TN 78-79 G 3
Dunlop 61 J 3
Dunmarra 158-159 F 3
Dunmore, PA 72-73 J 4
Dunn, NC 80-81 G 3
Dunnellon, FL 80-81 b 2
Dunning, NE 68-69 FG 5
Dunning, Chicago-, IL 83 II b 1
Dunnville 72-73 FG 3
Dunolly 160 F 6
Dunphy, NV 66-67 E 5
Dunqul 173 B 6
Dunqulah 164-165 KL 5
Dunqunāb 164-165 M 4
Duns 119 E 4
Dunseith, ND 68-69 F 1
Dunsmuir, CA 66-67 B 5
Duolun = Doloon Nuur 142-143 LM 3
Duong Đông = Phu Quôc 150-151 D 7
Duo Qi = Ting Jiang 146-147 F 9
Duozhu 146-147 E 10
Dupang Ling 146-147 C 9
Duparquet 62 M 2
Dūpenau 130 I a 1
Duperré = 'Ayn Daflah 166-167 GH 1
Duperre, Pulau-pulau 150-151 G 11
Dupleix = Dāmus 166-167 G 1
Dupleix Range = Tanglha 142-143 FG 5
Dupont, IN 70-71 H 6
Dupree, SD 68-69 F 3
Dupuyer, MT 66-67 G 1
Duqqi, Al-Qāhirah-ad- 170 II b 1
Duque de Bragança 172 C 3
Duque de Caxias 92-93 L 9
Duque de York, Isla — 111 A 8
Duquesne, PA 72-73 G 4
Du Quoin, IL 70-71 F 6-7
Durack Range 158-159 E 3
Duragan 136-137 F 2
Duran, NM 76-77 B 5
Durance 120-121 K 7
Durand, MI 72-73 E 3
Durand, WI 70-71 E 3
Durango, CO 64-65 E 4
Durango [MEX] 64-65 EF 6
Durango, Victoria de — 64-65 F 7
Durañona 106-107 G 6
Durant, MS 78-79 DE 4
Durant, OK 64-65 G 5
Durazno [ROU, administrative unit] 106-107 JK 4
Durazno [ROU, place] 111 E 4
Durazno, Cuchilla Grande del — 106-107 JK 4
Durazno, El — 106-107 E 6
Durazzo = Durrës 122-123 H 5
Durban 172 F 7
Durbanville 174-175 C 7
Durbe 124-125 C 5
Duren Tiga, Jakarta- 154 IV b 2
Durg 138-139 H 7
Durga nuur = Döröö nuur 142-143 GH 2
Durgapūr [BD] 141 B 3
Durgapur [IND] 134-135 O 6
Durgerdam 128 I b 1
Durham, KS 68-69 H 6
Durham, NC 64-65 L 4
Durham [CDN] 72-73 F 2
Durham [GB] 119 EF 4
Durham Downs 160 E 1
Dūrinzeik 141 E 7
Durkee, OR 66-67 E 3
Durmitor 122-123 H 4
Durness 119 D 2
Duro, Serra do — 98-99 P 10-11
Durrel 63 J 3
Durrës 122-123 H 5
Dur Sargon = Khorsabad 136-137 K 4
Dur Sharrukīn = Khorsabad 136-137 K 4
Dursunbey 136-137 C 3
Durt = Chanch 142-143 J 1
D'urt'uli 124-125 U 6
Duru [ZRE, place] 171 B 1
Duru [ZRE, river] 171 B 1
Durūz, Jabal ad- 134-135 D 4
D'Urville Island 161 E 5
Dušak 134-135 J 3
Dūsan 166-167 J 2
Dušanbe 134-135 K 3
Dušeti 126-127 M 5
Dusey River 62 F 2
Dūsh 173 B 5
Du Shan [TJ, mountain] 144-145 B 2
Dushan [TJ, place] 146-147 F 6
Du Shan = Lu Shan 146-147 FG 3
Dusheng 146-147 F 2
Du Shui = Du He 146-147 C 5
Düsseldorf 118 C 3
Dustin, OK 76-77 FG 5
Dustin Gol 146-147 A 2
Dutch Habor 52 D 35
Dutch John, UT 66-67 J 5
Dutou 146-147 D 9
Dutsen Wai 168-169 H 3
Dutton, MT 66-67 H 2
Dutton, Mount — 74-75 G 3-4
Duvan 132-133 K 6
Duved 116-117 E 6
Duvefjord 116-117 l 4
Duvernay 82 I a 1
Duveyrier = Dūfirī 166-167 F 3
Duvivier = Būshqūf 166-167 K 1
Duwayd, Ad- 134-135 E 5
Ḍuwayḥin, Dawhat aḍ- 134-135 G 6
Duwaym, Ad- 164-165 L 6
Duwayr, Ad- 173 B 4
Duxun 146-147 F 10
Duya, El — 94-95 F 5
Duyun 142-143 K 6
Duyūrah, Qaṭṭārat ad- 136-137 C 7
Dūz 166-167 L 3
Düzce 136-137 D 2
Duzerville = Al-Ḥajar 166-167 KL 1
Dvārka = Dwārka 138-139 B 6
Dvina, Severnaja — 132-133 G 5
Dvinsk = Daugavpils 124-125 EF 6
Dvinskaja guba 132-133 F 4-5
Dvorchangaj 142-143 J 2
Dvuch Cirkov, gora — 132-133 gh 4
Dwangwa 171 C 6
Dwārāhāt 138-139 G 3
Dwari Bay = Ise-wan 144-145 L 5
Dwārka 138-139 B 6
Dwarsberge 174-175 G 3
Dwarsrand 174-175 J 4
Dwarsrivier 174-175 H 2
Dwight, IL 70-71 F 5
Dwight D. Eisenhower Park 85 III c 1
Dworp 128 II a 2
Dworshak Reservoir 66-67 F 2
Dwyka 174-175 D 7
Dyaul Island 148-149 gh 5
Dychtau, gora — 126-127 L 5
Dyer, Cabo — 108-109 AB 7
Dyer, Cape — 56-57 YZ 4
Dyereiland 174-175 C 8
Dyer Island = Dyereiland 174-175 C 8
Dyer Plateau 53 BC 30
Dyers Bay 72-73 F 2
Dyersburg, TN 64-65 J 4
Dyersdale, TX 85 III bc 1
Dyersville, IA 70-71 E 4
Dyje 118 H 4
Dyker Beach Park 82 III b 3
Dylewska Gora 118 JK 2
Dyment 62 C 3
Dymer 126-127 E 1
Dyrhólaey 116-117 d 3
Dyrnesvågen 116-117 B 6
Dysselsdorp 174-175 E 7
Dzacha 142-143 H 4
Dza Chhu 142-143 H 5
Dzag 142-143 H 2
Džagdy, chrebet — 132-133 YZ 7
Dzahar es Soûq = Tahār as-Sūq 166-167 DE 2
Džalal-Abad 134-135 L 2
Džalilabad 126-127 O 7
Džalinda 132-133 XY 7
Džambajskij, ostrov — 126-127 OP 3
Džambejty 132-133 J 7
Džambul [SU ← Frunze] 132-133 MN 9
Džambul [SU ↖ Gurjev] 126-127 P 3
Džambul, gora — 132-133 N 9
Džangil'da = Turgaj 132-133 L 8
Džankoj 126-127 G 4
Džanybek 126-127 N 2
Dzaoudzi 172 J 4
Džardžan 132-133 X 4
Džargalant 142-143 LM 2
Džargalant = Chovd 142-143 G 2
Džarkent = Panfilov 132-133 OP 9
Dzartaj Dabas nuur 142-143 JK 4
Džarylgač, ostrov — 126-127 F 3-4
Dzasag = Xinjie 146-147 B 2
Dzaudžikau = Ordžonikidze 126-127 M 5
Džava 126-127 LM 5
Dzavchan [Mongolia, administrative unit = 4 ◁] 142-143 H 2
Dzavchan [Mongolia, place] 142-143 G 2
Dzavchan gol 142-143 H 2
Džebrail 126-127 N 7
Džedy 132-133 M 8
Dzei Chhu 142-143 H 5-6
Dzenzik, mys — 126-127 H 3
Dzērbene 124-125 E 5
Džermuk 126-127 M 7
Dzerzhinsk = Dzeržinsk 124-125 O 5
Dzeržinsk [SU, Belorusskaja SSR] 124-125 F 7
Dzeržinsk [SU, Rossijskaja SFSR] 132-133 GH 6
Dzeržinsk [SU, Ukrainskaja SSR] 126-127 CD 1
Dzeržinskij 113 V d 3
Dzeržinskij = Narjan-Mar 132-133 JK 4
Dzeržinskogo, PkiO im. — 113 V c 2
Džetygara 132-133 L 7
Džezkazgan 132-133 M 8
Dzhambul = Džambul 132-133 MN 9
Dzhardzhan = Džardžan 132-133 X 4
Dzhargalantu = Chovd 142-143 G 2
Dzhugdzhur Mountains = chrebet Džugdžur 132-133 Z-b 6
Działdowo 118 K 2
Dzibchalantu = Uliastaj 142-143 H 2
Dzibgalantu = Uliastaj 142-143 H 2
Dziedzice 118 J 4
Džikimde 132-133 X 6
Dzilam de Bravo 86-87 Q 7
Dzioua = Dibwah 166-167 J 3
Dzirgalantu = Chovd 142-143 G 2
Dzitbalche 86-87 PQ 7
Džizak 134-135 K 2
Dzöjtön nuur 142-143 G 4
Dz'ol' 124-125 T 3
Džubchulant = Uliastaj 142-143 H 2
Džugdžur, chrebet — 132-133 Z-b 6
Džūkste 124-125 D 5
Dzul'fa 126-127 M 7
Dzum Bulag = Džargalant 142-143 LM 2
Dzungaria = Junggarhiya 142-143 EF 2
Džungarskij Alatau, chrebet — 132-133 O 9-P 8
Džurin 126-127 D 2
Džusaly 132-133 L 8
Dzüsten Öls 142-143 F 2
Dzüünbajan 142-143 KL 3
Dzuunmod 142-143 K 2
Džvari 126-127 L 5

E

Eabamet Lake 62 F 2
Eads, CO 68-69 E 6
Eagar, AZ 74-75 J 5
Eagle, AK 58-59 R 4
Eagle, CO 68-69 C 6
Eagle, NE 68-69 H 5
Eagle Bend, MN 70-71 C 2
Eagle Butte, SD 68-69 F 3
Eagle Grove, IA 70-71 D 4
Eaglehill Creek 61 DE 5
Eagle Island 61 J 4
Eagle Lake, ME 72-73 M 1
Eagle Lake, TX 76-77 F 8
Eagle Lake [CDN] 62 C 3
Eagle Lake [USA, California] 66-67 C 5
Eagle Lake [USA, Maine] 72-73 M 1
Eagle Mountains 76-77 B 7
Eagle Nest, NM 76-77 B 4
Eagle Pass, TX 64-65 FG 6
Eagle Passage 108-109 K 9
Eagle Point, OR 66-67 B 4
Eagle Rapid 62 CD 2
Eagle River, AK 58-59 N 6
Eagle River, MI 70-71 F 2
Eagle River, WI 70-71 F 3
Eagle River [CDN] 62 C 3
Eagle Summit 58-59 P 4
Eagle Tail Mountains 74-75 G 6
Eagleville, CA 66-67 CD 5
Ea Hleo 150-151 F 6
Ea Krong 150-151 FG 6
Ealing, London- 129 II a 1
Ear Falls [CDN, place] 62 C 2
Ear Falls [CDN, river] 62 C 2
Earlimart, CA 74-75 D 5
Earlington, KY 70-71 G 7
Earlton 62 LM 3
Earlville, IL 70-71 F 5
Earlwood, Sydney- 161 I a 2
Early, IA 70-71 C 4
Earn 119 DE 3
Earn Lake 58-59 U 5
Earth, TX 76-77 C 5
Earth, Altar of the — 155 II b 2
Easley, SC 80-81 E 3
East Anglian Heights 119 F 6-G 5
East Angus 72-73 L 2
East Arlington, MA 84 I ab 2
East Atlanta, Atlanta-, GA 85 II c 2
East Australian Basin 156-157 GH 7
East Barnet, London- 129 II b 1
East Bay 78-79 E 6
East Bengal = Mashraqī Bangāl 134-135 O 5-P 6
East Bernard, TX 76-77 FG 8
Eastborne 119 G 6
East Boston, Boston-, MA 84 I b 2
East Brady, PA 72-73 G 4
East Braintree, MA 84 I c 3
East Broughton 72-73 L 1
East Caicos 88-89 L 4
East Cape [NZ] 158-159 P 7
East Cape [USA] 58-59 s 7
East Caroline Basin 156-157 G 4
East Chicago, IN 70-71 G 5
East China Sea 142-143 N 6-O 5
East Cleveland, OH 72-73 EF 4
East Coast 161 GH 4
East Coulée 61 BC 5
East Detroit, MI 84 II c 2
East Elmhurst, New York-, NY 82 III c 2
East Ely, NV 74-75 F 3
Eastend 66-67 J 1
East End, Metairie-, LA 85 I b 1
Easter Island 156-157 M 6
Eastern [EAK] 172 G 1-2
Eastern [GH] 168-169 E 4
Eastern [WAL] 168-169 C 3
Eastern [Z] 172 F 4
Eastern Ghats 134-135 M 8-N 7
Eastern Group = Lau Group 148-149 b 2
Eastern Indian Antarctic Basin 50-51 O-Q 8
Eastern Native, Johannesburg- 170 V b 2
Eastern Province = Nègenangira Palāna = 5 ◁ 140 E 6
Eastern Sayan Mountains = Vostočnyj Sajan 132-133 R 6-T 7
Eastern Sierra Madre = Sierra Madre Oriental 64-65 F 6-G 7
Easter Plateau 156-157 L-N 6
Easterville 61 J 4
East Falkland 111 E 8
East Falls, Philadelphia-, PA 84 III b 1
East Falls Church, Arlington-, VA 82 II a 2
East Fork Andreafsky 58-59 FG 5
East Fork Chandalar 58-59 P 2
East Fork Des Moines River 70-71 C 4
East Fork Sevier River 74-75 GH 4
East Fork White River 70-71 GH 6
East Frisian Islands = Ostfriesische Inseln 118 C 2
Eastgate, NV 74-75 DE 3
East Glacier Park, MT 66-67 G 1
East Grand Forks, MN 68-69 H 1-2
East Ham, London- 129 II c 1
East Hampton, NY 72-73 KL 4
East Helena, MT 66-67 H 2
East Island 148-149 h 7
East Lamma Channel 155 I a 2
Eastland, TX 76-77 E 6
Eastland Center 84 II c 2
East Lansdowne, PA 84 III b 2
East Lansing, MI 70-71 H 4
East Liverpool, OH 72-73 F 4
East London = Oos-Londen 172 EF 8
East Los Angeles, CA 83 III d 1
East Lynn, WV 72-73 E 5
East-Main 56-57 V 7
Eastmain River 56-57 VW 7
Eastman, GA 80-81 E 4
East Marin Island 83 I b 1
East Moline, IL 70-71 EF 5
East New York, New York-, NY 82 III c 2-3
Easton, MD 72-73 HJ 5
Easton, PA 72-73 J 4
Easton, WA 66-67 C 2
East Orange, NJ 72-73 J 4
Eastover, SC 80-81 F 4
East Pacific Ridge 156-157 M 5-6
East Palatka, FL 80-81 c 2
East Pass 78-79 G 6
East Pine 60 G 2
East Point, GA 64-65 K 5
Eastport 63 K 3
East Potomac Park 82 II a 2
East Prairie, MO 78-79 E 2
East Richmond, CA 83 I c 1
East River 82 III bc 2
East Saint Louis, IL 64-65 HJ 4
East Siberian Ridge 52 B 36-1
East Siberian Sea 132-133 d-h 3
East Tavaputs Plateau 74-75 J 3
East Watertown, MA 84 I ab 2
East Weymouth, MA 84 I c 3
Eastwick, Philadelphia-, PA 84 III b 2
Eastwood, Sydney- 161 I a 1
Eastwood Park 85 III b 2
Eaton, CO 68-69 D 5
Eaton, OH 70-71 H 6
Eaton, Lake — 158-159 EF 4
Eatonia 61 D 5
Eaton Rapids, MI 70-71 H 4
Eatonton, GA 80-81 E 4
Eatonville, WA 66-67 BC 2
Eaubonne 129 I c 2
Eau Claire, WI 64-65 H 3
Eauripik 148-149 M 5
Ébano 86-87 L 6
Ebara, Tōkyō- 155 III b 2
Ebba Ksoūr = Abbat Quṣūr 166-167 L 1-2
Ebbert Furr House 85 III b 1
Eben Junction, MI 70-71 G 2
Eber gölü 136-137 D 3
Eberswalde-Finow 118 F 2
Ebertswil 128 IV b 2
Ebetsu 144-145 b 2
Ebi nuur 142-143 E 3
Ebmatingen 128 IV b 1
Ebola 172 D 1
Ēboli 122-123 F 5
Ebolowa 164-165 G 8
Ebon 208 G 2
Ebony 172 BC 6
Eboue, Stade — 170 IV a 1
Ebrāhīmābād [IR ↗ Arāk] 136-137 O 5
Ebrāhīmābād [IR ↓ Qazvīn] 136-137 N 5
Ebro 120-121 G 8
Ebro, Delta del — 120-121 H 8
E. Bustos 106-107 C 4
Ebute-Metta, Lagos- 170 III b 2
Ebuṭṭābād 134-135 L 4
Ecatepec de Morelos 91 I c 1
Ecbatana = Hamadān 134-135 F 3-4
Eceabat 136-137 AB 2
Ech Chèbba = Ash-Shābah 166-167 M 2
ech Chema'ia = Ash-Shamā'iyah 166-167 B 3
ech Chiadma = Ash-Shiādmā' 166-167 B 4
Echeng 146-147 E 6
Echeta, WY 68-69 CD 3
Echigo sammyaku 144-145 M 4-N 3
Echo, OR 66-67 D 3
Echo, UT 66-67 H 5
Echo, Lake — 160 c 3
Echo Bank 64-65 P 7
Echo Cliffs 74-75 H 4
Echuca 158-159 H 7
Écija 120-121 E 10
Ecilda Paullier 106-107 J 5
Eckenheim, Frankfurt am Main- 128 III b 1
Eckington, Washington-, DC 82 II ab 1
Eclipse Spund 56-57 UV 3
Ečmiadzin 126-127 M 6
Economy 63 DE 5
Ecoporanga 100-101 D 10
Écorce, Lac de l' 72-73 HJ 1
Ecorse, MI 84 II b 3
Écouen 129 I c 1
Ecuador 92-93 CD 5
Ecuador = Équateur 172 CD 1
Ēd [ETH] 164-165 N 6
Eda, Yokohama- 155 III a 2
Edam 61 D 4
Edcouch, TX 76-77 EF 9
Ed Damur = Ad-Dāmūr 136-137 F 6
Eḍ Ḍaou = Aḍ-Ḍaw 136-137 G 5
ed Dâr el Beïḍâ' = Ad-Dār al-Bayḍā' 164-165 BC 2
ed Deffa = Aḍ-Ḍiffah 164-165 J 2
Ed Dehībet = Adh-Dhahībah 166-167 M 3
Ed-Dehna = Ad-Dahnā' 134-135 E 5-F 6
Ed Deir = Ad-Dayr 173 C 5
Eddies Cove 63 HJ 2
Eddington Gardens, PA 84 III d 1
Ed Diweir = Ad-Duwayr 173 B 4
Eddy, MT 66-67 F 2
Eddy, TX 76-77 F 7
Eddystone, PA 84 III b 2
Eddystone Point 160 d 2
Eddyville, KY 78-79 EF 2
Eddyville, NE 68-69 G 5
Ede [WAN] 168-169 G 4
Edéa 164-165 G 8
Edeia 102-103 H 2
Edeien el-Murzūq = Ṣaḥrā' Marzūq 164-165 G 3-4
Edeien-'Ubārī = Ṣaḥrā' Awbārī 164-165 G 3
Eden 158-159 JK 7
Eden, MT 66-67 H 2
Eden, NC 80-81 G 2
Eden, TX 76-77 E 7
Eden, WY 66-67 J 4
Edenburg [ZA, Oranje-Vrystaat] 174-175 FG 5
Edenburg [ZA, Transvaal] 170 V b 1
Edendale [ZA, Natal] 174-175 HJ 5
Edendale [ZA, Transvaal] 170 V bc 1
Eden Park 154 II b 2
Edenton, NC 80-81 H 2
Edenvale 170 V bc 1
Edenville 174-175 G 4
Eder 118 D 3
Ederet 142-143 JK 2
Edessa 122-123 JK 5
Edessa = Urfa 134-135 D 3
Edeyin el Murzuq = Sahrā' Marzūq 164-165 G 3-4
Edeyin Ubari = Ṣaḥrā' Awbārī 164-165 G 3
Edgar, NE 68-69 H 5
Edgar, WI 70-71 EF 3
Edgard, LA 78-79 D 5-6
Edgartown, MA 72-73 L 4
Edgefield, SC 80-81 EF 4
Edge Island = Edgeøya 116-117 l 5-6
Edgeley, ND 68-69 G 2
Edgell Island 56-57 Y 5
Edgemont, SD 68-69 E 4
Edgeøya 116-117 l 5-6
Edgerton, MN 70-71 BC 4
Edgerton, WI 70-71 F 4
Edgewater Park, NJ 84 III d 1
Edgewood, IL 70-71 F 6
Edgewood Park, New Orleans-, LA 85 I b 2
Edgware, London- 129 II a 1
Edina 168-169 C 4
Edina, MO 70-71 DE 5
Edinburg, IN 70-71 H 6
Edinburg, MS 78-79 E 4
Edinburg, TX 64-65 G 6
Edinburgh 119 E 4
Edirne 134-135 B 2
Edison, GA 78-79 G 5
Edison, WA 66-67 B 1
Edisto Island, SC 80-81 FG 4
Edisto River 80-81 F 4
Edithburgh 160 C 5
Edjelé = Ibjīl 164-165 F 3
Edmond, OK 76-77 F 5
Edmonds, WA 66-67 BC 2
Edmonton 56-57 NO 7
Edmonton, KY 70-71 H 7
Edmonton, London- 129 II b 1
Edmore, MI 70-71 H 4
Edmore, ND 68-69 G 1
Edmundston 56-57 X 8
Edna, TX 76-77 F 8
Edna Bay, AK 58-59 w 9
Edo 155 III c 2
Edo = Tōkyō 142-143 QR 4
Edogawa, Tōkyō- 155 III c 1
Edough = Idūgh 166-167 K 1
Edremit 134-135 B 3
Edremit körfezi 136-137 B 3
Edrī = Adrī 164-165 G 3
Edsbyn 116-117 F 7
Edsel Ford Range 53 B 22-23
Edson 56-57 N 7
Eduardo Castex 111 D 5
Eduvigis, La — 104-105 G 10
Edward Island 70-71 F 1
Edwards, CA 74-75 E 5
Edwards, MS 78-79 D 4
Edwards Creek 158-159 G 5
Edwards Plateau 64-65 FG 5
Edwardsville, IL 70-71 F 6
Edward VIIth Peninsula 53 B 21-22
Edziza Peak 58-59 W 8
Edzná 86-87 PQ 8
Eek, AK 58-59 FG 6
Eek River 58-59 G 6
'Eelbuur 164-165 b 3
Eel River [USA, California] 66-67 AB 5
Eel River [USA, Indiana] 70-71 GH 5
Eel Xamurre 164-165 bc 2
Eensaamheidpan = Eenzamheidpan 174-175 D 4
Eenzamheidpan 174-175 D 4
Eesti = Estnische Sozialistische Sowjetrepublik 124-125 EF 4
Eesti = Estonian Soviet Socialist Republic 124-125 EF 4
Efate 158-159 N 3
Efes = Ephesos 136-137 B 4
Efeso = Ephesos 136-137 B 4
Effingham, IL 64-65 F 4
Efrichu = Evrýchu 136-137 E 5
Efrikemer 154 I a 2
Efu = Idfu 164-165 L 3
Ēgadi, Isole — 122-123 DE 6
Egaña [RA] 106-107 H 6
Egaña [ROU] 106-107 J 4
Eganville 72-73 H 2
Egawa 155 III c 3
Egbe [WAN, Kwara] 168-169 G 3
Egbe [WAN, Ogun] 170 III a 1
Egbert, WY 68-69 D 5
Ege denizi 134-135 A 2-B 3
Egedesminde = Auslait 56-57 Za 4
Egegik, AK 58-59 J 7
Egegik River 58-59 HJ 7
Egeland, ND 68-69 G 1
Egenbüttel 130 I a 1
Eger 118 K 5
Egetswil 128 IV b 1
Egg [CH, mountain] 128 IV b 1
Eggers Ø 56-57 bc 6
Egg Harbor City, NJ 72-73 J 5
Egg Island 58-59 G 5
Egg Lake [CDN, Quebec] 56-57 W 7
Egg Lake [CDN, Saskatchewan] 61 F 3
Egijin gol 142-143 J 1-2
Egil 136-137 HJ 3
Egilsstadhir 116-117 f 2
Eglab, El — = Aghlāb 164-165 CD 3
Eglinton Island 56-57 MN 2
Egmont, Mount — 158-159 O 7
Egmont Bay 63 D 4
Egmont National Park 161 E 4
Egoji, Kelay — 164-165 N 6
Egošinskaja 124-125 QR 3
Egrā 138-139 L 7
Egremont 60 L 2
Eğret 136-137 D 3
Eğridir 134-135 C 3
Eğridir gölü 136-137 D 4
Eğrigöz dağı 136-137 C 3
Éguas, Rio das — 100-101 B 7
Egypt 164-165 KL 3
Egyptian Museum 170 II b 1
Eha Amufu 168-169 G 4
Eh-Eh, Riacho — 104-105 GH 9
Ehestorf 130 I a 2
Ehime 144-145 J 6
Eiche 130 III c 1
Eichstätt 118 E 4
Eid 116-117 AB 7
Eidelstedt, Hamburg- 130 I a 1
Eidfjord 116-117 B 7
Eidsvåg 116-117 BC 6
Eidsvoll 116-117 D 7
Eidsvollfjellet 116-117 j 5
Eifel 118 C 3
Eiffel, Tour — 129 I c 2
Eige, Carn — 119 D 3
Eigersund 116-117 A 8
Eigg 119 C 3
Eight Degree Channel 176 ab 1
Eights Coast 53 B 27-28
Eighty Mile Beach 158-159 D 3
Eilat = Ēlat 134-135 C 5
Eilbeck, Hamburg- 130 I b 1
Eildon Reservoir 158-159 J 7
Eilerts de Haan Gebergte 92-93 H 4
Eil Roba 172 GH 1
Eimsbüttel, Hamburg- 130 I a 1
Einasleigh 158-159 HJ 3
Einasleigh River 158-159 H 3
Eindhoven 120-121 K 3
Eindpaal 174-175 C 3
Einmé 141 D 7
Eiriksjökull 116-117 cd 2
Eiriksstadhir 116-117 f 2
Eiru, Rio — 96-97 F 5
Eirunepé 92-93 EF 6
Eiseb 172 C 6
Eisenach 118 E 3
Eisenerz 118 G 5
Eisenhower, Mount — 60 K 4
Eisenhüttenstadt 118 FG 2
Eisenstadt 118 H 5
Eišiškės 124-125 E 6
Eisleben 118 E 3
Eissendorf, Hamburg- 130 I a 2
Eiwugen = Saint Lawrence Island 56-57 BC 5
Ejeda 172 H 6
Ejer Bavnehøj 116-117 C 9-10
Ejido 94-95 F 3
Ejigbo 170 III a 1
Ejin Horo Qi 146-147 BC 2
Ejura 168-169 E 4
Ekalaka, MT 68-69 D 3
Ekang 168-169 H 4
Ekbatana = Hamadān 134-135 F 3-4
Ekece = Liz 136-137 JK 3
Ekecek dağı 136-137 EF 3
Ekenäs 116-117 K 7-8
Ekenie 168-169 G 4
Eket 168-169 G 4
Ekiatapskij chrebet 132-133 jk 4
Ekibastuz 132-133 NO 7
Ekimčan 132-133 Z 7
Ekoda, Tōkyō- 155 III ab 1
Ekonda 132-133 TU 4
Eksåra 154 II a 2
Eksere 136-137 DE 4
Eksjö 116-117 F 9

Ektagh Altai = Mongol Altajn nuruu 142-143 F-H 2
Ekwan River 56-57 U 7
Ekwok, AK 58-59 J 7
El Abadia = Al Ab'ādīyah 166-167 G 1
El Abed-Larache = Al-Ābid al-'Arsh 164-165 F 3
El-Abiod-Sidi-Cheikh = Al-Abyaḍ 166-167 G 3
El 'Achârâ = Al-'Asharah 136-137 J 5
El-Affroun = Al-'Afrūn 166-167 H 1
Elafonēsu, Stenòn — 122-123 K 7
El Águila 106-107 D 5
El Aguilar 104-105 D 8
el 'Aïoûn = Al-'Ayūn Dra'ah [MA, Agādīr] 166-167 A 5
el 'Aïoûn = Al-'Ayūn Dra'ah [MA, Ujdah] 166-167 E 2
el Aïoun du Draâ = Al-'Ayūn Dra'ah 166-167 A 5
El Aiun = Al-'Ayūn 164-165 B 3
El 'Ajam = Al-'Ajam 136-137 G 6
Ēlakkibeṭṭa = Cardamom Hills 140 C 5-6
El Álamo [MEX, Nuevo León] 76-77 E 9
El Almagre 86-87 J 4
El Alto [PE] 96-97 A 4
El Alto [RA] 104-105 D 11
Ēlāmala = Cardamom Hills 140 C 5-6
Ēlāmalai = Cardamom Hills 140 C 5-6
Elamanchili 140 F 2
Ela Medo = Ēl Medo 164-165 N 7
El Amparo 94-95 E 6
El Amparo de Apure 94-95 F 3
Elandsfontein 170 V c 2
Elands Height 174-175 H 6
Elandshoek 174-175 J 3
Elandsrivier [ZA ◁ Krokodilrivier] 174-175 G 3
Elandsrivier [ZA ◁ Olifantsrivier] 174-175 H 3
Elandsvlai 174-175 C 7
Elanga 174-175 H 6
El Angel 96-97 C 1
El Aouinet = Al-Awaynāt 166-167 KL 2
El Apartadero 91 III c 3
el 'Aqeila = Al-'Uqaylah 164-165 H 2
el 'Araïch = Al-'Arā'ish 164-165 C 1
El Arañado 106-107 F 3
el Arb'â' Amrân = Tamdah 166-167 B 3
El Arco 86-87 D 3
El-Aricha = Al-'Arīshah 166-167 F 2
El-Arrouch = Al-Harūsh 166-167 K 1
El Aspero, Cerro — 106-107 D 2
Elassón 122-123 K 6
Ēlat 134-135 C 5
Elato 148-149 N 5
El-Auja = Qēẓī'ōt 136-137 F 7
El Avila, Cerro — 91 II b 1
Elâzığ 134-135 D 3
El Azraq = Azraq ash-Shīshān 136-137 G 7
El Azulejo 76-77 D 9
Elba 122-123 D 4
Elba, AL 78-79 FG 5
Elba, ID 66-67 G 4
Elba, NE 68-69 G 5
El Bajío 64-65 F 7
El Banco 92-93 E 3
El Barco [PE] 96-97 A 4
El Barreal 106-107 DE 2
Elbasan 122-123 HJ 5
Elbaşı 136-137 FG 3
El Baúl 92-93 F 3
Elbe 118 D 1-2
El Beidā' = Al-Bayḍā' 164-165 J 2
El Beqā' = Al-Biqā' 136-137 FG 5-6
Elberton, GA 80-81 E 3
El Beşīrē = Buşayrah 136-137 J 5
Elbeuf 120-121 H 4
El Bisaliya = Al-Baṣalīyat Qiblī 173 C 5
Elbistan 136-137 G 3
Elbląg 118 J 1
El Bolsón 108-109 D 3
El Bordo = Patía 94-95 C 6
el Boroûj = Al-Burūj 166-167 C 3
El Bouerda = Al-Bū'irḍah 166-167 C 5
Elbow 61 E 5
Elbow Lake, MN 70-71 BC 2
El Brasil 76-77 D 9
El'brus, gora — 126-127 L 5
Elbtunnel 130 I a 1
Elbūr 172 J 1
Elburgon 171 C 3
El-Burro 76-77 D 8
Elburs = Reshteh Kūhhā-ye Alborz 134-135 G 3
Elburz = Reshteh Kūhhā-ye Alborz 134-135 G 3
Elburz Mountains 134-135 G 3
El Caburé 104-105 E 10
El Cadillal, Embalse — 104-105 D 10
El Cain 108-109 E 3
El Cajon, CA 74-75 E 6
El Caldén 106-107 DE 3
El Callao 94-95 L 4
El Campo, TX 76-77 F 8
El Cantón 94-95 F 4
El Caracol 91 I d 1
El Caribe [YV, Anzoátegui] 94-95 J 3
El Caribe [YV, Distrito Federal] 91 II c 1
El Carmelo 94-95 EF 2
El Carmen [BOL, Beni] 104-105 E 3-4
El Carmen [BOL, Santa Cruz] 104-105 G 6
El Carmen [CO, Amazonas] 94-95 H 7
El Carmen [CO, Chocó] 94-95 C 5
El Carmen [CO, Norte de Santander] 94-95 E 3
El Carmen [EC] 96-97 B 2
El Carmen [PY] 102-103 AB 4
El Carmen de Bolívar 92-93 DE 3
El Ceibal 104-105 E 10
El Centro 94-95 E 4
El Centro, CA 64-65 CD 5
El Cerrito 94-95 CD 6
El Cerrito, CA 83 I c 1
El Cerro 92-93 G 8
El Chacay 106-107 BC 5
El Chacho 106-107 E 3
El Chaco 96-97 C 2
El Chaparro 94-95 J 3
Elche 120-121 G 9
El-Chedādī = Ash-Shiddādī 136-137 J 4
Elcho Island 158-159 G 2
El Chorillo 106-107 DE 4
El Chorro 104-105 C 6
El Cisne 106-107 G 3
El Coco 64-65 b 3
El Cocuy 92-93 E 3
El Cojo [YV, place] 91 II b 1
El Cojo [YV, river] 91 II b 1
El Cojo, Punta — 91 II b 1
El Colorado [RA, Chaco] 104-105 G 10
El Colorado [RA, Santiago del Estero] 106-107 F 1
El Cóndor 108-109 E 9
El Contador 91 I d 1
El Corazón 96-97 B 2
El Corcovado 108-109 D 4
El Corozo 91 II b 1
El Coyte 108-109 D 5
El Crucero 94-95 J 2-3
El Cuervo Grande 76-77 B 7
El Cuil 94-95 B 6
El Cuy 111 C 5
Elda 120-121 G 9
El Descanso 86-87 B 1
El Desemboque 86-87 D 2
El Desierto 104-105 B 8
El Desmonte 104-105 E 8
El Diamante 91 III a 2
El Difícil 92-93 E 3
El'dikan 132-133 a 5
El Dividive 94-95 F 3
El Diviso [CO, Nariño] 94-95 B 7
El Diviso [CO, Putumayo] 94-95 D 7
El Divisorio 106-107 G 7
El-Djedeïda = Al-Jadīdah 166-167 L 1
El Djem = Al-Jamm 166-167 M 2
El Doctor 86-87 C 2
Eldon, IA 70-71 DE 5
Eldon, MO 70-71 D 6
Eldon, WA 66-67 B 2
Eldora, IA 70-71 D 4
El Dorado, AR 64-65 H 5
El Dorado, AR 64-65 H 5
Eldorado, IL 70-71 F 7
El Dorado, KS 68-69 H 7
Eldorado, OK 76-77 E 5
Eldorado, TX 76-77 D 7
Eldorado [BR] 102-103 HJ 6
El Dorado [CO] 92-93 E 4
Eldorado [MEX] 86-87 G 5
El Dorado [RA] 106-107 G 5
Eldorado [RA, Misiones] 111 EF 3
El Dorado [YV] 92-93 G 3
Eldorado, Aeropuerto — 91 III ab 2
Eldorado Mountains 74-75 F 5
El Dorado Park 83 III d 3
El Dorado Springs, MO 70-71 CD 7
Eldoret 172 G 1
El Durazno 106-107 E 6
El Duya 94-95 F 5
Electra, TX 76-77 E 5
Electric Mills, MS 78-79 E 4
Electric Peak 66-67 H 3
Elefantes, Golfo — 108-109 BC 6
Elefantes, Rio dos — 174-175 K 2-3
Elefantina = Elephantine 164-165 L 4
Éléfants, Réserve aux — 172 E 1
El Eglab = Aghlāb 164-165 CD 3
Elei, Wādī — = Wādī Ilay 173 D 7
Elekmonar 132-133 Q 7
Elektrostal' 124-125 M 5-6
El Empedrado 94-95 FG 3
Elena [RA] 106-107 E 4
El Encanto 94-95 GH 5
El Encuentro 96-97 E 8
Eleodoro Lobos 106-107 E 4
Elephanta Island 140 A 1
Elephant Butte Reservoir 76-77 A 6
Elephantine 164-165 L 4
Elephant Island 53 CD 31
Elephant Pass = Āṇayirāvu 140 E 6
Elephant Point, AK 58-59 G 3
el 'Erg = Al-'Irq 164-165 J 3
El Ergh = Al-'Irq 164-165 J 3
Elesbão Veloso 100-101 C 4
El Escorial 120-121 EF 8
Eleşkirt = Zidikân 136-137 K 3
El Estor 86-87 Q 10
Elets = Jelec 124-125 M 7
El Eulma = Al-'Ulmah 166-167 J 1
Eleuthera Island 64-65 LM 6
Elevi = Görele 136-137 H 2
Elewijt 128 II b 1
El Faijum = Al-Fayyūm 164-165 KL 3
El-Fâsher = Al-Fāshir 164-165 K 6
El Fayum = Al-Fayyūm 164-165 KL 3
El Ferrol de Caudillo 120-121 C 7
Elfin Cove, AK 58-59 TU 7
El Ford, Cerro — 108-109 D 9
El Fortín 106-107 F 3
El Forzado 106-107 D 4
El-Fourât = Al-Furāt 136-137 H 5
El Fuerte 86-87 F 4
El Furrial 94-95 K 3
El Galpón 104-105 D 9
el Gâra = Al-Gārah 166-167 C 3
el-Gatrun = Al-Qaṭrūn 164-165 GH 4
el Gedid = Sabhah 164-165 G 3
El-Geneina = Al-Junaynah 164-165 J 6
El Gezira = Al-Jazīrah 164-165 L 6
El Ghâb = Al-Ghāb 136-137 G 5
Elghena = Algēna 164-165 M 5
El Ghôr = Al-Ghūr 136-137 F 7
El Ghurdaqa = Al-Ghardaqah 164-165 L 3
Elgin, IL 64-65 J 3
Elgin, ND 68-69 F 2
Elgin, NE 68-69 G 5
Elgin, NV 74-75 F 4
Elgin, OR 66-67 E 3
Elgin, TX 76-77 F 7
Elgin [CDN] 63 D 5
Elgin [GB] 119 E 3
El-Goléa = Al-Gulī'ah 164-165 E 2
El Golfo de Santa Clara 86-87 C 2
Elgon, Mount — 172 F 1
El Goran 164-165 N 7
El Grullo 86-87 H 8
El Guapo 94-95 HJ 2
El Guarapo 91 II b 1
El Guarda 91 I a 2
El Guardamonte 104-105 D 10
El Guayabo [CO] 94-95 E 4
El Guayabo [YV] 94-95 EF 3
El Guettar = Al-Qaṭṭār 166-167 J 2
El Hadjar = Al-Ḥajar 166-167 KL 1
El-Hadjira = Al-Ḥajīrah 166-167 J 3
El Hagunia = Al-Haqūnīyah 164-165 B 3
el Ḥâjeb = Al-Ḥājab 166-167 D 3
El Hamada = Al-Hammadah 166-167 FG 4
El-Hamel = Al-Ḥāmil 166-167 J 2
El Ḥammâmèt = Al-Ḥammāmāt 166-167 M 1
El Haouâria = Al-Hawārīyah 166-167 M 1
el Ḥaouz = Al-Ḥawūz 166-167 B 4
El Harrach 170 I b 2
El Ḥaṣâḥeïṣa = Al-Ḥuṣayḥiṣah 164-165 L 6
El-Hasètchè = Al-Hasakah 134-135 D 3
El Hatillo [YV, place] 91 II c 2
El Hatillo [YV, river] 91 II c 2
El-Heir = Qaṣr al-Ḥayr 136-137 H 5
El Ḥencha = Al-Hanshah 166-167 M 2
El Hermel = Al-Harmal 136-137 G 5
el Hobra = Al-Habrah 166-167 J 3
el Hoṣeima = Al-Ḥusaymah 164-165 D 1
Elhovo 122-123 M 4
El Huecu 106-107 B 6
Eli, NE 68-69 F 4
Eliasville, TX 76-77 E 6
Elida, NM 76-77 C 6
El 'Idisât = Al-'Udaysāt 173 C 5
El Idrissia = Al-Idrīsīyah 166-167 H 2
Elie [CDN] 61 K 6
Eliki 164-165 F 6
Elila 172 E 2
Elim, AK 58-59 FG 4
Elim [ZA] 174-175 C 8
Eling Hu = Ngoring Tsho 142-143 H 4-5
Elisa 106-107 G 3
Elisabethbaai 174-175 A 4
Elisabeth Reef 158-159 L 5
Elisabethville = Lubumbashi 172 E 4
Elisenau 130 III c 1
Elisenvaara 124-125 GH 3
Elista 126-127 M 3
El-'Itmânîya = Al-'Uthmānīyah 173 BC 4
Eliúpolis 113 IV b 2
Elizabeth, IL 70-71 EF 4
Elizabeth, LA 78-79 C 5
Elizabeth, NJ 72-73 J 4
Elizabeth, Adelaide- 158-159 G 6
Elizabeth, Cape — 72-73 LM 3
Elizabeth, Cape — = Cape Pillar 158-159 J 8
Elizabeth Bay = Elisabethbaai 174-175 A 4
Elizabeth City, NC 80-81 H 2
Elizabeth-Port, NJ 82 III a 3
Elizabethton, TN 80-81 EF 2
Elizabethtown, KY 70-71 H 7
Elizabethtown, NC 80-81 G 3
Elizabethtown, NY 72-73 JK 2
Elizeu Martins 100-101 C 5
el Jadīda = Al-Jadīdah 164-165 C 2
El-Jafr = Al-Jafr 134-135 D 4
El Jaralito 76-77 B 9
El Jauf = Al-Jawf 164-165 J 4
El-Jebelein = Al-Jabalayn 164-165 L 6
el Jebīlèt = Al-Jabīlat 166-167 BC 4
El Jīzah = Al-Jīzah 136-137 FG 7
el Jofra Oasis = Wāḥāt al-Jufrah 164-165 GH 3
El Juile 86-87 N 9
Elk 118 L 2
Elk, CA 74-75 B 3
Elk, WA 66-67 E 1
Elkader, IA 70-71 E 4
El Kala = Al-Qal'ah 164-165 F 1
El-Kāmlīn = Al-Kamilīn 164-165 L 5
El-Kantara = Al-Qanṭarah 166-167 J 2
El-Katif = Al-Qaṭīf 134-135 F 5
el Kbab = Al-Qabāb 166-167 D 3
Elk City, ID 66-67 F 3
Elk City, OK 76-77 E 5
Elk Creek, CA 74-75 B 3
Elkedra 158-159 G 4
el Kelaa des Srarhna = Al-Qal'at as-S'rāghnah 166-167 C 3-4
Elkford 60 K 4
Elk Grove, CA 74-75 C 3
El-Khalīl = Al-Halīl 136-137 F 7
El-Khandaq = Al-Khandaq 164-165 KL 5
El-Khârga = Al-Khārījah 164-165 L 3
Elkhart, IN 70-71 GH 5
Elkhart, KS 76-77 D 4
Elkhart, TX 76-77 G 7
El-Khartūm Baḥrī = Al-Kharṭūm Baḥrī 164-165 L 5
El-Khaṭāṭba = Al-Haṭāṭibah 173 B 2
Elkhead Mountains 68-69 C 5
el Khemīs = Al-Khamīs 166-167 C 3
el Khemīs = Hamīs az-Zāmāmrah 166-167 B 3
el Khemīs = Sūq al-Khamīs as-Sāḥil 166-167 C 2
el Khemīs = Sūq al-Khamīs Banī 'Arūs 166-167 D 2
el Khemīssèt = Khamīssāt 166-167 CD 3
el Khemīs Zemâmra = Hamīs az-Zāmāmrah 166-167 B 3
El Khenachich 164-165 D 4
Elkhorn 61 H 5
Elkhorn, WI 70-71 F 4
Elkhorn Peak 66-67 H 2
Elkhorn Peaks 66-67 H 4
Elkhorn River 68-69 G 4
El Khroub = Al-Khurub 166-167 K 1
Elki 136-137 K 4
Elkin, NC 80-81 F 2
Elkins, NM 76-77 BC 6
Elkins, WV 72-73 FG 5
Elkins Park, PA 84 III c 1
Elk Mountain 68-69 C 5
Elko 66-67 F 1
Elko, NV 64-65 C 3
Elkol, WY 66-67 H 5
Elk Point 61 C 4
Elk Point, SD 68-69 H 4
Elk Rapids, MI 70-71 H 3
El Krenachich = El Khenachich 164-165 D 4
Elk Ridge 74-75 J 4
Elk River 66-67 F 1
Elk River, ID 66-67 EF 2
Elk River, MN 70-71 D 3
El Kseur = Al-Qaṣr 166-167 J 1
el Ksiba = Al-Q'sībah 166-167 CD 3
Elk Springs, CO 68-69 BC 5
Elkton, KY 78-79 F 2
Elkton, MD 72-73 HJ 5
Elkton, OR 66-67 B 4
Elkton, SD 68-69 H 3
Ēlla 140 E 7
El Ladiqiya = Al-Lādhiqīyah 134-135 CD 3
El-Lagodei = Qardho 134-135 F 9
El Lagowa = Al-Laqawah 164-165 K 6
Ellamar, AK 58-59 O 6
Ellāṅdu = Yellandu 140 E 2
Ellaville, GA 78-79 G 4
Ellef Ringnes Island 56-57 Q 2
El-Lejâ'a = Al-Lajā' 136-137 G 6
Ellen, Mount — 74-75 H 3
Ellendale, ND 68-69 G 2-3
El Lenguaraz 106-107 H 6-7
Ellensburg, WA 66-67 C 2
Ellenville, NY 72-73 J 4
Ellerbe, NC 80-81 G 3
Ellerbek 130 I a 1
Ellerslie, PA 84 III d 1
Ellesmere Island 52 B 27-A 26
Ellice Islands 156-157 H 5
Ellichpur = Achalpur 138-139 F 7
Ellijay, GA 78-79 G 3
Ellikane 168-169 H 2
Ellinwood, KS 68-69 G 6
Elliot 172 E 8
Elliotdale = Xhora 174-175 H 6
Elliot Lake [CDN, lake] 62 B 1
Elliot Lake [CDN, place] 56-57 U 8
Elliott 158-159 F 3
Elliott Knob 72-73 G 5
Ellis, ID 66-67 F 3
Ellis, KS 68-69 G 6
Ellis Land 82 III b 2
Elliston [AUS] 158-159 F 6
Elliston [CDN] 63 K 3
Ellisville, MS 78-79 E 5
El Lobo 96-97 A 4
Ellon 119 E 3
Ellora 138-139 E 7
Ellore = Elūru 134-135 N 7
Elloree, SC 80-81 F 4
Ellsinore, MO 78-79 D 2
Ellsworth, KS 68-69 G 6
Ellsworth, ME 72-73 M 2
Ellsworth, WI 70-71 D 3
Ellsworth Highland 53 B 28-25
El Lucero [MEX] 76-77 C 10
El Lucero [YV] 94-95 G 4
Ellwood City, PA 72-73 F 4
Elma 61 KL 6
Elma, IA 70-71 D 4
Elma, WA 66-67 B 2
El-Mabrouk = Al-Mabrūk 166-167 G 5
El Macao 88-89 M 5
Elma dağı [TR, mountain Ankara] 136-137 E 3
Elma dağı [TR, mountain Antalya] 136-137 CD 4
Elmadağı [TR, place] 136-137 E 3
El Maestro, Laguna — 106-107 J 6
El-Mahder = 'Ayn al-Qasr 166-167 K 2
El Mahia 164-165 D 4
El Maïa = Al-Māyah 166-167 G 3
El Maitén 108-109 D 4
Elmalı [TR, Antalya] 136-137 CD 4
Elmalı [TR, İstanbul] 154 I b 2
El Mamoun 168-169 E 1
El Mango 94-95 H 7
El-Mansour = Al-Manṣūr 166-167 F 6
El Manteco 92-93 G 3
El Manzano [RA] 106-107 E 3
El Manzano [RCH] 106-107 B 5
El Marsa 170 I b 1
El Marucho 106-107 BC 7
El Matrimonio 76-77 C 9
El Mayoco 108-109 D 4
El Mayor 74-75 F 6
Elm Creek 61 JK 6
Elm Creek, NE 68-69 G 5
El Medjdel = Ashqĕlōn 136-137 F 7
Ēl Medo 164-165 N 7
El Meghaier = Al-Mighāir 166-167 J 3
Elmer, MO 70-71 D 6
El Merdja = Al-Marjah 166-167 H 2
el-Merq = Al-Marj 164-165 J 2
Elmers End, London- 129 II b 2
El Metlaoui = Al-Mitlawī 164-165 F 2
El Mèthīn = Al-Māṭlīn 166-167 M 1
El Meṭouïa = Al-Miṭūyah 166-167 LM 3
El Mezeraa = Al-Mazra'ah 166-167 K 2
el Mḥamīd = Al-Maḥamīd 166-167 D 5
Elmhurst, IL 70-71 FG 5
El Miamo 94-95 L 4
El Miedo 94-95 F 5
El Milagro 111 C 4
El Milia = Al-Mīlīyah 166-167 JK 1
Elmira, CA 74-75 C 3
Elmira, ID 66-67 E 1
Elmira, MI 70-71 H 3
Elmira, NY 64-65 L 3
Elmira [CDN, Ontario] 72-73 F 3
Elmira [CDN, Prince Edward I.] 63 E 4
El Mirador 86-87 P 9
el-Mja'ra = Al-M'jarah 166-167 D 2
Elm Lake 68-69 G 3
El Moknin = Al-Muknīn 166-167 M 2
El Molinito 91 I b 2
El Molino 91 III c 2
El Monasterio 94-95 H 3
El Monastir = Al-Manastīr 166-167 M 2
Elmont, NY 82 III d 2
El Monte 104-105 D 7
El Monte, CA 83 III d 1
El Monte Airport 83 III d 1
El Moral 76-77 D 8
Elmore 160 G 6
el Morhân = Al-Mughrān 166-167 C 2
El Moro 106-107 H 7
El Morro 106-107 E 4
Elm Park, London- 129 II c 1
El Mreïti = Al-M'rāītī 164-165 C 4
Elmshorn 118 DE 2
Elmvale 72-73 G 2
Elmwood, IL 70-71 EF 5
Elmwood, OK 76-77 D 4
Elmwood, Philadelphia-, PA 84 III b 2
Elmwood Canal 85 I a 1
Elmwood Cemetery 84 II b 2
Elmwood Park 83 II a 1
Elne 120-121 J 7
El Nemlèt = An-Namlāt 166-167 KL 2
El Nido 148-149 G 4
El Nihuil 106-107 C 5
El Oasis 91 II ab 1
El-Obeidh = Al-Ubayyiḍ 164-165 KL 6
E. Lobos 106-107 E 4
Eloğlu 136-137 G 4
Elói Mendes 102-103 K 4
Elordi 106-107 F 5
el Ordi = Dunqulah 164-165 KL 5
El Oro [EC] 96-97 AB 3
El Oro [MEX, Coahuila] 76-77 C 9
El Oro [MEX, México] 86-87 K 8
Elorza 92-93 F 3
El Oso 94-95 J 5
El-Oued = Al-Wād 164-165 F 2
El Oûssel'tia = Al-Ūssaltīyah 166-167 LM 2
El-Oustaïa = Al-Uṭāyah 166-167 J 2
El-Outaïa = Al-Uṭāyah 166-167 J 2
Eloy, AZ 74-75 H 6
El Pacífico 94-95 C 4
El Pajarito 108-109 E 4
El Pájaro 94-95 E 2
El Palimito 86-87 H 5
El Palmar [BOL] 104-105 D 7
El Palmar [CO] 94-95 G 6
El Palmar [YV, Bolívar] 94-95 L 3-4
El Palmar [YV, Caracas] 91 II b 1
El Pampero 106-107 E 5
El Pantanoso, Arroyo — 110 III a 2
El Pao [YV, Anzoátegui] 94-95 J 3
El Pao [YV, Bolívar] 92-93 G 3
El Pao [YV, Cojedes] 94-95 GH 3
El Paraíso 106-107 GH 4
El Paso 92-93 E 3
El Paso, IL 70-71 F 5
El Paso, TX 64-65 E 5
El Paují 91 II c 2
El Pensamiento 106-107 G 7
El Peregrino 106-107 FG 5
El Perú 104-105 C 3
El Petén 64-65 H 8
Elphinstone Island 150-151 AB 6
Elphinstone Island = Pulau-pulau Duperre 150-151 G 11
Elphinstone Island = Tharawthèdangyī Kyūn 150-151 AB 6
El Pico 92-93 G 8
El Pilar 94-95 K 2
El Pinar, Parque Nacional — 91 II b 2
El Pingo 106-107 H 3
El Pintado 104-105 F 9
El Piquete 104-105 D 9
Ēlpiṭiya 140 E 7
El Pluma 108-109 DE 6
El Pluma, Cañadón — 108-109 D 6
El Pluma, Cordón — 108-109 D 6
El Pocito 104-105 E 4
El Portal, CA 74-75 CD 4
El Portugues 92-93 D 6
El Porvenir [CO] 94-95 G 6
El Porvenir [MEX] 76-77 AB 7
El Potosí 86-87 K 5
El Potossí 86-87 K 5
El Potrero 76-77 B 8
El Potro, Cerro — 106-107 C 2
El Pozo 86-87 F 2
El Presto 104-105 F 4
El Progreso [GCA] 86-87 P 10
El Progreso [Honduras] 64-65 J 8
El Progreso [PE] 96-97 E 9
El Puente [BOL, Santa Cruz] 104-105 E 5
El Puente [BOL, Tarija] 104-105 D 7
El Puerto de Santa Maria 120-121 D 10
El Puesto 104-105 C 10
El Qairouân = Al-Qayrawān 164-165 FG 1
El Qaṣṣerîn = Al-Qaṣrayn 164-165 F 1-2
el Qbâb = Al-Qabāb 166-167 D 3
El-Qedhâref = Al-Qaḍārif 164-165 M 6
el Qela'a es 'Srarhnâ = Al-Qal'at as-S'rāghnah 166-167 C 3-4
el Qenîtra = Al-Q'nitrah 164-165 C 2
El-Qoseir = Al-Quṣayr 164-165 L 3
El-Qoubayât = Al-Qubayyāt 136-137 G 5
El-Qousaïr = Al-Quṣayr 136-137 G 5
El Qsâbî = Al-Qaṣābī 166-167 D 3
El Qsour = Al-Quṣūr 166-167 L 2
El Quebrachal 104-105 DE 9
Elquí, Río — 106-107 B 3
El Rastreador 106-107 F 4
El Rastro 94-95 H 3
El Real 88-89 H 10
El Recado 106-107 FG 5
El Refugio 94-95 E 6
El Reno, OK 64-65 G 4
El Retamo 106-107 D 3-4
el Rharb = Al-Gharb 166-167 C 2
El Rhraïba = Al-Ghraybah 166-167 LM 2
El Rincon 91 III b 2
El Rodeo 94-95 J 3
El Rosario [YV, Bolívar] 94-95 J 4
El Rosario [YV, Zulia] 94-95 E 3
Elrose 61 D 5
El-Rouṭbé = Ar-Ruṭbah 136-137 G 6
Elroy, WI 70-71 E 4
El Salado 108-109 F 7
El Salitre 91 III b 1
El Salto 64-65 E 7
El Saltón 111 B 7
El Salvador [ES] 64-65 J 9
El Salvador [RCH] 104-105 B 10
El Samán de Apure 94-95 G 4
El Santuario 94-95 F 5
Elsas 70-71 J 1
El Sauce 88-89 C 8
El Sauz 86-87 G 3
El Sauzal 74-75 E 7
Elsberry, MO 70-71 E 6
Elsburg 170 V c 2
Elsburgspruit 170 V c 2
El Segundo, CA 83 III b 2
Elsengrund, Berlin- 130 III c 2
Elsinore, CA 74-75 E 6
Elsmore, KS 70-71 C 7
El Sobrante, CA 83 I c 1
El Socorro [MEX] 76-77 C 9
El Socorro [RA] 106-107 G 4
El Socorro [YV] 94-95 J 3
El Sombrerito 106-107 H 2
El Sombrero [RA] 106-107 H 1
El Sombrero [YV] 92-93 F 3
El Sosneado 106-107 BC 5
Elstal 130 III a 1
Elsternwick, Melbourne- 161 II bc 2
Elstree 129 II a 1
El Sueco 86-87 GH 3
El Sunchal 106-107 D 2
El Tablazo 94-95 F 2
El Tablón [CO, Nariña] 94-95 C 7
El Tablón [CO, Sucre] 94-95 D 3
El Taj = At-Tāj 164-165 J 4
El Tajín 86-87 M 7
El Tala [RA, San Luis] 106-107 D 4
El Tala [RA, Tucumán] 104-105 D 9-10
El Tambo [CO, Cauca] 92-93 D 4
El Tambo [CO, Nariño] 94-95 C 7
El Tambo [EC] 96-97 B 3
El Tejar 106-107 G 5
El Teleno 120-121 D 7
El Temazcal 86-87 LM 5
El Teniente 111 BC 4
Eltham, London- 129 II c 2
El Tigre [CO] 94-95 F 4
El Tigre [YV] 92-93 G 3
Eltingville, New York-, NY 82 III ab 3
El Tío 111 D 4
El Toba, Arroyo — 106-107 GH 2
El Toco 94-95 J 3
El Tocuyo 92-93 F 3
El Tofo 106-107 B 2
El'ton 126-127 N 2
Elton, LA 78-79 C 5
El'ton, ozero — 126-127 N 2
Eltopia, WA 66-67 D 2
El Tránsito 106-107 B 2
El Trebol 106-107 G 4
El Trigo 106-107 H 5
El Trino 94-95 E 6
El Triunfo 106-107 G 5
El Tuito 86-87 H 7
El Tunal 104-105 D 9
El Tunal, Parque Distrital de — 91 III b 4
El Turbio 111 B 8
Eluan Bi = Oluan Pi 146-147 H 11
Elūru 134-135 N 7
Elva 124-125 F 4
El Valle 94-95 C 4
El Valle, Río — 91 II b 2
Elvanlar = Eşme 136-137 C 3
Elvas 120-121 D 9
El Venado 94-95 G 4
Elverum 116-117 DE 7
Elvesis 122-123 K 6
El Viejo, Cerro — 94-95 E 4
El Vigia 92-93 E 3
Elvira 92-93 E 6
Elvira, Cape — 56-57 P 3
El Volcán 106-107 BC 4
El Wak 172 H 1
Elwell Lake 66-67 H 1
Elwood, IN 70-71 H 5
Elwood, NE 68-69 FG 5
Elwood, Melbourne- 161 II b 2
El Wuz = Al-Wazz 164-165 L 5
Elwyn, PA 84 III a 2
Ely 119 G 5
Ely, MN 70-71 DE 2
Ely, NV 64-65 D 4
El Yagual 94-95 G 4
Elyria, OH 72-73 E 4
El Ysian Park 83 III c 1
El Zanjón 106-107 E 1
El Zig-Zag 91 II b 1
El Zurdo 108-109 D 8
Emagusheni = Magusheni 174-175 H 6
Ema jõgi 124-125 F 4
Emāmzādeh 'Abbās 136-137 MN 6
Emān 116-117 F 9
Emangak, AK 58-59 E 5
Emba [SU, place] 132-133 K 8
Emba [SU, river] 132-133 K 8
Embalse Cabra Corral 104-105 D 9
Embalse Cerros Colorados 106-107 C 7
Embalse de Cijara 120-121 E 9
Embalse de Escaba 106-107 DE 1
Embalse de Guárico 94-95 H 3
Embalse de Guri 94-95 K 4
Embalse del Nihuil 106-107 C 5
Embalse del Río Negro 111 E 4
Embalse del Río Tercero 106-107 E 4
Embalse El Cadillal 104-105 D 10
Embalse el Chocón 106-107 C 7
Embalse Escaba 104-105 CD 10
Embalse Ezequiel Ramos Mexia 106-107 C 7
Embalse Florentino Ameghino 108-109 F 5
Embalse La Mariposa 91 II b 2
Embalse Río Hondo 106-107 E 1
Embalse Salto Grande 111 E 4
Embarcación 111 D 2
Embarí, Río — 94-95 H 8
Embarrass, MN 70-71 D 2
Embarrass River 70-71 FG 6
Embenčime 132-133 ST 4
Embetsu 144-145 b 1
Embira, Rio — 98-99 C 9
Emblem, WY 68-69 B 3
Emborai, Baía do — 100-101 AB 1
Emboscada 102-103 D 6
Embrach 128 IV b 1
Embu 172 G 2
Embuguaçu 102-103 J 5
Emden 118 C 2
Emei Shan 142-143 J 6
Emel gol 142-143 E 2
Émerainville 129 I d 2
Emerald 158-159 J 4
Emerson 68-69 H 1
Emerson, AR 78-79 C 4
Emerson, MI 70-71 H 2
Emery, UT 74-75 H 3
Emeryville, CA 83 I c 1-2
Emesa = Ḥims 134-135 D 4
Emet 136-137 C 3
Emi 132-133 S 7
Emigrant, MT 66-67 H 3
Emigrant Gap, CA 74-75 C 3
Emigrant Pass 66-67 E 5

Emigrant Peak 66-67 H 3
Emigrant Valley 74-75 F 4
Emiiganur = Emmiganūru 140 C 3
Emi Koussi 164-165 H 5
Emi Kusi = Emi Koussi 164-165 H 5
Emilia 106-107 G 3
Emìlia-Romagna 122-123 C-E 3
Emilio Ayarza 106-107 GH 5
Emilio Lamarca 108-109 H 3
Emilio Mitre 106-107 D 6
Emilio R. Coni 106-107 H 3
Emilio V. Bunge 106-107 F 5
Emine, nos — 122-123 MN 4
Eminence, KY 70-71 H 6
Eminence, MO 78-79 D 2
Eminönü, İstanbul- 154 I ab 2
Emirdağ 136-137 D 3
Emir dağları 136-137 D 3
Emirhan 136-137 GH 3
Emita 158-159 J 7-8
Emjanyana = Mjanyana
174-175 GH 6
Emma 106-107 G 6
Emmast = Emmaste 124-125 D 4
Emmaste 124-125 D 4
Emmen 120-121 L 2
Emmet 158-159 HJ 4
Emmet, ID 66-67 E 4
Emmetsburg, IA 70-71 C 4
Emmiganūru 140 C 3
Emory, TX 76-77 G 6
Emory Peak 76-77 C 8
Emory University 85 II c 2
Empalme 64-65 DE 6
Empangeni 172 F 7
Empedrado [RA] 111 E 3
Empedrado [RCH] 106-107 A 5
Empedrado, El — 94-95 FG 3
Empexa, Salar de — 104-105 B 7
Empire 64-65 b 2
Empire Dock 154 III ab 2
Empire State Building 82 III c 2
Èmpoli 122-123 D 4
Emporia, KS 64-65 G 4
Emporia, VA 80-81 H 2
Emporium, PA 72-73 G 4
Empress 61 C 5
Ems 118 C 2
Emsdale 72-73 G 2
Emumägi 124-125 F 4
Emu Park 158-159 K 4
En, Mui — = Mui Yên 150-151 G 6
Ena 144-145 L 5
Enare = Inari 116-117 M 3
Encampment, WY 68-69 C 5
Encantada, Sierra de la — 76-77 C 8
Encantadas, Serra das —
106-107 L 3
Encantado 106-107 M 2
Encantado, Rio de Janeiro- 110 I b 2
Encantanda, Sierra de la —
86-87 J 3-4
Encanto 98-99 N 10
Encanto, Bogotá-El — 91 III b 4
Encanto, El — 94-95 GH 5
Encarnación 111 E 3
Encarnacion de Díaz 86-87 JK 7
Encheng 146-147 EF 3
Enchi 164-165 D 7
Encinal 86-87 L 3
Encinal, TX 76-77 E 8
Encinitas, CA 74-75 E 6
Encino 94-95 E 4
Encino, NM 76-77 B 5
Encino, TX 76-77 E 9
Encontrados 92-93 E 3
Encruzilhada 100-101 D 8
Encruzilhada do Sul 106-107 L 3
Encuentro, El — 96-97 E 8
Endako 56-57 LM 7
Endau [EAK] 171 D 3
Endau [MAL] 148-149 D 6
Endau-Kluang 150-151 D 11
Endau-Kota Tinggi 150-151 D 11-12
Endeh 148-149 H 8
Endeh, Teluk — 152-153 O 10
Enderbury 208 JK 3
Enderby 60 H 4
Enderby Land 53 C 5-6
Endere Langar 142-143 E 4
Enderlin, ND 68-69 H 2
Enders Reservoir 68-69 F 5
Endevour Strait 158-159 H 2
Endicott, NE 68-69 H 5
Endicott, NY 72-73 H 3
Endicott Mountains 56-57 F 4
Endimari, Rio — 98-99 E 9
Ene, Río — 92-93 E 7
Enemutu 98-99 HJ 2
Energia 111 E 5
Enez 136-137 B 2
Enfer, Portes de l' 172 E 3
Enfidaville = An-N'fidah
166-167 LM 1
Enfield, CT 72-73 K 4
Enfield, IL 70-71 F 6
Enfield, NC 80-81 H 2
Engabeni = Nqabeni 174-175 J 6
Engadin 118 DE 5
Engano = Pulau Enggano
148-149 D 8
Engaño, Bahía — 108-109 G 4
Engaño, Cabo — 88-89 MN 5
Engaru 144-145 c 1
Engativá 91 III b 2
Engcobo 174-175 GH 6
Enge, Zürich- 128 IV b 1
Engelhard, NC 80-81 HJ 3
Engels 124-125 Q 8
Engelwood, CO 68-69 D 6
Engen 60 E 3
Engenheiro Beltrao 102-103 F 5
Engenho, Ilha do — 110 I c 2
Engenho Nova, Rio de Janeiro-
110 I b 2
Enggano, Pulau — 148-149 D 8
Enghien-les-Bains 129 I c 2
Engizek dağı 136-137 G 4
England, AR 78-79 D 3
Engle, NM 76-77 A 6
Englee 63 HJ 2
Englehart 62 M 3
Englewood, KS 76-77 DE 4
Englewood, NJ 82 III c 1
Englewood, Chicago-, IL 83 II b 2
Englewood Cliffs, NJ 82 III c 1
Englischer Garten 130 II b 2
English, IN 70-71 G 6
English Bay, AK 58-59 L 7
English Bāzār 138-139 LM 5
English Channel 114-115 H 6-J 5
English Coast 53 B 29-30
English Company's Islands
158-159 G 2
English River [CDN, place] 70-71 E 1
English River [CDN, river] 62 BC 2
English Turn, LA 85 I c 2
Englschalking, München- 130 II bc 2
Engongqi Hu = Ngangtse Tsho
138-139 L 2
Eng-Têng = Yongding 146-147 F 9
'Ên-Hazeva 136-137 F 7
Enid, OK 64-65 G 4
Enid, Mount — 158-159 C 4
Enid Lake 78-79 E 3
Enid Reservoir = Enid Lake
78-79 E 3
Eniwa 144-145 b 2
Enkeldoorn = Chivu 172 F 5
Enken, mys — 132-133 b 6
Enköping 116-117 G 8
Enmelen 132-133 kl 4
Enna 122-123 F 7
Ennadai Lake 56-57 Q 5
En Nebek = An-Nabk 134-135 D 4
Ennedi 164-165 J 5
En Nefud = An-Nafūd 134-135 E 5
en Nekhīla = An-Nakhīlah
166-167 E 2
Ennersdale 174-175 H 5
En Nfīda = An-N'fīdah
166-167 M 1
Enngonia 158-159 HJ 5
En Nkheila 173 B 4
Ennis 119 B 5
Ennis, MT 66-67 H 3
Ennis, TX 76-77 F 6
Enniscorthy 119 C 5
Enniskillen 119 C 4
Ennistimon 119 B 5
en Nôfilia = An-Nawfalīyah
164-165 H 2
Enns 118 G 5
Eno 116-117 O 6
Enontekiö 116-117 K 3
Enos = Enez 136-137 B 2
Enping 146-147 D 10
Enrekang 152-153 NO 7
Enrique Carbó 106-107 H 4
Enrique Lage = Imbituba
102-103 H 8
Enriquillo 88-89 L 6
Enriquillo, Lago — 88-89 L 5
Enschede 120-121 L 2
Enseada, Cachoeiro — 98-99 J 10
Enseada da Praia Grande 110 I c 2
Enseada de Botafogo 110 I bc 2
Enseada de Icaraí 110 I c 2
Ensenada [MEX] 64-65 C 5
Ensenada [RA] 106-107 J 5
Ensenada, La — 108-109 H 3
Ensenada de Calabozo 94-95 F 2
Ensenada de Docampadó 94-95 C 5
Ensenada de la Broa 88-89 EF 3
Ensenada de Tibugá 92-93 D 3
Ensenada Ferrocarril 76-77 F 10
Enshi 142-143 K 5
Enshih = Enshi 142-143 K 5
Enshū nada 144-145 LM 5
Ensign, KS 68-69 F 7
Enso = Svetogorsk 124-125 G 3
Entebbe 172 F 1
Entenbühl 118 F 4
Enterprise, AL 78-79 G 5
Enterprise, MS 78-79 E 4
Enterprise, OR 66-67 E 3
Enterprise, UT 74-75 G 4
Entiat, WA 66-67 C 2
Entiat Mountains 66-67 C 1-2
Entiat River 66-67 C 1-2
Entinas, Punta de las —
120-121 F 10
Entrada, Punta — 108-109 EF 8
Entrance Island, AK 58-59 V 8
Entrecasteaux, Point d'
158-159 BC 6
Entrecasteaux, Récife d'
158-159 M 3
Entre Rios [BOL] 92-93 G 9
Entre Rios [BR, Amazonas] 98-99 J 7
Entre Rios [BR, Bahia] 92-93 M 7
Entre Rios [BR, Pará] 98-99 LM 7
Entre Ríos [RA] 111 E 4
Entre-Rios = Malemo 172 G 4
Entre Ríos, Cordillera — 64-65 J 9
Entre Rios de Minas 102-103 K 4
Entrevias, Madrid- 113 III b 2
Entro, AZ 74-75 G 5
Entroncamento [BR] 106-107 K 2
Entroncamento [P] 120-121 CD 9
Entronque Huizache 86-87 K 6
Enugu 164-165 F 7
Enumclaw, WA 66-67 C 2
Enurmino 132-133 l 4
Envigado 94-95 D 4
Envira 92-93 EF 6
Enxadas, Ilha das — 110 I bc 2
Enxian = Encheng 146-147 EF 3
'Ên-Yahav 136-137 F 7
Enyellé 172 C 1
Enz 118 D 4
Enzan 144-145 M 5
Enzeli = Bandar-e Anzalī
134-135 FG 3
Eōlie o Lìpari, Ìsole — 122-123 F 6
Epe [WAN] 168-169 FG 4
Epecuén, Laguna — 106-107 F 6
Épeiros 122-123 J 6
Epéna 172 C 1
Épernay 120-121 J 4
Ephesos 136-137 B 4
Ephraim, UT 74-75 H 3
Ephrata, PA 72-73 H 4
Ephrata, WA 66-67 D 2
Epi 158-159 N 3
Epídauros 122-123 K 7
Epifania = Hamāh 134-135 D 3
Épinal 120-121 L 4
Epiphania = Hamāh 134-135 D 3
Épiphanie, l' 72-73 K 2
Epira 92-93 H 3
Epirus = Épeiros 122-123 J 6
Episcopi Bay = Kólpos Episkopês
136-137 E 5
Episkopês, Kólpos — 136-137 E 5
Eppegem 128 II b 1
Eppendorf, Hamburg- 130 I a 1
Epping, ND 68-69 E 1
Epping, Sydney- 161 I a 1
Epping Forest 129 II c 1
Epsom Downs, Houston-, TX
85 III b 1
Epulu 171 B 2
Epu-Pel 106-107 E 6
Epuyén 108-109 D 4
Équateur 172 CD 1
Equatoria = Gharb al-Istiwāīyah
164-165 KL 7
Equatorial Channel 176 a 3
Equatorial Guinea 164-165 FG 6
Erachh 138-139 G 5
Eraclea = Ereğli 134-135 C 2
Erakchiouen 168-169 E 1
Érákleion 113 IV b 1
Erakleion = Hērákleion 122-123 L 8
Erandol 138-139 E 7
Erāwadī Myit 148-149 C 2
Erāwadī Myitwanyā 148-149 BC 3
Erāwadī Taing 148-149 B 3
Erbaa 136-137 G 2
Erçek 136-137 K 3
Erçek gölü 136-137 K 3
Ercilla 106-107 A 7
Erciş 136-137 K 3
Erciyas dağı 134-135 D 3
Érd 118 J 5
Erdek 136-137 B 2
Erdek körfezi 136-137 B 2
Erdemli 136-137 F 4
Erdenecagaan 142-143 LM 2
Erdenheim, PA 84 III b 1
Erde Plateau = Erdi 164-165 J 5
Erdi 164-165 J 5
Erè 96-97 E 3
Erê, Campos — 102-103 F 6
Erebato, Río — 94-95 J 5
Erebus, Mount — 53 B 17-18
Erebus and Terror Gulf 53 C 31
Ereencav 142-143 M 2
Ereen Chabarg 142-143 EF 3
Ereğli [TR, Konya] 136-137 EF 4
Ereğli [TR, Zonguldak] 134-135 C 2
Erego 172 G 5
Erenhot = Erlian 142-143 L 3
Erenköy, İstanbul- 154 I b 3
Erepecu, Lago de — 92-93 H 5
Eresós 122-123 L 6
Erexim 111 F 3
Erfenisdam 174-175 G 5
Erfoûd = Arfūd 166-167 D 4
Erfurt 118 E 3
'Erg, el — = Al-'Irq 164-165 J 3
Ergani 136-137 H 3
Erg Bouraghet = 'Irq Buraghat
166-167 L 6
Erg Chech = Irq ash-Shāsh
164-165 D 3-4
Erg d'Admer = 'Irq Admar
164-165 F 4
Erg el Anngueur = 'Irq al-'Anqar
166-167 G 3-H 4
Erge-Muora-Sisse, ostrov — =
ostrov Arga-Muora-Sise
132-133 XY 3
Ergene nehri 136-137 B 2
Erg er Raoui = 'Irq ar-Rawī
164-165 D 3
Ergh, El — = Al-'Irq 164-165 J 3
Erg labès = 'Irq Yābis 166-167 EF 6
Erg Ighidi = Şahrā' al-Igīdi
164-165 CD 3
Erg Igidi = Şahrā' al-Igīdi
164-165 CD 3
Erg in Sakkane 164-165 D 4
Erg Issaouane = 'Irq Isāwuwan
164-165 F 3
Erg labès = 'Irq Yā'bis
166-167 EF 6
Ergli 124-125 E 5
Erg Sedra, Hassi — = Hāssī 'Irq
Sidrah 166-167 H 4
Erg Tihodaïne = 'Irq Tahūdawīn
166-167 K 7
Er Hai 142-143 J 6
Êrh-ch'iang = Charqiliq 142-143 F 4
Êrh-lien = Erlian 142-143 L 3
Erhlin 146-147 H 10
Eric 63 D 2
Érice 122-123 E 6
Erick, OK 76-77 E 5
Erie, CO 68-69 D 5-6
Erie, IL 70-71 EF 5
Erie, KS 70-71 C 7
Erie, ND 68-69 H 2
Erie, PA 64-65 K 3
Erie, Lake — 64-65 KL 3
Erieau 72-73 F 3
Erie Canal 72-73 G 3
'Erigaabo 164-165 b 1
Erik Eriksenstredet 116-117 m-o 5
Eriksdale 61 JK 5
Erimo misaki = Erimo-saki
142-143 RS 3
Erimo-saki 142-143 RS 3
Erin, TN 78-79 F 2
Erin Dzab = Ereencav 142-143 M 2
Erinpura 138-139 D 5
Erin Tal 142-143 L 3
Erith, London- 129 II c 2
Erito, Salto del — 94-95 K 4
Eritrea = Ērtira 164-165 M 5-N 6
Erize 106-107 F 6
Ērkāḍ = Yercaud 140 CD 5
Erkinis 136-137 JK 2
Erkizan = Ahlat 136-137 K 3
Erlangen 118 E 4
Erldunda 158-159 F 5
Erlenbach [CH] 128 IV b 2
Erlian 142-143 L 3
Erlin = Erhlin 146-147 H 10
E. R. Mejías 104-105 F 9
Ermelindo Matarazo, São Paulo-
110 II bc 1
Ermelo [ZA] 172 EF 7
Ermenak 136-137 E 4
Ermington, Sydney- 161 I a 1
Ermite, l' 128 II ab 2
Érmo = Gediz çayı 136-137 C 3
Ermont 129 I bc 2
Ernākulam, Cochin- 140 BC 5-6
Ernestina 106-107 H 5
Ernest Sound 58-59 w 8-9
Erode 134-135 M 8
Eromanga [AUS] 158-159 H 5
Eromanga [Vanuatu] 158-159 NO 3
Erongo 172 C 6
Erpe 130 III c 2
Erqiang = Charqiliq 142-143 F 4
Er Rahel = Hāssī al-Ghallah
166-167 F 2
Erramalai = Erramala Range
140 CD 3
Erramala Range 140 CD 3
Er Reba'a = Ar-Rub'ah 166-167 L 1
Er Redeyef = Ar-R'dayif
164-165 F 2
Er-Reşâfé = Rişāfah 136-137 H 5
Er Riad = Ar-Riyāḍ 134-135 F 6
Er-Ridisiya = Ar-Radīsīyat Baḥrī
173 C 5
er Rīf = Ar-Rīf 166-167 DE 2
Errigal 119 BC 4
Erris Head 119 AB 4
Er-Rôḍā = Ar-Rawḍah 173 B 4
Errol, NH 72-73 L 2
Errol Island 78-79 E 6
Er-Roşeireş = Ar-Ruşayriş
164-165 LM 6
Ersāma 138-139 L 7
Ersekë 122-123 J 5
Erskine, MN 70-71 BC 2
Ersoum el Lil, Hassi — = Hāssī
Arsum al-Lil 166-167 H 6
Ertil' 124-125 N 8
Ertira 164-165 M 5-N 6
Ertvågøy 116-117 BC 6
Eruh = Dih 136-137 K 4
Erval ↘ Bajé 106-107 L 4
Erval, Serra do — 106-107 LM 3
Ervália 102-103 L 4
Erwin, NC 80-81 G 3
Erwin, TN 80-81 E 2
Erýmanthos 122-123 JK 7
Erzerum = Erzurum 134-135 E 2-3
Erzgebirge 118 F 3
Erzhausen 128 III a 2
Erzin 132-133 S 7
Erzincan 134-135 D 3
Erzurum 134-135 E 2-3
Erzurum-Kars yaylâsı 136-137 JK 2
Esan-saki 144-145 b 3
Esashi [J ↑ Asahikawa] 144-145 c 1
Esashi [J ← Hakodate]
144-145 ab 3
Esbjerg 116-117 C 10
Esbo = Espoo 116-117 L 7
Escaba, Embalse — 104-105 CD 10
Escaba, Embalse de —
106-107 DE 1
Escada 100-101 G 5
Escalante, UT 74-75 H 4
Escalante, Islas — 96-97 AB 3
Escalante Desert 74-75 G 3-4
Escalante River 74-75 H 4
Escalón 86-87 H 4
Escanaba, MI 64-65 J 2
Escanaba River 70-71 G 2-3
Eschbach [D, river] 128 III b 1
Eschborn 128 III a 1
Eschenried 130 II a 1
Eschersheim, Frankfurt am Main-
128 III a 1
Eschscholtz Bay 58-59 G 3
Eschwege 118 DE 3
Esclusas de Gatún 64-65 b 2
Esclusas de Miraflores 64-65 b 3
Esclusas de Pedro Miguel 64-65 b 2
Escobal 64-65 ab 2
Escobar 102-103 D 6
Escoma 104-105 B 4
Escondida, La — 104-105 G 10
Escondido, CA 74-75 E 6
Escorial, El — 120-121 EF 8
Escoumins, les — 63 B 3
Escoumins, Rivière — 63 B 3
Escuadrón 201, Ixtapalapa- 91 I c 2
Escudo de Veraguas 88-89 F 10
Escuinapa de Hidalgo 64-65 E 7
Escuintla 64-65 H 9
Escutári = İstanbul-Üsküdar
134-135 BC 2
Eseka 168-169 H 5
Esendere = Bajirge 136-137 L 4
Esenler 154 I a 2
Esenli 136-137 G 2
Eşfahān 134-135 G 4
Esher 129 II a 2
Eshowe 172 F 7
Esh-Shaubak = Ash-Shawbak
136-137 F 7
Eshtehārd 136-137 O 5
Eska, AK 58-59 N 6
Eskifjördhur 116-117 g 2
Eskiköy 136-137 D 4
Eskilstuna 116-117 G 8
Eskimo Lakes 56-57 K 4
Eskimo Point 56-57 S 5
Eskipazar 136-137 E 2
Eskişehir 134-135 C 2-3
Esla 120-121 E 8
Eslāmābād 134-135 F 4
Eslöv 116-117 E 10
Eşme 136-137 C 3
Esmeralda [BR] 106-107 M 1-2
Esmeralda [MEX] 76-77 C 9
Esmeralda, Cordón — 108-109 C 6
Esmeralda, Isla — 108-109 B 7
Esmeralda, La — [CO, Amazonas]
94-95 J 6
Esmeralda, La — [CO, Meta]
94-95 F 6
Esmeralda, La — [PY] 111 D 2
Esmeralda, La — [YV] 94-95 F 3
Esmeraldas [EC, administrative unit]
96-97 B 1
Esmeraldas [EC, place] 92-93 CD 4
Esmeraldas, Río — 92-93 D 4
Esmond, ND 68-69 G 1
Esna = Isnā 164-165 L 3
Esnagami Lake 62 F 2
Esnagi Lake 70-71 H 1
Espanola 62 L 3
Espanola, NM 76-77 AB 5
Española, Isla — 92-93 B 5
Esperança 171 D 6
Espartillar 106-107 F 6
Esparto, CA 74-75 BC 3
Espenberg, AK 58-59 EF 3
Espenberg, Cape — 58-59 F 3
Espera Feliz 102-103 M 4
Esperança 100-101 FG 4
Esperança, Serra da —
102-103 G 6-7
Esperance 158-159 D 6
Esperance Bay 158-159 D 6
Esperantina 100-101 C 2
Esperantinópolis 100-101 B 3
Esperanza [CDN] 60 D 5
Esperanza [MEX] 86-87 M 8
Esperanza [PE, Huanuco] 96-97 C 6
Esperanza [PE, Loreto] 96-97 D 5
Esperanza [RA, Santa Cruz] 111 B 8
Esperanza [RA, Santa Fé] 111 D 4
Esperanza, Bogotá-La — 91 III c 3
Esperanza, La — [BOL]
104-105 EF 4
Esperanza, La — [C] 88-89 DE 3
Esperanza, La — [CO] 94-95 a 2
Esperanza, La — [Honduras]
88-89 BC 7
Esperanza, La — [RA, La Pampa]
106-107 D 6
Esperanza, La — [RA, Río Negro]
108-109 E 3
Esperanzas, Las — 76-77 D 9
Espichel, Cabo de — 120-121 C 9
Espigão, Serra do — 102-103 G 7
Espigão Mestre 100-101 A 6-C 8
Espigas 106-107 G 6
Espinal 92-93 DE 4
Espinazo 76-77 D 9
Espinhaço, Serra do — 92-93 L 8
Espinilho, Serra do — 106-107 K 2
Espinillo 111 E 2
Espino 94-95 HJ 3
Espinosa 100-101 C 8
Espírito Santo 92-93 L 9-M 8
Espírito Santo 158-159 MN 3
Espírito Santo, Bahía del —
86-87 R 8
Espíritu Santo, Cabo —
108-109 EF 9
Espíritu Santo, Isla — 86-87 EF 5
Espiye 136-137 H 2
Esplanada 92-93 M 7
Espoo 116-117 L 7
Espumoso 106-107 L 2
Espungabera 172 F 6
Esqueda 86-87 F 2
Esquel 111 B 6
Esquias 88-89 C 7
Esquimalt 56-57 M 8
Esquina 106-107 H 2-3
Esquiú 106-107 E 2
Es-Saïd = Aş-Şa'īd 164-165 L 3-4
eş Şaouïra = Aş-Şawīrah
164-165 BC 2
Es-Saqasiq = Az-Zaqazīq
164-165 KL 2
Essé [RFC] 168-169 J 4
Essen 118 C 3
Essenbeek 128 II a 2
Essendon, Melbourne- 161 II b 1
Essendon, Mount — 158-159 D 4
Essendon Airport 161 II b 1
Es Sened = As-Sanad
166-167 L 2
Essequibo 98-99 L 1-3
Essequibo River 92-93 H 4
Es Sers = As-Sars 166-167 L 1
Essex, CA 74-75 F 5
Essex, MT 66-67 G 1
Essex, VT 72-73 K 2
Essex Junction, VT 72-73 K 2
Es-Simbillâwein = As-Sinbillāwayn
173 BC 2
Essington, PA 84 III b 2
Es Skhīrra = Aş-Şahīrah
166-167 M 2
es Skhoûr = Sukhūr ar-Rihāmnah
166-167 BC 3
Essling, Wien- 113 I c 2
Esslingen 118 D 4
Esso 132-133 e 6
Es-Suweis = As-Suways
164-165 L 2-3
Est 168-169 F 2
Est, Île de l' 63 F 4
Estaca de Bares, Punta de la —
120-121 D 6-7
Estacas 106-107 H 3
Estación Kilómetro 31 110 III b 1
Estación Kilómetro 45 110 III a 2
Estación Pichi Ciego = Pichi Ciego
111 C 4
Estación Vanega 86-87 K 6
Estāda, Ābe — 134-135 K 4
Estadio Azteca 91 I c 3
Estadio Bernabeu 113 III ab 2
Estadio de Beisbol 91 II b 2
Estádio do Pacaembu 110 II b 2
Estadio Nacional 91 II b 2
Estadio Olímpico 91 I b 3
Estado, Parque do — 110 II b 2
Estados, Isla de los — 111 D 8
Estaire 72-73 F 1
Estância 92-93 M 7
Estancia, NM 76-77 AB 5
Estancia Ocampo-cué
102-103 D 5
Estarca 104-105 E 7
Estcourt 174-175 HJ 5
Este 122-123 D 3
Este, Parque Nacional de —
91 II b 2
Este, Punta del — 106-107 K 5
Esteban, Cabo — 108-109 B 8
Esteban A. Gascón 106-107 F 6
Esteban de Urizar 104-105 DE 8
Esteban Echeverría 110 III b 2
Esteban Echeverría-Monte Grande
110 III b 2
Esteban Rams 106-107 G 2
Estela 106-107 F 7
Estelí 64-65 J 9
Estella 120-121 F 7
Estelle, LA 85 I b 2
Estelline, TX 76-77 D 5
Estepona 120-121 E 10
Esterhazy 56-57 Q 7
Estero, FL 80-81 c 3
Estero Bay 74-75 C 5
Esteros 102-103 B 5
Esteros, Arroyos y — 102-103 D 6
Esteros del Batel 106-107 HJ 2
Esteros del Iberá 111 E 3
Esteros del Miriñay 106-107 J 2
Esteros del Santa Lucía
106-107 HJ 1-2
Esteros Grandes 106-107 G 2
Estes Park, CO 68-69 D 5
Estevan 56-57 Q 7
Estevan Group 60 BC 3
Estherville, IA 70-71 C 4
Estill, SC 80-81 F 4
Estiva, Riacho da — 100-101 B 4-5
Estomba 106-107 G 7
Estonia 124-125 D-F 4
Estor, El — 86-87 Q 10
Estrada, La — 120-121 C 7
Estrada Panamericana
102-103 H 5-6
Estrecho Asia 108-109 BC 8
Estrecho de Drake 111 B-D 9
Estrecho de Le Maire 111 C 9-D 8
Estrecho de Magallanes 111 AB 8
Estrecho de San Carlos = Falkland
Sound 111 DE 8
Estrecho Nelson 111 AB 8
Estreito 106-107 M 3
Estreito, Serra do — 100-101 C 6
Estrela 106-107 M 2
Estrêla, Serra da — [BR]
100-101 D 4
Estrela, Serra da — [P]
120-121 CD 8
Estrêla dos Anapurus 100-101 C 2
Estrela do Sul 102-103 J 3
Estrella, AZ 74-75 G 6
Estrella [MEX] 86-87 C 2
Estrella, Cerro de la — 91 I c 2
Estrella, La — 106-107 D 6
Estrella, Punta — 86-87 C 2
Estrella Nueva 104-105 E 5
Estrema [BR ↖ Cruzeiro do Sul]
96-97 E 5
Estrema [BR ↙ Rio Branco]
98-99 C 10
Estremadura 120-121 C 9
Estremoz 120-121 D 9
Estrondo, Serra do — 92-93 K 6
Estuário do Rio Amazonas
92-93 JK 4
Ēṭā = Etah 138-139 G 4
Etadunna 158-159 G 5
Etah 56-57 W 2
Etah = Etāwah 134-135 M 5
Étampes 120-121 HJ 4
Etawa = Bīnā 138-139 G 5
Etāwah [IND, Rājasthān] 138-139 F 5
Etāwah [IND, Uttar Pradesh]
138-139 G 4
Etawney Lake 61 K 2
Eterikan, proliv — 132-133 ab 3
Eternity Range 53 BC 30
Ethan, SD 68-69 GH 4
Ethel, MS 78-79 E 4
Ethel, Khorb el — = Khurb al-Athil
166-167 CD 5
Ethelbert 61 H 5
Ethiopia 164-165 MN 7
Ethnikón Museio 113 IV a 2
Ethnikos Kēpos 113 IV ab 2
Etivluk River 58-59 J 2
Etna, CA 66-67 B 5
Etna, Monte — 122-123 F 7
Etna, Mount — = Mazui Ling
150-151 G 3
Etnesjøen 116-117 AB 8
Etobikoke 72-73 G 3
Étoile du Congo 172 E 4
Etolin, Cape — 58-59 D 6
Etolin Island 58-59 w 8
Etolin Strait 56-57 C 5-6
Eton [AUS] 158-159 J 4
Etorofu = ostrov Iturup 132-133 c 9
Etosha Game Park 172 C 5
Etosha Pan 172 C 5
Etowah, TN 78-79 G 3
Etrī, Jebel — = Jabal Itrī 173 D 7
Etruria 106-107 F 4
Etter, TX 76-77 CD 4
Etterbeek 128 II b 1-2
Etzatlán 86-87 HJ 7
Etzikom 66-67 H 1
Etzikom Coulée 66-67 GH 1
Eua 208 J 5
Euabalong 160 GH 4
Eubank, KY 70-71 H 7
Euboea = Kai Évboia
122-123 K 6-L 7
Eucalyptus, les — 170 I b 2
Euch, Rass el — = Ra's al-'Ishsh
166-167 KL 2
Eucla 158-159 E 6
Euclid, OH 72-73 F 4
Euclides da Cunha 92-93 M 7
Eucumbene, Lake — 160 J 6
Eudistes, Lac des — 63 D 2
Eudora, AR 78-79 D 4
Eufaula, AL 78-79 G 5
Eufaula, OK 76-77 G 5
Eufaula Lake, NM 76-77 A 6
Eufaula Reservoir 76-77 G 5
Eufemio Uballes 106-107 GH 6
Eufrasio Loza 106-107 F 2
Eugene, OR 64-65 B 3
Eugenia, Punta — 64-65 C 6
Eugenio Bustos 106-107 C 4
Eugênio Penzo 102-103 E 5
Euice, NM 76-77 C 6
Eulma, El — = Al-'Ulmah
166-167 J 1
Eulo 158-159 J 5
Eunice, LA 78-79 C 5
Eupen 120-121 KL 3
Euphrat = Nahr al-Furāt
134-135 E 4
Euphrates = Nahr al-Furāt
134-135 E 4
Eupora, MS 78-79 E 4
EUR, Roma- 113 II b 2
Eurajoki 116-117 J 7
Eurasia Basin 50-51 K-O 1
Eure 120-121 H 4
Eureka, AK 58-59 MN 4
Eureka, CA 64-65 AB 3
Eureka, IL 70-71 F 5
Eureka, KS 68-69 H 7
Eureka, MT 66-67 F 1
Eureka, NV 74-75 EF 3
Eureka, SD 68-69 G 3
Eureka, UT 74-75 G 2-3
Eureka, WA 66-67 D 2
Eureka [CDN] 56-57 T 1
Eureka [ZA] 174-175 J 3
Eureka Acres, Houston-, TX 85 III b 1
Eureka Roadhouse, AK 58-59 NO 6
Eureka Sound 56-57 TU 2
Eureka Springs, AR 78-79 C 2
Eureupoucigne, Chaîne d' 98-99 M 3
Euroa 160 G 6
Europa [BR] 98-99 D 8
Europa, Île — 172 H 6
Europa, Picos de — 120-121 E 7
Europa, Point — 120-121 E 10
Europe 50-51 K-M 3
Eusebia 106-107 G 3
Eusebio Ayala 102-103 D 6
Euskadi [E] 120-121 F 7
Euskadi [RA] 106-107 D 6
Eustis, FL 80-81 c 2
Eustis, NE 68-69 FG 5
Eutaw, AL 78-79 F 4
Eutsuk Lake 60 D 3
Eva, OK 76-77 CD 4
Evalyn Wilson Park 85 III c 2
Evangelista 106-107 LM 2
Evangelistas, Islas — 108-109 B 9
Evans, Lac — 62 N 1
Evans, Mount — [CDN] 60 J 5
Evans, Mount — [USA, Colorado]
68-69 D 6
Evans, Mount — [USA, Montana]
66-67 G 2
Evans Head 158-159 K 5
Evans Strait 56-57 U 5
Evanston, IL 70-71 G 4
Evanston, WY 66-67 H 5
Evansville, AK 58-59 LM 3

Evansville, IL 70-71 F 6
Evansville, IN 64-65 J 4
Evansville, WI 70-71 F 4
Evant, TX 76-77 EF 7
Evaporación, Planta de — 91 I d 1
Evaristo 106-107 L 3
Evart, MI 70-71 H 4
Evaton 174-175 G 4
Évboia, Kai — 122-123 K 6-L 7
Evboïkós Kólpos 122-123 KL 6
Eveleth, MN 70-71 D 2
Evenequên 94-95 K 5
Evenki Autonomous Area 132-133 R-T 5
Evensk 132-133 e 5
Everard, Cape — 158-159 JK 7
Everard, Lake — 158-159 F 6
Everard Park 158-159 F 5
Everard Ranges 158-159 F 5
Everest, Mount — = Sagarmatha 142-143 F 6
Everett, GA 80-81 F 5
Everett, MA 84 I b 2
Everett, WA 64-65 B 2
Everett, Mount — 72-73 K 3
Everglades 64-65 K 6
Everglades, FL 80-81 c 4
Everglades National Park 64-65 K 6
Evergreen, AL 78-79 F 5
Evergreen Park, IL 83 II a 2
Evergreen Plaza, Chicago-, IL 83 II ab 2
Eversem 128 II ab 1
Evesboro, NJ 84 III d 2
Evinayong 164-165 G 8
Evje 116-117 BC 8
Évora 120-121 CD 9
Évreux 120-121 H 4
Evrýchu 136-137 E 5
Evrykhou = Evrýchu 136-137 E 5
Évzonos 113 IV b 2

Ewan, WA 66-67 E 2
Ewan Lake 58-59 P 5
Ewaso Ngiro 172 G 2
Ewell 129 II a 2
Ewing, KY 72-73 E 5
Ewing, MO 70-71 E 5-6
Ewing, NE 68-69 G 4
Ewing, VA 80-81 E 2
Ewo 172 BC 2

Exaltación [BOL] 92-93 F 7
Exaltación [BR] 104-105 C 2
Excelsior 174-175 G 5
Excelsior Mountains 74-75 D 3
Excelsior Springs, MO 70-71 CD 6
Excursion Inlet, AK 58-59 U 7
Exe 119 E 6
Executive Committee Range 53 B 24
Exeland, WI 70-71 E 3
Exelberg 113 I ab 1
Exeter, CA 74-75 D 4
Exeter, MO 78-79 C 2
Exeter, NE 68-69 H 5
Exeter, NH 72-73 L 3
Exeter [CDN] 72-73 F 3
Exeter [GB] 119 E 6
Exhibition Building 161 II b 1
Exira, IA 70-71 C 5
Exmoor Forest 119 E 6
Exmore, VA 80-81 HJ 2
Exmouth 119 E 6
Exmouth Gulf [AUS, bay] 158-159 B 4
Exmouth Gulf [AUS, place] 158-159 B 4
Expedition Range 158-159 J 4
Exploits River 63 HJ 3
Explorer Mount 58-59 FG 7
Extrema 102-103 JK 5
Extremadura 120-121 D 9-E 8
Exu 100-101 E 4
Exuma Island, Great — 64-65 L 7
Exuma Sound 64-65 L 7

Eyasi, Lake — 172 FG 2
Eyehill Creek 61 C 4
Eyjafjardhar 116-117 d 2
Eyjafjördhur 116-117 d 1
Eyl 164-165 b 2
Eynihal 136-137 CD 4
Eynsford 129 II c 2
Eyota, MN 70-71 D 3-4
Eyrarbakki 116-117 c 3
Eyre 158-159 E 6
Eyre, Lake — 158-159 G 5
Eyre, Seno — 111 B 7
Eyre North, Lake — 160 C 2
Eyre Peninsula 158-159 G 6
Eyre South, Lake — 160 C 2
Eyüp, İstanbul- 154 I a 2

Ezeiza, Aeropuerto Internacional de — 110 III b 2
Ezequiel Ramos Mejías 104-105 F 9
Ezequiel Ramos Mexía, Embalse — 106-107 C 7
Ezine 136-137 B 3
Ezinepazar = Zigala 136-137 G 2
Ezpeleta, Quilmes- 110 III c 2
Ezraa = Izra' 136-137 G 6
Ežva 124-125 S 3
Ez-Zagazig = Az-Zaqāzīq 164-165 KL 2
Ez Zemoul el Akbar = Az-Zamūl al-Akbar 166-167 K 5-L 4

F

Fáb. das Chitas, Rio de Janeiro- 110 I b 2
Fabens, TX 76-77 AB 7
Faber, Mount — 154 III a 2
Fabriano 122-123 E 4
Facatativá 94-95 D 5
Fachi 164-165 G 5
Facundo 108-109 DE 5
Fada 164-165 J 5
Fada-n'Gourma 164-165 DE 6
Faddeja, zaliv — 132-133 UV 2
Faddejevskij, ostrov — 132-133 b-d 2
Faddeyev Island = ostrov Faddejevskij 132-133 b-d 2
Fadghāmī 136-137 J 5
Fadiffolu Atoll 176 ab 1
Fadu N'Gurma = Fada-n'Gourma 164-165 DE 6
Faenza 122-123 D 3
Færingehavn 56-57 a 5
Faeroe Iceland Ridge 114-115 FG 3
Fafa 168-169 F 2
Fafan = Fafen 164-165 N 7
Fafanlap 148-149 K 7
Fafen 164-165 N 7
Faga 168-169 F 2
Făgăraş 122-123 L 3
Fagatoga 148-149 c 1
Fagernes 116-117 C 7
Fagersta 116-117 FG 7-8
Fagibin, Lake — = Lac Faguibine 164-165 CD 5
Fagnano, Lago — 108-109 EF 10
Faguibine, Lac — 164-165 CD 5
Fagundes [BR, Pará] 92-93 H 6
Fagundes [BR, Paraíba] 100-101 FG 4
Fahala 176 a 2
Fahl, Ouèd el — = Wādī al-Faḥl 166-167 HJ 4
Faḥl, Wādī al- 166-167 HJ 4
Fähna = Väana 124-125 E 4
Fahraj 134-135 H 5
Fahrlander See 130 III a 2
Faḥṣ, Al- 166-167 LM 1
Faial 204-205 DE 5
Faïd 173 C 2
Faïḍāt = Fayḍāt 136-137 HJ 5
Faifo = Hôi An 150-151 G 5
Faijum, El — = Al-Fayyūm 164-165 KL 3
Fair 106-107 H 6
Fairbairn Park 161 II b 1
Fairbank, AZ 74-75 H 7
Fairbanks, AK 56-57 G 5
Fairbanks, Houston-, TX 85 III a 1
Fairburn, GA 78-79 G 4
Fairburn, SD 68-69 E 4
Fairbury, IL 70-71 F 5
Fairbury, NE 64-65 G 3
Fairchild, WI 70-71 E 3
Fairfax, AL 78-79 G 4
Fairfax, MN 70-71 C 3
Fairfax, MO 70-71 C 5
Fairfax, OK 76-77 F 4
Fairfax, SC 80-81 F 4
Fairfax, SD 68-69 G 4
Fairfield, AL 78-79 F 4
Fairfield, CA 74-75 BC 3
Fairfield, IA 70-71 E 5
Fairfield, ID 66-67 F 4
Fairfield, IL 70-71 F 6
Fairfield, ME 72-73 M 2
Fairfield, MT 66-67 H 2
Fairfield, ND 68-69 E 2
Fairfield, TX 76-77 FG 7
Fairfield, Melbourne- 161 II c 1
Fairgrounds 85 I b 2
Fairholm, WA 66-67 AB 1
Fairhope, AL 78-79 F 5
Fair Isle 119 F 2
Fairlie 158-159 NO 8
Fair Meadows, Houston-, TX 85 III b 1
Fairmont, MN 70-71 C 4
Fairmont, NC 80-81 G 3
Fairmont, NE 68-69 H 5
Fairmont, WV 72-73 F 5
Fairmont Hot Springs 60 K 4
Fairmount, ND 68-69 H 2-3
Fairmount Park 84 III b 1-2
Fair Oaks, AR 78-79 D 3
Fairplay, CO 68-69 CD 6
Fair Play, MO 70-71 D 7
Fairport, NY 72-73 H 3
Fairport Harbor, OH 72-73 F 4
Fairview 60 H 1
Fairview, KS 70-71 C 6
Fairview, MT 68-69 D 2
Fairview, OK 76-77 E 4
Fairview, UT 74-75 H 3
Fairway Hills, MD 82 II a 1
Fairway Rock 58-59 C 4
Fairweather, Cape — 58-59 ST 7
Fairweather, Mount — 56-57 J 6
Fais 206-207 S 9
Faisalābād 134-135 L 4
Faith, SD 68-69 EF 3
Faizābād 134-135 N 5
Fajansovyj 124-125 K 6
Fajardo 88-89 O 5
Fajj Mazallah 166-167 JK 1
Fajr, Wādī — 134-135 D 5
Fakaofo 208 J 3
Fakel 124-125 T 5
Fakfak 148-149 K 7
Fakīragrām 138-139 MN 4
Fak Tha 150-151 C 3-4
Falaba 168-169 C 3
Faladyé 168-169 C 2
Falaise, Cap — = Mui Đa Du'ng 150-151 EF 3
Falaise de Tiguidit 168-169 GH 1
Fālākāta 138-139 M 4
Falam = Hpalam 148-149 B 2
Fălciu 122-123 MN 2
Falckner 108-109 F 3
Falcón 94-95 FG 2
Falcon, Cap — = Rā's Falkun 166-167 F 2
Falcon, Cape — 66-67 A 3
Falcone, Capo — 122-123 BC 5
Falcon Island 62 B 3
Falcon Reservoir 64-65 G 6
Falda, La — 106-107 E 3
Faléa 168-169 C 2
Falémé 164-165 B 6
Falemé = Falémé 164-165 B 6
Falenki 124-125 S 4
Faleru, Órmos — 113 IV a 2
Falešty 126-127 C 3
Falfurrias, TX 76-77 E 9
Falher 60 J 2
Falkenberg [DDR] 118 F 3
Falkenberg [S] 116-117 DE 9
Falkenberg, Berlin- 130 III c 1
Falkenhagener See 130 III a 1
Falkenhagen-Ost 130 III a 1
Falkenhagen-West 130 III a 1
Falkirk 119 E 3-4
Falkland Islands 111 DE 8
Falkland Sound 111 DE 8
Falkonéra 122-123 KL 7
Falköping 116-117 EF 8
Falkun, Rā's — 166-167 F 2
Falkville, AL 78-79 F 3
Fällanden 128 IV b 1
Fallbrook, CA 74-75 E 6
Fall Line Hills [USA, Alabama] 78-79 E 3
Fall Line Hills [USA, Georgia] 80-81 D-F 4
Fallon, MT 68-69 D 2
Fallon, NV 64-65 C 4
Fall River, MA 64-65 MN 3
Fall River Lake 70-71 BC 7
Fall River Mills, CA 66-67 C 5
Falls Church, VA 82 II a 2
Falls City, NE 70-71 C 5
Falls City, OR 66-67 B 3
Falls City, TX 76-77 EF 8
Falls Creek 160 H 6
Fallūjah, Al- 136-137 JK 6
Falmouth 119 D 6
Falmouth, KY 70-71 H 6
Falmouth, MA 72-73 L 4
Falsa Chipana, Punta — 104-105 A 7
False Bay = Valsbaai [ZA, Kaapland] 172 C 8
False Bay = Valsbaai [ZA, Natal] 174-175 K 4
False Cabo de Hornos 108-109 E 10
False Cape 80-81 c 2
False Divi Point 140 E 3
False Pass, AK 58-59 ab 2
False Point 134-135 O 6
Falster 116-117 E 10
Falsterbo 116-117 E 10
Faltbush, New York-, NY 82 III c 3
Falterona, Monte — 122-123 DE 4
Fălticeni 122-123 M 2
Falucho 106-107 E 5
Falun 116-117 F 7
Famagusta = Ammóchōstos 134-135 CD 3
Famagusta Bay = Kólpos Ammochōstu 136-137 EF 5
Famatina 106-107 D 2
Famatina, Sierra de — 106-107 D 2
Family Lake 62 B 2
Fana 168-169 D 2
Fanchang 146-147 G 6
Fancheng = Xiangfan 142-143 L 5
Fanchih = Fanshi 146-147 D 2
Fanegas 106-107 H 2
Fang 150-151 B 3
Fangak 164-165 L 7
Fangasso 168-169 DE 2
Fangcheng [TJ, Guangdong] 150-151 G 2
Fangcheng [TJ, Henan] 142-143 L 5
Fang-ch'êng = Fangcheng 150-151 G 2
Fangfeng 146-147 E 3
Fanghsien = Fang Xian 146-147 C 5
Fanglan = Jiangcun 146-147 D 2
Fangliao 146-147 H 10
Fangshan [TJ, Beijing] 146-147 E 2
Fangshan [TJ, Shanxi] 146-147 C 3
Fang-shan = Fengchiang 146-147 H 10
Fang Shan = Huoshan 146-147 F 6
Fang Xian 146-147 C 5
Fan-hsien = Fan Xian 146-147 E 4
Fanjiacun = Beijing-Huangtugang 155 II ab 2
Fanning 156-157 K 4
Fanning Trench 156-157 J 4-K 5
Fanø [DK] 116-117 C 10
Fano [I] 122-123 E 4
Fanshan 146-147 C 3
Fanshi 146-147 D 2
Fan Si Pan 148-149 D 2
Fant, Al- 173 B 3
Fanṭās, Gebel el — = Jabal al-Finṭās 173 B 6
Fan Xian 146-147 E 4
Fanyu = Panyu 146-147 D 10
Fanzhi = Fanshi 146-147 D 2
Faqīh Bin Ṣālaḥ, Al- 166-167 C 3
Fāqūs 173 BC 2
Farā', Al- 136-137 J 4
Faraba 168-169 C 2
Farabana 168-169 C 3
Faraday Seamount Group 114-115 C 5-6
Faradje 172 E 1
Faradofay 172 J 7
Farafangana 172 J 6
Farāfirah, Al-Qaṣr al- 164-165 K 3
Farāfirah, Wāḥāt al- 164-165 K 3
Farāh 134-135 J 4
Farāh Rōd 134-135 J 4
Farako 168-169 D 2
Farallón, Cabo — = Cabo Santa Elena 64-65 J 9
Farallon de Pajaros 206-207 S 7
Farallon Islands 74-75 B 4
Faranah 164-165 BC 6
Farasān, Jazā'ir — 134-135 E 7
Faraulep 148-149 M 5
Farāyid, Jabal al- 173 D 6
Fārbisganj = Forbesganj 138-139 L 4
Farewell, AK 58-59 KL 5
Farewell, MI 72-73 D 3
Farewell, Cape — 158-159 O 8
Farewell, Cape — = Kap Farvel 56-57 c 6
Farewell Field 84 II b 2
Fargo, GA 80-81 E 5
Fargo, ND 64-65 G 2
Fargo, OK 76-77 E 4
Faria 110 I b 2
Farias Brito 100-101 E 4
Faribault, MN 70-71 D 3
Farīdābād 138-139 F 3
Farīdkot 138-139 E 2
Farīdpūr [BD] 138-139 M 6
Faridpur [IND] 138-139 G 3
Fārigh, Wādī al- 164-165 HJ 2-3
Farim 164-165 AB 6
Farina 158-159 G 6
Farinha, Rio — 100-101 A 4
Fāris 134-135 G 6
Farka 168-169 F 2
Farlane 62 BC 2
Farmer City, IL 70-71 F 5
Farmersburg, IN 70-71 G 6
Farmerville, LA 78-79 C 4
Farmington, CA 74-75 C 4
Farmington, IA 70-71 DE 5
Farmington, IL 70-71 EF 5
Farmington, ME 72-73 LM 2
Farmington, MN 70-71 D 3
Farmington, MO 70-71 EF 7
Farmington, NM 74-75 J 4
Farmington, UT 66-67 GH 5
Farmsen, Hamburg- 130 I b 1
Farmville, NC 80-81 H 3
Farmville, VA 80-81 G 2
Farnborough, London- 129 II c 2
Farnham [CDN] 72-73 K 2
Farnsworth, TX 76-77 D 4
Faro [BR] 92-93 H 5
Faro [P] 120-121 CD 10
Faro [RA] 106-107 G 7
Faro [RFC] 164-165 G 7
Faro, Punta di — 122-123 F 6
Faro de Avión 120-121 CD 7
Farofa, Serra da — 106-107 MN 2
Fårön 116-117 H 9
Farquhar Islands 172 JK 4
Farrars Creek 158-159 H 4-5
Farrell, PA 72-73 F 4
Farrer Park 154 III b 2
Far Rockawa, New York-, NY 82 III d 3
Farroupilha 106-107 M 2
Farrukhābād 134-135 M 5
Fārs 134-135 G 4-5
Fársala 122-123 K 6
Farshūṭ 173 BC 4
Farsia = Ḥāssī al-Farsīyah 166-167 B 6
Farsīyah, Ḥāssī al- 166-167 B 6
Farson, WY 66-67 J 4
Farsund 116-117 B 8
Fartak, Rā's — 134-135 G 7
Fartura 102-103 H 5
Fartura, Serra da — 102-103 FG 7
Farvel, Kap — 56-57 c 6
Farwell, MI 70-71 H 4
Farwell, TX 76-77 C 5
Fas 164-165 CD 2
Fasā 134-135 G 5
Fasanerie-Nord, München- 130 II b 1
Fasaneriesee 130 II b 1
Fasangarten, München- 130 II b 2
Fasano 122-123 G 5
Fāsher, El- = Al-Fāshir 164-165 K 6
Fāshir, Al- 164-165 K 6
Fashn, Al- 164-165 KL 3
Fashoda = Kūdūk 164-165 L 6-7
Fåskrúdhsfjördhur 116-117 fg 2
Fastov 126-127 D 1
Fatagar, Tanjung — 148-149 K 7
Fatahgarh = Fatehgarh 138-139 G 4
Fatahpur = Fatehpur [IND, Bihār] 138-139 K 5
Fatahpur = Fatehpur [IND, Rājasthān] 134-135 L 5
Fatahpur = Fatehpur [IND, Uttar Pradesh ↘ Kānpur] 138-139 H 5
Fatahpur = Fatehpur [IND, Uttar Pradesh ↗ Lucknow] 138-139 H 4
Fatako 168-169 C 3
Fatala 168-169 B 3
Fatehābād [IND, Haryana] 138-139 E 3
Fatehābād [IND, Uttar Pradesh] 138-139 G 4
Fatehgarh 138-139 G 4
Fatehpur [IND, Bihār] 138-139 K 5
Fatehpur [IND, Rājasthān] 134-135 L 5
Fatehpur [IND, Uttar Pradesh ↘ Kānpur] 138-139 H 5
Fatehpur [IND, Uttar Pradesh ↗ Lucknow] 138-139 H 4
Fatehpur [Nepal] 138-139 L 4
Fatež 124-125 K 7
Fatḥa, Al- = Al-Fatḥah 134-135 E 3
Father Lake 62 O 2
Fatick 168-169 A 2
Fatih, İstanbul- 154 I a 2
Fatih Mehmet Camiî 154 I a 2
Fatikli 136-137 G 4
Fátima 120-121 C 9
Fatima, Bogotá- 91 III b 3
Fatima do Sul 102-103 E 5
Fatkong = Fogang 146-147 D 10
Fatmah, Bi'r — 136-137 K 5
Fatsa 136-137 G 2
Fat Tau Point 155 I b 2
Fatuma 171 B 4
Faucett, MO 70-71 C 6
Faucilles, Monts — 120-121 K 5-L 4
Faulkton, SD 68-69 G 3
Făurei 122-123 M 3
Fauresmith 174-175 F 5
Fauro 148-149 j 6
Fauske 116-117 F 4
Faust 60 K 2
Faust, UT 66-67 G 5
Faustino M. Parera 106-107 H 4
Faval, Porto do — 100-101 B 1
Fåvang 124-125 K 6
Favara 122-123 E 7
Faversham 119 G 6
Favignana 122-123 DE 7
Favoriten, Wien- 113 I b 2
Favourable Lake 62 C 1
Fāw, Al- 136-137 N 7-8
Fawāt 166-167 M 7
Fawkner, Melbourne- 161 II b 1
Fawkner Park 161 II b 2
Fawnie Range 60 E 3
Fawn River 56-57 T 7
Faxaflói 116-117 b 2
Faxinal 102-103 G 5
Fay, OK 76-77 E 5
Faya = Largeau 164-165 HJ 5
Fayala 172 C 2
Faya-Largeau 164-165 H 5
Fayḍābād 134-135 KL 3
Fayḍāt 136-137 HJ 5
Fayette, AL 78-79 F 4
Fayette, IA 70-71 E 4
Fayette, MO 70-71 D 6
Fayette, MS 78-79 D 5
Fayetteville, AR 64-65 H 4
Fayetteville, NC 64-65 L 4-5
Fayetteville, OH 72-73 E 5
Fayetteville, TN 78-79 F 3
Fāyid = Fā'id 173 C 2
Faylakah, Jazīrat — 136-137 N 8
Fayṣalīyah, Al- 136-137 KL 7
Faysh Khābūr 136-137 JK 4
Fayum, El — = Al-Fayyūm 164-165 KL 3
Fayyūm, Al- 164-165 KL 3
Fayzabad = Faizābād 134-135 N 5
Fāzilka 138-139 E 2
Fazrārah, Buḥayrat — 166-167 K 1
Fazzān 164-165 GH 3

Fdayrik 164-165 B 4

Fear, Cape — 64-65 L 5
Feather Falls, CA 74-75 C 3
Feather River 74-75 C 3
Feather River, North Fork — 74-75 C 2-3
Featherston 158-159 P 8
Featherville, ID 66-67 F 4
Febre 106-107 GH 4
Febrero, Parque 3 de — 110 III b 1
Fécamp 120-121 H 4
Fechenheim, Frankfurt am Main- 128 III b 1
Fédala = Al-Muḥammadīyah 166-167 C 3
Federación 106-107 HJ 3
Federal 111 E 4
Federal Capital Territory = 1 ◁ 164-165 F 7
Federal Capital Territory = Australian Capital Territory 158-159 J 7
Federal Dam, MN 70-71 CD 2
Federick Hills 158-159 G 2
Federico Lacroze 110 III b 1
Fedje 116-117 A 7
Fedjedj, Chott el — = Shaṭṭ al-Fijāj 166-167 L 2-3
Fedj-M'zala = Fajj Mazallah 166-167 JK 1
Fedosejevskaja 124-125 N 2
Fedotova, kosa — 126-127 G 3
Fedovo 124-125 M 2
Fehmarn 118 E 1
Feia 100-101 B 8
Feia, Lagoa — 92-93 L 9
Feicheng 146-147 F 3
Feidong 146-147 F 6
Feiheji 146-147 E 5
Feihekou = Feiheji 146-147 E 5
Fei-hsi = Feixi 146-147 F 6
Feihsien = Fei Xian 146-147 FG 4
Feijó 92-93 E 6
Feira de Santana 92-93 LM 7
Feisabad = Faizābād 134-135 N 5
Feitoria, Ilha da — 106-107 LM 3
Feixi 146-147 F 6
Fei Xian 146-147 FG 4
Feixiang 146-147 E 3
Fei-yün Chiang = Feiyun Jiang 146-147 GH 8
Feiyun Jiang 146-147 GH 8
Feke = Asmaca 136-137 F 4
Felâhiye 136-137 F 3
Felanitx 120-121 J 9
Feldberg 118 C 5
Feldioara 122-123 L 3
Feldkirch 118 DE 5
Feldmochinger See 130 II ab 1
Feliciano, Arroyo — 106-107 H 3
Felidu Atoll 176 a 2
Felipe Carillo Puerto 64-65 J 8
Felipe Solá 106-107 F 6-7
Felipe Yofré 106-107 HJ 2
Felixlândia 102-103 K 3
Felixton 174-175 JK 5
Félix U. Gómez 86-87 H 2
Feller Heights 60 G 2
Fellowship, NJ 84 III d 2
Fellsmere, FL 80-81 c 3
Felt, OK 76-77 C 4
Feltham, London- 129 II a 2
Felton, CA 74-75 B 4
Felton, MN 68-69 H 2
Feltre 122-123 D 2
Femund 116-117 D 6
Femundsenden 116-117 D 7
Fenaria 168-169 C 3
Fencheng 146-147 C 4
Fenelon Falls 72-73 G 2
Fener, İstanbul- 154 I a 2
Fenerbahçe Stadyumu 154 I b 3
Fener burnu 154 I b 3
Fénérive = Fenoarivo Atsinanana 172 JK 5
Fengâri 122-123 L 5
Fengcheng [TJ, Jiangxi] 146-147 E 7
Fengcheng [TJ, Liaoning] 142-143 N 3
Fengchiang 146-147 H 10
Fêng-chieh = Fengjie 142-143 K 5
Fêng-ch'iu = Fengqiu 146-147 E 4
Fengchuan 146-147 C 10
Fengdu 142-143 K 5-6
Fêng-fêng = Fengfeng 146-147 DE 3
Fêng-hsin = Fengxin 146-147 E 7
Fenghua 146-147 H 7
Fêng-hua = Fenghua 146-147 H 7
Fenghuang 146-147 B 8
Fengjie 142-143 K 5
Fengjun = Fengrun 146-147 FG 2
Fengkai 146-147 C 10
Fengkieh = Fengjie 142-143 K 5
Fengliang 146-147 F 10
Fenglin [RC] 146-147 H 10
Fenglin [TJ] 146-147 H 7
Fenglingdu 146-147 C 4
Fêng-ling-tu = Fenglingdu 146-147 C 4
Fengming Dao 144-145 C 3
Fêng-ming Tao = Fengming Dao 144-145 C 3
Fengning 142-143 M 3
Fengqiu 146-147 E 4
Fengrun 146-147 FG 2
Fengshan [RC] 146-147 GH 10
Feng Shan [TJ] 146-147 B 5
Fengshun 146-147 EF 10
Fengsien = Feng Xian 142-143 K 5
Fengtai 146-147 F 5
Fengtai, Beijing- 155 II a 2
Fengtaiqu, Beijing- 155 II ab 2
Fengting 146-147 G 9
Fengtu = Fengdu 142-143 K 5-6
Fengxian [TJ, Jiangsu ↓ Shanghai] 146-147 H 6
Feng Xian [TJ, Jiangsu ↖ Xuzhou] 146-147 F 4
Feng Xian [TJ, Shaanxi] 142-143 K 5
Fengxin 146-147 E 7
Fengyang 146-147 F 5
Fengyüan 146-147 H 9
Fen He 142-143 L 4
Fên Ho = Fen He 142-143 L 4
Fên-hsi = Fenxi 146-147 C 3
Fenī 141 B 4
Feni = Fenyi 146-147 E 8
Feniak Lake 58-59 HJ 2
Feni Islands 148-149 h 5
Fénix Grande, Río — 108-109 D 6
Fenner 61 C 5
Fennimore, WI 70-71 E 4
Fennville, MI 70-71 G 4
Fenoarivo Atsinanana 172 JK 5
Fenshui Ling 144-145 D 2-3
Fensi = Fenxi 146-147 C 3
Fenton, LA 78-79 C 5
Fenton, MI 70-71 J 4
Fenway Park 84 I b 2
Fenxi 146-147 C 3
Fenyang 142-143 L 4
Fenyi 146-147 E 8
Feodosija 126-127 G 4
Feou-ning = Funing 142-143 MN 5
Fer, Cap de — = Rā's al-Ḥadīd 166-167 K 1
Fer, Point au — 78-79 D 6
Férai 122-123 M 5
Ferbitz 130 III a 2
Ferdows 134-135 H 4
Fère, la — 120-121 J 4
Fergana 134-135 L 2-3
Ferganskaja dolina 134-135 L 2
Ferghana = Fergana 134-135 L 2-3
Fergus 72-73 F 3
Fergus Falls, MN 64-65 GH 2
Fergusson Island 148-149 h 6
Feriâna = Firyānah 166-167 L 2
Ferias, Bogotá-Las — 91 III b 2
Ferkane = Firgān 166-167 K 2
Ferkéssédougou 164-165 CD 7
Ferlo [SN, landscape] 164-165 AB 5
Ferlo [SN, river] 168-169 B 2
Fermo 122-123 E 4
Fermoselle 120-121 DE 8
Fermoy 119 B 5
Fernandes Belo 100-101 AB 1
Fernandes Pinheiro 102-103 G 6
Fernández 106-107 F 1
Fernandina, FL 80-81 c 1
Fernandina, Isla — 92-93 A 4-5
Fernando de Noronha 92-93 N 5
Fernando de Noronha, Ilha — 92-93 N 5
Fernando de Trejo y Sanabria, Colonia — 102-103 E 6
Fernandópolis 102-103 GH 4
Fernando Póo, Isla de — = Bioko 164-165 F 8
Ferndale 170 V a 1
Ferndale, CA 66-67 A 5
Ferndale, MI 84 II b 2
Ferndale, WA 66-67 B 1
Fernie 66-67 F 1
Fernlee 160 H 2
Fernley, NV 74-75 D 3
Fernmeldeturm Frankfurt 128 III a 1
Fernsehturm 130 II b 1
Fernwood, ID 66-67 EF 2
Ferokh 140 B 5
Ferozepore 138-139 E 2
Ferrara 122-123 DE 3
Ferré 106-107 G 5
Ferreira [ZA] 174-175 G 5
Ferreira Gomes 92-93 J 4
Ferreñafe 92-93 D 6
Ferrer Point 60 D 5
Ferriday, LA 78-79 D 5
Ferris, TX 76-77 F 6
Ferro = Hierro 164-165 A 3
Ferrol, Peninsula de — 92-93 CD 6
Ferrol de Caudillo, El — 120-121 C 7
Ferros 102-103 L 3
Ferry, AK 58-59 N 4
Ferryville = Manzil Būrgībah 166-167 L 1
Fertile, MN 68-69 H 2
Fes = Fās 164-165 CD 2
Feshi 172 C 3
Fessenden, ND 68-69 FG 2
Festus, MO 70-71 E 6
Fête Bové 168-169 B 2
Feteşti 122-123 M 3
Fethiye 134-135 B 3
Fethiye körfezi 136-137 C 4
Fetisovo 134-135 G 2
Fetlar 119 F 1
Fetzara, Lac — = Buḥayrat Fazrārah 166-167 K 1
Feucherolles 129 I ab 2
Feuerland 111 C 8
Feuêt = Fawāt 166-167 M 7
Fevat = Fawāt 166-167 M 7
Fevzipaşa 136-137 G 4
Fez = Fas 164-165 CD 2
Fezzan = Fazzān 164-165 GH 3

Fiambalá 104-105 C 10
Fiambalá, Río — 104-105 C 10
Fianarantsoa 172 J 6
Fichtelgebirge 118 EF 3
Ficksburg 174-175 GH 5
Ficuar 96-97 A 4
Fidalgo, Rio — 100-101 C 4
Fidelandia 100-101 D 10
Fidenza 122-123 D 3
Field 72-73 FG 1
Field, NM 76-77 A 5
Fielding 61 E 4
Field Museum 83 II b 1
Fier 122-123 H 5
Fier, Porțile de — 122-123 K 3
Fife Ness 119 E 3
Fīfī, Al- 164-165 J 6
Figalo, Cap — = Rā's Fīqālu 166-167 F 2
Figeac 120-121 J 6
Fighting Island 84 II b 3
Figig = Fijij 164-165 D 2
Figueira, Cachoeira — 98-99 J 9
Figueira da Foz 120-121 C 8
Figueiras 106-107 L 3
Figueras 120-121 J 7
Figuîg = Fijīj 164-165 D 2
Figuras, Serra das — 100-101 B 6
Fijāj, Shaṭṭ al- 166-167 L 2-3
Fiji 148-149 ab 2
Fiji Basin 156-157 H 6
Fiji Islands 148-149 ab 2
Fijīj 164-165 D 2
Fila = Vila 158-159 N 3
Filabres, Sierra de los — 120-121 F 10
Filadelfia [BR, Acre] 96-97 G 7
Filadélfia [BR, Goiás] 92-93 K 6
Filadelfia [PY] 111 D 2
Filadu 140 A 7
Filamana 168-169 CD 3
Filchner-Schelfeis 53 A 30-B 33
Filer, ID 66-67 F 4
Filiaşi 122-123 K 3
Filiátai 122-123 J 6
Filiatrá 122-123 J 7
Filicudi 122-123 F 6
Fili-Mazilovo, Moskva- 113 V b 3
Filingué 164-165 E 6
Filipevila = Sakīkdah 164-165 F 1
Filippiás 122-123 J 6
Filipstad 116-117 EF 8
Fillmore 61 G 6
Fillmore, CA 74-75 D 5
Fillmore, UT 74-75 G 3
Filyos çayı 136-137 E 2
Fimi 172 C 2
Finaalspan 170 V c 2

Financial District, New York-, NY 82 III bc 3
Finch 72-73 J 2
Finchley, London- 129 II b 1
Fındık 136-137 JK 4
Fındıklı 136-137 J 2
Findlay, OH 64-65 K 3
Fine Arts, Museum of — [USA, Boston] 84 I b 2
Fine Arts, Museum of — [USA, Houston] 85 III b 1
Fingal, ND 68-69 H 2
Finger, Cerro — 108-109 C 9
Finger Lake 62 C 1
Finger Lakes 64-65 L 3
Fingoè 172 F 5
Fingoland 174-175 GH 7
Finike 136-137 D 4
Finisterre, Cabo de — 120-121 BC 7
Fink Creek, AK 58-59 F 4
Finke 158-159 FG 5
Finkenkrug-Süd 130 III a 1
Finke River 158-159 G 5
Finland 116-117 K 7-M 4
Finland, MN 70-71 E 2
Finland, Gulf of — 114-115 N 4-O 3
Finlay Forks 60 EF 1
Finlay Mountains 76-77 B 7
Finlay Ranges 60 E 1
Finlay River 56-57 LM 6
Finley, ND 68-69 H 2
Finmark 70-71 F 1
Finnegan 61 BC 5
Finnis, Cape — 160 B 4
Finnmark 116-117 K 3-N 2
Finnmarksvidda 116-117 KL 3
Finn Mount 58-59 J 6
Finnskogene 116-117 E 7
Finnsnes 116-117 GH 3
Finschhafen 148-149 N 8
Finse 116-117 B 7
Finspång 116-117 FG 8
Finsteraarhorn 118 CD 5
Finsterwalde 118 FG 3
Finṭās, Jabal al- 173 B 6
Fiordland National Park 158-159 N 8-9
Fiordo Comau 108-109 C 4
Fiorito, Lomas de Zamora- 110 III b 2
Fiqāļu, Rā's — 166-167 F 2
Fırat nehri 134-135 D 3
Firebag River 61 C 2
Firebaugh, CA 74-75 C 4
Fire Boat Station 85 III b 2
Fire Island 58-59 M 6
Firenze 122-123 D 4
Fire River 70-71 HJ 1
Firesteel, SD 68-69 F 3
Firgān 166-167 K 2
Firindah 166-167 G 2
Firkessedougou = Ferkéssédougou 164-165 CD 7
Firmat 106-107 G 4
Firminópolis 102-103 GH 2
Firovo 124-125 J 5
Firoza 138-139 C 3
Fīrozābād 134-135 M 5
Fīrōzpur = Ferozepore 138-139 E 2
Firth of Clyde 119 D 4
Firth of Forth 119 EF 3
Firth of Lorne 119 CD 3
Firth of Tay 119 E 3
Firth River 58-59 R 2
Fīrūzābād [IR, Fārs] 134-135 G 5
Fīrūzābād [IR, Lorestān] 136-137 MN 6
Firvale 60 DE 3
Firyānah 166-167 L 2
Fischbek, Hamburg- 130 I a 2
Fischbeker Heide 130 I a 2
Fischteiche 130 II c 1
Fish Creek 58-59 LM 1
Fisher, MN 68-69 H 2
Fisher Bay 61 K 5
Fishermans Island 80-81 J 2
Fishermens Bend, Melbourne- 161 II b 1
Fisher Strait 56-57 U 5
Fishguard & Goodwick 119 D 5-6
Fishing Lake 61 G 5
Fishing Point 80-81 J 2
Fish Lake Valley 74-75 DE 4
Fish River 58-59 F 4
Fish River = Visrivier 174-175 B 3
Fisk, MO 78-79 D 2
Fiskåfjället 116-117 F 5
Fiske 61 D 5
Fiskenæsset = Qeqertarssuatsiaq 56-57 a 5
Fiskivötn 116-117 c 2
Fišt, gora — 126-127 J 5
Fitalancao 108-109 D 3
Fitchburg, MA 72-73 KL 3
Fittri, Lac — 164-165 H 6
Fitzgerald, GA 80-81 E 5
Fitz Hugh Sound 60 D 4
Fitzmaurice River 158-159 EF 2
Fitzpatrick 72-73 K 1
Fitz Roy 111 C 7
Fitzroy, Melbourne- 161 II b 1
Fitz Roy, Monte — 111 B 7
Fitzroy Crossing 158-159 DE 3
Fitzroy River [AUS, Queensland] 158-159 JK 4
Fitzroy River [AUS, Western Australia] 158-159 DE 3
Fitzwilliam Island 62 KL 4
Fitzwilliam Strait 56-57 NO 2
Fiume = Rijeka 122-123 F 3
Five Cowrie Creek 170 III b 2
Five Dunes 174-175 D 4
Five Miles Rapids 66-67 D 2
Fizi 172 E 2
Fizuli 126-127 N 7
Fkih 'Ben Ṣālaḥ = Al-Faqīh Bin Ṣālaḥ 166-167 C 3
Flå 116-117 C 7
Fladelfia 104-105 B 2
Flagler, CO 68-69 E 6
Flagstaff, AZ 64-65 D 4
Flagstaff Lake 72-73 L 2
Flagstaff Siphaqeni 172 EF 8
Flagstone 66-67 F 1
Flaherty Island 56-57 U 6
Flakensee 130 III cd 2
Flakstadøy 116-117 E 3
Flåm 116-117 B 7
Flamand = Arak 164-165 E 3
Flambeau Flowage 70-71 E 2
Flamborough Head 119 FG 4
Flamenco 104-105 A 10
Flamengo, Ponta do — 100-101 G 3
Flamengo, Serra do — 100-101 E 4
Fläming 118 F 2-3
Flaming Gorge Reservoir 66-67 J 5
Flamingo, FL 80-81 c 4
Flamingo, Teluk — 148-149 L 8
Flaminia, Via — 113 II b 1
Flanders 62 C 3
Flanders = Vlaanderen 120-121 J 3
Flandes 94-95 D 5
Flandreau, SD 68-69 H 3
Flanigan, NV 66-67 D 5
Flannan Isles 119 BC 2
Flasher, ND 68-69 F 2
Flat, AK 58-59 HJ 5
Flatey 116-117 b 2
Flateyri 116-117 ab 1
Flathead Indian Reservation 66-67 FG 2
Flathead Lake 64-65 CD 2
Flathead Mountains = Salish Mountains 66-67 F 1-2
Flathead River 66-67 F 1
Flat Island = Pulau Subi 150-151 G 11
Flatonia, TX 76-77 F 8
Flat River, MO 70-71 E 7
Flattery, Cape — [AUS] 158-159 J 2
Flattery, Cape — [USA] 66-67 A 1
Flat Top Mountain 80-81 F 2
Flaxman Island 58-59 P 1
Flax Pond 84 I c 2
Flaxton, ND 68-69 E 1
Flaxville, MT 68-69 D 1
Flèche, la — 120-121 GH 5
Flecheira, Serra da — 100-101 B 8
Fleetwood 119 E 5
Fleischhacker Zoo 83 II ab 2
Flekkefjord 116-117 AB 8
Fleming, CO 68-69 E 5
Flemingsburg, KY 72-73 E 5
Flemington, Melbourne- 161 II b 1
Flemington Racecourse 161 II b 1
Flen 116-117 G 8
Flensburg 118 DE 1
Flers 120-121 G 4
Flesher, MT 66-67 G 2
Fletcher, OK 76-77 EF 5
Fleur de Lys 63 HJ 2
Fleur de May, Lac — 63 D 2
Fleuve 168-169 B 1-2
Fleuve Saint-Laurent 56-57 W 8-9
Flinders Bay 158-159 BC 6
Flinders Island [AUS, Bass Strait] 158-159 J 7
Flinders Island [AUS, Great Australian Bight] 158-159 F 6
Flinders Range 158-159 G 6
Flinders River 158-159 H 3-4
Flin Flon 56-57 Q 7
Flint, MI 64-65 K 3
Flint [GB] 119 E 5
Flint [island] 156-157 K 6
Flintdale 62 G 2
Flint Hills 68-69 H 6-7
Flint River [USA, Georgia] 78-79 G 5
Flint River [USA, Michigan] 72-73 E 3
Flomaton, AL 78-79 F 5
Floodwood, MN 70-71 D 2
Flora 116-117 A 7
Flora, IL 70-71 F 6
Flora, OR 66-67 E 3
Florala, AL 78-79 F 5
Floral Park, NY 82 III de 2
Florânia 100-101 F 4
Floreana 92-93 AB 5
Floreana, Isla — 92-93 A 5
Florence, AL 64-65 J 5
Florence, AZ 74-75 H 6
Florence, CA 83 III c 2
Florence, CO 68-69 D 6
Florence, KS 68-69 H 6
Florence, OR 66-67 A 4
Florence, SC 64-65 L 5
Florence, SD 68-69 H 3
Florence, WI 70-71 F 3
Florence = Firenze 122-123 D 4
Florence Junction, AZ 74-75 H 6
Florencia [BOL] 104-105 C 2
Florencia [CO] 92-93 DE 4
Florencia [RA] 106-107 H 2
Florencia, La — 104-105 EF 9
Florencio Sánchez 106-107 J 4-5
Florencio Varela 110 III c 2
Florencio Varela-Gobernador Monteverde 110 III c 2
Florentino Ameghino 108-109 G 4
Florentino Ameghino, Embalse — 108-109 F 5
Flôres [BR] 100-101 EF 4
Flores [GCA] 64-65 J 8
Flores [RI] 148-149 H 8
Flores [ROU] 106-107 J 4
Flores, Arroyo de las — 106-107 GH 5-6
Flores, Buenos Aires- 110 III b 1
Flores, Isla de — 106-107 K 5
Flores, Las — [RA, Buenos Aires] 111 E 5
Flores, Las — [RA, Salta] 104-105 E 9
Flores, Las — [RA, San Juan] 106-107 C 3
Florescência 98-99 D 9
Florescênia 96-97 G 6
Flores Island 60 D 5
Flores Sea 148-149 GH 8
Floressee 148-149 GH 8
Floresta, Buenos Aires- 110 III b 1
Floresta Amazônica 92-93 E-H 6
Florešty 126-127 CD 3
Floresville, TX 76-77 EF 8
Floriano 92-93 L 6
Floriano Peixoto 98-99 DE 9
Florianópolis 111 G 3
Florida, NM 76-77 A 6
Florida [C] 88-89 GH 4
Florida [CO] 94-95 C 6
Florida [ROU, administrative unit] 106-107 JK 4
Florida [ROU, place] 111 E 4
Florida [USA] 64-65 K 5-6
Florida [ZA] 170 V a 1
Florida, Cape — 80-81 cd 4
Florida, La — [CO, Cundinamarca] 91 III a 2
Florida, La — [CO, Nariño] 94-95 C 7
Florida, La — [PE] 96-97 F 3
Florida, Straits of — 64-65 K 7-L 6
Florida, Vicente López- 110 III b 1
Florida Bay 64-65 K 7
Floridablanca 94-95 E 4
Florida City, FL 80-81 c 4
Florida Island 148-149 jk 6
Florida Keys 64-65 K 6-7
Florido, Río — 76-77 B 8-9
Florien, LA 78-79 C 5
Flŏrina 122-123 J 5
Florissant, MO 70-71 EF 6
Flottbek, Hamburg- 130 I a 1
Flotten Lake 61 D 3
Flourtown, PA 84 III b 1
Flowerpot Island 72-73 F 2
Flower's Cove 63 HJ 2
Flower Station 72-73 H 2
Floyd, NM 76-77 C 5
Floyd, VA 80-81 F 2
Floyd, Mount — 74-75 G 5
Floydada, TX 76-77 D 5-6
Floyd River 70-71 BC 4
Flughafen Hamburg-Fuhlsbüttel 130 I ab 1
Flughafen München-Riem 130 II c 2
Flughafen Tegel 130 III b 1
Flughafen Tempelhof 130 III b 2
Flughafen Wien-Schwechat 113 I c 2
Flughafen Zürich-Kloten 128 IV b 1
Flugplatz Aspern 113 I c 2
Flugplatz Gatow 130 III a 2
Flume Creek, AK 58-59 Q 4
Flumendosa 122-123 C 6
Flushing = Vlissingen 120-121 J 3
Flushing, New York-, NY 82 III d 2
Flushing Airport 82 III d 2
Flushing Meadow Park 82 III c 2
Flying Fish, Cape — 53 BC 26
Fly River 148-149 M 8
F. M. Butzel Field 84 II ab 2
Fô 168-169 D 3
Foam Lake 61 G 5
Foça [TR] 136-137 B 3
Foča [YU] 122-123 H 4
Foca, Punta — 108-109 G 6
Foch 60 E 4
Fo-chan = Foshan 142-143 L 7
Fochi 164-165 H 5
Fochville 174-175 G 4
Focşani 122-123 M 3
F'odorovka [SU, Kazachskaja SSR] 124-125 ST 8
F'odorovka [SU, Rossijskaja SFSR] 124-125 RS 7
Fogang 146-147 D 10
Fòggia 122-123 F 5
Fogo [Cape Verde] 204-205 E 7
Fogo [CDN] 63 J 3
Fogo Island 56-57 a 8
Föhr 118 D 1
Foix [F, landscape] 120-121 H 7
Foix [F, place] 120-121 H 7
Fo-kang = Fogang 146-147 D 10
Fokino 124-125 K 7
Folcroft, PA 84 III b 2
Folda [N, Nordland] 116-117 F 4
Folda [N, Nord-Trøndelag] 116-117 D 5
Folégandros 122-123 L 7
Foley, AL 78-79 F 5
Foley, MN 70-71 CD 3
Foleyet 62 K 2
Foley Island 56-57 V 4
Folgefonni 116-117 B 7-8
Folger, AK 58-59 JK 5
Foligno 122-123 E 4
Folkestone 119 G 6
Folkston, GA 80-81 E 5
Folldal 116-117 CD 6
Follett, TX 76-77 D 4
Folsom, CA 74-75 C 3
Folsom, NM 76-77 C 4
Folsom, PA 84 III b 2
Folteşti 122-123 MN 3
Fombonou 168-169 F 2
Fominskoje [SU ↗ Vologda] 124-125 O 4
Fonda, IA 70-71 C 4
Fonda, NY 72-73 J 3
Fondaq = Al-Funduq 166-167 D 2
Fond-du-Lac 56-57 PQ 6
Fond du Lac, WI 64-65 J 3
Fond du Lac Indian Reservation 70-71 D 2
Fond du Lac Mountains 70-71 E 2
Fond du Lac River 56-57 Q 6
Fondeadero Mazarredo 108-109 F 6
Fondi 122-123 E 5
Fondouk = Lakhḍarīyah 166-167 H 1
Fonsagrada 120-121 D 7
Fonseca [CO] 94-95 E 2
Fonseca [PE] 96-97 F 3
Fonseca, Golfo de — 64-65 J 9
Fontainebleau [F] 120-121 J 4
Fontainebleau [ZA] 170 V a 1
Fontana, Lago — 108-109 D 5
Fonte Boa 92-93 F 5
Fonteneau, Lac — 63 F 2
Fontenelle Reservoir 66-67 HJ 4
Fontibón 91 III ab 2
Fontur 116-117 fg 1
Fonualei 148-149 c 2
Foochow = Fengdu 142-143 K 5-6
Foochow = Fujian 142-143 MN 6
Foochow = Fuzhou 142-143 MN 6
Foothills 60 J 3
Footscray, Melbourne- 161 II b 1
Foping 146-147 AB 5
Foraker, Mount — 56-57 F 5
Forbes 158-159 J 6
Forbes, ND 68-69 G 3
Forbes, Mount — 60 J 4
Forbesganj 138-139 L 4
Forbes Island = Kawre Kyūn 150-151 B 7
Ford, KS 68-69 G 7
Ford, KY 70-71 H 7
Ford, Cape — 158-159 E 2
Ford City, CA 74-75 D 5
Ford City, Chicago-, IL 83 II a 2
Førde 116-117 AB 7
Ford Lake 74-75 F 6
Ford Plant 84 II b 3
Ford River 70-71 G 2-3
Fords Bridge 158-159 HJ 5
Fordsburg, Johannesburg- 170 V b 2
Fordsville, KY 70-71 G 7
Fordyce, AR 78-79 C 4
Forécariah 164-165 B 7
Forel, Mont — 56-57 d 4
Förelles-Attily 129 I d 3
Forest, MS 78-79 E 4
Forest, OH 72-73 E 4
Forest [CDN] 72-73 E 3
Foresta 100-101 E 5
Forestal, La — 111 E 2
Forestburg 61 BC 4
Forest Center, MN 70-71 E 2
Forest City, IA 70-71 D 4
Forest City, NC 80-81 EF 3
Forest Heights, MD 82 II ab 2
Forest Hills Cemetery 84 I b 3
Forestier Peninsula 160 d 3
Forest Lake, MN 70-71 D 3
Forest Oaks, Houston-, TX 85 III bc 2
Forest Park, GA 85 II bc 3
Forest Park [USA, New York] 82 III c 2
Forest Park [USA, San Francisco] 83 II a 1
Forest Park Cemetery 85 III b 2
Forest View, IL 83 II a 2
Forestville 63 B 3
Forestville, MD 82 II b 2
Forestville, Parc provincial de — 63 B 3
Forest West, Houston-, TX 85 III b 1
Forêt de Saint-Germain 129 I b 2
Forêt de Soignes 128 II b 2
Forêt Réserve 170 IV a 1
Forez, Monts du — 120-121 J 6
Forfar 119 E 3
Forgan, OK 76-77 D 4
Fork Mountain, TN 78-79 G 2
Forks, WA 66-67 A 1-2
Forlandsundet 116-117 hj 5
Forlì 122-123 DE 3
Forman, ND 68-69 H 2
Formentera 120-121 H 9
Formentor, Cabo — 120-121 J 8
Formiga 92-93 K 9
Formile Run 82 II a 2
Formosa [BR, Bahia] 100-101 E 5
Formosa [BR, Goiás] 92-93 K 8
Formosa [BR, Paraná] 102-103 F 6
Formosa [BR, Piauí] 100-101 C 4
Formosa [RA, administrative unit] 104-105 F 8-G 9
Formosa [RA, place] 111 E 3
Formosa = Taiwan 142-143 N 7
Formosa, Ilha de — 168-169 AB 3
Formosa, Serra — 92-93 HJ 7
Formosa Bay 171 E 3
Formosa Strait = Taiwan Haihsia 142-143 M 7-N 6
Formoso 98-99 O 10
Formoso, Rio — 100-101 B 7
Formoso de Rio Preto 100-101 B 6
Fornæs 116-117 D 9
Foro Romano 113 II b 2
Forqlôs = Furqlūs 136-137 G 5
Forrest, IL 70-71 F 5
Forrest [AUS] 158-159 E 6
Forrest [CDN] 61 J 5
Forrest City, AR 78-79 D 3
Forrester Island 58-59 vw 9
Forsan, TX 76-77 D 6
Forsayth 158-159 H 3
Forsmo 116-117 G 6
Forssa 116-117 K 7
Forstenried, München- 130 II ab 2
Forstenrieder Park 130 II a 2
Forster 160 L 4
Forst Erkner 130 III c 2
Forst Kasten 130 II a 2
Forst Klövensteen 130 I a 1
Forsyth, GA 80-81 E 4
Forsyth, MI 70-71 G 2
Forsyth, MT 68-69 C 2
Forsyth, Isla — 108-109 B 5
Fort 'Abbās 138-139 D 3
Fort Albany 56-57 U 7
Fortaleza [BOL] 104-105 C 3
Fortaleza [BR, Acre] 96-97 E 6
Fortaleza [BR, Amazonas] 98-99 C 8
Fortaleza [BR, Ceará] 92-93 M 5
Fortaleza [BR, Rondônia] 98-99 G 10
Fortaleza, Paso de la — 96-97 C 7
Fortaleza, Río de la — 96-97 C 7
Fortaleza do Ituxi 98-99 EF 8
Fortaleza dos Nogueiras 100-101 A 4
Fort Apache Indian Reservation 74-75 HJ 5
Fort-Archambault = Sarh 164-165 H 7
Fort Assiniboine 60 K 2
Fort Atkinson, WI 70-71 F 4
Fort Bayard = Zhanjiang 142-143 L 7
Fort Beaufort 174-175 G 7
Fort Belknap Agency, MT 68-69 B 1
Fort Belknap Indian Reservation 68-69 B 1
Fort Benton, MT 66-67 H 2
Fort Berthold Indian Reservation 68-69 EF 2
Fort Black 61 DE 3
Fort Bragg, CA 74-75 AB 3
Fort Bragg, NC 80-81 G 3
Fort Branch, IN 70-71 G 6
Fort Bridger, WY 66-67 HJ 5
Fort Bruce = Pībōr 164-165 L 7
Fort Brussaux = Markounda 164-165 H 7
Fort-Charlet = Jannah 164-165 FG 4
Fort Chimo 56-57 X 6
Fort Chipewyan 56-57 OP 6
Fort Cobb, OK 76-77 E 5
Fort Collins, CO 64-65 EF 3
Fort-Coulonge 72-73 H 2
Fort-Crampel = Kaga Bandoro 164-165 HJ 7
Fort-Dauphin = Faradofay 172 J 7
Fort Davis, TX 76-77 C 7
Fort Defiance, AZ 74-75 J 5
Fort-de-France 64-65 O 9
Fort de Kock = Bukittinggi 148-149 CD 7
Fort-de-Polignac = Illizi 166-167 L 6
Fort Deposit, AL 78-79 F 4-5
Fort-de-Possel = Possel 164-165 H 7
Fort Dodge, IA 64-65 GH 3
Fort Dupont Park 82 II b 2
Fort Duquesne = Pittsburg, Pa. 64-65 KL 3
Forte 100-101 A 8
Forteau 63 H 2
Forte Coimbra = Coimbra 102-103 D 3
Forte de Copacabana 110 I bc 2
Fort Edward 174-175 HJ 2
Fort Edward, NY 72-73 K 3
Forte Lami = N'Djamena 164-165 GH 6
Fort Erie 72-73 G 3
Fortescue River 158-159 C 4
Forte Veneza 98-99 D 8
Fort Fairfield, ME 72-73 MN 1
Fort-Flatters = Burj 'Umar Idrīs 164-165 EF 3
Fort Frances 56-57 S 8
Fort Fraser 60 EF 2
Fort Fred Steele, WY 68-69 C 5
Fort Gaines, GA 78-79 G 5
Fort-Gardel = Zaouatallaz 164-165 F 3-4
Fort George River 56-57 V 7
Fort Gibson, OK 76-77 G 5
Fort Gibson Lake 76-77 G 4
Fort Glenn, AK 58-59 mn 4
Fort Good Hope 56-57 L 4
Fort Grahame 60 E 1
Fort Grey 158-159 H 5
Forth, Firth of — 119 EF 3
Fort Hall, ID 66-67 G 4
Fort Hall = Murang'a 172 G 2
Fort Hall Indian Reservation 66-67 GH 4
Fort Harrison = Hsadôn 141 EF 3
Forthassa-Rharbia = Furtāsāt al-Gharbīyah 166-167 F 3
Fort Hertz = Pūdāō 148-149 C 1
Fort Hope 62 E 2
Fort Huachuca, AZ 74-75 H 7
Fortim 100-101 EF 3
Fortín, El — 106-107 F 3
Fortín Aroma 102-103 B 4
Fortín Ávalos Sánchez 102-103 BC 5
Fortín Ayacucho 102-103 BC 3
Fortín Ballivián 102-103 AB 5
Fortín Capitán Demattei 102-103 B 5
Fortín Capitán O. R. Ortellado 102-103 C 5
Fortín Carlos Antonio López 102-103 C 4
Fortín Coronel Hermosa 102-103 BC 5
Fortín Coronel Martínez 102-103 C 5
Fortín 1 de Mayo 106-107 B 7
Fortín Falcón 111 DE 2
Fortín Florida 102-103 C 4
Fortín Galpón 102-103 C 3
Fortín Garrapatal 102-103 B 4
Fortín General Aquino 102-103 C 6
Fortín General Bruguez 102-103 C 6
Fortín General Delgado 102-103 C 6
Fortín General Díaz [PY, Boquerón] 102-103 B 5
Fortín General Díaz [PY, Olimpo] 102-103 CD 4
Fortín General Mendoza 102-103 B 4
Fortín General Pando 102-103 C 3
Fortín Hernandarias 102-103 AB 4
Fortín Lavalle 111 D 3
Fortín Linares 102-103 B 5
Fortín Madrejón 111 D 2
Fortín Mayor Rodríguez 102-103 B 5
Fortín Muariscal López 102-103 C 5
Fortín Nueva Asunción 102-103 B 4
Fortín Olavarría 106-107 F 5
Fortín Orihuela 102-103 C 5
Fortín Paredes 104-105 G 6
Fortín Pilcomayo 111 DE 2
Fortín Príncipe de Beira = Príncipe da Beira 92-93 G 7
Fortín Puente Ayala 102-103 C 5
Fortín Ravelo 92-93 G 8
Fortín Río Verde 102-103 C 5
Fortín Rojas Silva 102-103 C 5
Fortín Sargento Primero Leyes 104-105 G 9
Fortín Soledad 104-105 F 9
Fortín Sorpresa 102-103 C 5-6
Fortín Suárez Arana 92-93 G 8
Fortín Teniente Martínez 102-103 C 4
Fortín Toledo 102-103 B 5
Fortín Uno 111 CD 5
Fortín Valois Rivarola 102-103 BC 5
Fortín Zenteno 102-103 BC 5
Fort Jackson 174-175 GH 7
Fort Jaco 128 II b 2
Fort Jameson = Chipata 172 F 4
Fort Johnston = Mangoche 172 G 4
Fort Jones, CA 66-67 B 5
Fort Kent 61 C 3
Fort Kent, ME 72-73 M 1
Fort Klamath, OR 66-67 BC 4
Fort Knox, KY 64-65 J 4
Fort-Lallemand = Burj al-Aḥmad 166-167 K 4
Fort-Lamy = N'Djamena 164-165 GH 6
Fort-Laperrine = Tamanrāsat 164-165 EF 4
Fort Laramie, WY 68-69 D 4
Fort Lauderdale, FL 64-65 KL 6
Fort Lee, NJ 82 III c 1
Fort Lewis, WA 66-67 B 2
Fort Liard 56-57 M 5
Fort Liberté 88-89 KL 5
Fort Lupton, CO 68-69 D 5
Fort MacDowell Indian Reservation 74-75 H 6
Fort MacKay 61 BC 2
Fort-Mac-Mahon = Burj Ban Būlʿīd 164-165 E 3
Fort MacMurray 56-57 O 6
Fort MacNair 82 II a 2
Fort MacPherson 56-57 JK 4
Fort Madison, IA 64-65 H 3
Fort Maguire 172 FG 4
Fort Mahan Park 82 II b 2
Fort Manning = Mchinji 172 F 4
Fort Meade, FL 80-81 bc 3
Fort Mill, SC 80-81 F 3
Fort-Miribel = Burj Mahībal 166-167 H 5
Fort Mohave Indian Reservation 74-75 F 5
Fort Morgan, AL 78-79 EF 5
Fort Morgan, CO 68-69 E 5
Fort Munro 138-139 B 2-3
Fort Myer, Arlington-, VA 82 II a 2
Fort Myers, FL 64-65 K 6
Fort Nassau = Albany, NY 64-65 LM 3
Fort-National = Arb'ā Nāyat Īrāthan 166-167 J 1
Fort Nelson 56-57 M 6
Fort Nelson River 56-57 M 6
Fort Norman 56-57 L 4-5
Fort Ogden, FL 80-81 c 3
Fort Payne, AL 78-79 G 3
Fort Peck, MT 68-69 C 1
Fort Peck Indian Reservation 68-69 CD 1
Fort Peck Lake 64-65 E 2
Fort Pierce, FL 64-65 KL 6
Fort Pierre, SD 68-69 F 3
Fort Plain, NY 72-73 J 3
Fort Portal 172 F 1
Fort Providence 56-57 N 5
Fort Qu'Appelle 61 FG 5
Fort Randolph 64-65 b 2
Fort Reliance 56-57 P 5
Fort Resolution 56-57 O 5
Fortress Mountain 66-67 HJ 3
Fort Richardson, AK 58-59 N 6
Fort Ripley, MN 70-71 CD 2
Fort Rock, OR 66-67 C 4
Fort Rosebery = Mansa 172 E 4
Fort Ross, CA 74-75 B 3
Fort-Rousset = Owando 172 C 2
Fort Rupert 56-57 V 7
Fort-Saint = Burj al-Ḥaṭṭabah 164-165 F 2
Fort Saint James 56-57 M 7
Fort Saint John 56-57 M 6
Fort Sandeman = Appozai 134-135 K 4
Fort Saskatchewan 56-57 NO 7
Fort Scott, KS 70-71 C 7
Fort Selkirk 56-57 JK 5
Fort Sendeman = Appozai 134-135 K 4
Fort-Ševčenko 126-127 OP 4
Fort Severn 56-57 T 6
Fort Seward, CA 66-67 B 5
Fort Sherman 64-65 ab 2
Fort Sibut = Sibut 164-165 H 7
Fort Simpson 56-57 M 5
Fort Smith 56-57 OP 5
Fort Smith, AR 64-65 H 4
Fort Stanton Park 82 II b 2
Fort Steele 60 K 5
Fort Stockton, TX 64-65 F 5
Fort Sumner, NM 76-77 B 5
Fort Supply, OK 76-77 E 4
Fort Thomas, AZ 74-75 HJ 6
Fort Thompson, SD 68-69 FG 3
Fort Totten Indian Reservation 68-69 G 2
Fort Towson, OK 76-77 G 5
Fort-Trinquet = Bīr Umm Qarayn 164-165 B 3
Fortuna 106-107 E 5
Fortuna, CA 66-67 AB 5
Fortuna, ND 68-69 E 1
Fortuna Lodge = Marshall, AK 58-59 FG 6
Fortune 63 HJ 4
Fortune Bay 56-57 Z 8
Fort Valley, GA 80-81 DE 4
Fort Vermilion 56-57 NO 6
Fort Victoria = Nyanda 172 F 5-6
Fortville, IN 70-71 H 6
Fort Walton Beach, FL 78-79 F 5
Fort Washakie, WY 68-69 B 4
Fort Wayne, IN 64-65 JK 3
Fort Wayne Military Museum 84 II b 3
Fort Wellington 98-99 K 1
Fort William [IND] 154 II b 2
Fort Wingate, NM 74-75 J 5
Fort Worth, TX 64-65 G 5
Fort Yates, ND 68-69 F 2
Fortymile 58-59 RS 4
Fortymile, Middle Fork — 58-59 Q 4
Fortymile, North Fork — 58-59 QR 4
Fortymile, West Fork — 58-59 Q 5
Fortymile River 58-59 R 4
Fort Yukon, AK 56-57 GH 4
Forum 83 III bc 2
Forward 61 F 6
Forzado, El — 106-107 D 4
Fosca 94-95 E 5
Fosforitnaja 124-125 ST 4
Foshan 142-143 L 7
Fosheim Peninsula 56-57 U 1-2
Fosna 116-117 CD 6
Foso 168-169 E 4
Fossano 122-123 BC 3
Fossberg 116-117 BC 7
Fossil, OR 66-67 C 3
Fosston, MN 70-71 BC 2
Foster 72-73 K 2
Foster River 61 F 2
Fostoria, OH 72-73 E 4
Fotan 146-147 FG 9
Foucauld = Awlād Abū 166-167 BC 3
Foucheng = Fucheng 146-147 F 3
Fougamou 172 B 2
Fougères 120-121 G 4
Fouke, AR 78-79 C 4
Foula 119 E 1
Foul Bay = Khalīj Umm al-Kataf 173 D 6
Foul Point = Pahan Tuḍuwa 140 E 6
Foulpointe = Mahavelona 172 JK 5
Foulwind, Cape — 158-159 NO 8
Fouman = Fūman 136-137 N 4
Foumban 164-165 G 7
Foum Taṭāouîn = Taṭāwīn 164-165 G 2
Foundiougne 164-165 A 6
Fountain, CO 68-69 D 6
Fountain Creek 68-69 D 6
Fouping = Fuping 146-147 E 2
Fourât, El- = Al-Furāt 136-137 H 5
Fourche Mountains 76-77 GH 5
Fourchette, MT 68-69 BC 2
Fourchu 63 FG 5
Four Corners, WY 68-69 D 3-4
Fourcroy, Cape — 158-159 E 2
Fouriesburg 174-175 H 5
Four Mountains, Islands of — 58-59 lm 4
Fournier, Lac — 63 D 2
Fourou 168-169 D 3
Fourqueux 129 I b 2
Fourteen Mile Point 70-71 F 2
Fourteen Streams = Veertien Strome 174-175 F 4-5
Foushan = Fushan 146-147 C 4
Fouta Djalon 164-165 B 6
Foux, Cap-à- 88-89 K 5
Foveaux Strait 158-159 N 9
Fowl Cay 88-89 H 2
Fowler, CO 68-69 D 6
Fowler, IN 70-71 G 5
Fowler, MI 70-71 H 4
Fowler, MT 66-67 H 1
Fowlers Bay 158-159 F 6
Fowlerton, TX 76-77 E 8
Fowling = Fengdu 142-143 K 5-6
Fowl Meadow Reservation 84 I b 3
Fowning = Funing 142-143 MN 5
Fox, AK 58-59 O 4
Fox Bay 63 F 3
Fox Chase, Philadelphia-, PA 84 III c 1
Fox Chase Manor, PA 84 III c 1
Fox Creek 60 J 2
Foxe Basin 56-57 UV 4
Foxe Channel 56-57 UV 4-5
Foxe Peninsula 56-57 V 5
Fox Islands 52 D 35
Foxpark, WY 68-69 CD 5

Fox River [USA, Illinois] 70-71 F 5
Fox River [USA, Wisconsin] 70-71 FG 3
Foxton 161 F 5
Fox Valley 61 D 5
Foxworth, MS 78-79 DE 5
Foye 168-169 B 3
Foyle, Lough — 119 C 4
Foyn, Cape — 53 C 30
Foynes 119 B 5
Foynøya 116-117 mn 4
Foz de Breu 98-99 B 9
Foz do Aripuanã = Novo Aripuanã 92-93 G 6
Foz do Embira = Envira 92-93 EF 6
Foz do Iguaçu 111 F 3
Foz do Jurupari 98-99 CD 8
Foz do Jutaí 98-99 E 6
Foz do Riozinho 92-93 E 6
Foz do Tarauacá 96-97 G 5

Frado, Monte do — 102-103 K 5
Fraga [RA] 106-107 E 4
Fragua, La — 111 D 3
Fraile Muerto 106-107 K 4
Frailes, Cordillera de los — 104-105 CD 6
Framnesfjella 53 C 7
Franca [BR, Bahia] 100-101 D 6
Franca [BR, São Paulo] 92-93 K 9
Francavilla Fontana 122-123 GH 5
France 120-121 H 4-K 6
Francês, Pico — 108-109 E 10
Frances Peak 66-67 J 3-4
Franceville 172 B 2
Franche-Comté 120-121 KL 5
Franchetti 166-167 G 2
Francia 106-107 J 4
Francis 61 G 5
Francis Case, Lake — 64-65 FG 3
Francisco Beltrão 102-103 F 6-7
Francisco Borges 106-107 J 2-3
Francisco de Orellana 96-97 EF 3
Francisco Escárcega 86-87 P 8
Francisco I. Madero [MEX ↗ Torreón] 76-77 C 10
Francisco I. Madero [MEX ↗ Victoria de Durango] 86-87 H 5
Francisco Madero 106-107 FG 5
Francisco Magnano 106-107 F 5
Francis M. Law Park 85 III b 2
Francistown 172 E 6
Franco, Serra do — 100-101 E 3-4
Franco da Rocha 102-103 J 5
François 63 H 4
François, Le — 88-89 Q 7
François Joseph, Chutes — 172 C 3
François Lake 60 DE 3
Franconia, VA 82 II a 2
Franconian Alb = Fränkische Alb 118 E 3-4
Franconville 129 I b 2
Francquihaven = Ilebo 172 D 2
Francs Peak 68-69 B 3-4
Frankenwald 118 E 3
Frankford, Philadelphia-, PA 84 III c 1
Frankfort 174-175 H 4
Frankfort, IN 70-71 G 5
Frankfort, KS 68-69 H 6
Frankfort, KY 64-65 K 4
Frankfort, MI 70-71 G 3
Frankfort = Frankfurt am Main 118 D 3
Frankfurt am Main 118 D 3
Frankfurt am Main-Berkersheim 128 III b 1
Frankfurt am Main-Bockenheim 128 III a 1
Frankfurt am Main-Bonames 128 III ab 1
Frankfurt am Main-Eckenheim 128 III b 1
Frankfurt am Main-Eschersheim 128 III a 1
Frankfurt am Main-Fechenheim 128 III b 1
Frankfurt am Main-Ginnheim 128 III a 1
Frankfurt am Main-Goldstein 128 III a 1
Frankfurt am Main-Griesheim 128 III a 1
Frankfurt am Main-Harheim 128 III b 1
Frankfurt am Main-Hausen 128 III a 1
Frankfurt am Main-Kalbach 128 III a 1
Frankfurt am Main-Nied 128 III a 1
Frankfurt am Main-Nieder Erlenbach 128 III b 1
Frankfurt am Main-Niederrad 128 III a 1
Frankfurt am Main-Niederursel 128 III a 1
Frankfurt am Main-Oberrad 128 III b 1
Frankfurt am Main-Preungesheim 128 III b 1
Frankfurt am Main-Riederwald 128 III b 1
Frankfurt am Main-Rödelheim 128 III a 1
Frankfurt am Main-Sachsenhausen 128 III ab 1
Frankfurt am Main-Schwanheim 128 III a 1
Frankfurt am Main-Seckbach 128 III b 1
Frankfurt am Main-Sindlingen 128 III a 1
Frankfurt am Main-Sossenheim 128 III a 1
Frankfurt am Main-Unterliederbach 128 III a 1
Frankfurt am Main-Zeilsheim 128 III a 1
Frankfurter Stadtwald 128 III a 1, b 1
Frankfurt/Oder 118 G 2
Fränkische Alb 118 E 3-4
Frankland, Cape — 160 c 1
Franklin 174-175 H 6
Franklin, AK 58-59 QR 4
Franklin, GA 78-79 G 4
Franklin, IN 70-71 GH 6
Franklin, KY 78-79 F 2
Franklin, LA 78-79 D 6
Franklin, MO 70-71 D 6
Franklin, NC 80-81 E 3
Franklin, NE 68-69 G 5
Franklin, NH 72-73 L 3
Franklin, OH 72-73 DE 5
Franklin, PA 72-73 G 4
Franklin, TN 78-79 F 3
Franklin, TX 76-77 F 7
Franklin, VA 80-81 H 2
Franklin, WV 72-73 G 5
Franklin, District of — 56-57 N-V 3
Franklin, Point — 58-59 H 1
Franklin Bay 56-57 L 3-4
Franklin Canyon Reservoir 83 III b 1
Franklin Delano Roosevelt Lake 64-65 C 2
Franklin D. Roosevelt Park 84 III b 2
Franklin Island 53 B 17-18
Franklin Mountains [CDN] 56-57 L 4-M 5
Franklin Mountains [USA] 58-59 P 2
Franklin Park 84 I b 3
Franklin Park, VA 82 II a 1
Franklin Roosevelt Park, Johannesburg- 170 V a 1
Franklin Strait 56-57 R 3
Franklinton, LA 78-79 DE 5
Franklinton, NC 80-81 G 2
Franklinville, NY 72-73 GH 3
Franklyn, Mount — 161 E 6
Frannie, WY 68-69 B 3
Franschhoek 174-175 C 7
Fransfontein 172 BC 6
Franz 70-71 H 1
Franz Josef Land = zemľa Franz Joseph 132-133 H 2-M 1
Franz Joseph, zemľa — 132-133 H-M 2
Frasca, Capo de — 122-123 BC 6
Frascati 122-123 E 5
Fraser Basin 60 EF 2
Fraserburg 172 D 8
Fraserburgh 119 EF 3
Fraserburgweg = Leeu Gamka 174-175 D 7
Fraserdale 62 KL 2
Fraser Island = Great Sandy Island 158-159 KL 4-5
Fraser Lake [CDN, lake] 60 E 2
Fraser Lake [CDN, place] 60 E 3
Fraser Plateau 56-57 M 7
Fraser Range 158-159 D 6
Fraser River 56-57 MN 7
Frauenkirche 130 II b 2
Frauental 128 IV a 2
Fray Bentos 111 E 4
Fray Luis Beltrán 106-107 E 7
Fray Marcos 106-107 JK 5
Fraysât, Bin al- 166-167 E 3
Frazer, MT 68-69 CD 1
Freda, MI 70-71 F 2
Frederic, WI 70-71 D 3
Frederica 116-117 CD 10
Frederick, MD 72-73 H 5
Frederick, OK 76-77 E 5
Frederick, SD 68-69 G 3
Fredericksburg, TX 76-77 E 7
Fredericksburg, VA 72-73 GH 5
Frederick Sound 58-59 vw 8
Fredericktown, MO 70-71 EF 7
Frederico Westphalen 106-107 L 1
Fredericton 56-57 X 8
Frederikshåb = Pâmiut 56-57 ab 5
Frederikshamn = Hamina 116-117 M 7
Frederikshavn 116-117 D 9
Frederiksted 88-89 O 6
Fredersdorf [DDR, Frankfurt] 130 III cd 1
Fredersdorf-Nord 130 III c 1
Fredonia 94-95 D 5
Fredonia, AZ 74-75 G 4
Fredonia, KS 70-71 BC 7
Fredonia, NY 72-73 G 3
Fredonyer Peak 66-67 C 5
Fredrikstad 116-117 D 8
Freeburg, MO 70-71 DE 6
Freedom, OK 76-77 E 4
Freel Peak 74-75 CD 3
Freels, Cape — 63 K 3
Freeman River 60 K 2
Freemansundet 116-117 l 5
Freeport 88-89 G 1
Freeport, IL 70-71 F 4
Freeport, TX 76-77 G 8
Freer 86-87 L 4
Freer, TX 76-77 E 9
Free Soil, MI 70-71 GH 3
Freetown 164-165 B 7
Freewater, OR 66-67 D 3
Freeway Manor, Houston-, TX 85 III bc 2
Freezeout Mountains 68-69 C 4
Fregenal de la Sierra 120-121 D 9
Freguesia, Rio de Janeiro- [BR ↑ Rio de Janeiro] 110 I bc 1
Freguesia, Rio de Janeiro- [BR ↑ Rio de Janeiro] 110 I a 2
Freiberg 118 F 3
Freiburg im Breisgau 118 C 4-5
Freie Universität Berlin 130 III b 2
Freimann, München- 130 II b 1
Freire 111 B 5
Freirina 106-107 B 2
Freising 118 E 4
Freistadt 118 G 4
Fréjus 120-121 L 7
Fremantle, Perth- 158-159 BC 6
Fremont, CA 74-75 C 4
Fremont, MI 70-71 GH 4
Fremont, NE 64-65 G 3
Fremont, OH 72-73 E 4
Fremont Island 66-67 G 5
Fremont River 74-75 H 3
French, NM 76-77 B 4
Frenchburg, KY 72-73 E 6
French Guiana 92-93 J 4
French Island 160 G 7
French Lick, IN 70-71 G 6
Frenchman, NV 74-75 D 3
Frenchman Bay 72-73 MN 2
Frenchman Creek 68-69 EF 5
Frenchman River 68-69 B 1
Frenchmans Cap 160 bc 3
French Shore 56-57 Z 7-8
French Somaliland = Djibouti 164-165 N 6
Frenda = Firindah 166-167 G 2
Frentones, Los — 111 D 3
Fresco, Rio — 98-99 N 8
Freshfield, Cape — 53 C 16
Fresh Pond 84 I ab 2
Fresia 108-109 C 3
Fresnes 129 I c 2
Fresnillo de Gonzalez Echeverria 86-87 J 6
Fresno, CA 64-65 BC 4
Fresno [CO] 94-95 D 5
Fresno Peak 76-77 BC 8
Fresno Reservoir 68-69 AB 1
Frette, la — 129 I b 2
Freycinet Peninsula 158-159 J 8
Freyre 106-107 F 3
Fria 164-165 B 6
Fría, La — 92-93 E 3
Friant, CA 74-75 D 4
Friar Point, MS 78-79 D 3
Frias 111 CD 3
Fribourg 118 C 5
Friday Harbor, WA 66-67 B 1
Fridenfeld = Komsomoľskoje 126-127 N 1
Friedenau, Berlin- 130 III b 2
Friedhof Altona 130 I a 1
Friedrichsfelde 174-175 AB 1-2
Friedrichsfelde, Berlin- 130 III c 1-2
Friedrichshafen 118 DE 5
Friedrichshain, Berlin- 130 III b 1
Friedrichstrasse 130 III b 1
Friend, KS 68-69 F 6
Friern Barnet, London- 129 II b 1
Fries, VA 80-81 F 2
Frijoles 64-65 b 2
Frio, Kaap — 172 B 5
Friona, TX 76-77 C 5
Frisco City, AL 78-79 F 5
Frisco Mountain 74-75 G 3
Frisia 106-107 E 5
Fritch, TX 76-77 D 5
Fritjof Nansen Land = zemľa Franz Joseph 132-133 H-M 2
Friuli-Venèzia Giulia 122-123 E 2
Fr. Madero 106-107 FG 5
Fr. Magnano 106-107 F 5
Frobisher 68-69 EF 1
Frobisher Bay [CDN, bay] 56-57 X 5
Frobisher Bay [CDN, place] 56-57 X 5
Frobisher Lake 61 DE 2
Frog Lake 61 C 4
Frohavet 116-117 C 5-6
Frohnau, Berlin- 130 III b 1
Froid, MT 68-69 D 1
Frolovo 126-127 L 2
Fromberg, MT 68-69 B 3
Frome 119 E 6
Frome, Lake — 158-159 GH 6
Frome Downs 158-159 GH 6
Fronteiras 92-93 L 6
Frontera 64-65 H 8
Frontera, Punta — 86-87 O 8
Frontignan 120-121 JK 7
Frontino 94-95 C 4
Front Range 64-65 E 3-4
Front Royal, VA 72-73 GH 5
Frosinone 122-123 E 5
Frostburg, MD 72-73 G 5
Frostproof, FL 80-81 c 3
Frotet, Lac — 62 O 1
Fröttmaninger Heide 130 II b 1
Frövi 116-117 F 8
Frøya 116-117 C 6
Fröya Bank 116-117 B 6
Frozen Strait 56-57 U 4
Fruita, CO 74-75 J 3
Fruitland, ID 66-67 E 3
Fruitland, UT 66-67 H 5
Frunze 132-133 NO 9
Fruška gora 122-123 H 3
Frutal 102-103 H 3-4
Frutillar 108-109 C 3
Fruto, CA 74-75 B 3
Fryusu 168-169 E 3

Fua Mulaku Island 176 a 3
Fu'an 142-143 MN 6
Fucha, Río — 91 III b 3
Fucheng 146-147 F 3
Fucheu = Fuzhou 142-143 MN 6
Fu-chien = Fujian 142-143 M 6
Fuchin = Fujin 142-143 P 2
Fu-ch'ing = Fuqing 142-143 MN 6
Fuchow = Fuzhou 142-143 MN 6
Fuchskauten 118 CD 3
Fuchū 155 III a 1
Fuchuan 146-147 C 9
Fu-ch'un Chiang = Fuchun Jiang 146-147 G 7
Fuchun Jiang 146-147 G 7
Fudai 144-145 NO 2-3
Fuding 146-147 H 8
Fuego, Tierra del — [RA, administrative unit] 111 C 8
Fuego, Tierra del — [RA, landscape] 110 C 8
Fuego, Volcán de — 64-65 H 9
Fuente 76-77 D 8
Fuente de San Esteban, La — 120-121 DE 8
Fuentes del Coyle 108-109 D 8
Fuentes de Oñoro 120-121 D 8
Fuerte, El — 86-87 F 4
Fuerte, Río — 64-65 E 6
Fuerte Bulnes 111 B 8
Fuerte Olimpo 111 E 2
Fuerteventura 164-165 B 3
Fufeng 146-147 AB 4
Fuglöy Bank 114-115 M 1
Fugou 146-147 E 4-5
Fugu 146-147 C 2
Fugui Jiao = Fukuei Chiao 146-147 H 9
Fu He 146-147 EF 7
Fu-hsien = Fu Xian [TJ, Liaoning] 142-143 N 4
Fu-hsien = Fu Xian [TJ, Shaanxi] 146-147 B 3
Fu-hsien = Fuxin 142-143 N 3
Fu-hsien Hu = Fuxian Hu 142-143 J 7
Fu-i Shui = Fuyi Shui 146-147 C 8
Fujairah, Al- = Al-Fujayrah 134-135 H 5
Fujayrah, Al- 134-135 H 5
Fuji 144-145 M 5
Fujian 142-143 M 6
Fu Jiang 142-143 K 5
Fujin 142-143 P 2
Fujinomiya 144-145 M 5
Fujioka 144-145 M 4
Fuji-san 142-143 Q 4-5
Fujisawa 144-145 MN 5
Fujiwara 155 III c 1
Fuji-Yoshida 144-145 M 5
Fukae = Fukue 144-145 G 6
Fukagawa 144-145 bc 2
Fukagawa, Tôkyô- 155 III b 2
Fûkah 136-137 B 7
Fukien = Fujian 142-143 M 6
Fu-kou = Fugou 146-147 E 4-5
Fuku = Fugu 146-147 C 2
Fukuchiyama 144-145 K 5
Fukue 144-145 G 6
Fukuei Chiao 146-147 H 9
Fukue-shima 144-145 G 6
Fukui 142-143 Q 4
Fukuoka [J, Fukuoka] 142-143 OP 5
Fukuoka [J, Iwate] 144-145 N 2
Fukura = Nandan 144-145 K 5
Fukushima [J, Fukushima] 142-143 R 4
Fukushima [J, Hokkaidô] 144-145 b 3
Fukushima [J, Nagano] 144-145 L 5
Fukuyama 144-145 J 5
Fûlah, Al- 164-165 K 6
Fulaikā', Jazirat — = Jazirat Faylakah 136-137 N 8
Fulda, MN 70-71 C 4
Fulda [D, place] 118 D 3
Fulda [D, river] 118 D 3
Fulham, London- 129 II b 2
Fuli 146-147 H 10
Fulidu Channel 176 a 2
Fuliji 146-147 F 5
Fuling 142-143 K 6
Fullerton, KY 72-73 E 5
Fullerton, NE 68-69 GH 5
Fulton 106-107 H 6
Fulton, AR 78-79 C 4
Fulton, CA 74-75 B 3
Fulton, KY 78-79 E 2
Fulton, LA 78-79 C 5
Fulton, MO 70-71 DE 6
Fulton, MS 78-79 E 3
Fulton, NY 72-73 H 3
Fulton River 60 D 2
Fûm al-Ḥasan 166-167 B 5
Fûman 136-137 N 4
Fumban = Foumban 164-165 G 7
Fūmch'ŏn = Kŭmch'on 144-145 F 3
Fumel 120-121 H 6
Fûm Z'gid 166-167 C 4
Funa 170 IV a 2
Funabashi 144-145 MN 5
Funabashi-Kaijin 155 III c 1
Funabashi-Maebara 155 III d 1
Funabashi-Tsudanuma 155 III d 1
Funabashi-Yonegasaki 155 III d 1
Funafuti 208 H 3
Funagawa = Oga 144-145 M 3
Funan 146-147 E 5
Funatsu = Kamioka 144-145 L 4
Funchal 164-165 A 2
Fundación 92-93 E 2
Fundão [BR] 92-93 LM 8
Fundão [P] 120-121 D 8
Fundão, Ilha do — 110 I b 2
Funduq, Al- 166-167 D 2
Fundy, Bay of — 56-57 X 8-9
Funhalouro 172 FG 6
Funing [TJ, Hebei] 146-147 G 2
Funing [TJ, Jiangsu] 142-143 MN 5
Funing = Xiapu 146-147 GH 8
Funing Wan 146-147 H 8
Funiu Shan 146-147 D 5
Funkley, MN 70-71 C 2
Funkturm Berlin 130 III b 1
Funter, AK 58-59 U 7
Funtua 164-165 F 6
Funza 91 III a 2
Fuoping = Foping 146-147 AB 5
Fuping [TJ, Hebei] 146-147 E 2
Fuping [TJ, Shaanxi] 146-147 B 4
Fuqing 142-143 MN 6
Fúquene, Laguna de — 94-95 E 5
Furancungo 172 F 4
Furano 144-145 c 2
Furât, Al- 134-135 DE 3
Furât, Nahr al- 134-135 E 4
Furât, Shaṭṭ al- 136-137 LM 7
Fūr Ghūrū = Fdayrik 164-165 B 4
Furman 61 B 6
Furmanov 124-125 N 5
Furmanovka [SU, Kazachskaja SSR] 132-133 N 9
Furmanovo 126-127 OP 2
Furnas, Represa de — 92-93 K 9
Furnas, Rio de Janeiro- 110 I b 2
Furneaux Group 158-159 J 7-8
Furness 61 CD 4
Fûrnoi 122-123 M 7
Furqlûs 136-137 G 5
Furrial, El — 94-95 K 3
Fürstenfeld 118 GH 5
Fürstenried, Schloss — 130 II a 2
Fürstenwalde 118 FG 2
Furtâsât al-Gharbîyah 166-167 F 3
Fürth 118 E 4
Further India 50-51 OP 5
Furubira 144-145 b 2
Furukamappu = Južno-Kuriľsk 132-133 c 9
Furukawa 144-145 N 3
Furutone 155 III c 1
Fury and Hecla Strait 56-57 TU 4
Fusagasugá 94-95 D 5
Fusan = Pusan 142-143 OP 4
Fuse = Higasiôsaka 144-145 KL 5
Fushan [TJ, Guangdong] 150-151 GH 3
Fushan [TJ, Jiangsu] 146-147 H 6
Fushan [TJ, Shandong] 146-147 H 3
Fushan [TJ, Shanxi] 146-147 C 4
Fu-shan-shih = Fushan 150-151 GH 3
Fushi = Yan'an 142-143 K 4
Fushing Bay 82 III c 2
Fu Shui = Fu He 146-147 EF 7
Fushun 142-143 NO 3
Fushuncheng 144-145 DE 2
Fusien = Fu Xian 142-143 N 4
Fusin = Fuxin 142-143 N 3
Fusong 142-143 O 3
Füssen 118 E 5
Fu-sung = Fusong 144-145 F 1
Futa Djalon = Fouta Djalon 164-165 B 6
Futalaufquen, Lago — 108-109 CD 4
Futaleufú 108-109 D 4
Futaleufú, Río — 108-109 D 4
Futamata 144-145 L 5
Futamatagawa, Yokohama- 155 III a 3
Futaoi-jima 144-145 H 5
Futatsubashi, Yokohama- 155 III a 3
Fu Tau Chao 155 I b 2
Fu-ting = Fuding 146-147 H 8
Futrono 108-109 C 3
Futsing = Fuqing 142-143 MN 6
Futuna 148-149 b 1
Fu-t'un Ch'i = Futun-Xi 146-147 F 8
Futun-Xi 146-147 F 8
Fuwah 173 B 2
Fu Xian [TJ, Liaoning] 142-143 N 4
Fu Xian [TJ, Shaanxi] 146-147 B 3
Fuxian Hu 142-143 J 7
Fuxin 142-143 N 3
Fuyang [TJ, Anhui] 142-143 M 5
Fuyang [TJ, Hangzhou] 146-147 G 6
Fuyang = Fuchuan 146-147 C 9
Fuyang He 146-147 E 3
Fu-yang Ho = Fuyang He 146-147 E 3
Fuyi Shui 146-147 C 8
Fuyu [TJ, Heilongjiang] 142-143 NO 2
Fuyu [TJ, Jilin] 142-143 NO 2
Fu-yü = Fuyu 142-143 NO 2
Fuyuan 142-143 P 2
Fuzhou [TJ, Fujian] 142-143 MN 6
Fuzhou [TJ, Jianxi] 142-143 M 6
Fuzhoucheng 142-143 N 4
Fuziji = Buzi 146-147 G 5

Fyn 116-117 D 10
Fyzabad = Faizābād 134-135 N 5

G

Ga 168-169 E 3
Gaalka'yo 164-165 b 2
Gaarowe 164-165 b 2
Gaasbeek 128 II a 2
Gaasp 128 I b 2
Gabakoro 168-169 D 2
Gabarouse 63 FG 5
Gabba' 164-165 c 2
Gabbs Valley 74-75 DE 3
Gabbs Valley Range 74-75 DE 3
Gabela [Angola] 172 BC 4
Gaberones = Gaborone 172 DE 6
Gabès = Qābis 164-165 FG 2
Gabes, Gulf of — = Khalīj al-Qābis 164-165 G 2
Gabiarra 100-101 E 9
Gabilan Range 74-75 C 4
Gabîlat = Jabîlat 166-167 BC 4
Gabinyânah = Jabinyânah 166-167 M 2
Gabon 172 AB 2
Gaborone 172 DE 6
Gaboto 106-107 G 4
Gabriel Antunes Maciel, Serra — 98-99 G 10-11
Gabrovo 122-123 L 4
Gabseľga 124-125 K 2
Gachalá 94-95 E 5
Gache 146-147 D 10
Gachsārān 134-135 G 4
Gackle, ND 68-69 G 2
Gacko 122-123 H 4
Gada [RN] 168-169 G 2
Gada [WAN] 168-169 G 2
Gad'ač 126-127 FG 1
Gadādhar 138-139 M 4
Gadag 140 B 3
Gaḍaga = Gadag 140 B 3
Gaḍahinglaj = Gadhinglaj 140 B 2
Gadake = Garthog 138-139 H 2
Gadap = Karāchī 134-135 K 6
Gāḍarvārā = Gādarwāra 138-139 G 6
Gādarwāra 138-139 G 6
Gaḍavāla = Gadwāl 140 C 2
Gaḍavāla = Munīrābād 140 BC 3
Gaḍchirōlī = Garhchiroli 138-139 GH 7
Gäddede 116-117 F 5
Gaḍhī = Garhi 138-139 E 6
Gadhinglaj 140 B 2
Gadîdah, Al- = Al-Jadîdah [MA] 164-165 C 2
Gadîdah, Al- = Al-Jadîdah [TN] 166-167 L 1
Gadjouan 168-169 J 4
Gado Bravo, Ilha do — 100-101 C 6
Gado Bravo, Serra do — 100-101 A 4-5
Gadrā 134-135 L 5
Gadsby 61 BC 4
Gadsden, AL 64-65 J 5
Gadwāl 140 C 2
Găeşti 122-123 L 3
Gaeta 122-123 E 5
Gaeta, Golfo di — 122-123 E 5
Gaf, Bir el — = Bi'r al-Qaf 164-165 H 3
Gafārah = Jafārah 166-167 M 3
Gaferut 206-207 S 9
Gaffney, SC 80-81 F 3
Gäfle = Gävle 116-117 G 7
Ga'fōur = Qa'fūr 166-167 L 1
Gafṣa = Qafṣah 166-167 L 2
Gagarin 124-125 K 6
Gage, NM 74-75 JK 6
Gage, OK 76-77 E 4
Gage Park, Chicago-, IL 83 II a 2
Gagere 168-169 G 2
Gagino 124-125 P 6
Gagliano del Capo 122-123 GH 6
Gagnoa 164-165 C 7
Gagnon 56-57 X 7
Gagny 129 I d 2
Gago Coutinho = Lungala N'Guimbo 172 D 4
Gagra 126-127 JK 5
Gagšor 124-125 S 3
Gahan 106-107 GH 5
Gahmar 138-139 J 5
Gahnpa 164-165 C 7
Gaia = Gayā 134-135 NO 5-6
Gaiab 174-175 C 4
Gaíba, Lagoa — 102-103 D 2
Gaibanda = Gāybāndā 138-139 M 5
Gaibes 174-175 B 5
Gaiharā = Mangawān 138-139 H 5
Gaika 138-139 MN 2
Gail 118 F 5
Gail, TX 76-77 D 6
Gaima 148-149 M 8
Gaimán 111 C 6
Gainesville, FL 64-65 K 6
Gainesville, GA 64-65 K 5
Gainesville, MO 78-79 C 2
Gainesville, TX 64-65 G 5
Gairdner, Lake — 158-159 G 6
Gai Xian 144-145 CD 2
Gaizina kalns 124-125 EF 5
Gajavāla = Gajwel 140 D 2
Gaji 168-169 H 3
Gajny 132-133 J 5
Gājol 138-139 M 5
Gajsin 126-127 D 2
Gajutino 124-125 M 4
Gajvoron 126-127 D 2
Gajwel 140 D 2
Gakarosa 174-175 E 4
Gakona, AK 58-59 P 5
Gakugsa 124-125 L 3
Galāchipā 141 B 4
Galadi = Geladī 164-165 O 7
Gala Hu = Kalba Tsho 138-139 M 3
Galán 94-95 E 4
Galán, Cerro — 111 C 3
Galana 172 GH 2
Galashiels 119 E 4
Galata, İstanbul- 154 I a 2
Galata Köprüsü 154 I ab 2
Galaṭi 122-123 MN 3
Galatia, KS 68-69 G 6
Galatina 122-123 H 5
Galatsion 113 IV a 1
Galatz = Galaṭi 122-123 MN 3
Galax, VA 80-81 F 2
Galbeed = Waqooyi-Galbeed 164-165 a 1
Gal'bstadt = Moločansk 126-127 GH 3
Galdhøpiggen 116-117 BC 7
Galea 148-149 J 6
Galeana 86-87 G 2
Galeão, Punta do — 110 I b 2
Galeão, Rio de Janeiro- 110 I b 1
Galena, AK 56-57 E 4-5
Galena, IL 70-71 E 4
Galena, MO 78-79 C 2
Galena Park, TX 85 III bc 2
Galeota Point 94-95 L 2
Galera, Punta — [CO] 94-95 D 2
Galera, Punta — [EC] 92-93 C 4
Galera, Punta — [RCH] 111 AB 6
Galera, Rio — 104-105 FG 4
Galera Point 64-65 OP 9
Galeria Acquasona 113 II a 1-2
Galesburg, IL 64-65 HJ 3
Galesville, WI 70-71 E 3
Galeta, Isla — 64-65 b 2
Galeta Island 64-65 b 2
Galeton 62 L 1
Galeton, PA 72-73 H 4
Galēwela 140 E 7
Gal-Guduud 164-165 b 2-3
Galheirão, Rio — 100-101 B 7
Galheiros 100-101 A 7
Gali 126-127 K 5
Gália 102-103 H 5
Galič [SU, Rossijskaja SFSR] 132-133 G 6
Galič [SU, Ukrainskaja SSR] 126-127 B 2
Galicia 120-121 CD 7
Galicja 118 J-L 4
Galičskaja vozvyšennosť 124-125 N 5-O 4
Galilee, Lake — 158-159 HJ 4
Galilee, Sea of — = Yam Kinneret 134-135 D 4
Galileia 102-103 M 3
Galineau, Rivière — 72-73 J 1
Galion, OH 72-73 E 4
Galípoli = Gelibolu 134-135 B 2
Galissonnière, Lac la — 63 E 2
Galisteo 106-107 G 3
Galiṭah, Gazā'ir — = Jazā'ir Jaliṭah 166-167 L 1
Galiṭah, Qanāt — = Qanāt Jaliṭah 166-167 L 1
Galite, Canal de la — = Qanāt Jaliṭah 166-167 L 1
Galite, Îles de la — = Jazā'ir Jaliṭah 166-167 L 1
Galiuro Mountains 74-75 H 6
Gâlla 134-135 MN 9
Gallabat = Qallābāt 164-165 M 6
Galladi = Geladī 164-165 O 7
Gallareta, La — 106-107 G 2
Gallatin, MO 70-71 D 6
Gallatin, TN 78-79 F 2
Gallatin Gateway, MT 66-67 H 3
Gallatin Peak 66-67 H 3
Gallatin River 66-67 H 3
Gallaudet College 82 II b 2
Galle = Gâlla 134-135 MN 9
Galle, Lac — 63 G 2
Gállego, Río — 120-121 G 7
Gallegos, NM 76-77 C 5
Gallegos, Río — 111 BC 8
Galliate 122-123 C 3
Gallina Mountains 76-77 A 5
Gallinas, Punta — 92-93 E 2
Gallipoli 122-123 GH 5
Gallipoli = Gelibolu 134-135 B 2
Gallipolis, OH 72-73 E 5
Gällivare 116-117 J 4
Gallo Mountains 74-75 J 5-6
Galloo Island 72-73 H 3
Galloupes Point 84 I c 2
Galloway 119 DE 4
Gallup, NM 64-65 E 4
Galmūḍe 140 EF 7
Gal Oya [CL, place] 140 E 6
Gal Oya [CL, river] 140 E 7
Galpón, El — 104-105 D 9
Galšir 142-143 L 2
Galt, CA 74-75 C 3
Galva, IL 70-71 EF 5
Galvarino 106-107 A 7
Galveston, TX 64-65 H 6
Galveston Bay 64-65 H 6
Galveston Island 76-77 G 8
Gálvez [RA] 111 D 4
Gálvez, Río — 96-97 E 4
Galway 119 B 5
Galway Bay 119 B 5
Gam, Pulau — 148-149 JK 7
Gâm, Sông — 150-151 E 1
Gāmā = Gāwān 138-139 KL 5
Gamane = Bertoua 164-165 G 8
Gamarra 94-95 E 3
Gamas, Las — 106-107 G 2
Gāmāsiyāb, Rūd-e — 136-137 MN 5
Gamay 106-107 E 6
Gambaga 164-165 D 6
Gambang 150-151 D 11
Gambeila = Gambēla 164-165 L 7
Gambēla 164-165 L 7
Gambell, AK 56-57 BC 5
Gambetta = Tawrah 166-167 KL 1
Gambhīr 138-139 F 4
Gambia [WAG, river] 168-169 A 2
Gambia [WAG, state] 164-165 AB 6
Gambie 164-165 B 6
Gambir, Jakarta- 154 IV a 1
Gambir, Poulo — = Cu Lao Poulo Gambir 150-151 GH 6
Gâmbita 94-95 E 4-5
Gamboa 64-65 b 2
Gamboa, Rio de Janeiro- 110 I b 2
Gamboma 172 C 2
Gambos 172 BC 4
Gameleira 100-101 G 5
Gameleira, Ponta do — 100-101 G 3
Gameleira, Serra da — 100-101 C 4

Gameleira da Lapa 100-101 C 7
Gamerco, NM 74-75 J 5
Game Reserve Number 1 172 CD 5
Game Reserve Number 2 172 BC 5
Gamkab 174-175 B 5
Gamkarivier 174-175 D 7
Gamlakarleby = Kokkola 116-117 K 6
Gamleby 116-117 FG 9
Gamm, Al- = Al-Jamm 166-167 M 2
Gammāl = Jammāl 166-167 M 2
Gamoep 174-175 C 5
Gamova, mys — 144-145 H 1
Gampaha 140 DE 7
Gampoḷa 140 E 7
Gamsah = Jamsah 173 C 4
Gamtoos 174-175 F 7
Gāmūr al-Kabīr, Al- = Al-Jāmūr al-Kabīr 166-167 M 1
Gamvik 116-117 N 2
G'amyš, gora — 126-127 N 6
Gan [Maldive Is., island] 176 a 2
Gan [Maldive Is., place] 176 a 3
Gana = Ghana 164-165 DE 7
Ganaane, Webi — 164-165 N 8
Ganado, AZ 74-75 J 5
Ganado, TX 76-77 F 8
Ganā'in = Janā'in 166-167 LM 4
Ganale Dorya = Genale 164-165 N 7
Gananoque 72-73 H 2
Ganaram 168-169 H 2
Ganāveh 134-135 FG 5
Gancedo 104-105 F 10
Gancevići 124-125 EF 7
Gancheng 150-151 G 3
Ganchhendzönga = Gangchhendsönga 134-135 O 5
Gand = Gent 120-121 JK 3
Ganda 172 B 4
Gandadiwata, Gunung — 152-153 NO 7
Gandai 138-139 H 7
Gandajika 172 DE 3
Gandak 134-135 NO 5
Gandak, Burhi — 138-139 K 4-5
Gandak, Buria — = Burhi Gandak 138-139 K 4-5
Gaṇḍak, Kālī — 138-139 JK 4
Gandak, Old — = Burhi Gandak 138-139 K 4-5
Gândara [RA] 106-107 H 5
Gandāvā 138-139 A 3
Gander 56-57 a 8
Gander Lake 63 J 3
Gander River 63 J 3
Gandesa 120-121 H 8
Gāndhi Dhām 138-139 C 6
Gandhinagar 138-139 D 6
Gāndhi Sāgar 138-139 E 5
Gandi 168-169 G 2
Gandia 120-121 GH 9
Gandilans Provincial Forest 62 B 3
Gandoī = Gondia 138-139 H 7
Gandu 100-101 E 7
Ganfūdah = Janfūdah 166-167 E 2
Gang [TJ] 138-139 M 3
Gangā 134-135 M 5
Ganga, Mouths of the — 134-135 OP 6
Gangākher 138-139 F 8
Gan Gan 111 C 6
Gangán, Pampa de — 108-109 EF 4
Gangānagar 134-135 LM 5
Gangāpur [IND, Mahārāshtra] 138-139 E 8
Gangāpur [IND, Rājasthān] 138-139 E 5
Gangara 168-169 G 2
Gangārāmpur 138-139 M 5
Gangaw 141 D 4
Gangāwati 140 C 3
Gangchhendsönga 134-135 O 5
Gangchhu 138-139 L 3
Gangchhung Gangri 138-139 K 2-3
Gangdhār 138-139 E 6
Ganges = Gangā 134-135 M 5
Ganges Canyon 134-135 O 6-7
Gang He = Sha He 146-147 E 3
Gangīr, Rūdkhāneh ye — 136-137 LM 6
Ganglung Gangri 138-139 HJ 2
Gangma Zong = Khampa Dsong 138-139 M 3
Gangmezhen = Longgang 146-147 GH 5
Gangoh 138-139 F 3
Gangotri [IND, mountain] 138-139 G 2
Gangotri [IND, place] 138-139 G 2
Gangou 144-145 B 2
Gangouzhen = Gangou 144-145 B 2
Gangpur 138-139 F 4
Gang Ranch 60 F 4
Gangrinpochhe 138-139 H 2
Gangshan = Kangshan 146-147 GH 10
Gangtalê 140 E 6
Gangthog 134-135 O 5
Gangtö Gangri 142-143 G 6
Gangtok = Gangthog 134-135 O 5
Gangtun 144-145 C 2
Gan He 142-143 N 1
Ganh Hao = Lo Than 150-151 E 8
Ganjām 138-139 K 8
Ganjiakou, Beijing- 155 II a 2
Gan Jiang 142-143 LM 6
Gannan Zangzu Zizhizhou 142-143 J 5
Gannaor = Gunnaur 138-139 G 3
Gannāvaram 140 E 2
Gannett, ID 66-67 FG 4
Gannett Peak 64-65 E 3
Gannvalley, SD 68-69 G 3-4
Ganquan 146-147 B 3
Gansbaai 174-175 C 8
Ganso Azul 96-97 D 5
Gansu 142-143 G 3-J 4
Ganta = Gahnpa 164-165 C 7
Gantang 146-147 B 10
Gantheaume Bay 158-159 B 5
Gantian 146-147 D 8
Gan'uškino 126-127 O 3
Ganxian = Ganzhou 142-143 LM 6
Ganyesa 174-175 F 4
Ganyu 146-147 G 4
Ganzhe = Minhou 146-147 G 8
Ganzhou 142-143 LM 6
Gao 164-165 D 5
Gao'an 142-143 LM 6
Gaobu 146-147 F 8
Gaochun 146-147 G 6
Gaocun 146-147 E 7
Gaodianzi 146-147 BC 6
Gaofu = Gaobu 146-147 F 8
Gaohebu 146-147 F 6
Gaojabu 146-147 C 2
Gaojiabao = Gaojiabu 146-147 C 2
Gaojiafang 146-147 D 7
Gaokeng 146-147 DE 8
Gaolan Dao 146-147 D 11
Gaoligong Shan 142-143 H 6
Gaoling 146-147 B 4
Gaomi 146-147 G 3
Gaopi 146-147 F 9
Gaoping 146-147 D 4
Gaoqiao = Gaoqiaozhen 144-145 C 2
Gaoqiaozhen 144-145 C 2
Gaoqing 146-147 FG 3
Gaosha 146-147 C 8
Gaoshan 146-147 G 9
Gaoshun = Gaochun 146-147 G 6
Gaotai 142-143 H 4
Gaotang 146-147 F 3
Gaoua 164-165 D 6
Gaoual 164-165 B 6
Gaoxiong = Kaohsiung 142-143 MN 7
Gaoyang 146-147 E 2
Gaoyao = Zhaoqing 146-147 D 10
Gaoyi 146-147 E 3
Gaoyou 146-147 G 5
Gaoyou Hu 146-147 G 5
Gaoyuan 146-147 F 3
Gaozhou 146-147 C 11
Gap 120-121 L 6
Gar = Garthog 138-139 H 2
Gar, Bir el — = Bi'r al-Qaf 164-165 H 3
Gâra, el — = Al-Gārah 166-167 C 3
Garabaldi Provincial Park 60 F 4-5
Garabato 106-107 GH 2
Garachiné 88-89 GH 10
Garachiné, Punta — 94-95 B 3
Gar'ad 164-165 bc 2
Garaet et Tarf = Qar'at at-Tarf 166-167 K 2
Garah 160 JK 2
Gārah, Al- 166-167 C 3
Garalo 168-169 D 3
Garamba, Parc national de la — 172 EF 1
Garam-bi = Oluan Pi 146-147 H 11
Garanhuns 92-93 M 6
Garaoṭhā = Garautha 138-139 G 5
Garapa, Serra da — 100-101 C 7
Garapuava 102-103 J 2
Gararu 100-101 F 5-6
Gara Samuil 122-123 M 4
Gār aş-Şallaḥ = Ghār aş-Şallah 166-167 E 3
Garautha 138-139 G 5
Garayalde 108-109 F 5
Garb, Gebel el — = Jabal Nafusah 164-165 G 2
Garbahaarrey 164-165 N 8
Garbatella, Roma- 113 II b 2
Garba Tula 171 D 2
Garber, OK 76-77 F 4
Garberville, CA 66-67 B 5
Garbyāng 138-139 H 2
Garça 102-103 H 5
Garças, Rio das — 102-103 F 1
Garces Navas 91 III b 2
Garches 129 I b 2
Garcias 92-93 J 9
Gard 120-121 K 6-7
Garda 122-123 D 3
Garda, Lago di — 122-123 D 3
Gardabani 126-127 M 6
Gardaneh-ye Chūl 136-137 MN 6
Gardelegen 118 E 2
Garden, MI 70-71 G 3
Gardena, CA 83 III c 2
Garden City, AL 78-79 F 3
Garden City, KS 64-65 F 4
Garden City, TX 76-77 D 7
Garden District, New Orleans-, LA 85 I b 2
Garden Grove, CA 74-75 D 6
Garden Island 70-71 H 3
Garden Oaks, Houston-, TX 85 III b 1
Garden Reach 138-139 LM 6
Garden Reach-Bartala 154 II a 2
Garden River 70-71 HJ 2
Garden State Race Track 84 III cd 2
Gardenton 62 A 3
Gardenvale, Melbourne- 161 II c 2
Garden Valley, ID 66-67 F 3
Gardey 106-107 H 6
Gardēz 134-135 K 4
Gardhsskagi 116-117 b 2
Gardiner 62 L 2
Gardiner, ME 72-73 M 2
Gardiner, MT 66-67 H 3
Gardiners Bay 72-73 KL 4
Gardiners Creek 161 II c 2
Gardner 208 J 3
Gardner, CO 68-69 D 7
Gardner, IL 70-71 F 5
Gardner, MA 72-73 KL 3
Gardner, ND 68-69 H 2
Gardnerville, NV 74-75 D 3
Gardu = Garthog 138-139 H 2
Gardula-Gidole = Gīdolē 164-165 M 7
Gareloi Island 58-59 t 6-7
Garenne-Colombes, la — 129 I bc 2
Garet el Djenoun = Qārat al-Junūn 166-167 J 7
Gare Windsor Forum 82 I b 2
Garfield, NJ 82 III b 1
Garfield Heights, OH 72-73 F 4
Garfield Mountain 66-67 G 3
Garfield Park 83 II a 1
Gargaliánoi 122-123 J 7
Gargano 122-123 FG 5
Gargano, Testa del — 122-123 G 5
Gargantua, Cape — 70-71 H 2
Gargar 136-137 L 3
Gargar, Īstgāh-e — 136-137 N 7
Garges-lès-Gonesse 129 I c 2
Gargia 116-117 K 3
Gargouna 168-169 F 2
Garhākota 138-139 G 6
Garhchiroli 138-139 H 7
Garhi 138-139 E 6
Garhī Khairo 138-139 AB 3
Garhī Yāsin 138-139 B 4
Garhjāt Hills 138-139 K 7
Garho 138-139 A 5
Garhvā = Garwa 138-139 J 5
Garhvāl = Garhwāl 138-139 G 2
Garhwāl 138-139 G 2
Gari [WAN] 168-169 H 2
Garian = Ghayān 164-165 G 2
Garib 174-175 B 2
Garibaldi 106-107 M 2
Garibaldi, OR 66-67 B 3
Garibaldi Provincial Park 66-67 B 1
Garies 172 C 8
Garinais 174-175 C 4
Garissa 172 GH 2
Gariya, Calcutta- 154 II b 3
Garkha 138-139 K 5
Garko 168-169 H 3
Garland, NC 80-81 G 3
Garland, TX 76-77 F 6
Garland, UT 66-67 G 5
Garma, De la — 106-107 G 6-7
Garmashīn, 'Ain — = 'Ayn Jarmashīn 173 B 5
Garmisch-Partenkirchen 118 E 5
Garner, IA 70-71 D 4
Garnet, MT 66-67 G 2
Garnett, KS 70-71 C 6
Garoet = Garut 152-153 G 9
Gārō-Khāsī Jayantiyā Pahāṛiyan = Khāsi-Jaintia Hills 141 BC 3
Garonne 120-121 G 6
Garoo = Gāru 138-139 K 6
Garopaba 111 G 3
Garot 138-139 E 5
Garou, Lac — 168-169 E 1
Garoua 164-165 G 7
Garoumele 168-169 J 2
Garré 106-107 F 6
Garretson, SD 68-69 H 4
Garrett, IN 70-71 H 5
Garrick 61 F 4
Garrison, MT 66-67 G 2
Garrison, ND 68-69 F 2
Garruchos 106-107 K 2
Garry Lake 56-57 Q 4
Garsīf 166-167 E 3
Garson Lake 61 CD 2
Garstedt 130 I a 1
Gartempe 120-121 H 5
Garth 61 C 3
Gartog 142-143 E 5
Gartok = Gartog 142-143 E 5
Gāru 138-139 K 6
Garua = Garoua 164-165 G 7
Garupá 106-107 K 1
Garut 152-153 G 9
Garvie Mountains 161 C 7
Garwa 138-139 J 5
Garwood, TX 76-77 F 8
Gary, IN 64-65 J 3
Gary, SD 68-69 H 3
Garza 106-107 F 2
Garza Garcia 86-87 K 5
Garzan = Zok 136-137 J 3
Garze 142-143 J 5
Garze Zangzu Zizhizhou 142-143 HJ 5
Garzón [CO] 92-93 DE 4
Garzón [ROU] 106-107 K 5
Garzón, Laguna — 106-107 K 5
Gasan-Kuli 134-135 G 3
Gascogne 120-121 GH 7
Gasconade River 70-71 E 6
Gascoyne, ND 68-69 E 2
Gascoyne, Mount — 158-159 C 4
Gascoyne River 158-159 C 5
Gashaka 164-165 G 7
Gashua 168-169 H 2
Gāsigānv = Gasigaon 141 D 2
Gasigaon 141 D 2
Gasmata 148-149 gh 6
Gaspar 102-103 H 7
Gaspar, Selat — 148-149 E 7
Gaspar Campos 106-107 D 5
Gasparilla Island 80-81 b 3
Gaspar Rodriguez de Francia 102-103 BC 5
Gaspé 56-57 Y 8
Gaspé, Baie de — 63 DE 3
Gaspé, Cap — 56-57 Y 8
Gaspé, Péninsule de — 56-57 XY 8
Gaspé Passage 56-57 XY 8
Gaspésie, Parc provincial de la — 63 CD 3
Gassan [HV] 168-169 E 2
Gas-san [J] 144-145 MN 3
Gassaway, WV 72-73 F 5
Gaston, OR 66-67 B 3
Gastonia, NC 64-65 K 4
Gastre 111 C 6
Gastre, Pampa de — 108-109 E 4
Gašuun Gov' 142-143 G 3
Gašuun nuur 142-143 HJ 3
Gat = Ghat 164-165 G 3
Gáta, Akrōtērion — 136-137 E 5
Gata, Cabo de — 120-121 FG 10
Gata, Sierra de — 120-121 D 8
Gatčina 132-133 DE 6
Gate City, VA 80-81 E 2
Gateshead 119 EF 4
Gates of the Mountains 66-67 H 2
Gatesville, TX 76-77 F 7
Gateway, CO 74-75 J 3
Gateway, MT 66-67 F 1
Gateway, OR 66-67 C 3
Gatico 104-105 A 8
Gâtinais 120-121 J 4
Gâtine, Hauteurs de — 120-121 G 5
Gatineau 72-73 J 2
Gatineau, Rivière — 72-73 J 1-2
Gatineau Park 72-73 HJ 2
Gato Negro 91 II b 1
Gatooma = Kadoma 172 E 5
Gatos 100-101 B 7
Gatrun, el- = Al-Qaṭrūn 164-165 GH 4
Gattikon 128 IV b 2
Gatun 64-65 b 2
Gatun, Barrage de — = Presa de Gatún 64-65 ab 2
Gatún, Brazo de — 64-65 b 2
Gatún, Esclusas de — 64-65 b 2
Gatún, Lago de — 64-65 b 2
Gatún, Presa de — 64-65 ab 2
Gatún, Río — 64-65 b 2
Gatun Arm = Brazo de Gatún 64-65 b 2
Gatuncillo 64-65 b 2
Gatuncillo, Río — 64-65 b 2
Gatun Dam = Presa de Gatún 64-65 ab 2
Gatun Lake = Lago de Gatún 64-65 b 2
Gatun Locks = Esclusas de Gatún 64-65 b 2
Gatvand 136-137 N 6
Gatyana 174-175 H 7
Gauani = Gewani 164-165 N 6
Gaud-e Zirrāh = Gawd-e Zere 134-135 J 5
Gauer Lake 61 K 2
Gauhati 134-135 P 5
Gauja 124-125 EF 5
Gaula 116-117 D 6
Gauley Mountain 72-73 F 5
Gaurama 106-107 LM 1
Gauribidanūr 140 C 4
Gauri Phānta 138-139 H 3
Gaurīpur 141 B 3
Gaurisankar = Jomotsering 134-135 O 5
Gaurīshankar = Jomotsering 134-135 O 5
Gaurnadi 141 AB 4
Gausta 116-117 C 8
Gausvik 116-117 G 3
Gávdos 122-123 L 8
Gávea, Rio de Janeiro- 110 I b 2
Gave de Pau 120-121 G 7
Gāveh Rūd 136-137 M 5
Gavião [BR] 100-101 E 6
Gaviao, Rio — 100-101 D 8
Gāvilgaḍ Ḍoṅgar = Gāwilgarh Hills 138-139 FG 7
Gavins Reservoir = Lewis and Clark Lake 68-69 H 4
Gaviota, CA 74-75 C 5
Gaviotas 106-107 F 7
Gävle 116-117 G 7
Gävleborg 116-117 G 6-7
Gavrilov-Jam 124-125 MN 5
Gavrilovo [SU, Archangel'skaja Oblast'] 124-125 Q 2
Gavrilov-Posad 124-125 N 5
Gawachab 174-175 B 4
Gāwān 138-139 KL 5
Gawd-e Zere 134-135 J 5
Gāwilgarh Hills 138-139 FG 7
Gawler 158-159 G 6
Gawler Ranges 158-159 G 6
Gawon Gulbi 168-169 G 2
Gay, MI 70-71 F 2
Gaya [DY] 164-165 E 6
Gaya [IND] 134-135 NO 5-6
Gayaza 171 B 3
Gāybāndā 138-139 M 5
Gaylord, MI 70-71 H 3
Gaylord, MN 70-71 C 3
Gayndah 158-159 K 5
Gaypón 108-109 D 8
Gaza 172 F 6
Gaza = Ghazzah 134-135 C 4
Gazā'ir Galiṭah = Jazā'ir Jaliṭah 166-167 L 1
Gazalkent 132-133 MN 9
Gazelle, CA 66-67 B 5
Gazelle Peninsula 148-149 h 5
Gazi 171 D 4
Gaziantep 134-135 D 3
Gaziantep yaylâsı 136-137 GH 4
Gazibenli 136-137 F 3
Gaziler = Bardız 136-137 K 2
Gazipaşa 136-137 E 4
Gazīpur = Ghāzīpur 138-139 J 5
Gāziyābād = Ghāziābād 138-139 F 3
Gbarnga 164-165 C 7
Gboko 168-169 H 4
Gdańsk 118 J 1
Gdańska, Zatoka — 118 J 1
Gdov 124-125 FG 4
Gdyel = Qadayal 166-167 F 2
Gdynia 118 HJ 1
Gearhart Mountain 66-67 C 4
Geary, OK 76-77 E 5
Geba, Canal do — 168-169 AB 3
Geba, Rio de — 164-165 AB 6
Gebal = Jubayl 136-137 F 5
Gebe, Pulau — 148-149 J 7
Gebeit = Jubayt 164-165 M 4
Gebel Archenū = Jabal Arkanū 164-165 J 4
Gebel Auenat = Jabal al-'Uwaynāt 164-165 K 4
Gebel Beida = Jabal Bayḍā' 173 D 6
Gebel Catarina = Jabal Katrīnah 164-165 L 3
Gebel Druso = Jabal ad-Durūz 134-135 D 4
Gebel el Fanṭās = Jabal al-Finṭās 173 B 6
Gebel el Garb = Jabal Nafusah 164-165 G 2
Gebel el-'Igma = Jabal al-'Ajmah 164-165 L 3
Gebel es Sabaa = Qārat as-Sab'ah 164-165 H 3
Gebel es-Sebā' = Qārat as-Sab'ah 164-165 H 3
Gebel es Sôdâ = Jabal as-Sawdā' 164-165 GH 3
Gebel eth Thabt = Jabal ath-Thabt 173 CD 3
Gebel Halāl = Jabal Hilāl 173 CD 2
Gebel Katerîna = Jabal Katrīnah 164-165 L 3
Gebel Mu'tiq = Jabal Mu'tiq 173 C 4
Gebel Na'âg = Jabal Nī'āj 173 C 6
Gebel Nugruş = Jabal Nuqruş 173 D 5
Gebel Yi'allaq = Jabal Yu'alliq 173 C 2
Gebiz = Macar 136-137 D 4
Gebo, WY 68-69 B 4
Gebze 136-137 C 2
Gedaref = Al-Qadārif 164-165 M 6
Geddes, SD 68-69 G 4
Gedi 172 G 2
Gedid, el — = Sabhah 164-165 G 3
Gedikbulak = Canik 136-137 K 3
Gediz 136-137 C 3
Gediz çayı 136-137 C 3
Gediz nehri 136-137 B 3
Gedmar Chhu 138-139 M 2
Gēdo [ETH] 164-165 M 7
Gedo [SP] 164-165 N 8
Gedser 116-117 DE 10
Gedū Hka 141 E 2
Geelong 158-159 H 7
Geelvink Channel 158-159 B 5
Geerlisberg 128 IV b 1
Geese Bank 132-133 GH 3
Geetvlei 174-175 D 4
Geeveston 158-159 J 8
Géfyra 122-123 K 5
Gegari Canal = Nahr Begārī 138-139 B 3
Gegeen gol = Gen He 142-143 N 1
Ge Hu 146-147 G 6
Geidam 164-165 G 6
Geikie Island 62 E 2
Geikie River 61 F 2
Geilo 116-117 C 7
Geiranger 116-117 B 6
Geiselgasteig 130 II b 2
Geislingen 118 D 4
Geita 172 F 2
Geitsaub = Keitsaub 174-175 C 2
Gejiu 142-143 J 7
Gela 122-123 F 7
Geladi 164-165 O 7
Gelai 171 D 3
Gelam, Pulau — 152-153 H 7
Gelang, Tanjung — 150-151 D 11
Gelendost 136-137 D 3
Gelendžik 126-127 HJ 4
Gelib = Jilib 172 H 1
Gelibolu 134-135 B 2
Gelidonya burnu 136-137 D 4
Gellibrand, Point — 161 II b 2
Gel'm'azov 126-127 EF 2
Gelora, Jakarta- 154 IV a 2
Gelsenkirchen 118 C 3
Geluk 174-175 F 4
Geluksburg 174-175 H 5
Gem 61 B 5
Gem, Lake — 85 II a 2
Gemas 148-149 D 6
Gemena 172 C 1
Gemerek 136-137 G 3
Gemiyanı 136-137 F 2
Gemlik 136-137 C 2
Gemlik körfezi 136-137 C 2
Gemona del Friuli 122-123 E 2
Gemsa = Jamsah 173 C 4
Gemsvlakte 174-175 C 4
Gemu Gofa 164-165 M 7
Genadendal 174-175 CD 7-8
Genale 164-165 N 7
Genç 136-137 J 3
Gendarme Barreto 108-109 D 8
Geneina, El- = Al-Junaynah 164-165 J 6
General Acha 111 CD 5
General Alvear [RA, Buenos Aires] 111 DE 5
General Alvear [RA, Mendoza] 111 C 4-5
General Arenales 106-107 G 5
General Artigas 102-103 DE 7
General Ballivián 104-105 E 8
General Belgrano [Antarctica] 53 B 32-33
General Belgrano [RA] 106-107 H 5
General Bernardo O'Higgins 53 C 31
General Cabrera 106-107 EF 4
General Câmara 106-107 M 2
General Campos 106-107 H 3
General Capdevila 104-105 EF 10
General Carneiro [BR, Mato Grosso] 102-103 F 1
General Carneiro [BR, Paraná] 102-103 G 7
General Carrera, Lago — 108-109 CD 6
General Cepeda 86-87 JK 5
General Conesa [RA, Buenos Aires] 106-107 J 6
General Conesa [RA, Río Negro] 111 CD 6
General Cruz 106-107 A 6
General D. Cerri 106-107 F 7
General Deheza 111 D 4
General Delgado 102-103 D 7
General Enrique Mosconi 111 D 2
General Eugenio A. Garay 102-103 AB 4
General Farfán 96-97 C 1
General Galarza 106-107 H 4
General Guido 111 E 5
General José de San Martín 111 E 3
General Juan Madariaga 111 E 5
General La Madrid 111 D 5
General Lavalle 111 E 5
General Levalle 106-107 EF 4
General Lorenzo Vintter 111 D 6
General Machado = Camacupa 172 C 4
General Mansilla 106-107 J 5
General Manuel Campos 106-107 EF 6
General Martín Miguel de Güemes 111 CD 2
General Nicolás H. Palacios 108-109 H 3
General Obligado 104-105 G 10
General O'Brien 106-107 G 5
General Paunero = Paunero 106-107 E 4
General Paz 106-107 H 5
General Pico 111 D 5
General Pinedo 111 D 3
General Pinto 106-107 FG 5
General Pirán 106-107 J 6
General Pizarro 104-105 E 9
General Plaza Gutierrez 96-97 BC 3
General Racedo 106-107 G 3-4
General Racedo, Valle — 108-109 E 4
General Roca 111 C 5
General Rondeau 106-107 F 7
General Saavedra 104-105 E 5
General Salgado 102-103 G 4
General San Martín [RA, Buenos Aires] 106-107 H 5
General San Martín [RA, La Pampa] 106-107 F 6-7
General San Martín-Caseros 110 III b 1
General San Martín-Villa Ballester 110 III b 1
General San Martín-Villa Bosch 110 III b 1
General San Martín-Villa José L. Suárez 110 III b 1
General San Martín-Villa Lynch 110 III b 1
General Santos 148-149 HJ 5
General Sarmiento 110 III a 1
General Sarmiento-Bella Vista 110 III ab 1
General Sarmiento-Campo de Mayo 110 III b 1
General Sarmiento-Grand Bourg 110 III a 1
General Sarmiento-los Polvorines 110 III ab 1
General Sarmiento-Muñiz 110 III a 1
General Sarmiento-Piñero 110 III a 1
General Sarmiento-Tortuguitas 110 III a 1
General Sarmiento-Villa de Mayo 110 III a 1
General Toševo 122-123 N 4
General Trías 86-87 GH 3
General Urquiza, Buenos Aires- 110 III b 1
General Vargas 106-107 K 2
General Viamonte 106-107 G 5
General Villamil = Playas 92-93 C 5
General Villegas 111 D 4-5
General Vintter, Lago — 108-109 D 4-5
Genesee, ID 66-67 E 2
Genesee River 72-73 GH 3
Geneseo, IL 70-71 E 5
Geneseo, KS 68-69 G 6
Geneseo, NY 72-73 H 3
Geneshuaya, Arroyo — 104-105 C 3
Geneva, AL 78-79 G 5
Geneva, NE 68-69 H 5
Geneva, NY 72-73 H 3
Geneva, OH 72-73 F 4
Geneva = Genève 118 C 5
Geneva, Lake — = Léman 118 C 5
Genève 118 C 5
Genghiz Khan, Wall of — 142-143 LM 2
Genhe [TJ, place] 142-143 N 1
Gen He [TJ, river] 142-143 N 1
Geničesk 126-127 G 3
Genil 120-121 E 10
Genk 120-121 K 3
Genkai nada 144-145 GH 6
Gennargentu, Monti del — 122-123 C 5-6
Gennevilliers 129 I c 2
Genoa 158-159 J 7
Genoa, IL 70-71 F 4
Genoa, NE 68-69 GH 5
Genoa, WI 70-71 E 4
Genoa = Gênova 122-123 C 3
Genoa, Arroyo — 108-109 D 5
Gênova 122-123 C 3
Gênova, Golfo di — 122-123 C 4
Genovesa, Isla — 92-93 B 4
Gent 120-121 JK 3
Genteng 148-149 E 8
Genteng, Tanjung — 152-153 FG 9
Gentilly, New Orleans-, LA 85 I c 1
Gentilly Terrace, New Orleans-, LA 85 I b 1
Gentilly Woods, New Orleans-, LA 85 I b 1
Genting 150-151 FG 11
Genting, Tanjung — 152-153 F 6
Gentio do Ouro 100-101 C 6
Genval 128 II b 2
Genzan = Wŏnsan 142-143 O 4
Geographe Bay 158-159 BC 6
Geographe Channel 158-159 B 4-5
Geokčaj 126-127 NO 6
Geok-Tepe 134-135 H 3
Georai = Gevrai 138-139 E 8
George 172 D 8
George, Lake — [AUS] 158-159 JK 7
George, Lake — [EAU] 172 F 2
George, Lake — [RWA] 171 B 3
George, Lake — [USA, Alaska] 58-59 PQ 5
George, Lake — [USA, Florida] 80-81 c 2
George, Lake — [USA, New York] 72-73 K 3
George, zemľa — 132-133 F-H 1
George Gills Range 158-159 F 4
George Island 108-109 JK 9
George River [CDN] 56-57 XY 6
George River [USA] 58-59 J 5
George S. Patton Park 84 II b 3
Georges River 161 I a 2
Georges River Bridge 161 I a 2-3
Georgetown, CA 74-75 C 3
Georgetown, DE 72-73 J 5
Georgetown, GA 78-79 G 5
Georgetown, ID 66-67 H 4
Georgetown, IL 70-71 G 6
Georgetown, KY 70-71 H 6
Georgetown, OH 72-73 E 5
Georgetown, SC 80-81 G 4
Georgetown, TX 76-77 F 7
Georgetown [AUS, Queensland] 158-159 H 3
George Town [AUS, Tasmania] 158-159 J 8
George Town [BS] 88-89 HJ 3
Georgetown [CDN, Ontario] 72-73 G 3
Georgetown [CDN, Prince Edward I.] 63 E 4
Georgetown [GB] 88-89 F 5
Georgetown [GUY] 92-93 H 3
Georgetown [WAG] 168-169 B 2
Georgetown [WV] 88-89 Q 8
George Town = Pinang 148-149 CD 5
Georgetown, Washington-, DC 82 II a 1
Georgetown of New Orleans, New Orleans-, LA 85 I bc 1
Georgetown University 82 II a 2
George Washington Birthplace National Monument 72-73 H 5
George Washington Bridge 82 III c 1
George Washington University 82 II a 2
George West, TX 76-77 E 8
Georgia 64-65 K 5
Georgia, South — 111 J 8
Georgia, Strait of — 56-57 M 8
Georgia at Atlanta, University of — 85 II bc 2
Georgiana, AL 78-79 F 5
Georgia National Guard 85 II bc 2
Georgian Bay 56-57 U 8-9
Georgian Soviet Socialist Republic 134-135 EF 2
Georgias del Sur, Islas — = South Georgia 111 J 8
Georgijevka 132-133 P 8
Georgijevsk 126-127 LM 4
Georgijevskoje 124-125 P 4
Georgina River 158-159 G 4
Georgswerder, Hamburg- 130 I b 1
Georg von Neumayer 53 B 36
Gera 118 EF 3
Gerais, Chapado dos — 92-93 K 8
Geral, Serra — [BR, Bahia ↓ Caculé] 100-101 C 8
Geral, Serra — [BR, Bahia ↖ Jequié] 100-101 D 7
Geral, Serra — [BR, Goiás] 100-101 A 6
Geral, Serra — [BR, Rio Grande do Sul ↖ Porto Alegre] 111 F 3
Geral, Serra — [BR, Rio Grande do Sul ↑ Porto Alegre] 106-107 M 2
Geral, Serra — [BR, Santa Catarina] 111 F 3
Geral, Serra — = Serra Grande 98-99 P 10
Geraldine 161 D 6-7
Geraldine, MT 66-67 HJ 2

Geraldton [AUS] 158-159 B 5
Geraldton [CDN] 56-57 T 8
Gerantahbawah 152-153 M 10
Gĕrasappa = Gersoppa 140 B 3
Gerasdorf bei Wien 113 I b 1
Gerasimovka 132-133 N 6
Gercif = Garsīf 166-167 E 2
Gercüş 136-137 J 4
Gerdakānehbālā 136-137 M 5
Gerdine, Mount — 56-57 F 5
Gerdview 170 V c 2
Gerede [TR, Bolu] 136-137 E 2
Gerede [TR, Eskişehir] 136-137 D 2
Gerede çayı 136-137 E 2
Gergebil' 126-127 N 5
Gering, NE 68-69 E 5
Gerlach, NV 66-67 D 5
Gerlachovský štít 118 JK 4
Gerli, Avellaneda- 110 III b 2
Gĕrlogubī 164-165 NO 7
Germania 106-107 FG 5
Germansen Landing 60 E 2
Germantown, TN 78-79 E 3
Germantown, Philadelphia-, PA 84 III b 1
Germany 118 C-F 2-4
Germencik 136-137 B 4
Germī 136-137 N 3
Germiston 172 E 7
Gern, München- 130 II b 2
Ger'nsy = Goris 126-127 N 7
Geroldswil 128 IV a 1
Gerona 120-121 J 8
Gerrard 60 J 4
Gers 120-121 H 7
Gersoppa 140 B 3
Gerstle River 58-59 P 5
Gertak Sanggui, Tanjung — 150-151 BC 10
Géryville = Al-Bayadh 166-167 G 3
Gerze 136-137 F 2
Gethsémani 63 F 2
Gettysburg, PA 72-73 H 5
Gettysburg, SD 68-69 G 3
Getulina 102-103 GH 4
Getúlio Vargas 106-107 LM 1
Getz Ice Shelf 53 B 23-24
Geuda Springs, KS 76-77 F 4
Geureudong, Gunung — 152-153 B 3
Geuzenveld, Amsterdam- 128 I a 1
Gevar ovası 136-137 L 4
Gevaş 136-137 K 3
Gevgelija 122-123 K 5
Gevrai 138-139 E 8
Gewanī 164-165 N 6
Geyang = Guoyang 146-147 F 5
Geyik dağı 136-137 E 4
Geylang, Singapore- 154 III b 2
Geyser, MT 66-67 H 2
Geyser, Banc du — 172 J 4
Geysir 116-117 c 2
Geyve 136-137 D 2
Gezira, El — = Al-Jazīrah 164-165 L 6
Gezir el-Ikhwân = Jazā'ir al-Ikhwān 173 D 4
Gezîret Mirâr = Jazīrat Marīr 173 DE 6
Gezir Qeisûm = Jazā'ir Qaysūm 173 CD 4

Ghāb, Al- 136-137 G 5
Ghâb, El — = Al-Ghāb 136-137 G 5
Ghāb, Jabal — 136-137 H 5
Ghabāt al-Mushajjarīn 166-167 F 2-G 1
Ghadai = Ghaday 136-137 M 8
Ghadâmes = Ghadāmis 164-165 FG 2-3
Ghadāmis 164-165 FG 2-3
Ghaday 136-137 M 8
Ghadūn, Wādī — 134-135 G 7
Ghaeratganj = Ghairatganj 138-139 G 6
Ghafargāon 138-139 N 5
Ghafsāi 166-167 D 2
Ghaggar 138-139 E 3
Ghāghara 134-135 N 5
Ghaibīḍero 138-139 A 4
Ghairatganj 138-139 G 6
Ghallah, Bi'r — 173 C 3
Ghalvāḍ = Gholvad 138-139 D 7
Gham'ā 166-167 J 3
Ghamal, Ḥāssī — 166-167 J 4
Ghana 164-165 DE 7
Ghanāīn Bū Rizq 166-167 F 3
Ghanamī, Ḥāssī al- 166-167 JK 4
Ghāndhi Sāgar 138-139 E 5
Ghānim, Jazīrat — 173 C 4
Ghanzi 172 D 6
Ghār, Al- 166-167 L 5
Ghār ad-Dimā' 166-167 L 1
Ghār al-Milḥ 166-167 M 1
Ghārāpuri = Elephanta Island 140 A 1
Gharaq as-Sulṭānī, Al- 173 AB 3
Ghār aṣ-Ṣallah 166-167 E 3
Gharb, Al- 166-167 C 2
Gharb al-Istiwā'iyah 164-165 KL 7
Gharbī, Jabal — 136-137 H 5
Gharbī, Jazīrat al- 166-167 M 2
Gharbī, Wādī al- 166-167 G 3-4
Ghardan, Bi'r — 166-167 K 2
Ghardaqah, Al- 164-165 L 3
Ghardāyah 164-165 E 2
Ghardimaou = Ghār ad-Dimā' 166-167 L 1
Ghardūār 141 C 2
Ghārgāňv = Ghārgaon 138-139 E 8
Ghārgaon 138-139 E 8
Ghargoda 138-139 J 6
Ghārib, Jabal — 164-165 L 3
Gharīd 166-167 K 3
Ghāris [DZ] 166-167 J 7
Gharīs [MA] 166-167 D 4
Gharīs, Al- 166-167 G 2
Gharīs, Wād — 166-167 D 3-4
Ghāro 138-139 A 5
Gharqābād 136-137 NO 5
Gharsa, Chott el — = Shaṭṭ al-Jarsah 166-167 KL 2
Gharyān 164-165 G 2
Ghassoul = Ghasul 166-167 G 3
Ghasul 166-167 G 3
Ghaswani 138-139 F 5
Ghat 164-165 G 3
Ghāṭ'ā', Al- 136-137 J 5
Ghātāl 138-139 L 6
Ghātampur 138-139 GH 4
Ghāṭīgāňv = Ghātīgaon 138-139 F 4
Ghātīgaon 138-139 F 4
Ghatol 138-139 E 6
Ghatprabha 140 B 2
Ghats, Eastern — 134-135 M 8-N 7
Ghats, Western — 134-135 L 6-M 8
Ghāṭshilā = Ghātsīla 138-139 L 6
Ghātsīla 138-139 L 6
Ghawdex 122-123 F 7
Ghayḍah, Al- [ADN ← Sayḥūt] 134-135 FG 7-8
Ghayḍah, Al- [ADN ↗ Sayḥūt] 134-135 G 7
Ghazāl, 'Ayn al- [ET] 173 B 5
Ghazal, 'Ayn al- [LAR] 164-165 J 4
Ghazawāt 164-165 D1
Ghazeil, Bîr el — = Bi'r al-Ghuzayl 166-167 M 5
Ghāziābād 138-139 F 3
Ghāzīpur 138-139 J 5
Ghazīr = Jazīr 136-137 F 5
Ghaz köl 142-143 G 4
Ghazni 134-135 K 4
Ghazzah 134-135 C 4
Ghedo = Gêdo 164-165 M 7
Ghent = Gent 120-121 JK 3
Gheorghe Gheorghiu-Dej 122-123 M 2
Gheorghieni 122-123 LM 2
Gheorghiu-Dej 126-127 JK 1
Gherāsahan 138-139 K 4
Gherdi 140 B 2
Gheris, Oued — = Wād Gharīs 166-167 D 3-4
Gherla 122-123 KL 2
Gherlogubi = Gerlogubī 164-165 NO 7
Ghiedo = Gêdo 164-165 M 7
Ghigner = Gīnīr 164-165 N 7
Ghimbi = Gimbī 164-165 M 7
Ghinah, Wādī al- 136-137 G 7-8
Ghio, Lago — 108-109 D 6
Ghir, Cap — = Rā's Ghīr 166-167 AB 4
Ghir, Cape — = Rā's Ghīr 166-167 AB 4
Ghīr, Rā's — 166-167 AB 4
Ghod 140 B 1
Gholvad 138-139 D 7
Ghôr, El — = Al-Ghūr 136-137 F 7
Ghōṛāsahan = Gherāsahan 138-139 K 4
Ghosi 138-139 J 4
Ghost River [CDN ↗ Dryden] 62 D 2
Ghost River [CDN ↑ Hearst] 62 H 2
Ghotāru 138-139 C 4
Ghotkī 138-139 B 3-4
Ghoumerassen = Ghumrāssin 166-167 M 3
Ghraybah, Al- 166-167 LM 2
Ghriss = Al-Gharīs 166-167 G 2
Ghubbat al-Qamar 134-135 G 7
Ghubbat Ṣauqirah = Dawḥat as-Sawqirah 134-135 H 7
Ghughri 138-139 H 6
Ghugri 138-139 L 5
Ghūgus 138-139 G 8
Ghuja 142-143 E 3
Ghumrāssin 166-167 M 3
Ghūr, Al- 136-137 F 7
Ghurarah 166-167 FG 5
Ghūrāyah 166-167 GH 1
Ghurd Abū Muḥarrik 164-165 KL 3
Ghurd al-Baghl 166-167 K 4
Ghurdaqa, El — = Al-Ghardaqah 164-165 L 3
Ghurrah, Shaṭṭ al- 166-167 M 2
Ghūryān 134-135 J 4
Ghuzayl, Bi'r al- 166-167 M 5

Gia Lai, Cao Nguyên — 150-151 G 5
Gia Nghia 150-151 F 7
Giannitsá 122-123 K 5
Giannutri 122-123 D 4
Giant Mountains 118 GH 3
Giant's Castle 174-175 H 5
Giant's Castle National Park 174-175 H 5
Gia Rai 148-149 E 5
Giardino Zoologico 113 II b 1
Giarre 122-123 F 7
Gibara 88-89 HJ 4
Gibbon, NE 68-69 G 5
Gibbon, OR 66-67 D 3
Gibbonsville, ID 66-67 G 3
Gibbsboro, NJ 84 III d 2
Gibbs City, MI 70-71 F 2
Gibbs City, WI 70-71 F 2
Gibbstown, NJ 84 III b 3
Gibeil = Jubayl 173 C 3
Gibeon [Namibia, administrative unit] 174-175 C 3
Gibeon [Namibia, place] 172 C 7
Gibraltar 120-121 E 10
Gibraltar, Strait of — 120-121 DE 11
Gibsland, LA 78-79 C 4
Gibson City, IL 70-71 F 5
Gibson Desert 158-159 DE 4
Gidajevo 124-125 ST 4
Gidan Mountains = Kolymskij nagorje 132-133 g 4-e 5
Giddalūr 140 D 3
Giddalūru = Giddalūr 140 D 3
Giddings, TX 76-77 F 7
Gideon, MO 78-79 DE 2
Gidgealpa 160 DE 1
Gīdolē 164-165 M 7
Gien 120-121 J 5
Giesing, München- 130 II b 2
Giessen 118 D 3
Giesshübl 113 I a 2
Giffard, Lac — 62 N 1
Gifu 142-143 Q 4
Gigant 126-127 K 3
Giganta, Sierra de la — 64-65 D 6-7
Gigantes, Cerro los — 106-107 E 3
Gigantes, Llanos de los — 86-87 HJ 3
Giglio 122-123 D 4
Gigüela 120-121 F 9
Gihân, Râs — = Rā's al-Bālā'im 173 C 3
Giheina = Juhaynah 173 B 4
Gihu = Gifu 142-143 Q 4
Gijón 120-121 E 7
Gil [BR] 106-107 M 2
Gil [RA] 106-107 G 7
Gila Bend, AZ 74-75 G 6
Gila Cliff 74-75 J 6
Gila Cliff Dwellings National Monument 74-75 J 6
Gila Desert 64-65 D 5
Gilâm = Jihlam 138-139 D 2
Gila Mountains 74-75 J 6
Gīlān 134-135 FG 3
Gīlān, Sarāb-e — 136-137 LM 5
Gīlān-e Gharb 136-137 LM 5
Gilardo Dam 72-73 K 1
Gila River 64-65 D 5
Gila River Indian Reservation 74-75 GH 6
Gilbert 106-107 H 4
Gilbert, Isla — 108-109 D 10
Gilbert, Mount — 58-59 o 3
Gilbert Islands 208 H 2-3
Gilbertown, AL 78-79 E 5
Gilbert River [AUS, place] 158-159 H 3
Gilbert River [AUS, river] 158-159 H 3
Gilbués 92-93 K 6
Gilby, ND 68-69 H 1
Gildford, MT 68-69 A 1
Gilead 174-175 H 2
Gilf Kebir Plateau = Haḍbat al-Jilf al-Kabīr 164-165 K 4
Gilgandra 158-159 J 6
Gilgat = Gilgit 134-135 L 3
Gilgil 171 CD 3
Gilgit 134-135 L 3
Gilindire 136-137 E 4
Gil Island 60 C 3
Gill, CO 68-69 D 5
Gillam 56-57 S 6
Gillen, Lake — 158-159 D 5
Gilles, Lake — 160 C 4
Gillespie, IL 70-71 EF 6
Gillett, AR 78-79 D 3
Gillett, WI 70-71 F 3
Gillette, WY 68-69 D 3
Gillon Point 58-59 p 6
Gilman, IA 70-71 D 5
Gilman, IL 70-71 FG 5
Gilman, WI 70-71 E 3
Gilmer, TX 76-77 G 6
Gilmore, GA 85 II b 1
Gilmore, ID 66-67 G 3
Gilolo = Halmahera 148-149 J 6
Gilroy, CA 74-75 G 4
Giluwe, Mount — 148-149 M 8
Gimbala, Jebel — = Jabal Marrah 164-165 JK 6
Gimbī 164-165 M 7
Gimli 62 A 2
Gimma = Jīma 164-165 M 7
Gimpu 148-149 GH 7
Gineifa = Junayfah 173 C 2
Ginevrabotnen 116-117 kl 5
Gin Ganga = Ging Ganga 140 E 7
Gingee 140 D 4
Ging Ganga 140 E 7
Gingindlovu 174-175 J 5
Gīngiova 122-123 KL 4
Gīnīr 164-165 N 7
Ginnheim, Frankfurt am Main- 128 III a 1
Ginyer = Gīnīr 164-165 N 7
Ginza, Tōkyō- 155 III b 1
Gioia del Colle 122-123 G 5
Giông Riêng = Kiên Binh 150-151 E 8
Giông Trôm 150-151 F 7-8
Giovi, Passo dei — 122-123 C 3
Gippsland 158-159 J 7
Gîr, Hammadat al- 166-167 E 4
Gīr, Wādī — 166-167 E 4
Girard, IL 70-71 F 6
Girard, KS 70-71 C 7
Girard, OH 72-73 F 4
Girard, PA 72-73 F 3-4
Girard, TX 76-77 D 6
Girardet 106-107 F 1
Girardot 92-93 E 4
Girardota 94-95 D 4
Giravān = Girwān 138-139 H 5
Girdwood, AK 58-59 N 6
Giren = Jīma 164-165 M 7
Giresun 134-135 D 2
Giresun dağları 136-137 H 2
Girge = Jirjā 164-165 L 3
Gīr Hills 138-139 C 7
Giri 172 C 1
Giridih 134-135 O 6
Girilambone 160 H 3
Girishk 134-135 J 4
Girna 138-139 E 7
Girnār Hills 138-139 C 7
Girón [CO] 94-95 E 4
Girón [EC] 96-97 B 3
Gironde 120-121 G 6
Girsovo 124-125 RS 4
Girvan 119 D 4
Girvas [SU, Karel'skaja ASSR] 124-125 J 2
Girvas [SU, Rossijskaja SFSR] 116-117 O 4
Girvas, vodopad — 124-125 J 2
Girvin 61 EF 5
Girvin, TX 76-77 C 7
Girwān 138-139 H 5
Gisasa River 58-59 H 4
Gisborne 158-159 P 7
Giscome 60 FG 2
Gisenyi 172 E 2
Gislaved 116-117 E 9
Gisr ash-Shughur 136-137 G 5
Gīṣṣar 166-167 C 3
Gitega 172 EF 2
Giuba = Webi Ganaane 172 H 1
Giuba, Isole — 172 H 2
Giulianova 122-123 EF 4
Giumbo = Jumbo 172 H 2
Giūra 122-123 L 6
Giurgiu 122-123 L 4
Giustiniana, Roma-La — 113 II ab 1
Givet 120-121 K 3
Giyani 174-175 J 2
Giždųvan 132-133 L 9
Gizeh = Al-Jīzah 164-165 KL 3
Gizhigin Bay = Gižiginskaja guba 132-133 e 5
Gižiga 132-133 f 5
Gižiginskaja guba 132-133 e 5
Gīzmel 136-137 M 5
Gizo 148-149 j 6
Gižycko 118 KL 1

Gjersvik 116-117 E 5
Gjiri i Drinit 122-123 H 5
Gjirokastër 122-123 HJ 5
Gjögurtá 116-117 d 1
Gjøvik 116-117 D 7
Gjuhës, Kepi i — 122-123 H 5

Glace Bay 56-57 YZ 8
Glacier Bay 58-59 TU 7
Glacier Bay National Monument 56-57 J 6
Glacier Mount 58-59 QR 4
Glacier National Park [CDN] 60 J 4
Glacier National Park [USA] 64-65 CD 2
Glacier Peak 66-67 C 1
Gladbrook, IA 70-71 D 4
Glade Park, CO 74-75 J 3
Gladesville, Sydney- 161 I a 1
Gladstone, MI 70-71 G 3
Gladstone [AUS, Queensland] 158-159 K 4
Gladstone [AUS, South Australia] 158-159 G 6
Gladstone [CDN] 61 J 5
Gladwin, MI 70-71 H 4
Gladwyne, PA 84 III b 1
Glady, WV 72-73 G 5
Glāma 116-117 b 2
Glamis, CA 74-75 F 6
Glasco, KS 68-69 H 6
Glasgow 119 DE 4
Glasgow, KY 70-71 H 7
Glasgow, MO 70-71 D 6
Glasgow, MT 68-69 C 1
Glaslyn 61 D 4
Glassboro, NJ 72-73 J 5
Glass Mountains 76-77 C 7
Glattbrugg 128 IV b 1
Glauchau 118 F 3
Glavnyj Kut 126-127 N 5
Glazier, TX 76-77 D 4
Glazok 124-125 N 7
Glazov 132-133 J 6
Gleeson, AZ 74-75 J 7
Gleisdorf 118 GH 5
Glen 174-175 G 5
Glen, NE 68-69 E 4
Glen Afton 72-73 FG 1
Glenboro 61 J 6
Glenbrook 160 K 4
Glenbrook Valley, Houston-, TX 85 III b 2
Glen Canyon 74-75 H 4
Glencoe, MN 70-71 C 3
Glencoe [CDN] 72-73 F 3
Glencoe [ZA] 174-175 HJ 5
Glendale, AZ 64-65 D 5
Glendale, CA 64-65 C 5
Glendale, NV 74-75 F 4
Glendale, OR 66-67 B 4
Glendale, Washington-, DC 82 II b 2
Glendale Cove 60 E 4
Glendevey, CO 68-69 D 5
Glendive, MT 68-69 D 2
Glendo, WY 68-69 D 4
Glendon 61 C 3
Glendora, NJ 84 III c 2
Glenelg 160 E 6
Glengyle 158-159 GH 4
Glen Innes 158-159 K 5
Glen Lyon, PA 72-73 HJ 4
Glen Mar Park, MD 82 II a 1
Glenmora, LA 78-79 C 5
Glen More 119 D 3
Glenmorgan 158-159 JK 5
Glennallen, AK 58-59 P 5
Glennie, MI 70-71 J 3
Glenns Ferry, ID 66-67 F 4
Glenolden, PA 84 III b 2
Glenora 58-59 W 8
Glenore 158-159 H 3
Glen Riddle, PA 84 III a 2
Glen Ridge, NJ 82 III a 2
Glenrio, NM 76-77 C 5
Glenrock, WY 68-69 D 4
Glen Rose, TX 76-77 F 6
Glens Falls, NY 72-73 K 3
Glen Shannon, Houston-, TX 85 III a 2
Glenside 174-175 J 5
Glenside, PA 84 III c 1
Glentworth 68-69 C 1
Glenville, MN 70-71 D 4
Glenwood, AR 78-79 C 3
Glenwood, IA 70-71 C 5
Glenwood, MN 70-71 C 3
Glenwood, OR 66-67 B 3
Glenwood, WA 66-67 C 2
Glenwood Cemetery 85 III b 1
Glenwood Springs, CO 68-69 C 6
Glenwoodville 60 L 5
Gleta, La — = Ḥalq al-Wad 166-167 M 1
Glicério 102-103 LM 5
Glidden 61 D 5
Glidden, WI 70-71 E 2
Glide, OR 66-67 B 4
Glienicke 130 III a 2
Glina 122-123 G 3
Glinka 124-125 J 6
Glint ustup 124-125 E-J 4
Glittertind 116-117 C 7
Głiwice 118 J 3
Globe, AZ 64-65 D 5
Globino 126-127 F 2
Gloggnitz 118 G 5
Głogów 118 GH 3
Glomfjord 116-117 EF 4
Glomma 116-117 D 7
Glommersträsk 116-117 HJ 5
Glória 92-93 M 6
Gloria, La — [CO] 92-93 E 3
Gloria, La — [RA] 106-107 F 6
Glória, Rio de Janeiro- 110 I b 2
Gloria de Dourados 102-103 EF 5
Glória do Goitá 100-101 G 4-5
Glorieta, NM 76-77 B 5
Glorieuses, Îles — 172 J 4
Glorioso Islands = Îles Glorieuses 172 J 4
Glosam 174-175 E 5
Gloster, MS 78-79 D 5
Glotovka 124-125 Q 7
Glotovo 124-125 RS 2
Gloucester, MA 72-73 L 3
Gloucester City, NJ 72-73 J 5
Glouchester 119 E 6
Glouster, OH 72-73 EF 5
Glouster, Cabo — 108-109 BC 10
Gloversville, NY 72-73 J 3
Glovertown 63 J 3
Glubacha 124-125 V 4
Glubokij 126-127 K 2
Glubokoje [SU, Belorusskaja SSR] 124-125 F 6
Glubokoje [SU, Kazachskaja SSR] 132-133 P 7
Gluchov 124-125 J 8
Gluša 124-125 G 7
Glusk 124-125 G 7
Glyndon, MN 68-69 H 2

Gmelinka 126-127 N 1
Gmünd 118 G 4
Gmunden 118 FG 5

Gnaday 136-137 M 8
Gnezdovo 124-125 H 6
Gniezno 118 H 2
Gniloj Tikič 126-127 E 2
Gnowangerup 158-159 C 6

Goa 134-135 L 7
Goageb [Namibia, place] 172 C 7
Goageb [Namibia, river] 174-175 B 4
Goālpara 141 B 2
Goanikontes 174-175 A 2
Goaso 164-165 D 7
Goba [ETH] 164-165 N 7
Goba [Mozambique] 174-175 K 4
Gobabis 172 C 6
Goba La 138-139 K 2
Gobas 174-175 C 4
Gobernador Ayala 106-107 CD 6
Gobernador Costa 108-109 D 5
Gobernador Crespo 106-107 G 3
Gobernador Duval 106-107 DE 7
Gobernador Gálvez 106-107 GH 4
Gobernador Gregores 111 BC 7
Gobernador Ingeniero Valentín Virasoro 106-107 J 2
Gobernador Mansilla 106-107 H 4
Gobernador Monteverde, Florencio Varela- 110 III c 2
Gobernador Moyano 108-109 D 8
Gobernador Piedra Buena 104-105 D 10
Gobi 142-143 H-L 3
Gobindganj 138-139 K 4
Gobindpur 138-139 K 6
Gobō 144-145 K 6
Gochas 174-175 C 3
Gockhausen 128 IV b 1
Go Công 150-151 F 7
Goḍāgāri 138-139 M 5
Godār-e Shāh 136-137 MN 5
Godarpura 138-139 F 6
Go Dâu Ha 150-151 F 7
Godāvari 134-135 N 7
Godāvari Delta 134-135 N 7
Godāvari Plain 138-139 EF 8
Godbout 63 C 3
Godda 138-139 L 5
Goddo 92-93 HJ 4
Goddua = Ghuddawah 164-165 G 3
Goderich 72-73 EF 3
Godfrey's Tank 158-159 E 4
Godhavn = Qeqertarssuq 56-57 Za 4
Godhra 138-139 D 6
Godoy [RA] 106-107 G 4
Godoy Cruz 111 BC 4
Gods Lake [CDN, lake] 56-57 S 7
Gods Lake [CDN, place] 56-57 S 7
Godthåb = Nûk 56-57 a 5
Godwin Austen, Mount — = K2 134-135 M 3
Goede Hoop, De — 98-99 K 2
Goeje Gebergte, De — 98-99 L 3
Goela 138-139 E 4
Goéland, Lac — 62 N 2
Goeree 120-121 J 3
Goethehaus 128 III ab 1
Goetheturm 128 III b 1
Goffs, CA 74-75 F 5
Gogebic, Lake — 70-71 F 2
Gogebic Range 70-71 EF 2
Goggiam = Gojam 164-165 M 6
Gogland, ostrov — 124-125 F 3
Gogra = Ghāghara 134-135 N 5
Gogrial = Qūqriāl 164-165 K 7
Gohad 138-139 G 4
Gohāna 138-139 F 3
Goharganj 138-139 F 6
Gohilwār 138-139 C 7
Gohpur 141 C 2
Goiabal 96-97 F 4
Goiana 92-93 MN 6
Goiandira 92-93 K 8
Goiânia 92-93 JK 8
Goianinha 100-101 G 4
Goiás [BR, administrative unit] 92-93 J 8-K 7
Goiás [BR, place] 92-93 JK 8
Goiatuba 92-93 JK 8
Goicoechea, Isla de — = New Island 108-109 J 8
Goidu 176 a 2
Goio Erê 102-103 F 6
Goioxim 102-103 FG 6
Gojam 164-165 M 6
Gojjam = Gojam 164-165 M 6
Gojrā 138-139 D 2
Gokāk 140 B 2
Gōkāka = Gokāk 140 B 2
Gökbel 136-137 C 4
Gökçe 136-137 A 2
Gökçe ada 136-137 AB 2
Gôkhteik 141 E 4
Gökırmak 136-137 F 2
Gokokuji Temple 155 III b 1
Gokōmutsumi 155 III c 1
Göksu [TR, place] 136-137 K 3
Göksu [TR, river] 136-137 FG 4
Göksu bendi 154 I b 2
Göksu deresi 154 I b 2
Göksun 136-137 G 3
Göksu nehir 134-135 C 3
Gök tepe 136-137 C 4
Gokurt 138-139 A 3
Gokwe 172 E 5
Gol 116-117 C 7
Gola 138-139 K 6
Golabari, Howrah- 154 II b 2
Golāghāt 141 CD 2
Golā Gokarannāth 138-139 H 3
Golaja Pristan' 126-127 F 3
Golakganj 138-139 MN 4
Golāshkerd 134-135 H 5
Gölbaşı [TR, Adıyaman] 136-137 G 4
Gölbaşı [TR, Ankara] 136-137 E 3
Golconda, IL 70-71 F 7
Golconda, NV 66-67 E 5
Gölcük [TR, Kocaeli] 136-137 CD 2
Gøldap 118 L 1
Gold Bar 60 F 1
Gold Beach, OR 66-67 A 4
Gold Bridge 60 F 4
Goldburg, ID 66-67 G 3
Gold Butte, MT 66-67 H 1
Gold Coast [AUS] 158-159 K 5
Gold Coast [GH] 164-165 DE 8
Gold Coast-Southport 160 LM 1
Gold Creek, AK 58-59 N 5
Golden 60 J 4
Golden, ID 66-67 F 3
Golden, IL 70-71 E 5
Golden Bay 161 E 5
Golden City, MO 70-71 C 7
Goldendale, WA 66-67 C 3
Golden Ears Provincial Park 60 F 5
Golden Gate 64-65 B 4
Golden Gate Bridge 83 I b 2
Golden Gate Fields Race Track 83 I bc 1
Golden Gate Park 83 I ab 2
Golden Hinde 60 E 5
Golden Meadow, LA 78-79 D 6
Golden Prairie 61 D 5
Golden Vale 119 BC 5
Golders Green, London- 129 II b 1
Goldfield, NV 74-75 E 4
Gold Hill, UT 66-67 G 5
Goldküste 164-165 D 8-E 7
Gold Point, NV 74-75 E 4
Gold River 60 D 5
Goldsand Lake 61 H 2
Goldsboro, NC 64-65 L 4-5
Goldsmith, TX 76-77 C 6-7
Goldstein, Frankfurt am Main- 128 III a 1
Goldsworthy, Mount — 158-159 CD 4
Goldthwaite, TX 76-77 E 7
Göle = Merdenik 136-137 K 2
Goléa, El- = Al-Gulī'ah 164-165 E 2
Golec-In'aptuk, gora — = gora In'aptuk 132-133 UV 6
Golec-Longdor, gora — = gora Longdor 132-133 W 6
Golela 172 F 7
Goleniów 118 G 2
Goleta, CA 74-75 D 5
Golf du Lion 120-121 JK 7
Golfe de Bejaïa = Khalīj Bijāyah 166-167 1
Golfe de Bonny 164-165 F 8
Golfe de Bougie = Khalīj Bijāyah 166-167 J 1
Golfe de Bou Grara = Khalīj Bū Ghrārah 166-167 M 3
Golfe de Honduras 64-65 J 8
Golfe de la Gonâve 64-65 M 8
Golfe de los Mosquitos 64-65 K 10
Golfe de Tadjoura 164-165 N 6
Golfe du Saint-Laurent = Gulf of Saint Lawrence 56-57 Y 8
Golfe Nuevo 111 D 6
Golfete de Coro 94-95 F 2
Golfito 64-65 K 10
Golf Links 161 II c 1
Golfo Almirante Montt 108-109 C 8
Golfo Aranci 122-123 CD 5
Golfo Corcovado 108-109 C 4
Golfo de Almería 120-121 F 10
Golfo de Ancud 111 B 6
Golfo de Arauco 106-107 A 6
Golfo de Batabanó 64-65 K 7
Golfo de Cádiz 120-121 D 10
Golfo de Cariaco 94-95 JK 2
Golfo de Chiriquí 64-65 K 10
Golfo de Cupica 92-93 D 3
Golfo de Fonseca 64-65 J 9
Golfo de Guacanayabo 64-65 L 7
Golfo de Guafo 111 B 6
Golfo de Guayaquil 92-93 C 5
Golfo del Darién 92-93 D 3
Golfo de los Coronados 108-109 BC 3
Golfo del Papagayo 64-65 J 9
Golfo de Mazarrón 120-121 G 10
Golfo de Montijo 88-89 F 11
Golfo de Morrosquillo 92-93 D 2-3
Golfo de Nicoya 64-65 J 9
Golfo de Panamá 64-65 L 10
Golfo de Paria 92-93 G 2
Golfo de Parita 88-89 FG 10
Golfo de Penas 111 AB 7
Golfo de San Jorge 120-121 H 8
Golfo de San Miguel 88-89 G 10
Golfo de Santa Clara, El — 86-87 C 2
Golfo de Tehuantepec 64-65 GH 8
Golfo de Urabá 92-93 D 3
Golfo de Valencia 120-121 H 9
Golfo de Venezuela 92-93 E 2
Golfo di Càgliari 122-123 C 6
Golfo di Castellammare 122-123 E 6
Golfo di Gaeta 122-123 E 5
Golfo di Gènova 122-123 C 4
Golfo di Manfredònia 122-123 FG 5
Golfo di Nàpoli 122-123 EF 5
Golfo di Policastro 122-123 F 5-6
Golfo di Salerno 122-123 F 5
Golfo di Sant'Eufèmia 122-123 FG 6
Golfo di Squillace 122-123 G 6
Golfo di Tàranto 122-123 G 5
Golfo di Venèzia 122-123 E 3
Golfo Dulce 64-65 K 10
Golfo Elefantes 108-109 BC 6
Golfo Ladrillero 108-109 AB 7
Golfo San Esteban 108-109 B 6
Golfo San Jorge 111 CD 7
Golfo San José 108-109 G 4
Golfo San Matías 111 D 6
Golfo Tres Montes 108-109 B 6
Golfo Trinidad 108-109 B 7
Golfo Triste 94-95 GH 2
Golf parc 170 IV a 1
Gölhisar 136-137 C 4
Goliad, TX 76-77 F 8
Goljanovo, Moskva- 113 V d 2
Gölköy = Kuşluyan 136-137 G 2
Gollel 174-175 J 4
Göllü = Çoğun 136-137 F 3
Gölmarmara 136-137 BC 3
Golmo 142-143 GH 4
Goloby 124-125 E 8
Golodnaja step' = Betpak-Dala 132-133 MN 8
Golog Zangzu Zizhizhou 142-143 HJ 5
Golog Zizhizhou 142-143 HJ 5
Golondrina 106-107 G 2
Golondrinas, Arroyo — 106-107 G 2
Golovanovo 124-125 N 6
Golovinščino 124-125 OP 7
Golovnin, AK 58-59 F 4
Golovnin Bay 58-59 F 4
Golovnin Mission, AK 58-59 F 4
Golpāyegān 134-135 G 4
Gölpazarı 136-137 D 2
Golspie 119 E 2-3
Gol Tappeh 136-137 L 4
Golubi 124-125 NO 4
Golubovka 126-127 G 2
Golungo Alto 172 B 3
Golva, ND 68-69 E 2
Gölveren 136-137 E 4
Golynki 124-125 H 6
Golyšmanovo 132-133 MN 6
Goma 172 E 2
Gomang Tsho 138-139 M 2
Gomati 134-135 N 5
Gomba 171 D 5
Gombari 171 B 2
Gombe [EAT] 172 F 2
Gombe [WAN] 164-165 G 6
Gombe, Kinshasa- 170 IV a 1

Gombe, Pointe de la — 170 IV a 1
Gombi 168-169 J 3
Gomel' 124-125 H 7
Gömele 136-137 D 2
Gomel'-Novobelica 124-125 H 7
Gomera 164-165 A 3
Gomes, Serra do — 98-99 P 9
Gómez, Lagunas de — 106-107 G 5
Gómez Farías 86-87 G 3
Gómez Palacio 64-65 EF 6
Gómez Rendón 96-97 A 3
Gonābād 134-135 H 4
Gonaïves 64-65 M 8
Gonam [SU, place] 132-133 Z 6
Gonam [SU, river] 132-133 Y 6
Gonâve, Golfe de la — 64-65 M 8
Gonâve, Île de la — 64-65 M 8
Gonbād-e Kavus = Gonbad-e Qābūs 134-135 H 3
Gonbad-e Qābūs 134-135 H 3
Gonda 138-139 HJ 4
Gondal 138-139 C 7
Gondar = Gonder 164-165 M 6
Gonder 164-165 M 6
Gondia 138-139 H 7
Gōṅdiyā = Gondia 138-139 H 7
Gondjakammā = Gundlakamma 140 DE 3
Gōṇḍvānā = Gondwānā 138-139 GH 6
Gondwānā 138-139 GH 6
Gönen 136-137 B 2
Gonesse 129 I c 2
Gong'an 146-147 D 6-7
Gongcheng 146-147 C 9
Gongdu = Guangdu 146-147 DE 7
Gongga Shan 142-143 J 6
Gongguan 146-147 B 11
Gonghui 146-147 C 9
Gongjiatun = Gangtun 144-145 C 2
Gongke Zong = Gongkar Dsong 138-139 N 3
Gonglee 168-169 C 4
Gongliao = Kungliao 146-147 HJ 9
Gongoh = Gangoh 138-139 F 3
Gongoji 100-101 E 8
Gongoji, Rio — 100-101 DE 8
Gongoji, Serra do — 92-93 LM 7-8
Gongola 164-165 G 6
Gongshan 141 F 2
Gong Shui 146-147 E 9
Gong Xian 146-147 D 4
Gongyingzi 144-145 BC 2
Gongzhuling = Huaide 142-143 NO 3
Goñi 106-107 J 4
Goniądz 118 L 2
Gonja 171 D 4
Gono-kawa 144-145 J 5
Gonoura 144-145 G 6
Gonzales, CA 74-75 C 4
Gonzales, LA 78-79 D 5
Gonzales, TX 76-77 F 8
González [MEX] 86-87 L 6
González [ROU] 106-107 J 5
González Catán, La Matanza- 110 III b 2
González Moreno 106-107 F 5
González Suárez 96-97 D 3
Gonzanamá 92-93 D 5
Goobies 63 JK 4
Goodenough, Cape — 53 C 13
Goodenough Island 148-149 gh 6
Good Hope [CDN] 60 D 4
Good Hope [ZA] 174-175 DE 6
Good Hope, Cape of — 172 C 8
Good Hope, Washington-, DC 82 II b 2
Goodhope Bay 58-59 F 3
Goodhouse 172 C 7
Gooding, ID 66-67 F 4
Goodland, KS 68-69 F 6
Goodman, WI 70-71 F 3
Goodnews, AK 58-59 FG 7
Goodnews Bay 58-59 FG 7
Goodnews River 58-59 G 7
Goodooga 160 HJ 2
Goodpaster River 58-59 P 4
Goodsoil 61 D 3
Goodwater 68-69 E 1
Goodwell, OK 76-77 CD 4
Goolgowi 160 G 4
Goomalling 158-159 C 6
Goona = Guna 134-135 M 6
Goondiwindi 158-159 JK 5
Goonyella 158-159 J 4
Goose Bay [CDN, British Columbia] 60 D 4
Goose Bay [CDN, Newfoundland] 56-57 Y 7
Gooseberry Creek 68-69 B 3-4
Goose Creek 66-67 FG 4
Goose Island 82 II a 2
Goose Lake [CDN] 61 H 3
Goose Lake [USA] 64-65 B 3
Goose River [CDN] 60 J 2
Goose River [USA] 68-69 H 2
Gooti 140 C 3
Gopālganj [BD] 138-139 M 6
Gopālganj [IND] 138-139 K 4
Gopat 138-139 J 5
Gopīballabhpur 138-139 L 6
Gopiballavpur = Gopīballabhpur 138-139 L 6
Go Quao 148-149 DE 5
gora Agoj 126-127 J 4
gora Aksoran 132-133 O 8
gora Aragac 126-127 M 6
gora Babadag 126-127 O 6
gora Bazardʼuzi 126-127 N 6
gora Belen'kaja 124-125 QR 7
gora Belucha 132-133 Q 8
gora Besšoky 134-135 G 2
gora Blednaja 132-133 M 2
gora Bol'šije Abuli 126-127 LM 6
gora Burun-Šibertuj 132-133 UV 8
Gor'ačegorsk 132-133 Q 6
Gor'ačevodskij 126-127 L 4-5
gora Chalab 126-127 M 6
Gor'ačij Kl'uč 126-127 J 4
gora Čuguš 126-127 JK 5
Goradiz 126-127 N 7
gora Dombaj-Ul'gen 126-127 KL 5
gora D'ubrar 126-127 O 6
gora Dvuch Cirkov 132-133 gh 4
gora Dychtau 126-127 L 5
gora Džambul 132-133 N 9
gora Dzeržinskaja 124-125 F 7
gora El'brus 126-127 L 5
gora Fišt 126-127 J 5
gora G'amyš 126-127 N 6
gora Golec-In'aptuk = gora In'aptuk 132-133 UV 6
gora Golec-Longdor = gora Longdor 132-133 W 6
Goragorskij 126-127 M 5
gora Goverla 126-127 B 2
gora Ička 124-125 S 8
gora In'aptuk 132-133 UV 6
gora Innymnej 132-133 kl 4
gora Išerim 132-133 K 5
gora Jamantau 132-133 K 7
gora Jenašimskij Polkan 132-133 RS 6
gora Kammenik 124-125 HJ 5
gora Kapydžik 126-127 M 7
gora Kazbek 126-127 M 5
gora Kelil'vun 132-133 g 4
Gorakhpur = Gorakhpoor 134-135 N 5
gora Ko 132-133 a 8
gora Kojp 124-125 W 2
Gorakpur = Gorakhpoor 134-135 N 5
gora K'um'urk'oj 126-127 O 7
gora Lenina 113 V d 2
gora Longdor 132-133 W 6
gora Lopatina 132-133 b 7
gora Manas 132-133 N 9
gora Melovskaja 124-125 NO 2
gora Mengulek 132-133 Q 7
gora Mepisckaro 126-127 L 6
Goram Islands = Kepulauan Seram-laut 148-149 K 7
gora Mogila Bel'mak 126-127 H 3
Goran, El — 164-165 N 7
gora Narodnaja 132-133 L 5
gora Nerojka 132-133 KL 5
Gorantla 140 CD 4
gora Oblačnaja 132-133 Za 9
gora Pajjer 132-133 L 4
gora Pobeda 132-133 c 4
gora Potčurk 124-125 T 2
gora Roman-Koš 126-127 FG 4
gora Šachdag 126-127 O 6
gora Šapsucho 126-127 J 4
gora Šchara 126-127 L 5
gora Skalistyi Golec 132-133 WX 6
gora Sochor 132-133 TU 7
gora Stoj 126-127 A 2
gora Strižament 126-127 L 4
gora Tardoki-Jani 132-133 a 8
gora Tchab 126-127 J 4
gora Tebulosmta 126-127 M 5
gora Tel'posiz 132-133 K 5
gora Topko 132-133 a 6
gora Uilpata 126-127 L 5
gora Ulutau 132-133 M 8
gora Ušba 126-127 L 5
gora Vozvraščenija 132-133 b 8
gora Vysokaja 132-133 a 8
gora Zamkova 124-125 EF 7
Gorbačevo 124-125 L 7
Gorbatov 124-125 O 5
Gorbea 108-109 C 2
Gorchs 106-107 H 5
Gorda, Punta — [RCH] 104-105 A 6
Gorda, Punta — [YV, Distrito Federal] 91 II b 1
Gorda, Punta — [YV, Guajira] 94-95 F 1
Gördes 136-137 C 3
Gordium 136-137 DE 3
Gordon, AK 58-59 R 2
Gordon, GA 80-81 E 4
Gordon, NE 68-69 E 4
Gordon, TX 76-77 E 6
Gordon, WI 70-71 E 2
Gordon, Isla — 108-109 E 10
Gordon, Lake — 160 bc 3
Gordon Downs 158-159 E 3
Gordon Feld Park 85 III b 2
Gordon Lake 61 C 2
Gordons Corner, MD 82 II b 2
Gordonsville, VA 72-73 G 5
Gordonvale 158-159 J 3
Gorè [Chad] 164-165 H 7
Gorē [ETH] 164-165 M 7
Gore [NZ] 158-159 N 9
Gore Bay 62 K 4
Görele 136-137 H 2
Göreme 136-137 F 3
Gore Mountain 72-73 L 2
Gore Point 58-59 M 7
Gorgān 134-135 GH 3
Gorgān, Rūd-e — 134-135 GH 3
Gorgona, Isla — 92-93 D 4
Gorgora 164-165 M 6
Gorgoram 168-169 H 2
Gori 126-127 M 5-6
Gōrībidnūru = Gauribidanūr 140 C 4
Gori Cheboa 171 E 2
Goricy 124-125 L 5
Goris 126-127 N 7
Gorizia 122-123 E 3
Gorka 124-125 N 3
Gorki [SU, Belorusskaja SSR] 124-125 H 6
Gorki [SU, Rossijskaja SFSR] 132-133 M 4
Gorki = Gor'kij 132-133 GH 6
Gor'kij 132-133 GH 6
Gor'ko-Solonoje, ozero — 126-127 MN 2
Gor'kovskoje vodochranilišče 132-133 GH 6
Görlitz 118 G 3
Gorlovka 126-127 J 2
Gorlowka = Gorlovka 126-127 J 2
Gorman, CA 74-75 D 5
Gorman, TX 76-77 E 6
Gorn'ak 124-125 M 7
Gorna Or'ahovica 122-123 LM 4
Gornji Milanovac 122-123 J 3
Gorno-Altai Autonomous Region = 9 ◁ 132-133 Q 7
Gorno-Altajsk 132-133 Q 7
Gorno Badakhshan Autonomous Region 134-135 L 3
Gornozavodsk 132-133 b 8
Gornyj 124-125 R 8
Gornyj Balyklej 126-127 M 2
Gornyj Tikič 126-127 DE 2
Gorochov 126-127 B 1
Gorochovec 124-125 O 5
Gorodec 124-125 O 5
Gorodenka 126-127 B 2
Gorodišče [SU, Belorusskaja SSR Brestskaja Oblast'] 124-125 EF 7
Gorodišče [SU, Belorusskaja SSR Mogil'ovskaja Oblast'] 124-125 G 7
Gorodišče [SU, Rossijskaja SFSR Leningradskaja Oblast'] 124-125 J 4
Gorodišče [SU, Rossijskaja SFSR Penzenskaja Oblast'] 124-125 P 7
Gorodišče [SU, Ukrainskaja SSR] 126-127 E 2
Gorodn'a 124-125 H 8
Gorodnica 126-127 C 1
Gorodok [SU, Belorusskaja SSR] 124-125 GH 6
Gorodok [SU, Rossijskaja SFSR] 124-125 H 4
Gorodok [SU, Ukrainskaja SSR Chmel'nickaja Oblast'] 126-127 C 2
Gorodok [SU, Ukrainskaja SSR L'vovskaja Oblast'] 126-127 AB 2
Gorodok = Zakamensk 132-133 T 7
Goroka 148-149 N 8
Gorom = Gorom-Gorow 164-165 DE 6
Gorom-Gorow 164-165 DE 6
Gorongosa, Serra de — 172 FG 5
Gorontalo 148-149 H 6
Gorostiaga 106-107 H 5
Gorrahei = Korahe 164-165 NO 7
Gors, De — 128 I b 1
Goršečnoje 126-127 J 1
Gort 119 B 5
Gorutuba, Rio — 102-103 L 1
gory Byrranga 132-133 Q 3-V 2
Goryn' 124-125 F 8
Gorzów Wielkopolski 118 GH 2
Gōsāiṅgāṅv = Gossaigāon 138-139 MN 4
Gosaingāon = Gossaigāon 138-139 MN 4
Gōsāiṅthān = Gōsainthang Ri 138-139 KL 3
Gōsainthang Ri 138-139 KL 3
Gosai Than = Gōsainthang Ri 138-139 KL 3
Gose Elbe 130 I b 2
Gosen [DDR] 130 III c 2
Gosen [J] 144-145 M 4
Gosener Graben 130 III c 2
Gosford-Woy Woy 158-159 K 6
Gosforth Park 170 V c 2
Gosforth Park Race Course 170 V b 2
Goshem 174-175 F 3-4
Goshen, CA 74-75 D 4
Goshen, IN 70-71 H 5
Goshen, NY 72-73 J 4
Goshen Hole 68-69 D 4-5
Goshogawara 144-145 MN 2
Goshute Indian Reservation 74-75 F 3
Goslar 118 DE 3
Gospić 122-123 F 3
Gosport 119 F 6
Gosport, IN 70-71 G 6
Goss, MS 78-79 DE 5
Gossas 168-169 A 2
Gossi 168-169 E 2
Gostini 124-125 EF 5
Gostynin 118 J 2
Gosyogahara = Goshogawara 144-145 MN 2
Göta älv 116-117 D 9-E 8
Göta kanal 116-117 EF 8
Götaland 116-117 E-G 9
Göteborg 116-117 D 9
Göteborg och Bohus 116-117 D 8
Gotha 118 E 3
Gothenburg, NE 68-69 FG 5
Gotland [S, administrative unit] 116-117 H 9
Gotland [S, island] 116-117 H 9
Götland = Götaland 116-117 E-G 9
Gotland Deep 114-115 M 4
Gotō-rettō 142-143 O 5
Gotska Sandön 116-117 HJ 8
Gōtsu 144-145 HJ 5
Gottert 128 IV a 2
Göttingen 118 DE 3
Gottwaldov [SU] 126-127 H 2
Götzenhain 128 III b 1
Goubangzi 144-145 CD 2
Goubéré 164-165 K 7
Gouda [ZA] 174-175 C 7
Goudge 106-107 CD 5
Goudiry 164-165 B 6
Goudreau 70-71 H 1
Goufi, Djebel el — = Jabal Ghūfī 166-167 KL 1
Gough 204-205 G 13
Gough, GA 80-81 E 4
Gouin Reservoir 56-57 VW 8
Goulatte, La — = Ḥalq al-Wad 166-167 M 1
Goulbi, Vallée du — 168-169 G 2
Goulburn 158-159 J 6
Goulburn Islands 158-159 F 2
Gould, AR 78-79 D 4
Gould, CO 68-69 CD 5
Gould, Sierra — 106-107 E 7
Gould Bay 53 B 31-32
Gould City, MI 70-71 GH 2
Goulette, la — = Ḥalq al-Wad 166-167 M 1
Goulimīm = Gulimīn 164-165 BC 3
Goulimime = Gulimīn 166-167 AB 5
Gouloumbo 168-169 B 2
Goundaï 168-169 H 1
Goundam 164-165 D 5
Goungo 168-169 F 2
Gouph, De — = Die Koup 174-175 E 7
Gourara = Ghurarah 166-167 FG 5
Gouraya = Ghūrāyah 166-167 GH 1
Gouré 164-165 G 6
Gouripur = Gaurīpūr 138-139 N 5
Gourits 174-175 D 8
Gouritz River = Gourits 174-175 D 8
Gourjhāmar 138-139 G 6
Gourma 164-165 E 6
Gourma-Rharous 164-165 D 5
Gouro 164-165 H 5
Gourrâma = Gurrāmah 166-167 DE 3
Goussainville 129 I c 1
Gouvernement, Maison du — 170 IV a 1
Gouvernement, Palais du — 170 IV a 1
Gouverneur, NY 72-73 J 2
Gouwa 172 E 8
Gōvā = Goa 134-135 L 7
Govālpāṛā = Goālpāra 138-139 N 4
Gov'altaj ◁ 142-143 H 3
Gov'altajn Nuruu 142-143 H 2-J 3
Govan 61 F 5
Gove, KS 68-69 F 6
Govena, mys — 132-133 g 6
Govenlock 68-69 B 1
Goverla, gora — 126-127 B 2
Governador, NM 76-77 A 4
Governador, Ilha do — 110 I b 1
Governador Dix-Sept Rosado 100-101 F 3
Governador Valadares 92-93 L 8
Government House [AUS] 161 II b 1
Government House [SGP] 154 III ab 2
Governors Island 82 III b 2
Governor's Mansion 85 II b 1
Govind Ballabh Pant Sāgar 138-139 J 5-6
Gōvindganj = Gobindganj 138-139 K 4
Govind Sāgar 138-139 F 2
Gowanda, NY 72-73 G 3
Gowan River 61 L 3
Gower Peninsula 119 DE 6
Gowrie, IA 70-71 C 4
Goya 111 E 3
Goyelle, Lac — 63 F 2
Goyllarisquizga 96-97 D 7
Göynücek 136-137 F 2
Göynük 136-137 D 2
Göynük = Oğnut 136-137 J 3
Goz-Beïda 164-165 J 6
Goze Delčev 122-123 KL 5
Gozha Tsho 142-143 E 4
Goz Regeb = Qawz Rajab 164-165 M 5
Göz tepe 154 I b 2
Graaff-Reinet 172 DE 8
Graafwater 174-175 C 7
Grabo [CI] 168-169 D 4
Grabouw 174-175 C 8
Graça Aranha 100-101 BC 3
Grã-Canária = Gran Canaria 164-165 A 3
Grace, ID 66-67 H 4
Gracefield 72-73 H 1
Graceville, FL 78-79 G 5
Graceville, MN 68-69 H 3
Grachovo 124-125 ST 5
Graciianópolis 102-103 G 4
Gracias 88-89 B 7
Gracias a Dios, Cabo — 64-65 K 8
Graciosa [P] 204-205 DE 5
Gračovka 124-125 T 7
Gradaús 92-93 J 6
Gradaús, Serra dos — 92-93 JK 6
Gräddö 116-117 H 8
Gradižsk 126-127 F 2
Grady, AR 78-79 D 3
Grady, NM 76-77 C 5
Graettinger, IA 70-71 C 4
Grafton 158-159 K 5
Grafton, IL 70-71 E 6
Grafton, ND 68-69 H 1
Grafton, WV 72-73 FG 5
Grafton, Islas — 108-109 C 10
Gragoatá, Niterói- 110 I c 2
Grah, Gunung — 150-151 C 10
Graham 70-71 E 1
Graham, CA 83 III c 2
Graham, NC 80-81 G 2-3
Graham, TX 76-77 E 6
Graham, Mount — 64-65 DE 5
Graham Bell, ostrov — 132-133 MN 1
Graham Island 56-57 JK 7
Graham Lake 60 KL 1
Graham Moore, Cape — 56-57 V-X 3
Graham River 60 F 1
Grahamstad = Grahamstown 172 E 8
Grahamstown 172 E 8
Graïba = Al-Ghraybah 166-167 LM 2
Graig, AK 58-59 w 9
Grain Coast 164-165 B 7-C 8
Grainfield, KS 68-69 F 6
Grainger 60 L 4
Grajagan 152-153 KL 10
Grajagan, Teluk — 152-153 KL 10
Grajaú 92-93 K 6
Grajau, Rio — [BR, Acre] 96-97 E 6
Grajaú, Rio — [BR, Maranhão] 92-93 K 5-6
Grajaú, Rio de Janeiro- 110 I b 2
Grajewo 118 L 2
Grajvoron 126-127 G 1
Gramado 106-107 M 2
Gramalote [CO, Bolívar] 94-95 D 4
Gramalote [CO, Norte de Santander] 94-95 E 3-4
Grambûsa, Akrōtḗrion — 122-123 K 8
Gramilla 104-105 D 10
Grámmos 122-123 J 5
Grampian Mountains 119 DE 3
Granada, CO 68-69 E 6-7
Granada [CO] 94-95 E 6
Granada [E] 120-121 F 10
Granada [NIC] 64-65 JK 9
Granadero Baigorria 106-107 GH 4
Gran Altiplanicie Central 111 BC 7
Gran Bajo [RA, La Pampa] 106-107 D 6
Gran Bajo [RA, Santa Cruz] 111 C 7
Gran Bajo del Gualicho 108-109 G 3
Gran Bajo de San Julián 108-109 E 7
Granbori 98-99 L 3
Gran Bretaña 91 III ab 4
Granbury, TX 76-77 EF 6
Granby 56-57 W 8
Granby, CO 68-69 CD 5
Granby, Lake — 68-69 D 5
Gran Canaria 164-165 AB 3
Gran Chaco 111 D 3-E 2
Gran Cordón Nevado 108-109 C 7
Grand Bahama Island 64-65 L 6
Grand Ballon 120-121 L 5
Grand Bank 63 HJ 4
Grand Bassa 168-169 C 4
Grand Bassa = Buchanan 164-165 B 7
Grand-Bassam 164-165 D 7-8
Grand Bay [CDN, bay] 70-71 F 1
Grand Bay [CDN, place] 63 C 5
Grand Beach 62 A 2
Grand-Bourg 64-65 OP 8
Grand Bourg, General Sarmiento- 110 III a 1
Grand-Bruit 63 G 4
Grand Caicos 88-89 L 4
Grand Canal 119 BC 5
Grand Canary = Gran Canaria 164-165 AB 3
Grand Canyon 64-65 D 4
Grand Canyon, AZ 74-75 GH 4
Grand Canyon National Monument 74-75 G 4
Grand Canyon National Park 64-65 D 4
Grand Cayman 64-65 KL 8
Grand Centre 61 C 3
Grand Chenier, LA 78-79 C 6
Grand Coulee, WA 66-67 D 2
Grand Coulee [CDN] 61 F 5
Grand Coulee [USA] 66-67 D 2
Grand Coulee Dam 64-65 BC 2
Grand Coulee Equalizing Reservoir = Banks Lake 66-67 D 2
Grande-Anse 63 D 4
Grande Cache 60 H 3
Grande Comore = Ngazidja 172 H 4
Grande de Paulino, Ilha — 100-101 CD 2
Grande Dépression Centrale 172 CD 2
Grande-Entrée 63 F 4
Grande Île de Criques 170 IV b 1-2
Grande Île de la Ndjili 170 IV b 1
Grande Prairie 56-57 N 6-7
Grand Erg de Bilma 164-165 G 5
Grande-Rivière 63 DE 3
Grande Ronde, OR 66-67 B 3
Grande Ronde River 66-67 E 2-3
Grandes de Lípez, Río — 104-105 C 7-8
Gran Desierto 64-65 D 5
Grandes Landes 120-121 G 6-7
Grande-Terre 88-89 Q 6
Grandfalls, TX 76-77 C 7
Grand Falls [CDN] 56-57 Za 8
Grand Falls [EAK] 171 D 3
Grand Falls [USA] 74-75 H 5
Grand Falls = Churchill Falls 56-57 XY 7
Grandfather Mountain 80-81 F 2
Grandfield, OK 76-77 E 5
Grand Forks 66-67 D 1
Grand Forks, ND 64-65 G 2
Grand Gedeh 168-169 CD 4
Grand Haven, MI 70-71 G 4
Grandioznyj, pik — 132-133 RS 7
Grand Island, NE 64-65 G 3
Grand Island [USA, Louisiana] 78-79 E 5
Grand Island [USA, Michigan] 70-71 G 2
Grand Island [USA, New York] 72-73 G 3
Grand Isle 72-73 K 2
Grand Isle, LA 78-79 D 6
Grand Junction, CO 64-65 DE 4
Grand Junction, TN 78-79 E 3
Grand Lac Amer = Al-Buḥayrat al-Murrat al-Kubrá 173 C 2
Grand Lac du Nord 63 C 2
Grand Lac Germain 63 C 2
Grand-Lahou 164-165 CD 7-8
Grand Lake, CO 68-69 CD 5
Grand Lake [CDN] 63 D 5
Grand Lake [USA, Louisiana] 78-79 D 6
Grand Lake [USA, Maine] 72-73 N 2
Grand Lake [USA, Michigan] 70-71 J 3
Grand Lake [USA, Ohio] 70-71 H 5
Grand Ledge, MI 70-71 H 4
Grand Manan Island 63 C 5
Grand Marais, MI 70-71 GH 2
Grand Marais, MN 70-71 EF 2
Grand Mécatina, Île du — 63 G 2
Grand'Mère 72-73 K 1
Grand Mesa 68-69 C 6
Grândola 120-121 C 9
Grand Paradiso 122-123 B 3
Grand-Popo 164-165 E 7
Grand Portage, MN 70-71 F 2
Grand Portage Indian Reservation 70-71 EF 2
Grand Prairie, TX 76-77 F 6
Grand Rapids, MI 64-65 J 3
Grand Rapids, MN 70-71 D 2
Grand Rapids [CDN, Alberta] 60 L 1
Grand Rapids [CDN, Manitoba] 61 J 4
Grand River [CDN] 72-73 FG 3
Grand River [USA, Michigan] 70-71 GH 4
Grand River [USA, Missouri] 70-71 D 6
Grand River [USA, South Dakota] 64-65 F 2
Grand River, North Fork — 68-69 E 3
Grand River, South Fork — 68-69 E 3
Grand River Valley 74-75 J 3
Grand Saline, TX 76-77 G 6
Grand Santi 98-99 LM 2
Grand Teton National Park 66-67 H 3-4
Grand Teton Peak 64-65 D 3
Grand Traverse Bay 70-71 H 3
Grand Trunk Pacific Railway = Candian National Railways 56-57 PQ 7
Grand Turk 88-89 L 4
Grand Turk Island 88-89 L 4
Grand Union Canal 129 II a 1-2
Grand Valley, CO 68-69 B 6
Grandview 61 H 5
Grand View, ID 66-67 EF 4
Grandview, MO 70-71 C 6
Grandview, WA 66-67 D 2
Grand Wash Cliffs 74-75 FG 5
Graneros [RA] 104-105 D 10
Graneros [RCH] 106-107 B 4-5
Grange, La — 158-159 D 3
Grange Hill, London- 129 II c 1
Granger, TX 76-77 F 7
Granger, WA 66-67 CD 2
Granger, WY 66-67 J 5
Grängesberg 116-117 F 7
Grangeville, ID 66-67 EF 3
Gran Guardia 104-105 G 9
Granite, CO 68-69 CD 6
Granite, OK 76-77 E 5
Granite, OR 66-67 D 3
Granite Bay 60 E 4
Granite City, IL 70-71 EF 6
Granite Downs 158-159 F 5
Granite Falls, MN 70-71 C 3
Granite Island [USA, Gulf of Alaska] 58-59 N 7
Granite Island [USA, Lake Superior] 70-71 G 2
Granite Mountains 74-75 F 5
Granite Peak [USA, Montana] 64-65 E 2
Granite Peak [USA, Utah] 66-67 G 5
Granite Range [USA, Alaska] 58-59 QR 6
Granite Range [USA, Nevada] 66-67 D 5
Granites, The — 158-159 F 4
Granite Springs Valley 66-67 D 5
Graniteville, SC 80-81 F 4
Granja 92-93 L 5
Granja, Bogotá-La — 91 III b 2
Granjas de Techo, Bogotá- 91 III b 3
Gran Laguna Salada 108-109 EF 5
Granma 88-89 H 4
Gran Malvina = West Falkland 111 D 8
Gränna 116-117 F 8
Gran Pajonal 96-97 D 7
Gran Pampa Pelada 92-93 F 9
Gran Pampa Salada 104-105 C 7
Gran Rio 98-99 L 3
Gran Sabana, La — 92-93 G 3
Gran Salitral 106-107 D 6
Gran San Bernardo 122-123 B 3
Gran Sasso 122-123 E 4
Grant 62 F 2
Grant, FL 80-81 c 3
Grant, MT 66-67 G 3
Grant, NE 68-69 F 5
Grant, Mount — [USA, Clan Alpine Mountains] 74-75 DE 3
Grant, Mount — [USA, Wassuk Range] 74-75 D 3
Grant City, MO 70-71 C 5
Grant Creek, AK 58-59 L 4
Grant Land 52 A 25-27
Grant Park 85 II b 2
Grant Range 74-75 F 3
Grants, NM 64-65 E 4
Grantsburg, WI 70-71 D 3
Grants Cabin, AK 58-59 M 6
Grants Pass, OR 66-67 B 4
Grantsville, UT 66-67 G 5
Grantsville, WV 72-73 F 5
Granum 66-67 G 1
Granville 120-121 G 4
Granville, ND 68-69 F 1
Granville Lake 61 HJ 2
Grão-Mogol 102-103 L 2
Grão Pará, Parque Nacional — 98-99 O 6
Grape Island 84 I c 3
Grapeland, TX 76-77 G 7
Grarem = Qarārim 166-167 K 1
Graskop 174-175 J 3
Grass Creek, WY 68-69 B 4
Grasse 120-121 L 7
Grasset, Lac — 62 MN 2
Grass Lake, CA 66-67 B 5
Grass Range, MT 68-69 B 2
Grassridge Dam 174-175 F 6
Grass River 61 K 2-3
Grass River Provincial Park 61 H 3
Grass Valley, CA 74-75 C 3
Grass Valley, OR 66-67 C 3
Grassy 158-159 H 8
Grassy Knob 72-73 F 5-6
Grassy Lake 66-67 H 1
Grassy Narrows 62 C 2
Gratangen 116-117 GH 3
Gravatá 92-93 M 6
Gravataí 106-107 M 2
Graveland, 's- 128 I b 2
Gravelbourg 61 E 6
Gravenbruch 128 III b 1
Gravenhage, 's- 120-121 JK 2
Gravenhurst 72-73 G 2
Grave Peak 66-67 F 2
Gravesend 160 JK 2
Gravesend, New York-, NY 82 III c 3
Gravette, AR 76-77 G 4
Graviña, Punta — 108-109 FG 5
Gravina di Pùglia 122-123 G 5
Grawn, MI 70-71 H 3
Gray 120-121 K 5
Gray, GA 80-81 E 4
Gray, OK 76-77 D 4
Grayling, AK 58-59 GH 5
Grayling, MI 70-71 H 3
Grayling Fork 58-59 QR 3
Grays Harbor 66-67 AB 2
Grayson 61 G 5
Grayson, KY 72-73 E 5
Grays Peak 68-69 CD 6
Grayville, IL 70-71 FG 6
Graz 118 G 5
Gr'azi 124-125 M 7
Gr'aznoje 124-125 M 6-7
Gr'azovec 124-125 MN 4
Grdelica 122-123 JK 4
Great Abaco Island 64-65 L 6
Great Artesian Basin 158-159 GH 4-5
Great Australian Bight 158-159 E 6-G 7
Great Bahama Bank 64-65 L 6-7
Great Bak River = Groot-Brakrivier 174-175 E 8
Great Barrier Island 158-159 P 7
Great Barrier Reef 158-159 H 2-K 4
Great Basin 64-65 CD 3-4
Great Bay 72-73 J 5
Great Bear Lake 56-57 MN 4
Great Bear River 56-57 LM 4-5
Great Belt = Store Bælt 116-117 D 10
Great Bend, KS 64-65 FG 4
Great Berg River = Groot Bergrivier 174-175 C 7
Great Bitter Lake = Al-Buḥayrat al-Murrat al-Kubra 173 C 2
Great Britain 114-115 H 4-5
Great Central 60 E 5
Great Cloche Island 62 KL 3
Great Divide Basin 68-69 BC 4
Great Dividing Range 158-159 H-K 3-7
Great Driffield 119 FG 4-5
Great Eastern Erg = Al-'Irq al-Kabīr ash-Sharqī 164-165 F 2-3
Greater Antilles 64-65 K 7-N 8
Greater Khingan Range 142-143 M 3-N 1
Greater Leech Lake Indian Reservation 70-71 CD 2
Greater Sunda Islands 148-149 E-H 7-8
Great Exuma Island 64-65 L 7
Great Fall 94-95 L 5
Great Falls, MT 64-65 DE 2
Great Falls, SC 80-81 F 3
Great Falls [CDN] 62 AB 2
Great Falls [GUY] 98-99 H 2
Great Falls [USA] 66-67 H 2
Great Fish River = Groot Visrivier [Namibia] 174-175 B 4
Great Fish River = Groot Visrivier [ZA ◁ Hoë Karoo] 174-175 D 6
Great Fish River = Groot Visrivier [ZA ◁ Indian Ocean] 174-175 G 7
Great Guana Cay 88-89 H 2
Great Inagua Island 64-65 M 7

Great Karas Mountains = Groot Karasberge 172 C 7
Great Karoo = Groot Karoo 172 D 8
Great Kei = Kepulauan Kai 148-149 K 8
Great Kei River = Groot Keiriviер 172 EF 8
Great Kills, New York-, NY 82 III b 3
Great Lake 158-159 J 8
Great Meteor Tablemount 50-51 H 4
Great Namaqua Land = Namaland 172 C 7
Great Natuna = Pulau Bunguran 148-149 E 6
Great Neck, NY 82 III d 2
Great Nicobar 134-135 P 9
Great Northern Pacific Railway 64-65 DE 2
Great Northern Peninsula 56-57 Z 7-8
Great Oasis = Al-Wāḥāt al-Khārīyah 164-165 KL 3-4
Great Oyster Bay 160 d 3
Great Peconic Bay 72-73 K 4
Great Plains 64-65 E 2-F 5
Great Ruaha 172 G 3
Great Sacandaga Lake 72-73 JK 3
Great Salt Desert = Dasht-e Kavīr 134-135 GH 3
Great Salt Lake 64-65 D 3
Great Salt Lake Desert 64-65 D 3
Great Salt Plains Reservoir 76-77 EF 4
Great Sand Dunes National Monument 68-69 CD 7
Great Sand Sea = Libysche Wüste 164-165 J 3-L 4
Great Sandy Desert [AUS] 158-159 DE 4
Great Sandy Desert [USA] 64-65 BC 3
Great Sandy Hills 61 D 5
Great Sandy Island 158-159 KL 4-5
Great Slave Lake 56-57 NO 5
Great Smoky Mountains 80-81 E 3
Great Smoky Mountains National Park 80-81 E 3
Great Swinton Island = Hswindan Kyûnmyâ 150-151 AB 7
Great Ums = Groot-Ums 174-175 C 2
Great Usutu 174-175 J 4
Great Valley 80-81 D 3
Great Victoria Desert 158-159 EF 5
Great Wall 142-143 K 4
Great Western Erg = Al-'Irq al-Kabīr al-Gharbī 164-165 D 3-E 2
Great Whale River 56-57 VW 6
Great Winterhoek = Groot Winterhoek 174-175 C 7
Great Yarmouth 119 GH 5
Grebenâ 122-123 J 5
Grebeni 124-125 R 4
Greboun, Mont — 164-165 F 4-5
Grecco 106-107 J 4
Greco, Cape — = Akrōtḗrion Grḗko 136-137 F 5
Gredos, Sierra de — 120-121 E 8
Greece 122-123 J 7-L 5
Greeley, CO 64-65 F 3
Greeley, NE 68-69 G 5
Greely Fiord 56-57 UV 1
Green 62 E 2
Green Bay 64-65 J 2-3
Green Bay, WI 64-65 J 3
Greenbelt Park 82 II b 1
Greenbrae, CA 83 I a 1
Greenbrier River 72-73 FG 5
Greenbush, MN 70-71 BC 1
Green Cape 160 K 6
Greencastle, IN 70-71 G 6
Greencastle, PA 72-73 GH 5
Green City, IA 70-71 D 5
Green Cove Springs, FL 80-81 bc 1
Greene, IA 70-71 D 4
Greeneville, TN 80-81 E 2
Greenfield, CA 74-75 C 4
Greenfield, IA 70-71 C 5
Greenfield, IN 70-71 H 6
Greenfield, MA 72-73 K 3
Greenfield, MO 70-71 CD 7
Greenfield, OH 72-73 E 5
Greenfield, TN 78-79 E 2
Greenfield Park 82 I c 2
Greenfields Village, NJ 84 III c 3
Greenford, London- 129 II a 1
Greenhorn Mountains 74-75 D 5
Greening 62 O 2
Green Island [AUS] 158-159 J 3
Green Island [HK] 155 I a 2
Green Island [USA] 58-59 O 6
Green Islands 148-149 hj 5
Green Lake [CDN] 61 E 3
Green Lake [USA] 70-71 F 4
Greenland 52 BC 23
Greenland, MI 70-71 F 2
Greenland Basin 50-51 JK 2
Greenland Sea 52 B 20-18
Green Mountain Reservoir 68-69 C 6
Green Mountains [USA, Vermont] 72-73 K 2-3
Green Mountains [USA, Wyoming] 68-69 C 4
Greenock 119 D 4
Green Pond, SC 80-81 F 4
Greenport, NY 72-73 K 4
Green Ridge, PA 84 III a 2
Green River, UT 74-75 H 3
Green River, WY 66-67 J 5
Green River [USA, Illinois] 70-71 F 5
Green River [USA, Kentucky] 70-71 G 7
Green River [USA, Wyoming] 64-65 E 3-4
Green River Basin 64-65 DE 3
Greens Bayou 85 III c 1
Greensboro, AL 78-79 F 4
Greensboro, GA 80-81 E 4
Greensboro, NC 64-65 L 4
Greensburg, IN 70-71 H 6
Greensburg, KS 68-69 G 7
Greensburg, KY 70-71 H 7
Greensburg, PA 72-73 G 4
Greenside, Johannesburg- 170 V b 1
Green Swamp 80-81 G 3
Greenup, IL 70-71 FG 6
Greenup, KY 72-73 E 5
Greenvale 158-159 HJ 3
Greenville 164-165 C 7-8
Greenville, AL 78-79 F 5
Greenville, CA 66-67 C 5
Greenville, FL 80-81 E 5
Greenville, IL 70-71 F 6
Greenville, IN 72-73 D 4
Greenville, KY 70-71 G 7
Greenville, ME 72-73 LM 2
Greenville, MI 70-71 H 4
Greenville, MS 64-65 HJ 5
Greenville, NC 64-65 L 4
Greenville, OH 70-71 H 5
Greenville, PA 72-73 F 4
Greenville, SC 64-65 K 5
Greenville, TX 64-65 GH 5
Greenwater Lake 70-71 E 1
Greenwater Lake Provincial Park 61 G 4
Greenway 68-69 G 1
Greenway, SD 68-69 G 3
Greenwich, OH 72-73 E 4
Greenwich, London- 119 FG 6
Greenwich Village, New York-, NY 82 III b 2
Greenwood 66-67 D 1
Greenwood, AR 76-77 GH 5
Greenwood, IN 70-71 GH 6
Greenwood, MA 84 I b 2
Greenwood, MS 64-65 HJ 5
Greenwood, SC 64-65 K 5
Greenwood, WI 70-71 E 3
Greenwood Cemetery [USA, Atlanta] 85 II b 2
Greenwood Cemetery [USA, New Orleans] 85 I b 2
Greenwood Cemetery [USA, Philadelphia] 84 III d 1
Greer, ID 66-67 EF 2
Greer, SC 80-81 E 3
Greeson, Lake — 78-79 C 3
Gregório, Rio — 98-99 C 8
Gregory, SD 68-69 G 4
Gregory, Lake — 158-159 GH 5
Gregory Downs 158-159 G 3
Gregory Range 158-159 H 3
Gregory River 158-159 G 3
Gregory Salt Lake 158-159 E 3-4
Greifswald 118 F 1
Grein 118 G 4
Greinerville 171 B 4
Greiz 118 EF 3
Grḗko, Akrōtḗrion — 136-137 F 5
Gremicha 132-133 F 4
Grenå 116-117 D 9
Grenada 64-65 O 9
Grenada, MS 78-79 E 4
Grenada Lake 78-79 E 4
Grenada Reservoir = Grenada Lake 78-79 E 4
Grenadines 64-65 O 9
Grenelle, Paris- 129 I c 2
Grenen 116-117 D 9
Grenfell [AUS] 160 HJ 4
Grenfell [CDN] 61 G 5
Grenivík 116-117 de 2
Grenoble 120-121 KL 6
Grenola, KS 76-77 F 4
Grenora, ND 68-69 E 1
Grenvill, Cape — 158-159 H 2
Grenville 94-95 L 1
Grenville, NM 76-77 C 4
Grenville, SD 68-69 H 3
Gresham Park 85 II c 2
Grésillons, les — 129 I b 2
Gressy 129 I d 2
Gretna 68-69 H 1
Gretna, LA 64-65 HJ 6
Grevy, Isla — 108-109 F 10
Grey, De — 158-159 CD 4
Greybull, WY 68-69 BC 3
Greybull River 68-69 B 3
Grey Islands 56-57 Za 7
Grey Islands Harbour 63 J 2
Greylingstad 174-175 H 4
Greylock, Mount — 72-73 K 3
Greymont, Johannesburg- 170 V a 1
Greymouth 158-159 O 8
Grey Range 158-159 H 5
Grey River 63 H 4
Grey River, De — 158-159 CD 4
Greytown 174-175 J 5
Greytown = Bluefields 64-65 K 9
Gribanovskij 126-127 KL 1
Gribbell Island 60 C 3
Gribingui 164-165 H 7
Gridley, CA 74-75 C 3
Griekwaland-Oos 174-175 H 6
Griekwaland-Wes 172 D 7
Griekwastad 174-175 E 5
Griesheim, Frankfurt am Main- 128 III a 1
Griffin 61 G 6
Griffin, GA 64-65 K 5
Griffin Point 58-59 QR 1
Griffith 158-159 J 6
Grigoriopol' 126-127 D 3
Grik 150-151 C 10
Grim, Cape — 158-159 H 8
Grimajlov 126-127 BC 2
Grimari 164-165 HJ 7
Grimes, CA 74-75 C 3
Grimma 118 F 3
Grimsby [CDN] 72-73 G 3
Grimsby [GB] 119 FG 5
Grimsey 116-117 d 1
Grimshaw 60 HJ 1
Grimstad 116-117 C 8
Grímsvötn 116-117 e 2
Grindavík 116-117 b 3
Grindsted 116-117 C 10
Grindstone Buttes 68-69 F 3
Grinnell, IA 70-71 D 5
Grinnell Land 56-57 UV 1-2
Grinnell Peninsula 56-57 RS 2
Grinzing, Wien- 113 I b 1
Griqualand East = Griekwaland-Oos 174-175 H 6
Griqualand West = Griekwaland-Wes 172 D 7
Griquatown = Griekwastad 174-175 E 5
Gris, Kuala — 150-151 D 10
Griswold, IA 70-71 C 5
Grita, La — 94-95 F 3
Grīva [SU, Lietuva] 124-125 F 6
Griva [SU, Rossijskaja SFSR] 124-125 S 3
Grīz = Kříz 166-167 L 2
Groais Island 63 J 2
Gröbenried 130 II a 1
Grobina 124-125 C 5
Groblersdal 174-175 H 3
Groblershoop 174-175 DE 5
Grodno 124-125 DE 7
Grodz'anka 124-125 G 7
Groenrivier [ZA ◁ Atlantic Ocean] 174-175 B 6
Groenrivier [ZA ◁ Ongersrivier] 174-175 E 6
Groenriviermond 174-175 B 6
Groenwaterrivier 174-175 E 5
Groesbeck, TX 76-77 F 7
Grœtavær 116-117 FG 3
Grogol, Kali — 154 IV a 2
Grogol Petamburan, Jakarta- 154 IV a 1
Groix, Île de — 120-121 F 5
Groll Seamount 50-51 H 6
Grombalia = Qrunbālīyah 166-167 M 1
Gronau 128 III b 1
Gronbâlia = Qrunbālīyah 166-167 M 1
Grong 116-117 E 5
Groningen [NL] 120-121 L 2
Groningen [SME] 92-93 HJ 3
Gronsdorf 130 II c 2
Groom, TX 76-77 D 5
Groot Bergrivier 174-175 C 7
Groot-Bijgaarden 128 II a 1
Groot Bosmanland 174-175 CD 5
Groot-Brakrivier 174-175 E 8
Groot Brukkaros 172 C 7
Grootdoring 174-175 E 5
Grootdrink 174-175 D 5
Groote Eylandt 158-159 G 2
Groote River = Grootrivier [ZA ◁ Gourits] 174-175 D 7
Groote Riviеr = Grootrivier [ZA ◁ Sint Francisbaai] 174-175 F 7
Grootfontein 172 C 5
Groot Karasberge 172 C 7
Groot Karoo 172 D 8
Groot Keirivier 172 EF 8
Groot Letaba 174-175 J 2
Groot-Marico 174-175 G 3
Groot Rietrivier 174-175 D 6-7
Grootrivier [ZA ◁ Gourits] 174-175 D 7
Grootrivier [ZA ◁ Sint Francisbaai] 174-175 F 7
Grootrivierhoogte 174-175 EF 7
Groot Shingwedzi 174-175 J 2
Groot Shingwidzi = Groot Shingwedzi 174-175 J 2
Groot-Spelonke 174-175 HJ 2
Groot Swartberge 174-175 DE 7
Groot-Ums 174-175 C 2
Groot Visrivier 172 C 7
Grootvlei 174-175 H 4
Grootvloer 174-175 D 5
Groot Winterhoek 174-175 C 7
Grosa, Punta — 120-121 H 9
Groslay 129 I c 2
Gros Morne [CDN] 63 H 3
Gros-Morne [RH] 88-89 K 5
Gros Morne National Park 56-57 Za 8
Grosnyj = Groznyj 126-127 M 5
Gross Borstel, Hamburg- 130 I a 1
Grossenbrode 118 E 1
Grosse Pointe, MI 84 II c 2
Grosse Pointe Farms, MI 84 II c 2
Grosse Pointe Park, MI 84 II c 2
Grosse Pointe Woods, MI 84 II c 2
Grosser Arber 118 F 3
Grosser Beerberg 118 E 3
Grosse Tet, LA 78-79 D 5
Grosseto 122-123 D 4
Grossglockner 118 F 5
Grosshadern, München- 130 II a 2
Grosshesselohe 130 II b 2
Grossjedlersdorf, Wien- 113 I b 1
Gross Moor 130 I b 2
Grossmünster 128 IV b 1
Grossos 100-101 F 3
Grossziethen [DDR, Potsdam] 130 III b 2
Grosvenor, Lake — 58-59 K 7
Gros Ventre River 66-67 H 4
Grote IJ-polder 128 I a 1
Grote Molenbeek 128 II a 1
Grotli 116-117 BC 6
Groton, NY 72-73 H 3
Groton, SD 68-69 GH 3
Grottoes, VA 72-73 G 5
Grouard 60 JK 2
Groundhog River 62 K 2
Grouse, ID 66-67 G 4
Grouse Creek, UT 66-67 G 5
Grouse Creek Mountain 66-67 FG 3
Grove City, PA 72-73 FG 4
Grove Hill, AL 78-79 F 5
Groveland, CA 74-75 CD 4
Grover, CO 68-69 DE 5
Grover, WY 66-67 H 4
Grover City, CA 74-75 C 5
Groveton, TX 76-77 G 7
Grovont, WY 66-67 H 4
Growler, AZ 74-75 FG 6
Growler Mountains 74-75 G 6
Grozny = Groznyj 126-127 M 5
Groznyj 126-127 M 5
Grū', Wād — 166-167 C 3
Grudovo 122-123 M 4
Grudziądz 118 J 2
Gruesa, Punta — 104-105 A 7
Grulla, TX 76-77 E 9
Grullo, El — 86-87 H 8
Grumantbyen 116-117 jk 5
Grumeti 171 C 3
Grumo Appula 122-123 G 5
Grünau [Namibia] 172 C 7
Grundarfjördhur 116-117 ab 2
Grundy, VA 80-81 EF 2
Grundy Center, IA 70-71 D 4
Grunewald [D] 130 III a 2
Grunewald, Berlin- 130 III b 2
Grunidora, Llanos de la — 86-87 JK 5
Grünwalder Forst 130 II b 2
Grušino 124-125 P 4
Gruta, La — 102-103 F 7
Gruver, TX 76-77 D 4
Gryfice 118 G 2
Gryllefjord 116-117 G 3
Grymes Hill, New York-, NY 82 III b 3
Grytviken 111 J 8

Gşaiba = Quşaybah 136-137 J 5

Gua 138-139 K 6
Guacanayabo, Golfo de — 64-65 L 7
Guacang Shan = Kuocang Shan 146-147 H 7
Guacara 94-95 GH 2
Guacarí 94-95 C 6
Guacas 94-95 F 4
Guachaca 94-95 E 2
Guachara 94-95 G 4
Guacharos, Las Cuevas de los — 94-95 CD 7
Guachi, Cerro — 106-107 C 2
Guachipas 104-105 D 9
Guachiria, Río — 94-95 F 5
Guachochi 86-87 G 4
Guaçu 102-103 E 5
Guaçu, Rio — 102-103 F 6
Guaçuí 102-103 M 4
Guadalajara [E] 120-121 F 8
Guadalajara [MEX] 64-65 EF 7
Guadalaviar 120-121 G 8
Guadalcanal [Solomon Is.] 148-149 j 6
Guadalcanal Gela = Guadalcanal 148-149 j 6
Guadales 106-107 D 5
Guadalete 120-121 DE 10
Guadalimar 120-121 F 9
Guadalope 120-121 G 8
Guadalquivir 120-121 E 10
Guadalupe, CA 74-75 C 5
Guadalupe [BOL] 104-105 DE 6
Guadalupe [CO] 94-95 D 4
Guadalupe [E] 120-121 E 9
Guadalupe [MEX ↗ San Luis Potosí] 86-87 KL 6
Guadalupe [MEX ↑ San Luis Potosí] 86-87 K 6
Guadalupe [MEX, Baja California] 86-87 B 2
Guadalupe [MEX, Coahuila] 76-77 D 9
Guadalupe [MEX, Nuevo León] 64-65 FG 6
Guadalupe [MEX, Zacatecas] 86-87 JK 6
Guadalupe [PE] 96-97 B 5
Guadalupe, Basilica de — 91 I c 2
Guadalupe, Isla de — 64-65 C 6
Guadalupe, Sierra de — [E] 120-121 E 9
Guadalupe, Sierra de — [MEX] 91 I c 1
Guadalupe Bravos 86-87 G 2
Guadalupe del Norte 91 I c 1
Guadalupe Mountains [USA → El Paso] 76-77 B 6-7
Guadalupe Peak 64-65 F 5
Guadalupe River 76-77 F 8
Guadalupe Victoria 86-87 J 5
Guadalupe y Calvo 86-87 G 4
Guadalupita, NM 76-77 B 4
Guadarrama [YV] 94-95 GH 3
Guadarrama, Sierra de — 120-121 EF 8
Guadeloupe 64-65 O 8
Guadeloupe Passage 64-65 O 8
Guadiana 120-121 D 10
Guadiana Menor 120-121 F 10
Guadix 120-121 F 10
Guadur = Gwādar 134-135 J 5
Guafo, Golfo de — 111 B 6
Guafo, Isla — 111 AB 6
Guai 148-149 L 7
Guaiba 106-107 M 3
Guaíba, Rio — 106-107 M 3
Guaicui 102-103 K 2
Guaicuras 102-103 D 4
Guainía 94-95 FG 6
Guainía, Río — 92-93 F 4
Guaiquinima, Cerro — 92-93 G 3
Guaíra [BR, Paraná] 111 F 2
Guaíra [BR, São Paulo] 102-103 H 4
Guairá [PY] 102-103 D 6-7
Guaira, La — 94-95 H 2
Guaire, Río — 91 II b 2
Guaitecas, Islas — 111 AB 6
Guajaba, Cayo — 88-89 H 4
Guajará 98-99 J 7
Guajará-Mirim 92-93 FG 7
Guajeru 100-101 D 8
Guajira 94-95 E 2
Guajira, Península de — 92-93 E 2
Guala, Punta — 108-109 C 4
Gualaceo 96-97 B 3
Gualala, CA 74-75 B 3
Gualán 86-87 Q 10
Gualaquiza 92-93 D 5
Gualeguay 111 E 4
Gualeguay, Río — 106-107 H 4
Gualeguaychú 111 E 4
Gualicho, Bajo del — 108-109 G 4
Gualicho, Gran Bajo del — 108-109 G 3
Gualicho, Salina del — 108-109 G 3
Gualior = Gwalior 134-135 M 5
Gualjaina 108-109 D 4
Gualjaina, Río — 108-109 D 4
Guallatiri, Volcán — 104-105 B 6
Gualqui 106-107 A 6
Guam 206-207 S 8
Guamá [BR] 98-99 P 5
Guama [YV] 94-95 G 2
Guamá, Rio — 100-101 A 2
Guamal [CO, Magdalena] 94-95 DE 3
Guamal [CO, Meta] 94-95 E 5
Guamal, Quebrada — 91 II b 1
Guamani, Cordillera de — 96-97 AB 4
Guamblin, Isla — 111 A 6
Guamini 106-107 F 6
Guamo [CO] 94-95 D 5
Guamo [YV] 94-95 E 3
Guamote 96-97 B 2
Guampí, Serra de — 94-95 J 4-5
Guamúchil 86-87 FG 5
Guamués, Río — 94-95 C 7
Gua Musang 150-151 CD 10
Gu'an 146-147 F 2
Guaña 92-93 G 4
Guanabara, Baía de — 102-103 L 5
Guanacache, Lagunas de — 106-107 CD 4
Guanaco, Bajo del — 108-109 E 6
Guanahacabibes, Península de — 88-89 D 4
Guanahani = San Salvador 64-65 M 7
Guanaja 88-89 D 6
Guanajutao 64-65 F 7
Guanambi 100-101 C 8
Guanani 94-95 E 3
Guanape 94-95 J 3
Guanare 92-93 F 3
Guanare, Río — 94-95 G 3
Guanarito 92-93 F 3
Guanay, Cerro — 94-95 H 5
Guandacol 106-107 C 2
Guandacol, Río — 106-107 C 2
Guandian 146-147 G 5
Guandong Bandao 144-145 C 3
Guandu 146-147 DE 7
Guane 64-65 K 7
Guang'an 142-143 K 5
Guangchang 142-143 M 6
Guangde 146-147 G 6
Guangdong 142-143 L 7
Guangfeng 146-147 G 7
Guanghai 142-143 L 7
Guanghua 142-143 L 5
Guangji 142-143 M 6
Guangling 146-147 E 2
Guanglu Dao 144-145 D 3
Guangnan 142-143 JK 7
Guangning 146-147 D 10
Guangping 146-147 E 3
Guangrao 146-147 G 3
Guangshan 146-147 E 5
Guangshui 146-147 E 6
Guangxi Zhuangzu Zizhiqu 142-143 KL 7
Guangyuan 142-143 K 5
Guangze 146-147 F 8
Guangzhou 142-143 LM 7
Guangzhou Wan = Zhanjiang Gang 142-143 L 7
Guanhães 102-103 L 3
Guanipa, Mesa de — 94-95 J 3
Guanipa, Río — 94-95 K 3
Guan Jiang 146-147 C 9
Guankou = Minhou 146-147 G 8
Guannan 146-147 G 4
Guano 96-97 B 2
Guanoco 94-95 K 2
Guano Islands = Penguin Eilanden 174-175 A 3-5
Guano Lake 66-67 D 4
Guanqumen, Beijing- 155 II b 2
Guanshui 144-145 E 2
Guanta [RCH] 106-107 B 2
Guanta [YV] 94-95 J 2
Guantánamo 64-65 LM 7-8
Guantao 146-147 E 3
Guantou Jiao 150-151 G 2
Guan Xian 146-147 E 3
Guanyang 146-147 C 9
Guanyintang 146-147 CD 4
Guanyun 142-143 MN 5
Guapay, Río — 104-105 E 5
Guapé 102-103 K 4
Guapí 92-93 D 4
Guapiara 102-103 H 6
Guápiles 88-89 E 9
Guapó 102-103 H 2
Guapo, El — 94-95 HJ 2
Guaporé 106-107 LM 2
Guaporé = Rondônia 92-93 G 7
Guaporé, Rio — [BR ◁ Rio Mamoré] 92-93 G 7
Guaporé, Rio — [BR ◁ Rio Taquari] 106-107 L 2
Guaqui 92-93 F 8
Guará [BR, Rio Grande do Sul] 106-107 K 3
Guará [BR, São Paulo] 102-103 J 4
Guará, Rio — 100-101 B 7
Guarabira 92-93 MN 6
Guaraçai 102-103 G 4
Guaracarumbo 91 II b 1
Guaraciaba do Norte 100-101 D 3
Guaraji 102-103 G 6
Guaramirim 102-103 H 7
Guaranda 92-93 D 5
Guaranésia 102-103 J 4
Guarani 102-103 L 4
Guaraniaçu 102-103 F 6
Guarantã 102-103 H 4
Guarapiranga, Barragem do — 110 II a 3
Guarapiranga, Reservatório de — 110 II a 3
Guarapo, El — 91 II b 1
Guarapuava 111 F 3
Guarapuavinha 102-103 G 6
Guaraqueçaba 102-103 HJ 6
Guararé 110 II c 3
Guararapes 102-103 G 4
Guararema 102-103 JK 5
Guaratinga 100-101 E 9
Guaratinguetá 92-93 KL 9
Guaratuba 111 G 3
Guaratuba, Baía de — 102-103 HJ 6
Guarayos, Llanos de — 92-93 G 8
Guarda 120-121 D 8
Guarda, El — 91 I a 2
Guardafui = 'Asayr 134-135 G 8
Guardamonte, El — 104-105 D 10
Guarda-Mor 102-103 J 2
Guardatinajas 94-95 H 3
Guardia, La — [BOL] 104-105 E 5
Guardia, La — [RA] 106-107 E 2
Guardia, La — [RCH] 106-107 C 1
Guardia Escolta 106-107 F 2
Guardia Mitre 108-109 H 3
Guardián, Cabo — 108-109 FG 7
Guardian Brito, Isla — 108-109 C 10
Guardo 120-121 E 7
Guarenas 94-95 H 2
Guariba 102-103 H 4
Guaricana, Pico — 102-103 H 6
Guarico 94-95 G 3
Guárico, Embalse de — 94-95 H 3
Guarico, Punta — 88-89 JK 4
Guárico, Río — 94-95 H 3
Guarita, Rio — 106-107 L 1
Guarrojo, Río — 94-95 F 5
Guarujá 102-103 JK 5-6
Guarulhos 92-93 K 9
Guarulhos-Cidade Brasil 110 II b 1
Guarulhos-Vila Cocaia 110 II b 1
Guarulhos-Vila Galvão 110 II b 1
Guarulhos-Vila Macedo 110 II b 1
Guasacaví, Cerro — 94-95 G 6
Guasapampa, Sierra de — 106-107 E 3
Guasave 64-65 E 6
Guasayán, Sierra de — 104-105 D 10-11
Guascama, Punta — 92-93 D 4
Guasdualito 92-93 EF 3
Guasipati 92-93 G 3
Guastalla 122-123 D 3
Guatapará 102-103 J 4
Guatavita 94-95 E 5
Guatemala [GCA, place] 64-65 HJ 9
Guatemala [GCA, state] 64-65 HJ 8
Guatemala Basin 156-157 N 4
Guateque 94-95 E 5
Guatimozin 106-107 FG 4
Guatire 94-95 H 2
Guatisimiña 94-95 K 5
Guatraché 106-107 F 6
Guatraché, Laguna — 106-107 F 6
Guatrochi 108-109 G 4
Guavatayoc, Laguna de — 104-105 CD 8
Guaviare 94-95 EF 6
Guaviare, Río — 92-93 F 4
Guaviravi 106-107 J 2
Guaxupé 92-93 K 9
Guayabal [C] 88-89 H 4
Guayabal [YV] 94-95 H 4
Guayabero, Río — 94-95 E 6
Guayabo, El — [CO] 94-95 E 4
Guayabo, El — [YV] 94-95 EF 3
Guayabones 94-95 F 3
Guayacán 106-107 B 2-3
Guayaguayare 94-95 L 2
Guayama 88-89 N 6
Guayana = Guyana 92-93 H 3-4
Guayaneco, Archipiélago — 108-109 AB 6
Guayapo, Río — 94-95 H 5
Guayaquil 92-93 CD 5
Guayaquil, Golfo de — 92-93 C 5
Guayaramerín 92-93 F 7
Guayas 96-97 AB 3
Guayas, Río — [CO] 94-95 D 7
Guayas, Río — [EC] 96-97 B 3
Guaycurú 106-107 GH 2
Guaycurú, Río — 102-103 C 7
Guayllabamba, Río — 94-95 B 1
Guaymas = Heroica Guaymas 64-65 D 6
Guayquiraró 106-107 H 3
Guayquiraró, Río — 106-107 H 3
Guazapares 86-87 FG 4
Guba 172 E 4
guba Buor-Chaja 132-133 Z 3
Gubacha 132-133 K 6
guba Mašigina 132-133 HJ 3
Guban 164-165 ab 1
Gubanovo = Vereščagino 132-133 JK 6
Gubbi 140 C 4
Gùbbio 122-123 E 4
Gubdor 124-125 V 3
Guben 118 G 3
Gubio 168-169 J 2
Gubkin 126-127 H 1
Gucheng [TJ, Hebei] 146-147 EF 3
Gucheng [TJ, Hubei] 146-147 C 5
Gucheng [TJ, Shanxi] 146-147 CD 4
Gučin Us 142-143 J 2
Gucun 146-147 F 8
Gūḍalūr [IND ↖ Coimbatore] 140 C 5
Gūḍalūr [IND ↙ Madurai] 140 C 6
Gūḍalūr = Cuddalore 134-135 MN 8
Gūḍam = Gūḍem 140 F 2
Gudāri 138-139 JK 8
Gudauta 126-127 K 5
Gudbrandsdal 116-117 CD 7
Gūḍem 140 F 2
Gudenå 116-117 CD 9
Gudermes 126-127 N 5
Gudibanda 140 CD 4
Gudivāda 140 E 2
Gudiyāttam 140 D 4
Gudong 141 F 3
Güdül 136-137 E 2
Gūḍūr 134-135 MN 8
Gūḍūru = Gūḍūr 134-135 MN 8
Guéckédou 164-165 BC 7
Gué de Constantine, le — 170 I ab 2
Guéguen, Lac — 62 N 2
Guéjar, Río — 94-95 E 6
Guékédou-Kankan 168-169 C 3
Guelma = Qalmah 164-165 F 1
Guelph 56-57 UV 9
Guémar = Qamār 166-167 K 3
Guéna 168-169 D 3
Guéné 164-165 E 6
Guenfouda = Janfūdah 166-167 E 2
Guenguel, Río — 108-109 D 5-6
Guentras, Région des — = Al-Qanṭarah 166-167 J 3
Güeppi 96-97 D 2
Güepsa 94-95 E 4
Guéra, Pic de — 164-165 H 6
Güer Aike 108-109 DE 8
Guerara = Al-Qarārah 166-167 J 3
Guerdane, Bir — = Bi'r Ghardan 166-167 K 2
Güere, Río — 94-95 J 3
Guerèda 164-165 J 6
Guerém 100-101 E 7
Guéret 120-121 H 5
Guernsey 119 E 7
Guernsey, WY 68-69 D 4
Guerrero [MEX, administrative unit] 64-65 FG 8
Guerrero [MEX, place Coahuila] 76-77 D 8
Guerrero [MEX, place Tamaulipas] 76-77 E 9
Guerrero Negro 86-87 CD 3-4
Guersīf = Garsīf 166-167 E 2
Guerzim = Qarzīm 166-167 F 5
G'uesevo 122-123 K 4
Guettar, El — = Al-Qaṭṭār 166-167 J 2
Guettara = Qaṭṭārah 166-167 E 4
Guettara, Aïn El — 164-165 D 4
Guetter, Chott el — = Shaṭṭ al-Qaṭṭār 166-167 L 2
Gueydan, LA 78-79 C 5-6
Gueyo 168-169 D 4
Guge 164-165 M 7
Gugging 113 I b 1
Gughe = Guge 164-165 M 7
Gugong Palace Museum 155 II b 2
Gūha = Gua 138-139 K 6
Guhāgar 140 A 2
Guia 92-93 H 8
Guia Lopes 102-103 J 4
Guia Lopes da Laguna 102-103 DE 4
Guiana Basin 50-51 G 5
Guiana Brasileira 92-93 G-J 4-5
Guiana Highlands = Macizo de las Guyanas 92-93 F 3-J 4
Guibes 174-175 B 4
Guichi 142-143 M 5
Guichicovi 86-87 N 9
Guichón 106-107 J 4
Guidder = Guider 164-165 G 6-7
Guide 142-143 J 4
Guider 164-165 G 6-7
Guiding 142-143 K 6
Guidong 146-147 D 8
Guier, Lac de — 164-165 AB 5
Guiglo 164-165 C 7
Güigüe 94-95 H 2-3
Gui He = Kuai He 146-147 F 5
Guija 174-175 K 3
Gui Jiang 146-147 C 9-10
Guiji Shan 146-147 H 7
Guildford 119 F 6
Guilin 142-143 KL 6
Guimarães [BR] 92-93 L 5
Guimarães [P] 120-121 C 8
Guimaras Island 148-149 H 4
Guimbalete 76-77 C 9
Guinan Zhou = Qiannon Zizhizhou 142-143 K 6
Guinea 164-165 B 6-C 7
Guinea, Gulf of — 164-165 C-F 8

Guinea Basin 50-51 J 5
Guinea Bissau 164-165 AB 6
Guinea Rise 50-51 JK 6
Güines [C] 64-65 K 7
Guingamp 120-121 F 4
Guinia 168-169 H 2
Guiones, Punta — 88-89 CD 10
Guioumbale Rapides 168-169 E 3
Guiping 142-143 KL 7
Guiqi = Guixi 146-147 F 7
Guir, Hamada du — = Hammadat al-Gīr 166-167 E 4
Guīr, Ouèd — = Wādī Gīr 166-167 E 4
Güira de Melena 88-89 E 3
Guiratinga 102-103 F 2
Güiria 94-95 K 2
Guīsser = Gīşşar 166-167 C 3
Guixi 146-147 F 7
Gui Xian 146-147 B 10
Guiyang [TJ, Guizhou] 142-143 K 6
Guiyang [TJ, Hunan] 142-143 L 6
Güiza, Río — 94-95 BC 7
Guizhou 142-143 JK 6
Gujarāt 134-135 L 6
Gujerat = Gujarāt 134-135 L 6
Gujiang 146-147 E 8
Gūjrānwāla 134-135 L 4
Gujrāt 134-135 L 4
Gük Tappah 136-137 L 5
Gulabarga = Gulburga 134-135 M 7
Gul'ajevo, Archangel'sk- 124-125 N 1
Gul'ajpole 126-127 H 3
Gulampaja, Sierra — 104-105 C 10
Gulargambone 160 J 3
Gulbān at-Ṭaiyārāt, Bīr — = Qulbān aṭ-Ṭayyārāt 136-137 JK 5
Gulbene 124-125 F 5
Gulburga 140 C 2
Guledagudda 140 B 2
Guleicheng = Duxun 146-147 F 10
Gülek = Çamalan 136-137 F 4
Gulf Beach, FL 78-79 F 5
Gulf Coastal Plain 64-65 G 6-J 5
Gulf of Boothia 56-57 ST 3-4
Gulf of Cambay 134-135 L 6
Gulf of Carpentaria 158-159 GH 2
Gulf of Kutch 134-135 KL 6
Gulf of Maine 64-65 N 3
Gulf of Mannar 134-135 M 9
Gulf of Papua 148-149 MN 8
Gulf of Saint Lawrence 56-57 Y 8
Gulf of Santa Catalina 74-75 DE 6
Gulf of Sirte = Khalīj as-Surt 164-165 H 2
Gulfport, FL 80-81 b 3
Gulfport, MS 64-65 J 5
Gulf Saint Vincent 158-159 G 6-7
Gulgong 160 JK 4
Gulinīm 164-165 BC 3
Gulistan 132-133 M 9
Gulkana, AK 58-59 OP 5
Gul'kevići 126-127 K 4
Gullbringu-Kjósar 116-117 b 2-c 3
Gullfoss 116-117 d 2
Gulliver, MI 70-71 GH 2
Gull Lake [CDN] 60 KL 3
Gull Lake [USA] 70-71 C 2
Gullrock Lake 62 BC 2
Güllük 136-137 B 4
Gulma 168-169 FG 2
Gülmīmā 166-167 D 4
Gülnar = Anaypazari 136-137 E 4
Gulph Mills, PA 84 III a 1
Gulrān 134-135 J 3
Gülšehir 136-137 F 3
Gulu 172 F 1
Guma Bazar 142-143 D 4
Gumaral 94-95 E 5
Gumbiro 171 C 5
Gumel 168-169 H 2
Gumla 138-139 K 6
Gumma 144-145 M 4
Gummi 168-169 G 2
Gümrü = Leninakan 126-127 LM 6
Gümtī 141 B 4
Gumti = Gomati 134-135 N 5
Gümüşane 134-135 D 2
Gümüşane dağları 136-137 H 2
Gümüşhacıköy 136-137 F 2
Gümüşköy 154 I a 1
Guna 134-135 M 6
Gunabad = Gonābād 134-135 H 4
Günar = Anaypazari 136-137 E 4
Gunchū = Iyo 144-145 J 6
Gundardehi 138-139 H 7
Gundlakamma 140 DE 3
Gundlupet 140 C 5
Guṇḍulupēṭā = Gundlupet 140 C 5
Gündüzlü 136-137 G 2
Güney 136-137 C 3
Güney = Kırık 136-137 J 2
Güneydoğu Toroslar 134-135 DE 3
Gungu 172 C 3
Gunib 126-127 N 5
Gunisao Lake 62 A 1
Gunisao River 62 A 1
Gunnaur 138-139 G 3
Gunnbjørn Fjeld 56-57 ef 4
Gunnedah 158-159 K 6
Gunnison, CO 64-65 E 4
Gunnison, UT 74-75 H 3
Gunnison Island 66-67 G 5
Gunnison River 68-69 BC 6
Gunt 132-133 L 3
Güntakal 134-135 M 7
Guntersville, AL 78-79 F 3
Guntersville Lake 78-79 FG 3
Guntūr 134-135 MN 7
Guṇṭūru = Guntūr 134-135 MN 7
Gunung Abong-Abong 152-153 B 3
Gunung Agung 148-149 G 8
Gunung Api 152-153 N 10
Gunungapi, Pulau — 148-149 J 8
Gunung Bagahak 152-153 N 3
Gunung Bandahara 152-153 BC 4
Gunung Batubrok 152-153 L 5
Gunung Benom 150-151 CD 11
Gunung Besar [MAL] 150-151 D 11
Gunung Besar [RI] 152-153 LM 7
Gunung Bintang 150-151 C 10
Gunung Bitang 152-153 D 3
Gunung Blumut 148-149 D 6
Gunung Bubu 150-151 C 10
Gunung Chamah 150-151 C 10
Gunung Cikuray 152-153 G 9
Gunung Dempo 148-149 D 7
Gunung Gandadiwata 152-153 NO 7
Gunung Geureudong 152-153 B 3
Gunung Grah 150-151 C 10
Gunung Inerie 148-149 H 8
Gunung Jaya 148-149 L 7
Gunung Kaba 152-153 E 7
Gunung Kambuno 152-153 O 7
Gunung Katopasa 152-153 O 6
Gunung Kerinci 148-149 D 7
Gunung Kinabalu 148-149 G 5
Gunung Kongkemul 152-153 M 5
Gunung Korbu 148-149 D 5-6
Gunung Lantee 152-153 M 10
Gunung Lawit [MAL] 150-151 D 10
Gunung Lawit [RI] 148-149 F 6
Gunung Ledang 150-151 D 11
Gunung Leuser 148-149 C 6
Gunung Lompobatang 152-153 NO 8
Gunung Magdalena 152-153 M 3
Gunung Malino 152-153 O 5
Gunung Marapi 152-153 D 6
Gunung Masurai 152-153 DE 7
Gunung Mekongga 148-149 H 7
Gunung Melta 152-153 M 3
Gunung Menyapa 152-153 M 5
Gunung Merbabu 152-153 J 9
Gunung Mulu 148-149 FG 6
Gunung Murud 152-153 LM 4
Gunung Muryo 152-153 J 9
Gunung Mutis 148-149 H 8
Gunung Niapa 152-153 M 5
Gunung Niut 148-149 E 6
Gunung Ophir = Gunung Ledang 150-151 D 11
Gunung Pangrango 152-153 G 9
Gunung Patuha 152-153 G 9
Gunung Pesagi 152-153 F 8
Gunung Peuetsagu 152-153 B 3
Gunung Rantekombola 148-149 GH 7
Gunung Rinjani 148-149 G 8
Gunung Saran 152-153 J 6
Gunung Sarempaka 152-153 L 6
Gunung Semeru 148-149 F 8
Gunung Sibuatan 152-153 BC 4
Gunung Sinabung 152-153 C 4
Gunungsitoli 148-149 C 6
Gunung Slamet 152-153 H 9
Gunung Sorikmarapi 152-153 C 5
Gunung Tahan 148-149 D 6
Gunung Talakmau 152-153 CD 5-6
Gunung Talang 152-153 D 6
Gunung Tambora 148-149 G 8
Gunung Tampulonanjing 152-153 CD 5
Gunung Tokala 152-153 O 6
Gunung Trus Madi 152-153 M 3
Gunung Wanggamet 152-153 NO 10-11
Gunung Wani 152-153 P 8
Gunupur 138-139 JK 8
Gunupura = Gunupur 138-139 JK 8
Gunworth 61 DE 5
Gunzan = Kunsan 142-143 O 4
Guocian = Yuanping 146-147 D 2
Guo He 146-147 F 5
Guo Xian 146-147 D 2
Guozhen 146-147 D 7
Gūra = Gūrha 134-135 L 5
Gurage 164-165 M 7
Guraghe = Gurage 164-165 M 7
Guramakuṇḍa = Gurramkonda 140 D 4
Gurara 168-169 G 3
Gurd Abū Muḥarrik 164-165 KL 3
Gurdāspur 134-135 M 4
Gurdon, AR 78-79 C 4
Gurdžaani 126-127 M 6
Gurgaon 138-139 F 3
Gurguéia, Rio — 92-93 L 6
Gūrha 134-135 L 5
Guri, Embalse de — 94-95 K 4
Gurinhatã 102-103 GH 3
Gurjev 126-127 PQ 3
Gurjevsk 132-133 Q 7
Gurk 118 G 5
Gurkha 138-139 K 3-4
Gurlha Mandhātā 138-139 H 2
Gurma = Gourma 164-165 E 6
Gürpınar = Kıgzı 136-137 K 3
Gurrāmah 166-167 DE 3
Gurramkonda 140 D 4
Gurskøy 116-117 A 6
Gurudaspur = Gurdāspur 134-135 M 4
Gurumanas 174-175 B 2
Gurun [MAL] 148-149 D 5
Gürün [TR] 136-137 G 3
Gurupá 92-93 J 5
Gurupá, Ilha Grande de — 92-93 J 5
Gurupi 98-99 O 10
Gurupi, Cabo — 98-99 PQ 5
Gurupi, Rio — 92-93 K 5
Gurupi, Serra do — 92-93 K 5-6
Gurushikhar = Guru Sikhar 138-139 D 5
Guru Sikhar 138-139 D 5
Gurvansajchan 142-143 K 2
Gurzuf 126-127 G 4
Gusau 164-165 F 6
Gus'-Chrustal'nyj 124-125 N 6
Gusev 118 L 1
Gushan 144-145 D 3
Gusher, UT 66-67 J 5
Gushi 142-143 M 5
Gushiago 168-169 E 3
Gusinaja guba 132-133 cd 3
Gusinaja Zemľa, poluostrov — 132-133 HJ 3
Gusino 124-125 H 6
Gustav Adolf land 116-117 l 5
Gustavo 104-105 F 2
Gustavo A. Madero, Ciudad de México- 91 l c 2
Gustavo Díaz Ordaz 86-87 L 4
Gustavo Sotelo 86-87 D 2
Gustavus, AK 58-59 U 7
Gustav V land 116-117 kl 4
Gustine, CA 74-75 C 4
Güstrow 118 EF 2
Gus'-Železnyj 124-125 N 6
Gutaj 132-133 U 7-8
Gutenberg 106-107 F 2
Gutenko Mountains 53 B 30
Güterfelde 130 III a 2
Guterres 106-107 J 3
Gütersloh 118 CD 3
Guthrie, KY 78-79 F 2
Guthrie, OK 76-77 F 5
Guthrie, TX 76-77 D 6
Guthrie Center, IA 70-71 CD 5
Gutian 146-147 G 8
Gutiérrez 104-105 E 6
Gutiérrez, Tuxtla — 64-65 H 8
Guttenberg, IA 70-71 E 4
Guttenberg, NJ 82 III bc 2
Guṭṭi = Gooti 140 C 3
Guty 126-127 G 1
Guulin 142-143 H 2
Guvāhāṭi = Gauhati 134-135 P 5
Güyan = Kılaban 136-137 K 4
Guyana 92-93 H 3-4
Guyanas, Macizo de las — 92-93 F 3-J 4
Guyandot River 72-73 EF 5
Guyenne 120-121 G-J 6
Guyi = Miluo 142-143 L 6
Guymon, OK 76-77 D 4
Guynemer 61 J 5
Guyotville = 'Ayn Binyān 166-167 H 1
Guyra 158-159 K 6
Guysborough 63 EF 5
Guzhang 146-147 BC 7
Guzhen 146-147 F 5
Guzhu 146-147 E 10
Guzmán 86-87 G 2
Guzmán, Ciudad — 64-65 F 8
Guzmán, Laguna de — 86-87 G 2
Gvalior = Gwalior 134-135 M 5
Gvāliyar = Gwalior 134-135 M 5
Gvardejskoje [SU, Ukrainskaja SSR] 126-127 G 4
Gwa 148-149 B 3
Gwa Au 141 D 7
Gwabegar 158-159 JK 6
Gwadabawa 168-169 G 3
Gwādar 134-135 J 5
Gwai 172 E 5
Gwalia 158-159 D 5
Gwalior 134-135 M 5
Gwaliyar = Gwalior 134-135 M 5
Gwanda 172 E 6
Gwane 172 E 1
Gwasero 168-169 F 3
Gwda 118 H 2
Gweru 172 E 5
Gwydir River 158-159 J 5
Gyamda Dsong 142-143 G 5
Gyanchhung 138-139 M 2
Gyangtse 142-143 FG 6
Gyanyima 138-139 H 2
Gyáros 122-123 L 7
Gyda 132-133 O 3
Gydanskaja guba 132-133 O 3
Gydanskij poluostrov 132-133 OP 3-4
Gympie 158-159 K 5
Gyobingauk = Kyōbingauk 141 DE 6
Gyöngyös 118 J 5
Győr 118 H 5
Gypsum, KS 68-69 H 6
Gypsum Palace 160 G 4
Gypsumville 61 J 5
Gýtheion 122-123 K 7
Gyula 118 K 5

H

Haafuun 164-165 c 1
Haafuun, Raas — 134-135 G 8
Haag, Den — = 's-Gravenhage 120-121 JK 2
Haakon VII land 116-117 hj 5
Ha'apai 208 J 4
Haapajärvi 116-117 LM 6
Haapamäki 116-117 KL 6
Haapsalu 124-125 D 4
Haardt 118 CD 4
Haarlem [NL] 120-121 JK 2
Haarlem [ZA] 174-175 E 7
Hābā, Bi'r — 136-137 H 5
Habana, La — 64-65 K 7
Habarana 140 E 6
Habarane = Habaraṇa 140 E 6
Habārūt 134-135 G 7
Habaswein 171 DE 2
Habay 56-57 N 6
Ḥabbānīyah 136-137 K 6
Ḥabbānīyah, Hawr al- 136-137 K 6
Habbārīyah 136-137 JK 6
Ḥabīb, Wādī — 173 BC 4
Ḥabībah, Juzur al- 166-167 F 2
Habibas, Îles — = Juzur al-Ḥabībah 166-167 F 2
Haboro 144-145 b 1
Habrah, Al- 166-167 J 3
Habrat Najid 136-137 K 7
Hacheim, Bîr — = Bi'r al-Ḥukayyim 164-165 J 2
Hachijō-jima 142-143 Q 5
Hachinohe 142-143 R 3
Hachiōji 144-145 M 5
Hachirō-gata 144-145 MN 3
Hachita, NM 74-75 J 7
Hacıbektaş 136-137 F 3
Hacıköy 136-137 F 2
Hacısaklı 136-137 E 4
Hack, Mount — 158-159 G 6
Hackberry, AZ 74-75 G 5
Hackensack, MN 70-71 CD 2
Hackensack, NJ 82 III b 1
Hackensack River 82 III b 2
Hackett 61 B 4
Hackleburg, AL 78-79 EF 3
Ha Côi 150-151 F 2
Ḥad, Al- 166-167 D 2
Hāḍabhāṅgā = Harbhanga 138-139 K 7
Hadagalli 140 BC 3
Hadal 'Awāb, Jabal — 173 D 7
Haḍbarāh 134-135 H 7
Haḍbat al-Jilf al-Kabīr 164-165 K 4
Ḥadd, Rā's al — 134-135 HJ 6
Haddār, Al- 134-135 EF 6
Haddock 60 J 3
Haddonfield, NJ 84 III c 2
Haddon Heights, NJ 84 III c 2
Haddummati Atoll 176 ab 2
Hadejia [WAN, place] 164-165 G 6
Hadejia [WAN, river] 164-165 F 6
Ḥadera 136-137 F 6
Hadersdorf, Wien- 113 I ab 2
Haderslev 116-117 C 10
Hadgāńv = Hadgaon 138-139 F 8
Hadgaon 138-139 F 8
Ḥadīd, Rā's — 166-167 AB 4
Ḥadīd, Rā's al- 166-167 K 1
Hadım 136-137 E 4
Ḥadītah, Al- 134-135 F 4
Hadjaj, Bir el — = Bi'r al-Hajāj 166-167 F 6
Hadjar, El — = Al-Ḥajar 166-167 KL 1
Hâdjeb el 'Aïoûn = Ḥājib al-'Ayūn 166-167 L 2
Hadjira, El- = Al-Ḥajīrah 166-167 J 3
Hadjout = Ḥajut 164-165 E 1
Hadley Bay 56-57 P 3
Hadong [ROK] 144-145 FG 5
Ha Đông [VN] 148-149 E 2
Ḥād Qurt 166-167 D 2
Ḥaḍr, Al- 136-137 K 5
Hadramaut = Ḥaḍramawt 134-135 F 7
Ḥaḍramaut, Wādī — = Wādī al-Musīlah 134-135 FG 7
Ḥaḍramawt 134-135 F 7
Hadseløy 116-117 EF 3
Hadu 172 GH 2
Ḥaḍūr Shu'ayb 134-135 EF 7
Hadweenzic River 58-59 NO 3
Haedarganj = Haidargarh 138-139 H 4
Haedo 106-107 HJ 4
Haedo, Cuchilla de — 111 E 4
Haeju 142-143 O 4
Haeju-man 144-145 E 4
Haemi 144-145 F 4
Haenam 144-145 F 5
Haenertsburg 174-175 H 2-3
Haengyŏng 144-145 GH 1
Ḥafar al- Bāṭin, Al- 134-135 F 5
Haffah 136-137 FG 5
Hafford 61 E 4
Ḥaffūz 166-167 L 2
Hafik 136-137 G 3
Hafızbey 136-137 D 4
Hāflāng = Hāflong 141 C 3
Hāflong 141 C 3
Hafnarfjördhur 116-117 bc 2
Hafoûz = Ḥaffūz 166-167 L 2
Haft Gel 134-135 FG 4
Hāgā 141 C 4
Hagadera = Alanga Arba 172 GH 1
Haga-Haga 174-175 H 7
Hagari 140 C 3
Hagemeister Strait 58-59 G 7
Hagen 118 C 3
Hagenbecks Tierpark 130 I a 1
Hagensborg 60 D 3
Hageri 124-125 E 4
Hagerman, ID 66-67 F 4
Hagerman, NM 76-77 B 6
Hagermeister Island 56-57 D 6
Hagerstown, MD 72-73 GH 5
Hagersville 72-73 F 3
Hagfors 116-117 EF 7-8
Haggers = Hageri 124-125 E 4
Hagi [IS] 116-117 b 2
Hagi [J] 144-145 H 5
Hagiá 122-123 K 6
Hagía Barbara 113 IV a 2
Ha Giang 148-149 DE 2
Hagía Paraskevē [GR, Athēnai] 113 IV b 1
Hagia Sophia 154 I ab 2
Hágion Óros 122-123 L 5
Hágios Andréa, Akrōtērion — 136-137 F 5
Hágios Evstrátios 122-123 L 6
Hágios Geṓrgios 122-123 KL 7
Hágios Iōánnēs, Akrōtērion — 122-123 LM 8
Hágios Iōánnis Rentes 113 IV a 2
Hágios Nikólaos 122-123 LM 8
Hagiwara 144-145 L 5
Hague 61 E 4
Hague, ND 68-69 FG 2
Hague, Cap de la — 120-121 G 4
Hague, The — = 's-Gravenhage 120-121 JK 2
Haguenau 120-121 L 4
Hagues Peak 68-69 CD 5
Hagui = Hagi 144-145 H 5
Hagunia, El — = Al-Haqūniyah 164-165 B 3
Haha 206-207 S 7
Hahnville, LA 78-79 D 6
Ha Hoa 150-151 E 2
Hai, Ko — 150-151 B 9
Ḥāi, Ouèd el — = Wād al-Ḥāy 166-167 E 2
Hai'an [TJ, Guangdong] 142-143 KL 7
Hai'an [TJ, Jiangsu] 146-147 H 5
Haiao-hsien = Xiao Xian 146-147 F 4
Haib [ZA, place] 174-175 C 5
Haib [ZA, river] 174-175 BC 5
Haibei Zangzu Zizhizhou 142-143 H-J 4
Haicheng 144-145 D 2
Haicheng = Longhai 146-147 FG 9
Ḥaidarābād 134-135 KL 5
Haidargarh 138-139 H 4
Haiderabad = Hyderābād 134-135 M 7
Haiderbad = Ḥaidarābād 134-135 KL 5
Haidhausen, München- 130 II b 2
Haidian, Beijing- 155 II a 2
Haidianqu, Beijing- 155 II ab 2
Hai'dra = Haydrah 166-167 L 2
Hai Du'o'ng 148-149 E 2
Haifa = Ḥēfa 134-135 CD 4
Haifeng 142-143 M 7
Haifong = Hai Phong 148-149 E 2
Haig, Mount — 66-67 F 1
Haigler, NE 68-69 F 5-6
Hai He 146-147 F 2
Hai He = Sanggan He 146-147 D 2
Hai Ho = Hai He 146-147 F 2
Haikang 142-143 KL 7
Haikangsuo = Qishui 146-147 B 11
Haikou 142-143 L 7-8
Hai-k'ou = Hangchun 146-147 H 10
Haikow = Haikou 142-143 L 7-8
Ḥā'il 134-135 E 5
Hai-la-êrh = Hailar 142-143 M 2
Hailākāndi 141 C 3
Hailar 142-143 M 2
Hailar He 142-143 MN 2
Hailey, ID 66-67 F 4
Hailing Dao 146-147 CD 11
Hailong 142-143 O 3
Hai-long Tao = Hailing Dao 146-147 CD 11
Hailun 142-143 O 2
Hailuoto 116-117 L 5
Haimen [TJ, Guangdong] 146-147 F 10
Haimen [TJ, Jiangsu] 142-143 N 5
Haimen [TJ, Zhejiang] 142-143 N 6
Haimen Wan 146-147 F 10
Haimur Wells = Ābār Ḥaymūr 173 CD 6
Hainan = Hainan Dao 142-143 KL 8
Hainan Dao 142-143 KL 8
Hainan Strait = Qiongzhou Haixia 142-143 KL 7
Hai-nan Tao = Hainan Dao 142-143 KL 8
Hainan Zangzu Zizhizhou 142-143 H 5-J 4
Hainan Zizhizhou 142-143 K 8
Hainan Zui = Baohu Jiao 146-147 C 11
Hainaut 120-121 JK 3
Haines, AK 56-57 JK 6
Haines, OR 66-67 DE 3
Haines City, FL 80-81 c 2
Haines Junction 56-57 J 5
Hainesport, NJ 84 III de 2
Haining 146-147 H 6
Hai Phong 148-149 E 2
Ḥais = Ḥays 134-135 E 8
Haitan Dao = Pingtan Dao 142-143 MN 6
Hai-t'an Hsia = Haitan Xia 146-147 G 9
Haitan Xia 146-147 G 9
Haïti 64-65 M 8
Haiti = Hispaniola 64-65 MN 8
Haitou 150-151 G 3
Hai-t'ou = Haitou 150-151 G 3
Hai Van, Đeo — 150-151 G 4
Haixi Monggolzu Zangzu Kazakzu Zizhizhou 142-143 GH 4, G 5
Haiyā = Hayyā 164-165 M 5
Haiyan [TJ, Guangdong] 146-147 D 11
Haiyan [TJ, Hangzhou] 146-147 H 6
Haiyang 146-147 H 3
Haiyang Dao 144-145 D 3
Hai-yang Tao = Haiyang Dao 144-145 D 3
Haiyanjie = Haiyan 146-147 D 11
Haizhou 142-143 M 5
Haizhou Wan 146-147 G 4
Ḥājab, Al- 166-167 D 3
Hajāj 166-167 G 1
Hajāj, Bi'r al- 166-167 F 6
Ḥajar, Al- [DZ] 166-167 KL 1
Ḥajar, Al- [Oman] 134-135 H 6
Hajara, Al- = Ṣaḥrā' al-Hijārah 136-137 JK 8
Hajdúböszörmény 118 KL 5
Ḥājeb, el — = Al-Ḥājab 166-167 D 3
Ḥājib al-'Ayūn 166-167 L 2
Ḥājjī Āqa = Bostānābād 136-137 M 4
Hajiki-saki 144-145 M 3
Hājīpur 138-139 K 5
Hajīr, Jabal — 134-135 G 8
Ḥajīrah, Al- 166-167 J 3
Ḥājī Sa'īd, Kūh-e — 136-137 M 4
Ḥājj 173 DE 3
Ḥajjah 134-135 E 7
Hajjār, Al- 164-165 EF 4
Ḥājjīābād 134-135 H 5
Hajnówka 118 L 2
Hājo 141 B 2
Hajo-do 144-145 F 5
Hajsyn = Gajsin 126-127 D 2
Hajut 164-165 E 1
Hajvoron = Gajvoron 126-127 D 2
Haka = Hāgā 141 C 4
Hakenfelde, Berlin- 130 III a 1
Hakkâri 136-137 KL 4
Hakkâri = Çölemerik 136-137 K 4
Hakkâri dağları 136-137 K 4
Hakken san 144-145 KL 5
Hak Kok Tau 155 I b 2
Hakodate 142-143 R 3
Hakos 174-175 B 2
Hakskeenpan 174-175 D 4
Hakui 144-145 L 4
Haku-san [J ↗ Ōno] 144-145 L 4
Haku-san [J ↓ Ōno] 144-145 L 5
Ha Kwai Chung 155 I a 1
Ḥāla 138-139 B 5
Ḥalab 134-135 D 3
Ḥalabān 134-135 E 6
Ḥalabcha = Sirwān 136-137 LM 5
Ḥalabīyah 136-137 H 5
Hala Hu = Char nuur 142-143 H 4
Ḥalā'ib 164-165 M 4
Ḥalāib, Jazā'ir — 173 E 6
Halāl, Gebel — = Jabal Hilāl 173 CD 2
Hālār 138-139 BC 6
Halawa, HI 78-79 d 2
Halāwata 140 D 7
Ḥalbā 136-137 FG 5
Halberstadt 118 E 3
Halbrite 68-69 E 1
Haldā 141 B 4
Halden 116-117 D 8
Haldensleben 118 E 2
Haldvānī = Haldwāni 138-139 G 3
Haldwāni 138-139 G 3
Hale 106-107 G 5
Hale, Mount — 158-159 C 5
Haleakala Crater 148-149 ef 3
Ḥaleb = Ḥalab 134-135 D 3
Halebid 140 BC 4
Hale Center, TX 76-77 CD 5
Hales Lake 85 II c 3
Haleyville, AL 78-79 F 3
Half Assini 168-169 E 4
Halfāyah, Al- 136-137 M 7
Halfeti 136-137 GH 4
Ḥalfīn, Wādī — 134-135 H 6
Hal Flood Range 53 B 23
Half Moon Bay 161 II b 2
Halfway Mount 58-59 K 6
Halfway River 60 FG 1
Halfway Street, London- 129 II c 2
Ḥalī = Khay' 134-135 E 7
Halia 138-139 J 5
Haliburton 72-73 G 2
Haliburton Highlands 62 MN 4
Haliç [TR] 154 I a 2
Halicarnassus = Bodrum 136-137 B 4
Ḥālidah, Bi'r — 136-137 B 7
Halifax, VA 80-81 G 2
Halifax [CDN] 56-57 Y 9
Halifax Bay 158-159 J 3
Ḥalīl, Al- 136-137 F 7
Ḥalīl Rūd 134-135 H 5
Halim, Jakarta- 154 IV b 2
Halimiye 136-137 E 4
Halim Perdanakusuma Airport 154 IV b 2
Haliyāl 140 B 3
Haliyāḷā = Haliyāl 140 B 3
Halkett, Cape — 58-59 LM 1
Hall 118 E 5
Hall, MT 66-67 G 2
Hall, Cabo — 108-109 G 10
Hall, ostrov — 132-133 KL 1
Halland 116-117 E 9
Hallandale, FL 80-81 c 4
Halla-san 144-145 F 6
Halle 118 EF 3
Halleck, NV 66-67 F 5
Hällefors 116-117 F 8
Hallein 118 F 5
Hallerbos 128 II a 2
Hallettsville, TX 76-77 F 8
Halley Bay 53 B 33-34
Halliday, ND 68-69 E 2
Hallingdal 116-117 C 7
Hallingskarvet 116-117 BC 7
Hall Lake 56-57 U 4
Hällnäs 116-117 H 5
Hallock, MN 68-69 H 1
Hallowell, ME 72-73 M 2
Hall Peninsula 56-57 X 5
Halls Bayou 85 III c 1
Hallsberg 116-117 F 8
Halls Creek 158-159 E 3
Hallstavik 116-117 H 7-8
Halmahera 148-149 J 6
Halmahera, Laut — 148-149 J 7
Halmeu 122-123 K 2
Halmstad 116-117 E 9
Halmyrós 122-123 K 6
Hālol 138-139 D 6
Ha Long, Vinh — 150-151 F 2
Halonnēsos 122-123 KL 6
Ḥalq al-Wad 166-167 M 1
Halsey, NE 68-69 F 5
Hälsingland 116-117 F 7-G 6
Halstad, MN 68-69 H 2
Haltiatunturi 116-117 J 3
Halvad 138-139 C 6
Halvar = Halvad 138-139 C 6
Halvmåneøya 116-117 lm 6
Halvorgate 61 E 5
Halyč = Galič 126-127 B 2
Hâlys = Kızılırmak 134-135 D 3
Ham [Namibia] 174-175 C 5
Ham, Wādī al- 166-167 HJ 2
Hama = Ḥamāā 136-137 G 5
Hamab = Hamrivier 174-175 C 5
Ḥamād, Al- 136-137 H 6-J 7
Hamad, Birkat — 136-137 KL 7
Hamada 144-145 HJ 5
Hamada, El — = Al-Hammadah 166-167 FG 4
Hamada, Région de — = Al-Hammadah 166-167 HJ 4
Hamada de la Daoura = Hammadat ad-Dawrah 166-167 DE 5
Hamada de Tindouf = Hammadat Tindūf 166-167 B 6-C 5
Hamada de Tinrhert = Hammadat Tinghīrt 164-165 FG 3
Hamada du Dra = Hammadat ad-Dara' 164-165 CD 3
Hamada du Guir = Hammadat al-Gīr 166-167 E 4
Hamada el Homra = Al-Ḥamādat al-Ḥamrā' 164-165 G 2-3
Hamâda ez Zegher = Ḥammadat az-Zaghir 166-167 M 6
Hamada Mangeni 164-165 G 4
Hamadān 134-135 F 3-4
Hamada Tounassine = Hammadat Tūnasīn 166-167 D 5
Hamadia = Ḥamādīyah 166-167 GH 2
Ḥamādīyah 166-167 GH 2
Ḥamāh 134-135 D 3
Hamajima 144-145 L 5
Hamamatsu 142-143 Q 5
Hamamatu = Hamamatsu 142-143 Q 5
Haman 136-137 F 3
Hamanaka 144-145 d 2
Hamana ko 144-145 L 5
Hamar 116-117 D 7
Hamar, ND 68-69 G 2
Ḥamār, Al- 136-137 M 8
Ḥamar, Dār — 164-165 K 6
Hamār, Wādī — 136-137 H 4
Hamarikyū Garden 155 III b 2
Hamas = Ḥamāh 134-135 D 3
Hamasaka 144-145 K 5
Ḥamāṭah, Jabal — 164-165 LM 4
Hama-Tombetsu 144-145 c 1
Hamatonbetu = Hama-Tombetsu 144-145 c 1
Hambantoṭa 140 E 7
Hamberg 170 V a 2
Hambergbreen 116-117 k 6
Hamber Provincial Park 56-57 N 7
Hamburg, AR 78-79 CD 4
Hamburg, CA 66-67 B 5
Hamburg, IA 70-71 BC 5
Hamburg, NY 72-73 G 3
Hamburg, PA 72-73 HJ 4
Hamburg [D] 118 E 2
Hamburg [ZA] 174-175 G 7
Hamburg-Allermöhe 130 I b 2
Hamburg-Alsterdorf 130 I ab 1
Hamburg-Bahrenfeld 130 I a 1
Hamburg-Barmbek 130 I b 1
Hamburg-Bergstedt 130 I b 1
Hamburg-Berne 130 I b 1
Hamburg-Billbrook 130 I b 1
Hamburg-Billstedt 130 I b 1
Hamburg-Billwerder Ausschlag 130 I b 1
Hamburg-Bramfeld 130 I b 1
Hamburg-Cranz 130 I a 1
Hamburg-Eidelstedt 130 I a 1
Hamburg-Eilbeck 130 I b 1
Hamburg-Eimsbüttel 130 I a 1
Hamburg-Eissendorf 130 I a 2
Hamburg-Eppendorf 130 I a 1
Hamburg-Farmsen 130 I b 1
Hamburg-Fischbek 130 I a 2
Hamburg-Flottbek 130 I a 1
Hamburg-Fuhlsbüttel, Flughafen — 130 I ab 1
Hamburg-Georgswerder 130 I b 1
Hamburg-Gross Borstel 130 I a 1
Hamburg-Hamm 130 I b 1
Hamburg-Hammerbrook 130 I b 1
Hamburg-Harvestehude 130 I a 1
Hamburg-Hausbruch 130 I a 2
Hamburg-Heimfeld 130 I a 2
Hamburg-Horn 130 I b 1
Hamburg-Hummelsbüttel 130 I b 1
Hamburg-Iserbrook 130 I a 1
Hamburg-Jenfeld 130 I b 1
Hamburg-Kirchdorf 130 I b 2
Hamburg-Klein Grasbrook 130 I ab 1
Hamburg-Klostertor 130 I b 1
Hamburg-Lemsahl-Mellingstedt 130 I b 1
Hamburg-Lokstedt 130 I a 1
Hamburg-Marienthal 130 I b 1
Hamburg-Meiendorf 130 I b 1
Hamburg-Moorburg 130 I a 2
Hamburg-Moorfleet 130 I b 1

Hamburg-Moorwerder 130 I b 2
Hamburg-Neuenfelde 130 I a 1
Hamburg-Neugraben 130 I a 2
Hamburg-Neuland 130 I ab 2
Hamburg-Niendorf 130 I a 1
Hamburg-Nienstedten 130 I a 1
Hamburg-Ochsenwerder 130 I b 2
Hamburg-Ohlsdorf 130 I b 1
Hamburg-Ohlstedt 130 I b 1
Hamburg-Oldenfelde 130 I b 1
Hamburg-Osdorf 130 I a 1
Hamburg-Othmarschen 130 I a 1
Hamburg-Ottensen 130 I a 1
Hamburg-Poppenbüttel 130 I b 1
Hamburg-Rahlstedt 130 I b 1
Hamburg-Reitbrook 130 I b 2
Hamburg-Rissen 130 I a 1
Hamburg-Ronneburg 130 I ab 2
Hamburg-Rothenburgsort 130 I b 1
Hamburg-Rotherbaum 130 I a 1
Hamburg-Sankt Georg 130 I ab 1
Hamburg-Sankt Pauli 130 I a 1
Hamburg-Sasel 130 I b 1
Hamburg-Schnelsen 130 I a 1
Hamburg-Spadenland 130 I b 2
Hamburg-Steilshoop 130 I b 1
Hamburg-Steinwerder 130 I a 1
Hamburg-Stellingen 130 I a 1
Hamburg-Sülldorf 130 I a 1
Hamburg-Tatenberg 130 I b 2
Hamburg-Tonndorf 130 I b 1
Hamburg-Uhlenhorst 130 I b 1
Hamburg-Veddel 130 I b 1
Hamburg-Waltershof 130 I a 1
Hamburg-Warwisch 130 I b 2
Hamburg-Wellingsbüttel 130 I b 1
Hamburg-Wilstorf 130 I a 2
Hamburg-Winterhude 130 I b 1
Hamch'ang 144-145 G 4
Ham-ch'uan = Hanchuan 146-147 DE 6
Ḥamḍ, Wādī al — 134-135 D 5
Ḥamdah 134-135 E 7
Ḥamdānīyah, Al- 136-137 G 5
Hämeen lääni 116-117 KL 7
Hämeenlinna 116-117 L 7
Ha Mei Wan 155 I a 2
Hamel, El- = Al-Ḥāmil 166-167 J 2
Hamelin = Hameln 118 D 2
Hamelin Pool [AUS, bay] 158-159 B 5
Hamelin Pool [AUS, place] 158-159 BC 5
Hameln 118 D 2
Hamersley Range 158-159 C 4
Ham-gang = Namhan-gang 144-145 F 4
Hamgyŏng-namdo 144-145 FG 2-3
Hamgyŏng-pukto 144-145 G 2-H 1
Hamhŭng 142-143 O 3-4
Hami 142-143 G 3
Ḥamīdīyah 136-137 F 5
Ḥāmil, Al- 166-167 J 2
Hamilton, AK 58-59 F 5
Hamilton, AL 78-79 EF 3
Hamilton, KS 68-69 H 6-7
Hamilton, MI 70-71 GH 4
Hamilton, MO 70-71 CD 6
Hamilton, MT 66-67 F 2
Hamilton, NY 72-73 J 3
Hamilton, OH 64-65 K 4
Hamilton, TX 76-77 E 7
Hamilton, WA 66-67 C 1
Hamilton [AUS] 158-159 H 7
Hamilton [Bermuda Islands] 64-65 O 5
Hamilton [CDN] 56-57 V 9
Hamilton [NZ] 158-159 OP 7
Hamilton, Mount — 74-75 F 3
Hamilton City, CA 74-75 BC 3
Hamilton Inlet 56-57 Z 7
Hamilton River [AUS, Queensland] 158-159 GH 4
Hamilton River [AUS, South Australia] 158-159 FG 5
Hamilton River = Churchill River 56-57 Y 7
Hamilton Sound 63 JK 3
Hamilton Square, NJ 72-73 J 4
Hamina 116-117 M 7
Ḥamīr, Wādī — [IRQ] 136-137 JK 7
Ḥamīr, Wādī — [Saudi Arabia] 136-137 J 7
Hamīrpur [IND, Himāchal Pradesh] 138-139 F 2
Hamīrpur [IND, Uttar Pradesh] 138-139 H 5
Ḥamīs, Al- = Al-Khamīs 166-167 C 3
Ḥamīs az-Zāmāmrah 166-167 B 3
Ḥamīssāt = Khamīssāt 166-167 CD 3
Hamitabad = Isparta 134-135 C 3
Hamiz, le — 170 I b 2
Hamiz, Oued el — 170 I b 2
Hamlet, NC 80-81 G 3
Hamlets, London- 129 II b 1
Hamlin, TX 76-77 D 6
Hamm 118 CD 3
Hamm, Hamburg- 130 I b 1
Hamma-Bouziane = Ḥammā Būziyān 166-167 JK 1
Ḥammā Būziyān 166-167 JK 1
Hammadah, Al- [DZ → Ghardāyah] 166-167 FG 4
Hammadah, Al- [DZ ← Ghardāyah] 166-167 HJ 4
Hammadat ad-Dawrah 166-167 DE 5
Ḥammadat al-Gīr 166-167 E 4
Ḥammadat az-Zaghir 166-167 M 6
Hammadat Tindūf 166-167 BC 5-6
Hammadat Tinghīrt 164-165 FG 3
Hammadat Tūnasīn 166-167 D 5
Ḥāmmah, Al- 166-167 L 3
Ḥammāl, Wādī al — = Wādī 'Ajaj 136-137 J 5
Ḥammām = Makhfir al-Ḥammān 136-137 H 5
Ḥammām, Al- 136-137 C 7
Ḥammām an-Nīf 166-167 M 1
Ḥammāmāt, Al- 166-167 M 1
Ḥammāmāt, Khalīj al- 164-165 G 1
Hammamet = Ḥammāmāt 166-167 K 2
Ḥammāmēt, El — = Al-Ḥammāmāt 166-167 M 1
Ḥammān, Al- 166-167 D 3
Ḥammān Awlād 'Alī 166-167 K 1
Hammanskraal 174-175 H 3
Hammar, Bahar el — = Bahr al-Aḥmar 166-167 GH 6
Ḥammār, Hawr al- 134-135 F 4
Hamme [B, Brabant] 128 II a 1
Hammelaḥ, Yam — 136-137 F 7
Hammerbrook, Hamburg- 130 I b 1
Hammerdal 116-117 F 6
Hammerfest 116-117 KL 2
Hammersmith, London- 129 II ab 2
Hammett, ID 66-67 F 4
Hammillēwa 140 E 6
Hammon, OK 76-77 E 5
Hammond, IN 64-65 J 3
Hammond, LA 78-79 D 5
Hammond, MT 68-69 D 3
Hammond, OR 66-67 AB 2
Hammond Bay 70-71 HJ 3
Hammond Heights, NJ 84 III c 3
Hammonton, NJ 72-73 J 5
Ham Ninh 150-151 E 7
Hampden 63 H 3
Hampstead [CDN, New Brunswick] 63 CD 5
Hampstead [CDN, Quebec] 82 I ab 2
Hampstead, London- 129 II b 1
Hampton 63 D 5
Hampton, AR 78-79 C 4
Hampton, FL 80-81 bc 2
Hampton, IA 70-71 D 4
Hampton, NH 72-73 L 3
Hampton, OR 66-67 C 4
Hampton, SC 80-81 F 4
Hampton, VA 80-81 H 2
Hampton, London- 129 II a 2
Hampton Tableland 158-159 E 6
Ḥamrā', Al- [Saudi Arabia] 134-135 D 6
Ḥamrā', Al- [SYR] 136-137 G 5
Ḥamrā', Al-Ḥammādat al- 164-165 G 2-3
Hamra, Oued el — = Wād al-Ḥamrā' 166-167 B 6
Ḥamrā', Wād al- 166-167 B 6
Ḥamrīn, Jabal — 136-137 KL 5
Hamrivier 174-175 C 5
Hamsah, Bi'r al- = Bi'r al-Khamsah 164-165 K 2
Hams Fork 66-67 H 4-5
Ham Tân 150-151 FG 7
Hamtramck, MI 84 II b 2
Ḥāmūl, Al- 173 B 2
Hamun = Daryācheh Sīstān 134-135 HJ 4
Hāmūn-e Jāz Mūreyān 134-135 H 5
Hāmūn-e Lōra 134-135 JK 5
Hāmūn-i Māshkel 134-135 J 5
Hamur 136-137 K 3
Ḥamza, Al — = Qawām al-Ḥamzah 136-137 L 7
Hana, HI 78-79 de 2
Hānagal 140 C 3
Hanak = Ortahanak 136-137 K 2
Hanākīyah, Al — 134-135 E 6
Hanalei, HI 78-79 c 1
Hanamaki 144-145 N 3
Hanamiplato 174-175 B 3
Hanam Plateau = Hanamiplato 174-175 B 3
Hanang 172 G 2
Hanazura-oki = Sukumo wan 144-145 J 6
Hanceville 60 F 4
Hancheng 146-147 C 4
Hancheu = Hangzhou 142-143 MN 5
Han Chiang = Han Jiang 146-147 F 9-10
Hanchuan 146-147 DE 6
Han-chuang = Hanzhuang 146-147 F 4
Hancock, MI 70-71 F 2
Hancock, NY 72-73 J 3-4
Handa 144-145 L 5
Handae-ri 144-145 FG 2
Handan 142-143 LM 4
Handaq, Al- = Al-Khandaq 164-165 KL 5
Handeni 172 G 3
Handrān 136-137 L 4
Handsworth 61 G 6
Haneda, Tōkyō- 155 III b 2
Hanford, CA 74-75 D 4
Hanford Works United States Atomic Energy Commission Reservation 66-67 D 2
Hangai = Changajn nuruu 142-143 HJ 2
Hāngal 140 B 3
Hangala = Hāngal 140 B 3
Hang Chat 150-151 B 3
Hang-chou Wan = Hangzhou Wan 146-147 H 6
Hangchow = Hangzhou 142-143 MN 5
Hangchun 146-147 H 10
Hanggin Qi 146-147 B 2
Hang Hau 155 I b 2
Hang-hsien = Hangzhou 142-143 MN 5
Han Giang 150-151 F 4
Hanging Rock 160 H 5
Hangjinqi = Hanggin Qi 146-147 B 2
Hangklip, Cape — = Kaap Hangklip 174-175 C 8
Hangklip, Kaap — 174-175 C 8
Hängö 116-117 K 8
Hangu 142-143 M 4
Hanguang 146-147 D 9
Hāngwēlla 140 E 7
Hangzhou 142-143 MN 5
Hangzhou Wan 146-147 H 6
Hani 136-137 J 3
Ḥanīfah, Wādī — 134-135 F 6
Hanīfrah = Khanīfrah 166-167 D 3
Ḥanīyah, Al- 136-137 LM 8
Han Jiang 146-147 F 9-10
Ḥank, Al- 164-165 C 3-4
Hankewicze = Gancevići 124-125 EF 7
Hankey 174-175 F 7
Hankha 150-151 BC 5
Hankinson, ND 68-69 H 2-3
Hanko = Hangö 116-117 K 8
Hankou, Wuhan- 142-143 LM 5
Hankow = Wuhan-Hankou 142-143 LM 5
Hanksville, UT 74-75 H 3
Hanku = Hangu 142-143 M 4
Hanley Falls, MN 70-71 C 3
Hann, Mount — 158-159 E 3
Hanna 56-57 O 7
Hanna, WY 68-69 C 5
Hannaford, ND 68-69 GH 2
Hannah, ND 68-69 G 1
Hannegev 136-137 F 7
Hannibal, MO 64-65 H 3-4
Hannō 144-145 M 5
Hannover 118 D 2
Hanōbukten 116-117 F 10
Ha Nôi 148-149 DE 2
Hanoi = Ha Nôi 148-149 DE 2
Ḥanōt Yōna = Khān Yūnūs 136-137 EF 7
Hanover, KS 68-69 H 6
Hanover, MT 68-69 B 2
Hanover, NH 72-73 KL 3
Hanover, PA 72-73 H 5
Hanover, VA 80-81 H 2
Hanover [CDN] 72-73 F 2
Hanover [ZA] 174-175 F 6
Hanover = Hannover 118 D 2
Hanover, Isla — 111 AB 8
Hanover Road = Hanoverweg 174-175 F 6
Hanoverweg 174-175 F 6
Hansard 60 G 2
Hansboro, ND 68-69 G 1
Hānsdiha 138-139 L 5
Hansen 70-71 HJ 1
Hansenfjella 53 BC 6
Hanshah, Al- 166-167 M 2
Hanshan 146-147 G 6
Hanshīr Labnah 166-167 M 1
Hanshou 146-147 C 7
Han Shui 142-143 K 5
Hānsi 138-139 EF 3
Hanson River 158-159 F 4
Hānsot 138-139 D 7
Hantan = Handan 142-143 LM 4
Hantu, Kampung — = Kampung Limau 150-151 CD 10
Hantu, Pulau — 154 III a 2
Hanumāngarh 138-139 E 3
Hanumānnagar 138-139 L 4
Hanwell, London- 129 II a 2
Hanwella = Hāngwēlla 140 E 7
Hanworth, London- 129 II a 2
Hanyang, Wuhan- 142-143 L 5
Hanyin 146-147 B 5
Hanzhong 142-143 K 5
Hanzhuang 146-147 F 4
Haocheng 146-147 F 5
Haofeng = Hefeng 146-147 BC 7
Haoli = Hegang 142-143 OP 2
Haora = Howrah 134-135 O 6
Haouach 164-165 J 5
Haouāria, El — = Al-Hawārīyah 166-167 M 1
Haouds, Région d' = Al-Ḥawḍ 166-167 J 4
Ḥaouz, el — = Al-Ḥawūz 166-167 B 4
Haoxue 146-147 D 6
Haparanda 116-117 KL 5
Hapch'ŏn 144-145 FG 5
Hapeville, GA 85 II c 2
Hāpoli 141 C 2
Happy, TX 76-77 D 5
Happy Camp, CA 66-67 C 5
Happy Valley Race Course 155 I b 2
Hapsal = Haapsalu 124-125 D 4
Hāpur 138-139 F 3
Ḥaql 134-135 CD 5
Haqūnīyah, Al- 164-165 B 3
Ḥaraḍ 134-135 F 6
Haragi 155 III c 1
Harahan, LA 85 I a 2
Haraiyā 138-139 J 4
Haramachi 144-145 N 4
Haram Dāgh 136-137 M 4
Haranomachi = Haramachi 144-145 N 4
Hara nur = Char nuur 142-143 G 2
Ḥarapā 138-139 D 2
Harappa = Ḥarapā 138-139 D 2
Harappanahalli = Harpanahalli 140 BC 3
Harardêre = Xarardeere 164-165 b 3
Harare 172 F 5
Ḥarāsīs, Jiddat al — 134-135 H 6-7
Hara Ulsa nur = Char us nuur 142-143 G 2
Ḥarawa 164-165 N 6-7
Hārbāng 141 BC 5
Harbel 168-169 C 4
Harbhanga 138-139 K 7
Harbin 142-143 O 2
Harbor Beach, MI 72-73 E 3
Harbor Springs, MI 70-71 H 3
Harbour Breton 63 HJ 4
Harbourdale, Houston-, TX 85 III b 1
Harbour Deep 63 H 2
Harbours, Bay of — 108-109 K 9
Harburger Berge 130 I a 2
Hard [CH] 128 IV b 1
Harda 138-139 F 6
Hardangerfjord 116-117 A 8-B 7
Hardangervidda 116-117 BC 7
Hardee, MS 78-79 D 4
Hardeeville, SC 80-81 F 4
Hardesty, OK 76-77 D 4
Hardeveld 174-175 C 6
Hardey River 158-159 C 4
Hardin, IL 70-71 E 6
Hardin, MO 70-71 D 6
Hardin, MT 68-69 C 3
Harding 172 EF 8
Harding Icefield 58-59 MN 6
Hardinsburg, KY 70-71 GH 7
Hardisty 61 C 4
Hardoi 138-139 H 4
Hardvār = Hardwār 134-135 M 4
Hardwār 134-135 M 4
Hardwick, VT 72-73 K 2
Hardy, AR 78-79 D 2
Hardy = 'Ayn al-Bayḍā 166-167 GH 2
Hardy, Peninsula — 111 BC 9
Hardy, Río — 74-75 F 6
Hare Bay 63 J 2
Harefield, London- 129 II a 1
Hareidlandet 116-117 A 6
Ḥarer [ETH, administrative unit] 164-165 NO 7
Ḥarer [ETH, place] 164-165 N 7
Hargeisa = Hargeysa 164-165 a 2
Hargeysa 164-165 a 2
Hargill, TX 76-77 EF 9
Hargla 124-125 F 5
Hargrave Lake 61 J 3
Harheim, Frankfurt am Main- 128 III b 1
Hari, Batang — 148-149 D 7
Hariāna 138-139 E 2
Ḥarīb 134-135 EF 7-8
Haribes 174-175 B 3
Haribongo, Lac — 168-169 E 1
Haridwar = Hardwār 134-135 M 4
Harihar 140 B 3
Harihara = Harihar 140 B 3
Hariharpur Garhī 138-139 K 4
Hārīj 138-139 C 6
Harike 138-139 E 2
Ḥarim 136-137 G 4
Harima nada 144-145 K 5
Harimgye 144-145 G 4
Hārinahaḍagali = Hadagalli 140 BC 3
Haringey, London- 129 II b 1
Haringhata = Hiranghātā 138-139 M 6-N 7
Haripād 140 C 6
Haripāda = Haripād 140 C 6
Haripura = Hirijūr 140 C 4
Harirōd 134-135 J 4
Haris 174-175 B 2
Harisal 138-139 F 7
Harischandra Range 140 B 1
Ḥāritah, Al- 136-137 M 7
Ḥarīz al-Faqī, Bi'r — 166-167 M 4
Härjedalen 116-117 E 6-F 7
Harjel = Hargla 124-125 F 5
Harker Village, NJ 84 III bc 2
Harkov = Char'kov 126-127 H 1-2
Harlaching, München- 130 II b 2
Harlan, IA 70-71 C 5
Harlan, KY 80-81 E 2
Harlan County Lake 68-69 G 5-6
Harlech 60 K 3
Harlem, GA 80-81 E 4
Harlem, LA 85 I ab 2
Harlem, MT 68-69 B 1
Harlem, New York-, NY 82 III c 2
Harlingen 120-121 K 2
Harlingen, TX 64-65 G 6
Harlington, London- 129 II a 2
Harlowton, MT 68-69 B 2
Harlu = Charlu 124-125 H 3
Harmal, Al- 136-137 G 5
Harmancık = Çardı 136-137 C 3
Harmanli 122-123 LM 5
Harmonville, PA 84 III b 1
Harmony, ME 72-73 M 2
Harmony, MN 70-71 DE 4
Harnai = Harnāy 138-139 A 2
Harnāy 138-139 A 2
Harney Basin 64-65 BC 3
Harney Lake 66-67 D 4
Harney Peak 68-69 E 4
Härnösand 116-117 GH 6
Haro 120-121 F 7
Haro, Cabo — 64-65 D 6
Harold Byrd Range 53 A 25-22
Harold Hill, London- 129 II c 1
Haro Strait 66-67 B 1
Harpanahalli 140 BC 3
Harper 164-165 C 8
Harper, KS 76-77 EF 4
Harper, OR 66-67 E 4
Harper, TX 76-77 E 7
Harper, Mount — [CDN] 58-59 RS 4
Harper, Mount — [USA] 58-59 PQ 4
Harpers Ferry, WV 72-73 GH 5
Harper Woods, MI 84 II c 2
Harpster, ID 66-67 F 2-3
Harquahala Mountains 74-75 G 6
Harquahala Plains 74-75 G 6
Harrach, El — 170 I b 2
Harrach, Oued el — 170 I b 2
Ḥarrah, Al — 134-135 D 4
Harraiya = Haraiyā 138-139 J 4
Harran [TR] 136-137 H 4
Harrar = Ḥarer 164-165 N 7
Ḥarrat al-Kishb 134-135 E 6
Ḥarrat al-'Uwayriḍ 134-135 D 5
Ḥarrat ash-Shahbā' 136-137 G 6-7
Ḥarrat Khaybar 134-135 DE 5
Ḥarrat Nawāṣīf 134-135 E 6
Ḥarrat Rahaṭ 134-135 DE 6
Harrawa = Ḥarawa 164-165 N 6-7
Harrell, AR 78-79 C 4
Harricanaw River 56-57 V 7-8
Harriman, TN 78-79 G 3
Harrington, DE 72-73 J 5
Harrington, WA 66-67 DE 2
Harrington Drain 84 II c 1-2
Harrington Harbour 56-57 Z 7
Harris [CDN] 61 E 5
Harris [GB] 119 C 3
Harris, Lake — 160 B 3
Harrisburg, IL 70-71 F 7
Harrisburg, NE 68-69 E 5
Harrisburg, OR 66-67 B 3
Harrisburg, PA 64-65 L 3
Harris County Cemetery 85 III c 1
Harrismith 172 E 7
Harrison, AR 78-79 C 2
Harrison, ID 66-67 E 2
Harrison, MI 70-71 H 3
Harrison, MT 66-67 H 3
Harrison, NE 68-69 E 4
Harrison, NJ 82 III b 2
Harrison, Cape — 56-57 Z 7
Harrison Bay 58-59 LM 1
Harrisonburg, VA 72-73 G 5
Harrison Lake 66-67 BC 1
Harrisonville, MO 70-71 C 6
Harris Ridge = Lomonosov Ridge 52 A
Harriston 72-73 F 3
Harriston, MS 78-79 D 5
Harrisville, MI 72-73 E 2
Harrisville, WV 72-73 F 5
Harrodsburg, KY 70-71 H 7
Harrogate 119 F 4-5
Harrold, SD 68-69 G 3
Harrow, London- 119 F 6
Harrow on the Hill, London- 129 II a 1
Harry Strunk Lake 68-69 FG 5
Har Sagī 136-137 F 7
Harsīn 136-137 M 5
Harşıt deresi 136-137 H 2
Harstad 116-117 FG 3
Harsūd 138-139 F 6
Harsvik 116-117 D 5
Hart 68-69 D 1
Hart, MI 70-71 G 4
Hart, TX 76-77 CD 5
Hart, Cape — 160 D 5-6
Hartbeesfontein 174-175 G 4
Hartbeespoortdam 174-175 GH 3
Hartbeesrivier 174-175 D 5
Hartebeespoort Dam = Hartbeespoortdam 174-175 GH 3
Hartenggole He = Chaaltyn gol 142-143 GH 4
Hartford, AL 78-79 G 5
Hartford, CT 64-65 M 3
Hartford, KY 70-71 G 7
Hartford, MI 70-71 G 4
Hartford, NJ 84 III d 2
Hartford, WI 70-71 F 4
Hartford City, IN 70-71 H 5
Hartington, NE 68-69 H 4
Hart Island 82 III d 1
Hart-Jaune, Rivière — 63 BC 2
Hartlepool 119 F 4
Hartley, IA 70-71 C 4
Hartley, TX 76-77 C 5
Hartley = Chegutu 172 EF 5
Hartline, WA 66-67 D 2
Hartman, AR 78-79 C 3
Hartmannshofen, München- 130 II ab 1
Hart Mountain 66-67 D 4
Hartney 68-69 F 1
Hartselle, AL 78-79 F 3
Hartshorne, OK 76-77 G 5
Harts Range 158-159 FG 4
Hartsrivier 172 DE 7
Hartsville, SC 80-81 FG 3
Hartsville, TN 78-79 FG 2
Hartwell, GA 80-81 E 3
Hartwell Lake 80-81 E 3
Harty 62 K 2
Harūj al-Aswad, Al- 164-165 H 3
Harumi International Sample Fair Hall 155 III b 2
Hārūnābād [IND] 138-139 D 3
Hārūnābād [IR] 136-137 N 4
Haruniye 136-137 G 4
Harūr 140 D 4
Harūsh, Al- 166-167 K 1
Hārūt Rōd 134-135 J 4
Harvard, CA 74-75 E 5
Harvard, IL 70-71 F 4
Harvard, NE 68-69 GH 5
Harvard Bridge 84 I b 2
Harvard University 84 I b 2
Harvestehude, Hamburg- 130 I a 1
Harvey 158-159 C 6
Harvey, IL 70-71 G 5
Harvey, LA 85 I b 2
Harvey, ND 68-69 FG 2
Harvey Canal 85 I b 2
Harwell 119 F 6
Harwich 119 G 6
Harwich, MA 72-73 LM 4
Harwood, TX 76-77 F 8
Harwood Heights, IL 83 II a 1
Haryana 134-135 M 5
Harz 118 E 3
Ḥāṣ, Jabal al- 136-137 G 5
'Ḥasā', Al — 134-135 F 5
Ḥasā, Wādī al- [JOR, Al-Karak] 136-137 F 7
Ḥasā, Wādī al- [JOR, Ma'ān] 136-137 G 7
Ḥaṣāḥeïṣa, El — = Al-Ḥuṣayḥiṣah 164-165 L 6
Ḥasakah, Al- 134-135 D 3
Ḥāsana = Hassan 134-135 M 8
Hasançelebi 136-137 GH 3
Hasan dağı 136-137 EF 3
Hasankale 136-137 J 2-3
Hasanparti 140 D 1
Hāsanpartti = Hasanparti 140 D 1
Hasanpur 138-139 FG 3
Ḥasb, Sha'īb — 134-135 E 4
Hasdo 138-139 J 6
Haselbach [A] 113 I ab 1
Haselhorst, Berlin- 130 III a 1
Hasenheide 130 III b 2
Hasenkamp 106-107 GH 3
Hasètchè, El- = Al-Hasakah 134-135 D 3
Hashdo = Hasdo 138-139 J 6
Hashemiya, Al — = Al-Hāshimīyah 136-137 L 6
Hāshimīyah, Al- 136-137 L 6
Hashimoto 144-145 K 5
Hashīr 136-137 K 4
Hashtpar 136-137 N 4
Hashtrūd 136-137 M 4
Hashun Shamo = Gašuun Gov' 142-143 G 3
Ḥāsī aṭ-Ṭawīl, Al- 166-167 K 4-5
Hasib, Sha'ib — = Sha'īb Ḥasb 134-135 E 4
Haskell, OK 76-77 G 5
Haskell, TX 76-77 E 6
Haskovo 122-123 L 5
Hasköy, İstanbul- 154 I a 2
Ḥasmat 'Umar, Bi'r — 173 CD 7
Hassa 136-137 G 4
Hassan 134-135 M 8
Hassayampa River 74-75 G 6
Hassell, NM 76-77 B 5
Hassel Sound 56-57 R 2
Hasselt 120-121 K 3
Ḥāssī al-Aḥmar 166-167 E 3
Ḥāssī al-Bayrāt 166-167 B 6
Ḥāssī al-Farsīyah 166-167 B 6
Ḥāssī al-Ghallah 166-167 F 2
Ḥāssī al-Ghanamī 166-167 JK 4
Ḥāssī al-Hajar 166-167 J 4
Ḥāssī al-'Iz 166-167 G 4
Ḥāssī al-Khābī 166-167 D 5
Ḥāssī al-Mamūrah 166-167 F 4
Ḥāssī al-Qaṭṭār 164-165 K 2
Ḥāssī 'Ambarūsī 166-167 F 6
Hassi Ambrosini = Ḥāssī 'Ambarūsī 166-167 F 6
Ḥāssī ar-Raml 164-165 E 2
Ḥāssī Arsum al-Līl 166-167 H 6
Ḥāssī 'Asīqāl 166-167 L 6-7
Hassi Assiguel = Ḥāssī 'Asīqāl 166-167 L 7
Ḥāssī 'Ayn Aghyūl 166-167 M 6
Ḥāssī Baljabbūr 166-167 K 5
Ḥāssī Ban 'Aysh 166-167 J 4
Ḥāssī Barakram 166-167 J 3
Ḥāssī Barbūshī 166-167 E 5
Hassi Barouda = Ḥāssī Bārudah 166-167 GH 5
Ḥāssī Bārudah 166-167 GH 5
Hassi bel Guebbour = Ḥāssī Baljabbūr 166-167 K 5
Ḥassī Ben Baṭā'ī = Ḥāssī Bin Baṭā'ī 166-167 AB 5
Hassi ben Yaïch = Ḥāssī Ban 'Aysh 166-167 J 4
Hassi Berbouchi = Ḥāssī Barbūshī 166-167 E 5
Hassi Berrekrem = Ḥāssī Barakram 166-167 J 3
Ḥāssī Bin Baṭā'ī 166-167 AB 5
Ḥāssī Boū Haiāra = Ḥāssī Bū Ḥayārah 166-167 D 4
Hassi Bou Khelala = Ḥāssī Bū al-Khallalah 166-167 F 4
Hassi Bou Zid = Ḥāssī Bū Zīd 166-167 G 4
Ḥāssī Bū al-Khallalah 166-167 G 2-3
Ḥāssī Bū Ḥayārah 166-167 D 4
Ḥāssī Bū Zīd 166-167 GH 4
Hassi Chaamba = Ḥāssī Sha'ambah 166-167 D 5
Hassi Cheikh = Ḥāssī Shaykh 166-167 G 4
Hassi Djafar = Ḥāssī Ja'far 166-167 H 4
Hassi Djafou = Ḥāssī Jafū 164-165 E 2
Hassi Djebilet = Ḥāssī Jabīlāt 166-167 BC 6
Hassi Djemel = Ḥāssī Ghamal 166-167 J 4
Hassi Djeribia = Ḥāssī Jarībīyah 166-167 J 4
Ḥāssī el Amar = Ḥāssī al-Aḥmar 166-167 E 3
Hassi el Azz = Ḥāssī al-'Iz 166-167 G 4
Ḥassī el Beïrât = Ḥāssī al-Bayrāt 166-167 B 6
Hassi-el-Ghella = Ḥāssī al-Ghallah 166-167 F 2
Hassi-el-Hadjar = Ḥāssī Ja'far 166-167 J 4
Hassi el Khebi = Ḥāssī al-Khābī 166-167 D 5
Hassi el Mamoura = Ḥāssī al-Mamūrah 166-167 F 4
Hassi el Rhenami = Ḥāssī al-Ghanamī 166-167 JK 4
Hassi Erg Sedra = Ḥāssī 'Irq Sidrah 166-167 H 4
Hassi Ersoum el Lil = Ḥāssī Arsum al-Līl 166-167 H 6
Ḥāssī Ghamal 166-167 J 4
Hassi Imoulaye = Ḥāssī Īmūlāy 166-167 L 5
Ḥāssī Īmūlāy 166-167 L 5
Hassi 'In Aquiel = Ḥāssī 'Ayn Aghyūl 166-167 M 6
Hassi-Inifel = Ḥāssī Īnīfīl 164-165 E 2-3
Ḥāssī Īnīfīl 164-165 E 2-3
Ḥāssī 'Irq Sidrah 166-167 H 4
Ḥāssī Jabīlāt 166-167 C 6
Ḥāssī Ja'far 166-167 H 4
Ḥāssī Jafū 164-165 E 2
Ḥāssī Jarībīyah 166-167 J 4
Hassi Lebeirat = Ḥāssī al-Bayrāt 166-167 AB 6
Ḥāssī Madakkan 166-167 EF 5
Ḥāssī Māī ad-Darwāwī 166-167 K 3
Hassi Mana = Ḥāssī Manāh 166-167 E 5
Ḥāssī Manāh 166-167 E 5
Ḥāssī Mastūr 166-167 GH 4
Ḥāssī Mas'ūd 164-165 F 2
Ḥāssī Maṭmāṭ 166-167 K 3
Hassi Mdakane = Ḥāssī Madakkan 166-167 EF 5
Hassi-Messaoud = Ḥāssī Mas'ūd 164-165 F 2
Hassi Mestour = Ḥāssī Mastūr 166-167 GH 4
Hassi Mey ed Dahraoui = Ḥāssī Māī ad-Darwāwī 166-167 K 3
Hassi Morra = Ḥāssī Murrah 166-167 EF 4
Ḥāssī Murrah 166-167 E 4
Ḥāssī Nashū 166-167 H 4
Hassi Nechou = Ḥāssī Nashū 166-167 H 4
Ḥāssī Ouenzgā = Ḥāssī Wanz'gā' 166-167 E 2
Hassi Ouskir = Ḥāssī Uskir 166-167 F 4
Hassi-R'Mel = Ḥāssī ar-Raml 164-165 E 2
Ḥāssī Sarāt 166-167 H 5
Ḥāssī Sha'ambah 166-167 D 5
Ḥāssī Shaykh 166-167 G 4
Ḥāssī Shiqq 164-165 B 3
Hassi Souf = Ḥāssī Ṣūf 166-167 F 5
Ḥāssī Ṣūf 166-167 F 5
Ḥāssī Tādīsat 166-167 K 6
Hassi Tadnist = Ḥāssī Tādīsat 166-167 K 6
Hassi Tafesrit = Ḥāssī Tafzirt 166-167 K 7
Ḥāssī Tafzirt 166-167 K 7
Ḥāssī Tarārah 166-167 GH 6
Ḥāssī Tartārat 166-167 K 4
Hassi-Tatrat = Ḥāssī Tartārat 166-167 K 4
Ḥāssī Tawārij 166-167 JK 4
Hassi Teraga = Ḥāssī Tarārah 166-167 GH 6
Ḥāssī Tighintūrīn 166-167 H 6
Hassi Tiguentourine = Ḥāssī Tighintūrīn 166-167 H 6
Hassi Tin Khéouné = Ḥāssī Tīn Quwānīn 166-167 L 7
Ḥāssī Tīn Quwānīn 166-167 L 7
Hassi Tiouklenine = Ḥāssī Tiyūkulīn 166-167 J 6
Ḥāssī Tiyūkulīn 166-167 J 6
Hassi Touareg = Ḥāssī Tawārij 166-167 JK 4
Ḥāssī Tūkāt Nakhlah 166-167 A 6
Ḥāssī Uskir 166-167 F 4
Ḥāssī Wanz'gā' 166-167 E 2
Ḥāssī Zegdoū = Ḥāssī Zighdū 166-167 D 5
Ḥāssī Zighdū 166-167 D 5
Ḥāssī Zūq 164-165 B 4
Hässleholm 116-117 EF 9
Hastings, FL 80-81 c 2
Hastings, MI 70-71 H 4
Hastings, MN 70-71 D 3
Hastings, NE 64-65 G 3
Hastings [GB] 119 G 6
Hastings [NZ] 158-159 P 7
Hasuur = Hazuur 174-175 C 4
Hasvik 116-117 JK 2
Haswell, CO 68-69 E 6
Hāta 138-139 J 4
Haṭā = Hatta 138-139 G 5
Hatâb, Ouêd — = Wād al-Ḥatāb 166-167 L 2
Ḥaṭab, Wād al- 166-167 L 2
Ḥaṭab, Wādī al- 173 C 7
Hat'ae-do 144-145 E 5
Ha Tân 150-151 E 3
Haṭāṭibah, Al- 173 B 2
Hatay 136-137 G 4
Hatch, NM 76-77 A 6
Hatch, UT 74-75 G 4
Hatches Creek 158-159 G 4
Hatchet Bay 88-89 HJ 2
Hatchie River 78-79 E 3
Hat Creek, WY 68-69 D 4
Haţeg 122-123 K 3
Hatfield [AUS] 160 F 4
Hathaway, MT 68-69 CD 2
Hat Hin = Mu'o'ng Hat Hin 150-151 D 1-2
Hāthras 134-135 M 5

Hatia = Hâtiya 141 B 4
Hatia Islands = Hâtiya Dīpsamuh 141 B 4
Ha Tiên 150-151 E 7
Hatillo, El — [YV, place] 91 II c 2
Hatillo, El — [YV, river] 91 II c 2
Haṭīnā-Māļiyā = Mālia 138-139 C 7
Ha Tinh 150-151 EF 3
Hatinohe = Hachinohe 142-143 R 3
Hatip 136-137 E 4
Hâtiya 141 B 4
Hâtiya Dīpsamuh 141 B 4
Hatizyô zima = Hachijō-jima 142-143 Q 5
Hātkanagale 140 B 2
Hatkanangale = Hātkanagale 140 B 2
Hat Nhao 150-151 F 5
Hato Corozal 94-95 F 4
Ha-tongsan-ni 144-145 F 3
Hatscher, Cerro — 108-109 C 7
Hat Sieo = Si Satchanalai 150-151 B 4
Hatsutomi 155 III c 1
Hatta 138-139 G 5
Hatteras, NC 80-81 J 3
Hatteras, Cape — 64-65 LM 4
Hatteras Island 64-65 LM 4
Hattfjelldal 116-117 F 5
Hattiesburg, MS 64-65 J 5
Hattingspruit 174-175 HJ 5
Haṭṭīyah 136-137 F 8
Hatton 56-57 P 7
Hatton, ND 68-69 H 2
Hatton = Heṭan 140 E 7
Hatvan 118 JK 5
Hat Yai 148-149 D 5
Hauchab 174-175 A 3
Haud = Hāwd 164-165 NO 7
Hâu Đu'c 150-151 G 5
Haugesund 116-117 A 8
Hâu Giang 150-151 E 7
Hauhungaroa Range 161 F 4
Haukadalur 116-117 c 2
Haukeligrend 116-117 B 8
Haukipudas 116-117 L 5
Haukivesi 116-117 N 6-7
Haukivuori 116-117 M 6-7
Haultain River 61 E 2
Haumonía 104-105 F 10
Haungtharaw Myit 150-151 B 4
Hauptbahnhof Hamburg 130 I ab 1
Hauptbahnhof München 130 II b 2
Hauptfriedhof Öjendorf 130 I b 1
Hauptikon 128 IV ab 2
Ḥaurā = Ḥawrah 134-135 F 7
Ḥaurā = Howrah 134-135 O 6
Ḥaurā, Al — = Al-Ḥawrah 134-135 F 8
Hauraki Gulf 158-159 OP 7
Ḥauṣah = Ḥawṣah 136-137 G 8
Hausbruch, Hamburg- 130 I a 2
Hausen, Frankfurt am Main- 128 III a 1
Hausen am Albis 128 IV b 2
Hausruck 118 F 4
Haussee 130 III c 1
Haussonvillers = Nāṣirīyah 166-167 HJ 1
Hautavaara = Chautavara 124-125 J 2
Haute-Kotto 164-165 J 7
Hauterive 63 B 3
Haute-Sangha 164-165 H 8
Hautes Plateaux = Nijād al-'Alī 164-165 D 2-E 1
Hauteurs de Gâtine 120-121 G 5
Haut-Mbomou 164-165 K 7
Haut-Ransbeek 128 II b 2
Hauts-Bassins 168-169 D 3
Haut-Zaïre 172 E 1
Hauz = Al-Ḥawūz 166-167 B 4
Havana, FL 78-79 G 5
Havana, IL 70-71 E 5
Havana, ND 68-69 H 3
Havana = La Habana 64-65 K 7
Havasu Lake 74-75 FG 5
Have Bank, La — 63 D 6
Havel 118 F 2
Ḥavelī 138-139 D 2
Havelock 72-73 GH 2
Havelock, NC 80-81 H 3
Havenbuurt 128 I b 1
Haverford, PA 84 III b 1
Haverford College 84 III b 1
Haverford Township Park 84 III a 2
Haverfordwest 119 D 6
Haverhill, MA 72-73 L 3
Haverhill, NH 72-73 KL 3
Hāveri 140 B 3
Havering, London- 129 II c 1
Haverstraw, NY 72-73 JK 4
Havertown, PA 84 III ab 2
Havilhanları 136-137 J 3
Havlíčkův Brod 118 G 4
Havøysund 116-117 L 2
Havre, MT 64-65 DE 2
Havre, le — 120-121 GH 4
Havre-Aubert 63 F 4
Havre de Grace, MD 72-73 HJ 5
Havre-Saint-Pierre 56-57 Y 7
Havsa 136-137 B 2
Havza 136-137 F 2
Hawai = Hawaii 148-149 ef 4
Hawaii 148-149 ef 4
Hawaiian Gardens, CA 83 III d 3
Hawaiian Islands 148-149 d 3-e 4
Hawaiian Ridge 156-157 JK 3
Hawaii Volcanoes National Park 78-79 e 3
Hawal 168-169 J 3
Hawarden 61 E 5
Hawarden, IA 68-69 H 4
Hawārīyah, Al- 166-167 M 1
Hawash, Wadi — = Haouach 164-165 J 5
Ḥawashīyah, Wādī — 173 C 3
Ḥawātah, Al- 164-165 LM 6
Hāwd 164-165 NO 7
Ḥawḍ, Al- [DZ] 166-167 J 4
Ḥawḍ, Al- [RIM] 164-165 C 5
Ḥawḍ al-Gharbī, Al- 168-169 C 1
Ḥawḍ ash-Sharqī, Al- 168-169 D 1
Hawea, Lake — 161 C 7
Hawera 158-159 OP 7
Hawesville, KY 70-71 G 7
Hawi, HI 78-79 e 2
Hawick 119 E 4
Ḥawīzah, Hawr al- 136-137 M 7
Hawke, Cape — 158-159 K 6
Hawke Bay 158-159 P 7
Hawker 158-159 G 6
Hawkes, Mount — 53 A 32-33
Hawke's Bay 161 G 4
Hawkesbury 72-73 J 2
Hawkesbury Island 60 C 3
Hawkes Pond 84 I b 1
Hawk Inlet, AK 58-59 U 7
Hawkins, WI 70-71 E 3
Hawkinsville, GA 80-81 E 4
Hawk Junction 62 J 2
Hawk Lake 62 C 3
Hawks, MI 70-71 HJ 3
Hawksbill Cay 88-89 H 2
Hawk Springs, WY 68-69 D 5
Hawley, MN 70-71 BC 2
Hawley, TX 76-77 E 6
Ḥawrah 134-135 F 7
Ḥawrah, Al- 134-135 F 8
Hawr al-Ḥabbānīyah 136-137 K 6
Hawr al-Ḥammār 134-135 F 4
Hawr al-Ḥawīzah 136-137 M 7
Hawr al-Jiljilah 136-137 L 6
Ḥawrān, Wādī — 134-135 E 4
Hawr ar-Razazah 136-137 KL 6
Hawr as-Sa'dīyah 136-137 M 6
Hawr as-Sanīyah 136-137 M 7
Hawr as-Suwayqīyah 136-137 LM 6
Hawr Awdah 136-137 M 7
Hawr Dalmaj 136-137 L 6
Haw River 80-81 G 3
Ḥawṣah 136-137 G 8
Ḥawsh 'Īsā 173 B 2
Hawston 174-175 C 8
Ḥawṭah, Al- = Al-Ḥillah 134-135 F 6
Hawthorn, FL 80-81 bc 2
Hawthorn, Melbourne- 161 II c 1
Hawthorne, CA 83 III b 2
Hawthorne, NV 74-75 D 3
Hawthorne Municipal Airport 83 III bc 2
Hawthorne Race Track 83 II a 1-2
Ḥawūz, Al- 166-167 B 4
Haxby, MT 68-69 C 2
Haxtun, CO 68-69 E 5
Hay [AUS] 158-159 HJ 6
Hay, Mount — 58-59 T 7
Ḥāy, Wād al- 166-167 E 2
Hayabuchi 155 III a 2
Hayang 144-145 G 5
Haycock, AK 58-59 G 4
Haydar dağı 136-137 DE 4
Haydarpaşa, İstanbul- 154 I b 3
Hayden, AZ 74-75 H 6
Hayden, CO 68-69 C 5
Haydrah 166-167 L 2
Hayes, LA 78-79 C 5
Hayes, SD 68-69 F 3
Hayes, London- [GB, Bromley] 129 II bc 2
Hayes, London- [GB, Hillingdon] 129 II a 1
Hayes, Mount — 56-57 G 5
Hayes Center, NE 68-69 F 5
Hayes Glacier 58-59 L 6
Hayes Halvø 56-57 XY 2
Hayes River 56-57 S 6
Ha Yeung 155 I b 2
Hayfield, MN 70-71 D 4
Hayfork, CA 66-67 B 5
Hay Lake = Habay 56-57 N 6
Hay Lakes 61 B 4
Hay-les-Roses, l' 129 I c 2
Haylow, GA 80-81 E 5
Haymana 136-137 E 3
Haymana yaylâsı 136-137 E 3
Ḥaymūr, Ābār — 173 CD 6
Ḥaymūr, Wādī — 173 C 6
Haynesville, LA 78-79 C 4
Hayneville, AL 78-79 F 4
Hayrabolu 136-137 B 2
Hayrabolu deresi 136-137 B 2
Hayrat 136-137 J 2
Hayrīr, Al- 166-167 L 7
Hay River [AUS] 158-159 G 4
Hay River [CDN, place] 56-57 NO 5
Hay River [CDN, river] 56-57 N 6
Hays 134-135 E 8
Hays, KS 64-65 G 4
Hays, MT 68-69 B 2
Ḥaysī, Bi'r al- 173 D 3
Hay Springs, NE 68-69 E 4
Haystack Mountain 72-73 K 3
Haystack Peak 74-75 G 3
Hayti, MO 78-79 E 2
Hayti, SD 68-69 H 3
Hayton's Falls 171 CD 3
Hayward, CA 74-75 BC 4
Hayward, WI 70-71 E 2
Haywood 61 J 6
Ḥayy, Al- 134-135 F 4
Ḥayyā 166-165 M 5
Hazak 136-137 J 4
Hazārān, Kūh-e — = Kūh-e Hezārān 134-135 H 5
Hazard, KY 64-65 K 4
Hazārībāgh 138-139 K 5-6
Hazārībāgh Range 138-139 JK 6
Ḥazawzā' 136-137 GH 7
Hazebrouck 120-121 J 3
Hazel Creek River 62 A 2
Hazel Green, IL 83 II a 2
Hazel Park 84 II b 2
Hazel Park, MI 84 II b 2
Hazel Park Race Track 84 II b 2
Hazelton Mountains 60 CD 2
Hazelton Peak 68-69 C 3
Hazen, AR 78-79 D 3
Hazen, ND 68-69 F 2
Hazen, NV 74-75 D 3
Hazen Strait 56-57 OP 2
Hazīm, Al- 136-137 G 7
Ḥazimī, Wādī al- 136-137 J 6
Hazipur = Hājīpur 138-139 K 5
Hazlehurst, GA 80-81 E 5
Hazlehurst, MS 78-79 D 5
Hazleton, PA 72-73 J 4
Hazlett, Lake 158-159 E 4
Ḥazm, Al- 173 E 3
Hazo 136-137 J 3
Hazro 136-137 J 3
Hazul, Al- = Al-Huzul 136-137 K 8
Hazuur 174-175 C 4
Hazzān an-Naṣr 173 C 6
Headland, AL 78-79 G 5
Headquarters, ID 66-67 F 2
Heads, The — 66-67 A 4
Healdsburg, CA 74-75 B 3
Healdton, OK 76-77 F 5
Healesville 160 GH 6
Healy, AK 58-59 N 5
Healy, KS 68-69 F 6
Healy Lake 58-59 P 5
Healy River 58-59 P 4
Heard 50-51 N 8
Hearne, TX 76-77 F 7
Hearst 56-57 U 8
Hearst Island 53 BC 30-31
Heart Butte 68-69 EF 2
Heart Butte Reservoir = Lake Tschida 68-69 EF 2
Heart River 68-69 F 2
Heart's Content 63 K 4
Heath, Río — 96-97 G 8
Heath Point 63 F 3
Heaven, Temple of — 155 II b 2
Heavener, OK 76-77 G 5
Hebbronville, TX 76-77 E 9
Hebei 142-143 LM 4
Heber, UT 66-67 H 5
Heber Springs, AR 78-79 C 3
Hebgen Lake 66-67 H 3
Hebi 146-147 E 4
Hebo, OR 66-67 AB 3
Hebrides, Sea of the — 119 C 3
Hebron, ND 68-69 EF 2
Hebron, NE 68-69 H 5
Hebron [CDN] 56-57 Y 6
Hebron [ZA] 174-175 H 3
Hebron = Al-Ḥalīl 136-137 F 7
Hebron = Windsorton 174-175 F 5
Hecate Strait 56-57 K 7
Heceta Head 66-67 A 3
Heceta Island 58-59 vw 9
Hecheng 146-147 D 11
Hechuan 142-143 JK 5
Hecla 62 A 2
Hecla, SD 68-69 GH 3
Hecla and Griper Bay 56-57 O 2
Hectorspruit 174-175 JK 3
Hede 116-117 E 6
He Devil Mountain 66-67 E 3
Hedien = Khotan 142-143 DE 4
Hedingen 128 IV a 2
Hedjas 134-135 D 5-6
Hedley 66-67 CD 1
Hedley, TX 76-77 D 5
Hedmark 116-117 D 6-E 7
Hedrick, IA 70-71 D 5
Heerlen 120-121 KL 3
Hefei 142-143 M 5
Hefeng 146-147 BC 7
Heffron Park 161 I b 2
Heflin, AL 78-79 G 4
Hegang 142-143 OP 2
Hegbach 128 III b 2
Hegnau 128 IV b 1
Hēgumenítsa 122-123 J 6
He Hu = Ge Hu 146-147 G 6
Heian-hokudō = P'yŏngan-pukto 144-145 E 2-3
Heian-nandō = P'yŏngan-namdo 144-145 EF 3
Ḥeidarābād = Ḥeydarābād 136-137 L 4
Heide [D] 118 D 1
Heide [Namibia] 174-175 B 2
Heidelberg, MS 78-79 E 5
Heidelberg [D] 118 D 4
Heidelberg [ZA, Kaapland] 174-175 D 8
Heidelberg [ZA, Transvaal] 174-175 H 4
Heidelberg, Melbourne- 161 II c 1
Heidoti 98-99 K 2
Ḥeifa 134-135 CD 4
Height of Land 63 A 5
Hei-ho = Aihui 142-143 O 1
Heijo = P'yŏngyang 142-143 NO 4
Heilar He = Chajlar gol 142-143 N 1-2
Heilbron 174-175 GH 4
Heilbronn 118 D 4
Heiligensee, Berlin- 130 III a 1
Heilongjiang [TJ, administrative unit] 142-143 M-P 2
Heilong Jiang [TJ, river] 142-143 O 1
Heilsberg 128 III b 1
Hei-lung Chiang = Heilong Jiang 142-143 O 1
Heilung Kiang = Heilong Jiang 142-143 O 1
Heimaey 116-117 c 3
Heimfeld, Hamburg- 130 I a 2
Heine Creek, AK 58-59 N 4
Heinersdorf, Berlin- 130 III b 1
Heinola 116-117 M 7
Heinsburg 61 C 4
Heinze Bay = Bôlkyīywā 150-151 A 5
Heir, El- = Qaṣr al-Ḥayr 136-137 H 5
Heishan 144-145 CD 2
Ḥeisī, Bīr el- = Bi'r al-Ḥaysī 173 D 3
Hejaz 131 G 7-8
Hejaz = Al-Hijaz 134-135 D 5-6
Hejian 146-147 EF 2
Hejiang [TJ, place] 146-147 C 11
He Jiang [TJ, river] 146-147 C 10
Hejie 146-147 C 9
Hejin 146-147 C 4
Hekimdağ = Taşköprü 136-137 D 3
Hekimhan 136-137 G 3
Hekla 116-117 d 3
Hekou = Hekouji 146-147 F 5
Hekouji 146-147 F 5
Hekpoort 174-175 G 3
Helagsfjället 116-117 E 6
Helder, Den — 120-121 K 2
Hele 150-151 H 3
Helechos, Cañada de los — 91 I b 2
Helem 141 C 2
Helen, Mount — 74-75 E 4
Helena, AR 64-65 H 5
Helena, GA 80-81 E 4
Helena, MT 64-65 D 2
Helena, OK 76-77 E 4
Helendale, CA 74-75 E 5
Helenenau 130 III c 1
Helen Reef 148-149 K 6
Heleysund 116-117 I 5
Helgeland 116-117 E 5-F 4
Helgoland 118 C 1
Helicoide, Caracas- 91 II b 2
Helicoide de la Roca Tarpeya 91 II b 2
Heligoland = Helgoland 118 C 1
Heligoland Bay 118 C 1
Helikôn 122-123 K 6
He Ling 150-151 G 3
Heliopolis 170 II b 1
Heliopolis = Al-Qahīrah-Miṣr al-Jadīdah 173 BC 2
Heliopolis = Ḥammān Awlād 'Alī 166-167 K 1
Heliqi = Helixi 146-147 G 6
Heliu = Heliuji 146-147 F 5
Heliuji 146-147 F 5
Helix, OR 66-67 D 3
Helixi 146-147 G 6
Hella 116-117 c 3
Hellabrunn, Tierpark — 130 II b 2
Helleland 116-117 B 8
Hellenikón, Aerolimên — 113 IV a 2
Hellepoort = Portes de l'Enfer 172 E 3
Hellersdorf, Berlin- 130 III c 1
Hellín 120-121 G 9
Hell-Ville 172 J 4
Helmand Rōd 134-135 K 4
Helmeringhausen 174-175 B 3-4
Helmet Mount 58-59 P 3
Helmond 120-121 KL 3
Helmsdale 119 E 2
Helmstedt 118 E 2
Helmville, MT 66-67 G 2
Helodranon'i Mahajamba 172 J 4-5
Helodranon'i Narinda 172 J 4
Helodrona Antongila 172 JK 5
Helong 142-143 O 3
Helper, UT 74-75 H 3
Helpmekaar 174-175 J 5
Helsingborg 116-117 DE 9
Helsingfors = Helsinki 116-117 L 7
Helsingør 116-117 DE 9
Helsinki 116-117 L 7
Helska, Mierzeja — 118 J 1
Heluo = Hele 150-151 H 3
Helvécia [BR] 100-101 E 9
Helvecia [RA] 106-107 G 3
Helvetia 174-175 G 5
Helwāk 140 A 2
Ḥelwān = Ḥulwān 164-165 L 3
Hemagiri 138-139 J 6-7
Hemāvati 140 B 4
Hemet, CA 74-75 E 6
Hemingford, NE 68-69 E 4
Hemphill, TX 78-79 C 5
Hempstead, NY 72-73 K 4
Hempstead, TX 76-77 F 7
Hempstead Harbor 82 III d 1-e 2
Hempstead Lake State Park 82 III de 2
Henan 142-143 L 5
Henares 120-121 F 8
Henashi-saki 144-145 M 2
Henbury 158-159 F 4
Ḥencha, El — = Al-Hanshah 166-167 M 2
Henchīr Lebna = Hanshīr Labnah 166-167 M 1
Henchow = Hengyang 142-143 L 6
Hendawashi 171 C 3
Hendaye 120-121 FG 7
Hendek 136-137 D 2
Henderson, KY 64-65 J 4
Henderson, NC 80-81 G 2
Henderson, NV 74-75 F 4
Henderson, TN 78-79 E 3
Henderson, TX 76-77 G 6
Henderson [RA] 106-107 G 6
Henderson Bay 72-73 H 2-3
Hendersonville, NC 80-81 E 3
Hendersonville, TN 78-79 F 2
Hendon, London- 129 II b 1
Hendriktop 98-99 K 2
Hendrik Verwoerd Dam 174-175 FG 6
Hendrina 174-175 HJ 4
Heng'ang = Hengyang 142-143 L 6
Heng-chan = Hengyang 142-143 L 6
Heng-chou = Heng Xian 142-143 K 7
Hengdong 146-147 D 8
Hengduan Shan 142-143 H 6
Hengelo 120-121 L 2
Hengfeng 146-147 F 7
Henghsien = Heng Xian 142-143 K 7
Heng Sha 146-147 HJ 6
Hengshan [TJ, Hunan] 142-143 L 6
Hengshan [TJ, Shaanxi] 146-147 B 3
Heng Shan [TJ, Shanxi] 146-147 D 2
Hengshan = Hengyang 142-143 L 6
Hengshui 142-143 LM 4
Heng Xian 142-143 K 7
Hengyang 142-143 L 6
Henik Lake = South Henik Lake 56-57 R 5
Henlopen, Cape — 72-73 J 5
Henly, TX 76-77 E 7
Hennebont 120-121 F 5
Hennenman 174-175 G 4
Hennersdorf [A] 113 I b 2
Hennesberget 116-117 E 4
Hennessey, OK 76-77 F 4
Henning, MN 70-71 C 2
Henrietta, TX 76-77 E 6
Henrietta Maria, Cape — 56-57 U 6
Henriette, ostrov — 132-133 ef 2
Henrique de Carvalho = Saurimo 172 D 3
Henry, IL 70-71 F 5
Henry, NE 68-69 DE 4
Henry, SD 68-69 H 3
Henry, Cape — 80-81 J 2
Henry, Mount — 66-67 F 1
Henryetta, OK 76-77 FG 5
Henry Kater Peninsula 56-57 XY 4
Henry Mountains 74-75 H 3-4
Henrys Fork 66-67 H 3-4
Hensall 72-73 F 3
Henson Creek 82 II b 2
Henty 160 H 5
Henzada = Hinthāda 148-149 BC 3
Heping 146-147 E 9
Hepo = Jiexi 146-147 E 10
Heppner, OR 66-67 D 3
Heppner Junction, OR 66-67 CD 3
Hepu 142-143 K 7
Hepworth 72-73 F 2
Hequ 146-147 C 2
Heraclea 122-123 G 5
Heraclea = Ereğli 134-135 C 2
Hēradhsflói 116-117 fg 2
Hēradhsvötn 116-117 d 2
Hērákleia 122-123 L 7
Hērákleia = Ereğli 134-135 C 2
Hērákleion 122-123 L 8
Herakol dağı 136-137 K 4
Herald, ostrov — 52 B 36
Heras, Las — [RA, Mendoza] 106-107 C 4
Heras, Las — [RA, Santa Cruz] 111 C 7
Herāt 134-135 J 4
Herbert 61 E 5
Herbert C. Legg Lake 83 III d 1
Herbert Island 58-59 I 4
Herbertsdale 174-175 DE 8
Hérbertville 62 PQ 2
Herb Lake 61 HJ 3
Herblay 129 I b 2
Hercegnovi 122-123 H 4
Herchmer 61 L 2
Hercilio, Rio — 102-103 GH 7
Heredia 88-89 DE 9
Hereford, TX 76-77 C 5
Hereford [GB] 119 E 5
Hereford [RA] 106-107 F 5
Herefoss 116-117 C 8
Herero 174-175 C 2
Hereroland 172 CD 6
Herferswil 128 IV a 2
Herford 118 D 2
Herglad = Hirglah 166-167 M 1
Herington, KS 68-69 H 6
Heri Rud = Harī Rūd 134-135 J 4
Herīs 136-137 M 3
Heritage Range 53 B 28-A 29
Herkimer, NY 72-73 J 3
Herlen He 142-143 M 2
Herlitzka 106-107 H 1
Herman, MN 70-71 BC 3
Hermanas 86-87 K 4
Hermanas, NM 74-75 JK 7
Hermanas, Las — 106-107 G 6
Herman Barnett Stadium 85 III b 2
Herman Brown Park 85 III bc 1
Herma Ness 119 F 1
Hermann, MO 70-71 E 6
Hermann Eckstein Park 170 V b 1
Hermann Park 85 III b 2
Hermannsburg [AUS] 158-159 F 4
Hermannskogel 113 I b 1
Hermanos, Cerro — 108-109 C 6
Hermansverk 116-117 B 7
Hermansville, MI 70-71 G 3
Hermanus 174-175 C 8
Hermel, El — = Al-Harmal 136-137 G 5
Hermes, Cape — = Kaap Hermes 174-175 H 6
Hermes, Kaap — 174-175 H 6
Hermidale 160 H 3
Hermiston, OR 66-67 D 3
Hermitage 63 HJ 4
Hermitage, AR 78-79 C 4
Hermitage Bay 63 H 4
Hermite, Isla — 111 C 9
Hermit Islands 148-149 N 7
Hermleigh, TX 76-77 D 6
Hermōn = Jabal as-Sayk̲h 136-137 FG 6
Hérmos = Gediz çayı 136-137 C 3
Hermosa, SD 68-69 E 4
Hermosa, La — 94-95 F 5
Hermosa Beach, CA 83 III b 2
Hermosillo 64-65 D 6
Hermoso Campo 104-105 F 10
Hermúpolis 122-123 L 7
Hernals, Wien- 113 I b 2
Hernandarias 111 F 3
Hernández 106-107 GH 4
Hernando 106-107 EF 4
Hernando, MS 78-79 E 3
Hernan M. Miraval 104-105 EF 10
Herndon, KS 68-69 F 6
Herning 116-117 C 9
Héroes Chapultepec, Ciudad de México- 91 I c 2
Héroes de Churubusco, Ixtapalapa- 91 I c 2
Heroica Alvarado = Alvarado 64-65 GH 8
Heroica Caborca 64-65 D 5
Heroica Cárdenas 86-87 O 8-9
Heroica Guaymas 64-65 D 6
Heroica Matamoros = Matamoros 64-65 G 6
Heroica Nogales 64-65 D 5
Heroica Puebla de Zaragoza = Puebla de Zaragoza 64-65 G 8
Heroica Tlapacoyan 86-87 M 7-8
Heroica Veracruz = Veracruz 64-65 GH 8
Heroica Zitácuaro 86-87 K 8
Heron, MT 66-67 F 1
Heron Bay 70-71 G 1
Herong 146-147 CD 6
Heron Lake 70-71 C 4
Hérons, Île aux — 82 I b 2
Herowabad = Khalkhāl 136-137 N 4
Herradura 104-105 G 10
Herradura, La — 108-109 F 7
Herreid, SD 68-69 FG 3
Herrera [E] 120-121 F 7
Herrera [PA] 88-89 F 10
Herrera [RA, Entre Ríos] 106-107 H 4
Herrera [RA, Santiago del Estero] 106-107 F 2
Herrera del Duque 120-121 E 9
Herrera de Pisuerga 120-121 EF 7
Herrera Vegas 106-107 G 6
Herrick 158-159 J 8
Herrin, IL 70-71 F 7
Herrington Island 72-73 DE 5
Herrington Lake 70-71 H 7
Herriot 61 H 2
Herrliberg 128 IV b 2
Herschel [CDN, island] 58-59 S 2
Herschel [CDN, place] 61 D 5
Herschel [ZA] 174-175 G 6
Herschel Island 56-57 J 3-4
Hersham 129 II a 2
Hersilia 106-107 G 2-3
Herson = Cherson 126-127 F 3
Hertford 119 FG 6
Hertford, NC 80-81 H 2
Hertogenbosch, 's- 120-121 KL 3
Hertzogville 174-175 F 5
Hervey Bay 158-159 K 4-5
Hervey-Jonction 72-73 K 1
Herzliya 173 D 1
Herzog-Ernst-Bucht 53 B 32-33
Heshjīn 136-137 N 4
Heshui [TJ, Gansu] 146-147 B 4
Heshui [TJ, Guangdong] 146-147 CD 10
Heshun 146-147 D 3
Hesperia, CA 74-75 E 5
Hesperus, CO 68-69 BC 7
Hess Creek 58-59 N 4
Hesse = Hessen 118 D 3
Hessen 118 D 3
Hess Mount 58-59 O 5
Hesteyri 116-117 b 1
Heston, London- 129 II a 2
Heṭan 140 E 7
Hetian [TJ, Fujian] 146-147 F 9
Hetian [TJ, Guangdong] 146-147 E 10
Het IJ 128 I a 1
Het Nieuwe Meer 128 I a 1-2
Hetou 146-147 B 11
Het Sas 128 II b 1
Het Schouw 128 I b 1
Hettinger, ND 68-69 E 2-3
Hettipoḷa 140 DE 7
Heuglin, Kapp — 116-117 lm 5
Heul, De — 128 I a 1
Heuningspruit 174-175 G 4
Heuningvleisoutpan 174-175 E 4
Heves 118 K 5
Hewlett, NY 82 III d 3
Hexi 146-147 F 9
He Xian [TJ, Anhui] 146-147 G 6
He Xian [TJ, Guangxi Zhuangzu Zizhiqu] 142-143 L 7
Hexigten Qi 142-143 M 3
Hexrivier 174-175 C 7
Hexrivierberge 174-175 C 7
Hext, TX 76-77 E 7
Hextable 129 II c 2
Hexue = Haoxue 146-147 D 6
Heyang [TJ, Shaanxi] 146-147 C 4
Heyang [TJ, Shandong] 146-147 G 4
Heyburn Lake 76-77 F 4-5
Ḥeydarābād 136-137 L 4
Heyuan 146-147 E 10
Heywood [AUS] 160 EF 7
Hezārān, Kūh-e- 134-135 H 5
Heze 142-143 M 4
Hezelton 56-57 L 6
Hialeah, FL 80-81 c 4
Hiawatha, KS 70-71 C 6
Hiawatha, UT 74-75 H 3
Hibbing, MN 64-65 H 2
Hibbs, Point — 160 b 3
Hibiya Park 155 III b 1-2
Hichiro-wan = zaliv Terpenija 132-133 b 8
Hickman, KY 78-79 E 2
Hickman, NE 68-69 H 5
Hickman, NM 74-75 JK 5
Hickman, Mount — 58-59 x 8
Hickmann 104-105 E 8
Hickory, NC 80-81 F 3
Hickory, Lake — 80-81 F 3
Hickory Hills, IL 83 II a 2
Hicksville, OH 70-71 H 5
Hico, TX 76-77 EF 6
Hidaka 144-145 c 2
Hidaka-sammyaku 144-145 c 2
Hidalgo [MEX, Coahuila] 76-77 DE 9
Hidalgo [MEX, Hidalgo] 64-65 G 7
Hidalgo [MEX, Tamaulipas] 86-87 L 5
Hidalgo, Ciudad — 86-87 K 8
Hidalgo, Salinas de — 86-87 JK 6
Hidalgo del Parral 64-65 EF 6
Hida sammyaku 144-145 L 4-5
Hiddensee 118 F 1
Hidden Valley, TX 85 III b 1
Hidrolândia 102-103 H 2
Hiem, Mu'o'ng — 150-151 D 2
Hienghène 158-159 MN 4
Hiệp Đu'c 150-151 G 5
Hierápetra 122-123 L 8
Hierisós 122-123 KL 5
Hieropolis = Manbij 136-137 GH 4
Hierra, La — 106-107 H 3
Hierro 164-165 A 3
Hietzing, Wien- 113 I b 2
Higashiōizumi, Tōkyō- 155 III a 1
Higasiōsaka 144-145 KL 5
Higbee, MO 70-71 D 6
Higgins, TX 76-77 D 4
Higgins Lake 70-71 H 3
Higham Hill, London- 129 II b 1
High Atlas 164-165 CD 2
Highflats 174-175 J 6
High Hill River 61 L 3
High Island 70-71 GH 3
High Island, TX 76-77 GH 8
High Island = Pulau Serasan 150-151 G 11
High Junk Peak 155 I b 2
Highland, IL 70-71 F 6
Highland, WA 66-67 E 2
Highland Acres, Houston-, TX 85 III b 1
Highland Ind. Park North, Houston-, TX 85 III b 1
Highland Park 84 I c 1
Highland Park, IL 70-71 G 4
Highland Park, MI 72-73 E 3
Highland Park, Los Angeles-, CA 83 III c 1
Highland Peak 74-75 F 4
Highmore, SD 68-69 G 3
High Point, NC 64-65 KL 4
High Prairie 56-57 NO 6
High River 60 KL 4
Highrock 61 HJ 3
High Rock Lake 80-81 FG 3
Highrock Lake [CDN, Manitoba] 61 H 3
Highrock Lake [CDN, Saskatchewan] 61 F 2
High Springs, FL 80-81 b 2
Highwood, MT 66-67 H 2
Highwood Peak 66-67 H 2
Higuera, La — 106-107 B 2
Higuerote 94-95 HJ 2
Hiidenmaa = Hiiumaa 124-125 CD 4
Hiiumaa 124-125 CD 4
Hijārah, Ṣahrā' al- [IRQ] 136-137 L 7
Hijārah, Ṣaḥrā' al- [Saudi Arabia] 136-137 JK 8
Ḥijāz, Al- 134-135 D 5-6
Ḥijāzah 173 C 5
Hijo = Tagum 148-149 J 5
Hijos, Cerro los — 96-97 B 5
Hikari 144-145 H 6
Hikkaḍuwa 140 DE 7
Hiko, NV 74-75 F 4
Hikone 144-145 L 5
Hiko-san 144-145 H 6
Hikurangi [NZ, mountain] 161 H 3-4
Hikurangi [NZ, place] 161 F 2
Hilāl, Jabal — 173 CD 2
Hilālī, Wādī al- 136-137 J 7
Hilario Ascasubi 106-107 F 7
Hilbert, WI 70-71 FG 3
Hildesheim 118 DE 2
Hilger, MT 68-69 B 2
Hill, MT 66-67 H 1
Hillah, Al- [IRQ] 134-135 E 4
Ḥillah, Al- [Saudi Arabia] 134-135 F 6
Hill Bāndh = Panchēt Pahāṛ Bāndh 138-139 L 6
Hill City, ID 66-67 F 4
Hill City, KS 68-69 G 6
Hill City, MN 70-71 D 2
Hill City, SD 68-69 E 3-4
Hill Crest, PA 84 III b 1
Hillcrest Cemetery 85 II b 2
Hillcrest Heights, MD 82 II b 2
Hillerød 116-117 DE 10
Hillī 138-139 M 5

Hillman, MN 70-71 D 2-3
Hillmond 61 D 4
Hills, MN 68-69 H 4
Hillsboro, GA 80-81 E 4
Hillsboro, IL 70-71 F 6
Hillsboro, NC 80-81 G 2
Hillsboro, ND 68-69 H 2
Hillsboro, NH 72-73 L 3
Hillsboro, NM 76-77 A 6
Hillsboro, OH 72-73 E 5
Hillsboro, OR 66-67 B 3
Hillsboro, TX 76-77 F 6
Hillsboro Canal 80-81 c 3
Hillsborough Bay 63 E 4
Hillsdale, MI 70-71 H 5
Hillside, AZ 74-75 G 5
Hillside, NJ 82 III a 2
Hillsport 70-71 H 1
Hillston 158-159 HJ 6
Hillsville, VA 80-81 F 2
Hilltop 174-175 H 5
Hilltop, NJ 84 III c 3
Hillwood, VA 82 II a 2
Hilmänd, Därya-ye- = Helmand Röd 134-135 K 4
Hilmar, CA 74-75 C 4
Hilo, HI 148-149 ef 4
Hilsa 138-139 K 5
Hilshire Village, TX 85 III a 2
Hilton Head Island 80-81 F 4
Hilts, CA 66-67 B 5
Hilu-Babor = Īlubabor 164-165 LM 7
Hilvan = Karaçurun 136-137 H 4
Hilversum 120-121 K 2
Himāchal Pradesh 134-135 M 4
Himālaya 134-135 L 4-P 5
Himālchūli 138-139 K 3
Himatnagar 138-139 D 6
Himeji 142-143 P 5
Himes, WY 68-69 B 3
Hime-saki 144-145 M 3
Himeville 174-175 H 5
Himezi = Himeji 142-143 P 5
Himi 144-145 L 4
Ḥimṣ 134-135 D 4
Hinai 144-145 N 2
Hinako, Pulau-pulau — 152-153 B 5
Hinche 88-89 KL 5
Hinchinbrook Entrance 58-59 OP 6
Hinchinbrook Island [AUS] 158-159 J 3
Hinchinbrook Island [USA] 58-59 OP 6
Hinckley, MN 70-71 D 2-3
Hinckley, UT 74-75 G 3
Hinḍaon = Hindaun 138-139 F 4
Hindaun 138-139 F 4
Hindes, TX 76-77 E 8
Hindi 138-139 K 4
Hindia, Lautan — 148-149 B 6-D 8
Hindīyah, Al- 136-137 KL 6
Hindoli 138-139 E 5
Hinds Lake 63 H 3
Hindūbāgh 134-135 K 4
Hindū Kush 134-135 KL 3
Hindupur 134-135 M 8
Hindupura = Hindupur 134-135 M 8
Hindustan 134-135 M 5-O 6
Hindusthān = Hindustan 134-135 M 5-O 6
Hines, FL 80-81 b 2
Hines, OR 66-67 D 4
Hines Creek 56-57 N 6
Hinesville, GA 80-81 F 5
Hingan = Ankang 146-147 B 5
Hinganghāt 138-139 G 7
Hingham, MA 84 I c 3
Hingham Bay 84 I c 3
Hinghsien = Xing Xian 146-147 C 2
Hinghwa = Putian 142-143 M 6
Hinghwa = Xinghua 146-147 GH 5
Hinghwa Wan = Xinghua Wan 146-147 G 9
Hingīr = Hemagiri 138-139 J 6-7
Hingjen = Xingren 142-143 K 6
Hingkwo = Xingguo 146-147 E 8
Hingol 134-135 K 5
Hingoli 134-135 M 7
Hingshan = Xingshan 146-147 C 6
Hingtang = Xingtang 146-147 E 2
Hingurakgoḍa 140 E 6-7
Hınıs 136-137 J 3
Hinkley, CA 74-75 E 5
Hinlopenstretet 116-117 kl 5
Hinna = Īmī 164-165 N 7
Hinnøy 116-117 FG 3
Hino, Yokohama- 155 III a 3
Hinojo 106-107 GH 6
Hinojosa del Duque 120-121 E 9
Hinomi-saki 144-145 J 5
Hinṣ 136-137 J 2
Hinsdale, MT 68-69 C 1
Hinterbrühl 113 I ab 2
Hinteregg 128 IV b 2
Hinterrhein 118 D 5
Hinthāda 148-149 BC 3
Hinton, WV 80-81 F 2
Hinton [CDN] 56-57 N 7
Hınzır burnu 136-137 F 4
Hınzır dağı 136-137 FG 3
Hipocapac 96-97 F 10
Hipódrome Argentino 110 III b 1
Hipódromo de la Rinconada 91 II b 2
Hipódromo de las Americas 91 I b 2
Hipódromo de la Zarzuela 113 III a 2
Hipódromo de México 91 I bc 2
Hipódromo de Techo 91 III b 3
Hipólito 86-87 K 5
Hipólito Yrigoyen 106-107 D 4
Hippodrome de Al-Jazā'ir 170 I b 2
Hippodrome de Longchamp 129 I bc 2
Hippodrome de Tremblay 129 I cd 2
Hippodrome de Vincennes 129 I c 2
Hippodrome Saint-Cloud 129 I b 2
Hippo Regius = Annābah 164-165 F 1
Hiraan 164-165 ab 3
Hirado 144-145 G 6
Hirado-shima 144-145 G 6
Hirakawa 155 III d 3
Hirākūd Reservoir 138-139 J 7
Hīrāphāṭā 138-139 M 6-N 7
Hīrāpur 138-139 G 5
Ḥirāsah, Rā's al- 166-167 K 1
Hirata 144-145 J 5
Hirato jima = Hirado-shima 144-145 G 6
Hiratori 144-145 c 2
Hireimis, Qârat el — = Qārat Huraymis 136-137 B 7
Hirekerūr 140 B 3
Hirfanlı barajı 136-137 E 3
Hirgis Nur = Chjargas nuur 142-143 GH 2
Hirglah 166-167 M 1
Hīrlāu 122-123 M 2
Hirondelles, Cap des — = Mui Yên 150-151 G 6
Hirono 144-145 N 4
Hiroo 144-145 c 2
Hirosaki 142-143 QR 3
Hiroshima 142-143 P 5
Hirosima = Hiroshima 142-143 P 5
Hirota-wan 144-145 NO 3
Hirr, Wādī al- 136-137 K 7
Hirschau [D, Oberbayern] 130 II b 1
Hirschgarten, Berlin- 130 III c 2
Hirschstetten, Wien- 113 I bc 2
Hirslanden, Zürich- 128 IV b 1
Hirson 120-121 K 4
Hirtshals 116-117 C 9
Hirzel 128 IV b 2
Hisaka-jima 144-145 G 6
Hisār 134-135 M 5
Ḥiṣār, Kohe — 134-135 K 4
Hisarönü 136-137 DE 2
Ḥismā 173 DE 3
Ḥismet 'Umar, Bīr — = Bi'r Ḥasmat 'Umar 173 CD 7
Hispaniola 64-65 MN 8
Hissār = Hisār 134-135 M 5
Ḥiṣṣar, Kūh-e- = Kōhe Ḥiṣār 134-135 K 4
Histiaía 122-123 K 6
Hisua 138-139 K 5
Hīt 136-137 K 6
Hita 144-145 H 6
Hitachi 142-143 R 4
Hitachi-Ōta = Hitati-Ōta 144-145 N 4
Hitati = Hitachi 142-143 R 4
Hitchland, TX 76-77 D 4
Hite, UT 74-75 H 4
Hitoyoshi 144-145 H 6
Hitra 116-117 C 6
Hitteren = Hitra 116-117 C 6
Hiuchi-dake 144-145 M 4
Hiuchi-nada 144-145 J 5
Hiw 173 C 4-5
Hiwasa 144-145 K 6
Hiyoshi, Yokohama- 155 III a 2
Hizan = Karasu 136-137 K 3
Hjälmaren 116-117 FG 8
Hjälmar Lake = Hjälmaren 116-117 FG 8
Hjelmelandsvågen 116-117 AB 8
Hjelmsøy 116-117 L 2
Hjørring 116-117 C 9
Hka, Nam — 141 F 5
Hkabè 141 E 6
Hkākabo Rāzī 141 EF 1
Hkarônwa 141 F 8
Hkaunglanbū 141 F 2
Hkaungzaunggwei 150-151 B 5
Hkaw, Lûy — 141 F 5
Hkayan 141 E 7
Hkin'ū 141 D 4
Hkweibûm 148-149 B 2
Hlabisa 174-175 JK 5
Hlaingbwè 148-149 C 3
Hlatikulu 174-175 J 4
Hlegu = Hlīgū 141 E 7
Hleo, Ea — 150-151 F 6
Hlīgū 141 E 7
Hlobane 174-175 J 4
Hlobyne = Globino 126-127 F 2
Hluhluwe 174-175 K 5
Hluhluwe Game Reserve 174-175 JK 4-5
Hluingbwe = Hlaingbwè 148-149 C 3
Hluti 174-175 J 4
Hmelnizkij = Chmel'nickij 126-127 C 2
Ho 164-165 E 7
Hoa Binh 148-149 DE 2
Hoachanas 174-175 C 2
Hoa Đà 150-151 G 7
Hoadley 60 K 3
Hoai Nho'n 148-149 E 4
Hoangho = Huang He 142-143 L 4
Hoang Sa, Quân Đao — 148-149 F 5
Hoarusib 172 B 5
Hoback Peak 66-67 H 4
Hōban 141 F 4
Hobart 158-159 J 8
Hobart, IN 70-71 G 5
Hobart, OK 76-77 E 5
Hobbs, NM 64-65 F 5
Hobbs Coast 53 B 23
Hobe Sound, FL 80-81 cd 3
Hobetsu 144-145 bc 2
Hobhouse 174-175 G 5
Hōbin 141 E 3
Hobo 94-95 D 6
Hoboken, NJ 82 III b 2
Hōbôn 141 E 5
Hobra, el — = Al-Habrah 166-167 J 3
Hobrechtsfelde 130 III c 1
Hobro 116-117 C 9
Hōbsögöl Dalay = Chövsgöl nuur 142-143 J 1
Hobsons Bay 161 II b 2
Hobyaa 164-165 b 2
Hochbrück 130 II b 1
Hochfeld = Hoëveld [ZA, Oranje-Vrystaat] 174-175 G 5-H 4
Hochfeld = Hoëveld [ZA, Transvaal] 174-175 HJ 4
Hochgolling 118 FG 5
Ho-ch'i = Hexi 146-147 F 9
Ho-chiang = Hejiang 146-147 C 11
Ho Chiang = He Jiang 146-147 C 10
Ho-chien = Hejian 146-147 EF 2
Hoching = Hejin 146-147 C 4
Hochow = Hechuan 142-143 K 5-6
Hochstadt [D] 128 III b 1
Ho-ch'ü = Hequ 146-147 C 2
Ho Chung 155 I b 1
Hochwan = Hechuan 142-143 K 5-6
Hoc Môn 150-151 F 7
Hoda, Lûy- 141 E 6
Hodal [IND] 138-139 F 4
Ḥoddua = Ghuddawah 164-165 G 3
Hodeida = Al-Ḥudaidah 134-135 E 8
Ḥōḍein, Wādī — = Wādī Ḥuḍayn 173 D 6
Hodgdon, ME 72-73 MN 1
Hodge, LA 78-79 C 4
Hodgenville, KY 70-71 GH 7
Hodgson 61 JK 5
Hodh = Al-Ḥawḍ 164-165 C 5
Hódmezővásárhely 118 K 5
Hodna, Chott el — = Ash-Shaṭṭ al-Hudnah 164-165 EF 1
Hodna, Monts du — = Jibal al-Hudnah 166-167 J 1-2
Hodna, Plaine du — = Sahl al-Hudnah 166-167 J 2
Hodogaya, Yokohama- 155 III a 3
Hodzana River 58-59 N 3
Hoef, De — 128 I a 2
Hoë Karoo 174-175 C-F 6
Hoek van Holland, Rotterdam- 120-121 JK 3
Hoengsŏng 144-145 FG 4
Hoeryŏng 144-145 G 1
Hoeve 128 II a 1-2
Hoëveld [ZA, Oranje-Vrystaat] 174-175 G 5-H 4
Hoëveld [ZA, Transvaal] 174-175 HJ 4
Hoey 61 F 4
Hoeyang 144-145 F 3
Hof 118 E 3
Hofbräuhaus 130 II b 2
Hofburg 113 I b 2
Höfdhakaupstadhur 116-117 cd 2
Hofei = Hefei 142-143 M 5
Hoffman, MN 70-71 BC 3
Hofmeyr [Namibia] 174-175 C 3
Hofmeyr [ZA] 174-175 FG 6
Höfn 116-117 f 2
Hofors 116-117 FG 7
Ḥofrat en Naḥās = Ḥufrat an-Naḥās 164-165 JK 7
Hofsjökull 116-117 d 2
Hofsós 116-117 d 2
Hofstade 128 II b 1
Hofstande = Hofstade 128 II b 1
Hōfu 144-145 H 5-6
Hofuf = Al-Hufūf 134-135 FG 5
Höganäs 116-117 E 9
Hogan Island 160 c 1
Hogansville, GA 78-79 G 4
Hogatza River 58-59 K 3
Hogback Mountain [USA, Montana] 66-67 GH 3
Hogback Mountain [USA, Nebraska] 68-69 E 5
Hogeland, MT 68-69 B 1
Hogem Range 60 D 1-E 2
Hogg Park 85 III b 1
Hog Island [USA, Michigan] 70-71 H 3
Hog Island [USA, Virginia] 80-81 J 2
Hog River, AK 58-59 K 3
Hoha 174-175 H 6
Hohe Acht 118 C 3
Hohenschönhausen, Berlin- 130 III c 1
Hohenwald, TN 78-79 F 3
Hohenzollernkanal 130 III b 1
Hoher Atlas 164-165 CD 2
Hoher Berg [D, Hessen] 128 III b 1
Hohe Tauern 118 F 5
Hohhot = Huhehaote 142-143 L 3
Hoh-kai = Ohōtsuku-kai 144-145 cd 1
Hoholitna River 58-59 J 6
Hohpi = Hebi 146-147 E 4
Ho-hsien = He Xian 142-143 L 7
Hohsien = He Xian 146-147 G 9
Ho-hsüeh = Haoxue 146-147 D 6
Hôi An 150-151 G 5
Hoifung = Haifeng 142-143 M 7
Hoihong = Haikang 142-143 KL 7
Hoima 172 F 1
Hoion = Hai'an 142-143 KL 7
Hoisbüttel 130 I b 1
Hoisington, KS 68-69 G 6
Hôi Xuân 150-151 E 2
Ho-jung = Herong 146-147 CD 6
Hōketçe 136-137 G 3
Hokien = Hejian 146-147 EF 2
Hokitika 158-159 NO 8
Hokkaidō [J, administrative unit] 144-145 bc 2
Hokkaidō [J, island] 142-143 RS 3
Hokkō = Peichiang 146-147 H 10
Hoku = Hequ 146-147 C 2
Hokuoka = Fukuoka 142-143 OP 5
Hokuriku 144-145 L 5-M 4
Holākērē = Holalkere 140 C 3
Holalkere 140 C 3
Holanda 104-105 D 4
Hólar 116-117 d 2
Holbæk 116-117 D 10
Holbox, Isla — 86-87 R 7
Holbrook 160 H 5
Holbrook, AZ 74-75 HJ 5
Holbrook, ID 66-67 G 4
Holden 61 BC 4
Holden, MO 70-71 CD 6
Holden, UT 74-75 G 3
Holdenville, OK 76-77 F 5
Holdich 108-109 EF 5
Holdrege, NE 68-69 G 5
Holē-Narasīpura = Hole Narsipur 140 C 4
Hole Narsipur 140 C 4
Holgate, OH 70-71 HJ 5
Holguín 64-65 L 7
Holiday Forest, Houston-, TX 85 III c 1
Holiday Lake Amusement Park 84 III d 1
Holikachuk, AK 58-59 H 5
Ho Ling = He Ling 150-151 G 3
Holitna River 58-59 J 6
Ho-liu = Heliuji 146-147 F 5
Höljes 116-117 E 7
Hollam's Bird Island = Hollams Voëleiland 174-175 A 3
Hollam's Bird Islands = Hollams Voëleilanden 174-175 H 3
Hollams Voëleiland 174-175 A 3
Holland, MI 70-71 GH 4
Holland [CDN] 61 J 6
Holland, Singapore- 154 III a 2
Hollandale, MS 78-79 D 4
Hollandia = Jayapura 148-149 M 7
Hollick-Kenyon Plateau 53 AB 25-26
Holliday, TX 76-77 E 6
Hollidaysburg, PA 72-73 G 4
Hollis, OK 76-77 E 5
Hollis, New York-, NY 82 III d 2
Hollister, CA 74-75 C 4
Hollister, ID 66-67 F 4
Hollister, MO 78-79 C 2
Hollmann, Cape — 148-149 gh 5
Holly, MI 72-73 E 3
Holly Bluff, MS 78-79 D 4
Holly Hill, FL 80-81 c 2
Holly Hill, SC 80-81 F 4
Holly Ridge, NC 80-81 H 3
Holly Springs, MS 78-79 E 3
Hollywood, FL 64-65 KL 6
Hollywood, PA 84 III c 1
Hollywood, Los Angeles-, CA 64-65 BC 5
Hollywood Bowl 83 III b 1
Hollywood Cemetery [USA, Atlanta] 85 II b 2
Hollywood Cemetery [USA, Houston] 85 III b 1
Hollywood Park Race Track 83 III bc 2
Holman Island 56-57 NO 3
Hólmavík 116-117 c 2
Holmdene 174-175 H 4
Holmes, PA 84 III b 2
Holmes, Mount — 66-67 H 3
Holmesburg, Philadelphia-, PA 84 III c 1
Holmes Run 82 II a 2
Holmestrand 116-117 CD 8
Holmfield 68-69 G 1
Holmsund 116-117 J 6
Holo Islands = Sulu Archipelago 148-149 H 5
Holoog 174-175 BC 4
Holopaw, FL 80-81 c 2
Holroyd River 158-159 H 2
Holsnøy 116-117 A 7
Holstebro 116-117 C 9
Holstein, IA 70-71 C 4
Holsteinsborg = Sisimiut 56-57 Za 4
Holston River 80-81 E 2
Holt, AL 78-79 F 4
Holt, FL 78-79 F 5
Holten, KS 70-71 C 6
Holten Bank 116-117 C 5
Holtville, CA 74-75 F 6
Holtyre 62 LM 2
Holung = Helong 144-145 G 1
Holy Cross, AK 56-57 DE 5
Holy Cross Bay = zaliv Kresta 132-133 k 4
Holy Cross Hospital 84 II bc 2
Holyhead 119 D 5
Holyoke, CO 68-69 E 5
Holyoke, MA 72-73 K 3
Holyrood, KS 68-69 G 6
Holy Sepulchre Cemetery 84 III b 1
Holysloot 128 I b 1
Holzminden 118 D 3
Homalin = Hōnmalin 141 D 3
Homberg 128 II b 2
Hombori 164-165 D 5
Hombre Muerto, Salar del — 104-105 C 9
Hôme 155 III d 1
Home, OR 66-67 E 3
Home Bay 56-57 XY 4
Homebush Bay 161 I a 1-2
Homedale, ID 66-67 E 4
Homel = Gomel' 124-125 H 7
Home Owned Estates, Houston-, TX 85 III c 1
Homer, AK 56-57 F 6
Homer, LA 78-79 C 4
Homer, MI 70-71 H 4
Homer, NY 72-73 H 3
Homerville, GA 80-81 E 5
Homesglen, Melbourne- 161 II c 2
Homestead 158-159 HJ 4
Homestead, FL 80-81 c 4
Hometown, IL 83 II a 2
Homewood, AL 78-79 F 4
Hominy, OK 76-77 F 4
Hommoku, Yokohama- 155 III ab 3
Homnābād 140 C 2
Homoine 172 FG 6
Homoljske Planine 122-123 J 3
Ḥomra, Al- = Al-Ḥumrah 164-165 L 6
Homra, Hamada el — = Al-Ḥamādat al-Ḥamrā' 164-165 G 2-3
Ḥomṣ = Al-Khums 164-165 GH 2
Ḥomṣ = Ḥimṣ 134-135 D 4
Hon, Cu Lao — = Cu Lao Thu 148-149 EF 4
Honai 144-145 J 6
Honan = Henan 142-143 L 5
Honaunau, HI 78-79 de 3
Honāvar 140 B 3
Hōnāvara = Honāvar 140 B 3
Honaz dağı 136-137 C 4
Honbetsu 144-145 cd 2
Hon Chông 150-151 E 7
Honda 92-93 E 3
Honda, Bahía — 94-95 EF 1
Honda, La — 94-95 C 4
Honda Bay 148-149 G 5
Hondeklipbaai [ZA, bay] 174-175 B 6
Hondeklipbaai [ZA, place] 174-175 B 6
Hondeklip Bay = Hondeklipbaai 174-175 B 6
Hondo, NM 76-77 B 6
Hondo, TX 76-77 E 8
Hondo [J] 144-145 H 6
Hondo [MEX] 76-77 D 9
Hondo = Honshū 142-143 PQ 4
Honduras 64-65 J 9
Honduras, Cabo de — 64-65 JK 8
Honduras, Golfe de — 64-65 J 8
Hondzocht 128 II a 2
Honesdale, PA 72-73 J 4
Honeydew 170 V a 1
Honey Grove, TX 76-77 FG 6
Honey Island, TX 76-77 G 7
Honey Lake 66-67 C 5
Honfleur 120-121 H 4
Hon Gai 150-151 F 2
Hong'an 146-147 E 6
Hongch'ŏn 144-145 FG 4
Hong-do 144-145 E 5
Hōngg, Zürich- 128 IV ab 1
Honghai Wan 146-147 E 10
Hong He [TJ, Henan] 146-147 E 5
Hong He [TJ, Inner Mongolian Aut. Reg.] 146-147 CD 1
Hong He [TJ, Yunnan] 142-143 J 7
Honghe Hanizu Yizu Zizhizhou 142-143 J 7
Hong Hu [TJ, lake] 146-147 D 7
Honghu [TJ, place] 142-143 L 6
Hongjiang 142-143 KL 6
Hong Jiang = Wu Shui 146-147 BC 8
Hong Kong 142-143 LM 7
Hong Kong Stadium 155 I b 2
Honglai 146-147 G 9
Hongliu He 146-147 B 3
Hongluoxian 144-145 C 2
Hongmiao, Beijing- 155 II b 2
Hongmoxian = Hongluoxian 144-145 C 2
Hông Ngư 150-151 E 7
Hongō, Tōkyō- 155 III b 1
Hongqizhen 150-151 G 3
Hong Sa = Mu'o'ng Hong Sa 150-151 C 3
Hongshan = Maocifan 146-147 D 6
Hongshui He 142-143 K 6-7
Hongsŏng 144-145 F 4
Hongtong 146-147 C 3
Hongū 144-145 K 6
Hongwŏn 144-145 FG 2-3
Hongyōtoku 155 III c 1
Hongze 146-147 G 5
Hongze Hu 146-147 G 5
Honiara 148-149 jk 6
Honjo 144-145 MN 3
Honjo, Tōkyō- 155 III b 1
Hon Khoai 150-151 E 8
Hon Khoi, Vung — 150-151 G 6
Hōnmalin 141 D 3
Hon Mê 150-151 EF 3
Honmonji Temple 155 III b 2
Honnāli 140 B 3
Honningsvåg 116-117 LM 2
Honokaa, HI 78-79 e 2
Honokohua, HI 78-79 d 2
Honolulu, HI 148-149 e 3
Honório Gurgel, Rio de Janeiro- 110 I a 2
Hōnow 130 III c 1
Hon Panjang 148-149 D 5
Ho'n Quan = An Lôc 150-151 F 7
Hon Rai 150-151 E 8
Honshū 142-143 PQ 4
Honsyû = Honshū 142-143 PQ 4
Hon Tre 150-151 G 6
Hon Vong Phu = Nui Vong Phu 150-151 G 6
Hon Way 150-151 D 8
Honye 174-175 F 3
Hood = Isla Española 92-93 B 5
Hood, Mount — 64-65 B 2
Hood Canal 66-67 B 2
Hood Point 158-159 CD 6
Hood River, OR 66-67 C 3
Hooghly 138-139 LM 7
Hoogli = Hoogly 138-139 LM 7
Hoogte 174-175 H 4
Hook, London- 129 II a 2
Hooker, OK 76-77 D 4
Hooker, Bi'r — 173 B 2
Hooker Creek 158-159 F 3
Hook Island 158-159 J 4
Hook of Holland = Rotterdam-Hoek van Holland 120-121 JK 3
Hoonah, AK 56-57 JK 6
Hoopa, CA 66-67 B 5
Hoopa Valley Indian Reservation 66-67 AB 5
Hooper, CO 68-69 D 7
Hooper, NE 68-69 H 5
Hooper, UT 66-67 G 5
Hooper Bay 58-59 DE 6
Hooper Bay, AK 58-59 DE 6
Hoopeston, IL 70-71 G 5
Hoopstad 174-175 F 4
Hoosier 61 CD 5
Hoover, SD 68-69 E 3
Hoover, TX 76-77 D 5
Hoover Dam 64-65 D 4
Hopa 136-137 J 2
Hope 66-67 C 1
Hope, AK 58-59 N 6
Hope, AR 64-65 H 5
Hope, AZ 74-75 G 6
Hope, IN 70-71 H 6
Hope, KS 68-69 H 6
Hope, NM 76-77 B 6
Hope, Ben — 119 D 2
Hopedale 56-57 YZ 6
Hopefield 174-175 C 7
Hopeh = Hebei 142-143 LM 4
Hope Island 72-73 F 2
Hopelchén 86-87 PQ 8
Hopen 52 B 16
Hopes Advance, Cape — 56-57 X 5
Hopetoun [AUS, Victoria] 158-159 H 7
Hopetoun [AUS, Western Australia] 158-159 D 6
Hopetown 172 D 7
Hopewell, VA 80-81 H 2
Ho-pi = Hebi 146-147 E 4
Hopi Indian Reservation 74-75 H 4-5
Hopin = Hōbin 141 E 3
Ho-p'ing = Heping 146-147 E 9
Hôpital Brugmann 128 II a 1
Hopkins, Lake — 158-159 E 4
Hopkinsville, KY 64-65 J 4
Hopland, CA 74-75 B 3
Ho-p'o-hsü = Jiexi 146-147 E 10
Hopong = Hōbôn 141 E 5
Hoppo = Hepu 142-143 K 7
Hopu = Hepu 142-143 K 7
Ho-p'u = Hepu 142-143 K 7
Hoquiam, WA 66-67 AB 2
Hōr Abū Ḥijār = Khawr Abū Ḥajār 136-137 L 7
Hōr al-Ḥwaiza = Hawr al-Ḥawīzah 136-137 M 7
Hōr al-Jiljila = Hawr al-Jiljilah 136-137 L 6
Hōrān, Wādī — = Wādī Ḥawrān 134-135 E 4
Horanā 140 DE 7
Horasan 136-137 K 2
Hōr as-Saffāf = Birkat as-Saffāf 136-137 M 7
Horburg 60 K 3
Hörby 116-117 E 10
Horcasitas 86-87 H 3
Horcón, Bahía — 106-107 AB 4
Horcón de Piedra, Cerro — 106-107 B 4
Horcones 104-105 D 9
Horcones, Río — 104-105 D 9
Hordaland 116-117 A 8-B 7
Hordio = Hurdiyo 134-135 G 8
Höri 128 IV ab 1
Horicon, WI 70-71 F 4
Horinouchi, Tōkyō- 155 III ab 1
Horizontina 106-107 KL 1
Horlick Mountains 53 A 26-27
Hormoz 134-135 H 5
Hormoz, Tangeh — 134-135 H 5
Hormuz, Strait of — = Tangeh Hormoz 134-135 H 5
Horn [IS] 116-117 bc 1
Horn, Cape — = Cabo de Hornos 111 CD 9
Horn, Hamburg- 130 I b 1
Horn, Îles — 148-149 b 1
Hornafjördhur 116-117 f 2
Hornavan 116-117 GH 4
Hornbeck, LA 78-79 C 5
Hornchurch, London- 129 II c 1
Hörnefors 116-117 H 6
Hornell, NY 72-73 H 3
Hornepayne 62 J 2
Horner Rennbahn 130 I b 1
Hornillas 76-77 B 9-10
Horn Island 78-79 E 5
Hornkranz 174-175 B 2
Horn Mountains [CDN] 56-57 MN 5
Horn Mountains [USA] 58-59 H 6
Hornos, Cabo de — 111 CD 9
Hornos, False Cabo de — 108-109 E 10
Horn Pond 84 I b 2
Horn Reefs = Blåvands Huk 116-117 BC 10
Hornsea 119 FG 5
Hornsey, London- 129 II b 1
Hornsund 116-117 jk 6
Hornsundtind 116-117 k 6
Horobetsu 144-145 b 2
Hōr Ōda = Hawr Awdah 136-137 M 7
Horodenka = Gorodenka 126-127 B 2
Horodnyca = Gorodnica 126-127 C 1
Horodok = Gorodok [SU, Chmel'nickaja Oblast'] 126-127 C 2
Horodok = Gorodok [SU, L'vovskaja Oblast'] 126-127 AB 2
Horodyšče = Gorodišče 126-127 E 2
Horonobe 144-145 bc 1
Horowupotāna 140 E 6
Horqueta 111 E 2
Horqueta, La — [YV, Bolívar] 94-95 L 4
Horqueta, La — [YV, Monagas] 94-95 K 3
Horquetas, Las — 108-109 D 7
Horquilla 104-105 G 10
Horsburgh's Island = Zādetkale Kyûn 150-151 AB 7
Horse Branch, KY 70-71 G 7
Horse Cave, KY 70-71 H 7
Horse Creek, WY 68-69 D 5
Horse Creek [USA, Colorado] 68-69 E 6
Horse Creek [USA, Wyoming] 68-69 D 5
Horsefly 60 G 3
Horsehead Lake 68-69 FG 2
Horseheads, NY 72-73 H 3
Horse Islands 63 J 2
Horsens 116-117 CD 10
Horse Race Course of Jakarta 154 IV b 2
Horseshoe 158-159 C 5
Horse Shoe Bend, ID 66-67 EF 4
Horse Springs, NM 74-75 JK 6
Horsham [AUS] 158-159 H 7
Horstermeer 128 I b 2
Horta [Açores] 204-205 E 5
Hortaleza, Madrid- 113 III b 2
Horten 116-117 D 8
Hortensia 106-107 G 5
Horto Florestal 110 II b 1
Horton, KS 70-71 C 6
Horton River 56-57 M 4
Horwood Lake 62 K 3
Horzum-Armutlu = Gölhisar 136-137 C 4
Hosadurga = Hosdrug 140 B 4
Hosadurga = Hosdurga 140 C 4
Hōsakōṭṭē = Hoskote 140 CD 4
Hosanagar = Hosanagara 140 B 4
Hosanagara 140 B 4
Hosapēṭa = Hospet 140 C 3
Hosdrug 140 B 4
Hosdurga 140 C 4
Hose, Pegunungan — 152-153 K 4-L 5
Hoṣeima, el — = Al-Ḥusaymah 164-165 D 1
Ḥoseinābād = Īlām 134-135 F 4
Ḥoseynābād 136-137 M 5
Hoseyniyeh 136-137 MN 6
Hoshan = Hecheng 146-147 D 10
Hoshangābād 138-139 FG 6
Hoshiārpur 138-139 EF 2
Hoshingo Mdogo 171 DE 3
Ḥōsh 'Īsā = Hawsh 'Īsā 173 B 2
Hōshiyārpur = Hoshiārpur 138-139 EF 2
Ho-shui = Heshui [TJ, Gansu] 146-147 B 4
Ho-shui = Heshui [TJ, Guangdong] 146-147 CD 10
Hoshun = Heshun 146-147 D 3
Hoskote 140 CD 4
Hosmer, SD 68-69 G 3
Hospet 140 C 3
Hospital 106-107 B 4
Hospital, Cuchilla del — 106-107 K 3
Hospitalet de Llobregat 120-121 J 8
Hosta Butte 74-75 JK 5
Hoste, Isla — 111 C 9
Hosūr 140 C 4
Hot 148-149 C 3
Hotan = Khotan 142-143 DE 4
Hotazel 174-175 E 4
Hotchkiss, CO 68-69 C 6
Hot Creek Valley 74-75 E 3
Hotel Humboldt 91 II b 1
Hotel Punta del Lago 108-109 CD 7
Hotham Inlet 58-59 FG 3
Hotien = Khotan 142-143 DE 4
Hot'ien-hsü = Hetian 146-147 E 10
Hoting 116-117 G 5
Hotong Qagan Nur 146-147 B 2
Hot Springs, AR 64-65 H 5
Hot Springs, MT 66-67 F 2
Hot Springs, NC 80-81 E 3
Hot Springs, SD 68-69 E 4
Hot Springs, VA 80-81 G 2
Hot Springs Cove 60 D 5
Hotspur Seamount 100-101 FG 9
Hot Sulphur Springs, CO 68-69 CD 5
Hottah Lake 56-57 N 4
Hottentot Bay = Hottentotsbaai 174-175 A 4
Hottentot Reserve 174-175 B 3-4
Hottentotsbaai 174-175 A 4
Hottingen, Zürich- 128 IV b 1

Hot Wells, TX 76-77 B 7
Hou = Mu'o'ng Ou Neua 150-151 CD 1
Houakhong 150-151 C 2
Houaphan 150-151 DE 2
Houei Sai = Ban Huei Sai 150-151 C 2
Hougang 146-147 D 6
Hough, OK 76-77 D 4
Houghton, MI 70-71 F 2
Houghton Lake 70-71 H 3
Houilles 129 I b 2
Houiung 146-147 H 9
Houjian = Hougang 146-147 D 6
Houlka, MS 78-79 E 3
Houlong = Houlung 146-147 H 9
Houlton, ME 72-73 MN 1
Houma 142-143 L 4
Houma, LA 64-65 H 6
Houmaïmâ, Bîr — = Bi'r Ḩumaymah 136-137 HJ 5
Houmen = Meilong 146-147 E 10
Houmet es Soûq = Ḩūmat as-Sūq 166-167 M 3
Houmont Park, TX 85 III c 1
Houms 174-175 C 5
Houndé 164-165 D 6
Ho'u'ng Thuy 150-151 FG 4
Hounslow, London- 129 II a 2
House of Government 155 I ab 2
Houses of Parliament 129 II b 2
Houston 60 D 2
Houston, MS 78-79 E 4
Houston, TX 64-65 G 5-6
Houston, University of — 85 III b 2
Houston-Acre Homes, TX 85 III b 1
Houston-Afton Oaks, TX 85 III b 2
Houston-Airline Village, TX 85 III b 1
Houston-Allendale, TX 85 III bc 2
Houston-Almeda, TX 85 III b 2
Houston-Arlington Heights, TX 85 III c 2
Houston-Basin Ind Dist, TX 85 III b 2
Houston-Bayou Bend, TX 85 III ab 1
Houston-Bayou Woods, TX 85 III b 1
Houston-Beverly Hills, TX 85 III c 2
Houston-Blueridge, TX 85 III b 2
Houston-Braeburn Gardens, TX 85 III a 2
Houston-Braeburn Glen, TX 85 III a 2
Houston-Braeburn Valley, TX 85 III a 2
Houston-Braes Heights, TX 85 III b 2
Houston-Brays Village, TX 85 III a 2
Houston-Briarcroft, TX 85 III b 2
Houston-Briarmeadow, TX 85 III a 2
Houston-Campbell Woods, TX 85 III a 1
Houston-City Gardens, TX 85 III b 1
Houston-Cole Creek Manor, TX 85 III ab 1
Houston-Crestmond Park, TX 85 III b 2
Houston-Epsom Downs, TX 85 III b 1
Houston-Eureka Acres, TX 85 III b 1
Houston-Fairbanks, TX 85 III a 1
Houston-Fair Meadows, TX 85 III b 1
Houston-Forest Oaks, TX 85 III bc 2
Houston-Forest West, TX 85 III b 1
Houston-Freeway Manor, TX 85 III bc 2
Houston-Garden Oaks, TX 85 III b 1
Houston Gardens, Houston-, TX 85 III b 1
Houston-Glenbrook Valley, TX 85 III b 2
Houston-Glen Shannon, TX 85 III a 2
Houston-Harbourdale, TX 85 III b 1
Houston-Highland Acres, TX 85 III b 1
Houston-Highland Ind. Park North, TX 85 III b 1
Houston-Holiday Forest, TX 85 III c 1
Houston-Home Owned Estates, TX 85 III c 1
Houston-Houston Gardens, TX 85 III b 1
Houston-Houston Skyscraper Shadows, TX 85 III b 2
Houston-Huntington, TX 85 III b 1
Houston-Independence Heights, TX 85 III b 1
Houston-Kashmere Gardens, TX 85 III b 1
Houston-Kings Court, TX 85 III b 2
Houston-Knob Oaks, TX 85 III a 1
Houston-Knollwood Village, TX 85 III b 2
Houston-Lakeside Estates, TX 85 III a 2
Houston-Lakeside Forest, TX 85 III a 1
Houston-Lakeview, TX 85 III a 1
Houston-Larchmont, TX 85 III b 2
Houston-Lincoln City, TX 85 III b 1
Houston-Lindale Park, TX 85 III b 1
Houston-Little York, TX 85 III b 1
Houston-Long Point Woods, TX 85 III a 1
Houston-Main Saint Gardens, TX 85 III ab 2
Houston-Mayfair, TX 85 III b 2
Houston-Meadow Brook, TX 85 III bc 2
Houston-Meadow Creek Village, TX 85 III b 2
Houston-Meyerland, TX 85 III b 2
Houston Music Theatre 85 III a 2
Houston-Northbrook, TX 85 III b 2
Houston-Oak Forest, TX 85 III b 1
Houston-Pamela Heights, TX 85 III b 2
Houston-Park Place, TX 85 III b 2
Houston-Pinemont Plaza, TX 85 III b 1
Houston-Plaza del Oro, TX 85 III b 2
Houston-Port Houston Turning, TX 85 III b 1
Houston-Reedwoods, TX 85 III b 2
Houston-Rentur, TX 85 III a 2
Houston-Ridgecrest, TX 85 III a 1
Houston-River Forest, TX 85 III a 1
Houston-Riveroaks, TX 85 III b 2
Houston-Rosedale Gardens, TX 85 III b 1
Houston-Rustling Oaks, TX 85 III a 1
Houston-Scenic Woods, TX 85 III b 1
Houston-Shadow Oaks, TX 85 III a 1
Houston-Shady Acres, TX 85 III b 1
Houston-Sharpstown, TX 85 III b 2
Houston Ship Canal 85 III c 2
Houston Skill Center 85 III b 2
Houston Skyscraper Shadows, Houston-, TX 85 III b 2
Houston-Songwood, TX 85 III bc 1
Houston-Southern Oaks, TX 85 III b 2
Houston-South Main Estates, TX 85 III ab 2
Houston-Sugar Valley, TX 85 III b 2
Houston-Sunset Heights, TX 85 III b 1
Houston-Tanglewood, TX 85 III b 1
Houston Technical Institute 85 III b 2
Houston-Timber Acres, TX 85 III b 1
Houston-Timbergrove Manor, TX 85 III b 1
Houston-Townley Place, TX 85 III b 1
Houston-Trinity Gardens, TX 85 III b 1
Houston-Uptown Business Park, TX 85 III b 2
Houston-Walnut Bend, TX 85 III a 2
Houston-Westbury, TX 85 III b 2
Houston-White Oak Acres, TX 85 III b 1
Houston-Willow Bend, TX 85 III b 2
Houston-Willow Brook, TX 85 III b 2
Houston-Wilshire, TX 85 III b 1
Houston-Windsor Village, TX 85 III b 2
Houston-Wood Lake, TX 85 III a 2
Houston-Wood Shadows, TX 85 III c 1
Houtem 128 II b 1
Houtkraal 174-175 F 6
Houtman Abrolhos 158-159 B 5
Houz Solṭān, Karavānsarā-ye — = Daryācheh Ḥowḍ Solṭān 136-137 O 5
Hoven, SD 68-69 G 3
Hover, WA 66-67 D 2
Hovland, MN 70-71 EF 2
Hovrah = Howrah 134-135 O 6
Howar = Wādī Huwār 164-165 K 5
Howard, KS 68-69 H 7
Howard, SD 68-69 H 3-4
Howard Beach, New York-, NY 82 III cd 3
Howard City, MI 70-71 H 4
Howard University 82 II a 1
Howe, ID 66-67 G 4
Howe, Cape — 158-159 K 7
Howell, MI 70-71 HJ 4
Howells, NE 68-69 H 5
Howes, SD 68-69 E 3
Howe Sound 66-67 B 1
Howick [CDN] 72-73 K 2
Howick [ZA] 174-175 J 5
Howland 156-157 J 4
Howley 63 H 3
Howrah 134-135 O 6
Howrah-Bāntra 154 II ab 2
Howrah-Belur 154 II b 2
Howrah Bridge 154 II ab 2
Howrah-Golabari 154 II b 2
Howrah-Kona 154 II a 2
Howrah-Liluah 154 II b 2
Howrah-Nibria 154 II a 2
Howrah-Salkhia 154 II b 2
Howrah-Sibpur 154 II a 2
Hoxie, AR 78-79 D 2-3
Hoxie, KS 68-69 F 6
Hoy 119 E 2
Hōya [J] 155 III a 1
Hoyang = Heyang [TJ, Shaanxi] 146-147 C 4
Ho-yang = Heyang [TJ, Shandong] 146-147 G 4
Høyanger 116-117 B 7
Hoyle 62 L 2
Hōyokaikō = Bungo-suidō 142-143 P 5
Hoyos [CO] 94-95 E 8
Hoyran gölü 136-137 D 3
Höytiäinen 116-117 N 6
Hoyuan = Heyuan 146-147 E 10
Hozat 136-137 H 3
Hpā'an 148-149 C 3
Hpābya 141 EF 8
Hpāgyaw 141 E 7
Hpalā 141 F 2
Hpalam 148-149 B 2
Hpālan, Lûy — 141 F 5
Hpāpûn 141 E 6-7
Hparûzô 141 E 6
Hpaungbyin 141 D 3
Hpawret Reletkyā 150-151 B 7
Hpeigôn 141 E 6
Hpôhwaik 141 C 4
Hpwāwaubû 141 E 6
Hpyābôn 141 D 7
Hpyū 148-149 C 3

Hradec Králové 118 GH 3
Hrochei La 142-143 DE 5
Hrochei La = Shipki La 138-139 G 2
Hron 118 J 4

Hsadôn 141 EF 3
Hsālingyī 141 D 4-5
Hsamī 141 C 5
Hsan, Lûy — 141 E 5
Hsandaushin 141 C 6
Hsatthwā [BUR, Magwe Taing] 141 D 6
Hsatthwā [BUR, Ragaing Taing] 141 D 7
Hsatung = Thādôn 141 E 5
Hsaw 141 D 5
Hsawnghsup = Thaungdût 141 D 3
Hsay Walad 'Alī Bābī 164-165 B 5
Hsei, Lûy — 141 F 4
Hseikhpyû 141 D 5
Hsenwi = Theimnī 141 EF 4
Hsia-chiang = Xiajiang 146-147 E 8
Hsia-ching = Xiajing 146-147 EF 3
Hsiachwan Tao = Xiachuan Dao 146-147 D 11
Hsia-ho = Xiahe 142-143 J 4
Hsia-hsien = Xia Xian 146-147 C 4
Hsia-kuan = Xiaguan 142-143 J 6
Hsia-mên = Xiamen 142-143 M 7
Hsi-an 142-143 K 5
Hsi-an = Xi'an 142-143 K 5
Hsiang Chiang = Xiang Jiang 146-147 D 8
Hsiang-chou = Xiangzhou 146-147 G 3
Hsiang-ho = Xianghe 146-147 F 2
Hsiang-hsiang = Xiangxiang 146-147 D 8
Hsiang-kang = Hong Kong 142-143 LM 7
Hsiang-shan = Xiangshan 146-147 HJ 7
Hsiang-shui-k'ou = Xiangshui 146-147 G 4
Hsiang-yang = Xiangyang 142-143 L 5
Hsiang-yang-chên = Xiangyangzhen 144-145 E 1
Hsiang-yin = Xiangyin 146-147 D 7
Hsiang-yüan = Xiangyuan 146-147 D 3
Hsiao-ch'ang-shan Tao = Xiaochang-shan Dao 144-145 D 3
Hsiao-chiang = Pubei 146-147 B 10
Hsiao-ch'ing Ho = Xiaoqing He 146-147 G 3
Hsiao-hung-t'ou Hsü = Hsiaolan-Hsü 146-147 H 11
Hsiao-i = Xiaoyi 146-147 C 3
Hsiao-kan = Xiaogan 146-147 D 6
Hsiaolan-Hsü 146-147 H 11
Hsiao-ling Ho = Xiaoling He 144-145 C 2
Hsiao-shan = Xiaoshan 146-147 H 6
Hsiao Shui = Xiao Shui 146-147 C 8-9
Hsiao-wei-hsi = Weixi 141 F 2
Hsiatanshui Chi 146-147 H 10
Hsia-tien = Xiadian 146-147 H 3
Hsia-tung = Xiadong 142-143 H 3
Hsia-yang = Xiayang 146-147 FG 8
Hsi-ch'ang = Xichang [TJ, Guangdong] 150-151 G 2
Hsi-ch'ang = Xichang [TJ, Sichuan] 142-143 J 6
Hsi-ch'ê = Xiche 146-147 B 7
Hsi Chiang = Xi Jiang 142-143 L 7
Hsi-ch'uan = Xichuan 142-143 L 5
Hsi-chuang-tsun = Wutai 146-147 D 2
Hsieh-ma-ho = Xiemahe 146-147 C 6
Hsien-chü = Xianju 146-147 H 7
Hsien-chung = Xianzhong 146-147 DE 7
Hsien-fêng = Xianfeng 146-147 B 7
Hsien-hsia Ling = Xiangxia Ling 146-147 G 7
Hsien-hs'ien = Xian Xian 142-143 M 4
Hsien-ning = Xianning 146-147 E 7
Hsien-yang = Xianyang 142-143 K 5
Hsien-yu = Xianyou 146-147 G 9
Hsi-fei Ho = Xifei He 146-147 EF 5
Hsi-fêng-k'ou = Xifengkou 144-145 B 2
Hsi-hsien = She Xian 142-143 M 5-6
Hsi-hsien = Xi Xian [TJ, Henan] 146-147 E 5
Hsi-hsien = Xi Xian [TJ, Shanxi] 142-143 L 4
Hsi-hu = Wusu 142-143 EF 3
Hsi-hua-shih = Xihua 146-147 E 5
Hsi-liao Ho = Xar Moron He 142-143 MN 3
Hsilo Chi 146-147 H 10
Hsin, Nam — 141 F 5
Hsin-an = Xin'an 146-147 F 8
Hsinbaungwè 141 D 6
Hsin-ch'ang = Xinchang 146-147 H 7
Hsin-chao = Xinzhao 146-147 A 2
Hsincheng 146-147 HJ 9
Hsin-ch'êng = Xincheng 146-147 EF 2
Hsin-chêng = Xinzheng 146-147 DE 4
Hsin Chiang = Xin Jiang 146-147 F 7
Hsin-chiang = Xinjiang Uygur Zizhiqu 142-143 D-F 3
Hsin-ch'iang = Xinqiang 146-147 D 7
Hsin-chou = Xinzhou 146-147 E 6
Hsinchu 142-143 N 6-7
Hsin-ch'üan = Xinquan 146-147 F 9
Hsindau [BUR, Magwe Taing] 141 D 5
Hsindau [BUR, Mandale Taing] 141 E 4
Hsin-fêng = Xinfeng [TJ, Guangdong] 146-147 E 9
Hsin-fêng = Xinfeng [TJ, Jiangxi] 146-147 E 9
Hsingaleinganti 141 D 3
Hsing-an = Xing'an 146-147 C 9
Hsingaung 141 CD 6
Hsing-ch'êng = Xingcheng 144-145 C 2
Hsing-hsien = Xing Xian 146-147 C 2
Hsing-hua = Xinghua 146-147 GH 5
Hsing-hua Wan = Xinghua Wan 146-147 G 9
Hsing-jên = Xingren 142-143 K 6
Hsing-kuo = Xingguo 146-147 E 8
Hsing-ning = Xingning 142-143 M 7
Hsing-p'ing = Xingping 146-147 B 4
Hsing-shan = Xingshan 146-147 C 6
Hsing-t'ang = Xingtang 146-147 E 2
Hsing-t'ian = Xingtian 146-147 G 8
Hsing-tzū = Xingzi 146-147 F 7
Hsingya 141 C 6
Hsin-hai-lien = Haizhou 142-143 M 5
Hsin-ho = Xinhe [TJ, Hebei] 146-147 E 3
Hsin-ho = Xinhe [TJ, Shandong] 146-147 G 3
Hsin-hsiang = Xinxiang 142-143 LM 4
Hsin-hsien = Shen Xian 146-147 E 2
Hsin-hsien = Xin Xian [TJ, Henan] 146-147 E 6
Hsin-hsien = Xin Xian [TJ, Shanxi] 146-147 D 2
Hsin-hsing = Xinxing 146-147 D 10
Hsinhua 146-147 H 10
Hsin-hua = Xinhua 142-143 L 6
Hsin-hui = Xinhui 146-147 D 10
Hsin-i = Xinyi 146-147 C 10
Hsi-ning = Xining 142-143 J 4
Hsi-ning = Yangyuan 146-147 E 1
Hsin-kan = Xingan 146-147 E 8
Hsin-kao Shan = Yu Shan 142-143 N 7
Hsinking = Changchun 142-143 NO 3
Hsin-liao Ho = Xiliao He 142-143 N 3
Hsin-li-t'un = Xinlitun 144-145 CD 1-2
Hsin-lo = Xinle 142-143 LM 4
Hsin-min = Xinmin 144-145 D 1-2
Hsinnamaung Taung 141 DE 6
Hsin-ning = Xinning 146-147 C 8
Hsin-pin = Xinbin 144-145 E 2
Hsin-t'ai = Xintai 146-147 FG 4
Hsin-t'ien = Xintian 146-147 CD 9
Hsin-ts'ai = Xincai 142-143 LM 5
Hsin-tu = Xindu 142-143 L 7
Hsin-yang = Xinyang 142-143 LM 5
Hsin-yeh = Xinye 146-147 D 5
Hsinying 146-147 H 10
Hsin-yü = Xinyi 146-147 C 10
Hsin-yü = Xinyu 146-147 E 8
Hsioa-fêng = Xiaofeng 146-147 G 6
Hsipaw = Thibaw 141 E 4
Hsi-p'ing = Xiping [TJ ↓ Luohe] 146-147 DE 5
Hsi-p'ing = Xiping [TJ ↖ Xichuan] 146-147 C 5
Hsi-shui = Xishui [TJ, place] 146-147 E 6
Hsi Shui = Xi Shui [TJ, river] 146-147 E 6
Hsi-ta-ch'uan = Xidachuan 144-145 FG 2
Hsi-tsang = Tsang 138-139 LM 3
Hsi-t'uan = Dafeng 146-147 H 5
Hsiu-i = Xuyi 146-147 G 5
Hsiung-êrh Shan = Xiong'er Shan 146-147 C 5-D 4
Hsiu-ning = Xiuning 146-147 FG 7
Hsiu-shan = Xiushan 146-147 B 7
Hsiu Shui = Xiushui 146-147 E 7
Hsi-wu = Xiuwu 146-147 D 4
Hsi-yang = Xiyang [TJ, Fujian] 146-147 F 9
Hsi-yang = Xiyang [TJ, Shanxi] 146-147 D 3
Hsüan-ên = Xuan'en 146-147 B 6-7
Hsüan-hua = Xuanhua 142-143 LM 3
Hsüan-wei = Xuanwei 142-143 J 6
Hsuchang = Xuchang 142-143 L 5
Hsü-chou = Xuzhou 142-143 M 5
Hsueh Shan 146-147 H 9
Hsümbārabûm 148-149 C 1
Hsün-ch'êng = Xuancheng 146-147 G 6
Hsün Ho = Xun He 146-147 B 5
Hsün-hua = Xunhua 142-143 J 4
Hsün-wu = Xunwu 146-147 E 9
Hsün-yang = Xunyang 146-147 B 5
Hsü-p'u = Xupu 146-147 C 8
Hsü-shui = Xushui 146-147 E 2
Hsü-wên = Xuwen 146-147 BC 11
Hswindan Kyûnmyā 150-151 AB 7

Htâhônā 141 E 3
Htâlawgyī 141 F 3
Htandabin [BUR, Bawlei Myit] 141 DE 7
Htandabin [BUR, Sittaung Myit] 141 E 6
Htaugaw 141 F 3
Htâwei 148-149 C 4
Htâwei Myit 150-151 B 5
Htawgaw = Htaugaw 141 F 3
Htīgyaing 141 E 4
Htilin 141 D 5
Htilôn 141 E 7
Htinzin 141 D 4
Htônbô 141 D 6
Htûchaung 141 E 6

Hu, Nam — = Nam Ou 150-151 D 2
Hua'an 142-143 M 6
Huab 172 B 6
Huabu 146-147 G 7
Huacachina 96-97 CD 9
Huacaña 96-97 DE 9
Huacana, La — 86-87 JK 8
Huachacalla 104-105 BC 6
Huachamacari, Cerro — 94-95 HJ 6
Huachi [BOL] 104-105 E 4
Huachi [PE] 92-93 D 5
Huachi [TJ] 146-147 AB 3
Huachi, Lago — 104-105 E 4
Huachis 96-97 D 6
Huacho 92-93 D 7
Huachos 96-97 D 8
Huaco 106-107 C 3
Huacrachuco 92-93 D 6
Huafou = Huabu 146-147 G 7
Huagaruancha 92-93 DE 7
Hua Hin 150-151 B 6
Hua-hsien = Hua Xian [TJ, Guangdong] 146-147 D 10
Hua-hsien = Hua Xian [TJ, Henan] 142-143 LM 4
Hua-hsien = Hua Xian [TJ, Shaanxi] 146-147 BC 4
Huahua, Río — 88-89 DE 7
Huaiá-Miço, Rio — 98-99 M 10
Huai'an 142-143 MN 5
Huaibei 146-147 F 4-5
Huaibin 146-147 E 5
Huai-chi = Huaiji 142-143 L 7
Huaide 142-143 NO 3
Huaidian = Shenqiu 146-147 E 5
Huai He 142-143 M 5
Huaihua 146-147 B 8
Huai-jên = Huairen 146-147 D 2
Huaiji 142-143 L 7
Huai-jou = Huairou 146-147 F 1
Huainan 142-143 M 5
Huaining = Anqing 142-143 M 5
Huairen 146-147 D 2
Huairou 146-147 F 1
Huai Samran 150-151 E 5
Huai Thap Than 150-151 D 5
Huaitiquina, Portezuelo de — 104-105 C 8
Huaiyang 146-147 E 5
Huaiyin 142-143 M 5
Huai-yin = Qingjiang 142-143 M 5
Huai Yot 150-151 B 9
Huaiyuan 146-147 F 5
Huai-yüan = Hengshan 146-147 B 3
Huaiyu Shan 146-147 F 7
Huajuapan de León 86-87 LM 9
Huakhong = Houakhong 150-151 C 2
Hualalai 78-79 e 3
Hualañe 106-107 B 5
Hualfin 104-105 C 10
Hualian = Hualien 142-143 N 7
Hualien 142-143 N 7
Huallabamba, Río — 96-97 C 5
Huallaga, Río — 92-93 D 6
Huallanca 92-93 D 6
Hualpai Indian Reservation 74-75 G 5
Hualpai Mountains 74-75 G 5
Huamachuco [PE ↖ Trujillo] 96-97 B 5
Huamachuco [PE ↗ Trujillo] 96-97 BC 5
Huamantia 86-87 M 8
Huambo [Angola, administrative unit] 172 C 4
Huambo [Angola, place] 172 C 4
Huamparâ 96-97 C 8
Huamuco, Cadena de — 96-97 C 6
Huamuni 104-105 C 6
Hu'a Mu'o'ng 148-149 D 2-3
Huanay 104-105 BC 4
Huancabamba 92-93 CD 6
Huancache, Sierra — 108-109 DE 4
Huancane [BOL] 104-105 C 6
Huancané [PE] 92-93 F 8
Huancapi 96-97 D 8
Huancapón 96-97 C 7
Huancarama 96-97 E 8
Huanca Sancos 96-97 D 8
Huancavelica [PE, administrative unit] 96-97 D 8
Huancavelica [PE, place] 92-93 DE 7
Huancayo 92-93 DE 7
Huanchaca 104-105 C 7
Huanchaca, Cerro — 104-105 C 7
Huanchaca, Serranía de — 92-93 G 7
Huan Chiang = Huan Jiang 146-147 A 3
Huanchillas 106-107 F 4
Huang'an = Hong'an 146-147 E 6
Huangbai 144-145 F 2
Huangbei = Huangpi 146-147 E 6
Huang-chou = Huanggang 146-147 E 6
Huangchuan 146-147 E 5
Huanggang 146-147 E 6
Huanggang = Raoping 146-147 F 10
Huang He 142-143 L 4
Huang He = Chatan gol 142-143 K 3
Huang He = Ma Chhu 142-143 J 4
Huanghe Kou 146-147 G 2
Huangheyan 142-143 H 5
Huang Ho = Chatan gol 142-143 K 3
Huang Ho = Huang He 142-143 L 4
Huang Ho = Ma Chhu 142-143 J 4
Huang-ho-yen = Huangheyan 142-143 H 5
Huang-hsien = Huang Xian 142-143 MN 4
Huanghua 146-147 F 2
Huanghuadian 144-145 D 2
Huang-hua-tien = Huanghuadian 144-145 D 2
Huangji = Huangqi 146-147 GH 8
Huang-kang = Huanggang 146-147 E 6
Huang-kang = Raoping 146-147 F 10
Huanglaomen 146-147 E 7
Huangling 146-147 B 4
Huangliu 150-151 G 3
Huanglong 146-147 BC 4
Huanglongtan 146-147 C 5
Huanglongzhen = Huanglongtan 146-147 C 5
Huanglujiao 152-153 KL 2
Huang-lung = Huanglong 146-147 BC 4
Huang-lung-chên = Huanglongtan 146-147 C 5
Huangmao Jian 146-147 G 8
Huangmei 146-147 EF 6
Huangnan Zangzu Zizhizhou 142-143 J 4-5
Huangpi 146-147 E 6
Huangqi 146-147 GH 8
Huangshahe 146-147 C 8
Huang-sha-ho = Huangshahe 146-147 C 8
Huang Shan 146-147 F 7-G 6
Huangshi 142-143 LM 5
Huangshijiang = Huangshi 142-143 LM 5
Huang Shui = Huang He 146-147 E 5-6
Huangsi, Beijing- 155 II b 2
Huangtang Hu 146-147 E 6-7
Huang-tang Hu = Huangtang Hu 146-147 E 6-7
Huangtugang, Beijing- 155 II ab 2
Huang-t'u-liang-tzû = Huangtuliangzi 144-145 B 2
Huangtuliangzi 144-145 B 2
Huangtuzhai = Yangqu 146-147 D 2
Huanguelén 111 D 5
Huang Xian 142-143 MN 4
Huangxian = Xinhuang 146-147 B 8
Huangyan 146-147 H 7
Huangyang = Huangyangsi 146-147 C 8
Huangyangsi 146-147 C 8
Huangyao Shan = Shengsi Liedao 146-147 J 6
Huang-yen = Huangyan 146-147 H 7
Huangyuan = Thangkar 142-143 J 4
Huani, Laguna — 88-89 E 7
Huan-jên = Huanren 144-145 E 2
Huan Jiang 146-147 A 3
Huanren 144-145 E 2
Huanshan = Yuhuan 146-147 H 7
Huan Shan = Yuhuan Dao 146-147 H 7
Huanta 92-93 E 7
Huantai 146-147 FG 3
Huantan 146-147 D 6
Huantraicó, Sierra de — 106-107 C 6
Huánuco [PE, administrative unit] 96-97 CB 6
Huánuco [PE, place] 92-93 D 6-7
Huanza 96-97 C 7
Huanzo, Cordillera de — 96-97 E 9
Huaphong = Houaphan 150-151 DE 2
Huapi, Montañas de — 88-89 D 8
Huara 111 BC 1-2
Huaral 96-97 C 7
Huaráz 92-93 D 6
Huari 96-97 D 7
Huaribamba 96-97 D 8
Huarmaca 96-97 B 4
Huarmey 92-93 D 7
Huarmey, Río — 96-97 B 7-C 6
Huarpes, Los — 106-107 D 5
Huasaga 96-97 C 3
Huasaga, Río — 96-97 C 3
Hua Sai 150-151 C 8
Huascaran = Nevado Huascaran 92-93 D 6
Huascha 106-107 E 3
Huasco 111 B 3
Huasco, Río — 106-107 B 2
Huasco, Salar de — 104-105 B 7
Hua Shan 142-143 L 5
Huashi 146-147 D 8
Huata 96-97 BC 6
Huatabampo 64-65 DE 6
Huatunas, Lagunas — 104-105 C 3
Huauchinango 64-65 G 7
Huaunta, Laguna — 88-89 E 8
Huaura, Río — 96-97 C 7
Hua Xian [TJ, Guangdong] 146-147 D 10
Hua Xian [TJ, Henan] 142-143 LM 4
Hua Xian [TJ, Shaanxi] 146-147 BC 4
Hu'a Xiêng 150-151 E 3
Huayasa 96-97 FG 10
Huayhuash, Cordillera — 96-97 C 7
Huayin 146-147 C 4
Huayllilas 96-97 C 6
Huayllay 96-97 C 7
Huayuan [TJ, Hubei] 146-147 E 6
Huayuan [TJ, Hunan] 146-147 B 7
Huayuri, Pampa de — 96-97 D 9
Ḩubâra, Wâdî — = Wādī al-Asyūṭī 173 B 4
Hubbaḷi = Hubli 134-135 M 7
Hubbard, IA 70-71 D 4
Hubbard, TX 76-77 F 7
Hubbard, Mount — 56-57 J 5
Hubbard Lake 70-71 HJ 3
Hubei 142-143 KL 5
Hubert 60 D 2
Hubli 134-135 M 7
Hucal 106-107 EF 6
Hucal, Valle de — 106-107 E 6
Huch'ang 144-145 F 2
Hu-chou = Wuxing 142-143 MN 5
Huchuento, Cerro — 64-65 E 7
Ḩudaybû = Ṭamrīdah 134-135 GH 8
Ḩudaydah, Al- 134-135 E 8
Ḩuḍayn, Wādī — 173 D 6
Huddersfield 119 F 5
Huddle Park 170 V b 1
Huddur Hadama 172 H 1
Hudiksvall 116-117 G 7
Hudnah, Ash-Shaṭṭ al- 164-165 EF 1
Hudnah, Jibal al- 166-167 J 1-2
Hudnah, Sahl al- 166-167 J 2
Hudson 62 CD 2
Hudson, CO 68-69 D 5
Hudson, MI 70-71 H 5
Hudson, NM 76-77 C 5
Hudson, NY 72-73 JK 3
Hudson, WI 70-71 D 3
Hudson, Cerro — 111 B 7
Hudson Bay [CDN, bay] 56-57 S-U 5-6
Hudson Bay [CDN, place] 61 GH 4
Hudson Canyon 72-73 KL 5
Hudson Falls, NY 72-73 K 3
Hudson Hope 60 G 1
Hudson Mountains 53 B 27
Hudson River 64-65 M 3
Hudson Strait 56-57 WX 5
Hudwin Lake 62 B 1
Huê 148-149 E 3
Huechucuicui, Punta — 108-109 B 3
Huechulafquén, Lago — 108-109 D 2
Hueco Mountains 76-77 AB 7
Huecu, El — 106-107 B 6
Huedin 122-123 K 2
Huehuetenango 86-87 P 10
Huei Si = Ban Huei Sai 150-151 C 2
Huejúcar 86-87 J 6
Huejuquilla el Alto 86-87 HJ 6
Huejutla 86-87 KL 6-7
Huelva 120-121 D 10
Huentelauquén 106-107 AB 3
Huequi, Península — 108-109 C 4
Huércal-Overa 120-121 FG 10
Huerfano River 68-69 D 7
Huerta, La — 106-107 AB 4
Huerta, Sierra de la — 106-107 D 3
Huesca 120-121 G 7
Huéscar 120-121 F 10
Hueso, Sierra del — 76-77 B 7
Huetamo de Núñez 86-87 K 8
Huey P. Long Bridge 85 I a 2
Ḩufrat an-Naḩās 164-165 JK 7
Hufūf, Al- 134-135 FG 5
Huggins Island 58-59 K 4
Hughenden 158-159 H 4
Hughes, AK 58-59 K 3
Hughes, AR 78-79 D 3
Hughes Airport 83 III b 2
Hugli = Hooghly 138-139 LM 7
Hugo, CO 68-69 E 6
Hugo, OK 76-77 G 5-6
Hugoton, KS 76-77 D 4
Huguan 146-147 D 3
Huhehaote 142-143 L 3
Huhsien = Hu Xian 146-147 B 4
Hui'an 146-147 G 9
Huiarau Range 161 G 4
Huibplato 172 C 7
Huichang 146-147 E 9
Hui-chi Ho = Huiji He 146-147 E 4
Huich'ŏn 142-143 O 3
Hui-chou = She Xian 142-143 M 5-6
Huidong 146-147 E 10
Huiji He 146-147 E 4
Huila [Angola, administrative unit] 172 BC 4
Huila [Angola, place] 172 B 5
Huila [CO] 94-95 D 6
Huila, Nevado del — 92-93 D 4
Huilai 146-147 F 10
Huiling Shan = Hailing Dao 146-147 CD 11
Huillapima 104-105 CD 11
Huilong = Huilongsi 146-147 C 8
Huilongsi 146-147 C 8
Huimbayoc 96-97 D 5
Huimin 146-147 F 3
Huinan 142-143 O 3
Huinca Renancó 106-107 EF 5
Huinganco 106-107 B 6

uintil 106-107 B 3
uipulco, Tlalpan- 91 I c 3
uiqi Shan = Guiji Shan
146-147 H 7
uitong 146-147 B 8
uitongqiao 141 F 3
ui-tsê = Huize 142-143 J 6
uittinen 116-117 K 7
ui-t'ung = Huitong 146-147 B 8
ui Xian 142-143 JK 5
uixquilucan de Degollado 91 I a 2
uixtla 64-65 H 8
uiyang 142-143 LM 7
uize 142-143 J 6
uizhongsi = Beijing-Datun
155 II b 2
uizingen 128 II a 2
ujūrābād = Huzūrābād 140 D 1
ujūrnagara = Huzūrnagar
140 DE 2
ukayyim, Bi'r al- 164-165 J 2
ūker, Bīr — = Bi'r Hooker 173 B 2
ukeri 140 B 2
ukkēri = Hukeri 140 B 2
ukou [RC] 146-147 H 9
ukou [TJ] 146-147 F 7
ūksan-chedo 144-145 E 5
ūksan-jedo = Hūksan-chedo
144-145 E 5
Hu-kuan = Huguan 146-147 D 3
Hukui = Fukui 142-143 Q 4
Hukuntsi 172 D 6
Hukusima = Fukushima
142-143 R 4
Hulah Lake 76-77 F 4
Hulan 142-143 O 2
Hulayfā' 134-135 E 5
Hulett, WY 68-69 D 3
Hulha Negra 106-107 L 3
Huli 140 B 3
Hull, IL 70-71 E 6
Hull, MA 84 I c 3
Hull, ND 68-69 F 2-3
Hull [CDN] 56-57 V 8
Hull [Kiribati] 208 J 3
Hull, Kingston upon — 119 FG 5
Hull Mountain 74-75 B 3
Hulu 148-149 HJ 6
Huludao 144-145 C 2
Hulu He 146-147 B 3-4
Hu-lu Ho = Hulu He 146-147 B 3-4
Hulun = Hailar 142-143 M 2
Hulun Nur 142-143 M 2
Hulun nuur 142-143 M 2
Hu-lu-tao = Huludao 144-145 C 2
Hulwān 164-165 L 3
Huma 142-143 O 1
Humacao 88-89 N 6-O 5
Humadu 176 a 2
Hu-ma-êrh Ho = Huma He
142-143 NO 1
Huma He 142-143 NO 1
Humahuaca 111 C 2
Humaitá [BR] 92-93 G 6
Humaitá [PY] 102-103 C 7
Humansdorp 172 DE 8
Ḥūmat as-Sūq 166-167 M 3
Ḥumayḍah, Al- 173 D 3
Humaym 134-135 GH 6
Ḥumaymah, Bi'r — 136-137 HJ 5
Humbe 172 B 5
Humber 119 G 5
Humberto de Campos 92-93 L 5
Humble, TX 76-77 G 7-8
Humboldt, AZ 74-75 GH 5
Humboldt, IA 70-71 C 4
Humboldt, NE 70-71 BC 5
Humboldt, NV 66-67 D 5
Humboldt, SD 68-69 H 4
Humboldt, TN 78-79 E 3
Humboldt [CDN] 56-57 PQ 7
Humboldt [RA] 106-107 G 3
Humboldt, Hotel — 91 II b 1
Humboldt, Mount — 158-159 N 4
Humboldt, Planetario — 91 II c 2
Humboldt Bay 66-67 A 5
Humboldt Gletscher 56-57 Y 2
Humboldthain 130 III b 1
Humboldtkette 142-143 H 4
Humboldt Park 83 II a 1
Humboldt Range 66-67 D 5
Humboldt River 64-65 C 3
Humboldt River, North Fork —
66-67 F 5
Humboldt Salt Marsh 74-75 DE 3
Humboldt-Universität 130 III b 1
Humedad, Isla — 64-65 a 2
Humelgem 128 II b 1
Humenli = Taiping 146-147 D 10
Humenné 118 KL 4
Hůmera 113 III a 2
Hume Reservoir 158-159 J 7
Humeston, IA 70-71 D 5
Humīr = Khumīr 166-167 L 1
Hummelsbüttel, Hamburg- 130 I b 1
Humos, Cabo — 106-107 A 5
Humos, Isla — 108-109 BC 5
Humpata 172 B 5
Humphrey, ID 66-67 GH 3
Humphrey, NE 68-69 H 5
Humphreys, Mount — 74-75 D 4
Humphreys Peak 64-65 D 4
Humptulips, WA 66-67 B 2
Ḥumrah, Al- 164-165 L 6
Humrat al-Baṭin 136-137 KL 8
Hums, Al- = Al-Khums
164-165 GH 2
Humurgān 136-137 J 2
Hūn 164-165 H 3
Hun, Mu'o'ng — = Mu'o'ng Houn
150-151 C 2
Húnaflói 116-117 c 1-2
Hunagund = Hungund 140 C 2
Hunan 142-143 L 6
Hunan = Runan 146-147 E 5
Huncal 106-107 B 6
Hun Chiang = Hun Jiang
144-145 E 2
Hunchun 142-143 P 3
Hūṇḍēsh 138-139 G 2
Hunedoara 122-123 K 3
Hungarian Plain = Alföld
118 J 5-L 4
Hungary 118 H-K 5
Hung-chiang = Hongjiang
142-143 KL 6
Hungerford [AUS] 160 G 2
Hunghai Wan = Honghai Wan
146-147 E 10
Hung Ho = Hong He [TJ, Henan]
146-147 E 5
Hung Ho = Hong He [TJ, Inner
Mongolian Aut. Reg.]
146-147 CD 1
Hung Ho = Hong He [TJ, Yunnan]
142-143 J 7
Hu'ng Hoa 150-151 E 2
Hung Hom, Kowloon- 155 I b 2
Hung Hu = Honghu 142-143 L 6
Hungkiang = Hongjiang
142-143 KL 6
Hung-lai = Honglai 146-147 G 9
Hung-liu Ho = Hongliu He
146-147 B 3
Hŭngnam 142-143 O 4
Hungry = Lima Village, AK
58-59 K 6
Hungry Horse Reservoir 66-67 G 1
Hung-shan = Maocifan
146-147 D 6
Hung-shui Ho = Hongshui He
142-143 K 6-7
Hung-tsê Hu = Hongze Hu
146-147 G 5
Hung-tung = Hongtong
146-147 C 3
Hungund 140 C 2
Hu'ng Yên 150-151 EF 2
Hun He 144-145 D 2
Hun Ho = Hun He 144-145 D 2
Hunissoutpan 174-175 C 6
Hunjani 172 F 5
Hunjiang [TJ, place] 144-145 F 2
Hun Jiang [TJ, river] 144-145 E 2
Ḥunkurāb, Rā's — 173 D 5
Hunsberge 174-175 B 4
Hunsrück 118 C 3-4
Hunsūr 140 C 4
Hunsūru = Hunsūr 140 C 4
Hunte 118 D 2
Hunter, KS 68-69 G 6
Hunter, ND 68-69 H 2
Hunter, Île — 158-159 O 4
Hunter Au 141 C 6
Hunter Island 60 C 4
Hunter Island Park 70-71 E 1
Hunter Islands 158-159 H 8
Hunter River 160 K 4
Hunters, WA 66-67 DE 1
Hunter's Bay = Hunter Au 141 C 6
Hunters Creek Village, TX 85 III bc 2
Hunters Hill, Sydney- 161 I ab 2
Hunters Point 83 I b 2
Hunting Bayou 85 III c 1-2
Huntingburg, IN 70-71 G 6
Huntingdon 119 F 5
Huntingdon, PA 72-73 GH 4
Huntingdon, TN 78-79 E 2-3
Huntingdon [CDN] 72-73 JK 2
Hunting Island 80-81 F 4
Hunting Park 84 III c 1
Huntington, IN 70-71 H 5
Huntington, OR 66-67 E 3
Huntington, TX 76-77 G 7
Huntington, UT 74-75 H 3
Huntington, WV 64-65 K 4
Huntington, Houston-, TX 85 III b 1
Huntington Beach, CA 74-75 DE 6
Huntington Park, CA 83 III c 2
Huntington Woods, MI 84 II ab 2
Huntley, MT 68-69 B 3
Hunt Mountain 68-69 BC 3
Hunts Inlet 60 B 2
Huntsville 72-73 G 2
Huntsville, AL 64-65 J 5
Huntsville, AR 78-79 C 2
Huntsville, MO 70-71 D 6
Huntsville, TX 64-65 GH 5
Hu'n Xiêng Hu'ng = Mu'o'ng Hu'n
Xiêng Hu'ng 150-151 D 2
Hun Yeang 154 III b 1
Hunyuan 146-147 D 2
Hunyung 144-145 H 1
Hunzā = Bāltit 134-135 L 3
Huo-ch'iu = Huoqiu 146-147 F 5
Huohou Shan 146-147 DE 10
Huo-hsien = Huo Xian
146-147 CD 3
Hu'o'ng Khê 150-151 E 3
Huon Gulf 148-149 N 8
Huon Peninsula 148-149 N 8
Huoqiu 146-147 F 5
Huoshan 146-147 F 6
Huo Shan = Huo Xian
146-147 CD 3
Huoshao Dao = Huoshao Tao
146-147 H 10
Huoshao Tao 146-147 H 10
Huo Xian 146-147 CD 3
Hupeh = Hubei 142-143 KL 5
Hura 138-139 L 6
Hūrānd 136-137 M 3
Huraybah, Al- 134-135 F 7
Huraymis, Qārat — 136-137 B 7
Hurd, Cape — 72-73 EF 2
Hurdiyo 164-165 c 1
Hure Qi 142-143 N 3
Huribgah = Khuribgah 164-165 C 2
Huritu Huasi 106-107 F 1
Hurjādah = Al-Ghardaqah
164-165 L 3
Hurkett 70-71 F 1
Hurley, MS 78-79 E 5
Hurley, NM 74-75 J 6
Hurley, SD 68-69 H 4
Hurley, WI 70-71 E 2
Hurlingham, Morón- 110 III b 1
Hurma çayı 136-137 G 3
Huron, CA 74-75 C 4
Huron, OH 72-73 E 4
Huron, SD 64-65 G 3
Huron, Lake — 64-65 K 2-3
Huron Mountains 70-71 FG 2
Hurricane, UT 74-75 G 4
Hurstville, Sydney- 161 I a 2
Hurtsboro, AL 78-79 G 4
Hurunui River 161 E 6
Hurzuf = Gurzuf 126-127 G 4
Húsavík 116-117 e 1
Ḥuṣayḥiṣah, Al- 164-165 L 6
Ḥusaymah, Al- 164-165 D 1
Ḥusayniyah, Al- 134-135 EF 7
Hüseyinli 136-137 EF 2
Hushuguan = Xuguanzhen
146-147 H 6
Hu-shu-kuan = Xuguanzhen
146-147 H 6
Hushyārpur = Hoshiārpur
138-139 EF 2
Huşi 122-123 MN 2
Huskisson 160 K 5
Huskvarna 116-117 F 9
Huslia, AK 58-59 J 4
Huslia River 58-59 J 3
Hussar 61 B 5
Hussein Dei 170 I b 2
Husum 118 D 1
Hutan Melintang 150-151 C 11
Hutanopan 148-149 CD 6
Hutchinson, KS 64-65 G 4
Hutchinson, MN 70-71 C 3
Hutchinsons Island 80-81 cd 3
Hutch Mountain 74-75 H 5
Hütteldorf, Wien- 113 I b 2
Huttig, AR 78-79 CD 4
Hut-t'o Ho = Hutuo He
146-147 D 2
Hutton 60 G 3
Hutuo He 146-147 D 2
Huty = Guty 126-127 G 1
Huundz 174-175 C 4
Huutokoski 116-117 M 6
Hüvek 136-137 H 4
Huwan = Xuwan 146-147 F 8
Huwār, Wādī — 164-165 K 5
Huwei 146-147 H 10
Hu Xian 146-147 B 4
Huxley, Mount — 58-59 R 6
Huy 120-121 K 3
Huyamampa 106-107 EF 1
Hüyük 136-137 D 4
Huzgan 136-137 MN 7
Huzhou = Wuxing 142-143 MN 5
Huzi san = Fuji-san 142-143 Q 4-5
Huzul, Al- 136-137 K 8
Huzūrābād 140 D 1
Huzūrnagar 140 DE 2
Hvalsbakur 116-117 g 2
Hval Sund 56-57 WX 2
Hvammsfjördhur 116-117 bc 2
Hvammstangi 116-117 c 2
Hvar 122-123 G 4
Hveragerdhi 116-117 c 2
Hvitá [IS, Árnes] 116-117 c 2
Hvitá [IS, Mýra] 116-117 c 2
Hvitárvatn 116-117 d 2
Hvolsvöllur 116-117 cd 3
Hwaak-san 144-145 F 3-4
Hwaan = Hua'an 146-147 F 9
Hwach'ŏn 144-145 F 3
Hwach'ŏn-ni 144-145 FG 3
Hwafeng = Hua'an 146-147 F 9
Hwahsien = Hua Xian [TJ,
Guangdong] 146-147 D 10
Hwahsien = Hua Xian [TJ, Shaanxi]
146-147 BC 4
Hwaian = Huai'an 142-143 MN 5
Hwaiyang = Huaiyang 146-147 E 5
Hwaiyuan = Huaiyuan 146-147 F 5
Ḥwaiza, Hōr al- = Hawr al-Ḥawīzah
136-137 M 7
Hwangchwan = Huangchuan
146-147 E 5
Hwange 172 E 5
Hwanggan 144-145 FG 4
Hwanghae-namdo 144-145 E 3-4
Hwanghae-pukto 144-145 EF 3
Hwangho = Huang He 142-143 L 4
Hwanghsien = Huang Xian
142-143 MN 4
Hwangju 144-145 EF 3
Hwangkang = Huanggang
146-147 E 6
Hwangmei = Huangmei
146-147 EF 6
Hwangyen = Huangyan
146-147 H 7
Hwangyuan = Thangkar
142-143 J 4
Hwantai = Huantai 146-147 FG 3
Hwap'yŏng 144-145 F 2
Hwasun 144-145 F 5
Hwayin = Huayin 146-147 C 4
Hwè-An 141 E 6
Hweian = Hui'an 146-147 G 9
Hweichow = She Xian
142-143 M 5-6
Hweilai = Huilai 146-147 F 10
Hweimin = Huimin 146-147 F 3
Hweitseh = Huize 142-143 J 6
Hwèrāō 141 E 6
Hwohsien = Huo Xian
146-147 CD 3
Hwoshan = Huoshan 146-147 F 6
Hyades, Cerro — 108-109 C 6
Hyannis, NE 68-69 F 4-5
Hyattsville, MD 82 II b 1
Hybart, AL 78-79 F 5
Hybla 72-73 H 2
Hydaburg, AK 58-59 w 9
Hyden 158-159 C 6
Hyden, KY 72-73 E 6
Hyde Park, VT 72-73 K 2
Hyde Park [AUS] 161 I b 2
Hyde Park [GB] 129 II b 1-2
Hyde Park, Boston-, MA 84 I b 3
Hyde Park, Chicago-, IL 83 II b 2
Hyde Park, Los Angeles-, CA
83 III c 2
Hyder 60 B 2
Hyder, AZ 74-75 G 6
Hyderābād 134-135 M 7
Hyderabad = Ḥaidarābād
134-135 KL 5
Hydra 122-123 K 7
Hydraulic 60 FG 3
Hydro, OK 76-77 E 5
Hyères 120-121 L 7
Hyères, Îles d' 120-121 L 7
Hyesanjin 142-143 O 3
Hyland Post 58-59 XY 8
Hyltebruk 116-117 E 9
Hyndman, PA 72-73 G 5
Hyndman Peak 66-67 FG 4
Hyōgo 144-145 K 5
Hyŏnch'on 144-145 G 2
Hyŏpch'ŏn = Hapch'ŏn
144-145 FG 5
Hypsárion 122-123 L 5
Hyrra-Banda 164-165 J 7
Hyrum, UT 66-67 H 5
Hyrynsalmi 116-117 N 5
Hysham, MT 68-69 C 2
Hyūga 144-145 H 6
Hyvinkää 116-117 L 7
Ḥzimī, Wādī al- = Wādī al-Ḥazimī
136-137 J 6

I

Iabès, Erg — = 'Irq Yābis
166-167 EF 6
Iaciara 100-101 A 8
Iaco, Rio — 92-93 EF 7
Iaçu 92-93 L 7
Ialomița 122-123 M 3
Ialu = Yalu Jiang 144-145 EF 2
Iapi 100-101 D 8
Iapó, Rio — 102-103 G 6
Iapu 102-103 L 3
Iara [BR] 100-101 E 4
Iarauarune, Serra — 98-99 HJ 4
Iaripo 98-99 L 4
Iași 122-123 M 2
Iati 100-101 F 5
Iauaretê 98-99 D 4
Iaundé = Yaoundé 164-165 G 8
Iavello = Yabēlo 164-165 M 7-8
Ib 138-139 JK 6
Iba [RP] 148-149 G 3
Iba = Ib 138-139 JK 6
Ibadan 164-165 E 7
Ibagué 92-93 DE 4
Ibahos Island 146-147 H 11
Ibaiti 102-103 G 5
Ibáñez 106-107 H 6
Ibar 122-123 J 4
Ibaraki 144-145 N 4
Ibare 106-107 K 3
Ibare, Río — 104-105 D 4
Ibarra 92-93 D 4
Ibarreta 111 E 3
Ibb 134-135 E 8
Iberá, Esteros del — 111 E 3
Iberá, Laguna — 106-107 J 2
Iberia [PE, Loreto] 96-97 D 4
Iberia [PE, Madre de Dios] 96-97 G 7
Iberian Basin 50-51 HJ 3
Iberville 72-73 K 2
Iberville, Lac d' 56-57 W 6
Ibese 170 III b 1
Ibi [WAN] 164-165 F 7
Ibiá 92-93 J 8
Ibiaçucê 100-101 CD 8
Ibiagui 100-101 BC 7
Ibiaí 102-103 K 2
Ibiajara 100-101 C 7
Ibiapina 100-101 D 2
Ibiaporã 100-101 D 7
Ibib, Wādī — 173 D 6
Ibibobo 104-105 E 7
Ibicaraí 92-93 M 7-8
Ibicuã 100-101 E 3
Ibicuí [BR, Bahia] 100-101 E 8
Ibicuí [BR, Rio Grande do Sul]
106-107 J 2
Ibicuí, Rio — 111 E 3
Ibicuy 111 E 4
Ibimirim 100-101 F 5
Ibipeba 100-101 C 6
Ibipetuba 92-93 KL 7
Ibipitanga 100-101 C 7
Ibiquera 100-101 D 7
Ibirá 102-103 H 4
Ibiraci 102-103 J 4
Ibiraçu 100-101 D 10
Ibirajuba 100-101 FG 5
Ibirama 102-103 H 7
Ibirapitanga 100-101 E 8
Ibirapuã 100-101 D 3
Ibirapuera, São Paulo- 110 II ab 2
Ibirapuitã, Rio — 106-107 K 2-3
Ibirarema 102-103 GH 5
Ibirataia 100-101 E 7-8
Ibirizu, Río — 104-105 D 5
Ibirocaí 106-107 J 2
Ibirubá 106-107 L 2
Ibitanhém 100-101 DE 9
Ibitiara 100-101 C 7
Ibitilá 100-101 D 6
Ibitinga 102-103 H 4
Ibitira 100-101 CD 8
Ibiuna 102-103 J 5
Ibiza [E, island] 120-121 H 9
Ibiza [E, place] 120-121 H 9
Ibjili 164-165 F 3
Ibn Hānī, Rā's — 136-137 F 5
Ibn Ṣuqayh, 'Uqlat — 136-137 M 8
Ibo 171 E 6
Ibo = Sassandra 164-165 C 7
Ibotirama 92-93 L 7
'Ibrā 134-135 H 6
İbradı 136-137 D 4
Ibrāhīm, Jabal — 134-135 E 6
Ibrāhīmīyah, Qanāl al- 173 B 3
İbrahimpaşa tepe 154 I b 1
Ibrāhīmpatan 140 D 2
İbrala 136-137 E 4
Ibresi 124-125 Q 6
'Ibrī 134-135 H 6
Ibshawāy 173 B 3
Ibu 148-149 J 6
Ibusuki 144-145 H 7
Ica [PE, administrative unit]
96-97 D 8-9
Ica [PE, place] 92-93 D 7
Iča [SU] 132-133 e 6
Ica = Ambrolauri 126-127 L 5
Içá, Rio — 92-93 F 5
Ica, Tablazo de — 96-97 CD 9
Icabarú 92-93 G 4
Icamaquã, Rio — 106-107 K 2
Içana 92-93 F 4
Içana, Rio — 92-93 F 4
Icaño 106-107 E 2
Icaparra, Barra de — 102-103 J 6
Icapuí 100-101 F 3
Icaraí, Enseada de — 110 I c 2
Icaraima 102-103 F 5
Icatu 92-93 L 5
Icatu, Rio — 100-101 C 6
İçel 136-137 EF 4
İçel = Mersin 134-135 C 3
Iceland 116-117 cd 2
Iceland Basin 114-115 CD 4
Iceland Jan Mayen Ridge
114-115 F 2
İçerenköy, İstanbul- 154 I b 3
Ichāgarh 138-139 K 6
Ichalkaranji 140 B 2
Ichang = Yichang 142-143 L 5
Ichang = Yizhang 146-147 D 9
Ich Bogd uul 142-143 J 3
Ich Cajdamyn nuur 142-143 GH 4
Ichchāpuram 138-139 K 8
Ichchhāgarh = Ichāgarh
138-139 K 6
Ichchhālkaranji 140 AB 2
Ichchhāvar = Ichhāwar 138-139 F 6
Ich Chogosoor 142-143 GH 5
I-ch'êng = Yicheng 146-147 C 4
Icheng = Yizheng 146-147 G 5
Icheu 168-169 G 4
Ichhāwar 138-139 F 6
Ichibusa-yama 144-145 H 6
Ichigualasto 106-107 D 3
Ichihara 144-145 N 5
Ichikawa 144-145 MN 5
Ichikawa-Kōnodai 155 III c 1
Ichikawa-Sugano 155 III c 1
Ichikawa-Wakamiya 155 III c 1
Ichikawa-Yawata 155 III c 1
Ichinohe 144-145 N 2
Ichinomya 144-145 L 5
Ichinoseki 142-143 QR 4
Ichoa, Río — 104-105 D 4
Ich'ŏn [North Korea] 144-145 F 3
Ich'ŏn [ROK] 142-143 O 4
Ichow = Linyi 142-143 M 4
Ichuan = Yichuan [TJ, Henan]
146-147 D 4
Ichuan = Yichuan [TJ, Shaanxi]
146-147 BC 3
Ichun = Yichun [TJ, Heilongjiang]
142-143 O 2
Ichun = Yichun [TJ, Jiangxi]
142-143 LM 6
I-chün = Yijun 146-147 B 4
Ichuña 96-97 F 10
Ičinskaja sopka = Velikaja Ičinskaja
sopka 132-133 e 6
Ička, gora — 124-125 S 8
Ičky = Sovetskij 126-127 G 4
Icla 104-105 D 6
İçme 136-137 H 3
Ičn'a 126-127 F 1
Icó 100-101 E 4
Iconha 102-103 M 4
Icoraci 98-99 O 5
Icorea 94-95 bc 2
Icy Bay 58-59 R 7
Icy Cape 56-57 D 3
Icy Strait 58-59 U 7
Ida 174-175 G 6
Ida, LA 76-77 GH 6
Ida = Kaz dağ 136-137 B 3
Ida, Anou n' = 'Anu an-Na'īdah
166-167 K 6
Ida, Mount — = Ídē Óros
122-123 L 8
Idabel, OK 76-77 G 6
Idad, Qārat al- 136-137 C 8
Ida Grove, IA 70-71 C 4
Idah 164-165 F 7
Idaho 64-65 C 2-D 3
Idaho City, ID 66-67 F 4
Idaho Falls, ID 64-65 D 3
Idalia 174-175 J 4
Idalia, CO 68-69 E 6
Idalou, TX 76-77 D 6
Idanha, OR 66-67 BC 3
Idar-Oberstein 118 C 4
'Idd, Al- 134-135 G 6
'Idd al-Ghanam 164-165 J 6
Iddo, Lagos- 170 III b 2
'Ided, Qâret el — = Qārat al-Idad
136-137 C 8
Idel' 124-125 JK 1
Ídē Óros 122-123 L 8
Iderijn gol 142-143 HJ 2
Idfū 164-165 L 4
Idget, Djebel — = Jabal 'Ikdat
166-167 B 4
'Idhaim, Nahr al- = Shaṭṭ al-'Uzaym
136-137 L 5
Idi 148-149 C 5-6
İdil = Hazak 136-137 J 4
Idiofa 172 C 3
'Idīsāt, El — = Al-'Udaysāt 173 C 5
Iditarod, AK 58-59 H 5
Iditarod River 58-59 H 5
Idjen, Tanah Tinggi — =
Tanahtinggiijen 148-149 r 9-10
Idjerane, Djebel — = Jabal Ijrān
166-167 H 6
Idkū, Buḥayrat — 173 B 2
Idlib 134-135 D 3
Idogaya, Yokohama- 155 III a 3
Idria, CA 74-75 C 4
Idria = Idrija 122-123 J 5
Idrica 124-125 G 5
Idrija 122-123 EF 2
İdris dağı 136-137 E 2
Idrīsīyah, Al- 166-167 H 2
Idrissia, El — = Al-Idrīsīyah
166-167 H 2
Idūgh 166-167 K 1
Idutywa 174-175 H 7
Idylwood, VA 82 II a 2
Idževan 126-127 M 6
Iepê 102-103 G 5
Ieper 120-121 J 3
Ierapetra = Hierápetra 122-123 L 8
Iesi 122-123 E 4
Iesk = Jesk 126-127 J 3
Ifakara 172 G 3
'Ifāl, Wādī al- 173 D 3
Ifalik 148-149 MN 5
Ifanadiana 172 J 6
Ife 164-165 EF 7
I-fêng = Yifeng 146-147 E 7
Ifèrouane 164-165 F 5
Ifetesene = Jabal Tibissah
166-167 J 7
Iffley 158-159 H 3
Iforas, Adrar des — 164-165 E 4-5
Ifrān 166-167 D 3
Igaci 100-101 F 5
Igalula 172 F 3
Igan 152-153 J 4
Igana 168-169 F 4
Iganga 172 F 1
Igangan 168-169 F 4
Iganmu, Lagos- 170 III b 2
Igaporã 100-101 C 7
Igara 100-101 DE 6
Igaraçu 100-101 G 4
Igara Paraná, Río — 94-95 E 8
Igarapava 92-93 K 9
Igarapé-Açu 92-93 K 5
Igarape Grande 100-101 B 3
Igarapé-Mirim 92-93 K 5
Igarité 92-93 L 7
Igarka 132-133 Q 4
Igarra 168-169 G 4
Igarzábal 106-107 F 7
Igatimi 102-103 E 6
Igatpuri 138-139 D 8
Igbobi 170 III b 1
Igbologun 170 III ab 2
Igbo Tako 168-169 G 4
Iğdır 136-137 KL 3
Igharghar, Wed — = Wādī Irhāran
166-167 J 6
Igharm 166-167 B 4
Ighil-Izane = Ghālizān 164-165 E 1
Ighil M'Goun = Ighil M'Gūn
164-165 C 2
Ighil M'Gūn 164-165 C 2
Ighlī 166-167 E 4
Igichuk Hill 58-59 FG 3
Igīdi, Erg — = Ṣaḥrā' al-Igīdi
164-165 CD 3
Igiugig, AK 58-59 JK 7
Iglās 138-139 FG 4
Iglesia [RA] 106-107 C 3
Iglèsias 122-123 C 6
Iglesias, Cerro — 108-109 EF 6
Iglesiente 122-123 C 6
Igli = Ighlī 166-167 E 4
'Igma, Gebel el- = Jabal al-'Ajmah
164-165 L 3
Ignace 70-71 E 1
Ignacio, CA 74-75 B 3
Ignacio, CO 68-69 C 7
Ignalina 124-125 EF 6
Ignatovka 124-125 Q 7
İğneada burnu 136-137 C 2
Igny 129 I b 3
Igo, CA 66-67 B 5
Igodovo 124-125 O 4
Igomo 172 F 3
Igra 124-125 T 5
Igreja, Morro da — 102-103 H 8
Igreja Nova 100-101 F 6
Igrim 132-133 L 5
Igrumaro 171 C 4
Iguá 100-101 D 8
Iguaçu, Parque Nacional do —
102-103 EF 6
Iguaçu, Rio — 111 F 3
Iguaje, Mesas de — 94-95 E 7
Igualada 120-121 H 8
Iguala de la Independencia
64-65 G 8
Iguana, Sierra de la — 76-77 D 9
Iguape 111 G 2
Iguapé, Ponta de — 100-101 EF 2
Iguará, Rio — 100-101 C 3
Iguaraci 100-101 F 4
Iguariaçá, Serra do — 106-107 K 2
Iguatama 102-103 K 4
Iguatemi 102-103 E 5
Iguatemi, Rio — 102-103 E 5
Iguatu 92-93 M 6
Iguazú, Cataratas del — 111 F 3
Iguéla 172 A 2
Igula 171 C 4
Igumale 168-169 GH 4
Igvak, Cape — 58-59 f 1
Ihavandiffulu Atoll 176 a 1
Ihenkari 154 II a 1
Ihing = Yixing 146-147 GH 6
I Ho = Yi He 146-147 G 4
Ihosy 172 J 6
İhsangazi 136-137 E 2
İhsaniye = Eğret 136-137 D 3
Ihsien = Yi Xian [TJ, Anhui]
146-147 F 7
Ihsien = Yi Xian [TJ, Hebei]
146-147 E 2
I-hsien = Yi Xian [TJ, Liaoning]
144-145 C 2
I-hsing = Yixing 146-147 GH 6
Ihtiman 122-123 KL 4
I-huang = Yihuang 146-147 F 8
Ihwang = Yihuang 146-147 F 8
Iida 144-145 L 5
Iida = Suzu 144-145 L 4
Iide-san 144-145 M 4
Iijoki 116-117 LM 5
Iisalmi 116-117 M 6
Iitomi 155 III c 3
Iizuka 144-145 H 6
IJ, Het — 128 I a 1
Ijara 172 H 2
Ijebu Igbo 168-169 FG 4
Ijebu Ode 168-169 FG 4
Ijesa-Tedo 170 III a 2
Ijiri 155 III c 3
Ijjill, Kidyat — 164-165 B 4
Ijrān, Jabal — 166-167 H 6
IJssel 120-121 KL 2
IJsselmeer 120-121 K 2
IJ-tunnel 128 I ab 1
Ijuí 106-107 KL 2
Ijuí, Rio — 106-107 K 2
Ik 124-125 T 6
Ikaalinen 116-117 K 7
Ikanga 171 D 3
Ikaría 122-123 LM 7
Ikatan, AK 58-59 b 2
'Ikdat, Jabal — 166-167 B 4
Ikeda [J, Hokkaidō] 144-145 c 2
Ikeda [J, Shikoku] 144-145 JK 5-6
Ikegami, Tōkyō- 155 III b 2
Ikeja 164-165 E 7
Ikela 172 D 2
Ikelemba 172 C 1
Ikhīl 'm Goûn = Ighil M'Gūn
164-165 C 2
Ikhwān, Gezir el- = Jazā'ir al-Ikhwān
173 D 4
Ikhwān, Jazā'ir al- 173 D 4
Iki 144-145 G 6
Ikindži-Jalama = Jalama
126-127 O 6
Ikire 168-169 G 4
Iki suidō 144-145 GH 6
Ikitsuki-shima 144-145 G 6
İkizdere = Çağrankaya 136-137 J 2
Ikkerre 164-165 F 7
Ikolik, Cape — 58-59 f 1
Ikom 168-169 H 4
Ikoma 172 F 2
Ikonde 171 B 4
Ikonium = Konya 134-135 C 3
Ikopa 172 J 5
Ikorec 126-127 JK 1
Ikorodu 168-169 F 4
Ikot Ekpene 168-169 G 4
Ikoto 171 C 1
Ikoyi, Lagos- 170 III b 2
Ikoyi Island 170 III b 2
Ikoyi Prison 170 III b 2
Ikpikpuk River 56-57 F 3-4
Ikr'anoje 126-127 N 3
Ikša 124-125 L 5
Ikuata 170 III b 2
Ikungi 171 C 4
Ikungu 171 C 4
Ikuno 144-145 K 5
Ikushumbetsu 144-145 bc 2
Ikuta 155 III a 2
Ikutha 171 D 3
Ila 168-169 G 4
Ilabaya 96-97 F 10
Ilagan 148-149 H 3

Ilāhābād = Allahābād 134-135 N 5
Ilak Island 58-59 t 7
Ila La Tortuga 92-93 FG 2
Īlām [IR] 134-135 F 4
Ilam [Nepal] 138-139 L 4
Īlām va Poshtkuh = 2 ◁ 134-135 F 4
Ilan 146-147 H 9
Ilan = Yilan 142-143 OP 2
Ilangali 172 FG 3
Ilanskij 132-133 S 6
Ilaro 164-165 E 7
Ilatane 168-169 G 1
Ilave, Rio — 96-97 G 10
Ilay, Wādī — 173 D 7
Ilayāngudi 140 D 6
Ilchuri Alin = Yilehuli Shan 142-143 NO 1
Île à la Crosse 61 D 3
Île à la Crosse, Lac — 61 E 3
Île Alright 63 F 4
Île Amherst 63 F 4
Île Anvers 53 C 30
Île aux Allumettes 72-73 H 2
Île aux Coudres 63 A 4
Île aux Hérons 82 I b 2
Ilebo 172 D 2
Île Brabant 53 C 30
Île Brion 63 F 4
Île Charcot 53 C 29
Île Chergui = Jazīrat ash-Sharqī 166-167 M 2
Île Chesterfield 172 H 5
Ileckaja Zaščita = Sol'-Ileck 132-133 JK 7
Île Clipperton 64-65 E 9
Île de Corps Mort 63 E 4
Île de Dorval 82 I a 2
Île-de-France 120-121 HJ 4
Île de Groix 120-121 F 5
Île de la Gonâve 64-65 M 8
Île de la Table = Đao Cai Ban 148-149 E 2
Île de la Tortue 64-65 M 7
Île de la Visitation 82 I b 1
Île de Montréal 82 I a 2-b 1
Île de Noirmoutier 120-121 F 5
Île de Ré 120-121 G 5
Île de Sainte Helène 82 I b 1
Île des Chins = Jazā'ir al-Kilāb 166-167 M 1
Île des Singes 170 IV a 1
Île des Sœurs 82 I b 2
Île de Verte 82 I bc 1
Île de Yeu 120-121 F 5
Île du Diable 92-93 J 3
Île du Grand Mécatina 63 G 2
Île du Petit Mécatina 63 G 2
Île du Teléphone 170 IV a 1-2
Île Europa 172 H 6
Île Hunter 158-159 O 4
Île Jésus 82 I a 1
Île Joinville 53 C 31
Ilek [SU, Kurskaja Oblast'] 126-127 G 1
Ilek [SU, Orenburgskaja Oblast' place] 124-125 T 8
Ilek [SU, Orenburgskaja Oblast' river] 124-125 T 8
Ileksa 124-125 L 2
Île Lifou 158-159 N 4
Île Maré 158-159 N 4
Île Marina = Espiritu Santo 158-159 MN 3
Île Matthew 158-159 O 4
Île Mbamou 170 IV b 1
Île Nightingale = Đao Bach Long Vi 150-151 F 2
Île Ouvéa 158-159 N 4
Île Pamanzi-Bé 172 J 4
Île Parisienne 72-73 D 1
Île Plane = Al-Jazīrah 166-167 F 2
Île Plane = Jazīrat al-Maṭrūḥ 166-167 M 1
Île Rachgoun = Jazīrat Rāshqūn 166-167 EF 2
Ileret 171 D 1
Île Royale = Cape Breton Island 56-57 X-Z 8
Île Sainte-Marie = Nosy Boraha 172 K 5
Île Saint-Ignace 70-71 FG 1
Îles Belep 158-159 M 3
Îles Cani = Jazā'ir al-Kilāb 166-167 M 1
Îles Chesterfield 158-159 L 3
Îles de Boucherville 82 I bc 1
Îles de la Galite = Jazā'ir Jaliṭah 166-167 L 1
Îles de la Madeleine 56-57 Y 8
Îles de Los 168-169 B 3
Îles de Pins 158-159 N 4
Îles des Saintes 88-89 PQ 7
Îles du Salut 98-99 MN 2
Îles Glorieuses 172 J 4
Ilesha 164-165 EF 7
Îles Habibas = Juzur al-Ḥabībah 166-167 F 2
Îles Horn 148-149 b 1
Îles Kerkenna = Jazur Qarqannah 164-165 G 2
Îles Kuriate = Jazā'ir Qūryāt 166-167 M 2
Îles Loyauté 158-159 N 4
Îles Marquises 156-157 L 5
Îles Paracels = Quân Đao Tây Sa 148-149 F 3
Îles Saloum 168-169 A 2
Îles Sandja 170 I b 1
Îles Toumotou 156-157 K 5-L 6
Îles Tristao 168-169 B 3
Îles Tuamotu 156-157 K 5-L 6
Îles Tubuai 156-157 K 6
Îles Wallis 148-149 b 1
Ilet' = Krasnogorskij 124-125 R 5
Île Tidra 164-165 A 5
Île Vaté = Efate 158-159 N 3
Île Victoria = Victoria Island 56-57 O-Q 3
'Ilfag = 'Afag 136-137 L 6
Ilford 56-57 RS 6
Ilford, London- 129 II c 1
Ilfracombe 119 D 6
Ilgaz 136-137 E 2
Ilgaz dağlar 136-137 EF 2
Ilgin 136-137 DE 3
Ilha Anajás 98-99 N 5
Ilha Apeuzinho 100-101 B 1
Ilha Aramacá 94-95 c 3
Ilha Bailique 98-99 O 4
Ilhabela 102-103 K 5
Ilha Benguérua 174-175 L 1
Ilha Caçumba 100-101 E 9
Ilha Caravela 168-169 A 3
Ilha Casa de Pedras 110 I c 1
Ilha Caviana 92-93 K 4
Ilha Comprida [BR, Atlantic Ocean] 111 G 2-3
Ilha Comprida [BR, Rio de Janeiro] 110 I b 3
Ilha Comprida [BR, Rio Paraná] 102-103 G 4
Ilha Curuá 98-99 NO 4
Ilha da Alfavaca 110 I b 3
Ilha da Âncora 102-103 M 5
Ilha da Conceição 110 I c 2
Ilha da Feitoria 106-107 LM 3
Ilha da Laguna 98-99 N 5
Ilha da Laje 110 I c 2
Ilha da Pombeba 110 I b 2
Ilha das Canárias 92-93 L 5
Ilha das Cobras 110 I bc 2
Ilha das Couves 102-103 K 5
Ilha das Duas Onças 102-103 F 5
Ilha das Enxadas 110 I bc 2
Ilha da Silva 98-99 F 5
Ilha das Onças 98-99 K 6
Ilha das Palmas 110 I b 3
Ilha das Peças 111 G 3
Ilha da Trindade 92-93 NO 9
Ilha da Vitória 102-103 K 5
Ilha de Ataúro 148-149 J 8
Ilha de Cananeia 102-103 J 6
Ilha de Cotunduba 110 I c 2
Ilha de Formosa 168-169 AB 3
Ilha de Itaparica 100-101 E 7
Ilha de Maracá 92-93 JK 4
Ilha de Marajó 92-93 JK 5
Ilha de Mutuoca 100-101 B 1
Ilha de Orango 164-165 A 6
Ilha de Santa Bárbara 110 I b 2
Ilha de Santa Catarina 111 G 3
Ilha de Santa Cruz 110 I c 2
Ilha de Santana 92-93 L 5
Ilha de Santo Amaro 102-103 JK 6
Ilha de São Francisco 102-103 HJ 7
Ilha de São Luís 100-101 BC 1-2
Ilha de São Sebastião 92-93 KL 9
Ilha de Tinharé 100-101 E 7
Ilha do Arvoredo 102-103 HJ 7
Ilha do Bananal 92-93 J 7
Ilha do Bazaruto 172 G 6
Ilha do Caju 100-101 CD 2
Ilha do Caldeirão 98-99 D 7
Ilha do Cardoso 102-103 J 6
Ilha do Careiro 98-99 J 6
Ilha do Engenho 110 I c 2
Ilha do Fundão 110 I b 2
Ilha do Gado Bravo 100-101 C 6
Ilha do Governador 110 I b 1
Ilha do Meio 110 I b 3
Ilha do Mel 102-103 H 6
Ilha do Pacoval 98-99 K 6
Ilha do Príncipe 164-165 F 8
Ilha do Rijo 110 I c 1
Ilha dos Alcatrazes 102-103 K 6
Ilha do Saravatá 110 I b 1
Ilha dos Búzios 102-103 K 5
Ilha dos Caranguejos 100-101 B 2
Ilha dos Macacos 98-99 N 5
Ilha dos Porcos 102-103 K 5
Ilha do Viana 110 I c 2
Ilha Fernando de Noronha 92-93 N 5
Ilha Grande [BR, Amazonas] 98-99 F 5
Ilha Grande [BR, Rio de Janeiro] 92-93 L 9
Ilha Grande [BR, Rio Grande do Sul] 106-107 M 3
Ilha Grande = Ilha das Sete Quedas 111 EF 2-3
Ilha Grande, Baía da — 102-103 K 5
Ilha Grande de Gurupá 92-93 J 5
Ilha Grande de Jutai 98-99 O 6
Ilha Grande de Paulino 100-101 CD 2
Ilha Grande de Santa Isabel 92-93 L 5
Ilha Grande ou das Sete Quedas 92-93 HJ 9
Ilha Inhaca 174-175 K 4
Ilha Irmãos 100-101 B 1
Ilha Janaucu 92-93 JK 4
Ilha Javari 98-99 E 5
Ilha Jurupari 98-99 NO 4
Ilha Mangunça 100-101 B 1
Ilha Maracá 92-93 G 4
Ilha Mariana 174-175 K 3
Ilha Mexiana 92-93 K 4-5
Ilha Mucunambiba 100-101 C 1-2
Ilha Mututi 98-99 N 5
Ilha Naipo 94-95 G 6
Ilha Pedro II 94-95 H 7
Ilha Providencia 94-95 J 8
Ilha Queimada 98-99 N 5
Ilha Queimada Grande 102-103 J 6
Ilha Rata 92-93 N 5
Ilhas, Cachoeira — 98-99 JK 5
Ilhas Angoche 172 GH 5
Ilha Santa Ana 102-103 M 5
Ilha São Jorge 100-101 B 1
Ilha São Tomé 164-165 F 8-9
Ilhas Cagarras 110 I b 3
Ilhas del Cisne = Swan Islands 64-65 K 8
Ilhas de Sao João 92-93 L 5
Ilhas Desertas 164-165 A 2
Ilhas dos Corais 102-103 HJ 6
Ilha Seca 110 I b 2
Ilhas Itacolomi 102-103 H 6
Ilhas Martim Vaz 92-93 O 9
Ilhas Quirimba 172 H 4
Ilhas Selvagens 164-165 A 2
Ilhas Três Irmãos 102-103 H 7
Ilha Tamaquari 98-99 F 5
Ilha Tupinambaranas 92-93 H 5
Ilhavo 120-121 C 8
Ilheo Bay, Port de — = Sandvisbai 174-175 A 2
Ilherir = Al-Hayrīr 166-167 L 7
Ilhéus 92-93 M 7
Ilhinha, Cachoeira — 98-99 K 5
Ili [SU] 132-133 O 8
Ili [TJ] 142-143 E 3
Ili = Gulja 142-143 E 3
Iliamna, AK 58-59 K 7
Iliamna Bay 58-59 L 7
Iliamna Lake 56-57 E 6
Iliamna Volcano 56-57 EF 5
Iliç 136-137 H 3
Iliff, CO 68-69 E 5
Iligan 148-149 H 5
Iligan Bay 152-153 PQ 1
Ilihuli Shan = Ilchuri Alin 142-143 NO 1
Ilion, NY 72-73 J 3
Ilion = Troia 134-135 B 3
Ilio Point 78-79 d 2
Ilisós 113 IV b 2
Ilivit Mountains 58-59 G 5
Iljič 132-133 M 9
Il'ič'ovsk [SU, Nachičevanskaja ASSR] 126-127 M 7
Il'ič'ovsk [SU, Ukrainskaja SSR] 126-127 E 3
Iljincy 126-127 D 2
Il'jino 124-125 H 6
Il'jinskij [SU ↑ Južno-Sachalinsk] 132-133 b 8
Il'jinskij [SU ↖ Perm'] 124-125 U 4
Il'jinsko-Podomskoje 124-125 QR 3
Il'jinsko-Zaborskoje 124-125 OP 5
Ilkāl 140 C 3
Illampu, Nevado — 92-93 F 8
Illana Bay 152-153 P 2
Illapel 111 B 4
Illecas 86-87 JK 6
Illela 168-169 G 2
Iller 118 E 4
Illesca, Cerro — 96-97 A 4-5
Illimani, Nevado de — 92-93 F 8
Illinci = Iljincy 126-127 D 2
Illiniza 96-97 B 2
Illinois 64-65 HJ 3
Illinois, University of — 83 II ab 1
Illinois Institute of Technology 83 II b 1
Illinois Peak 66-67 F 2
Illinois River 64-65 HJ 3-4
Illizi 166-167 L 6
Illmo, MO 78-79 E 2
Illo 168-169 F 3
Illovo Beach 174-175 J 6
Illubabor = Īlubabor 164-165 LM 7
Il'men', ozero — 132-133 E 6
Ilnik, AK 58-59 cd 1
Ilo 92-93 E 8
Ilo, Rada de — 92-93 E 8
Iloca 106-107 A 5
Iloilo 148-149 H 4
Ilopango, Lago de — 88-89 B 8
Ilorin 164-165 E 7
Ilosva = Iršava 126-127 A 2
Ilôt Cône = Kâs Moul 150-151 D 7
Ilovajsk 126-127 J 3
Ilovatka 126-127 MN 1
Ilovatnyj = Ilovatka 126-127 MN 1
Ilovľa [SU, place] 126-127 LM 2
Ilovľa [SU, river] 126-127 M 1
Ilp, Den — 128 I ab 1
Il'pyrskij 132-133 f 5-6
Il'skij 126-127 J 4
Īlubabor 164-165 LM 7
Ilūkste 124-125 EF 6
Ilula 171 C 3
Iluyana Potosí, Nevado — 104-105 B 5
Ilwaco, WA 66-67 AB 2
Ilwaki 148-149 J 8
Ilyč 124-125 V 2
Iłża 118 K 3

Imabari 144-145 J 5-6
Imabetsu 144-145 N 2
Imabu, Rio — 98-99 K 5
Imaculda 100-101 F 4
Imagane 144-145 ab 2
Imaichi 144-145 M 4
Imajō 144-145 KL 5
Imajuku, Yokohama- 155 III a 3
Imāmganj = Chhatarpur 138-139 K 5
Imán, Sierra del — 106-107 K 1
Imandra, ozero — 132-133 E 4
Imari 144-145 GH 6
Imaruí 102-103 H 8
Imata 96-97 F 9
Imataca, Serranía de — 92-93 G 3
Imatra 116-117 N 7
Imatra vallinkoski 116-117 N 7
Imaz, Bajo — 106-107 E 7
Imazu 144-145 KL 5
Imazuasayama 155 III d 3
Imbābah 173 B 2
Imbābah Bridge 170 II b 1
Imbabura 96-97 B 1
Imbaimadai 92-93 G 3
Imbituba 102-103 H 8
Imbituva 102-103 G 6
Imbros = İmroz 136-137 A 2
Imbuí, Punta do — 110 I c 2
Imbuíra 100-101 D 8
Imedrhâs, Jbel — = Jabal Imīdghās 166-167 D 4
I-mên = Yimen 146-147 F 5
Imeral, Adrâr n' = Jabal Mūriq 166-167 CD 3
Imeri, Serra — 92-93 F 4
Imfal = Imphāl 134-135 P 6
Imī 164-165 N 7
Imīdghās, Jabal — 166-167 D 4
Imilac 111 C 2
Imilshil 166-167 D 3
Imīn Tānūt 166-167 B 4
Imirhou, Oued — = Wādī Imirhu 166-167 L 7
Imirhu, Wādī — 166-167 L 7
Imišli 126-127 NO 7
Imja-do 144-145 E 5
Imjin-gang 144-145 F 3
Imlay, NV 66-67 DE 5
Imlay City, MI 72-73 E 3
Immokalee, FL 80-81 c 3
Immyŏng-dong 144-145 G 2
Imnaha River 66-67 E 3
Imo 164-165 F 7
Imola 122-123 D 3
Imore 170 III a 2
Imotski 122-123 G 4
Imoulaye, Hassi — = Ḥāssī Imūlāy 166-167 L 5
Imouzzer des Ida-Outanane = Sūq al-Khamīs 166-167 B 4
Imoûzzer Kandar = Imūzzar al-Kandar 166-167 D 3
Impendhle = Impendle 174-175 HJ 5
Impendle 174-175 HJ 5
Imperatriz 92-93 K 6
Impéria 122-123 C 4
Imperial, CA 74-75 F 6
Imperial, NE 68-69 F 5
Imperial, TX 76-77 C 7
Imperial [CDN] 61 F 5
Imperial [PE] 96-97 C 8
Imperial, Río — 106-107 A 7
Imperial Dam 74-75 F 6
Imperial Mills 61 C 3
Imperial Palace 155 III b 1
Imperial Valley 64-65 CD 5
Impfondo 172 C 1
Imphāl 134-135 P 6
Impilachti 124-125 H 3
Imp'o 144-145 FG 5
İmralı 136-137 C 2
İmranlı 136-137 GH 3
İmron 136-137 H 3
Imthān 136-137 G 6
Imūlāy, Ḥāssī — 166-167 L 5
Imuris 86-87 E 2
Imuruan Bay 148-149 G 4
Imuruk Basin 58-59 DE 4
Imuruk Lake 58-59 F 4
Imūzzar al-Kandar 166-167 D 3
Imūzzar al-Kandar 166-167 D 3
Imvani 174-175 G 7
Imwŏnjin 144-145 G 4

Ina [J] 144-145 LM 5
In'a [SU, place] 132-133 b 6
In'a [SU, river] 132-133 c 5
In Abangarit 164-165 F 5
In-Abeg 164-165 D 4
Inácio Dias, Morro — 110 I ab 2
Inácio Martins 102-103 G 6
Inajá 100-101 F 5
Inajá, Rio — 98-99 N 9
Inajá, Serra do — 98-99 N 9
In Alay 164-165 D 5
In Amênas = 'Ayn Umannās 164-165 F 3
Inanda 170 V b 1
Inanudak Bay 58-59 m 4
Inanwatan 148-149 K 7
Inâouên, Ouéd — = Wād Ināwīn 166-167 D 2
Iñapari 92-93 EF 7
In'aptuk, gora — 132-133 UV 6
'In Aquiel, Hassi — = Ḥāssī 'Ayn Aghyūl 166-167 M 6
In Areī 168-169 F 1
Inari [SF, lake] 116-117 MN 3
Inari [SF, place] 116-117 M 3
Inaru River 58-59 J 1
Inatsuke, Tōkyō- 155 III b 1
Inauini, Rio — 98-99 D 9
Inawashiro 144-145 MN 4
Inawashiro ko 144-145 MN 4
Ināwīn, Wād — 166-167 D 2
In Azaoua 164-165 F 4
In Azaoua = 'Ayn 'Azāwah 166-167 K 7
'In 'Azar = 'Ayn 'Azar 166-167 M 5
Inazkān 166-167 B 4
In-Belbel = 'Ayn Balbāl 166-167 G 6
Inca 120-121 J 9
Inca, Cerro del — 104-105 BC 7
Incaguasi 106-107 B 2
Incahuasi, Salina de — 104-105 C 9
İnce burun 134-135 C 2
İncekum burnu 136-137 EF 4
İncesu 136-137 F 3
Inch'ŏn 144-145 F 4
Inchupalla 96-97 G 9
Inchwe 174-175 G 2
Incienso 106-107 B 3
İncili 136-137 D 2
İncir burun 136-137 G 2
Incirköy, İstanbul- 154 I b 2
Incomáti, Rio — 174-175 K 3
Incoronata = Kornat 122-123 F 4
Incudine, l' 122-123 C 5
Indaiá 100-101 E 7
Indaia, Rio — 102-103 K 3
Indaiá Grande, Rio — 102-103 F 3
Indaial 102-103 H 7
Indaiatuba 102-103 J 5
Indaor = Indore 134-135 M 6
Indāpur 140 B 1
Indau 141 E 3
Indaugyī Aing 141 E 3
Indaur = Indore 134-135 M 6
Indaw 141 E 5
Indaw = Indau 141 D 4
Indawgyi, Lake — = Indaugyī Aing 141 E 3
Indé 76-77 B 10
Indel Airpark 84 III d 1
In Délimane 168-169 F 2
Independence, CA 74-75 D 4
Independence, IA 70-71 E 4
Independence, KS 76-77 FG 4
Independence, LA 78-79 D 5
Independence, MO 64-65 H 4
Independence, OR 66-67 B 3
Independence Heights, Houston-, TX 85 III b 1
Independence Mountains 66-67 EF 5
Independence National Historical Park 84 III c 2
Independence Valley 66-67 F 5
Independencia [BOL] 104-105 C 5
Independência [BR] 100-101 D 3
Independencia [PY, Boquerón] 102-103 AB 4
Independencia [PY, Guairá] 102-103 DE 6
Independencia [RA] 106-107 G 2
Independencia [MEX] 74-75 F 6
Independencia, Bahía de la — 96-97 C 8-9
Independencia, Islas — 92-93 D 7
Inder, ozero — 126-127 PQ 2
Inderagiri, Batang — 148-149 D 7
Inderborskij 126-127 P 2
Index, WA 66-67 C 2
Index Mount 58-59 PQ 2
Indi 140 BC 2
India 134-135 L-O 6
India, Bassas da — 172 GH 6
Indiana 64-65 J 3-4
Indiana, PA 72-73 G 4
Indianapolis, IN 64-65 J 4
Indian Head 61 FG 5
Indian Lake [USA, Michigan] 70-71 G 2-3
Indian Lake [USA, Ohio] 72-73 E 4
Indian Mountain 66-67 H 4
Indian Museum 154 II b 2
Indian Ocean 50-51 N-O 6-7
Indianola, IA 70-71 D 5
Indianola, MS 78-79 D 4
Indianola, NE 68-69 F 5
Indianópolis 102-103 J 3
Indianópolis, São Paulo- 110 II b 2
Indian Peak 74-75 G 3
Indian River [CDN] 62 N 2
Indian River [USA, Alaska] 58-59 KL 4
Indian River [USA, Florida] 64-65 K 6
Indian Springs, NV 74-75 F 4
Indian Springs, VA 82 II a 2
Indian Valley, ID 66-67 E 3
Indiga 132-133 HJ 4
Indigirka 132-133 bc 4
Indio, CA 74-75 E 6
Indio, Punta — 106-107 J 5
Indio, Río — 64-65 c 2
Indio Rico 106-107 G 7
Índios 102-103 G 7
Índios, Cachoeira dos — 92-93 G 4
Indispensable Strait 148-149 k 6
Indo = Sindh 134-135 L 4
Indonesia 148-149 D-K 7
Indonesian Bazaar 154 IV a 2
Indore 134-135 M 6
Indramaiu = Indramayu 148-149 E 8
Indramayu 148-149 E 8
Indramayu, Tanjung — 152-153 H 9
Indrāvati 134-135 N 7
Indre 120-121 H 5
Indre Arna 116-117 AB 7
Indura 124-125 DE 7
Indūra = Nizāmābād 134-135 M 7
Indus = Sengge Khamba 142-143 DE 5
Indus = Sindh 134-135 L 4
Indus Canyon 134-135 K 6
Indwe [ZA, place] 174-175 G 6
Indwe [ZA, river] 174-175 G 6
İnebolu 136-137 E 2
İnegöl 136-137 C 2
Inerie, Gunung — 148-149 H 8
Inès Indart 106-107 G 5
Ineul 122-123 L 2
İnevi 136-137 E 3
Inezgan = Inazkān 166-167 B 4
Inezgane = Inazkān 166-167 B 4
In-Ezzane = 'Ayn 'Azzān 164-165 G 4
Infanta, Cape — = Kaap Infanta 174-175 D 8
Infanta, Kaap — 174-175 D 8
Infantas 94-95 E 4
Infanzón 104-105 D 11
In Farghas 168-169 F 1
Infernão, Cachoeira do — 92-93 G 6
Inferninho, Caocheira — 98-99 H 9
Infiernillo, Presa del — 86-87 JK 8
Ing, Nam Mae — 150-151 C 2-3
Ingá [BR] 100-101 G 4
Ingabū 141 D 7
In-Gall 164-165 F 5
Ingapirca 96-97 B 3
Ingende 172 C 2
Ingeniero Balloffet 106-107 C 5
Ingeniero Beaugey 106-107 FG 5
Ingeniero Budge, Lomas de Zamora- 110 III b 2
Ingeniero Foster 106-107 E 5
Ingeniero Guillermo N. Juárez 104-105 EF 8
Ingeniero Gustavo André 106-107 CD 4
Ingeniero Jacobacci 111 BC 6
Ingeniero Julián Romero 106-107 DE 7
Ingeniero Luiggi 106-107 E 5
Ingeniero Luis A. Huergo 106-107 D 7
Ingeniero Montero 104-105 E 5
Ingeniero Pablo Nogues 110 III a 1
Ingeniero White 106-107 F 7
Ingenika Mine 60 E 1
Ingenio, Río del — 96-97 D 9
Ingenio Santa Ana 106-107 DE 1
Ingenstrem Rocks 58-59 q 6
Ingersoll 72-73 F 3
Ingham 158-159 J 3
Ingle, CA 74-75 C 4
Inglefield Bredning 56-57 XY 2
Inglefield Land 56-57 XY 2
Ingles, Bogotá- 91 III b 4
Ingleshire, TX 85 III a 1
Ingleside, San Francisco-, CA 83 I b 2
Inglewood 158-159 K 5
Inglewood, CA 74-75 D 6
Inglis 61 H 5
Inglutalik River 58-59 G 4
Ingōgā Būm 141 E 3
Ingogo 174-175 HJ 4
Ingolf 62 B 3
Ingólfshöfdhi 116-117 ef 3
Ingolstadt 118 EF 4
Ingomar, MT 68-69 C 2
Ingonisch 63 F 4
Ingøy 116-117 KL 2
Ingrebourne 129 II c 1
Ingrid Christensen land 53 BC 8
In Guezzam = 'Ayn Qazzān 164-165 EF 5
Ingul 126-127 F 3
Ingulec 126-127 F 2
Ingwavuma [ZA, place] 174-175 JK 4
Ingwavuma [ZA, river] 174-175 J 4
Inhaca, Ilha — 174-175 K 4
Inhaca, Península — 174-175 K 4
Inhambane [Mozambique, administrative unit] 172 FG 6
Inhambane [Mozambique, place] 172 G 6
Inhambane, Baía de — 174-175 L 2
Inhambupe 92-93 M 7
Inhambupe, Rio — 100-101 E 6
Inhaminga 172 FG 5
Inhamuns 100-101 DE 3
Inhandui 106-107 JK 2
Inhapim 102-103 LM 3
Inharrime 172 G 6
Inharrime, Rio — 174-175 L 3
Inhas = 'Ayn Unaḥḥās 166-167 HJ 6
Inhaúma, Rio de Janeiro- 110 I b 2
Inhaúma, Serra do — 100-101 B 3
Inhaumas 100-101 B 7
Inhobim 100-101 D 8
Inhulec' = Ingulec 126-127 F 3
Inhuma 100-101 D 4
Inhumas 102-103 H 2
Inhung-ni 144-145 F 3
Inírida, Río — 92-93 F 4
Inishowen Peninsula 119 C 4
Injune 158-159 J 5
Inkerman 158-159 H 3
Inkermann = Wādī Rāhīyu 166-167 G 2
Inklin 58-59 V 7
Inklin River 58-59 V 7
Inkom, ID 66-67 GH 4
Inland Lake 58-59 H 3
Inland Sea = Seto-naikai 142-143 P 5
Inle Aing 141 E 5
Inn 118 E 5
Innamincka 160 E 1
Inner Mongolian Autonomous Region 142-143 K 3-M 2
Inner Port Shelter 155 I b 1
Inner Sound 119 D 3
Innisfail [AUS] 158-159 J 3
Innisfail [CDN] 60 L 3
Innoko River 58-59 H 5
Innoshima 144-145 J 5
Innsbruck 118 E 5
Innymnej, gora — 132-133 kl 4
Ino 144-145 J 6
Inocência 102-103 FG 3
Inokashira Park 155 III a 1
Inomino-misaki 144-145 J 6
Inongo 172 C 2
İnönü 136-137 D 3
Inoucdjouac 56-57 V 6
Inowrocław 118 HJ 2
Inquisivi 92-93 F 8
In-Rhar = 'Ayn Ghar 166-167 G 6
Inriville 106-107 F 4
In-Salah = 'Ayn Ṣāliḥ 164-165 E 3
Insar 124-125 P 7
Inscription, Cape — 158-159 B 5
Inscription Point 161 I b 2
Insein = Inzein 148-149 C 3
Instituto Butantã 110 II a 2
Instituto Politécnico Nacional 91 I c 1-2
Inta 132-133 KL 4
Intake, MT 68-69 D 2
In Tallak 168-169 F 1
In Tebezas 168-169 F 1
In Tedeini = 'Ayn Tādīn 164-165 E 4
In Témégui 168-169 F 1
Intendente Alvear 106-107 F 5
Interamericana, Carretera — 88-89 E 10
Interior, SD 68-69 F 4
Interior Plateau 60 D 2-F 4
Interlagos, São Paulo- 110 II a 3
Interlaken 118 CD 5
International Amphitheatre 83 II b 2
International Falls, MN 70-71 D 1
Intersection, Mount — 60 G 3
Inthanon, Doi — 148-149 C 3
Intiyaco 111 DE 3
Intracoastal Waterway 78-79 C 6
Intuto 96-97 D 3
Inubō saki 144-145 N 5
Inútil, Bahía — 111 BC 8
Inuvik 56-57 K 4
Inuya, Río — 96-97 E 7
In'va 124-125 U 4
Invalides 129 I c 2
Inveja, Serra da — 100-101 F 5
Invercargill 158-159 NO 9
Inverell 158-159 K 5
Inverleigh 158-159 H 3
Invermere 60 J 4
Inverness, FL 80-81 b 2
Inverness [CDN] 63 F 4
Inverness [GB] 119 DE 3
Inverurie 119 EF 3
Inverway 158-159 EF 3
Investigator Group 160 AB 4
Investigator Strait 158-159 FG 7
Inwa 141 D 5
Inwood, NY 82 III d 3
Inxu 174-175 H 6
Inyak Island = Ilha Inhaca 174-175 K 4
Inyak Peninsula = Península Inhaca 174-175 K 4
Inyangani 172 F 5
Inyan Kara Mountain 68-69 D 3
Inyokern, CA 74-75 DE 5
Inyo Mountains 74-75 DE 4
Inza [SU, place] 132-133 H 7
Inza [SU, river] 124-125 PQ 7
Inžavino 124-125 O 7
Inzein 148-149 C 3
Inzersdorf, Wien- 113 I b 2
Inzia 172 C 3
Inzūtzūt 141 E 3

Iō 206-207 S 7
Ioánnina 122-123 J 6
Iō-jima 144-145 H 7
Iō-jima = Volcano Islands 206-207 S 7
Iola, KS 70-71 C 7
Iola, TX 76-77 FG 7
Iolotan' 134-135 J 3
Iona, ID 66-67 H 4
Iona, SD 68-69 G 4
Ione, CA 74-75 C 3
Ione, OR 66-67 D 3
Ione, WA 66-67 E 1
Ionen 128 IV a 2
Ionia, MI 70-71 H 4
Ionian Basin 164-165 HJ 1-2
Ionian Islands 122-123 H 6-J 7
Ionian Sea 114-115 M 8
Ionti = Joontoy 172 H 2
Iony, ostrov — 132-133 b 6
Iori 126-127 N 6
Iorskoje ploskogorje 126-127 MN 6
Íos 122-123 L 7
Iosser 124-125 T 2
Iota, LA 78-79 C 5
Iowa 64-65 H 3
Iowa, LA 78-79 C 5
Iowa City, IA 70-71 E 5
Iowa Falls, IA 70-71 D 4
Iowa Park, TX 76-77 E 5-6
Iowa River 70-71 E 5

Ipadu, Cachoeira — 92-93 F 4
Ipameri 92-93 K 8
Ipanema 102-103 M 3
Ipanema, Rio — 100-101 F 5
Ipanema, Rio de Janeiro- 110 I b 2
Ipanoré, Cachoeira — 94-95 GH 7
Iparia 92-93 E 6
Ipatinga 100-101 C 10
Ipatovo 126-127 L 4
Ipauçu 102-103 H 5
Ipaumirim 100-101 E 4
Ipecaetá 100-101 E 7
Ipel' 118 J 4
Ipewik River 58-59 E 2
Ipiales 94-95 C 7
Ipiaú 92-93 M 7
Ipin = Yibin 142-143 JK 6
Ipirá 100-101 E 7
Ipiranga [BR, Acre] 96-97 F 6
Ipiranga [BR, Amazonas ↗ Benjamin Constant] 92-93 F 5
Ipiranga [BR, Amazonas ↑ Benjamin Constant] 98-99 D 6
Ipiranga [BR, Paraná] 102-103 G 6
Ipiranga, São Paulo- 110 II b 2
Ipiranga do Piauí 100-101 D 4
Ipixuna 92-93 KL 5
Ipixuna, Rio — [BR ◁ Rio Juruá] 96-97 E 5
Ipixuna, Rio — [BR ◁ Rio Purus] 92-93 G 6

Ipoh 148-149 D 6
Iporã [BR, Goiás] 92-93 J 8
Ipora [BR, Mato Grosso do Sul] 102-103 F 5
Iporanga 102-103 H 6
Ippodrom 113 V b
Ippodromo 113 II b 2
Ippodromo Capanelle 113 II bc 2
Ippy 164-165 J 7
İpsala 136-137 B 2
Ipsario = Hypsárion 122-123 L 5
Ipsvoorde 128 II b 1
Ipswich, SD 68-69 G 3
Ipswich [GB] 119 G 5
Ipswich, Brisbane- 158-159 K 5
Ipu 92-93 L 5
Ipubi 100-101 D 4
Ipueiras 92-93 L 5
Iput' 124-125 H 7

Iqlīt 173 C 5
Iquique 111 B 2
Iquiri, Morro — 102-103 H 7
Iquiri, Rio — 98-99 E 9
Iquitos 92-93 E 5
Iquitos, Isla — 96-97 E 3

Iraan, TX 76-77 D 7
Iracema [BR, Acre] 98-99 D 9
Iracema [BR, Amazonas] 98-99 D 8
Iracema [BR, Ceará] 100-101 E 3
Iracema [BR, Rondônia] 98-99 H 9
Iracoubo 92-93 J 3
Irago-suidō 144-145 L 5
Irago-zaki 144-145 L 5
Iraí 106-107 L 1
Irajá 110 I b 1-2
Irajá, Rio de Janeiro- 110 I b 1
Irak 134-135 D-F 4
Irak = Arāk 134-135 F 4
Iraklion = Hērákleion 122-123 L 8
Irala [PY] 111 EF 3
Irala [RA] 106-107 G 5
Iramaia 100-101 D 7
Iran 134-135 F-H 4
Iran = Ilan 146-147 H 9
Iran, Pegunungan — 152-153 L 4-5
Iran, Plateau of — 50-51 MN 4
Iranaitivu = Iraneitivu 140 DE 6
Iraneitivu 140 DE 6
Irani, Rio — 102-103 F 7
Īrānshāh 136-137 M 4
Īrānshahr 134-135 HJ 5
Iraola 106-107 H 6
Irapa 92-93 G 2
Iraporanga 100-101 D 7
Irapuato 64-65 F 7
'Irāq Arabī 136-137 L 6-M 7
Iraquara 100-101 D 7
Irará 100-101 E 6-7
Irarrarene = Irharharān 164-165 F 3
Irati 111 F 3
Irau, Tanjong — 154 III b 1
Irauçuba 100-101 E 2
Irawadi = Erāwadī Myit 148-149 C 2
Irazú, Volcán — 64-65 K 9
Irazusta 106-107 H 4
Irbeni väin 124-125 CD 5
Irbid 134-135 D 4
Irbit 132-133 L 6
Irecê 92-93 L 7
Ireland 119 BC 5
Irene 111 D 5
Iretama 102-103 F 6
Irgalem = Yirga 'Alem 164-165 M 7
Irgāñiv = Kuru 138-139 K 6
Irgiz 132-133 L 8
Irharharān 164-165 F 3
Irherm = Igharm 166-167 B 4
Irhyang-dong 144-145 GH 2
Iri 144-145 F 4-5
Irian, Teluk — 148-149 KL 7
Iriba 164-165 J 5
Iricoumé, Serra — 98-99 K 4
Iriga 148-149 H 4
Irikī 166-167 C 5
Iringa 172 G 3
Iringo 168-169 E 3
Irinjālakuda 140 BC 5
Iriomote-jima 142-143 N 7
Iriomote zima = Iriomote-jima 142-143 N 7
Iriri, Rio — 92-93 J 5
Irish Sea 119 D 5
Irituia 92-93 K 5
Irivi Novo, Rio — 98-99 M 9
Iriyamazu 155 III d 3
Irkljev 126-127 EF 2
Irkutsk 132-133 TU 7
Irma 61 C 4
Irmak 136-137 E 3
Irmãos, Ilha — 100-101 B 1
Irmingersee 56-57 d-f 5
Iro, Lac — 164-165 HJ 7
Īrōḍ = Erode 134-135 M 8
Irona 88-89 D 7
Iron Baron 160 C 4
Iron Bridge 62 K 3
Iron City, TN 78-79 F 3
Iron Cove 161 I ab 2
Iron Creek, AK 58-59 E 4
Irondequoit, NY 72-73 H 3
Iron Gate = Porțile de Fier 122-123 K 3
Iron Knob 158-159 G 6
Iron Mountain 74-75 G 4
Iron Mountain, MI 70-71 FG 3
Iron Mountain, WY 68-69 D 5
Iron River, MI 70-71 F 2
Iron River, WI 70-71 E 2
Ironside, OR 66-67 DE 3
Ironton, MO 70-71 E 7
Ironton, OH 72-73 E 5
Ironwood, MI 64-65 HJ 2
Iroquois, SD 68-69 H 3
Iroquois Falls 56-57 U 8
Irō saki 144-145 M 5
Irpen' [SU, place] 126-127 E 1
Irpen' [SU, river] 126-127 DE 1
'Irq, Al- 164-165 J 3
Irq Admar 164-165 F 4
Irq Aftut 166-167 DE 6
'Irqah 134-135 F 8
'Irq al-'Anqar 166-167 G 3-H 4
'Irq al-Kabīr al-Gharbī, Al- 164-165 D 3-E 2
'Irq al-Kabīr ash-Sharqī, Al- 164-165 F 2-3
'Irq ar-Rawī 164-165 D 3
'Irq ash-Shāsh 164-165 D 3-4
'Irq Buraghat 166-167 L 6
'Irq Isāwuwan 164-165 F 3
'Irq Sidrah, Ḥāssī — 166-167 H 4
'Irq Tahūdawīn 166-167 K 7
'Irq Yābis 166-167 EF 6
Irrawaddy = Erāwadī Myit 148-149 C 2
Irricana 60 L 4
Irruputunco, Volcán — 104-105 B 7
Irša 126-127 D 1
Iršava 126-127 A 2
Irtyš 132-133 N 6
Irtyšskoje 132-133 NO 7
Irumu 172 E 1
Irún 120-121 G 7
Irupana 104-105 C 5
Iruya 111 CD 2
Iruya, Río — 104-105 D 8
Irvine 61 CD 6
Irvine, KY 72-73 E 6
Irving, TX 76-77 F 6
Irving Park, Chicago-, IL 83 II b 1
Irvington, KY 70-71 G 7
Irvington, NJ 82 III a 2
Irwin, ID 66-67 H 4
Irwin, NE 68-69 EF 4
Irwŏl-san 144-145 G 4
Iryānah 166-167 M 1

Īs, Jabal — 173 D 6
Isa 168-169 G 2
Isabel, SD 68-69 F 3
Isabela 148-149 H 5
Isabela, Isla — 92-93 A 5
Isabela, La — 88-89 FG 3
Isabella, CA 74-75 D 5
Isabella, MN 70-71 E 2
Isabella, Cordillera — 64-65 J 9
Isabella Lake 74-75 D 5
Isabel Victoria = Colonia Isabel Victoria 106-107 H 2
Isachsen 56-57 Q 2
Isachsen, Cape — 56-57 OP 2
Ísafjarðhardjúp 116-117 b 1
Isa Fjord = Ísafjardhadjúp 116-117 b 1
Ísafjördhur 116-117 b 1
Isagateto 170 III a 1
Isahara = Isahaya 144-145 GH 6
Isahaya 144-145 GH 6
Isakly 124-125 S 6
Isakogorka, Archangel'sk- 124-125 MN 1
Isan 138-139 G 4
Isana, Río — 94-95 F 7
Isando 170 V c 1
Isangi 172 D 1
Isar 118 F 4
'Isāwīyah, Al- 134-135 D 4
Isāwuwan, 'Irq — 164-165 F 3
Iscayachi 104-105 D 7
Isca Yacú 104-105 D 10
Ischia 122-123 E 5
Iscuandé 94-95 BC 6
Iscuandé, Río — 94-95 C 6
Ise [J] 144-145 L 5
Išejevka 124-125 QR 6
Iseo 122-123 D 3
Iserbrook, Hamburg- 130 I a 1
Isère 120-121 K 6
Isère, Pointe — 92-93 J 3
Išerim, gora — 132-133 K 5
Iseri-Osun 170 III a 1
Isèrnia 122-123 F 5
Iset' 132-133 L 6
Ise-wan 144-145 L 5
Iseyin 164-165 E 7
Isezaki 144-145 M 4
Isfahan = Eşfahān 134-135 G 4
İsfendiyar dağları 134-135 CD 2
Isfjorden 116-117 j 5
İshaklı 136-137 D 3
I-shan = Yishan 142-143 K 7
Isherton 98-99 J 3
Ishibashi 144-145 N 3
Ishigaki-shima 142-143 NO 7
Ishikari 144-145 b 2
Ishikari gawa 144-145 b 2
Ishikari-wan 144-145 b 2
Ishikawa 144-145 L 4
Ishinomaki 144-145 N 3
Ishinomaki wan 144-145 N 3
Ishioka 144-145 N 4
Ishizuchino san 144-145 J 6
Ishpeming, MI 70-71 G 2
'Ishsh, Ra's al- 166-167 KL 2
I-shui = Yishui 146-147 G 4
Ishurdi 138-139 M 6
Ishwarīpur 138-139 M 6
Isiboro, Río — 104-105 D 5
Isidoro 100-101 E 4
Isidro Casanova, La Matanza- 110 III b 2
Isigaki sima = Ishigaki-shima 142-143 NO 7
Isigny-sur-Mer 120-121 G 4
Işık dağı 136-137 E 2
Isil'kul' 132-133 N 7
Išim [SU, place] 132-133 M 6
Išim [SU, river] 132-133 M 7
Išimbaj 132-133 K 7
Isimbira 171 BC 4
Išimskaja step' 132-133 N 6-7
Isiolo 172 G 1
Isipingo Beach 174-175 J 5-6
Isiro 172 E 1
Isisford 158-159 H 4
Isispynten 116-117 mn 5
Iskandar 132-133 M 9
İskandarīyah, Al- 164-165 KL 2
Iskar 122-123 L 4
Iskardū = Skardū 134-135 M 3
Iškejevo 124-125 S 6
İskele 136-137 F 4
İskenderun 134-135 D 3
İskenderun körfezi 136-137 F 4
İskilip 136-137 F 2
Iskitim 132-133 P 7
Iskorost' = Korosten' 126-127 D 1
Iskushuban 164-165 bc 1
Iskut River 60 B 1
Isla 86-87 N 8
Islá, La — [PE] 96-97 D 9
Isla, La — [RA] 106-107 DE 3
Isla, Salar de la — 104-105 B 9
Isla Águila = Speedwell Island 108-109 JK 9
Isla Alta 102-103 D 7
Isla Altamura 86-87 F 5
Isla Angamos 108-109 B 7
Isla Ángel de la Guarda 64-65 D 6
Isla Antica 94-95 K 2
Isla Apipé Grande 106-107 J 1
Isla Barro Colorado 64-65 b 2
Isla Beata 64-65 M 8
Isla Benjamin 108-109 BC 5
Isla Bermejo 106-107 FG 7
Isla Blanca 86-87 R 7
Isla Bougainville = Lively Island 108-109 KL 9
Isla Byron 108-109 B 6
Isla Caballos 106-107 J 3
Isla Cabrera 120-121 J 9
Isla Cacahual 94-95 BC 5
Isla Campana 111 A 7
Isla Campo Rico 106-107 G 4
Isla Caneima 94-95 L 3
Isla Cangrejo 94-95 L 3
Isla Capitán Aracena 108-109 D 10
Isla Carlos 111 B 8
Isla Carmen 64-65 DE 6
Isla Cedros 64-65 C 6
Isla Cerralvo 64-65 E 7
Isla Chaffers 108-109 BC 5
Isla Chañaral 111 B 3
Isla Chatham 111 B 8
Isla Chaves = Isla Santa Cruz 92-93 AB 5
Isla Choele Choel Grande 106-107 DE 7
Isla Christmas 108-109 D 10
Isla Clarence 111 B 8
Isla Clarión 86-87 C 8
Isla Clemente 108-109 B 5
Isla Coche 94-95 K 2
Isla Coiba 64-65 K 10
Isla Conejera 120-121 J 9
Isla Contoy 86-87 R 7
Isla Contreras 111 AB 8
Isla Corocoro 94-95 LM 4
Isla Covadonga 108-109 BC 9
Isla Creciente 86-87 DE 5
Isla Cresciente 86-87 DE 5
Isla-Cristina 120-121 D 10
Isla Cubagua 94-95 J 2
Isla Cuptana 108-109 C 5
Isla Curuzú Chalí 106-107 H 3
Isla Dawson 111 BC 8
Isla de Borbón = Pebble Island 108-109 K 8
Isla de Chiloé 111 AB 6
Isla de Corisco 164-165 F 8
Isla de Cozumel 64-65 J 7
Isla de Fernando Póo = Bioko 164-165 F 8
Isla de Flores 106-107 K 5
Isla de Goicoechea = New Island 108-109 J 8
Isla de Guadalupe 64-65 C 6
Isla de la Bahía 64-65 J 8
Isla del Aire 120-121 K 9
Isla de la Juventud 64-65 K 7
Isla de la Nieve 106-107 H 2
Isla de la Plata 92-93 C 5
Isla del Caño 88-89 DE 10
Isla del Carmen 86-87 OP 8
Isla del Coco 92-93 B 3
Isla de Lobos 106-107 K 5
Isla de los Césares 108-109 HJ 3
Isla de los Estados 111 D 8
Isla de los Riachos 108-109 HJ 3
Isla del Pillo 106-107 G 4
Isla del Rey 64-65 L 10
Isla del Rosario 94-95 CD 2
Isla del Rosario = Carass Island 108-109 J 8
Isla del Sol 104-105 B 4-5
Isla de Margarita 92-93 G 2
Isla de Ometepe 64-65 J 9
Isla de Providencia 92-93 C 2
Isla de Roatán 64-65 J 8
Isla Desolación 111 AB 8
Isla Desterrada 86-87 Q 6
Isla Diego de Amagro 111 A 8
Isla Dragonera 120-121 HJ 9
Isla Dring 108-109 B 5
Isla Duque de York 111 A 8
Isla Esmeralda 108-109 B 7
Isla Española 92-93 B 5
Isla Espíritu Santo 86-87 EF 5
Isla Fernandina 92-93 A 4-5
Isla Floreana 92-93 A 5
Isla Forsyth 108-109 B 5
Isla Fuerte 94-95 C 3
Isla Galeta 64-65 b 2
Isla Genovesa 92-93 B 4
Isla Gilbert 108-109 D 10
Isla Gordon 108-109 E 10
Isla Gorgona 92-93 D 4
Isla Grande de Tierra del Fuego 108-109 D-F 9-10
Isla Grevy 108-109 F 10
Isla Guafo 111 AB 6
Isla Guamblin 111 A 6
Isla Guardian Brito 108-109 C 10
Isla Hanover 111 AB 8
Isla Hermite 111 C 9
İslâhiye 136-137 G 4
Isla Holbox 86-87 R 7
Isla Hoste 111 C 9
Isla Humedad 64-65 a 2
Isla Humos 108-109 BC 5
Isla Iquitos 96-97 E 3
Isla Isabela 92-93 A 5
Isla Jabalí 108-109 HJ 3
Isla James 108-109 B 5
Isla Javier 108-109 B 6
Isla Jorge = George Island 108-109 JK 9
Isla Jorge Montt 108-109 B 8
Isla Juan Gallegos 64-65 b 2
Isla Juan Stuven 111 A 7
Isla La Blanquilla 92-93 G 2
Isla Largo Remo 64-65 b 2
Isla La Sola 94-95 K 2
Isla Lennox 111 C 9
Isla Level 108-109 B 5
Isla Luz 108-109 BC 5
Islāmābād 134-135 L 4
Islāmābād = Anantnāg 134-135 M 4
Isla Madre de Dios 111 A 8
Isla Magdalena 111 B 6
Isla Malpelo 92-93 C 4
Isla Manuel Rodriguez 108-109 BC 9
Isla Marchena 92-93 AB 4
Isla Margarita 94-95 D 3
Isla María Cleofas 86-87 G 7
Isla María Madre 64-65 E 7
Isla María Magdalena 64-65 E 7
Isla Mariusa 94-95 L 3
Isla Melchor 111 AB 7
Isla Merino Jarpa 108-109 BC 6
Islāmkoț 138-139 C 5
Isla Mocha 111 B 5
Isla Monserrate 86-87 E 5
Islamorada, FL 80-81 c 4
Isla Mornington 111 A 7
Islāmpur 138-139 K 5
Islāmpur = Urun Islāmpur 140 B 2
Isla Mujeres 86-87 R 7
Isla Nalcayec 108-109 C 6
Isla Naos 64-65 bc 3
Isla Navarino 111 C 9
Island Barn Reservoir 129 II a 2
Island City, OR 66-67 E 3
Island Falls 62 L 2
Island Falls, ME 72-73 M 1-2
Island Lagoon 158-159 G 6
Island Lake [CDN, lake] 56-57 RS 7
Island Lake [CDN, place] 62 BC 1
Island María = Bleaker Island 108-109 K 9
Island Mountain, CA 66-67 B 5
Island Park, ID 66-67 H 3
Island Park Reservoir 66-67 H 3
Island Pond, VT 72-73 KL 2
Islands, Bay of — [CDN] 63 G 3
Islands, Bay of — [NZ] 158-159 OP 7
Islands of Four Mountains 58-59 lm 4
Isla Noir 111 B 8
Isla Nueva 111 C 9
Isla Núñez 108-109 BC 9
Isla O'Brien 108-109 D 10
Isla Orchila 92-93 F 2
Isla Patricio Lynch 111 A 7
Isla Pedro González 94-95 B 3
Isla Pérez 86-87 PQ 6
Isla Piazzi 108-109 BC 8
Isla Picton 108-109 F 10
Isla Pinta 92-93 A 4
Isla Prat 108-109 B 7
Isla Puná 92-93 C 5
Isla Quilán 108-109 B 4
Isla Quinchao 108-109 C 4
Isla Quiriquina 106-107 A 6
Isla Raya 88-89 FG 11
Isla Refugio 108-109 C 4
Isla Riesco 111 B 8
Isla Rivero 108-109 B 5
Isla Rojas 108-109 C 5
Isla Rowlett 108-109 B 5
Isla San Benedicto 64-65 DE 8
Isla San Benito 86-87 BC 3
Isla San Cristóbal 92-93 B 5
Isla San Jerónimo 106-107 H 2
Isla San José [MEX] 64-65 DE 6
Isla San José [PA] 88-89 G 10
Isla San José = Weddell Island 111 D 8
Isla San Juanico 86-87 G 7
Isla San Lorenzo [MEX] 86-87 D 3
Isla San Lorenzo [PE] 92-93 D 7
Isla San Marcos 86-87 DE 4
Isla San Rafael = Beaver Island 108-109 J 8
Isla San Salvador 92-93 A 5
Isla San Sebastian 86-87 DE 3
Isla Santa Catalina 86-87 EF 5
Isla Santa Cruz [EC] 92-93 AB 5
Isla Santa Cruz [MEX] 86-87 E 5
Isla Santa Inés 111 B 8
Isla Santa Magdalena 86-87 D 5
Isla Santa Margarita 64-65 D 7
Isla Santa María 106-107 A 6
Isla Saona 64-65 N 8
Islas Baleares 120-121 H 9-K 8
Islas Cabo Verde 50-51 H 5
Islas Camden 108-109 C 10
Islas Canarias 164-165 A 3
Islas Caracas 94-95 J 2
Islas Chafarinas 166-167 EF 2
Islas Chauques 108-109 C 4
Islas Chimanas 94-95 J 2
Islas Columbretes 120-121 H 9
Islas de Alhucemas 166-167 E 2
Islas de Barlovento 64-65 OP 8-9
Islas de Coronados 74-75 E 6
Islas de la Bahía 64-65 J 8
Islas de las Lechiguanas 106-107 H 4
Islas del Maíz 64-65 K 9
Islas de los Choros 106-107 B 2
Islas del Pasaje = Passage Islands 108-109 J 8
Islas de Revillagigedo 64-65 D 8
Islas de San Bernardo 94-95 CD 3
Islas Desertores 108-109 C 4
Islas Diego Ramírez 111 C 9
Isla Serrano 108-109 B 7
Islas Escalante 96-97 AB 3
Islas Evangelistas 108-109 B 9
Islas Georgias del Sur = South Georgia 111 J 8
Islas Grafton 108-109 C 10
Islas Guaitecas 111 AB 6
Isla Simpson 108-109 C 5
Islas Independencia 92-93 D 7
Islas Las Aves 92-93 F 2
Islas Londonderry 111 B 9
Islas Los Frailes 94-95 K 2
Islas Los Hermanos 94-95 JK 2
Islas Los Monjes 92-93 EF 2
Islas Los Roques 92-93 F 2
Islas Los Testigos 92-93 G 2
Islas Magill 108-109 C 10
Islas Marías 64-65 E 7
Isla Socorro 64-65 DE 8
Isla Soledad = East Falkland 111 E 8
Islas Pájoros 106-107 B 2
Islas Rennell 108-109 B 8-C 9
Islas Revillagigedo 86-87 C-E 8
Isla Stewart 111 B 8-9
Islas Torres 106-107 L 5
Isla Stosch 111 A 7
Islas Vallenar 108-109 B 5
Islas Wollaston 111 C 9
Islas Wood 108-109 E 10
Isla Taboga 64-65 bc 3
Isla Taboguilla 64-65 bc 3
Isla Talavera 106-107 J 1
Isla Talcan 108-109 C 4
Isla Tenquehuen 108-109 B 5
Isla Teresa 108-109 C 5
Isla Tiburón 64-65 D 6
Isla Tortuguilla 94-95 C 3
Isla Traiguén 108-109 C 5
Isla Tranqui 108-109 C 4
Isla Trinidad 111 D 5
Isla Trinidad = Sounders Island 108-109 J 8
Isla Turuepano 94-95 K 2
Isla Urabá 64-65 bc 3
Isla van der Meulen 108-109 B 7
Isla Venado 64-65 b 3
Isla Verde [CO] 94-95 D 2
Isla Verde [RA] 106-107 E 2
Isla Vidal Gormaz 108-109 B 8-9
Isla Vigía = Keppel Island 108-109 K 8
Isla Wellington 111 AB 7
Isla Wollaston 108-109 F 10
Isla Wood 106-107 F 7
Islay 119 C 4
Islay, Pampa de — 96-97 F 10
Islay, Punta — 96-97 E 10
Isla Yaciretá 102-103 D 7
Isla Zorra 64-65 b 2
Isle 120-121 H 6
Isle au Haut 72-73 M 2-3
Isle of Dogs 129 II b 2
Isle of Lewis 119 C 2
Isle of Man 119 DE 4
Isle of Wight 119 F 6
Isle Royale 64-65 J 2
Isle Royale National Park 70-71 F 2
Isles Dernieres 78-79 D 6
Isles of Scilly 119 C 7
Isleta, NM 76-77 A 5
Isleton, CA 74-75 C 3
Isleworth, London- 129 II a 2
Islington, MA 84 I a 3
Islington, London- 129 II b 1
Islón 106-107 B 2
Ismailia = Al-Ismā'īlīyah 164-165 L 2
Ismā'īlīyah, Al- 164-165 L 2
Ismā'īlīyah, Tur'at al- 170 II b 1
Ismailly 126-127 O 6
Ismay, MT 68-69 D 2
Ismetpaşa 136-137 H 3
Isna 164-165 L 3
Isnotú 94-95 F 3
Isogo, Yokohama- 155 III a 3
Isohama = Ōarai 144-145 N 4
Isoka 172 F 4
Isola Lampedusa 164-165 G 1
Isola Linosa 164-165 G 1
Isola Pianosa 122-123 D 4
Isola Salina 122-123 F 6
Isola Vulcano 122-123 F 6
Isole Égadi 122-123 DE 6
Isole Eólie o Lipari 122-123 F 6
Isole Giuba 172 H 2
Isole Ponziane 122-123 E 5
Isole Trèmiti 122-123 F 4
Isolo 170 III a 1
Ispahān = Eşfahān 134-135 G 4
İsparta 134-135 C 3
Isperih 122-123 M 4
İspir 136-137 J 2
Israel 134-135 CD 4
Israelite Bay 158-159 DE 6
Issa 124-125 P 7
Issano 92-93 H 3
Issaouane, Erg — = 'Irq Isāwuwan 164-165 F 3
Issati 168-169 F 3
Isser, Ouèd — = Wādī Yassar 166-167 H 1
Issia 168-169 D 4
Issoudun 120-121 HJ 5
Issyk-Kul', ozero — 142-143 M 3
Istādah, Āb-e- = Ābe Estāda 134-135 K 4
İstanbul 134-135 BC 2
İstanbul-Anadoluhisarı 154 I b 2
İstanbul-Anadolukavağı 154 I b 1
İstanbul-Bakırköy 136-137 C 2
İstanbul-Balat 154 I a 2
İstanbul-Balmumcu 154 I b 2
İstanbul-Bebek 154 I b 2
İstanbul-Beşiktaş 154 I b 2
İstanbul-Beykoz 136-137 C 2
İstanbul-Beylerbeyi 154 I b 2
İstanbul-Beyoğlu 154 I a 2
İstanbul boğazı 154 I b 1-2
İstanbul-Bostancı 154 I b 3
İstanbul-Boyacıköy 154 I b 2
İstanbul-Büyükada 136-137 C 2
İstanbul-Büyükdere 154 I b 2
İstanbul-Çapa 154 I a 2
İstanbul-Çengelköy 154 I b 2
İstanbul-Chiangir 154 I ab 2
İstanbul-Çubuklu 154 I b 2
İstanbul-Doğancılar 154 I b 2
İstanbul-Eminönü 154 I ab 2
İstanbul-Erenköy 154 I b 3
İstanbul-Eyüp 154 I a 2
İstanbul-Fatih 154 I a 2
İstanbul-Fener 154 I a 2
İstanbul-Galata 154 I a 2
İstanbul-Hasköy 154 I a 2
İstanbul-Haydarpaşa 154 I b 3
İstanbul-İçerenköy 154 I b 3
İstanbul-İncirköy 154 I b 2
İstanbul-İstinye 154 I b 2
İstanbul-Kadıköy 136-137 C 2
İstanbul-Kandilli 154 I b 2
İstanbul-Kanlica 154 I b 2
İstanbul-Kartal 136-137 C 2
İstanbul-Kefeliköy 154 I b 2
İstanbul-Kızıltoprak 154 I b 3
İstanbul-Kuruçeşme 154 I b 2
İstanbul-Kuzguncuk 154 I b 2
İstanbul-Orhaiye 154 I b 2
İstanbul-Paşabahce 154 I b 2
İstanbul-Rumelihisarı 154 I b 2
İstanbul-Rumelikavağı 154 I b 1
İstanbul-Sarıyer 136-137 C 3
İstanbul-Skutari = İstanbul-Üsküdar 134-135 BC 2
İstanbul-Tarabya 154 I b 2
İstanbul-Topkapı 154 I a 2
İstanbul-Umuryeri 154 I b 2
İstanbul-Üsküdar 134-135 BC 2
İstanbul-Vaniköy 154 I b 2
İstanbul-Yedikule 154 I a 3
İstanbul-Yenikapı 154 I a 3
İstanbul-Yeniköy 154 I b 2
İstanbul-Zeytinburnu 154 I a 3
Īstgāh-e Bīsheh 136-137 N 6
Īstgāh-e Gargar 136-137 N 7
Īstgāh-e Keshvar 136-137 N 6
Īstgāh-e Parandak 136-137 O 5
Isthilart 106-107 HJ 3
İstinye, İstanbul- 154 I b 2
Istisu 126-127 MN 7
Istmina 92-93 D 3
Istmo Carlos Ameghino 108-109 G 4
Istmo de Médanos 94-95 G 2
Istmo de Ofqui 108-109 B 6
Istmo de Panamá 64-65 L 9-10
Istmo de Tehuantepec 64-65 GH 8
Isto, Mount — 58-59 Q 2
Istra [SU] 124-125 L 6
Istranca dağları 136-137 B 1-C 2
Istria 122-123 EF 3
Isunba 170 III a 2
Isvestia Islands = ostrova Izvestij CIK 132-133 OP 2

Itá 102-103 D 6
Itabaiana 100-101 F 6
Itabaianinha 92-93 M 7
Itabaina 92-93 M 6
Itabapoana 102-103 M 4
Itabapoana, Rio — 102-103 M 4
Itabashi, Tōkyō- 155 III ab 1
Itaberá 102-103 H 5
Itaberaba 92-93 L 7
Itaberaí 92-93 JK 8
Itabira 102-103 L 3
Itabirito 102-103 L 4
Itaboraí 102-103 L 5
Itabuna 92-93 M 7
Itacaiúnas, Rio — 92-93 JK 6
Itacajá 98-99 P 9
Itacambira, Pico — 102-103 L 2
Itacambiruçu, Rio — 102-103 L 2
Itacaré 92-93 M 7
Itacira 100-101 D 7
Itacoatiara 92-93 H 5
Itacolomi, Ilhas — 102-103 H 6
Itacolomi, Pico — 92-93 L 9
Itacolomi, Ponta — 100-101 BC 1-2
Itacolomi, Saco de — 110 I b 1
Itacuaí, Rio — 96-97 F 5
Itacurubí del Rosario 102-103 D 6
Itaetê 92-93 L 7
Itaguá 100-101 D 4
Itaguaçu 100-101 D 10
Itaguaí 102-103 KL 5
Itaguara 102-103 K 4
Itaguari, Rio — 100-101 B 8
Itaguatins 92-93 K 6
Itaguí 94-95 D 4
Itaguyry 102-103 E 6
Itahuania, Cerros de — 96-97 F 8
Itaí 111 G 2
Itaíba 100-101 F 5
Itá Ibaté 106-107 J 1
Itaiçaba 100-101 F 3
Itaim, Rio — 100-101 D 4
Itaimbé 100-101 D 10
Itaimbey, Río — 102-103 E 6
Itainópolis 100-101 D 4
Itaiópolis 102-103 H 7
Itaipava, Cachoeira — [BR, Rio Araguaia] 92-93 K 6
Itaipava, Cachoeira — [BR, Rio Xingu] 92-93 J 5
Itaipe 100-101 D 7
Itaipu, Ponta — 102-103 J 6
Itaituba 92-93 H 5
Itajaí 111 G 3
Itajaí, Rio — 102-103 H 7
Itajaí do Sul, Rio — 102-103 H 7
Itajaí-Mirim, Rio — 102-103 H 7
Itají 100-101 E 9
Itajibá 100-101 E 8
Itajubá 92-93 K 9
Itajuípe 92-93 LM 7
Itaka 132-133 W 7
Īṭal, Wādī — 166-167 J 2-3
Itala = 'Adale 172 J 1
Itala, Río — 106-107 A 6
Itálica 120-121 DE 10
Italó 106-107 F 5
Italy 122-123 C 3-F 5
Italy, TX 76-77 F 6
Itamaraju 100-101 E 9
Itamarandiba 102-103 L 2
Itamataré 100-101 A 2
Itambacuri 102-103 M 3
Itambacuri, Rio — 102-103 M 3
Itambé 92-93 L 8
Itambé, Pico de — 102-103 L 3
Itamirim 100-101 C 8
Itamoji 102-103 J 4
Itamotinga 100-101 DE 5
Itanagra 100-101 EF 7
Itanhaém 102-103 J 6
Itanhandu 102-103 K 5
Itanhauã, Rio — 98-99 F 7
Itanhém 100-101 D 3
Itanhém, Rio — 100-101 E 9
Itanhomi 102-103 M 3
Itany 92-93 J 4
Itaocara 92-93 L 9
Itapaci 92-93 JK 7
Itapagé 92-93 LM 5
Itaparanã, Rio — 98-99 G 8
Itaparica, Ilha de — 100-101 E 7
Itapé [BR] 100-101 E 8
Itapé [PY] 102-103 D 6
Itapebi 92-93 M 8
Itapeim 100-101 EF 3
Itapeipu 100-101 D 6
Itapemirim 92-93 LM 9
Itapercerica 102-103 K 4
Itaperuna 102-103 LM 4
Itapetim 100-101 F 4
Itapetinga 92-93 LM 8
Itapetininga 111 G 2
Itapeva 111 G 2
Itapeva, Lagoa — 106-107 MN 2
Itapevi 106-107 K 2
Itapicuru [BR ↑ Alagoinhas] 100-101 EF 6
Itapicuru [BR ← Jequié] 100-101 D 7
Itapicuru, Rio — [BR, Bahia] 92-93 M 7
Itapicuru, Rio — [BR, Maranhão] 92-93 L 5
Itapicuru, Serra — 92-93 KL 6
Itapicuru Açu, Rio — 100-101 DE 6
Itapicurumirim 92-93 L 5
Itapicurumirim, Rio — 100-101 DE 6
Itapicuruzinho, Rio — 100-101 C 3
Itapina 100-101 D 10
Itapinima 98-99 H 7
Itapinima, Raudal — 94-95 F 7
Itapipoca 92-93 M 5
Itapira 92-93 K 9
Itapiranga 102-103 F 7
Itapirapuã, Pico — 102-103 H 6
Itapitocaí 106-107 J 2
Itapiúna 100-101 E 3
Itápolis 102-103 H 4
Itapora 102-103 E 4-5
Itaporanga [BR, Paraíba] 100-101 EF 4
Itaporanga [BR, São Paulo] 102-103 H 5
Itaporanga d'Ajuda 100-101 F 6
Itapuã [BR] 106-107 M 3
Itapúa [PY] 102-103 DE 7
Itapuí 102-103 H 5
Itaquaí, Rio — 98-99 C 7
Itaquatiara, Riacho — 100-101 D 5
Itaqui 111 E 3
Itarantim 100-101 DE 8
Itararé 102-103 H 6
Itararé, Rio — 102-103 H 5
Itarema 100-101 E 2
Itariri 102-103 J 6
Itārsi 134-135 M 6
Itarumã 102-103 G 3
Itasca, TX 76-77 F 6
Itasca, Lake — 64-65 G 2
Itatí 106-107 H 1
Itatiba 102-103 J 5

Itatina, Serra dos — 102-103 J 6
Itatinga 102-103 H 5
Itatique 104-105 E 7
Itatira 100-101 E 3
Itatuba 92-93 G 6
Itauçu 102-103 H 2
Itaueira 100-101 C 4
Itaueira, Rio — 100-101 C 4-5
Itaúna 102-103 K 4
Itaúnas 100-101 E 10
Iṭāva = Bīna 138-139 G 5
Iṭāvā = Etāwah 138-139 F 5
Itawa = Etāwah 134-135 M 5
Itbayat Island 146-147 H 11
Ite 96-97 F 10
Itebero 171 AB 3
Itel, Ouèd — = Wādī Īṯal 166-167 J 2-3
Itende 171 C 4
Itenes, Rio — 104-105 E 3
Ithaca, MI 70-71 H 4
Ithaca, NY 64-65 L 3
Ithaca = Ithákē 122-123 J 6
Ithákē 122-123 J 6
Ithan Creek 84 III a 1
Ithrā = Itrah 136-137 G 7
Itigi 172 F 3
Itimbiri 172 D 1
Itinga [BR, Maranhão] 98-99 P 7
Itinga [BR, Minas Gerais] 102-103 M 2
Itinga da Serra 100-101 DE 6
Itinoseki = Ichinoseki 142-143 QR 4
Itiquira 92-93 J 8
Itiquira, Rio — 92-93 H 8
Itirapina 102-103 J 5
Itire 170 III ab 1
Itiruçu 92-93 L 7
Itiúba 92-93 M 7
Itkillik River 58-59 M 2
'Itmāniya, El- = Al-'Uthmānīyah 173 BC 4
Itō 144-145 M 5
Itoigawa 144-145 L 4
Itoikawa = Itoigawa 144-145 L 4
Itororó 100-101 DE 8
Itrah 136-137 G 7
Itrī, Jabal — 173 D 7
Iṭsā 173 B 3
Itschnach 128 IV b 2
Itsjang = Yichang 142-143 L 5
Itterbeek 128 II a 1
Itu [BR] 102-103 J 5
Itu [WAN] 168-169 G 4
I-tu = Yidu 142-143 M 4
Itu = Yidu 146-147 C 6
Ituaçu 92-93 L 7
Ituango 94-95 D 4
Ituberá 100-101 E 7
Itueta 102-103 M 3
Ituí, Rio — 92-93 E 6
Ituim 106-107 M 2
Ituiutaba 102-103 H 3
Itula 172 E 2
Itulilik, AK 58-59 J 6
Itumbiara 92-93 K 8
Itumbiara, Represa de — 102-103 H 3
Itumirim 102-103 K 4
Ituna 61 G 5
Ituni Township 92-93 H 3
Itupeva 100-101 D 3
Itupiranga 92-93 JK 6
Ituporanga 102-103 H 7
Iturama 102-103 GH 3
Ituri 172 E 1
Iturregui 106-107 G 6
Iturup, ostrov — 132-133 c 8
Ituverava 102-103 J 4
Ituxi, Rio — 92-93 F 6
Ituzaingó 106-107 J 1
Ituzaingó, Morón- 110 III b 1
Īṯzar 166-167 D 3
Itzawisis 174-175 C 4
Itzehoe 118 D 1-2
Iuiú 100-101 C 8
Iuka, MS 78-79 E 3
Iúna 100-101 D 11
Iva, SC 80-81 E 3
Ivacevičì 124-125 E 7
Ivaí, Rio — 111 F 2
Ivaiporã 102-103 G 6
Ivajlovgrad 122-123 M 5
Ivalo 116-117 M 3
Ivalojoki 116-117 M 3
Ivan, AR 78-79 C 4
Ivancevo 124-125 S 4
Ivančina 124-125 TU 3
Ivangorod 124-125 G 4
Ivanhoe 158-159 H 6
Ivanhoe, MN 70-71 BC 3
Ivanhoe, Melbourne- 161 II c 1
Ivanhoe River 62 K 2-3
Ivaniči 126-127 B 1
Ivankov 126-127 DE 1
Ivan'kovo [SU, Kalininskaja Oblast'] 124-125 L 5
Ivanof Bay, AK 58-59 cd 2
Ivano-Frankovsk 126-127 B 2
Ivanov 126-127 D 2
Ivanovka [SU, Rossijskaja SFSR] 124-125 T 7
Ivanovka [SU, Ukrainskaja SSR] 126-127 E 3
Ivanovo [SU, Belorusskaja SSR] 124-125 E 7
Ivanovo [SU, Rossijskaja SFSR] 132-133 FG 6
Ivanovo, Voznesensk- = Ivanovo 132-133 FG 6
Ivanovskaja 124-125 UV 3
Ivanovskoje, Moskva- 113 V d 2
Ivanowsky 106-107 F 6
Ivantejevka [SU, Saratovskaja Oblast'] 124-125 R 7
Ivanuškova 132-133 UV 6
Ivaščenkovo = Čapajevsk 132-133 HJ 7
Ivatuba 102-103 FG 5
Ivdel' 132-133 L 5
Ivenec 124-125 F 7
Ivigtût 56-57 b 5
Ivindo 172 B 1
Ivinheima 102-103 F 5
Ivinheima, Rio — 92-93 J 9
Ivisaruk River 58-59 G 1-2
Iviza = Ibiza 120-121 H 9
Ivje 124-125 E 7
Ivnica 126-127 D 1
Ivohibe 172 J 6
Ivón 104-105 C 2
Ivón, Río — 104-105 C 2
Ivory Coast [RI, landscape] 164-165 CD 8
Ivory Coast [RI, state] 164-165 CD 7
Ivot 124-125 K 7
Ivrea 122-123 B 3
Ivrindi 136-137 B 3
Ivry-sur-Seine 129 I c 2
Ivuna 171 C 5
Iwadate 144-145 MN 2
Iwaizumi 144-145 NO 3
Iwaki 144-145 N 4
Iwaki yama 144-145 N 2
Iwakuni 144-145 J 5
Iwamizawa 142-143 R 3
Iwanai 144-145 b 2
Iwanowo = Ivanovo 132-133 FG 6
Iwanuma 144-145 N 3
Iwata 144-145 LM 5
Iwate [J, administrative unit] 144-145 N 2-3
Iwate [J, place] 144-145 N 3
Iwate-yama 144-145 N 3
Iwo 164-165 E 7
Iwō-jima = Iō-jima 144-145 H 7
Iwōn 144-145 G 2
Iwopin 168-169 G 4
Iwu = Yiwu 146-147 GH 7
Ixiamas 92-93 F 7
Ixopo 172 EF 8
Ixtacalco 91 I c 2
Ixtacalco-Agrícola Oriental 91 I c 2
Ixtacalco-Agrícola Pantitlán 91 I c 2
Ixtacalco-San Andrés Tetepilco 91 I c 2
Ixtapalapa 91 I c 2
Ixtapalapa-Avante 91 I c 3
Ixtapalapa-Escuadrón 201 91 I c 2
Ixtapalapa-Héroes de Churubusco 91 I c 2
Ixtapalapa-Los Reyes 91 I c 2
Ixtapalapa-San Felipe Terremotos 91 I c 2
Ixtapalapa-Santa Cruz Meyehualco 91 I c 2
Ixtapalapa-Santa Martha Acatitla 91 I cd 2
Ixtapalapa-Santiago Acahualtepec 91 I c 2
Ixtapalapa-Tepalcates 91 I c 2
Ixtayutla 86-87 M 9
Ixtepec 64-65 G 8
Ixtlán del Río 86-87 HJ 7
I-yang = Yiyang [TJ, Hunan] 142-143 L 6
Iyang = Yiyang [TJ, Jiangxi] 146-147 F 7
I-yang = Yiyang [TJ, Jiangxi] 146-147 F 7
Iyang, Pegunungan — 152-153 K 9
Iyo 144-145 J 6
Iyomishima 144-145 J 6
Iyonada 144-145 HJ 6
I-yüan = Yiyuan 146-147 G 3
Iž 124-125 T 5
'Iz, Ḥāssī al- 166-167 G 4
Izabal, Lago de — 64-65 HJ 8
Izalco 64-65 H 9
Izamal 86-87 Q 7
Izashiki = Sata 144-145 H 7
Iz'aslav 126-127 C 1
Izaviknek River 58-59 F 6
Izberbaš 126-127 NO 5
Izdeškovo 124-125 JK 6
Izembek Bay 58-59 b 2
Iževsk 132-133 J 6
Izhevsk = Iževsk 132-133 J 6
Izigan, Cape — 58-59 n 4
Izki 134-135 H 6
Ižma [SU, place] 132-133 J 4
Ižma [SU, river] 132-133 J 5
Izmail 126-127 D 4
Izmajlovo 124-125 Q 7
Izmajlovo, Moskva- 113 V d 2
Izmajlovskij PkiO 113 V d 2
Izmalkovo 124-125 LM 7
İzmir 134-135 B 3
İzmir körfezi 136-137 B 3
İzmit 134-135 BC 2
İzmit körfezi 136-137 C 2
İznik 136-137 C 2
İznik gölü 136-137 C 2
Izobil'nyj 126-127 KL 4
Izoplit 124-125 KL 5
Izozog 104-105 E 6
Izozog, Bañados de — 92-93 G 8
Izra' 136-137 G 6
Izúcar de Matamoros 86-87 LM 8
Izu hantō 144-145 M 5
Izuhara 144-145 G 5
Iz'um 126-127 H 2
Izumi 144-145 H 6
Izumi, Yokohama- 155 III a 3
Izumo 144-145 J 5
Izu-shotō 142-143 QR 5
Izu syotō = Izu-shotō 142-143 QR 5
Izvestij CIK, ostrova — 132-133 OP 2

J

Ja = Dja 164-165 G 8
Jaab Lake 62 K 1
Jaagupi 124-125 E 4
Jaani, Järva- 124-125 EF 4
Ja Ayun = Ya Ayun 150-151 G 6
Jāb, Tall — 136-137 G 6
Jabal, Baḥr al- 164-165 L 7
Jabalā 166-167 D 2
Jabal 'Abd al-'Azīz 136-137 HJ 4
Jabal Abū Ḍahr 173 D 6
Jabal Abū Dhi'āb 173 D 5
Jabal Abū Ḥamāmīd 173 D 5
Jabal Abū Ḥarbah 173 C 4
Jabal Abū Jamal 164-165 M 6
Jabal Abū Jurdī 173 D 6
Jabal Abū Rijmayn 136-137 H 5
Jabal aḍ-Ḍāyah 166-167 F 2
Jabal ad-Dūgh 166-167 F 3
Jabal ad-Durūz 134-135 D 4
Jabal Aghlāghal 166-167 G 6
Jabal Ajā 134-135 E 5
Jabal 'Ajlūn 136-137 FG 6
Jabal al-Abyaḍ, Al- 166-167 L 1
Jabal al-Aḍīriyāt 136-137 G 7
Jabal al-Aḥmar 173 B 3
Jabal al-'Ajmah 164-165 L 3
Jabal al-Akhḍar [LAR] 164-165 J 2
Jabal al-Akhḍar [Oman] 134-135 H 6
Jabal al-Anṣārīyah 136-137 G 5
Jabal al-'Askar 166-167 L 2
Jabal al-'Aṣr 173 B 6
Jabal al-Awrās 166-167 JK 2
Jabal al-Barqah 173 C 5
Jabal al-Batrā 136-137 F 8
Jabal al-Bishrī 136-137 H 5
Jabal al-Farāyid 173 D 6
Jabal al-Finṭās 173 B 6
Jabal al-Gulūd 166-167 M 1
Jabal al-Ḥāṣ 136-137 G 5
Jabal al-Jalālat al-Baḥrīyah 173 BC 3
Jabal al-Jalālat al-Qiblīyah 173 C 3
Jabal al-Jaw'alīyāt 136-137 G 7
Jabal al-Jiddī 173 C 2
Jabal al-Julūd 166-167 M 1
Jabal al-Kurā' 166-167 J 2
Jabal al-Kusūm 166-167 J 3
Jabal al-Lawz 134-135 D 5
Jabal al-Majradah 166-167 KL 1
Jabal al-Manār 134-135 EF 8
Jabal al-Mūdīr 166-167 HJ 7
Jabal al-Muqattam 170 II b 1-c 2
Jabal al-Qamar 134-135 G 7
Jabal al-Qṣūr 166-167 M 3
Jabal al-Titrī 166-167 H 1-2
Jabal al-'Urf 173 C 4
Jabal al-'Uwaynāt 164-165 K 4
Jabal al-Wāqif 173 B 6
Jabal al-Wārshanīs [DZ, mountain] 166-167 G 1-2
Jabal al-Wārshanīs [DZ, mountains] 166-167 GH 2
Jabal Ankūr 173 DE 7
Jabal an-Namāshah 166-167 K 2
Jabal an-Nasir 164-165 F 4
Jabal Ardar Gwagwa 173 D 6
Jabal Arkanū 164-165 J 4
Jabal ar-Ruwāq 136-137 G 5-6
Jabal as-Sarj 166-167 L 2
Jabal as-Sawdā' 164-165 GH 3
Jabal aṣ-Ṣayda' 166-167 G 2
Jabal as-Saykh 136-137 FG 6
Jabal as-Sibā'ī 173 CD 5
Jabal as-Simḥām 134-135 GH 7
Jabal Asūtarībah 173 E 7
Jabal 'Ataqah 173 C 2-3
Jabal ath-Thabt 173 CD 3
Jabal at-Tanf 136-137 H 6
Jabal aṭ-Ṭayr 134-135 E 7
Jabal at-Tīh 164-165 L 3
Jabal aṭ-Ṭubayq 134-135 D 5
Jabal Awlād Nāīl 166-167 H 2
Jabal 'Ayashī 164-165 CD 2
Jabalayn, Al- 164-165 L 6
Jabal 'Aysa 166-167 F 3
Jabal Azūrkī 166-167 C 4
Jabal az-Zāb 166-167 J 2
Jabal az-Zāwiyah 136-137 G 5
Jabal az-Zūjitīn 166-167 L 1-2
Jabal Bābūr [DZ, mountain] 166-167 J 1
Jabal Bābūr [DZ, mountains] 166-167 J 1
Jabal Banī 164-165 C 2-3
Jabal Bāqir 136-137 F 8
Jabal B'athar Zajū 173 C 7
Jabal Bayḍā' 173 D 6
Jabal Būdhīyah 173 C 3
Jabal Bū Iblān 166-167 D 3
Jabal Bū Kāhil 166-167 HJ 2
Jabal Bū Khaḍrah 166-167 KL 2
Jabal Bū Naṣr 166-167 E 3
Jabal Bū Ramlī 166-167 L 2
Jabal Buwārah 173 D 3
Jabal Dafdaf 173 D 3
Jabal Dibbāgh 173 D 4
Jabal Dīrah 166-167 H 1
Jabal Ghāb 136-137 H 5
Jabal Gharbī 136-137 H 5
Jabal Ghārib 164-165 L 3
Jabal Hadal 'Awāb 173 D 7
Jabal Hajir 134-135 G 8
Jabal Ḥamātah 164-165 LM 4
Jabal Ḥamrīn 136-137 KL 5
Jabal Hilāl 173 CD 2
Jabali, Isla — 108-109 HJ 3
Jabal Ibrāhīm 134-135 E 6
Jabal Ijrān 166-167 H 6
Jabal 'Ikdat 166-167 B 4
Jabal Īmīdghās 166-167 D 4
Jabal Īs 173 D 6
Jabal Itrī 173 D 7
Jabal Jirays 173 D 7
Jabal Jūrgāy 164-165 JK 6
Jabal Kalāt 173 D 6
Jabal Kasal 166-167 G 3
Jabal Katrīnah 164-165 L 3
Jabal Kharaz 134-135 E 8
Jabal Korbiyāy 173 D 6
Jabal Kutunbul 134-135 E 7
Jabal Loubnān = Jabal Lubnān 136-137 FG 5-6
Jabal Lubnān 136-137 FG 5-6
Jabal Lubnān ash-Sharqī 136-137 G 5-6
Jabal Ma'azzah 173 C 2
Jabal Ma'did 166-167 J 2
Jabal Mahmil 166-167 K 2
Jabal Ma'rafāy 173 D 6
Jabal Marrah 164-165 JK 6
Jabal Mazhafah = Jabal Buwārah 173 D 3
Jabal Mazi 166-167 F 3
Jabal M'ghīlah 166-167 L 2
Jabal Mishbīh 164-165 L 4
Jabal Mōāb 136-137 F 7
Jabal Mu'askar 166-167 D 3
Jabal Mubārak 136-137 F 8
Jabal Mudaysīsāt 136-137 G 7
Jabal Muqsim 173 CD 6
Jabal Mūrig 166-167 CD 3
Jabal Murrah 166-167 L 2
Jabal Mu'tiq 173 C 4
Jabal Nafusah 164-165 G 2
Jabal Nasīyah 173 C 6
Jabal Ni'āj 173 C 6
Jabal Nuqruṣ 173 D 5
Jabalón 120-121 F 9
Jabalpur 134-135 MN 6
Jabal Qarn at-Tays 173 C 6
Jabal Qarnayt 134-135 E 6
Jabal Qaṭrānī 173 B 3
Jabal Qaṭṭār 173 C 4
Jabal Rām 136-137 F 8
Jabal R'bāṭah 166-167 L 2
Jabal Ṣabāyā 134-135 E 7
Jabal Ṣaghrū' 164-165 C 2
Jabal Ṣahrā 173 CD 4
Jabal Salālah 173 D 7
Jabal Salmah 134-135 E 5
Jabal Sanām 136-137 M 7
Jabal Shaḥāmbī 164-165 F 1-2
Jabal Shā'ib al-Banāt 164-165 L 3
Jabal Shammar 134-135 E 5
Jabal Shār [Saudi Arabia] 173 D 4
Jabal Shā'r [SYR] 136-137 GH 5
Jabal Shīlyah 164-165 F 1
Jabal Shindidāy 173 E 6
Jabal Sinjār 136-137 JK 4
Jabal Sīrwah 166-167 C 4
Jabal Talju 164-165 K 6
Jabal Tanūshfī 166-167 F 2
Jabal Tāriq, Bughāz — 164-165 CD 1
Jabal Tasasah 166-167 F 2
Jabal Tashrīrt 166-167 J 2
Jabal Tazzikā' 166-167 DE 2
Jabal Tibissah [DZ] 166-167 J 7
Jabal Tibissah [TN] 166-167 L 2
Jabal Tidighīn 166-167 D 2
Jabal Tilimsān 166-167 F 2
Jabal Tishāro 166-167 JK 2
Jabal Tubqāl 164-165 C 2
Jabal Ṭummō 164-165 G 4
Jabal Ṭuwayq 134-135 F 6
Jabal 'Ubkayk 164-165 M 4
Jabal Ūdah 164-165 M 4
Jabal Umm aṭ-Ṭuyūr al-Fawqānī 173 D 6
Jabal Umm 'Inab 173 C 5
Jabal Umm Naqqāṭ 173 CD 5
Jabal Umm Shāghir 173 B 6
Jabal 'Unayzah 134-135 DE 4
Jabal Wārqzīz 164-165 C 3
Jabal Yu'alliq 173 C 2
Jabal Zubayr 173 C 4
Jabaquara, São Paulo- 110 II b 2
Jabavu, Johannesburg- 170 V a 2
Jabīlat, Al- 166-167 BC 4
Jabīlāt, Ḥāssī — 166-167 C 6
Jabinyānah 166-167 M 2
Jabjabah, Wādī — 173 C 7
Jablah 136-137 F 5
Jablanica [AL] 122-123 J 5
Jablanica [BG] 122-123 L 4
Jablanica [YU] 122-123 G 4
Jablunca Pass = Jablunkovsky průsmyk 118 J 4
Jablunkovský průsmyk 118 J 4
Jaboatão 100-101 G 5
Jabotablon 94-95 CD 4
Jabung, Tanjung — 148-149 DE 7
Jabuticabal 92-93 K 9
Jabuticatubas 102-103 L 3
Jaca 120-121 G 7
Jacaf, Canal — 108-109 C 5
Jaçanã, São Paulo- 110 II b 1
Jacaqua 106-107 K 2
Jacaraci 100-101 C 8
Jacaraí, Rio — 100-101 D 2
Jacarandá 100-101 E 8
Jacaraú 100-101 G 4
Jacaré, Rio — [BR, Bahia] 92-93 L 6-7
Jacaré, Rio — [BR, Minas Gerais] 102-103 K 4
Jacaré, Travessão — 98-99 O 10
Jacareacanga 98-99 JK 8
Jacarei 92-93 K 9
Jacarepaguá, Rio de Janeiro- 110 I ab 2
Jacaretinga 98-99 J 9
Jacarèzinho 102-103 H 5
Jáchal = San José de Jáchal 111 C 4
Jáchal, Río — 106-107 C 3
Jachhen 142-143 E 5
Jachroma 124-125 L 5
Jáchymov 118 F 3
Jaciara 102-103 E 1
Jacinto 100-101 D 3
Jacinto Aráuz 106-107 F 7
Jacinto City, TX 85 III bc 1
Jaciparaná 92-93 G 6
Jaciparana, Rio — 98-99 F 9-10
Jackfish 70-71 G 1
Jackfish Lake 61 DE 4
Jackhead Harbour 61 K 5
Jackman Station, ME 72-73 L 2
Jacksboro, TX 76-77 EF 6
Jackson, AL 78-79 F 5
Jackson, CA 74-75 C 3
Jackson, GA 80-81 DE 4
Jackson, KY 72-73 E 6
Jackson, LA 78-79 D 5
Jackson, MI 64-65 JK 3
Jackson, MN 70-71 C 4
Jackson, MO 70-71 F 7
Jackson, MS 64-65 HJ 5
Jackson, MT 66-67 G 3
Jackson, OH 72-73 E 5
Jackson, TN 64-65 J 4
Jackson, WY 66-67 H 4
Jackson, ostrov — 132-133 H-K 1
Jackson Head 158-159 N 8
Jackson Heights, New York-, NY 82 III c 2
Jackson Lake 66-67 H 4
Jackson Manion 62 CD 2
Jackson Mountains 66-67 D 5
Jackson Park [CDN] 84 II bc 3
Jackson Park [USA] 83 II b 2
Jackson Prairie 78-79 E 4
Jacksonville, AL 78-79 FG 4
Jacksonville, FL 64-65 KL 5
Jacksonville, IL 70-71 EF 6
Jacksonville, NC 80-81 H 3
Jacksonville, OR 66-67 B 4
Jacksonville, TX 76-77 G 6-7
Jacksonville Beach, FL 80-81 F 5
Jäckvik 116-117 G 4
Jacmel 64-65 M 8
Jacobina 92-93 L 7
Jacob Island 58-59 d 2
Jacob Lake, AZ 74-75 GH 4
Jacobs 62 E 2
Jacobsdal 174-175 F 5
Jaconda 86-87 J 8
Jacques Cartier 82 I bc 1
Jacques Cartier, Mount — 63 D 3
Jacques Cartier, Pont — 82 I b 1
Jacques Cartier, Rivière — 63 A 4
Jacques Cartier Passage 56-57 Y 7-8
Jacu 100-101 A 7
Jacu, Rio — 100-101 G 4
Jacuí [BR, Minas Gerais] 102-103 J 4
Jacuí [BR, Rio Grande do Sul] 106-107 L 2-3
Jacuí, Rio — 106-107 L 2
Jacuípe, Rio — 92-93 LM 7
Jacuizinho 106-107 L 2
Jacumba, CA 74-75 EF 6
Jacundá 92-93 K 5
Jacundá, Rio — 98-99 N 6
Jacupiranga 102-103 HJ 6
Jacura 94-95 G 2
Jacureconga, Cachoeira — 100-101 A 2
Jacurici, Rio — 100-101 E 6
Jacutinga 102-103 J 5
Jacuzão, Cachoeiro — 98-99 O 8
Jadā, Sha'īb — = Sha'īb al-Judā' 136-137 LM 7-8
Jadabpur, Calcutta- 154 II b 3
Jadaf, Wādī al- 134-135 E 4
Jadaf al-Jadaf 136-137 J 6
Jaddangi 140 F 2
Jaddī 166-167 JK 2
Jaddī, Wādī — 164-165 E 2
Jade 118 D 2
Jadīd, Berzekh el — = Rā's al-Jadīd 166-167 E 2
Jadīd, Bi'r — 166-167 K 3
Jadīd, Rā's al- 166-167 E 2
Jadīda, el — = Al-Jadīdah 164-165 C 2
Jadīdah, Al- [MA] 164-165 G 2
Jadīdah, Al- [TN] 166-167 L 1
Jadīd Rā's al-Fīl 164-165 K 6
Jado = Jādū 164-165 G 2
Jadotville = Likasi 172 E 4
Jadrin 124-125 Q 6
Jādū 164-165 G 2
Jaén [E] 120-121 F 10
Jaén [PE] 96-97 B 4
Jaenagar = Jaynagar 138-139 L 4
Jæren 116-117 A 8
Jaesalmēr = Jaisalmer 134-135 KL 5
Jafa, Tel Aviv- = Tel Aviv-Yafō 134-135 C 4
Ja'far, Ḥāssī — 166-167 H 4
Jāfarābād [IND, Gujarāt] 138-139 C 7
Jafarābād [IND, Mahārāshtra] 138-139 EF 7
Ja'farābād [IR] 134-135 F 3
Jāfarah 166-167 M 3
Jaffa, Cape — 160 D 6
Jaffatin = Jazā'ir Jiftūn 173 CD 4
Jaffna = Yāpanaya 134-135 MN 9
Jaffna Lagoon = Yāpanē Kalapuwa 140 E 6
Jaffray 66-67 F 1
Jafr, Al- [JOR, place] 134-135 D 4
Jafr, Al- [JOR, river] 136-137 G 7
Jafr, El- = Al-Jafr 134-135 D 4
Jāfrābād = Jāfarābād 138-139 C 7
Jafū, Ḥāssī — 164-165 E 2
Jafū, Wādī — 166-167 H 4
Jagādhari = Jagādhri 138-139 F 2
Jagādhri 138-139 F 2
Jagalūr 140 C 3
Jagalūru = Jagalūr 140 C 3
Jagannāthpur 154 II a 1
Jagatsingpur 138-139 KL 7
Jagatsiṅhpur = Jagatsingpur 138-139 KL 7
Jagdalpur 134-135 N 7
Jagdīspur 138-139 K 5
Jagersfontein 174-175 F 5
Jaggayyapeta 140 E 2
Jaghbūb, Al- 164-165 J 3
Jaghiagh, Wādī — 136-137 J 4
Jaghjagh, Ouâdî — = Wādī Jaghiagh 136-137 J 4
Jagir = Yelandūr 140 C 4
Jagl'ajarvi 124-125 H 2
Jagodnoje 132-133 cd 5
Jagog Tsho 142-143 F 5
Jago River 58-59 Q 2
Jagotin 126-127 E 1
Jagraon 138-139 E 2
Jagst 118 DE 4
Jagtiāl 134-135 M 7
Jagua, La — 92-93 E 3
Jaguapitã 102-103 G 5
Jaguaquara 100-101 E 7
Jaguarão 111 F 4
Jaguarari 92-93 LM 7
Jaguaretama 100-101 E 3
Jaguari 106-107 K 2
Jaguari, Rio — 106-107 K 2
Jaguariaíva 102-103 H 6
Jaguaribe 100-101 E 3
Jaguaribe, Rio — 92-93 M 6
Jaguaripe 100-101 E 7
Jaguaruana 100-101 F 3
Jaguaruna 102-103 H 8
Jagüé 106-107 C 2
Jagüé, Río del — 111 C 3
Jagüeles, Cañadón de los — 106-107 D 7
Jagüey Grande 88-89 F 3
Jahānābād 138-139 K 5
Jahāzpur 138-139 E 5
Jahīrābād = Zahīrābād 140 C 2
Jahotyn = Jagotin 126-127 E 1
Jahrah, Al- 134-135 F 5
Jahrom 134-135 G 5
Jaianary, Cachoeira — 94-95 J 7
Jaicós 92-93 L 6
Jaijon 138-139 F 2
Jailolo 148-149 J 6
Jaime Prats 106-107 CD 5
Jaintgaḍa = Jaintgarh 138-139 K 6
Jaintgarh 138-139 K 6
Jaintiapur = Jaintiyāpūr 141 BC 3
Jaintiyāpūr 141 BC 3
Jaipur [IND, Assam] 141 D 2
Jaipur [IND, Rājasthān] 134-135 M 5
Jaipūr Hāṭ 138-139 M 5
Jaisalmer 134-135 KL 5
Jaitāran 138-139 DE 4
Jaja 132-133 Q 6
Jajah, Al- 173 B 5
Jājarkot 138-139 HJ 3
Jājarm 134-135 H 3
Jajce 122-123 G 3
Jajin, Kampung — 150-151 D 10
Jājpur 138-139 L 7
Jajva [SU, place] 124-125 V 4
Jajva [SU, river] 124-125 V 4
Jakan, mys — 132-133 j 4
Jakarta 148-149 E 8
Jakarta, Teluk — 152-153 G 8-9
Jakarta-Ancol 154 IV ab 1
Jakarta-Binaria 154 IV b 1
Jakarta-Bintaro 154 IV a 2
Jakarta-Cedong 154 IV b 2
Jakarta-Cempaka Putih 154 IV b 2
Jakarta-Cilandak 154 IV a 2
Jakarta-Cililitan 154 IV b 2
Jakarta-Cilincing 154 IV b 1
Jakarta-Cipete 154 IV a 2
Jakarta-Duren Tiga 154 IV b 2
Jakarta-Gambir 154 IV a 1
Jakarta-Gelora 154 IV a 2
Jakarta-Grogol Petamburan 154 IV a 1
Jakarta-Halim 154 IV b 2
Jakarta-Jatinegara 154 IV b 2
Jakarta-Kebayoran Baru 154 IV a 2
Jakarta-Kebon Jeruk 154 IV a 2
Jakarta-Kemang 154 IV a 2
Jakarta-Kemayoran 154 IV b 1
Jakarta-Klender 154 IV b 2
Jakarta-Koja 154 IV b 1
Jakarta-Kramat Jati 154 IV b 2
Jakarta-Mampang Prapatan 154 IV a 2
Jakarta-Manggarai 154 IV b 2
Jakarta-Matraman 154 IV b 2
Jakarta-Menteng 154 IV ab 2
Jakarta-Palmerah 154 IV a 2
Jakarta-Pancoran 154 IV b 2
Jakarta-Pasar Minggu 154 IV ab 2
Jakarta-Pejagalan 154 IV a 1
Jakarta-Penjaringan 154 IV a 1
Jakarta-Pluit 154 IV a 1
Jakarta-Pulo Gadung 154 IV b 2
Jakarta-Rawamangun 154 IV b 2
Jakarta-Sawa Besar 154 IV ab 1
Jakarta-Senen 154 IV b 2
Jakarta-Setia Budi 154 IV ab 2
Jakarta-Simpruk 154 IV a 2
Jakarta-Slipi 154 IV a 2
Jakarta-Sunda Kelapa 154 IV ab 1
Jakarta-Sunter 154 IV b 1
Jakarta-Taman Sari 154 IV a 1
Jakarta-Tambora 154 IV a 1
Jakarta-Tanah Abang 154 IV a 2
Jakarta-Tanjung Prick 154 IV b 1
Jakarta-Tebet 154 IV b 2
Jākhal 138-139 E 3
Jakhao = Jakhau 138-139 B 6
Jakhau 138-139 B 6
Jakima = Lachdenpochja 124-125 GH 3
Jakkalawater 174-175 A 2
Jakobsdal = Jacobsdal 174-175 F 5
Jakobshavn = Jlulissat 56-57 ab 4
Jakobstad 116-117 JK 6
Jakobstadt = Jēkabpils 124-125 E 5
Jakovlevo 126-127 H 1
Jakovo 124-125 T 3
Jakša 132-133 K 5
Jakšanga 124-125 PQ 4
Jakšur-Bodja 124-125 T 5
Jakutsk 132-133 Y 5
Jal, NM 76-77 C 6
Jaladah, Al- 134-135 F 7
Jālālābād 138-139 GH 4
Jālālābad = Jalāl Kōt 134-135 KL 4
Jalālat al-Baḥrīyah, Jabal al- 173 BC 3
Jalālat al-Qiblīyah, Jabal al- 173 C 3
Jalāl Kōt 134-135 KL 4
Jalālpur [IND] 138-139 J 4
Jalālpūr [PAK] 138-139 C 3
Jalama 126-127 O 6
Jalāmīd, Al- 136-137 HJ 7
Ja'lan 134-135 H 6
Jalandar = Jullundur 134-135 LM 4
Jalandhar = Jullundur 134-135 LM 4
Jalangi 138-139 M 5
Jalan Kayu 154 III b 1
Jalaon = Jalaun 138-139 G 4
Jalapa 86-87 Q 10
Jalapa Enríquez 64-65 GH 8
Jalārpet 140 D 4
Jalaun 138-139 G 4
Jalawlā' 136-137 L 5
Jalca, La — 96-97 C 5
Jāle 138-139 K 4
Jales 102-103 G 4
Jalesar 138-139 G 4
Jaleshvara = Jaleswar 138-139 L 7
Jaleswar [IND] 138-139 L 7
Jaleswar [Nepal] 138-139 KL 4
Jalgāñv = Jālgaon [IND ← Bhusāwal] 134-135 M 6
Jalgāñv = Jālgaon [IND → Bhusāwal] 138-139 F 7
Jālgaon [IND ← Bhusāwal] 134-135 M 6
Jālgaon [IND → Bhusāwal] 138-139 F 7
Jalhāk, Al- 164-165 L 6
Jalīb, Maqarr al- 136-137 J 6
Jalībah 136-137 M 7
Jalib Shahab 136-137 M 7
Jalingo 164-165 G 7
Jalisco 64-65 EF 7
Jalitah, Jazā'ir — 166-167 L 1
Jaliṭah, Qanāt — 166-167 L 1
Jallekān 136-137 N 6
Jālna 134-135 M 7
Jalon = Jalaun 138-139 G 4
Jalón, Río — 120-121 G 8
Jalo Oasis = Wāḥāt Jālū 164-165 J 3
Jālor 138-139 D 5
Jalore = Jālor 138-139 D 5
Jalostotitlán 86-87 J 7
Jalpa 86-87 J 7
Jalpaiguri 138-139 M 4
Jalpan 86-87 KL 6-7
Jalpug 126-127 D 3-4
Jalpug, ozero — 126-127 D 4
Jalta 126-127 G 4
Jaltenango 86-87 O 10
Jaltuškov 126-127 C 2
Jalu = Yalu Jiang 144-145 EF 2
Jālū, Wāḥāt — 164-165 J 3
Jaluit 208 G 2
Jama [EC] 96-97 A 2
Jama = Silyānah 166-167 L 1
Jama, Salina de — 104-105 C 8
Jamaame 164-165 N 8
Jamaari 168-169 H 3
Jamaat 142-143 E 2
Jamā'at al-Ma'yuf 136-137 M 7
Jamaica 64-65 L 8
Jamaica, New York-, NY 82 III d 2
Jamaica Bay 82 III cd 3
Jamaica Channel 64-65 L 8
Jamaica Plain, Boston-, MA 84 I b 3
Jamaika 64-65 L 8
Jamakhaṇḍi = Jamkhandi 134-135 LM 7
Jamal, poluostrov — 132-133 MN 3
Jamālīyah, Al-Qāhirah-al- 170 II b 1
Jamalo-Neneckij Nacional'nyj Okrug = Yamalo-Nenets Autonomous Area 132-133 M-O 4-5
Jamālpur [BD] 138-139 M 5
Jamālpur [IND] 138-139 L 5
Jamantau, gora — 132-133 K 7
Jamanxim, Rio — 92-93 H 6
Jamari 98-99 G 9
Jamari, Rio — 92-93 G 6
Jamaši 124-125 S 6
Jambeli, Canal de — 96-97 AB 3

Jambi [RI, administrative unit = 5 ◁] 148-149 D 7
Jambi [RI, place] 148-149 D 7
Jambol 122-123 M 4
Jambuair, Tanjung — 152-153 BC 3
Jambūr 136-137 L 5
Jambusar 138-139 D 6
Jamdena, Pulau — 148-149 K 8
James, Isla — 108-109 B 5
James Bay 56-57 UV 7
James Bay, Parc provincial de — 62 M 1
James Craik 106-107 F 4
James Island = Bāda Kyûn 150-151 B 7
James Range 158-159 F 4
James River [USA ◁ Chesapeake Bay] 64-65 L 4
James River [USA ◁ Missouri River] 64-65 G 2
Jamestown, KS 68-69 H 6
Jamestown, KY 70-71 H 7
Jamestown, ND 64-65 G 2
Jamestown, NY 64-65 L 3
Jamestown, OH 72-73 E 5
Jamestown, TN 78-79 G 2
Jamestown [AUS] 160 D 4
Jamestown [Saint Helena] 204-205 G 10
Jamestown [ZA] 174-175 G 6
Jamestown Reservoir 68-69 G 2
Jamikunta 140 D 1
Jamīlah 166-167 J 1
Jaminaua, Rio — 96-97 F 6
Jām Jodhpur 138-139 BC 7
Jamkhandi 134-135 LM 7
Jāmkhed 140 B 1
Jamm 124-125 G 4
Jamm, Al- 166-167 M 2
Jammāl 166-167 M 2
Jammalamadugu 140 D 3
Jammerbugt 116-117 C 9
Jammerdrif 174-175 G 5
Jammu 134-135 LM 4
Jammu and Kashmīr 134-135 LM 3-4
Jamnā = Yamuna 134-135 MN 5
Jāmnagar 134-135 L 6
Jāmner 138-139 E 7
Jamnotri 138-139 G 2
Jampol' [SU, Chmel'nickaja Oblast'] 126-127 C 2
Jampol' [SU, Vinnickaja Oblast'] 126-127 D 2
Jāmpūr 134-135 KL 5
Jamsah 173 C 4
Jämsänkoski 116-117 L 7
Jamshedpur 134-135 NO 6
Jamsk 132-133 de 6
Jāmtāra 138-139 L 5-6
Jämtland 116-117 E-G 6
Jämtlands Sikås 116-117 F 6
Jamūi 138-139 L 5
Jamūnā [BD] 138-139 M 5
Jamuna [IND] 141 C 2
Jamundí 94-95 C 6
Jāmūr al-Kabīr, Al- 166-167 M 1
Jamursba, Tanjung — 148-149 K 7
Jana 132-133 Z 4
Janagāñv = Jangaon 140 D 2
Janai 154 II a 1
Janā'in 166-167 LM 4
Janaperi, Rio — 92-93 G 4
Janaúba 92-93 L 8
Janaucu, Ilha — 92-93 JK 4
Janaul 132-133 JK 6
Jandaia 102-103 GH 2
Jandaia do Sul 102-103 G 5
Jandaq 134-135 GH 4
Jandiatuba, Rio — 92-93 F 5-6
Jandowae 158-159 K 5
Janeiro, Rio de — 100-101 B 6
Janemale 98-99 L 3
Janesville, CA 66-67 C 5
Janesville, WI 70-71 F 4
Jang 141 B 2
Jangada 102-103 G 7
Jangamo 174-175 L 3
Jangaon 140 D 2
Jangarej 132-133 L 4
Jangi 138-139 G 2
Jangijul' 132-133 M 9
Jangipur 138-139 LM 5
Janglung 138-139 H 2
Jangmu 138-139 LM 3
Jango 102-103 E 4
Jangory 124-125 LM 2
Jangri Tsho 138-139 JK 2
Jang Thang 142-143 E-G 5
Jangtse Chhu 138-139 J 2
Jangtsekiang = Chang Jiang 142-143 K 5-6
Jānī Beyglū 136-137 M 3
Janīn 136-137 F 6
Janisjarvi, ozero — 124-125 H 3
Jānjgīr 138-139 J 6
Janji = Gingee 140 D 4
Jan Kemp 174-175 F 4
Jan Lake 61 G 3
Jan Mayen 52 B 19-20
Jan Mayen Ridge 114-115 H 1-2
Jannah 164-165 FG 4
Jano-Indigirskaja nizmennost' 132-133 Z-c 3
Jānoshalma 118 J 5
Janoviči 124-125 H 6
Janovka = Ivanovka 126-127 E 3
Janowo = Jonava 124-125 E 6
Jānsath 138-139 F 3
Jansenville 174-175 F 7
Janskij 132-133 Za 4
Janskij zaliv 132-133 Za 3
Jan Smuts = Johannesburg Airport 170 V c 1
Jantarnyj 118 J 1
Jantra 122-123 M 4
J. Antunes, Serra — 98-99 G 10-11
Januária 92-93 KL 8
Jan von Riebeeck Park 170 V ab 1
Jao-ho = Raohe 142-143 P 2
Jaonpur = Jaunpur 134-135 N 5
Jaoping = Raoping 146-147 F 10
Jaora 138-139 E 6
Jaorā = Jora 138-139 F 4
Jaoyang = Raoyang 146-147 EF 2
Jao-yang Ho = Raoyang He 144-145 D 2
Japan 142-143 P 5-R 3
Japan Sea 142-143 P 4-Q 3
Japan Trench 156-157 G 3
Japão, Serra do — 100-101 F 5-6
Japara 148-149 F 8
Jāpharābād = Jafarābād 138-139 EF 7
Japonskoje more 132-133 a 9
Japurá, Rio — 92-93 F 5
Jāpvo, Mount — 141 CD 3
Jaqué 94-95 B 4
Jaquí 96-97 D 9
Jaquirana 106-107 M 2
Jar 124-125 T 4
Jara, La — 120-121 E 9
Jarā', Wādī al- 166-167 H 6
Jarābulus 136-137 GH 4
Jarādah 164-165 D 2
Jaraguá 102-103 H 1
Jaraguá, São Paulo- 110 II a 1
Jaraguá, Serra do — 102-103 H 7
Jaraguá do Sul 102-103 H 7
Jaraguari 92-93 HJ 8-9
Jaralito, El — 76-77 B 9
Jaramillo 108-109 F 6
Jaranpada = Jarpara 138-139 K 7
Jaransk 132-133 H 6
Jarānwāla 138-139 D 2
Jararaca, Cachoeira — 102-103 G 6
Jarārah, Wādī — 173 D 6
Jarau 106-107 J 3
Jarauçu, Rio — 98-99 M 5-6
Jarāwī, Al- 136-137 H 7
Jarbah, Jazīrat — 164-165 G 2
Jarbidge, NV 66-67 F 5
Jarcevo [SU, Jenisej] 132-133 R 5
Jarcevo [SU, Smolenskaja Oblast'] 124-125 J 6
Jardim [BR, Ceará] 100-101 E 4
Jardim [BR, Mato Grosso do Sul] 102-103 D 4
Jardim América, São Paulo- 110 II ab 2
Jardim Botânico, Rio de Janeiro- 110 I b 2
Jardim Botânico do Rio de Janeiro 110 I b 2
Jardim da Aclimação 110 II b 2
Jardim de Piranhas 100-101 F 4
Jardim do Seridó 100-101 F 4
Jardim Paulista, São Paulo- 110 II ab 2
Jardim Zoológico do Rio de Janeiro 110 I b 2
Jardim Zoológico do São Paulo 110 II b 2
Jardín Balbuena, Ciudad de México- 91 I c 2
Jardín Botánico de Bogotá 91 III b 2-3
Jardín Botánico de Caracas 91 II b 1-2
Jardin botanique 82 I b 1
Jardin d'Essai 170 I ab 1
Jardin du Luxembourg 129 I c 2
Jardines de la Reina 64-65 L 7
Jardines Flotantes 91 I C 3
Jardinésia 102-103 H 3
Jardines Lookout 155 I b 2
Jardinópolis 102-103 J 4
Jardín Zoológico de México 91 I b 2
Jardin zoologique Angrigon 82 I b 2
Jardin zoologique de Brazzaville 170 IV a 1
Jardin zoologique de Kinshasa 170 IV a 1
Jarega 124-125 TU 2
Jarenga [SU, place] 124-125 R 2
Jarenga [SU, river] 124-125 R 2
Jarensk 132-133 H 5
Jares'ki 126-127 FG 2
Jari, Rio — 92-93 J 5
Jaria Jhangjail = Jariyā Jhanjāyl 141 B 3
Jarībīyah, Ḥāssī — 166-167 J 4
Jarīd, Shaṭṭ al- 164-165 F 2
Jarilla 106-107 D 4
Jarina, Rio — 98-99 M 10
Jarīr, Wādī — 134-135 E 5-6
Jarita, La — 86-87 KL 4
Jariyā Jhanjāyl 141 B 3
Jarjīs 166-167 M 3
Jarkand = Yarkand 142-143 D 4
Jarkovo 132-133 M 6
Jarmashīn, 'Ayn — 173 B 5
Jarnema 124-125 MN 2
Jarny 120-121 K 4
Jarocin 118 H 2-3
Jarok, ostrov — 132-133 a 3
Jaroslavl' 132-133 FG 6
Jarosław 118 L 3-4
Jaroso, CO 68-69 D 7
Jarpara 138-139 K 7
Järpen 116-117 E 6
Jarrāḥī, Rūd-e — 136-137 N 7
Jarry, Parc — 82 I b 1
Jarsah, Shaṭṭ al- 166-167 KL 2
Jar-Sale 132-133 MN 4
Jartum = Al-Kharṭūm 164-165 L 5
Jaru 92-93 G 7
Jaru, Reserva Florestal de — 98-99 GH 9
Jaru, Rio — 98-99 G 10
Järva-Jaani 124-125 EF 4
Järvenpää 116-117 L 7
Jarvie 60 L 2
Jarvis 156-157 J 5
Jarygino 124-125 K 6
Jasdan 138-139 C 6
Jasel'da 124-125 E 7
Jasenevo, Moskva- 113 V b 3
Jasenskaja kosa 126-127 HJ 3
Jashpurnagar 138-139 JK 6
Jasikan 168-169 F 4
Jasin 150-151 D 11
Jasinovataja 126-127 H 2
Jāsk 134-135 H 5
Jaškino 124-125 T 7
Jaškul' 126-127 M 3
Jasnogorsk 124-125 LM 6
Jasnyj 132-133 Y 7
Jasonhalvøy 53 C 30-31
Jason Islands 111 D 8
Jasonville, IN 70-71 G 6
Jasper, AL 78-79 F 4
Jasper, AR 78-79 C 2-3
Jasper, FL 80-81 b 1
Jasper, GA 78-79 G 3
Jasper, IN 70-71 G 6
Jasper, MN 68-69 H 4
Jasper, MO 76-77 G 4
Jasper, TX 76-77 GH 7
Jasper [CDN, Alberta] 56-57 N 7
Jasper [CDN, Ontario] 72-73 J 2
Jasper National Park 56-57 N 7
Jasrāsar 138-139 D 4
Jaṣṣān 136-137 L 6
Jassy = Iaşi 122-123 M 2
Jastrebac 122-123 J 4
Jastrebovka 126-127 H 1
Jászberény 118 JK 5
Jataí [BR ↘ Arrais] 100-101 A 7
Jataí [BR ↙ Rio Verde] 92-93 J 8
Jatapu, Rio — 92-93 H 5
Jatāra 138-139 G 5
Jataúba 100-101 F 4
Jatei 102-103 E 5
Jath 140 B 2
Jati [BR] 100-101 E 4
Jāti [PAK] 138-139 B 5
Jatibarang 152-153 H 9
Jatinegara, Jakarta- 154 IV b 2
Játiva 120-121 G 9
Jatni 138-139 K 7
Jatobá 92-93 JK 5
Jatoi Janūbī 138-139 C 3
Jat Potī = Kārēz 134-135 K 4
Jatunhuasi 96-97 CD 8
Jaú 92-93 K 9
Jaú, Cachoeira do — 98-99 OP 10
Jaú, Rio — 92-93 G 5
Jaua, Meseta de — 94-95 J 5
Jau'alīyāt, Jebel el- = Jabal al-Aḏiriyāt 136-137 G 7
Jauari, Serra — 98-99 M 5
Jauf, Al- = Al-Jawf 134-135 DE 5
Jauf, El — = Al-Jawf 164-165 J 4
Jauja 92-93 DE 7
Jaula, La — 106-107 C 5
Jaumave 86-87 L 6
Jaunde = Yaoundé 164-165 G 8
Jaunjelgava 124-125 E 5
Jaunpiebalga 124-125 F 5
Jaunpur 134-135 N 5
Jaura = Jora 138-139 F 4
Jauru 102-103 E 3
Jauru, Rio — [BR ◁ Rio Coxim] 102-103 EF 3
Jauru, Rio — [BR ◁ Rio Paraguai] 102-103 CD 2
Jauza 113 V c 2
Java 98-99 L 2
Jāvad = Jāwad 138-139 E 5
Javādi Hills 140 D 4
Javaés, Serra dos — 98-99 O 10
Java Head = Tanjung Lajar 148-149 DE 8
Javaj, poluostrov — 132-133 NO 3
Javalambre 120-121 G 8
Javari, Cachoeira do — 98-99 LM 5
Javari, Ilha — 98-99 E 5
Javari, Rio — 92-93 E 6
Java Sea 148-149 EF 8
Javhār = Jawhār 134-135 L 7
Javier, Isla — 108-109 B 6
Javlenka 132-133 M 7
Javor 122-123 HJ 4
Javorov 126-127 A 2
Jāvrā = Jaora 138-139 E 6
Jawa = Java 148-149 EF 8
Jawa Barat = 11 ◁ 148-149 E 8
Jāwad 138-139 E 5
Jaw'alīyāt, Jabal al- 136-137 G 7
Jawa Tengah = 12 ◁ 148-149 E 8
Jawa Timur = 14 ◁ 148-149 F 8
Jawf, Al- [LAR] 164-165 J 4
Jawf, Al- [Saudi Arabia] 134-135 DE 5
Jawf, Al- [Y] 134-135 EF 7
Jawhār 134-135 L 7
Jawi 152-153 H 6
Jawor 118 H 3
Jaxartes = Syrdarja 134-135 K 2
Jay, OK 76-77 G 4
Jaya, Gunung — 148-149 L 7
Jayanca 96-97 B 5
Jayapatna 138-139 J 8
Jayapura 148-149 M 7
Jayawijaya, Pegunungan — 148-149 LM 7
Jaydebpur 141 B 3
Jay Em, WY 68-69 D 4
Jaygaḍ = Jaygarh 140 A 2
Jaygarh 140 A 2
Jāyid 136-137 J 6
Jaynagar [IND, Bihār] 138-139 L 4
Jaynagar [IND, West Bengal] 138-139 M 6
Jaypur = Jaipur [IND, Assam] 141 D 2
Jaypur = Jaipur [IND, Rājasthān] 134-135 M 5
Jaypura = Jeypore 134-135 N 7
Jayton, TX 76-77 D 6
Jaza'ir, Al- [DZ] 164-165 E 1
Jaza'ir, Al- [IRQ] 136-137 M 7
Jazā'ir al-Ikhwān 173 D 4
Jazā'ir al-Kilāb 166-167 M 1
Jazā'ir az-Zubayr 134-135 E 7-8
Jazā'ir Farasān 134-135 E 7
Jazā'ir Ḥalāib 173 E 6
Jazā'ir Jalitah 166-167 L 1
Jazā'ir Jiftūn 173 CD 4
Jazā'ir Khūrīyā Mūrīyā 134-135 H 7
Jazā'ir Qaysūm 173 CD 4
Jazā'ir Qūryāt 166-167 M 2
Jazā'ir Siyāl 173 E 6
Jazīr 136-137 F 5
Jazīra, Al- = Arḍ al-Jazīrah 134-135 E 3-F 4
Jazīrah, Al- [DZ] 166-167 F 2
Jazīrah, Al- [IRQ] 136-137 J 5
Jazīrah, Al- [Sudan] 164-165 L 6
Jazīrah, Arḍ al- 134-135 E 3-F 4
Jazīrah Warraq al-Hadar 170 II b 1
Jazīrat al-Gharbī 166-167 M 2
Jazīrat al-Maṣīrah 134-135 HJ 6
Jazīrat al-Maṭrūḥ 166-167 M 1
Jazīrat al-'Uwaynidhīyah 173 DE 4
Jazīrat an Na'mān = Jazīrat an-Nu'mān 173 D 4
Jazīrat an-Nu'mān 173 D 4
Jazīrat ash-Sharqī 166-167 M 2
Jazīrat Būbīyan 134-135 FG 5
Jazīrat Faylakah 136-137 N 8
Jazīrat Fulaikā' = Jazīrat Faylakah 136-137 N 8
Jazīrat Ghānim 173 C 4
Jazīrat Jarbah 164-165 G 2
Jazīrat Kanā'is 166-167 M 2
Jazīrat Kubbar 136-137 N 8
Jazīrat Marīr 173 DE 6
Jazīrat Muhammad 170 II b 1
Jazīrat Mukawwa' 173 DE 6
Jazīrat Rāshqūn 166-167 EF 2
Jazīrat Safājā 173 D 4
Jazīrat Ṣanāfīr 173 D 4
Jazīrat Shakir 164-165 LM 3
Jazīrat Tīrān 173 D 4
Jazīrat Umm Quṣur 173 D 3-4
Jazīrat Wādī Jimāl 173 D 5
Jazīrat Zabarjad 173 DE 6
Jazīreh Ābādān 136-137 N 7-8
Jazīreh Dārā 136-137 N 7
Jazīreh-Qeshm 134-135 H 5
Jazīreh Qūyūn 136-137 L 4
Jazīreh-ye Khārk 134-135 FG 5
Jazīreh-ye Kīsh 134-135 G 5
Jāz Mūreyān, Hāmūn-e — 134-135 H 5
Jazur Qarqannah 164-165 G 2
Jaz'va 124-125 V 3
Jazykovo [SU, Baškirskaja ASSR] 124-125 U 6
Jazykovo [SU, Uljanovskaja Oblast'] 124-125 Q 6
Jazzīn 136-137 F 6

Jbel Azoûrkî = Jabal Azūrkī 166-167 C 4
Jbel Boû Naṣr = Jabal Bū Naṣr 166-167 E 3
Jbel ed Doûh = Jabal ad-Dūgh 166-167 F 3
Jbel Imedrhâs = Jabal Īmīdghās 166-167 D 4
Jbel Mâsker = Jabal Mu'askar 166-167 D 3
Jbel Ṣarhrô' = Jabal Ṣaghrū' 164-165 C 2
Jbel Ṭâroq, Bôrhâz — = Bughāz Jabal Ṭāriq 164-165 CD 1
Jbel Tazzeka = Jabal Tazzikā' 166-167 DE 2
Jbel Toubqâl = Jabal Tubqāl 164-165 C 2

Jean, NV 74-75 F 5
Jeanerette, LA 78-79 D 6
Jeanette, ostrov — 132-133 ef 2
Jean Lafitte, LA 85 I b 2
Jebail = Jubayl 136-137 F 5
Jebalā = Jabalā' 166-167 D 2
Jebba 164-165 E 7
Jebba = Al-Jabhah 166-167 D 2
Jebel Anaiza = Jabal Unayzah 134-135 DE 4
Jebel Andidanob = Jabal Asūtarībah 173 E 7
Jebel Arkenu = Jabal Arkanū 164-165 J 4
Jebel Chā'r = Jabal Shā'r 136-137 GH 5
Jebel ech Charqî = Jabal ar-Ruwāq 136-137 G 5-6
Jebel ed Dargagā = Jabal Ardar Gwagwa 173 D 6
Jebelein, El- = Al-Jabalayn 164-165 L 6
Jebel el-Jau'alīyāt = Jabal al-Aḏiriyāt 136-137 G 7
Jebel el Sauda = Jabal as-Sawdā' 164-165 GH 3
Jebel esh Sharqi = Jabal Lubnān ash-Sharqī 136-137 G 5-6
Jebel Etrī = Jabal Itrī 173 D 7
Jebel Gimbala = Jabal Marrah 164-165 JK 6
Jebel Obkeik = Jabal 'Ubkayk 164-165 M 4
Jebel 'Ōda = Jabal Ūdah 164-165 M 4
Jebel Teljō = Jabal Talju 164-165 K 6
Jebel Tenf = Jabal at-Tanf 136-137 H 6
Jebel Tisiten = Jabal Tīdīghīn 166-167 D 2
Jeberos 96-97 C 4
Jebīlēt, el — = Al-Jabīlat 166-167 BC 4
Jeblé = Jablah 136-137 F 5
Jechegnadzor 126-127 M 7
Jeddah = Jiddah 134-135 D 6
Jedincy 126-127 C 2
Jedlesee, Wien- 113 I b 1
Jed'ma 124-125 O 3
Jędrzejów 118 K 3
Jedway 60 B 3
Jefara = Az-Zāwīyah 164-165 G 2
Jeffara = Jafārah 166-167 M 3
Jeffers, MN 70-71 C 3
Jefferson, CO 68-69 D 6
Jefferson, GA 80-81 E 3
Jefferson, IA 70-71 C 4-5
Jefferson, LA 85 I ab 2
Jefferson, MT 66-67 GH 2
Jefferson, OH 72-73 F 4
Jefferson, OR 66-67 B 3
Jefferson, TX 76-77 G 6
Jefferson, WI 70-71 F 4
Jefferson, Mount — [USA, Nevada] 74-75 E 3
Jefferson, Mount — [USA, Oregon] 66-67 C 3
Jefferson, Village, VA 82 II a 2
Jefferson City, MO 64-65 H 4
Jefferson City, TN 80-81 E 2
Jefferson Park, Chicago-, IL 83 II a 1
Jeffersonville, GA 80-81 E 4
Jeffersonville, IN 70-71 H 6
Jeffrey Depth 158-159 F 7
Jefremov 124-125 LM 7
Jega 168-169 G 2
Jegorjevsk 132-133 FG 6
Jegorlyk 126-127 K 4
Jegorlykskaja 126-127 K 3
Jegyrjach 132-133 M 5
Jēhlam = Jihlam 134-135 L 4
Jehlum = Jihlam 134-135 L 4
Jehol = Chengde 142-143 M 3
Jeinemeni, Cerro — 108-109 C 6
Jeja 126-127 J 3
Jejsk 126-127 J 3
Jejuí Guazú, Río — 102-103 DE 6
Jejuri 140 B 1
Jēkabpils 124-125 E 5
Jekatarinburg = Sverdlovsk 132-133 L 6
Jekaterinfel'd = Bolnisi 126-127 M 6
Jekaterinodar = Krasnodar 126-127 J 4
Jekaterinoslav = Dnepropetrovsk 126-127 GH 2
Jekaterinovka [SU, Primorskij Kraj] 144-145 J 1
Jekaterinovka [SU, Saratovskaja Oblast'] 124-125 OP 7
Jekaterinštadt = Marx 124-125 Q 8
Jekimoviči 124-125 J 6
Jekubābād 134-135 K 5
Jekyakarta = Yogyakarta 148-149 EF 8
Jelan' [SU, place] 126-127 L 1
Jelan' [SU, river] 126-127 L 1
Jelanec 126-127 E 3
Jelan'-Kolenovskij 126-127 K 1
Jelchovka 124-125 S 7
Jelec 124-125 M 7
Jelenia Góra 118 GH 3
Jelenovka = Sevan 126-127 M 6
Jelenskij 124-125 K 7
Jelfa = Jilfah 164-165 E 2
Jelgava 124-125 DE 5
Jelgavkrasti 124-125 DE 5
Jeli, Kampung — 150-151 CD 10
Jelizavetgrad = Kirovograd 126-127 EF 2
Jelizavetpol' = Kirovabad 126-127 N 6
Jelizavety, mys — 132-133 b 7
Jelizovo [SU, Belorusskaja SSR] 124-125 G 7
Jelizovo [SU, Rossijskaja SFSR] 132-133 e 7
Jellico, TN 78-79 G 2
Jellicoe 62 F 3
Jel'n'a 124-125 J 6
Jeloga 124-125 T 4
Jelovo 124-125 U 5
Jelpačicha 124-125 UV 5
Jelšanka 124-125 Q 8
Jel'sk 124-125 G 8
Jelva 124-125 S 2
Jema = Djema 164-165 K 7
Jema Chhu 138-139 J 2
Jema eṭ Tolba = Jimā'h aṭ-Ṭulbah 166-167 D 2
Jemaja, Pulau — 148-149 DE 6
Jemaluang 150-151 DE 11
Jem'ā Sha'īm Thlēthā' = Jimā' 'Shā'im 166-167 B 3
Jemāt = Jimāt 166-167 B 6
Jember 152-153 K 9-10
Jembiani 171 DE 4
Jembongan, Pulau — 148-149 G 5
Jemca [SU, place] 124-125 N 2
Jemca [SU, river] 124-125 N 2
Jemeck 132-133 G 5
Jemeljanovka 124-125 H 2
Jemeljanovo 124-125 K 5
Jemen 134-135 E 7-8
Jementah 150-151 D 11
Jementau 132-133 N 7
Jemez Pueblo, NM 76-77 A 5
Jemmapes = 'Azzābah 166-167 K 1
Jempang, Danau — 152-153 LM 6
Jena 118 E 3
Jena, LA 78-79 CD 5
Jenakijevo 126-127 J 2
Jenašimskij Polkan, gora — 132-133 RS 6
Jendoûba = Jundūbah 166-167 L 1
Jenera, Kampung — 150-151 C 10
Jenfeld, Hamburg- 130 I b 1
Jên Ho = Ren He 146-147 B 5
Jenhsien = Ren Xian 146-147 E 3
Jên-hua = Renhua 146-147 D 9
Jenischpark 130 I a 1
Jenisej 132-133 Q 4
Jenisej, Bol'šoj — 132-133 S 7
Jenisej, Malyj — 132-133 RS 7
Jenisejsk 132-133 R 6
Jenisejskij kr'až 132-133 R 5-6
Jenisejskij zaliv 132-133 OP 3
Jenkins, KY 80-81 E 2
Jenkins Corner, MD 82 II b 2
Jenkintown, PA 84 III c 1
Jenkiu = Renqiu 142-143 M 4
Jenner 61 C 5
Jenner, CA 74-75 B 3
Jennings, KS 68-69 F 6
Jennings, LA 78-79 C 5
Jennings, MT 66-67 F 1
Jenny Lind Island 56-57 Q 4
Jenotajevka 126-127 N 3
Jensen, UT 66-67 J 5
Jensen Beach, FL 80-81 cd 3
Jens Munk Island 56-57 UV 4
Jens Munks Ø 56-57 cd 5
Jenud = Gorē 164-165 M 7
Jen'uka 132-133 X 6
Jeol = Chengde 142-143 M 3
Jeppener 106-107 HJ 5
Jequeri 102-103 L 4
Jequié 92-93 L 7
Jequitaí 92-93 L 8
Jequitaí, Rio — 102-103 K 2
Jequitinhonha 100-101 D 3
Jequitinhonha, Rio — 92-93 L 8
Jerâblous = Jarābulus 136-137 GH 4
Jerachtur 124-125 N 6
Jerâda = Jarādah 164-165 D 2
Jerantut 148-149 D 6
Jerba = Jazīrat Jarbah 164-165 G 2
Jerbogač'on 132-133 U 5
Jerčevo 124-125 MN 3
Jeremejevo [SU, Komi ASSR] 124-125 V 2
Jérémie 64-65 M 8
Jeremoabo 92-93 M 6-7
Jerevan 126-127 M 6
Jerez de García Salinas 64-65 F 7
Jerez de la Frontera 120-121 DE 10
Jerez de los Caballeros 120-121 D 9
Jergeni 126-127 M 2-3
Jericho [AUS] 158-159 J 4
Jericho [ZA] 174-175 GH 3
Jericho = Arīha 136-137 F 7
Jericó 94-95 CD 5
Jeridoaquara, Ponta — 100-101 DE 2
Jerik = Ilovatka 126-127 MN 1
Jerilderie 160 G 5
Jermak 132-133 O 7
Jermakovskoje 132-133 R 7
Jermī 136-137 L 4
Jeroaquara 102-103 G 1
Jerofej Pavlovič 132-133 X 7
Jerome, AZ 74-75 G 5
Jerome, ID 66-67 F 4
Jeropol 132-133 g 4
Jersey 119 E 7
Jersey City, NJ 64-65 M 3-4
Jersey Shore, PA 72-73 H 4
Jersey Village, TX 85 III a 1
Jerseyville, IL 70-71 E 6
Jeršiči 124-125 J 7
Jerteh 150-151 D 10
Jerumenha 92-93 L 6
Jerusalem = Yĕrūshālayim 134-135 CD 4
Jeruslan 126-127 N 1
Jervis, Monte — 108-109 B 7
Jervis Bay 158-159 K 7
Jervois Range 158-159 G 4
Jerzovka 126-127 M 2
Jesenice 122-123 EF 2
Jeseník 118 H 3
Jesil' 132-133 M 7
Jessalange 171 D 5
Jessaur = Jessore 134-135 O 6
Jesse H. Jones House 85 III b 2
Jessej 132-133 T 4
Jesselton = Kota Kinabalu 148-149 FG 5
Jessentuki 126-127 L 4
Jessica 66-67 C 1
Jesso = Hokkaidō 142-143 RS 3
Jessore 134-135 O 6
Jestro, Webi — = Weyb 164-165 N 7
Jesuit Bend, LA 85 I b 3
Jesup, GA 80-81 EF 5
Jesup, IA 70-71 DE 4
Jesús 102-103 E 7
Jésus, Île — 82 I a 1
Jesús Carranza 86-87 N 9
Jesús María [CO] 94-95 E 5
Jesús María [MEX] 86-87 HJ 6
Jesús María [RA] 111 D 4
Jesús María, Boca de — 86-87 M 5
Jet, OK 76-77 E 4
Jetait 61 H 2
Jetmore, KS 68-69 FG 6
J. E. Torrent = Torrent 106-107 J 2
Jetpur 138-139 C 7
Jevdino 124-125 S 2
Jevgora 124-125 J 2
Jevlach 126-127 N 6
Jevlaševo 124-125 Q 7
Jevpatorija 126-127 F 4
Jewell, IA 70-71 D 4
Jewell, KS 68-69 GH 6
Jewell, Arlington-, VA 82 II a 2
Jewish Autonomous Region = 13 ◁ 132-133 Z 8
Jeypore 134-135 N 7
Ježicha 124-125 Q 4
Jezioro Mamry 118 K 1
Jezioro Śniardwy 118 K 2
Jez'ovo [SU, Udmurtskaja ASSR] 124-125 T 4
Jezovo [SU, Vologodskaja Oblast'] 124-125 M 3
Jez'ovo-Čerkessk = Čerkessk 126-127 L 4
Jēzurī = Jejuri 140 B 1
Jezus-Eik 128 II b 2
Jezzīn = Jazzīn 136-137 F 6

Jhābua 138-139 E 6
Jhagadia 138-139 D 7
Jhagaḍiyā = Jhagadia 138-139 D 7
Jha Jha 138-139 L 5
Jhajjar 138-139 F 3
Jhalakāṭī 141 B 4
Jhālāvāṛ = Jhālawār 138-139 EF 5
Jhālāwār [IND, landscape] 138-139 C 6
Jhālawār [IND, place] 138-139 EF 5
Jhalidā 138-139 KL 6
Jhālod 138-139 E 6
Jhālrapātan 138-139 F 5
Jhang Maghiana = Jhang-Maghiyāna 134-135 L 4
Jhang-Maghiyāna 134-135 L 4
Jhanīdāh 138-139 M 6
Jhanjhārpur 138-139 L 4
Jhānsi 134-135 M 5
Jhāpa 138-139 L 4
Jhārgrām 138-139 L 6
Jharia 138-139 L 6
Jhārsuguda 134-135 NO 6
Jharsugura = Jhārsuguda 134-135 NO 6
Jhavānī = Jhawani 138-139 K 4
Jhawani 138-139 K 4
Jhelum = Jihlam 134-135 L 4
Jhenida = Jhanīdāh 138-139 M 6
Jhīl Manchhar 138-139 A 4
Jhīl Marav 138-139 B 3
Jhinjhūvāda 138-139 C 6
Jhorīgāṅ = Jorigām 138-139 J 8
Jhūnjhunu 138-139 E 3
Jhūṭhī Divi Antarīp = False Divi Point 140 E 3

Jiading 146-147 H 6
Jiaganj 138-139 M 5
Jiahe 146-147 D 9
Jiali = Lharugö 142-143 G 5
Jiali = Qionghai 142-143 L 8
Jialing Jiang 142-143 K 5
Jialu He 146-147 E 4
Jialuo Shankou = Kar La 138-139 MN 3
Jiamusi 142-143 P 2
Ji'an [TJ, Jiangxi] 142-143 LM 6
Ji'an [TJ, Jilin] 144-145 EF 2
Jianchang [TJ → Benxi] 144-145 E 2
Jianchang [TJ ← Jinzhou] 144-145 B 2
Jianchangying 146-147 G 1
Jiande 146-147 G 7
Jiangcun 146-147 D 2
Jiangdu 146-147 G 5
Jiangdu = Yangzhou 142-143 M 5
Jiange 142-143 JK 5
Jianghong 146-147 B 11
Jianghua 146-147 C 9
Jiangkou [TJ, Guangxi Zhuangzu Zizhiqu] 146-147 C 10
Jiangkou [TJ, Guizhou] 146-147 B 8
Jiangkou [TJ, Hubei] 146-147 C 6
Jiangkou [TJ, Hunan] 146-147 C 8
Jiangle 146-147 F 8
Jiangling 142-143 L 5
Jiangmen 142-143 L 7
Jiangnan = Shankou 146-147 C 7
Jiangning 146-147 G 6
Jiangpu 146-147 G 5
Jiangshan 146-147 G 7
Jiangsu 142-143 MN 5
Jiangtai, Beijing- 155 II bc 2
Jiangxi 142-143 LM 6
Jiang Xian 146-147 CD 4
Jiangyin 146-147 H 6
Jiangyong 146-147 C 9
Jianhe [TJ, place] 146-147 B 8
Jian He [TJ, river] 144-145 D 2
Jianhu 146-147 G 5
Jianli 146-147 D 7
Jianning 146-147 F 8
Jian'ou 142-143 M 6
Jianping 144-145 B 2
Jianqian He 146-147 BC 5
Jianshi 146-147 B 6
Jianshui 142-143 J 7
Jianyang [TJ, Fujian] 142-143 M 6
Jianyang [TJ, Sichuan] 142-143 JK 5
Jiaocheng 146-147 CD 3
Jiaohekou 146-147 B 4
Jiaokou 146-147 C 3
Jiaoling 146-147 EF 9
Jiaonan 146-147 G 4
Jiao Xi 146-147 G 8

Jiao Xian 142-143 M 4
Jiaozhou Wan 146-147 H 3-4
Jiaozou 142-143 L 4
Jia Qi = Jiao Xi 146-147 G 8
Jia Qi = Xiao Xi 146-147 GH 7-8
Jiaqian = Jia Xian 146-147 C 2
Jiashan [TJ, Anhui] 146-147 G 5
Jiashan [TJ, Zhejiang] 146-147 H 6
Jiāwān 138-139 J 5
Jia Xian [TJ, Henan] 146-147 D 5
Jia Xian [TJ, Shanxi] 146-147 C 2
Jiaxing 142-143 N 5
Jiayi = Chiayi 142-143 MN 7
Jiayu 146-147 D 6-7
Jiayuguan 142-143 H 4
Jiazi 146-147 F 10
Jibal al-Hudnah 166-167 J 1-2
Jibāl al-Quṣūr 166-167 FG 3
Jibāl an-Nūbah 164-165 KL 6
Jibhalanta = Uliastaj 142-143 H 2
Jibiya 168-169 G 2
Jibóia 98-99 D 4
Jibou 122-123 K 2
Jicarilla Apache Indian Reservation 76-77 A 4
Jičín 118 G 3
Jidaidat Ḥāmir = Judayyīat Ḥāmir 136-137 J 7
Jidāmī, Bi'r al- 173 C 4
Jiddah 134-135 D 6
Jiddat al Ḥarāsīs 134-135 H 6-7
Jiddī, Jabal al- 173 C 2
Jido 134-135 P 5
Jidole = Gīdolē 164-165 M 7
Jiekkevarre 116-117 H 3
Jie Shan = Wudang Shan 146-147 C 5
Jieshi 146-147 E 10
Jieshi Wan 146-147 E 10
Jieshou [TJ, Anhui] 146-147 E 5
Jieshou [TJ, Guangxi Zhuangzu Zizhiqu] 146-147 C 9
Jieshou [TJ, Jiangsi] 146-147 G 5
Ješjavrre 116-117 L 3
Jiexi 146-147 E 10
Jiexiu 146-147 CD 3
Jieyang 146-147 F 10
Jiftūn, Jazā'ir — 173 CD 4
Jiggithai Tsho 142-143 F 4
Jih-chao = Rizhao 146-147 G 4
Jihlam [PAK, place] 134-135 L 4
Jihlam [PAK, river] 134-135 L 4
Jihlava 118 G 4
Jījiga 164-165 N 7
Jījīli 164-165 F 1
Jil, Al- 136-137 KL 7
Jilava, Bucureşti- 122-123 M 5
Jilemutu 142-143 N 1
Jilf al-Kabīr, Haḍbat al- 164-165 K 4
Jilib 164-165 N 8
Jilīb Bākūr = Qalīb Bākūr 136-137 L 8
Jilidah, Al- = Al-Jaladah 134-135 F 6-7
Jilin [TJ, administrative unit] 142-143 N 2-O 3
Jilin [TJ, place] 142-143 O 3
Jiljila, Hōr al- = Hawr al-Jiljilah 136-137 L 6
Jiljilah, Hawr al- 136-137 L 6
Jill, Al- = Al-Jil 136-137 KL 7
Jilong = Chilung 142-143 N 6
Jīma 164-165 M 7
Jimā'h aṭ-Ṭulbah 166-167 D 2
Jimaja = Pulau Jemaya 148-149 DE 6
Jimāl, Wādī — 173 D 5
Jimā 'Shā'im 166-167 B 3
Jimāt 166-167 B 6
Jimbolia 122-123 J 3
Jiménez [MEX, Chihuahua] 64-65 F 6
Jiménez [MEX, Coahuila] 76-77 D 8
Jimeta 168-169 J 3
Jiminghe 146-147 E 6
Jimma = Jīma 164-165 M 7
Jimnah 166-167 L 3
Jimo 146-147 H 3
Jim River 58-59 M 3
Jimulco 86-87 J 5
Jinaḥ 173 B 5
Jinan 142-143 M 4
Jincheng 142-143 L 4
Jīnd 138-139 F 3
Jindabyne 160 J 6
Jing'an 146-147 E 7
Jing'anji 146-147 F 4
Jingbian 146-147 B 3
Jingbo Hu 142-143 O 3
Jingchuan 142-143 K 4
Jingde 146-147 G 6
Jingdezhen 142-143 M 6
Jingdong 142-143 J 7
J. Ingenieros 110 III b 2
Jinggu 142-143 J 7
Jinghai 146-147 F 2
Jinghe [TJ, place] 142-143 E 3
Jing He [TJ, river] 146-147 B 4
Jinghong 142-143 J 7
Jingji = Jingzhi 146-147 G 3
Jingjiang 146-147 H 5-6
Jingjiang = Tongguan 146-147 D 7
Jingle 146-147 CD 2
Jingmen 146-147 CD 6
Jingning 142-143 K 4
Jing Shan [TJ, mountains] 146-147 C 6
Jingshan [TJ, place] 146-147 D 6
Jingshi = Jinshi 142-143 L 6
Jingtai 142-143 J 4
Jingtian 146-147 E 8
Jing Xian [TJ, Anhui] 146-147 G 6
Jing Xian [TJ, Hebei] 146-147 EF 3
Jing Xian [TJ, Hunan] 146-147 B 8
Jingxing 146-147 DE 2
Jingyang 146-147 B 4
Jingyu 144-145 F 1
Jingyuan 142-143 JK 4
Jingzhen = Xinchengbu 142-143 K 4
Jingzheng = Jiyiz 146-147 C 4
Jingzhi 146-147 G 3
Jingziguan 146-147 C 5
Jinhua 142-143 MN 6
Jiniiang = Quanzhou 142-143 MN 6-7
Jining [TJ, Inner Mongolian Aut. Reg.] 142-143 L 3
Jining [TJ, Shandong] 142-143 M 4
Jinja 172 F 1
Jin Jiang [TJ ◁ Gan Jiang] 146-147 E 7
Jin Jiang [TJ ◁ Quanzhou Gang] 146-147 FG 9
Jinjing 146-147 D 7
Jinjing He = Jinqian He 146-147 BC 5
Jinkou 146-147 E 6
Jinlanshi = Jinlansi 146-147 D 8
Jinlansi 146-147 D 8
Jinmen = Kinmen Dao 142-143 M 7
Jinmu Jiao = Jintu Jiao 142-143 KL 8
Jinniu 146-147 E 6-7
Jinotega 64-65 J 9
Jinotepe 88-89 C 9
Jinping 146-147 B 8
Jinqi = Jinxi 146-147 F 8
Jin Qi = Jin Xi 146-147 F 8
Jinsen = Inch'ŏn 142-143 O 4
Jinsha Jiang 142-143 J 6
Jinshan 146-147 H 6
Jinshi 142-143 L 6
Jinshi = Jianshi 146-147 B 6
Jintan 146-147 G 6
Jintian 146-147 E 8
Jintu Jiao 142-143 KL 8
Jintūr 138-139 F 8
Jin Xi [TJ, Fujian] 146-147 F 8
Jinxi [TJ, Jiangsi] 146-147 F 8
Jinxi [TJ, Liaoning] 144-145 C 2
Jin Xian [TJ, Hebei] 146-147 E 2
Jinxian [TJ, Jiangxi] 146-147 F 7
Jin Xian [TJ, Liaoning ↗ Jinzhou] 144-145 C 2
Jin Xian [TJ, Liaoning ↑ Lüda] 142-143 N 4
Jinxiang [TJ, Shandong] 146-147 EF 4
Jinxiang [TJ, Zhejiang] 146-147 H 8
Jinxiu 146-147 C 9
Jinyuan 146-147 D 3
Jinyun 146-147 H 7
Jinzhai 146-147 E 6
Jinzhou 142-143 N 3
Jiparaná, Rio — 92-93 G 6-7
Jipijapa 92-93 C 5
Jiqi = Jixi 146-147 G 6
Jirādū 166-167 M 1
Jirays, Jabal — 173 D 7
Jiren = Jīma 164-165 M 7
Jirgalanta = Chovd 142-143 G 2
Jiriid 164-165 b 2
Jirijirimo, Raudal — 94-95 F 8
Jirira 104-105 B 6
Jirjā 164-165 L 3
Jīroft 134-135 H 5
Jiruá 106-107 K 1-2
Jirwān 134-135 G 6
Jishar 146-147 C 4
Jishi Shan = Amnyemachhen Gangri 142-143 HJ 5
Jishou 146-147 B 7
Jishui 146-147 E 8
Jisr ech Chaghoûr = Gisr ash-Shughūr 136-137 G 5
Jitan 146-147 E 9
Jitaúna 100-101 E 7-8
Jitra 150-151 C 9
Jiu 122-123 K 3
Jiuchangjiang = Changcheng 150-151 G 3
Jiuchaoxian = Chao Xian 146-147 FG 6
Jiudaoliang 146-147 BC 6
Jiufeng Shan 146-147 G 8
Jiugan'en = Gancheng 150-151 G 3
Jiugang, Beijing- 155 II b 3
Jiugong'an = Nanping 146-147 D 7
Jiugou = Jiukou 146-147 D 6
Jiuhe 146-147 E 10
Jiujiang [TJ, Guangdong] 146-147 D 10
Jiujiang [TJ, Jiangxi] 142-143 M 6
Jiukou 146-147 D 6
Jiuling Shan 146-147 E 7
Jiulong = Kowloon 142-143 LM 7
Jiulong Jiang 146-147 F 9
Jiulong Shan 146-147 G 7
Jiulong Xi 146-147 F 8
Jiunantian = Nantian 146-147 HJ 7
Jiuquan 142-143 H 4
Jiurongcheng 146-147 J 3
Jiushan Liedao 146-147 J 7
Jiusiyang = Siyang 146-147 G 5
Jiuxian 146-147 D 5
Jiuxiangcheng 146-147 E 5
Jiuxian He 146-147 F 9
Jiuxianqiao, Beijing- 155 II bc 2
Jiuyuhang 146-147 GH 6
Jiwā', Al- 134-135 G 6
Jīwānī 134-135 J 5-6
Jixi [TJ, Anhui] 146-147 G 6
Jixi [TJ, Heilongjiang] 142-143 P 2
Ji Xian [TJ, Hebei → Beijing] 146-147 F 1
Ji Xian [TJ, Hebei ↘ Shijiazhuang] 146-147 E 3
Ji Xian [TJ, Henan] 146-147 E 4
Ji Xian [TJ, Shanxi] 146-147 C 3
Jiyāganj = Jiaganj 138-139 M 5
Jiyang [TJ, Fujian] 146-147 FG 8
Jiyang [TJ, Shandong] 146-147 F 3
Jiyi 146-147 C 4
Jiyizhen = Jiyi 146-147 C 4
Jiyuan 146-147 D 4
Jiyun He 146-147 F 2
Jīzah, Al- [ET] 164-165 KL 3
Jīzah, Al- [JOR] 136-137 FG 7
Jīzah, El — = Al-Jīzah 136-137 FG 7
Jīzān 134-135 E 7
Jize 146-147 E 3
Jizl, Wādī al- 134-135 D 5
J. J. Almeyra 106-107 H 5
J. Jorba 106-107 E 4
Jlaiba = Jalībah 136-137 M 7
Jllovo Beach 174-175 J 6
Jlullssat 56-57 ab 4
Joaçaba 111 F 3
Jōai = Jowai 141 C 3
Joaíma 100-101 D 3
Joal 168-169 A 2
Joana Peres 92-93 JK 5
Joanes 98-99 O 5
Joanina 100-101 D 8
Joaninha, Serra da — 100-101 D 3
Joanna Spring 158-159 DE 4
João 92-93 J 5
João Amaro 100-101 D 7
João Câmara 100-101 G 3
João de Almeida = Chibia 172 B 5
João do Vale, Serra — 100-101 F 3-4
João Lisboa 98-99 P 7
João Monlevale 102-103 L 3
João Pessoa 92-93 N 6
João Pinheiro 102-103 JK 2
Joaquim Felício 92-93 KL 8
Joaquim Murtinho 102-103 GH 6
Joaquim Távora 102-103 GH 5
Joaquín V. González 111 D 3
Jobal Island = Jazā'ir Qaysūm 173 CD 4
Jobat 138-139 E 6
Job Peak 74-75 D 3
Jo-ch'iang = Charqiliq 142-143 F 4
Jockey 88-89 DE 8
Jocolí 111 C 4
Jodhpur 134-135 L 5
Jodiya Bandar 138-139 C 6
Jodpur = Jodhpur 134-135 L 5
Joe Kelly Butler Stadium 85 III b 2
Joensuu 116-117 NO 6
Joerg Plateau 53 B 29-30
Joes, CO 68-69 E 6
Jõesuu, Narva- 124-125 FG 4
Joe W. Brown Memorial Park 85 I c 1
Jofane 172 F 6
Joffre, Mount — 60 K 4
Jofra Oasis, el — = Wāḥāt al-Jufrah 164-165 GH 3
Jogbani 138-139 L 4
Jõgeva 124-125 F 4
Jog Falls 140 B 3
Joggins 63 D 5
Jogīghopa 141 B 2
Jogindamagar 138-139 F 1-2
Jogipet 140 CD 2
Jögödseer Chijd = Erdenecagaan 142-143 LM 2
Jogyakarta = Yogyakarta 148-149 EF 8
Jõhana 144-145 L 4
Johanna Island = Anjouan 172 HJ 4
Johannesburg 172 E 7
Johannesburg Airport 170 V c 1
Johannesburg-Albertynsville 170 V a 2
Johannesburg-Auckland Park 170 V ab 2
Johannesburg-Baragwanath 170 V a 2
Johannesburg-Bellevue 170 V b 2
Johannesburg-Booysens 170 V ab 2
Johannesburg-Bramley 170 V b 1
Johannesburg-Craighall 170 V b 1
Johannesburg-Craighall Park 170 V b 1
Johannesburg-Crosby 170 V a 2
Johannesburg-Diepkloof 170 V a 2
Johannesburg-Eastern Native 170 V b 2
Johannesburg-Franklin Roosevelt Park 170 V a 1
Johannesburg-Greenside 170 V b 1
Johannesburg-Greymont 170 V a 1
Johannesburg-Jabavu 170 V a 2
Johannesburg-Kew 170 V b 1
Johannesburg-Klipriviersoog 170 V a 2
Johannesburg-Linden 170 V ab 1
Johannesburg-Linksfield 170 V b 1
Johannesburg-Linmeyer 170 V b 2
Johannesburg-Lombardy 170 V b 1
Johannesburg-Malvern 170 V b 2
Johannesburg-Mayfair 170 V b 2
Johannesburg-Meadowlands 170 V a 2
Johannesburg-Melville 170 V ab 2
Johannesburg-Meredale 170 V a 2
Johannesburg-Mofolo 170 V a 2
Johannesburg-Mondeor 170 V ab 2
Johannesburg-Nancefield 170 V a 2
Johannesburg-New Canada 170 V a 2
Johannesburg-Newclare 170 V a 2
Johannesburg-Northcliff 170 V a 1
Johannesburg-Norwood 170 V b 1
Johannesburg-Oaklands 170 V b 1
Johannesburg-Ophirton 170 V b 2
Johannesburg-Orlando 170 V a 2
Johannesburg-Paarlshoop 170 V a 2
Johannesburg-Paradise Hill 170 V b 2
Johannesburg-Park Town 170 V b 2
Johannesburg-Pimville 170 V a 2
Johannesburg-Regents Park 170 V b 2
Johannesburg-Rivasdale 170 V a 2
Johannesburg-Robertsham 170 V ab 2
Johannesburg-Rosettenville 170 V b 2
Johannesburg-Sandringham 170 V b 1
Johannesburg-Selby 170 V b 2
Johannesburg-South Hills 170 V b 2
Johannesburg-Soweto 174-175 G 4
Johannesburg-Turffontein 170 V b 2
Johannesburg-Willowdene 170 V a 2
Johannesburg-Yeoville 170 V b 2
Johanneskirchen, München- 130 II bc 1
Johannisthal, Berlin- 130 III c 2
Johi [GUY] 92-93 H 4
Johi [PAK] 138-139 A 4
Johilla 138-139 H 6
John A. White Park 85 II b 2
John Day, OR 66-67 D 3
John Day River 66-67 C 3
John Day River, Middle Fork — 66-67 D 3
John Day River, North Fork — 66-67 D 3
John Day River, South Fork — 66-67 D 3
John F. Kennedy Center 82 II a 2
John F. Kennedy International Airport 82 III d 3
John F. Kennedy National Historical Site 84 I b 2
John F. Kennedy Stadium 84 III bc 2
John MacLaren Park 83 I b 2
John Martin Reservoir 68-69 E 6-7
John River 58-59 L 3
Johnson, KS 68-69 F 7
Johnson, Pico de — 86-87 DE 3
Johnsonburg, PA 72-73 G 4
Johnson City, NY 72-73 J 3
Johnson City, TN 64-65 K 4
Johnson City, TX 76-77 E 7
Johnsonville, SC 80-81 G 4
Johnston, SC 80-81 F 4
Johnston Lakes 158-159 D 6
Johnstown, NY 72-73 JK 3
Johnstown, PA 64-65 L 3-4
John T. Brechtel Memorial Park 85 I b 2
John T. Mason Park 85 III b 2
John Tyler Arboretum 84 III a 2
Johor 150-151 D 11
Johor Baharu 148-149 DE 6
Johor Strait 154 III ab 1
Jõhvi 124-125 F 4
Joinvile 111 G 3
Joinville, Île — 53 C 31
Joinville-le-Pont 129 I cd 2
Joka, South Suburbs- 154 II a 3
Jōkāu 164-165 L 7
Jokkmokk 116-117 HJ 4
Joko = Yoko 164-165 G 7
Jokohama = Yokohama 142-143 QR 4
Jökulsa á Brú 116-117 f 2
Jökulsá á Fjöllum 116-117 ef 2
Jolfā 134-135 F 3
Joliet, IL 64-65 J 3
Joliette 56-57 W 8
Joliette, ND 68-69 H 1
Joliette, Parc provincial de — 62 OP 3
Jolliet, Lacs — 62 N 1
Joló 148-149 H 5
Joló Island 148-149 H 5
Jombang 152-153 K 9
Jomo Gangkar 138-139 MN 3
Jomo Lhari 138-139 M 4
Jomotsering 134-135 O 5
Jomu 171 C 3
Jomuro 168-169 E 4
Jonava 124-125 E 6
Jones, Cape — 56-57 UV 7
Jonesboro, AR 64-65 H 4
Jonesboro, GA 78-79 G 4
Jonesboro, IL 70-71 F 7
Jonesboro, LA 78-79 C 4
Jones Islands 58-59 N 1
Jones Point 82 II a 2
Jonesport, ME 72-73 N 2
Jones Sound 56-57 TU 2
Jonesville, AK 58-59 N 6
Jonesville, LA 78-79 CD 5
Jonesville, MI 70-71 H 4-5
Jongkha 142-143 F 6
Joniškėlis 124-125 DE 5-6
Joniškis 124-125 DE 5
Jonkersberg 174-175 DE 7
Jönköping 116-117 EF 9
Jönköpings län 116-117 EF 9
Jonquière 56-57 WX 8
Jonzac 120-121 G 6
Joontoy 172 H 2
Joowhar 164-165 ab 3
Jo'ōyu Ri 138-139 L 3
Joplin, MO 64-65 H 4
Joplin, MT 66-67 H 1
Jóquei Clube [BR, Rio de Janeiro] 110 I b 2
Jóquei Clube [BR, São Paulo] 110 II a 2
Jora 138-139 F 4
Jorasanko, Calcutta- 154 II b 2
Jordan 134-135 D 4
Jordan, MN 70-71 D 3
Jordan, MT 68-69 C 2
Jordan = Nahr ash-Sharī'ah 136-137 F 6-7
Jordan Creek 66-67 E 4
Jordânia 100-101 D 8
Jordan Valley, OR 66-67 E 4
Jordão, Rio — 102-103 G 6
Jorf = Jurf 166-167 D 4
Jorf el Mellâḥ = Jurf al-Malḥā' 166-167 D 2
Jorge, Cabo — 108-109 B 8
Jorge, Isla — = George Island 108-109 JK 9
Jorge Montt, Isla — 108-109 B 8
Jorge Newbery, Aeroparque — 110 III b 1
Jorhāt 134-135 PQ 5
Jorigām 138-139 J 8
Jörn 116-117 J 5
Jornada del Muerto 76-77 A 6
Jorong 152-153 L 7-8
Jortom 124-125 Q 2
Jos 164-165 F 7
José A. Guisasola 106-107 G 7
José Bahía Casás 108-109 H 3
José Battle y Ordóñez 106-107 K 4
José Bonifácio [BR, Rondônia] 98-99 H 11
José Bonifácio [BR, São Paulo] 102-103 H 4
José C. Paz, Sarmiento- 110 III a 1
José de Freitas 100-101 C 3
José de San Martín 111 BC 6
José Enrique Rodó 106-107 J 4
José Gonçalves 100-101 D 8
José La Haye 102-103 D 6
Joselândia [BR, Maranhão] 100-101 B 3
Joselândia [BR, Mato Grosso] 102-103 DE 2
José María Blanco 106-107 F 6
José Mármol, Almirante Brown- 110 III b 2
José M. Micheo 106-107 H 5
José Otávio 106-107 K 3
José Pedro, Rio — 102-103 M 3-4
José Pedro Varela 106-107 KL 4
Joseph, OR 66-67 E 3
Joseph, Lac — 56-57 XY 7
Joseph, Lake — 72-73 G 2
Joseph Bonaparte Gulf 158-159 E 2
Joseph City, AZ 74-75 H 5
José S. Arévalo 106-107 H 5
Joshīmath 138-139 G 2
Joshīpur 138-139 L 7
Joṣhīpura = Joshīpur 138-139 L 7
Joshua Tree, CA 74-75 E 5
Joshua Tree National Monument 64-65 CD 5
Joškar-Ola 132-133 H 6
Joson Bulag = Altaj 142-143 H 2
Jos Plateau 164-165 E 6-7
Josselin 120-121 F 5
Jostedalsbreen 116-117 B 7
Jotajana 94-95 L 3
Jotunheimen 116-117 BC 7
Joubertina 174-175 EF 7
Joûniyé = Jūnīyah 136-137 F 6
Jourdanton, TX 76-77 E 8
Joutsa 116-117 LM 7
Jouy-en-Josas 129 I b 2
Jouy-le-Moutier 129 I b 1
Jovellanos 88-89 F 3
Jowai 141 C 3
Jow Kār 136-137 N 5
Joya, La — [BOL] 104-105 C 5
Joya, La — [PE] 96-97 F 10
Joyous Pavillon Park 155 II b 2
Joypur = Jaipur 141 D 2
J. Prats 106-107 CD 5
J. S. Arévalo 106-107 H 5
Juaba 98-99 O 6
Juan Aldama 64-65 F 7
Juan Amarillo 91 III b 2
Juan Anchorena, San Isidro- 110 III b 1
Juan A. Pradere 111 D 5
Juan B. Alberdi 106-107 G 5
Juan B. Arruabarrena 106-107 H 3
Juan Bautista Alberdi 104-105 CD 10
Juan B. Molina 106-107 G 4
Juancheng 146-147 E 4
Juancho 106-107 J 6
Juan de Fuca, Strait of — 56-57 LM 8
Juan de Garay 106-107 E 7
Juan del Monte 96-97 C 5
Juan de Mena 102-103 D 6
Juan de Nova 172 H 5
Juan Díaz 64-65 c 2
Juan E. Barra 106-107 G 6
Juan Escutia, Ciudad Netzahualcoyotl- 91 I C 2
Juan Fernández Ridge 156-157 N 6
Juan Gallegos, Isla — 64-65 b 2
Juan G. Bazán 104-105 F 9
Juan Godoy 106-107 B 1
Juan Gonzalez Romero, Ciudad de México- 91 I c 2
Juan Guerra 96-97 C 5
Juan J. Albornoz 108-109 E 7
Juan J. Almeyra 106-107 H 5
Juanjiang 146-147 D 7
Juan Jorba 106-107 E 4
Juan José Castelli 111 DE 3
Juan J. Paso 106-107 F 5
Juanjuí 92-93 D 6
Juankoski 116-117 N 6
Juan L. Lacaze 106-107 J 5
Juan Llerena 106-107 E 4
Juan N. Fernández 106-107 H 7
Juan Pujol 106-107 HJ 3
Juan Stuven, Isla — 111 A 7
Juan W. Gez 106-107 DE 4
Juarci 100-101 D 7
Juárez [MEX ↑ Chihuahua] 64-65 E 5
Juárez [MEX ↖ Chihuahua] 86-87 F 2
Juárez, Oaxaca de — 64-65 GH 8
Juárez, Sierra de — 64-65 C 5
Juarzon 168-169 C 4
Juatinga, Ponta do — 92-93 L 9
Juàzeirinho 100-101 F 4
Juazeiro 92-93 L 6
Juazeiro do Norte 92-93 M 6
Jūbā 164-165 L 8
Jubail, Al- = Al-Jubayl al-Baḥrī 134-135 FG 5
Jubal, Madiq — = Jazīrat Shadwan 164-165 LM 3
Jubayl [ET] 173 C 3
Jubayl [RL] 136-137 F 5
Jubayl al-Baḥrī, Al- 134-135 FG 5
Jubayt 164-165 M 4
Jubba = Jubbah 136-137 K 6
Jubbabe Hoose 172 H 2
Jubbada Hoose ◁ 4 164-165 N 8
Jubbade Dhexe 164-165 N 8
Jubbah 136-137 K 6
Jubbulpore = Jabalpur 134-135 MN 6
Jubeil = Jubayl 136-137 F 5
Jubilee Lake 158-159 E 5
Jubilee Reservoir 155 I a 1
Jubileo 106-107 H 3
Júcar 120-121 G 9
Juçara 102-103 F 5
Juçaral, Rio — 100-101 C 2
Júcaro 88-89 G 4
Jucás 92-93 LM 6
Juchitán de Zaragoza 64-65 GH 8
Juchmači 124-125 RS 6
Juchnov 124-125 K 6
Jucurucu, Rio — 100-101 DE 9
Jucurutu 100-101 F 3-4
Judā', Sha'īb al- 136-137 L 8-M 7
Judas, Punta — 88-89 D 10
Judayyīdat-Ar'ar 134-135 DE 4
Judayyīdat Ḥāmir 136-137 J 7
Judea 174-175 BC 2
Judenburg 118 G 5
Judge Haway, Mount — 66-67 BC 1
Judino = Petuchovo 132-133 M 6
Judino, Kazan'- 124-125 R 6
Judith, Point — 72-73 L 4
Judith Basin 68-69 AB 2
Judith Bassin 66-67 HJ 2
Judith Gap, MT 68-69 B 2
Judith Mountains 68-69 B 2
Judorna 132-133 a 6
Judys Lake 85 II b 3
Juejiang = Rudong 146-147 H 5
Juerana 100-101 E 9
Jufrah, Wāḥāt al- 164-165 GH 3
Jug [SU, place] 124-125 V 5
Jug [SU, river] 124-125 Q 3
Juggernaut = Purī 134-135 O 7
Jugiong 160 J 5
Jugo-Kamskij 124-125 UV 5
Jugorskij poluostrov 132-133 L 4
Jugorskij Šar, proliv — 132-133 L 4-M 3
Jugydtydor 124-125 T 2
Juhaym 136-137 L 8
Juhaynah 173 B 4
Ju He = Ju Shui 146-147 C 6
Juhua Dao 144-145 C 2
Juian = Rui'an 146-147 H 8
Juichang = Ruichang 146-147 E 7
Juigalpa 88-89 D 8
Juikin = Ruijin 142-143 M 6
Juile, El — 86-87 N 9
Juisui 146-147 H 10
Juiz de Fora 92-93 KL 9
Jujul 96-97 C 7
Jujuy 111 C 2
Jujuy = San Salvador de Jujuy 111 CD 2
Jujuy, San Salvador de — 111 CD 2
Jukagirskoje ploskogorje 132-133 de 4
Jukamenskoje 124-125 T 5
Jukao = Rugao 142-143 N 5
Jukoupu 146-147 C 8
Juksejevo 124-125 TU 4
Jukskei 170 V b 1
Jukte 132-133 TU 5
Jula 124-125 P 2
Julaca 92-93 F 9
Julcamarca, Cordillera de — 96-97 D 8
Julesburg, CO 68-69 EF 5
Juli 92-93 F 8
Júlia [BR] 98-99 DE 5
Juliaca 92-93 E 8
Julia Creek 158-159 H 4
Julian, CA 74-75 E 6
Julian Alps 122-123 EF 2
Julianatop 98-99 K 3
Julianehåb = Qaqortoq 56-57 b 5
Jülich 118 C 3
Julimes 76-77 B 8
9 de Julio, Bahía = King George Bay 108-109 J 8
Júlio de Castilhos 106-107 L 2
Júlio Furtado, Parque — 110 I b 2
Julio María Sanz 106-107 KL 4
Juliuhe 144-145 D 1
Julius, AK 58-59 N 4
Jullundur 134-135 LM 4
Julu 146-147 E 3
Julundur = Jullundur 134-135 LM 4
Julu Rayeu 152-153 BC 3
Jumaima, Al — = Al-Jumaymah 136-137 KL 8
Jumaymah, Al- 136-137 KL 8
Jumbe Salim's 171 D 5
Jumbilla 92-93 D 6
Jumbo 172 H 2
Jumbo, Raas — 172 H 2
Jume, Languna — 106-107 FG 4
Jumilla 120-121 G 9
Jumla 138-139 J 3
Jumna = Yamunā 134-135 MN 5
Jumnotri = Jamnotri 138-139 G 2
Jun = Jun Xian 146-147 C 5
Junāgaḍa = Jūnāgarh 138-139 J 8
Junagadh 134-135 KL 6
Jūnāgarh 138-139 J 8
Junagarh = Junagadh 134-135 KL 6
Junan 146-147 G 4
Junayfah 173 C 2
Junaynah, Al- 164-165 J 6
Juncal, Cerro — 106-107 BC 4
Junction, TX 76-77 E 7
Junction, UT 74-75 G 3
Junction City, AR 78-79 C 4
Junction City, KS 64-65 G 4
Jundah 158-159 H 4
Jundiaí 102-103 J 5
Jundtion City, OR 66-67 B 3
Juneau, AK 56-57 K 6
Juneau, WI 70-71 F 4
Junee 160 H 5
June Lake, CA 74-75 D 4
Jungar Qi 146-147 C 2
Jungcheng = Rongcheng 146-147 EF 2
Jungfernheide 130 III b 1
Jungfernheide, Volkspark — 130 III b 1
Jungghariyā 142-143 EF 2
Jung-hsien = Rong Xian 146-147 C 10
Jungo, NV 66-67 D 5
Jungshāhī 138-139 A 5
Jun-ho-chi = Runheji 146-147 F 5
Juniata, Philadelphia-, PA 84 III c 1
Juniata River 72-73 H 4
Junín [EC] 96-97 A 2
Junín [PE, administrative unit] 96-97 D 7
Junín [PE, place] 92-93 D 7
Junín [RA, Buenos Aires] 111 D 4
Junín [RA, Mendoza] 106-107 C 4
Junín, Lago de — 96-97 C 7
Junín de los Andes 111 BC 5
Junio, La Matanza-20 de — 110 III a 2
Juniper Mountains 74-75 G 5
Jūnīyah 136-137 F 6
Juniye = Jūnīyah 136-137 F 6
Junjik River 58-59 OP 2
Junnar 138-139 DE 8
Juno, TX 76-77 D 7
Junqoley 164-165 L 7
Junqueiro 100-101 F 5
Junsele 116-117 G 6
Junta, La — [BOL] 104-105 F 4
Junta, La — [MEX] 86-87 G 3
Juntas 106-107 B 3
Junten = Sunch'ŏn 142-143 O 4-5
Juntura, OR 66-67 DE 4
Junturas, Las — 106-107 F 3
Junun 150-151 C 10
Junxian = Xun Xian 146-147 E 4
Jupaguá 100-101 B 6
Juparanã, Lagoa — 100-101 DE 10
Jupiá, Represa de — 92-93 J 9
Jupiter River 63 E 3
Juquiá 102-103 J 6
Jūr, Nahr al- 164-165 K 7
Jūr, Nahr el — = Nahr al-Jūr 164-165 K 7
Jura [CH] 118 BC 5
Jura [GB] 119 D 3-4
Jura, Sound of — 119 D 4
Jurab = Djourab 164-165 H 5
Juradó 94-95 C 4
Juraiba, Al — = Al-Juraybah 136-137 KL 8
Juramento, Río — 104-105 D 9
Juratiški 124-125 EF 6
Juraybah, Al- 136-137 KL 8
Jurbarkas 124-125 D 6
Jurborg = Jurbarkas 124-125 D 6
Jurdī, Wādī — 173 C 4
Juréia, Praia da — 102-103 J 6
Jurema 100-101 F 5
Juremal 100-101 D 5
Jurf 166-167 D 4
Jurf ad-Darāwish 136-137 FG 7
Jurf al-Malḥā' 166-167 D 2
Jurf ed Darāwīsh = Jurf ad-Darāwish 136-137 FG 7
Jurga 132-133 P 6
Jūrgāy, Jabal — 164-165 JK 6
Jurien Bay 158-159 B 6
Juries, Los — 111 D 3
Jurino 124-125 PQ 5
Juriti 98-99 KL 6
Jurja 124-125 R 4
Jurjevec 132-133 G 6
Jurjev-Pol'skij 124-125 MN 5
Jurjurah 164-165 EF 1
Jurla 124-125 U 4
Jurlovka 124-125 N 7
Jurmala 124-125 DE 5
Jurong 146-147 G 6
Juruá 98-99 EF 6
Juruá, Rio — 92-93 F 6
Juruázinho, Rio — 96-97 FG 5
Juruena 92-93 H 7
Juruena, Rio — 92-93 H 6-7
Jurujuba, Punta de — 110 I c 2

Jurumirim, Represa de — 102-103 H 5
Jurupari, Ilha — 98-99 NO 4
Jurupari, Rio — 96-97 F 5-G 6
Jusepín 94-95 K 3
Jushan = Rushan 146-147 H 3
Ju Shui 146-147 C 6
Juškozero 132-133 E 5
Jussey 120-121 K 5
Justa 126-127 N 3
Justice, Palais de — 128 II ab 1-2
Justiceburg, TX 76-77 D 6
Justo Daract 111 CD 4
Jus'va 124-125 U 4
Jutaí [BR, Amazonas] 98-99 D 7
Jutaí [BR, Pernambuco] 100-101 D 5
Jutaí, Ilha Grande de — 98-99 O 6
Jutaí, Rio — 92-93 F 5
Jutaí, Serra do — 98-99 M 5
Jutaza 124-125 T 6
Jüterbog 118 F 2-3
Jūthī Antarīp = False Point 134-135 O 6
Juti 102-103 E 5
Jutiapa 64-65 HJ 9
Juticalpa 64-65 J 9
Jutland 116-117 C 9-10
Ju-tung = Rudong 146-147 C 11
Juuka 116-117 N 6
Juuru 124-125 E 4
Juva 116-117 MN 7
Juventud, Isla de la — 64-65 K 7
Juwā' 166-167 KL 5
Juwārah, Al- 134-135 H 7
Ju Xian 142-143 M 4
Juye 146-147 F 4
Ju-yüan = Ruyuan 146-147 D 9
Juža 124-125 O 5
Jūzān 136-137 N 5
Južnaja Kel'tma 124-125 U 3
Južna Morava 122-123 JK 4
Južno-Kuril'sk 132-133 c 9
Južno-Sachalinsk 132-133 bc 8
Južnyj, mys — 132-133 e 6
Južnyj An'ujskij chrebet = An'ujskij chrebet 132-133 fg 4
Južnyj Bug 126-127 E 3
Južnyj port 113 V c 3
Južnyj Ural 132-133 K 7-L 6
Juzovka = Doneck 126-127 H 2-3
Južsib 132-133 L 7
Juzur al-Ḥabībah 166-167 F 2
Juzur Ṭawīlah 173 CD 4

Jyājpura = Jājpur 138-139 L 7
Jyavan = Jiāwān 138-139 J 5
Jyekunde = Chhergundo 142-143 H 5
Jyväskylä 116-117 L 6

K

K 2 134-135 M 3

Ka 164-165 F 6
Kaain Veld = Kaiingveld 174-175 D 6-E 5
Kaala 78-79 c 2
Kaalkaroo 174-175 C 6
Kaamanen 116-117 M 3
Kaap Colombine 174-175 B 7
Kaap Frio 172 B 5
Kaap Hangklip 174-175 C 8
Kaap Hermes 174-175 H 6
Kaap Infanta 174-175 D 8
Kaap Kruis 172 B 6
Kaapland 172 DE 8
Kaapmuiden 174-175 J 3
Kaapplato 172 D 7
Kaapprovinsie = Kaapland 172 DE 8
Kaap Recife 174-175 FG 8
Kaap Seal 174-175 E 8
Kaap Sint Blaize 174-175 E 8
Kaap Sint Martin 174-175 B 7
Kaapstad 172 C 8
Kaaschka 134-135 HJ 3
Kaba [WAL] 168-169 B 3
Kaba, Gunung — 152-153 E 7
Kabaena, Pulau — 148-149 H 8
Kabaena, Selat — 152-153 O 8
Kabahaydar = Kalecik 136-137 H 4
Kabāla [GR] 122-123 L 5
Kabala [WAL] 164-165 B 7
Kabale 172 EF 2
Kabali 152-153 OP 6
Kabalo 172 E 3
Kabambare 172 E 2
Kabango 171 B 5
Kabanjahe 150-151 B 11
Kabansk 132-133 U 7
Kabara 168-169 E 1
Kabardino-Balkar Autonomous Soviet Socialist Republic 126-127 LM 5
Kabare [RCB] 172 E 2
Kabare [RI] 148-149 K 7
Kabarnet 171 CD 2
Kabarṭal 166-167 F 5
Kabba 164-165 F 7
Kabbani 140 C 4-5
Kåbdalis 116-117 J 4
Kabelega Falls 172 F 1
Kabelega Falls National Park 172 F 1
Kabenung Lake 70-71 H 1
Kaberamaido 171 C 2
Kabertene = Kabarṭal 166-167 F 5
Kabetogama Lake 70-71 D 1
Kabilcevaz 136-137 J 3
Kabinakagami Lake 70-71 H 1
Kabinakagami River 62 G 3
Kabin Buri 148-149 D 4
Kabinchaung 150-151 B 6
Kabinda 172 DE 3
Kabinda = Cabinda 172 B 3
Kabingyaung = Kabinchaung 150-151 B 6
Kabir 152-153 Q 10
Kabīr, Wāw al- 164-165 H 3
Kabīr, Zāb al- 136-137 K 4
Kabīr Kūh 134-135 F 4
Kabīwāla 138-139 C 2
Kabkābīyah 164-165 J 6
Kabo 164-165 H 7
Kabobo 171 B 4
Kabompo 172 D 4
Kabongo 172 DE 3
Kabosa Island = Kabūzā Kyûn 150-151 AB 6
Kaboûdia, Râss — = Rā's Qabūdīyah 166-167 M 2
Kabudārāhang 136-137 N 5
Kābul 134-135 K 4
Kabunda 171 B 6
Kaburuang, Pulau — 148-149 J 6
Kabūzā Kyûn 150-151 AB 6
Kabwe 172 E 4
Kača 126-127 F 4
Kačalinskaja 126-127 M 2
Kačanovo 124-125 FG 5
K'achana = Kafan 126-127 N 7
Kachchh = Kutch 134-135 K 6
Kacheliba 171 C 2
Ka-Chem = Malyj Jenisej 132-133 RS 7
Kachemak Bay 58-59 M 7
Kachgar = Qāshqār 142-143 CD 4
Kachhār = Cāchār 141 C 3
Kachi 126-127 N 6
Kachia 168-169 G 3
Kachin Pyinnei 148-149 C 1-2
Kachkatt = Yūssufīyah 166-167 B 3
Kachovka 126-127 F 3
Kachovskoje vodochranilišče 126-127 F 3
K'achta 132-133 U 7
Kaçkar dağı 136-137 J 2
Kačug 132-133 U 7
Kadada 124-125 Q 7
Kadaingdi 148-149 C 3
Kadaingti = Kadaingdi 148-149 C 3
Kadaiyanallūr 140 C 6
Kadaiyyanallūr = Kadaiyanallūr 140 C 6
Kadan Kyûn 148-149 C 4
Kaḍappa = Cuddapah 134-135 M 8
Kādarī = Kadiri 140 D 3
Kade [GH] 164-165 D 7
Kade [Guinea] 168-169 B 2
Kadei 164-165 H 8
Kadgoron = Ardon 126-127 M 5
Kadhdhāb, Sinn al- 173 BC 6
Kadi 138-139 D 6
Kadievka = Stachanov 126-127 J 2
Kadıköy, İstanbul- 136-137 C 2
Kadina 160 CD 4-5
Kadınhanı 136-137 E 3
Kadiolo 168-169 D 3
Kādīpur 138-139 J 4
Kadiri 140 D 3
Kadirli 136-137 FG 4
Kadiyevka = Stachanov 126-127 J 2
Kadmat Island 134-135 L 8
Kadnikov 124-125 N 4
Ka-do 144-145 E 3
Kadoka, SD 68-69 F 4
Kadoma 172 E 5
Kadon 150-151 E 5
Kadugli = Kāduqlī 164-165 KL 6
Kaduj 124-125 L 4
Kaduna [WAN, administrative unit] 168-169 G 3
Kaduna [WAN, place] 164-165 F 6
Kāduqlī 164-165 KL 6
Kaḍūr 140 BC 4
Kaḍūru = Kaḍūr 140 BC 4
Kadwāha 138-139 F 5
Kadyj 124-125 O 5
Kadykšan 132-133 C 5
Kadžaran 126-127 N 7
Kaech'i-ri 144-145 G 2
Kaemŏr = Kaimur Hills 138-139 HJ 5
Kaena Point 78-79 c 2
Kaeng Khoi 150-151 C 5
Kaerānā = Kairāna 138-139 F 3
Kaesarganj = Kaisarganj 138-139 H 4
Kaesŏng 142-143 O 4
Kaethal = Kaithal 138-139 F 3
Kāf 134-135 D 4
Kāf, Al- 164-165 F 1
Kafan 126-127 N 7
Kafanchan 164-165 F 7
Kaférévs, Akrōtérion — 122-123 L 6
Kafferrivier 174-175 FG 5
Kaffraria = Transkei 172 E 8
Kaffrine 164-165 AB 6
Kafr ash-Shaykh 173 B 2
Kafr az-Zayyāt 173 B 2
Kafta 164-165 M 6
Kafu 172 F 1
Kafue [Z, place] 172 E 5
Kafue [Z, river] 172 E 5
Kafue Flats 172 E 5
Kafue National Park 172 E 4-5
Kafulwa 171 B 5
Kaga 144-145 L 4
Kaga Bandoro 164-165 HJ 7
Kāgal 140 B 2
Kagamil Island 58-59 lm 4
Kagan 134-135 J 3
Kaganovič = Popasnaja 126-127 J 2
Kagarlyk 126-127 E 2
Kagati Lake 58-59 GH 7
Kagawa 144-145 JK 5
Kagera 172 F 2
Kagera, Parc national de la — 172 F 2
Kagera Magharibi 172 F 2
Kagi = Chiayi 142-143 MN 7
Kagianagami Lake 62 F 2
Kâğıthane [TR, place] 154 I ab 2
Kâğıthane [TR, river] 154 I a 2
Kağızman 136-137 K 2
Kagmār 164-165 L 6
Kāgna 140 C 2
Kagoro 164-165 F 7
Kagoshima 142-143 OP 5
Kagoshima wan 144-145 H 7
Kagosima = Kagoshima 142-143 OP 5
Kagran, Wien- 113 I b 2
Kagul [SU, place] 126-127 D 4
Kaguyak, AK 58-59 g 1
Kahā 138-139 BC 3
Kahalgāṅv = Colgong 138-139 L 5
Kahal Tābalbalah 166-167 EF 5
Kahal Tabelbala = Kaḥal Tābalbalah 166-167 EF 5
Kahama 172 F 2
Kahān 138-139 B 3
Kahayan, Sungai — 148-149 F 7
Kahemba 172 C 3
Kahia 172 E 3
Kahiltna Glacier 58-59 M 5
Kahlā [IR] 136-137 N 5
Kahlenberg 113 I b 1
Kahler Asten 118 D 3
Kahlotus, WA 66-67 D 2
Kahoka, MO 70-71 DE 5
Kahoku-gata 144-145 L 4
Kahoolawe 148-149 e 3
Kahraman 154 I b 3
Kahroṛ 138-139 C 3
Kahta = Kölük 136-137 H 4
Kahuku, HI 78-79 d 2
Kahuku Point 78-79 cd 2
Kahului, HI 78-79 d 2
Kahurangi Point 161 DE 5
Kai, Kepulauan — 148-149 K 8
Kaiama 164-165 E 7
Kaiashk River 62 E 3
Kaibab Indian Reservation 74-75 G 4
Kaibab Plateau 74-75 G 4
Kai Besar, Pulau — 148-149 K 8
K'ai-chien = Nanfeng 146-147 C 10
Kaidong = Tongyu 142-143 N 3
Kaieteur Falls 92-93 GH 3
Kaí Évboia 122-123 K 6-L 7
Kaifeng 142-143 LM 5
K'ai-fong = Kaifeng 142-143 LM 5
Kaihsien = Kai Xian 146-147 B 6
Kaihua 146-147 G 7
Kaihwa = Wenshan 142-143 JK 7
Kaiingveld 174-175 D 6-E 5
Kaijian = Nanfeng 146-147 C 10
Kaijin, Funabashi- 155 III c 1
Kaikalūr 140 E 2
Kaikalūru = Kaikalūr 140 E 2
Kai Kecil, Pulau — 148-149 K 8
Kaikohe 158-159 O 7
Kaikoura 158-159 O 8
Kaila Hu = Kalba Tsho 138-139 M 3
Kailahun 168-169 C 3
Kailasahar = Kailāshahar 141 C 3
Kailas Gangri = Kailash Gangri 142-143 E 5
Kailāsh = Gangrinpochhe 138-139 H 2
Kailāshahar 141 C 3
Kailash Gangri 142-143 E 5
Kailu 142-143 N 3
Kailua, HI 78-79 de 3
Kaimana 148-149 K 7
Kaimanawa Mountains 161 G 4
Kaimganj 138-139 G 4
Kaimon-dake 144-145 H 7
Kaimur Hills 138-139 HJ 5
Kainan 144-145 K 5
Kainantu 148-149 N 8
Kaining = Port Canning 138-139 M 6
Kainji Dam 164-165 EF 6-7
Kainji Reservoir 168-169 G 3
Kainoma Hill 168-169 G 2
Kainsk = Kujbyšev 132-133 O 6
Kaioba 152-153 P 8
Kaipara Harbour 158-159 O 7
Kaiparowits Plateau 74-75 H 4
Kaiping [TJ, Guangdong] 146-147 D 10
Kaiping [TJ, Hebei] 146-147 G 2
Kaira 138-139 D 6
Kairāna 138-139 F 3
Kairiru 148-149 M 7
Kairouan = Al-Qayrawān 164-165 FG 1
Kairuku 148-149 N 8
Kaisarganj 138-139 H 4
Kaisariané 113 IV b 2
Kaisariyah = Caesarea 136-137 F 6
Kaiserebersdorf, Wien- 113 I b 2
Kaiser Peak 74-75 D 4
Kaiserslautern 118 CD 4
Kaiser-Wilhelm-Gedächtniskirche 130 III b 1-2
Kaiser-Wilhelm II.-Land 53 C 9-10
Kaishū = Haeju 142-143 O 4
Kait, Tanjung — 152-153 G 7
Kaitaia 158-159 O 7
Kai Tak Airport 155 I b 2
Kaitangata 158-159 NO 9
Kaithal 138-139 F 3
Kaitum älv 116-117 HJ 4
Kaiwi Channel 78-79 d 2
Kai Xian 146-147 B 6
Kaiyuh Mountains 58-59 H 5-J 4
Kaizanchin = Hyesanjin 142-143 O 3
Kaj 124-125 T 4
Kajaani 116-117 MN 5
Kajabbi 158-159 H 4
Kājakay 134-135 JK 4
Kajakent 126-127 N 5
Kajan 152-153 P 10
Kajang [MAL] 150-151 CD 11
Kajang [RI] 148-149 H 8
Kajasula 126-127 M 4
Kajiado 172 G 2
Kājīrangā = Kāziranga 141 C 2
Kajnar [SU, Kazachskaja SSR] 132-133 O 8
Kajsajmas 126-127 P 1
Kākā 164-165 L 6
Kakaban, Pulau — 152-153 N 4
Kakabeka Falls 70-71 EF 1
Kakabia, Pulau — 152-153 P 9
Kakagi Lake 62 C 3
Kakamas 172 D 7
Kakamega 172 FG 1
Kakarka = Sovetsk 132-133 H 6
Kakata 164-165 B 7
Kākatpur 138-139 L 7-8
Kākaṭpura = Kākatpur 138-139 L 7-8
Kakbil = Karaoğlan 136-137 H 3
Kākdwip 138-139 LM 7
Kake 144-145 J 5
Kake, AK 58-59 w 8
Kakegawa 144-145 LM 5
Kakelwe 171 B 4
Kakhea = Kakia 174-175 E 3
Kakhonak, AK 58-59 K 7
Kakia 172 D 6-7
Kaki Bukit 150-151 BC 9
Kākināda 134-135 N 7
Käkisalmi = Prioz'orsk 132-133 DE 5
Kakogawa 144-145 K 5
Kakonko 171 B 3
Kākosi Metrāna Road 138-139 CD 5
Kakpin 168-169 E 3
Kaktovik, AK 58-59 Q 1
Kakuda 144-145 N 4
Kakulu 171 AB 4
Kakuma 172 FG 1
Kakunodate 144-145 N 3
Kakwa River 60 H 2
Kala 171 B 5
Kala, El — = Al-Qal'ah 164-165 F 1
Kalaa Djerda = Qal'at al-Jardah 166-167 L 2
Kalaa Kebira = Al-Qal'at al-Kabīrah 166-167 M 2
Kalaat es Senam = Qal'at Sinān 166-167 L 2
Kalabahi 148-149 H 8
Kalabakan 152-153 M 3
Kalabo 172 D 5
Kalábryta 122-123 K 6
Kalābsha 164-165 L 4
Kalač 126-127 K 1
Kalač-na-Donu 126-127 L 2
Kalādān 141 C 4
Kaladan = Kulādan Myit 141 C 5
Kaladar 72-73 H 2
Kalādgi 140 B 2
Ka Lae 148-149 e 4
Kālaghātagi = Kalghatgi 140 B 3
Kalagôk Kyûn 141 E 8
Kalāhāndi 138-139 J 8
Kalahari = Kalahari Desert 172 CD 6
Kalahari Desert 172 CD 6
Kalahari Gemsbok National Park 172 D 7
Kālahasti 140 D 4
Kalakan 132-133 W 6
Kaḷam 140 C 1
Kalama, WA 66-67 B 2-3
Kalamākion 113 IV a 2
Kalamáta 122-123 JK 7
Kalamazoo, MI 64-65 J 3
Kalamazoo River 70-71 H 4
Kaḷamba = Kaḷam 140 C 1
Kalamba La 138-139 M 2
Kalambau, Pulau — 152-153 L 8
Kalambo Falls 172 F 3
Kalamitskij zaliv 126-127 F 4
Kalamnūri 138-139 F 8
Kalampáka 122-123 JK 6
Kalamu, Kinshasa- 170 IV a 2
Kalana 168-169 CD 3
Kalančak 126-127 F 3
Kalang 141 C 2
Kalangali 171 C 4
Kalankpa, Mount — 168-169 F 3
Kalannie 158-159 C 6
Kalanshyū, Serīr — 164-165 J 3
Kalao, Pulau — 152-153 O 9
Kalaotao, Pulau — 148-149 H 8
Kalā Oya 140 E 6
Kalar 132-133 W 6
Kalārā Kyûn 150-151 AB 7
Kalaraš 126-127 D 3
Kalasin [RI] 148-149 F 6
Kalasin [T] 148-149 D 3
Kalašnikovo 124-125 K 5
Kalat = Qalāt 134-135 K 5
Kalāt, Jabal — 173 D 6
Kalâtdlit nunât 56-57 b 2-c 5
Kalāt-i Ghilzay 134-135 K 4
Kalatrava 168-169 H 5
Kaļau = Lansdowne 138-139 G 3
Kalaupapa, HI 78-79 d 2
Kalaus 126-127 L 4
Kālāvad 138-139 C 6
Kal'azin 124-125 LM 5
Kalbach, Frankfurt am Main- 128 III a 1
Kalbashar 138-139 M 3
Kalba Tsho 138-139 M 3
Kalbīyah, Sabkhat — 166-167 M 2
Kaldıdağ 136-137 F 4
Kale [TR, Denizli] 136-137 C 4
Kale [TR, Gümüşane] 136-137 H 2
Kale = Eynihal 136-137 CD 4
Kalecik [TR, Ankara] 136-137 E 2
Kalecik [TR, Urfa] 136-137 H 4
Kalegauk Island = Kalagôk Kyûn 141 E 8
Kalegosilik River 58-59 N 2-O 1
Kalehe 172 E 2
Kalemie 172 E 3
Kalemma 171 CD 3
Kalemyō 141 D 4
Kalenyj 126-127 P 2
Kale Sultanie = Çanakkale 134-135 B 2
Kaletwa 148-149 B 2
Kaleva, MI 70-71 GH 3
Kalevala 132-133 E 4
Kalewa 148-149 BC 2
Kaleybar 136-137 M 3
Kålfafell 116-117 de 2-3
Kálfafellsstadhur 116-117 f 2
Kalgačicha 124-125 L 2
Kalgan = Zhangjiakou 142-143 L 3
Kalgary, TX 76-77 D 6
Kalghatgi 140 B 3
Kalgin Island 58-59 M 6
Kalgoorlie 158-159 D 6
Kalhāt 134-135 H 6
Kali [Guinea] 168-169 C 2
Kali [IND] 138-139 G 4
Kālī [Nepal] 138-139 H 3
Kali = Sangha 172 C 1-2
Kaliakra, nos — 122-123 N 4
Kalianda 152-153 F 8
Kali Angke 154 IV a 1
Kalibo 148-149 H 4
Kali Brantas 152-153 JK 9
Kali Buaran 154 IV b 2
Kali Cakung 154 IV b 1-2
Kālī Gaṇḍak 138-139 JK 4
Kāliganj [BD → Calcutta] 138-139 M 6
Kāliganj [BD ↑ Jessaur] 138-139 M 6
Kalighat, Calcutta- 154 II ab 2
Kalighat Temple 154 II b 2
Kali Grogol 154 IV a 2
Kalikātā = Calcutta 134-135 O 6
Kali Krukut 154 IV a 2
Kalima 172 E 2
Kalimala 140 E 1
Kali Mampang 154 IV a 2
Kalimantan 148-149 F 7-G 6
Kalimantan Barat = 5 ◁ 148-149 F 7
Kalimantan Selatan = 9 ◁ 148-149 G 7
Kalimantan Tengah = 8 ◁ 148-149 F 7
Kalimantan Timur = 10 ◁ 148-149 G 6
Kālimpong 138-139 M 4
Kalimpŏṅg = Kālimpong 138-139 M 4
Kālīnadi 140 B 3
Kālingia 138-139 K 7
Kalinin 132-133 EF 6
Kaliningrad 118 K 1
Kalinino [SU, Arm'anskaja SSR] 126-127 M 6
Kalinino [SU, Rossijskaja SFSR] 124-125 UV 5
Kalininsk [SU, Moldavskaja SSR] 126-127 C 2
Kalininsk [SU, Rossijskaja SFSR] 124-125 P 8
Kalininskoje 126-127 F 3
Kalinkoviči 124-125 G 7
Kalinku 171 C 5
Kalinovka 126-127 D 2
Kali Pesanggrahan 154 IV a 2
Kalipur 154 II a 1
Kali Sekretaris 154 IV a 2
Kāli Sindh 138-139 F 5-6
Kalisizo 171 BC 3
Kalispell, MT 64-65 CD 2
Kali Sunter 154 IV b 1
Kalisz 118 J 3
Kalisz Pomorski 118 GH 2
Kalitva 126-127 K 2
Kaliua 172 F 2-3
Kalix älv 116-117 JK 4
Kāliyāganj 138-139 M 5
Kalkāli Ghāt 141 C 3
Kalkan 136-137 C 4
Kalkaska, MI 70-71 H 3
Kalkfeld 172 C 6
Kalkfontein 174-175 D 2
Kalkfontein = Karasburg 172 C 7
Kalkfonteindam 174-175 F 5
Kalk Plateau = Kalkplato 174-175 C 3
Kalkplato 174-175 C 3
Kalkrand 172 C 6
Kalksburg, Wien- 113 I ab 2
Kalksee 130 III cd 2
Kalkuni 98-99 K 2
Kallafo = Ķelafo 164-165 N 7
Kallakkurichchi 140 D 5
Kallands, AK 58-59 L 4
Kallang 154 III b 2
Kallar 140 C 6
Kallaste 124-125 F 4
Kallidaikurichchi 140 C 6
Kallipolis = Gelibolu 134-135 B 2
Kallithéa [GR, Attikē] 113 IV a 2
Kallsjön 116-117 E 6
Kallūr 140 E 2
Kallūru = Kallūr 140 E 2
Kalmar 116-117 G 9
Kalmar län 116-117 FG 9
Kalmarsund 116-117 G 9
Kal'mius 126-127 HJ 3
Kalmunai = Galmūṇē 140 EF 7
Kalmyckaja Avtonomnaja Sovetskaja Socialističeskaja Respublika = Kalmyk Autonomous Soviet Socialist Republic 126-127 MN 3
Kalmyckij Bazar = Privolžskij 126-127 NO 3
Kalmyk Autonomous Soviet Socialist Republic 126-127 MN 3
Kalmykovo 132-133 J 8
Kalnai 138-139 J 6
Kalnciems 124-125 DE 5
Kalnī 141 B 3
Kalnibolotskaja 126-127 JK 3
Kaloko 172 E 3
Kālol 138-139 D 6
Kalola 171 B 5
Kalomo 172 E 5
Kalonje 171 B 6
Kalpa 138-139 G 2
Kalpeni Island 134-135 L 8
Kālpi 138-139 G 4
Kalpiṭiya 140 D 6
Kal Sefīd 136-137 M 5
Kālsi 138-139 F 2
Kalskag, AK 58-59 G 6
Kalsūbai 138-139 DE 8
Kaltag, AK 58-59 H 4
Kaltasy 124-125 U 6
Kaltenbrünnlberg 113 I ab 2
Kaluga 124-125 KL 6
Kalukalukuang, Pulau — 152-153 MN 8
Kalulaui = Kahoolawe 148-149 e 3
Kalundborg 116-117 D 10
Kalundu 171 B 3
Kalungwishi 171 B 5
Kaluš 126-127 B 2
Kalutara 134-135 MN 9
Kalvān 138-139 E 7
Kalvarija 124-125 D 6
Kalwad = Kālāvad 138-139 C 6
Kalwākurti 140 D 2
Kalwan = Kalvān 138-139 E 7
Kalyāṇadurga = Kalyāndrug 140 C 3
Kalyāndrug 140 C 3
Kalyāni 140 C 2
Kálymnos 122-123 M 7
Kam [WAN] 168-169 H 3
Kam, Nam — 150-151 E 4
Kāma [BUR] 141 D 6
Kama [CDN] 70-71 G 1
Kama [RCB] 172 E 2
Kama [SU, place] 124-125 TU 5
Kama [SU, river] 132-133 J 6
Kamae 144-145 HJ 6
Kamaeura = Kamae 144-145 HJ 6
Kamagaya 155 III cd 1
Kamaggas Mountains = Komaggasberge 174-175 B 5-6
Kâmaing 141 E 3
Kamaishi 142-143 R 4
Kamaishi wan 144-145 NO 3
Kamaisi = Kamaishi 142-143 R 4
Kamakou 78-79 d 2
Kamalampakea 171 B 4
Kamālāpuram 140 D 3
Kamalāpuramu = Kamālāpuram 140 D 3
Kamalasai 150-151 D 4
Kamalia = Kamāliya 138-139 D 2
Kamāliya 138-139 D 2
Kamalpur 141 BC 3
Kamamaung 141 E 7
Kāman [IND] 138-139 F 4
Kaman [TR] 136-137 E 3
Kamane, Se — 150-151 F 5
Kamarān 134-135 E 7
Kamar Bay = Ghubbat al-Qamar 134-135 G 7
Kāmāreddi 140 CD 1
Kamareddy = Kāmāreddi 140 CD 1
Kamarhati 138-139 M 6
Kamarl'u = Artašat 126-127 M 7
Kamata, Tōkyō- 155 III b 2
Kamba [WAN] 168-169 FG 3
Kamba [ZRE] 172 D 2
Kambakkoddai = Kambākōṭṭē 140 E 6
Kambākōṭṭē 140 E 6
Kambal'naja sopka = Velikaja Kambalnaja sopka 132-133 e 7
Kambalnaja sopka, Velikaja — 132-133 e 7
Kambam 140 C 6
Kambang 152-153 D 6
Kambangan, Nusa — 152-153 H 9-10
Kambar 138-139 AB 4
Kambarka 124-125 U 5
Kambia 164-165 B 7
Kambing, Pulau — = Ilha de Ataúro 148-149 J 8
Kambja 124-125 F 4
Kambove 172 E 4
Kambuno, Gunung — 152-153 O 7
Kamčatka 132-133 e 6-7
Kamčatskij poluostrov 132-133 fg 6
Kamčatskij zaliv 132-133 f 6
Kamchatka = Kamčatka 132-133 e 6-7
Kamčija 122-123 M 4
Kamčugskij 124-125 O 3
Kameari, Tōkyō- 155 III c 1
Kameido, Tōkyō- 155 III bc 1
Kamela, OR 66-67 D 3
Kamenec 124-125 D 7
Kamenec-Podol'skij 126-127 C 2
Kāmeng 141 C 2
Kameng Frontier Division = Kāmeng 141 C 2
Kamenjak, Rt — 122-123 E 3
Kamenka [SU, Rossijskaja SFSR Mezenskaja guba] 132-133 G 4
Kamenka [SU, Rossijskaja SFSR Penzenskaja Oblast'] 124-125 OP 7
Kamenka [SU, Rossijskaja SFSR Voronežskaja Oblast'] 126-127 J 1
Kamenka-Bugskaja 126-127 B 1
Kamenka-Dneprovskaja 126-127 G 3
Kamen'-Kaširskij 124-125 E 8
Kamen'-na-Obi 132-133 OP 7
Kamennogorsk 124-125 GH 3
Kamennomostskij 126-127 K 4
Kamennomostskoje 126-127 L 5
Kamennyj Jar 126-127 M 2
Kamenskaya = Kamensk-Šachtinskij 126-127 K 2
Kamenskij 126-127 MN 1
Kamenskoje [SU, Rossijskaja SFSR] 132-133 fg 5
Kamenskoje = Dneprodzeržinsk 126-127 FG 2
Kamensk-Šachtinskij 126-127 K 2
Kamensk-Ural'skij 132-133 LM 6
Kamenz 118 FG 3
Kameoka 144-145 K 5
Kameshli = Al-Qāmishlīyah 134-135 E 3
Kameškovo 124-125 N 5
Kāmēt 134-135 M 4
Kamiah, ID 66-67 EF 2
Kamiakatsuka, Tōkyō- 155 III ab 1
Kamians'ke = Dneprodzeržinsk 126-127 FG 2
Kamiasao, Kawasaki- 155 III a 2
Kamień Pomorski 118 G 2
Kamiesberge 174-175 BC 6
Kamieskroon 174-175 B 6
Kamihongo, Matsudo- 155 III c 1
Kamiishihara, Chōfu- 155 III a 2
Kamiiso 144-145 b 3
Kami Jiao 146-147 B 11
Kamikawa 144-145 c 2
Kamikitazawa, Tōkyō- 155 III a 2
Kami-Koshiki-shima 144-145 G 7
Kāmil, Al- 134-135 H 6
Kamilīn, Al- 164-165 L 5
Kamina 172 DE 3
Kaministikwia 70-71 EF 1
Kaminokuni 144-145 ab 3
Kaminoshima 144-145 G 5
Kaminoyama 144-145 N 3
Kamishak Bay 58-59 KL 7
Kamishakujii, Tōkyō- 155 III a 1
Kamishiki 155 III c 1
Kami-Sihoro 144-145 c 2
Kamitsushima 144-145 G 5
Kamituga 171 AB 3
Kamiyaku 144-145 H 7
Kam Keut 150-151 E 3
Kam Ko't = Kam Keut 150-151 E 3
Kamla 138-139 L 4-5
Kāmlīn, El- = Al-Kamilīn 164-165 L 5
Kamliun, Cape — 58-59 e 1
Kamloops 56-57 MN 7
Kamloops Plateau 60 G 4-5
Kammanassierivier 174-175 E 7
Kammenik, gora — 124-125 HJ 5
Kammuri yama 144-145 HJ 5
Kamnasie River = Kammanassierivier 174-175 E 7
Kamniokan 132-133 V 6
Kamo [J] 144-145 M 4
Kamo [SU] 126-127 M 6
Kamoa Mountains 98-99 J 4
Kamoenai 144-145 ab 2
Kamortā Drīp = Camorta Island 134-135 P 9
Kamoshida, Yokohama- 155 III a 2
Kamp 118 G 4
Kampala 172 F 1
Kampar 148-149 D 6
Kampar, Sungai — 152-153 DE 5
Kamparkalns 124-125 D 5
Kampe 168-169 G 3
Kampemha 171 AB 5
Kamphaeng Phet 150-151 BC 4
Kampli 140 C 3
Kamp'o 144-145 G 5
Kampo = Campo 164-165 F 8
Kampolombo, Lake — 172 E 4
Kampong Amoy Quee 154 III b 1
Kampong Batak 154 III b 1
Kampong Kitin 154 III ab 1
Kampong Kranji 154 III a 1
Kampong Pinang 154 III b 1
Kampong Sungai Jurong 154 III a 1
Kampong Sungei Tengah 154 III b 1
Kampong Tanjong Penjuru 154 III a 2
Kampong Yio Chu Kang 154 III b 1
Kampot 148-149 D 4
Kāmptee 138-139 G 7
Kampti 168-169 E 3
Kampuchéa = Kambodscha 148-149 DE 4
Kampulu 171 B 5
Kampung Baning 150-151 D 10
Kampung Buloh 150-151 D 10
Kampung Cherating 150-151 D 10
Kampung Datok 150-151 D 11
Kampung Hantu = Kampung Limau 150-151 CD 10
Kampung Jajin 150-151 D 10
Kampung Jeli 150-151 CD 10
Kampung Jenera 150-151 C 10
Kampung Kuala Ping 150-151 D 10
Kampung Lenga = Lenga 150-151 D 11
Kampung Pasir Besar 148-149 D 6
Kampung Raja 150-151 D 10
Kāmrūp 141 B 2
Kamsack 61 GH 5
Kamsar 168-169 B 3

Kamskoje Ustje 124-125 R 6
Kamskoje vodochranilišče
132-133 K 6
Kamuchawie Lake 61 G 2
Kamuda 98-99 HJ 2
Kamudi [EAK] 171 D 3
Kamuḍi [IND] 140 D 6
Kamuela = Waimea, HI 78-79 e 2-3
Kamui-misaki 144-145 ab 2
Kamunars'ke = Kommunarsk
126-127 J 2
Kāmyārān 136-137 M 5
Kamyšin 126-127 M 1
Kamyšlov 132-133 L 6
Kamyš-Zar'a 126-127 H 3
Kamyz'ak 126-127 O 3
Kan [BUR] 141 D 4
Kan [SU] 132-133 S 6-7
Kana, Bukit — 152-153 K 4
Kanaal Brussel-Charleroi 128 II a 2
Kanaal van Willebroek 128 II b 1
Kanaaupscow River 56-57 VW 7
Kanab, UT 74-75 G 4
Kanab Creek 74-75 G 4
Kānad = Kannad 138-139 E 7
Kanada = Kannada Pathār
140 BC 3
Kanadej 124-125 Q 7
Kanaga Island 58-59 u 6-7
Kanaga Strait 58-59 u 7
Kanagawa 144-145 M 5
Kanagawa, Yokohama- 155 III a 3
Kanaima Falls 94-95 L 4
Kanaio, HI 78-79 d 2
Kanā'is, Jazīrat — 166-167 M 2
Kanā'is, Rā's al- 136-137 BC 7
Kanakanak, AK 58-59 H 7
Kanakapura 140 C 4
Kanala = Canala 158-159 N 4
Kanal im. Moskvy 113 V b 2
kanal Moskvy 124-125 L 5
Kanamachi, Tōkyō- 155 III c 1
Kan'ān 136-137 L 6
Kananga 172 D 3
Kanara = Kannada Pathār 140 BC 3
Kanarraville, UT 74-75 G 4
Kanaš 132-133 H 6
Kanasvā = Kanwās 138-139 F 5
Kanava 124-125 U 3
Kanawha River 72-73 EF 5
Kanazawa 142-143 Q 4
Kanbalū 141 D 4
Kanbauk 150-151 AB 5
Kanbetlet 141 CD 5
Kanchanaburi 148-149 C 4
Kancheepuram = Kānchipuram
134-135 MN 8
Kanchenjunga = Gangchhendsönga
134-135 O 5
Kan Chiang = Gan Jiang
146-147 E 8
Kanchibia 171 B 5
Kānchipuram 134-135 MN 8
Kanchor 150-151 DE 6
Kanchow = Zhangye 142-143 J 4
Kānchrāpāṛā 138-139 M 6
Kanchriech 150-151 E 7
Kanchuan = Ganquan 146-147 B 3
K'anda 124-125 M 1
Kanda, Tōkyō- 155 III b 1
Kandahār [AFG] 134-135 K 4
Kandahār [IND] 140 C 1
Kandal [K, administrative unit]
150-151 E 7
Kandal [K, place] 148-149 DE 4
Kandalakša 132-133 EF 4
Kandalakšskaja guba 132-133 EF 4
Kandangan 148-149 FG 7
Kandau = Kandava 124-125 D 5
Kandava 124-125 D 5
Kandavu 148-149 a 2
Kandé 168-169 F 3
Kāndhla 138-139 F 3
Kandī [BUR] 141 E 6
Kandi [DY] 164-165 E 6
Kāndī [IND] 138-139 LM 6
Kandi, Tanjung — 152-153 O 5
Kandiaro = Kandiyāro 138-139 B 4
Kandika 168-169 B 2
Kandik River 58-59 R 4
Kandilli, İstanbul- 154 I b 2
Kandıra 136-137 D 2
Kandiyāro 138-139 B 4
Kandla 134-135 L 6
Kandos 158-159 JK 6
Kandoûsī = Kandūsī 166-167 E 2
Kāndra 138-139 KL 6
Kandreho 172 J 5
Kandukūr 140 D 3
Kandukūru = Kandukūr 140 D 3
Kandūleh 136-137 M 5
Kandulu 171 D 5
Kandūsī 166-167 E 2
Kandy = Maha Nuwara
134-135 N 9
Kane, PA 72-73 G 4
Kane, WY 68-69 BC 3
Kane Basin 56-57 WX 2
Kanektok River 58-59 G 7
Kanem 164-165 H 6
Kaneohe, HI 78-79 d 2
Kanev 126-127 E 2
Kanevskaja 126-127 J 3
Kaneyama 144-145 M 4
Kang 172 D 6
Kangaba 168-169 CD 3
Kangal 136-137 G 3
Kangar 148-149 D 5
Kangaroo Island 158-159 G 7
Kangaruma 98-99 J 2
Kangāvar 136-137 M 5
Kāngayam 140 C 5
Kangding 142-143 J 5-6
Kangean, Pulau — 148-149 G 8
Kangerdlugssuaq [Greenland, bay]
56-57 ef 4
Kangerdlugssuaq [Greenland, place]
56-57 ab 4
Kangetet 172 G 1
Kanggye 142-143 O 3
Kanggyŏng 144-145 F 4
Kanghwa 144-145 F 4
Kanghwa-do 144-145 EF 4
Kanghwa-man 144-145 E 4
Kangik, AK 58-59 GH 1
Kangjin 144-145 F 5
Kangkar Jemaluang = Jemaluang
150-151 DE 11
Kangkar Lenggor = Lenggor
150-151 D 11
Kangkar Masai 154 III b 1
Kangnŭng 144-145 G 4
Kango 172 B 1
Kāngpokpi 141 C 3
Kāngra 138-139 F 1
Kāngsā 141 B 3
Kangsar, Kuala — 148-149 CD 6
Kangshan 146-147 GH 10
Kangsŏ 144-145 E 3
Kanhan 138-139 G 6-7
Kanhar 138-139 J 5-6
Kan Ho = Gan He 142-143 N 1
Kanī [BUR] 141 D 4
Kani [RB] 174-175 D 3
Kaniāh 138-139 K 7
Kaniama 172 DE 3
Kaniapiskau Lake 56-57 W 7
Kaniapiskau River 56-57 X 6
Kaniet Islands 148-149 N 7
Kanigiri 140 D 3
Kānī Masī 136-137 K 4
Kanin, poluostrov — 132-133 GH 4
Kanin Nos 132-133 G 4
Kanireş 136-137 J 3
Kanita 144-145 N 2
Kankakee, IL 64-65 J 3
Kankakee River 70-71 G 5
Kankan 164-165 C 6
Kankasanturē 140 E 6
Kankauli 140 A 2
Kānker 138-139 H 7
Kankesanturai = Kankasanturē
140 E 6
Kankō = Hamhŭng 142-143 O 3-4
Kankō = Hŭngnam 142-143 O 4
Kankossa = Kankūssah
164-165 B 5
Kan-kou-chên = Gango
144-145 B 2
Kānksā = Mānkur 138-139 L 6
Kankūssah 164-165 B 5
Kankwi 174-175 D 3
Kankyō-hokudō = Hamgyŏng-pukto
144-145 G 2-H 1
Kankyō-nandō = Hamgyŏng-namdo
144-145 FG 2-3
Kanlica, İstanbul- 154 I b 2
Kannad 138-139 E 7
Kannada Pathār 140 BC 3
Kannanūr = Cannanore
134-135 LM 8
Kannauj 138-139 G 4
Kannoj = Kannauj 138-139 G 4
Kannapolis, NC 80-81 F 3
Kannara = Kannada Pathār
140 BC 3
Kannauj 138-139 G 4
Kan-ngen = Gancheng 150-151 G 3
Kanniyākumāri 140 C 6-7
Kannod 138-139 F 6
Kannoj = Kannauj 138-139 G 4
Kannus 116-117 K 6
Kano [WAN, administrative unit]
168-169 H 3
Kano [WAN, place] 164-165 F 6
Kano [WAN, river] 168-169 H 3
Kanoji 144-145 J 5
Kanona 171 B 6
Kanopolis Lake 68-69 H 6
Kanorado, KS 68-69 EF 6
Kanosh, UT 74-75 G 3
Kanouri 164-165 G 6
Kanowit 152-153 JK 4
Kanoya 144-145 H 7
Kānpur 134-135 MN 5
Kańsāī = Kāsai 138-139 L 6
Kansas 64-65 FG 4
Kansas, OK 76-77 G 4
Kansas City, KS 64-65 GH 4
Kansas City, MO 64-65 H 4
Kansas River 64-65 G 4
Kansk 132-133 S 6
Kansŏng 144-145 G 3
Kansu = Gansu 142-143 G 3-J 4
Kantalahti = Kandalakša
132-133 EF 4
Kantalai = Gangtalē 140 E 6
Kantang 150-151 B 9
Kan-t'ang = Gantang 146-147 B 10
Kantani = Centane 174-175 H 7
Kantara = Al-Qanṭarah 173 C 2
Kantara, El- = Al-Qanṭarah
166-167 J 2
Kantchari 164-165 E 6
Kantemirovka 126-127 JK 2
Kantharalak 150-151 E 5
Kanthararom 150-151 E 5
Kantharawichai 150-151 D 4
Kānthi = Contai 138-139 L 7
Kantishna, AK 58-59 M 5
Kantishna River 58-59 M 4
Kantō 144-145 MN 4
Kantō sammyaku 144-145 M 4-5
Kanuchuan Lake 62 EF 1
Kanukov = Privolžskij 126-127 NO 3
Kanuku Mountains 98-99 J 3
Kanuma 144-145 M 4
Kanuparti 140 E 3
Kanuri = Kanouri 164-165 G 6
Kanus 174-175 C 4
Kanuti River 58-59 L 3
Kaṇvās = Kanwās 138-139 F 5
Kanwās 138-139 F 5
Kanyākumārī Antarīp = Cape
Comorin 134-135 M 9
Kanyama 171 B 2
Kanye 172 DE 6-7
Kanyu = Ganyu 146-147 G 4
Kan-yü = Ganyu 146-147 G 4
Kanzanlı 136-137 F 4
Kao-an = Gao'an 142-143 LM 6
Kao-chia-fang = Gaojiafang
146-147 D 7
Kaohsiung 142-143 MN 7
Kao-i = Gaoyi 146-147 E 3
Kaokoveld 172 B 5-6
Kaolack 164-165 A 6
Kaolak River 58-59 G 2
Kaolan = Lanzhou 142-143 JK 4
Kao-lan Tao = Gaolan Dao
146-147 D 11
Kao-li-kung Shan = Gaoligong Shan
142-143 H 6
Kaoling = Gaoling 146-147 B 4
Kaomi = Gaomi 146-147 G 3
Kaoping = Gaoping 146-147 D 4
Kao Sai 155 I b 1
Kao-sha = Gaosha 146-147 C 8
Kaosiung = Kaohsiung
142-143 MN 7
Kaotai = Gaotai 142-143 H 4
Kaotang = Gaotang 146-147 F 3
Kao-tien-tzŭ = Gaodianzi
146-147 BC 6
Kao-ts'un = Gaocun 146-147 E 7
Kaotwe 174-175 E 2
Kaouar 164-165 G 5
Kaoyang = Gaoyang 146-147 E 2
Kaoyu = Gaoyou 146-147 G 5
Kao-yüan = Gaoyuan 146-147 F 3
Kao-yu Hu = Gaoyou Hu
146-147 G 5
Kapaa, HI 78-79 c 1
Kap'a-do 144-145 F 6
Kapadvanj 138-139 D 6
Kapagere 148-149 N 8-9
Kap Alexander 56-57 WX 2
Kapalı Çarşı 154 I ab 2
Kapanga 172 D 3
Kap Arkona 118 F 1
Kapas, Pulau — 150-151 D 10
Kapāsan 138-139 E 5
Kapasin = Kapāsan 138-139 E 5
Kapatu 171 B 5
Kap Brewster 52 BC 20-21
Kapčagajskoje vodochranilišče
134-135 O 9
Kap Dan 56-57 d 4
Kapela 122-123 F 3
Kapellerfeld 113 I c 1
Kapenguria 171 C 2
Kap Farvel 56-57 c 6
Kapfenberg 118 G 5
Kapıdağı yarımadası 136-137 BC 2
Kapingamarangi 208 F 2
Kapinnie 160 B 5
Kapiri Mposhi 172 E 4
Kapiskau Lake 62 G 1
Kapiskau River 62 G 1-2
Kapit 148-149 F 6
Kapiti Island 161 F 5
Kaplan, LA 78-79 C 5-6
Kaplanova = Babajurt 126-127 N 5
Kap Morris Jesup 52 A 19-23
Kapoe 150-151 B 8
Kāpōētā 164-165 L 8
Kapona 172 E 3
Kapongolo 171 AB 4
Kaporo 168-169 B 3
Kapos 118 J 5
Kaposvár 118 HJ 5
Kapotn'a, Moskva- 113 V d 3
Kapoudia, Ras — = Rā's Qabūdīyah
166-167 M 2
Kapp Bessels 116-117 lm 5
K'appesel'ga 124-125 JK 2
Kapp Heuglin 116-117 lm 5
Kapp Linné 116-117 j 5
Kapp Melchers 116-117 m 6
Kapp Mohn 116-117 m 5
Kapp Norvegia 53 B 34-35
Kapp Platen 116-117 lm 4
Kapp Weyprecht 116-117 l 5
Kapsan 144-145 FG 2
Kapsowar 171 CD 2
Kapsukas 124-125 D 6
Kapuas, Sungai — [RI, Kalimantan
Barat] 148-149 F 6
Kapuas, Sungai — [RI, Kalimantan
Tengah] 152-153 L 6
Kapuas Hulu, Pegunungan —
152-153 K 5
Kapucijnenbos 128 II b 2
Kapunda 160 D 5
Kapūrthala 138-139 E 2
Kapur Utara, Pegunungan —
152-153 JK 9
Kapuskasing 56-57 U 8
Kapuskasing River 62 FG 3
Kapustin Jar 126-127 MN 2
Kaputar, Mount — 160 JK 3
Kaputir 171 C 2
Kapvāhā = Kadwāha 138-139 F 5
Kapydžik, gora — 126-127 M 7
Kap York 56-57 X 2
Kara 132-133 LM 4
Kara = Karrā 138-139 K 6
Karaali 136-137 E 3
Karababa dağı 136-137 FG 3
Karabanovo 124-125 M 5
Karabaš 124-125 T 6
Karabekaul 134-135 JK 3
Karabiğa 136-137 B 2
Kara-Bogaz-Gol, zaliv —
134-135 G 2
Karab Shahibīyah 166-167 C 6
Karabük 134-135 C 2
Kara burun [TR] 136-137 AB 3
Karaburun = Ahırlı 136-137 B 3
Karabutak 132-133 L 8
Karaca 136-137 H 2
Karacabey 136-137 C 2
Karaca dağ [TR, Ankara] 136-137 E 3
Karaca dağ [TR, Konya] 136-137 E 4
Karacadağ [TR, Urfa] 136-137 H 4
Karaca dağ = Kaynak 136-137 H 4
Karačajevsk 126-127 KL 5
Karacaköy 136-137 C 2
Karačala 126-127 O 7
Karačarovo, Moskva- 113 V cd 3
Karacasu 136-137 C 4
Karačev 124-125 K 7
Karachayevo-Cherkess Autonomous
Region 126-127 KL 5
Karāchī 134-135 K 6
Karaçurun 136-137 H 4
Karād 140 B 2
Karadağ 136-137 E 4
Kara deniz 134-135 B-D 2
Karadeniz boğazı 134-135 BC 2
Karādkah 166-167 G 3
Karadoğan 136-137 DE 2
Karafuto = Sachalin 132-133 b 7-8
Karagaj 124-125 U 4
Karagajly 132-133 NO 8
Karagan 126-127 P 4
Karaganda 132-133 NO 8
Kar'agino = Fizuli 126-127 N 7
Karaginskij, ostrov — 132-133 fg 6
Karaginskij zaliv 132-133 fg 6
Karagoua 164-165 G 6
Karahal = Karhal 138-139 G 4
Karahallı 134-135 C 3
Karahasanlı = Sadıkali 136-137 F 3
Karai = Ban Karai 150-151 F 4
Karaikkāl = Kārikāl 134-135 MN 8
Kāraikkudi 140 D 5
Kāraikuḍi = Kāraikkudi 140 D 5
Karaira = Karera 138-139 G 5
Karaisalı = Çeceli 136-137 F 4
Karaitivu = Kāreitivu 140 DE 6
Karaj 134-135 G 3
Karak 150-151 CD 11
Karak, Al- 134-135 D 4
Karakāla = Kārkal 140 B 4
Karakāla = Perdūru 140 B 4
Karakallı 136-137 KL 3
Kara-Kalpak Autonomous Soviet
Socialist Republic 202-203 UV 7
Karakeçi = Mizar 136-137 H 4
Karakeçili 136-137 E 3
Karakelong, Pulau — 148-149 J 6
Karaklis = Kirovakan 126-127 LM 6
Karakoçan = Tepe 136-137 HJ 3
Karakoram 134-135 L 3-M 4
Karakoram Pass = Qaramurun
davan 134-135 MN 3
Karakorē 164-165 MN 6
Karakorum = Char Chorin
142-143 J 2
Karaköse 134-135 E 3
Karakubstroj = Komsomol'skoje
126-127 HJ 3
Karakumskij kanal 134-135 J 3
Karakumy 134-135 HJ 3
Karākūrū, Nahr al- 168-169 C 1-2
Karalat 126-127 O 4
Karam = Karin 164-165 O 6
Karama, Sungai — 152-153 N 6-7
Karaman 134-135 C 3
Karaman = Çameli 136-137 C 4
Karambu 152-153 LM 7
Karamea 161 DE 5
Karami 168-169 H 3
Karamian, Pulau — 148-149 F 8
Karamürsel 136-137 C 2
Karamyševo 124-125 G 5
Karanambo 98-99 J 3
Karand 136-137 M 5
Karang = Gunung Chamah
150-151 C 10
Karangagung 152-153 F 7
Karangania 141 C 2
Karang Besar 152-153 N 5
Karanja 138-139 F 7
Karanjia 138-139 KL 7
Karanlık bendi 154 I a 1
Karaṇpur 138-139 D 3
Karantinmoje = Privolžskij
126-127 NO 3
Karaoğlan 136-137 H 3
Karaoli = Karauli 138-139 F 4
Karapınar 136-137 E 4
Karas, Pulau — 148-149 K 7
Karasaj 126-127 O 2
Karasberge, Groot — 172 C 7
Karasberge, Klein — 174-175 C 4
Karasburg 172 C 7
Kara Sea 132-133 L 3-Q 2
Karasgāńv = Karasgaon
138-139 F 7
Karasgaon 138-139 F 7
Kara Shar = Qara Shahr
142-143 F 3
Kara Shar = Qara Shahr
142-143 F 3
Karasjok 116-117 L 3
Karasjokka 116-117 L 3
Karas Mountains, Great — = Groot
Karasberge 172 C 7
Karas Mountains, Little — = Klein
Karasberge 174-175 C 4
Kara Strait = proliv Karskije Vorota
132-133 J-L 3
Karasu [SU] 126-127 N 6
Karasu [TR, place] 136-137 K 3
Karasu [TR, river] 136-137 J 3
Karasu = İncili 136-137 D 2
Karasu = Salavat 136-137 F 2
Karasu-Aras dağları 134-135 E 2-3
Karasu-Bazar = Belogorsk
126-127 G 4
Karasuk 132-133 O 7
Karataş = İskele 136-137 F 4
Karataş burnu 136-137 F 4
Karatau 132-133 N 9
Karatau, chrebet — 132-133 MN 9
Karativu 140 D 6
Karatobe 132-133 J 8
Karatoya 138-139 M 5
Karatsu 144-145 G 6
Karaul 132-133 P 3
Karauli 138-139 F 4
Karaussa Nor = Char us nuur
142-143 G 2
Karavansaraj = Idževan
126-127 M 6
Karavānsarā-ye Ḥouz Solṭān =
Daryācheh Ḥowẓ Solṭān
136-137 O 5
Karayazı = Bayraktar 136-137 JK 3
Karayün 136-137 G 3
Karažal 132-133 N 8
Karbalā' 134-135 E 4
Karben-Rendel 128 III b 1
Karcag 118 K 5
Kardeljevo 122-123 G 4
Kardítsa 122-123 JK 6
Kardiva Channel 176 a 1-2
Kärdla 124-125 D 4
Kardymovo 124-125 J 6
Kărdžali 122-123 L 5
Karee 174-175 G 5
Kareeberge 172 D 8
Kareima = Kuraymah 164-165 L 5
Kāreitivu 140 DE 6
Karelia 124-125 GH 2-3
Karelian Autonomous Soviet Socialist
Republic 132-133 E 4-5
Karel'skaja Avtonomnaja Sovetskaja
Socialističeskaja Respublika =
Karelian Autonomous Soviet
Socialist Republic 132-133 E 4-5
Karelstad = Charlesville 172 D 3
Karema 172 F 3
Karen = Karin Pyinnei 148-149 C 3
Karenni = Karin Pyinnei
148-149 C 3
Karera [IND ↓ Ajmer] 138-139 E 5
Karera [IND ← Jhānsi] 138-139 G 5
Karesuando 116-117 JK 3
Karet = Qārrāt 164-165 C 4
Karēz 134-135 K 4
Kargalinskaja 126-127 MN 5
Kargat 132-133 P 6
Kargi [EAK] 171 D 2
Kargi [TR] 136-137 F 2
Kargopol' 132-133 F 5
Karhāḍ = Karād 140 B 2
Karhal 138-139 G 4
Karhula 116-117 M 7
Kari = Kadi 138-139 D 6
Karia ba Mohammed = Qaryat Bā
Muḥammad 166-167 D 2
Kariba, Lake — 172 E 5
Kariba Dam 172 E 5
Kariba Gorge 172 EF 5
Kariba-yama 144-145 ab 2
Karibib 172 C 6
Kariega 174-175 E 7
Karigasniemi 116-117 LM 3
Kārikāl 134-135 MN 8
Karikari, Cape — 161 EF 1
Karima = Kuraymah 164-165 L 5
Karīmah, Wādī al- 166-167 F 3
Kārimangalam 140 D 4
Karimata, Pulau-pulau —
148-149 E 7
Karimata, Selat — 148-149 E 7
Karīmganj 141 C 3
Karīmnagara = Karīmnagar 140 D 1
Karimon Java Islands = Pulau-pulau
Karimunjawa 148-149 EF 8
Karimunjawa, Pulau-pulau —
148-149 EF 8
Karin 164-165 O 6
Karin Pyinnei 148-149 C 3
Karis 116-117 KL 7-8
Karisimbi, Mont — 172 E 2
Kariya 144-145 L 5
Karjaa = Karis 116-117 KL 8
Karjat [IND → Bombay] 140 A 1
Karjat [IND ↖ Kurduvādi] 140 B 1
Kārkal 140 B 4
Karkamış 136-137 G 4
Karkar 164-165 b 2
Karkar Island 148-149 N 7
Karkh 138-139 A 4
Karkheh, Rūd-e — 136-137 N 6-7
Karkinitskij zaliv 126-127 F 4
Karkkila 116-117 KL 7
Karkūk = Kirkūk 134-135 EF 3
Kar La [TJ] 138-139 MN 3
Karl Alexander, ostrov —
132-133 H-K 1
Karliova = Kanireş
136-137 J 3
Karlobag 122-123 F 3
Karlovac 122-123 F 3
Karlovka 126-127 G 2
Karlovy Vary 118 F 3
Karlsborg 116-117 F 8
Karlsfeld 130 II a 1
Karlshamn 116-117 F 9
Karlshof 130 III c 2
Karlskoga 116-117 F 8
Karlskrona 116-117 FG 9
Karlsruhe 118 D 4
Karlsruhe, ND 68-69 F 1
Karlstad 116-117 EF 8
Karlstad, MN 68-69 H 1
Karluk, AK 58-59 K 8
Karluk Lake 58-59 f 1
Karmah 164-165 L 5
Karmāla 140 B 1
Karmāḷēṅ = Karmāla 140 B 1
Karmanovo [SU, Rossijskaja SFSR]
124-125 K 6
Karmøy 116-117 A 8
Karnak, IL 70-71 F 7
Karnak, Al- 173 C 5
Karnāl 134-135 M 5
Karnāli 138-139 H 3
Karnāli, Mūgu — 138-139 J 3
Karṇāphuli 141 BC 4
Karnaprayāg 138-139 G 2
Karnataka 134-135 M 7-8
Karṇāṭaka Paṭhār = Kannada Pathār
140 BC 3
Karnes City, TX 76-77 EF 8
Karnobat 122-123 M 4
Kärnten 118 FG 5
Karnūlu = Kurnool 134-135 M 7
Karoi 172 E 5
Karokobe 171 B 2
Karompa, Pulau — 152-153 OP 9
Karondh = Kalāhāndi 138-139 J 8
Karonga 172 F 3
Karoo, Groot — 172 D 8
Karoo, Hoë — 174-175 C-F 6
Karoo, Klein — 172 D 8
Karoonda 160 DE 5
Karor 138-139 C 2
Kārōra 164-165 M 5
Karosa 148-149 G 7
Karow, Berlin- 130 III b 1
Kárpas 136-137 EF 5
Kárpathos [GR, island] 122-123 M 8
Kárpathos [GR, place] 122-123 M 8
Karpeddo 171 D 2
Karpenēsion 122-123 JK 6
Karpinsk = Krasnoturjinsk
132-133 L 5-6
Karpogory 124-125 P 1
Karrā 138-139 K 6
Karrats Fjord 56-57 Za 3
Karree = Karee 174-175 G 5
Kars 134-135 E 2
Karsakpaj 132-133 M 8
Karsantı 134-135 F 4
Kārsava 124-125 F 5
Karši 134-135 K 3
Karşıyaka 136-137 B 3
Karsiyāng = Kurseong
138-139 LM 4
Karskije Vorota, proliv —
132-133 J-L 3
Karsovaj 124-125 T 4
Karsun 124-125 Q 6
Kartabu 98-99 J 1
Kartal, İstanbul- 136-137 C 2
Kartal tepe 154 I a 1
Kartaly 132-133 KL 7
Karti = Kadi 138-139 D 6
Kartlijskij chrebet 126-127 M 5-6
Karu = Karkh 138-139 A 4
Karumba 158-159 H 3
Kārumbhar Island 138-139 B 6
Karumwa 171 C 3
Kārūn, Rūd-e — 134-135 FG 4
Karunāgapaḷḷi 140 C 6
Karunagapally = Karunāgapaḷḷi
140 C 6
Karuṇḍa = Kalāhāndi 138-139 J 8
Karungi 116-117 K 4-5
Karungu 171 C 3
Karūr 140 CD 5
Karvai = Korwai 138-139 FG 5
Karvī = Karwi 138-139 H 5
Karvinā 118 J 4
Kārwār 134-135 L 8
Karwi 138-139 H 5
Karyai 122-123 KL 5
Karžaz 166-167 F 5
Kaş 134-135 BC 3
Kasa = Ui-do 144-145 E 5
Kasaba [TR] 136-137 J 3
Kasaba [Z] 171 B 5
Kasaba = Turgutlu 136-137 BC 3
Kasabonika Lake 62 E 1
Kasache 171 C 6
Kasai [IND] 138-139 L 6
Kasai [ZRE] 172 C 2
Kasai, Tōkyō- 155 III c 2
Kasai-Occidental 172 CD 2-3
Kasai-Oriental 172 DE 2-3
Kasaji 172 D 4
Kasal, Jabal — 166-167 G 3
Kasama 172 F 4
Kasan = Kazan' 132-133 HJ 6
Kasanda 171 BC 2
Kasane 172 DE 5
Kasanga 172 F 3
Kasaoka 144-145 J 5
Kāsaragod 140 B 4
Kāsargōḍ = Kāsaragod 140 B 4
Kasary 126-127 K 2
Kasatochi Island 58-59 j 4
Kasa-Vubu, Kinshasa- 170 IV a 2
Kasba 138-139 L 5
Kasba, Calcutta- 154 II b 2
Kasbah, Al-Jazā'ir- 170 I a 1
Kasba Lake 56-57 Q 5
Kasba Patāspur 138-139 L 6
Kasba Tadla = Qaṣ'bat Tādlah
166-167 C 3
Kaseda 144-145 H 7
Kasegaluk Lagoon 58-59 EF 2
Kasempa 172 DE 4
Kasenga 172 E 4
Kasenyi 172 EF 1
Kasese 172 EF 1
Kaset Wisai 150-151 D 5
Kasewe 168-169 B 3
Kāsganj 138-139 G 4
Kasha 171 E 3
Kashabowie 70-71 EF 1
Kāshān 134-135 G 4
Kashega, AK 58-59 n 4
Kashegelok, AK 58-59 J 6
Kashgar = Qashqar 142-143 CD 4
Kashghariya 142-143 DE 4
Kashi 142-143 D 4
Kashi = Qäshqär 142-143 CD 4
Kashima 144-145 GH 6
Kashing = Jiaxing 142-143 N 5
Kashio, Yokohama- 155 III a 3
Kāshīpur [IND, Orissa] 138-139 J 8
Kāshīpur [IND, Uttar Pradesh]
138-139 G 3
Kāshīpura = Kāshīpur 138-139 J 8
Kashishi 171 B 6
Kashishibog Lake 62 E 3
Kashiwagi, Tōkyō- 155 III b 1
Kashiwazaki 144-145 LM 4
Kashkān, Rūdkhāneh-ye —
136-137 N 6
Kashmar 134-135 H 3-4
Kashmere Gardens, Houston-, TX
85 III b 1
Kashmīr 134-135 LM 4
Kashmīr, Jammu and —
134-135 LM 3-4
Kashmor 134-135 O 5
Kashqar = Qäshqär 142-143 CD 4
Kash Rūd = Khāsh Rōd
134-135 J 4
Kasia 138-139 JK 4
Kasiāri 138-139 L 6
Kasigao 171 D 3
Kasigluk, AK 58-59 F 6
Kasilof, AK 58-59 M 6
Kasimov 132-133 G 7
Kašin 124-125 L 5
Kāšira 124-125 LM 6
Kasirota = Pulau Kasiruta
148-149 J 7
Kasiruta, Pulau — 148-149 J 7
Kasivobara = Severo-Kuril'sk
132-133 de 7
Kasiyā = Kasia 138-139 JK 4
Kaskaskia River 70-71 F 6
Kaskinen = Kaskö 116-117 J 6
Kaskö 116-117 J 6
Kâs Kong 150-151 D 7
Kaslo 60 J 5
Kâs Moul 150-151 D 7
Kasongan 152-153 K 6-7
Kasongo 172 E 2
Kasongo-Lunda 172 C 3
Kásos 122-123 M 8
Kasossa, Tanjung — 152-153 N 10
Kaspi 126-127 M 5-6
Kaspijsk 126-127 NO 5
Kaspijskij 126-127 N 4
Kaširovka, Syzran'- 124-125 R 7
Kaspl'a 124-125 HJ 6
Kasnk 136-137 K 3
Kâs Rong 150-151 D 7
Kâs Rong Sam Lem 150-151 D 7
Kassai = Kasai 172 C 2
Kassalā 164-165 M 5
Kassama 168-169 C 2
Kassándra 122-123 K 5-6
Kassel 118 D 3
Kasserine = Al-Qasrayn
164-165 F 1-2
Kastamonu 134-135 CD 2
Kastamum = Kastamonu
134-135 CD 2
Kâs Tang 150-151 D 7
Kasteli Selianou = Palaiochŏra
122-123 KL 8
Kastélion 122-123 K 8
Kastellórizon = Mégistē
136-137 C 4
Kasten, Forst — 130 II a 2
Kastoria 122-123 J 5
Kastornoje 124-125 LM 8
Kasulu 172 F 2
Kasumiga ura 144-145 N 5
Kasumkent 126-127 O 6
Kasumpti 138-139 F 2
Kasungu 172 F 4
Kasungu National Park 171 C 6
Kasur = Qaṣūr 134-135 L 4
Kasvā = Kasba 138-139 L 5
Kataba 172 DE 5
Katahdin, Mount — 64-65 MN 2
Kaṭaka = Cuttack 134-135 NO 6
Katako-Kombe 172 D 2
Katakturuk River 58-59 P 2
Katakumba 172 D 3
Katalla, AK 58-59 P 6
Katami sammyaku 144-145 c 1-2
Katana 171 B 3
Katanga 132-133 T 5-6
Katanga = Shaba 172 DE 3
Katāngi 138-139 G 7
Katangli 132-133 b 7
Katanning 158-159 C 6
Kātapuram 140 E 1
Katar 134-135 G 5
Katārnian Ghat 138-139 H 3
Katav-Ivanovsk 132-133 K 7
Katāwāz 134-135 K 4
Katberg 174-175 G 7
Katbergpas 174-175 G 7
Katchal Island 134-135 P 9
Katchall Island 148-149 B 5
Katedupa, Pulau — 152-153 PQ 8
Kateel River 58-59 H 4
Katenga 172 E 3
Katera 171 BC 3
Katerîna, Gebel — = Jabal Katrīnah
164-165 L 3
Katerinē 122-123 K 5
Katerynoslav = Dnepropetrovsk
126-127 GH 2

Kates Needle 56-57 KL 6
Katete 172 F 4
Katghora 138-139 J 6
Kathā 148-149 C 2
Katherina, Gebel — = Jabal Katrīnah 164-165 L 3
Katherine 158-159 F 2
Kāthgodām 138-139 G 3
Kāthiāwār 134-135 K 6
Kathlambagebirge = Drakensberge 172 E 8-F 7
Kathleen Lake 70-71 J 2
Kathleen Lakes 58-59 T 6
Kathor 138-139 D 7
Kathua 171 D 3
Kati 164-165 C 6
Katif, El- = Al-Qaṭīf 134-135 F 5
Katihār 134-135 O 5
Katimik Lake 61 J 4
Katiola 164-165 CD 7
Katkop 174-175 D 6
Katkopberge 174-175 C 6-D 5
Katkop Hills = Katkopberge 174-175 C 6-D 5
Katmai, Mount — 56-57 F 6
Katmai Bay 58-59 K 8
Katmai National Monument 56-57 EF 6
Kātmāndu 134-135 NO 5
Katni [IND] 138-139 H 6
Katni [SU] 124-125 QR 5
Káto Achaïa 122-123 J 6
Kātol 138-139 G 7
Katomba 158-159 JK 6
Katong, Singapore- 154 III b 2
Katonga 171 B 2-3
Katoomba 160 JK 4
Katoomba = Blue Mountains 158-159 JK 6
Katopasa, Gunung — 152-153 O 6
Katowice 118 J 3
Katra 138-139 K 4
Katrancık dağı 136-137 D 4
Katrīnah, Jabal — 164-165 L 3
Katrineholm 116-117 G 8
Katsina 164-165 F 6
Katsina Ala [WAN, place] 164-165 F 7
Katsina Ala [WAN, river] 168-169 H 4
Katsuda 144-145 N 4
Katsumoto 144-145 G 6
Katsushika, Tōkyō- 155 III bc 1
Katsuta, Yokohama- 155 III a 2
Katsuura 144-145 N 5
Katsuyama 144-145 L 4
Katta = Katsuta 144-145 N 4
Kattakurgan 134-135 K 2-3
Kattegat 116-117 D 9
Katupa 152-153 N 10
Kaṭvā = Kātwa 138-139 LM 6
Kātwa 138-139 LM 6
Katwe 171 B 3
Katwoude 128 I b 1
Katy, TX 76-77 G 8
Kau, Teluk — 148-149 J 6
Kauai 148-149 e 3
Kauai Channel 148-149 e 3
Kaudeteunom 152-153 A 3
Kaufbeuren 118 E 5
Kaufman, TX 76-77 FG 6
Kaugama 168-169 H 2
Kauhajoki 116-117 JK 6
Kau I Chau 155 I a 2
Kaukasus Mountains 126-127 J 4-N 6
Kaukauna, WI 70-71 F 3
Kaukauveld 172 D 5
Kaukkwe Chaung 141 E 3
Kaukurus 174-175 C 2
Kaula 78-79 b 2
Kaulakahi Channel 78-79 b 1-c 2
Kauliranta 116-117 KL 4
Kaulsdorf, Berlin- 130 III c 1-2
Kaulsdorf-Süd, Berlin- 130 III c 2
Kaulun = Kowloon 142-143 LM 7
Kau Lung Peak 155 I b 1
Kau Lung Tong, Kowloon- 155 I b 1
Kau-mi = Gaomi 146-147 G 3
Kaunakakai, HI 78-79 d 2
Kauna Point 78-79 de 3
Kaunas 124-125 DE 6
Kaunata 124-125 F 5
Kaunch = Konch 138-139 G 4-5
Kaur 168-169 B 2
Kaura Namoda 164-165 F 6
Kauriāla Ghāt 138-139 H 3
Kau Sai Chau 155 I b 1
Kautokeino 116-117 KL 3
Kau Wa Kang 155 I a 1
Kavajë 122-123 H 5
Kavak [TR, Samsun] 136-137 FG 2
Kavak [TR, Sivas] 136-137 G 3
Kavalga Island 58-59 t 7
Kávali 140 DE 3
Kaval'kan 132-133 a 6
Kavaratti 134-135 L 8
Kavaratti Island 134-135 L 8
Kavardhā = Kawardha 134-135 N 6
Kavarna 122-123 N 4
Kāverī = Cauvery 140 C 5
Kaverī Ḍeltā = Cauvery Delta 140 D 5
Kāvi 138-139 D 6
Kavieng 148-149 h 5
Kavik River 58-59 O 2
Kavīr, Dasht-e — 134-135 GH 4
Kavīr-e Khorāsān = Dasht-e Kavīr 134-135 GH 4
Kāvīr-e Khorāsān = Kavīr-e Namak-e Mīghān 134-135 H 4
Kavīr-e Lūt 132-133 J 5
Kavīr-e Mīghān 136-137 N 5
Kavīr-e Namak-e Mīghān 134-135 H 4
Kavirondo Gulf 171 C 3
Kavkaz 126-127 H 4
Kavkaz, Malyj — 126-127 L 5-N 7
Kavkazskij zapovednik 126-127 K 5
Kavu 171 B 4
Kaw 92-93 J 4
Kawa 141 E 7
Kawagoe 144-145 M 5
Kawaguchi 144-145 MN 4-5
Kawaharada = Sawata 144-145 M 3-4
Kawaihae, HI 148-149 e 3
Kawaihoa Point 78-79 b 2
Kawaikini 78-79 c 1
Kawakawa 161 F 2
Kawamata 144-145 N 4
Kawambwa 172 EF 3
Kawanoe 144-145 J 5-6
Kawardha 134-135 N 6
Kawasaki 142-143 QR 4
Kawasaki-Chitose 155 III a 2
Kawasaki-Daishi 155 III b 2
Kawasaki-Kamiasao 155 III a 2
Kawasaki-ko 155 III b 2
Kawasaki-Kosugi 155 III ab 2
Kawasaki-Maginu 155 III a 2
Kawasaki-Maruko 155 III b 2
Kawasaki-Mizonokuchi 155 III a 2
Kawasaki-Nakanoshima 155 III a 2
Kawasaki-Nogawa 155 III a 2
Kawasaki-Oda 155 III b 2
Kawasaki-Shinjō 155 III a 2
Kawasaki Stadium 155 III b 2
Kawashima, Yokohama- 155 III a 3
Kawashiri-misaki 144-145 H 5
Kawawa, Yokohama- 155 III a 2
Kaweka 161 G 4
Kawene 70-71 E 1
Kawewe 171 AB 5
Kawgareik 141 F 7
Kawich Range 74-75 E 3-4
Kawimbe 172 F 3
Kawinaw Lake 61 J 4
Kawkareik = Kawgareik 141 F 7
Kawlin 148-149 C 2
Kawm Umbū 164-165 L 4
Kawnipi Lake 70-71 E 1
Kawn Ken = Khon Kaen 148-149 D 3
Kawre Kyûn 150-151 B 7
Kawthaung 148-149 C 4
Kaya [HV] 164-165 D 6
Kaya [J] 144-145 K 5
Kaya [RI] 148-149 G 6
Kayadibi 136-137 F 3
Kayak Island 56-57 H 6
Kāyalpatnam 140 D 6
Kayambi 172 F 3
Kayamganj = Kaimganj 138-139 G 4
Kayan = Hkayan 141 E 7
Kayan, Sungai — 152-153 M 4
Kāyānakuḷam = Kāyankulam 140 C 6
Kāyankulam 140 C 6
Kayā Pyinnei 148-149 C 3
Kaya-san 144-145 G 5
Kaycee, WY 68-69 C 4
Kayenta, AZ 74-75 H 4
Kayes 164-165 B 6
Kayhaydi 164-165 B 5
Kayis dağı 154 I bc 3
Kaymas 136-137 D 2
Kaynak 136-137 H 4
Kaynar 136-137 G 3
Kaynaslı 136-137 D 2
Kayoa, Pulau — 148-149 J 6
Kaypak = Serdar 136-137 G 4
Kay Point 58-59 S 2
Kayser Gebergte 98-99 K 3
Kayseri 134-135 D 3
Kaysville, UT 66-67 GH 5
Kayuadi, Pulau — 152-153 O 9
Kayuagung 148-149 DE 7
Kayuapu 152-153 E 8
Kayville 61 F 6
Kazach 126-127 M 6
Kazachskaja Sovetskaja Socialističeskaja Respublika = Kazakh Soviet Socialist Republic 132-133 J-P 8
Kazachskij Melkosopočnik 132-133 M-P 7-8
Kazachstan = Aksaj 132-133 J 7
Kazačinskoje [SU, Jenisej] 132-133 R 6
Kazačinskoje [SU, Kirenga] 132-133 U 6
Kazačje 132-133 a 3
Kazakh Soviet Socialist Republic 132-133 J-P 8
Kazakhstan 114-115 T-V 6
Kazakhstan = Kazakh Soviet Socialist Republic 132-133 J-P 8
Kazakh Uplands = Kazachskij Melkosopočnik 132-133 M-P 7-8
Kazamoto = Katsumoto 144-145 G 6
Kazan' [SU, Kirovskaja Oblast'] 124-125 RS 4
Kazan' [SU, Tatarskaja ASSR] 132-133 HJ 6
Kazandağ 136-137 K 3
Kazandžik 134-135 GH 3
Kazan'-Judino 124-125 R 6
Kazanka [SU, Rossijskaja SFSR] 124-125 R 5-6
Kazanka [SU, Ukrainskaja SSR] 126-127 F 3
Kazanlak 122-123 L 4
Kazan Lake 61 D 3
Kazanovka 124-125 M 7
Kazan-rettō = Volcano Islands 206-207 RS 7
Kazan River 56-57 Q 5
Kazanskaja 126-127 K 2
Kazanskoje [SU, Zapadno-Sibirskaja nizmennost'] 132-133 M 6
Kazantip, mys — 126-127 G 4
Kazatin 126-127 D 2
Kazaure 168-169 GH 2
Kazbegi 126-127 M 5
Kazbek, gora — 126-127 M 5
Kazer, Pico — 108-109 F 10
Kāzerūn 134-135 G 5
Kažim 124-125 ST 3
Kazi-Magomed 126-127 O 6
Kāẓimīyah, Baghdâd-Al- 136-137 L 6
Kazimoto 171 D 5
Kazincbarcika 118 K 4
Kāziranga 141 C 2
Kazlų Rūda 124-125 DE 6
Kaztalovka 126-127 O 2
Kazū 141 E 3
Kazumba 172 D 3
Kazungula 172 E 5
Kazvin = Qazvīn 134-135 FG 3
Kazym 132-133 M 5
Kbab, el — = Al-Qabāb 166-167 D 3
Kbaisa = Kubaysah 136-137 K 6
Kbal Damrei 150-151 E 5
Kbīr Kūh 134-135 F 4
Kdey, Kompong — = Phum Kompong Kdey 150-151 E 6
Kea 122-123 L 7
Keaau, HI 78-79 e 3
Kealaikahiki Channel 78-79 d 2
Kealakekua Bay 78-79 de 3
Keams Canyon, AZ 74-75 H 5
Kê An = Kê Sach 150-151 EF 8
Kearney, NE 64-65 G 3
Kearny, NJ 82 III b 2
Keat Hong 154 III a 1
Keban 136-137 H 3
Keban barajı 136-137 H 3
Kebāng 134-135 PQ 5
Kebanyoran 152-153 G 9
Kebayoran Baru, Jakarta- 154 IV a 2
Kebbi = Sokoto 164-165 EF 6
Kébémer 164-165 A 5
Kebili = Qabilī 166-167 L 3
Kebkābiya = Kabkābīyah 164-165 J 6
Kebnekajse 116-117 H 4
Kebon Jeruk, Jakarta- 154 IV a 2
Kebumen 148-149 E 8
Kebyang 138-139 JK 2
Keçiborlu 136-137 D 4
Keçilik 154 I b 1
Kecskemét 118 J 5
Keda 126-127 K 6
Kedabek 126-127 M 6
Kedah 150-151 C 9-10
Kédainiai 124-125 DE 6
Kedārnāth 138-139 G 2
Keddie, CA 74-75 C 2-3
Kedia d'Idjil = Kidyat Ijjill 164-165 B 4
Kediri 148-149 F 8
Kédougou 164-165 B 6
Keegans Bayou 85 III a 2
Keele Peak 56-57 KL 5
Keeler, CA 74-75 E 4
Keele River 56-57 L 5
Keeley Lake 61 D 3
Keeling Basin 50-51 OP 6
Keelung = Chilung 142-143 N 6
Keene, NH 72-73 KL 3
Keeseville, NY 72-73 K 2
Keetmanshoop 172 C 7
Keewatin 62 B 3
Keewatin, District of — 56-57 RS 4-5
Keewatin River 61 H 2
Keezhik Lake 62 E 2
Kefa 164-165 M 7
Kefallēnia 122-123 J 6
Kéfalos 122-123 M 7
Kefamenanu 148-149 HJ 8
Kef-el-Ahmar = Kaff al-Aḥmar 166-167 G 3
Kefeliköy, İstanbul- 154 I b 2
Keferdiz 136-137 G 4
Keffi 168-169 G 3
Kefil, Al- = Al-Kifl 136-137 L 6
Kéfisiá 122-123 KL 6
Kéfisós 113 IV a 1
Keflavík 116-117 b 2-3
Kef Mahmel = Jabal Mahmil 166-167 K 2
Ke Ga, Mui — 150-151 FG 7
Kégalla 140 E 7
Kegaska 63 F 2
Kegel = Keila 124-125 E 4
Kégueur Terbi 164-165 H 4
Kegul'ta 126-127 M 3
Kehl 118 CD 4
Kei 171 B 2
Kei Islands = Kepulauan Kai 148-149 K 8
Keiki-dō = Kyŏnggi-do 144-145 F 4
Keila 124-125 E 4
Keilor, Melbourne- 161 II b 1
Keimoes 174-175 D 5
Kei Mouth 174-175 H 7
Kein-Bijgarten 128 II a 2
Keishō-hokudō = Kyŏngsang-pukto 144-145 G 4
Keishō-nandō = Kyŏngsang-namdo 144-145 FG 5
Keiskamahoek = Keiskammahoek 174-175 G 7
Keiskammahoek 174-175 G 7
Keiskammarivier 174-175 G 7
Keitele 116-117 LM 6
Keith [AUS] 158-159 GH 7
Keith [GB] 119 E 3
Keith Arm 56-57 M 4
Keithsburg, IL 70-71 E 5
Keithville, LA 76-77 GH 6
Keitsaub 174-175 C 2
Keitū = Keytū 136-137 N 5
Kejimkujik National Park 63 D 5
Kēkaṛī = Kekri 138-139 E 5
Kēkirāwa 140 E 6
Kekri 138-139 E 5
Kela 168-169 C 3
Kelaa des Mgouna = Qal'at M'gūnā' 166-167 C 4
Kelaa des Srarhna, el — = Al-Qal'at as-S'rāghnah 166-167 C 3-4
Kelafo 164-165 N 7
Kelai 140 A 7
Kelan 146-147 C 2
Kelantan 150-151 CD 10
Kelantan, Sungei — 150-151 CD 10
Kelay Abe 164-165 N 6
Kelay Egoji 164-165 N 6
Kelay Tana 164-165 M 6
Kelbia, Sebkhet — = Sabkhat Kalbīyah 166-167 M 2
Keles 136-137 C 3
Kelfield 61 D 5
Kelford, NC 80-81 H 2
Kelibia = Qalībīyah 166-167 M 1
Kelifely, Causse du — 172 HJ 5
Kelif'vun, gora — 132-133 g 4
Kelingkang, Bukit — 152-153 J 5
Kelkit = Çiftlik 136-137 H 2
Kelkit çayı 136-137 G 2
Kellé 172 B 1-2
Keller Lake 56-57 M 5
Kellett, Cape — 56-57 L 3
Kelleys Island 72-73 E 4
Kelleys Islands 72-73 E 4
Kelliher 61 G 5
Kelliher, MN 70-71 C 1-2
Kellogg, ID 66-67 EF 2
Kelloselkä 116-117 N 4
Kelly, Mount — 58-59 EF 2
Kelly River 58-59 F 2
Kelm = Kelmė 124-125 D 6
Kelmė 124-125 D 6
Kélo 164-165 H 7
Kelowna 56-57 N 7-8
Kelsey Bay 60 D 4
Kelso, CA 74-75 F 5
Kelso, WA 66-67 B 2
Kelso [ZA] 172 F 8
Kelton Pass 66-67 G 5
Kelu 146-147 C 11
Keluang 150-151 D 11-12
Kelulun He = Herlen He 142-143 M 2
Kelushi = Kelu 146-147 C 11
Kelvin, AZ 74-75 H 6
Kelvington 61 G 4
Kelvin Island 62 E 3
Kem' [SU, place] 132-133 E 4
Kemā 142-143 H 6
Kemabong 152-153 LM 3
Kê-Macina 164-165 C 6
Kemah 136-137 H 3
Kemaliye [TR, Erzincan] 136-137 H 3
Kemaliye [TR, Trabzon] 136-137 H 2
Kemalpaşa [TR, Artvin] 136-137 J 2
Kemalpaşa [TR, İzmir] 136-137 B 3
Kemanai = Towada 144-145 N 2
Kemang, Jakarta- 154 IV a 2
Kemayoran, Jakarta- 154 IV b 1
Kemayoran Airport 154 IV b 1
Kembalpūr 134-135 L 4
Kembani 152-153 P 6
Kembolcha 164-165 MN 6
Kemena, Sungei — 152-153 K 4
Kemer [TR, İstanbul] 154 I bc 2
Kemer [TR, Muğla] 136-137 C 4
Kemer = Eskiköy 136-137 D 4
Kemerovo 132-133 PQ 6
Kemi 116-117 L 5
Kemijärvi [SF, lake] 116-117 MN 4
Kemijärvi [SF, place] 116-117 M 4
Kemijoki 116-117 L 4-5
Kemijoki = Kem' 132-133 E 4
Kem Kem = Qamqam 166-167 D 4
Keml'a 124-125 P 6
Kemmerer, WY 66-67 H 5
Kemnay 61 H 6
Kémo-Gribingui 164-165 H 7
Kemp, TX 76-77 F 6
Kemp, Lake — 76-77 E 6
Kemp Land 53 C 6
Kemp Peninsula 53 B 31
Kempsey 158-159 K 6
Kempt, Lac — 72-73 JK 1
Kempten 118 E 5
Kempton Park 170 V c 1
Kemptthal 128 IV b 1
Kemptville 72-73 HJ 2
Kemubu 150-151 D 10
Ken 138-139 H 5
Kena 124-125 M 2
Kena = Qinā 164-165 L 3
Kenadsa = Qanādsah 166-167 E 4
Kenai, AK 56-57 F 5
Kenai Lake 58-59 N 6
Kenai Mountains 56-57 F 6-G 5
Kenai Peninsula 56-57 FG 5
Kenamo 56-57 L 7
Kenansville, FL 80-81 c 3
Kenaston 61 EF 5
Kenbridge, VA 80-81 GH 2
Kendal [GB] 119 E 4
Kendal [RI] 152-153 J 9
Kendal [ZA] 174-175 H 4
Kendall, KS 68-69 F 7
Kendallville, IN 70-71 H 5
Kendari 148-149 H 7
Kendawangan 148-149 F 7
Kendeng, Pegunungan — 152-153 JK 9
Kendikolu 176 a 1
Kendong Si = Mendong Gonpa 138-139 K 2
Kēndrāpaḍā = Kendrāpāra 134-135 O 6
Kendrāpāra 134-135 O 6
Kendrew 174-175 F 7
Kendrick, ID 66-67 E 2
Kendu 171 C 3
Kēndujhar = Keonjhargar 138-139 KL 7
Kenedy, TX 76-77 EF 8
Kenega = Kenegha 174-175 H 6
Kenegha 174-175 H 6
Kenema 164-165 B 7
Kenesaw, NE 68-69 G 5
Kenge 172 C 2
Keng Kabao 150-151 E 4
Keng Kok 150-151 E 4
Keng Phao = Ban Keng Phao 150-151 F 5
Keng That Hai = Ban Keng That Hai 150-151 EF 4
Kengtung = Kyöngdôn 148-149 CD 2
Kenhardt 172 D 7
Kenia 172 G 1
Kenibuna Lake 58-59 L 6
Kéniéba 164-165 B 6
Kenitra = Al-Q'nitrah 164-165 C 2
Kenli 146-147 G 3
Kenmare, ND 68-69 EF 1
Kenmare [IRL, place] 119 B 6
Kenmare [IRL, river] 119 A 6
Kenmore, NY 72-73 G 3
Kenna, NM 76-77 BC 6
Kennebec, SC 68-69 FG 4
Kennebec River 72-73 LM 2
Kennebunk, ME 72-73 L 3
Kennedy 61 GH 5
Kennedy, Mount — 56-57 J 5
Kennedy Channel 56-57 WX 1-2
Kennedy Taungdeik 141 CD 4
Kennedy Town, Victoria- 155 I a 2
Kenner, LA 78-79 D 5-6
Kennett, MO 78-79 DE 2
Kennewick, WA 66-67 D 2
Kenney Dam 56-57 M 7
Kennicott, AK 58-59 Q 6
Kénogami 63 A 3
Kenogami River 62 G 2
Kenogamissi Falls 62 L 2-3
Keno Hill 56-57 JK 5
Kenonisca, Lac — 62 NO 1
Kenora 56-57 S 8
Kenosha, WI 64-65 J 3
Kenova, WV 72-73 E 5
Kenozero 124-125 M 2
Kensal, ND 68-69 G 2
Kensett, AR 78-79 D 3
Kensington 63 E 4
Kensington, CA 83 I c 1
Kensington, New York-, NY 82 III c 3
Kensington, Philadelphia-, PA 84 III c 2
Kensington and Chelsea, London- 129 II b 2
Kent 119 G 6
Kent, MN 68-69 H 2
Kent, OH 72-73 F 4
Kent, OR 66-67 C 3
Kent, TX 76-77 B 7
Kent, WA 66-67 B 2
Kent, Washington-, DC 82 II a 1
Kenta Canal 85 I b 3
Kentau 132-133 M 9
Kent Group 160 cd 1
Kent Junction 63 D 4
Kentland, IN 70-71 G 5
Kenton, OH 72-73 E 4
Kenton, OK 76-77 C 4
Kent Park 170 V b 1
Kent Peninsula 56-57 P 4
Kentucky 64-65 JK 4
Kentucky Lake 64-65 J 4
Kentucky River 70-71 H 6
Kent Village, MD 82 II b 1
Kentville 63 D 5
Kentwood, LA 78-79 D 5
Kenya 172 GH 1
Kenya, Mount — 172 G 1-2
Keokuk, IA 64-65 H 3
Keo Neua, Đeo — 150-151 E 3
Keonjhargar 138-139 KL 7
Keosauqua, IA 70-71 E 5
Kep 150-151 E 7
Kêpe = Quepem 140 B 3
Kepi i Gjuhës 122-123 H 5
Kępno 118 J 3
Keppel Bay 158-159 K 4
Keppel Harbour 154 III ab 2
Keppel Island 108-109 JK 8
Kepsut 136-137 C 3
Kepulauan Aju 148-149 K 6
Kepulauan Alor 152-153 Q 10
Kepulauan Anambas 148-149 E 6
Kepulauan Aru 148-149 K 8
Kepulauan Asia 148-149 K 6
Kepulauan Babar 148-149 JK 8
Kepulauan Balangan = Pulau-pulau Balabalangan 148-149 G 7
Kepulauan Banda 148-149 J 7
Kepulauan Banggai 148-149 H 7
Kepulauan Batu 148-149 C 7
Kepulauan Bunguran Selatan 148-149 E 6
Kepulauan Bunguran Utara 148-149 E 6
Kepulauan Kai 148-149 K 8
Kepulauan Leti 148-149 J 8
Kepulauan Lingga 148-149 DE 7
Kepulauan Mapia 148-149 KL 6
Kepulauan Mentawai 148-149 CD 7
Kepulauan Perhentian 150-151 D 10
Kepulauan Riau 148-149 DE 6
Kepulauan Sabalana 152-153 N 9
Kepulauan Salabangka 152-153 P 7
Kepulauan Sangihe 148-149 J 6
Kepulauan Sangkarang 152-153 N 8
Kepulauan Sembilan 150-151 C 10
Kepulauan Seram-laut 148-149 K 7
Kepulauan Solor 152-153 P 10
Kepulauan Sula 148-149 HJ 7
Kepulauan Talaud 148-149 J 6
Kepulauan Tanimbar 148-149 K 8
Kepulauan Tenga 148-149 G 8
Kepulauan Togian 148-149 H 7
Kepulauan Tukangbesi 148-149 H 8
Kerākat = Kirākat 138-139 J 5
Kerakda = Karādkah 166-167 G 3
Kerala 134-135 M 8-9
Kerang 158-159 H 7
Kerasūs = Giresun 134-135 D 2
Keratsínion 113 IV a 2
Kerava 116-117 L 7
Kerbi = Poliny-Osipenko 132-133 a 7
Kerby, OR 66-67 B 4
Kerč' 126-127 H 4
Kerčenskij poluostrov 126-127 GH 4
Kerčenskij proliv 126-127 H 4
Kerčevskij 124-125 UV 4
Kerch = Kerč' 126-127 H 4
Kerč'omja 124-125 T 3
Kereda = Karera 138-139 E 5
Kerema 148-149 N 8
Kerempe burnu 136-137 E 1
Keren 164-165 M 5
Kerens, TX 76-77 F 6
Kerewan 168-169 A 2
Kerga 124-125 PQ 2
Kerguelen 50-51 N 8
Kerguelen-Gaussberg Ridge 50-51 N 8-O 9
Kericho 171 C 3
Kerinci, Gunung — 148-149 D 7
Kerio 171 D 2
Keriske 132-133 Z 4
Keriya 142-143 E 4
Keriya Darya 142-143 E 4
Kerkbuurt 128 I b 1
Kerkenah Island = Juzur Qarqannah 164-165 G 2
Kerkenna, Îles — = Jazur Qarqannah 164-165 G 2
Kerkhoven, MN 70-71 C 3
Kerki 134-135 K 3
Kérkyra [GR, island] 122-123 H 6
Kérkyra [GR, place] 122-123 H 6
Kerling 116-117 de 2
Kerlingarfjöll 116-117 d 2
Kerma = Karmah 164-165 L 5
Kerma, Oued — 170 I a 2
Kermadec Islands 158-159 PQ 6
Kermadec Tonga Trench 156-157 J 5-6
Kermān 134-135 H 4
Kerman, CA 74-75 CD 4
Kermānshāh 134-135 F 4
Kermānshāhān = 1 ◁ 134-135 F 4
Kerme körfezi 136-137 B 4
Kermit, TX 76-77 C 7
Kernaka 168-169 G 2
Kern River 74-75 D 5
Kernville, CA 74-75 D 5
Kérouané 164-165 C 7
Kerpe burnu 136-137 D 2
Kerrick, TX 76-77 C 4
Kerrobert 61 D 4-5
Kerrville, TX 76-77 E 7
Kersaint, Đao — 150-151 FG 2
Kershaw, SC 80-81 F 3
Kersley 60 F 3
Kertamulia 152-153 H 6
Kerulen = Cherlen gol 142-143 L 2
Kerūr 140 B 3
Kerzaz = Karzāz 166-167 F 5
Kerženec 124-125 P 5
Kesabpūr 138-139 M 6
Kê Sach 150-151 EF 8
Kesagami Lake 62 L 1
Kesagami River 62 LM 1
Keşan 136-137 B 2
Kesâne = Keşan 136-137 B 2
Keşap 136-137 H 2
Kesariya 138-139 K 4
Ke Sāt 150-151 F 2
Kesennuma 144-145 NO 3
Keshan 142-143 O 2
Keshod 138-139 BC 7
Keshorai Pātan 138-139 EF 5
Keshvar, Īstgāh-e — 136-137 N 6
Kesinga 138-139 J 7
Kesiyārī = Kasiāri 138-139 L 6
Keskin 136-137 E 3
Keski-Suomen lääni 116-117 L 6
Kes'ma 124-125 L 4
Kesrā = Kisrā 166-167 L 2
Kestell 174-175 H 5
Kesten'ga 132-133 E 4
Kestenga 116-117 OP 5
Kestep 136-137 C 4
Keston, London- 129 II c 2
Keszthely 118 H 5
Ket' 132-133 P 6
Keta 164-165 E 7
Keta, ozero — 132-133 QR 4
Ketam, Pulau — 154 III b 1
Ketama = Kitāmah 166-167 D 2
Ketapang [RI, Java] 152-153 K 9
Ketapang [RI, Kalimantan] 148-149 EF 7
Ketaun 152-153 D 7
Ketchikan, AK 56-57 K 6
Ketchum, ID 66-67 F 4
Kete Krachi 164-165 DE 7
Keṭī Bandar 138-139 A 5
Ketik River 58-59 H 2
Ketil, Kuala — 150-151 C 10
Ketok Mount 58-59 J 7
Ketou 168-169 F 4
Kętrzyn 118 K 1-2
Kettering, OH 72-73 DE 5
Kettharin Kyûn 148-149 C 4
Kettle Falls, WA 66-67 DE 1
Kettle Point 72-73 EF 3
Kettle River [CDN] 66-67 D 1
Kettle River [USA] 70-71 D 2
Kettle River Range 66-67 D 1
Ketumbaine 171 D 3
Ketungau, Sungai — 152-153 J 5
Kevin, MT 66-67 H 1
Kevir = Kavīr-e Namak-e Mīghān 134-135 GH 4
Kew 88-89 KL 4
Kew, Johannesburg- 170 V b 1
Kew, Melbourne- 161 II c 1
Kewanee, IL 70-71 F 5
Kewaunee, WI 70-71 G 3
Keweenaw Bay 70-71 FG 2
Keweenaw Peninsula 64-65 J 2
Keweenaw Point 70-71 G 2
Keweigek 98-99 H 2
Kewir = Kavīr-e Namak-e Mīghān 134-135 GH 4
Kexholm = Prioz'orsk 132-133 DE 5
Keyaluvik, AK 58-59 E 6
Keya Paha River 68-69 FG 4
Keyes, OK 76-77 C 4
Key Harbour 72-73 F 2
Keyhole Reservoir 68-69 D 3
Key Junction 72-73 F 2
Key Largo 80-81 cd 4
Key Largo, FL 80-81 c 4
Keyser, WV 72-73 G 5
Keystone, SD 68-69 E 4
Keysville, VA 80-81 G 2
Keytū 136-137 N 5
Key West, FL 64-65 K 7
Kez 124-125 T 5
Kezar Stadium 83 I b 2
Kežma 132-133 T 6
Kežmarok 118 K 4
Kgokgole 174-175 E 4
Kgokgolelaagte = Kgokgole 174-175 E 4
Kgun Lake 58-59 EF 6
Khaanzuur, Raas — 164-165 ab 1
Khabarovsk = Chabarovsk 132-133 a 8
Khābī, Ḥāssī al- 166-167 D 5
Khabīr, Zāb al- = Zāb al-Kabīr 136-137 K 4
Khabra Najid = Habrat Najid 136-137 K 7
Khābūr, Nahr al- 134-135 E 3
Khābūrah, Al- 134-135 H 6
Khachraud = Khāchrod 138-139 E 6
Khāchrod 138-139 E 6
Khadiāla = Khariār 138-139 J 7
Khādir Dvīp = Khadīr Island 138-139 C 6
Khadīr Island 138-139 C 6
Khadra, Daïet el — = Ḍayat al-Khaḍrah 166-167 BC 6
Khadrah, Ḍayat al- 166-167 BC 6
Kha Dsong 138-139 M 4
Khaer = Khair 138-139 F 4
Khāgā 138-139 H 5
Khagaria 138-139 L 5
Khahrat Burqah 136-137 GH 6
Khaibar = Shurayf 134-135 D 5
Khaibar, Kotal — 134-135 L 4
Khalīj as-Sintirā', Al- 164-165 A 4
Khailung La 138-139 KL 2
Khair 138-139 F 4
Khairābād 134-135 N 5
Khairāgarh [IND, Madhya Pradesh] 138-139 H 7
Khairāgarh [IND, Uttar Pradesh] 138-139 FG 4
Khairpūr [PAK, Punjab] 134-135 K 5
Khairpūr [PAK, Sindh] 138-139 D 3
Khaitri = Khetri 138-139 E 3
Khajuha 138-139 H 4
Khakass Autonomous Region = 10 ◁ 132-133 R 7
Khalafābād 136-137 N 7
Khalaf al-Allāh 166-167 G 2
Khālāpur 140 A 1
Khālda, Bīr — = Bi'r Hālidah 136-137 B 7
Khalfallah = Khalaf al-Allāh 166-167 G 2
Khalīdj Toûnis = Khalīj at-Tūnisī 166-167 M 1
Khalifah, Al-Qāhirah-al- 170 II b 1
Khalig Bômba = Khalīj al-Bunbah 164-165 J 2
Khalīg es Suweis = Khalīj as-Suways 164-165 L 3
Khalīg Sidra = Khalīj as-Surt 164-165 H 2
Khalīj Abū Hashū'ifah 136-137 BC 7
Khalīj Abū Qīr 173 B 2
Khalīj al-'Aqabah 134-135 C 5
Khalīj al-'Arab 136-137 C 7
Khalīj al-Bunbah 164-165 J 2
Khalīj al-Ḥammāmāt 164-165 G 1
Khalīj al-Maṣīrah 134-135 H 6-7
Khalīj al-Qābis 164-165 G 2
Khalīj as-Surt 164-165 H 2
Khalīj as-Suways 164-165 L 3
Khalīj aṭ-Ṭīnah 173 C 2
Khalīj at-Tūnisī 166-167 M 1

Khalīj Bijāyah 166-167 J 1
Khalīj Bū Ghrārah 166-167 M 3
Khalīj Bū Th'rārah 166-167 M 3
Khalīj Sonmiyānī 134-135 J 6-K 5
Khalīj Umm al-Kataf 173 D 6
Khalīj Wahrān 166-167 F 2
Khalīl, El- = Al-Halīl 136-137 F 7
Khalīlābād 138-139 J 4
Khaliq tau 142-143 E 3
Khāliṣ, Al- 136-137 L 6
Khalkhāl 136-137 N 4
Khalki = Chálkē 122-123 M 7
Khalūf, Al- 134-135 H 6
Kham 142-143 H 5
Khāmam = Khammam 140 E 2
Khamāsīn, Al- 134-135 EF 6
Khambat = Cambay 134-135 L 6
Khambhalia = Khambhāliya 138-139 B 6
Khambhāliya 138-139 B 6
Khambhāt = Cambay 134-135 L 6
Khambhāt nī Khāḍī = Gulf of Cambay 134-135 L 6
Khāmgāňv = Khāmgaon 138-139 F 7
Khāmgaon 138-139 F 7
Khamir 134-135 E 7
Khamīs, Al- 166-167 C 3
Khāmis, Ash-Shallāl al- 164-165 L 5
Khamīs-Milyānah 166-167 H 1
Khamīssāt 166-167 CD 3
Kham Khuan Kaeo 150-151 E 5
Khamlā Chhu = Subansiri 141 D 2
Khammam 140 E 2
Khammouane 150-151 E 3-4
Khamnop 150-151 D 7
Khampa Dsong 142-143 F 6
Khamphô = Ban Khamphô 150-151 F 5
Khamsa, Bīr el- = Bi'r al-Khamsah 164-165 K 2
Khamsha, Bi'r al- 164-165 K 2
Khan 174-175 A 2
Khan, Nam — 150-151 D 2-3
Khān al-Baghdādī 136-137 K 6
Khānāpur [IND, Karnataka] 140 B 3
Khānāpur [IND, Madhya Pradesh] 140 B 2
Khānāpura = Khānāpur 140 B 3
Khānaqīn = Khāniqīn 136-137 L 5
Khān az-Zabīb 136-137 G 7
Khand = Khanda 138-139 J 7
Khanda 138-139 J 7
Khandāla [IND ↓ Pune] 140 AB 1
Khandāla [IND ↖ Pune] 140 A 1
Khandaq, Al- 164-165 KL 5
Khandaq, El- = Al-Khandaq 164-165 KL 5
Khaṅḍavā = Khandwa 134-135 M 6
Khānderi Island 140 A 1
Khāndêsh 138-139 E 7
Khāndhar 138-139 F 4
Khandhkot = Qandkoṭ 138-139 B 3
Khands = Khanda 138-139 J 7
Khandwa 134-135 M 6
Khānewāl 138-139 CD 2
Khan ez Zābib = Khān az-Zabīb 136-137 G 7
Khangai = Changajn nuruu 142-143 HJ 2
Khāngaṛh 138-139 C 3
Khanga-Sidi-Nadji = Khanqat Sīdī Nājī 166-167 K 2
Khang Khay 150-151 D 3
Khangmar [TJ ↓ Gyangtse] 138-139 M 3
Khangmar [TJ ↘ Mendong Gonpa] 138-139 K 2
Khanh Hoa = Diên Khanh 150-151 G 6
Khanh Hu'ng 150-151 E 8
Khania = Chaniá 122-123 KL 8
Khanīfrah 166-167 D 3
Khanion Bay = Kólpos Chaniõn 122-123 KL 8
Khāniqīn 134-135 F 4
Khānpur [IND, Calcutta] 154 II a 2
Khānpur [IND, Rajasthān] 138-139 F 5
Khānpūr [PAK, Punjab] 138-139 AB 3
Khānpūr [PAK, Sindh] 134-135 KL 5
Khanqat Sīdī Nājī 166-167 K 2
Khanshalah 164-165 F 1
Khantan = Kuantan 148-149 D 6
Khanty-Mansi Autonomous Area 132-133 L-P 5
Khanty-Mansiysk = Chanty-Mansijsk 132-133 M 5
Khanu Woralaksaburi 150-151 B 4
Khān Yūnūs 173 CD 2
Khanzi 172 D 6
Khanzi = Ghanzi 172 D 6
Khānzūr, Ras — = Raas Khaanzuur 164-165 ab 1
Khao Chamao 150-151 C 6
Khao Khieo 150-151 C 6
Khao Laem 150-151 C 5
Khao Langkha Tuk 150-151 B 8
Khao Luang [T ← Nakhon Si Thammarat] 148-149 CD 5
Khao Luang [T ← Thap Sakae] 150-151 B 7
Khao Mokochu 150-151 B 5
Khao Pa Cho = Doi Lang Ka 150-151 B 3
Khao Pha Napo 150-151 BC 4
Khao Phanom Bencha 150-151 B 8
Khao Soi Dao 150-151 B 9
Khao Soi Dao Tai 150-151 CD 6
Khao Song Khwae = Khaungzaunggwei 150-151 B 5
Khao Toei Yai 150-151 B 7
Khao Yai 150-151 B 5
Khao Yoi 150-151 B 6
Kha Panang = Ban Kha Panang 150-151 F 6
Khar 138-139 G 1-2
Kharāb, Al- 134-135 EF 7
Khārāghoḍa 138-139 CD 6
Kharagpur [IND, Bihār] 138-139 L 5
Kharagpur [IND, West Bengal] 134-135 O 6
Kharan Kalat = Khārān Qalāt 134-135 K 5
Khārān Qalāt 134-135 K 5
Kharar 138-139 F 2
Kharār = Lādnun 138-139 E 4
Kharaz, Jabal — 134-135 E 8
Kharbin = Harbin 142-143 O 2
Khardah 154 II b 1
Khardam = Khar 138-139 H 2
Khārepātan 140 A 2
Khārga, El- = Al-Khārijah 164-165 L 3
Khārga, Wāḥāt el- = Al-Wāḥāt al-Khārijah 164-165 KL 3-4
Khargaon = Khargon 138-139 E 7
Khargon 138-139 E 7
Khaṛgpur = Kharagpur 138-139 L 5
Khāri 138-139 E 5
Khariār 138-139 J 7
Kharībārī 138-139 M 4
Kharīfūt 134-135 G 7
Khārijah, Al- 164-165 L 3
Khārijah, Al-Wāḥāt al- 164-165 KL 3-4
Kharīṭ, Wādī al- 173 CD 5
Kharīṭ, Wādī el- = Wādī al-Kharīṭ 173 CD 5
Kharj, Al- 134-135 F 6
Khārk, Jazīreh-ye — 134-135 FG 5
Kharkheh, Rūd-e — 136-137 M 6
Kharkov = Char'kov 126-127 H 1-2
Kharora 138-139 HJ 7
Khar Rūd 136-137 N 5
Kharsāwān 138-139 K 6
Kharsūaṅ = Kharsāwān 138-139 K 6
Khartoum = Al-Kharṭum 164-165 L 5
Khartoum North = Al-Kharṭūm Baḥrī 164-165 L 5
Khartshang 138-139 M 2
Kharṭūm, Al- 164-165 L 5
Kharṭūm Baḥri, Al- 164-165 L 5
Kharṭūm Baḥri, El- = Al-Kharṭūm Baḥrī 164-165 L 5
Khaṣab, Al- 134-135 H 5
Khashm al-Makhrūq 136-137 J 7
Khashm al-Qirbah 164-165 LM 6
Khāsh Rōd 134-135 J 4
Khāsi-Jaintia Hills 141 BC 3
Khaṭāṭba, El- = Al-Haṭāṭibah 173 B 2
Khātēgāňv = Khātegaon 138-139 F 6
Khātegaon 138-139 F 6
Khaṭṭ, Wād al- 164-165 B 3
Khāvarī, Āẕarbāyejān-e- 134-135 EF 3
Khāvda 138-139 B 6
Khawr 'Abd Allāh 136-137 N 8
Khawr Abū Ḥajār 136-137 L 7
Khawr al-Amaīyah 136-137 N 8
Khawr al-Fakkān 134-135 H 5
Khawr az-Zubayr 136-137 MN 7
Khawr Rūrī 134-135 G 7
Khawr Unib 173 D 7
Khay' 134-135 E 7
Khaybar, Ḥarrat — 134-135 DE 5
Khazhung Tsho 142-143 F 5
Khāzir, Nahr al- 136-137 K 4
Khazir Su = Nahr al-Khāzir 136-137 K 4
Khazzan an-Naṣr 164-165 L 4
Khebi, Hassi el — = Ḥāssī al-Khābī 166-167 D 5
Khê Bô 150-151 E 3
Khechmā = Al-Bogham 136-137 J 5
Khed [IND ↑ Pune] 140 AB 1
Khed [IND ↙ Pune] 140 A 2
Khēḍā = Kaira 138-139 D 6
Khed Brahma 138-139 D 5
Khedir, Al — = Khiḍr Dardash 136-137 L 7
Khekra 138-139 F 3
Khemarat 148-149 DE 3
Khem Belder = Kyzyl 132-133 R 7
Khemīs, el — = Al-Khamīs 166-167 C 3
Khemīs, el — = Hamīs az-Zāmāmrah 166-167 B 3
Khemīs, el — = Sūq al-Khamīs as-Sāḥil 166-167 C 2
Khemīs, el — = Sūq al-Khamīs Banī 'Arūs 166-167 D 2
Khemis-Milana = Khamīs Milyānah 166-167 H 1
Khemīssēt, el — = Khamīssāt 166-167 CD 3
Khemīs Zemāmra, el — = Hamīs az-Zāmāmrah 166-167 B 3
Khenachich, El — 164-165 D 4
Khenachich, Oglat — 164-165 D 4
Khenchela = Khanshalah 164-165 F 1
Khenīfra = Khanīfrah 166-167 D 3
Khentei Nuruu = Chentin nuruu 142-143 K 2
Khera = Kaira 138-139 D 6
Khērāgaṛh = Khairāgarh 138-139 FG 4
Kherālu 138-139 D 6
Kheri 138-139 H 4
Kherson = Cherson 126-127 F 3
Khētaṛī = Khetri 138-139 E 3
Khetri 138-139 E 3
Khewāṛī 138-139 B 4
Khiching 138-139 K 7
Khiḍr Dardash 136-137 L 7
Khiehshow = Jieshou 146-147 E 5
Khieo, Khao — 150-151 C 6
Khilchipur 138-139 F 5
Khios = Chíos 122-123 L 6
Khipro 138-139 B 5
Khīrābād = Khairābād 134-135 N 5
Khirbat Kilwa 136-137 G 8
Khiri Ratthanikhom 150-151 B 8
Khirr, Wādī al- 134-135 E 4
Khlong Luang 150-151 C 5
Khlong Thom 150-151 B 9
Khlung 150-151 D 6
Khmel'nyc'kij = Chmel'nickij 126-127 C 2
Khoai, Hon — 150-151 E 8
Khobdo = Chovd 142-143 G 2
Khobso Gol = Chövsgöl nuur 142-143 J 1
Khökh Nuur = Chöch nuur 142-143 H 4
Kho Khot Kra 148-149 CD 4
Khok Kloi 150-151 AB 8
Khok Kong = Ban Khôk Kong 150-151 E 5
Kho Kong 150-151 D 7
Khok Samrong 150-151 C 5
Khomām 136-137 NO 4
Khomas Highland = Khomasplato 172 C 6
Khomasplato 172 C 6
Khomeyn 136-137 NO 6
Khomodimo 174-175 EF 2
Khon Buri 150-151 D 5
Khondāb 136-137 N 5
Khong [LAO] 150-151 EF 5
Khong [T] 150-151 D 5
Khong Chiam 150-151 E 5
Khong Sedone 148-149 E 3
Khon Kaen 148-149 D 3
Khon Sawan 150-151 CD 5
Khorāsān 134-135 H 3-4
Khorāsān, Kāvīr-e — = Kavīr-e Namak-e Mīghān 134-135 H 4
Khorat = Nakhon Ratchasima 148-149 D 3-4
Khorb el Ethel = Khurb al-Athil 166-167 CD 5
Khore 174-175 E 2
Khorel 154 II a 1
Khoribari = Kharībārī 138-139 M 4
Khōrmāl = Hūrmāl 136-137 LM 5
Khōr Onib = Khawr Unib 173 D 7
Khorramābād [IR, Lorestān] 134-135 FG 4
Khorramābād [IR, Māzandarān] 136-137 O 4
Khorramshahr 134-135 F 4
Khorsabad 136-137 K 4
Khosrovī 136-137 L 5
Khosrowābād [IR, Hamadān] 136-137 N 5
Khosrowābād [IR, Kordestan] 136-137 M 5
Khotan 142-143 DE 4
Khotan darya 142-143 E 3-4
Khoti 174-175 E 3
Khotol Mount 58-59 J 4
Khoumīr = Khumīr 166-167 L 1
Khouribga = Khurībgah 166-167 C 2
Khowai 141 B 3
Khraicia 170 I a 2
Khram Yai, Ko — 150-151 C 5
Khroub, El — = Al-Khurub 166-167 K 1
Khroumirie = Khumīr 166-167 L 1
Khrū 141 C 2
Khuan Khanun 150-151 BC 9
Khubai Gangri 138-139 J 3
Khudian = Khudiyān 138-139 E 2
Khudiyān 138-139 E 2
Khuff 134-135 E 6
Khuis 174-175 D 4
Khukhan 150-151 E 5
Khükhe Noor = Chöch nuur 142-143 H 4
Khuldābād 138-139 E 7-8
Khulnā 138-139 M 6
Khumīr 166-167 L 1
Khums, Al- 164-165 GH 2
Khungsharyar 138-139 K 2
Khunti 138-139 K 6
Khun Yuam 150-151 AB 3
Khurai 138-139 G 5
Khurasan = Khorāsān 134-135 H 3-4
Khurayṣ 134-135 F 5
Khurb al-Athil 166-167 CD 5
Khūr-e Mūsā 136-137 N 7-8
Khuria Tank 138-139 H 6
Khurībgah 166-167 C 2
Khūrīyā Mūrīyā, Jazā'ir — 134-135 H 7
Khurja 138-139 F 3
Khurmah, Al- 134-135 E 6
Khūrmāl 136-137 LM 5
Khurr, Wādī al- = Wādī al-Khirr 136-137 K 7
Khurub, Al- 166-167 K 1
Khushāb 134-135 L 4
Khuẓdār 134-135 K 5
Khūzestān 134-135 F 4
Khuzistan = Khuzestan 134-135 F 4
Khvāf 134-135 J 4
Khvostof Island 58-59 s 6
Khvoy 134-135 EF 3
Khwae Noi, Mae Nam — 150-151 B 5-6
Khwāf = Khvāf 134-135 J 4
Khyatthin 141 D 4
Khyber Pass = Kotal Khāibar 134-135 L 4
Khyetentshering 142-143 G 5
Kiabakari 171 C 3
Kiama 160 K 5
Kiambi 172 E 3
Kiamichi Mountains 76-77 G 5
Kiamichi River 76-77 G 5-6
Kiamusze = Jiamusi 142-143 P 2
Kian = Ji'an 142-143 LM 6
Kiana, AK 58-59 G 3
Kiangling = Jiangling 146-147 CD 6
Kiangning = Nanjing 142-143 M 5
Kiangshan = Jiangshan 146-147 G 7
Kiangsi = Jiangxi 142-143 LM 6
Kiangsu = Jiangsu 142-143 MN 5
Kiangtu = Jiangdu 146-147 G 5
Kiangyin = Jiangyin 146-147 H 6
Kiantajärvi 116-117 N 5
Kiaohsien = Jiao Xian 142-143 M 4
Kiating = Jiading 146-147 H 6
Kiawah Island 80-81 FG 4
Kiayu = Jiayu 146-147 D 6-7
Kiayukwan = Jiuquan 142-143 H 4
Kibaha = Bagamoyo 172 G 3
Kibale 171 B 2
Kibali 172 EF 1
Kibamba 172 E 2
Kibangou 172 B 2
Kibarty = Kybartai 124-125 D 6
Kibau 172 FG 3
Kibaya 172 G 3
Kiberashi 171 D 4
Kiberege 172 G 3
Kibiti 171 D 4
Kiboko 171 D 3
Kibombo 172 E 2
Kibondo 172 F 2
Kıbrıscık = Karadoğan 136-137 DE 2
Kibungu 172 F 2
Kibuye 171 AB 5
Kibwezi 172 G 2
Kičevo 122-123 J 5
Kichčik 132-133 de 7
Kichha 138-139 G 3
Kichijōji, Musashino- 155 III a 1
Kichinev = Kišin'ov 126-127 D 3
Kicking Horse Pass 56-57 NO 7
Kičmengskij Gorodok 124-125 P 3
Kidal 164-165 E 5
Kidaroupérou 168-169 F 3
Kidatu 172 G 3
Kidderpore, Calcutta- 154 II ab 2
Kidd's Beach 174-175 GH 7
Kidepo National Park 172 F 1
Kidete 171 D 4
Kidira 164-165 B 6
Kidjaboun 168-169 EF 3
Kidnappers, Cape — 161 GH 4
Kido 155 III d 1
Kidston 158-159 H 3
Kidul, Pegunungan — 152-153 J 9-K 10
Kidyat Ijjill 164-165 B 4
Kiekeberg 130 I a 2
Kiekebusch 130 III c 2
Kiel 118 E 1
Kiel, WI 70-71 F 4
Kiel Canal = Nord-Ostsee-Kanal 118 D 1-2
Kielce 118 K 3
Kieler Bucht 118 E 1
Kiên An 150-151 F 2
Kienan = Qian'an 146-147 G 1
Kiên Binh 150-151 E 8
Kiên Hung = Go Quao 148-149 DE 5
Kienkiang = Qianjiang 146-147 B 7
Kienli = Jianli 146-147 D 7
Kienning = Jian'ou 142-143 M 6
Kienshih = Jianshi 146-147 B 6
Kienshui = Jianshui 142-143 J 7
Kienteh = Jiande 146-147 G 7
Kienwerder 130 III a 2
Kierling 113 I b 1
Kierunavaara 116-117 J 4
Kiestinki = Kesten'ga 132-133 E 4
Kieta 148-149 j 6
Kiewietskuil 174-175 E 7
Kīfah 164-165 B 5
Kifaya 168-169 B 2
Kiffa = Kīfah 164-165 B 5
Kifl, Al- 136-137 L 6
Kifrī 136-137 L 5
Kigali 172 F 2
Kigalik River 58-59 K 2
Kiganga 171 C 4
Kiğı = Kasaba 136-137 J 3
Kigluaik Mountains 58-59 DE 4
Kigoma 172 E 2
Kigosi 171 B 3
Kıgzı 136-137 K 3
Kiha = Kwiha 164-165 MN 6
Kihambatang 152-153 K 6
Kihelkonna 124-125 D 4
Kihindi 171 D 5
Kihnu 124-125 D 4
Kiholo, HI 78-79 e 3
Kihowera 171 D 5
Kihsien = Qi Xian [TJ, Henan] 146-147 E 4
Kihsien = Qi Xian [TJ, Shanxi] 146-147 D 3
Kihti = Skiftet 116-117 J 7
Kihurio 171 D 4
Kii hantō 142-143 Q 5
Kiik-Atlama, mys — 126-127 GH 4
Kii sammyaku 144-145 KL 5-6
Kii-suidō 142-143 PQ 5
Kijang 144-145 G 5
Kijev 126-127 DE 1
Kijevka [SU, Kazachskaja SSSR] 132-133 N 7
Kijevka [SU, Rossijskaja SFSR] 144-145 J 1
Kijevskoje vodochranilišče 126-127 E 1
Kijik, AK 58-59 K 6
Kikerino 124-125 G 4
Kikiakrorak River 58-59 L 2
Kikinda 122-123 J 3
Kiknur 124-125 Q 5
Kikombo 171 CD 4
Kikonai 144-145 B 3
Kikori 148-149 M 8
Kikuna, Yokohama- 155 III a 2
Kikus 124-125 V 3
Kikwit 172 C 3
Kil 116-117 E 8
Kilāb, Jazā'ir al- 166-167 M 1
Kilaban 136-137 K 4
Kilakkarai 140 D 6
Kilambé, Cerro — 88-89 CD 8
Kilātes, Berzekh el — = Rā's Qilātis 166-167 E 2
Kilauea Crater 148-149 ef 4
Kil'azi 126-127 O 6
Kilbuck Mountains 56-57 E 5-D 6
Kilchu 144-145 G 2
Kilcoy 158-159 K 5
Kildinstroj 116-117 PQ 3
Kildonan 172 F 5
Kilemary 124-125 Q 5
Kilembe 171 B 2
Kilemon 174-175 D 2
Kilgore, ID 66-67 GH 3
Kilgore, TX 76-77 G 6
Kili 208 G 2
Kilifi 172 GH 2
Kiligwa River 58-59 H 2
Kilija 126-127 D 4
Kilimanjaro [EAT, administrative unit] 172 G 2
Kilimanjaro [EAT, mountain] 172 G 2
Kilimatinde 172 FG 3
Kilin = Jilin 142-143 N 2-O 3
Kilingi-Nõmme 124-125 E 4
Kilinochchi 140 E 6
Kilis 136-137 G 4
Kiliuda Bay 58-59 g 1
Kiliyanūr 140 DE 4
Kilkee 119 AB 5
Kilkenny 119 C 5
Kilkis 122-123 K 5
Killala Lake 70-71 G 1
Killam 61 C 4
Killarney [AUS] 160 L 2
Killarney [CDN] 68-69 FG 1
Killarney [IRL] 119 B 5
Killdeer 68-69 C 1
Killdeer, ND 68-69 E 2
Killdeer Mountains 68-69 E 2
Killeen, TX 76-77 F 7
Killiecrankie Pass 119 E 3
Killik 136-137 G 3
Killik River 58-59 KL 2
Killin 119 D 3
Killinek Island 56-57 Y 5
Killington Peak 72-73 K 3
Kill van Kull 82 III b 3
Killybegs 119 B 4
Kilmarnock 119 DE 4
Kil'mez' [SU, place Kirovskaja Oblast'] 124-125 S 5
Kil'mez' [SU, place Udmurtskaja ASSR] 124-125 S 5
Kil'mez' [SU, river] 124-125 S 5
Kilmichael, MS 78-79 E 4
Kilmore 160 G 6
Kilo 171 B 2
Kilombero 172 G 3
Kilómetro 106-107 C 5
Kilómetro 31, Estación — 110 III b 1
Kilómetro 45, Estación — 110 III a 2
Kilómetro 642 104-105 F 9
Ki-long = Chilung 142-143 N 6
Kilosa 172 G 3
Kilossa = Kilosa 172 G 3
Kilpisjärvi 116-117 J 3
Kilrea 119 C 4
Kilrush 119 B 5
Kiltān Island 134-135 L 8
Kilunga 168-169 J 3
Kilwa 172 E 3
Kilwa, Khirbat — 136-137 G 8
Kilwa Kisiwani 172 GH 3
Kilwa-Kissiwni = Kilwa Kisiwani 172 GH 3
Kilwa Kivinje 172 GH 3
Kilwa-Kiwindje = Kilwa Kivinje 172 GH 3
Kim, CO 68-69 E 7
Kim [MAL] 154 III b 1
Kim [RFC] 168-169 H 4
Kimaam 148-149 L 8
Kimali 171 C 3
Kimama, ID 66-67 G 4
Kimasozero 116-117 O 5
Kimba 160 C 4
Kimball, MN 70-71 C 3
Kimball, NE 68-69 E 5
Kimball, SD 68-69 G 4
Kimball, Mount — 58-59 PQ 5
Kimbe 148-149 gh 6
Kimbe Bay 148-149 h 6
Kimberley [AUS] 158-159 E 3
Kimberley [CDN] 56-57 NO 8
Kimberley [ZA] 172 DE 7
Kimberly, NV 74-75 F 3
Kimchaek 142-143 OP 3
Kimch'ŏn 142-143 O 4
Kimen = Qimen 146-147 F 7
Kimhandu 171 D 4
Kimje 144-145 F 5
Kimkang = Chengmai 142-143 KL 8
Kimōlos 122-123 L 7
Kimparana 168-169 D 2
Kimpoku san 144-145 LM 3
Kimry 132-133 F 6
Kim So'n 150-151 F 2
Kimuenza 172 C 2
Kinabalu, Gunung — 148-149 G 5
Kinabatangan, Sungei — 152-153 M 3
Kinak Bay 58-59 F 7
Kinapusan Island 152-153 O 3
Kinārsāni 140 E 2
Kinaskan Lake 58-59 WX 8
Kinbasket Lake 60 HJ 4
Kincaid, KS 70-71 C 6
Kincardine [CDN] 72-73 F 2
Kinchinjunga = Gangchhendsönga 134-135 O 5
Kincolith 60 BC 2
Kinda = Kinh Đu'c 150-151 F 7
Kindan Būm 141 E 2
Kindandai 152-153 P 6
Kindat = Kintat 141 D 4
Kinder, LA 78-79 C 5
Kindersley 56-57 P 7
Kindia 164-165 B 6
Kindu 172 E 2
Kinel' 132-133 J 7
Kinel'skije jary 124-125 ST 7
Kinešma 132-133 G 6
Kingabwa, Kinshasa- 170 IV b 2
King and Queen Court House, VA 80-81 H 2
King Charles Land = Kong Karlsland 116-117 mn 5
Kingchow = Jiangling 142-143 L 5
King Christian IX Land = Kong Christian den IX[s] Land 52 C 22
Kingchwan = Jingchuan 142-143 K 4
King City, CA 74-75 C 4
King City, MO 70-71 C 5
King Cove, AK 58-59 bc 2
King Edward VIIIth Gulf 53 C 6-7
King Edward VIIth Land = Edward VIIth Peninsula 53 B 21-22
King Edward VIIth Plateau = Dronning Maud fjellkjede 53 A
Kingfisher, OK 76-77 F 5
King Frederik VIII Land = Kong Frederik den VIII[s] Land 52 B 21
King Frederik VI Land = Kong Frederik den VI[s] Kyst 52 C 23
King George Bay 108-109 J 8
King George Island 53 CD 30-31
King George Sound 158-159 CD 7
King George's Reservoir 129 II bc 1
King George VI, Falls 94-95 L 5
King George VIth Sound 53 B 29-30
King George VI, Taman Kebangsaan — 150-151 D 10
King George V[th] Land 53 BC 15-16
King Hill, ID 66-67 F 4
Kinghsien = Jing Xian 146-147 G 6
Kingisepp [SU, Eesti] 124-125 D 4
Kingisepp [SU, Rossijskaja SFSR] 124-125 G 4
King Island [AUS] 158-159 H 7
King Island [CDN] 60 D 3
King Island [USA] 58-59 C 4
King Island = Kadan Kyūn 148-149 C 4
Kingku = Jinggu 142-143 J 7
King Lear 66-67 D 5
King Leopold Ranges 158-159 DE 3
Kingman, AZ 74-75 FG 5
Kingman, KS 68-69 GH 7
Kingmen = Jingmen 146-147 CD 6
King Mountain [USA, Oregon] 66-67 D 4
King Mountain [USA, Texas] 76-77 C 7
King of Prussia, PA 84 III a 1
King of Prussia Plaza 84 III a 1
Kingoonya 158-159 G 6
King Oscar Land 56-57 TU 2
Kingrī 138-139 B 2
King Salmon, AK 58-59 JK 7
King Salmon River [CDN ◁ Egegik Bay] 58-59 J 7
King Salmon River [CDN ◁ Nushagak River] 58-59 HJ 6
Kingsbury Green, London- 129 II a 1
Kings Canyon National Park 74-75 D 4
Kingscote 158-159 G 7
Kingscourt 119 C 5
Kings Court, Houston-, TX 85 III b 2
Kingsford Smith Airport 161 I ab 2
Kingsland, GA 80-81 F 5
Kingsland, TX 76-77 E 7
Kingsley 174-175 J 4
Kingsley, IA 70-71 BC 4
King's Lynn 119 FG 5
Kings Mountain, NC 80-81 F 3
King Sound 158-159 D 3
King's Park 155 I b 2
Kings Peaks 64-65 DE 3
Kings Point, NY 82 III d 2
Kingsport 63 D 5
Kingsport, TN 80-81 E 2
Kings River 74-75 CD 4
Kingston, MO 70-71 C 6
Kingston, NY 72-73 JK 4
Kingston, OK 76-77 F 5-6
Kingston, PA 72-73 HJ 4
Kingston, WA 66-67 B 2
Kingston [CDN] 56-57 Y 9
Kingston [JA] 64-65 L 8
Kingston [NZ] 158-159 N 9
Kingston Peak 74-75 EF 5
Kingston SE 158-159 G 7
Kingston upon Hull 119 FG 5
Kingstown [IRL] 119 CD 5
Kingstown [West Indies] 64-65 O 9
Kingstree, SC 80-81 G 4
Kingsville, TX 64-65 G 6
Kingsville, Melbourne- 161 II b 1
Kingswood 174-175 F 4
King William Island 56-57 R 4
King William's Town 172 E 8
Kingwood, WV 72-73 G 5
Kingyang = Qingyang 142-143 K 4
Kingyuan = Yishan 142-143 K 7
Kingyun = Qingyun 146-147 F 3
Kinh Đu'c 150-151 F 7
Kinhwa = Jinhua 142-143 MN 6
Kinibalu = Mount Kinabalu 148-149 G 5
Kınık 136-137 B 3
Kinistino 61 F 4
Kinkala 172 B 2
Kinkazan tō 144-145 NO 3
Kinmen = Kinmen Dao 142-143 M 7
Kinmen Dao 142-143 M 7
Kinmount 72-73 G 2
Kinmundy, IL 70-71 F 6
Kinnaird's Head 119 F 3
Kinneret, Yam — 134-135 D 4
Kino kawa 144-145 K 5
Kinomoto = Kumano 144-145 L 6
Kinoosao 61 GH 2
Kinosaki 144-145 K 5
Kinross 119 E 3
Kinsale 119 B 6
Kinsella 61 BC 4
Kinselmeer 128 I b 1
Kinsey, MT 68-69 D 2
Kinshan = Jinshan 146-147 H 6
Kinshasa 172 C 2
Kinshasa, Aéroport de — 170 IV ab 1
Kinshasa-Banda-Lungwa 170 IV a 1-2
Kinshasa-Barumbu 170 IV a 1
Kinshasa-Binza 170 IV a 2
Kinshasa-Bumbu 170 IV a 2
Kinshasa-Djelo-Binza 170 IV a 2
Kinshasa-Gombe 170 IV a 1
Kinshasa-Kalamu 170 IV a 2
Kinshasa-Kasa-Vubu 170 IV a 2
Kinshasa-Kingabwa 170 IV b 2
Kinshasa-Kintambo 170 IV a 2
Kinshasa-Limete 170 IV b 2
Kinshasa-Lingwala 170 IV a 1
Kinshasa-Makala 170 IV a 2
Kinshasa-Masina 170 IV b 2
Kinshasa-N'dolo 170 IV b 1
Kinshasa-Ngaba 170 IV ab 2
Kinshasa-Ngaliema 170 IV a 2
Kinshasa-Ngiri-Ngiri 170 IV a 2
Kinshasa-Présidence 170 IV a 1
Kinsien = Jin Xian 142-143 N 4
Kinsley, KS 68-69 G 7
Kinston, NC 64-65 L 4
Kintambo, Kinshasa- 170 IV a 2
Kintambo, Rapides de — 170 IV a 1
Kintampo 164-165 D 7
Kintan = Jintan 146-147 G 6
Kintap 148-149 G 7
Kintat 141 D 4
Kin-tcheou = Jinzhou 142-143 N 3
Kintinian 168-169 C 3
Kintinku 171 C 4
Kintyre 119 D 4
Kinuso 60 K 2
Kinvat = Kinwat 138-139 FG 8
Kinwat 138-139 FG 8
Kinyangiri 171 C 4
Kinyeti 171 C 1
Kiokluk Mount 58-59 HJ 6
Kiokluk Mountains 58-59 H 6
Kios = Gemlik 136-137 C 2
Kioshan = Queshan 142-143 L 5
Kiosk 72-73 G 1
Kioto = Kyōto 142-143 PQ 4
Kiowa, CO 68-69 D 6
Kiowa, KS 76-77 E 4
Kiowa, OK 76-77 FG 5
Kiowa Creek 68-69 D 5-6
Kipawa 72-73 G 1
Kipawa, Lac — 72-73 G 1
Kipawa, la Reserve de — 72-73 G 1
Kipembawe 172 F 3
Kipengere 171 C 5
Kipeta 171 B 5
Kipili 172 F 3
Kipini 172 H 2
Kipling 61 G 5
Kipnuk, AK 58-59 EF 7
Kipp 66-67 G 1
Kiptopeke, VA 80-81 J 2
Kipushi 172 E 4
Kir'a 124-125 Q 6
Kirākat 138-139 J 5
Kirakira 148-149 k 7
Kirandul 140 E 1
Kīranūr [IND ↑ Neyveli] 140 D 5
Kīranūr [IND ↙ Thanjāvar] 140 D 5
Kiraoli 138-139 F 4
Kirāvalī = Kiraoli 138-139 F 4
Kiraz 136-137 C 3
Kırbaşı 136-137 DE 2-3
Kirbyville, TX 76-77 GH 7
Kirchdorf, Hamburg- 130 I b 2
Kirenga 132-133 U 6
Kirensk 132-133 U 6
Kirgali 136-137 H 4
Kirghiz Soviet Socialist Republic 134-135 LM 2
Kirgis Nor = Chjargas nuur 142-143 GH 2
Kirgiz Kizilsu Zizhizhou 142-143 CD 3-4

Kirgizskaja Sovetskaja Socialističeskaja Respublika = Kirghiz Soviet Socialist Republic 134-135 LM 2
Kirgizskij chrebet 134-135 LM 2
Kiri 172 C 2
Kiribati 178-179 S 6
Kiries East = Kiries-Oos 174-175 C 4
Kiries-Oos 174-175 C 4
Kiries Wes = Kiries West 174-175 C 4
Kiries West 174-175 C 4
Kırık 136-137 J 2
Kırıkhan 136-137 G 4
Kirikiri Prisons 170 III a 2
Kırıkkale 134-135 C 2-3
Kirillov 132-133 F 6
Kirillovka 126-127 G 3
Kirin = Jilin [TJ, administrative unit] 142-143 N 2-O 3
Kirin = Jilin [TJ, place] 142-143 O 3
Kirindi Oya 140 E 7
Kirin-do 144-145 E 4
Kirishima-yama 144-145 H 7
Kiriši 124-125 J 4
Kiris-Ost = Kiries-Oos 174-175 C 4
Kiris-West = Kiries West 174-175 C 4
Kirit = Jiriid 164-165 O 7
Kiriwina Islands = Trobriand Islands 148-149 h 6
Kirka 136-137 D 3
Kırkağaç 136-137 BC 3
Kirkcaldy 119 E 3
Kirkcudbright 119 DE 4
Kirkenes 116-117 O 3
Kırkgeçit = Kasrık 136-137 K 3
Kirkjuból 116-117 g 2
Kirkland, TX 76-77 D 5
Kirkland Lake 56-57 U 8
Kırklareli 134-135 B 2
Kirksville, MO 64-65 H 3
Kirkūk 134-135 EF 3
Kirkwall 119 E 2
Kirkwood 172 DE 8
Kirkwood, MO 70-71 E 6
Kirkwood, NJ 84 III cd 3
Kirkwood, Atlanta-, GA 85 II c 2
Kirlangıç burnu = Gelidonya burnu 136-137 D 4
Kirman = Kermān 134-135 H 4
Kirmir çayı 136-137 E 2
Kirobası = Mağara 136-137 EF 4
Kirongwe 171 DE 4
Kirov [SU, Kalužskaja Oblast'] 124-125 K 6
Kirov [SU, Kirovskaja Oblast'] 132-133 HJ 6
Kirova, zaliv — 126-127 O 7
Kirova, zapovednik — 126-127 O 7
Kirovabad 126-127 N 6
Kirovakan 126-127 LM 6
Kirov-Kominternovskij 124-125 RS 4
Kirovo-Čepeck 124-125 S 4
Kirovograd 126-127 EF 2
Kirovsk [SU, Azerbajdžanskaja SSR] 126-127 O 7
Kirovsk [SU, Rossijskaja SFSR ↓ Murmansk] 132-133 EF 4
Kirovsk [SU, Rossijskaja SFSR Leningradskaja Oblast'] 124-125 H 4
Kirovskij [SU, Kazachskaja SSR] 132-133 O 9
Kirovskij [SU, Rossijskaja SFSR ↓ Astrachan'] 126-127 O 4
Kirovskij [SU, Rossijskaja SFSR ↖ Petropavlovsk-Kamčatskij] 132-133 de 7
Kirpil'skij liman 126-127 HJ 4
Kirs 132-133 J 6
Kirsanov 124-125 O 7
Kırşehir 134-135 C 3
Kırsırkaya 154 I a 1
Kirstonia 174-175 E 3
Kīrthar, Koh — 134-135 K 5
Kirthar Range = Koh Kīrthar 134-135 K 5
Kirtland, NM 74-75 J 4
Kiruna 116-117 HJ 4
Kiruru 148-149 KL 7
Kirwin, KS 68-69 G 6
Kirwin Reservoir 68-69 G 6
Kiryū 144-145 M 4
Kiržač 124-125 M 5
Kisa 116-117 F 8-9
Kisabi 171 B 4-5
Kisakata 144-145 M 3
Kisaki 171 D 4
Kisale, Lac — 172 E 3
Kisangani 172 E 1
Kisangire 172 G 3
Kisar, Pulau — 148-149 J 8
Kisaralik River 58-59 G 6
Kisaran 150-151 B 11
Kisarawe 172 G 3
Kisarazu 144-145 MN 5
Kisarazu Air Base 155 III c 3
Kisbey 61 G 6
Kisel'ovsk 132-133 Q 7
Kisen = Hŭich'ŏn 142-143 O 3
Kisengwa 172 E 3
Kišen'ki 126-127 G 2
Kisenyi = Gisenyi 172 E 2
Kisgegas 60 D 2
Kish 136-137 L 6
Kīsh, Jazīreh-ye — 134-135 G 5
Kishan = Ch'i-shhan 146-147 H 10
Kishanganj 138-139 LM 4-5
Kishangarh [IND ↗ Ajmer] 138-139 E 4
Kishangarh [IND ↑ Rāmgarh] 138-139 C 4
Kishb, Ḥarrat al- 134-135 E 6
Kishi 168-169 F 3
Kishikas River 62 CD 1
Kishinev = Kišin'ov 126-127 D 3
Kishiwada 144-145 K 5
Kishm = Qeshm [IR, landscape] 134-135 H 5
Kishm = Qeshm [IR, place] 134-135 H 5
Kishorganj 141 B 3
Kishui = Jishui 146-147 E 8
Kisigo 171 C 4
Kisii 172 F 2
Kisiju 171 D 4
Kısıklı 154 I b 2
Kišin'ov 126-127 D 3
Kısır dağı 136-137 K 2
Kiska Island 52 D 1
Kiskatinaw River 60 G 2
Kiska Volcano 58-59 r 6
Kiskittogisu Lake 61 J 3
Kiskitto Lake 61 J 3
Kiskunfélegyháza 118 JK 5
Kiskunhalas 118 J 5
Kislovodsk 126-127 L 5
Kismaanyo 172 H 2
Kismayu = Kismaanyo 172 H 2
Kismet, KS 76-77 D 4
Kiso gawa 144-145 L 5
Kiso sammyaku 144-145 L 5
Kispiox River 60 C 2
Kisrā 166-167 L 2
Kisreka 116-117 O 5
Kissangire = Kisangire 172 G 3
Kissaraing Island = Kettharin Kyūn 148-149 C 4
Kissenje = Gisenyi 172 E 2
Kissenji = Gisenyi 172 E 2
Kisserawe = Kisarawe 172 G 3
Kissidougou 164-165 BC 7
Kissimmee, FL 80-81 c 2
Kissimmee, Lake — 80-81 c 2-3
Kissimmee River 80-81 c 3
Kissinger 66-67 A 1
Kississing Lake 61 H 3
Kistna = Krishna 134-135 M 7
Kistufell 116-117 f 2
Kisumu 172 FG 2
Kisvárda 118 KL 4
Kiswere 171 D 5
Kita 164-165 C 6
Kita, Tōkyō- 155 III b 1
Kitaaoyagi 155 III d 2
Kita Daitō-jima 142-143 P 6
Kita-Daitō zima = Kita-Daitō-jima 142-143 P 6
Kitagō 144-145 H 7
Kitai = Qitai 142-143 FG 3
Kita-Ibaraki 144-145 N 4
Kita Iwojima = Kita-Io 206-207 S 7
Kitakami 144-145 N 3
Kitakami gawa 142-143 R 4
Kitakami kōti 144-145 N 2-3
Kitakata 144-145 MN 4
Kita-Kyūshū 142-143 OP 5
Kita-Kyūsyū = Kita-Kyūshū 142-143 OP 5
Kitale 172 G 1
Kita lo 206-207 S 7
Kitāmah 166-167 D 2
Kitami 142-143 R 3
Kita ura 144-145 N 4
Kitčan 132-133 Y 5
Kit Carson, CO 68-69 E 6
Kitchener 56-57 U 9
Kitchigama, Rivière — 62 M 1
Kitchioh = Jieshi 146-147 E 10
Kitchioh Wan = Jieshi Wan 146-147 E 10
Kitee 116-117 O 6
Kitega = Gitega 172 EF 2
Kitendwe 171 B 4
Kitengela Game Reserve 171 D 3
Kitgum 172 F 1
Kithāmah 166-167 D 2
Kitimat 56-57 L 7
Kitinen 116-117 LM 3
Kitkatla 60 B 3
Kitlope River 60 D 3
Kitsansara 124-125 GH 3
Kitseh = Jize 146-147 E 3
Kitsuki 144-145 H 6
Kittanning, PA 72-73 G 4
Kittery, ME 72-73 L 3
Kitthareng = Kettharin Kyūn 148-149 C 4
Kittilä 116-117 L 4
Kittūr 140 B 3
Kitty Hawk, NC 80-81 J 2
Kitu 171 A 4
Kitui 172 G 2
Kituku 171 B 4
Kitumbini 171 DE 5
Kitunda 172 F 3
Kitwanga 60 C 2
Kitwe 172 E 4
Kityang = Jieyang 146-147 F 10
Kitzbühel 118 EF 5
Kitzingen 118 E 4
Kiuchuan = Jiuquan 142-143 H 4
Kiuhsien = Qiu Xian 146-147 E 3
Kiukiang = Jiujiang 142-143 M 6
Kiulong Kiang = Jiulong Jiang 146-147 F 9
Kiunga 148-149 M 8
Kiung-chow = Qiongshan 142-143 L 8
Kiungchow Hai-hsia = Qiongzhou Haixia 142-143 KL 7
Kiuruvesi 116-117 M 6
Kiushiu = Kyūshū 142-143 P 5
Kiu Tsui Chau 155 I b 1
Kivač, vodopad — 124-125 J 2
Kivalina, AK 58-59 E 3
Kivalina River 58-59 E 2-3
Kivalo 116-117 L 5-M 4
Kivercy 126-127 B 1
Kiveriči 124-125 L 5
Kivu 172 E 2
Kivu, Lac — 172 EF 2
Kiwalik, AK 58-59 FG 3
Kiyang = Qiyang 146-147 CD 8
Kiyāt = Khay' 134-135 E 7
Kiyev = Kijev 126-127 DE 1
Kiyose 155 III a 1
Kiyosumi Garden 155 III b 1
Kizel 132-133 K 6
Kizema 124-125 P 3
Kiziba 171 C 2
Kızılcahamam 136-137 E 2
Kızılçakcak = Akkaya 136-137 K 2
Kızılırmak 134-135 D 3
Kızılırmak = Hüseyinli 136-137 EF 2
Kiziljurt 126-127 N 5
Kızılkaya 136-137 E 4
Kizil Khoto = Kyzyl 132-133 R 7
Kızılkoca = Şefaatli 136-137 F 3
Kizil Orda = Kzyl-Orda 132-133 M 9
Kizilsu Kirgiz Zizhizhou 142-143 C 4-D 3
Kızıltepe 136-137 J 4
Kızıltoprak, İstanbul- 154 I b 3
Kızılveran 136-137 F 2
Kizl'ar 126-127 N 5
Kizl'arskij zaliv 126-127 N 4
Kizner 124-125 S 5
Kızören 136-137 E 3
Kizyl-Arvat 134-135 H 3
Kizyl-Atrek 134-135 G 3
Kjækan 116-117 K 3
Kjerringøy 116-117 EF 4
Kjøllefjord 116-117 MN 2
Kjøpsvik 116-117 G 3
Klaarstroom 174-175 E 7
Kladno 118 FG 3
Kladovo 122-123 K 3
Kladow, Berlin- 130 III a 2
Klaeng 150-151 C 6
Klagenfurt 118 G 5
Klaipėda 124-125 C 6
Klamath, CA 66-67 A 5
Klamath Falls, OR 64-65 B 3
Klamath Mountains 64-65 B 3
Klamath River 64-65 B 3
Klamono 148-149 K 7
Klang, Ko — 150-151 AB 8
Klang, Pulau — 150-151 C 11
Klappan River 58-59 X 8
Klapper = Pulau Deli 148-149 DE 8
Klarälven 116-117 E 7
Kl'asticy 124-125 G 6
Klatovy 118 F 4
Klaver = Klawer 172 C 8
Kl'avlino 124-125 ST 6
Klawer 172 C 8
Klawock, AK 58-59 w 9
Klay = Bomi Hills 164-165 B 7
Kl'az'ma 124-125 N 5
Kleck 124-125 F 7
Kleena Kleene 60 E 3
Kleides 136-137 F 5
Kleinbeeren 130 III b 2
Kleinbegin 174-175 D 5
Klein Bosmanland 174-175 C 5
Kleiner Ravensberg 130 III a 2
Klein Gerau 128 III a 2
Klein Glienicke, Volkspark — 130 III a 2
Klein Grasbrook, Hamburg- 130 I ab 1
Kleinhadern, München- 130 II a 2
Klein Jukskei 170 V b 1
Klein-Karas 174-175 C 4
Klein Karasberge 174-175 C 4
Klein Karoo 172 D 8
Klein Letaba 174-175 J 2
Klein Moor 130 I b 2
Klein Namakwaland 174-175 B 5
Kleinpoort 174-175 F 7
Klein Rietrivier 174-175 D 6-7
Klein Roggeveld 174-175 D 7
Kleinschönebeck 130 III c 2
Kleinsee 174-175 B 5
Klein Swartberge 174-175 D 7
Kleinziethen 130 III b 2
Kléla 168-169 D 3
Klemtu 60 C 3
Klender, Jakarta- 154 IV b 2
Klerksdorp 172 E 7
Klery Creek, AK 58-59 GH 3
Klešcevo 124-125 M 2
Klesov 124-125 F 8
Kletn'a 124-125 J 7
Klēts kalns 124-125 F 5
Kletskij 126-127 L 2
Klevan' 126-127 BC 1
Kleve 118 BC 3
Kleven' 126-127 F 1
Kličev 124-125 G 7
Klickitat, WA 66-67 C 3
Klickitat River 66-67 C 2-3
Klidhes Island = Kleides 136-137 F 5
Klimoviči 124-125 HJ 7
Klimovo 124-125 J 7
Klimovsk 124-125 L 6
Klin 132-133 F 6
Klinaklini Glacier 60 E 4
Klincovka 124-125 R 8
Klincy 124-125 J 7
Klinovec 118 F 3
Klintehamn 116-117 GH 9
Klipdale 174-175 C 8
Klipdam 174-175 C 4
Klipkrans 174-175 E 7
Klippan 116-117 E 9
Klippebjergene = Rocky Mountains 56-57 L 5-P 9
Klippiga bergen = Rocky Mountains 56-57 L 5-P 9
Klipplaat 174-175 F 7
Klippoortje 170 V c 2
Kliprivier [ZA, Drakensberge] 174-175 H 4
Kliprivier [ZA, Johannesburg] 170 V a 2
Klipriviersberg 170 V b 2
Klipriviersoog, Johannesburg- 170 V a 2
Kliprugberg 174-175 C 6
Kliprug Kop = Kliprugberg 174-175 C 6
Kłodzko 118 H 3
Klomp 128 I b 2
Klondike 56-57 HJ 5
Klong, Mae — = Mae Nam Klong 150-151 CD 3-4
Klong, Nam Mae — = Nam Mae Ngat 150-151 B 3
Klosterneuburg 118 GH 4
Klostertor, Hamburg- 130 I b 1
Klotz, Mount — 58-59 R 4
Klövensteen, Forst — 130 I a 1
Kluane 58-59 ST 6
Kluane Lake 56-57 J 5
Kluane National Park 58-59 RS 6
Kl'učevskaja sopka = Velikaja Kl'učevskaja sopka 132-133 f 6
Kluchor = Karačajevsk 126-127 KL 5
Kluchorskij, pereval — 126-127 K 5
Kl'uči 132-133 f 6
Kluczbork 118 HJ 3
Klukwan, AK 58-59 U 7
Klumpang, Teluk — 152-153 M 7
Klutina Lake 58-59 OP 6
Kmeit = Al-Kumayt 136-137 M 6
Knabengruver 116-117 B 8
Knapp, WI 70-71 DE 3
Kn'aščiny 124-125 K 5
Kneïss, Djezîret = Jazīrat Kanā'is 166-167 M 2
Knewstubb Lake 60 E 3
Kneža 122-123 L 4
Knife River 68-69 EF 2
Knife River, MN 70-71 DE 2
Knight Inlet 60 E 4
Knight Island 58-59 N 6
Knin 122-123 FG 3
Knippa, TX 76-77 E 8
Knjaževac 122-123 K 4
Knobel, AR 78-79 D 2
Knob Lake = Schefferville 56-57 X 7
Knob Oaks, Houston-, TX 85 III a 1
Knolls, UT 66-67 G 5
Knollwood Village, Houston-, TX 85 III b 2
Knonau 128 IV a 2
Knōssós 122-123 L 8
Knowles, OK 76-77 DE 4
Knowles, Cape — 53 B 30-31
Knowltonwood, PA 84 III a 2
Knox 208 H 2
Knox, IN 70-71 G 5
Knox City, TX 76-77 DE 6
Knox Land 53 C 11
Knoxville, IA 70-71 D 5
Knoxville, TN 64-65 K 4
Knuckles 140 E 7
Knud Rasmussen Land 52 B 25-A 21
Knysna 172 D 8
Ko, gora — 132-133 a 8
Koba 152-153 G 7
Kob'aj 132-133 Y 5
Kobakof Bay 58-59 j 4-5
Kobayashi 144-145 H 6-7
Kobbegem 128 II a 1
Kobdo = Chovd 142-143 G 2
Kōbe 142-143 PQ 5
Kobeberge 174-175 C 6
Kobe Mountains = Kobeberge 174-175 C 6
København 116-117 DE 10
Koberivier 174-175 C 6
Kobin 136-137 J 4
Koblenz 118 C 3
Kobo 164-165 MN 6
Koboža [SU, place] 124-125 K 4
Kobra [SU, place] 124-125 S 3
Kobra [SU, river] 124-125 S 4
Kobrin 124-125 E 7
Kobroör, Pulau — 148-149 KL 8
Kobrur = Pulau Kobroör 148-149 KL 8
Kobuk, AK 58-59 J 3
Kobuk River 56-57 E 4
Kobuleti 126-127 K 6
Koca çay [TR ◁ Apolyont gölü] 136-137 C 3
Koca çay [TR ◁ Manyas gölü] 136-137 B 3
Koca çay [TR ◁ Mediterranean Sea] 136-137 C 4
Kocaeli 136-137 CD 2
Koca ırmak 136-137 E 2
Kočani 122-123 K 5
Kocapinar = Ömerin 136-137 JK 4
Koçarlı 136-137 B 4
Kocatas tepe 154 I b 1-2
Kočečum 132-133 ST 4
Kočen'ga 124-125 O 3
Kočetovka 124-125 N 7
Kočevje 122-123 F 3
Kočevo 124-125 TU 4
Ko Chan 150-151 AB 8
Kochana = Kočani 122-123 K 5
Kŏch'ang 144-145 F 5
Ko Chang [T, Andaman Sea] 150-151 B 8
Ko Chang [T, Gulf of Thailand] 148-149 D 4
Kochanovo 124-125 GH 6
Koch Bihār = Cooch Behār 138-139 M 4
Kochchi-Kaṇayannūr = Cochin 134-135 M 9
Kōchi 142-143 P 5
Kochig = Khiching 138-139 K 7
Kōchiṅgā = Khiching 138-139 K 7
Koch Island 56-57 V 4
Ko-chiu = Gejiu 142-143 J 7
Kochma 124-125 N 5
Kochow = Maoming 142-143 L 7
Koch Peak 66-67 H 3
Kochtel = Kohtla 132-133 D 6
Kočki 132-133 P 7
Kočkoma 124-125 JK 1-2
Kočubej 126-127 N 4
Koḍagu = Coorg 140 BC 4
Kodaikānal 140 C 5
Kōḍaṅgala = Korangal 140 C 2
Kōdangauk 141 C 5
Kodār 140 DE 2
Kodarma 138-139 K 5
Koddiyar Bay = Koḍḍiyār Warāya 140 E 6
Koḍḍiyār Warāya 140 E 6
Kodiak, AK 56-57 F 6
Kodiak Island 56-57 F 6
Koḍikāmam 140 E 6
Kōḍikkarai Antarīp = Point Calimere 134-135 MN 8
Kodima 124-125 O 2
Kodinār 138-139 C 7
Kodino 132-133 F 5
Kōdit Taung 141 D 6
Kodiyakkarai 140 DE 5
Kodōk = Kūdūk 164-165 L 6-7
Kodomari-misaki 144-145 MN 2
Kodori 126-127 K 5
Kodorskij, pereval — 126-127 MN 5
Kodorskij chrebet 126-127 KL 5
Kodumūru 140 C 3
Kodyma [SU, river] 126-127 E 3
Koeberg 174-175 C 5
Koegas 174-175 E 5
Koegrabie 174-175 D 5
Koekenaap 174-175 C 6
Koel 138-139 J 5
Koel, North — = Koel 138-139 J 5
Koel, South — 138-139 K 6
Kōenji, Tōkyō- 155 III ab 1
Koes 172 C 7
Koesan 144-145 FG 4
Koettlitz Glacier 53 B 15-16
Kofa Mountains 74-75 FG 6
Koffiefontein 174-175 F 5
Kofiau, Pulau — 148-149 JK 7
Koforidua 164-165 DE 7
Kofouno 168-169 F 2
Kōfu 142-143 Q 4
Koga 144-145 M 4
Kogane-saki = Henashi-saki 144-145 M 2
Kogarah, Sydney- 161 I a 2
Kogarah Bay 161 I a 2-3
Køge 116-117 DE 10
Kōgen-dō = Kangwŏn-do 144-145 F 3-G 4
Kogil'nik 126-127 D 3
Kogoluktuk River 58-59 J 3
Kogon 168-169 B 3
Kogoni 168-169 D 2
Kogota 144-145 N 3
Kogrukluk River 58-59 H 6
Kōgūm-do 144-145 F 5
Kogunsan-kundo 144-145 EF 5
Ko Hai 150-151 B 9
Kohāṭ 134-135 L 4
Kohe Ḥişār 134-135 K 4
Kohīma 134-135 P 5
Kohistān Sulaimān 134-135 KL 4-5
Koh Kīrthar 134-135 K 5
Koh Kong 148-149 D 4
Koh Lakhī 138-139 A 4-5
Köhlbrand 130 I a 1
Kohler Range 53 B 25
Kohlū 138-139 B 3
Kōhoku, Yokohama- 155 III a 2
Kohtla-Järve 132-133 D 6
Kōhu = Kōfu 142-143 Q 4
Koichab 174-175 AB 4
Koichabpan 174-175 A 4
Koide 144-145 M 4
Koīl, Dakshiṇī — = South Koel 138-139 K 6
Koīl, Uttarī — = Koel 138-139 J 5
Koilkuntla 140 D 3
Kōisanjaq = Kūysanjaq 136-137 L 4
Koishikawa, Tōkyō- 155 III b 1
Koitere 116-117 O 6
Koivisto = ostrov Bol'šoj Ber'ozovyj 124-125 FG 3
Koivisto = Primorsk 124-125 G 3
Koiwa, Tōkyō- 155 III c 1
Koja, Jakarta- 154 IV b 1
Kojdanov = Dzeržinsk 124-125 F 7
Kōje 144-145 G 5
Kōje-do 144-145 G 5
Kojgorodok 132-133 HJ 5
Kojp, gora — 124-125 W 2
Kojsug 126-127 JK 3
Kok, Nam — 150-151 B 2-3
Kōkai = Kanggye 142-143 O 3
Kōkai-hokudō = Hwanghae-pukto 144-145 EF 3
Kōkai-nandō = Hwanghae-namdo 144-145 E 3-F 4
Kokand 134-135 L 2-3
Kokanee Glacier Provincial Park 66-67 E 1
Kokaral, ostrov — 132-133 L 8
Kokatha 160 B 3
Kokčetav 132-133 MN 7
Kŏk-dong = Irhyang-dong 144-145 GH 2
Kokechik Bay 58-59 D 6
Kokemäenjoki 116-117 JK 7
Ko Kha 150-151 B 3
Ko Khram Yai 150-151 C 5
Koki 168-169 AB 2
Kokiu = Gejiu 142-143 J 7
Kok-Jangak 134-135 L 2
Kokkaniseri = Kokkānisseri 140 B 4
Kokkānisseri 140 B 4
Kokkola 116-117 K 6
Ko Klang 150-151 AB 8
Koknese 124-125 E 5
Koko 168-169 G 3
Kokoda 148-149 N 8
Kōkō Kyūn 148-149 B 4
Kokolik River 58-59 G 2
Kokomo, IN 64-65 JK 3
Kokonau 148-149 L 7
Koko Noor = Chöch nuur 142-143 H 4
Koko Nor = Chöch nuur 142-143 H 4
Kokonselkä 116-117 N 7
Kokorevka 124-125 K 7
Kokos, Pulau-pulau — 152-153 A 4
Koko Shili = Chöch Šili uul 142-143 FG 4
Kokpekty 132-133 P 8
Kokrines, AK 58-59 K 4
Kokrines Hills 58-59 KL 4
Kokšaal-Tau, chrebet — 134-135 M 2
Koksan 144-145 F 3
Koks Bāzār 134-135 P 6
Kokšen'ga 124-125 O 3
Kök shal 142-143 D 3
Koksoak River 56-57 X 6
Koksŏng 144-145 F 5
Koksovyj 126-127 K 2
Kokstad 174-175 H 6
Kōk Tappa = Gūk Tappah 136-137 L 5
Kokubo = Kokubu 144-145 H 7
Kokubu 144-145 H 7
Ko Kut 148-149 D 4
Kokwok River 58-59 HJ 7
Kōl = Alīgarh 134-135 M 5
Kola [SU, place] 132-133 E 4
Kola [SU, river] 116-117 P 3
Kola, Pulau — 148-149 KL 8
Kolachel 140 C 6
Kolachil = Kolachel 140 C 6
Ko Ladang 150-151 B 9
Kolahun 168-169 C 3
Kolaka 148-149 H 7
Koḷamba 134-135 MN 9
Kolamo [SU] 126-127 AB 2
Kolārom 118 J 5
Ko Lamphuk, Laem — = Laem Talumphuk 150-151 C 8
Ko Lan 150-151 C 6
Kolan = Kelan 146-147 C 2
Kolanjīn = Kulanjīn 136-137 N 5
Ko Lanta 150-151 B 9
Kōlāpura = Kolhāpur 140 D 2
Kolār 134-135 M 8
Kolāras 138-139 F 5
Kolār Gold Fields 134-135 M 8
Kolari 116-117 KL 4
Kōlāru = Kolār 134-135 M 8
Kolašin 122-123 H 4
Ko Latang = Ko Ladang 150-151 B 9
Kolāyat 138-139 D 4
Kolbio 172 H 2
Kolbuszowa 118 KL 3
Kol'čugino 124-125 MN 5
Kol'čugino = Leninsk-Kuzneckij 132-133 Q 6-7
Kolda 164-165 B 6
Kolding 116-117 C 10
Kole 172 D 2
Koléa = Al-Qulʻah 166-167 H 1
Kolebira 138-139 K 6
Kolepom, Pulau — 148-149 L 8
Koležma 124-125 KL 1
Kolgaon = Colgong 138-139 L 5
Kolguev Island = ostrov Kolgujev 132-133 GH 4
Kolgujev, ostrov — 132-133 GH 4
Kolhān 138-139 KL 6
Kolhāpur [IND, Andhra Pradesh] 140 D 2
Kolhāpur [IND, Mahārāshtra] 134-135 L 7
Koli 116-117 N 6
Ko Libong 150-151 B 9
Koliganek, AK 58-59 J 7
Kolīn 118 G 3-4
Kolka 124-125 D 5
Kolkasrags 124-125 D 5
Kolki 126-127 B 1
Kōllam = Quilon 134-135 M 9
Kollangod 140 C 5
Kōllankōḍ = Kollangod 140 C 5
Kollegāl 140 C 4
Kolleru Lake 140 E 2
Koll-e Semnan 134-135 GH 3
Kolliṭam = Coleroon 140 D 5
Kollumúli 116-117 fg 2
Kolmanskop 174-175 A 4
Köln 118 C 3
Kolno 118 K 2
Koło 118 J 2
Koloa, HI 78-79 c 2
Kolobovo 124-125 N 5
Kołobrzeg 118 GH 1
Kolodn'a 124-125 HJ 6
Kologriv 132-133 G 6
Kolokani 164-165 C 6
Kolombangara 148-149 j 6
Kolombo = Koḷamba 134-135 MN 9
Kolomenskoje, Moskva- 113 V c 3
Kolomna 124-125 LM 6
Kolomyja 126-127 B 2
Kolondiéba 168-169 D 3
Kolonie Buch, Berlin- 130 III b 1
Kolonie Lerchenau, München- 130 II b 1
Kolonie Neuhönow 130 III cd 1
Kolonodale 148-149 H 7
Kolosib 141 C 3
Kolosovka 132-133 N 6
Kolossia 171 CD 2
Kolp' [SU ◁ Suda] 124-125 K 4
Kolpaševo 132-133 P 6
Kolpino 124-125 H 4
Kolpny 124-125 L 7
Kólpos Akrōtḗriu 136-137 E 5
Kólpos Ammochṓstu 136-137 EF 5
Kólpos Chaniṓn 122-123 KL 8
Kólpos Chrysochū́s 136-137 E 5
Kólpos Episkopē̂s 136-137 E 5
Kólpos Mirampéllu 122-123 LM 8
Kólpos Mórfu 136-137 E 5
Kólpos Orfánu 122-123 KL 5
Kólpos Petaliṓn 122-123 L 7
Kolpūr 138-139 A 3
Kol'skij poluostrov 132-133 EF 4
Koltubanovskij 124-125 T 7
Koluel Kayke 108-109 EF 6
Kolufuri 176 a 2
Kölük 136-137 H 4
Kolumadulu Channel 176 a 2
Kolva 124-125 V 3
Kolwezi 172 DE 4
Kolyma 132-133 de 4
Kolymskaja nizmennost' 132-133 de 4
Kolymskoje nagorje 132-133 e 4-f 5
Kolyšlej 124-125 P 7
Kom 122-123 K 4
Komadugu Gana 164-165 G 6
Komadugu Yobe 164-165 G 6
Komae 155 III a 2
Komaga-dake 144-145 b 2
Komagane 144-145 LM 5
Komaga take 144-145 M 4
Komaggasberge 174-175 B 5-6
Komaggas Mountains = Komaggasberge 174-175 B 5-6
Komagome, Tōkyō- 155 III b 1
K'o-mai = Kemā 142-143 H 6
Ko Mak [T, Gulf of Thailand] 150-151 D 7
Ko Mak [T, Thale Luang] 150-151 C 9
Komandorskije ostrova 132-133 f 6-g 7
Komarin 124-125 H 8
Komarno [SU] 126-127 AB 2
Komárom 118 J 5
Komarovo [SU, Archangel'skaja Oblast'] 124-125 Q 3
Komarovo [SU, Kirovskaja Oblast'] 124-125 RS 4
Komarovo [SU, Novgorodskaja Oblast'] 124-125 JK 4
Komati 174-175 J 3-4
Komatipoort 172 F 7
Komatsu 144-145 L 4
Komatsugawa, Tōkyō- 155 III c 1
Komatsujima = Komatsushima 144-145 K 5-6
Komatsushima 144-145 K 5-6
Komazawa Ground 155 III a 2
Komba, Pulau — 152-153 P 9
Kombe, Katako- 172 D 2
Kombissiguiri 168-169 E 2
Kombol = Kompot 148-149 H 6
Kombolcha = Kembolcha 164-165 MN 6
Komchai Meas 150-151 E 7
Kome [EAT] 171 C 3
Kome [EAU] 171 C 3
Kome [RB] 174-175 E 3
Komga 174-175 GH 7
Komgha = Komga 174-175 GH 7
Komi Autonomous Soviet Socialist Republic 132-133 JK 5
Komi Avtonomnaja Sovetskaja Socialističeskaja Respublika = Komi Autonomous Soviet Socialist Republic 132-133 JK 5
Komillā 134-135 P 6
Kōminā = Kumund 138-139 J 7
Komine 168-169 H 4
Komintern = Marganec 126-127 G 3
Komintern = Novošachtinsk 126-127 J 3
Kominternovskij, Kirov- 124-125 RS 4
Kominternovskoje 126-127 E 3
Komi-Permyak Autonomous Area = 1 ◁ 132-133 J 6
Kommadagga 174-175 F 7
Kommunarsk 126-127 J 2
Kommunizma, pik — 134-135 L 3
Komodo, Pulau — 148-149 G 8
Komodougou 168-169 C 3
Komoe 164-165 D 7
Kōm Ombō = Kawm Umbū 164-165 L 4
Komono 172 B 2
Komoran, Pulau — 148-149 L 8
Komoro 144-145 M 4
Komotēnē 122-123 L 5
Kompasberg 174-175 F 6
Kompong Bang 150-151 E 6
Kompong Cham 148-149 E 4
Kompong Chhnang 148-149 D 4
Kompong Chikreng 150-151 E 6
Kompong Chrey 150-151 E 7

Kompong Kdey = Phum Kompong Kdey 150-151 E 6
Kompong Kleang 148-149 DE 4
Kompong Prasath 150-151 E 6
Kompong Râu 150-151 EF 7
Kompong Som 148-149 D 4
Kompong Som, Sremot — 150-151 D 7
Kompong Speu 148-149 D 4
Kompong Sralao 150-151 E 5
Kompong Taches 150-151 E 6
Kompong Thmâr 150-151 E 6
Kompong Thom 148-149 DE 4
Kompong Trabek [K, Kompong Thom] 150-151 E 6
Kompong Trabek [K, Prey Veng] 150-151 E 7
Kompong Trach [K, Kampot] 150-151 E 7
Kompong Trach [K, Svay Rieng] 150-151 E 7
Kompot 148-149 H 6
Komrat 126-127 D 3
Komsa 132-133 Q 5
Komsberg 174-175 D 7
Komsberge 174-175 D 7
Komsomolec 132-133 L 7
Komsomolec = Džambul 126-127 P 3
Komsomolec, ostrov — 132-133 P-R 1
Komsomolec, zaliv — 134-135 G 1
Komsomolets = ostrov Komsomolec 132-133 P-R 2
Komsomol'sklvanovo 124-125 N 5
Komsomol'skij [SU, Kalmyckaja ASSR] 126-127 N 4
Komsomol'skij [SU, Neneckij NO] 132-133 KL 4
Komsomol'sk-na-Amure 132-133 a 7
Komsomol'skoje [SU, Rossijskaja SFSR] 126-127 N 1
Komsomol'skoje [SU, Ukrainskaja SSR] 126-127 HJ 3
Komsomol'skoj Pravdy, ostrova — 132-133 U-W 2
Ko Muk 150-151 B 9
Kōmun-do 144-145 F 5
Komusan 144-145 G 1
Kon 138-139 J 5
Kona 164-165 D 6
Kona, Howrah- 154 II a 2
Konagkend 126-127 O 6
Konakovo 124-125 L 5
Konārak 138-139 L 8
Konawa, OK 76-77 F 5
Konaweha, Sungai — 152-153 O 7-P 8
Konch 138-139 G 4-5
Koncha = Kontcha 164-165 G 7
Konche darya 142-143 F 3
Konda 132-133 M 6
Kondagāñv = Kondagaon 138-139 H 8
Kondagaon 138-139 H 8
Kondalwādi 140 C 1
Kondapalle 140 E 2
Kondapalli = Kondapalle 140 E 2
Kondhāli 138-139 G 7
Kondiaronk, Lac — 72-73 H 1
Kondinskoje = Okt'abr'skoje 132-133 M 5
Kondirskoje 132-133 M 6
Kondoa 172 G 2
Kondolole 172 E 1
Kondopoga 132-133 EF 5
Kondostrov 124-125 L 1
Kondurča 124-125 S 6
Koné 158-159 M 4
Konec-Kovdozero 116-117 O 4
Koness River 58-59 P 2
Konevo 124-125 M 2
Kong 168-169 D 3
Kong, Kâs — 150-151 D 7
Kong, Mae Nam — 148-149 D 3
Kong, Mé — 148-149 E 4
Kong, Nam — 150-151 F 5
Kong, Sé — [K] 150-151 F 5-6
Kong, Se — [LAO] 150-151 F 5
Kongakut River 58-59 QR 2
Kongcheng 146-147 F 6
Kong Christian den IXs Land 56-57 de 4
Kong Christian den Xs Land 52 B 21-22
Kong Frederik den VIIIs Land 52 B 21
Kong Frederik den VIs Kyst 56-57 c 5
Kongga Zong = Gongkar Dsong 138-139 N 3
Konghow = Jiangkou 146-147 C 10
Kongju 144-145 F 4
Kong Karls land 116-117 mn 5
Kongkemul, Gunung — 152-153 M 5
Kong Leopold og Dronning Astrid land 53 BC 9
Kongmoon = Xinhui 146-147 D 10
Kongolo 172 E 3
Kongōr 164-165 L 7
Kongoussi 168-169 E 2
Kongpo 142-143 G 6
Kongsberg 116-117 C 8
Kongsøya 116-117 n 5
Kongsvinger 116-117 DE 7
Kongwa 172 G 3
Kongyu Tsho 138-139 HJ 2
Kōnha-dong 144-145 F 2
Koni, poluostrov — 132-133 d 6
Konia 168-169 C 3-4
Konin 118 J 2
Koning 174-175 E 4
Konjic 122-123 GH 4
Könkämä älv 116-117 J 3
Konkan 140 A 1-3
Konken = Khon Kaen 148-149 D 3
Konkiep = Goageb 172 C 7
Konkobiri 168-169 F 3
Konkouré 168-169 B 3
Konna = Kona 164-165 D 6
Konnagar 154 II b 1
Kōnodai, Ichikawa- 155 III c 1
Konongo 168-169 E 4
Konoša 132-133 G 5
Konotop 126-127 F 1
Konpāra 138-139 J 6
Kon Plong 150-151 G 5
Konradshöhe, Berlin- 130 III a 1
Konstabel 174-175 CD 7
Konstantinograd = Krasnograd 126-127 G 2
Konstantinovka 126-127 H 2
Konstantinovsk 126-127 K 3
Konstantinovskij [SU, Moskovskaja Oblast'] 124-125 MN 5
Konstanz 118 D 5
Konta 140 E 2
Kontagora 164-165 F 6
Kontcha 164-165 G 7
Kontiomäki 116-117 N 5
Kon Tom 150-151 F 4
Kontrashibuna Lake 58-59 KL 6
Kontum 148-149 E 4
Konur = Sulakyurt 136-137 E 2
Konya 134-135 C 3
Konya ovası 136-137 E 4
Konyševka 124-125 K 8
Konza 171 D 3
Koog aan de Zaan, Zaanstad- 128 I a 1
Kooigoedvlaktes 174-175 C 6
Kookhuis 174-175 FG 7
Kookynie 158-159 D 5
Koolau Range 78-79 cd 2
Kooloonong 160 F 5
Koonap 174-175 G 7
Koonibba 160 AB 3
Koopmansfontein 174-175 EF 5
Koorawatha 160 J 5
Koosharem, UT 74-75 H 3
Kootenai = Kootenay 56-57 N 8
Kootenai Falls 66-67 F 1
Kootenai River 64-65 C 2
Kootenay 56-57 N 8
Kootenay Lake 60 J 4-5
Kootenay National Park 60 J 4
Kootenay River 66-67 E 1
Kootjieskolk 174-175 D 6
Kopaonik 122-123 J 4
Kōpargāñv = Kopargaon 138-139 E 8
Kopargaon 138-139 E 8
Kópasker 116-117 ef 1
Kopatkeviči 124-125 G 7
Kópavogur 116-117 bc 2
Kopejsk 132-133 L 6-7
Koper 122-123 EF 3
Kopervik 116-117 A 8
Kopeysk = Kopejsk 132-133 L 6-7
Ko Phai 150-151 C 6
Ko Phangan 148-149 CD 5
Ko Phayam 150-151 B 8
Ko Phra Thong 150-151 AB 8
Ko Phuket 148-149 C 5
Köping 116-117 FG 8
Koporje 124-125 G 4
Koppa 140 B 4
Koppal 140 C 3
Koppang 116-117 D 7
Kopparberg 116-117 EF 7
Koppeh Dāgh 134-135 HJ 3
Kopperå 116-117 D 6
Koppies 174-175 G 4
Koprivnica 122-123 G 2
Köprüırmağı 136-137 D 4
Köprülü = Tito Veles 122-123 JK 5
Ko Pu 150-151 B 9
Kopyčincy 126-127 B 2
Kopyl' 124-125 F 7
Kopys' 124-125 H 6
Kora 138-139 L 5
Koraa, Djebel el — = Jabal al-Kurā' 166-167 J 2
Korab 122-123 J 5
Korahe 164-165 NO 7
Koraka burnu 136-137 B 3
Kor'akskaja sopka = Velikaja Kor'akskaja sopka 132-133 ef 7
Kor'akskoje nagorje 132-133 j-f 5
Koram = Korem 164-165 M 6
Korangal 140 C 2
Korannaberge 174-175 E 4
Korapun 148-149 h 6
Koraput 140 F 1
Korarou, Lac — 164-165 D 5
Korat = Nakhon Ratchasima 148-149 D 3-4
Koratagere 140 C 4
Koratalā = Koratla 140 D 1
Koratla 140 D 1
Ko Rawi 150-151 B 9
Kor'ažma 124-125 Q 3
Korba 138-139 J 6
Korba = Qurbah 166-167 M 1
Korbiyāy, Jabal — 173 D 6
Korbous = Qurbūş 166-167 M 1
Korbu, Gunung — 148-149 D 5-6
Korçë 122-123 J 5
Korčino 132-133 P 7
Korčula 122-123 G 4
Kordestān 134-135 D 3
Kordofān = Kurdufān al-Janūbīyah 164-165 KL 6
Korea Bay = Sŏhan-man 142-143 NO 4
Korea Strait = Chōsen-kaikyō 142-143 O 4-5
Korec 126-127 C 1
Kōrēgāñv = Koregaon 140 B 2
Koregaon 140 B 2
Korein = Al-Kuwayt 134-135 F 5
Korem 164-165 M 6
Korenevo 126-127 G 1
Korenovsk 126-127 J 4
Koret 172 D 1
Korf 132-133 g 5
Korgu = Coorg 140 BC 4
Kōṛhā = Kora 138-139 L 5
Korhogo 164-165 C 7
Kori Creek 138-139 B 6
Korienzé 168-169 E 2
Kōṛī Khāḍī = Kori Creek 138-139 B 6
Korima, Ouèd el — = Wādī al-Karīmah 166-167 F 3
Korinthiakòs Kólpos 122-123 JK 6
Kórinthos 122-123 K 7
Kori Nullah = Kori Creek 138-139 B 6
Kőrishegy 118 HJ 5
Kōriyama 142-143 QR 4
Korkino 132-133 L 7
Korkodon 132-133 de 5
Korkuteli 136-137 D 4
Korla 142-143 F 3
Korma 124-125 H 7
Kormack 62 K 3
Kormakitēs, Akrōtērion — 136-137 E 5
Kornat 122-123 F 4
Kornetspruit 174-175 G 5-6
Kornouchovo 124-125 RS 6
Kornsjø 116-117 DE 8
Koro [CI] 168-169 D 3
Koro [FJI] 148-149 a 2
Koro [HV] 168-169 E 2
Koroča 126-127 H 1
Köroğlu tepesi 136-137 DE 2
Korogwe 172 G 3
Koromo = Toyota 144-145 L 5
Korōneia, Límnē — 122-123 K 5
Korong Vale 160 F 6
Korop 126-127 F 1
Koror 148-149 KL 5
Körös 118 K 5
Koro Sea 148-149 ab 2
Korosko = Wādī Kuruskū 173 C 6
Korosten' 126-127 D 1
Korostyšev 126-127 D 1
Korotojak 126-127 J 1
Koro-Toro 164-165 H 5
Korotovo 124-125 L 4
Korovin Island 58-59 cd 2
Korovino 126-127 H 1
Korovinski, AK 58-59 j 4
Korovin Volcano 58-59 jk 4
Korowelang, Tanjung — 152-153 H 9
Korpilombolo 116-117 JK 4
Korppoo 116-117 JK 7
Korsakov 132-133 b 8
Korsakovo 124-125 L 7
Korsør 116-117 D 10
Kōrṭagērē = Koratagere 140 C 4
Kortenberg 128 II b 1
Kōrtī = Kūrtī 164-165 L 5
Kortneros 124-125 ST 3
Kortrijk 120-121 J 3
Kor'ukovka 124-125 J 8
Korumburra 160 GH 7
Korvā = Korba 138-139 J 6
Korvala 124-125 K 3
Korwai 138-139 FG 5
Koryak Autonomous Area 132-133 g 5-e 6
Korydallós 113 IV a 2
Kōs [GR, island] 122-123 M 7
Kōs [GR, place] 122-123 M 7
Kosa [SU, place] 124-125 U 4
Kosa [SU, river] 124-125 U 4
kosa Arabatskaja Strelka 126-127 G 3-4
kosa Fedotova 126-127 G 3
Koš-Agač 132-133 Q 7-8
Kosaja Gora 124-125 L 6
Kosaka 144-145 N 2
Kō-saki 144-145 G 5
Ko Samae San 150-151 C 6
Ko Samaesan = Ko Samae San 150-151 C 6
Ko Samet 150-151 C 6
Ko Samui 148-149 D 5
Košary 126-127 F 1
Koščagyl 134-135 G 1
Koscian 118 H 2
Kościerzyna 118 HJ 1
Kosciusko, MS 78-79 E 4
Kosciusko, Mount — 158-159 J 7
Kosciusko Island 58-59 vw 9
Köse 136-137 H 2
Köse dağı 136-137 GH 2
Kosgi 140 C 2
K'o-shan = Keshan 142-143 O 2
Koshigi = Kosgi 140 C 2
Koshigi = Kosigi 140 C 3
K'o-shih = Qāshqār 142-143 CD 4
Koshiki-rettō 144-145 G 7
Kōshū = Kwangju 142-143 O 4
Kōsī = Aruṇ 134-135 O 5
Kōsī = Sapt Kosi 134-135 O 5
Kosī, Dudh — 138-139 L 4
Kosi, Lake — = Kosimeer 174-175 K 4
Kosī, Sūn — 134-135 O 5
Kosī, Tambā — 138-139 L 4
Kosibaai 174-175 K 4
Košice 118 K 4
Ko Sichang 150-151 C 6
Kosigi 140 C 3
Kosimeer 174-175 K 4
Kosino [SU, Kirovskaja Oblast'] 124-125 S 4
Kosino [SU, Moskovskaja Oblast'] 113 V d 3
Kosi Reservoir 138-139 L 4
Koški [SU] 132-133 M 3
Kosju 132-133 KL 4
Koslan 132-133 H 5
Kosmos, WA 66-67 BC 2
Kosmynino 124-125 N 5
Koso Gol = Chövsgöl nuur 142-143 J 1
Kosŏng [North Korea] 142-143 O 4
Kōsŏng [ROK] 144-145 G 5
Kosŏng-ni 144-145 F 6
Kosov 126-127 B 2
Kosovo 122-123 J 4
Kosovo polje 122-123 J 4
Kosovska Mitrovica 122-123 J 4
Kosse, TX 76-77 F 7
Kossou 168-169 D 4
Kossovo 124-125 E 7
Koster 174-175 G 3
Kōsti = Kūstī 164-165 L 6
Kostino [SU ↓ Igarka] 132-133 Q 4
Kostopol' 126-127 C 1
Kostroma [SU, place] 132-133 G 6
Kostroma [SU, river] 124-125 N 4
Kostrzyn 118 G 2
Kost'ukoviči 124-125 HJ 7
Kosugi, Kawasaki- 155 III ab 2
Ko Sukon 150-151 B 9
Kosum Phisai 150-151 D 4
Kos'va 124-125 V 4
Koszalin 118 H 1
Kőszeg 118 H 5
Kota [IND] 134-135 M 5
Kota [MAL] 150-151 C 10
Kotaagung 148-149 D 8
Kota Baharu 148-149 D 5
Kotabaru 148-149 G 7
Kotabaru = Jayapura 148-149 M 7
Kota Belud 148-149 G 5
Kotabumi 148-149 DE 7
Koṭ Addū 138-139 C 2
Kotah = Kota 134-135 M 5
Kot'ajevka 126-127 O 3
Kota Kinabalu 148-149 FG 5
Kota Kota 172 F 4
Kotal Bolān 134-135 K 5
Kotal Khāibar 134-135 L 4
Ko Ta Luang 150-151 B 8
Koṭal Wākhjīr 134-135 LM 3
Kotamobagu 148-149 HJ 6
Ko Tao 150-151 BC 7
Kotapāt 138-139 J 8
Kotatengah 148-149 D 6
Kotawaringin 152-153 JK 7
Koṭchāndpūr 138-139 M 6
Koṭ Chuṭṭa 138-139 C 3
Koṭ Dijī 138-139 B 4
Kōṭdvārā = Kotdwāra 138-139 G 3
Kotdwāra 138-139 G 3
Kotel 122-123 M 4
Kotel'nič 132-133 H 6
Kotel'nikovo 126-127 L 3
Kotel'nyj, ostrov — 132-133 Za 2-3
Kotel'va 126-127 G 1
Ko Terutao 148-149 C 5
Kothi 138-139 H 5
Kothráki = Kythréa 136-137 E 5
Kotido 172 F 1
Koṭ Imāmgaṛh 138-139 B 4
Kotjeskolk = Kootjieskolk 174-175 D 6
Kotka 116-117 M 7
Kot Kapūra 138-139 E 2
Kot Kāsim 138-139 F 3
Kotkhāi 138-139 F 2
Kotla 138-139 F 1
Kotl'arevskaja = Majskij 126-127 M 5
Kotlas 132-133 H 5
Kotlik, AK 58-59 F 5
Kotlovan 124-125 K 4
Kōto, Tōkyō- 155 III b 1
Kotolnoi Island = Kotel'nyj ostrov 132-133 Za 2
Kotooka 144-145 N 2
Kotor 122-123 H 4
Kotor Varoš 122-123 G 3
Kotovo [SU, Saratovskaja Oblast'] 126-127 M 1
Kotovsk [SU, Rossijskaja SFSR] 124-125 N 7
Kotovsk [SU, Ukrainskaja SSR] 126-127 D 3
Kotowana Watobo, Teluk — 152-153 P 9
Kot Pūtli 138-139 F 4
Kotra 138-139 D 5
Koṭ Rādha Kishan 138-139 DE 2
Kotri [IND, place] 138-139 E 5
Kotri [IND, river] 138-139 H 8
Koṭrī [PAK] 134-135 K 5
Koṭ Rum 138-139 BC 3
Koṭ Samāba 138-139 C 3
Kotta = Kotla 138-139 F 1
Kottagūdem 134-135 N 7
Kottai Malai 140 C 6
Kōṭṭapaṭṭaṇam = Allūru Kottapatnam 140 E 3
Kottārakara 140 C 6
Kottātukuḷam = Kuttāttukulam 140 C 6
Koṭṭayādi = Kuttyādi 140 B 5
Kottayam 140 C 6
Kotte 140 DE 7
Kotto 164-165 J 7
Kottūru 140 BC 3
Kotuj 132-133 T 3
Kotujkan 132-133 U 3
Kotum 136-137 K 3
Kotzebue, AK 56-57 D 4
Kotzebue Sound 56-57 CD 4
Kouango 164-165 HJ 7
Kouara Débé 168-169 F 2
Kouba 164-165 H 5
Kouba, Al-Jazā'ir- 170 I ab 2
Kouchibouguac National Park 63 D 4
Koudougou 164-165 D 6
Kouéré 168-169 E 3
Koueveldberge 174-175 EF 7
Koufra, Oasis de — = Wāḥāt al-Kufrah 164-165 J 4
Kougaberge 174-175 EF 7
Kougarivier 174-175 F 7
Kougarok Mount 58-59 E 4
Kouilou 172 B 2
Koukdjuak River 56-57 W 4
Koula-Moutou 172 B 2
Koulen 148-149 DE 4
Koulikoro 164-165 C 6
Koumantou 168-169 D 3
Koumass = Kumasi 164-165 D 7
Koumbia 168-169 E 3
Koumra 164-165 H 7
Koundian 168-169 C 2
Koun-Fao 168-169 E 4
Koungheul 164-165 B 6
Kouniana 168-169 D 2
Kounradskij 132-133 O 8
Kountze, TX 76-77 G 7
Kouoro 168-169 D 3
Koup 174-175 D 7
Koup, Die — 174-175 E 7
Kou-pang-tzŭ = Goubangzi 144-145 CD 2
Koupéla 164-165 D 6
Kourba = Qurbah 166-167 M 1
Kourou 92-93 J 3
Kourouninkoto 168-169 C 2
Kouroussa 164-165 BC 6
Koutiala 164-165 C 6
Kouveld Berge = Koueveldberge 174-175 EF 7
Kouvola 116-117 M 7
Kouyou 172 BC 2
Kovdor 132-133 DE 4
Kovdozero 116-117 OP 4
Kovel' 124-125 E 8
Kovero 116-117 O 6
Kovik 56-57 V 5
Kovilpatti 140 C 6
Kovl'ar 126-127 M 6
Kovno = Kaunas 124-125 DE 6
Kovpyta 126-127 E 1
Kovrov 132-133 G 6
Kovūr 140 DE 3
Kovvūr 140 E 2
Kōvvūru = Kovūr 140 DE 3
Kovylkino 124-125 O 6
Kovža [SU, place] 124-125 L 3
Kovža [SU, river] 124-125 L 3
Kovžinskij Zavod 124-125 L 3
Kowas 174-175 BC 2
Kowloon 142-143 LM 7
Kowloon Bay 155 I b 2
Kowloon-Chung Wan 155 I a 1
Kowloon-Hung Hom 155 I b 2
Kowloon-Kau Lung Tong 155 I b 1
Kowloon-Pak Uk 155 I b 1
Kowloon-Sham Shui Po 155 I a 2
Kowloon-Tsim Sha Tsui 155 I a 2
Kowloon-Yau Mai Ti 155 I a 2
Kowŏn 142-143 O 4
Ko Yai 150-151 C 9
Kōyalkuṇtalā = Koilkuntla 140 D 3
Koyama, Tōkyō- 155 III b 2
Kōyaṁpattūr = Coimbatore 134-135 M 8
Ko Yao Yai 150-151 B 9
Köyceğiz = Yüksekkum 136-137 C 4
Kōyilpaṭṭi = Kovilpatti 140 C 6
Kōyikōṭa = Calicut 134-135 LM 8
Koyna 140 A 2
Koyuk, AK 58-59 G 4
Koyuk River 58-59 FG 4
Koyukuk, AK 58-59 HJ 4
Koyukuk, Middle Fork — 58-59 M 3
Koyukuk, North Fork — 58-59 M 3
Koyukuk, South Fork — 58-59 M 3
Koyukuk Island 58-59 J 4
Koyukuk River 56-57 EF 4
Koyulhisar 136-137 GH 2
Köyyeri 136-137 G 3
Koža [SU, river] 124-125 M 2
Kozan 136-137 F 4
Kozánē 122-123 J 5
Kozara 122-123 G 3
Kozelec 126-127 E 1
Kozel'ščina 126-127 F 2
Kozel'sk 124-125 K 6
Kozi 171 DE 3
Koźle 118 HJ 3
Kozloduj 122-123 K 4
Kozlovka [SU, Čuvašskaja ASSR] 124-125 QR 6
Kozlovka [SU, Voronežskaja Oblast'] 126-127 K 1
Kozlovo [SU ↘ Kalinin] 124-125 KL 5
Kozlovo [SU → Vyšnij Voloč'ok] 124-125 K 5
Kozluk = Hazo 136-137 J 3
Koz'mino [SU ↗ Kotlas] 124-125 QR 3
Koz'mino [SU ↘ Nachodka] 144-145 J 1
Koz'modemjansk [SU, Jaroslavskaja Oblast'] 124-125 M 5
Koz'modemjansk [SU, Marijskaja ASSR] 124-125 Q 5
Kožozero 124-125 M 2
Kožuchovo, Moskva- 113 V c 3
Kozukue, Yokohama- 155 III a 2
Kōzu-shima 144-145 M 5
Kožva 132-133 K 4
Kpalimé 164-165 E 7
Kpandu 164-165 DE 7
Kra, Isthmus of — = Kho Kot Kra 148-149 CD 4
Kra, Kho Khot — 148-149 CD 4
Kraainem 128 II b 1
Kraairivier 174-175 G 6
Kraankuil 174-175 F 5
Krabbé 106-107 G 6
Krabi 148-149 C 5
Kra Buri 148-149 C 4
Krachar 150-151 DE 6
Kragerø 116-117 C 8
Kragujevac 122-123 J 3
Krai, Kuala — 148-149 D 5
Krailling 130 II a 2
Krakatao = Anak Krakatau 148-149 DE 8
Krakatau, Anak — 148-149 DE 8
Krakor 150-151 DE 6
Kraków 118 JK 3
Kralanh 150-151 D 6
Kralendijk 64-65 N 9
Kraljevo 122-123 J 4
Kramat Jati, Jakarta- 154 IV b 2
Kramatorsk 126-127 H 2
Krambit 150-151 D 10
Kramfors 116-117 G 6
Krampnitz 130 III a 2
Krampnitzsee 130 III a 2
Kranichstein, Darmstadt- 128 III b 2
Kranichstein, Staatsforst — 128 III b 2
Kranidion 122-123 K 7
Kranj 122-123 F 2
Kranji 154 III a 1
Kransfontein 174-175 H 5
Kranskop [ZA, mountain] 174-175 H 4
Kranskop [ZA, place] 174-175 J 5
Kranzberg [Namibia] 174-175 A 1
Krapina 122-123 FG 2
Krapivna [SU, Smolenskaja Oblast'] 124-125 JK 6
Kras 122-123 EF 3
Krasavino 132-133 GH 5
Krasilov 126-127 C 2
Krasilovka 126-127 DE 1
Kraskino 144-145 H 1
Krāslava 124-125 F 6
Krasnaja Gora [SU, Br'anskaja Oblast'] 124-125 HJ 7
Krasnaja Gorbatka 124-125 NO 6
Krasnaja Pol'ana [SU Kirovskaja Oblast'] 124-125 S 5
Krasnaja Pol'ana [SU Krasnodarskaja Oblast'] 126-127 K 5
Krasnaja Sloboda 124-125 F 7
Kraśnik 118 L 3
Krasnoarmejsk [SU, Kazachskaja SSR] 132-133 MN 7
Krasnoarmejsk [SU, Saratovskaja Oblast'] 126-127 M 1
Krasnoarmejsk, Volgograd- 126-127 M 2
Krasnoarmejskaja 126-127 J 4
Krasnoarmejskij 126-127 L 3
Krasnoarmejskoje = Červonoarmejskoje 126-127 GH 3
Krasnoborsk 124-125 P 3
Krasnodar 126-127 J 4
Krasnodon 126-127 JK 2
Krasnofarfornyj 124-125 HJ 4
Krasnogorodskoje 124-125 G 5
Krasnogorsk 124-125 L 5-6
Krasnogorskij 124-125 R 5
Krasnogorskoje 124-125 T 5
Krasnograd 126-127 G 2
Krasnogvardejsk 134-135 K 3
Krasnogvardejsk = Gatčina 132-133 DE 6
Krasnogvardejskoje [SU, Rossijskaja SFSR Stavropol'skaja Oblast'] 126-127 KL 4
Krasnogvardejskoje [SU, Rossijskaja SFSR Voronežskaja Oblast'] 126-127 HJ 1
Krasnogvardejskoje [SU, Ukrainskaja SSR] 126-127 G 4
Krasnoil'sk = Mežirečje 126-127 B 2
Krasnoj Armii, proliv — 132-133 ST 1
Krasnojarsk 132-133 R 6
Krasnoje [SU, Rossijskaja SFSR Kirovskaja Oblast'] 124-125 QR 4
Krasnoje [SU, Rossijskaja SFSR Lipeckaja Oblast'] 124-125 M 7
Krasnoje [SU, Rossijskaja SFSR Vologodskaja Oblast'] 124-125 O 4
Krasnoje [SU, Ukrainskaja SSR] 126-127 B 2
Krasnoje Selo 124-125 GH 4
Krasnokamensk 132-133 W 7-8
Krasnokamsk 132-133 K 6
Krasnokutsk 126-127 G 1
Krasnolesnyj 124-125 M 8
Krasnonamenskij 132-133 M 7
Krasnookt'abr'skij [SU, Marijskaja ASSR] 124-125 Q 5
Krasnookt'abr'skij [SU, Volgogradskaja Oblast'] 126-127 M 2
Krasnookt'abr'skij, Moskva- 113 V b 2
Krasnopavlovka 126-127 H 2
Krasnoperekopsk 126-127 FG 3-4
Krasnopolje [SU, Belorusskaja SSR] 124-125 H 7
Krasnopolje [SU, Ukrainskaja SSR] 126-127 G 1
Krasnosel'kup 132-133 OP 4
Krasnoslobodsk [SU, Mordovskaja ASSR] 124-125 O 6
Krasnoslobodsk [SU, Volgogradskaja Oblast'] 126-127 M 2
Krasnoturjinsk 132-133 L 5-6
Krasnoufimsk 132-133 K 6
Krasnoural'sk 132-133 L 6
Krasnovišersk 132-133 K 5
Krasnovodsk 134-135 G 2-3
Krasnovodskoje plato 134-135 G 2
Krasnoyarsk = Krasnojarsk 132-133 R 6
Krasnozatonskij 124-125 ST 3
Krasnozavodsk 124-125 LM 5
Krasnyj = Možga 132-133 J 6
Krasnyj Bogatyr' 124-125 N 5
Krasnyj Cholm 124-125 L 4
Krasnyj Čikoj 132-133 UV 7
Krasnyj Dolginec 126-127 P 4
Krasnyje Baki 124-125 P 5
Krasnyje Četai 124-125 Q 6
Krasnyje Okny 126-127 D 3
Krasnyje Tkači 124-125 MN 5
Krasnyj Jar [SU, Astrachanskaja Oblast'] 126-127 NO 3
Krasnyj Jar [SU, Kujbyševskaja Oblast'] 124-125 S 7
Krasnyj Jar [SU, Volgogradskaja Oblast'] 126-127 M 1
Krasnyj Kut 126-127 N 1
Krasnyj Liman 126-127 HJ 2
Krasnyj Luč 126-127 J 2
Krasnyj Okt'abr' [SU, Vladimirskaja Oblast'] 124-125 M 5
Krasnyj Okt'abr' [SU, Volgogradskaja Oblast'] 126-127 M 2
Krasnyj Profintern 124-125 MN 5
Krasnyj Rog 124-125 J 7
Krasnyj Steklovar 124-125 R 5
Krasnyj Stroitel, Moskva- 113 V c 3
Krasnyj Sulin 126-127 K 3
Krasnyj Tekstil'ščik 126-127 M 1
Krasnyj Voschod 124-125 NO 6
Krasnystaw 118 L 3
Kratié 148-149 E 4
Krau 150-151 D 11
Krau, Kuala — 150-151 D 11
Krauchmar 150-151 E 6
Kraulshavn = Nûgssuaq 56-57 YZ 3
Kravanh, Phnom — 150-151 D 6-7
Krawang 148-149 E 8
Krawang, Tanjung — 152-153 G 8
kr'až Čekanovskogo 132-133 XY 3
kr'až Vetrenyj Pojas 124-125 K-M 2
Kreb Chehiba = Karab Shahibīyah 166-167 C 6
Krebs, OK 76-77 G 5
Krebu = Kamparkalns 124-125 D 5
Krečetovo 124-125 M 3
Krečevicy 124-125 HJ 4
Kreefte Bay = Groenriviermond 174-175 B 6
Kreewu kalns = Krievu kalns 124-125 CD 5
Krefeld 118 BC 3
Kreider = Al-Khaydar 166-167 G 2
Krekatok Island 58-59 D 5
Kremenčug 126-127 F 2
Kremenčugskoje vodochranilišče 126-127 EF 2
Kremenec 126-127 BC 1
Kreml' 113 V c 2
Kremlin-Bicêtre 129 I c 2
Kremmling, CO 68-69 C 5
Kremnica 118 J 4
Krems 118 G 4
Krenachich, El — = El Khenachich 164-165 D 4
Krenachich, Oglat — = Oglat Khenachich 164-165 D 4
Krēnē = Çeşme 136-137 B 3
Krenitzin Islands 58-59 no 3
Kress, TX 76-77 D 5
Kresta, zaliv — 132-133 k 4
Krestcy 124-125 HJ 4
Krestovaja guba 132-133 H-K 3
Krestovyj, pereval — 126-127 M 5
Kresty [SU, Moskovskaja Oblast'] 124-125 L 6
Krētē 122-123 L 8
Kretinga 124-125 C 6
Kreuzberg, Berlin- 130 III b 2
Kribi 164-165 F 8
Kričev 124-125 H 7
KXVIII Ridge 50-51 O 7
Kriel 174-175 H 4
Krieng 150-151 F 6
Krievu kalns 124-125 CD 5
Krige 174-175 C 8
Kriós, Akrōtērion — 122-123 K 8
Krishna 134-135 M 7
Krishna Delta 134-135 N 7
Krishnagiri 140 D 4
Krishnanagar 138-139 M 6
Krishnapur 138-139 M 5
Krishnarāja Sāgara 140 BC 4
Krishnarājapet 140 C 4
Kristiansand 116-117 BC 8
Kristianstad 116-117 F 9-10
Kristianstads län 116-117 E 9-F 10
Kristiansund 116-117 B 6
Kristiinankaupunki = Kristinestad 116-117 J 6
Kristineberg 116-117 H 5
Kristinehamn 116-117 EF 8
Kristinestad 116-117 J 6
Kriva Palanka 122-123 JK 4
Krivaja kosa 126-127 HJ 3
Kriviči 124-125 F 6
Krivoi Rog = Krivoj Rog 126-127 F 3
Krivoj Pojas 124-125 LM 2
Krivoj Rog 126-127 F 3

Krivoy Rog = Krivoj Rog 126-127 F 3
Kříz 166-167 L 2
Križevci [YU, Bilo gora] 122-123 G 2
Krk 122-123 F 3
Krnov 118 HJ 3
Krochino 124-125 M 3
Kroh 150-151 C 10
Krohnwodoke = Nyaake 164-165 C 8
Krokodilrivier [ZA ◁ Marico] 174-175 G 3
Krokodilrivier [ZA ◁ Rio Incomáti] 174-175 J 3
Krokodilsbrug 174-175 JK 3
Krok Phra 150-151 BC 5
Kroksfjardharnes 116-117 c 2
Krolevec 126-127 F 1
Kromdraai [ZA ↘ Standerton] 174-175 H 4
Kromdraai [ZA ↖ Witbank] 174-175 H 3
Kromme Mijdrecht [NL, place] 128 I a 2
Kromme Mijdrecht [NL, river] 128 I a 2
Kromme River = Kromrivier 174-175 C 6
Kromrivier [ZA, place] 174-175 E 6
Kromrivier [ZA, river] 174-175 C 6
Kromy 124-125 K 7
Krong Po'kô = Dak Po'kô 150-151 F 5
Kronoberg 116-117 EF 9
Kronockaja sopka = Velikaja Kronockaja sopka 132-133 ef 7
Kronockij, mys — 132-133 f 7
Kronockij zaliv 132-133 f 7
Kronoki 132-133 f 7
Kronprins Christians Land 52 AB 20-21
Kronprinsesse Mærtha land 53 B 35-1
Kronprins Frederiks Bjerge 56-57 de 4
Kronprins Olav land 53 C 5
Kronštadt 124-125 G 3-4
Kroonstad 172 E 7
Kropotkin 126-127 K 4
Krosno 118 K 4
Krosno Odrzańskie 118 G 2-3
Krotoszyn 118 H 3
Krotovka 124-125 S 7
Krottingen = Kretinga 124-125 C 6
Krotz Springs, LA 78-79 D 5
Kroya 152-153 H 9
Krueng Teunom 152-153 AB 3
Kruger National Park 172 F 6-7
Krugers 174-175 F 5
Krugersdorp 172 E 7
Krugloi Point 58-59 pq 6
Krugloje 124-125 G 6
Kruglyži 124-125 QR 4
Krui 148-149 D 8
Kruidfontein 174-175 D 7
Kruis, Kaap — 172 B 6
Krujë 122-123 HJ 5
Krukut, Kali — 154 IV a 2
Krulevščina 124-125 FG 6
Krummensee [DDR] 130 III c 1
Krung Thep, Ao — 150-151 C 6
Krupki 124-125 G 6
Krupunder See 130 I a 1
Krusenstern, Cape — 58-59 EF 3
Kruševac 122-123 J 4
Kruševo 122-123 J 5
Krutaja 124-125 U 2
Krutec 124-125 M 3
Kruzof Island 58-59 v 8
Krylatskoje, Moskva- 113 V ab 2
Krylovskaja ↑ Tichoreck 126-127 JK 3
Krym 126-127 FG 4
Krymsk 126-127 HJ 4
Krymskaja Oblast' 126-127 FG 4
Krymskije gory 126-127 FG 4
Krymskij zapovednik 126-127 G 4
Krynica 118 K 4
Krzyż 118 H 2

Ksabi = Al-Qaṣābī [DZ] 166-167 F 5
Ksabi = Al-Qaṣābī [MA] 166-167 D 3
Ksar ben Khrdache = Banī Khaddāsh 166-167 LM 3
Ksar-Chellala = Qaṣr Shillalah 166-167 H 1
Ksar-el-Boukhari = Qaṣr al-Bukharī 164-165 E 1
Ksar el Kebir = Al-Qaṣr al-Kabīr 164-165 C 1
Ksar es Seghir = Al-Qaṣr aṣ-Ṣaghīr 164-165 D 2
Ksar es Souk = Al-Qaṣr as-Sūq 164-165 K 2
Ksel, Djebel — = Jabal Kasal 166-167 G 3
Ksenjevka 132-133 WX 7
Kseur, El — = Al-Qaṣr 166-167 J 1
Kshatrapur = Chatrapur 138-139 K 8
Kshwan Mountain 60 C 2
Ksiba, el — = Al-Q'sībah 166-167 CD 3
Ksoum, Djebel el — = Jabal al-Kusūm 166-167 J 2
Ksour = Al-Quṣūr 166-167 L 2
Ksour, Monts des — = Jibāl al-Quṣūr 166-167 FG 3
Ksour Essaf = Quṣūr as-Sāf 166-167 M 2
Ksour Sidi Aïch = Quṣūr Sīdī 'Aysh 166-167 L 2
Kstovo 124-125 P 5
Ksyl-Orda = Kzyl-Orda 132-133 M 8-9
Ktēma 136-137 E 5
Ktesiphon 136-137 L 6
Ktima = Ktēma 136-137 E 5

Kuah 150-151 BC 9
Kuai He 146-147 F 5
Kuaiji Shan = Guiji Shan 146-147 H 7
Kuala 150-151 B 11
Kuala Belait 148-149 F 6
Kuala Brang 148-149 D 5-6
Kuala Dungun 148-149 D 6
Kuala Gris 150-151 D 10
Kuala Kangsar 148-149 CD 6
Kualakapuas 148-149 F 7
Kuala Kelawang 150-151 D 11
Kuala Ketil 150-151 C 10
Kuala Krai 148-149 D 5
Kuala Krau 150-151 D 11
Kuala Kubu Baharu 150-151 C 11
Kualakurun 152-153 K 6
Kualalangsa 148-149 C 6
Kuala Lipis 150-151 D 10
Kuala Lumpur 148-149 D 6
Kuala Marang 150-151 D 10
Kuala Masai 154 III b 1
Kuala Merang 148-149 D 5
Kuala Nal 150-151 CD 10
Kuala Nerang 150-151 C 9
Kualapembuang 152-153 K 7
Kualaperbaungan = Rantaupanjang 150-151 B 11
Kuala Perlis 148-149 CD 5
Kuala Pilah 150-151 D 11
Kuala Rompin 150-151 D 11
Kuala Selangor 148-149 D 6
Kuala Setiu = Setiu 150-151 D 10
Kualasimpang 152-153 B 3
Kuala Trengganu 148-149 DE 5
Kualu, Sungai — 150-151 BC 11
Kuamut 152-153 M 3
Kuan = Gu'an 146-147 F 2
Kuancheng 144-145 B 2
Kuan Chiang = Guan Jiang 146-147 C 9
Kuandang 148-149 H 6
Kuandang, Teluk — 152-153 P 5
Kuandian 144-145 E 2
Kuang-an = Guang'an 142-143 K 5
Kuang-ch'ang = Guangchang 142-143 M 6
Kuangchou = Guangzhou 142-143 L 7
Kuang-chou Wan = Zhanjiang Gang 142-143 L 7
Kuang-fêng = Guangfeng 146-147 G 7
Kuang-hai = Guanghai 142-143 L 7
Kuang-hsi = Guangxi Zhuangzu Zizhiqu 142-143 KL 7
Kuang-hsin = Shangrao 142-143 M 6
Kuang-jao = Guangrao 146-147 G 3
Kuang-ling = Guangling 146-147 E 2
Kuang-lu Tao = Guanglu Dao 144-145 D 3
Kuang-nan = Guangnan 142-143 JK 7
Kuang-ning = Guangning 146-147 D 10
Kuango = Kwango 172 C 2-3
Kuang-p'ing = Guangping 146-147 E 3
Kuang-shan = Guangshan 146-147 E 5
Kuang-shui = Guangshui 146-147 E 6
Kuangsi = Guangxi Zhuangzu Zizhiqu 142-143 KL 7
Kuang-tê = Guangde 146-147 G 6
Kuang-tsê = Guangze 146-147 F 8
Kuangtung = Guangdong 142-143 L 7
Kuang-yüan = Guangyuan 142-143 K 5
Kuanhsien = Guan Xian 146-147 E 3
Kuan-shan = Lilung 146-147 H 10
Kuantan 148-149 D 6
Kuantan, Batang — = Batang Inderagiri 148-149 D 7
Kuan-t'ao = Guantao 146-147 E 3
K'uan-tien = Kuandian 144-145 E 2
Kuan-t'ou Chiao = Guantou Jiao 150-151 G 2
Kuan-tung Pan-tao = Guandong Bandao 144-145 C 3
Kuan-yang = Guanyang 146-147 C 9
Kuan-yin-t'ang = Guanyintang 146-147 CD 4
Kuan-yün = Guanyun 142-143 MN 5
Kub [SU] 126-127 V 4
Kub [ZA] 174-175 B 3
Kuba [C] 64-65 KL 7
Kuba [SU] 126-127 O 6
Kuban' 126-127 J 4
Kubango = Rio Cubango 172 C 5
Kubaysah 136-137 K 6
Kubbar, Jazīrat — 136-137 N 8
Kubbum 164-165 J 6
Kubena 124-125 N 3
Kubenskoje 124-125 M 4
Kubenskoje, ozero — 124-125 M 4
Kuberle 126-127 KL 3
Kubiskowberge 174-175 C 6
Kubli Hill 168-169 FG 3
Kubn'a 124-125 Q 6
Kubokawa 144-145 J 6
Kubolta 126-127 C 2
Kuboos = Richtersveld 174-175 B 5
Kubu Bahru = Kuala Kubu Baharu 150-151 C 11
Kubumesaai 152-153 L 5
Kučevo 122-123 J 3
Kucha 142-143 E 3
Kuchāman 138-139 E 4
Ku-chang = Guzhang 146-147 BC 7
Kuche = Kucha 142-143 E 3
Ku-chên = Guzhen 146-147 F 5
Kucheng = Gucheng 146-147 C 5
Ku-ch'êng = Gucheng 146-147 EF 3
Kuchengtze = Qitai 142-143 FG 3
Ku-chiang = Gujiang 146-147 E 8
Kuchinarai 150-151 E 4
Kuchinda 138-139 K 7
Kuching 148-149 F 6
Kuchinoerabu-jima 144-145 GH 7
Kuchino-shima 144-145 G 7
Kuchow = Quzhou 146-147 E 3
Ku-chu = Guzhu 146-147 E 10
Küçük Ağrı dağı 136-137 L 3
Küçükbakkal 154 I b 3
Küçükköy 154 I a 2
Küçüksu = Kotum 136-137 K 3
Küçükyozgat = Elma dağı 136-137 E 3
Kuda 138-139 C 6
Kūdachi 140 B 2
Kudahuvadu Channel 176 a 2
Kudāl 140 A 2-3
Kuḍaligī = Kūdligi 140 C 3
Kudamatsu 144-145 H 5-6
Kudat 148-149 G 5
Kuḍḍlā = Kandla 134-135 L 6
Kudelstaart 128 I a 2
Kudever' 124-125 G 5
Kudiakof Islands 58-59 b 2
Kudiraimukha = Kudremukh 140 B 4
Kūdligi 140 C 3
Kudō = Taisei 144-145 ab 2
Kudobin Islands 58-59 c 1
Kudremukh 140 B 4
Kūdūk 164-165 L 6-7
Kudumalapshwe 174-175 F 2
Kudus 152-153 J 9
Kudymkar 132-133 JK 6
Kuei-ch'i = Guixi 146-147 F 7
Kuei Chiang = Gui Jiang 146-147 C 9-10
Kuei-ch'ih = Guichi 142-143 M 5
Kueichou = Guizhou 142-143 JK 6
Kuei-chou = Zigui 146-147 C 6
Kuei-lin = Guilin 142-143 KL 6
Kuei-p'ing = Guiping 142-143 KL 7
K'uei-t'an = Kuitan 146-147 E 10
Kuei-tê = Guide 142-143 J 4
Kuei-ting = Guiding 142-143 K 6
Kuei-tung = Guidong 146-147 D 8
Kuei-yang = Guiyang [TJ, Guizhou] 142-143 K 6
Kuei-yang = Guiyang [TJ, Hunan] 142-143 L 6
Kuerhlei = Korla 142-143 F 3
Kūfah, Al- 136-137 L 6
Kufra = Wāḥāt al-Kufrah 164-165 J 4
Kufrah, Wāḥāt al- 164-165 J 4
Kufra Oasis = Wāḥāt al-Kufrah 164-165 J 4
Küfre 136-137 K 3
Kufstein 118 F 5
Kugrua River 58-59 H 1
Kugruk River 58-59 F 4
Kugururok River 58-59 G 2
Kūh, Pīsh-e — 136-137 M 6
Kūhak 134-135 J 5
Kuh dağı = Kazandağ 136-137 K 3
Kūhdasht 136-137 M 6
Kūh-e Alvand 134-135 FG 4
Kūh-e Beyābān 134-135 H 5
Kūh-e Bozqūsh 136-137 M 4
Kūh-e Chelleh Khāneh 136-137 N 4
Kūh-e Dalāk 136-137 N 4
Kūh-e Damāvand 134-135 G 3
Kūh-e Darband 134-135 H 4
Kūh-e Dīnār 134-135 G 4
Kūh-e Ḥājī Sa'īd 136-137 M 4
Kūh-e Hazārān = Kūh-e Hezārān 134-135 H 5
Kūh-e Hezārān 134-135 H 5
Kūh-e-Ḥiṣṣar = Kōhe Ḥiṣār 134-135 K 4
Kūh-e Mānesht 136-137 M 6
Kūh-e Marzu 136-137 M 6
Kūh-e Mīleh 136-137 M 6
Kūh-e Mīshāb 136-137 L 3
Kūh-e Qal'eh 136-137 N 6
Kūh-e Qotbeh 136-137 M 6
Kūh-e Safīd = Kūh-e Sefīd 136-137 M 5-N 6
Kūh-e Sahand 136-137 M 4
Kūh-e Sefīd 136-137 M 5-N 6
Kūh-e Shāhān 136-137 LM 5
Kūh-e Sīāh = Kūh-e Marzu 136-137 M 6
Kūh-e Tafresh 136-137 NO 5
Kūh-e Taftān 134-135 J 5
Kūhhā-ye Chehel-e Chashmeh 136-137 M 5
Kūhhā-ye Sābālān 136-137 M 3
Kūhha-ye Ṭavālesh 136-137 MN 3
Kūhhā-ye Zāgros 134-135 F 3-4
Kūhīn 136-137 N 4
Kuhmo 116-117 NO 5
Kuibis = Guibes 174-175 B 4
Kuiepan 174-175 DE 4
Kuis 174-175 B 3
Kuiseb 174-175 B 2
Kuitan 146-147 E 10
Kuito 172 C 4
Kuitozero 116-117 O 5
Kuiu Island 56-57 K 6
Kuivaniemi 116-117 L 5
Kuja 132-133 G 4
Kujal'nickij liman 126-127 E 3
Kujang-dong 144-145 EF 3
Kujawy 118 J 2
Kujbyšev [SU, Kujbyševskaja Oblast'] 132-133 HJ 7
Kujbyšev [SU, Om'] 132-133 O 6
Kujbyšev [SU, Tatarskaja ASSR] 124-125 R 6
Kujbyševka-Vostočnaja = Belogorsk 132-133 YZ 7
Kujbyševo 126-127 J 3
Kujbyševskoje vodochranilišče 132-133 HJ 7
Kujeda 124-125 U 5
Kujgenkol' 126-127 NO 2
Kuji 142-143 R 3
Kujto, ozero — 132-133 E 5
Kujulik Bay 58-59 e 1
Kujumba 132-133 S 5
Kujū-san 144-145 H 6
Kuk 58-59 H 1
Kukaklek Lake 58-59 K 7
Kukami 174-175 E 3
Kukānār 140 E 1
Kukarka = Sovetsk 132-133 H 6
Kukatush 62 KL 2
Kukawa 164-165 G 6
Kuke 172 D 6
Kukiang = Qujiang 146-147 D 9
Kukkus = Privolžskoje 126-127 MN 1
Kukmor 124-125 S 5
Kukong 174-175 E 3
Kukpowruk River 58-59 F 2
Kukpuk River 58-59 DE 2
Kukshi 138-139 E 6
Kukukus Lake 70-71 E 1
Kukumane Kraal 174-175 F 2
Kuku Noor = Chöch nuur 142-143 H 4
Kukup 152-153 E 5
Kula [BG] 122-123 K 4
Kula [TR] 136-137 C 3
Kula [YU] 122-123 H 3
Kul'ab 134-135 K 3
Kulādan 141 C 5
Kulādan Myit 141 C 5
Ku-la-gauk = Kalagôk Kyûn 141 E 8
Kulagino 126-127 P 2
Kulai 150-151 D 12
Kulaiburu 138-139 K 6
Kulal 171 D 2
Kulaly, ostrov — 126-127 O 4
Kulāma Taunggyā 150-151 B 7
Kulambangra = Kolombangara 148-149 j 6
Kulanjīn 136-137 N 5
Kular, chrebet — 132-133 Z 4
Kulasekharapatnam 140 D 6
Kulasekharapaṭṭaṇam = Kulasekharapatnam 140 D 6
Kulaura 134-135 P 6
Kuldīga 124-125 CD 5
Kuldja = Gulja 142-143 E 3
Kuldo 60 CD 2
Kulebaki 124-125 O 6
Kulên, Phnom — 150-151 DE 6
Kulfo 168-169 G 3
Kulgera 158-159 F 5
Kulha Gangri 142-143 G 6
Kulhakangri = Kalha Gangri 138-139 N 3
Kulhakangri = Kulha Gangri 142-143 G 6
Kuligi 124-125 T 4
Kulik, Lake — [USA ↑ Kuskokwim River] 58-59 G 6
Kulik, Lake — [USA ↓ Kuskokwim River] 58-59 H 7
Kulikoro = Koulikoro 164-165 C 6
Kulikovka 126-127 E 1
Kulikovo Pole 124-125 LM 7
Kulim 150-151 C 10
Kulittalai 140 D 5
Kuliyāpiṭiya 140 DE 7
Kulja = Ghulja 142-143 E 3
Kullanchāvadi 140 DE 5
Kullen 116-117 E 9
Küllu 136-137 J 3
Kullū = Kulu 138-139 F 2
Küllük = Güllük 136-137 B 4
Kulm, ND 68-69 G 2
Kulmbach 118 E 3
Kuloj [SU, place] 124-125 O 3
Kuloj [SU, river] 124-125 O 3
Kulotino 124-125 J 4
Kulp 136-137 J 3
Kulpahār 138-139 G 5
Kulpawn 168-169 E 3
Kul'sary 132-133 J 8
Kulti 138-139 L 6
Kultuk 132-133 T 7
Kulu [IND] 138-139 F 2
Kulu [TR] 136-137 E 3
Kulu = Julu 146-147 E 3
Kuludu Faro 176 a 1
Kulukak Bay 58-59 H 7
Kulumadau 148-149 h 6
Kulunda 132-133 OP 7
Kulundinskaja step' 132-133 O 7
Kuḷuttalai = Kulittalai 140 D 5
Kulwin 160 F 5
Kum = Qom 134-135 G 4
Kuma [J] 144-145 J 6
Kuma [SU] 126-127 N 4
Kuma [TJ] 138-139 M 3
Kumagaya 144-145 M 4
Kumai 152-153 J 7
Kumai, Teluk — 148-149 F 7
Kumaishi 144-145 ab 2
Kumaka 98-99 J 3
Kumakahi, Cape — 78-79 e 3
Kumamba, Pulau-pulau — 148-149 LM 7
Kumamoto 142-143 P 5
Kumano 144-145 L 6
Kumano-nada 144-145 L 5-6
Kumanovo 122-123 JK 4
Kumārsaen = Kumhārsain 138-139 F 2
Kumasi 164-165 D 7
Kumaun 134-135 M 4
Kumayt, Al- 136-137 M 6
Kumba 164-165 F 8
Kumbakale 148-149 j 6
Kumbakonam 134-135 MN 8
Kumbe 148-149 LM 8
Kumbher 138-139 H 3
Kumbhir 141 C 3
Kumbukkan Oya 140 E 7
Kŭmch'ŏn 144-145 F 3
Kŭmch'ŏn = Kimch'ŏn 142-143 O 4
Kŭmē [SU] 141 E 5
Kumeny 124-125 RS 4
Kumertau 132-133 K 7
Kŭm-gang 144-145 F 4
Kŭmgang-san 144-145 FG 3
Kumhārsain 138-139 F 2
Kŭmhwa 144-145 F 3
Kumini-dake 144-145 H 6
Kumizawa, Yokohama- 155 III a 3
Kŭmje = Kimje 144-145 F 5
Kumla 116-117 F 8
Kumluca 136-137 D 4
Kummerfeld 130 I a 1
Kŭmnyŏng 144-145 F 6
Kumo 168-169 H 3
Kŭmo-do 144-145 FG 5
Kumo-Manyčskaja vpadina 126-127 K 3-M 4
Kumon Range = Kūmûn Taungdan 148-149 C 1
Kumphawapi 148-149 D 3
Kŭmsan 144-145 F 4
Kumta 140 B 3
Kumuch 126-127 N 5
Kumul = Hami 142-143 G 3
Kumund 138-139 J 7
Kūmûn Taungdan 148-149 C 1
K'um'urk'oj, gora — 126-127 O 7
Kuna River 58-59 J 2
Kunašir, ostrov — 132-133 c 9
Kunatata Hill 168-169 H 4
Kūnavaram 140 E 2
Kunayt, Al- 136-137 M 6
Kuncevo, Moskva- 124-125 L 6
Kunda [IND] 138-139 H 5
Kunda [SU] 124-125 F 4
Kundabwika Falls 171 B 5
Kuṅḍāpura = Condapoor 134-135 L 8
Kundelungu 172 E 3-4
Kundelungu, Parc National de — 171 AB 5
Kundgol 140 B 3
Kundiawa 148-149 M 8
Kundla 138-139 C 7
Kunduk = ozero Sasyk 126-127 DE 4
Kundur, Pulau — 148-149 D 6
Kunduz 134-135 K 3
Kunene 172 B 5
Kungā 138-139 M 7
Kung-ch'êng = Gongcheng 146-147 C 9
K'ung-ch'êng = Kongcheng 146-147 F 6
Kungej-Alatau, chrebet — 132-133 O 9
Kunghit Island 60 B 3
Kung-hsien = Gong Xian 146-147 D 4
Kung-hui = Gonghui 146-147 C 9
Kung-kuan = Gongguan 146-147 B 11
Kungliao 146-147 HJ 9
Kungok River 58-59 H 1
Kungrad 132-133 K 9
Kungsbacka 116-117 DE 9
Kung-shan = Gongshan 141 F 2
Kung Shui = Gong Shui 146-147 E 9
Kungu 172 C 1
Kungur 132-133 K 6
Kŭngyangŏn 141 E 7
Kung-ying-tsŭ = Gongyingzi 144-145 BC 2
Kunie = Île des Pins 158-159 N 4
Kunigal 140 C 4
Kuṇigala = Kunigal 140 C 4
Kunja 124-125 H 5
Kunlŏn 148-149 C 2
Kunlun Shan 142-143 D-H 4
Kunming 142-143 J 6
Kunming Hu 155 II a 2
Kunnamangalam 140 BC 5
Kunnamkulam 140 BC 5
Kunnūr = Coonor 140 C 5
Kunsan 142-143 O 4
Kunsan-man 144-145 F 5
Kunshan 146-147 H 6
Kunthī Kyûn 150-151 A 7
Kuntillā, Al- 173 D 3
Kunu 138-139 F 5
Kuṅwāri = Kunwāri 138-139 F 4
Kunwāri 138-139 F 4
K'ŭnyŏnp'yŏng-do = Tae-yŏnp'yŏng-do 144-145 E 4
Kunyu Shan 146-147 H 3
Kuocang Shan 146-147 H 7
Kuo Ho = Guo He 146-147 F 5
Kuo-hsien = Yuanping 146-147 D 2
Kuolisma 124-125 HJ 2
Kuopio 116-117 M 6
Kupa 122-123 FG 3
Kupang 148-149 H 9
Kup'ansk 126-127 H 2
Kupanskoje 124-125 M 5
Kup'ansk-Uzlovoj 126-127 HJ 2
Kuparuk River 58-59 N 1-2
Kupferteich 130 I b 1
Kupino 132-133 O 7
Kupiškis 124-125 E 6
Kuppili 140 FG 1
Kupreanof Island 56-57 K 6
Kupreanof Point 58-59 d 2
Kupreanof Strait 58-59 KL 7
Kura [SU ◁ Caspian Sea] 126-127 MN 6
Kura [SU ◁ Nogajskaja step'] 126-127 M 4
Kurā', Jabal al- 166-167 J 2
Kura-Araksinskaja nizmennost' 126-127 NO 6-7
Kurahashi-jima 144-145 J 5
Kuramo Waters 170 III b 2
Kuranami 155 III cd 3
Kurāndvād 140 B 2
Kurashiki 144-145 J 5
Kuratovo 124-125 R 3
Kuraymah 164-165 L 5
Kurayoshi 144-145 JK 5
Kurbali dere 154 I b 3
Kurchahan Hu = Chagan nuur 142-143 L 3
Kur Chhu 141 B 2
K'urdamir 126-127 O 6
Kurdeg 138-139 K 6
Kurdikos Naumiestis 124-125 D 6
Kurdistan = Kordestān 134-135 F 3
Kurdufān al-Janūbīyah 164-165 KL 6
Kurdufān ash-Shimālīyah 164-165 KL 5-6
Kurduvādi 140 B 1
Kure [J] 142-143 P 5
Küre [TR] 136-137 E 2
Kūreh-ye Meyāneh 136-137 M 5
Kurejka [SU, place] 132-133 PQ 4
Kurejka [SU, river] 132-133 QR 4
Kuremäe 124-125 F 4
Kuressaare = Kingisepp 124-125 D 4
Kurgan 132-133 M 6
Kurganinsk 126-127 K 4
Kurganovka 124-125 U 4
Kurgan-T'ube 134-135 KL 3
Kuria 208 H 2
Kuria Muria Island = Jazā'ir Khūrīyā Mūrīyā 134-135 H 7
Kuriate, Îles — = Jazā'ir Qūryāt 166-167 M 2
Kuṛigrām 138-139 M 5
Kurikka 116-117 JK 6
Kurikoma yama 144-145 N 3
Kuril Islands 142-143 S 3-T 2
Kurilovka 126-127 O 1
Kuril'sk 132-133 c 8
Kuril'skije ostrova 142-143 S 3-T 2
Kuril Trench 156-157 GH 2
Kurinskaja kosa 126-127 O 7
Kurinskaja Kosa = Kurkosa 126-127 O 7
Kurja 124-125 V 3
Kürkcü 136-137 E 4
Kurkino [SU, Moskva] 113 V a 2
Kurkosa 126-127 O 7
Kurkur 173 C 6
Kurle = Korla 142-143 F 3
Kurleja 132-133 WX 7
Kurlovskij 124-125 N 6
Kurmanajevka 124-125 ST 7
Kurman-Kemel'či = Krasnogvardejskoje 126-127 G 4
Kurmuk 164-165 L 6
Kurnell, Sydney- 161 I b 3
Kurnool 134-135 M 7
Kurobe 144-145 L 4
Kuroishi 144-145 N 2
Kuromatsunai 144-145 b 2
Kurosawajiri = Kitakami 144-145 N 3
Kuro-shima 144-145 G 7
Kurovskoje 124-125 M 6
Kurow [NZ] 161 CD 7
Kursavka 126-127 L 4
Kuršėnai 124-125 D 5
Kurseong 138-139 LM 4
Kursī 136-137 J 4
Kursk 124-125 KL 8
Kurskaja kosa 118 K 1
Kurskij zaliv 118 K 1
Kuršumlija 122-123 J 4
Kurşunlu [TR, Çankırı] 136-137 E 2
Kurtalan = Misriç 136-137 J 4
Kurthasanlı 136-137 E 3
Kūrtī 164-165 L 5
Kurtoğlu burnu 136-137 C 4
Kuru [IND] 138-139 K 6
Kurucaşile 136-137 E 2
Kuruçay 136-137 H 3
Kuruçeşme, İstanbul- 154 I b 2
Kurukkuchālai 140 D 6
Kurukshetra 138-139 F 3
Kuruman 172 D 7
Kuruman Heuvels 174-175 E 4
Kurume [J, Honshū] 155 III a 1
Kurume [J, Kyūshū] 144-145 H 6
Kurumkan 132-133 V 7
Kuruṇegala 134-135 MN 9
Kurung Tāl = Kurung Tank 138-139 J 6
Kurung Tank 138-139 J 6
Kurun-Ur'ach 132-133 a 6
Kurupa Lake 58-59 KL 2
Kurupa River 58-59 K 2
Kurupukari 92-93 H 4
Kuruskū, Wādī — 173 C 6
Kuryongp'o 144-145 G 5
Kus 150-151 E 7
Kuşadası 136-137 B 4
Kuşadası körfezi 136-137 B 4
Kusakaki-shima 144-145 G 7
Kusal = Kuusalu 124-125 E 4
Kusary 126-127 O 6
Kusatsu 144-145 KL 5
Kusawa Lake 58-59 T 6
Kusawa River 58-59 T 6
Kusaybah, Bi'r — 164-165 K 4
Kuščinskij 126-127 N 6
Kuščëvskaja 126-127 JK 3
Kusgölü 136-137 BC 2
Kushālgarh 138-139 E 6
Ku-shan = Gushan 144-145 D 3
Kusheriki 168-169 G 3
Kushih = Gushi 142-143 M 5
Kushikino 144-145 GH 7
Kushima 144-145 H 7
Kushimoto 144-145 K 6
Kushiro 142-143 RS 3
Kūshkak 136-137 NO 5
Kushtagi 140 C 3
Kushtaka Lake 58-59 PQ 6
Kushtia = Kushṭiyā 138-139 M 6
Kushṭiyā 138-139 M 6
Kushui 142-143 G 3
Kusilvak Mount 58-59 EF 6
Kusiro = Kushiro 142-143 RS 3
Kusiyārā 141 BC 3
Kuška 134-135 J 3
Kuskokwim, North Fork — 58-59 KL 5
Kuskokwim, South Fork — 58-59 KL 5
Kuskokwim Bay 56-57 D 6
Kuskokwim Mountains 56-57 EF 5
Kuskokwim River 56-57 DE 5
Kuskovo, Moskva- 113 V d 3
Kuşluyan 136-137 G 2
Kusmā 138-139 J 3
Kusmi 138-139 J 6
Kušmurun 132-133 LM 7
Kušnarenkovo 124-125 U 6
Kusnezk = Kuzneck 132-133 H 7
Kusŏng 144-145 E 2-3
Kustāgī = Kushtagi 140 C 3
Kustanaj 132-133 LM 7
Kustatan, AK 58-59 M 6
K'ustendil 122-123 K 4
Küstenkanal 118 CD 2
Kūstī 164-165 L 6
Kusu 144-145 H 6
Kušum 126-127 P 1
Kusūm, Jabal al- 166-167 J 2
Kusuman 150-151 E 4
Kusumba 154 II b 3
K'us'ur 132-133 Y 3
Kušva 132-133 K 6
Kūt, Al- 134-135 F 4
Kut, Ko — 148-149 D 4
Kūt 'Abdollāh 136-137 N 7
Kutacane 150-151 AB 11
Kütahya 134-135 BC 3
Kutai 148-149 G 6
Kutais 126-127 J 4
Kutaisi 126-127 L 5
Kut-al-Imara = Al-Kūt 134-135 F 4
Kutaradja = Banda Aceh 148-149 BC 5
Kutch 134-135 K 6
Kutch, Gulf of — 134-135 KL 6
Kutch, Rann of — 134-135 KL 6
Kutchan 144-145 b 2
Kutcharo-ko 144-145 d 2
Kutchi Hill 168-169 H 3
Kutien = Gutian 146-147 G 8
Kutina 122-123 G 3
Kutiyāna 138-139 BC 7
Kuṭiyāttam = Gudiyāttam 140 D 4
Kutkašen 126-127 N 6
Kutno 118 J 2
Kutru 138-139 H 8
Kutsing = Qujing 142-143 J 6
Kutta-jo Qabr 138-139 A 4
Kuttāttukulam 140 C 6
Kuttuparamb = Kūttuparamba 140 B 5
Kūttuparamba 140 B 5
Kuttyādi 140 B 5
Kutu 172 C 2
Kutubdia Island = Kutubdiyā Dīp 141 B 5
Kutubdiyā Dīp 141 B 5
Kutum 164-165 J 6
Kutunbul, Jabal — 134-135 E 7
Kutuzof, Cape — 58-59 c 1
Kuusalu 124-125 E 4
Kuusamo 116-117 N 5
Kuusankoski 116-117 M 7
Kuvandyk 132-133 K 7
Kuvšinovo 124-125 K 5
Kuwaima Falls 98-99 H 1-2
Kuwait 134-135 F 5
Kuwana 144-145 L 5
Kuwayt, Al- 134-135 F 5
Kuwo = Quwo 146-147 C 4
Kuyang = Quyang 146-147 E 2
Kuyeh = Juye 146-147 F 4
Kuye He 146-147 C 2
K'u-yeh Ho = Kuye He 146-147 C 2
Kūysanjaq 136-137 L 4
Kuyucak 136-137 C 4
Kuyung = Jurong 146-147 G 6
Kuyuwini River 98-99 J 3
Kužener 124-125 R 5
Kuženkino 124-125 J 5
Kuzguncuk, İstanbul- 154 I b 2
Kuzitrin River 58-59 EF 4
Kuz'minki, Moskva- 113 V cd 3
Kuz'movka 132-133 QR 5
Kuzneck 132-133 H 7
Kuzneckij Alatau 132-133 Q 6-7

Kuzneck-Sibirskij = Novokuzneck 132-133 Q 7
Kuznetsk = Kuzneck 132-133 H 7
Kuzomen' 132-133 F 5
Kuzucubelen 136-137 EF 4

Kvænangen 116-117 J 2
Kvailāndi = Quilāndi 140 B 5
Kvaløy 116-117 KL 2
Kvalsund 116-117 KL 2
Kvalvågen 116-117 k 6
Kvareli 126-127 MN 6
Kvarken 116-117 J 6
Kvarner 122-123 F 3
Kvarnerić 122-123 F 3
Kverkfjöll 116-117 ef 2
Kvichak, AK 58-59 J 7
Kvichak Bay 58-59 J 7
Kvichak River 58-59 J 7
Kvigtind 116-117 EF 5
Kvikne 116-117 D 6
Kvirily = Zestafoni 126-127 L 5
Kvitøya 116-117 no 4

Kwa 172 C 2
Kwabhaca 174-175 H 6
Kwaggablad 174-175 EF 4
Kwai 174-175 D 3
Kwair, Al — = Al-Quwayr 136-137 K 4
Kwakel, De — 128 I a 2
Kwakhanai 172 D 6
Kwakoegron 98-99 L 2
Kwakwani 98-99 JK 2
Kwakwasa 168-169 GH 3
Kwale 171 D 4
Kwa Mbonambi 174-175 K 5
Kwambonambi = Kwa Mbonambi 174-175 K 5
Kwamouth 172 C 2
Kwa Mtoro 171 CD 4
Kwangan = Guang'an 142-143 K 5
Kwangando 171 D 3
Kwangchang = Guangchang 142-143 M 6
Kwangch'on 144-145 F 4
Kwangchow = Guangzhou 142-143 L 7
Kwanghua = Guanghua 142-143 L 5
Kwangjao = Guangrao 146-147 G 3
Kwangju 142-143 O 4
Kwango 172 C 2-3
Kwangsi = Guangxi Zhuangzu Zizhiqu 142-143 KL 7
Kwangteh = Guangde 146-147 G 6
Kwangtseh = Guangze 146-147 F 8
Kwangtung = Guangdong 142-143 L 7
Kwangyuan = Guangyuan 142-143 K 5
Kwania, Lake — 171 C 2
Kwanmo-bong 144-145 G 2
Kwanto = Kantō 144-145 MN 4
Kwanyun = Guanyun 142-143 MN 5
Kwanza 172 C 3-4
Kwanza, Rio — 172 B 3
Kwara 164-165 E 6-F 7
Kwataboahegan River 62 KL 1
Kwatta 134-135 K 4
Kwazulu 172 F 7
Kwedia 174-175 F 3
Kweiang = Guiyang 142-143 K 6
Kweichih = Guichi 142-143 M 5
Kweichow = Fengjie 142-143 K 5
Kweichow = Guizhou 142-143 JK 6
Kweichow Island = Weizhou Dao 150-151 G 2
Kweichu = Guiyang 142-143 K 6
Kweilin = Guilin 142-143 KL 6
Kweiping = Guiping 142-143 KL 7
Kweiteh = Shangqiu 142-143 LM 5
Kweiyang = Guiyang 142-143 K 6
Kwekwe 172 E 5
Kwenge 172 C 3
Kwenlun = Kunlun Shan 142-143 D-H 4
Kwesang-bong 144-145 G 2
Kwethluk, AK 56-57 DE 5
Kwethluk River 58-59 G 6
Kwidzyn 118 J 2
Kwigillingok, AK 56-57 D 6
Kwigluk Island 58-59 E 7
Kwiguk, AK 58-59 E 5
Kwiha 164-165 MN 6
Kwikpak, AK 58-59 E 5
Kwilu 172 C 2
Kwinana 158-159 BC 6
Kwingauk 141 D 7
Kwinhagak = Quinhagak, AK 58-59 FG 7
Kwinitsa 60 C 2
Kwohsien = Juanping 146-147 D 2
Kwonai 168-169 G 3
Kwong Eng 152-153 LM 9
Kwonghoi = Guanghai 142-143 L 7
Kwun Tong 155 I b 2

Kyaikdôn 141 F 7-8
Kyaikhkamī 141 E 7
Kyaikhtau 141 DE 7
Kyaikhtīrō Burā 141 E 7
Kyaikkamī = Kyaikhkamī 141 E 7
Kyaiklat 141 D 7
Kyaikmaraw 141 EF 7
Kyaiktō 148-149 C 3
Kya-in = Kyā'inzeikkyī 141 EF 7
Kyā'inzeikkyī 141 EF 7
Kyaka 171 B 3
Kyancutta 158-159 G 6
Kyangdam 138-139 L 2
Kyangin 141 D 6
Ky Anh 150-151 F 3
Kyaring Tsho [TJ, Qinghai] 142-143 H 5
Kyaring Tsho [TJ, Xizang Zizhiqu] 142-143 F 5
Kyaukhpyū 141 C 6
Kyaukhsī 148-149 C 2
Kyaukkyī 141 E 6
Kyaukmè 141 E 4
Kyaukpandaung [BUR, Magwe Taing] 141 D 6
Kyaukpandaung [BUR, Mandale Taing] 141 D 5
Kyaukse = Kyaukhsī 148-149 C 2
Kyauksit 141 E 5-6
Kyauktan 141 E 7
Kyauktan = Kyaikhtau 141 DE 7
Kyauktau 141 C 5
Kyauktaw = Kyauktau 141 C 5
Kyaunggôn 141 D 7
Kybartai 124-125 D 6
Kydōniai = Ayvacık 136-137 B 3
Kyebang-san 144-145 G 4
Kyeindalī 141 D 6-7
Kyeintali = Kyeindalī 141 D 6-7
Kyezīmanzan 148-149 C 2
Kyid Chhu 138-139 N 3
Kyirong 138-139 K 3
Kykaukpyu = Kyaukhpyū 141 C 6
Kylâbyin 141 D 7
Kyle of Lochalsh 119 D 3
Kyllênē 122-123 J 7
Kýmē 122-123 L 6
Kymen lääni 116-117 MN 7
Kymijoki 116-117 M 7
Kynö = Kihnu 124-125 D 4
Kynuna 158-159 H 4
Kyôbingauk 141 DE 6
Kyoga, Lake — 172 F 1
Kyogami, Cape — = Kyōga-saki 144-145 K 5
Kyōga-saki 144-145 K 5
Kyogle 160 L 2
Kyŏmip'o = Songnim 142-143 O 4
Kyôn 141 E 5
Kyônbyau 141 D 7
Kyôndô 141 EF 7
Kyong = Kyôn 141 E 5
Kyôngadûn 141 D 7
Kyŏngan-ni 144-145 F 4
Kyôngdôn 148-149 CD 2
Kyŏnggi-do 144-145 F 4
Kyonghŭng 144-145 H 1
Kyŏngju 142-143 OP 4
Kyônglaung 141 C 5
Kyŏngnyŏlbi-yŏlto 144-145 E 4
Kyŏngsan 144-145 G 5
Kyŏngsang-pukto 144-145 G 4
Kyŏngsan-namdo 144-145 FG 5
Kyŏngsŏng 144-145 GH 2
Kyŏngsŏng = Sŏul 142-143 O 4
Kyŏngwŏn 144-145 H 1
Kyonpyaw = Kyônbyau 141 D 7
Kyōto 142-143 PQ 4
Kyparissia 122-123 J 7
Kyparissiakòs Kólpos 122-123 J 7
Kyrà Panagia 122-123 KL 6
Kyrēneia 136-137 E 5
Kyrenia = Kyrēneia 136-137 E 5
Kyrkanda 124-125 P 3
Kyrksæterøra 116-117 C 6
Kyrkslätt 116-117 L 7
Kyrönjoki 116-117 K 6
Kyštovka 132-133 O 6
Kyštym 132-133 L 6
Kysykkamys 126-127 P 2
Kýthēra 122-123 K 7
Kythêron, Stenòn — 122-123 K 7-8
Kýthnos 122-123 L 7
Kythréa 136-137 E 5
Kytyl-Žura 132-133 Y 5
Kyūgôk 148-149 C 2
Kyuguot Sound 60 D 5
Kyûndôn 141 DE 5
Kyûnhla 141 D 4
Kyuquot 60 D 4
Kyūshū 142-143 P 5
Kyushu Ridge 142-143 P 6-Q 7
Kyūshū sammyaku 144-145 H 6
Kyūsyū = Kyūshū 142-143 P 5
Kywèbwè 141 E 6
Kywong 160 H 5
Kyzyl 132-133 R 7
Kyzyl-Kija 134-135 L 2-3
Kyzylkum 132-133 LM 9
Kyzyl-Mažalyk 132-133 QR 7
Kyzylsu 134-135 L 3

Kzyl-Orda 132-133 M 9

L

Laa 118 H 4
La'ā', Al- = Al-Lu'ā'ah 136-137 L 7
La Adelia 106-107 EF 7
Laaer Berg 113 I b 2
La Alameda 76-77 CD 8
La Albufera 120-121 GH 9
La Alcarria 120-121 F 8
La Amarga, Laguna — 106-107 DE 7
La Angelina 106-107 E 5
La Antigua, Salina — 106-107 DE 2-3
Laar [B] 128 II b 1
La Aragonesa 108-109 E 7
La Argentina 106-107 H 4
La Armuña 120-121 DE 8
Laas'aanood 164-165 b 2
Laas Qoray 164-165 b 1
La Asturiana 106-107 E 6
La Asunción 92-93 G 2
Laaswarwar 164-165 bc 2
La Aurora 106-107 EF 1
Laba 168-169 G 2
La Babia 76-77 CD 8
la Baie 63 A 3
La Bajada 108-109 E 7
La Banda 111 D 3
La Bañeza 120-121 DE 7
La Barca 86-87 J 7
Labardén 106-107 H 6
La Barge, WY 66-67 HJ 4
La Barre, Balneario — 106-107 L 4
la Baule-Escoublac 120-121 F 5
Labbezanga 164-165 E 5-6
Labchhung Gangri 138-139 K 2
Labchhung Tsho 138-139 K 2
Labe [CS] 118 G 3
Labé [Guinea] 164-165 B 6
La Beba 106-107 G 5
Labelle 72-73 J 1
La Belle, FL 80-81 c 3
La Belle, MO 70-71 DE 5
Labengke, Pulau — 152-153 P 7
Laberge, Lake — 58-59 U 6
Laberinto, Punta — 106-107 FG 7
Labertino, Bahía del — = Adventures Sound 108-109 K 9
Labi 152-153 L 3
Labiar = Al Abyār 166-167 A 5
Labin 122-123 F 3
Labinsk 126-127 K 4
Labis 148-149 D 6
La Blanquilla, Isla — 92-93 G 2
La Boca 64-65 b 3
La Bomba 86-87 C 2
La Bonita 96-97 C 1
La Boquilla, Presa — 86-87 GH 4
Laborde 106-107 F 4
Labota 148-149 H 7
Labougle 106-107 HJ 3
Laboulaye 111 D 4
Labrador, Coast of — 56-57 YZ 6-7
Labrador Basin 50-51 G 3
Labrador City 56-57 X 7
Labrador Peninsula 56-57 V 6-Y 7
Labrador Sea 56-57 Y-a 5-6
La Brava, Laguna — 106-107 F 4
Lábrea 92-93 G 6
Labrieville 63 B 3
la Brive 128 II b 2
la Broquerie 61 KL 6
Labuan, Pulau — 148-149 FG 5
Labuha 148-149 J 7
Labuhan 148-149 E 8
Labuhanbajo 148-149 GH 8
Labuhanbatu 150-151 BC 11
Labuhanbilik 148-149 CD 6
Labuhan haji 152-153 B 4
Labuhanmarege 152-153 O 9
Labuk, Sungei — 152-153 M 2-3
Labuk, Teluk — 152-153 M 2
Labūttā 141 D 7
Labytnangi 132-133 M 4
Laĉa, ozero — 124-125 M 3
La Cabral 106-107 G 3
La Cal 104-105 G 6
Lac à la Croix 63 A 2
La Calandria 106-107 H 3
Lac Alaotra 172 J 5
Lac Albanel 62 P 1
La Caldera 104-105 D 9
La Calera 106-107 B 4
La California 106-107 FG 4
Lac-Allard 63 E 2
La Campiña [E, Andalucia] 120-121 E 10
La Campiña del Henares 120-121 F 8
La Cañada 106-107 F 1
La Canada Verde Creek 83 III d 2
La Candelaria 104-105 D 10
Lac Andou 72-73 H 1
La Canoa 94-95 JK 3
La Capilla 96-97 B 4
Lácar, Lago — 108-109 D 3
La Carlota [RA] 111 D 4
La Carlota, Aeropuerto — 91 II bc
La Carolina [E] 120-121 F 9
La Carolina [RA] 106-107 G 4
La Carreta 106-107 FG 6
Lac Assal 164-165 N 6
Lac Assinica 62 O 1
Lac Atticonipi 63 G 2
La Cautiva [BOL] 104-105 EF 6
La Cautiva [RA, Córdoba] 106-107 E 4
La Cautiva [RA, San Luis] 106-107 D 4
Lac aux Sangsues 72-73 GH 1
Lac Bertê 63 BC 2
Lac Bienville 56-57 W 6
Lac Bigot 63 D 2
Lac-Bouchette 62 P 2
Lac Boulain 63 F 3
Lac Briconnet 63 F 2
Lac Brochet 63 B 3
Lac Brochu 62 OP 2
Lac Bureau 62 O 2
Lac Cacaoui 63 C 2
Laccadive Islands 134-135 L 9
Lac Camachigama 62 NO 3
Lac Caribou = Rentiersee 56-57 Q 6
Lac Carrière 72-73 H 1
Lac Cayar = Ar-R'kīz 164-165 AB 5
Lac Chibougamau 62 OP 2
Lac Comencho 62 O 1
Lac Courte Oreilles Indian Reservation 70-71 E 3
Lac Debo 164-165 D 5
Lac Decelles 62 M 3
Lac de Guier 164-165 AB 5
Lac de la Robe Noir 63 E 2
Lac de la Surprise 62 O 2
Lac De Morhiban 63 E 2
Lac de Neuchâtel 118 C 5
Lac des Augustines 72-73 J 1
Lac des Bois 56-57 M 4
Lac des Eudistes 63 D 2
Lac des Mille Lacs 70-71 EF 1
Lac des Montagnes 62 O 1
Lac des Trente et un Milles 72-73 HJ 1
Lac du Bonnet 62 AB 2
Lac du Flambeau Indian Reservation 70-71 E 2-3
Lac du Male 62 O 2
Lac Dumoine 72-73 H 1
Lac-Édouard 62 PQ 3
La Ceiba [Honduras] 64-65 J 8
La Ceiba [YV] 92-93 E 3
La Ceja 94-95 D 5
Lacepede Islands 158-159 D 3
La Cesira 106-107 F 4
Lac Evans 62 N 1
Lacey, WA 66-67 B 2
Lac Faguibine 164-165 CD 5
Lac Fetzara = Buḥayrat Fazrārah 166-167 K 1
Lac Fittri 164-165 H 6
Lac Fleur de May 63 D 2
Lac Fonteneau 63 F 2
Lac Fournier 63 D 2
Lac-Frontiere 63 A 4
Lac Frotet 62 O 1
Lac Galle 63 G 2
Lac Garou 168-169 E 1
Lac-Gatineau 72-73 HJ 1
Lac Giffard 62 N 1
Lac Goéland 62 N 2
Lac Goyelle 63 F 2
Lac Grasset 62 MN 2
Lac Guéguen 62 N 2
Lachaqui 96-97 C 7
Lac Haribongo 168-169 E 1
La Chaux-de-Fonds 118 C 5
La Chauya Cocha 96-97 D 6
Lachdenpochja 124-125 GH 3
Lachhmangarh 138-139 F 4
Lachhmangarh Sīkar 138-139 E 4
Lachine 72-73 JK 2
Lachine, Canal — 82 I b 2
Lachine, Rapides de — 82 I b 2
La Chivera 91 II b 1
Lachlan River 158-159 HJ 6
La Chorrera [CO] 94-95 E 8
La Chorrera [PA] 64-65 b 3
L'achoviči 124-125 EF 7
Lac-Humqui 63 C 3
Lachute 72-73 JK 2
Lac Île à la Crosse 61 E 3
Lačin 126-127 N 7
la Ciotat 120-121 K 7
Lac Iro 164-165 HJ 7
La Cita 91 III c 1
La Citadelle 88-89 K 5
Lac Joseph 56-57 XY 7
Lackawanna, NY 72-73 G 3
Lac Kempt 72-73 JK 1
Lac Kenonisca 62 NO 1
Lac Kipawa 72-73 G 1
Lac Kisale 172 E 3
Lac Kivu 172 EF 2
Lac Kondiaronk 72-73 H 1
Lac Korarou 164-165 D 5
Lac la Bardeliere 62 OP 1
Lac la Biche 61 BC 3
Lac La Biche [CDN, place] 61 C 3
Lac la Croix 70-71 DE 1
Lac Lady Beatrix 62 N 1
Lac la Galissonnière 63 E 2
Lac la Hache 60 G 4
Lac la Martre 56-57 MN 5
Lac la Plonge 61 E 3
Lac la Ronge 56-57 Q 6
Lac la Ronge Provincial Park 61 F 3
Lac la Trêve 62 O 2
Lac Léopold II = Mai Ndombe 172 C 2
Lac Long 72-73 J 1
Lac Lucie 62 M 1
Lac Macamic 62 M 2
Lac Magpie 63 D 2
Lac Maicasagi 62 N 1
Lac Malartic 62 N 2
Lac Manicouagan 63 BC 2
Lac Manouane [CDN ↑ Québec] 63 A 2
Lac Manouane [CDN ← Québec] 72-73 J 1
Lac Manouanis 63 AB 2
Lac Marceau 63 CD 2
Lac Matagami 62 N 2
Lac Maunoir 56-57 M 4
Lac Maupertuis 62 PQ 1
Lac Memphremagog 72-73 KL 2
Lac Menaskwagama 63 EF 2
Lac Mesgouez 62 O 1
Lac Mishagomish 62 NO 1
Lac Mitchinamecus 72-73 J 1
Lac Mobutu-Sese-Seko 172 F 1
Lac Montcevelles 63 FG 2
Lac Musquaro 63 F 2
Lac Nemiscau 62 N 1
Lac Niangay 168-169 E 2
La Cocha 104-105 D 10
La Cocha, Laguna — 94-95 C 7
Lac Ogascanan 72-73 GH 1
Lac Olga 62 N 2
La Colina 106-107 G 6
Lacolle 72-73 K 2
La Colonia 108-109 C 6
La Colorada 86-87 EF 3
Lacombe 56-57 O 7
Lac Onangué 172 AB 2
La Concepción 92-93 E 2
Laconia, NH 72-73 L 3
Lac Onistagane 63 A 2
Lacoochee, FL 80-81 b 2
Lac Opataka 62 O 1
Lac Opatawaga 62 N 1
La Copelina 106-107 D 6
Lac Opémisca 62 O 1
La Copeta 106-107 G 6
La Cordobesa 106-107 J 4
La Coronilla 106-107 L 4
La Coruña 120-121 C 7
La Costa 106-107 D 4
la Courneuve 129 I c 2
Lac Parent 62 N 2
Lac Peribonca 63 A 2
Lac Piacouadie 63 A 2
Lac Plétipi 63 A 2
Lac Poisson Blanc 72-73 J 1-2
Lac Poulin de Courval 63 AB 3
Lac Poutrincourt 62 O 2
Lac Preissac 62 M 2
Lac Puskitamika 62 N 2
Lacq 120-121 G 7
Lac Quévillon 62 N 2
Lac qui Parle 68-69 H 3
La Crescent, MN 70-71 E 4
La Criolla 106-107 G 3
La Cristina 94-95 E 6
Lac R'kīz = Ar-R'kīz 164-165 AB 5
Lac Rohault 62 O 2
La Crosse, KS 68-69 G 6
Lacrosse, WA 66-67 E 2
La Crosse, WI 64-65 H 3
La Cruz [CO] 94-95 C 7
La Cruz [CR] 88-89 CD 9
La Cruz [MEX] 76-77 B 9
La Cruz [RA] 106-107 J 2
La Cruz [ROU] 106-107 JK 4
La Cruz de Taratara 94-95 G 2
Lac-Saguay 72-73 J 1
Lac Sainte-Louis 82 I a 2
Lac Saint François 72-73 L 2
Lac Saint-Jean 56-57 W 8
Lac Saint Patrice 72-73 H 1
Lac Saint-Pierre 72-73 K 1
Lac Seul 56-57 S 7
Lac Seul [CDN, place] 62 C 2
Lac Simard 72-73 G 1
Lacs Jolliet 62 N 1
Lac Soscumica 62 N 1
Lac Taureau 72-73 K 1
Lac Tauredu 62 OP 3
Lac Tchad 164-165 G 6
Lac Témiscamie 62 PQ 1
Lac Temiscouata 63 BC 4
Lac Tesecav 62 O 1
Lac Tumba 172 C 2
Lac Turgeon 62 M 2
La Cueva 94-95 E 2
La Culebra 94-95 H 3
Lacul Razelm 122-123 N 3
La Cumbre [RA] 106-107 E 3
La Cumbre [YV] 91 II b 1
Lac Upemba 172 E 3
Lac Waswanipi 62 N 2
Lac Woeonichi 62 O 1
Lac Woollett 62 P 1
Lada, Teluk — 152-153 F 9
Ladainha 102-103 LM 2
Ladākh 134-135 M 4
Ladākh Range 134-135 M 3-4
Ladan 126-127 F 1
Ladang, Ko — 150-151 B 9
La Danta 94-95 L 4
Ladário 102-103 D 3
Ladchhung 138-139 M 4
Ladder Creek 68-69 F 6
Laddonia, MO 70-71 E 6
Ladera Heights, CA 83 III b 2
La Desirade 88-89 Q 6
Lādhiqīyah, Al- 134-135 CD 3
Lâdik 136-137 FG 2
Ladiqiya, El — = Al-Lādhiqīyah 134-135 CD 3
Ladismith 172 D 8
Ladner 66-67 B 1
Lādnun 138-139 E 4
Ladoga, IN 70-71 G 6
Ladoga, Lake — = Ladožskoje ozero 132-133 E 5
La Dorada 92-93 E 3
La Dormida 106-107 D 4
Ladožskoje ozero 132-133 E 5
Ladrillero, Golfo — 108-109 AB 7
Ladrillero, Monte — 108-109 CD 9
Ladrones Peak 76-77 A 5
Ladron Mountains 76-77 A 5
Ladue River 58-59 R 5
La Dulce 106-107 H 7
La Dulce, Laguna — 106-107 D 7
L'ady [SU, Gor'kovskaja Oblast'] 124-125 P 5
L'ady [SU, Pskovskaja Oblast'] 124-125 G 4
Lady Beatrix, Lac — 62 N 1
Ladybrand 172 E 7
Lady Evelyn Lake 72-73 F 1
Lady Franklinfjord 116-117 k 4
Lady Frere 174-175 G 6
Lady Grey 174-175 G 6
Lady Newnes Ice Shelf 53 B 18-17
Ladysmith, WI 70-71 E 3
Ladysmith [CDN] 66-67 AB 1
Ladysmith [ZA] 172 EF 7
Lae [PNG] 148-149 N 8
La Eduvigis 104-105 G 10
Laeken, Parc de — 128 II b 1
Laem, Khao — 150-151 C 5
Laem Ko Lamphuk = Laem Talumphuk 150-151 C 8
Laem Ngop 150-151 D 6
Laem Pho 148-149 D 5
Laem Pracham Hiang 150-151 B 7
Laem Si 150-151 B 8
Laem Sing 150-151 CD 6
Laem Talumphuk 150-151 C 8
La Encantada, Cerro de — 64-65 C 5
La Ensenada 108-109 H 3
Lærdalsøyri 116-117 BC 7
La Escondida 104-105 G 10
La Esmeralda [CO, Amazonas] 94-95 J 6
La Esmeralda [CO, Meta] 94-95 F 6
La Esmeralda [PY] 111 D 2
La Esmeralda [YV] 94-95 F 3
Læsø 116-117 D 9
La Esperanza [BOL] 104-105 EF 4
La Esperanza [C] 88-89 DE 3
La Esperanza [CO] 94-95 a 2
La Esperanza [Honduras] 88-89 BC 7
La Esperanza [RA, La Pampa] 106-107 D 6
La Esperanza [RA, Río Negro] 108-109 E 3
La Estrada 120-121 C 7
La Estrella 106-107 D 6
Lafagu 168-169 G 3
La Falda 106-107 E 3
Lafayette, AL 78-79 G 4
La Fayette, GA 78-79 G 3
Lafayette, IN 64-65 J 3
Lafayette, LA 64-65 H 5-6
Lafayette, TN 78-79 FG 2
Lafayette Hill, PA 84 III b 1
la Fère 120-121 J 4
Laferrere, La Matanza- 110 III b 2
Lafia 164-165 F 7
Lafiagi 164-165 EF 7
Laflamme, Rivière — 62 N 2
la Flèche 120-121 GH 5
Laflèche [CDN, Quebec] 82 I c 2
Laflèche [CDN, Saskatchewan] 61 E 6
La Florencia 104-105 EF 9
La Florida [CO, Cundinamarca] 91 III a 2
La Florida [CO, Nariño] 94-95 C 7
La Florida [PE] 96-97 F 3
La Florida, Parque — 91 III b 2
La Follette, TN 78-79 G 2
Lafontaine, Parc — 82 I b 1
Laforest 62 L 3
La Forestal 111 E 2
La Fragua 111 D 3
Lafreriere Park 85 I a 2
la Frette 129 I b 2
La Fría 92-93 E 3
La Fuente de San Esteban 120-121 DE 8
La Gallareta 106-107 G 2
Lagan 116-117 E 9
Lagan' = Kaspijskij 126-127 N 4
la Garenne-Colombes 129 I bc 2
Lagarfljót 116-117 f 2
La Garita Mountains 68-69 C 6-7
Lagarterito 64-65 b 2
Lagarto 100-101 F 6
Lagarto = Palmas Bellas 64-65 a 2
Lagbar 168-169 B 2
Lageadinho 102-103 G 7
Lågen 116-117 CD 7
Lager Döberitz 130 III a 1
Laghi Amari = Al-Buḥayrat al-Murrat al-Kubrá 173 C 2
Laghouat = Al-Aghwāt 164-165 E 2
Lagi = Ham Tân 150-151 FG 7
Lagič 126-127 O 6
Lāgin 141 F 2
La Gleta = Ḥalq al-Wad 166-167 M 1
La Gloria [CO] 92-93 E 3
La Gloria [RA] 106-107 F 6
Lågneset 116-117 j 6
Lagoa Açu 100-101 B 2
Lagoa Amaramba = Lagoa Chiuta 172 G 4
Lagoa Bonita 102-103 EF 5
Lagoa Carapebus 102-103 M 5
Lagoa Chiuta 172 G 4
Lagoa Chuali 174-175 K 3
Lagoa Clara 100-101 C 7
Lagoa da Canoa 100-101 F 5
Lagoa da Rebeca 102-103 BC 1
Lagoa da Reserva 106-107 M 3
Lagoa da Tijuca 110 I ab 2
Lagoa de Araruama 102-103 L 5
Lagoa de Mostardas 106-107 M 3
Lagoa de Parnaguá 100-101 B 6
Lagoa de Prata 102-103 K 4
Lagoa do Caiuvá 106-107 LM 4
Lagoa do Capão do Poncho 106-107 MN 3
Lagoa do Pacheco 106-107 L 4
Lagoa do Peixe 106-107 M 3
Lagoa dos Barros 106-107 M 2
Lagoa dos Patos 111 F 4
Lagoa dos Quadros 106-107 MN 2
Lagoa Feia 92-93 L 9
Lagoa Gaíba 102-103 D 2
Lago Aiapuá 98-99 G 7
Lagoa Itapeva 106-107 MN 2
Lagoa Juparanã 100-101 DE 10
Lago Aluminé 106-107 B 7
Lagoa Mangueira 111 F 4
Lagoa Maricá 102-103 L 5
Lagoa Marrângua 174-175 L 3
Lago Amauã 92-93 G 5
Lagoa Mirim 111 F 4
Lago Aníbal Pinto 108-109 C 8-9
Lagoão 106-107 L 2
Lagoa Pequena 106-107 LM 3
Lagoa Piti 174-175 K 4
Lagoa Poelela 174-175 L 3
Lagoa Preta 100-101 D 8
Lago Arari 98-99 O 5
Lago Argentino 111 B 8
Lagoa Rodrigo de Freitas 110 I b 2
Lagoa Santa 102-103 L 3
Lagoa Uberaba 102-103 D 2
Lago Auquinco 106-107 C 6
Lagoa Vermelha 106-107 M 2
Lago Badajos 92-93 G 5
Lago Banamana 174-175 KL 2
Lago Blanco [RA] 108-109 D 5
Lago Blanco [RCH] 108-109 E 10
Lago Brava 106-107 C 2
Lago Buenos Aires 111 B 7
Lago Buenos Aires, Meseta del — 108-109 D 6
Lago Calafquen 108-109 C 2
Lago Canacari 98-99 J 6
Lago Cardiel 111 B 7
Lago Cardiel [RA, place] 108-109 D 7
Lago Chepelmut 108-109 F 10
Lago Club de Los Lagortos 91 III bc 2
Lago Cochrane 108-109 C 6
Lago Colhué Huapí 111 C 7
Lago Colico 106-107 AB 7
Lago Comprida = Lagoa Nova 92-93 J 4
Lago da Pedra 100-101 B 3
Lago de Chapala 64-65 F 7
Lagodechi 126-127 MN 6
Lago de Chungara 104-105 B 6
Lago de Coipasa 104-105 C 6
Lago de Erepecu 92-93 H 5
Lago de Gatún 64-65 b 2
Lagodei, El- = Qardho 134-135 F 9
Lago de Ilopango 88-89 B 8
Lago de Izabal 64-65 HJ 8
Lago de Junin 96-97 C 7
Lago del Budi 106-107 A 7
Lago de los Arroyos 104-105 D 3
Lago del Toro 108-109 C 8
Lago de Managua 64-65 J 9
Lago de Maracaibo 92-93 E 2-3
Lago de Nicaragua 64-65 JK 9
Lago de Pátzcuaro 86-87 JK 8
Lago de Poopó 92-93 F 8
Lago de San Luis 104-105 D 3
Lago de Texcoco 91 I cd 1
Lago de Valencia 92-93 F 2
Lago de Vilama 104-105 C 8
Lago de Xochimilco 91 I c 3
Lago di Bolsena 122-123 DE 4
Lago di Bracciano 122-123 DE 4
Lago di Como 122-123 C 2-3
Lago di Garda 122-123 D 3
Lago do Coari 98-99 G 6-7
Lago do Junco 100-101 B 3
Lago dos Cajueiros 100-101 CD 2
Lago Dulce 108-109 E 6
Lago Enriquillo 88-89 L 5
Lago Fagnano 108-109 EF 10
Lago Fontana 108-109 D 5
Lago Futalaufquen 108-109 CD 4
Lago General Carrera 108-109 CD 6
Lago General Vintter 108-109 D 4-5
Lago Ghio 108-109 D 6
Lago Grande 113 III a 2
Lago Grande do Curuai 98-99 L 6
Lago Huachi 104-105 E 4
Lago Huechulafquen 108-109 D 2
Lago Lácar 108-109 D 3
Lago Lagunillas 96-97 F 9
Lagolândia 102-103 H 1
Lago La Plata 108-109 D 5
Lago Llanquihue 111 B 6
Lago Madden 64-65 b 2
Lago Madruba 98-99 J 6
Lago Maggiore 122-123 C 2-3
Lago Mapiripán 94-95 EF 6
Lago Menéndez 108-109 D 4
Lago Menzalé = Buḥayrat al-Manzilah 173 BC 2
Lago Musters 111 BC 7
Lago Nahuel Huapí 111 B 6
Lagonegro 122-123 FG 5
Lago Niassa = Lake Malawi 172 F 4
Lago Novo 92-93 J 4
Lago Ofhidro 108-109 E 9
Lago O'Higgins 108-109 C 7
Lago Paciba 94-95 H 6
Lago Panguipulli 108-109 CD 2
Lago Pastos Grandes 104-105 C 7
Lago Pellegrini 106-107 CD 7
Lago Petén Itzá 86-87 Q 9
Lago Piorini 92-93 G 5
Lago Pitari 104-105 F 3
Lago Posadas 108-109 D 6
Lago Pozuelos 104-105 CD 8
Lago Presidente Ríos 108-109 B 6
Lago Pueyrredón 111 B 7
Lago Puyehue 108-109 C 3
Lago Quiroga 108-109 D 7
Lago Ranco 111 B 6
Lago Ranco [RCH, place] 108-109 C 3
Lago Rimachi 96-97 C 4
Lago Rogagua 92-93 F 7
Lago Rogoaguado 92-93 F 7
Lago Rupanco 108-109 CD 3
Lagos [P] 120-121 C 10
Lagos [WAN] 164-165 E 7
Lagos, Los — [RCH, administrative unit] 108-109 C 3-4
Lagos, Los — [RCH, place] 108-109 C 2
Lagosa 172 EF 3
Lago Salitroso 108-109 D 6
Lago San Martín 111 B 7
Lago San Nicolás 104-105 D 3
Lagos-Apapa 170 III b 2
Lagos-Apese 170 III b 2
Lagos de Moreno 64-65 F 7
Lagos-Ebute-Metta 170 III b 2
Lagos Harbour 170 III b 2
Lagos-Iddo 170 III b 2
Lagos-Iganmu 170 III b 2
Lagos-Ikoyi 170 III b 2
Lagos Island 170 III b 2

Lagos Lagoon 170 III b 2
Lagos-New Lagos 170 III b 1
Lagos-Surulere 170 III b 1
Lagosta = Lastovo 122-123 G 4
Lagos Terminus 170 III b 2
Lago Strobel 108-109 D 7
Lagos-Yaba 170 III b 1
Lago Tábua 100-101 C 2
Lago Tar 108-109 D 7
Lago Titicaca 92-93 F 8
Lago Todos los Santos 108-109 CD 3
Lago Toronto 86-87 GH 4
Lago Traful 108-109 D 3
Lago Trasimeno 122-123 DE 4
Lago Tromen 108-109 D 2
La Goulatte = Ḥalq al-Wad 166-167 M 1
la Goulette = Ḥalq al-Wad 166-167 M 1
Lago Varuá Ipana 94-95 EF 7
Lago Varvarco Campos 106-107 B 6
Lago Verde [BR] 100-101 B 2
Lago Verde [RA] 108-109 E 4
Lago Viedma 111 B 7
Lago Viedma [RA, place] 108-109 C 7
Lago Villarrica 108-109 C 2
Lagowa, El — = Al-Laqawah 164-165 K 6
Lago Xiriri 98-99 L 5
Lågøya 116-117 k 4
Lago Yehuin 108-109 EF 10
Lago Yelcho 108-109 C 4
Lago Ypoá 102-103 D 6
Lago Yulton 108-109 C 5
Lago Yusala 104-105 C 3
La Grande, OR 66-67 D 3
La Grange 158-159 D 3
La Grange, GA 64-65 JK 5
Lagrange, IN 70-71 H 5
La Grange, KY 70-71 H 6
La Grange, NC 80-81 H 3
La Grange, TX 76-77 F 7-8
Lagrange, WY 68-69 D 5
La Gran Sabana 92-93 G 3
La Grita 94-95 F 3
La Gruta 102-103 F 7
Lagua da Canabrava 100-101 D 6
La Guaira 94-95 H 2
La Guardia [BOL] 104-105 E 5
La Guardia [RA] 106-107 E 2
La Guardia [RCH] 106-107 C 1
La Guardia Airport 82 III c 2
Laguboti 150-151 B 11
Laguna, NM 76-77 A 5
Laguna [BR] 111 G 3
Laguna [PE] 96-97 B 5
Laguna, Ilha da — 98-99 N 5
Laguna, La — [PA ↑ Panamá] 64-65 b 2
Laguna, La — [PA ← Panamá] 64-65 b 3
Laguna, La — [RA] 106-107 F 4
Laguna 8 de Agosto 106-107 F 7
Laguna 8 de Agosto 108-109 H 2
Laguna Alsina 106-107 F 6
Laguna Arapa 96-97 FG 9
Laguna Ayarde 104-105 F 9
Laguna Beach, CA 74-75 DE 6
Laguna Blanca [RA, Formosa] 104-105 G 9
Laguna Blanca [RA, Neuquén] 106-107 B 7
Laguna Blanca [RA, Río Negro] 108-109 E 3
Laguna Blanca, Sierra — 104-105 C 10
Laguna Blanco 108-109 D 9
Laguna Caburgua 108-109 D 2
Laguna Cáceres 104-105 GH 6
Laguna Caimán 94-95 G 6
Laguna Campos 102-103 B 4
Laguna Cari Laufquen Grande 108-109 E 3
Laguna Castillos 106-107 KL 5
Laguna Chaira 94-95 D 7
Laguna Chasicó 106-107 F 7
Laguna Chichancanab 86-87 Q 8
Laguna Chicuaco 94-95 G 6
Laguna Concepción [BOL → Santa Cruz de la Sierra] 104-105 F 5
Laguna Concepción [BOL ↑ Santa Cruz de la Sierra] 104-105 E 4
Laguna Coronda 106-107 G 3-4
Laguna Curicó 108-109 G 3
Laguna Dam 74-75 FG 6
Laguna de Agua Brava 86-87 GH 6
Laguna de Babícora 86-87 FG 3
Laguna de Bacalar 86-87 Q 8
Laguna de Boyeruca 106-107 AB 5
Laguna de Caratasca 64-65 K 8
Laguna de Chiriquí 64-65 K 9-10
Laguna de Cuitzeo 86-87 K 8
Laguna de Fúquene 94-95 E 5
Laguna de Guavatayoc 104-105 CD 8
Laguna de Guzmán 86-87 G 2
Laguna de Jaco 76-77 C 9
Laguna del Abra 108-109 H 3
Laguna de la Laja 106-107 B 6
Laguna del Caimanero 86-87 G 6
Laguna del Carrizal 106-107 H 7
Laguna del Cisne 106-107 FG 2
Laguna del Maule 106-107 B 6
Laguna del Monte 106-107 H 5
Laguna de los Cisnes 108-109 D 6
Laguna de los Patos 106-107 F 3
Laguna de los Porongos 106-107 F 2-3
Laguna del Palmar 106-107 G 2
Laguna del Sauce 106-107 K 5
Laguna de Luna 106-107 J 2
Laguna de Monte 106-107 F 6
Laguna de Palo Parada 106-107 E 2
Laguna de Patos 86-87 GH 2
Laguna de Perlas 88-89 E 8
Laguna de Rocha 106-107 K 5
Laguna de Santiaguillo 86-87 H 5
Laguna de Tacarigua 94-95 J 2
Laguna de Tamiahua 64-65 G 7
Laguna de Términos 64-65 H 8
Laguna de Unare 94-95 J 2
Laguna de Vichuquén 106-107 AB 5
Laguna de Villarrica 106-107 AB 7
Laguna El Maestro 106-107 J 6
Laguna Epecuén 106-107 F 6
Laguna Escondida, Bajo de la — 108-109 F 2-G 3
Laguna Garzón 106-107 K 5
Laguna Grande [RA, Chubut] 108-109 F 4
Laguna Grande [RA, Santa Cruz lake] 108-109 E 6
Laguna Grande [RA, Santa Cruz place] 108-109 D 7
Laguna Guatraché 106-107 F 6
Laguna Huani 88-89 E 7
Laguna Huaunta 88-89 E 8
Laguna Iberá 106-107 J 2
Laguna La Amarga 106-107 DE 7
Laguna la Bella 102-103 B 6
Laguna La Brava 106-107 F 4
Laguna La Cocha 94-95 C 7
Laguna La Dulce 106-107 D 7
Laguna Larga 106-107 F 3
Laguna La Salada Grande 106-107 J 6
Laguna Limpia [RA ↖ Resistencia] 111 DE 3
Laguna Limpia [RA ↓ Resistencia] 106-107 H 1
Laguna Llancanelo 106-107 C 5
Laguna Lleulleu 106-107 A 7
Laguna Lorisccota 96-97 G 10
Laguna Los Chilenos 106-107 F 6
Laguna Madre 64-65 G 6-7
Laguna Mandioré 104-105 GH 6
Laguna Mar Chiquita 111 D 4
Laguna Melincué 106-107 G 4
Laguna Mountains 74-75 E 6
Laguna Negra [RA] 104-105 F 9
Laguna Negra [ROU] 106-107 L 4-5
Laguna Ocho de Agosto 106-107 F 7
Laguna Ojo de Liebre 86-87 CD 4
Laguna Paiva 106-107 G 3
Laguna Parinacochas 96-97 DE 9
Laguna Piranè 104-105 G 9
Lagunas [PE] 92-93 DE 6
Lagunas [RCH] 111 BC 2
Lagunas, Las — 106-107 E 5
Laguna Salada [MEX] 86-87 C 1
Laguna Salada [RA, Buenos Aires] 106-107 H 7
Laguna Salada [RA, Córdoba] 106-107 F 3
Laguna Salada [RA, La Pampa] 106-107 E 6
Laguna San Ignacio 86-87 D 4
Laguna Santa Catalina 110 III b 2
Laguna Saridú 94-95 GH 6
Laguna Atacavi 94-95 H 6
Lagunas de Gómez 106-107 G 5
Lagunas de Guanacache 106-107 CD 4
Lagunas Huatunas 104-105 C 3
Laguna Sirven 108-109 E 6
Lagunas Las Tunas Grandes 106-107 F 5-6
Lagunas Saladas 106-107 F 2
Laguna Superior 64-65 H 8
Laguna Tarabillas 76-77 B 7
Laguna Trinidad 102-103 B 4
Laguna Tunaima 94-95 E 7
Laguna Tunas Chicas 106-107 F 6
Laguna Uinamarca 104-105 B 5
Laguna Urre Lauquen 106-107 E 7
Laguna Uvá 94-95 F 6
Laguna Verá 111 E 3
Laguna Yema 111 D 2
Laguna Ypacaraí 102-103 D 6
Lagundu, Tanjung — 152-153 N 10
Lagunetas 94-95 F 3
Lagunillas [BOL] 104-105 E 6
Lagunillas [RCH] 106-107 B 4
Lagunillas [YV, Mérida] 94-95 F 3
Lagunillas [YV, Zuila] 94-95 F 2
Lagunillas, Lago — 96-97 F 9
Lagunita Country Club, La — 91 II c 2
Lagunitas 94-95 F 2
La Habana 64-65 K 7
Lahad Datu 148-149 G 5-6
Lahaina, HI 78-79 d 2
Laham [RI] 148-149 G 6
Laham [RN] 168-169 G 2
Lahan, Nong — 150-151 E 4
Lahār 138-139 G 4
Lāharpur 138-139 H 4
Lahat 148-149 D 7
Lāhaur 134-135 L 4
La Have Bank 63 D 6
Lahe = Lahei 141 D 2
Lahei 141 D 2
La Hermosa 94-95 F 5
La Herradura 108-109 F 7
Lahewa 148-149 C 6
La Hierra 106-107 H 3
La Higuera 106-107 B 2
Laḥij 134-135 EF 8
Lāhījān 134-135 FG 3
Lahir 138-139 B 8
Lahn 118 D 3
Laholm 116-117 E 9
Laholms bukten 116-117 E 9
La Honda 94-95 C 4
Lahontan Reservoir 74-75 D 3
Lahore = Lāhaur 134-135 L 4
La Horqueta [YV, Bolívar] 94-95 L 4
La Horqueta [YV, Monagas] 94-95 K 3
Lahrī 138-139 AB 3
Lahti 116-117 LM 7
La Huacana 86-87 JK 8
La Huerta 106-107 AB 5
Laï 164-165 H 7
Lai, Mui — 150-151 F 4
Lai'an 146-147 G 5
Laibin 146-147 B 10
Lai Châu 148-149 D 2
Lai Chi Kok, Victoria- 155 I a 1
Lai-chou Wan = Laizhou Wan 146-147 G 3
Laidley 160 L 1
Laifeng 146-147 B 7
Lai Hka = Lechā 148-149 C 2
Laikot 141 C 3
Lailā = Laylā 134-135 F 6
Lailān = Laylān 136-137 L 5
Laim, München- 130 II ab 2
Lainé 168-169 C 3
Laingsburg 172 CD 8
Lainz, Wien- 113 I b 2
Lainzer Tiergarten 113 I ab 2
Lai-pin = Laibin 146-147 B 10
Laipo = Lipu 142-143 KL 7
Laird, CO 68-69 E 5
Lais [RI, Celebes] 152-153 O 5
Lais [RI, Sumatra] 152-153 DE 7
La Isabela 88-89 FG 3
Laisamis 171 D 2
Laiševo 124-125 RS 6
Laishui 146-147 E 2
La Islá [PE] 96-97 D 9
La Isla [RA] 106-107 DE 3
Laiwu 146-147 F 3
Laixi 146-147 H 3
Laiyang 146-147 H 3
Laiyuan 142-143 LM 4
Lai-yüan = Laiyuan 142-143 LM 4
Laizhou Wan 146-147 G 3
Laja 104-105 B 5
Lajā', Al- 136-137 G 6
Laja, Laguna de la — 106-107 B 6
Laja, Río de la — 106-107 AB 6
La Jagua 92-93 E 3
La Jalca 96-97 C 5
La Jara 120-121 E 9
La Jara, CO 68-69 CD 7
La Jarita 86-87 KL 4
Lajas, Las — 106-107 B 7
La Jaula 106-107 C 5
Laje [BR ↙ Salvador] 100-101 E 7
Laje [BR ↖ Senhor do Bonfim] 100-101 D 6
Laje, Cachoeira da — 98-99 L 5
Laje, Ilha da — 110 I c 2
Lajeado 106-107 LM 2
Lajeado, Cachoeira do — 98-99 N 10
Lajedo 100-101 F 5
Lajedo Alto 100-101 DE 7
Laje dos Santos 102-103 JK 6
Lajes [BR, Rio Grande do Norte] 92-93 M 6
Lajes [BR, Santa Catarina] 111 F 3
Lajinha 102-103 M 4
Lajitas, TX 76-77 C 8
Lajitas, Las — [RA] 104-105 DE 9
Lajitas, Las — [YV] 94-95 J 4
Lajkovac 122-123 HJ 3
La Jolla, CA 74-75 E 6
La Joya, NM 76-77 A 5
La Joya [BOL] 104-105 C 5
La Joya [PE] 96-97 F 10
Lajtamak 132-133 M 6
La Junta, CO 64-65 F 4
La Junta [BOL] 104-105 F 4
La Junta [MEX] 86-87 G 3
Lak Boggai 171 D 2
Lak Bor 172 G 1
Lak Dera 172 H 1
Lak Dima 171 E 2
Lake, WY 66-67 H 3
Lake, The — 88-89 K 4
Lake Abert 66-67 CD 4
Lake Abitibi 56-57 UV 8
Lake Acraman 158-159 FG 6
Lake Albert 158-159 GH 7
Lake Aleknagik 58-59 H 7
Lake Alexandrina 158-159 GH 7
Lake Alma 68-69 D 1
Lake Alma = Harlan County Reservoir 68-69 G 5-6
Lake Almanor 66-67 C 5
Lake Amadeus 158-159 F 4
Lake Amboseli 171 D 3
Lake Andes 68-69 G 4
Lake Andes, SD 68-69 G 4
Lake Arthur, LA 78-79 C 5
Lake Arthur, NM 76-77 B 6
Lake Ashtabula = Baldhill Reservoir 68-69 GH 2
Lake Athabasca 56-57 OP 6
Lake Auld 158-159 D 4
Lake Austin 158-159 C 5
Lake Avalon 76-77 BC 6
Lake Ballard 158-159 D 5
Lake Bangweulu 172 EF 4
Lake Barcroft 82 II a 2
Lake Baringo 171 D 2
Lake Barkley 78-79 EF 2
Lake Barlee 158-159 C 5
Lake Benmore 161 D 7
Lake Benton, MN 70-71 BC 3
Lake Berryessa 74-75 B 3
Lake Beverley 58-59 H 7
Lake Bistineau 78-79 C 4
Lake Blanche [AUS, South Australia] 158-159 GH 5
Lake Blanche [AUS, Western Australia] 158-159 D 4
Lake Bolac 160 F 6
Lake Borgne 78-79 E 5-6
Lake Bowdoin 68-69 C 1
Lake Brooks 58-59 K 7
Lake Butler, FL 80-81 b 1
Lake Cadibarrawirracanna 160 AB 2
Lake Callabonna 158-159 G 5
Lake Calumet 83 II b 2
Lake Carey 158-159 D 5
Lake Cargelligo 158-159 J 6
Lake Carnegie 158-159 D 5
Lake Cataouatche 85 I a 2
Lake Chamo = Tyamo 164-165 M 7
Lake Champlain 64-65 LM 3
Lake Charles, LA 64-65 H 5
Lake Charlevoix 70-71 H 3
Lake Chelan 66-67 C 1
Lake Chilwa 172 G 5
Lake Chiuta 172 G 4
Lake Chrissie = Chrissiesmeer 174-175 J 4
Lake City, CO 68-69 C 6
Lake City, FL 80-81 b 1
Lake City, IA 70-71 C 4
Lake City, MI 70-71 H 3
Lake City, MN 70-71 D 3
Lake City, SC 80-81 G 4
Lake City, SD 68-69 H 3
Lake Claire 56-57 O 6
Lake Clark 58-59 K 6
Lake Coleridge 161 D 6
Lake Cormorant, MS 78-79 DE 3
Lake Cowal 158-159 J 6
Lake Cowan 158-159 D 6
Lake Cowichan 66-67 AB 1
Lake Crescent 66-67 B 1
Lake Crowley 74-75 D 4
Lake Crystal, MN 70-71 C 3
Lake Cumberland 70-71 H 7
Lake C. W. MacConaughy 68-69 E 5
Lake Darling 68-69 F 1
Lake Dey Dey 158-159 F 5
Lake Diefenbaker 61 E 5
Lake Disappointment 158-159 DE 4
Lake Dora 158-159 D 4
Lake Dow 172 D 6
Lake Dundas 158-159 D 6
Lake Eaton 158-159 EF 4
Lake Echo 160 c 3
Lake Erie 64-65 KL 3
Lake Eucumbene 160 J 6
Lake Everard 158-159 F 6
Lake Eyasi 172 FG 2
Lake Eyre 158-159 G 5
Lake Eyre North 160 C 2
Lake Eyre South 160 C 2
Lakefield, MN 70-71 C 4
Lakefield [AUS] 158-159 H 2-3
Lakefield [ZA] 170 V c 2
Lake Forest, New Orleans-, LA 85 I c 1
Lake Francis Case 64-65 FG 3
Lake Frome 158-159 GH 6
Lake Gairdner 158-159 G 6
Lake Galilee 158-159 HJ 4
Lake Gem 85 II a 2
Lake Geneva, WI 70-71 F 4
Lake George, NY 72-73 JK 3
Lake George [AUS] 158-159 JK 7
Lake George [EAU] 172 F 2
Lake George [RWA] 171 B 3
Lake George [USA, Alaska] 58-59 PQ 5
Lake George [USA, Florida] 80-81 c 2
Lake George [USA, New York] 72-73 K 3
Lake Gillen 158-159 D 5
Lake Gilles 160 C 4
Lake Gogebic 70-71 F 2
Lake Gordon 160 bc 3
Lake Grace 158-159 C 6
Lake Granby 68-69 D 5
Lake Greeson 78-79 C 3
Lake Gregory 158-159 GH 5
Lake Grosvenor 58-59 K 7
Lake Harbour 56-57 WX 5
Lake Harris 160 B 3
Lake Havasu City, AZ 74-75 FG 5
Lake Hawea 161 C 7
Lake Hickory 80-81 F 3
Lake Hopkins 158-159 E 4
Lake Huron 64-65 K 2-3
Lake Indawgyi = Indaugyi Aing 141 E 3
Lake Itasca 64-65 G 2
Lake Jackson, TX 76-77 G 8
Lake Joseph 72-73 G 2
Lake Kampolombo 172 E 4
Lake Kariba 172 E 5
Lake Kemp 76-77 E 6
Lake King 158-159 CD 6
Lake Kissimmee 80-81 c 2-3
Lake Kosi = Kosimeer 174-175 K 4
Lake Kulik [USA ↑ Kuskokwim River] 58-59 G 6
Lake Kulik [USA ↓ Kuskokwim River] 58-59 H 7
Lake Kwania 171 C 2
Lake Kyoga 172 F 1
Lake Laberge 58-59 U 6
Lake Lanao 148-149 HJ 5
Lakeland, FL 64-65 K 6
Lakeland, GA 80-81 E 5
Lake Lefroy 158-159 D 6
Lake Louise 58-59 O 5
Lake Louise [CDN] 60 JK 4
Lakelse 60 C 2
Lake Macdonald [AUS] 158-159 E 4
Lake MacDonald [CDN] 66-67 FG 1
Lake Macfarlane 158-159 G 6
Lake Machattie 158-159 GH 4
Lake Mackay 158-159 E 4
Lake MacLeod 158-159 B 4
Lake MacMillan 76-77 BC 6
Lake Macquarie 160 KL 4
Lake Magadi 171 D 3
Lake Maitland 158-159 D 5
Lake Malawi 172 F 4
Lake Malombe 172 G 4
Lake Manapouri 158-159 N 9
Lake Manitoba 56-57 R 7
Lake Manyara 172 G 2
Lake Margherita = Abaya 164-165 M 7
Lake Marion 80-81 F 4
Lake Maurepas 78-79 D 5
Lake Maurice 158-159 EF 5
Lake Mead 64-65 D 4
Lake Mead National Recreation Area 74-75 FG 4
Lake Melville 56-57 YZ 7
Lake Meramangye 158-159 F 5
Lake Merced 83 I b 2
Lake Meridith 76-77 D 5
Lake Merrit 83 I c 2
Lake Michigan 64-65 J 2-3
Lake Mills, IA 70-71 D 4
Lake Mills, WI 70-71 F 4
Lake Minchumina 58-59 L 5
Lake Minchumina, AK 58-59 L 5
Lake Minigwal 158-159 D 5
Lake Minnewaska 70-71 C 3
Lake Minto 56-57 V 6
Lake Mistassini 56-57 W 7
Lake Monger 158-159 C 5
Lake Moore 158-159 C 5
Lake Moultrie 80-81 F 4
Lake Murray [PNG] 148-149 M 8
Lake Murray [USA] 80-81 F 3
Lake Muskoka 72-73 G 2
Lake Mweru 172 E 3
Lake Natron 172 G 2
Lake Neale 158-159 F 4
Lake Nerka 58-59 H 7
Lake Ngami 172 D 6
Lake Nipigon 56-57 ST 8
Lake Nipissing 56-57 UV 8
Lake Nunavaugaluk 58-59 H 7
Lake Oahe 64-65 F 2
Lake Odessa, MI 70-71 H 4
Lake of Bays 72-73 G 2
Lake of the Ozarks 64-65 H 4
Lake of the Woods 56-57 R 8
Lake Ohau 161 CD 7
Lake Okeechobee 64-65 K 6
Lake Ontario 64-65 L 3
Lake Oswego, OR 66-67 B 3
Lake O'The Cherokees 76-77 G 4
Lake Owyhee 66-67 E 4
Lake Panache 62 L 3
Lake Park, IA 70-71 C 4
Lake Pedder 160 bc 3
Lake Philippi 158-159 G 4
Lake Pine, NJ 84 III de 2
Lake Placid, FL 80-81 c 3
Lake Placid, NY 64-65 M 3
Lake Pleasant, NY 72-73 J 3
Lake Poinsett 68-69 H 3
Lake Pontchartrain 64-65 HJ 5
Lakeport, CA 74-75 B 3
Lake Powell 64-65 D 4
Lake Poygan 70-71 F 3
Lake Preston, SD 68-69 H 3
Lake Providence, LA 78-79 D 4
Lake Pukaki 161 D 7
Lake Quannapowitt 84 I b 1
Lake Range 66-67 D 5
Lake Rebecca 158-159 D 6
Lake Rukwa 172 F 3
Lake Saint Ann 60 K 3
Lake Saint Clair 56-57 U 9
Lake Saint John = Lac Saint Jean 56-57 W 8
Lake Saint Joseph 56-57 ST 7
Lake Saint Lucia = Sint Luciameer 172 F 7
Lake Saint Martin 61 JK 5
Lake Sakakawea 64-65 F 2
Lake Salisbury 172 FG 1
Lake Salvador 78-79 D 6
Lake Semiole 78-79 G 5
Lakes Entrance 160 HJ 6
Lake Sewell = Canyon Ferry Reservoir 66-67 H 2
Lakeshore, New Orleans-, LA 85 I b 1
Lake Sibayi = Sibayameer 174-175 K 4
Lakeside, AZ 74-75 J 5
Lakeside, NE 68-69 E 4
Lakeside, OR 66-67 A 4
Lakeside, UT 66-67 G 5
Lakeside, VA 80-81 H 2
Lakeside Estates, Houston-, TX 85 III a 2
Lakeside Forest, Houston-, TX 85 III a 1
Lake Sidney Lanier 80-81 DE 3
Lake Simcoe 56-57 V 9
Lake Sinclair 80-81 E 4
Lake Sorell 160 c 2
Lake Stephanie = Thew Bahir 164-165 M 8
Lake Summer 76-77 B 5
Lake Superior 64-65 HJ 2
Lake Superior Provincial Park 62 G 4
Lake Tahoe 64-65 BC 4
Lake Tanganyika 172 E 2-F 3
Lake Taupo 158-159 P 7
Lake Te Anau 158-159 N 9
Lake Telaquana 58-59 L 6
Lake Terrace, New Orleans-, LA 85 I b 1
Lake Texoma 64-65 G 5
Lake Tillery 80-81 FG 3
Lake Timagami 72-73 F 1
Lake Torrens 158-159 G 6
Lake Toxaway, NC 80-81 E 3
Lake Traverse 68-69 H 3
Lake Travis 76-77 EF 7
Lake Tschida 68-69 EF 2
Lake Turkana 172 G 1
Lake Tyrell 158-159 H 7
Lake Tyrrell 160 F 5
Lake Victor, TX 76-77 E 7
Lake Victoria [AUS] 160 E 4
Lake Victoria [lake] 172 F 2
Lakeview, MI 70-71 H 4
Lakeview, OR 66-67 C 4
Lakeview, Chicago-, IL 83 II ab 1
Lakeview, Houston-, TX 85 III a 1
Lakeview, New Orleans-, LA 85 I b 1-2
Lake Village, AR 78-79 D 4
Lake Vista, New Orleans-, LA 85 I b 1
Lake Volta 164-165 DE 7
Lake Waccamaw 80-81 G 3
Lake Waikaremoana 161 G 4
Lake Wakatipu 161 C 7
Lake Wales, FL 80-81 c 3
Lake Wanaka 161 C 7
Lake Waukarlycarly 158-159 D 4
Lake Way 158-159 D 5
Lake Wells 158-159 D 5
Lake White 158-159 E 4
Lake Winnebago 70-71 F 3-4
Lake Winnipeg 56-57 R 7
Lake Winnipegosis 56-57 R 7
Lake Winnipesaukee 72-73 L 3
Lakewood, CA 83 III d 2
Lakewood, CO 68-69 D 6
Lakewood, NJ 72-73 J 4
Lakewood, NM 76-77 B 6
Lakewood, NY 72-73 G 3
Lakewood, OH 72-73 EF 4
Lakewood East, New Orleans-, LA 85 I c 1
Lakewood Park 85 II b 2
Lake Woods 158-159 F 3
Lakewood Stadium 85 II b 2
Lake Worth, FL 64-65 KL 6
Lake Wright 158-159 EF 5
Lake Yamma Yamma 158-159 H 5
Lake Yeo 158-159 D 5
Lake Younghusband 160 BC 3
Lake Zwai = Ziway 164-165 M 7
Lakhadsweep 134-135 L 8
Lakhdar, Ouèd — = Wād al-Akhdar 166-167 C 4
Lakhdaria = Lakhḍarīyah 166-167 H 1
Lakhḍarīyah 166-167 H 1
Lakhī, Koh — 138-139 A 4-5
Lakhīmpur [IND, Assam] 141 D 2
Lakhīmpur [IND, Uttar Pradesh] 138-139 H 4
Lakhipur [IND ↘ Alīpur Duār] 138-139 N 4-5
Lakhipur [IND ← Imphāl] 141 C 3
Lakhnādaun = Lakhnādon 138-139 G 6
Lakhnādon 138-139 G 6
Lakhnaū = Lucknow 134-135 MN 5
Lakhpat 138-139 B 6
Lakhtar 138-139 CD 6
Lakin, KS 68-69 F 7
Lakin = Lāgin 141 F 2
Lakinskij 124-125 M 5
Lakkhīsarāy = Luckeesarai 138-139 KL 5
Lakonia, Gulf of — = Lakōnikós Kólpos 122-123 K 7
Lakōnikós Kólpos 122-123 K 7
Lakota 168-169 D 4
Lakota, IA 70-71 CD 4
Lakota, ND 68-69 G 1
Lak Sao 150-151 E 3
Laksar 138-139 G 3
Laksefjord 116-117 M 2
Lakselv 116-117 L 2
Lakṣhadvīp = Lakshadweep 134-135 L 8
Lākshām 141 B 4
Lakshettipet 140 D 1
Lakshmanpur 138-139 J 6
Lakshmeshwar 140 B 3
Lakshmikāntapur 138-139 M 6
Lakshmīpur [BD] 140 F 1
Lakshmīpūr [IND] 141 B 4
Lālāghāt 141 C 3
La Laguna [PA ↑ Panamá] 64-65 b 2
La Laguna [PA ← Panamá] 64-65 b 3
La Laguna [RA] 106-107 F 4
La Lagunita Country Club 91 II c 2
Lâlapaşa 136-137 B 2
La Lara 168-169 H 5
Lalaua 172 G 4
Lālbāg 138-139 M 5
Lalbagh = Lālbāg 138-139 M 5
La Leonesa 104-105 G 10
Lālganj [IND, Bihār] 138-139 K 5
Lālganj [IND, Uttar Pradesh] 138-139 J 5
Lālgolā = Krishnapur 138-139 M 5
Lālguḍi 140 D 5
Lālī 136-137 N 6
Lalībela 164-165 M 6
La Libertad [EC] 96-97 A 3
La Libertad [PE] 96-97 BC 5
La Ligua 111 B 4
La Lima 88-89 B 7
La Linea 120-121 E 10
Lalitpur 138-139 G 5
Lālmanīr Hāṭ 138-139 M 5
La Lobería 108-109 H 3
La Loche 56-57 P 6
La Loche West 61 CD 2
La Loma 104-105 D 7
Lālpur 138-139 BC 6
Lal'sk 124-125 QR 3
Lālsot 138-139 F 4
La Luisa 106-107 GH 5
La Luz, NM 76-77 AB 6
Lâm [VN] 150-151 F 2
La Macolla 94-95 F 1
La Madrid 104-105 D 10
Lamadrid [MEX] 76-77 D 9
La Magdalena Atlipac 91 I d 2
La Magdalena Contreras 91 I b 3
La Magdalena Puerto Nare 94-95 D 4
Lamaing 141 EF 8
Lama-Kara 168-169 F 3
la Malbaie 63 AB 4
Lamaline 63 J 4
La Mancha 120-121 F 9
Lamandau, Sungai — 152-153 J 6-7
Lamar, CO 68-69 E 6
Lamar, MO 70-71 C 7
La Mariposa, Embalse — 91 II b 2
La Mariscala 106-107 K 5
La Maroma 106-107 DE 5
Lamarque 106-107 E 7
La Marque, TX 76-77 G 8
La Marquesa 91 I a 3
La Maruja 106-107 E 5
Lamas 96-97 C 5
La Mata 94-95 E 3
La Matanza 110 III b 2
La Matanza-20 de Junio 110 III a 2
La Matanza-Aldo Bonzi 110 III b 2
La Matanza-Ciudad General Belgrano 110 III b 2
La Matanza-González Catán 110 III b 2
La Matanza-Isidro Casanova 110 III b 2
La Matanza-Laferrere 110 III b 2
La Matanza-Rafael Castillo 110 III b 2
La Matanza-Ramos Mejía 110 III b 1
La Matanza-San Justo 110 III a 1
La Matanza-Tablada 110 III b 2
La Matanza-Tapiales 110 III b 2
La Matanza-Villa Madero 110 III b 2
Lama Temple 155 II b 2
Lambaréné 172 B 2
Lambari 102-103 K 4
Lambasa 148-149 a 2
Lambayeque [PE, administrative unit] 96-97 AB 5
Lambayeque [PE, place] 92-93 CD 6
Lambert, MS 78-79 DE 3
Lambert, MT 68-69 D 2
Lambert Glacier 53 B 8
Lambertsbaai 174-175 BC 7
Lamberts Bay = Lambertsbaai 174-175 BC 7
Lambeth, London- 129 II b 2
Lambi Kyûn 148-149 C 4
Lambouti 168-169 F 3
Lambton, Cape — 56-57 M 3
L'amca 124-125 L 1
Lam Chi 150-151 D 5
Lam Chiang Krai 150-151 C 5
Lāmding = Lumding 134-135 P 5
Lam Dom Noi 150-151 E 5
Lam Dom Yai 150-151 E 5
Lamé 164-165 G 7
Lame Deer, MT 68-69 C 3
Lamego 120-121 D 8
Lameguapi, Punta — 108-109 BC 3
La Merced [PE] 96-97 D 7
La Merced [RA] 104-105 D 11
la Mère et l'Enfant = Nui Vong Phu 150-151 G 6
La Mesa, CA 74-75 E 6
La Mesa, NM 76-77 A 6
Lamesa, TX 76-77 D 6
Lamèzia Terme 122-123 FG 6
Lamía 122-123 K 6
La Miel 94-95 G 3
L'amin 132-133 N 5
La Mirada, CA 83 III d 2
La Misión 74-75 E 6
Lamma Island = Pok Liu Chau 155 I a 2
Lamni 138-139 H 6
Lamo = Lamu 172 H 2
Lamobagar Gola 138-139 L 4
Lamoille, NV 66-67 F 5
La Moine, CA 66-67 B 5
Lamona, WA 66-67 D 2
Lamon Bay 148-149 H 4
Lamond, Washington-, DC 82 II a 1
Lamoni, IA 70-71 CD 5
Lamont, CA 74-75 D 5
Lamont, ID 66-67 H 3-4
Lamont, WY 68-69 C 4
La Montaña [E] 120-121 DE 7
La Montaña [PE] 92-93 E 5-6
La Montañita [CO] 94-95 D 7
La Montañita [YV] 94-95 F 2
La Mora 106-107 D 5
Lamoriciere = Awlād Mīmūn 166-167 F 2
La Morita 76-77 B 8
Lamotrek 148-149 N 5
La Mott, PA 84 III c 1
La Moure, ND 68-69 GH 2
La Moyne 82 I c 1
Lampa [PE] 92-93 EF 8
Lampa [RCH] 106-107 B 4
Lampang 148-149 C 3
Lampasas, TX 76-77 E 7
Lampazos de Naranjo 86-87 K 4
Lampedusa 122-123 E 8
Lampedusa, Isola — 164-165 G 1
Lam Phao 150-151 D 4
Lamphun 150-151 B 3
Lampi Island = Lambi Kyûn 148-149 C 4
Lam Plai Mat 150-151 D 5
Lampman 68-69 E 1
Lampung 148-149 DE 7

Lam Se Bai 150-151 E 4-5
Lamskoje 124-125 LM 7
Lamŭ [BUR] 141 D 6
Lamu [EAK] 172 H 2
Lamud 96-97 BC 5
La Mula 76-77 B 8
Lâm Viên, Cao Nguyên — 150-151 G 6-7
Lamy, NM 76-77 B 5
Lan' 124-125 F 7
Lan, Ko — 150-151 C 6
Lan, Lûy — 141 E 6
La Nacional 106-107 E 5
Lanai 148-149 e 3
Lanai City, HI 78-79 d 2
Lanao, Lake — 148-149 HJ 5
La Nava de Ricomalillo 120-121 E 9
Lancang Jiang 142-143 HJ 7
Lancaster 119 E 4
Lancaster, CA 74-75 DE 5
Lancaster, IA 70-71 D 5
Lancaster, KY 70-71 H 7
Lancaster, MN 68-69 H 1
Lancaster, NH 72-73 L 2
Lancaster, OH 72-73 E 5
Lancaster, PA 72-73 HJ 4
Lancaster, SC 80-81 F 3
Lancaster, WI 70-71 E 4
Lancaster Sound 56-57 TU 3
Lančchuti 126-127 K 5
Lancheu = Lanzhou 142-143 JK 4
Lan-ch'i = Lanxi [TJ, Hubei] 146-147 E 6
Lan-ch'i = Lanxi [TJ, Zhejiang] 146-147 G 7
Lanchou = Lanzhou 142-143 JK 4
Lanchow = Lanzhou 142-143 JK 4
Lancian = Lan Xian 146-147 C 2
Lanciano 122-123 F 4
Lanco 108-109 C 2
Lancun 142-143 N 4
Landa, ND 68-69 F 1
Lan Dao = Danhao Dao 146-147 DE 10
Landau 118 D 4
Landauk 141 E 2
Landeck 118 E 5
Landego 116-117 EF 4
Lander, WY 68-69 B 4
Landerneau 120-121 E 4
Lander River 158-159 F 4
Landeta 106-107 F 3-4
Landi 168-169 C 3
Landis 61 D 4
Landover Hills, MD 82 II b 1
Landri Sales 100-101 BC 4
Landrum, SC 80-81 E 3
Landsberg am Lech 118 E 4
Land's End [CDN] 56-57 LM 2
Land's End [GB] 119 CD 6
Landshut 118 F 4
Landskrona 116-117 E 10
Landsmeer 128 I ab 1
Lane Cove, Sydney- 161 I ab 1
Lane Cove National Park 161 I a 1
La Negra 106-107 H 6
Lanett, AL 78-79 G 4
La Nevada 106-107 FG 6
Lanfeng = Lankao 146-147 E 4
La Nga, Sông — 150-151 F 7
Langao 146-147 B 5
Langara 152-153 P 7-8
Langara Island 60 A 2
L'angasovo 124-125 RS 4
Langat, Sungei — 150-151 C 11
Langberge 174-175 E 4-5
Langbu Tsho 138-139 K 2
Lang Cây 150-151 E 2
Lang Chanh 150-151 E 2
Langchhen Khamba 142-143 DE 5
Lang-ch'i = Langxi 146-147 G 6
Langchung = Langzhong 142-143 JK 5
Langdon, ND 68-69 G 1
Langdon, Washington-, DC 82 II b 1
Langebaan 174-175 BC 7
Langeberge [ZA ← Hoë Karro] 174-175 C 6
Langeberge [ZA ↙ Klein Karro] 174-175 CD 7
Langeland 116-117 D 10
Langen = Langao 146-147 B 5
Langen, Staatsforst — 128 III b 2
Langenburg 61 GH 5
Langer See [DDR] 130 III c 2
Langerŭd 136-137 O 4
Langer Wald 128 III b 1
Langford, SD 68-69 H 3
Langford, Seno — 108-109 C 9
Langjökull 116-117 cd 2
Lang Ka, Doi — 150-151 B 3
Langkawi, Pulau — 148-149 C 5
Langkha Tuk, Khao — 150-151 B 8
Langklip 174-175 D 5
Langkon 152-153 M 2
Langkrans 174-175 J 4
Langley, VA 82 II a 1
Langlois, OR 66-67 A 4
Langma Dsong 138-139 M 2
Langnau am Albis 128 IV b 2
Langngag Tsho = Rakasdal 138-139 H 2
Langon 120-121 G 6
Langøy 116-117 F 3
Lang Phô Rang 150-151 E 1
Langping 146-147 C 6
Langres 120-121 K 5
Langres, Plateau de — 120-121 K 5
Langruth 61 J 5
Langsa 148-149 C 6
Lang Shan = Char Narijn uul 142-143 K 3
Lang So'n 148-149 E 2
Lang Suan 150-151 B 8
Lang Tâm 150-151 F 4
Langtans udde 53 C 31
Langtao = Landauk 141 E 2
Langtry, TX 76-77 D 8
Lângu [IND] 138-139 J 3
Langu [MAL] 150-151 B 9
Languedoc 120-121 J 7-K 6
Langueyú 106-107 H 6
Languna Jume 106-107 FG 4
Langwied, München- 130 II a 1
Langwieder See 130 II a 1
Langxi 146-147 G 6
Langzhong 142-143 JK 5
Lan Hsü 142-143 N 7
Laniel 72-73 G 1
Lanigan 61 F 5
Lanín, Parque Nacional — 108-109 D 2-3
Lanín, Volcán — 111 B 5
La Niña 106-107 G 5
Lânja 140 A 2
Lânjěn = Lânja 140 A 2
Lanji 138-139 H 7
Lankao 146-147 E 4
Lankou 146-147 E 10
Lankwitz, Berlin- 130 III b 2
Lannion 120-121 F 4
Lan Saka 150-151 B 8
Lansdale, PA 72-73 J 4
Lansdowne 138-139 G 3
Lansdowne, PA 84 III b 2
Lansdowne House 62 F 1
L'Anse, MI 70-71 F 2
Lansford, ND 68-69 F 1
Lanshan 146-147 D 9
Lansing, IA 70-71 E 4
Lansing, MI 64-65 K 3
Lanta, Ko — 150-151 B 9
Lan Tao = Danhao Dao 146-147 DE 10
Lantee, Gunung — 152-153 M 10
Lanteri 106-107 H 2
Lantian 146-147 B 4
Lantian = Lianyuan 146-147 C 8
Lantianchang 155 II a 2
Lantianchang, Beijing- 155 II a 2
Lan-t'ien = Lantian 146-147 B 4
Lan-ts'ang Chiang = Lancang Jiang 142-143 HJ 7
Lan-ts'un = Lancun 142-143 N 4
Lanús 110 III b 2
Lanús-Caraza 110 III b 2
Lanusei 122-123 C 6
Lanús-Monte Chingolo 110 III bc 2
Lanús-Remedios de Escalada 110 III b 2
Lanús-Villa Diamante 110 III b 2
Lanxi [TJ, Hubei] 146-147 E 6
Lanxi [TJ, Zhejiang] 146-147 G 7
Lan Xian 146-147 C 2
Lanzarote 164-165 B 3
Lanzhou 142-143 JK 4
Lao, Nam Mae — 150-151 B 3
Laoag 148-149 GH 3
Lao Bao 150-151 F 4
Lao-chung-chi = Laozhong 146-147 E 5
Laodicea = Al-Lâdhiqīyah 134-135 CD 3
Laoha He 144-145 B 2
Lao-ha Ho = Laoha He 144-145 B 2
Laohekou = Guanghua 142-143 L 5
Laohokow = Guanghua 142-143 L 5
Lao-hu-k'ou = Hukou 146-147 H 9
Laohumiao, Beijing- 155 II b 2
Laohushan 144-145 BC 2
Lao Kay 148-149 D 2
Laolong = Longchuan 146-147 E 9
Laon 120-121 J 4
Laona, WI 70-71 F 3
Lao Pi 150-151 D 3
Laopukou 146-147 B 9
Laora 148-149 H 7
Laoriā-Nandangarh = Thori 138-139 K 4
La Oroya 92-93 D 7
Laos 148-149 D 2-3
Laoshan 142-143 N 4
Laoshan Wan 146-147 H 3
Lao-t'ieh-shan-hsi Chiao = Laotieshanxi Jiao 144-145 C 3
Laotieshanxi Jiao 146-147 H 2
Lâoû', Ouèd — = Wâd Lâû' 166-167 D 2
Laozhong 146-147 E 5
Lapa 111 FG 3
Lapa, Campos de — 102-103 GH 6
Lapa, Rio de Janeiro- 110 I b 2
Lapa, São Paulo- 110 II a 2
Lapachito 104-105 G 10
La Palca 104-105 D 6
La Palma, CA 83 III d 2
La Palma [CO] 94-95 D 5
La Palma [E] 164-165 A 3
La Palma [PA] 88-89 GH 10
La Paloma [RCH] 106-107 B 3
La Paloma [ROU, Durazno] 106-107 K 4
La Paloma [ROU, Rocha] 111 F 4
La Paloma, Cerro — 106-107 C 4
La Pampa 106-107 DE 6
La Panza Range 74-75 CD 5
La Para 106-107 F 3
La Paragua 92-93 G 3
Lapasset = Sīdī al-Akhḍar 166-167 FG 1
La Pastoril = Colonia La Pastoril 106-107 DE 6
la Patte-d'Oie 129 I b 1-2
La Paz [BOL, administrative unit] 104-105 B 3-C 5
La Paz [BOL, place] 92-93 F 8
La Paz [Honduras] 88-89 C 7
La Paz [MEX, Baja California Sur] 64-65 DE 7
La Paz [MEX, San Luis Potosí] 86-87 K 6
La Paz [RA, Entre Ríos] 111 DE 4
La Paz [RA, Mendoza] 111 C 4
La Paz [ROU] 106-107 J 5
La Paz [YV] 94-95 E 2
La Paz, Bahía de — 64-65 DE 7
La Pedrera 92-93 EF 5
Lapeer, MI 72-73 E 3
La Pelada 106-107 G 3
La Peña 106-107 AB 6
La Perla 86-87 HJ 3
La Perouse 61 K 3
La Pérouse, proliv — 132-133 b 8
La Perouse, Sydney- 161 I b 2
La Pérouse Strait = proliv la Pérouse 142-143 R 2
La Pesca 86-87 M 6
Lápēthos 136-137 E 5
La Picada 106-107 G 3
La Piedad Cavadas 86-87 JK 7
Lapine, OR 66-67 C 4
Lapin lääni 116-117 L-N 4
Lapinlahti 116-117 MN 6
La Pintada 94-95 A 3
Lapithos = Lápēthos 136-137 E 5
Laplace, LA 78-79 D 5
Laplacette 106-107 G 5
Laplae 150-151 BC 4
Laplan 96-97 C 5
Lapland 116-117 F 5-N 3
Laplandskij zapovednik 116-117 OP 4
La Plant, ND 68-69 F 3
La Plant, SD 68-69 F 3
La Plata, IA 70-71 D 5
La Plata, MD 72-73 H 5
La Plata, MO 70-71 D 5
La Plata [CO] 92-93 D 4
La Plata [RA] 111 E 5
La Plata, Lago — 108-109 D 5
La Playosa 106-107 F 4
La Pointe, WI 70-71 E 2
La Poma 111 C 2
La Porte, IN 70-71 G 5
Laporte, PA 72-73 H 4
La Porte, TX 76-77 G 8
La Porte City, IA 70-71 DE 4
La Porteña, Salinas — 106-107 EF 7
La Posta 106-107 F 3
Lapovo 122-123 J 3
Lappajärvi 116-117 KL 6
Lappeenranta 116-117 N 7
Lappi 116-117 L 5
La Prairie 82 I bc 2
Laprida [RA, Buenos Aires] 111 D 5
Laprida [RA, Santiago del Estero] 106-107 E 2
La Primavera 106-107 D 6
La Pryor, TX 76-77 DE 8
Lâpseki 136-137 B 2
Lapteva Strait = proliv Dmitrija Lapteva 132-133 a-c 3
Laptev Sea 132-133 V 2-Z 3
Lapua 116-117 K 6
La Puebla 120-121 J 9
La Puerta [RA, Catamarca] 104-105 D 11
La Puerta [RA, Córdoba] 106-107 F 3
La Puerta [YV] 94-95 F 3
La Puntilla 92-93 C 5
La Purísima 86-87 DE 4
Lapush, WA 66-67 A 2
Lâp Vo 150-151 E 7
Łapy 118 L 2
Laqawah, Al- 164-165 K 6
Lâqiyat al-Arba'in 164-165 K 4
La Quemada 86-87 J 6
La Querencia 106-107 H 3
la Queue-en-Brie 129 I d 2
La Quiaca 111 CD 2
Lār 134-135 G 5
Lara 94-95 FG 2
Larache = Al-'Arā'ish 164-165 C 1
Laramie, WY 64-65 EF 3
Laramie Peak 68-69 D 4
Laramie Plains 68-69 D 4-5
Laramie Range 64-65 E 3
Laramie River 68-69 D 4-5
Laranjal 98-99 K 7
Laranjal Paulista 102-103 HJ 5
Laranjeiras 100-101 F 6
Laranjeiras, Rio de Janeiro- 110 I b 2
Laranjeiras do Sul 111 F 3
Larantuka 148-149 H 8
Larat, Pulau — 148-149 K 8
La Raya, Ciénage — 94-95 D 3
Lärbro 116-117 H 9
Larchmont, Houston-, TX 85 III b 2
Larch River 56-57 W 6
Larder Lake 62 M 2
Lare 171 D 2
Laredo, IA 70-71 D 5-6
Laredo, TX 64-65 G 6
La Reforma [RA, Buenos Aires] 106-107 H 5
La Reforma [RA, La Pampa] 106-107 DE 6
La Reforma [YV] 94-95 L 4
la Reine 62 M 2
la Réserve de Assinica 62 O 1
la Réserve de Chibougamau 62 OP 2
la Réserve de Kipawa 72-73 G 1
la Réserve de Mistassini 62 P 1
Lārestān 134-135 GH 5
Largeau = Faya-Largeau 164-165 H 5
Largō 138-139 L 3
Largo Remo, Isla — 64-65 b 2
Largo Remo Island 64-65 b 2
Lariang 148-149 G 7
Lariang, Sungai — 152-153 N 6
La Rica 106-107 H 5
Lari Larian, Pulau — 152-153 MN 7
Larimore, ND 68-69 GH 2
Larino 122-123 F 5
La Rioja [E] 120-121 F 7
La Rioja [RA, administrative unit] 106-107 D 2
La Rioja [RA, place] 111 C 3
Lárisa 122-123 K 6
Laristan = Lārestān 134-135 GH 5
Larjak 132-133 OP 5
Lärkāna 134-135 K 5
Larkspur, CO 68-69 D 6
Larnaka = Lárnax 134-135 C 4
Lárnax 134-135 C 4
Larne 119 D 4
Larned, KS 68-69 G 6
La Robla 120-121 E 7
la Rochelle 120-121 G 7
la Roche-sur-Yon 120-121 G 5
Larocque 62 L 2
la Roda 120-121 F 9
La Romana 64-65 J 8
la Ronge 56-57 P 6
La Rosita 86-87 K 3
Larrey Point 158-159 C 3
Larrimah 158-159 F 3
Larroque 106-107 H 4
Larry's River 63 F 5
Lars Christensen land 53 BC 7
Larsen Bay, AK 58-59 fg 1
Larsen is-shelf 53 C 30-31
Larslan, MT 68-69 CD 1
Larson 70-71 E 1
Larteh 168-169 H 4
Lartigau 106-107 G 7
La Rubia 111 D 4
Larut, Pegunungan — 150-151 C 10
Larvik 116-117 D 8
Lasa = Lhasa 142-143 G 6
La Sabana [CO] 94-95 G 6
La Sábana [RA] 106-107 H 1
La Sabana [YV] 94-95 H 2
Las Acequias 106-107 EF 4
La Sagra 120-121 EF 8
La Sal, UT 74-75 J 3
La Salada Grande, Laguna — 106-107 J 6
Las Alicias 91 I a 3
La Salle, CO 68-69 D 5
La Salle, IL 70-71 F 5
La Salle [CDN, Montréal] 82 I b 2
La Salle [CDN, Windsor] 84 II b 3
La Salle College 84 III c 1
Las Animas 76-77 C 9
Las Animas, CO 68-69 E 6-7
Las Armas 106-107 HJ 6
la Sarre 56-57 V 8
Las Arrias 106-107 F 3
Las Aves, Islas — 92-93 F 2
Las Avispas 106-107 G 2
Las Bonitas 92-93 FG 3
Las Breñas 104-105 F 10
Las Cabras 106-107 B 5
Lascan, Volcán — 104-105 C 8
Las Cañas 104-105 D 11
Las Cañas, Bahía — 106-107 A 5
Lascano 106-107 KL 4
Lascar, CO 68-69 D 7
Las Cascadas 64-65 b 2
Las Casuarinas 106-107 CD 3
Las Catitas 106-107 CD 4
Las Catonas, Arroyo — 110 III a 1
Las Cejas 111 D 3
Las Chacras 106-107 BC 6
Las Chapas 108-109 F 4
Las Choapas 86-87 NO 9
la Scie 63 J 2
Las Conchas 104-105 G 5
Las Condes 106-107 B 4
Las Cruces 64-65 b 2
Las Cruces, NM 64-65 E 5
Las Cuevas 106-107 BC 4
Las Cuevas de los Guacharos 94-95 CD 7
la Selle 88-89 KL 5
La Seña 106-107 D 4
La Serena [E] 120-121 E 9
La Serena [RCH] 111 B 3
Las Esperanzas 76-77 D 9
la Seyne-sur-Mer 120-121 K 7
Las Flores [RA, Buenos Aires] 111 E 5
Las Flores [RA, Salta] 104-105 E 9
Las Flores [RA, San Juan] 106-107 C 3
Las Gamas 106-107 G 2
Lāsgird = Lāsjerd 134-135 G 3
Lashburn 61 D 4
Las Heras [RA, Mendoza] 106-107 C 4
Las Heras [RA, Santa Cruz] 111 C 7
Las Hermanas 106-107 G 6
Lashio = Lâshō 148-149 C 2
Lâsh Juwayn 134-135 J 4
Lashkar = Gwalior 134-135 M 5
Lashkar Satma 142-143 F 4
Lâshō 148-149 C 2
Las Horquetas 108-109 D 7
La Sierra [ROU] 106-107 K 5
La Sierrita 94-95 EF 2
La Sila 122-123 G 6
La Silveta, Cerro — 111 B 8
Lasíthion 122-123 L 8
Lāsjerd 134-135 G 3
Las Julianas, Presa — 91 I b 2
Las Junturas 106-107 F 3
L'askel'a 124-125 H 3
Las Lagunas 106-107 E 5
Las Lajas 106-107 B 7
Las Lajas, Cerro — 106-107 B 7
Las Lajitas [RA] 104-105 DE 9
Las Lajitas [YV] 94-95 J 4
Las Lomitas 111 D 2
Lašma 124-125 N 6
Las Majadas 94-95 J 4
la Smala des Souassi = Zamâlat as-Suwâsī 166-167 M 2
Las Malvinas 106-107 C 5
Las Marianas 106-107 H 5
Las Marias 91 II bc 2
Las Marismas 120-121 D 10
Las Martinetas 106-107 G 6
Las Mercedes 92-93 F 3
Las Mesteñas 76-77 B 8
Las Minas, Bahía — 64-65 b 2
Las Nieves 76-77 B 9
Las Norias 76-77 C 8
Las Nutrias 106-107 H 7
La Sola, Isla — 94-95 K 2
La Solita 94-95 F 3
Lasolo 152-153 OP 7
Lasolo, Teluk — 148-149 H 7
Las Ortegas, Arroyo — 110 III b 2
La Sortija 106-107 G 7
Las Ovejas 106-107 B 6
Las Palmas 102-103 E 6
Las Palmas de Gran Canaria 164-165 AB 3
Las Palmeras 106-107 G 3
Las Palmitas 106-107 J 2
Las Palomas 86-87 FG 2
Las Palomas, NM 76-77 A 6
Las Parejas 106-107 G 4
Las Peñas 106-107 F 3
Las Perlas 88-89 E 8
Las Petacas 106-107 F 3
Las Petas 104-105 G 5
Las Petas, Río — 104-105 G 5
La Spèzia 122-123 C 3
Las Piedras [BOL] 104-105 C 2
Las Piedras [ROU] 106-107 J 5
Las Piedras [YV, Delta Amacuro] 94-95 L 3
Las Piedras [YV, Guárico] 94-95 H 3
Las Piedras [YV, Merida] 94-95 F 3
Las Playas 96-97 A 4
Las Plumas 111 C 6
Lasqueti Island 66-67 A 1
Las Rosanas 106-107 G 4
Las Salinas 96-97 C 7
Lassance 92-93 KL 8
Lassen Peak 64-65 B 3
Lassen Volcanic National Park 66-67 C 5
Las Tablas 88-89 FG 11
Lastarria 108-109 C 2
Lastarria, Volcán — 104-105 B 9
Last Chance, CO 68-69 DE 6
Las Termas 111 CD 3
Las Tinajas 102-103 A 7
Last Mountain Lake 61 F 5
Las Tortillas 76-77 E 9
Las Tórtolas, Cerro — 106-107 BC 2
Las Toscas 106-107 K 4
Las Totoras 106-107 E 4
Lastoursville 172 B 2
Lastovo 122-123 G 4
Lastra 106-107 G 6
Las Tres Matas 94-95 J 3
Las Tres Vírgenes 64-65 D 6
Las Trincheras 92-93 FG 3
Las Tunas [C] 88-89 H 4
Las Tunas [RA] 106-107 G 3
Las Tunas Grandes, Lagunas — 106-107 F 5-6
Las Varillas 111 D 4
Las Vegas 94-95 G 3
Las Vegas, NM 64-65 EF 4
Las Vegas, NV 64-65 C 4
Las Vegas Bombing and Gunnery Range 74-75 EF 4
Las Ventanas 94-95 H 4
Las Zorras 96-97 B 7
Lata 104-105 A 8
la Tabatière 63 G 2
Latacunga 92-93 D 5
Latady Island 53 BC 29
Latagħāṭ = Lālāghāt 141 C 3
La Tagua 94-95 D 8
Latakia = Al-Lādhiqīyah 134-135 CD 3
Latang, Ko — = Ko Ladang 150-151 B 9
la Tapa 106-107 F 1
Latchford 72-73 FG 1
Late 148-149 c 2
La Tebaida 94-95 D 5
Latehār 138-139 K 6
Laṭerī = Leteri 138-139 F 5
la Teste 120-121 G 6
La Teta 91 III bc 4
Lat Hane = Ban Lat Hane 150-151 CD 2
Lāthi 138-139 C 7
La Tina 96-97 B 4
Latina [I] 122-123 E 5
Latina, Madrid- 113 III a 2
Latinos, Ponta dos — 106-107 L 4
Latium = Lâzio 122-123 E 4-5
La Tola 92-93 D 4
La Toma 111 C 4
La Tordilla = Colonia La Tordilla 106-107 F 3
La Tortuga, Ila — 92-93 FG 2
Latouche, AK 58-59 N 7-O 6
Latouche Island 58-59 NO 7
La Tranca 106-107 D 4
La Trinidad 94-95 G 3
La Trinidad de Arauca 94-95 G 4
Latrobe 160 c 2
Latrobe, PA 72-73 G 4
Latsauk = Ratsauk 141 E 5
Latua 152-153 D 8
La Tunia 94-95 E 7
la Tuque 56-57 W 8
Lātūr 140 C 1
Latvia 124-125 C-F 5
Lat Yao 150-151 B 5
Lau 168-169 H 3
Lau Bangap 150-151 AB 11
Lauca, Río — 104-105 B 6
Lauder [CDN] 68-69 F 1
Lauderdale 160 c 3
Lauderdale, MS 78-79 E 4
Laudo, Cumbre del — 104-105 B 10
Lauenburg/Elbe 118 E 2
Laughing Fish Point 70-71 G 2
Laughlan Islands 148-149 h 6
Laughlin Peak 76-77 BC 4
Lau Group 148-149 b 2
La-un 150-151 B 7
Launceston [AUS] 158-159 J 8
Launceston [GB] 119 D 6
Launġa = Londa 140 B 3
Launglōn 150-151 AB 6
Launglōnbôk Kyûnzu 150-151 A 6
La Unión [BOL] 104-105 F 4
La Unión [CO, Nariño] 94-95 C 7
La Unión [CO, Valle del Cauca] 94-95 C 5
La Unión [E] 120-121 G 10
La Unión [ES] 64-65 J 9
La Unión [MEX] 86-87 K 9
La Unión [PE, Huánuco] 92-93 D 6-7
La Unión [PE, Piura] 96-97 A 4
La Unión [RCH] 111 B 6
La Unión [YV] 94-95 GH 3
Laupahoehoe, HI 78-79 e 3
Laura 158-159 H 3
Laura = Lavry 124-125 F 5
La Urbana 92-93 F 3
Laurel 152-153 M 8
Laurel, DE 72-73 J 5
Laurel, IN 70-71 H 6
Laurel, MD 72-73 H 5
Laurel, MS 64-65 J 5
Laurel, MT 68-69 B 3
Laurel, NE 68-69 H 4
Laurel, OH 72-73 D 5
Laurel, Mount — 84 III d 2
Laureles [PY] 102-103 D 7
Laureles [ROU] 106-107 JK 3
Laurel Hill 72-73 G 4-5
Laurel Hill, FL 78-79 F 5
Laurel Lake 85 II a 1
Laurel Springs, NJ 84 III c 3
Laurelton, New York-, NY 82 III d 3
Laurens, IA 70-71 C 4
Laurens, SC 80-81 EF 3
Laurentian Plateau 56-57 V 8-X 7
Laurentides, Parc provincial des — 56-57 W 8
Lauri 138-139 GH 5
La Uribe 91 III c 1
Laurie Island 53 C 32
Laurie River 61 H 2
Laurinburg, NC 80-81 G 3
Lauritsala 116-117 N 7
Laurium, MI 70-71 F 2
Lauro Müller 102-103 H 8
Lausanne 118 C 5
Lausitzer Gebirge 118 G 3
Laut, Pulau — [RI, Selat Makasar] 148-149 G 7
Laut, Pulau — [RI, South China Sea] 148-149 E 6
Lautan Hindia 148-149 B 6-D 8
Lautaro 106-107 A 7
Laut Halmahera 148-149 J 7
Laut Kecil, Pulau-pulau — 148-149 G 7-8
Lautoka 148-149 a 2
Laut Sulawesi 148-149 GH 6
Laut Tawar 152-153 B 3
Lauwater 174-175 C 2
Lauzon 63 A 4
Lava, NM 76-77 A 6
Lava Bads 74-75 JK 5
Lava Beds [USA, New Mexico ← Oscura Peak] 76-77 A 6
Lava Beds [USA, New Mexico ↑ Tularosa Basin] 76-77 AB 6
Lava Beds [USA, New Mexico ← United Pueblos Indian Reservation] 74-75 JK 5
Lava Beds [USA, Oregon ↘ Cedar Mountains] 66-67 E 4
Lava Beds [USA, Oregon ← Harney Basin] 66-67 C 4
Lava Beds [USA, Oregon ↘ Steens Mountain] 66-67 D 4
Lava Beds National Monument 66-67 C 5
Lavaisse 106-107 E 4
Laval [CDN] 56-57 VW 8
Laval [F] 120-121 G 4
La Valdesa 64-65 b 3
Laval-des-Rapides 82 I a 1
Lavalle [RA, Corrientes] 106-107 H 2
Lavalle [RA, Santiago del Estero] 106-107 E 2
Lavalleja [ROU, administrative unit] 106-107 K 4-5
Lavalleja [ROU, place] 106-107 J 3
Lavansaari = ostrov Moščnyj 124-125 FG 4
Lavapié, Punta — 111 AB 5
Laveaga Peak 74-75 C 4
La Vega [DOM] 64-65 MN 8
La Veguita 94-95 FG 3
La Vela de Coro 92-93 F 2
Lavelanet 120-121 HJ 7
La Venta 86-87 NO 8
La Ventana 86-87 KL 6
La Ventura 86-87 K 5
La Venturosa 94-95 G 4
La Vera 120-121 E 8
La Verde 106-107 E 5
La Verkin, UT 74-75 G 4
Laverlochère 72-73 G 1
Laverne, OK 76-77 DE 4
La Vernia, TX 76-77 EF 8
la Verrière 129 I a 3
Laverton 158-159 D 5
La Veta, CO 68-69 D 7
La Víbora 76-77 C 9
La Victoria [CO, Bogotá] 94-95 CD 5
La Victoria [CO, Valle del Cauca] 91 III a 3
La Victoria [YV] 94-95 H 2
Lavina, MT 68-69 B 2
La Viña [PE] 92-93 D 6
La Viña [RA] 111 C 3
Lavinia 102-103 G 4
La Violeta 106-107 GH 4
La Virginia 94-95 D 5
La Vista, GA 85 II c 1
La Viticola 106-107 F 7
Lavongai = New Hanover 148-149 gh 5
Lavonia, GA 80-81 E 3
Lavra = Monê Lávras 122-123 L 5
Lavrador = Labrador Peninsula 56-57 V 6-Y 7
Lavras 92-93 L 9
Lavras da Mangabeira 100-101 E 4
Lavras do Sul 106-107 L 3
Lavrentija 58-59 B 4
Lávrion 122-123 KL 7
Lavry 124-125 F 5
Lawa 92-93 J 4
La Ward, TX 76-77 F 8
Lawas 152-153 L 3
Lawashi River 62 H 1
Lawbida 141 E 6
Lawele 152-153 P 8
Lawen, OR 66-67 D 4
Lawers, Ben — 119 DE 3
Lawgi 158-159 K 4
Lawit, Gunung — [MAL] 150-151 D 10
Lawit, Gunung — [RI] 148-149 F 6
Lawn, TX 76-77 E 6
Lawndale, CA 83 III b 2
Lawndale, Chicago-, IL 83 II a 1
Lawndale, Philadelphia-, PA 84 III c 1
Lawnhill 60 B 3
Lawnside, NJ 84 III c 2
Lawnview Cemetery 84 III c 1
Lawowa 148-149 H 7
Lawqah 136-137 K 8
Lawra 164-165 D 6
Lawrence, KS 70-71 C 6
Lawrence, MA 72-73 L 3
Lawrence, NE 68-69 GH 5
Lawrence, NY 72-73 K 4
Lawrenceburg, IN 70-71 H 6
Lawrenceburg, KY 70-71 H 6-7
Lawrenceburg, OH 72-73 D 5
Lawrenceburg, TN 78-79 F 3
Lawrenceville, GA 80-81 DE 4
Lawrenceville, IL 70-71 G 6
Lawrenceville, VA 80-81 H 2
Laws, CA 74-75 D 4
Lawson, CO 68-69 CD 6
Lawton, OK 64-65 G 5
Lawz, Jabal al- 134-135 D 5
Laxå 116-117 F 8
Lay, CO 68-69 C 5
Laya 168-169 B 3
Lāyalpūr = Faisalābād 134-135 L 4
Layar, Tanjung — 148-149 DE 8
Laylā 134-135 F 6
Laylān 136-137 L 5
Layshi = Leshī 141 D 3
Layton, UT 66-67 G 5
Laž 124-125 R 5
La Zanja 106-107 F 6
Lazão, Ponta — 100-101 C 2
Lazarevo [SU, Chabarovskij kraj] 132-133 ab 7
Lazarevskoje, Soči- 126-127 J 5
Lázaro Cárdenas 86-87 C 2
Lazaro Cardenas, Presa — 86-87 H 5
Lazdijai 124-125 D 6
Lázio 122-123 E 4-5
Lazzarino 106-107 H 6
Lbiščensk = Čapajevo 126-127 P 1
Lea Canal 129 II b 1
Léach, Phum — 150-151 DE 6
Leach Island 70-71 H 2
Leachville, AR 78-79 D 3
Lead, SD 64-65 F 3
Leader 61 D 5
Leadore, ID 66-67 G 3
Leadville, CO 68-69 C 6
Leaf Rapids 61 J 2
Leaf River [CDN, Manitoba] 62 A 1
Leaf River [CDN, Quebec] 56-57 W 6
Leakesville, MS 78-79 E 5
Leakey, TX 76-77 E 8
Leaksville, NC 80-81 G 2
Leal = Lihula 124-125 DE 4
Leamington 72-73 E 3-4
Leamington, UT 74-75 GH 3
Le'an 146-147 E 8
Leander, TX 76-77 EF 7
Leandro N. Alem [RA, Misiones] 106-107 K 1
Leandro N. Alem [RA, San Luis] 106-107 D 4
Le'an Jiang 146-147 F 7
Leavenworth, KS 70-71 C 6
Leavenworth, WA 66-67 C 2
Leavitt Peak 74-75 D 3
Łeba 118 H 1
Lebádeia 122-123 K 6
Lebam, WA 66-67 B 2

Lebanon 134-135 D 4
Lebanon, IN 70-71 G 5
Lebanon, KS 68-69 G 6
Lebanon, KY 70-71 H 7
Lebanon, MO 70-71 D 7
Lebanon, NE 68-69 F 5
Lebanon, NH 72-73 KL 3
Lebanon, OH 70-71 H 6
Lebanon, OR 66-67 B 3
Lebanon, PA 72-73 H 4
Lebanon, SD 68-69 FG 3
Lebanon, TN 78-79 FG 2
Lebanon Junction, KY 70-71 H 7
Leb'ažje [SU, Kazachskaja SSR] 132-133 O 7
Leb'ažje [SU, Rossijskaja SFSR] 132-133 M 6
Lebed'an' 124-125 M 7
Lebedin 126-127 G 1
Lebeirat, Hassi — = Ḥāssī al-Bayrāt 166-167 AB 6
Lebesby 116-117 M 2
Lebir, Sungei — 150-151 D 10
Lébithia 122-123 M 7
le Blanc-Mesnil 129 I c 2
Leblon, Rio de Janeiro- 110 I b 2
Lebo 172 D 1
Lebo, KS 70-71 BC 6
Lebomboberge 174-175 JK 2-4
Lèbōn 148-149 B 2
Lebon Régis 102-103 G 7
Lębork 118 H 1
Lebowa-Kgomo 174-175 H 3
Lebranche Canal 85 I a 2
Lebrija 120-121 DE 10
Lebú 111 B 5
Lecce 122-123 H 5
Lecco 122-123 C 3
Le Center, MN 70-71 D 3
Lech 118 E 4
Lechā 141 E 5
Lechang 146-147 D 9
le Chenoit 128 II b 2
le Chesnay 129 I b 2
Lechiguanas, Islas de las — 106-107 H 4
Lecompte, LA 78-79 C 5
le Creusot 120-121 K 5
Lectoure 120-121 H 7
Lecueder 106-107 E 5
Ledākshi = Lepākshi 140 C 4
Ledang, Gunung — 150-151 D 11
Ledao Sha = Xinliao Dao 146-147 C 11
Ledaunggan 141 E 7
Ledo 141 D 2
Ledong 150-151 G 3
Ledong = Lotung 146-147 HJ 9
Leduc 56-57 O 7
Lee, MA 72-73 K 3
Leech Lake 70-71 C 2
Leedey, OK 76-77 E 5
Leeds 119 F 5
Leeds, AL 78-79 F 4
Leeds, ND 68-69 G 1
Leer 118 C 2
Leesburg, FL 80-81 bc 2
Leesburg, ID 66-67 FG 3
Leesburg, VA 72-73 H 5
Lee's Summit, MO 70-71 C 6
Lee Statue 85 I b 2
Leesville, LA 78-79 C 5
Leeton 158-159 J 6
Leeudoringstad 174-175 G 4
Leeu Gamka 174-175 D 7
Leeupoort 174-175 G 3
Leeuwarden 120-121 KL 2
Leeuwin, Cape — 158-159 B 6
Leeuwin Rise 158-159 A 8-B 7
Leeuwpan 170 V c 2
Leeuwpoort = Leeupoort 174-175 G 3
Lee Vining, CA 74-75 D 4
Leeward Islands 64-65 O 8
Lefini 172 C 2
Lefka = Lévka 136-137 E 5
Lefors, TX 76-77 D 5
Le François 88-89 Q 7
Lefroy, Lake — 158-159 D 6
Legaspi 148-149 H 4
Legaupi = Legaspi 148-149 H 4
Leghorn = Livorno 122-123 CD 4
Legion of Honor, Palace of the — 83 I b 2
Legnica 118 GH 3
Le Grand, Cape — 158-159 D 6
le Gué de Constantine 170 I ab 2
Leguizamón 106-107 F 5
Legya = Leigyā 141 E 5
Leh 134-135 M 4
Leham, Ouèd el — = Wādī al-Ham 166-167 HJ 2
le Hamiz 170 I b 2
le Havre 120-121 GH 4
Lehi, UT 66-67 GH 5
Lehliu 122-123 M 3
Lehlū, Bir — = Al-Bi'r al-Ahlū 166-167 B 6
Lehrte 118 DE 2
Lehua [TJ] 146-147 EF 7
Lehua [USA] 78-79 b 1
Lehui = Zhongyuan 150-151 H 3
Lehututu 172 D 6
Leiah = Leya 134-135 L 4
Leibnitz 118 G 5
Leicester 119 F 5
Leichhardt, Sydney- 161 I ab 2
Leichhardt Range 158-159 J 4
Leichhardt River 158-159 GH 3
Lei-chou Pan-tao = Leizhou Bandao 142-143 L 7
Lei-chou Wan = Leizhou Wan 146-147 C 11
Leiden 120-121 K 2
Leie 120-121 J 3
Leigaing 141 D 5
Leigh Creek 158-159 G 6
Leighton, AL 78-79 F 3
Leigyā 141 E 5
Leikanger 116-117 A 6
Leik Kyūn 141 CD 8
Leimbach, Zürich- 128 IV ab 2
Leimebamba 96-97 C 5
Lei Mwe = Lūymwe 141 F 5
Leine 118 D 3
Leinster 119 C 5
Leipoldtville 174-175 C 7
Leipsic, OH 70-71 HJ 5
Leipsic = Leipzig 118 F 3
Leipsói 122-123 M 7
Leipzig 118 F 3
Leiranger 116-117 F 4
Leiria 120-121 C 9
Lei Shui 146-147 D 8-9
Leisler, Mount — 158-159 EF 4
Leismer 61 C 3
Leitchfield, KY 70-71 GH 7
Leiter, WY 68-69 C 3
Leitha 118 H 5
Leith Harbour 111 J 8
Lei U Mun 155 I b 2
Leiva, Cerro — 94-95 D 6
Leiwe 141 DE 6
Leiyang 142-143 L 6
Leizhou Bandao 142-143 L 7
Leizhou Wan 146-147 C 11
Lejââ, El- = Al-Lajā' 136-137 G 6
Lejasciems 124-125 F 5
Lek 120-121 K 3
Leka 116-117 D 5
Lekef = Al-Kāf 164-165 F 1
Lekemti = Nekemtē 164-165 M 7
Leksand 116-117 F 7
Leksozero 124-125 H 2
Leksula 148-149 J 7
Lekuru 174-175 E 3
Lel = Lēh 134-135 M 4
Lela, TX 76-77 D 5
Leland, MI 70-71 GH 3
Leland, MS 78-79 D 4
Leland Elk Rapids, MI 72-73 D 2
Lel'čicy 124-125 FG 8
Leleiwi Point 78-79 e 3
Lelekovka 126-127 EF 2
Leleque 111 B 6
Leleque, Cordón — 108-109 D 4
Leling 146-147 F 3
Lelingluan 148-149 K 8
Lely Gebergte 98-99 L 2
Lema, Sierra de — 94-95 L 4
Lemahabang 148-149 E 8
Léman 118 C 5
le Mans 120-121 H 4-5
Le Marchand 108-109 E 8
Le Marie, Estrecho de — 111 C 9-D 8
Le Mars, IA 70-71 BC 4
Lembale 171 BC 4
Lemberg 61 G 5
Leme 102-103 J 5
Leme, Rio de Janeiro- 110 I bc 2
le Mesnil-Amelot 129 I d 1
le Mesnil-le-Roi 129 I b 2
Lemesós 134-135 C 4
Lemhi, ID 66-67 G 3
Lemhi Range 66-67 G 3
Lemhi River 66-67 G 3
Leming, TX 76-77 E 8
Lemitar, NM 76-77 A 5
Lemland 116-117 J 8
Lemmenjoen kansallispuisto 116-117 LM 3
Lemmon, SD 68-69 E 3
Lemmon, Mount — 74-75 H 6
Lēmnos 122-123 L 6
le Mont-Saint-Michel 120-121 FG 4
Lemoore, CA 74-75 CD 4
Lemouissate, Bir — = Bi'r al-M'wisāt 166-167 A 7
Lemoyne, NE 68-69 F 5
Lemrō Myit 141 C 5
Lemsahl-Mellingstedt, Hamburg- 130 I b 1
Lemsford 61 D 5
Lemukutan, Pulau — 152-153 GH 5
Lemvig 116-117 C 9
Lemyeth'hnā 141 D 7
Lemyethna = Lemyeth'hnā 141 D 7
Lena 132-133 W 5-6
Lena, LA 78-79 C 5
Lena, MS 78-79 E 4
Lena, OR 66-67 D 3
Lençóis 92-93 L 7
Lençóis, Baía dos — 100-101 B 1
Lençóis Grandes 100-101 C 2
Lençóis Paulista 102-103 H 5
Lenda 171 B 2
Lendery 132-133 E 5
Lenga 150-151 D 11
Lenger 132-133 MN 9
Lengerskij = Georgijevka 132-133 P 8
Lenggor 150-151 D 11
Lengshuijiang 146-147 C 8
Lengshuitan 146-147 C 8
Lengua de Vaca, Punta — 111 B 4
Lenguaraz, El — 106-107 H 6-7
Lenina, gora — 113 V d 2
Lenina, pik — 134-135 L 3
Lenina, Stadion im. — 113 V b 3
Leninabad 134-135 KL 2-3
Leninakan 126-127 LM 6
Leningrad 132-133 E 5-6
Leningradskaja 126-127 J 3
Lenino 126-127 G 4
Lenino = Leninsk-Kuzneckij 132-133 Q 6-7
Lenino, Moskva- 113 V c 3
Leninogorsk 132-133 P 7
Leninsk 126-127 M 2
Leninskaja Sloboda 124-125 P 5-6
Leninskij [SU Marijskaja ASSR] 124-125 P 5
Leninsk-Kuzneckij 132-133 Q 6-7
Leninsk-Kuznetsk = Leninsk-Kuzneckij 132-133 Q 6-7
Leninskoje 124-125 Q 4
Lenkoran' 126-127 O 7
Lennep, MT 66-67 H 2
Lennewaden = Lielvārde 124-125 E 5
Lennox, CA 83 III b 2
Lennox, SD 68-69 H 4
Lennox, Isla — 111 C 9
Lennoxville 72-73 L 2
Lenoir, NC 80-81 F 3
Lenoir City, TN 78-79 G 3
Lenola, NJ 84 III d 2
Lenora, KS 68-69 FG 6
Lenorah, TX 76-77 CD 6
Lenore 61 H 6
Lenox, IA 70-71 C 5
Lens 120-121 J 3
Lensk 132-133 V 5
Lentini 122-123 F 7
Lentvaris 124-125 E 6
Lenyā Myit 150-151 B 7
Lèo 164-165 D 6
Leoben 118 G 5
Leola, AR 78-79 C 3
Leola, SD 68-69 G 3
Leoma, TN 78-79 F 3
Leominster, MA 72-73 KL 3
Leon, IA 70-71 D 5
León [E, landscape] 120-121 E 7-8
León [E, place] 120-121 E 7
León [MEX] 64-65 F 7
León [NIC] 64-65 J 9
Leon, Cerro — 102-103 B 4
León, Cerro del — 64-65 G 8
Leon, Montes de — 120-121 D 7
León, Pays de — 120-121 E 4
Leonardtown, MD 72-73 H 5
Leonardville 172 C 6
Leona River 76-77 E 8
Leoncito, Cerro — 106-107 C 2
Leone, Valle — 108-109 G 2
Leones 106-107 F 4
Leones, Parque Nacional de los — 91 I b 3
Leonesa, La — 104-105 G 10
Leongatha 160 G 7
Leoni 102-103 G 7
Leonídion 122-123 K 7
Leonora 158-159 D 5
Leon River 76-77 E 7
Leontovich, Cape — 58-59 b 2
Leo Pargial 138-139 G 1
Leopoldau, Wien- 113 I b 1
Léopold II, Lac — = Mai Ndombe 172 C 2
Leopoldina 102-103 L 4
Leopoldo de Bulhões 102-103 H 2
Leopoldsdorf 113 I b 2
Leopoldstadt, Wien- 113 I b 2
Leopoldville = Kinshasa 172 C 2
Leoses 98-99 F 10
Leoti, KS 68-69 F 6
Leovo 126-127 D 3
Lepākshi 140 C 4
Lepanto, AR 78-79 D 3
Lepar, Pulau — 148-149 E 7
Lepel' 124-125 G 6
Leper Colony = Balboa Heights 64-65 b 3
le Perreux-sur-Marne 129 I d 2
Le Pessis-Bouchard 129 I b 1-2
Lephepe 172 DE 6
Lépi = Caála 172 C 4
Lepihue 108-109 C 3
le Pin 129 I d 2
Leping 142-143 M 6
Lepl'avo 126-127 E 2
le Plessis-Trévise 129 I d 2
Lepreau 63 C 5
Lepsy 132-133 O 8
Leptis magna 164-165 GH 2
le Puy 120-121 J 6
Lequeitio 120-121 F 7
Lēr 164-165 KL 7
Léraba 168-169 D 3
le Raincy 129 I d 2
Lerdo de Tejada 86-87 N 8
Léré [Chad] 164-165 G 7
Léré [RMM] 168-169 D 2
Lere [WAN] 168-169 H 3
le Relais 63 A 4
Leribe 174-175 H 5
Lérida [CO, Tolima] 94-95 D 5
Lérida [CO, Vaupés] 92-93 E 4
Lérida [E] 120-121 H 8
Lerik 126-127 O 7
Lerma 120-121 F 7-8
Lerma, Acueducto de — 91 I b 2
Lermá, Valle de — 104-105 D 9
Lermontov 126-127 L 4
Léros 122-123 M 7
Leroy 61 F 4
Le Roy, IL 70-71 F 5
Le Roy, MI 72-73 D 2
Le Roy, MI 70-71 H 3
Le Roy, MN 70-71 D 4
Le Roy, NY 72-73 GH 3
Le Roy, WY 66-67 H 5
Lértora 106-107 F 5
Lerwick 119 F 1
les Abymes 64-65 O 8
les Andelys 120-121 H 4
Lésbos 122-123 L 6
Les Cayes 64-65 M 8
Leščevo = Charovsk 132-133 G 6
les Clayes-sous-Bois 129 I a 2
les Escoumins 63 B 3
les Eucalyptus 170 I b 2
les Grésillons 129 I b 2
Leshan 142-143 J 6
Leshī 141 D 3
Lésigny 129 I d 3
Lesina = Hvar 122-123 G 4
Lesistyje Karpaty 118 KL 4
Lesken 126-127 L 5
Leskovac 122-123 J 4
Leslie 174-175 H 4
Leslie, AR 78-79 C 3
Leslie, ID 66-67 G 4
Leslie, MI 70-71 H 4
les Méchins 63 C 3
Lesnoj [SU ↓ Murmansk] 132-133 EF 4
Lesnoj [SU, Kirovskaja Oblast'] 132-133 J 6
Lesnoje [SU, Rossijskaja SFSR] 124-125 K 4
Lesobeng 174-175 H 5
Lesotho 172 E 7
Lesozavodsk 132-133 Za 8
Lesozavodskij 116-117 P 4
les Pavillons-sous-Bois 129 I cd 2
les Pins Maritimes 170 I b 2
les Quatre Chemins 170 I b 2
les Sables-d'Olonne 120-121 FG 5
Lesser Antilles 92-93 FG 2
Lesser Khingan = Xiao Hinggan Ling 142-143 O 1-P 2
Lesser Slave Lake 56-57 O 6
Lesser Sunda Islands 148-149 GH 8
le Stéhoux 128 II a 2
Lester, IA 68-69 H 4
Lester, PA 84 III b 2
Le Sueur, MN 70-71 D 3
Lešukonskoje 132-133 H 5
Leszno 118 H 3
Letaba [ZA, place Drakensberge] 174-175 J 2
Letaba [ZA, place Kruger National Park] 174-175 J 2
Letaba [ZA, river] 172 F 6
Letcher, SD 68-69 G 4
Letellier 68-69 H 1
Leteri 138-139 F 5
Lethā Taung 141 C 4
Lethbridge 56-57 O 8
Lethem 92-93 H 4
le Thillay 129 I c 1
Lê Thuy 150-151 F 4
Leti, Kepulauan — 148-149 J 8
Letiahau 172 D 6
Letičev 126-127 C 2
Leticia 92-93 EF 5
Leting 146-147 G 2
Letjesbosch = Letjiesbos 174-175 DE 7
Letjiesbos 174-175 DE 7
Letka [SU, place] 124-125 R 4
Letka [SU, river] 124-125 R 4
Letn'aja Stavka 126-127 L 4
Letnerečenskij 124-125 JK 1
Letohatchee, AL 78-79 F 4
Letong 150-151 E 11
Letpadan = Letpandan 148-149 C 3
Letpandan 148-149 C 3
le Tréport 120-121 H 3
Letsûtau Kyûn 150-151 AB 7
Leucite Hills 68-69 B 5
Leuser, Gunung — 148-149 C 6
Leuven 120-121 K 3
Levallois-Perret 129 I c 2
Levan, UT 74-75 H 3
Levanger 116-117 D 6
Levantine Basin 164-165 KL 2
Lėvanzo 122-123 DE 6
Levasseur = Bi'r Shuhadā' 166-167 K 2
Level, Isla — 108-109 B 5
Levelland, TX 76-77 C 6
Levelock, AK 58-59 J 7
Levent 136-137 G 3
Leveque, Cape — 158-159 D 3
Lever, Rio — 98-99 N 10
le Verdon-sur-Mer 120-121 G 6
Leverett Glacier 53 A 24-22
Leverger = San Antônio do Leverger 102-103 DE 1
Leverkusen 118 C 3
le Vert-Galant 129 I d 2
le Vésinet 129 I b 2
Levice 118 J 4
Levick, Mount — 53 B 16-17
Levin 158-159 P 8
Levinópolis 102-103 K 1
Lévis 56-57 W 8
Levittown, PA 72-73 J 4
Lévka 136-137 E 5
Levká Óré 122-123 KL 8
Lévkara 136-137 E 5
Levkás [GR, island] 122-123 J 6
Levkás [GR, place] 122-123 J 6
Levkōsia 134-135 C 3
Levokumskoje 126-127 M 4
Levski 122-123 L 4
Levskigrad 122-123 L 4
Lev Tolstoj 124-125 M 7
Levubu 174-175 J 2
Lewapaku 152-153 NO 10
Lewe = Leiwe 141 DE 6
Lewellen, NE 68-69 EF 5
Lewes, DE 72-73 J 5
Lewinsville, VA 82 II a 1
Lewinsville Heights, VA 82 II a 1
Lewis, Butt of — 119 C 2
Lewis, Isle of — 119 C 2
Lewis and Clark Lake 68-69 H 4
Lewisburg, KY 78-79 F 2
Lewisburg, PA 72-73 H 4
Lewisburg, TN 78-79 F 3
Lewisburg, WV 80-81 F 2
Lewisdale, MD 82 II b 1
Lewisham, London- 129 II b 2
Lewis Hills 63 G 3
Lewis Pass 158-159 O 8
Lewisporte 63 J 3
Lewis Range 64-65 D 2
Lewis River 66-67 BC 2
Lewiston, ID 64-65 C 2
Lewiston, ME 64-65 MN 3
Lewiston, MI 70-71 HJ 3
Lewiston, UT 66-67 H 5
Lewistown, IL 70-71 EF 5
Lewistown, MT 68-69 B 2
Lewistown, PA 72-73 GH 4
Lewisville, AR 78-79 C 4
Lewisville, TX 76-77 F 6
Lexington, KY 64-65 K 4
Lexington, MO 70-71 D 6
Lexington, MS 78-79 DE 4
Lexington, NC 80-81 FG 3
Lexington, NE 68-69 G 5
Lexington, TN 78-79 E 3
Lexington, TX 76-77 F 7
Lexington, VA 80-81 G 2
Lēxúrion 122-123 J 6
Leya 134-135 L 4
Leyden = Leiden 120-121 K 2
Leydsdorp 172 F 6
Leyte 148-149 J 4
Leyton, London- 129 II b 1
Leža [SU, place] 124-125 N 4
Ležajsk 118 L 3
Lezama [RA] 106-107 J 5
Lezama [YV] 94-95 H 3
Lezhë 122-123 H 5
Ležnevo 124-125 N 5
L'gov 124-125 K 8
Lhagö Gangri 138-139 L 3
Lhamolatse La 138-139 HJ 2
Lhamopäkargola = Lamobagar Gola 138-139 L 4
Lha Ri 142-143 E 5
Lharugö 142-143 G 5
Lhasa 142-143 G 6
Lhatse Dsong 142-143 F 6
Lhokkruet 148-149 BC 6
Lhokseumawe 148-149 C 5
Lholam 138-139 M 2
Lho Nagpo = Lo Nagpo 141 D 2
Lhophu 138-139 M 2
Lhunpo Gangri 142-143 EF 5-6
Lhuntse 141 B 2
Li 150-151 B 4
Liakhof Islands = Novosibirskije ostrova 132-133 Z-e 2
Liancheng 146-147 F 9
Liangcheng 146-147 GH 4
Liang-ch'iu = Liangqiu 146-147 FG 4
Lianggezhuang 146-147 E 2
Lianghekou 146-147 B 7
Liang-ho-k'ou = Lianghekou 146-147 B 7
Liangjiadian 144-145 CD 3
Liang-ko-chuang = Lianggezhuang 146-147 E 2
Liangqiu 146-147 FG 4
Liangshan 146-147 EF 4
Liangshan Yizu Zizhizhou 142-143 J 6
Liangshan Zizhizhou 142-143 J 6
Liangtian [TJ, Guangxi Zhuangzu Zizhiqu] 146-147 BC 10
Liangtian [TJ, Hunan] 146-147 D 9
Liang-t'ien = Liangtian 146-147 D 9
Liang Xiang 142-143 LM 4
Liangxiangzhen 142-143 LM 4
Liangyuan 146-147 F 5
Liangzi Hu 146-147 E 6
Lianhua 142-143 L 6
Lianhua Chi 155 II a 2
Lianhua He 155 II a 2
Lianhua Shan 146-147 E 10
Lianjiang [TJ, place Fujian] 146-147 G 8
Lianjiang [TJ, place Guangdong] 142-143 KL 7
Lian Jiang [TJ, river ⊲ Bei Jiang] 146-147 D 9
Lian Jiang [TJ, river ⊲ Gan Jiang] 146-147 E 9
Lian Jiang = Ping Jiang 146-147 E 8
Liannan 146-147 D 9
Lianozovo, Moskva- 113 V c 2
Lianping 142-143 LM 7
Lianshan 146-147 CD 9
Lianshan = Manyunjie 141 E 3
Lianshanguan 144-145 D 2
Lianshui [TJ, place] 146-147 G 5
Lian Shui [TJ, river] 146-147 CD 8
Liantang 146-147 E 7
Lian Xian 146-147 D 9
Lianyuan 146-147 C 8
Lianyungang 142-143 MN 5
Lianyun Shan 146-147 D 7
Lianzhen 146-147 F 7
Liaocheng 142-143 LM 4
Liao-chung = Liaozhong 144-145 D 2
Liaodong Bandao 142-143 N 4
Liaodong Wan 142-143 MN 3-4
Liao He 144-145 D 1
Liao Ho = Liao He 144-145 D 1
Liaoning 142-143 MN 3
Liaosi = Liaoxi 142-143 N 3
Liaotung = Liaodong Bandao 142-143 N 4
Liaotung, Gulf of — = Liaodong Wan 142-143 M 5-N 4
Liaotung Wan = Liaodong Wan 142-143 N 4
Liaoxi 142-143 N 3
Liaoyang 142-143 N 3
Liaoyuan 142-143 NO 3
Liaoyuan = Shuangliao 142-143 N 3
Liard River 56-57 M 5
Liat, Pulau — 152-153 G 7
Liaunim = Liaoning 142-143 MN 3
Libano [CO] 94-95 D 5
Líbano [RA] 106-107 G 6
Libanon 134-135 D 4
Libao 146-147 H 5
Libby, MT 66-67 F 1
Libby Reservoir 66-67 F 1
Libebe = Andara 172 D 5
Libenge 172 C 1
Liberal, KS 64-65 F 4
Liberata 102-103 G 7
Liberator Lake 58-59 HJ 2
Liberdade 96-97 F 7
Liberdade, Rio — [BR, Acre] 96-97 E 5-6
Liberdade, Rio — [BR, Mato Grosso] 98-99 M 10
Liberdade, São Paulo- 110 II b 2
Liberec 118 G 3
Liberia [CR] 88-89 D 9
Liberia [LB] 164-165 BC 7
Liberia Basin 50-51 J 5
Liberio Luna 106-107 E 4
Libertad [PE] 96-97 D 5
Libertad [RA] 106-107 HJ 3
Libertad [ROU] 106-107 J 5
Libertad [YV, Barinas] 94-95 G 3
Libertad [YV, Cojedes] 94-95 G 3
Libertad, La — [EC] 96-97 A 3
Libertad, La — [PE] 96-97 BC 5
Libertad, Merlo- 110 III a 2
Libertador General San Martín [RA, Jujuy] 104-105 D 8
Libertador General San Martín [RA, Misiones] 102-103 E 7
Libertador General San Martín = San Martín 106-107 E 4
Libertas 174-175 G 5
Liberty, AK 58-59 R 4
Liberty, IN 70-71 H 6
Liberty, KY 70-71 H 7
Liberty, MO 70-71 C 6
Liberty, NY 72-73 J 4
Liberty, OH 72-73 D 5
Liberty, TX 76-77 G 7-8
Liberty, WA 66-67 C 2
Liberty, Statue of — 82 III b 2
Liberty Acres, CA 83 III b 2
Liberty Bell Race Track 84 III c 1
Libong, Ko — 150-151 B 9
Libourne 120-121 GH 6
Libres del Sud 106-107 J 5
Libreville 172 AB 1
Libya 164-165 G-J 3
Libyan Desert 164-165 J 3-L 4
Licānia 100-101 DE 2
Licantén 111 B 4
Licata 122-123 E 7
Lice 136-137 J 3
Licenciado Matienzo 106-107 H 6
Lichangshan Liedao 144-145 D 3
Li-ch'ang-shan Lieh-tao = Lichangshan Liedao 144-145 D 3
Licheng 146-147 D 3
Li-ch'i = Lixi 146-147 E 7
Li-chia-chuang = Lijiazhuang 146-147 G 4
Li-chiang = Lijiang 142-143 J 6
Li-chia-tu = Lijiadu 146-147 F 7
Li-chin = Lijin 146-147 G 3
Lichinga 172 G 4
Lichoslavl' 124-125 K 5
Lichovskoj 126-127 JK 2
Lichtenburg 172 DE 7
Lichuan [TJ, Hubei] 146-147 B 6
Lichuan [TJ, Jiangxi] 146-147 F 8
Licínio de Almeida 100-101 C 8
Licking, MO 70-71 E 7
Licosa, Punta — 122-123 F 5
Licuri 100-101 D 7
Lida 124-125 E 7
Lida, NV 74-75 E 4
Lidām, Al- = Al-Khamāsīn 134-135 EF 6
Lidcombe, Sydney- 161 I a 2
Lidfontein 174-175 C 3
Lidgerwood, ND 68-69 H 2
Lidingö 116-117 H 8
Lídinon, Akrōtērion — 122-123 L 8
Lidköping 116-117 E 8
Lido di Ostia, Roma- 122-123 DE 5
Lieau, Nam — = Ea Hleo 150-151 F 6
Liebenbergsvleirivier 174-175 H 4-5
Liechtenstein 118 D 5
Liedao 146-147 J 6
Liederbach 128 III a 1
Liège 120-121 K 3
Lieksa 116-117 NO 6
Lieli 128 IV a 1
Lielupe 124-125 D 5
Lielvārde 124-125 E 5
Lienartville 172 E 1
Lien-chên = Lianzhen 146-147 F 3
Lien-ch'êng = Liancheng 146-147 F 9
Lien-chiang = Lianjiang [TJ, Fujian] 146-147 G 8
Lien-chiang = Lianjiang [TJ, Guangdong] 142-143 KL 7
Lien Chiang = Ping Jiang 146-147 E 8
Lien-hsien = Lian Xian 146-147 D 9
Lien-hua = Lianhua 142-143 L 6
Lienhwa = Lianhua 142-143 L 6
Lienkong = Lianjiang 146-147 G 8
Lienping = Lianping 146-147 E 9
Lien-shan-kuan = Lianshanguan 144-145 D 2
Lienshui = Lianshui [TJ, place] 146-147 G 5
Lien Shui = Lian Shui [TJ, river] 146-147 CD 8
Lien-t'ang = Liantang 146-147 E 7
Lienyun = Lianyungang 146-147 GH 4
Lienyunkang = Lianyungang 142-143 MN 5
Lien-yün Shan = Lianyun Shan 146-147 D 7
Lienz 118 F 5
Liepāja 124-125 C 5
Liepna 124-125 F 5
Lie-shan = Manyunjie 141 E 3
Liesing [A ⊲ Schwechat] 113 I b 2
Lietuva = Lithuanian Soviet Socialist Republic 124-125 DE 6
Lievenhof = Līvāni 124-125 F 5
Lièvre, Rivière du — 72-73 J 1
Liezen 118 FG 5
Lifi Mahuida 111 C 6
Lifīyah, Al- 136-137 K 7
Lifou, Île — 158-159 N 4
Lifu = Île Lifou 158-159 N 4
Lifubu 171 B 5
Liganga 171 C 5
Ligat = Līgatne 124-125 E 5
Līgatne 124-125 E 5
Light, Cape — 53 B 30-31
Lightning Ridge 160 HJ 2
Ligonha, Rio — 172 G 5
Ligthouse Beach 170 III ab 2
Ligua, Bahía la — 106-107 AB 4
Ligua, La — 111 B 4
Ligùria 122-123 B 4-C 3
Ligurian Sea 114-115 K 7
Li He 146-147 D 5
Lihir Group 148-149 h 5
Li Ho = Li He 146-147 D 5
Lihsien = Li Xian [TJ, Hebei] 146-147 E 2
Lihsien = Li Xian [TJ, Hunan] 146-147 C 7
Lihua = Litang 142-143 J 5
Lihuang = Jinzhai 146-147 E 6
Lihue, HI 78-79 c 2
Lihula 124-125 DE 4
Lijiadu 146-147 F 7
Lijiang 142-143 J 6
Lijiaping 146-147 CD 8
Lijiazhuang 146-147 G 4
Lijin 146-147 G 3
Lijnden 128 I a 1
Lik, Nam — 150-151 D 3
Likasi 172 E 4
Likati 172 D 1
Likely 60 G 3
Likely, CA 66-67 C 5
Likhāpāni 141 DE 2
Likiang = Lijiang 142-143 J 6
Likino-Dulevo 124-125 M 6
Likoma Island 172 FG 4
Likoto 172 D 2
Likouala [RCB ⊲ Sangha] 172 C 1
Likouala [RCB ⊲ Zaïre] 172 C 1
Likuala = Likouala [RCB ⊲ Sangha] 172 C 1
Likuala = Likouala [RCB ⊲ Zaïre] 172 C 1
Likupang 148-149 J 6
Liland 116-117 G 3
Lilbourn, MO 78-79 E 2
Liling 146-147 D 8
Lille 120-121 J 3
Lille Bælt 116-117 CD 10
Lille-Ballangen 116-117 G 3
Lillehammer 116-117 D 7
Lille Namaland = Klein Namakwaland 174-175 B 5
Lillesand 116-117 C 8
Lillestrøm 116-117 D 7-8
Lillian Lake 63 F 2
Lilliput 174-175 H 2
Lillooet 60 FG 4
Lillooet Range 60 F 4-G 5
Lilongwe [MW, place] 172 F 4
Lilongwe [MW, river] 171 C 6
Lilo Viejo 104-105 E 10
Liluah, Howrah- 154 II b 2
Lilung 146-147 H 10
Lilydale 160 c 2
Lim 122-123 H 4
Lima, MT 66-67 G 3
Lima, OH 64-65 K 3
Lima [P] 120-121 C 8
Lima [PE, administrative unit] 96-97 C 7-8
Lima [PE, place] 92-93 D 7
Lima [PY] 102-103 D 5
Lima [RA] 106-107 H 5
Lima = Dsayul 142-143 H 6
Lima, La — 88-89 B 7
Lima, Punta — 96-97 D 10
Lima Campos 100-101 E 4
Lima Duarte 102-103 L 4
Liman-Beren, ozero — 126-127 M 3
Limão, Cachoeira do — 92-93 J 6
Limão, São Paulo- 110 II ab 1
Lima Qundao = Dangan Liedao 146-147 E 10-11
Lima Reservoir 66-67 GH 3
Limarí, Río — 106-107 B 3
Limasol = Lemesós 134-135 C 4
Limassol = Lemesós 134-135 C 4
Lima Village, AK 58-59 K 6
Limay, Río — 111 C 5
Limay Mahuida 111 C 5
Limbang 148-149 FG 6
Limbani 96-97 G 9
Limbaži 124-125 E 5
Limbdi 138-139 CD 6

Limburg 118 D 3
Limchow = Hepu 142-143 K 7
Limeil-Brévennes 129 I cd 3
Limeira 92-93 K 9
Limerick 119 B 5
Limestone River 61 L 2
Limete, Kinshasa- 170 IV b 2
Limfjorden 116-117 D 9
Limia 120-121 C 8-D 7
Li Miao Zhou = Hainan Zangzu Zizhizhou 142-143 K 8
Limietskop 174-175 D 6
Limin = Thásos 122-123 L 5
Liminka 116-117 L 5
Limkong = Lianjiang 142-143 KL 7
Limmen Bight 158-159 G 2
Límnē 122-123 K 6
Límnē Begorĩtis 122-123 JK 5
Límnē Bistõnis 122-123 L 5
Límnē Boibēïs 122-123 K 6
Límnē Bólbē 122-123 K 6
Límnē Korõneia 122-123 K 5
Límnē Mégalē Prēspa 122-123 J 5
Límnē Trichõnis 122-123 J 6
Limoeiro 100-101 G 4
Limoeiro do Norte 100-101 E 3
Limoges [CDN] 72-73 J 2
Limoges [F] 120-121 H 6
Limón 64-65 K 9-10
Limon, CO 68-69 E 6
Limón, Bahía — 64-65 b 2
Limon Bay 64-65 b 2
Limón Verde, Cerro — 104-105 B 8
Limoquije 104-105 D 4
Limousin 120-121 HJ 6
Limoux 120-121 J 7
Limpia, Laguna — [RA ↖ Resistencia] 111 DE 3
Limpia, Laguna — [RA ↓ Resistencia] 106-107 H 1
Limpopo 172 E 6
Limpopo, Represa do — 174-175 K 3
Limpopo, Rio — 174-175 K 3
Limpoporivier 174-175 H 2
Limu 146-147 C 9
Lin 122-123 J 5
Lin, Lûy — 141 EF 4
Lin'an 146-147 G 6
Linan = Jianshui 142-143 J 7
Linares [CO] 92-93 D 4
Linares [E] 120-121 F 9
Linares [MEX] 64-65 G 7
Linares [RCH] 111 B 5
Linares, Los — 106-107 F 2
Linau Balui Plateau 152-153 L 4
Lin-Calel 106-107 G 7
Lincang 142-143 HJ 7
Lincheng 146-147 E 3
Lincheng = Xuecheng 146-147 F 4
Lin-ch'i = Linqi 146-147 D 4
Lin-chiang = Linjiang [TJ, Fujian] 146-147 G 8
Lin-chiang = Linjiang [TJ, Jilin] 142-143 O 3
Lin-ch'ing = Linqing 142-143 M 4
Linchow = Hepu 142-143 K 7
Linchu = Linqu 146-147 G 3
Linchuan = Fuzhou 142-143 MN 6
Lin-ch'üan = Linquan 146-147 E 5
Lincoln, CA 74-75 C 3
Lincoln, IL 70-71 F 5
Lincoln, KS 68-69 G 6
Lincoln, ME 72-73 M 2
Lincoln, NE 64-65 G 3
Lincoln, NH 72-73 KL 2
Lincoln, NM 76-77 B 6
Lincoln [GB] 119 F 5
Lincoln [RA] 111 D 4
Lincoln Center 82 III c 2
Lincoln City, IN 70-71 G 6
Lincoln City, Houston-, TX 85 III b 1
Lincolnia Heights, VA 82 II a 2
Lincoln Memorial 82 II a 2
Lincoln Memorial Park Cemetery 85 II b 2
Lincoln Memorial Park Center 85 II b 2
Lincoln Museum 82 II ab 2
Lincoln Park, MI 72-73 E 3
Lincoln Park [USA, Chicago] 83 II b 1
Lincoln Park [USA, New York] 82 III b 2
Lincoln Park [USA, San Francisco] 83 I ab 2
Lincoln Sea 52 A 24-25
Lincolnton, NC 80-81 F 3
Lind, WA 66-67 D 2
Linda [SU] 124-125 P 5
Linda, Serra — 100-101 D 8
Lindale, GA 78-79 G 3
Lindale, TX 76-77 G 6
Lindale Park, Houston-, TX 85 III b 1
Lindau [CH] 128 IV b 1
Lindau [D] 118 D 5
Linde [SU] 132-133 X 4
Linden, AL 78-79 F 4
Linden, IN 70-71 G 5
Linden, MA 84 I b 2
Linden, NJ 82 III a 3
Linden, TN 78-79 F 3
Linden, TX 76-77 G 6
Linden, Johannesburg- 170 V ab 1
Linden Airport 82 III a 3
Lindenberg [DDR, Frankfurt] 130 III c 1
Lindenwold, NJ 84 III d 3
Lindesberg 116-117 F 8
Lindesnes 116-117 B 9
Lindfield, Sydney- 161 I ab 1
Lindi [EAT] 172 G 3-4
Lindi [ZRE] 172 E 1
Lindian 142-143 NO 2
Lindley 174-175 GH 4
Líndos 122-123 N 7
Lindozero 124-125 J 2
Lindsay 72-73 G 2
Lindsay, CA 74-75 D 4
Lindsay, MT 68-69 D 2
Lindsay, OK 76-77 F 5
Lindsborg, KS 68-69 H 6
Linea, La — 120-121 E 10
Lineville, AL 78-79 G 4
Lineville, IA 70-71 D 5
Linfen 142-143 L 4
Lingadaw 141 D 5
Lingâla 140 E 1-2
Linganamakki Reservoir 140 B 3-4
Lingao 142-143 K 8
Lingao Jiao 150-151 G 3
Lingasugar = Lingsugūr 140 C 2
Lingayen Gulf 148-149 GH 3
Lingbao 146-147 C 4
Lingbi 146-147 F 5
Ling Chiang = Ling Jiang 146-147 H 7
Lingchuan 146-147 BC 9
Lingding Yang = Zhujiang Kou 146-147 D 10
Ling Dsong 138-139 N 3
Linge [BUR] 148-149 C 2
Lingeh = Bandar-e Lengeh 134-135 GH 5
Lingen 118 C 2
Lingga 152-153 J 5
Lingga, Kapulauan — 148-149 DE 7
Lingga, Pulau — 148-149 DE 7
Linghong Kou 146-147 G 4
Ling-hsien = Ling Xian 146-147 DE 8
Lingle, WY 68-69 D 4
Lingling 142-143 L 6
Lingman Lake 62 C 1
Lingmar 142-143 F 5-6
Ling'ö 138-139 L 3
Lingpao = Lingbao 146-147 C 4
Lingpi = Lingbi 146-147 F 5
Lingqiu 146-147 E 2
Lingshan 146-147 B 10
Lingshan Dao 146-147 H 4
Lingshanwei 146-147 H 4
Lingshi 146-147 C 3
Lingshih = Lingshi 146-147 C 3
Lingshou 146-147 E 2
Lingshui 150-151 GH 3
Lingsugūr 140 C 2
Lingtse 138-139 M 4
Linguère 164-165 AB 5
Lingwala, Kinshasa- 170 IV a 1
Ling Xian [TJ, Hunan] 146-147 DE 8
Ling Xian [TJ, Shandong] 146-147 F 3
Lingyang 146-147 F 6
Lingyuan 144-145 B 2
Ling-yüan = Lingyuan 144-145 B 2
Lingyun 142-143 K 7
Linhai 142-143 N 6
Linhares 92-93 LM 8
Linh Cam 148-149 E 3
Linhe 142-143 K 3
Lin-ho = Linhe 142-143 K 3
Lin-hsi = Linxi 142-143 M 3
Lin-hsia = Linxia 142-143 J 4
Lin-hsien = Lin Xian [TJ, Henan] 146-147 DE 3
Linhsien = Lin Xian [TJ, Shanxi] 146-147 C 3
Linhuaiguan 146-147 FG 5
Lin-huai-kuan = Linhuaiguan 146-147 FG 5
Lin-huan-chi = Linhuanji 146-147 F 5
Linhuanji 146-147 F 5
Lin-i = Linyi [TJ ↑ Jinan] 146-147 F 3
Lini = Linyi [TJ ↗ Xuzhou] 142-143 M 4
Linjiang [TJ, Fujian] 146-147 G 8
Linjiang [TJ, Jilin] 142-143 O 3
Linju = Linru 146-147 D 4
Linkebeek 128 II b 2
Linkiang = Linjiang 146-147 G 8
Linköping 116-117 FG 8
Linkou 142-143 OP 2
Linkow = Linkou 142-143 OP 2
Linkowo = Linkuva 124-125 D 5
Linksfield, Johannesburg- 170 V b 1
Linkuva 124-125 D 5
Linli 142-143 L 6
Linmeyer, Johannesburg- 170 V b 2
Linn, KS 68-69 H 6
Linn, MO 70-71 E 6
Linn, TX 76-77 E 9
Linn, Mount — 66-67 B 5
Linné, Kapp — 116-117 j 5
Linnhe, Loch — 119 D 3
Linosa 122-123 E 8
Linosa, Ìsola — 164-165 G 1
Linqi 146-147 D 4
Linqing 142-143 M 4
Linqu 146-147 G 3
Linquan 146-147 E 5
Linru 146-147 D 4
Lins 92-93 JK 9
Linshan = Zhouxiang 146-147 H 6
Linshu 146-147 G 4
Linsia = Linxia 142-143 J 4
Linsin = Linxia 142-143 J 4
Lintan 142-143 J 5
Lintao 142-143 J 4
Lintien = Lindian 142-143 NO 2
Linton, IN 70-71 G 6
Linton, ND 68-69 FG 2
Lintong 146-147 B 4
Linton-Jonction 72-73 KL 1
Lintsing = Linqing 142-143 M 4
Lintung = Lintong 146-147 B 4
Linwood, PA 84 III a 3
Linwri = Limbdi 138-139 CD 6
Linwu 146-147 D 9
Linxi 142-143 M 3
Linxia 142-143 J 4
Linxia Huizu Zizhizhou 142-143 J 4
Lin Xian [TJ, Henan] 146-147 DE 3
Lin Xian [TJ, Shanxi] 146-147 C 3
Linxiang 146-147 D 7
Linyanti 172 D 5
Linyi [TJ, Shandong ↑ Jinan] 146-147 F 3
Linyi [TJ, Shandong ↗ Xuzhou] 142-143 M 4
Linyi [TJ, Shanxi] 146-147 C 4
Linying 146-147 D 5
Linyou 146-147 AB 4
Linyu = Linyou 146-147 AB 4
Linyu = Shanhaiguan 144-145 BC 2
Linz 118 FG 4
Lio Matoh 152-153 L 4
Lion, Golf du — 120-121 JK 7
Lionárisson 136-137 F 5
Lion River = Löwenrivier 174-175 C 4
Lion Rock Tunnel 155 I b 1
Lions, Gulf of — = Golfe du Lion 120-121 JK 7
Lions Head 72-73 F 2
Liouesso 172 BC 1
Liozno 124-125 H 6
Li-pao = Libao 146-147 H 5
Lipari 122-123 F 6
Lipari Islands = Ìsole Eòlie o Lìpari 122-123 F 6
Lipatkain 152-153 D 5
Lipeck 124-125 M 7
Lípez, Cordillera de — 92-93 F 9
Lipin Bor 124-125 LM 3
Liping 142-143 K 6
Lipis, Kuala — 150-151 D 10
Lipkany 126-127 C 2
Lipljan 122-123 J 4
Lipno 118 J 2
Lipova 122-123 J 2
Lippe 118 C 3
Lippstadt 118 D 3
Lipscomb, TX 76-77 D 4
Lipton 61 G 5
Lipu 142-143 KL 7
Lique, Sierra de — 104-105 D 6-7
Lira 172 F 1
Liranga 172 C 2
Lircay 96-97 D 8
Lisala 172 D 1
Līsār 136-137 N 3
Lisboa 120-121 C 9
Lisbon, ND 68-69 H 2
Lisbon, OH 72-73 F 4
Lisbon = Lisboa 120-121 C 9
Lisbon, Rock of — = Cabo da Roca 120-121 C 9
Lisburn 119 CD 4
Lisburne, Cape — 56-57 C 4
Liscomb 63 F 5
Lishan 146-147 D 6
Lishi 142-143 L 4
Lishih = Lishi 142-143 L 4
Li Shui [TJ, Hunan] 146-147 C 7
Lishui [TJ, Jiangsu] 146-147 G 6
Lishui [TJ, Zhejiang] 142-143 MN 6
Lishui = Limu 146-147 C 9
Lisičansk 126-127 J 2
Lisieux 120-121 H 4
Liski = Gheorghiu-Dej 126-127 JK 1
Lisle, NY 72-73 HJ 3
Lismore [AUS] 158-159 K 5
Lismore [CDN] 63 E 5
Lismore [IRL] 119 C 5
Lista 116-117 B 8
Lister, Mount — 53 B 17
Listowel [CDN] 72-73 F 3
Listowel [IRL] 119 B 5
Litan 142-143 J 5
Litang 142-143 K 7
Līṭānī, Nahr al- 136-137 F 6
Litchfield, CA 66-67 CD 5
Litchfield, IL 70-71 F 6
Litchfield, MN 70-71 C 3
Litchfield, NE 68-69 G 5
Litchville, ND 68-69 G 2
Līth, Al- 134-135 E 6
Lithgow 158-159 K 6
Lithuania 124-125 CE 6
Litin 126-127 D 2
Litinon, Cape — = Akrōtḗrion Lídinon 122-123 L 8
Litke 132-133 ab 7
Litóchōron 122-123 K 5
Litoměřice 118 G 3
Litomyšl 118 GH 4
Litoral, Cordillera del — 91 II bc 1
Litovko 132-133 Za 8
Litsin = Lijin 146-147 G 3
Little Abaco Island 88-89 GH 1
Little Abitibi Lake 62 L 2
Little Abitibi River 62 L 1-2
Little Andaman 134-135 P 8
Little Barrier Island 161 F 3
Little Bay de Noc 70-71 G 3
Little Belt = Lille Bælt 116-117 CD 10
Little Belt Mountains 66-67 H 2
Little Bighorn River 68-69 C 3
Little Black River 58-59 Q 3
Little Blue River 68-69 G 5
Little Bow River 61 B 5
Little Bullhead 62 A 2
Little Carpathians = Malé Karpaty 118 H 4
Little Cayman 64-65 KL 8
Little Churchill River 61 L 2
Little Colorado River 64-65 DE 5
Little Creek 84 II c 3
Little Current 62 KL 4
Little Current River 62 FG 2
Little Darby Creek 84 III a 1
Little Desert 160 E 6
Little Falls, MN 70-71 C 2-3
Little Falls, NJ 82 III a 1
Little Falls, NY 72-73 J 3
Little Falls Dam 82 II a 1
Littlefield, AZ 74-75 G 4
Littlefield, TX 76-77 CD 6
Littlefork, MN 70-71 D 1
Little Fork River 70-71 D 1
Little Fort 60 G 4
Little Grande Lake 63 H 3
Little Grand Rapids 62 B 1
Little Hong Kong 155 I b 2
Little Humboldt River 66-67 E 5
Little Inagua Island 88-89 K 4
Little Karas Mountains = Klein Karasberge 174-175 C 4
Little Karroo = Klein Karoo 174-175 DE 7
Little Kiska Island 58-59 rs 7
Little Koniuji Island 58-59 d 2
Little Lake, CA 74-75 E 5
Little Longlac 62 F 3
Little Mecatina River 56-57 YZ 7
Little Melozitna River 58-59 L 4
Little Minch 119 C 3
Little Missouri River 68-69 E 2
Little Mount Ararat = Küçük Ağrı dağı 136-137 L 3
Little Nahant, MA 84 I c 2
Little Namaqua Land = Klein Namakwaland 174-175 B 5
Little Neck Bay 82 III d 2
Little Nicobar 134-135 P 9
Little Osage River 70-71 C 7
Little Pee Dee River 80-81 G 3-4
Little Powder River 68-69 D 3
Little Rann 138-139 C 6
Little River, KS 68-69 GH 6
Little Rock, AR 64-65 H 5
Littlerock, CA 74-75 DE 5
Little Rock, WA 66-67 B 2
Little Rock Mountains 66-67 J 1-2
Little Rocky Mountains 68-69 B 1-2
Little Ruaha 171 C 4-5
Little Sable Point 70-71 G 4
Little Salmon Lake 58-59 U 5
Little Sanke River 68-69 B 5
Little Sioux River 70-71 C 4
Little Sitkin Island 58-59 s 7
Little Smoky 60 J 2
Little Smoky River 60 J 2
Little Smoky Valley 74-75 F 3
Little Snake River 66-67 J 5
Little Timber Creek 84 III bc 2
Little Tinicum Island 84 III b 2
Littleton 129 II a 2
Littleton, CO 68-69 D 6
Littleton, NC 80-81 GH 2
Littleton, NH 72-73 L 2
Little Traverse Bay 70-71 H 3
Little Valley, NY 72-73 G 3
Little Vince Bayou 85 III b 2
Little White Bayou 85 III c 1
Little Wood River 66-67 FG 4
Little York, Houston-, TX 85 III b 1
Litunde 171 CD 6
Liucheng 146-147 B 9
Liu-chia-tzū = Liujiazi 144-145 C 2
Liuchow = Liuzhou 142-143 K 7
Liu-ch'üan = Liuquan 146-147 F 4
Liu-chuang = Liuzhuang 146-147 GH 5
Liuhe [TJ, Henan] 146-147 E 4
Liuhe [TJ, Jiangsu] 146-147 H 6
Liuhe [TJ, Jilin] 144-145 E 1
Liuhe = Luhe 146-147 G 5
Liuheng Dao 146-147 J 7
Liu-hêng Tao = Liuheng Dao 146-147 J 7
Liu-ho = Liuhe [TJ, Henan] 146-147 E 4
Liu-ho = Liuhe [TJ, Jiangsu] 146-147 H 6
Liu-ho = Liuhe [TJ, Jilin] 144-145 E 1
Liu-ho = Luhe 146-147 G 5
Liujiazi 144-145 C 2
Liulihezhen 146-147 EF 2
Liu-li-ho = Liulihezhen 146-147 EF 2
Liulitun = Beijing-Xinghuo 155 II bc 2
Liuquan 146-147 F 4
Liurbao 144-145 D 2
Liushouying 146-147 G 2
Liuwa Plain 172 D 4
Liuyang 146-147 D 7
Liuzhou 142-143 K 7
Liuzhuang 146-147 GH 5
Līvāni 124-125 F 5
Lively Island 108-109 KL 9
Livengood, AK 58-59 N 4
Live Oak, FL 80-81 b 1
Live Oak, LA 85 I b 3
Livermore, CA 74-75 C 4
Livermore, IA 70-71 CD 4
Livermore, KY 70-71 G 7
Livermore, Mount — 64-65 F 5
Livermore Falls, ME 72-73 LM 2
Liverpool [CDN] 63 D 5-6
Liverpool [GB] 119 E 5
Liverpool Bay [CDN] 56-57 L 3-4
Liverpool Range 158-159 JK 6
Livingston, AL 78-79 EF 4
Livingston, KY 72-73 DE 6
Livingston, MT 66-67 H 3
Livingston, TN 78-79 G 2
Livingston, TX 76-77 G 7
Livingstone 172 E 5
Livingstone Creek 58-59 UV 6
Livingstone Memorial 172 F 4
Livingstone Mountains 172 F 3-4
Livingstonia 171 C 5
Livingstonia = Chiweta 172 F 4
Livingston Island 53 CD 30
Livno 122-123 G 4
Livny 124-125 L 7
Livonia, MI 72-73 E 3
Livorno 122-123 CD 4
Livramento = Santana do Livramento 106-107 K 3
Livramento do Brumado 100-101 CD 7
Livry-Gargan 129 I d 2
Liwale 172 G 3
Liwung, Ci — 154 IV a 1
Lixi 146-147 E 7
Li Xian [TJ, Hebei] 146-147 E 2
Li Xian [TJ, Hunan] 146-147 C 7
Lixin 146-147 F 5
Liyang 146-147 G 6
Liyepaya = Liepāya 124-125 C 6
Lî Yûbû 164-165 K 7
Liz 136-137 JK 3
Lizarda 92-93 K 6
Lizard Head Peak 66-67 J 4
Lizard Point 119 D 7
Lizerorta 124-125 C 5
Ljubljana 122-123 F 2
Ljungan 116-117 G 6
Ljungby 116-117 FG 9
Ljusdal 116-117 FG 7
Ljusnan 116-117 F 6-7
Ljusne 116-117 G 7
Llahuin 106-107 B 3
Llaima, Volcán — 106-107 B 7
Llajta Mauca 106-107 F 2
Llallagua 104-105 C 6
Llamara, Salar de — 104-105 B 7
Llamellín 92-93 D 6
Llamuco 106-107 B 3
Llancanelo, Laguna — 106-107 C 5
Llancanelo, Salina — 106-107 C 5
Llandrindod Wells 119 E 5
Llanes 120-121 E 7
Llangefni 119 D 5
Llanito, Petare-El — 91 II c 2
Llano, TX 76-77 E 7
Llano de la Magdalena 64-65 D 6-7
Llano Estacado 64-65 F 5
Llano Estacado, Bluffs of — 76-77 C 5
Llano River 76-77 E 7
Llanos, Los — 94-95 C 7
Llanos, Sierra de los — 106-107 D 3
Llanos de Chiquitos 92-93 G 8
Llanos de Guarayos 92-93 G 8
Llanos de la Grunidora 86-87 JK 5
Llanos de la Rioja 106-107 DE 2
Llanos del Orinoco 92-93 E 4-F 3
Llanos de los Caballos Mesteños 76-77 BC 8
Llanos de los Gigantes 86-87 HJ 3
Llanos de Yari 94-95 D 7
Llanquihue, Lago — 111 B 6
Llanura Costera del Golfo 86-87 L-N 5-8
Llanura Costera del Pacifico 86-87 E-H 2-7
Llapo 96-97 B 6
Llareta, Paso de las — 106-107 BC 4
Llarretas, Cordillera de las — 106-107 C 4-5
Llata 92-93 D 6
Llavallol, Lomas de Zamora- 110 III b 2
Llaylla 96-97 D 7
Llay-Llay 106-107 B 4
Llera de Canales 86-87 L 6
Llerena 120-121 DE 9
Lleulleu, Laguna — 106-107 A 7
Lleyn Peninsula 119 D 5
Llica 104-105 B 6
Llico [RCH, Arauco] 106-107 A 6
Llico [RCH, Curicó] 106-107 A 5
Llobregat 120-121 H 7-8
Llorena, Punta — = Punta San Pedro 64-65 K 10
Lloró 94-95 C 5
Lloron, Cerro — 86-87 H 7
Lloyd Bay 158-159 H 2
Lloyd Lake 61 D 2
Lloydminster 56-57 OP 7
Llullaillaco, Volcán — 111 C 2-3
L. Luna 106-107 E 4
Lluta, Río — 104-105 B 6
Lô, Sông — 150-151 E 2
Loa, UT 74-75 H 3
Loa, Caleta — 104-105 A 7
Loa, Río — 111 BC 2
Loan = Le'an 146-147 E 8
Lo-an = Ledong 150-151 G 3
Loanda = Luanda 172 B 3
Loange 172 D 2-3
Loango 172 B 2
Loba, Brazo de — 94-95 D 3
Loban' 124-125 S 5
Lobatse 172 DE 7
Lobaye 164-165 H 8
Lobería [RA, Buenos Aires] 111 E 5
Lobería [RA, Chubut] 108-109 H 4
Lobería, La — 108-109 H 3
Lobería, Punta — 106-107 AB 3
Lobito 172 B 4
Lobitos 96-97 A 4
Lob nuur 142-143 G 3
Lobo 168-169 D 4
Lobo, El — 96-97 A 4
Lobos 106-107 H 5
Lobos, Cayo — 86-87 R 8
Lobos, Isla de — 106-107 K 5
Lobos, Point — 83 I a 2
Lobos, Punta — [RA] 108-109 G 4
Lobos, Punta — [RCH, Atacama] 106-107 B 2
Lobos, Punta — [RCH, Tarapacá ↑ Iquique] 104-105 A 6
Lobos, Punta — [RCH, Tarapacá ↓ Iquique] 104-105 A 7
Lobos, Punta de — 106-107 A 5
Lobstick Lake 56-57 Y 7
Locate, MT 68-69 D 2
Lôc Binh 150-151 F 2
Lo Chau [HK] 155 I b 2
Loch Awe 119 D 3
Loche, La — 56-57 P 6
Lo-ch'êng = Luocheng 146-147 B 9
Loche West, La — 61 CD 2
Loch Garman = Wexford 119 C 5
Lochgilphead 119 D 3
Lochham, München- 130 II a 2
Lochhausen, München- 130 II a 1
Lochiel 174-175 J 4
Lo-ch'ing = Yueqing 142-143 N 6
Lo-ch'ing Ho = Luoqing Jiang 146-147 B 9
Lo-ch'ing Wan = Yueqing Wan 146-147 H 7-8
Loch Linnhe 119 D 3
Loch Lomond 119 D 3
Loch Maree 119 D 3
Lochnagar 119 E 3
Loch Ness 119 D 3
Lochsa River 66-67 F 2
Loch Shin 119 D 2
Lo-ch'uan = Luochuan 146-147 B 4
Lochvica 126-127 F 1
Lock 160 BC 4
Lockeport 63 D 6
Lockes, NV 74-75 F 3
Lockesburg, AR 76-77 GH 6
Lockhart 160 H 5
Lockhart, AL 78-79 F 5
Lockhart, TX 76-77 F 8
Lock Haven, PA 72-73 H 4
Lockney, TX 76-77 D 5
Lockport, LA 78-79 D 6
Lockport, NY 72-73 G 3
Lockwood, MO 76-77 GH 4
Lôc Ninh 148-149 E 4
Locri 122-123 G 6
Locust Creek 70-71 D 5
Lod 136-137 F 7
Lodejnoje Pole 124-125 JK 3
Lodge, Mount — 58-59 T 7
Lodge Creek 68-69 B 1
Lodge Grass, MT 68-69 C 3
Lodgepole, NE 68-69 E 5
Lodgepole Creek 68-69 D 5
Lodhrān 138-139 C 3
Lodi 122-123 C 3
Lodi, CA 74-75 C 3
Lodi, NJ 82 III b 1
Lodi, WI 70-71 F 4
Lodi = Ayni 136-137 JK 4
Loding = Luoding 146-147 C 10
Lødingen 116-117 F 3
Lodja 172 D 2
Lodwar 172 G 1
Łódź 118 J 3
Loei 148-149 D 3
Loenersloot 128 I b 2
Loeriesfontein 174-175 C 6
Lo-fang = Luotang 146-147 E 8
Loffa 168-169 C 4
Loffa River 164-165 B 7
Lofoten 116-117 E 3-4
Lofoten Basin 114-115 JK 1
Lofthus 116-117 B 7
Lofty Range, Mount — 158-159 G 6
Lofusa 171 C 2
Log 126-127 LM 2
Loga [RN] 168-169 F 2
Logan, IA 70-71 BC 5
Logan, KS 68-69 G 6
Logan, NE 68-69 F 5
Logan, NM 76-77 C 5
Logan, OH 72-73 E 5
Logan, UT 64-65 D 3
Logan, WV 80-81 EF 2
Logan, Mount — [CDN, Quebec] 63 C 3
Logan, Mount — [CDN, Yukon Territory] 56-57 HJ 5
Logan, Philadelphia-, PA 84 III c 1
Logandale, NV 74-75 F 4
Logan Glacier 58-59 RS 6
Logan International Airport 84 I c 2
Logan Island 62 E 2
Logan Mountains 56-57 L 5
Logansport, IN 64-65 J 3
Logansport, LA 78-79 C 5
Logan Square, Chicago-, IL 83 II a 1
Loge, Rio — 172 B 3
Loginjag 124-125 T 3
Lognes 129 I d 2
Logojsk 124-125 FG 6
Logone 164-165 H 7
Logroño [E] 120-121 F 7
Logroño [RA] 106-107 G 2
Løgstør 116-117 C 9
Logtāk Lake 141 CD 3
Lohārdaga 134-135 N 6
Lohārdaggā = Lohārdaga 134-135 N 6
Lohāru 138-139 EF 3
Lohāvat = Lohāwat 138-139 D 4
Lohāwat 138-139 D 4
Lōhit = Luhit 134-135 Q 5
Lohja 116-117 KL 7
Löhme [DDR, Frankfurt] 130 III c 1
Lo Ho = Luo He [TJ ◁ Huang He] 146-147 CD 4
Lo Ho = Luo He [TJ ◁ Wei He] 146-147 B 4
Lohtaja 116-117 K 5
Lo-hua = Lehua 146-147 EF 7
Lohumbo 171 C 3
Lohusuu 124-125 F 4
Loi, Phou — 150-151 D 2
Loibl 118 G 5
Loica 106-107 B 4-5
Loikaw = Lûykau 148-149 C 3
Loimaa 116-117 K 7
Loir 120-121 G 5
Loire 120-121 H 5
Loiya 171 C 2
Loja [E] 120-121 E 10
Loja [EC, administrative unit] 96-97 AB 4
Loja [EC, place] 92-93 D 5
Lojev 124-125 H 8
Loji 148-149 J 7
Lojno 124-125 T 4
Lo-jung = Luorong 142-143 K 7
Loka 171 B 1
Lokan tekojärvi 116-117 MN 3
Lokāpur 140 B 2
Lokbatan 126-127 O 6
Lokčim 124-125 ST 3
Lokichoggio 171 C 1
Lokila 171 C 1
Lokitaung 172 FG 1
Lokka 116-117 MN 4
Lokn'a 124-125 H 5
Loko 168-169 G 3-4
Lokoja 164-165 F 7
Lokolo 172 CD 2
Lokoloko, Tanjung — 152-153 O 7
Loko Mountains 168-169 C 3
Lokossa 168-169 F 4
Lokot' 124-125 K 7
Lo-k'ou = Luokou 146-147 E 8
Loksa 124-125 E 4
Loks Land 56-57 Y 5
Lokstedt, Hamburg- 130 I a 1
Lokwabe 174-175 DE 3
Lōl, Nahr — = Nahr Lūl 164-165 K 7
Lola, Mount — 74-75 C 3
Loleta, CA 66-67 A 5
Lolgorien 171 C 3
Loling = Leling 146-147 F 3
Loliondo 171 C 3
Lol Laikumaiki 171 D 4
Lolland 116-117 D 10
Lolmuryoi 171 D 4
Lolo 172 B 2
Lolo, MT 66-67 F 2
Lolobau 148-149 h 5
Loloda 148-149 J 6
Lolodorf 168-169 H 5
Lolui 171 C 3
Lom [BG] 122-123 K 4
Lom [RFC] 164-165 G 7
Loma 168-169 C 4
Loma, MT 66-67 H 1-2
Loma, ND 68-69 G 1
Loma, La — 104-105 D 7
Loma Blanca 106-107 E 7
Loma Bonita 86-87 MN 8-9
Loma Cerro Blanco 108-109 F 4
Loma de Cochicó 106-107 D 6
Loma de la Chiva 106-107 C 7
Loma de los Cristales 106-107 B 2
Loma de los Tigres 106-107 DE 6
Lomadi 148-149 C 3
Loma Farías 106-107 C 7
Loma Linda 91 I b 2
Lomami 172 DE 2
Loma Mountains 164-165 B 7
Loma Negra [RA, Buenos Aires] 106-107 G 6
Loma Negra [RA, La Pampa] 106-107 E 6
Loma Negra [RA, Río Negro] 106-107 DE 7
Loma Penitente 108-109 D 9
Loma Redonda 106-107 DE 6
Lomas [PE] 92-93 E 8
Lomas [ROU] 106-107 KL 5
Lomas, Bahía — 108-109 E 9
Lomas, Los — 96-97 A 4
Lomas, Río — 96-97 D 9
Loma San Martín 108-109 E 2
Lomas Atlas 106-107 D 6
Lomas Blancas 106-107 CD 4
Lomas Chapultepec, Ciudad de México- 91 I b 2
Lomas Coloradas 108-109 F 4
Lomas de Vallejos 102-103 D 7
Lomas de Zamora 106-107 H 5
Lomas de Zamora-Banfield 110 III b 2
Lomas de Zamora-Fiorito 110 III b 2
Lomas de Zamora-Ingeniero Budge 110 III b 2
Lomas de Zamora-La Salada 110 III b 2
Lomas de Zamora-Llavallol 110 III b 2
Lomas de Zamora-Temperley 110 III b 2
Lomas de Zamora-Turdera 110 III b 2
Loma Verde 106-107 H 5
Lomax, IL 70-71 E 5
Lomba das Cutapines 104-105 E 2
Lombard, MT 66-67 H 2
Lombarda, Serra — 92-93 J 4
Lombardia 122-123 C 3-D 2
Lombardy = Lombardia 122-123 C 3-D 2
Lombardy, Johannesburg- 170 V b 1

Lomblem = Pulau Lomblen 148-149 H 8
Lomblen, Pulau — 148-149 H 8
Lombok 152-153 M 10
Lombok, Pulau — 148-149 G 8
Lombok, Selat — 148-149 G 8
Lomé 164-165 E 7
Lomela [ZRE, place] 172 D 2
Lomela [ZRE, river] 172 D 2
Lometa, TX 76-77 E 7
Lomié 164-165 G 8
Lomita, CA 83 III c 3
Lomitas, Las — 111 D 2
Lom Khao 150-151 C 4
Lomond 61 B 5
Lomond, Ben — [AUS] 160 cd 2
Lomond, Loch — 119 D 3
Lomonosov 124-125 G 4
Lomonosova, MTU im. — 113 V b 3
Lomonosov Ridge 52 A
Lomonosovskij 132-133 M 7
Lomphat 150-151 F 6
Lompobatang, Gunung — 152-153 NO 8
Lompoc, CA 74-75 C 5
Lompoul 168-169 A 2
Lom Raet = Thoen 150-151 B 4
Lom Sak 148-149 D 3
Łomża 118 L 2
Lôn, Lũy — 141 E 5
Lo Nagpo 141 D 2
Lonan = Luonen 146-147 C 4
Lonaula 140 A 1
Loncoche 111 B 5
Loncomilla, Rio — 106-107 AB 5
Loncopue 106-107 B 7
Lonco Vaca 108-109 E 3
Londa 140 B 3
Londlani 171 C 3
London, KY 72-73 DE 6
London, OH 72-73 E 5
London, TX 76-77 E 7
Lŏndôn [BUR] 141 E 3
London [CDN] 56-57 UV 9
London [GB] 119 G 6
London-Acton 129 II a 1
London-Addington 129 II b 2
London-Arkley 129 II b 1
London-Atte Bower 129 II c 1
London-Balham 129 II b 2
London-Barking 129 II c 1
London-Barkingside 129 II c 1
London-Barnes 129 II a 2
London-Barnet 129 II b 1
London-Battersea 129 II b 2
London-Beacontree 129 II c 1
London-Beckenham 129 II b 2
London-Bermondsey 129 II b 2
London-Bethnal Green 129 II b 1
London-Bexley 129 II c 2
London-Brent 129 II a 1
London-Brentford 129 II a 2
London-Camberwell 129 II b 2
London-Camden 129 II b 1
London-Canning Town 129 II c 1
London-Carshalton 129 II b 2
London-Catford 129 II c 2
London-Cheam 129 II b 2
London-Chelsfield 129 II c 2
London-Chessington 129 II a 2
London-Chingford 129 II bc 1
London-Chislehurst 129 II c
London-Chiswick 129 II ab 2
London-City 129 II b 1
London-Crayford 129 II c 2
London-Croydon 119 FG 7
London-Dagenham 129 II c 1
London-Deptford 129 II b 2
Londonderry 119 C 4
Londonderry, Cape — 158-159 E 2
Londonderry, Islas — 111 B 9
London-Ealing 129 II a 1
London-East Barnet 129 II b 1
London-East Ham 129 II c 1
London-Edgware 129 II a 1
London-Edmonton 129 II b 1
London-Elmers End 129 II b 2
London-Elm Park 129 II c 1
London-Eltham 129 II c 2
London-Erith 129 II c 2
London-Farnborough 129 II c 2
London-Feltham 129 II a 2
London-Finchley 129 II b 1
London-Friern Barnet 129 II b 1
London-Fulham 129 II b 2
London-Golders Green 129 II b 1
London-Grange Hill 129 II c 1
London-Greenford 129 II a 1
London-Greenwich 119 FG 6
London-Halfway Street 129 II c 2
London-Hamlets 129 II b 1
London-Hammersmith 129 II ab 2
London-Hampstead 129 II b 1
London-Hampton 129 II a 2
London-Hanwell 129 II a 2
London-Hanworth 129 II a 2
London-Harefield 129 II a 1
London-Haringey 129 II b 1
London-Harlington 129 II a 2
London-Harold Hill 129 II c 1
London-Harrow 119 F 6
London-Harrow on the Hill 129 II a 1
London-Havering 129 II c 1
London-Hayes [GB, Bromley] 129 II bc 2
London-Hayes [GB, Hillingdon] 129 II a 1
London Heathrow Airport 129 II a 2
London-Hendon 129 II b 1
London-Heston 129 II a 2
London-Higham Hill 129 II b 1
London-Hook 129 II a 2
London-Hornchurch 129 II c 1
London-Hornsey 129 II b 1
London-Hounslow 129 II a 2
London-Ilford 129 II c 1
London-Isleworth 129 II a 2
London-Islington 129 II b 1
London-Kensington and Chelsea 129 II b 2
London-Keston 129 II c 2
London-Kingsbury Green 129 II a 1
London-Lambeth 129 II b 2
London-Lewisham 129 II b 2
London-Leyton 129 II b 1
London-Longford 129 II a 2
London-Merton 129 II b 2
London-Mill Hill 129 II b 1
London-Mitcham 129 II b 2
London-Morden 129 II b 2
London-Mottingham 129 II c 2
London-Newham 129 II c 1
London-New Malden 129 II ab 2
London-Noak Hill 129 II c 1
London-Northolt 129 II a 1
London-Northwood 129 II a 1
London-Notting Hill 129 II b 1
London-Orpington 129 II c 2
London-Paddington 129 II b 1
London-Park Royal 129 II ab 1
London-Penge 129 II b 2
London-Petersham 129 II a 2
London-Pinner 129 II a 1
London-Poplar 129 II bc 1
London-Purley 129 II b 2
London-Putney 129 II b 2
London-Rainham 129 II c 1
London-Redbridge 129 II c 1
London-Romford 129 II c 1
London-Ruislip 129 II a 1
London-Saint Marylebone 129 II b 1
London-Saint Pancras 129 II b 1
London-Saint Paul's Cray 129 II c 2
London-Sanderstead 129 II b 2
London-Selhurst 129 II b 2
London-Shooters Hill 129 II c 2
London-Shoreditch 129 II b 1
London-Sidcup 129 II c 2
London-Silvertown 129 II c 2
London-Soho 129 II b 1
London-Southall 129 II a 1
London-Southgate 129 II b 1
London-Southwark 129 II b 2
London-Stanmore 129 II a 1
London-Stepney 129 II b 1
London-Stoke Newington 129 II b 1
London-Stratford 129 II c 1
London-Streatham 129 II b 2
London-Sudbury 129 II a 1
London-Surbiton 129 II a 2
London-Sutton 129 II b 2
London-Teddington 129 II a 2
London-Thornton Heath 129 II b 2
London-Tooting Graveney 129 II b 2
London-Tottenham 119 FG 6
London-Totteridge 129 II b 1
London-Tower 129 II b 1
London-Twickenham 129 II a 2
London-Uxbridge 129 II a 1
London-Wallington 129 II b 2
London-Waltham Forest 129 II bc 1
London-Walthamstow 129 II b 1
London-Wandsworth 129 II b 2
London-Wanstead 129 II c 1
London-Wealdstone 129 II a 1
London-Wembley 129 II a 1
London-Wennington 129 II c 2
London-West Drayton 129 II a 2
London-Westham 119 FG 6
London-Westminster 129 II b 2
London-West Wickham 129 II b 2
London-Willesden 129 II b 1
London-Wimbledon 119 F 6
London-Woodford 129 II c 1
London-Wood Green 129 II b 1
London-Yiewsley 129 II a 1
Londres 104-105 C 10
Londrina 111 FG 2
Lone Mountain 74-75 E 4
Lone Oak, TX 76-77 FG 6
Lone Pine, CA 74-75 DE 4
Lonerock, OR 66-67 D 3
Lone Rock, WI 70-71 EF 4
Lone Star 60 HJ 1
Lonetree, WY 66-67 H 5
Lone Wolf, OK 76-77 E 5
Long, AK 58-59 K 4
Long [T] 150-151 B 3
Long, ostrova de — 132-133 c-e 2
Longa [Angola] 172 C 4
Longá, Rio — 100-101 D 2
Long Akah 152-153 L 4
Long Atip 152-153 L 4
Longavi 106-107 B 5
Longavi, Baños de — 106-107 B 6
Longavi, Nevado — 106-107 B 6
Longbangun 152-153 L 5
Long Bay [AUS] 161 I b 2
Long Bay [USA] 64-65 L 5
Long Beach, CA 64-65 BC 5
Long Beach, NY 82 III d 3
Long Beach Municipal Airport 83 III d 3
Longboat Key 80-81 b 3
Long Branch, NJ 72-73 JK 4
Long Cay 88-89 J 3
Longchamp, Hippodrome de — 129 I bc 2
Longchuan [TJ, Dehong Daizu Zizhizhou] 142-143 H 7
Longchuan [TJ, Guangdong] 146-147 E 9
Longchuang Jiang 141 F 3
Long Creek, OR 66-67 D 3
Long Ditton 129 II a 2
Longdor, gora — 132-133 W 6
Long Eddy, NY 72-73 J 4
Longfellow, TX 76-77 C 7
Longford [AUS] 158-159 J 8
Longford [IRL] 119 BC 5
Longford, London- 129 II a 2
Longgang 146-147 GH 5
Longhai 146-147 FG 9
Long Hu 146-147 F 7
Longhua 142-143 M 3
Longhui 146-147 C 8
Longido 171 D 3
Lôngin 141 E 3
Longiram 148-149 G 6-7
Long Island, KS 68-69 G 6
Long Island [BS] 64-65 LM 7
Long Island [CDN] 56-57 UV 7
Long Island [PNG] 148-149 N 7-8
Long Island [USA, Massachusetts] 84 I c 3
Long Island [USA, New York] 64-65 M 3-4
Long Island City, New York-, NY 82 III c 2
Long Island Sound 72-73 K 4
Long Jiang 146-147 B 9
Longjing 144-145 G 1
Longkou 146-147 GH 3
Longkou Wan 146-147 GH 3
Longlac 62 F 3
Long Lake, WI 70-71 F 3
Long Lake [CDN, Ontario] 70-71 G 1
Long Lake [CDN, Yukon Territory] 58-59 T 6
Long Lake [USA, Alaska] 58-59 K 6
Long Lake [USA, Michigan] 70-71 J 3
Long Lake [USA, North Dakota] 68-69 G 2
Long Lama 152-153 L 4
Longleaf, LA 78-79 C 5
Longling 142-143 H 7
Longmen [TJ ↗ Guangzhou] 146-147 E 10
Longmen [TJ ↓ Haikou] 150-151 H 3
Longmire, WA 66-67 C 2
Longmont, CO 68-69 D 5
Long Murum 152-153 KL 4
Longnan 142-143 LM 7
Longnawan 148-149 FG 6
Longonot 171 D 3
Long Pine, NE 68-69 G 4
Longping = Longyao 146-147 E 3
Long Point [CDN, Lake Winnipeg] 61 J 4
Long Point [CDN, Ontario] 72-73 FG 3
Long Point [NZ] 161 CD 8
Long Point Bay 72-73 FG 3
Long Point Woods, Houston-, TX 85 III a 1
Long Prairie, MN 70-71 C 2-3
Longqi = Zhangzhou 142-143 M 7
Longquan 142-143 M 6
Longquan Xi 146-147 G 7-8
Long Range Mountains 56-57 Z 7-8
Longreach 158-159 H 4
Longshan 146-147 B 7
Longsheng [TJ ↖ Guilin] 146-147 BC 9
Longsheng [TJ ↙ Wuzhou] 146-147 C 10
Longs Peak 64-65 E 3
Longtan [TJ, Hunan] 146-147 C 8
Longtan [TJ, Jiangsu] 146-147 G 5
Long Teru 152-153 L 4
Long Thanh 150-151 G 7
Longtian 146-147 G 9
Longton, KS 76-77 FG 4
Longueuil 72-73 K 2
Longvalley, SD 68-69 F 4
Long Valley [USA, California] 74-75 D 4
Long Valley [USA, Nevada] 66-67 D 5
Longview, TX 64-65 GH 5
Longview, WA 64-65 B 2
Longxi 142-143 J 4-5
Long Xuyên 148-149 DE 4
Longyan 146-147 F 9
Longyao 146-147 E 3
Longyearbyen 116-117 jk 5
Longyou 142-143 M 6
Longzhen 142-143 O 2
Lo-ning = Luoning 146-147 C 4
Lonja 122-123 G 3
Lonjak, Bukit — 152-153 JK 5
Lonkin = Lôngin 141 E 3
Lônlê 141 C 4
Lonoke, AR 78-79 CD 3
Lonquimay 106-107 B 7
Lønsdal 116-117 F 4
Lons-le-Saunier 120-121 K 5
Lonton = Lôndôn 141 E 3
Lontra 98-99 N 7
Lontra, Rio — 102-103 F 4
Lontué, Rio — 106-107 B 5
Loogootee, IN 70-71 G 6
Lookout, Cape — [USA, North Carolina] 64-65 L 5
Lookout, Cape — [USA, Oregon] 66-67 A 3
Lookout Mount 58-59 H 5
Lookout Mountain 66-67 E 3
Lookout Mountains [USA, Alabama] 78-79 G 3
Lookout Mountains [USA, Washington] 66-67 BC 2
Lookout Pass 66-67 F 2
Lookout Ridge 58-59 HJ 2
Lookwood Hills 58-59 JK 3
Loolmalasin 171 CD 3
Loon 70-71 F 1
Loongana 158-159 E 6
Loon Lake [CDN, Alberta] 60 K 1
Loon Lake [CDN, Saskatchewan] 61 D 4
Loon River [CDN, Alberta] 61 A 2
Loon River [CDN, Manitoba] 61 H 2
Loon Straits 62 A 2
Loop, Chicago-, IL 83 II b 1
Loop Head 119 A 5
Loosdrechtse plassen 128 I b 2
Lôp, Ya — 150-151 F 6
Lopandino 124-125 K 7
Lopatin 126-127 NO 5
Lopatina, gora — 132-133 b 7
Lopatino 124-125 PQ 7
Lopatino = Volžsk 132-133 H 6
Lop Buri 148-149 D 4
Loperot 171 C 2
López [CO] 94-95 C 6
López [PE] 96-97 D 6
López [RA] 106-107 H 6
Lopez, Cap — 172 A 2
Loping = Leping 142-143 M 6
Lo-p'ing = Xiyang 146-147 D 3
Lop Noor = Lob nuur 142-143 G 3
Lop Nor = Lob nuur 142-143 G 3
Lopori 172 D 1
Lopphavet 116-117 JK 2
Lopp Lagoon 58-59 D 3-4
Lopt'uga 124-125 QR 2
Lopydino 124-125 ST 3
Lô Qui Hô, Đeo — = Đeo Hai Yân 150-151 D 1
Lōra, Hāmūn-e — 134-135 JK 5
Lora, Punta — 106-107 A 5
Lora, Rio — 94-95 E 3
Lora Creek 158-159 FG 5
Lora del Río 120-121 E 10
Lorain, OH 64-65 K 3
Loralai = Lorālāy 134-135 K 4
Lorālāy 134-135 K 4
Lorca 120-121 G 10
Lord Howe Island 158-159 LM 6
Lord Howe Islands = Ontong Java Islands 148-149 j 6
Lord Howe Rise 158-159 M 5-7
Lord Mayor Bay 56-57 ST 4
Lordsburg, NM 74-75 J 6
Lorena 92-93 KL 9
Lorengau 148-149 N 7
Lorestān 134-135 F 4
Loreto [BOL] 92-93 G 8
Loreto [BR, Amazonas] 98-99 F 5
Loreto [BR, Maranhão] 92-93 K 6
Loreto [CO] 92-93 EF 5
Loreto [EC] 96-97 C 2
Loreto [MEX, Baja California Norte] 64-65 D 6
Loreto [MEX, Zacatecas] 86-87 JK 6
Loreto [PE] 96-97 C-E 4
Loreto [PY] 102-103 D 5
Loreto [RA] 106-107 J 1
Lorette 61 K 6
Lorian Swamp 172 GH 1
Lorica 92-93 D 3
Lori dere 136-137 HJ 2
Lorient 120-121 F 5
Lorimor, IA 70-71 C 5
Loring, MT 68-69 C 1
Loripongo 96-97 FG 10
Loris, SC 80-81 G 3
Lorisccota, Laguna — 96-97 G 10
Lorne, Firth of — 119 CD 3
Loro 92-93 F 4
Loro Huasi 104-105 B 9
Loros, Los — 111 BC 3
Lörrach 118 C 5
Lorraine 120-121 KL 4
Lort, Cabo — 108-109 B 5
Lorugumu 171 C 2
Los, Îles de — 168-169 B 3
Losada, Rio — 94-95 D 6
Los Aguacatas 91 II c 1
Los Alamitos 106-107 C 5
Los Alamitos, CA 83 III d 3
Los Alamos, CA 74-75 C 5
Los Alamos, NM 64-65 E 4
Los Alamos [MEX] 86-87 J 3
Los Alamos [RCH] 106-107 A 6
Los Aldamas 76-77 E 9
Los Alerces, Parque Nacional — 108-109 D 4
Los Amores 111 DE 3
Los Andes 111 B 4
Los Angeles 83 III c 2
Los Angeles, CA 64-65 BC 5
Los Angeles, TX 76-77 E 8
Los Angeles [RA] 106-107 GH 5
Los Angeles [RCH] 111 B 5
Los Angeles, Bahía de — 86-87 CD 3
Los Angeles Aqueduct 74-75 DE 5
Los Angeles-Bel Air, CA 83 III b 1
Los Angeles-Boyle Heights, CA 83 III c 1
Los Angeles-Brentwood Heights, CA 83 III ab 1
Los Angeles-Century City, CA 83 III b 1
Los Angeles County Art Museum 83 III b 1
Los Angeles-Highland Park, CA 83 III c 1
Los Angeles-Hollywood, CA 64-65 BC 5
Los Angeles-Hyde Park, CA 83 III c 2
Los Angeles International Airport 83 III b 2
Los Angeles-Mar Vista, CA 83 III b 1
Los Angeles-Miracle Mile, CA 83 III bc 1
Los Angeles-Pacific Palisades, CA 83 III a 1
Los Angeles-Palms, CA 83 III b 1
Los Angeles-Playa de Rey, CA 83 III b 2
Los Angeles-Venice, CA 83 III b 2
Los Angeles-Watts, CA 83 III c 2
Los Angeles-Westchester, CA 83 III b 2
Los Angeles-West Los Angeles, CA 83 III b 1
Los Angeles-Westwood, CA 83 III b 1
Los Antiguos 108-109 D 6
Losap 208 F 2
Los Baños 96-97 F 11
Los Banos, CA 74-75 C 4
Los Blancos [RA] 111 D 2
Los Cardos 106-107 G 4
Los Cerillos 106-107 E 3
Los Chilenos, Laguna — 106-107 F 6
Los Cisnes 106-107 F 4
Los Cocos 94-95 KL 4
Los Colorados 106-107 D 2
Los Comales 76-77 E 9
Los Cóndores 106-107 EF 4
Los Conquistadores 106-107 H 3
Los Correas 106-107 J 5
Los Coyotes Indian Reservation 74-75 E 6
Los Cusis 104-105 D 4
Los Dos Caminos 91 II c 2
Losevo 124-125 H 5
Los Frailes, Islas — 94-95 K 2
Los Frentones 111 D 3
Los Gatos, CA 74-75 C 4
Los Glaciares, Parque Nacional — 108-109 C 7-8
Lo-shan = Luoshan 146-147 E 5
Los Hermanos, Islas — 94-95 JK 2
Los Huarpes 106-107 D 5
Lošinj 122-123 F 3
Los Jazmines, Presa — 91 I b 2
Los Juríes 111 D 3
Loskopdam 174-175 H 3
Los Lagortos, Lago Club de — 91 III bc 2
Los Lagos [RCH, administrative unit] 108-109 C 3-4
Los Lagos [RCH, place] 108-109 C 2
Los Linares 106-107 F 2
Los Llanos 94-95 C 7
Los Lomas 96-97 A 4
Los Loros 111 BC 3
Los Lunas, NM 76-77 A 5
Los Menucos 108-109 EF 3
Los Mochis 64-65 E 6
Los Molinos, CA 66-67 BC 5
Los Molles 106-107 BC 5
Los Monjes, Islas — 92-93 EF 2
Los Muermos 108-109 C 3
Los Nietos, CA 83 III d 2
Los Novillos 106-107 K 3-4
Los Palacios 88-89 DE 3
Los Pasos 94-95 D 7
Los Pirpintos 111 D 3
Los Pozos 106-107 E 3
Los Proceres, Monumento a — 91 II b 2
Los Quirquinchos 106-107 G 4
Los Ralos 104-105 D 10
Los Reartes 106-107 E 3
Los Reyes 91 I d 2
Los Reyes de Salgado 86-87 J 8
Los Ríos 96-97 B 2
Los Roques, Islas — 92-93 F 2
Los Santos 88-89 F 11
Los Sauces 106-107 A 6
Lossiemouth 119 E 3
Los Surgentes 106-107 FG 4
Los Taques 94-95 F 2
Lost Creek 68-69 B 4
Los Telares 106-107 F 2
Los Teques 92-93 F 2
Los Testigos, Islas — 92-93 G 2
Lost Hills, CA 74-75 D 5
Lost Lake 85 III c 1
Los Tres Chañares, Planicie — 106-107 EF 7
Lost River, AK 58-59 D 4
Lost River Range 66-67 FG 3
Lost Springs, WY 68-69 D 4
Lost Trail Pass 66-67 G 3
Los Vientos 111 BC 2
Los Vilos 111 B 4
Lot [B] 128 II a 2
Lot [F] 120-121 H 6
Lota 111 B 5
Lotagipi Swamp 172 FG 1
Lothair 174-175 J 4
Lothair, MT 66-67 H 1
Lo Than 150-151 E 8
Lo-tien = Luotian 146-147 E 6
Loting = Leting 146-147 G 2
Loting = Luoding 146-147 C 10
Lotlake 174-175 E 2
Lotmozero 116-117 NO 3
Lotošino 124-125 K 5
Lotsani 174-175 G 2
Lott, TX 76-77 F 7
Lotung 146-147 HJ 9
Lo-tung = Ledong 150-151 G 3
Loubad 174-175 H 3
Loubnān, Jabal — = Jabal Lubnān 136-137 FG 5-6
Loubomo 172 B 2
Louchi 132-133 E 4
Loudéac 120-121 F 4
Loudi 146-147 C 8
Loudonville, OH 72-73 EF 4
Louellen, KY 80-81 E 2
Loufan 146-147 C 2
Louga 164-165 A 5
Louge [RA] 106-107 G 6
Loughborough Kyûn 150-151 AB 7
Lough Corrib 119 B 5
Lough Derg 119 BC 5
Lougheed Island 56-57 PQ 2
Lough Foyle 119 C 4
Lough Neagh 119 C 4
Lough Ree 119 C 5
Loughton 129 II c 1
Louisa, VA 72-73 GH 5
Louis Armstrong Park 85 I b 2
Louisbourg 56-57 Z 8
Louisburg, NC 80-81 G 2
Louise, TX 76-77 F 8
Louise, Lake — 58-59 O 5
Louise Island 60 B 3
Louiseville 72-73 K 1
Louis-Gentil = Yūssufīyah 166-167 B 3
Louisiade Archipelago 148-149 h 7
Louisiana 64-65 H 5
Louisiana, MO 70-71 E 6
Louisiana Point 76-77 GH 8
Louisiana Superdome 85 I b 2
Louis Trichardt 172 EF 6
Louisville, CO 68-69 D 6
Louisville, GA 80-81 E 4
Louisville, IL 70-71 F 6
Louisville, KY 64-65 JK 4
Louisville, MS 78-79 E 4
Louisville, NE 68-69 H 5
Loulan = Loulanyiyi 142-143 F 3
Loulanyiyi 142-143 F 3
Loulé 120-121 C 10
Loup City, NE 68-69 G 5
Loup River 64-65 G 3
Lourdes [CDN] 63 G 3
Lourdes [F] 120-121 G 7
Lourenço 98-99 N 3
Lourenço Marques = Maputo 172 F 7
Lourenço Marques, Baía de — = Baía do Maputo 172 F 7
Lou Shui 146-147 C 7
Lousia, KY 72-73 E 5
Louth [AUS] 158-159 HJ 6
Louth [GB] 119 FG 5
Lou-ti = Loudi 146-147 C 8
Louvain = Leuven 120-121 K 3
Louviers 120-121 H 4
Louviers, CO 68-69 D 6
Louvre 129 I c 2
Louwsburg 174-175 J 4
Lo Vargas 106-107 B 5
Lovászi 118 H 5
Lovat' 124-125 H 5
Lovéa 150-151 D 6
Loveč 122-123 L 4
Lovelady, TX 76-77 G 7
Loveland, CO 68-69 D 5
Loveland, OH 70-71 H 6
Lovell, WY 68-69 B 3
Lovell Island 84 I c 3
Lovelock, NV 66-67 D 5
Lovenia, Mount — 66-67 H 5
Loverna 61 CD 5
Loviisa = Lovisa 116-117 M 7
Lovilia, IA 70-71 D 5
Loving, NM 76-77 BC 6
Lovingston, VA 80-81 G 2
Lovington, IL 70-71 F 6
Lovington, NM 76-77 C 6
Lovisa 116-117 M 7
Lovl'a 124-125 R 4
Lövskär = ostrov Moščnyj 124-125 FG 4
Lóvua 172 D 4
Low 72-73 HJ 2
Low, Cape — 56-57 T 5
Lowa 172 E 2
Low Cape 58-59 f 1
Lowder Brook 84 I a 3
Lowell, ID 66-67 F 2
Lowell, IN 70-71 G 5
Lowell, MA 64-65 M 3
Lowell, MI 70-71 H 4
Lowell, OR 66-67 B 4
Löwenrivier 174-175 C 4
Lower Adamson 174-175 G 6
Lower Arrow Lake 66-67 D 1
Lower Austria = Niederösterreich 118 F-H 4
Lower Bay 82 III b 3
Lower Brule Indian Reservation 68-69 F 3
Lower California 86-87 B 2-E 5
Lower California = Baja California 64-65 C 5-D 7
Lower Egypt = Mişr-Baḥrī 173 BC 2
Lower Guinea 50-51 K 5-6
Lower Hutt 158-159 OP 8
Lower Kalskag, AK 58-59 G 6
Lower Laberge 58-59 U 6
Lower Lake 66-67 CD 5
Lower Lake, CA 74-75 B 3
Lower Lough Erne 119 BC 4
Lower Pakamp Lake 84 I ab 2
Lower Peninsula 64-65 JK 3
Lower Plenty, Melbourne- 161 II c 1
Lower Red Lake 70-71 C 2
Lower Saxony = Niedersachsen 118 C-E 2
Lower Tonsina, AK 58-59 PQ 6
Lower Tunguska = Nižn'aja Tunguska 132-133 Q 4-R 5
Lower Woolgar 158-159 H 3
Lowestoft 119 GH 5
Łowicz 118 J 2
Lowlands 119 D 4-E 3
Lowman, ID 66-67 F 3
Low Rocky Point 160 b 3
Lowville, NY 72-73 J 3
Loxton 160 E 5
Loyalton, CA 74-75 C 3
Loyalton, SD 68-69 G 3
Loyalty Islands = Îles Loyauté 158-159 N 4
Loyang = Luoyang 142-143 L 5
Loyauté, Îles — 158-159 N 4
Loyola, Punta — 108-109 E 8
Loyola Marymount University 83 III b 2
Loyola University 85 I b 2
Loyuan = Luoyuan 146-147 G 8
Lo-yüan = Luoyuan 146-147 G 8
Lozada 106-107 E 3
Lozère 120-121 J 6
Loznica 122-123 H 3
Lozovaja 126-127 H 2
Lozym 124-125 S 3
Luʿāʿah, Al- 136-137 L 7
Luacano 172 D 4
Luachimo 172 D 3
Luala 172 E 3
Lualaba 172 E 3
Luama 172 E 2
Luambe 171 C 6
Lu'an 142-143 M 5
Luân Châu 150-151 D 2
Luancheng [TJ, Guangxi Zhuangzu Zizhiqu] 146-147 B 10
Luancheng [TJ, Hebei] 146-147 E 3
Luanchuan 146-147 C 5
Luanda 172 B 3
Luando, Rio — 172 C 4
Luang, Khao — [T ← Nakhon Si Thammarat] 148-149 CD 5
Luang, Khao — [T ← Thap Sakae] 150-151 B 7
Luang, Nam — 150-151 D 4
Luang, Thale — 148-149 D 5
Luanginga, Rio — 172 D 4
Lu'ang Prabang 148-149 D 3
Luangue, Rio — 172 C 3
Luangwa 172 F 4
Luangwa Valley Game Reserve 172 F 4
Luan He 146-147 G 2
Luan Ho = Luan He 146-147 G 2
Luan-hsien = Luan Xian 146-147 G 2
Luannan 146-147 G 2
Lua Nova 98-99 K 7
Luanping 142-143 M 3
Luanshya 172 E 4
Luan Toro 106-107 E 6
Luan Xian 142-143 M 4
Luapula 172 E 4
Luarca 120-121 D 7
Luatizi, Rio — 171 D 6
Luau 172 D 4
Lubaantun 86-87 Q 9
Lubań [PL] 118 G 3
L'uban' [SU, Belorusskaja SSR] 124-125 FG 7
L'uban' [SU, Rossijskaja SFSR] 124-125 H 4
Lubāna 124-125 F 5
Lubānas ezers 124-125 F 5
Lubandaye 171 B 4
Lubang Islands 148-149 G 4
Lubango 172 B 4
Lub'any 124-125 S 5
L'ubar 126-127 C 2
Lübars, Berlin- 130 III b 1
L'ubaševka 126-127 E 3
Lubaynī, Baḥr al- 170 II ab 2
Lubbock, TX 64-65 F 5
L'ubča 124-125 F 7
L'ubeč 124-125 H 8
Lübeck 118 E 2
Lubefu [ZRE, place] 172 D 2
Lubefu [ZRE, river] 172 D 2
L'ubercy 124-125 LM 6
Lubero 172 E 2
L'ubešov 124-125 E 8
Lubika 171 B 4
Lubilash 172 D 3
L'ubim 124-125 N 4
L'ubimovka [SU, Kurskaja Oblast'] 126-127 G 1
Lubin 118 H 3
L'ubinskij 132-133 N 6
Lublin 118 L 3
Lubliniec 118 J 3
L'ublino, Moskva- 113 V cd 3
Lubnān, Jabal — 136-137 FG 5-6
Lubnān ash-Sharqī, Jabal — 136-137 G 5-6
Lubny 126-127 F 1-2
L'ubochna 124-125 K 7
L'ubomi' 124-125 DE 8
Lubosalma 124-125 HJ 2
L'ubotin 126-127 GH 2
Lubu 146-147 D 10
Lubudi [ZRE, place] 172 E 3
Lubudi [ZRE, river] 172 DE 3
Lubuhanmaringgai 152-153 FG 8
Lubuklinggau 148-149 D 7
Lubukpakam 150-151 B 11
Lubuksikaping 148-149 CD 6
Lubumbashi 172 E 4
Lubutu 172 E 2
Lubwe 171 B 5
L'ubytino 124-125 J 4
Luc An Châu 150-151 E 1
Lucania, Mount — 56-57 HJ 5
Lucas, IA 70-71 D 5
Lucas, KS 68-69 G 6
Lucas, Punta — = Cape Meredith 111 D 8
Lucas Channel = Main Channel 62 L 4
Lucas González 106-107 H 4
Lucas Monteverde 106-107 GH 5
Lucca 122-123 D 4
Lucea 88-89 G 5
Lucedale, MS 78-79 E 5
Lucélia 102-103 G 4
Lucena [E] 120-121 E 10
Lucena [RP] 148-149 H 4
Lučenec 118 J 4
Lucera 122-123 F 5

Lucerna 96-97 G 8
Lucerne, IA 70-71 D 5
Lucerne = Luzern 118 CD 5
Lucerne, Lake — = Vierwaldstätter See 118 D 5
Lucerne Lake 74-75 E 5
Lucerne Valley, CA 74-75 E 5
Lucero, El — [MEX] 76-77 C 10
Lucero, El — [YV] 94-95 G 4
Luch [SU, river] 124-125 O 5
Lu-chai = Luzhai 146-147 B 9
Lucheng 146-147 D 3
Lucheringo 171 CD 6
Lu-ch'i = Luxi 146-147 C 7
Luchiang 146-147 H 9
Lu-chiang = Lujiang 146-147 F 6
Lu-chou = Hefei 142-143 M 5
Luchow = Lu Xian 142-143 K 6
Luchthaven Schiphol 128 I a 2
Luchuan 142-143 KL 7
Luchwan = Luchuan 142-143 KL 7
Luci 152-153 J 7
Lucia, CA 74-75 C 4
Lucialva 104-105 G 4
Luciara 98-99 N 10
Lucie 98-99 K 3
Lucie, Lac — 62 M 1
Lucin, UT 66-67 G 5
Lucio V. Mansilla 106-107 E 2
Lucipara, Pulau-pulau — 148-149 J 8
Lucira 172 B 4
Luck, WI 70-71 D 3
Luck [SU] 126-127 B 1
Luckeesarai 138-139 KL 5
Luckenwalde 118 F 2
Luckhoff 174-175 F 5
Lucknow [CDN] 72-73 F 3
Lucknow [IND] 134-135 MN 5
Lucky Lake 61 E 5
Luc Nam 150-151 F 2
Lucrecia, Cabo — 88-89 J 4
Lucy, NM 76-77 B 5
Luda [SU] 124-125 M 1
Lüda [TJ] 142-143 N 4
Lüda-Dalian 142-143 N 4
Lüda-Lüshun 142-143 MN 4
Ludden, ND 68-69 G 2
Ludell, KS 68-69 F 6
Lüderitz [Namibia] 172 BC 7
Lüderitzbaai 172 BC 7
Ludgate 72-73 F 2
Ludhiāna 134-135 M 4
Ludhiyāna = Ludhiāna 134-135 M 4
Ludington, MI 70-71 G 4
L'udinovo 124-125 K 7
Ludlow, CA 74-75 EF 5
Ludlow, CO 68-69 D 7
Ludlow, SD 68-69 E 3
Ludogorie 122-123 M 4
Ludowici, GA 80-81 F 5
Luduş 122-123 KL 2
Ludvika 116-117 F 7
Ludwigsburg 118 D 4
Ludwigsfeld, München- 130 II ab 1
Ludwigshafen 118 CD 4
Ludwigslust 118 E 2
Ludza 124-125 F 5
Luebo 172 D 3
Lueders, TX 76-77 E 6
Luemba 171 B 3
Luembe, Rio — 172 D 3
Luena 172 D 4
Luena, Rio — 172 D 4
Luena Flats 172 D 4
Luepa 94-95 L 5
Lufeng 142-143 M 7
Lufingen 128 IV b 1
Lufira 172 E 3-4
Lufkin, TX 64-65 H 5
Lug 138-139 G 2
Luga [SU, place] 132-133 D 6
Luga [SU, river] 132-133 D 6
Lugana de Santa Maria 86-87 G 2
Lugano 118 D 5
Lugansk = Vorošilovgrad 126-127 JK 2
Luganville 158-159 N 3
Lugard's Falls 171 D 3
Lugela 172 G 5
Lugenda, Rio — 172 G 4
Lugh Ferrandi = Luuq 164-165 N 8
Luginino 124-125 K 5
Lugo [E] 120-121 D 7
Lugo [I] 122-123 D 3
Lugoj 122-123 JK 3
Lugones 106-107 F 2
Luhayyah, Al- 134-135 E 7
Luhe [TJ] 146-147 G 5
Luhit 134-135 Q 5
Luhsien = Lu Xian 142-143 K 6
Lu Hu 146-147 E 6
Lu-i = Luyi 146-147 E 5
Luiana, Rio — 172 D 5
Luichow = Haikang 142-143 KL 7
Luichow Peninsula = Leizhou Bandao 142-143 L 7
Luik = Liège 120-121 K 3
Luilaka 172 D 2
Luimneach = Limerick 119 B 5
Luirojoki 116-117 M 4
Luisa, La — 106-107 GH 5
Luís Alves 102-103 H 7
Luis Correia 100-101 D 2
Luís Correira 92-93 L 5
Luís Domingues 100-101 AB 1
Luís Gomes 100-101 E 4
Luishia 172 E 4
Luisiânia 102-103 G 4
Luiza 172 D 3
Luizhou Jiang = Leizhou Wan 146-147 C 11
Luján [RA, Buenos Aires] 111 E 4
Luján [RA, Mendoza] 106-107 C 4
Luján [RA, San Luis] 106-107 DE 4
Lujenda = Rio Lugenda 172 G 4
Lujiang 146-147 F 6
Lujiang = Lu-chiang 146-147 H 9
Lujiapuzi 144-145 D 2
Lukanga 171 B 6
Lukanga Swamp 172 E 4
Lukašek 132-133 Z 7
Luk Chau [HK, island] 155 I a 2
Luk Chau [HK, place] 155 I a 2
Lukenie 172 C 2
Lukenie Supérieure, Plateau de la — 172 D 2
Lukfung = Lufeng 142-143 M 7
Lukiang = Lujiang 146-147 F 6
Lukimwa 171 D 5
Lukino 124-125 L 7
Lukmeshwar = Lakshmeshwar 140 B 3
Lukojanov 124-125 P 6
Lukolela 172 C 2
Lukou 146-147 D 8
Lukovit 122-123 L 4
Lukovnikovo 124-125 K 5
Łuków 118 L 3
L'uksemburg-Gruzinskij = Bolnisi 126-127 M 6
L'ukšudja 124-125 T 5
Lukuga 172 E 3
Lukuledi 171 D 5
Lukull, mys — 126-127 F 4
Lukulu 171 B 6
Lukunga 170 IV a 2
Lukusashi 171 B 6
Lūl, Nahr — 164-165 K 7
Lula, MS 78-79 D 3
Luleå 116-117 JK 5
Lule älv 116-117 J 4-5
Lulebargas = Lüleburgaz 136-137 B 2
Lüleburgaz 136-137 B 2
Luliani = Luliyānī 138-139 E 2
Luling, TX 76-77 F 8
Luliyānī 138-139 E 2
Lulong 146-147 G 2
Lulonga 172 C 1
Lulua 172 D 3
Luluabourg = Kananga 172 D 3
Lulung = Lulong 146-147 G 2
Luma 171 D 6
Lumajang 152-153 K 10
Lumb 106-107 H 7
Lumbala 172 D 4
Lumber River 80-81 G 3
Lumberton, MS 78-79 E 5
Lumberton, NC 64-65 L 5
Lumberton, NM 68-69 C 7
Lumbo 172 H 4-5
Lumby 60 H 4
Lumding 134-135 P 5
Lumege = Cameia 172 D 4
Lumeje 172 D 4
Lüm Fiord = Limfjorden 116-117 D 9
Lumpkin, GA 78-79 G 4
Lumsden 161 C 7
Lumu 148-149 G 7
Lumut 148-149 D 5
Lumut, Pulau — 150-151 C 11
Lumut, Tanjung — 152-153 FG 7
Lün 142-143 K 2
Lün, Lüy — 141 F 5
Luna 138-139 B 6
Luna, NM 74-75 J 6
Luna, Laguna de — 106-107 J 2
Lūnāvāda 138-139 D 6
Lunawada = Lūnāvāda 138-139 D 6
Lund 116-117 E 10
Lund, NV 74-75 F 3
Lund, UT 74-75 G 3-4
Lunda 172 CD 3
Lunda, Kasongo- 172 C 3
Lundar 61 K 5
Lundazi [Z, place] 172 F 4
Lundazi [Z, river] 171 C 6
Lundi [ZW, place] 172 F 6
Lundi [ZW, river] 172 F 6
Lundy 119 D 6
Lüneburg 118 E 2
Lüneburger Heide 118 DE 2
Luneburg Heath = Lüneburger Heide 118 DE 2
Lunenburg 56-57 Y 9
Lunéville 120-121 L 4
Lung 138-139 N 3
Lunga [Z] 172 E 4
Lunga = Dugi Otok 122-123 F 4
Lunga Game Reserve 172 DE 4
Lungala N'Guimbo 172 CD 4
Lung-chên = Longzhen 142-143 O 2
Lung Chiang = Long Jiang 146-147 B 9
Lung-chiang = Qiqihar 142-143 N 2
Lung-ching-ts'un = Longjing 144-145 G 1
Lung-ch'uan = Longchuan 141 EF 3
Lungchuan = Longquan 146-147 G 7
Lung-chuan = Suichuan 142-143 L 6
Lung-ch'uang Chiang = Longchuang Jiang 141 F 3
Lung-hsi = Longxi 142-143 J 4-5
Lung-hua = Longhua 144-145 AB 2
Lung-hui = Longhui 146-147 C 8
Lungi 168-169 B 3
Lungkar Gangri 138-139 K 2-3
Lungkar Gonpa 138-139 JK 2
Lungkar La 138-139 JK 2
Lung-ki = Zhangzhou 142-143 M 7
Lung-k'ou = Longkou 146-147 GH 3
Lung-kuan Hu = Long Hu 146-147 F 7
Lunglê = Lungleh 134-135 P 6
Lungleh 134-135 P 6
Lungler = Lônlê 141 C 4
Lungling = Longling 142-143 H 7
Lungma Ri 138-139 L 2
Lungmen = Longmen 146-147 E 10
Lung-mêng-shih = Longmen 150-151 H 3
Lung-nan = Longnan 142-143 LM 7
Lungshan = Longshan 146-147 B 7
Lung-shêng = Longsheng [TJ ↖ Guilin] 146-147 BC 9
Lung-shêng = Longsheng [TJ ↙ Wuzhou] 146-147 C 10
Lung-shih = Ninggang 146-147 DE 8
Lungsi = Longxi 142-143 J 4-5
Lung-t'an = Longtan 146-147 C 8
Lung-t'ien = Longtian 146-147 G 9
Lungué-Bungo, Rio — 172 D 4
Lung-yen = Longyan 146-147 F 9
Lungyu = Longyou 142-143 M 6
Lūni [IND, place] 138-139 D 4
Lūni [IND, river] 134-135 L 5
Lūnī [PAK] 138-139 BC 2
Lūni Marusthal 138-139 CD 5
Luninec 124-125 F 7
Lunino 124-125 P 7
Lunjevka 124-125 V 4
Lūnkaransar 138-139 DE 3
Lunno 124-125 E 7
Lunsemfwa 172 EF 4
Lunsklip 174-175 H 3
Luntai = Buquq 142-143 E 3
Lunyuk 152-153 M 10
Luochang = Lechang 146-147 D 9
Luocheng 146-147 B 9
Luochuan 146-147 B 4
Luoding 146-147 C 10
Luoding Jiang 146-147 C 10
Luodou Sha 150-151 H 2
Luofang 146-147 E 8
Luofu 171 B 3
Luohe [TJ, place] 146-147 E 5
Luo He [TJ, river ◁ Huang He] 146-147 CD 4
Luo He [TJ, river ◁ Wei He] 146-147 B 4
Luokou 146-147 E 8
Luombwa 171 B 6
Luonan 146-147 C 4
Luong, Pou — 150-151 E 2
Luongo 171 B 5
Luoning 146-147 C 4
Luoqing 146-147 BC 9
Luorong 142-143 K 7
Luoshan 146-147 E 5
Luotian 146-147 E 6
Luoyang 142-143 L 5
Luoyuan 146-147 G 8
Luozi 172 B 2
Lupa 171 C 5
Lupar, Sungei — 152-153 J 5
Lupilichi 171 C 5
Łupkowska, Przełęcz — 118 L 4
Lupolovo, Mogil'ov- 124-125 H 7
Lu-pu = Lubu 146-147 D 10
Luputa 172 D 3
Luque [PY] 102-103 D 6
Luray, VA 72-73 G 5
Luribay 104-105 C 5
Lurio 171 E 6
Lúrio, Rio — 172 GH 4
Luristan = Lorestān 134-135 F 4
Luro 106-107 F 6
Lurup, Hamburg 130 I a 1
Lusaka 172 E 5
Lusambo 172 D 2
Luscar 60 J 3
Lusenga Flats 172 E 3
Lushan [TJ, Henan] 146-147 D 5
Lu Shan [TJ, Jiangxi] 142-143 M 6
Lu Shan [TJ, Shandong] 146-147 FG 3
Lu Shan = Yi Shan 146-147 G 3
Lushi 146-147 C 4
Lu-shih = Lushi 146-147 C 4
Lushnjë 122-123 H 5
Lushoto 172 G 2
Lushui 141 F 2-3
Lüshun, Lüda- 142-143 MN 4
Lüsi 146-147 H 5
Lusien = Lu Xian 142-143 K 6
Lusikisiki 174-175 H 6
Lusk, WY 68-69 D 4
Luso = Moxico 172 CD 4
Lussanvira 102-103 G 4
Lussino = Lošinj 122-123 F 3
Lustheim 130 II b 1
Lustre, MT 68-69 D 1
Lü-szŭ = Lüsi 146-147 H 5
Lūţ, Dasht-e — 134-135 H 4
Lü-Tao = Huoshao Tao 146-147 H 10
Lutcher, LA 78-79 D 5-6
Lutembwe 171 C 6
Luther, MI 70-71 H 3
Luther, OK 76-77 F 5
Lutie, TX 76-77 D 5
Luthe 174-175 E 2
Luton 119 F 6
Lutong 148-149 F 6
Lutsk = Luck 126-127 B 1
Luttig 174-175 E 7
Lutunguru 171 B 3
Lützow-Holm bukt 53 C 4-5
Lutzputs 174-175 D 5
Luuq 164-165 N 8
Luverne, AL 78-79 F 5
Luverne, IA 70-71 CD 4
Luverne, MN 68-69 H 4
Luvua 172 E 3
Luwegu 172 G 3
Luwingu 172 F 4
Luwu 148-149 GH 7
Luwuk 148-149 H 7
Luxembourg [L, place] 120-121 KL 4
Luxembourg [L, state] 120-121 KL 4
Luxembourg, Jardin du — 129 I c 2
Luxi [TJ, Hunan] 146-147 C 7
Luxi [TJ, Yunnan] 141 F 3
Lu Xian 142-143 K 6
Luxico, Rio — 172 CD 3
Luxor = Al-Uqşur 164-165 L 3
Luxora, AR 78-79 DE 3
Lu Xun Museum 155 II b 2
Luyang 144-145 C 2
Luya Shan 146-147 CD 2
Lûy Hkaw 141 F 5
Lûy-Hoda 141 E 6
Lûy Hpālam 150-151 B 2
Lûy Hpālan 141 F 5
Lûy Hsan 141 E 5
Lûy Hsei 141 E 4
Luyi 146-147 E 5
Lûykau 148-149 C 3
Lûy Lan 141 E 6
Lûy Lin 141 EF 4
Lûylin 148-149 C 2
Lûy Lôn 141 E 5
Lûy Lûn 141 F 5
Lûylûn Taungdan 141 E 4
Lûy Maw [BUR, Kachin Pyinnei] 141 E 3
Lûy Maw [BUR, Shan Pyinnei] 141 E 5
Lûy Mû 141 F 4
Lûymwe 150-151 B 2
Lûy Myèbûm 141 E 3
Lûy Pan 141 E 4
Lûy Pannaung 150-151 C 2
Lûy Taunggyaw 141 E 4
Luz [BR] 92-93 K 8
Luz, Isla — 108-109 BC 5
Luza [SU, place] 132-133 H 5
Luza [SU, river] 124-125 Q 3
Luzern 118 CD 5
Luzhai 146-147 B 9
Luzhuba = Hetian 146-147 F 9
Luziânia 102-103 HJ 2
Luzilândia 100-101 C 2
Luzk = Luck 126-127 B 1
Lužma 124-125 H 2
Lužniki, Moskva- 113 V b 3
Luzón 148-149 H 3
Luzón Strait 148-149 H 2
L'vov 126-127 AB 2
Lwa = Mostva 124-125 F 8
Lwancheng = Luancheng 146-147 E 3
Lwanhsien = Luan Xian 142-143 M 4
Lweje = Lwîgyi 141 E 3
Lwela 171 B 5
Lwîgyi 141 E 3
Lwîthangalan 141 C 5
Lwow = L'vov 126-127 AB 2
Lyallpur = Faisalābād 134-135 L 4
Lyan Shan 141 F 3-4
Lyantonde 171 B 3
Lybrook, NM 76-77 A 4
Lyčkovo 124-125 J 5
Lycksele 116-117 H 5
Lydda = Lod 136-137 F 7
Lydell Wash 74-75 G 4
Lydenburg 172 EF 7
Lyell Island 60 B 3
Lyell Range 161 E 5
Lykabettós 113 IV ab 2
Lykwati 171 C 4
Lyle, MN 70-71 D 4
Lyle, WA 66-67 C 3
Lyles, TN 78-79 F 3
Lyleton 68-69 F 1
Lyme Bay 119 E 6
Lymva 124-125 T 2
Lynbrook, NY 82 III de 3
Lynch, KY 80-81 E 2
Lynch, NE 68-69 G 4
Lynchburg, VA 64-65 L 4
Lynches River 80-81 FG 3
Lynden, WA 66-67 B 1
Lyndhurst 160 D 3
Lyndon, KS 70-71 C 6
Lyndonville, VT 72-73 KL 2
Lyngenfjord 116-117 J 2-3
Lyngseiden 116-117 HJ 3
Lynhurst, NJ 82 III b 2
Lynn, IN 70-71 H 5
Lynn, MA 72-73 L 3
Lynn Canal 58-59 U 7
Lynndyl, UT 74-75 G 3
Lynnewood Gardens, PA 84 III bc 1
Lynn Harbor 84 I c 2
Lynn Haven, FL 78-79 G 5
Lynn Lake 56-57 Q 6
Lynn Woods Reservation 84 I c 1
Lynton 61 C 2
Lyntupy 124-125 F 6
Lynwood, CA 83 III c 2
Lyon 120-121 K 6
Lyon Park, Arlington-, VA 82 II a 2
Lyons, CO 68-69 D 5
Lyons, GA 80-81 E 4
Lyons, IL 83 II a 2
Lyons, KS 68-69 GH 6
Lyons, NE 68-69 H 5
Lyons, NY 72-73 H 3
Lyons = Lyon 120-121 K 6
Lyons River 158-159 C 4
Lysá hora 118 J 4
Lysekil 116-117 D 8
Lyserort = Lizerorta 124-125 C 5
Lysite, WY 68-69 C 4
Lyskovo 132-133 GH 6
Łysogory 118 K 3
Ly So'n, Dao — = Cu Lao Rê 150-151 G 5
Lyster 63 A 4
Lys'va 132-133 K 6
Lyswa = Lys'va 132-133 K 6
Lyttelton [NZ] 161 E 6
Lyttelton [ZA] 174-175 H 3
Lytton [CDN, British Columbia] 60 G 4
Lytton [CDN, Quebec] 72-73 HJ 1

M

Ma, Sông — 150-151 E 2
Mā, Wād al- 164-165 C 4
Ma'abūs = Tazarbū 164-165 J 3
Ma'adī, Al-Qāhirah-al- 170 II b 2
Maâdid, Djebel — = Jabal Ma'ḍīd 166-167 J 2
Maalaea, HI 78-79 d 2
Maalam 150-151 FG 7
Maalloûla = Ma'lūlā 136-137 G 6
Ma'ān [JOR] 134-135 D 4
Maan [TR] 136-137 H 4
Ma'anīyah, Al- 134-135 E 4
Ma'an Liedao 146-147 J 6
Ma-an Lieh-tao = Ma'an Liedao 146-147 J 6
Maanselkä 116-117 L 3-N 4
Maanshan 146-147 G 6
Maarianhamina = Mariehamn 116-117 HJ 7
Ma'ārik, Wādī — 136-137 H 7
Ma'arrah, Al- 136-137 G 4
Ma'arrat an-Nu'mān 136-137 G 5
Maas 120-121 K 3
Maastricht 120-121 K 3
Ma'ātin 'Uwayqilah 136-137 C 7
Ma'aziz 166-167 CD 3
Ma'azzah, Jabal — 173 C 2
Mababe Depression 172 D 5
Mabalane 172 F 6
Mabana 171 B 2
Mabang Gangri 142-143 DE 5
Mabaruma 92-93 H 3
Mabein 141 E 4
Mabella 70-71 EF 1
Maben, MS 78-79 E 4
Mabi 146-147 D 4
Mabicun = Mabi 146-147 D 4
Mabogwe 171 B 4
Mabrouk 164-165 D 5
Mabrouk, El- = Al-Mabrūk 166-167 G 5
Mabruck = Mabrouk 164-165 D 5
Mabrūk, Al- 166-167 G 5
Mabton, WA 66-67 CD 2
Mabua Sefhubi 174-175 E 3
Mabudis Island 146-147 H 11
Mabuki 172 F 2
Mača 132-133 W 6
Macá, Monte — 111 B 7
Maçacará 100-101 E 6
Macachín 106-107 F 6
Macacos, Ilha dos — 98-99 N 5
Macacos, Rio — 100-101 A 8
MacAdam 63 C 5
Macaé 92-93 L 9
Macaé à Campos, Canal de — 102-103 M 4-5
Macagua, Presa — 94-95 K 3
Macaíba 100-101 G 3
Macajuba 100-101 D 7
MacAlester, OK 64-65 GH 5
MacAlister, NM 76-77 C 5
MacAllen, TX 64-65 G 6
Macalogne 171 C 6
MacAlpine Lake 56-57 PQ 4
Macambará 106-107 JK 2
Macamic 62 M 2
Macamic, Lac — 62 M 2
Macao = Macau 142-143 L 7
Macao, El — 88-89 M 5
Macapá [BR, Amapá] 92-93 J 4
Macapá [BR, Amazonas] 98-99 E 9
Macaparana 100-101 G 4
Macaquara, Cachoeira — 98-99 M 4
Macar 136-137 D 4
Macará 92-93 CD 5
Macaracuay, Petare- 91 II c 2
Maçaranduba, Cachoeira — 92-93 J 4-5
Macarani 92-93 LM 8
Macarena, Serranía de la — 94-95 DE 6
Mácareo, Caño — 94-95 L 3
Macari 96-97 F 9
Maçaroca 100-101 D 5
MacArthur, OH 72-73 E 5
MacArthur Bridge 84 II c 2
MacArthur River 158-159 G 3
Macas 92-93 D 5
Macassar = Ujung Pandang 148-149 G 8
Macau [BR] 92-93 M 5-6
Macau [Macau] 142-143 L 7
Macauã, Rio — 98-99 D 9
Macaúba 92-93 J 7
Macaúbas 100-101 C 7
Macauley 208 J 6
Macayari 92-93 E 4
Macaza, Rivière — 72-73 J 1-2
MacBee, SC 80-81 F 3
MacBride 60 GH 3
MacCall, ID 66-67 EF 3
MacCamey, TX 76-77 C 7
MacCammon, ID 66-67 G 4
MacCarthy, AK 58-59 Q 6
Macchu Picchu 92-93 E 7
MacClellanville, SC 80-81 G 4
Macclenny, FL 80-81 b 1
Macclesfield Bank 148-149 FG 3
MacClintock, ostrov — 132-133 H-K 1
MacClintock Channel 56-57 Q 3
MacCloud, CA 66-67 BC 5
Maccluer, Teluk — = Teluk Berau 148-149 K 7
MacClure, PA 72-73 H 4
MacClure Strait 56-57 MN 2-3
MacClusky, ND 68-69 F 2
MacColl, SC 80-81 G 3
MacComb, MS 64-65 H 5
MacConnellsburg, PA 72-73 GH 5
MacConnelsville, OH 72-73 F 5
MacCook, NE 64-65 F 3
MacCormick, SC 80-81 EF 4
MacCormick Place 83 II b 1
MacCracken, KS 68-69 G 6
MacCreary 61 J 5
MacCullough, AL 78-79 F 5
MacCurtain, OK 76-77 G 5
MacDade, TX 76-77 F 7
MacDavid, FL 78-79 F 5
MacDermitt, NV 66-67 DE 5
Macdhui, Ben — 62 DE 3
Macdhui, Ben — [LS] 174-175 GH 6
Macdiarmid 70-71 FG 1
MacDonald 50-51 N 8
MacDonald, KS 68-69 F 6
Macdonald, Lake — [AUS] 158-159 E 4
MacDonald, Lake — [CDN] 66-67 FG 1
MacDonald Peak 66-67 G 2
Macdonnell Ranges 158-159 F 4
MacDonough, GA 80-81 DE 4
MacDouall Peak 158-159 F 5
MacDougall Sound 56-57 R 2-3
MacDowell Lake 62 C 1
MacDowell Peak 74-75 GH 6
Macedo 106-107 J 6
Macedonia 122-123 JK 5
Maceió 92-93 MN 6
Maceió, Ponta do — 100-101 F 3
Macenta 164-165 C 7
Macenta Malý 168-169 C 3
Macerata 122-123 E 4
Macfarlane, Lake — 158-159 G 6
MacGaffey, NM 74-75 J 5
MacGehee, AR 78-79 D 4
MacGill, NV 74-75 F 3
MacGillivray Falls 60 F 4
MacGill University 82 I b 1
MacGivney 63 C 4
MacGrath, AK 56-57 EF 5
MacGrath, MN 70-71 D 2
Macgregor 61 J 6
MacGregor, MN 70-71 D 2
MacGregor, TX 76-77 F 7
MacGregor Lake 61 B 5
Mac Gregor Park 85 III b 2
MacGuire, Mount — 66-67 F 3
Machacamarca 104-105 C 6
Machachi 92-93 D 5
Machačkala 126-127 NO 5
Machadinho, Rio — 104-105 E 1
Machado 102-103 K 4
Machado, Serra do — [BR, Amazonas] 98-99 H 8-9
Machado, Serra do — [BR, Ceará] 100-101 E 3
Machadodorp 174-175 J 3
Machagai 104-105 F 10
Machaila 172 F 6
Machakos 172 G 2
Machala 92-93 CD 5
Machambet 126-127 P 3
Ma-chan = Mazhan 146-147 G 3
Machaneng 172 E 6
Machang 150-151 D 10
Machanga 172 G 6
Machango 94-95 F 3
Macharadze 126-127 KL 6
Machareti 104-105 E 7
Machattie, Lake — 158-159 GH 4
Machatuine 174-175 K 3
Machava 174-175 K 3
Machaze 172 F 6
Macheng 146-147 E 6
MacHenry, ND 68-69 G 2
Mācherla 140 D 2
Ma Chha 142-143 HJ 5
Machhalipaṭṭaṇam = Bandar 134-135 N 7
Machhīshar 138-139 HJ 5
Ma Chhu [Bhutan] 138-139 MN 4
Ma Chhu [TJ] 142-143 J 4
Ma-chiang = Majiang 146-147 C 10
Machias, ME 72-73 N 2
Machiche = Maxixe 174-175 L 2
Machiques 92-93 E 2-3
Ma-chi-t'ang = Majitang 146-147 C 7
Machunguel 174-175 L 2
Machupo, Rio — 104-105 D 3
Machwe 174-175 E 2
Macia [Mozambique] 172 F 7
Maciá [RA] 106-107 H 4
Macias Nguema = Bioko 164-165 F 8
Maciel [PY] 102-103 D 7
Maciel [RA] 106-107 G 4
Măcin 122-123 N 3
Macina 164-165 CD 6
MacIntire, IA 70-71 D 4
MacIntosh 62 C 3
MacIntosh, SD 68-69 F 3
MacIntyre Bay 70-71 F 1
Macizo de las Guyanas 92-93 F 3-J 4
Mack, CO 74-75 J 3
Maçka = Cevizlik 136-137 H 2
MacKague 61 FG 4
Mackay 158-159 J 4
Mackay, ID 66-67 G 4
Mackay, Lake — 158-159 E 4
MacKay Lake [CDN, Northwest Territories] 56-57 O 5
MacKay Lake [CDN, Ontario] 70-71 G 1
MacKay River 61 BC 2
Mac Kean 208 J 3
MacKee, KY 72-73 DE 6
MacKeesport, PA 64-65 KL 3
MacKenzie, AL 78-79 F 5
MacKenzie, TN 78-79 E 2
Mackenzie [CDN, British Columbia] 60 F 2
MacKenzie [CDN, Ontario] 70-71 F 1
Mackenzie [GUY] 92-93 H 3
Mackenzie, District of — 56-57 L-P 5
Mackenzie Bay 56-57 J 4
MacKenzie Bridge, OR 66-67 BC 3
Mackenzie Highway 56-57 N 6
MacKenzie Island 62 BC 2
Mackenzie King Island 56-57 OP 2
Mackenzie Mountains 56-57 J 4-L 5
Mackenzie River 56-57 KL 4
Mackinac, Straits of — 70-71 H 3
Mackinaw City, MI 70-71 H 3
Mackinaw River 70-71 F 5
MacKinlay 158-159 H 4
MacKinley, Mount — 56-57 F 5
MacKinley Park, AK 58-59 N 5
MacKinney, TX 76-77 F 6
Mackinnon Road 172 GH 2
MacKirdy 70-71 FG 1
MacKittrick, CA 74-75 D 5
Macklin 61 D 4
Macksville 158-159 K 6
Maclaren River 58-59 O 5
MacLaughlin, SD 68-69 F 3
MacLean, TX 76-77 D 5
Maclean [AUS] 158-159 K 5
MacLean [USA] 82 II a 1
MacLeansboro, IL 70-71 F 6
Macleantown 174-175 GH 7
Maclear 172 E 8
Macleay River 160 L 3
MacLennan 56-57 N 6
MacLennan, Río — 108-109 F 9-10
Macleod 66-67 G 1
MacLeod, Lake — 158-159 B 4
MacLeod Bay 56-57 OP 5
MacLeod Lake 60 F 2
MacLeod River 60 J 3-K 2
MacLoughlin Peak 66-67 B 4
Maclovio Herrera 86-87 H 3
Mac-Mahon = 'Ayn Tūtah 166-167 J 2
MacMechen, WV 72-73 F 5
MacMillan, Lake — 76-77 BC 6
Macmillan River 58-59 U 5
MacMinnville, OR 66-67 B 3
MacMinnville, TN 78-79 FG 3
MacMorran 61 D 5
MacMunn 61 L 6
MacMurdo 53 B 16-17
MacMurdo Sound 53 B 17
MacNary, AZ 74-75 J 5
MacNary, TX 76-77 B 7
MacNeill, MS 78-79 E 5
Macoa, Serra — 98-99 JK 4
Macolla, La — 94-95 F 1
Macolla, Punta — 94-95 F 1
Macomb, IL 70-71 E 5
Macomb Mall 84 II c 1
Macomia 172 GH 4
Macon, GA 64-65 K 5
Macon, MO 70-71 D 6
Macon, MS 78-79 E 4
Mâcon [F] 120-121 K 5
Macondo 172 D 4
Macorís, San Francisco de — 64-65 MN 8
Macorís, San Pedro de — 64-65 N 8
Macoun 68-69 E 1
Macoun Lake 61 G 2
Macouria 98-99 M 2
MacPherson, KS 68-69 H 6
Macquarie 160 c 2-3
Macquarie, Lake — 160 KL 4
Macquarie Harbour 158-159 HJ 8
Macquarie Islands 53 D 16
Macquarie Ridge 50-51 Q 8
Macquarie River 158-159 J 6
MacRae 58-59 U 6
MacRae, GA 80-81 E 4
MacRitchie Reservoir 154 III ab 1
MacRoberts, KY 80-81 E 2
MacRobertson Land 53 BC 6-7
MacTavish Arm 56-57 N 4
MacTier 72-73 FG 2
Macuçaua 98-99 C 8
Macuco 102-103 L 4
Macuco, Cachoeira — 102-103 GH 4
Macujer 94-95 E 7
Macuma, Río — 96-97 C 3
Macumba 158-159 G 5
Macupari, Río — 104-105 C 3
Macururé 100-101 E 5
Macusani 92-93 E 7
Macuspana 86-87 O 9
Macuto 94-95 H 2
Macúzari, Presa — 86-87 F 4
MacVicar Arm 56-57 MN 4-5
Mā'dabā 136-137 F 7
Madadi 164-165 J 5
Madagascar 172 H 6-J 5
Madagascar Basin 50-51 M 7

Madagascar Ridge 50-51 M 7
Madā'in Şālih 134-135 D 5
Maḍakalapūwa 134-135 N 9
Madakasira 140 C 4
Madakkan, Ḥāssī — 166-167 EF 5
Madale 168-169 H 4
Madalena 100-101 E 3
Madam 168-169 E 3-4
Madama 164-165 G 4
Madampe 140 D 7
Madan 122-123 L 5
Madanapalle 140 D 4
Madang 148-149 N 8
Madania, Al-Jazā'ir-El — 170 I a 2
Madaniyin 164-165 FG 2
Madanpur 138-139 G 5
Madaoua 164-165 F 6
Madāqin 166-167 H 3
Mādāri Hāt 138-139 M 4
Madārīpūr 141 AB 4
Madauk 141 E 7
Madavā = Mandāwa 138-139 E 3
Madawaska [CDN, New Brunswick] 63 B 4
Madawaska [CDN, Ontario] 72-73 GH 2
Madawaska River 72-73 H 2
Madawrūsh 166-167 K 1
Madaya = Mattayā 141 E 4
Madaya River = Nam Bei 141 E 4
Maddagiri = Madhugiri 140 C 4
Maddalena 122-123 C 5
Madden, Lago — 64-65 b 2
Madden, Presa de — 64-65 b 2
Madden Dam = Presa de Madden 64-65 b 2
Madden Lake = Lago Madden 64-65 b 2
Maddikera 140 C 3
Maḍḍikkērē = Maddikera 140 C 3
Maddox Park 85 II b 2
Maddūr 140 C 4
Maddūru = Maddūr 140 C 4
Madeira 164-165 A 2
Madeira = Arquipélago da Madeira 164-165 A 2
Madeira, Arquipélago da — 164-165 A 2
Madeira, Río — 92-93 G 6
Madeirinha, Rio — 98-99 H 9
M'adel' 124-125 F 6
Madeleine, Îles de la — 56-57 Y 8
Madelia, MN 70-71 C 3-4
Madeline, CA 66-67 C 5
Madeline Island 70-71 E 2
Madeline Plains 66-67 C 5
Maden 136-137 H 3
Maden = Madenhanları 136-137 J 2
Maden adası = Alibey adası 136-137 B 3
Maden dağları 136-137 H 3
Madenhanları 136-137 J 2
Madera 64-65 E 6
Madera, CA 74-75 CD 4
Madera, Sierra — 76-77 C 7
Madera, Sierra de la — 86-87 F 2-3
Madero, Ciudad — 64-65 G 7
Maḍgāňv = Margao 140 A 3
Mādha 140 B 1
Māghēň = Mādha 140 B 1
Madhepura 138-139 L 5
Madhipura = Madhepura 138-139 L 5
Madhol = Mudhol 138-139 FG 8
Madhra 140 E 2
Madhubani 138-139 L 4
Madhugiri 140 C 4
Madhūmatī 138-139 M 6
Madhupur 138-139 L 5
Madhūpūr Jangal 141 B 3
Madhupur Jungle = Madhūpūr Jangal 138-139 N 5
Madhya Andamān = Middle Andaman 134-135 P 8
Madhyama Palāna ⊲ 140 E 7
Madhyamgram 154 II b 1
Madhya Pradesh 134-135 MN 6
Madi = Marsengdi 138-139 K 3
Madian 146-147 F 5
Madibira 171 C 5
Madibogo 174-175 F 4
Ma'did, Jabal — 166-167 J 2
Madidi, Río — 92-93 F 7
Madill, OK 76-77 F 5
Madimba 172 C 2-3
Madimele 174-175 D 2
Madina 168-169 C 2
Madina do Boé 164-165 B 6
Madīnah, Al- [IRQ] 136-137 M 7
Madīnah, Al- [Saudi Arabia] 134-135 DE 6
Madinani 168-169 D 3
Madinat ash-Sha'ab 134-135 EF 8
Madingou 172 B 2
Madiq Jubal = Jazīrat Shadwan 164-165 LM 3
Mādirā = Madhra 140 E 2
Madison, FL 80-81 b 1
Madison, GA 80-81 E 4
Madison, IN 70-71 H 6
Madison, KS 68-69 H 6
Madison, ME 72-73 LM 2
Madison, MN 70-71 BC 3
Madison, NE 68-69 H 5
Madison, SD 68-69 H 3
Madison, WI 64-65 HJ 3
Madison, WV 72-73 F 5
Madison Heights, MI 84 II b 1
Madison Park 85 III b 2
Madison Range 66-67 H 3
Madison River 66-67 H 3
Madison Square Garden 82 III c 2
Madisonville, KY 70-71 FG 7
Madisonville, TX 76-77 G 7
Madiun 148-149 F 8
Madiyi 146-147 C 7
Mādjen Bel'abbès = Māghin Bin al-'Abbās 166-167 L 2
Madjerda, Quèd — = Wad Majradah 164-165 F 1
Madjori 168-169 F 3
Madley, Mount — 158-159 D 4
Madoc 72-73 H 2
Mado Gashi 172 G 1
Madona 124-125 F 5
Madonela 174-175 H 6
Madonie 122-123 EF 7
Madou = Matou 146-147 H 10
Madra dağı 136-137 B 3
Madrakah, Rā's al- 134-135 H 7
Madras 134-135 N 8
Madras, OR 66-67 C 3
Madrās = Tamil Nadu 134-135 M 8-9
Madrasta = Madrās 134-135 N 8
Madre, Laguna — 64-65 G 6-7
Madre, Sierra — [MEX] 64-65 H 8
Madre, Sierra — [RP] 148-149 H 3
Madre de Dios [PE, administrative unit] 96-97 FG 7
Madre de Dios [PE, place] 92-93 EF 7
Madre de Dios, Isla — 111 A 8
Madre de Dios, Río — 92-93 F 7
Madrid, IA 70-71 D 5
Madrid, NE 68-69 F 5
Madrid, NM 76-77 AB 5
Madrid [CO] 94-95 D 5
Madrid [E] 120-121 EF 8
Madrid, La — 104-105 D 10
Madrid-Aravaca 113 III a 2
Madrid-Arganzuela 113 III a 2
Madrid-Barajas 113 III b 2
Madrid-Buenavista 113 III ab 2
Madrid-Campamento 113 III a 2
Madrid-Canillas 113 III b 2
Madrid-Canillejas 113 III b 2
Madrid-Carabanchel Alto 113 III a 2
Madrid-Centro 113 III a 2
Madrid-Chamartin 113 III ab 2
Madrid-Chamberi 113 III a 2
Madrid-Ciudad Lineal 113 III b 2
Madrid-Cuatro Vientos 113 III a 2
Madrid-Entrevias 113 III b 2
Madrid-Hortaleza 113 III b 2
Madrid-Latina 113 III a 2
Madrid-Moratalaz 113 III b 2
Madrid-Orcasitas 113 III a 2
Madrid-Palomeras 113 III b 2
Madrid-Peña Grande 113 III a 2
Madrid-Progresso 113 III ab 2
Madrid-Pueblo Nuevo 113 III b 2
Madrid-Puente Vallecas 113 III b 2
Madrid-Retiro 113 III ab 2
Madrid-San Fermín 113 III ab 2
Madrid-Tetuán 113 III a 2
Madrid-Usera 113 III a 2
Madrid-Valdebeba 113 III b 2
Madrid-Ventas 113 III ab 2
Madrid-Vicálvaro 113 III b 2
Madrid-Villaverde Bajo 113 III ab 2
Madrīsah 166-167 G 2
Mad River 66-67 B 5
Madrona, Sierra — 120-121 EF 9
Madruba, Lago — 98-99 J 6
Madu, Pulau — 152-153 OP 9
Madūbī 141 C 5
Madura 158-159 E 6
Madura = Madurai 134-135 M 9
Madura = Pulau Madura 148-149 F 8
Madura, Pulau — 148-149 F 8
Madura, Selat — 152-153 KL 9
Madurai 134-135 M 9
Madurai Malaikal 140 CD 5
Madurāntakam 140 DE 4
Maduranthakam = Madurāntakam 140 DE 4
Madureira, Rio de Janeiro- 110 I ab 2
Madūru Oya 140 E 7
Mádytos = Eceabat 136-137 AB 2
Madyūnah 166-167 C 3
Maē = Mahe 134-135 M 8
Mae Ai 150-151 B 2-3
Maebara, Funabashi- 155 III d 1
Maebashi 144-145 M 4
Mae Chaem 150-151 B 3
Mae Chan 150-151 B 2
Mae Hong Son 150-151 AB 3
Maekal = Maikala Range 138-139 H 6-7
Mae Khlong = Samut Songkhram 150-151 C 6
Mae Klong, Mae Nam - 150-151 F 7-8
Mae Klong = Mae Nam Klong 150-151 CD 3-4
Mae Klong = Samut Songkhram 150-151 C 6
Mae Klong, Mae Nam — 150-151 B 5-6
Mae La Noi 150-151 AB 3
Mae Nam Bang Pakong 150-151 C 6
Mae Nam Chao Phraya 148-149 CD 3-4
Mae Nam Khong 148-149 D 3
Mae Nam Khwae Noi 150-151 B 5-6
Mae Nam Kong 148-149 D 3
Mae Nam Mae Klong 150-151 B 5-6
Mae Nam Mai 141 EF 7
Mae Nam Mai = Mae Nam Moei 150-151 B 4
Mae Nam Moei 150-151 B 4
Mae Nam Mun 148-149 D 3
Mae Nam Nan 148-149 D 3
Mae Nam Pa Sak 150-151 C 4-5
Mae Nam Pattani 150-151 C 9
Mae Nam Ping 148-149 C 3
Mae Nam Sai Buri 150-151 C 9-10
Mae Nam Songkhram 150-151 DE 3-4
Mae Nam Suphan = Mae Nam Tha Chin 150-151 C 5-6
Mae Nam Tapi 150-151 B 8
Mae Nam Tha Chin 150-151 C 5-6
Mae Nam Wang 150-151 B 3
Mae Nam Yom 148-149 CD 3
Maengbu-san 144-145 F 2
Maeno, Tōkyō- 155 III b 1
Maenpurī = Mainpuri 138-139 G 4
Mae Phrik 150-151 B 4
Mae Ramat 150-151 B 4
Mae Rim 150-151 B 3
Mae Sai 148-149 CD 2
Mae Sariang 148-149 C 3
Mae Sot 150-151 B 4
Maestra, Sierra — 64-65 L 7-8
Mae Suai 150-151 B 3
Mae Taeng 150-151 B 3
Mae Tha 150-151 B 3
Mae Thot 150-151 B 4
Maevatanana 172 J 5
Maewo 158-159 N 3
Mae Yuam 150-151 A 3
Mafeking [CDN] 61 H 4
Mafeking = Mmabatho 172 DE 7
Mafeteng 174-175 G 5
Maffra 160 H 7
Mafia Channel 171 D 4-5
Mafia Island 172 GH 3
Mafra [BR] 111 FG 3
Mafraq, Al- 136-137 G 6
Mafrenso 100-101 D 5
Mafupa 172 E 4
Magadan 132-133 CD 6
Magadi 172 G 2
Magadi, Lake — 171 D 3
Magadoxo = Muqdiisho 164-165 O 8
Magalhães de Almeida 100-101 C 2
Maḥallat al-Kubra, Al- 164-165 L 2
Magaliesberge 174-175 G 3
Magallanes, Caracas-Los — 91 II b 1
Magallanes, Estrecho de — 111 AB 8
Magallanes, Península — 108-109 C 8
Magallanes y Antártica Chilena 108-109 B 7-E 10
Magaḷrēḍēñ = Mangalvedha 140 B 2
Maganguê 92-93 E 3
Mağara 136-137 EF 4
Mağara = Höketçe 136-137 G 3
Magaria 164-165 F 6
Magariños 102-103 B 5
Magatoberge 174-175 J 2
Magato Mountains = Magatoberge 174-175 J 2
Magaw 141 E 2
Magazine Mountain 78-79 C 3
Magburaka 164-165 B 7
Magdagači 132-133 Y 7
Magdala [RA] 106-107 G 6
Magdalena, NM 76-77 A 5
Magdalena [BOL] 92-93 G 7
Magdalena [CO] 94-95 D 2
Magdalena [MEX, Baja California Sur] 86-87 DE 4
Magdalena [RA] 106-107 J 5
Magdalena, Bahía — 64-65 D 7
Magdalena, Bahía de — 94-95 C 5-6
Magdalena, Gunung — 152-153 M 3
Magdalena, Isla — 111 B 6
Magdalena, Llano de la — 64-65 D 6-7
Magdalena, Río — [CO] 92-93 E 2-3
Magdalena, Río — [MEX] 64-65 D 5
Magdalena, Río de la — 91 I b 3
Magdalena Atlipac, La — 91 I d 2
Magdalena Contreras, La — 91 I b 3
Magdalena Puerto Nare, La — 94-95 DE 4
Magdalen Islands = Îles de la Madeleine 56-57 Y 8
Magdeburg 118 E 2
Magee, MS 78-79 DE 5
Mageik, Mount — 58-59 K 7
Magelang 148-149 EF 8
Magerøy 116-117 M 2
Magersfontein 174-175 F 5
Magga Range 53 B 35-36
Maggiolo 106-107 FG 4
Maghāghah 173 B 3
Maghayra', Al- 134-135 G 6
Māghin Bin al-'Abbās 166-167 L 2
Maghnia = Maghnīyah 166-167 F 2
Maghnīyah 166-167 F 2
Maghrah, Al- 136-137 C 7
Magi = Maji 164-165 M 7
Magic Reservoir 66-67 F 4
Magill, Islas — 108-109 C 10
Maginu, Kawasaki- 155 III a 2
Magliana 113 II a 2
Magliana, Roma- 113 II ab 2
Maglie 122-123 H 5
Magna, UT 66-67 GH 5
Magnesia = Manisa 134-135 B 3
Magness, AR 78-79 D 3
Magnetic Island 158-159 J 3
Magnitogorsk 132-133 KL 7
Magnolia, AR 78-79 C 4
Magnolia, MS 78-79 D 5
Magnolia, NJ 84 III c 2
Magnor 116-117 DE 7-8
Magny-les-Hameaux 129 I b 3
Magoè 172 F 5
Magog 72-73 KL 2
Magome, Tōkyō- 155 III b 2
M'agostrov 124-125 KL 1
Magoura = Maqūrah 166-167 F 2
Magpie 63 D 2
Magpie, Lac — 63 D 2
Magpie, Rivière — 63 D 2
Magpie River 70-71 H 1
Magrath 66-67 G 1
Magreb = Al-Maghrib 164-165 C 3-D 2
Magu, Rio — 100-101 C 2
Maguari, Cabo — 92-93 K 4-5
Magude 172 F 6-7
Maguí 94-95 B 7
Magumeri 168-169 J 2
Māgura 138-139 M 6
Magusheni 174-175 H 6
Magwe 148-149 BC 2
Magwe Taing 141 D 5-6
Mahābād 134-135 F 3
Mahābaleshwar 140 A 2
Mahābalipuram 140 E 4
Mahābhārat Lekh 134-135 NO 5
Mahabo 172 HJ 6
Mahabūbābād = Mahbūbābād 140 DE 2
Maha Chana Chai 148-149 DE 3
Mahād 140 A 1
Mahādeo Hills 138-139 G 6
Mahādeopur 140 DE 1
Mahadeo Range 140 B 1-2
Mahādēvapura = Mahādeopur 140 DE 1
Mahādēv Pahāṛiyān = Mahādeo Hills 138-139 G 6
Mahagi 172 F 1
Mahaicony 92-93 H 3
Mahajamba, Helodranon'i — 172 J 4-5
Mahājan 138-139 D 3
Mahajanga 172 J 5
Mahakam, Sungai — 148-149 G 6-7
Mahalapye 172 E 6
Mahālcharī 141 BC 4
Mahālingpur 140 B 2
Maham 138-139 F 3
Maḥamīd, Al- 166-167 D 5
Mahānadi 134-135 N 6
Mahānadi Delta 134-135 O 7
Mahānanda 138-139 L 4-5
Mahanoro 172 J 5
Maha Nuwara 134-135 N 9
Maha Oya [CL, place] 140 E 7
Maha Oya [CL, river] 140 DE 7
Mahārājganj [IND ↗ Gorakhpoor] 138-139 J 4
Mahārājganj [IND ↘ Lucknow] 138-139 H 4
Mahārāshtra [IND, administrative unit] 138-139 D 8-G 7
Mahārāshtra [IND, landscape] 134-135 M 7
Maharatta = Mahārāshtra 138-139 D 8-G 7
Mahārī, Al- = Al-Muhārī 136-137 L 7
Mahārī, Sha'īb al- 136-137 KL 7
Maḥāriq, Al- 173 B 5
Maḥaris, Al- 166-167 M 2
Maharpur 138-139 M 6
Mahāsamand = Mahāsamund 138-139 J 7
Mahāsamund 138-139 J 7
Maha Sarakham 148-149 D 3
Mahato 171 E 5
Maḥaṭṭat 1 173 B 7
Maḥaṭṭat 2 173 BC 7
Maḥaṭṭat 3 173 BC 7
Maḥaṭṭat 4 173 C 7
Maḥaṭṭat al-Hilmīyah, Al-Qāhirah- 170 II bc 1
Mahawa 134-135 M 9
Mahawēli Ganga 140 E 7
Mahbūbābād 140 DE 2
Mahbūbnagar 140 CD 2
Mahd adh-Dhahab 134-135 E 6
Mahder, El- = 'Ayn al-Qasr 166-167 K 2
Mahdia 92-93 H 3
Mahdīyah 166-167 C 2
Mahdīyah, Al- 164-165 G 1
Mahe [IND] 134-135 M 8
Mahé [Seychelles] 204-205 N 9
Mahé Archipelago = Seychelles 50-51 MN 6
Mahebūbnagara = Mahbūbnagar 140 CD 2
Mahendragarh 138-139 EF 3
Mahendra Giri [IND, Orissa] 138-139 JK 8
Mahendra Giri [IND, Tamil Nadu] 140 C 6
Mahendranagar 138-139 H 3
Mahendra Parvata = Eastern Ghats 134-135 M 8-N 7
Mahenge 172 G 3
Maher 62 L 2
Mahēsāṇā = Mehsāna 134-135 L 6
Maheshtala 154 II a 3
Mahēshvar = Maheshwar 138-139 E 6
Maheshwar 138-139 E 6
Maheson Island 62 A 2
Mahi 138-139 D 6
Māhī = Mahe 134-135 M 8
Mahia, El — 164-165 D 4
Mahia Peninsula 158-159 P 7
Mahiāri 154 II a 2
Mahīdpur = Mehidpur 138-139 E 6
Māhīm 138-139 D 8
Mahina 168-169 C 2
Mahindi 171 D 5
Mahirija = Al-Ma'irīgah 166-167 E 2-3
Mahlabatini 174-175 J 5
Mahlaing 141 D 5
Mahlsdorf-Süd, Berlin- 130 III c 2
Mahmedabad = Mēhmadābād 138-139 D 6
Mahmel, Kef — = Jabal Mahmil 166-167 K 2
Mahmil, Jabal — 166-167 K 2
Maḥmūdīyah, Al- 136-137 L 6
Mahmudiye 136-137 D 3
Mahmut bendi 154 I a 1
Māhneshān 136-137 M 4
Mahnomen, MN 70-71 BC 2
Maho = Mahawa 134-135 M 9
Mahoba 138-139 GH 5
Mahogany Mountain 66-67 E 4
Mahón [E] 120-121 K 9
Mahon [HV] 168-169 D 3
Mahone Bay 63 DE 5
Mahrī 138-139 A 4
Mahroni 138-139 G 5
Mahtowa, MN 70-71 D 2
Mahu = Mhow 138-139 E 6
Mahuida, Campana — 108-109 E 4
Mahukona, HI 78-79 de 2
Mahuta 171 D 5
Mahuva 138-139 CD 7
Mahwah 138-139 F 4
Mai, Mae Nam — = Mae Nam Moei 150-151 B 4
Maïa, El — = Al-Māyah 166-167 G 3
Māi ad-Darwāwī, Ḥāssī — 166-167 K 3
Maiándros = Büyük Menderes nehri 136-137 B 4
Maiaú, Ponta — 98-99 P 5
Maicasagi, Lac — 62 N 1
Maicasagi, Rivière — 62 NO 1
Mai Chai 150-151 BC 3
Maichaila 172 F 6
Maichen 146-147 B 11
Maicoa 94-95 E 2
Maicuru, Rio — 92-93 J 5
Mā'idah, Ḍāya al- 166-167 D 4
Maidalpur 138-139 J 8
Maidālpura = Maidalpur 138-139 J 8
Maidān = Maydān 136-137 L 5
Maidan, Calcutta- 154 II ab 2
Maīdān Akbas = Maydān Ikbis 136-137 G 4
Maidī = Maydī 134-135 E 7
Maidstone [CDN] 61 D 4
Maidstone [GB] 119 G 6
Maidstone, Melbourne- 161 II b 1
Maiduguri 164-165 G 6
Maiella 122-123 F 4
Maigaiti = Marqat Bazar 142-143 D 4
Maigualida, Serranía de — 92-93 F 3-G 4
Maihar 138-139 H 5
Maijdī 134-135 P 6
Mai-kai-t'i = Marqat Bazar 142-143 D 4
Maikala Range 138-139 H 6-7
Maikal Mountains = Maikala Range 138-139 H 6-7
Maiko 172 E 1-2
Maiko, Parc national de — 172 E 2
Maikona 171 D 2
Maikoor, Pulau — 148-149 K 8
Mailan 138-139 J 6
Mailāni 138-139 H 3
Maillín, Arroyo de — 106-107 F 2
Mailsī 138-139 CD 3
Maimacheng = Altanbulag 142-143 K 1-2
Maimansingh 134-135 OP 5-6
Main [D] 118 D 4
Ma'īn [Y] 134-135 EF 7
Maināguri 138-139 M 4
Main Barrier Range 158-159 H 6
Main Centre 61 E 5
Main Channel 62 L 4
Maindargi 140 C 2
Mai Ndombe 172 C 2
Maine [F] 120-121 GH 4
Maine [USA] 64-65 MN 2
Maine, Gulf of — 64-65 N 3
Mainemēnē = Menemen 136-137 B 3
Maïné-Soroa 164-165 G 6
Maingay Island = Zaraw Kyūn 150-151 AB 6
Mainggūn 141 E 2
Mainggwè 141 D 3
Maingy Island = Zaraw Kyūn 150-151 AB 6
Mainland [GB, Orkney] 119 DE 2
Mainland [GB, Shetland] 119 F 1
Main Pass 78-79 E 6
Mainpat Hills 138-139 J 6
Mainpur 138-139 J 7
Mainpuri 138-139 G 4
Main River 63 H 3
Main Saint Gardens, Houston-, TX 85 III ab 2
Maintirano 172 H 5
Mainz 118 D 3-4
Mainzer Berg 128 III b 2
Maio 204-205 E 7
Maioca 104-105 H 4
Maipo, Río — 106-107 B 4
Maipo, Volcán — 111 C 4
Maipú [RA, Buenos Aires] 111 E 5
Maipú [RA, Mendoza] 106-107 C 4
Maipú [RCH] 106-107 B 4
Maipures 92-93 F 3
Maiquetía 92-93 F 2
Maiquetía, Aeropuerto — 91 II b 1
Maiquinique 100-101 D 8
Mairabāri 141 C 2
Mairi 100-101 D 6
Ma'irījah, Al- 166-167 E 2-3
Mairipotaba 102-103 H 2
Mairta = Merta 138-139 DE 4
Maisarī, Al- = Al-Maysarī 136-137 H 7
Maisí, Cabo — 64-65 M 7
Maiskhāl Dīp 141 B 5
Maisome 171 C 3
Maison du Gouvernement 170 IV a 1
Maisonneuve, Parc de — 82 I b 1
Maisons-Alfort 129 I c 2
Maisons-Laffitte 129 I b 2
Maisūru = Mysore 134-135 M 8
Mait = Mayd 134-135 F 8
Maitén, El — 108-109 D 4
Maitencillo 106-107 B 3
Maitland 158-159 K 6
Maitland, Lake — 158-159 D 5
Maíz, Islas del — 64-65 K 9
Maizefield 174-175 H 4
Maizuru 142-143 Q 4
Maja 132-133 Za 6
Majadas, Las — 94-95 J 4
Majagual 92-93 E 3
Majal, Bi'r — 173 C 6
Majane 174-175 D 3
Majari, Rio — 98-99 H 3
Majarr al-Kabīr, Al- 136-137 M 7
Majdal = Ashqēlōn 136-137 F 7
Majé 102-103 L 5
Majene 148-149 G 7
Majes, Río de — 96-97 F 10
Majevica 122-123 H 3
Mājhgāň = Mājhgaon 138-139 K 6
Mājhgaon 138-139 K 6
Maji 164-165 M 7
Majiadian = Madian 146-147 F 5
Majiang 146-147 C 10
Maji Moto 172 F 3
Majitang 146-147 C 7
Majja 132-133 Z 5
Majkain 132-133 O 7
Majkop 126-127 K 4
Majkor 124-125 U 4
Majma'ah 134-135 F 5
Majn 132-133 h 5
Majna 124-125 Q 6
Majngy-Pil'gyn = Mejnypil'gyno 132-133 j 5
Majoli 92-93 H 4
Majorca = Mallorca 120-121 J 9
Major Isidoro 100-101 F 5
Major Pablo Lagerenza 111 DE 1
Major Peak 76-77 C 7
Majradah, Jabal al- 166-167 KL 1
Majradah, Wad — 164-165 F 1
Majskij 126-127 M 5
Majunga = Mahajanga 172 J 5
Majuriā 98-99 F 8
Majuro 208 H 2
Mak, Ko — [T, Gulf of Thailand] 150-151 D 7
Mak, Ko — [T, Thale Luang] 150-151 C 9
Maka 168-169 AB 2
Makah Indian Reservation 66-67 A 1
Makala, Kinshasa- 170 IV a 2
Makale 152-153 N 7
Makale = Mekele 164-165 MN 7
Makallè 104-105 G 10
Makalle = Mekelē 164-165 M 6
Makālu 138-139 L 4
Makalut = Makālu 138-139 L 4
Makampi 171 C 5
Makanya 171 D 4
Makapuu Point 78-79 d 2
Makarfi 168-169 G 3
Makar-Ib 124-125 RS 2
Makarjev 124-125 OP 5
Makarjevo 124-125 P 5
Makarov 132-133 b 8
Makarska 122-123 G 4
Makasar = Ujung Pandang 148-149 G 8
Makasar, Selat — 148-149 G 6-7
Makassar = Ujung Pandang 148-149 G 8
Makassar Strait = Selat Makasar 148-149 G 6-7
Makat 132-133 J 8
Makatini Flats 174-175 K 4
Makedonía 122-123 JK 5
Makedonija 122-123 B-D 4
Makejevka 126-127 HJ 2
Make-jima 144-145 H 7
Makeni 164-165 B 7
Makeyevka = Makejevka 126-127 HJ 2
Makgadikgadi Salt Pan 172 DE 6
Makhachkala = Machačkala 126-127 NO 5
Makham 150-151 D 6
Makhatal = Makhtal 140 C 2
Makhfir al-Ḥammān 136-137 H 5
Makhiruq, Wādī el- = Wādī al-Makhrūq 136-137 G 7
Makhmūr 136-137 K 5
Makhrūq, Khashm al- 136-137 J 7
Makhrūq, Wādī al- 136-137 G 7
Makhtal 140 C 2
Makian, Pulau — 148-149 J 6
Makīlī, Al- 164-165 J 2
Makin 208 H 2
Makinsk 132-133 MN 7
Makinson Inlet 56-57 UV 2
M'akit 132-133 d 5
Makka = Makkah 134-135 DE 6
Makkah 134-135 DE 6
Makkaur 116-117 O 2
Maklakovo 132-133 R 6
Maklautsi 174-175 H 2
Maknāsī, Al- 166-167 L 2
Maknassi = Al-Maknāsī 166-167 L 2
Makó 118 K 5
Makokibatan Lake 62 F 2
Makoko 171 C 4
Makokou 172 B 1
Makomezawa 155 III cd 1
Makona 168-169 C 3
Makoop Lake 62 D 1
Makoua 172 BC 1-2
Makounda = Markounda 164-165 H 7
Makragéfyra = Uzunköprü 136-137 B 2
Makrai 138-139 F 6
Makran = Mokrān 134-135 HJ 5
Makrāna 134-135 L 5
Makrónēsos 122-123 L 7
M'aksa 124-125 M 4
Maks al-Baḥrī, Al- 173 AB 5
Maks al-Qiblī, Al- 164-165 L 4
Maksaticha 124-125 KL 5
Maks el-Baharī = Al-Maks al-Baḥrī 173 AB 5
Makteir = Maqṭayr 164-165 BC 4
Makthar 166-167 L 2
Mākū 136-137 L 3
Mākū Chāy 136-137 L 3
Makuhari 155 III d 2
Makumbako 171 C 5
Makumbi 172 CD 3
Makunudu 176 a 1
Makurazaki 144-145 GH 7
Makurdi 164-165 F 7
Makushin, AK 58-59 n 4
Makushin Bay 58-59 n 4
Makushin Volcano 58-59 n 4
Makuyuni 171 D 3
Makwassie 174-175 F 4
Makwie 168-169 BC 3
Māl 138-139 M 4
Māla [IND] 140 C 5
Mala [PE] 96-97 C 8
Mala = Malaita 148-149 k 6
Malabar Coast 134-135 L 8-M 9
Malabo 164-165 F 8
Malabriga 106-107 H 2
Mal Abrigo 106-107 J 5
Malacacheta [BR, Minas Gerais] 102-103 LM 2
Malacacheta [BR, Roraima] 94-95 L 6
Malacca = Malaiische Halbinsel 148-149 C 5-D 6
Malacca, Strait of — 148-149 C 5-D 6
Malad City, ID 66-67 G 4
Maladeta 120-121 H 7
Malaga, NM 76-77 B 6
Málaga [CO] 92-93 E 3
Málaga [E] 120-121 E 10
Malagarasi [EAT, place] 171 B 4
Malagarasi [EAT, river] 172 F 2
Malagas = Malgas 174-175 D 8
Malagueño 106-107 E 3
Malaḥ, Al- 166-167 F 2
Malah, Sabkhat al- 166-167 F 5
Malaija = Melayu 148-149 D 6
Malaita 148-149 k 6
Malaja Beloz'orka 126-127 G 3
Malaja Ob' 132-133 M 5-L 4
Malaja Sejdemincha = Kalininskoje 126-127 F 3
Malaja Serdoba 124-125 P 7
Malaja Višera 132-133 E 6
Malaja Viska 126-127 E 2
Malaja Znamenka = Kamenka-Dneprovskaja 126-127 G 3
Malaka, Selat — 152-153 A 3
Malakāl 164-165 L 7
Mālākaṇḍ 134-135 L 4
Malakoff 129 I c 2
Mala Krsna 122-123 J 3
Malalaling 172 D 7
Malam = Maalam 150-151 FG 7
Malamala 152-153 O 7
Malanādu 140 B 3-4
Mālanchā 138-139 M 7
Malanchwane 174-175 D 3
Malang 148-149 F 8
Malange 172 C 3
Malangen 116-117 H 3
Malangowa = Malangwa 138-139 K 4
Malangwa 138-139 K 4
Malanzán 106-107 D 3
Malaoṭ = Malaut 138-139 E 2
Malappuram 140 BC 5
Malapuram = Malappuram 140 C 5
Mälaren 116-117 G 8
Malargüe 111 C 5
Mälar Lake = Mälaren 116-117 G 8
Malartic 56-57 V 8
Malartic, Lac — 62 N 2
Malaspina 111 C 6-7
Malaspina Glacier 56-57 H 5-6
Malatia = Malatya 134-135 D 3
Malatosh Lake 61 F 3
Malatya 134-135 D 3
Malatya dağları 136-137 G 4-H 3
Malaut 138-139 E 2
Malavalli 140 C 4
Malāvī 136-137 MN 6
Malavi = Malawi 172 FG 4
Malawali, Pulau — 152-153 M 2
Malawi 172 FG 4
Malawi, Lake — 172 F 4
Malayagiri 134-135 O 6
Malayalam Coast = Malabar Coast 134-135 L 8-M 9
Malaya Parvata = Eastern Ghats 134-135 M 8-N 7
Malay Archipelago 50-51 O 5-Q 6
Malāyer 134-135 F 4
Malāyer, Rūdkhāneh-ye — 136-137 N 5
Malay Peninsula 148-149 C 5-D 6
Malaysia 148-149 D-F 6
Malayu = Melayu 148-149 D 6

Malazgirt 136-137 K 3
Malbaie, la — 63 AB 4
Malbaza 168-169 G 2
Malbon 158-159 H 4
Malbooma 160 AB 3
Malbork 118 J 1-2
Malbrán 106-107 F 2
Malcanio, Cerro — 104-105 CD 9
Malcèsine 122-123 D 3
Malchow, Berlin- 130 III bc 1
Malcolm River 58-59 RS 2
Malden 156-157 K 5
Malden, MA 72-73 L 3
Malden, MO 78-79 DE 2
Malden River 84 I b 2
Maldive Islands 176 F 3
Maldives = Malediven 140 A 7
Maldonado [ROU, administrative unit] 106-107 K 5
Maldonado [ROU, place] 111 F 4
Maldonado, Punta — 64-65 FG 8
Maldonado-cué 102-103 D 5
Male [Maldive Is.] 178-179 N 5
Male, Lac du — 62 O 2
Maléas, Akrōtḗrion — 122-123 K 7
Male Atoll 176 a 2
Mālēgāñv = Mālegaon 134-135 LM 6
Mālegaon 134-135 LM 6
Male Island 176 a 2
Maleize 128 II b 2
Male Karpaty 118 H 4
Malek Kandī 136-137 M 4
Malekula 158-159 N 3
Malela 172 E 2
Malelane 174-175 J 3
Malemo 172 G 4
Malena 106-107 E 4
Malen'ga 124-125 KL 2
Malepeque Bay 63 E 4
Māler Kotla 138-139 EF 2
Maleza 94-95 G 5
Malgas 174-175 D 8
Malghīr, Shaṭṭ — 164-165 F 2
Malgobek 126-127 M 5
Malgrat 120-121 J 8
Malhada 100-101 C 8
Malḥah 136-137 K 5
Malhār 138-139 J 7
Malhārgarh 138-139 E 5
Malheur Lake 66-67 D 4
Malheur River 66-67 E 4
Mali [Guinea] 168-169 B 2
Mali [RMM] 164-165 C 6-D 5
Mālia [IND] 138-139 C 7
Maliangping 146-147 C 6
Malian He 146-147 A 4
Ma-lien Ho = Malian He 146-147 A 4
Māliḥ, Sabkhat al- 166-167 M 3
Malihābād 138-139 H 4
Mali Hka 141 E 2
Malije Derbety 126-127 M 3
Malik, Wādī al- 164-165 KL 5
Maliköy 136-137 E 3
Mali Kyûn 148-149 C 4
Mali Mamou 168-169 BC 3
Malimba, Monts — 171 B 4
Malin, OR 66-67 C 4
Malin [SU] 126-127 D 1
Malinaltepec 86-87 L 9
Malinau 148-149 G 6
Malindi 172 H 2
Malines = Mechelen 120-121 K 3
Malingping 152-153 G 9
Malin Head 119 C 4
Malinké 168-169 B 2
Malino, Gunung — 152-153 O 5
Malinyi 171 CD 5
Malipo 142-143 J 7
Malita 148-149 HJ 5
Malītah 166-167 M 2
Maliwûn 150-151 B 7
Māliya 138-139 C 6
Māḷiyā = Mālia 138-139 C 7
Malizarathseik 150-151 AB 6
Malizayatseik = Malizarathseik 150-151 AB 6
Maljamar, NM 76-77 C 6
Malka 126-127 L 5
Malkangiri 140 EF 1
Malkāpur [IND ↘ Bhusāwal] 138-139 EF 7
Malkāpur [IND ↖ Kolhāpur] 140 A 2
Malkara 136-137 B 2
Małkinia Górna 118 L 2
Mallacoota Inlet 160 JK 6
Mallāg, Wād — 166-167 L 1-2
Mallāḥ, Wād al- 166-167 C 3
Mallaig 119 D 3
Mallakastër 122-123 HJ 5
Mallama 94-95 BC 7
Mallampalli 140 DE 1
Mallānvan = Mallānwān 138-139 H 4
Mallānwān 138-139 H 4
Mallapunyah 158-159 G 3
Mallawī 173 B 4
Malleco, Río — 106-107 AB 7
Mallės Venosta 122-123 D 2
Mallet 102-103 G 6
Mallicolo = Malekula 158-159 N 3
Mallīt 164-165 K 6
Mallorca 120-121 J 9
Mallow 119 B 5
Malmberget 116-117 J 4
Malmedy 120-121 L 3
Malmesbury [ZA] 172 C 8
Malmö 116-117 E 10
Malmöhus 116-117 E 9-10
Malmyž 124-125 S 5
Malnad = Mālanādu 140 B 3-4
Maloarchangel'sk 124-125 L 7
Maloca 92-93 H 4
Maloca Macu 98-99 G 3
Malojaroslavec 124-125 KL 6
Maloje Karmakuly 132-133 HJ 3
Malole 171 B 5
Malombe, Lake — 172 G 4
Malone, NY 72-73 J 2
Maloney Reservoir 68-69 F 5
Malonga 172 D 4
Malosofijevka 126-127 G 2
Malošujka 124-125 L 2
Malova 154 I a 2
Malovata 126-127 D 3
Måløy 116-117 A 7
Mal Paso 106-107 E 1
Malpelo, Isla — 92-93 C 4
Malprabha 140 B 3
Mālpura 138-139 E 4
Mal'qat al-Wīdān 166-167 E 2
Māḷshiras = Mālsiras 140 B 2
Mālsiras 140 B 2
Malta, ID 66-67 G 4
Malta, MT 68-69 C 1
Malta [BR] 100-101 F 4
Malta [M] 122-123 EF 8
Malta [SU] 124-125 F 5
Maltahöhe 172 C 6
Maltepe 136-137 B 2
Malu 148-149 k 6
Maluku ◁ 148-149 J 7
Ma'lūlā 136-137 G 6
Malumba 172 E 2
Malumfashi 168-169 G 3
Malumteken 148-149 h 5
Malunda 152-153 N 7
Malung 116-117 E 7
Mālūr 140 CD 4
Mālūru = Mālūr 140 CD 4
Malūṭ 164-165 L 6
Maluti Mountains 174-175 GH 5
Mālvan 134-135 L 7
Malvern, AR 78-79 C 3
Malvern, IA 70-71 C 5
Malvern, Johannesburg- 170 V b 2
Malvern, Melbourne- 161 II c 2
Malvérnia 172 F 6
Malvinas 106-107 H 2
Malvinas, Las — 106-107 C 5
Mālwa 134-135 M 6
Malya 171 C 3
Malyj Irgiz 124-125 R 7
Malyj Jenisej 132-133 RS 7
Malyj Kavkaz 126-127 L 5-N 7
Malyj L'achovskij, ostrov — 132-133 bc 3
Malyj Tajmyr, ostrov — 132-133 UV 2
Malyj Uzen' 126-127 O 2
Mama 132-133 V 6
Mamadyš 124-125 S 6
Mamahatun 136-137 J 3
Mama Kassa 168-169 J 2
Mamanguape 100-101 G 4
Mamasa 148-149 G 7
Mamasa, Sungai — 152-153 N 7
Mambai 100-101 A 8
Mambasa 172 E 1
Mamberamo 148-149 L 7
Mambere = Carnot 164-165 H 8
Mambirima Falls 171 B 6
Mambone = Nova Mambone 172 G 6
Mameigwess Lake 62 EF 1
Mamera, Caracas- 91 II b 2
Mamfe 164-165 F 7
Māmī, Rā's — 134-135 GH 8
Mamisonskij, pereval — 126-127 L 5
Mammamattawa 62 G 2
Mâmmola 122-123 G 6
Mammoth, AZ 74-75 H 6
Mammoth Cave National Park 70-71 G 7
Mammoth Hot Springs, WY 66-67 H 3
Mamoi = Mawei 146-147 G 8-9
Mamoneiras, Serra das — 98-99 P 7-8
Mamonovo 118 JK 1
Mamoré, Rio — 92-93 FG 7-8
Mamou 164-165 B 6
Mamou Macenta 168-169 BC 3
Mamoura, Hassi el — = Ḥāssī al-Mamūrah 166-167 F 4
Mamouroudougou 168-169 C 3
Mampang, Kali — 154 IV a 2
Mampang Prapatan, Jakarta- 154 IV a 2
Mampawah 148-149 E 6
Mampi = Sepopa 172 D 5
Mampong 164-165 D 7
Mamre 174-175 C 7
Mamry, Jezioro — 118 K 1
Mamuel Choique 108-109 DE 3
Mamuil Malal, Paso — 108-109 CD 2
Mamuíra, Cachoeira — 98-99 P 6
Mamuju 148-149 G 7
Mamūrah, Ḥāssī al- 166-167 F 4
Mamuru, Rio — 98-99 K 6
Man [CI] 164-165 C 7
Mān [IND] 140 B 2
Man, Isle of — 119 DE 4
Man, Nam ~ 150-151 C 4
Mana, HI 78-79 c 1
Mana [French Guiana, place] 92-93 J 3
Mana [French Guiana, river] 98-99 M 2
Mana, Hassi — = Ḥāssī Manāh 166-167 E 5
Manaas 142-143 F 3
Manabí 96-97 AB 2
Manacacías, Río — 94-95 E 5-6
Manacapuru 92-93 G 5
Manacor 120-121 J 9
Manado 148-149 H 6
Managua 64-65 J 9
Managua, Lago de — 64-65 J 9
Manāh, Ḥāssī — 166-167 E 5
Manakara 172 J 6
Mana La 138-139 G 2
Manāli 138-139 F 1
Manāmadurai 140 D 6
Manāmah, Al- 134-135 G 5
Manambaho 172 HJ 5
Manambolo 172 H 5
Manam Island 148-149 N 7
Manamo, Caño — 92-93 G 3
Mananara [RM, place] 172 J 5
Mananara [RM, river] 172 J 6
Mananjary 172 J 6
Manankoro 168-169 D 3
Manantenina 172 J 6
Manantiales 111 BC 8
Manapire, Río — 94-95 H 3
Manapouri, Lake — 158-159 N 9
Manappārai 140 D 5
Manāqil, Al- 164-165 L 6
Manar = Maner 138-139 K 5
Manār, Jabal al- 134-135 EF 8
Manās [IND] 141 B 2
Manás [PE] 96-97 C 7
Manas, gora — 132-133 N 9
Manāsa 138-139 E 5
Mānasārovar = Mapham Tsho 142-143 E 5
Manāṣif, Al- 136-137 J 5
Manasquan, NY 72-73 JK 4
Manastīr, Al- 166-167 M 2
Manatí [CO] 94-95 D 2
Manatí [Puerto Rico] 88-89 N 5
Manattala 140 BC 5
Manātu 138-139 K 5
Man'aung 141 C 6
Man'aung Reletkyā 141 CD 6
Manaure, Punta — 94-95 E 2
Manaus 92-93 H 5
Man'aung Kyûn 148-149 B 3
Mānāvadar 138-139 C 7
Manāvar = Manāwar 138-139 E 6
Manavgat 136-137 D 4
Mānavī = Mānvi 140 C 2-3
Manawan Lake 61 G 3
Manāwar [DZ] 166-167 E 4
Manāwar [IND] 138-139 E 6
Manayunk, Philadelphia-, PA 84 III b 1
Manbanbyet 141 EF 4
Mānbāzār 138-139 L 6
Manbij 136-137 G 4
Mancelona, MI 70-71 H 3
Mancha, La — 120-121 F 9
Mancha Khiri 150-151 D 4
Manchan 142-143 G 2
Manchar 138-139 DE 8
Mancherāl 140 D 1
Manchester, CT 72-73 K 4
Manchester, GA 78-79 G 4
Manchester, IA 70-71 E 4
Manchester, KS 68-69 H 6
Manchester, KY 72-73 DE 6
Manchester, MI 70-71 H 4
Manchester, NH 64-65 MN 3
Manchester, OK 76-77 EF 4
Manchester, TN 78-79 FG 3
Manchester, VT 72-73 K 3
Manchester [BOL] 104-105 BC 2
Manchester [GB] 119 EF 5
Manchhar, Jhīl — 138-139 A 4
Manchouli = Manzhouli 142-143 M 2
Manchuanguan 146-147 BC 5
Man-ch'uan-kuan = Manchuanguan 146-147 BC 5
Manchuria 142-143 N-P 2
Manchuria = Manzhou 142-143 N-P 2
Máncora 92-93 C 5
Máncora = Puerto Máncora 92-93 C 5
Mancos, CO 74-75 J 4
Mānd 138-139 J 6
Mand, Rūd-e- = Rūd-e Mond 134-135 G 5
Manda [BD] 138-139 M 5
Manda [EAT, Iringa] 172 FG 4
Manda [EAT, Mbeya] 171 C 4
Mandab, Bāb al- 134-135 E 8
Mandabe 172 H 6
Mandacaru 100-101 D 8
Mandaguari 102-103 G 5
Mandai 138-139 B 3
Mandai, Bukit — 154 III a 1
Mandal [Mongolia] 142-143 K 2
Mandal [N] 116-117 B 8-9
Mandalay = Mandale 148-149 C 2
Mandalay = Mandale Taing 141 DE 5
Mandale Taing 141 DE 5
Māndalgarh 138-139 E 5
Mandalgov' 142-143 JK 2
Mandalī 136-137 L 6
Mandalika = Pulau Mondoliko 152-153 J 9
Mandal Ovoo 142-143 JK 3
Mandalya körfezi 136-137 B 4
Mandalyat = Selimiye 136-137 B 4
Mandan, ND 68-69 F 2
Mandaon 148-149 H 4
Mandapeta 140 EF 2
Mandar 148-149 G 7
Mandar, Tanjung — 152-153 N 7
Mandar, Teluk — 148-149 G 7
Mandara, Monts — 164-165 G 6-7
Mandas 122-123 C 6
Mandasor 134-135 LM 6
Mandav Hills = Girnār Hills 138-139 C 7
Māṇḍavī = Māndvi 134-135 K 6
Mandāwa 138-139 E 3
Mandeb, Bab al- = Bāb al-Mandab 134-135 E 8
Manderson, WY 68-69 BC 3
Mandeville 88-89 GH 5
Mandeville, LA 78-79 DE 5
Māndhātā = Godarpura 138-139 F 6
Mandi 134-135 M 4
Mandiana 168-169 C 3
Mandi Dabwāli 138-139 E 3
Mandidzudzure 172 F 5-6
Mandimba 172 G 4
Manding 164-165 C 6
Manding Plateau 168-169 C 3
Mandioli, Pulau — 148-149 J 7
Mandioré, Laguna — 104-105 GH 6
Mandiroba 100-101 C 8
Mandī Sādiqganj 138-139 D 2
Mandiyuti, Sierra de — 104-105 E 7
Mandla 134-135 N 6
Mandolegüe, Cordillera — 106-107 B 6
Mandor 152-153 H 5
Mandrael 138-139 F 4
Mandria 136-137 E 5
Mandritsara 172 J 5
Mandrūp 140 B 2
Maṅdsaor 134-135 LM 6
Mandsaur = Maṅdsaor 134-135 LM 6
Mandui = Māndvi 134-135 K 6
Mandurah 158-159 BC 6
Manduri 102-103 H 5
Mandúria 122-123 G 5
Māndvi [IND, Gujarāt ↙ Bhuj] 134-135 K 6
Māndvi [IND, Gujarāt → Surat] 138-139 D 7
Māndvi [IND, Mahārāshtra] 138-139 D 8
Mandya 140 C 4
Mané [HV] 168-169 E 2
Mane Grande 94-95 F 3
Manendragarh 138-139 HJ 6
Manenguba, Mount — 168-169 H 4
Maner [IND, place] 138-139 K 5
Māner [IND, river] 140 D 1
Māneru = Māner 140 D 1
Mānesht, Kūh-e — 136-137 M 6
Manevići 124-125 E 8
Manfalūṭ 173 B 4
Manfredònia 122-123 FG 5
Manfredònia, Golfo di — 122-123 FG 5
Manga [BR] 92-93 L 7
Manga [RN] 164-165 G 6
Mangabeiras, Chapada das — 92-93 K 6-L 7
Mangai 172 C 2
Mangalagiri 140 E 2
Mangaldai 141 BC 2
Mangaldēī = Mangaldai 141 BC 2
Mangalia 122-123 N 4
Mangalkot 138-139 LM 6
Mangalmé 164-165 HJ 6
Mangalore 134-135 L 8
Mangaḷūru = Mangalore 134-135 L 8
Mangalvedha 140 B 2
Manganore 174-175 E 5
Māṅgāñv = Māngaon 140 A 1
Māngaon 140 A 1
Mangaratiba 102-103 K 5
Mangas, NM 74-75 J 5
Mangawān 138-139 H 5
Mangde Chhu 141 B 2
Mangeni, Hamada — 164-165 G 4
Manggar 148-149 E 7
Manggarai, Jakarta- 154 IV b 2
Manggyŏng-dong 144-145 GH 1
Mangham, LA 78-79 CD 4
Mangi 172 E 1
Mangkalihat, Tanjung — 148-149 GH 6
Mang Kung Uk 155 I b 2
Manglaralto 96-97 A 2
Manglares, Cabo — 92-93 CD 4
Mango 164-165 E 6
Mango, El — 94-95 H 7
Mangoche 172 G 4
Mangoky 172 H 6
Mangole, Pulau — 148-149 J 7
Mangoli = Pulau Mangole 148-149 J 7
Māngrol [IND, Gujarāt] 138-139 BC 7
Māngrol [IND, Rājasthān] 138-139 F 5
Mangrove, Punta — 64-65 F 8
Mangrullo, Cuchilla — 106-107 KL 4
Mangrūl Pīr 138-139 F 7
Mang-shih = Luxi 141 F 3
Mangšlaksij zaliv 126-127 P 4
Mangu 170 IV b 2
Manguari 98-99 D 5
Mangueigne 164-165 J 6
Mangueira, Lagoa — 111 F 4
Mangueirinha 102-103 F 6
Mangue Seco 100-101 F 6
Mangui 142-143 O 1
Manguinho, Ponta do — 92-93 M 7
Mangum, OK 76-77 E 5
Mangunça, Baía de — 100-101 B 1
Mangunça, Ilha — 100-101 B 1
Mangyai 142-143 G 4
Mang Yang, Đeo — 150-151 G 5
Mangyichaung 141 C 5
Mangyšlak, plato — 134-135 G 2
Manhā 100-101 A 7
Manhasset, NY 82 III d 2
Manhattan, KS 64-65 G 4
Manhattan, MT 66-67 H 3
Manhattan, NV 74-75 E 3
Manhattan Beach, CA 74-75 D 6
Manhattan State Beach 83 III b 2
Manhatten, New York-, NY 82 III bc 2
Manhiça 174-175 K 3
Manhuaçu 92-93 L 9
Manhuaçu, Rio — 102-103 M 3
Manhumirim 102-103 LM 4
Mani [CO] 92-93 E 4
Mani [TJ] 142-143 F 5
Mani, Quebrada de — 104-105 B 7
Mānī', Wādī al- 136-137 J 5-6
Mania 172 J 6
Maniaçu 100-101 C 7
Maniamba 172 FG 4
Manibūra Myit 141 C 4
Manica [Mozambique, administrative unit] 172 5-6 F
Manica [Mozambique, place] 172 F 5
Manica e Sofala 172 F 5-6
Manicaland 172 F 5
Maniçauá-Miçu, Rio — 98-99 LM 10
Manicoré 92-93 G 6
Manicoré, Rio — 98-99 H 8
Manicouagan 63 B 2
Manicouagan, Lac — 63 BC 2
Manicouagan, Rivière — 56-57 X 7-8
Manicuaré 94-95 J 2
Maniema 171 AB 4
Manigotagan 62 AB 2
Manigotagan River 62 AB 2
Manihāri 138-139 L 5
Manihiki 156-157 JK 5
Manika, Plateau de la — 172 E 3-4
Mānikganj 138-139 MN 6
Mānikhawa 138-139 B 2
Manila 148-149 H 3-4
Manila, UT 66-67 HJ 5
Manila Bay 148-149 GH 4
Manilla 160 K 3
Manilla, IA 70-71 C 5
Manimba, Masi- 172 C 2
Maninjau, Danau — 152-153 CD 6
Manipur [IND, administrative unit] 134-135 P 5-6
Manipur [IND, river] 141 C 3
Manipur = Imphāl 134-135 P 6
Manipur Hills 141 CD 3
Maniqui, Río — 104-105 C 4
Manisa 134-135 B 3
Manislee River 72-73 D 2
Manistee, MI 70-71 G 3
Manistee River 70-71 H 3
Manistique, MI 70-71 GH 2
Manistique Lake 70-71 H 2
Manitoba 56-57 Q-S 6
Manitoba, Lake — 56-57 R 7
Manito Lake 61 D 4
Manitou 68-69 G 1
Manitou, Rivière — 63 D 2
Manitou Island 70-71 G 2
Manitou Islands 70-71 G 3
Manitou Lake 62 L 4
Manitou Lakes 70-71 D 1
Manitou Lakes 62 C 3
Manitoulin Island 56-57 U 8
Manitou Springs, CO 68-69 D 6
Manitouwadge 56-57 T 8
Manitowoc, WI 64-65 J 3
Maniitsoq 56-57 Za 4
Maniwaki 56-57 V 8
Maniyāchchi 140 CD 6
Maniyāhū = Mariāhu 138-139 J 5
Manizales 92-93 D 3
Manja 172 H 6
Manjacaze 172 F 6-7
Manjarābād 140 B 4
Manjeri 140 BC 5
Manjeshwara 140 B 4
Manjhanpur 138-139 H 5
Manjīl 136-137 N 4
Manjimup 158-159 C 6
Mānjlēgāñv = Manjlegaon 138-139 EF 8
Manjlegaon 138-139 EF 8
Mānjra 134-135 M 7
Manjuli Island 141 D 2
Mankāchar 138-139 MN 5
Mānkaḍnachā = Mānkarnācha 138-139 K 7
Mānkarnācha 138-139 K 7
Mankato, KS 68-69 GH 6
Mankato, MN 64-65 H 3
Mankayane 174-175 J 4
Mankeṛa 138-139 C 2
Mankono 164-165 C 7
Mankota 68-69 C 1
Mankoya 172 D 4
Mankūb 166-167 E 3
Mānkulam 140 E 6
Mānkur 138-139 L 6
Manley Hot Springs, AK 58-59 M 4
Manlu He 150-151 BC 2
Man-lu Ho = Manlu He 150-151 BC 2
Manly, IA 70-71 D 4
Manly, Sydney- 161 I b 1
Manly Warringah War Memorial Park 161 I b 1
Manmād 138-139 E 7
Manna 148-149 D 7
Mannahill 160 DE 4
Mannar = Mannārama [CL, island] 140 DE 6
Mannar = Mannārama [CL, place] 140 DE 6
Mannar, Gulf of — 134-135 M 9
Mannārama [CL, island] 140 DE 6
Mannārama [CL, place] 140 DE 6
Mannārgudi 140 D 5
Mannār Khāṛī = Gulf of Mannar 134-135 M 9
Manneken Pis 128 II ab 1
Manneru 140 D 3
Mannheim 118 D 4
Manning, AR 78-79 C 3
Manning, IA 70-71 C 5
Manning, ND 68-69 E 2
Manning, SC 80-81 FG 4
Manning Provincial Park 66-67 C 1
Mannington, WV 72-73 F 5
Man'niyah, Al — = Al-Ma'anīyah 134-135 E 4
Mannswörth 113 I bc 2
Mannville 61 C 4
Mano [WAL, place] 168-169 B 3-4
Mano [WAL, river] 168-169 C 4
Manoa [BR] 98-99 F 9
Manoa [YV] 94-95 L 3
Manoharpur 138-139 K 6
Manohar Thāna 138-139 F 5
Manokotak, AK 58-59 H 7
Manokwari 148-149 K 7
Manoli 140 B 3
Manombo 172 H 6
Manono 172 E 3
Manor, TX 76-77 F 7
Manorhaven, NY 82 III d 1
Mano River 168-169 C 4
Manouane, Lac — [CDN ↑ Québec] 63 A 2
Manouane, Lac — [CDN ← Québec] 72-73 J 1
Manouane, Rivière — 63 A 2-3
Manouanis, Lac — 63 AB 2
Manpaka 170 IV a 1
Manp'ojin 144-145 F 2
Manpur 138-139 H 7
Manqalah 164-165 L 7
Manresa 120-121 HJ 8
Mans, le — 120-121 H 4-5
Mānsa [IND, Gujarāt] 138-139 D 6
Mānsa [IND, Punjab] 138-139 E 3
Mansa [ZRE] 172 E 4
Mansa Konko 168-169 B 2
Mansalar = Pulau Musala 148-149 C 6
Mansar 138-139 G 7
Mansavillagra 106-107 K 4
Mansaya = Masaya 64-65 J 9
Mansel Island 56-57 U 5
Manseriche, Pongo de — 92-93 D 5
Mansfield, AR 76-77 G 5
Mansfield, LA 78-79 C 4
Mansfield, MO 78-79 C 2
Mansfield, OH 64-65 K 3
Mansfield, PA 72-73 H 4
Mansfield, WA 66-67 D 2
Mansfield [AUS] 160 H 6
Mansfield [GB] 119 F 5
Mansi = Manzī [BUR, Kachin Pyinnei] 141 E 3
Mansi = Manzī [BUR, Sitkaing Taing] 141 D 3
Manso, Rio — 92-93 J 7-8
Manson, IA 70-71 C 4
Manson Creek 60 E 2
Mansour, El — = Al-Manṣūr 166-167 F 6
Mansoura = Al-Manṣūrah 166-167 HJ 1
Manṣūr, Al- 166-167 F 6
Mansura, LA 78-79 C 5
Manṣūrābād = Mehrān 136-137 M 6
Manṣūrah, Al- [DZ] 166-167 HJ 1
Manṣūrah, Al- [ET] 164-165 L 2
Maṅsūrī = Mussoorie 138-139 G 2
Manṣūrīyah, Al- 136-137 L 5
Manta 92-93 C 5
Manta, Bahía de — 92-93 C 5
Mantalingajan, Mount — 148-149 G 5
Mantanani, Pulau — 152-153 LM 2
Mantaro, Río — 92-93 E 7
Mante, Ciudad — 64-65 G 7
Manteca, CA 74-75 C 4
Mantecal [YV, Apure] 94-95 G 4
Mantecal [YV, Bolívar] 94-95 J 4
Manteco, El — 92-93 G 3
Mantena 102-103 M 3
Mantenópolis 100-101 D 10
Manteo, NC 80-81 J 3
Mantes 168-169 B 3
Mantes-la-Jolie 120-121 H 4
Man Tha = Manthī 141 E 3-4
Manthani 140 D 1
Manthī 141 E 3-4
Manti, UT 74-75 H 3
Mantiqueira, Serra da — 92-93 KL 9
Manto 88-89 C 7
Manton, MI 70-71 H 3
Mantova 122-123 D 3
Mantsinsari 124-125 H 3
Mänttä 116-117 L 6
Mantua = Mantova 122-123 D 3
Mantua Creek 84 III b 3
Mantua Terrace, NJ 84 III b 3
Mantung 160 E 5
Manturovo [SU, Kostromskaja Oblast'] 124-125 P 4
Manturovo [SU, Kurskaja Oblast'] 126-127 H 1
Mäntyharju 116-117 M 7
Mäntyluoto 116-117 J 7
Mantzikert = Malazgirt 136-137 K 3
Manū 92-93 E 7
Manū, Rio — 96-97 F 7-8
Manua 208 K 4
Manuan 72-73 J 1
Manuel 86-87 LM 6
Manuel, Punta — 106-107 A 7
Manuel Alves, Rio — 98-99 OP 10
Manuel Benavides 86-87 HJ 3
Manuel Derqui 106-107 H 1
Manuelito, NM 74-75 J 5
Manuel Jorge, Cachoeira — 98-99 LM 7
Manuel Luís, Recife — 100-101 BC 1
Manuel Ribas 102-103 G 6
Manuel Rodriguez, Isla — 108-109 BC 9
Manuel Urbano 98-99 CD 9
Manuel Viana 106-107 K 2
Manuelzinho 92-93 HJ 6
Manui, Pulau — 152-153 P 7
Manuk, Pulau — 148-149 K 8
Mānūk, Tall — 136-137 H 6
Manukau 158-159 OP 7
Manukau Harbour 158-159 O 7
Manumukh 141 BC 3
Manurini, Río — 104-105 C 3
Manuripe, Río — 96-97 G 7
Manus 148-149 N 7
Manushūnash 166-167 K 2
Manvath = Mānwat 138-139 F 8
Mānvi 140 C 2-3
Manville, WY 68-69 D 4
Mānwat 138-139 F 8
Many, LA 78-79 C 5
Manyal Shīhah 170 II b 2
Manyara, Lake — 172 G 2
Manyas = Maltepe 136-137 B 2
Manyč 126-127 K 3
Manyč-Gudilo, ozero — 126-127 L 3
Manyčskaja vpadina, Kumo- 126-127 K 3-M 4
Manyonga 171 C 3-4
Manyoni 172 F 3
Manyunjie 141 E 3
Manzai 134-135 KL 4
Manzanares [E, place] 120-121 F 9
Manzanares [E, river] 120-121 F 8
Manzanares, Canal del — 113 III b 2-3
Manzanillo [C] 64-65 L 7
Manzanillo [MEX] 64-65 EF 8
Manzanillo, Punta — 64-65 L 9-10
Manzano, El — [RA] 106-107 E 3
Manzano, El — [RCH] 106-107 B 5
Manzano Mountains 76-77 A 5
Manzanza 171 B 4
Manzhouli 142-143 M 2
Manzī [BUR, Kachin Pyinnei] 141 E 3
Manzī [BUR, Sitkaing Taing] 141 D 3
Manzikert = Malazgirt 136-137 K 3
Manzilah, Al- 173 BC 2
Manzilah, Buḥayrat al- 173 BC 2
Manzil Būrgībah 166-167 L 1
Manzil Shākir 166-167 M 2
Manzil Tamīm 166-167 M 1
Manzini 172 F 7
Manzovka 132-133 Z 9
Mao 164-165 H 6
Mao, Nam — = Nam Wa 150-151 C 3
Maobi Tou = Maopi Tou 146-147 H 11
Maocifan 146-147 D 6
Maodahā = Maudaha 138-139 GH 5
Maoka = Cholmsk 132-133 b 8
Maoke, Pegunungan — 148-149 LM 7
Maoli 138-139 D 5
Maoming 142-143 L 7
Maoming = Gaozhou 146-147 C 11
Maoping = Xiangzikou 146-147 CD 7
Maopi Tou 146-147 H 11
Mao Songsang 141 D 3
Maotanchang 146-147 F 6
Maowei Hai = Qinzhou Wan 150-151 G 2
Mapaga 148-149 G 7
Mapai 172 F 6
Maparari 94-95 G 2
Maparuta 94-95 L 5
Mapastepec 86-87 O 10
Mapham Tsho 142-143 E 5
Mapham Yumtsho = Mapham Tsho 142-143 E 5
Mapi 148-149 L 8
Mapia, Kepulauan — 148-149 KL 6
Mapichí, Serranía de — 92-93 F 3-4
Mapimí 86-87 HJ 5
Mapimí, Bolsón de — 64-65 F 6
Maping 146-147 D 6
Ma-p'ing = Liuzhou 142-143 K 7
Mapinggang = Maping 146-147 D 6
Mapinhane 172 FG 6
Mapire 92-93 G 3
Mapireme 98-99 LM 4
Mapiri 104-105 B 4
Mapiri, Río — [BOL ◁ Río Abuñá] 104-105 C 2
Mapiri, Río — [BOL ◁ Río Beni] 104-105 B 4
Mapiripán, Lago — 94-95 EF 6
Mapiripan, Salto — 92-93 E 4
Ma-pi-ts'un = Mabi 146-147 D 4
Maple Beach, PA 84 III d 1
Maple Creek 61 D 6
Maple Meadow Brook 84 I ab 1
Maple Shade, NJ 84 III cd 2
Maplesville, AL 78-79 F 4
Mapleton, IA 70-71 BC 4
Mapleton, MN 70-71 D 4
Mapleton, OR 66-67 AB 3
Mapoon 158-159 H 2
Mapor, Pulau — 152-153 F 5
Maporal 94-95 F 4
Maporillal 94-95 F 4
Mappi = Mapi 148-149 L 8
Maprik 148-149 M 7
Māpuca 140 A 3
Mapuera, Rio — 92-93 H 5
Mapula 171 D 6
Mapulanguene 174-175 K 3
Mapulau, Rio — 98-99 G 3-4

Mapumulo 174-175 J 5
Maputa 174-175 K 4
Maputo [Mozambique, landscape] 174-175 K 4
Maputo [Mozambique, place] 172 F 7
Maputo, Baía do — 172 F 7
Maputo, Rio — 174-175 K 4
Ma'qalā' 134-135 F 5
Maqām Sīdī Shaykh 166-167 G 2
Maqarr al-Jalīb 136-137 J 6
Maqarr an-Na'ām 136-137 HJ 7
Ma'qil, Al- 136-137 M 7
Maqinchao 111 C 6
Maqnā 173 D 3
Maqṭayr 164-165 BC 4
Maquan He = Tsangpo 142-143 EF 6
Maquela do Zombo 172 BC 3
Maqueze 172 F 6
Maquie 96-97 D 5
Maquinista Levet 106-107 D 4
Maquoketa, IA 70-71 E 4
Maquoketa River 70-71 E 4
Māqūrah 166-167 F 2
Maqwa', Al- 136-137 M 8
Mar, Serra do — 111 G 2-3
Mara [EAT, administrative unit] 172 FG 2
Mara [EAT, place] 171 C 3
Mara [EAT, river] 172 F 2
Mara [GUY] 98-99 K 1-2
Mara [PE] 96-97 E 9
Mara [RI] 152-153 O 8
Maraã 92-93 F 5
Marabá 92-93 K 6
Marabitanas 92-93 F 4
Maracá 98-99 N 3
Maracá, Ilha — 92-93 G 4
Maracá, Ilha de — 92-93 JK 4
Maraca, Rio — 98-99 N 5
Maracaçumé 100-101 AB 2
Maraçacumé, Rio — 100-101 AB 1-2
Maracaí 102-103 G 5
Maracaibo 92-93 E 2
Maracaibo, Lago de — 92-93 E 2-3
Maracaju 92-93 H 9
Maracaju, Serra de — 92-93 H 9-J 8
Maracanã [BR, Pará] 92-93 K 5
Maracanã [BR, Rio de Janeiro] 110 I b 2
Maracanaquará, Planalto — 98-99 M 5
Maracás 100-101 D 7
Maracás, Chapada de — 100-101 DE 7
Maracay 92-93 F 2
Maracó Grande, Valle de — 106-107 EF 6
Marādah 164-165 H 3
Maradi 164-165 F 6
Marādoh = Mariado 138-139 G 5
Ma'rafāy, Jabal — 173 D 6
Mara Game Reserve 172 FG 2
Marāghah, Al- 173 B 4
Marāgheh 134-135 F 3
Maragoji 100-101 G 5
Maragojipe 100-101 E 7
Marahoué 168-169 D 3
Marahuaca, Cerro — 92-93 FG 4
Marahué, Parc National de la — 168-169 D 4
Maraial 100-101 G 6
Maraisburg 170 V a 2
Marais des Cygnes River 70-71 C 6
Marais Poitevin 120-121 G 5
Marajó, Baía de — 92-93 K 4-5
Marajó, Ilha de — 92-93 JK 5
Marakabeis 174-175 GH 5
Marākand 136-137 L 3
Marakei 208 H 2
Marakkānam 140 DE 4
Maralal 172 G 1
Maral Bashi 142-143 D 3-4
Maralinga 158-159 F 6
Maramasike 148-149 k 6
Maramba = Livingstone 172 E 5
Marambaia, Restinga da — 92-93 L 9
Marampa 164-165 B 7
Maran [BUR] 150-151 B 7
Maran [MAL] 148-149 D 6
Mārān = Mohājerān 136-137 N 5
Marana, AZ 74-75 H 6
Maranboy 158-159 F 2
Marand 136-137 L 3
Marandellas = Marondera 172 F 5
Marang = Maran 150-151 B 7
Marang, Kuala — 150-151 D 10
Maranguape 92-93 M 5
Maranhão 92-93 KL 5-6
Marānhaṭ = Morānhāt 141 D 2
Maranoa River 158-159 J 5
Marañón, Río — 92-93 DE 5
Marapanim 98-99 P 5
Marapi, Gunung — 152-153 D 6
Marapi, Rio — 98-99 K 4
Mar Argentino 111 D 7-E 5
Maraş 134-135 D 3
Maraşalçakmak 136-137 H 3
Mărăşeşti 122-123 M 3
Mārath 166-167 M 3
Maratha = Mahārāshtra [IND, administrative unit] 134-135 L 7-M 6
Maratha = Mahārāshtra [IND, landscape] 134-135 M 7
Marathon, FL 80-81 c 4
Marathon, TX 76-77 C 7
Marathon [CDN] 56-57 T 8
Marathón [GR] 122-123 KL 6
Maratua, Pulau — 148-149 G 6
Maraú [BR, Bahia] 100-101 E 8
Marau [BR, Rio Grande do Sul] 106-107 L 2
Marauiá, Rio — 98-99 F 4-5
Marauni 148-149 k 7
Marav, Jhīl — 138-139 B 3
Maraval 94-95 K 2
Marawī 164-165 L 5
Maray 96-97 C 7
Marayes 106-107 D 3
Mar'ayt 134-135 G 7
Maraza 126-127 O 6
Marbella 120-121 E 10
Marble, CO 68-69 C 6
Marble Bar 158-159 CD 4
Marble Canyon, AZ 74-75 H 4
Marble Falls, TX 76-77 E 7
Marble Gorge 74-75 H 4
Marble Hall 172 E 7
Marburg 118 D 3
Marcali 118 H 5
Marcapata 96-97 F 8
Marcaria 122-123 D 3
Marceau, Lac — 63 CD 2
Marceline, MO 70-71 D 6
Marcelino 92-93 F 5
Marcelino Escalada 106-107 G 3
Marcelino Ramos 106-107 LM 1
Marcellus, MI 70-71 H 4
Marcellus, WA 66-67 D 2
Marcha [SU, place] 132-133 X 5
Marcha [SU, river] 132-133 W 5
Marchand [CDN] 68-69 H 1
Marchand [ZA] 174-175 D 5
Marchand = Ar-Rummānī 166-167 C 3
Marchand, Le — 108-109 E 8
Marche [F] 120-121 HJ 5
Marche [I] 122-123 E 4
Marchena 120-121 E 10
Marchena, Isla — 92-93 AB 4
Mar Chiquita [RA, Buenos Aires ← Junín] 106-107 G 5
Mar Chiquita [RA, Buenos Aires ↑ Mar del Plata] 106-107 J 6
Mar Chiquita [RA, Médanos] 106-107 J 6
Mar Chiquita [RA, Pampas] 106-107 G 5
Mar Chiquita, Laguna — 111 D 4
Marco 100-101 D 2
Marcos Juárez 106-107 F 4
Marcos Paz 106-107 H 5
Marcoule 120-121 K 6
Marcus, IA 70-71 BC 4
Marcus = Minami Tori 156-157 G 3
Marcus Baker, Mount — 56-57 G 5
Marcus Hook, PA 84 III a 3
Marcus Island = Minami Tori 156-157 G 3
Marcus Necker Ridge 156-157 G 3-J 4
Marcy, Mount — 72-73 JK 2
Mardān 134-135 L 4
Mar de Ajó 106-107 J 6
Mar del Plata 111 E 5
Mar del Sur 106-107 HJ 7
Mardin 134-135 E 3
Mardin eşiği 136-137 J 4
Maré, Île — 158-159 N 4
Mare, Muntele — 122-123 K 2
Marebe = Mā'rib 134-135 F 7
Marechal C. Rondon 102-103 EF 6
Marechal Deodoro 100-101 G 5
Maree, Loch — 119 D 3
Mareeba 158-159 HJ 3
Mareeg 164-165 b 3
Mareetsane 174-175 F 4
Mareil-Marly 129 I b 2
Maremma 122-123 D 4
Marena 164-165 B 6
Marengo, IA 70-71 D 5
Marengo, IN 70-71 G 6
Marengo, WA 66-67 DE 2
Marengo = Ḥajut 164-165 E 1
Marenisco, MI 70-71 F 2
Mares, De — 94-95 DE 4
Māreth = Mārath 166-167 M 3
Marèttimo 122-123 DE 7
Marevo 124-125 HJ 5
Marfa, TX 76-77 B 7
Marfa', Al- = Al-Maghayrā' 134-135 G 6
Marfino 126-127 O 3
Marg, Dasht-e — 134-135 J 4
Margao 140 A 3
Margaret Bay 60 D 4
Margarita 111 D 3
Margarita, Isla — 94-95 D 3
Margarita, Isla de — 92-93 G 2
Margarita Belén 104-105 G 10
Margate [ZA] 174-175 J 6
Margento 94-95 D 3
Margeride, Monts de la — 120-121 J 6
Margherita 171 B 2
Margherita = Jamaame 172 H 1
Margherita, Lake — = Abaya 164-165 M 7
Margie 61 C 3
Margie, MN 70-71 D 1
Margilan 134-135 L 2
Margoh, Dasht-e — = Dasht-e Marg 134-135 J 4
Margosatubig 152-153 P 2
Marguerite, Baie — 53 C 29-30
Marguerite, Rivière — 63 C 2
Maria [CDN] 63 D 3
María, Island — = Bleaker Island 108-109 K 9
María, Monte — = Mount Maria 108-109 K 8
Maria, Mount — 108-109 K 8
María Chiquita 64-65 b 2
María Cleofas, Isla — 86-87 G 7
Maria de Fé 102-103 K 5
Maria de Suari 96-97 D 4
Mariado 138-139 G 5
María Elena 111 BC 2
María Enrique, Altos de — 64-65 bc 2
Maria Enzersdorf am Gebirge 113 I b 2
Maria Eugenia 106-107 G 3
Mariāhu 138-139 J 5
María Ignacia 106-107 H 6
Maria Island [AUS, Northern Territory] 158-159 G 2
Maria Island [AUS, Tasmania] 158-159 J 8
Mariakani 171 D 3
María la Baja 94-95 D 3
Maria-Lanzendorf 113 I b 2
María Madre, Isla — 64-65 E 7
María Magdalena, Isla — 64-65 E 7
Mariampolė = Kapsukas 124-125 D 6
Mariana 102-103 L 4
Mariana, Ilha — 174-175 K 3
Mariana Islands 206-207 S 7-8
Marianao 64-65 K 7
Marianas, Las — 106-107 H 5
Mariana Trench 156-157 G 4
Marianna, AR 78-79 D 3
Marianna, FL 78-79 G 5
Mariano Acosta, Merlo- 110 III a 2
Mariano I. Loza 106-107 HJ 2
Mariano J. Haedo, Morón- 110 III b 1
Mariano Machado = Ganda 172 B 4
Mariano Moreno 106-107 BC 7
Mariano Moreno, Moreno- 110 III a 1
Marianopolis 100-101 B 3
Mariano Roldán 106-107 GH 6
Mariano Unzué 106-107 G 6
Mariánské Lázně 118 F 4
Mariapiri, Mesa de — 94-95 FG 6
Marías, Islas — 64-65 E 7
Marías, Las — 91 II bc 2
Marias Pass 64-65 D 2
Marias River 66-67 H 1
María Teresa 106-107 FG 4-5
Mari Autonomous Soviet Socialist Republic = 3 ◁ 132-133 H 6
Maria van Diemen, Cape — 158-159 O 6
Maria Velha, Cachoeira — 98-99 K 7
Mariazell 118 G 5
Mā'rib 134-135 F 7
Maribondo, Cachoeira do — 102-103 H 4
Maribor 122-123 F 2
Maribyrnong River 161 II b 1
Marica [BG, place] 122-123 LM 4
Marica [BG, river] 122-123 L 4
Maricá [BR] 102-103 L 5
Maricá, Lagoa — 102-103 L 5
Marico [ZA, landscape] 174-175 FG 3
Marico [ZA, river] 174-175 G 3
Maricopa, AZ 74-75 G 6
Maricopa, CA 74-75 D 5
Maricopa Indian Reservation 74-75 G 6
Maricourt 56-57 W 5
Maricunga, Salar de — 104-105 B 10
Marīdī 164-165 KL 8
Marié, Rio — 92-93 F 5
Marie-Galante 64-65 OP 8
Mariehamn 116-117 HJ 7
Mariendorf, Berlin- 130 III b 2
Marienfelde, Berlin- 130 III b 2
Marienhöhe, Waldpark — 130 I a 1
Mariental 172 C 6
Marienthal, Hamburg- 130 I b 1
Mariestad 116-117 E 8
Marietta, GA 64-65 K 5
Marietta, OH 72-73 F 5
Marietta, OK 76-77 F 6
Marieville 72-73 K 2
Mariga 168-169 G 3
Marigot [Anguilla] 88-89 P 5
Marigot [WD] 88-89 Q 7
Mariinsk 132-133 Q 6
Mariinskij Posad 124-125 QR 5
Marii Prončiščevoj, buchta — 132-133 VW 2
Mariiupil = Ždanov 126-127 H 3
Marijec 124-125 R 5
Marijskaja Avtonomnaja Sovetskaja Socialističeskaja Respublika = Mari Autonomous Soviet Socialist Republic 132-133 H 6
Marikana 174-175 G 3
Mari Lauquén 106-107 F 6
Marília 92-93 JK 9
Mari Luan, Valle — 106-107 E 7
Marina 60 H 1
Marina, Île — = Espíritu Santo 158-159 MN 3
Marina del Rey 83 III b 2
Marina del Rey, CA 83 III b 2
Marina di Gioiosa Iònica 122-123 G 6
Marina North Beach, San Francisco-, CA 83 I b 2
Marin City, CA 83 I a 1
Marinduque Island 148-149 H 4
Marine City, MI 72-73 E 3
Marine Park 84 I bc 2
Mariners Harbor, New York-, NY 82 III ab 3
Marinette, WI 64-65 J 2
Maringa [BR] 102-103 FG 5
Maringa [ZRE] 172 D 1
Marin Headlands State Park 83 I ab 2
Marin Mall, CA 83 I ab 1
Mariño [RA] 104-105 D 10
Marino = Pristen' 126-127 H 1
Marin Peninsula 83 I a 1-b 2
Mario, Monte — 113 II b 1
Marion 53 E 4
Marion, AL 78-79 F 4
Marion, IA 70-71 E 4
Marion, IL 70-71 F 7
Marion, IN 70-71 H 5
Marion, KS 68-69 H 6
Marion, KY 70-71 F 7
Marion, LA 78-79 C 4
Marion, MI 70-71 H 3
Marion, MT 66-67 F 1
Marion, NC 80-81 EF 3
Marion, ND 68-69 G 2
Marion, OH 72-73 E 4
Marion, SC 80-81 G 3
Marion, SD 68-69 H 4
Marion, TX 76-77 EF 8
Marion, VA 80-81 F 2
Marion, WI 70-71 F 3
Marion, Lake — 80-81 F 4
Marion Island 53 E 4
Marion Junction, AL 78-79 F 4
Maripa 92-93 FG 3
Maripasoula 92-93 J 4
Mariposa, CA 74-75 D 4
Mariposa, Sierra — 104-105 B 8
Mariposas 106-107 B 5
Mariquita [BR] 100-101 B 7
Mariquita [CO] 94-95 D 5
Marīr, Jazīrat — 173 DE 6
Mariscala, La — 106-107 K 5
Marisco, Punta do — 110 I b 3
Marismas, Las — 120-121 D 10
Maritime 168-169 F 4
Maritime Alps = Alpes Maritimes 120-121 L 6
Maritsa = Marica 122-123 L 4
Mari-Turek 124-125 RS 5
Mariupol' = Ždanov 126-127 H 3
Mariusa, Caño — 94-95 L 3
Mariusa, Isla — 94-95 L 3
Marīvān 136-137 M 5
Marīyah, Al- 134-135 G 6
Marj, Al- 164-165 J 2
Marjaayoûn = Marj Uyūn 136-137 FG 6
Marjah, Al- 166-167 H 2
Mārjamaa 124-125 E 4
Marjan = Wāza Khwā 134-135 K 4
Marjevka 132-133 M 7
Marjina Gorka 124-125 FG 7
Marj Uyūn 136-137 F 6
Marka [SP] 164-165 NO 8
Markādā' 136-137 J 5
Markala 168-169 D 2
Markalasta 124-125 UV 2
Mārkāpur 140 D 3
Mārkāpura = Mārkāpur 140 D 3
Markazī, Ostān-e — 134-135 E 3-F 4
Markdale 72-73 F 2
Marked Tree, AR 78-79 D 3
Markha = Marcha 132-133 W 5
Markham 72-73 G 3
Markham, WA 66-67 AB 2
Markham, Mount — 53 A 15-16
Mārkhandī 138-139 G 8
Markkëri = Mercāra 134-135 M 8
Markleeville, CA 74-75 CD 3
Markounda 164-165 H 7
Markovo [SU, Čukotskij NO] 132-133 gh 5
Marks, MS 78-79 D 3
Marks = Marx 124-125 Q 8
Marksville, LA 78-79 CD 5
Marktredwitz 118 EF 3-4
Marlborough [AUS] 158-159 JK 4
Marlborough [NZ] 161 EF 5-6
Marlette, MI 72-73 E 3
Marlin, TX 76-77 F 7
Marlinton, WV 72-73 FG 5
Marlo 160 J 6
Marlow, OK 76-77 F 5
Marlow Heights, MD 82 II b 2
Marlton, NJ 84 III d 2
Marlton-Medford Airport 84 III d 2
Marly-le-Roi 129 I b 2
Marmagao 134-135 L 7
Marmande 120-121 H 6
Marmara adası 134-135 B 2
Marmara boğazı 154 I ab 3
Marmara denizi 134-135 B 2
Marmarâs = Marmaris 136-137 C 4
Marmarica = Barqat al-Baḥrīyah 164-165 JK 2
Marmaris 136-137 C 4
Marmarth, ND 68-69 E 2
Marmelão, Cachoeira — 98-99 KL 7
Marmeleiro 102-103 F 6
Marmelos, Rio dos — 92-93 G 6
Mar Menor 120-121 G 10
Marmet, WV 72-73 F 5
Marmion Lake 70-71 E 1
Marmolada 122-123 DE 2
Marmolejo, Cerro — 106-107 BC 4
Marmot Bay 58-59 L 7-8
Marmot Island 58-59 M 7
Mar Muerto 86-87 NO 9
Marne 120-121 JK 4
Marne au Rhin, Canal de la — 120-121 K 4
Marneuli 126-127 M 6
Marnia = Maghnīyah 166-167 F 2
Maroa 94-95 H 6
Maroa, IL 70-71 F 5
Maroantsetra 172 JK 5
Marocco, IN 70-71 G 5
Marokko 164-165 C 3-D 2
Marolles-en-Brie 129 I d 3
Maroma, La — 106-107 DE 5
Marondera 172 F 5
Maroni 92-93 J 3-4
Maroona 160 F 6
Maros [RI] 148-149 GH 7-8
Marosvasarhely = Tîrgu Mureş 122-123 L 2
Maroua 164-165 G 6
Maroubra, Sydney- 161 I b 2
Maroubra Bay 161 I b 2
Marouini 98-99 LM 3
Marovoay 172 J 5
Marowijne [SME, administrative unit] 98-99 L 2-3
Marowijne [SME, river] 92-93 J 3-4
Marqat Bazar 142-143 D 4
Marquand, MO 70-71 E 7
Marquard 174-175 G 5
Marques, Petare-El — 91 II c 2
Marquesa, La — 91 I a 3
Marquesas Keys 80-81 b 4
Marquês de Valença = Valença 102-103 KL 5
Marquette, IA 70-71 E 4
Marquette, MI 64-65 J 2
Marquette Park 83 II a 2
Marrah, Jabal — 164-165 JK 6
Marrâkech = Marrākush 164-165 C 2
Marrakesh = Marrākush 164-165 C 2
Marrākush 164-165 C 2
Marrângua, Lagoa — 174-175 L 3
Marrawah 158-159 H 8
Marrecas, Serra das — 100-101 D 5
Marree 158-159 G 5
Marrero, LA 85 I b 2
Marrickville, Sydney- 161 I ab 2
Marromeu 172 G 5
Marrupa 172 G 4
Marsā, Al- 166-167 M 1
Marsa, El — 170 I b 1
Marsā 'Alam 173 D 5
Marsā al-Burayqah 164-165 HJ 2
Marsā-Ban-Mahīdī 166-167 EF 2
Marsabit 172 G 1
Marsabit Game Reserve 171 D 2
Marsala 122-123 E 7
Mars al-Kabīr 166-167 F 1-2
Marsā Maṭrūḥ 164-165 K 2
Marsā Sha'b 164-165 M 4
Marsa Sūsa = Sūsah 164-165 J 2
Marseille 120-121 K 7
Marseilles 174-175 G 5
Marseilles, IL 70-71 F 5
Marseilles = Marseille 120-121 K 7
Marsengdi 138-139 K 3
Marsfjället 116-117 F 5
Marsh, MT 68-69 D 2
Marshall 168-169 C 4
Marshall, AK 58-59 FG 6
Marshall, AR 78-79 C 3
Marshall, IL 70-71 FG 6
Marshall, MI 70-71 H 4
Marshall, MN 70-71 BC 3
Marshall, MO 70-71 D 6
Marshall, NC 80-81 E 3
Marshall, OK 76-77 F 4
Marshall, TX 64-65 H 5
Marshall, Mount — 72-73 G 5
Marshall Basin 162 J 3
Marshall Islands 156-157 H 4
Marshalltown, IA 70-71 D 4
Marshall Trench 156-157 H 4
Marshfield, MO 78-79 C 2
Marshfield, WI 70-71 EF 3
Marshfield = Coos Bay, OR 64-65 AB 3
Marsh Harbour 88-89 H 1
Mars Hill, ME 72-73 MN 1
Marsh Island 78-79 CD 6
Marsing, ID 66-67 E 4
Marsland, NE 68-69 E 4
Marsqui 63 D 3
Marstrand 116-117 D 9
Mart, TX 76-77 F 7
Martaban = Mōktama 148-149 C 3
Martapura [RI, Borneo] 152-153 L 7
Martapura [RI, Sumatra] 152-153 EF 8
Marte, Campo de — 110 II b 2
Marten 60 K 2
Marten, Rivière — 62 O 1
Martensdale, IA 70-71 D 5
Martensøya 116-117 I 4
Marthaguy Creek 160 H 3
Martha's Vineyard 64-65 MN 3
Martī 88-89 H 4
Martigny 118 C 5
Martigues 120-121 K 7
Martīl 166-167 D 2
Martimprey-du-Kiss = Aḥfir 166-167 EF 2
Martim Vaz, Ilhas — 92-93 O 9
Martin 118 J 4
Martin, SD 68-69 EF 4
Martin, TN 78-79 E 2
Martín Colman 106-107 H 6
Martín de Loyola 106-107 DE 5
Martinetas, Las — 106-107 G 6
Martínez, San Isidro- 110 III b 1
Martínez de Hoz = Coronel Martínez de Hoz 106-107 FG 5
Martínez de la Torre 86-87 M 7
Martínez del Tineo 104-105 E 8
Martín Fierro 106-107 H 6
Martinho Campos 102-103 K 3
Martinique 64-65 OP 9
Martinique Passage 88-89 Q 7
Martin Lake 78-79 FG 4
Martinópolis 102-103 G 5
Martin Peninsula 53 B 25-26
Martin Point 56-57 H 3
Martin River 60 JK 1
Martins 100-101 EF 4
Martinsburg, WV 72-73 GH 5
Martinsdale, MT 66-67 H 2
Martins Ferry, OH 72-73 F 4
Martinsried 130 II a 2
Martinsville, IN 70-71 G 6
Martinsville, VA 80-81 G 2
Marton 158-159 OP 8
Martos 120-121 EF 10
Martre, Lac la — 56-57 MN 5
Martuk 132-133 K 7
Martuni [SU, Arm'anskaja SSR] 126-127 M 6
Martuni [SU, Azerbajdžanskaja SSR] 126-127 N 7
Marua = Maroua 164-165 G 6
Maruai 98-99 H 3
Marucho, El — 106-107 BC 7
Marudi 152-153 KL 3
Marudi Mountains 98-99 J 3
Marugame 144-145 J 5
Marui 148-149 M 7
Maruim 92-93 M 7
Maruja, La — 106-107 E 5
Maruko, Kawasaki- 155 III b 2
Marungu 172 EF 3
Marvão 120-121 D 9
Mārvāṛ = Mārwār [IND, landscape] 134-135 L 5
Mārvāṛ = Mārwār [IND, place] 134-135 L 5
Marvel, AR 78-79 D 3
Marvine, Mount — 74-75 H 3
Mar Vista, Los Angeles-, CA 83 III b 1
Marwan, Shaṭṭ — 166-167 JK 2-3
Marwānah 166-167 J 2
Mārwār [IND, landscape] 134-135 L 5
Mārwār [IND, place] 134-135 L 5
Marwayne 61 CD 4
Marwitz [DDR] 130 III a 1
Marx 124-125 Q 8
Mary 134-135 J 3
Mary, Cordón de — 106-107 BC 6
Maryborough [AUS, Queensland] 158-159 K 5
Maryborough [AUS, Victoria] 158-159 HJ 7
Marydale 174-175 DE 5
Maryfield 61 GH 6
Mary Kathleen 158-159 GH 4
Maryland [LB] 168-169 CD 4
Maryland [USA] 64-65 L 4
Maryneal, TX 76-77 D 6
Mary Rvier 158-159 F 2
Marystown 63 J 4
Marysvale, UT 74-75 GH 3
Marysville 63 C 4-5
Marysville, KS 68-69 H 6
Marysville, OH 72-73 E 4
Marysville, WA 66-67 BC 1
Maryum La 138-139 J 2
Maryūṭ, Buḥayrat — 173 AB 2
Maryvale 158-159 HJ 3
Maryville, CA 74-75 C 3
Maryville, MO 70-71 C 5
Maryville, TN 80-81 DE 3
Marzahn, Berlin- 130 III c 1
Marzo, Cabo — 92-93 D 3
Marzu, Kūh-e- 136-137 M 6
Marzūq 164-165 G 3
Marzūq, Ṣaḥrā' — 164-165 G 3-4
Maṣabb Dumyāṭ 173 BC 2
Maṣabb Rashīd 173 B 2
Masai 154 III b 1
Masai Mara Game Reserve 171 C 3
Masai Steppe 172 G 2
Masaka 172 F 2
Masākin 166-167 M 2
Masalima, Pulau-pulau 152-153 M 8
Masamba 152-153 O 7
Masampo = Masan 142-143 O 4-5
Masan 142-143 O 4-5
Masandam, Rā's — 134-135 H 5
Masaoṛhī = Masaurhi 138-139 K 5
Masardis, ME 72-73 M 1
Masasi 172 G 4
Masaurhi 138-139 K 5
Masavi 92-93 G 8
Masaya 64-65 J 9
Masba 168-169 J 3
Masbat = Masbate 148-149 H 4
Masbate 148-149 H 4
Mascara = Mū'askar 164-165 E 1
Mascarene Basin 50-51 M 6
Mascarene Islands 204-205 N 10-11
Mascarene Plateau 50-51 MN 6
Mascasín 106-107 D 3
Maschwanden 128 IV a 2
Mascote 100-101 E 8
Masefield 68-69 C 1
Maserti 136-137 J 4
Maseru 172 E 7
Mashala 172 D 2-3
Mashash, Bīr — = Bi'r Mushāsh 136-137 G 7
Mashhad 134-135 HJ 3
Mashike 144-145 b 2
Māshkel, Hāmūn-i — 134-135 J 5
Mashkode 70-71 HJ 2
Mashonaland North 172 EF 5
Mashonaland South 172 EF 5
Mashowingrivier 174-175 E 4
Mashra'a Aṣfā 166-167 G 2
Mashrā' ar-Raqq 164-165 K 7
Mashra' Bin Abū 166-167 C 3
Mashraḥ 166-167 DE 6
Mashrah' Bin al-Q'sīr 166-167 CD 2
Mashraqī Bangāl 134-135 O 5-P 6
Mashrūkah, Qārat al- 136-137 C 7
Mashū-ko 144-145 d 2
Mašigina, guba — 132-133 HJ 3
Masīlah, Wādī al- 134-135 F 7
Masi-Manimba 172 C 2
Masin 148-149 L 8
Masina, Kinshasa- 170 IV b 2
Masindi 172 F 1
Masīrābād 138-139 A 4
Maṣīrah, Jazīrat al- 134-135 HJ 6
Maṣīrah, Khalīj al- 134-135 H 6-7
Masisi 171 B 3
Masjed Soleymān 134-135 FG 4
Maskanah 136-137 GH 4-5
Mâsker, Jbel — = Jabal Mu'askar 166-167 D 3
Masoala, Cap — 172 K 5
Masoller 106-107 J 3
Mason, MI 70-71 H 4
Mason, TN 78-79 E 3
Mason, TX 76-77 E 7
Mason, WI 70-71 E 2
Mason, WY 66-67 HJ 4
Mason City, IA 64-65 H 3
Mason City, IL 70-71 F 5
Mason Creek 84 III d 2
Masonville, NJ 84 III d 2
Masonville, VA 82 II a 2
Maspeth, New York-, NY 82 III c 2
Masqaṭ 134-135 H 6
Masrakh 138-139 K 4
Maṣr el-Gedīda = Al-Qahīrah-Miṣr al-Jadīdah 173 B 2
Maṣrif al-Muḥīt 170 II a 1
Mass, MI 70-71 F 2
Massa 122-123 D 3
Massachusetts 64-65 M 3
Massachusetts, University of — 84 I b 3
Massachusetts Bay 64-65 MN 3
Massachusetts Institute of Technology 84 I b 2
Massadona, CO 68-69 B 5
Massakori = Massakory 164-165 H 6
Massakory 164-165 H 6
Massa Marittima 122-123 D 4
Massangena 172 F 6
Massango 172 C 3
Massangulo 171 C 6
Massapê 100-101 D 2
Massasi = Masasi 172 G 4
Massaua = Mitsiwa 164-165 MN 5
Massawa = Mitsawa 164-165 MN 5
Massena, NY 72-73 J 2
Massenheim 128 III b 1
Massénya 164-165 H 6
Massering 174-175 D 2
Masset 56-57 K 7
Masset Inlet 60 A 3
Massey 62 KL 3
Massif Central 120-121 J 6
Massif Décou-Décou 98-99 LM 2
Massif de la Hotte 88-89 JK 5
Massif Mbam 168-169 H 4
Massillon, OH 72-73 F 4
Massina = Macina 164-165 CD 6
Massinga 172 G 6
Massingir 174-175 JK 2
Massoche 174-175 K 2
Masson 72-73 J 2
Masson Island 53 C 10
Massy 129 I c 3
Mastabah 134-135 D 6
Masters, CO 68-69 D 5
Masterton 158-159 P 8
Mastigouche, Parc provincial de — 62 P 3
Mastung 134-135 K 5
Mastūr, Ḥāssī — 166-167 GH 4
Mastūrah 134-135 D 6
Masuda 144-145 H 5
Māsūleh 136-137 N 4
Masurai, Gunung — 152-153 DE 7
Masuria = Pojezierze Mazurskie 118 K 2-L 1
Māsvaḍ = Mhasvād 140 B 2
Maṣyāf 136-137 G 5
Māt [IND] 138-139 F 4
Mata, La — 94-95 E 3
Mata Amarilla 108-109 D 7
Mataban, Cape — = Akrōtērion Tainaron 122-123 K 7
Matabeleland 172 E 5-6
Mataca, Serranía de — 104-105 D 6
Matachewan 62 L 3
Matacuni, Río — 94-95 J 6
Mata da Corda, Serra da — 92-93 K 8
Mata de São João 100-101 E 7
Matadi 172 B 3
Matador 61 DE 5
Matador, TX 76-77 D 5-6
Matagalpa 64-65 J 9
Matagami 56-57 V 8
Matagami, Lac — 62 N 2
Matagamon, ME 72-73 M 1
Matagania 168-169 C 2
Matagorda, TX 76-77 G 8
Matagorda Bay 64-65 GH 6
Matagorda Island 64-65 G 6
Matagorda Peninsula 76-77 FG 8
Mata Grande 100-101 F 5
Maṭāi = Maṭāy 173 B 3
Mataj 132-133 O 8
Matak 152-153 G 4
Matak = Pulau Matak 150-151 F 11
Matak, Pulau — 150-151 F 11
Matakana Island 161 G 3
Matala 172 C 4
Matalaque 96-97 F 10
Mātale 140 E 7
Matam 164-165 B 5
Matamatá, Cachoeira — 98-99 HJ 8
Matameye 168-169 H 2
Matamoros [MEX, Coahuila] 64-65 F 6
Matamoros [MEX, Tamaulipas] 64-65 G 6

Maṭamūr, Al- 166-167 M 3
Matana, Danau — 152-153 O 7
Ma'tan as-Sarrah 164-165 J 4
Matancillas 111 B 4
Matandu 171 D 5
Matane 56-57 X 8
Matane, Parc provincial de — 63 C 3
Mata Negra 94-95 K 3
Matankari 168-169 FG 2
Ma'tan Oweiqila = Ma'ātin 'Uwayqilah 136-137 C 7
Ma'tan Shârib 136-137 C 7
Matanuska, AK 58-59 MN 6
Matanuska River 58-59 NO 6
Matanza [CO] 94-95 E 4
Matanza [RA] 106-107 H 5
Matanza, La — 110 III b 2
Matanza, Rio — 110 III b 2
Matanzas 64-65 K 7
Matanzilla, Pampa de la — 106-107 C 6
Matão 102-103 H 4
Matão, Serra do — 92-93 J 6
Matapalo, Cabo — 64-65 K 10
Matapédia, Rivière — 63 C 3
Mataporquera 120-121 E 7
Mataquito, Río — 106-107 B 5
Mātara [CL] 134-135 N 9
Matarà [RA] 106-107 F 2
Mataraca 100-101 G 4
Mataram 148-149 G 8
Matarani 92-93 E 8
Mataranka [AUS] 158-159 F 2
Matarīyah, Al Qāhirah-al- 170 II bc 1
Matārkah 166-167 E 3
Mataró 120-121 J 8
Matas, Serra das — 100-101 DE 3
Matatiele 172 E 8
Mataura River 161 C 7-8
Mataven, Río — 94-95 G 5
Maṭāy 173 B 3
Mategua 92-93 G 7
Matehuala 64-65 F 7
Matelândia 102-103 EF 6
Matemo 171 E 6
Matera 122-123 G 5
Mátészalka 118 KL 4-5
Matetsi 172 E 5
Māṭeur = Māṭir 164-165 FG 1
Mateus Leme 102-103 K 3
Mather, CA 74-75 D 4
Māthērān 138-139 D 8
Matheson 62 L 2
Matheson, CO 68-69 E 6
Mathews, VA 80-81 H 2
Mathis, TX 76-77 EF 8
Mathiston, MS 78-79 E 4
Mathon Tonbo = Htônbô 141 D 6
Mathura 134-135 M 5
Mati 148-149 J 5
Matiakouali 168-169 F 2
Mātiāli 138-139 M 4
Matiari = Matiyārī 138-139 B 5
Matias Barbosa 102-103 L 4
Matias Cardoso 100-101 C 8
Matías Hernández 64-65 bc 2
Matias Olimpio 100-101 C 2
Matías Romero 86-87 N 9
Maticora, Río — 94-95 F 2
Ma-ti-i = Madiyi 146-147 C 7
Matilde 102-103 M 4
Matimana 171 D 5
Matimbuka 172 G 4
Matina 100-101 C 7
Matinenda Lake 62 K 3
Matinha 100-101 B 2
Matinicus Island 72-73 M 3
Māṭir 164-165 FG 1
Matiwane 174-175 HJ 5
Matiyārī 138-139 B 5
Matjesfontein = Matjiesfontein 174-175 D 7
Matjiesfontein 174-175 D 7
Mātla 138-139 M 7
Maṭlā', Al- 136-137 M 8
Matlabas [ZA, place] 174-175 G 3
Matlabas [ZA, river] 174-175 G 3
M'atlevo 124-125 K 6
Mātlī 138-139 B 5
Matlīlī 166-167 H 3
Mātlīn, Al- 166-167 M 1
Matlock 61 K 5
Matlock, WA 66-67 B 2
Maṭmāṭ, Ḥāssī — 166-167 K 3
Maṭmāṭah 166-167 L 3
Mato, Cerro — 94-95 J 4
Mato, Serranía de — 94-95 J 4
Matobe 152-153 D 7
Matochkin Shar = proliv Matočkin Šar 132-133 KL 3
Matočkin Šar 132-133 KL 3
Matočkin Šar, proliv — 132-133 KL 3
Matões 100-101 C 3
Mato Grosso [BR, Acre] 98-99 C 9
Mato Grosso [BR, Mato Grosso administrative unit] 92-93 HJ 7
Mato Grosso [BR, Mato Grosso place] 92-93 H 7-8
Mato Grosso, Planalto do — 92-93 HJ 7
Mato Grosso do Sul 92-93 HJ 8-9
Matola 174-175 K 3-4
Matombo 171 D 4
Matope 172 FG 5
Matopo Hills 172 E 6
Matorrales 106-107 F 3
Matos, Río — 104-105 CD 4
Matos Costa 102-103 G 7
Matosinhos [BR] 102-103 K 3
Matosinhos [P] 120-121 C 8
Matoso, Punta do — 110 I b 1
Matou 146-147 H 10
Matoury 98-99 M 2
Mato Verde 100-101 C 8
Mátra 118 JK 5
Matra = Mathurā 134-135 M 5
Maṭraḥ 134-135 H 6
Matraman, Jakarta- 154 IV b 2
Matraville, Sydney- 161 I b 2
Matrimonio, El — 76-77 C 9
Matriz de Camarajibe 100-101 G 6
Maṭroûḥ, Djezîrat el — = Jazīrat al-Maṭrūḥ 166-167 M 1
Maṭrūḥ = Marsā Maṭrūḥ 164-165 K 2
Maṭrūḥ, Jazīrat al- 166-167 M 1
Maṭrūḥ, Marsā — 164-165 K 2
Matsang Tsangpo 138-139 J 2-K 3
Matsap 174-175 E 5
Matsudo 155 III c 1
Matsudo-Kamihongo 155 III c 1
Matsudo-Yagiri 155 III c 1
Matsue 142-143 P 4
Matsugashima 155 III d 2
Ma-tsui Ling = Mazui Ling 150-151 G 3
Matsumae 144-145 ab 3
Matsumoto 144-145 LM 4
Matsunami = Suzu 144-145 L 4
Matsusaka 144-145 KL 5
Matsu Tao 142-143 MN 6
Matsuwa = Matua 206-207 T 5
Matsuyama 144-145 J 6
Mattagami River 56-57 U 7-8
Mattaldi 106-107 E 5
Mattamuskeet Lake 80-81 HJ 3
Mattapan, Boston-, MA 84 I b 3
Mattawa 72-73 G 1
Mattawamkeag, ME 72-73 MN 2
Mattawin, Rivière — 72-73 K 1
Mattayā 141 E 4
Matterhorn [USA] 66-67 F 5
Matthew, Île — 158-159 O 4
Matthews Peak 172 G 1
Matthew Town 88-89 JK 4
Maṭṭī, Sabkhat — 134-135 G 6
Mattice 62 H 3
Matto Grosso = Mato Grosso 92-93 HJ 7
Matu 152-153 J 4
Matua [RI] 148-149 F 7
Matua [SU] 206-207 T 5
Matucana 92-93 D 7
Matue = Matsue 142-143 P 4
Matugama 140 E 7
Matugusanos 106-107 C 3
Matuku 148-149 ab 2
Matumoto = Matsumoto 142-143 Q 4
Matūn 134-135 KL 4
Matundu 172 D 1
Matura = Mathurā 134-135 M 5
Maturín 92-93 G 2-3
Maturucá 98-99 H 2
Matuyama = Matsuyama 142-143 P 5
Matvejevka 124-125 TU 7
Matvejev Kurgan 126-127 J 3
Matvejevskoje, Moskva- 113 V b 3
Mau [IND ↙ Allahabad] 138-139 H 5
Mau [IND ↗ Vārānasi] 138-139 J 5
Maū = Mhow 138-139 E 6
Mauá [BR] 102-103 J 5
Maúa [Mozambique] 172 G 4
Mauá, Salto — 102-103 G 6
Maubeuge 120-121 JK 3
Mauchī 141 E 6
Maud, OK 76-77 F 5
Maud, TX 76-77 G 6
Maudaha 138-139 GH 5
Maude 160 G 5
Maudin Sûn 141 CD 8
Maudlow, MT 66-67 H 2
Maud Seamount 53 C 1
Mau-é-ele 174-175 L 3
Mauer, Wien- 113 I ab 2
Maués 92-93 H 5
Maués-Açu, Rio — 92-93 H 5
Mauganj 138-139 H 5
Mauhan 148-149 C 2
Maui 148-149 e 3
Maukmei 141 E 5
Maulaik 141 D 4
Maulamyaing 148-149 C 3
Maulamyainggyûn 141 D 7
Maule 106-107 AB 5
Maule, Laguna del — 106-107 B 6
Maule, Río — 106-107 AB 5
Maulin = Mol Len 141 D 3
Maullín 111 B 6
Maullín, Río — 108-109 C 3
Maulvī Bāzār 141 B 3
Maumee, OH 72-73 DE 4
Maumee River 70-71 H 5
Maumere 148-149 H 8
Maun [RB] 172 D 5
Mauna Kea 148-149 e 4
Mauna Loa 148-149 e 4
Mauna Loa, HI 78-79 d 2
Maūnāth Bhanjan = Mau 138-139 J 5
Mauneluk River 58-59 K 3
Maungdaw 148-149 B 2
Maungmagan Kyûnzu 150-151 A 5
Mauni, Río — 96-97 G 10
Maunoir, Lac — 56-57 M 4
Maupertuis, Lac — 62 PQ 1
Maupin, OR 66-67 C 3
Maur 128 IV b 1
Mauralakitan 152-153 E 7
Mau Rānīpur 138-139 G 5
Maurepas, Lake — 78-79 D 5
Maurice, Lake — 158-159 EF 5
Mauriceville, TX 76-77 GH 7
Mauricie, Parc national de — 62 P 3
Mauricio Mayer 106-107 E 6
Mauritania 164-165 BC 4
Mauriti 100-101 E 4
Mauritius 178-179 MN 7
Maury Mountains 66-67 C 3
Mausembi 152-153 O 10
Mauston, WI 70-71 EF 4
Mautong 148-149 H 6
Mava 148-149 M 8
Mavaca, Río — 94-95 J 6
Mavago 172 G 4
Mavānā = Mawāna 138-139 F 3
Mavaricani, Raudal — 94-95 G 6
Māvelikara 140 C 6
Mavinga 172 CD 5
Mavlāni = Mailāni 138-139 H 3
Māvlī = Maoli 138-139 D 5
Mavrobouni 113 IV b 2
Mavzolej V. I. Lenina 113 V c 2-3
Maw, Lûy — [BUR, Kachin Pyinnei] 141 E 3
Maw, Lûy — [BUR, Shan Pyinnei] 141 E 5
Mawa 172 E 1
Mawāgū 141 F 2
Mawai 150-151 DE 12
Mawāna 138-139 F 3
Mawasangka 152-153 OP 8
Mawei 146-147 G 8-9
Mawer 61 E 5
Mawhun = Mauhan 148-149 C 2
Mawk Mai = Maukmei 141 E 5
Mawlaik = Maulaik 141 D 4
Mawson 53 C 7
Max, ND 68-69 F 2
Maxacalis 100-101 D 3
Maxaranguape 100-101 G 3
Maxbass, ND 68-69 F 1
Maxcanú 86-87 P 7
Maxesibeni 174-175 H 6
Maxey Park 85 III c 1
Maximo 171 D 6
Máximo Paz 106-107 H 5
Maxixe 174-175 L 2
Maxstone 68-69 CD 1
Maxville 72-73 J 2
Maxville, MT 66-67 G 2
Maxwell, CA 74-75 B 3
May, ID 66-67 G 3
May, OK 76-77 E 4
Maya, Pulau — 148-149 E 7
Mayādīn 136-137 J 5
Mayaguana Island 64-65 M 7
Mayagüez 64-65 N 8
Mayah, Al- 166-167 G 3
Mayama 172 BC 2
Maya Maya = Aéroport de Brazzaville 170 IV a 1
Maya Mountains 64-65 J 8
Mayang 146-147 B 8
Mayang-do 144-145 G 2-3
Mayanja 171 BC 2
Mayapán 64-65 J 7
Mayari 88-89 HJ 4
Mayas, Caracas-Las — 91 II b 2
Māyavaram = Māyūram 140 D 5
Maybell, CO 68-69 B 5
Mayd 164-165 b 1
Maydān 136-137 L 5
Maydān Ikbis 136-137 G 4
Maydena 158-159 J 8
Maydī 134-135 E 7
Mayence = Mainz 118 D 3-4
Mayenne [F, place] 120-121 G 4
Mayenne [F, river] 120-121 G 4-5
Mayer, AZ 74-75 G 5
Mayerthorpe 60 K 3
Mayesville, SC 80-81 F 3-4
Mayfair 61 E 4
Mayfair, Houston-, TX 85 III b 2
Mayfair, Johannesburg- 170 V b 2
Mayfair, Philadelphia-, PA 84 III c 1
Mayfield, ID 66-67 F 4
Mayfield, KY 78-79 E 2
Mayhill, NM 76-77 B 6
Maymaneh 134-135 JK 3
Maymyo = Memyō 148-149 C 2
Maynard, WA 66-67 B 2
Maynas 92-93 DE 5
Māyni 140 B 2
Mayo 150-151 C 9
Mayo, FL 80-81 b 1-2
Mayo, Cerro — 108-109 D 5
Mayo, Río — [PE] 96-97 C 4
Mayo, Río — [RA] 108-109 D 5
Mayoco, El — 108-109 D 4
Mayodan, NC 80-81 FG 2
Mayo Landing 56-57 JK 5
Mayor, El — 74-75 F 6
Mayor Buratovich 106-107 F 7
Mayor Island 161 G 3
Mayotte 172 H 4
Mayoumba 172 AB 2
May Point, Cape — 72-73 J 5
Maypuco 96-97 D 4
Mayrhofen 118 EF 5
Maysarī, Al- 136-137 H 7
Maysville, KY 72-73 E 5
Maysville, MO 70-71 C 6
Maysville, NC 80-81 H 3
Maytown 158-159 HJ 3
Mayu, Pulau — 148-149 J 6
Mayū Myit 141 C 5
Mayunga 172 E 2
Mayurākshī 138-139 LM 6
Māyūram 140 D 5
Mayū Taungdan 141 C 5
Mayville, ND 68-69 H 2
Mayville, NY 72-73 G 3
Maywood, CA 83 III c 2
Maywood, NE 68-69 F 5
Maywood, NJ 82 III b 1
Mayyit, Baḥr al- 134-135 D 4
Maza 106-107 F 6
Mazabuka 172 E 5
Mazagan = Al-Jadīdah 164-165 C 2
Mazagão 92-93 J 5
Mazáka = Kayseri 134-135 D 3
Mazalet 168-169 H 1
Mazamet 120-121 J 7
Mazán 96-97 E 3
Mazan = Villa Mazán 111 C 3
Mazán, Río — 96-97 E 3
Māzandarān 134-135 GH 3
Mazār, Al- 136-137 F 7
Mazar, Ouèd — = Wādī Mazār 166-167 G 3
Mazār, Wādī — 166-167 G 3
Mazara del Vallo 122-123 DE 7
Mazār-i-Sharīf 134-135 K 3
Mazarredo 108-109 F 6
Mazarredo, Fondeadero — 108-109 F 6
Mazarrón 120-121 G 10
Mazarrón, Golfo de — 120-121 G 10
Mazar tagh 142-143 D 4
Mazaruni River 98-99 HJ 1
Mazatenango 64-65 H 9
Mazatlán 64-65 E 7
Mazatuni River 94-95 L 4
Mazatzal Peak 74-75 H 5
Mažeikiai 124-125 D 5
Mazeppabaai 174-175 H 7
Mazeppa Bay = Mazeppabaai 174-175 H 7
Mazgirt 136-137 H 3
Mazhafah, Jabal — = Jabal Buwārah 173 D 3
Mazhan 146-147 G 3
Mazi, Jabal — 166-167 F 3
Mazıdağı = Samrah 136-137 J 4
Mazimchopes, Rio — 174-175 K 3
Mazirbe 124-125 CD 5
Mazoco 171 C 5
Mazo Cruz 96-97 G 10
Mazomanie, WI 70-71 F 4
Mazr'a, Al- 136-137 F 7
Mazra'ah, Al- 166-167 K 2
Mazsalaca 124-125 E 5
Māzū 136-137 N 6
Mazui Ling 150-151 G 3
Mazūnzūt 141 E 2
Mazurskie, Pojezierze — 118 K 2-L 1
Mazzūnah, Al- 166-167 L 2

Mbabane 172 F 7
Mbacké 168-169 B 2
M'Baiki 164-165 H 8
Mbala 172 F 3
Mbalabala 172 EF 6
Mbale 172 F 1
M'Balmayo 164-165 G 8
Mbam 168-169 H 4
Mbam, Massif — 168-169 H 4
Mbamba Bay 171 C 5
Mbamou, Île — 170 IV b 1
Mbamou, Pointe — 170 IV a 1
Mbandaka 172 C 1-2
Mbanga 164-165 FG 8
Mbanza Congo 172 B 3
Mbanza Ngungu 172 B 2-3
Mbaracayú, Cordillera de — 102-103 E 5-6
Mbarangandu [EAT, place] 171 D 5
Mbarangandu [EAT, river] 171 D 5
Mbarara 172 F 2
Mbari 164-165 J 7
M'Bé 172 C 2
Mbemkuru 172 GH 3
Mbenkuru 171 D 5
Mbeya [EAT, mountain] 171 C 5
Mbeya [EAT, place] 172 F 3
M'Bigou 172 B 2
Mbin 164-165 F 8
M'Binda 172 B 2
Mbindera 171 D 5
Mbinga 171 C 5
Mbini [Equatorial Guinea, administrative unit] 164-165 G 8
Mbini [Equatorial Guinea, river] 168-169 H 5
Mbizi 172 F 6
Mbogo's 171 C 4
Mbomou 164-165 J 7-8
Mbonge 168-169 H 4
M'Boro 171 AB 2
M'Bour 164-165 A 6
Mbozi 171 C 5
Mbud 164-165 B 5
Mbuji-Mayi 172 D 3
Mbulu 171 C 3
Mburu 171 C 5
Mburucuyá 111 E 3
Mbuyapey 102-103 D 7

Mccheta 126-127 M 6
Mcensk 124-125 L 7
Mcherrah = Mashraḥ 166-167 DE 6
Mchinga 172 GH 3
Mchinji 172 F 4
M'Chouneche = Manushūnash 166-167 K 2
M'Clintok 58-59 U 6

Mdaina, Al- = Al-Madīnah 136-137 M 7
Mdakane, Hassi — = Ḥāssī Madakkan 166-167 EF 5
Mdandu 171 C 5
M'dīlah, Al- 166-167 L 2
M'Dourouch = Madawrūsh 166-167 K 1

Mê, Hon — 150-151 EF 3
Meacham, OR 66-67 D 3
Mead, WA 66-67 E 2
Mead, Lake — 64-65 D 4
Meade, KS 68-69 F 7
Meade Peak 66-67 H 4
Meade River 58-59 J 1
Meade River, AK 58-59 J 1
Meadow, TX 76-77 CD 6
Meadowbank Park 161 I a 1
Meadow Brook, Houston-, TX 85 III bc 2
Meadow Creek Village, Houston-, TX 85 III b 2
Meadow Lake 56-57 P 7
Meadow Lake Provincial Park 61 D 3
Meadowlands, Johannesburg- 170 V a 2
Meadows, The —, TX 85 III a 2
Meadow Valley Range 74-75 F 4
Meadow Valley Wash 74-75 F 4
Meadville, PA 72-73 FG 4
Meaford 72-73 F 2
Mealy Mountains 56-57 Z 7
Meander 152-153 N 1
Meandro = Büyük Menderes nehri 136-137 B 4
Mearim, Rio — 92-93 L 5
Meath Park 61 F 4
Meat Mount 58-59 G 2
Meaux 120-121 J 4
Mebote 172 F 6
Mebreije, Rio — = Rio M'Bridge 172 B 3
Mebridege, Rio — 172 B 3
Meca = Makkah 134-135 DE 6
Mecaya, Río — 94-95 D 7
Mecca, CA 74-75 EF 6
Mecca = Makkah 134-135 DE 6
Mechanicsburg, PA 72-73 H 4
Mechanicville, NY 72-73 K 3
Meched = Mashhad 134-135 HJ 3
Mechelen 120-121 K 3
Mechems = M'shams 166-167 BC 6
Méchéria = Mishrīyah 164-165 DE 2
Méchins, les — 63 C 3
Mechlin = Mechelen 120-121 K 3
Mechongué 106-107 HJ 7
Mechraa Asfa = Mashra'a Aṣfā 166-167 G 2
Mechra' 'Ben 'Abou = Mashra' Bin Abū 166-167 C 3
Mechra' 'Ben el Qṣīrī = Mashra' Bin al-Q'sīrī 166-167 CD 2
Mechren'ga 124-125 N 2
Meçitözü 136-137 F 2
Mecklenburg-Vorpommern 118 EF 2
Mecklenburger Bucht 118 EF 1
Mecrihan 136-137 H 4
Mecsek 118 J 5
Mecúfi 172 H 4
Mecula 172 G 4
Meḍachala = Medchal 140 D 2
Medaguine = Madāqīn 166-167 H 3
Medak [IND] 140 D 1
Medan 148-149 C 6
Medanitos 104-105 C 10
Médano, Punta — 108-109 H 3
Médanos [RA, Buenos Aires landscape] 106-107 G 7-J 6
Médanos [RA, Buenos Aires place] 111 D 5
Médanos [RA, Entre Ríos] 106-107 H 4
Médanos, Istmo de — 94-95 G 2
Medanosa, Punta — 111 CD 7
Medaryville, IN 70-71 G 5
Mēdawachchiya 140 DE 6
Medchal 140 D 2
Médéa = Midyah 166-167 H 1
Medeiros Neto 100-101 D 3
Medellín [CO] 92-93 D 3
Medellín [RA] 111 D 3
Medelpad 116-117 FG 6
Medenīn = Madanīyīn 164-165 FG 2
Medetsiz 134-135 C 3
Medford, MA 72-73 L 3
Medford, OK 76-77 F 4
Medford, OR 64-65 B 3
Medford, WI 70-71 EF 3
Medford Hillside, MA 84 I b 2
Medfra, AK 58-59 K 5
Medgidia 122-123 N 3
Media, PA 84 III a 2
Médiadillet 168-169 E 1
Media Luna 106-107 D 5
Medianeira 102-103 E 6
Mediano 120-121 H 7
Mediapolis, IA 70-71 E 5
Mediaș 122-123 L 2
Medical Lake, WA 66-67 DE 2
Medicanceli 120-121 F 8
Medicine Bow, WY 68-69 C 5
Medicine Bow Mountains 68-69 CD 5
Medicine Bow Peak 64-65 EF 3
Medicine Bow River 68-69 CD 5
Medicine Hat 56-57 O 7
Medicine Lake 68-69 DE 1
Medicine Lake, MT 68-69 D 1
Medicine Lodge 60 J 3
Medicine Lodge, KS 76-77 EF 4
Medicine Mound, TX 76-77 E 5
Medina, ND 68-69 G 2
Medina, TX 76-77 E 8
Medina [BR] 102-103 M 2
Medina [CO] 94-95 E 5
Médina [WAG] 168-169 B 2
Medina = Al-Madīnah 134-135 DE 6
Medina del Campo 120-121 E 8
Medina de Rioseco 120-121 E 8
Medina River 76-77 E 8
Medinas, Río — 104-105 D 10
Medina-Sidonia 120-121 DE 10
Medininkai 124-125 E 6
Medinīpur = Midnapore 134-135 O 6
Medio, Arroyo del — 106-107 G 4
Mediodía 94-95 EF 8
Medioûna = Madyūnah 166-167 C 3
Mediterranean Sea 114-115 J 8-O 9
Medjdel, El — = Ashqĕlōn 136-137 F 7
Medjèz el Bâb = M'jaz al-Bāb 166-167 L 1
Mednogorsk 132-133 K 7
Mednoje 124-125 K 5
Mednyj, ostrov — 52 D 2
Médoc 120-121 G 6
Medora, KS 68-69 H 6
Medora, ND 68-69 E 2
Medstead 61 DE 4
Medur = Mettūr 140 C 5
Medvedica [SU ◁ Don] 124-125 P 7
Medvedkovo, Moskva- 113 V c 2
Medvedok 124-125 S 5
Medvedovskaja 126-127 J 4
Medvežij, ostrova — 132-133 f 3
Medvežjegorsk 132-133 EF 5
Medyn' 124-125 KL 6
Medžibož 126-127 C 2
Meekatharra 158-159 C 5
Meeker, CO 68-69 C 5
Meeker, OK 76-77 F 5
Meelpaeg Lake 63 H 3
Meerut 134-135 M 5
Mēga [ETH] 164-165 M 8
Mega [RI] 148-149 K 7
Mega, Pulau — 152-153 D 8
Megálē Prespa, Límnē — 122-123 J 5
Megalópolis 122-123 JK 7
Megālo Sofráno 122-123 M 7
Meganom, mys — 126-127 G 4
Mégantic 72-73 L 2
Mégara 122-123 K 6-7
Megāsini 138-139 L 7
Meghaier, El — = Al-Mighāir 166-167 J 3
Meghalaya 134-135 P 5
Mēghāsana = Megāsini 138-139 L 7
Meghnā 141 B 4
Megion 132-133 O 5
Mégiscane, Rivière — 62 NO 2
Mégistē 136-137 C 4
Megler, WA 66-67 B 2
Megrega 132-133 E 5
Meguro 155 III b 2
Meguro, Tōkyō- 155 III b 2
Mehadia 122-123 K 3
Mehar 138-139 A 4
Mehdia = Mahdīyah 164-165 E 1
Mehepur = Maharpur 138-139 M 6
Meherrin River 80-81 H 2
Mehidpur 138-139 E 6
Me Hka 141 EF 3
Mehkar 138-139 F 7
Mehmadābād 138-139 D 6
Mehndāval = Mehndāwal 138-139 J 4
Mehndāwal 138-139 J 4
Mehrabān 136-137 M 3-4
Mehrān 136-137 M 6
Mehrow 130 III c 1
Mehsāna 134-135 L 6
Meia Ponte, Rio — 92-93 K 8
Meicheng 146-147 G 7
Mei-ch'i = Meixi 146-147 G 6
Mei-chou Wan = Meizhou Wan 146-147 G 9
Meidling, Wien- 113 I b 2
Meiendorf, Hamburg- 130 I b 1
Méier, Rio de Janeiro- 110 I b 2
Meighen Island 56-57 RS 1
Meihekou = Shanchengzhen 144-145 EF 1
Mei-hsien = Mei Xian 146-147 EF 9
Meiji Shrine 155 III b 1
Meikhtīlā 148-149 BC 2
Meiktila = Meikhtīlā 148-149 BC 2
Meiling Guan = Xiaomei Guan 142-143 LM 6
Meilin Jiang = Lian Jiang 146-147 E 9
Meilong 146-147 E 10
Meiningen 118 E 3
Meio, Ilha do — 110 I b 3
Meio, Rio do — 100-101 B 7
Meiqi = Meixi 146-147 G 6
Meissen 118 F 3
Meiten = Meitene 124-125 DE 5
Meitene 124-125 DE 5
Meixi 146-147 G 6
Mei Xian 142-143 M 7
Meizhou Wan 146-147 G 9
Meja 138-139 J 5
Mejicana, Cumbre de — 111 C 3
Mejillón, Punta — 108-109 G 3
Mejillones 111 B 2
Mejillones del Sur, Bahía de — 104-105 A 8
Mejnypil'gyno 132-133 j 5
Meka Galla 171 D 2
Mekambo 172 B 1
Mekelē 164-165 M 6
Mekerrhane, Sebkha — = Sabkhat Mukrān 164-165 E 3
Mekhar = Mehkar 138-139 F 7
Mekhtar 138-139 B 2
Meknès = Miknās 164-165 C 2
Mê Kong 148-149 E 4
Mekong, Mouths of the — = Cu'a Sông Cu'u Long 148-149 E 5
Mekongga, Gunung — 148-149 H 7
Mekongga, Pegunungan — 152-153 O 7
Mekoryuk, AK 58-59 D 6
Mekran = Mokrān 134-135 HJ 5
Mékrou 164-165 E 6
Mel, Ilha do — 102-103 H 6
Mel, Serra do — 100-101 F 3
Melagênai 124-125 F 6
Melāgiri Hills 140 C 4
Mélah, Sebkhet el — = Sabkhat al-Māliḥ 166-167 M 3
Melah, Sebkra el — = Sabkhat al-Malah 166-167 F 5
Melaka [MAL, administrative unit] 150-151 D 11
Melaka [MAL, place] 148-149 D 6
Melaka, Selat — 148-149 CD 6
Melalap 152-153 LM 3
Melanesia 156-157 F 4-H 5
Melanieskop 174-175 H 5
Mēlas 122-123 L 7
Melawi, Sungai — 152-153 K 6
Melayu 148-149 D 6
Melba, ID 66-67 E 4
Melbourne, AR 78-79 D 2-3
Melbourne, FL 80-81 c 2
Melbourne [AUS] 158-159 H 7
Melbourne, University of — 161 II b 1
Melbourne-Airport West 161 II b 1
Melbourne-Albion 161 II b 1
Melbourne-Altona 161 II ab 2
Melbourne-Avondale Heights 161 II b 1
Melbourne-Balwyn 161 II c 1
Melbourne-Bentleigh 161 II c 2
Melbourne-Box Hill 161 II c 1-2
Melbourne-Braybrook 161 II b 1
Melbourne-Brighton 161 II bc 2
Melbourne-Brooklyn 161 II ab 1-2
Melbourne-Brunswick 161 II b 1
Melbourne-Camberwell 161 II c 2
Melbourne-Canterbury 161 II c 1
Melbourne-Caulfield 161 II c 2
Melbourne Cemetery 161 II b 1
Melbourne-Chadstone 161 II c 2
Melbourne-Coburg 161 II b 1
Melbourne-Collingwood 161 II bc 1
Melbourne-Doncaster 161 II c 1
Melbourne-Elsternwick 161 II bc 2
Melbourne-Elwood 161 II b 2
Melbourne-Essendon 161 II b 1
Melbourne-Fairfield 161 II c 1
Melbourne-Fawkner 161 II b 1
Melbourne-Fishermens Bend 161 II b 1
Melbourne-Fitzroy 161 II b 1
Melbourne-Flemington 161 II b 1
Melbourne-Footscray 161 II b 1
Melbourne-Gardenvale 161 II c 2
Melbourne-Hawthorn 161 II c 1
Melbourne-Heidelberg 161 II c 1
Melbourne-Homesglen 161 II c 2
Melbourne-Ivanhoe 161 II c 1
Melbourne-Keilor 161 II b 1
Melbourne-Kew 161 II c 1
Melbourne-Kingsville 161 II b 1
Melbourne-Lower Plenty 161 II c 1
Melbourne-Maidstone 161 II b 1
Melbourne-Malvern 161 II c 2
Melbourne-Moorabbin 161 II c 2
Melbourne-Mount Waverley 161 II c 2
Melbourne-Newport 161 II b 2
Melbourne-Northcote 161 II c 1
Melbourne-Notting Hill 161 II c 2
Melbourne-Nunawading 161 II c 1
Melbourne-Oakleigh 161 II c 2
Melbourne-Ormond 161 II c 2
Melbourne-Pascoe Vale 161 II b 1
Melbourne-Port Melbourne 161 II b 1-2
Melbourne-Prahran 161 II bc 2
Melbourne-Preston 161 II bc 1
Melbourne-Regent 161 II bc 1
Melbourne-Richmond 161 II bc 1
Melbourne-Rosanna 161 II c 1
Melbourne-Saint Kilda 161 II b 2
Melbourne-South Melbourne 161 II b 1-2
Melbourne-Spotswood 161 II b 1
Melbourne-Sunshine 161 II ab 1
Melbourne-Templestowe 161 II c 1
Melbourne-Thornbury 161 II bc 1
Melbourne-Toorak 161 II c 2
Melbourne-Werribee 160 FG 6
Melbourne-Williamstown 161 II b 2
Melbourne-Yarraville 161 II b 1
Melbu 116-117 F 3
Melchers, Kapp — 116-117 m 6
Melchor, Isla — 111 AB 7
Melchor de Mencos 86-87 Q 9
Melchor Múzquiz 64-65 F 6
Meldrim, GA 80-81 F 4
Meldrum Bay 62 K 3
Meleda = Mljet 122-123 G 4
Meleiro 106-107 N 2
Melekgon 174-175 D 4
Melendiz dağları 136-137 F 3
Melenki 124-125 N 6
Melero 106-107 F 2
Melfi [Chad] 164-165 H 6
Melfi [I] 122-123 F 5
Melfort 56-57 Q 7
Melgaço, Barão de — 104-105 F 3
Melik, Wadi el — = Wādī al-Malik 164-165 KL 5
Melili 171 CD 6
Melilia = Melilla 164-165 D 1
Melilla 164-165 D 1
Melimoyu, Monte — 111 B 6
Melinca 108-109 C 4
Melincué 106-107 G 4
Melincué, Laguna — 106-107 G 4
Melinde = Malindi 172 H 2
Melintang, Danau — 152-153 LM 6
Melipilla 111 B 4

Melita 68-69 F 1
Meľita = Maľitah 166-167 M 2
Melitene = Malatya 134-135 D 3
Melito di Porto Salvo 122-123 FG 7
Melitopol' 126-127 G 3
Melk 118 G 4
Melkbosch Point = Melkbospunt 174-175 B 5
Melkbospunt 174-175 B 5
Mellâḥ, Ouêd el — = Wād al-Mallāḥ 166-167 C 3
Mellavāgu 140 D 2
Mellêg, Ouêd — = Wād Mallāg 166-167 L 1-2
Mellen, WI 70-71 E 2
Mellerud 116-117 E 8
Mellette, SD 68-69 G 3
Mellīţ = Mallīţ 164-165 K 6
Mellizo Sur, Cerro — 111 B 7
Mellwood, AR 78-79 D 3
Melmoth 174-175 J 5
Mel'nica-Podol'skaja 126-127 C 2
Mělník 118 G 3
Mel'nikovo [SU ← Tomsk] 132-133 P 6
Melo [RA] 106-107 F 5
Melo [ROU] 111 F 4
Melo, Cordillera de — 106-107 AB 7
Meloco 171 D 6
Melole 152-153 O 10
Meloupey 150-151 E 6
Melovoje 126-127 JK 2
Melovoj Syrt 124-125 T 7
Melovskaja, gora — 124-125 NO 2
Melozitna River 58-59 KL 4
Melqa el Ouîdân = Mal'qat al-Wīdān 166-167 E 2
Melrhir, Chott — = Shaţţ Malghīr 164-165 F 2
Melrose, MA 84 I b 2
Melrose, MN 70-71 C 3
Melrose, MT 66-67 G 3
Melrose, NM 76-77 C 5
Melrose, New York-, Ny 82 III c 2
Melrose Highlands, MA 84 I b 2
Melrose Park 85 III b 1
Melrose Park, PA 84 III c 1
Melsetter = Mandidzudzure 172 F 5-6
Melstone, MT 68-69 BC 2
Melta, Gunung — 152-153 M 3
Meltaus 116-117 L 4
Melton Mowbray 119 F 5
Meluan 152-153 K 5
Meluco 171 D 6
Melun 120-121 J 4
Melunga 172 C 5
Melūr 140 D 5
Melūţ = Malūţ 164-165 L 6
Melville 61 G 5
Melville, LA 78-79 D 5
Melville, MT 66-67 HJ 2
Melville, Cape — 158-159 HJ 2
Melville, Johannesburg- 170 V ab 2
Melville, Lake — 56-57 YZ 7
Melville Bay 158-159 G 2
Melville Bugt 56-57 X-Z 2
Melville Hills 56-57 M 4
Melville Island [AUS] 158-159 F 2
Melville Island [CDN] 56-57 N-P 2
Melville Peninsula 56-57 U 4
Melville Sound = Viscount Melville Sound 56-57 O-Q 3
Memala 148-149 F 7
Memba 172 H 4
Memboro 148-149 G 8
Memel 174-175 H 4
Memmingen 118 DE 5
Memochhutshan 138-139 KL 3
Memorial Coliseum and Sports Arena 83 III c 1
Memorial Park 85 III b 1
Memorial Stadium 84 I b 2
Memphis 164-165 L 3
Memphis, IA 70-71 D 5
Memphis, TN 64-65 HJ 4
Memphis, TX 76-77 D 5
Memphremagog, Lac — 72-73 KL 2
Memuro 144-145 c 2
Memyō 148-149 C 2
Mena 126-127 F 1
Mena, AR 76-77 G 5
Menaa = Mana'ah 166-167 JK 2
Menado = Manado 148-149 H 6
Menafra 106-107 J 4
Ménaka 164-165 E 5
Menam = Mae Nam Chao Phraya 148-149 CD 3-4
Menan Khong 148-149 D 3
Me-nan-Kwa-noi = Mae Nam Khwae Noi 150-151 B 5-6
Menarandra 172 HJ 6-7
Menard, MT 66-67 H 3
Menard, TX 76-77 DE 7
Menasha, WI 70-71 F 3
Menaskwagama, Lac — 63 EF 2
Menbij = Manbij 136-137 G 4
Mencheong = Wenchang 150-151 H 3
Mencué 108-109 E 3
Mendawai, Sungai — 152-153 K 7
Mende 120-121 J 6
Mendenhall, MS 78-79 E 4-5
Mendenhall, Cape — 58-59 DE 7
Mendes Pimentel 100-101 D 10
Mendez [EC] 92-93 D 5
Méndez [MEX] 86-87 L 5
Mendī [ETH] 164-165 M 7
Mendi [PNG] 148-149 M 8
Mendocino, CA 74-75 AB 3
Mendocino, Cape — 64-65 AB 3
Mendocino Fracture Zone 156-157 KL 3
Mendocino Range 66-67 AB 5
Mendol, Pulau — 148-149 D 6
Mendong Gonpa 142-143 F 5
Mendota, CA 74-75 C 4
Mendota, IL 70-71 F 5
Mendoza [PA] 64-65 b 2
Mendoza [PE] 96-97 C 5
Mendoza [RA, administrative unit] 106-107 CD 5
Mendoza [RA, place] 111 C 4
Mendoza, Río — 106-107 C 4
Mendung 152-153 E 5
Mêné 172 C 1
Mene de Mauroa 92-93 E 2
Menemen 136-137 B 3
Menéndez 106-107 J 4
Menéndez, Lago — 108-109 D 4
Menéndez, Paso de — 108-109 CD 4
Ménerville = Tinyah 166-167 H 1
Menetué 108-109 D 2
Mengalum, Pulau — 152-153 L 2
Mengcheng 146-147 F 5
Mêng-chia-lou = Mengjialou 146-147 CD 5
Mengdingjie 141 F 4
Mengen [TR] 136-137 E 2
Mengene dağı 136-137 KL 3
Menggala 148-149 E 7
Menggongshi 146-147 C 8
Menggudai 146-147 B 2
Mengjiailou 146-147 CD 5
Mengjiang 146-147 C 10
Mengjin 146-147 D 4
Mêng-kung-shih = Menggongshi 146-147 C 8
Mengla 150-151 C 2
Menglian 141 F 4
Mêng-lien = Menglian 141 F 4
Mengoûb = Mankûb 166-167 E 3
Mengpeng 150-151 C 2
Meng Shan [TJ, mountains] 146-147 FG 4
Mengshan [TJ, place] 146-147 C 9
Mêng-ting = Mengdingjie 141 F 4
Mengtze = Mengzi 142-143 J 7
Mengulek, gora — 132-133 Q 7
Mengyin 146-147 FG 4
Mengzi 142-143 J 7
Menilmontant, Paris- 129 I c 2
Menindee 158-159 H 6
Menindee Lake 160 EF 4
Meninos, Ribeirão dos — 110 II b 2
Menjawak, Pulau — = Pulau Rakit 152-153 H 8
Menlo, KS 68-69 F 6
Menno, SD 68-69 H 4
Mennonietenbuurt 128 I a 2
Menominee, MI 70-71 G 3
Menominee Indian Reservation 70-71 F 3
Menominee River 70-71 FG 3
Menomonee Falls, WI 70-71 F 4
Menomonie, WI 70-71 DE 3
Menongue 172 C 4
Menorca 120-121 K 8
Menoreh, Pegunungan — 152-153 J 9
Menouarar = Manāwar 166-167 E 4
Mense = Misar 138-139 H 2
Menshikova, Cape — = mys Men'šikova 132-133 KL 3
Men'šikova, mys — 132-133 KL 3
Mentasta Mountains 58-59 Q 5
Mentawai, Kepulauan — 148-149 CD 7
Mentawai, Selat — 152-153 C 6-D 7
Mentawai Islands = Kepulauan Mentawai 148-149 CD 7
Mentekab 148-149 D 6
Menteng, Jakarta- 154 IV ab 2
Menterschwaige, München- 130 II b 2
Mentok = Muntok 148-149 DE 7
Mentolat, Monte — 108-109 C 5
Menton 120-121 L 7
Mentougou 146-147 E 2
Mên-t'ou-kou = Mentougou 146-147 E 2
Mentzdam 174-175 F 7
Menucos, Bajo de los — 108-109 F 2-3
Menucos, Los — 108-109 EF 3
Menūha, Bêer- 136-137 F 7
Menyapa, Gunung — 152-153 M 5
Menzalé, Lago — = Buḥayrat al-Manzilah 173 BC 2
Menzel Boûrguîba = Manzil Būrgībah 166-167 L 1
Menzel Chaker = Manzil Shākir 166-167 M 2
Menzelinsk 124-125 T 6
Menzie, Mount — 58-59 V 6
Menzies 158-159 D 5
Menzies, Mount — 53 B 6-7
Meobbaai 174-175 A 3
Meob Bay = Meobbaai 174-175 A 3
Meoqui 64-65 E 6
Mepisckaro, gora — 126-127 L 6
Meponda 171 C 6
Meppel 120-121 KL 2
Meppen 118 C 2
Meqdādiya, Al- = Al-Miqdādīyah 136-137 L 6
Mequinenza 120-121 GH 8
Mequinez = Miknās 166-167 D 3
Mera [EC] 96-97 BC 2
Merak 152-153 G 8
Meramangye, Lake — 158-159 F 5
Merang, Kuala — 148-149 D 5
Merano 122-123 D 2
Merapoh 148-149 D 6
Merasheen 63 J 4
Mêraṭh = Meerut 134-135 M 5
Meratus, Pegunungan — 148-149 G 7
Merauke 148-149 LM 8
Merbabu, Gunung — 152-153 J 9
Merbau 150-151 BC 11
Merbein 160 EF 5
Merca = Marka 172 HJ 1
Mercaderes 94-95 C 7
Mercāra 134-135 M 8
Merced, CA 64-65 BC 4
Merced, La — [PE] 96-97 D 7
Merced, La — [RA] 104-105 D 11
Merced, Lake — 83 I b 2
Mercedario, Cerro — 111 BC 4
Mercedes, TX 76-77 EF 9
Mercedes [RA, Buenos Aires] 111 DE 4
Mercedes [RA, Corrientes] 111 E 3
Mercedes [RA, San Luis] 111 C 4
Mercedes [ROU] 111 E 4
Mercedes [YV] 94-95 L 4
Mercedes, Las — 92-93 F 3
Mercedes, Punta — 108-109 FG 7
Merceditas 106-107 B 2
Merced River 74-75 C 4
Mercer, WI 70-71 EF 2
Mercês 102-103 L 4
Merchantville, NJ 84 III c 2
Mercier 104-105 BC 2
Mercier-Lacombe = Safīzaf 166-167 F 2
Mercimekkale = Sakavi 136-137 J 3
Mercoal 60 J 3
Mercury Islands 161 FG 3
Mercy, Cape — 56-57 Y 5
Merdeka Palace 154 IV a 1-2
Merdenik 136-137 K 2
Merdja, El — = Al-Marjah 166-167 H 2
Meredale, Johannesburg- 170 V a 2
Meredith, Cabo — = Cape Meredith 111 D 8
Meredith, Cape — 111 D 8
Meredosia, IL 70-71 E 6
Mère et l'Enfant, la — = Nui Vong Phu 150-151 G 6
Merefa 126-127 H 2
Meregh = Mareeg 172 J 1
Merena = Espíritu Santo 158-159 MN 3
Merga = Nukhaylah 164-165 K 5
Mergenevo 126-127 P 2
Mergezhung 138-139 K 2
Mergui = Myeik 148-149 C 4
Mergui Archipelago = Myeik Kyūnzu 148-149 C 4
Merhrâoua = Mighrāwah 166-167 DE 3
Meriç = Büyük Doğanca 136-137 B 2
Meriç nehri 136-137 B 2
Merida [E] 120-121 D 9
Mérida [MEX] 64-65 J 7
Mérida [YV] 92-93 E 3
Mérida, Cordillera de — 92-93 EF 3
Meriden, CT 72-73 K 4
Meriden, WY 68-69 D 5
Meridian, ID 66-67 E 4
Meridian, MS 64-65 J 5
Meridian, TX 76-77 F 7
Meridith, Lake — 76-77 D 5
Mērikānam = Marakkānam 140 DE 4
Merimbula 160 JK 6
Meringur 158-159 H 6
Merino Jarpa, Isla — 108-109 BC 6
Merinos 106-107 J 4
Merion Station, PA 84 III b 2
Merir 148-149 K 6
Merissa = Madrīsah 166-167 G 2
Merka = Marka 164-165 ab 3
Merke [SU] 132-133 N 9
Merkel, TX 76-77 D 6
Merket Bazar = Marqat Bazar 142-143 D 4
Merla 126-127 G 1-2
Merlimau 150-151 D 11
Merlin, OR 66-67 B 4
Merlo [RA, Buenos Aires] 110 III a 1
Merlo [RA, San Luis] 106-107 E 4
Merlo Gómez 110 III b 2
Merlo-Libertad 110 III a 2
Merlo-Mariano Acosta 110 III a 2
Merlo-Pontevedra 110 III a 2
Merlo-San Antonio de Padua 110 III a 2
Merluna 158-159 H 2
Mermer = Alibardak 136-137 J 3
Merna, NE 68-69 G 5
Merna, WY 66-67 H 4
Méroua 168-169 F 2
Merouana = Marwānah 166-167 J 2
Merowê = Marawī 164-165 L 5
Merpatti 138-139 H 8
Merq, el- = Al-Marj 164-165 J 2
Merredin 158-159 C 6
Merrick 119 D 4
Merri Creek 161 II b 1
Merrill, IA 68-69 H 4
Merrill, MS 78-79 E 5
Merrill, OR 66-67 C 4
Merrill, WI 70-71 F 3
Merrillan, WI 70-71 E 3
Merrimack River 72-73 L 3
Merriman 174-175 E 6
Merriman, NE 68-69 EF 4
Merrionette Park, IL 83 II a 2
Merrit 56-57 M 7
Merrit, Lake — 83 I c 2
Merriwa 160 JK 4
Mer Rouge, LA 78-79 D 4
Merrymount Park 84 I bc 3
Merryville, LA 78-79 C 5
Merseburg 118 EF 3
Mers-el-Kébir = Mars al-Kabīr 166-167 F 1-2
Mersin [TR] 134-135 C 3
Mersing 148-149 D 6
Mers-les-Bains 120-121 H 3
Mērsrags 124-125 D 5
Merta 138-139 DE 4
Mērtān = Merta 138-139 DE 4
Merthyr Tydfil 119 DE 6
Merti 171 D 2
Merton, London- 129 II b 2
Mertz Glacier 53 C 15
Mertzon, TX 76-77 D 7
Meru [EAK] 172 G 1-2
Meru [EAT] 172 G 2
Meru = Gangrinpochhe 138-139 H 2
Merume Montains 98-99 H 1-J 2
Merume Mountains 94-95 L 4-5
Meru National Park 171 D 2
Merundung, Pulau — 152-153 H 4
Meruóca 100-101 D 2
Merv 134-135 J 3
Merv = Mary 134-135 J 3
Merwar = Mārwār 134-135 L 5
Merzifon 136-137 F 2
Merzouna = Al-Mazzūnah 166-167 L 2
Mesa, AZ 64-65 D 5
Mesa, NM 76-77 B 5-6
Mesa, Cerro — 108-109 D 7
Mesabi Range 64-65 H 2
Mesa Central = Mesa de Anáhuac 64-65 FG 7-8
Mesa Chupadera 76-77 A 5-6
Mesa de Anáhuac 64-65 FG 7-8
Mesa de Guanipa 94-95 J 3
Mesa del Rito Gaviel 76-77 C 6
Mesa de Mariapiri 94-95 FG 6
Mesa de San Carlos 86-87 C 3
Mesa de Yambí 92-93 E 4
Mesagne 122-123 GH 5
Mesa Montosa 76-77 B 5
Mesanak, Pulau — 152-153 F 5
Mesaniyeu, Sierra — 108-109 DE 3
Mesas de Iguaje 94-95 E 7
Mesa Verde National Park 74-75 J 4
Mescalero, NM 76-77 B 6
Mescalero Apache Indian Reservation 76-77 B 6
Mescalero Ridge 76-77 BC 6
Mescalero Valley 76-77 BC 6
Mescit dağı 136-137 J 2
Mescitli 136-137 JK 3
Meščora 124-125 MN 6
Meščorskij 113 V a 3
Meščovsk 124-125 K 6
Meščura 124-125 S 2
Meseied = Musā'id 166-167 A 5
Meseta de Jaua 94-95 J 5
Meseta de la Muerte 108-109 CD 7
Meseta de las Vizcachas 111 B 8
Meseta del Lago Buenos Aires 108-109 D 6
Meseta del Norte 64-65 F 6
Meseta del Viento 108-109 C 7
Meseta de Montemayor 111 C 6-7
Meseta de Somuncurá 111 C 6
Meseta de Zohlaguna 86-87 Q 8
Mesgouez, Lac — 62 O 1
Meshed = Mashhad 134-135 HJ 3
Meshhed = Mashhad 134-135 HJ 3
Meshkīn Shar 136-137 M 3
Meshra' er Req = Mashrā' ar-Raqq 164-165 K 7
Mesick, MI 70-71 H 3
Mesilinka River 60 E 1
Mesilla, NM 76-77 A 6
Meskanaw 61 F 4
Meskenê = Maskanah 136-137 GH 4-5
Meskiana = Miskyānah 166-167 K 2
Meškovskaja 126-127 K 2
Mesmiyê = Al-Mismīyah 136-137 G 6
Mesnil-Amelot, le — 129 I d 1
Mesnil-le-Roi, le — 129 I b 2
Mesolóngion 122-123 J 6
Mesopotamia [IRQ] 134-135 E 3-F 4
Mesopotamia [RA] 111 E 3-4
Mesquita 100-101 C 10
Mesquite, NV 74-75 F 4
Mesquite, TX 76-77 F 6
Messaad = Mis'ad 166-167 H 2
Messalo, Rio — 172 G 4
Messaoud, Oued — = Wādī Mas'ūd 166-167 F 5-6
Messaria 136-137 E 5
'Messeied = Musā'id 166-167 A 5
Messel 128 III b 2
Messeler Höhe 128 III b 2
Messênê [GR, place] 122-123 JK 7
Messênê [GR, ruins] 122-123 J 7
Messenhausen 128 III b 2
Messêniakós Kólpos 122-123 JK 7
Messier, Canal — 108-109 B 7
Messina [I] 122-123 F 6
Messina [ZA] 172 EF 6
Messina, Gulf of — = Messêniakós Kólpos 122-123 JK 7
Messina, Stretto di — 122-123 F 6-7
Messinge 171 C 5
Messojacha 132-133 O 4
Mesteñas, Las — 76-77 B 8
Mestia 126-127 L 5
Mestour, Hassi — = Ḥāssī Mastūr 166-167 GH 4
Mestre, Venèzia- 122-123 E 3
Mesudiye 136-137 G 2
Mesuji, Wai — 152-153 F 7-8
Meta 94-95 E 6
Meta, Río — 92-93 E 3
Metagama 62 L 3
Meta Incognita Peninsula 56-57 X 5
Metairie, LA 64-65 H 5-6
Metairie Cemetery 85 I b 1
Metairie-East End, LA 85 I b 1
Metalici, Munţii — 122-123 K 2
Metaline Falls, WA 66-67 E 1
Metameur = Al-Maṭamūr 166-167 M 3
Metán 111 D 3
Metangula 172 FG 4
Metapan 88-89 B 7
Metaponto 122-123 G 5
Metarica 171 D 6
Metechi 126-127 M 6
Meteghan 63 CD 5
Metema 164-165 M 6
Metéōra 122-123 J 6
Meteor Crater 74-75 H 5
Meteor Depth 50-51 HJ 8
Methouia = Al-Miṭhūyah 166-167 LM 3
Methow River 66-67 CD 1
Mê Thuôt = Ban Me Thuôt 148-149 E 4
Methy Lake 61 D 2
Méthymna 122-123 LM 6
Methy River 61 D 2
Metileo 106-107 EF 5
Metili-Chaamba = Matlīlī 166-167 H 3
Metinic Island 72-73 M 3
Metković 122-123 GH 4
Metlakatla, AK 56-57 KL 6
Metlaoui, El — = Al-Mitlawī 164-165 F 2
Métlîn, El — = Al-Mātlīn 166-167 M 1
Metolius, OR 66-67 C 3
Metorica 171 D 6
Meṭouia, El — = Al-Miṭūyah 166-167 LM 3
Metro 152-153 F 8
Metropolis, IL 70-71 F 7
Metropolitan Hospital Clinic 84 II b 2
Métsobon 122-123 J 6
Metter, GA 80-81 E 4
Mettharaw 141 F 7
Mettuppālaiyam 140 C 5
Mettūr 140 C 5
Meṭṭur Kuḷam = Stanley Reservoir 134-135 M 8
Metuge 171 E 6
Metulla 136-137 F 6
Metundo 171 E 5
Metz 120-121 L 4
Meudon 129 I b 2
Meulaboh 148-149 C 6
Meulen, Isla van der — 108-109 B 7
Meureudu 148-149 C 5
Meuse 120-121 K 4
Meusegem 128 II a 1
Mevume 174-175 L 2
Mēwār 138-139 DE 5
Mexcala, Río — = Río Balsas 64-65 F 8
Mexia, TX 76-77 F 7
Mexicali 64-65 C 5
Mexican Hat, UT 74-75 J 4
Mexican Plateau = Altiplanicie Mexicana 64-65 E 5-F 7
Mexico, ME 72-73 L 2
Mexico, MO 70-71 DE 6
Mexico [MEX, administrative unit] 86-87 KL 8
México [MEX, place] 64-65 G 8
Mexico [MEX, state] 64-65 E 6-G 8
México, Bogotá- 91 III b 4
Mexico, Gulf of — 64-65 G-J 7
Mexico Basin 64-65 H-J 6
Mexico Bay 72-73 H 3
México City = México 64-65 G 8
Meyādīn = Mayādīn 136-137 J 5
Meyāndowab 136-137 M 4
Meyāneh 134-135 F 3
Meyāneh, Kūreh-ye — 136-137 M 5
Meydān Dāgh 136-137 MN 4
Meydān-e Naftūn 136-137 N 7
Mey ed Dahraoui, Hassi — = Ḥāssī Māī ad-Darwwī 166-167 K 3
Meyerland, Houston-, TX 85 III b 2
Meyersdale, PA 72-73 G 5
Meyronne 61 E 6
Mézalīgōn 141 D 7
Mèzā Myit 141 E 3-4
Mezdra 122-123 KL 4
Meždurečenskij 132-133 LM 6
Meždušarskij, ostrov — 132-133 HJ 3
Mezen' [SU, place] 132-133 GH 4
Mezen' [SU, river] 132-133 H 5
Mézenc, Mont — 120-121 JK 6
Mezenskaja guba 132-133 G 4
Mezeraa, El — = Al-Mazra'ah 166-167 K 2
Mezgorje 126-127 A 2
Mezguiṭem = Mizgīṭim 166-167 E 2
Meziadin Lake 60 C 1
Mežirečje 126-127 B 2
Mezőkövesd 118 K 5
Mezoûna = Al-Mazzūnah 166-167 L 2
Mežpanje 124-125 P 6
Mezquital 86-87 H 6
Mfongosi = Mfongozi 174-175 J 5
Mfongozi 174-175 J 5
Mfwanganu 171 C 3
Mga 124-125 H 4
M'ghīlah, Jabal — 166-167 L 2
Mglin 124-125 J 7
M. Gómez 110 III b 2
Mḥamīd, el — = Al-Maḥamīd 166-167 D 5
Mhāpasā = Māpuca 140 A 3
Mhasalān = Mhasla 140 A 1
Mhasla 140 A 1
Mhasvād 140 B 2
M. Heilman Memorial Field 84 II c 2
M. Hidalgo, Presa — 86-87 F 4
Mhlatuze 174-175 J 5
Mhow 138-139 E 6
Mia, Wed — = Wādī Miyāh 164-165 EF 2
Miajadas 120-121 E 9
Miājlar 134-135 KL 5
Miali = Miao-li 146-147 H 9
Miami, AZ 74-75 H 6
Miami, FL 64-65 K 6
Miami, OK 76-77 G 4
Miami, TX 76-77 D 5
Miami Beach, FL 64-65 KL 6
Miami Canal 64-65 K 6
Miami River 70-71 H 6
Miamisburg, OH 70-71 H 6
Miami Shores, FL 80-81 cd 4
Miamo, El — 94-95 L 4
Mianchi 146-147 CD 4
Miāndou Āb = Meyāndowab 136-137 M 4
Miandrivazo 172 J 5
Miangas, Pulau — 148-149 J 5
Mianwali = Miyānwālī 134-135 L 4
Mian Xian 142-143 K 5
Mianyang [TJ, Hubei] 146-147 D 6
Mianyang [TJ, Sichuan] 142-143 J 5
Miao Dao 146-147 H 3
Miaodao Qundao 142-143 N 4
Miaoli 146-147 H 9
Miao Liedao = Miaodao Qundao 142-143 N 4
Miao-tzū = Miaozi 146-147 CD 5
Miaozi 146-147 CD 5
Miass 132-133 L 7
Miastko 118 H 1-2
Miaws, Bi'r — 173 D 6
Mica 174-175 J 3
Mica Creek 60 H 3
Mica Dam 60 H 3
Micaela Cascallares 106-107 G 7
Micay 92-93 D 4
Micha Cchakaja 126-127 KL 5
Michaia Ivanoviča Kalinina 124-125 P 4-5
Michajliki 124-125 K 5
Michajlov 124-125 M 6
Michajlovka [SU, Rossijskaja SFSR Astrachanskaja Oblast'] 126-127 N 3
Michajlovka [SU, Rossijskaja SFSR Kurskaja Oblast'] 124-125 KL 7
Michajlovka [SU, Rossijskaja SFSR Volgogradskaja Oblast'] 126-127 L 1
Michajlovka [SU, Ukrainskaja SSR] 126-127 G 3
Michajlovskaja 124-125 PQ 3
Michajlovskij 132-133 OP 7
Michajlovskoje [SU, Moskva] 113 V b 3
Michalitsion = Karacabey 136-137 C 2
Michalovce 118 KL 4
Mī Chaung 141 C 5
Michel 66-67 F 1
Michel Peak 60 D 3
Michelson, Mont — 56-57 GH 4
Michigamme Reservoir 70-71 FG 2
Michigan 64-65 J 2-K 3
Michigan, ND 68-69 G 1-2
Michigan, Lake — 64-65 J 2-3
Michigan City, IN 70-71 G 5
Michigan State Fair Grounds 84 II b 2
Michikamau Lake 56-57 Y 7
Michikenis River 62 E 1
Michipicoten Bay 70-71 H 2
Michipicoten Harbour 70-71 H 1-2
Michipicoten Island 56-57 T 8
Michnevo 124-125 LM 6
Michoacán 64-65 F 8
Micronesia [archipelago] 156-157 G-H 4
Micronesia [Micronesia, state] 148-149 MN 5
Mičurin 122-123 MN 4
Mičurinsk 124-125 N 7
Mida 171 DE 3
Midáeion = Eskişehir 134-135 C 2-3
Midai, Pulau — 148-149 E 6
Midalt 166-167 D 3
Midār 166-167 E 2
Midas, NV 66-67 E 5
Mid Atlantic Ridge 50-51 H 3-J 8
Middelburg [ZA, Kaapland] 172 DE 8
Middelburg [ZA, Transvaal] 172 EF 7
Middelfart 116-117 CD 10
Middelpos 174-175 D 6
Middelpost = Middelpos 174-175 D 6
Middel Roggeveld 174-175 D 7
Middelsten Boskant 128 II a 1
Middelveld [ZA, Kaapland] 174-175 E 5
Middelveld [ZA, Transvaal] 174-175 FG 4
Middelwit 174-175 G 3
Middle Alkali Lake 66-67 CD 5
Middle America Trench 156-157 MN 4
Middle Andaman 134-135 P 8
Middle Atlas = Al-Aṭlas al-Mutawassit 164-165 CD 2
Middle Bank 63 FG 5
Middlebro 70-71 C 1
Middlebury, VT 72-73 K 2
Middle Concho River 76-77 D 7
Middle East, The — 50-51 NO 4
Middle Fork Chandalar 58-59 O 2-3
Middle Fork Fortymile 58-59 Q 4
Middle Fork John Day River 66-67 D 3
Middle Fork Koyukuk 58-59 M 3
Middle Fork Salmon River 66-67 F 3
Middle Harbour 161 I b 1
Middle Head 161 I b 1
Middle Island = Ko Klang 150-151 AB 8
Middle Loup River 68-69 G 5
Middle Moscos = Maungmagan Kyūnzu 150-151 A 5
Middle Musquodoboit 63 E 5
Middleport, OH 72-73 E 5
Middle Rapids 61 BC 2
Middle Reservoir 84 I b 2
Middle Ridge 63 J 3
Middle River, MN 70-71 BC 1
Middle River Village 60 E 2
Middlesboro, KY 64-65 JK 4
Middlesbrough 119 F 4
Middlesex Fells Reservation 84 I b 2
Middleton, ID 66-67 E 4
Middleton, TN 78-79 E 3
Middleton [CDN] 63 D 5
Middleton [ZA] 174-175 F 7
Middleton, Mount — 62 N 1
Middleton Island 56-57 GH 6
Middleton Reef 158-159 L 5
Middletown, NJ 72-73 J 4
Middletown, NY 72-73 J 4
Middletown, OH 72-73 DE 5
Middle Water, TX 76-77 C 5
Middle West 64-65 F-J 3
Midelt = Midalt 166-167 D 3
Midhdharidhrah, Al- 164-165 A 5
Midhsandur 116-117 c 2
Midia = Midye 136-137 C 2
Mid-Illovo 174-175 J 5-6
Mid Indian Basin 50-51 NO 6
Midland 72-73 FG 2
Midland, CA 74-75 F 6
Midland, MI 70-71 H 4
Midland, SD 68-69 F 3
Midland, TX 64-65 F 5
Midland Beach, New York-, NY 82 III b 3
Midlandvale 61 B 5
Midlothian, TX 76-77 F 6
Mid Moscos = Maungmagan Kyūnzu 150-151 A 5
Midnapore 134-135 O 6
Midnapur = Midnapore 134-135 O 6
Midongy-atsimo 172 J 6
Midori, Yokohama- 155 III a 2
Mid Pacific Ridge 156-157 J 8-L 7
Midsayap 148-149 HJ 5
Midu 176 a 3
Midvale, ID 66-67 E 3
Midvale, UT 66-67 H 5
Midville, GA 80-81 E 4
Midway 156-157 J 3
Midway Islands 58-59 NO 1
Midway Range 60 H 5
Midwest, WY 68-69 CD 4
Midwest City, OK 76-77 F 5
Midyah 166-167 H 1
Midyān II 173 D 3
Midyat 136-137 J 4
Midye 136-137 C 2
Midżor 122-123 K 4
Mie 144-145 L 5
Miedo, El — 94-95 F 5
Międzyrec Podlaski 118 L 3
Miel, La — 94-95 G 3
Mielec 118 K 3
Mien-ch'ih = Mianchi 146-147 CD 4
Mienhsien = Mian Xian 142-143 K 5
Mienyang = Mianyang [TJ, Hubei] 146-147 D 6
Mien-yang = Mianyang [TJ, Sichuan] 142-143 J 5
Miercurea-Ciuc 122-123 L 2
Mieres 120-121 DE 7
Miersdorf 130 III c 2
Mierzeja Helska 118 J 1
Mierzeja Wislana 118 J 1
Mieso 164-165 N 7
Mifflintown, PA 72-73 H 4
Migamuwa 134-135 M 9
Migdal Ashqĕlōn = Ashqĕlōn 136-137 F 7
Migdal Gad = Ashqĕlōn 136-137 F 7
Mighāir 166-167 J 3
Mighāir, Al- 166-167 J 3
Mighān, Kavīr-e — 136-137 N 5
Mighrāwah 166-167 DE 3
Migole 171 CD 4
Miguel Alemán, Presa — 86-87 M 8
Miguel Alves 92-93 L 5
Miguel Burnier 102-103 L 4
Miguel Calmon 92-93 LM 7
Miguel Cané 106-107 F 6
Miguel Hidalgo, Ciudad de México- 91 I b 2
Miguel Hidalgo, Parque Nacional — 91 I a 3
Miguel Riglos 106-107 F 6
Migues 106-107 K 5
Migulinskaja 126-127 K 2
Migyaungyé 141 D 6

Mihajlovgrad 122-123 K 4
Mihalıççık 136-137 D 3
Mihara 144-145 J 5
Mi He 146-147 G 3
Mi He = Ming He 146-147 E 3
Mihintalē 140 E 6
Mihmandar 136-137 F 4
Mi Ho = Mi He 146-147 G 3
Miho wan 144-145 J 5
Mi-hsien = Mi Xian 146-147 D 4
Miito = Moyto 164-165 H 6
Mijares 120-121 G 8-9
Mijnden 128 I b 2
Mijriyyah, Al- 164-165 B 5
Mikaševiči 124-125 F 7
Mikata 144-145 K 5
Mikawa wan 144-145 L 5
Miki 144-145 K 5
Mikindani 172 H 4
Mikir Hills 141 C 2
Mikkaichi = Kurobe 144-145 L 4
Mikkeli 116-117 M 7
Mikkwa River 61 A 2
Miknās 164-165 C 2
Mikojan-Šachar = Karačajevsk 126-127 KL 5
Mikumi 171 D 4
Mikumi National Park 171 D 4
Mikun' 132-133 HJ 5
Mikuni 144-145 KL 4
Mila = Mīlah 164-165 F 1
Milaca, MN 70-71 D 3
Miladummadulu Atoll 176 ab 1
Milagres 100-101 E 4
Milagro 96-97 B 3
Milagro, El — 111 C 4
Mīlah 164-165 F 1
Milāḥah, Wādī — 173 C 4
Milājerd 136-137 N 5
Milak 138-139 G 3
Milam 138-139 H 2
Milan 91 III c 2
Milan, IA 70-71 D 5
Milan, MI 72-73 E 3
Milan, TN 78-79 E 3
Milan, WA 66-67 E 2
Milan = Milano 122-123 C 3
Milano 122-123 C 3
Milano, TX 76-77 F 7
Milâs 136-137 B 4
Milazzo 122-123 F 6
Milbank, SD 68-69 H 3
Milbanke Sound 60 C 3
Milbertshofen, München- 130 II b 1
Milbridge, ME 72-73 N 2
Milden 61 E 5
Mildred, MT 68-69 D 2
Mildura 158-159 H 6
Mīleh, Kūh-e — 136-137 M 6
150 Mile House 60 G 3
100 Mile House 60 G 4
Milepa 171 D 5
Miles 158-159 JK 5
Miles, TX 76-77 DE 7
Miles, WA 66-67 D 2
Miles City, MT 64-65 E 2
Milesville, SD 68-69 EF 3
Milet = Miletos 136-137 B 4
Mileto = Miletos 134-135 B 3
Miletos 134-135 B 3
Miletus = Miletos 134-135 B 3
Milford, CA 66-67 C 5
Milford, DE 72-73 J 5
Milford, MA 72-73 L 3
Milford, NE 68-69 H 5
Milford, NH 72-73 L 3
Milford, PA 72-73 J 4
Milford, UT 74-75 G 3
Milford Sound [NZ, bay] 158-159 N 8
Milford Sound [NZ, place] 161 B 7
Milgis 171 D 2
Milḥ, Qurayyāt al- 136-137 G 7
Mili 208 H 2
Milia, El — = Al-Mīlīyah 166-167 JK 1
Miliān, Ouèd — = Wād Milyān 166-167 LM 1
Miliana = Milyānah 166-167 GH 1
Milicz 118 H 3
Miling 158-159 C 6
Military Museum 155 II a 2
Milīyah, Al- 166-167 JK 1
Milk, Wādī el — = Wādī al-Malik 164-165 KL 5
Mil'kovo 132-133 ef 7
Milk River [CDN] 66-67 GH 1
Milk River [USA] 64-65 E 2
Milk River Ridge 66-67 G 1
Millares 104-105 D 6
Millau 120-121 J 6
Mill City, OR 66-67 B 3
Mill Creek [USA, New Jersey] 84 III d 1
Mill Creek [USA, Pennsylvania] 84 III b 1
Milledgeville, GA 80-81 E 4
Millegan, MT 66-67 H 2
Mille Lacs Lake 64-65 H 2
Millen, GA 80-81 F 4
Miller 174-175 E 7
Miller, MO 76-77 GH 4
Miller, NE 68-69 G 5
Miller, SD 68-69 G 3
Miller, Mount — 58-59 QR 6
Millerovo 126-127 K 2
Miller Peak 74-75 H 7
Millersburg, OH 72-73 EF 4
Millersburg, PA 72-73 H 4
Millerton Lake 74-75 D 4
Millertown 63 H 3
Millevaches, Plateau de — 120-121 HJ 6
Mill Hill, London- 129 II b 1
Millican, OR 66-67 C 4
Millicent 158-159 GH 7
Millington, TN 78-79 E 3
Millinocket, ME 72-73 M 2
Mill Island [Antarctica] 53 C 11
Mill Island [CDN] 56-57 V 5
Millmerran 158-159 K 5
Millport, AL 78-79 EF 4
Millry, AL 78-79 E 5
Mills, NM 76-77 B 4
Millston, WI 70-71 E 3
Millville, NJ 72-73 J 5
Millwood Lake 76-77 G 6
Milmont Park, PA 84 III a 2
Milne Bay 148-149 h 7
Milnesand, NM 76-77 C 6
Milnet 72-73 F 1
Milnor, ND 68-69 H 2
Milo, IA 70-71 D 5
Milo, ME 72-73 M 2
Milo, OR 66-67 B 4
Milo [CDN] 61 B 5
Milo [Guinea] 164-165 C 7
Milolii, HI 78-79 de 3
Milparinka 158-159 H 5
Milton, FL 78-79 F 5
Milton, MA 84 I b 3
Milton, ND 68-69 GH 1
Milton, OR 66-67 D 3
Milton, PA 72-73 H 4
Milton, WI 70-71 F 4
Milton, WV 72-73 E 5
Milton [CDN] 63 D 5
Milton [NZ] 161 CD 8
Miltonvale, KS 68-69 H 6
Milton Village, MA 84 I b 3
Miluo 142-143 L 6
Miluo Jiang 146-147 D 7
Mil'utinskaja 126-127 KL 2
Milverton 72-73 F 3
Milwaukee, WI 64-65 J 3
Milwaukee Depth 64-65 N 8
Milwaukie, OR 66-67 B 3
Milyān, Wād — 166-167 LM 1
Milyānah 166-167 GH 1
Mim 168-169 E 4
Miminiska Lake 62 E 2
Mimitsu 144-145 H 6
Mimongo 172 B 2
Mimosa 100-101 A 7
Mimoso do Sul 102-103 M 4
Mimôt 150-151 EF 7
Mina, NV 74-75 DE 3
Mina, SD 68-69 G 3
Mina [MEX] 76-77 D 9
Mina [RI] 152-153 Q 10-11
Mina, Ouèd — = Wādī Mīnā 166-167 G 2
Mīnā, Wādī — 166-167 G 2
Mīnā' al-Aḥmadī 136-137 N 8
Mīnā Bāzār 138-139 B 2
Min' 'Abd Allāh 136-137 N 8
Mina de São Domingos 120-121 D 10
Minago River 61 J 3
Minahasa 148-149 H 6
Minakami 144-145 M 4
Minaki 62 B 3
Minam, OR 66-67 E 3
Minamata 142-143 P 5
Minami, Yokohama- 155 III a 3
Minami Daitō-jima 142-143 P 6
Minami-Daitō zima = Minami-Daitō-jima 142-143 P 6
Minami-Io 206-207 S 7
Minami Iwo = Minami Io 206-207 S 7
Minami Io 206-207 S 7
Minamitane 144-145 H 7
Minami Tori 156-157 G 3
Minas 111 EF 4
Minas, Baruta-Las — 91 II b 2
Minas, Serra de — 102-103 L 3
Minas, Sierra de las — 86-87 PQ 10
Minas Basin 63 DE 5
Minas Cué 111 E 2
Minas de Corrales 106-107 K 3
Minas de Riotinto 120-121 DE 10
Minas do Mimoso 100-101 D 6
Minas Gerais 92-93 KL 8-9
Minas Novas 102-103 L 2
Minatare, NE 68-69 E 5
Minatitlán 64-65 H 8
Minato = Nakaminato 144-145 N 4
Minato, Tōkyō- 155 III b 2
Minbū 141 D 5
Minbyā 141 C 5
Mincha 106-107 B 3
Min Chiang = Min Jiang [TJ, Fujian] 146-147 G 8
Min Chiang = Min Jiang [TJ, Sichuan] 142-143 J 5-6
Min-ch'in = Minqin 142-143 J 4
Minchinābād 138-139 D 2
Min-ch'ing = Minqing 146-147 G 8
Minchinmávida, Volcán — 108-109 C 4
Min-ch'üan = Minquan 146-147 E 4
Minchumina, Lake — 58-59 L 5
Minco, OK 76-77 EF 5
Mindanao 148-149 J 5
Mindanao Sea 148-149 HJ 5
Mindanau = Mindanao 148-149 J 5
Mindat 141 C 5
Mindat Sakan = Mindat 141 C 5
Minden 118 D 2
Minden, IA 70-71 C 5
Minden, LA 78-79 C 4
Minden, NE 68-69 G 5
Minden, NV 74-75 D 3
Minderoo 158-159 C 4
Mindōn 141 D 6
Mindōn Myit 141 D 6
Mindoro 148-149 GH 4
Mindoro Strait 148-149 GH 4
Mindra, Vîrful — 122-123 KL 3
Mindživan 126-127 N 7
Mine 144-145 H 5
Mine Centre 62 C 3
Mineiga, Bi'r — = Bi'r Munayjah 173 D 6
Mineiros 102-103 F 2
Mineola, NY 72-73 K 4
Mineola, TX 76-77 G 6
Miner, MT 66-67 H 3
Mineral, CA 66-67 C 5
Mineral, WA 66-67 B 2
Mineral Mountains 74-75 G 3
Mineral'nyje Vody 126-127 L 4
Mineral Point, WI 70-71 EF 4
Mineral Wells, TX 76-77 EF 6
Minersville, UT 74-75 G 3
Minerva, OH 72-73 F 4
Minervino Murge 122-123 FG 5
Mingan 63 DE 2
Mingan, Rivière — 63 E 2
Mingan Islands 63 DE 2
Mingan Passage = Jacques Cartier Passage 56-57 Y 7-8
Mingary 160 E 4
Mingečaur 126-127 N 6
Mingečaurskoje vodochranilišče 126-127 N 6
Mingenew 158-159 C 5
Mingfeng = Niya Bazar 142-143 E 4
Minggang 146-147 E 5
Ming He 146-147 E 3
Mingin 141 D 4
Mingjiang = Minggang 146-147 E 5
Mingo Junction, OH 72-73 F 4
Mingoya 171 D 5
Mingxi 146-147 F 8
Minhla [BUR, Magwe Taing] 141 D 6
Minhla [BUR, Pègū Taing] 141 D 7
Minh Long 150-151 G 5
Minho [P, landscape] 120-121 C 8
Minho [P, river] 120-121 C 7
Minhou 146-147 G 8
Minhow = Fuzhou 142-143 MN 6
Min-hsien = Min Xian 142-143 J 5
Minicoy Island 134-135 L 9
Minidoka, ID 66-67 G 4
Minier, IL 70-71 F 5
Minigwal, Lake — 158-159 D 5
Minikkōy Dvīp = Minicoy Island 134-135 L 9
Minilya River 158-159 BC 4
Mininco 106-107 A 6
Miniota 61 H 5
Ministro João Alberto 92-93 J 7
Minitonas 61 H 4
Min Jiang [TJ, Fujian] 142-143 M 6
Min Jiang [TJ, Sichuan] 142-143 J 5-6
Minkébé 172 B 1
Min'kovo 124-125 O 4
Minle 142-143 J 4
Min-lo = Minle 142-143 J 4
Minna 164-165 F 7
Minneapolis, KS 68-69 H 6
Minneapolis, MN 64-65 GH 2-3
Minnedosa 61 J 5
Minnekahta, SD 68-69 E 4
Minneola, KS 68-69 FG 7
Minneota, MN 70-71 BC 3
Minnesota 64-65 H 2-3
Minnesota River 64-65 H 3
Minnewaska, Lake — 70-71 C 3
Minnewaukan, ND 68-69 G 1
Minnipa 160 B 4
Minnitaki Lake 62 CD 3
Mino [J] 144-145 L 5
Miño [P] 120-121 D 7
Miño, Volcán — 104-105 B 7
Mino-Kamo 144-145 L 5
Minong, WI 70-71 DE 2
Minonk, IL 70-71 F 5
Minorca = Menorca 120-121 K 8
Minot, ND 64-65 F 2
Minqin 142-143 J 4
Minqing 146-147 G 8
Minquan 146-147 E 4
Min Shan 142-143 J 5
Minshāt al-Bakkārī 170 II a 1
Minshāt Dahshūr 173 B 3
Minsin 141 D 3
Minsk 124-125 FG 7
Minster, OH 70-71 H 5
Mintaqat al-Wajh 166-167 K 4
Minto, AK 58-59 N 4
Minto [CDN, Manitoba] 68-69 FG 1
Minto [CDN, New Brunswick] 63 C 4
Minto [CDN, Yukon Territory] 58-59 T 5
Minto, Lake — 56-57 V 6
Minto Inlet 56-57 N 3
Minton 68-69 D 1
Minturn, CO 68-69 C 6
Minūf 173 B 2
Minusinsk 132-133 R 7
Minuto de Dios, Bogotá- 91 III b 2
Min Xian 142-143 J 5
Minyā, Al- 164-165 KL 3
Mio, MI 70-71 H 3
Mios Num 148-149 KL 7
Mios Waar 148-149 KL 7
Miqdādīyah, Al- 136-137 L 6
Miquelon, Saint-Pierre et — 56-57 Za 8
Miquon, PA 84 III b 1
Mir 124-125 F 7
Mira 122-123 DE 3
Mira, Río — [CO] 94-95 B 7
Mīrā', Wādī al- 136-137 HJ 7
Miracatu 102-103 J 6
Miracema 102-103 LM 4
Miracema do Norte 92-93 K 6
Miracle Mile, Los Angeles-, CA 83 III bc 1
Mirador [BR] 92-93 KL 6
Mirador [MEX] 91 I b 1
Mirador, El — 86-87 P 9
Miradouro 102-103 L 4
Miraflores [CO, Boyacá] 94-95 E 5
Miraflores [CO, Vaupés] 94-95 E 7
Miraflores [PA] 64-65 b 2
Miraflores [YV] 91 II b 1
Miraflores, Esclusas de — 64-65 b 3
Miraflores Locks = Esclusas de Miraflores 64-65 b 3
Miraí 102-103 L 4
Miraíma 100-101 DE 2
Miraj 140 B 2
Miralta 102-103 KL 2
Miramar 111 E 5
Miramichi Bay 63 D 4
Miramichi River 63 CD 4
Mirampéllu, Kólpos — 122-123 LM 8
Miranda [BR] 92-93 H 9
Miranda [RA] 106-107 H 6
Miranda [YV] 94-95 H 2
Miranda, Río — 92-93 H 9
Miranda de Ebro 120-121 F 7
Miranda do Douro 120-121 D 8
Mirande 120-121 H 7
Mirandela 120-121 D 8
Mirandiba 100-101 E 5
Mirando City, TX 76-77 E 9
Mirândola 122-123 D 3
Mirangaba 100-101 D 6
Mirante, Serra do — 102-103 GH 5
Mirante do Paranapanema 102-103 FG 5
Mira Pampa 106-107 F 5
Mirapinima 92-93 G 5
Mirassol 102-103 H 4
Mir-Bašir 126-127 N 6
Mirbāṭ 134-135 GH 7
Mirêar, Gezîret — = Jazīrat Marīr 173 DE 6
Mirebâlais 88-89 KL 5
Mīrganj 138-139 K 4
Mirgorod 126-127 FG 1-2
Miri 148-149 F 6
Miriālguda 140 D 2
Miri Hills 141 CD 2
Mirim, Lagoa — 111 F 4
Mirimire 94-95 G 2
Miriñay, Esteros del — 106-107 J 2
Miriñay, Río — 106-107 J 2
Mirinzal 100-101 B 1-2
Miriti 92-93 H 6
Miriti, Cachoeira — 98-99 J 8
Miritiparaná, Río — 94-95 F 8
Mirjāveh 134-135 J 5
Mirnyj [Antarctica] 53 C 10
Mirnyj [SU] 132-133 V 5
Mironovka 126-127 E 2
Mīrpūr Batoro 138-139 B 5
Mīrpūr Khāṣ 138-139 B 5
Mīrpūr Sākro 138-139 A 5
Mirror River 61 D 2
Mirslavl' 124-125 MN 5
Mirtağ 136-137 J 3
Miryang 144-145 G 5
Mirzaani 126-127 N 6
Mīrzāpur 134-135 N 5-6
Misāḥah, Bi'r — 164-165 K 4
Misaine Bank 63 G 5
Misaki 155 III d 1
Misān 136-137 M 6
Misantla 86-87 M 8
Misar 138-139 H 2
Misau [WAN, place] 168-169 H 3
Misau [WAN, river] 168-169 H 3
Miscouche 63 DE 4
Miscou Island 63 DE 4
Misgund 174-175 E 7
Mish'āb, Al- 134-135 F 5
Mishāb, Kūh-e — 136-137 L 3
Mishagomish, Lac — 62 NO 1
Mishagua, Río — 96-97 E 7
Mishan 142-143 P 2
Mishawaka, IN 70-71 GH 5
Mishawum Lake 84 I b 1
Mishbīḥ, Jabal — 164-165 L 4
Misheguk Mountain 58-59 G 2
Mi-shima 144-145 H 5
Mishomis 72-73 J 1
Mi Shui 146-147 D 8
Misima 148-149 h 7
Misión, La — 74-75 E 6
Misión del Divino Salvador 102-103 E 6
Misiones [PY] 102-103 D 7
Misiones [RA] 111 EF 3
Misiones, Sierra de — 102-103 EF 7
Misión Fagnano 108-109 F 10
Misión Franciscana Tacaaglé 104-105 G 9
Misión San Francisco de Guayo 94-95 L 3
Misis 136-137 F 4
Miskito, Cayos — 64-65 K 9
Miskito Cays = Cayos Miskitos 64-65 K 9
Miskolc 118 K 4
Miskyānah 166-167 K 2
Misli = Gölcük 136-137 F 3
Mismāḥ, Tall al — 136-137 G 6
Mismār 164-165 M 5
Mismīyah, Al- 136-137 G 6
Misoa 94-95 F 2
Misol = Pulau Misoöl 148-149 K 7
Misoöl, Pulau — 148-149 K 7
Misore = Mysore 134-135 M 8
Miṣr, Al- 164-165 KL 3
Miṣr al-Qadīmah, Al-Qāhirah- 170 II b 1
Misrātah 164-165 H 2
Miṣr-Baḥrī 173 BC 2
Miṣr el-Gedīda = Al-Qāhirah-Miṣr al-Jadīdah 173 BC 2
Misriç 136-137 J 4
Misrikh 138-139 H 4
Missale 171 C 6
Missanabie 70-71 HJ 1
Missão 100-101 C 7
Missão Velha 100-101 E 4
Missinaibi Lake 70-71 J 1
Missinaibi River 56-57 U 7
Mission, SD 68-69 F 4
Mission, TX 76-77 E 9
Mission, San Francisco-, CA 83 I b 2
Mission City 66-67 B 1
Mission Dolores 83 I b 2
Mission San Gabriel Arcangel 83 III d 1
Missippinewa Lake 70-71 GH 5
Missisicabi, Rivière — 62 M 1
Mississauga 72-73 G 3
Mississippi 64-65 J 5
Mississippi River 64-65 H 3
Mississippi River Bridge 85 I b 2
Mississippi River Delta 64-65 J 6
Mississippi Sound 78-79 E 5
Missões, Serra das — 100-101 D 4
Missolonghi = Mesolóngion 122-123 J 6
Missoula, MT 64-65 D 2
Missouri 64-65 H 3-4
Missouri City, TX 85 III a 2
Missouri River 64-65 G 3
Missouri Valley, IA 70-71 BC 5
Missūr 166-167 DE 3
Mistassibi, Rivière — 62 P 2
Mistassini 62 PQ 2
Mistassini, Lake — 56-57 W 7
Mistassini, la Réserve de — 62 P 1
Mistassini, Rivière — 62 P 2
Mistassini Post 62 OP 1
Mistelbach 118 H 4
Misti 96-97 F 10
Misumi 144-145 H 6
Misurāṭa = Misrātah 164-165 H 2
Mita, Punta de — 64-65 E 7
Mitai 144-145 H 6
Mitaka 155 III a 1
Mitare [CO] 94-95 F 6
Mitare [YV] 94-95 F 2
Mitcham, London- 129 II b 2
Mitchell, IN 70-71 G 6
Mitchell, NE 68-69 E 5
Mitchell, OR 66-67 CD 3
Mitchell, SD 64-65 G 3
Mitchell [AUS] 158-159 J 5
Mitchell [CDN] 72-73 F 3
Mitchell, Mount — 64-65 K 4
Mitchell Lake 78-79 F 4
Mitchell River [AUS, place] 158-159 H 3
Mitchell River [AUS, river] 158-159 H 3
Mitchinamecus, Lac — 72-73 J 1
Miteja 171 D 5
Miṭhankoṭ 138-139 BC 3
Miṭhī 138-139 B 5
Mithra 138-139 C 3
Mithrāu 134-135 KL 5
Miṭhūyah, Al- 166-167 LM 3
Mitidja = Mītīja 166-167 H 1
Mītīja 166-167 H 1
Mitilini = Mytilēnē 122-123 M 6
Mitino [SU, Moskovskaja Oblast'] 113 V a 2
Mi'tiq, Gebel — = Jabal Mu'tiq 173 C 4
Mitishto River 61 HJ 3
Mīt Jamr 173 B 2
Mitla 86-87 M 9
Mitlā, Wādī al- 166-167 K 2
Mitlawī, Al- 164-165 F 2
Mitliktavik, AK 58-59 G 1
Mito 142-143 R 4
Mitowa 171 D 5
Mitra, Monte de la — 168-169 H 5
Mitre 158-159 O 2
Mitre, Peninsula — 111 CD 8
Mitrofania Island 58-59 d 2
Mitrofanovka 126-127 JK 2
Mitry-le-Neuf 129 I d 2
Mitry-Mory 129 I d 2
Mitsinjo 172 J 5
Mitsio, Nosy — 172 J 4
Mitšiwa 164-165 MN 5
Mitsuke 144-145 M 4
Mitsumata 144-145 c 2
Mitsushima 144-145 G 5
Mitta, Oued el — = Wādī al-Mitlā 166-167 K 2
Mittelberg [CH] 128 IV b 2
Mittellandkanal 118 CD 2
Mittersendling 130 II b 2
Mitū 92-93 EF 4
Mitumba, Chaîne des — 172 E 3-4
Mitumba, Monts — 172 E 2
Miṭūyah, Al- 166-167 LM 3
Mitwaba 172 E 3
Mityana 171 BC 2
Mitzic 172 B 1
Mitzusawa 142-143 QR 4
Mixcoac, Presa de — 91 I b 2
Mixcoac, Villa Obregón- 91 I b 2
Mi Xian 146-147 D 4
Miyagi 144-145 N 3
Miyāh, Wādī — 164-165 EF 2
Miyāh, Wādī al- 173 C 5
Miyāh, Wādī al- = Wādī Jarīr 134-135 E 5-6
Miya kawa 144-145 L 5
Miyake-jima 142-143 QR 5
Miyake zima = Miyake-jima 142-143 QR 5
Miyako 144-145 N 3
Miyako-jima 142-143 O 7
Miyakonojō 142-143 P 5
Miyakonozyō = Miyakonojō 142-143 P 5
Miyako wan 144-145 NO 3
Miyako zima = Miyako-jima 142-143 O 7
Mīyāneh = Meyāneh 134-135 F 3
Miyanoura = Kamiyaku 144-145 H 7
Miyānwālī 134-135 L 4
Miyazaki 142-143 P 5
Miyazu 144-145 K 5
Miyet, Baḥr el- = Baḥr al-Mayyit 134-135 D 4
Miyoshi 144-145 J 5
Mizā, Wādī — 166-167 J 3
Mizāb, Al- 166-167 J 3
Mizar 136-137 H 4
Mizdah 164-165 G 2
Mizen Head 119 AB 6
Mizgītim 166-167 E 2
Mizhi 146-147 C 3
Mizil 122-123 M 3
Mizoč 126-127 BC 1
Mizo Hills 141 C 4
Mizonokuchi, Kawasaki- 155 III a 2
Mizoram 134-135 P 6
Mizpah, MN 70-71 CD 2
Mizpah, MT 68-69 D 2
Mizque 92-93 FG 8
Mizque, Río — 104-105 D 6
Mizue, Tōkyō- 155 III c 1
Mizur = Buron 126-127 M 5
Mizusawa 142-143 QR 4
Mjanyana 174-175 GH 6
Mja'ra, el- = Al-M'jarah 166-167 D 2
M'jārah, Al- 166-167 D 2
M'jaz al-Bāb 166-167 L 1
Mjölby 116-117 F 8
Mjøsa 116-117 D 7
Mkambati 174-175 HJ 6
Mkam-Sidi-Cheikh = Maqām Sīdī Shaykh 166-167 G 2
Mkata 171 D 4
Mkhili = Al-Makīlī 164-165 J 2
Mkobela 171 D 5
Mkokotoni 171 D 4
Mkondo 174-175 J 4
Mkondoa 171 D 4
Mkonga 171 CD 4
Mkulwe 171 C 5
Mkuranga 171 D 4
Mkushi 171 B 6
Mkusi = Mkuze 174-175 K 4
Mkuze [ZA, place] 174-175 JK 4
Mkuze [ZA, river] 174-175 K 4
Mkuze Game Reserve 174-175 K 4
Mkuzi = Mkuze 174-175 JK 4
Mladá Boleslav 118 G 3
Mladenovac 122-123 J 3
Mlangali 171 C 5
Mława 118 K 2
Mlayḥān, Bi'r — 136-137 H 4
Mlcusi Bay = Kosibaai 174-175 K 4
Mligazi 171 D 4
Mljet 122-123 G 4
Mmabatho 172 DE 7
Mnevniki, Moskva- 113 V b 2
Moa [C] 88-89 J 4
Moa [WAL] 168-169 C 4
Moa, Pulau — 148-149 J 8
Moa, Rio — 96-97 E 5
Moab, UT 74-75 J 3
Mōāb, Jabal — 136-137 F 7
Moaco, Rio — 96-97 G 6
Moak Lake 61 K 2-3
Moala 148-149 a 2
Moamba 172 F 7
Moapa, NV 74-75 F 4
Moba [WAN] 170 III b 2
Moba [ZRE] 172 E 3
Mobaye 164-165 J 8
Mobeetie, TX 76-77 D 5
Moberly, MO 64-65 H 4
Moberly Lake 60 FG 2
Mobert 70-71 H 1
Mobile, AL 64-65 J 5
Mobile Bay 64-65 J 5
Mobridge, SD 68-69 FG 3
Mobutu-Sese-Seko, Lac — 172 F 1
Moca = Al-Mukhā 134-135 E 8
Mocache 96-97 B 2
Mocajuba 92-93 K 5
Močališče 124-125 R 5
Moçambique [Mozambique, place] 172 H 4-5
Moçambique [Mozambique, state] 172 F 6-G 4
Moçambique, Canal de — 172 H 6-4
Moçâmedes 172 B 5
Mo Cay 150-151 F 7-8
Mocaya, Río — 94-95 E 7
Moccasin, MT 68-69 AB 2
Môc Châu 150-151 E 2
Mocha = Al-Mukhā 134-135 E 8
Mocha, Isla — 111 B 5
Mochara, Cordillera de — 104-105 D 7
Moche 96-97 B 6
Mochis, Los — 64-65 E 6
Môc Hoa 150-151 EF 7
Möch Sar'dag uul 142-143 HJ 1
Mochudi 172 E 6
Mocidade, Serra da — 98-99 GH 4
Mocidade, Sierra da — 94-95 KL 7
Mocímboa da Praia 172 GH 4
Mocksville, NC 80-81 F 3
Moclips, WA 66-67 A 2
Mocó, Rio — 98-99 E 6
Mocoa 92-93 D 4
Mococa 102-103 J 4
Mocoduene 174-175 L 2
Moções, Rio — 98-99 O 5
Mocoretá 106-107 HJ 3
Moçoró 92-93 M 6
Mocovi 106-107 H 2
Moctezuma 86-87 F 3
Moctezuma, Río — 86-87 F 2-3
Mocuba 172 G 5
Modane 120-121 L 6
Modāsa 138-139 D 6
Modderfontein [ZA, place] 170 V bc 1
Modderfontein [ZA, river] 170 V b 1
Modderpoort 174-175 G 5
Modderrivier [ZA, place] 174-175 F 5
Modderrivier [ZA, river] 174-175 F 5
Moddi 168-169 F 2
Model, CO 68-69 DE 7
Modelia, Bogotá 91 III b 2
Mòdena 122-123 D 3
Modena, UT 74-75 FG 4
Modestino Pizarro 106-107 E 5
Modesto, CA 64-65 BC 4
Modhera 138-139 D 6
Mòdica 122-123 F 7
Modjamboli 172 D 1
Mödling [A, river] 113 I b 2
Modoc Lava Bed 66-67 C 5
Modriča 122-123 H 3
Mô Đu'c 150-151 G 5
Modur dağı 136-137 L 4
Moeda 102-103 K 4
Moeda, Serra da — 102-103 KL 4
Moedig 174-175 J 3
Moei, Mae Nam — 150-151 B 4
Moengo 92-93 J 3
Möen Island = Møn 116-117 E 10
Moenkopi Wash 74-75 H 4
Moe-Yallourn 158-159 J 7
Moffat, CO 68-69 D 6-7
Moffen 116-117 j 4
Moffett, Mount — 58-59 u 6-7
Moffit, ND 68-69 F 2
Mofolo, Johannesburg- 170 V a 2
Moga 138-139 E 2
Mogadiscio = Muqdiisho 164-165 O 8
Mogadishu = Muqdiisho 164-165 O 8
Mogador = Aṣ-Ṣawīrah 164-165 BC 2
Mogalakwenarivier 172 E 6
Mogami gawa 144-145 MN 3
Mōgaung [BUR, place] 141 E 3
Mōgaung [BUR, river] 141 E 3
Mogdy 132-133 Z 7
Mogees, PA 84 III b 1
Mogeiro 100-101 G 4
Moggar = Al-Muqqār 166-167 K 3
Moghān, Dasht-e — 134-135 F 3
Moghrane = Al-Mughrān 166-167 C 2
Moghrar = Mughrār 166-167 F 3
Mogila Bel'mak, gora — 126-127 H 3
Mogilev = Mogil'ov 124-125 GH 7
Mogil'ov 124-125 GH 7
Mogil'ov-Lupolovo 124-125 H 7
Mogil'ov-Podol'skij 126-127 CD 2
Mogincual 172 H 5
Mogna, Sierra de — 106-107 C 3
Mogoča [SU, place] 132-133 WX 7
Mogočin 132-133 P 6
Mogod = Muq'ud 166-167 L 1
Mōgōk 141 E 4
Mogol 174-175 G 2
Mogollon Mountains 74-75 J 6
Mogollon Rim 74-75 H 5
Mogororo = Mongororo 164-165 J 6
Mogotes, Cerro de los — 106-107 C 2
Mogotes, Punta — 106-107 J 7
Mogotes, Sierra de — 106-107 E 2
Mogotón, Cerro — 88-89 C 8
Moguer 120-121 D 10
Mogyichaung = Mangyichaung 141 C 5
Mogzon 132-133 V 7
Mohács 118 J 6
Mohājerān 136-137 N 5
Mohaka River 161 G 4
Mohaleshoek 174-175 G 6
Mohall, ND 68-69 F 1
Mohammadabad = Muhammadābād [IND ↓ Gorakhpoor] 138-139 J 4
Mohammadabad = Muhammadābād [IND ↗ Vārāṇasī] 138-139 J 5
Mohammadia = Muḥammadīyah 164-165 DE 1
Mohammed, Ras — = Rā's Muḥammad 164-165 LM 4
Moḥammedia = Al-Muḥammadīyah 166-167 C 3
Moḥammerah = Khorramshar 134-135 F 4
Mohana 138-139 K 8
Mohanganj 141 B 3
Mohania 138-139 J 5
Mohaniyā = Mohania 138-139 J 5
Mohanlālganj 138-139 H 4
Mohawk, AZ 74-75 G 6
Mohawk, MI 70-71 FG 2
Mohawk River 72-73 J 3
Mohe 142-143 N 1
Mohéli = Mwali 172 H 4
Mohenjodaro = Mūan-jo Daṛo 138-139 AB 4
Mohican, Cape — 56-57 C 5

Mohilla = Mwali 172 H 4
Mohindergarh = Mahendragarh 138-139 EF 3
Mohine 174-175 K 3
Mohn, Kapp — 116-117 m 5
Moho 96-97 G 9
Mo-ho = Mohe 142-143 N 1
Mohol 140 B 2
Mohon Peak 74-75 G 5
Mohoro 172 G 3
Mō Ingyī 141 E 7
Mointy 132-133 N 8
Mo i Rana 116-117 F 4
Moira River 72-73 H 2
Mõisaküla 124-125 E 4
Moisès Ville 106-107 G 3
Moisie 63 CD 2
Moisie, Baie — 63 D 2
Moisie, Rivière — 56-57 X 7
Moissac 120-121 H 6
Moïssala 164-165 H 7
Moitaco 94-95 J 4
Mojave, CA 74-75 DE 5
Mojave Desert 64-65 C 4
Mojave River 74-75 E 5
Moji das Cruzes 92-93 KL 9
Mojiguaçu 102-103 J 5
Mojiguaçu, Rio — 102-103 HJ 4
Mojimirim 102-103 J 5
Mojiquiçaba 100-101 E 9
Mojjero 132-133 T 4
Mojo, Pulau — 148-149 G 8
Mojocaya 104-105 D 6
Mojokerto 148-149 F 8
Mojón, Cerro del — 106-107 CD 5
Mojotoro 104-105 D 6
Moju 98-99 L 6
Mōka 144-145 MN 4
Mokai 158-159 P 7
Mōkakchāng = Mokokchūng 141 D 2
Mokambo 172 E 4
Mokameh 138-139 K 5
Mokane, MO 70-71 DE 6
Mokatani 174-175 F 2
Mokau River 161 F 4
Mokeetsi = Mooketsi 174-175 J 2
Mokelumne Aqueduct River 74-75 C 3-4
Mokhāda 138-139 D 8
Mokhara = Mokhāda 138-139 D 8
Mokhotlong 174-175 H 5
Mokhrīssèt = Mukhrissat 166-167 D 2
Mokil 208 F 2
Moknin, El — = Al-Muknīn 166-167 M 2
Mokochu, Khao — 150-151 B 5
Mokokchūng 141 D 2
Mokolo 164-165 G 6
Mōkpalin 141 E 7
Mokp'o 142-143 O 5
Mokraja Ol'chovka 126-127 M 1
Mokrān 134-135 HJ 5
Mokrissèt = Mukhrissat 166-167 D 2
Mokrous 124-125 Q 8
Mokša 124-125 P 7
Mokšan 124-125 P 7
Mōktama 148-149 C 3
Mōktama Kwe 148-149 C 3
Moktok-to = Kyŏngnyŏlbi-yŏlto 144-145 E 4
Mola di Bari 122-123 G 5
Mōļakkālamuruvu = Hānagal 140 C 3
Molalla, OR 66-67 B 3
Molango 86-87 L 7
Molanosa 61 F 3
Molat 122-123 F 3
Moldary 132-133 O 7
Moldavia 122-123 M 2-3
Moldavian Soviet Socialist Republic 126-127 CD 3
Moldavskaja Sovetskaja Socialističeskaja Respublika = Moldavian Soviet Socialist Republic 126-127 CD 3
Molde 116-117 B 6
Moldes = Coronel Moldes 106-107 E 4
Moldova 122-123 M 2
Moldoviţa 122-123 L 2
Mole Creek 160 bc 2
Molenbeek 128 II a 1
Molepolole 172 DE 6
Molfetta 122-123 G 5
Molière = Burj Bū Na'amah 166-167 G 2
Molina 106-107 B 5
Molina de Segura 120-121 G 9
Moline, IL 64-65 HJ 3
Moline, KS 76-77 F 4
Molinito, El — 91 I b 2
Molino, FL 78-79 F 5
Molino, El — 91 II c 2
Molino do Rosas, Villa Obregón- 91 I b 2
Molinos 104-105 C 9
Moliro 172 EF 3
Molise 122-123 F 5
Mollāhāt 138-139 M 6
Mollakendi 136-137 H 3
Mollālar 136-137 M 4
Mollem 128 II a 1
Mol Len 141 D 3
Mollendo 92-93 E 8
Mollera, zaliv — 132-133 HJ 3
Molles 106-107 J 4
Molles, Los — 106-107 BC 5
Molles, Punta — 106-107 B 4
Mölndal 116-117 DE 9
Moločansk 126-127 GH 3
Moločnoje 124-125 M 4
Moločnoje, ozero — 126-127 G 3
Molócue 172 G 5
Molodečno 124-125 F 6
Molodežnaja 53 C 5
Molodogvardejcev 132-133 N 7
Molodoj Tud 124-125 JK 5
Mologa 124-125 L 5
Molokai 148-149 e 3
Molokovo 124-125 L 4
Moloma 124-125 R 4
Molong 158-159 J 6
Molopo 172 D 7
Molotovsk = Nolinsk 132-133 HJ 6
Molotovsk = Severodvinsk 132-133 FG 5
Moloundou 164-165 H 8
Molsgat 174-175 H 3
Molson 61 K 5
Molson Lake 61 K 3
Molt, MT 68-69 B 3
Molteno [ZA] 174-175 G 6
Molu, Pulau — 148-149 K 8
Moluccas 148-149 J 6-7
Molucca Sea 148-149 HJ 7
Molundu = Moloundou 164-165 H 8
Molvoticy 124-125 HJ 5
Moma [Mozambique] 172 G 5
Moma [SU] 132-133 bc 4
Momba 171 C 5
Mombaça 100-101 E 3
Mombasa 172 GH 2
Mombetsu 142-143 R 3
Mombongo 172 D 1
Momboyo 172 C 2
Mombuca, Serra da — 102-103 FG 3
Momčilgrad 122-123 L 5
Mōmeik 141 E 4
Momence, IL 70-71 G 5
Mōminābād = Ambājogāi 134-135 M 7
Mompós 94-95 D 3
Momskij chrebet 132-133 b 4-c 5
Møn 116-117 E 10
Mona 64-65 N 8
Mona, UT 74-75 GH 3
Mona, Canal de la — 64-65 N 8
Móna, Punta — 88-89 E 10
Monaco [MC, place] 120-121 L 7
Monaco [MC, state] 120-121 L 7
Monagas 94-95 K 3
Monaghan 119 C 4
Monahans, TX 64-65 F 5
Monango, ND 68-69 G 2
Monapo 172 H 4-5
Monarāgala 140 E 7
Monarch, MT 66-67 H 2
Monarch Mount 60 E 4
Monashee Mountains 56-57 N 7
Monas National Monument 154 IV ab 2
Monasterio 106-107 J 5
Monasterio, El — 94-95 H 3
Monastir = Bitola 122-123 J 5
Monastīr, El — = Al-Manastīr 166-167 M 2
Monastyrščina 124-125 HJ 6
Monay 94-95 F 3
Monbetsu 144-145 bc 2
Monča Guba = Mončegorsk 132-133 DE 4
Monção [BR] 92-93 K 5
Mončegorsk 132-133 DE 4
Mönchaltorf 128 IV b 2
Môn Chaung 141 D 5
Mönchchaan 142-143 L 2
Mönch Chajrchan uul 142-143 FG 2
Mönchengladbach 118 BC 3
Monchique, Serra de — 120-121 C 10
Moncks Corner, SC 80-81 FG 4
Monclova 64-65 F 6
Moncton 56-57 XY 8
Mond, Rūd-e — 134-135 G 5
Mondai 102-103 F 7
Mondamin, IA 70-71 BC 5
Monday, Río — 102-103 E 6
Mondego 120-121 CD 8
Mondego, Cabo — 120-121 C 8
Mondeodo 152-153 OP 7
Mondeor, Johannesburg- 170 V ab 2
Mondo 171 CD 4
Mondoliko, Pulau — 152-153 J 9
Mondoñedo 120-121 D 7
Mondovì 122-123 BC 3
Mondovi, WI 70-71 E 3
Mondragon 120-121 K 6
Monds Island 84 III b 2
Mondulkiri 150-151 F 6
Monē 141 EF 5
Monē Dafníon 113 IV a 1
Monē Kaisarian 113 IV b 2
Monē Lávras 122-123 L 5
Monembasia 122-123 K 7
Moneron, ostrov — 132-133 b 8
Mones Cazón 106-107 FG 6
Monessen, PA 72-73 G 4
Monet 62 O 2
Moneta, VA 80-81 G 2
Moneta, WY 68-69 C 4
Monett, MO 78-79 C 2
Monfalcone 122-123 E 3
Monfort 94-95 G 7
Monforte de Lemos 120-121 D 7
Monga [EAT] 171 D 5
Monga [ZRE] 172 D 1
Mongala 172 CD 1
Mongalla = Manqalah 164-165 L 7
Möngban 141 F 5
Möngbûn 141 E 5
Mongbwalu 171 B 2
Möngbyat 148-149 CD 2
Mong Cai 150-151 FG 2
Möngdôn 148-149 C 2
Monger, Lake — 158-159 C 5
Mönggan 150-151 C 2
Mönggôk 141 F 5
Mönggöng 141 E 5
Monggŭmp'o-ri 144-145 E 3
Mong Hkok = Mönggôk 141 F 5
Mong Hsat = Möngzat 141 F 5
Mong Hsu = Möngshū 141 F 5
Monghyr 134-135 O 5
Mongkol Borey, Stung — 150-151 D 6
Möng Kung = Monggöng 141 E 5
Möngman 141 F 4
Möng Nai = Mônè 141 EF 5
Möngnaung 141 EF 5
Möng Nawng = Möngnaung 141 EF 5
Möngnôn 141 F 5
Mongo [Chad] 164-165 H 6
Mongol Altajn Nuruu 142-143 F-H 2
Mongolia 142-143 H-L 2
Mongororo 164-165 J 6
Möng Pan = Möngban 141 F 5
Möng Pawn = Möngbûn 141 E 5
Möngshū 141 F 5
Möng Si = Möngzī 141 F 4
Möng Tun = Möngdôn 148-149 C 2
Mongu 172 D 5
Monguba 100-101 E 2
Möngwi 141 E 4
Möng Yai = Möngyei 141 F 4
Möngyan 150-151 B 2
Möngyaung 141 F 5
Möng Yawn = Möngyaung 141 F 5
Möngyei 141 F 4
Möngyin 141 E 4
Möngyu 150-151 C 2
Möngzat 141 F 5
Möngzī 141 F 4
Mo Nhai 150-151 F 2
Monhegan Island 72-73 M 3
Monico, WI 70-71 F 3
Monida Pass 66-67 GH 3
Monilla = Mwali 172 H 4
Monino 124-125 M 6
Moniquirá 94-95 E 5
Monitor 61 C 5
Monitor Range 74-75 E 3
Monkoto 172 D 2
Monmouth, IL 70-71 E 5
Monmouth, OR 66-67 B 3
Mônnaung 141 F 4
Mono 164-165 E 7
Mono, Punta del — 88-89 E 9
Monod = Sīdī 'Allāl al-Baḥrāwī 166-167 CD 2
Mono Island 148-149 j 6
Mono Lake 64-65 C 4
Monomoy Point 72-73 M 4
Monon, IN 70-71 G 5
Monòpoli 122-123 G 5
Monor 118 J 5
Mōnqalla = Manqalah 164-165 L 7
Monreale 122-123 E 6
Monroe 63 K 3
Monroe, GA 80-81 DE 4
Monroe, LA 64-65 H 5
Monroe, MI 72-73 E 3-4
Monroe, NC 80-81 F 3
Monroe, OR 66-67 B 3
Monroe, UT 74-75 GH 3
Monroe, VA 80-81 G 2
Monroe, WA 66-67 C 2
Monroe, WI 70-71 F 4
Monroe City, MO 70-71 DE 6
Monroeville, AL 78-79 F 5
Monroeville, IN 70-71 H 5
Monrovia 164-165 B 7
Mons 120-121 J 3
Monsalvo 106-107 J 6
Monsefú 96-97 AB 5
Monsèlice 122-123 DE 3
Monsenhor Gil 100-101 C 3
Monsenhor Hipólito 100-101 D 4
Monsenhor Tabosa 100-101 DE 3
MOnserrate 91 III c 3
Monserrate, Isla — 86-87 E 5
Mönsterås 116-117 FG 9
Montagnac = Ramshi 166-167 F 2
Montagnana 122-123 D 3
Montagne Pelée 64-65 O 8
Montagnes, Lac des — 62 O 1
Montagnes de la Trinité 98-99 M 2
Montagne Tremblante, Parc provincial de la — 56-57 VW 8
Montagu 174-175 D 7
Montague, CA 66-67 B 5
Montague, MI 70-71 G 4
Montague, TX 76-77 EF 6
Montague Island 56-57 G 6
Montague Strait 58-59 N 7-M 6
Montain View, WY 66-67 HJ 5
Mont Ami 171 B 2
Montana 64-65 DE 2
Montana, AK 58-59 MN 5
Montaña, La — [E] 120-121 DE 7
Montaña, La — [PE] 92-93 E 5-6
Montañas de Convento 96-97 B 1-2
Montañas de Huapí 88-89 D 8
Montañas de Onzole 96-97 B 1
Montanha 100-101 D 10
Montañita, La — [CO] 94-95 D 7
Montañita, La — [YV] 94-95 F 2
Montargis 120-121 J 5
Montauban 120-121 H 6
Montauk, NY 72-73 L 4
Montauk Point 72-73 L 4
Mont aux Sources 172 E 7
Montbard 120-121 K 5
Montbéliard 120-121 L 5
Mont Blanc 120-121 L 6
Montbrison 120-121 K 6
Mont Cameroun 164-165 F 8
Mont Canigou 120-121 J 7
Montceau-les-Mines 120-121 K 5
Mont Cenis, Col du — 120-121 L 6
Montcevelles, Lac — 63 FG 2
Mont Cinto 122-123 C 4
Montclair, NJ 82 III a 2
Mont-de-Marsan 120-121 GH 7
Mont Dore 120-121 J 6
Monte, El — 104-105 D 7
Monte, Laguna de — 106-107 F 6
Monte, Laguna del — 106-107 H 5
Monte Adam = Mount Adam 111 DE 8
Monteagudo [BOL] 104-105 E 6
Monteagudo [RA] 111 F 3
Monte Águila 106-107 A 6
Monte Albán 64-65 G 8
Monte Alegre [BR, Pará] 92-93 J 5
Monte Alegre [BR, Rio Grande do Norte] 100-101 G 4
Monte Alegre de Goiás 100-101 A 7
Monte Alegre de Minas 102-103 H 3
Monte Alegre do Piauí 100-101 B 5
Monte Alegro 106-107 LM 2
Monte Alto [BR] 102-103 H 4
Monte Alto, Serra de — 100-101 C 8
Monte Amiata 122-123 D 4
Monte Antenne 113 II b 1
Monte Aprazível 102-103 GH 4
Monte Aymond 108-109 E 9
Monte Azul 92-93 L 8
Monte Azul Paulista 102-103 H 4
Montebello 72-73 J 2
Montebello, CA 83 III d 1
Montebello Islands 158-159 BC 4
Monte Belo 102-103 J 4
Montebu = Mombetsu 142-143 R 3
Monte Buey 106-107 F 4
Monte Burney 108-109 C 9
Monte Cabra 64-65 b 3
Montecarlo 102-103 E 7
Monte Carmelo 102-103 J 3
Monte Caseros 111 E 4
Monte Catedral 108-109 BC 6
Montecatini Terme 122-123 D 4
Monte Cervati 122-123 F 5
Monte Chingolo, Lanús- 110 III bc 2
Monte Cimone 122-123 D 3
Monte Circeo 122-123 E 5
Monte Comán 111 C 4
Montecoral 106-107 JK 4
Monte Creek 60 GH 4
Montecristi 96-97 A 2
Montecristo [I] 122-123 D 4
Monte Cristo [RA] 106-107 EF 3
Monte da Divisa 102-103 J 4
Monte das Araras 102-103 J 4
Monte de la Mitra 168-169 H 5
Monte de los Gauchos 106-107 F 4
Monte do Frado 102-103 K 5
Monte Etna 122-123 F 7
Monte Falterona 122-123 DE 4
Montefiascone 122-123 DE 4
Monte Fitz Roy 111 B 7
Montego Bay 64-65 L 8
Monte Grande 106-107 B 3
Monte Grande, Esteban Echeverría- 110 III b 2
Montegut, LA 78-79 D 6
Monte Hermaso 106-107 G 7
Monteiro 100-101 F 4
Monte Jervis 108-109 B 7
Montejinni 158-159 F 3
Monte Ladrillero 108-109 CD 9
Montelíbano 94-95 D 3
Montélimar 120-121 K 6
Monte Lindo, Río — 102-103 CD 5
Monte Lindo Chico, Riacho — 104-105 G 9
Monte Lindo Grande, Río — 104-105 G 9
Monte Lirio 64-65 b 2
Montell, TX 76-77 D 8
Montello, NV 66-67 F 5
Montello, WI 70-71 F 4
Monte Macá 111 B 7
Monte Maíz 106-107 F 4
Monte María = Mount Maria 108-109 K 8
Monte Mario 113 II b 1
Montemayor, Meseta de — 111 C 6-7
Monte Melimoyu 111 B 6
Monte Mentolat 108-109 C 5
Montemorelos 64-65 G 6
Montenegro [BR] 106-107 M 2
Montenegro [CO] 94-95 CD 5
Montenegro [YU] 122-123 H 4
Monte Nievas 106-107 EF 5
Montenotte-au-Ténès = Sīdī 'Ukāskah 166-167 G 1
Monte Nuestra Señora 108-109 B 7
Monte Pascoal 100-101 E 9
Monte Pascoal, Parque National de — 100-101 E 9
Monte Pecoraro 122-123 FG 6
Monte Perdido 120-121 GH 7
Monte Pinón 64-65 b 2
Monte Pissis 106-107 C 1
Monte Plata 88-89 LM 5
Montepuez [Mozambique, place] 172 GH 4
Montepuez [Mozambique, river] 171 D 6
Montepulciano 122-123 D 4
Monte Quemado 111 D 3
Monte Rasu 122-123 C 5
Monterey, CA 64-65 B 4
Monterey, TN 78-79 G 2
Monterey, VA 72-73 G 5
Monterey Bay 64-65 B 4
Monterey Park, CA 83 III d 1
Montería 92-93 D 3
Montero 92-93 G 8
Monteros 104-105 D 10
Monte Rosa 122-123 BC 2-3
Monterrey [MEX] 64-65 FG 6
Montes, Punta — 108-109 E 8
Monte Saavedra 106-107 G 3
Monte Sacro, Roma- 113 II b 1
Montes Altos 100-101 A 3
Montesano, WA 66-67 B 2
Monte Sant'Angelo 122-123 FG 5
Monte Santo 92-93 M 7
Monte Santo de Minas 102-103 J 4
Monte Sarmiento 108-109 D 10
Montes Claros 92-93 KL 8
Montes de Leon 120-121 D 7
Montes de Oca 106-107 F 7
Montes de Toledo 120-121 E 9
Monte Sião 102-103 J 5
Montespaccato, Roma- 113 II a 2
Montesquieu = Madawrūsh 166-167 K 1
Monte Stokes 108-109 C 8
Monte Torres 111 D 4
Monte Tres Conos 108-109 D 9
Monte Tronador 111 B 6
Monte Vera 106-107 G 3
Montevideo 111 EF 4-5
Montevideo, MN 70-71 BC 3
Montevideo-Santiago Vázquez 106-107 J 5
Montevideo-Villa del Cerro 106-107 J 5
Montevidiu 102-103 G 2
Monte Viso 122-123 B 3
Monte Vista, CO 68-69 C 7
Monte Volturino 122-123 FG 5
Monte Vúlture 122-123 F 5
Monte Warton 108-109 C 9
Monte Yate 108-109 C 3
Monte Zeballos 108-109 D 6
Montezuma 102-103 L 1
Montezuma, GA 80-81 DE 4
Montezuma, IA 70-71 D 5
Montezuma, IN 70-71 G 6
Montezuma, KS 68-69 F 7
Montezuma Castle National Monument 74-75 H 5
Montfermeil 129 I d 2
Mont Forel 56-57 d 4
Montfort 120-121 FG 4
Montfort, WI 70-71 E 4
Montgeron 129 I c 3
Montgolfier = Raḥūyah 166-167 G 2
Montgomery, AL 64-65 J 5
Montgomery, LA 78-79 C 5
Montgomery, MN 70-71 D 3
Montgomery, WV 72-73 F 5
Montgomery = Sāhīwāl 134-135 L 4
Montgomery City, MO 70-71 E 6
Montgomery Pass 74-75 D 3
Mont Greboun 164-165 F 4-5
Monticello, AR 78-79 D 4
Monticello, FL 80-81 E 5
Monticello, GA 80-81 E 4
Monticello, IA 70-71 E 4
Monticello, IL 70-71 F 5
Monticello, IN 70-71 G 5
Monticello, KY 78-79 G 2
Monticello, MS 78-79 DE 5
Monticello, NM 76-77 A 6
Monticello, NY 72-73 J 4
Monticello, UT 64-65 DE 4
Monticello Reservoir = Lake Berryessa 74-75 B 3
Monti del Gennargentu 122-123 C 5-6
Montiel, Cuchilla de — 106-107 H 3
Montiel, Selva de — 106-107 H 3
Montigny-le-Bretonneux 129 I b 2
Montijo 120-121 D 9
Montijo, Golfo de — 88-89 F 11
Montilla 120-121 E 10
Monti Nebrodie 122-123 F 7
Monti Peloritani 122-123 F 6-7
Monti Sabini 122-123 E 4
Mont-Joli 63 B 3
Mont Karisimbi 172 E 2
Mont-Laurier 56-57 V 8
Montluçon 120-121 J 5
Montmagny [CDN] 63 AB 4
Montmagny [F] 129 I c 2
Montmartre 61 G 5
Montmartre, Paris- 129 I c 2
Mont Mézenc 120-121 JK 6
Mont Michelson 56-57 GH 4
Montmorency [CDN] 63 A 4
Montmorillon 120-121 H 5
Mont Nimba 164-165 C 7
Monto 158-159 K 4
Mont Opémisca 62 O 1-2
Montoro 120-121 E 9
Mont Oué 168-169 HJ 4
Montoya, NM 76-77 B 5
Montparnasse, Paris- 129 I c 2
Montpelier, ID 66-67 H 4
Montpelier, OH 70-71 H 5
Montpelier, VT 64-65 M 3
Montpellier 120-121 JK 7
Mont Perry 158-159 K 5
Montréal [CDN] 56-57 VW 8
Montréal, Île de — 82 I a 2-b 1
Montréal, Université de — 82 I b 1
Montréal-Ahuntsic 82 I b 1
Montréal-Bordeaux 82 I ab 1
Montréal-Cartierville 82 I a 1
Montréal-Côte-Visitation 82 I b 1
Montréal International Airport 82 I a 2
Montreal Island 70-71 H 2
Montreal Lake [CDN, lake] 61 F 3
Montreal Lake [CDN, place] 61 F 3
Montréal-Nord 82 I b 1
Montréal-Notre-Dame-des-Victoires 82 I b 1
Montréal-Ouest 82 I ab 2
Montreal River [CDN ◁ Lake Superior] 70-71 HJ 2
Montreal River [CDN ◁ North Saskatchewan River] 61 F 3
Montreal River [CDN ◁ Ottawa River] 72-73 FG 1
Montreal River Harbour 70-71 H 2
Montréal-Saint-Michel 82 I b 1
Montréal-Sault-au-Recollet 82 I b 1
Montréal-Tétreauville 82 I b 1
Montréal-Youville 82 I ab 1
Montreuil [F → Berck] 120-121 H 3
Montreuil [F → Paris] 120-121 J 4
Montreux 118 C 5
Montrose 119 EF 3
Montrose, AR 78-79 D 4
Montrose, CO 64-65 E 4
Montrose, PA 72-73 J 4
Montrose Harbor 83 II b 1
Montross, VA 72-73 H 5
Mont Rotondo 122-123 C 4
Montrouge-Gentilly 129 I c 2
Mont Royal [CDN, mountain] 82 I b 1
Mont-Royal [CDN, place] 82 I ab 1
Mont Royal, Parc du — 82 I b 1
Mont Royal Tunnel 82 I b 1
Mont-Saint-Michel, le — 120-121 FG 4
Mont-Saint-Pont 128 II b 2
Monts Baguezane 164-165 F 5
Monts Chic-Choqs 56-57 X 8
Monts de Daïa = Jabal aḍ-Ḍāyah 166-167 F 2
Monts de Droupolé 168-169 CD 4
Monts de la Margeride 120-121 J 6
Monts de Saïda = Jabal aṣ-Ṣāyda 166-167 G 2
Monts des Ksour = Jibāl al-Quṣūr 166-167 FG 3
Monts des Nementcha = Jabal an-Namāmshah 166-167 K 2
Monts des Ouled Naïl = Jabal Awlād Nāïl 166-167 H 2
Monts de Tebessa = Jabal Tibissah 166-167 L 2
Monts de Tlemcen = Jabal Tilimsān 166-167 F 2
Monts de Zeugitane = Jabal az-Zūgītīn 166-167 L 1-2
Monts du Charolais 120-121 K 5
Monts du Forez 120-121 J 6
Monts du Hodna = Jibal al-Hudnah 166-167 J 1-2
Monts du Titeri = Jabal al-Titrī 166-167 H 1-2
Monts du Toura 168-169 D 4
Monts du Vivarais 120-121 K 6
Monts du Zab = Jibal az-Zāb 166-167 J 2
Montseny 120-121 J 8
Montserrado 168-169 C 4
Montserrat [E] 120-121 H 8
Montserrat [West Indies] 64-65 O 8
Monts Faucilles 120-121 K 5-L 4
Montsinéry 92-93 J 4
Monts Malimba 171 B 4
Monts Mandara 164-165 G 6-7
Monts Mitumba 172 E 2
Monts Mugila 172 E 3
Monts Notre Dame 56-57 WX 8
Monts Shickshock = Monts Chic-Choqs 56-57 X 8
Mont Tamgak 164-165 F 5
Mont Tembo 168-169 H 5
Mont Tremblant Provincial Park = Parc provincial de la Montagne Tremblante 56-57 VW 8
Mont Valérien 129 I b 2
Mont Ventoux 120-121 K 6
Montverde Nuovo, Roma- 113 II b 2
Mont Wright 56-57 X 7
Monument, CO 68-69 D 6
Monument, NM 76-77 C 6
Monument, OR 66-67 D 3
Monumental Hill 68-69 D 3
Monument Mount 58-59 FG 4
Monumento a Los Proceres 91 II b 2
Monument Valley 74-75 H 4
Mōnyin 141 E 3
Mōnyō 141 D 7
Monyul 141 BC 2
Mōnywā 141 D 4
Monza 122-123 C 3
Monze 172 E 5
Monzón [E] 120-121 H 8
Monzón [PE] 96-97 C 6
Mooca, Ribeirão da — 110 II b 2
Mooca, São Paulo- 110 II b 2
Moody, TX 76-77 F 7
Moody Park 85 III b 1
Mooi River = Mooirivier 174-175 HJ 5
Mooirivier [ZA, place] 174-175 HJ 5
Mooirivier [ZA, river] 174-175 J 5
Mookane 174-175 G 2
Mooketsi 174-175 J 2
Mookhorn 80-81 J 2
Moolawatana 160 DE 2-3
Moolman 174-175 J 4
Moomba 160 E 2
Moon, Altar of the — 155 II ab 2
Moonaree 160 B 3
Moonbeam 62 KL 2
Moonda Lake 158-159 H 5
Moonee Valley Racecourse 161 II b 1
Moonie 160 K 1
Moonie River 160 J 1
Moon Island 84 I c 3
Moon National Monument, Craters of the — 66-67 G 4
Moon Sound = Suur väin 124-125 D 4
Moonta 158-159 G 6
Moora 158-159 C 6
Moorabbin, Melbourne- 161 II c 2
Moorburg, Hamburg- 130 I a 2
Moorcroft, WY 68-69 D 3
Moore, ID 66-67 G 4
Moore, MT 68-69 B 2
Moore, OK 76-77 F 5
Moore, TX 76-77 E 8
Moore, Cape — 53 BC 17
Moore, Lake — 158-159 C 5
Moore Creek, AK 58-59 J 5
Mooreland, OK 76-77 E 4
Moore Park 161 I b 2
Moores 106-107 F 5
Moorestown, NJ 84 III d 2
Mooresville, IN 70-71 G 6
Mooresville, NC 80-81 F 3
Moorfleet, Hamburg- 130 I b 1
Moorhead, MN 64-65 G 2
Moorhead, MS 78-79 D 4
Moorhead, MT 68-69 CD 3
Moorreesburg 174-175 C 7
Moorwerder, Hamburg- 130 I b 2
Moorwettern 130 I a 2
Moose, WY 66-67 H 4
Moose Factory 62 LM 1
Moosehead Lake 72-73 M 2
Mooseheart Mount 58-59 M 4
Moose Jaw 56-57 P 7
Moosejaw Creek 61 F 6
Moose Lake, MN 70-71 D 2
Moose Lake [CDN, lake] 56-57 R 7
Moose Lake [CDN, place] 61 HJ 4
Mooselookmeguntic Lake 72-73 L 2
Moose Mountain Creek 61 G 6
Moose Mountain Provincial Park 61 G 6
Moose Pass, AK 58-59 N 6
Moose River [CDN, place] 62 L 1
Moose River [CDN, river] 56-57 U 7
Moosomin 61 H 5
Moosonee 56-57 U 7
Moosrivier = Mosesrivier 174-175 H 3
Mopane 174-175 HJ 2
Mopani = Mopane 174-175 HJ 2
Mopeia 172 G 5
Mopipi 172 DE 6
Mopoy 94-95 F 4
Moppo = Mokp'o 142-143 O 5
Mopti 164-165 D 6
Mōq'od = Muq'od 166-167 L 1
Moquegua [PE, administrative unit] 96-97 F 10
Moquegua [PE, place] 92-93 E 8
Moquegua, Río — 96-97 F 10
Moquehuá 106-107 H 5
Moqur 134-135 K 4
Mora, MN 70-71 D 3
Mora, NM 76-77 B 5
Mora [E] 120-121 EF 9
Mora [RFC] 164-165 G 6
Mora [S] 116-117 F 7
Mora, Cerro — 106-107 B 5
Mora, La — 106-107 D 5
Morača 122-123 H 4
Morādābād 134-135 MN 5
Morada Nova 100-101 E 3
Morafenobe 172 H 5
Morais, Serra do — 100-101 E 4
Moral, El — 76-77 D 8
Moraleda, Canal de — 111 B 6-7
Morales [CO, Bolívar] 94-95 DE 3
Morales [CO, Cauca] 94-95 C 6
Morales, Arroyo — 110 III ab 2
Moram 140 C 2
Moramanga 172 J 5
Moran, KS 70-71 C 7
Moran, MI 70-71 H 2-3
Moran, TX 76-77 E 6
Moran, WY 66-67 H 4
Morānhāt 141 D 2
Morant Point 88-89 HJ 6
Morappur 140 D 4
Morās, Punta de — 120-121 D 6-7
Morass Point 61 J 4
Moratalaz, Madrid- 113 III b 2
Moratalla 120-121 FG 9
Moratuwa 140 D 7
Moraujana 94-95 L 4
Morava [CS] 118 H 4
Morava [YU] 122-123 J 3
Moravia, IA 70-71 D 5
Morawa 158-159 C 5
Morawhanna 92-93 H 3
Moray Firth 119 DE 3
Morbi = Morvi 138-139 C 6
Morcenx 120-121 G 6
Mordāb = Mordāb-e Pahlavī 136-137 N 4
Mordāb-e Pahlavī 136-137 N 4
Mordağı 136-137 L 4
Morden 68-69 GH 1
Morden, London- 129 II b 2
Mordino 124-125 S 3
Mordovian Autonomous Soviet Socialist Republic = 5 ◁ 132-133 H 7
Mordovo 124-125 N 7
Mordovskaja Avtonomnaja Sovetskaja Socialističeskaja Respublika = Mordovian Autonomous Soviet Socialist Republic 132-133 H 7
Mordovskij zapovednik 124-125 O 6
More, Ben — [GB, Mull] 119 C 3
More, Ben — [GB, Outer Hebrides] 119 C 3
Morea = Pelopónnēsos 122-123 JK 7
More Assynt, Ben — 119 DE 2

Moreau River 68-69 F 3
Moreau River, North Fork — 68-69 E 3
Moreau River, South Fork — 68-69 E 3
Morecambe Bay 119 E 4-5
Moree 158-159 J 5
Morehead, KY 72-73 E 5
Morehead City, NC 80-81 H 3
Morehouse, MO 78-79 E 2
Moreland, ID 66-67 G 4
Morelia 64-65 F 8
Morella [AUS] 158-159 H 4
Morella [E] 120-121 GH 8
Morelos [MEX, administrative unit] 64-65 G 8
Morelos [MEX, place Coahuila] 76-77 D 8
Morelos [MEX, place Zacatecas] 86-87 J 6
Morelos, Ciudad de México- 91 I c 2
Morena 138-139 G 4
Morenci, AZ 74-75 J 6
Morenci, MI 70-71 H 5
Moreno [BR] 92-93 M 6
Moreno [RA] 110 III a 1
Moreno, Bahía — 104-105 A 8
Moreno, Cerro — 106-107 K 1
Moreno, Sierra de — 104-105 B 7
Moreno-Mariano Moreno 110 III a 1
Moreno-Paso del Rey 110 III a 1
Møre og Romsdal 116-117 BC 6
Morerú, Río — 98-99 J 10
Moresby Channel 176 a 1
Moresby Island 56-57 K 7
Moreses, Pulau — 152-153 L 8
Mores Isle 88-89 GH 1
Moreton 158-159 H 2
Moreton Bay 160 L 1
Moreton Island 158-159 K 5
Mörfelden, Staatsforst — 128 III a 1
Mórfu 136-137 E 5
Mórfu, Kólpos — 136-137 E 5
Morgan 158-159 GH 6
Morgan, TX 76-77 F 6
Morgan City, LA 78-79 D 6
Morganfield, KY 70-71 G 7
Morgan Hill, CA 74-75 C 4
Morgan Park, Chicago-, IL 83 II ab 2
Morganton, NC 80-81 F 3
Morgantown, IN 70-71 G 6
Morgantown, KY 70-71 G 7
Morgantown, WV 72-73 FG 5
Morgat 120-121 E 4
Morgenzon 174-175 HJ 4
Morguilla, Punta — 106-107 A 6
Morhân, el — = Al-Mughrân 166-167 C 2
Morhar 138-139 K 5
Mori [J] 144-145 b 2
Mori [RI] 148-149 H 7
Mori = Kusu 144-145 H 6
Moriah, Mount — 74-75 FG 3
Moriarty, NM 76-77 AB 5
Morib 150-151 C 11
Moribaya 168-169 C 3
Morice Lake 60 D 2
Morice River 60 D 2
Moricetown 60 D 2
Morichal 94-95 F 4
Moricha Largo, Río — 94-95 K 3
Morija 174-175 G 5
Moriki 168-169 G 2
Morillo 104-105 E 8
Morin Creek 61 D 3-4
Morinville 60 KL 3
Morioka 142-143 R 4
Morisset 160 K 4
Morita, La — 76-77 B 8
Morizane = Yamakuni 144-145 H 6
Morjärv 116-117 K 4
Morkoka 132-133 V 4
Morlaix 120-121 F 4
Morland, KS 68-69 FG 6
Morley 60 K 4
Mormon Range 74-75 F 4
Morningside 170 V b 1
Morningside, MD 82 II b 2
Morningside, Atlanta-, GA 85 II bc 2
Mornington, Isla — 111 A 7
Mornington Island 158-159 G 3
Morno 168-169 E 3
Moro, OR 66-67 C 3
Moro, El — 106-107 H 7
Morobe 148-149 N 8
Morocco 164-165 C 3-D 2
Morochata 104-105 C 5
Morococha 96-97 CD 7
Morogoro 172 G 3
Moro Gulf 148-149 H 5
Morokwen = Morokweng 172 D 7
Morokweng 172 D 7
Moroleón 86-87 K 7
Morombe 172 H 6
Morón [C] 64-65 L 7
Mörön [Mongolia] 142-143 J 2
Morón [RA] 111 E 4
Morón [YV] 94-95 G 2
Morona 96-97 C 3
Morona, Río — 92-93 D 5
Morona Santiago 96-97 BC 3
Morón-Castelar 110 III ab 1
Morondava 172 H 6
Morón de la Frontera 120-121 E 10
Morón-El Palomar 110 III b 1
Morón-Hurlingham 110 III b 1
Moroni 172 H 4
Moroni, UT 74-75 H 3
Morón-Ituzaingó 110 III b 1
Morón-Mariano J. Haedo 110 III b 1
Moróno, Arroyo — 110 III b 1
Mörönus 142-143 G 5
Morotai, Pulau — 148-149 J 6
Moroto [EAU, mountain] 171 C 2
Moroto [EAU, place] 172 F 1
Morozovsk 126-127 KL 2
Morpará 100-101 C 6
Morpeth 119 F 4
Morphou = Mórfu 136-137 E 5
Morphou Bay = Kólpos Mórfu 136-137 E 5
Morra, Djebel — = Jabal Murrah 166-167 L 2
Morra, Hassi — = Ḥāssī Murrah 166-167 EF 4
Morrelganj 141 A 4
Morrestown Mall 84 III d 2
Morretes 102-103 H 6
Morrilton, AR 78-79 C 3
Morrinhos 100-101 DE 2
Morrinsville 158-159 OP 7
Morris 62 A 3
Morris, IL 70-71 F 5
Morris, MN 70-71 BC 3
Morris = Ban Mahdī 166-167 KL 1
Morris Brown College 85 II b 2
Morrisburg 72-73 J 2
Morris Jesup, Kap — 52 A 19-23
Morrison 106-107 F 4
Morrison, IL 70-71 EF 5
Morrison Canal 85 I bc 1
Morris Park 84 III a 2
Morristown, SD 68-69 EF 3
Morristown, TN 64-65 K 4
Morro, El — 106-107 E 4
Morroa 94-95 D 3
Morro Agudo 102-103 HJ 4
Morro Cacitúa 108-109 C 4
Morro da Boa Vista 102-103 K 5
Morro da Igreja 102-103 H 8
Morro d'Anta 100-101 DE 10
Morro das Flores 100-101 D 7
Morro da Taquara 110 I b 2
Morro de Puercos 88-89 FG 11
Morro do Caricó 110 I b 2
Morro do Chapéu 100-101 C 8
Morro do Chapéu [BR, place] 100-101 D 6
Morro do Cochrane 110 I b 2
Morro do Tabuleiro 102-103 H 7
Morro Grande 92-93 HJ 5
Morro Inácio Dias 110 I ab 2
Morro Iquiri 102-103 H 7
Mórrope 96-97 A 4-5
Morro Peñón 106-107 B 4
Morro Quatro Irmãos 104-105 F 5
Morros [BR, Bahia] 100-101 D 7
Morros [BR, Maranhão] 92-93 L 5
Morro Selado 102-103 JK 5
Morrosquillo, Golfo de — 92-93 D 2-3
Morrumbala 172 G 5
Morrumbene 172 G 6
Mors 116-117 C 9
Moršansk 124-125 NO 7
Mörsbacher Grund 128 III ab 2
Morse, TX 76-77 D 4
Mōrshī = Morsi 138-139 FG 7
Morsi 138-139 FG 7
Morsott = Mūrsuṭ 166-167 L 2
Mortandade, Cachoeira — 98-99 P 8
Mortara 122-123 C 3
Morteros 111 D 4
Mortes, Rio das — 102-103 K 4
Mortimer 174-175 F 7
Mortlake 160 F 7
Mortlock Islands 208 F 2
Morton, MN 70-71 C 3
Morton, PA 84 III b 2
Morton, TX 76-77 C 6
Mortugaba 100-101 C 8
Morumbi, São Paulo- 110 II a 2
Morundah 160 GH 5
Moruya 158-159 K 7
Morvan 120-121 K 5
Morven 158-159 J 5
Morvi 138-139 C 6
Morwell 158-159 J 7
Morzhovoi Bay 58-59 b 2
Moržovec, ostrov — 132-133 GH 4
Moša 124-125 N 2-3
Mosal'sk 124-125 K 6
Mosby, MT 68-69 C 2
Moschâton 113 IV a 2
Moščnyj, ostrov — 124-125 FG 4
Mosconi 106-107 G 5
Moscos, Mid — = Maungmagan Kyûnzu 150-151 A 5
Moscos, Southern — = Launglônbôk Kyûnzu 150-151 A 6
Moscovo = Moskva [SU, place] 132-133 F 6
Moscovo = Moskva [SU, river] 124-125 K 6
Moscow, ID 66-67 C 2
Moscow, KS 68-69 F 7
Moscow = Moskva 132-133 F 6
Mosēdis 124-125 CD 5
Mosel 118 C 4
Moselle 120-121 L 4
Mošenskoje 124-125 K 4
Mosera = Jazirat al-Maṣīrah 134-135 H 6
Mosera Bay = Khalīj al-Maṣīrah 134-135 H 6-7
Moses, NM 76-77 C 4
Moses Lake 66-67 D 2
Moses Lake, WA 66-67 D 2
Moses Point, AK 58-59 F 4
Mosesrivier 174-175 H 3
Mosetenes, Cordillera de — 104-105 C 5
Mosgiel 161 CD 7
Moshi [EAT] 172 G 2
Moshi [WAN] 168-169 G 3
Mosimane 174-175 D 3
Mosinee, WI 70-71 F 3
Mosi-Oa-Toenja 172 DE 5
Mosjøen 116-117 E 5
Moskal'vo 132-133 b 7
Moskenesøy 116-117 EF 4
Moskovskaja vozvyšennost 124-125 K-M 5-6
Moskva [SU, place] 132-133 F 6
Moskva [SU, river] 124-125 K 6
Moskva-Aminjevo 113 V b 3
Moskva-Babuškin 124-125 LM 5-6
Moskva-Bat'unino 113 V c 3
Moskva-Beskudnikovo 113 V bc 2
Moskva-Bir'ulovo 124-125 LM 6
Moskva-Bogorodskoje 113 V cd 2
Moskva-Borisovo 113 V cd 3
Moskva-Bratcevo 113 V ab 2
Moskva-Bratejevo 113 V cd 3
Moskva-Čerkizovo 113 V c 2
Moskva-Čer'omuski 113 V bc 3
Moskva-Čertanovo 113 V bc 3
Moskva-Chimki-Chovrino 113 V b 2
Moskva-Chorošovo 113 V b 2
Moskva-D'akovskoje 113 V c 3
Moskva-Davydkovo 113 V b 3
Moskva-Degunino 113 V b 2
Moskva-Derevlevo 113 V b 3
Moskva-Fili-Mazilovo 113 V b 3
Moskva-Goljanovo 113 V d 2
Moskva-Ivanovskoje 113 V d 2
Moskva-Izmajlovo 113 V d 2
Moskva-Jasenevo 113 V b 3
Moskva-Jugo-Zapad 113 V b 3
Moskva-Kapotn'a 113 V d 3
Moskva-Karačarovo 113 V cd 3
Moskva-Kolomenskoje 113 V c 3
Moskva-Kožuchovo 113 V c 3
Moskva-Krasnookt'abr'skij 113 V b 2
Moskva-Krasnyj Stroitel 113 V c 3
Moskva-Krylatskoje 113 V ab 2
Moskva-Kuncevo 124-125 L 6
Moskva-Kuskovo 113 V d 3
Moskva-Kuz'minki 113 V cd 3
Moskva-Lenino 113 V c 3
Moskva-Lianozovo 113 V c 2
Moskva-L'ublino 113 V cd 3
Moskva-Lužniki 113 V b 3
Moskva-Matvejevskoje 113 V b 3
Moskva-Medvedkovo 113 V c 2
Moskva-Mnevniki 113 V b 2
Moskva-Nagatino 113 V c 3
Moskva-Nikol'skoje 113 V b 3
Moskva-Nikulino 113 V b 3
Moskva-Novochovrino 113 V b 2
Moskva-Novogirejevo 113 V cd 2
Moskva-Novyje Kuz'minki 113 V cd 3
Moskva-Očakovo 113 V b 3
Moskva-Ostankino 113 V c 2
Moskva-Perovo 124-125 LM 6
Moskva-Petrovsko-Razumovskoje 113 V b 2
Moskva-Pokrovskoje 113 V c 3
Moskva-Pokrovsko-Strešnevo 113 V b 2
Moskva-Ramenka 113 V b 3
Moskva-Rostokino 113 V c 2
Moskva-Saburovo 113 V c 3
Moskva-Sadovniki 113 V c 3
Moskva-Serebr'anyj Bor 113 V ab 2
Moskva-Strogino 113 V ab 2
Moskva-Tatarovo 113 V ab 2
Moskva-Tekstil'ščiki 113 V c 3
Moskva-Toplyj Stan 113 V b 3
Moskva-Troice-Lykovo 113 V a 2
Moskva-Tusino 113 V b 2
Moskva-Uzkoje 113 V b 3
Moskva-Vešn'ak 113 V d 3
Moskva-Vychino 113 V d 3
Moskva-Zil 113 V c 3
Moskva-Z'uzino 113 V b 3
Moskvy, kanal — 124-125 L 5
Moskvy, Kanal im. — 113 V b 2
Mosman, Sydney- 161 I b 1
Mosmota 106-107 D 4
Mosolovo 124-125 N 6
Mosonmagyaróvár 118 HJ 5
Mospino 126-127 HJ 3
Mosquera 92-93 D 4
Mosquero, NM 76-77 BC 5
Mosquitia 64-65 K 8
Mosquito, Rio — 102-103 M 1-2
Mosquito Lagoon 80-81 c 2
Mosquitos, Costa de — 64-65 K 9
Mosquitos, Golfo de los — 64-65 K 10
Moss 116-117 D 8
Mossaka 172 C 2
Mossâmedes 102-103 GH 2
Mossbank 61 EF 6
Mosselbaai 172 D 8
Mossendjo 172 B 2
Mossi 164-165 D 6
Mossleigh 61 B 5
Mossman 158-159 HJ 3
Moss Point, MS 78-79 E 5
Moss Town 88-89 J 2
Mossul = Al-Mūṣil 134-135 E 3
Moss Vale 158-159 JK 6
Mossy River 61 G 3
Most 118 F 3
Mostaganem = Mustaghānam 164-165 DE 1
Mostar 122-123 GH 4
Mostardas 111 D 4
Mostardas, Lagoa de — 106-107 M 3
Mostardas, Ponta de — 106-107 M 3
Mosteiro 110 I bc 2
Mostiska 126-127 A 2
Mostva 124-125 F 8
Mosty 124-125 E 7
Mosul = Al-Mūṣil 134-135 E 3
Mosŭlp'o 144-145 EF 6
Mota 164-165 M 6
Motaba 172 C 1
Motacucito 104-105 F 5
Motagua, Río — 86-87 Q 10
Motala 116-117 F 8
Motalerivier 174-175 J 2
Motatán, Río — 94-95 F 3
Moth 138-139 G 5
Mother and Child = Nui Vong Phu 150-151 G 6
Mother Brook 84 I ab 3
Mother Goose Lake 58-59 e 1
Motherwell and Wishaw 119 DE 4
Motīhāri 134-135 NO 5
Motley, MN 70-71 C 2
Motocuruña 94-95 J 5
Motoichiba = Fuji 144-145 M 5
Motol' 124-125 E 7
Motomachi, Yokohama- 155 III a 3
Motomiya 144-145 N 4
Motovskij zaliv 116-117 PQ 3
Motril 120-121 F 10
Mott, ND 68-69 E 2
Mottinger, WA 66-67 D 2-3
Mottingham, London- 129 II c 2
Motueka 161 E 5
Motul de Felipe Carillo Puerto 64-65 J 7
Mōṭuṇ Raṇ = Rann of Kutch 134-135 KL 6
Motupe 96-97 B 5
Motygino 132-133 RS 6
Motyklejka 132-133 c 6
Mouchalagane, Rivière — 63 B 2
Mouḥīṭ, Baḥr el — = Al-Baḥr al-Muḥīṭ 166-167 A 4-B 2
Mouila 172 B 2
Mouilah = Mwīlaḥ 166-167 C 5
Mouka 164-165 J 7
Moulamein 158-159 HJ 6-7
Moulamein Creek 158-159 HJ 7
Moulapamok 150-151 EF 5
Moûlây Boû Chtâ' = Mūlāy Bū Shtā' 166-167 D 2
Moûlây Boû Selhâm = Mūlāy Bū Salhām 166-167 C 2
Moûlây Idrîss = Mūlāy Idrīs Zarahūn 166-167 D 2-3
Moulay-Slissen = Mūlāy Salīsan 166-167 F 2
Mould Bay 56-57 MN 2
Moulins 120-121 J 5
Moulmein = Maulamyaing 148-149 C 3
Moulmeingyun = Maulamyainggyūn 141 D 7
Moulouŷa, Ouèd — = Wād Mūlūyā 164-165 D 2
Moulton, AL 78-79 F 3
Moulton, IA 70-71 D 5
Moultrie, GA 64-65 K 5
Moultrie, Lake — 80-81 F 4
Mound City, IL 70-71 F 7
Mound City, KS 70-71 C 6
Mound City, MO 70-71 C 5
Mound City, SD 68-69 FG 3
Moundou 164-165 H 7
Moundsville, WV 72-73 F 5
Moundville, AL 78-79 F 4
Moung 148-149 D 4
Moungali, Brazzaville- 170 IV a 1
Mount, Cape — 168-169 C 4
Mount Adam 111 DE 8
Mount Adams 64-65 B 2
Mountain, WI 70-71 F 3
Mountainair, NM 76-77 A 5
Mountain City, NV 66-67 F 5
Mountain City, TN 80-81 EF 2
Mountain Grove, MO 78-79 C 2
Mountain Home, AR 78-79 C 2
Mountain Home, ID 66-67 F 4
Mountain Park 60 J 3
Mountain Park, OK 76-77 E 5
Mountain Pine, AR 78-79 C 3
Mountain View, AR 78-79 CD 3
Mountain View, GA 85 II b 3
Mountain View, HI 78-79 e 3
Mountain View, MO 78-79 D 2
Mountain View, OK 76-77 E 5
Mountain Village, AK 56-57 D 5
Mount Airy, NC 80-81 F 2
Mount Airy, Philadelphia-, PA 84 III b 1
Mount Albert Markham 53 AB 17-15
Mount Alida 174-175 J 5
Mount Allen 58-59 QR 5
Mount Aloysius 158-159 E 5
Mount Alverno, PA 84 III a 2
Mount Alverstone 58-59 S 6
Mount Ambition 58-59 W 8
Mount Amherst 158-159 E 3
Mount Amundsen 53 BC 11
Mount Apo 148-149 HJ 5
Mount Arkell 58-59 U 6
Mount Ashland 66-67 B 4
Mount Aspid 58-59 n 4
Mount Aspiring 158-159 N 8
Mount Assiniboine 56-57 NO 7
Mount Auburn Cemetery 84 I b 2
Mount Augustus 158-159 C 4
Mount Ayliff = Maxesibeni 174-175 H 6
Mount Ayr, IA 70-71 CD 5
Mount Baker 66-67 C 1
Mount Baldy 66-67 H 2
Mount Bamboulos 168-169 H 4
Mount Barker 158-159 C 6
Mount Barrington 158-159 K 6
Mount Batchawana 70-71 H 2
Mount Behn 158-159 E 3
Mount Benedict Cemetery 84 I a 3
Mount Berlin 53 B 23
Mount Binga 172 F 5
Mount Blackburn 56-57 H 5
Mount Bogong 158-159 J 7
Mount Bona 58-59 QR 6
Mount Bonaparte 66-67 D 1
Mount Brazeau 60 J 3
Mount Brockman 158-159 C 4
Mount Brooks 58-59 MN 5
Mount Brown 53 BC 9
Mount Bruce 158-159 C 4
Mount Brukkaros = Groot Brukkaros 172 C 7
Mount Buller 160 H 6
Mount Burgess 58-59 S 3
Mount Callahan 74-75 E 3
Mount Cameron 155 I ab 2
Mount Carleton 63 C 4
Mount Carmel, IL 70-71 FG 6
Mount Carmel, PA 72-73 H 4
Mount Carmel, UT 74-75 G 4
Mount Caroline Livermore 83 I b 1
Mount Caroll, IL 70-71 EF 4
Mount Chamberlin 58-59 P 2
Mount Chiginagak 58-59 e 1
Mount Cleveland 66-67 D 2
Mount Collins 62 L 3
Mount Collinson 155 I b 2
Mount Columbia 56-57 N 7
Mount Conner 158-159 F 5
Mount Cook [NZ] 158-159 NO 8
Mount Cook [USA] 58-59 RS 6
Mount Cowen 66-67 H 3
Mount Crillon 58-59 T 7
Mount Crysdale 60 F 2
Mount Dalgaranger 158-159 C 5
Mount Dall 58-59 LM 5
Mount Dalrymple 158-159 J 4
Mount Dana 74-75 D 4
Mount Darwin 172 F 5
Mount Deborah 58-59 O 5
Mount Deering 158-159 E 5
Mount Denison 58-59 KL 7
Mount Desert Island 72-73 MN 2
Mount Doonerak 56-57 FG 4
Mount Dora, FL 80-81 c 2
Mount Dora, NM 76-77 C 4
Mount Douglas 58-59 KL 7
Mount Douglas [AUS] 158-159 J 4
Mount Downton 60 E 3
Mount Draper 58-59 S 7
Mount Dutton 74-75 G 3-4
Mount Dutton [AUS] 160 BC 1
Mount Edgecumbe, AK 58-59 v 8
Mount Egmont 158-159 O 7
Mount Eisenhower 60 K 4
Mount Elbert 64-65 E 4
Mount Elgon 172 F 1
Mount Ellen 74-75 H 3
Mount Elliot = Selwyn 158-159 H 4
Mount Elliot Cemetery 84 II b 2
Mount Enid 158-159 C 4
Mount Ephraim, NJ 84 III c 2
Mount Erebus 53 B 17-18
Mount Essendon 158-159 D 4
Mount Etna = Mazui Ling 150-151 G 3
Mount Evans [CDN] 60 J 5
Mount Evans [USA, Colorado] 68-69 D 6
Mount Evans [USA, Montana] 66-67 G 2
Mount Everest = Sagarmatha 142-143 F 6
Mount Everett 72-73 K 3
Mount Faber 154 III a 2
Mount Fairweather 56-57 J 6
Mount Fletcher 174-175 H 6
Mount Floyd 74-75 G 5
Mount Foraker 56-57 F 5
Mount Forbes 60 J 4
Mount Forest 72-73 F 2-3
Mount Franklin 161 E 6
Mount Frere = Kwabhaca 174-175 H 6
Mount Gambier 158-159 GH 7
Mount Garnet 158-159 HJ 3
Mount Gascoyne 158-159 C 4
Mount Gerdine 56-57 F 5
Mount Gilbert 58-59 o 3
Mount Gilead, OH 72-73 E 4
Mount Giluwe 148-149 M 8
Mount Godwin Austen = K2 134-135 M 3
Mount Goldsworthy 158-159 CD 4
Mount Graham 64-65 DE 5
Mount Grant [USA, Clan Alpine Mountains] 74-75 DE 3
Mount Grant [USA, Wassuk Range] 74-75 D 3
Mount Greenwood, Chicago-, IL 83 II a 2
Mount Greylock 72-73 K 3
Mount Hack 158-159 G 6
Mount Hagen 148-149 M 8
Mount Haig 66-67 F 1
Mount Hale 158-159 C 5
Mount Hamilton 74-75 F 3
Mount Hann 158-159 E 3
Mount Harper [CDN] 58-59 RS 4
Mount Harper [USA] 58-59 PQ 4
Mount Harvard 68-69 C 6
Mount Hawkes 53 A 32-33
Mount Hay 58-59 T 7
Mount Hayes 56-57 G 5
Mount Hebron, CA 66-67 BC 5
Mount Helen 74-75 E 4
Mount Henry 66-67 F 1
Mount Hickman 58-59 x 8
Mount Holly, NJ 72-73 J 4-5
Mount Holmes 66-67 H 3
Mount Hood 64-65 B 2
Mount Hope, WV 80-81 F 2
Mount Hope [AUS, New South Wales] 160 GH 4
Mount Hope [AUS, South Australia] 158-159 FG 6
Mount Hope Cemetery 84 I b 3
Mount Horeb, WI 70-71 F 4
Mount Houston, TX 85 III b 1
Mount Hubbard 56-57 J 5
Mount Humboldt 158-159 N 4
Mount Humphreys 74-75 D 4
Mount Huxley 58-59 R 6
Mount Intersection 60 G 3
Mount Isa 158-159 G 4
Mount Isto 58-59 Q 2
Mount Jacques Cartier 63 D 3
Mount Jāpvo 141 CD 3
Mount Jefferson [USA, Nevada] 74-75 E 3
Mount Jefferson [USA, Oregon] 66-67 C 3
Mount Joffre 60 K 4
Mount Judge Haway 66-67 BC 1
Mount Kalankpa 168-169 F 3
Mount Kaputar 160 JK 3
Mount Katahdin 64-65 MN 2
Mount Katmai 56-57 F 6
Mount Kelly 58-59 EF 2
Mount Kennedy 56-57 J 5
Mount Kenya 172 G 1-2
Mount Kenya National Park 171 D 3
Mount Kimball 58-59 PQ 5
Mount Klotz 58-59 R 4
Mount Kosciusko 158-159 J 7
Mount Laurel 84 III d 2
Mount Laurel, NJ 84 III d 2
Mount Lavinia, Dehiwala- 134-135 M 9
Mount Leisler 158-159 EF 4
Mount Lemmon 74-75 H 6
Mount Levick 53 B 16-17
Mount Lincoln 68-69 CD 6
Mount Linn 66-67 B 5
Mount Lister 53 B 17
Mount Livermore 64-65 F 5
Mount Lodge 58-59 T 7
Mount Lofty Range 158-159 G 6
Mount Logan [CDN, Quebec] 63 C 3
Mount Logan [CDN, Yukon Territory] 56-57 HJ 5
Mount Lola 74-75 C 3
Mount Lovenia 66-67 H 5
Mount Lucania 56-57 HJ 5
Mount Lyell 160 b 2
Mount MacGuire 66-67 F 3
Mount MacKinley 56-57 F 5
Mount MacKinley National Park 56-57 FG 5
Mount Madley 158-159 D 4
Mount Mageik 58-59 K 7
Mount Magnet 158-159 C 5
Mount Manara 158-159 H 6
Mount Manenguba 168-169 H 4
Mount Mantalingajan 148-149 G 5
Mount Marcus Baker 56-57 G 5
Mount Marcy 72-73 JK 2
Mount Maria 108-109 K 8
Mount Markham 53 A 15-16
Mount Marshall 72-73 G 5
Mount Marvine 74-75 H 3
Mount Maunganui 161 G 3
Mount Menzie 58-59 V 6
Mount Menzies 53 B 6-7
Mount Middleton 62 N 1
Mount Miller 58-59 QR 6
Mount Mitchell 64-65 K 4
Mount Moffett 58-59 u 6-7
Mount Morgan 158-159 K 4
Mount Moriah 74-75 FG 3
Mount Morris, MI 70-71 HJ 4
Mount Morris, NY 72-73 H 3
Mount Mulanje 172 G 5
Mount Mulligan 158-159 H 3
Mount Mumpu 171 B 6
Mount Mussali = Muṣa Ali 164-165 N 6
Mount Myenmoletkhat = Myinmôylet'hkat Taung 150-151 B 6
Mount Napier 158-159 EF 3
Mount Nebo 74-75 H 3
Mount Needham 60 A 3
Mount Nesselrode 58-59 UV 7
Mount Nyiru 172 G 1
Mount Ogden 58-59 V 7
Mount Olga 158-159 EF 5
Mount Olive, NC 80-81 G 3
Mount Olivet Cemetery 84 II bc 2
Mount Olympus 66-67 B 2
Mount Ossa 158-159 J 8
Mount-Owen 161 E 5
Mount Paget 111 J 8
Mount Palgrave 158-159 C 4
Mount Panié 158-159 M 4
Mount Parker 155 I b 2
Mount Pattullo 60 C 1
Mount Peale 64-65 DE 4
Mount Picton 160 bc 3
Mount Pinos 74-75 D 5
Mount Pisgah 66-67 C 3
Mount Pleasant 80-81 G 2
Mount Pleasant, IA 70-71 E 5
Mount Pleasant, MI 70-71 H 4
Mount Pleasant, TN 78-79 F 3
Mount Pleasant, TX 76-77 G 6
Mount Pleasant, UT 74-75 H 3
Mount Plummer 58-59 GH 6
Mount Pulog 148-149 H 3
Mount Queen Bess 60 E 4
Mount Queen Mary 58-59 S 6
Mount Rainier 64-65 BC 2
Mount Rainier, MD 82 II b 1
Mount Rainier National Park 66-67 C 2
Mount Ratz 58-59 VW 8
Mount Remarkable 158-159 G 6
Mount Revelstoke National Park 60 HJ 4
Mount Rex 53 B 29
Mount Riley, NM 76-77 A 7
Mount Ritter 64-65 C 4
Mount Robe 160 E 3
Mount Robson 56-57 N 7
Mount Robson [CDN, place] 60 H 3
Mount Robson Provincial Park 60 H 3
Mount Roraima 92-93 G 3
Mount Rover 58-59 R 3
Mount Royal, NJ 84 III b 3
Mount Russell 58-59 LM 5
Mount Saint Elias 56-57 H 5
Mount Saint Helens 66-67 BC 2
Mount Salisbury 58-59 O 2
Mount Samuel 158-159 F 3
Mount Sanford 58-59 Q 5
Mount Scott [USA → Crater Lake] 64-65 B 3
Mount Scott [USA ↓ Pengra Pass] 66-67 BC 4
Mount Shasta 64-65 B 3
Mount Shasta, CA 66-67 B 5
Mount Shenton 158-159 D 5
Mount Sheridan 66-67 H 3
Mount Sidley 53 B 24
Mount Singleton 158-159 F 4
Mount Siple 53 B 24
Mount Sir Alexander 60 GH 2
Mount Sir James MacBrien 56-57 KL 5
Mount Sir Sanford 60 J 4
Mount Sir Thomas 158-159 EF 5
Mount Sir Wilfrid Laurier 60 GH 3
Mount Snowy 72-73 J 3
Mount Spranger 60 G 3
Mount Springer 62 O 2
Mount Spurr 58-59 LM 6
Mount Stanley 158-159 F 4
Mount Steele 58-59 RS 6
Mount Steller 58-59 Q 6
Mount Stenhouse 155 I a 2
Mount Sterling, IL 70-71 E 6
Mount Stewart 63 E 4
Mount Stimson 66-67 G 1
Mount Stokes 161 EF 5
Mount Sturt 158-159 H 5
Mount Swan 158-159 G 4
Mount Sylvester 63 J 3
Mount Takahe 53 B 25-26
Mount Talbot 158-159 E 5
Mount Tamboritha 160 H 6
Mount Tasman 161 CD 6
Mount Tatlow 60 F 4
Mount Taylor 76-77 A 5
Mount Tenabo 66-67 E 5
Mount Thielsen 66-67 BC 4
Mount Thynne 66-67 C 1
Mount Tipton 74-75 F 5
Mount Tobin 66-67 E 5
Mount Tom Price 158-159 C 4
Mount Tom White 58-59 PQ 6
Mount Torbert 58-59 LM 6
Mount Travers 161 E 5-6
Mount Trumbull 74-75 G 4
Mount Tutoko 161 BC 7
Mount Union 74-75 G 5
Mount Union, PA 72-73 H 4
Mount Usborne 111 E 8
Mount Vancouver 58-59 RS 6
Mount Veniaminof 58-59 d 1
Mount Vernon, GA 80-81 E 4
Mount Vernon, IA 70-71 E 5
Mount Vernon, IL 64-65 J 4
Mount Vernon, IN 70-71 FG 7
Mount Vernon, KY 70-71 H 7
Mount Vernon, NY 72-73 K 4
Mount Vernon, OH 72-73 E 4
Mount Vernon, OR 66-67 D 3
Mount Vernon, TX 76-77 G 6
Mount Vernon, WA 66-67 BC 1
Mount Victoria 148-149 N 8
Mount Victoria = Tomaniive 148-149 a 2
Mount Victory, OH 72-73 E 4
Mount Vinson 53 B 28
Mount Vsevidof 58-59 m 4
Mount Waddington 56-57 LM 7
Mount Washington 64-65 M 3
Mount Watt 158-159 E 5
Mount Waverley, Melbourne- 161 II c 2
Mount Weber 60 C 2
Mount Whaleback 158-159 CD 4
Mount Whewell 53 B 17-18
Mount Whipple 60 B 1
Mount Whitney 64-65 C 4
Mount Wilhelm 148-149 M 8
Mount Will 58-59 X 8
Mount Willibert 60 B 1
Mount Willoughby 158-159 F 5
Mount Wilson 68-69 BC 7
Mount Witherspoon 58-59 O 6
Mount Wood [CDN] 58-59 R 6
Mount Wood [USA] 66-67 J 3
Mount Woodroffe 158-159 F 5
Mount Wrangell 58-59 P 5
Mount Wrightson 74-75 H 7
Mount Wrottesley 66-67 B 1
Mount Yenlo 58-59 M 5
Mount Ziel 158-159 F 4
Mount Zirkel 68-69 C 5
Mouping = Muping 146-147 H 3
Moura [AUS] 158-159 JK 4
Moura [BR] 92-93 G 5
Moura [P] 120-121 D 9
Moura, Rio — 96-97 E 5-6
Mourão 120-121 D 9
Mourdi, Dépression du — 164-165 J 5
Mourdiah 164-165 C 6
Mouslimiyé = Muslimīyah 136-137 G 4
Moussoro 164-165 H 6
Moussy 106-107 H 2
Mouths of the Ganga 134-135 OP 6
Mouths of the River Niger 164-165 F 7-8

Moutiers 120-121 L 6
Moutohora 158-159 P 7
Moutong = Mautong 148-149 H 6
Moutsamoudou = Mutsamudu 172 HJ 4
Mouydir = Jabal al-Mūdīr 166-167 HJ 7
Móvano 76-77 C 9
Moville, IA 70-71 BC 4
Mowasi 98-99 J 2
Moweaqua, IL 70-71 F 6
Mowich, OR 66-67 BC 4
Mowming = Maoming 142-143 L 7
Moxico 172 CD 4
Moxotó, Rio — 100-101 F 5
Moya [PE] 96-97 D 8
Moyale 172 G 1
Moyamba 164-165 B 7
Mo-yang Chiang = Moyang Jiang 146-147 C 10-11
Moyang Jiang 146-147 C 10-11
Moye Dao 146-147 J 3
Mo-yeh Tao = Moye Dao 146-147 J 3
Moyie 66-67 F 1
Moyie Springs, ID 66-67 E 1
Moylan, PA 84 III a 2
Moyne, La — 82 I c 1
Moyo [BOL] 104-105 D 7
Moyo [EAU] 171 B 2
Moyo = Pulau Moyo 148-149 G 8
Moyobamba 92-93 D 6
Moyock, NC 80-81 HJ 2
Moyowosi 171 B 3-4
Møysalen 116-117 FG 3
Moyto 164-165 H 6
M'oža [SU ◁ Unža] 124-125 P 4
M'oža [SU ◁ Zapadnaja Dvina] 124-125 J 5-6
Možajsk 124-125 KL 6
Mozambique 172 F 6-G 4
Mozambique = Moçambique [Mozambique, place] 172 H 4-5
Mozambique = Moçambique [Mozambique, state] 172 F 6-G 4
Mozambique Basin 172 H 4
Mozambique Channel 172 H 4-6
Možary 124-125 N 7
Mozdok 126-127 M 5
Možga 132-133 J 6
Mozuli 124-125 G 5
Mozyr' 124-125 G 7
Mpampáeski = Babaeski 136-137 B 2
Mpanda 172 F 3
Mpepo 172 F 4
Mpika 172 F 4
Mpila, Brazzaville- 170 IV a 1
Mporokoso 172 EF 3
M'Pouya 172 C 2
Mpulungu 172 F 3
Mpurakasese 172 G 4
Mpwapwa 171 D 4
M'rāītī, Al- 164-165 C 4
Mrayyah, Al- 164-165 C 5
Mreïti, El — = Al-M'rāītī 164-165 C 4
M. R. Gomez, Presa — 86-87 L 4
Mrhaïer = Al-Mighāīr 166-167 J 3
Mrīmīna = M'rīmīnah 166-167 C 5
M'rīmīnah 166-167 C 5
Msagali 172 G 3
Msaïda = Musā'idah 136-137 M 7
Msāken = Masākin 166-167 M 2
M'samrīr 166-167 D 4
Msasa 171 B 3
Mseleni 174-175 K 4
M'shams 166-167 BC 6
M'shīgīg, Sabkhat al- 166-167 L 2
Msid, Djebel — = Jabal Masīd 166-167 L 1
M'Sila = M'sīlah 166-167 J 2
M'sīlah 166-167 J 2
Msta [SU, place] 124-125 K 5
Msta [SU, river] 132-133 E 6
Mstinskij Most 124-125 J 4
Mstislavl' 124-125 HJ 6
Mswega 171 D 5
Mtâ el Rhèrra, Chott — = Shaṭṭ al-Ghurrah 166-167 M 2
Mtakuja 172 F 3
Mtama 171 D 5
Mtatarivier 174-175 H 6
Mtimbo 171 D 5
Mtito Andei 171 D 3
Mtowabaga 171 C 3
Mtubatuba 174-175 K 5
MTU im. Lomonosova 113 V b 3
Mtwalume 174-175 J 6
Mtwara 172 H 4
Mu'o'ng Boum 150-151 D 1
Mu'o'ng Khoua 148-149 D 2
Mu'o'ng Lam [VN, Sông Ca] 150-151 E 3
Mu'o'ng Lam [VN, Sông Ma] 150-151 D 2
Mu'o'ng Son 150-151 D 2
Mu'o'ng Soum 150-151 D 3
Mualama 172 G 5
Muan 144-145 F 5
Mu'ang Ba = Ban Mu'ang Ba 150-151 E 4
Muang Phichai = Phichai 150-151 C 4
Muang Phrae 150-151 C 4
Muang Pua = Pua 150-151 C 3
Muang Samsip 150-151 E 5
Mūan-jo Daṛo 138-139 AB 4
Muar 148-149 D 6
Muar, Sungei — 150-151 D 12
Muara 152-153 D 6
Muaraaman 148-149 D 7
Muaraancalung 148-149 G 6
Muarabenangin 152-153 LM 6
Muarabungo 152-153 E 6
Muaraenim 148-149 D 7
Muarajuloi 152-153 L 6
Muaralasan 148-149 G 6
Muarapangean 152-153 M 4
Muarapayang 152-153 LM 6
Muaras 152-153 N 5
Muarasabak 152-153 E 6
Muarasiberut 148-149 C 7
Muaratebo 148-149 D 7
Muaratembesi 148-149 D 7
Muarateweh 148-149 FG 7
Muaratunan 152-153 M 6
Muarawahau 152-153 M 5
Mū'askar 164-165 E 1
Mu'askar, Jabal — 166-167 D 3
Mubārak, Jabal — 136-137 F 8
Mubārakpur 138-139 J 4
Mubende 172 F 1
Mubi 164-165 G 6
Mubur, Pulau — 152-153 FG 4
Mucajaí, Rio — 92-93 G 4
Mucajaí, Serra do — 92-93 G 4
Mucambo 100-101 D 2
Muchanes 104-105 C 4
Muchinga Mountains 171 BC 5
Muchino 124-125 S 4
Muchiri 104-105 E 6
Muchorskij 126-127 P 2
Muchtolovo 124-125 O 6
Mučkapskij 124-125 O 8
Muco, Rio — 94-95 F 5
Mucojo 172 H 4
Muconda 172 D 4
Mucoque 174-175 L 1
Mucuburi, Rio — 171 D 6
Mucuchachí 94-95 F 3
Mucuchíes 94-95 F 3
Mucucuaú, Rio — 98-99 H 4
Mucuim, Rio — 98-99 F 8
Mucujê 100-101 D 7
Mucunambiba, Ilha — 100-101 C 1-2
Mucur 136-137 F 3
Mucuri 92-93 M 8
Mucuri, Rio — 92-93 L 8
Mucurici 100-101 D 10
Mucuripe, Ponta de — 92-93 M 5
Mucusso 172 D 5
Muda, Sungei — 150-151 C 10
Mudagĕrĕ = Mudigere 140 B 4
Mudanjiang 142-143 OP 3
Mudanya 136-137 C 2
Mudawwarah, Al- 134-135 D 5
Mudaysīsāt, Jabal — 136-137 G 7
Mud Butte, SD 68-69 E 3
Muddanūru 140 D 3
Muddebihāl 140 BC 2
Muḍḍĕbihāla = Muddebihāl 140 BC 2
Muddo Gashi = Mado Gashi 172 G 1
Muddusnationalpark 116-117 J 4
Muddy Creek 74-75 H 3
Muddy Gap 68-69 C 4
Muddy Gap, WY 66-67 K 4
Muddy Peak 74-75 F 4
Mudgal 140 C 2
Mudgee 158-159 JK 6
Mudgere = Mudigere 140 B 4
Mudhol [IND, Karnataka] 140 B 2
Mudhol [IND, Mahārāshtra] 138-139 FG 8
Mudhola = Mudhol [IND, Karnataka] 140 B 2
Mudhola = Mudhol [IND, Mahārāshtra] 138-139 FG 8
Mudigere 140 B 4
Mūdīr, Jabal al- 166-167 HJ 7
Mudīriyat el Istwā'ya = Al-Istiwā'īyah 164-165 K-M 7
Mudīriyat esh Shimāliya = Ash-Shimālīyah 164-165 KL 5
Mudjuga 124-125 M 2
Mudkhed 138-139 F 8
Mud Lake 74-75 E 4
Mudōn 148-149 C 3
Mŭdros 122-123 L 6
Mudugh 164-165 b 2
Mudukulattūr 140 D 6
Mudūr 140 E 6
Mudurnu 136-137 D 2
Muecate 172 G 4
Mueda 172 G 4
Muendaze 171 E 6
Muermos, Los — 108-109 C 3
Muerte, Meseta de la — 108-109 CD 7
Muerto, Sierra del — 104-105 AB 9
Mufulira 172 E 4
Mufu Shan 146-147 E 7
Mugadok Taung 150-151 B 5
Muganskaja ravnina 126-127 O 7
Müggelberge 130 III c 2
Müggelheim, Berlin- 130 III c 2
Muggi Tsho 138-139 M 2
Mughal Bhīm = Jāti 138-139 B 5
Mughal Sarai 138-139 J 5
Mughayrā', Al- 136-137 G 8
Mughrān, Al- 166-167 C 2
Mughrār 166-167 F 3
Mugi 144-145 K 6
Mu' Gia, Đeo — 150-151 E 4
Múgica 86-87 JK 8
Mugila, Monts — 172 E 3
Muğla 134-135 B 3
Mugodžary 132-133 K 8
Mugodzharskie Mountains = Mugodžary 132-133 K 8
Mugombazi 171 B 4
Mugrejevskij 124-125 O 5
Mūgu 138-139 J 3
Mūgu Karnāli 138-139 J 3
Muhamdī 138-139 GH 4
Muḥammad, Rā's — 164-165 LM 4
Muhammadābād [IND ↓ Gorakhpoor] 138-139 J 4
Muhammadābād [IND ↗ Vārānasī] 138-139 J 5
Muḥammadī, Wādī — 136-137 K 6
Muḥammadīyah, Al- 166-167 C 3
Muḥammad Ṭulayb 173 B 5
Muhammed, Ras — = Rā's Muḥammad 164-165 LM 4
Muhārī, Al- 136-137 L 7
Muhārī, Sha'īb al- 136-137 KL 7
Muhembo 172 D 5
Muhinga = Muyinga 172 EF 2
Mühlau 128 IV a 2
Mühlbach 128 III a 2
Mühldorf 118 F 4
Mühlenau 130 I a 1
Mühlenbecker See 130 III b 1
Mühlhausen 118 E 3
Mühlig-Hoffmann-Gebirge 53 B 1-2
Mühlleiten 113 I c 2
Muhu 124-125 D 4
Muhuwesi 171 D 5
Mui Bai Bung 148-149 D 5
Mui Ba Lang An = Mui Batangan 148-149 EF 3
Mui Batangan 148-149 EF 3
Mui Ca Mau = Mui Bai Bung 148-149 D 5
Mui Cho'n Mây 150-151 G 4
Mui Đa Du'ng 150-151 EF 3
Mui Đa Năng 150-151 G 4
Muiderberg 128 I b 2
Mui Diêu 148-149 EF 4
Mui Dinh 148-149 E 4
Mui En = Mui Yên 150-151 G 6
Mui Ke Ga 150-151 FG 7
Mui Lai 150-151 F 4
Muir Glacier 58-59 T 7
Muirite 171 D 6
Mui Ron Ma 148-149 E 3
Muisne 96-97 A 1
Mui Yên 150-151 G 6
Muizenberg 174-175 BC 8
Muja 132-133 W 6
Mujeres, Isla — 86-87 R 7
Mujezerskij 132-133 E 5
Mujlad, Al — 164-165 K 6
Mujnak 132-133 K 9
Muju 144-145 F 4-5
Mujunkum 132-133 MN 9
Muk, Ko — 150-151 B 9
Muka = Mouka 164-165 J 7
Mukačovo 126-127 A 2
Mukah 148-149 F 6
Mukallā, Al- 134-135 FG 8
Mukawa 144-145 b 2
Mukawwa', Jazīrat — 173 DE 6
Mukdahan 148-149 D 3
Mukden = Shenyang 142-143 NO 3
Mukebo 171 AB 4
Mukeriān 138-139 E 2
Mukhā, Al- 134-135 E 8
Mukhalid = Nětanya 136-137 F 6
Mukher 140 C 1
Mukhriṣṣat 166-167 D 2
Mukinbudin 158-159 C 6
Muknīn, Al- 166-167 M 2
Mukōjima, Tōkyō- 155 III bc 1
Mukoko 171 BC 3
Mukomuko 148-149 D 7
Mukrān, Sabkhat — 164-165 E 3
Mukry 134-135 K 3
Muktāgācha 138-139 MN 5
Mukthsar = Muktsar 138-139 E 2
Muktināth 138-139 J 3
Muktsar 138-139 E 2
Mukumbi = Makumbi 172 D 3
Mükūs 136-137 K 3
Mukutawa River 62 A 1
Mūl 138-139 G 7
Mula [IND] 138-139 E 8
Mula, La — 76-77 B 8
Mulainagiri 134-135 LM 8
Mulaku Atoll 176 a 2
Mulan 142-143 O 2
Mulanje 172 G 5
Mulanje, Mount — 172 G 5
Mulapamok = Moulapamok 150-151 EF 5
Mulata 98-99 LM 5
Mulatas, Archipiélago de las — 94-95 B 3
Mulativu 140 E 6
Mulatos 94-95 C 3
Mulatos, Punta — 91 II b 1
Mūlāy Bū Salhām 166-167 C 2
Mūlāy Bū Shtā' 166-167 D 2
Mūlāy Idrīs Zarahūn 166-167 D 2-3
Mūlayit Taung 148-149 C 3
Mūlāy Salīsan 166-167 F 2
Mulbāgal 140 D 4
Mulberry, KS 70-71 C 7
Mulchatna River 58-59 JK 6
Mulchén 106-107 A 6
Muldoon, ID 66-67 G 4
Muldrow, OK 76-77 G 5
Muleba 171 BC 3
Mule Creek, NM 74-75 J 6
Mule Creek, WY 68-69 D 4
Mulegé 86-87 DE 4
Mules, Pulau — 152-153 O 10
Muleshoe, TX 76-77 C 5
Mulgrave 63 F 5
Mulgrave Hills 58-59 F 3
Mulgrave Island 158-159 H 2
Mulgubi 144-145 G 2
Mulhacén 120-121 F 10
Mulhall, OK 76-77 F 4
Mulhouse 120-121 L 5
Muli = Vysokogornyj 132-133 ab 7
Mulka 160 D 2
Mūlki 140 B 4
Mull 119 CD 3
Mullaitivu = Mulativu 140 E 6
Mullāmāṛi 140 C 2
Mullan, ID 66-67 EF 2
Mullan Pass 64-65 D 2
Mullen, NE 68-69 F 4
Mullens, WV 80-81 F 2
Müller, Pegunungan — 148-149 F 6
Müllerberg 116-117 I 6
Mullet Lake 70-71 H 3
Mullewa 158-159 C 5
Mulligan River 158-159 G 4-5
Mullin, TX 76-77 E 7
Mullingar 119 C 5
Mullins, SC 80-81 G 3
Mulobezi 172 DE 5
Mulshī = Waki 140 A 1
Mulshi Lake 140 A 1
Multai 138-139 G 7
Multān 134-135 L 4
Mulu, Gunung — 148-149 FG 6
Mulubāgala = Mulbāgal 140 D 4
Mulug 140 DE 1
Mulula, Wed — = Wād Mūlūyā 164-165 D 2
Mulungu 100-101 G 4
Mulungu do Morro 100-101 D 6
Mulūṣī, Bi'r al- 136-137 J 6
Mulūṣī, Shādir al- 136-137 HJ 6
Mūlūyā, Wād — 164-165 D 2
Muluzia 171 B 5
Mulvane, KS 68-69 H 7
Mulymja 132-133 LM 5
Mumbai = Bombay 134-135 L 7
Mumbwa 172 E 5
Mumeng 148-149 N 8
Mumford, TX 76-77 F 7
Mumpu, Mount — 171 B 6
Mumra 126-127 N 4
Mumtrak = Coodnews, AK 58-59 FG 7
Mū Myit 141 D 4
Mun, Mae Nam — 148-149 D 3
Muna [MEX] 86-87 Q 7
Muna [SU] 132-133 W 4
Muna, Pulau — 148-149 H 8
Muñani 96-97 G 9
Munasarowar Lake = Mapham Tsho 142-143 E 5
Munayjah, Bi'r — 173 D 6
Münchehofe [DDR, Frankfurt] 130 III c 2
München 118 EF 4
München-Allach 130 II a 1
München-Au 130 II b 2
München-Aubing 130 II a 2
München-Berg am Laim 130 II b 2
München-Bogenhausen 130 II b 2
München-Daglfing 130 II bc 2
München-Denning 130 II bc 2
München-Englschalking 130 II bc 2
München-Fasanerie-Nord 130 II b 1
München-Fasangarten 130 II b 2
München-Forstenried 130 II ab 2
München-Freimann 130 II b 1
München-Gern 130 II b 2
München-Giesing 130 II b 2
München-Grosshadern 130 II a 2
München-Haidhausen 130 II b 2
München-Harlaching 130 II b 2
München-Hartmannshofen 130 II ab 1
München-Johanneskirchen 130 II bc 1
München-Kleinhadern 130 II a 2
München-Kolonie Lerchenau 130 II b 1
München-Laim 130 II ab 2
München-Langwied 130 II a 1
München-Lochham 130 II a 2
München-Lochhausen 130 II a 1
München-Ludwigsfeld 130 II ab 1
München-Menterschwaige 130 II b 2
München-Milbertshofen 130 II b 1
München-Neuhausen 130 II b 2
München-Nymphenburg 130 II ab 1
München-Oberföhring 130 II b 1
München-Obermenzing 130 II a 1
München-Obersendling 130 II b 2
München-Perlach 130 II b 2
München-Pipping 130 II a 2
München-Ramersdorf 130 II b 2
München-Riem, Flughafen — 130 II c 2
München-Siedlung Hasenbergl 130 II b 1
München-Siedlung Neuherberg 130 II b 1
München-Steinhausen 130 II b 2
München-Thalkirchen 130 II b 2
München-Trudering 130 II bc 2
München-Untermenzing 130 II a 1
München-Untersendling 130 II b 2
München-Waldperlach 130 II bc 2
München-Zamdorf 130 II b 2
Munchique, Cerro — 94-95 C 6
Munch'ŏn 144-145 F 3
Muncie, IN 64-65 JK 3
Mundal = Mūndalam 140 DE 7
Mūndalam 140 DE 7
Mundare 61 BC 4
Mundaú 100-101 E 2
Mundaú, Ponta de — 100-101 E 2
Munday, TX 76-77 E 6
Münden 118 D 3
Mundergi 140 BC 3
Mundgod 140 B 3
Mundiwindi 158-159 CD 4
Mundo, Río — 120-121 F 9
Mundo Novo [BR, Bahia ↖ Feira de Santana] 100-101 D 6
Mundo Novo [BR, Bahia ↓ Itabuna] 100-101 E 9
Mundo Novo [BR, Mato Grosso do Sul] 102-103 E 5
Mundra 138-139 B 6
Mundrabilla 158-159 E 6
Mundubbera 158-159 JK 5
Muṇḍugōḍa = Mundgod 140 B 3
Muṇḍugōḍe = Mundgod 140 B 3
Mundurucânia, Reserva Florestal — 98-99 JK 8
Muṇḍvā = Mūndwa 138-139 DE 4
Mūndwa 138-139 DE 4
Muneru 140 E 2
Munfordville, KY 70-71 H 7
Mungallala Creek 158-159 J 5
Mungana 158-159 H 3
Mungaoli 138-139 FG 5
Mungari 172 F 5
Muṅgāvalī = Mungaoli 138-139 FG 5
Mungbere 172 E 1
Mungeli 138-139 H 6
Mungēr = Monghyr 134-135 O 5
Mungindi 158-159 J 5
Munhafaḍ al-Qaṭṭārah 164-165 K 2-3
Munhango 172 C 4
Munich = München 118 EF 4
Munim, Rio — 100-101 B 2
Munirābād 140 BC 3
Munising, MI 70-71 G 2
Muñiz, General Sarmiento- 110 III a 1
Munizaga 108-109 DE 9
Muniz Freire 102-103 M 4
Munk 61 L 3
Munkfors 116-117 EF 8
Munkhafad ath-Tharthār 134-135 E 4
Munksund 116-117 JK 5
Munnik 174-175 HJ 2
Muñoz 106-107 G 6
Muñoz Gamero, Península — 111 B 8
Munro, Vicente López- 110 III b 1
Munsan 144-145 F 4
Munsfjället 116-117 F 5
Munshiganj 141 B 4
Münster [D] 118 C 2-3
Munster [IRL] 119 B 5
Münsterer Wald 128 III b 2
Munte 148-149 G 6
Muntele Ceahlău 122-123 LM 2
Muntele Mare 122-123 K 2
Muntele Nemira 122-123 M 2
Munţii Banatului 122-123 JK 3
Munţii Bihor 122-123 K 2
Munţii Călimani 122-123 L 2
Munţii Metalici 122-123 K 2
Muntok 148-149 DE 7
Munyeru River = Manneru 140 D 3
Munyu 174-175 H 6
Munzur dağları 136-137 H 3
Muodoslompolo 116-117 K 4
Mu'one, Nam — 150-151 E 3
Mu'o'ng Beng 150-151 C 2
Mu'o'ng Bum = Mu'o'ng Boum 150-151 D 1
Mu'o'ng Hat Hin 150-151 D 1-2
Mu'o'ng Het 150-151 E 2
Mu'o'ng Hiem 150-151 D 2
Mu'o'ng Hong Sa 150-151 C 3
Mu'o'ng Houn 150-151 C 2
Mu'o'ng Hun = Mu'o'ng Houn 150-151 C 2
Mu'o'ng Hung 150-151 D 2
Mu'o'ng Hu'n Xiêng Hu'ng 150-151 D 2
Mu'o'ng Kau 150-151 E 5
Mu'o'ng Khay 150-151 CD 3
Muong Kwa = Mu'o'ng Khoua 148-149 D 2
Mu'o'ng Lat 150-151 E 2
Muong Mongne = Mu'o'ng Mu'gne 150-151 C 2
Mu'o'ng Mu'gne 150-151 C 2
Muong Ngeun 150-151 C 3
Mu'o'ng Ngoi 150-151 D 2
Mu'o'ng Nhie 150-151 D 1
Mu'o'ng Nông 150-151 F 4
Mu'o'ng Ou Neua 150-151 CD 1
Mu'o'ng Ou Tay 150-151 C 1
Mu'o'ng Pa 150-151 C 3
Mu'o'ng Pak Beng 148-149 D 2-3
Mu'o'ng Pak Tha 150-151 C 2
Mu'o'ng Phalane 150-151 E 4
Mu'o'ng Phieng 150-151 C 3
Mu'o'ng Phine 150-151 EF 4
Muong Plateau = Cao Nguyên Trung Phần 148-149 E 4
Mu'o'ng Sai 150-151 CD 2
Mu'o'ng Sen 150-151 E 3
Mu'o'ng Sen, Deo — 148-149 DE 3
Mu'o'ng Sing 150-151 C 2
Mu'o'ng Song Khone 150-151 E 4
Mu'o'ng Soui 150-151 D 3
Muong Soum = Mu'o'ng Soum 150-151 D 3
Mu'o'ng Thadeua 150-151 C 3
Mu'o'ng Tourakom 150-151 D 3
Mu'o'ng Va 150-151 D 2
Mu'o'ng Wapi 150-151 EF 5
Mu'o'ng Yo 150-151 C 2
Muonio 116-117 KL 4
Muonio älv 116-117 K 4
Mupa 141 C 3
Mupa Upare Hill 168-169 GH 3
Muping 146-147 H 3
Mup'yŏng-ni = Chŏnch'ŏn 144-145 F 2
Muqattam, Jabal al- 170 II b 1-c 2
Muqayshit 134-135 G 6
Muqayyar, Al- = Ur 134-135 F 4
Muqqār, Al- 166-167 K 3
Muqsim, Jabal — 173 CD 6
Muq'ud 166-167 L 1
Muquém, Vereda do — 100-101 C 6
Muqui 102-103 M 4
Muqur = Moqur 134-135 K 4
Mur 118 FG 5
Mura 122-123 FG 2
Murādābād = Morādābād 134-135 MN 5
Muradiye [TR, Manisa] 136-137 B 3
Muradiye [TR, Van] 136-137 KL 3
Muraenā = Morena 138-139 G 4
Murafa 126-127 CD 2
Muraina = Morena 138-139 G 4
Murakami 144-145 M 3
Murallón, Cerro — 111 B 7
Mūrān [IR] 136-137 N 7
Murang'a 172 G 2
Mur'anyo 164-165 bc 1
Murāši 132-133 H 6
Murat dağı 134-135 B 3
Murat dağları = Serafettin dağları 136-137 J 3
Murathüyügü 136-137 G 4
Murat nehri 134-135 E 3
Murauaú, Rio — 98-99 H 4
Muravera 122-123 CD 6
Muravl'anka [SU → RO] 124-125 N 7
Murayama 144-145 N 3
Muraywad, Al- 136-137 L 8
Murchison, Cape — 56-57 S 3
Murchisonberge 174-175 J 2
Murchison Falls = Kabelega Falls 172 F 1
Murchison Falls National Park = Kabelega Falls National Park 172 F 1
Murchisonfjord 116-117 k 4-5
Murchisonfjorden 116-117 kl 4
Murchison Island 62 EF 2
Murchison River 158-159 C 5
Murcia [E, landscape] 120-121 G 9-10
Murcia [E, place] 120-121 G 9-10
Murdale 60 G 1
Murdo, SD 68-69 F 4
Murdochville 56-57 XY 8
Murdock, FL 80-81 b 3
Mureş 122-123 K 2-3
Murfreesboro, AR 78-79 C 3
Murfreesboro, NC 80-81 H 2
Murfreesboro, TN 64-65 J 4
Murgab [SU, place] 134-135 L 3
Murgab [SU, river] 134-135 J 3
Murge 122-123 G 5
Murghābrōd 134-135 JK 3-4
Murghā Kibzai 138-139 B 2
Murgon 158-159 K 5
Muria = Gunung Muryo 152-153 J 9
Muriaé 92-93 L 9
Muriaé, Rio — 102-103 M 4
Murici 100-101 G 5
Muriel Lake 61 C 3
Mūrig, Jabal — 166-167 CD 3
Murikanḍi 140 E 6
Murindó 94-95 C 4
Müritz 118 F 2
Murkong Selek 141 D 2
Murlīganj 138-139 L 5
Murmansk 132-133 EF 4
Murmansk Rise 132-133 EF 2
Murmaši 132-133 E 4
Murmino 124-125 N 6
Muro, Capo di — 122-123 C 5
Muro Lucano 122-123 FG 5
Murom 132-133 G 6
Muromcevo 132-133 O 6
Muroran 142-143 R 3
Muros 120-121 C 7
Muroto 144-145 JK 6
Muroto zaki 144-145 K 6
Murphy, ID 66-67 E 4
Murphy, NC 78-79 G 3
Murphy, TN 80-81 D 3
Murphy Canal 85 I b 2
Murphysboro, IL 70-71 F 7
Murr, Bi'r — 173 B 6
Murrah, Ḥāssī — 166-167 E 4
Murrah, Jabal — 166-167 L 2
Murrat al-Kubrā, Al-Buḥayrat al- 173 C 2
Murrat el-Kubrā, Buḥeiret el — = Al-Buḥayrat al-Murrat al-Kubrā 173 C 2
Murray, KY 78-79 E 2
Murray, Lake — [PNG] 148-149 M 8
Murray, Lake — [USA] 80-81 F 3
Murray Bridge 160 D 5
Murray Fracture Zone 156-157 KL 3
Murray Harbour 63 EF 5
Murray Lake 85 II b 3
Murray River [AUS] 158-159 H 6-7
Murray River [CDN] 60 G 2
Murraysburg 174-175 E 6
Murri, Río — 94-95 C 4
Murrumbidgee River 158-159 HJ 6
Murrumburrah 160 J 5
Murshidābād 138-139 M 5
Mürsut 166-167 L 2
Murtazāpur 138-139 F 7
Murtijāpur = Murtazāpur 138-139 F 7
Murtle Lake 60 H 3
Murtoa 160 F 6
Muru, Rio — 96-97 F 6
Murud 140 A 1
Murud, Gunung — 152-153 LM 4
Murumush 174-175 E 3
Murundu 102-103 M 4
Murung, Sungai — 152-153 L 7
Murunkan 140 E 6
Murupara 158-159 P 7
Murupu 92-93 G 4
Murvārā = Murwāra 134-135 N 6
Murwāra 134-135 N 6
Murwillumbah 158-159 K 5
Murygino 124-125 R 4
Muryo, Gunung — 152-153 J 9
Murzūq = Marzūq 164-165 G 3
Mürzzuschlag 118 G 5
Muş 134-135 E 3
Mūsā, Khūr-e — 136-137 N 7-8
Muşa Ali 164-165 N 6
Musabeyli = Murathüyügü 136-137 G 4
Musāfirkhāna 138-139 H 4
Musā'id 166-167 A 5
Musā'idah 136-137 M 7
Mūsā Kḥel Bāzār 138-139 B 2
Musala 122-123 K 4
Musala, Pulau — 148-149 C 6
Musan 142-143 OP 3
Mūsa Qal'a 134-135 JK 4
Musashino 155 III a 1
Musashino-Kichijōji 155 III a 1
Musayʿīd 134-135 G 5-6
Musayyib, Al- 136-137 L 6
Musazade 136-137 J 2
Muscat = Masqaṭ 134-135 HJ 6
Muscatine, IA 70-71 E 5
Muscoda, WI 70-71 E 4
Muscongus Bay 72-73 M 3
Musées 128 II b 1
Museo 113 II b 2
Museo Arqueológico 113 III ab 2
Museo de Belles Artes 91 II b 1
Museo del Oro 91 III c 3
Museo del Prado 113 III a 2
Museo de Nariño 91 III b 3
Museo Nacional [BR] 110 I b 2
Museo Nacional [CO] 91 III c 3
Museo Nacional de Antropologia 91 I b 2
Museu do Ipiranga 110 II b 2
Museum of Fine Arts [USA, Boston] 84 I b 2
Museum of Fine Arts [USA, Houston] 85 III b 1
Museum of National History 155 II b 2
Museum of Natural Science 85 III b 2
Museum of Science and Industry 83 II b 2
Musgrave 158-159 H 2
Musgrave Ranges 158-159 F 5
Musgravetown 63 JK 3
Mushā 173 B 4
Mushāsh, Bi'r — 136-137 G 7
Mushie 172 C 2
Mushin 168-169 F 4
Mushkābād = Ebrāhīmābād 136-137 O 5
Mushora = Mushūrah 136-137 K 4
Mushūrah 136-137 K 4
Mūsi 140 D 2
Musi, Sungai — 148-149 D 7
Mūṣil, Al- 134-135 E 3
Musinia Peak 74-75 H 3
Musiri 140 D 5
Musisi 171 C 4
Musium Pusat Abri 154 IV a 2
Mūsiyān 136-137 M 6
Muskat = Masqaṭ 134-135 H 6
Muskeg Bay 70-71 C 1
Muskeg Lake 70-71 EF 1
Muskegon, MI 64-65 J 3
Muskegon Heights, MI 70-71 G 4
Muskegon River 70-71 GH 4
Muski, Al-Qāhirah-al- 170 II b 1
Muskingum River 72-73 EF 5
Muskogee, OK 64-65 GH 4
Muskoka, Lake — 72-73 G 2
Muslimīyah 136-137 G 4
Musl'umovo 124-125 T 6
Musmār = Mismār 164-165 M 5
Musoma 172 F 2
Musoshi 171 AB 5
Muş ovası 136-137 J 3
Musquaro, Lac — 63 F 2
Musquaro, Rivière — 63 F 2
Mussali, Mount — = Muşa Ali 164-165 N 6
Mussanāt, Al- 136-137 M 8
Mussau 148-149 N 7
Musselburgh 119 E 4
Musselshell River 64-65 E 2
Mussende 172 C 4
Mussoorie 138-139 G 2
Mussuma 172 D 4
Mustafābād 138-139 G 4
Mustafakemalpaşa 136-137 C 2-3
Mustaghānam 164-165 DE 1
Mustajevo 124-125 T 8
Mustāng 138-139 JK 3
Mustang, OK 76-77 EF 5
Mustang Island 76-77 F 9
Mustapha, Al-Jazā'ir- 170 I a 1
Musters, Lago — 111 BC 7
Mustique 88-89 Q 8
Mustla 124-125 EF 4
Mustvee 124-125 F 4
Mustwee = Mustvee 124-125 F 4
Musʿūd, Wādī — 166-167 F 5-6
Musu-dan 144-145 GH 2
Muswellbrook 158-159 K 6
Mut [ET] 164-165 K 3
Mut [TR] 136-137 E 4
Muta 171 A 3
Mutá, Ponta do — 100-101 E 7
Mutankiang = Mudanjiang 142-143 OP 3
Mutare 172 F 5
Mutās 100-101 C 8
Mutatá 94-95 C 4
Muthanna, Al- 136-137 L 7

Mu'tiq, Jabal — 173 C 4
Mutis, Gunung — 148-149 H 8
Mutki = Mirtağ 136-137 J 3
Muṭlah = Al-Maṭlāʿ 136-137 M 8
Mutsamudu 172 HJ 4
Mutshatsha 172 D 4
Mutsu 144-145 N 2
Mutsu-wan 144-145 N 2
Mutton Bay 63 G 2
Muttra = Mathurā 134-135 M 5
Muttupet 140 D 5
Mutuipe 100-101 E 7
Mutum 102-103 M 3
Mutum, Rio — 98-99 D 7
Mutum Biyu 168-169 H 3
Mutumparanã 104-105 D 1
Mutuoca, Ilha de — 100-101 B 1
Mutuoca, Ponta da — 100-101 B 1
Mutur = Mudūr 140 E 6
Mututi, Ilha — 98-99 N 5
Mūvattupula 140 C 5-6
Mūvāṭṭ'upuḻa = Mūvattupula 140 C 5-6
Muwaffaqīyah, Al- 136-137 L 6
Muwayḥ, Al- 134-135 E 6
Muwayliḥ, Al- 173 D 4
Muxima 172 B 3
Muyeveld 128 I b 2
Muyinga 172 EF 2
Muyumanu, Río — 96-97 G 7
Muyumba 172 E 3
Muyuquira 104-105 D 7
Muẓaffarābād 134-135 LM 4
Muẓaffargaṛh 134-135 L 4-5
Muzaffarnagar 134-135 M 5
Muzaffarpur 134-135 NO 5
Muzambinho 102-103 J 4
Muži 132-133 L 4
Muzo 94-95 D 5
Muzon, Cape — 58-59 w 9
Muz tagh 142-143 E 4
Muz tagh ata 142-143 D 4

Mvôlô 164-165 KL 7
Mvuma 172 F 5

Mwali 172 H 4
Mwambwa 171 C 5
Mwanamundia 171 DE 3
Mwanza [EAT] 172 F 2
Mwanza [ZRE] 172 E 3
Mwatate 171 D 3
Mwaya 172 F 3
Mwazya 171 BC 5
Mweka 172 D 2
Mwene-Ditu 172 D 3
Mwenga 172 E 2
Mwenzo 171 C 5
Mweru, Lake — 172 E 3
Mweru Swamp 172 E 3
Mwilah 166-167 C 5
Mwingi 171 D 3
Mwinilunga 172 DE 4
M'wīsāt, Bi'r al- 166-167 A 7
Mwitikira 171 C 4

Mya, Ouèd — = Wādī Miyāh 166-167 J 4
Myāchlār = Miājlar 138-139 C 4
Myaing 141 D 5
Myan'aung 148-149 BC 3
Myaung 141 D 5
Myaungmya 141 D 7
Myawadī 141 F 7
Myebôn 141 C 5
Myèbûm, Lûy — 141 E 3
Myeik 148-149 C 4
Myeik Kyûnzu 148-149 C 4
Myemûn 141 D 4
Myenmoletkhat, Mount — = Myinmôylet'hkat Taung 150-151 B 6
Myi Chhu 138-139 L 3
Myingyan 148-149 BC 2
Myinmoletkat Taung = Myinmôylet'hkat Taung 150-151 B 6
Myinmôylet'hkat Taung 150-151 B 6
Myinmû 141 D 5
Myinzaung 150-151 A 5
Myitkyinā 148-149 C 1
Myitngei Myit 141 E 4-5
Myitthā 141 E 5
Myittha = Manibûra Myit 141 C 4
Myitthā Myit 141 D 4
Myjeldino 124-125 U 3
Mykênai 122-123 K 7
Mýkonos 122-123 L 7
Mymensingh = Maimansingh 134-135 OP 6
Mynämäki 116-117 JK 7
Mynaral 132-133 N 8
Mynfontein 174-175 EF 6
Myntobe 126-127 O 3
Myōgyī 141 E 5
Myôhaung 141 C 5
Myohyang-sanmaek 144-145 E 3-F 2
Myōkō-zan 144-145 LM 4
Myŏngch'ŏn 144-145 GH 2
Myothā 141 D 5
Myōthit 141 D 5
Myōzam 141 D 3
Mýra 116-117 c 2
Myrdal 116-117 B 7
Mýrdalsjökull 116-117 d 3
Mýrdalssandur 116-117 d 3
Myre 116-117 F 3
Mýrina 122-123 L 6
Myrnam 61 C 4
Myrthle 72-73 G 2
Myrtle Beach, SC 80-81 G 4
Myrtle Creek, OR 66-67 B 4
Myrtleford 160 H 6
Myrtle Point, OR 66-67 AB 4
mys Aleksandra 132-133 ab 7
mys Alevina 132-133 cd 6
mys Aniva 132-133 b 8
mys Barykova 132-133 jk 5
mys Bering 132-133 k 5
mys Blossom 132-133 jk 3
mys Borisova 132-133 a 6
mys Buor-Chaja 132-133 Z 3
mys Čel'uskin 132-133 T-V 2
mys Chersonesskij 126-127 F 4
mys Crillon 132-133 b 8
mys Čukotskij 132-133 l 5
mys Dežneva 132-133 lm 4
mys Duga-Zapadnaja 132-133 bc 6
mys Dzenzik 126-127 H 3
Myšega 124-125 L 6
Mysen 116-117 D 8
mys Enken 132-133 b 6
mys Gamova 144-145 H 1
mys Govena 132-133 g 6
mys Jakan 132-133 j 4
mys Jelizavety 132-133 b 7
mys Južnyj 132-133 e 6
mys Kazantip 126-127 G 4
mys Kiik-Atlama 126-127 GH 4
Myškino 124-125 LM 5
mys Kronockij 132-133 f 7
Myślenice 118 JK 4
mys Lopatka 52 D 3
mys Lukull 126-127 F 4
mys Meganom 126-127 G 4
mys Men'šikova 132-133 KL 3
mys Navarin 132-133 jk 5
mys Nizkij 132-133 hj 5
mys Ol'utorskij 132-133 h 6
mys Omgon 132-133 e 6
Mysore 140 C 4
Mysovsk = Babuškin 132-133 U 7
mys Ozernoj 132-133 fg 6
mys Peek 58-59 C 4
mys Pesčanyj 126-127 P 5
mys Picunda 126-127 K 5
mys Russkij Zavorot 132-133 JK 4
mys Sagyndyk 126-127 P 4
mys Saryč 126-127 F 4
mys Šelagskij 132-133 gh 3
mys Serdce Kamen' 58-59 BC 3
mys Sivučij 132-133 fg 6
mys Skuratova 132-133 LM 3
mys Sporyj Navolok 132-133 M-O 2
mys Šupunskij 132-133 f 7
mys Sv'atoj Nos 132-133 ab 3
mys Tajgonos 132-133 ef 5
mys Taran 118 JK 1
mys Tarchankut 126-127 EF 4
mys Terpenija 132-133 bc 8
Mystic, IA 70-71 D 5
Mystic, SD 68-69 E 3
Mystic River 84 I b 2
Mystic River Bridge 84 I b 2
mys Tolstoj 132-133 e 6
mys T'ub-Karagan 126-127 OP 4
mys Uengan 132-133 LM 3
mys Vchodnoj 132-133 QR 3
Mysy 124-125 TU 3
Mys Želanija 132-133 MN 2
mys Z'uk 126-127 H 4
My Tho 148-149 E 4
Mytilênê 122-123 M 6
Mytišči 124-125 LM 5-6
Myton, UT 66-67 HJ 5
Mývatn 116-117 e 2

Mzab = Al-Mizāb 166-167 HJ 3
Mzab, Ouèd — = Wādī Mīzāb 166-167 J 3
Mzi, Djebel — = Jabal Mazī 166-167 F 3
Mziha 172 G 3
Mzimba 172 F 4
Mzuzu 171 C 5

N

Na, Nam — 150-151 D 1
Naab 118 F 4
Na'āg, Gebel — = Jabal Niʿāj 173 C 6
Naalehu, HI 78-79 e 3
Na'ām, Bi'r an- 136-137 G 7
Na'ām, Jabal Zarqat 173 D 6
Na'ām, Maqarr an- 136-137 HJ 7
Naama = Na'āmah 166-167 F 3
Na'āmah 166-167 F 3
Naantali 116-117 JK 7
Naas 119 C 5
Näätämöjoki 116-117 MN 3
Naauwpoort = Noupoort 172 DE 8
Naauwte, De — 174-175 DE 6
Nabā 141 E 3
Nababeep = Nababiep 174-175 B 5
Nababiep 174-175 B 5
Nabadwīp 138-139 LM 6
Nabah, Bi'r — 173 C 7
Nabarangapur = Nowrangapur 138-139 J 8
Nābaw 141 E 3
Nabč 142-143 G 4
Naberežnyje Čelny 124-125 T 6
Nabesna, AK 58-59 Q 5
Nabesna Glacier 58-59 Q 5
Nābeul = Nābul 164-165 G 1
Nābha 138-139 F 2
Nabiac 160 L 4
Nabīganj 141 B 3
Nabilatuk 171 C 2
Nabileque, Pantanal de — 102-103 D 3-4
Nabileque, Rio — 102-103 D 4
Nabīnagar 138-139 K 5
Nabire 148-149 L 7
Nabīsar 134-135 KL 5-6
Nabisipi, Rivière — 63 E 2
Nabk, An- [Saudi Arabia] 136-137 G 7
Nabk, An- [SYR] 134-135 D 4
Nāblus = Nābulus 136-137 F 6
Nabolo 168-169 E 3
Nabón 96-97 B 3
Naboomspruit 174-175 H 3
Nabordo 168-169 H 3
Nabou 168-169 C 3
Nabq 173 D 3
Nābul 164-165 G 1
Nābulus 136-137 F 6
Nabûn 141 C 4
Nabung = Nabûn 141 C 4
Nacaca 171 D 5
Naçala 172 H 4
Nacfa = Nakfa 164-165 M 5
Naches, WA 66-67 C 2
Nachičevan' 126-127 M 7
Nachingwea 172 GH 4
Náchna 138-139 C 4
Nachodka 132-133 Z 9
Nachoi 138-139 M 5
Nachol = Nachoi 138-139 M 5
Nachrači = Kondirskoje 132-133 M 6
Nachtigal Falls 168-169 HJ 4
Nacimiento 106-107 A 6
Nacimiento Mountains 76-77 A 4-5
Nacional, La — 106-107 E 5
Naciria = Nāṣirīyah 166-167 HJ 1
Nacka 116-117 H 8
Naco 86-87 EF 2
Naco, AZ 74-75 HJ 7
Nacogdoches, TX 76-77 G 7
Nacololo 171 D 6
Nacozari de Gracía 64-65 DE 5
Ñacuñán 106-107 D 5
Ñacunday 102-103 E 7
Ñacunday, Río — 102-103 E 6
Nadadores 76-77 D 9
Nadbai 138-139 F 4
Nådendal = Naantali 116-117 JK 7
Nadeždinsk = Serov 132-133 L 6
Nadhatah, An- 136-137 J 6
Nadiād 134-135 L 6
Nadina River 60 D 3
Nadiyā = Kishnanagar 138-139 M 6
Nadjaf, An- = An-Najaf 134-135 E 4
Nadjd = Najd 134-135 E 5-6
Nădlac 122-123 J 2
Nadoa = Dan Xian 142-143 K 8
Nâdôr = An-Nāḍūr 166-167 E 2
Nadqān 134-135 G 6
Nāḍūr, An- 166-167 E 2
Nadvoicy 124-125 K 2
Nadvornaja 126-127 B 2
Naenpur = Nainpur 138-139 H 6
Naenwa 138-139 EF 5
Næstved 116-117 DE 10
Na Fac 150-151 E 1
Nafada 164-165 G 6
Nafīs, Wād — 166-167 B 4
Nafishah 173 BC 2
Nafṭ, Āb i — 136-137 L 6
Nafṭah 166-167 K 3
Naftalan 126-127 N 6
Naft-e Sefīd 136-137 N 7
Naft-e Shāh 136-137 L 5-6
Nafṭ Hānah 136-137 L 5
Nafṭ Khāna = Nafṭ Hānah 136-137 L 5
Nafūd, An- 134-135 E 5
Nafūd ad-Daḥī 134-135 EF 6
Nafūd as-Sirr 134-135 E 5-F 6
Nafusah, Jabal — 164-165 G 2
Naga 148-149 H 4
Nagagami Lake 70-71 H 1
Nagahama [J, Ehime] 144-145 J 6
Nagahama [J, Shiga] 144-145 L 5
Naga Hills 141 D 2-3
Nagai 144-145 MN 3
Nagai Island 58-59 cd 2
Nāgāland 134-135 P 5
Nāgamangala 140 C 4
Nagano 142-143 Q 4
Naganohara 144-145 M 4
Nagaoka 142-143 Q 4
Nāgaor = Nāgaur 134-135 L 5
Nāgapattinam 134-135 MN 8
Nagā Pradesh = Nāgāland 134-135 P 5
Nagar 138-139 F 4
Nāgar = Nāgore 140 DE 5
Nagara gawa 144-145 L 5
Nagar Aveli = Dādra and Nagar Haveli 134-135 L 6
Nagar Devla 138-139 E 7
Nagare Angū 141 CD 7
Nagar Haveli, Dadra and — 134-135 L 6
Nāgari 140 E 4
Nāgari Hills 140 D 4
Nāgārjuna Sāgar 140 D 2
Nāgar Karnūl 140 D 2
Nāgarkōyil = Nāgercoil 134-135 M 9
Nagar Kurnool = Nāgar Karnūl 140 D 2
Nagar Pārkar 134-135 KL 6
Nagar Untāri 138-139 J 5
Nagasaki 142-143 O 5
Naga-shima [J, island] 144-145 GH 6
Nagashima [J, place] 144-145 L 5
Nagatino, Moskva- 113 V c 3
Nagato 144-145 H 5
Nagatsuda, Yokohama- 155 III a 2
Nāgaur 134-135 L 5
Nāgāvali 140 F 1
Nagayoshi 155 III d 3
Nāgbhīr 138-139 G 7
Nag Chhu 142-143 G 5
Nagchhu Dsong 142-143 G 5
Nagchhukha = Nagchhu Dsong 142-143 G 5
Nāgercoil 134-135 M 9
Nagīna 138-139 G 3
Nāginimara 141 D 2
Nāgīshōt = Nāqīshūt 164-165 L 8
Nāgod 138-139 H 5
Nagorje 124-125 M 5
Nagorno-Karabagh Autonomous Region 126-127 N 6
Nagornyj 132-133 Y 6
Nagorsk 124-125 S 4
Nagoudé 168-169 H 2
Nagoya 142-143 Q 4
Nāgpur 134-135 M 6
Nagtshang 138-139 LM 2
Nagura, Ras en — = Rā's an-Naqurah 136-137 F 6
Naguun Mörön 142-143 NO 1-2
Nagykanizsa 118 H 5
Nagykőrös 118 JK 5
Nagyvárad = Oradea 122-123 JK 2
Naha 142-143 O 6
Nahabuan 152-153 L 5
Nāhan 138-139 F 2
Nahanni National Park 56-57 LM 5
Nahant, MA 84 I c 2
Nahant Bay 84 I c 2
Nahari 144-145 JK 6
Nahariya 136-137 F 6
Nahariyya = Nahariya 136-137 F 6
Nahar Ouassel, Oued — = Wādī Wāsal 166-167 GH 2
Nahāvand 136-137 N 5
Nāhid, Bi'r — 136-137 C 7
Nahīlah, An- = An-Nakhīlah 166-167 E 2
Nahlin River 58-59 W 7
Nahr al-ʿĀṣī 136-137 G 5
Nahr al-Furāt 134-135 E 4
Nahr al-ʿIdhaim = Shaṭṭ al-ʿUzaym 136-137 L 5
Nahr al-Jūr 164-165 K 7
Nahr al-Karākūrū 168-169 C 1-2
Nahr al-Khābūr 134-135 E 3
Nahr al-Khāzir 136-137 K 4
Nahr al-Līṭānī 136-137 F 6
Nahr ar-Rahad 164-165 L 6
Nahr ash-Sharīʿah 136-137 F 6-7
Nahr ʿAṭbarah 164-165 LM 5
Nahr Balīh 136-137 H 4
Nahr Begārī 138-139 B 3
Nahr Beliḳh = Nahr Balīh 136-137 H 4
Nahr Dijlah 134-135 E 3
Nahr Diyālā 134-135 EF 4
Nahr el Jûr = Nahr al-Jūr 164-165 K 7
Nahr esh-Sherīʿah = Nahr ash-Sharīʿah 136-137 F 6-7
Nahr Lôl = Nahr Lūl 164-165 K 7
Nahr Lūl 164-165 K 7
Nahr Pībōr 164-165 L 7
Nahr Rohrī 138-139 B 4
Nahr Shalar 136-137 L 5
Nahr Sôbâṭ = As-Sûbâṭ 164-165 L 7
Nahr Sūl 164-165 K 7
Nahuelbuta, Cordillera de — 106-107 A 6-7
Nahuel Huapi 108-109 D 3
Nahuel Huapí, Lago — 111 B 6
Nahuel Huapí, Parque Nacional — 108-109 D 3
Nahuel Mapá 106-107 DE 5
Nahuel Niyue 108-109 F 3
Nahuel Rucá 106-107 J 6
Nahungo 171 D 5
Nahunta, GA 80-81 EF 5
Nāhyā 170 II a 1
Naica 76-77 B 9
Naicam 61 F 4
Naicó 106-107 E 6
Na'idah, 'Anu an- 166-167 K 6
Naiguatá 94-95 H 2
Naihāti 138-139 M 6
Nain [CDN] 56-57 Y 6
Nāʾīn [IR] 134-135 G 4
Naindi 148-149 a 2
Naini Tal 134-135 M 5
Nainpur 138-139 H 6
Nain Singh Range = Nganglong Gangri 142-143 E 5
Naipo, Ilha — 94-95 G 6
Nair = Ner 138-139 F 7
Nairn 119 E 3
Nairobi 172 G 2
Naissaar 124-125 E 4
Naivasha 172 G 2
Naiyyāttinkara = Neyyāttinkara 140 C 6
Najaf, An- 134-135 E 4
Najafābād 134-135 G 4
Najd 134-135 E 5-6
Najʿ Ḥammādī 173 BC 4-5
Najībābād 138-139 G 3
Najin 142-143 P 3
Najran 134-135 E 7
Najstenjarvi 124-125 J 2
Naju 144-145 F 5
Naka 155 III c 1
Naka = Io 206-207 S 7
Naka, Yokohama- 155 III a 3
Nakadōri-shima 144-145 G 6
Na Kae 150-151 E 4
Naka gawa 144-145 K 6
Nakajima 155 III c 3
Nakajō 144-145 M 3
Nakakido 155 III d 1
Nakaminato 144-145 N 4
Nakamura 144-145 J 6
Nakamura = Sōma 144-145 N 4
Nakanbu, Tōkyō- 155 III b 2
Nakano 144-145 M 4
Nakano, Tōkyō- 155 III ab 1
Nakano-shima 144-145 J 4
Nakanoshima, Kawasaki- 155 III a 2
Nakano-umi 144-145 J 5
Nakasato 144-145 N 2
Naka-Shibetsu 144-145 d 2
Nakasongola 171 C 2
Nakatane 144-145 H 7
Nakatsu 144-145 H 6
Nakatsukawa 144-145 L 5
Nakatsukawa = Nakatsugawa 144-145 L 5
Nakatu 144-145 H 6
Nakayama, Yokohama- 155 III a 2
Nakchamik Island 58-59 e 1
Naked Island 58-59 O 6
Nakfa 164-165 M 5
Nakhichevan Autonomous Soviet Socialist Republic 126-127 M 7
Nakhīlah, An- 166-167 E 2
Nakhīl, Bi'r — 136-137 K 5
Nakhl 173 C 3
Nakhlāy, Bi'r — 173 B 6
Nakhon Lampang = Lampang 148-149 C 3
Nakhon Nayok 150-151 C 5
Nakhon Pathom 148-149 CD 4
Nakhon Phanom 148-149 D 3
Nakhon Ratchasima 148-149 D 3-4
Nakhon Rat Sima 150-151 DE 4-5
Nakhon Sawan 148-149 CD 3
Nakhon Si Thammarat 148-149 CD 5
Nakhon Tai 150-151 C 4
Nakhtarāna 138-139 B 6
Nakina 56-57 T 7
Nakło nad Notecią 118 H 2
Naknek, AK 56-57 E 6
Naknek Lake 58-59 JK 7
Nakodar 138-139 E 2
Nakonde 171 C 5
Nakop 174-175 CD 5
Nakou 146-147 F 9
Nakpanduri 168-169 EF 3
Nakskov 116-117 D 10
Nakṭa = Naqaṭah 166-167 M 2
Naktong-gang 144-145 G 5
Nakur 138-139 F 3
Nakuru 172 G 2
Nakusp 60 J 4
Nakwaby 168-169 E 3
Nāl 134-135 K 5
Nalaguṇḍa = Nalgonda 140 D 2
Nalajch 142-143 K 2
Nalazi 174-175 K 3
Nalbāri 141 B 2
Nalcayec, Isla — 108-109 C 6
Nal'čik 126-127 L 5
Na Le = Ban Na Le 150-151 C 3
Nalgonda 140 D 2
Nalhāti 138-139 L 5
Nali 150-151 G 2
Nalitābāṛī 141 AB 3
Nallamala Range 140 D 2-3
Nallıhan 136-137 D 2
Nalôn 141 E 3
Nalung 138-139 M 3
Na Lu'ong = Ban Na Lu'ong 150-151 E 4
Nālūt 164-165 G 2
Nama 174-175 BC 3
Namacurra 172 G 5
Na'mah, An- 164-165 C 5
Nam Ak 141 E 5
Namak, Daryācheh — 134-135 G 4
Nāmakkal 140 D 5
Namakwaland 172 C 7
Namakwaland = Klein Namakwaland 174-175 B 5
Namakwaland, Klein — 174-175 B 5
Namakzār-e Khwāf 134-135 HJ 4
Namakzār-e Shahdād 134-135 H 4
Namaland 172 C 7
Namamugi, Yokohama- 155 III b 3
Na'mān, Jazīrat an — = Jazīrat an-Nu'mān 173 D 4
Namanga 172 G 2
Namangan 134-135 L 2
Na'māniyah, An- 136-137 L 6
Namanyere 172 F 3
Namapa 172 GH 4
Namaqua Land, Little — = Klein Namakwaland 174-175 B 5
Namarrói 172 G 5
Namasagali 172 F 1
Namasakata 171 D 5
Namāshah, Jabal an- 166-167 K 2
Namashu 138-139 J 3
Namatanai 148-149 h 5
Namatele 171 D 5
Namban 141 F 5
Nambanje 171 D 5
Nam Bei 141 E 4
Nam Beng 150-151 C 2
Nam Bô 148-149 DE 5
Nambour 158-159 K 5
Nam Cađinh = Nam Theun 150-151 E 3
Năm Căn 148-149 D 5
Nāmche Bāzār 138-139 L 4
Namchhe Bazār = Nāmche Bāzār 138-139 L 4
Nam Chi 150-151 DE 5
Nam Choed Yai = Kra Buri 148-149 C 4
Nam Choen 150-151 CD 4
Namch'ŏnjŏm 144-145 F 3
Namcy 132-133 Y 5
Nam Đinh 148-149 E 2-3
Namerikawa 144-145 L 4
Nametil 172 G 5
Namew Lake 61 G 3
Nam-gang 144-145 F 3
Namgôk 141 E 5
Namhae-do 144-145 G 5
Namhan-gang 144-145 F 4
Nam Hka 141 F 5
Namhkok = Namgôk 141 E 5
Namhoi = Foshan 142-143 L 7
Namhsan = Namzan 141 E 4
Nam Hsin 141 F 5
Nam Hu = Nam Ou 150-151 D 2
Nami 150-151 C 9
Namib = Namibwoestyn 172 B 5-C 7
Namib Desert = Namibwoestyn 172 B 5-C 7
Namibia 172 C 6
Namib-Naukluft Park 172 BC 6
Namibwoestyn 172 B 5-C 7
Namies 174-175 C 5
Namiziz 174-175 B 4
Namjabarba Ri 142-143 H 6
Nam Kam 150-151 E 4
Nam Khan 150-151 D 2-3
Nam Khan = Nangan 141 E 4
Nam Kok 150-151 B 2-3
Nam Kong 150-151 F 5
Namlan 141 E 4
Namlang River = Nam Ak 141 E 5
Namlāt, An- 166-167 KL 2
Namlea 148-149 J 7
Nam Lieau = Ea Hleo 150-151 F 6
Nam Lik 150-151 D 3
Namling Dsong 142-143 FG 6
Nam Luang 150-151 D 4
Nam Lwei 150-151 B 2
Nam Ma 150-151 D 1
Nammadū 141 E 4
Nam Madū Myit 141 EF 4
Nam Mae Chaem 150-151 B 3
Nam Mae Ing 150-151 C 2-3
Nam Mae Klong = Nam Mae Ngat 150-151 B 3
Nam Mae Lao 150-151 B 3
Nam Mae Ngat 150-151 B 3
Nam Mae Pai 150-151 B 3
Nam Mae Tun 150-151 B 4
Namman [BUR] 141 E 6
Nam Man [T, place] 150-151 C 4
Nam Man [T, river] 150-151 C 4
Nam Mao = Nam Wa 150-151 C 3
Nammeigôn 141 E 6
Nam Me Klong = Mae Nam Mae Klong 150-151 B 5-6
Nam-me Klong = Mae Nam Ma Klong 150-151 B 5-6
Nammokon = Nammeigôn 141 E 6
Nam Mu'one 150-151 E 3
Nam Na 150-151 D 1
Nam Ngum 150-151 D 3
Nam Nhiệp 150-151 D 3
Namoa = Nan'ao 146-147 F 10
Namoa = Nan'ao Dao 146-147 F 10
Namoi River 158-159 J 6
Namoluk 208 F 2
Namone = Ban Namone 150-151 D 3
Namorik 208 G 2
Nam Ou 150-151 D 1
Namous, Ouèd en — = Wādī an-Nāmus 164-165 D 2
Nampa 60 J 1
Nampa, ID 64-65 C 3
Nam Pak 150-151 D 2
Nampala 164-165 C 5
Nam Pat 150-151 C 4
Nam Phao = Ban Nam Phao 150-151 C 3
Nam Phong 150-151 CD 4
Nampo 142-143 NO 4
Namp'o'ae-san 144-145 G 2
Nampula 172 GH 5
Nam Pûn 141 E 5-6
Nampung 138-139 M 4
Namru He = Ru He 146-147 E 5
Nam Sane 150-151 D 3
Namsen 116-117 E 5
Nam Seng 150-151 D 2
Namsi 144-145 E 3
Nam Si = Nam Chi 150-151 DE 5
Nam Soen = Nam Choen 150-151 CD 4
Nam Som 150-151 CD 4
Namsos 116-117 DE 5
Nam Suong = Nam Seng 150-151 D 2
Nam Tae = Ban Nam Tao 150-151 C 4
Nam Tan 141 F 5
Nam Teng = Nam Tan 141 F 5
Nam Tha 148-149 D 2
Nam Theun 150-151 E 3
Nam Tho'n = Nam Theun 150-151 E 3
Nam Tia = Ban Nam Tia 150-151 D 3
Nam Tilû 141 E 5
Nam Tsho 142-143 G 5
Namtu = Nammadū 141 E 4
Namu [CDN] 60 D 4
Namu [Micronesia] 208 G 2
Nam U = Nam Ou 150-151 D 1
Namuli, Serra — 172 G 5
Namuling Zong = Namling Dsong 142-143 FG 6
Namulo 171 D 6
Namuno 171 D 6
Namur 120-121 K 3
Namur Lake 61 B 2
Nāmūs, Wādī an- 164-165 D 2
Nāmūs, Waw an- 164-165 H 4
Namutoni 172 C 5
Nam Wa 150-151 C 3
Namwala 172 E 5
Nam Wei 155 I b 1
Namwŏn 144-145 F 5
Nam Yao = Nam Madū Myit 141 EF 4
Namzan 141 E 4
Nan 148-149 D 3
Nan, Mae Nam — 148-149 D 3
Nana Candungo 172 D 4
Nanae 144-145 b 3
Nanafalia, AL 78-79 F 4
Nanaimo 56-57 M 8
N'an'ajo' 124-125 S 2
Nanam 144-145 GH 2
Nana-Mambéré 164-165 GH 7
Nan'an 146-147 G 9
Nanango 158-159 K 5
Nananib Plateau = Nananibplato 174-175 B 3
Nananibplato 174-175 B 3
Nanao [J] 144-145 L 4
Nan-ao [RC] 146-147 H 9
Nan'ao [TJ] 146-147 F 10
Nan'ao Dao 146-147 F 10
Nan-ao Tao = Nan'ao Dao 146-147 F 10
Nanao wan 144-145 L 4
Nanas Channel 154 III b 1
Nanau 171 E 1
Nanay 96-97 E 3
Nanay, Río — 92-93 E 5
Nanbē 141 E 6
Nancefield, Johannesburg- 170 V a 2
Nancha 142-143 O 2
Nanchang 142-143 LM 6
Nanchang = Nanchong 142-143 JK 5
Nan-chang = Nanzhang 146-147 CD 6
Nanchang He 155 II a 2
Nanchao = Nanzhao 146-147 D 5
Nancheng 142-143 M 6
Nan-ch'iao = Fengxian 146-147 H 6
Nan-ching = Nanjing [TJ, Fujian] 146-147 F 9
Nan-ching = Nanjing [TJ, Jiangsu] 142-143 M 5
Nanchino = Nanjing 142-143 M 5
Nan-chi Shan = Nanji Shan 146-147 H 8
Nanchong 142-143 JK 5
Nanchung = Nanchong 142-143 JK 5
Nancy 120-121 L 4
Nancy Creek 85 II b 1
Nanda Devi 134-135 MN 4
Nandalur 140 D 3
Nandan 144-145 K 5
Nandangaṛh, Laoriā- = Thori 138-139 K 4
Nandapur 140 F 1
Nandapura = Nandapur 140 F 1
Nānded 134-135 M 7
Nandeir = Nānded 134-135 M 7
Nāndgāṅv = Nāndgaon 138-139 E 7
Nāndgaon 138-139 E 7
Nandi [FJI] 148-149 a 2
Nandi [IND] 140 C 4
Nandigāma 140 E 2
Nandikotkūr 140 D 3
Nandikōṭṭakkūru = Nandikotkūr 140 D 3
N'andoma 132-133 G 5
Nanduan River 62 A 1
Ñandubay 106-107 GH 3
Ñanducita 106-107 G 3
Nandu He 150-151 H 3
Nāndūra 138-139 F 7
Nandurbār 134-135 L 6
Nandyāl 134-135 M 7
Nanfeng [TJ, Guangdong] 146-147 C 10
Nanfeng [TJ, Jiangxi] 146-147 F 8
Nangade 171 DE 5
Nanga-Eboko 164-165 G 8
Nangal 138-139 F 2
Nangan 141 E 4
Nan-gang = Nam-gang 144-145 F 3
Nangā Parbat 134-135 LM 3-4
Nangapinoh 148-149 F 7
Nangaraun 152-153 K 5
Nangariza, Río — 96-97 B 4
Nangatayab 152-153 J 6
Nang'-ch'ien = Nangqian 142-143 H 5
Nanggûn Bûm 141 F 2
Nangkhartse Dsong 138-139 N 3
Nangnim-sanmaek 144-145 F 2
Nangong 146-147 E 3
Nangqian 142-143 H 5
Nang Rong 150-151 D 5
Nanguan 146-147 D 3
Nangugī 141 E 7
Nanguneri 140 C 6
Nan Hai 142-143 L 8-M 7
Nanhai = Foshan 142-143 L 7
Nanhe [TJ, place] 146-147 E 3
Nan He [TJ, river] 146-147 C 5
Nan-ho = Nanhe [TJ, place] 146-147 E 3
Nan Ho = Nan He [TJ, river] 146-147 C 5
Nanhsien = Nan Xian 146-147 D 7
Nan-hsiung = Nanxiong 142-143 LM 6
Nanhuatang 146-147 C 5
Nanhui 146-147 HJ 6
Nanika Lake 60 D 3
Nānikon 128 IV b 1
Nañjanagūḍu = Nanjangūd 140 C 4
Nanjangūd 140 C 4
Nanjiangqiao 146-147 DE 7

Nanjih Tao = Nanri Qundao 146-147 G 9
Nanjing [TJ, Fujian] 146-147 F 9
Nanjing [TJ, Jiangsu] 142-143 M 5
Nanji Shan 146-147 H 8
Nankana = Nankāna Sahib 138-139 DE 2
Nankāna Sahib 138-139 DE 2
Nankang [TJ, Guangdong] 146-147 B 11
Nankang [TJ, Jiangxi] 146-147 E 9
Nan-kang = Xingzi 146-147 F 7
Nankhu 142-143 G 3
Nanking = Nanjing 142-143 M 5
Nankoku 144-145 JK 6
Nan-kuan = Nanguan 146-147 D 3
Nankung = Nangong 146-147 E 3
Nanlaoye Ling 144-145 E 2-F 1
Nanle 146-147 E 3-4
Nan Ling [TJ, mountains] 142-143 L 6-7
Nanling [TJ, place] 142-143 M 5
Nan-liu Chiang = Nanliu Jiang 146-147 B 10-11
Nanliu Jiang 146-147 B 10-11
Nan-lo = Nanle 146-147 E 3-4
Nanma 146-147 H 7
Nanmofang, Beijing- 155 II b 2
Nanning 142-143 K 7
Nannup 158-159 C 6
Na Noi 150-151 C 3
Nanpan Jiang 142-143 JK 7
Nānpāra 138-139 H 4
Nanpi 146-147 F 2
Nanping [TJ, Fujian] 142-143 M 6
Nanping [TJ, Hubei] 142-143 L 6
Nan-p'u Ch'i = Nanpu Xi 146-147 G 8
Nanpu Xi 146-147 G 8
Nanqi = Youxikou 146-147 G 8
Nanripo 171 D 6
Nanri Qundao 146-147 G 9
Nansei Islands = Nansei-shotō 142-143 N 7-O 6
Nansei-shotō 142-143 NO 6-7
Nansei syotō = Nansei-shotō 142-143 NO 6-7
Nansen Sound 56-57 ST 1
Nan Shan 142-143 HJ 4
Nansio 172 F 2
Nantai-san 144-145 M 4
Nan-tch'ang = Nanchang 142-143 LM 6
Nan-tch'eng = Nancheng 142-143 M 6
Nan-tch'ong = Nanchong 142-143 JK 5
Nantes 120-121 G 5
Nantian 146-147 HJ 7
Nantian Dao 146-147 HJ 7
Nanticoke, PA 72-73 HJ 4
Nanton 60 L 4
Nantong 142-143 N 5
Nantongjiao 152-153 K 2
Nantou [RC] 146-147 H 10
Nantou [TJ] 146-147 D 10
Nantsang = Nanchang 142-143 LM 6
Nantucket, MA 72-73 LM 4
Nantucket Island 64-65 N 3
Nantucket Sound 72-73 L 4
Nantung = Nantong 142-143 N 5
Nanty Glo, PA 72-73 G 4
Nanumanga 208 H 3
Nanumea 208 H 3
Nānuṅ Raṇ = Little Rann 138-139 C 6
Nanuque 92-93 LM 8
Nanushuk River 58-59 M 2
Nan Xian 146-147 D 7
Nanxiong 142-143 LM 6
Nanyang 142-143 L 5
Nanyangchang 155 II b 3
Nanyang Hu 146-147 F 4
Nanyi = Nancha 142-143 O 2
Nanyuan, Beijing- 155 II b 3
Nanyuki 172 G 1
Nanzhang 146-147 CD 6
Nanzhao 146-147 D 5
Nanzheng = Hanzhong 142-143 K 5
Nao, Cabo de la — 120-121 H 9
Naochow Tao = Naozhou Dao 146-147 C 11
Naoconane Lake 56-57 W 7
Naoetsu 144-145 LM 4
Naogang = Nowgong 138-139 G 5
Naogāṅv = Nowgong 141 C 2
Naogaon = Naugāon 138-139 M 5
Naōgata = Nōgata 144-145 H 6
Naoli He 142-143 P 2
Nao-li Ho = Naoli He 142-143 P 2
Naos 174-175 B 2
Naos, Isla — 64-65 bc 3
Naouā = Nawā 136-137 FG 6
Naozhou Dao 146-147 C 11
Napa, CA 74-75 B 3
Napabalana 152-153 P 8
Napaimiut, AK 58-59 H 6
Napakiak, AK 58-59 FG 6
Napaku 148-149 G 6
Napaleofú 106-107 H 6
Napan 148-149 L 7
Napanee 72-73 H 2
Napas 132-133 P 6
Napaseudut 52
Nape 148-149 DE 3
Napenay 104-105 F 10
Na Phao = Ban Na Phao 150-151 E 4
Napier [NZ] 158-159 P 7
Napier [ZA] 174-175 C 8
Napier, Mount — 158-159 EF 3
Napier Mountains 53 C 6
Napinka 68-69 F 1
Naples, FL 64-65 K 6
Naples, NY 72-73 H 3
Naples = Nàpoli 122-123 EF 5
Naples, Gulf of — = Golfo di Nàpoli 122-123 E 5
Napo 96-97 C 2
Napo, Río — 92-93 E 5
Napo, Serranía de — 96-97 C 2
Napoleon, ND 68-69 G 2
Napoleon, OH 70-71 HJ 5
Napoleonville, LA 78-79 D 5-6
Nàpoli 122-123 E 5
Nàpoli, Golfo di — 122-123 EF 5
Napostá 106-107 F 7
Nappanee, IN 70-71 GH 5
Napu 152-153 NO 10
Naqāda = Naqādah 173 C 5
Naqādah 173 C 5
Naqadeh 136-137 L 4
Naqatah 166-167 M 2
Nāqishūt 164-165 L 8
Naqrīn 166-167 K 2
Naque 102-103 L 3
Naqūrah, Rā's an- 136-137 F 6
Nara [J] 144-145 KL 5
Nārā [PAK] 134-135 K 5
Nara [RMM] 164-165 C 5
Naracoorte 158-159 GH 7
Naradhan 160 GH 4
Naraingarh = Nārāyangarh 138-139 F 2
Nārāinpur 138-139 H 8
Narāl 138-139 M 6
Narala = Norla 138-139 J 7
Naramata 66-67 D 1
Naranjal 96-97 B 3
Naranjal, Río — 96-97 B 3
Naranjas, Punta — 92-93 C 3
Naranjito 96-97 B 3
Naranjo 94-95 C 6
Narasannapeta 140 G 1
Narasapur 140 E 2
Narasāpura = Narsāpur 140 D 2
Narasāpuram = Narasapur 140 E 2
Narasaraopet 140 E 2
Narasarāvpēṭa = Narasaraopet 140 E 2
Narashino 155 III d 1
Narasiṅhpur = Narsimhapur 138-139 G 6
Narasīpaṭṭaṇam = Narsīpatnam 140 F 2
Narasīpura = Tirumakūḍal Narsipur 140 C 4
Narathiwat 148-149 DE 5
Nara Visa, NM 76-77 C 5
Nārāyaṇapēṭa = Nārāyanpet 140 C 2
Narāyanganj 134-135 OP 6
Nārāyangarh 138-139 F 2
Nārāyankher 140 CD 1-2
Nārāyanpet 140 C 2
Narbadā = Narmada 134-135 LM 6
Narberth, PA 84 III b 1
Narbonne 120-121 J 7
Narchhen 138-139 JK 3
Nardiganj 138-139 K 5
Nardò 122-123 GH 5
Naré 106-107 G 3
Narembeen 158-159 C 6
Naréna 168-169 C 2
Narendranagar 138-139 FG 2
Narew 118 K 2
Nargen = Naissaar 124-125 E 4
Nārgol 138-139 D 7
Nargund 140 B 3
Nargya 138-139 M 3
Nāṛī 134-135 K 5
Narib 174-175 B 3
Narimanabad 126-127 O 7
Narin 146-147 C 2
Narinda, Helodranon'i — 172 J 4
Narin Nur 146-147 AB 2
Nariño [CO, Antioquia] 94-95 D 5
Nariño [CO, Córdoba] 94-95 CD 3
Nariño [CO, Nariño] 94-95 BC 7
Nariño, Museo de — 91 III b 3
Narjan-Mar 132-133 JK 4
Narli 136-137 G 4
Narmada 134-135 LM 6
Narman 136-137 J 2
Nārnaol = Nārnaul 138-139 F 3
Nārnaul 138-139 F 3
Naroč' 124-125 F 6
Narodnaja, gora — 132-133 L 5
Naro-Fominsk 124-125 KL 6
Narok 172 G 2
Narooma 158-159 JK 7
Narop 174-175 B 3
Narovl'a 124-125 G 8
Nārowāl 138-139 E 1
Narrabri 158-159 JK 6
Narragansett Bay 72-73 L 4
Narrandera 158-159 J 6
Narran Lake 160 H 2
Narran River 160 H 2
Narrogin 158-159 C 6
Narromine 158-159 J 6
Narrows, OR 66-67 D 4
Narrows, VA 80-81 F 2
Narrows, The — 82 III b 3
Narsampet 140 DE 2
Narsāpur 140 D 2
Narsimhapur 138-139 G 6
Narsingdī 141 B 3-4
Narsinghgarh 138-139 F 6
Narsinghpur 138-139 K 7
Narsīpatnam 140 F 2
Narsipur = Tirumakūḍal Narsipur 140 C 4
Narssaq 56-57 bc 5
Narssarssuaq 56-57 bc 5
Narte de Santander 94-95 E 3-4
Nartkala 126-127 LM 5
Narubis 174-175 C 4
Narugas 174-175 C 5
Narugo 144-145 N 3
Narungombe 171 D 5
Naru-shima 144-145 G 6
Naruto 144-145 K 5
Narva [SU, place] 132-133 D 6
Narva [SU, river] 124-125 F 4
Narva Bay = Narva laht 124-125 F 4
Narváez 104-105 D 7
Narva-Jõesuu 124-125 FG 4
Narva laht 124-125 F 4
Narvānā = Narwāna 138-139 F 3
Narvik 116-117 G 3
Narvskoje vodochranilišče 124-125 G 4
Narwa = Narva 132-133 D 6
Narwāna 138-139 F 3
Narym 132-133 P 6
Naryn [SU, Kirgizskaja SSR place] 134-135 M 2
Naryn [SU, Kirgizskaja SSR river] 134-135 L 2
Naryn [SU, Rossijskaja SFSR] 132-133 S 7
Naryn = Taš-Kumyr 134-135 L 2
Narynkol 134-135 MN 2
Naryškino 124-125 K 7
Nasafjell 116-117 F 4
Nasaló 106-107 F 2
Na Sâm 150-151 F 1
Na San = Ban Na San 150-151 B 8
Nasarawa [WAN, Gongola] 168-169 J 3
Nasarawa [WAN, Plateau] 164-165 F 7
Nasaret = Nazĕrat 136-137 F 6
Năsăud 122-123 L 2
Nascente 100-101 D 4
Naschel 106-107 E 4
Naschitti, NM 74-75 J 4
Nash Harbor, AK 58-59 D 6
Nāshik = Nāsik 134-135 L 6-7
Nashiño, Río — 96-97 D 2
Nashū, Ḥāssī — 166-167 H 4
Nashua, MT 68-69 C 1
Nashua, NH 72-73 L 3
Nashu Bûm 141 E 3
Nashville, AR 76-77 GH 5
Nashville, GA 80-81 E 5
Nashville, IL 70-71 F 6
Nashville, KS 68-69 G 7
Nashville, MI 70-71 H 4
Nashville, TN 64-65 J 4
Nashville Basin 78-79 F 2
Nashwauk, MN 70-71 D 2
Nasia 168-169 E 3
Našice 122-123 H 3
Näsijärvi 116-117 KL 7
Nāsik 134-135 L 6-7
Nāṣir 164-165 L 7
Nasir, Jabal an- 164-165 F 4
Nasīrābād [IND] 138-139 E 4
Nasīrābad [PAK] 138-139 A 4
Nāsirīyah 166-167 HJ 1
Nāsirīyah, An- 134-135 F 4
Nāṣir Muḥammad 138-139 A 4
Nasiyah, Jabal — 173 C 6
Nas Nas Point = Melkbospunt 174-175 B 5
Nasondoye 172 DE 4
Na Song = Ban Na Song 150-151 E 4
Naṣr 173 B 3
Naṣr, An- 173 C 5
Naṣr, Hazzān an- 173 C 6
Naṣr, Khazzan an- 164-165 L 4
Nāṣrīyah 136-137 G 6
Nasrullāhganj = Nāsrūllāhganj 138-139 F 6
Nāsrullāhganj 138-139 F 6
Nassarawa = Nasarawa 164-165 F 7
Nassau [BS] 64-65 L 6
Nassau [island] 156-157 J 5
Nassau, Bahía — 111 C 9
Nassau Sound 80-81 c 1
Nass Basin 60 C 2
Nassenwil 128 IV a 1
Nässjö 116-117 F 9
Nass River 56-57 L 6-7
Nastapoka Islands 56-57 V 6
Nasva 124-125 GH 5
Nata 172 E 6
Na-ta = Dan Xian 142-143 K 8
Natagaima 92-93 DE 4
Natal [BR, Amazonas] 98-99 D 7
Natal [BR, Maranhão] 100-101 C 3
Natal [BR, Rio Grande do Norte] 92-93 MN 6
Natal [CDN] 66-67 F 1
Natal [RI] 148-149 C 6
Natal [ZA] 172 EF 7
Natal Basin 50-51 LM 7
Natalia, TX 76-77 E 8
Natalkuz Lake 60 E 3
Natal Ridge 172 G 8
Natanya = Nĕtanya 136-137 F 6
Natash, Wādī — 173 CD 5
Natashquan 63 EF 2
Natashquan River 56-57 Y 7
Natchez, MS 64-65 H 5
Natchitoches, LA 64-65 H 5
Na Thao 150-151 DE 3
Na Thawi 150-151 C 9
Nāthdvārā = Nāthdwāra 138-139 DE 5
Nāthdwāra 138-139 DE 5
Na Thon = Ban Nathon 150-151 F 4
Nathorst land 116-117 jk 6
Nathrop, CO 68-69 C 6
Nathu La 138-139 M 4
Nation, AK 58-59 QR 4
Nation, Palais de la — 128 II b 1
National Arboretum 82 II b 2
National City, CA 74-75 E 6
National City, MI 70-71 HJ 3
National History, Museum of — 155 II b 2
Nationalities, Cultural Palace of — 155 II b 2
National Library 154 II b 2
National Library of Peking 155 II b 2
National Museum of Singapore 154 III b 2
National Park 80-81 E 3
National Park, NJ 84 III bc 2
National Park of Tōkyō 155 III b 2
National Reactor Testing Station 66-67 G 4
National Stadium 170 III b 2
National Stadium of Singapore 154 III b 2
National Stadium of Tōkyō 155 III b 1-2
National Zoological Park 82 II ab 1
Nation River [CDN] 60 F 2
Nation River [USA] 58-59 R 4
Natitingou 164-165 E 6
Natividade 92-93 K 7
Natívitas 91 I c 3
Natmauk 141 D 5
Natogyi = Nwādōgyī 141 D 5
Natoma, KS 68-69 G 6
Nātong Dsong 142-143 G 6
Nāṭor 138-139 M 5
Natron, Lake — 172 G 2
Natrun, Bir el — = Wāḥāt al-'Aṭrūn 164-165 K 5
Naṭrūn, Wādī an- 173 AB 2
Natrun Lakes = Wādī an-Naṭrūn 173 AB 2
Nattalin 141 D 6
Nattam 140 D 5
Natuna Islands = Kepulauan Bunguran Utara 148-149 E 6
Natural Bridges National Monument 74-75 HJ 4
Naturaliste, Cape — 158-159 B 6
Natural Science, Museum of — 85 III b 2
Naturita, CO 74-75 J 3
Naṭuvangngāṭ = Nedumangād 140 C 6
Naucalpan de Juárez, Ciudad de — 91 I b 2
Nauchas = Naukhas 174-175 B 2
Na'u Chhu 138-139 J 2
Naufragados, Ponta — 102-103 HJ 7
Naugāon 138-139 M 5
Naugo Bûm 141 CD 4
Naugong = Nowgong 138-139 G 5
Nauja Vileika, Vilnius- 124-125 EF 6
Naukhas 174-175 B 2
Naulavaraa 116-117 N 6
Naulila 172 BC 5
Naunglôn 141 E 6
Nā'ūr 136-137 F 7
Nauru 156-157 H 5
Náusa 122-123 JK 5
Naushahro Fīroz 138-139 B 4
Nauški 132-133 U 7
Nauta 92-93 E 5
Nautanwā 138-139 J 4
Nautla 86-87 M 7
Nauvo 116-117 JK 7
Nava [MEX] 76-77 D 8
Navābganj = Nawābganj 138-139 H 4
Navādā = Nawāda 138-139 K 5
Nava de Ricomalillo, La — 120-121 E 9
Navajo, AZ 74-75 J 5
Navajo Indian Reservation 74-75 HJ 4
Navajo Mountain 74-75 H 4
Navajo Reservoir 68-69 C 7
Navākōṭ = Nawākot 138-139 K 4
Navalagunda = Navalgund 140 B 3
Naval Air Station [USA, New Orleans] 85 I b 2
Naval Air Station [USA, New York] 82 III c 3
Navalgarh = Nawalgarh 138-139 E 4
Navalgund 140 B 3
Naval Observatory 82 II a 1
Navan 119 C 5
Navangar = Jāmnagar 134-135 L 6
Navāṅshahar = Nawāshahr 138-139 F 2
Navāpur 138-139 DE 7
Navarin, mys — 132-133 jk 5
Navarino, Isla — 111 C 9
Navarra 120-121 G 7
Navarra, Bogotá- 91 III c 2
Navarre = Navarra 120-121 G 7
Navarro 106-107 H 5
Navašino 124-125 O 6
Navasota, TX 76-77 FG 7
Navasota River 76-77 F 7
Navassa Island 64-65 LM 8
Naver 119 D 2
Navia 120-121 D 7
Navidad 106-107 AB 4
Navio, Riacho do — 100-101 E 5
Navirai 102-103 E 5
Navl'a 124-125 K 7
Navlakhī = Nawlakhi 138-139 C 6
Navoi 132-133 M 9
Navoj 134-135 K 2
Navojoa 64-65 E 6
Navolato 64-65 E 7
Navoloki 124-125 NO 5
Návpaktos 122-123 JK 6
Návplion 122-123 K 7
Navrongo 164-165 D 6
Navşar 136-137 L 4
Navsāri 138-139 D 7
Navy Board Inlet 56-57 U 3
Navy Town, AK 58-59 p 6
Nawā 136-137 FG 6
Nawa = Naha 142-143 O 6
Nawābganj [BD] 138-139 M 5
Nawābganj [IND ↗ Bareilly] 138-139 G 3
Nawābganj [IND ↗ Lucknow] 138-139 H 4
Nawābshāh 134-135 K 5
Nawāda 138-139 K 5
Nawādhību 164-165 A 4
Nawadwip = Nabadwīp 138-139 LM 6
Nawai 138-139 EF 4
Nawākot [Nepal] 138-139 K 4
Nawa Koṭ [PAK] 138-139 C 3
Nawākshūt 164-165 A 5
Nawāl, Sabkhat an- 166-167 LM 2
Nāwalapiṭiya 140 E 7
Nawalgarh 138-139 E 4
Nawān Koṭ 138-139 C 2
Nawāpāra 138-139 J 7
Nawapur = Navāpur 138-139 DE 7
Nawari = Nahari 144-145 JK 6
Nawāshahr 138-139 F 2
Nawāṣīf, Ḥarrat — 134-135 E 6
Nawfalīyah, An- 164-165 H 2
Nawlakhi 138-139 C 6
Nawngchik = Nong Chik 150-151 C 9
Naws, Rā's — 134-135 H 7
Náxos [GR, island] 122-123 L 7
Náxos [GR, place] 122-123 L 7
Naxos [I] 122-123 F 7
Nayá, Río — 94-95 C 6
Naya Chor 138-139 B 5
Nayāgaḍa = Nayāgarh 138-139 K 7
Nayāgarh 138-139 K 7
Nayakot = Nawākot 138-139 K 4
Nayarit 64-65 EF 7
Nāy Band [IR, Banāder va Jazāyer-e Khalīj-e Fārs] 134-135 G 5
Nāy Band [IR, Khorāsān] 134-135 H 4
Nāy Band, Ra's-e — 134-135 G 5
Naylor, MO 78-79 D 2
Nayoro 144-145 c 1
Nayoro = Gornozavodsk 132-133 b 8
Nāyudupeta 140 DE 4
Nazacara 104-105 B 5
Nazan Bay 58-59 jk 4
Nazaré [BR, Amapá] 98-99 N 4
Nazaré [BR, Amazonas] 92-93 F 4
Nazaré [BR, Bahia] 92-93 M 7
Nazaré [BR, Pará] 98-99 M 8
Nazaré [P] 120-121 C 9
Nazaré = Nazĕrat 136-137 F 6
Nazaré da Mata 100-101 G 4
Nazaré do Piauí 100-101 C 4
Nazareno 104-105 D 7
Nazareth [PE] 96-97 B 4
Nazareth = Nazĕrat 136-137 F 6
Nazário 102-103 H 2
Nazarovka 124-125 N 6
Nazas, Río — 86-87 H 5
Nazca 92-93 DE 7
Nazca Ridge 156-157 N 6-O 5
Naze, The — = Lindesnes 116-117 B 9
Nazĕrat 136-137 F 6
Nazija 124-125 HJ 4
Nazilli 136-137 C 4
Nazimiye 136-137 HJ 3
Nazimovo 132-133 QR 6
Nazina 132-133 OP 5-6
Nāzira 141 D 2
Nažir Hāṭ 141 BC 4
Nazko 60 F 3
Nazko River 60 F 3
Nazlat as-Sammān 170 II ab 2
Nāzlū Rūd 136-137 L 4
Nazombe 171 D 5
Nazrēt 164-165 M 7
Nazwā 134-135 H 6
Nazyvajevsk 132-133 N 6
Nazzah 173 B 4
Nchanga 171 AB 6
Nchelenge 171 B 5
Ndabala 171 B 6
N'daghāmshah, Sabkhat — 164-165 AB 5
Ndai 148-149 k 6
Ndala 171 C 4
Ndalatando 172 BC 3
N'Dali 164-165 E 7
N'Dande 168-169 A 2
Ndélé 164-165 J 7
N'Dendé 172 B 2
Ndeni 148-149 l 7
Ndikiniméki 168-169 H 4
N'Dioum 168-169 B 1
N'djamena 164-165 GH 6
Ndjili 170 IV b 2
Ndjili, Grande Île de la — 170 IV b 1
Ndjolé [Gabon] 168-169 H 4
N'Djolé [RFC] 172 AB 2
Ndola 172 E 4
N'dolo = Aéroport de Kinshasa 170 IV a 1
N'dolo, Kinshasa- 170 IV b 1
Ndumu Game Reserve 174-175 K 4
Nduye 171 B 2
Ndwedwe 174-175 J 5
Ndye 171 B 2
Ndzuwani 172 HJ 4
Néa Filadélfeia 113 IV a 1
Neagh, Lough — 119 C 4
Neah Bay, WA 66-67 A 1
Néa Iōnía [GR, Athēnai] 113 IV b 1
Neale, Lake — 158-159 F 4
Neales 158-159 G 5
Néa Liósia 113 IV a 1
Neamati 141 D 2
Neápolis [GR, Grámmos] 122-123 J 5
Neápolis [GR, Pelopónnēsos] 122-123 K 7
Near Islands 52 D 1
Near North Side, Chicago-, IL 83 II b 1
Néa Smýrnē 113 IV a 2
Nebek, En — = An-Nabk 134-135 D 4
Nebeur = Nibr 166-167 L 1
Nebine Creek 158-159 J 5
Nebit-Dag 134-135 GH 3
Neblina, Pico da — 92-93 FG 4
Neblina, Pico de — 98-99 F 4
Neblina, Sierra de la — 94-95 HJ 7
Nebo 174-175 H 3
Nebo, Mount — 74-75 H 3
Nebolči 124-125 J 4
Nébou 168-169 E 3
Nebraska 64-65 FG 3
Nebraska City, NE 70-71 BC 5
Nebrodie, Monti — 122-123 F 7
Necadah, WI 70-71 E 3
Nechako Plateau 56-57 L 7
Neches, TX 76-77 G 7
Neches River 76-77 G 7
Nechi 94-95 D 3
Nechí, Río — 94-95 D 4
Nechou, Hassi — = Ḥāssī Nashū 166-167 H 4
Nechvorošča 126-127 G 2
Neckar 118 D 4
Necochea 111 E 5
Necocli 94-95 C 3
Nederhorst den Berg 128 I b 2
Nederland, TX 76-77 G 8
Nederlandse Antillen 88-89 M 8
Nedlitz, Potsdam- 130 III a 2
Nédroma = Nidrūmā 166-167 F 2
Nedumangād 140 C 6
Neebish Island 70-71 H 2
Needham, Mount — 60 A 3
Needle Peak 74-75 E 5
Needles 60 HJ 4-5
Needles, CA 74-75 F 5
Ñeembucú 102-103 CD 7
Neem-ka-Thana = Nīm ka Thāna 138-139 EF 4
Neemuch = Nīmach 138-139 E 5
Neenah, WI 70-71 F 3
Neepawa 56-57 R 7
Neerach 128 IV a 1
Nee Soon 154 III ab 1
Nefoussa, Djebel — = Jabal Nafusah 164-165 G 2
Nefta = Naftah 166-167 K 3
Neftečala = 26 Bakinskij Komissarov 126-127 OP 7
Neftegorsk 126-127 J 4
Neftejugansk 132-133 NO 5
Neftekamsk 124-125 U 5
Neftekumsk 126-127 M 4
Nefud = An-Nafūd 134-135 E 5
Nefud, En — = An-Nafūd 134-135 E 5
Nefzāoua = Nifzāwah 166-167 L 3
Negade = Naqādah 173 C 5
Négansi 168-169 F 3
Negapatam = Nāgapattinam 134-135 MN 8
Negara 148-149 FG 8
Negara, Sungai — 152-153 L 7
Negaunee, MI 70-71 G 2
Negeb = Negev 136-137 F 7
Negelē 164-165 MN 7
Nēgenagira Palāna ◁ 140 E 7
Negeribatin 152-153 F 8
Negeri Sembilan 150-151 CD 11
Negerpynten 116-117 l 6
Neggina 61 K 4
Neggio = Nejo 164-165 M 7
Neghilli = Negelē 164-165 MN 7
Negoiu 122-123 L 3
Negomane 171 D 5
Negombo = Mīgamuwa 134-135 M 9
Negoreloje 124-125 F 7
Negotin 122-123 K 3
Negra, La — 106-107 H 6
Negrais, Cape — = Nagare Angū 141 CD 7
Negreiros 104-105 B 6
Negribreen 116-117 k 5
Negrillos 104-105 B 6
Négrine = Naqrīn 166-167 K 2
Negritos 96-97 A 4
Negro Muerto 108-109 G 2
Negros 148-149 H 5
Negru Vodă 122-123 N 4
Neguac 63 D 4
Negueve = Negev 136-137 F 7
Nehalem, OR 66-67 B 3
Nehbandān 134-135 HJ 4
Nehe 142-143 NO 2
Nehonsey Brook 84 II b 3
Neiafu 148-149 c 2
Neibbān 141 D 7
Nei-chiang = Neijiang 142-143 JK 6
Nei-ch'iu = Neiqiu 146-147 E 3
Neidpath 61 E 5
Neihart, MT 66-67 H 2
Nei-hsiang = Neixiang 146-147 C 5
Neihuang 146-147 E 4
Neijiang 142-143 JK 6
Neikiang = Neijiang 142-143 JK 6
Neilburg 61 D 4
Neilersdrif 174-175 D 5
Neillsville, WI 70-71 E 3
Neineva 136-137 JK 5
Neiqiu 146-147 E 3
Neisse 118 G 3
Neiva 92-93 DE 4
Neixiang 146-147 C 5
Neja 132-133 G 6
Nejd = Najd 134-135 E 5-6
Nejo 164-165 M 7
Nékaounté 168-169 D 4
Nekemtē 164-165 M 7
Nekhīla, en — = An-Nakhīlah 166-167 E 2
Nekl'udovo [SU, Gor'kovskaja Oblast'] 124-125 O 5
Nekmard 138-139 M 5
Nekoosa, WI 70-71 F 3
Nekrasovskoje 124-125 N 5
Nekropolis 173 C 5
Neksø 116-117 F 10
Nelahālu 140 C 4
Nelamangala 140 C 4
Nelidovo 124-125 J 5
Neligh, NE 68-69 GH 4
Nel'kan 132-133 Za 6
Nellāyi 140 C 5
Nellikkuppam 140 DE 5
Nellore 134-135 MN 8
Nellūru = Nellore 134-135 MN 8
Nel'ma 132-133 ab 8
Nelson, AZ 74-75 G 5
Nelson, CA 74-75 C 3
Nelson, NE 68-69 G 5
Nelson, WI 70-71 E 3
Nelson [CDN] 56-57 N 8
Nelson [NZ, administrative unit] 161 E 5
Nelson [NZ, place] 158-159 O 8
Nelson [RA] 111 DE 4
Nelson, Estrecho — 111 AB 8
Nelson Forks 56-57 M 6
Nelson House 61 J 3
Nelson Island 56-57 C 5
Nelson Reservoir 68-69 BC 1
Nelson River 56-57 RS 6
Nelsonville, OH 72-73 E 5
Nelspoort 174-175 E 7
Nelspruit 172 F 7
Nem 124-125 U 3
Nema 124-125 S 5
Nemah, WA 66-67 B 2
Neman [SU, river] 124-125 E 7
Ne'māniya, An — = An-Na'mānīyah 136-137 L 6
Nemāwar 138-139 F 6
Nemenčine 124-125 E 6
Nementcha, Monts des — = Jabal an-Namāmshah 166-167 K 2
Nemira, Muntele — 122-123 M 2
Nemirov [SU, Vinnickaja Oblast'] 126-127 D 2
Nemiscau 62 N 1
Nemiscau, Lac — 62 N 1
Nemlèt, El — = An-Namlāt 166-167 KL 2
Nemocón 94-95 DE 5
Nemours = Ghazawat 164-165 D 1
Nemrut dağı 136-137 JK 3
Nemunas = Neman 124-125 E 7
Nemuro 142-143 S 3
Nemuro-kaikyō 144-145 d 1-2
Nemuro wan 144-145 d 2
Nemurs = Ghazawāt 164-165 D 2
Nenagh 119 BC 5
Nenana, AK 56-57 FG 5
Nenana River 58-59 N 4-5
Nenasi 150-151 D 11
Neneo Rucá 108-109 D 3
Nenets Autonomous Area 132-133 J-L 4
Nenjiang [TJ, place] 142-143 O 2
Nen Jiang [TJ, river] 142-143 N 2
Nen Jiang = Naguun Mörön 142-143 NO 1-2
Nenusa, Pulau-pulau — 148-149 J 6
Neodesha, KS 70-71 BC 7
Neoga, IL 70-71 F 6
Neola, UT 66-67 H 5
Néon Fálēron 113 IV a 2
Neopit, WI 70-71 F 3
Neópolis 100-101 F 6
Neosho, MO 76-77 G 4
Neosho River 64-65 G 4
Nepa 132-133 U 6
Nepal 134-135 NO 5
Nepalganj 138-139 H 3
Nepeña 96-97 B 6
Nephi, UT 74-75 GH 3
Nephin 119 B 4
Nepisiguit River 63 CD 4
Nepoko 172 E 1
Neponset River 84 I b 3
Neponsit, New York-, NY 82 III c 3
Neptune 61 FG 6
Ner [IND] 138-139 F 7
Nérac 120-121 H 6
Neragon Island 58-59 D 6
Nerang, Kuala — 150-151 C 9
Nerbudda = Narmada 134-135 LM 6
Nerča 132-133 W 7
Nerčinsk 132-133 W 7
Nerčinskij Zavod 132-133 W 7
Nerdva 124-125 U 4
Nerechta 124-125 N 5
Nerecó, Valle — 106-107 E 6
Nereta 124-125 E 5
Neretva 122-123 H 4
Neri 138-139 G 7
Nerima, Tōkyō- 155 III a 1
Neringa 124-125 C 6
Neriquinha = N'Riquinha 172 D 5

Neris 124-125 E 6
Nerka, Lake — 58-59 H 7
Nerl' [SU, place] 124-125 LM 5
Nerl' [SU, river] 124-125 LM 5
Ñermete, Punta — 92-93 C 6
Nero, ozero — 124-125 M 5
Nerojka, gora — 132-133 KL 5
Nerópolis 102-103 H 2
Nerskoje ploskogorje 132-133 c 5
Nes aan de Amstel 128 I a 2
Nesebâr 122-123 MN 4
Neškan 58-59 A 3
Neskaupstadhur 116-117 fg 2
Nesna 116-117 E 4
Ness, Loch — 119 D 3
Ness City, KS 68-69 FG 6
Nesselrode, Mount — 58-59 UV 7
Nestaocano, Rivière — 62 P 1-2
Nesterov [SU, L'vovskaja Oblast'] 126-127 AB 1
Nestor Falls 70-71 D 1
Nestoria, MI 70-71 FG 2
Néstos 122-123 L 5
Nesttun, Bergen- 116-117 AB 7
Nesvíž 124-125 F 7
Nětanya 136-137 F 7
Nethanya = Nětanya 136-137 F 7
Netherdale 158-159 J 4
Netherlands 120-121 J 3-L 2
Netrākonā 141 B 3
Netrāvati 140 B 4
Nettilling Lake 56-57 W 4
Nett Lake 70-71 D 1
Nett Lake Indian Reservation 70-71 D 1-2
Nettleton, MS 78-79 E 3
Netzahualcóyotl, Ciudad — 86-87 L 8
Netzahualcóyotl, Presa — 86-87 O 9
Neualbern, Wien- 113 I b 2
Neubeeren 130 III b 2
Neubrandenburg 118 F 2
Neuchâtel 118 C 5
Neuchâtel, Lac de — 118 C 5
Neuenfelde, Hamburg- 130 I a 1
Neuessling 113 I c 1
Neu Fahrland 130 III a 2
Neufchâteau [B] 120-121 K 4
Neufchateau [F] 120-121 KL 4
Neufchâtel-en-Bray 120-121 H 4
Neugraben, Hamburg- 130 I a 2
Neuhausen, München- 130 II b 2
Neuherberg 130 II b 1
Neu-Heusis 174-175 B 2
Neuhimmelreich 130 II a 1
Neuhönow, Kolonie — 130 III cd 1
Neuilly-sur-Marne 129 I d 2
Neuilly-sur-Seine 129 I bc 2
Neuland, Hamburg- 130 I ab 2
Neu Lindenberg 130 III c 1
Neumarkt 118 E 4
Neumünster 118 DE 1
Neunkirchen [A] 118 H 5
Neunkirchen [D] 118 C 4
Neuquén [RA, administrative unit] 106-107 BC 7
Neuquén [RA, place] 111 C 5
Neuquén, Río — 106-107 C 7
Neurara 104-105 B 9
Neuried [D, Bayern] 130 II a 2
Neurott 128 III a 1
Neuruppin 118 F 2
Neuschwabenland 53 B 36-2
Neuse River 80-81 H 3
Neusiedler See 118 H 5
Neustift am Walde, Wien- 113 I b 2
Neustrelitz 118 F 2
Neusüssenbrunn, Wien- 113 I bc 1
Neutral Zone 134-135 F 5
Neu-Ulm 118 E 4
Neu Vehlefanz 130 III a 1
Neuwaldegg, Wien- 113 I ab 2
Neuwied 118 CD 3
Neva [SU] 124-125 H 4
Nevada 64-65 CD 4
Nevada, IA 70-71 D 4-5
Nevada, MO 70-71 C 7
Nevada, La — 106-107 FG 6
Nevada City, CA 74-75 C 3
Nevada del Cocuy, Sierra — 94-95 E 4
Nevado, Cerro El — 92-93 E 4
Nevado, Sierra del — 111 C 5
Nevado Ancohuma 104-105 B 4
Nevado Cololo 92-93 F 7
Nevado de Acay 104-105 C 9
Nevado de Ampato 92-93 E 8
Nevado de Cachi 111 C 2
Nevado de Champara 96-97 C 6
Nevado de Colima 64-65 EF 8
Nevado de Cumbal 94-95 BC 7
Nevado de Illimani 92-93 F 8
Nevado del Huila 92-93 D 4
Nevado de los Palos 108-109 C 5
Nevado del Ruiz 92-93 DE 4
Nevado del Tolima 94-95 D 5
Nevado de Sajama 92-93 F 8
Nevado de Salcantay 96-97 E 8
Nevado de Toluca 64-65 FG 8
Nevado Huascaran 92-93 D 6
Nevado Illampu 92-93 F 8
Nevado Iluyana Potosí 104-105 B 5
Nevado Longaví 106-107 B 6
Nevado Ojos del Salado 111 C 3
Nevado Putre 104-105 B 6
Nevados de Chillán 106-107 B 6
Nevados de Condoroma 96-97 F 9
Nevados de Pomasi 96-97 F 9
Neve, Serra da — 172 B 4
Nevel' 124-125 G 5
Never 132-133 XY 7
Nevers 120-121 J 5
Nevinnomyssk 126-127 KL 4
Nevis 64-65 O 8
Nevis, MN 70-71 C 2
Nevis, Ben — 119 D 3
Nevjansk 132-133 KL 6
Nevşehir 134-135 C 3
Newala 172 G 4
New Albany, IN 64-65 J 4
New Albany, MS 78-79 E 3
New Alexandria, VA 82 II a 2
New Amalfi 174-175 H 6
New Amsterdam 92-93 H 3
Newark, DE 72-73 J 5
Newark, NJ 64-65 M 3
Newark, NY 72-73 H 3
Newark, OH 72-73 E 4
Newark [GB] 119 F 5
Newark Airport 82 III a 2
Newark Bay 82 III b 2
New Athens, IL 70-71 F 6
Newaygo, MI 70-71 H 4
New Bedford, MA 64-65 MN 3
Newberg, OR 66-67 B 3
New Bern, NC 64-65 L 4
Newbern, TN 78-79 E 2
Newberry, CA 74-75 E 5
Newberry, MI 70-71 H 2
Newberry, SC 80-81 F 3
New Bethesda = Nieu-Bethesda 174-175 F 6
New Bosten, OH 72-73 E 5
New Boston, IL 70-71 E 5
New Boston, OH 72-73 E 5
New Boston, TX 76-77 G 6
New Braunfels, TX 64-65 G 6
New Brighton, New York-, NY 82 III b 3
New Britain 148-149 gh 6
New Britain, CT 72-73 K 4
New Britain Bougainville Trench 148-149 h 6
New Brunswick 56-57 X 8
New Brunswick, NJ 72-73 J 4
New Buffalo, MI 70-71 G 5
Newburg, MO 70-71 E 7
Newburgh, NY 72-73 J 4
Newburgh [CDN] 72-73 H 2
Newbury 119 F 6
Newburyport, MA 72-73 L 3
New Caledonia 158-159 MN 3
New Canada, Johannesburg- 170 V a 2
New Carlisle 63 D 3
New Carrollton, MD 82 II b 1
Newcastel 63 CD 4
Newcastel Creek 158-159 F 3
New Castile = Castilla la Nueva 120-121 E 9-F 8
New Castle, CO 68-69 C 6
New Castle, IN 70-71 H 5-6
New Castle, OH 72-73 D 5
New Castle, PA 72-73 F 4
Newcastle, TX 76-77 E 6
Newcastle, VA 80-81 F 2
Newcastle, WY 68-69 D 4
Newcastle [AUS] 158-159 K 6
Newcastle [GB] 119 D 4
Newcastle [ZA] 172 EF 7
Newcastle Bay 158-159 H 2
Newcastle upon Tyne 119 EF 4
Newcastle Waters 158-159 F 3
Newclare, Johannesburg- 170 V a 2
Newcomb, NM 74-75 J 4
Newcomerstown, OH 72-73 F 4
Newdale, ID 66-67 H 4
Newdegate 158-159 CD 6
New Delhi 134-135 M 5
New Dorp, New York-, NY 82 III b 3
Newell, SD 68-69 E 3
Newell Lake 61 BC 5
Newellton, LA 78-79 D 4
New England, ND 68-69 E 2
New England [USA] 64-65 M 3-N 2
New England [ZA] 174-175 G 6
New England Range 158-159 K 5-6
Newenham, Cape — 56-57 D 6
Newfane, VT 72-73 K 3
Newfolden, MN 70-71 BC 1
Newfoundland [CDN, administrative unit] 56-57 Y 6-Z 8
Newfoundland [CDN, island] 56-57 Za 8
Newfoundland Bank 50-51 G 3
Newfoundland Basin 50-51 GH 3
Newfoundland Ridge 50-51 G 3-H 4
New Georgia 148-149 j 6
New Georgia Group 148-149 j 6
New Georgia Sound = The Slot 148-149 j 6
New Germany 63 D 5
New Glasgow 56-57 Y 8
New Glatz, MD 82 II a 2
New Guinea 148-149 L 7-M 8
New Guinea Rise 148-149 M 5-6
Newgulf, TX 76-77 G 8
Newhalem, WA 66-67 C 1
Newhalen, AK 58-59 K 7
Newhall, CA 74-75 D 5
Newham, London- 129 II c 1
New Hamilton, AK 58-59 F 5
New Hampshire 64-65 M 3
New Hampton, IA 70-71 DE 4
New Hanover [PNG] 148-149 gh 5
New Hanover [ZA] 174-175 J 5
New Harmony, IN 70-71 G 6
New Haven, CT 64-65 M 3
New Haven, IN 70-71 H 5
New Haven, KY 70-71 H 7
Newhaven [GB] 119 G 6
New Hebrides 158-159 NO 2-3
New Hebrides Basin 158-159 MN 2
New Hebrides Trench 158-159 N 2-3
New Hyde Park, NY 82 III de 2
New Iberia, LA 64-65 H 5-6
Newington 174-175 J 3
New Ireland 148-149 h 5
New Island 108-109 J 8
New Jersey 64-65 M 3
New Kensington, PA 72-73 G 4
Newkirk, OK 76-77 F 4
New Knockhock, AK 58-59 E 5
New Kowloon 155 I b 1
New Lagos, Lagos- 170 III b 1
New Lexington, OH 72-73 EF 5
Newlin, TX 76-77 D 5
New Liskeard 56-57 UV 8
New London, CT 72-73 KL 4
New London, MN 70-71 C 3
New London, MO 70-71 E 6
New London, WI 70-71 F 3
New Madrid, MO 78-79 E 2
New Malden, London- 129 II ab 2
Newman, CA 74-75 C 4
Newman, NM 76-77 AB 6
Newman Grove, NE 68-69 GH 5
Newmarket [CDN] 72-73 G 2
Newmarket [ZA] 170 V b 2
Newmarket Race Course 170 V b 2
New Martinsville, WV 72-73 F 5
New Meadows, ID 66-67 E 3
New Mecklenburg = New Ireland 148-149 h 5
New Melbourne Cemetery 161 II b 1
New Mexico 64-65 EF 5
Newnan, GA 78-79 G 4
New Norfolk 158-159 J 8
New Orleans, LA 64-65 HJ 5-6
New Orleans, University of — 85 I b 1
New Orleans-Algiers, LA 85 I b 2
New Orleans-Aurora Gardens, LA 85 I c 2
New Orleans-Edgewood Park, LA 85 I b 2
New Orleans-Garden District, LA 85 I b 2
New Orleans-Gentilly, LA 85 I c 1
New Orleans-Gentilly Terrace, LA 85 I b 1
New Orleans-Gentilly Woods, LA 85 I b 1
New Orleans-Georgetown of New Orleans, LA 85 I bc 1
New Orleans International Airport 85 I c 2
New Orleans-Lake Forest, LA 85 I c 1
New Orleans Lakefront Airport 85 I b 1
New Orleans-Lakeshore, LA 85 I b 1
New Orleans-Lake Terrace, LA 85 I b 1
New Orleans-Lakeview, LA 85 I b 1-2
New Orleans-Lake Vista, LA 85 I b 1
New Orleans-Lakewood East, LA 85 I c 1
New Orleans Museum of Art 85 I b 2
New Orleans-Park Timbers, LA 85 I b 2
New Orleans-Pontchartrain Beach, LA 85 I b 1
New Orleans-Tall Timbers, LA 85 I c 2
New Orleans-Vieux Carré, LA 85 I b 2
New Philadelphia, OH 72-73 F 4
New Philippines = Caroline Islands 206-207 RS 9
New Pine Creek, OR 66-67 C 4
New Plymouth 158-159 O 7
New Pomerania = New Britain 148-149 gh 6
Newport, AR 78-79 D 3
Newport, KY 64-65 K 4
Newport, ME 72-73 M 2
Newport, NH 72-73 KL 3
Newport, OR 66-67 A 3
Newport, RI 72-73 L 4
Newport, TN 80-81 E 2-3
Newport, TX 76-77 EF 6
Newport, VT 72-73 KL 2
Newport, WA 66-67 E 1
Newport [GB, I. of Wight] 119 F 6
Newport [GB, Severn] 119 E 6
Newport, Melbourne- 161 II b 2
Newport News, VA 64-65 L 4
New Port Richey, FL 80-81 b 2
New Providence Island 64-65 L 6-7
Newquay 119 D 6
New Quebec 56-57 V-X 6
New Quebec Crater 56-57 VW 5
New Raymer, CO 68-69 E 5
New Redruth 170 V b 2
New Richmond 63 D 3
New Richmond, WI 70-71 DE 3
New River 98-99 JK 3
New Roads, LA 78-79 D 5
New Rochelle, NY 72-73 K 4
New Rockford, ND 68-69 G 2
Newry 119 CD 4
New Salem, ND 68-69 F 2
New Sharon, IA 70-71 D 5
New Sharon, NJ 84 III c 3
New Siberia = ostrov Novaja Sibir' 132-133 de 3
New Siberian Islands = Novosibirskije ostrova 132-133 Z-f 2
New Smyrna Beach, FL 80-81 c 2
New South Wales 158-159 H-K 6
New South Wales, University of — 161 I b 2
New Stuyahok, AK 58-59 J 7
New Territories 155 I a 1
Newton 106-107 H 5
Newton, AL 78-79 G 5
Newton, IA 70-71 D 5
Newton, IL 70-71 F 6
Newton, KS 64-65 G 4
Newton, MA 72-73 L 3
Newton, MS 78-79 E 4
Newton, NC 80-81 F 3
Newton, NJ 72-73 J 4
Newton, TX 78-79 C 5
Newton Falls, NY 72-73 J 2
Newtontoppen 116-117 k 5
New Town, ND 68-69 E 1-2
Newtown, Sydney- 161 I ab 2
Newtownards 119 D 4
Newtown Square, PA 84 III a 2
New Ulm, MN 70-71 C 3
New Ulm, TX 76-77 F 8
New Underwood, SD 68-69 E 3
New Waterford 63 FG 4
New Westminster 56-57 MN 8
New World Island 63 J 3
New York 64-65 LM 3
New York, NY 64-65 M 3-4
New York-Arverne, NY 82 III d 3
New York-Astoria, NY 82 III c 2
New York-Auburndale, NY 82 III d 2
New York-Baychester, NY 82 III cd 1
New York-Bay Ridge, NY 82 III b 3
New York-Bedford Park, NY 82 III c 1
New York-Bedford-Stuyvesant, NY 82 III c 2
New York-Bellerose, NY 82 III d 2
New York-Bergen Beach, NY 82 III c 3
New York-Bloomfield, NY 82 III ab 3
New York-Borough Park, NY 82 III bc 3
New York-Breezy Point, NY 82 III c 3
New York-Bronx, NY 82 III c 1
New York-Brooklyn, NY 82 III bc 3
New York-Canarsie, NY 82 III c 3
New York-Castleton Corners, NY 82 III b 3
New York-College Point, NY 82 III cd 2
New York-East Elmhurst, NY 82 III c 2
New York-East New York, NY 82 III c 2-3
New York-Eltingville, NY 82 III ab 3
New York-Flatbush, NY 82 III c 3
New York-Far Rockawa, NY 82 III d 3
New York-Financial District, NY 82 III bc 3
New York-Flushing, NY 82 III d 2
New York-Gravesend, NY 82 III c 3
New York-Great Kills, NY 82 III b 3
New York-Greenwich Village, NY 82 III b 2
New York-Grymes Hill, NY 82 III b 3
New York-Harlem, NY 82 III c 2
New York-Hollis, NY 82 III d 2
New York-Howard Beach, NY 82 III cd 3
New York-Jackson Heights, NY 82 III c 2
New York-Jamaica, NY 82 III d 2
New York-Kensington, NY 82 III c 3
New York-Laurelton, NY 82 III d 3
New York-Long Island City, NY 82 III c 2
New York-Manhatten, NY 82 III bc 2
New York-Mariners Harbor, NY 82 III ab 3
New York-Maspeth, NY 82 III c 2
New York-Melrose, Ny 82 III c 2
New York-Midland Beach, NY 82 III b 3
New York Mountains 74-75 F 5
New York-Neponsit, NY 82 III c 3
New York-New Brighton, NY 82 III b 3
New York-New Dorp, NY 82 III b 3
New York-Oakwood, NY 82 III b 3
New York-Port Richmond, NY 82 III b 3
New York-Princes Bay, NY 82 III a 3
New York-Queens, NY 82 III cd 2
New York-Richmond, NY 82 III ab 4
New York-Richmond Valley, NY 82 III a 3
New York-Ridgewood, NY 82 III c 2
New York-Riverdale, NY 82 III c 1
New York-Rockway Park, NY 82 III c 3
New York-Rossville, NY 82 III a 3
New York-Saint Albans, NY 82 III d 2
New York-Sheepshead Bay, NY 82 III c 3
New York-Soundview, NY 82 III c 2
New York-South Beach, NY 82 III b 3
New York-South Brooklyn, NY 82 III bc 2
New York-Springfield, NY 82 III d 2
New York-Tottenville, NY 82 III a 3
New York-Travis, NY 82 III a 3
New York-Utopia, NY 82 III d 2
New York-Wakefield, NY 82 III cd 1
New York-Westchester, NY 82 III d 1
New York-Whitestone, NY 82 III d 2
New York-Williams Bridge, NY 82 III c 1
New York-Williamsburg, NY 82 III c 2
New York-Woodhaven, NY 82 III cd 2
New York-Woodside, NY 82 III c 2
New Zealand 158-159 N 8-O 7
Neyed = Najd 134-135 E 5-6
Ney Rey Park 85 I a 1
Neyrīz 134-135 G 5
Neyshābūr 134-135 H 3
Neyveli 140 D 5
Neyyāttinkara 140 C 6
Nezametnyj = Aldan 132-133 XY 6
Nežin 126-127 E 1
Nezlobnaja 126-127 L 4
Nezperce, ID 66-67 EF 2
Nez Perce Indian Reservation 66-67 EF 2
Nfida, En — = An-N'fidah 166-167 M 1
N'fidah, An- 166-167 M 1
Nfis, Ouèd — = Wād Nafīs 166-167 B 4
Ngaba, Kinshasa- 170 IV ab 2
Ngabang 148-149 EF 6
Ngabé 141 D 5
Ngabudaw 141 D 7
Ngaliema, Baie de — 170 IV a 1
Ngaliema, Kinshasa- 170 IV a 2
Ngamba, Brazzaville- 170 IV a 1
Ngambé [RFC → Douala] 168-169 H 4
N'Gambe [RFC → Foumban] 168-169 H 4
Ngamdo Tsonag Tsho 142-143 G 5
Ngami, Lake — 172 D 6
Ngamo Chhu 138-139 M 4
Ngamouéri 170 IV a 1
Ngan Chau 155 I ab 2
Ngang, Đeo — 150-151 F 3-4
Ngang Chhu = Shakad Chhu 138-139 M 2
Nganghouei = Anhui 142-143 M 5
Nganglaring Tso = Ngangiha Ringtsho 142-143 EF 5
Nganglong Gangri 142-143 E 5
Ngangtha Ringtsho 142-143 EF 5
Ngangtse Tsho 142-143 F 5
Ngan-yang = Anyang 142-143 LM 4
Ngao 148-149 CD 3
Ngaoundéré 164-165 G 7
Ngape = Ngabé 141 D 5
Ngaputaw = Ngabudaw 141 D 7
Ngara 171 B 3
Ngari = Ngarikorsum 138-139 HJ 2
Ngarikorsum 138-139 HJ 2
Ngat, Nam Mae — 150-151 B 3
Ngatik 208 F 2
Ngau 148-149 a 2
Ngaumdere = Ngaoundéré 164-165 G 7
Ngau Mei Hoi = Port Shelter 155 I b 1
Ngaundere = Ngaoundéré 164-165 G 7
Ngauruhoe 161 FG 4
Ngawi 152-153 J 9
Ngayôk Au 141 CD 7
Ngazidja 172 H 4
Ngerengere 171 D 4
Nghia Lô 150-151 E 2
Ngiri-Ngiri, Kinshasa- 170 IV a 2
Ngiro, Ewaso — 172 G 2
Ngiva 172 C 5
Ngoc Diêm 150-151 EF 3
Ngoc Linh 148-149 E 3
Ngoko 172 C 1
Ngomba 171 C 5
Ngome 174-175 J 4
Ngong 172 G 2
Ngong Shun Chau 155 I a 2
Ngoring Tsho 142-143 H 4-5
Ngorongoro Crater 172 FG 2
Ngouma 168-169 E 2
N'Gounié 172 B 2
Ngoura 164-165 H 6
Ngouri 164-165 H 6
N'Gourti 164-165 G 5
Ngoywa 172 F 3
Ngozi 171 B 3
Ngqeleni 174-175 H 6
N'Guigmi 164-165 G 6
Ngulu 148-149 L 5
Ngum, Nam — 150-151 D 3
Ngumu 168-169 H 4
Ngunga 171 C 3
Ngunza 172 B 4
N'Guri = Ngouri 164-165 H 6
Nguru 164-165 G 6
Nguti 168-169 H 4
Ngwanedzi 174-175 J 2
Nha Bang = Tinh Biên 150-151 E 7
Nhachengue 174-175 L 2
Nhambiquara 98-99 J 11
Nhamundá 98-99 K 6
Nhamundá, Rio — 98-99 K 5
Nha Nam 150-151 EF 2
Nha Trang 148-149 EF 4
Nhecolândia 92-93 H 8
Nhiêp, Nam — 150-151 D 3
Nhi Ha, Sông — 148-149 D 2
Nhill 158-159 H 7
Nhommarath 150-151 E 4
Nhu Pora 106-107 JK 2
Niafounké 164-165 D 5
Niagara Falls 64-65 KL 3
Niagara Falls, NY 64-65 L 3
Niagara River 72-73 G 3
Niagassola 168-169 C 2
Niagui 168-169 D 4
Niah 148-149 F 6
Ni'āj, Jabal — 173 C 6
Niamey 164-165 E 6
Niamina 168-169 D 2
Niamtougou 168-169 F 3
Nian Chu = Nyang Chhu 138-139 M 3
Niandan-Koro 168-169 C 3
Niangara 172 E 1
Niangay, Lac — 168-169 E 2
Niangua River 70-71 D 7
Nia-Nia 172 E 1
Nianqingtanggula Shan = Nyanchhenthanglha 142-143 G 5-6
Niapa, Gunung — 152-153 M 5
Nias, Pulau — 148-149 C 6
Niassa 172 G 4
Niassa = Malawi 172 FG 4
Niassa, Lago — = Lake Malawi 172 F 4
Niausa 141 D 2
Nibāk 134-135 G 6
Nibe 116-117 C 9
Niblinto 111 B 5
Nibr 166-167 L 1
Nibria, Howrah- 154 II a 2
Nicaragua 64-65 JK 9
Nicaragua, Lago de — 64-65 JK 9
Nicaro 64-65 L 7
Nice 120-121 L 7
Niceville, FL 78-79 F 5
Nicgale 124-125 F 5
Nichinan 144-145 H 7
Nicholasville, KY 70-71 H 7
Nichole = Nachoī 138-139 M 5
Nicholl's Town 88-89 GH 2
Nicholson [AUS] 158-159 E 3
Nicholson [CDN] 70-71 J 1-2
Nicholson River 158-159 G 3
Nickajack Creek 85 II a 1
Nickel Lake 62 C 3
Nickerie [GUY, administrative unit] 98-99 K 2-3
Nickerie [GUY, river] 98-99 K 2
Nickol Bay 158-159 C 4
Nicman 63 CD 2
Nicobar Islands 134-135 P 9
Nicolás, Canal — 64-65 KL 7
Nicolás Bruzone 106-107 EF 5
Nicolás Descalzi 106-107 G 7
Nicolet 72-73 K 1
Nicomedia = İzmit 134-135 BC 2
Nico Pérez 111 EF 4
Nicosia 122-123 F 7
Nicosia = Levkōsia 134-135 C 3
Nicoya 64-65 J 9
Nicoya, Golfo de — 64-65 J 9
Nicoya, Península de — 64-65 J 9-10
Nida 118 K 3
Nidadavole 140 E 2
Niḍḍavolu = Nidadavole 140 E 2
Nī Dillī = New Delhi 134-135 M 5
Nido, El — 148-149 G 4
Nidrūmā 166-167 F 2
Niebüll 118 D 1
Nied, Frankfurt am Main- 128 III a 1
Niederdorfelden 128 III b 1
Nieder Erlenbach, Frankfurt am Main- 128 III b 1
Niedere Tauern 118 FG 5
Niederglatt 128 IV b 1
Niederhasli 128 IV ab 1
Niederhöchstadt 128 III a 1
Nieder-Neuendorfer Kanal 130 III a 1
Niederösterreich 118 GH 4
Niederrad, Frankfurt am Main- 128 III a 1
Niedersachsen 118 C-E 2
Niederschöneweide, Berlin- 130 III b 2
Niederschönhausen, Berlin- 130 III b 1
Niedersteinmaur 128 IV a 1
Niederursel, Frankfurt am Main- 128 III a 1
Niederuster 128 IV b 1
Niederwaldpark 128 III a 2
Niederwil 128 IV a 2
Niekerkshoop 174-175 E 5
Niekerkshope = Niekerkshoop 174-175 E 5
Niéllé 168-169 D 3
Nieman = Neman 124-125 E 7
Niemba [ZRE, place] 171 B 4
Niemba [ZRE, river] 171 B 4
Niemen = Neman 124-125 E 7
Niena 168-169 D 3
Nienburg 118 D 2
Nienchentanglha = Nyanchhenthanglha 142-143 F 6-G 5
Niendorf, Hamburg- 130 I a 1
Niendorfer Gehege 130 I a 1
Nienstedten, Hamburg- 130 I a 1
Nietverdiend 174-175 G 3
Nieu-Bethesda 174-175 F 6
Nieuw Amsterdam [SME] 92-93 HJ 3
Nieuw-Antwerpen = Nouvelle-Anvers 172 CD 1
Nieuwe Meer 128 I a 2
Nieuwe Meer, Het — 128 I a 1-2
Nieuwendam, Amsterdam- 128 I b 1
Nieuwenrode 128 II ab 1
Nieuwersluis 128 I b 2
Nieuwer ter Aa 128 I b 2
Nieuwerust = Nuwerus 174-175 C 6
Nieuw Nickerie 92-93 H 3
Nieuwoudtville 172 C 8
Nieuwveld Range = Nuweveldberge 174-175 DE 7
Nieve, Isla de la — 106-107 H 2
Nieves = Nevis 64-65 O 8
Nieves, Las — 76-77 B 9
Niffur = Nippur 136-137 L 6
Nifisha = Nafīshah 173 C 2
Nifzāwah 166-167 L 3
Niğde 134-135 CD 3
Nigel 174-175 H 4
Niger [RN, administrative unit] 164-165 F 7
Niger [RN, river] 164-165 E 6
Niger [RN, state] 164-165 FG 5
Níger = Niger 164-165 FG 5
Nigeria 164-165 E-G 7
Nigerian Museum 170 III b 2
Nighāsan 138-139 H 3
Nighthawk, WA 66-67 D 1
Nighthawk Lake 62 L 2
Nightingale 61 B 5
Nightingale, Île — = Đao Bach Long Vi 150-151 F 2
Nightingale Island = Đao Bach Long Vi 150-151 F 2
Nigisaktuvik River 58-59 H 1
Nigrita 122-123 K 5
Nigtevecht 128 I b 2
Nigtmute, AK 58-59 E 6
Nigu River 58-59 JK 2
Nihah 136-137 J 2
Nihoa 78-79 b 1
Nihonbashi, Tōkyō- 155 III b 1
Nihonmatsu = Nihommatsu 144-145 N 4
Nihuil, El — 106-107 C 5
Niigata 142-143 Q 4
Niihama 144-145 J 5-6
Niihau 148-149 de 3
Niimi 144-145 J 5
Nii-shima 144-145 M 5
Niitsu 144-145 M 4
Nijād al-'Alī 164-165 D 2-E 1
Nijamābād = Nizāmābād 134-135 M 7
Nijmegen 120-121 KL 3
Nikabuna Lakes 58-59 JK 6
Nikaia [GR, Athēnai] 113 IV a 2
Nikawèraṭiya 140 DE 7
Nikel' 132-133 E 4
Nikēphorion = Ar-Raqqah 136-137 H 5
Nikhaib, An- = Nukhayb 134-135 E 4
Nikishka Numero 2, AK 58-59 M 6
Nikito-Ivdel'skoje = Ivdel' 132-133 L 5
Nikki 164-165 E 6-7
Nikolai, AK 58-59 KL 5
Nikolajev 126-127 EF 3
Nikolajevka [SU, Rossijskaja SFSR] 124-125 Q 7
Nikolajevka [SU, Ukrainskaja SSR] 126-127 F 3
Nikolajevo 124-125 G 4
Nikolajevsk 126-127 MN 1
Nikolajevsk = Pugačov 132-133 HJ 7
Nikolajevsk-na-Amure 132-133 b 7
Nikolajevskoje = Bautino 126-127 OP 4
Nikolassee, Berlin- 130 III a 2
Nikolajev = Nikolajev 126-127 EF 3
Nikolo-Ber'ozovka 124-125 U 5
Nikol'sk [SU, Penzenskaja Oblast'] 124-125 PQ 7
Nikol'sk [SU, Severnyje uvaly] 132-133 H 6
Nikolski, AK 58-59 m 4
Nikol'skij 132-133 M 8
Nikol'skoje [SU, Komandorskije ostrova] 132-133 fg 6
Nikol'skoje [SU, Volgogradskaja Oblast'] 126-127 MN 3
Nikol'skoje, Moskva- 113 V b 3
Nikomēdeia = İzmit 134-135 BC 2
Nikonga 171 B 3-4
Nikopol [BG] 122-123 L 4
Nikopol' [SU] 126-127 G 3
Nikosia = Levkōsia 134-135 C 3
Nik Pey 136-137 N 4
Niksar 136-137 G 2
Nikšić 122-123 H 4
Nikulino [SU, Perm'skaja Oblast'] 124-125 V 4
Nikulino, Moskva- 113 V b 3
Nīl, An- 164-165 L 5
Nīl, Baḥr an- 164-165 L 3-4
Nila, Pulau — 148-149 JK 8
Nīlagiri = Nīlgiri Hills 134-135 M 8
Nilakkottai 140 C 5
Nilakōṭṭai = Nilakkottai 140 C 5
Nīl al-Abyaḍ, An- 164-165 L 6
Nīl al-Azraq, An- [Sudan, administrative unit] 164-165 L 6
Nīl al-Azraq, An- [Sudan, river] 164-165 L 6
Nilambūr 140 C 5
Niland, CA 74-75 F 6
Nilandu Atoll 176 a 2
Nilanga 140 C 1
Nila Pahar = Blue Mountain 141 C 4
Nilarga = Nilanga 140 C 1
Nile = Bahr an-Nīl 164-165 L 3-4
Nile, Albert — 172 F 1
Niles, MI 70-71 G 5
Niles, OH 72-73 F 4
Nīleshwar 140 B 4
Nilgani 154 II b 1
Nīlgiri 138-139 L 7
Nīlgiri Hills 140 C 5
Nīl Burewāla 138-139 D 2
Nilo 98-99 B 9
Nīlphāmārī 138-139 M 5
Nimach 138-139 E 5
Nimaikha River = Me Hka 141 EF 3
Nimaima 94-95 D 5
Nimāpaḍā = Nimapāra 138-139 KL 7-8
Nimapāra 138-139 KL 7-8
Nimār 138-139 EF 7
Nimāvar = Nemāwar 138-139 F 6
Nimba 168-169 C 4
Nimba, Mont — 164-165 C 7
Nimbahera 138-139 E 5
Nîmes 120-121 JK 7
Nimiuktuk River 58-59 H 2
Nīm ka Thāna 138-139 EF 4
Nimmitabel 160 J 6
Nimnyrskij 132-133 Y 6
Nimrod, MT 66-67 G 2
Nimūlē 164-165 L 8
Niña, La — 106-107 G 5
Ninacaca 96-97 D 7
Ninawá = Ninive 136-137 K 4

Nindigully 160 J 2
Nine Degree Channel 134-135 L 9
Ninette 68-69 G 1
Nineve = Ninive 134-135 E 3
Ninfas, Punta — 111 D 6
Ning'an 142-143 OP 3
Ningbo 142-143 N 6
Ningcheng 144-145 B 2
Ning-chin = Ningjin [TJ ↗ Dezhou] 146-147 F 3
Ning-chin = Ningjin [TJ ↘ Shijiazhuang] 146-147 E 3
Ningde 142-143 M 6
Ningdu 142-143 M 6
Ninggang 146-147 DE 8
Ningguo 142-143 M 5
Ninghai 146-147 H 7
Ninghe 146-147 FG 2
Ning-ho = Ninghe 146-147 FG 2
Ninghsia, Autonomes Gebiet 142-143 H 3-K 4
Ning-hsiang = Ningxiang 142-143 L 6
Ninghsien = Ning Xian 142-143 K 4
Ninghua 142-143 M 6
Ninghwa = Ninghua 142-143 M 6
Ningjin [TJ ↗ Dezhou] 146-147 F 3
Ningjin [TJ ↘ Shijiazhuang] 146-147 E 3
Ning-kang = Ninggang 146-147 DE 8
Ningling 146-147 E 4
Ning-po = Ningbo 142-143 N 6
Ningshan 146-147 B 5
Ningsia = Ningxia 142-143 H 3-K 4
Ningsia Autonomous Region 142-143 JK 3-4
Ningteh = Ningde 142-143 M 6
Ningtsin = Ningjin 146-147 E 3
Ningtsing = Ningjin 146-147 F 3
Ninguta = Ning'an 142-143 OP 3
Ningwu 146-147 D 2
Ningxia 142-143 H 3-K 4
Ningxia Huizu Zizhiqu 142-143 JK 3-4
Ning Xian 142-143 K 4
Ningxiang 142-143 L 6
Ningyuan 146-147 CD 9
Ninh Binh 150-151 EF 2
Ninh Giang 148-149 E 2
Ninh Hoa [VN ↙ Chan Thô] 150-151 E 8
Ninh Hoa [VN ↑ Nha Trang] 148-149 EF 4
Ninigo Group 148-149 M 7
Ninilchik, AK 58-59 M 6
Ninive 134-135 E 3
Ninjintangla Shan = Nyanchhenthanglha 142-143 G 5-6
Nin Lan = Ban Nin Lan 150-151 E 3
Ninnis Glacier 53 C 16-15
Ninua = Ninive 134-135 E 3
Nioaque 102-103 E 4
Niobe, ND 68-69 E 1
Niobrara, NE 68-69 GH 4
Niobrara River 64-65 F 3
Niokolo-Koba, Parc National du — 164-165 B 6
Nioku 141 D 2
Niono 168-169 D 2
Nioro 168-169 C 2
Nioro-du-Rip 164-165 A 6
Nioro du Sahel 164-165 C 5
Niort 120-121 G 5
Niou 168-169 E 2
Nipani 140 B 2
Nipawin 56-57 Q 7
Nipawin Provincial Park 61 F 3
Nipe, Bahía de — 88-89 J 4
Nipepe 171 D 6
Nipigon 56-57 T 8
Nipigon, Lake — 56-57 ST 8
Nipigon Bay 70-71 FG 1
Nipigon-Onaman Game Reserve 62 F 2-3
Nipigon River 70-71 F 1
Nipissing, Lake — 56-57 UV 8
Nipisso 63 D 2
Nippers Harbour 63 J 3
Nippo, Yokohama- 155 III a 2
Nippur 136-137 L 6
Nipton, CA 74-75 F 5
Niquelândia 92-93 K 7
Niquero 88-89 GH 4
Niquivil 106-107 C 3
Nīr 136-137 N 3
Nīra 140 B 1
Nirasaki 144-145 M 5
Ñire-Có 106-107 C 6
Ñireguco, Río — 108-109 CD 5
Nirgua 94-95 G 2
Niriz, Dāryacheh i — = Daryācheh Bakhtegān 134-135 G 5
Nirka 124-125 J 3
Nirmal 138-139 G 8
Nirmala = Nirmal 138-139 G 8
Nirmāli 138-139 L 4
Nirsā 138-139 L 6
Niš 122-123 JK 4
Nisā', Wādī an- 166-167 J 3
Nişāb 134-135 E 5
Nişāb, An — = Anşāb 134-135 F 8
Nišava 122-123 K 4
Niscemi 122-123 F 7
Nischintapur 138-139 M 5
Nishi, Yokohama- 155 III a 3
Nishinomiya 144-145 K 5
Nishinoomote 144-145 H 7
Nishino shima 144-145 J 4
Nishio 144-145 L 5
Nishisonoki hantō 144-145 G 6
Nishiyama 144-145 M 4
Nishlik Lake 58-59 H 6
Nishtawn 134-135 G 7
Nishtūn = Nishtawn 134-135 G 7
Nisia-Floresta 92-93 MN 6
Nisibin = Nusaybin 134-135 E 3
Nisibis = Nusaybin 134-135 E 3
Niskey Lake 85 II a 2
Nisko 118 KL 3
Nisland, SD 68-69 E 3
Nisling Range 58-59 S 5-T 6
Nisling River 58-59 S 5
Nissan 116-117 E 9
Nisser 116-117 C 8
Nisutlin Plateau 56-57 K 5
Nisyros 122-123 M 7
Nitau = Nītaure 124-125 E 5
Nītaure 124-125 E 5
Niterói 92-93 L 9
Niterói-Armação 110 I c 2
Niterói-Centro 110 I c 2
Niterói-Gragoatá 110 I c 2
Nitra 118 J 4
Nitrito 106-107 B 7
Nitro, WV 72-73 F 5
Nitzgal = Nīcgale 124-125 F 5
Niuafo'ou 148-149 b 2
Niuatoputapu 148-149 c 2
Niue 156-157 J 5
Niulii, HI 78-79 e 2
Niut, Gunung — 148-149 E 6
Niutao 208 H 3
Niutou Shan = Nantian Dao 146-147 HJ 7
Niva 116-117 P 4
Nivāī = Nawai 138-139 EF 4
Nivās = Niwas 138-139 H 6
Nivernais 120-121 J 5
Niverville 61 K 6
Nivšera [SU, place] 124-125 T 2
Nivšera [SU, river] 124-125 T 2
Nivskij 132-133 E 4
Niwas 138-139 H 6
Nixon, TX 76-77 F 8
Niya Bazar 142-143 E 4
Nizāmābād 134-135 M 7
Nizamghāt 134-135 Q 5
Nizām Sāgar 134-135 M 7
Nižankoviči 126-127 A 2
Nizgal = Nīcgale 124-125 F 5
Nizhne Ilimsk = Nižne-Ilimsk 132-133 T 6
Nizhni Tagil = Nižnij Tagil 132-133 KL 6
Nizhniy Novgorod = Gor'kij 132-133 GH 6
Nizina, AK 58-59 Q 6
Nizina River 58-59 Q 6
Nizip 136-137 G 4
Nízke Tatry 118 JK 4
Nizki Island 58-59 pq 6
Nizkij, mys — 132-133 hj 5
Nižn'aja Omra 124-125 U 2
Nižn'aja Palomica 124-125 Q 4
Nižn'aja Peša 132-133 H 4
Nižn'aja Tojma 124-125 P 2
Nižn'aja Tunguska 132-133 TU 5
Nižn'aja Tura 132-133 K 6
Nižn'aja Voč' 124-125 TU 3
Nižneangarsk 132-133 UV 6
Nižne Čir 126-127 L 2
Nižnegorskij 126-127 G 4
Nižneilimsk 132-133 T 6
Nižneimbatskoje 132-133 QR 5
Nižneje Sančelejevo 124-125 RS 7
Nižnekamsk 132-133 J 7
Nižneleninskoje 132-133 Z 8
Nižnetroickij 124-125 TU 6
Nižneudinsk 132-133 S 7
Nižnevartovsk 132-133 O 5
Nižnij Baskunčak 126-127 N 2
Nižnije Serogozy 126-127 G 3
Nižnij Jenangsk 124-125 Q 4
Nižnij Karanlug = Martuni 126-127 M 6
Nižnij Lomov 124-125 OP 7
Nižnij Novgorod = Gor'kij 132-133 GH 6
Nižnij Oseredok, ostrov — 126-127 O 4
Nižnij Tagil 132-133 KL 6
Nizovaja 126-127 O 6
Nizy 126-127 G 1
Njala = Mono 164-165 E 7
Njardhvík 116-117 b 3
Njassa = Lake Malawi 172 F 4
Njeleli 174-175 J 2
Njemen = Neman 124-125 E 7
Njombe [EAT, place] 172 FG 3
Njombe [EAT, river] 172 F 3
Nkandhla = Nkandla 174-175 J 5
Nkandla 174-175 J 5
Nkata Bay = Nkhata Bay 172 F 4
Nkawkaw 168-169 E 4
Nkhata Bay 172 F 4
Nkiōna 122-123 K 6
N'Kogo 168-169 H 6
Nkongsamba 164-165 FG 8
Nkrēko, Ákra — = Akrōtērion Grēko 136-137 F 5
Nkululu 171 C 4
Nkwalini 174-175 J 5
Noachabeb 174-175 C 4
Noa Dihing 141 E 2
Noākhāli 141 B 4
Noak Hill, London- 129 II c 1
Noanama 92-93 D 4
Noatak, AK 56-57 D 4
Noatak River 56-57 DE 4
Nobeoka 142-143 P 5
Noblesfontein 174-175 E 6
Noblesville, IN 70-71 GH 5
Noborito 155 III a 2
Nobsa 94-95 E 5
Nockatunga 160 F 1
Nodales, Bahía de los — 108-109 G 7
Nodaway River 70-71 C 5
Noel, MO 76-77 G 4
Noel Paul's River 63 H 3
Noetinger 106-107 F 4
Noe Valley, San Francisco-, CA 83 I b 2
Nōfilia, en — = An-Nawfalīyah 164-165 H 2
Nogajsk = Primorskoje 126-127 H 3
Nogajskaja step' 126-127 MN 4
Nogal = Nugal 134-135 F 9
Nogales, AZ 64-65 D 5
Nogales [RCH] 106-107 B 4
Nogamut, AK 58-59 HJ 6
Nogat 118 J 1
Nōgata 144-145 H 6
Nogawa, Kawasaki- 155 III a 2
Nogent-sur-Marne 129 I cd 2
Noginsk 124-125 M 5-6
Nogoyá 111 DE 4
Noguchi 155 III d 1
Nogueira, Pampa — 108-109 E 2-3
Nohar 138-139 E 3
Nohaṭā = Nohta 138-139 G 6
Noheji 144-145 N 2
Nohta 138-139 G 6
Noi, Se — 150-151 E 4
Noir, Isla — 111 B 8
Noirmoutier, Île de — 120-121 F 5
Noiseau 129 I d 2
Noisy-le-Grand 129 I d 2
Noisy-le-Sec 129 I c 2
Nojima-saki 144-145 MN 5
Nojon 142-143 J 3
Nokha 138-139 D 4
Nokia 116-117 K 7
Nokilalaki 152-153 O 6
Nok Kuṇḍī 134-135 J 5
Nokomis 61 F 5
Nokomis, IL 70-71 F 6
Nokomis Lake 61 G 2
Nola [RCA] 164-165 H 8
No La [TJ] 138-139 K 3
Nolan, AK 58-59 M 3
Nolinsk 132-133 HJ 6
Nomamisaki 144-145 GH 7
Nome, AK 56-57 C 5
Nome, Cape — 58-59 E 4
No-min Ho = Nuomin He 142-143 N 2
Nõmme, Kilingi- 124-125 E 4
Nõmme, Reval- = Tallinn-Nõmme 124-125 E 4
Nõmme, Tallinn- 124-125 E 4
Nomo-saki 144-145 G 6
Nomtsas 174-175 B 3
Nomuka 208 J 5
Nonantum, MA 84 I ab 2
Nondalton, AK 58-59 K 6
Nondweni 174-175 J 5
Nong'an 142-143 NO 3
Nong Bua Lam Phu 150-151 D 4
Nong Chik 150-151 C 9
Nong Han 150-151 D 4
Nông Het 150-151 D 3
Nong Keun = Ban Nong Kheun 150-151 D 3
Nong Khae 150-151 C 5
Nong Khai 148-149 D 3
Nong Khayang 150-151 B 5
Nong Ko'n = Ban Nong Kheun 150-151 D 3
Nong Lahan 150-151 E 4
Nongoma 172 F 7
Nong Phai 150-151 C 5
Nŏngpŏ = Nongpoh 141 BC 3
Nongpoh 141 BC 3
Nong Ri 150-151 B 5
Nong Rua 150-151 D 4
Nongstoin 141 B 3
Nonni = Nen Jiang 142-143 O 1-2
Nono 106-107 E 3
Nonoaí 106-107 L 1
Nonoava 86-87 G 4
Nonogasta 106-107 D 2
Nonouti 208 H 3
Nonsan 144-145 F 4
Non Sang 150-151 D 4
Non Sung 150-151 D 5
Nonthaburi 150-151 C 6
Non Thai 150-151 CD 5
Nonvianuk Lake 58-59 K 7
Noordhollands kanaal 128 I b 1
Noordpunt 94-95 G 1
Noordzeekanaal 120-121 K 2
Noormarkku 116-117 JK 7
Noorvik, AK 56-57 DE 4
Nootka Island 56-57 L 8
Nootka Sound 60 D 5
Noqui 172 B 3
Nora [ETH] 164-165 MN 5
Nora [S] 116-117 F 8
Noranda 62 M 2
Noraŝen = Il'ičëvsk 126-127 M 7
Norbu 138-139 M 3
Norcatur, KS 68-69 F 6
Nórcia 122-123 E 4
Norcross, GA 78-79 G 4
Nordaustlandet 116-117 k-m 5
Nordcross, GA 80-81 DE 3
Nordegg = Brazeau 60 J 3
Norden 118 C 2
Nordenskiöld, archipelag — 132-133 RS 2
Nordenskiöld, zaliv — 132-133 JK 2
Nordenskiøldbukta 116-117 l 4
Nordenskiøld land 116-117 jk 6
Nordenskiold River 58-59 T 6
Norderelbe 130 I b 2
Nordfjord 116-117 AB 7
Nordfjorden 116-117 j 5
Nordfriesische Inseln 118 D 1
Nordhausen 118 E 3
Nordhorn 118 C 2
Nordhur-Ísafjardhar 116-117 b 1-2
Nordhur-Múla 116-117 f 2
Nordhur-Thingeyjar 116-117 ef 1-2
Nordkapp [N] 116-117 LM 2
Nordkapp [Svalbard] 116-117 k 4
Nordkinn 116-117 MN 2
Nordkjosbotn 116-117 HJ 3
Nordland 116-117 E 5-G 3
Nördlingen 118 E 4
Nord-Mossi, Plateaux du — 168-169 E 2
Nordos çayı 136-137 K 3
Nordostrundingen 52 A 18-20
Nord-Ostsee-Kanal 118 D 1-2
Nordre Kvaløy 116-117 H 2
Nordre Strømfjord 56-57 a 4
Nordrhein-Westfalen 118 CD 3
Nord-Trøndelag 116-117 DE 5
Nordvik 132-133 V 3
Nore 116-117 C 7
Norfolk, NE 64-65 G 3
Norfolk, VA 64-65 LM 4
Norfolk Island 158-159 N 5
Norfolk Lake 78-79 CD 2
Norfolk Ridge 158-159 N 6-O 7
Norheimsund 116-117 AB 7
Nori 132-133 N 4
Norias, TX 76-77 F 9
Norias, Las — 76-77 C 8
Norikura dake 144-145 L 4
Noril'sk 132-133 Q 4
Norische Alpen 118 FG 5
Norla 138-139 J 7
Norlina, NC 80-81 G 2
Normal, IL 70-71 F 5
Norman, AR 78-79 C 3
Norman, OK 64-65 G 4
Normanby 119 F 4
Normanby Island 148-149 h 7
Normandie 120-121 GH 4
Normandin 62 P 2
Normandy = Normandie 120-121 GH 4
Normangee, TX 76-77 F 7
Norman River 158-159 H 3
Normanton 158-159 H 3
Norman Wells 56-57 KL 4
Normetal 62 M 2
Nornalup 158-159 C 6-7
Noroeste, Brazo — 108-109 DE 10
Norquinco 111 B 6
Norra Bergnäs 116-117 H 4
Norra Storfjället 116-117 FG 5
Norrbotten [S, administrative unit] 116-117 G-K 4
Norrbotten [S, landscape] 116-117 J 5-K 4
Norrembega 62 L 2
Nørresundby, Ålborg- 116-117 CD 9
Norridge, IL 83 II a 1
Norris, MT 66-67 H 3
Norris Arm 63 J 3
Norris City, IL 70-71 F 7
Norris Lake 78-79 GH 2
Norristown, PA 72-73 J 4
Norrköping 116-117 G 8
Norrland 116-117 F-J 5
Norrtälje 116-117 H 8
Norseman 158-159 D 6
Norsk 132-133 Y 7
Norte, Brazo — 108-109 B 7
Norte, Cabo — 92-93 K 4
Norte, Canal do — 92-93 JK 4
Norte, Serra do — 92-93 H 7
North, SC 80-81 F 4
North, Cape — 56-57 YZ 8
North Adams, MA 72-73 K 3
North Albanian Alps = Alpet e Shiqërise 122-123 HJ 4
Northallerton 119 F 4
Northam [AUS] 158-159 C 6
Northam [ZA] 172 E 7
North America 50-51 DE 3
North American Basin 50-51 FG 4
Northampton, MA 72-73 K 3
Northampton [AUS] 158-159 B 5
Northampton [GB] 119 FG 5
North Andaman 134-135 P 8
North Arlington, NJ 82 III b 2
North Arm 56-57 NO 5
North Atlanta, GA 85 II b 2
North Augusta, SC 80-81 EF 4
North Australian Basin 50-51 P 6
North Balabac Strait 152-153 M 1
North Baltimore, OH 72-73 E 4
North Banda Basin 148-149 HJ 7
North Battleford 56-57 P 7
North Bay 56-57 UV 8
North Belcher Islands 56-57 U 6
North Bend, NE 68-69 H 5
North Bend, OR 66-67 A 4
North Bend, WA 66-67 C 2
North Bergen, NJ 82 III b 2
Northbrook, Houston-, TX 85 III b 2
Northbrook, ostrov — 132-133 GH 2
North Bruny 160 cd 3
North Caicos 88-89 L 4
North Canadian River 64-65 FG 4
North Cape [CDN] 63 E 4
North Cape [NZ] 158-159 O 6
North Cape [USA] 58-59 jk 4
North Cape = Nordkapp 116-117 LM 2
North Caribou Lake 56-57 ST 7
North Carolina 64-65 KL 4
North-Central Province = Uturė Mèda Palāna = 2 ◁ 140 E 6
North Channel [CDN] 56-57 U 8
North Channel [GB] 119 CD 4
North Charleston, SC 80-81 G 4
North Chicago, IL 70-71 G 4
Northcliff, Johannesburg- 170 V a 1
Northcliffe 158-159 C 6
Northcote, Melbourne- 161 II c 1
North Creek, NY 72-73 JK 3
North Dakota 64-65 FG 2
North Dum Dum 154 II b 2
North East, PA 72-73 FG 3
Northeast Branch 82 II b 1
Northeast Cape [USA] 58-59 CD 5
North East Carry, ME 72-73 LM 2
North Eastern 172 H 1-2
Northeastern University 84 I b 2
North-East Island = Nordaustlandet 116-117 k-m 5
Northeast Providence Channel 64-65 L 6
Northeim 118 DE 3
Northern [GH] 168-169 E 3
Northern [MW] 171 C 5-6
Northern [WAL] 168-169 BC 3
Northern [Z] 172 E 3-F 4
Northern Cheyenne Indian Reservation 68-69 C 3
Northern Indian Lake 61 K 2
Northern Ireland 119 C 4
Northern Light Lake 70-71 E 1
Northern Marianas 162 GH 2
Northern Pacific Railway 64-65 EF 2
Northern Province = Ash-Shimālīyah 164-165 KL 5
Northern Province = Uturė Palāna = 1 ◁ 140 E 6
Northern Sporades = Bóreioi Sporádes 122-123 KL 6
Northern Territory 158-159 FG 3-4
Northfield, MN 70-71 D 3
Northfield, VT 72-73 K 2
North Fiji Basin 158-159 O 2
North Foreland 119 GH 6
North Fork, CA 74-75 D 4
North Fork, ID 66-67 FG 3
North Fork Camp Creek 85 II a 3
North Fork Chandalar 58-59 N 2-3
North Fork Cimarron River 76-77 D 4
North Fork Clearwater River 66-67 F 2
North Fork Feather River 74-75 C 2-3
North Fork Fortymile 58-59 QR 4
North Fork Grand River 68-69 E 3
North Fork Humboldt River 66-67 F 5
North Fork John Day River 66-67 D 3
North Fork Koyukuk 58-59 M 3
North Fork Kuskokwim 58-59 KL 5
North Fork Moreau River 68-69 E 3
North Fork Mountain 72-73 G 5
North Fork Payette River 66-67 E 3
North Fork Peachtree Creek 85 II c 1
North Fork Powder River 68-69 C 4
North Fork Red River 76-77 E 5
North Fork Smoky Hill River 68-69 EF 6
North Fork Solomon River 68-69 FG 6
North Fox Island 70-71 H 3
North French River 62 L 1-2
North Frisian Islands = Nordfriesische Inseln 118 D 1
Northgate 68-69 EF 1
North Haycock 152-153 G 4
North Head [AUS] 161 I b 1
North Head [CDN] 63 C 5
North Horr 172 G 1
North Houston Heights, TX 85 III b 1
North Island [NZ] 158-159 P 7
North Island [USA] 80-81 G 4
North Islands 78-79 E 6
North Judson, IN 70-71 G 5
North Kamloops 60 GH 4
North Koel = Koel 138-139 J 5
North Korea 142-143 O 3-4
North Lakhimpur 141 CD 2
Northland 161 E 2
Northland, MI 70-71 G 2
North Land = Severnaja Zeml'a 132-133 ST 1-2
North Laramie River 68-69 D 4
North Las Vegas, NV 74-75 F 4
Northline Terrace, TX 85 III b 1
North Little Rock, AR 64-65 H 4-5
North Loup, NE 68-69 G 5
North Loup River 68-69 G 5
North Magnetic Pole 56-57 Q 3
North Magnetic Pole Area 52 B 29
North Malosmadulu Atoll 176 a 1
North Manchester, IN 70-71 H 5
Northmead 170 V c 2
North Miami, FL 80-81 cd 4
North Minch 119 C 3-D 2
North Moose Lake 61 HJ 3
North Natuna Islands = Kepulauan Bunguran Utara 148-149 E 6
North Negril Point 88-89 G 5
North New River Canal 80-81 c 3
Northolt, London- 129 II a 1
Northolt Aerodrome 129 II a 1
North Ossetian Autonomous Soviet Socialist Republic 126-127 LM 5
North Pacific Basin 156-157 H-K 2-3
North Pageh = Pulau Pagai Utara 148-149 C 7
North Palisade 64-65 C 4
North Park, Chicago-, IL 83 II a 1
North Pass 64-65 J 6
North Pease River 76-77 D 5
North Philadelphia, Philadelphia-, PA 84 III bc 2
North Philadelphia Airport 84 III c 1
North Platte, NE 64-65 F 3
North Platte River 64-65 F 3
North Point [AUS] 161 I b 1
North Point [USA] 72-73 E 2
North Point, Victoria- 155 I b 2
North Pole, AK 58-59 O 4
Northport, AL 78-79 F 4
Northport, MI 70-71 H 3
Northport, NE 68-69 E 5
Northport, WA 66-67 E 1
North Powder, OR 66-67 DE 3
North Quincy, MA 84 I bc 3
North Range 70-71 DE 2
North Reservoir 84 I b 2
North Rhine-Westphalia = Nordrhein-Westfalen 118 CD 3
North Richmond, CA 83 I b 1
North Riverside, IL 83 II a 1
North Rona 119 D 2
North Ronaldsay 119 EF 2
North Ryde, Sydney- 161 I a 1
North Sālmāra 141 B 2
North Santiam River 66-67 B 3
North Saskatchewan River 56-57 OP 7
North Sea 114-115 J 4
North Sea Channel = Noordzeekanaal 120-121 K 2
North Share Channel 83 II ab 1
North Shore Range 70-71 E 1-2
North Slape 58-59 G-N 2
North Star 60 HJ 1
North Stradbroke Island 158-159 K 5
North Stratford, NH 72-73 L 2
North Sydney 63 F 4
North Sydney, Sydney- 161 I b 1-2
North Taranaki Bight 158-159 O 7
North Thompson River 60 G 4-H 3
North Tonawanda, NY 72-73 G 3
North Truchas Peak 64-65 E 4
North Ubian Island 152-153 NO 2
North Uist 119 BC 3
Northumberland Islands 158-159 JK 4
Northumberland Strait 56-57 Y 8
North Umpqua River 66-67 B 4
North Utoy Creek 85 II b 2
North Valleystream, NY 82 III de 2
North Vancouver 66-67 B 1
North Vanlaiphai 141 C 4
North Vernon, IN 70-71 H 6
North Wabasca Lake 60 L 1
Northway, AK 58-59 QR 5
Northway Junction, AK 58-59 R 5
Northwest Australian Basin 50-51 OP 6
Northwest Branch 82 II b 1
North West Cape 158-159 B 4
North Western 172 DE 4
North-Western Province = Vayamba Palāna = 3 ◁ 140 E 7
Northwestern University 83 II b 1
North-West-Frontier 132-133 L 3-4
Northwest Highlands 119 D 2-3
Northwest Indian Ridge 50-51 N 5-6
Northwest Pacific Basin 156-157 G 3
Northwest Pacific Ridge 156-157 H 2-3
Northwest Passage 56-57 J-L 3
Northwest Territories 56-57 M-U 4
North Weymouth, MA 84 I c 3
North Wilkesboro, NC 80-81 F 2
Northwood, IA 70-71 D 4
Northwood, ND 68-69 H 2
Northwood, London- 129 II a 1
North York 72-73 G 3
Norton, KS 68-69 G 6
Norton, VA 80-81 E 2
Norton Bay 58-59 FG 4
Norton Point 82 III b 3
Norton Sound 56-57 D 5
Nortonville, ND 68-69 G 2
Norvegia, Kapp — 53 B 34-35
Norwalk, CA 83 III d 2
Norwalk, CT 72-73 K 4
Norwalk, MI 70-71 GH 3
Norwalk, OH 72-73 E 4
Norway 116-117 C 8-L 2
Norway, IA 70-71 DE 5
Norway, ME 72-73 L 2
Norway, MI 70-71 G 3
Norway House 56-57 R 7
Norwegian Basin 50-51 JK 2
Norwegian Bay 56-57 ST 2
Norwegian Sea 114-115 F-K 2
Norwegian Trench 114-115 K 4
Norwich, CT 72-73 KL 4
Norwich, NY 72-73 J 3
Norwich [CDN] 72-73 F 3
Norwich [GB] 119 G 5
Norwood, MN 70-71 CD 3
Norwood, NC 80-81 F 3
Norwood, NY 72-73 J 2
Norwood, OH 70-71 H 6
Norwood, PA 84 III b 2
Norwood, Johannesburg- 170 V b 1
Norwood Park, Chicago-, IL 83 II a 1
nos Emine 122-123 MN 4
Noshiro 142-143 QR 3
Nosiro = Noshiro 142-143 QR 3
nos Kaliakra 122-123 N 4
Nosovka 126-127 EF 1
Nosovščina 124-125 L 2
Nossa Senhora da Glória 100-101 F 6
Nossa Senhora das Dores 100-101 F 6
Nossa Senhora do Livramento 102-103 D 1
Nossa Senhora do Ó, São Paulo- 110 II ab 1
Nossa Senhora do Socorro 100-101 F 6
Nossegem 128 II b 1
Nossikon 128 IV b 2
Nossob 172 C 6
Nossobougou 168-169 D 2
Nošuľ 124-125 R 3
Nosy-Bé 172 J 4
Nosy Boraha 172 K 5
Nosy Mitsio 172 J 4
Nosy Radama 172 J 4
Nosy-Varika 172 J 6
Notch Peak 74-75 G 3
Noteč 118 G 2
Noto [I] 122-123 F 7
Noto [J] 144-145 L 4
Notodden 116-117 C 8
Noto hantō 142-143 Q 4
Noto-jima 144-145 L 4
Notoro-ko 144-145 d 1
Notre Dame 129 I c 2
Notre-Dame, Bois — 129 I d 2
Notre Dame, Monts — 56-57 WX 8
Notre Dame Bay 56-57 Z 8-a 7
Notre-Dame-des-Lourdes 61 JK 6
Notre-Dame-des-Victoires, Montréal- 82 I b 1
Notre-Dame-du-Lac 63 BC 4
Notre-Dame-du-Laus 72-73 J 1
Notre Dame du Nord 62 M 3
Nottawasaga Bay 72-73 F 2
Nottaway River 56-57 V 7
Nottingham 119 F 5
Nottingham Island 56-57 VW 5
Nottingham Park, IL 83 II a 2
Nottinghamroad 174-175 HJ 5
Notting Hill, London- 129 II b 1
Notting Hill, Melbourne- 161 II c 2
Nottoway River 80-81 H 2
Notuken Creek 61 E 6
Notwani 174-175 FG 3
Nouadhibou = Nawādhību 164-165 A 4
Nouakchott = Nawākshūt 164-165 A 5
Nouâl, Choṭṭ en — = Sabkhat an-Nawāl 166-167 LM 2
Noukloofberge 174-175 AB 3
Noukloof Mountains = Noukloofberge 174-175 AB 3
Nouméa 158-159 N 4
Noun 168-169 H 4
Noupoort 172 DE 8
Nous 174-175 C 5
Nous West = Nous 174-175 C 5
Nouvelle Amsterdam 50-51 NO 7
Nouvelle-Anvers 172 CD 1
Nova Almeida 100-101 DE 11
Nova Andradina 102-103 F 5
Nova Aripuanã 98-99 H 9
Novabad 134-135 L 3
Nova Cachoeirinha, São Paulo- 110 II ab 1
Nova Chaves = Muconda 172 D 4
Nova Cruz 92-93 MN 6
Nova Era 102-103 L 3
Nova Esperança 102-103 FG 5
Nova Europa 102-103 H 4
Nova Floresta 100-101 E 3
Nova Freixo = Cuamba 172 G 4
Nova Friburgo 102-103 L 5
Nova Gaia 172 C 3-4
Nova Goa = Panjim 134-135 L 7
Nova Gradiška 122-123 GH 3
Nova Granada 102-103 H 4
Nova Iguaçu 92-93 L 9
Nova Iorque 100-101 B 4
Nova Itarana 100-101 DE 7
Novaja Basan' 126-127 E 1
Novaja Buchara = Kagan 134-135 J 3
Novaja Kachovka 126-127 F 3
Novaja Kalitva 126-127 K 1
Novaja Kazanka 126-127 O 2
Novaja Ladoga 124-125 HJ 3
Novaja Odessa 126-127 EF 3
Novaja Pis'm'anka = Leninogorsk 132-133 J 7
Novaja Sibir', ostrov — 132-133 de 3
Novaja Usman' 126-127 J 1
Novaja Zeml'a 132-133 J 3-L 2
Nova Lamego 164-165 B 6
Nova Lima 92-93 L 8-9
Nova Lisboa = Huambo 172 C 4
Nova Londrina 102-103 F 5
Nova Lusitânia 172 F 5
Nova Mambone 172 G 6
Nova Olímpia 104-105 H 4
Nova Olinda [BR, Ceará] 100-101 E 4
Nova Olinda [BR, Pará] 98-99 N 8
Nova Olinda do Norte 98-99 J 6
Nova Petropolis 106-107 M 2
Nova Ponte 102-103 J 3
Nova Prata 106-107 M 2
Novara 122-123 C 3
Nova Russas 100-101 D 3
Nova Scotia 56-57 X 9-Y 8
Nova Sofala 172 FG 6
Nova Soure 100-101 E 6
Novato, CA 74-75 B 3
Nova Trento 102-103 H 7
Nova Venécia 100-101 D 10
Nova Viçosa 100-101 E 9
Nova Vida 98-99 G 10
Novaya Zemlya = Novaja Zeml'a 132-133 J 3-L 2
Novaya Zemlya Trough 132-133 K 3-L 2
Nova Zagora 122-123 LM 4
Nové Zámky 118 J 4
Novgorod 132-133 E 6
Novgorod-Severskij 124-125 J 8
Novi Bečej 122-123 J 3
Noviembre, 28 de — 108-109 CD 8
Novigrad 122-123 E 3
Novije Basy 126-127 G 1
Novije Belokoroviči 126-127 C 1
Novillos, Los — 106-107 K 3-4
Novinka [SU ↓ Leningrad] 124-125 H 4
Novi Pazar [BG] 122-123 M 4

Novi Pazar [YU] 122-123 J 4
Novi Sad 122-123 HJ 3
Nóvita 94-95 C 5
Novo Acôrdo 98-99 P 9-10
Novo Acre 100-101 D 7
Novoajdar 126-127 J 2
Novoaleksandrovskaja 126-127 K 4
Novoaleksejevka 126-127 G 3
Novoaltajsk 132-133 PQ 7
Novoanninskij 126-127 L 1
Novoarchangel'skoje 113 V b 1
Novoazovskoje 126-127 HJ 3
Novobelica, Gomel'- 124-125 H 7
Novobogatinskoje 126-127 P 3
Novobratcevskij 113 V a 2
Novočeremšansk 124-125 RS 6
Novočerkassk 126-127 K 3
Novochop'orskij 126-127 K 1
Novochovrino, Moskva- 113 V b 2
Novo Cruzeiro 102-103 M 2
Novodugino 124-125 K 6
Novoekonomičeskoje 126-127 H 2
Novogirejevo, Moskva- 113 V cd 2
Novograd-Volynskij 126-127 CD 1
Novogrigorjevka 126-127 G 3
Novogrudok 124-125 EF 7
Novo Hamburgo 111 FG 3
Novo Horizonte 102-103 H 4
Novoivanovskoje 113 V a 3
Novojel'n'a 124-125 EF 7
Novojerudinskij 132-133 RS 6
Novokazalinsk 132-133 L 8
Novokubansk 126-127 K 4
Novokujbyševsk 124-125 RS 7
Novokuzneck 132-133 Q 7
Novolazarevskaja 53 B 1
Novo-Mariinsk = Anadyr'
132-133 j 5
Novo Mesto 122-123 F 3
Novomirgorod 126-127 EF 2
Novomoskovsk [SU, Rossijskaja SFSR] 124-125 M 6
Novomoskovsk [SU, Ukrainskaja SSR] 126-127 GH 2
Novonikolajevsk = Novosibirsk
132-133 P 6-7
Novo-Nikolajevskaja 126-127 L 1
Novonikolajevskij 126-127 L 1
Novo Oriente 100-101 D 3
Novopiscovo 124-125 NO 5
Novopokrovka = Liski 126-127 J 1
Novopokrovskaja 126-127 K 4
Novopolock 124-125 G 6
Novopskov 126-127 J 2
Novor'ažsk 124-125 N 7
Novo Redondo = N'Gunza Kabolo 172 B 4
Novorepnoje 126-127 O 1
Novorossijsk 126-127 HJ 4
Novoržev 124-125 G 5
Novošachtinsk 126-127 J 3
Novoselje 124-125 G 4
Novosergijevka 124-125 T 7
Novoshachtinsk = Novošachtinsk 126-127 J 3
Novosibirsk 132-133 P 6-7
Novosibirskije ostrova 132-133 Z-f 2
Novosil' 124-125 L 7
Novosokol'niki 124-125 GH 5
Novos'olovo 132-133 R 6
Novotroick 132-133 K 7
Novo-Troickij Promysel = Balej
132-133 W 7
Novotroickoje [SU, Chersonskaja Oblast'] 126-127 FG 3
Novotroickoje [SU, Kirovskaja Oblast'] 124-125 Q 4
Novotulka 126-127 NO 1
Novotul'skij 124-125 LM 6
Novoukrainka 126-127 EF 2
Novo-Urgenč = Urgenč
132-133 L 9
Novouzensk 126-127 O 1
Novovasiljevka 126-127 GH 3
Novov'atsk 124-125 RS 4
Novov'azniki 124-125 NO 5
Novovoronežskij 126-127 JK 1
Novozavidovskij 124-125 L 5
Novozybkov 124-125 HJ 7
Novra 61 H 4
Novska 122-123 G 3
Novyj Bug 126-127 F 3
Novyj Bujan 124-125 RS 7
Novyje Burasy 124-125 PQ 7
Novyje Karymkary 132-133 MN 5
Novyje Kuz'minki, Moskva-
113 V cd 3
Novyje Sanžary 126-127 FG 2
Novyj Margelan = Fergana
134-135 L 2-3
Novyj Nekouz 124-125 LM 4-5
Novyj Oskol 126-127 HJ 1
Novyj Port 132-133 MN 4
Novyj Terek 126-127 N 5
Novyj Uštagan 126-127 O 3
Novyj Zaj 124-125 ST 6
Nowa Sól 118 G 3
Nowata, OK 76-77 G 4
Nowbarān 136-137 N 5
Nowe 118 J 2
Nowgong [IND, Assam] 141 C 2
Nowgong [IND, Madhya Pradesh] 138-139 G 5
Nowgorod = Novgorod
132-133 E 6
Nowitna River 58-59 K 4
Nowkash 136-137 MN 6
Nowlin, SD 68-69 F 3-4
Nowood Creek 68-69 C 3-4
Nowra 158-159 K 6
Nowrangapur 138-139 J 8
Nowy Korczyn 118 K 3
Nowy Sącz 118 K 4
Nowy Targ 118 K 4
Noxon, MT 66-67 F 1-2
Noya 120-121 C 7
Noyes Island 58-59 vw 9
Noyon 120-121 J 4
Nqabeni 174-175 J 6
Nqutu 174-175 J 5
N'Riquinha = Lumbala 172 D 5
Nsa, Ouèd en — = Wādī an-Nisā'
166-167 J 3
Nsanje 172 G 5
Nsawam 168-169 E 4
Nsefu 171 BC 6
Nsukka 164-165 F 7
Ntcheu 172 FG 4
Ntem 168-169 H 5
Ntywenka 174-175 H 6
Nuages, Col des — = Đeo Hai Van
150-151 G 4
Nuanetsi = Mwenezi 172 EF 6
Nuanetsi, Rio — 174-175 J 2
Nuāpaḍā = Nawāpāra 138-139 J 7
Nuatja 168-169 F 4
Nub 138-139 L 4
Nubah, An- 164-165 K-M 4-5
Nūbah, Aṣ-Ṣaḥrā' an- 164-165 LM 4
Nūbah, Jibāl an- 164-165 KL 6
Nubian Desert = Aṣ-Ṣaḥrā' an-
Nūbah 164-165 LM 4
Nubieber, CA 66-67 C 5
Nūbiya = An-Nubah
164-165 K-M 4-5
Ñuble, Río — 106-107 B 6
Nubra 138-139 GH 2
Nucha = Sheki 126-127 N 6
N'uchča 124-125 Q 2
Nu Chiang = Nag Chhu
142-143 G 5
Nu Chiang = Nu Jiang 141 F 2
N'učpas 124-125 S 3
Nucuray, Río — 96-97 D 4
Nudo Aricoma 96-97 FG 9
Nudo Ausangate 92-93 E 7
Nudo Coropuna 92-93 E 8
Nudo de Applobamba 104-105 B 4
Nudo de Paramillo 94-95 CD 4
Nueces River 64-65 G 6
Nueltin Lake 56-57 R 5
Nuestra Señora, Monte —
108-109 B 7
Nuestra Señora del Rosario de Caa Catí 106-107 J 1
Nueva Antioquia 92-93 EF 3
Nueva Atzacoalco, Ciudad de
México- 91 I c 2
Nueva California 106-107 CD 4
Nueva Casas Grandes 64-65 E 5
Nueva Chicago, Buenos Aires-
110 III b 1
Nueva Constitución 106-107 DE 5
Nueva Escocia 106-107 DE 4
Nueva Esparta 94-95 J 2
Nueva Esperanza 104-105 DE 10
Nueva Florida 94-95 G 3
Nueva Galia 106-107 E 5
Nueva Germania 111 E 2
Nueva Gerona 88-89 E 3-4
Nueva Granada 94-95 D 3
Nueva Harberton 108-109 F 10
Nueva Helvecia 106-107 J 5
Nueva Imperial 106-107 A 7
Nueva Lima 96-97 C 5
Nueva Lubecka 108-109 D 5
Nueva Ocotepeque 88-89 B 7
Nueva Orán, San Ramón de la —
111 CD 2
Nueva Palmira 106-107 HJ 4
Nueva Población 104-105 F 9
Nueva Pompeya, Buenos Aires-
110 III b 1
Nueva Providencia 64-65 b 2
Nueva Roma 106-107 F 7
Nueva Rosita 64-65 F 6
Nueva San Salvador 64-65 HJ 9
Nueva Vizcaya 106-107 H 3
Nueve de Julio [RA, Buenos Aires]
111 D 5
Nueve de Julio [RA, San Juan]
106-107 C 3
Nuevitas 88-89 H 4
Nuevo Berlín 106-107 HJ 4
Nuevo Chagres 64-65 ab 2
Nuevo Emperador 64-65 b 2
Nuevo Laredo 64-65 FG 6
Nuevo León 64-65 F 7-G 6
Nuevo Mamo 94-95 K 3
Nuevo Padilla 86-87 L 6
Nuevo Rocafuerte 92-93 D 5
Nuevo San Juan 64-65 b 2
Nuevo Trujillo 96-97 DE 6
Nuffar = Nippur 136-137 L 6
Nugaal 164-165 b 2
Nugruş, Gebel — = Jabal Nuqruş
173 D 5
Nûgssuaq 56-57 YZ 3
Nûgssuaq Halvø 56-57 a 3
Nuguria Islands 148-149 hj 5
Nugurue, Punta — 106-107 A 5
Nūh 138-139 F 3
Nuhaylah, An- 173 B 4
Nuhūd, An- 164-165 K 6
Nuhurowa = Pulau Kai Kecil
148-149 K 8
Nuhu Rowa = Pulau Kai Kecil
148-149 K 8
Nuhu Tjut = Pulau Kai Besar
148-149 K 8
Nuhu Yut = Pulau Kai Besar
148-149 K 8
Nui 208 H 3
Nuia 124-125 E 4
Nui Ba Ra = Phu'o'c Binh
150-151 F 7
Nui Đeo 148-149 E 2
Nui Hon Diên 150-151 G 7
Nui Mang 150-151 FG 4
Nui Vong Phu 150-151 G 6
N'uja [SU, place] 132-133 W 5
N'uja [SU, river] 132-133 V 5
Nu Jiang 141 F 2
Nu Jiang = Nag Chhu 142-143 G 5
Nujiang Lisuzu Zizhizhou
142-143 H 6
Nûk 56-57 a 5
Nuka Island 58-59 M 7
Nuka River 58-59 H 2
Nukey Bluff 160 BC 4
Nukhayb 134-135 E 4
Nukhaylah 164-165 K 5
Nukheila, Bîr — = Nukhaylah
164-165 K 5
N'uksenica 124-125 P 3
Nuku'alofa 208 J 5
Nukufetau 208 H 3
Nukulaelae 208 H 3
Nukumanu Islands 148-149 jk 5
Nukunau 208 H 3
Nukunono 208 J 3
Nukuoro 208 F 2
Nukus 132-133 KL 9
N'ukža 132-133 X 6-7
Nulato, AK 56-57 E 5
Nulato River 58-59 H 4
Nullagine 158-159 D 4
Nullarbor 158-159 EF 6
Nullarbor Plain 158-159 EF 6
Nuluk River 58-59 D 4
Num, Mios — 148-149 KL 7
Numakunai = Iwate 144-145 N 3
Numan 164-165 G 7
Nu'mān, Jazīrat an- 173 D 4
Numancia 120-121 F 8
Numata [J, Gunma] 144-145 M 4
Numata [J, Hokkaidō] 144-145 bc 2
Numata, Tōkyō- 155 III b 1
Numazu 144-145 M 5
Numedal 116-117 C 7-8
Numeia = Nouméa 158-159 N 4
Numero 1 Station = Maḥaṭṭat 1
173 B 7
Numero 2 Station = Maḥaṭṭat 2
173 BC 7
Numero 3 Station = Maḥaṭṭat 3
173 BC 7
Numero 4 Station = Maḥaṭṭat 4
173 C 7
Numfoor, Pulau — 148-149 KL 7
Numto 132-133 MN 5
Numurkah 160 G 6
Nunachuak, AK 58-59 J 7
Nunapitchuk, AK 58-59 F 6
Nunavakanuk River 58-59 E 5-6
Nunavak Anukslak Lake 58-59 FG 6
Nunavakpok Lake 58-59 F 6
Nunavaugaluk, Lake — 58-59 H 7
Nunawading, Melbourne- 161 II c 1
Nunchia 94-95 E 5
Nun Chiang = Nen Jiang
142-143 O 1-2
Nundle 160 K 3
Ñuñez, Buenos Aires- 110 III b 1
Ñuñez, Isla — 108-109 BC 9
Ñuñez del Prado 106-107 EF 3
Nungan = Nong'an 142-143 NO 3
Nungesser Lake 62 BC 2
Nungo 172 G 4
Nunica, MI 70-71 GH 4
Nunivak Island 56-57 C 6
Nunn, CO 68-69 D 5
Nuñoa 96-97 F 9
Nunyamo 58-59 BC 4
Nuomin He 142-143 N 2
Nuoro 122-123 C 5
Nuqrat as-Salmān = As-Salmān
136-137 L 7
Nuqruş, Jabal — 173 D 5
Nuquí 94-95 C 5
Nura 132-133 N 7
Nurakita 208 H 4
Nuratau, chrebet — 132-133 M 9
N'urba 132-133 W 5
Nur dağlan 136-137 G 4
Nuremburg = Nürnberg 118 E 4
Nürensdorf 128 IV b 1
Nūrestān 134-135 KL 3-4
Nuria, Altiplanicie de — 94-95 L 4
Nurlat 124-125 S 6
Nurlaty 124-125 R 6
Nurmes 116-117 N 6
Nürnberg 118 E 4
Nuruhak dağı 136-137 G 3
Nusa Barung 152-153 K 10
Nusa Kambangan 152-153 H 9-10
Nusa Penida 148-149 FG 8
Nusa Tenggara Barat = 16 ◁
148-149 G 8
Nusa Tenggara Timur = 17 ◁
148-149 H 8
Nusaybin 134-135 E 3
Nushagak Bay 58-59 H 7
Nushagak Peninsula 58-59 H 7
Nushagak River 56-57 E 5-6
Nu Shan 142-143 H 6
Nushki 134-135 K 5
Nussdorf, Wien- 113 I b 1
Nusuvidu = Nūzvīd 140 E 2
Nutak 56-57 Y 6
Nutley, NJ 82 III b 2
Nutrias = Puerto de Nutrias
92-93 EF 3
Nutrias, Las — 106-107 H 7
Nutt, NM 76-77 A 6
Nutzotin Mountains 56-57 H 5
Nuvākoṭ = Nuwākot 138-139 JK 3
N'uvčim 124-125 S 3
Nuwākot 138-139 JK 3
Nuwara Eliya 134-135 N 9
Nuwaybi' al-Muzayyinah 173 D 3
Nuweiba' = Nuwaybi' al-Muzayyinah
173 D 3
Nuwerus 174-175 C 6
Nuweveld 174-175 DE 6
Nuweveldberge 174-175 DE 7
Nuweveldrecks = Nuweveldberge
174-175 DE 7
Nuyakuk Lake 58-59 H 7
Nuyakuk River 58-59 HJ 7
Nuyts Archipelago 158-159 F 6
Nūzvīd 140 E 2
Nwa 168-169 H 4
Nwādōgyī 141 D 5
Nwatle 174-175 D 2
Nxai Pan National Park 172 DE 5
Nyaake 164-165 C 8
Nyaba 138-139 L 2
Nyac, AK 58-59 GH 6
Nya Chhu = Yalong Jiang
142-143 HJ 5
Nyahanga 172 F 2
Nyakahanga 172 F 2
Nyālā 164-165 J 6
Ny Ålesund 116-117 hj 5
Nyalikungu 171 C 3
Nyamandhlovu 172 E 5
Nyamasane 174-175 J 3
Nyambiti 172 F 2
Nyämlêll 164-165 K 7
Nyamtam 168-169 H 4
Nyamtumbu 172 G 4
Nyanchhenthanglha [TJ, mountains]
142-143 F 6-G 5
Nyanchhenthanglha [TJ, pass]
142-143 G 5-6
Nyanda 172 F 5
Nyanga 172 B 2
Nyang Chhu 138-139 M 3
Nyanji 171 BC 6
Nyanza [EAK] 172 F 1-2
Nyanza [RU] 171 B 4
Nyanza [RWA] 171 B 3
Nyasa = Lake Malawi 172 F 4
Nyasameer = Lake Malawi 172 F 4
Nyaungdôn 141 D 7
Nyaunglebin 148-149 C 3
Nyaungywe 141 E 5
Nyawalu 171 AB 3
Nyborg 116-117 D 10
Nybro 116-117 F 9
Nyda 132-133 N 4
Nyenasi 168-169 E 4
Nyenchentanglha =
Nyanchhenthanglha
142-143 F 6-G 5
Nyeri [EAK] 172 G 2
Nyeri [EAU] 171 B 2
Nyeweni 174-175 H 6
Ny Friesland 116-117 k 5
Nyika Plateau 172 F 3-4
Nyima 138-139 K 3
Nyinahin 168-169 E 4
Nyingzhi 138-139 N 3
Nyira Gonga 171 B 3
Nyírbátor 118 KL 5
Nyíregyháza 118 K 5
Nyiri Desert 171 D 3
Nyiro, Uoso — = Ewaso Ngiro
172 G 2
Nyiru, Mount — 172 G 1
Nyítra = Nitra 118 J 4
Nykarleby 116-117 K 6
Nykøbing Falster 116-117 DE 10
Nykøbing Mors 116-117 C 9
Nykøbing Sjælland 116-117 D 9-10
Nyköping 116-117 G 8
Nyland = Uusimaa 116-117 KL 7
Nylrivier 174-175 H 3
Nylstroom 172 E 6
Nymagee 160 H 4
Nymboida 160 L 2
Nymburk 118 G 3
Nymphenburg, München- 130 II ab 1
Nymphenburg, Schlosspark —
130 II ab 2
Nynäshamn 116-117 GH 8
Nyngan 158-159 J 6
Nyong 164-165 G 8
Nyonga 172 F 3
Nyrob 124-125 V 3
Nyrud 116-117 N 3
Nysa 118 H 3
Nysa Kłodzka 118 H 3
Nyslott = Savonlinna 116-117 N 7
Nyssa, OR 66-67 E 4
Nystad = Uusikaupunki
116-117 J 7
Nytva 132-133 JK 6
Nyūdō-saki 144-145 M 2
Nyuggö 138-139 K 3
Nyunzu 172 E 3
Nyuri 141 C 2
Nzebela 168-169 C 3-4
Nzega 172 F 2
N'Zérékoré 164-165 C 7
N'Zeto 172 B 3
Nzheledam 174-175 HJ 2
Nzi 168-169 D 4
Nzo 168-169 D 4
Nzoia 171 C 2
Nzoro 171 B 2

O

Oahe, Lake — 64-65 F 2
Oahu 148-149 e 3
Oakbank 158-159 H 6
Oak City, UT 74-75 G 3
Oak Creek, CO 68-69 C 5
Oakdale, CA 74-75 C 4
Oakdale, GA 85 II a 1
Oakdale, LA 78-79 C 5
Oakdale, NE 68-69 GH 4
Oakes, ND 68-69 G 2
Oakey 158-159 K 5
Oak Forest, Houston-, TX 85 III b 1
Oak Grove, LA 78-79 D 4
Oak Grove Cemetery 84 I b 2
Oakharbor, OH 72-73 E 4
Oak Harbor, WA 66-67 B 1
Oak Hill, FL 80-81 c 2
Oak Hill, WV 72-73 F 5-6
Oakhurst, TX 76-77 G 7
Oak Island 70-71 E 2
Oak Lake [CDN, lake] 61 H 6
Oak Lake [CDN, place] 61 H 6
Oakland, CA 64-65 B 4
Oakland, IA 70-71 C 5
Oakland, MD 72-73 G 5
Oakland, NE 68-69 H 5
Oakland, OR 66-67 B 4
Oakland Cemetery 85 II bc 2
Oakland City, IN 70-71 G 6
Oakland City, Atlanta-, GA 85 II b 2
Oaklands 160 GH 5
Oaklands, Johannesburg- 170 V b 1
Oak Lawn, IL 70-71 FG 5
Oaklawn, MD 82 II b 2
Oakleigh, Melbourne- 161 II c 2
Oakley, ID 66-67 FG 4
Oakley, KS 68-69 F 6
Oaklyn, NJ 84 III c 2
Oakover River 158-159 D 4
Oak Park, IL 70-71 G 5
Oak Park, MI 84 II a 2
Oak Park Cemetery 85 III b 1
Oakridge, OR 66-67 B 4
Oak Ridge, TN 64-65 K 4
Oak Valley, NJ 84 III b 3
Oakview, NJ 84 III bc 2
Oakville, LA 85 I b 3
Oakville [CDN, Manitoba] 61 JK 6
Oakville [CDN, Ontario] 72-73 G 3
Oakwilde, TX 85 III b 1
Oakwood, OK 76-77 E 5
Oakwood, TX 76-77 FG 7
Oakwood, New York-, NY 82 III b 3
Oamaru 158-159 O 9
Ōana 155 III d 1
Ōarai 144-145 N 4
Oas 174-175 C 2
Oasis, CA 74-75 DE 4
Oasis, NV 66-67 F 5
Oasis, El — 91 II ab 1
Oasis de Koufra = Wāḥāt al-Kufrah
164-165 J 4
Oates Land 53 B 16-17
Oatlands [AUS] 160 cd 3
Oatlands [ZA] 174-175 F 7
Oatley, Sydney- 161 I a 2
Oatley Park 161 I a 2
Oatman, AZ 74-75 F 5
Oaxaca 64-65 G 8
Oaxaca de Juárez 64-65 GH 8
Ob' 132-133 NO 5
Ob, Gulf of — = Obskaja guba
132-133 N 3-4
Oba [CDN] 70-71 HJ 1
Oba [Vanuatu] 158-159 N 3
Oba Lake 70-71 H 1
Obama 144-145 K 5
Oban [CDN] 61 D 4
Oban [GB] 119 D 3
Oban [NZ] 158-159 N 9
Obando 94-95 H 6
Oban Hills 168-169 H 4
Obara = Ōchi 144-145 J 5
Obdorsk = Salechard 132-133 M 4
Obeidh, El- = Al-Ubayyiḍ
164-165 KL 6
Oberá 111 F 3
Oberdorfelden 128 III b 1
Oberembrach 128 IV b 1
Oberengstringen 128 IV a 1
Oberföhring, München- 130 II b 1
Oberglatt 128 IV b 1
Oberhasli 128 IV ab 1
Oberhausen 118 C 3
Oberhöchstadt 128 III a 1
Oberlaa, Wien- 113 I b 2
Oberlin, KS 68-69 F 6
Oberlin, LA 78-79 C 5
Oberlisse, Wien- 113 I b 1
Oberlunkhofen 128 IV a 2
Obermeilen 128 IV b 2
Obermenzing, München- 130 II a 1
Oberon, ND 68-69 G 2
Oberösterreich 118 F-H 4
Oberpfälzer Wald 118 F 4
Oberrad, Frankfurt am Main-
128 III b 1
Oberrieden [CH] 128 IV b 2
Ober-Roden 128 III b 2
Oberschöneweide, Berlin- 130 III c 2
Obersendling, München- 130 II b 2
Oberstdorf 118 E 5
Obersteinmaur 128 IV a 1
Obertshausen 128 III b 1
Obervolta 164-165 DE 6
Oberwil 128 IV a 2
Obetz, OH 72-73 E 5
Obfelden 128 IV a 2
Obi, Pulau — 148-149 J 7
Obiaruku 168-169 G 4
Óbidos [BR] 92-93 HJ 5
Obihiro 144-145 c 2
Obil'noje 126-127 M 3
Obion, TN 78-79 E 2
Obirigbene 168-169 G 4
Obispos 94-95 FG 3
Obispo Trejo 106-107 F 3
Obitočnaja kosa 126-127 H 3
Obitočnyj zaliv 126-127 GH 3
Obitsu 155 III c 3
Objačevo 132-133 H 5
Obkeik, Jebel — = Jabal 'Ubkayk
164-165 M 4
Oblačnaja, gora — 132-133 Za 9
Oblivskaja 126-127 L 2
Obluče 132-133 Z 8
Obninsk 124-125 L 6
Obo 164-165 K 7
Oboa 171 C 2
Obobogorap 174-175 D 4
Obock 164-165 N 6
Obojan' 126-127 H 1
Obok = Obock 164-165 N 6
Obol' 124-125 G 6
Obonai = Tazawako 144-145 N 3
Obonga Lake 62 E 2
Oboz'orskij 124-125 N 2
Obra 118 G 2
Obrajes 104-105 BC 5
Obrayeri 88-89 DE 7
Obregón, Ciudad — 64-65 DE 6
Obrenovac 122-123 HJ 3
Obrian Peak = Trident Peak
66-67 D 5
O'Brien, Isla — 108-109 D 10
Obrovac 122-123 F 3
Obruk = Kızören 136-137 E 3
Obruk yaylâsı 136-137 E 3
Obščij Syrt 132-133 H-K 7
Observatório Astronômico [BR]
110 II b 2
Observatorio Astronomico [E]
113 III ab 2
Observatorio de México 91 I b 2
Observatory [AUS] 161 I b 2
Observatory of Greenwich 129 II c 2
Obskaja guba 132-133 N 3-4
Obuasi 164-165 D 7
Obuchi = Rokkasho 144-145 N 2
Obuchov 126-127 E 1
Obva 124-125 U 4
Očakovo, Moskva- 113 V b 3
Ocala, FL 64-65 K 6
Očamčire 126-127 K 5
Ocamo, Río — 94-95 J 6
Ocampo [MEX, Chihuahua] 86-87 F 3
Ocampo [MEX, Tamaulipas]
86-87 L 6
Ocaña [CO] 92-93 E 3
Ocaña [E] 120-121 F 9
Ocauçu 102-103 H 5
Ocean 208 GH 3
Ocean City, MD 72-73 J 5
Ocean City, NJ 72-73 J 5
Ocean Falls 56-57 L 7
Oceanlake, OR 66-67 AB 3
Oceanside, CA 64-65 C 5
Ocean Springs, MS 78-79 E 5
Ocean Strip 66-67 A 2
Ocha 132-133 b 7
Ochansk 124-125 U 5
Öchë 122-123 L 6
O-ch'êng = Echeng 146-147 E 6
Ochiai = Dolinsk 132-133 b 8
Ochiai, Tōkyō- 155 III b 1
Ochiltree 60 FG 3
Ochoa, NM 76-77 C 6
Ocho de Agosto, Laguna —
106-107 F 7
Ochogbo = Oshogbo 164-165 EF 7
Och'ŏng-do 144-145 E 4
Och'onjang 144-145 G 2
Ochota 132-133 b 5
Ochotsk 132-133 b 6
Ochotskij Perevoz 132-133 a 5
Ochre River 61 HJ 5
Ochsenwerder, Hamburg- 130 I b 2
Ochvat 124-125 J 5
Ochwe 174-175 D 2
Ocilla, GA 80-81 E 5
Ocipaco 91 I b 1-2
Ockelbo 116-117 G 7
Ocmulgee National Monument
80-81 E 4
Ocmulgee River 80-81 E 4-5
Ocoña 96-97 E 10
Ocoña, Río de — 96-97 E 10
Oconee River 80-81 E 4
Oconto, NE 68-69 FG 5
Oconto, WI 70-71 G 3
Oconto Falls, WI 70-71 FG 3
Oconto River 70-71 F 3
Oč'or 124-125 U 5
Ocotal 88-89 C 8
Ocotlán 64-65 F 7
Ocracoke Island 80-81 J 3
Octave, Rivière — 62 M 2
October Revolution Island = ostrov
Okt'abr'skoj Revol'ucii
132-133 Q-S 2
Octubre, Canal — 108-109 B 7
Ocucaje 96-97 D 9
Oculi 88-89 D 7
Ocumare de La Costa 94-95 H 2
Ocumare del Tuy 94-95 H 2
Ocuri 104-105 D 6
Oda [GH] 164-165 D 7
Ōda [J] 144-145 J 5
Ōda, Hôr — = Hawr Awdah
136-137 M 7
'Ōda, Jebel — = Jabal Ūdah
164-165 M 4
Oda, Kawasaki- 155 III b 2
Ódádhahraun 116-117 e 2
Ōdaejin 144-145 GH 2
Odanah, WI 70-71 E 2
Ōdate 144-145 N 2
Odawara 144-145 M 5
O'Day 61 L 2
Odaym 136-137 H 5
Odda 116-117 B 7
Odduchuddan = Oḍḍusuḍḍān
140 E 6
Oddur = Huddur Hadama 172 H 1
Oḍḍusuḍḍān 140 E 6
Odell, NE 68-69 H 5
Odem, TX 76-77 F 9
Odemira 120-121 C 10
Ödemis 136-137 BC 3
Odendaalsrus 172 E 7
Odense 116-117 D 10
Odensholm = Osmussaar
124-125 D 4
Odenwald 118 D 4
Oder 118 G 2
Oderzo 122-123 E 3
Odessa 126-127 E 3
Odessa, TX 64-65 F 5
Odessa, WA 66-67 D 2
Odienné 164-165 C 7
Odin, IL 70-71 F 6
Odincovo 124-125 L 6
Odioñgan 148-149 H 4
Odojevo 124-125 L 7
Ōdomari = Korsakov 132-133 b 8
O'Donnell, TX 76-77 D 6
Odorheiul Secuiesc 122-123 L 2
Odra 118 H 3
Odum, GA 80-81 E 5
Odweeyne 164-165 b 2
Odzala 172 BC 1
Oedenstockach 130 II c 2
Oeiras [BR] 100-101 C 4
Oelrichs, SD 68-69 E 4
Oelwein, IA 70-71 E 4
Oenpelli Mission 158-159 F 2
Oe-raro-do 144-145 F 5
Oerlikon, Zürich- 128 IV b 1
Oetikon 128 IV b 2
Oetling 104-105 F 10
Oetwil am See 128 IV b 2
Oetwil an der Limmat 128 IV a 1
Oeyŏn-do 144-145 F 4
Of = Solaklı 136-137 J 2
O'Fallon Creek 68-69 D 2
Ofani, Gulf of — = Kólpos Orfánu
122-123 KL 5
Ofanto 122-123 F 5
Ofcolaco 174-175 J 3
Offa 168-169 G 3
Offenbach 118 D 3
Offenbach-Bieber 128 III b 1
Offenbach-Bürgel 128 III b 1
Offenbacher Stadtwald 128 III b 1
Offenbach-Rumpenheim 128 III b 1
Offenbach-Tempelsee 128 III b 1
Offenburg 118 CD 4
Offenthal 128 III b 2
Ofhidro, Lago — 108-109 E 9
Oficina Alemania 104-105 AB 9
Oficina Domeyko 104-105 B 8
Oficina Rosario 104-105 A 9
Ofin [GH] 168-169 E 4
Ofin [WAN] 170 III b 1
Ofooué 172 B 2
Ofotfjord 116-117 G 3
Ōfunato 144-145 NO 3
Oga 144-145 M 3
Ōgada 144-145 J 6
Ogaden = Wigadēn 164-165 NO 7
Oga hantō 144-145 M 3
Ōgaki 144-145 L 5
Ogallala, NE 68-69 EF 5
Ogan 168-169 F 3
Ogarevka 124-125 L 7
Ogasawara-guntō = Bonin
206-207 RS 7
Ogascanan, Lac — 72-73 GH 1
Ogashi 144-145 N 3
Ogashi tōge 144-145 MN 3
Ōgawara 144-145 N 3-4
Ogawara ko 144-145 N 2
Ogbomosho 164-165 E 7
Ogden, IA 70-71 C 4
Ogden, KS 68-69 H 6
Ogden, UT 64-65 D 3
Ogden, Mount — 58-59 V 7
Ogdensburg, NY 64-65 LM 3
Ogeechee River 80-81 EF 4
Ogema 61 F 6
Ogema, MN 70-71 BC 2
Oger = Ogre 124-125 E 5
Ogi 144-145 M 4
Ogida = Hinai 144-145 N 2
Ogidigbe 168-169 G 4
Ogies 174-175 H 3-4
Ogilby, CA 74-75 F 6
Ogilvie 106-107 G 2
Ogilvie Mountains 56-57 J 4-5
Oginskij kanal 124-125 E 7
Ogla = 'Uqlah 166-167 AB 7
Oglala Strait 58-59 s 7
Oglat Beraber = 'Uqlat Barābir
166-167 E 4
Oglat Khenachich 164-165 D 4
Oglat Khenachich = Oglat
Khenachich 164-165 D 4
Oglat Sbita = 'Uqlāt as-Sabīyah
166-167 D 7
Oglesby, IL 70-71 F 5
Oglethorpe University 85 II bc 1
Oglio 122-123 CD 3

Ogliuga Island 58-59 t 7
Ognon 120-121 KL 5
Oğnut 136-137 J 3
Ogoja 164-165 F 7
Ogoki 62 G 2
Ogoki Lake 62 F 2
Ogoki Reservoir 62 E 2
Ogoki River 56-57 T 7
Ogon'ok 132-133 ab 6
Ogooué 172 B 2
Ogoyo 170 III b 2
Ogr = 'Uqr 164-165 K 6
Ogre 124-125 E 5
Ogué = Ogooué 172 B 2
Ogulin 122-123 F 3
Ogun 164-165 E 7
Ogurčinskij, ostrov — 134-135 G 3
Oguta 168-169 G 4
Oğuzeli 136-137 G 4
Ogwashi-Uku 168-169 G 4

Ohain 128 II b 2
Ohakune 158-159 P 7
Ohanet = Ūhānīt 166-167 L 5
Ōhara 144-145 N 5
Ōhasama 144-145 N 3
Ōhata 144-145 N 2
Ohau, Lake — 161 CD 7
Ohazama 144-145 N 3
O'Higgins [RA] 106-107 G 5
O'Higgins [RCH, administrative unit] 106-107 B 5
O'Higgins [RCH, place] 111 BC 2
O'Higgins, Lago — 108-109 C 7
Ohio 64-65 K 3
Ohio River 64-65 J 4
Ohlsdorf, Hamburg- 130 I b 1
Ohlsdorf, Zentralfriedhof — 130 I b 1
Ohlstedt, Hamburg- 130 I b 1
Ohogamiut, AK 58-59 G 6
Ohopoho 172 B 5
Ohōtuku-kai 144-145 cd 1
Ohře 118 G 3
Ohrid 122-123 J 5
Ohridsko Ezero 122-123 J 5
Ohrigstad 174-175 J 3
Ohuam 164-165 H 7
Ōhunato 144-145 NO 3

Ōi, Tōkyō- 155 III b 2
Oiapoque 92-93 J 4
Oiapoque, Rio — 92-93 J 4
Oiba 94-95 E 4
Ōi gawa 144-145 M 5
Oikhe 174-175 D 2
Oil Bay 58-59 L 7
Oil City, PA 64-65 L 3
Oildale, CA 74-75 D 5
Oilton, TX 76-77 E 9
Oio = Oyo 164-165 E 7
Oise 120-121 J 4
Ōita 144-145 H 6
Oiticica 100-101 D 3

'Ōja, Al- = Al-'Awjā 136-137 M 8
Ojai, CA 74-75 D 5
Ojat' 124-125 J 3
Ojeda 106-107 EF 5
Ojem = Oyem 164-165 G 8
Öjendorf, Hauptfriedhof — 130 I b 1
Öjendorfer See 130 I b 1
Ojika-shima 144-145 G 6
Ojinaga 64-65 EF 6
Ojiya 144-145 M 4
Ojm'akon 132-133 b 5
Ojm'akonskoje nagorje 132-133 b 5
Ojocaliente 86-87 J 6
Ojo de Agua = Villa Ojo de Agua 111 D 3
Ojo de Laguna 86-87 G 3
Ojo de Liebre, Laguna — 86-87 CD 4
Öjöngö Nuur = Ojorong nuur 142-143 F 2
Ojorong nuur 142-143 F 2
Ojos de Agua 108-109 E 3
Ojos del Salado, Nevado — 111 C 3
Ojrot-Tura = Gorno-Altajsk 132-133 Q 7
Ojtal = Merke 132-133 N 9

Oka [SU ◁ Bratskoje vodochranilišče] 132-133 T 7
Oka [SU ◁ Volga] 132-133 G 6
Oka [WAN] 168-169 G 4
Okaba 148-149 L 8
Okahandja 172 C 6
Okaihau 161 E 2
Okaloacoochee Slough 80-81 c 3
Okanagan Falls 66-67 D 1
Okanagan Lake 56-57 MN 8
Okano 172 B 1
Okanogan, WA 66-67 D 1
Okanogan Range 66-67 CD 1
Okanogan River 66-67 D 1
Okāra 138-139 D 2
Okarche, OK 76-77 F 5
Okatjevo 124-125 R 4
Okatumba 174-175 B 2
Okaukuejo 172 C 5
Okavango 172 C 5
Okavango Basin 172 D 5
Ōkawara = Ōgawara 144-145 N 3-4
Okaya 144-145 LM 4
Okayama 142-143 P 5
Okazaki 144-145 L 5
Okeechobee, FL 80-81 c 3
Okeechobee, Lake — 64-65 K 6
Okeene, OK 76-77 E 4
Okefenokee Swamp 64-65 K 5
Okemah, OK 76-77 F 5
Okene 164-165 F 7
Oke Odde 168-169 G 3
Oke Ogbe 170 III b 2
Oketo 144-145 c 2
Okha 134-135 K 6
Okhaldunga 138-139 L 4
Okhotsk = Ochotsk 132-133 b 6
Okhotsk, Sea of — 132-133 b-d 6-7
Ōkhpō 141 D 6
Okhrid = Ohrid 122-123 J 5
Okhrid Lake = Ohridsko Ezero 122-123 J 5
Oki 142-143 P 4
Okiep 174-175 BC 5
Okinawa 142-143 O 6
Okinawa-guntō 142-143 O 6
Okino Daitō-jima 142-143 P 7
Okino-Daitō zima = Okino-Daitō-jima 142-143 P 7
Okino-shima 144-145 J 6
Okino-Tori-shima 142-143 Q 7
Okino-Tori sima = Okino-Tori-shima 142-143 Q 7
Okkang-dong 144-145 E 2
Oklahoma 64-65 G 4
Oklahoma City, OK 64-65 G 4
Okmok Volcano 58-59 m 4
Okmulgee, OK 76-77 FG 5
Oknica 126-127 C 2
Okny, Krasnyje — 126-127 D 3
Okobojo Creek 68-69 F 3
Okok 171 C 2
Okokmilaga River 58-59 L 2
Okolona, MS 78-79 E 3-4
Okombahe 172 BC 6
Okoppe 144-145 c 1
Okotoks 60 L 4
Okoyo 172 BC 2
Okpilak River 58-59 PQ 2
Okrika 168-169 G 4
Oksenof, Cape — 58-59 a 2
Øksfjordjøkelen 116-117 JK 2
Okskij zapovednik 124-125 N 6
Oksko-Donskaja ravnina 124-125 NO 7-8
Oksovskij 124-125 M 2
Okstindan 116-117 F 5
Okt'abr'sk [SU, Kazachskaja SSR] 132-133 K 8
Okt'abr'sk [SU, Kujbyševskaja Oblast'] 124-125 R 7
Okt'abr'skaja magistral' 124-125 J 4-5
Okt'abr'skij [SU, Belorusskaja SSR] 124-125 G 7
Okt'abr'skij [SU, Rossijskaja SFSR Archangel'skaja Oblast'] 124-125 O 3
Okt'abr'skij [SU, Rossijskaja SFSR Baškirskaja ASSR] 132-133 JK 7
Okt'abr'skij [SU, Rossijskaja SFSR chrebet Džagdy] 132-133 Y 7
Okt'abr'skij [SU, Rossijskaja SFSR Ivanovskaja Oblast'] 124-125 N 5
Okt'abr'skij [SU, Rossijskaja SFSR Kirovskaja Oblast'] 124-125 R 4
Okt'abr'skij [SU, Rossijskaja SFSR Kostromskaja Oblast'] 124-125 OP 4
Okt'abr'skij [SU, Rossijskaja SFSR Kurskaja Oblast'] 126-127 H 1
Okt'abr'skij [SU, Rossijskaja SFSR R'azan'skaja Oblast' ↓ R'azan'] 124-125 M 7
Okt'abr'skij [SU, Rossijskaja SFSR R'azan'skaja Oblast' ↙ R'azan'] 124-125 M 6
Okt'abr'skij [SU, Rossijskaja SFSR Volgogradskaja Oblast'] 126-127 L 3
Okt'abr'skoje [SU, Chanty-Mansijskij NO] 132-133 M 5
Okt'abr'skoje [SU, Krymskaja Oblast'] 126-127 FG 4
Okt'abr'skoje = Žovtnevoje 126-127 EF 3
Okt'abr'skoj Revol'ucii, ostrov — 132-133 Q-S 2
Oktember'an 126-127 LM 6
Ōktwin 141 E 6
Ōkubo, Yokohama- 155 III a 3
Ōkuchi 144-145 H 6
Okujiri-shima 144-145 a 2
Okulovka 124-125 J 4
Okusawa, Tōkyō- 155 III ab 2
Okushiri = Okujiri-shima 144-145 a 2
Okuta 168-169 F 3
Okwa [WAN, place] 168-169 H 4
Okwa [WAN, river] 168-169 G 3

Ola, AR 78-79 C 3
Ola, ID 66-67 E 3
Ola [SU, Belorusskaja SSR] 124-125 G 7
Ola [SU, Rossijskaja SFSR] 132-133 d 6
Olaa = Keaau, HI 78-79 e 3
Ô Lac 150-151 F 8
Olaeta 106-107 F 4
Olaf Prydz bukt 53 C 8
Ólafsfjördhur 116-117 d 1
Ólafsvík 116-117 ab 2
Olancha Peak 74-75 D 4
Öland 116-117 G 9
Olanga 116-117 NO 4
Olaria, Rio de Janeiro- 110 I b 2
Olary 158-159 GH 6
Olascoaga 106-107 G 5
Olathe, KS 70-71 C 6
Olavarría 111 DE 5
Olbia 122-123 C 5
Ol'chon, ostrov — 132-133 U 7
Ol'chovatka 126-127 J 1
Ol'chovka 126-127 M 2
Ol'chovskij = Art'omovsk 132-133 R 7
Ol'chovyj = Koksovyj 126-127 K 2
Olcott, NY 72-73 G 3
Old Castile = Castilla la Vieja 120-121 E 8-F 7
Oldcastle 119 C 5
Old Chitambo = Livingstone Memorial 172 F 4
Old Crow 56-57 J 4
Old Crow River 58-59 RS 2
Oldeani [EAT, mountain] 172 FG 2
Oldeani [EAT, place] 172 G 2
Oldenburg 118 CD 2
Oldenfelde, Hamburg- 130 I b 1
Old Faithful, WY 66-67 H 3
Old Ford Bay 63 GH 2
Old Forge, NY 72-73 J 3
Old Fort 60 D 2
Old Gandak = Burhi Gandak 138-139 K 4-5
Old Gumbiro 172 G 3-4
Oldham 119 EF 5
Oldham, SD 68-69 H 3
Old Harbor, AK 58-59 fg 1
Old Hogem 60 E 2
Old Ironsides U.S. Frigate Constitution 84 I b 2
Old John Lake 58-59 P 2
Old Man on His Back Plateau 68-69 B 1
Oldman River 61 B 6
Old Market Square Area 85 III b 1
Ol Doinyo Lengai 171 C 3
Old Orchard Beach, ME 72-73 LM 3
Old Perlican 63 K 3
Old Rampart, AK 58-59 QR 3
Olds 60 KL 4
Old Town, ME 72-73 M 2
Old Wives 61 E 5
Old Wives Lake 61 F 5-6
Old Woman Mountains 74-75 F 5
Old Woman River 58-59 GH 5
Oldzijt 142-143 J 2
Olean, NY 72-73 G 3
O'Leary 63 D 4
Olecko 118 L 1
Ölegey = Ölgij 142-143 FG 2
Olene, OR 66-67 C 4
Olenek = Olen'ok 132-133 X 3
Olenij, ostrov — 132-133 O 3
Olenino 124-125 J 5
Olen'ok [SU, place] 132-133 V 4
Olen'ok [SU, river] 132-133 X 3
Olen'okskij zaliv 132-133 WX 3
Olen'ovka 126-127 F 4
Olenty 126-127 Q 1
Oléron, Île d' 120-121 G 6
Oleśnica 118 H 3
Olevsk 126-127 C 1
Ol'ga 132-133 a 9
Olga, Lac — 62 N 2
Olga, Mount — 158-159 EF 5
Olga Bay 58-59 f 1
Olgastretet 116-117 m 5
Ölgij 142-143 FG 2
Olhão 120-121 D 10
Olhava = Volchov 124-125 HJ 4
Ôlho d'Água, Serra — 100-101 E 5-F 4
Olib 122-123 F 3
Oliden 104-105 G 6
Olifantsfontein 174-175 H 3-4
Olifantshoek 174-175 E 4
Olifants Kloof 174-175 D 2
Olifantsrivier [Namibia] 172 C 6-7
Olifantsrivier [ZA, Kaapland] 174-175 C 7
Olifantsrivier [ZA, Transvaal] 172 F 6
Olifantsrivierberge 174-175 C 7
Oliktot Point 58-59 N 1
Olimarao 148-149 MN 5
Olimar Grande, Río — 106-107 KL 4
Olímpia 102-103 H 4
Olimpo 102-103 C 4
Olinalá 86-87 L 9
Olinda 92-93 N 6
Olindina 100-101 E 6
O-Ling Hu = Ngoring Tsho 142-143 H 4-5
Olio 158-159 H 4
Olita = Alytus 124-125 E 6
Oliva 120-121 GH 9
Oliva [RA] 106-107 F 4
Oliva, Cordillera de — 111 BC 3
Olivar de los Padres, Villa Obregón 91 I b 2
Olivares, Cordillera de — 106-107 C 3
Olivares de Júcar 120-121 F 9
Olive, MT 68-69 D 3
Olive Hill, KY 72-73 E 5
Oliveira 102-103 K 4
Oliveira dos Brejinhos 100-101 C 7
Olivença 100-101 E 8
Olivenza 120-121 D 9
Oliver 66-67 D 1
Oliver Lake 61 G 2
Oliveros 106-107 G 4
Olivet, MI 68-69 H 4
Olivia, MN 70-71 C 3
Olivos 110 III b 1
Olkusz 118 J 3
Olla, LA 78-79 C 5
Ollachea 96-97 F 8
Ollagüe 111 C 2
Ollantaitambo 96-97 E 8
Ollas Arriba 64-65 b 3
Ollie, MT 68-69 D 2
Ollita, Cordillera de — 111 B 4
Olmos [PE] 92-93 CD 6
Olmos [RA] 106-107 F 4
Olney, IL 70-71 FG 6
Olney, MT 66-67 F 1
Olney, TX 76-77 E 6
Olney, Philadelphia-, PA 84 III c 1
Olofström 116-117 F 9
Oloho-d'Agua do Seco 100-101 C 7
Oloibiri 168-169 G 4
Oloj 132-133 f 4
Ol'okma 132-133 X 5-6
Ol'okminsk 132-133 WX 5
Ol'okminskij stanovik 132-133 W 7-X 6
Ol'okmo-Čarskoje ploskogorje 132-133 WX 6
Olomane, Rivière — 63 F 2
Olomouc 118 H 4
Olön = Lün 142-143 K 2
Olonec 124-125 J 3
Olongapo 148-149 GH 4
Oloron-Sainte-Marie 120-121 G 7
Olot 120-121 J 7
Olov'annaja 132-133 W 7
Olpād 138-139 D 7
Ol'šany 126-127 G 1
Öls nuur 142-143 G 4
Olsztyn 118 K 2
Olt 122-123 L 3
Olta 106-107 D 3
Olte, Sierra de — 108-109 E 4
Olten 118 C 5
Oltenița 122-123 M 3
Olteț 122-123 KL 3
Olton, TX 76-77 C 5
Oltu 136-137 JK 2
Oluan Pi 146-147 H 11
Olur 136-137 K 2
Olustee, OK 76-77 E 5
Olutanga Island 152-153 P 2
Olute 170 III a 2
Ol'utorskij, mys — 132-133 h 6
Ol'utorskij poluostrov 132-133 h 5
Ol'utorskij zaliv 132-133 g 5-6
Olvera 120-121 E 10
Ol'viopol' = Pervomajsk 126-127 E 2
Olympia, WA 64-65 B 2
Olympia [GR] 122-123 J 7
Olympiagelände 130 II b 1
Olympiastadion 130 III a 1
Olympia Stadium 84 II b 2
Olympic Mountains 66-67 AB 2
Olympic National Park 66-67 A 2
Olympic Park 161 II bc 1
Olympic Stadium 154 IV a 2
Olympisch Stadion 128 I a 1
Ólympos [CY] 136-137 E 5
Ólympos [GR, mountain] 122-123 K 5-6
Ólympos [GR, place] 122-123 M 8
Olympus, Mount — 66-67 B 2
Olyphant, PA 72-73 J 4
Olyutorski Bay = Ol'utorskij zaliv 132-133 g 5-6
Olyvenhoutsdrif 174-175 D 5

Om' 132-133 O 6
Ōma 144-145 N 2
Ōmachi 144-145 L 4
Omae-zaki 144-145 M 5
Ōmagari 144-145 N 3
Om Ager = Om Hajer 164-165 M 6
Omagh 119 C 4
O. Magnasco 106-107 H 3
Omaguas 96-97 E 3-4
Omaha, NE 64-65 G 3
Omaha, TX 76-77 G 6
Omak, WA 66-67 D 1
Omak Lake 66-67 D 1
Omalo 126-127 M 5
Ōmalūr 140 CD 5
Oman 134-135 H 6-7
Oman, Gulf of — 134-135 HJ 6
Omar, WV 80-81 E 2
Omaruru 172 C 6
Ōma-saki 144-145 N 2
Omatako, Omuramba — 172 C 5-6
Omate 92-93 E 8
Ombella-Mpoko 164-165 H 7-8
Ombepera 172 B 5
Omboué 172 A 2
Ombrone 122-123 D 4
Ombú [RA] 106-107 G 3
Ombu [TJ] 138-139 J 2
Ombu = Umbu 142-143 F 5
Ombucito 106-107 J 2
Ombuctá 111 D 5
Ombúes de Lavalle 106-107 J 4-5
Omčak 132-133 c 5
Omdraaisvlei 174-175 E 6
Omdurmān = Umm Durmān 164-165 L 5
O-mei Shan = Emei Shan 142-143 J 6
Omemee, ND 68-69 F 1
Omeo 160 HJ 6
Omer, MI 70-71 HJ 3
Ōmerin 136-137 JK 4
Ōmerli = Maserti 136-137 J 4
Ometepe, Isla de — 64-65 J 9
Omgon, mys — 132-133 e 6
Om Hajer 164-165 M 6
Omia 96-97 C 5
Ōminato 144-145 N 2
Omineca Mountains 56-57 LM 6
Omineca River 60 D 1-E 2
Omiš 122-123 G 4
Ōmi-shima 144-145 H 5
Omitara 174-175 C 2
Ōmiya 144-145 M 4-5
Omkoi 150-151 B 4
Ommaney, Cape — 58-59 v 8
Ommanney Bay 56-57 Q 3
Omni 85 II b 2
Ömnödelger 142-143 KL 2
Ömnögov' ◁ 142-143 K 3
Omo [ETH] 164-165 M 7
Omo Bottego = Omo 164-165 M 7
Omoloj 132-133 Z 3
Omolon [SU, place] 132-133 e 5
Omolon [SU, river] 132-133 e 4-f 5
Ōmon 144-145 J 5
Ô Môn = Phong Phu 150-151 E 7
Omono-gawa 144-145 N 3
Ōmori, Tōkyō- 155 III b 2
Omsk 132-133 N 7
Omsukčan 132-133 de 5
Ōmu 142-143 R 3
Omu Aran 168-169 G 3
Omul 122-123 L 3
Ōmura 144-145 G 6
Omuramba Omatako 172 C 5-6
Ōmura wan 144-145 G 6
Omuta 142-143 OP 5
Omutninsk 132-133 J 6

Ona, FL 80-81 bc 3
Onaga, KS 70-71 BC 6
Onagawa 144-145 N 3
Onahama = Iwaki 144-145 N 4
Onakawana 62 KL 1
Onalaska, WA 66-67 B 2
Onaman Lake 62 F 3
Onamia, MN 70-71 D 2
Onancock, VA 80-81 HJ 2
Onangué, Lac — 172 AB 2
Onaping Lake 62 L 3
Onaqui, UT 66-67 G 5
Onarga, IL 70-71 FG 5
Onawa, IA 70-71 BC 4
Onaway, MI 70-71 HJ 3
Onças, Ilha das — 98-99 K 6
Onças, Serra das — 98-99 H 9-10
Oncativo 106-107 F 3
Once, Buenos Aires- 110 III b 1
Onch'on-ni = Onyang 144-145 F 4
Oncócua 172 B 5
Ondangua 172 C 5
Ondas, Rio das — 100-101 B 7
Ondekaremba 174-175 B 2
Onderstedorings 174-175 D 6
Ondo 164-165 EF 7
Öndörchaan 142-143 L 2
Öndör Han = Öndörchaan 142-143 L 2
Ondor Khan = Öndörchaan 142-143 L 2
Ondozero 124-125 J 2
One and Half Degree Channel 176 a 2
Onega [SU, place] 132-133 F 5
Onega [SU, river] 132-133 F 5
Onega, Lake — = Onežkoje ozero 132-133 EF 5
Onega Bay = Onežkaja guba 132-133 F 4-5
Oneida, NY 72-73 J 3
Oneida, TN 78-79 G 2
Oneida Lake 72-73 HJ 3
O'Neill, NE 68-69 G 4
Onekaka 161 E 5
Onekama, MI 70-71 G 3
Onekotan, ostrov — 52 E 3
Oneonta, AL 78-79 F 4
Oneonta, NY 72-73 J 3
One Tree Peak 76-77 B 6
Onežskaja guba 132-133 F 5
Onežskij bereg 124-125 LM 1
Onežskij poluostrov 132-133 F 5
Onežskoje ozero 132-133 EF 5
Ong 138-139 J 7
Ông Đốc, Sông — 150-151 E 8
Ongeluksrivier 174-175 C 7
Ongersrivier 174-175 E 6
Ongersrivierdam 174-175 E 6
Ongerup 158-159 C 6
Ongijn gol 142-143 J 2
Ongjin 142-143 NO 4
Ongkharak 150-151 C 5
Ong Lee 154 III a 1
Ongole 134-135 MN 7
Ōngūlu = Ongole 134-135 MN 7
Oni 126-127 L 5
Onib, Khōr — = Khawr Unib 173 D 7
Onibabo 168-169 FG 3
Onida, SD 68-69 FG 3
Onilahy 172 HJ 6
Onion Lake 61 D 4
Onishere 168-169 G 4
Onistagane, Lac — 63 A 2
Onitsha 164-165 F 7
Onjŏng 144-145 EF 2
Onjŏng-ni 144-145 E 3
Ōnnē 141 E 7
Ōno [J, Fukui] 144-145 L 5
Ōno [J, Tōkyō] 155 III c 1
Onoda 144-145 H 5-6
Onomichi 144-145 J 5
Onon gol 142-143 L 2
Onoto 94-95 J 3
Onotoa 208 H 3
Onpo Wan = Anpu Gang 146-147 B 11
Onseepkans 174-175 C 5
Onslow 158-159 C 4
Onslow Bay 64-65 L 5
Onsong 144-145 GH 1
Ontake san 144-145 L 5
Ontario 56-57 S 7-V 8
Ontario, CA 74-75 E 5
Ontario, OR 66-67 E 3
Ontario, Lake — 64-65 L 3
Ontario Peninsula 56-57 UV 9
Ontonagon, MI 70-71 F 2
Ontong Java Islands 148-149 j 6
Onverwacht 92-93 H 3
Onwul 168-169 H 4
Onzole, Montañas de — 96-97 B 1

Oodnadatta 158-159 G 5
Oogies = Ogies 174-175 H 3-4
O'okiep = Okiep 174-175 BC 5
Ooldea 158-159 F 6
Oolitic, IN 70-71 G 6
Oologah Lake 76-77 G 4
Ooratippra 158-159 G 4
Oos-Londen 172 E 8
Oostacamund = Ootacamund 140 C 5
Oostende 120-121 J 3
Oosterschelde 120-121 JK 3
Oostpunt 94-95 G 1
Oostzaan 128 I a 1
Oostzaan, Amsterdam- 128 I ab 1
Ootacamund 140 C 5
Ootsa Lake [CDN, lake] 60 E 3
Ootsa Lake [CDN, place] 60 E 3

Opal, WY 66-67 H 5
Opala [SU] 132-133 e 7
Opala [ZRE] 172 D 2
Opal City, OR 66-67 C 3
Opanāke 140 E 7
Oparino 132-133 H 6
Opasatika Lake 62 K 2
Opasatika River 62 K 2
Opasquia 62 C 1
Opataka, Lac — 62 O 1
Opatawaga, Lac — 62 N 1
Opatija 122-123 EF 3
Opava 118 H 4
Opawica, Rivière — 62 O 2
Opazatika Lake 70-71 J 1
Opelika, AL 78-79 G 4
Opelousas, LA 78-79 CD 5
Opémisca, Lac — 62 O 1
Opémisca, Mont — 62 O 1-2
Opeongo Lake 72-73 GH 2
Opera House [AUS] 161 I b 2
Opera House [USA] 83 I b 2
Opfikon 128 IV b 1
Ophalfen 128 II a 1
Opheim, MT 68-69 C 1
Ophir, AK 56-57 E 5
Ophir, OR 66-67 A 4
Ophir, Gunung — = Gunung Ledang 150-151 D 11
Ophira 173 D 4
Ophirton, Johannesburg- 170 V b 2
Ophthalmia Range 158-159 CD 4
Opienge 172 E 1
Oploca 104-105 D 7
Opobo 168-169 G 4
Opočka 124-125 G 5
Opoco 104-105 C 6
Opogadó 94-95 C 4
Opole 118 HJ 3
Opole Lubelskie 118 KL 3
Oporto = Porto 120-121 C 8
Oposn'a 126-127 G 2
Opotiki 161 G 4
Opp, AL 78-79 F 5
Oppa gawa 144-145 N 3
Oppdal 116-117 C 6
Oppeid 116-117 F 3
Oppland 116-117 C 6-D 7
Optima, OK 76-77 D 4
Opuba 168-169 G 4
Opunake 158-159 O 7

'Oqlat Sedra = 'Uqlat Şudrā' 166-167 E 3
'Oqlet Zembeur = Sabkhat al-M'shīgīg 166-167 L 2
'Oqr = 'Uqr 164-165 K 6
Oquawka, IL 70-71 E 5

Or, Côte d' 120-121 K 5
'Or, Wâdi — = Wādī Ur 173 B 6-7
Oradea 122-123 JK 2
Öræfajökull 116-117 e 2
Orahovica 122-123 GH 3
Or'ahovo 122-123 KL 4
Orai 138-139 G 5
Oraibi, AZ 74-75 H 5
Oramar 136-137 KL 4
Oran, MO 78-79 E 2
Orán = San Ramón de la Nueva Orán 111 CD 2
Oran = Wahrān 164-165 D 1
Oran, Sebkra d' = Khalīj Wahrān 166-167 F 2
Orange, CA 74-75 E 6
Orange, NJ 82 III a 2
Orange, TX 64-65 H 5
Orange, VA 72-73 GH 5
Orange [AUS] 158-159 J 6
Orange [F] 120-121 K 6
Orange [LS] 174-175 H 5
Orange = Oranje-Vrystaat 172 E 7
Orange, Cabo — 92-93 J 4
Orange Beach, AL 78-79 F 5
Orangeburg, SC 64-65 K 5
Orange City, IA 70-71 BC 4
Orange Cliffs 74-75 H 3
Orangedale 63 F 5
Orangefontein = Oranjefontein 174-175 GH 2
Orange Free State = Oranje-Vrystaat 172 E 7
Orange Grove, TX 76-77 EF 9
Orange Park, FL 80-81 bc 1
Orange River = Oranjerivier [ZA, place] 174-175 EF 5
Orange River = Oranjerivier [ZA, river] 172 D 7
Orangeville 72-73 FG 3
Orange Walk Town 86-87 Q 8-9
Orango, Ilha de — 164-165 A 6
Orani [RP] 148-149 GH 4
Oranienbaum = Lomonosov 124-125 G 4
Oranje = Oranjerivier 172 BC 7
Oranjefontein 174-175 GH 2
Oranje Gebergte 92-93 HJ 4
Oranje Gebergte = Pegunungan Jayawijaya 148-149 LM 7
Oranjemond 174-175 AB 5
Oranjerivier [ZA, place] 174-175 EF 5
Oranjerivier [ZA, river] 172 D 7
Oranjestad 64-65 NM 9
Oranjeville 174-175 GH 4
Oranje-Vrystaat 172 E 7
Orany = Varėna 124-125 E 6
Oranžerei 126-127 N 4
Oratório, Ribeirão do — 110 II bc 2
Orawia 158-159 N 9
Orbāța, Djebel — = Jabal R'bāțah 166-167 L 2
Orbetello 122-123 D 4
Orbost 158-159 J 7
Örbyhus 116-117 G 7
Orca, AK 58-59 P 6
Orca Bay 58-59 OP 6
Orcadas 53 CD 32
Orcasitas, Madrid- 113 III a 2
Orchard, ID 66-67 EF 4
Orchard, NE 68-69 GH 4
Orchard Homes, MT 66-67 F 2
Orchard View, NJ 84 III d 1
Orchila, Isla — 92-93 F 2
Orchómenos 122-123 K 6
Orchon gol 142-143 J 2
Ord, NE 68-69 G 5
Ördene 142-143 L 3
Orderville, UT 74-75 G 4
Ordi, el — = Dunqulah 164-165 KL 5
Ord Mountain 74-75 E 5
Ordóñez 106-107 F 4
Ordos 142-143 K 4
Ord River 158-159 E 3
Ordu 134-135 D 2
Ordu = Yayladağı 136-137 FG 5
Ordubad 126-127 MN 7
Ordway, CO 68-69 E 6
Ordžonikidze 126-127 M 5
Orealla 92-93 H 3
Oreana, NV 66-67 D 5
Örebro [S, administrative unit] 116-117 F 8
Örebro [S, place] 116-117 F 8
Orechov 126-127 G 3
Orechovo [SU, Kostromskaja Oblast'] 124-125 NO 4
Orechovo-Zujevo 132-133 FG 6
Orechovsk 124-125 GH 6
Oregon 64-65 BC 3
Oregon, IL 70-71 F 4-5
Oregon, MO 70-71 C 5-6
Oregon, WI 70-71 F 4
Oregon Butte 66-67 E 2
Oregon City, OR 66-67 B 3
Oregon Inlet 80-81 J 3
Öregrund 116-117 H 7
Orekhovo-Zuyevo = Orechovo-Zujevo 132-133 FG 6
Orel' 126-127 G 2
Orel = Or'ol 124-125 L 7
Orellana [PE, Amazonas] 96-97 BC 4
Orellana [PE, Loreto] 96-97 D 5
Orem, UT 66-67 H 5
Ore Mountains = Erzgebirge 118 F 3
Ören [TR] 136-137 BC 4
Orenburg 132-133 JK 7
Orenburgskaja Oblast' 124-125 T 7
Örencik 136-137 C 3
Orense [E] 120-121 D 7
Orense [RA] 106-107 H 7
Øresund 116-117 E 10
Orfa = Urfa 134-135 D 3
Orfánu, Kólpos — 122-123 KL 5
Organ Pipe Cactus National Monument 64-65 D 5
Órgãos, Serra dos — 102-103 L 5
Orgejev 126-127 D 3
Orgeval 129 I a 2
Orgtrud 124-125 N 5
Orhaiye, İstanbul- 154 I b 2
Orhaneli = Beyce 136-137 C 3
Orhangazi 136-137 C 2
Oriči 124-125 R 4
Orick, CA 66-67 A 5
Orient, SD 68-69 G 3
Orient, TX 76-77 D 7
Orient, WA 66-67 D 1
Oriental 86-87 M 8
Oriental, NC 80-81 H 3
Oriente [BR, Acre] 98-99 CD 9
Oriente [BR, São Paulo] 102-103 G 5
Oriente [C] 64-65 LM 7
Oriente [RA] 106-107 G 7
Orihuela 120-121 G 9
Orillia 56-57 V 9
Orin, WY 68-69 D 4
Orinduik 98-99 HJ 2
Orinoca 104-105 C 6
Orinoco, Delta del — 92-93 G 3
Orinoco, Llanos del — 92-93 E 4-F 3
Orinoco, Río — 92-93 F 3
Orion 66-67 H 1
Orion, IL 70-71 E 5
Orissa 134-135 N 7-O 6
Orissa Coast Canal 138-139 L 7
Oristano 122-123 C 6
Orito [CO, landscape] 94-95 D 7
Orito [CO, place] 94-95 C 7
Orituco, Río — 94-95 H 3
Orivesi [SF, lake] 116-117 N 6
Orivesi [SF, place] 116-117 L 7
Oriximiná 92-93 H 5
Orizaba 64-65 G 8
Orizaba, Pico de — 86-87 M 8
Orizaba, Pico de — = Citlaltépetl 64-65 G 8
Orizona 102-103 H 2
Orkanger 116-117 C 6
Orkney [GB] 119 EF 2
Orkney [ZA] 174-175 G 4
Orla, TX 76-77 BC 7

Orland, CA 74-75 B 3
Orlândia 102-103 J 4
Orlando, FL 64-65 K 6
Orlando, Johannesburg- 170 V a 2
Orleães 102-103 H 8
Orléanais 120-121 HJ 4-5
Orléans 120-121 HJ 5
Orleans, NE 68-69 G 5
Orléans, Île d' 63 A 4
Orléansville = Al-Asnām 164-165 E 1
Orlik 132-133 S 7
Orlinga 132-133 U 6
Orlov = Chalturin 132-133 H 6
Orlov Gaj 126-127 O 1
Orlovskij 126-127 L 3
Ormānjhi 138-139 K 6
Ormārā 134-135 JK 5
Ormesson-sur-Marne 129 I d 2
Ormoc 148-149 HJ 4
Ormond, Melbourne- 161 II c 2
Ormond, Point — 161 II b 2
Ormond Beach, FL 80-81 c 2
Órmos Faleru 113 IV a 2
Ormsby 72-73 GH 2
Ormsö = Vormsi 124-125 D 4
Ormuz, Strait of — = Tangeh Hormoz 134-135 H 5
Orne 120-121 G 4
Örnsköldsvik 116-117 H 6
Oro, El — [EC] 96-97 AB 3
Oro, El — [MEX, Coahuila] 76-77 C 9
Oro, El — [MEX, México] 86-87 K 8
Oro, Museo del — 91 III c 3
Oro, Río de — 104-105 G 10
Orobayaya 104-105 E 3
Orobó 100-101 G 4
Orobo, Serra do — 100-101 D 7
Oročen 132-133 Y 6
Orocó 100-101 E 5
Orocué 92-93 E 4
Orodara 164-165 CD 6
Orofino, ID 66-67 EF 2
Orogrande, NM 76-77 AB 6
Oro Ingenio 104-105 CD 7
Or'ol [SU] 124-125 L 7
Oroluk 208 F 2
Oromocto 63 C 5
Oron 168-169 H 4
Orongo 96-97 D 9
Orongo gol 142-143 F 2
Orono, ME 72-73 M 2
Oronoque 92-93 H 4
Oronoque River 98-99 K 3-4
Orontes = Nahr al-'Āṣī 136-137 G 5
Orope 92-93 E 3
Oroquieta 148-149 H 5
Oro-ri 144-145 F 2
Oros 92-93 M 6
Orós, Açude de — 100-101 E 4
Orosei 122-123 C 5
Orosháza 118 K 5
Orosi, Volcán — 64-65 JK 9
Orotukan 132-133 d 5
Orovada, NV 66-67 DE 5
Oroville, CA 74-75 C 3
Oroville, WA 66-67 D 1
Oroya 96-97 G 8
Oroya, La — 92-93 D 7
Orpha, WY 68-69 D 4
Orpington, London- 129 II c 2
Orpúa 94-95 C 5
Orr, MN 70-71 D 1
Orroroo 160 D 4
Orrville, OH 72-73 F 4
Orsa [S] 116-117 F 7
Orša [SU] 124-125 H 6
Orsha = Orša 124-125 H 6
Orsk 132-133 K 7
Orșova 122-123 K 3
Ørsta 116-117 AB 6
Ortaca 136-137 C 4
Ortahanak 136-137 K 2
Ortaköy [TR, Çorum] 136-137 F 2
Ortaköy [TR, Niğde ↑ Aksaray] 136-137 EF 3
Ortaköy [TR, Niğde ← Bor] 136-137 F 4
Ortega 94-95 D 6
Ortegal, Cabo — 120-121 CD 7
Orteguaza, Río — 94-95 D 7
Orthez 120-121 G 7
Ortiga, Cordillera de la — 106-107 BC 2
Ortigueira 120-121 CD 7
Orting, WA 66-67 BC 2
Ortiz [ROU] 106-107 K 5
Ortiz [YV] 94-95 H 3
Ortiz de Rozas 106-107 G 5
Ortler = Ortles 122-123 D 2
Ortles 122-123 D 2
Ortón, Río — 104-105 C 2
Ortona 122-123 F 4
Ortonville, MN 68-69 H 3
Orumbo 174-175 BC 2
Orūmīyeh 134-135 E 3
Orūmīyeh, Daryācheh-ye — 134-135 E 3
Orumo 171 C 2
Oruro [BOL, administrative unit] 104-105 BC 6
Oruro [BOL, place] 92-93 F 8
Orust 116-117 D 8
Orvieto 122-123 DE 4
Orville Escarpment 53 B 29-30
Oš [SU] 134-135 L 2
Osa [SU] 124-125 U 5
Osa [ZRE] 171 AB 3
Osa, Peninsula de — 64-65 JK 10
Osaco 102-103 J 5
Osage, IA 70-71 D 4
Osage, NJ 84 III d 2
Osage, WY 68-69 D 4
Osage City, KS 70-71 BC 6
Osage Indian Reservation 76-77 F 4
Osage River 64-65 H 4
Ōsaka 142-143 Q 5
Ōsaka wan 144-145 K 5
Osakis, MN 70-71 C 3
Osām 122-123 L 4
Osan 144-145 F 4
Ošarovo 132-133 S 5
Osawatomie, KS 70-71 C 6
Osborne 61 K 6
Osborne, KS 68-69 G 6
Osborne, Cerro — = Mount Usborne 111 E 8
Osby 116-117 EF 9
Osceola, AR 78-79 DE 3
Osceola, IA 70-71 D 5
Osceola, MO 70-71 D 6
Osceola, NE 68-69 H 5
Osceola, WI 70-71 D 3
Oscoda, MI 72-73 E 2
Oscura, Sierra — 76-77 A 6
Oscura Peak 76-77 A 6
Osdorf [DDR] 130 III b 2
Osdorf, Hamburg- 130 I a 1
Osdorp, Amsterdam- 128 I a 1
Ösel = Saaremaa 124-125 CD 4
Ōse-zaki 144-145 G 6
Osgood, IN 70-71 H 6
Oshamambe 144-145 b 2
Oshawa 56-57 V 9
Ō-shima [J, Hokkaidō] 144-145 a 3
Ō-shima [J, Nagasaki] 144-145 G 6
Ō-shima [J, Sizuoka] 144-145 M 5
Ō-shima [J, Wakayama] 144-145 KL 6
Oshima hantō 142-143 Q 3
Oshin 168-169 G 3
Oshkosh, NE 68-69 E 5
Oshkosh, WI 64-65 HJ 3
Oshnavīyeh 136-137 L 4
Oshoek 174-175 J 4
Oshogbo 164-165 EF 7
Oshtorān Kūh 136-137 N 6
Oshtorīnān 136-137 N 5
Oshun 168-169 G 4
Oshwe 172 CD 2
Ošib 124-125 U 4
Osijek 122-123 H 3
Osima hantō = Oshima-hantō 142-143 QR 3
Osinniki 132-133 Q 7
Osintorf 124-125 H 6
Osipenko = Berd'ansk 126-127 H 3
Osipoviči 124-125 G 7
Oskaloosa, IA 64-65 H 3
Oskaloosa, KS 70-71 C 6
Oskar II land 116-117 j 5
Oskarshamn 116-117 G 9
Oskelaneo 62 O 2
Oslo 116-117 D 8
Oslo, MN 68-69 H 1
Oslofjord 116-117 D 8
Osmānābād 140 C 1
Osmancık 136-137 F 2
Osmaneli 136-137 C 2
Osmaniye 136-137 FG 4
Osmānnagar 140 D 1
Ošm'any 124-125 EF 6
Os'mino 124-125 G 4
Osmussaar 124-125 D 4
Osnabrück 118 D 2
Osnaburgh House 62 D 2
Oso 171 B 3
Oso, WA 66-67 C 1
Oso, El — 94-95 J 5
Osogovski Planini 122-123 K 4
Osona 174-175 B 2
Ōsone 155 III d 3
Osório [RA] 106-107 M 2
Osorio [YV] 91 II b 1
Osório, Salto — 111 F 3
Osório Fonseca 98-99 JK 6
Osorno [RCH] 111 B 6
Osorno, Volcán — 111 B 6
Os'otr 124-125 M 6
Osowiec 118 L 2
Osoyoos 66-67 D 1
Osøyra 116-117 A 7
Ospika River 60 F 1
Ospino 94-95 G 3
Ossa 122-123 K 6
Ossa, Mount — 158-159 J 8
Ossabaw Island 80-81 F 5
Osse 168-169 G 4
Osseo, WI 70-71 E 3
Ossidinge = Mamfé 164-165 F 7
Ossineke, MI 70-71 J 3
Ossining, NY 72-73 K 4
Ossipee, NH 72-73 L 3
Ossipevsk = Berdičev 126-127 D 2
Ossora 132-133 f 6
Ostān-e Markazī 134-135 E 3-F 4
Ostankino, Moskva- 113 V c 2
Ostaškov 124-125 J 5
Ostbahnhof Berlin 130 III b 1
Oste 118 D 2
Ostend = Oostende 120-121 J 3
Ostende [RA] 106-107 J 6
Österbotten = Pohjanmaa 116-117 K 6-M 5
Österdalälven 116-117 E 7
Østerdalen 116-117 D 7
Östergötland 116-117 F 8-9
Osterley Park 129 II a 2
Östersund 116-117 F 6
Østfold 116-117 D 8
Ostfriedhof Ahrensfelde 130 III c 1
Ostfriesische Inseln 118 C 2
Östhammar 116-117 GH 7
Ostia Antica, Roma- 122-123 DE 5
Ost'or [SU, Rossijskaja SFSR place] 124-125 J 6
Ost'or [SU, Rossijskaja SFSR river] 124-125 J 7
Ost'or [SU, Ukrainskaja SSR place] 126-127 E 1
Ost'or [SU, Ukrainskaja SSR river] 126-127 F 1
Ostpark München 130 II b 2
Ostras 100-101 E 10
Ostrava 118 J 4
Ostróda 118 JK 2
Ostrog [SU] 126-127 C 1
Ostrogožsk 126-127 J 1
Ostrołęka 118 KL 2
Ostrov [CS] 118 H 4-5
Ostrov [SU] 124-125 G 5
ostrova Anjou 52 B 4-5
ostrova Arktičeskogo Instituta 132-133 OP 2
ostrova Belaja Zeml'a 132-133 L-N 1
ostrova de Long 132-133 c-e 2
ostrova Diomida 56-57 C 4-5
ostrova Dunaj 132-133 XY 3
ostrova Izvestij CIK 132-133 OP 2
ostrova Komsomol'skoj Pravdy 132-133 U-W 2
ostrova Medvežij 132-133 f 3
ostrova Petra 132-133 VW 2
ostrov Arakamčečen 132-133 l 5
ostrov Arga-Muora-Sise 132-133 XY 3
ostrova Sergeja Kirova 132-133 QR 2
ostrov Askol'd 144-145 J 1
ostrova Atlasova 132-133 de 7
ostrova T'ulenji 126-127 OP 4
ostrov Barsakel'mes 132-133 KL 8
ostrov Begičeva = ostrov Bol'šoj Begičev 132-133 VW 3
ostrov Bel'kovskij 132-133 Za 2
ostrov Belyj 132-133 MN 3
ostrov Bennett 132-133 cd 2
ostrov Bering 132-133 fg 7
ostrov Bol'ševik 132-133 T-V 2
ostrov Bol'šoj Klimeckij 124-125 KL 3
ostrov Bol'šoj Šantar 132-133 ab 7
ostrov Bol'šoj T'uters 124-125 FG 4
ostrov Bol'šoj Ver'ozovyj 124-125 FG 3
ostrov Bulla 126-127 O 6
ostrov Čečen' 126-127 N 4
ostrov Chiuma = Hiiumaa 124-125 CD 4
ostrov Dolgij 132-133 K 4
ostrov Džambajskij 126-127 OP 3
ostrov Džarylgač 126-127 F 3-4
ostrov Erge-Muora-Sisse = ostrov Arga-Muora-Sise 132-133 XY 3
ostrov Faddejevskij 132-133 b-d 2
ostrov Gogland 124-125 F 3
ostrov Graham Bell 132-133 MN 1
ostrov Hall 132-133 KL 1
ostrov Henriette 132-133 ef 2
ostrov Herald 52 B 36
ostrov Iony 132-133 b 6
ostrov Iturup 132-133 c 8
ostrov Jackson 132-133 H-K 1
ostrov Jarok 132-133 a 3
ostrov Jeanette 132-133 ef 2
ostrov Karaginskij 132-133 fg 6
ostrov Karl Alexander 132-133 H-K 1
ostrov Kokaral 132-133 L 8
ostrov Kolguev 132-133 GH 4
ostrov Komsomolec 132-133 P-R 1
ostrov Kotel'nyj 132-133 Za 2-3
ostrov Kulaly 126-127 O 4
ostrov Kunašir 132-133 c 9
ostrov MacClintock 132-133 H-K 1
ostrov Malyj L'achovskij 132-133 bc 3
ostrov Malyj Tajmyr 132-133 UV 2
ostrov Mednyj 52 D 2
ostrov Meždušarskij 132-133 HJ 3
ostrov Moneron 132-133 b 8
ostrov Moržovec 132-133 GH 4
ostrov Moščnyj 124-125 FG 4
ostrov Nižnij Oseredok 126-127 O 4
ostrov Northbrook 132-133 GH 2
ostrov Novaja Sibir' 132-133 de 3
ostrov Ogurčinskij 134-135 G 3
ostrov Okt'abr'skoj Revol'ucii 132-133 Q-S 2
ostrov Ol'chon 132-133 U 7
ostrov Olenij 132-133 O 3
ostrov Onekotan 52 E 3
ostrov Paramušir 132-133 de 7
ostrov Pesčanyj 132-133 WX 3
ostrov Petra I 53 C 27
ostrov Pioner 132-133 QR 2
ostrov Put'atina 144-145 J 1
ostrov Ratmanova 58-59 BC 4
ostrov Rikorda 144-145 H 1
ostrov Rudolf 132-133 JK 1
ostrov Russkij [SU, Japan Sea] 132-133 Z 9
ostrov Russkij [SU, Kara Sea] 132-133 RS 2
ostrov Salisbury 132-133 HJ 1
ostrov Salm 132-133 KL 2
ostrov Sengejskij 132-133 HJ 4
ostrov Sibir'akova 132-133 OP 3
ostrov Simušir 142-143 T 2
Ostrovskoje 124-125 NO 5
ostrov Šmidta 132-133 QR 1
ostrov Šokal'skogo 132-133 NO 3
ostrov Stolbovoj 132-133 Za 3
ostrov Sverdrup 132-133 O 3
ostrov T'ulenij 126-127 N 4
ostrov Ujedinenija 132-133 OP 2
ostrov Urup 132-133 cd 8
ostrov Ušakova 132-133 OP 1
ostrov Vajgač 132-133 KL 3
ostrov Valaam 124-125 H 3
ostrov Vil'kickogo [SU, East Siberian Sea] 132-133 de 2
ostrov Vil'kickogo [SU, Kara Sea] 132-133 NO 3
ostrov Vize 132-133 O 2
ostrov Vozroždenija 132-133 KL 9
ostrov Wrangel 132-133 hj 3
ostrov Žiloj 126-127 P 6
ostrov Žochova 132-133 de 2
ostrov Z'udev 126-127 O 4
Ostrowiec Świętokrzyski 118 KL 3
Ostrów Mazowiecka 118 KL 2
Ostrów Wielkopolski 118 HJ 3
Ostryna 124-125 E 7
Oststeinbek 130 I b 1
Osttirol 118 F 5
Ostuni 122-123 G 5
O'Sullivan Lake 62 F 2
O'Sullivan Reservoir = Potholes Reservoir 66-67 D 2
Osum 122-123 J 5
Osumi Channel = Ōsumi-kaikyō 142-143 P 5
Ōsumi-kaikyō 142-143 P 5
Ōsumi-shotō 142-143 OP 5
Ōsumisyotō = Ōsumi-shotō 142-143 OP 5
Osuna 120-121 E 10
Osvaldo Cruz 102-103 G 4
Osveja 124-125 G 5-6
Oswa = Ausa 140 C 1
Oswego, KS 76-77 G 4
Oswego, NY 64-65 L 3
Oswego = Lake Oswego, OR 66-67 B 3
Oświęcim 118 J 3-4
Ōta 144-145 M 4
Ōta = Mino-Kamo 144-145 L 5
Ōta, Tōkyō- 155 III b 2
Otadaonanis River 62 H 1
Otago 161 C 7
Otago Peninsula 158-159 O 9
Ōtahara = Ōtawara 144-145 N 4
Ōtake 144-145 HJ 5
Otaki 158-159 OP 8
Ōtakine yama 144-145 N 4
Otar 132-133 O 9
Otare, Cerro — 92-93 E 4
Otaru 142-143 QR 3
Otaru-wan = Ishikari-wan 144-145 b 2
Otatal, Cerro — 86-87 E 3
Otavalo 92-93 D 4
Otavi 172 C 5
Otawi = Otavi 172 C 5
Otepää 124-125 F 4
Oteros, Río — 86-87 F 4
Otgon Tenger uul 142-143 H 2
O'The Cherokees, Lake — 76-77 G 4
Othello, WA 66-67 D 2
Othmarschen, Hamburg- 130 I a 1
Othōnoi 122-123 H 6
Óthrys 122-123 K 6
Oti 164-165 E 7
Otimbingwe = Otjimbingue 174-175 B 2
Otis, CO 68-69 E 5
Otis, OR 66-67 B 3
Otish Mountains 56-57 W 7
Otjekondo 172 C 5
Otjimbingue 174-175 B 2
Otjiseva = Otjisewa 174-175 B 2
Otjisewa 174-175 B 2
Otjiwarongo 172 C 6
Otobe 144-145 b 2-3
Otofuke 144-145 c 2
Otog Qi 146-147 AB 2
Otoineppu 144-145 c 1
Otok = Otog Qi 146-147 AB 2
Otoskwin River 62 D 2
Otpor = Zabajkal'sk 132-133 W 8
Otra 116-117 B 8
Otradnaja 126-127 K 4
Otradnyj 124-125 S 7
Otranto 122-123 H 5
Otranto, Canale d' 122-123 H 5-6
Otsego, MI 70-71 GH 4
Ōtsu [J, Hokkaidō] 144-145 c 2
Ōtsu [J, Shiga] 144-145 KL 5
Ōtsuchi 144-145 NO 3
Otta 116-117 C 7
Ottakring, Wien- 113 I b 2
Ot't'apālam = Ottapallam 140 C 5
Ottapallam 140 C 5
Ottavia, Roma- 113 II a 1
Ottawa 56-57 V 8
Ottawa, IL 70-71 F 5
Ottawa, KS 70-71 C 6
Ottawa, OH 70-71 HJ 5
Ottawa Islands 56-57 U 6
Ottawa River 56-57 V 8
Ottenby 116-117 G 9
Ottensen, Hamburg- 130 I a 1
Otter 63 E 3
Otter, Peaks of — 80-81 G 2
Otter Creek 68-69 C 3
Otter Creek, FL 80-81 b 2
Otter Lake 72-73 G 2
Otter Lake, MI 72-73 E 3
Otter Passage 60 BC 3
Otter River 62 E 1
Ottikon 128 IV b 1
Ottosdal 174-175 F 4
Ottoshoop 174-175 FG 3
Ottumwa, IA 64-65 H 3
Otukamamoan Lake 62 C 3
Otumpa 104-105 EF 10
Otuquis, Bañados — 104-105 G 6
Otuquis, Río — 104-105 G 6
Oturkpo 164-165 F 7
Otuzco 92-93 D 6
Otway, Bahía — 111 AB 8
Otway, Cape — 158-159 H 7
Otway, Seno — 111 B 8
Otwock 118 K 2
Ötztaler Alpen 118 E 5
Ou, Nam — 150-151 D 1
Ouachita Mountains 64-65 GH 5
Ouachita River 64-65 H 5
Ouadaï 164-165 HJ 6
Ouadda 164-165 J 7
Ouādī Jaghjagh = Wādī Jaghiagh 136-137 J 4
Ouagadougou 164-165 D 6
Ouahigouya 164-165 D 6
Ouahila = Wahīlah 166-167 D 6
Ouahran = Wahrān 164-165 D 2
Ouahrān Sebkra d' = Khafij Wahrān 166-167 F 2
Ouaka 164-165 J 7
Oualata = Walātah 164-165 C 5
Oualidia = Wālidīyah 166-167 B 3
Ouallam 168-169 F 2
Oua n'Ahaggar, Tassili — = Tāsīlī Wān al-Hajjār 164-165 E 5-F 4
Ouanary 98-99 MN 2
Ouanda Djallé 164-165 J 7
Ouango = Kouango 164-165 HJ 7
Ouangolodougou 164-165 C 7
Ouaouizarht = Wāwīzaght 166-167 C 3
Ouareau, Rivière — 72-73 JK 1
Ouargla = Warqlā 164-165 F 2
Ouarsenis, Djebel — = Jabal al-Wārshanīs 166-167 GH 2
Ouarsenis, Massif de l' = Jabal al-Wārshanīs 166-167 GH 2
Ouarzāzāt = Warzazāt 166-167 C 4
Ouasiemsca, Rivière — 62 P 2
Ouassadou 168-169 B 2
Ouassel, Ouėd — = Wādī Wāsal 166-167 GH 2
Ouassou 168-169 B 3
Ouataouais, Rivière — 62 NO 3
Oubangui 172 C 1
Ou Chiang = Ou Jiang 146-147 H 7
Ouchougan Rapids 63 C 2
Oudeika 168-169 E 1
Oude Kerk 128 I a 1
Oude Meer 128 I a 2
Oudenaken 128 II a 2
Ouder-Amstel 128 I ab 2
Oudergem = Auderghem 128 II b 2
Oudje, Région de l' = Minṭaqat al-Wajh 166-167 K 4
Oud-Loosdrecht 128 I b 2
Oud-Over 128 I b 2
Oûdref = Udrif 166-167 LM 2-3
Oudtshoorn 172 D 8
Oué, Mont — 168-169 HJ 4
Oued, El- = Al-Wād 164-165 F 2
Ouėd Akka = Wād 'Aqqah 166-167 B 5
Ouėd Asouf Mellene = Wādī Asūf Malān 166-167 H 7
Ouėd-Athmenia = Wādī Athmānīyah 166-167 JK 1
Ouėd Attar = Wādī 'Aṭṭār 166-167 J 3
Ouėd Beht = Wād Baḥt 166-167 D 3
Ouėd Chāref = Wād Shārīf 166-167 E 3
Ouėd Chélif = Shilif 166-167 G 1
Ouėd Chenachane = Wādī Shanāshīn 166-167 E 7
Ouėd Djafou = Wādī Jafū 166-167 H 4
Ouėd Djedi = Wādī Jaddī 166-167 JK 2
Ouėd Draa = Wād Dra'ah 166-167 C 5
Ouėd ed Daoura = Wādī ad-Dawrah 166-167 DE 5
Ouėd ed Drâ = Wad Dra'ah 164-165 BC 3
Oued èl Abiod = Wādī al-Abyaḍ 166-167 JK 2
Ouėd-el-Abtal = Wādī al-Abṭāl 166-167 G 2
Ouėd el Djaret = Wādī al-Jarā' 166-167 H 6
Ouėd el Fahl = Wādī al-Faḥl 166-167 HJ 4
Ouėd el Hâi = Wād al-Ḥāy 166-167 E 2
Oued el Hamiz 170 I b 2
Oued el Hamra = Wād al-Ḥamrā' 166-167 B 6
Oued el Harrach 170 I b 2
Ouėd el Korima = Wādī al-Karīmah 166-167 F 3
Ouėd el Leham = Wādī al-Ham 166-167 HJ 2
Ouėd el Mellâh = Wād al-Mallāḥ 166-167 C 3
Ouėd el Mitta = Wādī al-Mitlā 166-167 K 2
Ouėd el Rharbi = Wādī al-Gharbī 166-167 G 3-4
Oued el Terro 170 I a 2
Ouėd en Namous = Wādī an-Nāmus 164-165 D 2
Ouėd en Nsa = Wādī an-Nisā' 166-167 J 3
Ouėd er Retem = Wādī ar-Ratam 166-167 J 3
Ouėd ez Zergoun = Wādī az-Zarqūn 166-167 H 3
Oued-Fodda = Wādī al-Fiḍḍah 166-167 GH 1
Oued Gheris = Wād Gharīs 166-167 D 3-4
Ouėd Hatâb = Wād al-Ḥaṭāb 166-167 L 2
Oued-Imbert = Ayn-al-Bard 166-167 F 2
Oued Imirhou = Wādī Īmirhu 166-167 L 7
Ouėd Inâouèn = Wād Īnāwīn 166-167 D 2
Ouėd Isser = Wādī Yassar 166-167 H 1
Ouėd Itel = Wādī Īṭal 166-167 J 2-3
Oued Kerma 170 I a 2
Ouėd Lakhdar = Wād al-Akhdar 166-167 C 4
Ouėd Lâoû' = Wād Lāū' 166-167 D 2
Oued-Marsa = Wādī Marsā 166-167 J 1
Ouėd Martin = Mārtīl 166-167 D 2
Ouėd Mazar = Wādī Mazār 166-167 G 3
Ouėd Mellėg = Wād Mallāg 166-167 L 1-2
Oued Messaoud = Wādī Mas'ūd 166-167 F 5-6
Ouėd Miliân = Wād Milyān 166-167 LM 1
Ouėd Mina = Wādī Mīnā 166-167 G 2
Ouėd Mouloûya = Wād Mūlūyā 164-165 D 2
Ouėd Mya = Wādī Miyāh 166-167 J 4
Ouėd Mzab = Wādī Mīzāb 166-167 J 3
Ouėd Nahar Ouassel = Wādī Wāsal 166-167 GH 2
Ouėd Nfis = Wād Nafīs 166-167 B 4
Oued Noûn = Wād Nūn 166-167 A 5
Ouėd Ouassel = Wādī Wāsal 166-167 GH 2
Ouėd Ouèrrhâ = Wād Warghah 166-167 D 2
Ouėd Oum er Rbia = Wād Umm ar-Rabīyah 164-165 C 2
Ouėd 'Rherîs = Wād Gharīs 166-167 D 3-4
Ouėd-Rhiou = Wādī Rāhīyu 166-167 G 2
Ouėd Saoura = Wādī as-Sāwrah 164-165 D 2-3
Ouėd Seboû = Wad S'bū' 166-167 D 2
Ouėd Seggueur = Wādī as-Sūqar 166-167 GH 3
Ouėd Sidi Moussa = Wādī Sīdī Mūsā 166-167 J 6
Ouėd Tafassasset = Wādī Tafāsasat 164-165 F 4
Ouėd Tarat = Wādī Tarāt 164-165 F 3
Ouėd Tekouiât = Wādī Tākwayat 164-165 E 4
Ouėd Tensîft = Wad Tansīft 164-165 C 2
Ouėd Tessâout = Wād Tissāūt 166-167 C 4
Ouėd Tilia = Wādī Tīlayah 166-167 G 6
Ouėd Timedjerdane = Wādī Tamajirdayn 166-167 G 7
Oued Tim Mersoï 164-165 F 5
Oued-Tletat = Wādī Thalāthah 166-167 F 2
Ouėd Todrha = Wād Tudghā' 166-167 D 4
Ouėd Touil = Wādī aṭ-Ṭawīl 166-167 H 2
Ouėd Zarga = Wādī az-Zargah 166-167 L 1
Ouėd Zarqa = Wādī az-Zargah 166-167 L 1
Ouėd Zegrir = Wādī Zāghrīr 166-167 J 3
Oued Zem = Wād Zam 164-165 C 2
Ouėd Zemoul = Wād Zimūl 166-167 C 5
Ouėd Zeroûd = Wād Zurūd 166-167 LM 2
Ouėd Zousfana = Wādī Zusfānah 166-167 EF 4
Oueïta 164-165 J 5
Ouelle 168-169 DE 4
Ouėmé [DY, administrative unit] 168-169 F 4
Ouėmé [DY, river] 164-165 E 7
Ouenkoro 168-169 E 2
Ouenza = Winzah 166-167 KL 1-2
Ouenzé, Brazzaville- 170 IV a 1
Ouèrrhâ, Ouėd — = Wād Warghah 166-167 D 2
Ouessa 168-169 E 3
Ouessant, Île d' 120-121 E 4
Ouesso 172 C 1
Ouezzân = Wazzān 164-165 C 2
Oufrane = Ūfran 166-167 G 5
Ougarta = Ūgharṭah 166-167 E 5
Ouham-Pendé 164-165 H 7
Ouidah 164-165 E 7
Ouina 164-165 G 7
Ouinarden 168-169 E 1
Ou Jiang 146-147 H 7
Ouke 168-169 F 3
Oukoop 128 I b 2
Oûlad Boû 'Alî = Walad Bū 'Alī 166-167 M 2
Oûlâd Saïd = Awlād Sa'īd 166-167 BC 3
Oulainen 116-117 L 5
Ouled-Djellal = Walad Ghalal 166-167 J 2
Ouled-Mimoun = Awlād Mīmūn 166-167 F 2
Ouled Naïl, Monts des — = Jabal Awlād Nāïl 166-167 H 2
Ouled-Rahmoun = Awlād Raḥmūn 166-167 K 1
Ouled Smar 170 I b 2
Oûlmès = Ūlmās 166-167 CD 3
Oulu 116-117 LM 5
Oulujärvi 116-117 M 5
Oulujoki 116-117 M 5
Oumache = Ūm'āsh 166-167 J 2
Oum-Chalouba 164-165 J 5
Oum ed Drouss, Sebka — = Sabkhat Umm ad-Durūs 164-165 B 4
Oum el Achâr = Umm al-'Ashār 166-167 B 5
Oum-el-Bouaghi = Umm al-Bawāghī 166-167 K 2
Oum el Krialat, Sebkhet — = Sabkhat Umm al-Khiyālāt 166-167 M 3
Oum er Rbia, Ouėd — = Wād Umm ar-Rabīyah 164-165 C 2
Oum-Hadjer 164-165 H 6
Oumm el Drouss, Sebkha — = Sabkhat Umm ad-Durūs 164-165 B 4
Oum Semaa = Umm aṣ-Ṣam'ah 166-167 L 3
Ounarha = Unāghāh 166-167 B 4
Ounasjoki 116-117 L 4
Ounastunturi 116-117 KL 3
Ounasvaara 116-117 LM 4
Ou Neua = Mu'o'ng Ou Neua 150-151 C 1
Ounianga-Kebir 164-165 J 5
Ountivou 168-169 F 4
Ouolossébougou 168-169 D 2
Ouplaas 174-175 E 7
Oupu 142-143 O 1
Ouray, CO 68-69 C 6-7
Ouray, UT 66-67 J 5
Ourcq, Canal de l' 129 I d 2
Ourém 92-93 K 5
Ouri 164-165 H 4
Ouricana 100-101 E 8
Ouricana, Serra da — 100-101 DE 8
Ouricuri 100-101 D 4
Ouricuri, Serra — 100-101 FG 5
Ourinhos 92-93 K 9
Ourique 120-121 C 10
Ourlal = Urlāl 166-167 J 2
Ouro 100-101 A 5
Ouro, Rio do — 100-101 B 6
Ouro Fino 102-103 J 5
Ouro Preto [BR, Minas Gerais] 92-93 L 9
Ouro Preto [BR, Pará] 98-99 LM 7
Ouro Preto, Rio — 98-99 F 10
Oûroum es Şoughrâ = Urūm aṣ-Ṣuġrah 136-137 G 4
Ourou Rapids 168-169 G 3
Ourthe 120-121 K 3
Ōu sammyaku 144-145 N 2-4
Ouse 119 FG 5
Ouskir, Hassi — = Ḥāssī Uskir 166-167 F 4
Oûssel'tia, El — = Al-Ūssaltīyah 166-167 LM 2
Ousseukh, Al- = 'Ayn Dhahab 166-167 G 2
Oust 120-121 F 5
Oustaïa, El- = Al-Uṭāyah 166-167 J 2
Outaïa, El- = Al-Uṭāyah 166-167 J 2
Outaouais, Rivière — 72-73 G 1
Outardes, Rivière aux — 56-57 X 7-8
Oûṭaṭ Oûlad el Ḥâj = Awṭāt Awlād al-Ḥājj 166-167 E 3
Ou Tay = Mu'o'ng Ou Tay 150-151 C 1
Outenickwaberge = Outenikwaberge 174-175 E 7
Outenikwaberge 174-175 E 7
Outeniquas Mountains = Outenikwaberge 174-175 E 7
Outer Hebrides 119 B 3-C 2
Outer Island 70-71 E 2
Outer Mission, San Francisco-, CA 83 I b 2
Outjo 172 C 6
Outlook 61 E 5
Outremont 82 I b 1
Ouvéa, Île — 158-159 N 4
Ouyen 158-159 H 6-7
Ouzinkie, AK 58-59 L 8
Ovacık = Hacısaklı 136-137 E 4
Ovacık = Maraşalçakmak 136-137 H 3
Ovadnoje 126-127 B 1
Ovalau 148-149 a 2
Ovalle 111 B 4
Ovamboland 172 BC 5
Ovana, Cerro — 94-95 H 5
Ovando, MT 66-67 G 2
Ovar 120-121 C 8
Ovejas, Cerro de las — 106-107 E 4
Ovejas, Las — 106-107 B 6
Over 130 I b 2
Overbrook, Philadelphia-, PA 84 III b 2
Overdiemen 128 I b 1
Overflowing River 61 GH 4
Overflowing River = Dawson Creek 61 H 4
Överkalix 116-117 K 4
Overland Park, MO 70-71 C 6
Overo, Volcán — 106-107 BC 5
Overton, NV 74-75 F 4
Overton, TX 76-77 G 6
Övertorneå 116-117 K 4
Ovett, MS 78-79 E 5
Ovid, CO 68-69 E 5

Ovidiopol' 126-127 E 3
Oviedo 120-121 DE 7
Oviedo, FL 80-81 c 2
Oviši 124-125 C 5
Ovo 171 B 2
Övre Soppero 116-117 J 3
Ovruč 126-127 D 1
Ovs'anov 126-127 P 1

Owando 172 C 2
Ōwani 144-145 N 2
Owase 144-145 L 5
Owashi = Owase 144-145 L 5
Owatonna, MN 70-71 D 3
Owego, NY 72-73 H 3
Oweiqila, Ma'ṭan — = Ma'āṭin 'Uwayqilah 136-137 C 7
Owen, WI 70-71 E 3
Owen, Mount- 161 E 5
Owendo 172 A 1
Owen Falls Dam 172 F 1
Owen Island = Ōwin Kyūn 150-151 AB 7
Owensboro, KY 64-65 J 4
Owen's Island = Ōwin Kyūn 150-151 AB 7
Owens Lake 74-75 E 4
Owen Sound 56-57 U 9
Owens River 74-75 D 4
Owens River Valley 74-75 D 4
Owen Stanley Range 148-149 N 8-9
Owensville, MO 70-71 E 6
Owenton, KY 70-71 H 6
Owerri 164-165 F 7
Owingsville, KY 72-73 DE 5
Ōwin Kyūn 150-151 AB 7
Owl Creek 68-69 B 4
Owl Creek Mountains 68-69 B 4
Owo 164-165 F 7
Oworonsoki 170 III b 1
Owosso, MI 70-71 HJ 4
Owyhee, Lake — 66-67 E 4
Owyhee Range 66-67 E 4
Owyhee River 64-65 C 3

Oxapampa 92-93 DE 7
Oxbow 68-69 EF 1
Oxelösund 116-117 G 8
Oxford, KS 76-77 F 4
Oxford, MI 72-73 E 3
Oxford, MS 78-79 E 3
Oxford, NC 80-81 G 2
Oxford, NE 68-69 G 5
Oxford, OH 70-71 H 6
Oxford [CDN] 63 E 5
Oxford [GB] 119 F 6
Oxford [NZ] 158-159 O 8
Oxford House 61 L 3
Oxford Junction, IA 70-71 E 4-5
Oxford Lake 61 KL 3
Oxford Peak 66-67 GH 4
Oxhey 129 II a 1
Oxkutzcab 86-87 Q 7
Oxley 158-159 H 6
Oxnard, CA 64-65 BC 5
Oxon Hill 82 II b 2
Oxon Run 82 II b 2
Oxshott 129 II a 2
Oxus = Amudarja 134-135 J 2

Oya 152-153 J 4
Ōyada, Tōkyō- 155 III bc 1
Oyalı = Dalavakasır 136-137 J 4
Oyama [CDN] 60 H 4
Oyama [J] 144-145 MN 4
Oyapock 98-99 M 3
Oyapock, Baie d' 98-99 N 2
Oyem 172 B 1
Oyen 61 C 5
Øyeren 116-117 D 8
Oyo [WAN, administrative unit] 164-165 E 7
Oyo [WAN, place] 168-169 F 4
Oyón 96-97 C 7
Oyotún 96-97 B 5
Øyrlandet 116-117 jk 6
Oyster Bay 161 I a 2-3
Oysterville, WA 66-67 A 2
Oyuklu = Yavı 136-137 J 3

Özalp = Karakallı 136-137 KL 3
Ozamiz 148-149 H 5
Ozark, AL 78-79 G 5
Ozark, AR 78-79 C 3
Ozark, MO 78-79 C 2
Ozark Plateau 64-65 H 4
Ozarks, Lake of the — 64-65 H 4
Özd 118 K 4
Ozernoj, mys — 132-133 fg 6
Ozernoj, zaliv — 132-133 f 6
ozero Agata 132-133 R 4
ozero Alakol' 132-133 P 8
ozero Alibej 126-127 E 4
ozero Aralsor 126-127 NO 2
ozero Bajkal 132-133 U 7
ozero Balchaš 132-133 NO 8
ozero Baskunčak 126-127 N 2
ozero Botkul' 126-127 N 2
ozero Čany 132-133 O 7
ozero Chanka 132-133 Z 9
ozero Chanskoje 126-127 J 3
ozero Chantajskoje 132-133 QR 4
ozero Chozapini 126-127 L 6
ozero Dadynskoje 126-127 M 4
ozero Donuzlav 126-127 F 4
ozero El'ton 126-127 N 2
ozero Gimol'skoje 124-125 J 2
ozero Gor'ko-Sol'onoje 126-127 MN 2
ozero Il'men' 132-133 E 6
ozero Imandra 132-133 E 4
ozero Inder 126-127 PQ 2
ozero Issyk-Kul' 142-143 M 3
ozero Jalpug 126-127 D 4
ozero Janisjarvi 124-125 H 3
ozero Keta 132-133 QR 4
ozero Kubenskoje 124-125 M 4
ozero Kujto 132-133 E 5
ozero Lača 124-125 M 3
ozero Liman-Beren 126-127 M 3
ozero Manyč-Gudilo 126-127 L 3
ozero Moločnoje 126-127 G 3
ozero Nero 124-125 M 5
ozero P'asino 132-133 QR 4
ozero Šagany 126-127 DE 4
ozero Šalkar 126-127 P 1
ozero Sasyk [SU, Krymskaja Oblast'] 126-127 F 4
ozero Sasyk [SU, Odesskaja Oblast'] 126-127 DE 4
ozero Sasykkol' 132-133 P 8
ozero Seletyteniz 132-133 N 7
ozero Seliger 124-125 J 5
ozero Sevan 126-127 M 6
ozero Sivaš 126-127 FG 3-4
ozero Tajmyr 132-133 TU 3
ozero Tengiz 132-133 M 7
ozero Tulos 124-125 H 2
ozero Vivi 132-133 R 4
ozero Vože 124-125 M 3
ozero Zajsan 132-133 P 8
ozero Žaltyr 126-127 P 3
Ozette Lake 66-67 A 1
Ozhiski Lake 62 EF 1
Ozieri 122-123 C 5
Ozinki 124-125 R 8
Ožmegovo 124-125 T 4
Ozona, TX 76-77 D 7
Ozorków 118 J 3
Oz'ornyj [SU → Orsk] 132-133 L 7
Oz'ory [SU, Belorusskaja SSR] 124-125 E 7
Oz'ory [SU, Rossijskaja SFSR] 124-125 M 6
Ozurgety = Macharadze 126-127 KL 6
Oz'utiči 126-127 B 1

P

Pa = Chongqing 142-143 K 6
Pa, Mu'o'ng — 150-151 C 3
Paan = Batang 142-143 H 6
Paan = Hpa'an 148-149 C 3
Paardekop = Perdekop 174-175 H 4
Paarl 172 C 8
Paarlshoop, Johannesburg- 170 V a 2
Paatene = Padany 124-125 J 2
Paauilo, HI 78-79 e 2
Paauwpan = Poupan 174-175 EF 6
Pabean 152-153 L 9
Pabianice 118 JK 3
Pabna 138-139 M 5-6
Pabradė 124-125 E 6
Pabur, Despoblado de — 96-97 A 4
Paca, Cachoeira — 98-99 H 4
Pacaás Novas, Rio — 104-105 D 2
Pacaás Novos, Serra dos — 98-99 FG 10
Pacaembu 102-103 G 4
Pacaembu, Estádio do — 110 II b 2
Pacahuaras, Río 104-105 CD 2
Pacaipampa 96-97 B 4
Pacajá, Rio — 98-99 N 6
Pacajus 92-93 M 5
Pacaltsdorp 174-175 E 8
Pacaraima, Serra — 92-93 G 4
Pacasmayo 92-93 CD 6
Pacatu 100-101 E 6
Pacatuba 100-101 E 2-3
Pacaya, Río — 96-97 D 4
Pačelma 124-125 O 7
Pachača 132-133 gh 5
Pachacamac 96-97 C 8
Pachāgarh 138-139 M 4
Pachao Tao 146-147 G 10
Pacheco 106-107 M 3
Pacheco, Lagoa do — 106-107 L 4
Pāchenār 136-137 N 4
Pachham Dvīp = Pachham Island 138-139 BC 6
Pachham Island 138-139 BC 6
Pachhāpur 140 B 2
Pachhāpura = Pachhāpur 140 B 2
Pachhār = Ashoknagar 138-139 F 5
Pachia 96-97 F 10
Pachino 122-123 F 7
Pachitea, Río — 96-97 D 6
Pachmarhi 138-139 G 6
Pacho 94-95 D 5
Pa Cho, Khao — = Doi Lang Ka 150-151 B 3
Pāchora 138-139 E 7
Pāchōrēēn = Pāchora 138-139 E 7
Pachpadrā 138-139 CD 5
Pachu = Maral Bashi 142-143 D 3-4
Pachuca de Soto 64-65 G 7
Pa'ch'unjang 144-145 F 3
Paciba, Lago — 94-95 H 6
Pacific 60 CD 2
Pacific, CA 74-75 C 3
Pacific, MO 70-71 E 6
Pacific Grove, CA 74-75 BC 4
Pacífico, El — 94-95 C 4
Pacific Ocean 156-157 G-L 4-6
Pacific Palisades, Los Angeles-, CA 83 III a 1
Pacific Range 60 D 4-F 5
Pacific Rim National Park 60 E 5
Pacitan 148-149 F 8
Packwood, WA 66-67 BC 2
Pacofi 60 B 3
Pacoti 100-101 E 3
Pacoval 92-93 J 5
Pacoval, Ilha do — 98-99 K 6
Pactriu = Chachoengsao 148-149 D 4
Pacu, Cachoeira do — 92-93 J 9
Padampur [IND, Orissa] 138-139 J 7
Padampur [IND, Punjab] 138-139 D 3
Padang 148-149 CD 7
Padang, Pulau — 148-149 D 6
Padang Besar 150-151 C 9
Padang Endau = Endau 148-149 D 6
Padangsidempuan 148-149 CD 6
Padangtikar, Pulau — 148-149 E 7
Padany 124-125 J 2
Padauiri, Rio — 92-93 G 4
Padaung = Pandaung 141 D 6
Padcaya 92-93 FG 9
Paddington, London- 129 II b 1
Paddockwood 61 F 4
Paden City, WV 72-73 F 5
Paderborn 118 D 3
Padibe 171 C 2
Pad Īdan 138-139 B 4
Padilla 92-93 G 8
Padmā = Gangā 138-139 M 6
Padmanābhapuram 140 C 6
Padmapura = Padampur 138-139 J 7
Pādova 122-123 DE 3
Pādra 138-139 D 6
Paḍraonā = Padrauna 138-139 JK 4
Padrauna 138-139 JK 4
Padre, Serra do — 100-101 E 4
Padre Island 64-65 G 6
Padre Marcos 100-101 D 4
Padre Paraíso 100-101 D 3
Padre Vieira 100-101 D 2
Padstow 119 D 6
Padua = Pādova 122-123 DE 3
Paducah, KY 64-65 J 4
Paducah, TX 76-77 D 5
Pādūkka 140 E 7
Paek-san 144-145 F 3
Paektu-san = Baitou Shan 144-145 FG 2
Paengnyŏng-do 144-145 DE 4
Paeroa 158-159 P 7
Paestum 122-123 F 5
Páez 94-95 CD 6
Páfos 136-137 E 5
Pafúri 172 F 6
Pafuri = Levubu 174-175 J 2
Pafuri Game Reserve 174-175 J 2
Pag 122-123 F 3
Paga Conta 98-99 L 7
Pagadian 148-149 H 5
Pagai, Pulau-pulau — 148-149 CD 7
Pagai Selatan, Pulau — 148-149 CD 7
Pagai Utara, Pulau — 148-149 C 7
Pagalu 204-205 H 9
Pagan 206-207 S 8
Pagan = Pugan 141 D 5
Pagancillo 106-107 CD 2
Paganzo 106-107 D 3
Pagar, Tanjong — 154 III b 2
Pagasētikós Kólpos 122-123 K 6
Pagatan 152-153 L 7
Page, AZ 74-75 H 4
Page, ND 68-69 H 2
Page, OK 76-77 G 5
Page, WA 66-67 D 2
Pagėgiai 124-125 CD 6
Pageh = Pulau-pulau Pagai 148-149 CD 7
Pageland, SC 80-81 F 3
Pager 171 C 2
Pagerdewa 152-153 F 7
Paget, Mount — 111 J 8
Pagi 148-149 M 7
Pagi = Pulau-pulau Pagai 148-149 CD 7
Pāgla 141 B 3
Pagoh 150-151 D 11
Pago Pago = Fagatogo 148-149 c 1
Pago Redondo 106-107 H 2
Pagosa Springs, CO 68-69 C 7
Paguate, NM 76-77 A 5
Pagukkū 141 D 5
Pagwachuan 62 FG 3
Pagwa River 62 G 2
Pahājärvi 116-117 K 7
Pahala, HI 78-79 e 3
Pahandut = Palangka-Raya 148-149 F 7
Pahang 150-151 D 10-11
Pahang, Sungei — 150-151 D 11
Pahan Tuḍuwa 140 E 6
Pahaska, WY 66-67 J 3
Pahāsu 138-139 FG 3
Pahiatua 161 F 5
Pahoa, HI 78-79 e 3
Pahokee, FL 80-81 c 3
Pahranagat Range 74-75 F 4
Pah River 58-59 K 3
Pahrock Range 74-75 F 3-4
Pahrump, NV 74-75 K 3
Pahsien = Chongqing 142-143 K 6
Pahute Peak 74-75 F 4
Pai 150-151 B 3
Pai, Nam Mae — 150-151 B 3
Paiaguás 102-103 D 3
Paiçandu 102-103 F 5
Paiçandu, Cachoeira — 92-93 J 5
Paicaví 106-107 A 6
Pai-cha = Baicha 146-147 E 7
Pai-ch'êng = Bai 142-143 E 3
Paicheng = Taoan 142-143 N 2
P'ai-chou = Paizhou 146-147 D 6
Paide 124-125 E 4
Pai Ho = Bai He 146-147 D 5
Pai-hsiang = Baixiang 146-147 E 3
P'ai-hsien = Pei Xian 142-143 M 5
Pai Hu = Bai Hu 146-147 F 6
Paiján 96-97 B 5
Päijänne 116-117 L 7
Paikan Tao 146-147 H 8
Pai Khoi Mounts = Paj-Choj 132-133 L 4
Paila, Río — 104-105 E 5
Pailin 150-151 D 6
Pailita 104-105 C 2
Paillaco 108-109 C 3
Pailolo Channel 78-79 d 2
Pai-lu Hu = San Hu 146-147 D 6
Paimbœuf 120-121 F 5
Paim Filho 106-107 M 1
Paimiut, AK 58-59 G 5-6
Paimpol 120-121 F 4
Painan 148-149 CD 7
Paine, Cerro — 111 B 8
Painel 102-103 G 7
Painesdale, MI 70-71 F 2
Painesville, OH 72-73 F 4
Painganga = Penganga 134-135 M 7
Painted Desert 74-75 H 4-5
Painted Rock Reservoir 74-75 G 6
Paint Lake 61 K 3
Paint Rock, TX 76-77 E 7
Paintsville, KY 80-81 E 2
Paipa 94-95 E 5
Pai-p'êng = Baipeng 146-147 B 9
Paipote 104-105 A 10
Pai-p'u = Baipu 146-147 H 5
País do Vinho 120-121 CD 8
Pai-sha = Baisha [TJ, Guangdong] 146-147 D 10
Pai-sha = Baisha [TJ, Hainan Zizhizhou] 150-151 G 3
Pai-sha = Baisha [TJ, Hunan] 146-147 D 8
Pai-shih Kuan = Baishi Guan 146-147 CD 9
Pai-shui = Baishui [TJ, Hunan] 146-147 C 8
Pai-shui = Baishui [TJ, Shaanxi] 146-147 B 4
Paisley, OR 66-67 C 4
Paisley [CDN] 72-73 F 2
Paisley [GB] 119 D 4
Paita 92-93 C 5-6
Paita, Bahía de — 96-97 A 4
Paithan 138-139 E 8
Paitou 146-147 GH 7
Pai-t'ou Shan = Baitou Shan 144-145 FG 2
Pai-tu = Baidu 146-147 F 9
Pai-t'u-ch'ang-mên = Baituchangmen 144-145 CD 2
Paituna, Rio — 98-99 L 5-6
Paiute Indian Reservation [USA, California] 74-75 D 4
Paiute Indian Reservation [USA, Utah] 74-75 FG 3
Paiva Couceiro = Gambos 172 BC 4
Paizhou 146-147 D 6
Paj 124-125 K 3
Paja 171 C 1-2
Pajala 116-117 K 4
Paján 96-97 A 2
Pajares 120-121 E 7
Pajarito 94-95 E 5
Pajarito, El — 108-109 E 4
Pájaro, El — 94-95 E 2
Pájaros, Punta — 111 B 3
Paj-Choj 132-133 L 4
Pajeú 100-101 B 8
Pajeú, Rio — 100-101 E 5
Pajjer, gora — 132-133 L 4
Pajonal, Cerro — 104-105 B 7
Pajonales, Salar de — 104-105 B 9
Pájoros, Islas — 106-107 B 2
Pak, Nam — 150-151 D 2
Paka [MAL] 148-149 D 6
Pakanbaru 148-149 D 6
Pakar, Tanjung — 152-153 O 8
Pakaraima Mountains 98-99 HJ 2
Pakaribarāwān = Pakribarāwān 138-139 KL 5
Pakariyā = Pākuria 138-139 L 5
Pakashkan Lake 70-71 EF 1
Pākaur 138-139 L 5
Pak Ban 150-151 D 2
Pak Beng = Mu'o'ng Pak Beng 148-149 D 2-3
Pak Chan 150-151 B 7
Pakch'ŏn 144-145 E 3
Pak Chong 150-151 C 5
Pakenham, Cabo — 108-109 AB 7
Pakenham Oaks 85 I c 2
Pa Kha = Ban Pa Kha 150-151 F 5
Pak Hin Boun 150-151 E 4
Pakhoi = Beihai 142-143 K 7
Pak Hop = Ban Pak Hop 150-151 C 3
Pakin 208 F 2
Pakistan 134-135 K 5-L 4
Pak Lay 148-149 D 3
Paklow = Beiliu 146-147 C 10
Pak Nam 150-151 B 7
Pakokku = Pagukkū 141 D 5
Pākpaṭṭan 138-139 D 2
Pak Phanang 150-151 C 8
Pak Phayun 150-151 C 9
Pakrac 122-123 G 3
Pakribarāwān 138-139 KL 5
Paks 118 J 5
Paksane 148-149 D 3
Pak Sang = Ban Pak Sang 150-151 D 3
Pakse 148-149 E 3
Pak Seng 150-151 D 2
Pak Sha Wan 155 I b 1
Pak Sha Wan Hoi 155 I b 1
Pak Song 150-151 EF 5
Pak Tha = Mu'o'ng Pak Tha 150-151 C 2
Pak Tho 150-151 BC 6
Pak Thone = Ban Pak Thone 150-151 F 5
Pak Thong Chai 150-151 CD 5
Pakuí, Rio — 102-103 K 2
Pak Uk, Kowloon- 155 I b 1
P'akupur 132-133 NO 5
Pākuria 138-139 L 5
Pakwach 171 B 2
Pakwash Lake 62 BC 2
Pakwe 174-175 H 2
Pala [BUR] 150-151 B 6
Pala [Chad] 164-165 H 7
Pala Camp 174-175 G 2
Palace of the Legion of Honor 83 I b 2
Palácio das Exposições 110 I b 2
Palacio de Bellas Artes 91 I c 2
Palacio Nacional [E] 113 III a 2
Palacio Nacional [MEX] 91 I c 2
Palacio Presidencial 91 III bc 3
Palacios, TX 76-77 F 8
Palacios [RA] 106-107 G 3
Palacios [YV] 94-95 H 3
Palacios, Los — 88-89 DE 3
Palagruža 122-123 G 4
Pālagūṇḍa = Palkonda Range 140 D 3-4
Palaiochôra 122-123 KL 8
Palaiokastrítsa 122-123 H 6
Palaiòn Fálēron 113 IV a 2
Palais de Justice 128 II ab 1-2
Palais de la Nation 128 II b 1
Palais du Gouvernement 170 IV a 1
Palais du Roi 128 II b 1
Palaiseau 129 I b 3
Pālakkāṭ = Pālghāt 134-135 M 8
Pālakollu 140 EF 2
Palala 174-175 H 2
Pālam [IND] 138-139 F 8
Palam [RI] 152-153 P 6
Palame 100-101 F 7
Palāmū = Daltonganj 134-135 N 6
Palamut 136-137 B 3
Palana [AUS] 160 c 1
Palana [SU] 132-133 ef 6
Palandöken dağı 136-137 J 3
Palāndur 138-139 H 7
Palanga 124-125 C 6
Palangka-Raya 148-149 F 7
Paḷani = Palni 140 C 5
Paḷani = Palni Hills 140 C 5
Pālanpur 134-135 L 6
Palapye 172 E 6
Palār 140 D 4
Palāri 138-139 GH 6
Palāsbāri 141 B 2
Palāshbāṛī = Palāsbāri 141 B 2
Palāstha 138-139 L 6
Palatka 132-133 d 5
Palatka, FL 80-81 c 2
Palau [I] 122-123 C 5
Palau [USA] 206-207 R 9
Palau Islands 148-149 K 5
Palauk 148-149 C 4
Palau Ridge 142-143 Q 8-P 9
Palavi = Palāviya 140 D 7
Palāviya 140 D 7
Palaw 148-149 C 4
Palawan 148-149 G 4-5
Palawan Passage 148-149 G 4-5
Pālayankoṭṭai 140 CD 6
Palazzo dello Sport 113 II b 2
Palazzolo Acrèide 122-123 F 7
Palca [PE, Junín] 96-97 D 7
Palca [PE, Puno] 96-97 F 9
Palca [RCH ↘ Arica] 104-105 B 6
Palca [RCH ↓ Arica] 104-105 AB 6
Palca, La — 104-105 D 6
Palca, Río de la — 106-107 C 2
Palco, KS 68-69 G 6
Paldiski 124-125 DE 4
Pale [SU] 124-125 E 5
Pale = Pulè 141 D 5
Palech 124-125 NO 5
Palekbang 150-151 D 9
Palel 141 D 3
Paleleh 148-149 H 6
Palema 124-125 Q 3
Palembang 148-149 DE 7
Palena, Río — 108-109 C 4-5
Palencia 120-121 E 7
Palenque [MEX] 64-65 H 8
Palenque [PA] 88-89 G 10
Palenque [YV] 94-95 H 3
Palermo, CA 74-75 C 3
Palermo [I] 122-123 E 6
Palermo [ROU] 106-107 K 4
Palermo, Buenos Aires- 110 III b 1
Palēru = Palleru 140 D 2
Palestina [BR, Acre] 104-105 C 2
Palestina [BR, São Paulo] 102-103 H 4
Palestina [MEX] 76-77 D 8
Palestina [RCH] 104-105 B 8
Palestine, TX 64-65 GH 5
Paletwa 141 C 5
Pālghar 138-139 D 8
Pālghāt 134-135 M 8
Palgrave, Mount — 158-159 C 4
Palgru Tsho 138-139 KL 3
Palhoça 102-103 H 7
Pali [IND, Madhya Pradesh] 138-139 J 6
Pāli [IND, Rājasthān] 138-139 D 5
Palian 150-151 B 9
Palikao = Tighinnif 166-167 G 2
Palimbang 152-153 PQ 2
Palimito, El — 86-87 H 5
Palisade, CO 68-69 BC 6
Palisade, MN 70-71 D 2
Palisade, NE 68-69 F 5
Palisade, NV 66-67 EF 5
Pālitāna 138-139 C 7
Paliyā 138-139 H 3
Palizada 86-87 OP 8
Pali Zong = Phagri Dsong 138-139 M 4
Paljakka 116-117 MN 5
Palk Bay 140 D 6
Palkino 124-125 O 4
Pālkonda 140 F 1
Palkonda Range 140 D 3-4
Pālkot 138-139 K 6
Palk Strait 134-135 MN 8-9
Palladam 140 C 5
Pāl-Lahaḍā = Pāl Lahara 138-139 K 7
Pāl Lahara 138-139 K 7
Pallao 96-97 C 7
Pallapalla 92-93 E 7
Pallar 104-105 D 2
Palla Road 174-175 G 2
Pallasovka 126-127 N 1
Pallastunturi 116-117 KL 3
Palleru 140 D 2
Pallini = Kassándra 122-123 K 5-6
Palliser, Cape — 158-159 P 8
Palliser Bay 161 F 5
Palma, NM 76-77 B 5
Palma [BR] 102-103 L 4
Palma [E] 120-121 J 9
Palma [Mozambique] 172 GH 4
Palma, Arroio da — 106-107 L 3
Palma, Bahía de — 120-121 J 9
Palma, La — [CO] 94-95 D 5
Palma, La — [E] 164-165 A 3
Palma, La — [PA] 88-89 GH 10
Palma, Rio — 98-99 P 11
Palma, Sierra de la — 76-77 D 9-10
Palmácia 100-101 E 3
Palmaner = Palmanēru 140 D 4
Palmanēru 140 D 4
Palmar [BOL] 104-105 E 7
Palmar [CR] 88-89 E 10
Palmar [RA] 106-107 H 3-4
Palmar, El — [BOL] 104-105 D 7
Palmar, El — [CO] 94-95 G 6
Palmar, El — [YV, Bolívar] 94-95 L 3-4
Palmar, El — [YV, Caracas] 91 II b 1
Palmar, Laguna del — 106-107 G 2
Palmar, Punta del — 106-107 L 5
Palmar, Río — [CO] 91 III c 4
Palmar, Río — [YV] 94-95 E 2
Palmarcito 104-105 E 9
Palmar de Cariaco 91 II b 1
Palmares 92-93 M 6
Palmares do Sul 111 FG 4
Palmarito [BOL] 104-105 F 6
Palmarito [YV] 94-95 F 4
Palmas 102-103 FG 7
Palmas = Pulau Miangas 148-149 J 5
Palmas, Cape — 164-165 C 8
Palmas, Caracas-Las — 91 I b 1
Palmas, Ilha das — 110 I b 3
Palmas, Las — 102-103 E 6
Palmas, Río las — 74-75 E 6
Palmas Bellas 64-65 a 2
Palmas de Gran Canaria, Las — 164-165 AB 3
Palmas de Monte Alto 100-101 C 8
Palma Soriano 64-65 LM 7
Palm Beach, FL 64-65 KL 6
Palmdale, CA 74-75 DE 5
Palmdale, FL 80-81 c 3
Palmeira 111 FG 3
Palmeira das Missões 106-107 L 1
Palmeira dos Índios 92-93 M 6
Palmeirais 92-93 L 6
Palmeiras 100-101 D 7
Palmeiras, Rio — 98-99 P 10-11
Palmeiras, Serra das — 100-101 F 5
Palmeirinha 100-101 F 5
Palmeirinhas, Ponta das — 172 B 3
Palmengarten 128 III ab 1
Palmer 53 C 30
Palmer, AK 56-57 G 5
Palmer, NE 68-69 GH 5
Palmer, TN 78-79 G 3
Palmer, Cape — 53 B 27
Palmerah, Jakarta- 154 IV a 2
Palmeras, Las — 106-107 G 3
Palmer Park 84 II b 2
Palmer River [AUS, Northern Territory] 158-159 F 4-5
Palmer River [AUS, Queensland] 158-159 H 3
Palmerston [CDN] 72-73 F 3
Palmerston [Cook Islands] 208 K 4
Palmerston [NZ] 158-159 O 9
Palmerston = Darwin 158-159 F 2
Palmerstone, Cape — 158-159 JK 4
Palmerston North 158-159 OP 8
Palmerton, PA 72-73 J 4
Palmerville 158-159 H 3
Palmetto, FL 80-81 b 3
Palmi 122-123 F 6
Palmira [BR] 102-103 GH 6
Palmira [CO, Casanare] 94-95 F 5
Palmira [CO, Valle del Cauca] 92-93 D 4
Palmira [RA] 106-107 C 4
Pālmīrās Antarīp = Palmyras Point 134-135 O 6
Palm Islands 158-159 J 3
Palmital 102-103 GH 5
Palmitas 106-107 J 4
Palmitas, Las — 106-107 J 2
Palm Point 168-169 G 4
Palms, Los Angeles-, CA 83 III b 1
Palm Springs, CA 74-75 E 6
Palmyra, MO 70-71 E 6
Palmyra, NJ 84 III c 2
Palmyra, NY 72-73 H 3
Palmyra [SYR] 134-135 D 4
Palmyras Point 134-135 O 6
Palni 140 C 5
Palni Hills 140 C 5
Pal'niki 124-125 U 3
Palo Alto, CA 74-75 B 4
Palo Blanco 76-77 D 9
Palo Duro Canyon 76-77 D 5
Palo Duro Creek 76-77 C 5
Paloh [MAL] 150-151 D 11
Paloh [RI] 148-149 E 6
Paloma, La — [RCH] 106-107 B 3
Paloma, La — [ROU, Durazno] 106-107 K 4
Paloma, La — [ROU, Rocha] 111 F 4
Paloma, Punta — 104-105 A 6
Palomani 92-93 EF 7
Palomar, Morón-El — 110 III b 1
Palomar Mountain 64-65 C 5
Palomas 106-107 J 3
Palomas, Las — 86-87 FG 2
Palomeras, Madrid- 113 III b 2
Palometas 104-105 E 5
Palomitas 104-105 D 9
Palomós 120-121 J 8
Pāloncha 140 E 2
Palo Negro [RA] 106-107 F 2
Palo Negro [YV] 94-95 H 2
Palo Parada, Laguna de — 106-107 E 2
Palo Pinto, TX 76-77 E 6
Palopo 152-153 O 7
Palora 96-97 C 2
Palos, Cabo de — 120-121 G 10
Palos, Nevado de los — 108-109 C 5
Palo Santo 104-105 G 9
Palos de la Frontera 120-121 D 10
Palo Seco 64-65 b 3
Palotina 102-103 F 6
Palouse, WA 66-67 E 2
Palouse Falls 66-67 D 2
Palouse River 66-67 DE 2
Palpa 96-97 D 9
Palti Tsho = Yangdog Tsho 138-139 N 3
Pältsa 116-117 J 3
Palu [RI] 148-149 G 7
Palu [TR] 136-137 H 3
Palu, Pulau — 152-153 O 10
Palu, Teluk — 152-153 N 6
Paluke 168-169 C 4
Palval = Palwal 138-139 F 3
Palwal 138-139 F 3
Pam 158-159 M 4
Pama 164-165 E 6
Pamangkat 148-149 E 6
Pamanukan 148-149 E 8
Pamanzi-Bé, Île — 172 J 4
Pamar 94-95 F 8
Pāmarru 140 E 2
Pam'ati 13 Borcov 132-133 R 6
Pamba 171 B 5
Pāmban 140 D 6
Pāmban Channel 140 D 6
Pāmban Island 140 D 6
Pambiyar 140 C 6
Pamekasan 152-153 K 9
Pamela Heights, Houston-, TX 85 III b 2
Pāmidi 140 C 3
Pamiers 120-121 H 7
Pamir 134-135 L 3
Pāmiut 56-57 ab 5
Pamlico River 80-81 H 3
Pamlico Sound 64-65 L 4
Pamoni 94-95 J 6
Pampa, TX 64-65 F 4
Pampa [BR] 100-101 D 3
Pampa [ROU] 106-107 JK 4
Pampa, La — 106-107 DE 6
Pampa Alta 106-107 DE 6
Pampa Aullagas 104-105 C 6
Pampa de Agnia 108-109 E 4
Pampa de Agnía [RA, place] 108-109 E 4
Pampa de Chunchanga 96-97 CD 9
Pampa de Cunocuno 96-97 E 10
Pampa de Gangán 108-109 EF 4
Pampa de Gastre 108-109 E 4
Pampa de Huayuri 96-97 D 9
Pampa de Islay 96-97 F 10
Pampa de la Clemesi 96-97 F 10
Pampa de la Matanzilla 106-107 C 6
Pampa del Asador 108-109 D 6-7
Pampa de las Salinas 106-107 D 3-4
Pampa de las Tres Hermanas 108-109 F 6
Pampa de la Varita 106-107 D 5
Pampa del Castillo 111 C 7
Pampa del Cerro Moro 108-109 F 6-7
Pampa del Chalia 108-109 D 5
Pampa del Infierno 104-105 F 10
Pampa de los Guanacos 104-105 EF 10
Pampa del Sacramento 92-93 D 6
Pampa del Setenta 108-109 E 6
Pampa del Tamarugal 111 C 1-2
Pampa del Tigre 106-107 D 5
Pampa de Salamanca 108-109 F 5
Pampa des Castillo 108-109 EF 5
Pampa de Talagapa 108-109 EF 4
Pampa de Tambogrande 96-97 DE 9
Pampa Grande [BOL] 92-93 G 8
Pampa Grande [RA] 104-105 D 9
Pampa Hermosa 96-97 D 7
Pampa Húmeda 111 D 4-5
Pampamarca, Río — 96-97 E 9
Pampānadī = Pambiyar 140 C 6
Pampa Nogueira 108-109 E 2-3

Pampanua 152-153 O 8
Pampa Pelada 108-109 EF 5
Pampas [PE, Huancavelica] 92-93 DE 7
Pampas [PE, Lima] 96-97 D 8
Pampas [RA] 111 D 4-5
Pampas, Río — [PE, Apurímac] 96-97 E 8-9
Pampas, Río — [PE, Ayacucho] 96-97 D 8
Pampas de Corobamba 96-97 B 4-C 5
Pampas de Sihuas 96-97 EF 10
Pampa Seca 111 CD 4-5
Pampa Sierra Overa 104-105 AB 9
Pampayār = Pambiyar 140 C 6
Pampeiro 106-107 K 3
Pampero, El — 106-107 E 5
Pampilhosa 120-121 C 8
Pampitas 104-105 D 3
Pamplona [CO] 92-93 E 3
Pamplona [E] 120-121 G 7
Pampoenpoort 174-175 E 6
Pampus 128 I b 1
Pan, Lûy — 141 E 4
Pan, Tierra del — 120-121 DE 7-8
Pana, IL 70-71 F 6
Panaca, NV 74-75 F 4
Panache, Lake — 62 L 3
Panadero 102-103 E 5
Panadura = Pānaduraya 140 D 7
Pānaduraya 140 D 7
Panagʹurište 122-123 KL 4
Panaitan, Pulau — 148-149 DE 8
Panaji = Panjim 134-135 L 7
Panama, OK 76-77 G 5
Panamá [BR] 102-103 H 3
Pānama [CL] 140 EF 7
Panamá [PA, administrative unit] 64-65 a 3-b 2
Panamá [PA, place] 64-65 bc 3
Panama [PA, state] 64-65 KL 10
Panamá, Bahía de — 64-65 bc 3
Panamá, Canal de — 64-65 b 2
Panamá, Golfo de — 64-65 L 10
Panama, Gulf of — = Golfo de Panamá 64-65 L 10
Panamá, Istmo de — 64-65 L 9-10
Panama Canal 88-89 FG 10
Panama City, FL 64-65 JK 5-6
Panamá Viejo 64-65 c 2
Panambí [BR, Misiones] 106-107 K 1
Panambi [BR, Rio Grande do Sul] 106-107 L 2
Pan-Americana, Rodovia — 102-103 H 5-6
Panamint Range 74-75 E 4
Panamint Valley 74-75 E 4-5
Panane = Ponnāni 140 B 5
Panao 92-93 D 6
Panaon Island 148-149 HJ 5
Panare 150-151 C 9
Panarukan 152-153 L 9
Panarūti = Panruti 140 D 5
Pana Tinani 148-149 h 7
Panay 148-149 H 4
Panbult 174-175 J 4
Pancake Range 74-75 EF 3
Panças 100-101 D 10
Pančevo 122-123 J 3
Pānchari Bāzār 141 BC 4
Pānchet Pahār Bāndh 138-139 L 6
Pānchgani 140 AB 2
Panchh = Pench 138-139 G 7
Panch Mahāls 138-139 DE 6
Panchmahals = Panch Mahāls 138-139 DE 6
Panchmarhi = Pachmarhi 138-139 G 6
Panchor 150-151 D 11
Pānchur 154 II a 2
Pancoran, Jakarta- 154 IV ab 2
Panda 172 F 6
Pandale, TX 76-77 D 7
Pandan 152-153 K 4
Pandanau 141 D 7
Pandan Reservoir 154 III a 2
Pandaung 141 D 6
Pāndavapura 140 C 4
Pan de Azucar [CO] 92-93 D 4
Pan de Azúcar [ROU] 106-107 K 5
Pan de Azúcar, Quebrada — 104-105 A 10-B 9
Pandeiros, Rio — 102-103 K 1
Pandėlys 124-125 E 5
Pāndharkawada 138-139 G 7
Pandharpur 134-135 LM 7
Pāndhurna 138-139 G 7
Pandie Pandie 158-159 GH 5
Pando [BOL] 104-105 BC 2
Pando [ROU] 106-107 JK 5
Pandora 88-89 E 10
Pándormos = Bandırma 134-135 B 2
Pʹandž 134-135 K 3
Panelas 100-101 FG 5
Panepistēmion 113 IV a 2
Panevėžys 124-125 E 6
Panfilov 132-133 OP 9
Panfilovo [SU, Ivanovskaja Oblastʹ] 124-125 N 5
Pangaîon 122-123 KL 5
Pangala 172 BC 2
Pangalanes, Canal des — 172 J 5-6
Pangandaran 152-153 H 9
Pangani [EAT, place Morogoro] 171 D 4
Pangani [EAT, place Tanga] 171 C 5
Pangani [EAT, river] 172 G 2
Pangbei = Erlian 142-143 L 3
Pangburn, AR 78-79 D 3
Pangeo 148-149 J 6
Pangi 172 E 2
Pangkajene 148-149 G 7
Pangkalanberandan 152-153 C 3
Pangkalanbuun 152-153 JK 7
Pangkalpinang 148-149 E 7
Pangkor, Pulau — 150-151 C 10
Pangnirtung 56-57 XY 4
Pangrango, Gunung — 152-153 G 9
Pāngri 140 C 1
Pangtara = Pindara 141 E 5
Panguipulli, Lago — 108-109 CD 2
Panguitch, UT 74-75 G 4
Pangururan 152-153 C 4
Pangutaran Group 148-149 GH 5
Pangutaran Island 152-153 NO 2
Pang Yang = Panyan 141 F 4
Panhāla 140 AB 2
Panhandle 56-57 JK 6
Panhandle, TX 76-77 D 5
Panī = Pauni 138-139 G 7
Panié, Mount — 158-159 M 4
Pānihāti 154 II b 1
Pānihāti-Sodpur 154 II b 1
Pānihāti-Sukchar 154 II b 1
Pānikota Island 138-139 C 7
Pānīpat 138-139 F 3
Pānj = Pʹandž 134-135 K 3
Panjāb = Punjab [IND] 134-135 LM 4
Panjāb = Punjab [PAK] 134-135 L 4
Panjalih 152-153 P 7
Panjang [RI, island] 150-151 G 11
Panjang [RI, place] 148-149 E 8
Panjang, Hon — 148-149 D 5
Panjang, Pulau — 152-153 H 4
Panjāw 134-135 K 4
Panjgūr 134-135 J 5
Pānjharā = Pānjhra 138-139 E 7
Pānjhra 138-139 E 7
Panjim 134-135 L 7
Panjnad 138-139 C 3
Panjwīn 136-137 L 5
Pankeborn 130 III c 1
Pankof, Cape — 58-59 b 2
Pankop 174-175 H 3
Pankshin 164-165 FG 7
Panlı 136-137 E 3
Panlôn 141 F 4
Pʹanmunjŏm 144-145 F 3-4
Panna 134-135 N 6
Panna Hills 138-139 H 5
Pannaung, Lûy — 150-151 C 2
Paṇo Āqil 138-139 B 4
Panoche, CA 74-75 C 4
Panopah 152-153 J 6
Panorama 102-103 FG 4
Panruti 140 D 5
Panshan 144-145 D 2
Panshkuṛa = Pānskura 138-139 L 6
Pānskura 138-139 L 6
Pantanal de Nabileque 102-103 D 3-4
Pantanal de São Lourenço 102-103 D 3-E 2
Pantanal do Rio Negro 92-93 H 8
Pantanal do Taquari 102-103 DE 3
Pantanal Mato-Grossense 92-93 H 8
Pantanaw = Pandanau 141 D 7
Pantano, AZ 74-75 H 6-7
Pantar 152-153 LM 7
Pantar, Pulau — 148-149 H 8
Pʹanteg 124-125 UV 3
Pantelleria [I, island] 122-123 E 7
Pantelleria [I, place] 122-123 DE 7
Panthā 141 D 4
Pantin 129 I c 2
Pantjurbatu = Kuala 150-151 B 11
Pantoja 92-93 DE 5
Pantokrátōr 122-123 H 6
Pánuco 86-87 LM 6-7
Pánuco, Río — 64-65 G 7
Panʹutino 126-127 H 2
Panvel 138-139 D 8
Panwel = Panvel 138-139 D 8
Panyan 141 F 4
Panyu 146-147 D 10
Panyu = Guangzhou 142-143 LM 7
Panyusu, Tanjung — 152-153 FG 6
Panzan 141 F 4
Pāo = Pahang 150-151 D 10-11
Pao, El — [YV, Anzoátegui] 94-95 J 3
Pao, El — [YV, Bolívar] 92-93 G 3
Pao, El — [YV, Cojedes] 94-95 GH 3
Pao, Río — [YV, Bolívar] 94-95 J 3
Pao, Río — [YV, Cojedes] 94-95 G 3
Paoan = Bao'an [TJ, Guangdong] 146-147 DE 10
Pao-an = Bao'an [TJ, Shaanxi] 146-147 BC 4
Pao-an = Zhuolu 146-147 E 1
Paochi = Baoji 142-143 K 5
Pao-ching = Baojing 142-143 K 6
Pao-ch'ing = Shaoyang 142-143 L 6
Pão de Açúcar 110 I c 2
Pão de Açúcar [BR, place] 100-101 F 5
Pao-fêng = Baofeng 146-147 D 5
Paokang = Baokang 146-147 C 6
Paoki = Baoji 142-143 K 5
Pàola 122-123 FG 6
Paola, KS 70-71 C 6
Paoli, IN 70-71 G 6
Paonia, CO 68-69 C 6
Paoning = Langzhong 142-143 JK 5
Paonta 138-139 F 2
Paoshan = Baoshan [TJ, Jiangsu] 146-147 H 6
Paoshan = Baoshan [TJ, Yunnan] 142-143 HJ 6
Paoteh = Baode 142-143 L 4
Paoti = Baodi 146-147 F 2
Pao-ting = Baoding 142-143 LM 4
Paotow = Baotou 142-143 KL 3
Paotsing = Baojing 142-143 K 6
Paotsing = Baoqing 142-143 P 2
Paoying = Baoying 142-143 M 5
Pápa 118 H 5
Papagaio, Rio — 98-99 J 11
Papagayo, Golfo del — 64-65 J 9
Papagayos, Río de los — 106-107 C 5
Pāpaghnī = Pāpāgni 140 D 3-4
Pāpāgni 140 D 3-4
Papago Indian Reservation 74-75 GH 6
Papaikou, HI 78-79 e 3
Papakura 161 F 3
Papalé 104-105 D 9
Pāpanāsam 140 C 6
Papanduva 102-103 G 7
Papantla de Olarte 64-65 G 7
Papatoetoe 158-159 OP 7
Papelón 94-95 G 3
Papelotte 128 II b 2
Papera 94-95 J 8
Paphos = Páfos 136-137 E 5
Pa-pien Chiang = Babian Jiang 142-143 J 7
Papíkion 122-123 L 5
Papilė 124-125 D 5
Papinau Labelle, Parc provincial de — 62 O 3-4
Paposo 104-105 A 9
Papua, Gulf of — 148-149 MN 8
Papua New Guinea 148-149 MN 7-8
Papudo 106-107 B 4
Papulovo 124-125 R 3
Papun = Hpāpûn 141 E 6-7
Papuri, Río — 94-95 F 7
Paquica, Cabo — 104-105 A 7
Paquicama 98-99 N 6
Pará [BR] 92-93 J 5
Para [SME] 98-99 L 2
Para [SU] 124-125 N 6-7
Pará = Belém 92-93 K 5
Para, La — 106-107 F 3
Pará, Rio — 102-103 K 3
Pará, Rio do — 92-93 JK 5
Parabel' 132-133 P 6
Paraburdoo 158-159 C 4
Paracale 148-149 H 4
Paracas 96-97 CD 8
Paracas, Península — 92-93 D 7
Paracatu 92-93 K 8
Paracatu, Rio — [BR ↖ Rio São Francisco] 102-103 K 3
Paracatu, Rio — [BR ↙ Rio São Francisco] 102-103 K 2
Paracels, Îles — = Quân Đao Tây Sa 148-149 F 3
Parachilna 160 D 3
Parachute Jump Tower 155 II b 2
Paraćin 122-123 J 4
Paracuru 92-93 M 5
Parada, Punta — 92-93 D 8
Parada El Chacay = El Chacay 106-107 BC 5
Parade, SD 68-69 F 3
Pará de Minas 100-101 B 10
Pārādip 138-139 L 7
Paradise, CA 74-75 C 3
Paradise, MT 66-67 F 2
Paradise, NV 74-75 F 4
Paradise Hill 61 D 4
Paradise Hill, Johannesburg- 170 V b 2
Paradise Valley 61 C 4
Paradise Valley, NV 66-67 E 5
Parado 152-153 N 10
Parafijevka 126-127 F 1
Paragominas 98-99 P 6
Paragould, AR 64-65 H 4
Paragua, La — 92-93 G 3
Paraguá, Río — [BOL] 92-93 G 7
Paragua, Río — [YV] 92-93 G 3
Paraguaçu 102-103 K 4
Paraguacu, Rio — 100-101 DE 7
Paraguaçu Paulista 102-103 G 5
Paraguai, Rio — 92-93 H 9
Paraguaipoa 92-93 E 2
Paraguaná, Península de — 92-93 F 2
Paraguarí [PY, administrative unit] 102-103 D 6-7
Paraguarí [PY, place] 111 E 3
Paraguay 111 DE 2
Paraguay, Río — 111 E 2
Paraíba 92-93 M 6
Paraíba, Rio — 92-93 M 6
Paraíba do Sul 102-103 L 5
Paraíba do Sul, Rio — 102-103 L 4
Paraibano 100-101 B 4
Paraibuna 102-103 K 5
Paraim 100-101 B 6
Paraim, Rio — 100-101 A 8
Parainen = Pargas 116-117 K 7
Paraíso [BR, Mato Grosso do Sul] 102-103 F 3
Paraiso [BR, Rondônia] 104-105 E 2
Paraíso [MEX] 86-87 O 8
Paraíso [PA] 64-65 b 2
Paraíso [YV] 94-95 G 3
Paraíso, El — 106-107 GH 4
Paraisópolis 102-103 K 5
Parakou 164-165 E 7
Parālkote 138-139 H 8
Paramagudi 140 D 6
Paramānkuḍi = Paramagudi 140 D 6
Paramaribo 92-93 HJ 3
Parambu 100-101 D 4
Paramillo, Nudo de — 94-95 CD 4
Paramirim 92-93 L 7
Paramirim, Rio — 100-101 C 7
Páramo Cruz Verde 91 III c 4
Páramo Frontino 94-95 C 4
Paramonga 92-93 D 7
Paramoti 100-101 E 3
Paramount, CA 83 III d 2
Paramušir, ostrov — 132-133 de 7
Paraná [BR, administrative unit] 111 FG 2
Paranã [BR, place] 92-93 K 7
Paraná [RA] 111 DE 4
Paraná, Rio — [BR ◁ Rio de la Plata] 92-93 J 9
Paraná, Rio — [BR ◁ Rio Turiaçu] 100-101 B 2
Paranã, Rio — [BR ◁ Tocantins] 92-93 K 7
Paraná, Río — [RA] 111 E 3-4
Paranacito 106-107 H 4
Paranácity 102-103 F 5
Paraná Copea 98-99 G 6
Paraná de las Palmas, Río — 106-107 H 4-5
Paraná do Ouro, Rio — 96-97 F 6
Paranaguá 111 G 3
Paranaguá, Baía de — 102-103 HJ 6
Paraná Guazú, Río — 106-107 H 4-5
Paranaíba 92-93 J 8
Paranaíba, Rio — 92-93 JK 8
Paraná Ibicuy, Río — 106-107 H 4
Paranaita, Rio — 98-99 K 9-10
Paranam 98-99 L 2
Paraná Mirim Pirajauana 98-99 E 5
Paranapanema 102-103 H 5
Paranapanema, Rio — 92-93 J 9
Paranapiacaba, Serra do — 92-93 G 2-3
Paranapura, Río — 96-97 C 4
Paranaquara, Serra — 98-99 M 5
Paranari 98-99 EF 5
Paranatama 100-101 F 5
Paraná Uraríá 98-99 JK 6
Paranavaí 111 F 2
Parandak, Īstgāh-e — 136-137 O 5
Paranggi Aru 140 E 6
Paraṅgippeṭṭai = Porto Novo 140 DE 5
Paranjang 144-145 F 4
Parāntij 138-139 D 6
Paraopeba 102-103 K 3
Paraopeba, Rio — 102-103 K 3
Parapeti, Río — 104-105 E 6
Parapol'skij dol 132-133 fg 5
Parapuã 102-103 G 4
Paraque, Cerro — 94-95 H 5
Pará Rise 50-51 GH 5
Parás [MEX] 76-77 E 9
Parás [PE] 96-97 D 8
Parasagaḍa = Manoli 140 B 3
Parasgaon 138-139 H 8
Parāsi 138-139 J 4
Parasnāth 138-139 L 6
Parasnath Jain Temple 154 II b 2
Parata, Pointe della — 122-123 BC 5
Parateca 100-101 C 7
Parati 102-103 K 5
Paratigi 100-101 E 7
Paratinga 92-93 L 7
Parauapebas, Rio — 98-99 NO 8
Paraúna 92-93 JK 8
Paravūr 140 C 6
Parayanālankulam 140 DE 6
Paraytepuy 94-95 L 5
Paray-Vieille-Poste 129 I c 3
Pārbati 134-135 M 5
Pārbatīpur 134-135 O 5
Parbatsar 138-139 E 4
Parbhani 138-139 F 8
Parbig 132-133 P 6
Parc de Laeken 128 II b 1
Parc de Maisonneuve 82 I b 1
Parc du Mont Royal 82 I b 1
Parchim 118 EF 2
Parc Jarry 82 I b 1
Parc Lafontaine 82 I b 1
Parc national Albert = Parc national Virunga 172 E 1-2
Parc National de Kundelungu 171 AB 5
Parc national de la Bamingui 164-165 HJ 7
Parc National de la Boucle du Baoulé 168-169 C 2
Parc national de la Garamba 172 EF 1
Parc national de la Kagera 172 F 2
Parc National de la Marahué 168-169 D 4
Parc national de la Salonga Nord 172 D 2
Parc national de la Salonga Sud 172 D 2
Parc national de Maiko 172 E 2
Parc National de Taï 168-169 D 4
Parc National du Niokolo-Koba 164-165 B 6
Parc national Mauricie 62 P 3
Parc national Virunga 172 E 1-2
Parc procincial de la Montagne Tremblante 56-57 VW 8
Parc provincial de Causapscal 63 C 3
Parc provincial de Dunière 63 C 3
Parc provincial de Forestville 63 B 3
Parc provincial de James Bay 62 M 1
Parc provincial de Joliette 62 OP 3
Parc provincial de la Gaspésie 63 CD 3
Parc provincial de la Vérendrye 56-57 V 8
Parc provincial de Mastiogouche 62 P 3
Parc provincial de Matane 63 C 3
Parc provincial de Papinau Labelle 62 O 3-4
Parc provincial de Port-Cartier-Sept-Îles 63 C 2
Parc provincial des Laurentides 56-57 W 8
Parc provincial des Rimouski 63 BC 3-4
Parcs National du W 164-165 E 6
Parczew 118 L 3
Pārḍī 138-139 D 7
Pardo 106-107 H 6
Pardo, Rio — [BR ◁ Atlantic Ocean] 92-93 L 8
Pardo, Rio — [BR ◁ Rio Grande] 102-103 H 4
Pardo, Rio — [BR ◁ Rio Paraná] 92-93 J 9
Pardo, Rio — [BR ◁ Rio São Francisco] 102-103 K 1
Pardubice 118 GH 3
Pare 152-153 K 9
Parecis, Campos dos — 92-93 H 7
Parecis, Chapada dos — 92-93 GH 7
Pareditas 106-107 C 4-5
Paredón 86-87 K 4-5
Paredones 106-107 AB 5
Parejas, Las — 106-107 G 4
Parelhas 92-93 M 6
Pare Mountains 171 D 3-4
Parenda 140 B 1
Parent 62 O 3
Parent, Lac — 62 N 2
Parentis-en-Born 120-121 G 6
Parepare 148-149 G 7
Parera 106-107 E 5
Parfenjevo 124-125 O 4
Parfino 124-125 HJ 4-5
Parga 122-123 J 6
Pargas 116-117 K 7
Pargi 140 C 2
Pargolovo 124-125 H 3
Parguaza 94-95 H 4
Pari, São Paulo- 110 II b 2
Paria 104-105 C 5
Paria, Golfo de — 92-93 G 2
Paria, Península de — 92-93 G 2
Pariaguán 94-95 J 3
Pariaman 148-149 CD 7
Paria River 74-75 H 4
Pariaxá, Cachoeira — 98-99 N 6
Pariči 124-125 G 7
Paricutín, Volcán — 64-65 F 8
Parika 92-93 H 3
Parima, Reserva Florestal — 94-95 K 6
Parima, Rio — 98-99 FG 3
Parima, Sierra — 92-93 G 4
Parimé, Rio — 98-99 H 3
Parinacochas, Laguna — 96-97 DE 9
Pariñas, Punta — 92-93 C 5
Pariṇḍā = Parenda 140 B 1
Parintins 92-93 K 5
Paripārit Kyûn 148-149 B 4
Paris 120-121 J 4
Paris, AR 78-79 C 3
Paris, ID 66-67 H 4
Paris, IL 70-71 G 6
Paris, KY 70-71 H 6
Paris, MO 70-71 DE 6
Paris, TN 78-79 E 2
Paris, TX 64-65 GH 5
Paris-Auteuil 129 I c 2
Paris-Belleville 129 I c 2
Paris-Bercy 129 I c 2
Paris-Charonne 129 I c 2
Paris-Grenelle 129 I c 2
Parish [RA] 106-107 H 6
Parish [ROU] 106-107 J 4
Paris-la Villette 129 I c 2
Paris-les Batignolles 129 I c 2
Paris-Menilmontant 129 I c 2
Paris-Montmartre 129 I c 2
Paris-Montparnasse 129 I c 2
Paris-Passy 129 I c 2
Paris-Quartier-Latin 129 I c 2
Paris-Reuilly 129 I c 2
Paris-Vaugirard 129 I c 2
Parita, Golfo de — 88-89 FG 10
Parit Buntar 150-151 C 10
Parkāl 140 D 1
Parkano 116-117 K 6
Parkchester, New York, NY 82 III cd 2
Park City, KY 70-71 GH 7
Park City, UT 66-67 H 5
Parkdale, OR 66-67 C 3
Parkdene 170 V c 2
Parker, AZ 74-75 FG 5
Parker, KS 70-71 C 6
Parker, SD 68-69 H 4
Parker, Mount — 155 I b 2
Parker Dam, CA 74-75 F 5
Parkersburg, IA 70-71 D 4
Parkersburg, WV 64-65 K 4
Parkers Creek 84 III d 2
Parkerview 61 G 5
Parkes 158-159 J 6
Park Falls, WI 70-71 E 3
Park Hill [AUS] 161 I b 1
Park Hill [CDN] 72-73 F 3
Parkhurst 60 F 4
Parkin, AR 78-79 D 3
Parkland 60 KL 4
Parklawn, VA 82 II a 2
Parkman 61 H 6
Parkman, WY 68-69 C 3
Park Place, Houston-, TX 85 III b 2
Park Range 64-65 E 3-4
Park Rapids, MN 70-71 C 2
Park Ridge, IL 70-71 FG 4
Park River 68-69 H 1
Park River, ND 68-69 H 1
Park Royal, London- 129 II ab 1
Parkside 61 E 4
Parkside, PA 84 III a 2
Parkside, San Fransisco-, CA 83 I b 2
Park Station 170 V b 2
Parkston, SD 68-69 GH 4
Parksville 66-67 A 1
Park Timbers, New Orleans-, LA 85 I b 2
Park Town, Johannesburg- 170 V b 2
Park Valley, UT 66-67 G 5
Park View, NM 76-77 A 4
Parlākimidi 134-135 NO 7
Parlament 113 I b 2
Parlī = Purli 140 C 1
Parliament House [AUS, Melbourne] 161 II bc 1
Parliament House [AUS, Sydney] 161 I b 2
Parliament House [RI] 154 IV a 2
Parma 122-123 D 3
Parma, ID 66-67 E 4
Parma, MO 78-79 E 2
Parma, OH 72-73 F 4
Parmana 94-95 J 4
Parnaguá 92-93 L 7
Parnaguá, Lagoa de — 100-101 B 6
Parnaíba 92-93 L 5
Parnaíba, Rio — 92-93 L 5
Parnaibinha, Rio — 100-101 AB 5
Parnamirim [BR, Pernambuco] 100-101 E 5
Parnamirim [BR, Rio Grande do Norte] 100-101 G 3
Parnarama 100-101 C 3
Parnassós 122-123 K 6
Pārner 138-139 E 8
Párnēs 122-123 K 6
Párnōn 122-123 K 7
Pärnu 124-125 E 4
Pärnu jõgi 124-125 E 4
Pāro 138-139 K 4
Paro Dsong 138-139 M 4
Paro Jong = Paro Dsong 138-139 M 4
Pārola 138-139 E 7
Pāroḷēṅ = Pārola 138-139 E 7
Paromaj 132-133 b 7
Parona = Fındık 136-137 JK 4
Paroo Channel 158-159 H 6
Paroo River 158-159 H 5
Páros 122-123 L 7
Parowan, UT 74-75 G 4
Parque 3 de Febrero 110 III b 1
Parque Almirante Guillermo Brown 110 III b 1
Parque da Água Branca 110 II ab 2
Parque de Beisbol 91 I c 2
Parque del Retiro 113 III ab 2
Parque del Venado 91 I c 2
Parque Distrital de El Tunal 91 III b 4
Parque Distrital de Timiza 91 III ab 3
Parque do Estado 110 II b 2
Parque Jabaquara 110 II b 2
Parque Júlio Furtado 110 I b 2
Parque La Florida 91 III b 2
Parque Nacional Canaima 94-95 KL 5
Parque Nacional Cerro de la Estrella 91 I c 2-3
Parque Nacional de Aparados da Serra 106-107 MN 2
Parque Nacional de Este 91 II b 2
Parque Nacional de los Leones 91 I b 3
Parque Nacional de São Joaquim 106-107 MN 2
Parque Nacional de Ubajara 100-101 D 2
Parque Nacional do Araguaia 98-99 NO 10
Parque Nacional do Cachimbo 98-99 K 8-9
Parque Nacional do Iguaçu 102-103 EF 6
Parque Nacional do Xingu 98-99 M 10
Parque Nacional el Ávila 91 II bc 1
Parque Nacional El Pinar 91 II b 2
Parque Nacional Grão Pará 98-99 O 6
Parque Nacional Lanín 108-109 D 2-3
Parque Nacional Los Alerces 108-109 D 4
Parque Nacional Los Glaciares 108-109 C 7-8
Parque Nacional Miguel Hidalgo 91 I a 3
Parque Nacional Nahuel Huapi 108-109 D 3
Parque Nacional Paulo Afonso 100-101 E 5
Parque National de Monte Pascoal 100-101 E 9
Parque Nacional de Porto Alexandre 172 B 5
Parque Popular de Diversiones 91 III bc 2-3
Parque Presidente Nicolás Avellaneda 110 III b 1
Parr, SC 80-81 F 3
Parral 111 B 5
Parral, Hidalgo del — 64-65 EF 6
Parramatta, Sydney- 161 I a 1
Parramatta River 161 I a 1-2
Parramore Island 80-81 J 2
Parras de la Fuente 64-65 F 6
Parravicini 106-107 HJ 6
Parṛī = Pauri 138-139 G 2
Parrita 88-89 D 10
Parrsboro 63 D 5
Parry 61 F 6
Parry, Cape — 56-57 M 3
Parry Bay 56-57 U 4
Parry Island 72-73 F 2
Parry Islands 56-57 M-R 2
Parryøya 116-117 kl 4
Parry Sound 62 L 4
Parsa = Persepolis 134-135 G 5
Parsnip River 56-57 M 6-7
Parsons, KS 64-65 G 4
Parsons, TN 78-79 E 3
Parsons, WV 72-73 G 5
Parson's Pond 63 GH 2-3
Partābpur 138-139 J 6
Parṭa [YU] 122-123 J 3
Partāpgarh 138-139 E 5
Pårtefjället 116-117 GH 4
Parthenay 120-121 GH 5
Partinico 122-123 E 6
Partizansk 132-133 Z 9
Partol = Bandar 138-139 H 3
Partridge, KS 68-69 GH 7
Partridge River 62 L 1
Partūḍ = Partūr 138-139 F 8
Partūr 138-139 F 8
Pārū = Pāro 138-139 K 4
Paru, Rio — [BR] 92-93 J 5
Parú, Río — [YV] 94-95 H 5
Parú, Serranía — 94-95 J 5
Parucito, Río — 94-95 J 5
Paru de Este, Río — 98-99 L 3-4
Paru de Oeste, Rio — 98-99 L 3-4
Parūr 140 C 5
Parur = Paravūr 140 C 6
Paruro 96-97 F 8
Parvān = Parwān 138-139 F 5
Pārvatī = Pārbati 134-135 M 5
Pārvatīpurom 134-135 N 7
Parwān 138-139 F 5
Parys 174-175 G 4
Paša 124-125 J 4
Paşabahçe, İstanbul- 154 I b 2
Pasadena, CA 64-65 C 5
Pasadena, TX 64-65 GH 6
Pasadena Memorial Stadium 85 III c 2
Pasaje 92-93 D 5
Pasaje, Islas del — = Passage Islands 108-109 J 8
Pasaje, Río — 104-105 D 9
Pasajes de San Juan 120-121 FG 7
Pa Sak, Mae Nam — 150-151 C 4-5
Pa Sâm = Nam Ma 150-151 D 1
Pa Sang 150-151 B 3
Pasarbantal 152-153 D 7
Pasar Minggu, Jakarta- 154 IV ab 2
Pasarwajo 152-153 P 8
Pascagama, Rivière — 62 O 2
Pascagoula, MS 64-65 J 5
Pascagoula River 78-79 E 5
Paşcani 122-123 M 2
Pasco, WA 66-67 D 2
Pasco [PE] 96-97 CD 7
Pasco [RA] 110 III b 2
Pascoal, Monte — 100-101 E 9
Pascoe Vale, Melbourne- 161 II b 1
Pascuales 96-97 AB 2-3
Pas de Calais 120-121 HJ 3
Pasewalk 118 FG 2
Pasewalk = Pasvalys 124-125 E 5
Pashāwar 134-135 KL 4
Pashchimī Bangāl = West Bengal 134-135 O 6
Pashid Haihsia 142-143 N 7
Pasi, Pulau — 152-153 O 9
Pʹasina 132-133 QR 3
Pasinler = Hasankale 136-137 J 2-3
Pʹasino, ozero — 132-133 QR 4
Pʹasinskij zaliv 132-133 PQ 3
Pasión, Río — 86-87 PQ 9
Pasir 154 III b 1
Pasir Besar = Kampung Pasir Besar 148-149 D 6
Pasir Gudang 154 III b 1
Pasir Mas 150-151 CD 9
Pasir Panjang 150-151 C 11
Pasir Panjang, Singapore- 154 III a 2
Pasirpengarayan 152-153 D 5
Pasir Puteh 150-151 D 10
Pasir Ris 154 III b 1
Pasitanete, Pulau — 152-153 O 8
Paska 62 F 2
Paskenta, CA 74-75 B 3
Paškovo 124-125 O 7
Paškovskij 126-127 J 4
Pasley, Cape — 158-159 D 6
Pasman [RA] 106-107 F 6
Pašman [YU] 122-123 F 4
Pasni 134-135 J 5
Paso, El — 92-93 E 3
Paso Ataques 106-107 K 3
Paso Caballos 86-87 PQ 9
Paso Chacabuco 108-109 D 3
Paso Codorníz 108-109 C 6
Paso Coihaique Alto 108-109 D 5
Paso Copahue 111 BC 5
Paso de Águila 108-109 D 6
Paso de Chonta 96-97 D 8
Paso de Chureo 106-107 B 6
Paso de Desecho 106-107 B 6
Paso de Indios 111 BC 6
Paso de la Cumbre 111 BC 4
Paso de la Fortaleza 96-97 C 7
Paso del Agua Negra 106-107 BC 3
Paso de la Patria 102-103 C 7
Paso del Arco 106-107 B 7
Paso de las Llareta 106-107 BC 4
Paso de los Algarrobos 106-107 D 6
Paso de los Indios 106-107 C 7
Paso de los Libres 111 E 3
Paso de los Toros 111 EF 4
Paso de los Vientos 64-65 M 7-8
Paso del Portillo 106-107 BC 3
Paso del Rey, Moreno- 110 III a 1
Paso del Sapo 108-109 E 4
Paso de Menéndez 108-109 CD 4
Paso de Peña Negra 106-107 C 2
Paso de Potrerillo 106-107 BC 2
Paso Limay 108-109 DE 3
Paso Mamuil Malal 108-109 CD 2

Paso Quichuapunta 96-97 C 6
Pasorapa 104-105 D 6
Paso Robles, CA 74-75 C 5
Pasos, Los — 94-95 D 7
Paso San Francisco 104-105 B 10
Paso Tranqueras 106-107 K 3
Paso Tromen 108-109 CD 2
Paspébiac 63 D 3
Pasquia Hills 61 G 4
Passage Islands 108-109 J 8
Passagem Franca 100-101 BC 4
Passaic, NJ 82 III b 1
Passa-Quatro 102-103 K 5
Passau 118 F 4
Passa Vinte 102-103 KL 5
Pass Cavallo 76-77 FG 8
Pàssero, Capo — 122-123 F 7
Passinho 106-107 M 3
Passkij Perevoz 124-125 JK 3
Passo Borman 102-103 F 7
Passo dei Giovi 122-123 C 3
Passo della Cisa 122-123 CD 3
Passo do Sertão 106-107 N 2
Passo Fundo 111 F 3
Passo Fundo, Río — = Río Guarita 106-107 L 1
Passo Novo 106-107 K 2
Passos 92-93 K 9
Passy, Paris- 129 I c 2
Pastaza 96-97 C 2
Pastaza, Río — 92-93 D 5
Pasteur 106-107 FG 5
Pasto 92-93 D 4
Pastol Bay 58-59 F 5
Pastora Peak 74-75 J 4
Pastoril, La — = Colonia La Pastoril 106-107 DE 6
Pastos Blancos 108-109 D 5
Pastos Bons 100-101 B 4
Pastos Grandes, Lago — 104-105 C 7
Pastrana, Bogotá- 91 III ab 3
Pastura, NM 76-77 B 5
Pasul Turnu Roșu 122-123 KL 3
Pasuruan 152-153 K 9
Pasvalys 124-125 E 5
Pasvikelv 116-117 NO 3
Pata [BOL] 104-105 B 4
Pata [SN] 168-169 B 2
Patacamaya 104-105 BC 5
Patache, Punta — 104-105 A 7
Pata de Gallo, Cerro — 96-97 B 6
Patadkal 140 BC 3
Patagonia 111 B 8-C 6
Patagonia, AZ 74-75 H 7
Patagonian Cordillera = Cordillera Patagónica 111 B 8-5
Patagonian Shelf 50-51 FG 8
Patagónica, Cordillera — 111 B 8-5
Patamuté 100-101 E 5
Pātan [IND, Bihār] 138-139 K 5
Pātan [IND, Gujarāt] 138-139 D 6
Pātan [IND, Madhya Pradesh] 138-139 G 6
Pātan [IND, Mahārāshtra] 140 A 2
Pātan [Nepal] 134-135 NO 5
Pātan = Sōmnath 138-139 C 7
Patana = Pattani 148-149 D 5
Pātānapuram = Pāttānapuram 140 C 6
Patane = Pattani 148-149 D 5
Patang = Batang 142-143 H 6
Pataodī = Pataudi 138-139 F 3
Pātapatnam 140 G 1
Pāta Polavaram 140 F 2
Patara-Širaki 126-127 N 6
Patargân, Daqq-e — 134-135 J 4
Pātarghāṭa 138-139 MN 6
Paṭāshpur = Kasba Patāspur 138-139 L 6
Patauá, Cachoeira — 98-99 HJ 9
Pataudi 138-139 F 3
Patay Rondos 96-97 C 6
Patáz 96-97 C 5
Patchewollock 160 EF 5
Patchogue, NY 72-73 K 4
Pategi 168-169 G 3
Patensie 174-175 F 7
Paternal, Buenos Aires-La — 110 III b 1
Paternò 122-123 F 7
Pateros, WA 66-67 D 1-2
Paterson 174-175 FG 7
Paterson, NJ 72-73 J 4
Paterson, WA 66-67 D 2-3
Pathalgaon 138-139 J 6
Pathanapuram = Pāttānapuram 140 C 6
Pathānkōt 138-139 E 1
Pāthardi 138-139 E 8
Paṭhārgānv = Pathalgaon 138-139 J 6
Paṭhārgānv = Pathārgaon 138-139 JK 4
Pātharghāta 141 AB 4
Patherri = Pāthardi 138-139 E 8
Pathfinder Reservoir 68-69 C 4
Pathiu 150-151 B 7
Pāthri 138-139 F 8
Pathum Thani 148-149 CD 4
Pāti 138-139 E 7
Patía, Río — 92-93 D 4
Patiāla 134-135 M 4
P'atichatki 126-127 FG 2
Patience Well 158-159 E 4
P'atigorsk 126-127 L 4
P'atigory 124-125 U 3
P'atimar 126-127 P 2
Paṭiyālā = Patiāla 134-135 M 4
Pātkai Range 141 D 2
Pāṭkurā = Tirtol 138-139 L 7
Paṭlāvad = Petlāwad 138-139 E 6
Patlong 174-175 H 6
Pátmos 122-123 M 7
Patna 134-135 O 5
Pāṭnāgaḍa = Patnāgarh 138-139 J 7
Patnāgarh 138-139 J 7
Patnītola 138-139 M 5
Patnos 136-137 K 3
Pato Branco 102-103 F 7
Pātoda 140 B 1
Patomskoje nagorje 132-133 V 6-W 6
Patos [BR, Ceará] 100-101 E 2
Patos [BR, Paraíba] 92-93 M 6
Patos [BR, Piauí] 100-101 D 4
Patos, Lagoa dos — 111 F 4
Patos, Laguna de — 86-87 GH 2
Patos, Laguna de los — 106-107 F 3
Patos, Ponta dos — 100-101 E 2
Patos, Portillo de los — 104-105 B 10
Patos, Río de los — 106-107 C 3-4
Patos de Minas 102-103 J 3
Pa-tou = Badou 146-147 F 3
Patquía 111 C 4
Pátrai 122-123 J 6
Patraïkós Kólpos 122-123 J 6-7
Patras = Pátrai 122-123 JK 6
Patras, Gulf of — = Patraïkós Kólpos 122-123 J 6-7
Patreksfjördhur 116-117 ab 2
Patria, Cerro — 108-109 G 5
Patricia, SD 68-69 F 4
Patricia [CDN, landscape] 56-57 S-U 7
Patricia [CDN, place] 61 C 5
Patricinio do Muriaé 102-103 LM 4
Patricio Lynch, Isla — 111 A 7
Patricios 106-107 G 5
Patrimônio 102-103 H 3
Patrimônio União 102-103 E 5
Patrocínio 92-93 K 8
Paṭṭadakal = Patadkal 140 BC 3
Patta Island 172 H 2
Paṭ'ṭakkōṭṭai = Pudukkottai 140 D 5
Pāttānapuram 140 C 6
Pattani 148-149 D 5
Pattani, Mae Nam — 150-151 C 9
Patte-d'Oie, la — 129 I b 1-2
Patten, ME 72-73 M 2
Patterson, CA 74-75 C 4
Patterson, GA 80-81 E 5
Patti 122-123 F 6
Patti [IND, Punjab] 138-139 E 2
Patti [IND, Uttar Pradesh] 138-139 J 5
Pattiá 92-93 D 4
Pattikonda 140 C 3
Patton, PA 72-73 G 4
Pattonsburg, MO 70-71 CD 5
Pattukkottai 140 D 5
Pattullo, Mount — 60 C 1
Patu 92-93 M 6
Paṭūākhālī 141 B 4
Patuca, Punta — 64-65 K 8
Patuca, Río — 64-65 J 9-K 8
Patuha, Gunung — 152-153 G 9
Patung = Badong 142-143 KL 5
Pātūr 138-139 F 7
Pátzcuaro, Lago de — 86-87 JK 8
Pa-tzŭ = Bazai 146-147 E 9
Pau 120-121 G 7
Pau Brasil 100-101 E 8
Pauca 96-97 BC 5
Paucartambo 96-97 F 8
Pau d'Arco 92-93 K 6
Pau dos Ferros 100-101 E 4
Pau Ferro 100-101 D 5
Pauillac 120-121 G 6
Pauini 98-99 E 8
Pauini, Rio — [BR ◁ Rio Purus] 98-99 D 8-9
Pauini, Rio — [BR ◁ Rio Unini] 98-99 G 5-6
Paují, El — 91 II c 2
Pauk 141 D 5
Paukhkaung 141 D 6
Paukkaung = Paukhkaung 141 D 6
Pauksa Taung 141 D 6
Pauktaw 141 C 5
Paula 106-107 G 6
Paula Freitas 102-103 G 7
Paula Pereira 102-103 G 6-7
Paulding, MS 78-79 E 4
Paulding, OH 70-71 H 5
Paulicéia, Diadema- 110 II b 3
Paulina, OR 66-67 D 3
Paulina Mountains 66-67 C 4
Paulino Neves 100-101 C 2
Paulis = Isiro 172 E 1
Paul Island [USA] 58-59 d 2
Paulista [BR, Paraíba] 100-101 F 4
Paulista [BR, Pernambuco] 92-93 MN 6
Paulista [BR, Zona litigiosa] 92-93 L 8
Paulistana 92-93 L 6
Paulo Afonso 100-101 E 5
Paulo Afonso, Cachoeira de — 92-93 M 6
Paulo Afonso, Parque Nacional — 100-101 E 5
Paulo de Faria 102-103 H 4
Paulo Frontin 102-103 G 7
Paulpietersburg 174-175 J 4
Paul Roux 174-175 GH 5
Paulsboro, NJ 84 III b 3
Pauls Hafen = Pāvilosta 124-125 C 5
Paulshof 130 III c 1
Paulskirche 128 III b 1
Paulson 66-67 DE 1
Pauls Valley, OK 76-77 F 5
Paunero 106-107 E 4
Paung 141 E 7
Paungbyin = Hpaungbyin 141 D 3
Paungde = Paungdī 148-149 BC 3
Paungdī 148-149 BC 3
Paunglaung Myit 141 E 5-6
Pauni 138-139 G 7
Pauri [IND, Madhya Pradesh] 138-139 F 5
Pauri [IND, Uttar Pradesh] 138-139 G 2
Paurito 104-105 E 5
Pausin 130 III a 1
Pauto, Río — 94-95 EF 5
Pāvagada 140 C 3
Pavai = Pawai 138-139 H 5
Pavant Mountains 74-75 G 3
Pavēh 136-137 M 5
Pavelec 124-125 M 7
Pavia 122-123 C 3
Pavillon 60 G 4
Pavillons-sous-Bois, les — 129 I cd 2
Pāvilosta 124-125 C 5
Pavino 124-125 PQ 4
Pavle 96-97 B 3
Pavlodar 132-133 O 7
Pavlof Bay 58-59 c 2
Pavlof Harbor, AK 58-59 bc 2
Pavlof Islands 58-59 c 2
Pavlof Volcano 58-59 b 2
Pavlograd 126-127 GH 2
Pavlovac 122-123 G 3
Pavlovo 124-125 O 6
Pavlovsk [SU, Leningradskaja Oblast'] 124-125 H 4
Pavlovsk [SU, Voronežskaja Oblast'] 126-127 K 1
Pavlovskaja 126-127 JK 3
Pavlovskij 124-125 U 5
Pavlovskij Posad 124-125 M 6
Pavlyš 126-127 F 2
Pavo, GA 80-81 E 5
Pavte 96-97 B 3
Pavullo nel Frignano 122-123 D 3
Pavuvu = Russell Islands 148-149 j 6
Pavy 124-125 G 4
Pawahku = Mawāgū 141 F 2
Pawai 138-139 H 5
Pawan, Sungai — 152-153 J 6
Pawāyan 138-139 GH 3
Pawhuska, OK 76-77 F 4
Pawleys Island, SC 80-81 G 4
Pawnee, CO 68-69 E 5
Pawnee, OK 76-77 F 4
Pawnee City, NE 70-71 BC 5
Pawnee River 68-69 FG 6
Paw Paw, MI 70-71 GH 4
Pawtucket, RI 72-73 L 4
Páxoi 122-123 J 6
Paxson, AK 58-59 OP 5
Paxson Lake 58-59 OP 5
Paxton, IL 70-71 FG 5
Paxton, NE 68-69 F 5
Payakumbuh 148-149 D 7
Paya Lebar 154 III b 1
Paya Lebar Airport 154 III b 1
Payan 152-153 L 6
Payette, ID 66-67 E 3
Payette River 66-67 E 3-4
Payette River, North Fork — 66-67 E 3
Payinzet Kyûn 150-151 AB 6
Paylani = Palni 140 C 5
Payne, OH 70-71 H 5
Payne Bay = Bellin 56-57 WX 5
Payne Lake 56-57 W 6
Payne River 56-57 W 6
Paynes Creek, CA 66-67 BC 5
Paynesville 168-169 C 4
Paynesville, MN 70-71 C 3
Payong, Tanjung — 152-153 K 4
Paysandú [ROU, administrative unit] 106-107 HJ 3-4
Paysandú [ROU, place] 111 E 4
Pays de Caux 120-121 H 4
Pays de León 120-121 E 4
Payson, AZ 74-75 H 5
Payson, UT 66-67 GH 5
Payún, Borde Alto del — 106-107 C 6
Payún, Cerro — 111 BC 5
Paz, La — [BOL, administrative unit] 104-105 B 3-C 5
Paz, La — [BOL, place] 92-93 F 8
Paz, La — [Honduras] 88-89 C 7
Paz, La — [MEX, Baja California Sur] 64-65 DE 7
Paz, La — [MEX, San Luís Potosí] 86-87 K 6
Paz, La — [RA, Entre Ríos] 111 DE 4
Paz, La — [RA, Mendoza] 111 C 4
Paz, La — [ROU] 106-107 J 5
Paz, La — [YV] 94-95 E 2
Paz, Río de la — 104-105 C 5
Paza, Ponta — 100-101 F 6
Pazagug 138-139 K 3
Pazar 136-137 J 2
Pazar = Şorba 136-137 E 2
Pazarcık [TR, Bilecik] 136-137 C 2-3
Pazarcık [TR, Maraş] 136-137 G 4
Pazardžik 122-123 KL 4
Pazaryeri = Pazarcık 136-137 C 2-3
Paz de Río 94-95 E 4
Pazña 104-105 C 6
Pčinja 122-123 J 4-5
Peabiru 102-103 F 5
Peabody, KS 68-69 H 6
Peabody, MA 84 I c 1
Peace River [CDN, place] 56-57 N 6
Peace River [CDN, river] 56-57 MN 6
Peach Island 84 II c 2
Peachland 66-67 CD 1
Peach Springs, AZ 74-75 G 5
Peachtree Creek 85 II b 1
Peachtree Creek, North Fork — 85 II c 1
Peachtree Creek, South Fork — 85 II c 2
Peachtree Hills, Atlanta-, GA 85 II b 1
Peacock Bay 53 B 26-27
Peaima Falls 98-99 H 1
Peake Creek 160 B 1-2
Peak Hill [AUS, New South Wales] 160 J 4
Peak Hill [AUS, Western Australia] 158-159 C 5
Peakhurst, Sydney- 161 I a 2
Peaks of Otter 80-81 G 2
Peale, Mount — 64-65 DE 4
Peam Chileang 150-151 EF 6
Peam Chor 150-151 E 7
Pèam Prous = Phum Peam Prous 150-151 D 6
Pearce, AZ 74-75 J 7
Peard Bay 58-59 H 1
Pearl 70-71 F 1
Pearl Harbor 148-149 e 3
Pearl River 64-65 H 5
Pearl River, LA 78-79 DE 5
Pearsall, TX 76-77 E 8
Pearson 106-107 G 4
Pearson, GA 80-81 E 5
Pearston 174-175 F 7
Peary Channel 56-57 R 2
Peary Land 52 A 21-23
Peavine Creek 85 II c 2
Pebane 172 G 5
Pebas 92-93 E 5
Pebble Island 108-109 K 8
Peć 122-123 J 4
Peçanha 102-103 L 3
Pecan Island, LA 78-79 C 6
Peças, Ilha das — 111 G 3
Pecatonica River 70-71 F 4
Pečenežin 126-127 B 2
Pečenga [SU, place] 132-133 E 4
Pechabun = Phetchabun 148-149 CD 3
Pechawar = Pashāwar 134-135 KL 4
Pechincha, Rio de Janeiro- 110 I ab 2
Pech Nil, Đeo — 150-151 E 7
Pechora Bay = Pečorskaja guba 132-133 JK 4
Pečora [SU, place] 132-133 K 4
Pečora [SU, river] 132-133 K 5
Pecoraro, Monte — 122-123 FG 6
Pečoro-Ilyčskij zapovednik 124-125 VW 2
Pečorskaja guba 132-133 JK 4
Pečorskaja magistral' 132-133 JK 5
Pečory 124-125 FG 5
Pecos, TX 64-65 F 5
Pecos River 64-65 F 5
Pécs 118 HJ 5
Peda Konda 140 E 2
Pedasí 88-89 FG 11
Peddapalli 140 D 1
Peddāpuram 140 F 2
Pedder, Lake — 160 bc 3
Peddie 174-175 G 7
Peddocks Island 84 I c 3
Pedee, OR 66-67 B 3
Pedernal, NM 76-77 B 5
Pedernal [PY] 102-103 D 5
Pedernal [RA] 106-107 H 3
Pedernales [DOM] 88-89 L 5-6
Pedernales [EC] 92-93 CD 4
Pedernales [RA] 106-107 GH 5
Pedernales [YV] 92-93 G 3
Pedernales, Salar de — 104-105 B 10
Pederneira, Cachoeira — 92-93 FG 6
Pederneiras 102-103 H 5
Pedernera 106-107 E 4
Pēḍgāṅv = Pedgaon 140 B 1
Pedgaon 140 B 1
Pedra 100-101 F 5
Pedra Azul 92-93 L 8
Pedra Branca 100-101 E 3
Pedra Corrida 102-103 L 3
Pedra da Amolar, Cachoeira da — 100-101 B 5
Pedra de Amolar 98-99 P 10
Pedras, Rio das — 100-101 AB 7
Pedras Altas 106-107 L 3
Pedras Altas, Coxilha — 106-107 L 3
Pedras de Fogo 100-101 G 4
Pedras de Maria da Cruz 102-103 K 1
Pedra Sêca, Cachoeira da — 98-99 M 9
Pedras Negras 92-93 G 7
Pedras Negras, Reserva Florestal — 98-99 G 11
Pedregal [PA] 64-65 c 2
Pedregal [YU] 94-95 F 2
Pedregal, Caracas-El — 91 II b 1
Pedregulho 102-103 J 4
Pedreira 102-103 J 5
Pedreiras 92-93 KL 5
Pedrera [ROU] 106-107 K 5
Pedrera, La — 92-93 EF 5
Pedro, Point — = Pēduru Tuḍuwa 134-135 N 9
Pedro Afonso 92-93 K 6
Pedro Avelino 100-101 F 3
Pedro Bay, AK 58-59 K 7
Pedro Cays 64-65 L 8
Pedro Chico 94-95 F 7
Pedro de Valdivia 111 BC 2
Pedro Díaz Colodrero 106-107 H 3
Pedro Dorado 94-95 F 7
Pedro E. Funes 106-107 F 4
Pedro Gomes 102-103 E 3
Pedro González 102-103 CD 7
Pedro González, Isla — 94-95 B 3
Pedro II 92-93 L 5
Pedro II, Ilha — 94-95 H 7
Pedro II, Serra de — 100-101 D 3
Pedro Juan Caballero 111 E 2
Pedro Leopoldo 102-103 K 3
Pedro Luro 106-107 F 7
Pedro Lustosa 102-103 FG 6
Pedro Miguel 64-65 b 2
Pedro Miguel, Esclusas de — 64-65 b 2
Pedro Miguel Locks = Esclusas de Pedro Miguel 64-65 b 2
Pedro P. Lasalle 106-107 G 6
Pedro Point = Pēduru Tuḍuwa 140 E 6
Pedro R. Fernández 111 E 3
Pedro Totolapan 86-87 MN 9
Pedro Vargas 106-107 C 5
Pedro Velho 100-101 G 4
Pedro Versiani 102-103 M 2
Pēduru Tuḍuwa [CL, cape] 134-135 N 9
Pēduru Tuḍuwa [CL, place] 140 E 6
Peebinga 158-159 H 6
Peebles, OH 72-73 E 5
Peebles [CDN] 61 G 5
Peebles [GB] 119 E 4
Pee Dee River 64-65 L 5
Peek, mys — 58-59 C 4
Peekskill, NY 72-73 K 4
Peel River 56-57 JK 4
Peel Sound 56-57 R 3
Peene 118 F 2
Peera Peera Poolanna Lake 158-159 G 5
Peerless, MT 68-69 D 1
Peerless Lake 60 K 1
Peetz, CO 68-69 E 5
Pegasano 106-107 E 5
Pegasus Bay 158-159 O 8
Pegram, ID 66-67 H 4
Pègū 148-149 C 3
Pègū Myit 141 E 7
Pegunungan Alas 152-153 B 4
Pegunungan Apo Duat 152-153 L 3-4
Pegunungan Barisan 152-153 D 6-E 8
Pegunungan Batui 152-153 OP 6
Pegunungan Iran 152-153 L 4-5
Pegunungan Iyang 152-153 K 9
Pegunungan Jayawijaya 148-149 LM 7
Pegunungan Kapuas Hulu 152-153 K 5
Pegunungan Kapur Utara 152-153 JK 9
Pegunungan Kendeng 152-153 JK 9
Pegunungan Kidul 152-153 J 9-K 10
Pegunungan Larut 150-151 C 10
Pegunungan Maoke 148-149 LM 7
Pegunungan Mekongga 152-153 O 7
Pegunungan Menoreh 152-153 J 9
Pegunungan Meratus 148-149 G 7
Pegunungan Müller 148-149 F 6
Pegunungan Pusat Gayo 152-153 B 3
Pegunungan Quarles 152-153 N 7
Pegunungan Schwaner 148-149 F 7
Pegunungan Serayu 152-153 H 9
Pegunungan Sewu 152-153 J 9-10
Pegunungan Sudirman 148-149 L 7
Pegunungan Takolekaju 152-153 N 6-O 7
Pegunungan Tamabo 152-153 L 4
Pegunungan Tanambo 152-153 L 4
Pegunungan Tengger 152-153 K 9-10
Pegunungan Tigapuluh 152-153 E 6
Pegunungan Tineba 152-153 O 6-7
Pègū Taing 141 DE 6-7
Pègū Yōma 141 DE 5-6
Pehpei = Beipei 142-143 K 6
Pehuajó 111 D 5
Pehuén-Có 106-107 G 7
Peian = Bei'an 142-143 O 2
Pei-chên = Beizhen 144-145 C 2
Peicheng 146-147 FG 4
Peichiang 146-147 H 10
Pei Chiang = Bei Jiang 146-147 D 10
Pei-chieh Ho = Beijie He 150-151 G 3
Pei-ch'uan Ho = Beichuan He 146-147 C 3
Pei-fei Ho = Beifei He 146-147 F 5
Peighambār Dāgh = Peyghambar Dāgh 136-137 N 4
Pei-hai = Beihai 142-143 K 7
P'ei-hsien = Pei Xian 142-143 M 5
Peikang = Peichiang 146-147 H 10
Pei-li = Beili 150-151 G 3
Pei-liu = Beiliu 146-147 C 10
Peinado, Cerro — 106-107 C 6
Peine 118 E 2
Pei-ngan = Bei'an 142-143 O 2
Peint 138-139 D 7
Peipei = Beipei 142-143 K 6
Pei-p'iao = Beipiao 144-145 C 2
Peiping = Beijing 142-143 LM 3-4
Peipsi Lake = Čudskoje ozero 132-133 D 6
Peiraiévs 122-123 K 7
Peirce, Cape — 58-59 FG 7
Peirce Reservoir 154 III a 1
Peisegem 128 II a 1
Pei Shan = Bei Shan 142-143 GH 3
Peitawu Shan 146-147 H 10
Peixe 92-93 K 7
Peixe, Lagoa do — 106-107 M 3
Peixe, Rio do — [BR, Bahia] 100-101 E 6
Peixe, Rio do — [BR, Goiás] 102-103 F 2
Peixe, Rio do — [BR, Minas Gerais ◁ Rio Preto] 102-103 L 4
Peixe, Rio do — [BR, Minas Gerais ◁ Rio Santo Antônio] 102-103 L 3
Peixe, Rio do — [BR, Santa Catarina] 102-103 G 7
Peixe, Rio do — [BR, São Paulo] 102-103 G 4
Peixes, Rio dos — 98-99 K 10
Pei Xian [TJ ↖ Xuzhou] 142-143 M 5
Pei Xian [TJ → Xuzhou] 146-147 FG 4
Peixoto, Represa do — 102-103 J 4
Pejagalan, Jakarta- 154 IV a 1
Pejantan, Pulau — 152-153 G 5
Pekalongan 148-149 EF 8
Pekan 148-149 D 6
Pe Kiang = Bei Jiang 146-147 D 10
Pekin, IL 70-71 F 5
Pekin, IN 70-71 GH 6
Pekin, ND 68-69 G 2
Peking = Beijing 142-143 LM 4
Peking University 155 II ab 2
Peking Workers' Stadium 155 II b 2
Peking Zoo 155 II ab 2
Pektubajevo 124-125 R 5
Pekul'nej, chrebet — 132-133 hj 4
Pelabuhanratu, Teluk — 152-153 FG 9
Pelada, La — 106-107 G 3
Pelada, Serra — 100-101 D 8
Pelado, Serra do — 100-101 F 4
Pelagosa = Palagruža 122-123 G 4
Pelahatchie, MS 78-79 E 4
Pelaihari 148-149 F 7
Pelalawan 152-153 E 5
Pelayo 94-95 K 3
Peleaga 122-123 K 3
Pelechuco, Río — 104-105 B 4
Peleduj 132-133 V 6
Pelée, Montagne — 64-65 O 8
Pelee Island 72-73 E 4
Pelee Point 72-73 E 4
Pelēnaion 122-123 LM 6
Peleng, Pulau — 148-149 H 7
Peleng, Selat — 152-153 P 6
Pelgrimsrus 174-175 J 3
Pelham, GA 80-81 D 5
Pelham Bay Park 82 III d 1
Pelham Manor, NY 82 III d 1
Pelican, AK 58-59 TU 8
Pelicana 106-107 B 2-3
Pelican Lake, WI 70-71 F 3
Pelican Lake [CDN] 61 H 4
Pelican Lake [USA] 70-71 D 1
Pelican Mountains 60 KL 2
Pelican Narrows 61 G 3
Pelican Rapids [CDN, Alberta] 60 L 2
Pelican Rapids [CDN, Saskatchewan] 61 H 4
Pelicurá 106-107 F 7
Pelikan Rapids, MN 68-69 H 2
Pēlion 122-123 K 6
Pelješac 122-123 G 4
Pelkosenniemi 116-117 MN 4
Pella, IA 70-71 D 5
Pella [ZA] 174-175 C 5
Pellado, Cerro — 106-107 B 5
Pell City, AL 78-79 FG 4
Pellegrini 106-107 F 6
Pellegrini, Lago — 106-107 CD 7
Pellegrino, Cozzo — 106-107 HJ 5
Pellendorf 113 I b 2
Pello 116-117 L 4
Pellston, MI 70-71 H 3
Pelly Bay 56-57 S 4
Pelly Crossing 58-59 T 5
Pelly Mountains 56-57 K 5
Pelly River 56-57 K 5
Pelmaḍulla 140 E 7
Pelokang, Pulau — 152-153 N 9
Peloncillo Mountains 74-75 J 6
Pelopónnēsos 122-123 JK 7
Peloritani, Monti — 122-123 F 6-7
Pelotas 111 F 4
Pelotas, Rio — 111 F 3
Pelque, Río — 108-109 D 8
Pelusium 173 C 2
Pelusium, Bay of — = Khalīj aṭ-Ṭīnah 173 C 2
Pelvoux 120-121 L 6
Pelym [SU, place] 132-133 L 6
Pelym [SU, river] 132-133 L 5
Pemadumcook Lake 72-73 M 2
Pemalang 148-149 EF 8
Pemanggil, Pulau — 150-151 E 11
Pematangsiantar 148-149 C 6
Pemba [EAT] 172 GH 3
Pemba [Mozambique] 172 H 4
Pemba [Z] 172 E 5
Pemberton [AUS] 158-159 C 6
Pemberton [CDN] 60 F 4
Pembina 56-57 NO 7
Pembina Forks 60 JK 3
Pembina Mountains 68-69 G 1
Pembina River 60 K 3
Pembine, WI 70-71 FG 3
Pembroke, GA 80-81 F 4
Pembroke [CDN] 64-65 L 2
Pembroke [GB] 119 D 6
Pembuang, Sungai — 152-153 K 6-7
Pemuco 106-107 AB 6
Pen 140 A 1
Peña, La — 106-107 AB 6
Peña, Sierra de la — 120-121 G 7
Peña Blanca 106-107 B 2
Penablanca, NM 76-77 AB 5
Peñafiel 120-121 EF 8
Peñagolosa 120-121 G 8
Peña Grande, Madrid- 113 III a 2
Penalva 100-101 B 2
Penamar 100-101 C 7
Peña Negra, Paso de — 106-107 C 2
Peña Negra, Punta — 92-93 C 5
Peña Nevada, Cerro — 64-65 FG 7
Penang = George Town 148-149 CD 5
Penang = Pinang 150-151 C 10
Penang, Pulau — = Pulau Pinang 150-151 BC 10
Penanjung, Teluk — 152-153 H 9-10
Penápolis 102-103 GH 4
Peñarroya 120-121 G 8
Peñarroya-Pueblonuevo 120-121 E 9
Peñas, Cabo — 108-109 F 9
Peñas, Cabo de — 120-121 E 7
Penas, Golfo de — 111 AB 7
Peñas, Las — 106-107 F 3
Peñas, Punta — 92-93 G 2
Peña Ubiña 120-121 DE 7
Penawawa, WA 66-67 E 2
Pench 138-139 G 7
Penck, Cape — 53 C 9
Penco 106-107 A 6
Pendembu 164-165 B 7
Pendências 100-101 F 3
Pender, NE 68-69 H 4
Pender Bay 158-159 D 3
Pendjab = Punjab [IND] 134-135 LM 4
Pendjab = Punjab [PAK] 134-135 L 4
Pendjari 168-169 F 3
Pendleton, OR 64-65 C 2
Pend Oreille Lake 66-67 E 1-2
Pend Oreille River 66-67 E 1
Pendroy, MT 66-67 GH 1
Pendžikent 134-135 K 3
Penēios 122-123 K 6
Penembangan, Pulau — 152-153 H 6
Penetanguishene 72-73 FG 2
Pengalengan 152-153 G 9
Penganga 134-135 M 7
Peng Chau 155 I a 2
Pengchia Hsü 146-147 HJ 9
Pengcuo Ling = Phuntshog Ling 138-139 M 3
Penge [ZA] 174-175 J 3
Penge [ZRE, Haut-Zaïre] 171 AB 2
Penge [ZRE, Kasai-Oriental] 172 DE 3
Penge, London- 129 II b 2
P'eng-hu 146-147 G 10
Penghu Dao = Penghu Tao 146-147 G 10
Penghu Liedao = Penghu Lieh-tao 142-143 M 7
Penghu Lieh-tao 142-143 M 7
Penghu Shuitao 146-147 GH 10
Penghu Tao 146-147 G 10
P'êng-hu Tao = Penghu Tao 146-147 G 10
Pengibu, Pulau — 152-153 G 5
Pengjia Xu = Pengchia Hsü 146-147 HJ 9
Pengkou 146-147 F 9
Penglai 142-143 N 4
Peng Lem = Dak Hon 150-151 F 5
Pengra Pass 66-67 BC 4
Penguin Eilanden 174-175 A 3-5
Penguin Islands = Penguin Eilanden 174-175 A 3-5
Pengze 142-143 M 6
Penha, Rio de Janeiro- 110 I b 1
Penha, São Paulo- 102-103 J 5
Penha de França, São Paulo- 110 II b 2
Penhall 62 H 3
Penhurst 70-71 H 1
Penida, Nusa — 148-149 FG 8
Peninga 124-125 HJ 2
Península Antonio Varas 108-109 C 8
Península Brecknock 111 B 8-9
Península Brunswick 111 B 8
Península Córdova 108-109 C 9
Península de Araya 94-95 JK 2
Península de Azuero 64-65 K 10
Península de Ferrol 92-93 CD 6
Península de Guajira 92-93 E 2
Península de Guanahacabibes 88-89 D 4
Península de Nicoya 64-65 J 9-10
Península de Osa 64-65 JK 10
Península de Paraguaná 92-93 F 2
Península de Paria 92-93 G 2
Península de Taitao 111 AB 7
Península de Yucatán 64-65 HJ 8
Península de Zapata 88-89 F 3
Península Duende 108-109 B 6
Península Dumas 108-109 E 10
Península Hardy 111 BC 9
Península Huequi 108-109 C 4
Península Inhaca 174-175 K 4
Península Magallanes 108-109 C 8
Península Mitre 111 CD 8
Península Muñoz Gamero 111 B 8
Península Paracas 92-93 D 7
Península Sisquelan 108-109 BC 6
Península Skyring 108-109 B 5
Península Staines 108-109 C 8
Península Tres Montes 111 A 7
Península Valdés 111 D 6
Península Valiente 88-89 F 10
Península Verde 106-107 FG 7
Península Videau 108-109 C 7
Península Wilcock 108-109 BC 8
Península de Gaspé 56-57 XY 8
Peñíscola 120-121 H 8
Penitente, Loma — 108-109 D 9

Penitente, Río — 108-109 D 9
Penitente, Serra do — 92-93 K 6
Pénjamo 86-87 K 7
Penjaringan, Jakarta- 154 IV a 1
Penki = Benxi 142-143 N 3
Penmarch, Pointe de — 120-121 E 5
Penn 61 E 4
Pennandurchfahrt = Chong Phangan 150-151 BC 8
Pennāru = Penner 140 D 3
Pennask Mountain 66-67 C 1
Penne 122-123 EF 4
Penner 140 D 3
Penn Hills, PA 72-73 G 4
Pennine Chain 119 E 4-F 5
Pennsauken, NJ 84 III c 2
Pennsauken Creek North Branch 84 III d 2
Pennsauken Creek South Branch 84 III d 2
Pennsauken Merchandise Mart 84 III cd 2
Pennsylvania 64-65 KL 3
Pennsylvania, University of — 84 III b 2
Penn Valley, PA 84 III b 1
Penn Wynne, PA 84 III b 2
Penny 60 G 3
Penn Yan, NY 72-73 H 3
Penny Highland 56-57 X 4
Pennypack Creek 84 III c 1
Pennypack Park 84 III c 1
Penny Strait 56-57 R 2
Peno 124-125 J 5
Penobscot Bay 72-73 M 2
Penobscot River 72-73 M 2
Peñón 106-107 B 3
Peñon, Cerro — 91 I c 3
Peñón de Vélez de la Gomera 166-167 DE 2
Penong 158-159 F 6
Penonomé 88-89 F 10
Penrith 119 E 4
Pensa = Penza 132-133 GH 7
Pensacola, FL 64-65 J 5
Pensacola Bay 78-79 F 5
Pensacola Mountains 53 A 33-34
Pensamiento 104-105 F 4
Pensamiento, El — 106-107 G 7
Pensiangan 152-153 M 3
Pensilvania 94-95 D 5
Pentagon 82 II a 2
Pentakota 140 F 2
Pentecoste 100-101 E 2
Pentecoste, Açude — 100-101 E 2
Pentecost Island 158-159 N 3
Pênth = Peint 138-139 D 7
Penthièvre = 'Ayn Bārd'ah 166-167 K 1
Penticton 56-57 N 8
Pentland Firth 119 E 2
Pentwater, MI 70-71 G 4
Penukonda 140 C 3
Penungah 152-153 M 3
Penunjok, Tanjung — 150-151 D 10
Penwegon = Pènweigôn 141 E 6
Pènweigôn 141 E 6
Penwell, TX 76-77 C 7
Penyu, Pulau-pulau — 148-149 J 8
Penza 132-133 GH 7
Penzance 119 CD 6
Penžina 132-133 g 5
Penzing, Wien- 113 I b 2
Penžinskaja guba 132-133 f 5
Peonias 91 II ab 1
Peoples Creek 68-69 B 1
Peoria, AZ 74-75 G 6
Peoria, IL 64-65 HJ 3
Peotillos 86-87 K 6
Peotone, IL 70-71 G 5
Pepani 174-175 E 3
Pepel 164-165 B 7
Peper Bay = Teluk Lada 152-153 F 9
Peperiguaçu, Rio — 102-103 F 7
Pepin, WI 70-71 D 3
Pepperdine University 83 III c 2
Peque 94-95 D 4
Pequeni, Río — 64-65 bc 2
Pequi 102-103 K 3
Pequiri, Rio — 102-103 E 2
Pequizeiro 98-99 O 9
Pequop Mountains 66-67 F 5
Pequot Lakes, MN 70-71 C 2
Perai 150-151 C 10
Perak 150-151 C 10-11
Perak, Sungei — 150-151 C 10
Perälä 116-117 JK 6
Peralillo 106-107 B 5
Peralta [ROU] 106-107 J 4
Perambalūr 140 D 5
Percas 106-107 F 2
Percé 63 DE 3
Perche 120-121 H 4
Percival Lakes 158-159 DE 4
Perdekop 174-175 H 4
Perdices 106-107 H 4
Perdido, Monte — 120-121 GH 7
Perdido Bay 78-79 F 5
Perdizes 102-103 J 3
Perdões 102-103 K 4
Perdue 61 E 4
Perdūru 140 B 4
Peredelkino 113 V a 3
Peregrino, El — 106-107 FG 5
Pereguete, Río — 64-65 b 3
Pereira 92-93 D 4
Pereira, Cachoeira — 98-99 KL 7
Pereira, Cachoeiro — 92-93 H 5
Pereira Barreto 102-103 G 4
Pereira d'Éça = N'Giva 172 C 5
Pereirinha 98-99 K 9
Pereiro 100-101 E 4
Perejaslav-Chmel'nickij 126-127 EF 1
Perekop 126-127 F 3
Perekop, Gulf of — = Karkinitskij zaliv 126-127 F 4
Perelazovskij 126-127 L 2
Perelik 122-123 L 5
Perel'ub 124-125 S 8
Peremul Par 134-135 L 8
Peremyšl' 124-125 L 6
Perené 96-97 D 7
Perené, Río — 96-97 D 7
Perenosa Bay 58-59 LM 7
Pereslavl'-Zalesskij 124-125 M 5
pereval Kluchorskij 126-127 K 5
pereval Kodorskij 126-127 MN 5
pereval Krestovyj 126-127 M 5
pereval Mamisonskij 126-127 L 5
Perevoz [SU ↗ Arzamas] 124-125 P 6
Perevoz [SU ↗ Bodajbo] 132-133 W 6
Pérez 106-107 G 4
Pérez, Isla — 86-87 PQ 6
Pergamino 111 D 4
Pergamon 136-137 B 3
Pergamos = Pergamon 136-137 B 3
Perham, MN 70-71 C 2
Perhentian, Kepulauan — 150-151 D 10
Perhonjoki 116-117 KL 6
Periá, Rio — 100-101 C 2
Peribonca, Lac — 63 A 2
Péribonca, Rivière — 56-57 W 7-8
Perico 111 CD 2
Perico, TX 76-77 C 4
Pericos 86-87 G 5
Pericumã, Rio — 100-101 B 2
Périgord 120-121 H 6
Perigoso, Canal — 92-93 K 4
Perigotville = 'Ayn al-Khabīrā 166-167 J 1
Périgueux 120-121 H 6
Perija, Sierra de — 92-93 E 2-3
Peril Strait 58-59 U 8
Perimetral Norte 94-95 J 7
Perim Island = Barīm 134-135 E 8
Perín = Colonia Perín 102-103 BC 6
Periperi de Poções 100-101 D 8
Periquito, Cachoeira do — 92-93 G 6
Peri suyu 136-137 J 3
Perito Moreno 111 BC 7
Peritoró 100-101 B 3
Peritos, Cachoeira — 98-99 GH 9
Periya 140 BC 5
Periyakuḷam 140 C 5
Periyāpaṭṭaṇa = Piriyāpatna 140 BC 4
Periyār 140 C 5
Periyar Lake 140 C 6
Perk 128 II b 1
Perkerson Park 85 II b 2
Perkins, OK 76-77 F 4-5
Perla, La — 86-87 HJ 3
Perlach, München- 130 II b 2
Perlas, Archipiélago de las — 64-65 KL 10
Perlas, Laguna de — 88-89 E 8
Perlas, Las — 88-89 E 8
Perlas, Punta de — 64-65 K 9
Perley, MN 68-69 H 2
Perlis 150-151 C 9
Perlis, Kuala — 148-149 CD 5
Perm' 132-133 K 6
Permas 124-125 P 4
Permé 88-89 H 10
Permskoje = Komsomol'sk-na-Amure 132-133 a 7
Perm-Zakamsk 124-125 UV 5
Perm-Zaozerje 124-125 UV 4
Pernambuco 92-93 LM 6
Pernambuco = Recife 92-93 N 6
Pernem 140 A 3
Pernik 122-123 K 4
Péronne 120-121 J 4
Peron Peninsula 158-159 B 5
Perouse, La — 61 K 3
Perovo, Moskva- 124-125 LM 6
Perovsk = Kzyl-Orda 132-133 M 9
Perow 60 D 2
Perpignan 120-121 J 7
Perrégaux = Muḥammadīyah 164-165 DE 1
Perreux-sur-Marne, le — 129 I d 2
Perrin, TX 76-77 EF 6
Perrine, FL 80-81 c 4
Perris, CA 74-75 E 6
Perry 70-71 H 2
Perry, FL 80-81 b 1
Perry, GA 80-81 E 4
Perry, IA 70-71 CD 5
Perry, NY 72-73 GH 3
Perry, OK 76-77 F 4
Perry Island 58-59 O 6
Perrysburg, OH 72-73 E 4
Perryton, TX 76-77 D 4
Perryvale 60 L 2
Perryville, AK 58-59 d 2
Perryville, AR 78-79 C 3
Perryville, MO 70-71 EF 7
Perşembe 136-137 G 2
Persepolis 134-135 G 5
Perseverancia 92-93 G 7
Persia = Iran 134-135 F-H 4
Persian Gulf 134-135 FG 5
Peršinskaja 124-125 N 3
Persip 174-175 C 3
Pertandangan, Tanjung — 152-153 D 4
Pertek 136-137 H 3
Perth [AUS, Tasmania] 160 c 2
Perth [AUS, Western Australia] 158-159 BC 6
Perth [CDN] 72-73 H 2
Perth [GB] 119 E 3
Perth Amboy, NJ 72-73 J 4
Perth-Andover 63 C 4
Perth-Fremantle 158-159 BC 6
Pertominsk 124-125 LM 1
Peru, IL 70-71 F 5
Peru, IN 70-71 GH 5
Peru [PE] 92-93 D 5-E 7
Perú [RA] 111 D 5
Perú, El — 104-105 C 3
Peru Basin 156-157 N 5
Peru Chile Trench 92-93 C 6-D 7
Perúgia 122-123 E 4
Perugorría 106-107 H 2
Peruíbe 111 G 2
Perundurai 140 C 5
Pervari = Hashır 136-137 K 4
Perveri 136-137 GH 4
Pervomajsk [SU, Rossijskaja SFSR] 124-125 OP 6
Pervomajsk [SU, Ukrainskaja SSR] 126-127 E 2
Pervomajskaja 124-125 T 3
Pervomajskij [SU, Rossijskaja SFSR Archangel'skaja Oblast'] 124-125 N 1
Pervomajskij [SU, Rossijskaja SFSR Tambovskaja Oblast'] 124-125 N 7
Pervoural'sk 132-133 KL 6
Pervyj Kuril'skij proliv 132-133 de 7
Perwenitz 130 III a 1
Perzhinsk, Gulf of — = zaliv Šelechova 132-133 e 5-6
Pesagi, Gunung — 152-153 F 8
Pesanggrahan, Kali — 154 IV a 2
Pèsaro 122-123 E 4
Pesca, La — 86-87 M 6
Pescada, Ponta da — 98-99 NO 3
Pescade, Pointe — 170 I a 1
Pescadero, CA 74-75 B 4
Pescador 100-101 D 10
Pescadores = Penghu Lieh-tao 142-143 M 7
Pescadores, Punta — 96-97 E 10
Pescadores Channel = Penghu Shuitao 146-147 GH 10
Pesčanaja 126-127 D 2
Pesčanoje 124-125 KL 2
Pesčanyj, mys — 126-127 P 5
Pesčanyj, ostrov — 132-133 WX 3
Pescara 122-123 F 4
Pèschici 122-123 FG 5
Peshawar = Pashāwar 134-135 KL 4
Peshtigo, WI 70-71 G 3
Peshtigo River 70-71 F 3
Peshwar = Pashāwar 134-135 KL 4
Peski [SU, Rossijskaja SFSR Moskovskaja Oblast'] 124-125 M 6
Peski [SU, Rossijskaja SFSR Voronežskaja Oblast'] 126-127 L 1
Peski [SU, Ukrainskaja SSR] 126-127 F 1
Peskovka [SU, Rossijskaja SFSR] 124-125 ST 4
Peskovka [SU, Ukrainskaja SSR] 126-127 DE 1
Pešnoj, poluostrov — 126-127 P 3
Pesočnoje 124-125 M 5
Pesqueira 100-101 F 5
Pessene 174-175 K 3
Pessis-Bouchard, le — 129 I b 1-2
Peštera 122-123 KL 4
Pestovo 124-125 K 4
Pestravka 124-125 R 7
Petacalco, Bahía — 86-87 JK 9
Petacas, Las — 106-107 F 3
Petah Tiqua = Petaḥ Tiqwa 136-137 F 6
Petaḥ Tiqwa 136-137 F 6
Petaliõn, Kólpos — 122-123 L 7
Petaluma, CA 74-75 B 3
Petare 94-95 H 2
Petare-Caurimare 91 II bc 2
Petare-El Llanito 91 II c 2
Petare-El Marques 91 II c 2
Petare-Macaracuay 91 II c 2
Petare-Santa Ana 91 II bc 2
Petas, Las — 104-105 G 5
Petatlán 86-87 K 9
Petauke 172 F 4
Petawana 72-73 H 2
Petén, El — 64-65 H 8
Petén Itzá, Lago — 86-87 Q 9
Petenwell Lake 70-71 F 3
Petenwell Reservoir = Petenwell Lake 70-71 F 3
Peterbell 70-71 J 1
Peterborough, NH 72-73 KL 3
Peterborough [AUS, South Australia] 158-159 GH 6
Peterborough [AUS, Victoria] 160 F 7
Peterborough [CDN] 56-57 V 9
Peterborough [GB] 119 FG 5
Peterhead 119 F 3
Peterhof = Petrodvorec 124-125 G 4
Peter I[st] Island = ostrov Petra I 53 C 27
Petermann Ranges 158-159 E 4-F 5
Peter Pond Lake 56-57 P 6
Petersbach 113 I b 2
Petersburg, AK 56-57 K 6
Petersburg, IL 70-71 F 5
Petersburg, IN 70-71 G 6
Petersburg, TN 78-79 F 3
Petersburg, TX 76-77 D 6
Petersburg, VA 64-65 L 4
Petersburg, WV 72-73 G 5
Petersburg = Leningrad 132-133 E 5-6
Peters Creek, AK 58-59 M 5
Petersham, London- 129 II a 2
Peter's Mine 98-99 J 1
Petersville, AK 58-59 M 5
Petilia Policastro 122-123 G 6
Petit Bois Island 78-79 E 5-6
Petit-Cap 63 DE 3
Petit-Étang 63 F 4
Petit-Goâve 88-89 K 5
Petitjean = Sīdī Qāsim 164-165 CD 2
Petit Lac Manicouagan 63 C 2
Petit Manan Point 72-73 N 2
Petit Mécatina, Île du — 63 G 2
Petit Mécatina, Rivière du — 63 FG 2
Petitot River 56-57 M 5-6
Petit-Rocher 63 CD 4
Petlād 138-139 D 6
Petlāwad 138-139 E 6
Petnahor 154 I a 1
Peto 64-65 J 7
Peton Forest School Park 85 II b 2
Petorca 111 B 4
Petoskey, MI 70-71 H 3
Petra [JOR] 136-137 F 7
Petra, ostrova — 132-133 VW 2
Petra I, ostrov — 53 C 27
Petra Velikogo, zaliv — 132-133 Z 9
Petre, Point — 72-73 H 3
Petrel Bank 58-59 st 6
Petrerito de la Noria 104-105 G 6
Petrič 122-123 K 5
Petrified Forest National Monument 74-75 J 5
Petrikov 124-125 G 7
Petrikovka 126-127 G 2
Pétriou = Chachoengsao 148-149 D 4
Petriščevo 124-125 KL 6
Petroaleksandrovsk = Turtkul' 132-133 L 9
Petrodvorec 124-125 G 4
Petrograd = Leningrad 132-133 E 5-6
Petrolândia 92-93 M 6
Petrólea 92-93 E 3
Petroleum, TX 76-77 E 9
Petrolia 72-73 E 3
Petrolia, CA 66-67 A 5
Petrolina [BR, Amazonas] 98-99 E 6
Petrolina [BR, Pernambuco] 92-93 L 6
Petrolina de Goiás 102-103 H 2
Petronila 106-107 G 3
Petropavlovskaja = Sabirabad 126-127 O 6-7
Petropavlovka 132-133 TU 7
Petropavlovsk 132-133 MN 7
Petropavlovskij = Achtubinsk 126-127 MN 2
Petropavlovsk-Kamčatskij 132-133 ef 7
Petropavlovsk-Kamchatskiy = Petropavlovsk-Kamčatskij 132-133 ef 7
Petrópolis 92-93 L 9
Petroquímica Estación Comferpet 108-109 F 5
Petros, TN 78-79 G 2
Petrosa 113 II b 2
Petroşeni 122-123 K 3
Petroskoi = Petrozavodsk 132-133 EF 5
Petrovaradin 122-123 HJ 3
Petrovka [SU, Kujbyševskaja Oblast'] 124-125 ST 7
Petrovka [SU, Vladivostok] 144-145 J 1
Petrovsk 124-125 P 7
Petrovskaja 126-127 HJ 4
Petrovskij Jam 124-125 KL 2
Petrovskij Zavod = Petrovsk-Zabajkal'skij 132-133 U 7
Petrovskoje [SU, Jaroslavskaja Oblast'] 124-125 M 5
Petrovskoje [SU, Moskva] 113 V d 4
Petrovskoje [SU, Tambovskaja Oblast'] 124-125 N 7
Petrovskoje = Balabino 126-127 G 3
Petrovsko-Razumovskoje, Moskva- 113 V b 2
Petrovsk-Port = Machačkala 126-127 NO 5
Petrovsk-Zabajkal'skij 132-133 U 7
Petrov Val 126-127 M 1
Petrozavodsk 132-133 EF 5
Petrúpolis 113 IV a 1
Petrusburg 174-175 F 5
Petrus Steyn 174-175 H 4
Petrusville 174-175 F 6
Petseri = Pečory 124-125 FG 5
Pettibone, ND 68-69 G 2
Pettigrew, AR 78-79 C 3
Pettus, TX 76-77 EF 8
Pettys Island 84 III c 2
Petuchovo 132-133 M 6
Peuetsagu, Gunung — 152-153 B 3
Peumo 111 B 4
Peureulak, Ujung — 152-153 BC 3
Peutie 128 II b 1
Pevek 132-133 gh 4
Peyghambar Dāgh 136-137 N 4
Peyrano 106-107 G 4
Peyton, CO 68-69 D 6
Pézenas 120-121 J 7
Pežma 124-125 N 3
Pezmog 124-125 ST 3
Pezones 104-105 G 5
Pfaffenhofen 118 E 4
Pfaffhausen 128 IV b 1
Pfannenstiel 128 IV b 2
Pfarrkirchen 118 F 4
Pfaueninsel 130 III a 2
Pforzheim 118 D 4
Pfungen 128 IV b 1
Phachi 150-151 C 5
Phāgi 138-139 E 4
Phagri Dsong 138-139 M 4
Phagvāŗā = Phagwāra 138-139 E 2
Phagwāra 138-139 E 2
Phai, Ko — 150-151 C 6
Phaisali 150-151 C 5
Phalaborwa 174-175 J 2
Pha Lai 150-151 F 2
Phalane = Mu'o'ng Phalane 150-151 E 4
Phalodi 134-135 L 5
Phaltan 134-135 LM 7
Pha Luat 150-151 C 4
Phālut Peak 138-139 LM 4
Pha Napo, Khao — 150-151 BC 4
Phanat Nikhom 150-151 C 6
Phangan, Chong — 150-151 BC 8
Pha-ngan, Chong — = Chong Phangan 150-151 BC 8
Phangan, Ko — 148-149 CD 5
Phanggong Tsho 142-143 DE 5
Phangnga 150-151 B 8
Phanna Nikhom 150-151 D 4
Phanom Bencha, Khao — 150-151 B 8
Phanom Dang Raek 148-149 DE 4
Phanom Phrai 150-151 DE 5
Phanom Sarakham 150-151 C 6
Phanom Thuan 150-151 B 5
Phan Rang 148-149 EF 4
Phan Ri = Hoa Da 150-151 G 7
Phan Thiet 148-149 E 4
Phao, Lam — 150-151 D 4
Pha Pet, Phou — 150-151 E 3
Pharendā 138-139 J 4
Pharokha = Ferokh 140 B 5
Pharr, TX 76-77 E 9
Pharu Tsangpo 138-139 LM 2
Phat Diêm 150-151 F 2-3
Phatthalung 148-149 D 5
Phayam, Ko — 150-151 B 8
Phayao 150-151 BC 3
Phaykkhaphum Phisai 148-149 D 3
Phayuha Khiri 150-151 C 5
Phelps, WI 70-71 F 2-3
Phelps Corner, MD 82 II b 2
Phelps Lake 80-81 H 3
Phen 150-151 D 4
Phenix City, AL 64-65 J 5
Phetchabun 148-149 CD 3
Phetchaburi 148-149 CD 4
Phiafay 150-151 EF 5
Phia May 150-151 F 5
Phibun Mangsahan 150-151 E 5
Phichai 150-151 C 4
Phichit 150-151 C 4
Philadelphia, MS 78-79 E 4
Philadelphia, PA 64-65 LM 3-4
Philadelphia [ET] 173 B 3
Philadelphia [ZA] 174-175 C 7
Philadelphia-Bridesburg, PA 84 III c 2
Philadelphia-Burholme, PA 84 III c 1
Philadelphia-Bustleton, PA 84 III c 1
Philadelphia-Chestnut Hill, PA 84 III b 1
Philadelphia-Crescentville, PA 84 III c 1
Philadelphia-East Falls, PA 84 III b 1
Philadelphia-Eastwick, PA 84 III b 2
Philadelphia-Elmwood, PA 84 III b 2
Philadelphia-Fox Chase, PA 84 III c 1
Philadelphia-Frankford, PA 84 III c 1
Philadelphia-Germantown, PA 84 III b 1
Philadelphia-Holmesburg, PA 84 III c 1
Philadelphia International Airport 84 III b 2
Philadelphia-Juniata, PA 84 III c 1
Philadelphia-Kensington, PA 84 III c 2
Philadelphia-Lawndale, PA 84 III c 1
Philadelphia-Logan, PA 84 III c 1
Philadelphia-Manayunk, PA 84 III b 1
Philadelphia-Mayfair, PA 84 III c 1
Philadelphia-Mount Airy, PA 84 III b 1
Philadelphia Naval Shipyard 84 III bc 2
Philadelphia-North Philadelphia, PA 84 III bc 2
Philadelphia-Olney, PA 84 III c 1
Philadelphia-Overbrook, PA 84 III b 2
Philadelphia-Richmond, PA 84 III c 2
Philadelphia-Roxborough, PA 84 III b 1
Philadelphia-Somerton, PA 84 III c 1
Philadelphia-South Philadelphia, PA 84 III bc 2
Philadelphia-Tacony, PA 84 III c 1
Philadelphia-Tioga, PA 84 III bc 1
Philadelphia-Wissinoming, PA 84 III c 1
Philip, SD 68-69 F 3
Philip Island 158-159 N 5
Philipp, MS 78-79 DE 4
Philippe-Thomas = Al-Mittawī 164-165 F 2
Philippeville 120-121 K 3
Philippeville = Sakīkdah 164-165 F 1
Philippi, WV 72-73 FG 5
Philippi, Lake — 158-159 G 4
Philippiada = Filippiás 122-123 J 6
Philippines 148-149 H 3-J 5
Philippolis 174-175 F 6
Philippopolis = Plovdiv 122-123 L 4
Philippsthal 130 III a 2
Philipsburg, MT 66-67 G 2
Philipsburg, PA 72-73 G 4
Philip Smith Mountains 56-57 GH 4
Philipstown 174-175 F 6
Phillaor = Phillaur 138-139 EF 2
Phillaur 138-139 EF 2
Phillip Island 160 G 7
Phillips, ME 72-73 L 2
Phillips, WI 70-71 E 3
Phillipsburg, KS 68-69 G 6
Phillipsburg, MO 70-71 D 7
Phillipsburg, NJ 72-73 J 4
Phillips Mountains 53 B 22-23
Philo, CA 74-75 B 3
Phimai 150-151 D 5
Phinlaung 141 E 5
Phippsøya 116-117 kl 4
Phitsanulok 148-149 D 3
Phnom Damrei 150-151 DE 7
Phnom Dangraek = Phanom Dong Raek 148-149 DE 4
Phnom Kravanh 150-151 D 6-7
Phnom Kulên 150-151 DE 6
Phnom Penh 148-149 D 4
Phnom Samkos 150-151 D 6
Phnom Ta Det 150-151 D 6
Pho, Laem — 148-149 D 5
Phô Binh Gia 150-151 EF 2
Phoenix 208 JK 3
Phoenix, AZ 64-65 D 5
Phoenix Basin 162 KL 4
Phoenix Islands 156-157 J 5
Phoenix Trench 156-157 J 5
Phoenixville, PA 72-73 HJ 4
Phon 150-151 D 5
Phong, Nam — 150-151 CD 4
Phong Điền 150-151 F 4
Phong Lộc 150-151 F 4
Phong Phu 150-151 E 7
Phong Saly 148-149 D 2
Phong Thanh = Cao Lanh 150-151 E 7
Phong Thong 150-151 DE 4
Phon Phisai 150-151 D 3
Phopāgāṛ = Phopāgaon 138-139 J 3
Phopāgaon 138-139 J 3
Pho Rang = Lang Phô Rang 150-151 E 1
Phorog Tsho 138-139 J 2
Phosphate Hill 158-159 GH 4
Photharam 150-151 B 6
Phou Bia 150-151 D 3
Phou Khao Khouai 150-151 D 3
Phou Loi 150-151 D 2
Phou Pha Pet 150-151 E 3
Phou Xai Lai Leng 150-151 DE 3
Phra Chedi Sam Ong 148-149 C 3-4
Phrae 150-151 C 3
Phra Nakhon Si Ayutthaya 148-149 D 4
Phran Kratai 150-151 B 4
Phra Thong, Ko — 150-151 AB 8
Phrom Buri 150-151 C 5
Phrom Phiram 150-151 C 4
Phsar Oudong 150-151 E 7
Phu Cat 150-151 G 5-6
Phu Cu'o'ng 150-151 F 7
Phu Diễn Châu 148-149 E 3
Phu Ding Den 150-151 F 5
Phu Đoan 150-151 E 2
Phugsum 138-139 KL 3
Phuket 148-149 C 5
Phuket, Ko — 148-149 C 5
Phu Khieo 150-151 D 4
Phu Khu'o'ng 150-151 F 7
Phu Kradung 150-151 CD 4
Phūl 138-139 E 2
Phu Lang Thu'o'ng = Băc Giang 150-151 F 2
Phulbāni 138-139 JK 7
Phulji 138-139 A 4
Phu Lôc 150-151 F 4
Phu Lôc = Thanh Tri 150-151 EF 8
Phūlpur 138-139 J 4
Phu Ly 148-149 E 2
Phum Damdek 150-151 DE 6
Phum Kompong Kdey 150-151 E 6
Phum Krasang 150-151 E 6
Phum Krek 150-151 E 7
Phum Léach 150-151 DE 6
Phum Peam Prous 150-151 D 6
Phum Rovieng 148-149 E 4
Phum Siembauk 150-151 E 6
Phum Treng 150-151 D 6
Phu My 150-151 G 5
Phunakha 134-135 OP 5
Phung Chhu 138-139 L 3
Phung Hiệp 150-151 E 8
Phungpo Tsho 138-139 L 2
Phu Nho Quan 150-151 EF 2
Phunphin 150-151 B 8
Phuntshog Ling 138-139 M 3
Phu'o'c Binh 150-151 F 7
Phu'o'c Lê 150-151 F 7
Phu'o'c Long 150-151 E 8
Phu'o'c Vinh 150-151 F 7
Phu Qui 150-151 E 3
Phu Quôc 150-151 D 7
Phu Quôc, Đao — 148-149 D 4
Phu Riêng 150-151 F 7
Phu Soai Dao 150-151 C 4
Phutha-Ditjhaba 174-175 H 5
Phu Tho 148-149 DE 2
Phu Tinh Gia 150-151 EF 3
Phutthaisong 150-151 D 5
Phu Wiang 150-151 CD 4
Phu Yên Binh 150-151 E 2
Phya Lat = Ban Phya Lat 150-151 D 2
Piacá 92-93 K 6
Piaçabuçu 100-101 F 6
Piacenza 122-123 C 3
Piacoá 94-95 K 3
Piacouadie, Lac — 63 A 2
Pialba 158-159 K 5
Piamonte 106-107 FG 4
Piancó 100-101 F 4
Piangil 158-159 H 7
Pianguan 146-147 C 2
Pianma 141 F 2
Pianosa, Ìsola — 122-123 D 4
Piara-Açu 98-99 M 9
Pias [PE] 96-97 C 5
Piaseczno 118 K 2
Piatã 100-101 D 7
Piatra 122-123 L 3
Piatra-Neamţ 122-123 M 2
Piauí 92-93 L 6
Piauí, Rio — 92-93 L 6
Piauí, Serra do — 100-101 CD 5
Piave 122-123 E 2
Piaxtla, Punta — 86-87 G 6
Piaxtla, Río — 86-87 G 6
Piazza Armerina 122-123 F 7
Piazzi, Isla — 108-109 BC 8
Pībōr 164-165 L 7
Pībōr, Nahr — 164-165 L 7
Pica 104-105 B 7
Picabo, ID 66-67 F 4
Picacho, AZ 74-75 H 6
Picacho, CA 74-75 F 6
Picacho, NM 76-77 B 6
Picacho, Cerro del — 91 I c 1
Picacho del Centinela 64-65 F 6
Picada, La — 106-107 G 3
Picados, Cerro dos 86-87 CD 3
Pičajevo 124-125 O 7
Picardie 120-121 HJ 4
Picayune, MS 78-79 E 5
Pic Baumann 168-169 F 4
Pic Bette 164-165 HJ 4
Pic de Guéra 164-165 H 6
Pic de Tibé 168-169 C 3
Pichalo, Punta — 104-105 A 6
Pichamán 106-107 A 5
Pichanal 111 CD 2
Pichanas 106-107 E 3
Pichelsdorf 130 III a 1
Picher, OK 76-77 G 4
Pichhōr 138-139 G 5
Pichi Ciego 111 C 4
Pichieh = Bijie 142-143 K 6
Pichilemú 111 B 4
Pichi Mahuida 106-107 E 7
Pichi Mahuida, Sierra — 106-107 E 7
Pichincha [EC, administrative unit] 96-97 B 1-2
Pichincha [EC, mountain] 96-97 B 2
Pichirhua 96-97 E 9
Pichis, Río — 96-97 D 7
Pichon = Ḥaffūz 166-167 L 2
Pichor 138-139 G 5
Pichtovka 132-133 P 6
Pickens, MS 78-79 DE 4
Pickens, SC 80-81 E 3
Pickerel 72-73 F 2
Pickerel Lake 70-71 E 1
Pickle Crow 56-57 ST 7
Pickle Lake 62 D 2
Pico 204-205 E 5
Pico, El — 92-93 G 8
Pico, Río — 108-109 D 5
Pico Baú 102-103 K 5
Pico Bolívar 92-93 E 3
Pico Cristóbal Colón 94-95 E 2
Pico da Bandeira 92-93 L 9
Pico da Neblina 92-93 FG 4
Pico da Piedade 102-103 L 3
Pico das Almas 100-101 CD 7
Pico da Tijuca 110 I b 2
Pico de Aneto 120-121 H 7
Pico de Itambé 102-103 L 3
Pico de Johnson 86-87 DE 3
Pico de Neblina 98-99 F 4
Pico de Orizaba 86-87 M 8
Pico de Orizaba = Citlaltépetl 64-65 G 8
Pico de Salamanca 108-109 F 5
Pico de São Tomé 168-169 G 5
Pico de Tancítaro 64-65 F 8
Pico de Teide 164-165 A 3
Pico Duarte 64-65 M 8
Pico Francés 108-109 E 10
Pico Guaricana 102-103 H 6
Pico Itacambira 102-103 L 2
Pico Itacolomi 92-93 L 9
Pico Itapirapuã 102-103 H 6
Pico Kazer 108-109 F 10
Picola 160 G 5
Pico Negro 104-105 B 6
Pico Oriental 91 II bc 1
Pico Redondo 98-99 G 3
Pico Rivera, CA 83 III d 2
Pico Rondon 98-99 G 4
Pico Ruivo 164-165 A 2
Picos 92-93 L 6
Pico Salamanca 108-109 F 5
Picos de Europa 120-121 E 7
Picos de Urbión 120-121 F 8
Pico Sira 96-97 D 6
Pico Truncado 111 C 7
Pico Turquino 64-65 L 8
Pic River 70-71 G 1
Picton [CDN] 72-73 H 2-3
Picton [NZ] 158-159 O 8
Picton, Isla — 108-109 F 10
Picton, Mount — 160 bc 3
Pictou 63 E 5
Pic Toussidé 164-165 H 4
Picture Butte 66-67 G 1
Picuí 92-93 M 6
Picunda, mys — 126-127 K 5
Picún Leufú 111 BC 5
Picún Leufú, Arroyo — 106-107 BC 7
Picún Leufú, Cerro — 106-107 C 7
Pidurutalāgala 134-135 N 9
Piedad Cavadas, La — 86-87 JK 7
Piedade, Pico da — 102-103 L 3
Piedade, Rio de Janeiro- 110 I b 2
Piedade, Serra da — 100-101 F 4

Piedade do Rio Grande 102-103 KL 4
Piedad Narvarte, Ciudad de México-91 I c 2
Piedecuesta 94-95 E 4
Pie de Palo 111 C 4
Pie de Palo, Sierra — 106-107 C 3
Piedmont 64-65 K 5-L 4
Piedmont, AL 78-79 G 4
Piedmont, SC 80-81 E 3
Piedmont, SD 68-69 E 3
Piedmont, WV 72-73 G 5
Piedmont Park 85 II bc 2
Piedra Azul 91 II b 1
Piedra Blanca, Sierra — 106-107 CD 7
Piedra Clavada 108-109 E 6
Piedra de Cocuy 94-95 H 7
Piedra del Águila 111 BC 6
Piedra Echada 106-107 F 7
Piedras 92-93 CD 5
Piedras, Banco — 106-107 J 5
Piedras, Las — [BOL] 104-105 C 2
Piedras, Las — [ROU] 106-107 J 5
Piedras, Las — [YV, Delta Amacuro] 94-95 L 3
Piedras, Las — [YV, Guárico] 94-95 H 3
Piedras, Las — [YV, Merida] 94-95 F 3
Piedras, Punta — 106-107 J 5
Piedras, Río — 64-65 b 2
Piedras, Río de las — 92-93 E 7
Piedras Coloradas 106-107 J 4
Piedras de Lobos, Punta — 106-107 AB 3
Piedras Negras 64-65 F 6
Piedra Sola 106-107 J 4
Piedritas 106-107 F 5
Pie Island 70-71 F 1
Pieksämäki 116-117 M 6
Pielinen 116-117 N 6
Piemonte 122-123 BC 3
Pienaarsrivier 174-175 GH 3
Piendamó 94-95 C 6
P'ien-kuan = Pianguan 146-147 C 2
Pierce, ID 66-67 F 2
Pierce, NE 68-69 H 4
Pierce City, MO 76-77 GH 4
Pierceville, KS 68-69 F 7
Piercy, CA 74-75 B 3
Pieres 106-107 H 7
Pierre, SD 64-65 F 3
Pierrefitte 129 I c 2
Pierre Lake 62 L 2
Pierrelaye 129 I b 1
Pierreville 72-73 K 1
Pierson 68-69 F 1
Pierson, FL 80-81 c 2
Piešťany 118 HJ 4
Pietarsaari = Jakobstad 116-117 JK 6
Pietermaritzburg 172 F 7
Pietersburg 172 E 6
Pietrasanta 122-123 CD 4
Piet Retief 174-175 J 4
Pietrosul [RO ↙ Borşa] 122-123 L 2
Pietrosul [RO ↙ Vatra Dornei] 122-123 L 2
Pigailoe 148-149 N 5
Pigeon, MI 72-73 E 3
Pigeon Bay 72-73 E 4
Pigeon Lake 60 L 3
Pigeon Point 74-75 B 4
Pigeon River [CDN, place] 70-71 F 1
Pigeon River [CDN, river] 62 A 1
Piggott, AR 78-79 D 2
Pigg's Peak 174-175 J 3
Pigüé 106-107 F 6
Pigüé, Arroyo — 106-107 F 6
Pigŭm-do 144-145 E 5
Pihāni 138-139 H 4
Pi He 146-147 F 6
Pihsien = Pei Xian 146-147 FG 4
Pihtipudas 116-117 LM 6
Pi-hu = Bihu 146-147 G 7
Pihuel, Volcán — 106-107 C 6
Pihyŏn 144-145 E 2
Piippola 116-117 LM 5
Pija, Sierra de — 64-65 J 8
pik Aborigen 132-133 cd 5
Pikal'ovo 124-125 JK 4
Pikangikum 62 C 2
pik Chan Tengri 134-135 MN 2
Pike Creek 84 II c 3
Pikelot 148-149 N 5
Pikes Peak 64-65 F 4
Piketberg 172 C 8
Piketberge 174-175 C 7
Piketon, OH 72-73 E 5
Pikeville, KY 80-81 E 2
Pikeville, TN 78-79 G 3
pik Grandioznyj 132-133 RS 7
Pikkenwynrots 174-175 B 5
pik Kommunizma 134-135 L 3
pik Lenina 134-135 L 3
Pikmiktalik, AK 58-59 FG 5
Pikou 144-145 D 3
pik Pobedy 134-135 MN 2
pik Sedova 132-133 J 3
pik Stalina = pik Kommunizma 134-135 L 3
Pikwitonei 61 K 3
Piła [PL] 118 H 2
Pila [RA] 106-107 H 6
Pilagá, Riacho — 104-105 G 9
Pilah, Kuala — 150-151 D 11
Pilane 174-175 FG 3
Pilanesberg 174-175 G 3
Pilāni 138-139 E 3
Pilão Arcado 92-93 L 7
Pilar [BR, Alagoas] 100-101 G 5
Pilar [BR, Paraíba] 100-101 G 4
Pilar [PY] 111 E 3
Pilar [RA, Buenos Aires] 106-107 H 5
Pilar [RA, Córdoba] 106-107 EF 3
Pilar [RA, Santa Fe] 106-107 G 3
Pilar, El — 94-95 K 2
Pilar do Sul 102-103 J 5
Pilas Group 148-149 H 5
Pilawa 118 K 3
Pilaya, Río — 104-105 D 7
Pilcaniyeu 111 BC 6
Pilcomayo, Río — [BR] 111 D 2
Pilcomayo, Río — [PY] 102-103 C 6
Pile Bay, AK 58-59 L 7
Pilgrim Gardens, PA 84 III b 2
Pilgrim Springs, AK 58-59 EF 4
Pil'gyn 132-133 jk 4
Pīlībhīt 138-139 GH 3
Pilica 118 K 3
Pillahuincó 106-107 G 7
Pillahuincó, Sierra de — 106-107 G 7
Pillar, Cape — 158-159 J 8
Pillar Island 155 I a 1
Pillaro 96-97 B 2
Pillings Pond 84 I b 1
Pillo, Isla del — 106-107 G 4
Pilmaiquén, Río — 108-109 C 3
Pilões 100-101 B 8
Pilões, Cachoeira dos — 98-99 OP 9
Pilões, Chapada dos — 102-103 J 2-3
Pilot Mountain, NC 80-81 F 2
Pilot Peak [USA, Absaroka Range] 66-67 HJ 3
Pilot Peak [USA, Gabbs Valley Range] 74-75 E 3
Pilot Peak [USA, Toano Range] 66-67 FG 5
Pilot Point, AK 58-59 HJ 8
Pilot Point, TX 76-77 F 6
Pilot Rock, OR 66-67 D 3
Pilot Station, AK 58-59 F 6
Pilottown, LA 78-79 E 6
Pilquiniyeu, Altiplanicie del — 108-109 E 3
Piltene 124-125 C 5
Pim 132-133 N 5
Pimba 158-159 G 6
Pimenta, Cachoeira do — 94-95 K 7
Pimenta Bueno 92-93 G 7
Pimental 98-99 J 7
Pimenteiras 100-101 D 4
Pimentel 96-97 AB 5
Pimmit Hills, VA 82 II a 2
Pimmit Run 82 II a 1-2
Pimpalner 138-139 D 7
Pimville, Johannesburg- 170 V a 2
Pin 141 F 5
Pin, le — 129 I d 2
Piña [PA] 64-65 a 2
Pina [SU] 124-125 E 7
Pinacate, Cerro del — 86-87 D 2
Pináculo, Cerro — 108-109 CD 8
Pinaleno Mountains 74-75 HJ 6
Pinamar 106-107 J 6
Pinamelayan 148-149 H 4
Pinang 150-151 BC 10
Pinang, Ci — 154 IV b 2
Pinang, Pulau — 150-151 BC 10
Pinar = Ören 136-137 BC 4
Pinarbaşı 136-137 G 3
Pinar del Río 64-65 K 7
Pinaré 102-103 G 6
Pinarhisar 136-137 B 2
Piñas [EC] 96-97 B 3
Pinas [RA] 106-107 E 3
Pincén 106-107 F 5
Pinchas 106-107 D 2
Pinchaung 141 D 5
Pincher Creek 66-67 FG 1
Pin Chiang = Bin Jiang 146-147 D 9-10
Pinckneyville, IL 70-71 F 6
Pinconning, MI 70-71 HJ 4
Pîncota 122-123 J 2
Pindaí 100-101 C 8
Pindamonhangaba 102-103 K 5
Pindar 138-139 G 2-3
Pindara 141 E 5
Pindaré, Rio — 92-93 K 5
Pindaré-Mirim 100-101 B 2
Pindo, Río — 96-97 C 2
Pindobaçu 100-101 D 6
Pindobal 98-99 O 6
Pindorama 102-103 H 4
Píndos Óros 122-123 J 5-6
Pindus = Píndos Óros 122-123 J 5-6
Pinduši 124-125 K 2
Piṇḍvārā = Pindwāra 138-139 D 5
Pindwāra 138-139 D 5
Pine, ID 66-67 F 4
Pine, Cape — 63 K 4
Pine Acres, NJ 84 III c 3
Pine Apple, AL 78-79 F 5
Pine Bluff, AR 64-65 H 5
Pinebluff Lake 61 G 3-4
Pine Bluffs, WY 68-69 D 5
Pine City, MN 70-71 D 3
Pine City, WA 66-67 E 2
Pine Creek [AUS] 158-159 F 2
Pine Creek [USA] 66-67 E 5
Pinedale, WY 66-67 J 4
Pine Falls 62 AB 2
Pine Forest Mountains 66-67 D 5
Pinega 132-133 H 5
Pine Grove, NJ 84 III d 2
Pine Hills 64-65 J 5
Pinehouse Lake 61 E 3
Pineimuta River 62 DE 1
Pine Island 80-81 b 3
Pine Island, MN 70-71 D 3
Pine Island Bay 53 B 26
Pine Islands 80-81 c 4
Pineland, TX 76-77 GH 7
Pinemont Plaza, Houston-, TX 85 III b 1
Pine Mountain [USA, Georgia] 78-79 G 4
Pine Mountain [USA, Kentucky] 80-81 DE 2
Pine Point 56-57 O 5
Pine Ridge 68-69 C 2-3
Pine Ridge, PA 84 III a 2
Pine Ridge, SD 68-69 E 4
Pine Ridge Indian Reservation 68-69 EF 4
Pine River, MN 70-71 CD 2
Pine River [CDN, place Manitoba] 61 HJ 5
Pine River [CDN, place Saskatchewan] 61 E 2
Pine River [CDN, river] 60 FG 2
Piñero, General Sarmiento- 110 III a 1
Pinerolo 122-123 B 3
Pines, Point of — 84 I c 2
Pines River 84 I c 2
Pines Run 84 III c 3
Pinetown 174-175 J 5
Pine Tree Brook 84 I b 3
Pine Valley, NJ 84 III d 3
Pine Valley Mountains 74-75 G 4
Pineville, KY 72-73 E 6
Pineville, LA 78-79 C 5
Piney [CDN] 70-71 BC 1
Piney Buttes 68-69 C 2
Piney Point Village, TX 85 III a 2
Ping, Kampung Kuala — 150-151 D 10
Ping, Mae Nam — 148-149 C 3
P'ing-chiang = Pingjiang 146-147 D 7
P'ing-ch'üan = Pingquan 144-145 B 2
Pingding 146-147 DE 3
Pingdingshan 146-147 D 5
Pingdong = Pingtung 142-143 N 7
Pingdu 146-147 G 3
Pinggu 146-147 F 1
Pinghai 146-147 E 10
P'ing-hai = Pinghai 146-147 G 9
Pinghe 146-147 F 9
P'ing-ho = Pinghe 146-147 F 9
P'ing-hsiang = Pingxiang 142-143 L 6
P'ing-hsien = Pingxiang 142-143 K 7
Pinghu 146-147 H 6
Pingi 146-147 F 4
Pingjiang [TJ, place] 146-147 D 7
Ping Jiang [TJ, river] 146-147 E 8
Pingkiang = Pingjiang 146-147 D 7
P'ing-ku = Pinggu 146-147 F 1
Pingle [CDN] 61 C 3
Pingle [TJ] 142-143 L 7
P'ing-leang = Pingliang 142-143 K 4
Pingli 146-147 B 5
Pingliang 142-143 K 4
Pingliang = Pingtung 142-143 N 7
Pinglo = Pingle 142-143 L 7
P'ing-lo = Pingluo 142-143 K 4
Pinglu [TJ, Henan] 146-147 C 4
Pinglu [TJ, Shanxi] 146-147 D 2
Pinglucheng 146-147 CD 2
Pingluo 142-143 K 4
Ping-ma Chiao = Lingao Jiao 150-151 G 3
Pingmar, Cape — = Lingao Jiao 150-151 G 3
Pingnan [TJ, Fujian] 146-147 G 8
Pingnan [TJ, Guangxi Zhuangzu Zizhiqu] 146-147 C 10
Pingo, El — 106-107 H 3
Pingquan 144-145 B 2
Pingree, ID 66-67 G 4
Pingree, ND 68-69 G 2
Pingrup 158-159 C 6
Pingshan 146-147 DE 2
Pingshan = Huidong 146-147 E 10
Pingshi [TJ, Guangdong] 146-147 D 9
Pingshi [TJ, Henan] 146-147 D 5
Pingshun 146-147 D 3
Pingsiang = Pingxiang 142-143 L 6
Pingtan 146-147 GH 9
Pingtan Dao 142-143 MN 6
Pingting = Pingding 146-147 DE 3
P'ing-ting-shan = Pingdingshan 146-147 D 5
Pingtung 142-143 N 7
Pingurbek Island 58-59 E 7
Ping-wang = Bingwang 150-151 G 3
Pingwu 142-143 J 5
Pingxiang [TJ, Guangxi Zhuangzu Zizhiqu] 142-143 K 7
Pingxiang [TJ, Jiangxi] 142-143 L 6
Pingyang 146-147 H 8
Pingyao 146-147 D 3
Pingyi 146-147 F 4
Pingyin 146-147 F 3
Pingyuan [TJ, Guangdong] 146-147 EF 9
Pingyuan [TJ, Shandong] 146-147 F 3
P'ing-yüan = Pingyuan 146-147 F 3
Pingyuan = Renju 146-147 E 9
Pinhal 92-93 K 9
Pinhão 102-103 G 6
Pinheiro 92-93 KL 5
Pinheiro, Ponta do — 102-103 H 7
Pinheiro Machado 106-107 L 3
Pinheiro Marcado 106-107 L 2
Pinheiros 110 II a 2
Pinheiros, São Paulo- 110 II a 2
Pinhsien = Bin Xian [TJ, Shaanxi] 146-147 AB 4
Pinhsien = Bin Xian [TJ, Shandong] 146-147 FG 3
Pinhuã, Rio — 98-99 F 8
Pini, Pulau — 148-149 C 6
Pinjarra 158-159 C 6
Pinkiang = Harbin 142-143 O 2
Pinkwan = Pianguan 146-147 C 2
Pinlebu = Pinlĭbū 141 D 3
Pinlĭbū 141 D 3
Pinnacles National Monument 74-75 C 4
Pinnaroo 158-159 H 7
Pinner, London- 129 II a 1
Pinon, CO 68-69 D 6
Pinon, NM 76-77 B 6
Piñón, Monte — 64-65 b 2
Pinos, Mount — 74-75 D 5
Pinos, Point — 74-75 BC 4
Pino Suárez, Tenosique de — 64-65 H 8
Pinrang 148-149 G 7
Pins, Îles de — 158-159 N 4
Pins, Pointe aux — 72-73 F 3
Pinsk 124-125 F 7
Pins Maritimes, les — 170 I b 2
Pinta, Isla — 92-93 A 4
Pintada [BR, Bahia] 100-101 C 6
Pintada [BR, Rio Grande do Sul] 111 F 4
Pintada, La — 94-95 A 3
Pintada, Serra — 100-101 E 4
Pintadas 100-101 E 6
Pintado, El — 104-105 F 9
Pintados 111 BC 2
Pintados, Salar de — 104-105 B 7
Pintasan 152-153 MN 3
Pinto [RA] 111 D 3
Pinto Butte 61 E 6
Pinto Creek 66-67 K 1
Pinturas, Río — 108-109 D 6
Pin'ug 124-125 QR 3
Pinware River 63 H 1-2
Pinzón 106-107 G 4-5
Pio XII 100-101 B 2
Pioche, NV 74-75 F 4
Pio IX 100-101 D 4
Piombino 122-123 D 4
Pión 96-97 B 5
Pioneer Island = ostrov Pioner 132-133 QR 2
Pioneer Mountains 66-67 G 3
Pioneer Park 170 V b 2
Pioner, ostrov — 132-133 QR 2
Pionki 118 K 3
Piorini, Lago — 92-93 G 5
Piorini, Rio — 92-93 G 5
Piotrków Trybunalski 118 J 3
Pipanaco, Salar de — 104-105 C 10-11
Pīpār 138-139 D 4
Pipérion 122-123 L 6
Pipestone 61 H 6
Pipestone, MN 70-71 BC 3
Pipestone Creek 61 GH 5
Pipestone River 62 DE 1
Pipinas 111 E 5
Pipmuacan, Réservoir — 63 A 3
Pipping, München- 130 II a 2
Pipra [IND → Darbhanga] 138-139 L 4
Pipra [IND ↖ Muzaffarpur] 138-139 K 4
Piqua, KS 70-71 C 7
Piqua, OH 70-71 H 5
Piquetberg = Piketberg 172 C 8
Piquetberge = Piketberge 174-175 C 7
Piquet Carneiro 100-101 E 3
Piquête 102-103 K 5
Piquete, El — 104-105 D 9
Piquiri, Rio — 111 F 2
Pira 168-169 F 3
Pira, Salto de — 88-89 D 8
Pirabeiraba 102-103 H 7
Piracaia 102-103 J 5
Piracanjuba 92-93 JK 8
Piracanjuba, Rio — 102-103 H 2
Piracicaba 102-103 HJ 5
Piracicaba, Rio — [BR, Minas Gerais] 102-103 L 4
Piracicaba, Rio — [BR, São Paulo] 102-103 J 5
Piracuruca 92-93 L 5
Piracuruca, Rio — 100-101 C 2-D 3
Piraeus = Peiraiévs 122-123 K 7
Piragiba 100-101 C 7
Piraí do Sul 111 G 2
Piraju 102-103 H 5
Pirajuí 92-93 K 9
Pīr 'Alī Emāmzādeh 136-137 N 6
Pirámide, Cerro — 108-109 C 7
Pirâmide de Ciuciulco 91 I b 3
Pirâmide de Santa Cecilia 91 I b 1
Pirâmide de Tenayuca 91 I b 1
Pirámide el Triunfo 104-105 F 9
Piran 122-123 E 3
Piran [YU] 136-137 J 3
Piranã, Serra — 100-101 G 4
Pirané 111 E 3
Pirané, Laguna — 104-105 G 9
Piranga 102-103 L 4
Piranga, Serra da — 98-99 MN 6
Piranhas 92-93 M 6
Piranhas, Cachoeira das — 98-99 HJ 9
Piranhas, Rio — [BR, Goiás ◁ Rio Caiapo] 102-103 G 2
Piranhas, Rio — [BR, Goiás ◁ Rio Grande do Norte] 98-99 O 9
Piranhas, Rio — [BR, Rio Grande do Norte] 92-93 M 6
Piranhinha, Serra — 100-101 B 1-2
Piranji, Rio — 100-101 E 3
Pirapemas 100-101 BC 2
Pirapetinga 102-103 L 4
Pirapó, Arroyo — 102-103 E 7
Pirapó, Rio — [BR] 102-103 F 5
Pirapó, Río — [PY] 102-103 D 7
Pirapó, Serra do — 106-107 K 2
Pirapora 92-93 L 8
Pirapora, Cachoeira — 104-105 G 2
Pirapòzinho 102-103 G 5
Piraputangas 102-103 D 3
Piraquara 102-103 H 6
Pirarajá 106-107 K 4
Pirarara, Cachoeira — 98-99 KL 5
Pirassununga 92-93 K 9
Pirates Island = Dao Tching Lan Xan 150-151 FG 2
Pir'atin 126-127 F 1
Piratini 106-107 L 3
Piratini, Rio — 106-107 K 2
Piratininga 102-103 H 5
Piratuba 111 F 3
Pirāvā = Pirāwa 138-139 EF 5
Pirawa 138-139 EF 5
Piray, Río — 104-105 E 5
Piray Guazú, Arroyo — 102-103 E 7
Pirayú 102-103 D 6
Pirčevan = Mindživan 126-127 N 7
Pireneus, Serra dos — 102-103 HJ 1
Pirenópolis 102-103 H 1
Pires do Rio 102-103 HJ 2
Pirganj 138-139 M 5
Piriápolis 106-107 K 5
Pirin 122-123 K 5
Piripá 100-101 D 8
Piripiri 92-93 L 5
Piritiba 100-101 D 6
Píritu [YV, Falcón] 94-95 G 2
Píritu [YV, Portuguesa] 94-95 G 3
Pirituba, São Paulo- 110 II a 1
Piriyāpatna 140 BC 4
Pirizal 102-103 D 2
Pirmasens 118 C 4
Pirna 118 F 3
Piro-bong 144-145 G 3
Pirogovka 124-125 J 8
Pirojpur 138-139 MN 6
Pirot 122-123 K 4
Pirovano 106-107 G 6
Pīr Patho 138-139 A 5
Pirpintos, Los — 111 D 3
Pirquita 106-107 D 4
Pirre, Cerro — 94-95 C 4
Pirsagat 126-127 O 7
Pirtleville, AZ 74-75 J 7
Piru 148-149 J 7
Pisa 122-123 D 4
Pisac 96-97 F 8
Pisagua 111 B 1
Pisanda 94-95 C 7
Pisco 92-93 D 7
Pisco, Bahía de — 92-93 D 7
Pisco, Río — 96-97 CD 8
Piscobamba 96-97 C 6
Piscop 129 I c 1
Písek 118 G 4
Pisgah, Mount — 66-67 C 3
Pishan = Guma Bazar 142-143 D 4
P'i-shan = Guma Bazar 142-143 D 4
Pīsh-e Kūh 136-137 M 6
Piso Firme 104-105 EF 3
Pisoridorp 98-99 L 3
Pispek = Frunze 132-133 NO 9
Pisquí, Río — 96-97 D 5
Pissis, Monte — 106-107 C 1
Pisticci 122-123 G 5
Pistòia 122-123 D 3-4
Pistolet Bay 63 J 2
Pistol River, OR 66-67 A 4
Pisuerga 120-121 E 7
Pisz 118 K 2
Pita 164-165 B 6
Pitalito 94-95 CD 7
Pitanga 102-103 G 6
Pitanga, Serra da — 102-103 G 6
Pitangui 102-103 K 3
Pītāpuram = Pithāpuram 140 F 2
Pitari, Lago — 104-105 F 3
Pitcairn 156-157 L 6
Piteå 116-117 J 5
Pite älv 116-117 HJ 5
Piterka 126-127 N 1
Piteşti 122-123 L 3
Pit-Gorodok 132-133 RS 6
Pithāpuram 140 F 2
Pithara 158-159 C 6
Pithoraāgaṛh = Pithorāgarh 138-139 H 3
Pithauragarh = Pithorāgarh 138-139 H 3
Pithorāgarh 138-139 H 3
Piti, Cerro — 111 C 2
Piti, Lagoa — 174-175 K 4
Pitigliano 122-123 D 4
Pitithang 138-139 L 4
Pitk'ajarvi 116-117 NO 3
Pitk'aranta 124-125 HJ 3
Pitkin, LA 78-79 C 5
Pitman River 58-59 XY 7
Pitmega River 58-59 E 2
Pito, Salina del — 108-109 E 4
Pit River 66-67 BC 5
Pitrufquén 106-107 A 7
Pitsani 174-175 F 3
Pitssville, WI 70-71 EF 3
Pitt Island [CDN] 56-57 KL 7
Pitt Island [NZ] 158-159 Q 8
Pittsboro, NC 80-81 G 3
Pittsburg, CA 74-75 C 3
Pittsburg, KS 64-65 H 4
Pittsburg, KY 80-81 D 2
Pittsburg, TX 76-77 G 6
Pittsburgh, PA 64-65 KL 3
Pittsfield, IL 70-71 E 6
Pittsfield, MA 72-73 K 3
Pittsfield, ME 72-73 M 2
Pittston, PA 72-73 J 4
Pittsworth 160 K 1
Pituil 106-107 D 2
P'i-tzŭ-wo = Pikou 144-145 D 3
Piuí 102-103 K 4
Piuka = Bifuka 144-145 c 1
Piura [PE, administrative unit] 96-97 AB 4
Piura [PE, place] 92-93 CD 6
Piura, Río — 96-97 A 4
Piute Peak 74-75 D 5
Piuthān 138-139 J 3
Piva 122-123 H 4
Pivijay 94-95 D 2
Pivka 122-123 F 3
Pivot 61 C 5
Pixuna, Rio — 98-99 G 8
Pi-yang = Biyang 146-147 D 5
Pizacoma 96-97 G 10
Pižma [SU, place] 124-125 Q 5
Pižma [SU, river] 124-125 QR 5
Pizzo 122-123 FG 6
Pjagina, poluostrov — 132-133 de 6
Pjana 124-125 P 6
PkiO im. Dzeržinskogo 113 V c 2
PkiO Sokol'niki 113 V c 2
P.K. le. Roux Dam 174-175 F 6
Plá 106-107 G 5
Place Bonaventure 82 I b 2
Place d'Eau-Electrique 170 IV a 1
Place de la Concorde 129 I c 2
Place de la Republique 129 I c 2
Place des Artes 82 I b 1
Place Metropolitaine Centre 82 I b 1
Placentia 63 J 4
Placentia Bay 56-57 Za 8
Placer de Guadalupe 86-87 H 3
Placerville, CA 74-75 C 3
Placerville, CO 68-69 B 6-7
Placetas 64-65 L 7
Place Versailles 82 I b 1
Plácido de Castro 92-93 F 7
Plácido Rosas 106-107 KL 4
Placilla 104-105 A 9
Placilla de Caracoles 104-105 B 8
Plai Mat, Lam — 150-151 D 5
Plain City, OH 72-73 E 4
Plaine de Tamlelt = Sahl Tāmlilt 166-167 E 3
Plaine du Hodna = Sahl al-Hudnah 166-167 J 2
Plains, GA 78-79 G 4-5
Plains, KS 76-77 D 4
Plains, MT 66-67 F 2
Plains, TX 76-77 C 6
Plainview, MN 70-71 DE 3
Plainview, NE 68-69 GH 4
Plainview, TX 64-65 F 5
Plainville, KS 68-69 G 6
Plainwell, MI 70-71 H 4
Plamqang 152-153 MN 10
Plana Cays 88-89 K 3
Planada, CA 74-75 CD 4
Planadas 94-95 D 6
Planaltina 92-93 K 8
Planalto 106-107 L 1
Planalto Brasileiro 92-93 KL 8
Planalto da Borborema 92-93 M 6
Planalto do Mato Grosso 92-93 HJ 7
Planalto Maracanaquará 98-99 M 5
Planchon, Portillo del — 106-107 B 5
Plane, Île — = Jazīrat al-Maṭrūḥ 166-167 M 1
Planegger Holz 130 II a 2
Planeta Rica 94-95 D 3
Planetario Humboldt 91 II c 2
Planetarium 85 III b 2
Planicie de los Vientos 106-107 E 7
Planicie Los Tres Chañares 106-107 EF 7
Plankinton, SD 68-69 G 4
Plano, TX 76-77 F 6
Planta de Evaporación 91 I d 1
Plantation, FL 80-81 c 3
Plant City, FL 80-81 b 2-3
Planten un Blomen 130 I a 1
Planteurs = Ghābat al-Mushajjarīn 166-167 F 2-G 1
Plao Sieng = Buôn Plao Sieng 150-151 FG 6
Plaquemine, LA 78-79 D 5
Plasencia 120-121 D 8
Plast 132-133 L 7
Plaster City, CA 74-75 EF 6
Plaster Rock 63 C 4
Plaston 174-175 J 3
Plastun 132-133 a 9
Plata, Cordón de — 106-107 C 4
Plata, Isla de la — 92-93 C 5
Plata, La — [CO] 92-93 D 4
Plata, La — [RA] 111 E 5
Plata, Río de la — 111 EF 5
Platanal 94-95 J 6
Plate, River — = Río de la Plata 111 E 4-F 5
Plateau Central = Cao Nguyên Trung Phần 148-149 E 4
Plateau de Basso 164-165 J 5
Plateau de la Lukenie Supérieure 172 D 2
Plateau de la Manika 172 E 3-4
Plateau de Langres 120-121 K 5
Plateau de Millevaches 120-121 HJ 6
Plateau de Trung Phần = Cao Nguyên Trung Phần 148-149 E 4
Plateau du Coteau des Prairies 64-65 G 2-3
Plateau du Coteau du Missouri 64-65 FG 2
Plateau du Djado 164-165 G 4
Plateau du Tademaït = Tādmāit 164-165 E 3
Plateau du Tampoketsa = Causse du Kelifely 172 HJ 5
Plateau of the Shotts = At-Tall 164-165 D 2-E 1
Plateau of Tibet = Jang Thang 142-143 E-G 5
Plateaux 168-169 F 4
Plateaux du Nord-Mossi 168-169 E 2
Platen, Kapp — 116-117 lm 4
Platero 102-103 D 7
Platinum, AK 56-57 D 6
Plato 94-95 D 3
plato Mangyšlak 134-135 G 2
plato Putorana 132-133 RS 4
plato Ust'urt 132-133 K 9
Platovskaja = Bud'onnovskaja 126-127 KL 3
Platrand 174-175 H 4
Platte, SD 68-69 G 4
Platte City, MO 70-71 C 6
Platte River [USA, Missouri, Iowa] 70-71 C 5
Platte River [USA, Nebraska] 64-65 FG 3
Platteville, CO 68-69 D 5
Platteville, WI 70-71 E 4
Platt National Park 76-77 F 5
Plattsburg, MO 70-71 C 6
Plattsburgh, NY 64-65 LM 3
Plattsmouth, NE 70-71 BC 5
Plauen 118 F 3
Pļaviņas 124-125 EF 5
Plavsk 124-125 L 7
Playa del Carmen 86-87 R 7
Playa de Rey, Los Angeles-, CA 83 III b 2
Playadito 106-107 JK 1
Playa Larga 88-89 F 3
Playas 92-93 C 5
Playas, Las — 96-97 A 4
Playa Vicente 86-87 N 9
Playgreen Lake 61 J 3-4
Playosa, La — 106-107 F 4
Plaza, ND 68-69 F 1
Plaza del Oro, Houston-, TX 85 III b 2
Plaza de Mayo 110 III b 1
Plaza de Toros 113 III b 2
Plaza Huincul 111 BC 5
Plaza Park, NJ 84 III d 1
Pleasant Grove, UT 66-67 H 5
Pleasant Hill, MO 70-71 C 6
Pleasanton, KS 70-71 C 6
Pleasanton, TX 76-77 E 8
Pleasant Ridge, MI 84 II b 2
Pleasant Valley, OR 66-67 E 3
Pleasant View, MA 64-65 DE 2
Pleasantville, NJ 72-73 JK 5
Pleiku 148-149 E 4
Pleniţa 122-123 K 3
Plenty, Bay of — 158-159 P 7
Plenty Creek 161 II c 1
Plentywood, MT 68-69 D 1
Pleščenicy 124-125 FG 6
Pleseck 132-133 G 5
Plessis-Trévise, le — 129 I d 2
Plessisville 72-73 KL 1
Pleszew 118 HJ 3
Plétipi, Lac — 63 A 2
Plettenbergbaai 174-175 E 8
Plettenberg Bay = Plettenbergbaai 174-175 E 8
Pleven 122-123 L 4
Plevna, MT 68-69 D 2
Plitvice 122-123 F 3
Plitvička Jezera 122-123 FG 3
Pljevlja 122-123 H 4
Płock 118 JK 2
Ploieşti 122-123 LM 3
Plomb du Cantal 120-121 J 6
Plomer 106-107 H 5
Plonge, Lac la — 61 E 3
Pl'os 124-125 N 5
Ploskoje [SU, Rossijskaja SFSR] 124-125 M 7
Ploskoš' 124-125 H 5
Plottier 106-107 CD 7
Plovdiv 122-123 L 4
Plover Islands 58-59 K 1
Pluit, Jakarta- 154 IV a 1
Pluma, El — 108-109 DE 6
Plumas, Las — 111 C 6
Plummer, ID 66-67 E 2
Plummer, MN 70-71 BC 2
Plummer, Mount — 58-59 GH 6
Plumtree 172 E 6
Plungė 124-125 CD 6
Plush, OR 66-67 D 4
Pl'ussa [SU, place] 124-125 G 4
Pl'ussa [SU, river] 124-125 G 4
Plymouth, CA 74-75 C 3
Plymouth, IN 70-71 GH 5
Plymouth, MA 72-73 L 4
Plymouth, NC 80-81 H 3
Plymouth, NH 72-73 KL 3
Plymouth, PA 72-73 HJ 4
Plymouth, WI 70-71 FG 4
Plymouth [GB] 119 DE 6
Plymouth [West Indies] 88-89 P 6
Plymouth Meeting, PA 84 III b 1
Plzeň 118 F 4
Pnom Penh = Phnom Penh 148-149 D 4
Pô [HV] 164-165 D 6
Po [I] 122-123 D 3
Pobé 164-165 E 7
Pobeda, gora — 132-133 c 4

Pobedino 132-133 b 8
Pobedy, pik — 134-135 MN 2
Población 102-103 C 4
Pobohe = Pohe 146-147 E 6
Pocahontas 60 HJ 3
Pocahontas, AR 78-79 D 2
Pocahontas, IA 70-71 C 4
Pocão, Salto — 98-99 L 5
Poção, Serra do — 100-101 F 4
Pocatello, ID 64-65 D 3
Poccha, Río — 96-97 C 6
Počep 124-125 J 7
Pocho, Sierra de — 106-107 E 3
P'och'ŏn 144-145 F 4
Pochutla 86-87 M 10
Pochval'nyj 132-133 cd 4
Pochvistnevo 124-125 ST 7
Pocillas 106-107 A 6
Pocinhos 100-101 FG 4
Počinki 124-125 P 6
Počinok [SU, Smolenskaja Oblast'] 124-125 J 6
Pocito, El — 104-105 E 4
Pocitos, Salar — 104-105 C 9
Pocklington Reef 148-149 j 7
Pocoata 104-105 C 6
Poço Comprido, Riacho — 100-101 C 5-E 6
Poço Danta, Serra — 100-101 EF 6
Poço das Trincheiras 100-101 F 5
Poções 92-93 LM 7
Pocomoke City, MD 72-73 J 5
Pocomoke Sound 80-81 HJ 2
Poconé 92-93 H 8
Poço Redondo 100-101 F 5
Poços [BR ↗ Ibotirama] 100-101 C 7
Poços [BR ← Remanso] 100-101 C 5
Poços de Caldas 92-93 K 9
Poço Verde 100-101 E 6
Podberezje 124-125 H 5
Podborovje 124-125 K 4
Podčinnyj 126-127 M 1
Poddorje 124-125 H 5
Podgorenskij 126-127 J 1
Podgorica = Titograd 122-123 H 4
Podgornoje 132-133 P 6
Podgorodnoje ↑ Dnepropetrovsk 126-127 G 2
Podile 140 D 3
Podkamennaja Tunguska 132-133 R 5
Podkova 122-123 L 5
Podol'sk 124-125 L 6
Podol'skaja vozvyšennost' 126-127 B 2-D 3
Podor 164-165 AB 5
Podosinovec 124-125 Q 3
Podporožje 132-133 EF 5
Podravska Slatina 122-123 GH 3
Podsosenje 124-125 NO 2
Podsvilje 124-125 FG 6
Podtesovo 132-133 R 6
Pod'uga 124-125 N 3
Podvoločisk 126-127 BC 2
Poelela, Lagoa — 174-175 L 3
Po-êrh-t'a-la Chou = Bortala Monggol Zizhizhou 142-143 E 2-3
Pofadder 172 CD 7
Pogamasing 62 L 3
Pogar 124-125 J 7
Poggibonsi 122-123 D 4
Pogibi 132-133 b 7
Pogoreloje Gorodišče 124-125 KL 5
Pogrebišče 126-127 D 2
Pogromni Volcano 58-59 a 2
Pogyndeno 132-133 fg 4
Poh 152-153 P 6
Poh, Teluk — 152-153 P 6
P'oha-dong 144-145 GH 2
Po Hai = Bo Hai 142-143 M 4
Pohai, Gulf of — = Bohai Haixia 142-143 N 4
Po-hai Hai-hsia = Bohai Haixia 142-143 N 4
Po-hai Wan = Bohai Wan 146-147 FG 2
P'ohang 142-143 OP 4
Pohe 146-147 E 6
Pohjanmaa 116-117 K 6-M 5
Pohjois-Karjalan lääni 116-117 N 6
Pōhrī = Pauri 138-139 F 5
Pohsien = Bo Xian 142-143 LM 5
Pohue Bay 78-79 e 3
Pöide 124-125 D 4
Poinsett, Lake — 68-69 H 3
Point Abbaye 70-71 FG 2
Point Alexander 158-159 G 2
Point Arena 74-75 AB 3
Point Arena, CA 74-75 AB 3
Point Arguello 74-75 C 5
Point au Fer 78-79 D 6
Point Baker, AK 58-59 w 8
Point Barrow 56-57 EF 3
Point Blaze 158-159 EF 2
Point Bonita 83 I a 2
Point Brown 160 A 4
Point Buchon 74-75 C 5
Point Cabrillo 74-75 AB 3
Point Calimere 134-135 MN 8
Point Cloates 158-159 B 4
Point Conception 64-65 B 5
Point Culver 158-159 DE 6
Point Detour 70-71 G 3
Pointe-à-la-Fregate 63 D 3
Pointe a la Hache, LA 78-79 E 6
Pointe-à-Maurier 63 G 2
Pointe-à-Pitre 64-65 O 8
Pointe au Baril Station 72-73 F 2
Pointe Aux Barques 72-73 E 2
Pointe aux Pins 72-73 F 3
Pointe Behágue 92-93 J 3-4
Pointe de Barfleur 120-121 G 4
Pointe de la Gombe 170 IV a 1
Pointe della Parata 122-123 BC 5
Pointe de Penmarch 120-121 E 5
Pointe des Consuls 170 I a 1
Pointe-des-Monts 63 C 3
Pointe du Bois 62 B 2
Pointe du Raz 120-121 E 4
Pointe Isère 92-93 J 3
Pointe Mbamou 170 IV a 1
Pointe-Noire 172 B 2
Pointe Pescade 170 I a 1
Pointe Saint Mathieu 120-121 E 4
Point Europa 120-121 E 10
Point Franklin 58-59 H 1
Point Gellibrand 161 II b 2
Point Harbor, NC 80-81 J 2
Point Hibbs 160 b 3
Point Judith 72-73 L 4
Point Lake 56-57 O 4
Point Lay, AK 58-59 EF 2
Point Leamington 63 J 3
Point Lobos 83 I a 2
Point Marion, PA 72-73 G 5
Point of Ayre 119 DE 4
Point of Pines 84 I c 2
Point of Rocks, WY 68-69 B 5
Point Ormond 161 II b 2
Point Pedro = Pēduru Tuḍuwa 134-135 N 9
Point Petre 72-73 H 3
Point Pinos 74-75 BC 4
Point Pleasant, NJ 72-73 JK 4
Point Pleasant, WV 72-73 EF 5
Point Prawle 119 E 6
Point Reyes 74-75 B 3-4
Point Richmond 83 I b 1
Point Roberts, WA 66-67 B 1
Point Saint George 66-67 A 5
Point San Pablo 83 I b 1
Point San Pedro 83 I b 1
Point Spencer 58-59 D 4
Point Sur 74-75 BC 4
Point Vicente 74-75 D 6
Point Westall 160 AB 4
Point Weyland 160 AB 4
Point Whidbey 160 B 5
Poipet 150-151 D 6
Poisson Blanc, Lac — 72-73 J 1-2
Poitevin, Marais — 120-121 G 5
Poitiers 120-121 H 5
Poitou 120-121 GH 5
Poivre, Côte du — = Malabar Coast 134-135 L 8-M 9
Poix 120-121 HJ 4
Pojarkovo 132-133 Y 8
Pojezierze Chełmińskre 118 J 2
Pojezierze Mazurskie 118 K 2-L 1
Pojige, Río — 104-105 D 4
Pojo [BOL] 104-105 D 5
Pokaran 138-139 C 4
Pokataroo 160 J 2
Pokča 124-125 V 2
Pokegama Lake 70-71 CD 2
Pok Fu Lam 155 I a 2
Pokhara 134-135 N 5
Pok Liu Chau 155 I a 2
Poko 172 E 1
Poko Mount 58-59 F 2
Pokrovka [SU ↖ Abdulino] 124-125 T 7
Pokrovka [SU ↘ Buzuluk] 124-125 T 8
Pokrovsk 132-133 Y 5
Pokrovsk = Engels 124-125 Q 8
Pokrovskoje [SU, Archangel'skaja Oblast'] 124-125 M 1
Pokrovskoje, Moskva- 113 V c 3
Pokrovskoje-Strešnevo, Moskva- 113 V b 2
Pokrovsk-Ural'skij 132-133 K 5
Pokšen'ga 124-125 O 2
Pola [SU, place] 124-125 H 5
Pola [SU, river] 124-125 J 5
Polacca Wash 74-75 H 5
Pola de Siero 120-121 E 7
Polādpur 140 A 1-2
Polān [IR] 134-135 J 5
Poland 118 H-L 3
Pol'any [SU, Moskovskaja Oblast'] 113 V b 4
Pol'arnyj [SU, Indigirka] 132-133 c 3
Pol'arnyj Ural 132-133 LM 4
Polar Plateau 53 A 31-6
Polathane 136-137 H 2
Polatlı 134-135 C 3
Polavaram 140 E 2
Polcirkeln 116-117 J 4
Polcura 106-107 B 6
Poldarsa 124-125 PQ 3
Polesje 124-125 E 8-H 7
Polessk 118 K 1
Polewali 152-153 N 7
Polgahawela 140 E 7
Pōlgyo 144-145 F 5
Poli 164-165 G 7
Poli = Boli 142-143 P 2
Policastro, Golfo di — 122-123 F 5-6
Police Headquarters 85 III b 1
Polillo Islands 148-149 H 3-4
Poliny Osipenko 132-133 a 7
Pólis 136-137 E 5
Polist' 124-125 H 5
Polk, PA 72-73 FG 4
Pollāchchi = Pollāchi 140 C 5
Pollāchi 140 C 5
Polledo 106-107 E 5
Pollensa 120-121 J 9
Pollino 122-123 G 5-6
Pollock, ID 66-67 E 3
Pollock, LA 78-79 C 5
Pollock, SD 68-69 FG 3
Pollockville 61 C 5
Polmak 116-117 N 2
Polna [SU] 124-125 G 4
Polnovo-Seliger 124-125 J 5
Polo, IL 70-71 F 5
Polo = Boluo 146-147 E 10
Polock 124-125 G 6
Pologi 126-127 H 3
Polonio, Cabo — 111 F 4
Polonnaruwa 140 E 7
Polonnoje 126-127 C 1
Polotn'anyj 124-125 KL 6
Polousnyj kr'až 132-133 bc 4
Polovniki 124-125 S 2
Polovo 124-125 J 5
Polson, MT 66-67 FG 2
Poltava 126-127 G 2
Poltavakaja = Krasnoarmejskaja 126-127 J 4
Poltorack = Aščhabad 134-135 HJ 3
Pōltsamaa 124-125 EF 4
Pol'udov Kamen' 124-125 V 3
Pol'udov kr'až 124-125 V 3
Poluj [SU, place] 132-133 MN 4
Poluj [SU, river] 132-133 M 4
Polunočnoje 132-133 L 5
poluostrov Gusinaja Zeml'a 132-133 HJ 3
poluostrov Jamal 132-133 MN 3
poluostrov Javaj 132-133 NO 3
poluostrov Kanin 132-133 GH 4
poluostrov Koni 132-133 d 6
poluostrov Pešnoj 126-127 P 3
poluostrov Pjagina 132-133 de 6
poluostrov Rybačij 132-133 EF 4
poluostrov Sara 126-127 O 7
poluostrov Tajgonos 132-133 f 5
poluostrov Tajmyr 132-133 R-U 2
poluostrov T'ub-Karagan 126-127 P 4
Polūr 140 D 4
Pōlva 124-125 F 4
Polvaredas 106-107 C 4
Polvorines, General Sarmiento-los — 110 III ab 1
Polýaigos 122-123 L 7
Polýchnitos 122-123 LM 6
Polýgyros 122-123 K 5
Polynesia 156-157 J 4-5
Poma, La — 111 C 2
Pomabamba 96-97 C 6
Pomán 104-105 C 11
Pomarão 120-121 D 10
Pomasi, Cerro de — 92-93 E 8
Pomasi, Nevados de — 96-97 F 9
Pomba, Rio — 102-103 L 4
Pombal [BR] 92-93 M 6
Pombal [P] 120-121 C 9
Pombeba, Ilha da — 110 I b 2
Pombetsu = Honbetsu 144-145 cd 2
Pomerania 118 G 2-H 1
Pomeranian Bay = Pommersche Bucht 118 FG 1
Pomeroy, OH 72-73 EF 5
Pomeroy, WA 66-67 E 2
Pomfret 174-175 E 3
Pomme de Terre River 70-71 C 2-3
Pommersche Bucht 118 FG 1
Pomona, CA 74-75 E 5-6
Pomona, KS 70-71 C 6
Pomona, MO 78-79 D 2
Pomona [Namibia] 174-175 A 4
Pomona [RA] 106-107 E 7
Pomorie 122-123 MN 4
Pomorskij bereg 124-125 K 1-L 2
Pomošnaja 126-127 E 2
Pomo Tsho 138-139 MN 3
Pomozdino 124-125 U 2
Pompano Beach, FL 80-81 cd 3
Pompeia 102-103 G 5
Pompeji 122-123 F 5
Pompeston Creek 84 III d 1-2
Pompéu 102-103 K 3
Pompeys Pillar, MT 66-67 JK 2
Ponape 208 F 2
Ponass Lake 61 F 4
Ponazyrevo 124-125 Q 4
Ponca, NE 68-69 H 4
Ponca City, OK 64-65 G 4
Ponca Creek 68-69 G 4
Ponce 64-65 N 8
Ponce de Leon, FL 78-79 FG 5
Ponce de Leon Bay 80-81 c 4
Poncha Springs, CO 68-69 C 6
Ponchatoula, LA 78-79 D 5
Ponda 140 B 3
Pondaung Range = Pônnyâ Taung 141 D 4-5
Pond Creek 68-69 E 6
Pond Creek, OK 76-77 F 4
Pondicheri = Pondicherry 134-135 MN 8
Pondicherry 134-135 MN 8
Pond Inlet [CDN, bay] 56-57 VW 3
Pond Inlet [CDN, place] 56-57 V 3
Pondo Dsong 142-143 G 5
Pondoland 174-175 H 6
Pondosa, CA 66-67 C 5
Pondosa, OR 66-67 E 3
Ponds Creek 161 II b 1
Ponedjel = Pandēlys 124-125 E 5
Ponferrada 120-121 D 7
Pong 148-149 CD 3
Pongba 138-139 K 2
Pong Klua 150-151 BC 3
Pongnim-ni = Pōlgyo 144-145 F 5
Pongo de Manseriche 92-93 D 5
Pongola [ZA, place] 174-175 J 4
Pongola [ZA, river] 172 F 7
Pongolapoortdam 174-175 JK 4
Ponizovje [SU, Smolenskaja Oblast'] 124-125 H 6
Ponley 150-151 E 6
Pônnâgyûn 141 C 5
Ponnaiyār 140 DE 5
Ponnāni [IND, place] 140 B 5
Ponnāni [IND, river] 140 C 5
Ponneri 140 E 4
Ponnūru 140 E 2
Pônnyâ Taung 141 D 4-5
Ponoj 132-133 FG 4
Ponoka 60 L 3
Ponomar'ovka 124-125 TU 7
Ponorogo 152-153 J 9
Ponta Albina 172 B 5
Ponta Alta do Norte 98-99 P 10
Ponta Anastácio 106-107 M 3
Ponta Apaga Fogo 100-101 E 7
Ponta Bojuru 106-107 M 3
Ponta Cantagalo 102-103 H 7
Ponta Christóvão Pereira 106-107 M 3
Ponta Corumiquara 100-101 E 2
Ponta Curuçá 98-99 P 5
Ponta da Baleia 100-101 E 9
Ponta da Barra 174-175 L 2
Ponta da Barra Falsa 174-175 L 2
Ponta da Cancela 100-101 G 4
Ponta da Mutuoca 100-101 B 1
Ponta da Pescada 98-99 NO 3
Ponta das Palmeirinhas 172 B 3
Ponta da Taquara 102-103 HJ 7
Ponta de Atalaia 98-99 P 5
Ponta de Corumbaú 100-101 E 9
Ponta de Iguapé 100-101 EF 2
Ponta Delgada 204-205 E 5
Ponta de Mostardas 106-107 M 3
Ponta de Mucuripe 92-93 M 5
Ponta de Mundaú 100-101 E 2
Ponta de Pedras 92-93 JK 5
Ponta de Regência 92-93 M 8
Ponta de Santa Rita 100-101 G 3
Ponta de Santo Antônio 100-101 GH 4
Ponta do Arpoador [BR, Rio de Janeiro] 110 I bc 2
Ponta do Arpoador [BR, São Paulo] 102-103 J 6
Ponta do Aruacá 100-101 B 1
Ponta do Boi 102-103 K 6
Ponta do Calcanhar 92-93 M 6-N 5
Ponta do Coconho 100-101 G 3
Ponta do Conselho 100-101 E 7
Ponta do Coqueiros 100-101 G 4
Ponta do Flamengo 100-101 G 3
Ponta do Gameleira 100-101 G 3
Ponta do Juatinga 92-93 L 9
Ponta do Maceió 100-101 E 3
Ponta do Manguinho 92-93 M 7
Ponta do Morro, Serra da — 100-101 C 7
Ponta do Mutá 100-101 E 7
Ponta do Pinheiro 102-103 H 7
Ponta dos Cajuás 92-93 M 5
Ponta dos Latinos 106-107 L 4
Ponta dos Patos 100-101 E 2
Ponta do Tapes 106-107 M 3
Ponta do Tubarão 100-101 FG 3
Ponta do Zumui 100-101 B 1
Ponta Grande 100-101 E 9
Ponta Grossa [BR, Amapá] 92-93 K 4
Ponta Grossa [BR, Ceará] 100-101 F 3
Ponta Grossa [BR, Paraná] 111 F 3
Ponta Itacolomi 100-101 BC 1-2
Ponta Itaipu 102-103 J 6
Ponta Jeridoaquara 100-101 DE 2
Pontal 102-103 HJ 4
Pontal, Rio do — 100-101 D 5
Ponta Lazão 100-101 C 2
Pontal dos Ilhéus 100-101 E 8
Pontalina 102-103 H 2
Ponta Maiaú 98-99 P 5
Ponta Naufragados 102-103 HJ 7
Ponta Negra 100-101 G 3
Ponta Negra = Pointe-Noire 172 B 2
Ponta Paza 100-101 F 6
Ponta Porã 92-93 HJ 9
Ponta Rasa 106-107 LM 3
Ponta Redonda 92-93 M 5
Pontarlier 120-121 KL 5
Ponta São Sebastião 172 G 6
Ponta São Simão 106-107 M 3
Pontas dos Tres Irmãos 92-93 M 6-N 5
Ponta Tabajé 92-93 LM 5
Ponta Tropia 100-101 D 2
Pontault-Combault 129 I d 2
Ponta Verde 100-101 G 5
Pont Champlain 82 I b 2
Pontchartrain, Lake — 64-65 HJ 5
Pontchartrain Beach, New Orleans-, LA 85 I b 1
Pontchartrain Park 85 I b 1
Pontchartrain Shores, LA 85 I a 1
Pont-du-Fahs = Al-Faḥṣ 166-167 LM 1
Ponte Alta do Bom Jesus 100-101 A 7
Ponte da Amizade 102-103 E 6
Ponte de Itabapoana 102-103 M 4
Ponte de Pedra [BR ↘ Cuiabá] 102-103 E 2
Ponte de Pedra [BR ↖ Diamantino] 92-93 H 7
Ponte Firme 102-103 JK 3
Ponteix 61 E 6
Ponte-Leccia 122-123 C 4
Ponte Nova 92-93 L 9
Ponte Presidente Costa e Silva 110 I bc 2
Pontes-e-Lacerda 92-93 H 8
Pontevedra 120-121 C 7
Pontevedra, Merlo- 110 III a 2
Ponthierville = Ubundu 172 DE 2
Pontiac, IL 70-71 F 5
Pontiac, MI 64-65 K 3
Pontianak 148-149 E 7
Pontic Mountains 134-135 C-E 2
Pontivy 120-121 F 4
Pont Jacques Cartier 82 I b 1
Ponto Galeria, Roma- 113 II a 2
Pontoise 120-121 HJ 4
Pontotoc, MS 78-79 E 3
Pontrèmoli 122-123 CD 3
Pont-Viau 82 I a 1
Pont Victoria 82 I b 2
Pony, MT 66-67 GH 3
Ponza 122-123 E 5
Ponziane, Isole — 122-123 E 5
Poochera 160 B 4
Poole 119 E 6
Pool Malebo 172 C 2
Poona = Pune 134-135 L 7
Pooncarie 158-159 H 6
Poopó 92-93 F 8
Poopó, Lago de — 92-93 F 8
Poorman, AK 58-59 K 4
Poortje = Poortjie 174-175 E 6
Poortjie 174-175 E 6
Pōōsaspea 124-125 DE 4
Popa = Pôpkâ Taungdeik 141 D 5
Popa = Pulau Kofiau 148-149 JK 7
Po-pai = Bobai 146-147 BC 10
Popasnaja 126-127 J 2
Popayán 92-93 D 4
Popeljany = Papilė 124-125 D 5
Popeys Pillar, MT 68-69 BC 2
Popigaj 132-133 UV 3
Popihe = Pohe 146-147 E 6
Popilta Lake 160 E 4
Po-p'ing = Boping 146-147 F 3
Pôpkâ Taungdeik 141 D 5
Poplar, MT 68-69 D 1
Poplar, WI 70-71 E 2
Poplar, London- 129 II bc 1
Poplar Bluff, MO 64-65 H 4
Poplar Hill 62 B 1
Poplar River [CDN] 62 A 1
Poplar River [USA] 68-69 D 1
Poplar River, West Fork — 68-69 CD 1
Poplarville, MS 78-79 E 5
Popocatépetl 64-65 G 8
Popof Island 58-59 cd 2
Popoh 152-153 J 10
Popokabaka 172 C 3
Popondetta 148-149 N 8
Popovo 122-123 M 4
Poppenbüttel, Hamburg- 130 I b 1
Poprad [CS, place] 118 K 4
Poprad [CS, river] 118 K 4
Pōpsŏngp'o 144-145 F 5
Poptun 86-87 Q 9
Porādaha 138-139 M 6
Porāli 134-135 K 5
Porangatu 92-93 K 7
Porbandar 134-135 K 6
Porbunder = Porbandar 134-135 K 6
Porce, Río — 94-95 D 4
Porcher Island 60 B 3
Porchov 124-125 G 5
Porciúncula 102-103 LM 4
Porco 104-105 D 6
Porcos, Ilha dos — 102-103 K 5
Porcos, Rio dos — 100-101 B 7
Porcupine, AK 58-59 T 7
Porcupine Creek 68-69 C 1
Porcupine Creek, AK 58-59 M 3
Porcupine Hills 60 K 4-5
Porcupine Mountain 56-57 Q 7
Porcupine Plain 61 G 4
Porcupine River 56-57 H 4
Pordenone 122-123 E 2-3
Pore 92-93 E 3
Porecatu 102-103 G 5
Porečje [SU, Belorusskaja SSR] 124-125 E 7
Porez 124-125 S 5
Pórfido, Punta — 108-109 G 3
Pori 116-117 J 7
Porirua 161 F 5
Porjus 116-117 HJ 4
Porlamar 92-93 G 2
Pornic 120-121 F 5
Poroma [BOL, Chuquisaca] 104-105 D 6
Poroma [BOL, La Paz] 104-105 C 4
Poronajsk 132-133 b 8
Porong, Stung — 150-151 E 6
Porongo, Cerro — 106-107 D 3
Porongos 106-107 L 2
Porongos, Laguna de los — 106-107 F 2-3
Poroshiri-dake 144-145 c 2
Porosozero 124-125 J 2
Porotos, Punta — 106-107 B 2
Porpoise Bay 53 C 13
Porquis Junction 62 L 2
Porsangerfjord 116-117 LM 2
Porsangerhalvøya 116-117 L 2
Porsea 150-151 B 11
Porsgrunn 116-117 CD 8
Porsuk çayı 136-137 D 3
Portachuelo 92-93 G 8
Portadown 119 C 4
Portage, AK 58-59 N 6
Portage, UT 66-67 G 5
Portage, WI 70-71 F 4
Portage-la-Prairie 56-57 R 8
Portage Park, Chicago-, IL 83 II b 1
Portal, ND 68-69 E 1
Port Alberni 56-57 LM 8
Port Albert [AUS] 160 H 7
Port Albert [CDN] 72-73 EF 3
Portalegre 120-121 D 9
Portales, NM 64-65 F 5
Port Alexander, AK 58-59 v 8
Port Alfred 172 E 8
Port Alice 60 D 4
Port Allegany, PA 72-73 GH 4
Port Allen, LA 78-79 D 5
Port Angeles, WA 66-67 B 1
Port Antonio 64-65 L 8
Port Armstrong, AK 58-59 v 8
Port Arthur 160 cd 3
Port Arthur, TX 64-65 H 6
Port Arthur = Lüda-Lüshun 142-143 MN 4
Port Ashton, AK 58-59 N 6
Port Augusta 158-159 G 6
Port au Port 63 G 3
Port au Port Bay 63 G 3
Port au Port Peninsula 63 G 3
Port-au-Prince 64-65 M 8
Port Austin, MI 72-73 E 2
Port-Bergé 172 J 5
Port Blair 134-135 P 8
Port Blandford 63 J 3
Port Borden 63 E 4
Port-Bou 120-121 J 7
Port-Bouet 168-169 DE 4
Port Brega = Marsā al-Burayqah 164-165 H 2
Port Burwell [CDN, Ontario] 72-73 F 3
Port Burwell [CDN, Quebec] 56-57 XY 5
Port Canning 138-139 M 6
Port Cartier 56-57 X 7
Port-Cartier-Sept-Îles, Parc provincial de — 63 C 2
Port Chalmers 158-159 O 9
Port Chilkoot 58-59 U 7
Port Clarence 58-59 D 4
Port Clements 60 AB 3
Port Clinton, OH 72-73 E 4
Port Colborne 72-73 G 3
Port Coquitlam 66-67 B 1
Port Curtis 158-159 K 4
Port Daniel 63 D 3
Port Darwin 111 E 8
Port Davey 158-159 HJ 8
Port de Ilheo Bay = Sandvisbai 174-175 A 2
Port de Kinshasa 170 IV a 1
Port-de-Paix 88-89 K 5
Port Dickson 150-151 C 11
Port Dunford = Buur Gaabo 172 H 2
Port Eads, LA 78-79 E 6
Porte d'Annam = Đeo Ngang 150-151 F 3-4
Porte des Morts 70-71 G 3
Port Edward [CDN] 60 B 2
Port Edward [ZA] 174-175 J 6
Porteira, Serra das — 100-101 F 5
Porteirinha 102-103 L 1
Portel [BR] 92-93 J 5
Portela 102-103 M 4
Port Elgin [CDN, New Brunswick] 63 DE 4-5
Port Elgin [CDN, Ontario] 72-73 F 2
Port Elizabeth 172 E 8
Porteña 106-107 FG 3
Porteño, Río — 104-105 G 9
Porterdale, GA 80-81 DE 4
Port Erin 119 D 4
Porterville 172 CD 8
Porterville, CA 74-75 D 4-5
Portes de l'Enfer 172 E 3
Port Essington 56-57 KL 7
Portete, Bahía de — 94-95 EF 1
Port-Étienne = Nawādhību 164-165 A 4
Portezuelo 106-107 B 1-2
Portezuelo Ascotán 104-105 BC 7
Portezuelo de Huaitiquina 104-105 C 8
Portezuelo de Socompa 104-105 B 9
Portezuelo Quilhuiri 104-105 B 6
Port Fairy 158-159 H 7
Port-Francqui = Ilebo 172 D 2
Port Fu'ad = Būr Sādāt 173 C 2
Port-Gentil 172 A 2
Port Gibson, MS 78-79 D 5
Port Graham, AK 58-59 M 7
Port-Gueydon = Azfūn 166-167 J 1
Port Harcourt 164-165 F 8
Port Hardy 56-57 L 7
Port Harrison = Inoucdjouac 56-57 V 6
Port Hawkesbury 63 F 5
Port Hedland 158-159 C 4
Port Heiden 58-59 d 1
Port Heiden, AK 58-59 de 1
Port Henry, NY 72-73 K 2-3
Port Herald = Nsanje 172 G 5
Porthill, ID 66-67 E 1
Port Hood 63 F 4
Port Hope 72-73 G 2-3
Port Hope, MI 72-73 E 3
Port Houston Turning, Houston-, TX 85 III b 1
Port Hudson, LA 78-79 D 5
Port Hueneme, CA 74-75 D 5
Port Huron, MI 64-65 K 3
Portile de Fier 122-123 K 3
Port Iljič 126-127 O 7
Portillo 106-107 B 4
Portillo, Cordón de — 106-107 C 4
Portillo, Paso del — 106-107 BC 3
Portillo de los Patos 104-105 B 10
Portillo del Planchon 106-107 B 5
Portillo Puyehue 108-109 CD 3
Portimão 120-121 C 10
Port Isabel, TX 76-77 F 9
Port Jackson [AUS] 161 I b 2
Port Jackson [NZ] 161 F 3
Port Jefferson, NY 72-73 K 4
Port Jervis, NY 72-73 J 4
Port Keats 158-159 EF 2
Port Kembla, Wollongong- 158-159 K 6
Port Kennedy, PA 84 III a 1
Port Kenny 158-159 F 6
Port Klang 150-151 C 11
Port Lairge = Waterford 119 C 5
Portland, IN 70-71 H 5
Portland, ME 64-65 MN 3
Portland, MI 70-71 H 4
Portland, OR 64-65 B 2
Portland, TN 78-79 F 2
Portland, TX 76-77 F 9
Portland [AUS, New South Wales] 160 JK 4
Portland [AUS, Victoria] 158-159 H 7
Portland [CDN] 72-73 HJ 2
Portland = Dyrhólaey 116-117 d 3
Portland, Cape — 160 c 2
Portland Canal 58-59 x 9
Portland Inlet 58-59 xy 9
Portland Island 161 H 4
Portland Point 88-89 H 6
Portland Promontory 56-57 UV 6
Port Laoise 119 C 5
Port Lavaca, TX 76-77 F 8
Port Lincoln 158-159 FG 6
Port Lions, AK 58-59 KL 8
Port Loko 164-165 B 7
Port Louis [MS] 204-205 N 11
Port-Lyautey = Al-Q'nitrah 164-165 C 2
Port Mac Donell 160 DE 7
Port MacNeill 60 D 4
Port Macquarie 160 L 3
Port Maitland 63 C 5-6
Port Maria 88-89 H 5
Port Mayaca, FL 80-81 c 3
Port Melbourne, Melbourne- 161 II b 1-2
Port-Menier 63 D 3
Port Moller 58-59 c 1-2
Port Moller, AK 58-59 cd 1
Port Moody 66-67 B 1
Port Moresby 148-149 N 8
Port Mouton 63 D 6
Port Musgrave 158-159 H 2
Port Natal = Durban 172 F 7
Port Neches, TX 78-79 C 6
Port Neill 160 C 5
Port Nellie Juan, AK 58-59 NO 6
Port Nelson [BS] 88-89 J 3
Port Nelson [CDN, bay] 56-57 S 6
Port Nelson [CDN, place] 56-57 S 6
Portneuf, Rivière — 63 AB 3
Port Neville 60 DE 4
Port Nolloth 172 C 7
Port Norris, NJ 72-73 J 5
Porto [BR] 100-101 C 2
Porto [P] 120-121 C 8
Porto Acre 92-93 F 6
Porto Alegre [BR, Bahia] 100-101 D 7
Porto Alegre [BR, Pará] 98-99 M 7
Porto Alegre [BR, Rio Grando do Sul] 111 FG 4
Porto Alegre do Sul 102-103 F 4
Porto Alexandre 172 B 5
Porto Alexandre, Parque National de — 172 B 5
Porto Amazonas 102-103 GH 6
Porto Amboim 172 B 4
Porto Amélia = Pemba 172 H 4
Porto Artur 92-93 HJ 7
Porto Barra do Ivinheima 102-103 EF 5
Porto Belo [BR] 102-103 H 7
Portobelo [PA] 64-65 b 1
Porto Bicentenário 98-99 G 10
Port O'Brien, AK 58-59 KL 8
Porto Britânia 102-103 EF 6
Porto Calvo 100-101 G 6
Porto Camargo 102-103 F 5
Porto Caneco 92-93 HJ 7
Porto Conceição 92-93 H 8
Porto da Fôlha 100-101 F 5-6
Porto das Caixas 102-103 L 5
Porto de Más 92-93 H 8
Porto de Mós [BR] 92-93 J 5
Porto 15 de Novembro 102-103 F 4
Porto do Faval 100-101 B 1
Porto do Lontra 98-99 M 7
Porto dos Gaúchos 98-99 K 10
Porto Empêdocle 122-123 E 7
Porto Esperança 104-105 F 3
Porto-Farina = Ghar al-Milḥ 166-167 M 1
Porto Feliz 102-103 J 5
Portoferráio 122-123 CD 4
Porto Ferreira 102-103 J 4
Porto Franco 92-93 K 6
Port of Spain 64-65 O 9
Porto Grande 98-99 N 4
Portogruaro 122-123 E 3
Porto Guareí 102-103 F 5
Port Okha = Okha 134-135 K 6
Portola, CA 74-75 C 3
Porto Lucena 106-107 K 1
Portom 116-117 J 6
Porto Mau 98-99 E 7
Porto Mendes 111 F 2
Porto Murtinho 102-103 D 4
Portonaccio, Roma- 113 II b 2
Porto Nacional 92-93 K 7
Porto Novo [DY] 164-165 E 7
Porto Novo [IND] 140 DE 5
Porto Novo Creek 170 III b 2
Porto Poet 98-99 L 4
Port Orchard, WA 66-67 B 2
Porto Real do Colégio 92-93 M 6-7
Port Orford, OR 66-67 A 4
Porto Rico 98-99 B 8
Porto Rubim 98-99 C 9
Porto Saide 96-97 E 6
Porto Santana 92-93 J 5
Porto Santo 164-165 AB 2
Porto São José 111 F 2

Porto Seguro 92-93 M 8
Porto Seguro, Cachoeira — 98-99 MN 8
Porto Tolle 122-123 E 3
Porto Tòrres 122-123 C 5
Porto União 111 F 3
Porto-Vecchio 122-123 C 5
Porto Velho 92-93 G 6
Porto Veloso 100-101 A 4
Portoviejo 92-93 C 5
Porto Villazón 104-105 F 3
Porto Walter 92-93 E 6
Portpatrik 119 D 4
Port Phillip Bay 158-159 H 7
Port Pirie 158-159 G 6
Port Radium 56-57 NO 4
Port Reading, NJ 82 III a 3
Port Renfrew 66-67 AB 1
Portrerillos 106-107 C 4
Port Rexton 63 K 3
Port Richmond, New York-, NY 82 III b 3
Port Rowan 72-73 F 3
Port Royal = Annapolis Royal 56-57 XY 9
Port Royal Sound 80-81 F 4
Port Safâga = Safâjah 164-165 L 3
Port Safety, AK 58-59 E 4
Port Said = Bûr Sa'îd 164-165 L 2
Port Saint Joe, FL 78-79 G 6
Port Saunders 63 H 2
Port-Say = Marsā-Ban-Mahīdī 166-167 EF 2
Port Shelter 155 I b 1
Port Shepstone 172 F 8
Port Simpson 60 BC 2
Portsmouth, NH 64-65 MN 3
Portsmouth, OH 64-65 K 4
Portsmouth, VA 64-65 L 4
Portsmouth [GB] 119 F 6
Portsmouth [West Indies] 88-89 PQ 7
Port Stanley 72-73 F 3
Port Stanley = Stanley 111 E 8
Port Stephens 108-109 J 9
Port Sûdân = Bûr Sûdân 164-165 M 5
Port Sulphur, LA 78-79 E 6
Port Swettenham = Port Klang 150-151 C 11
Port Talbot 119 DE 6
Port Tewfik = Bûr Tawfiq 173 C 3
Porttipahdan tekojärvi 116-117 LM 3-4
Port Townsend, WA 66-67 B 1
Portugal 120-121 C 10-D 8
Portugalete 120-121 F 7
Portugália = Luachimo 172 D 3
Portugues, El — 92-93 D 6
Portuguesa 94-95 G 3
Portuguesa, Río — 92-93 F 3
Port Union 63 K 3
Port-Vendres 120-121 J 7
Port Victoria [AUS] 160 C 5
Port Victoria [EUA] 172 F 1-2
Port Wakefield 160 CD 5
Port Washington, NY 82 III d 2
Port Washington, WI 70-71 G 4
Port Weld 148-149 CD 6
Port Wells 58-59 NO 6
Port Wing, WI 70-71 E 2
Porushottampur 138-139 K 8
Porvenir [RA] 106-107 FG 5
Porvenir [RCH] 108-109 DE 9
Porvenir [ROU] 106-107 HJ 4
Porvenir, El — [CO] 94-95 G 6
Porvenir, El — [MEX] 76-77 AB 7
Porvoo = Borgå 116-117 LM 7
Posadas [RA] 111 E 3
Posad-Pokrovskoje 126-127 F 3
Pošechonje-Volodarsk 124-125 MN 4
Posen, MI 70-71 J 3
Posesión, Bahía — 108-109 E 9
Poshan = Boshan 142-143 M 4
Posio 116-117 N 4
Posjet 132-133 Z 9
Poso 148-149 H 7
Poso, Danau — 152-153 O 6
Poso, Teluk — 152-153 O 6
Posof = Duğur 136-137 K 2
Posŏng 142-143 O 5
Posse 92-93 K 7
Possession Island = Possessions Eiland 174-175 A 4
Possessions Eiland 174-175 A 4
Possum Kingdom Reservoir 76-77 E 6
Post, OR 66-67 C 3
Post, TX 76-77 D 6
Posta, La — 106-107 F 3
Posta de San Martín 106-107 GH 4
Posta Lencinas 104-105 F 9
Postavy 124-125 F 6
Post Falls, ID 66-67 E 2
Postmasburg 172 D 7
Posto Fiscal Rolim de Moura 104-105 EF 3
Pôsto Indigena 98-99 H 5
Postojna 122-123 F 3
Poston, AZ 74-75 F 5
Postrervalle 104-105 E 6
Postville, IA 70-71 E 4
Poswol = Pasvalys 124-125 E 5
Poṭāngī = Pottangi 140 F 1
Potawatomi Indian Reservation 70-71 BC 6
Potchefstroom 172 E 7
Potčurk, gora — 124-125 T 2
Poté 102-103 M 2
Poteau, OK 76-77 G 5
Poteet, TX 76-77 E 8
Potenza 122-123 F 5
Potfontein 174-175 F 6
Potgietersrus 172 E 6
Pothea = Kálymnos 122-123 M 7
Potholes Reservoir 66-67 D 2
Poti [BR] 100-101 D 3
Poti [SU] 126-127 K 5
Poti, Rio — 100-101 CD 3
Potiraguá 100-101 E 8
Potiskum 164-165 G 6
Potlatch, ID 66-67 E 2
Potloer 174-175 D 6
Pot Mountain 66-67 F 2
Poto 152-153 O 10
Po To Au 155 I b 2
Po Toi Group 155 I b 2
Po Toi Island 155 I b 2
Potomac River 72-73 H 5
Potomac River, South Branch — 72-73 G 5
Potong Pasir, Singapore- 154 III b 1
Poto Poto, Brazzaville- 170 IV a 1
Potosi, MO 70-71 E 7
Potosí [BOL, administrative unit] 104-105 CD 7
Potosí [BOL, place] 92-93 F 8
Potosí [CO] 94-95 C 7
Potosí, El — 86-87 K 5
Potossí, El — 86-87 K 5
Potrerillo, Paso de — 106-107 BC 2
Potrerillos [Honduras] 86-87 R 10
Potrerillos [RCH] 111 C 3
Potrero, El — 76-77 B 8
Potrero, San Francisco-, CA 83 I b 2
Potsdam 118 F 2
Potsdam, NY 72-73 J 2
Potsdam-Bornim 130 III a 2
Potsdam-Bornstedt 130 III a 2
Potsdam-Cecilienhöhe 130 III a 2
Potsdam-Drewitz 130 III a 2
Potsdam-Nedlitz 130 III a 2
Pottangi 140 F 1
Potter, NE 68-69 E 5
Poṭṭokī 138-139 D 2
Potts Camps, MS 78-79 E 3
Potts Hill Reservoirs 161 I a 2
Pottstown, PA 72-73 J 4
Pottsville, PA 72-73 H 4
Pottuvil = Potuvil 134-135 N 7
Potuvil 134-135 N 7
Potzu 146-147 H 10
Pouce Coupe 60 GH 2
Poughkeepsie, NY 64-65 LM 3
Poulin de Courval, Lac — 63 AB 3
Poulo Condore = Côn So'n 150-151 F 8
Poulo Gambir = Cu Lao Poulo Gambir 150-151 GH 6
Poulo Gambir, Cu Lao — 150-151 GH 6
Pou Luong 150-151 E 2
Poŭn 144-145 F 4
Poung, Ban — 150-151 E 4
Poupan 174-175 EF 6
Pourtalé 106-107 G 6
Pouso 98-99 H 11
Pouso Alegre [BR, Mato Grosso] 92-93 H 7
Pouso Alegre [BR, Minas Gerais] 92-93 K 9
Pouté 168-169 B 2
Poutrincourt, Lac — 62 O 2
Povenec 124-125 K 2
Poveneckij zaliv 124-125 K 2
Póvoa de Varzim 120-121 C 8
Povo Novo 106-107 L 3
Povorino 126-127 L 1
Povraz adasi = Alibey adasi 136-137 B 3
Povungnituk 56-57 V 6
Powassan 72-73 G 1
Powder River, WY 68-69 C 4
Powder River [USA, Montana] 64-65 E 2
Powder River [USA, Oregon] 66-67 E 3
Powder River, North Fork — 68-69 C 4
Powder River, South Fork — 68-69 C 4
Powder River Pass 68-69 C 3
Powderville, MT 68-69 D 3
Powell, WY 68-69 B 3
Powell, Lake — 64-65 D 4
Powell Butte, OR 66-67 C 3
Powell Creek 158-159 FG 3
Powell Islands = South Orkneys 53 C 32
Powell River 56-57 M 8
Power, MT 66-67 H 2
Powers, MI 70-71 G 3
Powers, OR 66-67 AB 4
Powers Lake, ND 68-69 E 1
Powhatan, LA 78-79 C 5
Poxorêu 92-93 J 8
Poyang = Boyang 146-147 F 7
Poyang Hu 142-143 M 6
Poygan, Lake — 70-71 F 3
Poyraz 154 I b 1
Poyraz burnu 154 I b 1
Pozama 104-105 G 6
Pozantı 136-137 F 4
Požarevac 122-123 J 3
Poza Rica 64-65 G 7
Požeg 124-125 U 3
Poževrevicy 124-125 G 5
Poznań 118 H 2
Pozo, El — 86-87 F 2
Pozo Almonte 111 C 2
Pozo Anta 102-103 B 5
Pozoblanco 120-121 E 9
Pozo Borrado 106-107 G 2
Pozo Cercado 104-105 E 8
Pozo Colorado 102-103 D 6
Pozo del Molle 106-107 F 4
Pozo del Tigre 104-105 F 9
Pozo Dulce 106-107 F 2
Pozo Hondo [RA] 111 D 3
Pozos, Los — 106-107 E 3
Pozos, Punta — 108-109 G 6
Pozos Colorados 94-95 DE 2
Pozuelos 94-95 J 2
Pozuelos, Lago — 104-105 CD 8
Pozuzo 96-97 D 7
Požva 124-125 UV 4
Pozzallo 122-123 F 7
Pozzuoli 122-123 EF 5
Pra [WG] 164-165 D 7
Prabat Chean Chum 150-151 E 7
Praça Duque de Caxias 110 I bc 2
Praça Seca, Rio de Janeiro- 110 I a 2
Pracham Hiang, Laem — 150-151 B 7
Prachantakham 150-151 CD 5
Prachin Buri 150-151 C 5
Prachuap Khiri Khan 148-149 CD 4
Praděd 118 H 3
Pradera 94-95 CD 6
Prades 120-121 J 7
Prades, Sierra de los — 106-107 HJ 6-7
Prades Thai = Muang Thai 148-149 CD 3
Prado [BR] 92-93 M 8
Prado [CO] 94-95 D 6
Prado, Bogotá-El — 91 III c 2
Prado, Museo del — 113 III a 2
Prague, NE 68-69 H 5
Prague, OK 76-77 F 5
Prague = Praha 118 G 3
Praha 118 G 3
Prahran, Melbourne- 161 II bc 2
Praia 204-205 E 7
Praia da Juréia 102-103 J 6
Praia de Copacabana 110 I bc 2
Praia de Leste 102-103 H 6
Praia Grande 102-103 J 6
Praia Grande, Enseada da — 110 I c 2
Praião, Cachoeira do — 92-93 K 8
Praia Redonda 102-103 H 8
Prainha [BR, Amazonas] 92-93 G 6
Prainha [BR, Pará] 92-93 J 5
Prairie, ID 66-67 F 4
Prairie, La — 82 I bc 2
Prairie City, OR 66-67 D 3
Prairie Dog Creek 68-69 F 6
Prairie Dog Town Fork 76-77 DE 5
Prairie du Chien, WI 70-71 E 4
Prairie River 61 G 4
Prairies 56-57 Q 7-R 9
Prairies, Rivière des — 82 I ab 1
Prakhon Chai 150-151 D 5
Pran Buri 148-149 CD 4
Prangli 124-125 E 4
Prānhita 134-135 MN 7
Prāntij = Parāntij 138-139 D 6
Prapat 150-151 B 11
Prasat 150-151 D 5
Praskoveja 126-127 M 4
Prasonêsion, Akrōtērion — 122-123 MN 8
Prat, Isla — 108-109 B 7
Prata [BR, Goiás] 100-101 A 6
Prata [BR, Minas Gerais] 102-103 H 3
Prata [BR, Pará] 92-93 K 5
Prata, Riacho de — 100-101 C 4
Prata, Rio — 98-99 P 9
Prata, Rio da — [BR ◁ Rio Paracatu] 102-103 J 2
Prata, Rio da — [BR ◁ Rio Paranaíba] 102-103 H 3
Pratābgaṛh = Partāpgarh 138-139 E 5
Prata do Piauí 100-101 CD 3
Pratapgarh 138-139 H 5
Pratápolis 102-103 J 4
Pratas = Dongsha Qundao 142-143 LM 7
Prater 113 I b 2
Pratinha 102-103 J 3
Prato 122-123 D 4
Pratt 61 J 6
Pratt, KS 68-69 G 7
Prattville, AL 78-79 F 4
Pratudinho, Rio — 100-101 B 8
Pravara 138-139 E 8
Pravdinsk [SU, Volga] 124-125 O 5
Prawle, Point — 119 E 6
Praya 152-153 M 10
Pr'aža 124-125 JK 3
Preah Vihear 150-151 E 5-6
Prêbeza 122-123 J 6
Prečistoje [SU, Jaroslavskaja Oblast'] 124-125 MN 4
Precordillera 111 C 3-4
Predivinsk 132-133 R 6
Preeceville 61 G 4-5
Pregol'a 118 K 1
Pregonero 94-95 F 3
Pregradnaja 126-127 K 5
Preiļi 124-125 F 5
Preissac, Lac — 62 M 2
Prêk Chbar 150-151 F 6
Prêk Chhlong 150-151 F 6
Prêk Kak 150-151 E 6
Prêk Phnou 150-151 E 7
Prêk Sandek 150-151 E 7
Prêk Tê 150-151 F 6
Prelate 61 D 5
Premier 58-59 y 8
Premier Mine 174-175 H 3
Premio 63 D 2
Premont, TX 76-77 EF 9
Premuda 122-123 F 3
Prentice, WI 70-71 EF 3
Prentiss, MS 78-79 E 5
Prenzlau 118 FG 2
Prenzlauer Berg, Berlin- 130 III b 1
Přerov 118 H 4
Presa Alvaro Obregón 86-87 F 4
Presa de Gatún 64-65 ab 2
Presa de la Amistad 86-87 JK 3
Presa de la Angustora 86-87 O 9-10
Presa de las Adjuntas 86-87 LM 6
Presa del Infiernillo 86-87 JK 8
Presa de Madden 64-65 b 2
Presa de Mixcoac 91 I b 2
Presa La Boquilla 86-87 GH 4
Presa Las Julianas 91 I b 2
Presa Lazaro Cardenas 86-87 H 5
Presa Los Jazmines 91 I b 2
Presa Macagua 94-95 K 3
Presa Macúzari 86-87 F 4
Presa M. Hidalgo 86-87 F 4
Presa Miguel Alemán 86-87 M 8
Presa M. R. Gomez 86-87 L 4
Presa Netzahualcóyotl 86-87 O 9
Presa Presidente Aleman 86-87 M 8
Presa Tarango 91 I b 2
Presa V. Carranza 86-87 KL 4
Prescott 72-73 J 2
Prescott, AR 78-79 C 4
Prescott, AZ 64-65 D 5
Prescott, WI 70-71 D 3
Presedio of San Francisco 83 I b 2
Presho, SD 68-69 FG 4
Présidence, Kinshasa- 170 IV a 1
Presidencia de la Plaza 104-105 G 10
Presidencia Roca 104-105 G 10
Presidencia Roque Sáenz Peña 111 D 3
Presidente Aleman, Presa — 86-87 M 8
Presidente Alves 102-103 GH 5
Presidente Bernardes 102-103 G 4-5
Presidente Costa e Silva, Ponte — 110 I bc 2
Presidente Doctor G. Vargas 106-107 KL 4
Presidente Dutra 92-93 L 6
Presidente Epitácio 92-93 J 9
Presidente Hayes 102-103 CD 5
Presidente Hermes 92-93 G 7
Presidente Murtinho 102-103 F 1
Presidente Nicolás Avellaneda, Parque — 110 III b 1
Presidente Olegário 102-103 J 3
Presidente Prudente 92-93 J 9
Presidente Rios, Lago — 108-109 B 6
Presidente Venceslau 102-103 FG 4
Presidio, TX 64-65 F 6
Prešov 118 K 4
Prespa Lake = Prespansko jezero 122-123 J 5
Prespansko Ezero 122-123 J 5
Presque Isle, ME 64-65 N 2
Presque Isle Point 70-71 G 2
Press Lake 62 D 3
Prestea 164-165 D 7
Presto, El — 104-105 F 4
Preston, CA 74-75 B 3
Preston, ID 66-67 H 4
Preston, MN 70-71 DE 4
Preston, MO 70-71 D 7
Preston [AUS] 158-159 C 4
Preston [GB] 119 E 5
Preston, Melbourne- 161 II bc 1
Prestonsburg, KY 80-81 E 2
Prestwick 119 DE 4
Preto, Rio — [BR ◁ Rio Grande] 92-93 K 7
Preto, Rio — [BR ◁ Rio Madeira] 98-99 G 9
Preto, Rio — [BR ◁ Rio Munim] 100-101 C 2
Preto, Rio — [BR ◁ Rio Negro] 98-99 F 4
Preto, Rio — [BR ◁ Rio Paracatu] 92-93 K 8
Preto, Rio — [BR ◁ Rio Paraíba] 102-103 L 5
Preto, Rio — [BR ◁ Rio Paranaíba] 102-103 G 3
Preto do Igapó-Açu, Rio — 98-99 H 7
Pretoria 172 E 7
Pretoriuskop 174-175 J 3
Pretos Forros, Serra dos — 110 I b 2
Pretty Prairie, KS 68-69 GH 7
Preungesheim, Frankfurt am Main- 128 III b 1
Preveza = Prébeza 122-123 J 6
Préville 82 I c 2
Prévost-Paradol = Mashra'a Aşfā 166-167 G 2
Prey Lovea 150-151 E 7
Prey Nop 150-151 D 7
Prey Veng 148-149 E 4
Priargunsk 132-133 WX 7
Pribilof Islands 52 D 35-36
Příbram 118 G 4
Pribrežnyj chrebet 132-133 Za 6
Price 63 B 3
Price, UT 64-65 D 4
Price Island 60 C 3
Price River 74-75 H 3
Pricetown, LA 85 I a 2
Prichard, AL 64-65 J 5
Prichard, ID 66-67 EF 2
Pric'ornomorskaja nizmennost' 126-127 E-G 3
Pridneprovskaja nizmennost' 126-127 E-G 1-2
Pridneprovskaja vozvyšennost' 126-127 D-G 2
Priego de Córdoba 120-121 E 10
Priekulė 124-125 C 6
Prienai 124-125 DE 6
Prieska 172 D 7
Priest Lake 66-67 E 1
Priest Rapids Reservoir 66-67 CD 2
Priest River, ID 66-67 E 1
Prijedor 122-123 G 3
Prijutnoje 126-127 L 3
Prijutovo 124-125 T 7
Prikaspijskaja nizmennost' 126-127 M 4-Q 2
Prikolotnoje 126-127 H 1
Prikubanskaja nizmennost' 126-127 J 4
Prikumsk 126-127 LM 4
Prilep 122-123 J 5
Priluki [SU, Ukrainskaja SSR] 126-127 F 1
Prima Porta, Roma- 113 II b 1
Primavalle, Roma- 113 II ab 1
Primavera, La — 106-107 D 6
Primeira Cachoeira 98-99 J 5
Primeira Cruz 100-101 C 2
Primeiro de Maio 102-103 G 5
Primghar, IA 70-71 C 4
Primor 104-105 D 1
Primorsk [SU, Azerbajdžanskaja SSR] 126-127 O 6
Primorsk [SU, Rossijskaja SFSR] 124-125 G 3
Primorskij chrebet 132-133 TU 7
Primorsko-Achtarsk 126-127 HJ 3
Primorskoje [SU, Rossijskaja SFSR] 124-125 FG 3
Primorskoje [SU, Ukrainskaja SSR] 126-127 H 3
Primos, PA 84 III b 2
Primrose 170 V bc 2
Primrose Lake 61 D 3
Primrose River 58-59 U 6
Prince Albert 56-57 P 7
Prince Albert Mountains 53 B 16-17
Prince Albert National Park 56-57 P 7
Prince Albert Peninsula 56-57 NO 3
Prince Albert Road = Prins Albertweg 174-175 D 7
Prince Albert Sound 56-57 NO 3
Prince Alfred, Cape — 56-57 KL 3
Prince Alfred's Hamlet = Prins Alfred Hamlet 174-175 CD 7
Prince Charles Island 56-57 V 4
Prince Charles Range 53 B 7
Prince Edward Bay 72-73 H 2-3
Prince Edward Island 56-57 Y 8
Prince Edward Islands 53 E 4
Prince Edward Peninsula 72-73 H 2-3
Prince Frederick, MD 72-73 H 5
Prince George 56-57 M 7
Prince Gustav Adolf Sea 56-57 P 2
Prince Island = Pulau Panaitan 148-149 DE 8
Prince of Wales, Cape — 56-57 C 4-5
Prince of Wales Island [AUS] 158-159 H 2
Prince of Wales Island [CDN] 56-57 QR 3
Prince of Wales Island [USA] 56-57 JK 6
Prince of Wales Island = Pulau Pinang 150-151 BC 10
Prince of Wales Island = Wales Island 56-57 T 4
Prince of Wales Strait 56-57 N 3
Prince Patrick Island 56-57 M 2
Princeps Island = Payinzet Kyūn 150-151 AB 6
Prince Regent Inlet 56-57 ST 3
Prince Regent Luitpold Land = Prinzregent-Luitpold-Land 53 B 33-34
Prince Rupert 56-57 KL 7
Princesa Isabel 100-101 F 4
Princes Bay, New York-, NY 82 III a 3
Princess Anne, MD 72-73 J 5
Princess Astrid Land = Princesse Astrid land 53 B 1-2
Princess Charlotte Bay 158-159 H 2
Princess Elizabeth Land 53 BC 8-9
Princess Royal Island 56-57 L 7
Princeton 66-67 C 1
Princeton, CA 74-75 BC 3
Princeton, IA 70-71 D 5
Princeton, IL 70-71 F 5
Princeton, IN 70-71 G 6
Princeton, KY 78-79 F 2
Princeton, MI 70-71 G 2
Princeton, MN 70-71 D 3
Princeton, NJ 72-73 J 4
Princeton, WI 70-71 F 4
Princeton, WV 80-81 F 2
Prince William Sound 56-57 G 5
Príncipe, Ilha do — 164-165 F 8
Príncipe da Baira 92-93 G 7
Príncipe da Beira 92-93 G 7
Prineville, OR 66-67 C 3
Pringle, SD 68-69 E 4
Pringle, Punta — 108-109 Ab 6
Prins Albert 174-175 E 7
Prins Albertweg 174-175 D 7
Prins Alfred Hamlet 174-175 CD 7
Prins Christian Sund 56-57 c 5-d 6
Prinsep Island = Payinzet Kyūn 150-151 AB 6
Prinsesse Astrid land 53 B 1-2
Prinsesse Ragnhild land 53 B 3
Prins Harald land 53 B 4-C 5
Prinzapolca [NIC, place] 88-89 E 8
Prinzapolca [NIC, river] 88-89 D 8
Prinzregent-Luitpold-Land 53 B 33-34
Priokskij 124-125 M 6
Prior, Cabo — 120-121 C 7
Priozersk = Prioz'orsk 132-133 DE 5
Prioz'orsk 132-133 DE 5
Prip'at' 124-125 G 8
Pripet = Prip'at' 124-125 G 8
Pripol'arnyj Ural 132-133 KL 4-5
Prišib 126-127 O 7
Prišib = Leninsk 126-127 M 2
Pristen' 126-127 H 1
Priština 122-123 J 4
Pritchett, CO 68-69 E 7
Privas 120-121 K 6
Priverno 122-123 E 5
Privetnoje 126-127 G 4
Prividencia, Isla de — 92-93 C 2
Privodino 124-125 PQ 3
Privol'noje 126-127 EF 3
Privolžje 124-125 R 7
Privolžsk 124-125 N 5
Privolžskaja vozvyšennost' 124-125 P 8-Q 6
Privolžskij 126-127 NO 3
Privolžskoje 126-127 MN 1
Prizren 122-123 J 4
Probolinggo 148-149 F 8
Prochladnyj 126-127 LM 5
Procter 60 J 5
Proctor, TX 76-77 E 6-7
Proctor Creek 85 II b 2
Proddattūru = Proddatūr 134-135 M 8
Proddatūr 134-135 M 8
Professor Dr. Ir. W. J. van Blommesteinmeer 92-93 H 4
Progreso [MEX, Coahuila] 76-77 D 9
Progreso [MEX, Yucatán] 64-65 J 7
Progreso [RA] 111 D 4
Progreso [ROU] 106-107 J 5
Progreso, El — [GCA] 86-87 P 10
Progreso, El — [Honduras] 64-65 J 8
Progreso, El — [PE] 96-97 E 9
Progresso 106-107 L 2
Progresso, Madrid- 113 III ab 2
Prokopjevsk 132-133 Q 7
Prokopyevsk = Prokopjevsk 132-133 Q 7
Prokuplje 122-123 J 4
Proletarij 124-125 H 4
Proletarsk 126-127 KL 3
Proletarskij [SU, Belgorodskaja Oblast'] 126-127 GH 1
Proletarskij [SU, Moskovskaja Oblast'] 124-125 L 6
proliv de Long 132-133 j 3-4
proliv de Vries 142-143 S 2
proliv Dmitrija Lapteva 132-133 a-c 3
proliv Eterikan 132-133 ab 3
proliv Jugorskij Šar 132-133 L 4-M 3
proliv Karskije Vorota 132-133 J-L 3
proliv Krasnoj Armii 132-133 ST 1
proliv La Pérouse 132-133 b 8
proliv Matočkin Šar 132-133 KL 3
proliv Sannikova 132-133 ab 3
proliv Šokal'skogo 132-133 RS 2
proliv Vil'kickogo 132-133 S-U 2
Prome = Pyin 148-149 C 3
Promissão 102-103 H 4
Promissao, Represa de — 102-103 H 4
Promyslovka 144-145 J 1
Pron'a [SU, river ◁ Oka] 124-125 N 6
Pron'a [SU, river ◁ Sož] 124-125 H 7
Prončiščeva, bereg — 132-133 UV 2-3
Pronsk 124-125 M 6
Propriá 92-93 M 7
Propriano 122-123 C 5
Pros'anaja 126-127 H 2
Proserpine 158-159 J 4
Proskurov = Chmel'nickij 126-127 C 2
Prosna 118 J 3
Prospect, OR 66-67 B 4
Prospector 61 H 3-4
Prospect Park, PA 84 III b 2
Prospect Point 82 III d 1
Prospekt Park 82 III c 3
Prosser, WA 66-67 D 2
Prostějov 118 H 4
Protection, KS 76-77 E 4
Protem 174-175 D 8
Protva 124-125 L 6
Provadija 122-123 M 4
Provence 120-121 K 7-L 6
Providence, KY 70-71 G 7
Providence, RI 64-65 MN 3
Providence, Cape — [NZ] 158-159 MN 9
Providence, Cape — [USA] 58-59 ef 1
Providence Island 172 JK 3
Providence Mountains 74-75 F 5
Providencia 64-65 KL 9
Providencia, Ilha — 94-95 J 8
Providência, Serra da — 98-99 H 10
Providenciales Island 88-89 K 4
Providenija 132-133 kl 5
Provincetown, MA 72-73 LM 3
Provins 120-121 J 4
Provo, SD 68-69 E 4
Provo, UT 64-65 D 3
Provost 56-57 O 7
Prudentópolis 102-103 G 6
Prudenville, MI 70-71 H 3
Prudhoe Bay [CDN, bay] 58-59 NO 1
Prudhoe Bay [CDN, place] 56-57 G 3
Prudhoe Land 56-57 XY 2
Prüm 118 C 3
Prūnshī 141 C 6
Prupuk 152-153 J 9
Průsa = Bursa 134-135 B 2-3
Pruszków 118 K 2
Prut [SU, place] 126-127 D 3
Prut [SU, river] 126-127 C 3
Pruth 122-123 N 3
Pružany 124-125 E 7
Pryor, OK 76-77 G 4
Pryor Creek 68-69 B 3
Pryor Mountains 68-69 B 3
Przełęcz Dukielska 118 KL 4
Przełęcz Łupkowska 118 L 4
Przemyśl 118 L 4
Prževal'sk 134-135 M 2
Prževal'skoje 124-125 HJ 6
Przeworsk 118 L 3
Przylądek Rozewie 118 J 1
Psará 122-123 L 6
Psérimos 122-123 M 7
Psiol = Ps'ol 126-127 F 2
Pskov 124-125 G 5
Pskovskoje ozero 124-125 FG 4-5
Ps'ol 126-127 F 2
Psychikón 113 IV b 1
Pszczyna 118 J 3-4
Ptič' 124-125 FG 7
Ptolemaïs 122-123 J 5
Ptuj 122-123 FG 2
Pu, Ko — 150-151 B 9
Pŭa [RCH] 106-107 A 7
Pua [T] 150-151 C 3
Puale Bay 58-59 K 8
Puan 106-107 F 6
Pubei 146-147 B 10
Pu Bia = Phou Bia 150-151 D 3
Pucacuro, Río — 96-97 D 3
Pucallpa 92-93 E 6
Pucapamba 96-97 B 4
Pucara [BOL] 104-105 DE 6
Pucará [PE] 96-97 F 9
Pucará, Río — 96-97 F 9
Pucarani 92-93 F 8
Pucatrihue 108-109 BC 3
Pučež 124-125 O 5
Puchang Hai = Lob nuur 142-143 G 3
Pucheng [TJ, Fujian] 142-143 M 6
Pucheng [TJ, Shaanxi] 142-143 KL 4-5
Pucheng [TJ, Shandong] 146-147 E 4
Puchi = Puqi 142-143 L 6
P'u-chiang = Pujiang 146-147 G 7
Puchuzún 106-107 C 3
Puck 118 J 1
Pucón 108-109 D 2
Pŭdāō 148-149 C 1
Pudasjärvi 116-117 M 5
Pudem 124-125 T 4
Pŭdimadaka 140 F 2
Pudimoe 174-175 F 4
Puding, Cape — = Tanjung Puting 148-149 F 7
Pudino 132-133 OP 6
Pudož 132-133 F 5
Pudukkottai 140 D 5
Pudukōṭṭai = Pattukkottai 140 D 5
Puebla [MEX, administrative unit] 86-87 LM 8
Puebla [MEX, place] 64-65 G 8
Puebla, La — 120-121 J 9
Puebla de Sanabria 120-121 D 7
Puebla de Zaragoza 64-65 G 8
Pueblitos 106-107 GH 5
Pueblo, CO 64-65 F 4
Pueblo Bello 94-95 E 2
Pueblo Bonito, NM 74-75 JK 5
Pueblo Brugo 106-107 GH 3
Pueblo Hundido 111 BC 3
Pueblo Ledesma 104-105 D 8
Pueblo Libertador 106-107 H 3
Pueblo Moscas 106-107 H 4
Pueblonuevo [CO] 94-95 D 3
Pueblo Nuevo [PA] 64-65 b 2-3
Pueblo Nuevo [YV] 92-93 F 2
Pueblo Nuevo, Madrid- 113 III b 2
Pueblo Valley 74-75 HJ 6
Pueblo Viejo [CO] 92-93 F 4
Puebloviejo [EC] 96-97 B 2
Puelches 111 C 5
Puelén 106-107 D 6
Puelo, Río — 108-109 C 3
Puente, El — [BOL, Santa Cruz] 104-105 E 5
Puente, El — [BOL, Tarija] 104-105 D 7
Puente Alto 106-107 B 4
Puenteáreas 120-121 CD 7
Puente Batel 106-107 H 2
Puente de Ixtla 86-87 L 8
Puente del Inca 106-107 BC 4
Puente Vallecas, Madrid- 113 III b 2
Puerco, Rio — 76-77 A 5
Puerco River 74-75 J 5
Puercos, Morro de — 88-89 FG 11
Pu-êrh-ching = Burchun 142-143 F 2
Puerta, La — [RA, Catamarca] 104-105 D 11
Puerta, La — [RA, Córdoba] 106-107 F 3
Puerta, La — [YV] 94-95 F 3
Puerta de Vacas 106-107 C 4
Puerto Acosta 92-93 F 8
Puerto Adela 102-103 E 6
Puerto Aisén 111 B 7
Puerto Alegre [BOL] 92-93 G 7
Puerto Alegre [PY] 102-103 D 5
Puerto Alfonso 92-93 E 5
Puerto Ángel 86-87 MN 10
Puerto Antequera 102-103 D 6
Puerto Argentina 92-93 E 4
Puerto Armuelles 64-65 K 10
Puerto Arrecife 102-103 D 5
Puerto Arturo 94-95 E 6
Puerto Asís 92-93 D 4
Puerto Ayacucho 92-93 F 3
Puerto Bajo Pisagua 108-109 C 6
Puerto Baquerizo 92-93 B 5

Puerto Barrios 64-65 HJ 8
Puerto Barros 96-97 D 2
Puerto Bermejo 104-105 G 10
Puerto Bermúdez 96-97 D 7
Puerto Berrio 92-93 E 3
Puerto Bertrand 108-109 C 6
Puerto Bolognesi 96-97 E 7
Puerto Boyaca 94-95 D 5
Puerto Caballas 92-93 D 7
Puerto Caballo 102-103 C 4
Puerto Cabello 92-93 F 2
Puerto Cabezas 64-65 K 9
Puerto Cahuinari 94-95 F 8
Puerto Capaz = Al-Jabhah 166-167 D 2
Puerto Carlos 94-95 F 8
Puerto Carranza 94-95 bc 2
Puerto Carreño 92-93 F 3
Puerto Casado 111 E 2
Puerto Castilla 88-89 CD 6
Puerto Catay 96-97 F 6
Puerto Ceticayo 96-97 F 7
Puerto Chacabuco 108-109 C 5
Puerto Chicama 92-93 CD 6
Puerto Cisnes 111 B 6-7
Puertocitos 86-87 C 2
Puerto Clemente 96-97 D 7
Puerto Coig 108-109 E 8
Puerto Colombia 94-95 D 2
Puerto Constanza 106-107 H 4
Puerto Cooper 102-103 CD 5
Puerto Cortés [CR] 88-89 DE 10
Puerto Cortés [Honduras] 64-65 J 8
Puerto Cumarebo 92-93 F 2
Puerto Dalmacia 102-103 CD 6
Puerto de Cayo 96-97 A 2
Puerto de Chorrera 64-65 b 3
Puerto de Despeñaperros 120-121 F 9
Puerto de Hierro 94-95 K 2
Puerto de Lobos 74-75 G 7
Puerto del Rosario 164-165 B 3
Puerto de Nutrias 92-93 EF 3
Puerto de Santa Maria, El — 120-121 D 10
Puerto Deseado 111 CD 7
Puerto Eduardo 96-97 D 6
Puerto Elvira 111 E 2
Puerto Escalante 96-97 C 4
Puerto Escondido [CO] 94-95 C 3
Puerto Escondido [MEX] 86-87 LM 10
Puerto Esperidião 92-93 H 8
Puerto Estrella 92-93 E 2
Puerto Ferreira 102-103 D 7
Puerto Fonciere 102-103 D 5
Puerto Francisco de Orellana 96-97 C 2
Puerto Frey 92-93 G 7
Puerto Gaboto = Gaboto 106-107 G 4
Puerto Galileo 102-103 CD 6
Puerto Gisela 106-107 K 1
Puerto Grether 92-93 FG 8
Puerto Guaraní 102-103 CD 4
Puerto Gulach 102-103 B 5
Puerto Harberton 111 C 8
Puerto Heath 92-93 F 7
Puerto Huitoto 94-95 D 7
Puerto Ibáñez 108-109 CD 6
Puerto Iguazú 111 EF 3
Puerto Inca 96-97 D 6
Puerto Inírida = Obando 94-95 H 6
Puerto Inuya 96-97 E 7
Puerto Irigoyen 102-103 AB 5
Puerto Isabel 92-93 H 8
Puerto Izozog 104-105 E 6
Puerto Juárez 64-65 J 7
Puerto La Cruz 92-93 G 2
Puerto La Paz 104-105 E 8
Puerto Leda 102-103 C 4
Puerto Leguízamo 92-93 E 5
Puerto Lempira 88-89 DE 7
Puerto Libertad 86-87 D 3
Puerto Libertador General San Martín = Libertador General San Martín 102-103 E 7
Puerto Libre 94-95 C 4
Puerto Limón [CO, Meta] 94-95 E 6
Puerto Limón [CO, Putumayo] 94-95 C 7
Puertollano 120-121 EF 9
Puerto Lobos [MEX] 86-87 D 2
Puerto Lobos [RA] 111 C 6
Puerto Lopez [CO, Guajira] 94-95 F 2
Puerto López [CO, Meta] 94-95 E 5
Puerto López [EC] 96-97 A 2
Puerto Madero 86-87 O 10
Puerto Madryn 111 C 6
Puerto Mainiqui 96-97 E 7
Puerto Maldonado 92-93 EF 7
Puerto Mamoré 104-105 D 5
Puerto Manatí 88-89 H 4
Puerto México = Coatzacoalcos 64-65 H 8
Puerto Mihanovich 102-103 CD 4
Puerto Miranda 94-95 L 4
Puerto Miranhas 94-95 F 8
Puerto Montt 111 B 6
Puerto Mosquito 94-95 E 3
Puerto Napo 96-97 BC 2
Puerto Nare 94-95 E 7
Puerto Nariño 94-95 GH 5
Puerto Natales 111 B 8
Puerto Navarino 108-109 EF 10
Puerto Nuevo [CO] 92-93 F 3
Puerto Nuevo [PY] 102-103 C 4
Puerto Ordaz, Ciudad Guayana- 92-93 G 3
Puerto Ospina 94-95 D 7
Puerto Padre 88-89 HJ 4
Puerto Páez 92-93 F 3
Puerto Palma Chica 102-103 CD 4
Puerto Palmares 102-103 BC 4
Puerto Pardo [PE, Loreto] 96-97 C 3
Puerto Pardo [PE, Madre de Dios] 96-97 G 8
Puerto Patillos 104-105 A 7
Puerto Peñasco 86-87 CD 2
Puerto Pilcomayo 104-105 GH 9
Puerto Pilón 64-65 b 2
Puerto Pinasco 111 E 2
Puerto Piracuacito 106-107 H 2
Puerto Pirámides 111 D 6
Puerto Píritu 92-93 FG 2-3
Puerto Pizarro 92-93 E 5
Puerto Plata 64-65 M 8
Puerto Portillo 92-93 E 6
Puerto Potrero 88-89 CD 9
Puerto Prado 92-93 DE 7
Puerto Princesa 148-149 G 5
Puerto Providencia 96-97 F 7
Puerto Puyuguapi 108-109 C 5
Puerto Quellón 111 B 6
Puerto Quellón = Quellón 111 B 6
Puerto Quijarro 104-105 GH 5
Puerto Ramírez 111 B 6
Puerto Rápido 94-95 CD 7
Puerto Real 120-121 DE 10
Puerto Rey 94-95 C 3
Puerto Rico [BOL] 92-93 F 7
Puerto Rico [CO, Caquetá] 94-95 D 6
Puerto Rico [CO, Meta] 94-95 D 7
Puerto Rico [Puerto Rico] 64-65 N 8
Puerto Rico [YV] 94-95 L 4
Puerto Rico = Libertador General San Martín 102-103 E 7
Puerto Rico Trench 50-51 FG 4
Puerto Río Negro 102-103 CD 5
Puerto Rondón 92-93 E 3
Puerto Ruiz 106-107 H 4
Puerto Saavedra 106-107 A 7
Puerto Sábalo 94-95 E 8
Puerto Salgar 94-95 D 5
Puerto San Agostino 94-95 b 2
Puerto San Augustín 96-97 F 3
Puerto San José 108-109 GH 4
Puerto San Julián 111 C 7
Puerto Santa Cruz 111 C 8
Puerto Santa Cruz = Santa Cruz 111 C 8
Puerto Santa Elena 102-103 D 6
Puerto Santa Rita 102-103 D 5
Puerto San Vicente 102-103 E 6
Puerto Sastre 111 E 2
Puerto Saucedo 104-105 E 3
Puerto Siles 104-105 D 3
Puerto Stigh 108-109 B 6
Puerto Suárez 92-93 H 8
Puerto Supe 92-93 D 7
Puerto Tejada 92-93 D 4
Puerto Tirol 104-105 G 10
Puerto Tirol = Tirol 106-107 H 1
Puerto Torno 104-105 D 5
Puerto Trinidad 64-65 b 3
Puerto Umbría 94-95 C 7
Puerto Unzué 106-107 H 4
Puerto Vallarta 86-87 H 7
Puerto Varas 108-109 C 3
Puerto Vassupe 96-97 D 7
Puerto Victoria [PE] 92-93 DE 6
Puerto Victoria [RA] 102-103 E 7
Puerto Viejo 106-107 B 1
Puerto Vilelas 104-105 G 10
Puerto Wilches 92-93 E 3
Puerto Williams 111 C 9
Puerto Yartou 108-109 DE 9
Puerto Ybapobó 102-103 D 5
Puerto Yeruá 106-107 H 3
Puesto, El — 104-105 C 10
Puesto de Castro 106-107 F 3
Pueyrredón, Lago — 111 B 7
Puga 102-103 D 3
Pugačov 132-133 HJ 7
Pūgal 134-135 L 5
Pugan 141 D 5
Puger 152-153 K 10
Puget Sound 66-67 B 2
Pùglia 122-123 FG 5
Pugwash 56-57 Y 8
Pūhalepa 124-125 D 4
P'u-hsi = Puxi 146-147 G 9
P'u-hsien = Pu Xian 146-147 C 3
Pui, Doi — = Doi Suthep 150-151 B 3
Pui Kau 155 I a 2
Puinahua, Canal de — 96-97 D 4
Puisoyé 106-107 HJ 1
Pujehun 164-165 B 7
Pujiang 146-147 G 7
Pujilí 96-97 B 2
Pujŏn-ho 144-145 FG 2
Pukaki, Lake — 161 D 7
Puka Puka 156-157 L 5
Pukatawagan 61 H 3
Pukchin 144-145 E 2
Pukch'ŏng 142-143 O 3
Puket = Ko Phuket 148-149 C 5
Pukhan-gang 144-145 F 3-4
Pukou 146-147 G 5
Puksa 124-125 N 2
Puksoozero 124-125 N 2
Puksubæk-san = Ch'ail-bong 144-145 F 2
Pula 122-123 E 3
Pulacayo 92-93 F 9
Pulador 106-107 L 2
Pulandian = Xinjin 144-145 CD 3
Pulangpisau 152-153 L 7
Pulantien = Xinjin 144-145 CD 3
Pulānto 138-139 HJ 3
Pulap 148-149 N 5
Pular, Volcán — 111 C 2
Pulaski, NY 72-73 HJ 3
Pulaski, TN 78-79 F 3
Pulaski, VA 80-81 F 2
Pulaski, WI 70-71 F 3
Pulau Adi 148-149 K 7
Pulau Adonara 148-149 H 8
Pulau Airabu 152-153 G 4
Pulau Alang Besar 150-151 C 11
Pulau Alor 148-149 HJ 8
Pulau Ambelau 148-149 J 7
Pulau Ambon 148-149 J 7
Pulau Aur 150-151 E 11
Pulau Babi 152-153 B 4
Pulau Bacan 148-149 J 7
Pulau Bahulu 152-153 P 7
Pulau Balambangan 148-149 G 5
Pulau Bali 148-149 FG 8
Pulau Banawaja 152-153 N 9
Pulau Banggai 148-149 H 7
Pulau Banggi 148-149 G 5
Pulau Bangka 148-149 E 7
Pulau Bangkaru 152-153 B 4-5
Pulau Bangkulu 152-153 P 6
Pulau Batam 148-149 D 6
Pulau Batanta 148-149 JK 7
Pulau Batuatu 152-153 P 8
Pulau Batudaka 152-153 O 6
Pulau Bawal 152-153 H 7
Pulau Bawean 148-149 F 8
Pulau Belitung 148-149 E 7
Pulau Bengkalis 148-149 D 6
Pulau Benua 152-153 G 5
Pulau Berhala 150-151 DE 11
Pulau Besar 152-153 P 10
Pulau Biak 148-149 L 7
Pulau Biaro 148-149 J 6
Pulau Binongko 152-153 Q 8
Pulau Bintan 148-149 DE 6
Pulau Bisa 148-149 J 7
Pulau Bonerate 152-153 O 9
Pulau Brani 154 III b 2
Pulau Breueh 148-149 B 5
Pulau Bruit 152-153 J 4
Pulau Bukum 154 III a 2
Pulau Bukum Kechil 154 III a 2
Pulau Bum Bum 152-153 N 3
Pulau Bunguran 148-149 E 6
Pulau Bunyu 148-149 G 6
Pulau Buru 148-149 J 7
Pulau Busing 154 III a 2
Pulau Butung 148-149 H 7-8
Pulau Damar 148-149 J 8
Pulau Dayang Bunting 148-149 C 5
Pulau Deli 148-149 DE 8
Pulau Dewakang Besar 152-153 N 8
Pulau Doangdoangan Besar 152-153 M 8
Pulau Dumdum 152-153 G 5
Pulau Enggano 148-149 D 8
Pulau Gam 148-149 JK 7
Pulau Gebe 148-149 J 7
Pulau Gelam 152-153 H 7
Pulau Gunungapi 148-149 J 8
Pulau Hantu 154 III a 2
Pulau Jamdena 148-149 K 8
Pulau Jemaja 148-149 DE 6
Pulau Jembongan 148-149 G 5
Pulau Kabaena 148-149 H 8
Pulau Kaburuang 148-149 J 6
Pulau Kai Besar 148-149 K 8
Pulau Kai Kecil 148-149 K 8
Pulau Kakaban 152-153 N 4
Pulau Kakabia 152-153 P 9
Pulau Kalambau 152-153 L 8
Pulau Kalao 152-153 O 9
Pulau Kalaotao 148-149 H 8
Pulau Kalukalukuang 152-153 MN 8
Pulau Kambing = Ilha de Ataúro 148-149 J 8
Pulau Kangean 148-149 G 8
Pulau Kapas 150-151 D 10
Pulau Karakelong 148-149 J 6
Pulau Karamian 148-149 F 8
Pulau Karas 148-149 K 7
Pulau Karompa 152-153 OP 9
Pulau Kasiruta 148-149 J 7
Pulau Katedupa 152-153 PQ 8
Pulau Kayoa 148-149 J 6
Pulau Kayuadi 152-153 O 9
Pulau Ketam 154 III b 1
Pulaukijang 152-153 E 6
Pulau Kisar 148-149 J 8
Pulau Klang 150-151 C 11
Pulau Kobroor 148-149 KL 8
Pulau Kofiau 148-149 JK 7
Pulau Kola 148-149 KL 8
Pulau Kolepom 148-149 L 8
Pulau Komba 152-153 P 9
Pulau Komodo 148-149 G 8
Pulau Komoran 148-149 L 8
Pulau Kundur 148-149 D 6
Pulau Labengke 152-153 P 7
Pulau Labuan 148-149 FG 5
Pulau Langkawi 148-149 C 5
Pulau Larat 148-149 K 8
Pulau Lari Larian 152-153 MN 7
Pulau Laut [RI, Selat Makasar] 148-149 G 7
Pulau Laut [RI, South China Sea] 148-149 E 6
Pulau Lemukutan 152-153 GH 5
Pulau Lepar 148-149 E 7
Pulau Liat 152-153 G 7
Pulau Lingga 148-149 DE 7
Pulau Lomblen 148-149 H 8
Pulau Lombok 148-149 G 8
Pulau Lumut 150-151 C 11
Pulau Madu 152-153 OP 9
Pulau Madura 148-149 F 8
Pulau Maikoor 148-149 K 8
Pulau Makian 148-149 J 6
Pulau Malawali 152-153 M 2
Pulau Mandioli 148-149 J 7
Pulau Mangole 148-149 J 7
Pulau Mantanani 152-153 LM 2
Pulau Manui 152-153 P 7
Pulau Manuk 148-149 K 8
Pulau Mapor 152-153 F 5
Pulau Maratua 148-149 G 6
Pulau Matak 150-151 F 11
Pulau Maya 148-149 E 7
Pulau Mayu 148-149 J 6
Pulau Mega 152-153 D 8
Pulau Mendol 148-149 D 6
Pulau Mengalum 152-153 L 2
Pulau Menjawak = Pulau Rakit 152-153 H 8
Pulau Merundung 152-153 H 4
Pulau Mesanak 152-153 F 5
Pulau Miangas 148-149 J 5
Pulau Midai 148-149 E 6
Pulau Misoöl 148-149 K 7
Pulau Moa 148-149 J 8
Pulau Mojo 148-149 G 8
Pulau Molu 148-149 K 8
Pulau Mondoliko 152-153 J 9
Pulau Moreses 152-153 L 8
Pulau Morotai 148-149 J 6
Pulau Mubur 152-153 FG 4
Pulau Mules 152-153 O 10
Pulau Muna 148-149 H 8
Pulau Musala 148-149 C 6
Pulau Nias 148-149 C 6
Pulau Nila 148-149 JK 8
Pulau Numfoor 148-149 KL 7
Pulau Obi 148-149 J 7
Pulau Padang 148-149 D 6
Pulau Padangtikar 148-149 E 7
Pulau Pagai Selatan 148-149 CD 7
Pulau Pagai Utara 148-149 C 7
Pulau Palu 152-153 O 10
Pulau Panaitan 148-149 DE 8
Pulau Pangkor 150-151 C 10
Pulau Panjang 152-153 H 4
Pulau Pantar 148-149 H 8
Pulau Pasi 152-153 O 9
Pulau Pasitanete 152-153 O 8
Pulau Pejantan 152-153 G 5
Pulau Peleng 148-149 H 7
Pulau Pelokang 152-153 N 9
Pulau Pemanggil 150-151 E 11
Pulau Penang = Pulau Pinang 150-151 BC 10
Pulau Penembangan 152-153 H 6
Pulau Pengibu 152-153 G 5
Pulau Pinang 150-151 BC 10
Pulau Pini 148-149 C 6
Pulau-pulau Badas 152-153 G 5
Pulau-pulau Balabalangan 148-149 G 7
Pulau-pulau Banyak 148-149 C 6
Pulau-pulau Bawah 152-153 G 4
Pulau-pulau Hinako 152-153 B 5
Pulau-pulau Karimata 148-149 E 7
Pulau-pulau Karimunjawa 148-149 EF 8
Pulau-pulau Kokos 152-153 A 4
Pulau-pulau Kumamba 148-149 LM 7
Pulau-pulau Laut Kecil 148-149 G 7-8
Pulau-pulau Lucipara 148-149 J 8
Pulau-pulau Nenusa 148-149 J 6
Pulau-pulau Pagai 148-149 CD 7
Pulau-pulau Penyu 148-149 J 8
Pulau-pulau Seribu 148-149 E 7-8
Pulau-pulau Tambelan 148-149 E 6
Pulau-pulau Watubela 148-149 K 7
Pulau Puteran 152-153 L 9
Pulau Raas 148-149 FG 8
Pulau Rakit 152-153 H 8
Pulau Rangsang 148-149 D 6
Pulau Redang 150-151 D 10
Pulau Repong 152-153 FG 4
Pulau Rinja 148-149 G 8
Pulau Romang 148-149 J 8
Pulau Roti 148-149 H 9
Pulau Rumberpon 148-149 KL 7
Pulau Rupat 148-149 D 6
Pulau Sabaru 152-153 N 9
Pulau Sakeng 154 III a 2
Pulau Sakijang Bendera 154 III ab 2
Pulau Sakijang Pelepah 154 III b 2
Pulau Salawati 148-149 K 7
Pulau Salayar 148-149 H 8
Pulau Salebabu 148-149 J 6
Pulau Salembu Besar 148-149 FG 8
Pulau Sambit 152-153 N 5
Pulau Samosir 148-149 C 6
Pulau Sanding 152-153 D 7
Pulau Sangeang 148-149 GH 8
Pulau Sangihe 148-149 J 6
Pulau Sapudi 148-149 FG 8
Pulau Sapuka Besar 152-153 N 9
Pulau Satengar 152-153 M 9
Pulau Sawu 148-149 H 9
Pulau Sebangka 148-149 DE 6
Pulau Sebarok 154 III a 2
Pulau Sebatik 148-149 G 6
Pulau Sebuku 148-149 G 7
Pulau Sedanau 150-151 F 11
Pulau Sekala 152-153 M 9
Pulau Selaru 148-149 K 8
Pulau Seletar 154 III b 1
Pulau Seluan 150-151 F 10
Pulau Selui 152-153 G 7
Pulau Semakau 154 III a 2
Pulau Semau 148-149 H 9
Pulau Sembilan 150-151 B 10
Pulau Semeuluë 148-149 BC 6
Pulau Semiun 150-151 F 10
Pulau Sempu 152-153 K 10
Pulau Senebui 150-151 C 11
Pulau Sentosa 154 III a 2
Pulau Sepenjang 148-149 G 8
Pulau Serangoon 154 III b 1
Pulau Serasan 150-151 G 11
Pulau Seraya 150-151 G 11
Pulau Sermata 148-149 J 8
Pulau Serua 148-149 K 8
Pulau Serutu 152-153 H 6
Pulau Siantan 150-151 EF 11
Pulau Siau 148-149 J 6
Pulau Siberut 148-149 C 7
Pulau Sibu 150-151 E 11
Pulau Simatang 152-153 NO 5
Pulau Singkep 148-149 DE 7
Pulau Sipora 148-149 C 7
Pulau Sipura = Pulau Sipora 148-149 C 7
Pulau Siumpu 152-153 P 8
Pulau Solor 148-149 H 8
Pulau Subar Luat 154 III ab 2
Pulau Subi 150-151 G 11
Pulau Subi Kecil 152-153 H 4
Pulau Sulabesi 148-149 J 7
Pulau Supiori 148-149 KL 7
Pulau Tahulandang 148-149 J 6
Pulau Taliabu 148-149 HJ 7
Pulau Tambelan 152-153 GH 5
Pulau Tambolongang 152-153 NO 9
Pulau Tanahbala 148-149 C 7
Pulau Tanahjampea 148-149 H 8
Pulau Tanahmasa 148-149 C 6-7
Pulau Tanakeke 148-149 G 8
Pulau Tanjungbuayabuaya 152-153 N 5
Pulau Tapat 148-149 J 7
Pulau Tarakan 152-153 MN 4
Pulau Tebingtinggi 148-149 D 6
Pulau Tekukor 154 III b 2
Pulau Tenggol 150-151 DE 10
Pulau Teun 148-149 J 8
Pulau Tidore 148-149 J 6
Pulau Tifore 148-149 J 6
Pulau Tiga 152-153 L 3
Pulau Timbun Mata 152-153 N 3
Pulau Tinggi 150-151 E 11
Pulau Tinjil 148-149 E 8
Pulau Tioman 148-149 DE 6
Pulau Tjendana = Sumba 148-149 G 9
Pulau Tobalai 148-149 J 7
Pulau Togian 152-153 O 6
Pulau Tomea 152-153 PQ 8
Pulau Trangan 148-149 K 8
Pulau Tuangku 152-153 B 4
Pulau Ubin 154 III b 1
Pulau Unauna 152-153 O 6
Pulau Waigeo 148-149 K 6
Pulau Wangiwangi 152-153 PQ 8
Pulau Weh 148-149 BC 5
Pulau Wetar 148-149 J 8
Pulau Wokam 148-149 KL 8
Pulau Wowoni 148-149 H 7
Pulau Wunga 152-153 B 5
Pulau Yapen 148-149 L 7
Puławy 118 L 3
Pulé 141 D 5
Pulga 138-139 F 1-2
Pūlgāṅv = Pulgaon 138-139 G 7
Pulgaon 138-139 G 7
Pulí [CO] 94-95 D 5
Puli [RC] 146-147 H 10
Puli = Tash Qurghan 142-143 D 4
Pulicat 140 E 4
Pulicat Lake 140 E 4
Puḷikkaṭṭa = Pulicat 140 E 4
Pulivendla 140 D 3
Pulivēṇḍra = Pulivendla 140 D 3
Puliyangudi 140 C 6
Puliyankulama 140 E 6
Pullmann, WA 66-67 E 2
Pulo Anna 148-149 K 6
Pulog, Mount — 148-149 H 3
Pulo Gadung, Jakarta- 154 IV b 2
Pulozero 116-117 PQ 3
Púlpito, Punta — 86-87 E 4
Pułtusk 118 K 2
Pülümür 136-137 HJ 3
Pu-lun-t'o Hai = Ojorong nuur 142-143 F 2
Pulusuk 148-149 NO 5
Puluwat 148-149 NO 5
Pumasillo, Cerro — 96-97 E 8
Pumpkin Creek 68-69 D 3
Pumpville, TX 76-77 D 8
Pûn, Nam — 141 E 5-6
Puna [BOL] 104-105 D 6
Puná [EC] 92-93 CD 5
Puna [RA] 106-107 F 1
Puna = Pune 134-135 L 7
Puná, Isla — 92-93 C 5
Puna Argentina 111 C 2-3
Punākha = Phunakha 134-135 OP 5
Pūnalūr 140 C 6
Punalūra = Pūnalūr 140 C 6
Punan 152-153 L 5
Punata 92-93 F 8
Pûnbāgyin 141 F 6
Punchaw 60 F 3
Punchbowl, Sydney- 161 I a 2
Puncuri 96-97 B 6
Punda Milia 174-175 J 2
Punduga 124-125 N 3
Pune 134-135 L 7
Puṇĕṅ = Pune 134-135 L 7
Punganur = Punganūru 140 D 4
Punganūru 140 D 4
Pûngaya Bûm 141 D 2
Punggol [SGP, place] 154 III b 1
Punggol [SGP, river] 154 III b 1
Punggol, Tanjong — 154 III b 1
P'ungnam-ni 144-145 F 5
P'ungnyu-ri 144-145 F 2
P'ungsan 144-145 FG 2
Punia 172 E 2
Punilla, Cordillera de la — 106-107 B 2
Punilla, Sierra de la — 106-107 C 2
Puning 146-147 F 10
Punitaqui 106-107 B 3
Punjab [IND] 134-135 LM 4
Punjab [PAK] 134-135 L 4
Punkuḍutivu 140 DE 6
Puno 96-97 FG 9
Puno = San Carlos de Puno 92-93 EF 8
Punta Abreojos 64-65 CD 6
Punta Achira 106-107 A 6
Punta Aguja 92-93 C 6
Punta Alcade 106-107 B 2
Punta Alice 122-123 G 6
Punta Alta 111 D 5
Punta Ameghino 108-109 G 4
Punta Angamos 111 B 2
Punta Animas 104-105 A 10
Punta Anton Lizardo 86-87 N 8
Punta Arena de las Ventas 86-87 F 5-6
Punta Arenas 104-105 A 7
Punta Arenas [RCH, place] 111 BC 8
Punta Arvejas 106-107 A 7
Punta Asunción 106-107 G 7
Punta Atalaya 106-107 J 5
Punta Atlas 108-109 G 5
Punta Baja [MEX, Baja California Norte] 64-65 C 5
Punta Baja [MEX, Sonora] 86-87 DE 3
Punta Baja [RCH] 108-109 AB 7
Punta Baja [YV] 92-93 G 3
Punta Ballena 106-107 K 5
Punta Banda 64-65 C 5
Punta Bermeja 108-109 H 3
Punta Blanca 106-107 J 5
Punta Brava 106-107 JK 5
Punta Buenos Aires 108-109 G 4-H 3
Punta Burica 64-65 K 10
Punta Cabeza de Vaca 104-105 A 10
Punta Cachos 111 B 3
Punta Canoas 94-95 D 2
Punta Caracoles 88-89 G 11
Punta Cardón 94-95 F 2
Punta Caribana 92-93 D 3
Punta Carnero 106-107 A 6
Punta Carretas 96-97 C 9
Punta Casacajal 94-95 B 6
Punta Castro 108-109 G 4
Punta Catalina 108-109 EF 9
Punta Cautén 106-107 A 7
Punta Cero 108-109 H 4
Punta Chala 96-97 D 9
Punta Chiguao 108-109 C 4
Punta Clara 108-109 G 4
Punta Cobija 104-105 A 8
Punta Coco 94-95 C 6
Punta Coicoi 106-107 A 6
Punta Cornejo 96-97 E 10
Punta Cosigüina 64-65 J 9
Punta Cruces 94-95 C 4
Punta Curaumilla 106-107 AB 4
Punta da Armação 110 I c 2
Punta de Araya 94-95 J 2
Punta de Arenas 111 C 8
Punta de Bombón 96-97 EF 10
Punta de Coles 92-93 E 8
Punta de Díaz 111 BC 3
Punta de Jurujuba 110 I c 2
Punta de la Baña 120-121 H 8
Punta de la Estaca de Bares 120-121 D 6-7
Punta del Agua 106-107 CD 5
Punta de las Entinas 120-121 F 10
Punta del Diablo 106-107 L 5
Punta del Este 106-107 K 5
Punta Delgada [RA, cape] 108-109 H 4
Punta Delgada [RA, place] 111 D 6
Punta Delgada [RCH] 111 C 8
Punta del Lago, Hotel — 108-109 CD 7
Punta del Mono 88-89 E 9
Punta de Lobos 106-107 A 5
Punta de los Llanos 106-107 D 3
Punta del Palmar 106-107 L 5
Punta de Mata 94-95 K 3
Punta de Mita 64-65 E 7
Punta de Morás 120-121 D 6-7
Punta de Perlas 64-65 K 9
Punta de Salinas 92-93 D 7
Punta de San Bernardo 94-95 CD 3
Punta Descanso 86-87 B 1
Punta Desengaño 108-109 F 7
Punta Desnudez 106-107 H 7
Punta de Tarifa 120-121 DE 11
Punta de Tubiacanga 110 I b 1
Punta di Faro 122-123 F 6
Punta do Catalão 110 I b 2
Punta do Galeão 110 I b 2
Punta do Imbuí 110 I c 2
Punta do Marisco 110 I b 3
Punta do Matoso 110 I b 1
Punta Doña Maria 92-93 D 7
Punta Duao 106-107 A 5
Punta Dungeness 108-109 EF 9
Punta El Cojo 91 II b 1
Punta Entrada 108-109 EF 8
Punta Estrella 86-87 C 2
Punta Eugenia 64-65 C 6
Punta Falsa Chipana 104-105 A 7
Punta Foca 108-109 G 6
Punta Frontera 86-87 O 8
Punta Galera [CO] 94-95 D 2
Punta Galera [EC] 92-93 C 4
Punta Galera [RCH] 111 AB 6
Punta Gallinas 92-93 E 2
Punta Garachiné 94-95 B 3
Punta Gorda, FL 80-81 bc 3
Punta Gorda [BH] 64-65 J 8
Punta Gorda [NIC] 88-89 E 7
Punta Gorda [RCH] 104-105 A 6
Punta Gorda [YV, Distrito Federal] 91 II b 1
Punta Gorda [YV, Guajira] 94-95 F 1
Punta Gorda [YV, Zulia] 94-95 F 2
Punta Graviña 108-109 FG 5
Punta Grosa 120-121 H 9
Punta Grossa 110 I b 1
Punta Gruesa 104-105 A 7
Punta Guala 108-109 C 4
Punta Guarico 88-89 JK 4
Punta Guascama 92-93 D 4
Punta Guiones 88-89 CD 10
Punta Huechucuicui 108-109 B 3
Punta Indio 106-107 J 5
Punta Islay 96-97 E 10
Punta Judas 88-89 D 10
Punta Laberinto 106-107 FG 7
Punta Lameguapi 108-109 BC 3
Punta Lavapié 111 AB 5
Punta La Vieja 106-107 A 5
Punta Lengua de Vaca 111 B 4
Punta Licosa 122-123 F 5
Punta Lima 96-97 D 10
Punta Llorena = Punta San Pedro 64-65 K 10
Punta Lobería 106-107 AB 3
Punta Lobos [RA] 108-109 G 4
Punta Lobos [RCH, Atacama] 106-107 B 2
Punta Lobos [RCH, Tarapacá ↑ Iquique] 104-105 A 6
Punta Lobos [RCH, Tarapacá ↓ Iquique] 104-105 A 7
Punta Lora 106-107 A 5
Punta Loyola 108-109 E 8
Punta Lucas = Cape Meredith 111 D 8
Punta Macolla 94-95 F 1
Punta Mala 64-65 L 10
Punta Maldonado 64-65 FG 8
Punta Manaure 94-95 E 2
Punta Mangrove 64-65 F 8
Punta Manuel 106-107 A 7
Punta Manzanillo 64-65 L 9-10
Punta Médano 108-109 H 3
Punta Medanosa 111 CD 7
Punta Mejillón 108-109 G 3
Punta Mercedes 108-109 FG 7
Punta Mogotes 106-107 J 7
Punta Molles 106-107 B 4
Punta Mona 88-89 E 10
Punta Montes 108-109 E 8
Punta Morguilla 106-107 A 6
Punta Morro 111 B 3
Punta Mulatos 91 II b 1
Punta Naranjas 92-93 C 3
Punta Negra [PE] 92-93 C 6
Punta Negra [RA] 106-107 H 7
Punta Negra [ROU] 106-107 K 5
Punta Negra, Salar de — 104-105 B 9
Punta Ñermete 92-93 C 6
Punta Ninfas 111 D 6
Punta Norte 111 D 6
Punta Norte del Cabo San Antonio 111 E 5
Punta Nugurue 106-107 A 5
Punta Pájaros 111 B 3
Punta Paloma 104-105 A 6
Punta Parada 92-93 D 8
Punta Pariñas 92-93 C 5
Punta Patache 104-105 A 7
Punta Patuca 64-65 K 8
Punta Peña Negra 92-93 C 5
Punta Peñas 92-93 G 2
Punta Pequeña 86-87 D 4
Punta Pescadores 96-97 E 10
Punta Piaxtla 86-87 G 6
Punta Pichalo 104-105 A 6
Punta Piedras 106-107 J 5
Punta Piedras de Lobos 106-107 AB 3
Punta Pórfido 108-109 G 3
Punta Porotos 106-107 B 2
Punta Pozos 108-109 G 6
Punta Pringle 108-109 Ab 6
Punta Púlpito 86-87 E 4
Punta Quillagua 108-109 BC 3
Punta Quiroga 108-109 G 3-4
Punta Rasa 111 D 6
Puntarenas 64-65 K 9-10
Punta Rescue 108-109 B 6
Punta Reyes 94-95 B 6
Punta Rieles 102-103 C 5
Punta Roja 108-109 G 5
Punta Rosa 86-87 EF 4
Punta San Andrés 106-107 J 7
Punta San Blas 64-65 L 10
Punta San Carlos 86-87 C 3
Punta San Francisco Solano 92-93 D 3
Punta San Pablo 86-87 C 4
Punta San Pedro [CR] 64-65 K 10
Punta San Pedro [RCH] 104-105 A 9
Punta Santa Ana 96-97 D 9
Punta Santa María [MEX] 86-87 F 5
Punta Santa María [ROU] 106-107 KL 5
Punta San Telmo 86-87 HJ 8
Punta Scerpeddi 122-123 C 6
Punta Serpeddì 122-123 C 6
Punta Sierra 108-109 G 3
Puntas Negras, Cerro — 111 C 2
Punta Sur del Cabo San Antonio 111 E 5
Punta Talca 106-107 AB 4
Punta Taltal 104-105 A 9
Punta Tanaguarena 91 II c 1
Punta Tejada 106-107 G 7
Punta Tetas 111 B 2
Punta Tombo 108-109 G 5
Punta Topocalma 106-107 A 5
Punta Toro 106-107 AB 4
Punta Tucupel 106-107 A 6
Punta Tumbes 106-107 A 6
Punta Vacamonte 64-65 b 3
Punta Villa del Señor 106-107 AB 3
Punta Villarino 108-109 G 3
Punta Virgen 106-107 AB 3
Punta Weather 108-109 B 4
Punta Zamuro 94-95 G 2

Puntijao 96-97 E 7
Puntilla, La — 92-93 C 5
Puntillas 104-105 B 7
Puntodo, Cerro — 106-107 E 7
Punuk Islands 58-59 C 5
Punxsutawney, PA 72-73 G 4
Punyu = Guangzhou 142-143 LM 7
Puolanka 116-117 MN 5
Pup'yŏng-dong 144-145 G 2
Puqi 142-143 L 6
Puqian 146-147 C 11
Puquio 92-93 E 7
Puquios [RCH ↗ Antofagasta] 104-105 B 7
Puquios [RCH ↗ Arica] 111 C 1
Puquios [RCH ↗ Copiapó] 106-107 C 1
Pur 132-133 O 4
Purace, Volcán — 94-95 C 6
Purāndar = Purandhar 140 AB 1
Purandhar 140 AB 1
Purang 138-139 H 2
Pūranpur 138-139 H 3
Purau 152-153 O 7
Purcell, OK 76-77 F 5
Purcell Mount 58-59 J 3
Purcell Mountains 56-57 N 7-8
Purcell Mountains Provincial Park 60 JK 4
Purén 106-107 A 6-7
Purgatoire River 68-69 DE 7
Purgatory, AK 58-59 N 3
Puri 134-135 O 7
Purificación 94-95 D 6
Purísima, La — 86-87 DE 4
Purley, London- 129 II b 2
Purli 140 C 1
Purma Gómez 96-97 E 6
Purmerbuurt 128 I b 1
Purmerland 128 I ab 1
Pūrna [IND, place] 138-139 F 8
Purna [IND, river ◁ Godāvari] 138-139 F 8
Pūrna [IND, river ◁ Tāpti] 138-139 F 7
Pūrnagad 140 A 2
Purnea 134-135 O 5
Purniyā = Purnea 134-135 O 5
Pursat 148-149 D 4
Pursat, Stung — 150-151 D 6
Purthi Ghāt 138-139 J 3
Purubi 104-105 F 6
Puruê, Rio — 96-97 G 3
Purukcau 148-149 F 7
Purūlia 134-135 O 6
Puruliyā = Purūlia 134-135 O 6
Purus, Rio — 92-93 F 6
Purvā = Purwa 138-139 H 4
Purvis, MS 78-79 E 5
Purwa 138-139 H 4
Purwa, Tanjung — 152-153 KL 10
Purwakarta 148-149 E 8
Purwaredja = Purworejo 148-149 EF 8
Purwokerto 148-149 EF 8
Purworejo 148-149 EF 8
Puryŏng 144-145 GH 1-2
Pusa 152-153 J 5
Pusad 138-139 F 8
Pusan 142-143 OP 4
Pusat Abri, Musium — 154 IV a 2
Pusat Gayo, Pegunungan — 152-153 B 3
Pushi 146-147 BC 7
P'u-shih = Pushi 146-147 BC 7
Pushkar 138-139 E 4
Pushpagiri [IND, mountain] 140 B 4
Pushpagiri [IND, place] 140 D 4
Pusi 96-97 G 9
Puškin 132-133 DE 6
Puškino [SU, Azerbajdžanskaja SSR] 126-127 O 7
Puškino [SU, Rossijskaja SFSR Moskovskaja Oblast'] 124-125 LM 5
Puškino [SU, Rossijskaja SFSR Saratovskaja Oblast'] 126-127 N 1
Puškinskije Gory 124-125 G 5
Puskitamika, Lac — 62 N 2
Pušlachta 124-125 L 1
Püspökladány 118 K 5
Pustoška 124-125 G 5
Pusur 138-139 M 6
Put, De — = Die Put 174-175 E 6
Put, Die — 174-175 E 6
Putaendo 106-107 B 4
Putai 146-147 GH 10
Putana, Volcán — 104-105 C 8
Putao = Pudão 148-149 C 1
Put'atina, ostrov — 144-145 J 1
Puteaux 129 I b 2
Puteran, Pulau — 152-153 L 9
Puthein 148-149 B 3
Puthein Myit 141 D 7
Puṭhimaṛi 141 B 2
Putian 142-143 M 6
Putien = Putian 142-143 M 6
Putilovo 124-125 P 4
Putina 96-97 G 9
Puting, Tanjung — 148-149 F 7
Putivl' 126-127 F 1
Putla de Guerrero 86-87 M 9
Putnam 171 B 2
Putney, London- 129 II b 2
Putorana, plato — 132-133 RS 4
Putre 104-105 B 6
Putre, Nevado — 104-105 B 6
Putsonderwater 174-175 DE 5
Puttalam = Puttalama 134-135 M 9
Puttalama 134-135 M 9
Puttalam Kalapuwa 140 DE 6
Puttalam Lagoon = Puttalam Kalapuwa 140 DE 6
Puttgarden 118 E 1
Puttuchcheri = Pondicherry 134-135 MN 8
Puttūr [IND, Andhra Pradesh] 140 D 4
Puttūr [IND, Karnataka] 140 B 4
Puttūru = Puttūr [IND, Andhra Pradesh] 140 D 4
Puttūru = Puttūr [IND, Karnataka] 140 B 4
Putū 106-107 A 5
Putumayo [CO, administrative unit] 94-95 C 7-D 8
Putumayo [CO, place] 92-93 D 4-5
Putumayo, Río — 92-93 E 5
Pütürge = İmron 136-137 H 3
Putuskum = Potiskum 164-165 G 6
Putussibau 152-153 K 5
Putzbrunn 130 II c 2
Putzonderwater = Putsonderwater 174-175 DE 5
Pu-tzŭ = Potzu 146-147 H 10
Puulavesi 116-117 M 7
Puuwai, HI 78-79 b 2
Puvāṅyā = Pawāyan 138-139 GH 3
Pūvār 140 C 6
Puxi 146-147 G 9
Pu Xian 146-147 C 3
Puxico, MO 78-79 D 2
Puy, le — 120-121 J 6
Puyallup, WA 66-67 B 2
Puyang 146-147 E 4
P'u-yang Chiang = Puyang Jiang 146-147 H 7
Puyang Jiang 146-147 H 7
Puyango, Río — 96-97 A 4-B 3
Puy de Dôme 120-121 J 6
Puyehue [RCH, mountain] 108-109 C 3
Puyehue [RCH, place] 111 B 6
Puyehue, Lago — 108-109 C 3
Puyehue, Portillo — 108-109 CD 3
Puyo 92-93 D 5
Puyuguapi, Canal — 108-109 C 5
Puzla 124-125 U 2
Pwani 172 G 3
Pwehla 141 E 5
Pwela = Pwehla 141 E 5
Pweto 172 E 3
Pwllheli 119 D 5
Pyang 138-139 G 2
Pyanmalaw 141 D 8
Pyapon = Hpyābôn 141 D 7
Pyatigorsk = P'atigorsk 126-127 L 4
Pyaubwei 141 E 5
Pyawbwe = Pyaubwei 141 E 5
Pye Islands 58-59 MN 7
Pyelongyi = Pyīlôngyī 141 C 5
Pyhäjärvi 116-117 L 6
Pyhäjoki 116-117 L 5-6
Pyhäranta 116-117 JK 7
Pyhätunturi 116-117 M 4
Pyīlôngyī 141 C 5
Pyin 148-149 C 3
Pyingaing 141 D 4
Pyinmanā 148-149 C 3
Pyinshwā 141 D 7
Pyinzabu Kyūn 150-151 A 7
Pýlos 122-123 J 7
Pymatuning Reservoir 72-73 F 4
Pyŏktong 144-145 E 2
Pyŏngam-ni 144-145 F 5
P'yŏngan-namdo 144-145 EF 3
P'yŏngan-pukto 144-145 E 2-3
P'yŏngch'ang 144-145 G 4
P'yŏnggang 144-145 F 3
Pyŏnggok-tong 144-145 G 4
P'yŏnghae 144-145 G 4
P'yŏngnamjin 144-145 F 2
P'yŏngt'aek 144-145 F 4
P'yŏngt'ong 144-145 E 3
P'yŏngyang 142-143 NO 4
Pyote, TX 76-77 C 7
Pyramid, NV 66-67 D 5
Pyramid Lake 64-65 C 3
Pyramid Lake Indian Reservation 74-75 D 3
Pyrenees 120-121 G-J 7
Pyre Peak 58-59 k 4
Pyrgion 122-123 LM 6
Pýrgos [GR, Pelopónnēsos] 122-123 J 7
Pýrgos [GR, Sámos] 122-123 M 7
Pyrzyce 118 G 2
Pyšak 124-125 R 4
Pyščug 124-125 P 4
Pytalovo 124-125 FG 5
Pyu = Hpyū 148-149 C 3
Pyuthān = Piuthān 138-139 J 3

Q

Qā'al 'Umarī 136-137 G 7
Qa'āmiyāt, Al- 134-135 F 7
Qa'ara, Al- = Al-Qa'rah 136-137 J 6
Qabāb, Al- 166-167 D 3
Qabāil, Al- 166-167 HJ 1
Qābes = Qābis 164-165 FG 2
Qabilī 166-167 L 3
Qābis 164-165 FG 2
Qābis, Khalīj al- 164-165 G 2
Qabīt, Wādī — = Wādī Qitbīt 134-135 G 7
Qabr Hūd 134-135 FG 7
Qabūdiyah, Rā's — 166-167 M 2
Qachasnek 174-175 H 6
Qadārif, Al- 164-165 M 6
Qadayal 166-167 F 2
Qadīmah, Al- 134-135 DE 6
Qādir Karam 136-137 L 5
Qādisiyah, Al- 136-137 L 7
Qā'en 134-135 H 4
Qaf, Bi'r al- 164-165 H 3
Qafṣah 164-165 F 2
Qa'fūr 166-167 L 1
Qāhirah, Al- 164-165 KL 2
Qāhirah-Miṣr al-Jadīdah, Al- 173 BC 2
Qā'im, Al- 136-137 J 5
Qairouân, El — = Al-Qayrawān 164-165 FG 1
Qairwan = Al-Qayrawān 164-165 FG 1
Qaisā = Qaysā' 134-135 G 8
'Qala 'et el Djerdā' = Qal'at al-Jardah 166-167 L 2
Qala'et eṣ-Ṣenam = Qal'at Sinān 166-167 L 2
Qal'ah, Al- 164-165 F 1
Qal'āh-ye Shaharak = Shaharak 134-135 J 4
Qal'a-i-Bist 134-135 JK 4
Qal'a-i-Naw 134-135 J 3-4
Qal'a-i-Shahar 134-135 K 3
Qalāt 134-135 K 5
Qal'at al-'Azlam 173 D 4
Qal'at al-Jardah 166-167 L 2
Qal'at al-Kabīrah, Al- 166-167 M 2
Qal'at al-'Uwainid = Qal'at al-'Azlam 173 D 4
Qal'at as-S'rāghnah, Al- 166-167 C 3-4
Qal'at Bishah 134-135 E 6-7
Qal'at Dīzakh 136-137 L 4
Qal'at eḍ Ḍab'a = Ḍab'ah 136-137 G 7
Qal'at M'gūnā' 166-167 C 4
Qal'at Ṣāliḥ 136-137 M 7
Qal'at Sekar = Qal'at Sukkar 136-137 LM 7
Qal'at Sinān 166-167 L 2
Qal'at Sukkar 136-137 LM 7
Qal'at Tris 166-167 D 2
Qal'at 'Uneizah = 'Unayzah 136-137 FG 7
Qalb ar-Rīshāt 164-165 B 4
Qal'eh, Kūh-e — 136-137 N 6
Qal'eh Chāy 136-137 LM 4
Qal'eh Darreh 136-137 M 6
Qal'eh Sahar 136-137 N 7
Qalīb Bākūr 136-137 L 8
Qalībīyah 164-165 G 1
Qallābāt 164-165 M 6
Qalmah 164-165 F 1
Qalqīlyah 136-137 F 6
Qaltat Zammūr 164-165 B 3
Qalyūb 173 B 2
Qamār 166-167 K 3
Qamar, Ghubbat al- 134-135 G 7
Qamar, Jabal al- 134-135 G 7
Qamata 174-175 G 6
Qāmishlīyah, Al- 134-135 E 3
Qamqam 166-167 D 4
Qanādsah 166-167 E 4
Qanāl al-Ibrāhīmīyah 173 B 3
Qânâq 56-57 WX 2
Qanat as-Suways 164-165 L 2
Qanāt Djāliṭa = Qanāt Jaliṭah 166-167 L 1
Qanāt es-Suweis = Qanat as-Suways 164-165 L 2
Qanāt Jaliṭah = Qanāt Jaliṭah 166-167 L 1
Qanāt Jaliṭah 166-167 L 1
Qandahār = Kandahār 134-135 K 4
Qandala 164-165 b 1
Qandkoṭ 138-139 B 3
Qanṭarah, Al- [DZ, landscape] 166-167 J 3
Qanṭarah, Al- [DZ, place] 166-167 J 2
Qanṭarah, Al- [ET] 173 C 2
Qaqortoq 56-57 b 5
Qara Dāgh 136-137 L 5
Qara Dong 142-143 E 4
Qa'rah, Al- [IRQ] 136-137 J 6
Qārah, Al- [Saudi Arabia] 136-137 J 8
Qarah Dāgh 136-137 K 4
Qaramai 142-143 EF 2
Qaramurun davan 132-133 MN 3
Qarānqū, Rūd-e — 136-137 M 4
Qara Qash Darya 142-143 D 4
Qara Qorām = Karakoram 134-135 L 3-M 4
Qārārah, Al- 166-167 J 3
Qarārim 166-167 K 1
Qara Shahr 142-143 F 3
Qārat Ajnis 136-137 BC 8
Qārat al-Idad 136-137 C 8
Qārat al-Junūn 166-167 J 7
Qārat al-Mashrūkah 136-137 C 7
Qara Tappa 136-137 L 5
Qārat as-Sab'ah 164-165 H 3
Qar'at aṭ-Ṭarf 166-167 K 2
Qārat aṭ-Ṭarfāyah 136-137 BC 7
Qārat el Hireimis = Qārat Huraymis 136-137 B 7
Qārat Huraymis 136-137 B 7
Qar'at Jubab 136-137 J 5
Qardho 164-165 b 2
Qareh Āghāj 136-137 M 4
Qareh Būteh 136-137 M 4
Qareh Chāy 136-137 M 3
Qareh Dāgh 134-135 F 3
Qareh Ḍiyā' ad-Dīn 136-137 L 3
Qareh Sū [IR, Kermānshāhān] 136-137 M 5
Qareh Sū [IR, Tehrān] 136-137 N 5
Qāret el 'Ided = Qārat al-Idad 136-137 C 8
Qarghaliq 142-143 D 4
Qaria bā Moḥammed = Qaryat Bā Muḥammad 166-167 D 2
Qarliq Tagh 142-143 GH 3
Qarn at-Tays, Jabal — 173 C 6
Qarnayt, Jabal — 134-135 E 6
Qarqannah, Jazur — 164-165 G 2
Qārrāt Ṣaḥrā' al-Igīdi 164-165 C 4-D 3
Qārūn, Birkat — 164-165 KL 3
Qaryah 134-135 E 7
Qaryat al-'Ulyā 134-135 F 5
Qaryatayn, Al- 136-137 G 5
Qaryat Bā Muḥammad 166-167 D 2
Qarzīm 166-167 F 5
Qaṣab 136-137 K 4
Qaṣab = Al-Khaṣab 134-135 H 5
Qaṣab, Wādī — 173 C 4
Qaṣab, Wādī al- 136-137 K 4-5
Qaṣabah, Al- 136-137 B 7
Qaṣabeh 136-137 M 3
Qaṣābī, Al- 166-167 D 3
Qaṣba el Oualīdia = Wālidīyah 166-167 B 3
Qaṣbah, Rā's — 173 D 3-4
Qaṣ'bat Tādlah 166-167 C 3
Qāshqār 142-143 CD 4
Qāshqār darya 142-143 CD 4
Qasigiánguit 56-57 ab 4
Qaṣīm, Al- 134-135 E 5
Qaṣr, Al- [DZ] 166-167 J 1
Qaṣr, Al- [ET] 164-165 K 3
Qasr al-Bukharī 164-165 E 1
Qaṣr al-Burqū 136-137 GH 6
Qaṣr al-Ḥayr 136-137 H 5
Qaṣr al-Khubbāz 136-137 JK 6
Qaṣr 'Amīj 136-137 J 6
Qaṣr aṣ-Ṣabīyah 136-137 N 8
Qaṣrayn, Al- 164-165 F 1-2
Qaṣr Banī Walīd 164-165 G 2
Qaṣr Bilāl 136-137 M 8
Qaṣr-e Shīrīn 136-137 LM 5
Qaṣr Shillalah 166-167 H 2
Qaṣṣerīn, El — = Al-Qaṣrayn 164-165 F 1-2
Qastū 166-167 K 1
Qaṣūr 134-135 L 4
Qāsvīn = Qazvīn 134-135 FG 3
Qaṭanā 136-137 G 6
Qatar 134-135 G 5
Qaṭīf, Al- 134-135 F 5
Qaṭrānah, Al- 136-137 FG 7
Qaṭrānī, Jabal — 173 B 3
Qaṭrūn, Al- 164-165 GH 4
Qaṭṭār, Al- 166-167 J 2
Qaṭṭār, Ḥāssī al- 164-165 K 2
Qaṭṭār, Jabal — 173 C 4
Qaṭṭār, Shaṭṭ al- 166-167 L 2
Qattara Depression = Munhafaḍ al-Qaṭṭarah 164-165 K 2-3
Qaṭṭarah 166-167 E 4
Qaṭṭārah, Munhafaḍ al- 164-165 K 2-3
Qaṭṭārat ad-Duyūrah 136-137 C 7
Qaṭṭāret ad-Duyūrah 136-137 C 7
Qawām al-Ḥamzah 136-137 L 7
Qawz Rajab 164-165 M 5
Qay'īyah, Al- 134-135 E 6
Qayrawān, Al- 164-165 FG 1
Qaysā' 134-135 G 8
Qayṣūmah, Al- 134-135 F 5
Qaysūm, Jazā'ir — 173 CD 4
Qayyārah 136-137 K 5
Qazvīn 134-135 FG 3
Qbāb, el — = Al-Qabāb 166-167 D 3
Qebilī = Qabilī 166-167 L 3
Qedhāref, El- = Al-Qaḍārif 164-165 M 6
Qeisari = Caesarea 136-137 F 6
Qeisūm, Gezir — = Jazā'ir Qaysūm 173 CD 4
Qela'a es 'Srarhnā, el — = Al-Qal'at as-S'rāghnah 166-167 C 3-4
Qela'a Mgoûnā = Qal'at M'gūnā' 166-167 C 4
Qelībia = Qalībīyah 164-165 G 1
Qenā = Qinā 164-165 L 3
Qenā, Wādī — = Wādī Qinā 173 C 4
Qenaiṭrā = Qunayṭirah 136-137 FG 6
Qenfoūda = Janfūdah 166-167 E 2
Qenītra, el — = Al-Q'nitrah 164-165 C 2
Qeqertarssuatsiaq 56-57 a 5
Qeqertarssuq 56-57 Za 4
Qerqena, Djezîret — = Jazur Qarqannah 166-167 M 2
Qeshlāq 136-137 O 4-5
Qeshm 134-135 H 5
Qeshm = Jazīreh Qeshm 134-135 H 5
Qeshm, Jazīreh- 134-135 H 5
Qeṭaifē = Al-Quṭayfah 136-137 G 6
Qeṭṭār, Chott el — = Shaṭṭ al-Qaṭṭār 166-167 L 2
Qeydar 136-137 N 4
Qezel Owzan, Rūd-e — 134-135 F 3
Qĕẓi'ōt 136-137 F 7
Qian'an 146-147 G 1
Qiancheng 146-147 BC 8
Qiandongnan Zizhizhou 142-143 K 6
Qianjiang [TJ, Guangxi Zhuangzu Zizhiqu] 146-147 B 10
Qianjiang [TJ, Hubei] 142-143 L 5
Qianjiang [TJ, Sichuan] 142-143 K 6
Qianligang 146-147 G 7
Qiannon Zizhizhou 142-143 K 6
Qian Shan [TJ, mountains] 144-145 D 2-3
Qianshan [TJ, place] 146-147 F 6
Qianwei 144-145 C 2
Qianxi 146-147 G 1
Qian Xian 146-147 B 4
Qianyang 146-147 C 8
Qianyou He 146-147 B 5
Qiblī Qamūlā, Al- 173 C 5
Qichun 146-147 E 6
Qichun = Qizhou 146-147 E 6-7
Qidi Maghah 168-169 BC 2
Qidong [TJ, Hunan] 146-147 D 8
Qidong [TJ, Jiangsu] 146-147 H 6
Qidong [TJ, Shandong] 146-147 F 3
Qiduqou 142-143 GH 5
Qiemo = Chärchän 142-143 F 4
Qieshan = Yanshan 146-147 F 7
Qift 173 C 4-5
Qigou = Xikou 146-147 C 7
Qihe 146-147 F 3
Qihu = Chihu 146-147 H 9-10
Qikou 146-147 F 2
Qil'a Safed 134-135 J 5
Qil'a Saif'ullāh 138-139 B 2
Qilātis, Rā's — 166-167 E 2
Qilian Shan 142-143 HJ 4
Qilingou 146-147 B 3
Qilin Hu = Seling Tsho 142-143 FG 5
Qilizhen 146-147 B 4
Qimen 146-147 F 7
Qinā 164-165 L 3
Qinā, Wādī — 173 C 4
Qin'an 142-143 K 5
Qing'an 142-143 O 2
Qingcheng = Qing'an 142-143 O 2
Qingdao 142-143 N 4
Qingduizi 144-145 D 3
Qingfeng 146-147 E 4
Qinghai 142-143 GH 4
Qing Hai = Chöch nuur 142-143 H 4
Qinghe 146-147 E 3
Qinghecheng 144-145 E 2
Qinghemen 144-145 C 2
Qinghezhen 146-147 F 3
Qingjian 146-147 C 3
Qing Jiang [TJ, Hubei] 146-147 C 6
Qingjiang [TJ, Jiangsu] 142-143 M 5
Qingjiang [TJ, Jiangxi] 142-143 M 6
Qinglian 146-147 D 9
Qingliu 146-147 F 8
Qinglong 144-145 B 2
Qinglong He 144-145 B 2
Qingpu 146-147 H 6
Qingshuihe [TJ, place] 146-147 C 2
Qingshui He [TJ, river] 146-147 B 2
Qingshui Jiang 146-147 B 8
Qingshuitai 144-145 DE 1
Qingtian 146-147 H 7
Qing Xian 146-147 F 2
Qingxu 146-147 D 3
Qingyang [TJ, Anhui] 146-147 FG 6
Qingyang [TJ, Gansu] 142-143 K 4
Qingyuan [TJ, Fujian] 146-147 G 8
Qingyuan [TJ, Guangdong] 142-143 L 7
Qingyuan [TJ, Liaoning] 144-145 E 1
Qingyuan = Baoding 142-143 LM 4
Qingyun 146-147 F 3
Qingzhang Dongyuan 146-147 D 3
Qin He 142-143 L 4
Qinhuangdao 142-143 MN 3-4
Qin Ling 142-143 KL 5
Qinshui 146-147 D 4
Qin Xian 146-147 D 3
Qinyang 142-143 L 4
Qinyuan 146-147 D 3
Qinzhou 142-143 K 7
Qinzhou Wan 150-151 G 2
Qionghai 142-143 L 8
Qiongshan 142-143 L 8
Qiongzhong 150-151 GH 3
Qiongzhou Haixia 142-143 KL 7
Qiqihar 142-143 N 2
Qiraiya, Wādī — = Wādī Qurayyah 173 D 2
Qird'an, Bi'r al- 166-167 A 7
Qiryat Ata' 136-137 F 6
Qiryat Shemona 136-137 F 6
Qisha 150-151 G 2
Qishan = Chishan 146-147 H 10
Qishm = Qeshm [IR, island] 134-135 H 5
Qishm = Qeshm [IR, place] 134-135 H 5
Qishn 134-135 G 7
Qishrān 134-135 D 6
Qishui 146-147 B 11
Qislah 136-137 N 8
Qitai 142-143 FG 3
Qitbīt, Wādī — 134-135 G 7
Qiu Xian 146-147 E 3
Qixia 146-147 H 3
Qi Xian [TJ, Henan ↘ Kaifeng] 146-147 E 4
Qi Xian [TJ, Henan ↗ Xinxiang] 146-147 DE 4
Qi Xian [TJ, Shanxi] 146-147 D 3
Qixing Dao 146-147 H 8
Qiyang 146-147 CD 8
Qiyi 146-147 D 5
Qizan = Jīzān 134-135 E 7
Qizhou 146-147 E 6-7
Qizhou Liedao 150-151 H 3
Qizil Uzun = Rūd-e Qezel Owzan 134-135 F 3
Q'nitrah, Al- 164-165 C 2
Qohord 136-137 N 5
Qojūr 136-137 N 5
Qom 134-135 G 4
Qom Rūd 136-137 O 6
Qomul = Hami 142-143 G 3
Qoqriāl = Qūqriāl 164-165 K 7
Qōratū = Quraytū 136-137 L 5
Qorba = Qurbah 166-167 M 1
Qorbouṣ = Qurbūṣ 166-167 M 1
Qorveh 136-137 M 5
Qoseir, El- = Al-Quṣayr 164-165 L 3
Qōsh, Al- = Alqūsh 136-137 K 4
Qotbeh, Kūh-e — 136-137 M 6
Qoṭūr 134-135 E 3
Qoṭūr Chāy 136-137 L 3
Qoubayāt, El- = Al-Qubayyāt 136-137 G 5
Q'oûr = Qu'ūr 166-167 L 3
Qoûriāt, Djezir — = Jazā'ir Qūryāt 166-167 M 2
Qouṣair, El- = Al-Quṣayr 136-137 G 5
Qōz Regeb = Qawz Rajab 164-165 M 5
Q'runbālīyah 166-167 M 1
Qsābī, El — = Al-Qaṣābī 166-167 D 3
Qṣar al-Kabīr, Al- 164-165 C 1
Qṣar aṣ-Ṣaghīr, Al- 166-167 D 2
Qṣar as-Sūq = Ar-Rashidīyah 164-165 D 2
Qṣar Ben Khedāch = Banī Khaddāsh 166-167 LM 3
Q'ṣībah, Al- 166-167 CD 3
Qsour, El — = Al-Quṣūr 166-167 L 2
Qsoûr es Sâf = Quṣūr as-Sāf 166-167 M 2
Qṣoûr Sīdī 'Aïch = Quṣūr Sīdī 'Aysh 166-167 L 2
Qṣūr, Jabal al- 166-167 M 3
Quabbin Reservoir 72-73 K 3
Quadraro, Roma- 113 II bc 2
Quadros, Lagoa dos — 106-107 MN 2
Quakenbrück 118 CD 2
Quakertown, PA 72-73 J 4
Qual'at Īrīs 166-167 D 2
Quambatook 160 F 5
Quanah, TX 76-77 E 5
Quần Đao Hoang Sa 148-149 F 5
Quần Đao Tây Sa 148-149 EF 3
Quangbinh = Đông Ho'i 148-149 E 3
Quang Nam = Điện Ban 150-151 G 5
Quang Ngai 148-149 EF 3-4
Quang Tri 148-149 E 3
Quang Yên 148-149 E 2
Quan He 146-147 E 5
Quanjiao 146-147 FG 5
Quannan 146-147 E 9
Quannapowitt, Lake — 84 I b 1
Quantico, VA 72-73 H 5
Quanwan = Tsun Wan 155 I a 1
Quanxian = Quanzhou 142-143 KL 6
Quanxishi 146-147 D 8
Quanzhou [TJ, Fujian] 142-143 MN 6-7
Quanzhou [TJ, Guangxi Zhuangzu Zizhiqu] 142-143 KL 6
Quanzhou Gang 146-147 G 9
Qu'Appelle 61 G 5
Qu'Appelle River 56-57 Q 7
Quaraçu 100-101 D 8
Quaraí 106-107 J 3
Quarles, Pegunungan — 152-153 N 7
Quarnaro, Gulf of — = Kvarner 122-123 F 3
Quartier-Latin, Paris- 129 I c 2
Quartu Sant'Elena 122-123 C 6
Quartzsite, AZ 74-75 FG 6
Quatá 102-103 G 5
Quatis 102-103 K 5
Quatre Chemins, les — 170 I b 2
Quatro Irmãos 106-107 L 1
Quatro Irmãos, Morro — 104-105 F 5
Quatsino 60 D 4
Quatsino Sound 60 CD 4
Quay, NM 76-77 C 5
Qubayyāt, Al- 136-137 G 5
Qubba, Al-Qāhirah-al- 170 II b 1
Qūchān 134-135 H 3
Quchaq Bai 142-143 D 4
Qūchghār 134-135 F 3
Quds, Al- 136-137 F 7
Quealy, WY 66-67 J 5
Queanbeyan 158-159 JK 7
Quebec [CDN, administrative unit] 56-57 V-Y 7
Québec [CDN, place] 56-57 W 8
Quebra-Anzol, Rio — 102-103 J 3
Quebrachal, El — 104-105 DE 9
Quebracho 111 E 4
Quebrachos 106-107 F 2
Quebrada Azapa 104-105 B 6
Quebrada Chugchug 104-105 B 8
Quebrada de Aroma 104-105 B 6
Quebrada de Chiza 104-105 AB 6
Quebrada del Salado 104-105 A 10
Quebrada de Mani 104-105 B 7
Quebrada de Soga 104-105 B 6
Quebrada de Taltal 104-105 AB 9
Quebrada Doña Inés Chica 104-105 B 10
Quebrada Grande 106-107 B 2
Quebrada Guamal 91 II b 1
Quebrada Pan de Azúcar 104-105 A 10-B 9
Quebrada San Julian 91 II b 1
Quebrado San Andrés 106-107 BC 1
Quebra Pote 98-99 K 5
Queçaba 102-103 H 7
Quedal, Cabo — 111 AB 6
Quèd er Remad = Wādī Ban ar-Ramād 166-167 F 3
Quèd Guîr = Wādī Gīr 166-167 E 4
Quedlinburg 118 E 3
Quèd Madjerda = Wad Majradah 164-165 F 1
Queen Alexandra Range 53 A 17-15
Queen Bess, Mount — 60 E 4
Queen Charlotte 56-57 K 7
Queen Charlotte Bay 108-109 J 8
Queen Charlotte Islands 56-57 K 7
Queen Charlotte Sound 56-57 KL 7
Queen Charlotte Strait 56-57 L 7
Queen Elizabeth II Reservoir 129 II a 2
Queen Elizabeth Islands 56-57 N-V 2
Queen Elizabeth National Park = Ruwenzori National Park 172 EF 2
Queen Mary, Mount — 58-59 S 6
Queen Mary Coast = Queen Mary Land 53 C 10
Queen Mary Land 53 C 10
Queen Mary Reservoir 129 II a 2
Queen Maud Gulf 56-57 Q 4
Queen Maud Land = Dronning Maud land 53 B 36-4
Queen Maud's Range = Dronning Maud fjellkjede 53 A
Queens, New York-, NY 82 III cd 2
Queen's Channel 158-159 E 2
Queenscliff 160 G 7
Queensland 158-159 G-J 4
Queen's Mercy 174-175 H 6
Queenstown [AUS] 158-159 HJ 8
Queenstown [NZ] 158-159 N 8
Queenstown [ZA] 172 E 8
Queens Town, Singapore- 154 III a 2
Queens Village, New York, NY 82 III d 2
Queets, WA 66-67 A 2
Queguay 106-107 J 4
Queguay, Cuchilla de — 106-107 J 3
Queguay, Río — 106-107 J 4
Quehua 104-105 C 6
Quehué 106-107 E 6
Quehué, Valle de — 106-107 E 6
Queimada, Ilha — 98-99 N 5
Queimada, Serra — 102-103 J 5-6
Queimada Grande, Ilha — 102-103 J 6
Queimada Nova 100-101 D 5
Queimada Redonda, Serra — 100-101 E 4-5
Queimadas [BR, Bahia] 100-101 E 6
Queimadas [BR, Piauí] 100-101 C 5
Queimados, Serra dos — 104-105 E 1
Quela 172 C 3
Quelimane 172 G 5
Quella 106-107 AB 5-6
Quellen 108-109 C 4
Quelon 106-107 B 3
Quelpart = Cheju-do 142-143 NO 5
Queluz 102-103 K 5
Quemada, La — 86-87 J 6
Quemado, NM 74-75 J 5
Quemado, TX 76-77 D 8
Quemchi 108-109 C 4
Quemoy = Kinmen 146-147 G 9
Quemoy = Kinmen Dao 142-143 M 7
Quemú-Quemú 106-107 EF 6
Quenn City, IA 70-71 D 5
Quenuma 106-107 F 6
Quepem 140 B 3
Que Que = Kwekwe 172 E 5
Quequén 106-107 H 7
Quequeña 96-97 F 10
Quequén Grande, Río — 106-107 H 7
Queras, Río — 64-65 a 3
Querco 96-97 D 8
Quercy 120-121 H 6
Querencia, La — 106-107 H 3
Querência do Norte 102-103 F 5
Querero, Cachoeira — 98-99 K 4-5
Querétaro 64-65 FG 7
Quero [EC] 96-97 B 2
Quesada 120-121 F 10
Queshan 142-143 L 5
Quesnel 56-57 M 7
Quesnel Lake 60 G 3
Questa, NM 76-77 B 4
Quetena 104-105 C 8
Quetico 70-71 E 1
Quetico Lake 62 CD 3
Quetico Provincial Park 70-71 E 1
Quetta = Kwatta 134-135 K 4
Queue-en-Brie, la — 129 I d 2
Queule 108-109 C 2
Quevedo 96-97 B 2
Quevedo, Río — 96-97 B 2
Quévillon, Lac — 62 N 2
Quezaltenango 64-65 H 9
Quezon City 148-149 H 4
Quffah, Wādī al- 173 C 6
Qufou = Qufu 146-147 F 4
Qufu 146-147 F 4
Quiaca, La — 111 CD 2
Quiansu = Jiangsu 142-143 LM 6
Quibala 172 BC 4
Quibaxe 172 B 3
Quibdó 92-93 D 3
Quibell 62 C 2-3
Quiberon 120-121 F 5
Quibor 94-95 G 3
Quibray Bay 161 I b 3
Quichagua, Sierra de — 104-105 CD 8
Qui Châu 150-151 E 3
Quichuapunta, Paso — 96-97 C 6
Qui Dat 150-151 EF 4
Quidico 106-107 A 7
Quiindy 102-103 D 6
Quijingue 100-101 E 6
Quijotoa, AZ 74-75 GH 6
Quilán, Cabo — 108-109 B 4

Quilán, Isla — 108-109 B 4
Quilāndi 140 B 5
Quilcene, WA 66-67 B 2
Quilcó 106-107 G 6
Quilengues 172 BC 4
Quilhuiri, Portezuelo — 104-105 B 6
Quilimarí 111 B 4
Quilingou 146-147 B 3
Quilino 106-107 E 3
Quillabamba 96-97 E 8
Quillacas 104-105 C 6
Quillacollo 92-93 F 8
Quillagua 111 BC 2
Quillagua, Punta — 108-109 BC 3
Quillaicillo 106-107 AB 3
Quillalauquén, Sierra de — 106-107 G 6
Quill Lakes 56-57 Q 7
Quillón 106-107 A 6
Quillota 111 B 4
Quilmes 106-107 HJ 5
Quilmes, Sierra de — 104-105 C 10
Quilmes-Bernal 110 III c 2
Quilmes-Don Bosco 110 III c 2
Quilmes-Ezpeleta 110 III c 2
Quilmes-San Francisco Solano 110 III c 2
Quilon 134-135 M 9
Quilpie 158-159 H 5
Quilpué 106-107 B 4
Quimal, Cerro — 104-105 B 8
Quimar, Alto de — 94-95 C 3
Quimbele 172 C 3
Quime 104-105 C 5
Quimet 70-71 F 1
Quimilí 111 D 3
Quimome 104-105 F 5
Quimper 120-121 E 4-5
Quimperle 120-121 F 5
Quimpitirique 96-97 DE 8
Quimsachota, Cerro de — 104-105 B 5
Quimurcu, Cerros de — 104-105 AB 8
Quinault, WA 66-67 B 2
Quinault Indian Reservation 66-67 AB 2
Quince Mil 92-93 EF 7
Quinchao, Isla — 108-109 C 4
Quinchia 94-95 D 5
Quincy, CA 74-75 C 3
Quincy, FL 78-79 G 5
Quincy, IL 64-65 H 4
Quincy, MA 72-73 L 3
Quincy, WA 66-67 D 2
Quincy Bay 84 I c 3
Quindage 172 B 3
Quindío 94-95 D 5
Quines 111 C 4
Quinghua, Beijing- 155 II b 1
Quinghuayuan, Beijing- 155 II b 2
Quinhagak, AK 58-59 FG 7
Quinh Nhai 150-151 D 2
Qui Nho'n 148-149 EF 4
Quinigua, Serranía — 94-95 J 5
Quiñihual 106-107 G 6
Quinn, SD 68-69 EF 3
Quinn River 66-67 E 5
Quinn River Crossing, NV 66-67 DE 5
Quino 106-107 A 7
Quinta [BR] 106-107 L 4
Quinta [RCH] 106-107 B 5
Quintai 106-107 B 4
Quintanar de la Orden 120-121 F 9
Quintana Roo 64-65 J 7-8
Quinter, KS 68-69 FG 6
Quintero 106-107 B 4
Quinto, Río — 106-107 E 5
Quinton, OK 76-77 G 5
Quiongdong = Quionghai 142-143 L 8
Quipapá 100-101 FG 5
Quirigua 86-87 Q 10
Quirigua, Bogotá- 91 III b 2
Quirihue 106-107 A 6
Quirima 172 C 4
Quirimba, Ilhas — 172 H 4
Quirindi 160 K 3
Quirinópolis 102-103 G 3
Quiriquina, Isla — 106-107 A 6
Quiriquire 94-95 K 3
Quiroga [BOL] 104-105 D 6
Quiroga, Lago — 108-109 D 7
Quiroga, Punta — 108-109 G 3-4
Quirquinchos, Los — 106-107 G 4
Quirusillas 104-105 DE 6
Quiruvilca 96-97 BC 6
Quisiro 94-95 F 2
Quissanga 172 H 4
Quissico 172 FG 6
Quitaque, TX 76-77 D 5
Quiterajo 171 E 5
Quitéria, Rio — 102-103 G 3
Quitilipi 104-105 F 10
Quitman, GA 80-81 E 5
Quitman, MS 78-79 E 4
Quitman, TX 76-77 G 6
Quitman Mountains 76-77 B 7
Quito 92-93 D 5
Quivilla 96-97 C 6
Quixaba 100-101 C 6
Quixadá [BR, Ceará] 92-93 M 5
Quixada [BR, Rondônia] 98-99 G 10
Quixeramobim 92-93 M 5-6
Quixeré 100-101 EF 3
Qujiang 146-147 D 9
Qujiang = Shaoguan 142-143 L 6-7
Qujie 146-147 C 11
Qujing 142-143 J 6
Qūlāshgird = Golāshkerd 134-135 H 5
Qulay'ah, Rā's al- 136-137 N 8
Qulayb, Bi'r — 173 CD 5
Qulbān as-Sūfān 136-137 H 8
Qulbān aṭ-Ṭayyārāt 136-137 JK 5
Qulbān Layyah 136-137 M 8
Quleib, Bîr — = Bi'r Qulayb 173 CD 5
Qulʿah, Al- 166-167 H 1
Qulin, MO 78-79 D 2
Qull, Al- 166-167 K 1
Qūlonjī 136-137 L 4
Qum = Qom 134-135 G 4
Qumbu 174-175 H 6
Qum darya 142-143 F 3
Qum Köl 142-143 F 4
Qum tagh 142-143 G 4
Qumush 142-143 F 3
Qunāytirah 136-137 FG 6
Qundūz = Kunduz 134-135 K 3
Qunfudhah, Al- 134-135 DE 7
Qungur tagh 142-143 D 4
Qunluotuoyaozi = Zhangsanta 146-147 C 2
Quoin Point = Quoinpunt 174-175 C 8
Quoinpunt 174-175 C 8
Quoram = Korem 164-165 M 6
Quorn [AUS] 158-159 G 6
Quorn [CDN] 70-71 E 1
Qūqriāl 164-165 K 7
Quraynī, Al- 134-135 GH 6
Quraytū 136-137 L 5
Qurayyah, Al- 173 DE 3
Qurayyah, Wādī — 173 D 2
Qurayyāt al-Milḥ 136-137 G 7
Qurbah 164-165 M 1
Qurbūş 166-167 M 1
Qurdud 164-165 KL 6-7
Qūrênâ = Shaḥḥāt 164-165 J 2
Qurnah, Al- 136-137 M 7
Qurqul 168-169 B 2
Quruq Tagh 142-143 F 3
Qūryāt, Jazā'ir — 166-167 M 2
Qūş 173 C 5
Quşaybah 136-137 J 5
Quşay'ir 134-135 G 7-8
Quşayr, Al- [ET] 164-165 L 3
Quşayr, Al- [IRQ] 136-137 L 7
Quşayr, Al- [SYR] 136-137 G 5
Qushrān 134-135 D 6
Qushui = Chhushul 142-143 FG 6
Qūşīyah, Al- 173 B 4
Qustantīnah 164-165 F 1
Quşūr, Al- 166-167 L 2
Quşūr, Jibāl al- 166-167 FG 3
Quşūr as-Sāf 166-167 M 2
Quşūr Sīdī 'Aysh 166-167 L 2
Qutang 146-147 H 5
Quṭayfah, Al- 136-137 G 6
Quthing 174-175 G 6
Qu'ūr 166-167 L 3
Quwārib, Al- 164-165 A 5
Quwaymāt, Al- 136-137 GH 6
Quwayr, Al- 136-137 K 4
Quwayrah, Al- 136-137 F 8
Quwaysinā 173 B 2
Quwo 146-147 C 4
Qu Xian 142-143 M 6
Quyang [TJ, Hebei] 146-147 E 2
Quyang [TJ, Jiangxi] 146-147 E 8
Quynh Lu'u 150-151 EF 3
Quyon 72-73 H 2
Qūyūn, Jazīreh — 136-137 L 4
Quzhou 146-147 E 3
Quzi 146-147 A 3

Qytet Stalin 122-123 HJ 5

R

Raab 118 G 5
Raahe 116-117 L 5
Raakmoor 130 I b 1
Ra'an, Ar- 136-137 J 8
Raanes Peninsula 56-57 T 2
Raas, Pulau — 148-149 FG 8
Raas, Selat — 152-153 L 9
Raas Adado 164-165 b 1
Raasdorf 113 I c 2
Raas Haafuun 134-135 G 8
Raas Jumbo 172 H 2
Raas Khaanzuur 164-165 ab 1
Raas Sura 164-165 b 1
Rab 122-123 F 3
Raba [H] 118 H 5
Raba [RI] 148-149 G 8
Rabaçal 120-121 D 8
Rabat [M] 122-123 F 7
Rabat = Ar-Ribāṭ 164-165 C 2
Rabaul 148-149 h 5
Rabbit Ears Pass 68-69 C 5
R'abcevo 124-125 HJ 6
Rābigh 134-135 D 6
Rabindra Sarovar 154 II b 2
Rabnābād Dīpsamuh 141 B 5
Rabun Bald 80-81 E 3
Raccoon Island 84 III a 3
Raccoon Mountains = Sand Mountains 64-65 J 5
Raccoon River 70-71 C 4-5
Race, Cape — 56-57 a 8
Race Course of Calcutta 154 II ab 2
Race Course of Johor Baharu 154 III a 1
Race Course of Singapore 154 III a 1
Race Course of Tollygunge 154 II b 2
Raceland, LA 78-79 D 6
Rāchayā = Rāshayyā 136-137 FG 6
Rach Gia 148-149 DE 4-5
Rach Gia, Vung — 150-151 E 8
Rachgoun, Île — = Jazīrat Rāshqūn 166-167 F 2
Rachnā Doāb 138-139 D 2
Rachov 126-127 B 2
Racht = Rasht 134-135 FG 3
Racibórz 118 J 3
Racine, WI 64-65 J 3
Radā' [Y] 134-135 EF 8
Rada de Ilo 92-93 E 8
Rada de Tumaco 92-93 CD 4
Radal 106-107 A 7
Radama, Nosy — 172 J 4
Rada Tilly 108-109 F 5
Rădăuţi 122-123 L 2
Radebrück 130 III d 1
Radechov 126-127 B 1
Radford, VA 80-81 F 2
Rādhākishorepur 141 B 4
Rādhanpur 138-139 C 6
Rādhāpuram 140 CD 6
Radīsīyat Baḥrī, Ar- 173 C 5
Radisson 61 E 4
Radium 174-175 H 3
Radium Hot Springs 60 K 4
Radium Springs, NM 76-77 A 6
Radkersburg 118 GH 5
Radnor, PA 84 III a 1
Radom 118 K 3
Radomsko 118 JK 3
Radomyšl' 126-127 D 1
Radovicy 124-125 M 6
Radøy 116-117 A 7
Radul' 124-125 H 8
Radviliškis 124-125 DE 6
Radville 68-69 DE 1
Rae 56-57 NO 5
Rāe Bareli 134-135 N 5
Raeford, NC 80-81 G 3
Rae Isthmus 56-57 T 4
Rae Strait 56-57 RS 4
Rafael 106-107 A 6
Rafaela 111 D 4
Rafael Calzada, Almirante Brown- 110 III b 2
Rafael Castillo, La Matanza- 110 III b 2
Rafael del Encanto 92-93 E 5
Rafael Garcia 106-107 E 3
Rafael Obligado 106-107 G 5
Rafai 164-165 J 7-8
Rafḥah 134-135 E 5
Rafiganj 138-139 K 5
Rafsanjān 134-135 H 4
Rafter 61 H 3
Raft River 66-67 G 4
Raft River Mountains 66-67 G 5
Rāgā [Sudan] 164-165 K 7
Raga [TJ] 138-139 K 3
Ragaing Taing 141 C 5-D 7
Ragaing Yōma 148-149 B 2-3
Ragam 168-169 G 3
Rāgama 140 DE 7
Raga Tsangpo 138-139 L 3
Ragged Island 72-73 M 3
Ragged Island Range 88-89 J 3
Rāghugarh 138-139 F 5
Raghunāthpur [IND, Bihār] 138-139 K 4-5
Raghunāthpur [IND, West Bengal] 138-139 L 6
Ragland, AL 78-79 FG 4
Rago, KS 68-69 GH 7
Rago = Pag 122-123 F 3
Ragonvalia 94-95 E 4
Ragozino 132-133 O 6
Ragunda 116-117 FG 6
Ragusa 122-123 F 7
Ragusa = Dubrovnik 122-123 GH 4
Raguva 124-125 E 6
Raha 148-149 H 7
Rahāb, Ar- = Ar-Riḥāb 136-137 L 7
Rahad, Ar- 164-165 L 6
Rahad, Nahr ar- 164-165 L 6
Rahad al-Bardī 164-165 J 6
Rahaeng = Tak 148-149 C 3
Rahaṭ, Ḥarrat — 134-135 DE 6
Rahel, Er — = Ḥāssī al-Ghallah 166-167 F 2
Raḥḥālīyah, Ar- 136-137 K 6
Rahimatpur 140 B 2
Rahīmyār Khān 138-139 C 3
Rāhjerd 136-137 O 5
Rahlī = Rehli 138-139 G 6
Rahlstedt, Hamburg- 130 I b 1
Raḥmat, Āb-e — 136-137 N 6
Rahnsdorf, Berlin- 130 III c 2
Rahouia = Raḥūyah 166-167 G 2
Rahue 106-107 B 7
Rāhuri 138-139 E 8
Raḥūyah 166-167 G 2
Rahway River 82 III a 3
Rai, Hon — 150-151 E 8
Raiada, Serra da — 100-101 EF 4
Raiāitît, Wâdi — = Wādī Rayāytīt 173 D 6
Raices 106-107 H 3
Raichūr 134-135 M 7
RAI Congrescentrum 128 I ab 1
Raidāk 138-139 M 4
Raidat aş Şai'ar = Raydat aṣ-Ṣay'ar 134-135 F 7
Raidestós = Tekirdağ 134-135 B 2
Raiganj 138-139 M 5
Raigarh 134-135 N 6
Rāikot 138-139 E 2
Railroad Pass 74-75 E 3
Railroad Valley 74-75 F 3-4
Raimangal 138-139 M 7
Rāinagar 138-139 L 6
Rainbow 160 EF 5
Rainbow Bridge National Monument 74-75 H 4
Raincy, le — 129 I d 2
Rainham, London- 129 II c 1
Rainier, OR 66-67 B 2
Rainier, Mount — 64-65 BC 2
Rainsford Island 84 I c 3
Rainy Lake [CDN] 62 C 3
Rainy Lake [USA] 64-65 H 2
Rainy Pass Lodge, AK 58-59 L 5
Rainy River 62 B 3
Raippaluoto 116-117 J 6
Raipur [IND, Madhya Pradesh] 134-135 N 6
Raipur [IND, West Bengal] 138-139 L 6
Raipur = Rāypūr 141 B 4
Raipura 138-139 GH 6
Raisen 138-139 FG 6
Rāisinghnagar 138-139 D 3
Raith 70-71 F 1
Raivola = Roščino 124-125 G 3
Raiwind = Rāywind 138-139 DE 2
Raja, Kampung — 150-151 D 10
Raja, Ujung — 152-153 AB 4
Rajada 92-93 L 6
Rajado, Cerro — 106-107 C 2
Rajahmundry 134-135 N 7
Rājākhera 138-139 G 4
Rajakoski 116-117 N 3
Rājam = Rāzām 140 F 1
Rājamahēndri = Rajahmundry 134-135 N 7
Rājampet 140 D 3
Rājampēṭa = Rājampet 140 D 3
Rajang [RI, place] 152-153 J 4
Rajang [RI, river] 148-149 F 6
Rājanpūr 138-139 C 3
Rajaoli = Rajauli 138-139 K 5
Rājapālaiyam 134-135 M 9
Rājapāḷayam = Rājapālaiyam 134-135 M 9
Rājāpur [IND] 140 A 2
Rājāpur [Nepal] 138-139 H 3
Rājasthān 134-135 LM 5
Rājasthān Canal 138-139 D 3
Rajauli 138-139 K 5
Rajbārī 138-139 M 6
Raj Bhawan Temple 154 II b 2
Rajčichinsk 132-133 YZ 8
Rajeputana = Rājasthān 134-135 LM 5
Rajevskij 124-125 U 6
Rājgarh [IND, Madhya Pradesh] 138-139 F 5
Rājgaṛh [IND, Rājasthān ← Bhiwāni] 138-139 E 3
Rājgarh [IND, Rājasthān ↗ Jaipur] 138-139 F 4
Rājgīr 138-139 K 5
Rajgorodok 126-127 Q 2
Rajik 152-153 FG 7
Rājim 138-139 HJ 7
Rājkot 134-135 L 6
Rājmahāl Hills 138-139 L 5
Rājnāndgānv = Rāj Nāndgaon 138-139 H 7
Rāj Nāndgaon 138-139 H 7
Rajnandgaon = Rāj Nāndgaon 138-139 H 7
Rājpipla 138-139 D 7
Rājpur 138-139 E 7
Rājpura 138-139 F 2
Rājputana = Rājasthān 134-135 LM 5
Rājputānā = Rājasthān 134-135 LM 5
Rājshāhī 134-135 O 6
Rājula 138-139 C 7
Rajuña 94-95 J 5
Rājūra 138-139 G 8
Rakahanga 208 K 4
Rakaia 158-159 O 8
Rakaia River 161 D 6
Rakasdal 142-143 E 5
Rakata = Anak Krakatau 148-149 DE 8
Rakha La 138-139 L 4
Rakhni 138-139 B 2
Rakhshān 134-135 JK 5
Rakit, Pulau — 152-153 H 8
Rakitnoje 126-127 GH 1
Rakiura = Stewart Island 158-159 N 9
Rakops 172 D 6
Rakovník 118 F 3
Raksakiny 132-133 NO 5
Raksaul = Raxaul 138-139 K 4
Rakšino 124-125 U 4
Rakvere 124-125 F 4
Rakwāna 140 E 7
Raleigh 62 CD 3
Raleigh, NC 64-65 L 4
Raleigh, ND 68-69 F 2
Raleigh Bay 80-81 HJ 3
Raley 66-67 G 1
Ralik Chain 156-157 H 4
Ralls, TX 76-77 D 6
Ralos, Los — 104-105 D 10
Ralston, WY 68-69 B 3
Rām, Jabal — 136-137 F 8
Rama 88-89 D 8
Rāmachandrapuram 140 EF 2
Rāmachjāp = Rāmechhāp 138-139 KL 4
Ramādah 166-167 M 3
Ramadān Jamāl 166-167 K 1
Ramādī, Ar- 134-135 E 4
Ramaditas 104-105 B 7
Rāmadurga = Rāmdurg 140 B 2-3
Rāmagiri 138-139 JK 8
Rāmagiri-Udayagiri = Udayagiri 138-139 K 8
Ramah 56-57 Y 6
Ramah, NM 74-75 J 5
Ramalho, Serra do — 92-93 KL 7
Rām Allāh 136-137 F 7
Ramallo 106-107 G 4
Raman [T] 150-151 C 9
Raman [TR] 136-137 J 4
Rāmanagaram 140 C 4
Rāmanapeta 140 D 2
Rāmanāthapuram 140 D 6
Rāmanguli 140 B 3
Ramansdrif 174-175 C 5
Rāmānuj Ganj 138-139 J 6
Ramapo Deep 142-143 R 5
Rāmapura = Rāmpur 140 E 1
Ramasucha 124-125 J 7
Ramathlabama 174-175 F 3
Ramayón 106-107 G 3
Rambha 138-139 K 8
Rambi 148-149 b 2
Rambler Channel 155 I a 1
Ramblón 106-107 C 4
Rambrè 148-149 B 3
Rambrè Kyûn 148-149 B 3
Rāmchandrapur 138-139 KL 7
Rāmchandrapura = Rāmchandrapur 138-139 KL 7
Ramdā', Ar- 136-137 L 8
Ramdane-Djamal = Ramadān Jamāl 166-167 K 1
Rāmdurg 140 B 3
Rāmechhāp 138-139 KL 4
Ramenka, Moskva- 113 V b 3
Ramenskoje 124-125 M 6
Ramer, AL 78-79 F 4
Ramersdorf, München- 130 II b 2
Rāmêshvar = Rāmeshwar 138-139 F 5
Rāmêshvaram = Rāmeswaram 140 D 6
Rāmeshwar 138-139 F 5
Rameški 124-125 KL 5
Rāmeswaram 140 D 6
Rāmgangā 138-139 G 4
Rāmgaṛh [BD] 141 BC 4
Rāmgarh [IND, Bihār ↓ Bhāgalpur] 138-139 L 5
Rāmgarh [IND, Bihār ↗ Rānchi] 138-139 K 6
Rāmgarh [IND, Bihār → Vārānasi] 138-139 J 5
Rāmgaṛh [IND, Rājasthān → Bīkaner] 138-139 E 3
Rāmgarh [IND, Rājasthān ↖ Jaipur] 138-139 E 4
Rāmgarh [IND, Rājasthān ↖ Jodhpur] 138-139 C 4
Rāmhormoz 136-137 N 7
Ramīlas 166-167 D 5
Ramírez de Velazco 106-107 F 2
Ramis, Río — 96-97 FG 9
Ramitsogu 174-175 F 3
Ramiz Galvão 106-107 L 2
Ramla 136-137 F 7
Rammei 138-139 M 3
Ramnad = Rāmanāthapuram 140 D 6
Rāmnagar [IND ↗ Morādābād] 138-139 G 3
Rāmnagar [IND ↘ Vārānasi] 138-139 J 5
Ramon' 124-125 M 8
Ramon, NM 76-77 B 5
Ramona, CA 74-75 E 6
Ramón Lista 108-109 F 6
Ramón M. Castro 106-107 C 7
Ramón Santamarina 106-107 H 7
Ramón Trigo 106-107 K 4
Ramos 98-99 M 5
Ramos, Rio de Janeiro- 110 I b 2
Ramos Arizpe 86-87 K 5
Ramoshwani 174-175 D 2
Ramos Mejía, La Matanza- 110 III b 1
Ramos Otero 106-107 HJ 6
Ramoutsa 174-175 F 3
Rāmpāl 138-139 M 6
Rampart, AK 58-59 M 4
Rāmpur [IND, Andhra Pradesh] 140 E 1
Rāmpur [IND, Gujarāt] 138-139 DE 6
Rāmpur [IND, Himāchal Pradesh] 138-139 F 2
Rāmpur [IND, Orissa] 138-139 K 7
Rāmpur [IND, Uttar Pradesh → Morādābād] 134-135 MN 5
Rāmpur [IND, Uttar Pradesh ↓ Sahāranpur] 138-139 F 3
Rāmpura = Rāmpur 138-139 K 7
Rāmpur Hāt 138-139 L 5
Ramree = Rambrè 148-149 B 3
Ramree Island = Rambrè Kyûn 148-149 B 3
Rāmsanehīghāt 138-139 HJ 4
Ramsay 62 KL 3
Ramsay Lake 62 KL 3
Ramseur, NC 80-81 G 3
Ramsey 119 DE 4
Ramsey, IL 70-71 F 6
Ramsgate 119 G 6
Ramsgate, Sydney- 161 I a 2
Ramshi 166-167 F 2
Rāmtek 138-139 G 7
Ramthā, Ar- 136-137 FG 6
Ram Tsho 138-139 M 3
Ramu River 148-149 N 8
Ramuro, Río — 98-99 L 11
Raṇ, Mōṭuṅ — = Rann of Kutch 134-135 KL 6
Rānāghāt 138-139 M 6
Rānāhū 138-139 B 5
Rānāpur 138-139 D 5
Ranau 152-153 M 3
Ranau, Danau — 152-153 E 8
Ranāwa 138-139 B 7
Rancagua 111 BC 4
Rancharia 102-103 G 5
Rancheria 94-95 E 2
Ranchería, Río — 94-95 E 2
Ranchester, WY 68-69 C 3
Rānchi 134-135 O 6
Ranco, Lago — 111 B 6
Rancocas, NJ 84 III d 1
Rancocas Creek 84 III d 1
Rancocas Heights, NJ 84 III de 2
Rancocas Woods, NJ 84 III d 2
Rancul 106-107 E 5
Rand 160 H 5
Rand Airport 170 V b 2
Randazzo 122-123 F 7
Randberge [Namibia] 174-175 B 2
Randberge [ZA] 174-175 J 4
Randburg 170 V ab 1
Rānder 138-139 D 7
Randers 116-117 CD 9
Randijaur 116-117 HJ 4
Randolph, KS 68-69 H 6
Randolph, NE 68-69 H 4
Randolph, UT 66-67 H 5
Randolph, WI 70-71 F 4
Randon = Başbaş 166-167 KL 1
Randsburg, CA 74-75 DE 5
Randsfjord 116-117 D 7
Rand Stadium 170 V b 2
Randwick, Sydney- 161 I b 2
Randwick Racecourse 161 I b 2
Rāṇêbanūra = Rānībennur 134-135 M 8
Rāṇêbanūru = Rānībennur 134-135 M 8
Ranebennur = Rānībennur 134-135 M 8
Rāneswar 138-139 L 5
Ranfurly 61 C 4
Rangae 150-151 C 9
Rangāmāti 141 C 4
Rangárvalla 116-117 cd 3
Rangasa, Tanjung — 152-153 N 7
Rangaunu Bay 161 EF 2
Rang Chhu 138-139 MN 3
Rangeley, ME 72-73 L 2
Rangely, CO 66-67 J 5
Ranger, TX 76-77 E 6
Ranger Lake = Saymo Lake 70-71 J 2
Rangia 141 B 2
Rangiora 158-159 O 8
Rangiya = Rangia 141 B 2
Rangkasbitung 152-153 FG 9
Rangôn 148-149 BC 3
Rangôn Myit 141 E 7
Rangoon = Rangôn 148-149 BC 3
Rangoon River = Rangôn Myit 141 E 7
Rangpūr [BD] 138-139 M 5
Rangpūr [PAK] 138-139 C 2
Rangsang, Pulau — 148-149 D 6
Rangun = Rangôn 148-149 BC 3
Rānībennur 134-135 M 8
Rānībirta 138-139 LM 4
Ranier, MN 70-71 D 1
Rānīganj [IND, Bihār] 138-139 L 4
Rānīganj [IND, West Bengal] 138-139 L 6
Rānīkhet 138-139 G 3
Rānīpet 140 D 4
Rānīpur 138-139 B 4
Rānīshvar = Rāneswar 138-139 L 5
Rānivārā = Rānīwāra 138-139 CD 5
Rānīwāra 138-139 CD 5
Rānīyah 136-137 L 4
Rank, Ar- 164-165 L 6
Ranka 138-139 J 5-6
Rankin, TX 76-77 D 7
Rankins Springs 158-159 J 6
Rannersdorf 113 I b 2
Rann of Kutch 134-135 KL 6
Ranoke 62 L 1
Ranong 150-151 B 8
Ranot 150-151 C 9
Ranpur 138-139 K 7
Ranquelcó 106-107 E 5
Ransdorp 128 I b 1
Ransiki 148-149 K 7
Ransom, KS 68-69 FG 6
Rantau [MAL] 150-151 C 11
Rantau [RI] 152-153 L 7
Rantaupanjang 150-151 B 11
Rantauprapat 148-149 CD 6
Rantekombola, Gunung — 148-149 GH 7
Rantoul, IL 70-71 FG 5
Rānya = Rānīyah 136-137 L 4
Ranyah, Wādī — 134-135 E 6
Ranzī 141 D 2
Raobartsganj = Robertsganj 138-139 J 5
Rao Co 150-151 E 3
Raohe 142-143 P 2
Raoping 146-147 F 10
Raorī = Rori 138-139 E 3
Raoui, Erg er — = 'Irq ar-Rawī 164-165 D 3
Raoul 208 J 5
Raoyang 146-147 EF 2
Raoyang He 144-145 D 2
Rapa 156-157 K 6
Rāpaḍ = Rāpar 138-139 C 6
Rapallo 122-123 C 3
Rāpar 138-139 C 6
Rapel, Río — 106-107 B 4-5
Rapelje, MT 68-69 B 2-3
Rapelli 104-105 D 10
Raper, Cabo — 108-109 AB 6
Raper, Cape — 56-57 XY 4
Rapid City 61 H 5
Rapid City, SD 64-65 F 3
Rapide-Blanc 72-73 K 1
Rapides de Kintambo 170 IV a 1
Rapides de Lachine 82 I b 2
Rapides-des-Joachims 72-73 H 1
Rapides de Talanyené 168-169 E 3
Rapid River, MI 70-71 G 2-3
Rapid River [USA, Alaska] 58-59 R 3
Rapid River [USA, Minnesota] 70-71 C 1
Rapids 62 KL 1
Rāpina 124-125 F 4
Rapla 124-125 E 4
Rappahannock River 80-81 H 2
Rappang 152-153 NO 7
Rāpti [IND] 134-135 N 5
Rāpti [Nepal] 138-139 K 4
Rapulo, Río — 104-105 C 4
Rāpūr 140 D 3
Rāpūru = Rāpūr 140 D 3
Raqabat Zād 166-167 D 3
Raqqah, Ar- 134-135 DE 3
Rāqūbah 164-165 H 3
Raquette Lake 72-73 J 3
Raquette River 72-73 J 2
Rarotonga 156-157 J 6
Rā's, aḍ-Ḍab'ah 136-137 C 7
Ras, Riacho das — 100-101 C 7-8
Rasa [MAL] 150-151 C 11
Raša [YU] 122-123 EF 3
Rā's Abū Dārah 173 E 6
Rā's Abū Ġashwah 134-135 G 8
Rā's 'Adabīyah 173 C 3
Rā's ad-Dīmās 166-167 M 2
Rā's al-Abyaḍ 164-165 FG 1
Rā's 'Alam ar-Rūm 136-137 B 7
Rā's al-Arḍ 136-137 N 8
Rā's al-'Ayn 136-137 J 4
Rā's al-Baddūzzah 164-165 BC 2
Rā's al-Balā'im 173 C 3
Rā's al-Basīṭ 136-137 F 5
Rā's al Ḥadd 134-135 HJ 6
Rā's al-Ḥadīd 166-167 K 1
Rā's al-Ḥikmah 136-137 BC 7
Rā's al-Ḥirāsah 166-167 K 1
Ra's al-'Ishsh 166-167 KL 2
Rā's al-Jadīd 166-167 E 2
Rā's al-Kanā'is 136-137 BC 7
Rā's al-Khaymah 134-135 GH 5
Rasalkuṇḍā = Russelkanda 138-139 K 8
Rā's al-Mā' 166-167 F 2
Rā's al-Madrakah 134-135 H 7
Rā's al-Qulay'ah 136-137 N 8
Ra's al-Wād 164-165 E 1
Rā's al-Wardah 166-167 L 1
Rā's an-Naqb 134-135 D 4-5
Rā's an-Naqūrah 136-137 F 6
Rasappa = Riṣāfah 136-137 H 5
Rā's Ashaqār 166-167 CD 2
Rā's ash-Sharbithāt 134-135 H 7
Rā's ash-Shikk'ah 136-137 F 5
Rā's as-Sidr 173 C 3
Rā's at-Tannūrah 134-135 G 5
Râs Baghdâdî = Rā's Ḥunkurāb 173 D 5
Rā's Ba'labakk 136-137 G 5
Ras Benas = Rā's Banās 164-165 M 4
Rā's Būjarun 166-167 JK 1
Rā's Bū Jaydūr 164-165 AB 3
Râs Chekkâ = Rā's ash-Shikk'ah 136-137 F 5
Ras Dashen 164-165 M 6
Rā's Duqm 134-135 H 7
Ra's-e Bahrgān 136-137 N 7-8
Rās-e Barkan = Ra's-e Bahrgān 136-137 N 7-8
Raseiniai 124-125 D 6
Râs el 'Aïn = Rā's al-'Ayn 136-137 J 4
Ras el-Auf = Rā's Banās 164-165 M 4
Ras el Ma 168-169 D 1
Ra's-e Nāy Band 134-135 G 5
Ras en Nagura = Rā's an-Naqurah 136-137 F 6
Rā's Falkun 166-167 F 2
Rā's Fartak 134-135 G 7
Rā's Fiqālu 166-167 F 2
Rā's Ghārib 173 C 3
Rā's Ghīr 166-167 AB 4
Râs Gihân = Rā's al-Bālā'im 173 C 3
Rashad 164-165 L 6
Rā's Ḥadīd 166-167 AB 4
Rāshayyā 136-137 FG 6
Rashīd 173 B 2
Rashīd, Maşabb — 173 B 2
Rāshidīyah, Ar- 164-165 D 2
Rashin = Najin 142-143 P 3
Rāshīpuram = Rāsipuram 140 D 5
Rāshqūn, Jazīrat — 166-167 EF 2
Rasht 134-135 FG 3
Rā's Ḥunkurāb 173 D 5
Rā's Ibn Hānī 136-137 F 5
Rāsīpuram 140 D 5
Rasi Salai 150-151 E 5
Raška 122-123 J 4
Ras Kapoudia = Rā's Qabūdīyah 166-167 M 2
Ras Khānzūr = Raas Khaanzuur 164-165 ab 1
Rā's Māmī 134-135 GH 8
Rā's Masandam 134-135 H 5
Ras Mohammed = Rā's Muḥammad 164-165 LM 4
Rā's Muḥammad 164-165 LM 4
Ras Muhammed = Rā's Muḥammad 164-165 LM 4
Rā's Naws 134-135 H 7
Raso da Catarina 100-101 E 5
Rason Lake 158-159 D 5
Raspberry Island 58-59 KL 7
Rā's Qabūdīyah 166-167 M 2
Rā's Qaşbah 173 D 3-4
Rā's Qilātis 166-167 E 2
Rasra 138-139 JK 5
Rass, Ar- 134-135 E 5
Râss Addâr = Rā's aṭ-Ṭīb 164-165 G 1
Rā's Sarrāṭ 166-167 L 1
Râss el Abiaḍ = Rā's al-Abyaḍ 164-165 FG 1

Rass el Euch = Ra's al-'Ishsh 166-167 KL 2
Rass-el-Oued = Ra's al-Wād 164-165 E 1
Ras Shaka 171 E 3
Ra's Sīm 166-167 AB 4
Râss Kaboûdia = Ra's Qabūdiyah 166-167 M 2
Rasskazovo 124-125 NO 7
Râss Serrâṭ = Ra's Sarrāṭ 166-167 L 1
Rass Tourgueness = Ra's Turk an-Naṣṣ 166-167 M 3
Ra's Tafalnī 166-167 AB 4
Ra's Tarfāyah 164-165 B 3
Rastatt 118 D 4
Rastavica 126-127 D 2
Rastigaissa 116-117 LM 3
Rastreador, El — 106-107 F 4
Rastro 86-87 L 5
Rastro, El — 94-95 H 3
Ra's Turk an-Naṣṣ 166-167 M 3
Rasu, Monte — 122-123 C 5
Rāsvagarhī 138-139 K 3
Raswagarhi = Rāsvagarhī 138-139 K 3
Ra's Wūruq 164-165 D 1
Râs Za'farâna = Az-Za'farānah 173 C 3
Rata, Ilha — 92-93 N 5
Rata, Tanjung — 152-153 F 8
Ratak Chain 156-157 H 4
Ratam, Wādī ar- 166-167 J 3
Ratanakiri 150-151 F 5-6
Ratangarh [IND, Madhya Pradesh] 138-139 E 5
Ratangaṛh [IND, Rājasthān] 138-139 E 3
Ratanpur 138-139 HJ 6
Ratchaburi 148-149 C 4
Rāth 138-139 G 5
Rathedaung 141 C 5
Rathenow 118 F 2
Rathlin Island 119 C 4
Ratisbon = Regensburg 118 EF 4
Rätische Alpen 118 DE 5
Rat Island 58-59 s 7
Rat Islands 52 D 1
Ratka, Wādī ar- = Wādī ar-Ratqah 136-137 J 5-6
Ratlām 134-135 LM 6
Ratmanova, ostrov — 58-59 BC 4
Ratnagaṛh = Ratangarh 138-139 E 5
Ratnāgiri 134-135 L 7
Ratnapura = Ratnapūraya 140 E 7
Ratnapūraya 140 E 7
Ratno 124-125 E 8
Ratō = Lotung 146-147 HJ 9
Ratodero 138-139 B 4
Raton, NM 64-65 F 4
Ratqah, Wādī ar- 136-137 J 5-6
Rat Rapids 62 DE 2
Ratsauk 141 E 5
Rat Sima, Nakhon — 150-151 DE 4-5
Rattaphum 150-151 BC 9
Rattlesnake Creek 68-69 G 7
Rattlesnake Range 68-69 C 4
Rättvik 116-117 F 7
Ratua 138-139 LM 5
Ratz, Mount — 58-59 VW 8
Raualpindi = Rāwalpindī 134-135 L 4
Raub 150-151 C 11
Rauch 111 E 5
Rauchenwarth 113 I bc 2
Rauchfangswerder, Berlin- 130 III c 2
Raudal 94-95 D 4
Raudales 86-87 O 9
Raudal Itapinima 94-95 F 7
Raudal Jirijirimo 94-95 F 8
Raudal Mavaricani 94-95 G 6
Raudal Santa Rita 94-95 K 4
Raudal Yupurari 94-95 F 7
Raudhamelur 116-117 bc 2
Raudhatayn 136-137 M 8
Raufarhöfn 116-117 f 1
Raukumara Range 161 G 4-H 3
Raul Soares 102-103 L 4
Rauma 116-117 J 7
Raumo = Rauma 116-117 J 7
Raung Kalan 141 C 4
Raurkela 134-135 NO 6
Rausu 144-145 d 1-2
Ravalli, MT 66-67 F 2
Ravalpindi = Rāwalpindī 134-135 L 4
Ravānsar 136-137 M 5
Rāvar 134-135 H 4
Rava-Russkaja 126-127 AB 1
Ravendale, CA 66-67 CD 5
Ravenna 122-123 E 3
Ravenna, NE 68-69 G 5
Ravenna, OH 72-73 F 4
Ravensberg, Kleiner — 130 III a 2
Ravensburg 118 D 5
Ravenshoe 158-159 HJ 3
Ravensthorpe 158-159 D 6
Ravenswood 170 V c 2
Ravenswood, WV 72-73 F 5
Ravensworth 72-73 G 2
Ravensworth, VA 82 II a 2
Ravenwood, VA 82 II a 2
Rāver 138-139 EF 7
Rāvī 134-135 L 4
Rāwah 136-137 JK 5
Rāwalpindī 134-135 L 4
Rawamangun, Jakarta- 154 IV b 2
Rawa Mazowiecka 118 K 3
Rawāndūz 136-137 L 4
Rawḍah, Ar- 173 B 4
Rawd al-Faraj, Al-Qāhirah- 170 II b 1
Raw Hide Butte 68-69 D 4
Rawi 152-153 K 7
Rawī, 'Irq ar- 164-165 D 3
Rawi, Ko — 150-151 B 9
Rawicz 118 H 3
Rawlinna 158-159 E 6
Rawlins, WY 64-65 E 3
Rawlinson Range 158-159 E 4-5
Rawson [RA, Buenos Aires] 106-107 GH 5
Rawson [RA, Chubut] 111 CD 6
Rawwāfah, Ar- 173 E 4
Raxaul 138-139 K 4
Ray, MN 70-71 D 1
Ray, ND 68-69 E 1
Ray, Cape — 56-57 Z 8
Raya, Bukit — 148-149 F 7
Raya, Isla — 88-89 FG 11
Rāyabāga = Rāybāg 140 B 2
Rāyachoti 140 D 3
Rāyachūru = Raichūr 134-135 M 7
Rāyadrug 140 C 3
Rāyadurga = Rāyadrug 140 C 3
Rayāq 136-137 G 6
Rayāt 136-137 L 4
Rayāytīt, Wādī — 173 D 6
Rāybāg 140 B 2
Rāy Barēlī = Rāe Bareli 134-135 N 5
Raydat aṣ-Ṣay'ar 134-135 F 7
Rāyganj = Raiganj 138-139 M 5
Rāygaṛh = Raigarh 134-135 N 6
Rāykōṭ = Rāikot 138-139 E 2
Rāymangal = Raimangal 138-139 M 7
Raymond 66-67 G 1
Raymond, CA 74-75 D 4
Raymond, IL 70-71 F 6
Raymond, MS 78-79 D 4
Raymond, MT 68-69 D 1
Raymond, WA 66-67 B 2
Raymond Terrace 160 KL 4
Raymondville, TX 64-65 G 6
Ray Mountains 56-57 F 4
Rāynagar = Rāinagar 138-139 L 6
Rayne, LA 78-79 C 5
Raynesford, MT 66-67 H 2
Rayo Cortado 106-107 F 3
Rayong 148-149 D 4
Rāypūr 141 B 4
Rāypur = Raipur [IND, Madhya Pradesh] 134-135 N 6
Rāypur = Raipur [IND, West Bengal] 138-139 L 6
Ray River 58-59 M 4
Rāysen = Raisen 138-139 FG 6
Rāysiṅhagar = Rāisinghnagar 138-139 D 3
Rayton 174-175 H 3
Rayville, LA 78-79 CD 4
Rāywind 138-139 DE 2
Raz, Pointe du — 120-121 E 4
Rāzām 140 F 1
Razampeta = Rājampet 140 D 3
Rāzān [IR, Kermānshāhan] 136-137 N 5
Razan [IR, Lorestān] 136-137 N 6
R'azan' [SU] 124-125 M 6
R'azancevo 124-125 M 5
Razazah, Hawr ar- 136-137 KL 6
Razdan 126-127 M 6
Razdel'naja 126-127 E 3
Razdolinsk 132-133 R 6
Razdol'noje 126-127 F 4
Razeh 136-137 N 6
Razelm, Lacul — 122-123 N 3
Razgrad 122-123 M 4
Razor Hill 155 I b 1
R'ažsk 124-125 N 7

R'bāṭah, Jabal — 166-167 L 2
Rbāṭ Tinezoûlîn = Tinzūlīn 166-167 CD 4

R'dayif, Ar- 164-165 F 2

Rê, Cu Lao — 150-151 G 5
Ré, Île de — 120-121 G 5
Reaburn 61 K 5
Reading, MA 84 I b 2
Reading, PA 64-65 L 3
Reading [GB] 119 F 6
Reading Terminal 84 III bc 2
Read Island 56-57 O 4
Readstown, WI 70-71 E 4
Readville, Boston-, MA 84 I b 3
Real, El — 88-89 H 10
Real, Rio — 96-97 G 6
Real del Castillo 74-75 E 6-7
Real del Padre 106-107 D 5
Realengo, Rio de Janeiro- 102-103 L 5
Realeza 102-103 L 4
Realicó 111 CD 4-5
Realitos, TX 76-77 E 9
Real Sayana 106-107 F 2
Réam 148-149 D 4
Reamal = Riāmāl 138-139 K 7
Reartes, Los — 106-107 E 3
Reata 76-77 D 9
Reba'a, Er — = Ar-Rub'ah 166-167 L 1
Rebaa Ouled Yahia = Ar-Rub'ah 166-167 L 1
Rebbenesøy 116-117 GH 2
Rebbo 168-169 C 4
Rebeca, Lagoa da — 102-103 BC 1
Rebecca, Lake — 158-159 D 6
Rebel Hill, PA 84 III b 1
Rebia, Um er — = Wād Umm ar-Rabīyah 164-165 C 2
Rebiāna = Ribyānah 164-165 J 4
Rebiana Sand Sea = Ṣahrā Ribyānah 164-165 J 4
Rebojo, Cachoeira de — 98-99 J 9
Reboledo 111 EF 4
Reboly 124-125 H 2
Rebouças 102-103 G 6
Rebun-jima 142-143 QR 2
Recado, El — 106-107 FG 5
Recalde 111 D 5
Recherche, Archipelago of the — 158-159 D 6
Rechna Doab = Rachnā Doāb 138-139 D 2
Rechō Taung 148-149 C 4
Recht = Rasht 134-135 FG 3
Rečica 124-125 H 7
Recife 92-93 N 6
Recife, Cape — = Kaap Recife 174-175 FG 8
Recife, Kaap — 174-175 FG 8
Recife Manuel Luís 100-101 BC 1
Recinto 106-107 B 6
Recoleta, Buenos Aires- 110 III b 1
Reconquista 111 DE 3
Reconquista, Río — 110 III a 1
Recreio 102-103 L 4
Recreio, Serra do — 100-101 D 5
Recreo [RA, La Rioja] 111 CD 3
Recreo [RA, Santa Fe] 106-107 G 3
Recreo, Azcapotzalco-El — 91 I b 2
Rectificación del Riachuelo 110 III b 2
Rector, AR 78-79 D 2
Recuay 96-97 C 6
Reḡā'iyeh = Orūmīyeh 134-135 EF 3
Reḡā'iyeh, Daryācheh — = Daryācheh-ye Orūmīyeh 134-135 F 3
Redang, Pulau — 150-151 D 10
Red Bank, NJ 72-73 J 4
Red Bank Battle Monument 84 III b 2
Red Bay, TN 78-79 EF 3
Red Bay [CDN] 63 H 2
Redberry Lake 61 E 4
Red Bluff, CA 64-65 B 3
Red Bluff Lake 76-77 BC 7
Red Bluff Reservoir = Red Bluff Lake 76-77 BC 7
Redbridge, London- 129 II c 1
Red Bud, IL 70-71 EF 6
Red Butte 74-75 GH 5
Redby, MN 70-71 C 2
Redcliffe, Brisbane- 158-159 K 5
Red Cliffs 160 F 5
Red Cloud, NE 68-69 G 5
Redd City, MI 70-71 H 4
Red Deer 56-57 O 7
Red Deer Lake 61 H 4
Red Deer River 56-57 O 7
Reddersburg 174-175 G 5
Red Desert 68-69 B 4-5
Red Devil, AK 58-59 J 6
Reddick, FL 80-81 b 2
Redding, CA 64-65 B 3
Reddit 62 B 3
Redd Peak 68-69 D 4
Redelinghuis = Redelinghuys 174-175 C 7
Redelinghuys 174-175 C 7
Redenção 100-101 E 3
Redenção da Gurguéia 100-101 B 5
Redenção da Serra 102-103 K 5
Redeyef, Er — = Ar-R'dayif 164-165 F 2
Redfern, Sydney- 161 I b 2
Redfield, AR 78-79 C 3
Redfield, SD 68-69 G 3
Red Hill 158-159 HJ 7
Red Hills [USA, Alabama] 64-65 J 5
Red Hills [USA, Kansas] 68-69 G 7
Red House, NV 66-67 E 5
Redig, SD 68-69 E 3
Red Indian Lake 63 H 3
Redinha 100-101 G 3
Red Lake [CDN, lake] 62 B 2
Red Lake [CDN, place] 56-57 S 7
Red Lake [USA] 64-65 G 2
Red Lake Falls, MN 70-71 BC 2
Red Lake Indian Reservation 70-71 C 1-2
Red Lake River 68-69 H 1-2
Redlands, CA 74-75 E 5-6
Red Lion, PA 72-73 H 5
Red Lodge, MT 68-69 B 3
Redmond, OR 66-67 C 3
Red Mountain, CA 74-75 E 5
Red Mountain [USA, California] 66-67 B 5
Red Mountain [USA, Montana] 66-67 G 2
Rednitz 118 E 4
Red Oak, IA 70-71 C 5
Redon 120-121 F 5
Redonda, Loma — 106-107 DE 6
Redonda, Ponta — 92-93 M 5
Redondela 120-121 C 7
Redondo [BR] 96-97 F 6
Redondo, Cerro — 106-107 C 4
Redondo, Pico — 98-99 G 3
Redondo Beach, CA 74-75 D 6
Redoubt Volcano 58-59 L 6
Red Pheasant 61 DE 4
Red River 64-65 H 5
Red River = Sông Nhi Ha 148-149 D 2
Red River, North Fork — 76-77 E 5
Red River, Salt Fork — 76-77 E 5
Red River of the North 64-65 G 2
Redrock, AZ 74-75 H 6
Redrock, NM 74-75 J 6
Red Rock, OK 76-77 F 4
Red Rock [CDN] 60 F 3
Red Rock [USA] 83 I b 1
Red Rock Point 158-159 E 6
Red Run 84 II b 1
Red Sandstone Desert = Ad-Dahnā' 134-135 E 5-F 6
Red Sea 134-135 D 5-E 7
Red Springs, NC 80-81 G 3
Redstone 60 F 3
Redstone, MT 68-69 D 1
Red Tank 64-65 b 2
Reduto 100-101 G 3
Reḡvandeh 136-137 N 4
Redvers 68-69 F 1
Red Volta 168-169 E 3
Redwater Creek 68-69 D 2
Red Willow Creek 68-69 F 5
Red Wing, MN 70-71 D 3
Redwood City, CA 74-75 B 4
Redwood Falls, MN 70-71 C 3
Redwood Valley, CA 74-75 B 3
Ree, Lough — 119 C 5
Reece, KS 68-69 H 7
Reed City, MI 72-73 D 3
Reeder, ND 68-69 E 2
Reed Lake 61 H 3
Reedley, CA 74-75 D 4
Reedpoint, MT 68-69 B 3
Reedsburg, WI 70-71 EF 4
Reedsport, OR 66-67 AB 4
Reedwoods, Houston-, TX 85 III b 2
Reefton 158-159 O 8
Reese, MI 70-71 J 4
Reese River 74-75 E 3
Refā'ī, Ar- = Ar-Rifā'ī 136-137 M 7
Refaniye 136-137 H 3
Reform, AL 78-79 EF 4
Reforma, La — [RA, Buenos Aires] 106-107 H 5
Reforma, La — [RA, La Pampa] 106-107 DE 6
Reforma, La — [YV] 94-95 L 4
Refugio, TX 76-77 F 8
Refugio, El — 94-95 E 6
Refugio, Isla — 108-109 C 4
Reg Aftout = 'Irq Aflūt 166-167 DE 4
Regattastrecke München-Feldmoching 130 II b 1
Regen 118 F 4
Regência 92-93 M 8
Regência, Ponta de — 92-93 M 8
Regeneração 100-101 C 4
Regensberg 128 IV a 1
Regensburg 118 EF 4
Regent, ND 68-69 E 2
Regent, Melbourne- 161 II bc 1
Regente Feijó 102-103 G 5
Regent's Park 129 II b 1
Regents Park, Johannesburg- 170 V b 2
Regents Park, Sydney- 161 I a 2
Reggane = Rijān 164-165 E 3
Règgio di Calàbria 122-123 FG 6
Règgio nell'Emìlia 122-123 D 3
Reggoû = Riggū 166-167 E 3
Regina, MT 68-69 C 2
Regina [CDN] 56-57 Q 7
Régina [French Guiana] 92-93 J 4
Regina Beach 61 F 5
Région de Hamada = Al-Hammadah 166-167 HJ 4
Région de la Chebka = Shabkah 166-167 H 3-4
Région des Daïa = Ḍāyah 166-167 HJ 3
Région des Guentras = Al-Qanṭarah 166-167 J 3
Registan = Rīgestān 134-135 JK 4
Registro 111 G 2
Registro do Araguaia 102-103 FG 1-2
Regocijo 86-87 H 6
Regresso, Cachoeira — 92-93 HJ 5
Regueïbat = Ar-Ruqaybah 166-167 AB 7
Reguengos de Monsaraz 120-121 D 9
Regyin 141 D 7
Reh 142-143 M 3
Rehār = Rihand 138-139 J 5
Rehberge, Volkspark — 130 III b 1
Rehbrücke, Bergholz- 130 III a 2
Rehli 138-139 G 6
Rehoboth 172 C 6
Rehoboth Beach, DE 72-73 J 5
Rēḥōvōt 136-137 F 7
Rei = Rey 136-137 O 5
Reibell = Qaṣr Shillalah 166-167 H 2
Reichle, MT 66-67 G 3
Reid 158-159 E 6
Reidsville, NC 80-81 G 2
Reigate 119 FG 6
Reihoku 144-145 GH 6
Reims 120-121 JK 4
Reina Adelaida, Archipiélago — 111 AB 8
Reinbeck, IA 70-71 D 4
Reindeer Island 61 K 4
Reindeer Lake 56-57 Q 6
Reindeer Station, AK 58-59 GH 3
Reine, la — 62 M 2
Reinosa 120-121 E 7
Reinøy 116-117 H 2-3
Reisa 116-117 J 3
Reitbrook, Hamburg- 130 I b 2
Reitz 174-175 H 4
Rejaf 171 B 1
Relais, le — 63 A 4
Relalhuleu 86-87 OP 10
Relegem 128 II a 1
Relem, Cerro — 111 B 5
Reliance, SD 68-69 G 4
Reliance, WY 66-67 J 5
Relizane = Ghālizān 164-165 E 1
Rellano 76-77 B 9
Relmo 106-107 F 6
Reloj, Tlalpan-El — 91 I c 3
Reloncaví, Seno — 108-109 C 3
Remad, Ouèd er — = Wādī Ban ar-Ramād 166-167 F 3
Remada = Ramādah 166-167 M 3
Remansão 92-93 JK 5
Remanso 92-93 L 6
Remanso Grande 98-99 DE 10
Remarkable, Mount — 158-159 G 6
Rembang 152-153 J 9
Rembate = Lielvārde 124-125 E 5
Rembau 150-151 D 11
Rembrücken 128 III b 1
Remchi = Ramshi 166-167 F 2
Reme-Cô 106-107 F 6
Remédios [BR, Bahia] 100-101 C 7
Remédios [BR, Fernando de Noronha] 92-93 N 5
Remedios [CO] 94-95 D 4
Remedios, Santuario de los — 91 I b 2
Remedios de Escalada, Lanús- 110 III b 2
Rementai 152-153 E 8
Remer, MN 70-71 D 2
Remeshk 134-135 H 5
Remiendos 104-105 A 9
Remígio 100-101 FG 4
Remington, IN 70-71 G 5
Remington, VA 72-73 H 5
Rémire 92-93 J 3-4
Remiremont 120-121 KL 4
Remolina 96-97 F 4
Remontnaja = Dubovskoje 126-127 L 3
Remontnoje 126-127 L 3
Remote, OR 66-67 B 4
Rems 118 D 4
Remscheid 118 C 3
Remsen, NY 72-73 J 3
Remus, MI 70-71 H 4
Rena 116-117 D 7
Renaico 106-107 A 6
Renāla Khurd 138-139 D 2
Renascença 92-93 F 5
Renault = Sīdī Muḥammad Ban 'Alī 166-167 G 1
Rencontre East 63 J 4
Rendova Island 148-149 j 6
Rendsburg 118 DE 1
Rēnēia 122-123 L 7
Reneke, Schweizer- 174-175 F 4
Renfrew [CDN] 72-73 H 2
Rengam 150-151 D 12
Rengat 148-149 D 7
Rengo 106-107 B 5
Reng Tlāng 141 C 4-5
Ren He 146-147 B 5
Renhua 146-147 D 9
Reni 126-127 D 4
Renison 62 L 1
Renju 146-147 E 9
Renk = Al-Rank 164-165 L 6
Renmark 158-159 H 6
Rennell, Islas — 108-109 B 8-C 9
Rennell Island 148-149 k 7
Rennes 120-121 G 4
Rennick Glacier 53 C 16-17
Rennie 61 L 6
Rennie's Mill 155 I b 2
Rennplatz München-Daglfing 130 II c 2
Reno, ID 66-67 G 3
Reno, NV 64-65 C 4
Reno [I] 122-123 DE 3
Reno, El —, OK 64-65 G 4
Renohill, WY 68-69 C 4
Renosterkop [ZA, mountain] 174-175 H 3
Renosterkop [ZA, place] 174-175 E 7
Renosterrivier [ZA, river ◁ Groot Visrivier] 174-175 D 6
Renosterrivier [ZA, river ◁ Vaalrivier] 174-175 G 4
Renoville, CA 74-75 EF 5
Renovo, PA 72-73 H 4
Renqiu 142-143 M 4
Rensselaer, IN 70-71 G 5
Rensselaer, NY 72-73 JK 3
Renton, WA 66-67 B 2
Rentur, Houston-, TX 85 III a 2
Renville, MN 70-71 C 3
Renwer 61 H 4
Ren Xian 146-147 E 3
Reo 148-149 H 8
Repalle 140 E 2
Repartição 98-99 K 7
Repartimento 98-99 K 6
Repartimento, Rio — 98-99 E 7
Repartimento, Serra — 98-99 E 7
Repaupo, NJ 84 III b 3
Repelón 94-95 D 2
Repjevka 126-127 J 1
Repki 124-125 H 8
Repola = Reboly 124-125 H 2
Repong, Pulau — 152-153 FG 4
Reppisch 128 IV a 1-2
Represa da Boa Esperança 100-101 B 4
Represa de Água Vermelha 102-103 GH 3
Represa de Barra Bonita 102-103 HJ 5
Represa de Capivara 102-103 G 5
Represa de Estreito 102-103 J 4
Represa de Furnas 92-93 K 9
Represa de Itumbiara 102-103 H 3
Represa de Jaguara 102-103 J 3-4
Represa de Jupiá 92-93 J 9
Represa de Jurumirim 102-103 H 5
Represa de Promissão 102-103 H 4
Represa de São Simão 92-93 JK 8
Represa de Volta Grande 102-103 HJ 3-4
Represa de Xavantes 102-103 H 5
Represa do Limpopo 174-175 K 3
Represa do Peixoto 102-103 J 4
Reprêsa do Rio Grande 102-103 J 5
Represa Sobradinho 100-101 C 6-D 5
Represa Três Marias 102-103 K 3
Republic, MI 70-71 G 2
Republic, MO 78-79 C 2
Republic, WA 66-67 D 1
República 104-105 F 3
Republican River 64-65 G 3
Republican River, South Fork — 68-69 E 6
Republic Observatory 170 V b 2
Repulse Bay [AUS] 158-159 JK 4
Repulse Bay [CDN, bay] 56-57 T 4
Repulse Bay [CDN, place] 56-57 TU 4
Repunshiri = Rebun-jima 144-145 b 1
Reqba Zād = Raqabat Zād 166-167 D 3
Reqi = Ruoxi 146-147 E 7
Reqiang = Charqiliq 142-143 F 4
Reque, Río de — 96-97 B 5
Requena [E] 120-121 G 9
Requena [PE] 92-93 E 6
Requeña [YV] 94-95 J 3-4
Reriutaba 100-101 D 3
Reşadiye [TR, Muğla] 136-137 B 4
Reşadiye [TR, Tokat] 136-137 G 2
Reşadiye yarımadası 136-137 BC 4
Reṣāfé, Er- = Riṣāfah 136-137 H 5
Resa'iya = Orūmīyeh 134-135 EF 3
Resbaladero 96-97 E 6
Reschenpass 118 E 5
Rescue, Punta — 108-109 B 6
Resende [BR] 102-103 K 5
Resende Costa 102-103 K 4
Reserva 102-103 G 6
Reserva, Lagoa da — 106-107 M 3
Reserva Florestal Barotiré 98-99 MN 8
Reserva Florestal de Jaru 98-99 GH 9
Reserva Florestal do Rio Negro 94-95 G 7
Reserva Florestal Mundurucânia 98-99 JK 8
Reserva Florestal Parima 94-95 K 6
Reserva Florestal Pedras Negras 98-99 G 11
Reservatório de Guarapiranga 110 II a 3
Reserve 61 G 4
Reserve, NM 74-75 J 6
Réserve aux Éléfants 172 E 1
Réserve de Faune de Bouna 164-165 D 7
Réservoir Baskatong 72-73 J 1
Réservoir Cabonga 72-73 HJ 1
Réservoir Decelles 72-73 GH 1
Réservoir Dozois 72-73 H 1
Réservoir Pipmuacan 63 A 3
Rešetilovka 126-127 FG 2
Rešety 124-125 G 5
Resguardo 106-107 B 4
Resht = Rasht 134-135 FG 3
Reshteh Ālādāgh 134-135 H 3
Reshteh Kūhhā-ye Alborz 134-135 G 3
Resistencia 111 DE 3
Reşiţa 122-123 J 3
Resolana 106-107 C 5
Resolute 56-57 S 3
Resolution Island 56-57 Y 5
Resplandes 100-101 B 4
Resplendor 102-103 M 3
Restigouche River 63 C 4
Restinga da Marambaia 92-93 L 9
Restinga de Sefton 199 AB 7
Restinga Sêca 106-107 L 2
Reston 68-69 F 1
Restrepo 94-95 E 5
Restrepo, Bogotá- 91 III b 3
Reta 106-107 GH 7
Retamito 106-107 C 4
Retamo, El — 106-107 D 3-4
Retamosa 106-107 K 4
Retem, Ouèd er — = Wādī ar-Ratam 166-167 J 3
Rethe 130 I a 1
Rethel 120-121 K 4
Réthymnon 122-123 L 8
Retimo = Réthymnon 122-123 L 8
Retiro 110 I b 2
Retiro, Buenos Aires- 110 III b 1
Retiro, Madrid- 113 III ab 2
Retiro, Parque del — 113 III ab 2
Retowo = Rietavas 124-125 C 6
Reuilly, Paris- 129 I c 2
Reus 120-121 H 8
Reuss 118 D 5
Reut 126-127 D 3
Reutersbron 174-175 A 3
Reutlingen 118 D 4
Reva, SD 68-69 E 3
Revā = Narmada 134-135 LM 6
Reval = Tallinn 124-125 E 4
Reval-Nõmme = Tallinn-Nõmme 124-125 E 4
Revāṛī = Rewāri 138-139 F 3
Revda [SU, Srednij Ural] 132-133 KL 6
Revelation Mountains 58-59 KL 6
Revelstoke 56-57 N 7
Reventador 96-97 C 1
Revenue 61 D 4
Revere, MA 84 I b 2
Revere Beach, MA 84 I c 2
Revesby, Sydney- 161 I a 2
Revillagigedo, Islas — 86-87 C-E 8
Revillagigedo, Islas de — 64-65 D 8
Revillagigedo Island 56-57 KL 6
Revillo, SD 68-69 H 3
Rēvīvīm 136-137 F 7
Revoil-Beni-Ounif = Banī Wanīf 164-165 D 2
Rewa [IND] 138-139 H 5
Rewā = Narmada 134-135 LM 6
Rewāri 138-139 F 3
Rewa River 98-99 J 3
Rewda = Revda 132-133 KL 6
Rex, AK 58-59 N 4
Rex, Mount — 53 B 29
Rexburg, ID 66-67 H 4
Rexel Institute of Technology 84 III b 2
Rexford, MI 70-71 H 2
Rexford, MT 66-67 F 1
Rexton, MI 70-71 H 2
Rey, Arroyo del — 106-107 H 2
Rey, Isla del — 64-65 L 10
Reydon, OK 76-77 E 5
Reyên = Riyān 166-167 E 2
Reyes 104-105 C 4
Reyes, Ixtapalapa-Los — 91 I c 2
Reyes, Los — 91 I d 2
Reyes, Point — 74-75 B 3-4
Reyes, Punta — 94-95 B 6
Reyhanlı 136-137 G 4
Reykhólar 116-117 b 2
Reykholt 116-117 c 2
Reykjanes 116-117 b 3
Reykjanes Ridge 50-51 H 2-3
Reykjavík [CDN] 61 J 5
Reykjavík [IS] 116-117 bc 2
Reynaud 61 F 4
Reynolds, ID 66-67 E 4
Reynolds, IN 70-71 G 5
Reynolds Range 158-159 F 4
Reynoldsville, PA 72-73 G 4
Reynosa 64-65 G 6
Reynosa Tamaulipas, Azcapotzalco- 91 I b 2
Rezā'īyeh = Orūmīyeh 134-135 EF 3
Rēzekne 124-125 F 5
Rezina 126-127 D 3

R. Franco, Serra — 104-105 F 4

R'gâia = R'ghāyah 166-167 D 2
R'ghāyah 166-167 D 2

Rhaetian Alps = Rätische Alpen 118 DE 5
Rhafsâi = Ghafsāi 166-167 D 2
Rhar, In- = 'Ayn Ghar 166-167 G 6
Rharb, el — = Al-Gharb 166-167 C 2
Rharbi, Chott — = Ash-Shaṭṭ al-Gharbī 166-167 F 3
Rharbî, Djezîra el — = Jazīrat al-Gharbī 166-167 M 2
Rharbi, Ouèd el — = Wādī al-Gharbī 166-167 G 3-4
Rhâr ed Dimâ' = Ghār ad-Dimā' 166-167 L 1
Rhâr el Melḥ = Ghār al-Milḥ 166-167 M 1
Rhâr eṣ Ṣâllaḥ = Ghār aṣ-Ṣallaḥ 166-167 E 3
Rharis = Ghāris 166-167 J 7
Rharsa, Choṭṭ — = Shaṭṭ al-Jarsah 166-167 KL 2
Rheims = Reims 120-121 JK 4
Rhein 118 C 3
Rheine 118 C 2
Rheinland-Pfalz 118 CD 3-4
Rhemiles = Ramīlas 166-167 D 5
Rhenami, Hassi el — = Ḥāssī al-Ghanamī 166-167 JK 4
Rhenosterkop = Renosterkop 174-175 E 7
Rhenoster River = Renosterrivier 174-175 D 6
'Rheris = Gharīs 166-167 D 4
'Rheris, Ouèd — = Wād Gharīs 166-167 D 3-4
Rhine = Rhein 118 C 3
Rhinelander, WI 70-71 F 3
Rhineland-Palatinate = Rheinland-Pfalz 118 C 3-4
Rhino Camp 172 F 1
Rhīr, Berzekh — = Ra's Ghīr 166-167 AB 4
Rhode Island [USA, administrative unit] 64-65 MN 3
Rhode Island [USA, island] 72-73 L 4
Rhodes 174-175 G 6
Rhodes = Ródos 122-123 N 7
Rhodesdrif 174-175 H 2
Rhodes Memorial Hall 85 II b 2
Rhodes Park 170 V b 2
Rhodope Mountains 122-123 KL 5
Rhön 118 DE 3
Rhondda 119 E 6
Rhone [CH] 118 C 5
Rhône [F] 120-121 K 6
Rhône au Rhin, Canal du — 120-121 L 4-5
Rhoumerâssen = Ghumrāssin 166-167 M 3
Rhourde-el-Baguel = Ghurd al-Baghl 166-167 K 4
Rhraïba, El — = Al-Ghraybah 166-167 LM 2
Rhu, Tanjong — 154 III b 2

Riachão 92-93 K 6
Riachão das Neves 100-101 B 6
Riachão do Dantas 100-101 F 6
Riachão do Jacuípe 100-101 E 6
Riachão São Pedro 102-103 J 2
Riacho 100-101 D 10
Riacho, Rio — 100-101 D 4
Riacho Cariús 100-101 E 4
Riacho Conceição 100-101 D 4
Riacho Corrente 100-101 B 4-5
Riacho da Estiva 100-101 B 4-5
Riacho das Almas 100-101 FG 5

Riacho das Ras 100-101 C 7-8
Riacho da Vargem 100-101 E 5
Riacho da Vermelha 100-101 BC 4
Riacho de Prata 100-101 C 4
Riacho de Santana 100-101 C 7
Riacho do Brejo 100-101 C 5
Riacho do Navio 100-101 E 5
Riacho dos Cavalos 100-101 F 4
Riacho Eh-Eh 104-105 GH 9
Riacho Itaquatiara 100-101 D 5
Riacho Monte Lindo Chico
104-105 G 9
Riacho Pilagá 104-105 G 9
Riacho Poço Comprido
100-101 C 5-E 6
Riachos, Isla de los — 108-109 HJ 3
Riacho Salado 104-105 G 9
Riacho Santa Maria 100-101 C 5
Riacho São João 100-101 D 4
Riacho Yacaré Norte 102-103 C 5
Riachuelo 110 III b 1
Riachuelo, Rectificación del —
110 III b 2
Riad, Er — = Ar-Riyāḍ 134-135 F 6
Riāmāl 138-139 K 7
Riāng 134-135 P 5
Riau, Kepulauan — 148-149 DE 6
Ribadeo 120-121 D 7
Ribamar 100-101 BC 2
Ribas do Rio Pardo 92-93 J 9
Ribaṭ, Ar- 164-165 C 2
Ribatejo 120-121 C 9
Ribauè 172 G 4-5
Ribe 116-117 C 10
Ribeira [BR] 102-103 H 6
Ribeira [P] 120-121 C 7
Ribeira, Rio de Janeiro- 110 I c 1
Ribeira do Amparo 100-101 E 6
Ribeira do Iguape, Rio —
102-103 H 6
Ribeira do Pombal 100-101 E 6
Ribeirão [BR, Pernambuco]
92-93 MN 6
Ribeirão [BR, Rondônia] 92-93 FG 7
Ribeirão Aricanduva 110 II bc 2
Ribeirão Bonito 102-103 HJ 5
Ribeirão Branco 102-103 H 6
Ribeirão Claro 102-103 H 5
Ribeirão Cupecê 110 II b 2
Ribeirão da Mooca 110 II b 2
Ribeirão das Almas 102-103 JK 2
Ribeirão do Oratório 110 II bc 2
Ribeirão do Pinhal 102-103 G 5
Ribeirão do Salto 100-101 DE 8
Ribeirão dos Meninos 110 II b 2
Ribeirão Preto 92-93 K 9
Ribeirão Vermelho 102-103 K 4
Ribeira Taquaruçu 102-103 F 4
Ribeirinha, Rio — 102-103 H 6
Ribeiro Ariranha 102-103 F 2
Ribeiro Gonçalves 92-93 KL 6
Ribeirópolis 100-101 F 6
Ribeiro Tadarimana 102-103 E 2
Riberalta 92-93 F 7
Rib Lake 72-73 FG 1
Rib Lake, WI 70-71 EF 3
Ribo Parjul = Leo Pargial
138-139 G 1
Ribstone Creek 61 C 4
Ribyānah 164-165 J 4
Ribyānah, Ṣaḥrā' — 164-165 J 4
Rica, Cañada — 106-107 GH 1
Rica, La — 106-107 H 5
Ricardo Flores Magón 86-87 GH 2-3
Ricardo Franco, Rio — 104-105 E 2
Ricardo Gaviña 106-107 G 6
Ricaurte 94-95 C 7
Ricaurte, Bogotá- 91 III b 3
Riccione 122-123 E 3-4
Rice, CA 74-75 F 5
Riceboro, GA 80-81 F 5
Rice Lake 72-73 GH 2
Rice Lake, WI 70-71 E 3
Rice University 85 III b 2
Rīch = Ar-Rīsh 166-167 D 3
Richardsbaai 174-175 K 5
Richard's Bay 172 F 7
Richards Bay = Richardsbaai
174-175 K 5
Richardson, AK 58-59 OP 4
Richardson Bay 83 I ab 1
Richardson Mountains 56-57 J 4
Richardton, ND 68-69 EF 2
Richelieu, Rivière — 72-73 K 1-2
Richey, MT 68-69 D 2
Richfield, ID 66-67 FG 4
Richfield, KS 68-69 F 7
Richfield, MN 70-71 D 3
Richfield, UT 74-75 GH 3
Richford, VT 72-73 K 2
Richgrove, CA 74-75 D 5
Rich Hill, MO 70-71 C 6
Richland, GA 78-79 G 4
Richland, MO 70-71 D 7
Richland, MT 68-69 C 1
Richland, WA 64-65 C 2
Richland Balsam 80-81 E 3
Richland Center, WI 70-71 EF 4
Richlands, VA 80-81 F 2
Richland Springs, TX 76-77 E 7
Richmond, CA 64-65 B 4
Richmond, IN 64-65 JK 3-4
Richmond, KS 70-71 C 6
Richmond, KY 70-71 H 7
Richmond, MO 70-71 CD 6
Richmond, TX 76-77 FG 8
Richmond, VA 64-65 L 4
Richmond [AUS] 158-159 H 4
Richmond [CDN] 72-73 KL 2
Richmond [ZA, Kaapland] 172 D 8
Richmond [ZA, Natal] 172 F 7-8
Richmond, Melbourne- 161 II bc 1
Richmond, New York-, NY 82 III ab 4
Richmond, Philadelphia-, PA 84 III c 2
Richmond, Point — 83 I b 1
Richmond, San Francisco-, CA
83 I ab 2
Richmond Gulf 56-57 V 6
Richmond Hill, GA 80-81 F 5
Richmond Range 161 E 5
Richmond-San Rafael Bridge 83 I b 1
Richmond Valley, New York-, NY
82 III a 3
Rich Mountain 76-77 G 5
Richtberg 174-175 B 4
Richtersveld 174-175 B 5
Richterswil 128 IV b 2
Richton, MS 78-79 E 5
Richwood, OH 72-73 E 4
Richwood, WV 72-73 F 5
Rickmansworth 129 II a 1
Rico, CO 68-69 BC 7
Ricrán 96-97 D 7
Ridder = Leninogorsk 132-133 P 7
Riddle, ID 66-67 EF 4
Riddle, OR 66-67 B 4
Rideau Lake 72-73 H 2
Ridgecrest, CA 74-75 E 5
Ridgecrest, Houston-, TX 85 III a 1
Ridgefield, NJ 82 III c 1-2
Ridgefield Park, NJ 82 III b 1
Ridgeland, SC 80-81 F 4
Ridgely, TN 78-79 E 2
Ridgetown 72-73 F 3
Ridgeway, SC 80-81 F 3
Ridgewood, New York-, NY 82 III c 2
Ridgway, CO 68-69 BC 6
Ridgway, PA 72-73 G 4
Riḍi Bāzār = Riri Bāzār 138-139 J 4
Riding Mountain 61 HJ 5
Riding Mountain National Park
56-57 Q 7
Riḍīsiya, Er- = Ar-Raḍīsīyat Baḥrī
173 C 5
Ridley Creek 84 III a 2
Ridley Park, PA 84 III b 2
Ridvan = Alenz 136-137 J 4
Riebeek-Wes 174-175 C 7
Riebeek West = Riebeek-Wes
174-175 C 7
Riecito 94-95 G 4
Riederwald, Frankfurt am Main-
128 III b 1
Riedikon 128 IV b 2
Riedt 128 IV a 1
Riekertsdam 174-175 G 3
Riemerling 130 II c 2
Riesa 118 F 3
Riesbach, Zürich- 128 IV b 1
Riesco, Cordillera — 108-109 D 9
Riesco, Isla — 111 B 8
Riesi 122-123 F 7
Rietavas 124-125 C 6
Rietbron 174-175 E 7
Rietfontein 172 D 7
Rieth, OR 66-67 D 3
Rieti 122-123 E 4
Rietkuil 174-175 H 4
Rietrivier 174-175 F 5
Rīf = Ar-Rīf 164-165 CD 1-2
Rīf, Ar- [MA, administrative unit]
166-167 DE 2
Rīf, Ar- [MA, mountains]
164-165 CD 1-2
Rīf, er — = Ar-Rīf 166-167 DE 2
Rifā'ī, Ar- 136-137 M 7
Rifferswil 128 IV ab 2
Rifle, CO 68-69 C 6
Rifstangi 116-117 ef 1
Rift Valley 172 G 1
Rīga 124-125 E 5
Riga, Gulf of — = Rīgas Jūŗas Līcis
124-125 DE 5
Rīgas Jūŗas Līcis 124-125 DE 5
Rigby, ID 66-67 H 4
Rīgestān 134-135 JK 4
Riggins, ID 66-67 E 3
Riggū 166-167 E 3
Rigo 148-149 N 8
Rigolet 56-57 Z 7
Rīhāb, Ar- 136-137 L 7
Rihand 138-139 J 5
Riihimäki 116-117 L 7
Riiser-Larsen halvøy 53 C 4-5
Rijān 164-165 E 3
Rijeka 122-123 F 3
Rijksmuseum 128 I a 1
Rijo, Ilha do — 110 I c 1
Rijpfjord 116-117 l 4
Rikers Island 82 III c 2
Rikeze = Zhigatse 142-143 F 6
Rikorda, ostrov — 144-145 H 1
Riksgränsen 116-117 GH 3
Rikubetsu 144-145 c 2
Rikugien Garden 155 III b 1
Rikuzen-Takada 144-145 NO 3
Rila 122-123 K 4-5
Riley, KS 68-69 H 6
Rimac, Río — 96-97 C 7
Rimachi, Lago — 96-97 C 4
Rimah, Wādī ar- 134-135 E 5
Rimāl, Ar- = Ar-Rub' al-Khālī
134-135 F 7-G 6
Rimāl al-Abyaḍ 166-167 L 4
Rimbey 60 K 3
Rimini 122-123 E 3
Rîmnicu Sărat 122-123 M 3
Rîmnicu Vîlcea 122-123 L 3
Rimouski 56-57 X 8
Rimouski, Parc provincial des —
63 BC 3-4
Rimouski, Rivière — 63 B 3
Rim Rocky Mountains 66-67 C 4
Rincão 102-103 HJ 4
Rincón 108-109 D 8
Rincon, NM 76-77 A 6
Rincon, El — 91 III b 2
Rincón, Salina del — 104-105 C 8-9
Rinconada 111 C 2
Rinconada, Caracas-La — 91 II b 2
Rinconada, Hipódromo de la —
91 II b 2
Rincón de Baygorria 106-107 J 4
Rincón del Bonete 106-107 JK 4
Rincón del Diamante 108-109 C 3
Rincón de Romos 86-87 J 6
Rincon Peak 76-77 B 5
Rin'gang = Riāng 134-135 P 5
Ringas = Ringus 138-139 E 4
Ringerike-Hønefoss 116-117 CD 7
Ringgold, LA 78-79 C 4
Ringgold, TX 76-77 F 6
Ringim 168-169 H 2
Ringkøbing 116-117 BC 9
Ringling, MT 66-67 H 2
Ringling, OK 76-77 F 5
Ringold, OK 76-77 G 5
Ringus 138-139 E 4
Ringvassøy 116-117 H 3
Ringwood, OK 76-77 E 4
Riñihue [RCH, mountain]
108-109 C 2
Riñihue [RCH, place] 111 B 5-6
Rinja, Pulau — 148-149 G 8
Rinjani, Gunung — 148-149 G 8
Rio Abacaxis 98-99 J 7
Rio Abaeté 102-103 K 3
Río Abajo 64-65 bc 2
Río Abiseo 96-97 C 5
Rio Abunã 92-93 F 7
Rio Acaraú 100-101 D 2
Rio Acaray 102-103 E 6
Rio Acari 98-99 J 7-8
Rio Achuta 104-105 B 5
Rio Acima 102-103 L 4
Río Aconcagua 106-107 B 4
Rio Acre 92-93 F 6
Rio Açu 100-101 F 3
Rio Açú = Rio Piranhas 92-93 M 6
Rio Acuruauá 96-97 F 6
Río Agrio 106-107 B 7
Río Agua Caliente 104-105 E 4
Río Aguán 64-65 J 8
Río Aguanaval 86-87 J 5
Rio Aguapeí [BR, Mato Grosso]
102-103 C 1
Rio Aguapeí [BR, São Paulo]
102-103 G 4
Río Aguapey 106-107 J 1-2
Río Aguaray Guazú 102-103 D 6
Río Aguarico 96-97 C 2
Río Aguaytía 96-97 D 6
Río Águeda 120-121 D 8
Río Aiari 96-97 G 1
Río Aipena 96-97 CD 4
Río Ajaijú 94-95 E 7
Río Ajuana 94-95 J 8
Río Alalaú 92-93 G 5
Rio Alegre [BR, place] 102-103 D 2
Rio Alegre [BR, river] 102-103 C 1
Río Algodón 96-97 E 3
Río Alisos 86-87 E 2
Río Alonso 102-103 G 6
Río Alota 104-105 C 7
Río Alpercatas 92-93 KL 6
Río Altamachi 104-105 C 5
Río Altar 86-87 E 2
Río Alto Anapu 92-93 J 5
Río Aluminé 108-109 D 2
Río Amacuro 94-95 L 3
Río Amambaí 102-103 E 5
Río Amapari 98-99 M 4
Río Amazonas [BR] 92-93 HJ 5
Río Amazonas [PE] 92-93 E 5
Río Ameca 86-87 H 7
Río Amú 94-95 E 7
Río Anajás 98-99 N 5
Río Anamu 98-99 K 4
Río Anapali 96-97 E 7
Río Anari 104-105 E 2
Río Anauá 98-99 HJ 4
Río Anhanduí-Guaçu 102-103 EF 4
Río Anhanduizinho 102-103 EF 4
Río Apa 111 E 2
Río Apaporis 92-93 EF 5
Río Apedia 98-99 H 11
Río Apere 104-105 D 4
Río Apiacá 98-99 K 9
Río Apiaí 102-103 H 5
Río Apiaú 94-95 L 6
Río Aponguao 98-99 H 3
Río Aporé 92-93 J 8
Río Apure 92-93 F 3
Río Apurimac 92-93 E 7
Río Apurito 94-95 H 4
Río Aquidabán-mi 102-103 D 5
Río Aquidauana 102-103 D 3
Río Aquio 94-95 GH 6
Río Arabela 96-97 D 2-3
Río Arabopó 94-95 L 5
Río Araçá 98-99 G 4
Río Araçuaí 102-103 L 2
Río Aragón 120-121 G 7
Río Araguaia 92-93 J 7
Río Araguari [BR, Amapá] 92-93 J 4
Río Araguari [BR, Minas Gerais]
102-103 H 3
Río Arantes 102-103 GH 3
Río Arapey Chico 106-107 J 3
Río Arapey Grande 106-107 J 3
Río Arapiuns 98-99 L 6
Río Arauá [BR ◁ Rio Madero]
98-99 H 8
Río Arauã [BR ◁ Rio Purus]
98-99 F 9
Río Arauca 92-93 F 3
Río Ariari 94-95 E 6
Río Arinos 92-93 H 7
Río Ariporo 94-95 F 4
Río Aripuanã 92-93 G 6
Río Armería 86-87 HJ 8
Río Aro 94-95 K 4
Río Aros 86-87 F 3
Río Arraias [BR, Goiás] 100-101 A 7
Río Arraias [BR, Mato Grosso]
98-99 L 10-11
Río Arrecifes 106-107 G 5-H 4
Río Arrojado 100-101 B 7
Río Atelchu 98-99 L 11
Río Atibaia 102-103 J 5
Río Atoyac 86-87 L 8
Río Atrato 92-93 D 3
Río Atuel 106-107 D 5
Río Auati Paraná 92-93 F 5
Río Ayambis 96-97 BC 3
Río Aycheyacu 96-97 C 4
Río Azero 104-105 D 6
Río Azul [BR, Acre] 96-97 E 5
Río Azul [BR, Paraná] 102-103 G 6
Río Babahoyo 96-97 B 2-3
Río Bacajá 98-99 N 7
Río Bacamuchi 86-87 EF 2-3
Río Balsas 64-65 F 8
Río Balsas ó Mezcala 86-87 KL 8-9
Riobamba 92-93 D 5
Río Banabuiú 100-101 E 3
Río Barima 94-95 L 3
Río Barrancas 106-107 BC 6
Río Baudó 94-95 C 5
Río Bavispe 86-87 F 2-3
Río Belén 104-105 C 10-11
Río Beni 92-93 F 7
Río Benicito 104-105 D 2-3
Río Bento Gomes 102-103 D 2
Río Berlengas 100-101 C 4-5
Río Bermejo [RA ◁ Río Desaguadero]
106-107 C 3
Río Bermejo [RA ◁ Río Paraguay]
111 D 2
Río Bermejo = Río Colorado
106-107 D 2
Río Bermejo, Antiguo Cauce del —
104-105 F 9
Río Bermejo, Valle del —
106-107 CD 3
Río Bezerra 100-101 A 7
Río Biá 98-99 E 7
Río Bío Bío 111 B 5
Río Blanco [BR] 92-93 G 7
Río Blanco [CO, Magdalena]
94-95 D 3
Rioblanco [CO, Tolima] 94-95 D 6
Río Blanco [PE] 96-97 E 4
Río Blanco [RA] 106-107 C 2
Río Blanco [RCH] 106-107 BC 4
Río Blenque 96-97 B 2
Río Boa Sorte 100-101 B 7
Río Bobonaza 96-97 C 2
Río Boconó 94-95 G 3
Río Bogotá 91 III b 1
Río Bonito 102-103 L 5
Río Boopi 104-105 C 5
Río Boyuyumanu 104-105 B 2
Río Braço do Norte 102-103 H 7-8
Río Branco [BR, Acre] 98-99 D 9
Río Branco [BR, Amazonas]
92-93 F 6
Río Branco [BR, Bahia]
100-101 B 6-7
Río Branco [BR, Mato Grosso]
104-105 F 2
Río Branco [BR, Mato Grosso do Sul]
102-103 D 4
Río Branco [BR, Rio Branco]
92-93 G 4-5
Río Branco [BR, Rondônia]
98-99 F 9-G 10
Río Branco [ROU] 106-107 L 4
Río Branco do Sul 102-103 H 6
Río Bravo 76-77 D 8
Río Bravo, Ciudad — 86-87 LM 5
Río Bravo del Norte 64-65 E 5-F 6
Río Brilhante 102-103 E 4
Río Bueno [RCH, place] 108-109 C 3
Río Bueno [RCH, river] 108-109 C 3
Río Buranhém 100-101 DE 9
Río Buriti 104-105 G 3
Río Buriticupu 100-101 A 3
Río Caatinga 102-103 JK 2
Río Cabaçal 102-103 CD 1
Río Cachapoal 106-107 B 5
Río Cachoeira 100-101 E 8
Río Caçiporé 92-93 J 4
Río Caeté 98-99 D 9
Río Caguán 92-93 E 4
Río Cahuapanas 96-97 C 4
Río Cahuinari 94-95 EF 8
Río Caiapó 102-103 G 2
Río Caimito 64-65 b 3
Río Caine 104-105 D 6
Río Cais 100-101 D 3
Río Cal 104-105 G 6
Río Calçoene 98-99 N 3-4
Río Caleufú 108-109 D 3
Río Calvas 96-97 B 4
Río Camaquã 106-107 L 3
Río Camararé 98-99 J 11
Río Camarones 104-105 AB 6
Río Camisea 96-97 E 7
Río Campuya 96-97 DE 2
Río Candeias 98-99 G 9-10
Río Candelaria [BOL] 104-105 G 5
Río Candelaria [MEX] 86-87 P 8
Río Cañete 96-97 CD 8
Río Canindé 100-101 C 4
Río Canoas 102-103 G 7
Río Caño Quebrado [PA, Colón]
64-65 a 2
Río Caño Quebrado [PA, Panamá]
64-65 b 2-3
Río Cantu 102-103 F 6
Río Canumã 98-99 J 7
Río Canumã = Rio Sucunduri
92-93 H 6
Río Capahuari 96-97 C 3
Río Capanaparo 94-95 G 4
Río Capanema 102-103 F 6-7
Río Capim 92-93 K 5
Río Capitán Costa Pinheiro
104-105 GH 2
Río Capitão Cardoso 98-99 HJ 10
Río Caquetá 92-93 E 5
Río Carabaya 96-97 FG 9
Río Carabinami 98-99 G 6
Río Caracol 100-101 A 5-6
Río Caraná 104-105 G 3
Río Carapa 102-103 E 6
Río Cara-Paraná 94-95 E 8
Río Carapo 94-95 K 4
Río Carcarañá 106-107 FG 4
Río Caribe 86-87 P 8
Río Caribe [MEX] 86-87 P 8
Río Caribe [YV] 94-95 K 2
Río Caris 94-95 K 3
Río Caroní 92-93 G 3
Río Carrao 94-95 K 4
Río Caru 100-101 A 2
Río Casanare 92-93 E 3
Río Casas Grandes 64-65 E 5-6
Río Casca 102-103 L 4
Río Casiquiare 92-93 F 4
Río Casireni 96-97 E 8
Río Casma 96-97 BC 6
Río Cassai 172 CD 4
Río Catamayo 96-97 AB 4
Río Catatumbo 94-95 EF 3
Río Catete 98-99 LM 8
Río Catolé Grande 100-101 D 8
Río Catrimani 92-93 G 4
Río Cauaburi 98-99 E 4-F 5
Río Cauamé 94-95 L 6
Río Cauaxi 98-99 O 7
Río Cauca 92-93 E 3
Río Caura 92-93 G 3
Río Caurés 98-99 G 5
Río Cautário 98-99 FG 10
Río Caveiras 102-103 G 7
Río Caxiabatay 96-97 D 5
Río Cebollatí 106-107 K 4
Río Cenepa 96-97 B 4
Río César 94-95 E 2
Río Chadileuvú 106-107 DE 6
Río Chagres 64-65 bc 2
Río Chalía 108-109 DE 7
Río Chama 76-77 A 4
Río Chamaya 96-97 B 4-5
Río Chambira 96-97 D 3
Río Chambira 96-97 D 4
Río Champotón 86-87 P 8
Río Chancay 96-97 C 7
Río Chandless 98-99 C 9-10
Río Changane 172 F 6
Río Chapare 104-105 D 5
Río Chaschuil 104-105 B 10
Río Chayanta 104-105 CD 6
Río Chevejecure 104-105 C 4
Río Chiapa = Rio Grande 64-65 H 8
Río Chicama 96-97 B 5
Río Chicapa 172 D 3
Río Chiché 98-99 LM 9
Río Chico [RA, Chubut] 111 C 6
Río Chico [RA, Río Negro]
108-109 D 3
Río Chico [RA, Santa Cruz ◁ Bahia
Grande] 111 C 7
Río Chico [RA, Santa Cruz ◁ Río
Gallegos] 111 C 7
Río Chico [RA, Santa Cruz place]
111 C 7
Río Chico [YV] 92-93 F 2
Río Chico Carmen Silva 108-109 E 9
Río Chilete 96-97 B 5
Río Chillón 96-97 C 7
Río Chinchipe 96-97 B 4
Río Chingovo 174-175 K 2
Río Chipillico 96-97 A 4
Río Chipiriri 104-105 D 5
Río Chira 96-97 A 4
Río Chirgua 94-95 H 3
Río Chiulezi 171 D 5-6
Río Chiumbe 172 D 3
Río Chixoy 64-65 H 8
Río Choapa 106-107 B 3
Río Chopim 102-103 F 6-7
Río Choro [BOL] 104-105 D 5
Río Choró [BR] 100-101 E 3
Río Chubut 111 C 6
Río Chucunaque 94-95 C 3
Río Cinaruco 94-95 G 4
Río Cipó 102-103 L 3
Río Ciri 64-65 a 3
Río Cisnes 108-109 D 5
Río Cisnes [RCH, place] 108-109 D 5
Río Citaré 98-99 L 4
Río Claro [BOL] 104-105 BC 3
Río Claro [BR, Goiás ◁ Rio Araguaia]
92-93 J 8
Río Claro [BR, Goiás ◁ Rio Paranaíba]
92-93 J 8
Río Claro [BR, Mato Grosso]
102-103 D 2
Río Claro [BR, São Paulo]
102-103 J 5
Río Claro [TT] 64-65 O 9
Río Claro [YV] 94-95 G 3
Río Claro, Serra do — 102-103 G 2
Río Coari 92-93 G 5-6
Río Coca 96-97 C 2
Río Cocharcas 104-105 D 3-4
Río Coco 64-65 K 9
Río Codózinho 100-101 B 3
Río Coengua 96-97 E 7
Río Cofuini 98-99 K 4
Río Coig 108-109 D 8
Río Coig, Brazo Sur del —
108-109 D 8
Río Coité 100-101 E 6
Río Cojedes 94-95 G 3
Río Colca 92-93 E 8
Río Collón Curá 108-109 D 3
Río Colorado [BOL] 98-99 GH 11
Río Colorado [MEX] 64-65 CD 5
Río Colorado [RA, La Pampa] 111 C 5
Río Colorado [RA, La Rioja]
106-107 D 2
Río Colorado [RA, Neuquén Río
Negro] 111 D 5
Río Colorado [RA, Río Negro]
111 CD 5
Río Colorado, Delta del —
108-109 H 2
Rio Comprido, Rio de Janeiro
110 I b 2
Río Conambo 96-97 C 2
Rio Conceição 100-101 A 7
Río Conchos 64-65 EF 6
Rio Confuso 102-103 C 6
Río Conlara 106-107 E 4
Río Cononaco 96-97 C 2
Río Conorochite 94-95 H 6
Río Consata 104-105 B 4
Río Copalyacu 96-97 D 3
Río Copiapó 106-107 B 1
Río Coralaque 96-97 F 10
Río Corda 100-101 B 3-4
Río Coreaú 100-101 D 2
Río Corixa Grande 102-103 C 2
Río Corrente [BR, Bahia] 92-93 L 7
Río Corrente [BR, Bahia] 92-93 L 7
Río Corrente [BR, Goiás ◁ Rio Paraná]
100-101 A 8
Río Corrente [BR, Goiás ◁ Rio
Paranaíba] 102-103 G 3
Río Corrente [BR, Piauí] 100-101 D 3
Río Correntes 102-103 E 2
Río Corrientes [EC] 96-97 C 3
Río Corrientes [RA] 106-107 H 2
Río Corumbá 92-93 K 8
Río Corumbataí 102-103 G 6
Río Cosapa 104-105 B 6
Río Cotacajes 104-105 C 5
Río Cotegipe 102-103 F 6
Río Cotia 104-105 D 1
Río Coxim 102-103 E 3
Río Cravari 104-105 GH 3
Río Cravo Norte 94-95 F 4
Río Cravo Sur 94-95 EF 5
Río Crepori 98-99 K 7
Río Crisnejas 96-97 BC 5
Río Cruxati 100-101 E 2
Río Cruzes 108-109 C 2
Río Cuando 172 D 5
Río Cuango 172 C 3
Río Cuao 94-95 H 5
Río Cuarein 106-107 J 3
Río Cuarto [RA, place] 111 D 4
Río Cuarto [RA, river] 106-107 EF 4
Río Cubango 172 C 5
Río Cuchi 172 C 4-5
Río Cuchivero 94-95 J 4
Río Cuemani 94-95 E 7-8
Río Cuiabá 92-93 H 8
Río Cuieté 102-103 M 3
Río Cuilo 172 C 3
Río Cuito 172 CD 5
Río Cuiuni 98-99 G 5
Río Cujar 96-97 E 7
Río Culuene 92-93 J 7
Río Cuminá 92-93 H 5
Río Cuminapanema 98-99 L 4-5
Río Cunene 172 B 5
Río Curaçá 100-101 E 5
Río Curacó 106-107 E 7
Río Curanja 96-97 F 7
Río Curaray 92-93 D 5
Río Curicuriari 98-99 DE 5
Río Curimatá 100-101 B 5-6
Río Curiuja 96-97 E 7
Río Curuá [BR ◁ Rio Amazonas]
98-99 L 4-5
Río Curuá [BR ◁ Rio Iriri] 92-93 J 6
Río Curuá do Sul 98-99 LM 6
Río Curuaés 98-99 L 9
Río Curuá Una 98-99 L 6
Río Curuçá 98-99 C 7
Río Curuguá 96-97 F 4
Río Curucuinazá 104-105 GH 3
Río Curupaí 102-103 EF 5
Río Curuquetê 98-99 F 9
Río Cururu-Açu 98-99 K 9
Río Cusiana 94-95 E 5
Río Cutzamala 86-87 K 8
Río Cuvo 172 B 4
Río da Areia 102-103 F 5-6
Río da Cachoeira 110 I b 2
Río da Conceição 100-101 A 6
Río Dadache 174-175 K 2
Río Dange 172 B 3
Río da Prata [BR ◁ Rio Paracatu]
102-103 J 2
Río da Prata [BR ◁ Rio Paranaíba]
102-103 H 3
Río Daraá 94-95 J 7-8
Río das Antas [BR, place]
102-103 G 7
Río das Antas [BR, Rio Grande do Sul]
106-107 M 2
Río das Antas [BR, Santa Catarina]
102-103 F 7
Río das Arraias do Araguaia
98-99 N 9-O 8
Río das Balsas 100-101 B 4
Río das Éguas 100-101 B 7
Río das Garças 102-103 F 1
Río das Mortes 102-103 K 4
Río das Ondas 100-101 B 7
Río das Pedras 100-101 AB 7
Río das Pedras [BR] 102-103 J 5
Río das Pedras [Mozambique]
174-175 L 2
Río das Velhas 92-93 L 8
Río Daule 92-93 CD 5
Río da Várzea [BR, Paraná]
102-103 H 6-7
Río da Várzea [BR, Rio Grande do Sul]
106-107 L 1
Río de Bavispe 74-75 J 7
Río de Contas 92-93 L 7
Río de Contas, Serra do —
100-101 D 7-8
Río de Geba 164-165 AB 6
Río de Janeiro 100-101 B 6
Río de Janeiro [BR, administrative
unit] 92-93 LM 9
Río de Janeiro [BR, place] 92-93 L 9
Rio de Janeiro-Acari 110 I a 1
Rio de Janeiro-Aldeia Campista
110 I b 2
Rio de Janeiro-Alto da Boa Vista
110 I b 2
Rio de Janeiro-Andaraí 110 I b 2
Rio de Janeiro-Anil 110 I a 2
Rio de Janeiro-Bangu 102-103 L 5
Rio de Janeiro-Barra da Tijuca
110 I ab 3
Rio de Janeiro-Bento 110 I a 2
Rio de Janeiro-Boca do Mato
110 I b 2
Rio de Janeiro-Bonsucesso 110 I b 2
Rio de Janeiro-Botafogo 110 I b 2
Rio de Janeiro-Caju 110 I b 2
Rio de Janeiro-Cascadura 110 I ab 2
Rio de Janeiro-Catete 110 I b 2
Rio de Janeiro-Cidade de Deus
110 I ab 2
Rio de Janeiro-Cocotá 110 I b 1
Rio de Janeiro-Copacabana
110 I bc 2
Rio de Janeiro-Cordovil 110 I b 1
Rio de Janeiro-Dende 110 I b 1
Rio de Janeiro-Encantado 110 I b 2
Rio de Janeiro-Engenho Nova
110 I b 2
Rio de Janeiro-Fáb. das Chitas
110 I b 2
Rio de Janeiro-Freguesia [BR ↑ Rio
de Janeiro] 110 I bc 1
Rio de Janeiro-Freguesia [BR ↑ Rio
de Janeiro] 110 I a 2
Rio de Janeiro-Furnas 110 I b 2
Rio de Janeiro-Galeão 110 I b 1
Rio de Janeiro-Gamboa 110 I b 2
Rio de Janeiro-Gávea 110 I b 2
Rio de Janeiro-Glória 110 I b 2
Rio de Janeiro-Grajaú 110 I b 2
Rio de Janeiro-Honório Gurgel
110 I a 2
Rio de Janeiro-Inhaúma 110 I b 2
Rio de Janeiro-Ipanema 110 I b 2
Rio de Janeiro-Irajá 110 I b 1
Rio de Janeiro-Jacarepaguá
110 I ab 2
Rio de Janeiro-Jardim Botânico
110 I b 2
Rio de Janeiro-Lapa 110 I b 2
Rio de Janeiro-Laranjeiras 110 I b 2
Rio de Janeiro-Leblon 110 I b 2
Rio de Janeiro-Leme 110 I bc 2
Rio de Janeiro-Madureira 110 I ab 2
Rio de Janeiro-Méier 110 I b 2
Rio de Janeiro-Olaria 110 I b 2
Rio de Janeiro-Pechincha 110 I ab 2
Rio de Janeiro-Penha 110 I b 1
Rio de Janeiro-Piedade 110 I b 2
Rio de Janeiro-Praça Seca 110 I a 2
Rio de Janeiro-Ramos 110 I b 2
Rio de Janeiro-Realengo
102-103 L 5
Rio de Janeiro-Ribeira 110 I c 1
Rio de Janeiro-Santa Cruz
102-103 L 5
Rio de Janeiro-São Conrado
110 I b 2
Rio de Janeiro-São Cristovão
110 I b 2
Rio de Janeiro-Tijuca 110 I b 2
Rio de Janeiro-Vigário Geral
110 I b 1
Rio de Janeiro-Vila Balneária
110 I b 3
Rio de Janeiro-Vila Pedro II 110 I a 1
Rio de Janeiro-Zumbi 110 I b 1
Río de la Cal 104-105 G 6
Río de la Fortaleza 96-97 C 7
Río de la Laja 106-107 AB 6
Río de la Magdalena 91 I b 3
Río de la Palca 106-107 C 2
Río de la Paz 104-105 C 5
Río de la Plata 111 EF 5
Río de las Piedras 92-93 E 7
Río de la Turba 108-109 E 9-10
Río del Carmen [MEX] 86-87 G 2-3
Río del Carmen [RCH] 106-107 B 2
Río del Ingenio 96-97 D 9
Río del Jagüé 111 C 3
Río de los Papagayos 106-107 C 5
Río de los Patos 106-107 C 3-4
Río de los Sauces 106-107 E 4
Río del Valle 104-105 D 11
Río del Valle del Cura 106-107 C 2
Río de Majes 96-97 F 10
Río de Mala 96-97 C 8
Río Demini 92-93 G 4-5
Río de Ocoña 96-97 E 10
Río de Oro 104-105 G 10
Río de Oro [PY] 102-103 C 7
Río de Oro [YV] 94-95 E 3
Río de Reque 96-97 B 5
Río Desaguadero [BOL] 92-93 F 8
Río Desaguadero [RA] 106-107 D 4
Río de São Pedro 100-101 DE 5
Río Deseado 111 BC 7
Río Deseado, Valle del —
108-109 E 6
Rio Diamante 106-107 D 5
Rio Diamantino 102-103 F 2
Rio do Anil 110 I a 2
Rio do Antônio 100-101 C 8

Rio do Cobre 102-103 FG 6
Rio do Côco 98-99 O 9
Rio do Meio 100-101 B 7
Rio do Ouro 100-101 B 6
Rio do Pará 92-93 JK 5
Rio do Peixe [BR, Bahia] 100-101 E 6
Rio do Peixe [BR, Goiás] 102-103 F 2
Rio do Peixe [BR, Minas Gerais ◁ Rio Preto] 102-103 L 4
Rio do Peixe [BR, Minas Gerais ◁ Rio Santo Antônio] 102-103 L 3
Rio do Peixe [BR, Santa Catarina] 102-103 G 7
Rio do Peixe [BR, São Paulo] 102-103 G 4
Rio do Pires 100-101 C 7
Rio do Pontal 100-101 D 5
Rio do Prado 100-101 D 3
Rio do Sangue 92-93 H 7
Rio dos Bois 102-103 G 3
Rio dos Elefantes 174-175 K 2-3
Rio dos Marmelos 92-93 G 6
Rio do Sono [BR, Goiás] 92-93 K 6-7
Rio do Sono [BR, Minas Gerais] 102-103 K 2
Rio dos Peixes 98-99 K 10
Rio dos Porcos 100-101 B 7
Rio do Sul 111 G 3
Rio Dourados [BR, Mato Grosso do Sul] 102-103 E 5
Rio Dourados [BR, Minas Gerais] 102-103 J 3
Río Duda 94-95 D 6
Rio Duerê 98-99 O 10
Río Dulce 111 D 3-4
Rio Eiru 96-97 F 5
Río Elqui 106-107 B 3
Río El Valle 91 II b 2
Rio Embari 94-95 H 8
Rio Embira 98-99 C 9
Rio Endimari 98-99 E 9
Río Ene 92-93 E 7
Rio Erebato 94-95 J 5
Río Esmeraldas 92-93 D 4
Rio Farinha 100-101 A 4
Río Fénix Grande 108-109 D 6
Rio Ferro 98-99 L 11
Río Fiambalá 104-105 C 10
Rio Fidalgo 100-101 C 4
Río Florido 76-77 B 8-9
Rio Formoso 100-101 B 7
Rio Formoso [BR, Goiás] 98-99 O 10
Rio Formoso [BR, Pernambuco] 100-101 G 5
Rio Fresco 98-99 N 8
Río Fucha 91 III b 3
Río Fuerte 64-65 E 6
Río Futaleufú 108-109 D 4
Río Galera 104-105 FG 4
Rio Galheirão 100-101 B 7
Río Gállego 120-121 G 7
Río Gallegos 111 BC 8
Río Gálvez 96-97 E 4
Río Gatún 64-65 b 2
Río Gatuncillo 64-65 b 2
Rio Gaviao 100-101 D 8
Rio Gongoji 100-101 DE 8
Rio Gorutuba 102-103 L 1
Rio Grajau [BR, Acre] 96-97 E 6
Rio Grajaú [BR, Maranhão] 92-93 K 5-6
Río Grande [BOL, place Potosí] 104-105 C 7
Río Grande [BOL, place Santa Cruz] 104-105 E 5
Río Grande [BOL, river] 92-93 G 8
Rio Grande [BR, Minas Gerais] 92-93 K 8-9
Rio Grande [BR, Rio Grande do Sul] 111 F 4
Río Grande [MEX] 64-65 H 8
Río Grande [NIC, place] 88-89 E 8
Río Grande [NIC, river] 64-65 JK 9
Río Grande [PE] 96-97 D 9
Río Grande [RA, Jujuy] 104-105 D 8
Río Grande [RA, La Rioja] 106-107 D 2
Río Grande [RA, Neuquén] 106-107 C 6
Río Grande [RA, Tierra de Fuego river] 108-109 E 9
Río Grande [RA, Tierra del Fuego place] 111 C 8
Rio Grande [USA, Colorado] 76-77 AB 4
Rio Grande [USA, Texas] 64-65 FG 6
Río Grande [YV, place] 91 II b 1
Río Grande [YV, river] 94-95 L 3
Rio Grande, Barragem do — 110 II a 3
Río Grande, Ciudad — 86-87 J 6
Rio Grande, Reprêsa do — 102-103 J 5
Rio Grande, Salar de — 104-105 BC 9
Rio Grande City, TX 76-77 E 9
Río Grande de Santiago 64-65 F 7
Rio Grande do Norte 92-93 M 6
Rio Grande do Norte = Natal 92-93 MN 6
Rio Grande do Piauí 100-101 C 4
Rio Grande do Sul 111 F 3-4
Rio Grande Rise 50-51 GH 7
Río Grandes de Lípez 104-105 C 7-8
Rio Gregório 98-99 C 8
Rio Guachiria 94-95 F 5
Rio Guaçu 102-103 F 6
Rio Guaíba 106-107 M 3
Rio Guainía 92-93 F 4
Río Guaire 91 II b 2
Río Gualeguay 106-107 H 4
Rio Gualjaina 108-109 D 4
Rio Guamá 100-101 A 2
Río Guamués 94-95 C 7
Río Guanare 94-95 G 3
Río Guandacol 106-107 C 2
Río Guanipa 94-95 K 3
Río Guapay 104-105 E 5
Rio Guaporé [BR ◁ Rio Mamoré] 92-93 G 7
Rio Guaporé [BR ◁ Rio Taquari] 106-107 L 2
Rio Guará 100-101 B 7
Río Guárico 94-95 H 3
Rio Guarita 106-107 L 1
Río Guarrojo 94-95 F 5
Río Guaviare 92-93 F 4
Río Guayabero 94-95 E 6
Río Guayapo 94-95 H 5
Río Guayas [CO] 94-95 D 7
Río Guayas [EC] 96-97 B 3
Río Guaycurú 102-103 C 7
Río Guayllabamba 94-95 B 1
Río Guayquiraró 106-107 H 3
Río Guéjar 94-95 E 6
Río Guenguel 108-109 D 5-6
Río Güere 94-95 J 3
Río Güiza 94-95 BC 7
Rio Gurguéia 92-93 L 6
Rio Gurupi 92-93 K 5
Ríohacha 92-93 E 2
Río Hardy 74-75 F 6
Río Hato 88-89 FG 10
Río Heath 96-97 G 8
Rio Hercilio 102-103 GH 7
Río Hondo [BOL] 104-105 BC 4
Río Hondo [MEX, place] 91 I b 2
Río Hondo [MEX, river] 91 I c 1
Rio Hondo [USA, California] 83 III cd 2
Rio Hondo [USA, New Mexico] 76-77 B 6
Río Hondo, Embalse — 106-107 E 1
Río Horcones 104-105 D 9
Río Huahua 88-89 DE 7
Rio Huaiá-Miço 98-99 M 10
Río Huallabamba 96-97 C 5
Río Huallaga 92-93 D 6
Río Huarmey 96-97 B 7-C 6
Río Huasaga 96-97 C 3
Río Huasco 106-107 B 2
Río Huaura 96-97 C 7
Rio Iaco 92-93 EF 7
Rio Iapó 102-103 G 6
Río Ibare 104-105 D 4
Río Ibicuí 111 E 3
Rio Ibirapuitã 106-107 K 2-3
Río Ibirizu 104-105 D 5
Rio Içá 92-93 F 5
Rio Icamaquã 106-107 K 2
Rio Içana 92-93 F 4
Rio Icatu 100-101 C 6
Río Ichoa 104-105 D 4
Rio Igara Paraná 94-95 E 8
Rio Iguaçu 111 F 3
Rio Iguará 100-101 C 3
Rio Iguatemi 102-103 E 5
Rio Ijuí 106-107 K 2
Río Ilave 96-97 G 10
Rio Imabu 98-99 K 5
Río Imperial 106-107 A 7
Rio Inajá 98-99 N 9
Rio Inauini 98-99 D 9
Rio Incomáti 174-175 K 3
Rio Indaia 102-103 K 3
Rio Indaiá Grande 102-103 F 3
Río Indio 64-65 c 2
Rio Inhambupe 100-101 E 6
Rio Inharrime 174-175 L 3
Río Inírida 92-93 F 4
Río Inuya 96-97 E 7
Rio Ipanema 100-101 F 5
Rio Ipixuna [BR ◁ Rio Juruá] 96-97 E 5
Rio Ipixuna [BR ◁ Rio Purus] 92-93 G 6
Rio Iquiri 98-99 E 9
Rio Irani 102-103 F 7
Rio Iriri 92-93 J 5
Rio Irivi Novo 98-99 M 9
Río Iruya 104-105 D 8
Río Isana 94-95 F 7
Río Iscuandé 94-95 C 6
Río Isiboro 104-105 D 5
Rio Itabapoana 102-103 M 4
Rio Itacaiúnas 92-93 JK 6
Rio Itacambiruçu 102-103 L 2
Rio Itacuaí 96-97 F 5
Rio Itaguari 100-101 B 8
Rio Itaim 100-101 D 4
Rio Itaimbey 102-103 E 6
Rio Itajaí 102-103 H 7
Rio Itajaí do Sul 102-103 H 7
Rio Itajaí-Mirim 102-103 H 7
Rio Itala 106-107 A 6
Rio Itambacuri 102-103 M 3
Rio Itanhauã 98-99 F 7
Rio Itanhém 100-101 E 9
Rio Itaparaná 98-99 G 8
Rio Itapicuru [BR, Bahia] 92-93 M 7
Rio Itapicuru [BR, Maranhão] 92-93 L 5
Rio Itapicuru Açu 100-101 DE 6
Rio Itapicurumirim 100-101 DE 6
Rio Itapicuruzinho 100-101 C 3
Rio Itaquai 98-99 C 7
Rio Itararé 102-103 H 5
Rio Itaueira 100-101 C 4-5
Rio Itenes 104-105 E 3
Rio Itiquira 92-93 H 8
Rio Itui 92-93 E 6
Rio Ituxi 92-93 F 6
Rio Ivaí 111 F 2
Rio Ivinheima 92-93 J 9
Río Ivón 104-105 C 2
Rioja [PE] 92-93 D 6
Rioja [RCH] 104-105 B 8
Rioja, La — [E] 120-121 F 7
Rioja, La — [RA, administrative unit] 106-107 D 2
Rioja, La — [RA, place] 111 C 3
Rioja, Llanos de la — 106-107 DE 2
Rio Jacarai 100-101 D 2
Rio Jacaré [BR, Bahia] 92-93 L 6-7
Rio Jacaré [BR, Minas Gerais] 102-103 K 4
Rio Jacuni 94-95 J 6
Río Jáchal 106-107 C 3
Rio Jaciparana 98-99 F 9-10
Rio Jacu 100-101 G 4
Rio Jacuí 106-107 L 2
Rio Jacuípe 92-93 LM 7
Rio Jacundá 98-99 N 6
Rio Jacurici 100-101 E 6
Rio Jaguari 106-107 K 2
Rio Jaguaribe 92-93 M 6
Río Jalon 120-121 G 8
Rio Jamanxim 92-93 H 6
Rio Jamari 92-93 G 6
Rio Jaminaua 96-97 F 6
Rio Janaperi 92-93 G 4
Rio Jandiatuba 92-93 F 5-6
Rio Japurá 92-93 F 5
Rio Jarauçu 98-99 M 5-6
Rio Jari 92-93 J 5
Rio Jarina 98-99 M 10
Rio Jaru 98-99 G 10
Rio Jatapu 92-93 H 5
Rio Jaú 92-93 G 5
Rio Jauru [BR ◁ Rio Coxim] 102-103 EF 3
Rio Jauru [BR ◁ Rio Paraguai] 102-103 CD 2
Rio Javari 92-93 E 6
Río Jejuí Guazú 102-103 DE 6
Rio Jequitaí 102-103 K 2
Rio Jequitinhonha 92-93 L 8
Rio Jiparaná 92-93 G 6-7
Rio Jordão 102-103 G 6
Rio José Pedro 102-103 M 3-4
Rio Juçaral 100-101 C 2
Rio Jucurucu 100-101 DE 9
Río Juramento 104-105 D 9
Rio Juruá 92-93 F 6
Rio Juruázinho 96-97 FG 5
Rio Juruena 92-93 H 6-7
Rio Jurupari 96-97 F 5-G 6
Rio Jutaí 92-93 F 5
Rio Kwanza 172 B 3
Río Lagartos 86-87 QR 7
Rio Largo 92-93 MN 6
Río las Palmas 74-75 E 6
Río Las Petas 104-105 G 5
Río Lauca 104-105 B 6
Rio Lever 98-99 N 10
Rio Liberdade [BR, Acre] 96-97 E 5-6
Rio Liberdade [BR, Mato Grosso] 98-99 M 10
Rio Ligonha 172 G 5
Río Limarí 106-107 B 3
Río Limay 111 C 5
Rio Limpopo 174-175 K 3
Río Lluta 104-105 B 6
Río Loa 111 BC 2
Rio Loge 172 B 3
Río Lomas 96-97 D 9
Río Loncomilla 106-107 AB 5
Rio Longá 100-101 D 2
Rio Lontra 102-103 F 4
Río Lontué 106-107 B 5
Río Lora 94-95 E 3
Río Losada 94-95 D 6
Rio Luando 172 C 4
Rio Luanginga 172 D 4
Rio Luangue 172 C 3
Rio Luatizi 171 D 6
Rio Luembe 172 D 3
Rio Luena 172 D 4
Rio Lugenda 172 G 4
Rio Luiana 172 D 5
Río Luján 106-107 H 5
Rio Lunguè-Bungo 172 D 4
Rio Lúrio 172 GH 4
Rio Luxico 172 CD 3
Rio Macacos 100-101 A 8
Rio Macauã 98-99 D 9
Rio Machadinho 104-105 E 1
Río Machupo 104-105 D 3
Rio MacLennan 108-109 F 9-10
Rio Macuma 96-97 C 3
Rio Macupari 104-105 C 3
Rio Madeira 92-93 G 6
Rio Madeirinha 98-99 H 9
Rio Madidi 92-93 F 7
Rio Madre de Dios 92-93 F 7
Río Magdalena [CO] 92-93 E 2-3
Río Magdalena [MEX] 64-65 D 5
Rio Magu 100-101 C 2
Rio Maicuru 92-93 J 5
Río Maipo 106-107 B 4
Rio Majari 98-99 H 3
Río Malleco 106-107 AB 7
Rio Mamoré 92-93 FG 7-8
Rio Mamuru 98-99 K 6
Río Manacacías 94-95 E 5-6
Río Manapire 94-95 H 3
Rio Manhuaçu 102-103 M 3
Rio Manicauá-Miçu 98-99 LM 10
Rio Manicoré 98-99 H 8
Río Maniqui 104-105 C 4
Rio Manso 92-93 J 7-8
Río Mantaro 92-93 E 7
Río Manú 96-97 F 7-8
Rio Manuel Alves 98-99 OP 10
Río Manurini 104-105 C 3
Río Manuripe 96-97 G 7
Río Mapiri [BOL ◁ Río Abuña] 104-105 C 2
Río Mapiri [BOL ◁ Río Beni] 104-105 B 4
Rio Mapuera 92-93 H 5
Rio Mapulau 98-99 G 3-4
Rio Maputo 174-175 K 4
Rio Maraca 98-99 N 5
Rio Maraçacumé 100-101 AB 1-2
Río Marañón 92-93 DE 5
Rio Marapi 98-99 K 4
Rio Marauiá 98-99 F 4-5
Rio Mariê 92-93 F 5
Río Marine = Mārtil 166-167 D 2
Río Matacuni 94-95 J 6
Río Matanza 110 III b 2
Río Mataquito 106-107 B 5
Río Mataven 94-95 G 5
Río Maticora 94-95 F 2
Río Matos 104-105 CD 4
Rio Maués-Açu 92-93 H 5
Río Maule 106-107 AB 5
Río Maullín 108-109 C 3
Rio Mauni 96-97 G 10
Río Mavaca 94-95 J 6
Río Mayo [PE] 96-97 C 4
Río Mayo [RA] 108-109 D 5
Río Mayo [RA, place] 111 BC 7
Río Mazán 96-97 E 3
Rio Mazimchopes 174-175 K 3
Rio Mearim 92-93 L 5
Rio Mebreije = Rio M'Bridge 172 B 3
Rio Mebridege 172 B 3
Río Mecaya 94-95 D 7
Río Medinas 104-105 D 10
Rio Meia Ponte 92-93 K 8
Río Mendoza 106-107 C 4
Rio Messalo 172 G 4
Río Meta 92-93 E 3
Río Mexcala = Río Balsas 64-65 F 8
Río Mira [CO] 94-95 B 7
Rio Miranda 92-93 H 9
Río Miriñay 106-107 J 2
Rio Miritiparaná 94-95 F 8
Río Mishagua 96-97 E 7
Río Mizque 104-105 D 6
Rio Moa 96-97 E 5
Río Moaco 96-97 G 6
Río Mocaya 94-95 E 7
Rio Mocó 98-99 E 6
Rio Moções 98-99 O 5
Río Moctezuma 86-87 F 2-3
Rio Mojiguaçu 102-103 HJ 4
Río Monday 102-103 E 6
Río Monte Lindo 102-103 CD 5
Río Monte Lindo Grande 104-105 G 9
Río Moquegua 96-97 F 10
Rio Morerú 98-99 J 10
Río Moricha Largo 94-95 K 3
Río Morona 92-93 D 5
Río Mosquito 102-103 M 1-2
Río Motagua 86-87 Q 10
Río Motatán 94-95 F 3
Rio Moura 96-97 E 5-6
Rio Moxotó 100-101 F 5
Rio Mucajaí 92-93 G 4
Río Muco 94-95 F 5
Rio Mucuburi 171 D 6
Rio Mucucuaú 98-99 H 4
Rio Mucuim 98-99 F 8
Rio Mucuri 92-93 L 8
Río Muerto 104-105 F 10
Río Mulatos 92-93 F 8
Río Mundo 120-121 F 9
Río Muni = Mbini 164-165 G 8
Rio Munim 100-101 B 2
Rio Muruaaú 98-99 H 4
Rio Muriaé 102-103 M 4
Río Murri 94-95 C 4
Rio Muru 96-97 F 6
Rio Mutum 98-99 D 7
Rio Muyumanu 96-97 G 7
Río Nabileque 102-103 D 4
Río Ñacunday 102-103 E 6
Río Nanay 92-93 E 5
Río Nangaritza 96-97 B 4
Río Napo 92-93 E 5
Río Naranjal 96-97 B 3
Río Nashiño 96-97 D 2
Río Nayá 94-95 C 6
Río Nazas 86-87 H 5
Río Nechí 94-95 D 4
Rio Negrinho 102-103 H 7
Río Negro [BOL, place] 104-105 C 1
Río Negro [BOL, river ◁ Laguna Concepción] 104-105 E 4
Río Negro [BOL, river ◁ Río Madeira] 104-105 C 2
Rio Negro [BR, Amazonas] 92-93 G 5
Rio Negro [BR, Mato Grosso] 92-93 H 8
Rio Negro [BR, Mato Grosso do Sul] 102-103 D 3
Rio Negro [BR, Paraná place] 111 F 3
Rio Negro [BR, Paraná river] 102-103 H 7
Rio Negro [BR, Rio de Janeiro] 102-103 L 4
Rionegro [CO, Antioquia] 94-95 D 4
Rionegro [CO, Santander] 94-95 E 4
Río Negro [PY] 102-103 D 6
Río Negro [RA, Chaco] 104-105 G 10
Río Negro [RA, Río Negro administrative unit] 111 C 6
Río Negro [RA, Río Negro river] 111 D 5-6
Río Negro [RCH, place] 108-109 C 3
Río Negro [RCH, river] 108-109 C 3
Río Negro [ROU, administrative unit] 106-107 J 4
Río Negro [ROU, river] 111 EF 4
Río Negro [YV, Amazonas] 94-95 H 7
Río Negro [YV, Zulia] 94-95 E 3
Río Negro, Bogotá 91 III c 2
Río Negro, Embalse del — 111 E 4
Rio Negro, Pantanal do — 92-93 H 8
Rio Negro, Reserva Florestal do — 94-95 G 7
Río Neuquén 106-107 C 7
Rio Nhamundá 98-99 K 5
Rioni 126-127 KL 5
Río Ñireguco 108-109 CD 5
Rio Novo [BR, Amazonas] 96-97 F 4
Rio Novo [BR, Minas Gerais] 102-103 L 4
Rio Nuanetzi 174-175 J 2
Río Ñuble 106-107 B 6
Río Nucuray 96-97 D 4
Río Ocamo 94-95 J 6
Rio Oiapoque 92-93 J 4
Río Olimar Grande 106-107 KL 4
Río Orinoco 92-93 F 3
Río Orituco 94-95 H 3
Río Orteguaza 94-95 D 7
Río Ortón 104-105 C 2
Río Oteros 86-87 F 4
Río Otuquis 104-105 G 6
Rio Ouro Preto 98-99 F 10
Rio Pacaás Novas 104-105 D 2
Rio Pacajá 98-99 N 6
Río Pacaya 96-97 D 4
Río Pachitea 96-97 D 6
Rio Padauiri 92-93 G 4
Río Paila 104-105 E 5
Rio Paituna 98-99 L 5-6
Rio Pajeú 100-101 E 5
Rio Pakuí 102-103 K 2
Río Palena 108-109 C 4-5
Rio Palma 98-99 P 11
Río Palmar [CO] 91 III c 4
Río Palmar [YV] 94-95 E 2
Rio Palmeiras 98-99 P 10-11
Río Pampamarca 96-97 E 9
Río Pampas [PE, Apurímac] 96-97 E 8
Río Pampas [PE, Ayacucho] 96-97 D 8
Rio Pandeiros 102-103 K 1
Río Pánuco 64-65 G 7
Río Pao [YV, Bolívar] 94-95 J 3
Río Pao [YV, Cojedes] 94-95 G 3
Rio Papagaio 98-99 J 11
Río Papuri 94-95 F 7
Rio Pará 102-103 K 3
Rio Paracatu [BR ↖ Rio São Francisco] 102-103 K 2
Rio Paracatu [BR ↙ Rio São Francisco] 102-103 K 2
Río Paraguá [BOL] 92-93 G 7
Río Paragua [YV] 92-93 G 3
Rio Paraguacu 100-101 DE 7
Rio Paraguai 92-93 H 9
Río Paraguay 111 E 2
Rio Paraíba 92-93 M 6
Rio Paraíba do Sul 102-103 L 4
Rio Paraim 100-101 A 8
Rio Paramirim 100-101 C 7
Rio Paraná [BR ◁ Río de la Plata] 92-93 J 9
Rio Paraná [BR ◁ Rio Turiaçu] 100-101 B 2
Rio Paranã [BR ◁ Tocantins] 92-93 K 7
Río Paraná [RA] 111 E 3-4
Río Paraná, Delta del — 106-107 H 4-5
Río Paraná de las Palmas 106-107 H 4-5
Rio Paraná do Ouro 96-97 F 6
Río Paraná Guazú 106-107 H 4-5
Rio Paranaíba 92-93 JK 8
Río Paraná Ibicuy 106-107 H 4
Rio Paranaíta 98-99 K 9-10
Rio Paranapanema 92-93 J 9
Río Paranapura 96-97 C 4
Rio Paraopeba 102-103 K 3
Río Parapetí 104-105 E 6
Rio Parauapebas 98-99 NO 8
Rio Pardo [BR ◁ Atlantic Ocean] 92-93 L 8
Rio Pardo [BR ◁ Rio Grande] 102-103 H 4
Rio Pardo [BR ◁ Rio Paraná] 92-93 J 9
Rio Pardo [BR ◁ Rio São Francisco] 102-103 K 1
Rio Pardo [BR, Bahia] 92-93 L 8
Rio Pardo [BR, Mato Grosso] 92-93 J 9
Rio Pardo [BR, Minas Gerais] 102-103 K 1
Rio Pardo [BR, Rio Grande do Sul] 106-107 L 2-3
Rio Pardo [BR, São Paulo] 102-103 H 4
Rio Pardo de Minas 92-93 L 8
Rio Parima 98-99 FG 3
Rio Parimé 98-99 H 3
Rio Parnaíba 92-93 L 5
Rio Parnaibinha 100-101 AB 5
Rio Paru [BR] 92-93 J 5
Río Parú [YV] 94-95 H 5
Río Parucito 94-95 J 5
Rio Paru de Este 98-99 L 3-4
Rio Paru de Oeste 98-99 L 3-4
Río Pasaje 104-105 D 9
Río Pasión 86-87 PQ 9
Rio Passo Fundo = Rio Guarita 106-107 L 1
Río Pastaza 92-93 D 5
Río Patía 92-93 D 4
Río Patuca 64-65 J 9-K 8
Rio Pauini [BR ◁ Rio Purus] 98-99 D 8-9
Rio Pauini [BR ◁ Rio Unini] 98-99 G 5-6
Río Pauto 94-95 EF 5
Río Pelechuco 104-105 B 4
Rio Pelotas 111 F 3
Río Pelque 108-109 D 8
Río Penitente 108-109 D 9
Rio Peperiguaçu 102-103 F 7
Río Pequeni 64-65 bc 2
Rio Pequiri 102-103 E 2
Rio Perdido [BR, Goiás] 98-99 P 9
Rio Perdido [BR, Mato Grosso do Sul] 102-103 D 4
Rio Pereguete 64-65 b 3
Río Perené 96-97 D 7
Rio Periá 100-101 C 2
Rio Pericumã 100-101 B 2
Río Pescado 104-105 D 8
Rio Piauí 92-93 L 6
Río Piaxtla 86-87 G 6
Río Pichis 96-97 D 7
Río Pico 108-109 D 5
Río Piedras 64-65 b 2
Río Piedras [RA] 104-105 D 9
Río Pilaya 104-105 D 7
Río Pilcomayo [BR] 111 D 2
Río Pilcomayo [PY] 102-103 C 6
Río Pilmaiquén 108-109 C 3
Rio Pindaré 92-93 K 5
Río Pindo 96-97 C 2
Rio Pinhuã 98-99 F 8
Río Pinturas 108-109 D 6
Rio Piorini 92-93 G 5
Rio Piquiri 111 F 2
Rio Piracanjuba 102-103 H 2
Rio Piracicaba [BR, Minas Gerais] 102-103 L 4
Rio Piracicaba [BR, Minas Gerais, place] 102-103 L 3
Rio Piracicaba [BR, São Paulo] 102-103 J 5
Rio Piracuruca 100-101 C 2-D 3
Rio Piranhas [BR, Goiás ◁ Rio Caiapo] 102-103 G 2
Rio Piranhas [BR, Goiás ◁ Rio Grande do Norte] 98-99 O 9
Rio Piranhas [BR, Rio Grande do Norte] 92-93 M 6
Rio Piranji 100-101 E 3
Rio Pirapó [BR] 102-103 F 5
Río Pirapó [PY] 102-103 D 7
Rio Piratini 106-107 K 2
Río Piray 104-105 E 5
Río Pisco 96-97 CD 8
Río Pisqui 96-97 D 5
Río Piura 96-97 A 4
Rio Pixuna 98-99 G 8
Río Poccha 96-97 C 6
Río Pojige 104-105 D 4
Rio Pomba 102-103 L 4
Río Porce 94-95 D 4
Río Porteño 104-105 G 9
Río Portuguesa 92-93 F 3
Rio Poti 100-101 CD 3
Rio Prata 98-99 P 9
Rio Pratudinho 100-101 B 8
Rio Preto [BR ◁ Rio Grande] 92-93 K 7
Rio Preto [BR ◁ Rio Madeira] 98-99 G 9
Rio Preto [BR ◁ Rio Munim] 100-101 C 2
Rio Preto [BR ◁ Rio Negro] 98-99 F 4
Rio Preto [BR ◁ Rio Paracatu] 92-93 K 8
Rio Preto [BR ◁ Rio Paraíba] 102-103 L 5
Rio Preto [BR ◁ Rio Paranaíba] 102-103 G 3
Rio Preto, Serra do — 102-103 J 2
Rio Preto do Igapó-Açu 98-99 H 7
Río Primero [RA, place] 111 D 4
Río Primero [RA, river] 106-107 F 3
Río Pucacuro 96-97 D 3
Río Pucará 96-97 F 9
Río Puelo 108-109 C 3
Río Puerco 76-77 A 5
Rio Puruê 96-97 G 3
Rio Purus 92-93 F 6
Río Putumayo 92-93 E 5
Río Puyango 96-97 A 4-B 3
Rio Quebra-Anzol 102-103 J 3
Río Queguay 106-107 J 4
Río Quequén Grande 106-107 H 7
Río Queras 64-65 a 3
Río Quevedo 96-97 B 2
Río Quinto 106-107 E 5
Rio Quitéria 102-103 G 3
Río Ramis 96-97 FG 9
Rio Ramuro 98-99 L 11
Río Ranchería 94-95 E 2
Río Rapel 106-107 B 4-5
Río Rapulo 104-105 C 4
Río Real 96-97 G 6
Rio Real 92-93 M 7
Río Reconquista 110 III a 1
Rio Repartimento 98-99 E 7
Rio Riacho 100-101 D 4
Rio Ribeira do Iguape 102-103 H 6
Rio Ribeirinha 102-103 H 6
Rio Ricardo Franco 104-105 E 2
Río Rímac 96-97 C 7
Río Rojas 106-107 G 5
Rio Roosevelt 92-93 G 6-7
Río Rosario 104-105 D 9
Rio Rovuma 172 G 4
Rio Rubens 108-109 C 9-D 8
Ríos, Los — 96-97 B 2
Río Sabinas 86-87 JK 3
Río Saladillo [RA, Córdoba] 106-107 F 4
Río Saladillo [RA, Santiago del Estero] 106-107 EF 2
Río Saladillo = Río Cuarto 106-107 EF 4
Río Saladillo, Bañado del — 106-107 F 4
Río Salado [MEX] 86-87 L 4
Río Salado [RA, Buenos Aires] 106-107 G 5
Río Salado [RA, Catamarca ◁ Río Blanco] 106-107 C 2
Río Salado [RA, Catamarca ◁ Río Colorado] 104-105 C 11
Río Salado [RA, Santa Fe] 111 D 3
Rio Salado [USA] 76-77 A 5
Rio-Salado = Al-Malaḥ 166-167 F 2
Río Salí 104-105 D 10
Rio Salinas 102-103 L 2
Rio Salitre 100-101 D 6
Rio Sama 96-97 F 10
Rio Sambito 100-101 CD 4
Río Samborombón 106-107 J 5
Río Samiria 96-97 D 4
Rio San Carlos 102-103 C 5
Río San Cristóbal 91 III b 3
Río San Fernando [BOL] 104-105 G 5
Río San Fernando [MEX] 86-87 LM 5
Río San Francisco 104-105 D 8
Río Sangonera 120-121 G 10
Rio Sangrado 110 I b 2
Rio Sangutane 174-175 K 2-3
Río San Javier 106-107 GH 3
Río San Joaquín 104-105 E 3
Río San Jorge 94-95 D 3
Río San Juan [CO, Chocó] 94-95 C 5
Río San Juan [CO, Nariño] 94-95 B 7
Río San Juan [MEX] 86-87 L 5
Río San Juan [NIC] 64-65 K 9
Río San Juan [PE] 96-97 D 8
Río San Juan [RA] 106-107 C 3
Río San Lorenzo 86-87 G 5
Río San Martín 92-93 G 8
Río San Miguel [BOL] 92-93 G 7-8
Río San Miguel [EC] 96-97 C 1
Río San Miguel [MEX, Chihuahua] 86-87 G 4
Río San Miguel [MEX, Sonora] 86-87 E 2
Río San Pablo 104-105 E 4
Río San Pedro [GCA] 86-87 P 9
Río San Pedro [MEX, river ◁ Pacific Ocean] 86-87 H 6
Río San Pedro [MEX, river ◁ Río Conchos] 86-87 GH 4
Río San Ramón 104-105 F 4
Río San Salvador 106-107 J 4
Río Santa 96-97 B 6
Río Santa Cruz 108-109 E 7-F 8
Río Santa Lucía 106-107 H 2
Rio Santa Maria [BR ◁ Rio Corrente] 100-101 A 8
Rio Santa Maria [BR ◁ Rio Ibicuí] 106-107 K 3
Río Santa María [MEX ◁ Laguna de Santa María] 86-87 G 2-3
Río Santa María [MEX ◁ Río Tamuín] 86-87 K 7
Río Santa María [RA] 104-105 D 10
Rio Santana 100-101 C 5
Río Santiago [EC] 96-97 B 1
Río Santiago [PE] 96-97 C 3
Rio Santo Antônio [BR ◁ Paraguaçu] 100-101 D 7
Rio Santo Antônio [BR ◁ Rio de Contas] 100-101 CD 8
Rio Santo Antônio [BR ◁ Rio Doce] 102-103 L 3
Rio Santo Antônio [BR ◁ Rio Iguaçu] 102-103 F 6
Río Santo Corazón 104-105 G 5
Río Santo Domingo [MEX] 64-65 G 8
Río Santo Domingo [YV] 94-95 G 3
Rio São Bartolomeu 102-103 J 2
Rio São Benedito 98-99 KL 9
Rio São Domingos [BR ◁ Rio Mamoré] 104-105 D 3-E 2
Rio São Domingos [BR ◁ Rio Paraná] 100-101 A 7
Rio São Domingos [BR ◁ Rio Paranaíba] 102-103 G 3
Rio São Domingos [BR ◁ Rio Verde] 102-103 F 3
Rio São Francisco [BR ◁ Atlantic Ocean] 92-93 LM 6
Rio São Francisco [BR ◁ Rio Paraná] 102-103 EF 6
Rio São João [BR ◁ Rio de Contas] 100-101 CD 8
Rio São João [BR ◁ Rio Paraná] 102-103 F 5
Rio São José dos Dourados 102-103 G 4
Rio São Lourenço 102-103 DE 2
Rio São Manuel 98-99 K 9
Rio São Marcos 102-103 J 2
Rio São Mateus 100-101 D 10
Rio São Miguel 102-103 J 1-2
Rio São Nicolau 100-101 D 3
Rio São Onofre 100-101 C 7
Rio Sapão 100-101 B 6
Rio Sapucaí 102-103 HJ 4
Rio Sarare 94-95 F 4
Rio Saturnina 98-99 J 11
Río Sauce Chico 106-107 F 7
Río Sauce Grande 106-107 G 7
Rio Saueuina 104-105 G 3
Rio Save 172 F 6
Río Seco [MEX] 86-87 E 2
Río Seco [RA] 104-105 E 8
Río Seco, Bajo del — 108-109 EF 7
Río Sécure 104-105 C 4
Río Segovia = Río Coco 64-65 K 9
Río Segre 120-121 H 8
Río Segundo [RA, place] 106-107 F 3
Río Segundo [RA, river] 106-107 F 3
Río Segura 120-121 G 9
Rio Sepatini 98-99 E 9-F 8
Rio Sepotuba 102-103 D 1
Rio Sereno 98-99 P 8
Rio Sergipe 100-101 F 6
Rio Serreno 100-101 A 4
Rio Setúbal 102-103 L 2
Río Shehuen 108-109 DE 7
Río Sheshea 96-97 E 6
Río Siapo 94-95 HJ 7

Río Sico 88-89 D 7
Río Siete Puntas 102-103 C 5
Río Simpson 108-109 C 5
Río Sinaloa 86-87 FG 4-5
Río Singuédzi 174-175 J 2
Río Sinú 94-95 CD 3
Río Sipapo 94-95 H 5
Río Soacha 91 III a 4
Río Sogamoso 94-95 E 4
Río Solimões 92-93 G 5
Río Solimões 92-93 F 5
Río Sonora 64-65 D 6
Río Sotério 98-99 F 10
Río Steinen 92-93 J 7
Río Suaçuí Grande 102-103 L 3
Río Suapure 94-95 H 4
Río Suches 104-105 B 4
Ríosucio 92-93 D 3
Río Sucio 94-95 C 4
Río Sucunduri 92-93 H 6
Río Sucuriú 92-93 J 8
Río Suiá-Miçu 98-99 M 10-11
Río Suripá 94-95 F 4
Río Surumú 98-99 H 2-3
Río Taboco 102-103 E 4
Río Tacuarembó 106-107 K 4
Río Tacutú 98-99 HJ 3
Río Tahuamanú 96-97 G 7
Río Tamaya 96-97 E 6
Río Tambo [PE ◁ Pacific Ocean] 96-97 F 10
Río Tambo [PE ◁ Río Ucayali] 92-93 E 7
Río Tambopata 96-97 G 8
Río Tamboryacu 96-97 D 2
Río Tamuín 86-87 L 7
Río Tapajós 92-93 H 5
Río Tapauá 92-93 F 6
Río Tapenaga 106-107 H 1-2
Río Taperoá 100-101 F 4
Río Tapiche 96-97 D 5
Río Tapuió 100-101 B 3-4
Río Taquari [BR ◁ Río Jacuí] 106-107 M 2
Río Taquari [BR ◁ Río Paranapanema] 102-103 H 5
Río Taquari [BR ◁ Río Taquari Novo] 102-103 F 3
Río Taquari Novo 92-93 H 8
Río Tarauacá 92-93 E 6
Río Tareni 104-105 C 3
Río Tarvo 104-105 F 4
Río Tauini 98-99 J 4
Río Tayota 104-105 C 5-D 4
Río Tea [BR] 98-99 EF 5
Río Tebicuary 102-103 DE 7
Río Tebicuary-mi 102-103 D 6-7
Río Tefé 92-93 F 5
Río Teles Pires 92-93 H 6
Río Tembey 102-103 E 7
Río Ten Lira 104-105 H 4
Río Tercero [RA, place] 111 D 4
Río Tercero [RA, river] 106-107 F 4
Río Tercero, Embalse del — 106-107 E 4
Río Teuco 111 D 2-3
Río Teuquito 104-105 F 9
Río Teusaca 91 III c 3
Río Thalnepantla 91 I b 1
Río Tibají 102-103 G 6
Río Tietê 102-103 H 4
Río Tietê, Canal do — 110 II b 2
Río Tigre [EC] 92-93 D 5
Río Tigre [YV] 94-95 K 3
Río Tijamuchi 104-105 D 4
Río Tijucas 102-103 H 7
Río Tijuco 102-103 H 3
Río Timane 102-103 B 4
Río Timbó 102-103 G 7
Río Tinto 100-101 G 4
Río Tiputini 96-97 C 2
Río Tiquié 94-95 G 7
Río Tiznados 94-95 H 3
Río Toachi 96-97 B 1-2
Río Tocantins 92-93 K 5-6
Río Tocuco 94-95 E 3
Río Tocumen 64-65 c 2
Río Tocuyo 94-95 G 2
Río Todos os Santos 102-103 M 2
Río Toltén 108-109 C 2
Río Tomo 92-93 F 3
Río Traipu 100-101 F 5
Río Trinidad 64-65 b 3
Río Trombetas 92-93 H 5
Río Trombudo 106-107 N 1
Río Truandó 94-95 C 4
Río Tubarão 102-103 H 8
Río Tucavaca 104-105 G 6
Río Tucavaca [BOL, place] 104-105 G 6
Río Tuira 94-95 BC 3
Río Tulumayo 96-97 D 7
Río Tunjuelito 91 III a 3
Río Tunuyán 106-107 CD 4
Río Tuparro 94-95 G 5
Río Turbio [RA, place] 108-109 CD 8
Río Turbio [RA, river] 108-109 D 8
Río Turiaçu 100-101 B 1-2
Río Turvo [BR, Goiás] 102-103 G 2
Río Turvo [BR, Rio Grande do Sul] 106-107 L 1-2
Río Turvo [BR, São Paulo ◁ Rio Grande] 102-103 H 4
Río Turvo [BR, São Paulo ◁ Rio Paranapanema] 102-103 H 5
Río Uanetze 174-175 K 3
Río Uatumã 92-93 H 5
Río Uaupés 92-93 F 4
Río Ucayali 92-93 D 6
Río Ulúa 64-65 J 8
Río Una 100-101 G 5
Río Unare 94-95 J 3
Río Undumo 104-105 C 3
Río Uneiuxi 92-93 F 5
Río Unini 92-93 G 5
Río Upía 94-95 E 5
Río Uraricaá 94-95 K 6
Río Uraricoera 92-93 G 4
Río Uribante 94-95 F 4
Río Urique 86-87 G 4
Río Urituyacu 96-97 D 4
Río Uriuaná 98-99 N 6
Río Uruará 98-99 M 6
Río Urubamba 92-93 E 7
Río Urubaxi 98-99 F 5
Río Urubu 98-99 J 6
Río Urucu 98-99 FG 7
Río Urucuia 102-103 K 2
Río Uruçuí Preto 100-101 B 5
Río Uruçuí Vermelho 100-101 B 5
Río Uruguai 111 F 3
Río Uruguay [RA ◁ Río de la Plata] 111 E 3
Río Uruguay [RA ◁ Río Paraná] 102-103 E 6
Río Urupa 98-99 G 10
Río Usumacinta 64-65 H 8
Río Utcubamba 96-97 B 4
Río Uva 94-95 G 6
Riouw Archipel = Kepulauan Riau 148-149 DE 6
Río Vacacaí 106-107 L 2-3
Río Vacaria [BR, Mato Grosso do Sul] 102-103 E 4
Río Vacaria [BR, Minas Gerais] 102-103 L 2
Río Vallevicioso 96-97 BC 2
Río Vasa Barris 100-101 E 6
Río Vaupés 92-93 E 4
Río Velille 96-97 F 9
Río Ventuari 92-93 F 3
Río Verde [BOL] 104-105 F 4
Río Verde [BR, Bahia] 100-101 C 6
Río Verde [BR, Goiás ◁ Chapada dos Pilões] 102-103 J 2
Río Verde [BR, Goiás ◁ Rio Maranhão] 102-103 H 1
Río Verde [BR, Goiás ◁ Rio Paranaíba] 92-93 J 8
Río Verde [BR, Goiás ◁ Serra do Verdinho] 102-103 G 3
Río Verde [BR, Goiás place] 92-93 J 8
Río Verde [BR, Mato Grosso ◁ Rio Paraná] 92-93 J 9
Río Verde [BR, Mato Grosso ◁ Rio Teles Pires] 92-93 H 7
Río Verde [BR, Minas Gerais ◁ Represa de Furnas] 102-103 K 4
Río Verde [BR, Minas Gerais ◁ Rio Grande] 102-103 H 3
Ríoverde [EC] 96-97 B 1
Río Verde [MEX, Oaxaca] 64-65 G 8
Ríoverde [MEX, San Luis Potosí place] 86-87 KL 7
Río Verde [MEX, San Luis Potosí river] 86-87 L 7
Río Verde [PY] 111 E 2
Río Verde [RCH] 111 B 8
Río Verde de Mato Grosso 92-93 HJ 8
Río Verde do Sul 102-103 E 5
Río Verde Grande 100-101 C 8
Río Vermelho [BR, Goiás] 98-99 P 8-9
Río Vermelho [BR, Minas Gerais] 102-103 L 3
Río Vermelho [BR, Pará] 98-99 O 7-8
Río Vichada 92-93 F 4
Río Viejo 106-107 F 2
Río Vila Nova 98-99 MN 4
Río Vilcanota 96-97 F 8-9
Río Villegas 108-109 D 3
Río Vinchina 106-107 C 2
Río Virú 96-97 B 6
Río Vita 94-95 G 5
Río Vitor 96-97 F 10
Río Xapecó 102-103 F 7
Río Xapecózinho 102-103 FG 7
Río Xapuri 98-99 D 10
Río Xapuri 96-97 G 7
Río Xeriuini 98-99 G 4
Río Xié 98-99 E 4
Río Xingu 92-93 J 6
Río Xiruá 98-99 D 8
Río Yabebyry 102-103 D 7
Río Yacuma 104-105 C 4
Río Yaguarón 106-107 L 3-4
Río Yaguas 96-97 E 3
Río Yanatili 96-97 E 8
Río Yapacani 104-105 D 5
Río Yapella 94-95 E 4
Río Yaqui 64-65 E 6
Río Yaracuy 94-95 G 2
Río Yarí 92-93 E 4
Río Yasuní 96-97 C 2
Río Yata 104-105 D 3
Río Yatua 94-95 H 7
Río Yauca 96-97 D 9
Río Yauchari 96-97 C 3
Río Yavarí 92-93 E 5
Río Yavari-Mirim 96-97 E 4
Río Yavero 96-97 E 8
Río Yguazú 102-103 E 6
Río Yí 106-107 J 4
Río Ypané 102-103 D 5
Río Yuruá 96-97 E 6
Río Zacatula 86-87 JK 8
Río Zambeze 172 F 5
Río Zamora 96-97 B 3
Río Zanjón Nuevo 106-107 CD 3
Riozinho [BR, Acre] 104-105 B 1
Riozinho [BR, Amazonas place] 98-99 E 9
Riozinho [BR, Amazonas river] 98-99 E 6
Río Zuata 94-95 J 3
Río Zutiua 100-101 B 3
Riparia, WA 66-67 DE 2
Ripley, CA 74-75 F 6
Ripley, MS 78-79 E 3
Ripley, NY 72-73 G 3
Ripley, TN 78-79 E 3
Ripley, WV 72-73 F 5
Ripoll 120-121 J 7
Ripon, WI 70-71 F 4
Ripon [CDN] 72-73 J 2
Ripple Mountain 66-67 E 1
Riri Bāzār 138-139 J 4
Rişāfah 136-137 H 5
Rīšām 'Anayzah 173 C 2
Rīşānī, Ar- 164-165 D 2
Risaralda 94-95 CD 5
Risasi 172 E 2
Rīsh, Ar- 166-167 D 3
Rishīkesh 138-139 FG 2
Rishiri suidō 144-145 b 1
Rishiri tō 142-143 QR 2
Ri'shōn Lĕziyyōn 136-137 F 7
Rishra 154 II b 1
Rising Star, TX 76-77 E 6
Rising Sun, IN 70-71 H 6
Rising Sun, OH 72-73 D 5
Risiri 144-145 b 1
Risle 120-121 H 4
Rison, AR 78-79 CD 4
Risør 116-117 C 8
Rissen, Hamburg- 130 I a 1
Risso, Colonia — 102-103 D 5
Ristikent 116-117 O 3
Ristna neem 124-125 CD 4
Rithuggemphel Gonpa 138-139 M 3
Rito Gaviel, Mesa del — 76-77 C 6
Ritscherhochland 53 B 36
Ritter, Mount — 64-65 C 4
Rittman, OH 72-73 EF 4
Rittman,, OH 72-73 EF 4
Ritzville, WA 66-67 D 2
Riukiu = Ryūkyū 142-143 N 7-O 6
Riung 152-153 O 10
Riva [I] 122-123 D 3
Rivā [IND] 138-139 GH 5
Rivadavia [RA, Buenos Aires] 111 D 5
Rivadavia [RA, Mendoza] 106-107 C 4
Rivadavia [RA, Salta] 111 D 2
Rivadavia [RA, San Juán] 106-107 C 3
Rivadavia [RCH] 111 B 3
Rivalensundet 116-117 mn 5
Rivaliza 98-99 B 8
Rīvān = Rewa 138-139 H 5
Rivas [NIC] 88-89 CD 9
Rivas [RA] 106-107 H 5
Rivasdale, Johannesburg- 170 V a 2
Rivera [RA] 111 D 5
Rivera [ROU, administrative unit] 106-107 K 3
Rivera [ROU, place] 111 E 4
River aux Sables 62 K 3
Riverbank, CA 74-75 C 4
River Cess 164-165 BC 7
Riverdale, CA 74-75 D 4
Riverdale, New York-, NY 82 III c 1
River Falls, WI 70-71 D 3
River Forest 83 II a 1
River Forest, Houston-, TX 85 III a 1
Riverhead, NY 72-73 K 4
Riverhurst 61 E 5
Riverina 158-159 HJ 6-7
Rivermeade Creek 85 II b 1
River Niger, Mouths of the — 164-165 F 7-8
Rivero, Isla — 108-109 B 5
Riveroaks, Houston-, TX 85 III b 2
River of Ponds 63 GH 2
River Ridge, LA 85 I a 2
River Rouge 84 II ab 3
River Rouge, MI 84 II b 3
Rivers 164-165 F 7-8
Riversdal 172 D 8
Riversdale = Riversdal 172 D 8
Riverside 84 II c 3
Riverside, CA 64-65 C 5
Riverside, IL 83 II a 1
Riverside, NJ 84 III d 1
Riverside, OR 66-67 DE 4
Riverside, Atlanta-, GA 85 II b 2
Rivers Inlet 60 D 4
Riverton, NJ 84 III cd 1
Riverton, WY 68-69 B 4
Riverton [AUS] 158-159 G 6
Riverton [CDN] 62 A 2
Riverton [NZ] 161 BC 8
Riviera, TX 76-77 EF 9
Riviera Beach, FL 80-81 cd 3
Rivière Aguanus 63 F 2
Rivière-à-Pierre 72-73 KL 1
Rivière Ashuapmuchuan 62 P 2
Rivière-au-Renard 63 DE 3
Rivière-au-Tonnerre 63 D 2-3
Rivière-aux-Graines 63 D 2
Rivière aux Outardes 56-57 X 7-8
Rivière aux Sables 63 A 3
Rivière Basin 62 O 3
Rivière Batiscan 72-73 K 1
Rivière Bell 62 N 2
Rivière Betsiamites 63 B 3
Rivière-Bleue 63 B 4
Rivière Broadback 62 MN 1
Rivière Caopacho 63 C 2
Rivière Capitachouahe 62 N 2-3
Rivière Cascapédia 63 C 3
Rivière Chaudière 63 A 4-5
Rivière Claire = Sông Lô 150-151 E 2
Rivière Coulonge 72-73 H 1
Rivière des Prairies 82 I ab 1
Rivière du Chef 62 P 1-2
Rivière du Lièvre 72-73 J 1
Rivière-du-Loup 56-57 WX 8
Rivière Dumoine 72-73 H 1
Rivière du Petit Mécatina 63 FG 2
Rivière du Sault aux Cochons 63 B 3
Rivière Escoumins 63 B 3
Rivière Galineau 72-73 J 1
Rivière Gatineau 72-73 J 1-2
Rivière Hart-Jaune 63 BC 2
Rivière Jacques Cartier 63 A 4
Rivière Kitchigama 62 M 1
Rivière Laflamme 62 N 2
Rivière-la-Madelaine 63 D 3
Rivière Macaza 72-73 J 1-2
Rivière Magpie 63 D 2
Rivière Maicasagi 62 NO 1
Rivière Manicouagan 56-57 X 7-8
Rivière Manitou 63 D 2
Rivière Manouane 63 A 2-3
Rivière Marguerite 63 C 2
Rivière Marten 62 O 1
Rivière-Matane 63 C 3
Rivière Matapédia 63 C 3
Rivière Mattawin 72-73 K 1
Rivière Mégiscane 62 NO 2
Rivière Mingan 63 E 2
Rivière Missisicabi 62 M 1
Rivière Mistassibi 62 P 2
Rivière Mistassini 62 P 2
Rivière Moisie 56-57 X 7
Rivière Mouchalagane 63 B 2
Rivière Musquaro 63 F 2
Rivière Nabisipi 63 E 2
Rivière Nestaocano 62 P 1-2
Rivière Noire 72-73 H 1
Rivière Octave 62 M 2
Rivière Olomane 63 F 2
Rivière Opawica 62 O 2
Rivière Ouareau 72-73 JK 1
Rivière Ouasiemsca 62 P 2
Rivière Ouatouoais 62 NO 3
Rivière Outaouais 72-73 G 1
Rivière Pascagama 62 O 2
Rivière-Pentecôte 63 C 3
Rivière Péribonca 56-57 W 7-8
Rivière-Pigou 63 D 2
Rivière Portneuf 63 AB 3
Rivière Richelieu 72-73 K 1-2
Rivière Rimouski 63 B 3
Rivière Romaine 56-57 Y 7
Rivière Saguenay 56-57 WX 8
Rivière Saint-Augustin 63 G 2
Rivière Saint-Augustin Nord-Ouest 63 G 2
Rivière Sainte Marguerite 63 A 3
Rivière Saint François 72-73 K 1-2
Rivière Saint-Jean [CDN, Pen. de Gaspé] 63 D 3
Rivière-Saint-Jean [CDN, place] 63 D 2-3
Rivière-Saint-Jean [CDN, Quebec] 63 D 2
Rivière Saint-Maurice 56-57 W 8
Rivière Saint-Paul 63 H 2
Rivière Samaqua 62 P 1-2
Rivière Savane 63 A 2
Rivière Serpent 63 A 2-3
Rivière Shipshaw 63 A 3
Rivière Témiscamie 62 P 1
Rivière Turgeon 62 M 2
Rivière Vermillon 72-73 K 1
Rivière-Verte 63 BC 4
Rivière Wawagosic 62 M 2
Rivière Wetetnagani 62 N 2
Riviersonderend 174-175 CD 8
Rivoli 122-123 B 3
Rivungo 172 D 5
Riwan = Rewa 138-139 H 5
Riwa Pathar = Rīvā 138-139 GH 5
Riyad = Ar-Riyāḍ 134-135 F 6
Riyāḍ, Ar- 134-135 F 6
Riyadh = Ar-Riyāḍ 134-135 F 6
Riyān 166-167 E 2
Rize 134-135 E 2
Rize dağları 136-137 J 2
Rizhao 146-147 G 4
Rizokárpason 136-137 EF 5
Rizzuto, Cabo — 122-123 G 6
Rjukan 116-117 C 8
R'kīz, Ar- 164-165 AB 5
R'kīz, Lac — = Ar-R'kīz 164-165 AB 5
Rmel el Abiod = Rimāl al-Abyaḍ 166-167 L 4
Roachdale, IN 70-71 G 6
Road Town 88-89 O 5
Roald Amundsen Sea = Amundsen havet 53 BC 25-26
Roan Cliffs 74-75 J 3
Roan Creek 68-69 B 6
Roanne 120-121 K 5
Roanoke, AL 78-79 G 4
Roanoke, VA 64-65 KL 4
Roanoke Island 80-81 J 3
Roanoke Rapids, NC 80-81 H 2
Roanoke River 64-65 L 4
Roan Plateau 68-69 B 6
Roaring Fork 68-69 C 6
Roaring Springs, TX 76-77 D 6
Roatán, Isla de — 64-65 J 8
Roba el Khali = Ar-Rub' al-Hālī 134-135 F 7-G 6
Robalo 88-89 E 10
Robāţ 136-137 M 5
Robb 60 J 3
Robbah = Rubbah 166-167 K 3
Robbeneiland 174-175 BC 7
Robben Island = Robbeneiland 174-175 BC 7
Robberson, TX 76-77 E 9
Robbinsdale, MN 70-71 D 3
Robbins Island 160 b 2
Robe [NZ] 160 D 6
Robe, Mount — 160 E 3
Robeline, LA 78-79 C 5
Robe Noir, Lac de la — 63 E 2
Roberta, GA 80-81 DE 4
Robert J. Palenscar Memorial Airport 84 III cd 2
Robert Lee, TX 76-77 D 7
Roberto Payan 94-95 B 7
Roberts 106-107 G 5
Roberts, ID 66-67 GH 4
Roberts Creek Mountain 74-75 E 3
Robertsfors 116-117 J 5
Robertsganj 138-139 J 5
Robertsham, Johannesburg- 170 V ab 2
Roberts Mount 58-59 E 7
Robertson 174-175 C 7
Robertson, WY 66-67 HJ 5
Robertson Bay 53 BC 17-18
Robertsons øy 53 C 31
Robertson Stadium 85 III b 2
Roberts Park, IL 83 II a 2
Robertsport 164-165 B 7
Robertstown 160 D 4
Roberval 56-57 W 8
Robinette, OR 66-67 E 3
Robinson 58-59 U 6
Robinson, IL 70-71 G 6
Robinson, TX 76-77 F 7
Robinson Crusoe 199 AB 7
Robinson Island 53 C 30
Robinson Mountains 58-59 QR 6
Robinson Ranges 158-159 C 5
Robinson River 158-159 G 3
Robinvale 158-159 H 6
Robla, La — 120-121 E 7
Robles 106-107 EF 2
Roblin 61 H 5
Robsart 68-69 B 1
Robson, Mount — 56-57 N 7
Robstown, TX 76-77 F 9
Roby, TX 76-77 D 6
Roca, Cabo da — 120-121 C 9
Roçadas = Xangongo 172 C 5
Rocafuerte 96-97 A 2
Roca Kong 150-151 E 7
Roçalgate = Rās al Ḥadd 134-135 HJ 6
Rocamadour 120-121 HJ 6
Roca Partida 86-87 D 8
Rocas, Atol das — 92-93 N 5
Rocas Alijos 86-87 C 5
Rocas Cormoranes = Shag Rocks 111 H 8
Rocas Negras = Black Rock 111 H 8
Roca Tarpeya, Helicoide de la — 91 II b 2
Ročegda 124-125 O 2
Rocha [ROU, administrative unit] 106-107 KL 4
Rocha [ROU, place] 111 F 4
Rocha, Laguna de — 106-107 K 5
Rochedo 102-103 E 3
Rochefort 120-121 G 5-6
Rochelle, IL 70-71 F 5
Rochelle, LA 78-79 C 5
Rochelle, TX 76-77 E 7
Rochelle, la — 120-121 G 7
Roche-Percée 68-69 E 1
Rocheport, MO 70-71 D 6
Rochester, IN 70-71 GH 5
Rochester, MI 72-73 E 3
Rochester, MN 64-65 H 3
Rochester, NH 72-73 L 3
Rochester, NY 64-65 L 3
Roche-sur-Yon, la — 120-121 G 5
Rocio, Bogotá-El — 91 III bc 3-4
Rock, MI 70-71 G 2
Rock, The — 160 H 5
Rockall 114-115 EF 4
Rockall Plateau 114-115 E 4
Rockaway Beach 82 III cd 3
Rockaway Inlet 82 III c 3
Rockaway Point 82 III c 3
Rock Bay 60 E 4
Rock Creek, OR 66-67 CD 3
Rock Creek [USA ◁ Clark Fork River] 66-67 G 2
Rock Creek [USA ◁ Milk River] 68-69 C 1
Rock Creek [USA ◁ Potomac River] 82 II a 1
Rock Creek Park 82 II a 1
Rockdale, TX 76-77 F 7
Rockdale, Sydney- 161 I a 2
Rockdale Park 85 II b 2
Rockdale Park, Atlanta-, GA 85 II b 2
Rockefeller Center 82 III bc 2
Rockefeller Plateau 53 AB 23-24
Rock Falls, IL 70-71 F 5
Rockford, IA 70-71 D 4
Rockford, IL 64-65 HJ 3
Rockford, OH 70-71 H 5
Rockglen 68-69 CD 1
Rockham, SD 68-69 G 3
Rockhampton 158-159 JK 4
Rock Harbor, MI 70-71 FG 1
Rock Hill, SC 64-65 K 4-5
Rockingham 158-159 BC 6
Rockingham, NC 80-81 FG 3
Rockingham Bay 158-159 J 3
Rock Island, IL 64-65 HJ 3
Rock Island, WA 66-67 CD 2
Rock Lake 66-67 E 2
Rockland, ID 66-67 G 4
Rockland, ME 72-73 M 2-3
Rocklands Reservoir 158-159 H 7
Rockledge, PA 84 III c 1
Rockmart, GA 78-79 G 3
Rockport, IN 70-71 G 7
Rockport, MO 70-71 C 5
Rockport, TX 76-77 F 8
Rockport, WA 66-67 C 1
Rock Rapids, IA 70-71 BC 4
Rock River, WY 68-69 CD 5
Rock River [USA, Illinois] 70-71 F 4-5
Rock River [USA, Minnesota] 68-69 H 4
Rocksprings 86-87 KL 2-3
Rock Springs, AZ 74-75 GH 5
Rock Springs, MT 68-69 CD 2
Rocksprings, TX 76-77 D 7
Rock Springs, WY 64-65 E 3
Rockstone 92-93 H 3
Rockton, IL 70-71 F 4
Rock Valley, IA 70-71 BC 4
Rockville, IN 70-71 G 6
Rockville, MD 72-73 H 5
Rockville, OR 66-67 E 4
Rockwall, TX 76-77 F 6
Rockway Park, New York-, NY 82 III c 3
Rockwell City, IA 70-71 C 4
Rockwood, PA 72-73 G 5
Rockwood, TN 78-79 G 3
Rockwood Cemetery 161 I a 2
Rocky Boys Indian Reservation 68-69 B 1
Rocky Ford, CO 68-69 DE 6
Rockyford, SD 68-69 E 4
Rocky Island Lake 62 K 3
Rocky Mount, NC 80-81 H 2-3
Rocky Mount, VA 80-81 G 2
Rocky Mountain 66-67 G 2
Rocky Mountain House 60 K 3
Rocky Mountain National Park 64-65 EF 3
Rocky Mountains 56-57 L 5-P 9
Rocky Mountains Forest Reserve 60 JK 3-4
Rocky Mountain Trench 56-57 L 6-N 7
Rocky Point [USA, Alaska] 58-59 F 4
Rocky Point [USA, California] 66-67 A 5
Rocquencourt 129 I b 2
Rōḍā, Er- = Ar-Rawḍah 173 B 4
Roda, la — 120-121 F 9
Rodalquilar 120-121 FG 10
Rodaun, Wien- 113 I b 2
Rødberg 116-117 C 7
Rødby Havn 116-117 D 10
Roddickton 63 HJ 2
Rode 174-175 H 6
Rodeador 100-101 B 8
Rodeio 102-103 H 7
Rödelheim, Frankfurt am Main- 128 III a 1
Rodenpois = Ropaži 124-125 E 5
Rodeo 111 BC 4
Rodeo, NM 74-75 J 7
Rodeo, El — 94-95 J 3
Rodeo del Medío 106-107 C 4
Rodeo Viejo 106-107 E 4
Rodez 120-121 J 6
Roding [GB] 129 II c 1
Rodney 72-73 F 3
Rodney, Cape — 58-59 D 4
Rodniki 124-125 NO 5
Ródos [GR, island] 122-123 N 7
Ródos [GR, place] 122-123 N 7
Rodosto = Tekirdağ 134-135 B 2
Rodovia Pan-Americana 102-103 H 5-6
Rodovia Perimetral Norte 98-99 G 4
Rodovia Transamazônica 98-99 L 7
Rodrigo de Freitas, Lagoa — 110 I b 2
Rodrigues [BR] 98-99 B 8
Rodrigues [Mascarene Islands] 50-51 N 6-7
Rodríguez 76-77 D 9
Roebourne 158-159 C 4
Roebuck Bay 158-159 D 3
Roedtan 174-175 H 3
Roelofskamp 174-175 F 4
Roermond 120-121 K 3
Roeselare 120-121 J 3
Roe's Welcome Sound 56-57 T 4-5
Rogač'ov 124-125 H 7
Rogagua, Lago — 92-93 F 7
Rogaland 116-117 B 8
Rogers, AR 76-77 GH 4
Rogers, ND 68-69 G 2
Rogers, TX 76-77 F 7
Rogers City, MI 70-71 J 3
Rogerson, ID 66-67 F 4
Rogersville, TN 80-81 E 2
Roggeveld, Achter — = Agter Roggeveld 174-175 D 6
Roggeveld, Agter — 174-175 D 6
Roggeveld, Klein — 174-175 D 7
Roggeveld, Middel — 174-175 D 7
Roggeveldberge 174-175 C 6-D 7
Roggeveld Mountains = Roggeveldberge 174-175 C 6-D 7
Rognan 116-117 F 4
Rogoaguado, Lago — 92-93 F 7
Rogowo = Rogava 124-125 E 6
Rogue River 66-67 A 4
Rogue River Mountains 66-67 AB 4
Roha 140 A 1
Roha-Lalibela = Lalībela 164-165 M 6
Rohan 120-121 F 4
Rohanpūr 138-139 M 5
Rohault, Lac — 62 O 2
Rohil Khand 138-139 GH 3
Rohṛī 134-135 K 5
Rohṛī, Nahr — 138-139 B 4
Rohtak 134-135 M 5
Roi, Palais du — 128 II b 1
Roi Et 150-151 D 4
Roissy 129 I c 3
Roissy-en-France 129 I cd 1
Roja 124-125 D 5
Rojas 111 D 4
Rojas, Isla — 108-109 C 5
Rojas, Río — 106-107 G 5
Rojhān 138-139 BC 3
Rojhi Māta 138-139 BC 6
Rokan 152-153 D 5
Rokan, Sungai — 152-153 D 5
Rokel 168-169 B 3
Rokitnoje 124-125 F 8
Rokkasho 144-145 N 2
Rokugō, Tōkyō- 155 III b 2
Rokugō-saki = Suzu misaki 144-145 L 4
Roland 68-69 H 1
Roland, AR 78-79 C 3
Rolândia 102-103 G 5
Roldán 106-107 G 4
Roldanillo 94-95 C 5
Rolecha 108-109 C 3
Rolette, ND 68-69 FG 1
Rolfe, IA 70-71 C 4
Rolla 116-117 G 3
Rolla, KS 76-77 D 4
Rolla, MO 64-65 H 4
Rolla, ND 68-69 G 1
Rolleston 158-159 J 4
Rolleville 88-89 H 3
Rolling Fork, MS 78-79 D 4
Rolling Fork, TX 85 III a 1
Rollingwood, CA 83 I bc 1
Rollwald 128 III b 2
Roluos 150-151 DE 6
Rolvsøy 116-117 K 2
Rom [EAU] 171 C 2
Rom [N] 116-117 B 8
Roma [AUS] 158-159 J 5
Roma [I] 122-123 E 5
Roma [LS] 174-175 G 5
Roma-Acilia 113 II a 2
Roma-Bufalotta 113 II b 1
Roma-Casaletti Mattei 113 II a 2
Roma-Casal Morena 113 II c 2
Roma-Casalotti 113 II a 2
Roma-Castel Giubileo 113 II b 1
Roma-Cecchignola 113 II b 2
Roma-Centocelle 113 II bc 2
Roma-Ciampino 113 II c 2
Roma-Cinecittà 113 II b 2
Roma-Corviale 113 II ab 2
Roma-EUR 113 II b 2
Roma-Garbatella 113 II b 2
Romain, Cape — 80-81 G 4
Romaine, Rivière — 56-57 Y 7
Romainville 129 I c 2
Roma-La Giustiniana 113 II ab 1
Roma-Lido di Ostia 122-123 DE 5
Roma-Los Saenz, TX 76-77 E 9
Roma-Magliana 113 II ab 2
Roma-Monte Sacro 113 II b 1
Roma-Montespaccato 113 II a 2
Roma-Montverde Nuovo 113 II b 2
Roman 122-123 M 2
Romana, La — 64-65 J 8
Román Arreola 76-77 B 9
Romanche Deep 50-51 J 6
Romang 106-107 H 2
Romang, Pulau — 148-149 J 8
Românî = Rummānah 173 C 2
Romania 122-123 K-M 2
Roman-Koš, gora — 126-127 FG 4
Romano, Cape — 80-81 bc 4
Romano, Cayo — 64-65 L 7
Romanov = Dzeržinsk 126-127 CD 1
Romanovka [SU, Bur'atskaja ASSR] 132-133 V 7
Romanovka [SU, Saratovskaja Oblast'] 124-125 O 8
Romanovka = Bessarabka 126-127 D 3
Romanovskij = Kropotkin 126-127 K 4
Romans-sur-Isère 120-121 K 6
Romanvloer 174-175 D 6
Roman Wall 119 E 4
Romanzof, Cape — 56-57 C 5
Romanzof Mountains 58-59 PQ 2
Roma-Ostia Antica 122-123 DE 5
Roma-Ottavia 113 II a 1
Roma-Ponto Galeria 113 II a 2
Roma-Pontonaccio 113 II b 2
Roma-Prima Porta 113 II b 1
Roma-Primavalle 113 II ab 1
Roma-Quadraro 113 II bc 2
Roma-San Basilio 113 II b c 1
Roma-Santa Maria del Soccorso 113 II bc 2
Roma-Sant'Onofrio 113 II b 1
Roma-Settecamini 113 II c 1
Roma-Spinaceto 113 II b 2
Roma-Spizzichino 113 II ab 1
Roma-Tomba di Nerone 113 II ab 1
Roma-Tor di Quinto 113 II b 1
Roma-Tor Marancia 113 II b 1
Roma-Tor Pignatara 113 II b 2
Roma-Torre Gaia 113 II c 2
Roma-Torre Lupara 113 II c 1
Roma-Torre Nova 113 II c 2
Roma-Torre Vècchia 113 II a 1
Roma-Tor Sapienza 113 II c 2
Roma-Tufello 113 II b 1
Roma-Valcanuta 113 II ab 2
Roma-Villini 113 II a 2
Roma-Vitinia 113 II ab 2
Romblon 148-149 H 4
Rome, GA 64-65 J 5
Rome, NY 64-65 LM 3
Rome, OR 66-67 E 4
Rome = Roma 122-123 E 5
Romen = Romny 126-127 F 1
Romeo, MI 72-73 E 3
Römer 128 III ab 1
Romero, TX 76-77 C 5
Romford, London- 129 II c 1
Romilly-sur-Seine 120-121 J 4

Rommânî = Ar-Rummânî 166-167 C 3
Romney, WV 72-73 G 5
Romny 126-127 F 1
Rømø 116-117 C 10
Romodan 126-127 F 1
Romodanovo 124-125 P 6
Rompin, Sungei — 150-151 D 11
Romsdal 116-117 BC 6
Romsdalfjord 116-117 B 6
Ron [IND] 140 B 3
Ron [VN] 150-151 F 4
Rōṅ = Ron 140 B 3
Ronan, MT 66-67 FG 2
Roncador 102-103 F 6
Roncador, Serra do — 92-93 J 7
Roncador Reef 148-149 j 6
Roncesvalles [CO] 94-95 D 5
Roncesvalles [E] 120-121 G 7
Ronceverte, WV 80-81 F 2
Ronda 120-121 E 10
Ronda das Selinas 102-103 BC 1
Rondane 116-117 C 7
Rondebult 170 V c 2
Rondon 102-103 F 5
Rondôn = Puerto Rondón 92-93 E 3
Rondon, Pico — 98-99 G 4
Rondônia [BR, administrative unit] 92-93 G 7
Rondônia [BR, place] 92-93 G 7
Rondonópolis 92-93 HJ 8
Rong, Kâs — 150-151 D 7
Rong'an 146-147 B 9
Rongcheng [TJ, Hebei] 146-147 EF 2
Rongcheng [TJ, Shandong] 146-147 J 3
Rongcheng = Jiurongcheng 146-147 J 3
Ronge, la — 56-57 P 6
Ronge, Lac la — 56-57 Q 6
Rongjiang [TJ, place] 146-147 B 9
Rong Jiang [TJ, river] 146-147 B 9
Rong Kwang 150-151 C 3
Rong Sam Lem, Kâs — 150-151 D 7
Rongshui 146-147 B 9
Rongui 171 E 5
Rong Xian 146-147 C 10
Rongxu = Cangwu 146-147 C 10
Ron Ma, Mui — 148-149 E 3
Rønne 116-117 F 10
Ronne Bay 53 B 29
Ronneburg, Hamburg- 130 I ab 2
Ronneby 116-117 F 9
Ronne Entrance = Ronne Bay 53 B 29
Roodebank 174-175 H 4
Roodehoogte = Rooihoogte 174-175 F 6
Roodepoort 174-175 G 4
Roodhouse, IL 70-71 EF 6
Roof Butte 74-75 J 4
Rooiberg [ZA, Kaapland] 174-175 C 6
Rooiberg [ZA, Transvaal mountain] 174-175 H 2
Rooiberg [ZA, Transvaal place] 174-175 G 3
Rooiberge 174-175 H 5
Rooihoogte 174-175 F 6
Rooiwal 174-175 G 4
Roorkee 138-139 FG 3
Roosendaal en Nispen 120-121 K 3
Roosevelt, MN 70-71 C 1
Roosevelt, OK 76-77 E 5
Roosevelt, TX 76-77 DE 7
Roosevelt, UT 66-67 HJ 5
Roosevelt, WA 66-67 C 3
Roosevelt, Rio — 92-93 G 6-7
Roosevelt Field 84 II b 2
Roosevelt Island 53 AB 20-21
Roossenekal 174-175 H 3
Rootok Island 58-59 o 3-4
Root Portage 62 D 2
Root River 70-71 DE 4
Rōpar 138-139 F 2
Ropaži 124-125 E 5
Roper River 158-159 F 2
Roper River Mission 158-159 FG 2
Roper Valley 158-159 F 2-3
Ropi 116-117 J 3
Roquefort-sur-Soulzon 120-121 J 7
Roque Pérez 106-107 H 5
Roraima 92-93 GH 4
Roraima, Mount — 92-93 G 3
Rori 138-139 E 3
Rorke's Drift 174-175 J 5
Rorketon 61 J 5
Røros 116-117 D 6
Rørvik 116-117 D 5
Ros' 126-127 E 2
Rosa 172 F 3
Rosa, Cap — = Rā's al-Wardah 166-167 L 1
Rosa, Saco de — 110 I b 1
Rošal 124-125 MN 6
Rosales 106-107 F 5
Rosalia, WA 66-67 E 2
Rosalind 61 B 4
Rosalinda 96-97 E 8
Rosamond, CA 74-75 D 5
Rosamond Lake 74-75 DE 5
Rosa Morada 86-87 H 6
Rosanna, Melbourne- 161 II c 1
Rosans, Las — 106-107 G 4
Rosarca = Rusera 138-139 L 5
Rosário [BR] 92-93 L 5
Rosario [MEX, Coahuila] 76-77 C 9
Rosario [MEX, Durango] 86-87 H 4
Rosario [MEX, Sinaloa] 86-87 GH 6
Rosario [PE] 96-97 F 9
Rosario [PY] 102-103 D 6
Rosario [RA, Jujuy] 104-105 C 8
Rosario [RA, Santa Fe] 111 DE 4
Rosario [ROU] 106-107 J 5
Rosario [YV] 94-95 E 2
Rosario, El — [YV, Bolívar] 94-95 J 4
Rosario, El — [YV, Zulia] 94-95 E 3
Rosario, Isla del — 94-95 CD 2
Rosario, Isla del — = Carass Island 108-109 J 8
Rosario, Río — 104-105 D 9
Rosario de Arriba 86-87 C 2-3
Rosario de la Frontera 111 D 3
Rosario de Lerma 104-105 D 9
Rosario del Tala 111 E 4
Rosário do Sul 111 EF 4
Rosário Oeste 92-93 HJ 7
Rosario Villa Ocampo 86-87 H 4
Rosarito [MEX, Baja California Norte ↑ Santo Domingo] 86-87 CD 3
Rosarito [MEX, Baja California Norte ↓ Tijuana] 74-75 E 6
Rosarito [MEX, Baja California Sur] 86-87 E 4
Rosas [CO] 94-95 C 6
Rosas [E] 120-121 J 7
Rosa Zárate 96-97 B 1
Roščino 124-125 G 3
Roscoe, NY 72-73 J 4
Roscoe, SD 68-69 G 3
Roscoe, TX 76-77 D 6
Roscoff 120-121 EF 4
Roscommon 119 BC 5
Roscommon, MI 70-71 H 3
Rose 208 K 4
Rose, NE 68-69 G 4
Roseau 64-65 O 8
Roseau, MN 70-71 BC 1
Roseau River 70-71 BC 1
Roseberry River 62 C 1
Rosebery 158-159 HJ 8
Rose-Blanche 63 G 4
Roseboro, NC 80-81 G 3
Rosebud, TX 76-77 F 7
Rosebud Creek 68-69 C 3
Rosebud Indian Reservation 68-69 F 4
Rosebud Mountains 68-69 C 3
Roseburg, OR 66-67 B 4
Rosebury, Sydney- 161 I b 2
Rosecroft Raceway 82 II b 2
Rosedal, Coyoacán- 91 I c 2
Rosedale 61 B 5
Rosedale, NM 76-77 A 6
Rosedale Gardens, Houston-, TX 85 III b 1
Rose Hills Memorial Park 83 III d 1
Roşeireş, Er- = Ar-Ruşayriş 164-165 LM 6
Rose Lake 60 DE 2
Roseland, Chicago-, IL 83 II b 2
Roseland Cemetery 85 II b 2
Rosemary 61 BC 5
Rosemead, CA 83 III d 1
Rosemont, PA 84 III ab 1
Rosenberg, TX 76-77 FG 8
Rosenheim 118 EF 5
Rosenthal, Berlin- 130 III b 1
Rose Point 60 AB 2
Rose River 158-159 G 2
Roses 88-89 J 3
Rosetown 56-57 P 7
Rose Tree, PA 84 III a 2
Rosetta = Rashîd 173 B 2
Rosetta Mouth = Maşabb Rashîd 173 B 2
Rosette = Rashîd 173 B 2
Rosettenville, Johannesburg- 170 V b 2
Rose Valley 61 G 4
Rose Valley, PA 84 III a 2
Roseville, IL 70-71 E 5
Roseville, MI 72-73 E 3
Roseway Bank 63 D 6
Rose Wood 160 L 1
Rosholt, SD 68-69 H 3
Rosholt, WI 70-71 F 3
Rosiclare, IL 70-71 F 7
Rosignano Marittimo 122-123 CD 4
Rosignol 92-93 H 3
Roşiori-de-Vede 122-123 L 3-4
Rosita, La — 86-87 K 3
Roskilde 116-117 E 10
Rosl'atino 124-125 P 4
Roslavl' 124-125 J 7
Roslindale, Boston-, MA 84 I b 3
Roslyn, WA 66-67 C 2
Roslyn Lake 70-71 G 1
Rosmead 174-175 F 6
Ross 158-159 O 8
Ross, WY 68-69 D 4
Rossano 122-123 G 6
Rossau [CH] 128 IV ab 2
Rossel Island 148-149 hi 7
Rossem 128 II a 1
Ross Ice Shelf 53 AB 20-17
Rossieny = Raseiniai 124-125 D 6
Rossignol, Lake 63 D 5
Rossijskaja Sovetskaja Federativnaja Socialističeskaja Respublika = Russian Soviet Federated Socialist Republic 132-133 l-g 4
Rössing [Namibia] 174-175 A 2
Ross Island [Antarctica, Ross Sea] 53 B 17-18
Ross Island [Antarctica, Weddell Sea] 53 C 31
Ross Island [CDN] 56-57 R 7
Ross Island = Dōn Kyūn 150-151 AB 6
Rossland 66-67 DE 1
Rosslare 119 CD 5
Rosslyn 174-175 GH 3
Rosslyn, Arlington-, VA 82 II a 2
Rosso 164-165 A 5
Rossoš' 126-127 J 1
Rossouw 174-175 G 6
Rossport 70-71 G 1
Ross River 56-57 K 5
Ross Sea 53 B 20-18
Rosston, OK 76-77 E 4
Røssvatn 116-117 E 5
Røssvik 116-117 FG 4
Rossville 158-159 HJ 3
Rossville, GA 78-79 G 3
Rossville, IL 70-71 G 5
Rossville, New York-, NY 82 III a 3
Rosswood 60 C 2
Rosthern 61 E 4
Rostock 118 F 1
Rostock-Warnemünde 118 F 1
Rostokino, Moskva- 113 V c 2
Rostov 132-133 FG 6
Rostov-na-Donu 126-127 J 3
Roswell, NM 64-65 F 5
Rota 120-121 D 10
Rotan, TX 76-77 D 6
Rotberg 130 III bc 2
Rothaargebirge 118 D 3
Rothbury 119 EF 4
Rothenburg 118 DE 4
Rothenburgsort, Hamburg- 130 I b 1
Rotherbaum, Hamburg- 130 I a 1
Rothesay 119 D 4
Rothsay, MN 70-71 BC 2
Rothschwaige 130 II a 1
Roti, Pulau — 148-149 H 9
Roto 158-159 J 6
Rotondo, Mont — 122-123 C 4
Rotorua 158-159 P 7
Rottenfish River 62 C 1
Rotterdam 120-121 JK 3
Rotterdam-Hoek van Holland 120-121 JK 3
Rotti = Pulau Roti 148-149 H 9
Rotuma 208 H 4
Roubaix 120-121 J 3
Rouen 120-121 H 4
Rouffach = Ḥammā-Būziyān 166-167 JK 1
Rouïba = Ar-Ruwībah 166-167 H 1
Rouïna = Ruwīnah 166-167 GH 1
Rouissat = Ruwisiyat 166-167 J 4
Roukkula = Rovkuly 124-125 H 1
Roulers = Roeselare 120-121 J 3
Round Island = Ngau Chau 155 I ab 2
Round Lake 62 D 1
Round Mountain 158-159 K 6
Round Mountain, NV 74-75 E 3
Round Mountain, TX 76-77 E 7
Round Rock, TX 76-77 F 7
Round Spring, MO 78-79 D 2
Roundup, MT 68-69 B 2
Round Valley Indian Reservation 74-75 B 3
Rounga, Dar — 164-165 J 6-7
Roura 98-99 MN 2
Rousay 119 E 2
Rouses Point, NY 72-73 K 2
Roussillon 120-121 J 7
Routbé, El- = Ar-Ruṭbah 136-137 G 6
Rouxville 174-175 G 6
Rouyn 56-57 V 8
Rovaniemi 116-117 L 4
Rovdino 124-125 O 3
Roven'ki 126-127 J 2
Rover, Mount — 58-59 R 3
Rovereto 122-123 D 3
Roversi 106-107 FG 1
Rovigo 122-123 D 3
Rovigo = Būgarā 166-167 H 1
Rovinj 122-123 E 3
Rovkuly 124-125 H 1
Rovno 126-127 C 1
Rovuma, Rio — 172 G 4
Rowan Lake 62 C 3
Rowe, NM 76-77 B 5
Rowe Park 170 III b 2
Rowlett, Isla — 108-109 B 5
Rowley Island 56-57 UV 4
Rowley Shoals 158-159 C 3
Rowuma = Rio Rovuma 172 G 4
Rox, NV 74-75 F 4
Roxas 148-149 H 4
Roxboro, NC 80-81 G 2
Roxborough, Philadelphia-, PA 84 III b 1
Roxburgh [NZ] 158-159 N 9
Roxbury, Boston-, MA 84 I b 3
Roxie, MS 78-79 D 5
Roy, MT 68-69 B 2
Roy, NM 76-77 B 5
Roy, UT 66-67 G 5
Royal Botanic Gardens [AUS, Melbourne] 161 II bc 1-2
Royal Botanic Gardens [AUS, Sydney] 161 I b 2
Royal Canal 119 C 5
Royal Center, IN 70-71 G 5
Royal Natal National Park 174-175 H 5
Royal Oak Township, MI 84 II b 2
Royal Observatory 155 I ab 2
Royal Park 161 II b 1
Royal Society Range 53 B 15-16
Royalton, MN 70-71 CD 3
Royan 120-121 G 6
Roy Hill 158-159 CD 4
Røykenvik 116-117 D 7
Royse City, TX 76-77 F 6
Royston, GA 80-81 E 3
Roždestveno [SU, Kalininskaja Oblast'] 124-125 L 5
Roždestvenskoje 124-125 P 4
Rozel, KS 68-69 G 6
Rozenburg [NL, place] 128 I a 2
Rozendo 98-99 G 3
Rozet, WY 68-69 D 3
Rozewie, Przylądek — 118 J 1
Rožišče 126-127 B 1
Rožňava 118 K 4
Roztocze 118 L 3
Rtiščevo 124-125 O 7
Rt Kamenjak 122-123 E 3
Ruacana Falls 172 BC 5
Ruaha, Great — 172 G 3
Ruaha National Park 171 C 4
Ruahine Range 161 F 5-G 4
Ruanda = Rwanda 172 EF 2
Ruapehu 158-159 P 7
Ruapuke Island 161 C 8
Rub'ah, Ar- 166-167 L 1
Rubā'ī, Ash-Shallāl ar 164-165 L 5
Rub' al-Khālī = Ar-Rub'al-Khālī 134-135 F 7-G 6
Rub' al-Khālī, Ar- 134-135 F 7-G 6
Rubanovka 126-127 G 3
Rubbah 166-167 K 3
Rubcovsk 132-133 P 7
Rubeho 171 D 4
Rubens, Río — 108-109 C 9-D 8
Rubesibe 144-145 c 2
Rubežnoje 126-127 J 2
Rubi 172 E 1
Rubia, La — 111 D 4
Rubim 100-101 D 3
Rubio 94-95 E 4
Rubl'ovo 113 V a 2
Rubondo 171 BC 3
Rubtsovsk = Rubcovsk 132-133 P 7
Ruby, AK 56-57 EF 5
Ruby Lake 66-67 F 5
Ruby Mountains 66-67 F 5
Ruby Range [CDN] 58-59 ST 6
Ruby Range [USA] 66-67 G 3
Ruby Valley 66-67 F 5
Ruč 124-125 T 3
Rucanelo 106-107 E 6
Rucava 124-125 C 5
Rucheng 146-147 D 9
Ruchlovo = Skovorodino 132-133 XY 7
Rudall 160 BC 4
Rūdarpur 138-139 J 4
Rudauli 138-139 H 4
Rūdbār 136-137 N 4
Rūd-e Āqdogh Mīsh 136-137 M 4
Rūd-e Aras 136-137 L 3
Rūd-e Dez 136-137 N 6
Rūd-e Douāb = Qareh Sū 134-135 FG 3-4
Rūd-e Doveyrīch 136-137 M 6
Rūd-e Gāmāsiyāb 136-137 MN 5
Rūd-e Gorgān 134-135 GH 3
Rūd-e Jarrāḥī 136-137 N 7
Rūd-e Karkheh 136-137 N 6-7
Rūd-e Kārūn 134-135 FG 4
Rūd-e Kharkheh 136-137 M 6
Rūd-e-Mand = Rūd-e Mond 134-135 G 5
Rūd-e Mond 134-135 G 5
Rudensk 124-125 F 7
Rūd-e Qarānqū 136-137 M 4
Rūd-e Qezel Owzan 134-135 F 3
Rūd-e Sīrvān 136-137 M 5
Rūd-e Tātā'ū 136-137 LM 4
Rudewa 171 C 5
Rūd-e Zāb-e Kūchek 136-137 L 4
Rūd-e Zohreh 136-137 N 7
Rudge Ramos, São Bernardo do Campo- 110 II b 2-3
Rūdkhāneh Talvār 136-137 MN 5
Rūdkhāneh-ye Ābdānān 136-137 M 6
Rūdkhāneh ye Gangīr 136-137 LM 6
Rūdkhāneh-ye Kashkān 136-137 N 6
Rūdkhāneh-ye Malāyer 136-137 N 5
Rudki 126-127 A 2
Rudn'a [SU] 124-125 H 6
Rudnaja Pristan' 132-133 a 9
Rudnica 126-127 D 2
Rudničnyj 124-125 ST 4
Rudnyj 132-133 L 7
Rudog 142-143 D 5
Rudolf, ostrov — 132-133 JK 1
Rudolfshöhe 130 III d 1
Rudolfstetten-Friedlisberg 128 IV a 1
Rudong [TJ, Guangdong] 146-147 C 11
Rudong [TJ, Jiangsu] 146-147 H 5
Rudow, Berlin- 130 III b 2
Rūd Sar 136-137 O 4
Rudyard, MI 70-71 H 2
Rudyard, MT 66-67 H 1
Rueil-Malmaison 129 I b 2
Ruel 62 L 3
Ruffec 120-121 GH 5
Rufiji 172 G 3
Rufino 111 D 4
Rufisque 164-165 A 5-6
Rufunsa 172 EF 5
Rugao 142-143 N 5
Rugby 119 F 5
Rugby, ND 68-69 FG 1
Rügen 118 FG 1
Rugl'akov = Okt'abr'skij 126-127 L 3
Rugozero 124-125 J 1
Ru He 146-147 E 5
Ru He = Beiru He 146-147 D 4
Ruhea = Ruheya 138-139 M 4
Ruhelkhand = Rohil Khand 138-139 GH 3
Ruheya 138-139 M 4
Ruhlsdorf 130 III b 2
Ruhnu 124-125 D 5
Ruhr 118 D 3
Ruhudji 171 D 5
Ruhuhu 171 C 5
Rui'an 146-147 H 8
Rui Barbosa 100-101 D 7
Ruichang 146-147 E 7
Ruidoso, NM 76-77 B 6
Ruijin 142-143 M 6
Rūi Khāf = Khvāf 134-135 J 4
Ruinas, Valle de las — 108-109 EF 4
Ruislip, London- 129 II a 1
Ruisui = Juisui 146-147 H 10
Ruivo, Pico — 164-165 A 2
Ruiz 86-87 H 7
Ruiz, Nevado del — 92-93 DE 4
Ruiz Díaz de Guzmán 106-107 F 4
Rujewa 171 C 5
Rūjiena 124-125 E 5
Rujm Ṭal'at al-Jamā'ah 136-137 F 7
Rukas Tal Lake = Rakasdal 142-143 E 5
Rukhaimiyah, Ar- = Ar-Rukhaymīyah 136-137 L 8
Rukhaymīyah, Ar- 136-137 L 8
Ruki 172 C 1-2
Rukumkot 138-139 J 3
Rukungiri 171 B 3
Rukuru 171 C 5
Rukwa 172 F 3
Rukwa, Lake — 172 F 3
Rule, TX 76-77 E 6
Ruleville, MS 78-79 D 4
Rum 119 C 3
Ruma 122-123 H 3
Rumāh, Ar- 134-135 F 5
Rumahui 148-149 k 7
Rumaylah, Ar- 136-137 M 7
Rumaythah, Ar- 136-137 L 7
Rumbalara 158-159 FG 5
Rumberpon, Pulau — 148-149 KL 7
Rumbīk 164-165 K 7
Rum Cay 64-65 M 7
Rumeli burnu 154 I b 1
Rumelifeneri 154 I b 1
Rumelihisarı 154 I b 2
Rumelihisarı, İstanbul- 154 I b 2
Rumelija 122-123 LM 4
Rumelikavağı, İstanbul- 154 I b 1
Rumford, ME 72-73 L 2
Rumi Punco 104-105 D 10
Rum Jungle 158-159 F 2
Rümlang 128 IV ab 1
Rummānah 173 C 2
Rummānī, Ar- 166-167 C 3
Rumoe = Rumoi 144-145 b 2
Rumoi 142-143 R 3
Rumorosa 74-75 EF 6
Rumpenheim, Offenbach- 128 III b 1
Rumpi 171 C 5
Rum River 70-71 D 3
Rumsey 61 B 5
Rumula 158-159 HJ 3
Rumuruti 171 CD 2
Runan 146-147 E 5
Runanga 161 D 6
Runciman 106-107 FG 4
Rundeng 150-151 AB 11
Rundu 172 C 5
Rungan, Sungai — 152-153 K 6-7
Runge, TX 76-77 F 8
Rungis 129 I c 3
Rungu 171 AB 2
Rungwa [EAT, place] 172 F 3
Rungwa [EAT, river] 171 C 4
Rungwa East 171 BC 4
Rungwe Mount 172 F 3
Runheji 146-147 F 5
Runnemede, NJ 84 III c 2
Running Water Creek 76-77 CD 5
Runton Range 158-159 D 4
Ruo Shui 142-143 HJ 3
Ruoxi 142-143 M 6
Rupanco 108-109 C 3
Rupanco, Lago — 108-109 CD 3
Rūpar = Rōpar 138-139 F 2
Rupat, Pulau — 148-149 D 6
Rūpbās 138-139 F 4
Rupert, ID 66-67 G 4
Rupert Bay 62 M 1
Rupert House = Fort Rupert 56-57 V 7
Rupert River 56-57 VW 7
Rūpnagar 138-139 E 4
Ruppert Coast 53 B 21-22
Ruqaybah, Ar- 166-167 AB 7
Ruqī, Ar- 136-137 M 8
Rūrkalā = Raurkela 134-135 NO 5
Rurkī = Roorkee 138-139 FG 3
Rurrenabaque 92-93 F 7
Rusanovo 132-133 JK 3
Rusape 172 F 5
Ruşayriş, Ar- 164-165 LM 6
Rüschlikon 128 IV b 2
Ruse 122-123 LM 4
Rusera 138-139 L 5
Ruşeţu 122-123 M 3
Rush, CO 68-69 DE 6
Rushan 146-147 H 3
Rush Center, KS 68-69 G 6
Rush City, MN 70-71 D 3
Rush Creek 68-69 E 6
Rushford, MN 70-71 E 4
Rush Springs, OK 76-77 EF 5
Rushville, IL 70-71 E 5
Rushville, IN 70-71 H 6
Rushville, NE 68-69 E 4
Rusk, TX 76-77 G 7
Ruskin, NE 68-69 GH 5
Rusnė 124-125 C 6
Ruso 150-151 C 9
Ruso, ND 68-69 F 2
Russ = Rūsnė 124-125 C 6
Russa, South Suburbs- 154 II ab 3
Russas 92-93 M 5
Russelkanda 138-139 K 8
Russell, KS 68-69 G 6
Russell, MN 70-71 BC 3
Russell [CDN] 61 H 5
Russell [NZ] 158-159 OP 7
Russell, Mount — 58-59 LM 5
Russell Fiord 58-59 S 7
Russell Island 56-57 R 3
Russell Islands 148-149 j 6
Russell Lake 61 H 2
Russell Range 158-159 D 6
Russell Springs, KS 68-69 F 6
Russellville, AL 78-79 F 3
Russellville, AR 78-79 C 3
Russellville, KY 78-79 F 2
Russel Springs, KS 68-69 F 6
Russenes 116-117 L 2
Russian Mission, AK 58-59 G 6
Russian River 74-75 B 3
Russian Soviet Federated Socialist Republic 132-133 L-g 4
Russisi = Ruzizi 172 E 2
Russkij, ostrov — [SU, Japan Sea] 132-133 Z 9
Russkij, ostrov — [SU, Kara Sea] 132-133 RS 2
Russkij Aktaš 124-125 T 6
Russkij Zavorot, mys — 132-133 JK 4
Rust, De — 174-175 E 7
Rustāq, Ar- 134-135 H 6
Rustavi 126-127 M 6
Rust de Winterdam 174-175 H 3
Rustenburg 172 E 7
Rustenfeld 113 I b 2
Rustic Canyon 83 III a 1
Rustling Oaks, Houston-, TX 85 III a 1
Ruston, LA 64-65 H 5
Rūşū = Al-Quwārib 164-165 A 5
Rusufa = Rişāfah 136-137 H 5
Rusumu, Chutes — 171 B 3
Rusville 170 V c 1
Rutana 172 EF 2
Rutanzig 172 E 2
Ruṭbah, Ar- [IRQ] 134-135 DE 4
Ruṭbah, Ar- [SYR] 136-137 G 6
Ruteng 152-153 O 10
Rutgers University Camden Campus 84 III c 2
Ruth, NV 74-75 F 3
Rutherford, NJ 82 III b 2
Rutherfordton, NC 80-81 F 3
Ruth Glacier 58-59 M 5
Ruthin 119 E 5
Ruth Street Park 85 II b 2
Ruthven, IA 70-71 C 4
Rutland 60 H 5
Rutland, ND 68-69 H 2
Rutland, VT 64-65 M 3
Rutledge, PA 84 III b 2
Rutshuru 172 E 2
Rutter 72-73 F 1
Rutul 126-127 N 6
Ruvo di Pùglia 122-123 G 5
Ruvu [EAT, place] 171 D 4
Ruvu [EAT, river] 172 G 3
Ruvu = Pangani 172 G 2
Ruvuma [EAT, administrative unit] 172 G 4
Ruvuma [EAT, river] 171 C 5
Ruvuvu 171 B 3
Ruwāq, Jabal ar- 136-137 G 5-6
Ruwenzori 172 F 1
Ruwenzori National Park 172 EF 2
Ruwībah, Ar- 166-167 H 1
Ruwīnah 166-167 GH 1
Ruwisiyat 166-167 J 4
Ruwu = Pangani 172 G 2
Ruyang 146-147 D 4
Ruyuan 146-147 D 9
Ruza [SU, place] 124-125 KL 6
Ruzajevka 132-133 GH 7
Ružany 124-125 E 7
Ruzizi 172 E 2
Ružomberok 118 J 4
Rwanda 172 EF 2
Rwashamaire 171 B 3
Ryan, OK 76-77 F 5
Ryanggang-do 144-145 FG 2
Ryazan = R'azan' 124-125 M 6
Rybačij 118 K 1
Rybačij, poluostrov — 132-133 EF 4
Rybačje 132-133 NO 9
Rybinsk 132-133 F 6
Rybinskoje vodochranilišče 132-133 FG 6
Rybinsk Reservoir = Rybinskoje vodochranilišče 132-133 F 6
Rybnica 126-127 D 3
Rybnik 118 J 3
Rybnoje 124-125 M 6
Rycroft 60 H 2
Rydal, PA 84 III c 1
Rydalmere, Sydney- 161 I a 1
Ryde, Sydney- 161 I a 1
Ryder, ND 68-69 F 2
Ryderwood, WA 66-67 B 2
Rye, CO 68-69 D 7
Ryegate, MT 68-69 B 2
Rye Patch Reservoir 66-67 D 5
Rykaartspos 174-175 G 4
Ryke Yseøyane 116-117 m 6
Ryl'sk 126-127 G 1
Rynfield 170 V cd 1
Ryn-peski 126-127 OP 2-3
Ryōtsu 144-145 M 3
Rypin 118 J 2
Ryškany 126-127 C 3
Ryūkyū 142-143 N 7-O 6
Ryukyu Trench 142-143 P 6-R 7
Ržaksa 124-125 NO 7
Ržava = Pristen' 126-127 H 1
Rzeszów 118 KL 3
Ržev 124-125 K 5
Rzhev = Ržev 124-125 K 5
Ržiščev 126-127 E 2

S

Sá [BR] 92-93 L 8
Sa [T] 150-151 C 3
Saa [DY] 168-169 F 3
Saa [RFC] 168-169 H 4
Saale 118 E 3
Saalfeld 118 E 3
Saar 118 C 4
Saarbrücken 118 C 4
Saaremaa 124-125 CD 4
Saarijärvi 116-117 L 6
Saariselkä 116-117 MN 3
Saarland 118 C 4
Saarlouis 118 C 4
Saavedra 106-107 F 6
Saavedra, Buenos Aires- 110 III b 1
Saba' [DZ] 166-167 F 5
Saba [West Indies] 64-65 O 8
Sabaa, Gebel es — = Qārat as-Sab'ah 164-165 H 3
Šabac 122-123 H 3
Sabadell 120-121 J 8
Sabae 144-145 KL 5
Sabah 148-149 G 5
Sab'ah, Qārat as- 164-165 H 3
Sabak, Cape — 58-59 pq 6
Sabaki = Galana 172 GH 2
Sabālān, Kūhhā-ye — 136-137 M 3
Sabalana, Kepulauan — 152-153 N 9
Sabalgarh 138-139 F 4
Sabana 94-95 E 8
Sabana, Archipiélago de — 64-65 KL 7
Sabana, La — [CO] 94-95 G 6
Sabana, La — [RA] 106-107 H 1
Sabana, La — [YV] 94-95 H 2
Sabana de la Mar 88-89 M 5
Sabanalarga [CO, Atlántico] 92-93 DE 2
Sabanalarga [CO, Casanare] 94-95 E 5
Sabancuy 86-87 P 8
Sabaneta [CO] 94-95 CD 7
Sabaneta [YV, Falcón] 94-95 FG 2
Sabaneta [YV, Mérida] 94-95 F 3-4
Sabang [RI, Aceh] 148-149 C 5
Sabang [RI, Sulawesi Tengah] 152-153 N 5
Şabanözü 136-137 E 2
Sabará 102-103 L 3
Sabaragamuva Palāna ◁ 140 E 7
Sabaragamuva 140 E 7
Sābari 134-135 N 7
Sābar Kantha 138-139 D 6
Sābarmati 138-139 D 5-6
Sabaru, Pulau — 152-153 N 9
Sabaungte 141 C 4
Sabawngpi = Sabaungte 141 C 4
Sabaya 104-105 B 6
Şabāyā, Jabal — 134-135 E 7
Sab' Biyār 136-137 G 6
Şabbūrah 136-137 G 5
Sabetha, KS 70-71 BC 6
Sabhah 164-165 G 3
Sabhah, As- 136-137 H 5
Sabhat Ṭāwurghā 164-165 H 2
Sabi 172 F 6
Sabībah 166-167 L 2
Sabie [Mozambique] 174-175 K 3
Sabie [ZA] 174-175 J 3
Sabierivier 174-175 J 3
Sabīkhanh, As- 166-167 LM 2
Sabile 124-125 D 5
Sabina, OH 72-73 E 5
Sabinal, TX 76-77 E 8
Sabinal, Cayo — 88-89 H 4
Sabinas 64-65 F 6
Sabinas, Río — 86-87 JK 3
Sabinas Hidalgo 64-65 F 6
Sabine, TX 76-77 GH 8
Sabine Lake 78-79 C 6
Sabine land 116-117 k 5
Sabine Peninsula 56-57 OP 2
Sabine River 64-65 H 5
Sabini, Monti — 122-123 E 4
Sabinópolis 102-103 L 3
Sabinoso, NM 76-77 B 5
Sabioncello = Pelješac 122-123 G 4
Sabirabad 126-127 O 6-7
Şābirīyah, Aş- 136-137 M 8
Şabīyah, Qaşr aş- 136-137 N 8
Sabkhat Abā ar Rūs 134-135 GH 6
Sabkhat al-Bardawīl 173 C 2
Sabkhat al-Malah 166-167 F 5
Sabkhat al-Māliḥ 166-167 M 3
Sabkhat al-M'shīgīg 166-167 L 2
Sabkhat an-Nawāl 166-167 LM 2
Sabkhat aṭ-Ṭawīl 136-137 J 5
Sabkhat 'Ayn Balbālah 166-167 D 6
Sabkhat 'Azmātī 164-165 DE 3
Sabkhat Bā'ūrah 136-137 J 5
Sabkhat Kalbīyah 166-167 M 2
Sabkhat Maṭṭī 134-135 G 6
Sabkhat Mukrān 164-165 E 3
Sabkhat N'daghāmshah 164-165 AB 5
Sabkhat Shinshān 164-165 B 4
Sabkhat Sīdī al-Hānī 166-167 M 2
Sabkhat Tādit 166-167 M 3
Sabkhat Tīmīmūn 166-167 G 5
Sabkhat Tindūf 164-165 C 3
Sabkhat Umm ad-Durūs 164-165 B 4
Sabkhat Umm al-Khiyālāt 166-167 M 3
Sable 158-159 M 3
Sable, Cape — [CDN] 56-57 XY 9
Sable, Cape — [USA] 64-65 K 6
Sable Island [CDN] 56-57 Z 9
Sable Island [PNG] 148-149 hj 5

Sable Island Bank 63 F 5-6
Sable River 63 D 6
Sables, River aux — 62 K 3
Sables, Rivière aux — 63 A 3
Sables-d'Olonne, les — 120-121 FG 5
Sablinskoje 126-127 L 4
Šablykino 124-125 K 7
Saboeiro 100-101 E 4
Sabon-Birni 168-169 G 2
Sabon Gari 168-169 H 3
Sabonkafi 168-169 H 2
Saboûrâ = Šabbûrah 136-137 G 5
Sabrina Land 53 C 12-13
Sabsab 166-167 H 3
Sabtang Island 146-147 H 11
Sabt G'zūlah, As- 166-167 B 3
Sabt 'Imghāt 166-167 AB 4
Sabun 132-133 P 5
Sabunči, Baku- 126-127 OP 6
Sabuncu = Sabuncupınar 136-137 D 3
Sabuncupınar 136-137 D 3
Saburovo, Moskva- 113 V c 3
Şabyā', Aş- 134-135 E 7
Sābzawār = Shīndand 134-135 J 4
Sabzevār 134-135 H 3
Sacaba 92-93 F 8
Sacaca 92-93 F 8
Sacajawea Peak 66-67 E 3
Sácama 94-95 E 4
Sacanana 108-109 E 4
Sacanta 111 D 4
Sačchere 126-127 L 5
Sac City, IA 70-71 C 4
Sachalin 132-133 b 7-8
Sachalinskij zaliv 132-133 b 7
Sach'ang-ni 144-145 F 2
Šachdag, gora — 126-127 O 6
Sachigo Lake 62 CD 1
Sachigo River 56-57 S 6-7
Sachin 138-139 D 7
Sachnovščina 126-127 G 2
Sachojere 104-105 D 4
Šachova kosa 126-127 P 6
Šachovskaja 124-125 K 5-6
Šachrisabz 134-135 K 3
Sachsen 118 FG 3
Sachsen-Anhalt 118 EF 2-3
Sachsenhausen, Frankfurt am Main- 128 III ab 1
Šachtinsk 132-133 N 8
Šachty 126-127 K 3
Šachunja 132-133 GH 6
Sack [SU, Rossijskaja SFSR] 124-125 N 6
Sackets Harbor, NY 72-73 HJ 3
Sackville 63 DE 5
Saclay 129 I b 3
Saco 100-101 C 4
Saco, ME 72-73 L 3
Saco, MT 68-69 C 1
Saco Comprido, Serra — 100-101 B 7
Saco de Itacolomi 110 I b 1
Saco de Rosa 110 I b 1
Sacramento 102-103 J 3
Sacramento, CA 64-65 B 4
Sacramento, Pampa del — 92-93 D 6
Sacramento Mountains 64-65 EF 5
Sacramento River 64-65 B 3-4
Sacramento Valley 64-65 B 3-4
Sacré-Cœur 129 I c 2
Sac River 70-71 D 6
Sacrower See 130 III a 2
Sacsayhuaman 96-97 EF 8
Sadābād 138-139 FG 4
Sad ad-Dokan = Sadd ad-Dukān 136-137 L 4-5
Sa'dah 134-135 E 7
Sada-misaki 144-145 HJ 6
Sadani 172 G 3
Sadāseopet 140 C 2
Sadd ad-Darbandī Khan 136-137 L 5
Sadd ad-Diyālá 136-137 L 5
Sadd ad-Dukān 136-137 L 4-5
Sadd al-'Ālī 164-165 L 4
Sadd al-Bakhmah 136-137 L 4
Saddle Brook, NJ 82 III b 1
Saddle Hills 60 H 2
Saddle Mountain 66-67 G 4
Saddle Mountains 66-67 CD 2
Saddle Peak 66-67 H 3
Sa Dec 148-149 E 4
Sad el 'Aswān = Sadd al-'Ālī 164-165 L 3
Sadgora 126-127 BC 2
Saḍhēikalā = Saraikelā 138-139 KL 6
Sādhis, Ash-Shallāl as- 164-165 L 5
Sadıkali 136-137 F 3
Sadiola 168-169 C 2
Sādiqābād 138-139 C 3
Sadiya 134-135 Q 5
Sa'diyah, As- 136-137 L 5
Sa'diyah, Hawr as- 136-137 M 6
Sadlerochit River 58-59 P 2
Sado [J] 142-143 Q 4
Sado [P] 120-121 C 10
Sadon = Hsadôn 141 EF 3
Sadovniki, Moskva- 113 V c 3
Sadovoje 126-127 M 3
Ṣadr, Wādī — 173 D 3
Sādra 138-139 D 6
Sadrās 140 E 4
Ṣadrātah 166-167 K 1
Sādri 138-139 D 5
Šadrinsk 132-133 LM 6
Sæby 116-117 D 9
Saedpur = Saidpur 138-139 J 5
Saeki = Saiki 144-145 HJ 6
Saelānā = Sailāna 138-139 E 6
Şafā, Aş- 136-137 G 6
Şafā, Tulūl aş- 136-137 G 6
Safad = Ẓefat 134-135 D 4
Şafaḥ, Aş- 136-137 J 4
Şafājā 164-165 L 3
Şafājā, Jazīrat — 173 D 4
Safaji Island = Jazīrat Safājah 173 D 4
Şafāqis 164-165 FG 2
Şafār 134-135 J 4
Şafayn, 'Ard — 136-137 H 5
Safed Kōh 134-135 JK 4
Şaff, Aş- 173 B 3
Saffāf, Birkat as- 136-137 M 7
Saffāf, Hōr as- = Birkat as-Saffāf 136-137 M 7
Saffānīyah 134-135 F 5
Saffi = Asfī 164-165 C 2
Säffle 116-117 E 8
Safford, AZ 74-75 J 6
Saffron Walden 119 G 5-6
Safi = Asfī 164-165 C 2
Sāfīd, Kūh-e — = Kūh-e Sefīd 136-137 M 5-N 6
Sāfīd Kuh = Safed Kōh 134-135 JK 4
Sāfīd Rūd = Sefīd Rūd 136-137 N 4
Safīpur 138-139 H 4
Safīrah 136-137 G 4
Şafīsifah 166-167 F 3
Şāfītā' 136-137 G 5
Şafīzaf 166-167 F 2
Safonovo 124-125 J 6
Saforcada 106-107 G 5
Şafranbolu 136-137 E 2
Šafranovo 124-125 U 7
Şafrū 166-167 D 3
Şaft al-Laban 170 II ab 1
Saga 142-143 P 5
Sagae 144-145 MN 3
Sagaing = Sitkaing 148-149 D 2
Sagaing = Sitkaing Taing 148-149 B 2-C 1
Sagala 168-169 D 2
Sagami nada 142-143 Q 4-R 5
Saganoga Lake 70-71 E 1
Saganoseki 144-145 HJ 6
Šagany, ozero — 126-127 DE 4
Sāgar [IND, Karnataka] 140 B 3
Sāgar [IND, Mahārāshtra] 134-135 M 6
Sagara 144-145 M 5
Sāgara = Sāgar 140 B 3
Saga-ri 144-145 F 5
Sagar Island 138-139 LM 7
Sagarmatha 142-143 F 6
Sagauli 138-139 K 4
Sagavanirktok River 56-57 G 3-4
Sāgbāra 138-139 D 7
Sage, WY 66-67 H 5
Sage Creek 68-69 A 1
Sagerton, TX 76-77 E 6
Sage Zong = Sakha Dsong 142-143 F 6
Şaghīr, Zāb aş- 136-137 K 5
Şaghrū', Jabal — 164-165 C 2
Sagī, Har — 136-137 F 7
Sagigik Island 58-59 k 5
Sagileru 140 D 3
Saginaw, MI 64-65 K 3
Saginaw, TX 76-77 F 6
Saginaw Bay 64-65 K 3
Sagiz 132-133 JK 8
Sagobé 168-169 B 1
Šagonar 132-133 R 7
Sagoni 138-139 G 6
Sagra 120-121 F 10
Sagra, La — 120-121 EF 8
Sagres 120-121 C 10
Sagu 141 D 5
Saguache, CO 68-69 CD 6
Saguache Creek 68-69 C 6-7
Sagua la Grande 88-89 FG 3
Saguaro National Monument 74-75 H 6
Saguenay, Rivière — 56-57 WX 8
Sagunto 120-121 GH 9
Sāgvārā = Sāgwāra 138-139 DE 6
Sāgwāra 138-139 DE 6
Sagyndyk, mys — 126-127 P 4
Sahagún 120-121 E 7
Sahagún [CO] 94-95 D 3
Sahand, Kūh-e — 136-137 M 4
Sahār 138-139 K 5
Sahara 164-165 C-K 4
Saharan Atlas 164-165 D 2-F 1
Sahāranpur 134-135 M 4
Sahara Well 158-159 D 4
Saharsa 138-139 L 5
Saharunpore = Sahāranpur 134-135 M 4
Sahasrām = Sasarām 138-139 JK 5
Sahasvān = Sahaswān 138-139 G 3
Sahaswān 138-139 G 3
Sahatsakhan 150-151 D 4
Şahbā', Wādī aş- 134-135 F 6
Sahebganj = Sāhibganj 138-139 L 5
Sahel 168-169 E 2
Şahel = Sāhil 164-165 BC 5
Şahḥāt = Shaḥḥāt 164-165 J 2
Sāhibganj 138-139 L 5
Şāḥil 164-165 BC 5
Şāḥirah, Aş- 166-167 M 2
Sāhīwāl 134-135 L 4
Sahl al-Hudnah 166-167 J 2
Sahl Tāmlilt 166-167 E 3
Şaḥn, Aş- 136-137 K 7
Şaḥneh 136-137 M 5
Şaḥrā, Jabal — 173 C 4
Şaḥrā' al-Ḥijārah [IRQ] 136-137 L 7
Şaḥrā' al-Ḥijārah [Saudi Arabia] 136-137 JK 8
Şaḥrā' at-Tīh 164-165 L 2
Şaḥrā' Awbārī 166-167 G 3
Şaḥrā' Marzūq 164-165 G 3-4
Şaḥrā' Rībyānah 164-165 J 4
Sahuaripa 86-87 F 3
Sahuarita, AZ 74-75 H 7
Sahuayo 64-65 F 7-8
Sahuayo de José Maria Morelos 86-87 J 7-8
Sahyādri = Western Ghats 134-135 L 6-M 8
Sai 138-139 J 5
Sai, Mu'o'ng — 150-151 CD 2
Saibai Island 148-149 M 8
Sai Buri 148-149 D 5
Saiburi = Alor Setar 148-149 CD 5
Sai Buri, Mae Nam — 150-151 C 9-10
Saicã 106-107 K 3
Saichong = Xichang 150-151 G 2
Şa'īd, Aş- 164-165 L 3-4
Saïd, Es- = Aş-Şa'īd 164-165 L 3-4
Saïda = Şāyda' [DZ] 166-167 G 2
Şaïdâ = Şaydā [RL] 134-135 CD 4
Saïda, Monts de — = Jabal aş-Şayda 166-167 G 2
Sa'īdābād = Sīrjān 134-135 H 5
Saidaiji 144-145 JK 5
Saidapet 140 E 4
Sa'īd Bundās 164-165 JK 7
Sa'īdīyah, As- 166-167 EF 2
Sa'īdpūr [BD] 138-139 M 5
Saidpur [IND] 138-139 J 5
Saigō 144-145 J 4
Saigon = Thàn Phô Hô Chí Minh 148-149 E 4
Saiḥūt = Sayḥūt 134-135 G 7
Saijo 144-145 J 6
Saikai National Park = Gotō-rettō 144-145 G 6
Sai Kang 155 I b 1
Saikhoa Ghāt 141 DE 2
Saiki 144-145 HJ 6
Saila = Sāyla 138-139 C 6
Sailāna 138-139 E 6
Sailu 138-139 F 8
Saim 132-133 L 5
Saima 144-145 E 2
Saimaa 116-117 MN 7
Sai-ma-chi = Saima 144-145 E 2
Saimbeyli 136-137 FG 3
Sā'īn Dezh 136-137 M 4
Sainjang 144-145 E 3
Sāīn Qal'eh = Shāhīn Dezh 136-137 M 4
Saintala 138-139 J 7
Saint Albans, VT 72-73 K 2
Saint Albans, WV 72-73 EF 5
Saint Alban's [CDN] 63 H 4
Saint Albans, New York-, NY 82 III d 2
Saint-Amand-Mont-Rond 120-121 J 5
Saint-André, Cap — 172 H 5
Saint Andrew, FL 78-79 FG 5
Saint Andrew Bay 78-79 FG 6
Saint Andrew Point 78-79 FG 6
Saint Andrews 63 C 5
Saint Andrews, SC 80-81 FG 4
Saint Andrew's Cathedral 154 III b 2
Saint Ann, Lake — 60 K 3
Saint Anne, IL 70-71 FG 5
Saint Ann's Bay 88-89 H 5
Saint Anthony 56-57 Za 7
Saint Anthony, ID 66-67 H 4
Saint Antonio = Vila Real de Santo António 120-121 D 10
Saint Arnaud 160 F 6
Saint-Arnaud = Al-'Ulmah 166-167 J 1
Saint Augustin 63 G 2
Saint Augustin, Baie de — 172 H 6
Saint-Augustin, Rivière — 63 G 2
Saint Augustine, FL 64-65 KL 6
Saint-Augustin Nord-Ouest, Rivière — 63 G 2
Saint Austell 119 D 6
Saint-Avold 120-121 L 4
Saint Barbe 63 H 2
Saint Barbe Islands 63 J 2
Saint Barthélemy 64-65 O 8
Saint-Blaize, Cape — = Kaap Sint Blaize 174-175 E 8
Saint-Boniface 56-57 R 8
Saint-Brice-sous-Forêt 129 I c 1
Saint Bride's 63 J 4
Saint-Brieuc 120-121 F 4
Saint Brieux 61 F 4
Saint-Camille 63 A 4
Saint Catharines 56-57 UV 9
Saint Catherines Island 80-81 F 5
Saint Charles, ID 66-67 H 4
Saint Charles, MI 70-71 H 4
Saint Charles, MO 64-65 H 4
Saint-Charles = Ramdān-Jamāl 166-167 K 1
Saint Charles, Cape — 56-57 Za 7
Saint Christopher-Nevis 64-65 O 8
Saint Clair, LA 85 I c 2
Saint Clair, MI 72-73 E 3
Saint Clair, MO 70-71 E 6
Saint Clair, Lake — 56-57 U 9
Saint Clair River 72-73 E 3
Saint Clair Shores, MI 84 II c 2
Saint Clairsville, OH 72-73 F 4
Saint-Cloud 129 I b 2
Saint Cloud, FL 80-81 c 2
Saint Cloud, MN 64-65 H 2
Saint Croix 64-65 O 8
Saint Croix Falls, WI 70-71 D 3
Saint Croix River 70-71 D 2-3
Saint-Cyr-l'École 129 I b 2
Saint David Islands = Kepulauan Mapia 148-149 KL 6
Saint Davids, PA 84 III a 1
Saint David's [CDN] 63 G 3
Saint David's Head 119 CD 6
Saint-Denis [F] 120-121 J 4
Saint-Denis [Réunion] 204-205 N 11
Saint-Denis-du-Sig = Sig 166-167 F 2
Saint-Dié 120-121 L 4
Saint-Dizier 120-121 K 4
Sainte-Agathe-des-Monts 56-57 VW 8
Sainte Anne, Cathedrale — 170 IV a 1
Sainte-Anne-de-Beaupré 63 A 4
Sainte-Anne-de-la-Pocatière 63 AB 4
Sainte-Anne-des-Chênes 61 KL 6
Sainte-Anne-des-Monts 63 CD 3
Sainte Anne du la Congo 170 IV a 1
Sainte-Barbe-du-Tlélat = Wādī Thalāthah 166-167 F 2
Sainte-Catherine-d'Alexandrie 82 I b 2
Saint Edward, NE 68-69 GH 5
Sainte Genevieve, MO 70-71 E 6-7
Sainte Helène, Île de — 82 I b 1
Saint Elias, Cape — 58-59 P 7
Saint Elias, Mount — 56-57 H 5
Saint Elias Mountains 56-57 J 5-6
Saint-Élie 92-93 J 3-4
Saint Elmo, IL 70-71 F 6
Sainte-Louis, Lac — 82 I a 2
Sainte Marguerite, Rivière — 63 A 3
Sainte-Marie [CDN] 72-73 L 1
Sainte-Marie [Gabon] 172 B 2
Sainte-Marie [Martinique] 64-65 O 9
Sainte-Marie, Cap — 172 J 7
Sainte-Marie, Île — = Nosy Boraha 172 K 5
Saint-Ephrem 63 A 4
Sainte-Rose 88-89 PQ 6
Sainte Rose du Lac 61 J 5
Saintes 120-121 G 6
Saintes, Îles des — 88-89 PQ 7
Sainte-Thérèse 72-73 JK 2
Saint-Étienne 120-121 JK 6
Saint Faith's 174-175 J 6
Saint-Félicien 62 P 2
Saint-Flour 120-121 J 6
Saint Francis, KS 68-69 EF 6
Saint Francis, ME 72-73 M 1
Saint Francis, Cape — = Sealpunt 174-175 F 8
Saint Francis Bay = Sint Francisbaai 174-175 F 8
Saint Franciscus Bay = Sint Franziskusbaai 174-175 A 3
Saint Francis River 64-65 H 4
Saint Francisville, IL 70-71 FG 6
Saint Francisville, LA 78-79 D 5
Saint François, Lac — 72-73 L 2
Saint François, Rivière — 72-73 K 1-2
Saint François Mountains 70-71 E 7
Saint-Gabriel-de-Brandon 72-73 K 1
Saint Gall = Sankt Gallen 118 D 5
Saint-Gaudens 120-121 H 7
Saint George, GA 80-81 E 5
Saint George, SC 80-81 F 4
Saint George, UT 74-75 G 4
Saint George [AUS] 158-159 J 5
Saint George [CDN] 63 C 5
Saint George, Cape — 78-79 G 5
Saint George, Point — 66-67 A 5
Saint George Island 78-79 G 6
Saint George's [CDN, Newfoundland] 63 G 3
Saint-Georges [CDN, Quebec] 63 A 4
Saint-Georges [French Guiana] 92-93 J 4
Saint George's [WG] 64-65 O 9
Saint George's Bay [CDN, Newfoundland] 63 G 3
Saint George's Bay [CDN, Nova Scotia] 63 F 5
Saint George's Channel [GB] 119 C 6-D 5
Saint George's Channel [PNG] 148-149 h 5-6
Saint-Georges-de-Cacouna 63 B 4
Saint George Sound 78-79 G 6
Saint-Germain, Forêt de — 129 I b 2
Saint-Gilles-sur-Vie 120-121 FG 5
Saint-Girons 120-121 H 7
Saint Govan's Head 119 D 6
Saint-Gratien 129 I c 2
Saint Gregor 61 F 4
Saint Helena 204-205 G 10
Saint Helena, CA 74-75 B 3
Saint Helena Bay = Sint Helenabaai 172 C 8
Saint Helena Range 74-75 B 3
Saint Helena Sound 80-81 FG 4
Saint Helens, OR 66-67 B 3
Saint Helens, WA 66-67 B 2
Saint Helens [AUS] 160 d 2
Saint Helens [GB] 119 E 5
Saint Helens, Mount — 66-67 BC 2
Saint Helens Point 160 d 2
Saint Helier 119 E 7
Saint-Hyacinthe 56-57 W 8
Saint Ignace, MI 70-71 H 3
Saint-Ignace, Île — 70-71 FG 1
Saint Ignatius, MT 66-67 FG 2
Saint Isidore = Laverlochère 72-73 G 1
Saint James 61 K 6
Saint James, MI 70-71 H 3
Saint James, MN 70-71 C 3-4
Saint James, MO 70-71 E 6-7
Saint James, Cape — 56-57 K 7
Saint-Jean 56-57 W 8
Saint-Jean, Lac — 56-57 W 8
Saint-Jean, Rivière — [CDN, Pen. de Gaspé] 63 D 3
Saint-Jean, Rivière — [CDN, Quebec] 63 D 2
Saint-Jean-de-Luz 120-121 FG 7
Saint-Jérôme 72-73 JK 2
Saint Jo, TX 76-77 F 6
Saint Joe, AR 78-79 C 2
Saint Joe River 66-67 E 2
Saint John, KS 68-69 G 6-7
Saint John, ND 68-69 FG 1
Saint John [CDN] 56-57 X 8
Saint John [West Indies] 88-89 O 5
Saint John, Cape — 63 J 3
Saint John, Lake — = Lac Saint Jean 56-57 W 8
Saint John Bay 63 H 2
Saint John Island = Shangchuan Dao 146-147 D 11
Saint John Islands 63 H 2
Saint John River 56-57 X 8
Saint Johns, AZ 74-75 J 5
Saint Johns, MI 70-71 H 4
Saint John's [CDN] 56-57 a 8
Saint John's [West Indies] 64-65 O 8
Saint Johns = Saint-Jean 56-57 W 8
Saint Johnsbury, VT 72-73 K 2
Saint Johns River 80-81 c 1-2
Saint-Joseph 63 A 4
Saint Joseph, LA 78-79 D 5
Saint Joseph, MI 70-71 G 4
Saint Joseph, MO 64-65 GH 4
Saint Joseph, Lake — 56-57 ST 7
Saint Joseph Bay 78-79 G 6
Saint-Joseph-d'Alma = Alma 56-57 W 8
Saint Joseph Island [CDN] 70-71 HJ 2
Saint Joseph Island [USA] 76-77 F 8-9
Saint Joseph Point 78-79 G 6
Saint Joseph's College 84 III ab 2
Saint-Jovite 72-73 J 1
Saint-Junien 120-121 H 6
Saint Kilda 119 B 3
Saint Kilda, Melbourne- 161 II b 2
Saint-Lambert [CDN] 72-73 K 2
Saint-Lambert [F] 129 I b 3
Saint Laurent [CDN, place] 61 K 5
Saint-Laurent [CDN, river] 82 I a 1-2
Saint-Laurent, Fleuve — 56-57 W 8-9
Saint-Laurent, Golfe du — = Gulf of Saint Lawrence 56-57 Y 8
Saint-Laurent-du-Maroni 98-99 LM 2-3
Saint Lawrence [AUS] 158-159 J 4
Saint Lawrence [CDN] 63 J 4
Saint Lawrence, Cape — 63 F 4
Saint Lawrence, Gulf of — 56-57 Y 8
Saint Lawrence Island 56-57 BC 5
Saint Lawrence River 56-57 X 8
Saint-Léonard [CDN ↑ Montréal] 82 I b 1
Saint-Léonard [CDN ↗ Montréal] 72-73 KL 1
Saint-Léonard [CDN → Québec] 63 C 4
Saint-Leu-la-Forêt 129 I bc 1
Saint-Lô 120-121 G 4
Saint-Louis 164-165 A 5
Saint Louis, MI 70-71 H 4
Saint Louis, MO 64-65 H 4
Saint-Louis-de-Kent 63 D 4
Saint Louis Park, MN 70-71 D 3
Saint Louis River 70-71 D 2
Saint Lucia 64-65 O 9
Saint Lucia, Lake — = Sint Luciameer 172 F 7
Saint Lucia Bay = Sint Luciabaai 174-175 K 5
Saint Lucia Channel 88-89 Q 7
Saint Luke Island = Zădetkale Kyûn 150-151 AB 7
Saint Magnus Bay 119 EF 1
Saint-Malachie 63 A 4
Saint-Malo 120-121 FG 4
Saint-Mandé 129 I c 2
Saint-Marc [CDN] 72-73 K 1
Saint-Marc [RH] 88-89 K 5
Saint Margaret's Bay 63 DE 5
Saint Maries, ID 66-67 E 2
Saint Marks, FL 80-81 D 5
Saint Martin [island] 64-65 O 8
Saint Martin, Cape — = Kaap Sint Martin 174-175 B 7
Saint Martin, Lake — 61 JK 5
Saint Martin Bay 70-71 H 2-3
Saint Martin's [CDN] 63 D 5
Saint Martins Bay 72-73 D 1-2
Saint Martins Point = Kaap Sint Martin 174-175 B 7
Saint Mary Islands 63 G 2
Saint Mary Lake 66-67 G 1
Saint Marylebone, London- 129 II b 1
Saint Mary Peak 158-159 G 6
Saint Mary River 60 JK 5
Saint Marys, AK 58-59 F 5
Saint Marys, GA 80-81 F 5
Saint Marys, KS 70-71 BC 6
Saint Marys, MO 70-71 EF 7
Saint Marys, OH 70-71 H 5
Saint Marys, PA 72-73 G 4
Saint Marys, WV 72-73 F 5
Saint Marys [AUS] 158-159 J 8
Saint Mary's [CDN, Newfoundland] 63 K 4
Saint Mary's [CDN, Ontario] 72-73 F 3
Saint Mary's, Cape — 63 J 4
Saint Mary's Bay [CDN, Newfoundland] 63 JK 4
Saint Mary's Bay [CDN, Nova Scotia] 63 CD 5
Saint Mary's River [CDN] 63 E 5
Saint Marys River [USA] 64-65 K 2
Saint Mary's Seminary 85 III b 1
Saint Mathieu, Pointe — 120-121 E 4
Saint Matthew 132-133 I 5
Saint Matthew Island 56-57 B 5
Saint Matthew Island = Zādetkyī Kyûn 148-149 C 5
Saint Matthews, SC 80-81 F 4
Saint Matthias Group 148-149 NO 7
Saint-Maurice [F] 129 I c 2
Saint-Maurice, Rivière — 56-57 W 8
Saint Michael, AK 56-57 D 5
Saint Michael = São Miguel 204-205 E 5
Saint Michaels, AZ 74-75 J 5
Saint-Michel, Montréal- 82 I b 1
Saint-Michel-des-Saints 72-73 K 1
Saint-Nazaire 120-121 F 5
Saint-Nom-la-Bretèche 129 I b 2
Saint-Omer 120-121 HJ 3
Saintonge 120-121 G 6
Saint-Ouen 129 I c 2
Saint-Pacôme 63 AB 4
Saint-Pamphile 63 AB 4
Saint Pancras, London- 129 II b 1
Saint Paris, OH 70-71 HJ 5
Saint-Pascal 63 B 4
Saint Patrice, Lac — 72-73 H 1
Saint Paul, MN 64-65 H 2
Saint Paul, NE 68-69 G 5
Saint Paul, VT 80-81 E 2
Saint Paul [CDN] 56-57 O 7
Saint Paul [Saint Paul] 50-51 NO 7
Saint Paul, Cape — 168-169 F 4
Saint-Paul, Rivière — 63 H 2
Saint Paul Island 63 F 4
Saint Paul River 164-165 BC 7
Saint Pauls, NC 80-81 G 3
Saint Paul's Cathedral 129 II b 1
Saint Paul's Cray, London- 129 II c 2
Saint Peter, MN 70-71 CD 3
Saint Peter Port 119 E 7
Saint Peter's 63 F 5
Saint Petersburg, FL 64-65 K 6
Saint Petersburg = Leningrad 132-133 E 5-6
Saint-Pierre 82 I b 2
Saint-Pierre, Havre- 56-57 Y 7
Saint-Pierre, Lac — 72-73 K 1
Saint Pierre Bank 63 HJ 5-6
Saint-Pierre et Miquelon 56-57 Za 8
Saint Pierre Island 172 JK 3
Saint-Prix 129 I c 1
Saint-Quentin [CDN] 63 C 4
Saint-Quentin [F] 120-121 J 4
Saint-Raphaël 120-121 L 7
Saint-Raymond 72-73 KL 1
Saint Regis, MT 66-67 F 2
Saint-Rémi 72-73 J 1-2
Saint-Romuald 63 A 4
Saint Sebastian Bay = Sint Sebastianbaai 174-175 D 8
Saint-Sebastien, Cap — 172 J 4
Saint Shott's 63 K 4
Saint-Siméon 63 AB 4
Saint Simons Island 80-81 F 5
Saint Simons Island, GA 80-81 F 5
Saint Stephens, SC 80-81 G 4
Saint Terese, AK 58-59 U 7
Saint Thomas, ND 68-69 H 1
Saint Thomas [CDN] 72-73 F 3
Saint Thomas [West Indies] 64-65 NO 8
Saint Thomas, University of — 85 III b 2
Saint-Tite 72-73 K 1
Saint-Tropez 120-121 L 7
Saint-Ulric 63 C 3
Saint Vincent, MN 68-69 H 1
Saint Vincent [WV] 64-65 O 9
Saint Vincent = São Vicente 204-205 E 7
Saint Vincent, Gulf — 158-159 G 6-7
Saint-Vincent-de-Paul 82 I ab 1
Saint Vincent Island 78-79 G 6
Saint Vincent Passage 88-89 Q 7
Saint Walburg 61 D 4
Saint Xavier, MT 68-69 C 3
Saio = Dembī Dolo 164-165 LM 7
Sāipāl 138-139 H 3
Saipurū 104-105 E 6
Saiqi 146-147 G 8
Saira 106-107 F 4
Sairang 141 C 4
Sairme 126-127 L 6
Saishū = Cheju-do 144-145 F 6
Saitama 144-145 M 4
Saiteli = Kadinhanı 136-137 E 3
Saito 144-145 H 6
Sai Wan Ho, Victoria- 155 I b 2
Sai'wun = Say'ūn 134-135 F 7
Sai Ying Poon, Victoria- 155 I a 2
Sai Yok 150-151 B 5
Sajak Pervyj 132-133 O 8
Sajama 104-105 B 6
Sajama, Nevado de — 92-93 F 8
Sajan, Vostočnyj — 132-133 R 6-T 7
Sajan, Zapadnyj — 132-133 Q-S 7
Sajarī, Bi'r — 136-137 H 6
Sajchin 126-127 N 2
Šajgino 124-125 Q 5
Saji-dong 144-145 G 2
Sajmak 134-135 L 3
Sajmenskij kanal 124-125 G 3
Sajnšand 142-143 KL 3
Sajo 118 K 4
Sajram nuur 142-143 DE 3
Saka 171 D 3
Šākah 166-167 E 2
Sakai 142-143 Q 5
Sakaide 144-145 JK 5
Sakaiminato 144-145 J 5
Sakākah 134-135 E 4-5
Sakakawea, Lake — 64-65 F 2
Sakamachi = Arakawa 144-145 M 3
Sakami Lake 56-57 V 7
Sakania 172 E 4
Sakarya 136-137 D 2
Sakarya = Adapazarı 134-135 C 2
Sakarya nehri 134-135 C 2
Sakata 142-143 Q 4
Sakavi 136-137 J 3
Sakawa 144-145 J 6
Sakchu 144-145 E 2
Sakeng, Pulau — 154 III a 2
Saketa 148-149 J 7
Sakha Dsong 142-143 F 6
Sakhalin = ostrov Sachalin 132-133 b 7-8
Sakhalin, Gulf of — = Sachalinskij zaliv 132-133 b 7
Sakht-Sar 136-137 O 4
Saki 126-127 F 4
Sakijang Bendera, Pulau — 154 III ab 2
Sakijang Pelepah, Pulau — 154 III b 2
Sakīkdah 164-165 F 1
Sakinohama 144-145 K 6
Sakishima-guntō 142-143 NO 7
Sakisima guntō = Sakishima-guntō 142-143 NO 7
Sakkane, Erg in — 164-165 D 4
Sakoi = Sakwei 141 E 6
Sākoli 138-139 G 7
Sakon Nakhon 148-149 B 3
Sakonnet Point 72-73 L 4
Sakovlevskoje = Privolžsk 132-133 N 5
Sakraṇḍ 138-139 AB 4
Sakrivier [ZA, place] 172 CD 8
Sakrivier [ZA, river ◁ Agter Roggeveld] 174-175 D 6
Sakrivier [ZA, river ◁ De Bosbulten] 174-175 D 5
Sakti 138-139 J 6
Sakwei 141 E 6
Sakya Gonpa 138-139 LM 3
Sal [Cape Verde] 204-205 E 7
Sal [SU] 126-127 K 3
Sala 116-117 G 8
Salabangka, Kepulauan — 152-153 P 7
Salacgrīva 124-125 DE 5
Sala Consilina 122-123 F 5
Salada, Laguna — [MEX] 86-87 C 1
Salada, Laguna — [RA, Buenos Aires] 106-107 H 7
Salada, Laguna — [RA, Córdoba] 106-107 F 3
Salada, Laguna — [RA, La Pampa] 106-107 E 6
Salada, Lomas de Zamora-La — 110 III b 2
Saladas 106-107 H 2
Saladas, Lagunas — 106-107 F 2
Saladillo [RA, Buenos Aires] 111 DE 5
Saladillo [RA, San Luis] 106-107 E 4
Saladillo [RA, Santiago del Estero] 104-105 EF 11
Saladillo, Río — [RA, Córboda] 106-107 F 4
Saladillo, Río — [RA, Santiago del Estero] 106-107 EF 2
Salado 104-105 C 11
Salado, Bahía — 106-107 B 1
Salado, El — 108-109 F 7
Salado, Quebrada del — 104-105 A 10
Salado, Río — [MEX] 86-87 L 4
Salado, Río — [RA, Buenos Aires] 106-107 G 5
Salado, Río — [RA, Catamarca ◁ Río Blanco] 106-107 C 2
Salado, Río — [RA, Catamarca ◁ Río Colorado] 104-105 C 11
Salado, Río — [RA, Santa Fe] 111 D 3
Salado, Rio — [USA] 76-77 A 5
Salado, Valle del — 64-65 F 7
Salaga 164-165 D 7
Salah, In- = 'Ayn Şālih 164-165 E 3
Salāhuddīn 136-137 KL 5
Salair 132-133 PQ 7
Salairskij kr'až 132-133 PQ 7
Salajar = Pulau Kabia 148-149 H 8
Šalakuša 124-125 N 2
Salal 164-165 H 6
Salala 168-169 C 4
Şalālah 134-135 G 7
Salālah, Jabal — 173 D 7
Salamá 86-87 P 10
Salamanca, NY 72-73 G 3
Salamanca [E] 120-121 E 8
Salamanca [MEX] 86-87 K 7
Salamanca [RCH] 106-107 B 3
Salamanca, Cerro de la — 106-107 C 2
Salamanca, Pampa de — 108-109 F 5
Salamanca, Pico — 108-109 F 5
Salamat, Bahr — 164-165 H 6-7
Salāmatābād 136-137 M 5
Salamaua 148-149 N 8
Salamina [CO, Caldas] 94-95 D 5
Salamina [CO, Magdalena] 94-95 D 2
Salamis 122-123 K 7
Salamīyah 136-137 G 5
Salang = Ko Phuket 148-149 C 5
Salantai 124-125 CD 5
Salaqui 94-95 C 4
Salar de Antofalla 104-105 C 9-10
Salar de Arizaro 111 C 2
Salar de Ascotán 104-105 B 7
Salar de Atacama 111 C 2
Salar de Bella Vista 104-105 B 7

Salar de Cauchari 104-105 C 8
Salar de Chalviri 104-105 C 8
Salar de Chiguana 104-105 C 7
Salar de Coipasa 92-93 F 8
Salar de Empexa 104-105 B 7
Salar de Huasco 104-105 B 7
Salar de la Isla 104-105 B 9
Salar del Hombre Muerto 104-105 C 9
Salar de Llamara 104-105 B 7
Salar de Maricunga 104-105 B 10
Salar de Pajonales 104-105 B 9
Salar de Pedernales 104-105 B 10
Salar de Pintados 104-105 B 7
Salar de Pipanaco 104-105 C 10-11
Salar de Punta Negra 104-105 B 9
Salar de Río Grande 104-105 BC 9
Salar de Tara 104-105 C 8
Salar de Uyuni 92-93 F 9
Salar Grande 104-105 AB 7
Salar Pocitos 104-105 C 9
Salatan, Cape — = Tanjung Selatan 148-149 F 7
Salatiga 148-149 F 8
Salavat [SU] 132-133 K 7
Salavat [TR] 136-137 F 2
Salaverry 92-93 D 6
Salavina 106-107 F 2
Salawati, Pulau — 148-149 K 7
Salāya 138-139 B 6
Salayar, Pulau — 148-149 H 8
Salayar, Selat — 152-153 N 9-O 8
Sala y Gómez 156-157 M 6
Salazar, NM 76-77 A 5
Salazar [CO] 94-95 E 4
Salazar = N'Dala Tando 172 BC 3
Sālbani 138-139 L 6
Salcantay, Nevado de — 96-97 E 8
Salcedo 94-95 B 8
Salcedo = San Miguel 96-97 B 2
Salcha River 58-59 P 4
Šalčininkai 124-125 E 6
Saldaña [CO] 94-95 D 5
Saldanha [BR] 100-101 C 6
Saldanha [ZA] 172 C 8
Saldungaray 106-107 G 7
Saldus 124-125 D 5
Sale [AUS] 158-159 J 7
Sale [BUR] 141 D 5
Salé = Slā' 164-165 C 2
Salebabu, Pulau — 148-149 J 6
Salechard 132-133 M 4
Saleh, Teluk — 148-149 G 8
Şāleḥābād [IR ↖ Hamadān] 136-137 N 5
Şāleḥābād [IR ↙ Īlām] 136-137 M 6
Salekhard = Salechard 132-133 M 4
Salem, AR 78-79 D 2
Salem, FL 80-81 b 2
Salem, IL 70-71 F 6
Salem, IN 70-71 GH 6
Salem, MA 72-73 L 3
Salem, MO 70-71 E 7
Salem, NJ 72-73 J 5
Salem, OH 72-73 F 4
Salem, OR 64-65 B 2
Salem, SD 68-69 H 4
Salem, VA 80-81 F 2
Salem, WV 72-73 F 5
Salem [IND] 134-135 M 8
Salem [ZA] 174-175 G 7
Salem, Winston-, NC 64-65 KL 4
Salembu Besar, Pulau — 148-149 FG 8
Salemi 122-123 E 7
Salempur 138-139 JK 4
Sälen 116-117 E 7
Salentina 122-123 GH 5
Salerno 122-123 F 5
Salerno, Golfo di — 122-123 F 5
Saleye 168-169 E 3
Salford 119 E 5
Salgir 126-127 G 4
Salgótarján 118 J 4
Salgueiro 92-93 M 6
Salhyr = Nižnegorskij 126-127 G 4
Šali [DZ] 166-167 F 6
Šali [SU] 126-127 MN 5
Salí, Río — 104-105 D 10
Salibabu Islands = Kepulauan Talaud 148-149 J 6
Salida, CO 64-65 E 4
Şalīf, Aş- 134-135 E 7
Şāliḥīyah, Aş- [ET] 173 BC 2
Şāliḥīyah, Aş- [SYR] 136-137 J 5
Salihli 136-137 C 3
Salima 172 FG 4
Şalīmah, Wāḥāt — 164-165 K 4
Salin 141 D 5
Salina, KS 64-65 G 4
Salina, OK 76-77 G 4
Salina, UT 74-75 H 3
Salina, Isola — 122-123 F 6
Salina Cruz 64-65 G 8
Salina de Incahuasi 104-105 C 9
Salina de Jama 104-105 C 8
Salina del Bebedero 106-107 D 4
Salina del Gualicho 108-109 G 3
Salina del Pito 108-109 E 4
Salina del Rincón 104-105 C 8-9
Salina Grande 106-107 D 6
Salina Grandes 104-105 CD 8
Salina La Antigua 106-107 DE 2-3
Salina Llancanelo 106-107 C 5
Salinas, CA 64-65 B 4
Salinas [BOL] 104-105 D 7
Salinas [BR] 92-93 L 8
Salinas [EC] 92-93 C 5
Salinas [MEX] 86-87 H 8
Salinas [RCH] 104-105 B 8
Salinas, Cabo de — 120-121 J 9
Salinas, Las — 96-97 C 7
Salinas, Pampa de las — 106-107 D 3-4
Salinas, Punta de — 92-93 D 7
Salinas, Rio — 102-103 L 2
Salinas de Garci Mendoza 104-105 C 6
Salinas de Hidalgo 86-87 JK 6
Salinas de Trapalcó 108-109 F 2
Salinas Grandes [RA ↖ Córdoba] 111 C 4-D 3
Salinas Grandes [RA, Península Valdés] 108-109 GH 4
Salinas La Porteña 106-107 EF 7
Salinas Peak 76-77 A 6
Salinas River 74-75 C 4-5
Salinas Victoria 76-77 DE 9
Salin Chaung 141 D 5
Saline, LA 78-79 C 4
Saline River [USA, Arkansas] 78-79 CD 4
Saline River [USA, Kansas] 68-69 G 6
Saline Valley 74-75 E 4
Salingyi = Hsalingyi 141 D 4-5
Salinópolis 92-93 K 4-5
Sālīpur 138-139 L 7
Salisbury 119 EF 6
Salisbury, CT 72-73 K 3-4
Salisbury, MD 64-65 LM 4
Salisbury, MO 70-71 D 6
Salisbury, NC 64-65 KL 4
Salisbury = Harare 172 F 5
Salisbury, Lake — 172 FG 1
Salisbury, Mount — 58-59 O 2
Salisbury, ostrov — 132-133 HJ 1
Salisbury Island 56-57 VW 5
Salish Mountains 66-67 F 1-2
Salitre 96-97 B 2
Salitre, El — 91 III b 1
Salitre, Rio — 100-101 D 6
Salitre-cué 102-103 DE 7
Salitroso, Lago — 108-109 D 6
Saljany 126-127 O 7
Šalkar 126-127 PQ 1
Šalkar, ozero — 126-127 P 1
Şalkhad 136-137 G 6
Salkhia, Howrah- 154 II b 2
Salkum, WA 66-67 B 2
Salla 116-117 N 4
Salle, La — [CDN, Montréal] 82 I b 2
Salle, La — [CDN, Windsor] 84 II b 3
Salley, SC 80-81 F 4
Salliqueló 106-107 F 6
Sallisaw, OK 76-77 G 5
Sallyana 134-135 N 5
Salm, ostrov — 132-133 KL 2
Salmah, Jabal — 134-135 E 5
Salmān, As- 136-137 L 7
Salmanlı = Kayadibi 136-137 F 3
Salmanlı = Kaymas 136-137 D 2
Salmannsdorf, Wien- 113 I b 1
Salmān Pāk 136-137 L 6
Sālmāra, South — 138-139 N 5
Salmās 136-137 L 3
Salmi 132-133 E 5
Salmo 66-67 E 1
Salmon, ID 66-67 FG 3
Salmon Arm 60 H 4
Salmon Falls 66-67 F 4
Salmon Falls Creek 66-67 F 4
Salmon Falls Creek Lake 66-67 F 4
Salmon Fork 58-59 R 3
Salmon Gums 158-159 D 6
Salmon River [CDN, Acadie] 63 D 4
Salmon River [CDN, Anticosti I.] 63 E 3
Salmon River [USA, Alaska] 58-59 H 3
Salmon River [USA, Idaho] 64-65 CD 2
Salmon River, Middle Fork — 66-67 F 3
Salmon River, South Fork — 66-67 F 3
Salmon River Mountains 64-65 C 3-D 2
Salmon Village, AK 58-59 QR 3
Salo 116-117 K 7
Saloá 100-101 F 5
Salobel'ak 124-125 R 5
Salomé 100-101 F 5
Salon 138-139 H 4
Salonga 172 D 2
Salonga Nord, Parc national de la — 172 D 2
Salonga Sud, Parc national de la — 172 D 2
Salonika = Thessaloníkē 122-123 K 5
Salonika, Gulf of — = Thermaïkòs Kólpos 122-123 K 5-6
Salonta 122-123 JK 2
Salor 120-121 D 9
Salor = Pulau Sedanau 150-151 F 11
Saloum, Îles — 168-169 A 2
Saloum, Vallée du — 168-169 B 2
Salpausselkä 116-117 L-O 7
Salsacate 111 CD 4
Sal'sk 126-127 K 3
Šal'skij 124-125 KL 3
Salso 122-123 E 7
Salsomaggiore Terme 122-123 C 3
Salt, As- 136-137 F 6
Salta [RA, administrative unit] 104-105 C 9-E 8
Salta [RA, place] 111 CD 2
Salta Ginete, Serra do — 102-103 K 3
Salt Basin 76-77 B 7
Salt Chaukī 138-139 B 5
Saltcoats 61 GH 5
Salt Creek 68-69 C 4
Salten 116-117 F 4-G 3
Saltfjord 116-117 EF 4
Salt Flat 76-77 B 7
Salt Flat, TX 64-65 EF 5
Salt Fork Brazos River 76-77 D 6
Salt Fork Red River 76-77 E 5
Saltillo 64-65 FG 6
Salt Lake, NM 74-75 J 5
Salt Lake City, UT 64-65 D 3
Salt Lakes 158-159 CD 5
Salt Lick, KY 72-73 E 5
Salt Marsh = Lake MacLeod 158-159 B 4
Salto [BR] 102-103 J 5
Salto [RA] 111 DE 4
Salto [ROU, administrative unit] 106-107 J 3
Salto [ROU, place] 111 E 4
Salto, El — 64-65 E 7
Salto Ariranha 102-103 G 6
Salto da Divisa 92-93 LM 8
Salto das Estrelas 104-105 G 4
Salto das Sete Quedas [BR, Paraná] 102-103 E 6
Salto das Sete Quedas [BR, Rio Teles Pires] 92-93 H 6
Salto de Angostura I 92-93 E 4
Salto de Angostura II 92-93 E 4
Salto del Angel 92-93 G 3
Salto de las Rosas 106-107 CD 5
Salto del Erito 94-95 K 4
Salto de Pira 88-89 D 8
Salto do Aparado 102-103 G 6
Salto do Ubá 111 F 2
Salto Grande [BR] 102-103 H 5
Salto Grande [CO] 94-95 E 8
Salto Grande, Embalse — 111 E 4
Salto Grande del Uruguay 111 F 3
Saltoluokta 116-117 H 4
Salto Mapiripan 92-93 E 4
Salto Mauá 102-103 G 6
Salton, CA 74-75 F 6
Saltón, El — 111 B 7
Salton Sea 64-65 CD 5
Salto Osório 111 F 3
Salto Pocão 98-99 L 5
Sāltora 138-139 L 6
Salto Santiago 102-103 F 6
Salto Von Martius 92-93 J 7
Salt Pan Creek 161 I a 2
Salt River [USA, Arizona] 64-65 D 5
Salt River [USA, Kentucky] 70-71 H 6-7
Salt River [USA, Missouri] 70-71 E 6
Salt River = Soutrivier [ZA ◁ Atlantic Ocean] 174-175 B 6
Salt River = Soutrivier [ZA ◁ Grootrivier] 174-175 E 7
Salt River Indian Reservation 74-75 H 6
Saltspring Island 66-67 B 1
Saltville, VA 80-81 F 2
Salt Water Lake 154 II b 2
Saltykovka 124-125 P 7
Saluda, SC 80-81 EF 3
Saluen 142-143 H 6
Salūm, As- 164-165 K 2
Salūmbar 138-139 DE 5
Sālūr 140 F 1
Sālūru = Sālūr 140 F 1
Salus, AR 78-79 C 3
Salut, Îles du — 98-99 MN 2
Saluzzo 122-123 B 3
Salvación, Bahía — 108-109 B 8
Salvador 92-93 M 7
Salvador, El — [ES] 64-65 J 9
Salvador, El — [RCH] 104-105 B 10
Salvador, Lake — 78-79 D 6
Salvan = Salon 138-139 H 4
Salvatierra [MEX] 86-87 K 7
Salvation Army College 85 II b 2
Salvus 60 C 2
Salwā Baḥrī 173 C 5
Salween = Thanlwin Myit 148-149 C 2-3
Salyānā = Sallyana 134-135 N 5
Salyersville, KY 72-73 E 6
Salzach 118 F 4-5
Salzbrunn 172 C 6
Salzburg [A, administrative unit] 118 F 5
Salzburg [A, place] 118 F 5
Salzgitter 118 E 2-3
Salzwedel 118 E 2
Sama, Río — 96-97 F 10
Samacá 94-95 E 5
Sama de Langreo 120-121 E 7
Samae San, Ko — 150-151 C 6
Samaesan, Ko — = Ko Samae San 150-151 C 6
Sāmāguri 141 C 2
Samāh, Bi'r — 136-137 L 8
Samaipata 104-105 DE 6
Sāmalakōṭṭa = Sāmalkot 140 F 2
Samalayuca 76-77 A 7
Samales Group 152-153 O 3
Samalga Island 58-59 m 4
Sāmalkot 140 F 2
Samālūṭ 173 B 3
Samāna 138-139 F 2
Samaná, Bahía de — 64-65 N 8
Samaná, Cabo — 88-89 M 5
Samana Cay 88-89 K 3
Samānaḷakanda 134-135 N 9
Samanco, Bahía de — 96-97 B 6
Samandağ 136-137 F 4
Samán de Apure, El — 94-95 G 4
Samandéni 168-169 D 3
Samangān 134-135 K 3
Samani 142-143 R 3
Samaqua, Rivière — 62 P 1-2
Samar 148-149 J 4
Samara [SU, Rossijskaja SFSR] 132-133 J 7
Samara [SU, Ukrainskaja SSR] 126-127 G 2
Samara = Kujbyšev 132-133 HJ 7
Samarai 148-149 gh 7
Samarga 132-133 ab 8
Samariapo 94-95 H 5
Samarinda 148-149 G 7
Samarkand 134-135 K 3
Samarkand = Temirtau 132-133 N 7
Samaro 138-139 B 5
Sāmarrā' 134-135 E 4
Samāstipur 138-139 K 5
Samāwah, As- 134-135 EF 4
Sambaíba 100-101 B 4
Sambala 172 D 3
Sambaliung 148-149 G 6
Sambalpore = Sambalpur 134-135 N 6
Sambalpur [IND, Madhya Pradesh] 138-139 H 7
Sambalpur [IND, Orissa] 134-135 N 6
Sambar, Tanjung — 152-153 HJ 7
Sambas 148-149 E 6
Sambas, Sungai — 152-153 H 5
Sambava 172 K 4
Sambhal 134-135 M 5
Sāmbhar 138-139 E 4
Sāmbhar Salt Lake 138-139 E 4
Sambia 172 E 5-F 4
Sambit, Pulau — 152-153 N 5
Sambito, Rio — 100-101 CD 4
Sambo 168-169 E 3
Samboja 148-149 G 7
Sambongi = Towada 144-145 N 2
Sambor [K] 148-149 E 4
Sambor [SU] 126-127 A 2
Samborombón, Bahía — 111 E 5
Samborombón, Río — 106-107 J 5
Samborondón 96-97 AB 2
Sambre 120-121 K 3
Sambro Bank 63 E 6
Šamchal 126-127 N 5
Samch'ŏk 142-143 OP 4
Samch'ŏnp'o 144-145 FG 5
Šamchor 126-127 MN 6
Sam Creek, AK 58-59 Q 4
Samdŭng 144-145 F 3
Same [EAT] 172 G 2
Samet, Ko — 150-151 C 6
Samfya 171 B 5
Samḥah 134-135 G 8
Sam Houston Park 85 III b 1
Sami 138-139 C 3
Sami = Hsamī 141 C 5
Samia [RN] 168-169 H 2
Samia [WAN] 168-169 F 3
Samīm, Umm as- 134-135 H 6
Samiria, Río — 96-97 D 4
Sam Ka Tsun 155 I b 2
Samkos, Phnom — 150-151 D 6
Sammanturai = Sammantureyi 140 EF 7
Sammantureyi 140 EF 7
Sāmmār 166-167 E 2
Samnagjin 144-145 G 5
Sam Neua 148-149 D 2
Sam Ngam 150-151 BC 4
Sam Ngao 150-151 B 4
Samoa 148-149 c 1
Samoa, CA 66-67 A 5
Samoa Islands 148-149 c 1
Samoded 124-125 N 2
Samôn Chaung 141 DE 5
Samora = Zamora de Hidalgo 64-65 F 7-8
Sámos [GR, island] 122-123 M 7
Sámos [GR, place] 122-123 M 7
Samosir, Pulau — 148-149 C 6
Samothrákē 122-123 L 5
Šamovo 124-125 H 6
S'amozero 124-125 J 3
Sampacho 111 CD 4
Sampaga 152-153 N 7
Sampang 148-149 F 8
Samper de Calanda 120-121 G 8
Sampgāňv = Sampgaon 140 B 3
Sampgaon 140 B 3
Sampit 148-149 F 7
Sampit, Sungai — 152-153 K 7
Sampit, Teluk — 148-149 F 7
Sampués 94-95 D 3
Sampur 124-125 NO 7
Samrah 136-137 J 4
Samrāla 138-139 EF 2
Samran, Huai — 150-151 E 5
Sam Rayburn Lake 76-77 G 7
Samrong 148-149 D 4
Samshui = Sanshui 146-147 D 10
Samsø 116-117 D 10
Samson, AL 78-79 FG 5
Sâm So'n [VN] 150-151 EF 3
Samstipur = Samāstipur 138-139 K 5
Samsu 144-145 G 2
Samsun 134-135 D 2
Sam Teu 150-151 E 2-3
Samtredia 126-127 L 5
Samuel, Cachoeira do — 98-99 G 9
Samuel, Mount — 158-159 F 3
Samuhú 106-107 G 1
Samui, Chong — 150-151 BC 8
Samui, Ko — 148-149 D 5
Samundarī 138-139 D 2
Samur 126-127 O 6
Samurskij chrebet 126-127 N 6
Samutlu 136-137 E 3
Samut Prakan 148-149 D 4
Samut Sakhon 150-151 BC 6
Samut Songkhram 150-151 C 6
Samyä La 138-139 K 2
Š'amža 124-125 N 3
San [PL] 118 L 3
San [RMM] 164-165 CD 6
San, Sé — 150-151 F 6
Sanā [ADN] 134-135 FG 7
Saña [PE] 96-97 B 5
Şan'ā' [Y] 134-135 EF 7
Sana [YU] 122-123 G 3
Sanaag 164-165 b 2
Sānabād 136-137 N 4
Şanabū 173 B 4
Sanad, As- 166-167 L 2
SANAE 53 b 36-1
Şanāfir, Jazīrat — 173 D 4
Sanaga 164-165 G 8
San Agustín [BOL] 104-105 C 7
San Agustín [CO] 94-95 C 7
San Agustín [RA, Buenos Aires] 111 E 5
San Agustín [RA, Córdoba] 106-107 E 3
San Agustin, Arroyo — 104-105 CD 3
San Agustin, Cape — 148-149 J 5
San Agustín de Valle Fértil 106-107 D 3
Sanak Island 58-59 b 2
Sanām, As- 134-135 G 6
Sanām, Jabal — 136-137 M 7
San Ambrosio 199 B 6
Sanam Chai 150-151 C 6
Sanana = Pulau Sulabesi 148-149 J 7
Sānand 138-139 D 6
Sanandaj 134-135 F 3
Sanandita 104-105 E 7
Sanando 168-169 D 2
San Andreas, CA 74-75 C 3
San Andres [BOL] 104-105 D 4
San Andrés [CO, island] 64-65 KL 9
San Andrés [CO, place] 94-95 E 4
San Andrés, Punta — 106-107 J 7
San Andrés, Quebrado — 106-107 BC 1
San Andrés Atenco 91 I b 1
San Andrés de Giles 106-107 H 5
San Andres Mountains 64-65 E 5
San Andrés Tetepilco, Ixtacalco- 91 I c 2
San Andrés Totoltepec 91 I b 3
San Andres Tuxtla 64-65 GH 8
San Andrés y Providencia 88-89 F 8-9
Sananduva 106-107 M 1
San Angel 92-93 E 2-3
San Angelo, TX 64-65 FG 5
Sanangyi 146-147 BC 8
Sanankoroba 168-169 CD 2
San Anselmo, CA 74-75 B 4
San Anton 96-97 F 9
San Antonio, NM 76-77 A 6
San Antonio, TX 64-65 G 6
San Antônio [BOL] 104-105 C 3
San Antonio [CO, Guajira] 94-95 E 2
San Antonio [CO, Tolima] 94-95 D 6
San Antonio [CO, Valle del Cauca] 94-95 C 6
San Antonio [PE] 96-97 EF 4
San Antonio [PY] 102-103 D 5
San Antonio [RA, Catamarca] 106-107 E 2
San Antonio [RA, Corrientes] 106-107 J 2
San Antonio [RA, Jujuy] 104-105 D 9
San Antonio [RA, La Rioja] 106-107 D 3
San Antonio [RA, San Luis] 106-107 D 4
San Antonio [RCH] 111 B 4
San Antonio [ROU] 106-107 J 3
San Antonio [YV, Amazonas] 94-95 H 6
San Antonio [YV, Barinas] 94-95 G 3
San Antonio [YV, Monagas] 94-95 K 2-3
San Antonio, Cabo — [C] 64-65 K 7
San Antonio, Cabo — [RA] 106-107 J 6
San Antonio, Sierra de — 86-87 E 2-3
San Antonio Bay 76-77 F 8
San Antonio de Areco 106-107 H 5
San Antonio de Caparo 92-93 E 3
San Antonio de Esmoraca 104-105 C 7-8
San Antonio de Galipán 91 II b 1
San Antonio de Lípez 104-105 C 7
San Antonio de Litin 106-107 F 4
San Antonio de los Cobres 111 C 2
San Antonio de Padua, Merlo- 110 III a 2
San Antonio de Táchira 94-95 E 4
San Antonio de Tamanaco 94-95 HJ 3
San Antonio Mountain 76-77 B 7
San Antonio Oeste 111 CD 6
San Antonio Peak 74-75 E 5
San Antonio River 76-77 F 8
San Antonio Zomeyucan 91 I b 2
San Ardo, CA 74-75 C 4
Sanare 94-95 G 3
Sanatorium, TX 76-77 D 7
San Augustine, TX 76-77 GH 7
Sanāvād = Sanāwad 138-139 EF 6
Sanavirones 106-107 FG 2
Sanāw 134-135 G 7
Sanāwad 138-139 EF 6
Sanāwān 138-139 C 2
Sanbalpur = Sambalpur 134-135 N 6
San Bartolo [PE, Amazonas] 96-97 BC 4
San Bartolo [PE, Lima] 96-97 C 8
San Bartolo Ameyalco 91 I b 3
San Bartolomé, Cabo — 108-109 G 10
San Basilio 106-107 EF 4
San Basilio, Roma- 113 II b c 1
San Benedetto del Tronto 122-123 EF 4
San Benedicto, Isla — 64-65 DE 8
San Benedito 94-95 E 4
San Benito, TX 64-65 G 6
San Benito, Isla — 86-87 BC 3
San Benito Abad 94-95 D 3
San Benito Mountain 74-75 C 4
San Bernardino 91 II a 3
San Bernardino, CA 64-65 CD 5
San Bernardino, Caracas- 91 II b 1
San Bernardino Mountains 74-75 E 5
San Bernardo [CO] 94-95 CD 3
San Bernardo [RA, Buenos Aires] 106-107 G 6
San Bernardo [RA, Chaco] 104-105 F 10
San Bernardo [RCH] 111 BC 4
San Bernardo, Islas de — 94-95 CD 3
San Bernardo, Punta de — 94-95 CD 3
San Bernardo, Sierra de — 108-109 E 5
San Blas [MEX] 86-87 F 4
San Blas [RA] 106-107 D 2
San Blas, Archipiélago de — 88-89 GH 10
San Blas, Bahía de — 86-87 H 7
San Blas, Cape — 64-65 J 6
San Blas, Cordillera de — 64-65 L 10
San Blas, Punta — 64-65 L 10
San Borja 92-93 F 7
San Borja, Sierra de — 86-87 D 3
Sanborn, MN 70-71 C 3
Sanborn, ND 68-69 G 2
San Bruno Mountain 83 I b 2
San Buenaventura [BOL] 104-105 BC 4
San Buenaventura [MEX] 86-87 JK 4
San Buenaventura = Ventura, CA 74-75 D 5
San Buenaventura, Cordillera de — 104-105 BC 10
San Camilo 104-105 F 9
Sancang 146-147 H 5
San Carlos, AZ 74-75 H 6
San Carlos [CO, Antioquia Cord. Central] 94-95 D 4
San Carlos [CO, Antioquia R. Nechí] 94-95 D 4
San Carlos [CO, Córdoba] 94-95 D 3
San Carlos [MEX, Baja California Sur] 86-87 DE 5
San Carlos [MEX, Tamaulipas] 86-87 L 5
San Carlos [NIC] 88-89 D 9
San Carlos [PY] 102-103 D 5
San Carlos [RA, Córdoba] 106-107 E 3
San Carlos [RA, Corrientes] 106-107 JK 1
San Carlos [RA, Mendoza] 106-107 C 4
San Carlos [RA, Salta] 104-105 CD 9
San Carlos [RCH] 111 B 5
San Carlos [ROU] 106-107 K 5
San Carlos [RP, Luzón] 148-149 GH 3
San Carlos [RP, Negros] 148-149 H 4
San Carlos [YV, Cojedes] 92-93 F 3
San Carlos [YV, Zulia] 94-95 F 2
San Carlos, Bahía — 86-87 D 3-4
San Carlos, Estrecho de — = Falkland Sound 111 DE 8
San Carlos, Mesa de — 86-87 C 3
San Carlos, Punta — 86-87 C 3
San Carlos, Río — 102-103 C 5
San Carlos Bay 80-81 bc 3
San Carlos Centro 106-107 G 3
San Carlos de Bariloche 111 B 6
San Carlos de Bolívar 111 D 5
San Carlos del Meta 94-95 H 4
San Carlos de Puno 92-93 EF 8
San Carlos de Río Negro 92-93 F 4
San Carlos de Zulia 92-93 E 3
San Carlos Indian Reservation 74-75 HJ 6
San Carlos Lake 74-75 H 6
San Cayetano 106-107 H 7
San-ch'a = Sani 146-147 H 9
Sānchi 138-139 F 6
San-chiang = Sanjiang 146-147 B 9
Sānchor 138-139 C 5
Sanchore = Sānchor 138-139 C 5
San Clemente, CA 74-75 E 6
San Clemente [RCH] 106-107 AB 5
San Clemente del Tuyú 106-107 JK 6
San Clemente Island 64-65 BC 5
Sancos 96-97 E 8
San Cosme [PY] 102-103 D 7
San Cosme [RA] 106-107 H 1
San Cristóbal [BOL, Potosí] 104-105 C 7
San Cristóbal [BOL, Santa Cruz] 104-105 EF 3
San Cristóbal [CO, Amazonas] 92-93 E 5
San Cristóbal [CO, Bogotá] 91 III c 2
San Cristóbal [E] 113 III b 2
San Cristóbal [PA] 88-89 F 10
San Cristóbal [RA] 111 D 4
San Cristóbal [Solomon Is.] 148-149 k 7
San Cristóbal [YV] 92-93 E 3
San Cristóbal, Isla — 92-93 B 5
San Cristóbal, Río — 91 III b 3
San Cristóbal de las Casas 64-65 H 8
San Cristobal Wash 74-75 G 6
San Cristoval = San Cristóbal 148-149 k 7
Sancti Spíritu 106-107 F 5
Sancti-Spíritus [C] 64-65 L 7
Sančursk 124-125 Q 5
Sand 116-117 AB 8
Şandafā' 173 B 3
Sandai 148-149 F 7
Sandakan 148-149 G 5
Sandalwood Island = Sumba 148-149 G 9
Sandan 150-151 F 6
Sandane 116-117 AB 7
Sandanski 122-123 K 5
Sand Arroyo 68-69 E 7
Sanday 119 EF 2
Sandberg [ZA] 174-175 C 7
Sandbult 174-175 G 2
Sandefjord 116-117 D 8
Sanders, AZ 74-75 J 5
Sanderson, TX 76-77 C 7
Sanderstead, London- 129 II b 2
Sandersville, GA 80-81 E 4
Sandfish Bay = Sandvisbaai 174-175 A 2
Sandfontein [Namibia → Gobabis] 172 CD 6
Sandfontein [Namibia ↓ Karasburg] 174-175 C 5
Sandfontein [ZA] 174-175 H 2
Sandford Lake 70-71 E 1
Sandhornøy 116-117 EF 4
Sandia 92-93 F 7
Sandia Crest 76-77 AB 5
Sandiao Jiao = Santiao Chiao 146-147 HJ 9
Sandia Peak = Sandia Crest 76-77 AB 5
San Diego 76-77 B 8
San Diego, CA 64-65 C 5
San Diego, TX 76-77 E 9
San Diego, Cabo — 111 CD 8
San Diego Aqueduct 74-75 E 6
San Diego de Cabrutica 94-95 J 3
San Diego de la Unión 86-87 K 7
Sandıklı 136-137 CD 3
Sandıklı dağları 136-137 D 3
Sandīlā 138-139 H 4
Sanding, Pulau — 152-153 D 7
Sandīp [BD, island] 141 B 4
Sandīp [BD, place] 141 B 4
Sandīp, Ābnāi — 141 B 4
Sand Island 70-71 E 2
Sand Islands 58-59 DE 5
Sandja, Îles — 170 I b 1
Sand Key 80-81 b 3
Sand Lake [CDN, lake] 62 B 2
Sand Lake [CDN, place] 70-71 H 2
Sand Mountains 64-65 J 5
Sandnes 116-117 A 8
Sandoa 172 D 3
Sandomierz 118 K 3
Sandoná 94-95 C 7
San Donà di Piave 122-123 E 3
Sandouping 146-147 C 6
Sandover River 158-159 FG 4
Sandovo 124-125 L 4
Sandoway = Thandwe 148-149 B 3
Sand Point, AK 58-59 c 2
Sandpoint, ID 66-67 E 1
Sandras dağı 136-137 C 4
Sandringham 158-159 G 4
Sandringham, Johannesburg- 170 V b 1
Sand River 61 C 3
Sandrivier [ZA ◁ Krokodilrivier] 174-175 G 3
Sandrivier [ZA ◁ Limpopo] 174-175 H 2
Sandrivier [ZA ◁ Vetrivier] 174-175 G 5
Sandspit 60 B 3
Sand Springs, MT 68-69 C 2
Sand Springs, OK 76-77 F 4
Sandspruit [ZA ↑ Johannesburg] 170 V b 1
Sandspruit [ZA ↑ Welkom] 174-175 G 4
Sandstone 158-159 C 5
Sandstone, MN 70-71 D 2
Sand Tank Mountains 74-75 G 6
Sandton 170 V b 1
Sandu 146-147 E 7
Sandu Ao 146-147 GH 8
Sandūr [IND] 140 C 3
Sandur [IS] 116-117 ab 2
Sandūru = Sandūr 140 C 3
Sandusky, MI 72-73 E 3
Sandusky, OH 72-73 E 4
Sandusky Bay 72-73 E 4
Sandveld [Namibia] 172 CD 6
Sandveld [ZA] 174-175 C 6-7
Sandverhaar 174-175 B 4
Sandviken 116-117 G 7
Sandvisbaai 174-175 A 2
Sandwich, IL 70-71 F 5
Sandwich Bay = Sandvisbaai 174-175 A 2
Sandwip = Sandīp 141 B 4
Sandwip Channel = Ābnāi Sandīp 141 B 4
Sandwip Island = Sandīp 141 B 4
Sandwshin = Hsandaushin 141 C 6
Sandy, NV 74-75 F 5
Sandy Bay 61 G 3
Sandybeach Lake 62 CD 3
Sandy Cape [AUS, Queensland] 158-159 K 4
Sandy Cape [AUS, Tasmania] 160 ab 2
Sandy City, UT 64-65 D 3
Sandy Creek [USA, Georgia] 85 II a 2
Sandy Creek [USA, Wyoming] 66-67 J 4-5
Sandy Desert = Ar-Rub' al-Hālī 134-135 F 7-G 6

Sandy Hills 64-65 GH 5
Sandy Hook 72-73 K 4
Sandy Hook, KY 72-73 E 5-6
Sandy Key 80-81 c 4
Sandy Lake [CDN, lake Newfoundland] 63 H 3
Sandy Lake [CDN, lake Ontario] 56-57 S 7
Sandy Lake [CDN, place Alberta] 60 L 2
Sandy Lake [CDN, place Ontario] 62 C 1
Sandy Lake [CDN, place Saskatchewan] 61 E 2
Sandy Narrows 61 G 3
Sandy Ridge 80-81 E 2
Sandy River 66-67 BC 3
Sandy Run 84 III c 1
Sane, Nam — 150-151 D 3
San Eduardo 106-107 F 4
San Emilio 106-107 G 5
San Enrique 106-107 G 5
San Estanislao 111 E 2
San Esteban, Golfo — 108-109 B 6
San Esteban de Gormaz 120-121 F 8
San Fabián de Alico 106-107 B 6
San Felipe, NM 76-77 A 5
San Felipe [CO] 92-93 F 4
San Felipe [MEX, Baja California Norte] 86-87 C 2
San Felipe [MEX, Guanajuato] 86-87 K 7
San Felipe [PE] 96-97 B 4
San Felipe [RCH] 111 B 4
San Felipe [YV] 92-93 F 2
San Felipe, Bahía — 108-109 DE 9
San Felipe de Jesús, Ciudad de México- 91 I c 2
San Felipe de Puerto Plata = Puerto Plata 64-65 M 8
San Felipe Terremotos, Ixtapalapa- 91 I c 2
San Feliu de Guixols 120-121 J 8
San Félix [RCH] 199 A 6
San Félix [YV] 94-95 E 3
San Fermín, Madrid- 113 III ab 2
San Fernando, CA 74-75 D 5
San Fernando [BOL] 104-105 G 5
San Fernando [E] 120-121 D 10
San Fernando [MEX] 86-87 LM 5
San Fernando [RA] 111 E 4
San Fernando [RCH] 111 B 4
San Fernando [RP ↖ Baguio] 148-149 GH 3
San Fernando [RP ↖ Manila] 148-149 H 3
San Fernando [TT] 64-65 L 9
San Fernando [YV] 92-93 F 3
San Fernando, Bogotá- 91 III c 2
San Fernando, Río — [BOL] 104-105 G 5
San Fernando, Río — [MEX] 86-87 LM 5
San Fernando de Atabapo 92-93 F 4
San Fernando del Valle de Catamarca 111 C 3
San Fernando-Victoria 110 III b 1
Sånfjället 116-117 E 6
Sanford 61 K 6
Sanford, FL 64-65 K 6
Sanford, ME 72-73 L 3
Sanford, NC 80-81 G 3
Sanford, Mount — 58-59 Q 5
San Francisco, CA 64-65 AB 4
San Francisco [BOL] 104-105 D 4
San Francisco [CO] 94-95 D 5
San Francisco [ES] 88-89 BC 8
San Francisco [MEX, Coahuila] 76-77 C 9
San Francisco [MEX, Sonora] 86-87 D 2
San Francisco [PE] 96-97 B 4
San Francisco [RA] 111 D 4
San Francisco [YV] 94-95 EF 2
San Francisco, Arroyo — 110 III bc 2
San Francisco, Paso — 104-105 B 10
San Francisco, Presedio of — 83 I b 2
San Francisco, Río — 104-105 D 8
San Francisco, University of — 83 I b 2
San Francisco Bay 74-75 B 4
San Francisco-Bayview, CA 83 I b 2
San Francisco Chimalpa 91 I a 2
San Francisco-Chinatown, CA 83 I b 2
San Francisco Culhuacán, Coyoacán- 91 I c 3
San Francisco de Bellocq 106-107 GH 7
San Francisco de Conchos 76-77 B 9
San Francisco de la Caleta 64-65 bc 3
San Francisco de Laishi 102-103 C 7
San Francisco del Chañar 106-107 EF 2
San Francisco del Monte de Oro 106-107 D 4
San Francisco del Oro 64-65 E 6
San Francisco del Parapetí 92-93 G 8-9
San Francisco del Rincón 86-87 JK 7
San Francisco de Macorís 64-65 MN 8
San Francisco de Naya 94-95 C 6
San Francisco de Paula, Bahía — = Byron Sound 108-109 J 8
San Francisco de Paula, Cabo — 108-109 F 7
San Francisco de Tiznados 94-95 GH 3
San Francisco-Ingleside, CA 83 I b 2
San Francisco-Marina North Beach, CA 83 I b 2
San Francisco Maritime State Historic Park 83 I b 2
San Francisco-Mission, CA 83 I b 2
San Francisco-Noe Valley, CA 83 I b 2
San Francisco-Oakland Bay Bridge 83 I bc 2
San Francisco-Outer Mission, CA 83 I b 2
San Francisco Peaks 74-75 GH 5
San Francisco Plateau 64-65 D 4-E 5
San Francisco-Potrero, CA 83 I b 2
San Francisco-Richmond, CA 83 I ab 2
San Francisco River 74-75 J 6
San Francisco Solano, Punta — 92-93 D 3
San Francisco Solano, Quilmes- 110 III c 2
San Francisco State University 83 I ab 2
San Francisco-Stonestown, CA 83 I b 2
San Francisco-Sunset, CA 83 I b 2
San Francisco Tlaltenco 91 I cd 3
San Fransisco-Parkside, CA 83 I b 2
Sangā 148-149 C 2
Sanga = Sangha 172 C 1-2
San Gabriel, CA 83 III d 1
San Gabriel [EC] 92-93 D 4
San Gabriel [RA] 106-107 J 2
San Gabriel Mountains 74-75 DE 5
Sangagchhö Ling 142-143 G 6
Sangaly 124-125 O 3
Sangam 140 D 3
Sangameshwar 140 A 2
Sangamner 138-139 E 8
Sangamon River 70-71 EF 5
Sangan [PAK] 138-139 A 3
Sangan [RI] 152-153 K 4
Sangar 132-133 Y 5
Saṅgareḍḍigūḍam = Zangareḍḍigūḍem 140 E 2
Sangareddipet 140 CD 2
Sangaredi 168-169 B 3
Sangarh Nāla 138-139 C 2
Sangârios = Sakarya nehri 134-135 C 2
Sangasăr 136-137 L 4
Sangay 92-93 D 5
Sangboy Islands 152-153 O 2
Sangchih = Sangzhi 146-147 C 7
Sāṅgē = Sanguem 140 B 3
Sangeang, Pulau — 148-149 GH 8
Sangenjaya, Tōkyō- 155 III b 2
Sanger, CA 74-75 D 4
Sanger, TX 76-77 F 6
San Germán [Puerto Rico] 88-89 N 5-6
San Germán [RA] 106-107 F 7
Sanggabugdog 138-139 MN 3
Sanggan He 146-147 E 1
Sanggau 148-149 F 6
Sanggou Wan 146-147 J 3
Sangha 172 C 1-2
Sangihe, Kepulauan — 148-149 J 6
Sangihe, Pulau — 148-149 J 6
San Gil 94-95 E 4
Sang-i Māsha 134-135 K 4
San Giovanni in Laterano 113 II b 2
San Giovanni in Persiceto 122-123 D 3
Sangju 144-145 G 4
Sang-kan Ho = Sanggan He 146-147 E 1
Sangkapura 152-153 K 8
Sangkarang, Kepulauan — 152-153 N 8
Sangker, Stung — 150-151 D 6
Sangkha 150-151 DE 5
Sangkhla Buri 150-151 B 5
Sang-kou Wan = Sanggou Wan 146-147 J 3
Sangkulirang 148-149 G 6
Sangkulirang, Teluk — 148-149 G 6
Sāngli 134-135 LM 7
Sangmélima 164-165 G 8
Sangmobertheg La 138-139 K 2
Sangod 138-139 F 5
Sāngola 140 B 2
Sāṅgōlē = Sāngola 140 B 2
Sangolquí 96-97 B 2
Sangonera, Río — 120-121 G 10
San Gorgonio Mountain 74-75 E 5
Sangpo = Matsang Tsangpo 138-139 J 2-3
Sangrado, Rio — 110 I b 2
Sangre de Cristo Range 64-65 E 4
San Gregorio [PE] 96-97 D 7
San Gregorio [RA, Santa Fe] 106-107 FG 5
San Gregorio [RA, Santiago del Estero] 104-105 E 10
San Gregorio [RCH, Biobío] 106-107 B 6
San Gregorio [RCH, Magallanes y Antártica Chilena] 108-109 D 9
San Gregorio [ROU] 106-107 K 4
San Gregorio Atlapulco 91 I c 3
Sangre Grande 64-65 OP 9
Sangrūr 138-139 E 2
Sangsang 138-139 L 3
Sang Sôi, Se — 150-151 E 4
Sangsues, Lac aux — 72-73 GH 1
Sangū 141 C 5
Sangudo 60 K 3
Sangue, Cachoeira do — 98-99 L 7
Sangue, Rio do — 92-93 H 7
San Guillermo 106-107 FG 3
Sanguin River 168-169 C 4
San Gustavo 106-107 H 3
Sangutane, Rio — 174-175 K 2-3
Sangymgort 132-133 M 5
Sangzhi 146-147 C 7
Sanharó 100-101 F 5
San He [TJ, Anhui] 146-147 FG 5
Sanhe [TJ, Guangdong] 146-147 F 9
Sanhe [TJ, Hebei] 146-147 F 2
San Hilario 104-105 G 10
San Hipólito 86-87 CD 4
Sanho = Sanhe 146-147 F 2
San Hu 146-147 D 6
Sani 146-147 H 9
Sanibel Island 80-81 b 3
Sāni Bheri 138-139 J 3
San Ignacio, NM 76-77 B 5
San Ignacio [BOL ↗ La Paz] 92-93 F 7
San Ignacio [BOL ↗ Santa Cruz] 92-93 G 8
San Ignacio [MEX] 86-87 D 4
San Ignacio [PE] 96-97 B 4
San Ignacio [PY] 111 E 3
San Ignacio [RA, Buenos Aires] 106-107 HJ 6
San Ignacio [RA, Misiones] 106-107 K 1
San Ignacio, Laguna — 86-87 D 4
San Isidro [EC] 96-97 A 2
San Isidro [RA] 111 E 4
San Isidro, Catedral de — 113 III a 2
San Isidro-Acassuso 110 III b 1
San Isidro-Beccar 110 III b 1
San Isidro-Boulogne 110 III b 1
San Isidro-Juan Anchorena 110 III b 1
San Isidro-Martínez 110 III b 1
San Isidro-Villa Adelina 110 III b 1
Sanitatas 172 B 5
Sanīyah, Hawr as- 136-137 M 7
San Jacinto, CA 74-75 E 6
San Jacinto [CO, Bolívar] 94-95 D 3
San Jacinto [CO, Magdalena] 94-95 D 3
San Jacinto, Serranía de — 94-95 D 3
San Jacinto Mountains 74-75 E 6
San Jacinto River 85 III c 1
San Javier [BOL, Beni] 104-105 D 4
San Javier [BOL, Santa Cruz] 92-93 G 8
San Javier [RA, Córdoba] 106-107 E 4
San Javier [RA, Misiones] 111 EF 3
San Javier [RA, Santa Fe] 106-107 GH 3
San Javier [RCH] 106-107 AB 5
San Javier [ROU] 106-107 HJ 4
San Javier, Río — 106-107 GH 3
San Jerónimo 106-107 D 4
San Jerónimo, Isla — 106-107 H 2
San Jerónimo, Serranía de — 92-93 D 3
San Jerónimo Lidice, Villa Obregón- 91 I b 3
Sanjiao 146-147 C 3
Sanjō 144-145 M 4
San Joaquín [BOL] 92-93 FG 7
San Joaquín [CO] 94-95 E 4
San Joaquín [PY, Boquerón] 102-103 B 4
San Joaquín [PY, Caaguazú] 102-103 D 6
San Joaquín [RA] 106-107 F 5
San Joaquín [YV] 94-95 J 3
San Joaquín, Río — 104-105 E 3
San Joaquin River 64-65 BC 4
San Joaquin Valley 64-65 BC 4
San Jon, NM 76-77 C 5
San Jorge [NIC] 88-89 CD 9
San Jorge [RA, Buenos Aires] 106-107 G 6
San Jorge [RA, Santa Fe] 106-107 FG 3
San Jorge [ROU] 106-107 JK 4
San Jorge, Bahía de — 86-87 D 2
San Jorge, Golfo — 111 CD 7
San Jorge, Golfo de — 120-121 H 8
San Jorge, Río — 94-95 D 3
San Jose, CA 64-65 B 4
San José [BOL] 104-105 F 6
San José [CO, Guainía] 94-95 G 6
San José [CO, Meta] 94-95 E 6
San José [CR] 64-65 K 9-10
San José [GCA] 64-65 H 9
San José [PA] 64-65 b 3
San José [PY, Caaguazú] 102-103 D 6
San José [PY, Itapúa] 102-103 E 7
San José [RA, Catamarca] 106-107 E 2
San José [RA, Mendoza ↗ Mendoza] 106-107 C 4
San José [RA, Mendoza ↙ Mendoza] 106-107 C 4
San José [RA, Misiones] 106-107 K 1
San José [RA, Santiago del Estero] 106-107 F 2
San José [ROU, administrative unit] 106-107 J 5
San José [ROU, place] 111 E 4
San José [RP] 148-149 H 3
San José [YV, Distrito Federal] 91 II b 1
San José [YV, Sucre] 94-95 K 2
San José [YV, Zulia] 94-95 E 2
San José, Golfo — 108-109 G 4
San José, Isla — [MEX] 64-65 DE 6
San José, Isla — [PA] 88-89 G 10
San José, Isla — = Weddell Island 111 D 8
San José, Serranía de — 104-105 F 5-6
San José de Buenavista 148-149 H 4
San José de Chiquitos 92-93 G 8
San José de Chupiamonas 104-105 B 4
San José de Feliciano 106-107 H 3
San José de Galipán 91 II b 1
San José de Guanipa 94-95 JK 3
San José de Guaribe 94-95 HJ 3
San José de Jáchal 111 C 4
San José de la Dormida 106-107 F 3
San José de la Esquina 106-107 FG 4
San José de la Mariquina 108-109 C 2
San Jose de las Raíces 86-87 KL 5
San José de las Salinas 111 CD 4
San José del Cabo 64-65 E 7
San José del Guaviare 92-93 E 4
San José de los Molinos 96-97 D 8
San José del Palmar 94-95 CD 5
San José del Rincon 106-107 G 3
San José de Maipo 106-107 BC 4
San José de Ocuné 92-93 E 4
San Josef Bay 60 C 4
San José-mi 102-103 D 7
San Jose River 74-75 JK 5
San Juan [BOL, Potosí] 104-105 C 7
San Juan [BOL, Santa Cruz] 104-105 FG 5
San Juan [DOM] 88-89 L 5
San Juan [MEX] 76-77 D 9
San Juan [PE] 92-93 DE 8
San Juan [Puerto Rico] 64-65 N 8
San Juan [RA, administrative unit] 106-107 CD 3
San Juan [RA, place] 111 C 4
San Juan, Cabo — [Equatorial Guinea] 164-165 F 8
San Juan, Cabo — [RA] 111 D 8
San Juan, Río — [CO, Chocó] 94-95 C 5
San Juan, Río — [CO, Nariño] 94-95 B 7
San Juan, Río — [MEX] 86-87 L 5
San Juan, Río — [NIC] 64-65 K 9
San Juan, Río — [PE] 96-97 D 8
San Juan, Río — [RA] 106-107 C 3
San Juan Archipelago 66-67 B 1
San Juan Bautista [E] 120-121 H 9
San Juan Bautista [PY] 111 E 3
San Juan Bautista = Villahermosa 64-65 H 8
San Juan Bautista Ñeembucú 102-103 D 7
San Juan Bautista Tuxtepec 86-87 M 9-10
San Juan Chimalhuacan 91 I d 2
San Juan de Aragón, Bosque — 91 I c 2
San Juan de Aragón, Ciudad de México- 91 I c 2
San Juan de Aragón, Zoológico de — 91 I c 2
San Juán de Arama 94-95 E 6
San Juan de Dios 91 II b 1
San Juan de Guadalupe 86-87 J 5
San Juan de Guía, Cabo de — 92-93 DE 2
San Juan del César 94-95 E 2
San Juan del Norte 88-89 E 9
San Juan del Norte = Bluefields 64-65 K 9
San Juan del Norte, Bahía de — 64-65 K 9
San Juan del Oro 96-97 G 8
San Juan de los Cayos 94-95 GH 2
San Juan de los Lagos 86-87 J 7
San Juan de los Morros 92-93 F 3
San Juan del Piray 104-105 DE 7
San Juan del Río 86-87 KL 7
San Juan del Sur 88-89 CD 9
San Juan de Manapiare 94-95 H 5
San Juan de Salvamento 108-109 H 10
San Juanico, Isla — 86-87 G 7
San Juan Ixtayopan 91 I d 3
San Juan Mountains 64-65 E 4
San Juan Nepomuceno [CO] 94-95 D 3
San Juan Nepomuceno [PY] 102-103 E 7
San Juan Quiotepec 86-87 MN 9
San Juan River 64-65 E 4
San Juan Toltoltepec 91 I b 2
San Julián, Bahía — = Queen Charlotte Bay 108-109 J 8
San Julián, Gran Bajo de — 108-109 E 7
San Julian, Quebrada — 91 II b 1
San Justo [RA, Buenos Aires] 110 III b 2
San Justo [RA, Santa Fe] 111 D 4
San Justo, Aeródromo — 110 III b 2
San Justo, La Matanza- 110 III a 1
Sankaranāyinarkovil 140 C 6
Sankarani 168-169 C 3
Sankaridrug 140 CD 5
Sankeng 146-147 D 10
Sankh 138-139 K 6
Sankheda 138-139 D 6
Sankisen 144-145 cd 2
Sānkrāil 154 II a 2
Sankt Gallen 118 D 5
Sankt Georg, Hamburg- 130 I ab 1
Sankt Gotthard 118 D 5
Sankt Michel = Mikkeli 116-117 MN 7
Sankt Moritz 118 DE 5
Sankt Pauli, Hamburg- 130 I a 1
Sankt Pölten 118 G 4
Sankuru 172 D 2
San Lázaro 102-103 CD 5
San Lázaro, Cabo — 64-65 D 7
San Lázaro, Sierra — 86-87 EF 6
San Lázaro, Sierra de — 86-87 E 5-F 6
San Lorenzo [BOL ↙ Riberalta] 92-93 F 7
San Lorenzo [BOL ↑ Tarija] 92-93 FG 9
San Lorenzo [BOL, Beni] 104-105 D 4
San Lorenzo [CO, Nariño] 94-95 C 7
San Lorenzo [CO, Vaupés] 94-95 E 6
San Lorenzo [EC] 92-93 D 4
San Lorenzo [MEX, México] 91 I d 2
San Lorenzo [MEX, Veracruz] 86-87 N 9
San Lorenzo [PE] 96-97 C 4
San Lorenzo [PY] 102-103 D 6
San Lorenzo [RA, Corrientes] 106-107 H 2
San Lorenzo [RA, Santa Fe] 111 D 4
San Lorenzo [YV, Arauca] 94-95 F 4
San Lorenzo [YV, Falcón] 94-95 G 2
San Lorenzo [YV, Zulia] 92-93 E 3
San Lorenzo, Cabo de — 92-93 C 5
San Lorenzo, Cerro — 111 B 7
San Lorenzo, Isla — [MEX] 86-87 D 3
San Lorenzo, Isla — [PE] 92-93 D 7
San Lorenzo, Río — 86-87 G 5
San Lorenzo, Sierra de — 120-121 F 7
San Lorenzo Acopilco 91 I ab 3
San Lorenzo de Quinti 96-97 CD 8
San Lorenzo Tezonco 91 I c 3
Sanlúcar de Barrameda 120-121 D 10
San Lucas, CA 74-75 C 4
San Lucas [BOL] 104-105 D 7
San Lucas [EC] 96-97 B 3
San Lucas [MEX] 86-87 F 6
San Lucas [PE] 96-97 A 4
San Lucas, Cabo — 64-65 E 7
San Lucas, Serranía — 94-95 D 3-4
San Luis, CO 68-69 D 7
San Luis [C] 88-89 J 4
San Luis [CO, Bogotá] 91 III c 3
San Luis [CO, Tolima] 94-95 D 5
San Luis [GCA] 86-87 Q 9
San Luis [RA, administrative unit] 106-107 DE 4-5
San Luis [RA, place] 111 C 4
San Luis [RCH] 108-109 DE 9
San Luis [YV] 94-95 G 2
San Luis, Lago de — 104-105 D 3
San Luis, Sierra de — [RA] 106-107 DE 4
San Luis, Sierra de — [YV] 92-93 EF 2
San Luis de la Paz 86-87 KL 7
San Luis del Palmar 106-107 H 1
San Luis Gonzaga 86-87 C 3
San Luis Obispo, CA 64-65 B 4
San Luis Obispo Bay 74-75 C 5
San Luis Pass 76-77 G 8
San Luis Potosí 64-65 FG 7
San Luis Río Colorado 86-87 C 1
San Luis Valley 68-69 CD 7
San Manuel 106-107 H 6
San Manuel, AZ 74-75 H 6
San Marcial, NM 76-77 A 6
San Marco, Capo — 122-123 BC 6
San Marcos, TX 64-65 G 6
San Marcos [CO] 94-95 D 3
San Marcos [GCA] 86-87 OP 10
San Marcos [MEX] 86-87 L 9
San Marcos [RCH] 111 B 4
San Marcos, Isla — 86-87 DE 4
San Marcos, Sierra de — 76-77 CD 9
San Marino [RSM, place] 122-123 E 4
San Marino [RSM, state] 122-123 E 4
San Márquez 96-97 D 6
San Martín [BOL] 92-93 G 7-8
San Martín [CO] 94-95 E 6
San Martín [PE] 96-97 C 5
San Martín [RA, La Rioja] 111 C 3
San Martín [RA, Mendoza] 106-107 C 4
San Martín [RA, San Luis] 106-107 E 4
San Martín, Lago — 111 B 7
San Martín, Loma — 108-109 E 2
San Martín, Río — 92-93 G 8
San Martín de Alto Negro 106-107 DE 5
San Martín de los Andes 108-109 D 3
San Martín de Pangoa 96-97 D 7
San Mateo, CA 64-65 B 4
San Mateo [PE] 96-97 F 3
San Mateo [YV] 94-95 J 3
San Mateo Ixtatán 86-87 P 10
San Mateo Peak 64-65 E 5
San Mateo Tecoloapan 91 I b 1
San Mateo Tlaltenango 91 I b 2
San Matías 111 H 8
San Matías, Golfo — 111 D 6
Sanmaur 62 OP 3
San Mauricio 94-95 H 3
San Mayol 106-107 GH 7
Sanmen 146-147 H 7
San-mên-hsia = Sanmenxia 142-143 L 5
Sanmen Wan 146-147 HJ 7
Sanmenxia 142-143 L 5
San Miguel, AZ 74-75 H 7
San Miguel, CA 74-75 C 5
San Miguel, NM 76-77 B 6
San Miguel [BOL] 104-105 F 5
San Miguel [CO] 94-95 F 5
San Miguel [EC] 96-97 B 2
San Miguel [ES] 64-65 J 9
San Miguel [PA] 94-95 B 3
San Miguel [PE] 96-97 E 8
San Miguel [PY, Concepción] 102-103 D 5
San Miguel [PY, Misiones] 102-103 D 7
San Miguel [RA, Corrientes] 106-107 J 1
San Miguel [RA, Mendoza] 106-107 D 4
San Miguel [RA, Tucumán] 104-105 D 10
San Miguel [YV] 94-95 K 3
San Miguel, Cerro — 104-105 F 6
San Miguel, Golfo de — 88-89 G 10
San Miguel, Río — [BOL] 92-93 G 7-8
San Miguel, Río — [EC] 96-97 C 1
San Miguel, Río — [MEX, Chihuahua] 86-87 G 4
San Miguel, Río — [MEX, Sonora] 86-87 E 2
San Miguel, Sierra — 104-105 B 10
San Miguel de Allende 86-87 KL 7
San Miguel de Huachi 92-93 F 8
San Miguel del Monte 111 E 5
San Miguel de Pallaques 96-97 B 5
San Miguel de Tucumán 111 CD 3
San Miguel Island 74-75 C 5
San Miguelito [NIC] 88-89 D 9
San Miguelito [PA] 64-65 bc 3
San Miguel River 74-75 JK 3
Sanming 146-147 F 8
Sannār 164-165 L 6
San Narciso 148-149 GH 3
Sannaspos 174-175 G 5
Sannī 138-139 A 3
San Nicolás 96-97 D 9
San Nicolás, Bahía — 96-97 D 9
San Nicolás, Lago — 104-105 D 3
San Nicolás de los Arroyos 111 D 4
San Nicolas de los Garzas 86-87 KL 5
San Nicolas Island 64-65 BC 5
San Nicolás Totolapan 91 I b 3
San Nicolás Viejo 91 I ab 1
Sannikova, proliv — 132-133 ab 3
Sanniquellie 164-165 C 7
Sannohe 144-145 N 2
Sannois 129 I bc 2
Sannūr, Wādī — 173 B 3
Sañogasta 106-107 D 2
Sañogasta, Sierra de — 106-107 D 2
Sanok 118 L 4
San Onofre 94-95 D 3
San Pablito, Caracas- 91 II ab 2
San Pablo, CA 83 I bc 1
San Pablo [BOL, Potosí] 104-105 C 7
San Pablo [BOL, Santa Cruz] 104-105 E 4
San Pablo [RA] 108-109 F 10
San Pablo [RP] 148-149 H 4
San Pablo [YV] 94-95 J 3
San Pablo, Bogotá- 91 III a 2
San Pablo, Point — 83 I b 1
San Pablo, Punta — 86-87 C 4
San Pablo, Río — 104-105 E 4
San Pablo Bay 74-75 B 3
San Pablo Creek 83 I c 1
San Pablo de Balzar, Cordillera de — 96-97 AB 2
San Pablo Huitzo 86-87 M 9
San Pablo Reservoir 83 I c 1
San Pablo Ridge 83 I c 1
San Patricio 102-103 D 7
San Pedro [BOL, Chuquisaca] 104-105 D 6
San Pedro [BOL, Pando] 104-105 C 2
San Pedro [BOL, Potosí] 104-105 D 6
San Pedro [BOL, Santa Cruz ↗ Roboré] 104-105 G 5
San Pedro [BOL, Santa Cruz ↗ Santa Cruz] 92-93 G 8
San Pedro [BOL, Santa Cruz ↑ Trinidad] 92-93 G 7
San Pedro [CI] 168-169 D 4
San Pedro [EC] 96-97 B 3
San Pedro [MEX, Baja California Sur] 86-87 E 6
San Pedro [MEX, Chihuahua] 76-77 B 8
San Pedro [MEX, Durango] 76-77 AB 9
San Pedro [MEX, México] 91 I d 2
San Pedro [PE] 96-97 DE 4
San Pedro [PY, administrative unit] 102-103 D 5-6
San Pedro [PY, place] 111 E 2
San Pedro [RA, Buenos Aires] 111 E 4
San Pedro [RA, Misiones] 102-103 EF 7
San Pedro [RA, San Luis] 106-107 D 4
San Pedro [RA, Santiago del Estero] 111 C 3
San Pedro [RCH, O'Higgins] 106-107 B 4
San Pedro [RCH, Valparaíso] 106-107 B 4
San Pedro [YV, Anzoátegui] 94-95 K 3
San Pedro [YV, Bolívar] 94-95 K 4
San Pedro [YV, Caracas] 91 II c 1
San Pedro, Bahía de — 108-109 BC 3
San Pedro, Cerro — 108-109 C 4
San Pedro, Point — 83 I b 1
San Pedro, Punta — [CR] 64-65 K 10
San Pedro, Punta — [RCH] 104-105 A 9
San Pedro, Río — [GCA] 86-87 P 9
San Pedro, Río — [MEX, river ◁ Pacific Ocean] 86-87 H 6
San Pedro, Río — [MEX, river ◁ Río Conchos] 86-87 GH 4
San Pedro, Sierra de — 120-121 D 9
San Pedro, Volcán — 92-93 F 9
San Pedro Channel 74-75 D 6
San Pedro-cué 102-103 D 7
San Pedro de Arimena 94-95 F 5
San Pedro de Atacama 104-105 BC 8
San Pedro de Jujuy 104-105 D 9
San Pedro de la Cueva 86-87 F 3
San Pedro de las Colonias 64-65 F 6
San Pedro de Lloc 96-97 B 5
San Pedro del Paraná 102-103 DE 7
San Pedro de Macorís 64-65 N 8
San Pedro de Quemez 104-105 BC 7
San Pedro Mártir 91 I b 3
San Pedro Mártir, Sierra — 64-65 CD 5
San Pedro Mártir, Sierra de — 86-87 C 2
San Pedro Mountain 76-77 A 4
San Pedro Norte 106-107 E 3
San Pedro River 74-75 H 6
San Pedro Sula 64-65 J 8
San Pedro Taviche 86-87 M 9
San Pelayo 94-95 CD 3
San Perlita, TX 76-77 F 9
San Petro Xalostoc 91 I c 1
San Petro Zacatenco, Ciudad de México- 91 I c 1
San Pietro [I] 122-123 BC 6
San Pietro [V] 113 II b 2
San Quentin State Prison 83 I ab 1
San Quintín 86-87 BC 2
San Quintín, Bahía de — 86-87 BC 2
San Quintín, Cabo — 64-65 C 5
San Rafael, CA 64-65 B 4
San Rafael [BOL] 104-105 F 5
San Rafael [CO, Guainía] 94-95 G 6
San Rafael [CO, Vichada] 94-95 G 4-5
San Rafael [MEX] 91 I b 2
San Rafaél [PE] 96-97 CD 7
San Rafael [RA] 111 C 4
San Rafael [RCH] 106-107 B 5
San Rafael [YV] 94-95 EF 2
San Rafael, Bahía de — 86-87 D 3
San Rafael, Bogotá- 91 III b 4
San Rafael, Isla — = Beaver Island 108-109 J 8
San Rafael Bay 83 I b 1
San Rafael de Atamaica 94-95 H 4
San Rafael de Canaguá 94-95 F 3
San Rafael del Encanto 92-93 E 5
San Rafael Mountains 74-75 CD 5
San Rafael River 74-75 H 3
San Rafael Swell 74-75 H 3
San Ramón [BOL, Beni] 104-105 D 3
San Ramón [BOL, Santa Cruz] 104-105 E 5
San Ramón [NIC] 88-89 D 7
San Ramón [PE] 96-97 D 7
San Ramón [ROU] 106-107 K 5
San Ramón, Río — 104-105 F 4
San Ramón de la Nueva Orán 111 CD 2
Sanrao 146-147 F 10
San Remo 122-123 BC 4
San Román, Cabo — 92-93 EF 2
San Roque [RA] 106-107 H 2
San Rosendo 111 B 5
San Saba, TX 76-77 E 7
San Saba River 76-77 E 7
Sansalé 168-169 B 3
San Salvador [BS] 64-65 M 7
San Salvador [ES] 64-65 HJ 9
San Salvador [PY] 102-103 D 5
San Salvador [RA, Corrientes] 106-107 J 2
San Salvador [RA, Entre Ríos] 106-107 H 3
San Salvador, Cuchilla — 106-107 HJ 4
San Salvador, Isla — 92-93 A 5
San Salvador, Río — 106-107 J 4
San Salvador de Jujuy 111 CD 2
Sansanding 164-165 CD 6
Sansanding, Barrage — 168-169 D 2
Sansané Haoussa 168-169 F 2
Sansanné-Mango = Mango 164-165 E 6
San Sebastián [CO] 94-95 DE 8
San Sebastián [E] 120-121 FG 7
San Sebastián [RA] 111 C 8
San Sebastián [YV] 94-95 H 3
San Sebastián, Bahía — 108-109 EF 9
San Sebastian, Isla — 86-87 DE 3
San Sebastián de Buenavista 94-95 DE 3
San Sebastián de la Gomera 164-165 A 3
San Severo 122-123 F 5
Sansha Wan 146-147 GH 8
San Silvestre [BOL] 104-105 B 2
San Silvestre [YV] 92-93 EF 3
San Simeon, CA 74-75 C 5
San Simón 94-95 EF 3
San Simon, AZ 74-75 J 6
Sansing = Yilan 142-143 OP 2
San Solano 106-107 E 3
Sansuan Shan 146-147 H 7
Sansui 146-147 B 8
Santa, Río — 96-97 B 6
Santa Adélia 102-103 H 4
Santa Ana, CA 64-65 E 5
Santa Ana [BOL ↘ Roboré] 104-105 G 6
Santa Ana [BOL ↘ San Ignacio] 104-105 F 5

Santa Ana [BOL ↖ Trinidad] 92-93 F 7
Santa Ana [CO, Guainía] 92-93 F 4
Santa Ana [CO, Magdalena] 94-95 D 3
Santa Ana [EC] 96-97 A 2
Santa Ana [ES] 64-65 HJ 9
Santa Ana [MEX] 64-65 D 5
Santa Ana [RA, Entre Ríos] 106-107 J 3
Santa Ana [RA, Misiones] 106-107 K 1
Santa Ana [YV, Anzoátegui] 94-95 J 3
Santa Ana [YV, Falcón] 94-95 FG 2
Santa Ana, Ilha — 102-103 M 5
Santa Ana, Petare- 91 II bc 2
Santa Ana, Punta — 96-97 D 9
Santa Ana Delicias 94-95 E 4
Santa Ana Jilotzingo 91 I a 1
Santa Ana Mountains 74-75 E 6
Santa Anna, TX 76-77 E 7
Santa Apolonia 94-95 F 3
Santa Barbara, CA 64-65 BC 5
Santa Bárbara [BR, Mato Grosso] 102-103 C 1
Santa Bárbara [BR, Minas Gerais] 102-103 L 3-4
Santa Barbara [CO] 94-95 D 5
Santa Bárbara [Honduras] 88-89 BC 7
Santa Bárbara [MEX] 64-65 E 6
Santa Bárbara [RCH] 111 B 5
Santa Bárbara [YV ↘ Ciudad Guayana] 94-95 K 4
Santa Bárbara [YV ↙ Maturín] 92-93 G 3
Santa Bárbara [YV → San Cristóbal] 92-93 E 3
Santa Bárbara [YV → San Fernando de Atabapo] 92-93 F 4
Santa Bárbara, Ilha de — 110 I b 2
Santa Bárbara, Serra de — 92-93 J 9
Santa Bárbara, Sierra de — 104-105 D 8-9
Santa Barbara Channel 74-75 CD 5
Santa Bárbara do Sul 106-107 L 2
Santa Barbara Island 74-75 D 6
Santa Catalina [RA, Córdoba] 106-107 E 4
Santa Catalina [RA, Jujuy] 111 C 2
Santa Catalina [RA, Santiago del Estero] 106-107 E 2
Santa Catalina = Catalina 111 C 3
Santa Catalina, Gulf of — 74-75 DE 6
Santa Catalina, Isla — 86-87 EF 5
Santa Catalina, Laguna — 110 III b 2
Santa Catalina Island 64-65 BC 5
Santa Catarina 111 FG 3
Santa Catarina, Ilha de — 111 G 3
Santa Catarina, Sierra de — 91 I cd 3
Santa Catarina, Valle de — 74-75 EF 7
Santa Catarina de Tepehuanes 86-87 H 5
Santa Catarina Yecahuizotl 91 I d 3
Santa Cecília 102-103 G 7
Santa Cecilia, Pirámide de — 91 I b 1
Santa Cecília do Pavão 102-103 G 5
Santa Clara, CA 64-65 B 4
Santa Clara [BOL] 104-105 C 3
Santa Clara [C] 64-65 KL 7
Santa Clara [CO] 92-93 EF 5
Santa Clara [MEX, Chihuahua] 76-77 B 8
Santa Clara [MEX, Durango] 86-87 J 5
Santa Clara [PE] 96-97 D 4
Santa Clara [RA] 104-105 D 9
Santa Clara [ROU] 106-107 K 4
Santa Clara Coatitla 91 I c 1
Santa Clara de Buena Vista 106-107 G 3
Santa Clara de Saguier 106-107 G 3
Santa Coloma 106-107 H 5
Santa Comba = Cela 172 C 4
Santa Cruz, CA 64-65 B 4
Santa Cruz [BOL, administrative unit] 104-105 E-G 5
Santa Cruz [BOL, place] 92-93 G 8
Santa Cruz [BR, Amazonas ↙ Benjamin Constant] 96-97 E 4
Santa Cruz [BR, Amazonas ↗ Benjamin Constant] 96-97 G 3
Santa Cruz [BR, Amazonas ↙ Benjamin Constant] 98-99 BC 7
Santa Cruz [BR, Amazonas ↗ Benjamin Constant] 98-99 D 6
Santa Cruz [BR, Espírito Santo] 100-101 DE 10
Santa Cruz [BR, Rio Grande do Norte] 92-93 M 6
Santa Cruz [BR, Rondônia ↖ Ariquemes] 104-105 E 1
Santa Cruz [BR, Rondônia ↘ Mategua] 104-105 E 3
Santa Cruz [CR] 88-89 CD 9
Santa Cruz [MEX] 86-87 E 2
Santa Cruz [PE, Cajamarca] 96-97 B 5
Santa Cruz [PE, Huánuco] 96-97 C 6
Santa Cruz [PE, Loreto] 96-97 D 4
Santa Cruz [RA, La Rioja] 106-107 D 2
Santa Cruz [RA, Santa Cruz] 111 BC 7
Santa Cruz [RCH] 106-107 B 5
Santa Cruz [YV, Anzoátegui] 94-95 J 3
Santa Cruz [YV, Barinas] 94-95 F 3
Santa Cruz [YV, Zulia] 94-95 F 2
Santa Cruz, Ilha de — 110 I c 2
Santa Cruz, Isla — [EC] 92-93 AB 5
Santa Cruz, Isla — [MEX] 86-87 E 5
Santa Cruz, Río — 108-109 E 7-F 8
Santa Cruz, Rio de Janeiro- 102-103 L 5
Santa Cruz, Sierra de — 104-105 E 5-6
Santa Cruz Alcapixca 91 I c 3
Santa Cruz Cabrália 92-93 M 8
Santa Cruz das Palmeiras 102-103 J 4
Santa Cruz de Barahona = Barahona 64-65 M 8
Santa Cruz de Bucaral 94-95 G 2
Santa Cruz de Goiás 102-103 H 2
Santa Cruz de la Palma 164-165 A 3
Santa Cruz del Quiché 86-87 P 10
Santa Cruz del Sur 88-89 GH 4
Santa Cruz de Tenerife 164-165 A 3
Santa Cruz do Capibaribe 100-101 F 4-5
Santa Cruz do Monte Castelo 102-103 F 5
Santa Cruz do Piauí 100-101 D 4
Santa Cruz do Rio Pardo 102-103 H 5
Santa Cruz dos Angolares 168-169 G 5
Santa Cruz do Sul 111 F 3
Santa Cruz Island 64-65 BC 5
Santa Cruz Islands 148-149 I 7
Santa Cruz Meyehualco, Ixtapalapa- 91 I c 2
Santa Cruz Mountains 74-75 BC 4
Santa Cruz River 74-75 H 6
Santa de la Ventana 106-107 G 7
Santa Efigênia, São Paulo- 110 II b 2
Santa Elena [BOL] 92-93 G 9
Santa Elena [EC] 96-97 A 3
Santa Elena [PE] 92-93 E 5
Santa Elena [RA, Buenos Aires] 106-107 G 6
Santa Elena [RA, Entre Ríos] 106-107 H 3
Santa Elena, Bahía de — 96-97 A 2-3
Santa Elena, Cabo — 64-65 J 9
Santa Elena, Cerro — 108-109 G 5
Santa Elena de Uairén 92-93 G 4
Santa Eleodora 106-107 F 5
Santa Eudóxia 102-103 J 4
Santa Fe, NM 64-65 E 4
Santa Fé [BOL] 104-105 E 6
Santa Fé [C] 88-89 E 4
Santa Fe [RA, administrative unit] 106-107 G 2-4
Santa Fe [RA, place] 111 D 4
Santa Fé [RCH] 106-107 A 6
Santa Fe [YV] 94-95 J 2
Santa Fe, Villa Obregón- 91 I b 2
Santa Fé des Minas 102-103 K 2
Santa Fé do Sul 92-93 J 9
Santa Fe Pacific Railway 64-65 F 4
Santa Fe Springs, CA 83 III d 2
Santa Filomena 92-93 K 6
Santa Genoveva = Cerro las Casitas 64-65 E 7
Sāntāhār 138-139 M 5
Santa Helena [BR, Maranhão] 92-93 K 5
Santa Helena [BR, Pará] 92-93 H 5-6
Santa Helena [BR, Paraná] 102-103 E 6
Santa Helena de Goiás 102-103 G 2
Santai 142-143 JK 5
Santa Inês [BR, Bahia] 92-93 LM 7
Santa Inês [BR, Maranhão] 100-101 B 2
Santa Inês [YV] 94-95 G 2
Santa Inés, Isla — 111 B 8
Santa Isabel [BR] 104-105 F 3
Santa Isabel [EC] 96-97 B 3
Santa Isabel [PE] 96-97 F 8
Santa Isabel [RA, La Pampa] 111 C 5
Santa Isabel [RA, Santa Fe] 106-107 G 4
Santa Isabel [Solomon Is.] 148-149 jk 6
Santa Isabel = Malabo 164-165 F 8
Santa Isabel, Cachoeira de — 98-99 OP 8
Santa Isabel, Ilha Grande de — 92-93 L 5
Santa Isabel do Araguaia 92-93 K 6
Santa Isabel do Morro 92-93 J 7
Santa Juana [RCH] 106-107 A 6
Santa Juana [YV] 94-95 H 4
Santa Juliana 102-103 J 3
Santa Justina 106-107 F 1
Santa Lídia 102-103 C 5
Santāl Parganas 138-139 L 5
Santa Lucía [RA, Buenos Aires] 106-107 GH 4
Santa Lucía [RA, Corrientes] 106-107 H 2
Santa Lucía [RA, San Juan] 106-107 C 3
Santa Lucía [RA, Santa Cruz] 108-109 E 8
Santa Lucía [ROU] 106-107 J 5
Santa Lucía, Esteros del — 106-107 HJ 1-2
Santa Lucía, Río — 106-107 H 2
Santa Lucía, Sierra de — 86-87 D 4
Santa Lucia Range 74-75 C 4-5
Santa Luísa, Serra de — 102-103 E 3
Santaluz [BR, Bahia] 92-93 M 7
Santa Luz [BR, Piauí] 100-101 C 5
Santa Luzia [BR, Maranhão] 100-101 B 2
Santa Luzia [BR, Minas Gerais] 102-103 L 3
Santa Luzia [BR, Rondônia] 98-99 G 9
Santa Magdalena 106-107 EF 5
Santa Magdalena, Isla — 86-87 D 5
Santa Margarida 102-103 LM 4
Santa Margarita, CA 74-75 C 5
Santa Margarita [RA] 106-107 G 2
Santa Margarita, Isla — 64-65 D 7
Santa Margherita Ligure 122-123 C 3
Santa Maria, CA 64-65 B 5
Santa Maria [Açores] 204-205 E 5
Santa Maria [BOL] 104-105 E 4
Santa Maria [BR, Amazonas] 92-93 H 5
Santa Maria [BR, Rio Grande do Sul] 111 EF 3
Santa María [CO] 94-95 G 6
Santa Maria [PE, Amazonas] 96-97 B 5
Santa Maria [PE, Loreto] 92-93 E 5
Santa Maria [RA] 111 C 3
Santa Maria [Vanuatu] 158-159 N 2
Santa María [YV, Apure] 94-95 H 4
Santa María [YV, Zulia] 94-95 F 3
Santa Maria [Z] 171 B 5
Santa María, Bahía de — 86-87 F 5
Santa María, Boca — 86-87 M 5
Santa Maria, Cabo de — 120-121 CD 10
Santa Maria, Cabo de — = Cap Sainte-Marie 172 J 7
Santa María, Isla — 106-107 A 6
Santa María, Lugana de — 86-87 G 2
Santa María, Punta — [MEX] 86-87 F 5
Santa María, Punta — [ROU] 106-107 KL 5
Santa María, Riacho — 100-101 C 5
Santa Maria, Rio — [BR ◁ Rio Corrente] 100-101 A 8
Santa Maria, Rio — [BR ◁ Rio Ibicuí] 106-107 K 3
Santa María, Río — [MEX ◁ Laguna de Santa María] 86-87 G 2-3
Santa María, Río — [MEX ◁ Río Tamuín] 86-87 K 7
Santa María, Río — [RA] 104-105 D 10
Santa María Asunción Tlaxiaco 64-65 G 8
Santa Maria da Boa Vista 100-101 E 5
Santa Maria das Barreiras 92-93 JK 6
Santa Maria da Vitória 100-101 BC 7
Santa Maria de Ipire 92-93 F 3
Santa Maria de Itabira 100-101 C 10
Santa María de la Mina 104-105 EF 5
Santa María del Oro 86-87 GH 5
Santa Maria del Soccorso, Roma- 113 II bc 2
Santa Maria de Nanay 96-97 E 3
Santa Maria di Leuca, Capo — 122-123 H 6
Santa Maria do Pará 98-99 P 5
Santa Maria do Suaçuí 102-103 L 3
Santa Maria Madalena 102-103 LM 4
Santa Maria Maggiore [I, Roma] 113 II b 2
Santa Mariana 102-103 G 5
Santa María Otaes 86-87 GH 5
Santa María Tulpetlac 91 I c 1
Santa Marta [CO] 92-93 DE 2
Santa Marta, Baruta- 91 II b 2
Santa Marta, Ciénaga Grande de — 94-95 DE 2
Santa Marta, Sierra Nevada de — 92-93 E 2
Santa Marta Grande, Cabo — 102-103 H 8
Santa Martha Acatitla, Ixtapalapa- 91 I cd 2
Santa Maura = Levkás 122-123 J 6
Santa Monica, CA 64-65 BC 5
Santa Monica, TX 76-77 F 9
Santa Mónica, Caracas- 91 II b 2
Santa Monica Bay 83 III ab 2
Santa Monica Mountains 83 III ab 1
Santa Monica Municipal Airport 83 III b 1
Santa Monica State Beach 83 III a 1
Santana 92-93 L 7
Santana, Coxilha da — 111 E 3-F 4
Santana, Ilha de — 92-93 L 5
Santana, Rio — 100-101 C 5
Santana, São Paulo- 110 II b 1
Santana, Serra de — [BR, Bahia] 100-101 C 7
Santana, Serra de — [BR, Rio Grande do Norte] 100-101 F 3-4
Santana da Boa Vista 106-107 L 3
Santana de Patos 102-103 J 3
Santana do Araguaia 98-99 NO 9
Santana do Cariri 100-101 E 4
Santana do Ipanema 100-101 F 5
Santana do Livramento 111 EF 4
Santana do Matos 100-101 F 3
Santana dos Garrotes 100-101 EF 4
Santander [CO, Cauca] 92-93 D 4
Santander [CO, Meta] 94-95 D 6
Santander [CO, Santander] 94-95 DE 4
Santander [E] 120-121 F 7
Santander Jiménez 86-87 LM 5
Santang 152-153 M 6
Sant'Angelo, Castel — 113 II b 2
Sant'Antioco [I, island] 122-123 BC 6
Sant'Antioco [I, place] 122-123 BC 6
Santañy 120-121 J 9
Santa Paula, CA 74-75 D 5
Santa Pola, Cabo de — 120-121 GH 9
Santapura = Santpur 140 C 1
Santa Quitéria 100-101 DE 3
Santa Quitéria do Maranhão 100-101 C 2
Santa Regina 106-107 F 5
Santarém [BR] 92-93 J 5
Santarem [P] 120-121 C 9
Santaren Channel 64-65 L 7
Santa Rita, NM 74-75 J 6
Santa Rita [BR, Amazonas] 98-99 C 8
Santa Rita [BR, Paraíba] 92-93 MN 6
Santa Rita [YV, Guárica] 94-95 H 3
Santa Rita [YV, Zulia] 92-93 E 2
Santa Rita, Ponta de — 100-101 G 3
Santa Rita, Raudal — 94-95 K 4
Santa Rita, Serra de — 100-101 E 3
Santa Rita de Cássia 100-101 B 6
Santa Rita de Catuna 106-107 D 3
Santa Rita de Jacutinga 102-103 KL 5
Santa Rita do Araguaia 92-93 J 8
Santa Rita do Passa Quatro 102-103 J 4
Santa Rita do Sapucaí 102-103 K 5
Santa Rito do Weil 92-93 F 5
Santa Rosa, CA 64-65 B 4
Santa Rosa, NM 76-77 B 5
Santa Rosa [BOL, Beni ↘ Riberalta] 92-93 F 7
Santa Rosa [BOL, Beni ↙ Santa Ana] 104-105 C 4
Santa Rosa [BOL, Chuquisaca] 104-105 E 7
Santa Rosa [BOL, Pandó] 104-105 C 2
Santa Rosa [BOL, Santa Cruz] 104-105 E 5
Santa Rosa [BR, Acre] 92-93 EF 6
Santa Rosa [BR, Amazonas] 94-95 K 6
Santa Rosa [BR, Goiás] 100-101 A 8
Santa Rosa [BR, Rio Grande do Sul] 111 F 3
Santa Rosa [BR, Rondônia] 98-99 GH 10
Santa Rosa [CO, Cauca] 94-95 C 7
Santa Rosa [CO, Guainía] 92-93 EF 4
Santa Rosa [EC] 96-97 A 3
Santa Rosa [PE] 92-93 E 5
Santa Rosa [PY, Boquerón] 102-103 B 4
Santa Rosa [PY, Misiones] 102-103 D 7
Santa Rosa [RA, Corrientes] 106-107 HJ 2
Santa Rosa [RA, La Pampa] 111 CD 5
Santa Rosa [RA, Mendoza] 111 C 4
Santa Rosa [RA, Río Negro] 108-109 F 2
Santa Rosa [RA, San Luis] 111 C 4
Santa Rosa [RA, Santa Fe] 106-107 GH 3
Santa Rosa [RCH] 106-107 A 6-7
Santa Rosa [ROU] 106-107 JK 5
Santa Rosa [YV, Anzoátegui] 94-95 J 3
Santa Rosa [YV, Apure] 94-95 H 4
Santa Rosa [YV, Barinas] 94-95 G 3
Santa Rosa [YV, Lara] 94-95 F 2
Santa Rosa, Cordillera de — 106-107 C 2
Santa Rosa de Amanadona 94-95 H 7
Santa Rosa de Cabal 94-95 CD 5
Santa Rosa de Calamuchita 106-107 E 4
Santa Rosa de Copán 64-65 J 9
Santa Rosa de la Roca 104-105 F 5
Santa Rosa del Palmar 92-93 G 8
Santa Rosa de Osos 94-95 D 4
Santa Rosa de Río Primero 106-107 F 3
Santa Rosa de Viterbo 102-103 J 4
Santa Rosa Island [USA, California] 64-65 B 5
Santa Rosa Island [USA, Florida] 78-79 F 5
Santa Rosalía [MEX, Baja California Norte] 86-87 C 3
Santa Rosalía [MEX, Baja California Sur] 64-65 D 6
Santa Rosalía [YV] 94-95 J 4
Santa Rosalía de las Cuevas 86-87 G 3-4
Santa Rosalilia 86-87 C 3
Santa Rosa Range 66-67 E 5
Santa Rosa Wash 74-75 GH 6
Šantarskije ostrova 132-133 a 6-7
Santa Sylvina 111 DE 3
Santa Tecla = Nueva San Salvador 64-65 HJ 9
Santa Tecla, Serra de — 106-107 KL 3
Santa Teresa [BR] 102-103 M 3
Santa Teresa [MEX] 76-77 D 9
Santa Teresa [PE] 96-97 E 8
Santa Teresa [RA ↖ Rosario] 106-107 G 4
Santa Teresa [RA ↓ Rosario] 106-107 G 4
Santa Teresa [YV] 94-95 H 2
Santa Teresa, Cachoeira — 98-99 G 9-10
Santa Teresinha 100-101 DE 7
Santa Teresita 106-107 J 6
Santa União 98-99 O 10
Santa Victoria [RA ← Bermejo] 104-105 D 8
Santa Victoria [RA → Tartagal] 104-105 E 8
Santa Victoria, Sierra — 104-105 D 8
Santa Vitória 102-103 GH 3
Santa Vitória do Palmar 111 F 4
Santa Ynez, CA 74-75 CD 5
Santee River 80-81 G 4
San Telmo, Punta — 86-87 HJ 8
Sant'Eufêmia, Golfo di — 122-123 FG 6
Santiago [BR] 111 EF 3
Santiago [Cape Verde] 204-205 E 7
Santiago [DOM] 64-65 M 7
Santiago [EC] 96-97 BC 3
Santiago [MEX] 86-87 F 6
Santiago [PA] 64-65 K 10
Santiago [PY] 102-103 D 7
Santiago, Cabo — 108-109 AB 8
Santiago, Cerro — 88-89 EF 10
Santiago, Río — [EC] 96-97 B 1
Santiago, Río — [PE] 96-97 C 3
Santiago, Salto — 102-103 F 6
Santiago, Serranía de — 104-105 G 6
Santiago Acahualtepec, Ixtapalapa- 91 I c 2
Santiago de Chile 111 B 4
Santiago de Chocorvos 96-97 D 8
Santiago de Chuco 92-93 D 6
Santiago de Cuba 64-65 L 7-8
Santiago de Huata 104-105 B 5
Santiago de las Montañas 96-97 C 4
Santiago del Estero [RA, administrative unit] 102-103 AB 7
Santiago del Estero [RA, place] 111 CD 3
Santiago de Paracaguas 104-105 BC 3
Santiago di Compostela 120-121 CD 7
Santiago Ixcuintla 64-65 EF 7
Santiago Jamiltepec 86-87 LM 9
Santiagoma 92-93 H 8
Santiago Mountains 76-77 C 7-8
Santiago Papasquiaro 64-65 EF 6-7
Santiago Peak 76-77 C 8
Santiago Temple 106-107 F 3
Santiago Tepalcatlalpan 91 I c 3
Santiago Tepatlaxco 91 I ab 2
Santiago Vázquez, Montevideo- 106-107 J 5
Santiago Zapotitlán 91 I c 3
Santiaguillo, Laguna de — 86-87 H 5
Santiam Pass 66-67 BC 3
Santiao Chiao 146-147 HJ 9
San Tiburcio 86-87 K 5
Santigi 148-149 H 6
San Timoteo 94-95 F 3
Sāntipur 138-139 M 6
Santo, TX 76-77 E 6
Santo Agostinho, Cabo de — 100-101 G 5
Santo Amaro 92-93 M 7
Santo Amaro, Ilha de — 102-103 JK 6
Santo Amaro, São Paulo- 110 II a 2
Santo Amaro de Campos 102-103 M 5
Santo Anastácio 102-103 G 4
Santo André 92-93 K 9
Santo André = Isla de San Andrés 64-65 KL 9
Santo André-Utinga 110 II b 2
Santo André-Vila Bastos 110 II b 2
Santo Ângelo 111 EF 3
Santo Antão 204-205 E 7
Santo Antônio [BR, Pará] 98-99 O 6
Santo Antônio [BR, Rio Grande do Norte] 100-101 G 4
Santo Antônio [BR, Rio Grande do Sul] 106-107 MN 2
Santo Antônio [São Tomé and Príncipe] 164-165 F 8
Santo Antônio, Cachoeira — [BR, Rio Madeira] 92-93 FG 6
Santo Antônio, Cachoeira — [BR, Rio Roosevelt] 98-99 HJ 9
Santo Antônio, Ponta de — 100-101 GH 4
Santo Antônio, Rio — [BR ◁ Paraguaçu] 100-101 D 7
Santo Antônio, Rio — [BR ◁ Rio de Contas] 100-101 CD 8
Santo Antônio, Rio — [BR ◁ Rio Doce] 102-103 L 3
Santo Antônio, Rio — [BR ◁ Rio Iguaçu] 102-103 F 6
Santo Antônio da Platina 102-103 GH 5
Santo Antônio de Jesus 92-93 LM 7
Santo Antônio de Pádua 102-103 LM 4
Santo Antônio de Rio Verde 102-103 J 2
Santo Antônio do Içá 98-99 DE 6
Santo Antônio do Jacinto 100-101 DE 9
Santo Antônio do Leverger 102-103 DE 1
Santo Antônio do Monte 102-103 K 4
Santo Antônio do Sudoeste 102-103 F 7
Santo Antônio do Zaire = Soyo 172 B 3
Santo Corazón 92-93 H 8
Santo Corazón, Río — 104-105 G 5
Santo Domingo [DOM] 64-65 MN 8
Santo Domingo [MEX, Baja California Norte] 86-87 CD 3
Santo Domingo [MEX, Baja California Sur] 86-87 DE 5
Santo Domingo [MEX, San Luis Potosí] 86-87 K 6
Santo Domingo [NIC] 88-89 D 8
Santo Domingo [PE, Junín] 96-97 D 7
Santo Domingo [PE, Loreto] 96-97 CD 3
Santo Domingo [RA] 106-107 J 6
Santo Domingo, Río — [MEX] 64-65 G 8
Santo Domingo, Río — [YV] 94-95 G 3
Santo Domingo de Guzmán = Santo Domingo 64-65 MN 8
Santo Domingo de los Colorados 96-97 B 2
Santo Domingo Tehuantepec 64-65 G 8
Santo Eduardo 102-103 M 4
Santo Estêvão 100-101 E 7
San Tomé 94-95 JK 3
Santoña 120-121 F 7
Sant'Onofrio, Roma- 113 II b 1
Santorínē = Thēra 122-123 L 7
Santos 92-93 K 9
Santos, Baía de — 102-103 JK 6
Santos, Laje dos — 102-103 JK 6
Santos, Los — 88-89 F 11
Santos Dumont [BR, Amazonas] 98-99 D 8
Santos Dumont [BR, Minas Gerais] 102-103 KL 4
Santos Dumont, Aeroporto — 110 I c 2
Santos Lugares 104-105 E 10
Santos Tomás [BOL] 104-105 G 5
Santo Tomás [CO] 94-95 D 2
Santo Tomás [MEX] 86-87 B 2
Santo Tomás [PE] 92-93 E 7
Santo Tomás de Castilla 88-89 B 7
Santo Tomé [RA, Corrientes] 111 E 3
Santo Tomé [RA, Santa Fe] 106-107 G 3
Santpur 140 C 1
San-tu = Sandu 146-147 E 7
San-tu Ao = Sandu Ao 146-147 GH 8
Santuario, El — 94-95 F 5
Santuario de los Remedios 91 I b 2
Sanup Plateau 74-75 G 5
San Valentín, Cerro — 111 B 7
San Vicente [BOL] 104-105 C 7
San Vicente [CO] 94-95 E 4
San Vicente [ES] 64-65 J 9
San Vicente [RA, Buenos Aires] 106-107 H 5
San Vicente [RA, Córdoba] 106-107 E 3
San Vicente [RA, Santiago del Estero] 106-107 E 2
San Vicente [RCH] 106-107 B 5
San Vicente, Bahía — 106-107 A 6
San Vicente, Cabo — 108-109 FG 10
San Vicente de Caguán 94-95 D 6
San Víctor 111 E 4
San Vito, Capo — 122-123 E 6
Sānwer 138-139 E 6
San Xavier Indian Reservation 74-75 H 6-7
Sanya = Ya Xian 142-143 KL 8
San Yanaro 92-93 EF 4
Sanyang 146-147 E 8
Sanya Wan 150-151 G 3
San Ygnacio, TX 76-77 E 9
San Ysidro, CA 74-75 E 6
Sanyuan 146-147 B 4
Sanzao Dao 146-147 D 11
Sanza Pombo 172 C 3
São Bartolomeu, Rio — 102-103 J 2
São Benedito 100-101 D 3
São Benedito, Rio — 98-99 KL 9
São Benedito do Rio Preto 100-101 C 2
São Bento [BR, Amazonas] 96-97 E 4
São Bento [BR, Maranhão] 100-101 B 2
São Bento [BR, Rio Grande do Sul] 106-107 L 2
São Bento do Norte 100-101 F 3
São Bento do Sapucaí 102-103 JK 5
São Bento do Una 100-101 F 5
São Bernardo 92-93 L 5
São Bernardo do Campo 102-103 J 5
São Bernardo do Campo-Rudge Ramos 110 II b 2-3
São Borja 111 EF 3
São Caetano 100-101 FG 5
São Caetano do Odivelas 98-99 OP 5
São Caetano do Sul 102-103 JK 5
São Carlos [BR, Rondônia] 98-99 G 9
São Carlos [BR, Santa Catarina] 102-103 F 7
São Carlos [BR, São Paulo] 92-93 K 9
São Conrado, Rio de Janeiro- 110 I b 2
São Cristóvão 100-101 F 6
São Cristovão, Rio de Janeiro- 110 I b 2
São Desidério 100-101 B 7
São Diogo 100-101 B 5
São Domingos [BR, Espírito Santo] 100-101 D 10
São Domingos [BR, Santa Catarina] 102-103 F 7
São Domingos [Guinea Bissau] 164-165 A 6
São Domingos, Rio — [BR ◁ Rio Mamoré] 104-105 D 3-E 2
São Domingos, Rio — [BR ◁ Rio Paraná] 100-101 A 7
São Domingos, Rio — [BR ◁ Rio Paranaíba] 102-103 G 3
São Domingos, Rio — [BR ◁ Rio Verde] 102-103 F 3
São Domingos, Serra — 100-101 D 3-E 4
São Domingos, Serra de — 100-101 A 7-8
São Domingos do Maranhão 100-101 BC 3
São Domingos do Prata 102-103 L 3
São Felipe 98-99 H 3
São Felix [BR, Mato Grosso] 98-99 N 10
São Félix [BR, Rondônia] 104-105 F 1
São Félix de Balsas 100-101 B 5
São Félix do Piauí 100-101 C 3
São Félix do Xingu 92-93 J 6
São Fernando 98-99 F 7
São Fidélis 102-103 M 4
São Filipe 92-93 M 7
São Francisco 102-103 K 1
São Francisco, Baía de — 102-103 HJ 7
São Francisco, Cachoeira — 98-99 LM 7
São Francisco, Ilha de — 102-103 HJ 7
São Francisco, Rio — [BR ◁ Atlantic Ocean] 92-93 LM 6
São Francisco, Rio — [BR ◁ Rio Paraná] 102-103 EF 6
São Francisco, Serra — 100-101 D 5-6
São Francisco de Assis 106-107 K 2
São Francisco de Paula 106-107 M 2
São Francisco de Sales 102-103 H 3
São Francisco do Conde 100-101 E 7
São Francisco do Maranhão 100-101 C 4
São Francisco do Sul 111 G 3
São Gabriel 111 EF 4
São Gabriel da Palha 100-101 D 10
São Gonçalo 102-103 L 5
São Gonçalo do Abaeté 102-103 K 3
São Gonçalo do Sapucaí 102-103 K 4
São Gonçalo dos Campos 100-101 E 7
São Gotardo 92-93 KL 8
Sao Hill 171 C 5
São Inácio 102-103 FG 5
São Jerônimo 106-107 M 2-3
São Jerônimo, Serra de — 92-93 J 8
São Jerônimo da Serra 102-103 G 5
São João [BR, Amazonas] 98-99 E 5
São João [BR, Rondônia] 104-105 E 2
Sao João, Ilhas de — 92-93 L 5
São João, Riacho — 100-101 D 4
São João, Rio — [BR ◁ Rio de Contas] 100-101 CD 8
São João, Rio — [BR ◁ Rio Paraná] 102-103 F 5
São João, Serra de — [BR, Amazonas] 98-99 GH 9
São João, Serra de — [BR, Paraná] 102-103 G 6
São João Batista 100-101 B 2
São João da Barra 102-103 M 4
São João da Boa Vista 102-103 J 4-5
São João da Ponte 102-103 L 1
São João de Araguaia 98-99 O 7
São João del Rei 102-103 K 4
São João de Meriti [BR, place] 102-103 L 5
São João de Meriti [BR, river] 110 I ab 1
São João do Ivaí 102-103 FG 5-6
São João do Paraíso 102-103 LM 1
São João do Piauí 92-93 L 6
São João dos Patos 100-101 C 4
São João do Triunfo 102-103 G 6
São João Evangelista 102-103 L 3
São João Nepomuceno 102-103 L 4
São Joaquim [BR, Amazonas] 98-99 E 4-5
São Joaquim [BR, Santa Catarina] 106-107 MN 2
São Joaquim, Parque Nacional de — 106-107 MN 2
São Joaquim da Barra 102-103 J 4
São Jorge 204-205 DE 5
São Jorge, Ilha — 100-101 B 1
São José [BR, Mato Grosso] 98-99 M 10
São José [BR, Paraíba] 100-101 E 4
São José [BR, Santa Catarina] 102-103 H 7
São José, Baía de — 100-101 BC 2
São José da Laje 100-101 FG 5
São José da Tapera 100-101 F 5
São José de Mipibu 100-101 G 4
São José do Anauá 98-99 H 4
São José do Belmonte 100-101 E 4
São José do Campestre 100-101 G 4
São José do Egito 100-101 F 4
São José do Gurupi 100-101 A 1
São José do Norte 106-107 LM 3-4
São José do Peixe 100-101 C 4
São José do Piriá 100-101 A 1
São José do Prado 100-101 E 9
São José do Rio Pardo 102-103 J 4
São José do Rio Preto [BR, Rio de Janeiro] 102-103 L 5
São José do Rio Preto [BR, São Paulo] 92-93 JK 9
São José dos Campos 92-93 KL 9
São José dos Dourados, Rio — 102-103 G 4
São José dos Pinhais 102-103 H 6
São Leopoldo 106-107 M 2

São Lourenço [BR, Mato Grosso] 102-103 E 2
São Lourenço [BR, Minas Gerais] 102-103 K 5
São Lourenço, Pantanal de — 102-103 D 3-E 2
São Lourenço, Rio — 102-103 DE 2
São Lourenço, Serra — 102-103 E 2
São Lourenço da Mata 100-101 G 4
São Lourenço do Sul 106-107 LM 3
São Lucas 106-107 K 2
São Lucas, Cachoeira de — 98-99 J 9
São Luís 92-93 L 5
São Luís, Ilha de — 100-101 BC 1-2
São Luís de Cacianã 98-99 F 8
São Luís do Curu 100-101 E 2
São Luís do Purunã 102-103 H 6
São Luís do Quitunde 100-101 G 5
São Luís Gonzaga 106-107 K 2
São Manuel 102-103 H 5
São Manuel, Rio — 98-99 K 9
São Marcelino 94-95 H 7
São Marcelo 100-101 B 6
São Marcos [BR, Rio Grande do Sul] 106-107 M 2
São Marcos [BR, Roraima] 94-95 L 6
São Marcos, Baía de — 92-93 L 5
São Marcos, Rio — 102-103 J 2
São Mateus [BR, Espírito Santo] 92-93 M 8
São Mateus [BR, Pará] 98-99 O 7
São Mateus, Rio — 100-101 D 10
São Mateus do Sul 102-103 GH 6
São Miguel [Açores] 204-205 E 5
São Miguel [BR, Maranhão] 100-101 C 3
São Miguel [BR, Rio Grande do Norte] 100-101 E 4
São Miguel, Rio — 102-103 J 1-2
São Miguel Arcanjo 102-103 HJ 5
São Miguel das Matas 100-101 E 7
São Miguel das Missões 106-107 K 2
São Miguel d'Oeste 102-103 F 7
São Miguel dos Campos 100-101 FG 5
São Miguel dos Macacos 98-99 N 5
São Miguel do Tapuio 92-93 L 6
Saona, Isla — 64-65 N 8
Saône 120-121 K 5
Saoner 138-139 G 7
São Nicolau 204-205 E 7
São Nicolau, Rio — 100-101 D 3
São Onofre, Rio — 100-101 C 7
São Paulo [BR, administrative unit] 92-93 JK 9
São Paulo [BR, island] 178-179 H 5
São Paulo [BR, place Acre] 98-99 BC 9
São Paulo [BR, place Amazonas] 98-99 B 8
São Paulo-Aclimação 110 II b 2
São Paulo Alto da Mooca 110 II b 2
São Paulo Americanópolis 110 II b 3
São Paulo-Barra Funda 110 II b 2
São Paulo-Bela Vista 110 II b 2
São Paulo-Bom Rètiro 110 II b 2
São Paulo-Brás 110 II b 2
São Paulo-Brasilândia 110 II a 1
São Paulo-Butantã 110 II a 2
São Paulo-Cambuci 110 II b 2
São Paulo-Cangaiba 110 II b 2
São Paulo-Cantareira 110 II b 1
São Paulo-Casa Verde 110 II b 1
São Paulo-Consolação 110 II ab 2
São Paulo de Olivença 92-93 F 5
São Paulo do Potenji 100-101 G 3
São Paulo-Ermelindo Matarazo 110 II bc 1
São Paulo-Ibirapuera 110 II ab 2
São Paulo-Indianópolis 110 II b 2
São Paulo-Interlagos 110 II a 3
São Paulo-Ipiranga 110 II b 2
São Paulo-Jabaquara 110 II b 2
São Paulo-Jaçanã 110 II b 1
São Paulo-Jaraguá 110 II a 1
São Paulo-Jardim América 110 II ab 2
São Paulo-Jardim Paulista 110 II ab 2
São Paulo-Lapa 110 II a 2
São Paulo-Liberdade 110 II b 2
São Paulo-Limão 110 II ab 1
São Paulo-Mooca 110 II b 2
São Paulo-Morumbi 110 II a 2
São Paulo-Nossa Senhora do Ó 110 II ab 1
São Paulo-Nova Cachoeirinha 110 II ab 1
São Paulo-Pari 110 II b 2
São Paulo-Penha 102-103 J 5
São Paulo-Penha de França 110 II b 2
São Paulo-Pinheiros 110 II a 2
São Paulo-Pirituba 110 II a 1
São Paulo-Santa Efigênia 110 II b 2
São Paulo-Santana 110 II b 1
São Paulo-Santo Amaro 110 II a 2
São Paulo-Saúde 110 II b 2
São Paulo-Sé 110 II b 2
São Paulo-Socorro 110 II a 2
São Paulo-Tatuapé 110 II b 2
São Paulo-Tremembé 110 II b 1
São Paulo-Tucuruvi 110 II b 1
São Paulo-Vila Boaçava 110 II a 1
São Paulo-Vila Formosa 110 II bc 2
São Paulo-Vila Guilherme 110 II b 2
São Paulo-Vila Jaguara 110 II a 2
São Paulo-Vila Madalena 110 II a 2
São Paulo-Vila Maria 110 II b 2
São Paulo-Vila Mariana 110 II b 2
São Paulo-Vila Matilde 110 II bc 2
São Paulo-Vila Prudente 110 II b 2
São Pedro [BR, Amazonas ↘ Benjamin Constant] 96-97 G 4
São Pedro [BR, Amazonas ↗ Benjamin Constant] 96-97 G 3
São Pedro [BR, Amazonas ↘ Benjamin Constant] 98-99 D 7
São Pedro [BR, Amazonas ↗ Benjamin Constant] 98-99 D 6
São Pedro [BR, Amazonas ↘ São Joaquim] 94-95 H 8
São Pedro [BR, Rio Grande do Sul] 106-107 LM 2
São Pedro [BR, Rondônia] 98-99 GH 9
São Pedro [BR, São Paulo] 102-103 J 5
São Pedro, Riachão — 102-103 J 2
São Pedro, Rio de — 100-101 DE 5
São Pedro, Serra de — 100-101 E 4
São Pedro da União 102-103 J 4
São Pedro de Ferros 102-103 L 4
São Pedro de Viseu 98-99 NO 6
São Pedro do Cipa 102-103 E 2
São Pedro do Ivaí 102-103 FG 5
São Pedro do Piauí 100-101 C 3
São Pedro do Sul [BR] 106-107 K 2
São Rafael 100-101 F 3
São Raimundo das Mangabeiras 100-101 B 4
São Raimundo de Codó 100-101 C 3
São Raimundo Nonato 92-93 L 6
São Romão [BR, Amazonas] 92-93 F 6
São Romão [BR, Minas Gerais] 92-93 KL 8
São Roque 102-103 J 5
São Roque, Cabo de — 92-93 MN 6
São Salvador [BR, Acre] 98-99 B 8
São Salvador [BR, Rio Grande do Sul] 106-107 M 2
São Sebastião [BR, Pará] 98-99 M 7
São Sebastião [BR, São Paulo] 102-103 K 5
São Sebastião, Canal de — 102-103 K 5-6
São Sebastião, Ilha de — 92-93 KL 9
São Sebastião, Ponta — 172 G 6
São Sebastião do Boa Vista 98-99 O 5
São Sebastião do Paraíso 102-103 J 4
São Sebastião do Passé 100-101 E 7
São Sebastião do Umbuzeiro 100-101 F 4-5
São Sepé 106-107 L 3
São Simão 102-103 J 4
São Simão, Ponta — 106-107 M 3
São Simão, Represa de — 92-93 JK 8
São Tiago 98-99 K 5
São Tomás de Aquino 102-103 J 4
São Tomé [BR] 100-101 F 4
São Tomé [São Tomé and Principe] 164-165 F 8
São Tomé, Cabo de — 92-93 LM 9
São Tomé, Ilha — 164-165 F 8-9
São Tomé, Pico de — 168-169 G 5
São Tomé and Principe 164-165 F 8
Şaouîra, eş — = Aş-Şawîrah 164-165 BC 2
Saoula 170 I a 2
Saoura, Ouèd — = Wādī as-Sāwrah 164-165 D 2-3
São Vicente [BR, Goiás] 100-101 A 7
São Vicente [BR, São Paulo] 92-93 K 9
São Vicente [Cape Verde] 204-205 E 7
São Vicente, Cabo de — 120-121 C 10
São Vicente, Serra de — 104-105 G 4
São Vicente de Minas 102-103 K 4
São Vicente Ferrer 100-101 B 2
São Xavier, Serra de — 106-107 KL 2
Sápai 122-123 L 5
Sapão, Rio — 100-101 B 6
Sapateiro, Cachoeira do — 92-93 H 5
Sapé [BR] 100-101 G 4
Sape [RI] 148-149 G 8
Sape, Selat — 152-153 N 10
Sapele 164-165 EF 7
Sapello, NM 76-77 B 5
Sapelo Island 80-81 F 5
Şaphane dağı 136-137 C 3
Sapiéntza 122-123 J 7
Sapinero, CO 68-69 C 6
Sapiranga 106-107 M 2
Šapki 124-125 H 4
Sapo, Serranía del — 94-95 B 4
Sapopema 102-103 G 5
Saposoa 92-93 D 6
Sa Pout = Ban Sa Pout 150-151 C 2
Sapožok 124-125 N 7
Sappa Creek 68-69 F 6
Sapphire Mountains 66-67 G 2-3
Sappho, WA 66-67 AB 1
Sapporo 142-143 QR 3
Sapri 122-123 F 5
Šapsucho, gora — 126-127 J 4
Sapt Kosi 134-135 O 5
Sapucai, Rio — 102-103 HJ 4
Sapucaia 102-103 L 5
Sapucaia do Sul 106-107 M 2
Sapudi, Pulau — 148-149 FG 8
Sapudi, Selat — 152-153 L 9
Sapuka Besar, Pulau — 152-153 N 9
Sapulpa, OK 64-65 G 4
Sapulut 152-153 M 3
Sa Put = Ban Sa Pout 150-151 C 2
Sapwe 171 B 5
Saqasiq, Es- = Az-Zaqaziq 164-165 KL 2
Sa Qi = Jin Jiang 146-147 FG 9
Saqīyat al-Ḥamrā' 164-165 B 3
Saqīyat Makkī 170 II b 2
Saqīyat Sīdī Yūsuf 166-167 L 1
Şaqqārah 173 B 3
Saqqez 134-135 F 3
Saquarema 102-103 L 5
Saquisilí 96-97 B 2
Sara, poluostrov — 126-127 O 7
Sarāb 136-137 M 4
Sarāb-e Gīlān 136-137 LM 5
Saraburi 148-149 D 4
Sarafutsu 144-145 c 1
Saragossa = Zaragoza 120-121 G 8
Saraguro 92-93 D 5
Sarai [SU] 124-125 N 7
Saraikelā 138-139 KL 6
Sarajevo 122-123 H 4
Sarala 132-133 Q 7
Saramabila 171 AB 4
Saramacca 98-99 KL 2
Saramaṭī 134-135 P 5
Sarampiuni 104-105 B 4
Saran' [SU, Kazachskaja SSR] 132-133 N 8
Šaran [SU, Rossijskaja SFSR] 124-125 U 6
Sāran = Chhaprā 134-135 N 5
Saran, Gunung — 152-153 J 6
Saran Bay 58-59 p 6
Saranac Lake, NY 72-73 J 2
Saranda 171 C 4
Sarandë 122-123 HJ 6
Sarandi [BR] 106-107 L 1
Sarandí [ROU] 106-107 J 3
Sarandí, Arroyo — 106-107 H 2-3
Sarandí, Avellaneda- 110 III bc 2
Sarandí del Yí 111 EF 4
Sarandí Grande 106-107 J 4
Šaranga 124-125 Q 5
Sarangani Bay 148-149 HJ 5
Sarangani Islands 148-149 HJ 5
Sārangarh 138-139 J 7
Sārangpur 138-139 F 6
Saranlay 164-165 N 8
Saranpaul' 132-133 L 5
Saransk 132-133 GH 7
Saránta Ekklēsies = Kırklareli 134-135 B 2
Saranzal, Cachoeira — 98-99 H 8
Sara-Ostrov = Narimanabad 126-127 O 7
Saraphi 150-151 B 3
Sarapuí 102-103 J 5
Sarapul 132-133 J 6
Sarapul'skaja vozvyšennost' 124-125 T 5-6
Sarapul'skoje 132-133 a 8
Sararāt Sayyāl, Bi'r — 173 D 6
Sararāt Seiyit = Bi'r Sararāt Sayyāl 173 D 6
Sarare, Río — 94-95 F 4
Sarasa 106-107 G 4-5
Sarāskand = Hashtrūd 136-137 M 4
Sarasota, FL 64-65 K 6
Saraswati 138-139 C 6
Sarāt, Ḥāssī — 166-167 H 5
Sarata 126-127 D 3-4
Sarath 138-139 L 5
Saratoga, WY 68-69 C 5
Saratoga Springs, NY 64-65 M 3
Saratok 152-153 J 5
Saratov 124-125 PQ 8
Saratovskoje vodochranilišče 124-125 R 7
Sarāvān 134-135 J 5
Saravane 148-149 E 3
Saravatā, Ilha do — 110 I b 1
Saravena 94-95 F 4
Sarawak 148-149 F 6
Saray 136-137 B 2
Sarāyah 136-137 F 5
Saraykela = Saraikelā 138-139 KL 6
Sarayköy 136-137 C 4
Sarayū = Ghāghara 134-135 N 5
Sarbhōg = Sorbhog 141 B 2
Sarcelles 129 I c 2
Sār Cham 136-137 MN 4
Sarco 106-107 B 2
Sārda 138-139 H 3
Sardalas 164-165 G 3
Sardarabad = Oktember'an 126-127 LM 6
Sardārpur 138-139 E 6
Sardārshahar = Sardārshahr 134-135 L 5
Sardārshahr 134-135 L 5
Sar Dasht [IR, Khūzestān] 136-137 N 6
Sar Dasht [IR, Kordestān] 136-137 L 4
Sardegna 122-123 C 5
Sardes 136-137 C 3
Sardhāna 138-139 F 3
Sardinata 94-95 E 3
Sardinia, OH 72-73 E 5
Sardinia = Sardegna 122-123 C 5
Sardis, GA 80-81 EF 4
Sardis, MS 78-79 E 3
Sardis Lake 78-79 E 3
Sardis Reservoir = Sardis Lake 78-79 E 3
Sardonem' 124-125 P 2
Sard Rūd 136-137 LM 3
Sare 171 C 3
Sarek nationalpark 116-117 GH 4
Sarektjåkko 116-117 G 4
Sarempaka, Gunung — 152-153 L 6
Sar-e Pol-e Dhahāb 136-137 LM 5
Sarepta = Krasnoarmejsk 126-127 M 2
Sarepul 134-135 K 3
Sargasso Sea 64-65 N-P 6
Sargent, NE 68-69 G 5
Sargent Icefield 58-59 N 6
Sargento Lores 96-97 D 3
Sargento Paixão, Serra do — 104-105 F 2
Sargento Valinotti 102-103 B 4
Sargents, CO 68-69 C 6
Sargho, Djebel — = Jabal Şaghrū' 164-165 C 2
Sargoda = Sargodhā 134-135 L 4
Sargodhā 134-135 L 4
Sargon, Dur — = Khorsabad 136-137 K 4
Šargorod 126-127 CD 2
Sargur 140 C 4-5
Sarh 164-165 H 7
Sarhade Wākhān 134-135 L 3
Şarhrô', Jbel — = Jabal Şaghrū' 164-165 C 2
Sārī 134-135 G 3
Sariá 122-123 M 8
Saridú, Laguna — 94-95 GH 6
Sarıgöl 136-137 C 3
Sarıkamış 136-137 K 2
Sarıkavak = Kumluca 136-137 D 4
Sarıkavak = Kürkcü 136-137 E 4
Sarıkaya = Gömele 136-137 D 2
Sarıkaya = Haman 136-137 F 3
Sarikei 148-149 F 6
Sarina 158-159 J 4
Sarıoğlan 136-137 FG 3
Sarir 164-165 J 3
Sarīr Tibastī 164-165 H 4
Sarīshābārī 138-139 M 5
Sarita 106-107 L 4
Sarita, TX 76-77 F 9
Sarī Tappah 136-137 KL 5
Sariwŏn 142-143 O 4
Sarıyar barajı 136-137 D 2
Sarıyer, İstanbul- 136-137 C 3
Sarız = Köyyeri 136-137 G 3
Sarj, Jabal as- 166-167 L 2
Šarja 132-133 H 6
Sarjāpur 140 C 4
Sarjāpura = Sarjāpur 140 C 4
Sarjū = Ghāghara 134-135 N 5
Sark 119 E 7
Šarkan 124-125 T 5
Şarkîkaraağaç 136-137 D 3
Sarkin Pawa 168-169 G 3
Şarkışla 136-137 G 3
Šarkovščina 124-125 FG 6
Sarlat 120-121 H 6
Sarles, ND 68-69 G 1
Sarmaor = Sirmūr 138-139 F 2
Şărmăsag 122-123 K 2
Sarmi 148-149 L 7
Sarmiento 111 BC 7
Sarmiento, Cordillera — 108-109 C 8-9
Sarmiento, Monte — 108-109 D 10
Sarmiento-José C. Paz 110 III a 1
Sär mörön 142-143 MN 3
Särna 116-117 E 7
Sarneh 136-137 M 6
Sarnia 56-57 U 9
Sarny 124-125 F 8
Saroako 152-153 O 7
Sarolangun 148-149 D 7
Saroma-ko 144-145 c 1
Saron 174-175 C 7
Saronikòs Kólpos 122-123 K 7
Saros körfezi 136-137 B 2
Sarpa 126-127 M 3
Sarpi 126-127 K 6
Sarpinskije oz'ora 126-127 M 2-3
Šar Planina 122-123 J 4-5
Sarpsborg 116-117 D 8
Sar Qal'ah 136-137 L 5
Sarrah, Ma'tan as- 164-165 J 4
Sarrāţ, Rā's — 166-167 L 1
Sarre, la — 56-57 V 8
Sarrebourg 120-121 L 4
Sarreguemines 120-121 L 4
Sarria 120-121 D 7
Sarro, Djebel — = Jabal Şaghrū 164-165 C 2
Sars, As- 166-167 L 1
Šar Süm = Altay 142-143 F 2
Sartana = Primorskoje 126-127 H 3
Sartang 132-133 Z 4
Sartène 122-123 C 5
Sarthe 120-121 G 5
Sartrouville 129 I b 2
Saruhan = Manisa 134-135 B 2
Saruhanlı 136-137 B 3
Sārūq Chāy 136-137 M 4
Saruyama-zaki 144-145 L 4
Sarvār = Sarwār 138-139 E 4
S'arve = Sõrve 124-125 D 5
Sarwār 138-139 E 4
Saryč, mys — 126-127 F 4
Sary-Išikotrau 132-133 O 8
Saryngol 142-143 K 2
Saryozek 132-133 O 9
Saryšagan 132-133 N 8
Sarysu 132-133 M 8
Sarytaš [SU, Kazachskaja SSR] 126-127 P 4
Sary-Taš [SU, Tadžikskaja SSR] 134-135 L 3
S'as' 124-125 J 4
Sas, Het — 128 II b 1
Sāsabe 86-87 E 2
Sasaginnigak Lake 62 AB 2
Sasake, Yokohama- 155 III a 3
Sasar, Tanjung — 152-153 NO 10
Sasarām 138-139 JK 5
Sasardí Viejo 94-95 C 3
Sasebo 142-143 O 5
Sasel, Hamburg- 130 I b 1
Saskatchewan 56-57 PQ 6-7
Saskatchewan River 56-57 Q 7
Saskatoon 56-57 P 7
Saskylach 132-133 VW 3
Sasmik, Cape — 58-59 u 7
Sasolburg 174-175 G 4
Sason = Kabilcevaz 136-137 J 3
Sason dağları 136-137 J 3
Sasovo 124-125 NO 6
Saspamco, TX 76-77 E 8
Sassafras Mountain 80-81 E 3
Sassandra [CI, place] 164-165 C 7-8
Sassandra [CI, river] 164-165 C 7
Sàssari 122-123 C 5
Sassnitz 118 FG 1
Sasstown 168-169 C 4
S'as'stroj 124-125 J 3
Sastobe 132-133 MN 9
Sastre 106-107 FG 3
Sāsvad 140 AB 1
Sasyk, ozero — [SU, Krymskaja Oblast'] 126-127 F 4
Sasyk, ozero — [SU, Odesskaja Oblast'] 126-127 DE 4
Sasykkol', ozero — 132-133 P 8
Sasyktau 126-127 O 3
Sata 144-145 H 7
Satadougou 164-165 B 6
Satakunta 116-117 JK 7
Sata-misaki 142-143 OP 5
Satāna 138-139 E 7
Satanov 126-127 C 2
Satanta, KS 68-69 F 7
Sātāra 134-135 L 7
Satawal 148-149 N 5
Satawan 208 F 2
Satelite, Ciudad — 91 I b 1
Satengar, Pulau — 152-153 M 9
Satevó 86-87 G 3-4
Sathing Phra 150-151 C 9
Satiḍera 138-139 C 5
Saţīf 164-165 F 1
Saţīl 166-167 J 2
Satilla River 80-81 F 5
Satipo 92-93 DE 7
Satiri 168-169 D 3
Satırlar 136-137 C 4
Sātiro Dias 100-101 E 6
Saţīţan 166-167 G 3
Satka 132-133 KL 6
Satkania = Sātkāniya 141 BC 4
Sātkāniya 141 BC 4
Sātkhīrā 138-139 M 6
Satki 124-125 P 6
Satlaj 134-135 L 4
Satlaj = Langchhen Khamba 142-143 DE 5
Sätleg = Satlaj 134-135 L 4
Sātmāla Hills 138-139 DE 7
Satna 138-139 H 5
Sátoraljaújhely 118 K 4
Sātpura Range 134-135 L-N 6
Satsuma-hantō 144-145 GH 7
Sattahip 148-149 D 4
Saţţāt 164-165 C 2
Sattenapalle 140 DE 2
Sattēnpalli = Sattenapalle 140 DE 2
Sāttūr 140 CD 6
Satuk 150-151 D 5
Satul = Satun 150-151 BC 9
Satu Mare 122-123 K 2
Satun 150-151 BC 9
Šatura 124-125 M 6
Saturnina, Rio — 98-99 J 11
Saturnino M. Laspiur 106-107 F 3
Satyamangalam 140 C 5
Sauce [RA] 111 E 3-4
Sauce [ROU] 106-107 JK 5
Sauce, El — 88-89 C 8
Sauce, Laguna del — 106-107 K 5
Sauce Chico, Río — 106-107 F 7
Sauce Corto, Arroyo — 106-107 G 6
Sauce de Luna 106-107 H 3
Sauce Grande, Río — 106-107 G 7
Sauces, Los — 106-107 A 6
Sauce Viejo 106-107 G 3
Saucier, MS 78-79 E 5
Saucillo 86-87 H 3-4
Saucito 86-87 K 4
Sauda 116-117 B 8
Sauda, Jebel el — = Jabal a Sawdā' 164-165 GH 3
Sauda, Jebel el — = Jabal as-Sawdā' 164-165 GH 3
Saudade, Cachoeira da — 98-99 M 8
Saudade, Serra da — 102-103 K 3
Saudável 100-101 CD 7
Saúde 92-93 L 7
Saúde, São Paulo- 110 II b 2
Saudhárkrókur 116-117 d 2
Saudi Arabia 134-135 D 5-F 6
Saudi Kingdom = Saudi Arabia 134-135 D 5-F 6
Saueuina, Rio — 104-105 G 3
Saugeen Peninsula = Bruce Peninsula 72-73 F 2
Saugeen River 72-73 F 2
Saugerties, NY 72-73 JK 3
Saugor = Sāgar 134-135 M 6
Saugus, MA 84 I b 2
Saugus River 84 I c 2
Saūjbolāgh = Mahābād 134-135 F 3
Saujil 104-105 C 11
Sauk Centre, MN 70-71 C 3
Sauk City, WI 70-71 EF 4
Saukira Bay = Dawḥat as-Sawqirah 134-135 H 7
Sau Ki Wan, Victoria- 155 I b 2
Saukorem 148-149 K 7
Sauk Rapids, MN 70-71 CD 3
Saül 92-93 J 4
Šaul'der 132-133 M 9
Saulkrasti 124-125 DE 5
Saulspoort 174-175 G 3
Sault-au-Mouton 63 B 3
Sault-au-Recollet, Montréal- 82 I b 1
Sault aux Cochons, Rivière du — 63 B 3
Sault-Sainte-Marie 56-57 U 8
Sault Sainte Marie, MI 64-65 JK 2
Šaum'ani 126-127 M 6
Sau Mau Ping 155 I b 2
Saumlaki 148-149 K 8
Saumur 120-121 G 5
Saundatti 140 B 3
Şauqirah, Ghubbat — = Dawḥat as-Sawqirah 134-135 H 7
Saura, Wed — = Wādī as-Sāwrah 164-165 D 2-3
Saurāshtra 134-135 KL 6
Sauri Hill 168-169 G 3
Saurimo 172 D 3
Sausalito, CA 74-75 B 4
Sausar 138-139 G 7
Sausu 152-153 O 6
Sautar 172 C 4
Sautatá 94-95 C 4
Sauz, El — 86-87 G 3
Sauzal, El — 74-75 E 7
S'ava [SU] 124-125 Q 4
Sava [YU] 122-123 J 3
Savage, MT 68-69 D 2
Savage River 160 b 2
Savageton, WY 68-69 CD 4
Savai'i 148-149 c 1
Savāī Mādhōpur = Sawai Mādhopur 138-139 F 5
Savalou 164-165 E 7
Savane, Rivière — 63 A 2
Savanes 168-169 EF 3
Savanna, IL 70-71 E 4
Savannah, GA 64-65 KL 5
Savannah, MO 70-71 C 6
Savannah, TN 78-79 EF 3
Savannah Beach, GA 80-81 F 4
Savannah River 64-65 K 5
Savannakhet 148-149 DE 3
Savanna-la-Mar 88-89 G 5
Savanne 70-71 EF 1
Savant Lake [CDN, lake] 62 D 2
Savant Lake [CDN, place] 62 D 2
Sāvantvādi 140 AB 3
Savanūr 140 B 3
Savanūru = Savanūr 140 B 3
Sāvar = Sānwer 138-139 E 6
Savari = Sābarī 134-135 N 7
Savaştepe 136-137 B 3
Sāvda 138-139 E 7
Savé [DY] 164-165 E 7
Save [F] 120-121 H 7
Save, Rio — 172 F 6
Sāveh 134-135 G 3-4
Savery, WY 68-69 C 5
Savigliano 122-123 BC 3
Savin Hill, Boston-, MA 84 I b 3
Savinka 126-127 N 1
Savino [SU, Ivanovskaja Oblast'] 124-125 N 5
Savino-Borisovskaja 124-125 P 2
Sāvnēr = Saoner 138-139 G 7
Savo 116-117 M 6-7
Savoie 120-121 L 5-6
Sāvojbolāgh = Mahābād 134-135 F 3
Savona 122-123 C 3
Savonlinna 116-117 N 7
Savoy, MT 68-69 B 1
Savran' 126-127 DE 2
Şavşat = Yeniköy 136-137 K 2
Sävsjö 116-117 F 9
Savu = Pulau Sawu 148-149 H 9
Savukoski 116-117 N 4
Savur 136-137 J 4
Savu Sea 148-149 H 8
Saw = Hsaw 141 D 5
Şawāb, Wādī aş- 136-137 J 5
Sawa Besar, Jakarta- 154 IV ab 1
Sawahlunto 148-149 D 7
Sawai Mādhopur 138-139 F 5
Sawākīn 164-165 M 5
Sawang Daen Din 150-151 D 4
Sawankhalok 150-151 BC 4
Sawantwadi = Sāvantvādi 140 AB 3
Sawara 144-145 N 5
Sawata 144-145 M 3-4
Sawatch Mountains 64-65 E 4
Sawazaki-bana 144-145 LM 4
Sawbill 61 H 2
Sawdā', Jabal as- 164-165 GH 3
Sawdirī 164-165 K 6
Sawer = Sānwer 138-139 E 6
Sawi 150-151 B 7
Sawilo 168-169 C 4
Şawīrah, Aş- 164-165 BC 2
Sawknah 164-165 GH 3
Sawner = Saoner 138-139 G 7
Sawqirah 134-135 H 7
Sawqirah, Dawḥat as- 134-135 H 7
Şawrah, Aş- 173 D 4
Sāwrah, Wādī as- 164-165 D 2-3
Sawtooth Mount 58-59 MN 4
Sawtooth Mountains 66-67 FG 3
Sawtooth Range 66-67 C 1-2
Sawu, Pulau — 148-149 H 9
Şawwān, 'Ard aş- 136-137 G 7
Sawyer, KS 68-69 G 7
Saxon, WI 70-71 E 2
Saxony = Sachsen 118 F 3
Saxton, PA 72-73 GH 4
Say 164-165 E 6
Sayaboury 148-149 D 3
Sayalgudi = Sāyalkudi 140 D 6
Sāyalkudi 140 D 6
Sayán 96-97 C 7
Sayausí 96-97 B 3
Şayda' [DZ] 166-167 G 2
Şaydā [RL] 134-135 CD 4
Şayda', Jabal aş- 166-167 G 2
Şayhūt 134-135 G 7
Saykh, Jabal as- 136-137 FG 6
Sāyla 138-139 C 6
Saymo Lake 70-71 J 2
Sayn Shanda = Sajnšand 142-143 KL 3
Sayo = Dembī Dolo 164-165 LM 7
Şayq, Wādī — 134-135 F 8
Sayre, OK 76-77 E 5
Sayre, PA 72-73 H 4
Sayula 86-87 HJ 8
Say'ūn 134-135 F 7
Sazanit 122-123 H 5
Sāzīn 136-137 N 5
Sazonovo 124-125 K 4

Sba = Saba' 166-167 F 5
Sbartel, Berzekh — = Rā's Ashaqār 166-167 CD 2
Sbeïtla = S'bītlat 166-167 L 2
Sbība = Sabībah 166-167 L 2
Sbīkha = As-Sābirah 166-167 M 2
Sbita, Oglat — = 'Uqlāt as-Sabīyah 166-167 D 7
S'bītlat 166-167 L 2
S'bū', Wād — 164-165 CD 2

Scafell Pike 119 E 4
Scalloway 119 F 1
Scammon Bay 58-59 E 5-6
Scammon Bay, AK 58-59 E 6
Scandia 61 BC 5
Scandia, KS 68-69 H 6
Scandinavia 114-115 K 4-N 1
Scānia = Skåne 130 III b 1
Scapa 61 B 5
Scapa Flow 119 E 2
Scappoose, OR 66-67 B 3
Ščara 124-125 E 7
Scarborough [GB] 119 FG 4
Scarborough [TT] 64-65 OP 9
Scarpanto = Kárpathos 122-123 M 8
Scarsdale, LA 85 I c 2
Scarth 61 H 6
Sceaux 129 I c 2
Ščeglovsk = Kemerovo 132-133 PQ 6
Ščelejki 124-125 K 3
Scenic, SD 68-69 E 4
Scenic Woods, Houston-, TX 85 III b 1
Scerpeddi, Punta — 122-123 C 6
Schäferberg 130 III a 2
Schaffhausen 118 D 5
Schafflerhof 113 I c 2
Schafrivier 174-175 B 2
Schamelbeek 128 II a 2
Šchara, gora — 126-127 L 5
Schaumburg, IL 70-71 F 5
Schebschi Mountains 164-165 G 7
Schefferville 56-57 X 7
Schelde 120-121 J 3
Schell Creek Range 74-75 F 3
Schellingwoude 128 I b 1
Schenectady, NY 64-65 LM 3
Schenkenhorst 130 III a 2
Schepdaal 128 II a 1-2
Schildow 130 III b 1
Schiplaken 128 II b 1
Schíza 122-123 J 7
Schleinikon 128 IV a 1
Schleswig 118 DE 1
Schleswig-Holstein 118 D 1-E 2
Schloss Charlottenburg 130 III b 1
Schloss Fürstenried 130 II a 2
Schlosspark Nymphenburg 130 II ab 2
Schlüchtern 118 DE 3
Schmargendorf, Berlin- 130 III b 2
Schmidt Island = ostrov Šmidta 132-133 QR 1
Schnelsen, Hamburg- 130 I a 1
Schneppenhausen 128 III a 2
Schöfflisdorf 128 IV a 1
Scholle, NM 76-77 A 5
Schönberg [D, Hessen] 128 III a 1
Schöneck [D] 128 III b 1
Schönerlinde 130 III b 1
Schönfliess [DDR, Potsdam] 130 III b 1
Schönwalde [DDR, Potsdam] 130 III a 1
Schoombee 174-175 F 6
Schouten Island 160 d 3
Schouw, Het — 128 I b 1
Schouwen 120-121 J 3
Schrag, WA 66-67 D 2
Schreiber 70-71 G 1
Schuckmannsburg 172 D 5
Schuler 61 C 5
Schulpfontein Point = Skulpfonteinpunt 174-175 B 6
Schulzenhöhe 130 III cd 2
Schurz, NV 74-75 D 3
Schuyler, NE 68-69 H 5
Schuylkill River 84 III b 1
Schwabach 118 E 4
Schwabinger Bach 130 II bc 1
Schwäbische Alb 118 D 5-E 4
Schwäbisch Gmünd 118 DE 4
Schwäbisch Hall 118 DE 4
Schwamendingen, Zürich- 128 IV b 1
Schwandorf 118 F 4
Schwaner, Pegunungan — 148-149 F 7
Schwanheim, Frankfurt am Main- 128 III a 1
Schwänkelberg 128 IV a 1
Schwarzbach [D ◁ RO] 128 III a 2

Schwarze Elster 118 FG 3
Schwarzes Meer 126-127 E-J 5
Schwarzwald 118 D 4-5
Schwatka Mountains 56-57 EF 4
Schweinfurt 118 E 3
Schweinsand 130 I a 1
Schweitzergletscher 53 B 32-33
Schweizer Land 56-57 d 4
Schweizer-Reneke 174-175 F 4
Schwerin 118 E 2
Schwerzenbach 128 IV b 1
Schwyz 118 D 5
Sciacca 122-123 E 7
Scicli 122-123 F 7
Scie, la — 63 J 2
Science and Industry, Museum of — 83 II b 2
Ščigry [SU, Kurskaja Oblast'] 124-125 L 8
Scilly, Isles of — 119 C 7
Scioto River 72-73 E 5
Scipio, UT 74-75 G 3
Scobey, MT 68-69 D 1
Ščokino 124-125 M 6-7
Scone 160 K 4
Scoresby Land 52 B 21
Scoresby Sund [Greenland, bay] 52 B 20-21
Scoresbysund [Greenland, place] 52 B 20-21
Ščors 124-125 H 8
Scotia, CA 66-67 AB 5
Scotia Ridge 50-51 G 8
Scotland 119 D 3-E 4
Scotland, SD 68-69 GH 4
Scotland Neck, NC 80-81 H 2
Scotstown 72-73 L 2
Scott 53 B 17-18
Scott, Cape — 56-57 L 7
Scott, Mount — [USA → Crater Lake] 64-65 B 3
Scott, Mount — [USA ↓ Pengra Pass] 66-67 BC 4
Scottburgh 174-175 J 6
Scott Channel 60 C 4
Scott City, KS 68-69 F 6
Scottcrest Park 85 III b 2
Scott Glacier [Antarctica, Dronning Maud fjellkjede] 53 A 21-23
Scott Glacier [Antarctica, Knox Land] 53 C 11
Scottie Creek Lodge, AK 58-59 R 5
Scott Inlet 56-57 WX 3
Scott Island 53 C 19
Scott Islands 60 C 4
Scott Middle Ground 84 II c 2
Scott Mittle Ground 84 II bc 2
Scott Range 53 C 5-6
Scott Reef 158-159 D 2
Scott Run 82 II a 1
Scottsbluff, NE 64-65 F 3
Scottsboro, AL 78-79 FG 3
Scottsburg, IN 70-71 GH 6
Scottsburg = Scottburgh 174-175 J 6
Scottsdale 158-159 J 8
Scotts Head 88-89 Q 7
Scottsville, KY 78-79 F 2
Scottsville, VA 80-81 G 2
Scottville, MI 70-71 GH 4
Scranton, AR 78-79 C 3
Scranton, PA 64-65 LM 3
Scribner, NE 68-69 H 5
Ščučinsk 132-133 MN 7
Scunthorpe 119 FG 5
Scutari = İstanbul-Üsküdar 134-135 BC 2
Scutari = Shkodër 122-123 H 4
Scutari, Lake — = Skadarsko jezero 122-123 H 4
Scythopolis = Bet-Sheʾan 136-137 F 6
Sé, São Paulo- 110 II b 2
Seabra 100-101 D 7
Seadrift, TX 76-77 F 8
Seaford, DE 72-73 J 5
Seagraves, TX 76-77 C 6
Seagull Lake 70-71 E 1
Seaham 119 F 4
Sea Islands 64-65 K 5
Seal, Cape — = Kaap Seal 174-175 E 8
Seal, Kaap — 174-175 E 8
Sea Lake 160 F 5
Seal Cape 58-59 d 1
Seale, AL 78-79 G 4
Sea Lion Islands 111 E 8
Seal Islands 58-59 d 1
Seal Point = Sealpunt 174-175 F 8
Sealpunt 174-175 F 8
Seal River 56-57 R 6
Sealy, TX 76-77 F 8
Sea of the Hebrides 119 C 3
Seara 102-103 F 7
Searchlight, NV 74-75 F 5
Searchmont 70-71 HJ 2
Searcy, AR 78-79 CD 3
Searles Lake 74-75 E 5
Searsport, ME 72-73 M 2
Sears Tower 83 II b 1
Seaside, CA 74-75 C 4
Seaside, OR 66-67 B 3
Seaside Park, NJ 72-73 JK 5
Seaton 60 D 2
Seat Plesant, MD 82 II b 2
Seattle, WA 64-65 B 2
Sebáʿ, Gebel es- = Qārat as-Sabʿah 164-165 H 3
Sebago Lake 72-73 L 3
Se Bai, Lam — 150-151 E 4-5
Sebangan, Teluk — 148-149 F 7
Se Bang Fai 150-151 E 4
Se Bang Hieng 150-151 E 4
Sebangka, Pulau — 148-149 DE 6
Sebarok, Pulau — 154 III a 2
Sebaru 152-153 M 10
Sebastian, FL 80-81 c 3
Sebastian, Cape — 66-67 A 4
Sebastián Elcano 106-107 F 3
Sebastián Vizcaíno, Bahía — 64-65 CD 6
Sebastopol, CA 74-75 B 3
Sebatik, Pulau — 148-149 G 6
Sebba 168-169 F 2
Sebbara = Al-Gārah 166-167 C 3
Sebdou = Sībdū 166-167 F 2
Sebeka, MN 70-71 C 2
Šebekino 126-127 H 1
Sébékoro 168-169 C 2
Seben 136-137 D 2
Seberi 106-107 L 1
Sebeş 122-123 K 2-3
Sebes Körös 118 K 5
Sebewaing, MI 72-73 E 3
Sebež 124-125 G 5
Sebḥa = Sabhah 164-165 G 3
Şebinkarahisar 136-137 H 2
Sebka Oum ed Drouss = Sabkhat Umm ad-Durūs 164-165 B 4
Sebkha el Adhibat = Sabkhat Tādīt 166-167 M 3
Sebkha Oumm el Drouss = Sabkhat Umm ad-Durūs 164-165 B 4
Sebkhet el Mèlaḥ = Sabkhat al-Māliḥ 166-167 M 3
Sebkhet Kelbia = Sabkhat Kalbīyah 166-167 M 2
Sebkhet Oum el Krialat = Sabkhat Umm al-Khiyālāt 166-167 M 3
Sebkra Aïne Belbela = Sabkhat ʿAyn Balbālah 166-167 D 6
Sebkra Azzel Matti = Sabkhat ʿAzmātī 164-165 DE 3
Sebkra de Timimoun = Sabkhat Tīmīmūn 166-167 G 5
Sebkra de Tindouf = Sabkhat Tindūf 164-165 C 3
Sebkra el Melah = Sabkhat al-Malah 166-167 F 5
Sebkra Mekerrhane = Sabkhat Mukrān 164-165 E 3
Sebkret Tadet = Sabkhat Tādīt 166-167 M 3
Seboû, Ouèd — = Wad Sʼbūʼ 166-167 D 2
Sebree, KY 70-71 G 7
Sebring, FL 80-81 c 3
Sebseb = Sabsab 166-167 H 3
Sebta = Ceuta 164-165 CD 1
Sebt ʾImrhât = Sabt ʾImghāt 166-167 AB 4
Sebt Jzoûla = As-Sabt Gʼzūlah 166-167 B 3
Sebu = Wād Sbūʼ 166-167 D 2
Sebuku, Pulau — 148-149 G 7
Sebuku, Teluk — 148-149 G 6
Seburi-yama 144-145 H 6
Sebuyau 152-153 J 5
Secane, PA 84 III b 2
Secaucus, NJ 82 III b 2
Secen Chaan = Öndörchaan 142-143 L 2
Sečenovo 124-125 PQ 6
Sechelt 66-67 AB 1
Sechuan = Sichuan 142-143 J 5-6
Sechura 92-93 C 6
Sechura, Bahía de — 92-93 C 6
Sechura, Desierto de — 96-97 A 4-5
Seckbach, Frankfurt am Main- 128 III b 1
Secunderābād 134-135 M 7
Sécure, Río — 104-105 C 4
Sedalia 61 C 5
Sedalia, MO 70-71 D 6
Sedan, KS 76-77 F 4
Sedan [AUS] 158-159 G 6
Sedan [F] 120-121 K 4
Sedanau, Pulau — 150-151 F 11
Sedanka Island 58-59 no 4
Sedaw = Hsindau 141 E 4
Seddinsee 130 III c 2
Seddonville 158-159 O 8
Sedel'nikovo 132-133 O 6
Sedgwick, KS 68-69 H 7
Sédhiou 164-165 AB 6
Sedili Besar 150-151 E 12
Šedjenān = Sijnān 166-167 L 1
Šedok 126-127 K 4
Sedôktayā 141 D 5
Sĕdôm 136-137 F 7
Sedona, AZ 74-75 H 5
Sedone 150-151 EF 5
Sedova, pik — 132-133 J 3
Sedrata = Sadrātah 166-167 K 1
Šeduva 124-125 DE 6
Seebach, Zürich- 128 IV b 1
Seeberg [DDR] 130 III c 1
Seeburg [DDR] 130 III a 1
Seechelt Peninsula 66-67 AB 1
Seefeld, Zürich- 128 IV b 1
Seeheim [Namibia] 172 C 7
Seehof 130 III b 2
Seeis 172 C 6
Seekoegat 174-175 E 7
Seekoerivier 174-175 F 6
Seeley Lake, MT 66-67 G 2
Şefaatli 136-137 F 3
Sefadu 164-165 B 7
Seferihisar 136-137 B 3
Séfeto 168-169 C 2
Sefīd, Kūh-e — 136-137 M 5-N 6
Sefīd Rūd 136-137 N 4
Sefkat 136-137 H 3
Şefroû = Şafrū 166-167 D 3
Segama, Sungei — 152-153 MN 3
Segamat 150-151 D 11
Segendy 126-127 P 5
Segesta 122-123 E 7
Segewold = Sigulda 124-125 E 5
Segeža 132-133 EF 5
Segguedim = Séguédine 164-165 G 4
Seggueur, Ouèd — = Wādī as-Sūqar 166-167 GH 3
Sego, UT 74-75 J 3
Segorbe 120-121 G 9
Ségou 164-165 C 6
Segovary 124-125 O 2
Segovia, TX 76-77 E 7
Segovia [CO] 94-95 D 4
Segovia [E] 120-121 E 8
Segovia, Río — = Río Coco 64-65 K 9
Segozero 124-125 J 2
Segré 120-121 G 5
Segre, Río — 120-121 H 8
Segu = Ségou 164-165 C 6
Seguam Island 58-59 kl 4
Seguam Pass 58-59 k 4
Séguédine 164-165 G 4
Séguéla 164-165 C 7
Séguénéga 168-169 E 2
Seguí 106-107 G 3
Seguin, TX 64-65 G 6
Seguine Point 82 III a 3
Segula Island 58-59 s 6
Seguntur 152-153 MN 5
Segura, Río — 120-121 G 9
Segura, Sierra de — 120-121 F 9-10
Sehirköy = Şarköy 136-137 B 2
Sehl Tamlélt = Sahl Tāmlilt 166-167 E 3
Sehore 138-139 F 6
Sehwan = Sihwān 138-139 AB 4
Sehzade Camii 154 I a 2
Seibal 86-87 P 9
Seibert, CO 68-69 E 6
Seikpyu = Hseikhpyū 141 D 5
Seiland 116-117 K 2
Seiling, OK 76-77 E 4
Seinäjoki 116-117 K 6
Seine 120-121 H 4
Seine, Baie de la — 120-121 G 4
Seinlôngabā 141 E 3
Seishin = Chʼŏngjin 142-143 OP 3
Seishū = Chʼŏngju 142-143 O 4
Seistan = Sīstān 134-135 J 4
Seitovka 126-127 O 3
Seival 106-107 L 3
Seiyit, Sararât — = Biʾr Sararāt Sayyāl 173 D 6
Sejaka 152-153 M 7
Sejm 126-127 F 1
Sejmčan 132-133 d 5
Sejny 118 L 1
Sejrī, Bīr — = Biʾr Sajarī 136-137 H 6
Sejtler = Nižnegorskij 126-127 G 4
Seka 150-151 DE 4
Sekala, Pulau — 152-153 M 9
Se Kamane 150-151 F 5
Sekayam, Sungai — 152-153 J 5
Sekayu 152-153 EF 7
Seke 172 F 2
Sekenke 172 F 2
Sekhuma 174-175 E 3
Sekiu, WA 66-67 A 1
Sekondi-Takoradi 164-165 D 7-8
Sé Kong [K] 150-151 F 5-6
Se Kong [LAO] 150-151 F 5
Sekretaris, Kali — 154 IV a 2
Šeksna [SU, place] 124-125 M 4
Šeksna [SU, river] 124-125 M 4
Selado, Morro — 102-103 JK 5
Šelagskij, mys — 132-133 gh 3
Selah, WA 66-67 C 2
Sělam = Salem 134-135 M 8
Selama 150-151 C 10
Selangor 150-151 C 11
Selangor, Kuala — 148-149 D 6
Selaphum 150-151 DE 4
Selaru, Pulau — 148-149 K 8
Selat Alas 148-149 G 8
Selat Alor 152-153 PQ 10
Selatan, Tanjung — 148-149 F 7
Selat Bali 152-153 L 10
Selat Bangka 148-149 E 7
Selat Berhala 152-153 EF 6
Selat Bungalaut 152-153 C 6-7
Selat Butung 152-153 P 8
Selat Cempi 152-153 N 10
Selat Dampier 148-149 K 7
Selat Gaspar 148-149 E 7
Selat Kabaena 152-153 O 8
Selat Karimata 148-149 E 7
Selat Lombok 148-149 G 8
Selat Madura 152-153 KL 9
Selat Makasar 148-149 G 6-7
Selat Malaka 152-153 A 3
Selat Melaka 148-149 CD 6
Selat Mentawai 152-153 C 6-D 7
Selat Peleng 152-153 P 6
Selat Raas 152-153 L 9
Selat Salayar 152-153 N 9-O 8
Selat Sape 152-153 N 10
Selat Sapudi 152-153 L 9
Selat Sengkir 154 III ab 2
Selat Serasan 150-151 G 11
Selat Siberut 148-149 C 7
Selat Sipora 152-153 CD 7
Selat Sumba 148-149 GH 8
Selat Sunda 148-149 E 8
Selat Tioro 152-153 P 8
Selat Walea 152-153 P 6
Selat Wowotobi 152-153 P 10
Selat Yapen 148-149 L 7
Selawik, AK 56-57 DE 4
Selawik Lake 56-57 DE 4
Selawik River 58-59 H 3
Selbu 116-117 D 6
Selby 119 F 5
Selby, SD 68-69 FG 3
Selby, Johannesburg- 170 V b 2
Selchow [DDR, Potsdam] 130 III b 2
Selden, KS 68-69 F 6
Seldovia, AK 56-57 F 6
Selemdža 132-133 YZ 7
Selemiyé = Salamīyah 136-137 G 5
Selendi 136-137 C 3
Selenge [Mongolia, administrative unit = 11 ◁] 142-143 K 2
Selenge [Mongolia, place] 142-143 J 2
Selenge mörön 142-143 J 2
Selenn'ach 132-133 a 4
Selenodolsk = Zelenodol'sk 132-133 HJ 6
Sélestat 120-121 L 4
Seletar [SGP, place] 154 III b 1
Seletar [SGP, river] 154 III a 1
Seletar, Pulau — 154 III b 1
Seletar Reservoir 154 III a 1
Seletyteniz, ozero — 132-133 N 7
Seleucia = Silifke 134-135 C 3
Seleucia Pieria = Samandağ 136-137 F 4
Selévkeia = Silifke 134-135 C 3
Selfoss 116-117 c 3
Selfridge, ND 68-69 F 2
Selhurst, London- 129 II b 2
Šelichova, zaliv — 132-133 e 5-6
Seliger, ozero — 124-125 J 5
Seligman, AZ 74-75 G 5
Seligman, MO 78-79 C 2
Selim 136-137 K 2
Selīma, Wāḥat es — = Wāḥāt Şalīmah 164-165 K 4
Selimiye 136-137 B 4
Selingdo 138-139 M 2
Seling Tsho 142-143 FG 5
Selinus 122-123 E 7
Seliphug Gonpa 142-143 E 5
Selišče [SU ↖ RO] 124-125 J 5
Seližarovo 124-125 JK 5
Seljord 116-117 C 8
Selkirk [CDN] 56-57 R 7
Selkirk Island 61 J 4
Selkirk Mountains 56-57 N 7-8
Selle, la — 88-89 KL 5
Selleck, WA 66-67 C 2
Sells, AZ 74-75 H 7
Selma, AL 64-65 J 5
Selma, CA 74-75 D 4
Selma, NC 80-81 G 3
Selmer, TN 78-79 E 3
Selong 152-153 M 10
Selous Game Reserve 172 G 3
Šeltozero 124-125 K 3
Selty 124-125 T 5
Seluan, Pulau — 150-151 F 10
Selui, Pulau — 152-153 G 7
Selukwe 172 F 5
Seluma 152-153 E 8
Selva 111 D 3
Selva de Montiel 106-107 H 3
Selvagens, Ilhas — 164-165 A 2
Selvas 90 DE 3
Selvas del Río de Oro 104-105 G 10
Selway River 66-67 F 2
Selwyn 158-159 H 4
Selwyn Mountains 56-57 KL 5
Selwyn Range 158-159 GH 4
Selz, ND 68-69 G 2
Šemacha 126-127 O 6
Semakau, Pulau — 154 III a 2
Seman 122-123 H 5
Semangka, Teluk — 152-153 F 8
Semans 61 F 5
Semarang 148-149 F 8
Se Mat = Ban Se Mat 150-151 F 6
Sematan 152-153 H 5
Semau, Pulau — 148-149 H 9
Sembakung, Sungai — 152-153 M 3-4
Sĕmbaligudā = Semiligūda 140 F 1
Sembawang [SGP, place] 154 III ab 1
Sembawang [SGP, river] 154 III a 1
Sembawang Hills 154 III ab 1
Sembien 140 E 4
Sembilan, Kepulauan — 150-151 C 10
Sembilan, Pulau — 150-151 B 10
Sembodja = Samboja 148-149 G 7
Şemdinli = Navşar 136-137 L 4
Semenanjung Blambangan 152-153 L 10
Semenivka = Sem'onovka [SU, Černigov] 124-125 J 7
Semenivka = Sem'onovka [SU, Poltavskaja Oblast'] 126-127 F 2
Semenovka = Sem'onovka [SU, Černigov] 124-125 J 7
Semenovka = Sem'onovka [SU, Poltavskaja Oblast'] 126-127 F 2
Semeru, Gunung — 148-149 F 8
Semeuluë, Pulau — 148-149 BC 6
Semeyen = Simēn 164-165 M 6
Semibratovo 124-125 M 5
Semibugry 126-127 O 3
Semidi Islands 58-59 e 1-2
Semikarakorskij 126-127 K 3
Semiligūda 140 F 1
Semiluki 124-125 M 8
Seminoe Dam, WY 68-69 C 4
Seminoe Mountains 68-69 C 4
Seminoe Reservoir 68-69 C 4
Seminole, OK 76-77 F 5
Seminole, TX 76-77 C 6
Seminole, Lake — 78-79 G 5
Semipalatinsk 132-133 OP 7
Semipolki 126-127 E 1
Semirara Islands 148-149 H 4
Semisopochnoi Island 58-59 st 6
Semitau 152-153 J 5
Semium 152-153 GH 3
Semiun, Pulau — 150-151 F 10
Semka = Sangā 148-149 C 2
Semmering 118 GH 5
Semnān 134-135 G 3
Semnan, Koll-e — 134-135 GH 3
Semois 120-121 K 4
Šemonaicha 132-133 P 7
Sem'onov 124-125 P 5
Sem'onovka [SU, Černigovskaja Oblast'] 124-125 J 7
Sem'onovka [SU, Poltavskaja Oblast'] 126-127 F 2
Šemordan 124-125 S 5
Semporna 152-153 N 3
Sempu, Pulau — 152-153 K 10
Semu 171 C 3
Semuda 152-153 K 7
Šemyšejka 124-125 P 7
Sen, Mu'o'ng — 150-151 E 3
Sen, Stung — 150-151 E 6
Seña, La — 106-107 D 4
Sena Aisen 108-109 C 5
Senador Firmino 102-103 L 4
Senador Pompeu 92-93 LM 6
Senaisla = Sunaysilah 136-137 J 5
Senaja 152-153 M 2
Sena Madureira 92-93 F 6
Sĕnānāyaka Samudraya 140 E 7
Senanga 172 D 5
Senate 68-69 B 1
Senatobia, MS 78-79 E 3
Šenber 132-133 M 8
Sendai [J, Kagoshima] 144-145 GH 7
Sendai [J, Miyagi] 142-143 R 4
Sendelingsdrif 174-175 B 5
Sĕndhavā = Sendhwa 138-139 E 7
Sendhwa 138-139 E 7
Sene 164-165 D 7
Senebui, Pulau — 150-151 C 11
Seneca, KS 68-69 H 6
Seneca, MO 76-77 G 4
Seneca, NE 68-69 F 4-5
Seneca, OR 66-67 D 3
Seneca, SC 80-81 E 3
Seneca, SD 68-69 G 3
Seneca Falls, NY 72-73 H 3
Seneca Lake 72-73 H 3
Sened, Es — = As-Sanad 166-167 L 2
Sénégal [SN, river] 164-165 B 5
Sénégal [SN, state] 164-165 AB 6
Senegal = Sénégal 164-165 AB 6
Sénégal-Oriental 168-169 AB 2
Sénégambia 168-169 AB 2
Senekal 174-175 G 5
Senen, Jakarta- 154 IV b 2
Seney, MI 70-71 H 2
Seng, Nam — 150-151 D 2
Sengejskij, ostrov — 132-133 HJ 4
Sengés 102-103 H 6
Sengge Khamba 142-143 DE 5
Senggetö 138-139 H 2
Sengilej 124-125 R 7
Sengkang 152-153 O 8
Sengkir, Selat — 154 III ab 2
Sengkuang 154 III a 1
Senguerr, Río 108-109 D 5
Sengwe 172 E 5
Senhor do Bonfim 92-93 L 7
Senibong 154 III a 1
Senigallia 122-123 E 4
Senījān 136-137 N 5
Senillosa 106-107 C 7
Senirkent 136-137 D 3
Senj 122-123 F 3
Senja 116-117 G 3
Senjū, Tōkyō- 155 III b 1
Senkaku-shotō 142-143 N 6
Senkaku syotō = Senkaku-shotō 142-143 N 6
Şenkaya 136-137 K 2
Šenkursk 132-133 G 5
Senlis 120-121 J 4
Senmonorom 148-149 E 4
Sennār 164-165 L 6
Sennār = Sannār 164-165 L 6
Senneterre 62 N 2
Senno 124-125 G 6
Seno 148-149 DE 3
Seno Almirantazgo 108-109 DE 10
Seno Año Nuevo 108-109 E 10
Seno Choiseul = Choiseul Sound 108-109 KL 8
Seno Cronath 108-109 B 6
Seno Eyre 111 B 7
Se Noi 150-151 E 4
Senoia, GA 78-79 G 4
Senoka 154 III a 1
Seno Langford 108-109 C 9
Seno Otway 111 B 8
Seno Reloncaví 108-109 C 3
Seno Skyring 111 B 8
Sens 120-121 J 4
Sensfelder Tanne 128 III a 2
Senta 122-123 HJ 3
Šentala 124-125 S 6
Sentarum, Danau — 152-153 JK 5
Sentery 172 E 3
Sentinel, AZ 74-75 G 6
Sentinel Peak 60 G 2
Sentinel Range 53 B 28
Sentosa, Pulau — 154 III a 2
Sento-Sé 92-93 L 6
Senyavin Islands 208 F 2
Şenyurt = Derbesiye 136-137 J 4
Seo de Urgel 120-121 H 7
Seonāth 138-139 J 7
Seondha 138-139 G 4
Seoni 134-135 M 6
Seoni-Mālwa 138-139 F 6
Seorīnārāyan 138-139 J 7
Seoul = Sŏul 142-143 O 4
Separ, NM 74-75 J 6
Separation Well 158-159 D 4
Separ Shāhābād 136-137 MN 5
Sepasu 152-153 M 5
Sepatini, Rio — 98-99 E 9-F 8
Sepenjang, Pulau — 148-149 G 8
Sepetiba, Baía de — 102-103 KL 5
Šepetovka 126-127 C 1
Sepik River 148-149 M 7
Sepo La 138-139 M 3
Sepone 148-149 E 3
Sepopa 172 D 5
Sep'o-ri 144-145 F 3
Sepotuba, Rio — 102-103 D 1
Sept-Îles 56-57 X 7-8
Sept-Îles, Baie des — 63 CD 2-3
Sept Pagodes = Mahābalipuram 140 E 4
Sept Pagodes = Pha Lai 150-151 F 2
Sequim, WA 66-67 B 1
Sequoia National Park 64-65 C 4
Serachs 134-135 J 3
Şerafettin dağları 136-137 J 3
Serafimovič 126-127 L 2
Serafina, NM 76-77 B 5
Seram [IND] 140 C 2
Seram [RI] 148-149 JK 7
Seram-laut, Kepulauan — 148-149 K 7
Serampore 134-135 O 6
Seramsee 148-149 JK 7
Serang 148-149 E 8
Serang = Seram 148-149 JK 7
Serangoon 154 III b 1
Serangoon, Pulau — 154 III b 1
Serangoon Harbour 154 III b 1
Serasan, Pulau — 150-151 G 11
Serasan, Selat — 150-151 G 11
Serāyā = Sarāyah 136-137 F 5
Seraya, Pulau — 150-151 G 11
Serayu, Pegunungan — 152-153 H 9
Serbia 122-123 H 3-J 4
Serbka 126-127 E 3
Serchhung 138-139 L 3
Serdar 136-137 G 4
Serdce Kamen', mys — 58-59 BC 3
Serdéles = Sardalas 164-165 G 3
Serdj, Djebel es — = Jabal as-Sarj 166-167 L 2
Serdobsk 124-125 P 7
Serebr'ansk 132-133 P 8
Serebr'anyj Bor, Moskva- 113 V ab 2
Serebr'anyje Prudy 124-125 M 6
Sereda [SU, Jaroslavskaja Oblast'] 124-125 N 4
Sereda [SU, Moskovskaja Oblast'] 124-125 K 6
Seredina-Buda 124-125 JK 7
Seredka 124-125 FG 4
Seredr'anka 124-125 T 3
Serefiye = Dereköy 136-137 G 2
Şereflikoçhişar 136-137 E 3
Seregovo 124-125 S 2
Seremban 148-149 D 6
Šeremetjevka 124-125 S 6
Serena, La — [E] 120-121 E 9
Serena, La — [RCH] 111 B 3
Serengeti National Park 172 FG 2
Serengeti Plain 171 C 3
Serengka 152-153 J 6
Serenje 172 F 4
Serenli = Saranley 172 H 1
Sereno, Rio — 98-99 P 8
Seret 126-127 B 2
Ser'ga 124-125 V 5
Sergač 124-125 P 6
Sergeja Kirova, ostrova — 132-133 QR 2
Sergijev = Zagorsk 132-133 F 6
Serginy 132-133 LM 5
Sergiopolis = Riṣāfah 136-137 H 5
Sergipe 92-93 M 7
Sergipe, Rio — 100-101 F 6
Sergo = Kadijevka 126-127 J 2
Seria 148-149 F 6
Serian 152-153 J 5
Seribu, Pulau-pulau — 148-149 E 7-8
Seribudolok 150-151 B 11
Şerifali 154 I b 3
Sérifos 122-123 L 7
Serik 136-137 D 4
Seringa, Serra da — 92-93 J 6
Seringapatam = Srīrangapatnam 140 C 4
Seringapatap = Srīrangapatnam 140 C 4
Serīr Kalanshyū 164-165 J 3
Serji Gonpa 138-139 L 2
Šerkaly 132-133 M 5
Šerlovaja gora 132-133 W 7
Sermādevi 140 C 6
Sermata, Pulau — 148-149 J 8
Sermilik 56-57 d 4
Serna, De la — 106-107 E 5
Sernovodsk 124-125 ST 7
Sernur 124-125 R 5
Serodino 106-107 G 4
Serón [RCH] 106-107 B 3
Serov 132-133 L 6
Serowe 172 E 6
Ser'oža 124-125 O 6
Serpa 120-121 D 10
Serpa Pinto = Menongue 172 C 4
Serpeddì, Punta — 122-123 C 6
Serpent, Rivière — 63 A 2-3
Serpentine Hot Springs, AK 58-59 EF 4
Serpiente, Boca de la — 92-93 G 2-3
Serpnevoje 126-127 D 3
Serpuchov 124-125 L 6
Serpukhov = Serpuchov 124-125 L 6
Serra 100-101 D 11
Serra Acaraí 92-93 H 4
Serra Azul [BR, mountains] 98-99 L 5
Serra Azul [BR, place] 102-103 J 4
Serra Barauanã 98-99 H 3-4
Serra Bodoquena 92-93 H 9
Serra Bom Jesus da Gurguéia 92-93 L 6-7
Serra Bom Sucesso 102-103 KL 1
Serra Bonita 100-101 A 8
Serra Botucaraí 106-107 L 2
Serra Branca [BR, Maranhão] 100-101 B 3-4
Serra Branca [BR, Paraíba] 100-101 F 4
Serra Branca [BR, Pernambuco] 100-101 DE 4
Serra Branca [BR, Rio Grande do Norte] 100-101 E 4
Serra Canelas 100-101 AB 4
Serra Central 100-101 C 8
Serra Curicuriari 98-99 E 5
Serra Curral Novo 100-101 EF 6
Serra da Araruna 100-101 G 4
Serra da Aurora 104-105 F 1-2
Serra da Balança 100-101 E 4
Serra da Boa Vista 100-101 EF 4
Serra da Bocaina 102-103 GH 7-8
Serra da Caatinga 100-101 EF 3
Serra da Canabrava [BR, Rio Jucurucu] 100-101 DE 9
Serra da Cana Brava [BR, Rio São Onofre] 100-101 C 7
Serra da Canastra [BR, Bahia] 100-101 E 6
Serra da Canastra [BR, Minas Gerais] 92-93 K 9
Serra da Cangalha [BR, Goiás] 98-99 P 9
Serra da Cangalha [BR, Piauí] 100-101 D 3
Serra da Cantareira 110 II ab 1
Serra da Carioca 110 I b 2
Serra da Chela 172 B 5
Serra da Chibata 100-101 D 10-11
Serra da Cinta 92-93 K 6
Serra da Croeira 100-101 A 4
Serra da Cruz 100-101 A 5
Serra da Desordem 100-101 AB 2
Serra da Divisa 98-99 G 9
Serra da Esperança 102-103 G 6-7
Serra da Estrêla [BR] 100-101 D 4
Serra da Estrela [P] 120-121 CD 8
Serra da Farofa 106-107 MN 2
Serra da Fartura 102-103 FG 7
Serra da Flecheira 100-101 B 8
Serra da Gameleira 100-101 C 4
Serra da Garapa 100-101 C 7
Serra da Inveja 100-101 F 5
Serra da Joaninha 100-101 D 3
Serra da Mantiqueira 92-93 KL 9
Serra da Mata da Corda 92-93 K 8
Serra da Mocidade 98-99 GH 4
Serra da Moeda 102-103 KL 4
Serra da Mombuca 102-103 FG 3
Serra da Neve 172 B 4
Serra da Ouricana 100-101 DE 8
Serra da Piedade 100-101 F 4
Serra da Piranga 98-99 MN 6
Serra da Pitanga 102-103 G 6
Serra da Ponta do Morro 100-101 C 7
Serra da Providência 98-99 H 10
Serra da Raiada 100-101 EF 4
Serra das Almas 100-101 D 4
Serra das Alpercatas 100-101 B 3-4
Serra das Araras [BR, Maranhão] 98-99 P 8
Serra das Araras [BR, Mato Grosso] 92-93 J 8
Serra das Araras [BR, Minas Gerais] 102-103 K 1
Serra das Araras [BR, Paraná] 111 F 2-3
Serra da Saudade 102-103 K 3
Serra das Balanças 100-101 DE 3
Serra das Cordilheiras 98-99 OP 8
Serra das Divisões 92-93 JK 8
Serra das Encantadas 106-107 L 3
Serra das Figuras 100-101 B 6
Serra das Mamoneiras 98-99 P 7-8
Serra das Marrecas 100-101 D 5
Serra das Matas 100-101 DE 3
Serra das Missões 100-101 D 4
Serra das Onças 98-99 H 9-10
Serra das Palmeiras 100-101 F 5
Serra das Porteira 100-101 F 5
Serra das Suçuarana 100-101 B 8
Serra das Umburanas 100-101 F 5-G 4
Serra das Vertentes 100-101 E 2-3
Serra da Tabatinga 100-101 B 6
Serra da Taquara 102-103 F 1
Serra da Vassouras 100-101 E 4-5
Serra de Amambaí 102-103 E 5
Serra de Apucarana 111 F 2
Serra de Araraquara 102-103 HJ 4
Serra de Caçapava 106-107 L 3
Serra de Carauna 98-99 H 3
Serra de Gorongosa 172 FG 5
Serra de Guampi 94-95 J 4-5
Serra de Maracaju 92-93 H 9-J 8
Serra de Minas 102-103 L 3
Serra de Monchique 120-121 C 10
Serra de Monte Alto 100-101 C 8
Serra de Pedro II 100-101 D 3
Serra de Santa Bárbara 92-93 J 9
Serra de Santa Luisa 102-103 E 3
Serra de Santana [BR, Bahia] 100-101 C 7
Serra de Santana [BR, Rio Grande do Norte] 100-101 F 3-4
Serra de Santa Rita 100-101 E 3
Serra de Santa Tecla 106-107 KL 3

Serra de São Domingos 100-101 A 7-8
Serra de São Jerônimo 92-93 J 8
Serra de São João [BR, Amazonas] 98-99 GH 9
Serra de São João [BR, Paraná] 102-103 G 6
Serra de São Pedro 100-101 E 4
Serra de São Vicente 104-105 G 4
Serra de São Xavier 106-107 KL 2
Serra de Saudade 102-103 K 3
Serra de Tiracambu 92-93 K 5
Serra de Uruburetama 100-101 DE 2
Serra do Acapuzal 98-99 MN 5
Serra do Açuruá 100-101 C 6
Serra do Almeirim 98-99 M 5
Serra do Alto Uruguai 106-107 L 1
Serra do Ambrósio 102-103 L 3
Serra do Angical 100-101 B 6
Serra do Apiaú 92-93 G 4
Serra do Arelão 98-99 M 5
Serra do Batista [BR, Bahia] 100-101 D 6
Serra do Batista [BR, Piauí] 100-101 D 4
Serra do Baturité 100-101 E 3
Serra do Boi Preto 102-103 F 6
Serra do Boqueirão [BR, Bahia] 92-93 L 7
Serra do Boqueirão [BR, Pernambuco] 100-101 F 5
Serra do Boqueirão [BR, Piauí] 100-101 C 4
Serra do Boqueirão [BR, Rio Grande do Sul] 106-107 K 2
Serra do Braga 100-101 E 4
Serra do Cabral 102-103 K 2
Serra do Cachimbo 92-93 HJ 6
Serra do Café 100-101 G 6
Serra do Caiapó 102-103 FG 2
Serra do Canguçu 106-107 L 3
Serra do Cantu 102-103 FG 6
Serra do Caparão 92-93 L 8-9
Serra do Capitão-Mór 100-101 F 4-5
Serra do Caracol 100-101 C 5
Serra do Castelo 100-101 D 11
Serra do Catramba 100-101 F 6
Serra do Catuni 102-103 L 2
Serra do Chifre 92-93 L 8
Serra do Cipó 102-103 L 3
Serra do Cocalzinho 102-103 H 1
Serra do Covil 100-101 BC 6
Serra do Cuité 100-101 F 4
Serra do Curururi 98-99 MN 4
Serra do Diabo 102-103 F 5
Serra do Duro 98-99 P 10-11
Serra do Erval 106-107 LM 3
Serra do Espigão 102-103 G 7
Serra do Espinhaço 92-93 L 8
Serra do Espinilho 106-107 K 2
Serra do Estreito 100-101 C 6
Serra do Estrondo 92-93 K 6
Serra do Flamengo 100-101 E 4
Serra do Franco 100-101 E 3-4
Serra do Gado Bravo 100-101 A 4-5
Serra do Gomes 98-99 P 9
Serra do Gongoji 92-93 LM 7-8
Serra do Gurupi 92-93 K 5-6
Serra do Iguariaçá 106-107 K 2
Serra do Inajá 98-99 N 9
Serra do Inhaúma 100-101 B 3
Serra Dois Irmãos 92-93 L 6
Serra do Japão 100-101 F 5-6
Serra do Jaraguá 102-103 H 7
Serra do Jutaí 98-99 M 5
Serra do Machado [BR, Amazonas] 98-99 H 8-9
Serra do Machado [BR, Ceará] 100-101 E 3
Serra do Mar 111 G 2-3
Serra do Matão 92-93 J 6
Serra do Mel 100-101 F 3
Serra do Mirante 102-103 GH 5
Serra do Moa 96-97 E 5
Serra do Morais 100-101 E 4
Serra do Mucajaí 92-93 G 4
Serra do Navio 98-99 M 4
Serra do Norte 92-93 H 7
Serra do Orobo 100-101 D 7
Serra do Padre 100-101 E 4
Serra do Paranapiacaba 92-93 G 2-3
Serra do Pelado 100-101 F 4
Serra do Penitente 92-93 K 6
Serra do Piauí 100-101 CD 5
Serra do Pirapó 106-107 K 2
Serra do Poção 100-101 F 4
Serra do Ramalho 92-93 KL 7
Serra do Recreio 100-101 D 5
Serra do Rio Claro 102-103 G 2
Serra do Rio de Contas 100-101 D 7-8
Serra do Rio Preto 102-103 J 2
Serra do Roncador 92-93 J 7
Serra dos Aimorés 92-93 L 8
Serra do Salta Ginete 102-103 K 3
Serra dos Apiacás 92-93 H 6-7
Serra do Sargento Paixão 104-105 F 2
Serra dos Ausentes 106-107 M 1-2
Serra dos Bastioes 100-101 DE 4
Serra dos Baús 102-103 F 2-3
Serra dos Caiabis 92-93 H 7
Serra dos Carajás 92-93 J 5-6
Serra dos Cariris Novos 100-101 D 3-4
Serra dos Cristais 102-103 J 2
Serra dos Dourados 111 F 2
Serra dos Gradaús 92-93 JK 6
Serra do Sincorá 100-101 D 7
Serra dos Itatina 102-103 J 6
Serra dos Javaés 98-99 O 10
Serra dos Órgãos 102-103 L 5
Serra dos Pacaás Novos 98-99 FG 10
Serra dos Pireneus 102-103 HJ 1
Serra dos Pretos Forros 110 I b 2
Serra dos Queimados 104-105 E 1
Serra dos Surucucus 98-99 G 3
Serra dos Três Rios 110 I b 2
Serra dos Tucuns 100-101 D 2
Serra do Surucucus 94-95 K 6
Serra dos Xavantes 92-93 K 7
Serra do Tapirapé 98-99 N 10
Serra do Taquaral 100-101 D 8
Serra do Tombador [BR, Bahia] 100-101 D 6
Serra do Tombador [BR, Mato Grosso] 92-93 H 7
Serra do Trucará 98-99 N 7-O 6
Serra do Tucano 94-95 LM 6
Serra do Tumucumaque 92-93 HJ 4
Serra do Uacamparique 104-105 E 2
Serra do Uopiane 104-105 E 2-3
Serra Dourada 92-93 K 7
Serra do Uruçuí 92-93 K 7-L 6
Serra do Valentim 92-93 L 6
Serra do Verdinho 102-103 F 2-G 3
Serra Formosa 92-93 HJ 7
Serra Gabriel Antunes Maciel 98-99 G 10-11
Serra Geral [BR, Bahia ↓ Caculé] 100-101 C 8
Serra Geral [BR, Bahia ↖ Jequié] 100-101 D 7
Serra Geral [BR, Goiás] 100-101 A 6
Serra Geral [BR, Rio Grande do Sul ↖ Porto Alegre] 111 F 3
Serra Geral [BR, Rio Grande do Sul ↑ Porto Alegre] 106-107 M 2
Serra Geral [BR, Santa Catarina] 111 F 3
Serra Geral = Serra Grande 98-99 P 10
Serra Geral de Goiás 92-93 K 7
Serra Grande [BR, Bahia] 100-101 D 5
Serra Grande [BR, Ceará] 100-101 D 3
Serra Grande [BR, Goiás] 98-99 OP 7
Serra Grande [BR, Piauí → Picos] 100-101 D 4
Serra Grande [BR, Piauí ↓ Ribeiro Gonçalves] 100-101 B 4-5
Serra Grande [BR, Rondônia] 98-99 H 9-10
Serra Grande [BR, Roraima] 94-95 L 6
Serra Grande ou de Carauna 98-99 H 3
Sérrai 122-123 K 5
Serra Iarauarune 98-99 HJ 4
Serra Imeri 92-93 F 4
Serra Iricoumé 98-99 K 4
Serra Itapicuru 92-93 KL 6
Serra Janquara 102-103 D 1
Serra J. Antunes 98-99 G 10-11
Serra Jauari 98-99 M 5
Serra João do Vale 100-101 F 3-4
Serra Linda 100-101 D 8
Serra Lombarda 92-93 J 4
Serra Macoa 98-99 JK 4
Serrán 96-97 B 4
Serrana 102-103 J 4
Serra Namuli 172 G 5
Serra Negra [BR, Goiás] 98-99 P 10
Serra Negra [BR, Maranhão] 100-101 A 4
Serra Negra [BR, Minas Gerais] 102-103 L 2-3
Serra Negra [BR, São Paulo] 102-103 J 5
Serra Negra [BR, Sergipe] 100-101 F 5-6
Serrania Chepite 104-105 BC 4
Serrania Chiru Choricha 104-105 BC 4
Serrania de Abibe 94-95 C 3-4
Serrania de Ayapel 94-95 D 4
Serrania de Baudó 94-95 C 4-5
Serrania de Cuenca 120-121 F 8-G 9
Serrania de Huanchaca 92-93 G 7
Serrania de Imataca 92-93 G 3
Serrania de la Cerbatana 92-93 F 3
Serrania de la Macarena 94-95 DE 6
Serrania del Beu 104-105 BC 4
Serrania del Darién 88-89 H 10
Serrania del Sapo 94-95 B 4
Serrania de Maigualida 92-93 F 3-G 4
Serrania de Mapichí 92-93 F 3-4
Serrania de Mataca 104-105 D 6
Serrania de Mato 94-95 J 4
Serrania de Napo 96-97 C 2
Serrania de San Jacinto 94-95 D 3
Serrania de San Jerónimo 92-93 D 3
Serrania de San José 104-105 F 5-6
Serrania de Santiago 104-105 G 6
Serrania de Sicasica 104-105 BC 5
Serrania de Sunsas 104-105 G 5-6
Serrania de Tabasará 88-89 EF 10
Serrania Parú 94-95 J 5
Serrania Quinigua 94-95 J 5
Serrania San Lucas 94-95 D 3-4
Serranias del Burro 64-65 F 6
Serranias Turagua 94-95 J 4
Serrano 106-107 F 5
Serrano, Isla — 108-109 B 7
Serra Nova 104-105 E 1
Serra Ôlho d'Água 100-101 E 5-F 4
Serra Ouricuri 100-101 FG 5
Serra Pacaraima 92-93 G 4
Serra Paranaquara 98-99 M 5
Serra Pelada 100-101 D 8
Serra Pintada 100-101 E 4
Serra Piraná 100-101 G 4
Serra Piranhinha 100-101 B 1-2
Serra Poço Danta 100-101 EF 6
Serra Preta 100-101 E 7
Serra Queimada 102-103 J 5-6
Serra Queimada Redonda 100-101 E 4-5
Serra Repartimento 98-99 E 7
Serra R. Franco 104-105 F 4
Serraria 100-101 G 4
Serra Saco Comprido 100-101 B 7
Serra São Domingos 100-101 D 3-E 4
Serra São Francisco 100-101 D 5-6
Serra São Lourenço 102-103 E 2
Serrâț, Râss — = Râ's Sarrâț 166-167 L 1
Serra Tabatinga 98-99 GH 4
Serra Taborda 100-101 F 5
Serra Talhada 92-93 M 6
Serra Tepequem 94-95 L 6
Serra Uaçari 92-93 H 4
Serra Upanda 172 BC 4
Serra Uscana 104-105 B 6
Serra Verde 100-101 F 3
Serra Verde, Chapada da — 100-101 FG 3
Serra Vermelha [BR ↑ Avelino Lopes] 100-101 BC 5
Serra Vermelha [BR ↓ Bertolínia] 100-101 BC 4-5
Serrezuela 111 C 4
Serrilhada 106-107 K 3
Serrinha [BR ↑ Feira de Santana] 92-93 M 7
Serrinha [BR ↑ Guaratinga] 100-101 E 9
Serrita 100-101 E 4
Serro 102-103 L 3
Serrolândia 100-101 D 6
Sers, Es — = As-Sars 166-167 L 1
Sertânia 92-93 M 6
Sertanópolis 102-103 G 5
Sertão 92-93 L 7-M 6
Sertão de Camapuã 92-93 J 8-9
Sertãozinho 102-103 HJ 4
Serua, Pulau — 148-149 K 8
Serule 172 E 6
Seruna 138-139 D 3
Serutu, Pulau — 152-153 H 6
Seruwai 150-151 B 10
Servilleta, NM 76-77 AB 4
Servon 129 I d 3
Serxü 142-143 H 5
Sé San 150-151 F 6
Sešan 58-59 B 3
Se Sang Sôi 150-151 E 4
Sesayap 152-153 M 4
Sesayap, Sungai — 152-153 M 4
Seščinskij 124-125 J 7
Sese Islands 172 F 2
Sesepe 148-149 J 7
Sesfontein 172 B 5
Seshachalam Hills 140 CD 3
Sesheke 172 DE 5
Sesimbra 120-121 C 9
Šešma 124-125 S 6
Sesquilé 94-95 E 5
Sessa Aurunca 122-123 EF 5
Šestakovo 124-125 RS 4
Šeštokaj 124-125 D 6
Sestroreck 132-133 DE 5
Setagaya, Tôkyô- 155 III a 2
Setana 142-143 Q 3
Sète 120-121 J 7
Sete Barras 102-103 HJ 6
Sete Cidades 100-101 D 3
Sétéia 122-123 M 8
Sete Lagoas 102-103 KL 3
Setenta, Pampa del — 108-109 E 6
Sete Quedas, Salto das — [BR, Paraná] 102-103 E 6
Sete Quedas, Salto das — [BR, Rio Teles Pires] 92-93 H 6
Setermoen 116-117 H 3
Setesdal 116-117 B 8
Seti 138-139 H 3
Setia Budi, Jakarta- 154 IV ab 2
Sétif = Saṭīf 164-165 F 1
Setiu, Kuala — = Setiu 150-151 D 10
Setlagodi 174-175 F 4
Seto 144-145 L 5
Seto-naikai 142-143 P 5
Seṭṭât = Saṭṭât 164-165 C 2
Setté Cama 172 A 2
Settecamini, Roma- 113 II c 1
Sette-Daban, chrebet — 132-133 a 5
Settlers 174-175 H 3
Sētu Aṇaikkaṭṭ = Adam's Bridge 140 D 6
Setúbal 120-121 C 9
Setúbal, Baía de — 120-121 C 9
Setúbal, Rio — 102-103 L 2
Sētubandh = Adam's Bridge 140 D 6
Seul = Sŏul 142-143 O 4
Seul, Lac — 56-57 S 7
Sevan 126-127 M 6
Sevan, ozero — 126-127 M 6
Sevaruyo 104-105 C 6
Sevastopol' 126-127 F 4
Ševčenko 126-127 P 5
Ševčenkovo = Dolinskaja 126-127 F 2
Seven Emus 158-159 G 3
Seven Islands = Sept-Îles 56-57 X 7-8
Seven Pagodas = Mahābalipuram 140 E 4
Seven Pagodas = Pha Lai 150-151 F 2
Seventy Mile House 60 G 4
Severin 104-105 B 9
Severino Ribeiro 106-107 JK 3
Severn [GB] 119 E 6
Severn [ZA] 174-175 E 4
Severnaja 132-133 QR 4
Severnaja Dvina 132-133 G 5
Severnaja Kel'tma 124-125 U 3
Severnaja Semlja = Severnaja Zemľa 132-133 ST 1-2
Severnaja Sos'va 132-133 L 5
Severnaja Zemľa 132-133 ST 1-2
Severnaya Zemlya = Severnaja Zemľa 132-133 ST 1-2
Severnoje [SU ↑ Kujbyšev] 132-133 O 6
Severnoje [SU, Orenburgskaja Oblast'] 124-125 T 6
Severn River 56-57 T 6-7
Severnyj 132-133 LM 4
Severnyj čink = Donyztau 132-133 K 8
Severnyj Donec 126-127 J 2
Severnyje uvaly 132-133 HJ 5-6
Severnyj Kommunar 124-125 TU 4
Severnyj Ledovityj okean 132-133 J-c 1
Severnyj Ural 132-133 K 5-6
Severo-Bajkal'skoje nagorje 132-133 UV 6
Severodoneck 126-127 J 2
Severodvinsk 132-133 FG 5
Severo-Jenisejsk 132-133 RS 5
Severo-Kuril'sk 132-133 de 7
Severo-Sibirskaja nizmennost' 132-133 P-X 3
Severo-Vostočnyj-Bank = Bank 126-127 O 7
Severo-Zanonsk 124-125 M 6-7
Severy, KS 68-69 H 7
Sevier Desert 74-75 G 3
Sevier Lake 74-75 G 3
Sevier River 64-65 D 4
Sevier River, East Fork — 74-75 GH 4
Sevierville 80-81 E 3
Sevierville, TN 80-81 E 3
Sevigné 106-107 HJ 6
Sevilla 120-121 E 10
Sevilla [CO] 94-95 D 5
Sevlievo 122-123 L 4
Sevran 129 I d 2
Sèvre 120-121 G 5
Sèvres 129 I b 2
Sevsib 132-133 H 6
Sevsk 124-125 K 7
Sewa 164-165 B 7
Seward, AK 56-57 G 5-6
Seward, KS 68-69 G 6
Seward, NE 68-69 H 5
Seward Glacier 58-59 R 6
Seward Peninsula 56-57 CD 4
Sewell, Lake — = Canyon Ferry Reservoir 66-67 H 2
Sewu, Pegunungan — 152-153 J 9-10
Sexsmith 60 H 2
Sey 104-105 C 8
Seya, Yokohama- 155 III a 3
Seybaplaya 86-87 P 8
Seychelles 172 J 3
Seydhisfjördhur 116-117 fg 2
Seydişehir 136-137 D 4
Seyhan = Adana 134-135 D 3
Seyhan nehri 134-135 D 3
Seyitgazi 136-137 D 3
Seyla' 164-165 N 6
Seymour, IA 70-71 D 5
Seymour, IN 64-65 JK 4
Seymour, MO 78-79 C 2
Seymour, TX 76-77 E 6
Seymour, WI 70-71 F 3
Seymour [AUS] 160 G 6
Seymour [ZA] 174-175 G 7
Seymour Arm 60 H 4
Seyne-sur-Mer, la — 120-121 K 7
Seytan 154 I b 2
Sezze 122-123 E 5
Sfax = Ṣafāqis 164-165 FG 2
Sfîntu Gheorghe 122-123 LM 3
Sfîntu Gheorghe, Braţul — 122-123 N 3
Sfire = Safirah 136-137 G 4
Sfissifa = Safīsifah 166-167 F 3
Sfizef = Safīzaf 166-167 F 2
Sfoûk = Sufūq 136-137 J 4
's-Graveland 128 I b 2
's-Gravenhage 120-121 JK 2
Sha Alam 148-149 D 6
Sha'ambah, Ḥāssī — 166-167 D 5
Shaanxi 142-143 K 4-5
Shaba 172 DE 3
Shābah, Ash- 166-167 M 2
Shabakah, Ash- [IRQ, landscape] 136-137 K 7
Shabakah, Ash- [IRQ, place] 136-137 K 7
Shabani = Zvishavane 172 F 6
Shabbona, IL 70-71 F 5
Shabeelle, Webi — 164-165 N 8
Shabellaha Dhexe = 5 ◁ 164-165 b 3
Shabellaha Hoose = 3 ◁ 164-165 N 8
Shabēlle, Webi — = Wabī Shebelē 164-165 N 7
Shabka 138-139 J 2
Shabkah 166-167 H 3-4
Shabunda 172 E 2
Shābūnīyah 166-167 H 2
Shabuskwia Lake 62 E 2
Shabwah 134-135 F 7
Sha Ch'i = Sha Xi 146-147 F 8
Shackleton Ice Shelf 53 C 10
Shackleton Inlet 53 A 19-17
Shackleton Range 53 A 35-1
Shacun 146-147 E 8
Shādegān 136-137 N 7
Shadehill Reservoir 68-69 E 3
Shadi 146-147 E 8
Shādir al-Mulūṣī 136-137 HJ 6
Shadow Oaks, Houston-, TX 85 III a 1
Shadūzūt 141 E 3
Shady Acres, Houston-, TX 85 III b 1
Shady Lane Park 85 III b 1
Shafter, CA 74-75 D 5
Shafter, NV 66-67 F 5
Shafter, TX 76-77 B 8
Shagamu 168-169 F 4
Shageluk, AK 58-59 H 5
Shaglli 96-97 B 3
Shag Rocks 111 H 8
Shaguotun 144-145 C 2
Shāh, Godār-e — 136-137 MN 5
Shāhābād [IND, Andhra Pradesh] 140 CD 2
Shāhābād [IND, Maisūru] 134-135 M 7
Shāhābād [IND, Punjab] 138-139 F 2
Shāhābād [IND, Rājasthān] 138-139 F 5
Shāhābād [IND, Uttar Pradesh ↓ Rāmpur] 138-139 G 3
Shāhābād [IND, Uttar Pradesh ↓ Shāhjahānpur] 138-139 G 4
Shāhāda 138-139 E 7
Shaḥāmbī, Jabal — 164-165 F 1-2
Shaḥāmī 136-137 H 6
Shāhān, Kūh-e — 136-137 LM 5
Shaḥan, Wādī — = Wādī Shiḥan 134-135 G 7
Shāhāpur [IND, Karnataka] 140 B 3
Shāhāpur [IND, Mahārāshtra] 138-139 D 8
Shaharak 134-135 J 4
Shahbā 136-137 G 6
Shahbā', Ḥarrat ash- 136-137 G 6-7
Shāhbandar 138-139 AB 5
Shāhbāzpūr 141 B 4
Shāhdā = Shāhāda 138-139 E 7
Shahdād 134-135 H 4
Shahdād, Namakzār-e — 134-135 H 4
Shāhdadkoṭ 138-139 A 4
Shāhdaḍpūr 138-139 B 5
Shahdol 138-139 H 6
Shahe [TJ, Hebei place] 146-147 E 3
Sha He [TJ, Hebei river] 146-147 E 3
Shahe [TJ, Shandong] 146-147 G 3
Shahedian 146-147 D 5
Shāhganj 138-139 J 4-5
Shāhgaṛh 138-139 BC 4
Shāhī 134-135 G 3
Shahidulla Mazar 142-143 D 4
Shāhjahānpur 134-135 MN 5
Shaho = Shahe [TJ, Hebei place] 146-147 E 3
Sha Ho = Sha He [TJ, Hebei river] 146-147 E 5
Sha-ho = Shahe [TJ, Shandong] 146-147 G 3
Sha-ho-tien = Shahedian 146-147 D 5
Shāhpur [IND] 140 C 2
Shāhpūr [PAK] 138-139 B 3
Shāhpur = Shāhāpur 138-139 D 8
Shāhpura [IND, Madhya Pradesh ← Jabalpur] 138-139 G 6
Shāhpura [IND, Madhya Pradesh → Jabalpur] 138-139 H 6
Shāhpura [IND, Rājasthān] 134-135 L 5
Shāhpūrī Dīpsamuh 141 BC 5
Shahr-e Bābak 134-135 GH 4
Shahredā 134-135 G 4
Shahr-e Kord 134-135 G 4
Shahrestānbālā 136-137 NO 4
Shāhrig 138-139 A 2
Shāhrūd [IR, place] 134-135 GH 3
Shāh Rūd [IR, river] 136-137 NO 4
Shahsien = Sha Xian 146-147 F 8
Shahu 146-147 D 6
Shāhzand 136-137 N 6
Sha'īb Abū Marīs 136-137 L 7
Sha'īb al-'Ailī = Sha'īb al-'Aylī 136-137 H 7
Sha'īb al-'Aylī 136-137 H 7
Sha'īb al-Banāt, Jabal — 164-165 L 3
Sha'īb al-Judā' 136-137 L 8-M 7
Sha'īb al-Mahārī 136-137 KL 7
Sha'īb al-Muhārī 136-137 KL 7
Sha'īb al-Wallī 136-137 H 6
Sha'īb Ḥasb 134-135 E 4
Sha'īb Ḥasb = Sha'īb Ḥasb 134-135 E 4
Shaikhpura 138-139 KL 5
Sha'īt, Wādī — 173 C 5
Shājāpur 138-139 F 6
Shajianzi 144-145 E 2
Shaka, Ras — 171 E 3
Shakad Chhu 138-139 M 2
Shakar Bolāghī = Qara Būteh 136-137 M 4
Shakespeare Island 70-71 F 1
Shakhty = Šachty 126-127 K 3
Shakh yar 142-143 E 3
Shaki 164-165 E 7
Shakir, Jazīrat — 164-165 LM 3
Shakopee, MN 70-71 D 3
Shakotan misaki 144-145 b 2
Shakou 146-147 D 9
Shaktī = Sakti 138-139 J 6
Shaktoolik, AK 58-59 G 4
Shaktoolik River 58-59 G 4
Shakujii 155 III a 1
Shāl 136-137 N 5
Shala 164-165 M 7
Shalanbod 164-165 N 8
Shalang 146-147 C 11
Shalar, Nahr — 136-137 L 5
Shalar Rūd = Nahr Shalar 136-137 L 5
Shallāl, Ash- [ET, place] 164-165 L 3
Shallāl, Ash- [ET, river] 164-165 L 3
Shallālāt Ḍahrānīyah 166-167 G 3
Shallop 63 E 3
Shallotte, NC 80-81 G 3-4
Shallowater, TX 76-77 CD 6
Shālmārā, Dakshiṇ — = South Sālmāra 138-139 N 5
Shāmah, Ash- = Al-Ḥarrah 136-137 GH 7
Shamā'īyah, Ash- 166-167 B 3
Shāmbah 164-165 L 7
Shamgong 138-139 N 4
Shāmguṛī = Sāmāguri 141 C 2
Shāmīyah, Ash- 136-137 L 7
Shāmli 138-139 F 3
Shammar, Jabal — 134-135 E 5
Shamo = Gobi 142-143 H-K 3
Shamokin, PA 72-73 H 4
Shamrock, FL 80-81 b 2
Shamrock, TX 76-77 DE 5
Shāmshīr = Pāveh 136-137 M 5
Sham Shui Po, Kowloon- 155 I a 2
Shamūrah 166-167 K 2
Shamva 172 F 5
Shamwam 141 E 2
Shanāshīn, Wādī — 166-167 E 7
Shanchengzhen 144-145 EF 1
Shan-ch'iu = Shenqiu 146-147 E 5
Shandan 142-143 J 4
Shandī 164-165 L 5
Shandish, MI 72-73 DE 3
Shandong 142-143 M 4
Shandong Bandao 142-143 MN 4
Shangani 172 E 5
Shangbahe 146-147 E 6
Shangbangcheng 144-145 B 2
Shangcai 146-147 E 5
Shangcheng 146-147 E 6
Shang-chia-ho = Shangjiahe 144-145 E 2
Shang-ch'iu = Shangqiu 142-143 LM 5
Shangchuan Dao 142-143 L 7
Shangchwan Tao = Shangchuan Dao 146-147 D 11
Shangcigang = Beijingzi 144-145 DE 3
Shangdachen Shan = Dachen Dao 146-147 HJ 7
Shangfu 146-147 E 7
Shanggang 146-147 H 5
Shanggao 146-147 E 7
Shanghai 142-143 N 5
Shanghang 142-143 M 6-7
Shanghe 146-147 F 3
Shangho = Shanghe 146-147 F 3
Shanghsien = Shang Xian 142-143 KL 5
Shangjao = Shangrao 142-143 M 6
Shangjiahe 144-145 E 2
Shangkan 146-147 C 6
Shang-kang = Shanggang 146-147 H 5
Shang-kao = Shanggao 146-147 E 7
Shangkiu = Shangqiu 142-143 LM 5
Shangnan 146-147 C 5
Shangqiu 142-143 LM 5
Shangrao 142-143 M 6
Shangshe 146-147 D 2
Shang Xian 142-143 KL 5
Shangyou 146-147 E 9
Shangyu 146-147 H 6-7
Shang-yu = Shangyou 146-147 E 9
Shang-yü = Shangyu 146-147 H 7
Shangzhi 142-143 O 2
Shanhaiguan 142-143 MN 3
Shan-hai-kuan = Shanhaiguan 144-145 BC 2
Shan-hsi = Shaanxi 142-143 L 4-5
Shaniko, OR 66-67 C 3
Shaṅkarīdurgam = Sankaridrug 140 CD 5
Shankh = Sankh 138-139 K 6
Shankiu = Shanqiu 142-143 LM 5
Shankou [TJ, Guangdong] 146-147 BC 11
Shankou [TJ, Hunan] 146-147 C 7
Shankou [TJ, Jiangxi] 146-147 E 7
Shānmalī = Shāmli 138-139 F 3
Shanngaw Taungdan 141 EF 2-3
Shannon [IRL] 119 B 5
Shannon [ZA] 174-175 G 5
Shannon Airport 119 B 5
Shannon Bay 60 A 3
Shannon Ø 52 B 20
Shannontown, SC 80-81 FG 4
Shan Pyinnei 148-149 C 2
Shanqiu 146-147 E 5
Shanshan 142-143 G 3
Shansi = Shanxi 142-143 L 4
Shan-tan = Shandan 142-143 J 4
Shantangyi 146-147 BC 8
Shantar Islands = Šantarskije ostrova 132-133 a 6
Shāntipur = Sāntipur 138-139 M 6
Shantou 142-143 M 7
Shantow = Shantou 142-143 M 7
Shantung = Shandong 142-143 M 4
Shan-tung Chiao = Chengshan Jiao 146-147 J 3
Shanwa 171 C 3
Shanwei 146-147 E 10
Shanxi 142-143 L 4
Shan Xian 146-147 EF 4
Shanyang 146-147 B 5
Shanyin 142-143 L 4
Shaobo 146-147 G 5
Shaodong 146-147 C 8
Shaoguan 142-143 L 6-7
Shaohsing = Shaoxing 142-143 N 5-6
Shao-kuan = Qujiang 146-147 D 9
Shaol Lake 70-71 C 1
Shao-po = Shaobo 146-147 G 5
Shaotze = Wan Xian 142-143 K 5
Shaowu 142-143 M 6
Shaoxing 142-143 N 5-6
Shaoyang 142-143 L 6
Shapaja 96-97 C 5
Ṣhapura = Shāhpur 140 C 2
Shaqlāwah 136-137 L 4
Shaqqah 166-167 JK 2
Shaqqāt, Ash- 164-165 C 3
Shaqrā' 134-135 F 5
Shār, Jabal — [Saudi Arabia] 173 D 4
Sha'r, Jabal — [SYR] 136-137 GH 5
Sharafkhāneh 136-137 LM 3
Sharāh, Ash- 136-137 F 7
Sharan Jogīzai 138-139 B 2
Sharavati 140 B 3
Sharbithāt, Rā's ash- 134-135 H 7
Sharbot Lake 72-73 H 2
Shārdā = Sārda 138-139 H 3
Shari 144-145 d 2
Shari = Chari 164-165 H 6
Shārī', Bahr ash- = Buhayrat Shārī 136-137 L 5
Shārī, Buhayrat — 136-137 L 5
Sharī'ah 166-167 H 1
Sharī'ah, Nahr ash- 136-137 F 6-7
Shārib, Ma'ṭan — 136-137 C 7
Shari-dake 144-145 d 2
Shārif 166-167 H 2
Shārīf, Wād — 166-167 E 3
Shāriqah, Ash- 134-135 GH 5
Sharja = Ash-Shāriqah 134-135 GH 5
Shark Bay 158-159 B 5
Shark Point 161 I b 2
Sharmah, Ash- 173 D 3-4
Sharmah, Wādī ash- = Wādī Ṣadr 173 D 3
Sharm ash-Shaykh 173 D 4
Sharm Dumayj 173 DE 4
Sharm esh-Sheikh = Sharm ash-Shayh 173 D 4
Shar Mörön 146-147 C 1-2
Shar Mörön = Chatan gol 142-143 K 3
Sharon, KS 76-77 E 4
Sharon, PA 64-65 KL 3
Sharon Hill, PA 84 III b 2
Sharon Springs, KS 68-69 F 6
Sharps Run 84 III d 2
Sharpstown, Houston-, TX 85 III b 2
Sharpstown Country Club 85 III a 2
Sharq al-Istiwā'īyah 164-165 L 7-8
Sharqāṭ, Ash- 136-137 K 5
Sharqī, Ash-Shaṭṭ ash- 164-165 DE 2
Sharqī, Jazīrat ash- 166-167 M 2
Sharqi, Jebel esh — = Jabal Lubnān ash-Sharqī 136-137 G 5-6
Sharru 138-139 L 3
Sharrukīn, Dur — = Khorsabad 136-137 K 4
Sharshar 166-167 K 2
Sharuin = Shārwīn 166-167 F 5
Shārwīn 166-167 F 5
Shashamanna = Shashemene 164-165 M 7
Shashemenē 164-165 M 7
Shashi 142-143 L 5-6
Shasta, Mount — 64-65 B 3
Shasta Lake 66-67 B 5
Sha-ti = Shadi 146-147 E 8
Sha Tin 155 I b 1
Shaṭrah, Ash- 136-137 LM 7
Shaṭṭ al-'Arab 134-135 F 4
Shaṭṭ al-Fijāj 166-167 L 2-3
Shaṭṭ al-Furāt 136-137 LM 7
Shaṭṭ al-Gharbī, Ash- 166-167 F 3
Shaṭṭ al-Ghurrah 166-167 M 2
Shaṭṭ al-Jarīd 164-165 F 2
Shaṭṭ al-Jarsah 166-167 KL 2
Shaṭṭ al-Qaṭṭār 166-167 L 2
Shaṭṭ al-'Uzaym 136-137 L 5
Shaṭṭ Dijlah 134-135 F 4
Shaṭṭ Malghīr 164-165 F 2
Shaṭṭ Marwan 166-167 JK 2-3
Shattuck, OK 76-77 E 4
Shau = Wādī Huwār 164-165 K 5
Shaubak, Esh- = Ash-Shawbak 136-137 F 7
Shaukkôn 141 D 6
Shaunavon 66-67 J 1
Shaviovik River 58-59 O 2
Shavli = Šiauliai 124-125 D 6
Shaw 106-107 H 6
Shaw, MS 78-79 D 4
Shawan 146-147 G 8
Shawano, WI 70-71 F 3
Shawatun = Shaguotun 144-145 C 2
Shawbak, Ash- 136-137 F 7
Shawbridge 72-73 J 2
Shawinigan Sud 56-57 W 8
Shaw Island 58-59 L 7
Shāwīyah, Ash- 166-167 C 3
Shawnee, OK 64-65 G 4
Shawneetown, IL 70-71 F 7
Shawo 146-147 E 6
Shawocun, Beijing- 155 II a 2
Shaw River 158-159 C 4
Shawville 72-73 H 2
Sha Xi [TJ, Fujian] 146-147 F 8
Shaxi [TJ, Jiangxi] 146-147 G 7
Shaxi [TJ, Nanchang] 146-147 E 8
Sha Xian 142-143 M 6
Shayang 146-147 D 6

Shaykh, Ḥāssī — 166-167 G 4
Shaykh Aḥmad 136-137 J 4
Shaykh Hilāl 136-137 G 5
Shaykh Sa'd 136-137 M 6
Shaykh Ṣalāḥ 136-137 J 4
Shaykh 'Uthmān, Ash- 134-135 EF 8
Shayōg = Shyog 134-135 M 3-4
Shazhou 146-147 H 6
Shāẓī, Wādī ash- 136-137 J 7
Shcherbakov = Rybinsk 132-133 F 6
Shea 92-93 H 4
She'aiba, Ash- = Ash-Shu'aybah 136-137 M 7
Sheaville, OR 66-67 E 4
Shebelē, Wabī — 164-165 N 7
Sheboygan, WI 64-65 J 3
Shebu 146-147 C 10
Shediac 63 D 4
Shedin Peak 60 D 2
Sheduan Island = Jazīrat Shadwān 164-165 LM 3
Sheenborough 72-73 H 1-2
Sheenjek River 56-57 H 4
Sheep Creek 68-69 CD 4
Sheep Mountain 68-69 D 3
Sheep Mountains 68-69 CD 2
Sheep Peak 74-75 F 4
Sheep Range 74-75 F 4
Sheepshead Bay, New York-, NY 82 III c 3
Sheerness 61 C 5
Sheet Harbour 63 EF 5
Sheffield, AL 78-79 EF 3
Sheffield, IA 70-71 D 4
Sheffield, TX 76-77 CD 7
Sheffield [AUS] 160 c 2
Sheffield [GB] 119 F 5
Sheffield Lake 63 H 3
Shefoo = Yantai 142-143 N 4
Shēgāṅv = Shegaon 138-139 F 7
Shēgāṅv = Shegvaon 141 B 2
Shegaon 138-139 F 7
Sheḥamī = Shaḥamī 136-137 H 6
Sheho 61 G 5
Shehsien = She Xian 146-147 DE 3
Shê-hsien = She Xian [TJ, Anhui] 142-143 M 5-6
Shê-hsien = She Xian [TJ, Hebei] 146-147 DE 3
Shehuen, Río — 108-109 DE 7
Sheikh, Sharm esh- = Sharm ash-Shayh 173 D 4
Sheikh Othman = Ash-Shaykh 'Uthmān 134-135 F 8
Shekak River 70-71 H 1
Shekhar Dsong 142-143 F 6
Shekhpurā = Shaikhpura 138-139 KL 5
Sheki 126-127 N 6
Shekiak River 62 G 3
Shekki = Chixi 146-147 D 10-11
Shekkong = Shilong 146-147 B 11
Sheklukshuk Range 58-59 J 3
Sheklung = Shilong 146-147 DE 10
Shek O 155 I b 2
Shelār 136-137 N 6
Shelbina, MO 70-71 D 6
Shelburne [CDN, Nova Scotia] 63 D 6
Shelburne [CDN, Ontario] 72-73 FG 2
Shelburne Bay 158-159 H 2
Shelby, MI 70-71 G 4
Shelby, MS 78-79 D 4
Shelby, MT 66-67 H 1
Shelby, NC 64-65 K 4
Shelby, OH 72-73 E 4
Shelbyville, IL 70-71 F 6
Shelbyville, IN 70-71 H 6
Shelbyville, KY 70-71 H 6
Shelbyville, MO 70-71 DE 6
Shelbyville, TN 78-79 F 3
Sheldon 174-175 FG 7
Sheldon, IA 70-71 BC 4
Sheldon, MO 70-71 C 7
Sheldon, TX 85 III c 1
Sheldon, WI 70-71 E 3
Sheldon Reservoir 85 III c 1
Sheldons Point, AK 58-59 DE 5
Sheldrake 63 D 2
Shelikof Strait 56-57 EF 6
Shell, WY 68-69 C 3
Shell Beach, LA 78-79 E 6
Shellbrook 61 EF 4
Shell Creek [USA, Colorado] 66-67 J 5
Shell Creek [USA, Nebraska] 68-69 H 5
Shellem 168-169 J 3
Shelley, ID 66-67 GH 4
Shellharbour, Wollongong- 158-159 K 6
Shell Lake 61 E 4
Shell Lake, WI 70-71 E 3
Shellman, GA 78-79 G 5
Shell River 61 H 5
Shellrock River 70-71 D 4
Shelter, Port — 155 I b 1
Shelter Cove, CA 66-67 A 5
Shelter Island 155 I b 2
Shelton, WA 66-67 B 2
Shemankar 168-169 H 3
Shemichi Islands 58-59 pq 6
Shemya Island 58-59 q 6
Shenāfiya, Ash- = Ash-Shināfīyah 136-137 L 7
Shenandoah, IA 70-71 C 5
Shenandoah, PA 72-73 HJ 4
Shenandoah, VA 72-73 G 5
Shenandoah Mountains 72-73 G 5
Shenandoah National Park 72-73 GH 5
Shenandoah River 72-73 GH 5
Shenashan, Wed — = Wādī Shanāshīn 166-167 E 7
Shenchi 146-147 CD 2
Shenchih = Shenchi 146-147 CD 2
Shên-ching = Shenjing 146-147 D 10-11
Shendam 164-165 FG 7
Shendī = Shandī 164-165 L 5
Shendurni 138-139 E 7
Shengcai = Shangcai 146-147 E 5
Shenge 168-169 B 4
Sheng Xian 142-143 N 6
Shenhsien = Shen Xian 146-147 E 2
Shenhu 146-147 G 9
Shenhuguan 141 EF 3
Shenjing 146-147 D 10-11
Shenmu 142-143 L 4
Shennongjia 146-147 C 6
Sheno Hill 168-169 J 3
Shenpūchi Pass = Shipki La 138-139 G 2
Shenqiu 146-147 E 5
Shensa Dsong 142-143 FG 5
Shensi = Shaanxi 142-143 K 4-5
Shenton, Mount — 158-159 D 5
Shentseh = Shenze 146-147 E 2
Shentuan 146-147 G 4
Shen Xian 146-147 E 2
Shenyang 142-143 NO 3
Shenze 146-147 E 2
Shenzhen = Nantou 146-147 D 10
Sheo = Shiv 138-139 C 4
Sheopur 138-139 F 5
Sheopuri = Shivpuri 134-135 M 5
Shepahua 96-97 E 7
Shepard 60 KL 4
Shepherd, MT 68-69 B 2-3
Shepherd, TX 76-77 G 7
Shepparton 158-159 HJ 7
Sheptē 96-97 C 5
Sherborne [ZA] 174-175 F 6
Sherbro Island 164-165 B 7
Sherbrooke [CDN, Nova Scotia] 63 F 5
Sherbrooke [CDN, Quebec] 56-57 W 8
Sherburn, MN 70-71 C 4
Shereik = Ash-Shurayk 164-165 L 5
Shērgaṛh 138-139 CD 4
Sherghāti 138-139 K 5
Sherī'ah, Nahr esh- = Nahr ash-Sharī'ah 136-137 F 6-7
Sheridan, AR 78-79 C 3
Sheridan, MT 66-67 GH 3
Sheridan, OR 66-67 B 3
Sheridan, TX 76-77 F 8
Sheridan, WY 64-65 E 3
Sheridan, Mount — 66-67 H 3
Sheridan Lake, CO 68-69 E 6
Sherman, MS 78-79 E 3
Sherman, TX 64-65 G 5
Sherman Inlet 56-57 R 4
Sherman Mills, ME 72-73 MN 2
Sherman Mountain 66-67 EF 5
Sherpūr [BD ↗ Jamālpūr] 138-139 N 5
Sherpūr [BD ↙ Jamālpūr] 138-139 M 5
Sherridon 56-57 Q 6
Shertally 140 C 6
's-Hertogenbosch 120-121 KL 3
Sheru 138-139 L 3
Sherwood, ND 68-69 F 1
Sherwood Forest, CA 83 I c 1
Sherwood Forest, Atlanta-, GA 85 II bc 2
Sherwood Park 61 B 4
Sheshalik, AK 58-59 F 3
Sheshea, Río — 96-97 E 6
She Shui 146-147 E 6
Sheslay 58-59 W 7
Sheslay River 58-59 V 7
Shethātha = Shithāthah 136-137 K 6
Shetland 119 FG 1
Sheung Kwai Chung 155 I a 1
Shevaroy Hills 140 D 5
Shevgaon 138-139 E 8
Shewa 164-165 M 7
She Xian [TJ, Anhui] 142-143 M 5-6
She Xian [TJ, Hebei] 146-147 DE 3
Sheyang 146-147 H 5
Sheyang He 146-147 H 5
Sheyenne River 68-69 H 2
Sheykh Ḥoseyn 136-137 N 7
Shiādmā', Ash- 166-167 B 4
Shibām 134-135 F 7
Shibarghān 134-135 K 3
Shibata 144-145 M 4
Shibazaki, Chōfu- 155 III a 2
Shibecha 144-145 d 2
Shibei 146-147 G 8
Shibetsu [J ↑ Asahikawa] 144-145 c 1
Shibetsu [J ↖ Nemuro] 144-145 d 2
Shibetsu, Naka- 144-145 d 2
Shibicha, Ash- = Ash-Shabakah 136-137 K 7
Shibīgā 168-169 C 1
Shibīn al-Kawn 173 B 2
Shibīn al-Qanāṭir 173 B 2
Shib Kūh 134-135 G 5
Shibogama Lake 62 EF 1
Shibsāgar = Sibsāgar 141 D 2
Shibukawa 144-145 M 4
Shibushi 144-145 H 7
Shibushi-wan 144-145 H 7
Shibutami = Tamayama 144-145 N 3
Shibuya, Tōkyō- 155 III ab 2
Shicheng 146-147 F 8
Shicheng Dao 144-145 D 3
Shichuan Ding 146-147 CD 9
Shickshock, Monts — = Monts Chic-Choqs 56-57 X 8
Shidād, Umm ash- = Sabkhat Abā ar-Rūs 134-135 G-H 6
Shidao 146-147 J 3
Shiddādī, Ash- 136-137 J 4
Shideng 141 F 2
Shīdīyah, Ash- 136-137 FG 8
Shidlaghaṭṭā = Sidlaghatta 140 CD 4
Shields, ND 68-69 F 2
Shifshawn 164-165 CD 1
Shiga 144-145 KL 5
Shigatse = Zhigatse 142-143 F 6
Shiggāṉa = Shiggaon 140 B 3
Shiggāṅv = Shiggaon 140 B 3
Shiggaon 140 B 3
Shiḥan, Wādī — 134-135 G 7
Shih-ch'êng = Shicheng 146-147 F 8
Shih-ch'êng Tao = Shicheng Dao 144-145 D 3
Shih-ch'ien = Shiqian 142-143 K 6
Shih-chiu-so = Shijiusuo 146-147 G 4
Shih-ch'ü = Serxü 142-143 H 5
Shihchuan = Shiquan 142-143 K 5
Shih-chuang = Shizhuang 146-147 H 5
Shih-hsing = Shixing 146-147 E 9
Shih-k'ang = Shikang 146-147 B 11
Shih-lou = Shilou 146-147 C 3
Shihlung = Shilong [TJ, Guangdong] 146-147 DE 10
Shih-lung = Shilong [TJ, Guangxi Zhuangzu Zizhiqu] 146-147 B 10
Shihmen = Shimen 146-147 C 7
Shihnan = Enshi 142-143 K 5
Shih-pei = Shibei 146-147 G 8
Shih-p'ing = Shiping 142-143 J 7
Shih-p'u = Shipu 146-147 HJ 7
Shiḥr, Ash- 134-135 F 8
Shih-shou = Shishou 146-147 D 7
Shihtai = Shitai 146-147 F 6
Shih-têng = Shideng 141 F 2
Shihtsien = Shiqian 142-143 K 6
Shih-wan-ta Shan = Shiwanda Shan 150-151 F 2
Shijiao 146-147 C 11
Shijiazhuang 142-143 L 4
Shijiu Hu 146-147 G 6
Shika 138-139 B 6
Shikang 146-147 B 11
Shikārpur [IND, Bihār] 138-139 K 4
Shikārpur [IND, Karnataka] 140 B 3
Shikārpūr [PAK] 134-135 K 5
Shikhartse = Zhigatse 142-143 F 6
Shikine-chima 144-145 M 5
Shikk'ah, Rā's ash- 136-137 F 5
Shikohābād 138-139 G 4
Shikoku 142-143 P 5
Shikoku sammyaku 144-145 JK 6
Shikotan-tō 142-143 S 3
Shikotsu-ko 144-145 b 2
Shikou 146-147 G 3
Shilaong = Shillong 134-135 P 5
Shilchar = Silchar 134-135 P 6
Shilif 164-165 E 1
Shilipu 146-147 CD 6
Shilka = Šilka 132-133 W 7
Shillington, PA 72-73 HJ 4
Shillong 134-135 P 5
Shiloguṛī = Siliguri 134-135 O 5
Shiloh National Military Park and Cemetery 78-79 EF 3
Shilong [TJ, Guangdong] 146-147 DE 10
Shilong [TJ, Guangxi Zhuangzu Zizhiqu] 146-147 B 10
Shilong = Shajianzi 144-145 E 2
Shilou 146-147 C 3
Shilute = Šilutė 124-125 C 6
Shīlyah, Jabal — 164-165 F 1
Shimabara 144-145 H 6
Shimabara hantō 144-145 H 6
Shimada 144-145 M 5
Shima-hantō 144-145 L 5
Shimālīyah, Ash- 164-165 KL 5
Shimane 144-145 HJ 5
Shimane, Tōkyō- 155 III b 1
Shimen 146-147 C 7
Shimen = Shijiazhuang 142-143 LM 4
Shimenjie 146-147 F 7
Shimizu 142-143 Q 4-5
Shimizu = Tosashimizu 144-145 J 6
Shimlā = Simla 134-135 M 4
Shimminato 144-145 L 4
Shimo = Kyūshū 142-143 P 5
Shimoda 144-145 M 5
Shimodate 144-145 MN 4
Shimoga 134-135 LM 8
Shimoigusa, Tōkyō- 155 III a 1
Shimoizumi 155 III d 3
Shimokita-hantō 142-143 R 3
Shimo-Koshiki-chima 144-145 G 7
Shimoni 172 GH 2
Shimonoseki 142-143 P 5
Shimono-shima 144-145 G 5
Shimoshakujii, Tōkyō- 155 III a 1
Shimoyaku = Yaku 144-145 H 7
Shimo-Yūbetsu 144-145 cd 1
Shimpi = Shinbī 141 C 4
Shimsha 140 C 4
Shimura, Tōkyō- 155 III b 1
Shimushiru = ostrov Simušir 132-133 d 8
Shimushu = ostrov Šumšu 132-133 e 7
Shin, Loch — 119 D 2
Shināfīyah, Ash- 136-137 L 7
Shinagawa, Tōkyō- 155 III b 2
Shinaibeidong 146-147 H 7
Shinaingbā 141 E 2
Shinano gawa 144-145 M 4
Shināṣ 134-135 H 6
Shināy, Bi'r — 173 D 6
Shinbī 141 C 4
Shinbwīyan 148-149 C 1
Shīndand 134-135 J 4
Shindidāy, Jabal — 173 E 6
Shiner, TX 76-77 F 8
Shingbwiyang = Shinbwīyan 148-149 C 1
Shingishu = Sinŭiju 142-143 NO 3
Shingleton, MI 70-71 G 2
Shingletown, CA 66-67 C 5
Shing Shi Mun 155 I b 2
Shingu 144-145 KL 6
Shingwedzi 174-175 J 2
Shingwidzi = Shingwedzi 174-175 J 2
Shing'ya 138-139 L 2
Shining Tree 62 L 3
Shiniu Shan 146-147 G 9
Shinjiang = Xinjiang Uyghur Zizhiqu 142-143 D-G 3
Shinji-ko 144-145 J 5
Shinjō 142-143 QR 4
Shinjō = Hsincheng 146-147 HJ 9
Shinjō, Kawasaki- 155 III a 2
Shinjuku, Tōkyō- 155 III b 1
Shinkafe 168-169 G 2
Shinko = Chinko 164-165 J 7
Shinkō = Hsincheng 146-147 HJ 9
Shinkolobwe 172 E 4
Shinmau Sūn 150-151 AB 6
Shin-nan = Enshi 142-143 K 5
Shinnston, WV 72-73 F 5
Shinohara, Yokohama- 155 III a 3
Shinqīti 164-165 B 4
Shinshān, Sabkhat — 164-165 B 4
Shinshū = Chinju 142-143 O 4
Shinyanga 172 F 2
Shinyukugyoen Garden 155 III b 1
Shiobara 144-145 MN 4
Shiogama 144-145 N 3
Shionomi, Cape — = Shiono-misaki 144-145 K 6
Shiono-misaki 144-145 K 6
Shioya-misaki 144-145 N 4
Shiping 142-143 J 7
Ship Island 78-79 E 5
Shipki 138-139 G 2
Shipki La 138-139 G 2
Shippegan 63 D 4
Shippegan Island 63 DE 4
Shippensburg, PA 72-73 GH 4
Shiprock, NW 74-75 J 4
Shipshaw, Rivière — 63 A 3
Shipu 146-147 HJ 7
Shiqian 142-143 K 6
Shiqiao 146-147 CD 6
Shiqq, Ḥāssī — 164-165 B 3
Shiquan 142-143 K 5
Shiquan He = Sengge Khamba 142-143 DE 5
Shirahama 144-145 K 6
Shirahaṭṭi = Shirhatti 140 B 3
Shirakami-saki 144-145 MN 2
Shirakawa 144-145 N 4
Shirāla 140 B 2
Shirane-san 144-145 LM 5
Shiranuka 144-145 cd 2
Shiraoi 144-145 b 2
Shirataka 144-145 MN 3
Shīrāz 134-135 G 5
Shiraze-hyōga 53 B 4-5
Shirbīn 173 B 2
Shire 172 FG 5
Shiretoko hantō 144-145 d 1-2
Shiretoko-misaki 144-145 d 1
Shirgaon 138-139 D 8
Shirhatti 140 B 3
Shirīn Sū 136-137 N 5
Shiritoru = Makarov 132-133 b 8
Shiriya-saki 144-145 N 2
Shirley, AR 78-79 C 3
Shirley Basin 68-69 C 4
Shiro, TX 76-77 G 7
Shiroishi 144-145 N 3-4
Shiroḷ 140 B 2
Shirotori 144-145 L 5
Shirpur 138-139 E 7
Shirqāṭ, Ash- = Ash-Sharqāṭ 136-137 K 5
Shirshāll 166-167 GH 1
Shirūr = Sirūr 140 B 1
Shishaldin Volcano 58-59 a 2
Shishāwah 166-167 B 4
Shishi 146-147 G 9
Shishihone, Tōkyō- 155 III c 1
Shishikui 144-145 K 6
Shishmaref, AK 56-57 CD 4
Shishmaref Inlet 58-59 DE 3
Shishou 146-147 D 7
Shitai 142-143 M 5
Shithāthah 136-137 K 6
Shitouzhai 141 F 4
Shiv 138-139 C 4
Shivagangā = Sivaganga [IND, mountain] 140 C 4
Shivagangā = Sivaganga [IND, place] 140 D 6
Shivakāshī = Sivakāsi 140 CD 6
Shivālak Pahāṛiyān = Siwālik Range 134-135 M 4-N 5
Shivamagga = Shimoga 134-135 LM 8
Shivarāya = Shevaroy Hills 140 D 4
Shivnarāyan = Seorīnārāyan 138-139 J 7
Shivnāth = Seonāth 138-139 J 7
Shivpur = Sheopur 138-139 F 5
Shivpuri 134-135 M 5
Shivwits Indian Reservation 74-75 FG 4
Shivwits Plateau 74-75 G 4
Shiwanda Shan 150-151 F 2
Shiwa Ngandu 171 BC 5
Shixing 146-147 E 9
Shiyan 146-147 C 5
Shizhu 146-147 B 6
Shizhuang 146-147 H 5
Shizukawa 144-145 N 3
Shizunai 144-145 c 2
Shizuoka 144-145 LM 5
Shkodër 122-123 H 4
Shkumbīn 122-123 H 5
Shmayṭīyah 136-137 H 5
Shmidt Island = ostrov Šmidta 132-133 QR 1
Shoa = Shewa 164-165 M 7
Shoal Lake [CDN, lake] 62 B 3
Shoal Lake [CDN, place] 61 H 5
Shoals, IN 70-71 G 6
Shōbara 144-145 J 5
Shobo Tsho 138-139 J 2
Shōdo-shima 144-145 K 5
Shodu 142-143 H 5
Shoe Cove 63 J 3
Shokā = Changhua 146-147 H 9
Shokalsky Strait = proliv Šokal'skogo 132-133 RS 2
Shokambetsu-dake 144-145 b 2
Shokotsu 144-145 c 1
Sholāpur 134-135 M 7
Sholavandan = Cholavandan 140 C 5
Shomolu 170 III b 1
Shooters Hill, London- 129 II c 2
Shōra, Ash- = Ash-Shūr'a 136-137 K 5
Shoranūr 140 C 5
Shorāpur 134-135 M 7
Shoreacres 66-67 E 1
Shoreditch, London- 129 II b 1
Shorewood, WI 70-71 G 4
Shorkoṭ 138-139 CD 2
Shorru Tsho 138-139 L 2
Shortland Island 148-149 hj 6
Shoshone, CA 74-75 EF 5
Shoshone, ID 66-67 F 4
Shoshone Falls 66-67 FG 4
Shoshone Mountain 74-75 E 4
Shoshone Mountains 64-65 C 3-4
Shoshone River 68-69 B 3
Shoshoni, WY 68-69 BC 4
Shō-Tombetsu 144-145 c 1
Shott el Jerid = Shaṭṭ al-Jarīd 164-165 F 2
Shotts, Plateau of the — = At-Tall 164-165 D 2-E 1
Shouchang 146-147 G 7
Shouguang 146-147 G 3
Shou-hsien = Shou Xian 146-147 F 5
Shou-kuang = Shouguang 146-147 G 3
Shoulder Mount 58-59 Q 3
Shouning 146-147 G 8
Shoup, ID 66-67 F 3
Shou Xian 146-147 F 5
Shouyang 146-147 D 3
Showak = Shuwak 164-165 M 6
Showhsien = Shou Xian 146-147 F 5
Showkwang = Shouguang 146-147 G 3
Show Low, AZ 74-75 H 5
Showning = Shouning 146-147 G 8
Showyang = Shouyang 146-147 D 3
Shrangavarapukōṭṭā = Srungavarapukota 140 F 1
Shreveport, LA 64-65 H 5
Shrewsbury 119 E 5
Shrīgonda 140 B 1
Shrīgōṇḍēṅ = Shrīgonda 140 B 1
Shrīharikoṭṭa Prāydvīp = Sriharikota Island 140 E 4
Shrīkākulam = Srīkākulam 134-135 M 7
Shrī Mādhōpur = Sri Mādhopur 138-139 E 4
Shrīmōhangaṛh = Sri Mohangarh 138-139 C 4
Shrimushanam = Srīmushnam 140 D 5
Shringēri = Sringeri 140 B 4
Shrīnivāsapura = Srīnivāspur 140 D 4
Shrīperambattūr = Srīperumbūdūr 140 DE 4
Shrīpūr 141 B 3
Shrīrāmpur = Serampore 134-135 O 6
Shrīrangam = Srīrangam 134-135 M 8
Shrīraṅgapaṭṭaṇa = Srīrangapatnam 140 C 4
Shrīshailam = Srīsailam 140 D 2
Shrīvaikuṇṭham = Srīvaikuntam 140 CD 6
Shrīvalliputtūr = Srīvilliputtūr 140 C 6
Shrīvardhan = Srīvardhan 134-135 L 7
Shuaiba = Ash-Shu'aybah 136-137 M 7
Shuaiba = As-Su'aybah 136-137 M 7
Shuangcheng 142-143 NO 2
Shuang-ch'êng = Shuangcheng 142-143 NO 2
Shuangfeng 146-147 D 8
Shuanggou [TJ, Hubei] 146-147 D 5
Shuanggou [TJ, Jiangsu ↓ Suqian] 146-147 G 5
Shuanggou [TJ, Jiangsu ↘ Xuzhou] 146-147 FG 4
Shuang-kou = Shuanggou [TJ, Hubei] 146-147 D 5
Shuang-kou = Shuanggou [TJ, Jiangsu ↓ Suqian] 146-147 G 5
Shuang-kou = Shuanggou [TJ, Jiangsu ↘ Xuzhou] 146-147 FG 4
Shuangliao 142-143 N 3
Shuangpai 146-147 C 8-9
Shu'aybah, Ash- 136-137 M 7
Shu'bah, Ash- 136-137 L 8
Shubert, NE 70-71 BC 5
Shublik Mountains 58-59 P 2
Shubrā, Al-Qāhirah- 170 II b 1
Shubrā al-Khaymah 170 II b 1
Shubuta, MS 78-79 E 5
Shucheng 146-147 F 6
Shufu = Qāshqār 142-143 CD 4
Shugra = Shuqrā 134-135 F 8
Shuguri Falls 171 D 5
Shuhekou 146-147 B 5
Shu-ho-k'ou = Shuhekou 146-147 B 5
Shuidong = Dianbai 146-147 C 11
Shuifeng Supong Hu = Supung Hu 144-145 E 2
Shuigoutou = Laixi 146-147 H 3
Shuiji 146-147 G 8
Shuikou 142-143 M 6
Shujāābad 138-139 C 3
Shujālpur 138-139 F 6
Shullsburg, WI 70-71 EF 4
Shulu 146-147 E 3
Shumagin Islands 56-57 DE 6
Shuman House, AK 58-59 PQ 3
Shumla 86-87 K 3
Shumla, TX 76-77 D 8
Shumlūl, Ash- = Ma'qalā' 134-135 F 5
Shūnāmganj 141 B 3
Shun'an = Chun'an 146-147 G 7
Shunchang 146-147 FG 8
Shunde 146-147 D 10
Shungnak, AK 56-57 EF 4
Shungnak River 58-59 J 3
Shunhua = Chunhua 146-147 B 4
Shunking = Nanchong 142-143 JK 5
Shunsen = Ch'unch'ŏn 142-143 O 4
Shuntak = Shunde 146-147 D 10
Shunteh = Shunde 146-147 D 10
Shunteh = Xingtai 142-143 L 4
Shuo-hsien = Shuo Xian 146-147 D 2
Shuo Xian 146-147 D 2
Shuqrā' 134-135 F 8
Shūr, Āb-e — 136-137 N 7
Shūr'a, Ash- 136-137 K 5
Shurayf 134-135 D 5
Shurayk, Ash- 164-165 L 5
Shurugwi 172 EF 5
Shūsh 136-137 N 6
Shushan = Susa 136-137 N 6
Shushartie 60 CD 4
Shushong 174-175 G 2
Shūshtar 134-135 F 4
Shuswap Lake 60 H 4
Shutō 138-139 MN 3
Shuwak 164-165 M 6
Shuwayyib, Ash- 136-137 MN 7
Shuyak Island 58-59 LM 7
Shuyak Strait 58-59 L 7
Shuyang 142-143 M 5
Shuzenji 144-145 M 5
Shwāmūn 141 D 5
Shwangcheng = Shuangcheng 142-143 NO 2
Shwangliao = Liaoyuan 142-143 NO 3
Shwebō 148-149 C 2
Shwedaung 141 D 6
Shwegū 141 E 3
Shwegūn 141 E 7
Shwegyin 141 E 7
Shwelī Myit 141 E 4
Shwemyō 141 E 5
Shyog 134-135 M 3-4
Shyopur = Shivpuri 134-135 M 5
Si, Laem — 150-151 B 8
Siabu 152-153 C 5
Siāh, Kūh-e — = Kūh-e Marzu 136-137 M 6
Siāhdehān = Tākestān 136-137 NO 4
Siak, Sungai — 152-153 DE 5
Siakiang = Xiajiang 146-147 E 8
Siak Sri Indrapura 152-153 DE 5
Siakwan = Xiaguan 142-143 J 6
Sialcote = Siyālkoṭ 134-135 LM 4
Sialkot = Siyālkoṭ 134-135 LM 4
Sialsūk 141 C 4
Siam = Thailand 148-149 CD 3
Si'an 146-147 G 6
Sian = Xi'an 142-143 K 5
Siangcheng = Xiangcheng 146-147 E 5
Siangfan = Fangcheng 142-143 L 5
Siangho = Xianghe 146-147 F 2
Siangning = Xiangning 146-147 C 3-4
Siangtan = Xiangtan 142-143 L 6
Siangyang = Xiangyang 142-143 L 5
Siangyin = Xiangyin 146-147 D 7
Siangyuan = Xiangyuan 146-147 D 3
Sianquião = Xiang Jiang 146-147 D 8
Siantan, Pulau — 150-151 EF 11
Siaofeng = Xiaofeng 146-147 G 6
Siao Hingan Ling = Xiao Hinggan Ling 142-143 O 1-P 2
Siaohsien = Xiao Xian 146-147 F 4
Siaokan = Xiaogan 146-147 D 6
Siaoyi = Xiaoyi 146-147 C 3
Siapa 94-95 H 6
Siapo, Río — 94-95 HJ 7
Siargao Island 148-149 J 4-5
Siau, Pulau — 148-149 J 6
Šiauliai 124-125 D 6
Siazan' 126-127 O 6
Sībah, As- 136-137 N 7
Sībaī, Jabal as- 173 CD 5
Sibā'īyah, As- 173 C 5
Sibaj 132-133 K 7
Sibasa 174-175 J 2
Sibayameer 174-175 K 4
Sibayi, Lake — = Sibayameer 174-175 K 4
Sibbald 61 C 5
Sībdū 166-167 F 2
Šibenik 122-123 FG 4
Siberia 132-133 O-X 5
Siberimanua 152-153 C 7
Siberut, Pulau — 148-149 C 7
Siberut, Selat — 148-149 C 7
Sibī 134-135 K 5
Sibir'akova, ostrov — 132-133 OP 3
Sibirien 132-133 N-W 5
Sibiti [EAT] 171 C 3
Sibiti [RCA] 172 B 2
Sibiu 122-123 KL 3
Sibley, IA 70-71 BC 4
Sibley Provincial Park 70-71 F 1
Siboa 152-153 NO 5
Sibolga 148-149 C 6
Siborongborong 150-151 B 11
Sibpur, Howrah- 154 II a 2
Sibsāgar 141 D 2
Sibu 148-149 F 6
Sibu, Pulau — 150-151 E 11
Sibuatan, Gunung — 152-153 BC 4
Sibuco 152-153 OP 2
Sibū 'Gharb, As- 173 C 6
Sibuguey Bay 152-153 P 2
Sibuti 152-153 K 3
Sibutu Group 148-149 G 6
Sibutu Passage 152-153 N 3
Sibuyan Island 148-149 H 4
Sibuyan Sea 148-149 H 4
Siby 168-169 C 2
Sibyŏn-ni 144-145 F 3
Sica, Cascade de — 168-169 F 3
Sicamous 60 H 4
Sicasica 92-93 F 8
Sicasica, Serranía de — 104-105 BC 5
Sicasso = Sikasso 164-165 C 6
Sichang = Xichang 142-143 J 6
Sichang, Ko — 150-151 C 6
Šichany 124-125 Q 7
Sichem = Nābulus 136-137 F 6
Sichon 150-151 BC 8
Sichota-Alin = Sichote-Alin' 132-133 a 8-Z 9
Sichotė-Alin' 132-133 a 8-Z 9
Šichrany = Kanaš 132-133 H 6
Sichuan 142-143 J 5-6
Sichwan = Xichuan 142-143 L 5
Sicilia 122-123 EF 7
Sicily = Sicilia 122-123 EF 7
Sico, Río — 88-89 D 7
Sicuani 92-93 E 7
Sīdamo 164-165 MN 8
Sidamo-Borana = Sīdamo 164-165 MN 8
Sidao, Beijing- 155 II b 2
Sidaogou 144-145 F 2
Sidcup, London- 129 II c 2
Siddapur 140 B 3
Siddhapura = Siddapur 140 B 3
Siddipet 140 D 1
Siddipēṭa = Siddipet 140 D 1
Sideby 116-117 J 6
Sid-el-Hadj-Zaoui = Sīdī al-Ḥājj Zāwī 166-167 J 5
Sidéradougou 168-169 DE 3
Sidērókastron 122-123 K 5
Sideros, Akrōtērion — 122-123 M 8
Sidhaolī = Sidhauli 138-139 H 4
Sidhauli 138-139 H 4
Sidhi 138-139 H 5
Sidhout 140 D 3
Sidhpur 138-139 D 5-6
Sīdī 'Abd ar-Raḥmān 136-137 C 7
Sīdī-Aḥmadū 166-167 H 5
Sidi-Aïch = Sīdī Aysh 166-167 J 1
Sīdī 'Aīsá 166-167 EF 2
Sīdī al-Akḥdar 166-167 FG 1
Sīdī al-Ḥājj ad-Dīn 166-167 G 3
Sīdī al-Ḥājj Zāwī 166-167 J 5
Sīdī al-Hānī, Sabkhat — 166-167 M 2
Sīdī-'Alī Ban Yūb 166-167 F 2
Sidi-Ali-Ben-Youb = Sīdī 'Alī Ban Yūb 166-167 F 2
Sīdī 'Alī Bin Naṣr Allah 166-167 LM 2
Sīdī 'Allāl al-Baḥrawī 166-167 CD 2
Sīdī al-Muhthār 166-167 B 4
Sīdī 'Amur Bū Ḥajalah 166-167 LM 2
Sīdī 'Aysā 166-167 H 2
Sīdī 'Aysh 166-167 J 1
Sīdī az-Zūīn 166-167 B 4
Sīdī Ban al-'Abbas 164-165 DE 1
Sīdī Barrānī 164-165 K 2
Sidi-bel-Abbès = Sīdī Ban al-'Abbas 164-165 DE 1
Sīdī Binnūr 166-167 B 3
Sīdī Boūbker = Abū Bakr 166-167 F 2
Sīdī Bū al-Anwār 166-167 B 4
Sīdī Bū Ghadrah 166-167 B 3
Sīdī Bū Zīd 166-167 L 2
Sīdī Chemākh = Sīdī Shammakh 166-167 M 3
Sidi Chemmakh = Sīdī Shammakh 166-167 M 3

Sîdî Chiger = Sîdî Shigar 166-167 B 4
Sidi-el-Hadj-ed-Dine = Sîdî al-Hājj ad-Dīn 166-167 G 3
Sîdî Îfnî 164-165 B 3
Sîdî Ismā'il 166-167 B 3
Sidikalang 152-153 BC 4
Sidi-Lakhdar = Sîdî al-Akhḍar 166-167 FG 1
Sidi Makhlūf 166-167 H 2
Sîdî Manṣūr 166-167 L 2
Sidi-Marūf 166-167 K 1
Sidi-Mérouane = Sîdî Mīrwān 166-167 JK 1
Sidi-M'Hamed-Benali = Sîdî Muḥammad Ban Alī 166-167 G 1
Sîdî Mirwān 164-165 JK 1
Sidi M'Mamed, Al-Jazā'ir- 170 I a 1
Sidi Mokhtar = Sîdî al-Muhtār 166-167 B 4
Sidi Moussa = Sîdî Mūsá 166-167 B 3
Sidi Moussa, Ouèd — = Wādī Sîdî Mūsā 166-167 J 6
Sîdî Muhammad Ban 'Alī 166-167 G 1
Sîdî Mūsā 166-167 B 3
Sîdî Mūsā, Wādī — 166-167 J 6
Sîdî Naṣīr 166-167 L 1
Sidinginan 152-153 D 5
Sîdî Nṣīr = Sîdî Naṣīr 166-167 L 1
Sîdî Omar Boû Hadjila = Sîdî 'Amur Bū Ḥajalah 166-167 LM 2
Sidi Ouada 170 I b 2
Sîdî Qāsim 164-165 CD 2
Sîdî Raḥḥāl 166-167 C 4
Sîdî Sālim 173 B 2
Sîdî Shammakh 166-167 M 3
Sîdî Shigar 166-167 B 4
Sîdî Slîmân = Sîdî Sulīmān 166-167 CD 2
Sidi Smaïl = Sidi Ismā'il 166-167 B 3
Sîdî Sulīmān 166-167 CD 2
Sîdî Ṭla'a = Unāghāh 166-167 B 4
Sîdî 'Ukāskah 166-167 G 1
Sîdî Yaḥyā al-Gharb 166-167 CD 2
Sidi Youssef = Sāqīyat Sîdî Yusuf 166-167 L 1
Sidlaghatta 140 CD 4
Sidley, Mount — 53 B 24
Sidlī 138-139 N 4
Sidnaw, MI 70-71 F 2
Sidney 66-67 B 1
Sidney, IA 70-71 C 5
Sidney, MT 68-69 D 2
Sidney, NE 68-69 E 5
Sidney, NY 70-71 H 5
Sidney, OH 72-73 D 4
Sidobia 168-169 F 2
Sidoktaya = Sedôktayâ 141 D 5
Sidorovo 124-125 N 4
Sidr, As- 164-165 H 2
Sidr, Wādī — 173 C 3
Sidra = As-Surt 164-165 H 2-3
Sidra, Khalīg — = Khalīj as-Surt 164-165 H 2
Sidrolândia 92-93 HJ 9
Siebenhirten, Wien- 113 I b 2
Siedlce 118 L 2
Siedlung Hasenbergl, München- 130 II b 1
Siedlung Neuherberg, München- 130 II b 1
Sieg 118 C 3
Siegen 118 D 3
Siegessäule 130 III b 1
Siembok = Phum Siembauk 150-151 E 6
Siemensstadt, Berlin- 130 III b 1
Siemiatycze 118 L 2
Siem Pang 150-151 F 5
Siem Reap 148-149 D 4
Siena 122-123 D 4
Sienfeng = Xianfeng 146-147 B 7
Sienku = Xianju 146-147 H 7
Sienning = Xianning 146-147 E 7
Sienyang = Xianyang 142-143 K 5
Sieradz 118 J 3
Sierpc 118 JK 2
Sierra, La — [ROU] 106-107 K 5
Sierra, Punta — 108-109 G 3
Sierra Ambargasta 106-107 EF 2
Sierra Añueque 108-109 E 3
Sierra Apas 108-109 F 3-4
Sierra Auca Mahuida 106-107 C 6
Sierra Azul 106-107 BC 5-6
Sierra Balmaceda 108-109 DE 9
Sierra Blanca, TX 76-77 B 7
Sierra Blanca de la Totora 108-109 E 3-F 2
Sierra Blanca Peak 64-65 E 5
Sierra Brava [RA, mountains] 106-107 E 2
Sierra Brava [RA, place] 106-107 E 2
Sierra Calcatapul 108-109 E 4
Sierra Cañadón Grande 108-109 E 5
Sierra Carapacha Grande 106-107 DE 6-7
Sierra Cavalonga 104-105 C 8
Sierra Chata 108-109 FG 4
Sierra Chauchaiñeu 108-109 E 3
Sierra Chica [RA, mountains] 106-107 E 3
Sierra Chica [RA, place] 106-107 G 6
Sierra Choique Mahuida 106-107 E 7
Sierra Colorada 111 C 6
Sierra Cuadrada 108-109 E 5
Sierra Cupupira 94-95 J 6-7
Sierra da Mocidade 94-95 KL 7
Sierra de Agalta 64-65 J 8-9
Sierra de Aguas Calientes 104-105 C 9
Sierra de Aguilar 104-105 D 8
Sierra de Ahogayegua 64-65 b 2-3
Sierra de Alcaraz 120-121 F 9
Sierra de Alférez 106-107 KL 4
Sierra de Ambato 104-105 C 11
Sierra de Ancasti 106-107 E 2
Sierra de Aracena 120-121 D 10
Sierra de Azul 106-107 GH 6
Sierra de Baraqua 94-95 FG 2
Sierra de Calalaste 111 C 2-3
Sierra de Cañazas 88-89 G 10
Sierra de Cantantal 106-107 D 3-4
Sierra de Carapé 106-107 K 5
Sierra de Carmen Silva 108-109 E 9
Sierra de Catán-Lil 106-107 B 7
Sierra de Chachahuen 106-107 C 6
Sierra de Chañi 104-105 D 8-9
Sierra de Chepes 106-107 D 3
Sierra de Chiribiquete 94-95 E 7
Sierra de Coalcomán 86-87 J 8
Sierra de Cochinoca 104-105 D 8
Sierra de Comechingones 106-107 E 4
Sierra de Córdoba [RA] 111 C 4-D 3
Sierra de Cura Mala 106-107 FG 6-7
Sierra de Divisor 92-93 E 6
Sierra de Famatina 106-107 D 2
Sierra de Gata 120-121 D 8
Sierra de Gredos 120-121 E 8
Sierra de Guadalupe [E] 120-121 E 9
Sierra de Guadalupe [MEX] 91 I c 1
Sierra de Guadarrama 120-121 EF 8
Sierra de Guasapampa 106-107 E 3
Sierra de Guasayán 104-105 D 10-11
Sierra de Huantraicó 106-107 C 6
Sierra de Juárez 64-65 C 5
Sierra del Aconquija 104-105 CD 10
Sierra de la Encantada 76-77 C 8
Sierra de la Encantada 86-87 J 3-4
Sierra de la Giganta 64-65 D 6-7
Sierra de la Huerta 106-107 D 3
Sierra de la Iguana 76-77 D 9
Sierra de la Madera 86-87 F 2-3
Sierra de la Neblina 94-95 HJ 7
Sierra de la Palma 76-77 D 9-10
Sierra de la Peña 120-121 G 7
Sierra de la Punilla 106-107 C 2
Sierra de las Aguadas 106-107 BC 5
Sierra de las Minas 86-87 PQ 10
Sierra de las Tunas 106-107 G 6
Sierra de las Vacas 108-109 C 6-7
Sierra de la Ventana 111 D 5
Sierra del Carmen 86-87 J 3
Sierra del Centinela 104-105 D 8-9
Sierra del Cobre 104-105 C 8-9
Sierra de Lema 94-95 L 4
Sierra del Hueso 76-77 B 7
Sierra del Imán 106-107 K 1
Sierra de Lique 104-105 D 6-7
Sierra del Muerto 104-105 AB 9
Sierra del Nevado 111 C 5
Sierra del Norte 106-107 E 3
Sierra de los Alamitos 86-87 JK 4
Sierra de los Chacays 108-109 F 4
Sierra de los Cóndores 106-107 E 4
Sierra de los Filabres 120-121 F 10
Sierra de los Llanos 106-107 D 3
Sierra de los Prades 106-107 HJ 6-7
Sierra del Tandil 106-107 H 6
Sierra del Tigre 106-107 C 3
Sierra del Tlahualilo 76-77 C 9
Sierra del Volcán 106-107 H 6
Sierra del Zamura 94-95 K 5
Sierra de Mandiyutí 104-105 E 7
Sierra de Misiones 102-103 EF 7
Sierra de Mogna 106-107 C 3
Sierra de Mogotes 106-107 E 2
Sierra de Moreno 104-105 B 7
Sierra de Olte 108-109 E 4
Sierra de Outes 120-121 C 7
Sierra de Perija 92-93 E 2-3
Sierra de Pija 64-65 J 8
Sierra de Pillahuincó 106-107 G 7
Sierra de Pocho 106-107 E 3
Sierra de Quichagua 104-105 CD 8
Sierra de Quillalauquén 106-107 G 6
Sierra de Quilmes 104-105 C 10
Sierra de San Antonio 86-87 E 2-3
Sierra de San Bernardo 108-109 E 5
Sierra de San Borja 86-87 D 3
Sierra de San Lázaro 86-87 E 5-F 6
Sierra de San Lorenzo 120-121 F 7
Sierra de San Luís [RA] 106-107 DE 4
Sierra de San Luis [YV] 92-93 EF 2
Sierra de San Marcos 76-77 CD 9
Sierra de Sañogasta 106-107 D 2
Sierra de San Pedro 120-121 D 9
Sierra de San Pedro Mártir 86-87 C 2
Sierra de Santa Bárbara 104-105 D 8-9
Sierra de Santa Catarina 91 I cd 3
Sierra de Santa Cruz 104-105 E 5-6
Sierra de Santa Lucía 86-87 D 4
Sierra de Segura 120-121 F 9-10
Sierra de Tamaulipas 86-87 L 6
Sierra de Tartagal 104-105 E 8
Sierra de Tatul 106-107 B 2
Sierra de Tecka 108-109 D 4
Sierra de Tolox 120-121 E 10
Sierra de Tontal 106-107 C 3
Sierra de Tunuyan 111 C 4
Sierra de Ulapes 106-107 D 3-4
Sierra de Umango 106-107 C 2
Sierra de Unturán 94-95 J 7
Sierra de Uspallata 106-107 C 4
Sierra de Valle Fértil 106-107 CD 3
Sierra de Varas 104-105 B 9
Sierra de Velasco 106-107 D 2
Sierra de Vilgo 106-107 D 2-3
Sierra de Villicún 106-107 C 3
Sierra Diablo 76-77 B 7
Sierra Gorda 111 C 2
Sierra Gould 106-107 E 7
Sierra Grande [MEX] 86-87 H 3
Sierra Grande [RA, Córdoba] 106-107 E 3-4
Sierra Grande [RA, Río Negro mountains] 108-109 G 3
Sierra Grande [RA, Río Negro place] 111 C 6
Sierra Gulampaja 104-105 C 10
Sierra Huancache 108-109 DE 4
Sierra Laguna Blanca 104-105 C 10
Sierra Leone 164-165 B 7
Sierra Leone Basin 50-51 HJ 5
Sierra Leone Rise 50-51 HJ 5
Sierra Madera 76-77 C 7
Sierra Madre [MEX] 64-65 H 8
Sierra Madre [RP] 148-149 H 3
Sierra Madre [USA] 68-69 C 5
Sierra Madre del Sur 64-65 FG 8
Sierra Madre Mountains 74-75 CD 5
Sierra Madre Occidental 64-65 E 5-F 7
Sierra Madre Oriental 64-65 F 6-G 7
Sierra Madrona 120-121 EF 9
Sierra Maestra 64-65 L 7-8
Sierra Mariposa 104-105 B 8
Sierra Mesaniyeu 108-109 DE 3
Sierra Mochada 86-87 HJ 4
Sierra Mojada 86-87 J 4
Sierra Morena 120-121 D 10-E 9
Sierra Negra [RA ↘ Paso de Indios] 108-109 F 5
Sierra Negra [RA ↖ Paso de Indios] 108-109 DE 4
Sierra Negra [RA, Precordillera] 106-107 C 3
Sierra Nevada [E] 120-121 F 10
Sierra Nevada [RA] 108-109 E 4
Sierra Nevada [USA] 64-65 BC 4
Sierra Nevada [YV] 94-95 F 3
Sierra Nevada del Cocuy 94-95 E 4
Sierra Nevada de Santa Marta 92-93 E 2
Sierra Oscura 76-77 A 6
Sierra Pailemán 108-109 FG 3
Sierra Parima 92-93 G 4
Sierra Pereyra 106-107 G 3
Sierra Pichi Mahuida 106-107 E 7
Sierra Pie de Palo 106-107 C 3
Sierra Piedra Blanca 106-107 CD 7
Sierra Pinta 74-75 G 6
Sierra Rosada 108-109 E 4
Sierra Sabinas = Sierra de la Iguana 76-77 D 9
Sierra San Lázaro 86-87 EF 6
Sierra San Miguel 104-105 B 10
Sierra San Pedro Mártir 64-65 CD 5
Sierra Santa Victoria 104-105 D 8
Sierras Blancas 108-109 EF 2-3
Sierras de Zacatecas 86-87 JK 6
Sierras Pampeanas 111 C 3
Sierra Sumampa 106-107 F 2
Sierra Tapirapecó 92-93 FG 4
Sierra Taquetrén 108-109 E 4
Sierra Tarahumara 64-65 E 6
Sierra Telmo 104-105 D 8
Sierra Tepequem 98-99 GH 3
Sierra Valenzuela 104-105 A 8
Sierra Velluda 106-107 B 6
Sierra Vicuña Mackenna 104-105 AB 9
Sierra Vieja 76-77 B 7
Sierra Vizcaíno 64-65 D 6
Sierrita, La — 94-95 EF 2
Siesta Key 80-81 b 3
Siete Puntas, Río — 102-103 C 5
Sievering, Wien- 113 I b 1
Sifa, Cape — = Dahua Jiao 150-151 H 3
Sifa Point = Dahua Jiao 150-151 H 3
Sīf Fatimah, Bi'r — 166-167 L 4
Siffray 168-169 C 3
Sífnos 122-123 L 7
Sifton Pass 56-57 LM 6
Sig 166-167 F 2
Sigep 152-153 C 6
Sigep, Tanjung — 152-153 C 6
Sighetul Marmatiei 122-123 KL 2
Sighişoara 122-123 L 2
Sigiriya 140 E 7
Sigli 148-149 C 5
Siglufjördhur 116-117 d 1
Signai 62 N 2
Signal Hill 83 III cd 3
Signal Peak 74-75 FG 6
Signy 53 C 32
Sigoor 171 C 2
Sigourney, IA 70-71 DE 5
Sigsig 96-97 B 3
Sigtuna 116-117 GH 8
Siguiri 164-165 C 6
Sigulda 124-125 E 5
Sigurd, UT 74-75 H 3
Si He 146-147 F 4
Sihlwald 128 IV b 2
Sihong 146-147 G 5
Sihōr = Sehore 138-139 F 6
Sihora 138-139 H 6
Sihsien = She Xian 142-143 M 5-6
Sihsien = Xi Xian [TJ, Henan] 146-147 E 5
Sihsien = Xi Xian [TJ, Shanxi] 142-143 L 4
Sihuas 96-97 C 6
Sihuas, Pampas de — 96-97 EF 10
Sihui 146-147 D 10
Sihwān 138-139 AB 4
Siilinjärvi 116-117 M 6
Siinai = Sînâ' 164-165 L 3
Siirt 134-135 E 3
Siján 104-105 C 11
Sijerdijelach Jur'ach = Batamaj 132-133 YZ 5
Sijiao Shan 146-147 HJ 6
Sijiazi = Laohushan 144-145 BC 2
Sijnān 166-167 L 1
Sik 150-151 C 10
Sikandarābād 138-139 F 3
Sikandarābād = Secunderābād 134-135 M 7
Sikandrabad = Sikandarābād 138-139 F 3
Sikandra Rao 138-139 G 4
Sikao 148-149 C 5
Sīkar 138-139 E 4
Sikāripāra 138-139 L 5
Sikasso 164-165 C 6
Sikefti 136-137 KL 3
Sikeli 152-153 O 8
Sikem = Nābulus 136-137 F 6
Sikes, LA 78-79 C 4
Sikeston, MO 78-79 E 2
Sikhim = Sikkim 134-135 O 5
Sikhiu 148-149 D 4
Sikhoraphum 150-151 D 5
Sikhota Alin = Sichotė-Alin' 132-133 a 8-Z 9
Si Kiang = Xi Jiang 146-147 C 10
Siking = Xi'an 142-143 K 5
Sikinos 122-123 L 7
Sikiré 168-169 E 2
Šikirlykitaj = Suvorovo 126-127 D 4
Sikkim 134-135 O 5
Sikoku = Shikoku 142-143 P 5
Sikotan tō = Shikotan-tō 142-143 S 3
Sikt'ach 132-133 X 4
Siktyakh = Sikt'ach 132-133 X 4
Sikyȯn 122-123 K 7
Sil 120-121 D 7
Sila, La — 122-123 G 6
Šilador 124-125 R 3
Šilalė 124-125 D 6
Silao 86-87 K 7
Silasjaure 116-117 G 3-4
Silcharī Bāzār 141 BC 4
Silcox 61 L 2
Şile 136-137 C 2
Silencio 86-87 K 3
Siler City, NC 80-81 G 3
Sileru 140 E 2
Silesia 118 GH 3
Silesia, MT 68-69 B 3
Silfke = Silifke 134-135 C 3
Silgarhi Doti 134-135 N 5
Silghāt 141 C 2
Silhaṭ 138-139 P 5-6
Silifke 134-135 C 3
Siligir 132-133 V 4
Silīguri 134-135 O 5
Silípica 106-107 EF 2
Silistra 122-123 M 3
Silivri 136-137 C 2
Siljan 116-117 F 7
Šilka 132-133 W 7
Šilkan 132-133 c 6
Silkeborg 116-117 C 9
Sillajguai, Cordillera — 104-105 B 6
Silleiro, Cabo — 120-121 C 7
Silli 168-169 E 3
Sillyŏng 144-145 G 4
Šil'naja Balka 126-127 O 1
Siloam Springs, AR 76-77 G 4
Silondi 138-139 H 6
Silos 94-95 E 4
Šilovo [SU, R'azan'skaja Oblast'] 124-125 N 6
Šilovo [SU, Tul'skaja Oblast'] 124-125 M 7
Silsbee, TX 76-77 GH 7
Siltou 164-165 H 5
Siluas 152-153 H 5
Silumpur, Wai — 152-153 F 7
Siluria, AL 78-79 F 4
Šilutė 124-125 C 6
Silva 96-97 A 4
Silva, Ilha da — 98-99 F 5
Silva Jardim 102-103 LM 5
Silvan 136-137 J 3
Silvānī = Silwāni 138-139 G 6
Silvânia 102-103 H 2
Silva Porto = Bié 172 C 4
Silvāsa = Silvassa 138-139 D 7
Silvassa 138-139 D 7
Silverbell, AZ 74-75 H 6
Silverbow, MT 66-67 G 2-3
Silver City 64-65 b 2
Silver City, ID 66-67 E 4
Silver City, NM 64-65 E 5
Silver City, UT 74-75 G 3
Silver Creek 66-67 D 4
Silver Creek, MS 78-79 DE 5
Silver Creek, NE 68-69 H 5
Silver Creek, NY 72-73 G 3
Silver Lake, CA 74-75 EF 5
Silver Lake, OR 66-67 C 4
Silver Lake Reservoir 83 III c 1
Silver Mountain 70-71 EF 1
Silverpeak, NV 74-75 E 4
Silver Peak Range 74-75 E 4
Silverstreams 174-175 E 5
Silverthrone Mount 60 D 4
Silverton 158-159 H 6
Silverton, CO 68-69 C 7
Silverton, OR 66-67 B 3
Silverton, TX 76-77 D 5
Silvertown, London- 129 II c 2
Silves [BR] 98-99 J 6
Silves [P] 120-121 C 10
Silvia 94-95 C 6
Silvianópolis 102-103 K 5
Silvies River 66-67 D 4
Silwa Baḥarī = Salwá Baḥrī 173 C 5
Silwāni 138-139 G 6
Silyānah 166-167 L 1
Silyānah, Wād — 166-167 L 1-2
Sīm, Rā's — 166-167 AB 4
Simandou 168-169 C 3
Simanggang 148-149 F 6
Šimanovsk 132-133 Y 7
Simao 142-143 J 7
Simão Dias 100-101 F 6
Simard, Lac — 72-73 G 1
Simaria 138-139 K 5
Simatang, Pulau — 152-153 NO 5
Simav 136-137 C 3
Simav çayı 136-137 C 3
Simbillâwein, Es- = As-Sinbillâwayn 173 BC 2
Simbirsk = Uľjanovsk 132-133 H 7
Simcoe 72-73 FG 3
Simcoe, Lake — 56-57 V 9
Simēn 164-165 M 6
Simeonof Island 58-59 d 2
Simferopol' 126-127 G 4
Simhāchalam 140 F 2
Simḥām, Jabal as- 134-135 GH 7
Similkameen River 66-67 CD 1
Simingan = Samangān 134-135 K 3
Siming Shan 146-147 H 7
Simiti 92-93 E 3
Simi Valley, CA 74-75 D 5
Simiyu 171 C 3
Simizu = Shimizu 142-143 Q 4-5
Sim Kolodiaziv = Lenino 126-127 G 4
Simla 134-135 M 4
Simla, Calcutta- 154 II b 2
Simmesport, LA 78-79 CD 5
Simmie 61 D 6
Simms, MT 66-67 GH 2
Simoca 104-105 D 10
Simões 100-101 D 4
Simokita hantō = Shimokita-hantō 142-143 R 3
Simola 116-117 MN 7
Simonette River 60 HJ 2
Simonhouse Lake 61 H 3
Simonicha 124-125 TU 5
Simonoseki = Shimonoseki 142-143 P 5
Simonstad 172 C 8
Simonstown = Simonstad 172 C 8
Simoom Sound 60 D 4
Šimozero 124-125 K 3
Simpang 152-153 F 6
Simpang Bedok 154 III b 1-2
Simpang-kanan, Sungai — 150-151 AB 11
Simpang-kiri, Sungai — 152-153 B 4
Simplício Mendes 92-93 L 6
Simplon 118 CD 5
Simpruk, Jakarta- 154 IV a 2
Simpson, Cape — 58-59 KL 1
Simpson, Isla — 108-109 C 5
Simpson, Río — 108-109 C 5
Simpson Desert 158-159 G 4-5
Simpson Island 70-71 G 1
Simpson Islands 56-57 O 5
Simpson Peninsula 56-57 T 4
Simpson Strait 56-57 R 4
Simra 138-139 K 4
Simrishamn 116-117 F 10
Sims Bayou 85 III b 2
Šimsk 124-125 H 4
Simular = Pulau Simeuluë 148-149 BC 6
Simunul Island 152-153 NO 3
Simušir, ostrov — 142-143 T 2
Sīnā' [ET] 164-165 L 3
Sina [IND] 140 B 1
Sinabang 148-149 C 6
Sinabung, Gunung — 152-153 C 4
Sinadhapo = Dhuusa Maareeb 164-165 b 2
Sinai = Sīnā' 164-165 L 3
Sinaloa 64-65 E 6-7
Sinaloa, Río — 86-87 FG 4-5
Sinamaica 94-95 F 2
Sinan 142-143 K 6
Sinanju 144-145 E 3
Sinanpaşa 136-137 CD 3
Sinaru, AK 58-59 HJ 1
Sinaûen = Sīnāwan 164-165 G 2
Sīnāwan 164-165 G 2
Sinbaungwe = Hsinbaungwê 141 D 6
Sinbillāwayn, As- 173 BC 2
Sincan 136-137 GH 3
Sincanlı = Sinanpaşa 136-137 CD 3
Sincé 94-95 D 3
Sincelejo 92-93 DE 3
Sinch'ang 144-145 G 2
Sinchang = Xinchang 146-147 H 7
Sinch'ang-ni 144-145 F 3
Sincheng = Xincheng 146-147 EF 2
Sincheng = Xingren 142-143 K 6
Sinch'ŏn 144-145 E 3
Sincik = Birimşe 136-137 H 3
Sinclair Mills 60 G 2
Sincorá, Serra do — 100-101 D 7
Sind 134-135 M 5
Sind = Sindh 134-135 K 5
Sinda = Sindh 134-135 K 5
Sindagi = Sindgi 140 C 2
Sindangbarang 148-149 E 8
Sindelfingen 118 D 4
Sindgi 140 C 2
Sindh 134-135 K 5
Sindhnūr 140 C 3
Sindh Sāgar Doāb 138-139 C 2-3
Sindhu = Sindh 134-135 L 4
Sindhūli Garhi 138-139 KL 4
Sindi [IND] 138-139 G 7
Sindi [SU] 124-125 E 4
Sindıran 136-137 E 3
Sindırgı 136-137 C 3
Sindkhed 138-139 F 7-8
Sindkhēḍ = Sindkheda 138-139 E 7
Sindkheda 138-139 E 7
Sindlingen, Frankfurt am Main- 128 III a 1
Sin-do 144-145 DE 3
Sindri 138-139 L 6
Šindy = Sajmak 134-135 L 3
Sinegorje 124-125 S 4
Sinegorskij 126-127 K 3
Sinel'nikovo 126-127 G 2
Sines 120-121 C 10
Sines, Cabo de — 120-121 C 10
Sine-Saloum 168-169 AB 2
Sinfra 168-169 D 4
Sing, Mu'o'ng — 150-151 C 2
Singah 164-165 L 6
Singaing 141 E 5
Si-ngan = Xi'an 142-143 K 5
Singapore 148-149 DE 6
Singapore, Strait of — 148-149 DE 6
Singapore-Alexandra 154 III ab 2
Singapore-Geylang 154 III b 2
Singapore-Holland 154 III a 2
Singapore-Katong 154 III b 2
Singapore-Pasir Panjang 154 III a 2
Singapore Polytechnic 154 III b 2
Singapore-Potong Pasir 154 III b 1
Singapore-Queens Town 154 III a 2
Singapore-Tanglin Hill 154 III ab 2
Singapore-Toa Payoh Town 154 III b 1
Singapore-Wayang Satu 154 III ab 2
Singapur 148-149 DE 6
Singaraja 148-149 G 8
Singatoka 148-149 a 2
Singaung = Hsindau 141 D 5
Singaung = Hsingaung 141 CD 6
Sing Buri 148-149 D 3-4
Singen 118 D 5
Singes, Île des — 170 IV a 1
Singhbhūm 138-139 K 6
Singhpur 138-139 HJ 7
Singia 138-139 KL 5
Singida 172 F 2
Singkarak, Danau — 152-153 CD 6
Singkawang 148-149 E 6
Singkep, Pulau — 148-149 DE 7
Singkil 148-149 C 6
Singleton 158-159 K 6
Singleton, Mount — 158-159 F 4
Singora = Songkhla 148-149 D 5
Sin'gosan 144-145 F 3
Singri 141 C 2
Singtai = Xingtai 142-143 L 4
Singtze = Xingzi 146-147 F 7
Singū 141 E 4
Singuédzi, Rio — 174-175 J 2
Sin'gye 144-145 F 3
Sinhbhūm = Singhbhūm 134-135 NO 6
Sin-hiang = Xinxiang 142-143 LM 4
Si Nho = Ban Si Nhô 150-151 E 4
Sinho = Xinhe 146-147 E 3
Sinhsien = Xin Xian 142-143 L 4
Sinickaja 124-125 P 3
Sining = Xining 142-143 J 4
Siniqal, Baḥr — 168-169 B 2
Siniscola 122-123 CD 5
Sinjai 148-149 GH 8
Sinjār 136-137 J 4
Sinjār, Jabal — 136-137 JK 4
Sin-kalp'ajin 144-145 F 2
Sinkan = Xingan 146-147 E 8
Sinkāt 164-165 M 5
Sinkiang = Xinjiang 142-143 L 4
Sinkiang = Xinjiang Uygur Zizhiqu 142-143 G 3
Sinlo = Xinle 142-143 LM 4
Sinlungaba = Seinlôngabâ 141 E 3
Sinmak 144-145 F 3
Sinmi-do 144-145 E 3
Sinmin = Xinmin 144-145 D 1-2
Sinn al-Kadhdhāb 173 BC 6
Sinnamary [French Guiana, place] 92-93 J 3
Sinnamary [French Guiana, river] 98-99 M 2
Sinnar 138-139 DE 8
Sinneh = Sanandaj 134-135 F 3
Sinnhabhūm = Singhbhūm 134-135 NO 6
Sin Nombre, Cerro — 108-109 C 5-6
Sinnūris 173 B 3
Sinnyŏng = Sillyŏng 144-145 G 4
Sinoe 168-169 C 4
Sinoe = Greenville 164-165 C 7-8
Sinola = Chinhoyi 172 EF 5
Sinop 134-135 D 2
Sinope = Sinop 134-135 D 2
Sinp'o 142-143 O 3-4
Sinquim = Xi'an 142-143 K 5
Sinqunyane 174-175 H 5
Sinsiang = Xinxiang 142-143 LM 4
Sint-Agatha-Berchem = Berchem-Sainte-Agathe 128 II a 1
Sintang 148-149 F 6
Sint-Anna-Pede 128 II a 2
Sint Blaize, Kaap — 174-175 E 8
Sint-Brixius-Rode 128 II ab 1
Sint Eustatius 64-65 O 8
Sint Francisbaai 174-175 F 8
Sint Franziskusbaai 174-175 A 3
Sint-Gertruide-Pede 128 II a 2
Sint Helenabaai 172 C 8
Sint-Lambrechts-Woluwe = Woluwe-Saint-Lambert 128 II b 1
Sint Luciabaai 174-175 K 5
Sint Lucimeer 172 F 7
Sint-Martens-Bodegem 128 II a 1
Sint Martin, Kaap — 174-175 B 7
Sint Nicolaas 94-95 G 1
Sinton, TX 76-77 F 8
Sint-Pieters-Woluwe = Woluwe-Saint-Pierre 128 II b 1
Sintra [BR] 92-93 G 6
Sintra [P] 120-121 C 9
Sintsai = Xincai 142-143 LM 5
Sint Sebastianbaai 174-175 D 8
Sint-Stevens-Woluwe 128 II b 1
Sint-Ulriks-Kapelle 128 II a 1
Sinú, Río — 94-95 CD 3
Sin'ucha 126-127 E 2
Sinuk, AK 58-59 D 4
Sinuk River 58-59 DE 4
Sinwŏn-ni 144-145 E 3
Sinyang = Xinyang 142-143 LM 5
Sinyu = Xinyu 146-147 E 8
Sinzyō = Shinjō 142-143 QR 4
Sió 118 J 5
Siocon 152-153 OP 2
Sioma 172 D 5
Sion [CH] 118 C 5
Sion [PE] 96-97 C 5
Sioux City, IA 64-65 GH 3
Sioux Falls, SD 64-65 G 3
Sioux Lookout 56-57 S 7
Sioux Rapids, IA 70-71 C 4
Sipaliwini 98-99 K 3
Sipang, Tanjung — 152-153 J 5
Sipapo, Río — 94-95 H 5
Siparia 94-95 L 2
Šipčenski prohod 122-123 LM 4
Siphageni 172 EF 8
Sipí 94-95 C 5
Šipicyno 124-125 PQ 3
Siping 142-143 N 3
Sipitang 148-149 G 5-6
Sipiwesk 61 K 3
Sipiwesk Lake 61 K 3
Siple, Mount — 53 B 24
Sipolilo = Chiporiro 172 F 5
Sipora, Pulau — 148-149 C 7
Sipora, Selat — 152-153 CD 7
Si Prachan 150-151 BC 5
Sip Sông Châu Thai 148-149 D 2
Sipura, Pulau — = Pulau Sipora 148-149 C 7
Siqueira Campos 102-103 GH 5
Siquijor Island 148-149 H 5
Siquisique 92-93 F 2
Sira [IND] 140 C 4
Sira [N, place] 116-117 B 8
Sira [N, river] 116-117 B 8
Šira [SU] 132-133 QR 7
Sira, Pico — 96-97 D 6
Si Racha 150-151 C 6
Siracuas 111 D 2
Siracusa 122-123 F 7
Sirāguppa = Siruguppa 140 C 3
Sir'ajevo 126-127 E 3
Sirājganj 138-139 M 5
Sir Alexander, Mount — 60 GH 2
Sirama = Seram 140 C 2
Siran = Karaca 136-137 H 2
Sirasilla = Sirsilla 140 D 1
Sirāthu 138-139 H 5
Sirdar 66-67 E 1
Sir Edward Pellew Group 158-159 G 3
Siren, WI 70-71 D 3
Siret [RO, place] 122-123 M 2
Siret [RO, river] 122-123 M 3
Sirḥān, Wādī as — 134-135 D 4
Sirik, Tanjung — 152-153 J 4
Širinguši 124-125 O 7
Sirinhaém 100-101 G 5
Sirirskaja ravnina 132-133 L-P 5-6
Sir James MacBrien, Mount — 56-57 KL 5
Sīrjān 134-135 H 5
Sir John Hayes Island = Kûnthī Kyûn 150-151 A 7
Sīrkāzhi 140 DE 5
Sırkıntı 136-137 F 4
Sirmaur 138-139 H 5
Sirmaur = Sirmūr 138-139 F 2
Sirmūr 138-139 F 2
Sirmūr = Sirmaur 138-139 H 5
Şırnak 136-137 K 4
Sirohi 138-139 D 5
Sironcha 140 DE 1
Sironj 138-139 F 5
Sirpur 138-139 J 7
Sirr, Nafūd as- 134-135 E 5-F 6
Sirsa 134-135 LM 5
Sir Sanford, Mount — 60 J 4
Sirsi 140 B 3
Sirsilla 140 D 1
Sirte = Khalīj as-Surt 164-165 H 2
Sirte, Gulf of — = Khalīj as-Surt 164-165 H 2
Sir Thomas, Mount — 158-159 EF 5
Sirtica = As-Surt 164-165 H 2-3
Siruguppa 140 C 3
Sirūr 140 B 1
Şirvan = Küfre 136-137 K 3
Sīrvān, Rūd-e — 136-137 M 5
Sirvel 140 D 3
Sirvēlā = Sirvel 140 D 3
Sirven, Laguna — 108-109 E 6
Širvintos 124-125 E 6
Sirwah, Jabal — 166-167 C 4
Sirwān 136-137 LM 5
Sirwān, Ābi — 136-137 L 5
Sir Wilfrid Laurier, Mount — 60 GH 3
Sirya = Zeytinlik 136-137 JK 2
Sisak 122-123 G 3
Si Sa Ket 148-149 D 3-4
Sisal 86-87 P 7
Si Satchanalai 150-151 B 4
Si Sawat 150-151 B 5
Sishen 172 D 7
Sishuang Liedao 146-147 H 8
Sishui [TJ, Henan] 146-147 D 4
Sishui [TJ, Shandong] 146-147 F 4
Sisian 126-127 MN 7
Sisimiut 56-57 Za 4
Sisipuk Lake 61 H 3
Siskiyou, OR 66-67 B 4
Siskiyou Mountains 66-67 B 4-5

Si Songkhram 150-151 E 4
Sisophon 148-149 D 4
Sisquelan, Península — 108-109 BC 6
Sisseton, SD 68-69 H 3
Sisseton Indian Reservation 68-69 H 3
Sissili 168-169 E 3
Sīstān 134-135 J 4
Sīstān, Daryācheh — 134-135 HJ 4
Sīstān va Balūchestān 134-135 H 4-J 5
Sisteron 120-121 K 6
Sisters, OR 66-67 C 3
Siswa Bāzār 138-139 J 4
Sit' 124-125 L 4
Sita 168-169 B 3
Sitachwe 174-175 D 3
Sītāmarhi 138-139 K 4
Sītāmau 138-139 E 5-6
Sītāpur 138-139 H 4
Siteki 174-175 JK 4
Sithandone 150-151 EF 5
Sithōnia 122-123 K 5-6
Siting 146-147 D 3
Sítio da Abadia 92-93 K 7
Sítio do Mato 100-101 C 7
Sitio Grande 100-101 B 7
Sitio Novo [BR, Bahia] 100-101 E 7
Sitio Novo [BR, Maranhão] 100-101 A 3
Sitio Novo do Grajaú 100-101 A 3
Sitio Nuevo 94-95 D 2
Sitka, AK 56-57 J 6
Sitkaing 148-149 C 2
Sitkaing Taing 148-149 B 2-C 1
Sitkalidak Island 58-59 g 1
Sitkinak Island 58-59 g 1
Sitkinak Strait 58-59 fg 1
Šitkino 132-133 S 6
Sitn'aki 126-127 D 1
Sittang River = Sittaung Myit 141 E 6
Sittaung Myit 141 E 6
Sittwe 148-149 B 2
Siumbatu 152-153 P 7
Siumpu, Pulau — 152-153 P 8
Siunī = Seoni 134-135 M 6
Siunī-Mālwā = Seoni-Mālwa 138-139 F 6
Siuṛī = Sūri 138-139 L 6
Siushan = Xiushan 146-147 B 7
Siuslaw River 66-67 B 4
Siut = Asyūṭ 164-165 L 3
Siuxt = Džūkste 124-125 D 5
Siva [SU, place] 124-125 U 4
Siva [SU, river] 124-125 U 5
Sivaganga [IND, mountain] 140 C 4
Sivaganga [IND, place] 140 D 6
Sivakāsi 140 CD 6
Sivaki 132-133 Y 7
Sivān = Siwān 138-139 K 4
Sivānā = Siwāna 138-139 D 5
Sīvand 134-135 G 4
Sivāni = Siwāni 138-139 E 3
Sivas 134-135 D 3
Sivaš, ozero — 126-127 FG 3-4
Sivaslı 136-137 C 3
Siverek 136-137 H 4
Siverskij 124-125 H 4
Siverst 124-125 H 5
Sivin' 124-125 P 6
Sivrice 136-137 H 3
Sivrihisar 136-137 D 3
Sivučij, mys — 132-133 fg 6
Siwa 152-153 O 7
Sīwah 164-165 K 3
Sīwah, Wāḥāt — 164-165 K 3
Siwālik Range 134-135 M 4-N 5
Siwān 138-139 K 4
Siwāna 138-139 D 5
Siwāni 138-139 E 3
Siwni = Seoni 134-135 M 6
Siwni-Malwa = Seoni-Mālwa 138-139 F 6
Si Xian 146-147 FG 5
Sixtymile 58-59 RS 4
Siyāh Chaman 136-137 M 4
Siyāl, Jazā'ir — 173 E 6
Siyālkoṭ 134-135 LM 4
Siyang 146-147 G 5
Siyang = Xiyang 146-147 D 3

Sjælland 116-117 DE 10
Sjöbo 116-117 EF 10
Sjøvegan 116-117 GH 3
Sjuøyane 116-117 l 4

Skadarsko jezero 122-123 H 4
Skadovsk 126-127 F 3
Skagafjardhar 116-117 d 2
Skagafjördhur 116-117 c 1-d 2
Skagen 116-117 D 9
Skagens Horn = Grenen 116-117 D 9
Skagerrak 116-117 B 9-D 8
Skagit River 66-67 C 1
Skagway, AK 56-57 JK 6
Skaland 116-117 G 3
Skalap, Bukit — 152-153 KL 4
Skala-Podol'skaja 126-127 C 2
Skálar 116-117 f 1
Skálholt 116-117 cd 2
Skalistyj Golec, gora — 132-133 WX 6
Skanderborg 116-117 CD 9
Skåne 116-117 E 10
Skanör 116-117 E 10
Skara 116-117 E 8
Skaraborg 116-117 EF 8
Skardū 134-135 M 3
Skarżysko-Kamienna 118 K 3
Skaudvilė 124-125 D 6
Skaw, The — = Grenen 116-117 D 9
Skead 72-73 F 1
Skeena 60 BC 2
Skeena Mountains 56-57 L 6
Skeena River 56-57 L 6
Skegness 119 G 5
Skeidharársandur 116-117 e 3
Skeldon 98-99 K 2
Skellefteå 116-117 J 5
Skellefte älv 116-117 H 5
Skelleftehamn 116-117 JK 5
Skene 116-117 E 9
Skhīrra, Es — = Aṣ-Ṣahīrah 166-167 M 2
Skhoûr, es — = Sukhūr ar-Riḥāmnah 166-167 BC 3
Ski 116-117 D 8
Skíathos 122-123 K 6
Skidaway Island 80-81 F 5
Skidegate Inlet 60 AB 3
Skidel' 124-125 E 7
Skidmore, TX 76-77 EF 8
Skien 116-117 C 8
Skierniewice 118 K 3
Skiff 66-67 H 1
Skiftet 116-117 J 7
Skikda = Sakīkdah 164-165 F 1
Skilak Lake 58-59 M 6
Skipskjølen 116-117 NO 2
Skipskop 174-175 D 8
Skive 116-117 C 9
Skjalfandafljót 116-117 e 2
Skjálfandi 116-117 e 1
Skjervøy 116-117 J 2
Skjold 116-117 H 3
Sklad 132-133 X 3
Šklov 124-125 H 6
Skobelev = Fergana 134-135 L 2-3
Skógafoss 116-117 cd 3
Skokie, IL 70-71 FG 4
Skolpen Bank 114-115 OP 1
Skönvik 116-117 G 6
Skópelos 122-123 K 6
Skopin 124-125 M 7
Skopje 122-123 J 4-5
Skoplje = Skopje 122-123 J 4-5
Skorodnoje 126-127 H 1
Skoun 150-151 E 6
Skoûra = Ṣukhūrah 166-167 C 4
Skövde 116-117 EF 8
Skovorodino 132-133 XY 7
Skowhegan, ME 72-73 M 2
Skownan 61 J 5
Skrunda 124-125 CD 5
Skudeneshavn 116-117 A 8
Skuilte 170 V cd 1
Skukuza 172 F 7
Skul'any 126-127 C 3
Skull Valley, AZ 74-75 G 5
Skull Valley Indian Reservation 66-67 G 5
Skulpfonteinpunt 174-175 B 6
Skunk River 70-71 DE 5
Skuodas 124-125 CD 5
Skuratova, mys — 132-133 LM 3
Skutari, İstanbul- = İstanbul-Üsküdar 134-135 BC 2
Skutskär 116-117 GH 7
Skvira 126-127 D 2
Skwentna, AK 58-59 M 6
Skwentna River 58-59 LM 6
Skwierzyna 118 G 2
Skye 119 C 3
Skykomish, WA 66-67 C 2
Skyring, Península — 108-109 B 5
Skyring, Seno — 111 B 8
Skyrópula 122-123 KL 6
Skŷros 122-123 L 6

Slā' 164-165 C 2
Slabberts 174-175 H 5
Slagelse 116-117 D 10
Slagnäs 116-117 H 5
Slamet, Gunung — 152-153 H 9
Slana, AK 58-59 PQ 5
Slancy 116-117 N 8
Slangberge 174-175 D 6
Slănic 122-123 L 3
Slate Islands 70-71 G 1
Slater, CO 68-69 C 5
Slater, MO 70-71 D 6
Slatina 122-123 L 3
Slaton, TX 76-77 D 6
Slatoust = Zlatoust 132-133 K 6
Slav'anka 144-145 H 1
Slav'ansk 126-127 HJ 2
Slav'ansk-na-Kubani 126-127 J 4
Slave Coast 164-165 E 7
Slave Lake 60 K 2
Slave River 56-57 O 5-6
Slavgorod [SU, Belorusskaja SSR] 124-125 H 7
Slavgorod [SU, Rossijskaja SFSR] 132-133 O 7
Slavgorod [SU, Ukrainskaja SSR] 126-127 G 2
Slavkov u Brna 118 H 4
Slavonija 122-123 GH 3
Slavonska Požega 122-123 GH 3
Slavonski Brod 122-123 GH 3
Slavskoje [SU, Ukrainskaja SSR] 126-127 A 2
Slavuta 126-127 C 1
Slavyansk = Slav'ansk 126-127 HJ 2
Sławno 118 H 1
Slayton, MN 70-71 BC 3
Sledge Island 58-59 D 4
Sleemanābād 138-139 H 6
Sleeping Bear Point 70-71 G 3
Sleepy Eye, MN 70-71 C 3
Sleetmute, AK 56-57 E 5
Slidell, LA 78-79 E 5
Slide Mountain 72-73 J 3
Sliema 122-123 F 8
Sligeach = Sligo 119 B 4
Sligo 119 B 4
Sligo Branch 82 II ab 1
Slīmanābād = Sleemanābād 138-139 H 6
Slim Buttes 68-69 E 3
Slipi, Jakarta- 154 IV a 2
Slipi Orchid Garden 154 IV a 2
Slissen = Mūlay-Salīsan 166-167 F 2
Slite 116-117 H 9
Sliten = Zlītan 164-165 GH 2
Sliven 122-123 M 4
Slivnica 122-123 K 4
Sloan, IA 68-69 H 4
Sloboda = Liski 126-127 J 1
Slobodčikovo 124-125 QR 3
Slobodka [SU, Ukrainskaja SSR] 126-127 D 3
Slobodskoj 132-133 HJ 6
Slobodzeja 126-127 D 3
Slobozia 122-123 M 3
Slocan 66-67 E 1
Slocan Lake 66-67 E 1
Sloko River 58-59 V 7
Slomichino = Furmanovo 126-127 OP 2
Slonim 124-125 E 7
Slot, The — 148-149 j 6
Sloter plas 128 I a 1
Slotervaar, Amsterdam- 128 I a 1
Slough 119 F 6
Sloûk = Sulūk 136-137 H 4
Slovenia 122-123 F 3-G 2
Slovenské rudohorie 118 JK 4
Slovinka 124-125 O 4
Sluč' 126-127 C 1
Sluck 124-125 F 7
Sl'ud'anka 132-133 T 7
Sludka 124-125 S 3
Slunj 122-123 F 3
Słupsk 118 H 1
Slurry 174-175 FG 3

Smach 150-151 D 7
Smackover, AR 78-79 C 4
Smala des Souassi, la — = Zamālat as-Suwāsī 166-167 M 2
Småland 116-117 EF 9
Smalininkai 124-125 D 6
Small, ID 66-67 G 3
Small Point 72-73 M 3
S'marah 164-165 B 3
Smederevo 122-123 J 3
Smela 126-127 E 2
Smeloje 126-127 FG 1
Smeru = Gunung Semeru 148-149 F 8
Smethport, PA 72-73 G 4
Šmidta, ostrov — 132-133 QR 1
Smiley 61 D 5
Smiley, Cape — 53 B 29
Smiltene 124-125 EF 5
Smith [CDN] 56-57 O 6-7
Smith [RA] 106-107 G 5
Smith Arm 56-57 M 4
Smith Bay 58-59 KL 1
Smith Center, KS 68-69 G 6
Smithers 56-57 L 7
Smithfield 174-175 G 6
Smithfield, NC 80-81 G 3
Smithfield, UT 66-67 H 5
Smithfield, VA 80-81 H 2
Smith Inlet 60 CD 4
Smith Island [CDN] 56-57 V 5
Smith Island [USA] 80-81 H 4
Smith River 66-67 H 2
Smith River, CA 66-67 A 5
Smiths Creek Valley 74-75 E 3
Smith's Falls 56-57 V 9
Smiths Ferry, ID 66-67 EF 3
Smiths Grove, KY 70-71 G 7
Smith Sound 56-57 W 2
Smithton 158-159 HJ 8
Smithtown 160 L 3
Smithville, GA 80-81 DE 5
Smithville, TN 78-79 G 2
Smithville, TX 76-77 F 7-8
Smjörfjöll 116-117 f 2
Smögen 116-117 D 8
Smoke Creek Desert 66-67 D 5
Smoky Bay 160 A 4
Smoky Cape 160 L 3
Smoky Falls 62 K 1
Smoky Hill River 64-65 FG 4
Smoky Hill River, North Fork — 68-69 EF 6
Smoky Hills 68-69 G 6
Smoky Lake 61 BC 3
Smoky Mountains 66-67 F 4
Smoky River 56-57 N 7
Smøla 116-117 B 6
Smol'an 122-123 L 5
Smolensk 124-125 J 6
Smolenskaja vozvyšennost 124-125 H-K 6
Smoleviči 124-125 G 6
Smólikas 122-123 J 5
Smoot, WY 66-67 H 4
Smooth Rock Falls 62 L 2
Smoothrock Lake 62 DE 2
Smoothstone Lake 61 E 3
Smoothstone River 61 E 3
Smorgon' 124-125 F 6
Smotrič 126-127 C 2
Smyrna, GA 85 II a 1
Smyrna, TN 78-79 F 2-3
Smyrna = İzmir 134-135 B 3
Smyth, Canal — 108-109 B 8-C 9

Snaefell [GB] 119 D 4
Snæfell [IS] 116-117 f 2
Snæfellsjökull 116-117 ab 2
Snæfellsnes 116-117 b 2
Snag 56-57 HJ 5
Snaipol 150-151 E 7
Snake Creek [USA, Nebraska] 68-69 F 4
Snake Creek [USA, South Dakota] 68-69 G 3
Snake Range 74-75 F 3
Snake River [USA ◁ Columbia River] 64-65 C 2
Snake River [USA ◁ Croix River] 70-71 D 2-3
Snake River Canyon 66-67 E 3
Snake River Plains 64-65 D 3
Snake Valley 74-75 G 3
Snåsa 116-117 E 5
Sn'atyn 126-127 B 2
Sneeuberg 174-175 C 7
Sneeuberge 174-175 F 6
Sneeukop 174-175 C 7
Snežnoje 126-127 J 2
Śniardwy, Jezioro — 118 K 2
Sniežka 118 GH 3
Snigir'ovka 126-127 F 3
Snipe Lake 60 J 2
Snøhetta 116-117 C 6
Snohomish, WA 66-67 BC 2
Snoqualmie Pass 66-67 C 2
Snota 116-117 C 6
Snøtind 116-117 E 4
Snoul 150-151 F 6
Snov 124-125 H 8
Snowden, MT 68-69 D 1-2
Snowdon 119 DE 5
Snowdrift 56-57 OP 5
Snowflake, AZ 74-75 H 5
Snow Hill, MD 72-73 J 5
Snow Hill Island 53 C 31
Snow Lake 61 H 3
Snow Road 72-73 H 2
Snowshoe Peak 66-67 F 1
Snowtown 160 CD 4
Snowville, UT 66-67 G 5
Snowy Mountains 158-159 J 7
Snowy River 160 J 6
Snug Corner 88-89 K 3
Snyder, OK 76-77 E 5
Snyder, TX 64-65 F 5

Soacha 94-95 D 5
Soacha, Río — 91 III a 4
Soai Dao, Phu — 150-151 C 4
Soalala 172 HJ 5
Soanierana-Ivongo 172 JK 5
Soan-kundo 144-145 F 5
Soap Lake, WA 66-67 D 2
Soasiu 148-149 J 6
Soatá 94-95 E 4
Soavinandriana 172 J 5
Sobaek-sanmaek 144-145 F 5-G 4
Sōbāṭ, Nahr — = As-Sūbāṭ 164-165 L 7
Sobinka 124-125 N 6
Sobolev 124-125 S 8
Sobolevo 132-133 e 7
Sobo-zan 144-145 H 6
Sobozo 164-165 GH 4
Sobradinho [BR, Distrito Federal] 102-103 J 1
Sobradinho [BR, Pará] 98-99 K 7
Sobradinho [BR, Rio Grande do Sul] 106-107 L 2
Sobradinho, Represa — 100-101 C 6-D 5
Sobrado [BR] 92-93 J 6
Sobral [BR, Acre] 96-97 E 6
Sobral [BR, Ceará] 92-93 L 5
Soca [ROU] 106-107 K 5
Socavão 102-103 H 6
Socgorodok 126-127 J 1
Socha 92-93 E 3
Sochaczew 118 K 2
Soche = Yarkand 142-143 D 4
Sŏch'ŏn 144-145 F 4
Sochor, gora — 132-133 TU 7
Soči 126-127 J 5
Soči-Adler 126-127 J 5
Soči-Dagomys 126-127 J 5
Sociedade Hípica Paulista 110 II a 2
Society Islands 156-157 K 5
Soči-Lazarevskoje 126-127 J 5
Socompa, Portezuelo de — 104-105 B 9
Socompa, Volcán — 111 C 2
Socorro, NM 76-77 A 5-6
Socorro [BR] 102-103 J 5
Socorro [CO] 92-93 E 3
Socorro, El — [MEX] 76-77 C 9
Socorro, El — [RA] 106-107 G 4
Socorro, El — [YV] 94-95 J 3
Socorro, Isla — 64-65 DE 8
Socorro, São Paulo- 110 II a 2
Socoto = Sokoto 164-165 EF 6
Socotra = Suquṭrā' 134-135 G 8
Soc Trăng = Khanh Hu'ng 150-151 E 8
Socuéllamos 120-121 F 9
Sōdā, Gebel es — = Jabal as-Sawdā' 164-165 GH 3
Soda Creek 60 F 3
Soda Lake 74-75 F 5
Sodankylä 116-117 LM 4
Soda Springs, ID 66-67 H 4
Soddu = Sodo 164-165 M 7
Soddy, TN 78-79 G 3
Sodegaura 155 III c 3
Söderhamn 116-117 G 7
Söderköping 116-117 G 8
Södermanland 116-117 G 8
Södertälje 116-117 GH 8
Sōdirī = Sawdirī 164-165 K 6
Sodium 174-175 E 6
Sodo 164-165 M 7
Sodom = Sĕdōm 136-137 F 7
Sodpur, Pānihāti- 154 II b 1
Sodus, NY 72-73 H 3
Soe 152-153 Q 10
Soekmekaar 172 E 6
Soela väin 124-125 D 4
Soen, Nam — = Nam Choen 150-151 CD 4
Soest 118 D 3
Sœurs, Île des — 82 I b 2
Sofala, Baía de — 172 FG 6
Sofala, Manica e — 172 F 5-6
Sofia 172 J 5
Sofia = Sofija 122-123 K 4
Sofija 122-123 K 4
Sofijevka = Červonoarmejskoje 126-127 GH 3
Sofijsk 132-133 Z 7
Sofporog 116-117 O 5
Soga 171 D 4
Soga, Quebrada de — 104-105 B 6
Sogakofe 168-169 F 4
Sogamoso 92-93 E 3
Sogamoso, Río — 94-95 E 4
Soğanlı çayı 136-137 E 2
Sogndalstrand 116-117 B 8
Sognefjord 116-117 AB 7
Sogn og Fjordane 116-117 AB 7
Söğüt 136-137 D 2-3
Söğütlü dere 136-137 G 3
Sogwip'o 144-145 F 6
Sōhāg = Sawhāj 164-165 L 3
Sohāgpur [IND → Jabalpur] 138-139 H 6
Sohāgpur [IND ↙ Jabalpur] 138-139 G 6
Sŏhan-man 142-143 NO 4
Sohano 148-149 h 6
Sohar = Ṣuḥār 134-135 H 6
Sohela 138-139 J 7
Sohella = Sohela 138-139 J 7
Sohna 138-139 F 3
Soho, London- 129 II b 1
So-hŭksan-do 144-145 E 5
Soi Dao, Khao — 150-151 B 9
Soi Dao Tai, Khao — 150-151 CD 6
Soignes, Fôret de — 128 II b 2
Soissons 120-121 J 4
Soitué 106-107 CD 5
Sŏja 144-145 J 5
S'ojacha 132-133 N 3
Sojakpur 138-139 C 6
Sojat 138-139 D 5
Sojga 124-125 P 2
Sojiji Temple 155 III ab 2
Sojna [IND] 138-139 G 5
Šojna [SU] 132-133 G 4
Sŏjosŏn-man = Sŏhan-man 142-143 NO 4
Sok 124-125 S 6
Sokal' 126-127 B 1
Šokal'skogo, ostrov — 132-133 NO 3
Šokal'skogo, proliv — 132-133 RS 2
Söke 134-135 B 3
Sokhna = Sawknah 164-165 GH 3
Sokku Wan 155 I a 2
Sokloko 174-175 E 3
Sokodé 164-165 E 7
Sokol 132-133 G 6
Sokolij gory 124-125 S 7
Sokółka 118 L 2
Sokol'niki, PkiO — 113 V c 2
Sokolo 164-165 C 6
Sokołów Podlaski 118 L 2
Sokol'skoje 124-125 O 5
Sokotindji 168-169 F 3
Sokoto [WAN, administrative unit] 168-169 G 3
Sokoto [WAN, place] 164-165 EF 6
Sokoto [WAN, river] 164-165 E 6
Sokotra = Suquṭrā' 134-135 G 8
Sŏkpŏ 148-149 C 3
Sokskije jary 124-125 S 7-T 6
Sŏk-to 144-145 E 3
So Kun Tan 155 I a 1
Sol, Costa del — 120-121 EF 10
Sol, Isla del — 104-105 B 4-5
Solá [RA] 106-107 H 4
Sola de Vega 86-87 M 9
Solai 172 G 1-2
Solaklı 136-137 J 2
Solander, Cape — 161 I b 3
Solander Island 161 B 8
Solânea 100-101 G 4
Solanet 106-107 H 6
Sol'anka 124-125 RS 8
Solano, NM 76-77 BC 5
Solano, Bahía — 94-95 C 4
Sōlāpur = Sholāpur 134-135 M 7
Sol'cy 124-125 H 4
Soldedad 92-93 DE 2
Sol de Julio 106-107 F 2
Soldier Fields 83 II b 1
Soldotna, AK 58-59 M 6
Soledad, CA 74-75 C 4
Soledad [MEX] 76-77 D 9
Soledad [RA] 106-107 G 3
Soledad [RCH] 104-105 B 7
Soledad [YV] 92-93 G 3
Soledad, Isla — = East Falkland 111 E 8
Soledad Díez Gutiérrez 86-87 K 6
Soledade [BR, Amazonas] 98-99 D 8
Soledade [BR, Rio Grande do Sul] 106-107 L 2
Soledade [BR, Roraima] 98-99 H 3
Soledade, Cachoeira — 98-99 LM 7
Solesmes 120-121 G 5
Soleure = Solothurn 118 C 5
Soleymān, Takht-e — 136-137 O 4
Solfonn 116-117 B 8
Solheim 170 V b 2
Soligalič 124-125 NO 4
Soligorsk 124-125 F 7
Solihull 119 F 5
Solikamsk 132-133 K 6
Sol'-Ileck 132-133 JK 7
Solīmān = Sulaymān 166-167 M 1
Solimões, Rio — 92-93 G 5
Solingen 118 C 3
Solís [RA] 106-107 H 5
Solís [ROU] 106-107 K 5
Solita, La — 94-95 F 3
Solitaire 174-175 AB 2
Sollefteå 116-117 G 6
Sóller 120-121 J 9
Sollum = As-Salūm 164-165 K 2
Sol-lun = Solon 142-143 N 2
Solna 116-117 GH 8
Solnceva 113 V a 3
Solnečnogorsk 124-125 L 5
Solo 168-169 D 3
Solo = Surakarta 148-149 F 8
Sologne 120-121 HJ 5
Šologoncy 132-133 VW 4
Solok 148-149 D 7
Sololá 86-87 P 10
Solomennoje 124-125 K 3
Solomon, AK 58-59 E 4
Solomon, KS 68-69 H 6
Solomondale 174-175 HJ 2
Solomon Islands [archipelago] 148-149 h 6-k 7
Solomon Islands [Solomon Is., state] 148-149 kl 7
Solomon River 68-69 GH 6
Solomon River, North Fork — 68-69 FG 6
Solomon River, South Fork — 68-69 F 6
Solomons Basin 148-149 h 6
Solomon Sea 148-149 hj 6
Solon, IA 70-71 E 5
Solončak Šalkarteniz 132-133 L 8
Solong Cheer = Sulan Cheer 142-143 K 3
Sol'onoje Ozero 126-127 G 4
Solonópole 100-101 E 3
Solon Springs, WI 70-71 DE 2
Solor, Kepulauan — 152-153 P 10
Solor, Pulau — 148-149 H 8
Solothurn 118 C 5
Soloveckije ostrova 132-133 F 4
Šolta 122-123 G 4
Solṭān, Bīr — = Bi'r Sulṭān 166-167 L 3
Solṭānābād = Arāk 134-135 F 4
Solṭānīyeh 136-137 N 4
Soltau 118 DE 2
Soluch = Sulūq 164-165 J 2
Solun 142-143 N 2
Soluq = Sulūq 164-165 J 2
Solvay, NY 72-73 H 3
Sölvesborg 116-117 F 9
Sol'vyčegodsk 132-133 H 5
Solway Firth 119 DE 4
Solwezi 172 E 4
Solza 124-125 M 1
Sōma [J] 144-145 N 4
Soma [TR] 136-137 B 3
Somabhula 172 E 5
Somalia 164-165 N 8-O 7
Somali Basin 50-51 M 5-6
Sōmapēṭa = Sompeta 138-139 K 8
Sōma Tsangpo 138-139 K 2
Sombor 122-123 H 3
Sombrerete 86-87 J 6
Sombrerito, El — 106-107 H 2
Sombrero 88-89 P 5
Sombrero, El — [RA] 106-107 H 1
Sombrero, El — [YV] 92-93 F 3
Sombrio 106-107 N 4
Sombye 138-139 M 4
Şomcuta Mare 122-123 K 2
Somerdale, NJ 84 III c 2
Somero 116-117 K 7
Somers, MT 66-67 F 1
Somerset, CO 68-69 C 6
Somerset, KY 70-71 H 7
Somerset, PA 72-73 G 4-5
Somerset [AUS] 158-159 H 2
Somerset [CDN] 68-69 G 1
Somerset East = Somerset-Oos 172 DE 8
Somerset Island 56-57 S 3
Somerset-Oos 172 DE 8
Somerset-Wes 174-175 C 8
Somersworth, NH 72-73 L 3
Somerton, AZ 74-75 F 6
Somerton, Philadelphia-, PA 84 III c 1
Somerville, MA 72-73 L 3
Somerville, NJ 72-73 J 4
Somerville, TN 78-79 E 3
Somerville, TX 76-77 F 7
Someş 122-123 K 2
Somesbar, CA 66-67 B 5
Somkele 174-175 K 5
Somme 120-121 H 3
Sommerset, MD 82 II a 1
Somnāth 138-139 C 7
Sompeta 138-139 K 8
Somuncurá, Meseta de — 111 C 6
Son [IND] 134-135 N 6
Son, Mu'o'ng — 150-151 D 2
Sona 88-89 F 11
Sonahula 138-139 L 5
Sonai 141 C 4
Sonaimuri = Sonāymuṛī 141 B 4
Sonāmukhī 138-139 L 6
Sonār 138-139 GH 5
Sonāri 141 D 2
Sonāymuṛī 141 B 4
Sonbarsa 138-139 K 4
Sonbarsa Raj 138-139 L 5
Sŏnch'ŏn 144-145 E 3
Sondagsrivier 174-175 F 7
Sønderborg 116-117 CD 10
Sondershausen 118 E 3
Sondheimer, LA 78-79 D 4
Søndre Kvaløy 116-117 GH 3
Søndre Strømfjord 56-57 a 4
Søndre Strømfjord = Kangerdlugssuaq 56-57 ab 4
Sondrio 122-123 CD 2
Sonduga 124-125 NO 3
Sonepat 138-139 F 3
Sonepur 138-139 J 7
Song [MAL] 152-153 K 4
Song [T] 150-151 C 3
Songarh 138-139 D 7
Songbai 146-147 D 8
Sŏng Be 150-151 F 7
Sông Boung 150-151 F 5
Songbu 146-147 E 6
Sông Bung = Sông Boung 150-151 F 5
Sông Ca 150-151 E 3
Sông Câu 150-151 E 2
Sông Chảy 150-151 E 1
Sŏngch'on 144-145 F 3
Sông Chu 150-151 E 3
Sông Đa 148-149 D 2
Songea 172 G 4
Songfou = Songbu 146-147 E 6
Sông Gâm 150-151 E 1
Songhua Hu 142-143 O 3
Songhua Jiang 142-143 O 2
Sŏnghwan 144-145 F 4
Songjiang 142-143 N 5
Songjiangzhen 144-145 F 1
Sŏngjin = Kim Chak 142-143 OP 3
Songjŏng-ni 144-145 F 5
Songkhla 148-149 D 5
Sông Khôn = Ban Sông Khôn 150-151 E 3
Song Khone = Mu'o'ng Song Khone 150-151 E 4
Songkhram, Mae Nam — 150-151 DE 3-4
Songkla = Songkhla 148-149 D 5
Songkou 146-147 G 9
Sông La Nga 150-151 F 7
Sông Lô 150-151 E 2
Sông Ma 150-151 E 2
Songmen 146-147 H 7
Sŏngnae-ri = Inhung-ni 144-145 F 3
Song Nhi Ha 148-149 D 2
Songnim 142-143 O 4
Songo 172 BC 3
Sông Ông Đôc 150-151 E 8
Songpan 142-143 J 5
Song Phi Nong 150-151 BC 5
Songrougrou 168-169 B 2
Song Shan 146-147 D 4
Songtao 146-147 B 7
Sông Tra 150-151 G 5
Songwe 171 C 5
Songwood, Houston-, TX 85 III bc 1
Songxi 146-147 G 8
Song Xian 146-147 CD 4
So'n Ha 150-151 G 5
Sonhaolā = Sonahula 138-139 L 5
Sonhāt 134-135 N 6
So'n Hoa 150-151 G 6
Sŏnkach 138-139 F 6
Sonkatch = Sŏnkach 138-139 F 6
Sonkovo 132-133 F 6
So'n La 150-151 D 2
Sonmiani = Sonmiyānī 134-135 K 5
Sonmiyānī 134-135 K 5
Sonmiyānī, Khalīj — 134-135 J 6-K 5
Sonneberg 118 E 3
Sono, Rio do — [BR, Goiás] 92-93 K 6-7
Sono, Rio do — [BR, Minas Gerais] 102-103 K 2
Sonoita 86-87 D 2
Sonoma, CA 74-75 B 3
Sonoma Range 66-67 E 5
Sonora 64-65 DE 6
Sonora, AZ 74-75 H 6
Sonora, CA 74-75 C 3-4
Sonora, TX 76-77 D 7
Sonora Peak 74-75 D 3
Sonqor 136-137 M 5
Sonsón 92-93 DE 3
Sonsonate 64-65 HJ 9
Sonsorol 148-149 K 5
Sonstraal 174-175 E 4
So'n Tây 150-151 E 2
Sopachuy 104-105 D 6
Soperton, GA 80-81 E 4
Sop Hao 150-151 E 2
Sop Khao 150-151 D 3
Sŏp'o-ri 144-145 FG 2
Sopot 118 J 1
Sop Prap 150-151 B 4
Sopron 118 H 5
Sop's Arm Provincial Park 63 H 3
Sor 120-121 C 9
Sora 122-123 E 5
Sorab 140 B 3
Sŏraba = Sorab 140 B 3
Sorada 138-139 K 8
Sorāh 138-139 B 4
Sŏrak-san 144-145 G 3
Soraon 138-139 H 5
Sorapa 96-97 G 10
Sorata 104-105 B 4
Soraṭh 138-139 BC 7
Sŏrath = Jūnāgaḍh 134-135 KL 6
Ṣorba 136-137 E 2
Sorbas 120-121 FG 10
Sorbhog 141 B 2
Sorbonne 129 I c 2
Sordwanabaai 174-175 K 4
Sorel 56-57 W 8
Sorell 160 cd 3
Sorell, Cape — 158-159 HJ 8

Sorell, Lake — 160 c 2
Soren Arwa = Selat Yapen 148-149 L 7
Sørfonna 116-117 Im 5
Sòrgono 122-123 C 5
Sorgun = Büyük Köhne 136-137 F 3
Sörhād = Sarhade Wākhān 134-135 L 3
Soria 120-121 F 8
Soriano [ROU, administrative unit] 106-107 HJ 4
Soriano [ROU, place] 106-107 H 4
Sorikmarapi, Gunung — 152-153 C 5
Sørkapp 116-117 k 6
Sørkapp land 116-117 k 6
Sørkjosen 116-117 J 3
Sorø [DK] 116-117 D 10
Soro [IND] 138-139 L 7
Soro [YV] 94-95 K 2
Sorocaba 111 G 2
Soročinka [SU, Kazachskaja SSR] 126-127 PQ 3
Soročinsk 132-133 J 7
Soroka = Belomorsk 132-133 EF 5
Soroki 126-127 CD 2
Sorokino = Krasnodon 126-127 JK 2
Sorol 148-149 M 5
Soron 138-139 G 4
Sorong 148-149 K 7
Soroti 172 F 1
Sørøy 116-117 K 2
Sørøysund 116-117 K 2
Sorraia 120-121 C 9
Sør-Randane 53 B 2-3
Sorrento 122-123 F 5
Sorsele 116-117 G 5
Sør-Shetland = South Shetlands 53 C 30
Sorsogon 148-149 HJ 4
Sortavala 132-133 E 5
Sorte Gobi = Char Gov' 142-143 GH 3
Sortija, La — 106-107 G 7
Sortland 116-117 F 3
Sør-Trøndelag 116-117 CD 6
Sørvågen 116-117 E 4
Sõrve 124-125 D 5
Sõrve säär 124-125 CD 5
Šorža 126-127 M 6
Sosa [PY] 102-103 D 7
Sōsan 144-145 F 4
Soscumica, Lac — 62 N 1
Sosedka 124-125 O 7
Sosenka 113 V ab 4
Sosenki 113 V b 3
Soshigaya, Tōkyō- 155 III a 2
Sosneado, El — 106-107 BC 5
Sosnica 126-127 F 1
Sosnogorsk 132-133 JK 5
Sosnovka [SU, Kirovskaja Oblast'] 124-125 S 5
Sosnovka [SU, Tambovskaja Oblast'] 124-125 N 7
Sosnovka, Čeboksary- 124-125 QR 5
Sosnovo 124-125 H 3
Sosnovoborsk 124-125 Q 7
Sosnovo-Oz'orskoje 132-133 V 7
Sosnovyj Solonec 124-125 RS 7
Sosnowiec 118 J 3
Sossenheim, Frankfurt am Main- 128 III a 1
Sossusvlei 174-175 A 3
Šostka 124-125 J 8
Sōsura 144-145 H 1
Sos'va [SU ↘ Serov] 132-133 L 6
Sos'va [SU, Chanty-Mansijskij NO] 132-133 L 5
Sosyka 126-127 J 3
Sota 168-169 F 3
Sotara 94-95 C 6
Sotará, Volcán — 94-95 C 6
So-tch'ê = Yarkand 142-143 D 4
Sotério, Rio — 98-99 F 10
Sotkamo 116-117 N 5
Soto 106-107 E 3
Soto, Cerro de — 106-107 B 3
Sotra 116-117 A 7
Souakria 170 I b 2
Souanké 172 B 1
Ṣoûâr = Aṣ-Ṣuwār 136-137 J 5
Soubré 164-165 C 7
Soudan 158-159 G 4
Soudana 168-169 H 1
Souf = Ṣūf 166-167 K 3
Souf, Aïn — = 'Ayn Ṣūf 166-167 H 5
Souf, Hassi — = Ḥāssī Ṣūf 166-167 F 5
Soufrière 64-65 O 9
Sougueur = Sūgar 166-167 G 2
Souillac 120-121 H 6
Souk-Ahras = Sūq Ahrās 164-165 F 1
Souk el Arba des Aït Baha = Sūq al-Arba'ā' al-Aït Bāhā 166-167 B 4
Souk el Arba du Rhab = Sūq al-Arb'ā' 166-167 CD 2
Souk el Khemis = Bū Sālām 166-167 L 1
Souk el Tleta = As-Sars 166-167 L 1
Soukhouma = Ban Sukhouma 150-151 E 5
Sŏul 142-143 O 4
Souloungou 168-169 F 2
Soum, Muong — = Mu'o'ng Soum 150-151 D 3
Sound, The — 161 I b 1
Sound, The — = Öresund 116-117 E 10
Sounders Island 108-109 J 8
Sounding Creek 61 C 5
Sound of Jura 119 D 4
Soundview, New York-, NY 82 III c 2
Soûq el Arb'â' = Jundūbah 166-167 L 1
Soûq el Arba = Sūq al-Arb'ā' 166-167 C 2
Soûq el Khemîs = Bū Sālām 166-167 L 1
Soûq Jema'â' Oûlâd 'Aboû = Awlād Abū 166-167 BC 3
Sources, Mont aux — 172 E 7
Soure [BR] 92-93 K 5
Sour-el-Ghozlane = Sūr al-Ghuzlān 166-167 HJ 1
Souris, ND 68-69 F 1
Souris [CDN, Manitoba] 61 H 6
Souris [CDN, Prince Edward I.] 63 E 4
Souris River 56-57 Q 8
Sourlake, TX 76-77 G 7
Sousa 92-93 M 6
Soûssâ = Sūssah 136-137 J 5
Sousse = Sūsah 164-165 G 1
Sout 174-175 C 6
Sout Doringrivier 174-175 C 6
South Africa 172 D-F 7
Southall, London- 129 II a 1
South Alligator River 158-159 F 2
South America 50-51 FG 6
Southampton, NY 72-73 KL 4
Southampton [CDN] 72-73 F 2
Southampton [GB] 119 F 6
Southampton Island 56-57 TU 5
South Andaman 134-135 P 8
South Auckland-Bay of Plenty 161 FG 3-4
South Aulatsivik Island 56-57 YZ 6
South Australia 158-159 E-G 5-6
South Australian Basin 50-51 PQ 8
South Baldy 76-77 A 5-6
South Banda Basin 148-149 J 8
South Baymouth 62 K 4
South Beach, New York-, NY 82 III b 3
South Bend, IN 64-65 JK 3
South Bend, WA 66-67 B 2
South Bend Park 85 II b 2
South Boston, VA 80-81 G 2
South Boston, Boston-, MA 84 I b 2
South Boston High School 84 I bc 2
South Branch Potomac River 72-73 G 5
South Brooklyn, New York-, NY 82 III bc 2
South Bruny 160 cd 3
South Carolina 64-65 K 5
South Charleston, OH 72-73 E 5
South Charleston, WV 72-73 EF 5
South Chicago, Chicago-, IL 83 II b 2
South China Basin 148-149 FG 3-4
South China Sea 142-143 L 8-M 7
South Dakota 64-65 FG 3
South Dum Dum 134-135 OP 6
South East Cape 158-159 J 8
Southeast Indian Basin 50-51 OP 7
Southeast Pacific Basin 156-157 MN 7-8
Southeast Pass 78-79 E 6
South East Point 160 H 7
South El Monte, CA 83 III d 1
Southend [CDN] 56-57 PQ 6
Southend-on-Sea 119 G 6
Southern [WAL] 168-169 BC 4
Southern [Z] 172 E 5
Southern Alps 158-159 NO 8
Southern California, University of — 83 III c 1
Southern Cross 158-159 CD 6
Southern Indian Lake 56-57 R 6
Southern Moscos = Launglônbôk Kyûnzu 150-151 A 6
Southern Oaks, Houston-, TX 85 III b 2
Southern Pacific Railway 64-65 EF 5
Southern Pine Hills = Pine Hills 64-65 J 5
Southern Pines, NC 80-81 G 3
Southern Sierra Madre = Sierra Madre del Sur 64-65 FG 8
Southern Uplands 119 DE 4
Southern Ute Indian Reservation 68-69 BC 7
Southeyville 174-175 G 6
South Fiji Basin 158-159 OP 4-5
South Fork, CO 68-69 C 7
South Fork Clearwater River 66-67 F 3
South Fork Flathead River 66-67 G 2
South Fork Grand River 68-69 E 3
South Fork John Day River 66-67 D 3
South Fork Koyukuk 58-59 M 3
South Fork Kuskokwim 58-59 KL 5
South Fork Moreau River 68-69 E 3
South Fork Mountains 66-67 B 5
South Fork Owyhee River 66-67 E 4-5
South Fork Peachtree Creek 85 II c 2
South Fork Powder River 68-69 C 4
South Fork Republican River 68-69 E 6
South Fork Salmon River 66-67 F 3
South Fork Solomon River 68-69 F 6
South Fork White River 68-69 F 4
South Fox Island 70-71 GH 3
South Gate, CA 74-75 DE 6
Southgate, London- 129 II b 1
South Georgia 111 J 8
South Georgia Ridge 50-51 H 8
South Grand River 70-71 CD 6
South Haven, KS 76-77 F 4
South Haven, MI 70-71 G 4
South Head 161 I b 1-2
South Henik Lake 56-57 R 5
South Hill, VA 80-81 G 2
South Hills, Johannesburg- 170 V b 2
South Honshu Ridge 142-143 R 5-6
South Horr 172 G 1
South Houston, TX 85 III c 2
South Indian Lake [CDN, place] 61 J 2
South Indian Ridge 50-51 OP 8
South Island 158-159 OP 8
South Junction 70-71 BC 1
South Koel 138-139 K 6
South Korea 142-143 OP 4
Southland 161 BC 7
South Lawn, MD 82 II b 2
South Loup River 68-69 FG 5
South Lynnfield, MA 84 I c 1
Southmag 72-73 FG 2
South Magnetic Pole Area 53 C 14-15
South Main Estates, Houston-, TX 85 III ab 2
South Male Atoll 176 ab 2
South Malosmadulu Atoll 176 a 1-2
South Mangsi Island 152-153 MN 2
South Media, PA 84 III a 2
South Melbourne, Melbourne- 161 II b 1-2
South Milwaukee, WI 70-71 G 4
South Moose Lake 61 H 4
South Mountain 72-73 H 4-5
South Nahanni River 56-57 LM 5
South Natuna Islands = Kepulauan Bunguran Selatan 148-149 E 6
South Negril Point 88-89 G 5
South Ogden, UT 66-67 H 5
South Orkneys 53 C 32
South Ossetian Autonomous Region 126-127 LM 5
South Pacific Basin 156-157 KL 6-7
South Padre Island 76-77 F 9
South Pageh = Pulau Pagai Selatan 148-149 CD 7
South Paris, ME 72-73 L 2
South Pasadena, CA 83 III cd 1
South Pass [USA, Louisiana] 64-65 J 6
South Pass [USA, Wyoming] 64-65 E 3
South Philadelphia, Philadelphia-, PA 84 III bc 2
South Platte River 64-65 F 3
South Porcupine 62 L 2
Southport, NC 80-81 GH 3
Southport [AUS] 160 c 3
Southport, Gold Coast- 160 LM 1
South Portland, ME 72-73 LM 3
South Reservoir 84 I b 2
South River [CDN, place] 72-73 G 2
South River [CDN, river] 72-73 G 1-2
South River [USA] 85 II b 2
South Ronaldsay 119 EF 2
South Saint Paul, MN 70-71 D 3
South Sālmāra 138-139 N 5
South Sandwich Islands 53 CD 34
South Sandwich Trench 53 D 34
South San Gabriel, CA 83 III d 1
South Saskatchewan River 56-57 OP 7
South Seal River 61 J 2
South Shetlands 53 C 30
South Shields 119 F 4
South Shore, Chicago-, IL 83 II b 2
South Sioux City, NE 68-69 H 4
South Suburbs 138-139 LM 6
South Suburbs-Chakdaha 154 II ab 3
South Suburbs-Joka 154 II a 3
South Suburbs-Russa 154 II ab 3
South Suburbs-Satsuna 154 II a 3
South Suburbs-Thākurpukur 154 II a 3
South Sulphur River 76-77 G 6
South Taranaki Bight 158-159 O 7
South Tent 74-75 H 3
South Tyrol 122-123 D 2
South Uist 119 BC 3
South Umpqua River 66-67 B 4
Southview Cemetery 85 II bc 2
South Wabasca Lake 60 L 2
Southwark, London- 129 II b 2
South West Cape [AUS] 160 bc 3
Southwest Cape [NZ] 158-159 N 9
Southwest Cay 64-65 KL 9
Southwest Indian Basin 50-51 MN 7
Southwest Miramichi River 63 CD 4
Southwest Museum 83 III c 1
Southwest Pass [USA, Mississippi River Delta] 64-65 J 6
Southwest Pass [USA, Vermillion Bay] 78-79 C 6
South Williamsport, PA 72-73 H 4
Soutpansberge 172 EF 6
Soutrivier [ZA ◁ Atlantic Ocean] 174-175 B 6
Soutrivier [ZA ◁ Grootrivier] 174-175 E 7
Souzel 92-93 J 5
Sovdozero 124-125 J 2
Soven 106-107 E 5
Sovetsk [SU, Kaliningradskaja Oblast'] 118 K 1
Sovetsk [SU, Kirovskaja Oblast'] 132-133 H 6
Sovetskaja 126-127 KL 2
Sovetskaja Gavan' 132-133 ab 8
Sovetskij [SU, Rossijskaja SFSR] 124-125 G 3
Sovetskij [SU, Ukrainskaja SSR] 126-127 G 4
Sovetskoje [SU, Čečeno-Ingušskaja ASSR] 126-127 MN 5
Sovetskoje [SU, Saratovskaja Oblast'] 124-125 Q 8
Soviet Union 132-133 E-b 5
Sowden Lake 70-71 E 1
Soweto, Johannesburg- 174-175 G 4
Sōya [J, Hokkaidō] 144-145 b 1
Soya [J, Tōkyō] 155 III c 1
Sōya-kaikyō 142-143 R 2
Sōya misaki 144-145 bc 1
Söylemez = Mescitli 136-137 JK 3
Soyo 172 B 3
Soyopa 86-87 F 3
Sož 124-125 H 7
Sozing 138-139 M 4
Sozopol 122-123 MN 4
Spadenland, Hamburg- 130 I b 2
Spafarief Bay 58-59 FG 3
Spain 120-121 E 7-F 9
Špakovskoje 126-127 L 4
Spalato = Split 122-123 G 4
Spalding, ID 66-67 E 2
Spalding, NE 68-69 G 5
Spalding [AUS] 160 D 4
Spalding [GB] 119 FG 5
Spandauer Zitadelle 130 III a 1
Spangle, WA 66-67 E 2
Spanish Fork, UT 66-67 H 5
Spanish Head 119 D 4
Spanish Peak = West Spanish Peak 68-69 D 7
Spanish Town 64-65 L 8
Spanta, Akrōtērion — 122-123 KL 8
Sparbu 116-117 D 6
Spåre 124-125 D 5
Sparkman, AR 78-79 C 3-4
Sparks, GA 80-81 E 5
Sparks, NV 74-75 D 3
Sparta, GA 80-81 E 4
Sparta, IL 70-71 F 6
Sparta, MI 70-71 H 4
Sparta, NC 80-81 F 2
Sparta, TN 78-79 G 3
Sparta, WI 70-71 E 4
Sparta = Spártē 122-123 K 7
Spartanburg, SC 64-65 K 4-5
Spártē 122-123 K 7
Spartel, Cap — = Rā's Ashaqār 166-167 CD 2
Spartel, Cape — = Rā's Ashaqār 166-167 CD 2
Spartivento, Capo — [I, Calàbria] 122-123 G 7
Spartivento, Capo — [I, Sardegna] 122-123 G 6
Spasporub 124-125 R 3
Spassk = Kujbyšev 132-133 HJ 7
Spassk = Spassk-Dal'nij 132-133 Z 9
Spasskaja Guba 124-125 J 2
Spassk-Dal'nij 132-133 Z 9
Spasskoje [SU, Kostroma] 124-125 Q 4
Spassk-R'azanskij 124-125 N 6
Spatsizi River 58-59 X 8
Spearfish, SD 68-69 E 3
Spearhill 61 JK 5
Spearman, TX 76-77 D 4
Spearville, KS 68-69 G 7
Spectacle Island 84 I c 3
Spectrum 84 III bc 2
Speedwell Island 108-109 JK 9
Speising, Wien- 113 I b 2
Speke Gulf 172 F 2
Spelman College 85 II b 2
Speluzzi 106-107 EF 5
Spenard, AK 58-59 N 6
Spencer, IA 70-71 C 4
Spencer, ID 66-67 G 3
Spencer, IN 70-71 G 6
Spencer, NC 80-81 F 3
Spencer, SD 68-69 H 4
Spencer, WI 70-71 E 3
Spencer, WV 72-73 F 5
Spencer, Cape — [AUS] 158-159 G 7
Spencer, Cape — [USA] 58-59 T 7
Spencer, Point — 58-59 D 4
Spencerbaai 174-175 A 3
Spencer Bay = Spencerbaai 174-175 A 3
Spencer Gulf 158-159 G 6
Spencer Street Station 161 II b 1
Spencerville, OH 70-71 HJ 5
Spences Bridge 60 G 4
Spenser Mountains 161 E 6
Sperling 68-69 H 1
Spessart 118 D 3-4
Spétsai 122-123 K 7
Spey 119 E 3
Speyer 118 D 4
Spèzia, La — 122-123 C 3
Spezzano Albanese 122-123 G 6
Sphakia = Chṓra Sfakíōn 122-123 L 8
Sphinx 170 II a 2
Spicer Islands 56-57 UV 4
Spike Mount 58-59 QR 3
Spilimbergo 122-123 E 2
Spillimacheen 60 J 4
Spinaceto, Roma- 113 II b 2
Spin Bulgak 134-135 K 4
Spioenberg I 174-175 D 6
Spioenberg II 174-175 CD 6
Spirit Lake, IA 70-71 C 4
Spirit Lake, ID 66-67 E 1-2
Spirit Lake, WA 66-67 BC 2
Spirit River 60 H 2
Spiritwood 61 E 4
Spiro, OK 76-77 G 5
Spirovo 124-125 K 5
Spitak 126-127 LM 6
Spithamn = Pōōsaspea 124-125 DE 4
Spiti 138-139 FG 1
Spitsbergen 116-117 k 6-n 5
Spittal 118 F 5
Spizzichino, Roma- 113 II ab 1
Split 122-123 G 4
Split Lake [CDN, lake] 61 KL 2
Split Lake [CDN, place] 61 K 2
Split Rock, WY 68-69 C 4
Splügen 118 D 5
Spofford, TX 76-77 D 8
Spoği 124-125 F 5
Spokane, WA 64-65 C 2
Spokane Indian Reservation 66-67 DE 2
Spokane River 66-67 DE 2
Spokojnyj 132-133 YZ 6
Špola 126-127 E 2
Spoleto 122-123 E 4
Spong 150-151 E 6
Spooner, MN 70-71 C 1
Spooner, WI 70-71 E 3
Spoon River 70-71 E 5
Sporades 122-123 M 6-7
Sport, Palazzo dello — 113 II b 2
Sportsmans Park Race Track 83 II a 1
Sporyj Navolok, mys — 132-133 M-O 2
Spot Pond 84 I b 2
Spotswood, Melbourne- 161 II b 1
Spotted Horse, WY 68-69 D 3
Spotted Range 74-75 F 4
Sprague, WA 66-67 DE 2
Sprague River 66-67 C 4
Sprague River, OR 66-67 C 4
Spranger, Mount — 60 G 3
Spratly Islands = Quân Đao Hoang Sa 148-149 F 5
Spray, OR 66-67 D 3
Spree 118 G 3
Spreewald 118 F 2-G 3
Spremberg 118 G 3
Sprengisandur 116-117 de 2
Spring, TX 76-77 G 7
Spring Bay 66-67 G 5
Springbok 172 C 7
Springbokvlakte 174-175 H 3
Spring City, TN 78-79 G 3
Spring Creek Park 82 III c 3
Springdale, AR 76-77 GH 4
Springdale, MT 66-67 HJ 3
Springdale, NV 74-75 E 4
Springdale, UT 74-75 G 4
Springdale, WA 66-67 DE 1
Springer, NM 76-77 B 4
Springer, Mount — 62 O 2
Springerville, AZ 74-75 J 5
Springfield, CO 68-69 E 7
Springfield, GA 80-81 F 4
Springfield, ID 66-67 G 4
Springfield, IL 64-65 HJ 4
Springfield, KY 70-71 H 7
Springfield, MA 64-65 M 3
Springfield, MN 70-71 C 3
Springfield, MO 64-65 H 4
Springfield, OH 64-65 K 3-4
Springfield, OR 66-67 B 3
Springfield, PA 84 III ab 2
Springfield, SD 68-69 GH 4
Springfield, TN 78-79 F 2
Springfield, VA 82 II a 2
Springfield, VT 72-73 K 3
Springfield, New York-, NY 82 III d 2
Springfontein 174-175 FG 6
Springhill, LA 78-79 C 4
Spring Hill, TN 78-79 F 3
Spring Hope, NC 80-81 GH 3
Springhouse 60 FG 4
Spring Mill, PA 84 III b 1
Spring Mountains 74-75 F 4
Spring Pond 84 I c 2
Springs 172 E 7
Springside, NJ 84 III de 1
Springsure 158-159 J 4
Springton Reservoir 84 III a 2
Spring Valley, IL 70-71 F 5
Spring Valley, MN 70-71 D 4
Spring Valley, TX 85 III a 1
Spring Valley [USA] 74-75 F 3
Spring Valley [ZA] 174-175 G 7
Springview, NE 68-69 G 4
Springville, AL 78-79 F 4
Springville, NJ 84 III d 2
Springville, NY 72-73 G 3
Springville, UT 66-67 H 5
Sproat Lake 66-67 A 1
Sprucedale 72-73 G 2
Spruce Grove 60 KL 3
Spruce Knob 64-65 KL 4
Spruce Mountain 66-67 F 5
Spruce Pine, NC 80-81 EF 2
Spry, UT 74-75 G 4
Spur, TX 76-77 D 6
Spur Lake, NM 74-75 J 5-6
Spurr, Mount — 58-59 LM 6
Sputendorf bei Grossbeeren 130 III a 2
Spy Pond 84 I a 2
Squamish 66-67 B 1
Squantum, MA 84 I bc 3
Squaw Harbor, AK 58-59 c 2
Squaw Rapids Dam 61 G 4
Squaw River 62 F 2
Squaw Valley, CA 64-65 BC 4
Squillace, Golfo di — 122-123 G 6
Squirrel River 58-59 G 3
Sralao = Kompong Sralao 150-151 E 5
Srê Ântong = Phum Srê Ântong 150-151 F 6
Srê Chis 150-151 F 6
Sredinnyj chrebet 132-133 f 6-e 7
Sredna gora 122-123 L 4
Sredn'aja Achtuba 126-127 M 2
Srednekolymsk 132-133 d 4
Srednerusskaja vozvyšennost' 124-125 L 6-8
Sredne-Sibirskoje ploskogorje 132-133 R-W 4-5
Srednij Ural 132-133 KL 6
Sredsib 132-133 L 7-P 7
Srê Koki 150-151 F 6
Srem 118 H 2
Sremot Kompong Som 150-151 D 7
Sremska Mitrovica 122-123 H 3
Sremska Rača 122-123 H 3
Sreng, Stung — 150-151 D 5-6
Srêpok 150-151 F 6
Sretensk 132-133 W 7
Srê Umbell 148-149 D 4
Sriharikota Island 140 E 4
Srīkākulam 134-135 M 7
Srī Lanka 134-135 N 9
Sri Mādhopur 138-139 E 4
Sri Mohangarh 138-139 C 4
Srīmushnam 140 D 5
Srīnagar 134-135 LM 4
Sringeri 140 B 4
Srīnivāspur 140 D 4
Srīperumbūdūr 140 DE 4
Sripur = Shrīpūr 138-139 N 5
Srīrangam 134-135 M 8
Srīrangapatnam 140 C 4
Srīsailam 140 D 2
Srīvaikuntam 140 CD 6
Srīvardhan 134-135 L 7
Srīvilliputtūr 140 C 6
Środa Wielkopolski 118 HJ 2
Srungavarapukota 140 F 1
Sseu-p'ing = Siping 142-143 N 3
Ssongea = Songea 172 G 4
Staaken, Berlin- 130 III a 1
Staaten River 158-159 H 3
Staatsforst Kranichstein 128 III b 2
Staatsforst Langen 128 III b 2
Staatsforst Mörfelden 128 III a 1
Stachanov 126-127 J 2
Stackpool 62 L 3
Stack Skerry 119 D 2
Stade [CDN] 82 I b 1
Stade [D] 118 D 2
Stade de Kinshasa 170 IV a 1
Stade Eboue 170 IV a 1
Städel 128 III b 1
Stádio 113 IV a 2
Stadion Dinamo 113 V b 2
Stadion im. Lenina 113 V b 3
Stadio Olimpio 113 II b 1
Stadium 82 II b 2
Stadium 200 85 III b 2
Städjan 116-117 E 7
Stadlandet 116-117 A 6
Stadlau, Wien- 113 I b 2
Stadtpark Hamburg 130 I b 1
Stafford 119 E 5
Stafford, KS 68-69 G 7
Stafford, NE 68-69 G 4
Stafford, TX 85 III a 2
Staicele 124-125 E 5
Staines 129 II a 2
Staines, Península — 108-109 C 8
Staines Reservoir 129 II a 2
Staked Plain = Llano Estacado 64-65 F 5
Stalina, pik — = pik Kommunizma 134-135 L 3
Stalinabad = Dušanbe 134-135 K 3
Stalingrad = Volgograd 126-127 LM 2
Staliniri = Cchinvali 126-127 LM 5
Stalinka = Černovozavodskoje 126-127 FG 1
Stalino = Doneck 126-127 H 2-3
Stalino = Ošarovo 132-133 S 5
Stalinogorsk = Novomoskovsk 124-125 M 6
Stalinsk = Novokuzneck 132-133 Q 7
Stallikon 128 IV ab 2
Stallo, MS 78-79 E 4
Stalowa Wola 118 L 3
Stalwart 61 F 5
Stalwart Point = Stalwartpunt 174-175 G 7
Stalwartpunt 174-175 G 7
Stamboul 170 I b 1
Stambul = İstanbul 134-135 BC 2
Stamford 158-159 H 4
Stamford, CT 72-73 K 4
Stamford, TX 76-77 E 6
Stammersdorf, Wien- 113 I b 1
Stampriet 172 C 6
Stamps, AR 78-79 C 4
Stamsund 116-117 EF 3
Stanberry, MO 70-71 C 5
Stanbury Mountains 66-67 G 5
Stancy 124-125 G 4
Standerton 172 EF 7
Standing Rock Indian Reservation 68-69 F 2-3
Standish, MI 70-71 HJ 4
Stane = Stavnoje 126-127 A 2
Stanford, KY 70-71 H 7
Stanford, MT 66-67 H 2
Stanger 174-175 J 5
Stanislau = Ivano-Frankovsk 126-127 B 2
Stanislaus River 74-75 C 3-4
Stanke Dimitrov 122-123 K 4
Stanley, ID 66-67 F 3
Stanley, KY 70-71 G 7
Stanley, ND 68-69 E 1
Stanley, NM 76-77 AB 5
Stanley, WI 70-71 E 3
Stanley [AUS] 160 b 2
Stanley [CDN] 63 C 4
Stanley [Falkland Islands] 111 E 8
Stanley [HK] 155 I b 2
Stanley, Mount — 158-159 F 4
Stanley Mission 61 FG 3
Stanley Mound 155 I b 2
Stanley Pool = Pool Malebo 172 C 2
Stanley Reservoir 134-135 M 8
Stanleyville = Kisangani 172 E 1
Stanmore, London- 129 II a 1
Stann Creek 64-65 J 8
Stanovoj chrebet 132-133 X-Z 6
Stanovoje nagorje 132-133 VW 6
Stanthorpe 160 KL 2
Stanton, KY 72-73 E 6
Stanton, MI 70-71 H 4
Stanton, ND 68-69 F 2
Stanton, NE 68-69 H 5
Stanton, TX 76-77 CD 6
Stanwell 129 II a 2
Stanwick, NJ 84 III d 2
Stanwood, WA 66-67 B 1
Stapi 116-117 b 2
Stapleford Abbotts 129 II c 1
Staples, MN 70-71 C 2
Stapleton, NE 68-69 F 5
Star' 124-125 JK 7
Star, MS 78-79 DE 4
Star, NC 80-81 G 3
Starachowice 118 K 3
Staraja Buchara = Buchara 134-135 JK 3
Staraja Kulatka 124-125 Q 7
Staraja Ladoga 124-125 HJ 4
Staraja Majna 124-125 R 6
Staraja Matvejevka 124-125 T 6
Staraja Porubežka 124-125 RS 7
Staraja Račejka 124-125 QR 7
Staraja Russa 132-133 E 6
Staraja Toropa 124-125 HJ 5
Stara Pazova 122-123 J 3
Stara Zagora 122-123 L 4
Starbejevo 113 V b 1
Starbuck [CDN] 61 JK 6
Starbuck [island] 156-157 K 5
Star City, AR 78-79 D 4
Stargard Szczeciński 118 G 2
Starica 124-125 K 5
Starigrad 122-123 F 3
Starke, FL 80-81 bc 2
Starkey, ID 66-67 E 3
Starkville, CO 68-69 D 7
Starkville, MS 78-79 E 4
Starkweather, ND 68-69 G 1
Starnberg 118 E 4-5
Starnberger See 118 E 5
Starobel'sk 126-127 J 2
Starodub 124-125 J 7
Starogard Gdański 118 HJ 2
Staroizborsk 124-125 FG 5
Staroje 124-125 N 4
Starojurjevo 124-125 N 7
Starokonstantinov 126-127 C 2
Starominskaja 126-127 J 3
Staroščerbinovskaja 126-127 J 3
Starotimoškino 124-125 Q 7
Starotitarovskaja 126-127 H 4
Staroverčeskaja 124-125 QR 4
Staryj Bir'uz'ak 126-127 N 4
Staryje Dorogi 124-125 G 7
Staryj Krym 126-127 G 4
Staryj Oskol 126-127 HJ 1
Staryj Sambor 126-127 A 2
Staryj Terek 126-127 N 5
Stassfurt 118 E 3
Staszów 118 K 3
State Capitol 85 II bc 2
State College, PA 72-73 GH 4
State House [USA] 84 I b 2
State House [WAN] 170 III b 2
State Line, MS 78-79 E 5
Staten Island 72-73 JK 4
Staten Island = Isla de los Estados 111 D 8
Staten Island Airport 82 III b 3
Statenville, GA 80-81 E 5
Statesboro, GA 80-81 F 4
Statesville, NC 64-65 K 4
Statland = Stadland 116-117 A 6
Statue of Liberty 82 III b 2
Stauffer, OR 66-67 C 4
Staung, Stung — 150-151 E 6
Staunton, IL 70-71 F 6
Staunton, VA 64-65 KL 4
Stavanger 116-117 A 8
Stavely 60 KL 4
Stavern 116-117 CD 8
Stavka = Urda 126-127 N 2
Stavkoviči 124-125 G 5
Stavnoje 126-127 A 2
Stavropol' 126-127 KL 4
Stavropol' = Togliatti 132-133 H 7
Stavropol, Kraj — 202-203 R 6-7
Stavropol'skaja vozvyšennost' 126-127 K-M 4
Stavrós 122-123 K 5
Stawell 158-159 H 7
Stazione Termini 113 II b 2
Steamboat, NV 74-75 D 3
Steamboat Springs, CO 68-69 C 5
Stearns, KY 78-79 G 2
Stebbins, AK 58-59 F 5
Stedelijk Museum 128 I a 1
Steel Creek, AK 58-59 R 4
Steele, AL 78-79 F 4
Steele, MO 78-79 E 2
Steele, ND 68-69 FG 2
Steele, Mount — 58-59 RS 6
Steele Creek 161 II b 1
Steele Island 53 B 30-31
Steelpoort 172 EF 6
Steelpoortrivier 174-175 HJ 3
Steel River 70-71 G 1
Steelton, PA 72-73 H 4
Steelville, MO 70-71 E 7

Steenkampsberge 174-175 HJ 3
Steenkool 148-149 K 7
Steenokkerzeel 128 II b 1
Steensby Inlet 56-57 V 3
Steens Mountain 66-67 D 4
Steenstrups Gletscher 56-57 Za 2
Steephill Lake 61 G 2-3
Steep Island 155 I b 2
Steep Point 158-159 B 5
Steep Rock 61 J 5
Steep Rock Lake 70-71 DE 1
Ştefăneşti 122-123 M 2
Stefansson Island 56-57 OP 3
Steffen, Cerro — 108-109 D 5
Steflești 122-123 K 3
Stege 116-117 E 10
Stéhoux, le — 128 II a 2
Steiermark 118 G 5
Steilloopbrug 174-175 H 2
Steilshoop, Hamburg- 130 I b 1
Steinbach 61 K 6
Steinbach (Taunus) 128 III a 1
Steinberg [D, Hessen] 128 III b 1
Steinen, Rio — 92-93 J 7
Steinhatchee, FL 80-81 b 2
Steinhausen, München- 130 II b 2
Steinhuser Wald 128 IV ab 2
Steinkjer 116-117 DE 5
Steinkopf 174-175 BC 5
Steinmaur 128 IV a 1
Steinneset 116-117 m 6
Steins, NM 74-75 J 6
Steinstücken, Berlin- 130 III a 2
Steinwerder, Hamburg- 130 I a 1
Stekľanka 124-125 N 4
Stella 174-175 F 4
Stella, LA 85 I c 2
Stellaland 172 D 7
Stellarton 63 E 5
Stellenbosch 172 CD 8
Steller, Mount — 58-59 Q 6
Stellingen, Hamburg- 130 I a 1
Stendal 118 E 2
Stende 124-125 D 5
Stenhouse, Mount — 155 I a 2
Stenòn Elafonêsu 122-123 K 7
Stenòn Kythêron 122-123 K 7-8
Stensele 116-117 G 5
Stepan' 124-125 F 8
Stepanakert 126-127 N 7
Stepana Razina 124-125 P 6
Stepanavan 126-127 LM 6
Stephanie, Lake — = Thew Bahir 164-165 M 8
Stephansdom 113 I b 2
Stephen, MN 68-69 H 1
Stephens, AR 78-79 C 4
Stephens, Cape — 161 EF 5
Stephens Island 60 B 2
Stephenson, MI 70-71 G 3
Stephens Passage 58-59 U 7-V 8
Stephenville 56-57 YZ 8
Stephenville, TX 76-77 EF 6
Stephenville Crossing 63 GH 3
Stepn'ak 132-133 N 7
Stepney, London- 129 II b 1
Stepovak Bay 58-59 cd 2
Štepovka 126-127 G 1
Sterkspruit 174-175 G 6
Sterkstroom 172 E 8
Sterkwater 174-175 H 3
Sterley, TX 76-77 D 5
Sterling, AK 58-59 M 6
Sterling, CO 64-65 F 3
Sterling, IL 70-71 F 5
Sterling, KS 68-69 GH 6
Sterling, ND 68-69 FG 2
Sterling City, TX 76-77 D 7
Sterling Heights, MI 72-73 E 3
Sterling Landing, AK 58-59 K 5
Sterling Park, CA 83 I b 2
Sterlitamak 132-133 K 7
Sterrebeek 128 II b 1
Stettler 61 B 4
Steuben, MI 70-71 G 2
Steubenville, OH 64-65 K 3
Stevenson, AL 78-79 FG 3
Stevenson, WA 66-67 BC 3
Stevenson Lake 62 A 1
Stevenson River 158-159 FG 5
Stevens Point, WI 70-71 F 3
Stevens Village, AK 58-59 N 3-4
Stevensville, MT 66-67 FG 2
Steveston 66-67 B 1
Stewart, AK 56-57 KL 6
Stewart, MN 70-71 C 3
Stewart, NV 74-75 D 3
Stewart, Isla — 111 B 8-9
Stewart Island 158-159 N 9
Stewart Islands 148-149 k 6
Stewart River [CDN, place] 56-57 J 5
Stewart River [CDN, river] 56-57 JK 5
Stewartsville, MO 70-71 CD 6
Stewart Valley 61 DE 5
Stewartville, MN 70-71 D 4
Steynsburg 174-175 F 6
Steynsrus 174-175 G 4
Steyr 118 G 4
Steytlerville 174-175 EF 7
Stickney, IL 83 II a 2
Stickney, SD 68-69 G 4
Stierstadt 128 III a 1
Stigler, OK 76-77 G 5
Stikine Mountains = Cassiar Mountains 56-57 KL 6
Stikine Plateau 56-57 K 6
Stikine River 56-57 KL 6
Stikine Strait 58-59 w 8
Stilbaai 174-175 D 8
Stiles, TX 76-77 D 7
Still Run 84 III b 3
Stillwater, MN 70-71 D 3
Stillwater, OK 76-77 F 4
Stillwater Mountains 74-75 DE 3
Stilwell, OK 76-77 G 5
Stimson 62 L 2
Stimson, Mount — 66-67 G 1
Stinear Nunataks 53 BC 7
Stinnett, TX 76-77 D 5
Stintonville 170 V c 2
Štip 122-123 K 5
Stirling [CDN] 66-67 G 1
Stirling City, CA 74-75 C 3
Stirling Range 158-159 C 6
Stites, ID 66-67 EF 2
Stitten = Saṭīṭan 166-167 G 3
Stjernøy 116-117 K 2
Stjørdalshalsen 116-117 D 6
Stobi 122-123 J 5
Stochod 124-125 E 8
Stockdale, TX 76-77 EF 8
Stockdorf 130 II a 2
Stockerau 118 H 4
Stockett, MT 66-67 H 2
Stockholm 116-117 GH 8
Stockholm, ME 72-73 MN 1
Stockholms län 116-117 GH 8
Stockport 119 E 5
Stocks Seamount 92-93 N 7
Stockton, CA 64-65 BC 4
Stockton, IL 70-71 EF 4
Stockton, KS 68-69 G 6
Stockton, MO 70-71 D 7
Stockton Island 70-71 E 2
Stockton Islands 58-59 OP 1
Stockton on Tees 119 F 4
Stockton Plateau 76-77 C 7
Stockville, NE 68-69 FG 5
Stodolišče 124-125 J 6
Stoffberg 174-175 H 3
Stoj, gora — 126-127 A 2
Stojba 132-133 Z 7
Stoke Newington, London- 129 II b 1
Stoke on Trend 119 EF 5
Stokes, Bahía — 108-109 C 10
Stokes, Monte — 108-109 C 8
Stokes, Mount — 161 EF 5
Stokes Point 160 ab 2
Stokkseyri 116-117 c 3
Stokksnes 116-117 f 2
Stolac 122-123 GH 4
Stolbcy 116-117 M 11
Stolbcy 124-125 F 7
Stolbovaja 124-125 L 6
Stolbovoj, ostrov — 132-133 Za 3
Stolin 124-125 F 8
Stolpe-Dorf 130 III b 1
Stolzenfels [Namibia] 174-175 C 5
Ston 122-123 G 4
Stone Canyon Reservoir 83 III b 1
Stone City, CO 68-69 D 6
Stonecutters Island 155 I a 2
Stoneham, MA 84 I b 2
Stonehaven 119 EF 3
Stonehenge [AUS] 158-159 H 4
Stonehenge [GB] 119 EF 6
Stone Mountains 80-81 F 2
Stoner, CO 74-75 J 4
Stonestown, San Francisco-, CA 83 I b 2
Stonewall 61 K 5
Stonewall, TX 76-77 E 7
Stonington 53 C 30
Stonington, ME 72-73 M 2-3
Stony Brook Reservation 84 I b 3
Stony Creek, VA 80-81 H 2
Stonyford, CA 74-75 B 3
Stony Point [CDN] 61 K 4-5
Stony Point [USA] 72-73 H 3
Stony River 56-57 EF 5
Stony River, AK 58-59 JK 6
Stony Tunguska = Podkamennaja Tunguska 132-133 R 5
Stopnica 118 K 3
Stora Lulevatten 116-117 HJ 4
Stora Sjöfallet 116-117 H 4
Stora-Sjöfallets nationalpark 116-117 GH 4
Storavan 116-117 H 5
Stord 116-117 A 8
Store Bælt 116-117 D 10
Støren 116-117 CD 6
Storfjord 116-117 B 6
Storfjordbotn 116-117 LM 2
Storfjorden 116-117 k 6
Storlien 116-117 E 6
Storm Bay 158-159 J 8
Stormberg 174-175 FG 6
Stormberge 174-175 G 6
Storm Lake, IA 70-71 C 4
Stormsrivier 174-175 E 7-F 8
Stormy Lake 62 CD 3
Stornorrfors 116-117 HJ 6
Stornoway 119 CD 2
Storøya 116-117 n 4
Storoževsk 132-133 J 5
Storsjön 116-117 E 6
Storuman [S, lake] 116-117 G 5
Storuman [S, place] 116-117 G 5
Story City, IA 70-71 D 4
Stosch, Isla — 111 A 7
Stoughton 61 G 6
Stoughton, WI 70-71 F 4
Stout Lake 62 B 1
Strabane 119 C 4
Strafford, PA 84 III a 1
Straight Cliffs 74-75 H 4
Strait of Belle Isle 56-57 Z 7
Strait of Canso 56-57 YZ 8
Strait of Dover 119 GH 6
Strait of Georgia 56-57 M 8
Strait of Juan de Fuca 56-57 LM 8
Strait of Singapore 148-149 DE 6
Straits of Florida 64-65 K 7-L 6
Straits of Mackinac 70-71 H 3
Strakonice 118 FG 4
Stralsund 118 F 1
Strand 172 C 8
Stranda 116-117 c 1-2
Stranraer 119 D 4
Strasbourg [CDN] 61 F 5
Strasbourg [F] 120-121 L 4
Strasburg, CO 68-69 D 6
Strasburg, ND 68-69 FG 2
Strašeny 126-127 D 3
Stratford, CA 74-75 D 4
Stratford, CT 72-73 K 4
Stratford, NJ 84 III c 3
Stratford, SD 68-69 GH 3
Stratford, TX 76-77 CD 4
Stratford, WI 70-71 EF 3
Stratford [AUS] 160 H 7
Stratford [CDN] 56-57 U 9
Stratford [NZ] 161 F 4
Stratford, London- 129 II c 1
Stratford on Avon 119 F 5
Strathcona Procincial Park 66-67 A 1
Strathcona Provincial Park 60 DE 5
Strathfield, Sydney- 161 I a 2
Strathgordon 160 bc 3
Strathmoor, Detroit-, MI 84 II a 2
Strathmore [CDN] 60 L 4
Strathmore [GB] 119 E 3
Strathnaver 60 FG 3
Strathroy 72-73 F 3
Stratonis Turris = Caesarea 136-137 F 6
Stratton, CO 68-69 E 6
Stratton, ME 72-73 L 2
Stratton, NE 68-69 F 5
Straubing 118 F 4
Straw, MT 68-69 AB 2
Strawberry Mountains 66-67 D 3
Strawberry Park 85 III c 2
Strawberry Point, CA 83 I ab 1
Strawberry Point, IA 70-71 E 4
Strawberry River 66-67 H 5
Strawbridge Lake 84 III d 2
Strawn, TX 76-77 E 6
Streaky Bay [AUS, bay] 158-159 F 6
Streaky Bay [AUS, place] 158-159 FG 6
Streatham, London- 129 II b 2
Streator, IL 70-71 F 5
Strebersdorf, Wien- 113 I b 1
69th Street Center 84 III b 2
Streeter, ND 68-69 G 2
Streetman, TX 76-77 FG 7
30th Street Station 84 III b 2
Streich Mound 158-159 D 6
Strelka-Čun'a 132-133 T 5
Strenči 124-125 E 5
Stresa 122-123 C 3
Strešen' = Strašeny 126-127 D 3
Stretto di Messina 122-123 F 6-7
Strevell, ID 66-67 G 4
Strickland River 148-149 M 8
Stringtown, OK 76-77 FG 5
Strižament, gora — 126-127 L 4
Striži 124-125 R 4
Strobel, Lago — 108-109 D 7
Stroeder 111 D 6
Strofádes 122-123 J 7
Strogino, Moskva- 113 V ab 2
Strómboli 122-123 F 6
Stromsburg, NE 68-69 H 5
Strömstad 116-117 D 8
Strömsund 116-117 F 6
Ströms Vattudal 116-117 F 5-6
Stroner, WY 68-69 D 3
Strong, AR 78-79 C 4
Strong City, KS 68-69 H 6
Stronsay 119 EF 2
Stroud 119 EF 6
Stroud, OK 76-77 F 5
Stroudsburg, PA 72-73 J 4
Struer 116-117 C 9
Strugi Krasnyje 124-125 G 4
Struisbaai 174-175 D 8
Struma 122-123 K 5
Strumica 122-123 K 5
Strunino 124-125 M 5
Struys Bay = Struisbaai 174-175 D 8
Strydenburg 174-175 E 5
Strydomsvlei 174-175 E 7
Strydpoortberge 174-175 H 3
Stryj [SU, place] 126-127 A 2
Stryj [SU, river] 126-127 A 2
Strymŏn 122-123 K 5
Strzelecki Creek 160 E 2
Strzelno 118 HJ 2
Stuart, FL 80-81 c 3
Stuart, IA 70-71 C 5
Stuart, NE 68-69 G 4
Stuart, OK 76-77 FG 5
Stuart, VA 80-81 F 2
Stuart Island 56-57 D 5
Stuart Lake 56-57 M 7
Stuart Range 158-159 FG 5
Stubbenkammer 118 FG 1
Studenica 122-123 J 4
Studenka 124-125 G 6
Stumpy Point, NC 80-81 J 3
Stung Battambang = Stung Sangker 150-151 D 6
Stung Chikrang 150-151 E 6
Stung Chinit 150-151 E 6
Stung Daun Tri 150-151 D 6
Stung Mongkol Borey 150-151 D 6
Stung Porong 150-151 E 6
Stung Pursat 150-151 D 6
Stung Sangker 150-151 D 6
Stung Sen 150-151 E 6
Stung Sreng 150-151 D 5-6
Stung Staung 150-151 E 6
Stung Tanad 150-151 D 6
Stung Treng 148-149 E 4
Stupino 124-125 LM 6
Stura di Demonte 122-123 B 3
Sturge Island 53 C 17
Sturgeon Bay 61 JK 4
Sturgeon Bay, WI 70-71 G 3
Sturgeon Bay Canal 70-71 G 3
Sturgeon Falls [CDN, place] 72-73 FG 1
Sturgeon Falls [CDN, river] 62 L 2
Sturgeon Lake [CDN, Alberta] 60 J 2
Sturgeon Lake [CDN, Ontario] 62 D 3
Sturgeon Landing 61 H 3
Sturgeon River [CDN, Ontario] 72-73 F 1
Sturgeon River [CDN, Saskatchewan] 61 E 4
Sturgis, KY 70-71 G 7
Sturgis, MI 70-71 H 5
Sturgis, OK 76-77 C 4
Sturgis, SD 68-69 E 3
Sturt, Mount — 158-159 H 5
Sturt Creek 158-159 E 3
Sturt Desert 158-159 H 5
Sturt Plain 158-159 F 3
Stutterheim 172 E 8
Stuttgart 118 D 4
Stuttgart, AR 78-79 D 3
Stuurmen 174-175 CD 6
Stviga 124-125 F 8
Stykkisholm = Stykkishólmur 116-117 b 2
Stykkishólmur 116-117 b 2
Stylís 122-123 K 6
Styr' 126-127 B 1
Styria = Steiermark 118 G 5
Suaçuí Grande, Rio — 102-103 L 3
Suai 152-153 K 4
Suaita 94-95 E 4
Sûâkin = Sawâkin 164-165 M 5
Suan 144-145 F 3
Suancheng = Xuancheng 146-147 G 6
Suanen = Xuan'en 146-147 B 6-7
Süanhua = Xuanhua 142-143 LM 3
Suanhwa = Xuanhua 142-143 LM 3
Suan Phung 150-151 B 6
Suao 142-143 N 7
Su'ao = Suao 142-143 N 7
Suapi 104-105 C 4
Suapure, Río — 94-95 H 4
Suâr 138-139 G 3
Suardi 106-107 G 3
Suárez [CO, Cauca] 94-95 C 6
Suárez [CO, Tolima] 94-95 D 5
Suárez [ROU] 106-107 J 5
Suaruro, Cordillera de — 104-105 DE 7
Suasúa 94-95 L 4
Suba 91 III b 2
Subansiri 141 D 2
Šubarkuduk 132-133 K 8
Subar Luat, Pulau — 154 III ab 2
Subarnarekha 138-139 L 6
Sûbâţ, As — 164-165 L 7
Subate 124-125 EF 5
Subayhah 136-137 H 7
Subbat = Subate 124-125 EF 5
Subi, Pulau — 150-151 G 11
Subiaco 122-123 E 5
Subi Kecil, Pulau — 152-153 H 4
Sublett, ID 66-67 G 4
Sublette, KS 68-69 F 7
Subotica 122-123 HJ 2
Subugo 171 C 3
Suburban Canal 85 I a 1-2
Success 61 D 5
Suceava 122-123 LM 2
Sucesso 100-101 D 3
Suchaj nuur 142-143 GH 4
Suchana 132-133 W 4
Suchbaatar [Mongolia, administrative unit = 17] 142-143 L 2
Süchbaatar [Mongolia, place] 142-143 JK 1
Sucheng = Su Xian 142-143 M 5
Suches, Río — 104-105 B 4
Su-chia-t'un = Sujiatun 144-145 D 2
Su-ch'ien = Suqian 142-143 M 5
Suchiniči 124-125 K 6
Suchobezvodnoje 124-125 P 5
Suchodn'a 113 V a 2
Suchoj Liman 126-127 E 3
Suchona 132-133 G 6
Suchou = Xuzhou 142-143 M 5
Su-chou = Yibin 142-143 JK 6
Suchow = Xuzhou 142-143 M 5
Suchow = Yibin 142-143 JK 6
Suchumi 126-127 K 5
Sucio, Río — 94-95 C 4
Suckling, Cape — 58-59 Q 7
Sucre [BOL] 92-93 FG 8
Sucre [CO, Caquetá] 94-95 D 7
Sucre [CO, Sucre administrative unit] 94-95 D 3
Sucre [CO, Sucre place] 94-95 D 3
Sucre [EC] 96-97 A 2
Sucre [PE] 96-97 C 6
Sucre [YV] 94-95 K 2
Sucúa 96-97 B 3
Suçuarana 100-101 D 8
Suçuarana, Serra da — 100-101 B 8
Sucuaro 92-93 F 4
Sucun 146-147 G 4
Sucunduri, Rio — 92-93 H 6
Sucupira 100-101 C 4
Sucuriú, Rio — 92-93 J 8
Sucy-en-Brie 129 I d 2
Sûd = As-Sudd 164-165 L 7
Suda [SU, river] 124-125 L 4
Sudaj 124-125 O 4
Sudak 126-127 G 4
Sudan, TX 76-77 C 5
Sudan [landscape] 164-165 C-K 6
Sudan [Sudan, state] 164-165 J-L 6
Sudau 152-153 N 3
Sudayr 134-135 EF 5
Sudbišči 124-125 L 7
Sudbury [CDN] 56-57 U 8
Sudbury, London- 129 II a 1
Sudd, As — 164-165 L 7
Suddie 92-93 H 3
Süderelbe 130 I a 2
Sudhâgarh 140 A 1
Súdhavík 116-117 b 1
Sudhur-Múla 116-117 f 2
Sudhur-Thingeyjar 116-117 ef 2
Sudirman, Pegunungan — 148-149 L 7
Sudislavl' 124-125 NO 5
Sudogda [SU, place] 124-125 N 6
Sudong-ni = Changhang 144-145 F 4-5
Sudost' 124-125 J 7
Sud-Ouest 168-169 E 3
Sudr = Râ's as-Sidr 173 C 3
Sudr, Wâdî — = Wâdî Sidr 173 C 3
Sudža 126-127 G 1
Sue = Nahr Sûî 164-165 K 7
Sueca 120-121 G 9
Sueco, El — 86-87 GH 3
Suemez Island 58-59 w 9
Suez = As-Suways 164-165 L 3
Suez, Gulf of — = Khalîj as-Suways 164-165 L 3
Sûf 166-167 K 3
Şûf, 'Ayn — 166-167 H 5
Şûf, Ḥâssî — 166-167 F 5
Sûfân, Qulbân as- 136-137 H 8
Sûfeyân 136-137 LM 3
Suffield 61 C 5
Suffolk, VA 80-81 H 2
Suffolk Downs Race Track 84 I c 2
Suflíon 122-123 LM 5
Sufu = Qäshqär 142-143 CD 4
Sufûq 136-137 J 4
Šuga 132-133 N 4
Sugamo, Tôkyô- 155 III b 1
Sugano, Ichikawa- 155 III c 1
Sûgar 166-167 G 2
Sugar Creek 85 II b 2
Sugar Island 70-71 H 2
Sugarloaf Mountain 72-73 LM 2
Sugar Valley, Houston-, TX 85 III b 2
Suggi Lake 61 G 3
Suginami, Tôkyô- 155 III a 1
Sugita, Yokohama- 155 III a 3
Sugiyasu 144-145 H 6
Suğla gölü 136-137 DE 4
Šugozero 124-125 K 4
Sugut, Sungei — 152-153 M 2
Suguta 171 D 2
Sûhâj 164-165 L 3
Şuḥâr 134-135 H 6
Suhelîpâḍ = Suheli Par 134-135 L 8
Suheli Par 134-135 L 8
Suhl 118 E 3
Su-hsien = Su Xian 142-143 M 5
Şuhûrah 166-167 C 4
Şuhut 136-137 D 3
Sûî 138-139 B 3
Sûî, Nahr — 164-165 K 7
Suiá-Miçu, Rio — 98-99 M 10-11
Sui'an 146-147 G 7
Suichang 146-147 G 7
Sui-ch'i = Suixi 146-147 C 11
Sui Chiang = Sui Jiang 146-147 D 10
Suichuan 142-143 L 6
Sui-chung = Suizhong 144-145 C 2
Suichwan = Suichuan 142-143 L 6
Suide 142-143 KL 4
Suifenhe 142-143 OP 3
Sui He 146-147 F 4-5
Sui Ho = Sui He 146-147 F 4-5
Suihsien = Sui Xian [TJ, Henan] 146-147 E 4
Suihsien = Sui Xian [TJ, Hubei] 142-143 L 5
Suihua 142-143 O 2
Suihwa = Suihua 142-143 O 2
Sui Jiang 146-147 D 10
Suilai = Manaas 142-143 F 3
Suining [TJ, Hunan] 146-147 BC 8
Suining [TJ, Jiangsu] 146-147 FG 5
Suipacha 106-107 H 5
Suiping 146-147 D 5
Suir 119 C 5
Suiteh = Suide 142-143 KL 4
Suitland, MD 82 II b 2
Suixi [TJ, Anhui] 146-147 F 5
Suixi [TJ, Guangdong] 146-147 C 11
Sui Xian [TJ, Henan] 146-147 E 4
Sui Xian [TJ, Hubei] 142-143 L 5
Suiyuan 142-143 K 4-L 3
Sui-yüan = Suiyuan 142-143 K 4-L 3
Suizhong 144-145 C 2
Šuja [SU, Ivanovo] 132-133 G 6
Šuja [SU, Karel'skaja ASSR] 124-125 J 3
Sûjângarh 138-139 E 4
Sujâwal 138-139 B 5
Sujiatun 144-145 D 2
Šujostrov 124-125 K 1
Šujskoje 124-125 N 4
Sukabumi 148-149 E 8
Sukadana 148-149 EF 7
Sukadana, Teluk — 152-153 H 6
Sukagawa 144-145 MN 4
Sukaraja 148-149 F 7
Sukchar, Pânihâti- 154 II b 1
Sukch'ŏn 144-145 E 3
Sukhe Bator = Süchbaatar 142-143 JK 1
Şukhnah, Aṣ- 136-137 H 5
Sukhum = Suchumi 126-127 K 5
Sukhuma = Ban Soukhouma 150-151 E 5
Şukhûrah 166-167 C 4
Şukhûr ar-Rihâmnah 166-167 BC 3
Sûki, As- 164-165 L 6
Sukkertoppen = Manîtsoq 56-57 Za 4
Sukkothai 150-151 B 4
Sukkozero 124-125 J 2
Sukkur = Sukkhur 134-135 KL 5
Sûkḷî = Sukri 138-139 D 5
Sukoharjo 152-153 J 9
Sukon, Ko — 150-151 B 9
Sukri 138-139 D 5
Sukromľa 124-125 K 5
Sukses 172 C 6
Sukulu 171 C 2
Sukumo 144-145 J 6
Sukumo wan 144-145 J 6
Sul, Canal do — 92-93 K 4-5
Sula, MT 66-67 FG 3
Sula [SU] 126-127 F 1
Sula, Kepulauan — 148-149 HJ 7
Sulabesi, Pulau — 148-149 J 7
Sulaimân, Kohistân — 134-135 KL 4-5
Sulak [SU, place] 126-127 N 5
Sulak [SU, river] 126-127 N 5
Sulakyurt 136-137 E 2
Sulan Cheer 142-143 K 3
Sula Sgeir 119 C 2
Sulatna Crossing, AK 58-59 JK 4
Sulatna River 58-59 K 4
Šulavery = Šaum'ani 126-127 M 6
Sulawesi 148-149 G 7-H 6
Sulawesi, Laut — 148-149 GH 6
Sulawesi Selatan = 21 ◁ 148-149 G 7
Sulawesi Tengah = 19 ◁ 148-149 H 6
Sulawesi Tenggara = 20 ◁ 148-149 H 7
Sulawesi Utara = 18 ◁ 148-149 H 6
Sulaymân 166-167 M 1
Sulaymânîyah 134-135 EF 3
Sulaymîyah, As- 134-135 F 6
Sulayyil, As- 134-135 F 6
Şulb, Aş- 134-135 F 5
Sul'ca 124-125 Q 2
Sule He 142-143 H 4
Sule Skerry 119 D 2
Sulet = Solta 122-123 G 4
Süleymanlı 136-137 G 4
Sullivan, IL 70-71 F 6
Sulima 164-165 B 7
Sulimov = Čerkessk 126-127 L 4
Sulina 122-123 N 3
Sulina, Braţul — 122-123 N 3
Sulitjelma [N, mountain] 116-117 G 4
Sulitjelma [N, place] 116-117 FG 4
Sullana 92-93 C 5
Süllberg 130 I a 1
Sülldorf, Hamburg- 130 I a 1
Sulligent, AL 78-79 E 4
Sullivan, IN 70-71 G 6
Sullivan, MO 70-71 E 6
Sullivan Bay 60 D 4
Sullivan Canyon 83 III a 1
Sullivan Island = Lambi Kyûn 148-149 C 4
Sullivan Lake 61 C 5
Šul'mak = Novabad 134-135 L 3
Sulmona 122-123 E 4-5
Su-lo Ho = Sule He 142-143 H 4
Sulphur, LA 78-79 C 5
Sulphur, NV 66-67 D 5
Sulphur, OK 76-77 F 5
Sulphurdale, UT 74-75 G 3
Sulphur River 76-77 GH 6
Sulphur Springs, TX 76-77 G 6
Sulṭân, Bi'r — 166-167 L 3
Sultanabad = Arâk 134-135 F 4
Sultânâbâd = Osmânnagar 140 D 1
Sultan Ahmet Camii 154 I a 3
Sultan dağları 136-137 D 3
Sultan Hamud 171 D 3
Sultanhisar 136-137 BC 4
Sultan Mosque 154 III b 2
Sultânpur 134-135 N 5
Sultus 124-125 M 3
Sulu Archipelago 148-149 H 5
Suluca 136-137 F 2
Sulûk 136-137 H 4
Sülüklü 136-137 E 3
Sulukna River 58-59 K 5
Sul'ukta 134-135 KL 3
Suluova = Suluca 136-137 F 2
Sulûq 164-165 J 2
Sülüru 140 E 4
Sulu Sea 148-149 GH 5
Sulusee 148-149 GH 5
Sulwân 166-167 E 2
Sülz [D, river ◁ Mühlbach] 128 III b 2
Sulzbach (Taunus) 128 III a 1
Sulzberger Bay 53 B 21-22
Šumači 124-125 J 7
Sumaco, Volcán — 96-97 C 2
Šumadija 122-123 J 3-4
Sumalata 152-153 P 5
Sumampa 106-107 F 2
Sumampa, Sierra — 106-107 F 2
Sûmâr 136-137 L 6
Sumas, WA 66-67 BC 1
Sumatera = Sumatra 148-149 C 6-D 7
Sumatera Barat = 3 ◁ 148-149 D 7
Sumatera Selatan = 6 ◁ 148-149 D 7
Sumatera Tengah = Riau = 4 ◁ 148-149 D 6
Sumatera Utara = 2 ◁ 148-149 C 6
Sumatra 148-149 C 6-D 7
Sumatra, FL 78-79 G 5
Sumatra, MT 68-69 C 2
Sumaúma 92-93 G 6
Sumba 148-149 G 9
Sumba, Selat — 148-149 GH 8
Sumbawa 148-149 G 8
Sumbawa, Teluk — 152-153 M 10
Sumbawa Besar 148-149 G 8
Sumbawanga 172 F 3
Sümber 142-143 K 2
Sumbu 171 B 5
Sumbu Game Reserve 171 B 5
Sumburgh Head 119 F 2
Šumbut 124-125 S 6
Sumé 100-101 F 4
Šumen 122-123 M 4
Sumenep 152-153 KL 9
Šumerľa 124-125 PQ 6
Sumgait [SU, place] 126-127 O 6
Sumgait [SU, river] 126-127 O 6
Šumicha 132-133 L 6
Sumida, Tôkyô- 155 III bc 1
Sumidouro 102-103 L 5
Šumilino 124-125 G 6
Šumina 124-125 T 3
Sumisu-jima 142-143 R 5
Sumisu zima = Sumisu-jima 142-143 R 5
Şummân, Aş- [Saudi Arabia ↑ Ar-Riyâḍ] 134-135 F 5
Şummân, Aş- [Saudi Arabia ↘ Ar-Riyâḍ] 134-135 F 6
Summer, Lake — 76-77 B 5
Summerfield, TX 76-77 C 5
Summer Island 70-71 G 3
Summer Lake 66-67 C 4
Summer Lake, OR 66-67 C 4
Summerland 66-67 CD 1
Summerside 62 E 4
Summertown, TN 78-79 F 3
Summerville, SC 80-81 FG 4
Summerville, WV 72-73 F 5
Summit 64-65 b 2
Summit, AK 58-59 N 5
Summit, CA 74-75 E 5
Summit, IL 83 II a 2
Summit, MS 78-79 D 5
Summit, OR 66-67 B 3
Summit, SD 68-69 H 3
Summit Lake [CDN] 60 FG 2
Summit Lake [USA] 58-59 P 5
Summit Lake Indian Reservation 66-67 D 5
Summit Mountain 74-75 E 3
Summit Peak 68-69 C 7
Summt 130 III b 1
Summter See 130 III b 1
Sumner, IA 70-71 D 4
Sumner, MO 70-71 D 6
Sumner Strait 58-59 w 8
Sumoto 144-145 K 5
Sumozero 124-125 K 1-2
Šumperk 118 H 3-4
Sumprabum = Hsûmbârabûm 148-149 C 1
Sumpter, OR 66-67 DE 3
Sumrall, MS 78-79 E 5
S'umsi 124-125 ST 5
Sumskij Posad 124-125 K 1
Sumter, SC 64-65 KL 5
Sumy 126-127 G 1
S'un' 124-125 T 6
Sun, Altar of the — 155 II b 2
Suna [EAT] 171 C 4
Suna [SU, place] 124-125 S 5
Suna [SU, river] 124-125 J 2
Sunagawa 144-145 b 2
Sunâm 138-139 E 2
Sunamachi, Tôkyô- 155 III bc 1
Sunamganj = Shûnâmganj 141 B 3
Sunan 144-145 E 3
Sunato 171 DE 6
Sunaysilah 136-137 J 5
Sunburst, MT 66-67 H 1
Sunbury 129 II a 2
Sunbury, OH 72-73 E 4
Sunbury, PA 72-73 H 4
Sunchal, El — 106-107 D 2
Sunchales 106-107 G 3
Suncho Corral 111 D 3
Sunch'ŏn [North Korea] 144-145 E 3
Sunch'ŏn [ROK] 142-143 O 4-5
Sunchow = Guiping 142-143 KL 7
Suncook, NH 72-73 L 3
Sunda, Selat — 148-149 E 8
Sunda Kelapa, Jakarta- 154 IV ab 1
Sundance, WY 68-69 D 3
Sundar Ban = Sundarbans 134-135 OP 6
Sundarbans 134-135 OP 6
Sundargaḍa = Sundargarh 138-139 JK 6
Sundargarh 138-139 JK 6
Sunda Trench 50-51 P 6
Sunday Islands = Raoul 208 J 5
Sundays River = Sondagsrivier 174-175 F 7
Sunday Strait 158-159 D 3
Sundblad 106-107 F 5
Sundbyberg 116-117 G 8
Sunderbunds = Sundarbans 134-135 OP 6
Sunderland [CDN] 72-73 G 2
Sunderland [GB] 119 F 4
Sündiken dağları 136-137 D 2-3
Sundown [AUS] 158-159 F 5
Sundown [CDN] 68-69 H 1
Sundre 60 K 4
Sundsvall 116-117 GH 6
Sun'ga 124-125 K 2
Sungaianyar 152-153 M 7
Sungai Arut 152-153 J 6-7
Sungai Asahan 152-153 C 4
Sungai Bahau 152-153 LM 4
Sungai Bampu 152-153 C 4
Sungai Barumun 152-153 CD 5
Sungai Belayan 152-153 L 5

Sungai Berau 152-153 M 4
Sungaidareh 148-149 D 7
Sungaiguntung 152-153 E 5
Sungai Kahayan 148-149 F 7
Sungai Kampar 152-153 DE 5
Sungai Kapuas [RI, Kalimantan Barat] 148-149 F 6
Sungai Kapuas [RI, Kalimantan Tengah] 152-153 L 6
Sungai Karama 152-153 N 6-7
Sungai Kayan 152-153 M 4
Sungai Ketungau 152-153 J 5
Sungai Konaweha 152-153 O 7-P 8
Sungai Kualu 150-151 BC 11
Sungai Lamandau 152-153 J 6-7
Sungai Lariang 152-153 N 6
Sungailiat 152-153 G 6
Sungai Mahakam 148-149 G 6-7
Sungai Mamasa 152-153 N 7
Sungai Melawi 152-153 K 6
Sungai Mendawai 152-153 K 7
Sungai Murung 152-153 L 7
Sungai Musi 148-149 D 7
Sungai Negara 152-153 L 7
Sungai Pawan 152-153 J 6
Sungai Pembuang 152-153 K 6-7
Sungaipenuh 148-149 D 7
Sungaipinang 152-153 KL 6
Sungai Rokan 152-153 D 5
Sungai Rungan 152-153 K 6-7
Sungai Sambas 152-153 H 5
Sungai Sampit 152-153 K 7
Sungai Sekayam 152-153 J 5
Sungai Sembakung 152-153 M 3-4
Sungai Sesayap 152-153 M 4
Sungai Siak 152-153 DE 5
Sungai Simpang-kanan 150-151 AB 11
Sungai Simpang-kiri 152-153 B 4
Sungaisudah 152-153 K 5
Sungai Telen 152-153 M 5
Sungai Tembesi 152-153 E 6-7
Sungai Walahae 152-153 NO 8
Sungari 142-143 N 2-O 3
Sungari Reservoir = Songhua Hu 142-143 O 3
Sung-chiang = Songjiang 142-143 N 5
Sungei Baleh 152-153 K 5
Sungei Balui 152-153 KL 4
Sungei Dungun 150-151 D 10
Sungei Kelantan 150-151 CD 10
Sungei Kemena 152-153 K 4
Sungei Kinabatangan 152-153 M 3
Sungei Labuk 152-153 M 2-3
Sungei Langat 150-151 C 11
Sungei Lebir 150-151 D 10
Sungei Lupar 152-153 J 5
Sungei Muar 150-151 D 12
Sungei Muda 150-151 C 10
Sungei Nal = Kuala Nal 150-151 CD 10
Sungei Pahang 150-151 D 11
Sungei Patani 148-149 CD 5
Sungei Perak 150-151 C 10
Sungei Rompin 150-151 D 11
Sungei Segama 152-153 MN 3
Sungei Sugut 152-153 M 2
Sungei Terengganu 150-151 D 10
Sungguminasa 152-153 N 8
Sung-hsien = Song Xian 146-147 CD 4
Song hua Chiang = Songhua Jiang 142-143 N 2-O 3
Sŭngjibaegam 144-145 G 2
Sungkai 150-151 C 11
Sungkiang = Songjiang 142-143 N 5
Sung Kong Island 155 I b 2
Sung-k'ou = Songkou 146-147 G 9
Sung Men 150-151 C 3
Sung-mên = Songmen 146-147 H 7
Sung Noen 150-151 CD 5
Sung-t'ao = Songtao 146-147 B 7
Sungu 172 C 2
Sungurlu 136-137 F 2
Sunhing = Xinxing 146-147 D 10
Sunhwa = Xunhua 142-143 J 4
Sūnikon 128 IV a 1
Suning = Xiuning 146-147 FG 7
Súnion, Atrōtérion — 122-123 KL 7
Sunke = Xunke 142-143 O 2
Sūn Kosī 134-135 O 5
Sunnagyn, chrebet — 132-133 Y 6
Sunndalsøra 116-117 C 6
Sunniland, FL 80-81 c 3
Sunnūris = Sinnūris 173 B 3
Sunnyside, UT 74-75 H 3
Sunnyside, WA 66-67 CD 2
Sunnyside Park 85 III b 2
Sunnyvale, CA 74-75 B 4
Suno saki 144-145 M 5
Sunray, TX 76-77 D 4-5
Sunrise, AK 58-59 N 6
Sunrise, WY 68-69 D 4
Sun River 66-67 GH 2
Sunsas, Serranía de — 104-105 G 5-6
Sunset, San Francisco-, CA 83 I b 2
Sunset Country 160 E 5
Sunset Heights, Houston-, TX 85 III b 1
Sunset House 60 J 2
Sunset Prairie 60 G 2
Sunshine, Melbourne- 161 II ab 1
Sunstrum 62 C 2
Suntar 132-133 W 5
Suntar-Chajata, chrebet — 132-133 ab 5
Suntaug Lake 84 I b 1
Sûn Taung 141 D 5
Suntaži 124-125 E 5
Sunter, Jakarta- 154 IV b 1
Sunter, Kali — 154 IV b 1
Suntrana, AK 58-59 N 5
Suntsar 134-135 J 5
Sun Valley, ID 66-67 F 4
Sunyang = Xunyang 146-147 B 5
Sunyani 164-165 D 7
Suojarvi 132-133 E 5
Suojoki 124-125 J 2
Suokonmäki 116-117 KL 6
Suolahti 116-117 LM 6
Suomen selkä 116-117 K-N 6
Suomussalmi 116-117 N 5
Suō nada 144-145 H 6
Suonenjoki 116-117 M 6
Suong, Nam — = Nam Seng 150-151 D 2
Sūpa 140 B 3
Supai, AZ 74-75 G 4
Supaol = Supaul 138-139 L 4
Supaul 138-139 L 4
Supe 96-97 F 3
Superb 61 D 5
Superior, AZ 74-75 H 6
Superior, MT 66-67 F 2
Superior, NE 68-69 GH 5
Superior, WI 64-65 H 2
Superior, WY 68-69 B 5
Superior, Lake — 64-65 HJ 2
Superior, Valle — 108-109 FG 4
Suphan, Mae Nam — = Mae Nam Tha Chin 150-151 C 5-6
Suphan Buri 148-149 CD 4
Suphan dağı 136-137 K 3
Supiori, Pulau — 148-149 KL 7
Sup'ung-chŏsuji 144-145 E 2
Supung Hu 142-143 NO 3
Šupunskij, mys — 132-133 f 7
Sūq Ahrās 164-165 F 1
Sūq al-Arb'ā' 166-167 C 2
Sūq al-Arba'ā' al-Aīt Bāhā 166-167 B 4
Sūq al-Arb'ā' 'Ayāshah 166-167 CD 2
Sūq al-Hamīs = Sūq al-Khamīs 166-167 B 4
Sūq al-Hamīs as-Sāḥil = Sūq al-Khamīs as-Sāḥil 166-167 C 2
Sūq al Hamīs Banī 'Arūs = Sūq al-Khamīs Banī 'Arūs 166-167 D 2
Sūq al-Khamīs 166-167 B 4
Sūq al-Khamīs as Sāḥil 166-167 C 2
Sūq al-Khamis Banī 'Arūs 166-167 D 2
Suq ash-Shuyūkh 136-137 M 7
Suq ath-Thalāthah 166-167 C 2
Sūq at-Talātah = Sūq ath-Thalāthah 166-167 C 2
Suqian 142-143 M 5
Suquṭrā' 134-135 G 8
Ṣūr [Oman] 134-135 H 6
Ṣur [RL] 136-137 F 6
Sur, Point — 74-75 BC 4
Sura 124-125 Q 6
Sura, Calcutta- 154 II b 2
Sura, Raas — 164-165 b 1
Šurab 134-135 L 2
Surabaia = Surabaya 148-149 F 8
Surabaya 148-149 F 8
Surachany, Baku- 126-127 P 6
Suraḍā = Sorada 138-139 K 8
Sūrājpur 138-139 J 6
Surakarta 148-149 F 8
Sūr al-Ghuzlān 166-167 HJ 1
Şūrān 136-137 G 5
Surat [AUS] 158-159 J 5
Surat [IND] 134-135 L 6
Surate = Surat 134-135 L 6
Sūratgaṛh 138-139 DE 3
Surat Thani 148-149 CD 5
Suraž [SU, Belorusskaja SSR] 124-125 H 6
Suraž [SU, Rossijskaja SFSR] 124-125 J 7
Surbiton, London- 129 II a 2
Surcubamba 96-97 D 8
Sūrdāsh 136-137 L 5
Surendranagar 138-139 C 6
Šuren'ga 124-125 M 2
Suresnes 129 I b 2
Surf, CA 74-75 C 5
Surf Inlet 60 C 3
Surgāṇā 138-139 D 7
Surgentes, Los — 106-107 FG 4
Surgut [SU, Chanty-Mansijskij NO] 132-133 N 5
Surgut [SU, Kujbyšev] 132-133 J 7
Surguticha 132-133 PQ 5
Sūri 138-139 L 6
Suriāpet 140 D 2
Surigao 148-149 J 5
Surin 148-149 D 4
Suriname [SME, administrative unit] 98-99 L 2
Suriname [SME, state] 92-93 HJ 4
Suring, WI 70-71 F 3
Suripā 94-95 G 4
Suripá, Río — 94-95 F 4
Surkhet 138-139 H 3
Šurma 124-125 RS 5
Sürmene = Hurmurgān 136-137 J 2
Surnadalsøra 116-117 C 6
Surovikino 126-127 L 2
Surprêsa 98-99 F 10
Surprise, Lac de la — 62 O 2
Surprise Valley 66-67 CD 5
Surrey, ND 68-69 F 1
Surrey Canal 129 II b 2
Sur-Sari = ostrov Gogland 124-125 F 3
Sursk 124-125 PQ 7
Surskoje 124-125 Q 6
Surt 164-165 H 2
Surt, As- 164-165 H 2-3
Surt, Khalīj as- 164-165 H 2
Surtanāhū 138-139 BC 4
Surtsey 116-117 c 3
Surubim 100-101 G 4
Sürüç 136-137 H 4
Surucucus, Serra dos — 98-99 G 3
Suruga wan 144-145 M 5
Surukom 168-169 E 4
Surulangun 148-149 D 7
Surulere, Lagos- 170 III b 1
Surumú, Río — 98-99 H 2-3
Surwāya 138-139 FG 5
Šuryškary 132-133 M 4
Sūs, As- 166-167 B 4
Sūs, Wād — 166-167 B 4
Susa [CO] 94-95 DE 5
Susa [I] 122-123 B 3
Susa [IR] 136-137 N 6
Susa [J] 144-145 H 5
Šuša [SU] 126-127 N 7
Susa = Sūsah 164-165 G 1
Sušac 122-123 G 4
Sūsah [LAR] 164-165 J 2
Sūsah [TN] 164-165 G 1
Susaki 144-145 J 6
Susami 144-145 K 6
Susan = Susa 136-137 N 6
Susang = Durgapūr 141 B 3
Susanino 124-125 N 4
Susanville, CA 64-65 B 3
Sušč'ovo 124-125 GH 5
Suşehri 136-137 GH 2
Sushui = Xushui 146-147 E 2
Sušice 118 F 4
Susitna, AK 58-59 M 6
Susitna Lake 58-59 O 5
Susitna River 56-57 FG 5
Suslonger 124-125 R 5
Susner 138-139 F 6
Susong 146-147 F 6
Suspiro 106-107 K 3
Susquehanna, PA 72-73 HJ 4
Susquehanna River 72-73 H 5
Susques 111 C 2
Süssah 136-137 J 5
Süssenbrunn, Wien- 113 I bc 1
Sussex [CDN] 63 D 5
Sussex 119 FG 6
Sustut Peak 60 D 1
Susulatna River 58-59 K 5
Susuman 132-133 cd 5
Susung = Susong 146-147 F 6
Susurluk 136-137 C 3
Sütçüler 136-137 D 4
Suthep, Doi — 150-151 B 3
Sutherland, NE 68-69 F 5
Sutherland [CDN] 61 EF 4
Sutherland [ZA] 172 CD 8
Sutherland, Sydney- 161 I a 3
Sutherland Reservoir 68-69 F 5
Sutherlin, OR 66-67 B 4
Sutlej = Satlaj 134-135 L 4
Sutsien = Suqian 142-143 M 5
Su-ts'un = Sucun 146-147 G 4
Sutter Creek, CA 74-75 C 3
Sutton, NE 68-69 H 5
Sutton, WV 72-73 F 5
Sutton, London- 129 II b 2
Suttsu 144-145 ab 2
Sutvik Island 58-59 e 1
Suurberge [ZA ↑ Winterberge] 174-175 F 6
Suurberge [ZA ↙ Winterberge] 174-175 F 7
Suure-Jaani 124-125 E 4
Suur Manamägi 124-125 F 5
Suur väin 124-125 D 4
Suva 148-149 a 2
Suvadiva Atoll 176 ab 2
Suvainiškis 124-125 E 5
Suvorov [island] 156-157 JK 5
Suvorovo 126-127 D 4
Suwa 144-145 M 4
Suwa-ko 144-145 M 4-5
Suwałki 118 L 1
Suwalki = Vilkaviškis 124-125 D 6
Suwanna Phum 150-151 DE 5
Suwannee River 80-81 b 2
Suwannee Sound 80-81 b 2
Ṣuwār, Aṣ- 136-137 J 5
Suwaybit, As- 136-137 H 6
Suwaydā', As- 134-135 D 4
Suwayḥ 134-135 HJ 6
Suwayqīyah, Hawr as- 136-137 LM 6
Ṣuwayr 136-137 J 7
Ṣuwayrah, Aṣ- 136-137 L 6
Suways, As- 164-165 L 2-3
Suways, Khalīj as- 164-165 L 3
Suways, Qanat as- 164-165 L 2
Suweis, Es- = As-Suways 164-165 L 2-3
Suweis, Khalîg es — = Khalīj as-Suways 164-165 L 3
Suweis, Qanât es- = Qanat as-Suways 164-165 L 2
Suwen = Xuwen 146-147 BC 11
Suwŏn 142-143 P 4
Ṣuwwān, 'Arḍ eş — = 'Arḍ aṣ-Ṣawwān 136-137 G 7
Su Xian 142-143 M 5
Suxima = Tsushima 144-145 G 5
Suyut 150-151 E 2
Suzaka 144-145 M 4
Suzdal' 124-125 N 5
Suzhou 142-143 N 5
Suzu 144-145 L 4
Suzuka 144-145 L 5
Suzu misaki 144-145 L 4
Svalbard = Spitsbergen 116-117 k 6-o 5
Svanetskij chrebet 126-127 L 5
Svapa 124-125 K 8
Svappavaara 116-117 J 4
Svār = Suār 138-139 G 3
Svartenhuk Halvø 56-57 Za 3
Svartisen 116-117 EF 4
Sv'atoj Krest' = Prikumsk 126-127 LM 4
Sv'atoj Nos, mys — 132-133 ab 3
Svatovo 126-127 J 2
Svay Chek 150-151 D 6
Svay Daun Keo 150-151 D 6
Svay Rieng 148-149 E 4
Sveagruva 116-117 k 6
Svealand 116-117 E-G 7
Sveča 124-125 Q 4
Svedala 116-117 E 10
Sveg 116-117 F 6
Svelvik 116-117 CD 8
Švenčionėliai 124-125 EF 6
Svendborg 116-117 D 10
Svenskøya 116-117 mn 5
Šventoji 124-125 E 6
Sverdlovo [SU, Vologodskaja Oblast'] 124-125 MN 4
Sverdlovsk [SU, Rossijskaja SFSR] 132-133 L 6
Sverdlovsk [SU, Ukrainskaja SSR] 126-127 JK 2
Sverdrup, ostrov — 132-133 O 3
Sverdrup Islands 56-57 P-T 2
Svessa 124-125 JK 8
Svetac 122-123 F 4
Svetlaja 132-133 a 8
Svetlogorsk [SU, Belorusskaja SSR] 124-125 GH 7
Svetlograd 126-127 L 4
Svetlyj [SU → Orsk] 132-133 L 7
Svetogorsk 124-125 G 3
Svetozarevo 122-123 J 3-4
Svijaga 124-125 R 6
Svilengrad 122-123 LM 5
Svir' [SU, place] 124-125 F 6
Svir [SU, river] 132-133 EF 5
Svirica 124-125 J 3
Svirsk 132-133 T 7
Svir'stroj 124-125 J 3
Svisloč' [SU, place] 124-125 E 7
Svisloč' [SU, river ◁ Berezina] 124-125 FG 7
Svištov 122-123 L 4
Svoboda [SU] 124-125 KL 8
Svobodnyj [SU ↑ Belogorsk] 132-133 YZ 7
Svobodnyj [SU, Saratovskaja Oblast'] 124-125 PQ 7
Svobodnyy = Svobodnyj 132-133 YZ 7
Svolvær 116-117 F 3
Swabian Alb = Schwäbische Alb 118 D 5-E 4
Swabue = Shanwei 146-147 E 10
Swaib, As — = Ash-Shuwayyib 136-137 MN 7
Swaibit, As — = As-Suwaybit 136-137 H 6
Swain Post 62 C 2
Swain Reefs 158-159 K 4
Swains 208 JK 4
Swainsboro, GA 80-81 E 4
Şwaira, Aş — = Aş-Şuwayrah 136-137 L 6
Swakop 174-175 B 2
Swakopmund 172 B 6
Swale 119 F 4
Swalferort = Sõrve säär 124-125 CD 5
Swallow Islands 148-149 I 7
Swāmihalli 140 C 3
Swampscott, MA 84 I c 2
Swanage 119 F 6
Swan Hill 158-159 H 7
Swan Hills 56-57 N 7
Swan Lake [CDN] 61 H 4
Swan Lake [USA] 68-69 FG 3
Swanley 129 II c 2
Swannell Ranges 60 E 1
Swan Range 66-67 G 2
Swan River [CDN, place] 56-57 Q 7
Swan River [CDN, river ◁ Little Slave Lake] 60 K 2
Swan River [CDN, river ◁ Swan Lake] 61 H 4-5
Swansea 119 DE 6
Swansea, SC 80-81 F 4
Swans Island 72-73 M 2-3
Swanton, VT 72-73 K 2
Swanville, MN 70-71 C 3
Swar = Suār 138-139 G 3
Swartberg 174-175 H 6
Swartberge 172 D 8
Swarthmore College 84 III ab 2
Swartkops 174-175 F 7
Swartmodder 174-175 D 5
Swart Nossob 174-175 C 2
Swartplaas 174-175 G 4
Swartrand 174-175 B 3-4
Swartruggens [ZA, Kaapland] 174-175 F 7
Swartruggens [ZA, Transvaal] 174-175 G 3
Swart Umfolozi 174-175 J 4-5
Swasiland 172 F 7
Swāt 134-135 L 3-4
Swatow = Shantou 142-143 M 7
Swaziland 172 F 7
Sweden 116-117 F 8-K 4
Swede Run 84 III d 1-2
Swedesburg, PA 84 III ab 1
Swedru 168-169 E 4
Sweeny, TX 76-77 G 8
Sweetgrass, MT 66-67 GH 1
Sweet Home, OR 66-67 B 3
Sweetwater, TX 64-65 FG 5
Sweetwater River 68-69 B 4
Swellendam 172 D 8
Swenyaung 141 E 5
Świdnica 118 H 3
Świdwin 118 GH 2
Świebodzin 118 G 2
Świecie 118 HJ 2
Swift Current 56-57 P 7-8
Swift River 58-59 K 6
Swinburne, Cape — 56-57 R 3
Swindon 119 F 6
Swinoujście 118 G 2
Swinton Islands = Hswindan Kyûnmyâ 150-151 AB 7
Switzerland 118 CD 5
Sybaris 122-123 G 6
Sycamore, IL 70-71 F 4-5
Sychem = Nābulus 136-137 F 6
Syčovka 124-125 JK 6
Sydney [AUS] 158-159 K 6
Sydney [CDN] 56-57 Y 8
Sydney [Phoenix Islands] 208 JK 3
Sydney, University of — 161 I ab 2
Sydney-Ashfield 161 I a 2
Sydney-Auburn 161 I a 2
Sydney-Balmain 161 I b 2
Sydney-Bankstown 161 I a 2
Sydney-Beverly Hills 161 I a 2
Sydney-Bexley 161 I a 2
Sydney-Botany 161 I b 2
Sydney-Brookvale 161 I b 1
Sydney-Burwood 161 I a 2
Sydney-Campsie 161 I a 2
Sydney-Canterbury 161 I a 2
Sydney-Carlingford 161 I a 1
Sydney-Chatswood 161 I b 1
Sydney-Chullora 161 I a 2
Sydney-Concord 161 I a 2
Sydney-Crows Nest 161 I b 1
Sydney-Drummoyne 161 I a 2
Sydney-Earlwood 161 I a 2
Sydney-Eastwood 161 I a 1
Sydney-Epping 161 I a 1
Sydney-Ermington 161 I a 1
Sydney-Gladesville 161 I a 1
Sydney Harbour Bridge 161 I b 2
Sydney-Hunters Hill 161 I ab 2
Sydney-Hurstville 161 I a 2
Sydney-Kogarah 161 I a 2
Sydney-Kurnell 161 I b 3
Sydney-Lane Cove 161 I ab 1
Sydney-La Perouse 161 I b 2
Sydney-Leichhardt 161 I ab 2
Sydney-Lidcombe 161 I a 2
Sydney-Lindfield 161 I ab 1
Sydney-Manly 161 I b 1
Sydney-Maroubra 161 I b 2
Sydney-Marrickville 161 I ab 2
Sydney-Matraville 161 I b 2
Sydney Mines 63 FG 4
Sydney-Mosman 161 I b 1
Sydney-Newtown 161 I ab 2
Sydney-North Ryde 161 I a 1
Sydney-North Sydney 161 I b 1-2
Sydney-Oatley 161 I a 2
Sydney-Parramatta 161 I a 1
Sydney-Peakhurst 161 I a 2
Sydney-Punchbowl 161 I a 2
Sydney-Ramsgate 161 I a 2
Sydney-Randwick 161 I b 2
Sydney-Redfern 161 I b 2
Sydney-Regents Park 161 I a 2
Sydney-Revesby 161 I a 2
Sydney-Rockdale 161 I a 2
Sydney-Rosebury 161 I b 2
Sydney-Rydalmere 161 I a 1
Sydney-Ryde 161 I a 1
Sydney-Strathfield 161 I a 2
Sydney-Sutherland 161 I a 3
Sydney-Sylvania 161 I a 3
Sydney-Vaucluse 161 I b 2
Sydney-Waverly 161 I b 2
Sydney-Willoughby 161 I b 1
Sydney-Woollahra 161 I b 2
Syene = Aswān 164-165 L 4
Syfergat 174-175 G 6
Syktyvkar 132-133 J 5
Sylacauga, AL 78-79 F 4
Sylarna 116-117 E 6
Sylhet = Silhaṭ 134-135 P 6
Sylt 118 D 1
Sylva 124-125 V 4
Sylva, NC 80-81 E 3
Sylvan Grove, KS 68-69 G 6
Sylvania, GA 80-81 F 4
Sylvania, Sydney- 161 I a 3
Sylvan Lake 60 K 3
Sylvan Pass 66-67 H 3
Sylvester, GA 80-81 E 5
Sylvester, TX 76-77 DE 6
Sylvester, Mount — 63 J 3
Sylvia, KS 68-69 G 7
Sylviaberg 174-175 A 3
Sylvia Hill = Sylviaberg 174-175 A 3
Sym 132-133 Q 5
Sýmē 122-123 M 7
Syndasko 132-133 UV 3
Syowa 53 C 4-5
Syracuse, KS 68-69 F 6-7
Syracuse, NY 64-65 LM 3
Syrdarja 132-133 M 9
Syria 134-135 D 4
Syriam = Thanlyin 148-149 C 3
Syrian Desert 134-135 DE 4
Sýrna 122-123 M 7
Sýros 122-123 L 7
Syrskij 124-125 M 7
Sysladobsis Lake 72-73 MN 2
Sysola 124-125 S 3
Sysran = Syzran' 132-133 N 7
Syt'kovo 124-125 K 5
Sytynja 132-133 YZ 4
Syzran' 132-133 H 7
Syzran'-Kašpirovka 124-125 R 7
Szamos 122-123 K 2
Szamotuły 118 H 2
Szczecin 118 G 2
Szczecinek 118 H 2
Szczytno 118 K 2
Szechuan = Sichuan 142-143 J 6-K 5
Szeged 118 JK 5
Szehsien = Si Xian 146-147 FG 5
Székesfehérvár 118 J 5
Szekszárd 118 J 5
Szemao = Simao 142-143 J 7
Szeming = Xiamen 142-143 M 7
Szentes 118 K 5
Szeping = Siping 142-143 N 3
Szeskie Wzgórza 118 KL 1
Szolnok 118 K 5
Szombathely 118 H 5
Szū-an = Si'an 146-147 G 6
Szū-mao = Simao 142-143 J 7
Szū-ming Shan = Siming Shan 146-147 H 7
Szū-nan = Sinan 146-147 B 8
Szū-p'ing = Siping 142-143 N 3
Szū-shui = Sishui [TJ, Henan] 146-147 D 4
Szū-shui = Sishui [TJ, Shandong] 146-147 F 4
Szū-tao-kou = Sidaogou 144-145 F 2
Szū-t'ing = Siting 146-147 D 3

T

Ta = Da Xian 142-143 K 5
Tababela 96-97 B 2
Tabacal 104-105 D 8
Tabaco 148-149 H 4
Tabacundo 96-97 B 1
Tābah, Bi'r — 173 D 3
Tabajé, Ponta — 92-93 LM 5
Ṭābalbalah 166-167 E 5
Tābalkūzah 166-167 G 5
Tabang Chhu 141 B 2
Tabankort 164-165 D 5
Tabankulu 174-175 H 6
Tabar Islands 148-149 h 5
Tabarka = Ṭabarqah 164-165 F 1
Ṭabarqah 164-165 F 1
Ṭabas 134-135 H 4
Tabasará, Serranía de — 88-89 EF 10
Tabasco 64-65 H 8
Tabašino 124-125 QR 5
Tabatière, la — 63 G 2
Tabatinga [BR, Amazonas] 92-93 F 5
Tabatinga [BR, São Paulo] 102-103 H 4
Tabatinga, Serra — 98-99 GH 4
Tabatinga, Serra da — 100-101 B 6
Tabayin = Dīpéyin 141 D 4
Tabelbala = Tābalbalah 166-167 E 5
Tabelkoza = Tābalkūzah 166-167 G 5
Taber 56-57 O 7
Taberdga = Sharshar 166-167 K 2
Taberg 116-117 EF 9
Tabiazo 96-97 B 1
Tabira 100-101 F 4
Tabiteuea 208 H 3
Tablada, La Matanza- 110 III b 2
Tablang Dsong = Tāplejung 138-139 L 4
Tablas, Cabo — 106-107 AB 3
Tablas, Las — 88-89 FG 11
Tablas Island 148-149 H 4
Tāblat 166-167 H 1
Tablazo, El — 94-95 F 2
Tablazo de Ica 96-97 CD 9
Table, Île de la — = Đao Cai Ban 148-149 E 2
Table Bay = Tafelbaai 174-175 C 7
Table Cape 161 H 4
Table Island 155 I b 2
Table Mount 58-59 Q 2
Table Mount = Tafelberg 174-175 BC 8
Table Mountain 66-67 G 3
Table Rock 68-69 H 5
Table Rock Lake 78-79 C 2
Tablón, El — [CO, Nariña] 94-95 C 7
Tablón, El — [CO, Sucre] 94-95 D 3
Taboada [RA] 106-107 F 1-2
Taboco, Rio — 102-103 E 4
Taboga 64-65 b 3
Taboga, Isla — 64-65 bc 3
Taboguilla, Isla — 64-65 bc 3
Taboleiro 100-101 E 5
Tābor 118 G 4
Tabora 172 F 3
Tabor City, NC 80-81 G 3
Taborda, Serra — 100-101 F 5
Tabou 164-165 C 8
Tabris = Tabrīz 134-135 F 3
Tabrīz 134-135 F 3
Tábua, Lago — 100-101 C 2
Tabu-dong 144-145 G 4
Tabūk 134-135 D 5
Tabuleirinho, Cachoeira 98-99 K 5
Tabuleiro 98-99 JK 7
Tabuleiro, Morro do — 102-103 H 7
Täby 116-117 GH 8
Tabyn-Bogdo-Ola = Tavan Bogd uul 142-143 F 2
Tacabamba 96-97 B 5
Tacagua 91 II a 1
Tacaimbó 100-101 F 5
Tacambaro de Codallos 86-87 K 8
Tacaná, Volcán de — 86-87 O 10
Tacañitas 106-107 F 2
Tacaratu 100-101 EF 5
Tacarcuna, Cerro — 94-95 C 3
Tacarigua [YV, Nueva Esparta] 94-95 JK 2
Tacarigua [YV, Valencia] 94-95 GH 2-3
Tacarigua, Laguna de — 94-95 J 2
Tacau = Kaohsiung 142-143 MN 7
T'ačev 126-127 A 2
Ta-ch'ang-shan Tao = Dachangshan Dao 144-145 D 3
Tacheng = Chuguchak 142-143 E 2
T'a-ch'êng = Chuguchak 142-143 E 2
Tachi [RC ↘ Pingtung] 146-147 H 10
Tachi [RC ↙ Taipei] 146-147 H 9
Tachia 142-143 MN 7
Ta-ch'iao = Daqiao 146-147 E 7
Tachibana-wan 144-145 GH 6
Tachikawa 144-145 M 5
Tachin = Samut Sakhon 150-151 BC 6
Ta-ching = Dajing 146-147 H 7
Ta-ch'ing Shan = Daqing Shan 142-143 L 3
Táchira 94-95 EF 4
Tachiūmet = Takyūmit 166-167 LM 6
Ta-chou-Tao = Dazhou Dao 150-151 H 3
Tachrirt, Djebel — = Jabal Tashrīrt 166-167 J 2
Tachta 132-133 a 7
Tachta-Bazar 134-135 J 3
Tachtabrod 132-133 M 7
Tachtojamsk 132-133 de 5
Ta-ch'üan = Daquan 142-143 H 3
Tacima 100-101 G 4
Tacloban 148-149 HJ 4
Tacna [PE, administrative unit] 96-97 F 10
Tacna [PE, place] 92-93 E 8
Tacoma, WA 64-65 B 2
Taconic Range 72-73 K 3-4
Tacony, Philadelphia-, PA 84 III c 1
Tacony Creek 84 III c 1
Tacony Creek Park 84 III c 1
Taco Pozo 104-105 E 9
Tacora, Volcán — 111 C 1
Tacuaras 102-103 CD 7
Tacuarembó [ROU, administrative unit] 106-107 JK 4
Tacuarembó [ROU, place] 111 EF 4
Tacuarembó, Río — 106-107 K 4
Tacuatí 102-103 D 5
Tacuato 94-95 G 2
Tacuba, Ciudad de México- 91 I b 2
Tacubaya, Ciudad de México- 91 I b 2
Tacural 106-107 G 3
Tacuru 102-103 E 5
Tacutú, Rio — 98-99 HJ 3
Tāda Kaṇḍera 138-139 C 3
Tadami gawa 144-145 M 4
Tadarimana; Ribeiro — 102-103 E 2
Tadau = Tandā'ū 141 D 5
Tadein 150-151 B 5
Tademaït, Plateau du — = Tādmāit 164-165 E 3
Tādepallegūdem 140 E 2
Ta Det, Phnom — 150-151 D 6
Tadet, Sebkret — = Sabkhat Tādit 166-167 M 3
Tāḍipatri = Tādpatri 134-135 M 7-8
Tādīsat, Ḥāssī — 166-167 K 6
Tādit, Sabkhat — 166-167 M 3
Tadjemout = Tajmūt 166-167 H 7
Tādjerouïn = Tājarwīn 166-167 L 2
Tadjerouma = Tājrūmah 166-167 H 3
Tadjoura 164-165 N 6
Tadjoura, Golfe de — 164-165 N 6
Tādmāīt 164-165 E
Tadmur 134-135 D 4
Tadnist, Hassi — = Ḥāssī Tādīsat 166-167 K 6
Tadó 94-95 C 5
Tadoussac 56-57 X 8
Tādpatri 134-135 M 7-8
Tadum = Tradum 142-143 E 6
Tadzhik Soviet Socialist Republic 134-135 KL 3
T'aean 144-145 F 4
T'aebaek-san 144-145 G 4
T'aebaek-sanmaek 142-143 O 4
Taebu-do 144-145 F 4
T'aech'ŏn 144-145 E 3
Taech'ŏng-do 144-145 E 4
Taedong-gang 144-145 EF 3
Taegu 142-143 O 4
Tae-hŭksan-do 144-145 E 5
Taehwa-do 144-145 E 3
Taejŏn 142-143 O 4
Taejŏng 144-145 EF 6
Tae-muŭi-do 144-145 EF 4
Ta-êrh Hu = Dalaj Nur 142-143 M 3
T'aet'an 144-145 E 3
Tae-yŏnp'yŏng-do 144-145 E 4
Tafalla 120-121 G 7
Tafalnī, Rā's — 166-167 AB 4
Ta-fan = Dafan 146-147 E 7
Tafaraut = Ṭarfāyah 164-165 B 3
Tafāsasat, Wādī — 164-165 F 4
Tafassasset, Ouèd — = Wādī Tafāsasat 164-165 F 4
Tafassasset, Ténéré du — 164-165 FG 4
Tafdasat 164-165 F 3-4
Tafelbaai 174-175 C 7
Tafelberg [A] 113 I a 1
Tafelberg [SME] 98-99 K 3

Tafelberg [ZA, mountain] 174-175 BC 8
Tafelberg [ZA, place] 174-175 F 6
Tafelney, Cap — = Râs Tafalnî 166-167 AB 4
Tafesrit, Hassi — = Ḥâssî Tafzirt 166-167 K 7
Ṭafîlah, Aṭ- 136-137 F 7
Tâfîlâl't 166-167 DE 4
Tafinegoûlt = Tâfîngûlt 166-167 B 4
Tâfîngûlt 166-167 B 4
Tafí Viejo 111 C 3
Tafôrhalt = Tâfûghâh 166-167 E 2
Tafrannt = Tafrânt 166-167 D 2
Tafrânt 166-167 D 2
Tafrâût 166-167 B 5
Tafresh 136-137 N 5
Tafresh, Kûh-e — 136-137 NO 5
Taft, CA 74-75 D 5
Taft, OK 76-77 G 5
Taft, TX 76-77 F 8-9
Taftân, Kûh-e — 134-135 J 5
Tâfûghâh 166-167 E 2
Tafzirt, Ḥâssî — 166-167 K 7
Tagagawik River 58-59 H 4
Tagalak Island 58-59 j 5
Tagalgan 142-143 H 4
Taganrog 126-127 J 3
Taganrogskij zaliv 126-127 HJ 3
Tâgau 148-149 C 2
Tagaung 141 E 4
Tagawa = Takawa 144-145 H 6
Tagbilaran 148-149 H 5
Tag-Dheer 164-165 b 2
Tagelswangen 128 IV b 1
Taghbâlt 166-167 D 4
Taghbâlt, Wâd — 166-167 D 4
Taghghîsht 166-167 B 5
Tâghît 164-165 D 2
Tagiûra = Tâjûrâ' 164-165 G 2
Tagla Khar 138-139 H 2
Tagmar 138-139 M 3
Tagna 94-95 b 2
Tâgoûnît = Tâgûnît 166-167 D 5
Tagrag Tsangpo 138-139 L 2
Tagsut = Ṭahâr as-Sûq 166-167 DE 2
Tagtse 138-139 M 3
Tagu = Taegu 142-143 O 4
Tagua, La — 94-95 D 8
Taguatinga [BR, Distrito Federal] 92-93 K 8
Taguatinga [BR, Goiás] 92-93 K 7
Taguedoufat 168-169 H 1-2
Taguine = Tâḥîn 166-167 H 2
Tagula 148-149 h 7
Tagum 148-149 J 5
Tâgûnît 166-167 D 5
Tagus = Tajo 120-121 F 8
Tahâlah 166-167 D 2
Tahan, Gunung — 148-149 D 6
Tahara 144-145 L 5
Ṭahâr as-Sûq 166-167 DE 2
Tahat 164-165 F 4
Tahaungdam 141 E 1
Tahawndam = Tahaungdam 141 E 1
Tâhîn 166-167 H 2
Tahiti 156-157 K 5
Tahlequah, OK 76-77 G 5
Tahltan 58-59 W 7
Tahoe, Lake — 64-65 BC 4
Tahoe City, CA 74-75 C 3
Tahoe Valley, CA 74-75 CD 3
Tahoka, TX 76-77 D 6
Tahola, WA 66-67 A 2
Tahoua 164-165 F 6
Taḥrîr, At- 173 AB 2
Ta-hsien = Da Xian 142-143 K 5
Ta-hsin-tien = Daxindian 146-147 H 3
Tahsis 60 D 5
Ta Hsü = Chimei Hsü 146-147 G 10
Ta-hsüeh Shan = Daxue Shan 142-143 J 5-6
Ṭaḥṭâ 164-165 L 3
Tahtacı = Borlu 136-137 C 3
Tahtalı dağı 136-137 D 4
Tahtalı dağlar 136-137 F 4-G 3
Tahtsa Peak 60 D 3
Ta-hu = Tachia 142-143 MN 7
Tahua 104-105 C 6
Ta-hua Chiao = Dahua Jiao 150-151 H 3
Tahulandang, Pulau — 148-149 J 6
Tahuna 148-149 HJ 6
Ta-hung Shan = Dahong Shan 146-147 D 6
Ta-hu-shan = Dahushan 144-145 D 2
Taï 164-165 C 7
Taï, Parc National de — 168-169 D 4
Ta'ian [TJ, Liaoning] 144-145 D 2
Ta'ian [TJ, Shandong] 142-143 M 4
Tai Au Mun 155 I b 2
Taiba 168-169 A 2
Taibai 146-147 B 3
Taibai Shan 142-143 K 5
Taibei = Taipei 142-143 N 6-7
Taïbet-el-Gueblia = Ṭâyabat al-Janûbiyah 166-167 K 3
Taicang 146-147 H 6
T'ai-chou Wan = Taizhou Wan 146-147 H 7
Taichû = Taichung 142-143 N 7
Taichung 142-143 MN 7
T'ai-chung = Taichung 142-143 MN 7
T'ai-chung-hsien = Fêngyüan 146-147 H 9
Tâïdâlt 166-167 B 5
Taiden = Taejŏn 142-143 O 4
Taidong = Taitung 142-143 N 7
Taieri River 161 D 7
Ṭâ'if, Aṭ- 134-135 E 6
Taigu 142-143 L 4
Tai Hang, Victoria- 155 I b 2
Taihang Shan 142-143 LM 4
Taihape 161 FG 4
Taihe [TJ, Anhui] 146-147 E 5
Taihe [TJ, Jiangxi] 142-143 L 6
Taihei yô 144-145 K 7-O 3
Taihing = Taixing 142-143 N 5
T'ai-ho = Taihe [TJ, Anhui] 146-147 E 5
Taiho = Taihe [TJ, Jiangxi] 142-143 L 6
Taihoku = Taipei 142-143 N 6-7
Taihsien = Dai Xian 146-147 D 2
Tai Hu [TJ, lake] 142-143 MN 5
Taihu [TJ, place] 146-147 F 6
Taikang 146-147 E 4
Taiki 144-145 c 2
Taikkyi 141 DE 7
Tai Koo Shing, Victoria- 155 I b 2
Taiku = Taigu 142-143 L 4
Taikyu = Taegu 142-143 O 4
Tailai 142-143 N 2
T'ai-lai = Tailai 142-143 N 2
Tailem Bend 158-159 GH 7
Tailie 146-147 B 8
Tai Long Head 155 I b 2
Taim 111 F 4
Tai Muang 152-153 BC 1
Taimyr Lake = ozero Tajmyr 132-133 TU 3
Taimyr Peninsula = Tajmyr 132-133 S-U 2
Tain [GB] 119 D 3
Tain [GH] 168-169 E 4
Tainan 142-143 MN 7
T'ai-nan = Tainan 142-143 MN 7
Tainão = Tainan 142-143 MN 7
Tainaron, Akrôtêrion — 122-123 K 7
Taining 146-147 F 8
Tai No 155 I b 1
Taiô 102-103 GH 7
Taiobeiras 102-103 LM 1
T'ai-pai Shan = Taibai Shan 146-147 A 4-5
Taipale 116-117 N 6
Taipas 100-101 A 7
Taipeh = Taipei 142-143 N 6-7
Taipei 142-143 N 6-7
Taiping [MAL] 148-149 CD 5-6
Taiping [TJ, Anhui] 146-147 G 6
Taiping [TJ, Guangdong] 146-147 D 10
Taiping [TJ, Guangxi Zhuangzu Zizhiqu] 146-147 C 10
Taipingshao 144-145 E 2
Taiping Wan 146-147 G 3
Taiping Yang 142-143 O 8-R 5
Taipinsan = Miyako-jima 142-143 O 7
Taipu 100-101 G 3
Taisei 144-145 ab 2
Tai Seng 154 III b 2
Taisha 144-145 J 5
Tai Shan [TJ, mountains] 146-147 F 3
Taishan [TJ, place] 146-147 D 10
Tai Shan = Dai Shan 146-147 HJ 6
Taishan Liedao 146-147 H 8
Taishun 142-143 MN 6
Taisien = Tai Xian 146-147 H 5
Ta'iss = Ta'izz 134-135 E 8
Tai Tam Bay 155 I b 2
Taitam Peninsula 155 I b 2
Tai Tam Reservoirs 155 I b 2
Taitao, Cabo — 111 A 7
Taitao, Península de — 111 AB 7
T'ai-tchong = Taichung 142-143 MN 7
Taitô = Taitung 142-143 N 7
Taitô, Tôkyô- 155 III b 1
Taitsang = Taicang 146-147 H 6
Taitung 142-143 N 7
T'ai-tzŭ Ho = Taizi He 144-145 D 2
Taivalkoski 116-117 N 5
Taivassalo 116-117 JK 7
Taiwa 144-145 N 3
Tai Wai 155 I b 1
Tai Wan [HK] 155 I b 2
Taiwan [RC] 142-143 N 7
Taiwan Haihsia 142-143 M 7-N 6
Taiwan Haixia = Taiwan Haihsia 142-143 M 7-N 6
Taiwan Strait = Taiwan Haihsia 142-143 M 7-N 6
Tai Wan Tau 155 I b 2
Tai Xian 146-147 H 5
Taixing 142-143 N 5
Taiyanggong, Beijing- 155 II b 2
Taiyuan 142-143 L 4
T'ai-yüan = Taiyuan 142-143 L 4
Taiyue Shan 146-147 CD 3
Taizhong = Taichung 142-143 MN 7
Taizhou 142-143 MN 5
Taizhou Wan 146-147 H 7
Taizi He 144-145 D 2
Ta'izz 134-135 E 8
Tāj, At- 164-165 J 4
Taj, El — = At-Tāj 164-165 J 4
Tajan 148-149 F 7
Tajarḥî 164-165 G 4
Tâjarwîn 166-167 L 2
Tajdžinar nuur 142-143 GH 4
Tajga 132-133 PQ 6
Tajgonos, mys — 132-133 ef 5
Tajgonos, poluostrov — 132-133 f 5
Tajim, El — 86-87 M 7
Tajima 144-145 M 4
Tajique, NM 76-77 A 5
Tajis 134-135 G 8
Tajjal 138-139 B 4
Tajmura 132-133 ST 5
Tajmût [DZ, Jabal 'Amûr] 166-167 H 7
Tâjmût [DZ, Sahara] 166-167 H 3
Tajmyr, ozero — 132-133 TU 3
Tajmyr, poluostrov — 132-133 R-U 2
Tajmyrskij Nacional'nyj Okrug = Dolgano-Nenets Autonomous Area 132-133 P-U 3
Tajo 120-121 F 8
Tajpur 154 II a 1
Tâjrûmah 166-167 H 3
Tajsara, Cordillera de — 104-105 D 7
Tajšet 132-133 S 6
Tajsir 142-143 H 2
Tajumulco, Volcán de — 64-65 H 8
Tajuña 120-121 F 8
T'a-jung = Tarong 141 F 1-2
Tajûrâ' 164-165 G 2
Tak 148-149 C 3
Takâb 136-137 M 4
Takaba 171 E 2
Takachiho = Mitai 144-145 H 6
Takachu 174-175 DE 2
Takada 142-143 Q 4
Takada = Bungotakada 144-145 H 6
Takada = Rikuzen-Takata 144-145 NO 3
Takahagi 144-145 N 4
Takahashi 144-145 J 5
Takahashi-gawa 144-145 J 5
Takahe, Mount — 53 B 25-26
Takaido, Tôkyô- 155 III a 1
Takaishi 155 III a 2
Takalar 148-149 G 8
Takamatsu 142-143 PQ 5
Takamatu = Takamatsu 142-143 PQ 5
Takamori 144-145 H 6
Takanabe 144-145 H 6
Takane 155 III d 1
Takao = Kaohsiung 142-143 MN 7
Takaoka 142-143 Q 4
Takapuna 158-159 O 7
Takasaki 142-143 Q 4
Takataka 148-149 k 6
Takawa 144-145 H 6
Takayama 144-145 L 4
Takayanagi 155 III c 3
Takefu 144-145 KL 5
Takemachi = Taketa 144-145 H 6
Takengon 148-149 C 6
Takenotsuka, Tôkyô- 155 III b 1
Takéo 148-149 D 4
Take-shima [J ↖ Oki] 144-145 HJ 4
Take-shima [J, Ôsumi shotô] 144-145 H 7
Tâkestân 136-137 NO 4
Taketa 144-145 H 6
Takhini River 58-59 T 6
Takhli 150-151 C 5
Takhlîs, Bi'r — 173 AB 6
Takht-e Jämshîd = Persepolis 134-135 G 4
Takht-e Soleymân 136-137 O 4
Taki 155 III d 1
Takieta 168-169 H 2
Takikawa 144-145 b 2
Takinogawa, Tôkyô- 155 III b 1
Takinoue 144-145 c 1
Takipy 61 H 3
Takiyuak Lake 56-57 O 4
Takkuna neem 124-125 CD 4
Takla Lake 56-57 LM 6
Takla Landing 60 DE 2
Takla Makan 142-143 D-F 4
Takla Makan Chöli 142-143 D-F 4
Takla River 60 D 2
Tako-bana 144-145 J 5
Takolekaju, Pegunungan — 152-153 N 6-O 7
Takoradi = Sekondi-Takoradi 164-165 D 7-8
Takotna, AK 58-59 JK 5
Takslesluk Lake 58-59 F 6
Takslesluk Lake 58-59 F 6
Takua Pa 148-149 C 5
Takua Thung 150-151 B 8
Takû Glacier 58-59 U 7
Ta-ku Ho = Dagu He 146-147 H 3
Takum 168-169 H 4
Taku River 58-59 V 7
Tâkwayat, Wâdî — 164-165 E 4
Takyu = Taegu 142-143 O 4
Takyûmît 166-167 LM 6
Tala [ET] 173 B 2
Tala [MEX] 86-87 J 7
Tala [ROU] 106-107 K 5
Tâla = Tâlah 166-167 L 2
Tala, El — [RA, San Luis] 106-107 D 4
Tala, El — [RA, Tucumán] 104-105 D 9-10
Talacasto 111 C 4
Talagante 106-107 B 4
Talagapa 108-109 E 4
Talagapa, Pampa de — 108-109 EF 4
Talâgh 166-167 F 2
Tâlah 166-167 L 2
Tâlai [IND] 140 C 4
Ta Lai [VN] 150-151 F 7
Talaimannar = Taleimannârama 134-135 MN 9
Tâlâinot = Tâlâinût 166-167 D 2
Tâlâînût 166-167 D 2
Talâjâ 138-139 CD 7
Tal'menka 132-133 PQ 7
Talak 164-165 EF 5
Talakmau, Gunung — 152-153 CD 5-6
Talamanca, Cordillera de — 88-89 E 10
Talamba 138-139 D 2
Talampaya, Campo de — 106-107 CD 2-3
Talamuyuna 106-107 D 2
Talana 174-175 J 5
Talang, Gunung — 152-153 D 6
Tala Norte 106-107 F 3
Talanyené, Rapides de — 168-169 E 3
Tâlaqân 136-137 O 4
Talar, Tigre-El — 110 III b 1
Talara 92-93 C 5
Talas 132-133 N 9
Talasea 148-149 gh 6
Talasheri = Tellicherry 140 B 5
Talasheri = Tellicherry 140 B 5
Talâtâ', At- = Ath-Thâlâtha' [MA, Marrâkush] 166-167 BC 3-4
Talâtâ', At- = Ath-Thâlâtha' [MA, Miknâs] 166-167 D 2
Talata Mafara 168-169 G 2
Talat Chum = Wang Thong 150-151 C 4
Talaud, Kepulauan — 148-149 J 6
Talaut Islands = Kepulauan Talaud 148-149 J 6
Talavera, Isla — 106-107 J 1
Talavera de la Reina 120-121 E 8-9
Talawdî 164-165 L 6
Talawgyi = Htâlawgyi 141 E 3
Talberg 128 III b 1
Talbingo 160 J 5
Talbot, Cape — 158-159 E 2
Talbot, Mount — 158-159 E 5
Talbotton, GA 78-79 G 4
Talca 111 B 5
Talca, Punta — 106-107 AB 4
Talcan, Isla — 108-109 C 4
Tâlcher 138-139 K 7
Talco, TX 76-77 G 6
Talcuhuano 111 AB 5
Taldykuduk 126-127 O 1
Taldy-Kurgan 132-133 OP 8
Talegaon Dâbhâde 140 AB 1
Taleimannârama 134-135 MN 9
Tal-e Khosravî 134-135 G 4
Talembote = Tâlâînût 166-167 D 2
Talemzane = Tâlamzân 166-167 HJ 3
Talent, OR 66-67 B 4
Tâlera 138-139 E 5
Tale Sap = Thale Luang 148-149 D 5
Talghemt, Tizi 'n — = Tizi 'N Talrhemt 166-167 D 3
Talguppa 140 B 3
Tali = Dali [TJ, Shaanxi] 146-147 B 4
Tali = Dali [TJ, Yunnan] 142-143 HJ 6
Taliabu, Pulau — 148-149 HJ 7
Talibîyah, At- 170 II ab 2
Talica [SU, Kirov] 124-125 S 4
Talickij 124-125 Q 4
Talicnioc 96-97 D 7
Ta-lien = Lüda-Dalian 142-143 N 4
Tâlîganj = Tollygunge 138-139 M 6
Talîghmah 166-167 K 1
Talihina, OK 76-77 G 5
Ta-li Ho = Dali He 146-147 B 3
Tâlîkota 140 C 2
Talimâ 92-93 H 4
Talinay, Altos de — 106-107 B 3
Ta-ling Ho = Daling He 144-145 G 2
Talin Shan = Huaiyu Shan 146-147 F 7
Talîouîn = Talîwîn 166-167 C 4
Tâlîparamb = Taliparamba 140 B 4
Taliparamba 140 B 4
Talita 106-107 E 4
Taliwang 148-149 G 8
Talîwîn 166-167 C 4
Talju, Jabal — 164-165 K 6
Talkeetna, AK 58-59 M 5
Talkeetna Mountains 56-57 G 5
Talkeetna River 58-59 N 5
Talkheh Rûd 136-137 M 3
Talkôt 138-139 H 3
Talladega, AL 64-65 J 5
Tall adh-Dhakwah 136-137 G 6
Tall 'Afar 136-137 K 4
Tallahassee, FL 64-65 K 5
Tall al-Abyaḍ 136-137 H 4
Tall al-'Amârinah 173 B 4
Tall al Mismâḥ 136-137 G 6
Tallapoosa, GA 78-79 G 4
Tall as-Sam'ân 136-137 H 4
Tallassee, AL 78-79 G 4
Tall Bisah 136-137 G 5
Tallenga 96-97 C 6-7
Tall Ḥalaf 136-137 HJ 4
Tallî 138-139 B 3
Tallin = Tallinn 132-133 CD 6
Tallinn 132-133 CD 6
Tallinn-Nõmme 124-125 E 4
Tall Jâb 136-137 G 6
Tall Kalah 136-137 G 5
Tall Kayf 136-137 K 4
Tall Kujik 136-137 JK 4
Tall Mânûk 136-137 H 6
Tall Tâmir 136-137 J 4
Tall Timbers, New Orleans-, LA 85 I c 2
Tallulah, LA 78-79 D 4
Tall Umm Karâr 136-137 H 6
Tall 'Uwaynât 136-137 JK 4
Talmage 61 G 6
Tal'menka 132-133 PQ 7
Talmist 166-167 B 4
Talnach 132-133 QR 4
Tal'noje 126-127 E 2
Talo = Nantong 142-143 N 5
Taloda 138-139 DE 7
Talôdî = Talawdî 164-165 L 6
Taloga, OK 76-77 E 4
Talok 152-153 N 5
Talong Mai 150-151 F 6
Talovaja 126-127 K 1
Talpa, TX 76-77 E 7
Talpa de Allende 86-87 H 7
Talrhemt, Tizi N — 166-167 D 3
Talsara 138-139 K 6
Talsi 124-125 D 5
Talsinnt = Talsînt 166-167 E 3
Talsînt 166-167 E 3
Taltal 111 B 3
Taltal, Punta — 104-105 A 9
Taltal, Quebrada de — 104-105 AB 9
Taltson River 56-57 O 5
Ta Luang, Ko — 150-151 B 8
Taludaa 152-153 P 5
Taluk 152-153 D 6
Talumphuk, Laem — 150-151 C 8
Talvâr, Rûdkhâneh — 136-137 MN 5
Talvik 116-117 K 2
Talwat 166-167 C 4
Talwood 160 J 2
Talyawalka Creek 160 F 3-4
Talzazah 166-167 E 4
Tama, IA 70-71 D 5
Tama [J] 155 III b 2
Tama [RA] 106-107 D 3
Tamabo, Pegunungan — 152-153 L 4
Tamâdah 164-165 E 4
Tamagawa, Tôkyô- 155 III ab 2
Tamaghzah 166-167 KL 2
Tamajirdayn, Wâdî — 166-167 G 7
Tamala 124-125 O 7
Tamalameque 94-95 E 3
Tamale 164-165 D 7
Taman' [SU, Krasnodarskaja Oblast'] 126-127 H 4
Taman [SU, Perm'skaja Oblast'] 124-125 UV 4
Tamana [J] 144-145 H 6
Tamana [Kiribati] 208 H 3
Tamaná, Cerro — 94-95 CD 5
Ṭamanâr 166-167 B 4
Tamanârt, Wâd — 166-167 B 5
Tamanduateí 110 II b 2
Tamangueyú 106-107 H 7
Tamaniquá 98-99 F 6
Taman Kebangsaan 150-151 D 10
Taman Kebangsaan King George Vth 150-151 D 10
Tamano 144-145 JK 5
Tamanrâsat 164-165 EF 4
Tamanrâsat, Wâdî — 164-165 E 4
Taman Sari, Jakarta- 154 IV a 1
Tamanthi = Tamanzî 141 D 3
Tamanzî 141 D 3
Tamaqua, PA 72-73 J 4
Tamaquari, Ilha — 98-99 F 5
Tamar 138-139 K 6
Tâmara 94-95 E 5
Tamarugal, Pampa del — 111 C 1-2
Tamâsi 118 HJ 5
Tamâsîn 166-167 JK 3
Tamatama 94-95 HJ 6
Tamatave = Toamasina 172 JK 5
Tamaulipas 64-65 G 6-7
Tamaulipas, Sierra de — 86-87 L 6
Tamaya 106-107 B 3
Tamaya, Río — 96-97 E 6
Tamayama 144-145 N 3
Tamazula de Gordiano 86-87 J 8
Tamazunchale 86-87 KL 6-7
Tambach 171 CD 2
Tambacounda 164-165 B 6
Tambâ Kosî 138-139 L 4
Tambaqui 92-93 G 6
Tambaram 140 E 4
Tambaú 102-103 J 4
També 100-101 G 4
Tambej 132-133 N 3
Tambelan, Pulau — 152-153 GH 5
Tambelan, Pulau-pulau — 148-149 E 6
Tambería, Cerro — 106-107 C 2
Tamberías 106-107 C 3
Tambillo 96-97 B 5
Tambillos 106-107 B 3
Tambo [PE, Ayacucho] 96-97 DE 8
Tambo [PE, Cajamarca] 96-97 B 5
Tambo [PE, Loreto] 96-97 D 6
Tambo, El — [CO, Cauca] 92-93 D 4
Tambo, El — [CO, Nariño] 94-95 C 7
Tambo, El — [EC] 96-97 B 3
Tambo, Río — [PE ◁ Pacific Ocean] 96-97 F 10
Tambo, Río — [PE ◁ Río Ucayali] 92-93 E 7
Tambogrande, Pampa de — 96-97 DE 9
Tambo Gregoria 96-97 E 6
Tambohorano 172 H 5
Tambolongang, Pulau — 152-153 NO 9
Tambopata, Río — 96-97 G 8
Tambo Quemado 96-97 D 9
Tambora, Gunung — 148-149 G 8
Tambora, Jakarta- 154 IV a 1
Tambo Real 96-97 B 6
Tambores 106-107 JK 3
Tamboriaco 98-99 B 9
Tamboril 100-101 D 3
Tamboritha, Mount — 160 H 6
Tamboryacu, Río — 96-97 D 2
Tambov 124-125 N 7
Tâmbraparni 140 D 6
Tamburi 100-101 D 7
Tamč 142-143 G 2
Tam Cag Bulak = Tamsagbulag 142-143 M 2
Tam Cân = Câu Ke 150-151 EF 8
Tamchhog Khamba 138-139 J 2
Tamdah 166-167 B 3
Tam Đao 150-151 E 2
Tamdybulak 132-133 L 9
Tame 94-95 F 4
Tâmega 120-121 D 8
Tamel Aike 108-109 D 7
Tamerza = Tamaghzah 166-167 KL 2
Tamgak, Mont — 164-165 F 5
Tamgrût 166-167 D 4
Tamiahua, Laguna de — 64-65 G 7
Tamiami Canal 80-81 c 4
Tamiḷnâḍ = Carnatic 134-135 M 8-9
Tamil Nadu 134-135 M 8-9
Tamin 152-153 K 4
Ta'mîn, At- 136-137 KL 5
Taming = Daming 146-147 E 3
Tâmîr'z'qîd 164-165 AB 5
Tâmîyah 173 B 3
Tamiyanglayang 152-153 L 7
Tamjûl 166-167 J 1
Tam Ky 148-149 E 3
Tamlelt, Plaine de — = Sahl Tâmlilt 166-167 E 3
Tâmlilt al-Gadîd 166-167 C 4
Tamlûk 138-139 L 6
Tammerfors = Tampere 116-117 K 7
Tammisaari = Ekenäs 116-117 K 7
Tampa, FL 64-65 K 6
Tampa Bay 64-65 K 6
Tampere 116-117 KL 7
Tampico 64-65 G 7
Tampico, MT 68-69 C 1
Tampin 148-149 D 6
Tampines 154 III b 1
Tampoketsa, Plateau du — = Causse du Kelifely 172 HJ 5
Tampulonanjing, Gunung — 152-153 CD 5
Tâmralipti = Tâmluk 138-139 L 6
Tâmraparṇi = Tâmbraparni 140 D 6
Ṭamrîdah 134-135 G 8
Tamsagbulag 142-143 M 2
Tamsal = Tamsalu 124-125 F 4
Tamsalu 124-125 F 4
Tâmshikiṭ 164-165 BC 5
Tamshiyacu 96-97 E 3
Tamshiyacu 94-95 a 2-3
Tamû 141 D 3
Tamud = Thamûd 134-135 F 7
Tamuín, Río — 86-87 L 7
Tâmur 138-139 L 4
Tamworth [AUS] 158-159 K 6
Tamyang 144-145 F 5
Tan, Nam — 141 F 5
Tana [EAK] 172 GH 2
Tana [N, place] 116-117 N 2
Tana [N, river] 116-117 M 2-3
Tana [RCH] 104-105 B 6
Tana [Vanuatu] 158-159 N 3
Tana, Kelay — 164-165 M 6
Tanabe 144-145 K 6
Tanabi 102-103 H 4
Tanabu = Mutsu 144-145 N 2
Tanacross, AK 56-57 H 5
Tanad, Stung — 150-151 D 6
Tanadak Island 58-59 k 4
Tanada Lake 58-59 PQ 5
Ta n'Adar 164-165 F 5
Tanafjord 116-117 N 2
Tanaga Bay 58-59 t 7
Tanaga Island 52 D 36-1
Tanaga Pass 58-59 tu 7
Tanâgra 122-123 K 6
Tanaguarena 91 II c 1
Tanaguarena, Punta — 91 II c 1
Tanah Abang, Jakarta- 154 IV a 2
Tanahbala, Pulau — 148-149 C 7
Tanahbato 148-149 C 6
Tanahgrogot 148-149 G 7
Tanahjampea, Pulau — 148-149 H 8
Tanahmasa, Pulau — 148-149 C 6-7
Tanah Menah 148-149 D 5
Tanahmerah 148-149 LM 8
Tanah-tinggi Cameron 148-149 D 6
Tanah Tinggi Idjen = Tanahtinggiljen 148-149 r 9-10
Tanahtinggiljen 152-153 L 9-10
Tanai Kha = Taning Hka 141 E 2-3
Tanak, Cape — 58-59 m 4
Tanakeke, Pulau — 148-149 G 8
Tanakpur 138-139 GH 3
Tanal 168-169 E 2
Taṇamalwila 140 E 7
Tanambo, Pegunungan — 152-153 L 4
Tanami 158-159 E 3
Tanami Desert 158-159 F 3
Tân An [VN ↓ Ca Mâu] 150-151 E 8
Tân An [VN ↙ Thành Phô Hô Chí Minh] 150-151 F 7
Tân An = Hiệp Đưc 150-151 G 5
Tanana, AK 56-57 F 4
Tananarive = Antananarivo 172 J 5
Tanana River 56-57 G 5
Tânant = Tânânt 166-167 C 4
Tânânt 166-167 C 4
Tân Âp 148-149 E 3
Tana River 58-59 Q 6
Tânaro 122-123 B 3
Tanârût, Wâdî — 166-167 M 4-5
Tanashi 155 III a 1
Ṭanburah 164-165 K 7
Tancacha 106-107 F 4
Tân Châu 150-151 E 7
Tanchavur = Thanjâvar 134-135 MN 8
Tancheng 146-147 G 4
Tan Chiang = Dan Jiang 146-147 C 5
Tanchoj 132-133 TU 7
Tanch'ŏn 144-145 G 2
Tanchow = Dan Xian 142-143 K 8
Tancítaro, Pico de — 64-65 F 8
Tânda [IND ↘ Faizâbâd] 138-139 J 4
Tânda [IND ↗ Morâdâbâd] 138-139 G 3
Tandag 148-149 J 5
Tandaho = Tendaho 164-165 N 6
Ṭandârei 122-123 M 3
Tandâ'û 141 D 5
Tandianwali = Ṭândiyânwâla 138-139 D 2
Tandil 111 E 5
Tandil, Sierra del — 106-107 H 6
Ṭândiyânwâla 138-139 D 2
Ṭanḍo Âdam 138-139 B 5
Ṭanḍo Allahyâr 138-139 B 5
Ṭanḍo Bâgo 138-139 B 5
Ṭanḍo Jâm 138-139 B 5
Ṭanḍo Muhammad Khân 138-139 B 5
Tandou Lake 160 EF 4
Tandrârah 166-167 EF 3
Tandulâ Tâl = Tandula Tank 138-139 H 7
Tandula Tank 138-139 H 7
Tandun 152-153 D 5
Tândûr 140 C 2
Tandûru = Tândûr 140 C 2
Tanduy, Ci — 152-153 H 9
Tanega-shima 142-143 P 5
Tanega sima = Tanega-shima 142-143 P 5
Tanela 94-95 C 3
Tanen Taunggyi 150-151 B 3-5
Tanen Tong Dan 141 F 7
Tanew 118 L 3
Tanezrouft = Tânîzruft 164-165 DE 4
Ṭanezzûft, Uâdi — = Wâdî Tanizzuft 166-167 M 7
Tanf, Jabal at- 136-137 H 6
Tan-fêng = Danfeng 146-147 C 5
Tang, Kâs — 150-151 D 7
Tanga 172 G 3
Tangail = Ṭangâyal 134-135 O 6
Tanga Islands 148-149 h 5
Tangale Peak 168-169 H 3
Tanganyika, Lake — 172 E 2-F 3
Tangar = Thangkar 142-143 J 4
Tangará 111 F 3
Tangario National Park 161 F 4
Tangâyal 134-135 O 6
T'ang-chan = Tangshan 142-143 M 4
Tangdukou 146-147 C 8
Tangeh Hormoz 134-135 H 5
Tanger = Ṭanjah 164-165 C 1
Tangerang 152-153 G 9
Tanggalla 140 E 7-8
Tanggela Youmu Hu = Thangra Yumtsho 142-143 EF 5
Tanggu 142-143 M 4
Tanghe [TJ, place] 146-147 D 5
Tang He [TJ, river ◁ Bai He] 146-147 D 5
Tang He [TJ, river ◁ Baiyang Dian] 146-147 E 2
T'ang-ho = Tanghe [TJ, place] 146-147 D 5
T'ang Ho = Tang He [TJ, river ◁ Bai He] 146-147 D 5
T'ang Ho = Tang He [TJ, river ◁ Baiyang Dian] 146-147 E 2
T'ang-hsien-chên = Tangxianzhen 146-147 D 6
Tângi 138-139 K 8
Tangier 63 E 5
Tangiers = Ṭanjah 164-165 C 1
Tangier Sound 72-73 HJ 5
Tangjin 144-145 F 4
Tang Krasang 150-151 E 6
Tang La [TJ, Himalaya pass] 142-143 F 6
Tangla [TJ, Himalaya place] 138-139 K 3
Tang La [TJ, Tanglha] 142-143 G 5
Tangla = Tanglha 142-143 FG 5
Tanglewood, Houston-, TX 85 III b 1
Tanglha 142-143 FG 5
Tanglin Hill, Singapore- 154 III ab 2
Tang Phloch 150-151 DE 6-7
Tangshan 142-143 M 4
Tangshan = Dangshan 146-147 F 4
Tangshancheng 144-145 DE 2
Tangstedt 130 I a 1
Tangtou 146-147 G 4
Tangtu = Dangtu 146-147 G 6
T'ang-tu-k'ou = Tangdukou 146-147 C 8
Tangua 94-95 C 7
Tânguche 96-97 B 6
Tangueur, Bir — = Bi'r Tanqûr 166-167 L 4
Tanguieta 168-169 F 3
Tanguj 132-133 T 6
Tangung 152-153 LM 4
Tangutûru 140 E 3
Tangxi 146-147 G 7
Tang Xian 146-147 E 2
Tangxianzhen 146-147 D 6
Tangyiang = Dangyang 146-147 CD 6
Tangyin 146-147 E 4
Tangyuan 142-143 O 2
Tanhaçu 100-101 D 8
Tan Ho = Dan He 146-147 D 4
Tanhsien = Dan Xian 142-143 K 8
Tani 150-151 E 7
Tanimbar, Kepulauan — 148-149 K 8
Taning = Daning 146-147 C 3
Ta-ning = Wuxi 146-147 B 6

Taning Hka 141 E 2-3
Taninthārī 148-149 C 4
Taninthārī Kyūn 150-151 AB 6
Taninthārī Myitkyī 150-151 B 5-6
Taninthārī Taing 148-149 C 3-4
Taninthārī Taungdan 150-151 B 5-6
Tānīzruft 164-165 DE 4
Tanizzuft, Wādī — 166-167 M 7
Ṭanjah 164-165 C 1
Tanjay 148-149 H 5
Tanjong China 154 III ab 2
Tanjong Irau 154 III b 1
Tanjong Malim 148-149 D 6
Tanjong Pagar 154 III b 2
Tanjong Punggol 154 III b 1
Tanjong Rhu 154 III b 2
Tanjor = Thanjāvar 134-135 MN 8
Tanjung 148-149 G 7
Tanjung Api 152-153 O 6
Tanjung Aru 152-153 M 7
Tanjungbalai 148-149 CD 6
Tanjung Batikala 152-153 O 7
Tanjungbatu 152-153 MN 4
Tanjung Batubesar 152-153 N 10
Tanjung Batuk 152-153 P 10
Tanjung Beram 152-153 KL 3
Tanjung Berikat 152-153 G 7
Tanjung Besar 152-153 O 5
Tanjung Besi 152-153 O 10
Tanjungblitung 150-151 G 11
Tanjungbuayabuaya, Pulau — 152-153 N 5
Tanjung Bugel 152-153 J 9
Tanjung Cimiring 152-153 H 9-10
Tanjung Datu 148-149 E 6
Tanjung De Jong 148-149 L 8
Tanjung Fatagar 148-149 K 7
Tanjung Gelang 150-151 D 11
Tanjung Genteng 152-153 FG 9
Tanjung Genting 152-153 F 6
Tanjung Gertak Sanggui 150-151 BC 10
Tanjung Indramayu 152-153 H 9
Tanjung Jabung 148-149 DE 7
Tanjung Jambuair 152-153 BC 3
Tanjung Jamursba 148-149 K 7
Tanjung Kait 152-153 G 7
Tanjung Kandi 152-153 O 5
Tanjungkarang 148-149 DE 8
Tanjungkarang-Telukbetung 148-149 DE 8
Tanjung Kasossa 152-153 N 10
Tanjung Korowelang 152-153 H 9
Tanjung Krawang 152-153 G 8
Tanjung Lagundu 152-153 N 10
Tanjung Layar 148-149 DE 8
Tanjung Lokoloko 152-153 O 7
Tanjung Lumut 152-153 FG 7
Tanjung Mandar 152-153 N 7
Tanjung Mangkalihat 148-149 GH 6
Tanjung Pakar 152-153 O 8
Tanjungpandan 148-149 E 7
Tanjung Panyusu 152-153 FG 6
Tanjung Payong 152-153 K 4
Tanjung Penunjok 150-151 D 10
Tanjungperiuk 152-153 G 8-9
Tanjung Pertandangan 152-153 D 4
Tanjungpinang 148-149 DE 6
Tanjung Prick, Jakarta- 154 IV b 1
Tanjungpura 148-149 C 6
Tanjung Purwa 152-153 KL 10
Tanjungpusu 152-153 KL 5-6
Tanjung Puting 148-149 F 7
Tanjung Rangasa 152-153 N 7
Tanjung Ratu 152-153 F 8
Tanjungredeb 148-149 G 6
Tanjung Sambar 152-153 HJ 7
Tanjung Sasar 152-153 NO 10
Tanjung Selatan 148-149 F 7
Tanjung Selor 152-153 M 4
Tanjung Sigep 152-153 C 6
Tanjung Sipang 152-153 J 5
Tanjung Sirik 152-153 J 4
Tanjung Telukpunggur 152-153 DE 7-8
Tanjungtiram 150-151 B 11
Tanjung Unsang 152-153 N 3
Tanjung Vals 148-149 L 8
Tanjungwaringin 152-153 J 6
Tanjung Watupayung 152-153 P 10
Tankara 138-139 C 6
Tan Kena = Tān Kun 166-167 L 6
Tankersly, TX 76-77 D 7
Tankhala 138-139 DE 6-7
Tân Kol 150-151 F 5
Tankoro 168-169 F 2
Tān Kun 166-167 L 6
Tankwa 174-175 D 7
Tanlovo 132-133 NO 4
Tân My 150-151 G 7
Tännäs 116-117 E 6
Tannin 70-71 E 1
Tannūmah, At- 136-137 MN 7
Tannu-Ola 132-133 R 7
Tannu Tuva = Tuva Autonomous Soviet Socialist Republic 132-133 RS 7
Tano 164-165 D 7
Tanor = Tānūr 140 B 5
Tanoso 168-169 E 4
Tanot 138-139 C 4
Tanout 164-165 F 6
Tan Passage = Chong Tao 150-151 BC 8
Tanqua River = Tankwa 174-175 D 7
Tanque, AZ 74-75 J 6
Tanque Alvarez 76-77 C 9
Tanque Nova 100-101 C 7
Tanqūr, Bi'r — 166-167 L 4
Tanshui 142-143 N 6
Tan-shui = Danshui 146-147 E 10
Tanshui Chiang 146-147 H 9
Tansīft, Wad — 164-165 C 2
Tānsing 138-139 J 4
Ṭanṭā 164-165 KL 2
Tantabin = Htandabin [BUR, Bawlei Myit] 141 DE 7
Tantabin = Htandabin [BUR, Sittaung Myit] 141 E 6
Tantallon 61 GH 5
Ṭanṭan 166-167 A 5
Tantara 96-97 D 8
Tanti 106-107 E 3
Tantoyuca 86-87 LM 7
Tāntpur 138-139 F 4
Tanu 60 B 3
Tanuku 140 E 2
Tanunak, AK 58-59 E 6
Tānūr 140 B 5
Tanūshfī, Jabal — 166-167 F 2
Tanyan 141 F 4
Tan Yan = Kampung Jerangau 150-151 D 10
Tanyang 144-145 G 4
Tanyang = Danyang 146-147 G 6
Tanyeri 136-137 HJ 3
Tanzania 172 FG 3
Tanzī 141 D 4
Tanzilla River 58-59 W 7
Tao, Chong — 150-151 BC 8
Tao, Ko — 150-151 BC 7
Taoan 142-143 N 2
Tao'an = Baicheng 142-143 N 2
T'ao-chou = Lintan 142-143 J 5
Taocun 146-147 H 3
Tao-hsien = Dao Xian 146-147 C 9
Taohua Dao 146-147 J 7
Taojiang [TJ, place] 146-147 D 7
Tao Jiang [TJ, river] 146-147 E 9
Taole = Taoluo 146-147 G 4
Tao-li = Daoli 146-147 H 3
Taolihawa 138-139 J 4
Taoluo 146-147 G 4
Taoqi = Taoxi 146-147 F 6
Taormina 122-123 F 7
Taos, NM 64-65 E 4
Tao Shan = Peitawu Shan 146-147 H 10
Tao Shui = Dao Shui 146-147 E 6
T'ao-ts'un = Taocun 146-147 H 3
Taoudénni 164-165 D 4
Taouïala = Tāwaylah 166-167 G 3
Tâounât = Tāwnāt 166-167 D 2
Taoura = Tawrah 166-167 KL 1
Taourirt = Tāwrīrt 164-165 D 2
Ṭâouz = Ṭāūz 166-167 D 4
Taoxi 146-147 F 6
T'ao-yüan [RC] 146-147 H 9
Taoyuan [TJ] 146-147 C 7
Tapa 124-125 E 4
Tapa, la — 106-107 F 1
Tapacaré 102-103 B 3
Tapacari 104-105 C 5
Tapachula 64-65 H 9
Tapah 150-151 C 10
Tapajós, Rio — 92-93 H 5
Tapaktuan 148-149 C 6
Tapal 96-97 B 4
Tapalquén 106-107 G 6
Tapanadsum 138-139 L 2
Tapanahony 98-99 L 3
Tapanatepec 86-87 NO 9
Tapanuli, Teluk — 152-153 C 5
Tapara, Ilha Grande do 98-99 L 6
Tapará, Serra do 98-99 M 6
Ta-pa Shan = Daba Shan 142-143 KL 5
Tapat, Pulau — 148-149 J 7
Tapauá 92-93 FG 6
Tapauá, Rio — 92-93 F 6
Tapebicuá 106-107 J 2
Tapejara 106-107 LM 2
Tapenaga, Río — 106-107 H 1-2
Ta-p'êng = Dapeng 146-147 E 10
Tapepo 171 B 4
Tapera [BR, Rio Grande dol Sul] 106-107 L 2
Tapera [BR, Rondônia] 104-105 F 3
Tapera Pesoe 102-103 B 1
Taperoá [BR, Bahia] 92-93 M 7
Taperoá [BR, Paraíba] 100-101 F 4
Taperoá, Rio — 100-101 F 4
Tapes 106-107 M 3
Tapes, Ponta do — 106-107 M 3
Tapeta = Tappita 164-165 C 7
Taphane = Ban Taphane 150-151 E 5
Taphan Hin 150-151 C 4
Tāpī = Tāpti 134-135 M 6
Tapi, Mae Nam — 150-151 B 8
Tapia 104-105 F 6
Tapiales, La Matanza- 110 III b 2
Tapiantana Group 152-153 P 2
Tapiche, Río — 96-97 D 5
Ta-pieh Shan = Dabie Shan 142-143 M 5
Ta-p'ing-tsu = Huitongqiao 141 F 3
Tapini 148-149 N 8
Tapiocanga, Chapada do — 102-103 J 2
Tapira 94-95 G 7
Tapirapé, Serra do — 98-99 N 10
Tapirapecó, Sierra — 92-93 FG 4
Tapirapua 104-105 GH 4
Tapita = Tappita 164-165 C 7
Taplejung 138-139 L 4
Tapoa 168-169 F 2
Ta-p'o-ti = Dabaidi 146-147 E 8
Tappahannock, VA 72-73 H 5-6
Tappi-saki 144-145 MN 2
Tappita 164-165 C 7
Taps = Tapa 124-125 E 4
Tapsia, Calcutta- 154 II b 2
Tāpti 134-135 M 6
Tapuaenuku 158-159 O 8
Ta-pu-hsün Hu = Dabas nuur 142-143 H 4
Tapuiò, Rio — 100-101 B 3-4
Tapul Group 152-153 O 3
Tapuruquara 92-93 FG 5
Taqānat, At- 168-169 C 1
Ṭaqṭaq 136-137 L 5
Taquara, Morro da — 110 I b 2
Taquara, Ponta da — 102-103 HJ 7
Taquara, Serra da — 102-103 F 1
Taquaral, Serra do — 100-101 D 8
Taquaras 100-101 D 10
Taquarembó 106-107 L 2
Taquari [BR, Mato Grosso] 102-103 F 2
Taquari [BR, Rio Grande do Sul] 106-107 M 2
Taquari, Pantanal do — 102-103 DE 3
Taquari, Rio — [BR ◁ Rio Jacuí] 106-107 M 2
Taquari, Rio — [BR ◁ Rio Paranapanena] 102-103 H 5
Taquari, Rio — [BR ◁ Rio Taquari Novo] 102-103 F 3
Taquari Novo, Rio — 92-93 H 8
Taquaritinga 102-103 H 4
Taquaritinga do Norte 100-101 FG 4-5
Taquarituba 102-103 H 5
Taquaruçu, Ribeira — 102-103 F 4
Taques, Los — 94-95 F 2
Taquetrén, Sierra — 108-109 E 4
Taquiara 100-101 E 3
Tar, Lago — 108-109 D 7
Tara [AUS] 158-159 K 5
Tara [SU, place] 132-133 N 6
Tara [SU, river] 132-133 O 6
Tara [YU] 122-123 H 4
Tara, Salar de — 104-105 C 8
Tarabganj 138-139 HJ 4
Tarabillas, Laguna — 76-77 B 7
Tarabuco 92-93 FG 8
Ṭarābulus 164-165 GH 2
Ṭarābulus al-Gharb 164-165 G 2
Ṭarābulus ash-Shām 134-135 CD 4
Tarabya, İstanbul- 154 I b 2
Tarādehi 138-139 G 6
Tarago 160 J 5
Tarahumar, Altos de — 86-87 G 4-5
Tarahumara, Sierra — 64-65 E 6
Tarai 138-139 F 5
Tarāī = Terāi 134-135 NO 5
Taraika Bay = zaliv Terpenija 132-133 b 8
Tarairi 104-105 E 7
Tarakan 148-149 G 6
Tarakan, Pulau — 152-153 MN 4
Taraklı 136-137 D 2
Taraklija 126-127 D 4
Taralga 160 JK 5
Taram Darya = Tarim darya 142-143 E 3
Taran, mys — 118 JK 1
Tarāna 138-139 EF 6
Taranaki 161 F 4
Taranaquis 104-105 G 5
Tarangire National Park 171 D 3-4
Tarango, Presa — 91 I b 2
Taran Tāran = Tarn Tāran 138-139 E 2
Tàranto 122-123 G 5
Tàranto, Golfo di — 122-123 G 5
Tarapacá [CO] 94-95 c 2
Tarapacá [RCH, administrative unit] 104-105 B 6-7
Tarapacá [RCH, place] 104-105 B 6
Tarapoto 92-93 D 6
Tarāpur 138-139 D 8
Taraquá 92-93 F 4
Tarārah, Ḥāssī — 166-167 GH 6
Tarare 120-121 K 6
Tararua Range 161 F 5
Tarās 138-139 M 5
Tarašča 126-127 E 2
Tarascon 120-121 K 7
Tarasovo [SU, Archangel'skaja Oblast'] 124-125 N 2
Tarasovskij 126-127 K 2
Tarat, Ouèd — = Wādī Tarāt 164-165 F 3
Tarāt, Wādī — 164-165 F 3
Tarata [BOL] 104-105 C 5
Tarata [PE] 96-97 F 10
Tarātmīn 166-167 H 7
Tarauacá 92-93 E 6
Tarauacá, Rio — 92-93 E 6
Tarāvganj = Tarabganj 138-139 HJ 4
Tarawa 208 H 2
Tarayfāwī 136-137 J 7
Tarazona 120-121 G 8
Tarbagataij, chrebet — 132-133 PQ 8
Tarbagatay 142-143 EF 2
Tarbaj 171 E 2
Tarbes 120-121 H 7
Tarboro, NC 80-81 H 3
Tarchankut, mys — 126-127 EF 4
Tarcoola 158-159 FG 6
Tarcoon 160 H 3
Tardoire 120-121 H 6
Tardoki-Jani, gora — 132-133 a 8
Taree 158-159 K 6
Tareja 132-133 R 3
Tärendö 116-117 JK 4
Tareni, Río — 104-105 C 3
Tareraimbu, Cachoeira — 92-93 J 6
Tarf, Garaet et — = Qar'at at-Tarf 166-167 K 2
Ṭarfā', Wādī aṭ- 173 B 3
Ṭarfâia = Ṭarfāyah 166-167 AB 5-6
Ṭarfāwī, Bi'r — 136-137 K 5
Ṭarfāyah [MA, administrative unit] 166-167 AB 5-6
Ṭarfāyah [MA, place] 164-165 B 3
Ṭarfāyah, Qārat aṭ- 136-137 BC 7
Tarfāyah, Rā's — 164-165 B 3
Targane 168-169 G 1
Targhee Pass 66-67 H 3
Tārgīst 166-167 D 2
Târgovište 122-123 M 4
Târguîst = Tārgīst 166-167 D 2
Tarhbâlt = Taghbālt 166-167 D 4
Tarhit = Tāghīt 164-165 D 2
Tarhjicht = Taghghīsht 166-167 B 5
Tarhūnah 164-165 G 2
Tariâga = Manzil Shākir 166-167 M 2
Tariana 94-95 G 7
Tarian Ganga = Dariganga 142-143 L 2
Tarian Gol 146-147 B 1
Táriba 94-95 EF 4
Tarīf 134-135 G 6
Tarifa 120-121 E 10
Tarifa, Punta de — 120-121 DE 11
Tarija [BOL, administrative unit] 104-105 DE 7
Tarija [BOL, place] 92-93 G 9
Tarikere 140 B 4
Tarīm 134-135 F 7
Tarim darya 142-143 E 3
Tarime 171 C 3
Tarka 174-175 FG 7
Tarkastad 174-175 G 7
Tarkhan, Cape — = mys Tarchankut 126-127 EF 4
Tarkio, MO 70-71 C 5
Tarkio, MT 66-67 F 2
Tarkio River 70-71 C 5
Tarko-Sale 132-133 O 5
Tarkwa 164-165 D 7
Tarlac 148-149 H 3
Tarma [PE, Junín] 96-97 D 7
Tarma [PE, Loreto] 96-97 F 3
Ṭārmīyah, Aṭ- 136-137 KL 6
Tarn 120-121 H 7
Tärna 116-117 F 5
Tarnogskij Gorodok 124-125 O 3
Tarnopol' = Ternopol' 126-127 B 2
Tarnów 118 K 3
Tarn Tāran 138-139 E 2
Tarog Tsho 138-139 JK 2
Ṭārom 134-135 GH 5
Tarong 141 F 1-2
Taronga Zoological Park 161 I b 2
Taroom 158-159 JK 5
Târoûdânt = Tārūdānt 164-165 C 2
Tarpley, TX 76-77 E 8
Tarpon Springs, FL 80-81 b 2
Tarqui 96-97 B 2
Tarquínia 122-123 D 4
Tarragona 120-121 H 8
Tarrakoski 116-117 J 3
Tar River 80-81 H 3
Tarso = Tarsus 136-137 F 4
Tarso Emissi = Kégueur Terbi 164-165 H 4
Tarsus 136-137 F 4
Tarsusırmağı 136-137 F 4
Tartagal [RA, Salta] 111 D 2
Tartagal [RA, Santa Fe] 106-107 H 2
Tartagal, Sierra de — 104-105 E 8
Tartār, Wādī at- 136-137 K 5
Tartārat, Ḥāssī — 166-167 K 4
Tartas [SU] 132-133 O 6
Ṭarṭīn, Bi'r — 136-137 J 5
Tartu 124-125 F 4
Ṭarṭūs 134-135 D 4
Tārūdānt 164-165 C 2
Tarūfāwī, Bi'r — 136-137 K 6
Tarum, Ci — 152-153 G 9
Tarumirim 102-103 LM 3
Tarumizu 144-145 H 7
Tarusa [SU, place] 124-125 L 6
Tarutino 126-127 D 3
Tarutung 148-149 C 6
Tarvisio 122-123 E 2
Tarvita 104-105 D 6
Tarvo, Río — 104-105 F 4
Tasasah, Jabal — 166-167 F 2
Tasauz 132-133 K 9
Tasāwah 164-165 G 3
Taschereau 62 M 2
Taşçı 136-137 F 3
Tascosa, TX 76-77 C 5
Tasejevo 132-133 RS 6
Tasek Bera 150-151 D 11
Taseko River 60 F 4
Taşeli yaylâsı 136-137 E 4
Tasfaout = Tāsfāwat 166-167 F 5
Tāsfāwat 166-167 F 5
Tāsgāñv = Tāsgaon 140 B 2
Tasgaon 140 B 2
Ta Shan 146-147 D 8
Tashichhö Dsong = Thimbu 134-135 OP 5
Tashigong = Zhaxigang 142-143 DE 5
Tashigong Dsong 141 B 2
Tashi Gonpa 142-143 G 5
Ta-shih-ch'iao = Dashiqiao 144-145 D 2
Tashijong Dsong 134-135 P 5
Tashilhumpo = Zhaxilhünbo 142-143 F 6
Ṭashk, Daryācheh — 134-135 GH 5
Tashkent = Taškent 132-133 M 9
Tashota 62 F 2
Tash Qurghan 142-143 D 4
Tashrīrt, Jabal — 166-167 J 2
Tasikmalaja 148-149 E 8
Tāsīlah 166-167 B 5
Tāsīlī Wān Ahjār 164-165 F 3
Tāsīlī Wān al-Hajjār 164-165 E 5-F 4
Taškent 132-133 M 9
Taşköprü [TR, Eskişehir] 136-137 D 3
Taşköprü [TR, Kastamonu] 136-137 F 2
Taš-Kumyr 134-135 L 2
Tas-Kystabyt 132-133 bc 5
Tašla 124-125 T 8
Taşlı 154 I b 2
Taşlıcay 136-137 K 3
Tasman, Mount — 161 CD 6
Tasman Bay 158-159 O 8
Tasman Head 160 cd 3
Tasmania 158-159 HJ 8
Tasman Land 158-159 D 3-E 2
Tasman Mountains 161 E 5
Tasman Peninsula 160 d 3
Tasman Rise 50-51 R 8
Tasman Sea 158-159 K-N 7
Tasmin 126-127 EF 2
Taşova = Yemişenbükü 136-137 G 2
Tassila 168-169 D 2
Tâssîla = Tāsīlah 166-167 B 5
Tassili n'Ajjer = Tāsīlī Wān Ahjār 164-165 F 3
Tassili Oua n'Ahaggar = Tāsīlī Wān al-Hajjār 164-165 E 5-F 4
Taštagol 132-133 Q 7
Tastūr 166-167 L 1
Taštyp 132-133 Q 7
Tasu 60 B 3
Tasūj 136-137 L 3
Tata 118 J 5
Tatabánya 118 HJ 5
Ṭāṭah 166-167 BC 5
Ṭāṭah, Wād — 166-167 B 5
Ta-t'ang = Datang 146-147 B 9
Tatar 152-153 M 10
Tatar Autonomous Soviet Socialist Republic = 6 ◁ 132-133 J 6
Tatarbunary 126-127 D 4
Tatarka 124-125 G 7
Tatarovo, Moskva- 113 V ab 2
Tatarsk 132-133 NO 6
Tatarskaja Avtonomnaja Sovetskaja Socialističeskaja Respublika = Tatar Autonomous Soviet Socialist Republic 132-133 J 6
Tatar Strait 132-133 b 7-a 8
Tatau 152-153 K 4
Tātā'ū, Rūd-e — 136-137 LM 4
Tataurovo 124-125 O 4
Ṭāṭāwīn 164-165 G 2
Tate, Cabo — 108-109 BC 9
Tatenberg, Hamburg- 130 I b 2
Tateoka = Murayama 144-145 N 3
Tates Cairn 155 I b 1
Tateyama 144-145 M 5
Tateyamahōjō = Tateyama 144-145 M 5
Tathlina Lake 56-57 N 5
Tathlīth 134-135 E 7
Tathlīth, Wādī — 134-135 E 6-7
Tathong Channel 155 I b 2
Tathong Point 155 I b 2
Ta-tien = Dadian [TJ, Anhui] 146-147 F 5
Ta-tien = Dadian [TJ, Shandong] 146-147 G 4
Ta-t'ien = Datian 146-147 F 9
Tatiščevo 124-125 P 8
Tatitlek, AK 58-59 O 6
Tatla Lake 60 E 4
Tatlawiksuk River 58-59 K 5-6
Tatlayoko Lake 60 E 4
Tatlīt = Tathlīth 134-135 E 7
Tatlmain Lake 58-59 TU 5
Tatlow, Mount — 60 F 4
Tatman Mountain 68-69 B 3
Tatnam, Cape — 56-57 ST 6
Tatonduk River 58-59 R 4
Ta-t'ong = Datong 142-143 L 3
Tatos dağlar 136-137 J 2
Tatra = Tatry 118 JK 4
Tatran 142-143 EF 4
Tatry 118 JK 4
Tatsaitan = Tagalgan 142-143 H 4
Tatshenshini River 58-59 T 6-7
Tatsuno 144-145 K 5
Tatta = Ṭhaṭṭha 134-135 K 6
Tatuapé, São Paulo- 110 II b 2
Tatuí 102-103 J 5
Tatuk Lake 60 E 3
Ta-tu-k'ou = Dadukou 146-147 F 6
Tatul, Sierra de — 106-107 B 2
Tatum, NM 76-77 C 6
Tatum, TX 76-77 G 6
Tatums, OK 76-77 F 5
Tatung = Datong [TJ, Anhui] 146-147 F 6
Tatung = Datong [TJ, Shanxi] 142-143 L 3
Ta-t'ung Ho = Datong He 142-143 J 4
Tatvan 136-137 K 3
Tau 116-117 AB 8
Tauá 92-93 L 6
Taubaté 92-93 KL 9
Tauberbischofsheim 118 DE 4
Taučik 126-127 P 4
Tauene 174-175 K 3
Taufkirchen 130 II b 2
Tauini, Rio — 98-99 J 4
Taujskaja guba 132-133 cd 6
Taukum 132-133 O 9
Taumarunui 158-159 OP 7
Taumaturgo 92-93 E 6
Taum Sauk Mountain 70-71 E 7
Taunay 102-103 D 4
Taung 174-175 F 4
Taungdôngyī 141 E 6
Taungdwingyī 148-149 BC 2-3
Taunggôk 141 D 6
Taunggôk Taunggyā 141 D 6
Taunggyaw, Lûy — 141 E 4
Taunggyī 148-149 C 2
Taungma Taung 141 E 5
Taungmè 141 E 4
Taungngū 148-149 C 3
Taungnī 141 E 3
Taungs = Taung 174-175 F 4
Taungsûn 141 EF 8
Taungthā 141 D 5
Taungthônlôn 141 D 3
Taungup = Taunggôk 141 D 6
Taunsa 138-139 C 2
Taunton 119 E 6
Taunton, MA 72-73 L 4
Taunton Lake 84 III d 2
Taunton Lake, NJ 84 III de 2
Taunus 118 D 3
Taupo 158-159 P 7
Taupo, Lake — 158-159 P 7
Tauragė 124-125 D 6
Tauramena 94-95 E 5
Tauranga 158-159 P 7
Taureau, Lac — 72-73 K 1
Tauredu, Lac — 62 OP 3
Taurirt = Tāwrīrt 164-165 D 2
Taurovo 132-133 N 6
Taurus Mountains 134-135 C 3
Tausa [CO] 94-95 E 5
Taushqan Darya = Kök shal 142-143 D 3
Ṭāūz [MA] 166-167 D 4
Tauz [SU] 126-127 M 6
Tavai 102-103 E 3
Ṭavālesh, Kūhha-ye — 136-137 MN 3
Tavan Bogd uul 142-143 F 2
Tavares 100-101 F 4
Tavares, FL 80-81 c 2
Tavas = Yarangüme 136-137 C 4
Tavastehus = Hämeenlinna 116-117 L 7
Tavda [SU, place] 132-133 M 6
Tavda [SU, river] 132-133 L 6
Taveta 172 G 2
Taveuni 148-149 b 2
Ta Viang = Ban Ta Viang 150-151 D 3
Tavira 120-121 D 10
Tavistock, NJ 84 III c 2
Tavolara 122-123 CD 5
Tavoliere 122-123 F 5
Tavoy = Htāwei 148-149 C 4
Tavoy, Cape — = Shinmau Sûn 150-151 AB 6
Tavoy Island = Mali Kyûn 148-149 C 4
Tavoy Point = Shinmau Sûn 150-151 AB 6
Tavoy River = Htāwei Myit 150-151 B 5
Távros 113 IV a 2
Tavşanlı 136-137 C 3
Tavua 148-149 a 2
Ta-wa = Dawa 144-145 D 2
Tawake 168-169 D 4
Ta-wan = Dawan 146-147 B 10
Tawang = Tawan Hka 141 E 2
Ta-wang-chia Tao = Dawangjia Dao 144-145 D 3
Tawan Hka 141 E 2
Tawar, Laut — 152-153 B 3
Tawargiri 140 C 3
Tawārij, Ḥāssī — 166-167 JK 4
Tawas City, MI 70-71 J 3
Tawau 148-149 G 6
Ṭāwaylah 166-167 G 3
Ta-wên-k'ou = Dawenkou 146-147 F 3-4
Ṭawīl, Bi'r — 164-165 L 4
Ṭawīl, Sabkhat aṭ- 136-137 J 5
Ṭawīl, Wādī aṭ- 166-167 H 2
Ṭawīlah 166-167 C 7
Ṭawīlah, Juzur — 173 CD 4
Tawile Island = Juzur Ṭawīlah 173 CD 4
Tawitawi Group 152-153 NO 3
Tawi-tawi Island 148-149 GH 5
Ṭawkar 164-165 M 5
Tāwnāt 166-167 D 2
Tāwrīrt 164-165 D 2
Tawu 146-147 H 10
Tawûm Bûm 141 E 2
Ṭāwūq 136-137 L 5
Ṭāwūq Chāy 136-137 L 5
Ṭāwurgā, Sabhat — 164-165 H 2
Tawzar 164-165 F 2
Taxco de Alarcón 64-65 FG 8
Tay 119 E 3
Tay, Firth of — 119 E 3
Tayabamba 92-93 D 6
Ṭāyabat al-Janūbīyah 166-167 K 3
Ta-ya Ch'ün-tao = Qizhou Liedao 150-151 H 3
Ta-yang Ho = Dayang He 144-145 D 2
Taya Qundao = Qizhou Lidao 150-151 H 3
Ta-ya Wan = Daya Wan 146-147 E 10
Ṭayb al-Fāl 136-137 J 5
Tayeegle 164-165 ab 3
Ta-yeh = Daye 146-147 E 6
Tayepharba La 138-139 J 2
Taÿgetos 122-123 K 7
Ta-ying Chiang = Daying Jiang 141 EF 3
Tayishan = Guanyun 142-143 MN 5
Taylor 60 G 1
Taylor, AK 58-59 E 4
Taylor, AR 78-79 C 4
Taylor, NE 68-69 G 5
Taylor, TX 76-77 F 7
Taylor, Mount — 76-77 A 5
Taylor Mountains 58-59 J 6
Taylor Ridge 78-79 G 3
Taylor River 60 C 1
Taylor Springs, NM 76-77 BC 4
Taylorsville, KY 70-71 H 6
Taylorsville, MS 78-79 E 5
Taylorsville, NC 80-81 F 2-3
Taylorville, IL 70-71 F 6
Taymā' 134-135 D 5
Tayna 171 B 3
Tây Ninh 148-149 E 4
Tāynīst 166-167 DE 2
Tayoltita 86-87 GH 5
Tayota, Río — 104-105 C 5-D 4
Ṭayr, Jabal aṭ- 134-135 E 7
Taytay 148-149 GH 4
Tayu 152-153 J 9
Ta-yü = Dayu 142-143 L 6
Ta-yü Ling = Dayu Ling 146-147 DE 9
Tayung = Dayong 142-143 L 6
Ta-yü Shan = Dayu Shan 146-147 H 6
Taz 132-133 OP 4
Tazādīt 164-165 B 4
Tāzāh 164-165 D 2
Tazarbū 164-165 J 3
Tāzārīn 164-165 CD 2
Tazarine = Tāzārīn 164-165 CD 2
Tazawako 144-145 N 3
Taze = Tanzī 141 D 4
Tazenâkht = Tāznākht 166-167 C 4
Tázerbó = Tazarbū 164-165 J 3
Tazewell, TN 80-81 E 2
Tazewell, VA 80-81 F 2
Tazimina Lakes 58-59 KL 6-7
Tazlina Lake 58-59 OP 6
Tazna 104-105 C 7
Tāznākht 166-167 C 4
Tazolé 168-169 H 1
Tazovskaja guba 132-133 NO 4
Tazovskij 132-133 OP 4
Tazovskij poluostrov 132-133 NO 4
Tazu = Tīgazū 141 D 3
Tazūndam 141 E 1
Tazungdam = Tazūndam 141 E 1
Tazzait, Aïn — = 'Ayn Tazārat 166-167 JK 6
Tazzeka, Jbel — = Jabal Tazzikā' 166-167 DE 2
Tazzikā', Jabal — 166-167 DE 2

Tbilisi 126-127 M 6
T'bursuq 166-167 L 1

Tchab, gora — 126-127 J 4
Tchabal Nbabo 168-169 HJ 4
Tchad, Lac — 164-165 G 6
Tch'ang-cha = Changsha 142-143 L 6
Tchang-kia-k'eou = Zhangjiakou 142-143 L 3
Tch'ang-tch'ouen = Changchun 142-143 NO 3
Tchan-kiang = Zhanjiang 142-143 L 7
Tchaourou 168-169 F 3
Tch'eng-tö = Chengde 142-143 M 3
Tch'eng-tou = Chengdu 142-143 J 5
Tchentlo Lake 60 E 2
Tchertchen = Chärchän 142-143 F 4
Tchibanga 172 B 2
Tchien 164-165 C 7
Tching Lan Xan, Đao — 150-151 FG 2
Tchin Tabaraden 164-165 F 5
Tchong King = Chongqing 142-143 K 6
Tchula, MS 78-79 D 4
Tczew 118 J 1

Tea, Rio — [BR] 98-99 EF 5
Teacapan 86-87 GH 6
Teague, TX 76-77 F 7
Tê-an = De'an 146-147 EF 7
Te Anau, Lake — 158-159 N 9
Teaneck, NJ 82 III bc 1
Teano 122-123 F 5
Teapa 86-87 O 9
Teapot Dome 68-69 CD 4
Tea Tree Well 158-159 F 4
Te Awamutu 158-159 OP 7
Tebaida, La — 94-95 D 5
Tebas = Thēbai [ET] 164-165 L 3
Tebedu 152-153 J 5
Teberda 126-127 KL 5
Teberdinskij zapovednik 126-127 KL 5
Tebessa = Tibissah 164-165 F 1
Tebessa, Monts de — = Jabal Tibissah 166-167 L 2
Tebet, Jakarta- 154 IV b 2
Tebicuary, Río — 102-103 DE 7
Tebicuary-mi, Río — 102-103 D 6-7
Tebingtinggi [RI, Sumatera Selatan] 148-149 D 7
Tebingtinggi [RI, Sumatera Utara] 148-149 CD 6
Tebingtinggi, Pulau — 148-149 D 6
Tebleši 124-125 L 5
Ṭebourba = Ṭuburbah 166-167 L 1
Teboursouq = T'bursuq 166-167 L 1
Tebrau 154 III a 1
Tebulosmta, gora — 126-127 M 5
Tecate 64-65 C 5
Tecer dağları 136-137 G 3
Tê-ch'ing = Deqing 146-147 GH 6
Techis 142-143 E 3
Technical College of Kowloon 155 I b 2
Technische Universität Berlin 130 III b 1
Techo, Hipódromo de — 91 III b 3
Tecka 111 B 6
Tecka, Sierra de — 108-109 D 4
Teckla, WY 68-69 D 4

Tecolote, NM 76-77 B 5-6
Tecomán 64-65 F 8
Tecoripa 86-87 EF 3
Tecozautla 86-87 L 7
Tecuala 64-65 E 7
Tecuci 122-123 M 3
Tecumseh, MI 70-71 HJ 4
Tecumseh, NE 70-71 BC 5
Tedders = Tiddas 166-167 C 3
Teddington, London- 129 II a 2
Tedín Uriburu 106-107 H 6
Tedžen 134-135 J 3
Tees 119 EF 4
Teeswater 72-73 F 2-3
Tefariti = Atfāriti 166-167 A 7
Tefé 92-93 G 5
Tefé, Lago de 98-99 F 6
Tefé, Rio — 92-93 F 5
Tefedest = Tafdasat 164-165 F 3-4
Tefenni 136-137 C 4
Tegal 148-149 E 8
Tegeler See 130 III b 1
Tegelort, Berlin- 130 III ab 1
Tégerhi = Tajarhi 164-165 G 4
Tegernsee 118 EF 5
Tegheri, Bi'r — 166-167 M 6
Tegina 168-169 G 3
Tegineneng 152-153 F 8
Tegouma 168-169 H 2
Teguantepeque = Santo Domingo Tehuantepec 64-65 G 8
Tegucigalpa 64-65 J 9
Teguiddan Tessoum 168-169 G 1
Tegul'det 132-133 Q 6
Tehachapi, CA 74-75 D 5
Tehachapi Mountains 74-75 D 5
Tehachapi Pass 74-75 D 5
Tehama, CA 66-67 B 5
Tehata 138-139 M 6
Tehek Lake 56-57 R 4
Teheran = Tehrān 134-135 G 3
Téhini 168-169 E 3
Tehrān 134-135 G 3
Tehri 138-139 G 2
Tê-hsing = Dexing 146-147 F 7
Tê-hua = Dehua 146-147 G 9
Tehuacán 64-65 G 8
Tehuantepec, Golfo de — 64-65 GH 8
Tehuantepec, Istmo de — 64-65 GH 8
Tehuantepec, Santo Domingo — 64-65 G 8
Tehuelches 108-109 F 6
Teian = De'an 146-147 EF 7
Teide, Pico de — 164-165 A 3
Teixeira 100-101 F 4
Teixeira da Silva 172 C 4
Teixeiras 102-103 L 4
Tejada, Punta — 106-107 G 7
Tejar, El — 106-107 G 5
Tejkovo 124-125 N 5
Tejo 120-121 C 9
Tejon Pass 64-65 C 4-5
Teju 141 E 2
Tekağaç burun 136-137 B 4
Tekamah, NE 68-69 H 5
Te Kao 158-159 O 6
Tekāri 138-139 K 5
Tekax 86-87 Q 7
Teke [TR, landscape] 136-137 CD 4
Teke [TR, place] 136-137 C 2
Teke burnu [TR ↙ Çanakkale] 136-137 AB 2
Tekeli 132-133 O 9
Tekeli dağı 136-137 G 2
Tekirdağ 134-135 B 2
Tekkali 140 FG 1
Tekman 136-137 J 3
Teknaf = Ṭarfāyah 166-167 AB 5-6
Ṭeknāf 141 C 5
Tekoa, WA 66-67 E 2
Tekouiât, Oued — = Wādī Tākwayat 164-165 E 4
Tekstil'ščiki, Moskva- 113 V c 3
Teku 152-153 P 6
Te Kuiti 158-159 OP 7
Tekukor, Pulau — 154 III b 2
Tel 134-135 N 6
Tela 64-65 J 8
Tēla = Tel 134-135 N 6
Telaga Papan = Nenasi 150-151 D 11
Telagh = Talāgh 166-167 F 2
Telanaipura = Jambi 148-149 D 7
Telaquana, Lake — 58-59 L 6
Telares, Los — 106-107 F 2
Telavi 126-127 M 5-6
Tel Avive Jafa = Tel Aviv-Yafō 134-135 C 4
Tel Aviv-Yafō 134-135 C 4
Telechany 124-125 EF 7
Teleférico 91 II b 1
Telefomin 148-149 M 8
Telegapulang 152-153 K 7
Telegino 124-125 P 7
Telegraph Bay 155 I a 2
Telegraph Creek 56-57 K 6
Telegraph Point 160 L 3
Telegraph Range 60 F 3
Tel el-'Amarina = Tall al-'Amārinah 173 B 4
Tel el-'Amarna = Tall al-'Amārinah 173 B 4
Telemark 116-117 BC 8
Telemsès = Tlemcès 164-165 EF 5
Telén 106-107 E 6
Telen, Sungai — 152-153 M 5
Teleneštу 126-127 D 3
Teleno, El — 120-121 D 7
Téléphone, Île du — 170 IV a 1-2
Télergma = Talighmah 166-167 K 1
Telescope Peak 74-75 E 4
Teles Pires, Rio — 92-93 H 6
Teletaye 168-169 F 1
Telford 119 E 5
Telida, AK 58-59 L 5
Telig 164-165 D 4
Telijn nuur 142-143 F 2
Télimélé 164-165 B 6
Teljō, Jebel — = Jabal Talju 164-165 K 6
Telkwa 60 D 2
Tell, TX 76-77 D 5
Tell Abyad = Tall al-Abyaḍ 136-137 H 4
Tell Atlas 164-165 D 2-E 1
Tell Bīs = Tall Bisah 136-137 G 5
Tell City, IN 70-71 G 6-7
Tell Dekoûa = Tall adh-Dhakwah 136-137 G 6
Tell el-Amarna = Tall al-'Amārinah 173 B 4
Teller, AK 56-57 CD 4
Tell Ḥalaf = Tall Ḥalaf 136-137 HJ 4
Tellicherry 140 B 5
Tellico Plains, TN 78-79 G 3
Tellier 108-109 FG 6
Tellitcherri = Tellicherry 140 B 5
Tell Kalakh = Tall Kalah 136-137 G 5
Tell Kôttchak = Tall Kujik 136-137 JK 4
Tell Sem'ân = Tall as-Sam'ān 136-137 H 4
Telluride, CO 68-69 C 7
Tel'manovo 126-127 J 3
Tèlmést = Talmist 166-167 B 4
Telmo, Sierra — 104-105 D 8
Telocaset, OR 66-67 E 3
Telok Anson 148-149 CD 6
Telok Betong = Tanjungkarang-Telukbetung 148-149 DE 8
Telok Datok 150-151 C 11
Teloloapan 64-65 FG 8
Tēlos 122-123 M 7
Telouet = Talwat 166-167 C 4
Tel'posiz, gora — 132-133 K 5
Telsen 111 C 6
Telšiai 124-125 D 6
Teltowkanal 130 III a 2
Teluk Adang 152-153 M 6
Teluk Airhitam 152-153 HJ 7
Teluk Anson = Telok Anson 148-149 CD 6
Teluk Apar 152-153 M 7
Teluk Banten 152-153 G 8
Telukbatang 152-153 HJ 6
Teluk Berau 148-149 K 7
Telukbetung = Tanjungkarang 148-149 DE 8
Teluk Bone 148-149 H 7
Teluk Brunei 152-153 L 3
Teluk Buli 148-149 J 6
Telukdalam 148-149 C 6
Teluk Darvel 152-153 N 3
Teluk Datu 148-149 EF 6
Teluk Endeh 152-153 O 10
Teluk Flamingo 148-149 L 8
Teluk Grajagan 152-153 KL 10
Teluk Irian 148-149 KL 7
Teluk Jakarta 152-153 G 8-9
Teluk Kau 148-149 J 6
Teluk Klumpang 152-153 M 7
Teluk Kotowana Watobo 152-153 P 9
Teluk Kuandang 152-153 P 5
Teluk Kumai 148-149 F 7
Teluk Labuk 152-153 M 2
Teluk Lada 152-153 F 9
Teluk Lasolo 148-149 H 7
Teluk Maccluer = Teluk Berau 148-149 K 7
Teluk Mandar 148-149 G 7
Telukmeranti 152-153 E 5
Teluk Palu 152-153 N 6
Teluk Pelabuhanratu 152-153 FG 9
Teluk Penanjung 152-153 H 9-10
Teluk Poh 152-153 P 6
Teluk Poso 152-153 O 6
Telukpunggur, Tanjung — 152-153 DE 7-8
Teluk Saleh 148-149 G 8
Teluk Sampit 148-149 F 7
Teluk Sangkulirang 148-149 G 6
Teluk Sebangan 148-149 F 7
Teluk Sebuku 148-149 G 6
Teluk Semangka 152-153 F 8
Teluk Sukadana 152-153 H 6
Teluk Sumbawa 152-153 M 10
Teluk Tapanuli 152-153 C 5
Teluk Tolo 148-149 H 7
Teluk Tomini 148-149 H 7
Teluk Tomori 148-149 H 7
Teluk Waingapu 152-153 O 10
Tema 164-165 DE 7
Témacine = Tamāsīn 166-167 JK 3
Temangan 150-151 D 10
Temassinine = Burj 'Umar Idrīs 164-165 EF 3
Temax 86-87 Q 7
Temazcal, El — 86-87 LM 5
Tembeling 150-151 D 10
Tembellaga = Timboulaga 164-165 F 5
Tembenči 132-133 S 4
Tembesi, Sungai — 152-153 E 6-7
Tembey, Río — 102-103 E 7
Tembilahan 148-149 D 7
Temblador 94-95 K 3
Temblor Range 74-75 D 5
Tembo 168-169 H 3
Tembo, Mont — 168-169 H 5
Temboeland 174-175 GH 6
Tembuland = Temboeland 174-175 GH 6
Temecula, CA 74-75 E 6
Temelli = Samutlu 136-137 E 3
Tementfoust 170 I b 1
Temerloh 150-151 D 11
Temescal Canyon 83 III a 1
Temesvár = Timişoara 122-123 J 3
Téminos, Laguna de — 64-65 H 8
Temir 132-133 K 8
Temir-Chan-Šura = Bujnaksk 126-127 N 5
Temirtau [SU, Kazachskaja SSR] 132-133 N 7-8
Temirtau [SU, Rossijskaja SFSR] 132-133 Q 7
Témiscamie, Lac — 62 PQ 1
Témiscamie, Rivière — 62 P 1
Témiscaming 56-57 V 8
Temiscouata, Lac — 63 BC 4
Temkino 124-125 K 6
Temnikov 132-133 G 7
Temora 158-159 J 6
Temosachic 86-87 G 3
Témpē 122-123 K 6
Tempe, AZ 74-75 GH 6
Tempe, Danau — 148-149 GH 7
Tempelfelde 130 III c 1
Tempelsee, Offenbach- 128 III b 1
Temperley, Lomas de Zamora- 110 III b 2
Tèmpio Pausània 122-123 C 5
Temple 129 I a 1
Temple, OK 76-77 E 5
Temple, TX 64-65 G 5
Temple Bay 158-159 H 2
Temple City, CA 83 III d 1
Temple Hills, MD 82 II b 2
Temple of Confucius 155 II b 2
Temple of Heaven 155 II b 2
Templestowe, Melbourne- 161 II c 1
Templeton, IN 70-71 G 5
Temple University 84 III bc 2
Tempoal de Sánchez 86-87 KL 6-7
Temporal, Cachoeira — 92-93 J 7
Temr'uk 126-127 H 4
Temr'ukskij zaliv 126-127 H 4
Temsiyas 136-137 H 3
Temuco 111 B 5
Tena [CO] 92-93 D 5
Tena [EC] 94-95 C 8
Tenabo 86-87 P 7-8
Tenabo, NV 66-67 E 5
Tenabo, Mount — 66-67 E 5
Tenafly, NJ 82 III c 1
Tenaha, TX 76-77 G 7
Tenakee Springs, AK 58-59 U 8
Tenāli 134-135 N 7
Tenancingo 86-87 L 8
Tenasserim = Tanintharī 148-149 C 4
Tenasserim = Tanintharī Taing 148-149 C 3-4
Tenasserim Island = Tanintharī Kyûn 150-151 AB 6
Tenasserim River = Tanintharī Myitkyī 150-151 B 5-6
Tenayuca, Pirámide de — 91 I b 1
Tenda, Colle di — 122-123 B 3
Tendaho 164-165 N 6
Tendega = Tendeka 174-175 J 4
Ten Degree Channel 134-135 P 8
Tendeka 174-175 J 4
Tendrovskaja kosa 126-127 EF 3
Tendūf 166-167 C 3
Tendürek dağı 136-137 KL 3
Tenedos = Bozca ada 136-137 AB 3
Ténenkou 168-169 D 2
Tenente Portela 106-107 L 1
Ténéré 164-165 FG 4-5
Ténéré du Tafassasset 164-165 FG 4
Tenerife [CO] 94-95 D 3
Tenerife [E] 164-165 A 3
Ténès = Tanas 164-165 E 1
Tenessi = Tennessee River 78-79 F 3
Tenf, Jebel — = Jabal at-Tanf 136-137 H 6
Teng, Nam — = Nam Tan 141 F 5
Tenga, Kepulauan — 148-149 G 8
Tengcheng = Chengcheng 146-147 BC 4
Têng-ch'iao = Tengqiao 150-151 G 3
Tengchong 142-143 H 6-7
Tengchow = Penglai 146-147 H 3
Tengchung = Tengchong 142-143 H 6-7
Tenggarong 148-149 G 7
Tenggeli Hai = Nam Tsho 142-143 G 5
Tengger, Pegunungan — 152-153 K 9-10
Tenggol, Pulau — 150-151 DE 10
Tenghai = Chenghai 146-147 F 10
Tenghsien = Deng Xiang 146-147 D 5
Tenghsien = Teng Xian 142-143 M 4
Tengiz, ozero — 132-133 M 7
Tengqiao 150-151 G 3
Tengréla = Tingréla 164-165 C 6
Tengri Nuur = Nam Tsho 142-143 G 5
Tengtian 146-147 E 8
Teng-t'ien-tsên = Tengtian 146-147 E 8
Teng Xian 142-143 M 4
Teng Xiang 146-147 C 10
Teniente, El — 111 BC 4
Teniente F. Delgado 102-103 B 5
Teniente Matienzo 53 C 30-31
Teniente Ochoa 102-103 B 4
Teniente Origone 106-107 F 7
Teniente Rueda 102-103 B 4
Teniet-el-Haad = Thanīyat al-Ḥad 166-167 GH 2
Tenimber Islands = Kepulauan Tanimbar 148-149 K 8
Tenino, WA 66-67 B 2
Tenkāshi = Tenkāsi 140 C 6
Tenkāsi 140 C 6
Tenke 172 E 4
Ten'ki 124-125 R 6
Tenkiller Ferry Lake 76-77 G 5
Tenkodogo 164-165 DE 6
Tenleytown, Washington-, DC 82 II a 1
Ten Lira, Rio — 104-105 H 4
Tennant, CA 66-67 C 5
Tennant Creek 158-159 FG 3
Tenndrâra = Tandrārah 166-167 EF 3
Tennessee 64-65 JK 4
Tennessee River 64-65 J 4-5
Tennille, GA 80-81 E 4
Teno 106-107 B 5
Tenom 152-153 LM 3
Tēnos 122-123 L 7
Tenosique de Pino Suárez 64-65 H 8
Tenouchfi, Djebel — = Jabal Tanūshfī 166-167 F 2
Tenquehuen, Isla — 108-109 B 5
Tenryū gawa 144-145 L 5
Tensift, Ouèd — = Wad Tansīft 164-165 C 2
Ten Sleep 66-67 K 3-4
Ten Sleep, WY 68-69 C 3-4
Tenstrike, MN 70-71 C 2
Tenterfield 158-159 K 5
Ten Thousand Islands 64-65 K 6
Tentolomatinan 152-153 OP 5
Tenyueh = Tengchong 142-143 H 6-7
Teocaltiche 64-65 F 7
Teodoro Sampaio 102-103 D 5
Teodor Sampaio 102-103 F 5
Teófilo Otoni 92-93 L 8
Teofipol' 126-127 C 2
Teonthar 138-139 H 5
Teotepec, Cerro — 64-65 FG 8
Teotihuacán 86-87 L 8
Teotitlán del Camino 86-87 M 8
Tepa 148-149 J 8
Tepalcates, Ixtapalapa- 91 I c 2
Tepasto 116-117 L 3-4
Tepatitlán de Morelos 64-65 F 7
Tepe 136-137 HJ 3
Tepeji del Rio 86-87 L 8
Tepeköy [TR ↘ İzmir] 136-137 B 3
Tepepan, Tlalpan- 91 I c 3
Tepequem, Sierra — 98-99 GH 3
Tepic 64-65 EF 7
Tê-p'ing = Deping 146-147 F 3
Teplice 118 E 3
Teplovka 124-125 S 8
Teques, Los — 92-93 F 2
Tequila 86-87 J 7
Tēqūma 136-137 F 7
Ter 120-121 J 8
Tera [E] 120-121 D 8
Téra [RN] 164-165 E 6
Teradomari 144-145 M 4
Teraga, Hassi — = Ḥāssī Tarārah 166-167 GH 6
Terai 134-135 NO 5
Terang 160 F 7
Terangan = Pulau Trangan 148-149 K 8
Terayama, Yokohama- 155 III a 2
Terbuny 124-125 M 7
Tercan = Mamahatun 136-137 J 3
Terceira 204-205 E 5
Tercio, CO 68-69 D 7
Terechovka 124-125 HJ 7
Terek 126-127 N 5
Terek, Novyj — 126-127 N 5
Terek, Staryj — 126-127 N 5
Terek Autonomous Soviet Socialist Republic = Checheno-Ingush Autonomous Soviet Socialist Republic 126-127 MN 5
Terekli-Mekteb 126-127 M 4
Terekty = Karasaj 126-127 O 2
Terempa 150-151 EF 11
Terence 61 HJ 6
Teren'ga 124-125 R 7
Terengganu = Kuala Terengganu 148-149 DE 5
Terengganu, Sungei — 150-151 D 10
Terenos 102-103 E 4
Teresa, Isla — 108-109 C 5
Teresa Cristina 102-103 G 6
Teresina 92-93 L 6
Teresinha 92-93 J 4
Teresita 94-95 G 7
Tereška 124-125 Q 7
Teresópolis 102-103 L 5
Teressa Island 134-135 P 9
Terevinto 104-105 E 5
Terhazza [RMM, landscape] 164-165 CD 4
Terhazza [RMM, ruins] 164-165 CD 4
Teriberka [SU, place] 132-133 F 4
Terijoki = Zelenogorsk 124-125 GH 3
Terlingua, TX 76-77 C 8
Termas, Las — 111 CD 3
Termas de Puyehue 108-109 C 3
Termas de Tolguaca 106-107 B 7
Terme 136-137 G 2
Terme di Caracalla 113 II b 2
Termet 164-165 G 5
Termez 134-135 K 3
Terminal 106-107 J 5
Tèrmini Imerese 122-123 E 7-F 6
Termit = Termet 164-165 G 5
Tèrmoli 122-123 F 4-5
Ternate 148-149 J 6
Ternej 132-133 a 8
Terni 122-123 E 4
Ternopol' 126-127 B 2
Ternovka 124-125 P 7
Terny 126-127 F 2
Terpenija, mys — 132-133 bc 8
Terpenija, zaliv — 132-133 b 8
Terra Boa 102-103 F 5
Terra Buena Island 83 I b 2
Terrace 56-57 L 7
Terracina 122-123 E 5
Terrāk 116-117 E 5
Terra Nova 63 J 3
Terranova = Newfoundland 56-57 Za 8
Terranovo = Gela 122-123 F 7
Terra Roxa 102-103 H 4
Terra Roxa d'Oeste 102-103 EF 6
Terrassa 120-121 HJ 8
Terre Adélie 53 C 14-15
Terrebonne 72-73 K 2
Terrebonne, OR 66-67 C 3
Terrebonne Bay 78-79 D 6
Terre Clarie 53 C 14
Terre des Hommes 82 I b 1
Terre Haute, IN 64-65 J 4
Terrell, TX 64-65 G 5
Terrenceville 63 J 4
Terreros 91 III a 4
Terreton, ID 66-67 G 4
Territoire de Yukon = Yukon Territory 56-57 JK 4-5
Terro, Oued el — 170 I a 2
Terry, MT 68-69 D 2
Terrytown, LA 85 I b 2
Tersa 126-127 L 1
Tersizhan gölü 136-137 E 3
Terskej-Alatau, chrebet — 134-135 M 2
Terter 126-127 N 6
Terter = Mir-Bašir 126-127 N 6
Teruel [CO] 94-95 D 6
Teruel [E] 120-121 G 8
Terusan Banjir 154 IV a 1-2
Terutao, Ko — 148-149 C 5
Tesaua = Tasāwah 164-165 G 3
Tescott, KS 68-69 GH 6
Tesecav, Lac — 62 O 1
Teseney 164-165 M 5-6
Teshekpuk Lake 56-57 F 3
Teshikaga 144-145 d 2
Teshio 142-143 R 3
Teshio dake 144-145 c 2
Teshio-gawa 144-145 bc 1
Teshio-santi 144-145 bc 1
Tesijn gol 142-143 H 2
Tesio = Teshio 142-143 R 3
Teslin 56-57 K 5
Teslin Crossing 58-59 U 6
Teslin Lake 56-57 K 5
Teslin River 56-57 K 5
Tesouro 102-103 F 2
Tessala, Djebel — = Jabal Tasalah 166-167 F 2
Tessalit 164-165 E 4
Tessaoua 164-165 F 6
Tessâout, Ouèd — = Wād Tissāūt 166-167 C 4
Tessier 61 E 5
Tessolo 174-175 L 1
Test, Tīzī N — 166-167 B 4
Testa del Gargano 122-123 G 5
Teste, la — 120-121 G 6
Testoûr = Tastūr 166-167 L 1
Teta, La — 91 III bc 4
Tetagouche River 63 CD 4
Tetas, Punta — 111 B 2
Tete [Mozambique, administrative unit] 172 F 5
Tete [Mozambique, place] 172 F 5
Tête-à-la-Baleine 63 G 2
Teterboro Airport 82 III b 1
Tétéré 132-133 T 5
Teterev 126-127 D 1
Teteven 122-123 L 4
Tetlin, AK 58-59 Q 5
Tetlin Junction, AK 58-59 QR 5
Tetlin Lake 58-59 Q 5
Tetonia, ID 66-67 H 4
Teton Mountains 66-67 H 3-4
Teton River 66-67 H 2
Tetouan = Tiṭwān 164-165 CD 1
Tetovo 122-123 J 4-5
Tétreauville, Montréal- 82 I b 1
Tetuán = Tiṭwān 164-165 CD 1
Tetuán, Madrid- 113 III a 2
Tet'uche-Pristan' = Rudnaja Pristan' 132-133 a 9
Tet'uši 132-133 H 6-7
Teuco, Río — 111 D 2-3
Teufelsbach 174-175 B 2
Teufelsberg [D] 130 III ab 2
Teulada 122-123 C 6
Teul de González Ortega 86-87 J 7
Teulon 61 K 5
Teun, Pulau — 148-149 J 8
Teunom, Krueng — 152-153 AB 3
Teuquito, Río — 104-105 F 9
Teuri-tō 144-145 b 1
Teusaca, Río — 91 III c 3
Teutoburger Wald 118 C 2-D 3
Teutoburg Forest = Teutoburger Wald 118 C 2-D 3
Tèvere 122-123 E 4
Tèverya 136-137 F 6
Teviot 174-175 F 6
Tevriz 132-133 N 6
Te Waewae Bay 161 B 8
Tewanthar = Teonthar 138-139 H 5
Tewksbury Heights, CA 83 I c 1
Texada Island 66-67 A 1
Texarkana, AR 64-65 H 5
Texarkana, TX 64-65 GH 5
Texas [AUS] 158-159 K 5
Texas [USA] 64-65 FG 5
Texas City, TX 64-65 GH 6
Texas Medical Center 85 III b 2
Texas Southern University 85 III b 2
Texcoco 86-87 L 8
Texcoco, Lago de — 91 I cd 1
Texel 120-121 K 2
Texhoma, OK 76-77 D 4
Texico, NM 76-77 C 5
Texline, TX 76-77 C 4
Texoma, Lake — 64-65 G 5
Teyateyaneng 174-175 G 5
Teza 124-125 N 5
Tezanos Pinto 104-105 F 10
Tezaua = Tasāwah 164-165 G 3
Teziutlán 64-65 G 7-8
Tezpur 134-135 P 5
Tezzeron Lake 60 EF 2
Tha, Nam — 148-149 D 2
Thabana Ntlenyana 174-175 H 5
Thaba Nchu 174-175 G 5
Thabantshonyana = Thabana Ntlenyana 174-175 H 5
Thaba Putsoa [ZA, mountain] 174-175 GH 5
Thaba Putsoa [ZA, mountains] 174-175 G 5-6
Thābaung 141 D 7
Thabazimbi 172 E 6
Thabeikkyin 141 DE 4
Thablā La 138-139 K 3
Tha Bo 150-151 D 4
Thabt, Gebel eth — = Jabal ath-Thabt 173 CD 3
Thabt, Jabal ath- 173 CD 3
Thabye Tshākha Tsho 138-139 K 2
Thac Du'ot = Ban Thac Du'ot 150-151 F 5
Thachin = Samut Sakhon 150-151 BC 6
Tha Chin, Mae Nam — 150-151 C 5-6
Thach Xa Ha 150-151 F 4
Thadawleikkyī 150-151 B 6-7
Thadeua = Mu'o'ng Thadeua 150-151 C 3
Tha Do'a = Mu'o'ng Thadeua 150-151 C 3
Thadôn [BUR, Karin Pyinnei] 148-149 C 3
Thadôn [BUR, Shan Pyinnei] 141 E 5
Tha Dua 150-151 B 3-4
Thaerfelde 130 III c 1
Thagwebôlô 141 E 6
Thagyettaw 150-151 AB 6
Thai Binh 150-151 F 2
Thailand 148-149 CD 3
Thailand, Gulf of — 148-149 D 4-5
Thai Muang 150-151 AB 8
Thai Nguyên 150-151 EF 2
Thair 140 C 1
Thaj, Ath- 134-135 F 5
Tha Khanon = Khiri Ratthanikhom 150-151 B 8
Thakhek 148-149 DE 3
Thākuran 138-139 M 7
Thākurdwāra 138-139 G 3
Thākurgāon 134-135 O 5
Thākurmunda 138-139 L 7
Thākurpukur, South Suburbs- 154 II a 3
Thal [PAK] 134-135 L 4
Thala = Tālah 166-167 L 2
Thalabarivat 150-151 E 6
Thalang 150-151 B 8
Thalātha', Ath- [MA, Marrākush] 166-167 BC 3-4
Thalātha', Ath- [MA, Miknās] 166-167 D 2
Thale Luang 148-149 D 5
Tha Li 150-151 C 4
Thālith, Ash-Shallāl ath- 164-165 KL 5
Thalkirchen, München- 130 II b 2
Thallon 160 J 2
Thalmann, GA 80-81 F 5
Thalnepantla, Río — 91 I b 1
Thames [GB] 119 G 6
Thames [NZ] 158-159 P 7
Thames [RA] 106-107 F 6
Thames Ditton 129 II a 2
Thames River 72-73 F 3
Thamisatse 138-139 M 2
Tha Muang 150-151 BC 5-6
Thamūd 134-135 F 7
Tha Mun Ram 150-151 C 4
Thāna 138-139 D 8
Thanatpin 141 E 7
Thanbyūzayat 141 E 8
Thandaung 141 E 6
Thāndla 138-139 E 6
Thandwe 148-149 B 3
Thānē = Thāna 138-139 D 8
Thānesar 138-139 F 2-3
Thăng Binh 150-151 G 5
Thangkar 142-143 J 4
Thangra Tsho = Thangra Yumtsho 142-143 EF 5
Thangra Yumtsho 142-143 EF 5
Thanh Hoa 148-149 E 3
Thanh Moi 150-151 F 2
Thành Phô Hô Chí Minh 148-149 E 4
Thành So'n 150-151 F 7
Thanh Tri 150-151 EF 8
Thanīyat al-Had 166-167 GH 2
Thanjāvar 140 D 5
Than Kyûn 150-151 A 8
Thanlwin Myit 148-149 C 2-3
Thanlyin 148-149 C 3
Thāno Bulla Khān 138-139 AB 5
Than Uyên 150-151 DE 2
Thanyaburi 150-151 C 5-6
Tha Phraya 150-151 D 5
Tha Pla 150-151 C 4
Thap Put 150-151 B 8
Thapsacus = Dibsah 136-137 GH 5
Thap Sakae 150-151 B 7
Thap Than 150-151 B 5
Thap Than, Huai — 150-151 D 5
Thar 134-135 L 5
Tharād 138-139 C 5
Tharawthèdangyī Kyûn 150-151 AB 6
Tharetkun 141 D 3
Thargo Gangri 138-139 L 2
Thargomindah 158-159 H 5
Thargo Tsangpo 138-139 L 2
Thārī 138-139 B 4
Tharrawaddy = Thāyāwadī 141 DE 7
Tharrawaw = Thāyawaw 141 D 7
Tharsis 120-121 D 10
Tharthār, Bahr ath — = Munkhafad ath-Tharthār 134-135 E 4
Tharthār, Munkhafad ath- 134-135 E 4
Tharthār, Wādī ath- 136-137 K 5
Tha Rua 150-151 C 5
Tharwānīyah = Ath-Tharwānīyah 134-135 GH 6
Tharwānīyah, Ath- 134-135 GH 6
Tha Sa-an = Bang Pakong 150-151 C 6
Tha Sae 150-151 B 7
Tha Sala 150-151 B 8
Tha Song Yang 150-151 B 4
Thásos [GR, island] 122-123 L 5
Thásos [GR, place] 122-123 L 5
Tha Tako 150-151 C 5
Thatcher, AZ 74-75 HJ 6
Thatcher, CO 68-69 DE 7
Tha Thom 150-151 D 3
Thât Khê 150-151 F 1
Thaton = Thadôn 148-149 C 3
That Phanom 150-151 E 4
Ṯhaṭṭha 134-135 K 6
Tha Tum 150-151 D 5
Thaungdût 141 D 3
Tha Uthen 150-151 E 4
Thauval = Thoubal 141 D 3
Tha Wang Pha 150-151 C 3
Thawatchaburi 150-151 D 4-5
Tha Yang 150-151 B 6
Thāyāwadī 141 DE 7
Thāyawaw 141 D 7
Thayer, KS 70-71 C 7
Thayer, MO 78-79 D 2
Thayetchaung 150-151 B 6
Thayetmyō 141 D 6
Thayne, WY 66-67 H 4
Thāzī 148-149 C 2
Thbeng 148-149 DE 4
Thbeng Meanchey 148-149 DE 4
Thēbai [ET] 164-165 L 3
Thēbai [GR] 122-123 K 6
Thebe = Thēbai 164-165 L 3
Thebes = Thēbai [ET] 164-165 L 3
Thebes = Thēbai [GR] 122-123 K 6
The Bluff 88-89 H 2
The Brothers = Jazā'ir al-Ikhwān 173 D 4
The Brothers = Samḥah, Darsah 134-135 G 8
The Capitol 82 II ab 2
Thèchaung 150-151 B 7
The Cheviot 119 EF 4
The Coorong 158-159 G 7
The Dallas, OR 66-67 C 3
The Dalles, OR 66-67 C 3
The Dangs = Dāngs 138-139 D 7
Thèdaw 141 E 5
Thedford, NE 68-69 F 4-5
Thègôn 141 D 6
The Granites 158-159 F 4
The Heads 66-67 A 4
Theimnī 141 EF 4
The Lake 88-89 K 4
Thelepte 166-167 L 2
Thelon Game Sanctuary 56-57 PQ 5
Thelon River 56-57 Q 5
The Meadows, TX 85 III a 2
The Narrows 82 III b 3
Thenia = Tinyah 166-167 H 1
Theodore 158-159 JK 4-5
Theodore, AL 78-79 E 5
Theodore Roosevelt Island 82 II a 2
Theodore Roosevelt Lake 74-75 H 6
Theodore Roosevelt National Memorial Park 68-69 E 2
The Pas 56-57 Q 7
Thepha 150-151 C 9
Thēra 122-123 L 7
Theresienwiese 130 II b 2
Thermaïkòs Kólpos 122-123 K 5-6
Thermopolis, WY 68-69 B 4
Thermopýlai 122-123 K 6
The Rock 160 H 5
Theron Range 53 AB 34-36
Theronsville = Pofadder 172 CD 7
Thèrûr = Thair 140 C 1
Thèséion 113 IV a 2
The Slot 148-149 j 6
The Sound 161 I b 1
Thessalía 122-123 JK 6
Thessalon 70-71 J 2
Thessaloníkē 122-123 K 5
Thessaly = Thessalía 122-123 JK 6
Thetford 119 G 5
Thetford Mines 56-57 W 8
Thethaitāngar 138-139 K 6
Thethiyanagar = Thethaitāngar 138-139 K 6
The Thumbs 161 D 6
The Twins 161 D 5
The Two Rivers 61 G 3
Theun, Nam — 150-151 E 3

Theunissen 174-175 G 5
The Wash 119 G 5
Thiais 129 I c 2
Thībaw 141 E 4
Thibodaux, LA 78-79 D 6
Thicket Portage 61 K 3
Thickwood Hills 61 BC 2
Thief Lake 70-71 BC 1
Thief River Falls, MN 70-71 BC 1
Thiel 168-169 B 2
Thiel Mountains 53 A
Thielsen, Mount — 66-67 BC 4
Thieng, Ban — 150-151 CD 3
Thiers 120-121 J 6
Thiersville = Al-Gharīs 166-167 G 2
Thiès 164-165 A 6
Thiêu Hoa 150-151 E 3
Thieux 129 I d 1
Thika 171 D 3
Thikombia 148-149 b 2
Thillay, le — 129 I c 1
Thilogne 168-169 B 2
Thi Long 150-151 E 3
Thimbu 134-135 OP 5
Thinbôn Kyûn 141 C 5
Thingvallavatn 116-117 c 2
Thingvellir 116-117 c 2
Thio 158-159 N 4
Thionville 120-121 KL 4
Thirinam Tsho 138-139 K 2
Thiruvalla = Tiruvalla 140 C 6
Thisted 116-117 C 9
Thistilfjördhur 116-117 f 1
Thistle, UT 74-75 H 2-3
Thistle Creek 58-59 S 5
Thistle Island 158-159 G 7
Thjórsá 116-117 d 2
Thlèta Madârî, Berzekh — = Râ's Wūruq 164-165 D 1
Thlewiaza River 56-57 R 5
Thmail = Thumayl 136-137 K 6
Thmâr, Kompong — 150-151 E 6
Thmar Pouok 150-151 D 5-6
Thnīn Rīāt, Ath- 166-167 B 3
Thoen 150-151 B 4
Thogchhen 138-139 HJ 2
Thogdoragpa 142-143 F 5
Thogjalung 142-143 E 5
Tho'i Binh 150-151 E 8
Thomas, OK 76-77 E 5
Thomas, WV 72-73 G 5
Thomaston, GA 80-81 DE 4
Thomaston, TX 76-77 F 8
Thomasville, AL 78-79 EF 5
Thomasville, GA 64-65 K 5
Thomasville, NC 80-81 F 3
Thomochabgo 138-139 L 2
Thompson 56-57 R 6
Thompson, UT 74-75 HJ 3
Thompson, Cape — 58-59 D 2
Thompson Falls, MT 66-67 F 2
Thompson Island 84 I bc 3
Thompson Pass 58-59 P 6
Thompson Peak [USA, Colorado] 66-67 B 5
Thompson Peak [USA, Montana] 66-67 F 2
Thompson River [CDN] 60 G 4
Thompson River [USA] 70-71 D 5-6
Thompson's Falls 171 D 2-3
Thompsonville, MI 70-71 GH 3
Thomson 154 III b 1
Thomson, GA 80-81 E 4
Thomson Deep 158-159 KL 6
Tho'n, Nam — = Nam Theun 150-151 E 3
Thon Buri 148-149 CD 4
Thong Pha Phum 148-149 C 4
Thongsa Chhu = Mangde Chhu 138-139 N 4
Thongsa Dsong 141 B 2
Thôngwa 141 E 7
Thonon-les-Bains 120-121 L 5
Thonpa 138-139 M 3
Thoreau, NM 74-75 JK 5
Thorez 126-127 J 3
Thori 138-139 K 4
Thørisvatn 116-117 de 2
Thornbury, Melbourne- 161 II bc 1
Thorndale, TX 76-77 F 7
Thornton, CO 68-69 D 6
Thornton, IA 70-71 D 4
Thornton, WA 66-67 E 2
Thornton Beach 83 I a 2
Thornton Heath, London- 129 II b 2
Thornville 174-175 HJ 5
Thorofare, PA 84 III b 2
Thorp, WA 66-67 C 2
Thorshafn = Tórshavn 114-115 G 3
Thórshöfn 116-117 f 1
Thôt Nôt 150-151 E 7
Thoubal 141 D 3
Thousand Islands 72-73 HJ 2
Thousand Islands = Pulau-pulau Seribu 148-149 E 7-8
Thousand Spring Creek 66-67 F 5
Thovala = Tovāla 140 C 6
Thowa 172 G 2
Thrákē 122-123 LM 5
Three Creek, ID 66-67 F 4
Three Creeks 60 J 1
Three Forks, MT 66-67 H 3
Three Hummock Island 160 bc 2
Three Kings Islands 158-159 O 6
Three Lakes, WI 70-71 F 3
Threemile Rapids 66-67 F 3
Three Pagodas Pass = Phra Chedi Sam Ong 148-149 C 3-4
Three Points, Cape — 164-165 D 8
Three Rivers, MI 70-71 H 5
Three Rivers, NM 76-77 A 6
Three Rivers, TX 76-77 EF 8
Three Rivers = Trois-Rivières 56-57 W 8
Three Sisters [USA] 66-67 C 3
Three Sisters [ZA] 174-175 E 6
Three Sisters Range 58-59 WX 7
Three Springs 158-159 BC 5
Three Valley 60 HJ 4
Throckmorton, TX 76-77 E 6
Throgs Neck 82 III d 2
Thu, Cu Lao — 148-149 EF 4
Thubby = Abū Ẓabī 134-135 G 6
Thu Bôn 150-151 G 5
Thu Dau Môt = Phu Cu'o'ng 150-151 F 7
Thugsum 138-139 J 2
Thul [PAK ↘ Dāḏū] 138-139 B 4
Thul [PAK ↑ Shikārpūr] 138-139 B 3
Thule = Qânâq 56-57 W-X 2
Thumayl 136-137 K 6
Thumb, WY 66-67 H 3
Thumbs, The — 161 D 6
Thun 118 C 5
Thunder Bay [CDN] 56-57 ST 8
Thunder Bay [USA] 72-73 E 2
Thunder Butte Creek 68-69 EF 3
Thunderhouse Falls 62 K 1-2
Thunder Mount 58-59 G 2
Thung Saliam 150-151 B 4
Thung Song 150-151 B 8
Thu'ong Đu'c 150-151 FG 5
Thuqb al-Ḥājj 136-137 L 8
Thüringen 118 E 3
Thüringer Wald 118 E 3
Thuringia = Thüringen 118 EF 3
Thuringian Forest = Thüringer Wald 118 E 3
Thurloo Downs 160 F 2
Thurso [CDN] 72-73 J 2
Thurso [GB] 119 E 2
Thurston Island 53 BC 26-27
Thutade Lake 60 D 1
Thyatera = Akhisar 136-137 BC 3
Thyatira = Akhisar 136-137 BC 3
Thykkvibær 116-117 c 3
Thynne, Mount — 66-67 C 1
Thysville = Mbanza-Ngungu 172 B 3
Tiahuanaco 92-93 F 8
Tía Juana 94-95 F 2
Tian'anmen 155 II b 2
Tianbao 146-147 F 9
Tianchang 146-147 G 5
Tiandu 150-151 G 3
Tianeti 126-127 M 5
Tiangol 168-169 B 2
Tianguá 92-93 L 5
Tianhe [TJ, Guangxi Zhuangzu Zizhiqu] 146-147 B 9
Tianhe [TJ, Hubei] 146-147 C 5
Tianjin 142-143 M 4
Tianmen 146-147 D 6
Tianmu Shan 146-147 G 6
Tianshui 142-143 JK 5
Tiantai 146-147 H 7
Tiantan Park 155 II b 2
Tianzhu 146-147 B 8
Tianzhuangtai 144-145 CD 2
Tiaofeng 150-151 H 2
Tiaraju 106-107 K 3
Tiaret = Tiyārat 164-165 E 1
Tiassalé 164-165 CD 7
Tib 164-165 G 1
Tibaji 111 F 2
Tibaji, Rio — 102-103 G 6
Tībastī, Sarīr — 164-165 H 4
Tibati 164-165 G 7
Tībazah 166-167 H 1
Tibé, Pic de — 168-169 C 3
Ṭib el Fâl = Ṭayb al-Fāl 136-137 J 5
Tibell, Wādī — = Wādī at-Tubal 136-137 J 6
Tiberias = Ṭēvarya 173 D 1
Tibesti 164-165 H 4
Tibet, Plateau of — = Jang Thang 142-143 E-G 5
Tibetan Autonomous Region 142-143 E-G 5
Tibissah 164-165 F 1
Tibissah, Jabal — [DZ] 166-167 J 7
Tibissah, Jabal — [TN] 166-167 L 2
Tibnī 136-137 H 5
Tibooburra 158-159 H 5
Tibrikot 138-139 J 3
Tibû 94-95 E 3
Tibugá, Ensenada de — 92-93 D 3
Tiburon, CA 83 I b 1
Tiburón, Isla — 64-65 D 6
Tiburon Peninsula 83 I b 1
Tiburtina, Via — 113 II c 2
Tichao, Djebel — = Jabal Tīshāro 166-167 JK 2
Tichborne 72-73 H 2
Tichitt = Tīshīt 164-165 C 5
Tichka, Tīzī N — 166-167 C 4
Tichon'kaja Stancija = Birobidžan 132-133 Z 8
Tichoreck 126-127 JK 4
Tichvin 132-133 E 6
Tichvinka 124-125 JK 4
Tichvinskij kanal 124-125 K 4
Ticino [CH] 118 D 5
Ticino [RA] 106-107 F 4
Ticomán, Ciudad de México- 91 I c 1
Ticonderoga, NY 72-73 K 3
Ticul 64-65 J 7
Tidaholm 116-117 EF 8
Tidal Basin 82 II a 2
Tiddas 166-167 C 3
Tiddim = Tīdein 141 C 4
Tīdein 141 C 4
Tīdighīn, Jabal — 166-167 D 2
Tidikelt = Tidikilt 164-165 E 3
Tidioute, PA 72-73 G 4
Tidjikja = Tijiqjah 164-165 B 5
Tidore, Pulau — 148-149 J 6
Tidra, Île — 164-165 A 5
Tidwell Park 85 III b 1
Tiébissou 168-169 D 4
Tiechang 144-145 EF 2
Tiefwerder, Berlin- 130 III a 1
T'ieh-ling = Tieling 144-145 DE 1
Tiekel, AK 58-59 P 6
Tielinanmu Hu = Thirinam Tsho 138-139 K 2
Tieling 144-145 DE 1
T'ien-chia-an = Huainan 142-143 M 5
T'ien-chin = Tianjin 142-143 M 4
T'ien-chouei = Tianshui 142-143 JK 5
T'ien-chu = Tianzhu 146-147 B 8
T'ien-chuang-t'ai = Tianzhuangtai 144-145 CD 2
Tiền Giang 150-151 E 7
T'ien-ho = Tianhe 146-147 B 9
Tienkiaan = Huainan 142-143 M 5
Tienko 168-169 D 3
Tienmen = Tianmen 146-147 D 6
T'ien-pao = Tianbao 146-147 F 9
Tien Schan 142-143 C-G 3
Tien Shan 142-143 C-G 3
Tienshui = Tianshui 142-143 JK 5
Tientai = Tiantai 146-147 H 7
Tientsin = Tianjin 142-143 M 4
Tien-tu = Tiandu 150-151 G 3
Tiên Yên 148-149 E 2
Tierfontein 174-175 G 5
Tiergarten, Berlin- 130 III b 1
Tierp 116-117 G 7
Tierpark Berlin 130 III c 2
Tierpark Hellabrunn 130 II b 2
Tierpoortdam 174-175 G 5
Tierra Amarilla 106-107 BC 1
Tierra Amarilla, NM 76-77 A 4
Tierra Blanca [MEX, Chihuahua] 76-77 B 9
Tierra Blanca [MEX, Veracruz] 64-65 G 8
Tierra Blanca [PE] 96-97 D 5
Tierra Blanca Creek 76-77 CD 5
Tierra Colorada 86-87 L 9
Tierra Colorada, Bajo de los — 108-109 F 4
Tierra de Barros 120-121 D 9
Tierra de Campos 120-121 E 7-8
Tierra del Fuego [RA, administrative unit] 111 C 8
Tierra del Fuego [RA, landscape] 110 C 8
Tierra del Fuego, Isla Grande de — 108-109 D-F 9-10
Tierra del Pan 120-121 DE 7-8
Tierradentro 94-95 D 5
Tierralta 94-95 C 3
Tie Siding, WY 68-69 D 5
Tiétar 120-121 E 8
Tietê [BR, place] 102-103 J 5
Tietê [BR, river] 110 II a 2
Tietê, Rio — 102-103 H 4
Tieton, WA 66-67 C 2
Tiêu Cân 150-151 F 8
Tifariti = Atfārītī 164-165 B 3
Tiffany Mountain 66-67 CD 1
Tiffin, OH 72-73 E 4
Tifist, Bi'r — 166-167 M 4
Tiflat 166-167 C 3
Tiflis = Tbilisi 126-127 M 6
Tifore, Pulau — 148-149 J 6
Tifrīst 166-167 E 2
Tifton, GA 80-81 E 5
Tiga, Pulau — 152-153 L 3
Tigalda Island 58-59 o 3
Tigapuluh, Pegunungan — 152-153 E 6
Tigara = Point Hope, AK 58-59 D 2
Tigaras 150-151 B 11
Tigazû 141 D 3
Tiger Point 78-79 C 6
Tiger Ridge 85 I c 3
Tiger Stadium 84 II b 2
Tighennif = Tighinnīf 166-167 G 2
Tighighīmīn 166-167 H 6
Tighina = Bendery 126-127 D 3
Tighinnīf 166-167 G 2
Tighintūrīn 166-167 L 6
Tighintūrīn, Ḥāssī — 166-167 H 6
Tighzirt 166-167 J 1
Tigieglo = Tayeegle 172 H 1
Tigil' 132-133 e 6
Tigīt 166-167 A 5
Tignish 63 DE 4
Tigra = Tigrē 164-165 MN 6
Tigra, Bajo de la — 106-107 E 7
Tigrē [ETH] 164-165 MN 6
Tigre [RCH] 104-105 B 8
Tigre, Cordillera del — 106-107 C 3-4
Tigre, Dent du — = Dông Voi Mêp 148-149 F 4
Tigre, El — [CO] 94-95 F 4
Tigre, El — [YV] 92-93 G 3
Tigre, Río — [EC] 92-93 D 5
Tigre, Río — [YV] 94-95 K 3
Tigre, Sierra del — 106-107 C 3
Tigre-Don Torcuato 110 III b 1
Tigre-El Talar 110 III b 1
Tigres, Loma de los — 106-107 DE 6
Tigris = Nahr-Dijlah 134-135 E 3
Tigris = Shaṭṭ Dijlah 134-135 E 4
Tiguelguemine = Tighighīmīn 166-167 H 6
Tiguentourine = Tighintūrīn 166-167 L 6
Tiguentourine, Hassi — = Ḥāssī Tighintūrīn 166-167 H 6
Tigui 164-165 H 5
Tiguidit, Falaise de — 168-169 GH 1
Tiguila 168-169 E 2
Tigur 138-139 K 3
Tigyaing = Htigyaing 141 E 4
Tīh, Jabal at- 164-165 L 3
Tīh, Ṣaḥrā' at- 164-165 L 2
Tiham = Tihāmah 134-135 D 6-E 8
Tihāmah 134-135 D 6-E 8
Tihodaïne, Erg — = 'Irq Tahūdawīn 166-167 K 7
Ṭihrī = Tehri 138-139 G 2
Ti-hua = Ürümchi 142-143 F 3
Tihwa = Ürümchi 142-143 F 3
Tiirismaa 116-117 L 7
Tijamuchi, Río — 104-105 D 4
Tijāra 138-139 F 4
Tijeras, NM 76-77 A 5
Tijiqjah 164-165 B 5
Tijoca 92-93 K 5
Tijuana 64-65 C 5
Tijuca 100-101 B 5
Tijuca, Lagoa da — 110 I ab 2
Tijuca, Pico da — 110 I b 2
Tijuca, Rio de Janeiro- 110 I b 2
Tijucas 102-103 H 7
Tijucas, Baía de — 102-103 H 7
Tijucas, Rio — 102-103 H 7
Tijuco, Rio — 102-103 H 3
Tika 63 C 2
Tikal 64-65 J 8
Tikamgarh 138-139 G 5
Ṭikārī = Tekāri 138-139 K 5
Tikchik Lake 58-59 HJ 7
Tikhvin = Tichvin 132-133 E 6
Tikiklut, AK 58-59 J 1
Tikopia 158-159 N 2
Tikota 140 B 2
Tikrīt 136-137 K 5
Tiksi 132-133 Y 3
Tikšozero 116-117 OP 4
Tilādru 140 E 2
Tiladummati Atoll 176 a 1
Tilādūru = Tilādru 140 E 2
Tilaiya Reservoir 138-139 K 5
Tilama 106-107 B 4
Tilamuta 148-149 H 6
Tīlayah, Wādī — 166-167 G 6
Tilbeşar ovası 136-137 G 4
Tilburg 120-121 K 3
Tilbury 72-73 E 3
Tilcara 111 CD 2
Tilden, NE 68-69 H 4-5
Tilden, TX 76-77 E 8
Tilemsi 164-165 E 5
Tilhar 138-139 G 4
Tilia, Ouèd — = Wādī Tīlayah 166-167 G 6
Tiličiki 132-133 g 5
Tilimsān, Jabal — 166-167 F 2
Tilin = Htīlin 141 D 5
Tilisarao 106-107 E 4
Tillabéri 164-165 E 6
Tillamook, OR 66-67 B 3
Tillamook Bay 66-67 AB 3
Tillery, Lake — 80-81 FG 3
Tilley 61 C 5
Tillia 164-165 E 5
Tillsonburg 72-73 F 3
Tilmās 166-167 C 7
Tilomonte 104-105 B 8
Tilos = Tēlos 122-123 M 7
Tilpa 158-159 H 6
Tilrahmat 166-167 H 3
Tilrhemt = Tilrahmat 166-167 H 3
Tilston 68-69 F 1
Tiltil 106-107 B 4
Tīlū, Nam — 141 E 5
Tilvārā = Tilwāra 138-139 CD 5
Tilwāra 138-139 CD 5
Tim 126-127 H 1
Ṭīmā 173 B 4
Timagami 72-73 FG 1
Timagami, Lake — 72-73 F 1
Timah, Bukit — 154 III a 1
Timalūlīn 166-167 L 5
Timanā 92-93 D 4
Timane, Río — 102-103 B 4
Timanskij kr'až 132-133 J 5-H 4
Timaru 158-159 O 8
Timaševo [SU, Kujbyševskaja Oblast'] 124-125 S 7
Timaševsk 126-127 J 4
Timasova Gora 124-125 Q 3
Timassah 164-165 H 3
Timassanin = Burj 'Umar Idrīs 164-165 EF 3
Timbalier Bay 78-79 D 6
Timbalier Island 78-79 D 6
Timbara 96-97 B 3
Timbaúba 100-101 G 4
Timbaúva 106-107 KL 2-3
Timbédra = Tinbadghah 164-165 C 5
Timber, OR 66-67 B 3
Timber Creek, Houston-, TX 85 III b 1
Timber Creek North Branch 84 III c 2-3
Timbergrove Manor, Houston-, TX 85 III b 1
Timber Lake, SD 68-69 F 3
Timber Mountain 74-75 F 3
Timbío 94-95 C 6
Timbiquí 94-95 C 6
Timbiras 100-101 C 3
Timbó [BR, Rio de Janeiro] 110 I b 2
Timbó [BR, Santa Catarina] 102-103 H 7
Timbo [Guinea] 164-165 B 6
Timbó, Rio — 102-103 G 7
Timboulaga 164-165 F 5
Timbun Mata, Pulau — 152-153 N 3
Timedjerdane, Ouèd — = Wādī Tamajirdayn 166-167 G 7
Timehri 98-99 JK 1
Timellouine = Timalūlīn 166-167 L 5
Timgad = Timkād 166-167 K 2
Timḥadīt 166-167 D 3
Timia 164-165 F 5
Timimoun = Tīmīmūn 164-165 E 3
Timimoun, Sebkra de — = Sabkhat Tīmīmūn 166-167 G 5
Tīmīmūn 164-165 E 3
Tīmīmūn, Sabkhat — 166-167 G 5
Timiş 122-123 J 3
Timişoara 122-123 J 3
Timiza, Parque Distrital de — 91 III ab 3
Timkād 166-167 K 2
Tim Mersoï, Oued — 164-165 F 5
Timmins 56-57 U 8
Timmonsville, SC 80-81 G 3
Timmoudi = Tīmmūdī 164-165 D 3
Timon 92-93 L 6
Timonha 100-101 D 2
Timor 148-149 H 9-J 8
Timorante 100-101 E 4
Timor Sea 158-159 E 2
Timor Timur = 23 ◁ 148-149 J 8
Timor Trough 148-149 J 8
Timošino 124-125 L 3
Timote 106-107 F 5
Timotes 94-95 F 3
Timpahute Range 74-75 F 4
Timpas, CO 68-69 E 7
Timpson, TX 76-77 G 7
Timsāḥ, Buḥayrat at- 173 C 2
Timšer [SU, place] 124-125 U 3
Timšer [SU, river] 124-125 U 3
Tina 174-175 H 6
Tina, La — 96-97 B 4
Tinaco 94-95 G 3
Ṭīnah, Khalīj aṭ- 173 C 2
Tinajas, Las — 102-103 A 7
Tinakula 148-149 kl 7
Tinaquillo 94-95 G 3
Tinbadghah 164-165 C 5
Tin City, AK 58-59 D 4
Tincopalca 96-97 F 9
Tindivanam 140 DE 4
Tindouf = Tindūf 164-165 C 3
Tindouf, Hamada de — = Hammadat Tindūf 166-167 B 6-C 5
Tindouf, Sebkra de — = Sabkhat Tindūf 164-165 C 3
Tindūf 164-165 C 3
Tindūf, Hammadat — 166-167 BC 5-6
Tindūf, Sabkhat — 164-165 C 3
Tineba, Pegunungan — 152-153 O 6-7
Tin Edrin 168-169 E 1
Tinejdâd = Tinjdād 166-167 D 4
Tineo 120-121 D 7
Tin Essalak 164-165 E 5
Tinezoûlîn = Tinzūlīn 166-167 CD 4
Tin Fouchaye = Tīn Fūshay 166-167 L 5
Tinfouchi = Tīn Fūshī 166-167 D 5
Tīn Fūshay 166-167 L 5
Tīn Fūshī 166-167 D 5
Ting-an = Ding'an 150-151 H 3
Tingchei Dsong 138-139 LM 3
Tinggi, Pulau — 150-151 E 11
Tingha 160 K 2-3
Tinghing = Dingxing 146-147 E 2
Tinghīr 166-167 D 4
Tinghīrt, Hammadat — 164-165 FG 3
Ting-hsi = Dingxi 142-143 J 4
Tinghsien = Ding Xian 146-147 E 2
Ting-hsin = Dingxin 142-143 H 3
Ting-hsing = Dingxing 146-147 E 2
Ting Jiang 146-147 F 9
Ting Kau 155 I a 1
Tingling Shan = Qin Ling 142-143 KL 5
Tingmerkput Mount 58-59 FG 2
Ting-nan = Dingnan 146-147 E 9
Tingo 96-97 B 2
Tingo María 92-93 D 6
Tingpian = Dingbian 146-147 A 3
Tingréla 164-165 C 6
Tingri Dsong 142-143 F 6
Tingsiqiao 146-147 E 7
Tingsryd 116-117 F 9
T'ing-szŭ-ch'iao = Tingsiqiao 146-147 E 7
Tingtao = Dingtao 146-147 E 4
Tinguipaya 92-93 F 8
Tinguiririca, Volcán — 106-107 B 5
Tingvoll 116-117 BC 6
Tingwon 148-149 g 5
Ting-yüan = Dingyuan 146-147 F 5
Ting-yüan-ying = Bajan Choto 142-143 JK 4
Tinharé, Ilha de — 100-101 E 7
Tinh Biên 150-151 E 7
Tinhosa Island = Dazhou Dao 150-151 H 3
Tinicum Wildlife Preserve 84 III b 2
Tinjar, Batang — 152-153 L 4
Tinjdād 166-167 D 4
Tinjil, Pulau — 148-149 E 8
Tin Khéouné, Hassi — = Ḥāssī Tīn Quwānīn 166-167 L 7
Tinkisso 164-165 BC 6
Tinnevelly = Tirunelvēli 134-135 M 9
Tinogasta 111 C 3
Tinpak = Dianbai 146-147 C 11
Tīn Quwānīn, Ḥāssī — 166-167 L 7
Tinrhert, Hamada de — = Hammadat Tinghīrt 164-165 FG 3
Tinsukia 134-135 Q 5
Tintah, MN 68-69 H 2-3
Tin Tarābīn, Wādī — 164-165 F 4
Tin Tehoun 168-169 E 1
Tintina 111 D 3
Tintinara 160 E 5
Tinyah 166-167 H 1
Tīn Zakyū 166-167 JK 6-7
Tin Zekiou = Tīn Zakyū 166-167 JK 6-7
Tinzūlīn 166-167 CD 4
Tío, El — 111 D 4
Tioga, CO 68-69 D 7
Tioga, LA 78-79 C 5
Tioga, ND 68-69 E 1
Tioga, TX 76-77 F 6
Tioga, Philadelphia-, PA 84 III bc 1
Tiogo 168-169 E 2
Tioman, Pulau — 148-149 DE 6
Tionesta, CA 66-67 C 5
Tionesta, PA 72-73 G 4
Tioro, Selat — 152-153 P 8
Tioukeline, Hassi — = Ḥāssī Tiyūkulīn 166-167 J 6
Tiourinine = Tiyūrīnīn 166-167 K 7
Tipaza = Tībāzah 166-167 H 1
Tipp City, OH 70-71 H 6
Tippecanoe River 70-71 GH 5
Tipperā 141 B 3-4
Tipperary 119 BC 5
Tipton, CA 74-75 D 4
Tipton, IA 70-71 E 5
Tipton, IN 70-71 G 5
Tipton, MO 70-71 D 6
Tipton, OK 76-77 E 5
Tipton, WY 68-69 B 5
Tipton, Mount — 74-75 F 5
Tiptonville, TN 78-79 E 2
Tip Top Hill 70-71 GH 1
Tipttūru = Tiptūr 140 C 4
Tiptūr 140 C 4
Tiputini, Río — 96-97 C 2
Tiquaruçu 100-101 E 6-7
Tiquié, Rio — 94-95 G 7
Tiquisate 86-87 P 10
Tiracambu, Serra de — 92-93 K 5
Tiradentes 102-103 KL 4
Tira Fogo 98-99 G 9
Tīrān, Jazīrat — 173 D 4
Tirana = Tiranë 122-123 HJ 5
Tiranë 122-123 HJ 5
Tirāp 141 E 2
Tirapata 96-97 F 9
Tirap Frontier Division = Tirāp 141 E 2
Tirasduines 174-175 B 4
Tiras Mountains = Tirasplato 174-175 B 3-4
Tirasplato 174-175 B 3-4
Tiraspol' 126-127 D 3
Tiratimine = Tarātmīn 166-167 H 7
Tirbande Turkestān 134-135 JK 3
Tire 136-137 B 3
Tirebolu 136-137 H 2
Tiree 119 C 3
Tiree Passage 119 C 3
Tîrgovişte 122-123 L 3
Tîrgu Cărbuneşti 122-123 KL 3
Tîrgu Jiu 122-123 K 3
Tîrgu Mureş 122-123 L 2
Tîrgu Neamţ 122-123 LM 2
Tirhatimine = Tarātmīn 166-167 H 7
Tirhut 138-139 K 4
Tirich Mīr 134-135 L 3
Tirikuṇāmalaya 134-135 N 9
Tīrnabos 122-123 K 6
Tiro 168-169 C 3
Tirodi 138-139 G 7
Tirol 118 EF 5
Tirong Dsong 141 C 2
Tiros 102-103 K 3
Tirso 122-123 C 6
Tirthahalli 140 B 4
Tirtol 138-139 L 7
Tirúa 106-107 A 7
Tiruchchendur 134-135 M 9
Tiruchchirāppalli = Tiruchirāpalli 134-135 M 8
Tiruchendur = Tiruchchendur 134-135 M 9
Tiruchengodu 140 CD 5
Tiruchinkōṭṭai = Tiruchengodu 140 CD 5
Tiruchirāpalli 134-135 M 8
Tirukkoyilūr 140 D 5
Tirukkunamalai = Tirikuṇāmalaya 134-135 N 9
Tirukoilur = Tirukkoyilūr 140 D 5
Tirumakūdal Narsipur 140 C 4
Tirumangalam 140 CD 6
Tirumayam 140 D 5
Tirunelveli 134-135 M 9
Tirupati 134-135 M 8
Tiruppattur = Tiruppattūr 140 D 5
Tiruppattūr [IND ↙ Madurai] 140 D 5
Tiruppattūr [IND ↗ Salem] 140 D 4
Tiruppundi 140 DE 5
Tiruppūr 140 C 5
Tirūr = Trikkandiyur 140 B 5
Tiruttani 140 D 4
Tirutturaippūndi 140 DE 5
Tiruvādānai 140 D 6
Tiruvalla 140 C 6
Tiruvallūr 140 DE 4
Tiruvālūr 140 D 5
Tiruvanatapuram = Trivandrum 134-135 M 9
Tiruvannāmalai 140 D 4
Tiruvarur = Tiruvālūr 140 D 5
Tiruvatāmūr = Trevancore 140 C 6
Tiruvāyam = Tirumayam 140 D 5
Tiruvettipuram 140 D 4
Tiruvur = Tiruvūru 140 E 2
Tiruvūru 140 E 2
Tisa 122-123 J 3
Tisa = Tisza 118 K 5
Tisaiyanvilai 140 CD 6
Tīsamsīlt 166-167 G 2
Tisdale 56-57 Q 7
Tīshāro, Jabal — 166-167 JK 2
Tīshīt 164-165 C 5
Tishlah 164-165 AB 4
Tishomingo, MS 78-79 E 3
Tishomingo, OK 76-77 F 5
Tis Isat fwafwate 164-165 M 6
Tisiten, Jebel — = Jabal Tīdighīn 166-167 D 2
Tiškovka 126-127 E 2
Tismana 122-123 K 3
Tissah 166-167 D 2
Tissamaharama = Tissamahārāmaya 140 E 7
Tissamahārāmaya 140 E 7
Tissāūt, Wād — 166-167 C 4
Tissemsilt = Tīsamsīlt 166-167 G 2
Tistā 138-139 M 5
Tisza 118 K 5
Tit 166-167 G 6
Ṭītabar 141 D 2
Ṭītagarh 138-139 M 6
Titaluk River 58-59 K 2
Titālya 138-139 M 4
Tit-Ary 132-133 Y 3
Titemsi 164-165 E 5
Titeri, Monts du — = Jabal al-Tītrī 166-167 H 1-2
Titicaca, Lago — 92-93 F 8
Titlagarh 138-139 J 7
Titna River 58-59 L 4
Titograd 122-123 H 4
Titovo Užice 122-123 HJ 4
Titov Veles 122-123 JK 5
Titran 116-117 C 6
Titri, Jabal al- 166-167 H 1-2
Tittabawassee River 70-71 HJ 4
Titu [EAK] 171 D 2
Titule 172 DE 1
Titusville, FL 80-81 c 2
Titusville, PA 72-73 G 4
Tiṭwān 164-165 CD 1
Tiu Chung Chau 155 I b 1-2
Tiura Pipardih 138-139 JK 5
Tivaouane 164-165 A 5
Tiverton 119 E 6
Tivoli 122-123 E 5
Tixtla de Guerrero 86-87 L 9
Tiyāgai 140 D 5
Tiyārat 164-165 E 1
Tiyūkulīn, Ḥāssī — 166-167 J 6
Tiyūrīnīn 166-167 K 7
Tizapán, Villa Obregón- 91 I b 2
Tizimín 64-65 J 7
Tizi 'n Talghemt = Tizi 'N Talrhemt 166-167 D 3
Tīzī N Talrhemt 166-167 D 3
Tīzī N Test 166-167 B 4
Tīzī N Tichka 166-167 C 4
Tizi-Ouzou = Tīzī Wazū 164-165 E 1
Tīzī Wazū 164-165 E 1
Tiznados, Río — 94-95 H 3
Tiznīt 164-165 C 3
Tizoc 86-87 JK 5
Tjeggelvas 116-117 GH 4
Tjendana, Pulau — = Sumba 148-149 G 9
Tjertjen = Chărchăn 142-143 F 4
Tjirebon = Cirebon 148-149 E 8
Tjörn [IS] 116-117 c 2
Tjörn [S] 116-117 D 8-9
Tjörnes 116-117 e 1
Tjøtta 116-117 E 5
Tjumen = Tumen' 132-133 M 6
Tjuvfjorden 116-117 l 6
Tkibuli 126-127 L 5
Tkvarčeli 126-127 K 5
Tlacotalpan 86-87 N 8
Tlahuac 91 I c 3
Tlahualilo, Sierra del — 76-77 C 9
Tlahualilo de Zaragoza 76-77 C 9
Tlalnepantla de Comonfort 86-87 L 8
Tlalpan 91 I b 3
Tlalpan-El Reloj 91 I c 3
Tlalpan-Huipulco 91 I c 3
Tlalpan-Tepepan 91 I c 3
Tlalpan-Villa Coapa 91 I c 3
Tlapa de Comonfort 86-87 LM 9
Tlaquepaque 64-65 F 7
Tl'arata 126-127 N 5
Tlaxcala 64-65 G 8
Tlaxcala de Xicoténcatl 64-65 G 8
Tlaxiaco, Santa María Asunción — 64-65 G 8
Tlell 60 B 3
Tlemcen = Tilimsān 164-165 D 2
Tlemcen, Monts de — = Jabal Tilimsān 166-167 F 2
Tlemcès 164-165 EF 5
Tleta = Sūq ath-Thalāthah 166-167 C 2
Tleta Beni Oulid = Ath-Thālātha 166-167 D 2
Tleta Ketama = Kitāmah 166-167 D 2
Tlumač 126-127 B 2
Tluste = Tolstoje 126-127 B 2
Tmessa = Timassah 164-165 H 3
Tnine Riat = Ath-Thnīn Rīāt 166-167 B 3
Toachi, Río — 96-97 B 1-2
Toamasina 172 JK 5
Toano, VA 80-81 H 2
Toano Range 66-67 F 5
Toa Payoh Town, Singapore- 154 III b 1
Toay 106-107 E 6
Toba [J] 144-145 L 5
Toba [RA] 106-107 G 2
Toba, Danau — 148-149 C 6
Tobago 64-65 OP 9

Tobago, Trinidad and — 64-65 O 9-10
Tobalai, Pulau — 148-149 J 7
Tobar, NV 66-67 F 5
Tobarra 120-121 G 9
Tobas 106-107 F 2
Ṭoba Ṭek Singh 138-139 CD 2
Tobatí 102-103 D 6
Tobelo 148-149 J 6
Tobelumbang 152-153 OP 6
Tobermorey 158-159 G 4
Tobermory 72-73 EF 2
Tobi 148-149 K 6
Tobias, NE 68-69 H 5
Tobias Barreto 100-101 EF 6
Tobin, Mount — 66-67 E 5
Tobin Lake [CDN, lake] 61 G 4
Tobin Lake [CDN, place] 61 G 4
Tobique River 63 C 4
Tobi-shima 144-145 M 3
Tobli 168-169 C 4
Tobo 148-149 JK 7
Toboali 148-149 E 7
Tobol [SU, place] 132-133 L 7
Tobol [SU, river] 132-133 M 6
Toboli 148-149 H 7
Tobol'sk 132-133 MN 6
Tô Bông 150-151 G 6
Toborochi 104-105 E 6
Töbrang 138-139 K 3
Tobruch = Ṭubruq 164-165 J 2
Tobruk = Tubruq 164-165 J 2
Tobseda 132-133 J 4
T'ob'ulech 132-133 b 3
Tobys' 124-125 T 2
Tocache Nuevo 96-97 C 6
Tocaima 94-95 D 5
Tocantínia 92-93 K 6
Tocantinópolis 92-93 K 6
Tocantins, Rio — 92-93 K 5-6
Toccoa, GA 80-81 E 3
Tochigi 144-145 MN 4
Tochio 144-145 M 4
T'o-chi Tao = Tuoji Dao 146-147 H 2
Toch'o-do 144-145 E 5
Tochta 124-125 R 2
Tockoje 124-125 T 7
Toco [RCH] 111 C 2
Toco [TT] 94-95 L 2
Toco, El — 94-95 J 3
Tócome 91 II c 1
Toconao 104-105 C 8
Tocopilla 111 B 2
Tocorpuri, Cerro de — 92-93 F 9
Tocota 106-107 C 3
Tocqueville = Ra's al-Wād 164-165 E 1
Tocra = Ṭūkrah 164-165 HJ 2
Tocruyoc 96-97 F 9
Tocuco, Río — 94-95 E 3
Tocumen, Río — 64-65 c 2
Tocuyo, El — 92-93 F 3
Tocuyo, Río — 94-95 G 2
Tocuyo de La Costa 94-95 GH 2
Ṭoda Bhīm 138-139 F 4
Toda Rai Singh 138-139 E 4-5
Todatonten Lake 58-59 L 3
Todeli 148-149 H 7
Todenyang 171 C 1
Tödi [CH] 118 D 5
Todi [I] 122-123 E 4
Todmorden [AUS] 158-159 FG 5
Todness 92-93 H 3
To-dong 144-145 H 4
Todo-saki 144-145 O 3
Todos los Santos, Lago — 108-109 CD 3
Todos os Santos, Baía de — 92-93 M 7
Todos os Santos, Rio — 102-103 M 2
Todos Santos [BOL, Cochabamba] 92-93 F 8
Todos Santos [BOL, Pando] 104-105 C 3
Todos Santos [MEX] 64-65 D 7
Todos Santos, Bahía de — 86-87 B 2
Todrha, Ouèd — = Wād Tudghā' 166-167 D 4
Todro 171 B 2
Todupulai 140 C 6
Toei Yai, Khao — 150-151 B 7
Toejo 144-145 FG 3
Tōen = Tao-yüan 146-147 H 9
Toeng 150-151 C 3
Toèsse 168-169 E 3
Töez 94-95 C 6
Tofino 60 E 5
Tofo, El — 106-107 B 2
Tofte, MN 70-71 E 2
Tofty, AK 58-59 M 4
Tofua 208 J 4
Togi 144-145 L 4
Togiak, AK 58-59 GH 7
Togiak Bay 58-59 G 7
Togiak Lake 58-59 GH 7
Togiak River 58-59 GH 7
Togian, Kepulauan — 148-149 H 7
Togian, Pulau — 152-153 O 6
Togliatti 132-133 H 7
Togo 164-165 E 7
Togochale = Togotyalē 164-165 N 7
Togotyalē 164-165 N 7
Togtoh = Tugt 142-143 L 3-4
Togye-dong 144-145 G 4
Tōgyu-sen 144-145 FG 5
Tohāna 138-139 EF 3
Tohatchi, NM 74-75 J 5
Tohma çayı 136-137 G 3
Tohma suyu 136-137 GH 3
To Ho = Tuo He 146-147 F 5
Tohoku 144-145 N 2-4
Toiama = Toyama 142-143 Q 4
Toijala 116-117 K 7
Toili 148-149 H 7
Toi-misaki 144-145 H 7
Toiserivier 174-175 G 7
Toivola, MI 70-71 F 2
Toiyabe Range 74-75 E 3
Tojo 152-153 D 6
Tok [SU] 124-125 U 7
Tokachi-dake 144-145 c 2
Tokachi-gawa 144-145 c 2
Tōkagi 155 III c 1
Tokai 144-145 LM 5
Tokaj 118 K 4
Tokala 152-153 O 6
Tokala, Gunung — 152-153 O 6
Tōkamachi 144-145 M 4
Ṭōkar = Ṭawkar 164-165 M 5
Tokara-kaikyō 142-143 O 5-P 6
Tokara-rettō 142-143 OP 6
Tokarevka 124-125 N 8
Tokat 134-135 D 2
Tŏkchŏk-kundo 144-145 EF 4
Tŏkch'ŏn 144-145 F 3
Tokelau Islands 156-157 J 5
Toki 144-145 L 5
Tokio, TX 76-77 C 6
Tokio = Tōkyō 142-143 QR 4
Tokitsu = Toki 144-145 L 5
Tok Junction, AK 58-59 Q 5
Tokko 132-133 WX 6
Tok-kol 144-145 GH 2
Toklat, AK 58-59 MN 4
Tokmak [SU, Kirgizskaja SSR] 132-133 O 9
Tokmak [SU, Ukrainskaja SSR] 126-127 GH 3
Tōkō = Tungchiang 146-147 H 10
Tokolimbu 148-149 H 7
Tokong Boro 152-153 G 3
Tokoro 144-145 cd 1
Tokosun = Toksun 142-143 F 3
Tokra = Tūkrah 164-165 HJ 2
Toksun 142-143 F 3
Toktat River 58-59 MN 4
Tokuno-shima 142-143 O 6
Tokuno sima = Tokuno-shima 142-143 O 6
Tokushima 142-143 PQ 5
Tokusima = Tokushima 142-143 PQ 5
Tokuyama 144-145 HJ 5
Tōkyō 142-143 QR 4
Tōkyō-Adachi 155 III b 1
Tōkyō-Akabane 155 III b 1
Tōkyō-Akasaka 155 III b 1
Tōkyō-Amanuma 155 III a 1
Tōkyō-Aoyama 155 III b 2
Tōkyō-Arakawa 155 III b 1
Tōkyō-Asagaya 155 III a 1
Tōkyō-Asakusa 155 III b 1
Tōkyō-Azabu 155 III b 2
Tōkyō-Bunkyō 155 III b 1
Tōkyō-Chiyoda 155 III b 1
Tōkyō-Chūō 155 III b 1
Tōkyō-Denenchōfu 155 III ab 2
Tōkyō-Ebara 155 III b 2
Tōkyō-Edogawa 155 III c 1
Tōkyō-Ekoda 155 III ab 1
Tōkyō-Fukagawa 155 III b 2
Tōkyō-Ginza 155 III b 1
Tōkyō-Haneda 155 III b 2
Tōkyō-Higashiōizumi 155 III a 1
Tōkyō-Hongō 155 III b 1
Tōkyō-Honjo 155 III b 1
Tōkyō-Horinouchi 155 III ab 1
Tōkyō-Ikegami 155 III b 2
Tōkyō-Inatsuke 155 III b 1
Tōkyō International Airport 155 III b 2
Tōkyō-Itabashi 155 III ab 1
Tōkyō-Kamata 155 III b 2
Tōkyō-Kameari 155 III c 1
Tōkyō-Kameido 155 III bc 1
Tōkyō-Kamiakatsuka 155 III ab 1
Tōkyō-Kamikitazawa 155 III a 2
Tōkyō-Kamishakujii 155 III a 1
Tōkyō-Kanamachi 155 III c 1
Tōkyō-Kanda 155 III b 1
Tōkyō-Kasai 155 III c 2
Tōkyō-Kashiwagi 155 III b 1
Tōkyō-Katsushika 155 III bc 1
Tōkyō-Kita 155 III b 1
Tōkyō-ko 155 III b 2
Tōkyō-Kōenji 155 III ab 1
Tōkyō-Koishikawa 155 III b 1
Tōkyō-Koiwa 155 III c 1
Tōkyō-Komagome 155 III b 1
Tōkyō-Komatsugawa 155 III c 1
Tōkyō-Kōto 155 III b 1
Tōkyō-Koyama 155 III b 2
Tōkyō-Maeno 155 III b 1
Tōkyō-Magome 155 III b 2
Tōkyō-Meguro 155 III b 2
Tōkyō-Minato 155 III b 2
Tōkyō-Mizue 155 III c 1
Tōkyō-Mukōjima 155 III bc 1
Tōkyō-Nakanbu 155 III b 2
Tōkyō-Nakano 155 III ab 1
Tōkyō National Museum 155 III b 1
Tōkyō-Nerima 155 III a 1
Tōkyō-Nihonbashi 155 III b 1
Tōkyō-Numata 155 III b 1
Tōkyō-Ochiai 155 III b 1
Tōkyō-Ōi 155 III b 2
Tōkyō-Okusawa 155 III ab 2
Tōkyō-Ōmori 155 III b 2
Tōkyō-Ōta 155 III b 2
Tōkyō-Ōyada 155 III bc 1
Tōkyō-Rokugō 155 III b 2
Tōkyō-Sangenjaya 155 III b 2
Tōkyō-Senjū 155 III b 1
Tōkyō-Setagaya 155 III a 2
Tōkyō-Shibuya 155 III ab 2
Tōkyō-Shimane 155 III b 1
Tōkyō-Shimoigusa 155 III a 1
Tōkyō-Shimoshakujii 155 III a 1
Tōkyō-Shimura 155 III b 1
Tōkyō-Shinagawa 155 III b 2
Tōkyō-Shinjuku 155 III b 1
Tōkyō-Shishihone 155 III c 1
Tōkyō-Soshigaya 155 III a 2
Tōkyō-Sugamo 155 III b 1
Tōkyō-Suginami 155 III a 1
Tōkyō-Sumida 155 III bc 1
Tōkyō-Sunamachi 155 III bc 1
Tōkyō-Taitō 155 III b 1
Tōkyō-Takaido 155 III a 1
Tōkyō-Takenotsuka 155 III b 1
Tōkyō-Takinogawa 155 III b 1
Tōkyō-Tamagawa 155 III ab 2
Tōkyō-Toshima 155 III b 1
Tōkyō Tower 155 III b 2
Tōkyō-Toyotama 155 III a 1
Tōkyō-Ueno 155 III b 1
Tōkyō-Ukita 155 III c 1
Tōkyō wan 144-145 M 5
Tōkyō-Yōga 155 III a 2
Tōkyō-Yukigaya 155 III b 2
Tola, La — 92-93 D 4
Tolageak, AK 58-59 FG 1-2
Tolar, NM 76-77 C 5
Tolar, Cerro — 104-105 C 10
Tolar Grande 111 C 2
Tolbuhin 122-123 MN 4
Tole 88-89 F 10
Toledo, IA 70-71 D 4
Toledo, OH 64-65 K 3
Toledo, OR 66-67 B 3
Toledo [BOL] 104-105 C 6
Toledo [BR, Amazonas] 96-97 E 4
Toledo [BR, Paraná] 102-103 F 6
Toledo [E] 120-121 EF 9
Toledo [PE] 98-99 B 7
Toledo [RCH] 106-107 B 1
Toledo, Alto de — 96-97 F 9
Toledo, Montes de — 120-121 E 9
Toledo Bend Reservoir 76-77 GH 7
Tolenay 94-95 F 6
Tolentino [MEX] 86-87 K 6
Tolga = Ṭūljā 164-165 EF 2
Toliary 172 H 6
Tolima 94-95 D 5-6
Tolima, Nevado del — 94-95 D 5
Tōling 138-139 GH 2
Tolitoli 148-149 H 6
Toll'a, zaliv — 132-133 ST 2
Tolleson, AZ 74-75 G 6
Tolley, ND 68-69 EF 1
Tolloche 111 D 3
Tolly's Nullah 154 II b 3
Tolmač'ovo 124-125 G 4
Tolo, Teluk — 148-149 H 7
Toločin 124-125 G 6
Tolomosa 104-105 D 7
Tolono, IL 70-71 FG 6
Tolori 104-105 G 4
Tolosa 120-121 FG 7
Tolovana, AK 58-59 N 4
Tolovana River 58-59 N 4
Tolox, Sierra de — 120-121 E 10
Tolsan-do 144-145 FG 5
Tolstoj, mys — 132-133 e 6
Tolstoje 126-127 B 2
Toltén 111 B 5
Toltén, Río — 108-109 C 2
Tolú 94-95 D 3
Toluca, IL 70-71 F 5
Toluca, Nevado de — 64-65 FG 8
Toluca de Lerdo 64-65 FG 8
To-lun = Doloon Nuur 142-143 LM 3
Toma, La — 111 C 4
Tomah, WI 70-71 E 3-4
Tomahawk, WI 70-71 F 3
Tomakomai 142-143 R 3
Tomakovka 126-127 G 3
Tomamae 144-145 b 1
Tomaniive 148-149 a 2
Tomar [BR] 92-93 G 5
Tomar [P] 120-121 C 9
Tomar do Geru 100-101 F 6
Tomarovka 126-127 GH 1
Tomarrazón 94-95 E 2
Tomarza 136-137 F 3
Tomás Barrón 104-105 C 5
Tomaševka 124-125 DE 8
Tomás Gomensoro 106-107 J 3
Tomás Young 106-107 FG 2
Tomaszów Lubelski 118 L 3
Tomaszów Mazowiecki 118 K 3
Tomatlán 86-87 H 8
Tomave 104-105 C 7
Tomazina 102-103 H 5
Tomba di Nerone, Roma- 113 II ab 1
Tombador, Serra do — [BR, Bahia] 100-101 D 6
Tombador, Serra do — [BR, Mato Grosso] 92-93 H 7
Tomball, TX 76-77 G 7
Tombé 164-165 L 7
Tombes Royales = Lang Tâm 150-151 F 4
Tombetsu, Hama- 144-145 c 1
Tombetsu, Shō- 144-145 c 1
Tombigbee River 64-65 J 5
Tombo, Punta — 108-109 G 5
Tomboco 172 B 3
Tomboli 152-153 O 7
Tombos 102-103 L 4
Tombouctou 164-165 D 5
Tombstone, AZ 74-75 HJ 7
Tom Burke 174-175 G 2
Tomé 111 B 5
Tomea, Pulau — 152-153 PQ 8
Tomé-Açu 98-99 OP 6
Tömek = Aşağıpınarbaşı 136-137 E 3
Tomelilla 116-117 EF 10
Tomelloso 120-121 F 9
Tomiko 72-73 G 1
Tomini 148-149 H 6
Tomini, Teluk — 148-149 H 7
Tominian 168-169 D 2
Tomioka 144-145 N 4
Tomkinson Ranges 158-159 E 5
Tommot 132-133 Y 6
Tomo 92-93 F 4
Tomo, Río — 92-93 F 3
Tomolasta, Cerro — 106-107 DE 4
Tomori, Teluk — 148-149 H 7
Tompkins 61 D 5
Tompkinsville, KY 78-79 G 2
Tompo 132-133 a 5
Tomra 116-117 B 6
Tomsk 132-133 PQ 6
Toms River, NJ 72-73 JK 5
Tomtabakken 116-117 EF 9
Tom White, Mount — 58-59 PQ 6
Tô Myit 141 E 7
Tona [E] 94-95 E 4
Tonalá 64-65 H 8
Tonalea, AZ 74-75 H 4
Tonami 144-145 L 4
Tonantins 92-93 F 5
Tonasket, WA 66-67 D 1
Tonate 98-99 M 2
Tonbai Shan 142-143 L 5
Tonbridge 119 G 6
Tonda 148-149 M 8
Tønder 116-117 C 10
Tondern 70-71 H 1
Tondi 134-135 M 9
Tondibi 168-169 EF 1
Tone-gawa 144-145 N 5
Tonekābon 134-135 G 3
Tŏngā [Sudan] 164-165 L 7
Tonga [Tonga] 148-149 bc 2
Tongaat 174-175 J 5
Tonga Islands 156-157 J 5-6
Tongaland 172 F 7
Tong'an 146-147 G 9
Tongatapu 208 J 5
Tonga Trench 148-149 c 2
Tongbai 146-147 D 5
Tongch'ang 144-145 EF 2
Tongcheng [TJ, Anhui] 146-147 F 6
Tongcheng [TJ, Hubei] 146-147 DE 7
Tongcheng [TJ, Jiangsu] 146-147 G 5
Tong Chhu 138-139 M 3
T'ongch'ŏn 144-145 FG 3
Tongchuan 142-143 K 4
Tongdao 146-147 B 8
Tonggu 146-147 E 7
Tongguan [TJ, Hunan] 146-147 D 7
Tongguan [TJ, Shaanxi] 142-143 L 5
Tonggu Jiao 150-151 H 3
Tonggu Zhang 146-147 F 10
Tonghan-man 142-143 O 4
Tonghua 142-143 O 3
Tonghui He 155 II bc 2
Tongjosŏn-man = Tonghan-man 142-143 O 4
Tongkil Island 152-153 O 2
Tong La 138-139 L 3
Tongliao 142-143 N 3
Tongling 142-143 M 5
Tonglu 142-143 M 5-6
Tongmun'gŏ-ri 144-145 F 2
Tongoy 111 B 4
Tongoy, Bahía — 106-107 B 3
Tongphu 142-143 H 5
Tongpu = Tongphu 142-143 H 5
Tongren 142-143 K 6
Ṭongsā Jong = Thongsa Dsong 138-139 N 4
Tongshan 146-147 E 7
Tongshan = Dongshan 146-147 F 10
Tongshan Dao = Dongshan Dao 146-147 F 10
Tongshannei Ao 146-147 F 10
Tongshi 146-147 F 4
Tongue River 68-69 CD 2
Tong Xian 142-143 M 3-4
Tongxiang 146-147 H 6
Tongxu 146-147 E 4
Tongyang 144-145 F 3
Tongyang = Dongyang 146-147 H 7
T'ŏngyŏng = Ch'ungmu 144-145 G 5
Tongyu 142-143 N 3
Tonhon 150-151 E 7
Tonk 134-135 M 5
Tonkawa, OK 76-77 F 4
Tonki Cape 58-59 M 7
Tonkin 148-149 DE 2
Tonkin = Bắc Bô 148-149 D 2
Tonkin, Gulf of — 148-149 E 2-3
Tonlé Sap 148-149 D 4
Tonndorf, Hamburg- 130 I b 1
Tonneins 120-121 GH 6
Tonopah, NV 64-65 C 4
Tonorio, Volcán — 88-89 D 9
Tonosí 88-89 F 11
Tons 138-139 HJ 5
Tønsberg 116-117 CD 8
Tonsina, AK 58-59 P 6
Tonstad 116-117 B 8
Tontal, Sierra de — 106-107 C 3
Tontelbos 174-175 D 6
Tonya 136-137 H 2
Tŏnzan 141 C 4
Tonzona River 58-59 L 5
Tooele, UT 64-65 D 3
Tooligie 160 B 4
Toolik River 58-59 N 2
Toompine 160 G 1
Toora 160 H 7
Toora-Chem 132-133 S 7
Toorak, Melbourne- 161 II c 2
Tooting Graveney, London- 129 II b 2
Toowoomba 158-159 K 5
Topagoruk River 58-59 JK 1
Topeka, KS 64-65 G 4
Topia 86-87 G 5
Topkapi 154 I ab 2
Topkapı, İstanbul- 154 I a 2
Topki 132-133 PQ 6
Topko, gora — 132-133 a 6
Toplita 122-123 L 2
Toplyj Stan, Moskva- 113 V b 3
Topocalma, Punta — 106-107 A 5
Topock, AZ 74-75 F 5
Topoli 126-127 P 3
Topolobampo 64-65 E 6
Topolovgrad 122-123 M 4
Toponas, CO 68-69 C 5
Topozero 132-133 E 4
Toppenish, WA 66-67 C 2
Toprakkale 136-137 FG 4
Topsi 174-175 G 2
Ṭoqra = Ṭūkrah 164-165 HJ 2
Toqsun = Toksun 142-143 F 3
Toquepala 92-93 E 8
Toquerville, UT 74-75 G 4
Toquima Range 74-75 E 3
Tora [ZRE] 171 B 2
Torbalı = Tepeköy 136-137 B 3
Torbat-e Ḥeydarīyeh 134-135 HJ 3-4
Torbat-e Jām 134-135 J 3
Torbat-e Sheikh Jām = Torbat-e Jām 134-135 J 3
Torbay 119 E 6
Torbert, Mount — 58-59 LM 6
Torbino 124-125 J 4
Torch Lake 70-71 H 3
Torch River 61 FG 4
Torčin 126-127 B 1
Torcy 129 I d 2
Tordesillas 120-121 E 8
Tordilla, La — = Colonia La Tordilla 106-107 F 3
Tor di Quinto, Roma- 113 II b 1
Töre 116-117 K 5
Torekov 116-117 E 9
Torellbreen 116-117 j 6
Torell land 116-117 k 6
Toreo Campo Militar 91 I b 2
Torgau 118 F 3
Tori 164-165 L 7
Toribulu 152-153 O 6
Toriñana, Cabo — 120-121 C 7
Torino 122-123 BC 3
Tōrīt = Tūrīt 164-165 L 8
Torixoréu 102-103 F 2
Torkamān 136-137 M 4
Torkoviči 124-125 H 4
Tor Marancia, Roma- 113 II b 2
Tormes 120-121 D 8
Tormosin 126-127 L 2
Tornado Peak 60 K 5
Torneå = Tornio 116-117 L 5
Torne älv 116-117 K 4
Torneträsk 116-117 H 3
Torngat Mountains 56-57 Y 6
Tornio 116-117 L 5
Torno Largo 98-99 G 9
Tornquist 111 D 5
Toro [CO] 94-95 C 5
Toro [E] 120-121 E 8
Toro [ZRE] 171 B 2
Toro, Cerro del — 111 C 3
Toro, Lago del — 108-109 C 8
Toro, Punta — 106-107 AB 4
Torobuku 152-153 P 8
Torodi 164-165 E 6
Torodo 168-169 C 2
Torokina 148-149 hj 6
Toroku = Yünlin 146-147 H 10
Toronto 56-57 UV 9
Toronto, KS 70-71 C 7
Toronto, Lago — 86-87 GH 4
Toropalca 104-105 D 7
Toro Peak 74-75 E 6
Toropec 124-125 H 5
Tororo 172 F 1
Toros, Plaza de — 113 III b 2
Toros dağları 134-135 C 3
Torotoro 104-105 CD 6
Tor Pignatara, Roma- 113 II b 2
Torquato Severo 106-107 K 3
Torrance, CA 74-75 D 6
Torrance Municipal Airport 83 III b 3
Torre del Greco 122-123 F 5
Torre de Moncorvo 120-121 D 8
Torre Gaia, Roma- 113 II c 2
Torrelaguna 120-121 F 8
Torrelavega 120-121 E 7
Torre Lupara, Roma- 113 II c 1
Torre Nova, Roma- 113 II c 2
Torrens, Lake — 158-159 G 6
Torrens Creek 158-159 HJ 4
Torrent 106-107 J 2
Torrente 120-121 G 9
Torreón 64-65 F 6
Torreón de Cañas 76-77 B 9
Torres 111 G 3
Torres, Islas — 106-107 L 5
Torres de Alcalá = Qal'at Īrīs 166-167 D 2
Torres Islands 158-159 N 2
Torres Martinez Indian Reservation 74-75 E 6
Torres Strait 158-159 H 2
Torres Vedras 120-121 C 9
Torre Vécchia, Roma- 113 II a 1
Torrevieja 120-121 G 10
Torrijos 120-121 E 8-9
Torrington, CT 72-73 K 4
Torrington, WY 68-69 DE 4
Torrinha 102-103 HJ 5
Torsa 138-139 M 4
Tor Sapienza, Roma- 113 II c 2
Torsås 116-117 FG 9
Torsby 116-117 E 7
Tórshavn 114-115 G 3
Tortillas, Las — 76-77 E 9
Tortola 64-65 O 8
Tortolì 122-123 C 6
Tortona 122-123 C 3
Tortosa 120-121 H 8
Tortosa, Cabo de — 120-121 H 8
Tortue, Île de la — 64-65 M 7
Tortugas 106-107 FG 4
Tortuguero 88-89 E 9
Tortuguilla, Isla — 94-95 C 3
Tortuguitas, General Sarmiento- 110 III a 1
Tortum = Nihah 136-137 J 2
Ṭorūd 134-135 H 3
Torugart Davan 134-135 L 2
Torul = Ardasa 136-137 H 2
Toruń 118 J 2
Tõrva 124-125 E 4-5
Tory 119 B 4
Tory Hill 72-73 GH 2
Toržok 132-133 E 6
Torzym 118 G 2
Tos̆a [SU, place] 124-125 O 6
Tos̆a [SU, river] 124-125 O 6
Tosan = Chūbu 144-145 L 5-M 4
Tosashimizu 144-145 J 6
Tosa-wan 144-145 J 6
Toscana 122-123 D 4
Toscas, Las — 106-107 K 4
To-shima 144-145 M 5
Toshima, Tōkyō- 155 III b 1
Toshimaen Recreation Ground 155 III ab 1
Tosno 124-125 H 4
Tos nuur 142-143 H 4
T'o-so Hu = Tos nuur 142-143 H 4
Tosoncengel 142-143 H 2
T'osovo-Netyl'skij 124-125 H 4
Tosquita 106-107 E 4
Tossi 152-153 N 10
Tostado 111 D 3
Tõstamaa 124-125 D 4
Toston, MT 66-67 H 2
Tosu 144-145 H 6
Tosya 134-135 C 2
Totana 120-121 G 10
Toteng 172 D 6
Tothill 61 C 6
Tot'ma 132-133 G 5-6
Totogan Lake 62 E 1
Totonicapán 64-65 HJ 8-9
Totora [BOL, Cochabamba] 92-93 FG 8
Totora [BOL, Oruro] 104-105 BC 5
Totora, Cordillera de la — 106-107 BC 3
Totora, Sierra Blanca de la — 108-109 E 3-F 2
Totoral [RA] 106-107 D 3
Totoral [RCH] 106-107 B 1
Totoral [ROU] 106-107 J 4
Totoralejos 106-107 E 2
Totorapalca 104-105 D 6
Totoras, Las — 106-107 E 4
Totoya 148-149 ab 2
Totson Mount 58-59 J 4
Totsuka, Yokohama- 155 III a 3
Totta 132-133 a 6
Tottan Range 53 B 35-36
Totten Glacier 53 C 12
Tottenham [AUS] 158-159 J 6
Tottenham [CDN] 72-73 FG 2
Tottenham, London- 119 FG 6
Tottenville, New York-, NY 82 III a 3
Totteridge, London- 129 II b 1
Tottori 142-143 P 4
Totumal 94-95 E 3
Toṭupuyla = Todupulai 140 C 6
Tou 168-169 E 2
Ṭouāl 'Abā = Ṭuwāl 'Abā' 136-137 H 4
Touareg, Hassi — = Ḥāssī Tawāriq 166-167 JK 4
Touat = At-Tuwāt 164-165 DE 3
Touba [CI] 164-165 C 7
Touba [SN] 164-165 A 6
Toubqāl, Jbel — = Jabal Tubqāl 164-165 C 2
Toudao Jiang 144-145 F 1-2
Tougan 164-165 D 6
Touggourt = Tughghūrt 164-165 EF 2
Tougnifili 168-169 B 3
Tougouri 168-169 E 2
Tougue 168-169 C 3
Touho 158-159 N 4
Touil, Ouèd — = Wādī aṭ-Ṭawīl 166-167 H 2
Toukat = Hassī Tūkāt Nakhlah 166-167 A 6
Toukley 160 KL 4
Toukoto 164-165 BC 6
Tou-kou = Dougou 146-147 E 5
Toul 120-121 K 4
Toulépleu 164-165 C 7
Tou-lin = Yünlin 146-147 H 10
Toulon, IL 70-71 EF 5
Toulon [F] 120-121 KL 7
Toulon [ZA] 174-175 J 3
Touloûl, Dīret et — = Dīrat at-Tulūl 136-137 G 6
Touloûl eş Ṣafā = Tulūl aṣ-Ṣafā 136-137 G 6
Toulouse 120-121 HJ 7
Toummo 164-165 G 4
Toumodi 164-165 CD 7
Toumotou, Îles — 156-157 K 5-L 6
Tounan 146-147 H 10
Tounassine, Hamada — = Hammadat Tūnasīn 166-167 D 5
Toûnfit = Tūnfit 166-167 D 3
Toungo 168-169 HJ 3
Toungoo = Taungngū 148-149 C 3
Toûnis = Tūnis 164-165 FG 1
Toûnis, Khalîdj — = Khalīj at-Tūnisī 166-167 M 1
Toura, Monts du — 168-169 D 4
Touraine 120-121 H 5
Tourakom = Mu'o'ng Tourakom 150-151 D 3
Tourane = Đa Năng 148-149 E 3
Tourane, Cap — = Mui Đa Năng 150-151 G 4
Tour Eiffel 129 I c 2
Tourgueness, Rass — = Rā's Turk an-Naṣṣ 166-167 M 3
Tournai 120-121 J 3
Tournavista 96-97 D 6
Tournon 120-121 K 6
Touro Passo 106-107 J 2
Touros 92-93 MN 5-6
Toûroûg = Tūrūg 166-167 D 4
Tours 120-121 H 5
Tourville 63 AB 4
Toussidé, Pic — 164-165 H 4
Toussus-le-Noble 129 I b 3
T'ou-tao Chiang = Toudao Jiang 144-145 F 1-2
Touwsrivier [ZA, place] 174-175 D 7
Touwsrivier [ZA, river] 174-175 D 7
Töv ◁ 142-143 K 2
Tovāla 140 C 6
Tovar 94-95 F 3
Tovarkovskij 124-125 M 7
Tovmač = Tlumač 126-127 B 2
Tovqussaq 56-57 a 5
Tovste = Tolstoje 126-127 B 2
Towada 144-145 N 2
Towada-ko 144-145 N 2
Towanda, PA 72-73 H 4
Towani 174-175 G 2
Towari 152-153 O 8
Towdystan 60 E 3
Tower 129 II b 2
Tower, MN 70-71 D 2
Tower, London- 129 II b 1
Tower Bridge 129 II b 2
Towner, CO 68-69 E 6
Towner, ND 68-69 F 1
Townes Pass 74-75 E 4
Town Estates, NJ 84 III d 1
Town Hall 161 II b 1
Townley, NY 82 III a 2
Townley Place, Houston-, TX 85 III b 1
Townsend, GA 80-81 F 5
Townsend, MT 66-67 H 2
Townshend Island 158-159 K 4
Townsville 158-159 J 3
Towot 164-165 L 7
Towra Point 161 I b 3
Towson, MD 72-73 H 5
Towuti, Danau — 148-149 H 7
Toyah, TX 76-77 C 7
Toyahvale, TX 76-77 BC 7
Tōya-ko 144-145 b 2
Toyama 142-143 Q 4
Toyama-wan 142-143 Q 4
Toyohara = Južno-Sachalinsk 132-133 bc 8
Toyohashi 142-143 Q 5
Toyohasi = Toyohashi 142-143 Q 5
Toyoma 144-145 N 3
Toyonaka 144-145 K 5
Toyooka 144-145 K 5
Toyota 144-145 L 5
Toyotama 144-145 G 5
Toyotama, Tōkyō- 155 III a 1
Tôzeur = Tawzar 164-165 F 2
Tozitna River 58-59 LM 4
Tra, Sông — 150-151 G 5
Trabiju 102-103 H 5
Trabzon 134-135 DE 2
Tracadie 63 D 4
Trach, Kompong — [K, Kampot] 150-151 E 7
Trach, Kompong — [K, Svay Rieng] 150-151 E 7
Trachéia = Silifke 134-135 C 3
Tra Cu 148-149 E 5
Tracy 63 C 5
Tracy, CA 74-75 C 4
Trade Mart Tower 85 I b 2
Tradum 142-143 E 6
Træna 116-117 DE 4
Traer, IA 70-71 D 4
Trafalgar, Cabo de — 120-121 D 10
Trafâwî, Bi'r — 136-137 H 4
Traful, Lago — 108-109 D 3
Traição, Córrego — 110 II ab 2
Traiguén 106-107 A 7
Traiguén, Isla — 108-109 C 5
Trail 64-65 N 8
Trail, MN 70-71 C 2
Trail City, SD 68-69 F 3
Traill 106-107 G 3
Trainer, PA 84 III a 3
Traipu 100-101 F 5
Traipu, Rio — 100-101 F 5
Trairi 100-101 E 2
Trajanova vrata 122-123 L 4
Traka 174-175 E 7
Trakai 124-125 E 6
Trakan Phutphon 150-151 E 5
Trakya 136-137 AB 2
Tralach 150-151 E 7
Tralee 119 B 5
Trälleborg = Trelleborg 116-117 E 10
Tralung 138-139 GH 2
Tramandaí 106-107 MN 2
Tram Khnar 150-151 E 7
Tra Môn 150-151 F 7
Tra My = Hâu Đu'c 150-151 G 5
Tranås 116-117 F 8

Tranca, La — 106-107 D 4
Trancas 111 CD 3
Trang 150-151 B 9
Trangan, Pulau — 148-149 K 8
Trang Bang 150-151 EF 7
Trani 122-123 G 5
Trańkabâr = Tranquebar 140 DE 5
Trân Ninh, Cao Nguyên — 148-149 D 3
Tranquebar 140 DE 5
Tranqui, Isla — 108-109 C 4
Transamazônica, Rodovia — 98-99 L 7
Trans Canada Highway 56-57 P 7
Transcaucasia = Malyj Kavkaz 126-127 L 5-N 7
Transhimalaja = Transhimalaya 142-143 EF 5
Transhimalaya 142-143 EF 5
Transilvania 122-123 K-M 2
Transit istasyonu = Doğubayazıt 136-137 KL 3
Trânsito 106-107 F 3
Trânsito, El — 106-107 B 2
Transkasp 134-135 H 3
Transsib 132-133 L 6
Transturan 132-133 K 7
Transvaal 172 EF 6
Transylvanian Alps = Alpi Transilvaniei 122-123 KL 3
Tranum 150-151 CD 11
Tra Ôn 150-151 EF 7-8
Trapalcó 106-107 D 7
Trapalcó, Salinas de — 108-109 F 2
Trapandé, Baía de — 102-103 J 6
Trápani 122-123 E 6-7
Trapezûs = Trabzon 134-135 DE 2
Trappenfelde 130 III c 1
Trapper Peak 66-67 F 3
Trappes 129 I a 2
Traralgon 158-159 J 7
Trarza = At-Trârzah 164-165 AB 5
Trârzah, At- 164-165 AB 5
Trasimeno, Lago — 122-123 DE 4
Trás-os-Montes 120-121 D 8
Trás-os-Montes = Cucumbi 172 C 4
Trat 148-149 D 4
Traunstein 118 F 5
Trava, Cachoeira — 92-93 H 5
Travá, Cachoeira 98-99 K 5
Travancore 140 C 6
Travers, Mount — 161 E 5-6
Traverse, Lake — 68-69 H 3
Traverse City, MI 64-65 JK 2-3
Traverse Peak 58-59 GH 4
Travesía del Tunuyán 106-107 D 4-5
Travesía Puntana 106-107 DE 5
Travessão do Urubu 98-99 M 8
Travessão Jacaré 98-99 O 10
Tra Vingh 148-149 E 5
Tra Vinh = Phu Vinh 148-149 E 5
Travis, Lake — 76-77 EF 7
Travis, New York-, NY 82 III a 3
Trbovlje 122-123 F 2
Tre = Hon Tre 150-151 G 6
Tre, Hon — 150-151 G 6
Treasure Island 83 I b 2
Treasure Island Naval Station 83 I b 2
Treasury = Mono Island 148-149 j 6
Treat Island 58-59 JK 3
Třebíč 118 G 4
Trebinje 122-123 H 4
Trebisonda = Trabzon 134-135 DE 2
Trebol, El — 106-107 G 4
Trebolares 106-107 F 5
Trechado, NM 74-75 J 5
Trefâouî, Bîr — = Bi'r Trafâwî 136-137 H 4
Trego, MT 66-67 F 1
Trégorrois 120-121 F 4
Treherne 61 J 6
Treinta de Agosto 106-107 F 6
Treinta y Tres [ROU, administrative unit] 106-107 KL 4
Treinta y Tres [ROU, place] 111 F 4
Trekkopje 174-175 A 2
Trelew 111 C 6
Trelleborg 116-117 E 10
Tremadoc Bay 119 D 5
Tremblay, Hippodrome de — 129 I cd 2
Tremblay-lès-Gonesse 129 I d 2
Trembleur Lake 60 E 2
Tremedal 100-101 D 8
Tremembé 102-103 K 5
Tremembé, São Paulo- 110 II b 1
Trèmiti, Isole — 122-123 F 4
Tremonton, UT 66-67 G 5
Tremp 120-121 H 7
Trempealeau, WI 70-71 E 3-4
Trenary, MI 70-71 G 2
Trenčín 118 J 4
Trenel 106-107 E 5
Treng, Phum — 150-151 D 6
Trengganu 150-151 D 10
Trenque Lauquen 111 D 5
Trent = Trento 122-123 D 2
Trente et un Milles, Lac des — 72-73 HJ 1
Trentino-Alto Adige 122-123 D 2
Trento 122-123 D 2
Trenton 72-73 H 2
Trenton, FL 80-81 b 2
Trenton, IA 70-71 D 5
Trenton, MI 72-73 E 3
Trenton, NE 68-69 F 5
Trenton, NJ 64-65 M 3-4
Trenton, TN 78-79 E 3
Trepassey 63 K 4
Tréport, le — 120-121 H 3
Treptow, Berlin- 130 III b 2
Treptower Park 130 III b 2
Tres Algarrobos 106-107 F 5
Tres Altitos, Cerro — 106-107 C 4
Tres Árboles 106-107 J 4
Tres Arroyos 111 DE 5
Três Barras 102-103 GH 7
Tres Bôcas [BR] 98-99 C 7
Tres Bocas [YV] 94-95 E 3
Tres Cerros [RA, mountain] 108-109 D 4
Tres Cerros [RA, place] 108-109 F 7
Tres Conos, Monte — 108-109 D 9
Três Corações 92-93 KL 9
Tres Cruces [RA] 104-105 D 8
Tres Cruces [RCH] 106-107 B 2
Tres Cruces [ROU] 106-107 J 3
Tres Cruces, Cerro — 106-107 C 1
Tres de Febrero 110 III b 1
Tres de Febrero-Ciudadela 110 III b 1
Tres de Maio 106-107 KL 1
Tres Esquinas 92-93 DE 4
Tres Forcas, Cap — = Râ's Wūruq 164-165 D 1
Tres Hermanas, Pampa de las — 108-109 F 6
Três Irmãos, Cachoeira 98-99 F 9
Três Irmãos, Ilhas — 102-103 H 7
Tres Irmãos, Pontas dos — 92-93 M 6-N 5
Três Irmãos, Serra dos 98-99 F 9
Tres Isletas 104-105 F 10
Treska 122-123 J 5
Três Lagoas 92-93 J 9
Tres Lagos 111 B 7
Tres Lagunas 106-107 F 6
Tres Marias 102-103 K 3
Três Marias, Represa — 102-103 K 3
Tres Matas, Las — 94-95 J 3
Tres Montes, Golfo — 108-109 B 6
Tres Montes, Península — 111 A 7
Tres Morros 104-105 D 8
Tres Ollas 102-103 D 5
Três Passos 106-107 KL 1
Tres Picos 106-107 F 7
Tres Picos, Cerro — 111 B 6
Tres Piedras, NM 76-77 B 4
Três Pontas 102-103 K 4
Tres Porteñas 106-107 CD 4
Tres Pozos 106-107 FG 2
Tres Puentes 106-107 BC 1
Tres Puntas, Cabo — 111 CD 7
Três Rios 92-93 L 9
Tres Rios, Serra dos — 110 I b 2
Tres Unidos 96-97 D 4
Tres Virgenes, Las — 64-65 D 6
Tret'akovskaja galereja 113 V c 3
Treuer River = Macumba 158-159 G 5
Treungen 116-117 C 8
Trêve, Lac la — 62 O 2
Treviglio 122-123 C 3
Treviño 120-121 F 7
Treviso 122-123 E 3
Trézel = Sūgar 166-167 G 2
Treze Quedas 92-93 H 4
Triabunna 160 c 3
Triang 150-151 D 11
Triangle, ID 66-67 E 4
Triangulos, Arrecifes — 86-87 OP 7
Trianons 129 I b 2
Tribugá 94-95 C 5
Tribune 68-69 DE 1
Tribune, KS 68-69 F 6
Tricaó 106-107 CD 7
Trichaty 126-127 E 3
Trichônis, Límnē — 122-123 J 6
Trichūr 134-135 M 8
Trida 158-159 HJ 6
Tridell, UT 66-67 J 5
Trident Peak 66-67 D 5
Triel-sur-Seine 129 I b 2
Trier 118 C 4
Trieste 122-123 E 3
Trigo, El — 106-107 H 5
Tríkala 122-123 JK 6
Trikkandiyur 140 B 5
Trili 106-107 F 5
Trimân 138-139 B 3
Trinchera, CO 76-77 BC 4
Trincheras 86-87 E 2
Trincheras, Las — 92-93 FG 3
Trincomalee = Tirikuṇāmalaya 134-135 N 9
Trincomali = Tirikuṇāmalaya 134-135 N 9
Trindade [BR, Goiás] 102-103 H 2
Trindade [BR, Roraima] 98-99 H 4
Trindade = Trinidad [BOL] 92-93 G 7
Trindade = Trinidad [TT] 64-65 O 9
Trindade, Ilha da — 92-93 NO 9
Tring, Ban — = Buôn Hô 150-151 G 6
Trinidad, CA 66-67 A 5
Trinidad, CO 64-65 F 4
Trinidad, TX 76-77 FG 6
Trinidad, WA 66-67 CD 2
Trinidad [BOL, Beni] 92-93 G 7
Trinidad [BOL, Pando] 104-105 C 2
Trinidad [C] 64-65 KL 7
Trinidad [CO] 92-93 E 3
Trinidad [PY] 111 E 3
Trinidad [ROU] 111 E 4
Trinidad [TT] 64-65 O 9
Trinidad = Ilha da Trindade 92-93 NO 9
Trinidad, Bahía — 64-65 b 2
Trinidad, Baruta-La — 91 II b 2
Trinidad, Canal 108-109 B 7-8
Trinidad, Golfo — 108-109 B 7
Trinidad, Isla — 111 D 5
Trinidad, Isla — = Sounders Island 108-109 J 8
Trinidad, La — 94-95 G 3
Trinidad, Laguna — 102-103 B 4
Trinidad, Río — 64-65 b 3
Trinidad, Washington-, DC 82 II b 2
Trinidad and Tobago 64-65 O 9-10
Trinidad de Arauca, La — 94-95 G 4
Trinil 152-153 J 9
Trinité, Montagnes de la — 98-99 M 2
Trinity, TX 76-77 G 7
Trinity Bay 56-57 a 8
Trinity Center, CA 66-67 B 5
Trinity Gardens, Houston-, TX 85 III b 1
Trinity Islands 56-57 F 6
Trinity Mountains 66-67 B 5
Trinity Range 66-67 D 5
Trinity River [USA, California] 66-67 B 5
Trinity River [USA, Texas] 64-65 G 5
Trino, El — 94-95 E 6
Trio Island 155 I b 2
Trion, GA 78-79 G 3
Tripoli, WI 70-71 EF 3
Tripolis 122-123 K 7
Tripolis = Ṭarābulus al-Gharb 164-165 G 2
Tripolitania = Ṭarābulus 164-165 GH 2
Tripp, SD 68-69 GH 4
Tripps Run 82 II a 2
Tripura 134-135 P 6
Tripurāntakam 140 D 3
Trishshivaperūr = Trichūr 134-135 M 8
Trishūl = Trisūl 138-139 G 2
Trishūlī = Trisūli 138-139 K 3-4
Tristan da Cunha 204-205 FG 12
Tristao, Îles — 168-169 B 3
Tristeza, Cuchilla de la — 106-107 C 5
Trisūl 138-139 G 2
Trisūli 138-139 K 3-4
Tri Tôn 150-151 E 7
Triumph, MN 70-71 C 4
Triunfo [BOL] 98-99 E 9
Triunfo [BR] 100-101 E 4
Triunfo, El — 106-107 G 5
Triunfo, Pirâmide el — 104-105 F 9
Trivandrum 134-135 M 9
Trnava 118 H 4
Trobriand Islands 148-149 h 6
Trochu 60 L 4
Trofors 116-117 E 5
Trogir 122-123 FG 4
Troglav 122-123 G 4
Trôia [I] 122-123 F 5
Troia [TR] 134-135 B 3
Troice-Lykovo, Moskva- 113 V a 2
Troick 132-133 L 7
Troickoje [SU, Rossijskaja SFSR] 132-133 a 8
Troickoje [SU, Ukrainskaja SSR] 126-127 HJ 2
Troicko-Pečorsk 132-133 K 5
Troickosavsk = K'achta 132-133 U 7
Trois-Pistoles 63 B 3
Trois-Rivières 56-57 W 8
Trojan 122-123 L 4
Trojanski prohod 122-123 L 4
Trojekurovo [SU, Lipeckaja Oblast'] 124-125 M 7
Trollhättan 116-117 E 8
Trolltindan 116-117 B 6
Tromba Grande, Cabo — 100-101 E 8
Trombetas, Rio — 92-93 H 5
Trombudo, Rio — 106-107 N 1
Trombudo Central 102-103 H 7
Tromelin 204-205 N 10
Tromen, Cerro del — 106-107 B 6
Tromen, Lago — 108-109 D 2
Tromen, Paso — 108-109 CD 2
Trompsburg 174-175 FG 6
Troms 116-117 G-J 3
Tromsø 116-117 H 3
Tron 116-117 D 6
Trona, CA 74-75 E 5
Tronador, Monte — 111 B 6
Tronco 100-101 B 4
Trondheim 116-117 D 6
Trondheimfjord 116-117 CD 6
Tronoh 150-151 C 10
Troödos 134-135 C 4
Tropar'ovo, Moskva 113 V b 3
Tropêço Grande, Cachoeira de — 98-99 OP 11
Tropenmuseum 128 I b 1
Tropia, Ponta — 100-101 D 2
Tropic, UT 74-75 GH 4
Trosa 116-117 G 8
Trost'anec [SU, Sumskaja Oblast'] 126-127 G 1
Trost'anec [SU, Vinnickaja Oblast'] 126-127 D 2
Trotus 122-123 M 2
Troûmbâ = Turumbah 136-137 J 4
Troup, TX 76-77 G 6
Trout Creek 66-67 D 4
Trout Creek, MT 66-67 EF 2
Trout Creek, UT 74-75 G 3
Trout Lake, MI 70-71 H 2
Trout Lake [CDN, Alberta] 60 K 1
Trout Lake [CDN, Northwest Territories] 56-57 MN 5
Trout Lake [CDN, Ontario] 56-57 S 7
Trout Peak 68-69 B 3
Trout River 63 G 3
Trouwers Island = Pulau Tinjil 148-149 E 8
Trowbridge 119 EF 6
Troy, AL 64-65 J 5
Troy, ID 66-67 E 2
Troy, KS 70-71 C 6
Troy, MO 70-71 E 6
Troy, MT 66-67 F 1
Troy, NC 80-81 G 3
Troy, NY 64-65 M 3
Troy, OH 70-71 H 5
Troy, OR 66-67 E 3
Troy, PA 72-73 H 4
Troyes 120-121 K 4
Truandó, Río — 94-95 C 4
Trubčevsk 124-125 J 7
Trubetčino 124-125 M 7
Trucará, Serra do — 98-99 N 7-O 6
Truc Giang 150-151 F 7
Trucial Oman = United Arab Emirates 134-135 GH 6
Truckee, CA 74-75 CD 3
Truckee River 74-75 D 3
Trud [SU] 124-125 JK 5
Trudante = Tārūdānt 164-165 C 2
Trudering, München- 130 II bc 2
Trudfront 126-127 N 4
Trujillo [CO] 94-95 C 5
Trujillo [E] 120-121 DE 9
Trujillo [Honduras] 64-65 J 8
Trujillo [PE] 92-93 CD 6
Trujillo [YV] 92-93 EF 3
Trujillo, Ciudad — = Santo Domingo 64-65 MN 8
Truk 208 F 2
Trumann, AR 78-79 D 3
Trumbull, Mount — 74-75 G 4
Trung Bô 148-149 D 3-E 4
Trung Phân, Cao Nguyên — 148-149 E 4
Trung Phân, Plateau de — = Cao Nguyên Trung Phân 148-149 E 4
Truro, IA 70-71 D 5
Truro [CDN] 56-57 Y 8
Truro [GB] 119 D 6
Truscott, TX 76-77 E 6
Truskavec 126-127 A 2
Trus Madi, Gunung — 152-153 M 3
Truth or Consequences, NM 76-77 A 6
Trutnov 118 GH 3
Truxilho = Trujillo 64-65 J 8
Tryon, NE 68-69 F 5
Trysil 116-117 DE 7
Trysilelv 116-117 DE 7
Tsabong 172 D 7
Tsabrang 138-139 G 2
Tsaidam 142-143 GH 4
Tsai-Dam = Tsaidam 142-143 GH 4
Tsala Apopka Lake 80-81 bc 2
Tsamkong = Zhanjiang 142-143 L 7
Tsane 174-175 DE 3
Tsang 138-139 LM 3
Tsangpo 142-143 EF 6
Tsangwu = Wuzhou 142-143 L 7
Ts'ang-yüan = Cangyuan 141 F 4
Tsan-huang = Zanhuang 146-147 E 3
Tsaobis 174-175 A 2
Ts'ao-hsien = Cao Xian 146-147 E 4
Tsaoshui = Zhashui 146-147 B 5
Tsaratanana [RM, mountain] 172 J 4
Tsaratanana [RM, place] 172 J 5
Tsarskoye Selo = Puškin 132-133 DE 6
Tsau 172 D 6
Tsauchab 174-175 A 3
Tsau Tsau Flats 174-175 D 2
Tsavo [EAK, place] 172 G 2
Tsavo [EAK, river] 171 D 3
Tsavo National Park 172 G 2
Tschicoma Peak 76-77 AB 4
Tschida, Lake — 68-69 EF 2
Tsechang = Zichang 146-147 B 3
Tsekhung Tsho 138-139 L 2
Ts'ê-lo = Chira Bazar 142-143 DE 4
Tsengcheng = Zengcheng 146-147 D 10
Tseng Shue Tsai 155 I b 1
Tšerkassy = Čerkassy 126-127 EF 2
Tšernigov = Černigov 126-127 E 1
Tses 172 C 7
Tsesum 138-139 J 2
Tsethang 142-143 G 6
Tsetserlig = Cecerleg 142-143 J 2
Tseung Kwan 155 I b 2
Tshaidam 142-143 GH 4
Tshela 172 B 2-3
Tshikapa 172 CD 3
Tshimbo 171 B 4
Tshing Hai = Chöch nuur 142-143 H 4
Tshipa = Katakumba 172 D 3
Tshofa 172 DE 3
Tshomo Thritong 138-139 LM 3
Tsho Ngonpo = Chöch nuur 142-143 H 4
Tshopo 172 E 1
Tshuapa 172 D 2
Tshungu, Chutes — 172 DE 1
Tshwane 172 D 6
Tsiafajavona 172 J 5
Tsienkiang = Qianjiang 142-143 L 5
Tsihombe 172 HJ 7
Tsimlyanskaya = Čiml'ansk 126-127 KL 3
Tsimo = Jimo 146-147 H 3
Tsim Sha Tsui, Kowloon- 155 I a 2
Tsim Tsa Tsui 155 I ab 2
Tsinan = Jinan 142-143 M 4
Tsincheng = Jincheng 142-143 L 4
Tsinchow = Tianshui 142-143 JK 5
Tsineng 174-175 E 4
Tsinghai = Qinghai 142-143 GH 4
Tsingho = Qinghe 146-147 E 3
Tsinghu = Jinghe 142-143 E 3
Tsing Island 155 I a 1
Tsingkiang = Jingjiang 146-147 H 5-6
Tsingkiang = Qingjiang [TJ, Jiangsu] 142-143 M 5
Tsingkiang = Qingjiang [TJ, Jiangxi] 142-143 M 6
Tsinglo = Jingle 146-147 CD 2
Tsingpien = Jingbian 146-147 B 3
Tsingpu = Qingpu 146-147 H 6
Tsingtau = Qingdao 142-143 N 4
Tsingteh = Jingde 146-147 G 6
Tsingyuan = Baoding 142-143 LM 4
Tsingyun = Qingyuan 146-147 D 10
Tsinh Ho 150-151 D 1
Tsining = Jining 142-143 M 4
Tsining = Xining 142-143 J 4
Tsin Shui Wan 155 I b 2
Tsinsien = Jinxian 146-147 F 7
Tsinyang = Qinyang 142-143 L 4
Tsiroanomandidy 172 J 5
Tsitsa 174-175 H 6
Tsitsihar = Qiqihar 142-143 N 2
Tsitsikamaberge 174-175 EF 7
Tsivory 172 J 6
Tsiyang = Jiyang 146-147 F 3
Tsochuan = Zuoquan 146-147 D 3
Tsolo 174-175 H 6
Tsomo [ZA, place] 174-175 GH 7
Tsomo [ZA, river] 174-175 G 6-7
Tsôna 141 BC 2
Tsondab 174-175 A 2-3
Tsondabvlei 174-175 A 2
Tsorlū = Çorlu 136-137 B 2
Tsoshui = Zhashui 146-147 B 5
Tso Shui Wan 155 I b 2
Tsou-hsien = Zou Xian 146-147 F 4
Tsou-p'ing = Zouping 146-147 F 3
Tsou-shih = Zoushi 146-147 C 7
Tso-yün = Zuoyun 146-147 D 2
Tsu 142-143 Q 5
Tsubame 144-145 M 4
Tsuboi 155 III d 1
Tsuchiura 144-145 N 4
Tsudanuma, Funabashi- 155 III d 1
Tsugaru kaikyō 142-143 R 3
Tsū-hsing = Zixing 146-147 D 9
Tsukigata 144-145 b 2
Tsukumi 144-145 H 6
Tsuma = Saito 144-145 H 6
Tsumeb 172 C 5
Tsumis 174-175 B 2
Tsumispark 174-175 B 2
Tsunashima, Yokohama- 155 III a 2
Ts'ung-hua = Conghua 146-147 D 10
Tsung-hua = Zunhua 146-147 F 1
Tsunghwa = Conghua 146-147 D 10
Tsungjen = Chongren 146-147 EF 8
Tsungming = Chongming 142-143 N 5
Tsungteh = Chongde 146-147 H 6
Tsung-ts'un-hsü = Zongcun 146-147 D 8
Tsunhwa = Zunhua 146-147 F 1
Tsuno-shima 144-145 H 5
Tsun Wan 155 I a 1
Tsunyi = Zunyi 142-143 K 6
Tsuruga 144-145 KL 5
Tsurugi san 144-145 JK 6
Tsurumi 155 III ab 2
Tsurumi, Yokohama- 155 III a 2
Tsurumi-zaki 144-145 J 6
Tsuruoka 144-145 M 3
Tsurusaki 144-145 HJ 6
Tsushima 142-143 O 5
Tsushima-kaikyō 142-143 OP 5
Tsuyama 144-145 JK 5
Tsuyung = Chuxiong 142-143 J 7
Tswana 174-175 C 2
Tu = Tibesti 164-165 H 4
Tu = Tsu 142-143 Q 5
Tua 120-121 D 8
Tuamapu, Canal — 108-109 B 4-C 5
Tuamotu, Îles — 156-157 K 5-L 6
Tuamotu Basin 156-157 KL 6
Tuan, Ujung — 152-153 C 5
Tuanfeng 146-147 E 6
Tuần Giao 150-151 D 2
Tuangku, Pulau — 152-153 B 4
Tuan He 146-147 C 5
T'uan Ho = Tuan He 146-147 C 5
Tuan-shih = Duanshi 146-147 D 4
Tuapse 126-127 J 4
Tuaran 152-153 LM 2
Tubac, AZ 74-75 H 7
Tuba City, AZ 74-75 H 4
Tubal, Wādī at- 136-137 J 6
Tuban 148-149 F 8
Tubarão 111 G 3
Tubarão, Ponta do — 100-101 FG 3
Tubarão, Rio — 102-103 H 8
Tubau 148-149 F 6
Ṭubayq, Jabal aṭ- 134-135 D 5
Tubiacanga, Punta de — 110 I b 1
Tübingen 118 D 4
T'ub-Karagan, mys — 126-127 OP 4
T'ub-Karagan, poluostrov — 126-127 P 4
Tubqāl, Jabal — 164-165 C 2
Ṭubruq 164-165 J 2
Tubuai, Îles — 156-157 K 6
Ṭuburbah 166-167 L 1
Tucacas 92-93 F 2
Tucano 92-93 M 7
Tucano, Cachoeira — 94-95 G 7
Tucano, Serra do — 94-95 LM 6
Tucapel 106-107 AB 6
Tucapel, Punta — 106-107 A 6
Tucavaca 92-93 H 8
Tucavaca, Río — 104-105 G 6
Tuchang 146-147 H 9
Tucholskie, Bory — 118 HJ 2
Tucho River 58-59 X 7
Tucker Bay 53 B 18
Tuckerman, AR 78-79 D 3
Tuckerton, NJ 72-73 JK 5
Tuckum = Tukums 124-125 D 5
Tucson, AZ 64-65 D 5
Tucson Mountains 74-75 H 6
Tucuman 104-105 D 10
Tucumán = San Miguel de Tucumán 111 CD 3
Tucumán, San Miguel de — 111 CD 3
Tucumcari, NM 64-65 F 4
Tucumcari Mountain 76-77 C 5
Tucume 96-97 AB 5
Tucunduva 106-107 K 1
Tucuns 100-101 B 5
Tucuns, Serra dos — 100-101 D 2
Tucunuco 111 C 4
Tucuparé 98-99 L 7
Tucupido 94-95 J 3
Tucupita 92-93 G 3
Tucupita, Caño — 94-95 L 3
Tucuruí 92-93 K 5
Tucuruvi, São Paulo- 110 II b 1
Tucu Tucu 108-109 D 7
Tuddo = Tudu 124-125 F 4
Tudela 120-121 G 7
Tudghā', Wād — 166-167 D 4
Tudu 124-125 F 4
Tuela 120-121 D 8
Tuensang [IND, landscape] 141 D 2-3
Tuensang [IND, place] 141 D 2
Tuensang Frontier Division = Tuensang 141 D 2-3
Tueré, Rio 98-99 N 6-7
Tufello, Roma- 113 II b 1
Tufi 148-149 N 8
Tufts University 84 I b 2
Tugaru kaikyō = Tsugaru-kaikyō 142-143 R 3
Tugela [ZA, place] 174-175 J 5
Tugela [ZA, river] 172 F 7
Tugela Ferry 174-175 J 5
Tuggurt = Tughghūrt 164-165 EF 2
Tugh Fafan = Fafen 164-165 N 7
Tughghūrt 164-165 EF 2
Tugidak Island 58-59 f 1
Tugt 142-143 L 3-4
Tuguegarao 148-149 H 3
Tugur 132-133 a 7
Tuhai He 146-147 FG 3
Tuht 136-137 E 2
Tuichang 141 C 4
Tuilianpui = Tūīliyanpūī 141 C 4
Tūīliyanpūī 141 C 4
Tuindorp, Amsterdam- 128 I ab 1
Tuinplaas 174-175 H 3
Tuira, Río — 94-95 BC 3
Tuito, El — 86-87 H 7
Tujmazy 132-133 JK 7
Tuka 150-151 B 11
Tukalinsk 132-133 N 6
Tu-kan = Shangkan 146-147 C 6
Tukangbesi, Kepulauan — 148-149 H 8
Tūkāt Nakhlah, Ḥāssī — 166-167 A 6
Tukayyid 136-137 L 8
Tukchor 150-151 D 6
Tuklung, AK 58-59 H 7
Tūkrah 164-165 HJ 2
Tuktoyaktuk 56-57 JK 4
Tukums 124-125 D 5
Tukung, Bukit — 152-153 JK 6
Tukuyu 172 F 3
Tula [EAK] 171 D 3
Tula [MEX] 86-87 L 6
Tula [SU] 124-125 L 6
Tul'ači 124-125 RS 6
Tula de Allende 86-87 KL 6-7
Tulagi 148-149 jk 6
Tulaguen, Cerro — 106-107 B 3
Tulameen 66-67 C 1
Tulancingo 64-65 G 7
Tulane University 85 I b 2
Tulangbawang, Wai — 152-153 F 8
Tulare, CA 64-65 C 4
Tulare, SD 68-69 G 3
Tulare Lake 64-65 C 4
Tulare Lake Area 74-75 D 5
Tularosa, NM 76-77 A 6
Tularosa Basin 76-77 A 6
Tularosa Mountains 74-75 J 6
Tūlasi 140 EF 1
Tulbagh [ZA, mountain] 174-175 D 6
Tulbagh [ZA, place] 174-175 C 7
Tulcán 92-93 D 4
Tulcea 122-123 N 3
Tul'čin 126-127 D 2
Tulcingo de Valle 86-87 LM 8-9
Tuléar = Toliary 172 H 6
Tulelake, CA 66-67 C 5
Tulenij, ostrov — 126-127 N 4
Tulenji, ostrova — 126-127 OP 4
Tule River 74-75 D 4
Tule River Indian Reservation 74-75 D 4-5
Tul'gan 132-133 K 7
Tuli 172 E 6
Tulia, TX 76-77 D 5
Tūljā 164-165 EF 2
Tuljāpur 140 C 1-
Tūl Karm 136-137 F 6
Tul'kino 124-125 V 4
Tullahoma, TN 78-79 FG 3
Tullamore 160 H 4
Tulle 120-121 HJ 6
Tullibigeal 160 GH 4
Tully 158-159 J 3
Tulos, ozero — 124-125 H 2
Tulpan 132-133 K 5
Tulsa, OK 64-65 G 4
Tulsa = La Barge, WY 66-67 HJ 4
Tulsequah 58-59 V 7
Tulsi 138-139 KL 4
Tūlsi = Tūlasi 140 EF 1
Tulsīpur 138-139 J 4
Tuluá 92-93 D 4
Tulufan = Turpan 142-143 F 3
Tuluga River 58-59 M 2
Tuluksak, AK 58-59 G 6
Tulūl, Dīrat at- 136-137 G 6
Tulūl al-Ashāqif 136-137 G 6
Tulūl ash-Shaḥm 136-137 FG 8
Tulūl aṣ-Ṣafā 136-137 G 6
Tulum 86-87 R 7
Tulumaya 106-107 C 4
Tulumayo, Río — 96-97 D 7
Tulun 132-133 ST 7
Tulungagung 152-153 J 10
Tulun Mosque 170 II b 1
Tulu Welel 164-165 LM 7
Tulyehualco 91 I c 3
Tuma [SU, Kazachskaja SSR] 126-127 P 2
Tuma [SU, Rossijskaja SFSR] 124-125 N 6
Tumacacori National Monument 74-75 H 7
Tumaco 92-93 D 4
Tumaco, Rada de — 92-93 CD 4
Tuman'an 126-127 M 6
Tuman-gang 144-145 G 1
Tumanovo 124-125 L 6
Tumany 132-133 e 5
Tumba, Lac — 172 C 2
Tumbarumba 158-159 J 7
Tumbaya 104-105 D 8
Tumbes [EC, administrative unit] 96-97 A 3-4
Tumbes [EC, place] 92-93 C 5
Tumbes, Punta — 106-107 A 6
Tumboni 172 G 2
Tumby Bay 160 C 5
T'umen' [SU] 132-133 M 6
Tumen [TJ] 142-143 O 3
Tumen Jiang 144-145 G 1
Tumeremo 94-95 L 4
Tumiritinga 102-103 M 3
Tumkūr 134-135 M 8
Tumkūru = Tumkūr 134-135 M 8
Ṭummō, Jabal — 164-165 G 4
Tumpat 148-149 D 5
Tumsar 138-139 G 7
Tumu 164-165 D 6
Tumucumaque, Reserva Florestal 98-99 L 3-4
Tumucumaque, Serra do — 92-93 HJ 4
Tumupasa 104-105 C 4
Tumureng 92-93 G 3
Tumusla 104-105 D 7
Tumut 160 J 5
Tun, Nam Mae — 150-151 B 4
Tunaima, Laguna — 94-95 E 7
Tunal, Bogotá-El — 91 III b 4
Tunal, El — 104-105 D 9
Tunas, Coxilha das — 106-107 L 3
Tunas, Las — [C] 88-89 H 4
Tunas, Las — [RA] 106-107 G 3
Tunas, Sierra de las — 106-107 G 6
Tunas, Victoria de las — 64-65 L 7
Tunas Chicas, Laguna — 106-107 F 6
Tūnasīn, Hammadat — 166-167 D 5
Tunceli 136-137 H 3
Tunchang 150-151 GH 3
Tünchel 142-143 K 2
Tūndla 138-139 G 4
Tundrino 132-133 N 5
Tunduma 172 F 3
Tunduru 172 G 4
Tundža 122-123 M 4
Túnel Boquerón 91 II ab 1
Tūnfit 166-167 D 3
Tung 132-133 W 4
Tung-a = Dong'a 146-147 F 3
Tungabhadra 140 C 3
Tungabhadra Reservoir 140 C 3
Tung-an = Dong'an 146-147 C 8
Tungan = Tong'an 146-147 G 9
Tungaru = Tunqarū 164-165 L 6
Tung Chang 150-151 C 3
Tung-ch'êng = Tongcheng [TJ, Anhui] 146-147 F 6
Tung-ch'êng = Tongcheng [TJ, Hubei] 146-147 DE 7
Tung-ch'êng = Tongcheng [TJ, Jiangsu] 146-147 G 5
Tungchiang 146-147 H 10
Tung Chiang = Dong Jiang 146-147 DE 10
Tung-chou = Dali 146-147 B 4
Tung-chou = Nantong 142-143 N 5
Tungchow = Nantong 142-143 N 5
Tung-ch'uan = Tongchuan 142-143 K 4
Tungchwan = Huize 142-143 J 6
Tungchwan = Santai 142-143 JK 5
Tung-fang = Dongfang 142-143 K 8
Tung Hai = Dong Hai 142-143 NO 5-6
Tunghai Tao = Donghai Dao 146-147 C 11
Tunghiang = Tongxiang 146-147 H 6
Tung Ho = Dong He 146-147 A 3
Tung-hsiang = Dongxiang 146-147 F 7
T'ung-hsiang = Tongxiang 146-147 H 6
Tunghsien = Tong Xian 142-143 M 3-4

Tung-hsi-lien Tao = Dongxi Lian Dao 146-147 GH 4
T'ung-hsü = Tongxu 146-147 E 4
Tunghua = Tonghua 142-143 O 3
Tunghwa = Tonghua 142-143 O 3
Ţungī 141 B 4
Tungjen = Tongren 142-143 K 6
Tung-k'ou = Dongkou 146-147 C 8
Tung-ku = Tonggu 146-147 E 7
Tung-kuan = Dongguan 142-143 LM 7
Tungkuan = Dongguan 142-143 LM 7
T'ung-kuan = Tongguan 142-143 L 5
Tung-kuang = Dongguang 146-147 F 3
Tung Ku Chau 155 I b 2
T'ung-ku Chiao = Tonggu Jiao 150-151 H 3
Tung-liao = Tongliao 142-143 N 3
Tung-liu = Dongliu 146-147 F 6
Tunglu = Tonglu 142-143 M 5-6
Tung Lung 155 I b 2
Tung-pai = Tongbai 146-147 D 5
Tungping = Dongping 146-147 F 4
Tung-p'ing Hu = Dongping Hu 146-147 F 3-4
Tung-p'u = Tongphu 142-143 H 5
Tung-shan = Tongshan 146-147 E 7
Tungshan = Xuzhou 142-143 M 5
Tung-shêng = Dongsheng 142-143 K 4
Tung-shih = Tongshi 146-147 F 4
Tungsiang = Dongxiang 146-147 F 7
Tungtai = Dongtai 142-143 N 5
Tung-tao = Tongdao 146-147 B 8
Tung-t'ing Hu = Dongting Hu 142-143 L 6
Tung-t'ou Shan = Dongtou Shan 146-147 H 8
Tungtuang = Tônzan 141 C 4
Tungurahua 96-97 B 2
Tung-wei-shê = Penghu 146-147 G 10
Tung-yang = Dongyang 146-147 H 7
Tun-hua = Dunhua 142-143 O 3
Tun-huang = Dunhuang 142-143 GH 3
Tunhwang = Dunhuang 142-143 GH 3
Tuni 140 F 2
Tunia, La — 94-95 E 7
Tunica, MS 78-79 D 3
Tūnis 164-165 FG 1
Tunis, Gulf of — = Khalīj at-Tūnisī 166-167 M 1
Tunisi, Canale di — 122-123 D 7
Tūnisī, Khalīj at- 166-167 M 1
Tunisia 164-165 F 1-2
Tunj 164-165 K 7
Tunja 92-93 E 3
Tunjuelito, Bogotá- 91 III b 4
Tunjuelito, Río — 91 III a 3
Tunkhannock, PA 72-73 HJ 4
Tunki 88-89 D 8
Tunliu 146-147 D 3
Tunnsjø 116-117 E 5
Tunqarū 164-165 L 6
Tuntum 100-101 B 3
Tuntutuliak, AK 58-59 F 6
Tunupa, Cerro — 104-105 C 6
Tunuyán 106-107 C 4
Tunuyán, Río — 106-107 CD 4
Tunuyan, Sierra de — 111 C 4
Tunuyán, Travesía del — 106-107 D 4-5
Tunxi 142-143 M 6
Tuo He 146-147 F 5
Tuoji Dao 146-147 H 2
Tuokeqin = Thogchhen 138-139 HJ 2
Tuoketuo = Tugt 142-143 L 3
Tuokexun = Toksun 142-143 F 3
Tuokezheng = Thogchhen 138-139 HJ 2
Tuolin = Töling 138-139 GH 2
Tuolumne, CA 74-75 CD 4
Tuolumne River 74-75 CD 4
Tuoppajärvi = Topozero 132-133 E 4
Tuosuo Hu = Tos nuur 142-143 H 4
Tupã 92-93 JK 9
Tupaciguara 102-103 H 3
Tūp Āghāj 136-137 M 4
Tupambaé 106-107 K 4
Tupanatinga 100-101 F 5
Tupanciretã 111 F 3
Tu-p'ang Ling = Dupang Ling 146-147 C 9
Tuparai 106-107 JK 2
Tuparro, Río — 94-95 G 5
Tupelo, MS 64-65 J 5
Tupelo, OK 76-77 F 5
Tupi 94-95 G 2
Tupik [SU ↑ Mogoča] 132-133 WX 7
Tupik [SU ↗ Smolensk] 124-125 J 6
Tupim 100-101 D 7
Tupinambaranas, Ilha — 92-93 H 5
Tupirama 98-99 O 9
Tupiza 92-93 F 9
Tupper Lake, NY 72-73 J 2
Tupungato 106-107 C 4
Tupungato, Cerro — 111 BC 4
Tuque, la — 56-57 W 8
Túquerres 92-93 D 4
Ţūr, Aţ- 164-165 L 3
Tura [IND] 138-139 N 5
Tura [SU, place] 132-133 ST 5
Tura [SU, river] 132-133 L 6
Turā, Al-Qāhirah- 170 II b 2
Turabah 134-135 E 6
Turagua, Cerro — 94-95 J 4
Turagua, Serranías — 94-95 J 4
Turaiyūr 140 D 5
Turakom = Mu'o'ng Tourakom 150-151 D 3
Turan 132-133 R 7
Turan = Turanskaja nizmennosť 132-133 K 9-L 8
Turangi 161 FG 4
Turanian Plain = Turanskaja nizmennosť 132-133 K 9-L 8
Turanskaja nizmennosť 132-133 K 9-L 8
Tur'at al-Ismā'īlīyah 170 II b 1
Tur'at az-Zumar 170 II ab 1
Ţurayf 134-135 D 4
Turba, Río de la — 108-109 E 9-10
Turbaco 94-95 D 2
Turbat 134-135 J 5
Turbi 171 D 2
Turbio, El — 111 B 8
Turbo 92-93 D 3
Turbov 126-127 D 2
Turco 104-105 B 6
Turco, Cordillera de — 96-97 C 6
Turda 122-123 K 2
Turdera, Lomas de Zamora- 110 III b 2
Ţūreh 136-137 N 5
Turek 118 J 2
Turffontein, Johannesburg- 170 V b 2
Turffontein Race Course 170 V b 2
Turgaj [SU, place] 132-133 L 8
Turgaj [SU, river] 132-133 L 8
Turgajskaja ložbina 132-133 L 7
Turgel = Türi 124-125 E 4
Türgen Echin uul 142-143 FG 2
Turgeon, Lac — 62 M 2
Turgeon, Rivière — 62 M 2
Turgut 136-137 DE 3
Turgutlu 136-137 BC 3
Turhal 136-137 G 2
Türi 124-125 E 4
Turia 120-121 G 9
Turiaçu 92-93 K 5
Turiaçu, Baía de — 92-93 KL 5
Turiaçu, Rio — 100-101 B 1-2
Turiamo 94-95 GH 2
Turija 124-125 E 8
Turij Rog 132-133 Z 8
Turimiquire, Cerro — 94-95 JK 2
Turin 61 B 5-6
Turin = Torino 122-123 BC 3
Turinsk 132-133 L 6
Ţūrīt 164-165 L 8
Turja 124-125 S 2
Turka 126-127 A 2
Turkana 171 C 2
Turkana, Lake — 172 G 1
Turk an-Naşş, Rā's — 166-167 M 3
Türkeli = Gemiyanı 136-137 F 2
Türkeli adası 136-137 B 2
Turkestan 134-135 K-O 3
Turkey 134-135 B-E 3
Turkey, TX 76-77 D 5
Turkey River 70-71 E 4
Turki 124-125 O 8
Türkmen dağı 136-137 D 3
Turkmen-Kala 134-135 J 3
Turkmen Soviet Socialist Republic 134-135 HJ 2-5
Turks and Caicos Islands 88-89 KL 4
Turksib 132-133 P 7
Turks Islands 64-65 M 7
Turku 116-117 K 7
Turkwel 172 G 1
Türler See 128 IV ab 2
Turlock, CA 74-75 C 4
Turmalina 102-103 L 2
Turmerito 91 II b 2
Turmero 94-95 H 2
Turnagain, Cape — 161 G 5
Turnberry 61 GH 4
Turneffe Islands 64-65 J 8
Turner, MT 68-69 B 1
Turner, WA 66-67 E 2
Turner Valley 60 K 4
Turnhout 120-121 K 3
Turning Basin 85 III b 2
Turnor Lake 61 D 2
Turnu Măgurele 122-123 L 4
Turnu Roşu, Pasul — 122-123 KL 3
Turo 171 DE 3
Turon, KS 68-69 G 7
Tuross Head 160 K 6
Turov 124-125 FG 7
Turpan 142-143 F 3
Turpicotay, Cordillera de — 96-97 D 8
Turquino, Pico — 64-65 L 8
Turquoise Lake 58-59 KL 6
Turrell, AR 78-79 D 3
Tursāq 136-137 L 6
Turtkul' 132-133 L 9
Turtleford 61 D 4
Turtle Islands 168-169 B 4
Turtle Lake 61 D 4
Turtle Lake, ND 68-69 F 2
Turtle Lake, WI 70-71 D 3
Turtle Mountain 68-69 FG 1
Turtle Mountain Indian Reservation 68-69 G 1
Turton, SD 68-69 GH 3
Turuchansk 132-133 Q 4
Turuepano, Isla — 94-95 K 2
Ţūrūg 166-167 D 4
Turugart = Torugart Davan 134-135 L 2
Turumbah 136-137 J 4
Turun ja Poorin lääni 116-117 K 6-7
Turut = Ţorūd 134-135 H 3
Turuvekere 140 C 4
Turuvēkkērē = Turuvekere 140 C 4
Turvo, Rio — [BR, Goiás] 102-103 G 2
Turvo, Rio — [BR, Rio Grande do Sul] 106-107 L 1-2
Turvo, Rio — [BR, São Paulo ◁ Rio Grande] 102-103 H 4
Turvo, Rio — [BR, São Paulo ◁ Rio Paranapanema] 102-103 H 5
Tuscaloosa, AL 64-65 J 5
Tuscany = Toscana 122-123 D 4
Tuscarora, NV 66-67 E 5
Tuscola, IL 70-71 F 6
Tuscola, TX 76-77 E 6
Tuscumbia, AL 78-79 EF 3
Tuscumbia, MO 70-71 D 6
Tusenøyane 116-117 l 6
Tu Shan = Du Shan [TJ, mountain] 144-145 B 2
Tu-shan = Dushan [TJ, place] 146-147 F 6
Tu-shêng-chên = Dusheng 146-147 F 2
Tuside = Pic Toussidé 164-165 H 4
Tusima = Tsushima 142-143 O 5
Tusima kaikyō = Tsushima-kaikyō 142-143 OP 5
Tuskegee, AL 78-79 G 4
Tussey Mountain 72-73 GH 4
Tustna 116-117 B 6
Tustumena Lake 58-59 MN 6
Tutajev 124-125 M 5
Tutak 136-137 K 3
Tutang 146-147 F 7
Tuti 96-97 F 9
Tuticorin 134-135 M 9
Tutna Lake 58-59 K 6
Tutóia 100-101 C 2
Tutoko, Mount — 161 BC 7
Tutončana 132-133 R 4
Tu-t'ou = Dutou 146-147 D 9
Tutrakan 122-123 M 3-4
Tuttle, ND 68-69 FG 2
Tuttle, OK 76-77 F 5
Tuttle Creek Lake 68-69 H 6
Tuttle Lake 70-71 C 4
Tuttlingen 118 D 4-5
Tūttukkuḍi = Tuticorin 134-135 M 9
Tutubu 171 C 4
Tutuila 148-149 c 1
Tutupaca, Volcán — 92-93 E 8
Tutwiler, MS 78-79 D 3-4
Tuul gol 142-143 JK 2
Tuva Autonomous Soviet Socialist Republic 132-133 RS 7
Tuvalu 208 HJ 3
Tu Vu 150-151 E 2
Ţuwāl 'Aba' 136-137 H 4
Tuwāt, At- 164-165 DE 3
Ţuwayq, Jabal — 134-135 F 6
Ţuwaysah, Aţ- 164-165 K 6
Tuxedni Bay 58-59 L 6
Tuxedo, MD 82 II b 2
Tuxford 61 EF 5
Tuxie He = Tuhai He 146-147 FG 3
Tuxpan [MEX, Jalisco] 86-87 J 8
Tuxpan [MEX, Nayarit] 64-65 E 7
Tuxpán de Rodriguez Cano 64-65 G 7
Tuxtepec 86-87 M 8
Tuxtla Gutiérrez 64-65 H 8
Tuy 120-121 C 7
Tuy An 148-149 E 4
Tuya River 58-59 W 7
Tuyên Hoa 150-151 F 4
Tuyên Quang 150-151 E 2
Tuy Hoa 148-149 EF 4
Tuy Phong 150-151 G 7
Tūyserkān 136-137 N 5
Tuyun = Duyun 142-143 K 6
Tuzgölü 134-135 C 3
Ţuz Khurmātū 136-137 L 5
Tuzla [TR] 136-137 F 4
Tuzla [YU] 122-123 H 3
Tuzluca 136-137 K 2
Tūzlū Gol = Kavīr-e Mīghān 136-137 N 5
Tuzly 126-127 E 4
Tvedestrand 116-117 C 8
Tver' = Kalinin 132-133 EF 6
Tverca 124-125 K 5
Twaingnu 141 C 4
Twande 141 DE 7
Twante = Twande 141 DE 7
Tweed [CDN] 72-73 H 2
Tweed [GB] 119 E 4
Tweedsmuir Provincial Park 56-57 L 7
Tweeling 174-175 H 4
Twee Rivieren 174-175 D 4
Twelvemile Summit 58-59 OP 4
Twentieth Century Fox Studios 83 III b 1
Twenty-four Parganas = 24-Parganas 138-139 M 6-7
Twentynine Palms, CA 74-75 EF 5
Twentytwo Mile Village, AK 58-59 PQ 3
Twickenham, London- 129 II a 2
Twilight Cove 158-159 E 6
Twin Bridges, MT 66-67 GH 3
Twin Buttes Reservoir 76-77 D 7
Twin Falls, ID 64-65 CD 3
Twin Heads 158-159 E 4
Twin Islands 56-57 UV 7
Twin Lakes 58-59 KL 6
Twin Oaks, PA 84 III a 2
Twin Peaks [USA, Idaho] 66-67 F 3
Twin Peaks [USA, San Francisco] 83 I b 2
Twins, The — 161 DE 5
Twin Valley, MN 70-71 BC 2
Two Butte Creek 68-69 E 7
Two Buttes, CO 68-69 E 7
Twodot, MT 66-67 HJ 2
Two Harbors, MN 64-65 HJ 2
Two Hills 61 C 4
Two Rivers, WI 70-71 G 3
Tyagadurgam = Tiyāgai 140 D 5
Tyamo 164-165 M 7
Tyārīt, Wādī — 166-167 LM 4
Tyborøn 116-117 BC 9
Tyencha 164-165 M 7
Tyew Bahir 164-165 M 8
Tygda 132-133 Y 7
Tygh Valley, OR 66-67 C 3
Tylden 174-175 G 7
Tyler, MN 68-69 H 3
Tyler, TX 64-65 GH 5
Tyler Park, VA 82 II a 2
Tylertown, MS 78-79 DE 5
Tylösand 116-117 E 9
Tylovaj 124-125 T 5
Tym 132-133 P 6
Tymfréstós 122-123 JK 6
Tymovskoje 132-133 b 7
Tympákion 122-123 L 8
Tyndall, SD 68-69 H 4
Tyndinskij 132-133 XY 6
Tynemouth 119 F 4
Tynset 116-117 D 6
Tyonek, AK 58-59 M 6
Tyone River 58-59 O 5
Tyŏnthar = Teonthar 138-139 H 5
Tyŏsen kaikyō = Chŏsen-kaikyō 142-143 O 5
Tyre = Şūr 136-137 F 6
Tyrell, Lake — 158-159 H 7
Tyrifjord 116-117 CD 7
Tyrma 132-133 Z 7
Tyrnyauz 126-127 L 5
Tyrol = Tirol 118 EF 5
Tyrone, OK 76-77 D 4
Tyrone, PA 72-73 G 4
Tyros = Şūr 136-137 F 6
Tyrrell, Lake — 160 F 5
Tyrrhenian Sea 114-115 L 7-8
Tyry = Mindživan 126-127 N 7
Tysnesøy 116-117 A 7-8
Tytuvėnai 124-125 D 6
Tyumen = Tumen' 132-133 M 6
Tyuo River = Twaingnu 141 C 4
Tzaneen 172 F 6
Tz-ch'iu = Ziqiu 146-147 C 6
Tzechung = Zizhong 142-143 JK 5-6
Tzekam = Zijin 146-147 E 10
Tzekung = Zigong 142-143 JK 6
Tzekwei = Zigui 146-147 C 6
Tzitzikama Mountains = Tsitsikamaberge 174-175 EF 7
Tzŭ-ch'ang = Zichang 146-147 B 3
Tzŭ-chin = Zijin 146-147 E 10
Tz'ŭ-hsien = Ci Xian 146-147 E 3
Tzŭ-hu = Bajan Choto 142-143 JK 4
Tzŭ-kuei = Zigui 146-147 C 6
Tzŭ-kung = Zigong 142-143 JK 6
Tz'ŭ-li = Cili 146-147 C 7
Tzŭ Shui = Zi Shui 146-147 C 7
Tzŭ-ya Ho = Ziya He 146-147 F 2
Tzŭ-yang = Ziyang 146-147 B 5
Tzŭ-yüan = Ziyuan 146-147 C 8

U

U, Nam — = Nam Ou 150-151 D 1
Uacamparique, Serra do — 104-105 E 2
Uaçari, Serra — 92-93 H 4
Uaco Cungo 172 C 4
Uacuru, Cachoeira — 98-99 HJ 10
Uaddān = Waddān 164-165 H 3
Uadi-Halfa = Wādī Ḥalfā 164-165 L 4
Uádi Ṭanezzúft = Wādī Tanizzuft 166-167 M 7
Uádi Zemzen = Wādī Zamzam 164-165 G 2
Uagadugu = Ouagadougou 164-165 D 6
Uaianary, Cachoeira — 98-99 FG 4
Ualega = Welega 164-165 LM 7
Ualik Lake 58-59 H 7
Uanaraca 94-95 H 8
Uancheu = Wenzhou 142-143 N 6
Uanetze, Rio — 174-175 K 3
Uanle Uen = Wanleweeyn 172 H 1
Uarangal = Warangal 134-135 MN 7
Uari 98-99 K 8
Uaruma 94-95 G 7
Uaso Nyiro 171 D 2
Uatumã, Rio — 92-93 H 5
Uauá 92-93 M 6
Uáu el Chebir = Wādī Bay al-Kabīr 164-165 GH 2
Uáu en-Námús = Wāw an-Nāmūs 164-165 H 4
Uaupés 92-93 F 5
Uaupés, Rio — 92-93 F 4
Uaxactún 64-65 J 8
Uazzén = Wāzin 166-167 M 4
Ubá 92-93 L 9
Ubá, Cachoeira do — 98-99 MN 9
Ubá, Salto do — 111 F 2
Ubaí 102-103 K 2
Ubaíra 100-101 E 7
Ubaitaba 92-93 M 7
Ubajara 100-101 D 2
Ubajara, Parque Nacional de — 100-101 D 2
Ubajay 106-107 H 3
Ubalá 94-95 E 5
Ubangi 172 C 1
Ubari = Awbārī 164-165 G 3
'Ubārī, Edeien- = Şaḥrā' Awbārī 164-165 G 3
Ubatã 100-101 E 8
Ubaté 94-95 E 5
Ubatuba 102-103 K 5
Ubauro 138-139 B 3
Ubaye 120-121 L 6
'Ubaylah, Al- 134-135 G 6
Ubayyiḍ, Al- 164-165 KL 6
Ubayyiḍ, Wādī al- 136-137 K 6
Ube 142-143 P 5
Úbeda 120-121 F 9
Ubekendt Ø 56-57 a 3
Uberaba 92-93 K 8
Uberaba, Lagoa — 102-103 D 2
Uberlândia 92-93 K 8
Ubiaja 168-169 G 4
Ubin, Pulau — 154 III b 1
Ubiña, Peña — 120-121 DE 7
Ubiraitá 100-101 D 7
Ubiratã 102-103 F 6
'Ubkayk, Jabal — 164-165 M 4
Ubombo 174-175 JK 4
Ubon Ratchathani 150-151 E 5
Ubort' 124-125 FG 8
Ubsa Nur = Uvs nuur 142-143 G 1
Ubundu 172 DE 3
Ucacha 106-107 F 4
Ucami 132-133 S 5
Ucayali 96-97 D 4
Ucayali, Río — 92-93 D 6
Uch = Uchh 138-139 C 3
Uchh 138-139 C 3
Uchiko 144-145 J 6
Uchi Lake 62 C 2
Uchinoko = Uchiko 144-145 J 6
Uchinoura 144-145 H 7
Uchiura-wan 144-145 b 2
Uchiza 96-97 C 6
Uchta [SU, Archangel'sk] 124-125 M 3
Uchta [SU, Komi ASSR] 132-133 J 5
Uchta = Kalevala 132-133 E 4
Ūchturpan 142-143 DE 3
Ucluelet 60 E 5
Ucross, WY 68-69 C 3
Učur 132-133 Z 6
Uda [SU ◁ Čuna] 132-133 S 7
Uda [SU ◁ Selenga] 132-133 UV 7
Uda [SU ◁ Udskaja guba] 132-133 Z 7
Ūdah, Jabal — 164-165 M 4
Udaipur [IND ↗ Ahmadābād] 134-135 L 6
Udaipur [IND ↖ Jaipur] 138-139 E 4
Udaipur Garhi = Udaypur Gaṛhī 138-139 L 4
Udaj 126-127 F 1
Udala 138-139 L 7
Udalguri 141 C 2
Udamalpet 140 C 5
Udanguḍi = Udankudi 140 C 6
Udankudi 140 C 6
Udaquiola 106-107 H 6
Udayagiri [IND, Andhra Pradesh] 140 D 3
Udayagiri [IND, Orissa] 138-139 K 8
Udaypur Gaṛhī 138-139 L 4
'Udaysāt, Al- 173 C 5
Udbina 122-123 FG 3
Uddevalla 116-117 DE 8
Uddjaur 116-117 H 5
Udgīr 140 C 1
Udimskij 124-125 PQ 3
Údine 122-123 E 2
Udipi 134-135 L 8
Uḍīsā = Orissa 134-135 N 7-O 6
Udjidji = Ujiji 172 E 2-3
Udmurt Autonomous Soviet Socialist Republic = 2 ◁ 132-133 J 6
Udmurtskaja Avtonomnaja Sovetskaja Socialističeskaja Respublika = Udmurt Autonomous Soviet Socialist Republic 132-133 J 6
U-do 144-145 F 6
Udobnaja 126-127 K 4
Udomľa 124-125 K 5
Udon Thani 148-149 D 3
Udrif 166-167 LM 2-3
Udskaja guba 132-133 a 7
Uḍuppi = Udipi 134-135 L 8
Udža 132-133 W 3
Udžary 126-127 N 6
Uebonti 148-149 H 7
Ueda 144-145 M 4
Uedineniya Island = ostrov Ujedinenija 132-133 OP 2
Uegit = Wajid 172 H 1
Uele 172 D 1
Uelen 56-57 BC 4
Uelikon 128 IV b 2
Uelzen 118 E 2
Uengan, mys — 132-133 LM 3
Ueno 144-145 L 5
Ueno, Tōkyō- 155 III b 1
Ueno Parak 155 III b 1
Uere 172 E 1
Uerzlikon 128 IV ab 2
Uetikon 128 IV b 2
Uetliberg 128 IV ab 1
Ufa [SU, place] 132-133 K 7
Ufa [SU, river] 132-133 K 6
Ūfran 166-167 G 5
Ufťuga 124-125 Q 3
Ugak Bay 58-59 g 1
Ugak Island 58-59 gh 1
Ugāle 124-125 CD 5
Ugalen = Ugāle 124-125 CD 5
Ugalla 172 F 3
Ugamak Island 58-59 o 3
Ugamas 174-175 C 5
Uganda 172 F 1
Uganik Island 58-59 K 8
Ugarteche 106-107 C 4
Ugashik, AK 58-59 J 8
Ugashik Bay 58-59 HJ 8
Ugashik Lakes 58-59 J 8
Ugep 168-169 H 4
Ūgharṭah 166-167 E 5
Ugie 174-175 H 6
Ugleuralskij 124-125 V 4
Uglič 132-133 F 6
Ugljan 122-123 F 3
Uglovka 124-125 J 4
Ugogo 172 FG 3
Ugoľnyj = Beringovskij 132-133 j 5
Ugoma 171 B 3-4
Ugra [SU, place] 124-125 K 6
Ugra [SU, river] 124-125 K 6
Uguay 111 E 3
Uğurludağ = Kızılveran 136-137 F 2
Uha 172 F 2
Uha-dong 142-143 O 3
Uhlenhorst 174-175 B 2
Uhlenhorst, Hamburg- 130 I b 1
Uhrichsville, OH 72-73 F 4
Uibaí 100-101 C 6
Ui-do 144-145 E 5
Uíge 172 BC 3
Uijŏngbu 144-145 F 4
Uiju 144-145 E 2
Uil 132-133 J 8
Uilpata, gora — 126-127 L 5
Uinamarca, Laguna — 104-105 B 5
Uintah and Ouray Indian Reservation [USA ↓ East Tavaputs Plateau] 74-75 J 3
Uintah and Ouray Indian Reservation [USA ↓ Uinta Mountains] 66-67 HJ 5
Uinta Mountains 64-65 DE 3
Uiraponga 100-101 E 3
Uiraúna 100-101 E 4
Uisŏng 144-145 G 4
Uitdam 128 I b 1
Uitenhage 172 DE 8
Uitikon 128 IV a 1
Uj 132-133 L 7
Ujandina 132-133 b 4
Ujar 132-133 R 6
Ujda = Ujdah 164-165 D 2
Ujdah 164-165 D 2
Ujedinenija, ostrov — 132-133 OP 2
Ujhāni 138-139 G 3-4
Uji-guntō 144-145 G 7
Ujiji 172 E 2-3
Ujjaen = Ujjain 134-135 M 6
Ujjain 134-135 M 6
Ujunglamuru 152-153 NO 8
Ujung Pandang 148-149 G 8
Ujung Peureulak 152-153 BC 3
Ujung Raja 152-153 AB 4
Ujung Tuan 152-153 C 5
Ukamas = Ugamas 174-175 C 5
Ukara 171 C 3
'Ukāsh, Wādī — 136-137 J 5-6
Ukata 168-169 G 3
Ukerewe Island 172 F 2
Ukhrul 141 D 3
Ukiah, CA 64-65 B 4
Ukiah, OR 66-67 D 3
Ukimbu 172 F 3
Ukita, Tōkyō- 155 III c 1
Ukmergė 124-125 E 6
Ukonongo 172 F 3
Ukraina 126-127 F 3-J 2
Ukraine 114-115 O-Q 6
Ukrainian Soviet Socialist Republic 126-127 C-H 2
Ukrainskaja Sovetskaja Socialističeskaja Respublika = Ukrainian Soviet Socialist Republic 126-127 C-H 2
Uksora 124-125 NO 2
Ukumbi 172 F 3
Uku-shima 144-145 G 6
Ukwama 171 C 5
Ukwi 174-175 D 2
Ula 136-137 C 4
'Ulā', Al- 134-135 D 5
Ulaanbaatar 142-143 K 2
Ulaan Choto = Ulan Hot 142-143 N 2
Ulaangom 142-143 G 1-2
Ulaan mörön [TJ ◁ Dre Chhu] 142-143 G 5
Ulaan Mörön [TJ ◁ Kuye He] 146-147 BC 2
Ulaan uul 142-143 G 5
Ulak Island 58-59 t 7
Ulala = Gorno-Altajsk 132-133 Q 7
Ulamba 172 D 3
Ulan = Dulaan Chijd 142-143 H 4
Ulan Bator = Ulaanbaatar 142-143 K 2
Ulan Bator = Ulaan Bataar 142-143 K 2
Ulan-Burgasy, chrebet — 132-133 UV 7
Ulan-Erge 126-127 M 3
Ulan Gom = Ulaangom 142-143 G 1-2
Ulan Hot 142-143 N 2
Ulankom = Ulaangom 142-143 G 1-2
Ulan-Udė 132-133 U 7
Ulapes 111 C 4
Ulapes, Sierra de — 106-107 D 3
Ulaş 136-137 G 3
Ulastai = Uljastaj 142-143 H 2
Ulawa 148-149 k 6
Ul'ba 132-133 P 7
Ulchin 144-145 G 4
Ulcinj 122-123 H 5
Uldza = Bajan Uul 142-143 L 2
Üldzejt = Öldzijt 142-143 J 2
Uldz gol 142-143 L 2
Uleåborg = Oulu 116-117 L 5
Uleelheue 148-149 C 5
Ulen, MN 68-69 H 2
Ulete 172 G 3
Ulety 132-133 V 7
Ulge 172 BC 3
Ulhasnagar 134-135 L 7
Uliaga Island 58-59 m 4
Uliassutai = Uliastaj 142-143 H 2
Uliastai 142-143 H 2
Ulijasutai = Uliastaj 142-143 H 2
Ulindi 172 E 2
Ulingan 148-149 N 7
Ulīpūr 138-139 M 5
Ulja 132-133 b 6
Uljanovka 126-127 E 2
Uljanovsk 132-133 H 7
Uljinskij chrebet 132-133 ab 6
Ulkatcho 60 E 3
Ulla 124-125 G 6
Ulladulla 158-159 K 7
Ullin, IL 70-71 F 7
Ulloma 104-105 B 5
Ullsfjord 116-117 HJ 3
Ullŭn 106-107 C 3
Ullŭng-do 142-143 P 4
Ullyul 144-145 E 3
Ulm 118 D 4
Ulm, AR 78-79 D 3
Ulm, MT 66-67 H 2
Ulm, WY 68-69 C 3
'Ulmah, Al- 166-167 J 1
Ulmarra 160 L 2
Ūlmās 166-167 CD 3
Uløy 116-117 J 3
Ulpad = Olpād 138-139 D 7
Ulsan 142-143 OP 4
Ulster 119 C 4
Ulster Canal 119 C 4
Ultadanga, Calcutta- 154 II b 2
Ulu 132-133 Y 5
Ulúa, Río — 64-65 J 8
Ulubat gölü = Apolyont gölü 136-137 C 2
Ulu Bedok 154 III b 2
Ulubey 136-137 C 3
Ulubey = Gündüzlü 136-137 G 2
Uluborlu 136-137 D 3
Uluçınar = Arsuz 136-137 F 4
Uludağ 136-137 C 2-3
Ulugh Muz tagh 142-143 F 4
Uluguru Mountains 172 G 3
Ulukışla 136-137 F 4
Ulundi 174-175 J 5
Ulundurpettai = Kīranūr 140 D 5
Ulus 136-137 E 2
Ulutau 132-133 M 8
Ulutau, gora — 132-133 M 8
Ulverstone 160 bc 2
'Ulyā, Qaryat al- 134-135 F 5
Ulyastai = Uliastaj 142-143 H 2
Ulysses, KS 68-69 F 7
Ulysses, NE 68-69 H 5
Umala 92-93 F 8
Umal'tinskij 132-133 Z 7
Umán [MEX] 86-87 PQ 7
Uman' [SU] 126-127 DE 2
Umanak = Umánaq 56-57 ab 3
Umanak Fjord 56-57 Za 3
Umánaq 56-57 ab 3
Umango, Sierra de — 106-107 C 2
Umanskaja = Leningradskaja 126-127 J 3
Umarga 140 C 2
'Umarī, Qā'al — 136-137 G 7
Umaria 138-139 H 6
Umarkhed 138-139 F 8
Umarkher = Umarkhed 138-139 F 8
Umarkoţ 138-139 BC 5
Umarote 96-97 D 9
Ūm'āsh 166-167 J 2
Umatilla Indian Reservation 66-67 D 3
Umatilla River 66-67 D 3
Umba = Lesnoj 132-133 EF 4
Umbarger, TX 76-77 C 5
Umbarpāda 138-139 D 7
Umberto 1° 106-107 G 3
Umboi 148-149 N 8
Umbria 122-123 DE 4
Umbu [BR] 106-107 K 2
Umbu [TJ] 142-143 F 5
Umburanas 100-101 D 6
Umburanas, Serra das — 100-101 F 5-G 4
Umburatiba 100-101 D 3
Umbuzeiro 100-101 G 4
Umeå 116-117 HJ 6
Ume älv 116-117 H 5
Um er Rebia = Wād Umm ar-Rabīyah 164-165 C 2
Umet 124-125 O 7
Umfolozi 174-175 JK 5
Umfolozi Game Reserve 174-175 JK 5
Umgeni 174-175 J 5
Umhlatuzi = Mhlatuze 174-175 J 5
Umiat, AK 58-59 K 2
Umiris 98-99 J 7

Umkomaas [ZA, place] 174-175 J 6
Umkomaas [ZA, river] 174-175 J 6
Umkomanzi = Umkomaas 174-175 J 6
Umm ad-Durūs, Sabkhat — 164-165 B 4
Umm al-'Abīd 164-165 H 3
Umm al-'Ashār 166-167 B 5
Umm al-Bawāghī 166-167 K 2
Umm al-Kataf, Khalīj — 173 D 6
Umm al-Khiyālāt, Sabkhat — 166-167 M 3
Umm al-Qaywayn 134-135 GH 5
Umm ar-Rabīyah, Wād — 164-165 C 2
Umm ash-Shidād = Sabkhat Abā ar-Rūs 134-135 G-H 6
Umm aṣ-Ṣam'ah 166-167 L 3
Umm as-Samīm 134-135 H 6
Umm aṭ-Ṭuyūr al-Fawqānī, Jabal — 173 D 6
Umm aṭ-Ṭūẓ 136-137 K 5
Umm az-Zumūl 134-135 GH 6
Umm Badr 164-165 K 6
Umm Ball 164-165 K 6
Umm Bishtīt, Bi'r — 173 DE 6
Umm Bujmah 173 C 3
Umm Durmān 164-165 L 5
Umm el-'Abid 164-165 H 3
Umm Hagar = Om Hajer 164-165 M 6
Umm Hajer = Om Hajer 164-165 M 6
Umm Ḥibāl, Bi'r — 173 C 6
Umm 'Inab, Jabal — 173 C 5
Umm Kaddādah 164-165 K 6
Umm Karār, Tall — 136-137 H 6
Umm Keddāda = Umm Kaddādah 164-165 K 6
Umm Laǧǧ = Umm Lajj 134-135 D 5
Umm Lajj 134-135 D 5
Umm Naqqāṭ, Jabal — 173 CD 5
Umm Qaṣr 136-137 M 7
Umm Quṣur, Jazīrat — 173 D 3-4
Umm Rashrash = Ēlat 134-135 C 4
Umm Ruwābah 164-165 L 6
Umm Sa'īd, Bi'r — 173 CD 3
Umm Shāghir, Jabal — 173 B 6
Umnak Island 52 D 35-36
Umnak Pass 58-59 mn 4
Umniati 172 E 5
Umpqua River 66-67 AB 4
Umraniye 154 I b 2
Umrat 138-139 D 7
Umrēḍ = Umrer 138-139 G 7
Umrer 138-139 G 7
Umreth 138-139 D 6
'Umshaymin, Al- 136-137 H 6
Ūmsŏng 144-145 F 4
Umtali = Mutare 172 F 5
Umtata 172 E 8
Umtata River = Mtatarivier 174-175 H 6
Umtatarivier = Mtatarivier 174-175 H 6
Umtentweni 174-175 J 6
Umtwalumi = Mtwalume 174-175 J 6
Umuahia 168-169 G 4
Umuarama 102-103 F 5
Umuryeri, İstanbul- 154 I b 2
Umvoti 174-175 J 5
Umvuma = Mvuma 172 F 5
Umzimhlava 174-175 H 6
Umzimkulu [ZA, place] 174-175 H 6
Umzimkulu [ZA, river] 174-175 J 6
Umzimvubu 172 EF 8
Umzinto 174-175 J 6
Umzumbe 174-175 J 6
Umzumbi = Umzumbe 174-175 J 6

Una [BR] 92-93 M 8
Una [IND, Gujarāt] 138-139 C 7
Una [IND, Himāchal Pradesh] 138-139 F 2
Una [YU] 122-123 G 3
Una, Rio — 100-101 G 5
'Unāb, Wādī el- = Wādī al-'Unnāb 136-137 G 7-8
Unac 122-123 G 3
Unadilla, GA 80-81 DE 4
Unāghah 166-167 B 4
Unai 92-93 K 8
'Unaizah = 'Unayzah 134-135 E 5
Unaka Mountains 80-81 DE 3
Unalakleet, AK 56-57 D 5
Unalakleet River 58-59 GH 5
Unalaska, AK 58-59 n 4
Unalaska Bay 58-59 n 3-4
Unalaska Island 52 D 35
Unalga Island [USA, Delarof Islands] 58-59 t 7
Unalga Island [USA, Unalaska Island] 58-59 no 4
Unango 171 C 6
Unare, Laguna de — 94-95 J 2
Unare, Río — 94-95 J 3
Unauna, Pulau — 152-153 O 6
'Unayzah [JOR] 136-137 FG 7
'Unayzah [Saudi Arabia] 134-135 E 5
'Unayzah, Jabal — 134-135 DE 4
Uncía 92-93 F 8
Uncompahgre Peak 64-65 E 4
Uncompahgre Plateau 74-75 JK 3
Underberg 174-175 H 5
Underbool 160 E 5
Underground 85 II b 2
Underwood, ND 68-69 F 2
Undory 124-125 QR 6
Undozero 124-125 M 2
Undumo, Río — 104-105 C 3
Undurkhan = Öndörchaan 142-143 L 2
Uneča 124-125 J 7
Uneiuxi, Rio — 92-93 F 5
UNESCO 129 I c 2
Unga, AK 58-59 c 2
Unga Island 56-57 D 6
Ungalik, AK 58-59 G 4
Ungalik River 58-59 GH 4
Unga Strait 58-59 c 2
Ungava 56-57 V-X 6
Ungava Bay 56-57 X 6
Ungava Crater = New Quebec Crater 56-57 VW 5
Ungava Peninsula 56-57 VW 5
Ungeny 126-127 CD 3
Unggi 144-145 H 1
Uni 124-125 S 5
União 92-93 L 5
União da Vitória 102-103 G 7
União dos Palmares 92-93 MN 6
Unib, Khawr — 173 D 7
Unicorn Ridge 155 I b 1
Unidad Santa Fe, Villa Obregón- 91 I b 2
Unije 122-123 EF 3
Unimak, AK 58-59 a 2
Unimak Bight 58-59 ab 2
Unimak Island 52 D 35
Unimak Pass 58-59 o 3
Unini 96-97 E 7
Unini, Rio — 92-93 G 5
Union, MO 70-71 E 6
Union, MS 78-79 E 4
Union, OR 66-67 E 3
Union, SC 80-81 F 3
Union, WV 80-81 F 2
Unión [PY] 102-103 D 6
Unión [RA] 111 C 5
Union [Saint Vincent] 88-89 Q 8
Unión, La — [BOL] 104-105 F 4
Unión, La — [CO, Nariño] 94-95 C 7
Unión, La — [CO, Valle del Cauca] 94-95 C 5
Unión, La — [E] 120-121 G 10
Unión, La — [ES] 64-65 J 9
Unión, La — [MEX] 86-87 K 9
Unión, La — [PE, Huánuco] 92-93 D 6-7
Unión, La — [PE, Piura] 96-97 A 4
Unión, La — [RCH] 111 B 6
Unión, La — [YV] 94-95 GH 3
Union, Mount — 74-75 G 5
Union City, IN 70-71 H 5
Union City, NJ 82 III b 2
Union City, PA 72-73 FG 4
Union City, TN 78-79 E 2
Union Creek, OR 66-67 B 4
Uniondale 174-175 E 7
Uniondale Road = Uniondaleweg 174-175 E 7
Uniondaleweg 174-175 E 7
Union Depot 84 II b 3
Unión de Tula 86-87 HJ 7
Union Pacific Railway 64-65 E 3
Union Point, GA 80-81 E 4
Union Springs, AL 78-79 G 4
Union Station [USA, Houston] 85 III b 1
Union Station [USA, Los Angeles] 83 III c 1
Uniontown, AL 78-79 F 4
Uniontown, KY 70-71 G 7
Uniontown, PA 72-73 G 5
Unionville, IA 70-71 D 5
Unionville, NV 66-67 DE 5
United Arab Emirates 134-135 GH 6
United Kingdom 119 G 4-5
United Nations-Headquarters 82 III c 2
United Provinces = Uttar Pradesh 134-135 MN 5
United Pueblos Indian Reservation 76-77 A 5
United States 64-65 C-K 4
United States Atomic Energy Commission Reservation = National Reactor Testing Station 66-67 G 4
United States Naval Annex 84 I b 2
Unity 61 D 4
Unity, ME 72-73 M 2
Universal City, TX 76-77 E 8
Universal City Mall 84 II b 2
Universidad Catolica Andrés Bello 91 II b 2
Universidad Militar Latino Americana 91 I b 2
Universidad Nacional 91 III bc 3
Universitas Katolik Indonesia 154 IV ab 2
Universität München 130 II b 2
Universität Wien 113 I b 2
Universität Zürich 128 IV b 1
Université de Al-Jazā'ir 170 I a 1
Université de Montréal 82 I b 1
Üniversite İstanbul 154 I a 2
Universiteit van Amsterdam 128 I ab 1
University City, MO 70-71 E 6
University Gardens, NY 82 III d 2
University Heights, OH 72-73 F 4
University of Cairo 170 II b 1
University of Calcutta 154 II b 2
University of California [USA, Los Angeles] 83 III b 1
University of California [USA, San Francisco] 83 I c 1
University of Chicago 83 II b 2
University of Detroit 84 II b 2
University of Georgia at Atlanta 85 II bc 2
University of Hong Kong 155 I a 2
University of Houston 85 III b 2
University of Illinois 83 II ab 1
University of Indonesia 154 IV b 2
University of Lagos 170 III b 1
University of Massachusetts 84 I b 3
University of Melbourne 161 II b 1
University of New Orleans 85 I b 1
University of New South Wales 161 I b 2
University of Pennsylvania 84 III b 2
University of Saint Thomas 85 III b 2
University of San Francisco 83 I b 2
University of Singapore 154 III a 2
University of Southern California 83 III c 1
University of Sydney 161 I ab 2
University of the Americas 91 I b 2
University of Windsor 84 II b 3
University of Witwatersrand 170 V b 2
University Park, MD 82 II b 1
University Park, NM 76-77 A 6
Unja 124-125 W 3
Unjamwesi = Unyamwezi 172 F 2-3
'Unnāb, Wādī al- 136-137 G 7-8
Unnão 138-139 H 4
Unnāv = Unnão 138-139 H 4
U No'a = Mu'o'ng Ou Neua 150-151 CD 1
Unquillo 106-107 E 3
Unsan 144-145 E 2-3
Unsang, Tanjung — 152-153 N 3
Unsan-ni 144-145 EF 3
Unst 119 F 1
Unstrut 118 E 3
Unterbiberg 130 II b 2
Unterengstringen 128 IV a 1
Unterliederbach, Frankfurt am Main- 128 III a 1
Untermenzing, München- 130 II a 1
Untersendling, München- 130 II b 2
Unturán, Sierra de — 94-95 J 7
Unuk River 60 B 1
Unyamwezi 172 F 2-3
Ünye 136-137 G 2
Unža [SU ◁ Gor'kovskoje vodochranilišče] 124-125 P 4

Uolkitte = Welkītē 164-165 M 7
Uollega = Welega 164-165 LM 7
Uomán 94-95 K 5
Uopiane, Serra do — 104-105 E 2-3
Uoso Nyiro = Ewaso Ngiro 172 G 2
Uozu 144-145 L 4

Upanda, Serra — 172 BC 4
Upanema 100-101 F 3
Upardāng Gaṛhī 138-139 K 4
Upata 94-95 K 3
Upemba, Lac — 172 E 3
Upemba, Parc national de l' 172 E 3
Upernavik 56-57 Z 3
Upham, ND 68-69 F 1
Upham, NM 76-77 A 6
Upi 152-153 PQ 2
Upía, Río — 94-95 E 5
Upington 172 D 7
Upland, PA 84 III a 2
Upleta 138-139 C 7
Upnuk Lake 58-59 H 6
Upolokša 116-117 O 4
Upolu 148-149 c 1
Upolu Point 78-79 de 2
Upper 168-169 E 3
Upper Arrow Lake 60 J 4
Upper Austria = Oberösterreich 118 F-H 4
Upper Bay 82 III b 2-3
Upper Darby, PA 72-73 J 4-5
Upper Egypt = Aṣ-Ṣa'īd 164-165 L 3
Upper Guinea 50-51 JK 5
Upper Humber River 63 H 3
Upper Hutt 161 F 5
Upper Klamath Lake 66-67 BC 4
Upper Laberge 58-59 U 6
Upper Lake 66-67 C 5
Upper Lake, CA 74-75 B 3
Upper Musquodoboit 63 E 5
Upper Mystic Lake 84 I ab 2
Upper Nile = Aali an-Nīl 164-165 KL 7
Upper Peninsula 64-65 J 2
Upper Red Lake 70-71 C 1
Upper Sandusky, OH 72-73 E 4
Upper Seal Lake = Lac d'Iberville 56-57 W 6
Upper Volta = Burkina Faso 164-165 D 6
Uppland 116-117 G 7-H 8
Uppsala [S, administrative unit] 116-117 GH 7
Uppsala [S, place] 116-117 G 8
Upsala 70-71 E 1
Upsalquitch 63 C 4
Upstart Bay 158-159 J 3
Upton, KY 70-71 GH 7
Upton, WY 68-69 D 3
Uptown, Chicago-, IL 83 II ab 1
Uptown Business Park, Houston-, TX 85 III b 2

'Uqaylah, Al- 164-165 H 2
'Uqayr, Al- 134-135 FG 5
'Uqlah 166-167 AB 7
'Uqlat as-Sabīyah 166-167 D 7
'Uqlat Barābir 166-167 E 4
'Uqlat Ibn Ṣuqayh 136-137 M 8
'Uqlat Ṣudrā' 166-167 E 3
Uqṣur, Al- 164-165 L 3
Uquia 104-105 D 8

Ur 134-135 F 4
Ur, Wādī — 173 B 6-7
Urabá, Golfo de — 92-93 D 3
Urabá, Isla — 64-65 bc 3
Uracas = Farallon de Pajaros 206-207 S 7
Uracoa 94-95 K 3
Uraī = Orai 138-139 G 5
Urakawa 144-145 c 2
Ural 132-133 J 8
Ural, MT 66-67 F 1
Ural, Pol'arnyj — 132-133 LM 4
Ural, Pripol'arnyj — 132-133 KL 4-5
Ural, Severnyj — 132-133 K 5-6
Uralla 160 K 3
Uralmed'stroj = Krasnoural'sk 132-133 L 6
Urals 132-133 K 5-7
Ural'sk 132-133 J 7
Uran 140 A 1
Urana 160 GH 5
Urandangi 158-159 G 4
Urandi 92-93 L 7
Urania, LA 78-79 C 5
Uranium City 56-57 P 6
Uraricaá, Rio — 94-95 K 6
Uraricoera 98-99 H 3
Uraricoera, Rio — 92-93 G 4
Uraricuera 94-95 L 6
Ura-T'ube 134-135 K 3
Uravāguṇḍa = Uravakonda 140 C 3
Uravakonda 140 C 3
Uravan, CO 74-75 J 3
Urawa 142-143 QR 4
Urayasu 155 III c 2
'Uray'irah 134-135 F 5
'Urayyiḍah, Bi'r — 173 BC 3
Urazovo 126-127 J 1
Urbana, IL 70-71 FG 5
Urbana, OH 72-73 E 4
Urbana, La — 92-93 F 3
Urbano Santos 100-101 C 2
Urbe, Aeroporto dell' 113 II b 1
Urbino 122-123 E 4
Urbión, Picos de — 120-121 F 8
Urcos 92-93 E 7
Urda [SU] 126-127 N 2
Urdampilleta 106-107 G 6
Urdinarrain 106-107 H 4
Urdoma 124-125 R 3
Urdorf 128 IV a 1
Urdžar 132-133 P 8
Uren' 124-125 P 5
Ureparapara 158-159 N 2
Ures 64-65 DE 6
'Urf, Jabal al- 173 C 4
Urfa 134-135 D 3
Urfa yaylâsı 136-137 H 4
'Urf Umm Rashīd 173 D 5
Urga 132-133 K 9
Urga = Ulaanbaatar 142-143 K 2
Urgenč 132-133 L 9
Ürgüp 136-137 F 3
Uribante, Río — 94-95 F 4
Uribe 92-93 E 4
Uribe, La — 91 III c 1
Uribelarrea 106-107 H 5
Uribia 92-93 E 2
Uriburu 106-107 EF 6
Urica 94-95 JK 3
Urickij 124-125 K 7
Urickoje 132-133 M 7
Urikura 155 III c 3
Urilia Bay 58-59 a 2
Urim = Ur 134-135 F 4
Urimán 94-95 K 5
Uriondo 104-105 D 7
Urique, Río — 86-87 G 4
Urīsā = Orissa 134-135 N 7-O 6
Urisino 160 F 2
Uritorco, Cerro — 106-107 E 3
Urituyacu, Río — 96-97 D 4
Uruaná, Rio — 98-99 N 6
Urla 134-135 B 3
Urlāl 166-167 J 2
Urmannyj 132-133 M 5
Urmary 124-125 Q 6
Urmia = Daryācheh Orūmīyeh 134-135 F 3
Urmia = Reḍā'iyeh 134-135 EF 3
Urmia, Daryācheh — = Daryācheh Orūmīyeh 134-135 F 3
Uromi 168-169 G 4
Urrao 94-95 C 4
Urre Lauquen, Laguna — 106-107 E 7
Ursatjevskaja = Chavast 134-135 K 2
Ursine, NV 74-75 F 3-4
Urtigueira 102-103 G 6
Urt Mörön = Chadzaar 142-143 G 4
Uruaçu 92-93 K 7
Uruana 92-93 JK 8
Uruapan del Progreso 64-65 F 8
Uruará, Rio — 98-99 M 6
Urubamba 92-93 E 7
Urubamba, Río — 92-93 E 7
Urubaxi, Rio — 98-99 F 5
Urubicha 104-105 E 4
Urubici 102-103 H 7-8
Urubu, Cachoeira do — 98-99 OP 11
Urubu, Rio — 98-99 J 6
Urubu, Travessão do — 98-99 M 8
Uruburetama 100-101 E 2
Uruburetama, Serra de — 100-101 DE 2
Uruçanga 102-103 H 8
Urucará 92-93 H 5
Urucu, Rio — 98-99 FG 7
Uruçuca 100-101 E 8
Uruçuí 92-93 L 6
Uruçuí, Serra do — 92-93 K 7-L 6
Urucuia 102-103 K 2
Urucuia, Rio — 102-103 K 2
Uruçuí Preto, Rio — 100-101 B 5
Uruçuí Vermelho, Rio — 100-101 B 5
Urucurituba 92-93 H 5
Uruguai, Rio — 111 F 3
Uruguaiana 111 E 3
Uruguay 111 EF 4
Uruguay, Río — [RA ◁ Río de la Plata] 111 E 3
Uruguay, Río — [RA ◁ Río Paraná] 102-103 E 6
Uruguay, Salto Grande del — 111 F 3
Urumacó 94-95 F 2
Urūm aṣ-Ṣughrah 136-137 G 4
Urumbi 92-93 F 4
Ürümchi 142-143 F 3
Urumchi = Ürümchi 142-143 F 3
Urundi = Burundi 172 EF 2
Urunga 160 L 3
Ur'ung-Chaja 132-133 VW 3
Urun Islāmpur 140 B 2
Uruoca 100-101 D 2
Urup 126-127 K 4
Urup, ostrov — 132-133 cd 8
Urupa, Rio — 98-99 G 10
Urupês 102-103 H 4
Ur'upinsk 126-127 L 1
Uruppu = ostrov Urup 132-133 cd 8
'Urūq al-Mu'tariḍah, Al- 134-135 G 6-7
Uruquê 100-101 D 4
Uruša 132-133 X 7
Urus-Martan 126-127 M 5
Urussu 124-125 T 6
Urutágua 100-101 A 8
Urutaí 102-103 HJ 2
Uruyén 92-93 G 3
Urville, Île d' 53 C 31
Urville, Mer d' 53 C 14-15
Urville, Tanjung d' 148-149 L 7
Urziceni 122-123 M 3
Uržum 132-133 HJ 6

Usa 132-133 K 4
Ušači 124-125 G 6
Usagara 172 G 3
Uşak 134-135 B 3
Usakos 172 BC 6
Ušakova, ostrov — 132-133 OP 1
Usambara Mountains 171 D 4
Usango 171 C 4
Usaquén 91 III c 2
Ušba, gora — 126-127 L 5
Usborne, Mount — 111 E 8
Uscana, Serra — 104-105 B 6
Usedom 118 F 1-G 2
Usengo 171 B 4
Usera, Madrid- 113 III a 2
Usetsu = Noto 144-145 L 4
Usevia 171 B 4
'Usfān 134-135 D 6
Ushagat Island 58-59 L 7
Ushakova Island = ostrov Ušakova 132-133 OP 2
Ushakov Island = ostrov Ušakova 132-133 OP 1
Ushero 171 BC 4
Usherville 61 G 4
Ushibuka 144-145 GH 6
Ushibukuro 155 III c 3
Ushirombo 171 BC 3
Ushuaia 111 C 8
Usk 60 C 2
Usk, WA 66-67 E 1
Uskir, Ḥāssī — 166-167 F 4
Üsküdar, İstanbul- 134-135 BC 2
Uskumruköy 154 I b 1
Üsküp = Skopje 122-123 J 4-5
Usman' 124-125 MN 7
Usme 94-95 DE 5
Usno 106-107 D 3
Usoke 171 C 4
Usolje [SU, Perm'skaja Oblast'] 124-125 V 4
Usolje = Usolje-Sibirskoje 132-133 T 7
Usolje-Sibirskoje 132-133 T 7
Usolje-Solikamskoje = Berezniki 132-133 JK 6
Usolye Sibirskoye = Usolje-Sibirskoje 132-133 T 7
Usoro 168-169 G 4
Usouil 96-97 C 5
Uspallata 106-107 C 4
Uspallata, Sierra de — 106-107 C 4
Uspara, Cerro — 106-107 E 4
Uspenka 126-127 J 2
Ussagara = Usagara 172 G 3
Üssaltīyah, Al- 166-167 LM 2
Ussuri = Wusuli Jiang 142-143 P 2
Ussurijsk 132-133 Z 9
Ussurijskij zaliv 144-145 HJ 1
Usta 124-125 PQ 5
Ust'-Abakanskoje = Abakan 132-133 R 7
Ust'-Alekseyevo 124-125 Q 3
Ust'-Barguzin 132-133 UV 7
Ust'-Bol'šereck 132-133 de 7
Ust'-Buzulukskaja 126-127 L 1
Ust'-Čaun 132-133 h 4
Ust'-Cil'ma 132-133 J 4
Ust'-Čižapka 132-133 OP 6
Ust'-Čorna 126-127 AB 2
Ust'-Č'ornaja 124-125 ST 3
Ust'-Dolgaja 124-125 V 4
Ust'-Dolyssy 124-125 G 5
Ust'-Doneckij 126-127 K 3
Ust'-Džegutinskaja 126-127 KL 4
Ustica 122-123 E 6
Ust'-Ilimsk 132-133 T 6
Ustilug 126-127 B 1
Ust'-Ilyč 124-125 V 2
Ústí nad Labem 118 FG 3
Ustinovka 126-127 F 3
Ust'-Išim 132-133 N 6
Ustja 124-125 P 3
Ustje [SU, Vologodskaja Oblast'] 124-125 M 4
Ustje-Agapy = Agapa 132-133 Q 3
Ust'-Juribej 132-133 MN 4
Ustka 118 H 1
Ust'-Kamčatsk 132-133 f 6
Ust Kamchatsk = Ust'-Kamčatsk 132-133 f 6
Ust'-Kamenogorsk 132-133 OP 7-8
Ust'-Kan 132-133 PQ 7
Ust'-Karabula 132-133 S 6
Ust'-Karsk 132-133 W 7
Ust'-Kulom 132-133 JK 5
Ust'-Kut 132-133 U 6
Ust'-Labinsk 126-127 JK 4
Ust'-Luga 124-125 FG 4
Ust'-Maja 132-133 Z 5
Ust'-Nem 124-125 U 3
Ust'-Nera 132-133 b 5
Uštobe 132-133 O 8
Ust'-Orda = Ust'-Ordynskij 132-133 TU 7
Ust'-Ordynskij 132-133 TU 7
Ust-Ordynsky-Buryat Autonomous Area = 11 ◁ 132-133 T 7
Ust'-Oz'ornoje 132-133 Q 6
Ust'-Pinaga 124-125 NO 1
Ust'-Pinega 132-133 G 5
Ust'-Port 132-133 PQ 4
Ust'-Ščugor 132-133 K 5
Ust'-Šonoša 124-125 N 3
Ust Sysolsk = Syktyvkar 132-133 J 5
Ust'-Tatta 132-133 Za 5
Ust'-Tym 132-133 OP 6
Ust'-Ulagan 132-133 Q 7
Ust'-Unja 124-125 V 3
Ust'-Ura 124-125 P 2
Ust'urt, plato — 132-133 K 9
Ust'-Usa 132-133 K 4
Ust'užna 124-125 L 4
Ust'-Vačerga 124-125 QR 2
Ust'-Vajen'ga 124-125 O 2
Ust'-Vym' 124-125 S 2
Usu-dake 144-145 b 2
Usuki 144-145 HJ 6
Usuktuk River 58-59 J 1
Usule 171 C 4
Usulután 88-89 B 8
Usumacinta, Río — 64-65 H 8
Usumbura = Bujumbura 172 EF 2
Usun Apau Plateau 152-153 L 4
Usure 171 C 4
Usutu = Great Usutu 174-175 J 4
Usuyŏng 144-145 EF 5
Usu zan 144-145 b 2
Usv'aty 124-125 H 6

Utah 64-65 DE 4
Utah Lake 64-65 D 3
Utasinai 144-145 c 2
U Tay = Mu'o'ng Ou Tay 150-151 C 1
Uṭāyah, Al- 166-167 J 2
Utcubamba, Río — 96-97 B 4
Ute, IA 70-71 C 4
Ute Creek 76-77 C 5
Utegi 171 C 3
Ute Mountain Indian Reservation 74-75 J 4
Utena 124-125 E 6
Utengule 171 C 5
Ute Peak 74-75 J 4
Utete 172 G 3
Utevka 124-125 S 7
Uthai Thani 150-151 C 5
'Uthmānīyah, Al- 173 BC 4
U Thong 148-149 C 4
Uthumphon Phisai 150-151 DE 5
Utiariti 92-93 H 7
Utica 166-167 M 1
Utica, KS 68-69 F 6
Utica, MS 78-79 D 4
Utica, NY 64-65 LM 3
Utica, OH 72-73 E 4
Utiel 120-121 G 9
Utik Lake 61 KL 3
Utikuma Lake 60 K 2
Utinga 100-101 D 7
Utinga, Santo André- 110 II b 2
Utique = Utica 166-167 M 1
Utiura-wan 142-143 R 3
Utnūr 138-139 G 8
Utopia, AK 58-59 L 3-4
Utopia, TX 76-77 E 8
Utopia, New York-, NY 82 III d 2
Utorgoš 124-125 H 4
Utoy Creek 85 II b 2
Utracán 106-107 E 6
Utracán, Valle de — 106-107 E 6
Utraula 138-139 J 4
Utrecht [NL] 120-121 K 2
Utrecht [ZA] 174-175 J 4
Utrera 120-121 E 10
Utrillas 120-121 G 8
Utsjoki 116-117 M 3
Utsunomiya 142-143 QR 4
Utta 126-127 M 3
Uttamapālaiyam 140 C 6
Uttamapāḷayam = Uttamapālaiyam 140 C 6
Uttaradit 148-149 D 3
Uttar Andamān = North Andaman 134-135 P 8
Uttarī Koīl = Koel 138-139 J 5
Uttarkāshī 138-139 G 2
Uttar Lakhimpur = North Lakhimpur 141 CD 2
Uttarpāra-Kotrung 154 II ab 1
Uttar Pradesh 134-135 MN 5
Uttar Shālmārā = North Salmara 141 B 2
Uṭṭi = Ootacamund 140 C 5
Uttnoor = Utnūr 138-139 G 8
Utukok River 58-59 GH 2
Utunomiya = Utsunomiya 142-143 QR 4
Utupua 148-149 I 7
Uturė Mėda Palāna ◁ 140 E 6
Uturė Palāna ◁ 140 E 6
Utva 124-125 T 8

Uu = Wuhu 142-143 M 5
Uudenmaan lääni 116-117 K-M 7
Uusikaarlepyy = Nykarleby 116-117 K 6
Uusikaupunki 116-117 J 7
Uusimaa 116-117 KL 7

Ūva [CL] 140 E 7
Uva [SU] 124-125 T 5
Uvá, Laguna — 94-95 F 6
Uva, Río — 94-95 G 6
Uvaia 102-103 G 6
Uvalde, TX 64-65 G 6
Ūva Palāna ◁ 140 E 7
Uvarovo 124-125 NO 8
Uvat 132-133 M 6
Uvéa 148-149 b 1
Uvea = Île Ouvéa 158-159 N 4
Uvinza 172 F 2-3
Uvira 172 E 2
Uvod' 124-125 N 5
Uvs 142-143 G 2
Uvs nuur 142-143 G 1

Uwajima 142-143 P 5
'Uwayjā', Al- 134-135 G 6
Uwayl 164-165 K 7
'Uwaynāt, Jabal al- 164-165 K 4
'Uwaynidhīyah, Jazīrat al- 173 DE 4
'Uwayqīlah, Ma'ātin — 136-137 C 7
'Uwayriḍ, Ḥarrat al- 134-135 D 5
Uwaysit 136-137 GH 7
Uwazima = Uwajima 142-143 P 5
Uwimbi 172 FG 3
Uwinsa = Uvinza 172 F 2-3

Uxbridge 72-73 G 2
Uxbridge, London- 129 II a 1
Uxin Ju 146-147 B 2
Uxin Qi 146-147 B 2
Uxmal 64-65 J 7

Uyak Bay 58-59 KL 8
Uyere 168-169 G 4
Uyowa 171 BC 4
Uyu Myit 141 D 3
Uyuni 92-93 F 9
Uyuni, Salar de — 92-93 F 9

Už 126-127 D 1
Uza 124-125 P 7
'Uzaym, Shaṭṭ al- 136-137 L 5
'Uzayr, Al- 136-137 M 7
Uzbek Soviet Socialist Republic 134-135 J 2-K 3
Uzboj 134-135 H 2-3
Uzcudun 108-109 F 5
Uzda 124-125 F 7
Uzen', Bol'šoj — 126-127 O 2
Uzen', Malyj — 126-127 O 2
Uzès-le-Duc = Wādī-al-Abṭāl 166-167 G 2
Uzgen 134-135 L 2
Užgorod 126-127 A 2
Uzinki = Ouzinkie, AK 58-59 LM 8
Uzkoje, Moskva- 113 V b 3
Uzlovaja 124-125 LM 7
Uzlovoje 126-127 A 2
Uzundere 154 I b 1
Uzunköprü 136-137 B 2
Uzun yaylâ 136-137 G 3
Uzunye burnu 154 I b 1
Užur 132-133 QR 6

V

Vääkiö 116-117 N 5
Vaala 116-117 M 5
Vaalbrivier 174-175 EF 5
Vaaldam 172 E 7
Vaal-Harts-Weir 174-175 F 5
Vaal River = Vaalrivier 172 E 7
Vaalrivier 172 E 7
Vaalwater 172 E 6
Vääna 124-125 E 4
Vaasa 116-117 J 6
Vác 118 J 5
Vača [SU] 124-125 O 6
Vacacai 106-107 K 3
Vacacaí, Rio — 106-107 L 2-3
Vaca Cuá 106-107 HJ 2
Vaca Huañuna 106-107 F 1
Vacamonte, Punta — 64-65 b 3
Vacaria 111 F 3
Vacaria, Campos da — 106-107 M 2
Vacaria, Rio — [BR, Mato Grosso do Sul] 102-103 E 4
Vacaria, Rio — [BR, Minas Gerais] 102-103 L 2
Vacas, Sierra de las — 108-109 C 6-7
Vacaville, CA 74-75 BC 3
Vach [SU] 132-133 O 5
Vachš 134-135 K 3
Vachtan 124-125 Q 5
Vad 124-125 O 7
Vāda [IND] 138-139 D 8
Vaḍakara = Badagara 140 B 5
Vadakkancheri 140 C 5
Vāḍēn = Vāda 138-139 D 8
Vader, WA 66-67 B 2
Vadheim 116-117 A 7
Vaḍhvān = Wadhwān 134-135 L 6
Vadnagar 138-139 D 6

Vadōdarā 134-135 L 6
Vadsø 116-117 NO 2
Vadstena 116-117 F 8
Vaduz 118 D 5
Vaer = Weir 138-139 F 4
Værøy 116-117 E 4
Vafs 136-137 N 5
Vaga 124-125 O 2
Vagaj 132-133 M 6
Vågåmo 116-117 C 7
Vagaršapat = Ečmiadzin 126-127 M 6
Vaggeryd 116-117 EF 9
Vagino 124-125 S 4
Vågsfjord 116-117 G 3
Văh 118 H 4
Vaiden, MS 78-79 E 4
Vaigach Island = ostrov Vajgač 132-133 KL 3
Vaigai 140 D 6
Vaigat 56-57 a 3
Vaijāpur 138-139 E 8
Vaikam 140 C 6
Väinäjoki = Daugava 124-125 E 5
Vaippār 140 CD 6
Vairāgaḍ = Wairāgarh 138-139 H 7
Vaires-sur-Marne 129 I d 2
Vaithīshvarankollu 140 DE 5
Vaitupu Iu 208 HJ 3
Vajdaguba 116-117 OP 3
Vajen'ga 124-125 OP 2
Vajgač, ostrov — 132-133 KL 3
Vakaga 164-165 J 7
Vākārē 140 E 6
Vakfıkebir = Kemaliye 136-137 H 2
Valā = Vallabhipur 138-139 CD 7
Valaam, ostrov — 124-125 H 3
Vālachchenei 140 E 7
Valachia 122-123 K-M 3
Valadim = Mavago 172 G 4
Valaichchenai = Vālachchenai 140 E 7
Valais 118 C 5
Välåjåpēṭ = Wālājāpet 140 D 4
Valamaz 124-125 T 5
Val-Barrette 72-73 J 1
Valcanuta, Roma- 113 II ab 2
Valcheta 111 C 6
Valcheta, Arroyo — 108-109 F 3
Valdagno 122-123 D 3
Valdaj 124-125 J 5
Valdajskaja vozvyšennost' 124-125 H-K 5
Val d'Aosta 122-123 B 3
Valdebeba, Madrid- 113 III b 2
Valdebebas, Arroyo de — 113 III b 1
Valdemārpils 124-125 D 5
Valdemarsvik 116-117 G 8
Valdepeñas 120-121 F 9
Valderaduey 120-121 E 7-8
Valders, WI 70-71 FG 3
Valdés, Península — 111 D 6
Valdesa, La — 64-65 b 3
Valdez 96-97 B 1
Valdez, AK 56-57 G 5
Valdia = Weldya 164-165 M 6
Valdivia [CO] 94-95 D 4
Valdivia [RCH] 111 B 5
Valdivia, Bahía de — 108-109 C 2
Val-d'Or 56-57 V 8
Valdosta, GA 64-65 K 5
Valdres 116-117 C 7
Vale 126-127 L 6
Vale, OR 66-67 E 3-4
Vale, SD 68-69 E 3
Valea-lui-Mihai 122-123 K 2
Vålebru 116-117 D 7
Valegoculovo = Dolinskoje 126-127 DE 3
Valemont 60 H 3
Valença [BR, Bahia] 92-93 M 7
Valença [BR, Rio de Janeiro] 102-103 KL 5
Valença [P] 120-121 C 7-8
Valença = Valencia [YV] 92-93 F 2
Valença do Piauí 92-93 L 6
Valence 120-121 K 6
Valencia [E, landscape] 120-121 G 8-9
Valencia [E, place] 120-121 GH 9
Valencia [YV] 92-93 F 2
Valencia, Golfo de — 120-121 H 9
Valencia, Lago de — 92-93 F 2
Valencia de Alcántara 120-121 D 9
Valencia de Don Juan 120-121 E 7
Valenciennes 120-121 J 3
Valente 100-101 E 6
Valentim, Serra do — 92-93 L 6
Valentin 132-133 Za 9
Valentín Alsina, Avellaneda- 110 III b 1
Valentine, MT 68-69 B 2
Valentine, NE 68-69 F 4
Valentine, TX 76-77 B 7
Valenton 129 I c 2
Valenza 122-123 C 3
Valenzuela, Sierra — 104-105 A 8
Valera 92-93 E 3
Valera, TX 76-77 E 7
Valérien, Mont — 129 I b 2
Vale Verde 100-101 E 9
Valga 124-125 F 5
Valgāñv = Walgaon 138-139 F 7
Valhalla Mountains 66-67 DE 1
Vālia 138-139 D 7
Valiente, Península — 88-89 F 10
Valier, MT 66-67 G 1
Valikāndapuram 140 D 5
Valikāntapuram = Valikāndapuram 140 D 5
Valjyā = Vālia 138-139 D 7
Valjevo 122-123 H 3
Valka 124-125 EF 5
Valkeakoski 116-117 L 7
Valki 126-127 G 2
Vālkoṇḍa = Bālkonda 140 D 1
Vallabhipur 138-139 CD 7
Valladolid [E] 120-121 E 8
Valladolid [EC] 96-97 B 4
Valladolid [MEX] 64-65 J 7
Valle, AZ 74-75 G 5
Valle, Caracas-El — 91 II b 2
Valle, El — 94-95 C 4
Valle, Río del — 104-105 D 11
Vallecas, Canteras de — 113 III b 2
Vallecas, Cumbres de — 113 III b 2
Valle Chapalcó 106-107 E 6
Vallecillo 76-77 DE 9
Vallecito 106-107 D 3
Vallecito Mountains 74-75 E 6
Vallecito Reservoir 68-69 C 7
Valle Daza 106-107 E 6
Valle de Bandenas 86-87 H 7
Valle de Hucal 106-107 E 6
Valle de la Pascua 92-93 FG 3
Valle de las Ruinas 108-109 EF 4
Valle del Cauca 94-95 C 6
Valle del Cura, Río del — 106-107 C 2
Valle de Lermá 104-105 D 9
Valle del Río Bermejo 106-107 CD 3
Valle del Río Deseado 108-109 E 6
Valle del Rosario 86-87 GH 4
Valle del Salado 64-65 F 7
Valle de Maracó Grande 106-107 EF 6
Valle de Quehué 106-107 E 6
Valle de Santa Catarina 74-75 EF 7
Valle de Utracán 106-107 E 6
Valle de Zaragoza 76-77 B 9
Valledupar 92-93 E 2
Vallée du Goulbi 168-169 G 2
Vallée du Saloum 168-169 B 2
Vallée-Jonction 63 A 4
Valle Fértil 106-107 D 3
Valle Fértil, Sierra de — 106-107 CD 3
Valle General Racedo 108-109 E 4
Valle Grande [BOL] 92-93 G 8
Valle Grande [RA] 104-105 D 8
Valle Hermoso [MEX] 64-65 G 6
Valle Hermoso [RA] 108-109 E 5-6
Vallejo, CA 64-65 B 4
Valle Leone 108-109 G 2
Valle Longitudinal 106-107 A 6-B 5
Valle Mari Luan 106-107 E 7
Vallenar 111 B 3
Vallenar, Islas — 108-109 B 5
Valle Nerecó 106-107 E 6
Valles Calchaquíes 104-105 CD 9
Valle Superior 108-109 FG 4
Valletta 122-123 F 8
Vallevicioso, Río — 96-97 BC 2
Valley, NE 68-69 H 5
Valley, WY 66-67 J 3
Valley City, ND 68-69 GH 2
Valley Falls, KS 70-71 C 6
Valley Falls, OR 66-67 C 4
Valleyfield 56-57 VW 8
Valley Forge Historical State Park 84 III a 1
Valley Mills, TX 76-77 F 7
Valley of 10,000 Smokes 58-59 K 7
Valley of Willows, AK 58-59 JK 2
Valley Pass 66-67 FG 5
Valley River 61 H 5
Valley Stream, NY 82 III de 3
Valleyview 60 J 2
Valliant, OK 76-77 G 5-6
Vallican 60 J 5
Valli di Comàcchio 122-123 E 3
Vallimanca 106-107 G 6
Vallimanca, Arroyo — 106-107 G 5-6
Valls 120-121 H 8
Vallur = Vuyyūru 140 E 2
Vallūru = Vuyyūru 140 E 2
Val Marie 68-69 C 1
Valmiera 124-125 E 5
Valmont, NM 76-77 AB 6
Valmy, NV 66-67 E 5
Valnera 120-121 F 7
Välod 138-139 D 7
Valok 126-127 G 4
Valparai 140 C 5
Valparaiso, IN 70-71 G 5
Valparaiso, NE 68-69 H 5
Valparaíso [BR, Acre] 96-97 E 5-6
Valparaíso [BR, São Paulo] 102-103 G 4
Valparaíso [MEX] 86-87 HJ 6
Valparaíso [RCH] 111 B 4
Valpoy 140 AB 3
Vals, Tanjung — 148-149 L 8
Valsbaai [ZA, Kaapland] 172 C 8
Valsbaai [ZA, Natal] 174-175 K 4
Valsch, Cape — = Tanjung Vals 148-149 L 8
Valsetz, OR 66-67 B 3
Valsrivier 174-175 G 4
Vāltēru = Waltair 140 F 2
Valujki 126-127 J 1
Valverde [DOM] 88-89 L 5
Valverde [E] 164-165 A 3
Valverde del Camino 120-121 D 10
Vam Co Đông 150-151 EF 7
Vamizi 171 E 5
Vammala 116-117 K 7
Vamos Ver 98-99 OP 8
Vamsadhārā 140 G 1
Van 134-135 E 3
Van Alstyne, TX 76-77 F 6
Vananda, MT 68-69 C 2
Van Antwerp Playfield 84 II ab 2
Vanapartti = Wanparti 140 D 2
Van Asch van Wijck Gebergte 98-99 K 3-L 2
Vanavara 132-133 T 5
Van Buren, AR 76-77 G 5
Van Buren, ME 72-73 MN 1
Van Buren, MO 78-79 D 2
Văn Canh 150-151 G 6
Vanceboro, ME 72-73 N 2
Vanceboro, NC 80-81 H 3
Vanceburg, KY 72-73 E 5
Van Cortlandt Park 82 III c 1
Vancouver 56-57 M 8
Vancouver, WA 64-65 B 2
Vancouver, Mount — 58-59 RS 6
Vancouver Island 56-57 L 8
Vandalia, IL 70-71 F 6
Vandalia, MO 70-71 E 6
Vandavāshi = Wandiwāsh 140 D 4
Vandemere, NC 80-81 H 3
Vandenberg Air Force Base 74-75 C 5
Vanderbijlpark 174-175 G 4
Vanderbilt, TX 76-77 F 8
Vanderhoof 60 F 2
Vanderlei 100-101 C 7
Vanderlin Island 158-159 G 3
Van Diemen, Cape — 158-159 EF 2
Van Diemen Gulf 158-159 F 2
Van Diemensland = Tasmania 158-159 HJ 8
Van Diemen Strait = Ōsumi-kaikyō 142-143 P 5
Vändra 124-125 E 4
Vāndrā = Bāndra 134-135 L 7
Vandry 62 P 3
Vandyksdrif 174-175 H 4
Vandyš 124-125 N 3
Vänern 116-117 E 8
Vänersborg 116-117 E 8
Vang, Ban — 150-151 C 3
Vanga = Shimoni 172 GH 2
Vangaindrano 172 J 6
Van Gia = Van Ninh 150-151 G 6
Van gölu 134-135 E 3
Vangunu 148-149 j 6
Vang Vieng 150-151 D 3
Van Horn, TX 76-77 B 7
Van Houten, NM 76-77 B 4
Vanikoro Islands 148-149 I 7
Vaniköy, İstanbul- 154 I b 2
Vanimo 148-149 M 7
Vānīvilāsa Sāgara 140 C 4
Vāniyambādi 140 D 4
Vāṅkānēr = Wānkāner 138-139 C 6
Vankarem 132-133 k 4
van Keulenfjord 116-117 jk 6
Vankleek Hill 72-73 J 2
Văn Ly 150-151 F 2
Van Mai 150-151 E 2
van Mijenfjord 116-117 jk 6
Vännäs 116-117 HJ 6
Vannes 120-121 F 5
Van Ninh 150-151 G 6
Van Norman, MT 68-69 C 2
Vannøy 116-117 HJ 2
Van Reenen 174-175 H 5
Van Reenenspas 174-175 H 5
Vanrhynsdorp 172 CD 8
Vanrook 158-159 H 3
Vanryn Dam 170 V cd 1
Vansbro 116-117 EF 7
Vansittart Bay 158-159 E 2
Vansittart Island 56-57 U 4
Van Tassell, WY 68-69 D 4
Vanthli 138-139 C 7
Vanua Lava 158-159 N 2
Vanua Levu 148-149 b 2
Vanuatu 158-159 N 2-O 3
Vanves-Issy-les-Moulineaux 129 I c 2
Van Wert, OH 70-71 H 5
Vanwyksdorp 174-175 D 7
Vanwyksvlei 172 D 8
Van Yên 150-151 E 2
Vanzevat 132-133 M 5
Vanžil'kynak 132-133 P 5
Vapn'arka 126-127 D 2
Varadā 140 B 3
Vārāhi 138-139 C 6
Varakļāni 124-125 F 5
Varalé 168-169 E 3
Vārānasi 134-135 N 5
Varangal = Warangal 134-135 MN 7
Varangerbotn 116-117 N 2
Varangerfjord 116-117 NO 2-3
Varanger halvøya 116-117 NO 2
Varas, Sierra de — 104-105 B 9
Vārāsiunī = Wārāseoni 138-139 H 7
Varaždin 122-123 FG 2
Varazze 122-123 C 3
Varberg 116-117 DE 9
Vardannapet 140 D 2
Vardar 122-123 K 5
Varde 116-117 C 10
Vardenis 126-127 M 6
Vardhā = Wardha [IND, place] 134-135 M 6
Vardhā = Wardha [IND, river] 134-135 M 6
Vardø 116-117 O 2
Varegovo 124-125 M 5
Varela 106-107 D 5
Varella, Cap — = Mui Diêu 148-149 EF 4
Varella, Cape — = Mui Diêu 148-149 EF 4
Varēna 124-125 E 6
Vareš 122-123 H 3
Varese 122-123 C 3
Varfolomejevka 132-133 Z 9
Vargas Guerra 96-97 C 3
Vargas Island 60 DE 5
Vargem 102-103 J 5
Vargem, Riacho da — 100-101 E 5
Vargem Alta 102-103 M 4
Vargem Grande [BR, Amazonas] 98-99 DE 6
Vargem Grande [BR, Maranhão] 100-101 BC 2
Vargem Grande [BR, Piauí] 100-101 CD 5
Vargem Grande do Sul 102-103 J 4
Varginha 92-93 K 9
Varillas 111 B 2
Varillas, Las — 111 D 4
Varita, Pampa de la — 106-107 D 5
Varjegan 132-133 O 5
Varkaus 116-117 MN 6
Varlā = Yerla 140 B 2
Värmland 116-117 E 8
Värmlandsnäs 116-117 E 8
Varna [BG] 122-123 MN 4
Varna [IND] 140 A 2
Varnado, LA 78-79 E 5
Värnamo 116-117 F 9
Varnek 132-133 KL 4
Varney, NM 76-77 B 5
Varniai 124-125 D 6
Varnville, SC 80-81 F 4
Varoḍā = Warora 138-139 G 7
Varshalai 140 D 6
Varsinais Suomi 116-117 JK 7
Varšipel'da 124-125 L 2
Vartašen 126-127 N 6
Varto 136-137 J 3
Varuá Ipana, Lago — 94-95 EF 7
Vārud = Warud 138-139 FG 7
Varvarco 106-107 B 6
Varvarco Campos, Lago — 106-107 B 6
Varvarovka 126-127 E 3
Várzea, Rio da — [BR, Paraná] 102-103 H 6-7
Várzea, Rio da — [BR, Rio Grande do Sul] 106-107 L 1
Várzea Alegre [BR, Ceará] 100-101 E 4
Várzea Alegre [BR, Goiás] 98-99 O 9
Várzea da Palma 102-103 K 2
Várzea do Caldas 100-101 D 7
Várzea Grande 102-103 D 1
Varzeão 102-103 H 6
Várzeas 100-101 B 7
Vasa = Vaasa 116-117 J 6
Vasa Barris, Rio — 100-101 E 6
Vasai = Bassein 138-139 D 8
Vaşcău 122-123 K 2
Vasconcelos 106-107 M 3
Vashon Island 66-67 B 2
Vasilevići 124-125 G 7
Vasilevo 124-125 H 5
Vasilevo = Čkalovsk 124-125 O 5
Vasiljevka 126-127 G 3
Vasiljevo 124-125 R 5-6
Vasil'kov 126-127 E 1
Vasil'kovka 126-127 G 2
Vasil'sursk 124-125 Q 5
Vasknarva 124-125 F 4
Vaskojoki 116-117 LM 3
Vaslui 122-123 MN 2
Vasmat = Basmat 138-139 F 8
Vásquez 106-107 GH 7
Vassar 72-73 E 3
Vassar, MI 72-73 E 3
Vassouras 102-103 L 5
Vassouras, Serra da — 100-101 E 4-5
Vastan = Gevaş 136-137 K 3
Västerås 116-117 FG 8
Västerbotten [S, administrative unit] 116-117 F-J 5
Västerbotten [S, landscape] 116-117 H 6-J 5
Västerdalälven 116-117 EF 7
Västergötland 116-117 E 9-F 8
Västernorrland 116-117 GH 6
Västervik 116-117 G 9
Västmanland 116-117 FG 8
Vasto 122-123 F 4
Vas'ugan 132-133 O 6
Vas'uganje 132-133 N 5-O 6
Vas'utinskaja 124-125 PQ 2-3
Vasvár 118 H 5
Vasyugane Swamp = Vas'uganje 132-133 N 5-O 6
Vatè, Île — = Efate 158-159 N 3
Vatican City 122-123 DE 5
V'atka 132-133 H 6
V'atka = Kirov 132-133 HJ 6
Vatnajökull 116-117 e 2
Vatoa 208 J 4
Vatomandry 172 JK 5
Vatra Dornei 122-123 L 2
V'atskije Pol'any 132-133 HJ 6
V'atskij uval 124-125 R 5-S 4
Vättern 116-117 F 8
Vaucluse, Sydney- 161 I b 2
Vaucresson 129 I b 2
Vaughn, MT 66-67 H 2
Vaughn, NM 76-77 B 5
Vaugirard, Paris- 129 I c 2
Vauhallan 129 I b 3
Vaujours 129 I d 2
Vaupés 94-95 EF 7
Vaupés, Río — 92-93 E 4
Vauxhall 61 BC 5
Vaux-sur-Seine 129 I a 1
Våv 138-139 C 5
Vava'u Group 148-149 c 2
Vavoz 124-125 S 5
Vavuniya = Vavuniyāwa 140 E 6
Vavuniyāwa 140 E 6
Växjö 116-117 F 9
Vayalapāḍu = Vāyalpād 140 D 4
Vāyalpād 140 D 4
Vayamba Palāna ◁ 140 E 7
Vayanāṭ = Wynnad 140 C 5
Vayittiri 140 BC 5
Vazante 102-103 J 2
V'azemskij 132-133 Za 8
V'az'ma 124-125 JK 6
V'azniki 124-125 NO 5
V. Carranza, Presa — 86-87 KL 4
Veadeiros, Chapada dos — 92-93 K 7-8
Veblen, SD 68-69 H 3
Vecpiebalga 124-125 EF 5
Vedārranniyam 140 DE 5
Vēdavatī = Hagari 140 C 3
Veddel, Hamburg- 130 I b 1
Vedea 122-123 L 3
Vedia 111 D 4
Vedlozero 124-125 J 3
Veedersburg, IN 70-71 G 5
Veeravalli = Vīravaḷḷi 140 F 2
Veertien Strome 174-175 F 4-5
Vega 116-117 D 5
Vega, TX 76-77 C 5
Vega, Caracas-La — 91 II b 2
Vega, La — [DOM] 64-65 MN 8
Vega Bay 58-59 r 7
Vega de Granada 120-121 EF 10
Vega de Itata 106-107 A 6
Vega Point 58-59 r 7
Vegas, Las — 94-95 G 3
Veglio = Krk 122-123 J 5
Vegreville 56-57 O 7
Veguita, La — 94-95 FG 3
Veimandu Channel 176 a 2
Veinticinco de Mayo [RA, Buenos Aires] 106-107 GH 5
Veinticinco de Mayo [RA, Mendoza] 106-107 C 5
Veinticinco de Mayo [ROU] 106-107 J 5
Veintiocho de Mayo 96-97 B 3
Veiros 98-99 MN 6
Veis = Veys 136-137 N 7
Vejer de la Frontera 120-121 DE 10
Vejle 116-117 C 10
Veka Vekalla = Vella Lavella 148-149 j 6
Vekkam = Vaikam 140 C 6
Vel' 124-125 N 3
Vela, Cabo de la — 92-93 E 2
Vela de Coro, La — 92-93 F 2
Velasco, Sierra de — 106-107 D 2
Velasco Ibarra 96-97 B 2
Velásquez 94-95 D 4
Velay 120-121 JK 6
Velázquez 106-107 K 5
Velddrif 174-175 C 7
Veldurti 140 C 3
Velebit 122-123 F 3
Velet'ma 124-125 O 6
Vélez 94-95 E 4
Vélez-Málaga 120-121 EF 10
Vel'gija 124-125 JK 4
Velhas, Rio das — 92-93 L 8
Vělhēṅ = Welhe 140 A 1
Velho = Mágoè 172 F 5
Velikaja [SU ◁ Anadyrskij zaliv] 132-133 h 5
Velikaja [SU ◁ Pskovskoje ozero] 124-125 G 5
Velikaja Aleksandrovka 126-127 FG 3
Velikaja Belozʼorka 126-127 G 3
Velikaja Guba 124-125 KL 2
Velikaja Ičinskaja sopka 132-133 e 6
Velikaja Kambalnaja sopka 132-133 e 7
Velikaja Kľučevskaja sopka 132-133 f 6
Velikaja Kor'akskaja sopka 132-133 ef 7
Velikaja Kronockaja sopka 132-133 ef 7
Velikaja Lepeticha 126-127 FG 3
Velikaja Novoselka 126-127 H 3
Velikaja Znamenka 126-127 FG 3
Velikij Burluk 126-127 H 1
Velikije Luki 124-125 H 6
Velikij Šiveluč 132-133 f 6
Velikij Ust'ug 132-133 GH 5
Velikonda Range 140 D 3-4
Velikookt'abr'skij 124-125 JK 5
Veliko Tărnovo 122-123 L 4
Velille 96-97 F 9
Velille, Río — 96-97 F 9
Vélingara 168-169 B 2
Veliž 124-125 H 6
Vélizy-Villacoublay 129 I b 2
Velkije Mosty 126-127 B 1
Velkomstpynten 116-117 j 5
Vella Lavella 148-149 j 6
Vellār 140 D 5
Velletri 122-123 E 5
Velliguṇḍa = Velikonda Range 140 D 3-4
Vellore 134-135 M 8
Velloso 106-107 H 6
Velluda, Sierra — 106-107 B 6
Velluga 132-133 H 6
Velmerstot 118 D 3
Velodrome of Jakarta 154 IV b 2
Vel'sk 132-133 G 5
Velucá, Cerro — 88-89 D 7
Vēlūr = Vellore 134-135 M 8
Velva, ND 68-69 F 1-2
Vembanād Lake 140 C 6
Vembanād Peninsula 140 BC 6
Vemdalen 116-117 EF 6
Vempalle 140 D 3
Vempaḷḷi = Vempalle 140 D 3
Venado 94-95 J 6
Venado, El — 94-95 G 4
Venado, Isla — 64-65 b 3
Venado, Parque del — 91 I c 2
Venados Grandes 104-105 F 10
Venado Tuerto 111 D 4
Venamo, Cerro — 94-95 L 5
Venâncio Aires 106-107 L 2
Venango, NE 68-69 EF 5
Venator, OR 66-67 DE 4
Venceslau Brás 102-103 GH 5
Vendas Novas 120-121 C 9
Vendée 120-121 G 5
Vendôme 120-121 H 5
Veneta, OR 66-67 B 3-4
Venetia = Vèneto 122-123 DE 3
Venetie, AK 56-57 G 4
Venetie Landing, AK 58-59 OP 3
Veneto 122-123 DE 3
Veneza 98-99 C 9
Venèzia 122-123 E 3
Venèzia, Golfo di — 122-123 E 3
Venèzia-Mestre 122-123 E 3
Venèzia Tridentina = Trentino Alto Adige 122-123 D 2
Venezuela 92-93 FG 3
Venezuela, Golfo de — 92-93 E 2
Vēṅgaṅgā = Wainganga 134-135 MN 6-7
Vengerovo 132-133 O 6
Vengurlā 134-135 L 7
Vēṅgurlēṅ = Vengurla 134-135 L 7
Veniaminof, Mount — 58-59 d 1
Venice, FL 80-81 b 3
Venice, LA 78-79 E 6
Venice = Venèzia 122-123 E 3
Venice, Los Angeles-, CA 83 III b 2
Venkatagiri 140 D 4
Venkatāpuram 140 E 1
Venosa 122-123 F 5
Ven'ov 124-125 M 6
Vegta 124-125 CD 5
Venta, La — 86-87 NO 8
Venta de Baños 120-121 E 8
Ventana, La — 86-87 KL 6
Ventana, Sierra de la — 111 D 5
Ventanas 96-97 B 2
Ventanas, Las — 94-95 H 4
Ventania 102-103 G 6
Ventas, Madrid- 113 III ab 2
Ventersburg 174-175 G 5
Ventersdorp 174-175 G 4
Venterstad 174-175 F 6
Ventilla 104-105 C 5
Ventisquero, Cerro — 108-109 D 3
Ventnor 119 F 6
Ventoux, Mont — 120-121 K 6
Ventspils 124-125 C 5
Ventuari, Río — 92-93 F 3
Ventura, CA 74-75 D 5
Ventura, La — 86-87 K 5
Venturosa, La — 94-95 G 4
Venustiano Carranza 86-87 OP 9
Venustiano Carranza, Ciudad de México- 91 I c 2
Vera, TX 76-77 E 6
Vera [RA] 111 D 3
Vera, Bahía — 108-109 G 5
Vera, La — 120-121 E 8
Verá, Laguna — 111 E 3
Vera Cruz [BR, Bahia] 100-101 E 7
Vera Cruz [BR, Rondônia] 104-105 E 1
Vera Cruz [BR, São Paulo] 102-103 H 5
Veracruz [MEX, administrative unit] 64-65 G 7-8
Veracruz [MEX, place] 64-65 GH 8
Veraguas 88-89 F 10
Veraguas, Escudo de — 88-89 F 10
Veranópolis 111 F 3
Verāval 134-135 KL 6
Verbena, AL 78-79 F 4
Verbrande Brug 128 II b 1
Vercelli 122-123 C 3
Verchnij Rubez 124-125 L 3
Verchn'aja Amga 132-133 Y 6
Verchn'aja Chava 124-125 MN 8
Verchn'aja Chortica 126-127 G 3
Verchn'aja Jaz'va 124-125 V 3
Verchn'aja Kosa 124-125 T 4
Verchn'aja Maza 124-125 Q 7
Verchn'aja Tojma 132-133 GH 5
Verchn'aja Troica 124-125 L 5
Verchn'aja Volmanga 124-125 QR 4
Verchnebakanskij 126-127 H 4
Verchnečusovskije Gorodki 124-125 V 4
Verchnedvinsk 124-125 FG 6
Verchneimbatskoje 132-133 QR 5
Verchnejarkejevo 124-125 U 6
Verchneje Adimi 144-145 H 1
Verchnekamskaja vozvyšennost' 124-125 T 4
Verchne Ozernaja 132-133 f 6
Verchneudinsk = Ulan-Udė 132-133 U 7
Verchneural'sk 132-133 KL 7
Verchnesinkoje 132-133 RS 7
Verchnevil'ujsk 132-133 X 5
Verchnij Baskunčak 126-127 N 2
Verchnije Tatyšly 124-125 U 5
Verchnij Leb'ažinskij 126-127 N 3
Verchnij Mamon 126-127 K 1
Verchnij Trajanov val 126-127 D 3
Verchnij Ufalej 132-133 KL 6
Verchnij Uslon 124-125 R 6
Verchojansk 132-133 Za 4
Verchojanskij chrebet 132-133 Y 4-Z 5
Vercholedka 124-125 N 2
Verchopuja 124-125 NO 3
Verchošižemje 124-125 R 4-5
Verchovažje 124-125 O 3
Verchovje 124-125 L 7
Verchozim 124-125 Q 7
Verdalsøyra 116-117 DE 6
Verde, La — 106-107 E 5
Verde Grande, Rio — 100-101 C 8
Verden 118 D 2
Verde River 74-75 H 5
Verdi, NV 74-75 CD 3
Verdigre, NE 68-69 G 4
Verdinho, Serra do — 102-103 F 2-G 3
Verdon 120-121 L 7
Verdon-sur-Mer, le — 120-121 G 6
Verdun [CDN] 82 I b 2
Verdun [F] 120-121 K 4
Verdura 86-87 FG 5
Vereda de Côcos 100-101 B 7
Vereda do Cambueiro 100-101 B 6
Vereda do Muquém 100-101 C 6
Vereda Pimenteira 100-101 C 5-6
Veredas 102-103 K 3
Vereeniging 172 E 7
Vereja 124-125 L 6
Vérendrye, Parc provincial de la — 56-57 V 8
Vereščagino [SU ↓ Igarka] 132-133 QR 5
Vereščagino [SU ← Krasnokamsk] 132-133 JK 6
Verga, NJ 84 III bc 2
Verga, Cap — 168-169 B 3
Vergara [RA] 106-107 HJ 5
Vergara [ROU] 106-107 KL 4
Vergas, MN 70-71 BC 2
Vergeleë 174-175 F 3
Verín 120-121 D 8
Veríssimo 102-103 H 3
Veríssimo Sarmento 172 D 3
Verkhneudinsk = Ulan-Udė 132-133 U 7
Verkhoyansk = Verchojansk 132-133 Za 4
Verkhoyansk Mountains = Verchojanskij chrebet 132-133 Y 4-b 5
Verkola 124-125 P 2
Verkykerskop 174-175 H 4
Verlegenhuken 116-117 jk 4
Vermaas 174-175 FG 4
Vermilion 56-57 O 7
Vermilion, OH 72-73 E 4
Vermilion Bay 78-79 CD 6
Vermilion Cliffs 74-75 G 4
Vermilion Lake 70-71 D 2
Vermilion Range 70-71 DE 2
Vermilion River 70-71 D 1-2
Vermilion River 61 C 4
Vermillion, OH 72-73 E 4
Vermillion, SD 68-69 H 4
Vermillion Bay 62 C 3
Vermillon, Rivière — 72-73 K 1
Vermont 64-65 M 3
Vermont, IL 70-71 E 5
Vernadovka 124-125 O 7
Vernal, UT 66-67 J 5
Verneukpan [ZA, landscape] 174-175 D 5
Verneukpan [ZA, place] 174-175 D 6
Vernon, AZ 74-75 J 5
Vernon, CA 83 III c 1
Vernon, NV 66-67 D 5
Vernon, TX 64-65 FG 5
Vernon [CDN, British Colombia] 56-57 N 7
Vernon [CDN, Prince Edward I.] 63 E 4
Vernon [F] 120-121 H 4
Vernon = Onaqui, UT 66-67 G 5
Vernonia, OR 66-67 B 3
Vernouillet 129 I ab 2
Vernyj = Alma-Ata 132-133 O 9
Vero Beach, FL 80-81 cd 3
Verona 122-123 D 3
Verónica 106-107 J 5
Verrazano-Narrows Bridge 82 III b 3
Verrekykerskop = Verkykerskop 174-175 H 4
Verrière, la — 129 I a 3
Verrières-le-Buisson 129 I c 3
Versailles 120-121 HJ 4
Versailles, IN 70-71 H 6
Versailles, KY 70-71 H 6
Versailles, MO 70-71 D 6
Versailles, OH 72-73 D 5
Versailles, Buenos Aires- 110 III b 1
Versalles 104-105 E 3
Veršino-Darasunskij 132-133 VW 7
Verte, Île de — 82 I bc 1
Vertentes 100-101 G 6
Vertentes, Serra das — 100-101 E 2-3
Vert-Galant, le — 129 I d 2
Vertientes 88-89 G 4
Vértiz 106-107 F 5
Vērūl = Ellora 138-139 E 7
Verulam 174-175 J 5
Verviers 120-121 KL 3
Vervins 120-121 JK 4
Verwood 68-69 D 1
Vescovato 122-123 C 4
Veselí nad Lužnicí 118 G 4
Veselinovo 126-127 E 3
Veselovskoje vodochranilišče 126-127 K 3
Veselyj Kut 124-125 T 2
Vésinet, le — 129 I b 2
Vesjegonsk 132-133 F 6
Veškajma 124-125 Q 6
Veški [SU, Moskva] 113 V c 1
Ves'l'ana [SU, place] 124-125 S 2
Ves'l'ana [SU, river] 124-125 T 3
Vešn'ak, Moskva- 113 V d 3
Ves'oloje 126-127 G 3
Ves'olyj 126-127 K 3
Vesoul 120-121 KL 5
Vest-Agder 116-117 B 8
Vesterålen 116-117 FG 3
Vestfjorden 116-117 E 4-F 3
Vestfold 116-117 CD 8
Vestfonna 116-117 l 4
Véstia 102-103 G 4
Vestmannaeyjar 116-117 c 3

Vestspitsbergen 116-117 j-l 5
Vestur-Bardhastrandar 116-117 ab 2
Vestur-Húnavatn 116-117 cd 2
Vestur-Ísafjardhar 116-117 b 1-2
Vestur-Skaftafell 116-117 de 3
Vestvågøy 116-117 EF 3
Vesùvio 122-123 F 5
Vesuvius = Vesùvio 122-123 F 5
Veszprem 118 HJ 5
Vetāpālem 140 E 3
Vetka 124-125 H 7
Vetlanda 116-117 F 9
Vetluga [SU, place] 124-125 P 5
Vetluga [SU, river] 124-125 P 5
Vetlužskij 124-125 P 5
Vetralla 122-123 DE 4
Vetrenyj Pojas, kr'až — 124-125 K-M 2
Vetrivier 174-175 F 4
Vevay, IN 70-71 H 6
Vevay, OH 72-73 D 5
Veynes 120-121 K 6
Veyo, UT 74-75 G 4
Veys 136-137 N 7
Vézère 120-121 H 6
Vezirköprü 136-137 F 2

V. Gómez 106-107 F 5

Via Appia 113 II b 2
Via Aurelia 113 II a 2
Via Cassia 113 II a 1
Viacha 92-93 F 8
Via Flaminia 113 II b 1
Vialar = Tīsamsīlt 166-167 G 2
Viale 106-107 GH 3
Viamão 106-107 M 3
Viamonte 106-107 F 4
Vian, OK 76-77 G 5
Viana [BR, Espírito Santo] 100-101 D 11
Viana [BR, Maranhão] 92-93 K 5
Viana, Ilha do — 110 I c 2
Viana del Bollo 120-121 D 7
Viana do Castelo 120-121 C 8
Vianópolis 92-93 K 8
Viarèggio 122-123 CD 4
Via Tiburtina 113 II c 2
Vibank 61 G 5
Víbora, La — 76-77 C 9
Viborg 116-117 C 9
Viborg, SD 68-69 H 4
Viborg = Vyborg 132-133 DE 5
Vibo Valentia 122-123 FG 6
Vic 120-121 J 8
Vicálvaro, Madrid- 113 III b 2
Vicência 100-101 G 4
Vicente, Point — 74-75 D 6
Vicente Guerrero [MEX, Baja California Norte] 86-87 BC 2
Vicente Guerrero [MEX, Durango] 86-87 HJ 6
Vicente López 106-107 H 5
Vicente López-Carapachay 110 III b 1
Vicente López-Florida 110 III b 1
Vicente López-Munro 110 III b 1
Vicentina 102-103 E 5
Vicenza 122-123 D 3
Viceroy 68-69 D 1
Vichada 94-95 FG 5
Vichada, Río — 92-93 F 4
Vichadero 106-107 K 3
Viche 96-97 B 1
Vichigasta 106-107 D 2
Vichuquén 106-107 A 5
Vichuquén, Laguna de — 106-107 AB 5
Vichy 120-121 J 5
Vici, OK 76-77 E 4
Vicksburg, AZ 74-75 FG 6
Vicksburg, MI 70-71 H 4
Vicksburg, MS 64-65 HJ 5
Viçosa [BR, Alagoas] 100-101 F 5
Viçosa [BR, Minas Gerais] 102-103 L 4
Viçosa do Ceará 100-101 D 2
Victor, CO 68-69 D 6
Victor, ID 66-67 H 4
Victor, MT 66-67 F 2
Victor Harbor 158-159 G 7
Victor-Hugo = Ḥamādīyah 166-167 GH 2
Victoria, KS 68-69 G 6
Victoria, TX 64-65 G 6
Victoria [AUS] 158-159 HJ 7
Victoria [BOL] 104-105 G 6
Victoria [CDN] 56-57 M 8
Victoria [HK] 142-143 LM 7
Victoria [MAL] 148-149 FG 5
Victoria [PE] 96-97 D 5
Victoria [RA] 111 DE 4
Victoria [RCH, Araucanía] 111 B 5
Victoria [RCH, Magallanes y Antártica Chilena] 108-109 E 9
Victoria [SY] 204-205 N 9
Victoria [WAN] 164-165 F 8
Victoria [ZW] 172 F 6
Victoria, Ciudad — 64-65 G 7
Victoria, Île — = Victoria Island 56-57 O-Q 3
Victoria, La — [CO, Bogotá] 94-95 CD 5
Victoria, La — [CO, Valle del Cauca] 91 III a 3
Victoria, La — [YV] 94-95 H 2
Victoria, Lake — [AUS] 160 E 4
Victoria, Lake — [lake] 172 F 2
Victoria, Mount — 148-149 N 8
Victoria, Mount — = Tomaniive 148-149 a 2
Victoria, Pont — 82 I b 2
Victoria, San Fernando- 110 III b 1
Victoria and Albert Mountains 56-57 VW 1-2
Victoria Beach [CDN] 62 A 2
Victoria Beach [WAN] 170 III b 2
Victoria Cove 63 J 3
Victoria de Durango 64-65 F 7
Victoria de las Tunas 64-65 L 7
Victoria Harbour 155 I ab 2
Victoria Hill 88-89 JK 2
Victoria Island [CDN] 56-57 O-Q 3
Victoria Island [WAN] 170 III b 2
Victoria-Kennedy Town 155 I a 2
Victoria-Lai Chi Kok 155 I a 1
Victoria Lake [CDN] 63 H 3
Victoria Lake [ZA] 170 V b 2
Victoria Land 53 B 17-15
Victoria Memorial 154 II b 2
Victoria-North Point 155 I b 2
Victoria Park [GB] 129 II b 1
Victoria Park [HK] 155 I b 2
Victoria Peak 60 DE 4
Victoria Peak [HK] 155 I a 2
Victoria Peak [USA] 76-77 B 7
Victoria Point = Kawthaung 148-149 C 4
Victoria River 158-159 EF 3
Victoria River Downs 158-159 F 3
Victoria-Sai Wan Ho 155 I b 2
Victoria-Sai Ying Poon 155 I a 2
Victoria-Sau Ki Wan 155 I b 2
Victoria Strait 56-57 QR 4
Victoria-Tai Hang 155 I b 2
Victoria-Tai Koo Shing 155 I b 2
Victoria Taungdeik 141 CD 5
Victoriaville 72-73 KL 1
Victoria-Wan Chai 155 I ab 2
Victoria-Wes 172 D 8
Victoria West = Victoria-Wes 172 D 8
Victorica 111 C 5
Victorino 92-93 F 4
Victorino de la Plaza 106-107 F 6
Victorville, CA 74-75 E 5
Vičuga 132-133 G 6
Vicuña 106-107 B 2-3
Vicuña Mackenna 106-107 EF 4
Vicuña Mackenna, Sierra — 104-105 AB 9
Vicus 96-97 AB 4
Vida, MT 68-69 D 2
Vidal, CA 74-75 F 5
Vidal Gormaz, Isla — 108-109 B 8-9
Vidalia, GA 80-81 E 4
Vidalia, LA 78-79 D 5
Videau, Peninsula — 108-109 C 7
Videira 102-103 G 7
Videla 106-107 G 3
Vidim 132-133 T 6
Vidin 122-123 K 3-4
Vidio, Cabo — 120-121 DE 7
Vidisha 134-135 M 6
Vidlica 124-125 HJ 3
Vidor, TX 76-77 GH 7
Vidos 154 I a 2-3
Vidra 122-123 M 3
Vidzeme 124-125 EF 5
Vidzju 124-125 S 3
Vidzy 124-125 F 6
Viedma 111 D 6
Viedma, Lago — 111 B 7
Viena 96-97 D 7
Vienchan = Vientiane 148-149 D 3
Vienna, GA 80-81 E 4
Vienna, IL 70-71 F 7
Vienna, MO 70-71 E 6
Vienna, SD 68-69 H 3
Vienna, WV 72-73 F 5
Vienna = Wien 118 H 4
Vienne [F, place] 120-121 K 6
Vienne [F, river] 120-121 H 5
Vien Pou Kha 150-151 C 2
Vientiane 148-149 D 3
Viento, Cordillera del — 106-107 B 6
Viento, Meseta del — 108-109 C 7
Vientos, Los — 111 BC 2
Vientos, Paso de los — 64-65 M 7-8
Vientos, Planicie de los — 106-107 E 7
Vieques 64-65 N 8
Vierfontein 174-175 G 4
Vierwaldstätter See 118 D 5
Vierzon 120-121 J 5
Viesca 86-87 J 5
Viesīte 124-125 E 5
Vieste 122-123 G 5
Vietnam 148-149 D 2-E 4
Viêt Tri 148-149 E 2
Vieux Carré, New Orleans-, LA 85 I b 2
Vieux Fort 88-89 Q 8
Vievis 124-125 E 6
View, TX 76-77 E 6
View Park, CA 83 III bc 1
Vieytes 106-107 J 5
Viga 124-125 O 4
Viga, Cerro de la — 106-107 B 3
Vigan 148-149 GH 3
Vigário Geral, Rio de Janeiro- 110 I b 1
Vigia 92-93 K 5
Vigía, Cabo — 108-109 F 7
Vigía, El — 92-93 E 3
Vigia, Isla — = Keppel Island 108-109 K 8
Vigia Chico 86-87 R 8
Vigía de Curvaradó 94-95 C 4
Vignola 122-123 D 3
Vigo 120-121 C 7
Vigten Islands = Vikna 116-117 D 5
Vihārī 138-139 D 2
Vihowā 138-139 C 2
Vihren 122-123 K 5
Viipuri = Vyborg 132-133 DE 5
Viitasaari 116-117 LM 6
Vijāpur 138-139 D 6
Vijāpur = Bijāpur 134-135 LM 7
Vijayadurg 140 A 2
Vijayanagaram = Vizianagaram 134-135 NO 7
Vijayawāda 134-135 N 7
Vijaypur = Bijaipur 138-139 F 4
Vík 116-117 d 3
Vika 116-117 M 4
Vikārābād 140 C 2
Viking 56-57 O 7
Vikna 116-117 D 5
Vikøyri 116-117 B 7
Vila [RA] 106-107 G 3
Vil'a [SU] 124-125 O 6
Vila [Vanuatu] 158-159 N 3
Vila Arriaga = Bibala 172 B 4
Vila Artur de Paiva = Cubango 172 C 4
Vila Balneária, Rio de Janeiro- 110 I b 3
Vila Bastos, Santo André- 110 II b 2
Vila Bela 104-105 G 3
Vila Bittencourt 98-99 D 5
Vila Boaçava, São Paulo- 110 II a 1
Vila Cabral = Lichinga 172 G 4
Vila Cocaia, Guarulhos- 110 II b 1
Vila Conceição, Diadema- 110 II b 3
Vila Coutinho 172 F 4
Vila da Maganja 172 G 5
Vila de Aljustrel = Cangamba 172 C 4
Vila de Aviz = Oncócua 172 B 5
Vila de João Belo = Xai Xai 172 F 7
Vila de Manica = Manica 172 F 5
Vila de Sena 172 FG 5
Vila Fontes 172 G 5
Vila Fontes = Caia 172 G 5
Vila Formosa, São Paulo- 110 II bc 2
Vila Franca de Xira 120-121 C 9
Vila Galvão, Guarulhos- 110 II b 1
Vila General Machado = Coeli 172 C 4
Vila Gouveia = Catandica 172 F 5
Vila Guilherme, São Paulo- 110 II b 2
Vila Henrique de Carvalho = Saurimo 172 D 3
Vilaine 120-121 F 5
Vila Jaguara, São Paulo- 110 II a 2
Vila João de Almeida = Chibia 172 B 5
Vilaller 120-121 H 7
Vila Luísa 174-175 K 3
Vila Luso = Moxuco 172 CD 4
Vilama, Lago de — 104-105 C 8
Vila Macedo, Guarulhos- 110 II b 1
Vila Macedo do Cavaleiros = Andulo 172 C 4
Vila Madalena, São Paulo- 110 II a 2
Vila Marechal Carmona = Vige 172 C 3
Vila Maria, São Paulo- 110 II b 2
Vila Mariana, São Paulo- 110 II b 2
Vila Mariano Machado = Ganda 172 B 4
Vila Matilde, São Paulo- 110 II bc 2
Vilanculos 172 G 6
Viļāni 124-125 F 5
Vila Norton de Matos = Balombo 172 B 4
Vila Nova, Rio — 98-99 MN 4
Vila Nova do Seles 172 B 4
Vila Paiva Couceiro = Gambos 172 BC 4
Vila Pedro II, Rio de Janeiro- 110 I a 1
Vila Pereira d'Eça = N'Giva 172 C 5
Vila Pery = Manica 172 F 5
Vila Prudente, São Paulo- 110 II b 2
Vila Real 120-121 D 8
Vila Real de Santo António 120-121 D 10
Vilar Formoso 120-121 D 8
Vila Roçadas = Roçadas 172 C 5
Vilas, SD 68-69 H 3
Vila Salazar = N'Dala Tando 172 BC 3
Vila Teixeira da Silva = Bailundo 172 C 4
Vila Teixeira de Sousa = Luau 172 CD 4
Vilāttikuḷam 140 D 6
Vila Velha [BR, Amapá] 98-99 N 3
Vila Velha [BR, Espírito Santo] 92-93 LM 9
Vila Viçosa 120-121 D 9
Vilavila 104-105 C 7
Vilcabamba 96-97 E 8
Vilcabamba, Cordillera — 92-93 E 7
Vilcanota, Cordillera de — 96-97 E 8-F 9
Vilcanota, Río — 96-97 F 8-9
Vilcún 106-107 A 7
Viled' 124-125 R 3
Vilejka 124-125 F 6
Vilela 106-107 H 5
Vilelas 106-107 F 1
V. I. Lenina, Mavzolej — 113 V c 2-3
Vilgo, Sierra de — 106-107 D 2-3
Vil'gort [SU, Komi ASSR] 124-125 S 3
Vil'gort [SU, Perm'skaja Oblast'] 124-125 V 3
Vil'gort [SU, Syktyvkar] 132-133 HJ 5
Vilhelmina 116-117 G 5
Vilhena 92-93 G 7
Vilija 124-125 EF 6
Viljandi 124-125 E 4
Viljoenskroon 174-175 G 4
Vilkaviškis 124-125 D 6
Vil'kickogo, ostrov — [SU, East Siberian Sea] 132-133 de 2
Vil'kickogo, ostrov — [SU, Kara Sea] 132-133 NO 3
Vil'kickogo, proliv — 132-133 S-U 2
Vilkija 124-125 D 6
Vilkitsky Island = ostrov Vil'kickogo 132-133 NO 3
Vilkovo 126-127 D 4
Villa Abecia 92-93 FG 9
Villa Aberastain 106-107 C 3
Villa Acuña 76-77 D 8
Villa Acuña,, GA 78-79 G 3
Villa Ada 113 II b 1
Villa Adelina, San Isidro- 110 III b 1
Villa Ahumada 86-87 G 2
Villa Aldama 86-87 K 4
Villa Ana 106-107 H 2
Villa Ángela 111 D 3
Villa Atamisqui 106-107 F 2
Villa Atuel 106-107 CD 5
Villa Ballester, General San Martín- 110 III b 1
Villa Barilari, Avellaneda- 110 III b 2
Villa Bella 92-93 F 7
Villa Berthet 104-105 F 10
Villablino 120-121 D 7
Villa Borghese 113 II b 1-2
Villa Bosch, General San Martín- 110 III b 1
Villa Brana 102-103 A 7
Villa Bruzual 94-95 G 3
Villa Bustos 106-107 D 2
Villacañas [E] 120-121 F 9
Villa Cañás [RA] 106-107 G 5
Villacarillo 120-121 F 9
Villa Carlos Paz 106-107 E 3
Villa Castelli 106-107 CD 2
Villach 118 F 5
Villacidro 122-123 C 6
Villa Cisneros = Ad-Dakhlah 164-165 A 4
Villa Clara = Clara 106-107 H 3
Villa Coapa, Tlalpan- 91 I c 3
Villa Colón 106-107 CD 3
Villa Constitución [MEX] 86-87 E 5
Villa Constitución [RA] 106-107 GH 4
Villa Coronado 86-87 H 4
Villa Cristóbal Colón, Avellaneda- 110 III b 2
Villa Cura Brochero 106-107 E 3
Villada 120-121 E 7
Villa de Cos 86-87 J 6
Villa de Cura 92-93 F 2-3
Villa de la Quebrada 106-107 DE 4
Villa del Cerro, Montevideo- 106-107 J 5
Villa del Rosario 106-107 F 3
Villa del Señor, Punta — 106-107 AB 3
Villa del Totoral 106-107 EF 3
Villa de María 111 D 3
Villa de Mayo, General Sarmiento- 110 III a 1
Villa de Praga 106-107 E 4
Villa de Ramos 86-87 K 6
Villa Devoto, Buenos Aires- 110 III b 1
Villa Diamante, Lanús- 110 III b 2
Villa Dolores 111 C 4
Villa Domínguez = Domínguez 106-107 H 3
Villa Dominico, Avellaneda- 110 III c 2
Villa Doria Pamphili 113 II b 2
Villa El Chocón 106-107 C 7
Villa Elisa 106-107 H 4
Villa Escolar 104-105 G 10
Villa Federal = Federal 111 E 4
Villa Flores 86-87 O 9
Villa Florida 102-103 D 7
Villa Franca [PY] 102-103 CD 7
Villafranca del Bierzo 120-121 D 7
Villafranca de los Barros 120-121 DE 9
Villafranca del Penedès 120-121 H 8
Villa Frontadó 94-95 K 2
Villa Frontera 64-65 F 6
Villagarcía de Arosa 120-121 C 7
Village Green, PA 84 III a 2
Villa General Roca 106-107 D 4
Villa Gesell 106-107 J 6
Village Square, LA 85 I c 2
Villàggio Duca degli Abruzzi = Joowhar 172 J 1
Villa Grove, IL 70-71 FG 6
Villaguay 111 E 4
Villa Guillermina 106-107 H 2
Villa Gutiérrez 106-107 E 3
Villa Hayes 102-103 D 6
Villahermosa [MEX] 64-65 H 8
Villa Hernandarias 106-107 H 3
Villa Hidalgo 86-87 H 4
Villa Huidobro 106-107 E 5
Villa Industrial 104-105 B 5
Villa Iris 106-107 F 7
Villa Jiménez 106-107 E 1
Villa José L. Suárez, General San Martín- 110 III b 1
Villajoyosa 120-121 GH 9
Villa Krause 106-107 C 3
Villa La Angostura 108-109 D 3
Villa Larca 106-107 E 4
Villa Larroque = Larroque 106-107 H 4
Villaldama 76-77 D 9
Villa Lía 106-107 H 5
Villalonga 108-109 H 2
Villa López 76-77 B 9
Villa Lugano, Buenos Aires- 110 III b 2
Villa Luiza = Vila Luísa 174-175 K 3
Villa Lynch, General San Martín- 110 III b 1
Villa Madero, La Matanza- 110 III b 2
Villa Mantero 106-107 H 4
Villa María 111 D 4
Villa María Grande 106-107 H 3
Villa Maza = Maza 106-107 F 6
Villa Mazán 111 C 3
Villa Media Agua 106-107 CD 3
Villamil 92-93 A 5
Villa Minetti 106-107 G 2
Villa Moderna 106-107 E 5
Villa Montes 92-93 G 9
Villance, Cañada de — 106-107 D 4
Villa Nora 174-175 GH 2
Villanova, PA 84 III ab 1
Villanova i la Geltrú 120-121 HJ 8
Villanova University 84 III a 1
Villanueva, NM 76-77 B 5
Villanueva [CO, Bolívar] 94-95 D 2
Villanueva [CO, Guajira] 94-95 E 2
Villanueva [RA, Buenos Aires] 106-107 H 5
Villa Nueva [RA, Córdoba] 106-107 F 4
Villa Nueva [RA, Mendoza] 106-107 C 4
Villanueva de Córdoba 120-121 E 9
Villanueva de la Serena 120-121 E 9
Villanveva 86-87 J 6
Villa Obregón 91 I b 2
Villa Obregón-Alpes 91 I b 2
Villa Obregón-Mixcoac 91 I b 2
Villa Obregón-Molino do Rosas 91 I b 2
Villa Obregón-San Jerónimo Lidice 91 I b 3
Villa Obregón-Santa Fe 91 I b 2
Villa Obregón-Tizapán 91 I b 2
Villa Obregón-Unidad Santa Fe 91 I b 2
Villa Ocampo 111 DE 3
Villaodrid 120-121 D 7
Villa Ojo de Agua 111 D 3
Villa Oliva 102-103 D 6-7
Villapinzón 94-95 E 5
Villa Quesada 88-89 D 9
Villa Ramírez 106-107 GH 4
Villa Real, Buenos Aires- 110 III b 1
Villa Reducción 106-107 F 4
Villa Regina 106-107 D 7
Villa Rey 102-103 D 6
Villa Rica 104-105 C 2
Villarino, Punta — 108-109 G 3
Villa Rosario 94-95 E 4
Villarreal de los Infantes 120-121 GH 9
Villarrica [PY] 111 E 3
Villarrica [RCH] 108-109 C 2
Villarrica, Lago — 108-109 C 2
Villa Sáenz Peña, Buenos Aires- 110 III b 1
Villa San Isidro 106-107 CD 3
Villa San José 106-107 H 4
Villa San Martín 111 D 3
Villa Sarmiento 106-107 E 5
Villa Sauze 106-107 F 5
Villasboas 106-107 J 4
Villa Serrano 104-105 D 6
Villa Traful 108-109 D 3
Villa Trinidad 106-107 FG 3
Villa Tulumba 106-107 EF 3
Villa Unión [MEX, Coahuila] 76-77 D 8
Villa Unión [MEX, Sinaloa] 86-87 GH 6
Villa Unión [RA, La Rioja] 111 C 3
Villa Unión [RA, Santiago del Estero] 106-107 F 2
Villa Valeria 111 CD 4
Villaverde Bajo, Madrid- 113 III ab 2
Villavicencio [CO] 92-93 E 4
Villavicencio [RA] 106-107 C 4
Villaviciosa 120-121 E 7
Villa Victoria 86-87 J 8
Villavieja de Yeltes 120-121 D 8
Villa Viscara 104-105 D 6
Villazón [BOL, Chuquisaca] 104-105 E 7
Villazón [BOL, Potosí] 104-105 D 7-8
Villecresnes 129 I d 3
Villefranche-sur-Saône 120-121 K 5-6
Villejuif 129 I c 2
Ville-Marie 72-73 G 1
Villemomble 129 I cd 2
Villena 120-121 G 9
Villenes-sur-Seine 129 I a 2
Villeneuve-la-Garonne 129 I c 2
Villeneuve-le-Roi 129 I c 3
Villeneuve-Saint-Georges 120-121 J 4
Villeneuve-sur-Lot 120-121 H 6
Villeparisis 129 I d 2
Villepinte 129 I d 2
Ville Platte, LA 78-79 C 5
Villepreux 129 I b 2
Villers-le-Bel 129 I c 1
Villeta [CO] 94-95 D 5
Villeta [PY] 102-103 D 6
Villette, Paris-la — 129 I c 2
Villeurbanne 120-121 K 6
Villevaudé 129 I d 2
Villicún, Sierra de — 106-107 C 3
Villiers 174-175 H 4
Villiersdorp 174-175 C 7-8
Villiers-le-Bâcle 129 I b 3
Villiers-sur-Marne 129 I d 2
Villingen-Schwenningen 118 D 4
Villini, Roma- 113 II a 2
Villisca, IA 70-71 C 5
Villmanstrand = Lappeenranta 116-117 N 7
Villupuram 140 D 4-5
Vilnius 124-125 E 6
Vilnius-Nauja Vileika 124-125 EF 6
Vilos, Los — 111 B 4
Viloyo 104-105 C 6
Vilsandi 124-125 C 4
Vil'uj 132-133 W 5
Vil'ujsk 132-133 X 5
Vilyui = Vil'uj 132-133 X 5
Vimmerby 116-117 FG 9
Vimont 82 I a 1
Viña 106-107 G 4
Vina, CA 74-75 BC 3
Viña, La — [PE] 92-93 D 6
Viña, La — [RA] 111 C 3
Viña del Mar 111 B 4
Vinalhaven, ME 72-73 M 2-3
Viñalito, Bañados del — 104-105 E 9
Vinaroz 120-121 H 8
Vincennes 129 I c 2
Vincennes, IN 64-65 J 4
Vincennes Bay 53 C 11
Vinces 96-97 B 2
Vinchina 106-107 CD 2
Vinchina, Río — 106-107 C 2
Vinchos 96-97 D 8
Vinculo 91 III a 4
Vindelälven 116-117 H 5
Vindeln 116-117 HJ 5
Vindhya Achal = Panna Hills 138-139 H 5
Vindhya Range 134-135 L-N 6
Vineland, NJ 72-73 J 5
Vineyard Sound 72-73 L 4
Vinh = Xa-doai 148-149 E 3
Vinh Cam Ranh 150-151 G 7
Vinh Châu 150-151 EF 8
Vinh Ha Long 150-151 F 2
Vinh Hao = Tuy Phong 150-151 G 7
Vinh Linh 150-151 F 4
Vinh Lo'i 148-149 E 5
Vinh Long 148-149 E 4
Vinh Ninh = Ninh Giang 150-151 F 2
Vinho, País do — 120-121 CD 8
Vinh Phyên 150-151 EF 2
Vinh Thu'c, Đao — = Đao Kersaint 150-151 FG 2
Vinh Tuy 150-151 E 1
Vinh Yên 150-151 E 2
Vinings, GA 85 II b 1
Vinita, OK 76-77 G 4
Vinje 116-117 BC 8
Vinjhān 138-139 B 6
Vinkekuil 174-175 D 7
Vinkeveen 128 I b 2
Vinkeveense plassen 128 I b 2
Vinkovci 122-123 H 3
Vinnica 126-127 D 2
Vinnitsa = Vinnica 126-127 D 2
Vinson, Mount — 53 B 28
Vinsulla 60 GH 4
Vinte de Setembro 98-99 J 11
Vinton, IA 70-71 DE 4
Vinton, LA 78-79 C 5
Vinton, VA 80-81 G 2
Vinuguṇḍa = Vinukonda 140 DE 2
Vinukonda 140 DE 2
Viola, KS 68-69 H 7
Violeta, La — 106-107 GH 4
Vioolsdrif 174-175 B 5
Vipos 104-105 D 10
Vipya Mountains 171 C 5
Virac 148-149 H 4
Viradouro 102-103 HJ 4
Virājapāṭā = Virarājendrapet 140 BC 4
Viramgām 134-135 L 6
Viramgaon = Viramgām 134-135 L 6
Virandozero 124-125 KL 1
Viranşehir 136-137 H 4
Virarājendrapet 140 BC 4
Viravalli 140 F 4
Virbalis 124-125 D 6
Virden 61 H 6
Virden, IL 70-71 F 6
Virden, NM 74-75 J 6
Vire 120-121 G 4
Vîrful Mindra 122-123 KL 3
Virgem da Lapa 102-103 L 2
Virgen, Punta — 106-107 AB 3
Vírgenes, Cabo — 111 C 8
Virgina Hills, VA 82 II a 2
Virgin Gorda 88-89 OP 5
Virginia, IL 70-71 EF 6
Virginia, MN 64-65 H 2
Virginia [USA] 64-65 KL 4
Virginia [ZA] 174-175 G 5
Virginia, La — 94-95 D 5
Virginia Beach, VA 80-81 HJ 2
Virginia City, MT 66-67 GH 3
Virginia City, NV 74-75 D 3
Virginia Highlands, Arlington-, VA 82 II a 2
Virginia Mountains 74-75 D 3
Virginiatown 62 M 2
Virgin Islands 64-65 NO 8
Virgin Mountains 74-75 FG 4
Virginópolis 102-103 L 3
Virgin River 74-75 FG 4
Virgolândia 102-103 LM 3
Virihaure 116-117 G 4
Virmond 102-103 FG 6
Viroflay 129 I b 2
Viroqua, WI 70-71 E 4
Virovitica 122-123 G 3
Virtaniemi 116-117 MN 3
Virtsu 124-125 D 4
Virú 96-97 B 6
Virú, Río — 96-97 B 6
Virudunagar 140 CD 6
Viruḍunagaram = Virudunagar 140 CD 6
Virunga, Parc national — 172 E 1-2
Vis 122-123 G 4
Visagapatão = Vishākhapatnam 134-135 NO 7
Visakhapaṭṭaṇam = Vishākhapatnam 134-135 NO 7
Visalia, CA 74-75 D 4
Visapur 140 B 1
Visāvadar 138-139 C 7
Visayan Sea 148-149 H 4
Visby 116-117 GH 9
Visconde do Rio Branco 102-103 L 4
Viscount 61 F 4
Viscount Melville Sound 56-57 O-Q 3
Višegrad 122-123 H 4
Višera [SU, river ◁ Kama] 124-125 V 3
Višera [SU, river ◁ Vyčegda] 124-125 S 2
Višerskij kanal 124-125 HJ 4
Viseu [BR] 92-93 K 5
Viseu [P] 120-121 D 8
Vişeu-de-Sus 122-123 L 2
Vishākhapatnam 134-135 NO 7
Vishanpur = Bishenpur 134-135 P 6
Vishṇupur = Bishnupur 138-139 L 6
Vishvanāth = Bishnāth 141 C 2
Visim 124-125 V 4
Visitation, Île de la — 82 I b 1
Visnagar 138-139 D 6
Višnevec 126-127 B 2
Viso, Monte — 122-123 B 3
Visrivier 174-175 B 4
Vissannapeta 140 E 2
Vista Alegre [BR, Rio Amazonas] 98-99 H 4
Vista Alegre [BR, Rio Içana] 98-99 DE 4
Vista Alegre [PE] 96-97 B 5
Vista Alegre [RA, La Pampa] 106-107 D 6
Vista Alegre [RA, Neuquén] 106-107 C 7
Vista Bella 91 I b 1
Vista Nova 100-101 D 8
Vista Reservoir 66-67 F 5
Vistula = Wisła 118 K 3
Vit 122-123 L 4
Vita [IND] 140 B 2
Vita, Río — 94-95 G 5
Viṭe = Vita 140 B 2
Vitebsk 124-125 H 6
Viterbo 122-123 DE 4
Vitiaz Strait 148-149 N 8
Vitichi 92-93 F 9
Vitícola, La — 106-107 F 7
Viti Levu 148-149 a 2
Vitim 132-133 V 6
Vitimskoje ploskogorje 132-133 V 7
Vitinia, Roma- 113 II ab 2
Vitjaz Deep 142-143 S 3
Vitor 96-97 F 10
Vitor, Río — 96-97 F 10
Vitoria [BR, Espírito Santo] 92-93 LM 9
Vitória [BR, Pará] 98-99 MN 6
Vitoria [E] 120-121 F 7
Vitória, Ilha da — 102-103 K 5
Vitória da Conquista 92-93 L 7
Vitória de Santo Antão 100-101 G 5
Vitória do Mearim 100-101 B 2
Vitorino Freire 100-101 B 3
Vitoša Planina 122-123 K 4
Vitré 120-121 G 4
Vitry-le-François 120-121 K 4
Vitshumbi 171 B 3
Vittangi 116-117 JK 4
Vit Thu Lu 150-151 F 4
Vittòrio d'Africa = Shalanbod 172 HJ 1
Vittòrio Vèneto 122-123 E 2
Vitu Islands 148-149 g 5
Vivarais, Monts du — 120-121 K 6
Vivario 122-123 C 4
Vivero 120-121 D 7
Vivi 132-133 S 4
Vivi, ozero — 132-133 R 4
Vivian 61 K 6
Vivian, LA 76-77 GH 6
Vivian, SD 68-69 F 4
Vivoratá 111 E 5
Vivsta 116-117 G 6
Viyḷupuram = Villupuram 140 D 4-5
Vižaj 124-125 VW 3
Vižajskij zavod = Krasnovišersk 132-133 K 5
Vizcachas, Meseta de las — 111 B 8
Vizcaíno, Desierto de — 86-87 CD 4
Vizcaíno, Sierra — 64-65 D 6
Vize 136-137 B 2
Vize, ostrov — 132-133 O 2
Vizianagaram 134-135 NO 7
Vizinga 132-133 HJ 5
Vižnica 126-127 B 2

Vjatka = Kirov 132-133 HJ 6
Vjosë 122-123 HJ 5

Vlaanderen 120-121 J 3
Vladikavkaz = Ordžonikidze 126-127 M 5
Vladimir 132-133 FG 6
Vladimir Iljič Lenina 124-125 Q 7
Vladimirovka [SU, Kazachskaja SSR] 126-127 P 1
Vladimirovka [SU, Rossijskaja SFSR] 126-127 MN 2
Vladimirovka [SU, Ukrainskaja SSR Doneckaja Oblast'] 126-127 H 3
Vladimirovka [SU, Ukrainskaja SSR Nikolajevskaja Oblast'] 126-127 F 3
Vladimir Volynskij 126-127 B 1
Vladislavovka 126-127 G 4
Vladivostok 132-133 Z 9
Vladyčnoje 124-125 M 4
Vlakfontein 174-175 F 4
Vlasenica 122-123 H 3
Vlasotince 122-123 K 4
Vleifontein 174-175 D 7

Vlezenbeek 128 II a 2
Vlissingen 120-121 J 3
Vlorë 122-123 H 5
Vltava 118 G 4

Vochma [SU, place] 124-125 Q 4
Vochma [SU, river] 124-125 Q 4
Vochtoga 124-125 N 4
Vodla 124-125 L 3
Vodlozero 124-125 L 2
Vodnyj 124-125 T 2
vodopad Girvas 124-125 J 2
vodopad Kivač 124-125 J 2
Voëleiland 174-175 G 7
Vœune Sai 148-149 E 4
Vogas 104-105 F 1
Vogel Creek 85 III c 1
Vogelkop = Candravasih 148-149 K 7
Vogel Peak 168-169 HJ 3
Vogelsang, Winterthur- 128 IV b 1
Vogelsberg [D, mountain] 118 D 3
Vogelsberg [D, place] 128 III b 2
Vogelsdorf [DDR, Frankfurt] 130 III c 1
Voghera 122-123 C 3
Vohémar = Vohimarina 172 K 4
Vohibinany 172 JK 5
Vohimarina 172 K 4
Vohipeno 172 J 6
Voi [EAK, place] 172 G 2
Voi [EAK, river] 171 D 3
Voinjama 164-165 BC 7
Voiron 120-121 K 6
Vojejkov šelfovyj lednik 53 C 12-13
Vojkovo 126-127 F 4
Vojvodina 122-123 HJ 3
Voj-Vož 124-125 U 2
Volborg, MT 68-69 D 3
Volcán, Cerro — 108-109 E 5
Volcán, Cerro del — 106-107 BC 3
Volcán, El — 106-107 BC 4
Volcán, Sierra del — 106-107 H 6
Volcán Antofalla 104-105 BC 9
Volcán Antuco 106-107 B 6
Volcán Apagado 104-105 BC 8
Volcán Atitlán 64-65 H 9
Volcán Barú 64-65 K 10
Volcán Calbuco 108-109 C 3
Volcán Callaquén 106-107 B 6
Volcán Copiapó 106-107 C 1
Volcán Corcovado 111 B 6
Volcán Cosigüina 64-65 J 9
Volcán Cutanga 94-95 C 7
Volcán de Fuego 64-65 H 9
Volcán Descabezado Grande 106-107 B 5
Volcán de Tacaná 86-87 O 10
Volcán de Tajumulco 64-65 H 8
Volcán Domuyo 111 BC 5
Volcán Guallatiri 104-105 B 6
Volcán Irazú 64-65 K 9
Volcán Irruputunco 104-105 B 7
Volcán Lanín 111 B 5
Volcán Lascan 104-105 C 8
Volcán Lastarria 104-105 B 9
Volcán Llaima 106-107 B 7
Volcán Llullaillaco 111 C 2-3
Volcán Maipo 111 C 4
Volcán Minchinmávida 108-109 C 4
Volcán Miño 104-105 B 7
Volcano Bay = Uchiura-wan 144-145 b 2
Volcano Islands 206-207 RS 7
Volcán Orosi 64-65 JK 9
Volcán Osorno 111 B 6
Volcán Overo 106-107 BC 5
Volcán Paricutín 64-65 F 8
Volcán Pihuel 106-107 C 6
Volcán Pular 111 C 2
Volcán Purace 94-95 C 6
Volcán Putana 104-105 C 8
Volcán San Pedro 92-93 F 9
Volcán Socompa 111 C 2
Volcán Sotará 94-95 C 6
Volcán Sumaco 96-97 C 2
Volcán Tacora 111 C 1
Volcán Tinguiririca 106-107 B 5
Volcán Tonorio 88-89 D 9
Volcán Tutupaca 92-93 E 8
Volcán Viejo 88-89 C 8
Volchov [SU, place] 132-133 E 5-6
Volchov [SU, river] 124-125 HJ 4
Volchovstroj = Volchov 132-133 E 5-6
Volčja 126-127 H 2
Volčki 124-125 N 7
Volda 116-117 B 6
Voľdino 124-125 U 2
Volga [SU, place] 124-125 M 5
Volga [SU, river] 132-133 F 6
Volgodonsk 126-127 L 3
Volgo-Donskoj kanal 126-127 LM 2
Volgograd 126-127 LM 2
Volgograd-Beketovka 126-127 M 2
Volgograd-Krasnoarmejsk 126-127 M 2
Volgogradskoje vodochranilišče 126-127 MN 1-2
Volgoverchovje 124-125 J 5
Volhynia and Podolia, Hills of — = Volynskaja vozvyšennosť 126-127 BC 1
Volin, SD 68-69 H 4
Volketswil 128 IV b 1
Volkovysk 124-125 DE 7
Volksdorfer Wald 130 I b 1
Volkspark Hamburg 130 I a 1
Volkspark Jungfernheide 130 III b 1
Volkspark Klein Glienicke 130 III a 2
Volkspark Rehberge 130 III b 1
Volkspark Wuhlheide 130 III c 2
Volksrust 174-175 H 4
Volnovacha 126-127 H 3
Voločanka 132-133 R 3
Voloč'ok 124-125 NO 2
Volodarsk 124-125 O 5
Volodarsk, Pošechonje- 124-125 MN 4
Volodarsk-Volynskij 126-127 D 1
Vologda 132-133 FG 6
Vologino 126-127 P 1
Volokolamsk 124-125 KL 5
Volokonovka 126-127 HJ 1
Voloma 124-125 P 3
Vološka [SU, place] 124-125 MN 3
Vološka [SU, river] 124-125 M 3
Volosovo 124-125 G 4
Volosskaja Balakleja 126-127 JK 2
Volot 124-125 H 5
Volovec 126-127 A 2
Volovo 124-125 LM 7
Voložin 124-125 F 6
Voľsk 132-133 H 7
Volta [BR] 100-101 E 5
Volta [GH] 164-165 E 7
Volta, Black — 164-165 D 7
Volta, Lake — 164-165 DE 7
Volta, White — 164-165 D 7
Volta Grande 102-103 L 4
Volta Noire [HV, administrative unit] 168-169 E 2
Volta Noire [HV, river] 164-165 D 6
Volta Redonda 102-103 KL 5
Voltera 122-123 D 4
Voltti 116-117 K 6
Volturino, Monte — 122-123 FG 5
Volturno 122-123 F 5
Volubilis 164-165 C 2
Voluntad 106-107 G 6
Volynskaja Oblasť 124-125 DE 8
Volynskaja vozvyšennosť 126-127 BC 1
Volžsk 132-133 H 6
Volžskij 126-127 M 2
Vōma 124-125 D 4
Vona = Perşembe 136-137 G 2
Von Frank Mount 58-59 K 5
Vong Phu, Nui — 150-151 G 6
Vonguda 124-125 M 2
Von Martius, Salto — 92-93 J 7
von Otterøya 116-117 I 5
Vop' 124-125 J 6
Vopnafjördhur [IS, bay] 116-117 fg 2
Vopnafjördhur [IS, place] 116-117 f 2
Vorarlberg 118 DE 5
Vorderrhein 118 D 5
Vordingborg 116-117 D 10
Vorenža 124-125 K 2
Vorga 124-125 J 7
Vorjapauľ 132-133 L 5
Vorkuta 132-133 L 4
Vormsi 124-125 D 4
Vorochta 126-127 B 2
Vorogovo 132-133 QR 5
Vorona 124-125 O 7
Voroncovo [SU, Dudinka] 132-133 PQ 3
Voroncovo [SU, Pskovskaja Oblasť] 124-125 G 5
Voronež [SU, Rossijskaja SFSR place] 124-125 M 8
Voronež [SU, Rossijskaja SFSR river] 124-125 MN 7
Voronež [SU, Ukrainskaja SSR] 124-125 J 8
Voronezh = Voronež 124-125 M 8
Voronežskij zapovednik 124-125 MN 8
Voronino 124-125 P 4
Voronje [SU, Kirovskaja Oblasť] 124-125 ST 4
Voronok 124-125 J 7
Voronovo 124-125 E 6
Voropajevo 124-125 F 6
Vorošilovgrad = Vorošilovgrad 126-127 JK 2
Vorošilov = Ussurijsk 132-133 Z 9
Vorošilovgrad 126-127 JK 2
Vorotan 126-127 M 7
Vorožba 126-127 FG 1
Vorpommern 118 F 1-2
Vorskla 126-127 G 2
Võrtsjärv 124-125 E 4
Võru 124-125 F 5
Vorzeľ 126-127 E 1
Vosburg 174-175 E 6
Vösendorf 113 I b 2
Vosges 120-121 L 4-5
Voskapel 128 II b 1
Voskresensk 124-125 LM 6
Voskresenskoje [SU, Vologodskaja Oblasť ↑ Čerepovec] 124-125 LM 4
Voss 116-117 B 7
Vostočnyj 113 V d 2
Vostočnyje Karpaty 126-127 AB 2-3
Vostočnyj Sajan 132-133 R 6-T 7
Vostok [Antarctica] 53 B 11
Vostok [island] 156-157 K 5
Vostychoj = Jegyrjach 132-133 M 5
Votice 118 G 4
Votkinsk 132-133 J 6
Votkinskoje vodochranilišče 132-133 JK 6
Votuporanga 102-103 H 4
Vouga 120-121 C 8
Vouonkoro Rapides 168-169 E 3
Vožajeľ 124-125 S 2
Vožaoľ 124-125 RS 2
Vože, ozero — 124-125 M 3
Vožega 124-125 N 3
Vozgaly 124-125 S 4
Voznesenje 124-125 KL 3
Voznesensk 126-127 E 3
Voznesensk-Ivanovo = Ivanovo 132-133 FG 6
Voznesenskoje 124-125 O 6
Vozroždenija, ostrov — 132-133 KL 9
Vozvraščenija, gora — 132-133 b 8

Vraca 122-123 K 4
Vradijevka 126-127 E 3
Vranje 122-123 J 4
Vrbas [YU, place] 122-123 H 3
Vrbas [YU, river] 122-123 G 3
Vrede 174-175 H 4
Vredefort 174-175 G 4
Vredenburg 174-175 B 7
Vreed-en-Hoop 92-93 H 3
Vreeland 128 I b 2
Vriddachalam = Vriddhāchalam 140 D 5
Vriddhāchalam 140 D 5
Vrindāvan 138-139 F 4
Vrouwenakker 128 I a 2
Vrouwentroost 128 I a 2
Vršac 122-123 J 3
Vryburg 172 D 7
Vryheid 172 F 7

Vschody 124-125 JK 6
Vsetin 118 J 4
Vsevidof, Mount — 58-59 m 4
Vsevidof Island 58-59 m 4

Vu Ban 150-151 E 2
Vukovar 122-123 H 3
Vu Lao 150-151 DE 1
Vulcan 61 B 5
Vulcano, Ìsola — 122-123 F 6
Vu Liêt 150-151 E 3
Vùlture, Monte — 122-123 F 5
Vŭn = Wŭn 138-139 G 7
Vundik Lake 58-59 Q 3
Vung Bên Goi = Vung Hon Khoi 150-151 G 6
Vung Hon Khoi 150-151 G 6
Vung Liêm 150-151 EF 7
Vung Rach Gia 150-151 E 8
Vung Tau 150-151 F 7
Vuotso 116-117 M 3
Vuria 171 D 3
Vurnary 124-125 Q 6
Vuyyūru 140 E 2

Vyārā 138-139 D 7
Vyatka = Kirov 132-133 HJ 6
Vyazma = V'az'ma 124-125 K 6
Vyborg 132-133 DE 5
Vyčegda 132-133 J 5
Vyčegodskij 124-125 Q 3
Vychegda = Vyčegda 132-133 J 5
Vychino, Moskva- 113 V d 3
Vyg 124-125 K 2
Vygoda 126-127 AB 2
Vygozero 124-125 K 2
Vyksa 132-133 G 6
Vym' 124-125 S 2
Vypolzovo 124-125 J 5
Vyrica 124-125 H 4
Vyša 124-125 O 7
Vyshniy Volochek = Vyšnij Voloček 132-133 EF 6
Vyšnij Voloč'ok 132-133 EF 6
Vysock 124-125 G 3
Vysokaja, gora — 132-133 a 8
Vysokogornyj 132-133 ab 7
Vysokoje [SU, Belorusskaja SSR] 124-125 D 7
Vysokoje [SU, Rossijskaja SFSR] 124-125 K 5
Vysokovsk 124-125 KL 5
Vytegra 132-133 F 5

W

W, Parcs National du — 164-165 E 6

Wa 164-165 D 6
Wa, Nam — 150-151 C 3
Waajid 164-165 a 3
Waal 120-121 K 3
Waar, Mios — 148-149 KL 7
Wababimiga Lake 62 FG 2
Wabag 148-149 M 8
Wabamun 60 K 3
Wabana 56-57 a 8
Wabasca 60 L 1
Wabasca River 56-57 NO 6
Wabash, IN 70-71 H 5
Wabasha, MN 70-71 D 3
Wabash River 64-65 J 3
Wabassi River 62 F 1-2
Wabasso, MN 70-71 C 3
Wabeno, WI 70-71 F 3
Wabigoon 62 C 3
Wabimeig Lake 62 G 2
Wabī Shebelē 164-165 N 7
Wabowden 61 J 3
Wabu Hu 146-147 F 5
Wabuska, NV 74-75 D 3
Waccamaw, Lake — 80-81 G 3
Waccasassa Bay 80-81 b 2
Wachan = Wākhān 134-135 L 3
Wachenbuchen 128 III b 1
Waco 63 D 2
Waco, TX 64-65 G 5
Wād, Al- 164-165 F 2
Wada = Vāda 138-139 D 8
Wād ad-Dawarah 166-167 D 4
Wadah, Al- 173 D 6
Wād Aīt 'Aysā 166-167 E 3
Wād al-'Abīd 166-167 CD 3-4
Wād al-Akhḍar 166-167 C 4
Wād al-Ḥamrā' 166-167 B 6
Wād al-Ḥaṭāb 166-167 L 2
Wād al-Ḥāy 166-167 E 2
Wād al-Khaṭṭ 164-165 B 3
Wād al-Mā 164-165 C 4
Wād al-Mallāḥ 166-167 C 3
Wād an-Nayl 164-165 LM 6
Wād 'Aqqah 166-167 B 5
Wād Atūwi 164-165 B 4
Wād Awlaytīs 164-165 B 3
Wadayama 144-145 K 5
Wād Ayn Bin Tīlī 166-167 B 6-7
Wad Baḥt 166-167 D 3
Wād Bandah 164-165 K 6
Wād Bū Raghragh 166-167 C 3
Wād Dādis 166-167 C 4
Waddān 164-165 H 3
Waddiāram 140 D 2
Waddington, Mount — 56-57 LM 7
Wād Dra'ah 164-165 BC 3
Wadena 61 G 5
Wadena, MN 70-71 C 2
Wadesboro, NC 80-81 F 3
Wād Gharīs 166-167 D 3-4
Wād Grū' 166-167 C 3
Wād Ḥāmid 164-165 L 5
Wadhwān 134-135 L 6
Wādī, Bi'r al — 136-137 K 6
Wādī Abā' al-Qūr 136-137 J 7
Wādī Abū Ḥādd 173 D 7
Wādī Abū Jaḥaf 136-137 K 6
Wādī Abū Jīr 136-137 K 6
Wādī Abū Khārga = Wādī Abū Kharjah 173 BC 3
Wādī Abū Kharjah 173 BC 3
Wādī Abū Marw 173 C 6
Wādī ad-Dawāsir 134-135 EF 6
Wādī ad-Dawrah 166-167 DE 5
Wādī Ajaj 136-137 J 5
Wādī 'Akāsh = Wādī 'Ukāsh 136-137 J 5-6
Wādī al-Abtāl 166-167 G 2
Wādī al-Abyaḍ 166-167 JK 2
Wādī al-Afal = Wādī al-'Ifāl 173 D 3
Wādī al-'Ain = Wādī al-'Ayn 134-135 H 6
Wādī al-'Allāqī 173 C 6
Wādī al-'Aqabah 173 CD 2-3
Wādī al-'Arab 166-167 K 2
Wādī al-'Arabah 136-137 F 7
Wādī al-'Arīsh 173 C 2-3
Wādī al-Asyūṭī 173 B 4
Wādī al-Aṭrash 173 C 4
Wādī al-'Ayn 134-135 H 6
Wādī al-Bāṭin 134-135 F 5
Wādī al-Faḥl 166-167 HJ 4
Wādī al-Fārigh 164-165 HJ 2-3
Wādī al-Fiḍḍah 166-167 GH 1
Wādī al-Gharbī 166-167 G 3-4
Wādī al-Ghinah 136-137 G 7-8
Wādī al-Ham 166-167 HJ 2
Wādī al Ḥamḍ 134-135 D 5
Wādī al Ḥammāl = Wādī 'Ajaj 136-137 J 5
Wādī al-Ḥasā [JOR, Al-Karak] 136-137 F 7
Wādī al-Ḥasā [JOR, Ma'ān] 136-137 G 7
Wādī al-Ḥaṭab 173 C 7
Wādī al-Ḥazimī 136-137 J 6
Wādī al-Hilālī 136-137 J 7
Wādī al-Hirr 136-137 K 7
Wādī al-Ḥizimī = Wādī al-Ḥazimī 136-137 J 6
Wādī al-'Ifāl 173 D 3
Wādī al-Jadaf 134-135 E 4
Wādī al-Jarā' 166-167 H 6
Wādī al-Jizl 134-135 D 5
Wādī al-Karīmah 166-167 F 3
Wādī al-Kharīṭ 173 CD 5
Wādī al-Khirr 134-135 E 4
Wādī al-Khurr = Wādī al-Khirr 136-137 K 7
Wādī al-Makhrūq 136-137 G 7
Wādī al-Malik 164-165 KL 5
Wādī al-Mānī' 136-137 J 5-6
Wādī al-Masīlah 134-135 F 7
Wādī al-Mirā' 136-137 HJ 7
Wādī al-Mitlā 166-167 K 2
Wādī al-Miyāh 173 C 5
Wādī al-Miyāh = Wādī Jarīr 134-135 E 5-6
Wādī al-Qaṣab 136-137 K 4-5
Wādī al-Quffah 173 C 6
Wādī al-Ubayyiḍ 136-137 K 6
Wādī al-'Unnāb 136-137 G 7-8
Wādī al-Wirāj 173 B 3
Wādī 'Āmīj 136-137 J 6
Wādī an-Nāmūs 164-165 D 2
Wādī an-Naṭrūn 173 AB 2
Wādī an-Nisā' 166-167 J 3
Wādī 'Arabah 173 C 3
Wādī 'Ar'ar 136-137 J 7
Wādī ar-Ratam 166-167 J 3
Wādī ar-Ratka = Wādī ar-Ratqah 136-137 J 5-6
Wādī ar-Ratqah 136-137 J 5-6
Wādī ar-Rimah 134-135 E 5
Wādī ash-Sharmah = Wādī Ṣadr 173 D 3
Wādī ash-Shāzī 136-137 J 7
Wādī aṣ-Ṣahbā' 134-135 F 6
Wādī aṣ-Ṣawāb 136-137 J 5
Wādī as-Sāwrah 164-165 D 2-3
Wādī as Sirḥān 134-135 D 4
Wādī Asūf Malān 166-167 H 7
Wādī Athmāniyah 166-167 JK 1
Wādī ath-Tharthār 136-137 K 5
Wādī 'Aṭṭār 166-167 J 2
Wādī aṭ-Ṭarfā' 173 B 3
Wādī at-Tartār 136-137 K 5
Wādī at-Tawīl 166-167 H 2
Wādī at-Tubal 136-137 J 6
Wadi Azawak = Azaouak 164-165 E 5
Wādī Aẓlam 173 DE 4
Wādī az-Zargah 166-167 L 1
Wādī az-Zarqūn 166-167 H 3
Wādī Bad' 173 C 3
Wādī Bā'ir 136-137 G 7
Wādī Bay al-Kabīr 164-165 GH 2
Wādī Bayzaḥ 173 C 5
Wādī Bēzah = Wādī Bayzaḥ 173 C 5
Wādī Bīshah 134-135 E 6-7
Wādī Damā 173 DE 4
Wādī Di'īb 173 DE 6-7
Wādī Dufayt 173 D 6
Wādī Elei = Wādī Ilay 173 D 7
Wādī el-Kharīṭ = Wādī al-Kharīṭ 173 CD 5
Wādī el-Makhiruq = Wādī al-Makhrūq 136-137 G 7
Wadi el Melik = Wādī al-Malik 164-165 KL 5
Wādī el Milk = Wādī al-Malik 164-165 KL 5
Wādī el-'Unāb = Wādī al-'Unnāb 136-137 G 7-8
Wādī Fajr 134-135 D 5
Wādī Ghadūn 134-135 G 7
Wādī Gīr 166-167 E 4
Wādī Ḥabīb 173 BC 4
Wādī Ḥaḍramaut = Wādī al-Musīlah 134-135 FG 7
Wādī Ḥalfā 164-165 L 4
Wādī Ḥalfin 134-135 H 6
Wādī Ḥamar 136-137 H 4
Wādī Ḥamīr [IRQ] 136-137 JK 7
Wādī Ḥamīr [Saudi Arabia] 136-137 J 7
Wādī Ḥanīfah 134-135 F 6
Wādī Ḥawashīyah 173 C 3
Wādī Ḥawrān 134-135 E 4
Wādī Ḥaymūr 173 C 6
Wādī Ḥōḍein = Wādī Ḥuḍayn 173 D 6
Wādī Ḥōrān = Wādī Ḥawrān 134-135 E 4
Wādī Ḥubāra = Wādī al-Asyūṭī 173 B 4
Wādī Ḥuḍayn 173 D 6
Wādī Huwār 164-165 K 5
Wādī Ibib 173 D 6
Wādī Ilay 173 D 7
Wādī Imirhu 166-167 L 7
Wādī Iṭal 166-167 J 2-3
Wādī Jabjabah 173 C 7
Wādī Jaddī 164-165 E 2
Wādī Jafū 166-167 H 4
Wādī Jaghiagh 136-137 J 4
Wādī Jarārah 173 D 6
Wādī Jarīr 134-135 E 5-6
Wadi Jemal Island = Jazirat Wādī Jimāl 173 D 5
Wādī Jimāl 173 D 5
Wādī Jimāl, Jazīrat — 173 D 5
Wādī Jurdī 173 C 4
Wādī Kuruskū 173 C 6
Wādī Ma'ārik 136-137 H 7
Wādī Marsā 166-167 J 1
Wādī Mazār 166-167 G 3
Wādī Milāḥah 173 C 4
Wādī Mīnā 166-167 G 2
Wādī Miyāh 164-165 EF 2
Wādī Mizā 166-167 J 3
Wādī Muḥammadī 136-137 K 6
Wādī Mūs'ūd 166-167 F 5-6
Wādī Natash 173 CD 5
Wād Ināwin 166-167 D 2
Wādī 'Or = Wādī Ur 173 B 6-7
Wādī Qabīt = Wādī Qitbīt 134-135 G 7
Wādī Qaṣab 173 C 4
Wādī Qenā = Wādī Qinā 173 C 4
Wādī Qinā 173 C 4
Wādī Qiraiya = Wādī Qurayyah 173 D 2
Wādī Qitbīt 134-135 G 7
Wādī Qurayyah 173 D 2
Wādī Rāhīyu 166-167 G 2
Wādī Raiāītīt = Wādī Rayāytīt 173 D 6
Wādī Ranyah 134-135 E 6
Wādī Rayāytīt 173 D 6
Wādī Ṣadr 173 D 3
Wādī Sannūr 173 B 3
Wādī Ṣayq 134-135 F 8
Wādī Shahan = Wādī Shiḥan 134-135 G 7
Wādī Sha'īt 173 C 5
Wādī Shanāshīn 166-167 E 7
Wādī Shiḥan 134-135 G 7
Wādī Sīdī Mūsā 166-167 J 6
Wādī Sidr 173 C 3
Wādī Sudr = Wādī Sidr 173 C 3
Wādī Tafāsasat 164-165 F 4
Wādī Tākwayat 164-165 E 4
Wādī Tamajirdayn 166-167 G 7
Wādī Tamanrāsat 164-165 E 4
Wādī Tanārūt 166-167 M 4-5
Wādī Tanizzuft 166-167 M 7
Wādī Tarāt 164-165 F 3
Wādī Tathlīth 134-135 E 6-7
Wādī Thalāthah 166-167 F 2
Wādī Tibell = Wādī at-Tubal 136-137 J 6
Wādī Tilayah 166-167 G 6
Wādī Tīn Tarābīn 164-165 F 4
Wādī Tyārīt 166-167 LM 4
Wādī 'Ukāsh 136-137 J 5-6
Wādī Ur 173 B 6-7
Wādī Wardān 173 C 3
Wādī Yassar 166-167 H 1
Wādī Zāghrīr 166-167 J 3
Wādī Zamzam 164-165 G 2
Wādī Zaydūn 173 C 5
Wādī Zeidūn = Wādī Zaydūn 173 C 5
Wādī Zusfānah 166-167 EF 4
Wadki 138-139 G 7
Wād Lāū' [MA, place] 166-167 D 2
Wadley, GA 80-81 E 4
Wād Madanī 164-165 L 6
Wad Majradah 164-165 F 1
Wād Mallāg 166-167 L 1-2
Wād Milyān 166-167 LM 1
Wād Mūlūyā 164-165 D 2
Wād Nafīs 166-167 B 4
Wād Nūn 166-167 A 5
Wād S'bū' 164-165 CD 2
Wād Sharīf 166-167 E 3
Wād Silyānah 166-167 L 1-2
Wād Sūs 166-167 B 4
Wadsworth, NV 74-75 D 3
Wād Taghbālt 166-167 D 4
Wād Tamanārt 166-167 B 5
Wad Tansīft 164-165 C 2
Wād Ṭāṭah 166-167 B 5
Wād Tissāūt 166-167 C 4
Wād Tudghā' 166-167 D 4
Wadu Channel 176 a 2
Wād Umm ar-Rabīyah 164-165 C 2
Wād Warghah 166-167 D 2
Wād Zam 164-165 C 2
Wād Zimūl 166-167 C 5
Wād Zīz 166-167 D 4
Wād Zurūd 166-167 LM 2
Waegwan 144-145 G 4-5
Waelder, TX 76-77 F 8
Wa-fang-tien = Fu Xian 142-143 N 4
Wagal-bong = Maengbu-san 144-145 F 2
Wāgeima 141 D 7
Wageningen [SME] 92-93 H 3
Wager Bay 56-57 T 4
Waggaman, LA 85 I a 2
Wagga Wagga 158-159 J 7
Wagin 158-159 C 6
Wagina 148-149 j 6
Wagner, SD 68-69 G 4
Wagoner, OK 76-77 G 5
Wagon Mound, NM 76-77 B 4
Wagontire, OR 66-67 D 4
Wągrowiec 118 H 2
Waḥah 164-165 H 3
Wahai 148-149 J 7
Wāḥāt ad-Dākhilah 164-165 K 3
Wāḥāt al-'Aṭrūn 164-165 K 5
Wāḥāt al-Baḥarīyah 164-165 K 3
Wāḥāt al-Farāfirah 164-165 K 3
Wāḥāt al-Jufrah 164-165 GH 3
Wāḥāt al-Kufrah 164-165 J 4
Wāhāt el Cufra = Wāḥāt al-Kufrah 164-165 J 4
Wāḥāt el-Khārga = Al-Wāḥāt al-Khārijah 164-165 KL 3-4
Wāḥat es Selīma = Wāḥāt Ṣalīmah 164-165 K 4
Wāḥāt Jālū 164-165 J 3
Wāḥāt Ṣalīmah 164-165 K 4
Wāḥāt Sīwah 164-165 K 3
Wahilah 166-167 D 6
Wahlbergøya 116-117 k 5
Wahlenbergfjord 116-117 kl 5
Wahoo, NE 68-69 H 5
Wahpeton, ND 68-69 H 2
Wahrān 164-165 D 1
Wahrān, Khalīj — 166-167 F 2
Wah Wah Mountains 74-75 G 3
Wai 140 A 1-2
Waialua, HI 78-79 c 2
Waianae, HI 78-79 c 2
Waiau 161 E 6
Waiau River 161 E 6
Waidhofen an der Thaya 118 G 4
Waidmannslust, Berlin- 130 III b 1
Waifang Shan 146-147 C 5-D 4
Waigama 148-149 JK 7
Waigeo, Pulau — 148-149 K 6
Waigev = Pulau Waigeo 148-149 K 6
Waiheke Island 161 F 3
Waihi Beach 161 FG 3
Waihou River 161 F 3-4
Waikabubak 148-149 G 8
Waikaremoana, Lake — 161 G 4
Waikawa 161 CD 8
Waikerie 158-159 GH 6
Waimate 158-159 O 8
Waimea, HI [USA, Hawaii] 78-79 e 2-3
Waimea, HI [USA, Kanai] 78-79 c 2
Wai Mesuji 152-153 F 7-8
Wainganga 134-135 MN 6-7
Waingapu 148-149 GH 8
Waingapu, Teluk — 152-153 O 10
Waingmau 141 E 3
Waingmaw = Waingmau 141 E 3
Waini Point 92-93 H 3
Wainwright 61 C 4
Wainwright, AK 56-57 DE 3
Waipahu, HI 78-79 c 2
Waipara 161 E 6
Waipukurau 161 G 4-5
Wairāgarh 138-139 H 7
Wairau River 161 E 5
Wairoa 158-159 P 7
Wai Silumpur 152-153 F 7
Waitaki River 158-159 O 8
Waitara 158-159 OP 7
Waitarini = Baitarani 138-139 KL 7
Waitsap = Huaiji 142-143 L 7
Waitsburg, WA 66-67 D 2
Wai Tulangbawang 152-153 F 8
Waiwerang 152-153 P 10
Waiyeung = Huiyang 142-143 LM 7
Wajh, Al- 134-135 D 5
Wajima 144-145 L 4
Wak, El — 172 H 1
Waka 172 D 2
Wakamatsu = Aizu-Wakamatsu 144-145 M 4
Wakamatsu-shima 144-145 G 6
Wakamiya, Ichikawa- 155 III c 1
Wakasa 144-145 K 5
Wakasa-wan 144-145 K 5
Wakatipu, Lake — 161 C 7
Wakaw 61 F 4
Wakayama 142-143 Q 5
Wake 156-157 H 4
Wa Keeney, KS 68-69 G 6
Wakefield, KS 68-69 H 6
Wakefield, MA 84 I b 1
Wakefield, MI 70-71 F 2
Wakefield, NE 68-69 H 4
Wakefield, New York-, NY 82 III cd 1
Wake Forest, NC 80-81 G 3
Wakeham = Maricourt 56-57 W 5
Wakema = Wāgeima 141 D 7
Wākhān 134-135 L 3
Wākhjīr, Koṭal — 134-135 LM 3
Waki 140 A 1
Wakinosawa 144-145 N 2
Wakkanai 142-143 R 2
Wakkerstroom 174-175 J 4
Wakō 155 III a 1
Wakomata Lake 70-71 J 2
Wakool 160 G 5
Wākṣa = Wāqiṣah 136-137 K 7
Wakunai 148-149 j 6
Wakwayowkastic River 62 L 1-2
Walad Bū 'Alī 166-167 M 2
Walad Ghalal 166-167 J 2
Walahae, Sungai — 152-153 NO 8
Wālājāpet 140 D 4
Walakpa, AK 58-59 HJ 1
Wa'lan 164-165 E 4
Walapai, AZ 74-75 G 5
Walasmula 140 E 7
Walātah 164-165 C 5
Walātah, Ḍhar — 164-165 C 5
Walawē Ganga 140 E 7
Wałbrzych 118 H 3
Walcha 160 KL 3
Walcheren 120-121 J 3
Walcott 60 D 2
Walcott, ND 68-69 H 2
Walcott, WY 68-69 C 5
Wałcz 118 H 2
Waldacker 128 III b 1
Waldegg [CH] 128 IV a 1
Walden, CO 68-69 CD 5
Waldenau-Datum 130 I a 1
Walden Pond 84 I c 2
Walden Ridge 78-79 G 3
Waldfriedhof München 130 II ab 2
Waldhofen an der Ybbs 118 G 5
Waldo, AR 78-79 C 4
Waldo, FL 80-81 bc 2
Waldpark Marienhöhe 130 I a 1
Waldperlach, München- 130 II bc 2
Waldport, OR 66-67 A 3
Waldron, AR 76-77 GH 5
Waldstadion 128 III ab 1
Walea, Selat — 152-153 P 6
Wales, AK 56-57 C 4
Wales, MN 70-71 E 2
Wales Island 56-57 T 4
Walfergem 128 II a 1
Walgaon 138-139 F 7
Walgett 158-159 J 6
Walgreen Coast 53 B 26
Walhalla, MI 70-71 GH 3
Walhalla, ND 68-69 H 1
Walhalla, SC 80-81 E 3
Wālidīyah 166-167 B 3
Waligiro 171 DE 3
Walikale 172 E 2
Walker, MN 70-71 C 2
Walker, SD 68-69 F 3
Walkerbaai 174-175 C 8
Walker Bay = Walkerbaai 174-175 C 8
Walker Cove 58-59 x 9
Walker Lake [CDN] 61 K 3
Walker Lake [USA] 64-65 C 4
Walker Mountain 80-81 F 2
Walker Mountains 53 B 26-27
Walker River Indian Reservation 74-75 D 3
Walkerton 72-73 F 2
Walkerton, IN 70-71 G 5
Walkerville, MT 66-67 G 2
Walkite = Welkītē 164-165 M 7
Wall, SD 68-69 E 3-4
Wallace 72-73 GH 2
Wallace, ID 66-67 EF 2
Wallace, MI 70-71 G 3
Wallace, NC 80-81 GH 3
Wallace, NE 68-69 F 5
Wallaceburg 72-73 E 3
Wallal Downs 158-159 D 3-4
Wallangarra 160 KL 2
Wallaroo 158-159 G 6
Wallasey 119 E 5
Walla Walla, WA 64-65 C 2
Wallekraal 174-175 B 6
Wallel = Tulu Welēl 164-165 LM 7
Wallīj, Sha'īb al- 136-137 H 6
Wallingford, CT 72-73 K 4
Wallingford, PA 84 III a 2
Wallington, NJ 82 III b 1
Wallington, London- 129 II b 2
Wallis, TX 76-77 F 8
Wallis, Îles — 148-149 b 1
Wall Lake, IA 70-71 C 4
Wallowa, OR 66-67 E 3
Wallowa Mountains 66-67 E 3
Wallowa River 66-67 E 3
Wallula, WA 66-67 D 2
Walmer 174-175 F 7
Walney 119 E 4
Walnut, IL 70-71 F 5
Walnut, KS 70-71 C 7

Walnut, MS 78-79 E 3
Walnut Bend, Houston-, TX 85 III a 2
Walnut Canyon National Monument 74-75 H 5
Walnut Cove, NC 80-81 F 2
Walnut Creek 68-69 F 6
Walnut Grove, MO 70-71 D 7
Walnut Grove, MS 78-79 E 4
Walnut Park, CA 83 III c 2
Walnut Ridge, AR 78-79 D 2
Walod = Vālod 138-139 D 7
Walpole 158-159 NO 4
Walpole, NH 72-73 K 3
Walrus Islands 58-59 GH 7
Walsall 119 F 5
Walsenburg, CO 68-69 D 7
Walsh 158-159 H 3
Walsh, CO 68-69 E 7
Waltair 140 F 2
Walterboro, SC 80-81 F 4
Walter D. Stone Memorial Zoo 84 I b 2
Walter Reed Army Medical Center 82 II ab 1
Walters, OK 76-77 E 5
Waltersdorf [DDR] 130 III c 2
Waltershof, Hamburg- 130 I a 1
Waltham 72-73 H 2
Waltham Forest, London- 129 II bc 1
Walthamstow, London- 129 II b 1
Walthill, NE 68-69 H 4
Waltman, WY 68-69 C 4
Walton, IN 70-71 G 5
Walton, KY 70-71 H 6
Walton, NY 72-73 J 3
Walton-on-Thames 129 II a 2
Walton Run 84 III d 1
Walt Whiteman Homes, NJ 84 III bc 2
Walt Withman Bridge 84 III c 2
Walvisbaai [ZA, bay] 174-175 A 2
Walvisbaai [ZA, place] 172 B 6
Walvis Bay = Walvisbaai [ZA, bay] 174-175 A 2
Walvis Bay = Walvisbaai [ZA, place] 172 B 6
Walvis Ridge 50-51 K 7
Wamanfo 168-169 E 4
Wamba [EAK] 171 D 2
Wamba [WAN] 164-165 F 7
Wamba [ZRE, Bandundu] 172 C 3
Wamba [ZRE, Haut-Zaïre] 172 E 1
Wamego, KS 68-69 H 6
Wami 172 G 3
Wamlana 148-149 J 7
Wampū 88-89 D 7
Wanaaring 158-159 H 5
Wanaka, Lake — 161 C 7
Wan'an 146-147 E 8
Wanapiri 148-149 L 7
Wanapitei Lake 72-73 F 1
Wanapitei River 72-73 F 1
Wan Chai, Victoria- 155 I ab 2
Wanchuan = Zhangjiakou 142-143 L 3
Wanda 102-103 E 7
Wandarama 168-169 DE 3
Wanda Shan 142-143 P 2
Wandawasi = Wandiwāsh 140 D 4
Wandering River 60 L 2
Wandingzhen 141 EF 3
Wandiwāsh 140 D 4
Wandle 129 II b 2
Wan-do 144-145 F 5
Wandoan 158-159 JK 5
Wandse 130 I b 1
Wandsworth, London- 129 II b 2
Wanfu 144-145 D 2
Wanfu He 146-147 F 4
Wang, Mae Nam — 150-151 B 3
Wanganella 160 G 5
Wanganui 158-159 OP 7
Wanganui River 161 F 4
Wangaratta 158-159 J 7
Wangary 160 B 5
Wangasi 168-169 E 3
Wang-chia-ch'ang = Wangjiachang 146-147 C 7
Wang-chiang = Wangjiang 146-147 F 6
Wang Chin 150-151 B 4
Wangdu 146-147 E 2
Wangen [CH] 128 IV b 1
Wangen [D] 130 II a 2
Wangener Wald 128 IV b 1
Wanggamet, Gunung — 152-153 NO 10-11
Wangi 171 E 3
Wangiwangi, Pulau — 152-153 PQ 8
Wangjiachang 146-147 C 7
Wangjiang 146-147 F 6
Wangkiang = Wangjiang 146-147 F 6
Wang Lan 155 I b 2
Wangmudu 146-147 E 9
Wang Nua 150-151 B 3
Wangpang Yang 142-143 N 5
Wangpan Yang 146-147 H 6
Wang Saphung 150-151 CD 4
Wang Thong 150-151 C 4
Wangtu = Wangdu 146-147 E 2
Wangyemiao = Ulan Hot 142-143 N 2
Wanhsien = Wan Xian [TJ, Hebei] 146-147 E 2
Wanhsien = Wan Xian [TJ, Sichuan] 142-143 K 5
Wani, Gunung — 152-153 P 8
Wānkāner 138-139 C 6
Wankie = Hwange 172 E 5
Wankie National Park 172 E 5
Wanleweeyn 164-165 NO 8
Wannian 146-147 F 7
Wanning 142-143 L 8
Wannsee 130 III a 2
Wannsee, Berlin- 130 III a 2
Wanon Niwat 150-151 D 4
Wanparti 140 D 2
Wanshan Liehtao = Wanshan Qundao 146-147 DE 11
Wanshan Qundao 146-147 DE 11
Wanstead, London- 129 II c 1
Wantan 146-147 C 6
Wan-ta Shan-mo = Wanda Shan 142-143 P 2
Want'ing = Wandingzhen 141 EF 3
Wantsai = Wanzai 142-143 LM 6
Wan Xian [TJ, Hebei] 146-147 E 2
Wan Xian [TJ, Sichuan] 146-147 B 6
Wanyuan 146-147 B 5
Wanzai 142-143 LM 6
Wanzhi 146-147 G 6
Wapakoneta, OH 70-71 HJ 5
Wapanucka, OK 76-77 F 5
Wapato, WA 66-67 C 2
Wapawekka Lake 61 FG 3
Wapello, IA 70-71 E 5
Wapi = Mu'o'ng Wapi 150-151 EF 5
Wapikham Tong 150-151 E 5
Wapi Pathum 150-151 D 5
Wapiti, WY 68-69 B 3
Wapiti River 60 GH 2
Wapsipinicon River 70-71 E 5
Wa-pu He = Wabu Hu 146-147 F 5
Waqbā, Al- 136-137 L 8
Waqf, Al- 173 C 4
Wāqif, Jabal al- 173 B 6
Wāqiṣah 136-137 K 7
Waqooyi-Galbeed 164-165 a 1
War, WV 80-81 F 2
Wārāh 138-139 A 4
Warān 164-165 BC 4
Warangal 134-135 MN 7
Wārāseoni 138-139 H 7
Waratah 160 b 2
Waratah Bay 160 GH 7
Warba, MN 70-71 D 2
Warburton [AUS, place] 160 G 6
Warburton [AUS, river] 158-159 G 5
Wardah, Rā's al- 166-167 L 1
Wardān, Wādī — 173 C 3
Ward Cove, AK 58-59 x 9
Warden 174-175 H 4
Warden, WA 66-67 D 2
Wardere = Werdër 164-165 O 7
Wardha [IND, place] 134-135 M 6
Wardha [IND, river] 134-135 M 6
Ward Hunt, Cape — 148-149 N 8
Wardlow 61 C 5
Ware 56-57 LM 6
Ware, MA 72-73 KL 3
Waren [DDR] 118 F 2
Waren [RI] 148-149 L 7
Warghah, Wād — 166-167 D 2
Wari'ah, Al- 134-135 F 5
Warialda 158-159 K 5
Warin Chamrap 148-149 DE 3
Waring Mountains 58-59 GH 3
Waritchaphum 150-151 D 4
Wāriyapola 140 E 7
Warland, MT 66-67 F 1
Warman 61 E 4
Warmbad [Namibia, administrative unit] 174-175 BC 5
Warmbad [Namibia, place] 172 C 7
Warmbad [ZA] 172 E 6-7
Warmsprings, MT 66-67 G 2
Warm Springs, OR 66-67 C 3
Warm Springs, NV [USA ↓ Cherry Creek] 74-75 F 3
Warm Springs, NV [USA → Tonopah] 74-75 EF 3
Warm Springs Indian Reservation 66-67 C 3
Warm Springs Valley 66-67 C 5
Warnemünde, Rostock- 118 F 1
Warner 66-67 GH 1
Warner, SD 68-69 G 3
Warner Range 64-65 B 3
Warner Robins, GA 64-65 K 5
Warner Valley 66-67 CD 4
Warnes [BOL] 92-93 G 8
Warnes [RA] 106-107 G 5
Waropko 148-149 LM 8
Warora 138-139 G 7
Warpath River 61 J 4
Warqlā 164-165 F 2
Wārqzīz, Jabal — 164-165 C 3
Warra 158-159 K 5
Warracknabeal 160 F 6
Warragul 160 G 7
Warrāq al-'Arab 170 II b 1
Warraq al-Hadar, Jazīrah — 170 II b 1
Warrego River 158-159 J 5
Warren, AR 78-79 CD 4
Warren, AZ 74-75 J 7
Warren, ID 66-67 F 3
Warren, IL 70-71 EF 4
Warren, IN 70-71 H 5
Warren, MI 72-73 E 3
Warren, MN 68-69 H 1
Warren, OH 64-65 K 3
Warren, PA 72-73 G 4
Warren, TX 76-77 G 7
Warren [AUS] 160 HJ 3
Warren [CDN] 72-73 F 1
Warren Landing 61 J 4
Warrensburg, MO 70-71 CD 6
Warrenton 172 DE 7
Warrenton, GA 80-81 E 4
Warrenton, MO 70-71 E 6
Warrenton, NC 80-81 GH 2
Warrenton, OR 66-67 AB 2
Warrenton, VA 72-73 H 5
Warri 164-165 F 7
Warriner Creek 160 BC 2
Warrington, FL 78-79 F 5
Warrior, AL 78-79 F 4
Warrnambool 158-159 H 7
Warroad, MN 70-71 C 1
Warsaw, IL 70-71 E 5
Warsaw, IN 70-71 H 5
Warsaw, KY 70-71 H 6
Warsaw, MO 70-71 D 6
Warsaw, NC 80-81 GH 3
Warsaw, NY 72-73 GH 3
Warsaw = Warszawa 118 K 2
Wārshanīs, Jabal al- [DZ, mountain] 166-167 G 1-2
Wārshanīs, Jabal al- [DZ, mountains] 166-167 GH 2
Warszawa 118 K 2
Warta 118 HJ 2
Wartenberg, Berlin- 130 III c 1
Warton, Monte — 108-109 C 9
Wartrace, TN 78-79 F 3
Warud 138-139 FG 7
Warwick, GA 80-81 DE 5
Warwick, RI 72-73 L 4
Warwick [AUS] 158-159 K 5
Warwick [GB] 119 EF 5
Warwisch, Hamburg- 130 I b 2
Warzazāt 166-167 C 4
Wasa 60 K 5
Wasatch, UT 66-67 H 5
Wasatch Range 64-65 D 3-4
Wasbank 174-175 J 5
Wascana Creek 61 F 5
Waschbank = Wasbank 174-175 J 5
Wasco, CA 74-75 D 5
Wasco, OR 66-67 C 3
Wase 168-169 H 3
Waseca, MN 70-71 D 3
Wash, The — 119 G 5
Washago 72-73 G 2
Washakie Needles 68-69 B 4
Wāshaung 141 E 3
Washburn, ND 68-69 F 2
Washburn, TX 76-77 D 5
Washburn, WI 70-71 E 2
Washburn Lake 56-57 PQ 3
Washington, AK 58-59 vw 8
Washington, AR 76-77 GH 6
Washington, DC 64-65 LM 4
Washington, GA 80-81 E 4
Washington, IA 70-71 DE 5
Washington, IN 70-71 G 6
Washington, KS 68-69 H 6
Washington, MO 70-71 E 6
Washington, NC 80-81 H 3
Washington, PA 72-73 F 4
Washington [RA] 106-107 E 4
Washington [USA] 64-65 BC 2
Washington, Mount — 64-65 M 3
Washington-Anacostia, DC 82 II b 2
Washington-Bellevue, DC 82 II a 2
Washington-Brightwood, DC 82 II a 1
Washington-Brookland, DC 82 II b 1
Washington-Burleith, DC 82 II a 1
Washington-Capitol Hill, DC 82 II ab 2
Washington Cemetery 85 III b 1
Washington-Cleveland Park, DC 82 II a 1
Washington-Columbia Heights, DC 82 II a 1
Washington-Congress Heights, DC 82 II b 2
Washington-Deanewood, DC 82 II b 2
Washington-Eckington, DC 82 II ab 1
Washington-Georgetown, DC 82 II a 1
Washington-Glendale, DC 82 II b 2
Washington-Good Hope, DC 82 II b 2
Washington Island 70-71 G 3
Washington-Kent, DC 82 II a 1
Washington-Lamond, DC 82 II a 1
Washington-Langdon, DC 82 II b 1
Washington Monument 82 II a 2
Washington National Airport 82 II a 2
Washington Naval Station 82 II ab 2
Washington Park [USA, Atlanta] 85 II b 2
Washington Park [USA, Chicago] 83 II b 2
Washington-Tenleytown, DC 82 II a 1
Washington-Trinidad, DC 82 II b 2
Washington Virginia Airport 82 II a 2
Washita River 64-65 G 4-5
Washm, Al- 134-135 EF 5-6
Washow Bay 62 A 2
Wash Shahri 142-143 F 4
Wasilla, AK 58-59 N 6
Wasior 148-149 KL 7
Wasipe 168-169 E 3
Wāsit 136-137 L 6
Wāsiṭah, Al- 164-165 L 3
Waskada 68-69 F 1
Waskaiowaka Lake 61 K 2
Waskatenau 60 L 2
Waskesiu Lake 61 F 4
Waskish, MN 70-71 C 1
Waskom, TX 76-77 G 6
Wassamu 144-145 c 1-2
Wassberg 128 IV b 1
Wasser 174-175 C 4
Wassmannsdorf 130 III bc 2
Wassuk Range 74-75 D 3
Wasta, SD 68-69 E 3
Wasum 148-149 g 6
Waswanipi 62 N 2
Waswanipi, Lac — 62 N 2
Watabeag Lake 62 L 2
Watampone 148-149 GH 7
Watansoppeng 148-149 G 7
Wataru Channel 176 a 2
Wat Bot 150-151 C 4
Watchung Mountain 82 III a 1
Watcomb 62 D 3
Waterberg 172 C 6
Waterberge 174-175 GH 3
Waterbury, CT 72-73 K 4
Wateree River 80-81 F 3
Waterfall, AK 58-59 w 9
Waterford, CA 74-75 C 4
Waterford [CDN] 72-73 F 3
Waterford [IRL] 119 C 5
Waterford [ZA] 174-175 F 7
Watergang 128 I b 1
Waterhen Lake [CDN, Manitoba] 61 J 4
Waterhen Lake [CDN, Saskatchewan] 61 DE 3
Waterhen River 61 D 3
Waterkloof 174-175 F 6
Waterloo, IA 64-65 H 3
Waterloo, IL 70-71 EF 6
Waterloo, MT 66-67 G 3
Waterloo, NY 72-73 H 3
Waterloo [AUS] 158-159 EF 3
Waterloo [B] 120-121 K 3
Waterloo [CDN, Ontario] 72-73 F 3
Waterloo [CDN, Quebec] 72-73 K 2
Waterloo [WAL] 168-169 B 3
Waterpoort 174-175 H 2
Waterproff, LA 78-79 D 5
Waters, MI 70-71 H 3
Watersmeet, MI 70-71 F 2
Waterton Lakes National Park 60 KL 5
Waterton Park 60 KL 5
Watertown, MA 84 I ab 2
Watertown, NY 64-65 LM 3
Watertown, SD 64-65 G 2
Watertown, WI 70-71 F 4
Waterval-Boven 174-175 J 3
Water Valley, MS 78-79 E 3
Water Valley, TX 76-77 D 7
Waterval-Onder 174-175 J 3
Waterville, KS 68-69 H 6
Waterville, ME 64-65 N 3
Waterville, MN 70-71 D 3
Waterville, WA 66-67 CD 2
Waterways 56-57 OP 6
Waterworks Park 84 II c 2
Watford City, ND 68-69 E 2
Watganj, Calcutta- 154 II a 2
Wathaman River 61 G 2
Watino 60 J 2
Watkins Glen, NY 72-73 H 3
Watkinsville, GA 80-81 E 4
Watlam = Yulin 142-143 L 7
Watling Island = San Salvador 64-65 M 7
Watonga, OK 76-77 E 5
Watrous 61 F 5
Watrous, NM 76-77 B 5
Watsa 172 E 1
Watseka, IL 70-71 G 5
Wat Sing 150-151 BC 5
Watson 61 F 4
Watson, AR 78-79 D 4
Watson, UT 74-75 J 3
Watson Lake 56-57 L 5
Watsonville, CA 74-75 BC 4
Watt 128 IV a 1
Watt, Mount — 158-159 E 5
Wattegama 140 E 7
Watthana Nakhon 150-151 D 6
Watts, Los Angeles-, CA 83 III c 2
Watts Bar Lake 78-79 G 3
Watubela, Pulau-pulau — 148-149 K 7
Watu Bella Islands = Pulau-pulau Watubela 148-149 K 7
Watupayung, Tanjung — 152-153 P 10
Wau 148-149 N 8
Waubay, SD 68-69 H 3
Wauchope 160 L 3
Wauchula, FL 80-81 bc 3
Wau el Kebir = Wāw al-Kabīr 164-165 H 3
Wau en Namus = Wāw an-Nāmūs 164-165 H 4
Waugh 62 B 3
Waukarlycarly, Lake — 158-159 D 4
Waukeenah, FL 80-81 DE 5
Waukegan, IL 70-71 G 4
Waukesha, WI 70-71 F 4
Waukon, IA 70-71 E 4
Wauneta, NE 68-69 F 5
Waupaca, WI 70-71 F 3
Waupun, WI 70-71 F 4
Waurika, OK 76-77 F 5
Wausa, NE 68-69 H 4
Wausau, WI 64-65 J 2-3
Wausaukee, WI 70-71 FG 3
Wausawng = Wāshaung 141 E 3
Wauseon, OH 70-71 HJ 5
Wauthier-Braine 128 II a 2
Wautoma, WI 70-71 F 3
Wauwatosa, WI 70-71 F 4
Wav = Văv 138-139 C 5
Wave Hill 158-159 F 3
Waver 128 I a 2
Waverley 174-175 G 6
Waverly, IA 70-71 D 4
Waverly, NY 72-73 H 3
Waverly, OH 72-73 E 5
Waverly, SD 68-69 H 3
Waverly, TN 78-79 F 2
Waverly, VA 80-81 H 2
Waverly, Sydney- 161 I b 2
Waverly Hall, GA 78-79 G 4
Waverveen 128 I a 2
Wavre 128 II b 2
Waw [BUR] 141 E 7
Wāw [Sudan] 164-165 K 7
Wawa 70-71 H 1-2
Wawagosic, Rivière — 62 M 2
Wawaitin Falls 62 L 2
Wāw al-Kabīr 164-165 H 3
Waw an-Nāmūs 164-165 H 4
Wawina 88-89 D 7
Wāwīzaght 166-167 C 3
Wawota 61 GH 6
Waxahachie, TX 76-77 F 6
Waxell Ridge 56-57 H 5
Way, Hon — 150-151 D 8
Way, Lake — 158-159 D 5
Wayan, ID 66-67 H 4
Wayang Satu, Singapore- 154 III ab 2
Waycross, GA 64-65 K 5
Wayland, KY 80-81 E 2
Wayland, MI 70-71 H 4
Wayne, NE 68-69 H 4
Wayne, PA 84 III a 1
Wayne, WV 72-73 E 5
Waynesboro, GA 80-81 EF 4
Waynesboro, MS 78-79 E 5
Waynesboro, PA 72-73 H 5
Waynesboro, TN 78-79 F 3
Waynesboro, VA 72-73 G 5
Waynesburg, PA 72-73 FG 5
Wayne State University 84 II b 2
Waynesville, MO 70-71 DE 7
Waynesville, NC 80-81 E 3
Waynoka, OK 76-77 E 4
Wayside, TX 76-77 D 5
Waza 164-165 G 6
Wāza Khwā 134-135 K 4
Wāzin 166-167 M 4
Wāzīrābād = Balkh 134-135 K 3
Wazz, Al- 164-165 L 5
Wazzān 164-165 C 2
Wealdstone, London- 129 II a 1
Weapons Range 61 D 3
Weather, Punta — 108-109 B 4
Weatherford, OK 76-77 E 5
Weatherford, TX 76-77 F 6
Weaubleau, MO 70-71 D 7
Weaverville, CA 66-67 B 5
Webb 61 D 5
Webb, TX 76-77 E 9
Webbe Shibeli = Wābi Shebelē 164-165 N 7
Weber, Mount — 60 C 2
Webi Ganaane 164-165 N 8
Webi Jestro = Weyb 164-165 N 7
Webi Shabeelle 164-165 N 8
Webi Shabēlle = Wabī Shebelē 164-165 N 7
Webster 60 H 2
Webster, MA 72-73 KL 3
Webster, SD 68-69 H 3
Webster City, IA 70-71 D 4
Webster Reservoir 68-69 G 6
Webster Springs, WV 72-73 F 5
Weda 148-149 J 6
Weddell Island 111 D 8
Weddell Sea 156-157 PQ 8
Wedding, Berlin- 130 III b 1
Wed ed Daura = Wādī ad-Dawrah 166-167 DE 5
Wedel Jarlsberg land 116-117 j 6
Wedgeport 63 C 6
Wed Igharghar = Wādī Irhāran 166-167 J 6
Wed Mia = Wādī Miyāh 164-165 EF 2
Wed Mulula = Wād Mūlūyā 164-165 D 2
Wed Nun = Wād Nūn 166-167 A 5
Wedowee, AL 78-79 G 4
Wed Saura = Wādī as-Sāwrah 164-165 D 2-3
Wed Shenashan = Wādī Shanāshīn 166-167 E 7
Wed Zem = Wād Zam 164-165 C 2
Weed, CA 66-67 B 5
Weedon Centre 72-73 L 2
Weedville, PA 72-73 G 4
Weeks, LA 78-79 D 6
Weeksbury, KY 80-81 E 2
Weenen 174-175 J 5
Weenusk = Winisk 56-57 T 6
Weeping Water, NE 70-71 BC 5
Weerde 128 II b 1
Weesow 130 III c 1
Wee Waa 158-159 J 6
Wegendorf 130 III d 1
Wegener-Inlandeis 53 B 36-1
Weh, Pulau — 148-149 BC 5
Weichang 142-143 M 3
Weichou Tao = Weizhou Dao 146-147 B 11
Weiden 118 EF 4
Weidling 113 I b 1
Weifang 142-143 MN 4
Weigongcun, Beijing- 155 II ab 2
Weihai 142-143 N 4
Wei He [TJ ◁ Hai He] 142-143 M 4
Wei He [TJ ◁ Huang He] 142-143 K 5
Wei He [TJ ◁ Laizhou Wan] 146-147 G 3
Wei Ho = Wei He [TJ ◁ Hai He] 146-147 F 2
Wei Ho = Wei He [TJ ◁ Laizhou Wan] 146-147 G 3
Weihsien = Wei Xian 146-147 E 3
Wei-hsien = Yu Xian 146-147 E 2
Weilmoringle 160 H 2
Weimar 118 E 3
Weimar, TX 76-77 F 8
Weinan 146-147 B 4
Weiner, AR 78-79 D 3
Weining 142-143 JK 6
Weiningen 128 IV a 1
Weipa 158-159 H 2
Weir 138-139 G 4
Weir River 61 L 2
Weirton, WV 72-73 F 4
Weisburd 102-103 A 7
Weiser, ID 66-67 E 3
Weiser River 66-67 E 3
Weishan Hu 146-147 F 4
Weishi 146-147 E 4
Weisse Elster 118 F 3
Weissenfels 118 E 3
Weisskirchen [D] 128 III a 1
Weiss Knob 72-73 G 5
Weissrand Mountains = Witrandberge 174-175 C 3
Weitzel Lake 61 E 2
Weixi 141 F 2
Wei Xian [TJ, Hebei] 146-147 E 3
Wei Xian [TJ, Shandong] 146-147 G 3
Weiyang = Huiyang 142-143 LM 7
Weizhou Dao 146-147 B 11
Wejh = Al-Wajh 134-135 D 5
Wekusko 61 J 3
Wekusko Lake 61 J 3
Welaung 141 C 5
Welbourn Hill 158-159 F 5
Welch, TX 76-77 CD 6
Welch, WV 80-81 F 2
Welcome Monument 154 IV a 2
Weldon, NC 80-81 H 2
Weldona, CO 68-69 E 5
Weldon River 70-71 D 5
Weldya 164-165 M 6
Weleetka, OK 76-77 FG 5
Welega 164-165 LM 7
Welel, Tulu — 164-165 LM 7
Welgeleë 174-175 G 5
Welhe 140 A 1
Wēligama 140 E 7-8
Wēlimada 140 E 7
Welkītē 164-165 M 7
Welkom 172 E 7
Welland 72-73 G 3
Welland Canal 72-73 G 3
Wēllawāya 140 E 7
Wellesley Islands 158-159 GH 3
Wellesley Lake 58-59 RS 5
Wellingsbüttel, Hamburg- 130 I b 1
Wellington, CO 68-69 D 5
Wellington, KS 76-77 F 4
Wellington, NV 74-75 D 3
Wellington, OH 72-73 E 4
Wellington, TX 76-77 D 5
Wellington [AUS] 158-159 JK 6
Wellington [CDN] 72-73 H 3
Wellington [NZ, administrative unit] 161 F 4-G 5
Wellington [NZ, place] 158-159 OP 8
Wellington [ZA] 174-175 C 7
Wellington, Isla — 111 AB 7
Wellington Channel 56-57 S 2-3
Wellman, IA 70-71 E 5
Wellman, TX 76-77 C 6
Wells 60 G 3
Wells, MN 70-71 D 4
Wells, NE 68-69 F 4
Wells, NV 64-65 C 3
Wells, TX 76-77 G 7
Wells, Lake — 158-159 D 5
Wellsboro, PA 72-73 H 4
Wellsford 158-159 OP 7
Wells Gray Provincial Park 56-57 MN 7
Wells next the Sea 119 G 5
Wellston, OH 72-73 E 5
Wellsville, KS 70-71 C 6
Wellsville, MO 70-71 E 6
Wellsville, NY 72-73 H 3
Wellton, AZ 74-75 FG 6
Welo 164-165 MN 6
Wels 118 FG 4
Welsford 63 C 5
Welshpool 119 E 5
Wembere 172 F 2-3
Wembley 60 H 2
Wembley, London- 129 II a 1
Wembley Stadium [GB] 129 II a 1
Wembley Stadium [ZA] 170 V b 2
Wen'an 146-147 F 2
Wenasaga River 62 C 2
Wenatchee, WA 64-65 BC 2
Wenatchee Mountains 66-67 C 2
Wenchang 150-151 H 3
Wên-ch'ang = Wenchang 150-151 H 3
Wenchi 168-169 E 4
Wên-chou Wan = Wenzhou Wan 146-147 H 8
Wenchow = Wenzhou 142-143 N 6
Wendel, CA 66-67 CD 5
Wendell, ID 66-67 F 4
Wendell, NC 80-81 G 3
Wenden, AZ 74-75 G 6
Wendeng 146-147 J 3
Wendenschloss, Berlin- 130 III c 2
Wendling, OR 66-67 B 3
Wendover, UT 66-67 FG 5
Wendover, WY 68-69 D 4
Wendte, SD 68-69 F 3
Wener Lake = Vänern 116-117 E 8
Wengyuan 146-147 DE 9
Wen He 146-147 G 4
Wên-hsi = Wenxi 146-147 C 4
Wenling 146-147 H 7
Wennington, London- 129 II c 2
Wenquan 146-147 B 6
Wenshan 142-143 JK 7
Wenshang 146-147 F 4
Wenshan Zhuangzu Miaozu Zizhizhou 142-143 JK 7
Wenshi 146-147 C 9
Wên-shih = Wenshi 146-147 C 9
Wenshui 146-147 CD 3
Wên-su = Aqsu 142-143 E 3
Wenteng = Wendeng 146-147 J 3
Wentworth 158-159 H 6
Wentworth, SD 68-69 H 3-4
Wentzville, MO 70-71 E 6
Wenxi 146-147 C 4
Wenzhou 142-143 N 6
Wenzhou Wan 146-147 H 8
Wepener 172 E 7
Werdër [ETH] 164-165 O 7
Werftpfuhl 130 III cd 1
Wernecke Mountains 56-57 JK 5
Werner Lake 62 B 2
Wernigerode 118 E 3
Wernsdorf 130 III c 2
Wernsdorfer See 130 III c 2
Werra 118 D 3
Werribee, Melbourne- 160 FG 6
Werris Creek 158-159 K 6
Wesel 118 C 3
Weser 118 D 2
Weserbergland 118 D 2-3
Weser Hills = Weserbergland 118 D 2-3
Weskan, KS 68-69 F 6
Wesleyville 63 K 3
Wesleyville, PA 72-73 FG 3
Wessel, Cape — 158-159 G 2
Wessel Islands 158-159 G 2
Wesselsbron 174-175 G 4
Wessington, SD 68-69 G 3
Wessington Hills 68-69 G 3
Wessington Springs, SD 68-69 G 3-4
Wesson, MS 78-79 D 5
West, MS 78-79 E 4
West, TX 76-77 F 7
Westall, Point — 160 AB 4
West Allis, WI 70-71 FG 4
West Australian Basin 50-51 P 7
West Bank 136-137 F 6-7
West Bay 78-79 E 6
West Bend, IA 70-71 C 4
West Bend, WI 70-71 FG 4
West Bengal 134-135 O 6
West Berlin, NJ 84 III d 3
West Blocton, AL 78-79 F 4
Westboro, WI 70-71 E 3
Westbourne 61 J 5
West Branch, MI 70-71 HJ 3
Westbridge 66-67 D 1
West Bristol, PA 84 III d 1
Westbrook, ME 72-73 L 3
Westbrook, TX 76-77 D 6
Westbury, Houston-, TX 85 III b 2
West Butte 66-67 H 1
Westby, MT 68-69 D 1
Westby, WI 70-71 E 4
West Caicos Island 88-89 K 4
West Canal 85 III c 1
West Caroline Basin 156-157 FG 4
West Carson, CA 83 III c 2
Westchester, Los Angeles-, CA 83 III b 2
Westchester, New York-, NY 82 III d 1
Westcliffe, CO 68-69 D 6
West Collingswood, NJ 84 III c 2
West Collingswood Heights, NJ 84 III c 2
West Columbia, SC 80-81 F 4
West Columbia, TX 76-77 FG 8
West Conshohocken, PA 84 III b 1
Westcotville, NJ 84 III c 3
West Des Moines, IA 70-71 CD 5
West Drayton, London- 129 II a 2
West End 88-89 G 1
Westend, Atlanta-, GA 85 II b 2
Westerland 118 D 1
Westerly, RI 72-73 L 4
Western [EAK] 172 F 1
Western [GH] 168-169 E 4
Western [Z] 172 D 4
Western Area 168-169 B 3
Western Australia 158-159 C-E 4-5
Western Bank 63 E 6
Western Carpathians = Biele Karpaty 118 HJ 4
Western Ghats 134-135 L 6-M 8
Western Isles = Açores 204-205 E 5
Western Peninsula 62 B 3
Western Port 158-159 HJ 7
Westernport, MD 72-73 G 5
Western Sahara 164-165 A 4-B 3
Western Sayan Mountains = Zapadnyj Sajan 132-133 Q-S 7
Western Shoshone Indian Reservation 66-67 E 4-5
Western Sierra Madre = Sierra Madre Occidental 64-65 E 5-F 7
Westerschelde 120-121 J 3
Westerville, OH 72-73 E 4
Westerwald 118 CD 3
West European Basin 50-51 HJ 3
West Falkland 111 D 8
Westfall, OR 66-67 E 3-4
Westfield 63 C 5
Westfield, MA 72-73 K 3
Westfield, NY 72-73 G 3
Westfield, PA 72-73 H 4
West Fork, AR 76-77 GH 5
West Fork Des Moines River 70-71 C 4
West Fork Fortymile 58-59 Q 5
West Fork Poplar River 68-69 CD 1
West Fork White River 70-71 G 6
West Frankfort, IL 70-71 F 7
West Frisian Islands 120-121 KL 2
Westgate 158-159 J 5
Westham, London- 119 FG 6
Westhaven 128 I a 1
West Haven, CT 72-73 K 4
Westhoff, TX 76-77 F 8
West Hollywood, CA 83 III b 1
Westhope, ND 68-69 F 1
West Ice Shelf 53 C 9
Westindien 64-65 LM 7
West Indies 64-65 L-O 7
West Irian 148-149 K 7-L 8

West Jefferson, NC 80-81 F 2
West Lafayette, IN 70-71 G 5
Westlake, LA 78-79 C 5
Westlake, OR 66-67 A 4
Westland [NZ] 161 CD 6
Westland National Park 161 D 6
West Lanham Hills, MD 82 II b 1
West Laurel Hill Cemetery 84 III b 1
Westleigh 174-175 G 4
West Liberty, IA 70-71 E 5
West Liberty, KY 72-73 E 6
Westlock 60 L 2
West Los Angeles, Los Angeles-, CA 83 III b 1
West Manayunk, PA 84 III b 1
West Medford, MA 84 I b 2
West Memphis, AR 64-65 H 4
Westminster 174-175 G 5
Westminster, CO 68-69 D 6
Westminster, MD 72-73 H 5
Westminster, London- 129 II b 2
Westminster Abbey 129 II b 2
Westminster School 85 II b 1
West Monroe, LA 78-79 C 4
Westmont, CA 83 III c 2
Westmont, NJ 84 III c 2
Westmoreland, KS 68-69 H 6
Westmorland, CA 74-75 F 6
Westmount 82 I b 2
West Mountain 72-73 JK 3
West New York, NJ 82 III b 2
West Nicholson 172 EF 6
Weston, CO 68-69 D 7
Weston, ID 66-67 GH 4
Weston, MO 70-71 C 6
Weston, OR 66-67 D 3
Weston, WV 72-73 F 5
Weston [CDN] 72-73 G 3
Weston [MAL] 148-149 G 5
Weston-super-Mare 119 E 6
Westover, TX 76-77 E 6
West Palm Beach, FL 64-65 KL 6
West Pass 78-79 G 6
West Plains, MO 78-79 CD 2
West Point, GA 78-79 G 4
West Point, KY 70-71 H 7
West Point, MS 78-79 E 4
West Point, NE 68-69 H 5
West Point, NY 72-73 K 4
West Point, VA 80-81 H 2
West Point [CDN] 63 D 3
West Point [USA] 58-59 P 4
Westport, CA 74-75 AB 3
Westport, OR 66-67 B 2
Westport [CDN] 63 C 5
Westport [IRL] 119 AB 5
Westport [NZ] 158-159 O 8
West Pullman, Chicago-, IL 83 II b 2
Westray [CDN] 61 H 4
Westray [GB] 119 E 2
Westree 62 L 3
West Road River 60 EF 3
Westrode 128 II a 1
West Roxbury, Boston-, MA 84 I b 3
West Scotia Basin 50-51 G 8
West Somerville, MA 84 I b 2
West Spanish Peak 68-69 D 7
West Spitsbergen = Vestspitsbergen 116-117 j-l 5
West Union, IA 70-71 DE 4
West Union, OH 72-73 E 5
West Union, WV 72-73 F 5
West Unity, OH 70-71 H 5
West University Place, TX 85 III b 2
Westview Cemetery 85 II b 2
Westville, IL 70-71 G 5-6
Westville, NJ 84 III c 2
Westville, OK 76-77 G 4-5
Westville Grove, NJ 84 III c 2
West Virginia 64-65 KL 4
Westwater, UT 74-75 J 3
Westwego, LA 78-79 DE 6
West Whittier, CA 83 III d 2
West Wickham, London- 129 II b 2
Westwood, CA 66-67 C 5
Westwood, Los Angeles-, CA 83 III b 1
West Wyalong 160 H 4
West Yellowstone, MT 66-67 H 3
Westzaan, Zaanstad- 128 I a 1
Westzaner Overtoom 128 I a 1
Wetar, Pulau — 148-149 J 8
Wetaskiwin 56-57 NO 7
Wete 172 GH 3
Wetetnagani, Rivière — 62 N 2
Weti = Wete 172 GH 3
Wetlet 141 D 4
Wetmore, OR 66-67 D 3
Wet Mountains 68-69 D 6-7
Wetonka, SD 68-69 G 3
Wetter = Pulau Wetar 148-149 J 8
Wetter Lake = Vättern 116-117 E 8
Wettswil 128 IV a 1-2
Wetumpka, AL 78-79 FG 4
Wevok, AK 58-59 DE 2
Wewahitchka, FL 78-79 G 5-6
Wewak 148-149 M 7
Wewela, SD 68-69 G 4
Wewoka, OK 76-77 F 5
Wexford 119 C 5
Weyanoke, VA 82 II a 2
Weyb 164-165 N 7
Weybridge 129 II a 2
Weyburn 56-57 Q 8
Weyland, Point — 160 AB 4
Weymouth, MA 84 I c 3
Weymouth [CDN] 63 CD 5
Weymouth [GB] 119 EF 6
Weymouth, Cape — 158-159 HJ 2
Weymouth Back River 84 I c 3
Weymouth Fore River 84 I c 3
Weyprecht, Kapp — 116-117 l 5
Wezembeek-Oppem 128 II b 1
Whakatane 158-159 P 7
Whaleback, Mount — 158-159 CD 4
Whale River 56-57 X 6
Whales, Bay of — 53 B 19-20
Whalsay 119 F 1
Whangarei 158-159 OP 7
Wharton, TX 76-77 FG 8
What Cheer, IA 70-71 D 5
Wheatland, CA 74-75 C 3
Wheatland, WY 68-69 D 4
Wheatley, AR 78-79 D 3
Wheaton, MN 68-69 H 3
Wheeler, OR 66-67 AB 3
Wheeler, TX 76-77 D 5
Wheeler Islands 138-139 L 7
Wheeler Lake 78-79 F 3
Wheeler Peak [USA, Nevada] 64-65 CD 4
Wheeler Peak [USA, New Mexico] 64-65 E 4
Wheeler Ridge, CA 74-75 D 5
Wheeler River 61 F 2
Wheeling, WV 64-65 KL 4-5
Whelan 61 D 3-4
Whewell, Mount — 53 B 17-18
Whichaway Nunataks 53 A 34-1
Whidbey, Point — 160 B 5
Whidbey Island 66-67 B 1
Whiporie 160 L 2
Whipple, Mount — 60 B 1
Whiskey Gap 66-67 G 1
Whitby [CDN] 72-73 G 3
White, SD 68-69 H 3
White, Lake — 158-159 E 4
White Bay 56-57 Z 7
White Bear 61 DE 5
White Bear Lake, MN 70-71 D 3
White Bird, ID 66-67 EF 3
White Castle, LA 78-79 D 5
White City, FL 80-81 c 3
White City, KS 68-69 H 6
White Cliffs 158-159 H 6
White Cloud, MI 70-71 H 4
Whitecourt 60 K 2
White Deer, TX 76-77 D 5
White Earth, ND 68-69 E 1
White Earth Indian Reservation 70-71 C 2
White Eye, AK 58-59 O 3
Whiteface, TX 76-77 C 6
Whiteface Mountain 72-73 JK 2
Whitefish 62 L 3
Whitefish, MT 66-67 F 1
Whitefish Bay 70-71 H 2
Whitefish Bay, WI 70-71 G 4
Whitefish Falls 62 L 3
Whitefish Lake [CDN, Aleutian Range] 58-59 K 6
Whitefish Lake [CDN, Kilbuck Mts.] 58-59 GH 6
Whitefish Lake [CDN, Ontario] 70-71 F 1
Whitefish Lake [USA] 70-71 CD 2
Whitefish Point 70-71 H 2
Whitefish Point, MI 70-71 H 2
Whitefish Range 66-67 F 1
Whiteflat, TX 76-77 D 5
White Gull Lake 56-57 Y 6
White Hall, IL 70-71 EF 6
Whitehall, MI 70-71 G 4
Whitehall, MT 66-67 GH 3
Whitehall, NY 72-73 K 3
Whitehall, WI 70-71 E 3
Whitehaven 119 DE 4
White Hills 58-59 N 2
Whitehorse 56-57 JK 5
White Horse, CA 66-67 C 5
White Horse Pass 66-67 FG 5
White House 82 II a 2
White Island 161 G 3
White Island = Kvitøya 52 AB 15
White Lake, SD 68-69 G 4
White Lake, WI 70-71 F 3
White Lake [CDN] 70-71 H 1
White Lake [USA] 78-79 C 6
Whiteland, TX 76-77 E 7
Whitemark 160 cd 2
White Mountain, AK 56-57 D 5
White Mountains [USA, Alaska] 58-59 OP 4
White Mountains [USA, California] 74-75 D 4
White Mountains [USA, New Hampshire] 72-73 L 2
Whitemouth 61 KL 5-6
Whitemouth Lake 70-71 BC 1
White Nile = An-Nīl al-Abyaḍ 164-165 L 6
White Nossob = Wit Nossob 174-175 C 2
White Oak Acres, Houston-, TX 85 III b 1
White Oak Bayou 85 III ab 1
White Oak Park 85 III b 1
Whiteoak Swamp 80-81 H 3
White Otter Lake 62 CD 3
White Owl, SD 68-69 E 3
White Pass 58-59 U 7
White Pine, MT 66-67 F 2
White Pine Mountains 74-75 F 3
White Plains, NY 72-73 JK 4
White River, SD 68-69 F 4
White River [CDN, Ontario place] 70-71 H 1
White River [CDN, Ontario river] 70-71 GH 1
White River [CDN, Yukon Territory] 56-57 H 5
White River [USA, Alaska] 58-59 R 6
White River [USA, Arkansas] 64-65 H 4
White River [USA, California] 74-75 F 4
White River [USA, Colorado] 68-69 BC 5
White River [USA, Indiana] 70-71 G 6
White River [USA, South Dakota] 64-65 F 3
White River [USA, Texas] 76-77 D 6
White River = Witrivier 174-175 J 3
White River, East Fork — 70-71 GH 6
White River, South Fork — 68-69 F 4
White River, West Fork — 70-71 G 6
White River Plateau 68-69 C 6
White River Valley 74-75 F 3
White Rock, SD 68-69 H 3
White Russian Soviet Socialist Republic = Belorussian Soviet Socialist Republic 124-125 E-H 6-7
Whitesail Lake 60 D 3
White Salmon, WA 66-67 C 3
Whitesands = Witsand 174-175 D 8
White Sands National Monument 76-77 A 6
Whites Brook 63 C 4
White Sea 132-133 FG 4
Whiteshell Forest Reserve 61 KL 6
Whiteshell Provincial Park 62 B 2-3
Whiteside, Canal — 108-109 D 9-10
White Sox Park 83 II b 1-2
White Springs, FL 80-81 b 1
Whitestone, New York-, NY 82 III d 2
White Sulphur Springs, MT 66-67 H 2
White Swan, WA 66-67 C 2
Whitetail, MT 68-69 D 1
White Umfolozi = Wit Umfolozi 174-175 J 5
Whiteville, NC 80-81 G 3
Whiteville, TN 78-79 E 3
White Volta 164-165 D 7
Whitewater, CO 68-69 B 6
Whitewater, KS 68-69 H 7
Whitewater, MT 68-69 C 1
Whitewater, WI 70-71 F 4
Whitewater Baldy 64-65 E 5
Whitewater Lake 62 DE 2
Whitewood, SD 68-69 DE 3
Whitewright, TX 76-77 F 6
Whitfield 160 H 6
Whithorn 119 DE 4
Whiting, NJ 72-73 J 5
Whiting River 58-59 V 7
Whitla 61 C 6
Whitley City, KY 78-79 G 2
Whitman, ND 68-69 GH 1
Whitman, NE 68-69 F 4
Whitmire, SC 80-81 F 3
Whitmore Mountains 53 A
Whitney, NE 68-69 E 4
Whitney, OR 66-67 DE 3
Whitney, TX 76-77 F 7
Whitney, Mount — 64-65 C 4
Whitsett, TX 76-77 E 8
Whitsunday Island 158-159 JK 4
Whittier, AK 56-57 G 5
Whittier, CA 83 III d 2
Whittier College 83 III d 2
Whittier Narrows Dam 83 III d 1
Whittle, Cap de — 63 F 2
Whittlesea 160 G 6
Whitwell, TN 78-79 G 3
Wholdaia Lake 56-57 PQ 5
Whyalla 158-159 G 6

Wiang Pa Pao 150-151 B 3
Wiang Phran = Mae Sai 148-149 CD 2
Wiarton 72-73 F 2
Wibaux, MT 68-69 D 2
Wichian Buri 148-149 D 3
Wichita, KS 64-65 G 4
Wichita Falls, TX 64-65 FG 5
Wichita Mountains 76-77 E 5
Wick 119 E 2
Wickenburg, AZ 74-75 G 5-6
Wickersham, WA 66-67 BC 1
Wickes, AR 76-77 G 5
Wickham, Cape — 160 b 1
Wickliffe, KY 78-79 E 2
Wicklow 119 CD 5
Wicklow Mountains 119 C 5
Wide Bay 58-59 ef 1
Widen, WV 72-73 F 5
Widgiemooltha 158-159 D 6
Wi-do 144-145 F 5
Widŏn 141 C 5
Widyan, Al- 134-135 E 4
Więcbork 118 H 2
Wiegnaarspoort 174-175 E 7
Wieluń 118 J 3
Wien [A, place] 118 G 4
Wien [A, river] 113 I b 2
Wien-Altmannsdorf 113 I b 2
Wien-Azgersdorf 113 I b 2
Wien-Breitenlee 113 I bc 1
Wien-Donaufeld 113 I b 1
Wien-Donaustadt 113 I bc 2
Wien-Dornbach 113 I b 2
Wienerberg 113 I b 2
Wiener Neustadt 118 GH 5
Wienerwald 118 GH 4
Wien-Essling 113 I c 2
Wien-Favoriten 113 I b 2
Wien-Grinzing 113 I b 1
Wien-Grossjedlersdorf 113 I b 1
Wien-Hadersdorf 113 I ab 2
Wien-Hernals 113 I b 2
Wien-Hietzing 113 I b 2
Wien-Hirschstetten 113 I bc 2
Wien-Hütteldorf 113 I b 2
Wien-Inzersdorf 113 I b 2
Wien-Jedlesee 113 I b 1
Wien-Kagran 113 I b 2
Wien-Kaiserebersdorf 113 I b 2
Wien-Kalksburg 113 I ab 2
Wien-Lainz 113 I b 2
Wien Lake 58-59 M 4
Wien-Leopoldau 113 I b 1
Wien-Leopoldstadt 113 I b 2
Wien-Mauer 113 I ab 2
Wien-Meidling 113 I b 2
Wien-Neualbern 113 I b 2
Wien-Neustift am Walde 113 I b 2
Wien-Neusüssenbrunn 113 I bc 1
Wien-Neuwaldegg 113 I ab 2
Wien-Nussdorf 113 I b 1
Wien-Oberlaa 113 I b 2
Wien-Oberlisse 113 I b 1
Wien-Ottakring 113 I b 2
Wien-Penzing 113 I b 2
Wien-Rodaun 113 I b 2
Wien-Salmannsdorf 113 I b 1
Wien-Schwechat, Flughafen — 113 I c 2
Wien-Siebenhirten 113 I b 2
Wien-Sievering 113 I b 1
Wien-Speising 113 I b 2
Wien-Stadlau 113 I b 2
Wien-Stammersdorf 113 I b 1
Wien-Strebersdorf 113 I b 1
Wien-Süssenbrunn 113 I bc 1
Wieprz 118 L 3
Wierzbołowo = Virbalis 124-125 D 6
Wiesbaden 118 CD 3
Wiese Island = ostrov Vize 132-133 O 2
Wigadēn 164-165 NO 7
Wiga Hill 168-169 H 3
Wigan 119 E 5
Wiggins, CO 68-69 D 5
Wiggins, MS 78-79 E 5
Wight, Isle of — 119 F 6
Wijde Blik 128 I b 2
Wijdefjorden 116-117 j 5
Wilber, NE 68-69 H 5
Wilborn, MT 66-67 G 2
Wilbourn Hill 160 B 1
Wilbur, WA 66-67 D 2
Wilburton, OK 76-77 G 5
Wilcannia 158-159 H 6
Wilcock, Peninsula — 108-109 BC 8
Wilcox, NE 68-69 G 5
Wilczek, zemľa — 132-133 L-N 1
Wilczek land = zemľa Wilczek 132-133 L-N 1
Wildcat Canyon Regional Park 83 I c 1
Wilde, Avellaneda- 110 III c 2
Wilderness = Wildernis 174-175 E 7-8
Wildernis 174-175 E 7-8
Wild Horse Reservoir 66-67 F 5
Wild Lake 58-59 M 3
Wildpark West 130 III a 2
Wild Rice River 70-71 BC 2
Wild River 58-59 M 3
Wildrose, ND 68-69 E 1
Wild Rose, WI 70-71 F 3
Wildwood, FL 80-81 bc 2
Wildwood, NJ 72-73 J 5
Wildwood Lake 85 II a 2
Wilge 174-175 H 4
Wilgena 160 B 3
Wilgespruit 170 V a 1
Wilhelm, Mount — 148-149 M 8
Wilhelmina Gebergte 92-93 H 4
Wilhelmøya 116-117 l 5
Wilhelmshaven 118 CD 2
Wilhelmshorst [DDR] 130 III a 2
Wilhelmstadt, Berlin- 130 III a 1
Wilhelmstal 174-175 B 1
Wilkes 53 C 12
Wilkes Barre, PA 64-65 L 3
Wilkes Land 53 BC 12-14
Wilkie 56-57 P 7
Wilkinsburg, PA 72-73 G 4
Wilkinson Lakes 158-159 F 5
Will, Mount — 58-59 X 8
Willaccochee, GA 80-81 E 5
Willamette River 64-65 B 3
Willandra Billabong Creek 160 G 4
Willapa Bay 66-67 AB 2
Willard, CO 68-69 E 5
Willard, MT 68-69 D 2
Willard, NM 76-77 AB 5
Willard, OH 72-73 E 4
Willard, UT 66-67 GH 5
Willcox, AZ 74-75 HJ 6
Willebroek, Kanaal van — 128 II b 1
Willemstad [NA] 64-65 N 9
Willeroo 158-159 F 3
Willesden, London- 129 II b 1
William B. Hartsfield Atlanta International Airport 85 II b 3
William Creek 158-159 G 5
William Girling Reservoir 129 II bc 1
William Lake 61 J 3-4
William P. Hobby Airport 85 III b 2
Williams, AZ 74-75 G 5
Williams, CA 74-75 B 3
Williams Bridge, New York-, NY 82 III c 1
Williamsburg, IA 70-71 DE 5
Williamsburg, KY 80-81 DE 2
Williamsburg, New York-, NY 82 III c 2
Williams Lake 56-57 M 7
Williamson, WV 80-81 E 2
Williamsport, IN 70-71 G 5
Williamsport, PA 64-65 L 3
Williamston, NC 80-81 H 2-3
Williamstown, KY 70-71 H 6
Williamstown, Melbourne- 161 II b 2
Williamsville, MO 78-79 D 2
Willibert, Mount — 60 B 1
Willimantic, CT 72-73 K 4
Willingboro, NJ 84 III d 1
Willingboro Plaza 84 III d 1
Willingdon 61 B 4
Willis, TX 76-77 G 7
Willis Group 158-159 K 3
Willis Island 63 K 3
Williston 172 D 8
Williston, FL 80-81 b 2
Williston, ND 64-65 F 2
Williston, SC 80-81 F 4
Williston Lake 60 F 1-2
Willits, CA 74-75 B 3
Willmar, MN 70-71 C 3
Willmar Station 68-69 E 1
Willmersdorf [DDR, Frankfurt] 130 III c 1
Willmore Wilderness Provincial Park 60 H 3
Willoughby, OH 72-73 F 4
Willoughby, Sydney- 161 I b 1
Willow 56-57 F 5
Willow Bend, Houston-, TX 85 III b 2
Willow Brook, CA 83 III c 2
Willow Brook, Houston-, TX 85 III b 2
Willow Bunch 68-69 D 1
Willow Creek, AK 58-59 P 6
Willow Creek [USA, California] 66-67 C 5
Willow Creek [USA, Oregon] 66-67 D 3
Willowdene, Johannesburg- 170 V a 2
Willow Lake, SD 68-69 H 3
Willowlake River 56-57 MN 5
Willowmore 172 D 8
Willow Ranch, CA 66-67 C 5
Willow River 60 F 2
Willow River, MN 70-71 D 2
Willow Run, MI 72-73 E 3
Willows, CA 74-75 B 3
Willow Springs, MO 78-79 CD 2
Willow Waterhole Bayou 85 III ab 2
Will Rogers State Historical Park 83 III a 1
Willsboro, NY 72-73 K 2
Wills Point, LA 85 I bc 3
Wills Point, TX 76-77 FG 6
Willswood, LA 85 I a 2
Willunga 160 D 5
Wilmer, AL 78-79 E 5
Wilmersdorf, Berlin- 130 III b 2
Wilmington, DE 64-65 LM 4
Wilmington, IL 70-71 FG 5
Wilmington, NC 64-65 L 5
Wilmington, OH 72-73 E 5
Wilmington [AUS] 160 D 4
Wilmington [GB] 129 II c 2
Wilmot, AR 78-79 D 4
Wilmot, SD 68-69 H 3
Wilpattu 140 DE 6
Wilsall, MT 66-67 H 3
Wilshire, Houston-, TX 85 III b 1
Wilson, AR 78-79 D 3
Wilson, NC 64-65 L 4
Wilson, NY 72-73 G 3
Wilson, OK 76-77 F 5
Wilson Bluff 158-159 EF 6
Wilson City 88-89 H 1
Wilson Creek, WA 66-67 D 2
Wilson Creek Range 74-75 F 3
Wilson Lake 78-79 F 3
Wilson River 158-159 H 5
Wilsons Promontory 158-159 J 7
Wilsonville, NE 68-69 FG 5
Wilstorf, Hamburg- 130 I a 2
Wilton, ND 68-69 F 2
Wilton, WI 70-71 E 4
Wilton River 158-159 F 2
Wiluna 158-159 D 5
Wimbledon, ND 68-69 G 2
Wimbledon, London- 119 F 6
Wimborne 60 L 4
Wimmera 158-159 H 7
Wina = Ouina 164-165 G 7
Winamac, IN 70-71 G 5
Winburg 172 E 7
Winchell, TX 76-77 E 7
Winchester, ID 66-67 E 2
Winchester, IL 70-71 EF 6
Winchester, IN 70-71 H 5
Winchester, KY 72-73 DE 5
Winchester, MA 84 I ab 2
Winchester, TN 78-79 F 3
Winchester, VA 64-65 L 4
Winchester, WY 68-69 BC 4
Winchester [CDN] 72-73 J 2
Winchester [GB] 119 F 6
Winchester Bay, OR 66-67 A 4
Windber, PA 72-73 G 4
Wind Cave National Park 68-69 E 4
Winder, GA 80-81 E 3-4
Windesi 148-149 K 7
Windfern Forest, TX 85 III a 1
Windham, AK 58-59 V 8
Windhoek 172 C 6
Windigo Lake 62 D 1
Windigo River 62 D 1
Windmill Point 84 II c 2
Windom, MN 70-71 C 4
Windorah 158-159 H 5
Wind River, WY 68-69 B 4
Wind River [USA, Alaska] 58-59 O 2-3
Wind River [USA, Wyoming] 68-69 B 4
Wind River Indian Reservation 66-67 J 4
Wind River Range 64-65 DE 3
Windsor, CO 68-69 D 5
Windsor, MO 70-71 D 6
Windsor, NC 80-81 H 2
Windsor, ND 68-69 G 2
Windsor, VT 72-73 K 3
Windsor [AUS] 160 K 4
Windsor [CDN, Newfoundland] 63 HJ 3
Windsor [CDN, Nova Scotia] 63 D 5
Windsor [CDN, Ontario] 56-57 U 9
Windsor [CDN, Quebec] 72-73 KL 2
Windsor [GB] 119 F 6
Windsor [ZA] 170 V a 1
Windsor, University of — 84 II b 3
Windsor Airport 84 II c 3
Windsor Hills, CA 83 III bc 2
Windsorton 174-175 F 5
Windsor Village, Houston-, TX 85 III b 2
Windward Islands [West Indies] 64-65 O 9
Windy, AK 58-59 N 5
Winefred Lake 61 C 3
Winfield, AL 78-79 F 3-4
Winfield, IA 70-71 E 5
Winfield, KS 64-65 G 4
Winfred, SD 68-69 H 3-4
Wing, ND 68-69 F 2
Wingham 72-73 F 3
Wingham Island 58-59 P 6
Wingo, KY 78-79 E 2
Winifred, MT 68-69 B 2
Winifreda 106-107 E 6
Winisk 56-57 T 6
Winisk Lake 56-57 T 7
Winisk River 56-57 T 7
Wink, TX 76-77 C 7
Winkel [CH] 128 IV b 1
Winkel [NL] 128 I b 2
Winkelman, AZ 74-75 H 6
Winkelpos 174-175 G 4
Winkler 68-69 H 1
Winlock, WA 66-67 B 2
Winneba 164-165 D 7
Winnebago, MN 70-71 CD 4
Winnebago, Lake — 70-71 F 3-4
Winnemucca, NV 64-65 C 3
Winnemucca Lake 66-67 D 5
Winner, SD 68-69 G 4
Winnetka, IL 70-71 G 4
Winnett, MT 68-69 B 2
Winnfield, LA 78-79 C 5
Winnibigoshish Lake 70-71 CD 2
Winnie, TX 76-77 G 8
Winning Pool 158-159 B 4
Winnipeg 56-57 R 7
Winnipeg, Lake — 56-57 R 7
Winnipeg Beach 62 A 2
Winnipegosis 61 HJ 5
Winnipegosis, Lake — 56-57 R 7
Winnipeg River 56-57 RS 7
Winnipesaukee, Lake — 72-73 L 3
Winnsboro, LA 78-79 D 4
Winnsboro, SC 80-81 F 3
Winnsboro, TX 76-77 G 6
Winona, AZ 74-75 H 5
Winona, KS 68-69 F 6
Winona, MI 70-71 F 2
Winona, MN 64-65 H 3
Winona, MO 78-79 D 2
Winona, MS 78-79 DE 4
Winona, TX 76-77 G 6
Winona, WA 66-67 DE 2
Winschoten 120-121 L 2
Winslow, AR 76-77 G 5
Winslow, AZ 64-65 DE 4
Winslow, IN 70-71 G 6
Winslow, ME 72-73 M 2
Winsted, CT 72-73 K 4
Winston, MT 66-67 GH 2
Winston, OR 66-67 B 4
Winston-Salem, NC 64-65 KL 4
Winterberg [CH] 128 IV b 1
Winterberg [D] 118 D 3
Winterberge 174-175 FG 7
Winter Garden, FL 80-81 c 2
Winter Harbour 60 C 4
Winterhaven, CA 74-75 F 6
Winter Haven, FL 80-81 c 2
Winter Hill, MA 84 I b 2
Winterhude, Hamburg- 130 I b 1
Winter Park, CO 68-69 CD 6
Winter Park, FL 80-81 c 2
Winters, CA 74-75 C 3
Winters, TX 76-77 E 7
Winterset, IA 70-71 CD 5
Winterthur 118 D 5
Winterthur-Vogelsang 128 IV b 1
Winterthur-Wülflingen 128 IV b 1
Winterton [ZA] 174-175 H 5
Winterveld 174-175 E 6
Winthrop, MA 84 I c 2
Winthrop, ME 72-73 LM 2
Winthrop, MN 70-71 C 3
Winthrop, WA 66-67 C 1
Winton, MN 70-71 E 2
Winton, WA 66-67 C 2
Winton, WY 66-67 J 5
Winton [AUS] 158-159 H 4
Winton [NZ] 158-159 N 9
Winyah Bay 80-81 G 4
Winzah 166-167 KL 1-2
Wipkingen, Zürich- 128 IV b 1
Wirāj, Wādī al- 173 B 3
Wirrulla 158-159 FG 6
Wiscasset, ME 72-73 M 2
Wisconsin 64-65 H 2-J 3
Wisconsin Dells, WI 70-71 F 4
Wisconsin Rapids, WI 70-71 EF 3
Wisconsin River 64-65 HJ 3
Wisdom, MT 66-67 G 3
Wiseman, AK 56-57 FG 4
Wishart 61 FG 5
Wishek, ND 68-69 G 2
Wisła 118 K 3
Wislana, Mierzeja — 118 J 1
Wislany, Zalew — 118 J 1
Wisłok 118 KL 4
Wisłoka 118 K 4
Wismar 118 E 2
Wisner, LA 78-79 D 4-5
Wisner, NE 68-69 H 4-5
Wissahickon Creek 84 III b 1
Wissel, Danau — 148-149 L 7
Wissembourg 120-121 LM 4
Wissinoming, Philadelphia-, PA 84 III c 1
Wissmann, Chutes — 172 CD 3
Wissous 129 I c 3
Wistaria 60 D 3
Wister, OK 76-77 G 5
Wiswila 171 AB 5
Witbank 172 EF 7
Witberge 174-175 G 6
Witchekan Lake 61 E 4
Witdraai 174-175 D 4
Witelsbos 174-175 F 8
Witfonteinrand 174-175 G 3
Withernsea 119 FG 5
Witherspoon, Mount — 58-59 O 6
Witikon, Zürich- 128 IV b 1
Witkop 174-175 D 4
Witkoppies 174-175 H 4
Wit Nossob 174-175 C 2
Witpoort 174-175 G 4
Witpoortje 170 V a 1
Witputs 172 C 7
Witrandberge 174-175 C 3
Witrivier 174-175 J 3
Witsand 174-175 D 8
Witteberg 174-175 C 7
Witteberge 174-175 D 7
Witte-Els-Bosch = Witelsbos 174-175 F 8
Witten, SD 68-69 FG 4
Wittenau, Berlin- 130 III b 1
Wittenberg 118 F 3
Wittenberg, WI 70-71 F 3
Wittenberge 118 EF 2
Wittenoom 158-159 C 4
Wittlich 118 C 4
Wittmann, AZ 74-75 G 6
Wittstock 118 F 2
Witu 172 GH 2
Wit Umfolozi 174-175 J 5
Witung = Widŏn 141 C 5
Witvlei 172 C 6
Witwatersrand 174-175 G 3-H 4
Wivenhoe 61 L 2
Wiwŏn 144-145 F 2

Wkra 118 JK 2

Włocławek 118 J 2
Włodawa 118 L 3

Woburn, MA 84 I ab 2
Wodonga 160 H 6
Woeonichi, Lac — 62 O 1
Wohlthatmassiv 53 B 2
Wokam, Pulau — 148-149 KL 8
Woking 60 H 2
Wolbach, NE 68-69 G 5
Wolcott, NY 72-73 H 3
Woleai 148-149 M 5
Wolf Creek, MT 66-67 G 2
Wolf Creek, OR 66-67 B 4
Wolf Creek Pass 68-69 C 7
Wolfe City, TX 76-77 F 6
Wolfenbüttel 118 E 2
Wolff, Chutes — 172 D 3
Wolfforth, TX 76-77 C 6
Wolf Mountains 68-69 C 3
Wolf Point, MT 68-69 D 1
Wolf River 70-71 F 3
Wolfsburg 118 E 2
Wolfsgarten, Berlin- 130 III c 2
Wolfville 63 DE 5
Wolhuterskop 174-175 G 3
Wolin 118 G 2
Wolkitte = Welkītē 164-165 M 7
Wollaston, MA 84 I b 3
Wollaston, Isla — 108-109 F 10
Wollaston, Islas — 111 C 9
Wollaston Lake 56-57 PQ 6
Wollaston Lake Post 61 FG 1
Wollaston Peninsula 56-57 NO 3-4
Wollega = Welega 164-165 LM 7
Wollishofen, Zürich- 128 IV b 1
Wollo = Welo 164-165 MN 6
Wollogorang 158-159 G 3
Wollongong 158-159 K 6
Wollongong-Port Kembla 158-159 K 6
Wollongong-Shellharbour 158-159 K 6
Wolmaransstad 174-175 F 4
Wolo 152-153 O 7
Wolok = Hele 150-151 H 3
Wołów 118 H 3
Wolseley [AUS] 158-159 GH 7
Wolseley [CDN] 61 G 5
Wolseley [ZA] 174-175 C 7
Wolsey, SD 68-69 G 3
Wolstenholme 56-57 VW 5
Wolstenholme, Cape — 56-57 VW 5
Wolsztyn 118 GH 2
Woluwe-Saint-Lambert 128 II b 1
Woluwe-Saint-Pierre 128 II b 1
Wolverhampton 119 E 5
Wolverine, MI 70-71 H 3
Woman River 62 K 3
Wonder, OR 66-67 B 4
Wonderfontein 174-175 HJ 3
Wonderkop 174-175 G 4
Wŏngsŏng-dong 144-145 DE 3
Wŏnju 142-143 O 4
Wonogiri 152-153 J 9
Wonosari 148-149 F 8
Wŏnsan 142-143 O 4
Wonthaggi 158-159 HJ 7
Woocalla 160 C 3
Wood, SD 68-69 F 4
Wood, Isla — 106-107 F 7
Wood, Islas — 108-109 E 10
Wood, Mount — [CDN] 58-59 R 6

Wood, Mount — [USA] 66-67 J 3
Wood Bay 53 B 17-18
Woodbine, GA 80-81 F 5
Wood Buffalo National Park 56-57 O 6
Woodburn, OR 66-67 B 3
Woodbury, GA 78-79 G 4
Woodbury, NJ 72-73 J 5
Woodbury Creek 84 III bc 2
Woodbury Heights, NJ 84 III c 3
Woodbury Terrace, NJ 84 III c 2
Woodchopper, AK 58-59 PQ 4
Woodend 160 G 6
Woodfjorden 116-117 j 5
Woodford, London- 129 II c 1
Wood Green, London- 129 II b 1
Woodhaven, New York-, NY 82 III cd 2
Woodlake, CA 74-75 D 4
Wood Lake, NE 68-69 FG 4
Wood Lake, Houston-, TX 85 III a 2
Woodland, CA 74-75 BC 3
Woodland, WA 66-67 B 3
Woodland Park, CO 68-69 D 6
Woodlands 154 III a 1
Woodlands Cemetery 84 III b 2
Woodlark Island 148-149 h 6
Woodlawn, Chicago-, IL 83 II b 2
Woodlawn Cemetery [USA, Boston] 84 I b 2
Woodlawn Cemetery [USA, Detroit] 84 II b 2
Woodlawn Cemetery [USA, Houston] 85 III b 1
Woodlyn, PA 84 III a 2
Woodlynne, NJ 84 III c 2
Woodmere, NY 82 III d 3
Woodmere Cemetery 84 II b 3
Woodmont, MD 82 II a 1
Wood Mountain [CDN, mountain] 68-69 C 1
Wood Mountain [CDN, mountains] 61 E 6
Woodpecker 60 FG 3
Woodridge 70-71 BC 1
Wood-Ridge, NJ 82 III b 1
Wood River, IL 70-71 EF 6
Wood River, NE 68-69 G 5
Wood River [CDN] 61 E 5-6
Wood River [USA] 58-59 NO 4
Woodroffe, Mount — 158-159 F 5
Woodruff, SC 80-81 EF 3
Woodruff, UT 66-67 H 5
Woodruff, WI 70-71 F 3
Woods, Lake — 158-159 F 3
Woods, Lake of the — 56-57 R 8
Woodsboro, TX 76-77 F 8
Woodsfield, OH 72-73 F 5
Wood Shadows, Houston-, TX 85 III c 1
Woodside 158-159 J 7
Woodside, UT 74-75 H 3
Woodside, New York-, NY 82 III c 2
Woodson, AR 78-79 CD 3
Woodstock, IL 70-71 FG 4
Woodstock, VA 72-73 G 5
Woodstock, VT 72-73 K 3
Woodstock [AUS] 158-159 H 3
Woodstock [CDN, New Brunswick] 63 C 4
Woodstock [CDN, Ontario] 72-73 F 3
Woodsville, NH 72-73 KL 2
Woodville 158-159 P 8
Woodville, MS 78-79 D 5
Woodville, TX 76-77 G 7
Woodward, OK 64-65 G 4
Woody Island, AK 58-59 L 8
Woolgar, Lower — 158-159 H 3
Woolgoolga 160 L 3
Woollahra, Sydney- 161 I b 2
Woollett, Lac — 62 P 1
Wooltana 160 DE 3
Woomera 158-159 G 6
Woonsocket, RI 72-73 KL 4
Woonsocket, SD 68-69 GH 3
Wooramel 158-159 BC 5
Wooramel River 158-159 C 5
Wooster, OH 72-73 F 4
Worcester, MA 64-65 M 3
Worcester [GB] 119 E 5
Worcester [ZA] 172 CD 8
Worcester Range 53 B 17-15
Worden, OR 66-67 BC 4
Worfelden 128 III a 2
Workington 119 E 4
Worland, WY 68-69 C 3
Wormer [NL, landscape] 128 I a 1
Worms 118 CD 4
Woronara River 161 I a 2-3
Woronów = Voronovo 124-125 E 6
Wortel [Namibia] 174-175 B 2
Worth, IL 83 II a 2
Wortham, TX 76-77 F 7
Worthing 119 FG 6
Worthington, MN 70-71 C 4
Wosnesenski Island 58-59 c 2
Wou-han = Wuhan 142-143 L 5
Wou-hou = Wuhu 142-143 M 5
Wour 164-165 H 4
Wou-tcheou = Wuzhou 142-143 L 7
Wowoni, Pulau — 148-149 H 7
Wowotobi, Selat — 152-153 P 10
Wrakpunt 174-175 B 5
Wrangel, ostrov — 132-133 hj 3
Wrangell, AK 56-57 K 6
Wrangell, Mount — 58-59 P 5
Wrangell Island 58-59 w 8
Wrangell Mountains 56-57 H 5
Wrath, Cape — 119 D 2
Wray, CO 68-69 E 5
Wreck Point = Wrakpunt 174-175 B 5
Wrens, GA 80-81 E 4
Wright 60 G 4
Wright, Lake — 158-159 EF 5
Wright City, OK 76-77 G 5
Wrightson, Mount — 74-75 H 7
Wrightsville, GA 80-81 E 4
Wrigley 56-57 M 5
Wrigley Gulf 53 B 24
Writing on Stone Provincial Park 66-67 H 1
Wrocław 118 H 3
Wrottesley, Mount — 66-67 B 1
Wroxton 61 GH 5
Września 118 HJ 2
Wschowa 118 H 3
Wu'an 146-147 E 3
Wubin 158-159 C 5-6
Wubu 146-147 C 3
Wuchai = Wuzhai 146-147 C 2
Wuchang 142-143 O 3
Wuchang, Wuhan- 142-143 LM 5
Wucheng [TJ, Shandong] 146-147 EF 3
Wucheng [TJ, Shanxi] 146-147 C 3
Wu-ch'i = Wuqi [TJ, Shaanxi] 146-147 B 3
Wu-ch'i = Wuxi [TJ, Sichuan] 146-147 B 6
Wu-chiang = Wujiang [TJ, place] 146-147 H 6
Wu Chiang = Wu Jiang [TJ, river] 142-143 K 6
Wu-ch'iang = Wuqiang 146-147 E 2
Wu-ch'iao = Wuqiao 146-147 F 3
Wu-chih = Wuzhi 146-147 D 4
Wu-chih Shan = Wuzhi Shan 150-151 G 3
Wu-chou = Wuzhou 142-143 L 7
Wuchow = Wuzhou 142-143 L 7
Wuchuan [TJ, Guangdong] 146-147 C 11
Wuchuan [TJ, Guizhou] 142-143 K 6
Wuchuan [TJ, Inner Mongolian Aut. Reg.] 142-143 L 3
Wu-chung-pao = Wuzhong 142-143 K 4
Wuchwan = Wuchuan 146-147 C 11
Wudang Shan 146-147 C 5
Wudaogou 144-145 EF 1
Wudaokou = Beijing-Dongsheng 155 II ab 1
Wudi 142-143 M 4
Wudian 146-147 D 6
Wuding He 146-147 C 3
Wudu 142-143 J 5
Wuduhe 146-147 C 6
Wufeng 146-147 C 6
Wugang 142-143 L 6
Wugong 146-147 AB 4
Wugong Shan 146-147 D 8
Wuhan 142-143 L 5
Wuhan-Hankou 142-143 LM 5
Wuhan-Hanyang 142-143 L 5
Wuhan-Wuchang 142-143 LM 5
Wuhe 146-147 F 5
Wu hei 142-143 K 4
Wuhle 130 III c 1
Wuhlheide, Volkspark — 130 III c 2
Wu-ho = Wuhe 146-147 F 5
Wu-hsi = Wuxi 142-143 MN 5
Wu-hsiang = Wuxiang 146-147 D 3
Wu-hsüan = Wuxuan 146-147 B 10
Wuhu 142-143 M 5
Wuhua 146-147 E 10
Wu-i = Wuyi [TJ, Anhui] 146-147 G 5
Wu-i = Wuyi [TJ, Zhejiang] 146-147 G 7
Wu-i Shan = Wuyi Shan 142-143 M 6
Wujiang [TJ, place] 146-147 H 6
Wu Jiang [TJ, river] 142-143 K 6
Wujin = Changzhou 142-143 MN 5
Wukang 146-147 GH 6
Wukari 164-165 F 7
Wuki = Wuxi 146-147 B 6
Wukiao = Wuqiao 146-147 F 3
Wu-kung = Wugong 146-147 AB 4
Wuleidao Wan 146-147 HJ 3
Wülflingen, Winterthur- 128 IV b 1
Wuli 142-143 K 7
Wulian 146-147 G 4
Wuliang Shan 142-143 J 7
Wulik River 58-59 EF 3
Wu Ling 146-147 CD 4
Wuling He 142-143 P 2
Wuling Shan 146-147 B 8-C 7
Wulmsdorf 130 I a 2
Wulongij = Huaibin 146-147 E 5
Wulumuqi = Ürümchi 142-143 F 3
Wulun He = Dingzi Wan 146-147 H 3
Wumei Shan 146-147 E 7
Wūn 138-139 G 7
Wūndwin 141 DE 5
Wunga, Pulau — 152-153 B 5
Wuning 146-147 E 7
Wunnummin Lake 62 E 1
Wunstorf 118 D 2
Wuntho = Wūnzō 141 D 4
Wūnzō 141 D 4
Wupatki National Monument 74-75 GH 5
Wuping 146-147 F 9
Wuppertal [D] 118 C 3
Wuppertal [ZA] 174-175 C 7
Wūqbā, Al- = Al-Waqbā 136-137 L 8
Wuqi 146-147 B 3
Wuqiang 146-147 E 2
Wuqiao 146-147 F 3
Wur = Wour 164-165 H 4
Wurno 164-165 EF 6
Wūruq, Rā's — 164-165 D 1
Würzburg 118 DE 4
Wushan 146-147 BC 6
Wusheng 146-147 G 7
Wushi [TJ ↓ Shaoguan] 142-143 L 7
Wushi [TJ ↙ Zhanjiang] 146-147 BC 11
Wushi = Üchturpan 142-143 DE 3
Wu Shui [TJ ◁ Bei Jiang] 146-147 D 9
Wu Shui [TJ ◁ Yuan Jiang, Hongjiang] 146-147 BC 8
Wu Shui [TJ ◁ Yuan Jiang, Qiancheng] 146-147 B 8
Wusi = Wuxi 142-143 MN 5
Wusiang = Wuxiang 146-147 D 3
Wuskwatim Lake 61 J 3
Wusong 142-143 N 5
Wusu 142-143 EF 3
Wusuli Jiang 142-143 P 2
Wutai 146-147 D 2
Wutai Shan 142-143 L 4
Wu-tang Shan = Wudang Shan 146-147 C 5
Wuti = Wudi 142-143 M 4
Wu-ting = Huimin 146-147 F 3
Wu-ting Ho = Wuding He 146-147 C 3
Wutong 146-147 B 9
Wutongqiao 142-143 J 6
Wutong Shan = Wugong Shan 146-147 D 8
Wutsing = Wuqing 146-147 F 2
Wu-tu = Wudu 142-143 J 5
Wu-tu-ho = Wuduhe 146-147 C 6
Wūtwūn 141 E 4
Wuvulu 148-149 M 7
Wuwei [TJ, Anhui] 146-147 F 6
Wuwei [TJ, Gansu] 142-143 J 4
Wuxi 142-143 MN 5
Wuxian = Suzhou 142-143 N 5
Wuxiang 146-147 D 3
Wuxing 142-143 MN 5
Wuxue = Guangji 142-143 M 6
Wuyang [TJ, Henan] 146-147 D 5
Wuyang [TJ, Hunan] 146-147 C 8
Wuyi [TJ, Anhui] 146-147 G 5
Wuyi [TJ, Zhejiang] 146-147 G 7
Wuyiling 142-143 OP 2
Wuying 142-143 OP 2
Wuyi Shan 142-143 M 6
Wuyou 146-147 H 5
Wu-yu = Wuyou 146-147 H 5
Wuyuan [TJ, Inner Mongolian Aut. Reg.] 142-143 K 3
Wuyuan [TJ, Jiangxi] 146-147 FG 7
Wu-yüan = Wuyuan [TJ, Inner Mongolian Aut. Reg.] 142-143 K 3
Wu-yüan = Wuyuan [TJ, Jiangxi] 146-147 FG 7
Wuyun 142-143 O 2
Wu-yün = Wuyun 142-143 O 2
Wuz, El — = Al-Wazz 164-165 L 5
Wuzhai 146-147 C 2
Wuzhang = Wuchang 142-143 O 3
Wuzhen 146-147 C 6
Wuzhi 146-147 D 4
Wuzhi Shan 150-151 G 3
Wuzhong 142-143 K 4
Wuzhou 142-143 L 7
Wyandotte, MI 72-73 E 3
Wyandra 158-159 HJ 5
Wyanet, IL 70-71 F 5
Wyangala Reservoir 158-159 J 6
Wyara = Wyārā 138-139 D 7
Wyarno, WY 68-69 C 3
Wye 119 E 5
Wymark 61 E 5
Wymore, NE 68-69 H 5
Wynaad 140 C 5
Wynbring 158-159 F 6
Wyncote, PA 84 III c 1
Wyndham 158-159 E 3
Wyndmere, ND 68-69 H 2
Wyndmoor, PA 84 III b 1
Wynne, AR 78-79 D 3
Wynne Wood, OK 76-77 F 5
Wynnewood, PA 84 III b 2
Wynniatt Bay 56-57 O 3
Wynyard [AUS] 158-159 HJ 8
Wynyard [CDN] 61 FG 5
Wyola, MT 68-69 C 3
Wyoming 64-65 D-F 3
Wyoming, IL 70-71 F 5
Wyoming, MI 70-71 H 4
Wyoming Peak 66-67 H 4
Wyoming Range 66-67 H 4
Wyschki = Spoģi 124-125 F 5
Wysokie Litewskie = Vysokoje 124-125 D 7
Wytheville, VA 80-81 F 2

X

Xadded 164-165 b 1
Xa-doai 148-149 E 3
Xai Lai Leng, Phou — 150-151 DE 3
Xai Xai 172 F 7
Xalapa = Jalapa Enríquez 64-65 GH 8
Xalin 164-165 b 2
Xalisco = Jalisco 64-65 EF 7
Xamboiá 98-99 O 8
Xangongo 172 C 5
Xanh, Cu Lao — = Cu Lao Poulo Gambir 150-151 GH 6
Xánthē 122-123 L 5
Xanxerê 111 F 3
Xapecó 102-103 F 7
Xapecó, Rio — 102-103 F 7
Xapecózinho, Rio — 102-103 FG 7
Xaprui, Rio — 98-99 D 10
Xapuri 92-93 F 7
Xarardeere 164-165 b 3
Xar Moron He 142-143 MN 3
Xateturu, Cachoeira — 98-99 MN 8
Xauen = Shifshawn 164-165 CD 1
Xavantes 102-103 H 5
Xavantes, Represa de — 102-103 H 5
Xavantes, Serra dos — 92-93 K 7
Xavantina 102-103 F 4
Xaxim 102-103 F 7
Xcan 64-65 J 7
Xenia, IL 70-71 F 6
Xenia, OH 72-73 E 5
Xeriuini, Rio — 98-99 G 4
Xexi 146-147 F 9
Xhora 174-175 H 6
Xiachuan Dao 142-143 L 7
Xiadanshui Qi = Hsiatanshui Chi 146-147 H 10
Xiadian 146-147 H 3
Xiadong 142-143 H 3
Xiaguan [TJ, Henan] 146-147 C 5
Xiaguan [TJ, Yunnan] 142-143 J 6
Xiahe 142-143 J 4
Xiajiang 146-147 E 8
Xiajing 146-147 EF 3
Xiamen 142-143 M 7
Xiamen Gang 146-147 G 9
Xi'an 142-143 K 5
Xianfeng 146-147 B 7
Xiangcheng [TJ ↓ Xuchang] 146-147 DE 5
Xiangcheng [TJ ↘ Zhoukou] 146-147 E 5
Xiangfan 142-143 L 5
Xiangfen 146-147 C 3-4
Xianggang = Hong Kong 142-143 LM 7
Xianggang = Victoria 155 I a 2
Xianghe 146-147 F 2
Xianghua 146-147 GH 5
Xianghua Wan 146-147 G 9
Xiang Jiang 142-143 L 6
Xiangning 146-147 C 3-4
Xiangshan 146-147 HJ 7
Xiangshan Gang 146-147 HJ 7
Xiangshui 146-147 G 4
Xiangtan 142-143 L 6
Xiangxiang 146-147 D 8
Xiangxi Zizhizhou 142-143 KL 6
Xiangyang 142-143 L 5
Xiangyangzhen 144-145 E 1
Xiangyin 146-147 D 7
Xiangyuan 146-147 D 3
Xiangzhou [TJ, Guangxi Zhuangzu Zizhiqu] 146-147 B 9
Xiangzhou [TJ, Shandong] 146-147 G 3
Xiangzikou 146-147 CD 7
Xianju 146-147 H 7
Xianning 142-143 LM 6
Xianshui = Jieshou 146-147 C 9
Xianxia Ling 146-147 G 7
Xian Xian 142-143 M 4
Xianyang 142-143 K 5
Xianyou 146-147 G 9
Xianzhong 146-147 DE 7
Xiaochangshan Dao 144-145 D 3
Xiaochi 146-147 E 9
Xiaofeng 146-147 G 6
Xiaogan 146-147 D 6
Xiao Hinggan Ling 142-143 O 1-2
Xiaohongmen, Beijing- 155 II b 3
Xiaojiang 146-147 E 9
Xiaolangpu = Shantangyi 146-147 BC 8
Xiaoliangshan 144-145 D 1
Xiaoling He 144-145 C 2
Xiaomei Guan 142-143 LM 6
Xiaoqi = Xiaoxi 146-147 E 9
Xiaoqing He 146-147 G 3
Xiao Shan [TJ, mountains] 146-147 C 4
Xiaoshan [TJ, place] 146-147 H 6
Xiao Shui 146-147 C 8-9
Xiaoweixi = Weixi 141 F 2
Xiaowutai Shan 146-147 E 2
Xiao Xi 146-147 G 7-8
Xiao Xian 146-147 F 4
Xiaoyi 146-147 C 3
Xiapu 146-147 GH 8
Xiatangji 146-147 F 5
Xia Xian 146-147 C 4
Xiayang 146-147 FG 8
Xiayi 146-147 F 4
Xibahe = Beijing-Taiyanggong 155 II b 2
Xichang [TJ, Guangdong] 150-151 G 2
Xichang [TJ, Sichuan] 142-143 J 6
Xiche 146-147 B 7
Xichū 86-87 K 7
Xichuan 142-143 L 5
Xico, Cerro — 91 I d 3
Xicoco = Shikoku 142-143 P 5
Xicotepec de Juárez 86-87 LM 7
Xico Viejo 91 I d 3
Xidachuan 144-145 FG 2
Xi Dian = Baiyang Dian 146-147 EF 2
Xié, Rio — 98-99 E 4
Xiegar Zong = Shekhar Dsong 142-143 F 6
Xieji = Funan 146-147 E 5
Xiemahe 146-147 C 6
Xiêng Khouang 148-149 D 3
Xieng Kok = Ban Xiêng Kok 150-151 C 2
Xiengmai = Chiang Mai 148-149 C 3
Xiêng Mi 150-151 D 3
Xifei He 146-147 EF 5
Xifengkou 144-145 B 2
Xigezi = Zhigatse 142-143 F 6
Xiguit Qi 142-143 N 2
Xi Hu = Chengxi Hu 146-147 EF 5
Xihua 146-147 E 5
Xi Jiang 142-143 L 7
Xikou 146-147 C 7
Xile Qi = Hsilo Chi 146-147 H 10
Xiliao He 142-143 N 3
Xilin Hot 142-143 M 3
Ximeng 141 F 4
Ximo = Kyūshū 142-143 P 5
Ximucheng 144-145 D 2
Xin 'an [TJ, Henan] 146-147 D 4
Xin'an [TJ, Jiangxi] 146-147 F 8
Xin'an = Guannan 146-147 G 4
Xin'an Jiang 146-147 G 7
Xinavane 174-175 K 3
Xinbin 144-145 E 2
Xincai 142-143 LM 5
Xinchang 146-147 H 7
Xincheng 146-147 EF 2
Xincheng = Hsincheng 146-147 HJ 9
Xinchengbu 142-143 K 4
Xindi 144-145 B 2
Xindi = Honghu 142-143 L 6
Xindu 142-143 L 7
Xinfeng [TJ ↓ Fuzhou] 146-147 F 8
Xinfeng [TJ ↓ Ganzhou] 146-147 E 9
Xing'an [TJ, Guangxi Zhuangzu Zizhiqu] 146-147 C 9
Xingan [TJ, Jiangxi] 146-147 E 8
Xingang = Tanggu 142-143 M 4
Xingao Shan = Yu Shan 146-147 H 10
Xingcheng 144-145 C 2
Xingguo 146-147 E 8
Xinghua 146-147 GH 5
Xinghua Wan 146-147 G 9
Xinghuo, Beijing- 155 II b 2
Xingning 142-143 M 7
Xingping 146-147 B 4
Xingren 142-143 K 6
Xingshan 146-147 C 6
Xingtai 142-143 L 4
Xingtang 146-147 E 2
Xingtian 146-147 G 8
Xingu [BR, Amazonas] 92-93 F 6
Xingu [BR, Mato Grosso] 98-99 M 11
Xingu, Parque Nacional do — 98-99 M 10
Xingu, Rio — 92-93 J 6
Xing Xian 146-147 C 2
Xingzi 146-147 F 7
Xinhai = Huanghua 146-147 F 2
Xinhe [TJ, Hebei] 146-147 E 3
Xinhe [TJ, Shandong] 146-147 G 3
Xinhua 142-143 L 6
Xinhua = Hsinhua 146-147 H 10
Xinhuang 146-147 B 8
Xinhui 146-147 D 10
Xining 142-143 J 4
Xinjiang [TJ, place] 142-143 L 4
Xin Jiang [TJ, river] 146-147 F 7
Xinjiang = Xinjiang Uygur Zizhiqu 142-143 D-F 3
Xinjiang Uyghur Zizhiqu 142-143 D-G 3
Xinjiang Uygur Zizhiqu 142-143 D-F 3
Xinjie 146-147 B 2
Xinjin 144-145 CD 3
Xinjiulong = New Kowloon 155 I b 1
Xinkai He 142-143 N 3
Xinle 142-143 LM 4
Xinliao Dao 146-147 C 11
Xinlitun 144-145 CD 1-2
Xinmin 142-143 N 3
Xinning 146-147 C 8
Xinquan 146-147 F 9
Xinshao 146-147 C 8
Xinshi 146-147 D 8
Xintai 146-147 FG 4
Xintian 146-147 CD 9
Xinwen 146-147 F 4
Xin Xian [TJ, Henan] 146-147 E 6
Xinxian [TJ, Shanxi] 142-143 L 4
Xinxiang 142-143 LM 4
Xinxing 146-147 D 10
Xinyang 142-143 LM 5
Xinye 146-147 D 5
Xinyi [TJ, Guangdong] 146-147 C 10
Xinyi [TJ, Jiangsu] 146-147 G 4
Xinyu 146-147 E 8
Xinzhangzi 144-145 AB 2
Xinzhao Shan 146-147 AB 2
Xinzhen = Ba Xian 146-147 F 2
Xinzheng 146-147 DE 4
Xinzhou [TJ, Hainan Zizhizhou] 150-151 G 3
Xinzhou [TJ, Hubei] 146-147 E 6
Xinzhu = Hsinchu 142-143 N 7
Xiong'er Shan 146-147 C 5-D 4
Xiong Xian 146-147 F 2
Xiongyuecheng 144-145 CD 2
Xiping [TJ ↓ Luohe] 146-147 DE 5
Xiping [TJ ↖ Xichuan] 146-147 C 5
Xiquexique 92-93 L 7
Xiraz = Shīrāz 134-135 G 5
Xiriri, Lago — 98-99 L 5
Xiruá, Rio — 98-99 D 8
Xishuangbanna Daizu Zizhizhou 142-143 J 7
Xishuangbanna Zizhizhou ◁ 142-143 J 7
Xishui [TJ, place] 146-147 E 6
Xi Shui [TJ, river] 146-147 E 6
Xitianmu Shan = Tianmu Shan 146-147 G 6
Xitoli 168-169 B 3
Xiungyi = Xunyi 146-147 B 4
Xiuning 146-147 FG 7
Xiushan 146-147 B 7
Xiushui 146-147 E 7
Xiuwu 146-147 D 4
Xiuyan 144-145 D 2
Xixia 146-147 C 5
Xi Xian [TJ, Henan] 146-147 E 5
Xi Xian [TJ, Shanxi] 142-143 L 4
Xiyang [TJ, Fujian] 146-147 F 9
Xiyang [TJ, Shanxi] 146-147 D 3
Xiyang Dao 146-147 H 8
Xiyuqu, Beijing- 155 II a 2
Xizang = Tsang 138-139 LM 3
Xizhong Dao 144-145 C 3
Xizhuang, Beijing- 155 II b 2
Xochimilco 91 I c 3
Xochimilco, Lago de — 91 I c 3
Xochistlahuaca 86-87 L 9
Xochitenco 91 I cd 2
Xolapur = Sholāpur 134-135 M 7
Xom Cuc 150-151 EF 4
Xorroxó 100-101 E 5
Xpuhil 86-87 Q 8
Xuancheng 146-147 G 6
Xuancheng = Ningguo 146-147 G 6
Xuan'en 142-143 KL 5-6
Xuanhua 142-143 LM 3
Xuân Lôc 150-151 F 7
Xuanwei 142-143 J 6
Xuanwu Park 155 II b 2
Xuanwuqu, Beijing- 155 II ab 2
Xuchang 142-143 L 5
Xuddur 164-165 a 3
Xué 98-99 E 7
Xuecheng 146-147 F 4
Xuefeng Shan 146-147 C 7-8
Xuguanzhen 146-147 H 6
Xuguit Qi 142-143 N 2
Xuji = Shuiji 146-147 G 8
Xu Jiang 146-147 F 8
Xun He 146-147 B 5
Xunhua 142-143 J 4
Xunke 142-143 O 2
Xunwu 146-147 E 9
Xun Xian 146-147 E 4
Xunyang 146-147 B 5
Xunyangba 146-147 B 5
Xunyi 146-147 B 4
Xunyuecheng = Xiongyuecheng 144-145 CD 2
Xupu 146-147 C 8
Xushui 146-147 E 2
Xuwan 146-147 F 8
Xuwen 146-147 BC 11
Xuyan = Xiuyan 144-145 D 2
Xuyên Môc 150-151 F 7
Xuyi 146-147 G 5
Xuy Nông Chao 150-151 F 2
Xuzhou 142-143 M 5

Y

Yaak, MT 66-67 F 1
Ya'an 142-143 J 6
Yaapeet 160 EF 5
Ya Ayun 150-151 G 6
Yaba, Lagos- 170 III b 1
Yaba-College of Technology 170 III b 1
Yaballo = Yabēlo 164-165 M 7-8
Yabayo 168-169 D 4
Yabe, Yokohama- 155 III a 3
Yabebyry, Río — 102-103 D 7
Yabēlo 164-165 M 7-8
Yābis, 'Irq — 166-167 EF 6
Yablonovoi Mountains = Jablonovyj chrebet 132-133 U-W 7
Yabrīn 134-135 F 6
Yacaré Norte, Riacho — 102-103 C 5
Yachats, OR 66-67 A 3
Yacheng 142-143 K 8
Ya-chou = Ya'an 142-143 J 6
Yachow = Ya'an 142-143 J 6
Yacíretá, Isla — 102-103 D 7
Yacolt, WA 66-67 B 3
Yacopí 94-95 D 5
Yacuaboy, Colonia — 102-103 DE 7
Yacuiba 92-93 G 9
Yacuma, Río — 104-105 C 4
Yādagiri = Yādgir 140 C 2
Yādgir 140 C 2
Yadong 138-139 M 4
Ya Drang 150-151 F 6
Yafi 148-149 M 7
Yafō, Tel Aviv- 134-135 C 4
Yagda = Erdemli 136-137 F 4
Yagiri, Matsudo- 155 III c 1
Yağmurdere 136-137 HJ 2
Yaguachi Nuevo 96-97 B 3
Yagual, El — 94-95 G 4
Yaguara 94-95 D 6
Yaguarapara 94-95 K 2
Yaguarí 106-107 K 3
Yaguarón 102-103 D 6
Yaguarón, Río — 106-107 L 3-4
Yaguaru 104-105 E 4
Yaguas, Río — 96-97 F 3
Yahiko 144-145 M 4
Yahila 172 D 1
Yahk 66-67 EF 1
Ya Hleo = Ea Hleo 150-151 F 6
Yahuma 172 D 1
Yahyalı = Gazibenli 136-137 F 3
Yai, Khao — 150-151 B 5
Yai, Ko — 150-151 C 9
Yaichau = Ya Xian 142-143 KL 8
Yai-chou Wan = Yaizhou Wan 150-151 G 3
Yaila Mountains = Krymskije gory 126-127 FG 4
Yaizhou Wan 150-151 G 3
Yaizu 144-145 M 5
Yajalón 86-87 OP 9
Yājpura = Jājpur 138-139 L 7
Yakak, Cape — 58-59 u 7
Yakarta = Jakarta 148-149 E 8
Yakima, WA 64-65 BC 2
Yakima Indian Reservation 66-67 C 2
Yakima Ridge 66-67 CD 2
Yakima River 66-67 CD 2
Yakishiri-jima 144-145 b 1
Yakko 141 D 2
Yako 164-165 D 6
Yakō, Yokohama- 155 III b 2
Yakobi Island 58-59 T 8
Yakoko = Yapehe 172 DE 2
Yakrigourou 168-169 F 3
Ya Krong Bo'lah 150-151 F 5
Yakt, MT 66-67 F 1
Yak Tuḏuwa 140 DE 6
Yaku 144-145 H 7
Yakuendai 155 III d 1
Yakumo 144-145 b 2
Yaku-shima 142-143 P 5
Yaku sima = Yaku-shima 142-143 P 5
Yakutat, AK 56-57 HJ 6
Yakutat Bay 56-57 HJ 6
Yakut Autonomous Soviet Socialist Republic 132-133 U-b 4
Yakutsk = Jakutsk 132-133 Y 5
Yal 168-169 J 3
Yala [BUR] 148-149 D 5
Yāla [CL] 140 E 7
Yalal 166-167 G 2
Yalandūru = Yelandūr 140 C 4
Yalavarga = Yelbarga 140 BC 3
Yālbāng 138-139 H 2
Yale 66-67 C 1
Yale, MI 72-73 E 3
Yale, OK 76-77 F 4
Yale Point 74-75 J 4
Yalgoo 158-159 C 5
Yalí 94-95 D 4
Yalinga 164-165 J 7
Yallāmañchili = Elamanchili 140 F 2
Yallāpura = Yellāpur 140 B 3
Yalnızçam dağları 136-137 JK 2
Yalo 168-169 DE 2
Yalógo 168-169 EF 2
Yaloké 164-165 H 7
Yalong Jiang 142-143 J 6
Ya Lôp 150-151 F 6
Yalova 136-137 C 2
Yalta = Jalta 126-127 G 4
Yalu 142-143 N 2
Yalu Cangpu Jiang = Tsangpo 142-143 EF 6
Ya-lu Chiang = Yalu Jiang 144-145 EF 2
Yalu He 142-143 N 2
Ya-lu Ho = Yalu He 142-143 N 2
Yalu Jiang 142-143 O 3
Ya-lung Chiang = Yalong Jiang 142-143 J 6
Yalvaç 136-137 D 3
Yamada 144-145 NO 3
Yamada = Nankoku 144-145 JK 6
Yamaga 144-145 H 6
Yamagata 142-143 QR 4
Yamaguchi 144-145 HJ 5
Yamakuni 144-145 H 6
Yamalo-Nenets Autonomous Area 132-133 M-P 4
Yamal Peninsula = Jamal 132-133 MN 3
Yamanashi 144-145 M 5
Yamasaki 144-145 K 5
Yamato Bank 142-143 PQ 4
Yamato-sammyaku 53 B 4
Yambéring 164-165 B 6
Yambi, Mesa de — 92-93 E 4
Yāmbiū 164-165 K 8
Yambu = Kātmāndu 134-135 NO 5
Yamdok Tso = Yangdog Tsho 138-139 N 3
Yamethin = Yamīthin 148-149 C 2
Yam Hammelaḥ 136-137 F 7
Y'Ami Island 146-147 H 11
Yaminué = Arroyo Seco 108-109 F 3
Yamīthin 148-149 C 2
Yam Kinneret 134-135 D 4
Yamma Yamma, Lake — 158-159 H 5
Yammu = Jammu 134-135 LM 4
Yamón 96-97 B 4
Yamoussoukro 168-169 D 4
Yampa, CO 68-69 C 5
Yampa River 68-69 BC 5
Yampi Sound 158-159 D 3
Yamsay Mountain 66-67 C 4
Yamuduozuonake Hu = Ngamdo Tsonag Tsho 142-143 G 5
Yamuna 134-135 MN 5
Yamunā = Jamuna 141 C 2
Yamunānagar 138-139 F 2
Yamunōtri = Jamnotri 138-139 G 2
Yana 168-169 B 3
Yanac 160 E 6
Yanacancha 96-97 B 5
Yanagawa 144-145 H 6

Yanahuanca 96-97 C 7
Yanai 144-145 HJ 6
Yanaka 155 III d 3
Yanam 134-135 N 7
Yan'an 142-143 K 4
Yanaoca 92-93 E 7
Yanaon = Yanam 134-135 N 7
Yanatili, Río — 96-97 E 8
Yanbian 142-143 J 6
Yanbian Chaoxianzu Zizhizhou 142-143 OP 3
Yanbian Zizhizhou 144-145 GH 1
Yanbu' al-Baḥr 134-135 D 6
Yancapata 96-97 D 7
Yanchang 146-147 C 3
Yancheng [TJ, Henan] 146-147 E 5
Yancheng [TJ, Jiangsu] 142-143 N 5
Yan Chi 146-147 A 3
Yanchuan 142-143 KL 4
Yandama Creek 160 E 2
Yandoon = Nyaungdôn 141 D 7
Yane 106-107 A 6
Yanfolila 168-169 CD 3
Yangambi 172 DE 1
Yangang-do = Ryanggang-do 144-145 FG 2
Yangasso 168-169 D 2
Yangcheng 146-147 D 4
Yang-chiang = Yangjiang 142-143 L 7
Yang-chiao-kou = Yangjiaogou 146-147 G 3
Yangchuan = Yangquan 142-143 L 4
Yangchun 146-147 CD 10
Yangcun = Wuqing 146-147 F 2
Yangdog Tsho 138-139 N 3
Yangdŏk 144-145 F 3
Yangdong Tsho 142-143 G 6
Yanggu [ROK] 144-145 FG 3
Yanggu [TJ] 146-147 E 3
Yang-hsin = Yangsin 146-147 F 3
Yang-hsin = Yangxin 146-147 E 7
Yangi Hisar 142-143 CD 4
Yangjiang 142-143 L 7
Yangjiaogou 146-147 G 3
Yangjŏng-ni 144-145 F 4
Yangkiang = Yangjiang 142-143 L 7
Yangku = Taiyuan 142-143 L 4
Yangku = Yanggu 146-147 E 3
Yang-liu-ch'ing = Yangliuqing 146-147 F 2
Yangliuqing 146-147 F 2
Yangloudong 146-147 D 7
Yangmei 146-147 C 10
Yangping 146-147 C 6
Yangpu Gang 150-151 G 3
Yangp'yŏng 144-145 F 4
Yangqu 146-147 D 2
Yangquan 142-143 L 4
Yangsan 144-145 G 5
Yangshan 146-147 D 9
Yangshuling 144-145 B 2
Yangshuo 146-147 C 9
Yangsi 144-145 E 3
Yangsin = Yangxin 146-147 F 3
Yangso = Yangshuo 146-147 C 9
Yang Talat 150-151 D 4
Yangtze Kiang = Chang Jiang 142-143 K 5-6
Yangxi 146-147 E 8
Yangxin [TJ, Hubei] 146-147 E 7
Yangxin [TJ, Shandong] 146-147 F 3
Yangyang 142-143 O 4
Yangyuan 146-147 E 1
Yangzhong 146-147 GH 5
Yangzhou 142-143 M 5
Yangzhuoyong Hu = Yangdog Tsho 138-139 N 3
Yanhe [TJ, place] 146-147 B 7
Yan He [TJ, river] 146-147 BC 3
Yanina = Iôánnina 122-123 J 6
Yanji 142-143 O 3
Yanjin 146-147 DE 4
Yanjing 142-143 H 6
Yankee Stadium 82 III c 2
Yankton, SD 64-65 G 3
Yanku = Taiyuan 142-143 L 4
Yanling 146-147 DE 4
Yanna 158-159 J 5
Yanonge 172 D 1
Yân Oya 140 E 6
Yanping = Enping 146-147 D 10
Yanqi = Qara Shahr 142-143 F 3
Yanshan [TJ, Hebei] 146-147 F 2
Yanshan [TJ, Jiangxi] 146-147 F 7
Yanshi 146-147 D 4
Yanskoi Bay = Janskij zaliv 132-133 Za 3
Yantabulla 160 G 2
Yantai 142-143 N 4
Yanwa 141 F 2
Yanxi 142-143 L 6
Yanzhou 146-147 F 4
Yao 164-165 H 6
Yaoganhutun = Yaoqianhu 144-145 D 2
Yao-hsien = Yao Xian 146-147 B 4
Yao-kou = Yaowan 146-147 G 4
Yaolo 172 D 1
Yaoqianhu 144-145 D 2
Yaoundé 164-165 G 8
Yaowan 146-147 G 4
Yaowari 146-147 G 4
Yao Xian 146-147 B 4
Yao Yai, Ko — 150-151 B 9
Yap 206-207 R 9
Yapacana, Cerro — 94-95 H 6
Yapacani, Río — 104-105 D 5
Yāpanaya 134-135 MN 9
Yāpanē Kalapuwa 140 E 6
Yapehe 172 DE 2
Yapella, Río — 94-95 E 7
Yapen, Pulau — 148-149 L 7
Yapen, Selat — 148-149 L 7
Yapeyú 106-107 J 2
Yap Islands 148-149 L 5
Yapraklı = Tuht 136-137 E 2
Yaqui, Río — 64-65 E 6
Yaquina Head 66-67 A 3
Yaracuy 94-95 G 2
Yaracuy, Río — 94-95 G 2
Yaraka 158-159 H 4
Yaralıgoz dağı 136-137 EF 2
Yarang 150-151 C 9
Yarangüme 136-137 C 4
Yarani 168-169 D 3
Yarí, Llanos de — 94-95 D 7
Yarí, Río — 92-93 E 4
Yariga-take 142-143 Q 4
Yaring 150-151 C 9
Yaritagua 94-95 G 2
Yarkand 142-143 D 4
Yarkand darya 142-143 D 4-E 3
Yarmouth 56-57 X 9
Yarnell, AZ 74-75 G 5
Yāro Luṇḍ 138-139 B 4
Yaroslavl = Jaroslavl' 132-133 FG 6
Yarra Bend National Park 161 II c 1
Yarram 158-159 J 7
Yarraman 158-159 K 5
Yarra River 161 II c 1
Yarras 160 L 3
Yarraville, Melbourne- 161 II b 1
Yarrawonga 160 GH 6
Yarumal 92-93 D 3
Yarvicoya, Cerro — 104-105 B 6-7
Yasanyama 164-165 J 8
Yasawa Group 148-149 a 2
Yashi 168-169 G 2
Yashima 144-145 N 3
Yashiro-jima 144-145 J 6
Yasothon 150-151 E 5
Yass 158-159 J 6
Yassar, Wādī — 166-167 H 1
Yassıçal 144-145 J 5
Yasun burnu 136-137 GH 2
Yasuni 96-97 D 2
Yasuní, Río — 96-97 C 2
Yata 104-105 C 3
Yata, Río — 104-105 D 3
Yatağan 136-137 C 4
Yatakala 164-165 E 6
Yate, Monte — 108-109 C 3
Yates Center, KS 70-71 C 6-7
Yathkyed Lake 56-57 R 5
Yathung = Yadong 138-139 M 4
Yatina 104-105 D 7
Yatsu 155 III d 1
Yatsuga take 144-145 M 4-5
Yatsushiro 144-145 H 6
Yatsushiro-wan 144-145 H 6
Yatta Plateau 171 D 3
Yattī 166-167 B 7-C 6
Yatua, Río — 94-95 H 7
Yauca 96-97 D 9
Yauca, Río — 96-97 D 9
Yauchari, Río — 96-97 C 3
Yauco 88-89 N 6
Yau Mai Ti, Kowloon- 155 I a 2
Yaunde = Yaoundé 164-165 G 8
Yauri 96-97 F 9
Yautepec 86-87 L 8
Yau Tong 155 I b 2
Yau Ue Wan 155 I b 2
Yauyos 92-93 D 7
Yāval 138-139 E 7
Yavarí, Río — 92-93 E 5
Yavari-Mirim, Río — 96-97 E 4
Yavatmāḷ = Yeotmāl 138-139 FG 7
Yavello = Yabēlo 164-165 M 7-8
Yavero, Río — 96-97 E 8
Yavı [TR, Erzurum] 136-137 J 3
Yavi [TR, Sivas] 136-137 G 3
Yavi, Cerro — 92-93 F 3
Yaviza 94-95 C 3
Yavuzeli 136-137 G 4
Yawal = Yāval 138-139 E 7
Yawata, Ichikawa- 155 III c 1
Yawatahama 144-145 J 6
Yaw Chaung 141 D 5
Yawnghwe = Nyaungywe 141 E 5
Yaxchilán 64-65 H 8
Ya Xian 142-143 KL 8
Yayaköy = Palamut 136-137 B 3
Yayladağı 136-137 FG 5
Yayo 164-165 H 5
Yayuan 144-145 F 2
Yazd 134-135 G 4
Yazoo City, MS 78-79 D 4
Yazoo River 64-65 H 5
Ybytymí 102-103 D 6
Ycliff 62 D 2
Ye 148-149 C 3
Yeadon, PA 84 III b 2
Yebala = Jabalā 166-167 D 2
Ye-Buri midre Selate 164-165 N 5
Yebyū 150-151 B 5
Yecheng = Qarghaliq 142-143 D 4
Yech'ŏn 144-145 G 4
Yecla 120-121 G 9
Yécora 86-87 F 3
Yedashe = Yedāshī 141 E 6
Yedāshī 141 E 6
Yedikule, İstanbul- 154 I a 3
Yedo = Tōkyō 142-143 QR 4
Yegros 102-103 D 7
Yeh-ch'êng = Qarghaliq 142-143 D 4
Yeh-chih = Yanwa 141 F 2
Yeh-hsien = Ye Xian 146-147 D 5
Yeh Kyûn 141 C 6
Yehsien = Ye Xian 142-143 MN 4
Yehuin, Lago — 108-109 EF 10
Yei [Sudan, place] 164-165 L 8
Yei [Sudan, river] 171 B 1
Yeji [GH] 168-169 E 3
Yeji [TJ] 146-147 E 6
Yékia Sahal 164-165 H 5
Yelahanka 140 C 4
Yelandūr 140 C 4
Yelbāra 138-139 G 7
Yelbarga 140 BC 3
Yelcho, Lago — 108-109 C 4
Yele 168-169 BC 3
Yélimané 164-165 BC 5-6
Yelizavety, Cape — = mys Jelizavety 132-133 b 7
Yell 119 F 1
Yellamanchili = Elamanchili 140 F 2
Yellandu 140 E 2
Yellāpur 140 B 3
Yellāreḍḍi 140 CD 1
Yellareddy = Yellāreḍḍi 140 CD 1
Yellow Grass 61 FG 6
Yellowhead Highway 60 GH 3
Yellowhead Pass 56-57 N 7
Yellowknife 56-57 O 5
Yellow Medicine River 70-71 BC 3
Yellow Pine, ID 66-67 F 3
Yellow River 70-71 E 3
Yellow Sea 142-143 N 4
Yellowstone Lake 64-65 D 3
Yellowstone National Park 64-65 D 3
Yellowstone River 64-65 E 2
Yellowstone River, Clarks Fork — 68-69 B 3
Yellowtail Reservoir 66-67 JK 3
Yellville, AR 78-79 C 2
Yelwa 164-165 EF 6
Yemassee, SC 80-81 F 4
Yemen 134-135 E 7-8
Yemişenbükü 136-137 G 2
Yemyet In 141 D 4
Yen 150-151 C 10
Yên, Mui — 150-151 G 6
Yenangyat 141 D 5
Yenangyaung 148-149 BC 2
Yenanma 141 D 6
Yên Bay 148-149 DE 2
Yên Binh Xa 150-151 E 1
Yenchang = Yanchang 146-147 C 3
Yên Châu 150-151 E 2
Yencheng = Yancheng [TJ, Henan] 146-147 E 5
Yencheng = Yancheng [TJ, Jiangsu] 142-143 N 5
Yen-ch'i = Qara Shahr 142-143 F 3
Yen-chi = Yanji 142-143 O 3
Yen-chin = Yanjin 146-147 DE 4
Yen-ching = Yanjing 142-143 H 6
Yen-ch'uan = Yanchuan 142-143 KL 4
Yendi 164-165 DE 7
Yengan 141 E 5
Yengejeh 136-137 N 4
Yengema 168-169 C 3
Yengī Kand 136-137 MN 4
Yen-hai = Hsincheng 146-147 HJ 9
Yenho = Yanhe 146-147 B 7
Yeniçağa 136-137 DE 2
Yenice [TR, Çanakkale] 136-137 B 3
Yenice [TR, Mersin] 136-137 F 4
Yenice = Sındıran 136-137 E 3
Yeniceırmağı 136-137 FG 3
Yenidoğan, Ankara- 136-137 E 2
Yenikapı, İstanbul- 154 I a 3
Yeniköy [TR, Artvin] 136-137 K 2
Yeniköy, İstanbul- 154 I b 2
Yenimahalle 136-137 E 2-3
Yenipazar 136-137 BC 4
Yenişehir 136-137 C 2
Yenişehir, Ankara- 136-137 E 3
Yenisei = Jenisej 132-133 Q 4
Yenisei Bay = Jenisejskij zaliv 132-133 OP 3
Yeniyol 136-137 JK 2
Yenki = Qara Shahr 142-143 F 3
Yenki = Yanji 142-143 O 3
Yên Lac 150-151 E 3
Yenling = Yanling 146-147 DE 4
Yenlo, Mount — 58-59 M 5
Yenpien = Yanbian 142-143 J 6
Yenping = Nanping 142-143 M 6
Yen-shan = Yanshan 146-147 F 2
Yen-shih = Yanshi 146-147 D 4
Yentai = Yantai 142-143 N 4
Yentna River 58-59 M 5
Yeo, Lake — 158-159 D 5
Yeola 138-139 E 7
Yeotmāl 138-139 FG 7
Yeovil 119 E 6
Yeoville, Johannesburg- 170 V b 2
Yeppoon 158-159 K 4
Yerbal Nuevo 106-107 K 1
Yerbas 106-107 GH 6
Yercaud 140 CD 5
Yerevan = Jerevan 126-127 M 6
Yerington, NV 74-75 D 3
Yerköy 136-137 F 3
Yerla 140 B 2
Yermo 76-77 B 9
Yerna Tsho 142-143 F 5
Yerqiang = Yarkand 142-143 D 4
Yerres [F, place] 129 I d 3
Yeruá 106-107 H 3
Yerupaja 92-93 D 7
Yĕrūshālayim 134-135 CD 4
Yesagyō 141 D 5
Yesan 144-145 F 4
Yeşilhisar 136-137 F 3
Yeşilırmak 134-135 D 2
Yeşilova = Satırlar 136-137 C 4
Yeşilyurt = İsmetpaşa 136-137 H 3
Yeso, NM 76-77 B 5
Yesso = Hokkaidō 142-143 RS 3
Yeste 120-121 F 9
Yetman 160 K 2
Ye'ū 141 D 4
Yeu, Île de — 120-121 F 5
Yeungkong = Yangjiang 142-143 L 7
Yevpatoriya = Jevpatorija 126-127 F 4
Yewale = Yāval 138-139 E 7
Yew Mountain 72-73 F 5
Ye Xian [TJ, Henan] 146-147 D 5
Ye Xian [TJ, Shandong] 142-143 MN 4
Yezd = Yazd 134-135 G 4
Yezhi = Yanwa 141 F 2
Yezo = Hokkaidō 142-143 RS 3
Yezo Strait = Nemuro-kaikyō 144-145 d 1-2
Yguazú, Río — 102-103 E 6
Yhaty 102-103 D 6
Yhú 111 E 2
Yí, Río — 106-107 J 4
Yi'allaq, Gebel — = Jabal Yu'alliq 173 C 2
Yibin 142-143 JK 6
Yichang 142-143 L 5
Yicheng [TJ, Hubei] 142-143 L 5
Yicheng [TJ, Shanxi] 146-147 C 4
Yichuan [TJ, Henan] 146-147 D 4
Yichuan [TJ, Shaanxi] 146-147 BC 3
Yichun [TJ, Heilongjiang] 142-143 O 2
Yichun [TJ, Jiangxi] 142-143 LM 6
Yidda = Jiddah 134-135 D 6
Yidu [TJ, Hubei] 142-143 L 5
Yidu [TJ, Shandong] 142-143 M 4
Yiershi 142-143 MN 2
Yiewsley, London- 129 II a 1
Yifeng 146-147 E 7
Yiğılca = Cayırlıahmetçiler 136-137 D 2
Yi He [TJ, Henan] 146-147 D 4
Yi He [TJ, Shandong] 146-147 G 4
Yiheyuan Summer Palace 155 II a 1
Yihuang 146-147 F 8
Yijun 146-147 B 4
Yilan 142-143 OP 2
Yilan = Ilan 146-147 H 9
Yıldız dağı 136-137 G 2
Yıldızeli 136-137 G 3
Yilehuli Shan 142-143 NO 1
Yimen 146-147 F 5
Yinan 146-147 G 4
Yincheng 146-147 D 4
Yin-chiang = Yinjiang 146-147 B 7
Yinchuan 142-143 JK 4
Yindu He = Sengge Khamba 142-143 E 5
Yingcheng 146-147 D 6
Yingchuan 142-143 K 4
Yingde 142-143 L 7
Yingge Zui 150-151 G 3
Ying He 146-147 F 5
Ying Ho = Ying He 146-147 F 5
Yinghsien = Ying Xian 146-147 D 2
Yingjia 146-147 C 9
Yingjiang 141 E 3
Yingjisha = Yangi Hisar 142-143 CD 4
Ying-ko Tsui = Yingge Zui 150-151 G 3
Yingkou 142-143 N 3
Ying-k'ou = Yingkou 142-143 N 3
Yingkow = Yingkou 144-145 CD 2
Yingle Jiang = Anpu Gang 146-147 B 11
Yingpan 144-145 E 2
Yingshan [TJ → Nanchong] 142-143 K 5
Yingshan [TJ → Wuhan] 146-147 EF 6
Yingshan [TJ ↖ Wuhan] 146-147 D 6
Yingshang 146-147 EF 5
Yingtan 142-143 M 6
Ying-tê = Yingde 142-143 L 7
Ying Xian 146-147 D 2
Yining = Ghulja 142-143 E 3
Yining = Wutong 146-147 B 9
Yinjiang 146-147 B 7
Yinkeng 146-147 E 8
Yinkow = Yingkou 142-143 N 3
Yinmābin 141 D 4
Yin Xian 146-147 H 7
Yinxian = Ningbo 142-143 N 6
Yi-pin = Yibin 142-143 JK 6
Yirga-Alam = Yirga Alem 164-165 M 7
Yirga 'Alem 164-165 M 7
Yirŏl 164-165 L 7
Yi Shan [TJ, mountains] 146-147 G 3
Yishan [TJ, place] 142-143 K 7
Yishi = Linyi 146-147 C 4
Yishui 146-147 G 4
Yi-tcheou = Linyi 142-143 M 4
Yitu = Yidu 142-143 M 4
Yiwu [TJ, Yunnan] 150-151 C 2
Yiwu [TJ, Zhejiang] 146-147 GH 7
Yi Xian [TJ, Anhui] 146-147 F 7
Yi Xian [TJ, Hebei] 146-147 E 2
Yi Xian [TJ, Liaoning] 142-143 N 3
Yixian = Ye Xian 142-143 LM 4
Yixing 146-147 GH 6
Yiyang [TJ, Henan] 146-147 D 4
Yiyang [TJ, Hunan] 142-143 L 6
Yiyang [TJ, Jiangxi] 146-147 F 7
Yiyang = Ruyang 146-147 D 4
Yiyuan 146-147 G 3
Yizhang 146-147 D 9
Yizheng 146-147 G 5
Yläne 116-117 K 7
Ylikita 116-117 N 4
Ylivieska 116-117 L 5
Yllästunturi 116-117 KL 4
Ymēttós [GR, mountains] 113 IV b 2
Ymēttós [GR, place] 113 IV ab 2
Yndin 124-125 U 3
Yo, Mu'o'ng — 150-151 C 2
Yoakum, TX 76-77 F 8
Yocalla 104-105 D 6
Yochow = Yueyang 142-143 L 6
Yoder, WY 68-69 D 5
Yodoe 144-145 J 5
Yōga, Tōkyō- 155 III a 2
Yogan, Cerro — 111 BC 8
Yōgīguphā = Jogīghopa 138-139 N 4
Yōgipēṭa = Jogipet 140 CD 2
Yogyakarta [RI, administrative unit = 13 ◁] 148-149 EF 8
Yogyakarta [RI, place] 148-149 EF 8
Yoho National Park 60 J 4
Yoichi 144-145 b 2
Yokadouma 164-165 H 8
Yōkaichiba 144-145 N 5
Yokchi-do 144-145 G 5
Yokkaichi 142-143 Q 5
Yokkaiti = Yokkaichi 142-143 Q 5
Yoko 164-165 G 7
Yokohama 142-143 QR 4
Yokohama-Asahi 155 III a 3
Yokohama-Eda 155 III a 2
Yokohama-Futamatagawa 155 III a 3
Yokohama-Futatsubashi 155 III a 3
Yokohama-Hino 155 III a 3
Yokohama-Hiyoshi 155 III a 2
Yokohama-Hodogaya 155 III a 3
Yokohama-Hommoku 155 III ab 3
Yokohama-Idogaya 155 III a 3
Yokohama-Imajuku 155 III a 3
Yokohama-Isogo 155 III a 3
Yokohama-Izumi 155 III a 3
Yokohama-Kamoshida 155 III a 2
Yokohama-Kanagawa 155 III a 3
Yokohama-Kashio 155 III a 3
Yokohama-Katsuta 155 III a 2
Yokohama-Kawashima 155 III a 3
Yokohama-Kawawa 155 III a 2
Yokohama-Kikuna 155 III a 2
Yokohama-ko 155 III ab 3
Yokohama-Kōhoku 155 III a 2
Yokohama-Kozukue 155 III a 2
Yokohama-Kumizawa 155 III a 3
Yokohama-Midori 155 III a 2
Yokohama-Minami 155 III a 3
Yokohama-Motomachi 155 III a 3
Yokohama-Nagatsuda 155 III a 2
Yokohama-Naka 155 III a 3
Yokohama-Nakayama 155 III a 2
Yokohama-Namamugi 155 III b 3
Yokohama National University 155 III a 3
Yokohama-Nippo 155 III a 2
Yokohama-Nishi 155 III a 3
Yokohama-Ōkubo 155 III a 3
Yokohama-Sasake 155 III a 3
Yokohama-Seya 155 III a 3
Yokohama-Shinohara 155 III a 3
Yokohama-Sugita 155 III a 3
Yokohama-Terayama 155 III a 2
Yokohama-Totsuka 155 III a 3
Yokohama-Tsunashima 155 III a 2
Yokohama-Tsurumi 155 III a 2
Yokohama-Yabe 155 III a 3
Yokohama-Yakō 155 III b 2
Yokosuka 142-143 QR 4
Yokote 142-143 QR 4
Yola 164-165 G 7
Yolaina, Cordillera de — 88-89 D 9
Yolo 170 IV a 2
Yolombo 172 D 2
Yom, Mae Nam — 148-149 CD 3
Yōmagyō 141 E 6
Yomoso 91 III b 4
Yomou 168-169 C 4
Yonago 144-145 J 5
Yŏnan 144-145 EF 4
Yoncalla, OR 66-67 B 4
Yŏnch'ŏn 144-145 F 3
Yonegasaki, Funabashi- 155 III d 1
Yoneshiro-gawa 144-145 N 2
Yonezawa 142-143 QR 4
Yŏngam 144-145 F 5
Yongamp'o 144-145 E 3
Yong'an 142-143 M 6
Yongcheng 146-147 F 5
Yŏngch'ŏn 144-145 G 5
Yongchun 146-147 G 9
Yongcong 146-147 B 8
Yongdeng 142-143 J 4
Yongdian 144-145 E 2
Yongding 146-147 F 9
Yongding He 146-147 F 2
Yongdingmen, Beijing- 155 II b 2
Yŏngdŏk 144-145 G 4
Yŏngdong 144-145 F 4
Yongfeng 146-147 E 8
Yongfeng = Shuangfeng 146-147 D 8
Yongfu 146-147 B 9
Yonggok-tang 144-145 E 2
Yŏnghae 144-145 G 4
Yongha-ri 144-145 F 3
Yonghe 146-147 C 3
Yonghŭng 144-145 F 3
Yŏnghŭng-do 144-145 EF 4
Yŏngil-man 144-145 G 4
Yongji 142-143 L 5
Yongjia 146-147 H 7
Yongjia = Wenzhou 142-143 N 6
Yŏngju 144-145 G 4
Yongkang 146-147 H 7
Yongling 144-145 E 2
Yonglonghe 146-147 D 6
Yongming = Jiangyong 146-147 C 9
Yongnian 146-147 E 3
Yongning 142-143 J 6
Yongning = Nanning 142-143 K 7
Yong Peng 150-151 D 11-12
Yongqing 146-147 F 2
Yŏngsan 144-145 G 5
Yongshou 146-147 AB 4
Yongshun 146-147 B 7
Yongsui = Huayuan 146-147 B 7
Yongtai 142-143 M 6
Yŏngwŏl 144-145 G 4
Yŏngwŏn 144-145 F 3
Yongxin 146-147 E 8
Yongxing 146-147 D 8
Yongxiu 142-143 LM 6
Yongyang 146-147 E 8
Yŏngyu 144-145 E 3
Yonker 61 CD 4
Yonkers, NY 64-65 M 3
Yonne 120-121 J 5
Yopal 94-95 E 5
York, AL 78-79 E 4
York, ND 68-69 G 1
York, NE 68-69 H 5
York, PA 64-65 L 3-4
York, SC 80-81 F 3
York [AUS] 158-159 C 6
York [GB] 119 F 5
York, Cape — 158-159 H 2
York, Kap — 56-57 X 2
Yorke Peninsula 158-159 G 6
Yorketown 158-159 G 6-7
York Factory 56-57 S 6
York Harbour 63 G 3
York River 80-81 H 2
Yorkshire 119 F 4
York Sound 158-159 DE 2
Yorkton 56-57 Q 7
Yorktown, TX 76-77 F 8
Yorktown, VA 80-81 H 2
Yoro 88-89 C 7
Yorosso 168-169 D 2
Yoruba 168-169 FG 3
Yosemite National Park 74-75 D 4
Yosemite National Park, CA 64-65 C 4
Yoshida 144-145 J 6
Yoshii-gawa 144-145 K 5
Yoshino-gawa 144-145 JK 5
Yoshioka = Taiwa 144-145 N 3
Yōsō-do 144-145 F 6
Yösön Bulag = Altaj 142-143 H 2
Yost, UT 66-67 G 5
Yŏsu 142-143 O 5
Yotala 104-105 D 6
Yotaú 92-93 G 8
Yōtei-dake 144-145 b 2
You'anmen, Beijing- 155 II ab 2
Youanmi 158-159 C 5
Youghal 119 C 6
Youkounkoun 164-165 B 6
Youks-les-Bains = Ḥammāmāt 166-167 K 2
Young, AZ 74-75 H 5
Young [AUS] 158-159 J 6
Young [CDN] 61 F 5
Young [ROU] 106-107 J 4
Younghusband, Lake — 160 BC 3
Younghusband Penisland 160 D 5-6
Young Island 53 C 16-17
Youngstown 61 C 5
Youngstown, FL 78-79 G 5
Youngstown, OH 64-65 KL 3
Younts Peak 66-67 J 4
You Shui 146-147 BC 7
Youshuwan = Huaihua 146-147 B 8
Yoûsoufia = Yūssufīyah 166-167 B 3
Youth Recreation Park 154 II a 2
Youville, Montréal- 82 I ab 1
Youxi [TJ, place] 146-147 G 8
You Xi [TJ, river] 146-147 G 8-9
Youxian 146-147 D 8
Youxikou 146-147 G 8
Youyang 146-147 B 7
Youyu 146-147 D 1
Yowl Islands = Kepulauan Aju 148-149 K 6
Yoyang = Yueyang 142-143 L 6
Yŏyu 144-145 F 4
Yozgat 134-135 CD 3
Ypacaraí 102-103 D 6
Ypacaraí, Laguna — 102-103 D 6
Ypané, Río — 102-103 D 5
Ypê Jhú 102-103 E 5
Ypoá, Lago — 102-103 D 6
Ypres = Ieper 120-121 J 3
Ypsilanti, MI 72-73 E 3
Ypsilanti, ND 68-69 G 2
Yreka, CA 66-67 B 5
Ysabel = Santa Isabel 148-149 jk 6
Ysabel Channel 148-149 NO 7
Ysleta, TX 76-77 A 7
Yssel Lake = IJsselmeer 120-121 K 2
Ystad 116-117 E 10
Yu'alliq, Jabal — 173 C 2
Yuam, Mae - 141 E 6
Yuam, Mae — 150-151 A 3
Yuan'an 142-143 L 5
Yüan-an = Yuan'an 142-143 L 5
Yüan Chiang = Hong He 142-143 J 7
Yüan Chiang = Yuan Jiang 142-143 L 6
Yüan-chou = Yichun 142-143 LM 6
Yuanchow = Zhijiang 142-143 KL 6
Yuanjiang [TJ, place] 146-147 D 7
Yuan Jiang [TJ, river] 142-143 L 6
Yuankiang = Yuanjiang 146-147 D 7
Yüanlin 146-147 H 9-10
Yuanling 142-143 L 6
Yüan-ling = Yuanling 142-143 L 6
Yuanmou 142-143 J 6
Yuanping 142-143 L 4
Yuanqu 146-147 C 4
Yuanshi 146-147 E 3
Yüan-shih = Yuanshi 146-147 E 3
Yuan Shui 146-147 E 8
Yuantan [TJ, Guangdong] 146-147 D 10
Yuantan [TJ, Henan] 146-147 D 5
Yuanyang 146-147 DE 4
Yuba City, CA 64-65 B 4
Yūbari 142-143 R 3
Yuba River 74-75 C 3
Yūbetsu 144-145 d 2
Yūbetsu, Shimo- 144-145 cd 1
Yūbetu ↖ Kusiro 144-145 d 2
Yubineto 96-97 D 2
Yubo = Lī Yūbū 164-165 K 7
Yucatán 64-65 J 7
Yucatán, Península de — 64-65 HJ 8
Yucatan Basin 64-65 JK 8
Yucatan Channel = Canal de Yucatán 64-65 J 7
Yucca, AZ 74-75 F 5
Yuchān 104-105 DE 8
Yucheng [TJ, Henan] 146-147 EF 4
Yucheng [TJ, Shandong] 146-147 F 3
Yu-ch'i = Youxi [TJ, place] 146-147 G 8
Yu Ch'i = You Xi [TJ, river] 146-147 G 8-9
Yü-chiang = Yujiang 146-147 F 7
Yuci 142-143 L 4
Yudian = Keriya 142-143 E 4
Yudu 146-147 E 9
Yuegezhuang, Beijing- 155 II a 2
Yüeh-k'ou-chên = Yuekou 146-147 D 6
Yüeh-yang = Yueyang 142-143 L 6
Yuekou 146-147 D 6
Yueqing 142-143 N 6
Yueqing Wan 146-147 H 7-8
Yuetan = Altar of the Moon 155 II ab 2
Yueyang 142-143 L 6
Yugan 146-147 F 7
Yugor Strait = proliv Jugorskij Šar 132-133 L 4-M 3
Yugoslavia 122-123 F 3-J 5
Yü-hang = Jiuyuhang 146-147 G 6
Yuheng = Yucheng 146-147 F 3
Yü-hsien = Yu Xian [TJ, Hebei] 146-147 E 2
Yuhsien = Yu Xian [TJ, Henan] 146-147 D 4
Yü-hsien = Yu Xian [TJ, Henan] 146-147 D 4
Yuhsien = Yu Xian [TJ, Shanxi] 146-147 D 2
Yü-hsien = Yu Xian [TJ, Shanxi] 146-147 D 2
Yuhuan 146-147 H 7
Yuhuan Dao 146-147 H 7-8
Yuhuang 142-143 M 4
Yuhuang Ding 142-143 M 4
Yujiang [TJ, place] 146-147 F 7
Yu Jiang [TJ, river] 146-147 B 10
Yü-kan = Yugan 146-147 F 7
Yukarı Doğancılar 136-137 D 2
Yukarı Hadım = Hadım 136-137 E 4
Yukarı ova 136-137 FG 4
Yuki = Yuxi 146-147 G 9
Yukiang = Yujiang 146-147 F 7
Yukigaya, Tōkyō- 155 III b 2
Yuki Mount 58-59 JK 4
Yuki River 58-59 J 4
Yukon, Territoire de — = Yukon Territory 56-57 JK 4-5
Yukon Crossing 58-59 T 5
Yukon Delta 58-59 EF 5
Yukon Plateau 56-57 J 5
Yukon River 56-57 H 4
Yukon Territory 56-57 JK 4-5
Yüksekkum 136-137 C 4
Yüksekova = Dize 136-137 L 4
Yukuduma = Yokadouma 164-165 H 8
Yukuhashi 144-145 H 6
Yulee, FL 80-81 c 1
Yule River 158-159 C 4
Yüli [RC] 146-147 H 10
Yuli [WAN] 168-169 H 3
Yulin [TJ, Guangdong] 150-151 G 3
Yulin [TJ, Guangxi Zhuangzu Zizhiqu] 142-143 L 7
Yulin [TJ, Shaanxi] 142-143 KL 4
Yü-lin = Yulin [TJ, Guangdong] 150-151 G 3
Yü-lin = Yulin [TJ, Guangxi Zhuangzu Zizhiqu] 142-143 L 7
Yü-lin = Yulin [TJ, Shaanxi] 142-143 KL 4
Yulongxue Shan 142-143 J 6
Yulton, Lago — 108-109 C 5
Yü-lung Shan = Yulongxue Shan 142-143 J 6
Yuma, AZ 64-65 D 5
Yuma, CO 68-69 E 5
Yuma Desert 74-75 F 6
Yuma Indian Reservation 74-75 F 6
Yumare 94-95 G 2
Yumari, Cerro — 92-93 F 4
Yumbel 106-107 A 6
Yumbo 94-95 C 6
Yumen 142-143 H 4
Yumu Yumu 106-107 B 7
Yuna 158-159 BC 5
Yunak 136-137 D 3

Yunan 146-147 C 10
Yunaska Island 58-59 I 4
Yuncheng [TJ, Shandong] 146-147 EF 4
Yuncheng [TJ, Shanxi] 146-147 C 4
Yün-ch'êng = Yuncheng [TJ, Shandong] 146-147 EF 4
Yün-ch'êng = Yuncheng [TJ, Shanxi] 146-147 C 4
Yundan 141 F 2
Yundum 168-169 A 2
Yunfeng Shan = Xuefeng Shan 146-147 C 7-8
Yunfu 146-147 CD 10
Yungan = Yong'an 142-143 M 6
Yungas 92-93 FG 8
Yungay 106-107 AB 6
Yungchang = Baoshan 142-143 HJ 6
Yungcheng = Yongcheng 146-147 F 5
Yung-chi = Yongji 142-143 L 5
Yung-ch'ing = Yongqing 146-147 F 2
Yung-chou = Lingling 142-143 L 6
Yungchun = Yongchun 146-147 G 9
Yungfeng = Yongfeng 146-147 E 8
Yung-fu = Yongfu 146-147 B 9
Yungho = Yonghe 146-147 C 3
Yung-hsin = Yongxin 146-147 E 8
Yung-hsing = Yongxing 146-147 D 8
Yung-hsiu = Yongxiu 146-147 E 7
Yungkang = Yongkang 146-147 H 7
Yungki = Jilin 142-143 O 3
Yungkia = Yongjia 146-147 H 7
Yung-lung-ho = Yonglonghe 146-147 D 6
Yung-nien = Yongnian 146-147 E 3
Yung-ning = Yongning 142-143 J 6
Yung-shou = Yongshou 146-147 AB 4
Yung Shu Wan 155 I a 2
Yungsin = Yongxin 146-147 E 8
Yungtai = Yongtai 142-143 M 6
Yung-têng = Yongdeng 142-143 J 4
Yung-tien-ch'êng = Yongdian 144-145 E 2
Yung-ting = Yongding 146-147 F 9
Yung-ting Ho = Yongding He 146-147 F 2
Yungtsing = Yongqing 146-147 F 2
Yung-ts'ung = Yongcong 146-147 B 8
Yunguillo 94-95 C 7
Yunguyo 96-97 G 10
Yungxiao 142-143 M 7
Yung-yang = Yongyang 146-147 E 8
Yunhe 146-147 G 7
Yunhe = Lishui 142-143 MN 6
Yün-hsi = Yunxi 146-147 C 5
Yunhsien = Yun Xian 146-147 C 5
Yunkai Dashan 146-147 C 10
Yünlin 142-143 MN 7
Yunmeng 146-147 D 6
Yün-mêng = Yunmeng 146-147 D 6
Yunnan 142-143 HJ 7
Yunnan = Kunming 142-143 J 6
Yun Shui 146-147 D 6
Yün Shui = Yun Shui 146-147 D 6
Yunsiao = Yunxiao 142-143 M 7
Yunta 160 D 4
Yunxi 146-147 C 5
Yun Xian 146-147 C 5
Yunxiao 142-143 M 7
Yunyang 146-147 B 6
Yün-yang = Yun Xian 146-147 C 5
Yün-yang = Yunyang 146-147 B 6
Yünzalin Chaung 141 E 6-7
Yupixian = Yuxikou 146-147 G 6
Yupurari, Raudal — 94-95 F 7
Yuqueri 106-107 HJ 2
Yura [BOL] 104-105 C 7
Yura [PE] 96-97 F 10
Yura-gawa 144-145 K 5
Yurimaguas 92-93 D 6
Yuruá, Rio — 96-97 E 6
Yurung darya 142-143 DE 4
Yusala, Lago — 104-105 C 3
Yuşa tepesi 154 I b 2
Yuscarán 88-89 C 8
Yûsef, Baḥr — = Baḥr Yusuf 173 B 3
Yu Shan [RC] 142-143 N 7
Yushan [TJ] 146-147 FG 7
Yü-shan = Yushan 146-147 FG 7
Yü-shan-chên = Yushanzhen 146-147 B 7
Yushanzhen 146-147 B 7
Yushe 146-147 D 3
Yü-shih = Fugou 146-147 E 4-5
Yushu 142-143 O 3
Yushu = Chhergundo 142-143 H 5
Yu Shui = You Shui 146-147 BC 7
Yushu Zangzu Zizhizhou 142-143 GH 5
Yūssufīyah 166-167 B 3
Yusuf, Baḥr — 173 B 3
Yusufeli 136-137 J 2
Yūsufīyah, Al- 136-137 KL 6
Yutai 146-147 F 4
Yutian 146-147 F 2
Yü-tien = Keriya 142-143 E 4
Yutien = Yutian 146-147 F 2
Yü-t'ien = Yutian 146-147 F 2
Yuto 104-105 D 8
Yutsien = Yuxikou 146-147 G 6
Yü-tu = Yudu 146-147 E 9
Yuty 111 E 3
Yutze = Yuci 142-143 L 4
Yuweng Dao = Yüweng Tao 146-147 G 10
Yüweng Tao 146-147 G 10
Yuxi 146-147 G 9
Yu Xian [TJ, Hebei] 146-147 E 2
Yu Xian [TJ, Henan] 146-147 D 4
Yu Xian [TJ, Shanxi] 146-147 D 2
Yuxikou 146-147 G 6
Yuyaansha 152-153 L 1
Yuyang = Youyang 146-147 B 7
Yuyao 146-147 H 6
Yuyuan Tan 155 II a 2
Yuyuantan, Beijing- 155 II a 2
Yuzawa [J, Akita] 144-145 N 3
Yuzawa [J, Niigata] 144-145 M 4

Z

Zaachila 86-87 M 9
Zaaltajn Gov' 142-143 H 3
Zaandijk, Zaanstad- 128 I a 1
Zaanse Schans 128 I a 1
Zaanstad 120-121 K 2
Zaanstad-Koog aan de Zaan 128 I a 1
Zaanstad-Westzaan 128 I a 1
Zaanstad-Zaandijk 128 I a 1
Zāb, Jabal az- 166-167 J 2
Zab, Monts du — = Jibal az-Zāb 166-167 J 2
Zabajkal'sk 132-133 W 8
Zāb al-Kabīr 136-137 K 4
Zāb al-Khabīr = Zāb al-Kabīr 136-137 K 4
Zabarjad, Jazīrat — 173 DE 6
Zāb aṣ-Ṣaghīr 136-137 K 5
Zabdānī 136-137 G 6
Zāb-e Kūchek, Rūd-e — 136-137 L 4
Zabīd 134-135 E 8
Žabljak 122-123 H 4
Z'ablovo 124-125 T 4
Zabok 122-123 FG 2
Zabol 134-135 J 4
Zaburunje 126-127 P 3
Zabzugu 168-169 F 3
Zacapa 86-87 Q 10
Zacapu 86-87 K 8
Zacarevo 126-127 O 3
Zacatecas 64-65 F 7
Zacatecas, Sierras de — 86-87 JK 6
Zacatecoluca 88-89 B 8
Zacatula, Río — 86-87 JK 8
Zacoalco de Torres 86-87 J 7
Zadar 122-123 F 3
Zādetkale Kyûn 150-151 AB 7
Zādetkyî Kyûn 148-149 C 5
Zadonsk 124-125 M 7
Ẓafār = Ẓufār 134-135 G 7
Za'farānah, Az- 173 C 3
Zafra 120-121 D 9
Žagań 118 G 3
Žagarė 124-125 D 5
Zagazig, Ez- = Az-Zaqāzīq 164-165 KL 2
Zaghartā 136-137 F 5
Zaghir, Ḥammadat az- 166-167 M 6
Zaghlūl 166-167 F 6
Zaghouan = Zaghwān 166-167 M 1
Zaghouane = Zaghwān 166-167 M 1
Zāghrīr, Wādī — 166-167 J 3
Zaghūrah 164-165 C 2
Zaghwān 166-167 M 1
Zaglou = Zaghlūl 166-167 F 6
Zagnanado 164-165 E 7
Zāgôrā = Zaghūrah 164-165 C 2
Zagorodje 124-125 E 7
Zagorsk 132-133 F 6
Zagreb 122-123 FG 3
Zāgros, Kūhhā-ye — 134-135 F 3-4
Zagros Mountains = Kūhhā-ye Zāgros 134-135 F 3-4
Žagubica 122-123 J 3
Ẓahar 166-167 LM 3
Zāhedān 134-135 J 5
Ẓahīliqah, Az- 166-167 C 3
Zahirābād 140 C 2
Zahl, ND 68-69 E 1
Zaḥlah 136-137 F 6
Ẓahrān 134-135 E 7
Ẓahrān, Aẓ- 134-135 FG 5
Zahraz al-Gharbī 166-167 H 2
Zahraz ash-Sharqī 166-167 H 2
Zaidam = Tshaidam 142-143 GH 4
Zaire [Angola] 172 B 3
Zaïre [ZRE, river] 172 C 2
Zaïre [ZRE, state] 172 C-E 2
Zaječar 122-123 JK 4
Zajsan 132-133 P 8
Zajsan, ozero — 132-133 P 8
Zakamensk 132-133 T 7
Zakamsk, Perm- 124-125 UV 5
Zakarpatskaja Oblast' 126-127 A 2
Zakatal'skij zapovednik 126-127 N 6
Zakataly 126-127 N 6
Zākhū 134-135 E 3
Zako 164-165 J 7
Zakopane 118 JK 4
Zakouma 164-165 HJ 6
Zakroczym 118 K 2
Zákynthos [GR, island] 122-123 J 7
Zákynthos [GR, place] 122-123 J 7
Zala 118 H 5
Zalabīyah 136-137 HJ 5
Zalaegerszeg 118 H 5
Zalanga 168-169 H 3
Zalău 122-123 K 2
Zalazna 124-125 T 4
Zalegošč' 124-125 L 7
Zalew Wislany 118 J 1
Zalfānah, Bi'r — 166-167 HJ 3
Zālingei 164-165 J 6
zaliv Akademii 132-133 a 7
zaliv Aniva 132-133 b 8
zaliv Babuškina 132-133 de 6
zaliv Faddeja 132-133 UV 2
zaliv Kara-Bogaz-Gol 134-135 G 2
zaliv Kirova 126-127 O 7
zaliv Komsomolec 134-135 G 1
zaliv Kresta 132-133 k 4
zaliv Mollera 132-133 HJ 3
zaliv Nordenskiöld 132-133 JK 2
zaliv Ozernoj 132-133 f 6
zaliv Petra Velikogo 132-133 Z 9
zaliv Šelichova 132-133 e 5-6
zaliv Terpenija 132-133 b 8
zaliv Toll'a 132-133 ST 2
Zaltan 164-165 H 3
Žaltyr, ozero — 126-127 P 3
Zalučje 124-125 H 5
Zalūn 141 D 7
Zamālat as-Suwāsī 166-167 M 2
Zamālik, Al-Qāhirah-az- 170 II b 1
Zamānia 138-139 J 5
Žambaj 126-127 P 3
Zambeze, Rio — 172 F 5
Zambezi 172 EF 5
Zambézia 172 G 5
Zambia 172 E 5-F 4
Zamboanga 148-149 H 5
Zamboanga Peninsula 148-149 H 5
Zambrano 94-95 D 3
Zamdorf, München- 130 II b 2
Zamfara 164-165 E 6
Zami Myit 141 F 8
Zamjany 126-127 NO 3
Zamkova, gora — 124-125 EF 7
Zammār 136-137 K 4
Zammūrah 166-167 G 2
Zamora, CA 74-75 BC 3
Zamora [E] 120-121 E 8
Zamora [EC, administrative unit] 96-97 B 3
Zamora [EC, place] 92-93 D 5
Zamora, Río — 96-97 B 3
Zamora de Hidalgo 64-65 F 7-8
Zamość 118 L 3
Zamūl al-Akbar, Az- 166-167 K 5-L 4
Zamura, Sierra del — 94-95 K 5
Zamuro, Punta — 94-95 G 2
Zamzam, Wādī — 164-165 G 2
Žanadarja 132-133 L 9
Zanaga 172 B 2
Zanapa 136-137 F 4
Žanašu 126-127 O 3
Žanatas 132-133 MN 9
Záncara 120-121 F 9
Zandbult = Sandbult 174-175 G 2
Zanderij 98-99 L 2
Zandrivier = Sandrivier 174-175 G 3
Zane Hills 58-59 JK 3
Zanelli, Cerro — 108-109 C 9
Zanesville, OH 64-65 K 4
Zang = Xizang Zizhiqu 142-143 EF 5
Zangaréddigûdem 140 E 2
Zanhuang 146-147 E 3
Zania 174-175 C 2
Zanja, La — 106-107 F 6
Zanjān 134-135 F 3
Zanjānrūd 136-137 MN 4
Zanjón, El — 106-107 E 1
Zanjón de Oyuela 108-109 H 3
Zanjón Nuevo, Río — 106-107 CD 3
Zante = Zákynthos 122-123 J 7
Zanthus 158-159 D 6
Zanulje 124-125 R 3
Zanzash 166-167 H 2
Zanzibar 172 GH 3
Zanzibar and Pemba 172 GH 3
Zanzibar Island 172 GH 3
Zaokskoje 124-125 L 6
Zaoshi 146-147 C 7
Zaouatallaz 164-165 F 3-4
Zaouia-el-Kahla = Burj 'Umar Idrīs 164-165 EF 3
Zaouia Sidi Chiker = Sīdī Shigar 166-167 B 4
Zaouia Sidi Rahhal = Sīdī Raḥḥāl 166-167 C 4
Zâouiet el Mgaïz = Zāwiyat al-M'gāïz 166-167 M 1
Zâouiet el Mrhaïz = Zāwiyat al-M'gāïz 166-167 M 1
Zaoyang 146-147 D 5
Zaozerje, Perm- 124-125 UV 4
Zaozhuang 146-147 FG 4
Zap = Çığlı 136-137 K 4
Zapadnaja Dvina [SU, place] 124-125 HJ 5
Zapadnaja Dvina [SU, river] 124-125 FG 6
Zapadnaja Dvina = Daugava 124-125 E 5
Zapadna Morava 122-123 J 4
Zapadno-Sibirskaja ravnina 132-133 L-Q 5-6
Zapadnyj Sajan 132-133 Q-S 7
Zapadny port 113 V b 2
Zapala 111 BC 5
Zapaleri, Cerro — 111 C 2
Zapallar 106-107 B 4
Zaparinqui 104-105 F 10
Zapata 106-107 C 4
Zapata, TX 76-77 E 9
Zapata, Península de — 88-89 F 3
Zapatoca 94-95 E 4
Zapatosa, Ciénaga de — 94-95 E 3
Zapicán 106-107 K 4
Zapiga 111 BC 1
Zapiškis 124-125 D 6
Zapokrovskij 132-133 W 7
Zapopan 86-87 J 7
Zaporozhye = Zaporozje 126-127 G 3
Zaporožje 126-127 G 3
Zapotal 96-97 B 2
Zapotillo 96-97 A 4
zapovednik Beloveža skaja pušča 124-125 E 7
zapovednik Kirova 126-127 O 7
Zaqāzīq, Az- 164-165 KL 2
Zara [TR, Amasya] 136-137 F 2
Zara [TR, Sivas] 136-137 G 3
Zara = Zadar 122-123 F 3
Zaragoza [CO] 94-95 D 4
Zaragoza [E] 120-121 G 8
Zaragoza [MEX] 86-87 K 3
Zaragoza, Juchitán de — 64-65 GH 8
Zaragoza, Puebla de — 64-65 G 8
Zarajsk 124-125 M 6
Zarand-e Kohneh 136-137 O 5
Zarasai 124-125 EF 6
Zārate 111 E 4
Zaraw Kyûn 150-151 AB 6
Zaraza 92-93 F 3
Zarbāṭiya = Zurbāṭiyah 136-137 LM 6
Zardob 126-127 NO 6
Zarembo Island 58-59 w 8
Zareq 136-137 N 5
Zarhouân = Zaghwān 166-167 M 1
Zari 168-169 J 2
Zaria 164-165 F 6
Zarībat al-Wād 166-167 K 2
Zarisberge 172 C 6-7
Zarizyn = Volgograd 126-127 LM 2
Žarkamys 132-133 K 8
Žarkovskij 124-125 J 6
Žarma 132-133 OP 8
Zarqā', Az- 136-137 G 6
Zarqat, Nā'am, Jabal — 173 D 6
Zarqūn, Wādī az- 166-167 H 3
Zarrīnābād 136-137 N 5
Zarrīneh Rūd 136-137 LM 4
Zarskoje Selo = Puškin 132-133 DE 6
Zarubino 124-125 JK 4
Zaruma 96-97 B 3
Zarumilla 96-97 A 3
Zaruşat = Arpaçay 136-137 K 2
Žary 118 G 3
Žaryk 132-133 N 8
Zarzāītīn 166-167 L 5-6
Zarzaitine = Zarzāītīn 166-167 L 5-6
Zarzal 94-95 C 5
Zarzis = Jarjīs 166-167 M 3
Zarzuela, Hipódromo de la — 113 III a 2
Žašejek [SU ↙ Kandalakša] 116-117 O 4
Žašejek [SU ↑ Kandalakša] 116-117 P 4
Žaškov 126-127 E 2
Zasla 116-117 M 10
Zaslav = Iz'aslav 126-127 C 1
Zaslavľ 124-125 F 6
Zastron 174-175 G 6
Zat = Jath 140 B 2
Zatab ash-Shamah 136-137 GH 7
Žataj 132-133 YZ 5
Žatec 118 F 3
Žatīr, Az- 134-135 E 6-7
Zatišje 126-127 DE 3
Zatoka 126-127 E 3
Zatoka Gdańska 118 J 1
Zaugyi Myit 141 E 5
Zâuiet el Beidâ' = Al-Bayḍā' 164-165 J 2
Zavalia 106-107 G 5
Zavalla, TX 76-77 G 7
Zavetnoje 126-127 L 3
Zavety Iljiča 132-133 ab 8
Zavia = Az-Zāwiyah 164-165 G 2
Zavidoviči 122-123 GH 3
Zavitinsk 132-133 Y 7
Zāviyeh 136-137 L 3
Zavodoukovsk 132-133 M 6
Zavolžje 132-133 G 6
Zavolžsk 124-125 O 5
Zawgyi River = Zaugyi Myit 141 E 5
Zawi 172 EF 5
Zawia = Az-Zāwiyah 164-165 G 2
Zawīlah 164-165 H 3
Zāwiya al-M'gāïz 166-167 M 1
Zāwiyah, Az- 164-165 G 2
Zāwiyah, Jabal az- 136-137 G 5
Zāwiyat al-M'gāïz 166-167 M 1
Zāwiyat Nābit 170 II a 1
Zawr, Az- 136-137 N 8
Zayb, Bi'r — 136-137 K 6
Zaydūn, Wādī — 173 C 5
Zayetkôn 141 D 5
Zaytun, Al-Qāhirah-az- 170 II b 1
Zayū 166-167 E 2
Zbaraž 126-127 B 2
Zbaszyn 118 GH 2
Zborov 126-127 B 2
Zbruč 126-127 C 2
Ždanov 126-127 H 3
Ždanovsk 126-127 N 7
Zdolbunov 126-127 C 1
Zduńska Wola 118 J 3
Zealand 63 C 4
Zealand = Sjælland 116-117 DE 10
Zeballos 60 D 4
Zeballos, Monte — 108-109 D 6
Zebedānī = 'Zabdānī 136-137 G 6
Zebediela 174-175 H 3
Zeebrugge, Brugge- 120-121 J 3
Zeehan 158-159 HJ 8
Zeekoegat = Seekoegat 174-175 E 7
Zeekoe River = Seekoerivier 174-175 F 6
Zeeland, MI 70-71 GH 4
Zeerust 172 E 7
Zēfat 134-135 D 4
Zegdoû, Ḥâssî — = Ḥāssī Zighdū 166-167 D 5
Zegher, Hamâda ez — = Ḥammadat az-Zaghir 166-167 M 6
Zeghortâ = Zaghartā 136-137 F 5
Zegrir, Ouèd — = Wādī Zāghrīr 166-167 J 3
Zeidûn, Wâdî — = Wādī Zaydūn 173 C 5
Zeila = Seyla' 164-165 N 6
Zeilsheim, Frankfurt am Main- 128 III a 1
Žeimelis 124-125 DE 5
Zeitz 118 EF 3
Zeja [SU, place] 132-133 Y 7
Zeja [SU, river] 132-133 Y 7
Zekeriyaköy 154 I b 1
Zel'abova 124-125 E 7
Zelebiyé = Zalabīyah 136-137 HJ 5
Zelenaja Rošča 124-125 T 6
Zelenčukskaja 126-127 K 5
Zelenga 126-127 O 3
Zelenoborskij 116-117 P 4
Zelenodol'sk 132-133 HJ 6
Zelenogorsk 124-125 GH 3
Zelenograd 124-125 J 5
Zelenogradsk 118 K 1
Zelenokumsk 126-127 LM 4
Železnik 122-123 J 3
Železnodorožnyj [SU, Komi ASSR] 132-133 J 5
Železnogorsk 124-125 KL 7
Železnovodsk 126-127 L 4
Zelfana, Bir — = Bi'r Zalfānah 166-167 HJ 3
Zelijk = Zellik 128 II a 1
Zelinograd = Celinograd 132-133 MN 7
Zella = Zillah 164-165 H 3
Zellik 128 II a 1
Zélouân = Sulwān 166-167 E 2
Zeluán = Sulwān 166-167 E 2
Želudok 124-125 E 7
Zel'va 124-125 E 7
Zelwa = Zel'va 124-125 E 7
Zembeur, 'Oglet — = Sabkhat al-M'shīgīg 166-167 L 2
Zembra, Djezîra — = Al-Jāmūr al-Kabīr 164-165 M 1
Zemcy 124-125 J 5
Zemetčino 124-125 O 7
Zemio 164-165 JK 7
zeml'a Aleksandra I 53 C 29
zeml'a Alexandra 132-133 FG 1
zeml'a Bunge 132-133 b 2-3
zeml'a Franz Joseph 132-133 H-M 2
zeml'a George 132-133 F-H 1
Zemlandskij poluostrov 118 K 1
Zemľansk 124-125 M 8
zeml'a Wilczek 132-133 L-N 1
Zemmâr = Zammār 136-137 K 4
Zemmora = Zammūrah 166-167 G 2
Zémongo 164-165 J 7
Zemoul, Ouèd — = Wād Zimūl 166-167 C 5
Zemoul el Akbar, Ez — = Az-Zamūl al-Akbar 166-167 K 5-L 4
Zempoala 86-87 M 8
Zempoaltepec, Cerro — 64-65 GH 8
Zemun, Beograd- 122-123 HJ 3
Zemzen, Uâdi — = Wādī Zamzam 164-165 G 2
Zengcheng 146-147 D 10
Zenia, CA 66-67 B 5
Zenica 122-123 G 3
Zenina = Al-Idrīsīyah 166-167 H 2
Zen'kov 126-127 G 1
Zenón Pereyra 106-107 G 3
Zenshū = Chŏnju 142-143 O 4
Zentena 106-107 G 6
Zentralflughafen Schönefeld 130 III c 2
Zentralfriedhof Ohlsdorf 130 I b 1
Zentralfriedhof Wien 113 I b 2
Zephyrhills, FL 80-81 bc 2
Zeppelinheim 128 III a 1
Zeraïa = Zirāyah 166-167 JK 1
Zeravšan 134-135 K 3
Zeravšanskij chrebet 134-135 K 3
Zerbst 118 F 2-3
Zerdevka 124-125 N 8
Zere, Gawd-e — 134-135 J 5
Zerev 126-127 D 1
Zergoun, Ouèd ez — = Wādī az-Zarqūn 166-167 H 3
Zeribet-el-Ouèd = Zarībat al-Wād 166-167 K 2
Zernograd 126-127 K 3
Zeroûd, Ouèd — = Wād Zurūd 166-167 LM 2
Žešart 124-125 RS 2
Zesfontein = Sesfontein 172 B 5
Zeshou = Jieshou 146-147 G 5
Zestafoni 126-127 L 5
Zetland = Shetland 119 FG 1
Zeugitane, Monts de — = Jabal az-Zūgitīn 166-167 L 1-2
Zeuthener See 130 III c 2
Zevenhoven 128 I a 2
Zevgári, Akrōtērion — 136-137 E 5
Zevghari, Cape — = Akrōthērion Zevgári 136-137 E 5
Zeydikān = Zidikān 136-137 K 3
Zeytinburnu, Istanbul- 154 I a 3
Zeytinlik 136-137 JK 2
Zêzere 120-121 CD 9
Zgierz 118 J 3
Zgurovka 126-127 E 1
Zhahang = Tsethang 142-143 G 6
Zhajiang 146-147 D 8
Zhajin 146-147 E 7
Zhaling Hu = Kyaring Tsho 142-143 F 5
Zhangdu Hu 146-147 E 6
Zhangguangcai Ling 142-143 O 2-3
Zhang He 146-147 E 3
Zhanghua = Changhua 146-147 H 9
Zhanghuang 146-147 B 10
Zhangjiakou 142-143 L 3
Zhangjiapang 146-147 E 6
Zhangling 142-143 N 1
Zhangmutou 146-147 E 10
Zhangping 146-147 F 9
Zhangpu 146-147 F 9
Zhangqiao 146-147 F 5
Zhangqiu 146-147 F 3
Zhangsanta 146-147 C 2
Zhangsanying 144-145 AB 2
Zhang Shui 146-147 E 9
Zhangye 142-143 J 4
Zhangzhou 142-143 M 7
Zhangzi 146-147 D 3
Zhangzi Dao 144-145 D 3
Zhanhua 146-147 FG 3
Zhanjiang 142-143 L 7
Zhanjiang Gang 142-143 L 7
Zhao'an 146-147 F 10
Zhao'an Wan 146-147 F 10
Zhaocheng 146-147 C 3
Zhaocheng = Jiaocheng 146-147 CD 3
Zhaoping 146-147 C 9
Zhaoqing 146-147 D 10
Zhaotong 142-143 J 6
Zhao Xian [TJ, Hebei] 146-147 E 3
Zhao Xian [TJ, Shandong] 146-147 G 4
Zhaoyuan 146-147 H 3
Zhapo 146-147 C 11
Zhashui 146-147 B 5
Zhaxigang 142-143 DE 5
Zhaxilhünbo 142-143 F 6
Zhdanov = Ždanov 126-127 H 3
Zhecheng 146-147 E 4
Zhegao 146-147 F 6
Zhejiang 142-143 MN 6
Zhelang Jiao 146-147 E 10
Zheling Guan 142-143 L 6
Zhen'an 146-147 B 5
Zheng'an = Cheng'an 146-147 E 3
Zhengding 146-147 E 2
Zhenghe 146-147 G 8
Zhengjiayi 146-147 C 7
Zhengyang 146-147 E 5
Zhengyangguan 146-147 F 5
Zhengzhou 142-143 LM 5
Zhenhai 142-143 N 5-6
Zhenjiang 142-143 M 5
Zhenkang 141 F 4
Zhenping 146-147 D 5
Zhen Shui 146-147 DE 9
Zhentong 146-147 GH 5
Zhenxi = Bar Köl 142-143 G 3
Zhenyuan [TJ, Guizhou] 142-143 K 6
Zhenyuan [TJ, Yunnan] 142-143 J 7
Zhenyue = Yiwu 150-151 C 2
Zherong 146-147 GH 8
Zhidan 146-147 B 3
Zhigatse 142-143 F 6
Zhijiang [TJ, Hubei] 146-147 C 6
Zhijiang [TJ, Hunan] 142-143 KL 6
Zhikharkhunglung 142-143 F 5
Zhili 146-147 E 3-F 2
Zhitan 146-147 F 7
Zhitomir = Žitomir 126-127 D 1
Zhlobin = Žlobin 124-125 G 7
Zhob 138-139 B 2
Zhokhova Island = ostrov Žochova 132-133 de 2
Zhongcun 146-147 FG 4
Zhongdian 142-143 HJ 6
Zhongdu 146-147 B 9
Zhonghai 155 II b 2
Zhongmou 146-147 DE 4
Zhongshan 142-143 L 7
Zhongshan Park 155 II b 2
Zhongtiao Shan 146-147 CD 4
Zhongwei 142-143 JK 4
Zhongxiang 146-147 D 6
Zhongxin 146-147 E 9
Zhongyang 146-147 C 3
Zhongyang Shanmo = Chungyang Shanmo 142-143 N 7
Zhongyuan 150-151 H 3
Zhoucun 146-147 FG 3
Zhoudangfan 146-147 E 6
Zhoujiakou = Zhoukou 142-143 LM 5
Zhoukou 142-143 LM 5
Zhouning 146-147 G 8
Zhoushan Qundao 142-143 N 5
Zhouxiang 146-147 H 6
Zhouzhi 146-147 AB 4
Zhuanghe 144-145 D 3
Zhucheng 142-143 MN 4
Zhudong = Chutung 146-147 H 9
Zhuguang Shan 146-147 DE 8-9
Zhuhe = Shangzhi 142-143 O 2
Zhuji 142-143 N 6
Zhujia Jian 146-147 J 7
Zhujiang Kou 146-147 D 10
Zhulong He 146-147 E 2
Zhumadian 146-147 DE 5
Zhungruthugkha 138-139 K 3
Zhuolu 146-147 E 1
Zhuo Xian 146-147 E 2
Zhuozhang He 146-147 D 3
Zhuqiao 146-147 GH 3
Zhushan 142-143 KL 5
Zhushui He 146-147 EF 4
Zhutan 146-147 E 7
Zhuting 146-147 D 8
Zhuxi 146-147 BC 5
Zhuzhou 142-143 L 6
Ziarat = Ziyārat 138-139 A 2
Zia Town 168-169 D 4
Zīban 166-167 JK 2
Zibane = Zīban 166-167 JK 2
Zībār, Az- 136-137 KL 4
Zibo 142-143 M 4
Zichang 146-147 B 3
Zicheng 146-147 C 6
Zichuan 146-147 FG 3
Zidane 170 I b 2
Zidani most 122-123 F 2
Zidikān 136-137 K 3
Zid'ki 126-127 H 2
Ziegelwasser 113 I c 2
Ziegenhals [DDR] 130 III c 2
Ziel, Mount — 158-159 F 4
Zielona Góra 118 GH 2-3
Zierbeek 128 II a 1
Ziftá 173 B 2
Zigala 136-137 G 2
Žigalovo 132-133 U 7
Žigansk 132-133 X 4
Zighān 164-165 J 3
Zighdū, Ḥāssī — 166-167 D 5
Zighout-Youcef = Zighūt Yūsuf 166-167 K 1
Zighūt Yūsuf 166-167 K 1
Zigôn [BUR, Pègû Taing] 141 D 6
Zigôn [BUR, Ragaing Taing] 141 D 7
Zigong 142-143 JK 6
Ziguei 164-165 H 6
Zigui 146-147 C 6
Ziguinchor 164-165 A 6
Žiguli 124-125 R 7
Žigulʹovsk 124-125 R 7
Zig-Zag, El — 91 II b 1
Zihu = Bajan Choto 142-143 JK 4
Zihuatanejo 86-87 JK 9
Žijenbet 126-127 N 2
Zijin 142-143 M 7
Zikhrōn-Ya'aqov 136-137 F 6
Zil, Moskva- 113 V c 3
Zilāf 136-137 G 6
Zilair 132-133 K 7
Zilalet 168-169 GH 1
Zile 136-137 F 2
Žilina 118 J 4
Zillah 164-165 H 3
Zillah, WA 66-67 C 2
Žiloj 126-127 P 6
Žiloj, ostrov — 126-127 P 6
Zilfī, Az- 134-135 EF 5
Zilupe 124-125 FG 5
Zima 132-133 T 7
Zimane 174-175 K 2
Zimapán 86-87 KL 6-7
Zimbabwe [ZW, ruins] 172 F 6
Zimbabwe [ZW, state] 172 EF 5
Zimi 168-169 C 4
Zimkān, Āb-e — 136-137 LM 5
Zimme = Chiang Mai 148-149 C 3
Zimnicea 122-123 L 4
Zimovniki 126-127 L 3
Zimūl, Wād — 166-167 C 5
Zinder 164-165 F 6
Zingkaling Hkamti = Hsingaleinganti 141 D 3
Ziniaré 168-169 E 2
Zinqiang 146-147 D 7
Zintenhof = Sindi 124-125 E 4
Zion, IL 70-71 G 4
Zion National Monument 74-75 G 4
Zion National Park 74-75 G 4
Zionsville, IN 70-71 GH 6
Zipaquirá 92-93 E 3-4
Ziqiu 146-147 C 6
Zira 138-139 E 2
Žir'atino 124-125 J 7
Zirāyah 166-167 JK 1
Žirje 122-123 F 4
Žirnov 126-127 K 2
Žirnovsk 126-127 M 1
Zirrāh, Gaud-e — = Gawd-e Zere 134-135 J 5
Zi Shui 142-143 L 6
Zistersdorf 118 H 4
Žitkoviči 124-125 FG 7
Žitkovo 124-125 G 3
Žitkur 126-127 N 2
Žitomir 126-127 D 1
Zittau 118 G 3
Zitundo 174-175 K 4
Zitziana River 58-59 M 4
Zivank 136-137 E 3
Ziway 164-165 M 7
Zixi 146-147 F 8
Zixing 146-147 D 9
Ziya He 146-147 F 2
Ziyang 146-147 B 5
Ziyang = Yanzhou 146-147 F 4
Ziyārat 138-139 A 2
Ziyuan 146-147 C 8
Zīz, Wād — 166-167 D 4
Žizdra [SU, place] 124-125 K 7
Žizdra [SU, river] 124-125 K 7
Zizhong 142-143 JK 5-6
Zizhou 146-147 B 3
Zizō-zaki 144-145 J 5
Zlatica 122-123 KL 4
Zlatograd 122-123 L 5
Zlatopol' 126-127 E 2
Zlatoust 132-133 K 6
Zlatoustovsk 132-133 Za 7
Zlín 118 G 4

Zlitan 164-165 GH 2
Žlobin 124-125 GH 7
Złoczew 118 J 3
Złotów 118 H 2
Zlynka 124-125 H 7
Zmeinogorsk 132-133 P 7
Zmeinyj ostrov 126-127 E 4
Zmejevy gory 124-125 Q 7-8
Žmerinka 126-127 D 2
Zmijev = Gottwaldov 126-127 H 2
Zmijovka 124-125 L 7
Znamenka [SU, Rossijskaja SFSR Smolenskaja Oblast'] 124-125 K 6
Znamenka [SU, Rossijskaja SFSR Tambovskaja Oblast'] 124-125 N 7
Znamenka [SU, Ukrainskaja SSR] 126-127 F 2
Znamensk 118 K 1
Znamenskoje [SU, Orlovskaja Oblast'] 124-125 KL 7
Znojmo 118 GH 4
Zoar 174-175 D 7
Zóbuè 172 F 5
Žochova, ostrov — 132-133 de 2
Zogirma 168-169 FG 2
Zōgrafos 113 IV b 2
Zohlaguna, Meseta de — 86-87 Q 8
Zohreh, Rūd-e — 136-137 N 7
Zok 136-137 J 3
Zola Chāy 136-137 L 3-4
Žolkev = Nesterov 126-127 AB 1
Žolkva = Nesterov 126-127 AB 1
Zollikerberg 128 IV b 1
Zollikon 128 IV b 1
Zol'noje 124-125 RS 7
Zoločev [SU, Char'kovskaja Oblast'] 126-127 GH 1
Zoločev [SU, L'vovskaja Oblast'] 126-127 B 2
Zolotaja Gora 132-133 XY 7
Zolotar'ovka 124-125 P 7
Zolotonoša 126-127 F 2
Zomba 172 G 5
Zombi Nzoro 171 B 2
Zombo 172 F 5
Zonda 106-107 C 3
Zongcun 146-147 D 8
Zongo 172 C 1
Zonguldak 134-135 C 2
Zongwe 171 AB 4
Zoniënbos 128 II b 2
Zonūz 136-137 L 3
Zoo [SU] 113 V b 2
Zoo [USA, Chicago] 83 II b 1
Zoo [USA, New York] 82 III c 1
Zoo-Baba 168-169 J 1
Zoo Berlin 130 III b 1
Zoological Garden of Al-Qāhirah 170 II b 1
Zoological Gardens [AUS] 161 II b 1
Zoological Gardens [IND] 154 II ab 2
Zoological Gardens [USA, Houston] 85 III b 2
Zoological Gardens [USA, New Orleans] 85 I b 2
Zoological Gardens of Johannesburg 170 V b 1-2
Zoological Gardens of Johor Baharu 154 III a 1
Zoological Gardens of London 129 II b 1
Zoológico de San Juan de Aragón 91 I c 2
Zorgo 168-169 E 2
Zorra, Isla — 64-65 b 2
Zorras, Las — 96-97 B 7
Zorritos 96-97 A 3
Zortman, MT 68-69 B 2
Zorzor 164-165 C 7
Zou [DY, administrative unit] 168-169 F 4
Zou [DY, river] 168-169 F 4
Zouar 164-165 H 4
Zouping 146-147 F 3
Zousfana, Ouèd — = Wādī Zusfānah 166-167 EF 4
Zoushi 146-147 C 7
Zoutpansberge = Soutpansberge 172 EF 6
Zou Xian 146-147 F 4
Žovkva = Nesterov 126-127 AB 1
Žovtnevoje 126-127 EF 3
Zrenjanin 122-123 J 3
Zribet-el-Oued = Zarībat al-Wād 166-167 K 2
Zuar = Zouar 164-165 H 4
Zuata 94-95 J 3
Zuata, Río — 94-95 J 3
Zubaydīyah, Az- 136-137 L 6
Zubayr, Az- 136-137 M 7
Zubayr, Jabal — 173 C 4
Zubayr, Jazā'ir az- 134-135 E 7-8
Zubayr, Khawr az- 136-137 MN 7
Zubcov 124-125 K 5
Zubova Pol'ana 124-125 O 6
Zubovo 124-125 L 3
Zubovskaja = Ali-Bajramly 126-127 O 7
Zudañez 104-105 D 6
Z'udev, ostrov — 126-127 O 4
Zuénoula 164-165 C 7
Zuera 120-121 G 8
Ẓufār 134-135 G 7
Zug 118 D 5
Zugdidi 126-127 KL 5
Zug Island 84 II b 3
Zugspitze 118 E 5
Zuiderwoude 128 I b 1
Zuila = Zawīlah 164-165 H 3
Zuishavane 172 F 6
Zújar 120-121 E 9
Zujevka 124-125 S 4
Zujevo, Orechovo- 132-133 FG 6
Zūjitīn, Jabal az- 166-167 L 1-2
Z'uk, mys — 126-127 H 4
Z'ukajka 124-125 U 4
Žukovka 124-125 J 7
Žukovskij 124-125 M 6
Zukur 164-165 N 6
Žuldyz 126-127 O 2
Zulia 94-95 EF 2
Zululand 174-175 J 5-K 4
Zumar, Tur'at az- 170 II ab 1
Zumba 92-93 D 5
Zumbi, Rio de Janeiro- 110 I b 1
Zumbrota, MN 70-71 D 3
Zumikon 128 IV b 2
Zumpango 86-87 L 8
Zumui, Ponta do — 100-101 B 1
Zumūl, Umm az- 134-135 GH 6
Zunderdorp 128 I b 1
Zungeru 164-165 F 7
Zunhua 146-147 F 1
Zuni, NM 74-75 J 5
Zuni Indian Reservation 74-75 J 5
Zuni Mountains 74-75 JK 5
Zunnebeek 128 II a 2
Zunyi 142-143 K 6
Zuo'an 146-147 E 8
Zuo'anmen, Beijing- 155 II b 2
Zuoquan 146-147 D 3
Zuoyun 146-147 D 2
Županja 122-123 H 3
Zūq, Ḥāssī — 164-165 B 4
Zuqar = Zukur 164-165 N 6
Zūrābād 136-137 L 3
Zurak 168-169 H 3
Žuraviči 124-125 H 7
Zurbāṭīyah 136-137 LM 6
Zurdo, El — 108-109 D 8
Zürich 118 D 5
Zürich-Affoltern 128 IV ab 1
Zürich-Albisrieden 128 IV ab 1
Zürich-Altstetten 128 IV a 1
Zürich-Binz 128 IV b 1
Zürich-Enge 128 IV b 1
Zürich-Hirslanden 128 IV b 1
Zürich-Höngg 128 IV ab 1
Zürich-Hottingen 128 IV b 1
Zürich-Leimbach 128 IV ab 2
Zürich-Oerlikon 128 IV b 1
Zürich-Riesbach 128 IV b 1
Zürich-Schwamendingen 128 IV b 1
Zürichsee 118 D 5
Zürich-Seebach 128 IV b 1
Zürich-Seefeld 128 IV b 1
Zürich-Wipkingen 128 IV b 1
Zürich-Witikon 128 IV b 1
Zürich-Wollishofen 128 IV b 1
Zurmi 168-169 G 2
Zurnga Chhu 138-139 J 2
Zuru 164-165 F 6
Zurūd, Wād — 166-167 LM 2
Zurzuna 136-137 K 2
Zuša 124-125 L 7
Zusfānah, Wādī — 166-167 EF 4
Zutiua, Rio — 100-101 B 3
Žutovo = Okt'abr'skij 126-127 L 3
Zuun 128 II a 2
Zuwārah 164-165 G 2
Zuwe 174-175 F 2
Z'uzino, Moskva- 113 V b 3
Zvenigorodka 126-127 E 2
Zvenigovo 124-125 QR 6
Zviahel' = Novograd-Volynskij 126-127 CD 1
Zvolen 118 J 4
Zvornik 122-123 H 3
Zwai, Lake — = Ziway 164-165 M 7
Zwanenburg 128 I a 1
Zwartberg = Swartberg 174-175 H 6
Zwartkops = Swartkops 174-175 F 7
Zwartmodder = Swartmodder 174-175 D 5
Zweibrücken 118 C 4
Zwelitsha 174-175 G 7
Zwettl 118 G 4
Zwickau 118 F 3
Zwiesel 118 F 4
Zwillikon 128 IV a 2
Zwölfaxing 113 I b 2
Zwolle 120-121 L 2
Zwolle, LA 78-79 C 5
Zyōhana 144-145 L 4
Zyōzankei 144-145 b 2
Zyr'anka 132-133 cd 4
Zyr'anovsk 132-133 PQ 8
Żyrardów 118 K 2

Index Addenda

Afyon 134-135 C 3
Aizawal 134-135 P 6
Aktau 126 127 P 5

Babušara 126 127 K 5
Baharampur 134 135 O 6
Bakhtarān 134-135 F 4
Balbina, Represa — 92-93 H 5
Baleswar 134-135 O 6
Banaba 162 JK 4
Band Bābā, Kōh-i — 134-135 J 4
Band-i-Turkestān, Selselae-i- 134-135 JK 3
Bazarčulan 126-127 PQ 2
Bejlagan 126-127 N 7
Belzy 126-127 CD 3
Bender 126-127 D 3
Beruni 134-135 J 2
Bhadrak 134-135 O 6
Bhavnagar 134-135 L 6
Bil'assuvar 126-127 O 7
Biqā', Al- = 4 ◁ 136-127 G 6
Biqā', Sahl al- 136-137 F 6-G 5
Bir 134-135 M 7
Biškek 132-133 NO 9
Blagodarnyj 126-127 L 4
Boğazici 134-135 BC 2
Budennovsk 126-127 LM 4
Bushehr 134-135 G 5

Chaghcharān 134-135 JK 4
Chahār Burjak 134-135 J 4
Chişinău 126-127 D 3
Chudžand 134-135 K 2-L 3
Crimea Autonomous Region 126-127 FG 4
Czech Republic 118 F-H 4

Deh Shū 134-135 J 4
Dhule 134-135 L 6
Dimitrov 126-127 H 2
Dmitrovka 126-127 F 1
Dobrič 122-123 MN 4
Dubessar 126-127 D 3

Eritrea 164-165 M 5-N 6

G'andža 126-127 N 6
Gangtok 134-135 O 5
Gawdezereh 134-135 J 5
Gazi Mağusa 134-135 CD 3
Georgia [State] 134-135 EF 2
Gjumri 134-135 E 2
Gorakpur 134-135 N 5
Gorodovikovsk 126-127 KL 3

Hankendi 126-127 N 7
Haora 134-135 O 6
Hisār, Kōh-i — 134-135 K 4
Hubli-Dhawad 134-135 M 7

Issyk-Kul' 134-135 LM 2
Istāda-i-Moqur, Ābe — 134-135 K 4

Jabal Lubnān = 2 ◁ F 6 136-137
Jalālābad 134-135 KL 4
Jekaterinburg 132-133 L 6
Jhang Maghiyanah 134-135 L 4

Kachul 126-127 D 4
Kajakī 134-135 K 4
Kanchepuram 134-135 MN 7
Karamanmaraş 134-135 D 3
Khambhat 134-135 L 6
Khowst 134-135 KL 4
Kirgizia 134-135 LM 2
Konārak [IR] 134-135 HJ 5
Kuçovë 122-123 HJ 5
Kuressaare 124-125 D 4

Lahawr 134-135 L 4
Lāshe Jowayn 134-135 J 4
Lazurnoje 126-127 G 3
Leyah 134-135 L 4
Liski 126-127 JK 1
Lubnān al-Janūbī = 3 ◁ 136-137 F 6
Lubnān ash-Shimālī = 1 ◁ 136-137 G 5

Lugansk 126-127 JK 2

Machilipatnam 134-135 N 7
Mandsaur 134-135 LM 6
Margo, Dasht-i — 134-135 J 4
Marijampolė 124-125 D 6
Mariupol' 126-127 H 3
Markazī 134-135 F 3-G 4
Maymana 134-135 JK 3
Medinipur 134-135 O 6
Milet 134-135 B 3
Moldavia [state] 126-127 CD 3
Mukačevo 126-127 A 2
Munger 134-135 O 5
Nāsirīyah [IRQ] 134-135 F 4
Nižnevolžsk 126-127 N 3
Nižnij Novgorod 132-133 GH 6

Očamčira 126-127 K 5
Oneşti 122-123 M 2
Orchej 126-127 D 3
Ozurgati 126-127 KL 6

Palmas [BR, Tocantins] 92-93 K 6
Panaj 134-135 L 7
Panjāb 134-135 K 4
P'atimarskoje 126-127 P 2
Podgorica 122-123 H 4
Primorsk [Ukraine] 126-127 H 3
Purnia 134-135 O 5

Qala Shahr 134-135 K 3
Qandahār 134-135 K 4

Rourkela 134-135 NO 6
Russia 132-133 N-b 5

Safēd Kōh, Selsalae — 134-135 J 4-K 3
Samara 132-133 HJ 7
Šamkir 126-127 MN 6
Sankt Peterburg 132-133 E 5-6
Sanlı Urfa 134-135 D 3
Sare Pul 134-135 K 3
Šarur 126-127 M 7
Šeki 126-127 N 6
Senaki 126-127 KL 5
Sergijev Posad 132-133 F 6
Shāh Faidalabad 134-135 L 4
Shahrak 134-135 J 4
Simbirsk 132-133 H 7
Slovakia 112 H-K 4
Solapur 134-135 M 7
Spin Buldak 134-135 K 4

Tadzhikistan 134-135 KL 3
Thanjavur 134-135 MN 7
Tibet = Xizang 142-143 EF 5
Tiruchendur 134-135 M 9
Tocantins 92-93 K 5-6
Torez 126-127 J 2-3
Tribugá, Golfo de — 92-93 D 3
Troja = Truva 134-135 B 3
Truva 134-135 B 3
Tucuruí, Represa — 92-93 K 5
Turkmenistan 134-135 HJ 2-5
Tver' 132-133 EF 6

Udipi = Udupi 134-135 L 8
Udupi 134-135 L 8
Ungen 126-127 CD 3
Uštagan 126-127 O 3
Ust'-Džeguta 126-127 K 4
Uzbekistan 134-135 J 2-K 3
Užice 122-123 HJ 4

Veles 122-123 JK 5
Vladikavkaz 126-127 M 5
Vol'nansk 126-127 G 3

Wāzakhwā 134-135 K 4
White Russia 124-125 E-H 6-7

Xalapa 64-65 GH 8
Xizang 142-143 EF 4

Yamoussoukro 164-165 CD 7
Yasuj 134-135 G 4

Zarghun Shahr 134-135 K 4
Žarkent 132-133 OP 9
Zmijev 126-127 H 2